Places of Importance to Women Writers of the *British Isles*

COMPILED BY DEBORAH KENNEDY

North Sea

ATLANTIC OCEAN

Irish Sea

NORTH CHANNEL

ORKNEY ISLANDS

CAITHNESS

SUTHERLAND

ROSS & CROMARTY

MORAY FIRTH

NAIRN

MORAY

BANFF

KINCARDINE

ANGUS

PERTH

FIFE

KINROSS

CLACKMANNAN

STIRLING

Glasgow

Loch Lomond

DUMBARTON

R. Clyde

LANARK

Edinburgh

WEST LOTHIAN

EAST LOTHIAN

BERWICK

SELKIRK

ROXBURGH

R. Tweed

Berwick-upon-Tweed

NORTHUMBERLAND

Alnwick

Newcastle upon Tyne

R. Tyne

Durham

CO. DURHAM

R. Tees

Carlisle

CUMBERLAND

RYDAL MOUNT

Ambleside

Grasmere

Near Sawrey

WESTMORLAND

Lake District

Cockermouth

CRAIGENPUTTOCK

Gretna Green

DUMFRIES

KIRKCUDBRIGHT

Galloway

WIGTOWN

ARRAN I.

BUTE

ISLE of SKYE

INNER HEBRIDES

OUTER HEBRIDES

NORTH MINCH

LITTLE MINCH

LEWIS

ROSS

ISLE of MAN

INVERNESS

ARGYLL

GRAMPIAN MOUNTAINS

Highlands

Cheviot Hills

Pentland Hills

Lammermuir Hills

FIRTH OF FORTH

ULSTER

Northern Ireland

ANTRIM

Belfast

DOWN

TYRONE

FERMANAGH

MONAGHAN

CAVAN

LOUTH

MEATH

WESTMEATH

LONGFORD

LEITRIM

ROSCOMMON

MAYO

CONNAUGHT

CLARE

ARAN ISLANDS

DONEGAL BAY

Edgeworthstown

R. Boyne

R. Shannon

OFFALY

The county system in England, Scotland, Wales, and Northern Ireland underwent comprehensive changes in 1974; this map represents the earlier names and boundaries.

The Norton Anthology of Literature by Women

THIRD EDITION
VOLUME 1
THE MIDDLE AGES
THROUGH THE TURN OF THE CENTURY

True Womanhood
1. piety
2. purity
3. Submissiveness
4. domesticity

The true woman makes her husband a
better person by influence . . .
Simply because she is so pure & good.

The Norton Anthology
of Literature by Women

THIRD EDITION
VOLUME 1
The Middle Ages
Through the Turn of the Century

The Norton Anthology of Literature by Women
The Traditions in English

THIRD EDITION

VOLUME 1

THE MIDDLE AGES
THROUGH THE TURN OF THE CENTURY

Sandra M. Gilbert

UNIVERSITY OF CALIFORNIA, DAVIS

Susan Gubar

INDIANA UNIVERSITY

W • W • NORTON & COMPANY • *New York* • *London*

W. W. Norton & Company has been independent since its founding in 1923, when William Warder Norton and Mary D. Herter Norton first published lectures delivered at the People's Institute, the adult education division of New York City's Cooper Union. The Nortons soon expanded their program beyond the Institute, publishing books by celebrated academics from America and abroad. By mid-century, the two major pillars of Norton's publishing program—trade books and college texts—were firmly established. In the 1950s, the Norton family transferred control of the company to its employees, and today—with a staff of four hundred and a comparable number of trade, college, and professional titles published each year—W. W. Norton & Company stands as the largest and oldest publishing house owned wholly by its employees.

Composition by Binghamton Valley Composition.
Manufacturing by R. R. Donnelley—Crawfordsville.
Book design by Antonina Krass.
Project editor: Lory A. Frenkel.
Production manager: Benjamin Reynolds.

Library of Congress Cataloging-in-Publication Data

The Norton anthology of literature by women : the traditions in English /
[compiled by] Sandra M. Gilbert, Susan Gubar.—3rd ed.
p. cm.
Includes bibliographical references and index.
ISBN-13: 978-0-393-93013-9 (v. 1 : pbk.)
ISBN-10: 0-393-93013-0 (v. 1 : pbk.)
ISBN-13: 978-0-393-93014-6 (v. 2 : pbk.)
ISBN-10: 0-393-93014-9 (v. 2 : pbk.)

1. American literature—Women authors. 2. English literature—Women
authors. 3. Women—Literary collections. I. Gilbert, Sandra M.
II. Gubar, Susan, 1944–
PS508.W7N67 2007
820.8'09287—dc22
2006101170

W. W. Norton & Company, Inc., 500 Fifth Avenue, New York, N.Y. 10110
www.wwnorton.com

W. W. Norton & Company Ltd., Castle House, 75/76 Wells Street, London WIT 3QT

2 3 4 5 6 7 8 9 0

Contents

Literature of the Seventeenth and Eighteenth Centuries 123

Literature of the Nineteenth Century 407

Turn-of-the-Century Literature

Preface

> I think I was enchanted
> When first a sombre Girl -
> I read that Foreign Lady -
> The Dark - felt beautiful -

So wrote the brilliant American poet Emily Dickinson in the mid–nineteenth century, as she contemplated the literary achievements of "that Foreign Lady," the great British poet Elizabeth Barrett Browning, then living in exile in Italy. We begin our preface to the Third Edition of *The Norton Anthology of Literature by Women* with this tribute from one woman of letters to another because it emphasizes the international intellectual bonds that link readers and writers across time and space. In 1985, we began our Preface to the First Edition with Virginia Woolf's remark in *A Room of One's Own* that "books continue each other." Woolf, we noted, was urging her audience to contemplate the connections between the Restoration iconoclast Aphra Behn, the eighteenth-century lyricist Anne Finch, and the four great novelists of the nineteenth century—Jane Austen, Charlotte Brontë, Emily Brontë, and George Eliot—but by implication she was also arguing for the places occupied in her "fairly long series" by such American writers as Harriet Beecher Stowe and Dickinson. It was the tradition constituted by this series that the First Edition brought to a new audience of students and general readers.

Today, however, we can see more clearly just how complex and multifaceted Woolf's set of women writers really is. For during the years that have intervened between editions, the interlocked fields of women's studies, gender studies, feminist theory, queer theory, and cultural studies have evolved in ways we might not have anticipated in 1985. Throughout the past two decades, scholars have continued the excavation and assessment that provisionally defined women's literary history in the 1970s and '80s, and we are grateful to them for newly recovered works of literature, better edited texts, and new historical writings. In particular, however, we owe to them contributions that enrich the original pages of this anthology so dramatically as to have invited a crucial emendation in our subtitle: originally subtitled "The Tradition in English," with the Second Edition we began subtitling it "The Traditions in English" to signal a commitment to both mirror and serve the range of scholarly, critical, and pedagogic viewpoints that have enlivened feminist studies in a globalized era. Diversity itself has shaped the evolution of feminist criticism, from its early preoccupation with women's shared experiences to its more recent absorption in the complex issues and assumptions informing English-language texts by women writers of diverse geographical, cultural, racial, sexual, religious, and class origins and influences, just as diversity shaped the revisions of this anthology. The section-by-section

changes noted below convey the diversity in genre, in ethnic and geographical origins, and in representation of individual writers that characterize the Third Edition.

At the same time, this Third Edition of *The Norton Anthology of Literature by Women* continues to remind readers of Woolf's affirmation that "books continue each other." Like all historically oriented Norton anthologies, our volumes provide a broad chronological overview of their subject—an overview that enables readers to fully appreciate the female literary traditions that, for several centuries, have coexisted with, revised, and influenced male literary models. With 219 writers (61 new to the Third Edition), *The Norton Anthology of Literature by Women* chronicles both the evolution in and the revolutions of women's literature in the British Isles, the United States, Canada, Australia, India, Africa, the Caribbean, and other English-speaking regions from the fourteenth century to the present.

As what is essentially a course-in-a-book, the anthology maintains its original commitment to offering major works in their entirety. To Charlotte Brontë's *Jane Eyre* and Kate Chopin's *The Awakening,* both included complete, we have added a third novel, *Quicksand,* by Nella Larsen. We offer a wealth of complete longer prose fictions—Aphra Behn's *Oroonoko,* Eliza Haywood's *Fantomina,* Maria Edgeworth's *The Grateful Negro,* Jane Austen's *Love and Freindship,* George Eliot's *The Lifted Veil,* Rebecca Harding Davis's *Life in the Iron-Mills,* Willa Cather's *Coming, Aphrodite!,* and Carson McCullers's *Ballad of the Sad Café.* Drama has been similarly strengthened. To Susan Glaspell's pioneering *Trifles* and Caryl Churchill's innovative *Top Girls,* we add Margaret Edson's powerful and poignant full-length play, *Wit.* Longer verse selections include new versions of two narratives by Marie de France, translated by Dorothy Gilbert into rhymed octosyllabics especially for this volume, along with a number of complete long poems or poem cycles—notably Christina Rossetti's *Goblin Market,* H. D.'s "The Master," Edna St. Vincent Millay's *Sonnets from an Ungrafted Tree,* Muriel Rukeyser's "Käthe Kollwitz," Gwendolyn Brooks's "The Sundays of Satin-Legs Smith," Sylvia Plath's "Bee" sequence, and Marilyn Hacker's "Ballad of Ladies Lost and Found."

Taking into account the suggestions of countless teachers and students who used the anthology in many different educational settings, we have strengthened the representation of many "classic" or "standard" women writers. In some cases, we replaced earlier selections with more resonant texts; we now offer, for example, new prose works by such widely read authors as Elizabeth Gaskell, Louisa May Alcott, Sarah Orne Jewett, Mary E. Wilkins Freeman, Jean Rhys, Grace Paley, Nadine Gordimer, and Edna O'Brien. In other instances, we expanded representation of key authors such as Anne Bradstreet, Charlotte Smith, Frances Burney, Dorothy Wordsworth, Fanny Fern, George Eliot, Frances E. W. Harper, Charlotte Perkins Gilman, Charlotte Mew, Marianne Moore, Stevie Smith, Elizabeth Bishop, Margaret Walker, Ruth Stone, Judith Wright, Gwendolyn Brooks, Maxine Kumin, Adrienne Rich, Lucille Clifton, Eavan Boland, Rita Dove, and Louise Erdrich.

Section-by-Section Revisions

We have continued to organize these diverse writings chronologically, for we still believe that although conventional literary periodization does not always suit women's aesthetic past, the history of women's literary traditions does have significant historical phases of its own. Thus, here as in earlier editions, we have for the most part omitted references to the usual literary "ages" (i.e., Augustan, Romantic, Victorian) and instead have organized our authors by birth date into six eras, which our period introductions discuss in a way that makes clear the historical and thematic coherence of the material within each section. Since all of these periods are so dramatically affected by the manifold literary "traditions in English" that we represent, it will be useful to summarize the additions to each section, as well as to highlight the scope of each volume in the new two-volume format.

Volume 1

Literature of the Middle Ages and the Renaissance. Included for the first time are Marie de France's influential rhymed romances "Bisclavret" and "Yönec," in Dorothy Gilbert's lively and accessible new translations; Anne Askew's famous Newgate ballad; Martha Moulsworth's "Memorandum"; and Rachel Speght's passionate polemic against "Melastomus," the "cynical baiter of and foul-mouthed barker against Eve's sex." In addition, we have significantly expanded and enriched our representation of Julian of Norwich and Margery Kempe.

Literature of the Seventeenth and Eighteenth Centuries. Prose offerings newly include Sarah Kemble Knight's seventeenth-century "Journal of the Journey from Boston to N.Y.," and Judith Sargent Murray's polemic "On the Equality of the Sexes." Verse offerings have been greatly strengthened with the addition of eight new poets—Anne Ingram, Mary Leapor, Lucy Terry, Mary Alcock, Hannah More, Sarah Wentworth Morton, Helen Maria Williams, and Joanna Baillie—as well as expanded selections for Katherine Philips, Aphra Behn, Charlotte Smith, Lady Mary Wortley Montagu, and Phillis Wheatley.

Literature of the Nineteenth Century. This section has been enriched by three new poets whose popularity in their era gives them crucial historical importance: Felicia Hemans, Letitia Elizabeth Landon ("L.E.L"), and Adah Isaacs Menken. New prose works include Elizabeth Gaskell's "The Old Nurse's Story" and George Eliot's "Silly Novels by Lady Novelists," which highlights the conflicting forces that shaped the literary marketplace in which women poets and "lady novelists" were gaining ground in this period. New selections by Fanny Fern ("Blackwell's Island") and Louisa May Alcott ("How I Went Out to Service") offer insights into the lives of working-class women in the era; and expanded selections by Harriet Jacobs and Frances E. W. Harper facilitate the study of race relations and literary representation. Finally, the texts for Emily Dickinson poems are now those of the newly established Franklin edition, with the Johnson numbering retained for reference.

Turn-of-the-Century Literature. Major additions here include works by two African American writers: the theorist of education Anna Julia Cooper and the pioneering novelist, playwright, and journalist Pauline E. Hopkins. A diverse group of new poets has been newly added: the American Sarah

Morgan Bryan Piatt, the Victorian Augusta Webster, and the collaborative couple known as "Michael Field" (Katherine Harris Bradley and Edith Emma Cooper). Other, equally striking additions are two poets in the Jewish traditions—the American Emma Lazarus and the English Amy Levy—and the Native Canadian Pauline Johnson, a poet and writer of fiction.

Volume 2

Early-Twentieth-Century Literature. A new centerpiece of this section is Nella Larsen's eminently teachable short novel *Quicksand.* Larsen is joined by two other important new fiction writers: the Asian American writer Sui Sin Far (Edith Maud Eaton), and the British writer Charlotte Mew (hitherto represented only by poetry), as well as new fiction by Jean Rhys. In addition, the section includes the American poet-activist Genevieve Taggard, the Irish novelist and travel writer Kate O'Brien, and the American poet-critic Laura Riding—long absent because of her theoretical stance against anthologies, but now represented by verse and by the brilliant prose monologue "Eve's Side of It."

Later-Twentieth-Century and Contemporary Literature. As the table of contents moves toward the present moment, richly diverse writers of "global English" proliferate: the Jamaican poets Louise Bennett and Lorna Goodison, the aboriginal Australian poet Oodgeroo Noonuccal (Kath Walker), the American Israeli artist Shirley Kaufman, the Italian American Beat Generation writer Diane di Prima, the African American feminist June Jordan, the Dominican American writer Julia Alvarez, the Canadian experimentalist Anne Carson, the Irish poet Medbh McGuckian, the Guyanese-born British writer Grace Nichols, the Native American poet Joy Harjo, the Chinese American novelist and short story writer Gish Jen, the Italian American poet Kim Addonizio, the Chicana writers Sandra Cisneros and Helen María Viramontes, the Asian American poet Marilyn Chin, the British poet Carol Ann Duffy, the Irish poet Paula Meehan, the British writer of lesbian fiction Jeanette Winterson, the American playwright Margaret Edson, the Scottish poet Jackie Kay, and the Indian American short story writer Jhumpa Lahiri. Included for the first time, these artists help us foreground both the vitality and the variety of recent achievements by contemporary literary women, whose global English radiates around the world, as if to support the claim made by Julia Alvarez in her witty "Bilingual Sestina" that not everything gets said in the supposed mainstream of "snowy, blue-eyed, gum-chewing English."

The geographic diversity above is matched by the greater diversity of genres, including science fiction and fantasy by James Tiptree Jr. (Alice Sheldon) and Octavia Butler, the experimental poetry of Lyn Hejinian, and Toni Morrison's influential critical essay "Unspeakable Things Unspoken." This section also looks afresh at many widely taught women writers, offering revised and expanded selections for Stevie Smith, Elizabeth Bishop, Ruth Stone, Carolyn Kizer, Maxine Kumin, Adrienne Rich, and Rita Dove, as well as newly anthologized stories by Mavis Gallant, Grace Paley, Nadine Gordimer, Janet Frame, A. S. Byatt, and Anita Desai.

Of course, no anthology can pretend to completeness. Editors inevitably find themselves unable to trace the ongoing evolution of every literary movement and tradition. In addition, permissions problems sometimes lead to the

exclusion of important texts, as do space limitations. Thus we regret that inability to secure permission or financial constraints have made it impossible to reprint certain works we very much wanted, among them Virginia Woolf's *A Room of One's Own*, Adrienne Kennedy's play *A Movie Star Has to Star in Black and White*, and Toni Morrison's novel *The Bluest Eye*. Finally, we regret that we have not had room to include texts by countless women writers whose achievements we much admire. We are convinced, however, that the texts we have chosen will expand the contours of the canon. In addition, we continue to believe that whatever the subject, form, or provenance of our anthology's texts, we here reprint works whose historical, intellectual, or aesthetic significance clearly merits their inclusion.

Editorial Procedures

Adopting editorial procedures that have proved helpful in other Norton anthologies, we have in every case used what seemed to us the most accurate texts. In some instances, in order to make a work more easily accessible to the reader, we have modernized spelling and Americanized punctuation; otherwise, the spelling and punctuation of our texts is that of their authors or— as in the case of, say, Emily Brontë or Emily Dickinson—their best editors. After every selection we have indicated the date of first periodical or book publication (and, when appropriate, the date of a revised printing) on the right; whenever the facts are available, we have also indicated the date of composition on the left. Difficult allusions, foreign phrases, unfamiliar idioms, and arcane words have been glossed in annotations, many newly revised and expanded in this edition, at the bottom of the page. Whenever we found it necessary to present a text only in part, we have indicated internal cuts by three asterisks and prefaced the title of the work by the word "from." If we have supplied our own title for an excerpt, that title is enclosed in square brackets. Selected Bibliographies, extensively updated for this edition, are provided at the end of each volume to encourage and expedite further reading and research by students. Prepared by Deborah Kennedy, Saint Mary's University, and drawn by Adrian Kitzinger, three new endpaper maps, highlighting places of importance to women writers in the British Isles and North America and to women writers in English worldwide, provide a useful visual reference to the anthology's emphasis on global English literature. Finally, we have adopted a bolder typeface and redesigned the page, so as to make the text more readable.

We have tried to compose (and revise) headnotes and period introductions that are as lucid and informative as possible, providing necessary historical and biographical background without interposing our own critical interpretations between the reader and the text. Following our usual collaborative procedures, each of the two editors drafted approximately half of the headnotes, then exchanged and helped revise the drafts of the other editor. Two period introductions—those on the Literature of the Middle Ages and the Renaissance and on Later-Twentieth-Century and Contemporary Literature—originally written collaboratively, were revised separately, while the other period introductions were composed individually, then exchanged and revised: Susan Gubar drafted the introductions to the Seventeenth and Eighteenth Centuries and Turn-of-the-Century Literature, and revised the introduction to Later-Twentieth-Century and Contemporary Literature; Sandra

Gilbert drafted the introductions to Literature of the Nineteenth Century and Early-Twentieth-Century Literature, and revised the introduction to the Literature of the Middle Ages and the Renaissance.

Additional Resources

Following the model of several other Norton anthologies, the Third Edition introduces a two-volume format that has been welcomed by instructors and students for its flexibility and portability. The two-volume set accommodates the many instructors who use the anthology in a one-semester survey; it also opens up possibilities for using the individual volumes 1 or 2 for a variety of courses organized by period or topic, at levels from introductory to advanced.

Two new features give instructors even more flexibility: first, the publisher is making available the full list of 180 Norton Critical Editions, including the most frequently assigned novels—among them, Jane Austen's *Pride and Prejudice* and *Emma*, Mary Shelley's *Frankenstein*, Emily Brontë's *Wuthering Heights*, Edith Wharton's *The House of Mirth*, and Jean Rhys's *Wide Sargasso Sea*—to be packaged with the two-volume Third Edition, or either individual volume, for a low supplemental cost. Students thus can receive an authoritative, carefully annotated text accompanied by rich contextual and critical materials.

Second, in response to the call from adopters for more critical and theoretical texts, we have collaboratively edited a new companion reader, *Feminist Literary Theory and Criticism: A Norton Reader*. The *Reader*, the first anthology to trace the historical evolution of feminist writing about literature in English from the Middle Ages to the twenty-first century, includes more than one hundred writers in its three-part structure: Part 1, "Women Writers: On Writing," spans six centuries of historical documents (by 45 writers) about female literary creativity—from Christine de Pizan to Eavan Boland. Part 2, "Theory: On Gender and Culture," which focuses on the theoretical debates in the half century since Simone de Beauvoir articulated the idea of "alterity" in 1949, includes selections by 42 scholars and theorists. Part 3, "Practice: Representative Readings and Analyses," gathers contemporary critical interpretations of key literary works in six mini-casebooks: On Medieval Women, On Aphra Behn's *Oroonoko*, On Charlotte Brontë's *Jane Eyre*, On Emily Dickinson, On the Harlem Renaissance, and On Sylvia Plath. The mini-casebooks have been tailored to be integrated with central texts and authors in *The Norton Anthology of Literature by Women*. Flexibly designed both to aid instructors who want to integrate more criticism and theory into their literature survey and to serve as a core text for feminist theory and criticism courses, this reader may be packaged with the anthology at a substantial discount to students or ordered on its own.

With the Third Edition of *The Norton Anthology of Literature by Women*, the publisher expands its already extensive online resource—Norton Literature Online (wwnorton.com/literature)—the gateway to all of the outstanding literature resources available from Norton. Students will find there a deep and broad array of general resources, among them a glossary of literary terms, advice on writing about literature and using MLA documentation style, study aids and quizzes, an author portrait gallery featuring 400 authors, more than 100 maps, and over 90 minutes of recorded readings and musical selections. Access to Norton Literature Online is free with the password included in each new copy of the anthology.

With their passwords, students also gain access to a site specifically developed to support *The Norton Anthology of Literature by Women*. This website will feature six online topics focusing on cultural and literary contexts of the works in the anthology. Each cluster illuminates a key cultural or literary development by providing a tightly cohesive group of texts and images, annotated web links, and questions for writing and discussion.

Teaching with The Norton Anthology of Literature by Women: *A Guide for Instructors,* Third Edition, by Laura Runge, University of South Florida, has been reconceived and rewritten virtually from beginning to end to reflect the new scholarship and new approaches (cultural studies, colonial/postcolonial, psychoanalytic, etc.) to teaching women's literature; it also offers inventive, carefully developed suggestions for organizing thematic and genre-based courses. This guide is a more practical, easy-to-use reference than past versions; its author/work entries include an introductory teaching hook, a quick read section, teaching suggestions, and discussion questions and projects or research ideas. Teaching links between the anthology and the reader are highlighted throughout. A selected bibliography completes the guide.

We began these prefatory remarks with references to Emily Dickinson's tribute to Elizabeth Barrett Browning and Virginia Woolf's pioneering essay on women and fiction; we want to now acknowledge our deep intellectual indebtedness to the hundreds of teachers worldwide who have for the past several decades responded to Woolf's impassioned explanation that "we think back through our mothers if we are women" by laboring to recover the female literary inheritance that we have attempted to reconstitute here. For these additions, we are indebted not just to new scholarship but also to the suggestions of countless teachers and students who have used the earlier editions of the anthology in many different educational settings. To be more specific about our methods: through questionnaires completed by a broad range of colleagues, we ascertained which texts, because infrequently assigned, could be replaced by others in greater demand.

We have included a separate list of acknowledgments in which we thank the many teachers, critics, and scholars who prepared detailed critiques of our material, offered special textual suggestions, and took time to respond to the detailed questionnaire. Their ideas—like our own—seem to us to be a part of a larger and ongoing collective enterprise on the part of countless researchers to whom we must all be profoundly grateful.

We also want to express our gratitude to a number of research and secretarial assistants, institutions, colleagues, friends, and relatives whose aid facilitated our work on this edition. Specifically, we thank Jamie Horrocks, Augustus Rose, and Julie Wise for invaluable research assistance. A number of readers and reviewers helped us with suggestions, including Alison Booth, Mary Favret, Susan Fraiman, Linda Gardiner, Marilyn Hacker, Tricia Lootens, Deidre Lynch, Andrew Miller, Celeste Schenck, Hollis Seamon, and Yung-Sing Wu. At W. W. Norton, Annie Abrams, Eileen Connell, Lory Frenkel, Rivka Genesen, Neil Ryder Hoos, Debra Morton Hoyt, Benjamin Reynolds, Nancy Rodwan, and Catherine Spencer were consistently helpful. As always, moreover, we are grateful to our home institutions—the University of California, Davis, and Indiana University—for financial and secretarial support. In addition, we wish to thank a number of colleagues and friends— Joanna Feit Diehl, Dorothy Gilbert, Kenneth Gros Louis, Kieran Setiya, Mary Jo Weaver—for advice and assistance. Sandra Gilbert wishes to thank

the University of California, Davis, Humanities Institute and the Bogliasco Foundation for research and secretarial support; Susan Gubar would like to thank the Indiana University Distinguished Professors' fund for similar support, as well as Dean Kumble Subbaswamy and the College Arts and Humanities Institute. And we are as usual grateful to members of our innermost circles: our children—Roger, Katherine, and Susanna Gilbert and Marah and Simone Gubar—and our life companions—David Gale and Donald Gray.

Finally, though, our greatest debt is to several co-workers who in some sense helped author this book. Alice Falk's meticulous and scrupulous scholarship facilitated wise and detailed revisions of our annotations. Julia Reidhead's unflagging enthusiasm, support, and guidance buoyed us up at even our rockiest moments and made much of our work a great pleasure. The perpetually sagacious example of M. H. Abrams, Class of 1916 Professor Emeritus at Cornell and adviser on Norton anthologies, offered us a continual model of pedagogical and critical good sense. And perhaps most important of all, the late John Benedict, our first editor at Norton, continued to function (the way he always did) as a kind of muse whose spirit hovered over and sustained this project. His editorial expertise and personal brilliance inspired whatever was best in the First Edition, and it is to his memory that we rededicate our work on this Third Edition of *The Norton Anthology of Literature by Women*.

Acknowledgments

Among our many advisers and friends, the following were of special help in providing critiques of particular periods: Carolyn Dinshaw (New York University); Tricia Lootens (University of Georgia); Anne Mellor (University of California, Los Angeles); and Ruth Perry (MIT). We would also like to express appreciation to the teachers who provided reviews: Antoinette M. Aleccia (Montgomery College); Sharon Anthony (Montgomery College); Phyllis Ballata (Century College); Paula Barbour (Florida State University); Maria Belen Bistue (University of California, Davis); Perle Besserman (Illinois State University); Elyse M. Blankley (California State University–Long Beach); Suzanne Bost (Southern Methodist University); Paula R. Buck (Florida Southern College); Anne Charles (University of New Orleans); Nora Chase (Kingsboro Community College); Linda Daigle (Houston Community College); Michelle M. Davidson (Ivy Tech Community College–Columbus); Ron Di Constanzo (Long Beach City College); Angela Di Pace (Sacred Heart University); Regina Dilgen (Palm Beach Community College–Lake Worth); Cynthia Doherty (Harrisburg Area Community College); Helen Dunn (Sonoma State University); Nancy Fitzgerald (College of St. Scholastica); Katie Freeman (West Virginia Northern Community College); Cynthia Huff (University of Oklahoma); Norma Gillespie (Seminole State College); Christine Goold (Fort Lewis College); Pam Hardman (Western Washington University); Kathy Hickok (Iowa State University); Ondee Lerman Israel (Pace University); Nancy E. Johnson (SUNY—New Paltz); Dana Kinnison (University of Missouri); Diane Krantz (Weber State University); Ausra Kubilius (Southern New Hampshire University); Winifred Moranville (Simpson College); Rachel Nash (University of the Cariboo, British Columbia); Ann Norton (Saint Anselm College); Ellen Peel (San Francisco State University); Cathy Peppers (Idaho State University); Cathy Preston (University of Colorado); Jeanne M. Purdy (University of Minnesota–Morris); Lisa Robson (Brandon University, Manitoba); Deborah Sarbin (Clarion University); Bonnie Kime Scott (San Diego State University); Kathryn L. Seidel (University of Central Florida); Judy Slagle (East Tennessee State University); Marie Trevino (Michigan State University); Linda Wagner-Martin (University of North Carolina, Chapel Hill); Mary Katherine Wainwright (Manatee Community College); Kari Winter (University of Vermont); Teresa Winterhalter (Armstrong Atlantic State University); Yung-Hsing Wu (University of Louisiana at Lafayette); Sharon Yang (Worcester State College); and Bonnie Zimmerman (San Diego State University).

Acknowledgments

Among our many advisors and friends, the following were of special help in providing critiques of particular periods: Carmen Dinshaw (New York University), Zoë Carens (University of Georgia), Anne Walker (University of California, Los Angeles), and Ruth Perry (MIT). We would also like to express appreciation to the teachers who provided reviews: Antonema M. Nicola (Montgomery College), Sharon Arlinton (Montgomery College), Phyllis Ballata (Century College), Paula Barbour (Florida State University), Marti Reker Brame (University of California, Davis), Rene Bessaman (Illinois State University), Elyse M. Blankley (California State University, Long Beach), Suzanne Barr (Southern Methodist University), Paula R. Buck (Florida Southern College), Anne Charles (University of New Orleans), Nora Chase (King's Son Community College), Linda Diffile (Houston Community College), Michelle A. Daveston (DeTech Community College – Calumatus), Ron DiCostanzo (Long Beach City College), Angela D. Pace (Sawell Heart University), Reethal Dijon (Palm Beach Community College), Aaron Worth (Cinna Deberry (Harrisburg Area Community College), Helen Doern (Sonoma State University), Nancy Fitzgerald (College of St. Scholastica), Kate Freeman (West Virginia Northern Community College), Cynthia Hall (University of Oklahoma), Normie Gillespie (Seminole State College), Christine Gould (Front Lewis College), Pam Hardman (Western Washington University), Karin Hitchin (Iowa State University), Index Lennon Kinel (Pace University), Amy D. Johnson (SUNY – New Paltz), Dana Knighten (University of Missouri), Diane Krantz (Weber State University), Ason Lubitza (Southern New Hampshire University), Winifred Morgan (Ill. Skippan College), Rachel Nash (University of the Cariboo, British Columbia), Ann Ronan (Saint Anselm College), Ellen Peel (San Francisco State University), Cathy Peppers (Idaho State University), Cathy Preston (University of Colorado), Jeanne M. Purdy (University of Minnesota–Morris), Lisa Robson (Brandon University, Manitoba), Deborah Schein (Clarion University), Roppie Kline Scott (San Diego State University), Kathryn L. Seidel (University of Central Florida), Judy Slagle (East Tennessee State University), Maria Trevino (Michigan State University), Linda Wagner-Martin (University of North Carolina, Chapel Hill), Mary Suburbia Wainwright (Manatee Community College), Scott Winter (University of Vermont), Texas Wittreich (Texas Wittreich (Florida Atlantic State University), Ying-Hsiu Wu (University of California at Edwarten, Shinon), and (Worcester State College) and Bonnie Zimmerman (San Diego State University).

The Norton Anthology
of Literature by Women

THIRD EDITION
VOLUME 1
THE MIDDLE AGES
THROUGH THE TURN OF THE CENTURY

Literature of the Middle Ages and the Renaissance

MEDIEVAL AND RENAISSANCE HISTORY

The years that historians define as the Old English period, the Middle Ages, and the Renaissance constitute a time of important literary activity. From the first half of the eighth century, when scholars speculate that the great Anglo-Saxon epic called *Beowulf* was composed, to the years between 1386 and 1400, when Geoffrey Chaucer wrote his *Canterbury Tales,* to 1603, when Shakespeare's *Hamlet* was first printed in London, these ages produced a number of classics. Besides *Beowulf,* the Old English era saw the composition of such major poems as "The Dream of the Rood" and "The Wanderer." In the Middle Ages, besides the *Canterbury Tales,* artists created courtly romances such as *Sir Gawain and the Green Knight* (1374–1400), dream visions such as *Piers Plowman* (ca. 1372–89), and religious dramas, including *The Second Shepherd's Play* (ca. 1425) and *Everyman* (after 1485). Finally, the Renaissance years that fostered Shakespeare's astounding creativity also developed the talents of such poets as Edmund Spenser (*The Faerie Queene,* 1590, 1596, 1609), Christopher Marlowe (*Doctor Faustus,* 1604, 1616), Sir Philip Sidney (*Arcadia,* 1590, 1593), Thomas Wyatt, and Ben Jonson. It is significant, however, that most of the writers who flourished in these periods were men. When we turn to the literary history of women in these nine hundred years, we find no texts in the Old English period that have been definitively identified as composed by women, few by medieval women, and—in comparison to the great wave of male-authored texts produced in this period—comparatively few by Renaissance women.

The female writers whose works we include here suggest the kinds of women whose words have been preserved. Women's literature in Middle English is represented by just four somewhat shadowy figures: a mysterious Anglo-Norman aristocrat who composed compelling, versified romances (Marie de France), a religious recluse (Julian of Norwich), an eccentric preacher (Margery Kempe), and an enigmatic author of hunting and fishing handbooks, possibly a prioress (Juliana Berners), whose authorship has been intermittently disputed over the centuries. More prolific and better known, Renaissance women of letters are exemplified by nine complex and diverse figures. The most prominent among these were powerful aristocrats or in some way associated with the court: the poet, polemicist, and Protestant martyr Anne Askew, daughter of an old Lincolnshire family who shared her spiritual convictions with her friend and associate Katherine Parr, the wife of Henry VIII; Elizabeth I, the charismatic queen after whom the English Renaissance is named the "Elizabethan period"; Mary Sidney Herbert,

1

countess of Pembroke, the learned sister of the famous poet Sir Philip Sidney; Aemilia Lanyer, the bohemian wife of a court musician, whose patroness was the countess of Cumberland; Elizabeth Carey, the defiantly Catholic wife of a high-ranking nobleman; and Lady Mary Wroth, a niece of Mary Sidney Herbert and Sir Philip Sidney. By birth and breeding, all six had unusual access to education along with a sense of authority that contemporary society suppressed in most women. As for the other figures in our Renaissance grouping, these women too were arguably privileged in special ways. As the sister of a middle-class lawyer-poet, the witty Isabella Whitney moved in a supportively literary atmosphere; the pioneering feminist autobiographer Martha Moulsworth expressed pride in her genteel birth along with her father's status as an Oxford tutor; and the polemicist Rachel Speght was the well-educated daughter of a London minister.

What were the female contemporaries of these writers doing? We know of other medieval Englishwomen connected with the court who also made notable literary contributions. Dame Eleanor Hull (ca. 1394–1460) and Lady Margaret Beaufort (1443–1509), for instance, both produced translations of devotional texts. Dame Eleanor, whose father and husband served the royal family, translated a thirteenth-century French commentary on the Psalms as well as a French collection of prayers and meditations. Lady Margaret, the mother of Henry VII and grandmother of Henry VIII, rendered into English book 4 of the famous *Imitation of Christ*, a spiritual guide attributed to the medieval philosopher Thomas à Kempis (1380–1471), along with a pious work titled *The Mirror of Gold*. In addition, we know that a number of other wellborn medieval women were sufficiently literate to read and write letters, some of which are included in the cache of fifteenth-century documents, now known as the Paston Letters, that originally belonged to a family of Norfolk gentry. It has been speculated, moreover, that many anonymous medieval texts were authored by women who chose not to sign their works. "Anon. . . . was often a woman," proclaimed Virginia Woolf in 1929, as she mused on the rich horde of ballads and tales whose creators have never been identified. But even some spiritual meditations—such as the early-fifteenth-century vision of the afterlife known as "A Revelation Showed to a Holy Woman"—appear to have had female authors whose names have not been preserved.

When the Renaissance brought a newly secular interest in art and learning to England, increasing numbers of literary women took up their pens to write either for private circulation in aristocratic circles or, less often, for publication. The contemporaries of our Renaissance writers included such figures as the polemicist Jane Anger (fl. 1589) and such moralists as Elizabeth Grymeston (ca. 1563–1603) and Elizabeth Jocelin (1595–1622). Yet even in this more liberal period, the situation of most women was not conducive to creativity. In the words of the scholar Elaine Beilin, the "legal, theological and familial subjugation" of Renaissance women had "an inhibiting effect on women writers." As in the Middle Ages, most lived severely private lives in which, confined to the home—whether farm, castle, or convent—and constrained by cultural definitions of femininity, they had neither the experience of public life nor the expectation of an audience that would foster composition. As in the Middle Ages, too, it is likely that a number of the works women did produce were not thought worth saving, while others have

been handed down to us anonymously or in some cases, if saved, have not yet been discovered in the attics, abbeys, and libraries where they may still be stored. Finally, as some contemporary critics—among them Margaret Ezell and Laurie Finke—have incisively noted, our current model of "authorship" is derived from literary histories that began, from the eighteenth century onward, to trace publications in a commercial marketplace, but such a model is ill-suited to the literary circles in which more early women writers may have flourished than we have until quite recently realized.

Despite these caveats, however, it is notable that the medieval and Renaissance authors whose works we include here were all in one way or another spiritually or socially exceptional. Julian of Norwich, for instance, was a solitary visionary. Margery Kempe was impelled by inner voices to rebel against social conventions. Anne Askew was a Protestant rebel whose death at the stake was a newsworthy martyrdom that became a subject of ballads, sermons, and a widely circulated woodcut. Elizabeth I was England's most learned queen. Mary Sidney Herbert was the extraordinarily well-educated and wealthy patroness of many Elizabethan intellectuals, as was her niece, Mary Wroth. Isabella Whitney and Elizabeth Cary were among the very first Englishwomen to attempt composition in the genres of lyric poetry and verse tragedy, which had long been exclusively masculine preserves, and some scholars speculate that Aemilia Lanyer may actually have been the flirtatiously independent "dark lady" of Shakespeare's sonnets. Atypical in both education and intellectual authority, these women responded to spiritual movements and historical events about which most of their female counterparts were, at least publicly, silent.

Those events included a series of major political upheavals, a set of drastic social changes, and a dramatic succession of cultural transformations. Among the forces shaping early English history had been the fifth-century invasion of the country by the Germanic tribes of the Angles, the Saxons, and the Jutes as well as the eleventh-century conquest of the island by French (Norman) invaders, an event that brought Marie de France to England. The Anglo-Saxon language in which the heroic saga *Beowulf* is written had metamorphosed, because of the Norman conquest, into a range of French-influenced dialects called Middle English, dialects in which such major works as *Sir Gawain and the Green Knight, Piers Plowman,* and *The Canterbury Tales* were composed. As English evolved, moreover, it became an ever more viable alternative to the Latin that had long been used by chroniclers, theologians, and poets to signify the seriousness of their work. In particular, it became a language in which women such as Julian and Margery, who would probably never have studied Latin, could record their visions and lives.

But the lives that these women recorded must also have been determined by the shift from an essentially tribal Anglo-Saxon culture to a hierarchical society organized around a so-called feudal system in which serfs (peasants) swore loyalty to vassals (knights and landowners), who, in turn, pledged their allegiance to great lords, as well as by the slow disintegration of that system with the rise to power of a literate, mercantile, town-dwelling middle class. In addition, the lives of Julian and Margery (as well as the career of the woman known as Juliana Berners) must have been marked by the cultural centrality of the Roman Catholic Church, which increasingly dominated

English life and letters after the seventh-century conversion of the Anglo-Saxons to Christianity. Julian's mystical revelations were part of a long medieval tradition of spiritual meditations, while Margery's individualistic preachings reflect a tumultuous moment in Church history—a moment when a number of revolutionary monastic orders arose throughout Europe, demanding spiritual reform.

Even more than Marie, Julian, and Margery, the Renaissance authors included here were involved in crucial political, social, and cultural events. Indeed, Elizabeth I not only was shaped by such events but shaped them herself. By the time Elizabeth came to the throne, the Middle English of Julian and Margery had developed into something much closer to modern English, and as England was unified by Elizabeth's rule, the divergent dialects of the Middle Ages began to be consolidated into a single national language, laying the groundwork for the emergence of a national literature. Before Elizabeth's accession, moreover, the country, earlier divided by the fifteenth-century War of the Roses (which set the great houses of York and Lancaster against each other in a battle for the throne), had begun to be unified by two Tudor monarchs, Henry VII and Henry VIII. The most magnetic of the Tudor rulers, Elizabeth completed the transformation of what had been a comparatively fragmented feudal society into a centralized nation-state dominated by a single royal court. It was this court that facilitated literary production throughout the English Renaissance, and not insignificantly Mary Sidney Herbert, Aemilia Lanyer, and Mary Wroth were members of intermeshed courtly circles: Wroth was Herbert's niece, and Lanyer dedicated her poems to Herbert (as well as to other aristocrats), while Herbert dedicated hers to Elizabeth.

But these women were not just associated with the centralized authority of the court. Like Cary, they were also learned ladies who had the rare good fortune to be educated in the fashion recommended by the new movement called humanism—that is, they had studied the classics and had been trained in the intricacies of Renaissance rhetoric and logic. Elaborately paradoxical, stylistically ornate, and ingeniously allusive, their verse embodies the humanist passion for polemical skill and classical knowledge that was imported to England from Italy during the sixteenth century by such thinkers as Sir Thomas More, the English author of *Utopia* (1516), and Desiderius Erasmus, the Dutch-born author of *In Praise of Folly* (1509). The lives of these women also coincided with the secularization of culture brought about by humanism's renewal of interest in the pre-Christian classics of Greece and Rome, by the increasing substitution of the vernacular for churchly Latin, by the growing literacy of the non-Latin-speaking middle class, by the new nationalism of the aristocracy, and by the Reformation's questioning of papal power. As the English (Anglican) Church separated itself, on the one hand, from the Rome-dominated international hierarchy of Roman Catholicism and, on the other hand, from the German and Swiss Protestantism established by Luther and Calvin, it developed a distinctive national identity, with the English monarch replacing the pope as a central earthly symbol of sacred authority. This phenomenon, along with the rise of modern English and the dramatic strength of the queen, contributed to an extraordinary cultural vitality that expressed itself in the exuberant energy of Elizabethan literature, an energy that manifests itself in the words and works of all the Renaissance women discussed above.

Nevertheless, although their writings are infused with the energy of the age, these exceptional artists rarely aspired to rival their ambitious male contemporaries. To be sure, Wroth gained notoriety when she produced both a prose romance and a sonnet sequence in the mode of works for which her uncle, Sir Philip Sidney, had become famous, while Cary daringly inscribed a verse tragedy based on a tale told in the first century C.E. by the Jewish historian Josephus. But even such Renaissance aristocrats found themselves alienated and embattled in a culture that discouraged women from composing the kinds of epics, romances, lyrics, comedies, tragedies, and allegories that male poets, dramatists, and prose stylists circulated in manuscripts, staged in the theater, and published to critical acclaim throughout this dauntingly great age of English literature. And although some of the authors included here—notably Mary Herbert and Mary Wroth—moved in strikingly intellectual circles, few can be said to have belonged to literary communities comparable to the loosely organized groups of male writers who supported and encouraged the works of such artists as Marlowe, Shakespeare, and Jonson. That in representing the earliest writings of English women we have had to conflate the Old English era, the Middle Ages, and the Renaissance into a single "early" period is simply the most dramatic sign of women's literary marginality in the years from 700 to 1600. Perhaps further evidence of their aesthetic dilemma is revealed in the themes and dreams recorded by those women who did manage to write. For while the works of these artists mirror the varying spirits of their ages, they are also—no matter when they were written—frequently and distinctively concerned with the problems creativity posed for women, and they may therefore seem idiosyncratic when set against the texts of male contemporaries. Haunted by the images of women that men had constructed for them, these writers created a tradition that seeks either to redefine or to resign itself to male preconceptions about femininity. Specifically, in the years from the 1370s, when Julian began to describe her revelation of divine love in the *Book of Showings,* to the 1590s, when Mary Sidney Herbert undertook to translate the Psalms into English, women had to confront the misogyny of male theologians who sought to censure and silence them as well as an ideal of courtly love that glamorized and glorified them in ways that were sometimes problematic.

MEDIEVAL AND RENAISSANCE IMAGES OF WOMEN

"By God," exclaimed Chaucer's Wife of Bath in a famous passage from *The Canterbury Tales,*

> If wommen hadden writen stories,
> As clerkes han within hir oratories,
> They wolde han writen of men more wikkednesse
> Than al the merk of Adam may redresse.

Afflicted by the book of "wikked wives" from which her fifth husband persistently read to her every evening, this lively female character was responding to the tradition of misogyny that extended from early church fathers such as Saints Paul and Jerome to later theologians such as Augustine and Tertullian; it was, indeed, a tradition that would reach beyond her author's lifetime into the antifemale diatribes of the *Malleus Maleficarum (Hammer of*

Witches, 1486), a fifteenth-century German handbook for witch hunters, into the portrait of the dissembling seductress Duessa in Edmund Spenser's *The Faerie Queene*, and into the punitive subjugation of Kate in William Shakespeare's *The Taming of the Shrew* (1594). While it is clear that no book of "wikked wives" will ever stifle Chaucer's exuberant Wife, such texts may well have inhibited her real-life contemporaries. Though, as we have seen, the two periods were in many ways very different, in the Middle Ages and the Renaissance alike even the most talented literary women were constrained by cultural strictures which implied that any intellectual ambition might mean they were evil. Worse still, such would-be writers had to struggle against gender definitions suggesting that femaleness itself was an intrinsically debased and secondary condition.

Defining woman's essential nature, Tertullian, the third-century philosopher of asceticism, proclaimed that she is a "temple built over a sewer." About women's history and particularly the culpability of Eve, the first woman, whose rebellious eating of forbidden fruit led to the fall of all humanity, the thirteenth-century writer Jacques de Vitry declared: "Between Adam and God in Paradise there was but one woman and she had no rest until she had succeeded in banishing her husband from the garden of delights and in condemning Christ to the torment of the cross." About woman's biological character, the views of the first-century C.E. Roman scholar Pliny the Elder persisted: "Contact with [menstrual fluid] turns new wine sour, crops touched by it become barren[,] . . . the edge of steel and the gleam of ivory are dulled, hives of bees die, even bronze and iron are at once seized by rust, and a horrible smell fills the air." Nor were such views unique to the particular traditions out of which these three thinkers wrote. Anglo-Saxon culture, which predated Christianity in England, was oblivious of or hostile to women. Indeed, one of the few lyrics from this period that scholars have tentatively attributed to a woman—a piece called "The Wife's Lament" (ca. 900)—begins with an impassioned complaint: "I make this song sadly about myself, / about my life. I a woman say / I've been unhappy since I grew up" (translation by Willis Barnstone and Elene Kolb). In *Beowulf*, the age's major epic, moreover, women are objects of exchange, servants to men, monsters, or mothers of monsters. Similarly, the Greek philosopher Aristotle had argued in the fourth century B.C.E. that woman is a "deformity of nature." That pre-Christian definition, taken together with the Bible's excoriation of Eve, informed the work of such major medieval thinkers as St. Augustine and St. Thomas Aquinas, both of whom believed that women were physically and spiritually inferior to men.

But while Eve, the primordial female, was viewed as both secondary (created from Adam's rib) and destructive (a temptress who condemned humanity to death and degradation), she did have a positive counterpart: the mother of Christ, the Virgin Mary, who redeemed the world with the fruit of her womb. It might seem, then, that even though ambitious women were oppressed by what we now call "negative role models," they could gain strength from the sacred example of Mary. From the twelfth century to about the fifteenth, Mariolatry—the cult of the Virgin—swept Europe. As one historian has observed, "her miracles were on every lip" and "provided the stock themes for miracle plays," the festival dramas in which modern English theater had its origins. Indeed, in England, worship of the Blessed Mother seems

often to have taken precedence over devotion to the Father and the Son, so much so that some scholars have seen the adoration of Mary as a lingering remnant of earlier religions that worshipped the Great Goddess. Whatever its origins, Mariolatry gave rise in sermons, songs, plays, and poems to celebrations of the female body and soul that directly controverted contemporary monastic misogyny, works in which even the sin of Eve was justified because it resulted in the sanctity of Mary, mother of the Redeemer of that sin.

A popular Middle English lyric summarized this potentially feminist theory of what has been called the "fortunate fall," the idea that the calamity brought about by Eve's rebellion led to the redemption promised by Mary's sacred maternity:

> Ne hadde the appil take ben
> Ne hadde the appil take ben
> The appil taken ben,
> Ne hadde never our lady
> A ben hevene's quene
> Blessed be the time
> That appil take was
> Therefore we moun singen
> "Deo Gracias!"

Other poems celebrated the paradox of Mary's maidenly motherhood. The lyric that begins "I sing of a maiden / That is makelees" (matchless), for instance, affirms that "moder and maiden / Was nevere noon but she: / Wel may swich a lady / Godes moder be" (mother and maiden—i.e., virgin—was never none but she: well may such a lady God's mother be). Such texts implied that far from being man's inferior, woman, made in Mary's image, might be his superior. As one medieval theologian argued,

> Woman is to be preferred to man, to wit in material: Adam made from clay and Eve from side of Adam; in place: Adam made outside paradise and Eve w'in; in conception: a woman conceived God which a man did not do; in apparition: Christ appeared to a woman after the Resurrection, to wit the Magdalene; in exaltation: a woman is exalted above the choirs of angels, to wit the Blessed Mary. St. Bernadine even declares thus: "It is a great grace to be a woman: more women are saved than men."

What is most noteworthy here is that Mary's grace sanctifies all women, even an ostensibly fallen one such as Christ's disciple the reformed prostitute Mary Magdalene. Thus, though Mary herself may have been unique—"alone of all her sex," as the title of Marina Warner's useful study of Mariolatry has it—even ordinary women are not to be excluded from the queendom of heaven that she rules.

The implications of such a vindication of the female were far-reaching. First, they put in question the presuppositions of antifemale clerics and instigated a dialogue between misogynists like the author of the sardonic French *Quinze joies de mariage* (*The Fifteen Joys of Marriage*, 1480–90) and defenders of women like the Chaucer of *The Legend of Good Women*, a long poem praising female virtue. Second, they even transformed some of the philosophical foundations of Western literature. From Plato on, the European

worldview had been based on what A. O. Lovejoy called the "Great Chain of Being," a hierarchy of the created world that extended from God down through man to woman and then to animals, plants, and stones. With the ascendancy of Mary, however, came a seemingly subversive revision of this system of stratification. For some late medieval writers, it was a mortal woman, a blessed beloved such as Dante's Beatrice or Petrarch's Laura, who mediated between God and the writer in just the way that the immortal Mary mediated between God and man. Influenced by Mariolatry, these artists were also working out of a tradition of courtly love that functioned as a secular counterpoint to the cult of Our Lady. As early as the twelfth century, lyricists called troubadours in France and minnesingers in Germany had begun to praise the elegance and excellence of aristocratic ladies, to whom they swore fealty and dedicated their art. Their poems set a fashion that spread rapidly from the courts of France, Germany, and Italy to the English court and to the great castles of aristocrats in all these nations. Gottfried von Strassbourg's *Tristan*, part 1 of Guillaume de Loris's *Roman de la Rose* (*The Romance of the Rose*), Petrarch's sonnets to Laura, and Dante's *La Vita Nuova* (*The New Life*) marked the culmination of this tradition, which for the first time identified secular desire with spiritual love, the creation of poetry with the consecration of prayer. In *Tristan*, the Cave of Love is a sacred place; in *La Vita Nuova*, Beatrice is an earthly angel; in the *Roman de la Rose*, the rose, representative of the beloved lady, is an emblem of heavenly perfection. For all these poets, and for the knights who followed the fashion they set, love was—in the phrase of the noted medieval historian Eileen Power—"feudalized," for "the lover served his lady as humbly as the vassal served his lord."

Even during the Renaissance, when medieval feudalism had begun to disintegrate, the conventions of courtly love persisted in literature, if not in life. Sir Philip Sidney's prose narrative *Arcadia*, for instance, recounts the romances of knights and ladies in a pastoral realm where the art of love represents an aesthetic ideal, while his sonnet sequence *Astrophil and Stella* (1582) explores the poet-lover's feelings for his mistress on the assumption that such passionate emotions toward a beloved woman were the most appropriate subject for lyric poetry. Influenced by the highly stylized modes and elaborately romantic themes of "Petrarchanism," a literary movement that began in Italy with Petrarch and was brought to England by Sir Thomas Wyatt, Sidney was only one of the many major Renaissance poets who produced such sonnet cycles meditating on the rapture and torment of man's love for woman. Others included Edmund Spenser (*Amoretti*, 1595), Samuel Daniel (*Delia*, 1592), and Shakespeare (*Sonnets*, 1609). In the same years when these writers were composing their celebratory sonnets, moreover, Spenser's *The Faerie Queene* offered images of pure and powerful heroines such as Una, Gloriana, and Britomart. And throughout this period, poets regularly proclaimed their aesthetic indebtedness to the female divinities known as muses, first celebrated as sources of inspiration by the Greek and Roman writers whom many Renaissance poets strove to emulate.

Ennobling and empowering as the rhetoric of Mariolatry, the rhymes of courtly love, the sonnets of Petrarchanism, the allegorical figures of Spenser, and the concept of female muses might seem to have been for women, however, they still retained traces of the very misogyny they would appear to have

replaced. About Mary, after all, one lyric declared "moder and maiden / Was nevere noon but she": no earthly woman could achieve such paradoxical grandeur. As for courtly love, it too posed problems. Highly stylized and abstract, the poet's or knight's service to the lady was often merely lip service, even in literary works that praised her powers. Functioning as muse or mistress, the blessed damsel was usually no more than an object, albeit an object of worship. For the most part, she herself was granted no subjectivity, nor was she often portrayed as engaging in the kinds of heroic deeds that redeemed her lover.

Worse still, embedded in even the most chivalric texts are images of women as monsters and witches: any beautiful lady, these romances hint, may be a sorceress. In the medieval tale of *Sir Gawain and the Green Knight,* for instance, the hero is tested by a temptress whose wiles threaten his destruction and whose charms force him to confront his own mortality. Similarly, the medieval *Tristan* documents Tristan's death at the hands of a false Isolde even while it dramatizes the joys of the Cave of Love, and Sir Thomas Malory's fifteenth-century Arthurian cycle preserves the gestures of chivalry but also traces the way the disintegration of the Round Table is brought about by Queen Guinevere's faithlessness. Witches and bad ladies abound in medieval literature, and they are almost always associated with female sexuality, assertion, and creativity. No wonder, then, that Chaucer has his sexy, assertive, and creative Wife of Bath revise and reverse this association by telling the story of a knight who is tricked into wedding and bedding an aged crone and is rewarded for relinquishing his authority to her when she transforms herself into a beautiful lady.

Though Chaucer's *Wife of Bath's Tale* parodies the courtly romance to reveal its underlying misogyny, the Wife of Bath herself is a character out of another genre, which dwelled more frankly on the defects of women: the fabliau. In fact, this genre makes explicit the misogyny implicit in the courtly romance. Realistic and comic, fabliaux were folktales addressed to a bourgeois audience. Their plots generally turned on the machinations of cuckolding wives and cunning maids, while the resolutions they recommended for men who wanted to tame such shrews ranged from public humiliation to wife beating. At the same time, as Chaucer himself suggests in his envoi to *The Clerk's Tale,* which told the story of a famously submissive heroine called Patient Griselda, some writers implied, perhaps ironically and perhaps not, that women could avoid Griselda's hardships only by becoming savage "as is a tygre yond in Ynde" and, as one translation puts it, "clatter[ing] like a mill . . . to beat the male." Enormously popular throughout the Middle Ages, fabliaux formed the basis of a number of Chaucer's narratives, including *The Miller's Tale* and *The Nun's Priest's Tale,* the first a story of a faithless young wife and the second a tale of a henpecked rooster. Good-humored though they are—in each case the storyteller clearly feels as much sympathy for the wife as for the husband—these tales deflate romantic ideals of love by depicting the female as fleshly, shrewd, earthbound.

In the same way that medieval genres which seemed to praise women covertly implied critiques of femininity and were accompanied by franker treatments of the battle of the sexes in the fabliau, so too Renaissance epics, lyrics, and dramas castigated as well as celebrated key female figures. These writings suggest that below the surface of even the most honorific language

there may frequently be a secret hostility to women. Such heroines of *The Faerie Queene* as Una and Gloriana are shadowed, after all, by the sinister witch appropriately named Duessa, whose lovely facade cracks open to reveal the horror of "her neather parts, the shame of all her kind" as well as, "at her rompe," a "foxes taile, with dong all fowly dight" (decked). To be sure, *The Faerie Queene*'s heroes are often balanced by sinister or villainous male figures, but the evil of those characters is never so specifically associated with sexuality. Similarly, while Shakespeare used idealizing rhetoric to praise both Mr. W. H., who was the "onlie begetter" of his famous sonnet cycle, and the so-called dark lady to whom he also pledged erotic devotion in the cycle, he subverted that rhetoric only when he turned his attention to his mistress's femaleness. In particular, Sonnet 130 ("My mistress's eyes are nothing like the sun") ostensibly praises his beloved, but concedes that her breasts are "dun," her hair is "black wires," and her breath "reeks," while implying that such realistic descriptions should also be applied to many other women who are "belied with false compare"—that is, falsely and foolishly flattered by the metaphoric excesses of poetry.

Finally, for every Shakespeare heroine who is as ingenious and imaginative as Viola in *Twelfth Night* (1601) or as vigorously dutiful as Cordelia in *King Lear* (1606), there is a ferocious figure such as Lady Macbeth in *Macbeth* (1606) and Goneril and Regan in *King Lear*. Of course, Shakespeare's dramas also offer countless examples of villainous male characters: Iago in *Othello* (1603), Edmund in *King Lear*, and so on. But, again, the evil of such men is not usually identified with warped or excessive sexuality. By contrast, women such as Lady Macbeth, Goneril, and Regan are marked by monstrous female ambition or grotesque erotic energy. Lady Macbeth's perversity is manifested at one point by her plea "Come, . . . unsex me here" and at another by her admission that if she had sworn to do so, she would have "plucked" her nipple from her child's "boneless gums / And dashed [its] brains out." Similarly, the voracious lust for power and the sexual insatiability of Goneril and Regan are dramatized not only through their treatment of their aged father but also in their erotic intrigues with the bastard Edmund. Indeed, when in his madness the dispossessed King Lear proclaims that "Down from the waist" even dainty ladies are "Centaurs, / Though women all above. / But to the girdle do the Gods inherit. / Beneath is all the fiend's," his apparently insane misogyny seems ultimately sane in light of his two older daughters' viciousness. What clarifies the assumptions about the proper relations between the sexes that these plays dramatized, moreover, is that even attractively autonomous characters such as Viola in *Twelfth Night* and Rosalind in *As You Like It* (1600) must ultimately be stripped of their independence and brought to acquiesce in a husband's power. All's well that ends well, Shakespeare declared, but to "end well" a woman must, like Viola, become her lord's "mistress and his fancy's queen."

MEDIEVAL AND RENAISSANCE WOMEN'S LIVES

Did Shakespeare's plays reflect the reality of Renaissance women's lives? Did courtly romances mirror the lives of aristocratic medieval ladies, and did fabliaux tell the truth about ordinary women in the Middle Ages? By all

accounts, both Renaissance and medieval texts did and did not record real facts about female experience.

Women's Lives in the Middle Ages

Because feudal society was organized for war, it was essentially a masculine world in which great landlords preserved the integrity of their estates through the rule of primogeniture (the right of the eldest son to inherit property). As the historian Doris Stenton has explained, women generally passed from father to husband, with the age of marital consent for girls usually defined as twelve. Canon law (i.e., church law) permitted and sometimes even encouraged wife beating, while secular as well as religious legal tradition forbade divorce and, except under special circumstances, female ownership of property. Still, although women could not serve as judges, on juries, or in government councils, a widow could obtain some degree of power, for she usually received a third part of her husband's estate, and in 1215 King John promised such widows a measure of freedom from royal authority: they were no longer forced to remarry (as they had been before that year) according to the king's wishes. Yet their daughters continued to be wed at early ages in order to ensure the integrity of important estates, and even grown women could be summarily married off, against their own wishes, unless they could purchase from their feudal lords the right to choose their own husbands.

A number of great ladies did, however, have the power of patronage, a power to elevate poets and knights through financial as well as personal encouragement. From the eleventh century on, aristocratic women commissioned illuminated manuscripts for their own uses. Because they were usually untutored in Latin themselves and because they were often the primary tutors of the next generation, by the end of the Middle Ages such women had been influential in promoting vernacular translations of Latin religious works. As daughters, wives, and mothers, medieval ladies also helped guard their lords' manors, regularly organizing almsgiving, household budgets, clothing, and food for large families and retinues of servants and even, when their men were away, supervising farm affairs, lawsuits, and other estate business.

When a family like the Pastons in Norfolk rose by acquiring large landholdings, their sons were sent to Eton and Oxford and sometimes educated to enter the Inns of Court, while their daughters remained at home. Yet, as the late medieval family documents called the Paston Letters reveal, these fifteenth-century wives and daughters actively concerned themselves with the legal, educational, and moral welfare of their husbands and brothers. Similarly, the wives of middle-class English farmers were responsible for looking after their husbands' stock, making butter and cheese, helping in the fields, and producing cloth for the family from the wool of their own sheep. From the evidence of manorial court records, it is also clear that many widows independently farmed the holdings of their deceased husbands and engaged in litigation on their own behalf. Moreover, country women brewed and sold ale at a profit, while bourgeois and working-class women in towns and cities earned considerable sums of money from two other major home industries—textiles (spinning and weaving) and food production (brewing and baking); wives and so-called *femes sole* (widows and unmarried women)

also sometimes worked as leather sellers, wool merchants, shopkeepers, chandlers, shoemakers, bookbinders, and goldsmiths. Significantly, in 1469 the Crown awarded an annual salary of £10 to the first known English midwife, Margaret Cobbe, and in 1470 she attended the labor of Queen Elizabeth (1437–1483), wife of Edward IV (1442–1483). In addition, documents before 1200 listing needle artists refer almost exclusively to women: men's names did not appear until after 1200, and men began to dominate the lists only after production came to be centered in London. In the early Middle Ages, women were often active members of craft guilds (the counterpart of modern trade unions), but as the era progressed, female workers were less frequently admitted as full members of these organizations.

To be sure, whether the working-class girl was apprenticed at an early age as a child laborer or the aristocratic daughter was given by her father in a marriage that was essentially a business contract, the lives of both women were shaped by a male-controlled socioeconomic system. In addition, their lives were shadowed by the perils of childbearing that began early and ended late, by a high infant mortality rate, and by the never-ending cares of a household that had to be sustained and maintained at great physical cost to the woman. Worse still, the peace of both was frequently threatened by the virulent phenomenon of witch hunting, an activity that became increasingly ferocious between the fourteenth and the seventeenth centuries. The ratio of women to men accused of witchcraft ranged from twenty to one in some parts of Europe to one hundred to one in other areas. Like the Jew, the witch was blamed for social ills that, in the fourteenth century, included the Black Death (the plague) and the Hundred Years' War between England and France. Like the heretic, she was believed to worship strange gods, whose ways would undermine the authority of the established church. In this era, the *Malleus Maleficarum,* mentioned earlier, functioned with great efficiency as a handbook for witch hunters: the scholars Barbara Ehrenreich and Deirdre English have estimated that the total number of women tortured and executed during the period may have climbed into the millions.

It is hardly surprising, therefore, that a significant group of young women took refuge in the church. Some simply turned to prayer or meditation, but others entered convents, where they could educate themselves and tutor the daughters of wealthy families, where they were safe from harassment, and where their administrative as well as intellectual abilities were given scope. Medieval nunneries were usually poorer as well as smaller in number and in population than monasteries. Their official business, especially record keeping, was frequently carried on by male chaplains who were better educated than their female counterparts. Yet these institutions did serve as sanctuaries for the unmarried daughters of the nobility and even of the middle class. A Benedictine nun like the German writer Hrosvitha could pursue a serious literary career within the convent, producing hymns, Latin plays, and saints' lives. Moreover, although by the fifteenth century the nunneries of England were being faulted for worldly frivolity, and although most had in any case never been as powerful as the monasteries, a few had long been bastions of wealth. "If the Abbot of Glastonbury would marry the Abbess of Shaftesbury," observed one wit, "their heir would have more land than the King of England." While to most convents such a statement would not apply, even the poorest medieval nunneries clearly functioned as communities of

women, providing their inhabitants with an autonomy unmatched in the secular world.

Like most medieval women's lives, the lives of nuns are only partially reflected in the images of women that can be drawn from most medieval texts. The ladies to whom troubadours and other courtly poets swore fealty, for instance, did have the power of patronage, but that power was translated in works like *La Vita Nuova*, the *Roman de la Rose*, and *Sir Gawain and the Green Knight* into images of the beloved woman not as a financial investor but as a muse. Similarly, as we have seen, many bourgeois women were as enterprising and inventive as Chaucer's Wife of Bath, but their creative industry was reflected in *The Canterbury Tales'* characterization of a wife whose business is not, say, brewing but matrimony. Finally, a number of nuns did, like Chaucer's Prioress, achieve significant independence in the convent, but few were either as elegant or as frivolous as Chaucer's portrait of that figure might suggest; indeed, far from possessing such emblems of conspicuous consumption as the Prioress's well-fed lapdog and her expensive jewelry, most were obliged to support themselves as "educators" who functioned more as high-class babysitters than as real teachers. Thus, even though literary works did summarize some key contemporary visions of women, social historians must inevitably draw more information from guild records and legal documents than they do from courtly romances and fabliaux. As we will suggest, Renaissance scholars must depend on similar sources to supplement the images they find in plays, prose romances, and sonnet cycles.

Women's Lives in the Renaissance

During the Renaissance, women in England continued to be defined as either *femes sole* (unmarried or widowed women) or *femes covert* ("covered" or married women). Some of those who belonged to the first of these groups might have—as they had had in the Middle Ages—considerable freedom. Aristocratic widows could manage their own property; choose second, third, or fourth husbands; and handle marriage settlements for themselves. Middle-class widows could establish businesses, join guilds, enter into foreign trade, and even, in some cases, sue or be sued. Similarly, some of those who belonged to the second group were also surprisingly independent. Although as *femes covert* they had practically no legal rights, they were often entrusted by their husbands with major responsibilities. As in the Middle Ages, aristocratic wives supervised great estates, including large landholdings, and frequently functioned almost as the business partners of the men to whom they were married. Similarly, middle-class wives—like medieval bourgeoises—often shared in their husbands' mercantile enterprises or oversaw home industries (spinning, weaving, silk making, bookbinding, brewing) that could be quite remunerative.

In fact, the only Renaissance women who may be said to have been entirely without legal, economic, or social power of any kind were young unmarried women, especially girls from wealthy families, who might bring large financial settlements to their future husbands. These girls were frequently pressured or forced by their parents to enter into marriages of convenience to consolidate important estates. Worse still, if they had any property of their own, they were sometimes subject to abduction by unscrupulous adventurers

who would hold them as prisoners until they agreed to marry (and surrender their property). That this problem was no small matter is suggested by the fact that statutes to protect "ladies, gentlewomen, and other women sole" from such treatment were passed in 1453, 1557, and 1597; in that last year, as one historian reports, "maids . . . and widows with property were still being abducted and defiled or forced into marriage."

Of course, as in the Middle Ages, *all* women were enjoined to be submissive and modest in their relations to men. The Renaissance scholar Pearl Hogrefe observes that "Tudor women would have been models of chaste, passive obedience if they had only followed the advice given them in much didactic literature of the sixteenth century." But then, as the same writer also remarks, in this era as in so many others, there was a notable difference between the "ideal" woman and the real woman. Indeed, visiting England in 1592, Frederick, duke of Wirtemberg, wittily declared that "England is a paradise for women, a prison for servants, and a hell or purgatory for horses—for the females have great liberty and are almost like masters." Though ultimately his remark must be considered hyperbolic, he and a few other contemporaries—most notably the Protestant reformer John Knox, author of *The First Blast of the Trumpet against the Monstrous Regiment of Women* (1558)—thought the British Isles had "unnaturally" succumbed to the rule ("regiment") of women because England and Scotland were governed by queens such as Mary Tudor, Mary Stuart, and Elizabeth I, and because a few great ladies had considerable power in courtly circles.

Nevertheless, the average woman very likely did not feel that she lived in a "paradise." It is true that after 1500 a surprising number of aristocratic women began, for the first time, to receive the same kind of education in the classics that their brothers did; the unprecedented training in Greek and Latin that marked the upbringing of such women as Elizabeth I, Mary Sidney Herbert, and Elizabeth Cary was a strong positive consequence of the humanist Sir Thomas More's idea that both sexes were "equally suited for the knowledge of learning by which reason is cultivated." But most girls, even the very well born, received little education. In addition, although many middle-class women did undertake to carry on their own businesses, historians have demonstrated that in the years between 1485 and 1500 the numbers of such women declined drastically. Evidently, the rise of an increasingly ambitious group of male entrepreneurs institutionalized and professionalized work that had previously gone on somewhat informally, so that Renaissance men tended to take over guilds and industries where medieval women had earlier dominated or at least participated on an equal basis.

It should finally be noted that the power wielded by *femes covert* who joined with their husbands in the supervision of estates or businesses depended on the goodwill of the husbands. If a husband was brutal, oppressive, or merely indifferent, his wife had no legal recourse, because she had no rights of her own. Thus, though plays like Shakespeare's *The Taming of the Shrew* or *Twelfth Night* may subtly misrepresent the reality of most women's lives— the first exaggerating the Renaissance ideology of male dominance and the second glamorizing a portrait of female independence followed by an even more romantic vision of female surrender—both contain at least a modicum of truth. Because marriage was a woman's principal goal and the role of wife her primary role, she must always—with the unique exception of Elizabeth,

the "virgin" queen—define herself in relation to men. Given such a self-definition, however, it would be hard indeed for her to gain the intellectual authority required for writing serious works. Not surprisingly, then, even the most learned ladies often assumed secondary positions in relation to literary tradition: talented though they might have been, many became translators (of male texts) and patronesses (of male artists). As we will see, moreover, much female-authored writing adopted at least a surface stance of piety and decorum—in part, perhaps, because any female artist who flouted convention was sharply censured: when Lady Mary Wroth's long but unfinished prose romance *The Countess of Montgomery's Urania* appeared in 1621, it was greeted by a chorus of protest because, as the critic Barbara Lewalski has pointed out, it included disguised references to "scandals and personages of the Jacobean court." Understandably distressed, Lady Mary withdrew the work from circulation. Her decision dramatizes at least one of the more obvious ways in which a female literary career could be discouraged or deformed.

MEDIEVAL AND RENAISSANCE WOMEN WRITERS

Despite the sense of secondariness that had been instilled in so many medieval and Renaissance women, a yearning for a female community, together with a corollary vision of female power, informed much of the literature by women in this period. Such a yearning, for instance, characterized the work of perhaps the most prominent early European feminist, Christine de Pisan (1364–1429), whose *Le Livre de la Cité des Dames* (*The Book of the City of Ladies,* 1405) offered an unprecedented dream vision of a female utopia in which what Renaissance thinkers called "Women Worthies"—great women from all ages and nations—were gathered to prove the worthiness of women.

Participating in an early version of the French debate over femininity that was termed the *Querelle des Femmes* (quarrel about women), Christine assumed equality with male thinkers to contest Jean de Meun's misogynistic continuation (1269–78) of Guillaume de Loris's *Roman de la Rose,* a satire on women's wiles in which Jean scathingly repudiated the courtly humility toward the female Rose that was cultivated by his predecessor, Guillaume. Besides producing her fervent affirmation not just of the rights but also of the achievements of women, the widowed Christine wrote a number of other books and became, as a French scholar has noted, the first female "man of letters" to support herself (along with three children) by her pen. Yet like the writing of so many medieval and Renaissance women, her major feminist treatise was out of print from the sixteenth century to the twentieth. Nevertheless, despite its long neglect, *The City of Ladies* summarized a vision of female power that would also be recorded in various ways by such mystics as Julian of Norwich and Margery Kempe and such secular gentlewomen as Mary Sidney Herbert and Aemilia Lanyer.

Christine had Continental counterparts and descendants in, for instance, the devout Italian poet Vittoria Colonna (1490/92–1547) and the more worldly French sonneteer Louise Labé (1524–1566). But neither they nor the Englishwomen represented here can be said to have had professional literary careers comparable to hers. Whether they were cloistered like Julian

of Norwich, well-off like Margery Kempe, richly married like Mary Sidney Herbert, or precariously attached to the court like Aemilia Lanyer, these women were not in any modern sense "men of letters." On the contrary, several of them—notably Queen Elizabeth and Mary Sidney Herbert, countess of Pembroke—were themselves important literary patronesses. Others, among them Elizabeth Cary and Lady Mary Wroth, also contributed to the production of poetry by financing such male artists as Thomas Nashe, Ben Jonson, and John Donne. Although they wielded some power as patronesses, these English women of letters were almost always economically dependent on church or state. (An exception was Isabella Whitney, a daughter of the minor gentry whose sisters may actually have been in service in London.) Unlike the independent bourgeoise Christine de Pisan, then, most English women writers of the Middle Ages and the Renaissance frequently articulate conventionally submissive attitudes toward woman's "place" in the cultural scheme. As Elaine Beilin observes, "At a time when writing could be considered an inappropriate activity for women, the woman writer early on created a little island for herself in the literary stream by writing pious works." In fact, she argues, "many women took pains . . . to emphasize that they themselves were virtuous—specifically chaste, modest, and obedient—and that women, far from inheriting Eve's penchant for rebellion, were determined to redeem her through virtuous words and deeds." Such conservatism, she continues, "almost guaranteed that most women would not participate in the literary experimentation or secularization carried on by men of the period." Yet a passion not unlike Christine's frequently disrupted the careful decorum that so many of these Englishwomen cultivated. Julian redefined Christ as a mother; Kempe revised the rules of marriage to liberate herself from her husband, as did Askew; Herbert compared Queen Elizabeth to God; Lanyer justified the ways of Eve to man. Cary and Wroth dared to work in genres traditionally associated with the male imagination, while with imperious panache Whitney wittily "bequeathed" the entire city of London to her descendants. Similarly, Moulsworth took her own life story so seriously that she became an innovative autobiographer, and Speght daringly entered into a debate with the misogynistic "Melastomus," whom she reviled as a "foul-mouthed barker against Eve's sex." As for Queen Elizabeth herself, she provided a paradigm of female regality for all her contemporaries, and in her own verse, sparse though it was, she vaunted and flaunted her power, threatening to "poll" the "tops" (cut off the heads) of those who vexed her.

To be sure, all these women were extraordinary and extraordinarily fortunate—a point they themselves generally understood, for most of their female contemporaries had neither a medieval flowering nor a renaissance. If Shakespeare was the common man transformed into Western culture's most uncommon genius, he had no woman counterpart drawn, as he was, from the intellectually ambitious, aspiring middle class. In 1929, Virginia Woolf told us why. Had Shakespeare had a "wonderfully gifted sister," she explained in *A Room of One's Own*, the girl would have been given no education; her parents would have forced her to do dull domestic chores and tried to make her marry young; she would have run away to London, only to be seduced and abandoned by a predatory theatrical entrepreneur; finally, she would have died a suicide, though "the birds that sang in the hedge were not more musical than she was [and s]he had the quickest fancy, a gift like

her brother's, for the tune of words." But for the first sixteen hundred years after Jesus was born to Mary, Queen of Heaven, the tune of words was not fostered in women. Given that for the female imagination the so-called Dark Ages persisted well beyond the male-defined Renaissance, it is impressive enough that an extraordinarily talented set of writers implicitly chose to declare, with Aemilia Lanyer, that "Our mother Eve, who tasted of the tree . . . Was simply good" and therefore to dream, as Lanyer did, that women might "have our liberty again."

MARIE DE FRANCE
fl. 1170?

Ki Deu ad dune escience / E de parler bon' eloquence / Ne s'en deit taiser ne celer, / Ainz se deit volunters mustrer. Or, loosely translated, "To whom God gives intelligence, / And the great gift of eloquence, / Shouldn't hide or silence talent, / But show it and be valiant!" So wrote the mysterious medieval lady of letters known as Marie de France. Yet though Marie appears to have authored a number of compelling romances or "lays" while also translating and refashioning many classical fables, her identity remains a riddle.

This much is known: born in Normandy yet residing for many years in England, fluent in Latin and English as well as her native French, Marie was an aristocrat by blood and breeding who wrote her influential works in the dialect now known as Anglo-Norman. Some scholars, indeed, have speculated that Marie was the powerful abbess of Shaftesbury, who was the illegitimate daughter of Geoffrey of Anjou (1113–1151)—himself the founder of the Plantagenet dynasty of English kings—and therefore also sister of England's Henry II. In any case, whatever her genealogy, this mysterious *romancière* (creator of romances) was cultivated, authoritative, imaginative. And for many years, apparently, she lived in England, where she used the Anglo-Norman dialect to compose much-loved, highly popular tales of courtly love and fantastic catastrophe, tales that were widely read, recited, and imitated throughout her era.

Like her compatriot and contemporary, the famous French poet Chrétien de Troyes (fl. 1170), who wrote such classic romances as *Perceval* and *Erec and Enide*, the enigmatic Marie produced versified accounts of the enchantments and anxieties that surrounded the magical yet troubled court of Arthur, Guinevere, and their fabled knights. Her *lais* were probably transmitted orally rather than through written manuscripts, yet such transmission hardly diminished their popularity. Exploring heroes and heroines in revisionary depth, Marie shows that most of her romance characters are as conflicted as they are courtly: she depicts, with what one critic calls "startling economy," the splendors of the fantastic realm of Arthurian chivalry, along with the gender troubles that beset the genre in which such splendors were sometimes celebrated, sometimes satirized. In "Bisclavret," for instance, she dramatizes the woes (and ultimate triumphs) of a werewolf, while in "Yönec" she sets the tensions of a May-December marriage against a richly textured but problematic fairy-tale background.

Our translations and annotations here have been prepared by the scholar and poet Dorothy Gilbert, whose verse captures the verve and wit of Marie's original Anglo-Norman.

Bisclavret[1]

In Crafting Lays, I won't forget—
I mustn't—that of Bisclavret;
Bisclavret: so named in Breton;
But *Garwaf* in the Norman tongue.[2]

5 One used to hear, in times gone by—
it often happened, actually—
men became werewolves, many men,
and in the forest made their den.
A werewolf is a savage beast;
10 in his blood-rage, he makes a feast
of men, devours them, does great harms,
and in vast forests lives and roams.
Well, for now, let us leave all that;
I want to speak of Bisclavret.

15 In Brittany there lived a lord—
wondrous, the praise of him I've heard—
a good knight, handsome, known to be
all that makes for nobility.
Prized, he was, much, by his liege lord;
20 by all his neighbors was adored.
He'd wed a wife, a worthy soul,
most elegant and beautiful;
he loved her, and she loved him, too.
One thing she found most vexing, though.
25 During the week he'd disappear
for three whole days, she knew not where;
what happened to him, where he went.
His household, too, was ignorant.
He returned home again one day;
30 high-spirited and happy. She
straightway proceeded to inquire:
"My fair sweet friend," she said, "fair sire,
if I just dared, I'd ask of you
a thing I dearly wish to know,
35 except that I'm so full of fear
of your great anger, husband dear."
When he had heard this, he embraced her,

1. Translated and annotated by Dorothy Gilbert. Belief in lycanthropy—the existence of werewolves—was widespread in the Middle Ages, and werewolves figure often in folklore and also in literature: *lais*, romances, fabliaux, and beast fables. Versions of this story appear as early as in 1st-century C.E. Roman works by Pliny (*Natural History*) and Petronius (*The Satyricon*). Marie's story may well have contributed to later versions in the 13th and 14th centuries, such as the *Roman de Reynart le Contrefait*, where the hero is called Bisclarel and the king is Arthur.

2. Alfred Ewert derives the name *bisclavret* from the Breton *bleis lauaret*, "speaking wolf" (*Marie de France, Lais*, 172). Jean Rychner, in his perhaps even more authoritative edition, adds that the form *bisclavret* may derive from *bisc lavret*, which suggests a wolf in pants or breeches, a different human characteristic. He believes *garwaf* (with other variant spellings in the manuscripts) to be probably a scribal misspelling of the familiar *garolf* or *garou*(s), which both ultimately derive from earlier words (Old English, Franconian, Latin) meaning "man-wolf" (*Les Lais de Marie de France*, 252).

drew her to him, clasped and kissed her.
 "Lady," he said, "come, ask away!
40 Nothing you wish, dear, certainly
 I will not tell you, that I know."
 "Faith!" she said, "you have cured me so!
 But I have such anxiety,
 sire, on those days you part from me,
45 my heart is full of pain. I fear
 so much that I will lose you, dear.
 Oh, reassure me, hastily!
 If you do not, I soon will die.
 Tell me, dear husband; tell me, pray,
50 What do you do? Where do you stay?
 It seems to me you've found another!
 You wrong me, if you have a lover!"
 "Lady," he said, "have mercy, do!
 I'll have much harm in telling you.
55 I'd lose your love, if I should tell
 and be lost to myself, as well."
 Now when the wife was thus addressed,
 it seemed to her to be no jest.
 Oftimes she begged, with all her skill,
60 coaxing and flattering, until
 at last he told her all he did,
 the tale entire; kept nothing hid.
 "Dame, I become a bisclavret.
 in the great forest I'm afoot,
65 in deepest woods, near thickest trees,
 and live on prey I track and seize."
 When he had told the whole affair,
 she persevered; she asked him where
 his clothes were; was he naked there?
70 "Lady," he said, "I go all bare."
 "Tell me, for God's sake, where you put your clothes!"
 "Oh, I'll not tell you that:
 I would be lost, you must believe,
 if it were seen just how I live.
75 Bisclavret would I be, forever;
 never could I be helped then, never,
 till I got back my clothes, my own;
 that's why their cache must not be known."
 "Sire," said his lady in reply,
80 "more than all earth I love you. Why
 hide, why have secrets in your life?
 Why, why mistrust your own dear wife?
 That does not seem a loving thought.
 What have I done? What sin, what fault
85 has caused your fear, in any way?
 You must be fair! You have to say!"
 So she harassed and harried him
 So much, he finally gave in.
 "Lady," he said, "just by the wood,

90 just where I enter, by the road,
there's an old chapel. Now, this place
has often brought me help and grace.
There is a stone there, in the brush,
hollow and wide, beneath a bush.
95 In brush and under bush, I store
my clothes, till I head home once more."
 The lady was amazed to hear:
She blushed deep red, from her pure fear.
Terror, she felt, at this strange tale.
100 She thought what means she could avail
herself of how to leave this man.
She could not lie with him again.

 In these parts lived a chevalier
who had long been in love with her.
105 Much did he pray and sue, and give
largesse in service to his love;[3]
she had not loved him, nor had she
granted him any surety
that she, too, loved; but now she sent
110 this knight the news of her intent.
 "Friend," she wrote him, "rejoice, and know
that for which you have suffered so,
I grant you now without delay;
I'll not hold back in any way.
115 My body and my love I grant;
make me your mistress, if you want!"
 Kindly he thanked her, and her troth
accepted; she received his oath.
She told her lover how her lord
120 went to the wood, and what he did,
what he became, once he was there.
She told in detail how and where
to find the road and clothing cache;
and then she sent him for the stash.
125 Thus was Bisclavret trapped for life;
ruined, betrayed, by his own wife.
Because his absences were known,
people assumed he'd really gone,
this time, for good. They searched around,
130 enough, but he could not be found,
for all their inquiries. At last
everyone let the matter rest.
The lady wed the chevalier
who'd been so long in love with her.

3. I.e., the chevalier, doing service to his lady love in the courtly mode, performed acts of generosity (largesse) in honor of her, hoping to exalt his own spirit, be worthy of her, and earn her approval and her love.

135 A whole year, after this event,
thus passed. The king went out to hunt,
went to the forest straightaway,
there where the bisclavret now lay.
The hunting dogs were now unleashed
140 and soon they found the changeling beast.
All day they flung themselves at him,
all day pursued, both dogs and men;
they almost had him. Now they'd rend
and tear him; now he'd meet his end.
145 His eye, distinguishing, could see
the king; to beg his clemency
he seized the royal stirrup, put
a kiss upon the leg and foot.
The king, observing, felt great fear.
150 Calling his men, he cried, "Come here!"
"Lords!" he said, "Come and look at this!
See what a marvel is this kiss,
this humble, gracious gesturing!
That's a man's mind; it begs the king
155 for mercy. Now, drive back the hounds!
See that none strike or give it wounds.
This beast has mind; it has intent.
Come, hurry up! It's time we went.
I'll give protection for this beast.
160 And for today, the hunt has ceased."[4]

 The king had turned around, at that;
following him, the bisclavret
close by; he would not lose the king,
abandon him, for anything.
165 The king then led the beast, to bring
it to the castle, marveling,
rejoicing at it, for he'd never,
seen such a wondrous creature, ever.
He loved the wolf and held it dear
170 and he charged every follower
that, for his love, they guard it well
and not mistreat the animal.
No one must strike it; and, he'd said,
it must be watered and well fed.
175 Gladly his men now guarded it.
Among the knights, the bisclavret
now lived, and slept close by the king;
everyone loved it, cherishing

4. Perhaps an allusion to the famous story of Actaeon, well-known in the Middle Ages and the Renaissance through the immensely popular and influential *Metamorphoses* (ca. 10 C.E.) by the Roman poet Ovid. In that tale the unfortunate hunter Actaeon happens to see the goddess Diana bathing naked, and thereby enrages her; she turns him into a stag, and he is mauled to death by his own hounds. He has a human mind in a stag's body, but no opportunity to prove it and thus be recognized as human and saved.

its noble bearing and its charm.
180 It never wanted to do harm,
and where the king might walk or ride,
there it must be, just at his side,
wherever he might go or move;
so well it showed its loyal love.

185 What happened after that? Now, hear.
The king held court; he had appear
all barons, vassals; gave commands
to all who held from him their lands,
to help a festival take place,
190 serving with elegance and grace.
Among those chevaliers was he—
so richly dressed, so splendidly!—
who'd wed the wife of Bisclavret.
Little he knew or thought just yet
195 that he would find his foe so near!
Soon as he came, this chevalier,
to court, and Bisclavret could see
the man, he ran up furiously,
sank in his teeth, and dragged him close.
200 Many the injuries and woes
he would have suffered, but the king
called out commands, while brandishing
his staff. The beast rushed, twice, that day,
to bite the man; all felt dismay,
205 for none had seen the beast display
toward anyone, in any way,
such viciousness. There must be reason,
the household said, for him to seize on
the knight, who must have done him wrong;
210 the wish for vengeance seemed so strong.

 And so they let the matter rest
till the conclusion of the feast.
The barons took their leave, each one,
each to his castle and his home.
215 All my good judgment counsels me
he who was first to leave was he
set upon by the bisclavret.
Small wonder the beast had such hate!

 Not too long after this occurred
220 —such is my thought, so I have heard—
into the forest went the king—
so noble and so wise a being—
where he'd first found the bisclavret.
The animal was with him yet.
225 The night of this return, the king
took, in this countryside, lodging.
And this the wife of Bisclavret

well knew. Dressed fetchingly, she set
out, to have speech with him next day;
230 rich gifts were part of her display.
Bisclavret saw her come. No man
had strength to hold him as he ran
up to his wife in rage and fury.
Hear of his vengeance! Hear the story!
235 He tore her nose off, then and there.
What worse could he have done to her?
From all sides now, and full of threat
men ran and would have killed him, but
a wise man expeditiously
240 spoke to the king. "Listen to me!
He's been with you, this animal;
there is not one man of us all
who has not, long since, had to see
and travel with him, frequently,
245 and he has harmed no one, not once
shown viciousness nor violence
save just now, as you saw him do.
And by the faith I owe to you,
he has some bitter quarrel with her
250 and with her husband, her seigneur.
She was wife to that chevalier
whom you so prized, and held so dear,
who disappeared some time ago.
What happened, no one seems to know.
255 Put her to torture. She may state
something, this dame, to indicate
why the beast feels for her such hate.
Force her to speak! She'll tell it straight.
We've all known marvels, chanced to see
260 strange events, here in Brittany."
 The King thought this advice was fair;
and he detained the chevalier.
The lady, too, he held; and she
he put to pain and agony.
265 Part out of pain, part out of fear,
she made her former lord's case clear:
how she had managed to betray
her lord, and take his clothes away;
the story he had told to her,
270 what he became, and how, and where;
and how, when once his clothes were gone—
stolen—he was not seen again.
She gave her theory and her thought:
Surely this beast was Bisclavret.
275 These spoils, these clothes, the king demanded;
whether she would or no, commanded
that she go back and find them, get
and give them to the bisclavret.

When they were put in front of him
280 he didn't seem to notice them.
The king's wise man spoke up once more—
the one who'd counseled him before—
"Fair sire, this will not do at all!
We can't expect this animal,
285 in front of you, sire, to get dressed
and change his semblance of a beast.
You don't grasp what this means, my king!—
or see his shame and suffering.
Into your room have led this beast;
290 with him, his clothes. Let him get dressed;
For quite some time, leave him alone.
If he's a man, that is soon known!"[5]

 The king himself led the bisclavret;
and on him all the doors were shut.
295 They waited. And then finally
two barons, with the king, all three,
entered. What a discovery!
There on the king's bed, they could see
asleep, the knight. How the king ran
300 to the bed, to embrace his man,
kiss him, a hundred times and more!

 Quickly he acted to restore
his lands, as soon as possible;
more he bestowed than I can tell.
305 His wife was banished. She was chased
out of the country, and disgraced,
and chased out, traveling with her,
her mate and co-conspirator.

 Quite a few children had this dame,
310 who in their way achieved some fame
for looks, for a distinctive face;
numbers of women of her race—
it's true—were born without a nose.
Noseless they lived, the story goes.

315 And this same story you have heard
truly occurred; don't doubt my word.
I made this *lai* of Bisclavret
so no one, ever, will forget.

 ca. 1170

5. In many ancient and medieval stories of the supernatural, the change from supernatural creature to human and vice versa, the crossing of the border between human reality and something else, can be shrouded and obscure. The need for privacy can also be seen, as Robert Hanning and Joan Ferrante suggest, as a sign of regaining the virtue of modesty, and also of human dignity and propriety (*The Lais of Marie de France*, 104).

Yönec[1]

Since I've begun these lays, I'll not
cease when their work is difficult;
adventures, stories, known to me,
I'll put, all, in rhymed poetry.
5 First my desire and my intent
concerns Yönec, and I want
to tell his birth, and how his father
before him first came to his mother.
The man who fathered Yönec
10 had for his name Muldumarec.[2]

In Brittany, in times gone by,
there lived a rich man, elderly—
extremely—known as the seigneur
of Carẅent,[3] and honored there.
15 The city sits on Duelas,
where vessels, at one time, could pass.
Though this man was advanced in age
because of his good heritage
he took a wife; he hoped to breed,
20 and heirs would follow in his stead.

This young girl was of high estate,
courtly and wise; her beauty great;
for this rich man, a fine award.
He loved her loveliness, this lord.
25 Her beauty and nobility
made him guard her most carefully;
he'd shut her in his tower; her home
in that high place, a well-paved room.
He had a sister, old and lone,
30 widowed, with no lord of her own,
whom he'd placed with her in the tower
so he'd be surer of his power.
Women there were, I'm sure, that he
placed in a chamber separately;
35 The young wife never spoke with them
Without the leave of this old dame.

1. Translated and annotated by Dorothy Gilbert. The name is pronounced "Ee oh neck." In Marie's original French the name is given as "Iwenec" in line 6 and "Yvenec" in line 9; the existing manuscripts of the poem give several other variations of the name. It is thought to be derived from Old Celtic "Esugenus," or "descendant of Esus, god of thunder" (see A. Ewert's edition of Marie's *Lais*,). 2. Manuscript evidence (according to Ewert) suggests that the *lai* was once named after the father, not the son.

3. Pronounced "Caruwent," with three syllables, as is evident in the meter of Marie's original lines. Ewert comments: "Various attempts have been made to identify the scene of the lay. It would appear that, at least at one stage, the scene was laid in S. Wales and that *Carẅent* may be identified with Caerwent, the old Venta Silurum, which view would find support in the identification of *Karliun* with Caerleon [in Wales]. *Duelas* may be the name formerly given to the stream on which Caerwent lies."

And so passed more than seven years.
No children came. There were no heirs.
Shut in the tower, she could not leave,
40 no, not for friend or relative.
When her lord went to bed with her
no manservant dared enter there;
no porter dared to set alight
candles before his lord, at night.
45 Sadness surrounded her, these years;
weeping and sighing, frequent tears.
She lost her beauty in this way,
like one whose will has drained away
completely; she no longer cared.
50 Quick death she would have much preferred.

 April had come, when birds display
their loveliest songs, as is their way.
One morning early, the old lord
made ready to ride to the wood
55 and the old woman rose, too, for
after him she must shut the door.
She had performed her duty then.
The lord went off, with all his men.
The old dame, with her psalter, went
60 off to recite her prayers, and chant.

 Awake, in tears, the lady lay;
she saw the sun's warm clarity,
she saw that the old dame had gone
and she herself was left alone.
65 much she complained then, much she sighed,
made lamentation, moaned and cried.
 "Alas, that I was born, to be
cursed with this dreadful destiny!
Here in this prison tower I lie,
70 never to go out till I die.
Jealous old man, what's in his mind,
demented fool, that I'm confined
in this great prison! He's afraid,
constantly, that he'll be betrayed.
75 I cannot go to church, nor hear
the worship service offered there.
If I could speak with other folk,
enjoy their company and talk,
I'd make some semblance to my sire
80 of liking—far from my desire!
Cursed be my family, with those,
hateful, the lot of them, who chose
to give me to Sir Jealousy
and to his carcass marry me!
85 It's a strong rope I draw and pull—
he'll never, never die at all!

When he was baptized, this old sire,
they plunged him in Hell's river of fire—
hard sinews, veins he has! But good
90 blood runs inside them, live and red.
 Many times I've heard stories told
how it could be, in days of old,
in this same land, adventures fell
to folk, and helped the miserable.
95 Knights found young women, beautiful,
noble, withal desirable:
ladies found lovers of great price,
so handsome, valiant, courteous;
they were not blamed. And what had been
100 was never known, was never seen.
If such can be, if such was done,
such things fell out for anyone,
God, for whom all is possible,
grant it to me! My wish fulfill!"

105 Just as she spoke, lamenting so,
She saw, just by the small window
a great bird's shadow, stretched across;
she had no notion what it was.
It flew into the room. Bands bound
110 each foot;[4] a hawk, it seemed, around
five or six moltings.[5] Now before
the girl, it perched, upon the floor.
When it had rested there a bit
and she had had a look, then it
115 became a handsome, noble knight.
The lady marveled at the sight,
she trembled, shaken in her blood;
in terror, covered up her head.

 Most courteous was the chevalier;
120 It was he who first spoke to her.
 "Oh, lady, do not fear me so!
the hawk's a noble bird. Although
its secrets are obscure to you,
cherish, trust what you know is true,
125 and take me for your lover! Dame,
it is for that," he said, "I came.
I have long loved you. I have long
held in my heart desire—so strong!
No other woman has been my lover
130 and I shall never have another.
But I could not come to you in love—
out of my palace could not move—
had you yourself not summoned me.

4. I.e., the bands tied to hawks trained to hunt by falconers.

5. Hawks molt every year of their life except the first.

But now I can be your *ami*!⁶
135 The girl, encouraged by this talk,
uncovered now her head, and spoke,
responding. She would be his love
if he believed in God above;⁷
if so, there was no obstacle,
140 and then their love was possible.
For such was his great beauty, she
had never known that this could be,
or seen such beauty in a man.
Surely she never would again.
145 "Lady," he said, "You've spoken well.
Never, for anything at all,
would I wish any accusation
or have your doubt or your suspicion.
I worship most devotedly
150 our dear Creator. It is he
who saved us from the tragic plight
where Adam placed us, with the bite
of the bitter apple.⁸ God has been
—will ever be—for us in sin
155 both light and life. But if you fear
me still, summon your chaplain here.
Say you are ill; say that you want
that service and that sacrament
given the world by our dear Lord
160 by which we sinners all are cured.
I will assume your form, receive
the Host; and thus you will perceive
my credo, how I speak it then—
never will you have doubts again!"
165 And she replied; this was well said.
He lay beside her in the bed;
he did not wish to touch her, though,
embrace or kiss her, or make show of love.
 On the old dame's return
170 she saw the young girl lying prone
and told her: time to be astir!
She wished to bring her clothes to her.
 The lady said, no, she was sick;
send for the chaplain, and be quick,
175 he must at once come to her side!
Dying, she was, and terrified.
 "Patience, madame!" the old dame said.
"My lord has gone off to the wood;

6. Friend (*Ami/amie*); French in courtly usage, "lover." It could also be used as an address in situations of flirtation or gallantry (the feminine form is *amie*).
7. I.e., proved that he was not a devil or demon summoned after she has cursed her family and cas- tigated her husband. Ewert notes, "Supernatural beings are commonly made to seek to prove themselves Christians by partaking of the sacrament."
8. I.e., the forbidden fruit of the tree of knowledge (Genesis 3.2–6).

no one but me can enter here."
180 The lady was now seized by fear;
indeed she seemed to faint away.
The old dame saw, with great dismay,
opened the door, and straightaway
called for the priest without delay.
185 He came as quickly as might be,
Bringing the *corpus Domini*.[9]
 And thus the knight received the Host,
the wine, the blood of Jesus Christ;
the priest left. They were as before,
190 and the old woman closed the door.
Lady and knight lay nestled there;
never was such a handsome pair!

 They laughed and played awhile. They spoke
of their new love in lovers' talk,
195 the knight then took his leave, to go
back to his land. He said adieu;
softly she begged him to return,
to make another visit soon.
 "Lady," he said, "at your request
200 I'll come before an hour has passed;
but you must take great care and thought
that we are not surprised and caught.
The old dame will betray us, pry
night and day with her spying eye;
205 she will find out our love; for sure
she will tell all to the seigneur.
If this should happen as I say
and we're discovered in this way
I cannot leave, I cannot fly,
210 without it happening that I die."

 After this speech he went away,
leaving his sweetheart in great joy.
Next day she woke up hale and sound,
all week a sweet contentment found,
215 care and attention gave her body,
and she recovered all her beauty.
Now she was glad of her small space;
why seek out joy some other place!
Often she wished to call her love
220 and all their sweet communion have;
soon as her husband went away,
early and late, and night and day
she had her pleasure with her knight;
God grant these two a long delight!

9. The body of the Lord (Latin); the eucharistic bread.

225 Having such bliss and joy, to be
much in her lover's company,
her manner was much changed, and thus
her lord, astute and devious,
noticed her heart and spirit, her grace,
230 so different from her former ways.
He viewed his sister with suspicion;
met her one day for some discussion,
saying it was quite marvelous
how his wife seemed to act and dress.
235 What did this mean? What was the cause?
The old dame did not know, because
Madame spoke not with any other,
she did not have a friend or lover,
it was just that she seemed to be
240 all by herself more willingly.
She too had seen what change there was.
And the old lord responded thus:
"By faith! I think that's so!" said he.
Now you must do a thing for me:
245 tomorrow morning, when I'm gone,
and you have closed the doors again,
pretend that you yourself have gone
and leave her lying there alone.
You find yourself a secret spot;
250 watch keenly. See that you find out
where this thing comes from, what it is,
that brings our dame such joy and bliss."
They parted, done with this cabal.
Alas! What evil can befall
255 someone whom spies intend to get
entangled in the trap they've set!

Three days later, so I've heard,
the lord left—or it so appeared.
He told his wife he had a writ;
260 the king commanded him to court,
but swiftly he'd return to her.
He went; his sister shut the door,
and the old woman rose and hid
behind an arras, where she stood.
265 All she desired to hear and see
she could take in most easily.
The young wife lay in bed, awake,
full of desire and love's sweet ache
for her *ami*, her chevalier;
270 He came. He did not waste an hour.
What bliss and joy they made together
by speech, by deed, lover to lover!
Then they must rise, and it was done,
and he must go, this magic one.
275 The old dame saw the whole event,
saw how he came and how he went,

and wild with terror in her stalk
saw him first man and then a hawk.
 And when the lord was back again
280 most hastily, as was the plan—
she lost no time, but told her brother
all of the truth about this lover.
 Oh, fiercely anxious was this man!
Further traps now, and further plan
285 he made, to kill the chevalier;
prongs he had made of iron, that were
sharp at the tip and razor-keen;
beneath sweet heaven no worse have been.
When these had been prepared, in form
290 forklike—such tines could do most harm—
there in the window they were set,
the tines as close as they could get,
through which the chevalier must fly
when he made tryst with his *amie.*
295 God! How little suspects the knight
his foe's great treachery and spite!

 The day that followed, the old sire
rose before dawn, for his desire,
he said, was to go hunt. He went;
300 the old dame also rose, and sent
him forth, then bedward made her way.
Dark was not her idea of day.
The young dame wakened, rose, to see
him whom she loved so loyally;
305 said he could well come now, and seize
this time; they could be at their ease.
Soon as she'd spoken her request,
he came, without delay or rest,
swooping up to the window.
 But
310 there were the prongs. One of them cut
straight to the heart; in a great spout
his scarlet blood came leaping out.
It was his death wound. When he knew
he struggled free, and came on through.
315 He sat before her on the bed,
all of the bedclothes soaked with blood;
she saw the wound, she saw the flood,
anguished, dismayed, at how he bled.
 He said, "Sweet love, sweet *bele*[1] *amie,*
320 for my great love of you I die.
I warned you this would come to pass;
your beauty was the death of us."

 Hearing, she fainted and fell down
deathlike, a moment, in her swoon.

1. Beautiful (Anglo-Norman French).

325 But he consoled her tenderly;
grief was worth nothing, and, said he,
now she was pregnant. She would have
a son, most valiant and most brave;
he would restore her, bring her joy.
330 Yönec he'd be named, this boy;
he would avenge this treachery
and kill their mortal enemy.
 The knight could now no longer stay;
for his wound bled continuously,
335 and in great pain he left her side.
She followed. Dreadfully she cried,
tore through the window, leaped and fell.
Truly it was a miracle
she was not killed; it was a leap
340 of twenty feet, down from the keep.
Naked beneath her shift[2] she went,
followed the trace of blood, the spent
drops of it trickling from the wound
there on the road, so quickly found.
345 She kept straight on that road, until
in front of her she saw a hill,
an entrance in it, still the trace
of blood that moistened all the place.
Nothing beyond was visible.
350 But she was certain, through that hill
her love had gone. The track, the lead,
was not too plain. But, with due speed
she entered in that lightless place,
kept the right road, and kept her pace
355 until she came outside the hill.

 There was a meadow, beautiful,
its grasses stained with blood, and she
felt terror, now, increasingly.
But through this field she went, kept on;
360 nearby, she saw, there was a town.
On every side there was a wall;
there was not house, nor tower, nor hall
that did not seem of silver, all;
places so rich, so wonderful!
365 Close to the town, the nearer edge
were marsh and woods, and field and hedge;
and on the other side of town,
close to the keep, a river ran
encircling all. Berthed ships lay there;
370 three hundred sails and more there were.
 The lower gate lay open wide,
and so the lady went inside,
and still she followed blood, and still

2. A chemise, the shirtlike undergarment worn next to the skin.

all through the town she went, until
375 she reached the castle. No one there
spoke to her, or discovered her.
In the paved palace hall she found
blood on the floor and all around.
She saw a lovely room; went in,
380 and found a knight, asleep, within;
she knew him not. So, leaving him,
she went, and found a larger room;
a bed was in it, nothing more,
on it, a sleeping chevalier.
385 Out of this second chamber, too,
she went, and in a third, she knew
her lover.[3]
 On a bed with feet
of purest gold, he lay. No sheet
or quilt there I'd attempt to price;
390 or chandeliers, that would suffice
to burn all night, to burn all day;
worth a whole city's gold, I'd say.
 Instantly, in that sumptuous place
she knew her lover, knew his face;
395 in terror, she came toward him. Then
she fainted and fell over him.
He held her, he, so passionate;
often he cried out, cursing Fate.
When she'd made some recovery
400 he comforted her tenderly.
 "For God's sake, though, my *bele amie*,
get out of here! Go, sweetheart, flee!
Soon, love, by daybreak, I shall die.
There'll be deep grief, and great outcry;
405 if you are found, most certainly
you will be done great injury.
My people will know well the cost—
that through our love I have been lost.
I'm full of grief for you, and fear!"
410 The lady said: "Sweet friend, my dear,
I would much rather die right here
than at the hands of my seigneur;
if I return, he'll murder me!"
 The knight spoke reassuringly.
415 He gave her a small ring, and said
to guard it well, and if she did
—he carefully instructed her—
she need not fear, for her seigneur
would not keep what she'd done in mind,

3. As Ewert points out here, "The description of Muldumarec as a ruler of some supernatural realm which is reached through a hill not far from Caerwent is in contradiction with the latter part of the story (346ff.) where his domain is situated on the road from Caerwent to Caerleon." To many scholars this indicates the fusion of two versions of the tale, but he notes that "such contradictions are common in fairy tales."

420 nor keep her wretched and confined.
He gave into her hands his sword;
required of her her solemn word
it must not pass to any man
but she must keep it for their son.
425 And when he was of age, and grown,
a valiant knight, his courage known,
she must go to a festival,
leading her lord and son as well.
And to an abbey they would come
430 and in that abbey see a tomb.
There they'd be told a memory
of wrongful death and treachery.
She'd give the sword up to the son,
tell how he was conceived and born,
435 who fathered him. What he'd do then
they would soon see.
 The knight had shown
the lady all that must be done.
A rich *bliaut*,[4] a lovely gown
he gave her, said that she must wear;
440 and then he took his leave of her.
 She left then, carrying the ring,
and the sword, deeply comforting.
Out of the gate, out of the town,
no more than half a league, she'd gone,
445 when she could hear the bell, the toll,
and cries inside the castle wall,
for the seigneur, who was no more.
He must be dead now, she was sure.
 Grief overcame her. In a swoon,
450 four times, while walking, she fell down,
then she recovered and went on,
back toward the hill and tunnel. Soon
she entered, came on through, and found
herself once more in her own land.

455 With her old lord, and free of fear,
she lived for many a day and year.
He never shamed her, this old sir,
ridiculed or insulted her.

 The son was born, and lovingly
460 nourished and cherished, watchfully,
named Yönec. And in that land,
that kingdom, no man could be found
so handsome, valiant, brave; withal
so generous, so liberal.

4. A long tunic, laced at the sides, with long, full sleeves. It was the outermost garment of a fully dressed 12th-century Frenchwoman, worn over a *chainse*, a floor-length dress of linen or hemp with long tight sleeves (which was in turn worn over the chemise).

465 When he was grown, and time was right,
this fine young man was dubbed a knight.
When that was done, that very year
something else happened: listen, hear.

It was the feast of St. Aaron,[5]
470 which was observed at Caerleon
and many other towns. The lord
was summoned, and with due accord
gathered his friends up in a band,
which was the custom of the land.
475 His wife and son, most richly dressed,
accompanied him to the feast.

And so it was. They set out, though
they had no notion where to go.
A young man they brought with them showed
480 these festal seekers the right road.
They found a castle on their quest—
Surely on earth the loveliest!
Inside the wall an abbey lay
where the devoted work and pray,
485 and there the guide, the young valet
brought all his band to lodge and stay,
and in the room of the Abbé
they were served with great courtesy.
 Next morning they heard mass, and then
490 thought to go on their way again,
but the good Abbé prayed they'd stay;
he'd much to show, and much to say.
The sleeping rooms, they'd get to see,
the chapter house, refectory—
495 since they were lodged so graciously
the lord consented readily.

When they had dined, the following day,
the tour began. And on the way
just by the chapter house, they found
500 a large tomb. Cloth, with stripes, and round
wheel patterns, of a silk brocade,
gold-bordered, on the tomb was laid.
And at the feet, the sides, the head,
full twenty candles' light was shed,
505 the chandeliers were gold, the best,
the censers glowed with amethyst.[6]
All day they swung, and their perfume
honored the ornate, splendid tomb.
 The visitors made inquiry

5. One of the two famous saints of Caerleon, both natives martyred in the persecutions of the Emperor Diocletian (284–305); Aaron and Julian each had a church in Caerleon.
6. Probably silver censers studded with amethysts.

510 of their kind hosts; who could it be
whose tomb was such an honored place?
What man lay in such cherished space?
 Those whom they asked, the local folk
began to weep. But still they spoke:
515 here lay the best of chevaliers,
the strongest, proudest, and most fierce,
the handsomest, most loved of men
who in this world was ever born.
And of this country he'd been king—
520 never a courtlier was seen.
At Carwent his blood was spilled;
love for a lady got him killed.
 "Since then we have had no seigneur,
no king; but waited many a year
525 for the son he engendered. Thus
our own dear lord commanded us."

 The lady heard. The tale was done.
In a strong voice she called her son:
"Fair son," said she, "now have you heard
530 how God has called us here? This lord
who lies here is your father. He,
this greybeard, killed him wrongfully.
Now I entrust to you at last
this sword I've kept for long years past."
535 For all to hear, she now made known
how their seigneur had got a son;
how he was wont to come to her,
how her own lord betrayed them there.
 She told the truth to one and all;
540 then in a faint they saw her fall;
and there she died, upon the tomb;
never more spoke to anyone.
 When her son knew that she was dead,
he took his own stepfather's head.
545 Thus he avenged, with swordthrust, both
his father's and his mother's death.
When this had happened, and was known,
and the news spread throughout the town,
with all due honor she was borne
550 in a fair coffin, to the tomb.
There by her lover she was placed;
God give them both sweet peace and rest!
Before they left, with due accord
the folk made Yönec their lord.

555 Those who this tale of love had heard
made it a *lai,* long afterward.
Out of compassion they did so
for lovers' suffering and woe.

ca. 1170

JULIAN OF NORWICH
1342–ca. 1416

"Because I am a woman should I therefore believe that I ought not to tell you about the goodness of God since I saw at the time that it is his will that it be known?" Specifically, what Julian of Norwich saw were sixteen "showings," or direct experiences of God's goodness, which she described in a powerful spiritual meditation. While she considered herself "a woman, unlettered, feeble and frail," this first English woman of letters drew her authority from "the showing of Him who is Sovereign Teacher" and was thereby empowered to record her mystical visions in a prose remarkable for its brilliant transformations of images drawn from everyday experiences.

Julian's revelations occurred in two days of her thirtieth year, during a near-fatal illness when she experienced pity for Christ's suffering. After receiving last rites, she perceived a "sudden change" that was accompanied by the series of visions of Christ, which make up the substance of her book. A recluse or anchoress in St. Julian's Church, Norwich, Julian most likely underwent a rite of enclosure, which resembled a burial service for the soul that sought to die to the world in order to live more fully with Christ. In a cell attached to the church, probably with a maidservant, an anchoress like Julian could dedicate herself to solitary meditation and silent prayer. Little else is known about her, although she clearly had some renown as a pious woman, for she was visited by Margery Kempe, another visionary, who sought spiritual advice and counsel. Modesty, ignorance of Latin, or actual illiteracy may have caused Julian to consider herself "unlettered"; however, she drew on biblical imagery and on a range of books that included the works of Richard Rolle, *The Cloud of Unknowing*, and the *Ancren Riwle* (rules for the life of anchoresses), all popular religious texts in her time.

Two records of her revelations exist, either written by her or dictated to an amanuensis: a shorter account, which is thought to have been written first and which vividly presents the sixteen revelations, and a longer version, in which she records the growth in her understanding of the revelations over a period of some twenty years. The survival of a number of manuscripts may indicate the popularity of Julian's work, although after the Reformation it ceased to attract readers. The text modernized here by Edmund Colledge and James Walsh is from the longer version. In the context of Thomas Aquinas's assertion of the inferiority of women in his *Summa Theologica* (1265–77), Julian's description of the maternity of God may seem startling. Yet, as Caroline Walker Bynum has shown in *Jesus as Mother*, the image of "mother Jesus" flowered in twelfth-century works by Anselm of Canterbury and Bernard of Clairvaux. Throughout *A Book of Showings* (sometimes called *A Revelation of Divine Love*), Julian associated her "bodily" and "ghostly" visions of Christ with the "words [which] formed in my understanding." In the excerpt printed here, she describes how the mystical experiences felt to her physically and what she saw as she realized that "the Trinity is God, God is the Trinity." Additionally, she implies that the incarnation has a unique meaning for women, who can affirm their spirituality and creativity through imagery of conception, birth, and nurturance.

From A Book of Showings to the Anchoress Julian of Norwich[1]

Chapter 3

[THE FIRST REVELATION]

And when I was thirty year old and a half, God sent me a bodily sickness in the which I lay three days and three nights; and on the fourth night I took all my rites of holy church, and went[2] not to have liven till day. And after this I lay two days and two nights; and on the third night I weened[3] oftentimes to have passed, and so weened they that were with me. And yet in this I felt a great loathsomeness[4] to die, but for nothing that was on earth that me liketh to live for, ne[5] for no pain that I was afraid of, for I trusted in God of his mercy. But it was for I would have lived to have loved God better and longer time, that I might by the grace of that living have the more knowing and loving of God in the bliss of heaven. For me thought[6] all that time that I had lived here so little and so short in regard of[7] that endless bliss, I thought: Good Lord, may my living no longer be to thy worship?[8] And I understood by my reason and by the feeling of my pains that I should die; and I assented fully with all the will of my heart to be at God's will.

Thus I endured till day, and by then was my body dead from the middes downward, as to my feeling.[9] Then was I holpen[1] to be set upright, underset[2] with help, for to have the more freedom of my heart to be at God's will, and thinking on God while my life lasted. My curate was sent for to be at my ending, and before he came I had set up my eyen[3] and might not speak. He set the cross before my face and said: "I have brought the image of thy savior; look thereupon and comfort thee therewith." Me thought I was well, for my eyen was set upright into heaven, where I trusted to come by the mercy of God; but nevertheless I assented to set my eyen in the face of the crucifix, if I might, and so I did, for me thought I might longer dure to look even forth than right up.[4] After this my sight began to fail. It waxed as dark about me in the chamber as if it had been night, save in the image of the cross, wherein held a common light; and I wist[5] not how. All that was beside the cross was ugly and fearful to me as[6] it had been much occupied with fiends.

After this the over[7] part of my body began to die so farforth that unneth I[8] had any feeling. My most pain was shortness of breath and failing of life. Then went[9] I verily to have passed. And in this suddenly all my pain was taken from me, and I was as whole, and namely in the over part of my body, as ever I was before. I marvelled of this sudden change, for me thought that it was a privy working of God, and not of kind;[1] and yet by feeling of this ease I trusted never more to have lived, ne the feeling of this ease was no

1. The text is based on that given by Edmund Colledge, O.S.A., and James Walsh, S.J. for the Pontifical Institute of Mediaeval Studies, Toronto (1978), but it has been freely edited and modern spelling has been used where possible.
2. Thought.
3. Believed.
4. Reluctance.
5. Nor.
6. I thought.
7. In comparison with.
8. In your honor.
9. As it felt to me.
1. Helped.
2. Supported.
3. Eyes.
4. Persist in looking straight ahead longer than straight up.
5. Knew.
6. As if.
7. Upper.
8. To such an extent that I scarcely.
9. Thought.
1. Nature. "Privy": hidden.

full ease to me, for me thought I had liever[2] have been delivered of this world, for my heart was willfully set thereto.

Then came suddenly to my mind that I should desire the second wound of our Lord's gift and of his grace, that my body might be fulfilled with mind and feeling of his blessed passion, as I had before prayed,[3] for I would that his pains were my pains, with compassion and afterward longing to God. Thus thought me that I might with his grace have the wounds that I had before desired; but in this I desired never no bodily sight ne no manner showing of God, but compassion as me thought that a kind soul might have with our Lord Jesu, that for love would become a deadly[4] man. With him I desired to suffer, living in my deadly body, as God would give me grace.

Chapter 4

And in this suddenly I saw the red blood running down from under the garland, hot and freshly, plenteously and lively, right as it was in the time that the garland of thorns was pressed on his blessed head. Right so, both God and man, the same that suffered for me, I conceived truly and mightily that it was himself that shewed it me without any mean.[5]

And in the same showing suddenly the Trinity[6] fulfilled my heart most of joy, and so I understood it shall be in heaven without end to all that shall come there. For the Trinity is God, God is the Trinity. The Trinity is our maker, the Trinity is our keeper, the Trinity is our everlasting lover, the Trinity is endless joy and our bliss, by our Lord Jesu Christ, and in our Lord Jesu Christ. And this was showed in the first sight and in all, for where Jesu appeareth, the blessed Trinity is understand, as to my sight.[7] And I said, "*Benedicite dominus.*"[8] This I said for reverence in my meaning,[9] with a mighty voice, and full greatly was I astoned[1] for wonder and marvel that I had, that he that is so reverend and so dreadful will be so homely[2] with a sinful creature living in this wretched flesh.

Thus I took it for that time that our Lord Jesu of his courteous love would show me comfort before the time of my temptation; for me thought it might well be that I should by the sufferance of God and with his keeping be tempted of[3] fiends before I should die. With this sight of his blessed passion, with the godhead that I saw in my understanding, I knew well that it was strength enough to me, yea, and to all creatures living that should be saved, against all the fiends of hell, and against all ghostly[4] enemies.

In this he brought our Lady Saint Mary to my understanding; I saw her ghostly in bodily likeness, a simple maiden and a meek, young of age, a little waxen above a child,[5] in the stature as she was when she conceived. Also God showed me in part the wisdom and the truth of her soul, wherein I understood the reverend beholding, that she beheld her God, that is her maker, marvelling with great reverence that he would be born of her that

2. Rather.
3. One of the three gifts for which Julian had prayed (they were mortal sickness and the wounds of true contrition, loving compassion, and a willed desire for God).
4. Mortal.
5. Intermediary.
6. The first person of the Trinity is God, the second person is Jesus Christ, and the third is the Holy Spirit; all three, may bear the name God.

7. Is understood, as I see it.
8. Blessed be the Lord (Latin).
9. With reverent intention.
1. Astonished.
2. Familiar, at home with. "Dreadful": awe-inspiring.
3. By.
4. Spiritual.
5. Grown a little older than a child.

was a simple creature of his making. And this wisdom and truth, knowing the greatness of her maker and the littlehead[6] of herself that is made, made her to say full meekly to Gabriel: "Lo me here, God's handmaiden."[7] In this sight I did understand verily that she is more than all that God made beneath her in worthiness and in fullhead;[8] for above her is nothing that is made but the blessed manhood of Christ, as to my sight.

From *Chapter* 58

[JESUS AS MOTHER]

God the blessedful Trinity, which is everlasting being, right as he is endless fro without beginning,[9] right so it was in his purpose endless to make mankind,[1] which fair kind first was dight to[2] for his own son, the second person; and when he would,[3] by full accord of all the Trinity he made us all at once.[4] And in our making he knit us and oned[5] us to himself, by which oneing we be kept as clean[6] and as noble as we were made. By the virtue of that ilke[7] precious oneing we love our maker and like[8] him, praise and thank him, and endlessly enjoy[9] in him. And this is the working which is wrought continually in each soul that shall be saved, which is the godly will before said.

And thus in our making God almighty is our kindly[1] father, and god all wisdom is our kindly mother, with the love and the goodness of the Holy Ghost, which is all one God, one Lord. And in the knitting and in the oneing he is our very true spouse and we his loved wife[2] and his fair maiden, with which wife he was never displeased. For he sayeth: "I love thee and thou lovest me, and our love shall never part in two."

I beheld the working of all the blessed Trinity, in which beholding I saw and understood these three properties: The property of the fatherhood, and the property of the motherhood, and the property of the lordship in one God. In our father almighty we have our keeping and our bliss as anemptis[3] our kindly substance which is to us by our making fro without beginning.[4] And in the second person in wit[5] and wisdom we have our keeping as anemptis our sensuality[6] our restoring and our saving, for he is our mother, brother and savior And in our good lord the Holy Ghost we have our rewarding and our yielding for our living and our travail,[7] and endlessly overpassing[8] all that we desire in his marvelous courtesy of his high plenteous grace. For all our life is in three: in the first we have our being, and in the second we have our increasing, and in the third we have our fulfilling. The first is kind,[9] the second is mercy, the third is grace.

For the first[1] I saw and understood that the high might of the Trinity is

6. Littleness.
7. See Luke 1.38.
8. Fullness.
9. I.e., eternal.
1. I.e., his purpose to make humankind is also eternal.
2. Made for. "Kind": nature.
3. Wanted to.
4. All of us simultaneously.
5. United. The idea of oneness is further emphasized in the verb *oned* and the noun *oneing*.
6. Pure.
7. Same.
8. Please.

9. Rejoice.
1. Both "kind" and "natural."
2. I.e., Christ is the bridegroom and the human soul his spouse.
3. As regards. "Keeping": maintenance.
4. I.e., our natural created being, which is eternal. *Substance* is regarded by Julian as the eternal essence of being.
5. Intelligence.
6. Our sensual being (as opposed to substance).
7. Life and labor. "Yielding": payment.
8. Surpassing.
9. Nature.
1. For the first time.

our father, and the deep wisdom of the Trinity is our mother, and the great love of the Trinity is our lord; and all these have we in kind and in our substantial making. And furthermore I saw that the second person, which is our mother, substantially the same dearworthy person,[2] is now become our mother sensual,[3] for we be double of God's making, that is to say substantial and sensual. Our substance is the higher part, which we have in our father God almighty; and the second person of the Trinity is our mother in kind in our substantial making, in whom we be grounded and rooted, and he is our mother of mercy in our sensual taking.[4]

<p style="text-align:center">* * *</p>

From *Chapter 59*

[GOD THE MOTHER]

As truly as God is our Father, so truly is God our Mother, and he revealed that in everything, and especially in these sweet words where he says. I am he,[5] that is to say: I am he, the power and goodness of fatherhood; I am he, the wisdom and the lovingness of motherhood; I am he, the light and the grace which is all blessed love; I am he, the Trinity; I am he, the unity; I am he, the great supreme goodness of every kind of thing; I am he who makes you to love; I am he who makes you to long; I am he, the endless fulfilling of all true desires. For where the soul is highest, noblest, most honourable, still it is lowest, meekest and mildest.

And from this foundation in substance we have all the powers of our sensuality by the gift of nature, and by the help and the furthering of mercy and grace, without which we cannot profit. Our great Father, almighty God, who is being, knows us and loved us before time began. Out of this knowledge, in his most wonderful deep love, by the prescient eternal counsel of all the blessed Trinity he wanted the second person to become our Mother, our brother and our saviour. From this it follows that as truly as God is our Father, so truly is God our Mother. Our Father wills, our Mother works, our good Lord the Holy Spirit confirms. And therefore it is our part to love our God in whom we have our being, reverently thanking and praising him for our creation, mightily praying to our Mother for mercy and pity, and to our Lord the Holy Spirit for help and grace. For in these three is all our life: nature, mercy and grace, of which we have mildness, patience and pity, and hatred of sin and wickedness; for the virtues must of themselves hate sin and wickedness.

And so Jesus is our true Mother in nature by our first creation, and he is our true Mother in grace by his taking our created nature. All the lovely works and all the sweet loving offices of beloved motherhood are appropriated to the second person, for in him we have this godly will, whole and safe forever, both in nature and in grace, from his own goodness proper to him.

I understand three ways of contemplating motherhood in God. The first

2. The same beloved person with regard to our substance.
3. Mother of our physical being.
4. Taking on physicality.

5. In a series of visions in the previous chapters, Christ showed himself to Julian and spoke words that she then interprets in the later chapters.

is the foundation of our nature's creation; the second is his taking of our nature, where the motherhood of grace begins; the third is the motherhood at work. And in that, by the same grace, everything is penetrated, in length and in breadth, in height and in depth without end; and it is all one love.

Chapter 60

But now I should say a little more about this penetration, as I understood our Lord to mean: How we are brought back by the motherhood of mercy and grace into our natural place, in which we were created by the motherhood of love, a mother's love which never leaves us.

Our Mother in nature, our Mother in grace, because he wanted altogether to become our Mother in all things, made the foundation of his work most humbly and most mildly in the maiden's womb. And he revealed that in the first revelation, when he brought that meek maiden before the eye of my understanding in the simple stature which she had when she conceived; that is to say that our great God, the supreme wisdom of all things, arrayed and prepared himself in this humble place, all ready in our poor flesh, himself to do the service and the office of motherhood in everything. The mother's service is nearest, readiest and surest: nearest because it is most natural, readiest because it is most loving, and surest because it is truest. No one ever might or could perform this office fully, except only him. We know that all our mothers bear us for pain and for death. O, what is that? But our true Mother Jesus, he alone bears us for joy and for endless life, blessed may he be. So he carries us within him in love and travail, until the full time when he wanted to suffer the sharpest thorns and cruel pains that ever were or will be, and at the last he died. And when he had finished, and had borne us so for bliss, still all this could not satisfy his wonderful love. And he revealed this in these great surpassing words of love. If I could suffer more, I would suffer more.[6] He could not die any more, but he did not want to cease working; therefore he must needs nourish us, for the precious love of motherhood has made him our debtor.

The mother can give her child to suck of her milk, but our precious Mother Jesus can feed us with himself, and does, most courteously and most tenderly, with the blessed sacrament, which is the precious food of true life; and with all the sweet sacraments he sustains us most mercifully and graciously, and so he meant in these blessed words, where he said: I am he whom Holy Church preaches and teaches to you.[7] That is to say: All the health and the life of the sacraments, all the power and the grace of my word, all the goodness which is ordained in Holy Church for you, I am he.

The mother can lay her child tenderly to her breast, but our tender Mother Jesus can lead us easily into his blessed breast through his sweet open side, and show us there a part of the godhead and of the joys of heaven, with inner certainty of endless bliss. And that he revealed in the tenth revelation,[8] giving us the same understanding in these sweet words which he says: See, how I love you, looking into his blessed side, rejoicing.

6. In the ninth revelation, Christ spoke these words to Julian.
7. Spoken in the twelfth revelation.

8. In the tenth revelation Christ showed Julian a wound in his side, through which she saw "his blessed heart riven in two."

This fair lovely word "mother" is so sweet and so kind in itself that it cannot truly be said of anyone or to anyone except of him and to him who is the true Mother of life and of all things. To the property of motherhood belong nature, love, wisdom and knowledge, and this is God. For though it may be so that our bodily bringing to birth is only little, humble and simple in comparison with our spiritual bringing to birth, still it is he who does it in the creatures by whom it is done. The kind, loving mother who knows and sees the need of her child guards it very tenderly, as the nature and condition of motherhood will have. And always as the child grows in age and in stature, she acts differently, but she does not change her love. And when it is even older, she allows it to be chastised to destroy its faults, so as to make the child receive virtues and grace. This work, with everything which is lovely and good, our Lord performs in those by whom it is done.[9] So he is our Mother in nature by the operation of grace in the lower part, for love of the higher part. And he wants us to know it, for he wants to have all our love attached to him; and in this I saw that every debt which we owe by God's command to fatherhood and motherhood is fulfilled in truly loving God, which blessed love Christ works in us. And this was revealed in everything, and especially in the great bounteous words when he says: I am he whom you love.[1]

Chapter 61

And in our spiritual bringing to birth he uses more tenderness, without any comparison, in protecting us. By so much as our soul is more precious in his sight, he kindles our understanding, he prepares our ways, he eases our conscience, he comforts our soul, he illumines our heart and gives us partial knowledge and love of his blessed divinity, with gracious memory of his sweet humanity and his blessed Passion,[2] with courteous wonder over his great surpassing goodness, and makes us to love everything which he loves for love of him, and to be well satisfied with him and with all his works. And when we fall, quickly he raises us up with his loving embrace and his gracious touch. And when we are strengthened by his sweet working, then we willingly choose him by his grace, that we shall be his servants and his lovers, constantly and forever.

And yet after this he allows some of us to fall more heavily and more grievously than ever we did before, as it seems to us. And then we who are not all wise think that everything which we have undertaken was all nothing. But it is not so, for we need to fall, and we need to see it; for if we did not fall, we should not know how feeble and how wretched we are in ourselves, nor, too, should we know so completely the wonderful love of our Creator.

For we shall truly see in heaven without end that we have sinned grievously in this life; and notwithstanding this, we shall truly see that we were never hurt in his love, nor were we ever of less value in his sight. And by the experience of this falling we shall have a great and marvellous knowledge of

9. I.e., in disciplining her child the mother acts as an agent of God's will.
1. Spoken in the twelfth revelation.

2. The crucifixion, in which Christ sacrificed his own life as payment for humanity's sins.

love in God without end; for enduring and marvellous is that love which cannot and will not be broken because of offences.

And this was one profitable understanding; another is the humility and meekness which we shall obtain by the sight of our fall, for by that we shall be raised high in heaven, to which raising we might never have come without that meekness. And therefore we need to see it; and if we do not see it, though we fell, that would not profit us. And commonly we first fall and then see it; and both are from the mercy of God.

The mother may sometimes suffer[3] the child to fall and to be distressed in various ways, for its own benefit, but she can never suffer any kind of peril to come to her child, because of her love. And though our earthly mother may suffer her child to perish, our heavenly Mother Jesus may never suffer us who are his children to perish, for he is almighty, all wisdom and all love, and so is none but he, blessed may he be.

But often when our falling and our wretchedness are shown to us, we are so much afraid and so greatly ashamed of ourselves that we scarcely know where we can put ourselves. But then our courteous Mother does not wish us to flee away, for nothing would be less pleasing to him; but he then wants us to behave like a child. For when it is distressed and frightened, it runs quickly to its mother; and if it can do no more, it calls to the mother for help with all its might. So he wants us to act as a meek child, saying: My kind Mother, my gracious Mother, my beloved Mother, have mercy on me. I have made myself filthy and unlike you, and I may not and cannot make it right except with your help and grace.

And if we do not then feel ourselves eased, let us at once be sure that he is behaving as a wise Mother. For if he sees that it is profitable to us to mourn and to weep, with compassion and pity he suffers that until the right time has come, out of his love. And then he wants us to show a child's characteristics, which always naturally trusts in its mother's love in well-being and in woe. And he wants us to commit ourselves fervently to the faith of Holy Church, and find there our beloved Mother in consolation and true understanding, with all the company of the blessed. For one single person may often be broken, as it seems to him, but the entire body of Holy Church was never broken, nor ever will be without end. And therefore it is a certain thing, and good and gracious to will, meekly and fervently, to be fastened and united to our mother Holy Church, who is Christ Jesus. For the flood of mercy which is his dear blood and precious water is plentiful to make us fair and clean. The blessed wounds of our saviour are open and rejoice to heal us. The sweet gracious hands of our Mother are ready and diligent about us; for he in all this work exercises the true office of a kind nurse, who has nothing else to do but attend to the safety of her child.

It is his office to save us, it is his glory to do it, and it is his will that we know it; for he wants us to love him sweetly and trust in him meekly and greatly. And he revealed this in these gracious words: I protect you very safely.[4]

3. Allow.
4. Spoken in chapter 37 after the thirteenth revelation.

Chapter 86

[CONCLUSION]

This book is begun by God's gift and his grace, but it is not yet performed,[5] as to my sight. For charity, pray we all together with God's working, thanking, trusting, enjoying, for thus will our good Lord be prayed, but the understanding that I took in all his own meaning, and in the sweet words where he sayeth full merrily: "I am ground of thy beseeching." For truly I saw and understood in our Lord's meaning that he showed it for he will have it known more than it is. In which knowing he will give us grace to love him and cleave to him, for he beheld his heavenly treasure with so great love on earth that he will give us more light, and solace in heavenly joy, in drawing of our hearts fro sorrow and darkness which we are in.

And fro the time that it was showed, I desired oftentimes to wit[6] in what was our Lord's meaning. And fifteen year after and more, I was answered in ghostly understanding, saying thus: "What, wouldst thou wit thy Lord's meaning in this thing? Wit it well, love was his meaning. Who showeth it thee? Love. What showed he thee? Love. Wherefore showeth he it thee? For love. Hold thee therein, thou shalt wit more in the same. But thou shalt never wit therein other withouten end."

Thus was I learned,[7] that love is our Lord's meaning. And I saw full surely in this and in all, that ere God made us he loved us, which love was never slaked[8] ne never shall. And in this love he hath done all his works, and in this love he hath made all things profitable to us, and in this love our life is everlasting. In our making we had beginning, but the love wherein he made us was in him fro without beginning. In which love we have our beginning, and all this shall we see in God withouten end.

Deo gracias. Explicit liber revelacionum Julyane anacorite Norwyche, cuius anime propicietur deus.[9]

ca. 1390

5. Completed.
6. Know.
7. Taught.
8. Lessened.

9. Thanks be to God. This ends the book of revelations of Julian, anchorite of Norwich, for whose soul may god pray (Latin).

MARGERY KEMPE
ca. 1373–1438

When Margery Kempe visited Julian of Norwich, the aging anchoress and author of *A Book of Showings*, she sought "good counsel" about her own divine revelations. The forty-year-old Margery had decided, after almost twenty years of marriage and fourteen children, that she was meant to be married not to her husband but to Christ. While Julian confirmed Margery's grace, the anchoress also warned her visitor about "the language of the world, for the more despite, shame and reproof that ye have in

the world," Julian explained, "the more is your merit in the sight of God." What Julian seemed to understand in her "holy dalliance" with Margery was the vulnerability of a "sister" whose spirituality took a quite different form from her own, for Margery dramatically enacted her religious enthusiasm in the world. Indeed, dressed all in white, wearing a ring (engraved "Jesus Christ is my love"), frequently called to fast or weep, Margery traveled throughout England and went on pilgrimages to Jerusalem, Rome, Germany, and in the Baltic states. Not dedicated to the vow of silence, she reproved even the highest church officials for what she considered their moral lapses and preached to people wherever she found them. Whether her audience threatened to burn her at the stake as a heretic or promised to follow what they deemed her saintly tales and exhortations, Margery exhibited notable courage, inventiveness, and zeal, or so it seems in the major source we have of her life, *The Book of Margery Kempe*.

The same feisty energy that characterized Margery's life must have impelled her to originate the first extant autobiography in the vernacular. *The Book of Margery Kempe* was narrated to several scribes, who recorded what Kempe remembered about her adventures as a spiritual teacher. Margery did not focus on her youth in Lynn, where she was raised by a prosperous mayor named John Brunham, or her marriage in 1393 to John Kempe, a tax collector, brewer, and miller by turns. Instead, she began when she was twenty-one, pregnant, and in the midst of a disabling spiritual struggle, which she placed in the context of her visions of Christ, on the one hand, and her marital responsibilities, on the other. Margery's eventual marriage to Christ, which she attained by bargaining with her husband for freedom from sexual relations, evidently involved a sexualized relation with God not uncommon in the mystical tradition. While some scholars have diagnosed Kempe as hysterical, others have compared her brash vitality to the irreverence of Chaucer's candid Wife of Bath or her spiritual ecstasy to the intensity of St. Bridget of Sweden, who also claimed to have visions of being present at Christ's birth.

As the self-defined "creature" of her Creator, Margery recorded both mystical revelations and homely anecdotes. Invariably, she defended herself against the injunction, based on the teachings of St. Paul, that "no woman should preach," by explaining "I preach not sin; I come into no pulpit. I use but communication and good words, and that I will do while I live." Unlike the recluse Julian, who meditated exclusively on the growth of her spiritual understanding, Margery produced a lively, realistic narrative as well as an illuminating document of fifteenth-century society.

A modernization of *The Book of Margery Kempe* was not printed until 1936, when it was produced by W. Butler-Bowder. The modernized text included here comes from Lynne Staley's 1996 edition, which was used for the Norton Critical edition (2001).

From The Book of Margery Kempe[1]

Chapter 3

[ON FEMALE CELIBACY]

On a night, as this creature[2] lay in her bed with her husband, she heard a sound of melody so sweet and delectable, she thought, as if she had been in paradise. And therewith she started out of her bed and said, "Alas, that ever I did sin; it is full merry in heaven."

This melody was so sweet that it passed[3] all the melody that ever might be

1. The first two chapters of this spiritual autobiography recount Margery's earlier desires and ambitions, before her renunciation of the world.

2. I.e., Margery, who consistently refers to herself in the third person.

3. Surpassed.

heard in this world, without any comparison, and caused this creature when she heard any mirth or melody afterward to have full plenteous and abundant tears of high devotion with great sobbings and sighings after the bliss of heaven, not dreading the shames and the scorns of the wretched world. And ever after this draught[4] she had in her mind the mirth and the melody that was in heaven, so much that she could not well restrain herself from the speaking thereof. For, where she was in any company, she would say often-times, "It is full merry in heaven." And they who knew her governance before that time and now heard her speak so much of the bliss of heaven said unto her, "Why speak you so of the mirth that is in heaven; you know it not, and you have not been there anymore than we," and were angry with her for she would not hear any speak of worldly things, as they did and as she did before.

And after this time she had never desire to common fleshly with her husband, for the debt of matrimony[5] was so abominable to her that she had rather, she thought, eat or drink the ooze, the muck in the channel, than to consent to any fleshly commoning, save only for obedience. And so she said to her husband, "I may not deny you my body, but the love of my heart and my affection is drawn from all earthly creatures and set only in God."

He would have his will, and she obeyed with great weeping and sorrowing because she might not live chaste. And oftentimes this creature lived chaste, counseled her husband to live chaste, and said that they oftentimes, she knew well, had displeased God by their inordinate love and the great delectation that they both had in using[6] one another, and now it was good that they should, by both their wills and the consent of them both, punish and chastise themselves willfully by abstaining from their lust of their bodies. Her husband said it was good to do so, but he might not yet; he should when God would.[7] And so he used her as he had done before; he would not spare. And ever she prayed to God that she might live chaste, and three or four years after, when it pleased our Lord, he made a vow of chastity, as shall be written after, by the leave of Jesus.

And also, after this creature heard this heavenly melody, she did great bodily penance. She was shriven sometimes twice or three times a day, and especially of that sin which she so long had concealed and covered, as it is written in the beginning of the book.[8] She gave herself to great fasting and to great waking. She rose at two or three o'clock and went to church and was there in her prayers unto time of noon and also all the afternoon. And then was she slandered and reproved by many people because she kept so straight a living. Then she got herself a hair cloth from a kiln such as men use for drying malt and laid it in her kirtle as subtly and privily[9] as she might so that her husband should not spy it, nor did he; and yet she lay by him every night in his bed, and wore the hair cloth every day,[1] and bore children during that time.

Then she had three years of great labor with temptations which she bore as meekly as she could, thanking our Lord for all his gifts, and was as merry

4. Experience that she drank in.
5. I.e., sexual relations ("debt" can mean "duty"). "Common": have intercourse.
6. Having sexual intercourse with.
7. I.e., when God willed.
8. Chapter 1 made clear that Margery had not

made a practice of going to confession (i.e., being shriven). Her "sin" was that she had slandered her husband and herself and had desired wickedness.
9. Secretly. "Kirtle": skirt, gown.
1. I.e., as a hair shirt, worn next to the skin as a penance.

when she was reproved, scorned, or mocked for our Lord's love, and much more merry than she was before in the worship of the world. For she knew right well she had sinned greatly against God and was worthy of more shame and sorrow than any man could do to her, and the despite[2] of the world was the right way toward heaven, since Christ himself chose that way. All his apostles, martyrs, confessors, and virgins, and all who ever come to heaven, passed by the way of tribulation, and she desired nothing so much as heaven. Then was she glad in her conscience when she believed that she was entering the way that would lead her to the place that she most desired. And this creature had contrition and great compunction[3] with plenteous tears and many violent sobbings for her sins and for her unkindness against her maker. She recalled the unkindnesses of her childhood as our Lord would bring them to her memory full many a time. And then, she beholding her own wickedness, she might but sorrow and weep and ever pray for mercy and forgiveness. Her weeping was so plenteous and so continuing that many people thought that she might weep and leave off when she would, and therefore many men said she was a false hypocrite and wept for the world for succor and for worldly good. And then full many forsook her who had loved her before while she was in the world and would not know her, and ever she thanked God for all, nothing desiring but mercy and the forgiveness of sin.

Chapter 4

[HER TEMPTATION TO ADULTERY]

The first two years when this creature was thus drawn to our Lord, as for any temptations, she had great quiet of spirit. She might well endure fasting; it grieved her not. She hated the joys of the world. She felt no rebellion in her flesh. She was strong, as she thought, so that she dreaded no devil in hell, for she did such great bodily penance. She thought that she loved God more than he her. She was smitten with the deadly wound of vain glory and felt it not, for she desired many times that the crucifix should loose his hands from the cross and embrace her in token of love.

Our merciful Lord Christ Jesus, seeing this creature's presumption, sent her, as is written before, three years of great temptation, of which one of the hardest I purpose to write for an example for those who come after, so that they should not trust in their own selves, nor have joy in themselves as this creature had; for without doubt, our ghostly enemy sleeps not, but he full busily searches our complexions[4] and our dispositions, and wherever he finds us most frail, there, by our Lord's sufferance, he lays his snare, which may no man escape by his own power. And so he laid before this creature the snare of lechery when she thought that all fleshly lust had wholly been quenched in her. And for so long she was tempted with the sin of lechery for ought that she could do. And yet she was often shriven; she wore the hair cloth and did great bodily penance and wept many a bitter tear and prayed full often to our Lord that he would preserve her and keep her so she would not fall into temptation, for she thought she had rather be dead than consent

2. Contempt, defiance.
3. Remorse.

4. Temperament. "Ghostly enemy": the Devil.

thereto. And in all this time she had no lust to common with her husband, but it was very painful and horrible to her.

In the second year of her temptations it befell so that a man whom she loved well said unto her on Saint Margaret's Eve[5] before evensong that, despite anything, he would lie by her and have his lust of his body, and she should not withstand him, for, if he might not have his will that time, he said, he should else have it another time, she could not choose.

And he did it in order to prove[6] her, what she would do; but she thought that he had meant it in full earnest at that time and said but little about it. So they parted asunder for then and went both to hear evensong, for their church was Saint Margaret's. This woman was so labored with the man's words that she might not hear her evensong, nor say her Pater Noster,[7] or think any other good thought, but was more labored than ever she was before. The devil put in her mind that God had forsaken her, and else should she not have been so tempted. She believed the devil's persuasions and began to consent because she could think no good thought. Therefore thought she that God had forsaken her. And, when evensong was done, she went to the man before said so that he should have his lust, as she thought that he had desired, but he made such simulation[8] that she could not know his intent, and so they parted asunder for that night.

This creature was so labored[9] and vexed all that night that she knew never what she might do. She lay by her husband, and, whether to common with him, it was so abominable unto her that she might not endure it, and yet it was lawful unto her at a lawful time if she had wanted. But ever she was labored with the other man, whether to sin with him inasmuch he had spoken to her. At the last, through the inopportunity of temptation and the lack of discretion, she was overcome, and consented in her mind, and went to the man to learn if he would then consent to her. And he said he wouldn't for all the good in this world; he had rather been hewn as small as meat for the pot. She went away all shamed and confused within herself, seeing his stableness and her own unstableness.

Then thought she of the grace that God had given her before, how she had two years of great quiet of soul, repentance of her sin with many bitter tears of compunction, and a perfect will never to turn again to her sin, but rather, she thought, to be dead. And now she saw how she had consented in her will to do sin. Then she fell half in despair. She thought she would have been in hell for the sorrow that she had. She thought she was worthy of no mercy, for her consenting was so willfully done, nor never worthy to do him service because she was so false unto him. Nevertheless she was shriven many times and often, and did her penance, whatsoever her confessor would enjoin her to do, and was governed after the rules of the Church. That grace God gave this creature, blessed may he be, but he withdrew not her temptation but rather increased it, as she thought.

And therefore she knew that he had forsaken her and dared not trust to his mercy, but was labored with horrible temptations of lechery and of

5. I.e., the daily service of evening prayer on the evening before St. Margaret's feast day (July 20). St. Margaret was martyred for her determination not to lose her virginity.
6. Test.

7. Our Father (Latin); i.e., the Lord's Prayer (Matthew 6.9–13).
8. He feigned indifference; or, perhaps, he gave her conflicting signs of his desire.
9. Burdened, distressed.

despair nearly all the next year following, save our Lord of his mercy, as she said herself, gave her each day for the most part two hours of compunction for her sins with many bitter tears. And afterward she was labored with temptations of despair as she was before and was as far from feeling grace as those who had never felt any. And that might she not bear, and therefore always she despaired. Save for the time that she felt grace, her labors were so wonderful that she could hardly fare with them, but ever mourned and sorrowed as though God had forsaken her.

Chapter 11

[A SETTLEMENT WITH HER HUSBAND]

It befell upon a Friday on Midsummer Eve in right hot weather, as this creature was coming from York bearing a bottle with beer in her hand and her husband a loaf in his bosom, he asked his wife this question, "Margery, if there came a man with a sword and would smite off my head unless I should common naturally with you as I have done before, tell me the truth from your conscience—for you say you will not lie—whether would you suffer my head to be smote off or else suffer me to meddle with you again, as I did at one time?"

"Alas, sir," she said, "why move you this matter, and have we been chaste these eight weeks?"

"For I will know the truth of your heart."

And then she said with great sorrow, "Forsooth I had rather see you be slain than we should turn again to our uncleanness."

And he said again, "You are no good wife."

And then she asked her husband what was the cause that he had not meddled with her eight weeks before, since she lay with him every night in his bed. And he said he was so made afraid when he would have touched her that he dared do no more.

"Now, good sir, amend yourself and ask God mercy, for I told you nearly three years since that you should be slain suddenly,[1] and now is this the third year, and yet I hope I shall have desire. Good sir, I pray you grant me what I shall ask, and I shall pray for you that you shall be saved through the mercy of our Lord Jesus Christ, and you shall have more reward in heaven than if you wore a hair cloth or a jacket of mail.[2] I pray you, suffer me to make a vow of chastity in whatever bishop's hand that God will."

"No," he said, "that will I not grant you, for now may I use you without deadly sin and then might I not so."

Then she said again, "If it be the will of the Holy Ghost to fulfill what I have said, I pray God you may consent thereto; and, if it be not the will of the Holy Ghost, I pray God you never consent thereto."

Then went they forth toward Bridlington in right hot weather, the aforesaid creature having great sorrow and great dread for her chastity. And, as they came by a cross, her husband set himself down under the cross, calling his wife unto him and saying these words unto her, "Margery, grant me my

1. A prophecy made to her by Christ, as related in chapter 9.

2. Sometimes worn against the skin, like a hair shirt, for penance.

desire, and I shall grant you your desire. My first desire is that we shall lie still together in one bed as we have done before; the second, that you shall pay my debts before you go to Jerusalem; and the third, that you shall eat and drink with me on Fridays[3] as you were wont to do."

"No, sir," she said, "to break the Friday I will never grant you while I live."

"Well," he said, "then shall I meddle you again."

She prayed him that he would give her leave to make her prayers, and he granted it well. Then she kneeled down beside a cross in the field and prayed in this manner with great abundance of tears, "Lord God, you know all things; you know what sorrow I have had to be chaste in my body to you all these three years, and now might I have my wish, and I dare not for love of you. For, if I would break that manner of fasting which you commanded me, to keep the Friday without food or drink, I should now have my desire. But, blessed Lord, you know I will not go against your will, and great now is my sorrow unless I find comfort in you. Now; blessed Jesus, make your will known to me, unworthy, so that I may follow thereafter and fulfill it with all my might."

And then our Lord Jesus Christ with great sweetness spoke to this creature, commanding her to go again to her husband and pray him to grant her what she desired. "And he shall have what he desires. For, my worthy daughter, this was the cause that I bade you to fast, for you should the sooner obtain and get your desire, and now it is granted you. I wish no longer for you to fast, therefore I bid you in the name of Jesus eat and drink as your husband does."

Then this creature thanked our Lord Jesus Christ for his grace and his goodness, then rose up and went to her husband, saying unto him, "Sir, if it pleases you, you shall grant me my desire, and you shall have your desire. Grant me that you shall not come in my bed, and I grant you to requite your debts before I go to Jerusalem. And make my body free to God so that you never challenge me by asking the debt of matrimony after this day while you live, and I shall eat and drink on the Friday at your bidding."

Then said her husband again to her, "As free may your body be to God as it has been to me."

This creature thanked God greatly, rejoicing that she had her desire, praying her husband that they should say three Our Father's in the worship of the Trinity[4] for the great grace that he had granted them. And so they did, kneeling under a cross, and afterward they ate and drank together in great gladness of spirit. This was on a Friday on Midsummer Eve. Then went they forth toward Bridlington and also to many other countries and spoke with God's servants, both anchorites and recluses and many other of our Lord's lovers, with many worthy clerks, doctors of divinity, and bachelors also in many different places. And this creature to divers[5] of them showed her feelings and her contemplations, as she was commanded to do, to learn if any deceit were in her feelings.

3. Traditionally fast days (when food and drink was restricted) in the Catholic Church, because Jesus was crucified on a Friday.

4. I.e., God the Father, Son, and Holy Spirit, the three viewed as a unity.

5. Some number, sundry.

From *Chapter 18*

[A MEETING WITH JULIAN]

* * *

And then she was bidden by our Lord to go to an anchoress in the same city, who was called Dame Julian.[6] And so she did and showed her the grace that God put in her soul of compunction, contrition, sweetness and devotion, compassion with holy meditation and high contemplation, and full many holy speeches and dalliances[7] that our Lord spoke to her soul, and many wonderful revelations which she showed to the anchoress to learn if there were any deceit in them, for the anchoress was expert in such things and good counsel could give.

The anchoress, hearing the marvelous goodness of our Lord, highly thanked God with all her heart for his visitation, counseling this creature to be obedient to the will of our Lord God and fulfill with all her mights whatever he put in her soul if it were not against the worship of God and profit of her fellow Christians, for, if it were, then it were not the moving of a good spirit but rather of an evil spirit.

"The Holy Ghost moves never a thing against charity,[8] and, if he did, he would be contrary to his own self, for he is all charity. Also he moves a soul to all chasteness, for chaste livers are called the temple of the Holy Ghost,[9] and the Holy Ghost makes a soul stable and steadfast in the right faith and the right belief. And a double[1] man in soul is ever unstable and unsteadfast in all his ways. He that is evermore doubting is like the flood of the sea, which is moved and borne about with the wind, and that man is not likely to receive the gifts of God. What creature that has these tokens, he must steadfastly believe that the Holy Ghost dwells in his soul. And much more, when God visits a creature with tears of contrition, devotion, or compassion, he may and ought to believe that the Holy Ghost is in his soul. Saint Paul says that the Holy Ghost asks for us with unspeakable mournings and weepings,[2] that is to say, he makes us ask and pray with mournings and weepings so plenteously that the tears may not be numbered. There may no evil spirit give these tokens, for Jerome[3] says that tears torment more the devil than do the pains of hell. God and the devil are evermore contrary, and they shall never dwell together in one place, and the devil has no power in a man's soul. Holy Writ says that the soul of a righteous man is the seat of God, and so I trust, sister, that you are. I pray God grant you perseverance. Set all your trust in God and fear not the language of the world, for the more despite, shame, and reproof that you have in the world, the greater is your merit in the sight of God. Patience is necessary unto you for in that shall you keep your soul."

Much was the holy dalliance that the anchoress and this creature had by commoning in the love of our Lord Jesus Christ the many days that they were together.

* * *

6. Julian of Norwich (1342–ca. 1416); see above, p. 37.
7. Conversations.
8. Christian love.

9. See 1 Corinthians 6.19.
1. Duplicitous.
2. Romans 8.26.
3. St. Jerome (ca. 340–420), a church father.

From *Chapter 28*

[PILGRIMAGE]

* * *

And so they[4] went forth into the Holy Land till they might see Jerusalem. And, when this creature saw Jerusalem, riding on an ass, she thanked God with all her heart, praying him for his mercy that, as he had brought her to see this earthly city Jerusalem, he would grant her grace to see the blissful city Jerusalem above, the city of heaven. Our Lord Jesus Christ, answering to her thought, granted her to have her desire. Then, for joy that she had and the sweetness that she felt in the dalliance of our Lord, she was in point to have fallen off her ass, for she might not bear the sweetness and grace that God wrought in her soul. Then two German pilgrims went to her and kept her from falling, of which one was a priest. And he put spices in her mouth to comfort her, thinking she had been sick. And so they helped her forth to Jerusalem.

And, when she came there, she said, "Sirs, I pray you be not displeased though I weep sorely in this holy place where our Lord Jesus Christ was quick[5] and dead."

Then went they to the temple in Jerusalem,[6] and they were let in on the one day at evensong time and abided therein till the next day at evensong time.

Then the friars[7] lifted up a cross and led the pilgrims about from one place to another where our Lord had suffered his pains and his passions, every man and woman bearing a wax candle in their hand. And the friars always, as they went about, told them what our Lord suffered in every place. And the foresaid creature wept and sobbed so plenteously as though she had seen our Lord with her bodily eye suffering his Passion at that time. Before her in her soul she saw him verily by contemplation, and that caused her to have compassion. And when they came up onto the Mount of Calvary, she fell down so that she might not stand or kneel but wallowed and twisted with her body, spreading her arms abroad, and cried with a loud voice as though her heart should have burst asunder, for in the city of her soul she saw verily and freshly how our Lord was crucified. Before her face she heard and saw in her ghostly sight the mourning of our Lady,[8] of Saint John and Mary Magdalene, and of many others who loved our Lord. And she had so great compassion and so great pain to see our Lord's pain that she might not keep herself from crying and roaring though she should have died from it.

And this was the first cry that ever she cried in any contemplation. And this manner of crying endured many years after this time for aught that any man might do, and therefore suffered she much despite and much reproof. The crying was so loud and so wonderful that it made the people astonished unless they had heard it before or else they knew the cause of the crying. And she had them so often that they made her right weak in her bodily

4. A company of pilgrims, including Margery.
5. Living.
6. The Church of the Holy Sepulcher, built on the site where Jesus was entombed after his crucifixion; only a limited number of pilgrims were admitted at a time.

7. The Franciscans, whose convent joined the church.
8. The Virgin Mary; medieval art often portrays these three figures at the foot of Jesus' cross (see John 19.25–26). "Ghostly": spiritual.

mights, and, namely,[9] if she heard of our Lord's Passion. And sometimes, when she saw the crucifix, or if she saw a man or a beast, whether it were,[1] had a wound or if a man beat a child before her or smote a horse or another beast with a whip, if she might see it or hear it, she thought she saw our Lord being beaten or wounded just as she saw in the man or in the beast, as well in the field as in the town, and by herself alone, as well as among the people.

First when she had her cryings at Jerusalem, she had them often times, and in Rome also. And, when she came home into England, first at her coming home it came but seldom, as it were once in a month, afterward once in the week, afterward daily, and once she had fourteen on one day, and another day she had seven, and so as God would visit her, sometime in the church, sometime in the street, sometime in the chamber, sometime in the field when God would send them, for she knew never time nor hour when they should come. And they came never without passing great sweetness of devotion and high contemplation.

And, as soon as she perceived that she should cry, she would keep it in as much as she might, so that the people should not have heard it, for it annoyed them. For some said it was a wicked spirit vexed her; some said it was a sickness; some said she had drunk too much wine; some banned[2] her; some wished she had been in the harbor; some would she had been in the sea in a bottomless boat; and so each man as he thought. Other ghostly men loved her and favored her the more. Some great clerks[3] said our Lady cried never so, nor no saint in heaven, but they knew full little what she felt, nor would they not believe that she might have abstained from crying if she wished.

* * *

Chapter 52

[CHARGES OF HERESY]

There was a monk who should preach in York, who had heard much slander and much evil language of the said creature. And, when he should preach, there was a great multitude of people to hear him, and she was present with them. And so, when he was in his sermon, he rehearsed[4] many matters so openly that the people conceived well it was because of her, wherefore her friends that loved her well were full sorry and heavy thereof, and she was much the more merry, for she had matter to prove her patience and her charity wherethrough she trusted to please our Lord Christ Jesus. When the sermon was done, a doctor of divinity who loved her well, with many others also, came to her and said, "Margery, how have you done this day?"

"Sir," she said, "right well, blessed be God. I have cause to be right merry and glad in my soul that I may suffer anything for his love, for he suffered much more for me."

Anon[5] after came a man of good will who loved her right well, with his

9. Especially. "Right": very.
1. Wherever it might be.
2. Cursed.

3. Clergymen.
4. Repeated.
5. Immediately.

wife and others, and led her seven miles thence to the Archbishop of York, and brought her into a fair chamber, where came a good clerk, saying to the good man who had brought her thither, "Sir, why have you and your wife brought this woman hither? She shall steal away from you, and then shall you have shame of her."

The good man said, "I dare well say she will abide and be at her answering[6] with good will."

On the next day she was brought into the Archbishop's chapel, and there came many of the Archbishop's household, despising her, calling her "lollard"[7] and "heretic," and swearing many a horrible oath that she should be burnt. And she, through the strength of Jesus, said again to them, "Sirs, I fear you shall be burnt in hell without end unless you amend yourselves of your swearing of oaths, for you keep not the commandments of God. I would not swear as you do for all the good[8] of this world."

Then they went away as if they were ashamed. She then, making her prayer in her mind, asked grace so to conduct herself that day as was most pleasant to God and profit to her own soul and good example to her fellow Christians. Our Lord, answering her, said it should be right well. At the last, the said Archbishop came into the chapel with his clerks, and sharply he said to her, "Why go you in white? Are you a maiden?"

She, kneeling on her knees before him, said, "No, sir, I am no maiden; I am a wife."

He commanded his household to fetch a pair of fetters and said she should be fettered, for she was a false heretic. And then she said, "I am no heretic, nor shall you prove me one."

The Archbishop went away and let her stand alone. Then she made her prayers to our Lord God almighty to help her and succor her against all her enemies, ghostly and bodily, a long while, and her flesh trembled and quaked wonderfully so that she was fain to put her hands under her clothes so that it should not be espied.

Afterward the Archbishop came again into the chapel with many worthy clerks, among which was the same doctor[9] who had examined her before and the monk who had preached against her a little time before in York. Some of the people asked whether she were a Christian woman or a Jew; some said she was a good woman, and some said no. Then the Archbishop took his seat, and his clerks also, each of them in his degree,[1] many people being present. And in the time while the people were gathering together and the Archbishop taking his seat, the said creature stood all behind, making her prayers for help and succor against her enemies with high devotion, so long that she melted all into tears. And at the last she cried loudly therewith, so that the Archbishop and his clerks and many people had great wonder of her, for they had not heard such crying before. When her crying was passed, she came before the Archbishop and fell down on her knees, the Archbishop saying full roughly unto her, "Why weep you so, woman?"

6. I.e., of the charges against her.
7. A follower of the English religious reformer John Wycliffe (ca. 1330–1384); viewed by the Catholic Church as heretics, the Lollards were numerous in England in the late 14th and early 15th century.
8. Goods; money.
9. Learned divine.
1. According to his rank.

She, answering, said, "Sir, you shall wish some day that you had wept as sorely as I."

And then anon, after the Archbishop put to her the Articles of our Faith,[2] to which God gave her grace to answer well and truly and readily without any great study so that he might not blame her, then he said to the clerks, "She knows her faith well enough. What shall I do with her?"

The clerks said, "We know well that she knows the Articles of the Faith, but we will not suffer her to dwell among us, for the people have great faith in her dalliance, and perhaps she might pervert some of them."

Then the Archbishop said unto her, "I am badly informed of you; I hear said you are a right wicked woman."

And she said again, "Sir, so I hear said that you are a wicked man. And, if you are as wicked as men say, you shall never come into heaven unless you amend yourself while you are here."

Then he said full roughly, "Why, you, what say men of me?"

She answered, "Other men, sir, can tell you well enough."

Then said a great clerk with a furred hood, "Peace, you speak of yourself and let him be."

Afterward said the Archbishop to her, "Lay your hand on the book here before me and swear that you shall go out of my diocese as soon as you may."

"No, sir," she said, "I pray you, give me leave to go again into York to take my leave of my friends."

Then he gave her leave for one day or two. She thought it was too short a time, wherefore she said again, "Sir, I may not go out of this diocese so hastily, for I must tarry and speak with good men before I go, and I must, sir, with your leave, go to Bridlington and speak with my confessor,[3] a good man, who was the good prior's confessor, who is now canonized."

Then said the Archbishop to her, "You shall swear that you shall neither teach nor challenge the people in my diocese."

"No, sir, I shall not swear," she said, "for I shall speak of God and reprove those who swear great oaths wheresoever I go, unto the time that the pope and holy church have ordained that no man shall be so hardy[4] to speak of God, for God almighty forbids not, sir, that we shall speak of him. And also the gospel makes mention that, when the woman had heard our Lord preach, she came before him with a loud voice and said, 'Blessed be the womb that bore you and the teats that gave you suck. Then our Lord said again to her, 'Forsooth so are they blessed that hear the word of God and keep it.'[5] And therefore, sir, I think that the gospel gives me leave to speak of God."

"A, sir," said the clerks, "here know we well that she has a devil within her, for she speaks of the gospel."

Immediately a great clerk brought forth a book and laid Saint Paul for his part against her that no woman should preach.[6]

She, answering thereto, said, "I preach not, sir, I go in no pulpit. I use but communication and good words, and that will I do while I live."

Then said a doctor who had examined her beforetime, "Sir, she told me the worst tales of priests that ever I heard."

2. The Apostles' Creed, a statement of belief ascribed by tradition to the twelve apostles.
3. William Sleighholme, who was also confessor to St. John of Bridlington (d. 1379), recently canonized.
4. Bold.
5. Luke 11.27–28.
6. 1 Corinthians 14.34–35.

The bishop commanded her to tell that tale.

"Sir, by your reverence, I spoke but of one priest by way of example, who as I have learned went wayward in a wood through the sufferance of God for the profit of his soul until the night came upon him. He, destitute of his lodging, found a fair garden, in which he rested that night, having a fair pear tree in the midst all flourished with flowers and embellished, and blooms full delectable to his sight, where came a bear, great and violent, ugly to behold, shaking the pear tree and knocking down the flowers. Greedily this grievous beast ate and devoured those fair flowers. And, when he had eaten them, turning his tail end in the priest's presence, voided them out again at the shameful part.

"The priest, having great abomination of that loathly sight, conceiving great heaviness[7] for doubt of what it might mean, on the next day wandered forth on his way all heavy and pensive and fortuned to meet with a seemly aged man, like a palmer or a pilgrim, who inquired of the priest the cause of his heaviness. The priest, rehearsing the matter before written, said he conceived great dread and heaviness when he beheld that loathly beast befoul and devour such fair flowers and blooms and afterward so horribly devoid them before him at his tail end, and he not understanding what this might mean.

"Then the palmer, showing himself the messenger of God, thus addressed him, 'Priest, you yourself are the pear tree, somewhat flourishing and flowering through saying your service and administering the sacraments, though you do so undevotedly, for you take full little heed how you say your matins[8] and your service, just so it is blabbered to an end. Then go you to your mass without devotion, and for your sin have you full little contrition. You receive there the fruit of everlasting life, the sacrament of the altar, in full feeble disposition. Afterward all the day after you mis-spend your time, you give yourself to buying and selling, chopping and changing,[9] as if you were a man of the world. You sit at the ale, giving yourself to gluttony and excess, to lust of your body, through lechery and uncleanness. You break the commandments of God through swearing, lying, detraction, and backbiting, and the use of other such sins. Thus by your misgovernance,[1] like the loathly bear, you devour and destroy the flowers and blooms of virtuous living to your endless damnation and many men's hindering unless you have grace from repentance and amending.' "

Then the Archbishop liked well the tale and commended it, saying it was a good tale. And the clerk who had examined her beforetime, in the absence of the Archbishop, said, "Sir, this tale smites me to the heart."

The foresaid creature said to the clerk, "A, worshipful doctor, sir, in the place where my dwelling is mostly, is a worthy clerk, a good preacher, who boldly speaks against the misgovernance of the people and will flatter no man. He says many times in the pulpit, 'If any man is evil pleased with my preaching, note him well, for he is guilty.' And right so, sir," said she to the clerk, "fare you by me,[2] God forgive it you."

The clerk knew not well what he might say to her. Afterward the same

7. Sadness.
8. Morning prayers.
9. Bartering, exchanging.

1. Misconduct, misbehavior.
2. You behave with me.

clerk came to her and prayed her for forgiveness that he had been so against her. Also he prayed her specially to pray for him. And then anon after, the Archbishop said, "Where shall I find a man who might lead this woman from me?"

Quickly many young men started up, and every man said, "My Lord, I will go with her."

The Archbishop answered, "You are too young; I will not have you."

Then a good sober man from the Archbishop's household asked his Lord what he would give him if he should lead her. The Archbishop offered him five shillings, and the man asked for a noble.[3] The Archbishop, answering, said, "I will not spend so much on her body."

"Yes, good sir," said the said creature, "our Lord shall reward you right well again."

Then the Archbishop said to the man, "See, here is five shillings, and lead her fast out of this country."

She, kneeling down on her knees, asked his blessing. He, praying her to pray for him, blessed her and let her go.

Then she, going again to York, was received by many people and by full worthy clerks, who delighted in our Lord who had given her, not lettered, wit and wisdom to answer so many learned men without villainy or blame. Thanks be to God.

Chapter 76

[NURSING HER HUSBAND]

It happened on a time that the husband of the said creature, a man of great age passing three score years,[4] as he would have come down from his chamber barefoot and bare-leg, he slithered or else failed of his footing and fell down to the ground from the steps, with his head under him grievously broken and bruised, insomuch that he had in his head five rolls of soft material in the wounds[5] for many days while his head was healing. And, as God would, it was known to some of his neighbors how he had fallen down the steps, perhaps through the din and the rushing of his falling. And so they came to him and found him lying with his head under him, half on life,[6] all streaked with blood, never likely to have spoken with priest nor with clerk[7] unless by high grace and miracle. Then the said creature, his wife, was sent for, and so she came to him. Then was he taken up and his head was sewn, and he was sick a long time after, so that men thought that he should have been dead. And then the people said, if he died, his wife was worthy to be hanged for his death, forasmuch as she might have kept[8] him and did not.

They dwelled not together; they lay not together, for, as is written before, they both with one assent and with free will of the other had made a vow to live chaste. And therefore to avoid all perils they dwelled and sojourned in divers places where no suspicion should be had of their incontinence,[9] for first they dwelled together after they had made their vow, and then the people

3. A coin worth 6⅔ shillings.
4. I.e., more than 60 years old.
5. Inserted to encourage drainage.
6. Half alive.

7. I.e., to confess and receive last rites.
8. Taken care of.
9. Unchastity. "Divers": separate.

slandered them and said they used[1] their lust and their liking as they did before their vow-making. And, when they went out on pilgrimage or to see and speak with other ghostly creatures, many evil folk whose tongues were their own, lacking the dread and love of our Lord Jesus Christ, thought and said that they went rather to woods, groves, or valleys to use the lust of their bodies so that the people should not espy it nor know it. They, having knowledge how prone the people were to think evil of them, desiring to avoid all occasion, inasmuch as they might goodly, by their good will and their mutual consent, they parted asunder as touching their board[2] and their chambers, and went to board in divers places. And this was the cause that she was not with him and also that she should not be hindered from her contemplation.

And therefore, when he had fallen and grievously was hurt, as is said before, the people said, if he died, it was worthy that she answer for his death. Then she prayed to our Lord that her husband might live a year and she delivered from slander if it were his pleasure. Our Lord said to her mind, "Daughter, you shall have your boon, for he shall live, and I have wrought a great miracle for you that he was not dead. And I bid you take him home and keep him for my love."

She said, "No, good Lord, for I shall then not tend to you as I do now."

"Yes, daughter," said our Lord, "you shall have as much meed[3] for keeping him and helping him in his need at home as if you were in church to make your prayers. And you have said many times that you would fain keep me. I pray you now keep him for the love of me, for he has sometime fulfilled your will and my will both, and he has made your body free to me so that you should serve me and live chaste and clean, and therefore I will that you be free to help him at his need in my name."

"A, Lord," said she, "for your mercy grant me grace to obey your will and fulfill your will and let never my ghostly enemies have any power to hinder me from fulfilling your will."

Then she took home her husband with her and kept him years after, as long as he lived, and had full much labor with him, for in his last days he turned childish again and lacked reason so that he could not do his own easement by going to a stool, or else he would not, but, as a child, voided his natural digestion in his linen clothes where he sat by the fire or at the table, whether it were, he would spare no place. And therefore was her labor much the more in washing and wringing and her expense in making fires and hindered her full much from her contemplation, so that many times she should have been irked at her labor save she bethought herself of how she in her young age had full many delectable thoughts, fleshly lusts, and inordinate loves for his person.[4] And therefore she was glad to be punished with the same person and took it much the more easily and served him and helped him, as she thought, as she would have done Christ himself.

1436–38

1. Practiced.
2. Daily meals.
3. Reward.
4. Body.

JULIANA BERNERS
ca. 1388–?

Little is known of Juliana Berners (sometimes known as Juliana Barnes), who evidently authored a guide to hunting as well as several essays on beasts of the field that were included in an early treatise on these matters titled *The Book of St. Albans* (1486). Some scholars have identified her as the daughter of Sir James Berners, a favorite of Richard II, while others speculate that she lived at the manor of Julians Barnes. Still others claim that she was the prioress of Sopwell Abbey, near St. Albans, where she translated and versified two prose treatises on hunting as educational texts for upper-class children. In addition, she is thought to have composed a work on fly-fishing (*Treatyse of Fyshinge with an Angle*), a sport about which she roundly declared, "It will be a very great pleasure to see the fair bright shining-scaled fishes deceived by your crafty means and drawn to land." If, as is likely, Juliana Berners did in fact compose the portion of *The Book of St. Albans* from which our selection is drawn, she was perhaps the first Englishwoman in print and one of the first Englishwomen to work in what was to become a rich tradition of female-authored advice literature. She was apparently also, as a writer for *Sports Illustrated* noted in 1996, a pioneering theorist of fishing: "One of the flies depicted in her *Treatyse*, the 'stone flye,' is still being tied today."

 The excerpts printed here have been rendered into modern English by the scholar and translator Dorothy Gilbert, but their verse style preserves the terse vitality of the original. Frank and practical, these passages focus with remarkable clarity on the anatomy and physiology of game animals (the deer, the hare) as they were viewed by medieval thinkers. Like the other portions of *The Book of St. Albans* probably composed by Juliana Berners, they reveal that women in this period were rarely squeamish about the physical details of field and kitchen, hunt and home.

FROM THE BOOK OF ST. ALBANS[1]

Hunting Terminology

Beasts of Venery[2]

Wherever you fare by forest or fell[3]
My dear child, take heed how Tristram[4] doth you tell,
The kinds of animals for hunting that he knew,
Listen to your mother; she will teach them to you.
5 Four kinds of hunted animals there are:
The first of them is the hart;[5] the second is the hare;
 One of them is the boar;
 The wolf, too; and no more.

1. Modernized and annotated by Dorothy Gilbert.
2. Hunting. Game animals were classified either as "beasts of venery" or as "beasts of chase." The distinction appears to have been one of etiquette and tradition, not law, though it may be that a higher prestige was associated with the hunting of beasts of venery, since they were also listed as "beasts of the forest," i.e., beasts that were protected by the law that governed the royal forests, while they lived on land that formed part of the forest domain. Beasts of the chase, on the other hand, were protected only by the common law,

while they lived in a "chase" (enclosure).
3. A hill or ridge; here, probably a wild, elevated, or precipitous stretch of moorland or open pasture, as contrasted with a wooded area. The original has "by fryth or by fell," a conventional phrase meaning "by woods or by (open, high) hill."
4. Sir Tristram (or Tristan), in Arthurian tradition the lover of Isolde and nephew of King Mark, was famed for his consummate skill as a hunter and his knowledge of all the lore and etiquette of the subject.
5. Male red deer.

Beasts of the Chase

Wherever you go, on what plain, in what place,
I will tell you which are the beasts of the chase.
One of them is the buck, the other is the doe,
The fox and the marten and the wild roe,[6]
5 And you shall, my dear child, with the other beasts all,
Wherever you find them, "rascal"[7] them call,
 In woodland or fell,
 Or forest; this I tell.

Note Here the Age of a Hart

Now to speak of the hart, if you will learn it here,
You shall call him a calf, when his age is a year.
"Brocket" is what you call him when he is two,
"Spayad" when he is three; thus you learn what to do.
5 Call him a stag, when he is four,
At five, call him a great stag; mind your mother's lore.
 Call him a hart, when he is six;
Do so, my child, while you have your wits.

The Hare

Now to speak of the hare, my son, certainly
This beast shall be called king of all venery.
For all hunting's fine terms and brave blasts,[1] be aware,
Grow out of the tracking and finding of the hare.
5 For, my dear child, I can take it on hand[2]
He is the most wonderful beast in any land.
For he casts droppings, and pellets, he has suet and fat,[3]
Chews his cud constantly, and has front teeth that stick out.
And sometimes he is male, and like a male creature,
10 And sometimes he is female, and bears young by nature.[4]
And when he is female, and his young are formed within,
They grow in three stages, before he parts with them:
First rough, and then smooth, the two babies will be,
And then unformed lumps, during his pregnancy,[5]
15 When his phase is female.
 So I tell my tale.

6. Deer; a small, delicately formed Eurasian species, known in England from Anglo-Saxon times. "Marten": a thick-furred animal resembling a weasel.
7. Animals not hunted as game, e.g., skunks and badgers.
1. I.e., of the horn.
2. I guarantee, I undertake; I assure you.
3. Aristotle (*Hist. Anim.* 2.17) describes suet and fat as occurring in different animals: "those with teeth in both jaws have fat, those without have suet." Thus the hare may be unusual.
4. A belief in the hare's hermaphroditism and other sexual peculiarities—found in the Roman dramatist Terence's *Eunuchus* (161 B.C.E.; a common school text), in Latin encyclopedias, and in biblical commentary—seems to have been widespread in the Middle Ages and is thought even to have influenced Chaucer's *Pardoner's Tale* (1386–1400).
5. Both Aristotle (*Hist. Anim.* 6.33; ca. 340 B.C.E.) and the Roman Pliny (*Nat. Hist.* 8.81.217; 77 C.E.) state that a hare can conceive young while already pregnant or nursing. This belief probably gave rise to comments like Berners'.

The Reward for the Hounds

When your hounds by main force have the hare, and she's dead,
The hunter shall reward them then with the head,
The shoulders, flanks, bowels of the animal,
And all things in the belly save only the gall,
5 And the viscera; that
They do not get.
This reward for the dogs that is dealt out on the ground
Good hunters call the "hallow," the hare's parts for the hound.
Then the loins of the hare, look you do not forget,
10 But bring them to the kitchen, for the lord's meat.[6]
 And of this same hare
 Speak we no more.

More about the Hare: Why the Hare Voids Its Dung Standing Up, and Makes Pellets of It

"Yet, master, I would know, if you'll lend me your wit,
Why the hare voids dung standing, and makes pellets of it,
When all other hunted beasts, game generally,
Void standing or squatting, as we can see."
5 "That I can surely tell thee," the master answered then,
"Why the hare stands and makes pellets, as is known to men.
He stands because his body is so full of suet,
And he makes pellets, men say, because of all his fat.
And he crouches on his hocks when he lets it go—
10 No other game does that, as far as men know."
"How many beasts void standing, I would fain find out,
And also I would learn, how many of them squat?"
"To tell you that," said the master, "is a job done easily.
All beasts that bear suet, and stand upright, you must see,
15 Let their scat fall when they stand, you may be sure of that,
And other beasts—the squatting kind—get rid of it when they squat."

<div align="right">1486</div>

6. "Meete" in the original means "food, nourishment."

ANNE ASKEW
1521–1546

Polemicist, poet, and early Protestant martyr, Anne Askew was a woman of fierce
independence, lively imagination, and considerable theological sophistication. Born
and raised in an old Lincolnshire family that gave her an unusually good education,
she studied the Bible with special passion and engaged at an early age in scriptural
disputation with the local clergy. But at fifteen she was compelled to marry one

Thomas Kyme, although, already strong willed and a proto-feminist, she refused to accept either his surname or his Catholic faith. Eventually her husband turned her out of his house because of her beliefs. Leaving behind her two children, she journeyed to London, where she unsuccessfully sought a divorce and became even more deeply committed to religious dissent, preaching, distributing radical tracts, and working closely with other reformers, who even included Katharine Parr, the sixth and last wife of Henry VIII.

Arrested several times for her heterodox views, Askew consistently refused to repudiate her beliefs and was condemned to torture and execution. Yet despite four weeks of excruciating torment on the rack in the Tower of London, she remained steadfast in her Protestantism; nor would she reveal the names of her associates, although numerous clerics and government officials especially sought to force her to implicate Katharine Parr. When she was finally burned at the stake, Askew had been so crippled by torture that she had to be carried to the place of execution. Before she died, however, she smuggled an account of her experience to sympathetic friends. After her death it was included in John Foxe's *Acts and Monuments* (1563), also known as *Foxe's Book of Martyrs*; it has recently been republished as *The Examinations of Anne Askew*.

A vivid narrative, skillful polemic, and spiritual autobiography, *The Examinations* records Askew's defiant commitment to her unchangeable beliefs: "They said to me there that I was a heretic, and condemned by the law if I would stand in my opinion. I answered that I was no heretic, neither yet deserved I any death by the law of God. But as concerning [my faith], I would not, I said, deny it, because I knew it to be true." The same spirit of indomitable rebellion informs the combative "Ballad Which Anne Askewe Made and Sang When She Was in Newgate."

The Ballad Which Anne Askew Made and Sang When She Was in Newgate[1]

Like as the armèd knight
Appointed to the field,
With this world will I fight
And faith shall be my shield.[2]
5 Faith is that weapon strong
Which will not fail at need;
My foes therefore among
Therewith will I proceed.
 As it is had in strength
10 And force of Christ's way,
It will prevail at length
Though all the devils say nay.
 Faith in the father's old
Obtainèd rightwiseness[3]
15 Which make me very bold
To fear no world's distress.

1. After being arrested and examined for heresy in June 1545, Askew was released, but in June 1546 she was arrested again and tortured; she was burned at the stake in July. This ballad was included in two accounts of her ordeal, printed in 1546 and 1547, by John Bale, a Protestant bishop.

"Newgate": a London prison.
2. Ephesians 6.13–17 urges the Christian to put on "the whole armor of God," including "the shield of faith, wherewith ye shall be able to quench all the fiery darts of the wicked."
3. Righteousness.

I now rejoice in heart
And hope bid me do so,
For Christ will take my part
20 And ease me of my woe.
Thou sayst lord, who so kneck,[4]
To them wilt thou attend;
Undo therefore the lock
And thy strong power send.
25 More enemies now I have
Than hairs upon my head
Let them not me deprave,[5]
But fight thou in my stead.
On thee my care I cast
30 For all their cruel spite
I set not by their haste,[6]
For thou art my delight.
I am not she that list[7]
My anchor to let fall
35 For every drizzling mist
My ship substantial.
Not oft use I to write
In prose nor yet in rhyme,
Yet will I show one sight
40 That I saw in my time.
I saw a royal throne
Where Justice should have sit,
But in her stead was one
Of modie[8] cruel wit.
45 Absorbed[9] was rightwiseness
As of the raging flood;
Satan in his excess
Sucked up the guiltless blood.
Then thought I, Jesus lord,
50 When thou shalt judge us all,
Hard is it to record
On these men what will fall.
Yet lord I thee desire
For that[1] they do to me,
55 Let them not taste the hire[2]
Of their iniquity.[3]

1546

4. Knocks. Matthew 7.7: "Ask, and it shall be given you; seek, and ye shall find; knock, and it shall be opened unto you."
5. Defame.
6. I do not care about their rashness.
7. Chooses.
8. Haughty; angry.

9. Swallowed up.
1. What.
2. Recompense.
3. Compare the words of Jesus after he is crucified: "Father, forgive them; for they know not what they do" (Luke 23.34).

QUEEN ELIZABETH I
1533–1603

By 1558, when Elizabeth Tudor ascended the throne at the age of twenty-five, she was proficient in Greek and Latin as well as French, Italian, Spanish, and German. Her translations, speeches, and poems illustrate her political genius and her rhetorical ingenuity. She needed both of these assets, for she faced personal, political, and religious opposition to her rule. Her father, Henry VIII, had wanted a male heir, and her mother, Anne Boleyn, was executed on charges of adultery and treason when Elizabeth was three years old. The child had been declared illegitimate by Pope Clement VII, who refused to sanction her father's remarriage, and even after her supremacy had been established, she confronted public reservations about her unmarried state. As monarch, she was caught in the middle: she had to deal with a Protestant Parliament, papal objection to her legitimacy, and constant threat of war from the Catholic powers, Spain and France. As the head of the church established by her father, Elizabeth presided over an institution that, in its structure, doctrines, and rituals, was effectively Roman Catholic; Henry had simply replaced the pope as the supreme ruler of the church in England. Elizabeth was opposed on the one hand by Catholics, who resented Henry's rejection of papal supremacy, and on the other hand by Puritan Protestants, who believed that the church had not been sufficiently "purified" of its Roman Catholic elements. Neither Protestant nor Catholic, Elizabeth, to ensure peace in England, followed a middle course, which eventually prevailed and became Anglicanism.

Most historians agree that, paradoxically enough, Queen Elizabeth achieved complete sovereignty only after a papal condemnation of 1570 excommunicated her and released her subjects from their allegiance to her rule. Public opinion consolidated against her Catholic rival, Mary Queen of Scots, and in favor of Elizabeth, who quickly became the symbol of English nationalism. When, in 1588, she commanded land forces and supervised naval raids against a papal-financed Spanish fleet (the famous Armada) that was planning to invade Britain, she defeated the last pretender to the throne, Philip II of Spain. Her resulting popularity was enhanced by the diplomatic course she maintained in strengthening the Anglican Church to resist the influence of both the Catholics and the Puritans. During the prolific literary age that was named for her forty-five-year-long reign, she was celebrated in many poems and plays as a uniquely English embodiment of the female power associated with such biblical and mythological heroines as Judith, Esther, Diana, Astraea, Gloriana, and Minerva. In her own writing, moreover, she revealed the same witty intelligence that distinguishes so much Elizabethan literature.

The Doubt of Future Foes[1]

The doubt of future foes exiles my present joy,
And wit[2] me warns to shun such snares as threaten mine annoy;
For falsehood now doth flow, and subjects' faith doth ebb,
Which should not be if reason ruled or wisdom weaved the web.
5 But clouds of joys untried do cloak aspiring minds,

1. "The poem concerns Elizabeth's Roman Catholic cousin, Mary Stuart, Queen of Scotland, who in 1568 sought refuge in England from her rebellious subjects. Mary was the focus of several Roman Catholic conspiracies to place her on the English throne in place of Elizabeth. 'Doubt': fear" [Barbara Lewalski's note].
2. Intelligence.

Which turn to rain of late repent by changéd course of winds.
The top of hope supposed the root upreared shall be,[3]
And fruitless all their grafted[4] guile, as shortly ye shall see.
The dazzled eyes with pride, which great ambition blinds,
10 Shall be unsealed by worthy wights[5] whose foresight falsehood finds.
The daughter of debate that discord aye[6] doth sow
Shall reap no gain where former rule still peace hath taught to know.
No foreign banished wight shall anchor in this port;
Our realm brooks not seditious sects, let them elsewhere resort.
15 My rusty sword through rest shall first his edge employ
To poll their tops[7] that seek such change or gape[8] for future joy.

1570 1589

[Ah Silly Pug, Wert Thou So Sore Afraid][1]

Ah silly pug, wert thou so sore afraid,
Mourn not (my Wat[2]) nor be thou so dismayed,
It passeth fickle fortune's power and skill,
To force my heart to think thee any ill.
5 No fortune base thou sayest shall alter thee,
And may so blind a witch[3] so conquer me?
No no my pug, though fortune were not blind,
Assure thy self she could not rule my mind.
Fortune I know sometimes doth conquer kings
10 And rules & reigns on earth & earthly things,
But never think fortune can bear the sway,
If virtue watch & will not her obey.
Ne chose I thee by fickle fortune's rede,[4]
Ne she shall force me alter[5] with such speed
15 But if to try this mistress jest with thee,
. [6]
Pull up thy heart, suppress thy brackish[7] tears,
Torment thee not, but put away thy fears;
Dead to all joys & living unto woe,
Slain quite by her that ne're gave wiseman blow
20 Revive again & live without all dread,
The less afraid the better thou shalt speed.[8]

ca. 1578–88 1992

3. I.e., her enemies' unfounded hopes concentrate on the "top," or outcome of their schemes, while Elizabeth defeats them by pulling up their "roots."
4. Continues the botanical metaphor: her enemies have unsuccessfully tried to "graft" their plans onto roots that will not support them.
5. Men.
6. Always. "Discord" is the object of "sow."
7. To prune or crop the tops of trees, with an obvious suggestion of beheading.
8. Have a longing.
1. This poem was written in answer to one by Sir Walter Ralegh, probably "Fortune Hath Taken

Thee Away, My Love" (published 1589). "Silly": deserving pity or compassion; also foolish, defenseless, or lowly. "Pug": a term of endearment.
2. A diminutive of Walter.
3. I.e., fortune, often personified as a woman, and as blind or blindfolded.
4. Counsel. "Ne": neither.
5. To change. "Ne": nor.
6. A line of the poem may here be missing; or perhaps line 15, with its near-rhyme, is part of a triplet.
7. Salty.
8. Attain your purpose.

On Monsieur's Departure[1]

I grieve and dare not show my discontent,
I love and yet am forced to seem to hate,
I do, yet dare not say I ever meant,[2]
I seem stark mute but inwardly do prate.[3]
5 I am and not, I freeze and yet am burned,
Since from myself another self I turned.

My care is like my shadow in the sun,
Follows me flying, flies when I pursue it,
Stands and lies by me, doth what I have done.
10 His too familiar care doth make me rue it.
 No means I find to rid him from my breast,
 Till by the end of things[4] it be suppressed.

Some gentler passion slide into my mind,
For I am soft and made of melting snow;
15 Or be more cruel, love, and so be kind.
Let me or float or sink, be high or low.
 Or[5] let me live with some more sweet content,
 Or die and so forget what love ere meant.

1823

Speech to the Troops at Tilbury[1]

My loving people,

 We have been persuaded by some that are careful of[2] our safety, to take heed how we commit our selves to armed multitudes, for fear of treachery; but I assure you I do not desire to live to distrust my faithful and loving people.⟦Let tyrants fear, I have always so behaved myself that, under God, I have placed my chiefest strength and safeguard in the loyal hearts and good-will of my subjects;⟧and therefore I am come amongst you, as you see, at this time, not for my recreation and disport,[3] but being resolved, in the midst and heat of the battle, to live or die amongst you all; to lay down for my God, and for my kingdom, and my people, my honor and my blood, even in the dust.⟦I know I have the body but of a weak and feeble woman; but I have the heart and stomach of a king, and of a king of England too, and think foul scorn that Parma or Spain,[4] or any prince of Europe, should dare to invade the borders of my realm; to which rather than any dishonor shall grow by me, I myself will take up arms, I myself will be your general, judge, and

1. "Monsieur" has been identified as either the French duke of Anjou (1555–1584), with whom Elizabeth had negotiated marriage, or the earl of Essex (1567–1601), one of her favorite courtiers.
2. I.e., meant to do.
3. Chatter.
4. The Day of Judgment.
5. Either.
1. Delivered by Elizabeth to land forces that had assembled at Tilbury in anticipation of the landing of the Spanish Armada, a fleet of warships sent by

Philip II to invade England. That the Armada was defeated at sea, and so never reached England, does not diminish Elizabeth's courage in personally leading her troops.
2. Anxious for.
3. Entertainment.
4. Alessandro Farnese, duke of Parma (1545–1592), was expected to join Philip II, the king of Spain (1527–1598; r. 1556–98), in the Invasion of England.

rewarder of every one of your virtues in the field. I know already, for your forwardness you have deserved rewards and crowns;[5] and We do assure you in the word of a prince, they shall be duly paid you. In the mean time, my lieutenant general[6] shall be in my stead, than whom never prince commanded a more noble or worthy subject; not doubting but by your obedience to my general, by your concord in the camp, and your valour in the field, we shall shortly have a famous victory over those enemies of my God, of my kingdom, and of my people.

1588 1752

5. English coins; also possibly honorary titles. 6. Robert Dudley, earl of Leicester (1532–1588).

ISABELLA WHITNEY
fl. 1567–1573

"Till some household cares me tie, / My books and pen I will apply," declared the young Isabella Whitney in a verse letter to a married sister. The first Englishwoman to publish a book of poems, Whitney abbreviated her name to "Is. W." when she signed both her broadside *Copy of a Letter Lately Written in Meter, by a Young Gentlewoman: to her Unconstant Lover. With an Admonition to All Young Gentlewomen, and to all Other Maids in General to Beware of Men's Flattery* (1567) and her major collection, *A Sweet Nosegay or Pleasant Posy, Containing a Hundred and Ten Philosophical Flowers* (1573). Yet even so modest a signature was a daring gesture.

Born into a middle-class, Reformist family, Whitney appears to have had two brothers, including one who authored a collection of poems titled *A Choice of Emblems* (1586), along with several sisters who served in genteel London households. Little else is known of her life except that by 1600 she may have acquired a husband and two children. Her most ambitious work, "The Author . . . Maketh Her Will and Testament," is a mock will in which she bequeaths to the city of London all its most salient characteristics. Often sardonic in its portrayal of contemporary social institutions (shops, prisons, markets, Inns of Court), the poem records vivid details of daily life in urban sixteenth-century England, from the lucrative activities of tailors ("such as make the sweeping cloaks") to the unlucky lot of the mad (those in Bedlam who "out of tune do talk"). But despite Whitney's wit and vitality, her works have only recently begun to find their way back into print, with excerpts from *A Sweet Nosegay*, including her remarkable "Will and Testament," now republished in collections of Renaissance verse. The text we include here was rendered in modern English by the scholar and poet Mary Moore.

Will and Testament[1]

The author (though loath to leave the city) upon her friend's procurement is constrained to depart, wherefore she feigneth as she would die and maketh her will and testament, as followeth, with large legacies of such goods and

1. We are grateful for the editing and annotations by Mary Moore.

riches which she most abundantly hath left behind her, and thereof maketh
London sole executor to see her legacies performed.

A communication which the author had to London, before she made her will

The time is come I must depart
 from thee, ah, famous city:
I never yet to rue my smart[2]
 did find that thou hadst pity.
5 Wherefore, small cause there is that I
 would grieve from thee [to] go,
But many women foolishly,
 like me and other more,
Do such a fixèd fancy set
10 on those which least deserve
That long it is ere wit[3] we get
 away from them to swerve.
But Time with pity oft will tell,
 to those that will her try,
15 Whether it best be more to mell,[4]
 or utterly defy.
And now hath time me put in mind
 of thy great cruelness,
That never once a help would find
20 to ease me in distress.
Thou never yet wouldst credit give
 to board me for a year,
Nor with apparel me relieve
 except thou payèd were.[5]
25 No, no, thou never didst me good
 nor ever wilt, I know;
Yet am I in no angry mood,
 but will, or ere[6] I go,
In perfect love and charity
30 my testament here write,
And leave to thee such treasury
 as I in it recite.
Now stand aside and give me leave
 to write my latest will:
35 And see that none you do deceive
 of[7] that I leave them till.[8]

The manner of her will, and what she left to London and to all those in it at her departing

I whole in body and in mind
 but very weak in purse,

2. Regret my pain.
3. Intelligence.
4. Interfere, concern oneself.
5. I.e., to board and clothe her on credit.

6. Before.
7. Cheat out of.
8. To them.

Do make and write my testament
40 for fear it will be worse.[9]
And first I wholly do commend
 my soul and body eke[1]
To God the Father and the Son,
 so long as I can speak.
45 And after speech, my soul to him,
 and body to the grave,
Till time that all shall rise again,
 their judgment for to have.
And then I hope they both[2] shall meet
50 to dwell for aye in joy
Whereas I trust to see my friends
 released from all annoy.[3]
Thus have you heard touching my soul
 and body what I mean;
55 I trust you all will witness bear,
 I have a steadfast brain.
And now let me dispose such things
 as I shall leave behind,
That those which will receive the same
60 may know my willing mind.
I first of all to London leave,
 because I there was bred,
Brave buildings rare, of churches store,
 and Paul's to the head.[4]
65 Between the same, fair streets there be
 and people goodly store;
Because their keeping craveth cost,[5]
 I yet will leave hem more.
First, for their food, I butchers leave,
70 that every day shall kill;
By Thames you shall have brewers store,
 and bakers at your will.
And such as orders do observe,[6]
 and eat fish thrice a week,
75 I leave two streets full fraught[7] therewith;
 they need not far to seek.
Watling Street and Canwick Street
 I full of woolen leave,
And linen store in Friday Street
80 if they me not deceive.
And those which are of calling such
 that costlier they require,
I mercers[8] leave, with silk so rich

9. I.e., she later will not be whole in body and mind.
1. Also.
2. I.e., body and soul.
3. Trouble, hardship. "Whereas": where.
4. I.e., I leave to London fine buildings, a "store"

of many churches, and before them all St. Paul's.
5. Requires expenditure.
6. Those who are ministers or clergymen.
7. Supplied, filled.
8. Those who deal in textile fabrics, especially in costly materials.

as any would desire.
85 In Cheap,[9] of them they store shall find,
 and likewise in that street
 I goldsmiths leave, with jewels such
 as are for ladies meet.
 And plate to furnish cupboards with
90 full brave there shall you find,
 With purl of silver and of gold
 to satisfy your mind.
 With hoods, bongraces, hats, or caps,
 such store are in that street,
95 As if on tone side you should miss,
 the tother[1] serves you feat.
 For nets of every kind of sort,
 I leave within the pawn,[2]
 French ruffs, high purls, gorgets, and sleeves
100 of any kind of lawn.
 For purse or knives, for comb or glass,
 or any needful knack,
 I by the Stocks[3] have left a boy
 will ask you what you lack.
105 I hose do leave in Birchin Lane,
 of any kind of size,
 For women stitched, for men both trunks
 and those of Gascon guise,[4]
 Boots, shoes, or pantables good store,
110 Saint Martin's hath for you;
 In Cornwall,[5] there I leave you beds,
 and all that 'longs thereto.
 For women, shall you tailors have:
 by Bow, the chiefest dwell;
115 In every lane you some shall find
 can do indifferent well.[6]
 And for the men, few streets or lanes,
 but body-makers[7] be,
 And such as make the sweeping cloaks
120 with guards[8] beneath the knee.
 Artillery at Temple Bar
 and dagges at Tower Hill;
 Swords and bucklers of the best
 are nigh the Fleet until.
125 Now when thy folk are fed and clad
 with such as I have named,
 For dainty mouths and stomachs weak,
 some junkets[9] must be framed.

9. Cheapside Market, near St. Paul's.
1. "Tone . . . tother": the one . . . the other.
2. The upper walk or gallery of the Royal Exchange.
3. A market in the center of London.
4. Two kinds of breeches: trunk-hose (full and baglike) and gaskins (wide breeches).
5. "Cornwallish ground" in Vintry Ward.
6. Fairly well.
7. Makers of clothes for the body, tailors.
8. Stripes.
9. Confections or delicacies.

Wherefore, I 'pothecaries leave,
130 with banquets[1] in their shop;
Physicians also for the sick,
 diseases for to stop.
Some roisters still must bide in thee
 and such as cut it out,[2]
135 That with the guiltless quarrel will,
 to let their blood about.
For them I cunning surgeons leave,
 some plasters[3] to apply,
That ruffians may not still be hanged
140 nor quiet persons die.
For salt, oatmeal, candles, soap,
 or what you else do want,
In many places shops are full,
 I left you nothing scant.[4]
145 If they that keep what I you leave
 ask money when they sell it,
At Mint there is such store it is
 unpossible to tell[5] it.
At Steelyard store of wines there be,
150 your dullèd minds to glad,
And handsome men that must not wed
 except they leave their trade.[6]
They oft shall seek for proper girls,
 and some perhaps shall find
155 That need compels or lucre lures
 to satisfy their mind.
And near the same I houses leave
 for people to repair,
To bathe themselves, so to prevent
160 infection of the air.
On Saturdays I wish that those
 which all the week do drug
Shall thither trudge to trim them up
 on Sundays to look smug.
165 If any other thing be lacked
 in thee, I wish them look;
For there it is: I little brought,
 but nothing from thee took.
Now for the people in thee left,
170 I have done as I may,
And that the poor, when I am gone,
 have cause for me to pray,
I will to prisons portions leave,
 what though but very small,

1. Sweetmeats. "Pothecaries": apothecaries origi-
nally sold spices, preserves, and other commodities
besides drugs.
2. Flaunt, make a show. "Royst'rers": riotous or
swaggering fellows.

3. Medicated dressings.
4. I.e., plenty.
5. Count.
6. I.e., they are apprentices, who were not allowed
to marry.

175 Yet that they may remember me
 occasion be it shall.[7]
And first the Counter they shall have,
 lest they should go to wrack,
Some coggers and some honest men
180 that sergeants draw aback.
And such as friends will not them bail,
 whose coin is very thin,
For them I leave a certain hole,
 and little ease within.
185 The Newgate once a month shall have
 a sessions for his share,
Lest being heaped, infection might
 procure a further care.
And at those sessions some shall 'scape
190 with burning near the thumb,
And afterward to beg their fees[8]
 till they have got the sum.
And such whose deeds deserveth death,
 and twelve have found the same,
195 They shall be drawn up Holborn Hill
 to come to further shame.[9]
Well, yet to such I leave a nag
 shall soon their sorrows cease,
For he shall either break their necks
200 or gallop from the preace.
The Fleet not in their circuit is,
 yet if I give him nought,
It might procure his curse, ere I
 unto the ground be brought.
205 Wherefore I leave some papist old
 to underprop his roof,
And to the poor within the same,
 a box for their behoof.
What makes you standers-by to smile,
210 and laugh so in your sleeve,
I think it is because that I
 to Ludgate nothing give.
I am not now in case to lie,
 here is no place of jest:
215 I did reserve that for myself,
 if I my health possessed
And ever came in credit so
 a debtor for to be,
When days of payment did approach,
220 I thither meant to flee,
To shroud myself amongst the rest
 that choose to die in debt

7. I.e., perhaps the charity will cause those in prison to remember her in their prayers.
8. I.e., the discharge fees that prisoners were required to pay.
9. The road to Tyburn—the place of execution—ran by Holborn Hill.

Rather than any creditor
 should money from them get.
225 Yet 'cause I feel myself so weak
 that none me credit dare,
I here revoke, and do it leave
 some bankrupts to his share.
To all the bookbinders by Paul's,
230 because I like their art,
They every week shall money have
 when they from books depart.
Amongst them all, my printer must
 have somewhat to his share;
235 I will my friends these books to buy
 of him, with other ware.[1]
For maidens poor, I widowers rich
 do leave, that oft shall dote.
And by that means shall marry them,
240 to set the girls afloat.
And wealthy widows will I leave
 to help young gentlemen,
Which when you have, in any case
 be courteous to them then.
245 And see their plate[2] and jewels eke
 may not be marred with rust,
Nor let their bags[3] too long be full,
 for fear that they do burst.
To every gate under the walls
250 that compass thee about,
I fruitwives leave to entertain
 such as come in and out.
To Smithfield[4] I must something leave,
 my parents there did dwell:
255 So careless for to be of it,
 none would accompt it well.
Wherefore it thrice a week shall have
 of horse and neat good store;
And in his spittle blind and lame
260 to dwell for evermore.
And Bedlam[5] must not be forgot,
 for that was oft my walk:
I people there too many leave
 that out of tune do talk.
265 At Bridewell there shall beadles be,
 and matrons that shall still
See chalk well-chopped and spinning plied,
 and turning of the mill.
For such as cannot quiet be,
270 but strive for house or land,

1. I.e., her friends will use other goods to buy
books from her printer.
2. Goods made out of precious metal.
3. Money bags, purses.

4. West Smithfield, known for its horse market.
5. The hospital of St. Mary of Bethlehem, the oldest insane asylum in England.

At th'Inns of Court I lawyers leave
 to take their cause in hand.
And also leave I, at each Inn
 of Court or Chancery,
275 Of gentlemen a youthful rout[6]
 full of activity:
For whom I store of books have left
 at each bookbinder's stall,
And part of all that London hath
280 to furnish them withal.
And when they are with study cloyed,[7]
 to recreate their mind,
Of tennis courts, of dancing schools,
 And fence,[8] they store shall find.
285 And every Sunday at the least
 I leave, to make them sport,[9]
In divers places players[1] that
 of wonders shall report.
Now, London, have I (for thy sake),
290 within thee and without,
As comes into my memory
 dispersèd round about
Such needful things as they should have
 here left now unto thee:
295 When I am gone, with conscience
 let them dispersèd be.
And though I nothing namèd have
 to bury me withal,
Consider that above the ground
300 annoyance be I shall[2]
And let me have a shrouding sheet
 to cover me from shame,
And in oblivion bury me
 and never more me name.
305 Ringings[3] nor other ceremonies
 use you not for cost,
Nor at my burial make no feast,
 your money were but lost.
Rejoice in God that I am gone
310 out of this vale so vile,
And that of each thing left such store
 as may your wants exile.
I make thee sole executor, because
 I loved thee best.
315 And thee I put in trust to give
 the goods unto the rest.
Because thou shalt a helper need
 in this so great a charge,

6. A company; also, a disorderly crowd.
7. Disgusted or wearied with excess.
8. Fencing.
9. Amuse themselves.

1. Actors.
2. I shall be troublesome.
3. I.e., bell ringing.

I wish Good Fortune be thy guide, lest
320 thou shouldst run at large.
The happy days and quiet times
they both her servants be,
Which well will serve to fetch and bring
such things as need to thee.
325 Wherefore (good London) not refuse
for helper her to take:
Thus being weak and weary both,
an end here will I make.
To all that ask what end I made,
330 and how I went away,
Thou answer mayst: "like those which here
no longer tarry may."
And unto all that wish me well
or rue that I am gone,
335 Do me commend, and bid them cease
my absence for to moan.
And tell them further, if they would
my presence still have had,
They should have sought to mend my luck,
340 which ever was too bad.
So fare thou well a thousand times,
God shield thee from thy foe,
And still make thee victorious
of those that seek thy woe.
345 And, though I am persuade that I
shall never more thee see,
Yet to the last I shall not cease
to wish much good to thee.
This twenty of October, I,
350 in Anno Domini
A thousand five hundred seventy-three,
as almanacs descry,[4]
Did write this will with mine own hand
and it to London gave,
355 In witness of the standers-by
whose names if you will have,
Paper, Pen, and Standish[5] were
at that same present by,
With Time, who promised to reveal,
360 so fast as she could hie,[6]
The same, lest of my nearer kin
for any thing should vary:[7]
So finally I make an end,
no longer can I tarry.

1573

4. Make known.
5. Inkstand.
6. Speed, hasten.

7. I.e., so my relatives won't try to change anything in the will.

MARY SIDNEY HERBERT,
COUNTESS OF PEMBROKE
1561–1621

Mary Sidney Herbert is probably best known today as the sister of the poet Sir Philip Sidney and one of the sixteenth century's great patronesses of learning. But besides facilitating the work of others, she was herself a translator and poet of extraordinary skill. Aemilia Lanyer, dedicating her verse narrative of "the passion of Christ" to Herbert, self-deprecatingly admitted "many books she writes that are more rare," while other literary figures such as Edmund Spenser, John Donne, and Ben Jonson praised what Spenser called the "heavenly gifts and graces of her mind."

The third of seven children, Herbert was born at Tickenhall in Worcestershire, into an aristocratic family. Her father was the godson of Henry VIII and a close friend of Edward VI. Her mother was a lady in waiting to Queen Elizabeth, a post Mary herself was to fill between 1575 and 1577. Exceptionally well educated for her time—she knew Latin as well as French and Italian—she was always particularly close to her older brother Philip, with whom she shared a passion for literature. Married in 1577 to Henry Herbert, the earl of Pembroke, she settled with him at Wilton House, near Salisbury, one of the most majestic of England's stately homes, and in 1580, when Philip Sidney was temporarily exiled from Elizabeth's court, the poet made a number of long visits to her there. "In her time," remembered the seventeenth-century diarist John Aubrey, "Wilton House was like a college, there were so many learned and ingenious persons." It is likely that Philip wrote portions of his *Arcadia* and wrote or revised his *Apology for Poetry* when he was in residence. In addition—to name only a few other members of the Wilton House circle—the poet Samuel Daniel was employed as a tutor for the countess's sons, and the chemist Adrian Gilbert, half-brother of Sir Walter Raleigh, had a laboratory in the house.

After Philip was killed fighting in the Netherlands in 1586, his sister devoted herself to editing and publishing his poems, among them his verse translations of the psalms, although she also may have elegized him in several poems, including "The Doleful Lay of Clorinda" (1595, formerly attributed to Spenser). During the 1590s, the countess also began working on translations of her own, among them a version of Garnier's tragedy *Antoine* (1592) and an artful rendering of Petrarch's terza-rima *Trionfo del morte* (*The Triumph of Death*, 1599). But her most enduring accomplishment was a continuation of the English version of the psalms that her brother had begun before his death. Fascinating in its metrical variety and stanzaic inventiveness, the 150-psalm sequence—first published in its entirety in 1823—is a virtual compendium of Elizabethan verse strategies. Herbert's revisionary translations start with Psalm 44, and her style is brilliantly complex, as both *To the Thrice-Sacred Queen Elizabeth* (her dedication of the psalms to the queen) and her version of Psalm 58 suggest. Whether she wrote many other original poems is not known; a number of manuscripts may have been lost in a fire that destroyed the Wilton House library in 1647, twenty-six years after the countess's death. But even as it stands, Herbert's achievements in translation and versification justify both Lanyer's description of her as "a Lady whom Minerva [the goddess of wisdom] chose / To live with her in height of all respect" and the praise of her niece, the poet Mary Wroth, who considered her "as perfect in Poetry and all other Princely vertues as any woman that ever liv'd."

To the Thrice-Sacred Queen Elizabeth[1]

1

Even now that care[2] which on thy crown attends
And with thy happy[3] greatness daily grows
Tells me, thrice-sacred Queen, my muse offends,
And of respect to thee the line out goes.[4]
5 One instant will or willing can she lose[5]
I say not reading, but receiving rhymes,
On whom in chief dependeth to dispose[6]
What Europe acts in these most active times?

2

Yet dare I so, as humbleness may dare,
10 Cherish some hope they shall acceptance find;
Now weighing less thy state, lighter thy care,
But knowing more thy grace, abler thy mind.
What heavenly powers thee highest throne assigned,
Assigned thee goodness suiting that degree,[7]
15 And by thy strength thy burthen so designed,[8]
To others toil is exercise to thee.

3

Cares though still great, cannot be greatest still,
Business must ebb, though leisure never flow;
Then these the posts[9] of duty and goodwill
20 Shall press to offer what their senders[1] owe,
Which once in two, now in one subject go,
The poorer left, the richer rest[2] away,
Who better might (O might, ah word of woe)
Have given for me what I for him defray.[3]

4

25 How can I name whom sighing signs extend,[4]
And not unstop my tears' eternal spring?
But he did warp, I weaved this web to end;[5]
The stuff not ours, our work no curious[6] thing,
Wherein yet well we thought the Psalmist King

1. This poem was written to accompany a translation of the Psalms of David, begun by Herbert's brother Sir Philip Sidney and completed by Herbert after his death. Sidney was exiled from Elizabeth's court when he incurred her disfavor by counseling against a marriage with the duke of Anjou.
2. Burden.
3. Fortunate.
4. I.e., the meter is broken.
5. I.e., will she, or can she willingly, lose one instant?
6. Arrange, settle.
7. I.e., the throne.
8. I.e., those powers designated your responsibilities according to your strength.

9. The poems as sent to Elizabeth.
1. I.e., Herbert and the late Sidney. "Press": eagerly advance.
2. Perhaps a variation of "wrested," seized and pulled (by death). "The richer": Sidney.
3. Pay (metaphorically, present a tribute).
4. I.e., how can I name him (Sidney) to whom sighs, the signs of grief, are extended?
5. In clothmaking, to lay down the first set of threads (the warp), which is then intersected by another set (the woof). Herbert is referring to the fact that Sidney only began the Psalms, which she completed.
6. Accomplished, ingenious. "Stuff": raw material (i.e., the Bible).

30 How English denizened,[7] though Hebrew born,
Would to thy music undispleaséd sing,
Oft having worse, without repining worn;

5

And I the cloth in both our names present,
A livery robe to be bestowed[8] by thee;
35 Small parcel of the undischargéd rent,
From which no pains nor payments can us free.
And yet enough to cause our neighbors see
We will our best, though scanted[9] in our will;
And those nigh fields where sown they favors be
40 Unwealthy do, not else unworthy till.[1]

6

For in our work what bring we but thine own?
What English is, by many names is thine,
There humble laurels[2] in thy shadows grown
To garland others would themselves repine.[3]
45 Thy breast the cabinet, thy seat[4] the shrine,
Where muses[5] hang their vowéd memories;
Where wit, where art, where all that is divine
Conceivéd[6] best, and best defended lies.

7

Which if men did not (as they do) confess,[7]
50 And wronging worlds would otherwise consent,[8]
Yet here who minds so meet a patroness[9]
For authors' state or writings' argument?[1]
A King should only to a Queen be sent;
God's lovéd choice unto his chosen love;
55 Devotion to devotion's president;[2]
What all applaud, to her whom none reprove.

8

And who sees ought, but sees[3] how justly square[4]
His haughty ditties to thy glorious days?
How well beseeming thee his triumphs[5] are?

7. Naturalized as an English subject. I.e., if David ("the Psalmist King") were an English subject, he would willingly serve you, since he had served under a worse ruler (the tyrant Saul) without complaining.
8. Employed or stored. "Robe": courtly dress.
9. Limited, or possibly presumed to be inadequate (perhaps a reference to Elizabeth's anger at Sidney). "Will": desire to do.
1. I.e., we till the fields of your favor without shows of wealth (as in costly gifts), but otherwise worthily.
2. Leaves associated with poets and with victory.
3. I.e., the laurels themselves would complain at being worn by others, since all English art ultimately stems from Elizabeth.
4. Place of abode and of rulership. "Cabinet": small room.
5. In Greek mythology, nine daughters of Memory

who preside over the arts and all intellectual pursuits.
6. Understood. "Wit": intelligence.
7. I.e., if men did not agree that Elizabeth is the author of all English works.
8. Agree in their opinion. "Wronging": doing a great wrong.
9. I.e., who in England can remember so fitting a supporter?
1. Plot or meaning. "State": financial condition.
2. One who presides, leads (as queen, Elizabeth was the head of the Church of England). "Devotion . . . devotion": worship or prayer; the second use is closer to piety, devoutness.
3. I.e., who sees anything, who does not see?
4. A verb meaning "correspond," "fit."
5. Both victories and triumphal songs. "Beseeming": matching, resembling.

60 His hope, his zeal, his prayer, plaint, and praise,
Needless thy person[6] to their height to raise;
Less need to bend them down to thy degree;
These holy garments each good soul assays,[7]
Some sorting all, all sort[8] to none but thee.

9

65 For even thy rule is painted[9] in his reign;
Both clear in right; both nigh by wrong oppressed;[1]
And each at length (man crossing God in vain)
Possessed of place, and each in peace possessed.
Proud Philistines did interrupt his rest,
70 The foes of heaven no less have been thy foes;
He with great conquest, thou with greater blessed;
Thou sure to win, and he secure to lose.[2]

10

Thus hand in hand with him thy glories walk;
But who can trace them where alone they go?
75 Of thee who hemispheres on honor talk,[3]
And lands and seas thy trophies[4] jointly show.
The very winds did on thy party blow,
And rocks in arms thy foemen eft[5] defy.
But soft, my muse, thy pitch[6] is earthly love;
80 Forbear this heaven where only eagles fly.

11

Kings on a Queen enforced their states to lay;[7]
Mainlands for empire waiting on[8] an isle;
Men drawn by worth a woman to obey;
One moving all, herself unmoved the while;
85 Truth's restitution, vanity exile,
Wealth sprung of want, war held without annoy,[9]
Let subject be of some inspired style,
Till then the object of her subjects' joy.

12

Thy utmost[1] can but offer to her sight
90 Her handmaids' task, which most her will endears;[2]
And pray unto thy pains life from that light
Which lively light some, court and kingdom cheers,[3]

6. Self.
7. Tries on. "Holy garments": i.e., the Psalms.
8. A play on *sort*: (1) going through, (2) are appropriate.
9. Represented, figured.
1. Probably closer to "defeated" than in its modern meaning. Both Elizabeth and David reigned during times of war; their enemies, the Spanish and the Philistines, were perceived as enemies of the true religion. "Nigh": almost.
2. I.e., facing overwhelming odds against winning.
3. I.e., talk of your honor.
4. Victories. In 1588 England defeated the Spanish Armada, with the aid of the weather.
5. Probably a misprint for "oft." "Rocks": an allusion to David's killing of the Philistine Goliath with a single stone; here they represent cannonballs.

The rocks defy or challenge the foemen.
6. In music, a tone or level of dynamics. Here, the subject of the muse's song. Herbert feels she is not qualified to write of war, traditionally a male subject.
7. I.e., kings forced to place their states under Elizabeth's rule; Herbert is somewhat exaggerating Elizabeth's gains in power.
8. Obeying; also courting. "Empire": government.
9. Vexation.
1. I.e., Herbert's muse's greatest effort.
2. I.e., simple tokens of loyalty are more endearing to the queen than great works.
3. I.e., that lively light (Elizabeth) that is cheered by court and kingdom. The meaning of "some" here is not clear; it may be a misprint.

What[4] wish she may (far past her living peers
And rival still to Judah's faithful king)[5]
95 In more than he and more triumphant years,[6]
Sing what God doth, and do what men may sing.

1599 1962

Psalm 58 *Si Vere Utique*[1]

And call ye this to utter what is just
 You that of justice hold the sovereign throne?
And call ye this, to yield, O sons of dust,
 To wrongèd brethren every man his own?
5 O no! It is your long malicious will
 Now to the world to make by practice known
With whose oppression you the balance fill:
 Just to yourselves, indifferent else[2] to none.

But what could they, who even in birth declined[3]
10 From truth and right to lies and injuries?
To show the venom of their cankered[4] mind
 The adder's image scarcely can suffice;
Nay, scarce the aspic[5] may with them contend,
 On whom the charmer all in vain applies
15 His skilfull'st spells, aye missing of his end,
 While she, self-deaf and unaffected, lies.

Lord, crack their teeth! Lord, crush these lions' jaws!
 So let them sink as water in the sand.
When deadly bow their aiming fury draws,
20 Shiver[6] the shaft ere past the shooter's hand.
So make them melt as the dishousèd snail,
 Or as the embryo whose vital band
Breaks ere it holds, and formless eyes do fail
 To see the sun, though brought to lightful land.

25 O let their brood, a brood of springing thorns,
 Be by untimely rooting overthrown;
Ere bushes waxed, they push with pricking horns,[7]
 As fruits yet green are oft by tempest blown.
The good with gladness this revenge shall see
30 And bathe his feet in blood of wicked one
While all shall say, "The just rewarded be;
 There is a God that carves[8] to each his own."

1599 1820

4. Who (i.e., court and kingdom).
5. David. "Judah" is another name for Israel.
6. I.e., in a longer and more triumphant reign.
1. If truly certainly, the first words of Psalm 58 in the Vulgate Latin Bible. The first line of this psalm, in the King James version, reads, "Do ye indeed speak righteousness, O congregation?"

2. Otherwise impartial.
3. Deviated; sank.
4. Infected with evil.
5. Asp (like the adder, a poisonous snake).
6. Shatter.
7. Thorns. "Waxed": grew.
8. Apportions.

AEMILIA LANYER
1569–1645

Known in her own day as a woman "of distinguished . . . learning," Aemilia Lanyer spent much of her career at court during the reigns of Elizabeth I, James I, and Charles I. The daughter of Baptista Bassano, an Italian musician at the English court, and his common-law wife, Margaret Johnson, she became the mistress of the wealthy Henry Cary, Lord Hunsden, a nobleman forty-five years her elder, who "maintained [her] in great pomp," according to one contemporary source. When she became pregnant at the age of twenty-three, however, she was married off to Alphonso Lanyer, a royal musician, and soon after bore a son (presumably Cary's child). After her husband's death in 1613, she appears to have been involved with his relatives in various legal squabbles over his estate. Otherwise her history is shadowy, although the historian A. L. Rowse has argued that she may well have been the "Dark Lady" of Shakespeare's sonnets, the independent and impetuous mistress to whom the great playwright claimed he was hopelessly enthralled.

Whatever the truth about this poet's life, her verse is striking and accomplished, so much so that Rowse uses its radicalism as a basis for his assertion about her role in Shakespeare's poetry. In particular, her retelling of the biblical story of the Fall is a kind of pioneering vindication of the rights of "Our mother Eve," who, declares Lanyer, gave Adam "what she held most dear"—the fruit of knowledge—because she was "simply good." In fact, insists Lanyer, Eve's primordial female act of "betrayal" was performed in unconscious innocence, while men are more culpable because they consciously betrayed Jesus Christ to his crucifixion: "If one weak woman simply did offend, / This sin of yours hath no excuse, nor end." Significantly, in sketching out such a feminist version of two of Western culture's major legends, Lanyer outlined a pattern of revisionary mythmaking that was to be followed by many female descendants who may never even have read her work.

The selections printed here include both prose and verse examples of Lanyer's skill at theological argument. In addition, her elegant celebration of Cooke-ham—the country seat of her patroness, Margaret, countess of Cumberland—offers a vision of a kind of female paradise lost, even while it is also the first known English-language instance of a genre, the "country-house poem," in which such notable male artists as Ben Jonson ("To Penshurst," 1616) and Andrew Marvell (*Upon Appleton House*, written 1651) would also soon work.

From Salve Deus Rex Judaeorum[1]

To the Doubtful Reader[2]

Gentle Reader, if thou desire to be resolved, why I give this title, *Salve Deus Rex Judaeorum*, know for certain, that it was delivered unto me in sleep many years before I had any intent to write in this manner, and was quite out of my memory, until I had written the Passion of Christ, when immediately it came into my remembrance, what I had dreamed long before. And thinking it a significant token[3] that I was appointed to perform this work, I gave the very same words I received in sleep as the fittest title I could devise for this book.

1. Hail God, king of the Jews (Latin); a variant of the words fixed above Jesus when he was crucified.
2. Lanyer placed this explanation at the end of her volume. "Doubtful": doubting.
3. Sign.

To the Queen's Most Excellent Majesty[4]

Renowned Empress, and Great Britain's Queen,
Most gracious mother of succeeding kings;
Vouchsafe[5] to view that which is seldom seen,

A woman's writing of divinest things:
5 Read it fair Queen, though it defective be,
 Your Excellence can grace both it and me.

 * * *

Behold, great Queen, fair *Eve's* Apology,[6]
Which I have writ in honor of your sex,
75 And do refer unto your Majesty
To judge if it agree not with the Text:[7]
 And if it do, why are poor women blamed,
 Or by more faulty men so much defamed.

 * * *

My weak distempered brain and feeble spirits,
140 Which all unlearned have adventured, this
To write of Christ, and of his sacred merits,
Desiring that this book her[8] hands may kiss:
 And though I be unworthy of that grace,
 Yet let her blessed thoughts this book embrace.

145 And pardon me (fair Queen) though I presume
To do that which so many better can;
Not that I learning to myself assume,
Or that I would compare with any man:
 But as they are scholars, and by Art do write,
150 So Nature yields my soul a sad[9] delight.

And since all Arts at first from Nature came,
That goodly creature, mother of perfection
Whom *Jove's*[1] almighty hand at first did frame,
Taking both her and hers[2] in his protection:
155 Why should not she now grace my barren muse,
 And in a woman all defects excuse.

So peerless Princess humbly I desire,
That your great wisdom would vouchsafe t'omit[3]
All faults; and pardon if my spirits retire,
160 Leaving[4] to aim at what they cannot hit:

4. Anne of Denmark (1574–1619), the wife of James I and a notable patron of the arts. This was the first of eight poems that Lanyer addressed to women at court who were potential patrons.
5. Deign.
6. Defense.
7. I.e., the Bible (Genesis 1–3).
8. The queen's.

9. Solemn, serious.
1. I.e., God's (Jove or Jupiter was the supreme deity in Roman mythology).
2. I.e., both Nature and those close to her (especially women).
3. To overlook.
4. Declining, neglecting.

To write your worth, which no pen can express,
Were but t'eclipse[5] your fame, and make it less.

To the Virtuous Reader

Often have I heard, that it is the property of some women, not only to emulate the virtues and perfections of the rest, but also by all their powers of ill speaking, to eclipse the brightness of their deserved fame: now contrary to their custom, which men I hope unjustly lay to their charge, I have written this small volume, or little book, for the general use of all virtuous ladies and gentlewomen of this kingdom; and in commendation of some particular persons of our own sex, such as for the most part, are so well known to myself, and others, that I dare undertake Fame dares not to call any better. And this have I done, to make known to the world, that all women deserve not to be blamed though some forgetting they are women themselves, and in danger to be condemned by the words of their own mouths, fall into so great an error, as to speak unadvisedly against the rest of their sex; which if it be true, I am persuaded they can show their own imperfection in nothing more: and therefore could wish (for their own case, modesties, and credit) they would refer such points of folly, to be practiced by evil disposed men, who forgetting they were born of women, nourished of women, and that if it were not by the means of women, they would be quite extinguished out of the world, and a final end of them all, do like vipers deface the wombs wherein they were bred,[6] only to give way and utterance to their want of discretion and goodness. Such as these, were they that dishonored Christ his Apostles and Prophets, putting them to shameful deaths. Therefore we are not to regard any imputations, that they undeservedly lay upon us, not otherwise than to make use of them to our own benefits, as spur to virtue, making us fly all occasions that may color their unjust speeches to pass current. Especially considering that they have tempted even the patience of God himself, who gave power to wise and virtuous women, to bring down their pride and arrogancy. As was cruel Cesarus by the discreet counsel of noble Deborah, judge and prophetess of Israel: and resolution of Jael wife of Heber the Kenite:[7] wicked Haman, by the divine prayers and prudent proceedings of beautiful Hester:[8] blasphemous Holofernes, by the invincible courage, rare wisdom, and confident carriage of Judeth: and the unjust Judges, by the innocency of chaste Susanna:[9] with infinite others, which for brevity sake I will omit. As also in respect it pleased our Lord and Savior Jesus Christ, without the assistance of man, being free from original[1] and all other sins, from the time

5. To obscure.
6. Since antiquity, it was believed that unborn vipers gnawed their way out of the womb, killing their mother as they emerged (see Herodotus 3.109).
7. Deborah delivered Sisera, a Canaanite captain (i.e., a leader or "Caesar/Cesarus") and his army into the hand of Barak. Sisera fled to the tent of Jael, whose husband's house was at peace with the Canaanite king; she feigned friendship but then drove a tent spike through his temples into the ground while he slept (Judges 4).
8. Esther, the Jewish wife of Ahasuerus (Xerxes I), King of Persia, who foiled the plot of the king's

minister, Haman, to kill all the Jews in the kingdom (Esther 1–7).
9. Both stories are found in the Apocrypha. In the Book of Judith, the beautiful widow saved Judea by encouraging the attentions of the Assyrian general Holofernes and decapitating him while he was drunk. In the Book of Susannah, the beautiful and righteous widow, falsely accused of adultery by the two elders (the judges) whose sexual advances she had refused, is exonerated by the wise intervention of Daniel.
1. Original sin, state of sin of all humanity that resulted from the Fall of Adam and Eve.

of his conception, till the hour of his death, to be begotten of a woman, born of a woman, nourished of a woman, obedient to a woman; and that he healed women, pardoned women, comforted women: yea, even when he was in his greatest agony and bloody sweat, going to be crucified, and also in the last hour of his death, took care to dispose of a woman:[2] after his resurrection, appeared first to a woman, sent a woman[3] to declare his most glorious resurrection to the rest of his Disciples. Many other examples I could allege of divers faithful and virtuous women, who have in all ages, not only been confessors, but also endured most cruel martyrdom for their faith in Jesus Christ. All which is sufficient to enforce all good Christians and honorable-minded men to speak reverently of our sex, and especially of all virtuous and good women. To the modest censures of both which, I refer these my imperfect endeavors, knowing that according to their own excellent dispositions, they will rather, cherish, nourish, and increase the least spark of virtue where they find it, by their favorable and best interpretations, than quench it by wrong constructions. To whom I wish all increase of virtue, and desire their best opinions.

Eve's Apology in Defense of Women[4]

Now Pontius Pilate is to judge the cause[5]
Of faultless Jesus, who before him stands,
Who neither hath offended prince, nor laws,
Although he now be brought in woeful bands.
5 "O noble governor, make thou yet a pause,
Do not in innocent blood imbrue[6] thy hands;
 But hear the words of thy most worthy wife,[7]
 Who sends to thee, to beg her Savior's life.

"Let barbarous cruelty far depart from thee,
10 And in true justice take affliction's part;
Open thine eyes, that thou the truth mayest see.
Do not the thing that goes against thy heart,
Condemn not him that must thy Savior be;
But view his holy life, his good desert.
15 Let not us women glory in men's fall.[8]
 Who had power given to overrule us all.

"Till now your indiscretion sets us free,
And makes our former fault[9] much less appear;
Our mother Eve, who tasted of the tree,
20 Giving to Adam what she held most dear,
Was simply good, and had no power to see;[1]

2. Jesus asked his apostle John to care for ("dispose of") his mother, Mary (John 19.26–27).
3. Mary Magdalene (John 20.11–18).
4. Lanyer supplies the title for this subsection on her title page.
5. Case. Pilate was the Roman official who authorized Jesus' execution.
6. Stain.
7. Pilate's wife wrote a letter to her husband telling him of her dream that warned against harming Jesus (Matthew 27.19).
8. Of both Adam and Christ (perhaps also Pilate).
9. Eve traditionally is blamed for the tempting of Adam in Eden.
1. According to the Book of Genesis, Eve, the first woman, was persuaded by the serpent to eat fruit from the forbidden Tree of Knowledge, which she then gave to her husband, Adam. As punishment God banished Adam and Eve from the Garden of Eden and brought death into the world.

The after-coming harm did not appear:
 The subtle serpent that our sex betrayed
 Before our fall so sure a plot had laid

25 "That undiscerning ignorance perceived
 No guile or craft that was by him intended;
 For had she known of what we were bereaved,[2]
 To his request she had not condescended.[3]
 But she, poor soul, by cunning was deceived;
30 No hurt therein her harmless heart intended:
 For she alleged God's word, which he[4] denies,
 That they should die, but even as gods be wise.

"But surely Adam cannot be excused;
 Her fault though great, yet he was most to blame.
35 What weakness offered, strength might have refused;
 Being lord of all, the greater was his shame;
 Although the serpent's craft had her abused,
 God's holy word ought all his actions frame;[5]
 For he was lord and king of all the earth,
40 Before poor Eve had either life or breath,

"Who being framed[6] by God's eternal hand
 The perfectest man that ever breathed on earth,
 And from God's mouth received that strait[7] command,
 The breach whereof he knew was present death;
45 Yea, having power to rule both sea and land,
 Yet with one apple won to lose that breath[8]
 Which God had breathéd in his beauteous face,
 Bringing us all in danger and disgrace;

"And then to lay the fault on patience's back,
50 That we (poor women) must endure it all;
 We know right well he did discretion lack,
 Being not persuaded thereunto at all.[9]
 If Eve did err, it was for knowledge sake;
 The fruit being fair persuaded him to fall.
55 No subtle serpent's falsehood did betray him;
 If he would eat it, who had power to stay[1] him?

"Not Eve, whose fault was only too much love,
 Which made her give this present to her dear,
 That what she tasted he likewise might prove,[2]
60 Whereby his knowledge might become more clear;

2. Deprived, specifically of immortal life.
3. Yielded, acquiesced.
4. The referent is unclear; it may be either the serpent or Adam. In any case, Eve seems aware that the consequences of her act are mortality, but prefers godlike wisdom to immortal ignorance. "Alleged": cited, repeated.
5. Enclose, determine.

6. Made or fashioned.
7. Strict.
8. I.e., the breath of immortal life; see Genesis 2.7.
9. Adam took the fruit without Eve's saying anything (Genesis 3.6).
1. Prevent.
2. Experience.

He never sought her weakness to reprove
With those sharp words which he of God did hear;
 Yet met will boast of knowledge, which he took
 From Eve's fair hand, as from a learned book.

65 "If any evil did in her remain,
Being made of him,[3] he was the ground of all.
If one of many worlds[4] could lay a stain
Upon our sex, and work so great a fall
To wretched man by Satan's subtle train,[5]
70 What will so foul a fault amongst you all?[6]
 Her weakness did the serpent's words obey,
 But you in malice God's dear son betray,

"Whom, if unjustly you condemn to die,
Her sin was small to what you do commit.
75 All mortal sins[7] that do for vengeance cry
Are not to be compared unto it;
If many worlds would altogether try
By all their sins the wrath of God to get,
 This sin of yours surmounts them all as far
80 As doth the sun another little star[8]

"Then let us have our liberty again,
And challenge[9] to yourselves no sovereignty.
You came not in the world without our pain,
Make that a bar[1] against your cruelty;
85 Your fault being greater, why should you disdain
Our being your equals, free from tyranny?
 If one weak woman simply did offend,
 This sin of yours hath no excuse nor end,[2]

"To which, poor souls, we never gave consent
90 Witness, thy wife, O Pilate, speaks for all,
Who did but dream, and yet a message sent
That thou shouldest have nothing to do at all
With that just man;[3] which, if thy heart relent,
Why wilt thou be a reprobate with Saul[4]
95 To seek the death of him that is so good,
 For thy soul's health to shed his dearest blood?"

1611

3. Genesis 2.21–22 describes Eve being formed from Adam's rib.
4. The phrase suggests great quantities. I.e., one woman out of many.
5. Satan's serpentine arguments to Eve. Though later tradition identified Satan with the serpent, Genesis does not.
6. Implicitly, how great a stigma will your crime cast upon your sex?
7. Sins punishable by eternal damnation.

8. It was then assumed, on the Ptolemaic model, that the sun was actually larger than the stars.
9. Claim.
1. Check, prevention.
2. Purpose.
3. Jesus.
4. King of Israel who attempted to kill David, who had been his protégé (1 Samuel 18–19). "Reprobate": morally unprincipled person.

The Description of *Cooke-ham*

Farewell (sweet *Cooke-ham*) where I first obtained
Grace from the grace where perfect grace remained:[1]
And where the Muses[2] gave their full consent,
I should have power the virtuous to content:
5 Where princely palace willed me to indite,[3]
The sacred story of the soul's delight.
Farewell (sweet place) where virtue then did rest,
And all delights did harbor in her breast:
Never shall my sad eyes again behold
10 Those pleasures which my thoughts did then unfold:
Yet you (great Lady) Mistress of that place,
From whose desires did spring this work of grace;
Vouchsafe[4] to think upon those pleasures past,
As fleeting worldly joys that could not last:
15 Or, as dim shadows of celestial pleasures,
Which are desired above all earthly treasures.
Oh how (me thought) against[5] you thither came,
Each part did seem some new delight to frame!
The house received all ornaments to grace it,
20 And would endure no foulness to deface it.
The walks put on their summer liveries,
And all things else did hold like similes:[6]
The trees with leaves, with fruits, with flowers clad,
Embraced each other, seeming to be glad,
25 Turning themselves to beauteous canopies,
To shade the bright sun from your brighter eyes:
The crystal streams with silver spangles gracéd,
While by the glorious sun they were embracéd:
The little birds in chirping notes did sing,
30 To entertain both you and that sweet spring.
And *Philomela* with her sundry lays,[7]
Both you and that delightful place did praise.
Oh how me thought each plant, each flower, each tree
Set forth their beauties then to welcome thee:
35 The very hills right humbly did descend,
When you to tread upon them did intend.
And as you set your feet, they still did rise,
Glad that they could receive so rich a prize.
The gentle winds did take delight to be
40 Among those woods that were so graced by thee.
And in sad[8] murmur uttered pleasing sound,
That pleasure in that place might more abound:

1. I.e., favor from the noble person in whom perfect virtue remained. That person is Margaret, countess of Cumberland (d. 1616).
2. In Greek mythology, nine daughters of Memory who preside over the arts and all intellectual pursuits.
3. Write.
4. Grant.
5. Before; in anticipation of. "Me thought": it seemed to me.
6. Comparisons; i.e., different parts of nature are compared to the liveried servants of the countess of Cumberland. "Liveries": uniforms; distinctive dress.
7. Songs. "Philomela": the nightingale (from the name of the mournful woman who, according to Greek myth, was turned into this bird).
8. Heavy.

The swelling banks delivered all their pride,
When such a *Phoenix*[9] once they had espied.
45 Each arbor, bank, each seat, each stately tree,
Thought themselves honored in supporting thee.
The pretty birds would oft come to attend thee,
Yet fly away for fear they should offend thee:
The little creatures in the burrow by
50 Would come abroad to sport them in your eye;
Yet fearful of the bow in your fair hand,
Would run away when you did make a stand.
Now let me come unto that stately tree,
Wherein such goodly prospects you did see;
55 That oak that did in height his fellows pass,
As much as lofty trees, low growing grass:
Much like a comely cedar straight and tall,
Whose beauteous stature far exceeded all:
How often did you visit this fair tree,
60 Which seeming joyful in receiving thee,
Would like a palm tree spread his arms abroad,
Desirous that you there should make abode:
Whose fair green leaves much like a comely veil,
Defended *Phoebus*[1] when he would assail:
65 Whose pleasing boughs did yield a cool fresh air,
Joying[2] his happiness when you were there.
Where being seated, you might plainly see,
Hills, vales, and woods, as if on bended knee
They had appeared, your honor to salute,
70 Or to prefer some strange unlooked for suit:[3]
All interlaced with brooks and crystal springs,
A prospect fit to please the eyes of kings:
And thirteen shires[4] appeared all in your sight,
Europe could not afford much more delight.
75 What was there then but gave you all content,
While you the time in meditation spent,
Of their Creator's power, which there you saw,
In all his creatures held a perfect law;
And in their beauties did you plain descry,[5]
80 His beauty, wisdom, grace, love, majesty.
In these sweet woods how often did you walk,
With Christ and his Apostles there to talk;
Placing his holy writ in some fair tree,
To meditate what you therein did see:
85 With *Moses* you did mount his holy hill,[6]
To know his pleasure, and perform his will.
With lowly *David* you did often sing,
His holy hymns[7] to heaven's Eternal King.

9. A legendary bird, unique of its kind; it lives five hundred years, then burns to death and is reborn from the ashes.
1. Protected against the sun (identified here with Phoebus Apollo).
2. Rejoicing at.
3. Entreaty. "Prefer": present.
4. Counties.

5. Perceive, observe.
6. Mount Sinai, which Moses climbed to speak with God and to receive the Ten Commandments (Exodus 24).
7. Tradition remembers the biblical King David as a musician and poet, and he is credited with many of the poems in Psalms.

And in sweet music did your soul delight,
90 To sound his praises, morning, noon, and night.
With blessed *Joseph*[8] you did often feed
Your pinéd[9] brethren, when they stood in need.
And that sweet lady sprung from *Clifford*'s race,
Of noble *Bedford*'s blood, fair stem of grace;[1]
95 To honorable *Dorset* now espoused,
In whose fair breast true virtue then was housed:
Oh what delight did my weak spirits find
In those pure parts of her well framéd mind:
And yet it grieves me that I cannot be
100 Near unto her, whose virtues did agree
With those fair ornaments of outward beauty,
Which did enforce from all both love and duty.
Unconstant Fortune, thou art most to blame,
Who casts us down into so low a frame:
105 Where our great friends we cannot daily see,
So great a difference is there in degree.
Many are placed in those orbs of state,
Parters in honor,[2] so ordained by fate;
Nearer in show, yet farther off in love,
110 In which, the lowest always are above.[3]
But whither am I carried in conceit?
My wit too weak to conster[4] of the great.
Why not? although we are but born of earth,
We may behold the heavens, despising death;
115 And loving heaven that is so far above,
May in the end vouchsafe us entire love.
Therefore sweet Memory do thou retain
Those pleasures past, which will not turn again:
Remember beauteous *Dorset*'s former sports,[5]
120 So far from being touched by ill reports;
Wherein myself did always bear a part,
While reverend Love presented my true heart:
Those recreations let me bear in mind,
Which her sweet youth and noble thoughts did find:
125 Whereof deprived, I evermore must grieve,
Hating blind fortune, careless to relieve.[6]
And you sweet *Cooke-ham*, whom these ladies leave,
I now must tell the grief you did conceive[7]
At their departure; when they went away,
130 How everything retained a sad dismay:
Nay long before, when once an inkling came,
Methought each thing did unto sorrow frame:[8]

8. A son of Jacob; his brothers had sold him into slavery, but he became powerful in Egypt and later aided his family during a great famine (Genesis 37–47).
9. Wasted by hunger.
1. The countess of Cumberland's daughter, Anne (1590–1676); she was related to the Cliffords (earls of Cumberland) and the Russells (earls of Bedford), through her father and mother, and married Richard Sackville, earl of Dorset.
2. Those set apart in rank.
3. I.e., the one lower in rank is "above" the higher-born in loving more.
4. Construe, interpret. "Conceit": figure of language.
5. Pleasant pastimes. "Beauteous Dorset's": Anne's.
6. Having no care to rise again.
7. Take on.
8. Give shape to sorrow.

The trees that were so glorious in our view,
Forsook both flowers and fruit, when once they knew
135 Of your depart, their very leaves did wither,
Changing their colors as they grew together.
But when they saw this had no power to stay you,
They often wept, though speechless, could not pray[9] you;
Letting their tears in your fair bosoms fall,
140 As if they said, Why will ye leave us all?
This being vain, they cast their leaves away,
Hoping that pity would have made you stay:
Their frozen tops like age's hoary hairs,
Shows their disasters, languishing in fears:
145 A swarthy riveled rind[1] over all spread,
Their dying bodies half alive, half dead.
But your occasions[2] called you so away,
That nothing there had power to make you stay:
Yet did I see a noble grateful mind,
150 Requiting[3] each according to their kind,
Forgetting not to turn and take your leave
Of these sad creatures, powerless to receive
Your favor when with grief you did depart,
Placing their former pleasures in your heart;
155 Giving great charge to noble Memory,
There to preserve their love continually:
But specially the love of that fair tree,
That first and last you did vouchsafe to see:
In which it pleased you oft to take the air,
160 With noble *Dorset*, then a virgin fair:[4]
Where many a learned book was read and scanned
To this fair tree, taking me by the hand,
You did repeat the pleasures which had past,
Seeming to grieve they could no longer last.
165 And with a chaste, yet loving kiss took leave,
Of which sweet kiss I did it soon bereave:[5]
Scorning a senseless creature should possess
So rare a favor, so great happiness.
No other kiss it could receive from me
170 For fear to give back what it took of thee:
So I ungrateful creature did deceive[6] it,
Of that which you vouchsafed in love to leave it.
And though it often had given me much content,
Yet this great wrong I never could repent:
175 But of the happiest made it most forlorn,
To show that nothing's free from Fortune's scorn.
While all the rest with this most beauteous tree,
Made their sad consort[7] sorrow's harmony.
The flowers that on the banks and walks did grow,
180 Crept in the ground, the grass did weep for woe.

9. Beg.
1. Dark wrinkled bark.
2. Necessary business.
3. Rewarding.
4. I.e., before she was married.

5. I.e., by kissing the tree after the countess, Lanyer takes away the kiss for herself.
6. Cheat.
7. A set of musicians; more generally, company.

The winds and waters seemed to chide together,
Because you went away they know not whither:
And those sweet brooks that ran so fair and clear,
With grief and trouble wrinkled did appear.
185 Those pretty birds that wonted[8] were to sing,
Now neither sing, nor chirp, nor use their wing;
But with their tender feet on some bare spray,
Warble forth sorrow, and their own dismay.
Fair *Philomela* leaves her mournful ditty,
190 Drowned in dead sleep, yet can procure no pity:
Each arbor, bank, each seat, each stately tree,
Looks bare and desolate now for want[9] of thee;
Turning green tresses into frosty gray,
While in cold grief they wither all away.
195 The sun grew weak, his beams no comfort gave,
While all green things did make the earth their grave:
Each briar, each bramble, when you went away,
Caught fast your clothes, thinking to make you stay:
Delightful Echo wonted to reply
200 To our last words, did now for sorrow die:
The house cast off each garment that might grace it,
Putting on dust and cobwebs to deface it.
All desolation then there did appear,
When you were going whom they held so dear.
205 This last farewell to *Cooke-ham* here I give,
When I am dead thy name in this may live,
Wherein I have performed her noble hest,[1]
Whose virtues lodge in my unworthy breast,
And ever shall, so long as life remains,
210 Tying my heart to her by those rich chains.

1611

8. Accustomed. 1. The bidding of the countess of Cumberland.
9. Lack.

MARTHA MOULSWORTH
1577–16??

Through fifty-five couplets for her fifty-five years, Martha Moulsworth produced a verse autobiography in 1632 that was discovered at the beginning of the 1990s in the Beinecke Library at Yale University and published in 1993. The author of "The Memorandum of Martha Moulsworth, Widow" laments men's monopoly on higher education, while boasting of what women might achieve were they given proper schooling. Though men have two universities, if women had "but one," they "would in wit, and tongues surpass/All art that is, or ever was." Martha Moulsworth's last name comes from her third (and last) husband, Bevill Molesworth, who was a London goldsmith. She was born to Martha and Robert Dorsett in Oxfordshire, where her father was an Anglican priest and where she was early orphaned and raised by a

maternal grandmother and stepgrandfather. Sometimes compared to Chaucer's fictional Wife of Bath, Martha Moulsworth probably fictionalized parts of her accounts about her relationship to her father, her three husbands, their children, and her widowhood. The marginal brackets are her own annotations.

The Memorandum of Martha Moulsworth, Widow

November the 10th, 1632

The tenth day of the winter month November
A day which I must duly still remember,
Did open first these eyes, and showed this light,
Now on that day, upon that day I write. [*November the 10th, 1632*]
5 This season fitly willingly combines
The birthday of myself, and of these lines.
The time the clock, the yearly stroke is one [*My muse is a tell*
That clock by fifty five returns hath gone *clock,*[1] *and echoes every*
How few, how many warnings it will give *stroke with a coupled*
10 He only knows, in whom we are, and live. *rhyme so many times,*
In carnal state of sin original[2] *viz. 55. Acts 17.28 &*]
I did not stay one whole day natural.
The seal of grace in sacramental water
So soon had I, so soon become the daughter
15 Of earthly parents, and of heavenly Father.
Some christen late for state, the wiser rather.[3]

My name was Martha. Martha took much pain [*Luke 10.14*][4]
Our Savior Christ her guest to entertain.
God give me grace my inward house to dight[5]
20 That he with me may sup, and stay all night. [*Revelation 3.20*]
My father was a man of spotless fame [*Luke 24.29*]
Of gentle birth, and Dorset was his name.
He had, and left lands of his own possession;
He was of Levi's tribe by his profession.[6]
25 His mother Oxford knowing well his worth,
Arrayed in scarlet robe did send him forth.[7]
By him I was brought up in godly piety,
In modest cheerfulness, and sad[8] sobriety.
Nor only so, beyond my sex and kind
30 He did with learning Latin deck [my] mind.
And why not so? The muses females are,[9]
And therefore of us females take some care.
Two universities[1] we have of men,
O that we had but one of women then!

1. I.e., counts the hours.
2. The state of sin of all humanity that resulted from the Fall of Adam and Eve, which is taken away by baptism ("sacramental water").
3. Earlier. "State": pomp.
4. Actually, Luke 10.41; Martha was the sister who tended to her house-keeping while her sister Mary sat at Jesus' feet.
5. Decorate.
6. I.e., he performed religious duties (see Num-

bers 1.47–53). Moulsworth's father was a clergyman.
7. I.e., as a graduate, in the scarlet robes of a doctor of divinity.
8. Grave.
9. In Greek mythology, these nine daughters of Memory preside over the arts and all intellectual pursuits.
1. I.e., Oxford and Cambridge, which both date to the early 12th century.

35 O then that would in wit, and tongues surpass
All art of men that is, or ever was.
But I of Latin have no cause to boast
For want of use, I long ago it lost. *[Latin is not the most
marriage
metal]*

Had I no other portion to my dower
40 I might have stood a virgin to this hour,
But though the virgin Muses I love well,
I have long since bid virgin life farewell.
Thrice this right hand did holy wedlock plight
And thrice this left with pledged ring was dight.²
45 Three husbands me, and I have them enjoyed,
Nor I by them, nor they by me annoyed.
All lovely, loving all, some more, some less,
Though gone, their love and memory I bless.
Until my one and twentieth yeare of age
50 I did not bind myself in marriage *[I husband,
Mr. Nicholas Prynne,
April 18, 1598]*
My spring was late, some think that sooner love
But backward³ springs do oft the kindest prove.
My first knot⁴ held five years, and eight months more,
Then was a year set on my mourning score.⁵
55 My second bond ten years nine months did last *[2nd Mr. Thomas
Througood,
February 3, 1604]*
Three years eight months I kept a widow's fast.⁶
The third I took a lovely man, and kind,
Such comeliness in age we seldom find. *[3rd Mr. Bevull Moulsworth,
June 15, 1619]*
From Mortimers⁷ he drew his pedegree
60 Their arms he bore, not bought with herald's fee.⁸
Third wife I was to him, as he to me
Third husband was, in number we agree.
Eleven years and eight months his autumn lasted
A second spring,⁹ too soon away it hasted.
65 Was never man so buxom¹ to his wife,
With him I led an easy darling's life.
I had my will in house, in purse, in store,²
What would a woman old or young have more?

Two years almost outwearing since he died,
70 And yet, and yet my tears for him not dried.
I by the first, and last, some issue had
But root and fruit³ is dead, which makes me sad.
My husbands all on holidays did die
Such day, such way, they to the saints did hie.
75 This life is workday⁴ even at the best,
But Christian death, an holy day of rest.
The first, the first of Martyrs did befall,

2. Adorned.
3. Late.
4. Marriage bond.
5. Account.
6. I.e., abstained from marital comforts and pleasures.
7. An ancient noble family.
8. I.e., he did not buy, as many did, a phony ped-
igree and coat of arms from a corrupt official.
9. Though aging ("autumn") he enjoyed in marriage a renewed youth ("second spring").
1. Obliging.
2. Provision of household goods.
3. All her children, as well as their fathers ("root").
4. Days of labor.

St. Stephen's feast[5] to him was funeral.
The morrow after Christ our flesh did take,
80 This husband did his mortal flesh forsake.
The second on a double sainted day
To Jude, and Simon,[6] took his happy way.
This Simon as an ancient story saith
Did first in England plant the Christian faith. *[Nicerphorus,[7] History]*
85 Most sure it is that Jude in holy writ *[Jude, verse 3][8]*
Doth warn us to maintain, and fight for it,
In which all those that live, and die, may well
Hope with the saints eternally to dwell.
The last on St. Matthias day[9] did wend
90 Unto his home, and pilgrimage's end.
This feast comes in that season which doth bring
Upon dead winter's cold, a lively spring.
His body wintering in the lodge of death,
Shall feel a spring, with bud of life and breath,
95 And rise in incorruption, glory, power. *[1 Corinthians 15.42][1]*
Like to the body of our Savior. *[Philippians 3.21][2]*

In vain it were, profane it were for me
With sadness to ask which of these three *[Matthew 22.18][3]*
I shall call husband in the Resurrection,
100 For then shall all in glorious perfection,
Like to th'immortal heavenly angels live
Who wedlock's bonds do neither take nor give. *[[Matthew 22] verse*
But in the meantime this must be my care *30][4]*
Of knitting here a fourth knot to beware.
105 A threefold cord though hardly yet is broken, *[Ecclesiastes 4.12][5]*
Another ancient story doth betoken
That seldom comes a better.[6] Why should I
Then put my widowhood in jeopardy?
The virgin's life is gold, as clerks us tell,
110 The widow's silver. I love silver well!

1632 1993

5. December 26; for his martyrdom, see Acts 7.54–60.
6. October 28.
7. Nicephorus Callistus (ca. 1256–1335), a Byzantine historian who wrote an 18-volume church history. The story of Simon planting Christianity in England is repeated by Thomas Fuller in his *Church-History of Britain* (1655).
8. "Ye should earnestly contend for the faith which was once delivered unto the saints" (Jude 1.3).
9. February 24.
1. The body is said to be "sown in corruption" and "raised in incorruption" at the resurrection of the dead (1 Corinthians 15.42).

2. Christ is said to change "our vile body, that it may be fashioned like unto his glorious body" (Philippians 3.21).
3. Jesus denounced the "wickedness" of a question by the Pharisees in Matthew 22.18.
4. Asked about a woman married to seven, brothers in turn, Jesus replied that "in the resurrection they neither marry, nor are given in marriage, but are as the angels of God in heaven" (Matthew 22.30).
5. "A threefold cord is not quickly broken" (Ecclesiastes 4.12).
6. "Seldom comes the better?" was a proverb common in the period.

ELIZABETH CARY
1585–1639

One of the most precocious and prolific of Elizabethan women of letters, Elizabeth Tanfield Cary wrote her ambitious verse play, *The Tragedy of Mariam, the Faire Queene of Jewry*, at the age of seventeen. As a child, despite parental disapproval, she had taught herself a range of languages (including French, Latin, and Hebrew), completed a number of translations, and begun the wide reading in theology that resulted in her conversion to Catholicism in 1626. Married at fifteen or sixteen to Henry Cary, later Viscount Falkland, she bore him eleven children before he separated from her; in an effort to punish her for her conversion, he denied her financial support and custody of her children. Although the Privy Council later ordered her estranged husband to support her and the couple eventually reconciled, Cary remained a Roman Catholic, as did most of her children. One of her daughters, four of whom became Benedictine nuns in a French convent, produced a respectful and detailed account of her history, *The Lady Falkland: Her Life*; it is the first known biography of a woman writer but was not published until 1861.

Appearing in 1613, a decade after it was written, *Mariam* was the first full-length play by an Englishwoman to be circulated in print rather than in manuscript. An eloquent record of a woman's ambivalence toward marriage and male authority, the work is based on tales of Herod, his wife Mariam, and his sister Salome that are told in contemporary translations of *Jewish Antiquities,* written in the first century C.E. by the Jewish historian Josephus. The plot of the drama turns on Herod's perfidy and Mariam's resistance: appointed by Rome to rule the Jews, Herod leaves his wife, Doris, for Mariam, granddaughter of Hircanus, the rightful king, and then has Hircanus killed and Mariam's brother drowned; finally, after Salome convinces him that Mariam is trying to poison him, he condemns the heroine herself to death.

Significantly, Josephus portrays the "Queen of Jewry" as selfish and manipulative, while Cary depicts her as a noble rebel whose defiance of her husband heralds the new law of Christianity. Yet despite the piety that infused her art, this writer's rebellion against what she saw in both art and life as conjugal tyranny left her with a reputation of impropriety and unwomanliness. Two years after she died, one commentator declared that she was "a lady of a most masculine understanding, allayed with the passions and infirmities of her own sex"; as recently as 1962, another critic described her as a woman of "literary, masculine, and eccentric character." This criticism, even the more recent, may reflect the fact that unlike many of her female contemporaries, Cary had, in the words of her daughter's biography, "read very exceeding much: poetry of all kinds, ancient and modern, in several languages, all that ever she could meet; history very universally, especially all ancient Greek and Roman historians, and chroniclers whatsoever of her own country along with many other books usually forbidden."

From The Tragedy of Mariam, the Faire Queene of Jewry

From *Act* 3, *Scene* 3

[ON THE DUTIES OF A WIFE]

215 CHORUS. 'Tis not enough for one that is a wife
 To keep her[1] spotless from an act of ill:

1. I.e., herself.

But from suspicion she should free her life,
And bare herself of[2] power as well as will.
 'Tis not so glorious for her to be free,
220 As by her proper[3] self restrained to be.

When she hath spacious ground to walk upon,
Why on the ridge should she desire to go?
It is no glory to forbear alone[4]
Those things that may her honor overthrow.
225 But 'tis thankworthy if she will not take
 All lawful liberties for honor's sake.

That wife her hand against her fame doth rear,
That more than to her lord alone will give
A private word to any second ear,
230 And though she may with reputation live,
 Yet though most chaste, she doth her glory blot,
 And wounds her honor, though she kills it not.

When to their husbands they themselves do bind,
Do they not wholly give themselves away?
235 Or give they but their body, not their mind,
Reserving that, though best, for others' prey?[5]
 No sure, their thoughts no more can be their own,
 And therefore should to none but one be known.

Then she usurps upon another's right,
240 That seeks to be by public language graced:
And though her thoughts reflect with purest light,
Her mind if not peculiar[6] is not chaste.
 For in a wife it is no worse to find,
 A common[7] body than a common mind.

245 And every mind, though free from thought of ill,
That out of glory seeks a worth to show,
When any's ears but one therewith they fill,
Doth in a sort her pureness overthrow.
 Now Mariam had (but that to this she bent)[8]
250 Been free from fear, as well as innocent.

From *Act 4, Scene 8*

[MARIAM'S FATE]

525 MARIAM. Am I the Mariam that presumed so much,
And deemed my face must needs preserve my breath?
Ay, I it was that thought my beauty such,
As it alone could countermand my death.

2. I.e., keep herself from.
3. I.e., her own.
4. To only do without.
5. I.e., keeping their minds from their husbands

to be the prey of others.
6. Exclusively her own.
7. Shared, public.
8. I.e., if only she had inclined to this course.

Now death will teach me: he can pale as well
530 A cheek of roses as a cheek less bright,
And dim an eye whose shine doth most excel,
As soon as one that casts a meaner light.
Had not myself against myself conspired,
No plot, no adversary from without
535 Could Herod's love from Mariam have retired,[9]
Or from his heart have thrust my semblance out.
The wanton queen that never loved for love,
False Cleopatra, wholly set on gain,
With all her sleights did prove, yet vainly prove,[1]
540 For her the love of Herod to obtain.
Yet her allurements, all her courtly guile,
Her smiles, her favors, and her smooth deceit
Could not my face from Herod's mind exile,
But were with him of less than little weight.
545 That face and person that in Asia late
For beauty's goddess, Paphos' queen,[2] was ta'en:
That face that did captive great Julius' fate,
That very face that was Anthonius' bane,
That face that to be Egypt's pride was born,
550 That face that all the world esteemed so rare:
Did Herod hate, despise, neglect, and scorn,
When with the same, he Mariam's did compare.
This made that I improvidently wrought,
And on the wager even my life did pawn:
555 Because I thought, and yet but truly thought,
That Herod's love could not from me be drawn.
But now, though out of time,[3] I plainly see
It could be drawn, though never drawn from me,
Had I but with humility been graced,
560 As well as fair I might have proved me wise:
But I did think because I knew me chaste,
One virtue for a woman might suffice.
That mind for glory of our sex might stand,
Wherein humility and chastity
565 Doth march with equal paces hand in hand.
But one, if single seen, who setteth by?[4]
And I had singly one, but 'tis my joy,
That I was ever innocent, though sour:
And therefore can they but my life destroy,
570 My soul is free from adversary's power. [*Enter* DORIS[5]]
You princes great in power, and high in birth,
Be great and high, I envy not your hap:[6]
Your birth must be from dust, your power on earth;
In Heaven shall Mariam sit in Sara's lap.[7]

9. Withdrawn.
1. Try. Cleopatra (68–31 B.C.E.), queen of Egypt.
2. Aphrodite, the Greek goddess of love who was born in the sea near the island Paphos. Cleopatra first captured the love of Julius Caesar and then Mark Anthony, who ultimately was drawn by her into an unsuccessful war against Rome.
3. I.e., in the wrong time; too late.
4. Disregards.
5. Herod's first wife, whom he set aside so that he might marry Mariam.
6. Fortune.
7. The lap of Abraham's wife; i.e., with the blessed dead.

575 DORIS. Ay, Heaven—your beauty cannot bring you thither,
 Your soul is black and spotted, full of sin:
 You in adultery lived nine year together,
 And Heaven will never let adultery in.
 MARIAM. What art thou that dost poor Mariam pursue,
580 Some spirit sent to drive me to despair?
 Who sees for truth that Mariam is untrue?
 If fair she be, she is as chaste as fair.
 DORIS. I am that Doris that was once beloved,
 Beloved by Herod, Herod's lawful wife:
585 'Twas you that Doris from his side removed,
 And robbed from me the glory of my life.
 MARIAM. Was that adultery? Did not Moses say,
 That he that being matched did deadly hate:
 Might by permission put his wife away,
590 And take a more beloved to be his mate?[8]
 DORIS. What did he hate me for: for simple truth?
 For bringing beauteous babes, for love to him?
 For riches, noble birth, or tender youth?
 Or for no stain did Doris' honor dim?
595 Oh, tell me, Mariam, tell me if you know,
 Which fault of these made Herod Doris' foe?
 These thrice three years have I with hands held up,
 And bowéd knees fast nailéd to the ground,
 Besought for thee the dregs of that same cup,
600 That cup of wrath that is for sinners found.
 And now thou art to drink it: Doris' curse
 Upon thyself did all this wile[9] attend,
 But now it shall pursue thy children worse.
 MARIAM. Oh, Doris, now to thee my knees I bend,
605 That heart that never bowed to thee doth bow:
 Curse not mine infants, let it thee suffice,
 That Heaven doth punishment to me allow.
 Thy curse is cause that guiltless Mariam dies.
 DORIS. Had I ten thousand tongues, and every tongue
610 Inflamed with poison's power, and steeped in gall:
 My curses would not answer for my wrong,
 Though I in cursing thee employed them all.
 Hear thou that didst Mount [Gerizim] command,[1]
 To be a place whereon with cause to curse:
615 Stretch thy revenging arm, thrust forth thy hand,
 And plague the mother much: the children worse.
 Throw flaming fire upon the baseborn heads
 That were begotten in unlawful beds.
 But let them live till they have sense to know
620 What 'tis to be in miserable state:
 Then be their nearest friends their overthrow,
 Attended by they by suspicious hate.
 And, Mariam, I do hope this boy of mine

8. This is not quite what Moses says; see Deuter-
onomy 24.1–4.
9. While.

1. According to Deuteronomy 27.11–26, Moses
commanded his people to stand on Mount Gerizim
to bless and Mount Ebal to curse.

Shall one day come to be the death of thine. [*Exit.*]
625 MARIAM. Oh! Heaven forbid. I hope the world shall see,
This curse of thine shall be returned on thee:
Now, earth, farewell, though I be yet but young,
Yet I, methinks, have known thee too too long. [*Exit.*]

CHORUS. The fairest action of our human life
630 Is scorning to revenge an injury:
For who forgives without a further strife,
His adversary's heart to him doth tie.
 And 'tis a firmer conquest truly said,
 To win the heart than overthrow the head.

635 If we a worthy enemy do find,
To yield to worth, it must be nobly done:
But if of baser metal² be his mind,
In base revenge there is no honor won.
 Who would a worthy courage overthrow,
640 And who would wrestle with a worthless foe?

We say our hearts are great and cannot yield;
Because they cannot yield it proves them poor:
Great hearts are tasked beyond their power but seld,³
The weakest lion will the loudest roar.
645 Truth's school for certain doth this same allow,
 High-heartedness doth sometimes teach to bow.

A noble heart doth teach a virtuous scorn:
To scorn to owe a duty overlong,
To scorn to be for benefits forborne,⁴
650 To scorn to lie, to scorn to do a wrong,
 To scorn to bear an injury in mind,
 To scorn a freeborn heart slavelike to bind.

But if for wrongs we needs revenge must have,
Then be our vengeance of the noblest kind:
655 Do we his body from our fury save,
And let our hate prevail against our mind?
 What can 'gainst him a greater vengeance be,
 Than make his foe more worthy far than he?

Had Mariam scorned to leave a due unpaid,
660 She would to Herod then have paid her love:
And not have been by sullen passion swayed.
To fix her thoughts all injury above
 Is virtuous pride. Had Mariam thus been proved,⁵
 Long famous life to her had been allowed.

1602 1613

2. I.e., mettle; quality of disposition or character. 4. I.e., not to repay an obligation.
3. Seldom. 5. I.e., had she shown herself to be such a person.

MARY WROTH
1587?–1651/53

Aristocratic, controversial, and adventurous, Mary Wroth was a major literary heiress. Her father, Sir Robert Sidney (later earl of Leicester), was himself a reputable poet; even better known were her uncle, Sir Philip Sidney, and her aunt, Lady Mary Sidney Herbert, the countess of Pembroke. Perhaps inspired by such distinguished origins, she became the first Englishwoman to produce a full-length prose romance and the first to compose a sonnet sequence.

Raised in an atmosphere of wealth and privilege, Wroth was the eldest of four girls and two boys nurtured by fond parents, particularly a mother whom the poet Ben Jonson praised for her hospitality and generosity. "My Lady," wrote Sir Robert's steward, Rowland White, "sees [her children] well taught, and brought up in Learning, and Qualities, fitt for theire Birth and Condicion." The young Mary Sidney's happy childhood came to an end, however, when she entered into what was clearly an unhappy marriage with Sir Robert Wroth; Jonson remarked that she was "unworthily married to a jealous husband." Worse still, after Robert Wroth's untimely death in 1614, his widow was left with an infant son and a heavily indebted estate. Two years later her son died, and her indebtedness deepened when even his share of the estate was entailed away from her. As the critic Ann Rosalind Jones has observed, moreover, her difficulties were "probably intensified" by the long affair into which she then entered with her cousin William, earl of Pembroke, who became the father of her two surviving children.

From the perspective of her contemporaries, Wroth's literary career was at least as unconventional as her personal life. Her major work was the ambitious prose romance *The Countess of Montgomery's Urania* (1621), to which the sonnet sequence *Pamphilia to Amphilanthus* was appended. The structure and title of the *Urania* were modeled on *The Countess of Pembroke's Arcadia,* the most celebrated work by Mary Sidney Wroth's famous uncle. But because Wroth's romance was a kind of roman à clef it infuriated several courtiers whose thinly disguised portraits appeared in it. Most vituperative was one Lord Denny, who castigated the author for writing "lascivious tales and amorous toys," and circulated a poem reviling Wroth as "a hermaphrodite in show, in deed a monster." Though Wroth defended herself in a set of passionate "Railing Rimes"—including one in which she protested Denny's "spiteful words against a harmless book" and spiritedly countered that he himself was a "hermaphrodite in *sense,* in Art a monster"—she gained little support from others in her circle, and within six months withdrew the volume she had so boldly and hopefully published.

Paradoxically, the eponymous heroine of Wroth's work is a noble shepherdess based on an offstage character in Sir Philip Sidney's *Arcadia,* while Pamphilia, whose name means "all-loving" and who is the speaker of her sonnet sequence, represents female constancy, chastity, and "heroic virtue" in a fallen world. Indeed, as several critics have noted, Pamphilia's merits have much in common with the glories attributed to Elizabeth I herself: "shee is upright and just," remarks one of Wroth's characters, "in her government mild, and loving to her subjects," and "she hath . . . a brave and manlike spirit, and wondrous wise shee is." At the same time, throughout the technically accomplished and melodious verses in which this fictive woman of letters speaks, Wroth reveals the aesthetic potential of the woman poet even while, as Ann Jones puts it, she "expands the possibilities of a female poetic voice to encompass passion, purgation, and vision."

Of Wroth's later life little is known. Both her real romance with Pembroke and the scandal surrounding her prose romance evidently forced her withdrawal from the public sphere and in particular from active engagement in life at court. But she per-

sisted in her literary vocation, composing a continuation of the *Urania* along with a pastoral play titled *Love's Victory*, neither of which was published in her lifetime. Plagued by creditors, she sold off many of her own lands, managing her affairs with, as one biographer puts it, "considerable determination"—the same determination, no doubt, that had energized her pioneering art.

Most of the texts we reprint here have been modernized by the scholar and poet Mary Moore, to whom we are also indebted for some annotations.

Song[1]

Love what art thou? A vain thought
 In our minds by fant'sy wrought.
 Idle smiles did thee beget,
 While fond wishes made the net
5 Which so many fools have caught.

Love what art thou? Light and fair,
 Fresh as morning, clear as th' air.
 But too soon thy evening change
 Makes thy worth with coldness range;
10 Still thy joy is mixt with care.

Love what art thou? A sweet flower
 Once full blown,[2] dead in an hour.
 Dust in wind as staid[3] remains
 As thy pleasure or our gains,
15 If thy humor[4] change, to lour.

Love what art thou? Childish, vain,
 Firm as bubbles made by rain,
 Wantonness thy greatest pride.
 These foul faults thy virtues hide—
20 But babes can no staidness gain.

Love what art thou? Causeless cursed,
 Yet alas these not the worst:
 Much more of thee may be said.
 But thy law I once obeyed,
25 Therefore say no more at first.

1621

1. This is one of a group of poems that end the first book of *The Countess of Montgomery's Urania*; it is sung by a shepherdess to a shepherd.
2. In full bloom.
3. Fixed, permanent.
4. Whim.

From Pamphilia to Amphilanthus

1

When night's black mantle could most darkness prove,[1]
 And sleep, death's Image, did my senses hire[2]
 From knowledge of myself, then thoughts did move
 Swifter than those most swiftness need require:
5 In sleep, a chariot drawn by winged desire
 I saw, where sat bright Venus, Queen of love,
 And at her feet, her son,[3] still adding fire
 To burning hearts, which she did hold above;
But one heart flaming more than all the rest
10 The goddess held and put it to my breast.
 "Dear son, now shut,"[4] said she, "Thus must we win";
He her obeyed and martyred my poor heart;
 I, waking, hoped as dreams it would depart,
 Yet since, O me, a lover I have been.

8

Love, leave to urge: thou know'st thou hast the hand.[5]
 T'is cowardice to strive where none resist;
 Pray thee leave off; I yield unto thy band;[6]
 Do not thus still in thine own power persist;
5 Behold, I yield: let forces be dismissed;
 I am thy subject, conquered, bound to stand,
 Never they foe, but did thy claim assist,
 Seeking thy due of those who did withstand;[7]
But now it seems thou would'st I should thee love;
10 I do confess: t'was thy will made me choose,
 And thy fair shows made me a lover prove,
 When I my freedom did for pain refuse.
Yet this, Sir god: your boyship I despise:
Your charms I obey, but love not want[8] of eyes.

11

The weary traveler who, tired, sought
 In places distant far, yet found no end
 Of pain or labor nor his state to mend,[9]
 At last with joy is to his home back brought—
5 Finds not more ease, though he with joy be fraught[1]
 (When past is fear, content like souls ascend),[2]
 Than I, on whom new pleasures do descend,

1. Display; also, test.
2. Bribe.
3. Cupid, Roman god of love.
4. I.e., shut the flaming heart into Pamphilia's breast; also, because Cupid is associated with the darts or arrows of love, "shut" is here a pun on "shoot."
5. I.e., the upper hand. "Leave": omit, cease.

6. I.e., to your bond.
7. I.e., from those who resisted.
8. Lack. Cupid was sometimes depicted as blind or blindfolded.
9. I.e., nor any way to mend his state.
1. Supplied, filled.
2. When fear is past, contentment ascends like souls.

Which now as high as first born bliss[3] is wrought;
He tired with his pains, I, with my mind;
10 He all content receives by ease of limbs;
I, greatest happiness that I do find
Belief for faith,[4] while hope in pleasure swims;
Truth says it was wrong conceit bred my despite,[5]
Which once acknowledged brings my heart's delight.

24

When last I saw thee, I did not thee see;
 It was thine image, which in my thoughts lay
 So lively figured as no time's delay
 Could suffer[6] me in heart to parted be;
5 And sleep so favorable is to me
 As not to let thy loved remembrance stray,
 Lest that I, waking, might have cause to say
 There was one minute found to forget thee;
Then, since my faith is such, so kind my sleep
10 That gladly thee presents into my thought,
 And still true-lover-like thy face doth keep
 So[7] as some pleasure shadow-like is wrought,
Pity my loving, nay, of conscience, give
Reward to me, in whom thy self doth live.

25

Like to the Indians,[8] scorched with the sun,
 The sun, which they do as their God adore,
 So am I used by love, for ever more
 I worship him, less favors have I won;
5 Better are they who thus to blackness run
 And so can only whiteness' want deplore,
 Than, I, who, pale and white am with grief's store,[9]
 Nor can have hope but to see hopes undone;[1]
Besides, their sacrifice received is in sight
10 Of their chose[2] saint; mine hid as worthless rite.
 Grant me to see where I my offerings give;
Then let me wear the mark of Cupid's might
 In heart, as they in skin of Phoebus'[3] light,
 Not ceasing offerings to love while I live.

3. The joy of giving birth to one's first child. "Which": i.e., pleasures.
4. I.e., I receive belief through faith as he receives contentment from physical ease.
5. Disdain, ill-will. "Conceit": thought, idea (or perhaps a fanciful expression).
6. Permit.
7. Refers back to the lover's face (i.e., keep as it is) and forward as a conjunction (i.e., so pity my loving).

8. Inhabitants of India, or of the East more generally.
9. With storing grief.
1. Defeated (primary meaning); but Wroth spelled the word *undunn*, which also puns on *dun,* "dull and dark."
2. Chosen.
3. The sun, whose mark the Indians wear on their skin.

43

Night, welcome art thou to my mind distressed,
 Dark, heavy, sad, yet not more sad than I;
 Never could'st thou find fitter company
 For thine own humor[4] than I, thus oppressed.
5 If thou be dark, my wrongs still unredressed
 Saw never light, nor smallest bliss can spy;[5]
 If heavy, joy from me too fast doth hie,
 And care outgoes[6] my hope of quiet rest.
Then now in friendship, join with hapless me,
10 Who am as sad and dark as thou canst be,
 Hating all pleasure or delight of life;
Silence and grief, with thee I best do love,
 And from you three, I know I cannot move;
 Then let us live, companions without strife.

64

Love like a juggler comes to play his prize[7]
 And all minds draw his wonders to admire,
 To see how cunningly he, wanting[8] eyes,
 Can yet deceive the best sight of desire;
5 The wanton child, how he can feign his fire
 So prettily[9] as none sees his disguise,
 How finely do his tricks, while we fools hire
 The badge and office[1] of his tyrannies,
For in the end, such juggling he doth make
10 As he our hearts, instead of eyes, doth take;
 For men can only by their sleights abuse
The sight with nimble and delightful skill,
 But if he play, his gain is our lost will;
 Yet, childlike, we cannot his sports[2] refuse.

74

SONG

Love, a child, is ever crying;
 Please him, and he straight is flying;
 Give him, he the more is craving,
 Never satisfied with having;

5 His desires have no measure;
 Endless folly is his treasure;

4. Temperament; also, in ancient and medieval physiology, one of the four fluids that determine a person's temperament (the dark and heavy one is melancholy).
5. I.e., the speaker's unredressed wrongs are more thoroughly dark even than night.
6. Outstrips. "Hie": quickly depart.
7. His game, his part.
8. Lacking.
9. Skillfully.
1. I.e., the signs and service.
2. Games.

What he promiseth, he breaketh;
Trust not one word that he speaketh;

He vows nothing but false matter
10 And to cousen[3] you, he'll flatter;
Let him gain the hand, he'll leave you
And still glory to deceive you;

He will triumph in your wailing
And yet cause be of your failing;
15 These his virtues are and slighter
Are his gifts, his favors lighter;

Feathers are as firm in staying;
Wolves no fiercer in their preying.
As a child, then, leave him crying
20 Nor seek him so given to flying.

From *A Crown of Sonnets Dedicated to Love*[4]

77 [*First of the Corona*]

In this strange labyrinth, how shall I turn?
 Ways are on all sides, while the way, I miss;
 If to the right hand, there, in love I burn;
 Let me go forward, therein danger is;
5 If to the left, suspicion hinders bliss;[5]
 Let me turn back, shame cries I ought return,
 Nor faint, though crosses[6] with my fortunes kiss;
 Standstill is harder, although sure to mourn;[7]
Thus, let me take the right or left hand way,
10 Go forward, or stand still, or back retire,
 I must these doubts endure without allay[8]
 Or help, but travail find for my best hire;[9]
Yet that which most my troubled sense doth move
Is to leave all and take the thread of love.[1]

78 [*Second of the Corona*]

Is to leave all and take the thread of love,
 Which line straight leads unto the soul's content,
 Where choice delights with pleasure's wings do move,

3. I.e., cozen, "cheat"; possibly punning on *cousin*. Wroth's lover was her cousin William Herbert, who was the son of Mary Sidney Herbert, the countess of Pembroke.
4. Poems 77, 78, 79, and 89 are from a "crown" or "corona" of fourteen sonnets; in this sequence, the last line of each sonnet becomes the first line of the following one, until a circle is completed by the last line of the final poem, which is the same as the first line of the first one.
5. The left side was regarded as the unlucky side

for omens (in Latin, "left" is *sinister*).
6. Obstacles. "Faint": lose heart.
7. I.e., the speaker would mourn, and standstill would lead to mourning.
8. Abatement, lessening.
9. I.e., I find toil (travail, with a pun on "travel," then an alternate spelling) is my only reward.
1. I.e., as the mythological Greek hero Theseus found his way through Minos's labyrinth with the help of thread supplied by Ariadne, so for the speaker love will provide the way out.

And idle fantasy never room had lent;
5 When chaste thoughts guide us, then our minds are bent
To take that good which ills from us remove,
Light of true love, brings fruit which none repent,
But constant lovers seek and wish to prove;
Love is the shining star of blessings light,
10 The fervent fire of zeal,[2] the root of peace,
The lasting lamp, fed with the oil of right,
Image of faith, and womb for joy's increase.
Love is true virtue and his ends delight;
His flames are joys; his bands[3] true lovers' might.

79 [Third of the Corona]

His flames are joys, his bands, true lovers' might;
No stain is there but pure as purest white,
Where no cloud can appear to dim his light,
Nor spot defile, but shame will soon requite;[4]
5 Here are affections tried[5] by love's just might,
As gold by fire, and black discerned by white,
Error by truth, and darkness known by light,
Where faith is valued for love to requite;
Please him and serve him; glory in his might,
10 And firm he'll be as innocency white,[6]
Clear as the air, warm as sun beams, as day, light,[7]
Just as truth, constant as fate, joyed to requite;
Then love obey; strive to observe his might,
And be in his brave court a glorious light.

89 [Thirteenth of the Corona]

Free from all fogs but shining fair and clear,
Wise in all good and innocent in ill,
Where holy friendship is esteemed dear
With truth in love and justice in our will;
5 In love these titles only have their fill[8]
Of happy life, maintainer, and the mere
Defense of right, the punisher of skill
And fraud, from whence directions doth appear;
To thee, then, lord commander of all hearts,
10 Ruler of our affections, kind and just,
Great King of Love, my soul from feigned smarts
Or thought of change, I offer to your trust
This crown, my self, and all that I have more,
Except my heart which you bestowed before.

2. Like other imagery in this stanza, the word *zeal* has religious connotations.
3. Shackles.
4. Retaliate for, repay.
5. Proved.

6. I.e., love will be as firm as innocence is white.
7. I.e., warm as sun beams, warm as daylight, and light as day.
8. I.e., the titles are "fulfilled" as accurate descriptions.

91

SONG

Sweet, let me enjoy thy sight,
 More clear, more bright than morning sun,
Which in spring time gives delight[9]
 And by which summer's pride is won;

5 Present sight doth pleasures move,
 Which, in sad absence, we must miss,
But, when met again in love,
 Then twice redoubled is our bliss,

Yet this comfort absence gives—
10 And only faithful loving tries—
That, though parted, love's force lives
 As just[1] in heart as in our eyes,

But such comfort banish quite;
 Far sweeter is it still to find
15 Favor in thy loved sight,
 Which, present, smiles with joys combined

Eyes of gladness, lips of love,
 And hearts from passion not to turn,
But in sweet affections move
20 In flames of faith, to live and burn;

Dearest, then, this kindness give,
 And grant me life which is your sight,
Wherein I more blessed live
 Than graced with sun's fair light.

96

Late in the forest I did Cupid see
 Cold, wet, and crying, he had lost his way,
 And, being blind, was farther like to stray,
 Which sight a kind compassion bred in me;
5 I kindly took and dried him while that he,
 Poor child, complained he starved was with stay,[2]
 And pined for want of his accustomed prey,
 For none in that wild place his host would be;
I was glad of his finding, thinking sure[3]
10 This service should my freedom still procure,
 And in my arms I took him then unharmed,
Carrying him safe unto a Myrtle bower,
 But on the way he made me feel his power,
 Burning my heart, who had him kindly warmed.

9. Because seeing was thought to involve active emissions from the eyes, "sight" acts like the sun. The word *sight* also has its present meanings (the act of seeing or the thing seen).

1. I.e., just as.
2. With being stopped (i.e., from preying on lovers). "Starved": dying.
3. Surely.

103

My muse, now happy, lay thy self to rest;
 Sleep in the quiet of a faithful love;
 Write you no more but let these fantasies move
 Some other hearts; wake not to new unrest,
5 But, if you study, be those thoughts addressed
 To truth, which shall eternal goodness prove,
 Enjoying of true joy the most and best,
 The endless gain which never will remove;
Leave the discourse of Venus and her sun[4]
10 To young beginners, and their brains inspire
 With stories of great love, and from that fire,
 Get heat to write the fortunes they have won,
And thus leave off; what's past shows you can love;
Now let your constancy your honor prove.

1621

4. Both Venus' *son* Cupid and love as the *sun* of our lives.

RACHEL SPEGHT
ca. 1598–1630?

"For man was created of the dust of the earth, but woman was made of a part of man; after that he was a living soul: yet was she not produced from Adam's foot, to be his too low inferior, nor from his head to be his superior, but from his side, near his heart, to be his equal": Rachel Speght used biblical interpretation to challenge the misogynists of her day who were engaged in lively and lucrative pamphleteering. Like the earlier *querelles des femmes* in medieval France, the so-called Jacobean pamphlet wars attacked female depravity, inconstancy, ignorance, and irrationality. After the fencing instructor Joseph Swetnam published his *Arraignment of Lewd, Idle, Froward, and Unconstant Women* (1615) under the pseudonym Thomas Tell-Troth, Speght responded with *A Muzzle for Melastomus, The Cynical Baiter of, and Foul-mouthed Barker against Eve's Sex* (1617), which she boldly published under her own name. The title implies that the barking attacker, like a dog or a bear, needs a muzzle for his "melastomus," or black mouth. That Speght's appended subtitle characterizes her antagonist as "irreligious" reflects not only her invocation of scripture throughout her tract but also her background. Her father, a Calvinist clergyman, served as rector of St. Mary Magdalene and St. Clement churches in London; he published a number of his sermons and probably supported his daughter's educational and writing efforts. In *Mortalities Memorandum* (1621), Rachel Speght castigates readers who attributed *A Muzzle for Melastomus* to her father and provides a glimpse into the two women who were important to her development: her mother, who died before her second work was published, and her godmother, who was Mary Moundford, wife of the sometime bursar of King's College, Cambridge. Married probably in 1621 to William Procter and the mother of two children, Rachel Speght has become part of a lineage that evolved from Aemilia Lanyer to Mary Astell and Mary Wollstonecraft—a tradition of feminist polemic to which she contributed the idea that women must be considered flesh of men's flesh, bone of men's bone, and therefore co-partners in the human endeavor.

A Muzzle for Melastomus[1]

Not unto the Veriest Idiot That Ever Set Pen to Paper, but to the Cynical Baiter of Women, or Metamorphosed Misogunes,[2] Joseph Swetnam

From standing water, which soon putrifies, can no good fish be expected; for it produceth no other creatures but those that are venomous or noisome, as snakes, adders, and such like. Semblably,[3] no better stream can we look should issue from your idle corrupt brain, than that whereto the rough of your fury (to use your own words)[4] hath moved you to open the sluice. In which excrement of your roving cogitations you have used such irregularities touching concordance, and observed so disordered a method, as I doubt not to tell you, that a very accidence scholar[5] would have quite put you down in both. You appeare herein not unlike that painter, who seriously endeavoring to portray Cupid's bow, forgot the string: you for being greedy to botch up your mingle-mangle invective against women have not therein observed, in many places, so much as a grammar sense. But the emptiest barrel makes the loudest sound; and so we will account of[6] you.

Many propositions have you framed, which (as you think) make much against women, but if one would make a logical assumption, the conclusion would be flat against your own sex. Your dealing wants so much discretion, that I doubt whether to bestow so good a name as the dunce upon you: but minority[7] bids me keep within my bounds; and therefore I only say unto you, that your corrupt heart and railing tongue hath made you a fit scribe for the Devil.

In that you have termed your virulent foam *the Bear-baiting of Women,* you have plainly displayed your own disposition to be cynical,[8] in that there appears no other dog or bull to bait them, but your self. Good had it been for you to have put on that muzzle, which Saint James would have all Christians to wear; *Speak not evil one of another:*[9] and then had you not seemed so like the serpent Porphirus,[1] as now you do; which, though full of deadly poison, yet being toothless, hurteth none so much as himself. For you having gone beyond the limits not of humanity alone, but of Christianity, have done greater harm unto your own soul than unto women, as may plainly appear. First, in dishonoring of God by palpable blasphemy, wresting and perverting every place of Scripture, that you have alleged; which by the testimony of Saint Peter is to the destruction of them that so do.[2] Secondly, it appears by your disparaging of and opprobrious speeches against that excellent work of God's hands, which in his great love he perfected for the comfort of man. Thirdly, and lastly, by this your hodge-podge of heathenish sentences, similes, and examples, you have set forth your self in your right colours, unto the view of the world: and I doubt not but the judicious will account of you

1. The black-mouthed. This text has been modernized from the edition of Barbara Kiefer Lewalski by Alice Falk.
2. Hater of women (Greek).
3. Similarly.
4. Speght echoes a phrase in Swetnam's *Arraignment of Women* (1615).
5. I.e., a student learning Latin declensions and conjugations. "Concordance": grammatical concord or agreement.

6. Value.
7. Subordinacy.
8. To be a sneering fault-finder (from the Greek word meaning "dog").
9. James 4.11 [Speght's marginal note].
1. A snake mentioned in Edward Topsell, *The History of Serpents* (1608).
2. 1. Pet. 3.16 [margin]; in the King James version (KSV), 2 Peter 3.16. "Alleged": cited.

according to your demerit: as for the vulgar sort, which have no more learning than you have showed in your book, it is likely they will applaud you for your pains.

As to your *bugbear* or advice unto women, that whatsoever they do think of your work, they should conceal it, lest in finding fault, they bewray their galled backs to the world; in which you allude to that proverb, *Rub a galled horse, and he will kick:* Unto it I answer by way of apology,[3] that though every galled horse, being touched, doth kick; yet every one that kicks is not galled: so that you might as well have said, that because burnt folks dread the fire, therefore none fear fire but those that are burnt, as made that illiterate conclusion which you have absurdly inferred.

In your title leaf, you arraign none but lewd, idle, froward[4] and unconstant women, but in the sequel (through defect of memory as it seemeth) forgetting that you had made a distinction of good from bad, condemning all in general, you advise men to beware of and not to match with any of these six sorts of women, *viz.* good and bad, fair and foul, rich and poor: but this doctrine of devils Saint Paul foreseeing would be broached in the latter times, gives warning of.[5]

There also you promise a commendation of wise, virtuous, and honest women, when as in the subsequent, the worst words, and filthiest epithets that you can devise, you bestow on them in general, excepting no sort of women. Herein may you be likened unto a man, which upon the door of a scurvy[6] house sets this superscription, *Here is a very fair house to let:* whereas the door being opened, it is no better than a dog-hole and dark dungeon.

Further, if your own words be true, that you wrote with your hand, but not with your heart, then are you an hypocrite in print: but it is rather to be thought that your pen was the bewrayer of the abundance of your mind, and that this was but a little mortar to daub up against the wall, which you intended to break down.

The revenge of your railing work we leave to Him, who hath appropriated vengeance unto himself, whose pen-man hath included railers in the catalogue of them that shall not inherit God's kingdom,[7] and your self unto the mercy of that just Judge, who is able to save and to destroy.

Your undeserved friend,
RACHEL SPEGHT.

In Praise of the Author and Her Work

If little David that for Israel's sake,
 esteemed neither life nor limb too dear,
In that he did adventure without dread,
 to cast at him, whom all the host did fear,
5 A stone, which brought Goliah[8] to the ground,
 Obtain'd applause with songs and timbrels sound.

3. Defense. "Bewray": expose, unintentionally reveal.
4. Hard to please, refractory.
5. 1. Tim. 4.3 [margin].
6. Worthless.
7. For this "catalogue," which includes "revilers,"

see 1 Corinthians 6.9–10.
8. I.e., Goliath, the giant Philistine whom young David killed with a stone from a slingshot (1 Samuel 17). After his triumph, he was met by women singing and playing instruments (18.6–7; "timbrels" are tambourines).

Then let another young encombatant
 receive applause, and thanks, as well as he:
For with an enemy to women kind,
10 she hath encountered, as each wight[9] may see:
And with the fruit of her industrious toil,
To this Goliah she hath given the foil.

Admire her much I may, both for her age,
 and this her *Muzzle* for a black-mouth'd wight,
15 And praise her, and her work, to that desert,
 which unto them belongs of equal right
I cannot; only this I say, and end,
She is unto her sex a faithful friend.

<div align="right">PHILALETHES[1]</div>

If he that for his Country doth expose
 himself unto the fury of his foe,
Doth merit praise and due respect of those,
 for whom he did that peril undergo:
5 Then let the author of this *Muzzle* true
Receive the like, of right it is her due.

For she to shield her sex from slander's dart,
 and from invective obtrectation,[2]
Hath ventured by force of learning's art,
10 (in which she hath had education)
To combat with him, which doth shame his sex,
By offring feeble women to perplex.

<div align="right">PHILOMATHES[3]</div>

Praise is a debt, which doth of due belong
To those, that take the path of virtue's trace,
Meting[4] their ways and works by reason's rule,
Having their hearts so lightned with God's grace,
5 That willingly they would not him offend,
 But holily their lives begin and end.

Of such a pupil unto piety
As is describ'd, I do intend to speak,
A virgin young, and of such tender age,
10 As for encounter[5] may be deemed too weak,
 She having not as yet seen twenty years,
 Though in her carriage older she appears.

Her wit and learning in this present work,
More praise doth merit, than my quill can write:

9. Person.
1. Lover of truth (Greek).
2. Vituperative slander.

3. Lover of knowledge (Greek).
4. Measuring.
5. Battle, skirmish.

15 Her magnanimity deserves applaud,
 In ventring[6] with a fiery foe to fight:
 And now in fine, what shall I further say?
 But that she bears the triumph quite away.

<div align="right">FAVOUR[7] B.</div>

A Muzzle for Melastomus the Cynical Baiter of, and Foul-Mouthed Barker against Eve's Sex

Proverbs 18.22. He That Findeth a Wife, Findeth a Good Thing, and Receiveth Favour of the Lord

If lawful it be to compare the potter with his clay, or the architect with the edifice; then may I, in some part, resemble that love of God towards man, in creating woman, unto the affectionate care of Abraham for his son Isaac, who that he might not take to wife one of the daughters of the Canaanites, did provide him one of his own kindred.[8]

Almighty God, who is rich in mercy,[9] having made all things of nothing, and created man in his own image:[1] that is (as the Apostle expounds it), *In wisdom, righteousness and true holiness;*[2] *making him lord over all*: to avoid that solitary condition that he was then in, having none to commerce or converse withal[3] but dumb creatures, it seemed good unto the Lord, that as of every creature he had made male and female, and man only being alone without mate, so likewise to form an help meet for him.[4] Adam for this cause being cast into a heavy sleep, God extracting a rib from his side, thereof made, or built, Woman;[5] showing thereby, that man was as an unperfect building afore woman was made; and bringing her unto Adam, united and married them together.

Thus the resplendent love of God toward man appeared, in taking care to provide him an helper before he saw his own want,[6] and in providing him such an helper as should be meet for him. Sovereignty had he over all creatures, and they were all serviceable unto him; but yet afore woman was formed, there was not a meet help found for Adam.[7] Man's worthiness not meriting this great favour at God's hands, but his mercy only moving him thereunto: I may use those words which the Jews uttered when they saw Christ weep for Lazarus, *Behold how he loved him*:[8] Behold, and that with good regard, God's love; yea his great love, which from the beginning he hath borne unto man: which, as it appears in all things; so next, his love in Christ Jesus apparently in this; that for man's sake, that he might not be an unit, when all other creatures were for procreation dual, he created woman to be a solace unto him, to participate of his sorrows, partake of his pleasures, and as a good yokefellow bear part of his burden.[9] Of the excellency of this struc-

6. Venturing.
7. Supporter (from Latin *favor,* "partiality," "applause").
8. Gen. 24.4 [margin].
9. Ephe. 2.4 [margin].
1. Col. 3.30 [margin]; perhaps Colossians 3.10.
2. Ephe. 4.24 [margin].

3. To associate or talk with.
4. Gen. 2.20 [margin]. "Meet": suitable, proper.
5. Genesis 2.21.
6. Lack.
7. Gen. 2.20 [margin].
8. John 11.36 [margin].
9. 1. Cor. 11.9 [margin].

ture, I mean of women, whose foundation and original of creation, was God's love, do I intend to dilate.[1]

Of Woman's Excellency, with the Causes of Her Creation, and of the Sympathy Which Ought to Be in Man and Wife Each Toward Other

The work of creation being finished, this approbation thereof was given by God himself, that *All was very good:*[2] if all, then Woman, who, excepting man, is the most excellent creature under the canopy of heaven. But if it be objected by any.

First,[3] that woman, though created good, yet by giving ear to Satan's temptations, brought death and misery upon all her posterity.

Secondly,[4] that *Adam was not deceived, but that the woman was deceived, and was in the transgression.*[5]

Thirdly,[6] that Saint Paul saith, *It were good for a man not to touch a woman.*[7]

Fourthly,[8] and lastly, that of Solomon, who seems to speak against all of our sex; *I have found one man of a thousand, but a woman among them all have I not found,*[9] whereof in its due place.

To the first of these objections I answer;[1] that Satan first assailed the woman, because where the hedge is lowest, most easy it is to get over, and she being the weaker vessel[2] was with more facility to be seduced: like as a crystal glass sooner receives a crack than a strong stone pot. Yet we shall find the offence of Adam and Eve almost to parallel: for as an ambitious desire of being made like unto God was the motive which caused her to eat, so likewise was it his; as may plainly appear by that ironia, *Behold, man is become as one of us:*[3] not that he was so indeed; but hereby his desire to attain a greater perfection than God had given him was reproved. Woman sinned, it is true, by her infidelity in not believing the Word of God, but giving credit to Satan's fair promises, that *she should not die;*[4] but so did the man too: and if Adam had not approved of that deed which Eve had done, and been willing to tread the steps which she had gone, he being her head would have reproved her, and have made the commandment a bit to restrain him from breaking his Maker's injunction: For if a man burn his hand in the fire, the bellows that blowed the fire are not to be blamed, but himself rather, for not being careful to avoid the danger: yet if the bellows had not blowed, the fire had not burnt; no more is woman simply to be condemned for man's transgression: for by the free will, which before his fall he enjoyed, he might have avoided, and been free from being burnt, or singed with that fire which was kindled by Satan, and blown by Eve. It therefore served not his turn a whit, afterwards to say, *The woman which thou gavest me, gave me of the tree, and I did eat:*[5] for a penalty was inflicted upon him, as well as on the woman, the punishment of her transgression being particular to her own sex,[6] and to none but the female kind: but for the sin of man the whole earth

1. Write about.
2. Gen. 1.31 [margin].
3. 1 *Object.* [margin].
4. 2 *Object.* [margin].
5. 1. Tim. 2.14 [margin].
6. 3 *Object.* [margin].
7. 1. Cor. 7.1 [margin].
8. 4 *Object.* [margin].
9. Eccles. 7.30 [margin]; KJV, Ecclesiastes 7.28.

1. 1 *Object. answered* [margin].
2. A common description of women (e.g., see 1 Peter 3.7).
3. Gen. 3.22 [margin]. "Ironia": i.e., ironic (and thus untrue) declaration.
4. Gen. 3.4 [margin].
5. Genesis 3.12 [margin].
6. I.e., pain in childbirth (Genesis 3.16).

was cursed. And he being better able than the woman to have resisted temptation,[7] because the stronger vessel, was first called to account, to show that to whom much is given, of them much is required;[8] and that he who was the sovereign of all creatures visible should have yielded greatest obedience to God.

True it is (as is already confessed) that woman first sinned, yet find we no mention of spiritual nakedness till man had sinned: then it is said, *Their eyes were opened,*[9] the eyes of their mind and conscience; and then perceived they themselves naked, that is, not only bereft of that integrity, which they originally had, but felt the rebellion and disobedience of their members[1] in the disordered motions of their now corrupt nature, which made them for shame to cover their nakedness: then (and not afore) is it said that they saw it, as if sin were imperfect, and unable to bring a deprivation of a blessing received, or death on all mankind, till man (in whom lay the active power of generation) had transgressed. The offence therefore of Adam and Eve is by Saint Austin[2] thus distinguished, *the man sinned against God and himself, the woman against God, her self, and her husband:* yet in her giving of the fruit to eat had she no malicious intent towards him, but did therein show a desire to make her husband partaker of that happiness, which she thought by their eating they should both have enjoyed. This her giving Adam of that sauce, wherewith Satan had served her, whose sourness afore he had eaten, she did not perceive, was that which made her sin to exceed his: wherefore, that she might not of him, who ought to honour her,[3] be abhorred, the first promise that was made in Paradise, God makes to woman, that by her seed should the serpent's head be broken:[4] whereupon Adam calls her *Hevah,* life,[5] that as the woman had been an occasion of his sin, so should woman bring forth the Saviour from sin, which was in the fullness of time accomplished; by which was manifested, that he is a Saviour of believing women,[6] no less than of men, that so the blame of sin may not be imputed to his creature, which is good; but to the will by which Eve sinned, and yet by Christ's assuming the shape of man was it declared, that his mercy was equivalent to both sexes; so that by *Hevah's* blessed seed (as Saint Paul affirms)[7] it is brought to pass, that *male and female are all one in Christ Jesus.*

To the second objection I answer,[8] that the Apostle doth not hereby exempt man from sin, but only giveth to understand, that the woman was the primary transgressor and not the man; but that man was not at all deceived was far from his meaning: for he afterward expressly saith, that as *in Adam all die, so in Christ shall all be made alive.*[9]

For the third objection,[1] *It is good for a man not to touch a woman:* the Apostle makes it not a positive prohibition, but speaks it only because of the Corinths' present necessity,[2] who were then persecuted by the enemies of the Church, for which cause, and no other, he saith, *Art thou loosed from a wife? seek not a wife:* meaning whilst the time of these perturbations should

7. Genesis 3.17 [margin].
8. See Luke 12.48.
9. Genesis 3.7 [margin].
1. Sexual organs.
2. St. Augustine (354–430). The following commonplace seems to be derived from his sermon on Adam and Eve.
3. 1 Pet. 3.7 [margin].
4. Genesis 3.15 [margin].

5. Genesis 3.20. The Hebrew word *chava* means "life" or "living."
6. Galat. 4.4 [margin].
7. Galat. 3.28 [margin].
8. 2 *Objection answered* [margin].
9. 1. Cor. 15.22 [margin].
1. 3 *Objection answered* [margin].
2. 1 Cor. 7 [margin]. "Corinths": Corinthians.

continue in their heat; *but if thou art bound, seek not to be loosed: if thou marriest, thou sinnest not,* only increasest thy care: *for the married careth for the things of this world, And I wish that you were without care, that ye might cleave fast unto the Lord without separation: For the time remaineth, that they which have wives be as though they had none:* for the persecutors shall deprive you of them, either by imprisonment, banishment, or death; so that manifest it is, that the Apostle doth not hereby forbid marriage, but only adviseth the Corinths to forbear a while, till God in mercy should curb the fury of their adversaries. For (as Eusebius[3] writeth) Paul was afterward married himself, the which is very probable, being that interrogatively he saith,[4] *Have we not power to lead about a wife, being a sister, as well as the rest of the Apostles, and as the brethren of the Lord and Cephas?*[5]

The fourth and last objection,[6] is that of Solomon, *I have found one man among a thousand, but a woman among them all have I not found:*[7] for answer of which, if we look into the story of his life, we shall find therein a commentary upon this enigmatical sentence included: for it is there said, that Solomon had seven hundred wives, and three hundred concubines, which number connexed[8] make one thousand. These women turning his heart away from being perfect with the Lord his God, sufficient cause had he to say, that among the said thousand women found he not one upright.[9] He saith not, that among a thousand women never any man found one worthy of commendation, but speaks in the first person singularly, *I have not found,* meaning in his own experience: for this assertion is to be holden a part of the confession of his former follies, and no otherwise,[1] his repentance being the intended drift of Ecclesiastes.

Thus having (by God's assistance) removed those stones, whereat some have stumbled, others broken their shins, I will proceed toward the period[2] of my intended task, which is, to decipher the excellency of women: of whose creation I will, for order's sake observe; First, the efficient cause, which was God; Secondly, the material cause, or that whereof she was made; Thirdly, the formal cause, or fashion, and proportion of her feature; Fourthly and lastly, the final cause, the end or purpose for which she was made.[3] To begin with the first.

The efficient cause of woman's creation was Jehovah the Eternal; the truth of which is manifest in Moses his narration of the six days' works, where he saith, *God created them male and female:*[4] and David exhorting all *the earth to sing unto the Lord;* meaning, by a metonymy, earth, all creatures that live on the earth, of what nation or sex soever, gives this reason, *For the Lord hath made us.*[5] That work then cannot choose but be good, yea very good, which is wrought by so excellent a workman as the Lord:[6] for he being a

3. Bishop of Caesarea (ca. 260–ca. 340), early church historian.
4. 1. Corint. 9.5 [margin].
5. I.e., the apostle Peter (see John 1.42); *kephas* in Aramaic means "rock" (as does *petros* in Greek).
6. 4 *Object answered* [margin].
7. Eccles. 7.30 [margin]; KJV, Ecclesiastes 7.28.
8. Connected, joined together.
9. Pagnine [margin]. I.e., they were pagan, and thus unlikely to be "upright."
1. In no other way.
2. Final stage.
3. This terminology derives from Aristotle's *Phys-*

ics (ca. 340 B.C.E.), 2.3, which defines four meanings of *cause:* the material cause is the stuff out of which something is made, the formal cause is its pattern or structure, the efficient cause is the agent that makes change and thus imposes its form, and the final cause is its purpose.
4. Genesis 1.28 [margin]; KJV, verse 27. The authorship of the first five books of the Bible is traditionally ascribed to Moses.
5. Psal. 100.3 [margin]. See also verse 1. "Metonomy": figure of speech in which a thing's part or attribute stands for the thing itself.
6. Psal. 100.4 [margin]; KJV, verse 5.

glorious Creator, must needs effect[7] a worthy creature. Bitter water cannot proceed from a pleasant sweet fountain, nor bad work from that workman which is perfectly good, and in propriety, none but he.[8]

Secondly, the material cause, or matter whereof woman was made, was of a refined mould, if I may so speak: for man was created of the dust of the earth,[9] but woman was made of a part of man, after that he was a living soul: yet was she not produced from Adam's foot, to be his too low inferior; nor from his head to be his superior, but from his side,[1] near his heart, to be his equal; that where he is lord, she may be lady: and therefore saith God concerning man and woman jointly, *Let them rule over the fish of the sea, and over the fowls of the Heaven, and over every beast that moveth upon the earth:*[2] by which words, he makes their authority equal, and all creatures to be in subjection unto them both. This being rightly considered doth teach men to make such account of their wives, as Adam did of Eve, *This is bone of my bone, and flesh of my flesh:*[3] as also, that they neither do or wish any more hurt unto them, than unto their own bodies: for men ought to love their wives as themselves, because he that loves his wife, loves himself:[4] and never man hated his own flesh (which woman is) unless a monster in nature.

Thirdly, the formal cause, fashion, and proportion of woman was excellent: for she was neither like the beasts of the earth, fowls of the air, fishes of the sea, or any other inferior creature, but man was the only object which she did resemble. For as God gave man a lofty countenance, that he might look up toward Heaven, so did he likewise give unto woman. And as the temperature[5] of man's body is excellent, so is woman's. For whereas other creatures, by reason of their gross humours, have excrements for their habit,[6] as fowls, their feathers, beasts, their hair, fishes, their scales, man and woman only have their skin clear and smooth. And (that more is) in the image of God were they both created;[7] yea and to be brief, all the parts of their bodies, both external and internal, were correspondent and meet each for other.[8]

Fourthly and lastly, the final cause, or end, for which woman was made, was to glorify God, and to be a collateral[9] companion for man to glorify God, in using her body, and all the parts, powers, and faculties thereof, as instruments for his honour: as with her voice to sound forth his praises, like Miriam and the rest of her company;[1] with her tongue not to utter words of strife, but to give good counsel unto her husband, the which he must not despise. For Abraham was bidden to give ear to Sarah his wife.[2] Pilate was willed by his wife not to have any hand in the condemning of CHRIST;[3] and a sin it was in him, that he listened not to her: Leah and Rachel counseled Jacob to do according to the word of the Lord:[4] and the Shunamite put her husband

7. Make.
8. Math. 19.17 [margin]. "In propriety": in the strict sense; i.e., strictly speaking, only God is perfectly good.
9. Genesis 2.7 [margin]. "Mould": both pattern and loose earth.
1. Genesis 2.21.
2. Genesis 1.26 [margin].
3. Genesis 2.23 [margin].
4. Ephes. 5.28 [margin].
5. I.e., the balance of the four qualities (hot, dry, cold, wet); from Hippocrates (a Greek who wrote on medicine) in the 5th century B.C.E. onward, men were generally thought to be hot and dry,

while women were cold and wet (and thus inferior).
6. Garment.
7. Gen. 1.26 [margin]; KJV, verse 27.
8. Each was mutually adapted to and suitable for the other.
9. Ranking side by side with.
1. Exod. 15.20 [margin]. The prophetess Miriam and all the women sang a song of triumph to the Lord after the army of the pharaoh of Egypt was destroyed in the sea.
2. Genesis 21.12 [margin].
3. Math. 27.19 [margin].
4. Genesis 31.16 [margin].

in mind of harbouring the Prophet Elisha:[5] her hands should be open according to her ability, in contributing towards God's service, and distressed servants, like to that poor widow, which cast two mites into the treasury;[6] and as Mary Magdalen, Susanna, and Joanna the wife of Herod's steward,[7] with many other, which of their substance ministered unto CHRIST. Her heart should be a receptacle for God's Word, like Mary that treasured up the sayings of CHRIST in her heart.[8] Her feet should be swift in going to seek the Lord in his sanctuary, as Mary Magdalen made haste to seek CHRIST at his sepulchre.[9] Finally, no power external or internal ought woman to keep idle, but to employ it in some service of GOD, to the glory of her Creator, and comfort of her own soul.

The other end for which woman was made was to be a companion and helper for man; and if she must be an helper, and but an helper, then are those husbands to be blamed, which lay the whole burden of domestical affairs and maintenance on the shoulders of their wives. For, as yoke-fellows they are to sustain part of each other's cares, griefs, and calamities: but as if two oxen be put in one yoke, the one being bigger than the other, the greater bears most weight; so the husband being the stronger vessel is to bear a greater burden than his wife; and therefore the Lord said to Adam, *In the sweat of thy face shalt thou eat thy bread, till thou return to the dust.*[1] And Saint Paul saith, *That he that provideth not for his household is worse than an infidel.*[2] Nature hath taught senseless creatures to help one another; as the male pigeon, when his hen is weary with sitting on her eggs, and comes off from them, supplies her place, that in her absence they may receive no harm, until such time as she is fully refreshed.[3] Of small birds the cock always helps his hen to build her nest; and while she sits upon her eggs, he flies abroad to get meat for her, who cannot then provide any for her self. The crowing cockerel helps his hen to defend her chickens from peril, and will endanger himself to save her and them from harm.[4] Seeing then that these unreasonable creatures, by the instinct of nature, bear such affection each to other that without any grudge, they willingly, according to their kind, help one another, I may reason *à minore ad maius,*[5] that much more should man and woman, which are reasonable creatures, be helpers each to other in all things lawful, they having the law of God to guide them, his Word to be a lantern unto their feet, and a light unto their paths, by which they are excited to a far more mutual participation of each other's burden than other creatures. So that neither the wife may say to her husband, nor the husband unto his wife, I have no need of thee, no more than the members of the body may say so each to other,[6] between whom there is such a sympathy, that if one member suffer, all suffer with it: Therefore though God bade Abraham forsake his country and kindred, yet he bade him not forsake his wife, who being *Flesh of his flesh, and bone of his bone,*[7] was to be copartner with him

5. 2 Kings 4.9 [margin].
6. Luke 21.1–4.
7. Luke 8 [margin], verses 2–3.
8. Luke 1.51 [margin].
9. John 20.1 [margin].
1. Gen. 3.19 [margin].
2. 1. Tim. 5.8 [margin].
3. Revived by food and rest. According to the Roman scholar Pliny the Elder (23–79 C.E.), the female pigeon sits on the eggs from midday till morning; the male, the rest of the time (*Natural History* 10.79).

4. For the attention and comfort said to be rendered by these male birds to their mates, see Pliny, *Natural History* 10.52.
5. From the lesser to the greater (Latin). "Unreasonable": not endowed with reason.
6. 1. Cor. 12.21 [margin]; more generally, see verses 14–26.
7. Genesis 2.23 (said of Eve, by Adam). For God's instructions to Abraham, which do not mention his wife, see Genesis 12.1–3.

of whatsoever did betide him, whether joy or sorrow. Wherefore Solomon saith, *Woe to him that is alone;*[8] for when thoughts of discomfort, troubles of this world, and fear of dangers do possess him, he wants a companion to lift him up from the pit of perplexity, into which he is fallen:[9] for a good wife, saith Plautus,[1] is the wealth of the mind, and the welfare of the heart; and therefore a meet associate for her husband; and *Woman,* saith Paul, *is the glory of the man.*[2]

Marriage is a merri-age, and this world's Paradise, where there is mutual love. Our blessed Saviour vouchsafed to honour a marriage with the first miracle that he wrought,[3] unto which miracle matrimonial estate may not unfitly be resembled: for as Christ turned water into wine, a far more excellent liquor; which, as the Psalmist saith, *Makes glad the heart of man;*[4] so a single man is by marriage changed from a bachelor to a husband, a far more excellent title: from a solitary life unto a joyful union and conjunction, with such a creature as God hath made meet for man, for whom none was meet till she was made. The enjoying of this great blessing made Pericles[5] more unwilling to part from his wife, than to die for his country; and Antoninus Pius[6] to pour forth that pathetical exclamation against death, for depriving him of his dearly beloved wife, *O cruel hard-hearted death in bereaving me of her whom I esteemed more than my own life!* A virtuous woman, saith Solomon, *is the crown of her husband;*[7] by which metaphor he showeth both the excellency of such a wife, and what account her husband is to make of her: For a king doth not trample his crown under his feet, but highly esteems of it, gently handles it, and carefully lays it up, as the evidence of his kingdom; and therefore when David destroyed Rabbah he took off the crown from their king's head:[8] so husbands should not account their wives as their vassals, but as those that are heirs together of the grace of life[9] and with all lenity and mild persuasions set their feet in the right way, if they happen to tread awry, bearing with their infirmities, as Elkanah did with his wife's barrenness.[1]

The Kingdom of God is compared unto the marriage of a king's son:[2] John calleth the conjunction of Christ and his Chosen, a marriage:[3] and not a few but many times doth our blessed Saviour in the Canticles[4] set forth his unspeakable love towards his Church under the title of an husband rejoicing with his wife; and often vouchsafeth to call her his sister and spouse, by which is showed that with *God is no respect of persons,*[5] nations, or sexes: for whosoever, whether it be man or woman, that doth *believe in the Lord Jesus, such shall be saved.*[6] And if God's love even from the beginning had not been as great toward woman as to man, then would he not have preserved from

8. Eccles. 4.10 [margin].
9. Eccles. 4.10 [margin].
1. Roman writer of comedy (d. ca. 184 B.C.E.); the lines apparently paraphrase *Amphitryon* lines 839–42.
2. 1. Cor. 11.7 [margin].
3. John 2 [margin], a wedding at Cana in Galilee.
4. Psal. 104.15 [margin].
5. Athenian statesman (ca. 495–429 B.C.E.); the woman to whom he was famously devoted was not his wife (whom he divorced) but his mistress, the courtesan Aspasia, with whom he lived for many years.
6. Roman emperor (86–161 C.E.; emperor, 138–161), reknowned for his integrity. In memory of his wife, Faustina (d. 141), he set aside funds for the

care of orphaned girls and minted a series of commemorative coins.
7. Prov. 12.4 [margin].
8. 1. Chron. 20.2 [margin]. According to verse 1, Rabbah was destroyed not by David but by Joab (in 2 Samuel 12.29–30, David does fight as well as take the crown).
9. 1. Pet. 3.7 [margin].
1. 1. Sam. 1.17 [margin]. More to the point is verse 8.
2. Math. 22 [margin], verse 2.
3. Rev. 19.7 [margin].
4. The Song of Solomon, interpreted allegorically by Christians.
5. Rom. 2.11 [margin].
6. John 3.18 [margin].

the deluge of the old world as many women as men; nor would Christ after his resurrection have appeared unto a woman first[7] of all other, had it not been to declare thereby, that the benefits of his death and resurrection are as available, by belief, for women as for men; for he indifferently[8] died for the one sex as well as the other. Yet a truth ungainsayable is it, that the *Man is the woman's head;*[9] by which title yet of supremacy, no authority hath he given him to domineer, or basely command and employ his wife as a servant; but hereby is he taught the duties which he oweth unto her: for as the head of a man is the imaginer and contriver of projects profitable for the safety of his whole body; so the husband must protect and defend his wife from injuries: for he is her *head, as Christ is the Head of his Church,*[1] which he entirely loveth, and for which he gave his very life; the dearest thing any man hath in this world;[2] *Greater love than this hath no man, when he bestoweth his life for his friend,*[3] saith our Saviour: this precedent passeth[4] all other patterns, it requireth great benignity, and enjoineth an extraordinary affection, for *men must love their wives, even as Christ loved his Church.* Secondly, as the head doth not jar or contend with the members, which *being many,* as the Apostle saith, *yet make but one body;*[5] no more must the husband with the wife, but expelling all bitterness and cruelty[6] he must live with her lovingly, and religiously, honouring her as the weaker vessel.[7] Thirdly, and lastly, as he is her head, he must, by instruction, bring her to the knowledge of her Creator, that so she may be a fit stone for the Lord's building.[8] Women for this end must have an especial care to set their affections upon such as are able to teach them, that as they *grow in years, they may grow in grace, and in the knowledge of Christ Jesus our Lord.*[9]

Thus if men would remember the duties they are to perform in being heads, some would not stand a tip-toe[1] as they do, thinking themselves lords and rulers, and account every omission of performing whatsoever they command, whether lawful or not, to be matter of great disparagement, and indignity done them; whereas they should consider, that women are enjoined to submit themselves unto their husbands no otherways than as to the Lord;[2] so that from hence, for man, ariseth a lesson not to be forgotten, that as the Lord commandeth nothing to be done, but that which is right and good, no more must the husband; for if a wife fulfill the evil command of her husband, she obeys him as a tempter, as Sapphira did Ananias.[3] But lest I should seem too partial in praising women so much as I have (though no more than warrant from Scripture doth allow) I add to the premises, that I say not, all women are virtuous, for then they should be more excellent than men, sith[4] of Adam's sons there was Cain as well as Abel, and of Noah's, Cham as well as Sem;[5] so that of men as of women, there are two sorts, namely, good and

7. I.e., Mary Magdalene (Mark 16.9; John 20.11–18).
8. Equally.
9. 1. Cor. 11.3 [margin].
1. Ephe. 5.23 [margin].
2. Job 2.4 [margin].
3. John 15.13 [margin].
4. Surpasses.
5. 1. Cor. 12.20 [margin].
6. Col. 3.19 [margin].
7. 1. Pet. 3.7 [margin].
8. 1. Cor. 14.35 [margin].
9. 1. Pet. 3.18 [margin]. KJV, 2 Peter 3.18.

1. On tiptoe; i.e., artificially elevating themselves.
2. Ephes. 5 [margin], verse 22. "No otherways": not otherwise.
3. Actes 5.2 [margin]. Ananias's wife was privy to his wrongdoing when he "sold a possession, and kept back part of the price" (5.1–2).
4. Since.
5. Cain was cursed for killing his brother, Abel (Genesis 4.1–16); Ham (Cham) was cursed for seeing the nakedness of his father, while his brothers, Shem and Japheth, were blessed for covering him (Genesis 9.22–27).

bad, which in Matthew the five and twenty chapter, are comprehended under the name of sheep and goats.[6] And if women were not sinful, then should they not need a Saviour: but the Virgin Mary a pattern of piety, *rejoiced in God her Saviour:*[7] *ergo,* she was a sinner. In the Revelation the Church is called the Spouse of Christ;[8] and in Zechariah, wickedness is called a woman,[9] to show that of women there are both godly and ungodly: for Christ would not *purge his floor* if there were not chaff among the wheat;[1] nor should gold need to be fined,[2] if among it there were no dross. But far be it from any one, to condemn the righteous with the wicked,[3] or good women with the bad (as the Baiter of women doth): For though there are some scabbed[4] sheep in a flock, we must not therefore conclude all the rest to be mangy: and though some men, through excess, abuse God's creatures, we must not imagine that all men are gluttons; the which we may with as good reason do, as condemn all women in general for the offences of some particulars.[5] Of the good sort is it that I have in this book spoken, and so would I that all that read it should so understand me: for if otherwise I had done, I should have incurred that woe, which by the Prophet Isaiah is pronounced against them that *speak well of evil,*[6] and should have *justified the wicked, which thing is abominable to the Lord.*[7]

The Epilogue or Upshot of the Premises

Great was the unthankfulness of Pharaoh's butler unto Joseph; for though he had done him a great pleasure, of which the butler promised requital, yet was he quite forgotten of him:[8] but far greater is the ingratitude of those men toward God, that dare presume to speak and exclaim against Woman, whom God did create for man's comfort. What greater discredit can redound to a workman, than to have the man, for whom he hath made it, say, it is naught? or what greater discourtesy can be offered to one that bestoweth a gift, than to have the receiver give out, that he cares not for it: for he needs it not? And what greater ingratitude can be showed unto GOD than the opprobrious speeches and disgraceful invectives, which some diabolical natures do frame against women?

Ingratitude is and always hath been accounted so odious a vice, that Cicero[9] saith, *If one doubt what name to give a wicked man, let him call an ungrateful person, and then he hath said enough.* It was so detested among the Persians, as that by a law they provided, that such should suffer death as felons, which proved unthankful for any gift received. And *Love* (saith the Apostle) *is the fulfilling of the law:*[1] but where ingratitude is harbored, there love is banished. Let men therefore beware of all unthankfulness, but espe-

6. See Matthew 25.31–46, which describes how Christ on Judgment Day will separate the sheep— the blessed, who will enjoy eternal life—from the goats, sent into everlasting punishment.
7. Luke 1.47 [margin].
8. Revelation 21.2, 9.
9. Zach. 5.7 [margin]; KJV, verses 7–8.
1. See Luke 3.17.
2. Refined.
3. Gen. 18.25 [margin].
4. Afflicted with mange, a skin disease.
5. Individuals.

6. Esay 5.20 [margin]. "Esay": Isaiah.
7. Prov. 17.15 [margin].
8. Gen. 40.23 [margin]. "Pleasure": service. When both were imprisoned, Joseph had interpreted the butler's dream, but the butler forgot him when restored to his former position (verses 9–23).
9. Roman statesman and author (106–43 B.C.E.); in one of his letters to his brother, he wrote that the vice of ingratitude contains all other evils (*To Atticus* 8.4).
1. Rom. 13.10 [margin]. "The Apostle": Paul.

cially of the superlative ingratitude, that which is towards God, which is no way more palpably declared, than by the contemning[2] of and railing against women, which sin, of some men (if to be termed men) no doubt but God will one day avenge, when they shall plainly perceive, that it had been better for them to have been born dumb and lame, than to have used their tongues and hands, the one in repugning,[3] the other in writing against God's handiwork, their own flesh, women I mean, whom God hath made equal with themselves in dignity, both temporally and eternally, if they continue in the faith: which God for his mercy sake grant they always may, to the glory of their Creator, and comfort of their own souls, through Christ Amen.

To God only wise be glory now and for ever, AMEN.

1617

2. Despising. 3. Fighting against, opposing.

Literature of the Seventeenth
and Eighteenth Centuries

AN AGE OF CHANGE

In her fantasy, *Orlando* (1928), Virginia Woolf told the story of a writer, representing English literary history, who was born male during the Renaissance and started life as an Elizabethan, but turned into a woman in the second half of the seventeenth century. Her protagonist's sex change dramatizes a major event in the history of English letters—namely, the entrance of women into the literary marketplace. Throughout the seventeenth and eighteenth centuries, the printing press, invented in the fifteenth century, led to an expansion of literacy as well as a reconceptualization of the role of the author. Not insignificantly, a number of women began to write and publish just when the production of literature became commercialized, when the patron started to give way to the printer, and when the small courtly audience began to give way to a large reading public. For the first time, too, many of these women were not exceptionally privileged by virtue of their aristocratic rank or religious calling; some, indeed, were ordinary middle-class women.

What in *A Room of One's Own* (1929) Woolf considers "a change" of "greater importance than the Crusades or the Wars of the Roses"—the moment when the middle-class woman began to write—took place during an era of transition that is usually associated with the emergence of the modern world. Such vocations as law, medicine, science, journalism, and politics became professionalized in ways that would have been unimaginable before. On both sides of the Atlantic, the religious disputes of the seventeenth century gave way to the commercial growth of the eighteenth century: the Church of England was supplemented as a central cultural institution by the Bank of England, and the early Puritan settlers, pilgrims searching for an earthly paradise, were succeeded by American citizens determined to establish their economic independence. The religious, intellectual, and social movements that accompanied this transformation—Puritanism, empiricism, and urbanization—had a paradoxical and complex impact on women's lives. On the one hand, these movements overtly excluded women or further subjected them to male regulation; and yet, on the other hand, they implicitly provided precedents for questioning the conventional authorities who had defined women as the second sex. While women's contribution to production decreased when the English and American economies shifted from agriculture to manufacturing and commerce, the spread of education and the expansion of middle-class professions helped make possible the emergence of productive, publishing literary women, who began to form unique traditions of their own.

Put in the starkest terms, the seventeenth century was marked by political conflicts and religious disputes, while the eighteenth century was remarkable for its moderation, tolerance, and prosperity. Even the American Revolution at the end of the period could be said to dramatize optimistic assumptions about the common sense and morality of ordinary citizens as well as the secularization of civic activity. Nor did the loss of the colonies deter England from expanding and consolidating its empire elsewhere around the globe. Although the shifting of political power from the court to the city and of literary power from the patron to the printer cannot be assigned to a specific date, this transformation nevertheless distinguished the quite different atmospheres in which authors wrote and readers read at the beginning and end of this two-hundred-year span. As both producers and consumers, many women with literary aspirations and tastes began to participate with men in the literary marketplace and to agitate for their rights as citizens.

POLITICAL BACKGROUND

English Revolution and Consolidation

English political history in the seventeenth century, which has been characterized as "a history of hurts," included two revolutions within fifty years, two kings deposed and one killed, and an Anglican Church that was consolidated, overthrown, and rebuilt. Civil strife was a direct result of religious disputes dating back to the Reformation, when the Church of England separated from the Catholic Church, for radical reformers continued to believe that the church had to further "purify" itself of Catholic rites and creeds. Attacking the official Church of England, such Puritans fought for civic and religious freedom from the authority of the bishops and the authoritarianism of the Stuart kings, James I (r. 1603–25) and Charles I (r. 1625–49). They were, therefore, viewed as rebels both by moderate Protestants and by Catholics. But a crisis ensued when the Stuart monarchs aligned themselves with Rome, levied high taxes, and attempted to assert, as James I did, that "kings are not only God's lieutenants on earth, but even by God himself they are called gods." Many moderate Protestants in Parliament, elected representatives of men of property, united with the reformers against the Crown. By 1642, the struggle between Parliament and king—Puritans and Royalists, country and court—culminated in armed conflict. The execution of King Charles I in 1649 and the succession of Oliver Cromwell, the leader of the parliamentary army and lord protector of England (1653–58), hastened the rise to power of the middle class, led to the persecution of such supposedly tradition-bound groups as Anglicans and Catholics, and—perhaps most important—effectively ended belief in the divine right of kings.

Before, during, and after the English civil war, many Parliamentarians and Royalists feared the chaos associated with a growing number of radical Protestant sects. Such anxious citizens as Samuel Pepys and John Evelyn recorded the confusion of the times in their diaries. Pepys, for example, described a Royalist uncle condemned in the Tower of London while another uncle served as a captain in the parliamentary militia, and Evelyn protested against an anarchistic mechanic preaching "feculent stuff" from a church pulpit. Nevertheless, the political upheavals of the seventeenth century had

a liberating impact on the lives of some women, for the Puritan revolution created a crisis in which women on both sides were charged with new, unforeseen responsibilities. Royalists such as Margaret Cavendish, duchess of Newcastle, and Charlotte Stanley, countess of Derby, defended their homes against parliamentary armies or traveled back and forth between England and France on their husbands' behalf. Similarly, Puritans like Lucy Hutchinson and Quakers like Margaret Fell recorded their efforts to help their families survive in quickly shifting political circumstances. A number of female prophets—Lady Eleanor Davies, Mary Cary, and Anna Trapnell—dictated or composed their claims to divine inspiration. Still, women's virtual exclusion from political institutions meant that their role was confined mainly to personal influence in a time when revolutionary instability was followed first by conservative reaction and then by compromise.

Internal disputes among Parliamentarians, fear of fanaticism and the mob, desire for stability, and dislike of military rule resulted in the Restoration of the Stuart monarchy of Charles II (r. 1660–85). Whereas Catholic families and Royalist bishops had been persecuted under Cromwell, Puritans were excluded from positions of civil and religious authority during the reign of Charles II. In stark contrast to the Puritans, who had closed the theaters and instituted fines against swearing, drinking, and dancing, aristocratic courtiers in the Restoration quickly became infamous for the sexual freedom that was reflected in the comedies on the reopened stage, now performed regularly not only by actors but, for the first time, by actresses too. In spite of the courtly decadence associated with, for instance, Charles II's actress-mistress Nell Gwyn, the king had to conform to the policies of a Parliament that worked to strengthen England's trading and agricultural industries, for the balance of power had already begun to shift from the court to the city, from the king to two clashing political parties: the Tories, associated with a conservative aristocracy, and the Whigs, identified with the growing commercial class. When the restored Stuart monarchs again asserted their autonomy as well as their sympathy with Roman Catholicism, popular sentiment led to the so-called Glorious Revolution of 1688. Charles II's successor, James II (r. 1685–88), was forced to relinquish the crown to his Protestant daughter and her husband, a nonviolent change in government that promised an end to a century of violent upheaval and the beginning of a stable equilibrium. Also in 1689, a bill of rights placed limits on the king while affirming the supremacy of Parliament. John Dryden expressed the relieved optimism of the next generation when, in his "The Secular Masque" (1700), he exclaimed, " 'Tis well an old age is out, / And time to begin a new."

As divisive as these civil and religious disorders undoubtedly were, they had, by the middle of the eighteenth century, given way to a secularized, parliamentary government. Church and state had been effectively separated, and the Act of Toleration (1689) freed Dissenters (Protestants outside the Church of England) from religious persecution, although its toleration did not extend to Catholics. Parliament also joined Scotland with England and established the stability of royal succession. Religious toleration and governmental continuity were matched by freedom of the press and free trade. With Parliament now controlling taxation and foreign policy, England became the wealthiest world power. Throughout the eighteenth century, the authority of government continued to shift from the court to the Parliament and the

ministerial cabinet, an institution that took shape during the reign of Anne (1702–14) and became dominant during Sir Robert Walpole's long ministry (1721–42), in part because the three kings named George (1714–1820) were less than charismatic leaders. By midcentury, when the last Stuart heir was defeated in his effort to restore a more orthodox monarchy, mercantile interests were providing the impetus for a series of wars against France, which led to England's acquisition of an empire reaching from India to Gibraltar to Canada. Paradoxically, however, the very principles of religious toleration, civic autonomy, and vigorous mercantile development that infused eighteenth-century English growth would lead in America to a revolt against English rule.

The New World

The Puritans began to leave England before the English civil war. From 1629 to 1640, thousands, mostly from the middle classes, emigrated to New England in the hope of finding a place free from the religious persecution and economic harassment they associated with the Old World. After an arduous three-month voyage across the Atlantic, the emigrants embarked on what the colonist Samuel Danforth described as "an errand into the wilderness." They were strengthened to face the threats of illness, privation, wild animals, and homesickness by the conviction that they, like the tribe of Moses in search of the Promised Land, had entered into a divine covenant, which would enable them to build a holy "city on the hill" in the New World. Puritan leaders in the Massachusetts Bay Colony such as John Winthrop and Cotton Mather saw America as an ideal location for a "new Zion," a theocracy in which God's will could be carried out without interference from Anglican bishops or English monarchs.

Whether the impetus for settlement was predominantly religious, as in Pennsylvania, where the Quakers sought refuge, or financial, as in Virginia, with its profitable tobacco crop, many later colonists saw the New World as an inspiring, if sometimes bewildering, opportunity for development. Yet the eastern edge of the American continent was also being populated by convicts transported by British judges, indentured servants, and slaves sold to southern planters by English, French, Portuguese, and Spanish traders. By the 1770s and 1780s, seventy thousand African slaves were landed annually, half of them carried in British ships. Chained into overcrowded and filthy quarters, thousands of Africans died of smallpox, dysentery, insanity, and suicidal mutinies throughout the eighteenth century. Meanwhile, the number of colonists grew from 111,000 in 1670 to 1,600,000 by 1760. During the second half of the century, they were joined by additional Dutch, French Protestant, and German settlers. Together, the colonists appropriated the lands of the American Indians, who were forced either to migrate or to fight.

Economic impediments created by acts of Parliament led the colonists toward the independence movement. England's policy of taxation without representation fueled American resentment, and political resistance to George III reached new heights in a skeptical generation that no longer espoused the Puritanism of the pioneers: Benjamin Franklin, for example, began his publishing career by writing the *Silence Dogood Papers* (1722), a satire on Cotton Mather's *Bonifacius: An Essay . . . to Do Good* (1710). If

America was still viewed as "the most perfect society now existing in the world"—the sentiments expressed by the French settler Jean de Crévecoeur in 1782—it enjoyed that status precisely because of its freedom from the religious fervor prevalent in Europe, for "zeal in Europe is confined[,] . . . a grain of powder enclosed; here it burns away in the open air, and consumes without effect." Essayists and philosophers based their arguments for separation from England on the national identity of America, as did such poets as Philip Freneau and Hugh Henry Brackenridge when they delivered the collaborative *Poem on the Rising Glory of America* at the 1771 Princeton commencement. Attempts of the king and Parliament to control the political and economic life of the American colonies finally led to the revolution of 1776. That insurrection was also justified by English-born men such as Tom Paine and Joseph Priestley, who supported the inalienable rights of ordinary citizens as opposed to the tyrannies of kings, states, and churches. Their ideal had informed the English civil war, and it would profoundly affect not only the lives but the letters of women.

INTELLECTUAL AND SOCIAL BACKGROUND

Puritanism

Puritanism, which shaped English history and American identity throughout the seventeenth century, dramatically endowed the inner life of the self and the historical development of the state with divine significance. Early English and colonial Puritans believed that after the Fall, God had offered a covenant of grace through Christ to certain elect souls. Because God was thought to visit his grace directly on each of these individuals, the Puritans minimized the rule of church ritual and liturgy, emphasizing instead each individual's need to study the self, the world, and the Bible so as to attain spiritual certitude and moral rectitude. Advocating what the historian Christopher Hill has called "a doctrine of spiritual equality" ("one good man was as good as another, and better than a bad peer or bishop or king"), the Puritans in England posed the challenge of individual conscience to civil and religious institutions: they viewed the "Witness of the Indwelling Spirit" as a better spiritual authority than the Anglican Church, which, in the phrase of William Bradford, first governor of Plymouth, had not yet "purified" itself "to recover [its] primitive order, liberty, and beauty."

Besides raising the individual's conscience above the dictates of the church, the doctrine of predestination meant that "though none are Sav'd that wickednesse imbrace, / Yet none are Damn'd that have Inherent Grace"—or so it was interpreted by the colonial poet Edward Taylor in his *God's Determinations Touching His Elect* (composed 1685). Puritans could not earn grace through good works; however, English preachers like Thomas Taylor explained that "we teach that only doers shall be saved, and by their doing though not for their doing." In the cosmic drama of salvation that they witnessed in their private and public lives, therefore, Puritan poets and preachers were motivated by a high sense of moral purpose that paradoxically infused not only their struggle to wean the soul away from earthly desire but also their effort to serve the community through productive labor. While Puritanism thereby fostered self-education and spiritual introspec-

tion, it also contributed, as a number of sociologists have pointed out, to the rise of capitalism.

Before and after the civil war in England, the Puritans were stereotyped as sternly self-absorbed fanatics, opposed to the frivolity and idolatry of the arts. Both English and colonial writers did, in fact, express their distrust of the imagination, in much the same strain as Cotton Mather when, in 1726, he warned ministry students to "beware of a boundless and sickly appetite for the reading of the poems which now the rickety nation swarms withal." Yet the aim of Puritanism was not to obliterate imaginative literature but to turn it toward the search for evidences of God's grace. During the civil war, pulpit oratory and political pamphleteering resulted in a simpler, more functional prose style. Not just the bawdy satires of Ben Jonson and the melodramatic tragedies of John Webster but also the elaborately paradoxical poems of Richard Crashaw and John Donne were succeeded by introspective, spiritual meditations on biblical themes. The publication of the King James translation of the Bible in 1611 had already made that book more widely read than ever before. A close second in popularity during this period was John Bunyan's *The Pilgrim's Progress* (1678), a prose allegory written while Bunyan was in jail for his religious beliefs. Just as Bunyan in England stressed the virtues of faith and industry, so such American Puritans as John Winthrop and Cotton Mather traced the New World's mission in terms of God's covenant with humankind. A similar confidence that history develops according to a providential plan characterizes the highly popular captivity narrative authored by Mary Rowlandson, who witnessed her own and her children's injuries and escapes as divine signs of God's grand design.

In its emphasis on the importance of each soul, its association of atheism with illiteracy, and its concomitant commitment to the education of the laity, Puritanism allowed a number of women to explore and articulate the authority of their spiritual experiences. Although, as the historian Sheila Rowbotham has argued, Puritan culture reinforced the power of the father as the head of the family, it defined the wife as her husband's partner: her soul was equal to his in the sight of God. The stress on conscience, not only in Puritanism but also in other dissenting Protestant sects, meant that women were sometimes allowed to preach, as Jane Holmes, Anne Wentworth, and Margaret Fox did in the seventeenth century and as Ann Lee, Joanna Southcott, and Betty Gray did in the eighteenth century. Significantly, the Protestant mystic Jane Lead prophesied a female savior, a "woman clothed with the sun," while the Quaker Margaret Fell argued that Christ was the same in men and women, who could speak both of and for him. An early autobiographical narrative, *Some Account of the Fore Part of the Life of Elizabeth Ashbridge* (1774), typifies the ways in which spiritual introspection would empower American women to take responsibility for and control over their own lives. In addition, by implicitly granting authority to the female conscience as well as to the male, the self-consciousness of Puritanism made possible Anne Bradstreet's meditative poetry.

Nevertheless, like most Puritan women, Bradstreet was forbidden to participate publicly in the interpretation of scripture and excluded from the governing boards that ruled over civic and religious issues. Both English literary history and American social history provide evidence that as potentially liberating as Puritanism could be for women, it was embedded in a

male-dominated ideology that was hostile to women. The clash between the midwife-preacher Anne Hutchinson and the Puritan theocracy of Boston demonstrates just how threatening a woman preacher could seem, for Hutchinson was attacked by civil and religious authorities after she had attracted as many as sixty people to her discussions of the "indwelling Christ." Found guilty of heresy, she was excommunicated by the church and banished from the colony. Subsequent lecturers in Boston described an infant whom Hutchinson had miscarried in prison as a "monstrous birth" that "embodied her spiritual errors" and as "the work of the devil," an apelike being with horns and claws. Like that of Bradstreet's sister, who was also excommunicated for her preaching, the case of Hutchinson highlights the misogyny that informed the Salem witchcraft trials. Nineteen people and two dogs were hanged for witchcraft within the space of four months, and few people appear to have had the audacity of Sarah Good, who, when convicted during one such trial, cried out on the scaffold to the Reverend Nicholas Noye, "You are a liar. I am no more a witch than you are a wizard, and if you take away my life God will give you blood to drink."

In England, the two-edged implications of Puritan thought were probably best expressed by John Milton, who composed the age's principal hymn to matrimonial love in his epic poem *Paradise Lost* (1667, 1674). In the garden of Eden, Adam and Eve express pleasure at finding the mutuality of their desire for each other, for sexuality is the "perpetual fountain of domestic sweets," and Adam's higher reason is said to complement Eve's greater sensitivity. Drawing on Puritan arguments for freedom of choice in marriage and on the idea of the wife as a helpmate, Milton argued in a number of tracts that wives should be able to sue for divorce from husbands and that "unchastity" was worse in men than in women. Yet in *Paradise Lost*, Milton portrayed an Eve created out of and for Adam. Following the biblical story, moreover, he allotted culpability for the Fall to a woman who not only disobeys God's commandment but also refuses to stay in her proper place: "He for God only, she for God in him." Eve's fascination with Satan leads to the Fall and humankind's punishment: expulsion from paradise, mortality, and labor. Just as important, Eve's alliance with Satan is prefigured in the poem by the thralldom of the allegorical figure Sin, who also serves Satan and brings death into the world. To be sure, in the moral scheme of Milton's epic, Sin signifies a great deal more than maternity. But because she is the only mother in the work, it seems crucial that she foreshadows the painful maternity that is God's punishment of Eve. Embodying a horrific female generativity, Sin breeds innumerable hellhounds, animals that emerge from and return to her womb, where they bark and howl unseen. Milton's Puritan radicalism—his defense of regicide, republicanism, and freedom of the press—did not extend to women, as Mary Astell would point out when she wondered why a man so concerned about freedom did not "cry up liberty to poor female slaves." Images of women in *Paradise Lost* would haunt women writers from Mary Wollstonecraft to Charlotte Brontë, Virginia Woolf, and Laura Riding Jackson. As the scholar Hilda L. Smith has argued, however, the Puritan protest against tyranny that Milton articulated may have contributed to the rise of feminism, for in that protest women could witness their exclusion from even the most radical movement of their time.

Science and Rationalism

Perhaps, as some historians have suggested, it was precisely the civic and religious upheavals of the seventeenth century that gave rise to the belief that no single creed could be accepted over all the others. In any case, the tolerant pluralism that characterized eighteenth-century intellectual history was in part the result of direct challenges to traditional religion, challenges associated with the rise of mathematics, physics, and anatomy. The telescope, which furnished evidence of a Copernican universe, and the microscope, which provided proof of the corpuscular composition of the blood and thereby added the final support to Harvey's theory of circulation, were both invented in the seventeenth century, as were such instruments as the barometer and the thermometer. At the beginning of the century, Francis Bacon (1561–1626) emphasized the need to liberate knowledge from blind acceptance of Greek and medieval philosophies by testing authority against experience. Already in Bacon's time, poets and theologians like John Donne worried that the "new philosophy calls all in doubt: / The element of fire is quite put out," for the world seemed "all in pieces, all coherence gone." By the Restoration, science had become fashionable in court, and the Royal Society for the Improving of Natural Knowledge, a scientific institute, was founded with the motto *Nullius in verba*, "on the word of no one."

Although advances like Robert Boyle's (1627–1691) substitution of chemistry for medieval alchemy were viewed by many as a direct assault on religion, the scientists' investigations of physical experience were not unrelated to the Puritans' spiritual examination of personal experience. By the turn of the century, moreover, a number of empiricists sought to affirm the principles of a new faith based on the "laws" of nature that Sir Isaac Newton (1642–1727) had discovered by applying mathematics to physics. The result was Deism, a philosophy that viewed nature as a well-ordered mechanism in which God functioned only as a divine mechanic. Rejecting the need for supernatural revelation in general and for Christian doctrine in particular, the Deists assumed that logic and observation would allow them to deduce the intelligibility and coherence of the universe. Just as the philosopher John Locke (1632–1704) explained with confidence that "the works of nature in every part of them sufficiently evidence a Deity," so too Alexander Pope proclaimed in his *An Essay on Man* (1733), "All are but parts of one stupendous whole, / Whose body Nature is, and God the soul."

Both the new science and Deism exerted a profound effect on eighteenth-century literature. Gone were the baroque rhetorical flourishes of "false wit," replaced by what Jonathan Swift hailed as a "clear, masculine, and smooth" style. Inspiration was derided by English satirists as "enthusiasm," which was associated with the madness of the Puritans in particular and the Whigs in general, for some of the most prominent writers of this period were conservatives whose satire attempted to right the wrongs of an age descending into crass commercialism and individualism. Modeling their work on the poetry produced by Virgil and Horace in the Rome of Augustus (emperor 27 B.C.E.– 14 C.E.), these Augustan or neoclassical writers assumed that if nature had its laws then poetry probably did too. While literary critics began to enumerate the rules that regulated various genres, poets such as Dryden and Pope assumed that the classics best articulated general truths about the

nature of man, so that "Homer and Nature were," in fact, "the same." They chose the heroic couplet—two rhymed lines composed in iambic pentameter —for a discursive, public poetry that was as didactic as the new science was utilitarian.

While many of the satirists were pessimistic about the depravity of humanity and society, Pope's optimism in *An Essay on Man*—"Whatever IS, is RIGHT"—resembled the cheerful argument of the Whig philosopher Anthony Ashley Cooper, third earl of Shaftesbury. Because human nature is as well constructed as physical nature, Shaftesbury reasoned, an innate benevolence governs the moral instincts of human beings. The cult of feeling that would develop out of this idea was associated with the sympathetic tears that heroes and heroines alike shed from the 1720s on in sentimental comedies on the English stage. Paradoxically, however, Deism also contributed to the formation of what the title of a book by Tom Paine called "the age of reason" (1795). Paine's book began with the assertion that all institutions of faith have tyrannized over humankind, and it went on to attack the Bible, contrasting a corrupt Solomon (with his seven hundred wives and three hundred concubines) with an enlightened Benjamin Franklin, whose "mind was ever young, [whose] temper ever serene; science, that never grows gray, was always his mistress." The new secularism doubtless molded Benjamin Franklin and Thomas Jefferson, both of whom played important roles in the American version of the Royal Society. Indeed, Franklin's experiments in electricity reflected the sanguine practicality of his famous *Almanac* (1732– 57) and *Autobiography* (composed 1771–90), just as Jefferson's rejection of "superstition" in *The Life and Morals of Jesus of Nazareth* (extracted from the Gospels, ca. 1819–20) represented the same confidence in a well-regulated universe that inspired him to construct a government that would "govern least."

By the middle of the eighteenth century, the new empiricism had contributed to a general decline in traditional religion, which was only further accelerated in England by the complacency of the Anglican Church. On both sides of the Atlantic, the 1740s saw religious revivals that were clearly a reaction against the weakening of traditional faith. In England, John Wesley began to preach salvation through Christ to large middle- and working-class crowds in open-air meetings. Although his followers, known as Methodists, were initially ridiculed as illiterate fanatics, the spiritual fervor of this movement eventually had a major impact within the church, inspiring the growth of evangelicalism. In America, the first Great Awakening was led, in part, by the eminent American preacher Jonathan Edwards, and it too gave rise to a great number of what Edwards himself called "surprising conversions."

That Edwards was eventually forced to resign from his church by his own congregation, however, illustrates the changing religious temper of the times. The inductive method, respect for each individual's experience, and belief in the innate benevolence of the creator undermined the influences of Edwards's sovereign and arbitrary God. For all the severity of his sermon "Sinners in the Hands of an Angry God" (1741), moreover, Edwards himself wrote a scientific essay, "Of Insects," early in life; read John Locke at Yale College; and ended his career by returning to the mystical pantheism of his youth. Similarly, Wesley, who preached forty thousand sermons and traveled many thousands of miles on horseback, tried to keep his followers within the

Church of England and maintained a lively, observant journal that was published posthumously. In other words, even those thinkers who opposed the secularization of culture evinced the new fascination with documentation, which manifested itself in proliferating diaries, biographies, travelogues, histories, natural histories, and encyclopedias.

Not a few women lamented that men "refuse to let us know / What sacred Science doth impart." Yet, from Margaret Cavendish's scientific investigations to Sarah Frye Egerton's poem in praise of Robert Boyle and Mary Wortley Montagu's pioneering advocacy of inoculation, literary women were involved in the scientific revolution of their time. As with Puritanism, the impact of the new science on women's history was complex. On the one hand, as the scholar Carolyn Merchant has shown, Bacon's view that nature had to be "hounded in her wanderings"—that the scientist should "torture nature's secrets from her"—paralleled the widespread torture of witches in the early seventeenth century and reduced men's sense of responsibility to an earth no longer viewed as a nurturing mother. On the other hand, the materialistic philosophers associated with this revolution called into question the divine right of patriarchal authority. In his *Leviathan* (1651), Thomas Hobbes described the state of nature as a matriarchy in which "every woman that bears children, becomes both a mother and a lord." Although Hobbes argued that the predatory precultural state is bestial and must be replaced by the consent of men to the authority of a powerful king, his theory nevertheless undermined the idea of the father's natural ownership of the child, as did John Locke's direct attack on the "absolute arbitrary dominion of the father."

Just as important, Locke's psychological model of the mind as a tabula rasa (blank slate) implied that all knowledge is the result of sensuous experience. Besides opening up the discourse of rights and responsibilities, then, Locke paved a way to the realism that would enable many eighteenth-century women to record in letters and journals the private experiences that had shaped their development. Similarly, both the cult of sentimentality fostered by Deist benevolence and the religious revivals of the 1740s quickly became associated with women, who had, since Milton's time, been identified with an emotional receptivity thought to complement male rationalism: it is hardly insignificant that John Wesley, the founder of Methodism, was said to have acquired his new doctrines from his mother's preachings and that the sensitive heroine of Samuel Richardson's *Pamela* (1740), a best seller both in England and America, embodied the middle-class virtues of industry, moral integrity, and upward mobility. Yet the rise of the novel, which was so important to women's history, depended not only on the new empiricism and the cult of sentimentality but also on the formation of a middle-class reading public, a development that reflected the extraordinary growth of capitalism in the late eighteenth century.

Urbanization

As England moved from a predominantly rural economy of local farmers and yeomen to an industrial economy of large landholders and national markets, it became what the novelist Daniel Defoe called in 1724 "the most flourishing and opulent country in the world." After the founding of the Bank of England (1694) and the world's first stock exchange (1689) made possible

vast investments both in England and in the colonies, such inventions as Newcomen's steam pump (1712), Kay's flying shuttle (1733), Hargreaves's spinning jenny (1764), Arkwright's water frame (1764), and Cartwright's power loom (1785–87) began to transform the woolen industry, which manufactured England's most stable export. In addition, large landowners began consolidating open fields previously cultivated by tenant farmers; this process (called *enclosure*) permitted techniques of farming to be applied on a more productive scale, though it also turned many independent smallholders into agricultural laborers. As coal mining and ironworks grew, sustained by Watt's new steam engine (1769), the Midlands cities began to expand. With the shift of population to industrial towns, the English working class began to face the exploitative conditions that would give rise at the end of the century to trade unionism.

London remained the center of what was now the first of the industrialized countries. After the Great Fire of 1666 destroyed many sections of the city, the capital was rebuilt on a larger scale, and the architect Sir Christopher Wren established his reputation with St. Paul's Church while the painter William Hogarth gained renown with his portrayals of London street scenes. Celia Fiennes's *Through England on a Side Saddle in the Time of William and Mary* (ca. 1702) described the hazardous road conditions outside London in the late seventeenth century, but by the middle of the eighteenth century turnpikes and macadamized roads connected the capital to the rest of Great Britain, as did canals, which gave the country the most efficient system of transport it had known. A falling death rate after 1740 and a rising birth rate caused the population to grow steadily in the last decades of the eighteenth century. A similar growth spurt in America created three cities— Boston, New York, and Philadelphia—that were larger than any English towns other than London.

The growth of these urban centers throughout the eighteenth century was reflected in the cosmopolitan wit of much writing, which focused on topical social and political issues. The first daily newspapers—for instance, *The Daily Courant* (1702) in England and the *News-Letter* (1704) in Boston—as well as periodicals such as *The Spectator, The Gentleman's Magazine*, and *The American Magazine*, published reviews, stories, social instruction, and moral essays for the literati, who populated coffeehouses on both sides of the Atlantic. In addition, by the second decade of the eighteenth century there were already more than seventy printing and publishing shops in London. Although the Augustan wits leveled much of their satire against the mediocrity they associated with commercial writing, the literary marketplace had been transformed. "Writing," as Defoe explained in 1725, had "become a very considerable branch of the English commerce," a view corroborated by the fact that he sold eighty thousand copies of *The True-Born Englishman* (1700).

Pope was the first major English poet to support himself through the sales of his books, and his most influential successor, Dr. Samuel Johnson, the son of a Lichfield bookseller, was the first major author to establish his reputation through scholarship (his *Dictionary*, 1755), criticism (his *Lives of the Poets*, 1779–81), and conversational genius (preserved in James Boswell's *Life*, 1791). With the proliferation of publishing houses in America, American writers were less dependent on English acceptance than they had been

at the beginning of the century. But the threat to neoclassical standards posed by the commercialization of literature and the emergence of subscription sales and circulating libraries is probably best gauged by the growing popularity of a new form that was appropriately called the *novel*. Both Daniel Defoe, a journalist-turned-novelist who wrote about an entrepreneurial adventurer in *Robinson Crusoe* (1719), and Samuel Richardson, a printer-turned-novelist who wrote about an industrious servant girl in *Pamela*, articulated the bourgeois values of the large reading public who bought unprecedented numbers of their books.

Perhaps no other change had a greater impact on literary women than the demise of the older, more closed patronage system for the support of authors, and this change was instantaneous. After Charles II licensed two theatrical companies, women dramatists from Aphra Behn to Susannah Centlivre, Mary Pix, and Catherine Trotter began producing and publishing their own plays. Between 1695 and the death of Queen Anne in 1714, at least forty plays were written by women dramatists. Their work was probably made possible by mutual support as well as by changes in the theater itself, as its moral tone rose and increasing numbers of educated women attended performances. It was important, too, that in these years (unlike the Elizabethan era when players were all male) women were able to appear on stage as actresses. Aphra Behn was the first woman to write lines spoken by a woman specifically to women in a hit play that allowed her to earn sellout box-office receipts for two nights.

Behn's *Oroonoko* (1688), sometimes considered the first English novel, marks the beginning of the exceptionally popular prose fiction produced by women of letters. Although at times such writers as Behn, Delarivier Manley, and Eliza Haywood were criticized for their reliance on scandalous material, they gained fame from their productions of epistolary novellas and romantic narratives. Novelists, in particular, began to realize that literature was one of the few lucrative professions open to women, and economic need quickly became a defense for publication. As Sarah Fielding explained in the preface to *David Simple* (1744), "Perhaps the best excuse that can be made for a woman's venturing to write at all, is that which really produced this book; distress in her circumstances: which she could not so well remove by any other means in her power." While the poets Anne Bradstreet, Katherine Philips, and Phillis Wheatley depended on male relatives and friends to publish their books, historians like Catharine Macaulay and essayists like Elizabeth Montagu increasingly negotiated with booksellers and printers themselves. Eventually, the philanthropist Hannah More and the novelists Charlotte Smith and Susanna Rowson helped support their families by publishing numerous books not just on manners and morals but also on civic issues such as slavery and education. In addition, the predominantly middle-class women who frequented the circulating libraries provided such writers with an audience interested in the private lives of wives and daughters. Women participated vigorously in almost all of the major literary movements and genres in the eighteenth century, frequently supporting themselves in the process; however, their contributions remained distinctive, no doubt because of the myths and realities that differentiated the female experience from the male in this period.

IMAGES OF WOMEN

Literary ladies, no less than other women, had to confront the misogynist images of their sex still prevalent in their culture, for such popular writers as Joseph Swetnam continued to castigate women during the seventeenth century in phrases that harked back to medieval times: "Eagles eat not men till they are dead but women devour them alive, for a woman will pick thy pocket and empty thy purse, laugh in thy face and cut thy throat, they are ungrateful, perjured, full of fraud, flouting and deceit, unconstant, waspish, toyish, light, sullen, proud, discourteous, and cruel" (*The Arraignment of Lewd, Idle, Forward, and Unconstant Women*, 1615). During the period before the English civil war, conniving, ambitious ladies were frequently portrayed by Swetnam and his ilk, but patronesses and mistresses were also idealized in courtly poetry. Yet even in the many erotic and romantic verses of seventeenth-century lyricists, the visions of women that such works recorded were often projections of, on the one hand, male anxieties and, on the other hand, male desire. To be sure, great poems such as John Donne's 1633 "The Ecstasy," "A Valediction: Forbidding Mourning," and "The Relic" acknowledged female subjectivity and even argued that in their love the poet and his mistress transcended gender: "Difference of sex no more we knew," wrote Donne in "The Relic," "Than our guardian angels do." The same poet, however, tended to make an object out of woman; thus in "Elegy 19: To His Mistress Going to Bed" (1669), Donne possessively defined his beloved as "my America! my new-found-land, / My kingdom, safeliest when with one man manned." And whereas Donne celebrated his conquest of his mistress in terms of the laying of the land, in such sardonic pieces as "Song: Go and Catch a Falling Star" and "Woman's Constancy," both published in 1633, he argued that "No where/Lives a woman true, and fair."

In this regard, his attitudes were typical of those held by many of his contemporaries, who both reproached women for inconstancy and blamed them for unnatural eroticism. Ben Jonson's scathing "To Fine Lady Would-Be" (1616), for example, savagely excoriates a court lady for loving to make love but refusing to bear children, noting that "the world reputes you barren; but I know / Your 'pothecary, and his drug says no." Accusing her of using medicinal arts either to abort babies or prevent conception, Jonson concludes, "Write, then on thy womb, / Of the not born, yet buried, here's the tomb." But though Donne and Jonson reproached women for inconstancy or wanton sexuality, such poets as Andrew Marvell, Robert Herrick, and even Jonson himself censured women for clinging to virginity. Poems urging women to yield themselves to their lovers were so ubiquitous in the period as to constitute a literary tradition of their own. Exemplifying the so-called carpe diem (seize the day) theme, such verses urged the beloved to yield to the importunities of her lover before it was too late. Jonson's "Song: To Celia" (1606) argues that the lovers should "prove, / While we may, the sports of love" because "Time will not be ours forever; / He at length our good will sever"; Andrew Marvell's "To His Coy Mistress" (1681) explains that if his mistress does not yield herself, "worms shall / Try that long-preserved virginity"; and Robert Herrick's "To the Virgins, to Make Much of Time" (1648) notoriously advises young girls to "Gather ye rosebuds while ye may, / Old time is still a-flying." Yet during the Restoration, when comedies of manners

proliferated on the stage, a number of dramatists presented verbal duals between rakish men in sexual pursuit of women and witty heroines entertained by their own efforts to devise stratagems that might conquer the would-be conquerors.

Negative images of the gossiping shrew, the affected devout, or the proud prude proliferated in the seventeenth and early eighteenth centuries. As satire gained literary prominence, however, more artists drew on the classical writer Juvenal's *Satire* 6 to bemoan the demise of female fidelity, modesty, and purity, and to express their horror of female sexuality. "Let the porter, and the groom, / Things designed for dirty slaves; / Drudge in fair Aurelia's womb, / To get supplies for age and graves," John Wilmot, second earl of Rochester, exclaimed in "A Song" (1691), as if to illustrate the satirists' equation of the womb with the tomb. From John Oldham's "A Satire upon a Woman, Who by Her Falsehood and Scorn Was the Death of His Friend" (1678) to Jonathan Swift's "Strephon and Chloe" (1731) and "A Beautiful Young Nymph Going to Bed" (1734), verse portraits presented women as adulterous wantons, syphilitic prostitutes, and flirtatious coquettes: Oldham—who cursed his female subject as "Vil'st of that viler sex, who damn'd us all!"—was just as scatological in his depiction of women as Swift, who stripped away the makeup, clothing, perfume, and wigs that adorned women to reveal that "Celia, Celia, Celia shits!" ("The Lady's Dressing Room," 1732). Frequently using mock-pastoral conventions to uncover the filthy physicality of the contaminating whore who lurks behind the idealized shepherdess, the satirists projected onto the female figure their horror at materialistic acquisition, pride, and hypocrisy, a perversion of values that would eventually result in the death of culture. But while female inconstancy and physicality implied deceitfulness and death, they also meant, in Pope's famous line, that " 'Most women have no characters at all.' " It is hardly surprising, in the context established by his "Epistle 2: To a Lady" (1735), that the only female model Pope could imagine was described as a "contradiction," "a softer man."

As the century progressed, many thinkers came to counsel women, in the words of Lord Lyttleton, to

> Seek to be good, but aim not to be great:
> A woman's noblest station is retreat:
> Her fairest virtues fly from public sight,
> Domestic worth, that shuns too strong a light.

Satire gave way to sentiment, and popular pamphlets, conduct books, sermons, and essays began to analyze the proper duties of wives and daughters with the more genteel condescension of Lord Chesterfield, explaining that "women are but children of a larger growth." Middle-class women, now increasingly confined to the domestic sphere, were told by essayists like Richard Steele that all they have "to do in this world, is contained within the duties of a daughter, a sister, a wife, and a mother." As the literature about domestic conduct proliferated, it applied the ideal of politeness implicit in Augustan literature to women, who were now expected to be modest and decorous: the naturalist-poet Erasmus Darwin explained, "The Muses are young ladies; we expect to see them dressed."

Such literature also began to contribute to the sentimentality implicit in

Shaftesbury's Deism, creating a middle-class cult of weeping and delicacy in women praised for their emotional sensitivity as well as their purity and passivity. Sentimental fiction, as a number of critics have pointed out, featured moral ideals of gentleness and refined feelings that were considered feminine. By the time Richardson published *Pamela* and *Clarissa* (1747–48), the bourgeoisie had associated its moral superiority with the image of an angelic, chaste woman who was engaged in a struggle for supremacy with a predatory, masculine noble. Not every writer embraced this view: comic novelists like Henry Fielding continued to criticize Richardson's heroines as conniving upstarts, while pornographers like John Cleland continued to focus on the exotic pleasures provided by whores. But in countless popular novels imitating Richardson's astonishingly successful fiction, female characters were transformed from demonic sinners into domestic saints, much to the delight of the many middle-class women who read these works.

Clearly, both satires on female vice and celebrations of feminine virtue in the eighteenth century were informed by medieval portraits of a destructive Eve and a redemptive Mary. More striking, however, was the emergence of a new image of woman, a satiric portrait of the female artist, which constituted a reaction against the growing visibility of literary women. The late-seventeenth- and eighteenth-century attacks on literary ladies are important not only because they demonstrate why many women were unable to write or publish but also because they explain why those who did write and publish frequently felt it necessary to apologize for or justify their efforts. As the scholar Wendy Martin has explained, Puritan scorn for so-called scribbling women is aptly illustrated by Thomas Parker's 1650 condemnation of his sister: "Your printing of a book beyond the custom of your sex," Parker wrote in a public letter, "doth rankly smell." Similarly, as the literary historian Myra Reynolds has shown, both the plays and the poetry produced in England after the Restoration attacked women writers, readers, and speakers, who were consistently represented as mangling the language they wrote, read, or regurgitated. From a learned lady named "Bisarre" in George Farquhar's *The Inconstant* (1702) to Sophronia and Lady Wrangle in Colley Cibber's *The Refusal* (1721), female erudition was satirized as affectation. But feminine addiction to romantic literature was also attacked: Biddy Tipkins in Steele's *The Tender Husband* (1705), who would rather be called "Elismonda" or "Deidania," inhabits a hodgepodge world of shepherds, knights, and groves: she is a type of the "female Quixote" Charlotte Lennox would popularize in 1752, whose descendants were George Colman's Polly Honeycomb (*Polly Honeycomb*, 1760) and Richard Sheridan's Lydia Languish (*The Rivals*, 1775).

Just as the American Puritan John Winthrop had bemoaned the lot of a woman who had "fallen into a sad infirmity, the loss of her understanding, and reason, which had been growing upon her diverse years, by occasion of her giving herself wholly to reading and writing, and written many books" (1645), so too the Augustan satirists implied that reading and writing would derange weaker female minds. In *Three Hours after Marriage* (1717), Pope, Swift, and John Arbuthnot directly satirized the poet Anne Finch as Phoebe Clinket, a prototypical female dunce who proves the point Pope had made earlier in *The Rape of the Lock* (1714)—that "the poetic and the hysteric fit" are near allied in the female. Eliza Haywood, caricatured as a loose lady

novelist, is the prize in a pissing contest between hack writers and mercenary booksellers in one of Pope's early versions of *The Dunciad* (1728), while a monstrous Goddess of Criticism represents the self-indulgence of modern literature in Swift's *Tale of a Tub* (1704) and a nursing Goddess of Dullness is the deity of the hacks in the last book of *The Dunciad* (1743). Toward the end of the century, when Dr. Johnson compared a woman preacher to a dancing dog, or when he condemned portrait painting as improper in women because "public practice of any art . . . and staring in men's faces, is very indelicate in a female," he was assuming that "creativity" and "femininity" were contradictory terms.

WOMEN'S LIVES

While the literary woman was depicted as an anomalous character, all women in this period were burdened by the judgments prescribed by judicial authorities. In 1632 the author of *The Laws' Resolution of Women's Rights* succinctly explained that women "have nothing to do in constituting laws, of consenting to them, in interpreting of laws, or in hearing them interpreted . . . and yet they stand strictly tied to men's establishments, little or nothing excused by ignorance." Within the legal system throughout the seventeenth and eighteenth centuries, women were held to different standards of behavior than men and were punished more severely for departing from those standards. For example, mothers of stillborn babies could be charged with infanticide (if they could not produce witnesses to prove the child had been born dead) until 1803. So-called scolding women were punished with the "brank" (an iron framework caging the head) or the "ducking stool" (a chair with straps that was let down into a river) before 1809. As late as 1770 Parliament passed a statute declaring that "all women of whatever age, rank, profession, or degree, whether virgin maid or widow, that shall from and after such Act impose upon, seduce, and betray into matrimony any of His Majesty's subjects by means of scent, paints, cosmetics, washes, artificial teeth, false hair, Spanish wool, iron stays, hoops, high-heeled shoes, or bolstered hips, shall incur the penalty of the law now in force against witchcraft and like misdemeanours, and that the marriage upon conviction shall stand null and void."

The misogyny implicit in such a statute also informed laws unrelated to criminal offenses. Although an unmarried woman could own property and a widow was entitled to a portion of her deceased husband's estate, a married woman throughout this period could neither own property nor make a will, "for the husband is entitled to the fruits of his wife's labour." By virtue of the judicial concept of the *feme covert* ("covered" woman), the woman's legal existence was suspended by marriage: she was theoretically incorporated into the person of her husband, under whose protection she carried on all her activities. With no right to divorce and no rights with respect to her own children, she also had no rights over her own body, for English husbands could imprison wives in their houses until 1891. In America the concept of civil marriage resulted in a slightly more tolerant attitude toward divorce, and the patriarchal rule of primogeniture (the right of the oldest son to inherit the estate) was more erratic, but legal conditions for women were almost as difficult.

Although women clearly labored under legal disadvantages, both men and women in this period gained greater freedom in choosing a marriage partner. To be sure, in wealthy families marriage was often still settled through formal contracts, and a number of women were forced either to marry against their wishes or to wait many years for their fathers' consent. But many women were allowed to follow the dictates of their affection in choosing husbands. Both married and single aristocrats, including the duchess of Marlborough, intimate friend of Queen Anne, and Lady Hester Stanhope, niece of the prime minister William Pitt, exercised considerable political influence and lived luxurious, even adventurous, lives. Middle- and working-class single women, wives, and widows lost many of their previously important economic roles, however. For the middle class in particular, the assumption that husbands should support their wives gave rise to an ideology of female idleness, a belief that wives were symbols of their husbands' status by virtue of their leisure.

Many historians agree that working-class women lost much of their economic independence during the period when England and America moved from agricultural to industrial production. The specialization that accompanied industrialization meant that a number of home industries previously open to women (spinning, baking, preserving, sewing, farming, and brewing) steadily decreased. In the country, yeomen's wives tended to withdraw from agricultural labor; and in the city, journeymen's wives were less involved in their husbands' trades. Though women continued to work as brewsters and spinsters, they were beginning to be excluded from many other industries by the separation of the workplace from the home.

In America, of course, the lady on a southern plantation or the wife of a Massachusetts fisherman would be expected to help carry on her husband's business. When exploration and Indian wars resulted in labor shortages, women worked as crafts makers, innkeepers, and shopkeepers. In southern England, too, women continued to specialize in dairy and poultry work. But with the enclosures of the second half of the eighteenth century, as Sir Frederick Eden remarked in 1797, "the acquisition of the necessities of life required by a labourer's family, rest[ed] entirely in the husband." Working-class women could always become servants, yet even Dr. Johnson could not give Boswell a satisfactory reason why "women servants . . . have much lower wages than men servants" although "our female house servants work much harder than the male." Toward the end of the eighteenth century, women began laboring in the developing mills and factories; however, they generally earned only two-thirds of a man's pay.

Perhaps there is no better example of how professionalization excluded women than the struggle between midwives and physicians. In the sixteenth century, church examiners certified midwives; in the seventeenth century, greater emphasis was placed on medical knowledge, and examiners were frequently members of the College of Physicians. Two writers defended the autonomy of midwives: Jane Sharp, in *The Midwives Book* (1671), attempted to provide women with the anatomical information men received in universities, and Elizabeth Cellier, in *A Scheme for the Foundation of a Royal Hospital* (composed 1687), proposed a corporation that would establish standards for midwives. Yet, castigated as witches or incompetents, midwives were replaced throughout the eighteenth century by male physicians, both in lying-in hospitals and in middle-class homes. Using new instruments like

the forceps, and placing women in beds instead of on birthing stools, doctors, who worked under covers to protect women's modesty, were reminded in textbooks that "Degorges, one of the best obstetricians of his time, was blind." But despite their best efforts, infant mortality rates remained quite high throughout the period. None of Queen Anne's seventeen offspring out-lived her. Only about one child in four born in London survived in the early part of the eighteenth century. One baby died out of every fifteen born at the British Lying-In Hospital between 1749 and 1759.

The exclusion of midwives from the medical education that would have ensured their professional survival illustrates widespread acceptance of Lord Halifax's view that "there is inequality in the sexes, and that for the better economy of the world, the men, who were to be the lawgivers, had the larger share of reason bestowed upon them." Frequently reprinted in England and advertised extensively in colonial newspapers, Halifax's *The Lady's New-Year's Gift; or, Advice to a Daughter* (1688) was far more typical than, say, Defoe's advocacy of equalizing the educational opportunities of the sexes (*An Essay upon Projects,* 1697). Even within the increasingly popular boarding schools for middle-class girls in Defoe's time, a "liberal education" consisted mainly of embroidery, modeling in wax, painting on glass, and musical accomplish-ments, although some girls' schools did put on plays and teach cooking skills. Between 1698 and 1715, more than one hundred charity schools were estab-lished in London and Westminster, but most of the girls who attended were trained there for domestic service. There was, of course, no formal higher education for women of any class. Like Oxford and Cambridge, the American colleges founded in this period—the earliest being Harvard (1636), William and Mary (1693), Yale (1701), and Princeton (1746)—were closed to women.

As the anonymous author of *An Essay in Defence of the Female Sex* (1696) explained, "We are taught only our mother tongue, or perhaps French," while "the other sex by means of a more extensive education to the knowledge of the Roman and Greek languages, have a vaster field for the imaginations to rove in, and their capacities thereby enlarged." Yet with classical imitation, allusion, and translation playing a major role in neoclassical literature, a knowledge of Greek and Latin was virtually a prerequisite for poetic author-ship. When an exceptional woman like Elizabeth Elstob was encouraged by her family to become an Anglo-Saxon scholar, her publications did not save her from pecuniary difficulties after she lost that support: following her brother's death, the author of *The Rudiments of Grammar for the English-Saxon Tongue* (1715) was forced to become first a poorly paid teacher and then a dependent governess. Furthermore, such a learned woman was con-stantly cautioned, in the words of the moralist Dr. Gregory, to "keep [her learning] a profound secret, especially from the men, who generally look with a jealous and malignant eye on a woman of great parts or a cultivated under-standing" (*A Father's Legacy to His Daughters,* 1774). Still, in spite of such discouragement, by the 1760s in London a small circle of aristocratic ladies, imitating the salons of French hostesses, became renowned for learning and grace. Elizabeth Montagu, Elizabeth Carter, and Frances Boscawen were called "bluestockings," a phrase associated with the informality of their con-versational gatherings, where worsted stockings (as opposed to silk) could be worn. Montagu's *An Essay on the Writings and Genius of Shakespeare* (1769),

along with Catharine Macaulay's *History of England* (1763–83) and Hester Mulso Chapone's *Letters on the Improvement of the Mind* (1773), contributed to the growing recognition of women's intellectual abilities.

WOMEN'S NEW PROFESSION OF LETTERS

Although it subjected them to ridicule and censure, writing was one of the few professions open to middle-class women, one they could pursue in their homes with financial success. Some women—by virtue of their leisure—were able to follow Joseph Addison's advice that they should "apply themselves to letters," for "they have more spare time on their hands, and lead a more sedentary life" than men. Yet, constantly reminded of their inadequacies, not a few shared the views of the poet Mary Oxlie, who meditated anxiously on the impediments to female creativity posed by women's lack of education and their domestic preoccupations, and by the resentment that such confinement necessarily breeds:

> Perfection in a woman's work is rare;
> From an untroubled mind should verses flow;
> My discontents make mine too muddy show;
> And hoarse encumbrances of household care,
> Where these remain the Muses ne'er repair.

Because "all heroic actions, public employments, powerful governments and eloquent pleadings are denied our sex in this age," Margaret Cavendish believed that her own "restless" ambition caused her "to run upon every subject." Women who refused to submit to the distraction or the notoriety she suffered understandably wrote only in private and in forms considered "trivial," like Dorothy Osborne, whose observant, witty letters in the 1650s were meant for the sole audience of her lover, William Temple. Sara Kemble Knight's *Private Journal of a Journey from Boston to New York,* which was composed during 1704 and 1705 but not published until 1825, typified many diaries and autobiographies that were written by women who kept them as private or familial forms of communication. If women agreed to publication, it was often—as with Katherine Philips—"with the same reluctancy as I would cut off a limb to save my life," and frequently they published anonymously.

A few women writers, especially if protected by anonymity or rank, directly questioned male assumptions about female inferiority. The nameless author of a poem in praise of the poet Sarah Egerton, for example, declared in 1706, "No more let haughty man with fierce disdain, / Despise the product of a female brain." Later in the century, Mary Wortley Montagu explained her conviction, after reading *Gulliver's Travels,* that "if there was a commonwealth of rational horses (as Doctor Swift has supposed), it would be an established maxim among them that a mare could not be taught to pace." Later still, in a poem published in *The Gentleman's Magazine* (1771) to which the scholar Roger Gilbert has called attention, an anonymous literary lady complained of "Mr. Pope's characters of women":

> By custom doomed to folly, sloth, and ease,
> No wonder Pope such female triflers sees;

> But, would the satirist confess the truth,
> Nothing so like as male and female youth.

In verse, both Lady Mary Wortley Montagu and Anne Ingram defended women against the attacks of neoclassical satirists. But more frequently women's opinions were like those of the poet Anne Finch, who contrasted the "happy . . . race of men" with the sadness of female "ciphers," to lament the fact that "since the Fall (by our seducement wrought) / Ours is the greater loss as ours the greater fault." Finally, conservative writers such as Mrs. Chapone, Mrs. Trimmer, and Mrs. Barbauld accepted the view that their own literary success was an aberration: Hannah More advised girls to "aspire only to those virtues that are *peculiar to your sex;* follow your natural modesty, and think it your greatest commendation not to be talked of one way or another."

Yet even Hannah More changed her mind as the eighteenth century progressed, writing in 1799 that women's potential is unknown, for their minds have been as "stunted and cramped" as the "crippled" feet of Chinese women. In an age that equated reason with virtue, it was a protest against female miseducation that motivated and shaped a new form of writing. That new form had old roots; proposals to reform women's morals and manners drew on the earlier arguments of Anna von Schurman, whose *The Learned Maid; or, Whether a Maid May Be a Scholar?* was translated into English in 1659, and Bathsua Pell (Mrs. Makin), who published an essay to revive the "ancient education of gentlewomen" in 1673. From Mary Astell and Lady Mary Wortley Montagu to Catharine Macaulay, the foundation was laid for the radical vindication of women's rights that Mary Wollstonecraft published in 1792. In the crucible of revolutionary idealism associated with the French and the American revolutions, Wollstonecraft made the connection between the ideals of fraternity and those of sorority, much as Abigail Adams, wife of John Adams, did in letters that admonished her husband to "Remember the Ladies," for they were "determined to foment a Rebelion" and refused to be "bound by any Laws in which we have no voice, or Representation" (1776). In addition, Adams's compatriot Judith Sargent Murray produced a polemical tract against female miseducation, while one woman of letters, Helen Maria Williams, who witnessed the French Revolution firsthand during what became an extended sojourn in France, published influential and largely sympathetic accounts in *Letters Written in France in the Summer of 1790*, a work that earned her many admirers and, later, many detractors.

Like the polemicists, female poets both participated in and diverged from the literary conventions and genres established by their male contemporaries. Aphra Behn used the sexual license of the Restoration to satirize male impotence rather than female debauchery, while Anne Finch, who composed in all the conventional Augustan forms (song, satire, fable, tragedy), frequently resisted the closure of the heroic couplet in her verse and rejected the prevailing political didacticism for a more personal observation of nature. Katherine Philips's poems on the pleasures of female friendship are no less marked by her gender than is Lady Chudleigh's bitter attack on marriage in "To the Ladies" (1703). In a quite different mode, Anne Bradstreet placed her Puritan spiritual meditations in a domestic and maternal context, and Phillis Wheatley presented her decidedly pious poems in terms of her expe-

rience as a slave. On both sides of the Atlantic, then, women poets used and subverted the literary traditions they inherited from an overwhelmingly male-dominated literary history.

Though the classical forms and subjects of eighteenth-century verse were not always suited to an exploration of women's lives, the increasingly popular prose narratives of this period were ideal for such a project. At the end of the seventeenth and the beginning of the eighteenth century, narratives such as Behn's *Oroonoko,* Manley's *The Adventures of Rivella* (1714), and Haywood's *Love in Excess* (1719–20) combined romantic intrigue with adventure plots and achieved instant success; *Love in Excess,* for example, became the most popular novel in England besides *Robinson Crusoe.* Later, nonfictional prose included moralizing tracts, conduct books, and personal essays along with collections of letters; the letters of such aristocrats as Lady Russell and Mrs. Delaunay, for instance, were as popular as Hester Thrale's account of Dr. Johnson's life. The writers in this last group elevated social and literary gossip into a suitable subject of analysis, and as the critic Ian Watt has explained, it was only a small step from minute accounts of authentic experience to the production of what purported to be such an account. In addition, the realistic mode allowed female authors to record the domestic experiences of women, who were doubtless also encouraged to write in this mode by its very newness: unlike in poetry, in eighteenth-century fiction the speaking subject was not conventionally identified as male.

In other words, the significance of the female narrators invented by Defoe (in *Moll Flanders,* 1722, or *Roxana,* 1724) and Richardson (in *Pamela* or *Clarissa*) would not have been lost on women writers. Richardson, who presented his novels as collections of letters, and Defoe, who presented his as autobiographies, were fictionalizing genres already popular with women readers and writers. Richardson, in particular, involved a circle of female friends in his subtle analyses of emotional reactions, going so far as to send to a friend's daughters a copy of *Pamela* with blank pages interleaved for their corrections. Empowered by the extraordinary popularity of these books, especially with women readers, women writers began to produce their own heroines in novels of manners and Gothic romances. With the publication of commercially successful novels such as Frances Burney's *Evelina* (1778), Susanna Rowson's *Charlotte Temple* (1791), and Ann Radcliffe's *The Mysteries of Udolpho* (1794), the female imagination had found the forms and the themes that would sustain it for another, even more productive century. Often just as popular, the verse of Radcliffe's poetic contemporaries—Anna Letitia Barbauld, Charlotte Smith, Mary Robinson, and Joanna Baillie—exhibited a new sensibility in poetry at the end of the eighteenth century, one that literary historians associate with the rise of Romanticism. Expressing personal emotion, describing the beauty of the natural world, returning to the sonnet form, and displaying a fascination with the specificity of ordinary experiences, these writers influenced and were influenced by such male contemporaries as William Wordsworth and William Hazlitt, with whom they entered into an implicit dialogue.

As Virginia Woolf understood, the seventeenth century inaugurated a new age of female creativity. Literary women like Sarah Egerton were determined to reject the strictures of male contemporaries and to keep on writing: "My daring pen will bolder sallies make," she declared, "And like myself, an

unchecked freedom take." No monolithic voice emerges from the compositions of Egerton's diverse contemporaries and descendants. Tonal differences distinguish the more licentious productions of Eliza Haywood from the more respectable, domestic writings of Frances Burney; seventeenth-century female poets may have found it more difficult to find an audience than did eighteenth-century women novelists; the apparently humble apologies of Anne Bradstreet and Anne Finch contrast with the witty satires of Lady Mary Wortley Montagu. Obviously, too, the attacks against slavery mounted by an English writer like Aphra Behn cannot be conflated with those composed by Americans reacting to institutionalized slavery close at hand. However, by the middle of the eighteenth century, the female imagination had come into its own, a fact evidenced by some notable efforts to justify and commemorate a feminine canon. In 1748, Thomas Seward, the father of the poet Anna Seward, published *The Female Right to Literature;* in 1752, George Ballard compiled *Memoirs of Several Ladies of Great Britain who have been Celebrated for their Writings;* and in 1755, George Colman and Bonnell Thornton edited *Poems by Eminent Ladies,* an anthology in two volumes meant as "standing proof that great abilities are not confined to the men, and that genius often glows with equal warmth, and perhaps with more delicacy, in the breast of a female." No wonder, then, that by Queen Anne's reign Woolf's artistic heroine, Orlando, "was apt to think of poetry when she should have been thinking of taffeta." Although "there was something in the sneer of Mr. Pope, in the condescension of Mr. Addison . . . which took away her relish for the society of wits," Orlando creates a salon and discovers the pleasures of writing as a woman.

ANNE BRADSTREET
ca. 1612–1672

When she arrived in America in 1630, Anne Bradstreet later remembered, "I found a new world and new manners, at which my heart rose. But," she added, "after I was convinced it was the way of God, I submitted to it and joined to the church at Boston." Combining a rebellious spirit with the scrupulousness of conscience fostered by the Puritan community to which she belonged, her statement reveals both the independence and the integrity that characterized this woman whose *The Tenth Muse Lately Sprung Up in America* was to become the first collection of verse produced in the New World and, according to contemporary booksellers, one of the "most vendible"—i.e., one of the most salable—volumes in seventeenth-century London. Born in England, Bradstreet was raised in luxurious surroundings on the estates of the earl of Lincoln, where her father, Thomas Dudley, managed the nobleman's property. Both her parents were wellborn and well-bred; she herself was educated by private tutors and was evidently quite early given access to the earl's extensive library. In 1628, at the age of sixteen, she married Simon Bradstreet, a cultivated Cambridge graduate nine years her senior, who had also worked as the earl's steward. Her life in England would seem to have been one of easy elegance so that she might well, in that year, have looked forward to a comfortable and civilized future.

Besides being humane and genteel, however, the Dudley family were devout Puritans, for whom life's trials symbolized God's intention to educate the soul. As a child of six or seven, Bradstreet recalled in a memoir, "I began to make conscience of my ways," confessing that "as I grew up to be about 14 or 15, I found my heart more carnal, and sitting loose from God." Just before her marriage, she therefore continued, "the Lord laid His hand sore upon me and smote me with the smallpox." Even before her arrival in Puritan New England, then, she felt she had experienced considerable "affliction," and she had learned to see the world as a text in which the divine will was inscribed. Still, nothing in her English girlhood could have entirely prepared this disciplined young woman for the hardships of the wilderness outpost to which the whole Dudley family, including the recently married Bradstreets, journeyed in 1630, when Anne was eighteen. Like the other Massachusetts colonists, they had come to escape the political and religious persecutions to which Puritans were subject in the old country; and though they were of higher rank than most—indeed, both Bradstreet's father and her husband were to become governors of Massachusetts—they had to confront the same rigors that troubled all the settlers: famine and fever, severe winters and scorching summers, a savage coast and a mysterious new land that stretched, it must have seemed, indefinitely off to the west.

For the Dudleys and the Bradstreets, as for the other colonists, there was only one way to survive such difficulties with sanity and with what the Puritans called "grace": one clung to God and to the Bible that was his word, one ceaselessly examined experience to interpret its theological message, and one redefined life as a passionate pilgrimage to a better life after death. Inevitably, however, in defending themselves with such religious intensity against the dangers of the New World, the settlers became fiercely doctrinaire, and their righteously reiterated dogmas had some especially problematic implications for women. By God's will, the Puritans felt, woman was created as man's helpmate and subordinate; thus a good wife must be submissive and self-abnegating, renouncing what would seem to be egotistical ambitions and desires for intellectual self-advancement or self-fulfillment. Indeed, such desires were often seen as potentially dangerous. In 1645, John Winthrop, then the governor of the colony, wrote sorrowfully about "a godly young woman," who had gone mad by "giving herself wholly to reading and writing, and written many books." Less than a decade earlier, moreover, in 1637 and 1638, Winthrop's election as governor had facilitated the trial, imprisonment, and banishment of the unorthodox Anne Hutchinson, a woman well known to Anne Bradstreet: Hutchinson was accused of "traducing the ministers and their ministry" by preaching her own interpretations of Puritan theology.

Given such strictures against female ambition, it is no wonder that so far as biographers can tell, Bradstreet never attempted to publish her poetry in her own lifetime. Rather, in 1650 her brother-in-law, John Woodbridge, arranged without her knowledge (or so he claimed) to have *The Tenth Muse* printed in London. When he did so, he wrote a careful foreword, explaining that her verse was "the work of a woman, honoured and esteemed where she lives, for . . . her exact diligence in her place, and discreet managing of her family occasions, and . . . these poems are but the fruit of some few hours, curtailed from her sleep and other refreshments." And in fact, at this point, Bradstreet was the diligent mother of a growing family—she eventually had eight children—as well as the devoted wife of an increasingly prosperous settler. The poems collected in *The Tenth Muse* betray little overt rebellion against such a lot; although largely written before she was thirty, they do show considerable learning and literary ambition. Bradstreet had obviously studied the works of Sir Walter Ralegh and Sir Philip Sidney with care, and she was deeply influenced by Joshua Sylvester's translation of Guillaume du Bartas's *La Septmaine du Creation*, a compendious poem that appeared in English as *The Divine Weeks and Works* and that, in Bradstreet's own words, was marked by a mastery of "natural philosophy . . . grave divinity . . . high astronomy . . . anatomy . . . music and state policy." But perhaps precisely

because their composition had been so consciously scholarly and their author was so decorous, such poems as "The Humours," "The Ages of Man," and "The Four Monarchies" read like studiously versified notes rather than personal utterances.

Even in the 1650 edition of *The Tenth Muse*, though, we can discern if not a rebellion against woman's domestic "place," then a rising of the heart against female intellectual subordination. "The Prologue," for instance, claims to be the product of a "foolish, broken, blemished Muse," a talent "made . . . irreparable" by nature, for "men can do best, and women know it well." But at the same time, the poet allows herself a flash of anger. "I am obnoxious to each carping tongue / Who says my hand a needle better fits," she observes tartly, adding that "if what I do prove well, it won't advance, / They'll say it's stolen, or else it was by chance." The modesty of the poem's conclusion, in which Bradstreet renounces what would be an artist's natural desire to be crowned with the laurel or bay wreath of Apollo that traditionally announced a poet's success in favor of a coronet of domestic herbs ("Give thyme or parsley wreath, I ask no bays") can be seen as sardonic. Similarly, her fine elegy "In Honour of That High and Mighty Princess Queen Elizabeth of Happy Memory" may seem at first like a conventional celebration of royalty, full of rhetorical flourishes and elegant compliments. But again, a vein of feminist anger embedded in the work surfaces when the poet declares, "Nay masculines, you have thus taxed us long, / But she, though dead, will vindicate our wrong. / Let such as say our sex is void of reason / Know 'tis a slander now but once was treason." Clearly this diligent wife and mother knew her own worth, and in the "few hours, curtailed from her sleep and other refreshment" when she ostensibly wrote her poems, she confronted her role as domestic helpmate with a sharp wit.

Ultimately, however, Bradstreet's situation as wife and mother was to prove not an obstacle to creativity but an inspiration, for the poems and prose meditations she wrote after the 1650 publication of *The Tenth Muse* depended heavily on images and metaphors drawn from her life as a woman: the "thyme or parsley wreath" had energized her. Bradstreet's loving verses to her husband and affectionate addresses to her children—her "eight birds hatched in one nest"—along with her *Meditations Divine and Moral* and her famous "Upon the Burning of Our House" all show the ways in which, as she matured into "Mistress Anne Bradstreet," a powerful matron and patroness of the Massachusetts Bay Colony, the domestic and the theological merged and glowed in her mind, even God himself coming to be seen (in the *Meditations*) as a nursing mother or a "prudent mother" so that the converse of such a proposition might also be true: the nursing mother or the "prudent mother" might be considered analogous to God.

Anne Bradstreet died in 1672, after decades of intermittent "affliction" that she sought, in characteristic Puritan fashion, to transform into a divine education in such touching poems as her elegy "In Memory of My Dear Grandchild Anne Bradstreet," along with several other verses mourning untimely deaths. The second edition of *The Tenth Muse*, containing numerous additions to the 1650 volume (including many of her most notable writings), was not published until six years after her own death. As time went by, her reputation declined, so that by the nineteenth century, critics of American literature were defining her achievement as "a pitiful indication of the literary poverty of the days and land in which it was popular." Still, over the years, poets from the seventeenth-century writer Edward Taylor to the twentieth-century artists Conrad Aiken and John Berryman have rendered her respect in their various ways, with Berryman's "Homage to Mistress Bradstreet" (1953) constituting a major acknowledgment of her genius. For after all, as Adrienne Rich has argued, "to have written . . . the first good poems in America, while rearing eight children, lying frequently sick, keeping house at the edge of the wilderness, was to have managed a poet's range and extension within confines as severe as any American poet has confronted."

tone: sarcasm & sardonic
image: of self... "little ol' me
"simple I"

THE PROLOGUE / 147

The Prologue

1

To sing of wars, of captains, and of kings,
Of cities founded, commonwealths begun,
For my mean[1] pen are too superior things:
Or how they all or each their dates have run,[2]
5 Let poets and historians set these forth;
My obscure lines shall not so dim their worth.

2

But when my wondering eyes and envious heart
Great Bartas'[3] sugared lines do but read o'er,
Fool I do grudge the Muses did not part
10 'Twixt him and me that overfluent store;[4]
A Bartas can do what a Bartas will,
But simple I according to my skill.[5]

3

From schoolboy's tongue no rhetoric we expect,
Nor yet a sweet consort[6] from broken strings,
15 Nor perfect beauty where's a main defect:
My foolish, broken, blemished Muse so sings,
And this to mend, alas, no art is able,
'Cause nature made it so irreparable.

4

Nor can I, like that fluent sweet-tongued Greek,
20 Who lisped at first,[7] in future times speak plain.
By art he gladly found what he did seek,
A full requital of his striving pain.
Art can do much, but this maxim's most sure:
A weak or wounded brain admits no cure.

5

vulnerable
25 I am obnoxious to each carping[8] tongue
Who says my hand a needle better fits;
A poet's pen all scorn I should thus wrong,[9]

1. Humble, lowly.
2. I.e., how their sequences of events fell.
3. Guillaume du Bartas (1544–1590), author of _The Divine Weeks and Works_, an epic poem on Christian history.
4. I.e., I foolishly regret that the Muses (nine Greek goddesses of the arts, learning, and inspiration) did not equally divide their overflowing wealth between us.
5. I.e., a simple person like me can only do what she has the ability to do. "Will": desires.
6. Harmony. "Rhetoric": eloquent language.
7. The Greek orator Demosthenes (ca. 383–322 B.C.E.), who overcame a speech defect by placing pebbles in his mouth and addressing the sea.
8. Complaining. "Obnoxious": vulnerable, exposed.
9. I.e., all scornfully say I would wrong.

all of her work compiled in The Tenth Muse
that her brother supposedly published

For such despite they cast on female wits;[1]
If what I do prove well, it won't advance,[2]
30 They'll say it's stolen, or else it was by chance.

6

[handwritten: 9 muses were female...]

But sure the antique[3] Greeks were far more mild,
Else of our sex why feignéd they those nine,[4]
And poesy made Calliope's[5] own child?
So 'mongst the rest they placed the arts divine.
35 But this weak knot they[6] will full soon untie:
The Greeks did nought but play the fools and lie.[7]

7

Let Greeks be Greeks, and women what they are,
Men have precedency and still excel.
It is but vain unjustly[8] to wage war;
40 Men can do best, and women know it well.
Preeminence in all and each is yours;
Yet grant some small acknowledgement of ours.

8

[handwritten: addressing male critics]

And oh ye highflown quills that soar the skies,
And ever with your prey[9] still catch your praise,
45 If e'er you deign[1] these lowly lines your eyes,
Give thyme or parsley wreath, I ask no bays;[2] *[handwritten: what makes crown wreath]*
This mean and unrefinéd ore of mine
Will make your glistering gold but more to shine.

1650

In Honor of That High and Mighty Princess Queen Elizabeth[1] of Happy Memory

The Proem[2]

Although, great Queen, thou now in silence lie
Yet thy loud herald[3] Fame doth to the sky
Thy wondrous worth proclaim in every clime,
And so hath vowed while there is world or time.

1. Intelligence. "Despite": contempt.
2. Be any benefit. "Prove": turn out.
3. Ancient.
4. I.e., why did they invent the Muses?
5. The muse of epic poetry (which deals with the subjects described in ll. 1–2).
6. The speaker's critics. "Knot": argument.
7. This line anticipates what the critics will say.
8. On false premises.

9. Metaphorically, the poets' works. "Quills": pens made from birds' feathers; by association, poets.
1. Condescend to give.
2. Laurel leaves, associated with poets and victors.
1. Elizabeth Tudor, queen of England (1533–1603, r. 1558–1603).
2. Brief introductory verse.
3. Royal crier or messenger.

5 So great's thy glory and thine excellence,
The sound thereof rapts[4] every human sense,
That men account it no impiety
To say thou wert a fleshly deity.
Thousands bring offerings (though out of date)
10 Thy world of honors to accumulate;
'Mongst hundred hecatombs[5] of roaring verse,
Mine bleating stands before thy royal hearse.[6]
Thou never didst nor canst thou now disdain
T'accept the tribute of a loyal brain.
15 Thy clemency did erst[7] esteem as much
The acclamations of the poor as rich,
Which makes me deem my rudeness is no wrong,
Though I resound thy praises 'mongst the throng.

The Poem

No Phoenix[8] pen, nor Spenser's poetry,
20 No Speed's nor Camden's learned history,
Eliza's works, wars, praise, can e'er compact;[9]
The world's the theatre where she did act.
No memories nor volumes can contain
The 'leven Olympiads[1] of her happy reign,
25 Who was so good, so just, so learned, so wise,
From all the kings on earth she won the prize.
Nor say I more than duly is her due,
Millions will testify that this is true.
She hath wiped off th' aspersion of her sex,
30 That women wisdom lack to play the rex.[2]
Spain's monarch says not so, nor yet his host;[3]
She taught them better manners, to their cost.
The Salic law[4] in force now had not been,
If France had ever hoped for such a queen.
35 But can you, doctors,[5] now this point dispute.
She's argument enough to make you mute.
Since first the Sun did run his ne'er run race,
And earth had, once a year, a new old face,
Since time was time, and unmanly man,
40 Come show me such a phoenix if you can.
Was ever people better ruled than hers?

4. Enraptures.
5. Honorary tributes (literally, sacrificial slaughter, of animals).
6. Frame placed over a coffin or tomb for holding candles and epitaphs.
7. Formerly, at one time. "Clemency": leniency.
8. A mythical bird that immolates itself and is then reborn from its own ashes. Bradstreet associates the bird with the immortality of both great poetry and Elizabeth's name. "No": neither.
9. Condense, summarize. The allusions are to Edmund Spenser (1552–1599), major English poet; John Speed (1542–1629), English historian and mapmaker; and William Camden (1551–

1623), English historian.
1. The four-year period between Olympic games in ancient Greece; thus Elizabeth reigned for forty-four years.
2. King (Latin).
3. Army. Philip II (1527–1598; r. 1556–98) was king of Spain, Portugal, and the Netherlands; under his rule the Spanish Armada, a fleet of warships, attempted to invade England and was defeated in 1588.
4. Law forbidding women to inherit land; used in France and Spain to prevent the ascension of female monarchs.
5. Scholars.

Was ever land more happy freed from stirs[6]
Did ever wealth in England more abound?
Her victories in foreign coasts resound;
45 Ships more invincible than Spain's, her foe,
She wracked, she sacked,[7] she sunk his Armado;
Her stately troops advanced to Lisbon's wall,
Don Anthony[8] in's right there to install.
She frankly helped Frank's brave distressèd king;[9]
50 The states united[1] now her fame do sing.
She their protectrix was; they well do know
Unto our dread virago,[2] what they owe,
Her nobles sacrificed their noble blood,
Nor men nor coin she spared to do them good.
55 The rude untaméd Irish she did quell;
Before her picture the proud Tyrone[3] fell.
Had ever prince such counsellors as she?
Herself Minerva[4] caused them so to be.
Such captains and such soldiers never seen,
60 As were the subjects of our Pallas queen.
Her seamen though all straits the world did round;
Terra incognita[5] might know the sound.
Her Drake came laden home with Spanish gold;
Her Essex took Cadiz, their Herculean[6] hold.
65 But time would fail me, so my tongue would too,
To tell of half she did, or she could do.
Semiramis[7] to her is but obscure,
More infamy than fame she did procure.
She build her glory but on Babel's walls,[8]
70 World's wonder for a while, but yet it falls.
Fierce Tomris (Cyrus' headsman) Scythians' queen,[9]
Had put her harness off, had she but seen
Our Amazon in th' Camp of Tilbury,[1]
Judging all valor and all majesty
75 Within that princess to have residence,
And prostrate yielded to her excellence,
Dido,[2] first foundress of proud Carthage walls

6. Conflicts, wars.
7. Looted. "Wracked": destroyed.
8. Don Antonio of Crato (1531–1595), Philip II's unsuccessful rival for the throne of Portugal, supported by England and France.
9. Henri II (1553–1610; r. 1589–1610), king of France, whom Elizabeth aided generously with money and arms to fight Catholic rebels backed by Spain.
1. I.e., the Netherlands, aided by Elizabeth in wars against Spain.
2. Woman warrior. "Protectrix": female protector.
3. Hugh O'Neill (ca. 1540–1616), nobleman who, assisted by the Spanish, led the Irish rebellion against English rule; he was defeated at Kinsale in 1601.
4. The Roman virgin goddess of wisdom, war, and justice, known to the Greeks as Pallas Athena.
5. Unknown land (Latin).
6. Strong, mighty (because well-defended). Sir Francis Drake (1540–1596), English admiral and explorer. "Essex": Robert Devereaux (1566–1601), second earl of Essex, who captured the Spanish port Cádiz in 1596.
7. Assyrian queen (9th century B.C.E.), legendary builder of Babylon.
8. The great tower raised in the ancient city of Babylon (Genesis 11); to punish the builders' presumption, God confused their language and scattered them.
9. Tomyris, queen of a Scythian tribe that in 529 B.C.E. defeated Cyrus, founder of the Persian Empire; according to Herodotus (1.214), she had him beheaded.
1. Site of Elizabeth's famous speech to her troops (see above, p. 67); "Amazon": member of a mythical race of women warriors.
2. Queen of Carthage, an ancient city in North Africa; her abandonment by her lover Aeneas and subsequent self-immolation on her own funeral pyre are recounted in Virgil's epic The Aeneid (19 B.C.E.).

(Who living consummates her funerals),
A great Eliza, but compared with ours,
80 How vanisheth her glory, wealth, and powers.
Profuse, proud Cleopatra,[3] whose wrong name,
Instead of glory, proved her country's shame,
Of her what worth in stories to be seen,
But that she was a rich Egyptian queen.
85 Zenobya,[4] potent empress of the East,
And of all these without compare the best,
Whom none but great Aurelius[5] could quell;
Yet for our Queen is no fit parallel.
She was a phoenix queen, so shall she be,
90 Her ashes not revived, more phoenix she.
Her personal perfections, who would tell
Must dip his pen in th' Heleconian well,[6]
Which I may not; my pride doth but aspire
To read what others write and so admire.
95 Now say, have women worth? or have they none?
Or had they some, but with our Queen is't gone?
Nay masculines, you have thus taxed[7] us long,
But she, though dead, will vindicate our wrong.
Let such as say our sex is void of reason
100 Know 'tis a slander now but once was treason.
But happy England which had such a queen;
Yea happy, happy, had those days still been.
But happiness lies in the higher sphere,
Then wonder not Eliza moves not here.
105 Full fraught with honor, riches and with days
She set, she set, like Titan[8] in his rays.
No more shall rise or set so glorious sun
Until the heaven's great revolution,[9]
If then new things their old forms shall retain,
110 Eliza shall rule Albion[1] once again.

Her Epitaph

Here sleeps the queen, this is the royal bed
Of th' damask rose, sprung from the white and red,[2]
Whose sweet perfume fills the all-filling air.
This rose is withered, once so lovely fair.
115 On neither tree did grow such rose before,
The greater was our gain, our loss the more.

3. Queen of Egypt best known as mistress of the powerful Romans Julius Caesar and Mark Antony. (69–30 B.C.), Her name means "glory to the father" (or "fatherland") in Greek.
4. Queen of Palmyra (d. ca. 273 C.E.), an ancient city in Syria.
5. I.e., Aurelian, emperor of Rome (270–275 C.E.), who captured Zenobia and destroyed her kingdom.
6. Hipprocrene, a spring on Helicon, mountain home of the Muses; it was the source of poetic

inspiration.
7. Accused; blamed.
8. I.e., the sun.
9. The Day of Judgment.
1. Britain.
2. The colors of the two houses in the War of the Roses (1455–85). "Damask rose": a fragrant red rose, symbolic of the Tudors' union of the warring houses of York and Lancaster in, respectively, Elizabeth's mother, Anne Boleyn, and her father, Henry VIII.

Another

Here lies the pride of queens, pattern of kings,
So blaze[3] it, Fame, here's feathers for thy wings
Here lies the envied, yet unparalleled prince,
120 Whose living virtues speak (though dead long since).
If many worlds, as that fantastic framed,[4]
In every one be her great glory famed.

1650

The Author to Her Book[1]

Thou ill-formed offspring of my feeble brain,
Who after birth didst by my side remain,
Till snatched from thence by friends, less wise than true,
Who thee abroad, exposed to public view,
5 Made thee in rags, halting to th' press to trudge,
Where errors were not lessened (all may judge).
At thy return my blushing was not small,
My rambling brat (in print) should mother call,
I cast thee by as one unfit for light,
10 Thy visage was so irksome in my sight;
Yet being mine own, at length affection would
Thy blemishes amend, if so I could:
I washed thy face, but more defects I saw,
And rubbing off a spot still made a flaw.
15 I stretched thy joints to make thee even feet,[2]
Yet still thou run'st more hobbling than is meet;[3]
In better dress to trim thee was my mind,
But nought save homespun cloth i' th' house I find.
In this array 'mongst vulgars[4] may'st thou roam.
20 In critic's hands beware thou dost not come,
And take thy way where yet thou art not known
If for thy father asked, say thou hadst none;
And for thy mother, she alas is poor,
Which caused her thus to send thee out of door.

1678

3. Blazon, proclaim.
4. I.e., as that visionary or demented person theorized. This may be a reference to the Polish astronomer Nicolaus Copernicus (1473–1543), who challenged the Ptolemaic model of the universe, which placed the earth at the center, by asserting that the earth revolved around the sun along with the other planets.

1. Bradstreet's volume of poems *The Tenth Muse* was published in 1650 without her knowledge; this poem was probably written while she was preparing a revised second edition for publication.
2. I.e., metrical feet; thus, to smooth out the meter of the lines.
3. Appropriate, decorous.
4. Common people.

To My Dear and Loving Husband

[handwritten: His is mutual.]

[handwritten: He is Hott, but they are one.]

If ever two were one, then surely we.
If ever man were loved by wife, then thee; *[handwritten: I love you.]*
If ever wife was happy in a man, *[handwritten: you love me.]*
Compare with me ye women if you can.
5 I prize thy love more than whole mines of gold,
Or all the riches that the East doth hold.
My love is such that rivers cannot quench,
Nor ought but love from thee, give recompense.[1]
Thy love is such I can no way repay,
10 The heavens reward thee manifold[2] I pray. *[handwritten: Earthly love]*
Then while we live, in love let's so persevere, *[handwritten: will live]*
That when we live no more, we may live ever. *[handwritten: 4ever.]*

[handwritten: Not only does she love him, but she is glad that he returns it. He 'better !!!!']

1678

A Letter to Her Husband, Absent upon Public Employment

My head, my heart, mine eyes, my life, nay, more,
My joy, my magazine[1] of earthly store,
If two be one, as surely thou and I,
How stayest thou there, whilst I at Ipswich[2] lie?
5 So many steps, head from the heart to sever,
If but a neck, soon should we be together.
I, like the Earth this season, mourn in black,
My Sun is gone so far in's zodiac,[3]
Whom whilst I 'joyed, nor storms, nor frost I felt,
10 His warmth such frigid colds did cause to melt.
My chilled limbs now numbed lie forlorn:
Return, return, sweet Sol, from Capricorn;[4]
In this dead time, alas, what can I more
Than view those fruits which through thy heat I bore?
15 Which sweet contentment yield me for a space,
True living pictures of their father's face.
O strange effect! now thou art southward gone,
I weary grow the tedious day so long;
But when thou northward to me shalt return,
20 I wish my Sun may never set, but burn
Within the Cancer[5] of my glowing breast,
The welcome house of him my dearest guest.
Where ever, ever stay, and go not thence,
Till nature's sad decree shall call thee hence;

1. Can adequately return.
2. Many times.
1. Warehouse.
2. Town in Massachusetts, north of Boston.
3. The path of the sun and planets through the

heavens. "My Sun": her husband.
4. The tenth sign of the zodiac, which rises in winter. "Sol": the sun.
5. The fourth sign of the zodiac, which rises in summer.

25 Flesh of thy flesh, bone of thy bone,[6]
I here, thou there, yet both but one.

1678

In Reference to Her Children, 23 June, 1659

I had eight birds hatched in one nest,
Four cocks there were, and hens the rest.
I nursed them up with pain and care,
Nor cost, nor labor did I spare,
5 Till at the last they felt their wing,
Mounted the trees, and learned to sing;
Chief of the brood then took his flight
To regions far and left me quite.
My mournful chirps I after send,
10 Till he return, or I do end:
Leave not they nest, thy dam and sire,
Fly back and sing amidst this choir.
My second bird did take her flight,
And with her mate flew out of sight;
15 Southward they both their course did bend,
And seasons twain they there did spend,
Till after blown by southern gales,
They norward steered with filled sails.
A prettier bird was no where seen,
20 Along the beach among the treen.[1]
I have a third of color white,
On whom I placed no small delight;
Coupled with mate loving and true,
Hath also bid her dam adieu;
25 And where Aurora[2] first appears,
She now hath perched to spend her years.
One to the academy flew
To chat among that learned crew;
Ambition moves still in his breast
30 That he might chant above the rest,
Striving for more than to do well,
That nightingales he might excel.
My fifth, whose down is yet scarce gone,
Is 'mongst the shrubs and bushes flown,
35 And as his wings increase in strength,
On higher boughs he'll perch at length.
My other three still with me nest,
Until they're grown, then as the rest,
Or[3] here or there they'll take their flight,
40 As is ordained, so shall they light.

6. This line echoes Genesis 2:23. 2. In Roman mythology, the goddess of the dawn.
1. Trees. 3. Either.

If birds could weep, then would my tears
Let others know what are my fears
Lest this my brood some harm should catch,
And be surprised for want of watch,
45 Whilst pecking corn and void of care,
They fall un'wares in fowler's[4] snare,
Or whilst on trees they sit and sing,
Some untoward[5] boy at them do fling,
Or whilst allured with bell and glass,
50 The net be spread, and caught, alas.
Or lest by lime-twigs they be foiled,[6]
Or by some greedy hawks be spoiled.[7]
O would my young, ye saw my breast,
And knew what thoughts there sadly rest,
55 Great was my pain when I you bred,
Great was my care when I you fed,
Long did I keep you soft and warm,
And with my wings kept off all harm,
My cares are more and fears than ever,
60 My throbs such now as 'fore were never.
Alas, my birds, you wisdom want,
Of perils you are ignorant;
Oft times in grass, on trees, in flight,
Sore accidents on you may light.
65 O to your safety have an eye,
So happy may you live and die.
Meanwhile my days in tunes I'll spend,
Till my weak lays[8] with me shall end.
In shady woods I'll sit and sing,
70 And things that past to mind I'll bring.
Once young and pleasant, as are you,
But former toys (no joys) adieu.
My age I will not once lament,
But sing, my time so near is spent.
75 And from the top bough take my flight
Into a country beyond sight,
Where old ones instantly grow young,
And there with seraphims[9] set song;
No seasons cold, nor storms they see;
80 But spring lasts to eternity.
When each of you shall in your nest
Among your young ones take your rest,
In chirping language, oft them tell,
You had a dam that loved you well,
85 That did what could be done for young,
And nursed you up till you were strong,
And 'fore she once would let you fly,
She showed you joy and misery;

4. Bird catcher's.
5. Unruly, out of control.
6. I.e., defeated by birdlime (a sticky substance) spread on twigs.

7. Seized, destroyed.
8. Songs, poems.
9. Angels.

Taught what was good, and what was ill,
90 What would save life, and what would kill.
Thus gone, amongst you I may live,
And dead, yet speak, and counsel give:
Farewell, my birds, farewell adieu,
I happy am, if well with you.

1678

In Memory of My Dear Grandchild Anne Bradstreet, Who Deceased June 20, 1669, Being Three Years and Seven Months Old

With troubled heart and trembling hand I write,
The heavens have changed to sorrow my delight.
How oft with disappointment have I met,
When I on fading things my hopes have set.
5 Experience might 'fore this have made me wise,
To value things according to their price.
Was ever stable joy yet found below?
Or perfect bliss without mixture of woe?
I knew she was but as a withering flower,
10 That's here today, perhaps gone in an hour;
Like as a bubble, or the brittle glass,
Or like a shadow turning as it was.
More fool then I to look on that was lent
As if mine own, when thus impermanent.
15 Farewell dear child, thou ne'er shall come to me,
But yet a while, and I shall go to thee;
Meantime my throbbing heart's cheered up with this:
Thou with thy Savior art in endless bliss.

1678

For Deliverance from a Fever

When sorrows had begirt me round,
And pains within and out,
When in my flesh no part was found,[1]
Then didst Thou rid me out.[2]
5 My burning flesh in sweat did boil,
My aching head did break,
From side to side for ease I toil,
So faint I could not speak.
Beclouded was my soul with fear
10 Of Thy displeasure sore,
Nor could I read my evidence

1. I.e., no healthy part. 2. Rid me of illness, "Thou": God.

Which oft I read before.
"Hide not Thy face from me!" I cried,
"From burnings keep my soul.
15 Thou know'st my heart, and hast me tried;
I on Thy mercies roll."[3]
"O heal my soul," Thou know'st I said,
"Though flesh consume to nought,
What though in dust it shall be laid,
20 To glory 't shall be brought."
Thou heard'st, Thy rod Thou didst remove
And spared my body frail,
Thou show'st to me Thy tender love,
My heart no more might quail
25 O, praises to my mighty God,
Praise to my Lord, I say,
Who hath redeemed my soul from pit,
Praises to Him for aye.[4]

1867

From Meditations Divine and Moral

6

The finest bread hath the least bran, the purest honey the least wax, and the sincerest Christian the least self-love.

8

Downy beds make drowsy persons, but hard lodging keeps the eyes open; a prosperous state makes a secure Christian, but adversity makes him consider.

9

Sweet words are like honey: a little may refresh, but too much gluts the stomach.

10

Diverse children have their different natures: some are like flesh[1] which nothing but salt will keep from putrefaction, some again like tender fruits that are best preserved with sugar. Those parents are wise that can fit their nurture according to their nature.

12

Authority without wisdom is like a heavy axe without an edge: fitter to bruise than polish.

3. Trust.
4. Always. "Pit": hell.

1. Meat.

16

That house which is not often swept makes the cleanly inhabitant soon loathe it, and that heart which is not continually purifying itself is no fit temple for the spirit of God to dwell in.

19

Corn,[2] till it have passed through the mill and been ground to powder, is not fit for bread. God so deals with his servants: he grinds them with grief and pain till they turn to dust, and then are they fit manchet[3] for his mansion.

38

Some children are hardly weaned; although the teat be rubbed with worm-wood[4] or mustard, they will either wipe it off, or else suck down sweet and bitter together. So is it with some Christians: let God embitter all the sweets of this life, that so they might feed upon more substantial food, yet they are so childishly sottish[5] that they are still hugging and sucking these empty breasts that God is forced to hedge up their way with thorns or lay affliction on their loins that so they might shake hands with the world, before it bid them farewell.

39

A prudent mother will not clothe her little child with a long and cumber-some garment; she easily forsees what events it is like to produce, at the best, but falls and bruises or perhaps somewhat worse. Much more will the all-wise God proportion His dispensations according to the stature and strength of the person He bestows them on. Large endowments of honor, wealth, or a healthful body would quite overthrow some weak Christian; therefore God cuts their garments short to keep them in such a trim that they might run the ways of His commandment.

1867

Here Follows Some Verses upon the Burning of Our House July 10th, 1666. Copied out of a Loose Paper

> In silent night when rest I took
> For sorrow near I did not look
> I wakened was with thund'ring noise
> And piteous shrieks of dreadful voice.
> 5 That fearful sound of "Fire!" and "Fire!"
> Let no man know is my desire.
> I, starting up, the light did spy,

2. Wheat.
3. White bread made from the finest flour.
4. A bitter extract placed on a mother's breast

("teat") to wean her child from breast-feeding.
5. Foolish; self-indulgent.

And to my God my heart did cry
To strengthen me in my distress
10 And not to leave me succorless.[1]
Then, coming out, beheld a space[2]
The flame consume my dwelling place.
And when I could no longer look,
I blest His name that gave and took,[3]
15 That laid my goods now in the dust.
Yea, so it was, and so 'twas just.
It was His own, it was not mine,
Far be it that I should repine;[4]
He might of all justly bereft[5]
20 But yet sufficient for us left.
When by the ruins oft I passed
My sorrowing eyes aside did cast,
And here and there the places spy
Where oft I sat and long did lie:
25 Here stood that trunk, and there that chest,
There lay that store I counted best.
My pleasant things in ashes lie,
And them behold no more shall I.
Under thy roof no guest shall sit,
30 Nor at thy table eat a bit.
No pleasant tale shall e'er be told,
Nor things recounted done of old.
No candle e'er shall shine in thee,
Nor bridegroom's voice e'er heard shall be.
35 In silence ever shall thou lie,
Adieu, Adieu, all's vanity.[6]
Then straight I 'gin my heart to chide,
And did thy wealth on earth abide?
Didst fix thy hope on mold'ring dust?
40 The arm of flesh didst make thy trust?
Raise up thy thoughts above the sky
That dunghill mists away may fly.
Thou hast an house on high erect,
Framed by that mighty Architect,
45 With glory richly furnishéd,
Stands permanent though this be fled.
It's purchaséd and paid for too
By Him who hath enough to do.
A price so vast as is unknown
50 Yet by His gift is made thine own;
There's wealth enough, I need no more,
Farewell, my pelf,[7] farewell my store.
The world no longer let me love,
My hope and treasure lies above.

1867

1. Helpless.
2. In a short period of time.
3. Cf. Job 1.21: "The Lord gave, and the Lord hath taken away; blessed be the name of the Lord."
4. Complain.

5. I.e., he might have taken everything from us with good cause.
6. Empty, worthless.
7. Money, by implication stolen.

MARGARET CAVENDISH,
DUCHESS OF NEWCASTLE
1623–1673

"What a vision of loneliness and riot the thought of Margaret Cavendish brings to mind!" exclaimed Virginia Woolf in 1928. The author of "philosophical fancies" and scientific speculations, poems and plays, the woman who so bemused Woolf was born Margaret Lucas to an aristocratic Essex family where "all the brothers were valiant, and all the sisters virtuous;" and although many at court disliked her for her shyness and eccentricity, she became a maid of honor to the queen. In 1645 she married William Cavendish, duke of Newcastle, a Royalist soldier with whom she lived on the Continent in poverty and exile during Cromwell's reign. Thirty years older than she, the duke supported her aesthetic ambitions. After the Restoration, the couple returned to their English estate, where the childless duchess pursued her literary career with diligence. But although she published numerous books in her lifetime—including *Poems and Fancies* (1653), *Nature's Pictures Drawn by Fancie's Pencil* (1656), and *Plays Written by the thrice Noble, Illustrious and Excellent Princess, the Lady Marchioness of Newcastle* (1667)—most of Cavendish's contemporaries regarded her as a freak because of the oddity of her writings and the peculiarity of her dress. At a time when it was considered bold for women to produce even the tamest of compositions, "the crazy duchess" tried to combine metaphysical poetry with scientific speculation, philosophical meditation and utopian romance with autobiographical reflection. Many of her works were published at the Newcastles' own expense. Although praised by the philosopher Thomas Hobbes, she was judged to be "a mad, conceited, ridiculous woman" by the diarist Samuel Pepys. Dorothy Osborne, a seventeenth-century letter writer, believed "the poor woman is a little distracted, she could never have been so ridiculous else as to venture at writing books and in verse too."

Despite her undoubted strangeness, however, the duchess at her best produced some witty verse as well as some lively and thoughtful prose. Though her work was never as strong as the poetry of her American contemporary Anne Bradstreet, her imagery, like Bradstreet's, often drew on the realities of female life—fashion, cooking, housekeeping. In addition, her speculations on the meaning of femininity—in particular those dramatized in *Female Orations*—were unusually sophisticated in their acknowledgment of the complex problems posed by woman's cultural situation. Similarly, "The Poetess's Hasty Resolution" and "An Excuse for So Much Writ Upon My Verses" illuminate the anxieties authorship also instilled in Bradstreet. Clearly, Cavendish had scrutinized her own psychological reactions to the process of writing and used them to explore many other women's attitudes toward femininity and creativity.

The Poetess's Hasty Resolution

Reading my verses, I liked them so well,
Self-love did make my judgment to rebel.
Thinking them so good, I thought more to write;
Considering not how others would them like.
5 I writ so fast, I thought if I lived long,
A pyramid of fame to build thereon.
Reason observing which way I was bent,
Did stay my hand, and asked me what I meant;

Will you, said she, thus waste your time in vain,
On that which in the world small praise shall gain?
For shame leave off, said she, the Printer spare,
He'll lose by your ill poetry, I fear.
Besides the world hath already such a weight
Of useless books, as it is over fraught.[1]
Then pity take, do the world a good turn,
And all you write cast in the fire, and burn.
Angry I was, and Reason struck away,
When I did hear, what she to me did say.
Then all in haste I to the press it sent,
Fearing persuasion might my book prevent:
But now 'tis done, with grief repent do I,
Hang down my head with shame, blush, sigh, and cry.
Take pity, and my drooping spirits raise,
Wipe off my tears with handkerchiefs of praise.

1653

An Excuse for So Much Writ upon My Verses

Condemn me not for making such a coil[1]
About my book, alas it is my child.
Just like a bird, when her young are in nest,
Goes in, and out, and hops, and takes no rest;
But when their young are fledged,[2] their heads out peep,
Lord what a chirping does the old one keep.
So I, for fear, my strengthless child should fall
Against a door, or stool, aloud I call,
Bid have a care of such a dangerous place:
Thus write I much, to hinder all disgrace.

1653

Female Orations

I

Ladies, gentlewomen, and other inferior women, but not less worthy: I have been industrious to assemble you together, and wish I were so fortunate as to persuade you to make frequent assemblies, associations, and combinations[1] amongst our sex, that we may unite in prudent counsels, to make ourselves as free, happy, and famous as men; whereas now we live and die as if we were produced from beasts, rather than from men; for men are happy, and we women are miserable; they possess all the ease, rest, pleasure, wealth, power, and fame; whereas women are restless with labor, easeless

1. Laden. 2. Feathered.
1. Turmoil, stir. 1. Confederacies.

with pain, melancholy for want of pleasures, helpless for want of power, and die in oblivion, for want of fame. Nevertheless, men are so unconscionable and cruel against us that they endeavor to bar us of all sorts of liberty, and will not suffer us freely to associate amongst our own sex; but would fain bury us in their houses or beds, as in a grave. The truth is, we live like bats or owls, labor like beasts, and die like worms.

II

Ladies, gentlewomen, and other inferior women: The lady that spoke to you hath spoken wisely and eloquently, in expressing our unhappiness; but she hath not declared a remedy, or showed us a way to come out of our miseries; but, if she could or would be our guide, to lead us out of the labyrinth men have put us into, we should not only praise and admire her, but adore and worship her as our goddess: but alas! men, that are not only our tyrants but our devils, keep us in the hell of subjection, from whence I cannot perceive any redemption or getting out; we may complain and bewail our condition, yet that will not free us; we may murmur and rail against men, yet they regard not what we say. In short, our words to men are as empty sounds; our sighs, as puffs of winds; and our tears, as fruitless showers; and our power is so inconsiderable, that men laugh at our weakness.

III

Ladies, gentlewomen, and other inferior women: The former orations were exclamations against men, repining at their condition and mourning for our own; but we have no reason to speak against men, who are our admirers and lovers; they are our protectors, defenders, and maintainers; they admire our beauties, and love our persons; they protect us from injuries, defend us from dangers, are industrious for our subsistence, and provide for our children; they swim great voyages by sea, travel long journeys by land, to get us rarities and curiosities; they dig to the center of the earth for gold for us; they dive to the bottom of the sea for jewels for us: they build to the skies houses for us: they hunt, fowl, fish, plant, and reap for food for us. All which, we could not do ourselves; and yet we complain of men, as if they were our enemies, whenas[2] we could not possibly live without them, which shows we are as ungrateful as inconstant. But we have more reason to murmur against Nature, than against men, who hath made men more ingenious, witty,[3] and wise than women; more strong, industrious, and laborious than women; for women are witless and strengthless, and unprofitable creatures, did they not bear children.

Wherefore, let us love men, praise men, and pray for men; for without men, we should be the most miserable creatures that Nature hath made or could make.

IV

Noble ladies, gentlewomen, and other inferior women: The former oratoress says we are witless and strengthless; if so, it is that we neglect the one

2. While on the other hand. 3. Intelligent.

and make no use of the other, for strength is increased by exercise, and wit is lost for want of conversation. But to show men we are not so weak and foolish as the former oratoress doth express us to be, let us hawk, hunt, race, and do the like exercises that men have; and let us converse in camps,[4] courts, and cities; in schools, colleges, and courts of judicature; in taverns, brothels, and gaming houses; all of which will make our strength and wit known, both to men and to our own selves, for we are as ignorant of ourselves as men are of us. And how should we know ourselves, when we never made a trial of ourselves? Or how should men know us, when they never put us to the proof?[5] Wherefore my advice is, we should imitate men; so will our bodies and minds appear more masculine, and our power will increase by our actions.

V

Noble, honorable, and virtuous women: The former oration was to persuade us to change the custom of our sex, which is a strange and unwise persuasion, since we cannot change the nature of our sex, nor make ourselves men; and to have female bodies, and yet to act masculine parts, will be very preposterous and unnatural. In truth, we shall make ourselves like the defects of Nature, and be hermaphroditical,[6] neither perfect women, nor perfect men, but corrupt and imperfect creatures. Wherefore let me persuade you, since we cannot alter the nature of our persons, not to alter the course of our lives; but to rule so our lives and behaviors that we be acceptable and pleasing to God and men; which is, to be modest, chaste, temperate, humble, patient, and pious; also, be housewifely, cleanly, and of few words. All which will gain us praise from men and blessing from Heaven; love in this world and glory in the next.

VI

Worthy women: The former oratoress's oration endeavored to persuade us that it would not only be a reproach and disgrace, but unnatural, for women in their actions and behavior to imitate men: we may as well say it will be a reproach, disgrace, and unnatural to imitate the gods, which imitation we are commanded both by the gods and their ministers; and shall we neglect the imitation of men, which is more easy and natural than the imitation of the gods? For how can terrestrial creatures imitate celestial deities? Yet one terrestrial may imitate another, although in different sorts of creatures. Wherefore, since all terrestrial imitations ought to ascend to the better and not to descend to the worse, women ought to imitate men, as being a degree in nature more perfect than they themselves; and all masculine women ought to be as much praised as effeminate men to be dispraised; for the one advances to perfection, the other sinks to imperfection; that so, by our industry, we may come, at last, to equal men, both in perfection and power.

4. I.e., military camps. "Converse": keep company.
5. Test.
6. Male and female within one body (from the name in Greek legend of the son of the gods Hermes and Aphrodite, who was joined, in one body, with a nymph).

VII

Noble ladies, honorable gentlewomen, and worthy female-commoners:
The former oratoress's speech was to persuade us out of ourselves and to be
that which Nature never intended us to be, to wit, masculine. But why should
we desire to be masculine, since our own sex and condition is far the better?
For if men have more courage, they have more danger; and if men have more
strength, they have more labor than women have; if men are more eloquent
in speech, women are more harmonious in voice; if men be more active,
women are more graceful; if men have more liberty, women have more safety;
for we never fight duels nor battles; nor do we go long travels or dangerous
voyages; we labor not in building nor digging in mines, quarries, or pits, for
metal, stone, or coals; neither do we waste or shorten our lives with university
or scholastical studies, questions, and disputes; we burn not our faces with
smiths' forges or chemists'[7] furnaces; and hundreds of other actions which
men are employed in; for they would not only fade the fresh beauty, spoil
the lovely features, and decay the youth of women, causing them to appear
old, when they are young; but would break their small[8] limbs, and destroy
their tender lives. Wherefore women have no reason to complain against
Nature or the god of Nature, for although the gifts are not the same as they
have given to men, yet those gifts they have given to women are much better;
for we women are much more favored by Nature than men, in giving us such
beauties, features, shapes, graceful demeanor, and such insinuating and
enticing attractives,[9] that men are forced to admire us, love us, and be desir-
ous of us; insomuch that rather than not have and enjoy us, they will deliver
to our disposals their power, persons, and lives, enslaving themselves to our
will and pleasures; also, we are their saints, whom they adore and worship;
and what can we desire more than to be men's tyrants, destinies, and
goddesses?

1662

7. Alchemists'. 9. Attractive personal qualities.
8. Slender.

JANE LEAD
1624–1704

A mystic and spiritual autobiographer, the visionary writer Jane Lead was born Jane
Ward in Norfolk and educated "like other girls" until at the age of fifteen she heard
a miraculous voice speaking to her amid Christmas festivities and resolved to lead a
devotional life. When she was twenty-one, she married William Lead, a distant rela-
tive six years her senior, with whom she had four daughters. After his death, when
she was forty-six, she renewed her commitment to mystical theology and to what she
called "Spiritual Virginity." At around this time, moreover, she had the striking vision,
excerpted here, of a female figure whom the critic Catherine Smith regards as "Lead's
revision of Sophia, the Virgin Wisdom of God in esoteric theology and apocalyptic
tradition."

Already a student of the works of the radical German theologian Jacob Boehme (1575–1624), Lead now became even more passionately mystical, and in 1674 she moved into the household of Dr. John Pordage, the leader of one of the many Nonconformist congregations that were springing up in England around this time. In 1681, after Pordage's death, she began to publish her own spiritual writings; and in 1694, with the assistance of a young disciple, Dr. Francis Lee, she founded the Philadelphia Society, a Nonconformist group (like the Diggers and the Ranters) based on Boehme's teachings. Her books include *The Heavenly Cloud Now Breaking* (1681), *The Enochian Walks with God* (1694), and perhaps most important, the four-volume *A Fountain of Gardens, Watered by the Rivers of Divine Pleasure* (1697–1701). Although her works are primarily religious and she was not consciously a feminist, her writing was consistently energized by images of the magical woman within the soul who, she believed, would bring redemption to male and female spirits alike, and her metaphors of rebirth are distinctively feminine. Numerous excerpts from her books have now been posted online; their visions are so vivid that some commentators who believe in extraterrestrial visitations consider the events Lead reports "strikingly similar to modern accounts of abductions by UFOs."

From A Fountain of Gardens[1]

[*THE FIRST VISION*]

The first vision that appeared to me was in the month of April, 1670, which was on this wise[2]—

Being my lot at that time to visit a friend in a solitary country place, where I had great advantage of retirement, often frequenting lonely walks in a grove or wood, contemplating the happy state of the angelical world and how desirous I was to have my conversation there, my thoughts were much exercised upon Solomon's choice, which was to find out the noble stone of divine Wisdom;[3] for by acquainting myself with her, all desirable good in spiritual things would meet upon me. The report and fame that Solomon gave of Wisdom[4] did much excite me to seek her favor and friendship; demurring in myself from whence she was descended, still questioning whether she was a distinct being from the Deity or no? Which while in this debate within my mind, there came upon me an overshadowing bright cloud, and in the midst of it the figure of a woman, most richly adorned with transparent gold, her hair hanging down, and her face as the terrible crystal for brightness, but her countenance was sweet and mild. At which sight I was somewhat amazed, but immediately this voice came, saying, "Behold, I am God's eternal Virgin Wisdom, whom thou hast been inquiring after; I am to unseal the treasures of God's deep wisdom unto thee, and will be as Rebecca[5] was unto Jacob, a true natural mother; for out of my womb thou shalt be brought forth

1. The full title is *A Fountain of Gardens, Watered by the Rivers of Divine Pleasure, and Springing Up in All the Variety of Spiritual Plants; Blown Up by the Pure Breath into a Paradise.*
2. In this way.
3. In one biblical tradition, wisdom is personified as a woman, Sophia (Greek for "wisdom"), who represents the wisdom of God (see, e.g., Proverbs 8; 1 Corinthians 1.24). Here the biblical king Sol-

omon, noted for his wisdom, is associated with the legendary philosopher's stone, which was reputed to change base metals into gold.
4. See the apocryphal Wisdom of Solomon.
5. The mother of Jacob and his older twin Esau. She helped Jacob deceive his dying father, Isaac, into giving him the blessing that was promised to Esau (Genesis 27).

after the manner of a spirit, conceived and born again; this thou shalt know by a new motion of life, stirring and giving a restlessness, till wisdom be born within the inward parts of thy soul. Now consider of my saying till I return to thee again."

This vision took great impression on me, yet I kept it for the present hid, but it operated so much upon me, as indeed I was incapable to converse with any mortals; which was taken notice of, that some extraordinary thing had happened, for the which I begged my friend's excuse and desired that she would give me the liberty to be much alone, and to walk in the silent woods, where I might contemplate what had so lately happened. Now after three days, sitting under a tree, the same figure in greater glory did appear, with a crown upon her head, full of majesty, saying, "Behold me as thy mother, and know thou art to enter into covenant[6] to obey the new creation laws, that shall be revealed unto thee." Then did she hold out a golden book, with three[7] seals upon it, saying, "Herein lieth hidden the deep wonders of Jehovah's wisdom, which hath been sealed up, that none could or ever shall break up, but such as of her virgin offspring shall appear to be, who will her laws receive and keep, as they shall spring daily in the new heart and mind." This appearance and words was wonderfully sweet and refreshing in my soul; at which I bowed and prostrated at her feet, promising to be obedient to all her laws. So the vision shut up for that time.

Pondering this in my heart with great comfort, that this daystar[8] had visited me from on high, I returned to London to my own habitation, retiring myself from all my acquaintance, saving one person that was highly illuminated,[9] who encouraged me still to wait upon this vision, for he was acquainted with somewhat of this kind. So after six days the vision appeared again, with a train of virgin spirits, and with an angelical host; and called to me to come and see the virgin queen, with her first-born children; asking me whether I was willing to be joined amongst this virgin company? At which I replied, "All willing to offer up myself most free." Then immediately I was encompassed about with this heavenly host, and made a spirit of light. Then these words from the Virgin proceeded, saying, "I shall now cease to appear in a visible figure unto thee, but I will not fail to transfigure myself in thy mind and there open the spring of Wisdom and understanding, that so thou mayst come to know the only True God, in and by the formation of Christ, the anointed prophet in thee; that shall reveal great and wonderful things unto thee, that are to be made known and public in its time and day. Therefore be watchful, and to thy mother Wisdom's counsel give good heed, and thou shalt greatly prosper, and succeed the prophets and apostles to perfect what was left behind, for completing as to Christ the fullness of God's great mystery: so go on, and nothing fear or doubt; for I thy glass[1] for divine seeing shall evermore stand before thee." Then my spirit replied, "According to thy word let all this be fulfilled." And so this glory withdrew; but an inward glory did my heart fill, for a burning love to all of those heavenly beings did kindle within my heart vehemently.

6. Solemn agreement; here alluding to God's covenant with the Israelites (Genesis 6.18).
7. A mystic number—as in the Holy Trinity.

8. I.e., morning star.
9. Enlightened spiritually.
1. Lens.

[*THE SECOND VISION*]

In the Month of August

The mind of Wisdom thus opened itself in me, as I waited in my spirit upon her; she did show me what key would open the great mystery, which lay deeply hid in myself. It was wrought and carved out of such pure gold as had passed though many fires; many keys I had tried, but could not turn in this secret enclosed lock, but still it shut upon me, though I thought I had that key which was compounded of such metals as would have made its entrance, as love, faith, patience, humility,[2] which with strong supplication and prayer I presented, as the key of the work. All which was too short to reach it. Whereupon I was put to a loss altogether to seek how this gate should be opened, having compassed the Holy City,[3] and waited and tried every way, where I might find passage, circling from one path to another, from prayer to prayer, and from faith to faith; so that in good earnest I began to consider I had not found this wonderful key, for want[4] of which I might run out in waste all my days, and grope as in the dark, yet never find the door which opens into my true shepherd's fold.[5] Whereupon being cast into a deep astonishing silence and stillness, the word of Wisdom thus opened itself unto me: "Oh, thou deep searching spirit, marvel not thou hast been so long frustrated, for as to thy present state and dispensation, thou couldst never reach me to all eternity, for my birth in thee lies deeper than thy present gift of faith and prayer can open; thou hast with many others been in a great mistake. But in as much thou ownest and bewailest thy unskill-fulness, I will make known to thee what key will turn this great wheel of my Wisdom, so as it may move and manifest itself in thee through all thy properties,[6] if thou canst bid up to the price of it. For understand that it is compounded of all pure gold, subsisting in a burning furnace of many fires. And although this wonderful key is of Wisdom's carving out, and her free gift, yet, O thou seeking spirit, she will cost thee very dear, if ever thou obtainest her. Yet she goeth about seeking such as are worthy of her, and will show herself within the walls of the mind, and meet them in every thought that waits for her laws and counsel, and brings a kingdom which will be well worth thy selling all for. But the great thing," saith Wisdom, "now is to discipline and make thy spirit a cunning artist, to give it knowledge of what matter in number, weight, and measure this pure key is made up of, which is all pure deity in the number THREE, which is weighty indeed, being one exceeding weighty glory, fitting in the circle of the heavens within man's heart, measuring with the line of his power, the temple and inward court, with the worshippers therein. This is Wisdom's key, which will make our hands drop with sweet-smelling myrrh upon the handles of her lock." Which while I was opening her privy[7] door with this key, my soul failed within me, and I retained no strength; my sun of reason and the moon of my outward sense were folded up and withdrew. I knew nothing by myself, as to those working properties from nature and creature,[8] and the wheel of the motion

2. These echo some of the theological virtues.
3. I.e., the New Jerusalem of Revelation.
4. Lack.
5. Pen for sheep; the true shepherd is Christ.

6. I.e., personal qualities.
7. Private.
8. I.e., she knew nothing of her natural human functions.

standing still, another moved from a central fire;[9] so that I felt myself trans-
muted into one pure flame. Then came that word to me, "This is no other
than the gate of my eternal deep; canst thou subsist in this fiery region, which
is Wisdom's mansion where she meets with holy abstracted spirits, and gives
forth a fiery law, which if thereunto thou canst give heed, so as to come up
to her requirings, then no secret shall be withheld from thee." Thus far am
I admitted to come into the entrance of her house, where I must stop till I
hear further from her.

Now as I was attending to obtain a fresh visit, being entered into this first
mansion of her house,[1] to hear and learn further, she said on this wise, that
I was greatly beloved, and she would be my mother, and so should I own her
and call her, who would now be to me as Rebecca was to Jacob, to contrive
and put me in a way how I should obtain the birthright blessing. For if I
would apply myself to her doctrine, and draw my life's food from no other
breast, I should then know the recovery of a lost kingdom; at which salutation
I was dissolved and melted, the fervent heat of this love strongly impulsing
me to a resolve for to obey her in all things.

When pure oil from Wisdom's vessel stopping, it opened again not till
October the 20th in the morning watch; then heard I her voice thus,
"Sequester and draw out of thy animal sensitive life[2] that is too gross: I
cannot appear till that disappear. There must be spirit with spirit, light with
light." No sooner had I this caution, but I felt power which suspended the
active busy mind, which for a time was expired into silence. "Know then,"
said the same voice, "thou shalt supplant thy brother Esau, who according
to the figure, is a cunning hunter in the out-birth[3] and field of nature. While
he with his subtlety seeking it abroad in the wild properties of the external
region, I will now help thee to it near at hand, even in thy own enclosed
ground. There the true scapegoat[4] feeds, of which I will make savory meat,
such as God thy Father loves." Hearing this salutation from my late known
mother, I was deadly ravished in the spirit, in the light of the Lord, and
feared to return to the dark house of my outward senses again; which opened
a spring of intercession in me, that as one of the friends of the bridegroom[5]
I might hear his voice still, which indeed was so pleasant and sweet as I could
well have admitted of a dissolution of my elementary being, rather than this
conference should not still be maintained with this renowned pearl of wis-
dom. But I have learned to observe her time and seasons; I witness her
opening as in the twinkling of an eye, a pure bright, subtle, swift spirit, a
working motion, a circling fire, a penetrating oil.

1697–1701

9. I.e., as the wheel of ordinary motion stopped,
another wheel—that of Wisdom—moved from a
central fire.
1. See John 14:2: "In my Father's house are many
mansions" (i.e., abodes).
2. I.e., life of the senses.
3. Progeny, something brought forth.

4. Leviticus 16 commands that each year one goat
be sent into the wilderness as a live offering to the
Lord (the scapegoat) and another be sacrificed.
Lead may also be thinking of Christ as "the true
scapegoat" bearing the sins of the people.
5. I.e., Jesus.

KATHERINE PHILIPS
1632–1664

Known in her own day as "the Matchless Orinda," Katherine Philips was the daughter of John Fowler, a London merchant. In 1648 she married James Philips, a wealthy Puritan thirty-four years her senior, who shared some of her interests and supported her literary career. The couple resided at Cardigan Priory in Wales, but the young bride also spent a good deal of time in London. That James Philips was a prominent supporter of Cromwell (he signed Charles I's death warrant in 1649) while his wife remained a Royalist does not seem to have significantly troubled the relations between the pair, although Katherine's poetry records their political differences.

When Katherine Philips began writing verse shortly after her marriage, she quickly became the center of an intellectual circle called the Society of Friendship, in which each member was given a playfully neoclassical pseudonym. She herself was known as "Orinda" and her husband was called "Antenor," while her close friend Anne Owen, Viscountess Dungannon, was the original of the "Excellent Lucasia" to whom a number of Orinda's pieces on friendship are dedicated; another dear friend, Mary Aubrey, the recipient of "To Mrs. M. A. at Parting," was dubbed "Rosania."

Though Philips evidently did not herself seek to publish poems in her lifetime, her translation of Corneille's *La Mort de Pompée* (*The Death of Pompey*, 1643) was staged in Dublin and appeared in print soon after, in 1663. Her verses, circulated privately, received so much praise from such contemporary poets and intellectuals as Abraham Cowley, Jeremy Taylor, Henry Vaughan, and John Dryden that an unauthorized edition titled *Poems by the Incomparable Mrs. K.P.* was published in 1664. It was quickly withdrawn because of Philips's objections not only to publication per se but to "the falseness of the copies"—that is, the inadequate printing.

The mother of two children, one of whom died in infancy, Katherine Philips clearly had a "room of her own" in which to write and leisure for friendship as well as literary activity. As our selections indicate, she wrote on a wide range of subjects, including courtship, marriage, maternity, and mourning. But her most loving poems are addressed to female friends, suggesting the bonds that were beginning to develop between seventeenth-century intellectual women, who felt that they had found "all the world" in each other rather than in romanticized heroes. Nevertheless, the Matchless Orinda was admired by male as well as female readers. When she died of smallpox at only thirty-two, countless tributes appeared, eulogizing her. "If *Apollo* should design / A woman *Laureat* to make," declared Cowley in a flamboyant elegy, "Without dispute he would *Orinda* take."

Recent commentators have speculated that Philips's contemporaries saw her as a virtuous counterpart of the scandalous poet-playwright Aphra Behn, who was frequently vilified as a "shady lady." Yet though some of Philips's work was conventionally pious or sentimental, much of it was elegant and eloquent. Certainly her collection of plays and poems, posthumously assembled and printed under the supervision of Sir Charles Cotterell, a close friend, was extraordinarily popular. As the poet Anne Killigrew somewhat enviously remarked, musing on "Orinda's" reputation, "every laurel to her laurel bowed"—that is, every respected poet praised her artistry.

Friendship's Mystery, to My Dearest Lucasia[1]

Set by Mr. H. Lawes.[2]

1

Come, my Lucasia, since we see
 That miracles men's faith do move
By wonder and by prodigy,[3]
 To the dull, angry world let's prove
5 There's a religion in our love.

2

For though we were designed[4] t'agree,
 That fate no liberty destroys,
But our election[5] is as free
 As Angels, who with greedy choice
10 Are yet determined to their joys.

3

Our hearts are doubled by their loss,[6]
 Here mixture is addition grown;
We both diffuse, and both engross,[7]
 And we, whose minds are so much one,
15 Never, yet ever, are alone.

4

We court our own captivity,
 Then thrones more[8] great and innocent:
'Twere banishment to be set free,
 Since we wear fetters whose intent
20 Not bondage is, but ornament.

5

Divided joys are tedious found,
 And griefs united easier grow:
We are our selves but by rebound,[9]
 And all our titles shuffled so,
25 Both princes, and both subjects too.

6

Our hearts are mutual victims laid,
 While they (such power in friendship lies)
Are altars, priests, and offerings made,

1. Anne Owen (1633–1692), later Viscountess Dungannon.
2. Henry Lawes (1596–1662), a Royalist musician and composer.
3. Extraordinary event, omen.
4. Minded, resolved.
5. Exercise of deliberate choice. The mention of angels (line 9) suggests also the notion of "divine election," God's choice of some for eternal salvation.
6. I.e., each has lost her heart to the other.
7. Gather together, condense. "Diffuse": spread abroad, become diffused.
8. More than thrones.
9. Reflection.

And each heart which thus kindly dies,
30 Grows deathless by the sacrifice.

1655

To Mrs. M. A.[1] at Parting

I have examined and do find,
 Of all that favor me
There's none I grieve to leave behind
 But only only thee.
5 To part with thee I needs must die,
Could parting separate thee and I.

But neither chance nor compliment
 Did element[2] our love:
'Twas sacred sympathy was lent
10 Us from the choir above.
(That friendship fortune did create,
Still fears a wound from time or fate.)

Our changed and mingled souls are grown
 To such acquaintance now,
15 That if each would resume their own,
 Alas! we know not how.
We have each other so engrossed
That each is in the union lost.[3]

And thus we can no absence know,
20 Nor shall we be confined;
Our active souls will daily go
 To learn each other's mind.
Nay, should we never meet to sense,
Our souls would hold intelligence.[4]

25 Inspiréd with a flame divine,
 I scorn to court a stay;[5]
For from that noble soul of thine
 I ne'er can be away.
But I shall weep when thou dost grieve;
30 Nor can I die whilst thou dost live.

By my own temper I shall guess
 At thy felicity,
And only like my happiness
 Because it pleaseth thee.

1. Mary Aubrey (1631–1700), a friend of Philips from childhood and the first member of her "Society of Friendship."
2. I.e., form the elements of.

3. I.e., their two souls have become one.
4. Would still commune.
5. Postponement (of their parting).

35 Our hearts at any time will tell
If thou or I be sick or well.

All honor, sure, I must pretend,[6]
All that is good or great:
She that would be Rosania's[7] friend
40 Must be at least complete.
If I have any bravery,
'Tis cause I have so much of thee.

Thy leiger[8] soul in me shall lie,
And all thy thoughts reveal;
45 Then back again with mine shall fly,
And thence to me shall steal.
Thus still to one another tend:
Such is the sacred name of friend.

Thus our twin souls in one shall grow,
50 And teach the world new love,
Redeem the age and sex, and show
A flame fate dares not move:
And courting death to be our friend,
Our lives, together too, shall end.

55 A dew shall dwell upon our tomb
Of such a quality
That fighting armies, thither come,
Shall reconciléd be.
We'll ask no epitaph, but say:
60 ORINDA and ROSANIA.

1664

On the Death of My First and Dearest Child, Hector Philips, Borne the 23d of April, and Died the 2d of May 1655

Set by Mr. Lawes.[1]

1

Twice forty months in wedlock I did stay,[2]
Then had my vows crowned with a lovely boy.
And yet in forty days he dropped away;
O! swift vicissitude of human joy!

2

5 I did but see him, and he disappeared,
I did but touch the rosebud, and it fell;

6. Aspire to.
7. I.e., Mary Aubrey's.
8. Acting as a resident ambassador.

1. Henry Lawes (1596–1662), a Royalist musician and composer. No musical setting is extant.
2. Philips was married in August 1648.

A sorrow unforeseen and scarcely feared,
 So ill can mortals their afflictions spell.[3]

3

 And now (sweet babe) what can my trembling heart
10 Suggest to right my doleful fate or thee?
Tears are my muse, and sorrow all my art,
 So piercing groans must be thy elegy.

4

Thus whilst no eye is witness of my moan,
 I grieve thy loss (Ah, boy too dear to live!)
15 And let the unconcerned world alone,[4]
 Who neither will, nor can refreshment give.

5

An offering too for thy sad tomb I have,
 Too just a tribute to thy early hearse;
Receive these gasping numbers[5] to thy grave,
20 The last of thy unhappy mother's verse.

 1667

To Sir Amorous La Fool

Bless us, here's a do[1] indeed!
That she must so much courtship need.
Scorn sits so handsome on this face,
With such an unaffected grace,
5 That I could wish my sex were changed to be
A lover only of your cruelty.

Women, men say, are fools they know,
But what are they that call us so,
When their sighs and amorous ware,
10 But more serious follies are.[2]
What time we spend to curl and dress our hair,
You spend to think us, though we are not, fair.

What pretty dotage[3] call you this,
To weep and groan and glance and kiss;
15 Unkindness makes your heart to break,
And not a word of sense to speak,
And court the careless, when with far less pain,
Some wholesome milkmaid would say yours again.

 1667

3. Understand, decipher.
4. Spiritual restoration.
5. Lines of poetry.

1. Fuss.
2. "But . . . are": are but, are only.
3. Foolish affection.

A Married State

A married state affords but little ease:
The best of husbands are so hard to please.
This in wives' careful faces you may spell,
Though they dissemble[1] their misfortunes well.
5 A virgin state is crowned with much content,
It's always happy as it's innocent.
No blustering husbands to create your fears,
No pangs of childbirth to extort your tears,
No children's cries for to offend your ears,
10 Few worldly crosses to distract your prayers.
Thus are you freed from all the cares that do
Attend on matrimony and a husband too.
Therefore, madam, be advised by me:
Turn, turn apostate to love's levity.
15 Suppress wild nature if she dare rebel,
There's no such thing as leading apes in hell.[2]

1667

1. Disguise. "Spell": make out with difficulty.
2. The proverbial destiny of unmarried women. See Shakespeare's *Taming of the Shrew* (ca. 1592),
2.1.33–34: "I must dance barefoot on her wedding day, / And for your love to her lead apes in hell."

MARY ROWLANDSON
ca. 1636–1711

At dawn on February 10, 1676, Mary Rowlandson, her six-year-old daughter, and her two older children were captured by a group of New England Indians. Both Rowlandson and the six-year-old were wounded, and they were separated from the older children. Though a number of people, including Rowlandson's sister, were killed in the raid, her husband—a minister—survived because he was away from home. During a three-month imprisonment that followed, Rowlandson lived with the members of the Wampanoag woman Weetamoo's household, migrating with them into southwestern New Hampshire; visiting, when possible, with her son, Joseph, and her daughter, Mary; and coping with cold by reading a Bible that was given to her and with hunger by knitting or sewing in exchange for pancakes and bear meat. Her resiliency and survival skills seem to have surprised even herself: before the Indian raid she had believed that she would "choose rather to be killed by them than taken alive." But, she explains in a narrative that has since become a classic of frontier literature, "when it came to the trial my mind changed; their glittering weapons so daunted my spirit, that I chose rather to go along with those (as I may say) ravenous beasts, than that moment to end my days."

The raid on her house had been part of a yearlong series of attacks on colonial outposts led by Metacomet, or "Philip," as the white settlers called him. Rowlandson was understandably irate, if not racist, about the "merciless heathen" who taunted her and tormented her children. Yet even her account implies that the Wampanoag

were themselves starving and uprooted. In fact, what became known as "King Philip's War" was a futile effort on the part of the Native Americans to reclaim the homeland they had lost to Puritans like the Rowlandsons. By the time their struggle for independence was over in August 1676, three thousand of the Wampanoags and their allies had been killed. Three months before the war ended, Rowlandson was thankful that the Indian community assented to the ransom her husband offered for her, that several of its representatives provided a hood and scarf for her journey, and that during her captivity "not one of them ever offered me the least abuse of unchastity to me, in word or action."

After moving with her husband to Wethersfield, Connecticut, where he died in 1678, Rowlandson married Captain Samuel Talcott in 1679 and published her *Narrative* in 1682. It has remained a prototype of the captivity narrative, a popular American genre mined not only by early writers who experienced captivities in their lives but also by later novelists such as James Fenimore Cooper and William Faulkner, who composed fictionalized versions of the form.

Documenting, as it does, her shifting attitudes toward Native American culture, her capacity for endurance, and the Puritan rhetorical tradition, Rowlandson's captivity narrative, which she wrote for her surviving children, has been exceptionally popular, going through more than thirty editions since its first publication.

From A Narrative of the Captivity and Restoration of Mrs. Mary Rowlandson

The Third Remove[1]

The morning being come, they prepared to go on their way. One of the Indians got up upon a horse, and they set me up behind him, with my poor sick babe in my lap. A very wearisome and tedious day I had of it; what with my own wound, and my child's being so exceeding sick, and in a lamentable condition with her wound.[2] It may be easily judged what a poor feeble condition we were in, there being not the least crumb of refreshing that came within either of our mouths from Wednesday night to Saturday night, except only a little cold water. This day in the afternoon, about an hour by sun, we came to the place where they intended, *viz.* an Indian town, called Wenimesset, northward of Quabaug. When we were come, Oh the number of pagans (now merciless enemies) that there came about me, that I may say as David, "I had fainted, unless I had believed, etc." (Psalm 27:13).[3] The next day was the sabbath. I then remembered how careless I had been of God's holy time; how many sabbaths I had lost and misspent, and how evilly I had walked in God's sight; which lay so close unto my spirit, that it was easy for me see how righteous it was with God to cut off the thread of my life and cast me out of His presence for ever. Yet the Lord still showed mercy to me, and upheld me; and as He wounded me with one hand, so he healed me with the other. This day there came to me one Robert Pepper (a man belonging to Roxbury) who was taken in Captain Beers's fight,[4] and had been

1. I.e., departure. From February 12 to 27 Rowlandson and her captors stayed at a Native American village on the Ware River, near New Braintree. (All dates are given according to the Julian calendar, whose year began on March 25; add 11 days for the present Gregorian equivalent.)
2. During the raid, Rowlandson was shot in the side, and the child in her arms was shot in the hand and belly.
3. The verse continues, "to see the goodness of the Lord in the land of the living."
4. Captain Beers battled to rescue the garrison of Northfield, Massachusetts, on September 4, 1675.

now a considerable time with the Indians; and up with them almost as far as Albany, to see King Philip, as he told me, and was now very lately come into these parts. Hearing, I say, that I was in this Indian town, he obtained leave to come and see me. He told me he himself was wounded in the leg at Captain Beer's fight; and was not able some time to go, but as they carried him, and as he took oaken leaves and laid to his wound, and through the blessing of God he was able to travel again. Then I took oaken leaves and laid to my side, and with the blessing of God it cured me also; yet before the cure was wrought, I may say, as it is in Psalm 38:5–6, "My wounds stink and are corrupt, I am troubled, I am bowed down greatly, I go mourning all the day long." I sat much alone with a poor wounded child in my lap, which moaned night and day, having nothing to revive the body, or cheer the spirits of her, but instead of that, sometimes one Indian would come and tell me one hour that "your master will knock your child in the head," and then a second, and then a third, "your master will quickly knock your child in the head."

This was the comfort I had from them, miserable comforters are ye all, as he[5] said. Thus nine days I sat upon my knees, with my babe in my lap, till my flesh was raw again; my child being even ready to depart this sorrowful world, they bade me carry it out to another wigwam (I suppose because they would not be troubled with such spectacles) whither I went with a very heavy heart, and down I sat with the picture of death in my lap. About two hours in the night, my sweet babe like a lamb departed this life on Feb. 18, 1675. It being about six years, and five months old. It was nine days from the first wounding, in this miserable condition, without any refreshing of one nature or other, except a little cold water. I cannot but take notice how at another time I could not bear to be in the room where any dead person was, but now the case is changed; I must and could lie down by my dead babe, side by side all the night after. I have thought since of the wonderful goodness of God to me in preserving me in the use of my reason and senses in that distressed time, that I did not use wicked and violent means to end my own miserable life. In the morning, when they understood that my child was dead they sent for me home to my master's wigwam (by my master in this writing, must be understood Quanopin, who was a Sagamore,[6] and married King Philip's wife's sister; not that he first took me, but I was sold to him by another Narraganset Indian, who took me when first I came out of the garrison). I went to take up my dead child in my arms to carry it with me, but they bid me let it alone; there was no resisting, but go I must and leave it. When I had been at my master's wigwam, I took the first opportunity I could get to go look after my dead child. When I came I asked them what they had done with it; then they told me it was upon the hill. Then they went and showed me where it was, where I saw the ground was newly digged, and there they told me they had buried it. There I left that child in the wilderness, and must commit it, and myself also in this wilderness condition, to Him who is above all. God having taken away this dear child, I went to see my daughter Mary, who was at this same Indian town, at a wigwam not very far off, though we had little liberty or opportunity to see one another. She was

5. I.e., Job 16.2: "I have heard many such things: miserable comforters are ye all."
6. A subordinate chief among Algonquin Indians.

Quanopin was Weetamoo's husband; Rowlandson became her servant.

about ten years old, and taken from the door at first by a Praying Ind. and afterward sold for a gun. When I came in sight, she would fall aweeping; at which they were provoked, and would not let me come near her, but bade me be gone; which was a heart-cutting word to me. I had one child dead, another in the wilderness, I knew not where, the third they would not let me come near to: "Me (as he said) have ye bereaved of my Children, Joseph is not, and Simeon is not, and ye will take Benjamin also, all these things are against me."[7] I could not sit still in this condition, but kept walking from one place to another. And as I was going along, my heart was even overwhelmed with the thoughts of my condition, and that I should have children, and a nation which I knew not, ruled over them. Whereupon I earnestly entreated the Lord, that He would consider my low estate, and show me a token for good, and if it were His blessed will, some sign and hope of some relief. And indeed quickly the Lord answered, in some measure, my poor prayers; for as I was going up and down mourning and lamenting my condition, my son came to me, and asked me how I did. I had not seen him before, since the destruction of the town, and I knew not where he was, till I was informed by himself, that he was amongst a smaller parcel of Indians, whose place was about six miles off. With tears in his eyes, he asked me whether his sister Sarah was dead; and told me he had seen his sister Mary; and prayed me, that I would not be troubled in reference to himself. The occasion of his coming to see me at this time, was this: there was, as I said, about six miles from us, a small plantation of Indians, where it seems he had been during his captivity; and at this time, there were some forces of the Ind. gathered out of our company, and some also from them (among whom was my son's master) to go to assault and burn Medfield.[8] In this time of the absence of his master, his dame brought him to see me. I took this to be some gracious answer to my earnest and unfeigned desire. The next day, viz. to this, the Indians returned from Medfield, all the company, for those that belonged to the other small company, came through the town that now we were at. But before they came to us, Oh! the outrageous roaring and hooping that there was. They began their din about a mile before they came to us. By their noise and hooping they signified how many they had destroyed (which was at that time twenty-three.) Those that were with us at home were gathered together as soon as they heard the hooping, and every time that the other went over their number, these at home gave a shout, that the very earth rung again. And thus they continued till those that had been upon the expedition were come up to the Sagamore's wigwam; then, Oh, the hideous insulting[9] and triumphing that there was over some Englishmen's scalps that they had taken (as their manner is) and brought with them. I cannot but take notice of the wonderful mercy of God to me in those afflictions, in sending me a Bible. One of the Indians that came from Medfield fight, had brought some plunder, came to me, and asked me, if I would have a Bible, he had got one in his basket. I was glad of it, and asked him, whether he thought the Indians would let me read? He answered, yes. So I took the Bible, and in that melancholy time, it came into my mind to read first the 28th chapter of Deuteronomy,[1] which I did, and when I had read it, my dark heart wrought on

7. The lament of Jacob (Genesis 42.36).
8. This attack on Medfield, Massachusetts, took place on February 21.

9. Insolent boasting.
1. This chapter concerns God's blessings and curses on those who obey and disobey him.

this manner: that there was no mercy for me, that the blessings were gone, and the curses come in their room, and that I had lost my opportunity. But the Lord helped me still to go on reading till I came to Chap. 30, the seven first verses, where I found, there was mercy promised again, if we would return to Him by repentance;[2] and though we were scattered from one end of the earth to the other, yet the Lord would gather us together, and turn all those curses upon our enemies. I do not desire to live to forget this Scripture, and what comfort it was to me.

Now the Ind. began to talk of removing from this place, some one way, and some another. There were now besides myself nine English captives in this place (all of them children, except one woman). I got an opportunity to go and take my leave of them. They being to go one way, and I another, I asked them whether they were earnest with God for deliverance. They told me they did as they were able, and it was some comfort to me, that the Lord stirred up children to look to Him. The woman, *viz.* goodwife[3] Joslin, told me she should never see me again, and that she could find in her heart to run away. I wished her not to run away by any means, for we were near thirty miles from any English town, and she very big with child, and had but one week to reckon, and another child in her arms, two years old, and bad rivers there were to go over, and we were feeble, with our poor and coarse entertainment.[4] I had my Bible with me, I pulled it out, and asked her whether she would read. We opened the Bible and lighted on Psalm 27, in which Psalm we especially took notice of that, *ver. ult.,*[5] "Wait on the Lord, Be of good courage, and he shall strengthen thine Heart, wait I say on the Lord."

1682

2. "That then the Lord thy God will turn thy captivity, and have compassion upon thee, and will return and gather thee from all the nations" (Deuteronomy 30.3).
3. I.e., mistress of a house.
4. Food.
5. The last verse (Latin); here, verse 14.

APHRA BEHN
1640?–1689

Spy and playwright, traveler and wit, Aphra Behn was England's first professional woman writer. In an age when many women of letters were intellectual aristocrats such as Anne Finch, countess of Winchilsea, and Margaret Cavendish, duchess of Newcastle, wealthy ladies who claimed to write only for pleasure and "fame" among their friends, Behn was a middle-class widow who frankly wrote for money and public acclaim. Of uncertain parentage, she seems to have traveled to the West Indies at the age of sixteen when her father was appointed lieutenant governor of the sugar colony Surinam. Her adventures are said by some biographers to have included an involvement in a slave rebellion and a visit to a group of American Indians who had never before seen Europeans (though it should be remembered that her autobiographical accounts were composed to sell books, and therefore many of the facts of her life remain elusive). Returning to England in 1664, Behn was briefly married to a man about whom little is known except that he was a London merchant of Dutch ancestry, who very likely died in the terrible plague of 1665.

In 1666, widowed and casting about for some means of support, Behn entered the intelligence service of King Charles II, though as she later acknowledged, such "public toils of state affairs" were "unusual with my sex, or in my years." Assigned to work as a spy in Antwerp, she carried out her mission "remarkably well," according to Angeline Goreau, one of her biographers; but because the king's agents never paid her properly for her labors, she ended up spending some time in 1668 in a London debtors' prison. Apparently it was the trauma of this last experience that decided her on what was, for a woman, an unprecedented step: writing for money. By 1670, Aphra Behn's first play, *The Forced Marriage,* was successfully produced on the London stage.

From 1670 on, Behn's groundbreaking literary career was characterized by remarkable productivity. She had always been a literary young woman, a fluent diarist, and an enthusiastic reader of French romances. Now, as she became a professional playwright, she moved from writing somewhat derivative tragicomedies to producing farces in the style of such contemporaries as the comic dramatist William Wycherley. Altogether, during her years in the theater she wrote and published some fourteen plays, including *The Rover* (1677), *Sir Patient Fancy* (1678), *The Roundheads* (1681), and *The City Heiress* (1682). At the same time, Behn inquired, "What has poor woman done that she must be / Debarred from. . . . sacred poetry?" and demanded freedom to assert what society defined as "my masculine part, the poet in me." She was also composing and publishing a series of briskly witty verses, some marked by an erotic honesty that scandalized many of her readers. For although the Restoration circles in which she traveled permitted extraordinary license to male artists like Behn's libertine friend and patron the poet John Wilmot, earl of Rochester, the same circles expected women to remain decently silent about their own desires. As her poem "The Disappointment" suggests, however, Behn did not maintain such a silence, leading even a subsequent supporter like the writer Anne Finch to concede that "a little too loosely she writ."

In Behn's later years, the London theaters on which she had depended for her livelihood suffered a number of reverses, and her income from playwriting was severely reduced. Enterprising as ever, she turned her talents in yet another direction, writing and publishing a set of pioneering prose fictions—*Love Letters between a Nobleman and His Sister* (1684–85), *The Fair Jilt* (1688), *Agnes de Castro* (1688), and, most notably, *Oroonoko* (1688). Loosely based on "real life," with the revolutionary *Oroonoko* supposedly recounting Behn's early experiences in Surinam and including a passionate protest against the institution of slavery, these literary novelties were to play a part in the development of a new form, the novel, in which, as some critics have suggested, women of letters were to find a particularly important outlet. Part travel narrative, part memoir, part fantasy, part biography, *Oroonoko* is complex in its treatment of racial difference, yet ultimately Behn's sympathy for her heroic royal slave and her outrage against the injustice of slavery give the book extraordinary resonance. Following in her footsteps, such white women of letters as Maria Edgeworth and Elizabeth Barrett Browning (in England) along with Elizabeth Cady Stanton and Harriet Beecher Stowe (in the United States) produced polemics against the savagery of supposedly civilized societies that denied full humanity to all human beings. In so doing, they echoed the protests of African American contemporaries from Sojourner Truth to Frederick Douglass.

Behn died in pain and poverty within a year of the publication of *Oroonoko,* and her reputation was to be obscured or defaced for centuries after her death. Yet she had once again broken new ground. "All women together ought to let flowers fall upon the tomb of Aphra Behn," declared the author of *A Room of One's Own,* "for it was she who earned them the right to speak their minds." Her grave—somewhat surprisingly located in Westminster Abbey—is marked by a censorious stone that reads "Here lies a Proof that wit can never be / Defence against mortality." But Virginia Woolf's tribute to her memory was more apt than such a motto.

The Willing Mistress[1]

Amyntas led me to a grove,
　　Where all the trees did shade us;
The sun itself, though it had strove,
　　It could not have betrayed us.[2]
5　The place secured from human eyes
　　No other fear allows
But when the winds that gently rise
　　Do kiss the yielding boughs.

Down there we sat upon the moss,
10　　And did begin to play
A thousand amorous tricks,[3] to pass
　　The heat of all the day.
A many kisses did he give
　　And I returned the same,
15　Which made me willing to receive
　　That which I dare not name.

His charming eyes no aid required
　　To tell their softening tale;
On her that was already fired,[4]
20　　'Twas easy to prevail.
He did but kiss and clasp me round,
　　Whilst those his thoughts expressed:
And laid me gently on the ground;
　　Ah who can guess the rest?

　　　　　　　　　　　　　　　　　1673

Love Armed[1]

Love in fantastic triumph[2] sat
Whilst bleeding hearts around him flowed,
For whom fresh[3] pains he did create
And strange tyrannic power he showed.

5　From thy bright eyes he took the fires
Which round about in sport he hurled,
But 'twas from mine he took desires
Enough t'undo the amorous world.[4]

1. This song appears in Behn's play *The Dutch Lover*, where it is sung by a maidservant to her mistress.
2. I.e., revealed us to others.
3. Games, amusements.
4. I.e., made warm with desire.
1. A song in Behn's play *Abdelazer; or, The Moor's Revenge.* "Love" in this poem is Cupid, often

depicted during the Renaissance as a cruel and arbitrary god, armed with darts (see, e.g., the Maske of Cupid in Spenser's *The Faerie Queene* [1590], 3.12).
2. In a splendid procession.
3. New.
4. To destroy the world's lovers in the sufferings of desire.

From me he took his sighs and tears,
10 From thee his pride and cruelty;
From me his languishments and fears.
And every killing dart from thee.

Thus thou and I the God have armed
And set him up a deity;
15 But my poor heart alone is harmed,
Whilst thine the victor is, and free.

1676

The Disappointment[1]

One day the amorous Lysander,
By an impatient passion swayed,[2]
Surprised fair Cloris, that lovéd maid,
Who could defend herself no longer.
5 All things did with his love conspire;[3]
The gilded planet[4] of the day,
In his gay chariot drawn by fire,
Was now descending to the sea,
And left no light to guide the world
10 But what from Cloris' brighter eyes was hurled.

In a lone thicket made for love,
Silent as yielding maid's consent,
She with a charming languishment,
Permits his force, yet gently strove;[5]
15 Her hands his bosom softly meet,
But not to put him back designed,
Rather to draw 'em on inclined:
Whilst he lay trembling at her feet,
Resistance 'tis in vain to show:
20 She wants[6] the power to say—*Ah! what d'ye do?*

Her bright eyes sweet and yet severe,
Where love and shame confusedly strive,
Fresh vigor to Lysander give;
And breathing faintly in his ear,
25 She cried—*Cease, cease—your vain desire,*
Or I'll call out—what would you do?
My dearer honor[7] *even to you*
I cannot, must not give—Retire,[8]

1. Based on the first half of a French poem titled "L'Occasion perdue recouverte," i.e., the lost chance recovered.
2. By desire moved.
3. I.e., the outside world seemed to encourage his love.
4. The sun.
5. Struggled.
6. Lacks.
7. Virginity.
8. Leave.

Or take this life, whose chiefest part
30 I gave you with the conquest of my heart.

But he as much unused to fear,
As he was capable of love,
The blessed minutes to improve[9]
Kisses her mouth, her neck, her hair;
35 Each touch her new desire alarms;
His burning, trembling hand he pressed
Upon her swelling snowy breast,
While she lay panting in his arms.
All her unguarded beauties lie
40 The spoils and trophies of the enemy.

And now without respect or fear
He seeks the object of his vows
(His love no modesty allows)
By swift degrees advancing—where
45 His daring hand that altar[1] seized,
Where gods of love do sacrifice:
That awful throne, that paradise
Where rage is calmed, and anger pleased;
That fountain where delight still flows,
50 And gives the universal world repose.

Her balmy lips encountering his,
Their bodies, as their souls, are joined;
Where both in transports unconfined
Extend themselves upon the moss.
55 Cloris half dead and breathless lay;
Her soft eyes cast a humid light
Such as divides the day and night;
Or falling stars, whose fires decay:
And now no signs of life she shows,
60 But what in short-breathed sighs returns and goes.

He saw how at her length she lay;
He saw her rising bosom bare;
Her loose thin robes, through which appear
A shape designed for love and play;
65 Abandoned by her pride and shame
She does her softest joys dispense,
Offering her virgin innocence
A victim to love's sacred flame;
While the o'er-ravished shepherd lies
70 Unable to perform the sacrifice.

Ready to taste a thousand joys,
The too transported hapless swain[2]
Found the vast pleasure turned to pain;

9. Use profitably. 2. Unfortunate lover.
1. I.e., her genitals.

Pleasure which too much love destroys:
75 The willing garments[3] by he laid,
And heaven all opened to his view.
Mad to possess, himself he threw
On the defenseless lovely maid.
But oh what envying god conspires
80 To snatch his power, yet leave him the desire!

Nature's support (without whose aid
She can no human being give)
Itself now wants the art[4] to live;
Faintness its slackened nerves invade:
85 In vain th'enragéd youth essayed
To call its fleeting vigor back;
No motion 'twill from motion take;
Excess of love his love betrayed:
In vain he toils, in vain commands:
90 The insensible fell weeping in his hand.

In this so amorous cruel strife,
Where love and fate were too severe,
The poor Lysander in despair
Renounced his reason with his life:
95 Now all the brisk and active fire
That should the nobler part[5] inflame
Served to increase his rage and shame,
And left no spark for new desire:
Not all her naked charms could move
100 Or calm that rage that had debauched[6] his love.

Cloris returning from the trance
Which love and soft desire had bred,
Her timorous hand she gently laid
(Or guided by design or chance)
105 Upon that fabulous Priapus,[7]
That potent god, as poets feign:[8]
But never did young shepherdess,
Gathering the fern upon the plain,
More nimbly draw her fingers back,
110 Finding beneath the verdant[9] leaves a snake,

Than Cloris her fair hand withdrew,
Finding that god of her desires
Disarmed of all his awful fires,
And cold as flowers bathed in the morning dew.
115 Who can the nymph's confusion guess?
The blood forsook the hinder place,
And strewed[1] with blushes all her face,

3. I.e., hers.
4. Lacks the ability.
5. His reason, but also his impotent phallus.
6. Corrupted.
7. I.e., his phallus (from Priapus, the always-erect

Greek god of fertility).
8. Claim; pretend falsely.
9. Green. "Nimbly": quickly.
1. Scattered, covered. "Hinder place": her genitals.

Which both disdain and shame expressed:
And from Lysander's arms she fled,
120 Leaving him fainting on the gloomy bed.

Like lightning through the grove she hies,
Or Daphne² from the Delphic god;
No print upon the grassy road
She leaves, to instruct pursuing eyes.
125 The wind that wantoned³ in her hair
And with her ruffled garments played,
Discovered⁴ in the flying maid
All that the gods e'er made, if fair.
So Venus, when her love was slain,⁵
130 With fear and haste flew o'er the fatal plain.

The nymph's resentments none but I
Can well imagine or condole:
But none can guess Lysander's soul,
But those who swayed⁶ his destiny.
135 His silent griefs swell up to storms,
And not one god his fury spares;
He cursed his birth, his fate, his stars;
But more the shepherdess's charms,
Whose soft bewitching influence
140 Had damned him to the hell of impotence.

1680

On Her Loving Two Equally

I

How strong does my passion flow,
Divided equally twixt two?
Damon had ne'er subdued my heart
Had not Alexis took his part;
5 Nor could Alexis powerful prove,¹
Without my Damon's aid, to gain my love.

II

When my Alexis present is,
Then I for Damon sigh and mourn;
But when Alexis I do miss,
10 Damon gains nothing but my scorn.
But if it chance they both are by,²
For both alike I languish, sigh, and die.

2. In Greek myth, a nymph who escapes the lecherous pursuit of the god Apollo by turning into a laurel tree.
3. Played wildly, frolicked.
4. Uncovered, displayed.
5. Adonis, slain by a boar. Venus is the Roman goddess of love.
6. Governed, directed; compare line 2. "Those": i.e., the gods.
1. Show himself.
2. Near.

III

Cure then, thou mighty wingéd god,[3]
This restless fever in my blood;
15 One golden-pointed dart[4] take back:
But which, O Cupid, wilt thou take?
If Damon's, all my hopes are crossed;[5]
Or that of my Alexis, I am lost.

1684

To the Fair Clarinda, Who Made Love to Me, Imagined More than Woman[1]

Fair lovely maid, or if that title be
Too weak, too feminine for nobler thee,
Permit a name that more approaches truth:
And let me call thee lovely charming youth.
5 This last will justify my soft complaint,[2]
While that[3] may serve to lessen my constraint;
And without blushes I the youth pursue,
When so much beauteous woman is in view.
Against thy charms we struggle but in vain;
10 With thy deluding form thou givest us pain,
While the bright nymph betrays us to the swain.[4]
In pity to our sex sure thou wert sent,
That we might love, and yet be innocent:[5]
For sure no crime[6] with thee we can commit;
15 Or if we should—thy form excuses it.
For who that gathers fairest flowers believes
A snake lies hid beneath the fragrant leaves.

Thou beauteous wonder of a different kind,
Soft Cloris with the dear Alexis[7] joined;
20 Whene'er the manly part of thee would plead[8]
Thou tempts us with the image of the maid,
While we the noblest passions[9] do extend
The love to Hermes, Aphrodite the friend.[1]

1688

3. Cupid, the Roman god of love.
4. According to myth, Cupid shot darts of lead and of gold at the hearts of lovers, corresponding to false and true love, respectively.
5. Blocked, ruined.
1. I.e., as a hermaphrodite, a union of male and female in one body.
2. Declaration of love. "This last": the title of youth (male).
3. "That": the title of maid (female).
4. A male shepherd. That is, her feminine beauty induces us to surrender to her masculine aggres-
siveness.
5. I.e., virginal.
6. Sexual transgression.
7. Conventional names in pastoral poetry for a shepherdess and shepherd.
8. I.e., beg for sexual favors.
9. Love and friendship, sharply distinguished in the 18th century.
1. I.e., friendship. The Greek messenger god (Hermes) and the Greek goddess of love (Aphrodite), had a son, Hermaphroditus, whose body merged with that of a nymph.

Oroonoko, or The Royal Slave[1]

I do not pretend, in giving you the history of this royal slave, to entertain my reader with the adventures of a feigned hero, whose life and fortunes fancy may manage at the poet's pleasure, not in relating the truth, desire to adorn it with any accidents but such as arrived in earnest to him. And it shall come simply into the world, recommended by its own proper merits and natural intrigues, there being enough of reality to support it, and to render it diverting, without the addition of invention.

I was myself an eyewitness to a great part of what you will find here set down, and what I could not be witness of, I received from the mouth of the chief actor in this history, the hero himself, who gave us the whole trans-actions of his youth; and though I shall omit for brevity's sake a thousand little accidents of his life, which, however pleasant to us, where history was scarce and adventures very rare, yet might prove tedious and heavy to my reader, in a world where he finds diversions for every minute, new and strange. But we who were perfectly charmed with the character of this great man were curious to gather every circumstance of his life.

The scene of the last part of his adventures lies in a colony in America called Surinam,[2] in the West Indies.

But before I give you the story of this gallant slave, 'tis fit I tell you the manner of bringing them to these new colonies, for those they make use of there are not natives of the place; for those we live with in perfect amity, without daring to command 'em, but on the contrary caress 'em with all the brotherly and friendly affection in the world, trading with 'em for their fish, venison, buffaloes,[3] skins, and little rarities; as marmosets, a sort of monkey as big as a rat or weasel but of a marvelous and delicate shape, and has face and hands like a human creature, and *cousheries*,[4] a little beast in the form and fashion of a lion, as big as a kitten, but so exactly made in all parts like that noble beast, that it is it in miniature. Then for little parakeetoes, great parrots, macaws, and a thousand other birds and beasts of wonderful and surprising forms, shapes, and colors. For skins of prodigious snakes, of which there are some threescore yards in length, as is the skin of one that may be seen at his Majesty's antiquaries'; where are also some rare flies[5] of amazing forms and colors, presented to 'em by myself, some as big as my fist, some less, and all of various excellencies, such as art cannot imitate. Then we trade for feathers which they order into all shapes, make themselves little short habits of 'em, and glorious wreaths for their heads, necks, arms and legs, whose tinctures are unconceivable. I had a set of these presented to me, and I gave 'em to the King's theater, and it was the dress of the Indian Queen,[6] infinitely admired by persons of quality, and were unimitable. Besides these, a thousand little knacks and rarities in nature, and some of

1. The text, prepared by Joanna Lipking, is based on the 1688 edition, the sole edition published during Behn's lifetime. The critical edition of G. C. Duchovnay (1971), which collates the four 17th-century editions, has been consulted.
2. A British sugar colony on the South American coast south of Venezuela, later Dutch Guiana.
3. Wild oxen of various species.

4. A name appearing in local descriptions, but the animal is not clearly identified; possibly the *cujara* (Portuguese), a swamp rodent known as the rice rat.
5. Butterflies.
6. The title character in the 1664 heroic play by Sir Robert Howard and John Dryden, which was noted for its lavish production. There are contem-

art, as their baskets, weapons, aprons, et cetera. We dealt with 'em with beads of all colors, knives, axes, pins and needles, which they used only as tools to drill holes with in their ears, noses, and lips, where they hang a great many little things, as long beads, bits of tin, brass, or silver beat thin, and any shining trinket. The beads they weave into aprons about a quarter of an ell long, and of the same breadth,[7] working them very prettily in flowers of several colors of beads; which apron they wear just before 'em, as Adam and Eve did the fig leaves, the men wearing a long stripe of linen which they deal with us for. They thread these beads also on long cotton threads and make girdles to tie their aprons to, which come twenty times or more about the waist, and then cross, like a shoulder belt, both ways, and round their necks, arms, and legs. This adornment, with their long black hair, and the face painted in little specks or flowers here and there, makes 'em a wonderful figure to behold.

Some of the beauties which indeed are finely shaped, as almost all are, and who have pretty features, are very charming and novel; for they have all that is called beauty, except the color, which is a reddish yellow; or after a new oiling, which they often use to themselves, they are of the color of a new brick, but smooth, soft, and sleek. They are extreme modest and bashful, very shy and nice[8] of being touched. And though they are all thus naked, if one lives forever among 'em there is not to be seen an indecent action or glance; and being continually used to see one another so unadorned, so like our first parents[9] before the Fall, it seems as if they had no wishes; there being nothing to heighten curiosity, but all you can see you see at once, and every moment see, and where there is no novelty there can be no curiosity. Not but I have seen a handsome young Indian dying for love of a very beautiful young Indian maid; but all his courtship was to fold his arms, pursue her with his eyes, and sighs were all his language; while she, as if no such lover were present, or rather, as if she desired none such, carefully guarded her eyes from beholding him, and never approached him but she looked down with all the blushing modesty I have seen in the most severe and cautious of our world. And these people represented to me an absolute idea of the first state of innocence, before man knew how to sin. And 'tis most evident and plain that simple Nature is the most harmless, inoffensive, and virtuous mistress. 'Tis she alone, if she were permitted, that better instructs the world than all the inventions of man. Religion would here but destroy that tranquillity they possess by ignorance, and laws would but teach 'em to know offense, of which now they have no notion. They once made mourning and fasting for the death of the English governor, who had given his hand to come on such a day to 'em and neither came nor sent, believing when once a man's word was passed, nothing but death could or should prevent his keeping it. And when they saw he was not dead, they asked him what name they had for a man who promised a thing he did not do. The governor told them, such a man was a liar, which was a word of infamy to a gentleman. Then one of 'em replied, "Governor, you are a liar, and guilty of that infamy." They have a native justice which knows no fraud, and they understand no

porary records of "speckled plumes" and feather headdresses.

7. About a foot square.

8. Shy, reluctant. "Extreme": extremely.

9. I.e., Adam and Eve, who put on fig leaves only after they ate the fruit of the tree of knowledge (Genesis 3.6–7).

vice or cunning, but when they are taught by the white men. They have plurality of wives, which, when they grow old, they serve those that succeed 'em, who are young, but with a servitude easy and respected; and unless they take slaves in war, they have no other attendants.

Those on that continent where I was had no king, but the oldest war captain was obeyed with great resignation. A war captain is a man who has led them on to battle with conduct[1] and success, of whom I shall have occasion to speak more hereafter, and of some other of their customs and manners, as they fall in my way.

With these people, as I said, we live in perfect tranquillity and good understanding, as it behooves us to do, they knowing all the places where to seek the best food of the country and the means of getting it, and for very small and unvaluable trifles, supply us with what 'tis impossible for us to get; for they do not only in the wood and over the savannas, in hunting, supply the parts of hounds, by swiftly scouring through those almost impassable places, and by the mere activity of their feet run down the nimblest deer and other eatable beasts; but in the water one would think they were gods of the rivers, or fellow citizens of the deep, so rare an art they have in swimming, diving, and almost living in water, by which they command the less swift inhabitants of the floods. And then for shooting, what they cannot take, or reach with their hands, they do with arrows, and so admirable an aim that they will split almost a hair; and at any distance that an arrow can reach, they will shoot down oranges and other fruit, and only touch the stalk with the dart's point, that they may not hurt the fruit. So that they being, on all occasions, very useful to us, we find it absolutely necessary to caress 'em as friends, and not to treat 'em as slaves; nor dare we do other, their numbers so far surpassing ours in that continent.

Those then whom we make use of to work in our plantations of sugar are Negroes, black slaves altogether, which are transported thither in this manner. Those who want slaves make a bargain with a master or captain of a ship and contract to pay him so much apiece, a matter of twenty pound a head for as many as he agrees for, and to pay for 'em when they shall be delivered on such a plantation. So that when there arrives a ship laden with slaves, they who have so contracted go aboard and receive their number by lot; and perhaps in one lot that may be for ten, there may happen to be three or four men, the rest women and children. Or be there more or less of either sex, you are obliged to be contented with your lot.

Coramantien,[2] a country of blacks so called, was one of those places in which they found the most advantageous trading for these slaves, and thither most of our great traders in that merchandise trafficked; for that nation is very warlike and brave, and having a continual campaign, being always in hostility with one neighboring prince or other, they had the fortune to take a great many captives; for all they took in battle were sold as slaves, at least those common men who could not ransom themselves. Of these slaves so taken, the general only has all the profit; and of these generals, our captains and masters of ships buy all their freights.

The King of Coramantien was himself a man of a hundred and odd years

1. Aptitude for leadership.
2. Until 1665, a fortified British trading station on the Gold Coast of Africa, in modern-day Ghana. Persons transported from the region were called Cormantines and impressed many European observers by their beauty and bearing, their fierceness in war, and their extreme dignity in captivity or under torture.

old, and had no son, though he had many beautiful black wives; for most certainly there are beauties that can charm of that color. In his younger years he had had many gallant men to his sons, thirteen of which died in battle, conquering when they fell; and he had only left him for his successor one grandchild, son to one of these dead victors, who, as soon as he could bear a bow in his hand and a quiver at his back, was sent into the field, to be trained up by one of the oldest generals to war; where, from his natural inclination to arms and the occasions given him, with the good conduct of the old general, he became, at the age of seventeen, one of the most expert captains and bravest soldiers that ever saw the field of Mars.[3] So that he was adored as the wonder of all that world, and the darling of the soldiers. Besides, he was adorned with a native beauty so transcending all those of his gloomy[4] race that he struck an awe and reverence even in those that knew not his quality; as he did in me, who beheld him with surprise and wonder, when afterwards he arrived in our world.

He had scarce arrived at his seventeenth year, when fighting by his side, the general was killed with an arrow in his eye, which the Prince Oroonoko (for so was this gallant Moor[5] called) very narrowly avoided; nor had he, if the general, who saw the arrow shot, and perceiving it aimed at the Prince, had not bowed his head between, on purpose to receive it in his own body rather than it should touch that of the Prince, and so saved him.

'Twas then, afflicted as Oroonoko was, that he was proclaimed general in the old man's place; and then it was, at the finishing of that war, which had continued for two years, that the Prince came to court, where he had hardly been a month together from the time of his fifth year to that of seventeen; and 'twas amazing to imagine where it was he learned so much humanity; or to give his accomplishments a juster name, where 'twas he got that real greatness of soul, those refined notions of true honor, that absolute generosity, and that softness that was capable of the highest passions of love and gallantry, whose objects were almost continually fighting men, or those mangled or dead; who heard no sounds but those of war and groans. Some part of it we may attribute to the care of a Frenchman of wit and learning, who, finding it turn to very good account to be a sort of royal tutor to this young black, and perceiving him very ready, apt, and quick of apprehension, took a great pleasure to teach him morals, language, and science, and was for it extremely beloved and valued by him. Another reason was, he loved, when he came from war, to see all the English gentlemen that traded thither, and did not only learn their language but that of the Spaniards also, with whom he traded afterwards for slaves.

I have often seen and conversed with this great man, and been a witness to many of his mighty actions, and do assure my reader the most illustrious courts could not have produced a braver man, both for greatness of courage and mind, a judgment more solid, a wit more quick, and a conversation more sweet and diverting. He knew almost as much as if he had read much. He had heard of and admired the Romans; he had heard of the late civil wars in England, and the deplorable death of our great monarch,[6] and would

3. Roman god of war.
4. Of dark color.
5. Loosely used for any black-skinned person.
6. Charles I, beheaded in 1649 during England's civil war between the Royalists and Parliamentar-

ians. In 1688, this remark and others would have signaled Behn's ardent support of James II, the last of the Stuart kings, who would be forced into exile within the year.

discourse of it with all the sense and abhorrence of the injustice imaginable. He had an extreme good and graceful mien, and all the civility of a well-bred great man. He had nothing of barbarity in his nature, but in all points addressed himself as if his education had been in some European court.

This great and just character of Oroonoko gave me an extreme curiosity to see him, expecially when I knew he spoke French and English, and that I could talk with him. But though I had heard so much of him, I was as greatly surprised when I saw him as if I had heard nothing of him, so beyond all report I found him. He came into the room and addressed himself to me, and some other women, with the best grace in the world. He was pretty tall, but of a shape the most exact that can be fancied. The most famous statuary[7] could not form the figure of a man more admirably turned from head to foot. His face was not of that brown, rusty black which most of that nation are, but a perfect ebony or polished jet. His eyes were the most awful[8] that could be seen, and very piercing, the white of 'em being like snow, as were his teeth. His nose was rising and Roman, instead of African and flat; his mouth the finest shaped that could be seen, far from those great turned lips which are so natural to the rest of the Negroes. The whole proportion and air of his face was so noble and exactly formed that, bating[9] his color, there could be nothing in nature more beautiful, agreeable, and handsome. There was no one grace wanting that bears the standard of true beauty. His hair came down to his shoulders by the aids of art; which was by pulling it out with a quill and keeping it combed, of which he took particular care. Nor did the perfections of his mind come short of those of his person, for his discourse was admirable upon almost any subject; and whoever had heard him speak would have been convinced of their errors, that all fine wit is confined to the white men, especially those of Christendom, and would have confessed that Oroonoko was as capable even of reigning well, and of governing as wisely, had as great a soul, as politic maxims, and was as sensible[1] of power, as any prince civilized in the most refined schools of humanity and learning, or the most illustrious courts.

This prince, such as I have described him, whose soul and body were so admirably adorned, was (while yet he was in the court of his grandfather), as I said, as capable of love as 'twas possible for a brave and gallant man to be; and in saying that, I have named the highest degree of love, for sure, great souls are most capable of that passion.

I have already said, the old general was killed by the shot of an arrow, by the side of this prince, in battle, and that Oroonoko was made general. This old dead hero had one only daughter left of his race, a beauty that, to describe her truly, one need say only she was female to the noble male, the beautiful black Venus[2] to our young Mars, as charming in her person as he, and of delicate virtues. I have seen a hundred white men sighing after her, and making a thousand vows at her feet, all vain and unsuccessful. And she was, indeed, too great for any but a prince of her own nation to adore.

7. Sculptor.
8. Awe-inspiring, commanding profound respect.
9. Except for. The singling out of Africans with European looks or moral values is by no means unique to Behn; for example, Edward Long's 1774 *History of Jamaica* reports of the Cormantines that "their features are very different from the rest of the African Negroes, being smaller, and more of the European turn."
1. Cognizant, conscious. "Politic": shrewd, sagacious.
2. Roman goddess of love (in classical mythology, the lover of Mars).

Oroonoko coming from the wars (which were now ended), after he had made his court to his grandfather, he thought in honor he ought to make a visit to Imoinda, the daughter of his foster-father, the dead general; and to make some excuses to her, because his preservation was the occasion of her father's death; and to present her with those slaves that had been taken in this last battle, as the trophies of her father's victories. When he came, attended by all the young soldiers of any merit, he was infinitely surprised at the beauty of this fair queen of night, whose face and person was so exceeding all he had ever beheld; that lovely modesty with which she received him; that softness in her look, and sighs, upon the melancholy occasion of this honor that was done by so great a man as Oroonoko, and a prince of whom she had heard such admirable things: the awfulness[3] wherewith she received him, and the sweetness of her words and behavior while he stayed, gained a perfect conquest over his fierce heart, and made him feel the victor could be subdued. So that having made his first compliments, and presented her a hunded and fifty slaves in fetters, he told her with his eyes that he was not insensible of her charms; while Imoinda, who wished for nothing more than so glorious a conquest, was pleased to believe she understood that silent language of newborn love, and from that moment put on all her additions to beauty.

The prince returned to court with quite another humor than before; and though he did not speak much of the fair Imoinda, he had the pleasure to hear all his followers speak of nothing but the charms of that maid, insomuch that, even in the presence of the old king, they were extolling her and heightening, if possible, the beauties they had found in her. So that nothing else was talked of, no other sound was heard in every corner where there were whisperers, but "Imoinda! Imoinda!"

'Twill be imagined Oroonoko stayed not long before he made his second visit, nor, considering his quality, not much longer before he told her he adored her. I have often heard him say that he admired[4] by what strange inspiration he came to talk things so soft and so passionate, who never knew love, nor was used to the conversation[5] of women; but (to use his own words) he said, most happily some new and till then unknown power instructed his heart and tongue in the language of love, and at the same time, in favor of him, inspired Imoinda with a sense of his passion. She was touched with what he said, and returned it all in such answers as went to his very heart, with a pleasure unknown before. Nor did he use those obligations[6] ill that love had done him, but turned all his happy moments to the best advantage; and as he knew no vice, his flame aimed at nothing but honor, if such a distinction may be made in love; and especially in that country, where men take to themselves as many as they can maintain, and where the only crime and sin with woman is to turn her off, to abandon her to want, shame, and misery. Such ill morals are only practiced in Christian countries, where they prefer the bare name of religion, and, without virtue or morality, think that's sufficient. But Oroonoko was none of those professors, but as he had right notion of honor, so he made her such propositions as were not only and barely such; but contrary to the custom of his country, he made her vows

3. Reverence.
4. Marveled.

5. Company.
6. Benefits.

she should be the only woman he would possess while he lived; that no age or wrinkles should incline him to change, for her soul would be always fine and always young, and he should have an eternal idea in his mind of the charms she now bore, and should look into his heart for that idea when he could find it no longer in her face.

After a thousand assurances of his lasting flame, and her eternal empire over him, she condescended to receive him for her husband, or rather, received him as the greatest honor the gods could do her.

There is a certain ceremony in these cases to be observed, which I forgot to ask him how performed; but 'twas concluded on both sides that, in obedience to him, the grandfather was to be first made acquainted with the design, for they pay a most absolute resignation to the monarch, especially when he is a parent also.

On the other side, the old king, who had many wives and many concubines, wanted[7] not court flatterers to insinuate in his heart a thousand tender thoughts for this young beauty, and who represented her to his fancy as the most charming he had ever possessed in all the long race of his numerous years. At this character his old heart, like an extinguished brand, most apt to take fire, felt new sparks of love and began to kindle; and now grown to his second childhood, longed with impatience to behold this gay thing, with whom, alas! he could but innocently play. But how he should be confirmed she was this wonder, before he used his power to call her to court (where maidens never came, unless for the King's private use), he was next to consider; and while he was so doing, he had intelligence brought him that Imoinda was most certainly mistress to the Prince Oroonoko. This gave him some chagrin; however, it gave him also an opportunity, one day when the Prince was a-hunting, to wait on a man of quality, as his slave and attendant, who should go and make a present to Imoinda as from the Prince; he should then, unknown, see this fair maid, and have an opportunity to hear what message she would return the Prince for his present, and from thence gather the state of her heart and degree of her inclination. This was put in execution, and the old monarch saw, and burned. He found her all he had heard, and would not delay his happiness, but found he should have some obstacle to overcome her heart; for she expressed her sense of the present the Prince had sent her in terms so sweet, so soft and pretty, with an air of love and joy that could not be dissembled, insomuch that 'twas past doubt whether she love Oroonoko entirely. This gave the old king some affliction, but he salved it with this, that the obedience the people pay their king was not at all inferior to what they paid their gods; and what love would not oblige Imoinda to do, duty would compel her to.

He was therefore no sooner got to his apartment but he sent the royal veil to Imoinda, that is, the ceremony of invitation: he sends the lady he has a mind to honor with his bed a veil, with which she is covered, and secured for the King's use; and 'tis death to disobey, besides held a most impious disobedience.

'Tis not to be imagined the surprise and grief that seized this lovely maid at this news and sight. However, as delays in these cases are dangerous and

7. Lacked.

pleading worse than treason, trembling, and almost fainting, she was obliged to suffer herself to be covered and led away.

They brought her thus to court; and the King, who had caused a very rich bath to be prepared, was led into it, where he sat under a canopy, in state, to receive this longed-for virgin; whom he having commanded should be brought to him, they (after disrobing her) led her to the bath, and making fast the doors, left her to descend. The King, without more courtship, bade her throw off her mantle and come to his arms. But Imoinda, all in tears, threw herself on the marble, on the brink of the bath, and besought him to hear her. She told him, as she was a maid, how proud of the divine glory she should have been, of having it in her power to oblige her king; but as by the laws he could not, and from his royal goodness would not, take from any man his wedded wife, so she believed she should be the occasion of making him commit a great sin, if she did not reveal her state and condition, and tell him she was another's, and could not be so happy to be his.

The King, enraged at this delay, hastily demanded the name of the bold man that had married a woman of her degree without his consent. Imoinda, seeing his eyes fierce and his hands tremble (whether with age or anger, I know not, but she fancied the last), almost repented she had said so much, for now she feared the storm would fall on the Prince. She therefore said a thousand things to appease the raging of his flame, and to prepare him to hear who it was with calmness; but before she spoke, he imagined who she meant, but would not seem to do so, but commanded her to lay aside her mantle and suffer herself to receive his caresses; or by his gods, he swore that happy man whom she was going to name should die, though it were even Oroonoko himself. "Therefore," said he, "deny this marriage, and swear thyself a maid." "That," replied Imoinda, "by all our powers I do, for I am not yet known to my husband." " 'Tis enough," said the King; " 'tis enough to satisfy both my conscience and my heart." And rising from his seat, he went and led her into the bath, it being in vain for her to resist.

In this time the Prince, who was returned from hunting, went to visit his Imoinda, but found her gone; and not only so, but heard she had received the royal veil. This raised him to a storm, and in his madness they had much ado to save him from laying violent hands on himself. Force first prevailed, and then reason. They urged all to him that might oppose his rage, but nothing weighed so greatly with him as the King's old age, uncapable of injuring him with Imoinda. He would give way to that hope, because it pleased him most, and flattered best his heart. Yet this served not altogether to make him cease his different passions, which sometimes raged within him, and sometimes softened into showers. 'Twas not enough to appease him, to tell him his grandfather was old and could not that way injure him, while he retained that awful duty which the young men are used there to pay to their grave[8] relations. He could not be convinced he had no cause to sigh and mourn for the loss of a mistress he could not with all his strength and courage retrieve. And he would often cry, "O my friends! Were she in walled cities or confined from me in fortifications of the greatest strength, did enchantments or monsters detain her from me, I would venture through any hazard to free her. But here, in the arms of a feeble old man, my youth, my violent

8. Respected, influential.

love, my trade in arms, and all my vast desire of glory avail me nothing. Imoinda is as irrecoverably lost to me as if she were snatched by the cold arms of Death. Oh! she is never to be retrieved. If I would wait tedious years, till fate should bow the old king to his grave, even that would not leave me Imoinda free; but still that custom that makes it so vile a crime for a son to marry his father's wives or mistresses would hinder my happiness, unless I would either ignobly set an ill precedent to my successors, or abandon my country and fly with her to some unknown world, who never heard our story."

But it was objected to him that his case was not the same; for Imoinda being his lawful wife, by solemn contract, 'twas he was the injured man and might if he so pleased take Imoinda back, the breach of the law being on his grandfather's side; and that if he could circumvent him and redeem her from the Otan, which is the palace of the King's women, a sort of seraglio, it was both just and lawful for him so to do.

This reasoning had some force upon him, and he should have been entirely comforted, but for the thought that she was possessed by his grandfather. However, he loved so well that he was resolved to believe what most favored his hope, and to endeavor to learn from Imoinda's own mouth what only she could satisfy him in, whether she was robbed of that blessing which was only due to his faith and love. But as it was very hard to get a sight of the women (for no men ever entered into the Otan but when the King went to entertain himself with some one of his wives or mistresses, and 'twas death at any other time for any other to go in), so he knew not how to contrive to get a sight of her.

While Oroonoko felt all the agonies of love, and suffered under a torment the most painful in the world, the old king was not exempted from his share of affliction. He was troubled for having been forced by an irresistible passion to rob his son[9] of a treasure he knew could not but be extemely dear to him, since she was the most beautiful that ever had been seen, and had besides all the sweetness and innocence of youth and modesty, with a charm of wit surpassing all. He found that, however she was forced to expose her lovely person to his withered arms, she could only sigh and weep there, and think of Oroonoko; and oftentimes could not forbear speaking of him, though her life were, by custom, forfeited by owning her passion. But she spoke not of a lover only, but of a prince dear to him to whom she spoke, and of the praises of a man who, till now, filled the old man's soul with joy at every recital of his bravery, or even his name. And 'twas this dotage on our young hero that gave Imoinda a thousand privileges to speak of him without offending, and this condescension[1] in the old king that made her take the satisfaction of speaking of him so very often.

Besides, he many times inquired how the Prince bore himself; and those of whom he asked, being entirely slaves to the merits and virtues of the Prince, still answered what they thought conduced best to his service; which was to make the old king fancy that the Prince had no more interest in Imoinda, and had resigned her willingly to the pleasure of the King; that he diverted himself with his mathematicians, his fortifications, his officers, and his hunting.

This pleased the old lover, who failed not to report these things again to

9. I.e., grandson. 1. Gracious disregard of their dittering status.

Imoinda, that she might, by the example of her young lover, withdraw her heart, and rest better contented in his arms. But however she was forced to receive this unwelcome news, in all appearance with unconcern and content, her heart was bursting within, and she was only happy when she could get alone, to vent her griefs and moans with sighs and tears.

What reports of the Prince's conduct were made to the King, he thought good to justify as far as possibly he could by his actions, and when he appeared in the presence of the King, he showed a face not at all betraying his heart. So that in a little time, the old man being entirely convinced that he was no longer a lover of Imoinda, he carried him with him in his train to the Otan, often to banquet with his mistress. But as soon as he entered, one day, into the apartment of Imoinda with the King, at the first glance from her eyes, notwithstanding all his determined resolution, he was ready to sink in the place where he stood, and had certainly done so but for the support of Aboan, a young man who was next to him; which, with his change of countenance, had betrayed him, had the King chanced to look that way. And I have observed, 'tis a very great error, in those who laugh when one says a Negro can change color, for I have seen 'em as frequently blush, and look pale, and that as visibly as ever I saw in the most beautiful white. And 'tis certain that both these changes were evident, this day, in both these lovers. And Imoinda, who saw with some joy the change in the Prince's face, and found it in her own, strove to divert the King from beholding either by a forced caress, with which she met him, which was a new wound in the heart of the poor dying Prince. But as soon as the King was busied in looking on some fine thing of Imoinda's making, she had time to tell the Prince with her angry but love-darting eyes that she resented his coldness, and bemoaned her own miserable captivity. Nor were his eyes silent, but answered hers again, as much as eyes could do, instructed by the most tender and most passionate heart that ever loved. And they spoke so well and so effectually, as Imoinda no longer doubted but she was the only delight and the darling of that soul she found pleading in 'em its right of love, which none was more willing to resign than she. And 'twas this powerful language alone that in an instant conveyed all the thoughts of their souls to each other, that[2] they both found there wanted but opportunity to make them both entirely happy. But when he saw another door opened by Onahal, a former old wife of the King's who now had charge of Imoinda, and saw the prospect of a bed of state made ready with sweets and flowers for the dalliance of the King, who immediately led the trembling victim from his sight into that prepared repose, what rage, what wild frenzies seized his heart! which forcing to keep within bounds, and to suffer without noise, it became the more insupportable, and rent his soul with ten thousand pains. He was forced to retire to vent his groans, where he fell down on a carpet and lay struggling a long time, and only breathing now and then, "—O Imoinda!"

When Onahal had finished her necessary affair within, shutting the door, she came forth to wait till the King called; and hearing someone sighing in the other room, she passed on, and found the Prince in that deplorable condition, which she thought needed her aid. She gave him cordials, but all in vain, till finding the nature of his disease by his sighs and naming Imoinda.

2. So that.

She told him, he had not so much cause as he imagined to afflict himself, for if he knew the King so well as she did, he would not lose a moment in jealousy, and that she was confident that Imoinda bore, at this minute, part in his affliction. Aboan was of the same opinion, and both together persuaded him to reassume his courage; and all sitting down on the carpet, the Prince said so many obliging things to Onahal that he half persuaded her to be of his party. And she promised him she would thus far comply with his just desires, that she would let Imoinda know how faithful he was, what he suffered, and what he said.

This discourse lasted till the King called, which gave Oroonoko a certain satisfaction, and with the hope Onahal had made him conceive, he assumed a look as gay as 'twas possible a man in his circumstances could do; and presently after, he was called in with the rest who waited without. The King commanded music to be brought, and several of his young wives and mistresses came all together by his command to dance before him; where Imoinda performed her part with an air and grace so passing all the rest as her beauty was above 'em, and received the present ordained as a prize. The Prince was every moment more charmed with the new beauties and graces he beheld in this fair one. And while he gazed, and she danced, Onahal was retired to a window with Aboan.

This Onahal, as I said, was one of the cast[3] mistresses of the old king; and 'twas these (now past their beauty) that were made guardians or governants[4] to the new and the young ones, and whose business it was to teach them all those wanton arts of love with which they prevailed and charmed heretofore in their turn; and who now treated the triumphing happy ones with all the severity, as to liberty and freedom, that was possible, in revenge of those honors they rob them of; envying them those satisfactions, those gallantries and presents, that were once made to themselves, while youth and beauty lasted, and which they now saw pass regardless by, and were paid only to the bloomings. And certainly nothing is more afflicting to a decayed beauty than to behold in itself declining charms that were once adored, and to find those caresses paid to new beauties to which once she laid a claim; to hear 'em whisper as she passes by, "That once was a delicate woman." These abandoned ladies therefore endeavor to revenge all the despites[5] and decays of time on these flourishing happy ones. And 'twas this severity that gave Oroonoko a thousand fears he should never prevail with Onahal to see Imoinda. But, as I said, she was now retired to a window with Aboan.

This young man was not only one of the best quality,[6] but a man extremely well made and beautiful; and coming often to attend the King to the Otan, he had subdued the heart of the antiquated Onahal, which had not forgot how pleasant it was to be in love. And though she had some decays in her face, she had none in her sense and wit; she was there agreeable still, even to Aboan's youth, so that he took pleasure in entertaining her with discourses of love. He knew also that to make his court to these she-favorites was the way to be great, these being the persons that do all affairs and business at court. He had also observed that she had given him glances more tender and inviting than she had done to others of his quality. And now, when he saw

3. Cast-off.
4. Female teachers or chaperones.

5. Insults.
6. Rank.

that her favor could so absolutely oblige the Prince, he failed not to sigh in her ear and to look with eyes all soft upon her, and give her hope that she had made some impressions on his heart. He found her pleased at this, and making a thousand advances to him; but the ceremony ending and the King departing broke up the company for that day, and his conversation.

Aboan failed not that night to tell the Prince of his success, and how advantageous the service of Onahal might be to his amour with Imoinda. The Prince was overjoyed with this good news and besought him, if it were possible, to caress her so as to engage her entirely, which he could not fail to do, if he complied with her desires. "For then," said the Prince, "her life lying at your mercy, she must grant you the request you make in my behalf." Aboan understood him, and assured him he would make love[7] so effectually that he would defy the most expert mistress of the art to find out whether he dissembled it or had it really. And 'twas with impatience they waited the next opportunity of going to the Otan.

The wars came on, the time of taking the field approached, and 'twas impossible for the Prince to delay his going at the head of his army to encounter the enemy. So that every day seemed a tedious year till he saw his Imoinda, for he believed he could not live if he were forced away without being so happy. 'Twas with impatience, therefore, that he expected the next visit the King would make, and according to his wish, it was not long.

The parley of the eyes of these two lovers had not passed so secretly but an old jealous lover could spy it; or rather, he wanted not flatterers who told him they observed it. So that the Prince was hastened to the camp, and this was the last visit he found he should make to the Otan; he therefore urged Aboan to make the best of this last effort, and to explain himself so to Onahal that she, deferring her enjoyment of her young lover no longer, might make way for the Prince to speak to Imoinda.

The whole affair being agreed on between the Prince and Aboan, they attended the King, as the custom was, to the Otan, where, while the whole company was taken up in beholding the dancing and antic posture the women-royal made to divert the King, Onahal singled out Aboan, whom she found most pliable to her wish. When she had him where she believed she could not be heard, she sighed to him, and softly cried, "Ah, Aboan! When will you be sensible of my passion? I confess it with my mouth, because I would not give my eyes the lie; and you have but too much already perceived they have confessed my flame. Nor would I have you believe that because I am the abandoned mistress of a king, I esteem myself altogether divested of charms. No, Aboan; I have still a rest[8] of beauty enough engaging, and have learned to please too well not to be desirable. I can have lovers still, but will have none but Aboan." "Madam," replied the half-feigning youth, "you have already, by my eyes, found you can still conquer, and I believe 'tis in pity of me you condescend to this kind confession. But, Madam, words are used to be so small a part of our country courtship, that 'tis rare one can get so happy an opportunity as to tell one's heart, and those few minutes we have are forced to be snatched for more certain proofs of love than speaking and sighing: and such I languish for."

He spoke this with such a tone that she hoped it true, and could not

7. Woo. 8. Remnant.

forbear believing it; and being wholly transported with joy, for having sub-
dued the finest of all the King's subjects to her desires, she took from her
ears two large pearls and commanded him to wear 'em in his. He would have
refused 'em, crying, "Madam, these are not the proofs of your love that I
expect; 'tis opportunity, 'tis a lone hour only, that can make me happy." But
forcing the pearls into his hand, she whispered softly to him, "Oh! Do not
fear a woman's invention, when love sets her a-thinking." And pressing his
hand, she cried, "This night you shall be happy. Come to the gate of the
orange groves behind the Otan, and I will be ready, about midnight, to
receive you." 'Twas thus agreed, and she left him, that no notice might be
taken of their speaking together.

The ladies were still dancing, and the King, laid on a carpet, with a great
deal of pleasure was beholding them, especially Imoinda, who that day
appeared more lovely than ever, being enlivened with the good tidings Ona-
hal had brought her of the constant passion the Prince had for her. The
Prince was laid on another carpet at the other end of the room, with his eyes
fixed on the object of his soul; and as she turned or moved, so did they, and
she alone gave his eyes and soul their motions. Nor did Imoinda employ her
eyes to any other use than in beholding with infinite pleasure the joy she
produced in those of the Prince. But while she was more regarding him than
the steps she took, she chanced to fall, and so near him as that, leaping with
extreme force from the carpet, he caught her in his arms as she fell; and
'twas visible to the whole presence[9] the joy wherewith he received her. He
clasped her close to his bosom, and quite forgot that reverence that was due
to the mistress of a king, and that punishment that is the reward of a boldness
of this nature; and had not the presence of mind of Imoinda (fonder of his
safety than her own) befriended him, in making her spring from his arms
and fall into her dance again, he had at that instant met his death; for the
old king, jealous to the last degree, rose up in rage, broke all the diversion,
and led Imoinda to her apartment, and sent out word to the Prince to go
immediately to the camp, and that if he were found another night in court
he should suffer the death ordained for disobedient offenders.

You may imagine how welcome this news was to Oroonoko, whose unsea-
sonable transport and caress of Imoinda was blamed by all men that loved
him; and now he perceived his fault, yet cried that for such another moment,
he would be content to die.

All the Otan was in disorder about this accident; and Onahal was partic-
ularly concerned, because on the Prince's stay depended her happiness, for
she could no longer expect that of Aboan. So that ere they departed, they
contrived it so that the Prince and he should come both that night to the
grove of the Otan which was all of oranges and citrons, and that there they
should wait her orders.

They parted thus, with grief enough, till night, leaving the King in posses-
sion of the lovely maid. But nothing could appease the jealousy of the old
lover. He would not be imposed on, but would have it that Imoinda made a
false step on purpose to fall into Oroonoko's bosom, and that all things
looked like a design on both sides; and 'twas in vain she protested her inno-

9. Company.

cence. He was old and obstinate, and left her more than half assured that his fear was true.

The King going to his apartment sent to know where the Prince was, and if he intended to obey his command. The messenger returned and told him, he found the Prince pensive and altogether unpreparing for the campaign, that he lay negligently on the ground, and answered very little. This confirmed the jealousy of the King, and he commanded that they should very narrowly and privately watch his motions, and that he should not stir from his apartment but one spy or other should be employed to watch him. So that the hour approaching wherein he was to go to the citron grove, and taking only Aboan along with him, he leaves his apartment, and was watched to the very gate of the Otan where he was seen to enter, and where they left him, to carry back the tidings to the King.

Oroonoko and Aboan were no sooner entered but Onahal led the Prince to the apartment of Imoinda, who, not knowing anything of her happiness, was laid in bed. But Onahal only left him in her chamber, to make the best of his opportunity, and took her dear Aboan to her own, where he showed the heighth of complaisance for his prince, when, to give him an opportunity, he suffered himself to be caressed in bed by Onahal.

The Prince softly wakened Imoinda, who was not a little surprised with joy to find him there; and yet she trembled with a thousand fears. I believe he omitted saying nothing to this young maid that might persuade her to suffer him to seize his own, and take the rights of love; and I believe she was not long resisting those arms where she so longed to be; and having opportunity, night and silence, youth, love and desire, he soon prevailed, and ravished in a moment what his old grandfather had been endeavoring for so many months.

'Tis not to be imagined the satisfaction of these two young lovers; not the vows she made him that she remained a spotless maid till that night, and that what she did with his grandfather had robbed him of no part of her virgin honor, the gods in mercy and justice having reserved that for her plighted lord, to whom of right it belonged. And 'tis impossible to express the transports he suffered, while he listened to a discourse so charming from her loved lips, and clasped that body in his arms for whom he had so long languished; and nothing now afflicted him but his sudden departure from her; for he told her the necessity and his commands, but should depart satisfied in this, that since the old king had hitherto not been able to deprive him of those enjoyments which only belonged to him, he believed for the future he would be less able to injure him; so that abating the scandal of the veil, which was no otherwise so than that she was wife to another, he believed her safe, even in the arms of the King, and innocent; yet would he have ventured at the conquest of the world, and have given it all, to have had her avoided that honor of receiving the royal veil. 'Twas thus, between a thousand caresses, that both bemoaned the hard fate of youth and beauty, so liable to that cruel promotion. 'Twas a glory that could well have been spared here, though desired and aimed at by all the young females of that kingdom.

But while they were thus fondly employed, forgetting how time ran on, and that the dawn must conduct him far away from his only happiness, they heard a great noise in the Otan, and unusual voices of men; at which the Prince, starting from the arms of the frighted Imoinda, ran to a little battle-ax

he used to wear by his side, and having not so much leisure as to put on his habit, he opposed himself against some who were already opening the door; which they did with so much violence that Oroonoko was not able to defend it, but was forced to cry out with a commanding voice, "Whoever ye are that have the boldness to attempt to approach this apartment thus rudely, know that I, the Prince Oroonoko, will revenge it with the certain death of him that first enters. Therefore stand back, and know, this place is sacred to love and me this night; tomorrow 'tis the King's."

This he spoke with a voice so resolved and assured that they soon retired from the door, but cried, " 'Tis by the King's command we are come; and being satisfied by thy voice, O Prince, as much as if we had entered, we can report to the King the truth of all his fears, and leave thee to provide for thy own safety, as thou art advised by thy friends."

At these words they departed, and left the Prince to take a short and sad leave of his Imoinda, who, trusting in the strength of her charms, believed she should appease the fury of a jealous king by saying she was surprised, and that it was by force of arms he got into her apartment. All her concern now was for his life, and therefore she hastened him to the camp, and with much ado prevailed on him to go. Nor was it she alone that prevailed; Aboan and Onahal both pleaded, and both assured him of a lie that should be well enough contrived to secure Imoinda. So that at last, with a heart sad as death, dying eyes, and sighing soul, Oroonoko departed and took his way to the camp.

It was not long after the King in person came to the Otan, where, beholding Imoinda with rage in his eyes, he upbraided her wickedness and perfidy, and threatening her royal lover, she fell on her face at his feet, bedewing the floor with her tears and imploring his pardon for a fault which she had not with her will committed, as Onahal, who was also prostrate with her, could testify; that unknown to her, he had broke into her apartment, and ravished her. She spoke this much against her conscience, but to save her own life 'twas absolutely necessary she should feign this falsity. She knew it could not injure the Prince, he being fled to an army that would stand by him against any injuries that should assault him. However, this last thought of Imoinda's being ravished changed the measures of his revenge; and whereas before he designed to be himself her executioner, he now resolved she should not die. But as it is the greatest crime in nature amongst 'em to touch a woman after having been possessed by a son, a father, or a brother, so now he looked on Imoinda as a polluted thing, wholly unfit for his embrace; nor would he resign her to his grandson, because she had received the royal veil. He therefore removes her from the Otan, with Onahal; whom he put into safe hands, with order they should be both sold off as slaves to another country, either Christian or heathen; 'twas no matter where.

This cruel sentence, worse than death, they implored might be reversed; but their prayers were vain, and it was put in execution accordingly, and that with so much secrecy that none, either without or within the Otan, knew anything of their absence or their destiny.

The old king, nevertheless, executed this with a great deal of reluctancy; but he believed he had made a very great conquest over himself, when he had once resolved, and had performed what he resolved. He believed now that his love had been unjust, and that he could not expect the gods, or

Captain of the Clouds (as they call the unknown power), should suffer a better consequence from so ill a cause. He now begins to hold Oroonoko excused, and to say he had reason for what he did. And now everybody could assure the King how passionately Imoinda was beloved by the Prince; even those confessed it now, who said the contrary before his flame was abated. So that the King being old, and not able to defend himself in war, and having no sons of all his race remaining alive but only this, to maintain him on his throne; and looking on this as a man disobliged, first by the rape of his mistress, or rather wife; and now by depriving of him wholly of her, he feared, might make him desperate and do some cruel thing, either to himself or his old grandfather, the offender: he began to repent him extremely of the contempt he had, in his rage, put on Imoinda. Besides, he considered he ought in honor to have killed her for this offense, if it had been one. He ought to have had so much value and consideration for a maid of her quality as to have nobly put her to death, and not to have sold her like a common slave, the greatest revenge and the most disgraceful of any; and to which they a thousand times prefer death, and implore it, as Imoinda did, but could not obtain that honor. Seeing therefore it was certain that Oroonoko would highly resent this affront, he thought good to make some excuse for his rashness to him; and to that end he sent a messenger to the camp, with orders to treat with him about the matter, to gain his pardon, and to endeavor to mitigate his grief; but that by no means he should tell him she was sold, but secretly put to death, for he knew he should never obtain his pardon for the other.

When the messenger came, he found the Prince upon the point of engaging with the enemy; but as soon as he heard of the arrival of the messenger, he commanded him to his tent, where he embraced him and received him with joy; which was soon abated by the downcast looks of the messenger, who was instantly demanded the cause by Oroonoko, who, impatient of delay, asked a thousand questions in a breath, and all concerning Imoinda. But there needed little return, for he could almost answer himself of all he demanded, from his sighs and eyes. At last, the messenger casting himself at the Prince's feet, and kissing them with all the submission of a man that had something to implore which he dreaded to utter, he besought him to hear with calmness what he had to deliver to him, and to call up all his noble and heroic courage to encounter with his words, and defend himself against the ungrateful[1] things he must relate. Oroonoko replied, with a deep sigh and a languishing voice, "I am armed against their worst efforts—; for I know they will tell me, Imoinda is no more—and after that, you may spare the rest." Then, commanding him to rise, he laid himself on a carpet, under a rich pavilion, and remained a good while silent, and was hardly heard to sigh. When he was come a little to himself, the messenger asked him leave to deliver that part of his embassy which the Prince had not yet divined. And the Prince cried, "I permit thee—." Then he told him the affliction the old king was in, for the rashness he had committed in his cruelty to Imoinda; and how he deigned to ask pardon for his offense, and to implore the Prince would not suffer that loss to touch his heart too sensibly, which now all the gods could not restore him, but might recompense him in glory, which he

1. Offensive.

begged he would pursue; and that Death, that common revenger of all injuries, would soon even the account between him and a feeble old man.

Oroonoko bade him return his duty to his lord and master, and to assure him, there was no account of revenge to be adjusted between them; if there were, 'twas he was the aggressor, and that Death would be just and, maugre[2] his age, would see him righted; and he was contented to leave his share of glory to youths more fortunate and worthy of that favor from the gods. That henceforth he would never lift a weapon or draw a bow, but abandon the small remains of his life to sighs and tears, and the continual thoughts of what his lord and grandfather had thought good to send out of the world, with all that youth, that innocence, and beauty.

After having spoken this, whatever his greatest officers and men of the best rank could do, they could not raise him from the carpet, or persuade him to action and resolutions of life; but commanding all to retire, he shut himself into his pavilion all that day, while the enemy was ready to engage; and wondering at the delay, the whole body of the chief of the army then addressed themselves to him, and to whom they had much ado to get admittance. They fell on their faces at the foot of his carpet, where they lay and besought him with earnest prayers and tears to lead 'em forth to battle, and not let the enemy take advantages of them; and implored him to have regard to his glory, and to the world, that depended on his courage and conduct. But he made no other reply to all their supplications but this, that he had now no more business for glory; and for the world, it was a trifle not worth his care. "Go," continued he, sighing, "and divide it amongst you; and reap with joy what you so vainly prize, and leave me to my more welcome destiny."

They then demanded what they should do, and whom he would constitute in his room,[3] that the confusion of ambitious youth and power might not ruin their order and make them a prey to the enemy. He replied, he would not give himself the trouble—; but wished 'em to choose the bravest man amongst 'em, let his quality or birth be what it would. "For, O my friends!" said he, "it is not titles make men brave or good, or birth that bestows courage and generosity, or makes the owner happy. Believe this, when you behold Oroonoko, the most wretched and abandoned by fortune of all the creation of the gods." So turning himself about, he would make no more reply to all they could urge or implore.

The army, beholding their officers return unsuccessful, with sad faces and ominous looks that presaged no good luck, suffered a thousand fears to take possession of their hearts, and the enemy to come even upon 'em, before they would provide for their safety by any defense; and though they were assured by some, who had a mind to animate 'em, that they should be immediately headed by the Prince, and that in the meantime Aboan had orders to command as general, yet they were so dismayed for want of that great example of bravery that they could make but a very feeble resistance; and at last downright fled before the enemy, who pursued 'em to the very tents, killing 'em. Nor could all Aboan's courage, which that day gained him immortal glory, shame 'em into a manly defense of themselves. The guards that were left behind about the Prince's tent, seeing the soldiers flee before the enemy and scatter themselves all over the plain, in great disorder, made such out-

2. In spite of. Oroonoko is saying that he will die 3. Set in authority in his place.
first.

cries as roused the Prince from his amorous slumber, in which he had remained buried for two days without permitting any sustenance to approach him. But in spite of all his resolutions, he had not the constancy of grief to that degree, as to make him insensible of the danger of his army; and in that instant he leaped from his couch and cried, "—Come, if we must die, let us meet Death the noblest way; and 'twill be more like Oroonoko to encounter him at an army's head, opposing the torrent of a conquering foe, than lazily on a couch to wait his lingering pleasure, and die every moment by a thousand wrecking[4] thoughts; or be tamely taken by an enemy, and led a whining, lovesick slave to adorn the triumphs of Jamoan, that young victor, who already is entered beyond the limits I had prescribed him."

While he was speaking, he suffered his people to dress him for the field, and sallying out of his pavilion, with more life and vigor in his countenance than ever he showed, he appeared like some divine power descended to save his country from destruction; and his people had purposely put on him all things that might make him shine with most splendor, to strike a reverend awe into the beholders. He flew into the thickest of those that were pursuing his men, and being animated with despair, he fought as if he came on purpose to die, and did such things as will not be believed that human strength could perform, and such as soon inspired all the rest with new courage and new order. And now it was that they began to fight indeed, and so as if they would not be outdone even by their adored hero; who, turning the tide of the victory, changing absolutely the fate of the day, gained an entire conquest; and Oroonoko having the good fortune to single out Jamoan, he took him prisoner with his own hand, having wounded him almost to death.

This Jamoan afterwards became very dear to him, being a man very gallant and of excellent graces and fine parts; so that he never put him amongst the rank of captives, as they used to do, without distinction, for the common sale or market; but kept him in his own court, where he retained nothing of the prisoner but the name, and returned no more into his own country, so great an affection he took for Oroonoko; and by a thousand tales and adventures of love and gallantry flattered[5] his disease of melancholy and languishment, which I have often heard him say had certainly killed him, but for the conversation of this prince and Aboan, and the French governor he had from his childhood, of whom I have spoken before, and who was a man of admirable wit, great ingenuity and learning, all which he had infused into his young pupil. This Frenchman was banished out of his own country for some heretical notions he held, and though he was a man of very little religion, he had admirable morals and a brave soul.

After the total defeat of Jamoan's army, which all fled, or were left dead upon the place, they spent some time in the camp, Oroonoko choosing rather to remain a while there in his tents than enter into a palace or live in a court where he had so lately suffered so great a loss. The officers, therefore, who saw and knew his cause of discontent, invented all sorts of diversions and sports to entertain their prince; so that what with those amusements abroad and others at home, that is, within their tents, with the persuasions, arguments, and care of his friends and servants that he more peculiarly prized, he wore off in time a great part of that chagrin[6] and torture of despair which

4. Racking.
5. Soothed.

6. Melancholy.

the first efforts of Imoinda's death had given him. Insomuch as having received a thousand kind embassies from the King, and invitations to return to court, he obeyed, though with no little reluctancy; and when he did so, there was a visible change in him, and for a long time he was much more melancholy than before. But time lessens all extremes, and reduces 'em to mediums and unconcern; but no motives or beauties, though all endeavored it, could engage him in any sort of amour, though he had all the invitations to it, both from his own youth and others' ambitions and designs.

Oroonoko was no sooner returned from this last conquest, and received at court with all the joy and magnificence that could be expressed to a young victor, who was not only returned triumphant but beloved like a deity, when there arrived in the port an English ship.

This person[7] had often before been in these countries and was very well known to Oroonoko, with whom he had trafficked for slaves, and had used to do the same with his predecessors.

This commander was a man of a finer sort of address and conversation, better bred and more engaging than most of that sort of men are, so that he seemed rather never to have been bred out of a court than almost all his life at sea. This captain therefore was always better received at court than most of the traders to those countries were; and especially by Oroonoko, who was more civilized, according to the European mode, than any other had been, and took more delight in the white nations, and above all men of parts and wit. To this captain he sold abundance of his slaves, and for the favor and esteem he had for him, made him many presents, and obliged him to stay at court as long as possibly he could. Which the captain seemed to take as a very great honor done him, entertaining the Prince every day with globes and maps, and mathematical discourses and instruments; eating, drinking, hunting, and living with him with so much familiarity that it was not to be doubted but he had gained very greatly upon the heart of this gallant young man. And the captain, in return of all these mighty favors, besought the Prince to honor his vessel with his presence, some day or other, to dinner, before he should set sail; which he condescended to accept, and appointed his day. The captain, on his part, failed not to have all things in a readiness, in the most magnificent order he could possibly. And the day being come, the captain in his boat, richly adorned with carpets and velvet cushions, rowed to the shore to receive the Prince, with another longboat where was placed all his music and trumpets, with which Oroonoko was extremely delighted; who met him on the shore attended by his French governor, Jamoan, Aboan, and about a hundred of the noblest of the youths of the court. And after they had first carried the Prince on board, the boats fetched the rest off; where they found a very splendid treat, with all sorts of fine wines, and were as well entertained as 'twas possible in such a place to be.

The Prince, having drunk hard of punch and several sorts of wine, as did all the rest (for great care was taken they should want nothing of that part of the entertainment), was very merry, and in great admiration of the ship, for he had never been in one before; so that he was curious of beholding every place where he decently might descend. The rest, no less curious, who were not quite overcome with drinking, rambled at their pleasure fore and

7. The ship's captain.

aft, as their fancies guided 'em. So that the captain, who had well laid his design before, gave the word, and seized on all his guests; they clapping great irons suddenly on the Prince, when he was leaped down in the hold to view that part of the vessel, and locking him fast down, secured him. The same treachery was used to all the rest; and all in one instant, in several places of the ship, were lashed fast in irons, and betrayed to slavery. That great design over, they set all hands to work to hoise[8] sail; and with as treacherous and fair a wind, they made from the shore with this innocent and glorious prize, who thought of nothing less than such an entertainment.

Some have commended this act as brave in the captain; but I will spare my sense of it, and leave it to my reader to judge as he pleases.

It may be easily guessed in what manner the Prince resented this indignity, who may be best resembled to a lion taken in a toil; so he raged, so he struggled for liberty, but all in vain; and they had so wisely managed his fetters that he could not use a hand in his defense, to quit himself of a life that would by no means endure slavery, nor could he move from the place where he was tied to any solid part of the ship, against which he might have beat his head, and have finished his disgrace that way. So that being deprived of all other means, he resolved to perish for want of food. And pleased at last with that thought, and toiled and tired by rage and indignation, he laid himself down, and sullenly resolved upon dying, and refused all things that were brought him.

This did not a little vex the captain, and the more so because he found almost all of 'em of the same humor; so that the loss of so many brave slaves, so tall and goodly to behold, would have been very considerable. He therefore ordered one to go from him (for he would not be seen himself) to Oroonoko, and to assure him he was afflicted for having rashly done so unhospitable a deed, and which could not be now remedied, since they were far from shore; but since he resented it in so high a nature, he assured him he would revoke his resolution, and set both him and his friends ashore on the next land they should touch at; and of this the messenger gave him his oath, provided he would resolve to live. And Oroonoko, whose honor was such as he never had violated a word in his life himself, much less a solemn asseveration, believed in an instant what this man said, but replied, he expected for a confirmation of this to have his shameful fetters dismissed. This demand was carried to the captain, who returned him answer that the offense had been so great which he had put upon the Prince that he durst not trust him with liberty while he remained in the ship, for fear lest by a valor natural to him, and a revenge that would animate that valor, he might commit some outrage fatal to himself and the King his master, to whom his vessel did belong. To this Oroonoko replied, he would engage his honor to behave himself in all friendly order and manner, and obey the command of the captain, as he was lord of the King's vessel and general of those men under his command.

This was delivered to the still doubting captain, who could not resolve to trust a heathen, he said, upon his parole,[9] a man that had no sense or notion of the God that he worshipped. Oroonoko then replied, he was very sorry to hear that the captain pretended to the knowledge and worship of any gods who had taught him no better principles than not to credit as he would be

8. Hoist. 9. Word of honor.

credited; but they told him the difference of their faith occasioned that distrust. For the captain had protested to him upon the word of a Christian, and sworn in the name of a great god, which if he should violate, he would expect eternal torment in the world to come. "Is that all the obligation he has to be just to his oath?" replied Oroonoko. "Let him know I swear by my honor; which to violate, would not only render me contemptible and despised by all brave and honest men, and so give myself perpetual pain, but it would be eternally offending and diseasing all mankind, harming, betraying, circumventing and outraging all men; but punishments hereafter are suffered by one's self, and the world takes no cognizances whether this god have revenged 'em or not, 'tis done so secretly and deferred so long. While the man of no honor suffers every moment the scorn and contempt of the honester world, and dies every day ignominiously in his fame, which is more valuable than life. I speak not this to move belief, but to show you how you mistake, when you imagine that he who will violate his honor will keep his word with his gods." So turning from him with a disdainful smile, he refused to answer him, when he urged him to know what answer he should carry back to his captain; so that he departed without saying any more.

The captain pondering and consulting what to do, it was concluded that nothing but Oroonoko's liberty would encourage any of the rest to eat, except the Frenchman, whom the captain could not pretend to keep prisoner, but only told him he was secured because he might act something in favor of the Prince, but that he should be freed as soon as they came to land. So that they concluded it wholly necessary to free the Prince from his irons, that he might show himself to the rest; that they might have an eye upon him, and that they could not fear a single man.

This being resolved, to make the obligation the greater, the captain himself went to Oroonoko; where after many compliments, and assurances of what he had already promised, he receiving from the Prince his parole and his hand for his good behavior, dismissed his irons and brought him to his own cabin; where after having treated and reposed him a while, for he had neither eat[1] nor slept in four days before, he besought him to visit those obstinate people in chains, who refused all manner of sustenance, and entreated him to oblige 'em to eat, and assure 'em of their liberty the first opportunity.

Oroonoko, who was too generous not to give credit to his words, showed himself to his people, who were transported with excess of joy at the sight of their darling prince, falling at his feet and kissing and embracing 'em, believing, as some divine oracle, all he assured 'em. But he besought 'em to bear their chains with that bravery that became those whom he had seen act so nobly in arms; and that they could not give him greater proofs of their love and friendship, since 'twas all the security the captain (his friend) could have, against the revenge, he said, they might possibly justly take for the injuries sustained by him. And they all with one accord assured him, they could not suffer enough, when it was for his repose and safety.

After this they no longer refused to eat, but took what was brought 'em, and were pleased with their captivity, since by it they hoped to redeem the Prince, who, all the rest of the voyage, was treated with all the respect due to his birth, though nothing could divert his melancholy; and he would often

1. The past form of *eat*.

sigh for Imoinda, and think this a punishment due to his misfortune, in having left that noble maid behind him that fatal night, in the Otan, when he fled to the camp.

Possessed with a thousand thoughts of past joys with this fair young person, and a thousand griefs for her eternal loss, he endured a tedious voyage, and at last arrived at the mouth of the river of Surinam, a colony belonging to the King of England, and where they were to deliver some part of their slaves. There the merchants and gentlemen of the country going on board to demand those lots of slaves they had already agreed on, and, amongst those, the overseers of those plantations where I then chanced to be, the captain, who had given the word, ordered his men to bring up those noble slaves in fetters whom I have spoken of; and havin' put 'em some in one and some in other lots, with women and children (which they call pickaninnies), they sold 'em off as slaves to several merchants and gentlemen; not putting any two in one lot, because they would separate 'em far from each other, not daring to trust 'em together, lest rage and courage should put 'em upon contriving some great action, to the ruin of the colony.

Oroonoko was first seized on, and sold to our overseer, who had the first lot, with seventeen more of all sorts and sizes, but not one of quality with him. When he saw this, he found what they meant, for, as I said, he understood English pretty well; and being wholly unarmed and defenseless, so as it was in vain to make any resistance, he only beheld the captain with a look all fierce and disdainful, upbraiding him with eyes that forced blushes on his guilty cheeks; he only cried, in passing over the side of the ship, "Farewell, sir. 'Tis worth my suffering, to gain so true a knowledge both of you and of your gods by whom you swear." And desiring those that held him to forbear their pains, and telling 'em he would make no resistance, he cried, "Come, my fellow slaves; let us descend, and see if we can meet with more honor and honesty in the next world we shall touch upon." So he nimbly leaped into the boat, and showing no more concern, suffered himself to be rowed up the river with his seventeen companions.

The gentleman that bought him was a young Cornish gentleman whose name was Trefry, a man of great wit and fine learning, and was carried into those parts by the Lord—, Governor,[2] to manage all his affairs. He reflecting on the last words of Oroonoko to the captain, and beholding the richness of his vest,[3] no sooner came into the boat but he fixed his eyes on him; and finding something so extraordinary in his face, his shape and mien, a greatness of look and haughtiness in his air, and finding he spoke English, had a great mind to be inquiring into his quality and fortune; which, though Oroonoko endeavored to hide, by only confessing he was above the rank of common slaves, Trefry soon found he was yet something greater than he confessed, and from that moment began to conceive so vast an esteem for him that he ever after loved him as his dearest brother, and showed him all the civilities due to so great a man.

Trefry was a very good mathematician and a linguist, could speak French and Spanish; and in the three days they remained in the boat (for so long were they going from the ship to the plantation) he entertained Oroonoko

2. Lord Willoughby of Parham (ca. 1613–1666), coproprietor of Surinam by royal grant. John Trefry was his plantation overseer.
3. An outer garment or robe.

so agreeably with his art and discourse, that he was no less pleased with Trefry than he was with the Prince; and he thought himself at least fortunate in this, that since he was a slave, as long as he would suffer himself to remain so, he had a man of so excellent wit[4] and parts for a master. So that before they had finished their voyage up the river, he made no scruple of declaring to Trefry all his fortunes, and most part of what I have here related, and put himself wholly into the hands of his new friend, whom he found resenting all the injuries were done him, and was charmed with all the greatness of his actions; which were recited with that modesty and delicate sense as wholly vanquished him, and subdued him to his interest. And he promised him on his word and honor, he would find the means to reconduct him to his own country again, assuring him, he had a perfect abhorrence of so dishonorable an action, and that he would sooner have died than have been the author of such a perfidy. He found the Prince was very much concerned to know what became of his friends, and how they took their slavery; and Trefry promised to take care about the inquiring after their condition, and that he should have an account of 'em.

Though, as Oroonoko afterwards said, he had little reason to credit the words of a *backearary*,[5] yet he knew not why, but he saw a kind of sincerity and awful truth in the face of Trefry; he saw an honesty in his eyes, and he found him wise and witty enough to understand honor; for it was one of his maxims, a man of wit could not be a knave or villain.

In their passage up the river they put in at several houses for refreshment, and ever when they landed, numbers of people would flock to behold this man; not but their eyes were daily entertained with the sight of slaves, but the fame of Oroonoko was gone before him, and all people were in admiration of his beauty. Besides, he had a rich habit on, in which he was taken, so different from the rest, and which the captain could not strip him of, because he was forced to surprise his person in the minute he sold him. When he found his habit made him liable, as he thought, to be gazed at the more, he begged Trefry to give him something more befitting a slave, which he did, and took off his robes. Nevertheless, he shone through all; and his osenbrigs (a sort of brown holland[6] suit he had on) could not conceal the graces of his looks and mien, and he had no less admirers than when he had his dazzling habit on. The royal youth appeared in spite of the slave, and people could not help treating him after a different manner, without designing it. As soon as they approached him they venerated and esteemed him; his eyes insensibly commanded respect, and his behavior insinuated it into every soul. So that there was nothing talked of but this young and gallant slave, even by those who yet knew not that he was a prince.

I ought to tell you that the Christians never buy any slaves but they give 'em some name of their own, their native ones being likely very barbarous and hard to pronounce; so that Mr. Trefry gave Oroonoko that of Caesar,[7] which name will live in that country as long as that (scarce more) glorious one of the great Roman; for 'tis most evident, he wanted[8] no part of the

4. Intelligence.
5. White person or master; a variant of *backra*, from an Ibo word transported with the slaves to Surinam and the Caribbean.
6. Coarse cotton or linen; sometimes called *osna-*

burg, after a German cloth-manufacturing town.
7. Julius Caesar (100–44 B.C.E.), statesman general, notable writer, and victor in Rome's civil war.
8. Lacked.

personal courage of that Caesar, and acted things as memorable, had they been done in some part of the world replenished with people and historians that might have given him his due. But his misfortune was to fall in an obscure world, that afforded only a female pen to celebrate his fame; though I doubt not but it had lived from others' endeavors, if the Dutch, who immediately after his time took that country,[9] had not killed, banished, and dispersed all those that were capable of giving the world this great man's life, much better than I have done. And Mr. Trefry, who designed it, died before he began it, and bemoaned himself for not having undertook it in time.

For the future, therefore, I must call Oroonoko Caesar, since by that name only he was known in our western world, and by that name he was received on shore at Parham House, where he was destined a slave. But if the King himself (God bless him) had come ashore, there could not have been greater expectations by all the whole plantation, and those neighboring ones, than was on ours at that time; and he was received more like a governor than a slave. Notwithstanding, as the custom was, they assigned him his portion of land, his house, and his business, up in the plantation. But as it was more for form than any design to put him to his task, he endured no more of the slave but the name, and remained some days in the house, receiving all visits that were made him, without stirring towards that part of the plantation where the Negroes were.

At last he would needs go view his land, his house, and the business assigned him. But he no sooner came to the houses of the slaves, which are like a little town by itself, the Negroes all having left work, but they all came forth to behold him, and found he was that prince who had, at several times, sold most of 'em to these parts; and from a veneration they pay to great men, especially if they know 'em, and from the surprise and awe they had at the sight of him, they all cast themselves at his feet, crying out in their language, "Live, O King! Long live, O King!" and kissing his feet, paid him even divine homage.

Several English gentlemen were with him; and what Mr. Trefry had told 'em was here confirmed, of which he himself before had no other witness than Caesar himself. But he was infinitely glad to find his grandeur confirmed by the adoration of all the slaves.

Caesar, troubled with their over-joy and over-ceremony, besought 'em to rise and to receive him as their fellow slave, assuring them he was no better. At which they set up with one accord a most terrible and hideous mourning and condoling, which he and the English had much ado to appease; but at last they prevailed with 'em, and they prepared all their barbarous music, and everyone killed and dressed something of his own stock (for every family has their land apart, on which, at their leisure times, they breed all eatable things), and clubbing it together,[1] made a most magnificent supper, inviting their *Grandee Captain,* their prince, to honor it with his presence; which he did, and several English with him; where they all waited on him, some playing, others dancing before him all the time, according to the manners of their several nations, and with unwearied industry endeavoring to please and delight him.

9. In 1667 the Dutch attacked and conquered Surinam, and England ceded it by treaty in exchange for New York.
1. Contributing jointly.

While they sat at meat Mr. Trefry told Caesar that most of these young slaves were undone in love with a fine she-slave, whom they had had about six months on their land. The Prince, who never heard the name of love without a sigh, nor any mention of it without the curiosity of examining further into that tale, which of all discourses was most agreeable to him, asked how they came to be so unhappy as to be all undone for one fair slave. Trefry, who was naturally amorous and loved to talk of love as well as any-body, proceeded to tell him, they had the most charming black that ever was beheld on their plantation, about fifteen or sixteen years old, as he guessed; that for his part, he had done nothing but sigh for her ever since she came, and that all the white beauties he had seen never charmed him so absolutely as this fine creature had done; and that no man, of any nation, ever beheld her that did not fall in love with her; and that she had all the slaves perpet-ually at her feet, and the whole country resounded with the fame of Clemene, "for so," said he, "we have christened her. But she denies us all with such a noble disdain, that 'tis a miracle to see that she, who can give such eternal desires, should herself be all ice and all unconcern. She is adorned with the most graceful modesty that ever beautified youth; the softest sigher—that, if she were capable of love, one would swear she languished for some absent happy man; and so retired, as if she feared a rape even from the god of day,[2] or that the breezes would steal kisses from her delicate mouth. Her task of work some sighing lover every day makes it his petition to perform for her, which she accepts blushing and with reluctancy, for fear he will ask her a look for a recompense, which he dares not presume to hope, so great an awe she strikes into the hearts of her admirers." "I do not wonder," replied the Prince, "that Clemene should refuse slaves, being as you say so beautiful, but wonder how she escapes those who can entertain her as you can do; or why, being your slave, you do not oblige her to yield." "I confess," said Trefry, "when I have, against her will, entertained her with love so long as to be transported with my passion, even above decency, I have been ready to make use of those advantages of strength and force nature has given me. But oh! she disarms me with that modesty and weeping, so tender and so moving that I retire, and thank my stars she overcame me." The company laughed at his civility to a slave, and Caesar only applauded the nobleness of his passion and nature, since that slave might be noble or, what was better, have true notions of honor and virtue in her. Thus passed they this night, after having received from the slaves all imaginable respect and obedience.

The next day, Trefry asked Caesar to walk, when the heat was allayed, and designedly carried him by the cottage of the fair slave, and told him she whom he spoke of last night lived there retired. "But," says he, "I would not wish you to approach, for I am sure you will be in love as soon as you behold her." Caesar assured him he was proof against all the charms of that sex, and that if he imagined his heart could be so perfidious to love again, after Imoinda, he believed he should tear it from his bosom. They had no sooner spoke, but a little shock dog[3] that Clemene had presented her, which she took great delight in, ran out; and she, not knowing anybody was there, ran to get it in again, and bolted out on those who were just speaking of her.

2. The sun.
3. A long-haired dog or poodle, especially associated with women of fashion.

When seeing them, she would have run in again, but Trefry caught her by the hand and cried, "Clemene, however you fly a lover, you ought to pay some respect to this stranger" (pointing to Caesar). But she, as if she had resolved never to raise her eyes to the face of a man again, bent 'em the more to the earth when he spoke, and gave the Prince the leisure to look the more at her. There needed no long gazing or consideration to examine who this fair creature was; he soon saw Imoinda all over her; in a minute he saw her face, her shape, her air, her modesty, and all that called forth his soul with joy at his eyes, and left his body destitute of almost life: it stood without motion, and for a minute knew not that it had a being; and I believe he had never come to himself, so oppressed he was with over-joy, if he had not met with this allay,[4] that he perceived Imoinda fall dead in the hands of Trefry. This awakened him, and he ran to her aid and caught her in his arms, where by degrees she came to herself; and 'tis needless to tell with what transports, what ecstasies of joy, they both a while beheld each other, without speaking; then snatched each other to their arms; then gaze again, as if they still doubted whether they possessed the blessing they grasped; but when they recovered their speech, 'tis not to be imagined what tender things they expressed to each other, wondering what strange fate had brought 'em together again. They soon informed each other of their fortunes, and equally bewailed their fate; but at the same time they mutually protested that even fetters and slavery were soft and easy, and would be supported with joy and pleasure, while they could be so happy to possess each other and to be able to make good their vows. Caesar swore he disdained the empire of the world while he could behold his Imoinda; and she despised grandeur and pomp, those vanities of her sex, when she could gaze on Oroonoko. He adored the very cottage where she resided, and said that little inch of the world would give him more happiness than all the universe could do; and she vowed it was a palace, while adorned with the presence of Oroonoko.

Trefry was infinitely pleased with this novel,[5] and found this Clemene was the fair mistress of whom Caesar had before spoke; and was not a little satisfied that heaven was so kind to the Prince as to sweeten his misfortunes by so lucky an accident; and leaving the lovers to themselves, was impatient to come down to Parham House (which was on the same plantation) to give me an account of what had happened. I was as impatient to make these lovers a visit, having already made a friendship with Caesar, and from his own mouth learned what I have related; which was confirmed by his Frenchman, who was set on shore to seek his fortunes, and of whom they could not make a slave, because a Christian, and he came daily to Parham Hill to see and pay his respects to his pupil prince. So that concerning and interesting myself in all that related to Caesar, whom I had assured of liberty as soon as the Governor arrived, I hasted presently to the place where the lovers were, and was infinitely glad to find this beautiful young slave (who had already gained all our esteems, for her modesty and her extraordinary prettiness) to be the same I had heard Caesar speak so much of. One may imagine then we paid her a treble respect; and though, from her being carved in fine flowers and birds all over her body, we took her to be of quality before, yet when we knew Clemene was Imoinda, we could not enough admire her.

4. Check; abatement of force. 5. Novel event or piece of news.

I had forgot to tell you that those who are nobly born of that country are so delicately cut and rased[6] all over the forepart of the trunk of their bodies, that it looks as if it were japanned, the works being raised light high point round the edges of the flowers. Some are only carved with a little flower or bird at the sides of the temples, as was Caesar; and those who are so carved over the body resemble our ancient Picts,[7] that are figured in the chronicles, but these carvings are more delicate.

From that happy day Caesar took Clemene for his wife, to the general joy of all people; and there was as much magnificence as the country would afford at the celebration of this wedding: and in a very short time after she conceived with child, which made Caesar ever adore her, knowing he was the last of his great race. This new accident made him more impatient of liberty, and he was every day treating with Trefry for his and Clemene's liberty, and offered either gold or a vast quantity of slaves, which should be paid before they let him go, provided he could have any security that he should go when his ransom was paid. They fed him from day to day with promises, and delayed him till the Lord Governor should come; so that he began to suspect them of falsehood, and that they would delay him till the time of his wife's delivery and make a slave of that too, for all the breed is theirs to whom the parents belong. This thought made him very uneasy, and his sullenness gave them some jealousies[8] of him; so that I was obliged, by some persons who feared a mutiny (which is very fatal sometimes in those colonies, that abound so with slaves that they exceed the whites in vast numbers), to discourse with Caesar, and to give him all the satisfaction I possibly could; they knew he and Clemene were scarce an hour in a day from my lodgings, that they eat with me, and that I obliged 'em in all things I was capable of. I entertained him with the lives of the Romans, and great men, which charmed him to my company, and her with teaching her all the pretty works[9] that I was mistress of, and telling her stories of nuns, and endeavoring to bring her to the knowledge of the true God. But of all discourses Caesar liked that the worst, and would never be reconciled to our notions of the Trinity,[1] of which he ever made a jest; it was a riddle, he said, would turn his brain to conceive, and one could not make him understand what faith was. However, these conversations failed not altogether so well to divert him that he liked the company of us women much above the men, for he could not drink, and he is but an ill companion in that country that cannot. So that obliging him to love us very well, we had all the liberty of speech with him, especially myself, whom he called his Great Mistress; and indeed my word would go a great way with him. For these reasons, I had opportunity to take notice to him that he was not well pleased of late as he used to be, was more retired and thoughtful; and told him I took it ill he should suspect we would break our words with him, and not permit both him and Clemene to return to his own kingdom, which was not so long a way but when he was once on his voyage he would quickly arrive there. He made me some answers that showed a doubt in him, which made me ask him what advantage it would be to doubt. It would but give us a fear of him, and possibly compel us to

6. Incised. The carving is likened to figured lac-quer-work in the Japanese style and to elaborate "high point" lace.
7. A North British people appearing in histories of England and Scotland.

8. Suspicions.
9. Decorative needlework or other handiwork.
1. The unity in a single godhead of the Father, the Son, and the Holy Spirit, a basic Christian tenet.

treat him so as I should be very loath to behold; that is, it might occasion his confinement. Perhaps this was not so luckily spoke of me, for I perceived he resented that word, which I strove to soften again in vain. However, he assured me that whatsoever resolutions he should take, he would act nothing upon the white people; and as for myself and those upon that plantation where he was, he would sooner forfeit his eternal liberty, and life itself, that lift his hand against his greatest enemy on that place. He besought me to suffer no fears upon his account, for he could do nothing that honor should not dictate; but he accused himself for having suffered slavery so long; yet he charged that weakness on Love alone, who was capable of making him neglect even glory itself, and for which now he reproaches himself every moment of the day. Much more to this effect he spoke, with an air impatient enough to make me know he would not be long in bondage; and though he suffered only the name of a slave, and had nothing of the toil and labor of one, yet that was sufficient to render him uneasy; and he had been too long idle, who used to always in action and in arms. He had a spirit all rough and fierce, and that could not be tamed to lazy rest; and though all endeavors were used to exercise himself in such actions and sports as this world afforded, as running, wrestling, pitching the bar,[2] hunting and fishing, chasing and killing tigers[3] of a monstrous size, which this continent affords in abundance, and wonderful snakes, such as Alexander is reported to have encountered at the river of Amazons,[4] and which Caesar took great delight to overcome, yet these were not actions great enough for his large soul, which was still panting after more renowned action.

Before I parted that day with him, I got, with much ado, a promise from him to rest yet a little longer with patience, and wait the coming of the Lord Governor, who was every day expected on our shore; he assured me he would, and this promise he desired me to know was given perfectly in complaisance to me, in whom he had an entire confidence.

After this, I neither thought it convenient to trust him much out of our view, nor did the country, who feared him; but with one accord it was advised to treat him fairly, and oblige him to remain within such a compass, and that he should be permitted as seldom as could be to go up to the plantations of the Negroes or, if he did, to be accompanied by some that should be rather in appearance attendants than spies. This care was for some time taken, and Caesar looked upon it as a mark of extraordinary respect, and was glad his discontent had obliged 'em to be more observant[5] to him. He received new assurance from the overseer, which was confirmed to him by the opinion of all the gentlemen of the country, who made their court to him. During this time that we had his company more frequently than hitherto we had had, it may not be unpleasant to relate to you the diversions we entertained him with, or rather he us.

My stay was to be short in the country, because my father died at sea, and never arrived to possess the honor was designed him (which was lieutenant general of six and thirty islands, besides the continent[6] of Surinam) nor the

2. A game in which players compete in throwing a heavy bar or rod.
3. Wild cats, including the South American jaguar and cougar.
4. The Macedonian king Alexander the Great (356–323 B.C.E.) is supposed to have encountered

both snakes and Amazons (warrior women) in a campaign against India.
5. Showing more respect.
6. "Land not disjoined by the sea from other lands" (Johnson's *Dictionary*), i.e., the mainland portion.

advantages he hoped to reap by them; so that though we were obliged to continue on our voyage, we did not intend to stay upon the place. Though, in a word, I must say thus much of it, that certainly had his late Majesty, of sacred memory, but seen and known what a vast and charming world he had been master of in that continent, he would never have parted so easily with it to the Dutch. 'Tis a continent whose vast extent was never yet known, and may contain more noble earth than all the universe besides, for, they say, it reaches from east to west, one way as far as China and another to Peru. It affords all things both for beauty and use; 'tis there eternal spring, always the very months of April, May, and June; the shades are perpetual, the trees bearing at once all degrees of leaves and fruit, from blooming buds to ripe autumn: groves of oranges, lemons, citrons, figs, nutmegs, and noble aromatics, continually bearing their fragrancies. The trees appearing all like nosegays adorned with flowers of different kinds; some are all white, some purple, some scarlet, some blue, some yellow; bearing, at the same time, ripe fruit and blooming young, or producing every day new. The very wood of all these trees has an intrinsic value above common timber, for they are, when cut, of different colors, glorious to behold, and bear a price considerable, to inlay withal. Besides this they yield rich balm and gums, so that we make our candles of such an aromatic substance as does not only give a sufficient light, but, as they burn, they cast their perfumes all about. Cedar is the common firing, and all the houses are built with it. The very meat we eat, when set on the table, if it be native, I mean of the country, perfumes the whole room; especially a little beast called an armadilly, a thing which I can liken to nothing so well as a rhinoceros; 'tis all in white armor, so jointed that it moves as well in it as if it had nothing on; this beast is about the bigness of a pig of six weeks old. But it were endless to give an account of all the diverse wonderful and strange things that country affords, and which we took a very great delight to go in search of, though those adventures are oftentimes fatal and at least dangerous. But while we had Caesar in our company on these designs we feared no harm, nor suffered any.

As soon as I came into the country, the best house in it was presented me, called St. John's Hill. It stood on a vast rock of white marble, at the foot of which the river ran a vast depth down, and not to be descended on that side; the little waves still dashing and washing the foot of this rock made the softest murmurs and purlings in the world; and the opposite bank was adorned with such vast quantities of different flowers eternally blowing,[7] and every day and hour new, fenced behind 'em with lofty trees of a thousand rare forms and colors, that the prospect was the most ravishing that fancy can create. On the edge of this white rock, towards the river, was a walk or grove of orange and lemon trees, about half the length of the Mall[8] here, whose flowery and fruit-bearing branches met at the top and hindered the sun, whose rays are very fierce there, from entering a beam into the grove; and the cool air that came from the river made it not only fit to entertain people in, at all the hottest hours of the day, but refreshed the sweet blossoms and made it always sweet and charming; and sure the whole globe of the world cannot show so delightful a place as this grove was. Not all the gardens

7. Blooming.
8. Fashionable walk in St. James's Park in London.

of boasted Italy can produce a shade to outvie this, which nature had joined with art to render so exceeding fine; and 'tis a marvel to see how such vast trees, as big as English oaks, could take footing on so solid a rock and in so little earth as covered that rock; but all things by nature there are rare, delightful, and wonderful. But to our sports.

Sometimes we would go surprising,[9] and in search of young tigers in their dens, watching when the old ones went forth to forage for prey; and oftentimes we have been in great danger and have fled apace for our lives when surprised by the dams. But once, above all other times, we went on this design, and Caesar was with us, who had no sooner stolen a young tiger from her nest but, going off, we encountered the dam, bearing a buttock of a cow which he[1] had torn off with his mighty paw, and going with it towards his den. We had only four women, Caesar, and an English gentleman, brother to Harry Martin, the great Oliverian;[2] we found there was no escaping this enraged and ravenous beast. However, we women fled as fast as we could from it; but our heels had not saved our lives if Caesar had not laid down his cub, when he found the tiger quit her prey to make the more speed towards him, and taking Mr. Martin's sword, desired him to stand aside, or follow the ladies. He obeyed him, and Caesar met this monstrous beast of might, size, and vast limbs, who came with open jaws upon him; and fixing his awful stern eyes full upon those of the beast, and putting himself into a very steady and good aiming posture of defense, ran his word quite through his breast down to his very heart, home to the hilt of the sword. The dying beast stretched forth her paw, and going to grasp his thigh, surprised with death in that very moment, did him no other harm than fixing her long nails in his flesh very deep, feebly wounded him, but could not grasp the flesh to tear off any. When he had done this, he hallooed to us to return, which, after some assurance of his victory, we did, and found him lugging out the sword from the bosom of the tiger, who was laid in her blood on the ground; he took up the cub, and with an unconcern that had nothing of the joy or gladness of a victory, he came and laid the whelp at my feet. We all extremely wondered at his daring, and at the bigness of the beast, which was about the heighth of a heifer but of mighty, great, and strong limbs.

Another time, being in the woods, he killed a tiger which had long infested that part, and borne away abundance of sheep and oxen, and other things that were for the support of those to whom they belonged; abundance of people assailed this beast, some affirming they had shot her with several bullets quite through the body at several times, and some swearing they shot her through the very heart, and they believed she was a devil rather than a mortal thing. Caesar had often said he had a mind to encounter this monster, and spoke with several gentlemen who had attempted her, one crying, "I shot her with so many poisoned arrows," another with his gun in this part of her, and another in that; so that he, remarking all these places where she was shot, fancied still he should overcome her by giving her another sort of a wound than any had yet done; and one day said (at the table), "What trophies and garlands, ladies, will you make me, if I bring you home the heart of this

9. A military term for making sudden raids.
1. The very jarring mixture of pronouns in the two accounts of the tigers may perhaps suggest a reluctance to use a feminine pronoun in moments of extreme violence. The first account was left uncorrected in all four 17th-century editions.
2. Supporter of Oliver Cromwell, leader of the Parliamentarians.

ravenous beast that eats up all your lambs and pigs?" We all promised he should be rewarded at all our hands. So taking a bow, which he choosed out of a great many, he went up in the wood, with two gentlemen, where he imagined this devourer to be; they had not passed very far in it but they heard her voice, growling and grumbling, as if she were pleased with something she was doing. When they came in view, they found her muzzling in the belly of a new ravished sheep, which she had torn open; and seeing herself approached, she took fast hold of her prey with her forepaws and and set a very fierce raging look on Caesar, without offering to approach him, for fear at the same time of losing what she had in possession. So that Caesar remained as good while, only taking aim, and getting an opportunity to shoot her where he designed; 'twas some time before he could accomplish it, and to wound her and not kill her would but have enraged her more, and endangered him. He had a quiver of arrows at his side, so that if one failed he could be supplied; at last, retiring a little, he gave her opportunity to eat, for he found she was ravenous, and fell to as soon as she saw him retire, being more eager of her prey than of doing new mischiefs. When he going softly to one side of her, and hiding his person behind certain herbage that grew high and thick, he took so good aim that, as he intended, he shot her just into the eye, and the arrow was sent with so good a will and so sure a hand that it stuck in her brain, and made her caper and become mad for a moment or two; but being seconded by another arrow, he fell dead upon the prey. Caesar cut him open with a knife, to see where those wounds were that had been reported to him, and why he did not die of 'em. But I shall now relate a thing that possibly will find no credit among men, because 'tis a notion commonly received with us, that nothing can receive a wound in the heart and live; but when the heart of this courageous animal was taken out, there were seven bullets of lead in it, and the wounds seamed up with great scars, and she lived with the bullets a great while, for it was long since they were shot. This heart the conqueror brought up to us, and 'twas a very great curiosity, which all the country came to see, and which gave Caesar occasion of many fine discourses, of accidents in war and strange escapes.

At other times he would go a-fishing; and discoursing on that diversion, he found we had in that country a very strange fish, called a numb eel[3] (an eel of which I have eaten), that while it is alive, it has a quality so cold, that those who are angling, though with a line of never so great a length with a rod at the end of it, it shall, in the same minute the bait is touched by this eel, seize him or her that holds the rod with benumbedness, that shall deprive 'em of sense for a while; and some have fallen into the water, and others dropped as dead on the banks of the rivers where they stood, as soon as this fish touches the bait. Caesar used to laugh at this, and believed it impossible a man could lose his force at the touch of a fish, and could not understand that philosophy,[4] that a cold quality should be of that nature. However, he had a great curiosity to try whether it would have the same effect on him it had on others, and often tried, but in vain. At last the sought for fish came to the bait, as he stood angling on the bank; and instead of throwing away

3. Electric eel.
4. "Hypothesis or system upon which natural effects are explained" (Johnson's *Dictionary*).

the rod or giving it a sudden twitch out of the water, whereby he might have caught both the eel and have dismissed the rod, before it could have too much power over him, for experiment sake he grasped it but the harder, and fainting fell into the river; and being still possessed of the rod, the tide carried him, senseless as he was, a great way, till an Indian boat took him up, and perceived when they touched him a numbness seize them, and by that knew the rod was in his hand; which with a paddle (that is, a short oar) they struck away, and snatched it into the boat, eel and all. If Caesar were almost dead with the effect of this fish, he was more so with that of the water, where he had remained the space of going a league, and they found they had much ado to bring him back to life. But at last they did, and brought him home, where he was in a few hours well recovered and refreshed, and not a little ashamed to find he should be overcome by an eel, and that all the people who heard his defiance would laugh at him. But we cheered him up; and he being convinced, we had the eel at supper, which was a quarter of an ell[5] about and most delicate meat, and was of the more value, since it cost so dear as almost the life of so gallant a man.

About this time we were in many mortal fears about some disputes the English had with the Indians, so that we could scarce trust ourselves, without great numbers, to go to any Indian towns or place where they abode, for fear they should fall upon us, as they did immediately after my coming away; and that it was in the possession of the Dutch, who used 'em not so civilly as the English, so that they cut in pieces all they could take, getting into houses and hanging up the mother and all her children about her, and cut a footman I left behind me all in joints, and nailed him to trees.

This feud began while I was there, so that I lost half the satisfaction I proposed, in not seeing and visiting the Indian towns. But one day, bemoaning of our misfortunes upon this account, Caesar told us we need not fear, for if we had a mind to go, he would undertake to be our guard. Some would, but most would not venture; about eighteen of us resolved and took barge, and after eight days arrived near an Indian town. But approaching it, the hearts of some of our company failed, and they would not venture on shore; so we polled who would and who would not. For my part, I said if Caesar would, I would go; he resolved; so did my brother and my woman, a maid of good courage. Now none of us speaking the language of the people, and imagining we should have a half diversion in gazing only and not knowing what they said, we took a fisherman that lived at the mouth of the river, who had been a long inhabitant there, and obliged him to go with us. But because he was known to the Indians, as trading among 'em, and being by long living there become a perfect Indian in color, we, who resolved to surprise 'em by making 'em see something they never had seen (that is, white people), resolved only myself, my brother and woman should go; so Caesar, the fisherman, and the rest, hiding behind some thick reeds and flowers that grew on the banks, let us pass on towards the town, which was on the bank of the river all along. A little distant from the houses, or huts, we saw some dancing, others busied in fetching and carrying of water from the river. They had no sooner spied us but they set up a loud cry, that frighted us at first; we thought

it had been for those that should kill us, but it seems it was of wonder and amazement. They were all naked, and we were dressed so as is most commode[6] for the hot countries, very glittering and rich, so that we appeared extremely fine; my own hair was cut short, and I had a taffety cap with black feathers on my head; my brother was in a stuff[7] suit, with silver loops and buttons and abundance of green ribbon. This was all infinitely surprising to them, and because we saw them stand still till we approached 'em, we took heart and advanced, came up to 'em, and offered 'em our hands; which they took, and looked on us round about, calling still for more company; who came swarming out, all wondering and crying out "*Tepeeme*," taking their hair up in their hands and spreading it wide to those they called out to, as if they would say (as indeed it signified) "Numberless wonders," or not to be recounted, no more than to number the hair of their heads. By degrees they grew more bold, and from gazing upon us round, they touched us, laying their hands upon all the features of our faces, feeling our breasts and arms, taking up one petticoat, then wondering to see another; admiring our shoes and stockings, but more our garters, which we gave 'em, and they tied about their legs, being laced with silver lace at the ends, for they much esteem any shining things. In fine, we suffered 'em to survey us as they pleased, and we thought they would never have done admiring us. When Caesar and the rest saw we were received with such wonder, they came up to us; and finding the Indian trader whom they knew (for 'tis by these fishermen, called Indian traders, we hold a commerce with 'em, for they love not to go far from home, and we never go to them), when they saw him therefore they set up a new joy, and cried, in their language, "Oh! here's our *tiguamy*, and we shall now know whether those things can speak." So advancing to him some of 'em gave him their hands and cried, "*Amora tiguamy*," which is as much as, "How do you?" or "Welcome, friend," and all with one din began to gabble to him and asked if we had sense and wit; if we could talk of affairs of life and war, as they could do; if we could hunt, swim, and do a thousand things they use. He answered 'em, we could. Then they invited us into their houses, and dressed venison and buffalo for us; and going out, gathered a leaf of a tree called a *sarumbo* leaf, of six yards long, and spread it on the ground for a tablecloth; and cutting another in pieces instead of plates, setting us on little bow Indian stools, which they cut out of one entire piece of wood and paint in a sort of japan work. They serve everyone their mess on these pieces of leaves, and it was very good, but too high seasoned with pepper. When we had eat, my brother and I took out our flutes[8] and played to 'em, which gave 'em new wonder; and I soon perceived, by an admiration that is natural to these people, and by the extreme ignorance and simplicity of 'em, it were not difficult to establish any unknown or extravagant religion among them, and to impose any notions or fictions upon 'em. For seeing a kinsman of mine set some paper afire with a burning glass, a trick they had never before seen, they were like to have adored him for a god, and begged he would give them the characters or figures of his name, that they might oppose it against winds and storms; which he did, and they held it up in those seasons, and fancied it had a charm to conquer them, and kept it like a holy relic. They are very

6. Suitable.
7. Woven fabric, worsted.

8. Probably recorders.

superstitious, and called him the great *Peeie*, that is, prophet. They showed us their Indian *Peeie*, a youth of about sixteen years old, as handsome as nature could make a man. They consecrate a beautiful youth from his infancy, and all arts are used to complete him in the finest manner, both in beauty and shape. He is bred to all the little arts and cunning they are capable of, to all the legerdemain tricks and sleight of hand, whereby he imposes upon the rabble, and is both a doctor in physic and divinity; and by these tricks makes the sick believe he sometimes eases their pains, by drawing from the afflicted part little serpents, to odd flies, or worms, or any strange thing; and though they have besides undoubted good remedies for almost all their diseases, they cure the patient more by fancy than by medicines, and make themselves feared, loved, and reverenced. This young *Peeie* had a very young wife, who seeing my brother kiss her, came running and kissed me; after this they kissed one another, and make it a very great jest, it being so novel; and new admiration and laughing went round the multitude, that they never will forget that ceremony, never before used or known. Caesar had a mind to see and talk with their war captains, and we were conducted to one of their houses, where we beheld several of the great captains, who had been at council. But so frightful a vision it was to see 'em no fancy can create; no such dreams can represent so dreadful a spectacle. For my part I took 'em for hobgoblins or fiends rather than men; but however their shapes appeared, their souls were very humane and noble; but some wanted their noses, some their lips, some both noses and lips, some their ears, and others cut through each check with long slashes, through which their teeth appeared; they had other several formidable wounds and scars, or rather dismemberings. They had *comitas* or little aprons before 'em, and girdles of cotton, with their knives naked, stuck in it; a bow at their backs and a quiver of arrows on their thighs; and most had feathers on their heads of diverse colors. They cried *"Amora tiguamy"* to us at our entrance, and were pleased we said as much to 'em; they seated us, and gave us drink of the best sort and wondered, as much as the others had done before, to see us. Caesar was marveling as much at their faces, wondering how they should all be so wounded in war; he was impatient to know how they all came by those frightful marks of rage or malice, rather than wounds got in noble battle. They told us, by our interpreter, that when any war was waging, two men chosen out by some old captain whose fighting was past, and who could only teach the theory of war, these two men were to stand in competition for the generalship, or great war captain; and being brought before the old judges, now past labor, they are asked what they dare do to show they are worthy to lead an army. When he who is first asked, making no reply, cuts off his nose, and throws it contemptibly[9] on the ground; and the other does something to himself that he thinks surpasses him, and perhaps deprives himself of lips and an eye; so they slash on till one gives out, and many have died in this debate. And 'tis by a passive valor they show and prove their activity, a sort of courage too brutal to be applauded by our black hero; nevertheless he expresses his esteem of 'em.

In this voyage Caesar begot so good an understanding between the Indians and the English that there were no more fears or heart-burnings[1] during our stay, but we had a perfect, open, and free trade with 'em. Many things

9. With contempt. 1. Grudges.

remarkable and worthy reciting we met with in this short voyage, because Caesar made it his business to search out and provide for our entertainment, especially to please his dearly adored Imoinda, who was a sharer in all our adventures; we being resolved to make her chains easy as we could, and to compliment the Prince in that manner that most obliged him.

As we were coming up again, we met with some Indians of strange aspects; that is, of a larger size and other sort of features than those of our country. Our Indian slaves that rowed us asked 'em some questions, but they could not understand us; but showed us a long cotton string with several knots on it, and told us, they had been coming from the mountains so many moons as there were knots. They were habited in skins of a strange beast, and brought along with 'em bags of gold dust, which, as well as they could give us to understand, came streaming in little small channels down the high mountains when the rains fell; and offered to be the convoy to any body or persons that would go to the mountains. We carried these men up to Parham, where they were kept till the Lord Governor came. And because all the country was mad to be going on this golden adventure, the Governor by his letters commanded (for they sent some of the gold to him) that a guard should be set at the mouth of the river of Amazons[2] (a river so called, almost as broad as the river of Thames) and prohibited all people from going up that river, it conducting to those mountains of gold. But we going off for England before the project was further prosecuted, and the Governor being drowned in a hurricane, either the design died, or the Dutch have the advantage of it. And 'tis to be bemoaned what his Majesty lost by losing that part of America.

Though this digression is a little from my story, however since it contains some proofs of the curiosity and daring of this great man, I was content to omit nothing of his character.

It was thus for some time we diverted him; but now Imoinda began to show she was with child, and did nothing but sigh and weep for the captivity of her lord, herself, and the infant yet unborn, and believed if it were so hard to gain the liberty of two, 'twould be more difficult to get that for three. Her griefs were so many darts in the great heart of Caesar; and taking his opportunity one Sunday when all the whites were overtaken in drink, as there were abundance of several trades and slaves for four years[3] that inhabited among the Negro houses, and Sunday was their day of debauch (otherwise they were a sort of spies upon Caesar), he went pretending out of goodness to 'em to feast amongst 'em; and sent all his music, and ordered a great treat for the whole gang, about three hundred Negroes; and about a hundred and fifty were able to bear arms, such as they had, which were sufficient to do execution[4] with spirits accordingly. For the English had none but rusty swords that no strength could draw from a scabbard, except the people of particular quality, who took care to oil 'em and keep 'em in good order. The guns also, unless here and there one, or those newly carried from England, would do no good or harm; for 'tis the nature of that country to rust and eat up iron, or any metals but gold and silver. And they are very unexpert at the bow, which the Negroes and Indians are perfect masters of.

2. The mouth of the Amazon, in Brazil, is far distant from Surinam.
3. Tradesmen and whites who for crimes or debt were indentured for a fixed period.
4. Harm, slaughter.

Caesar, having singled out these men from the women and children, made an harangue to 'em of the miseries and ignominies of slavery, counting up all their toils and sufferings, under such loads, burdens, and drudgeries as were fitter for beasts than men, senseless brutes than human souls. He told 'em, it was not for days, months, or years, but for eternity; there was no end to be of their misfortunes. They suffered not like men, who might find a glory and fortitude in oppression, but like dogs that loved the whip and bell,[5] and fawned the more they were beaten. That they had lost the divine quality of men and were become insensible asses, fit only to bear; nay, worse: an ass, or dog, or horse, having done his duty, could lie down in retreat and rise to work again, and while he did his duty endured no stripes; but men, villainous, senseless men such as they, toiled on all the tedious week till Black Friday;[6] and then, whether they worked or not, whether they were faulty or meriting, they promiscuously, the innocent with the guilty, suffered the infamous whip, the sordid stripes, from their fellow slaves, till their blood trickled from all parts of their body, blood whose every drop ought to be revenged with a life of some of those tyrants that impose it. "And why," said he, "my dear friends and fellow sufferers, should we be slaves to an unknown people? Have they vanquished us nobly in fight? Have they won us in honorable battle? And are we by the chance of war become their slaves? This would not anger a noble heart, this would not animate a soldier's soul; no, but we are bought and sold like apes or monkeys, to be the sport of women, fools, and cowards, and the support of rogues, runagades,[7] that have abandoned their own countries for rapine, murders, thefts, and villainies. Do you not hear every day how they upbraid each other with infamy of life, below the wildest savages; and shall we render obedience to such a degenerate race, who have no one human virtue left to distinguish 'em from the vilest creatures? Will you, I say, suffer the lash from such hands?" They all replied, with one accord, "No, no, no; Caesar has spoke like a great captain, like a great king."

After this he would have proceeded, but was interrupted by a tall Negro of some more quality than the rest; his name was Tuscan; who bowing at the feet of Caesar, cried, "My lord, we have listened with joy and attention to what you have said, and, were we only men, would follow so great a leader through the world. But oh! consider, we are husbands and parents too, and have things more dear to us than life, our wives and children, unfit for travel in these unpassable woods, mountains, and bogs; we have not only difficult lands to overcome, but rivers to wade, and monsters to encounter, ravenous beasts of prey——." To this, Caesar replied that honor was the first principle in nature that was to be obeyed; but as no man would pretend to that, without all the acts of virtue, compassion, charity, love, justice, and reason, he found it not inconsistent with that to take an equal care of their wives and children as they would of themselves; and that he did not design, when he led them to freedom and glorious liberty, that they should leave that better part of themselves to perish by the hand of the tyrant's whip. But if there were a woman among them so degenerate from love and virtue to choose slavery before the pursuit[8] of her husband, and with the hazard of her life to share

5. Proverbial for something that distracts from comfort or pleasure, from the protective charm on chariots of triumphing generals in ancient Rome.
6. Here, a day of customary beating; more widely, a Friday bringing some notable disaster, from students' slang for examination day.
7. Renegades or fugitives.
8. Aim. "Degenerate": degenerated, debased.

with him in his fortunes, that such a one ought to be abandoned, and left as a prey to the common enemy.

To which they all agreed—and bowed. After this, he spoke of the impassable woods and rivers, and convinced 'em, the more danger, the more glory. He told them that he had heard of one Hannibal, a great captain, had cut his way through mountains of solid rocks;[9] and should a few shrubs oppose them, which they could fire before 'em? No, 'twas a trifling excuse to men resolved to die or overcome. As for bogs, they are with a little labor filled and hardened; and the rivers could be no obstacle, since they swam by nature, at least by custom, from their first hour of birth. That when the children were weary they must carry them by turns, and the woods and their own industry would afford them food. To this they all assented with joy.

Tuscan then demanded what he would do. He said, they would travel towards the sea, plant a new colony, and defend it by their valor; and when they could find a ship, either driven by stress of weather or guided by Providence that way, they would seize it and make it a prize, till it had transported them to their own countries; at least, they should be made free in his kingdom, and be esteemed as his fellow sufferers, and men that had the courage and the bravery to attempt, at least, for liberty; and if they died in the attempt it would be more brave than to live in perpetual slavery.

They bowed and kissed his feet at this resolution, and with one accord vowed to follow him to death. And that night was appointed to begin their march; they made it known to their wives, and directed them to tie their hamaca[1] about their shoulder and under their arm like a scarf, and to lead their children that could go, and carry those that could not. The wives, who pay an entire obedience to their husbands, obeyed, and stayed for 'em where they were appointed. The men stayed but to furnish themselves with what defensive arms they could get; and all met at the rendezvous, where Caesar made a new encouraging speech to 'em, and led 'em out.

But as they could not march far that night, on Monday early, when the overseers went to call 'em all together to go to work, they were extremely surprised to find not one upon the place, but all fled with what baggage they had. You may imagine this news was not only suddenly spread all over the plantation, but soon reached the neighboring ones; and we had by noon about six hundred men they call the militia of the county, that came to assist us in the pursuit of the fugitives. But never did one see so comical an army march forth to war. The men of any fashion would not concern themselves, though it were almost the common cause, for such revoltings are very ill examples, and have very fatal consequences oftentimes in many colonies. But they had a respect for Caesar, and all hands were against the Parhamites, as they called those of Parham plantation, because they did not, in the first place, love the Lord Governor, and secondly they would have it that Caesar was ill used, and baffled with;[2] and 'tis not impossible but some of the best in the country was of his counsel in this flight, and depriving us of all the slaves; so that they of the better sort would not meddle in the matter. The deputy governor,[3] of whom I have had no great occasion to speak, and who

9. The Carthaginian general (247–183 B.C.E.) and his troops literally hacked their way down the Alps into Italy to attack Rome.
1. Hammock.

2. Cheated.
3. William Byam (1623–1670; governor, 1654–67). There are recorded complaints against him for high-handedness and from him about insubordi-

was the most fawning fair-tongued fellow in the world and one that pretended the most friendship to Caesar, was now the only violent man against him; and though he had nothing, and so need fear nothing, yet talked and looked bigger than any man. He was a fellow whose character is not fit to be mentioned with the worst of the slaves. This fellow would lead his army forth to meet Caesar, or rather to pursue him; most of their arms were of those sort of cruel whips they call cat with nine tails; some had rusty useless guns for show, others old basket hilts[4] whose blades had never seen the light in this age, and others had long staffs and clubs. Mr. Trefry went along, rather to be a mediator than a conqueror in such a battle; for he foresaw and knew, if by fighting they put the Negroes into despair, they were a sort of sullen fellows that would drown or kill themselves before they would yield; and he advised that fair means was best. But Byam was one that abounded in his own wit[5] and would take his own measures.

It was not hard to find these fugitives; for as they fled they were forced to fire and cut the woods before 'em, so that night or day they pursued 'em by the light they made and by the path they had cleared. But as soon as Caesar found he was pursued, he put himself in posture of defense, placing all the women and children in the rear, and himself with Tuscan by his side, or next to him, all promising to die or conquer. Encouraged thus, they never stood to parley, but fell on pell-mell upon the English, and killed some and wounded a good many, they having recourse to their whips as the best of their weapons. And as they observed no order, they perplexed the enemy so sorely with lashing 'em in the eyes; and the women and children seeing their husbands so treated, being of fearful cowardly dispositions, and hearing the English cry out, "Yield and live, yield and be pardoned," they all run in amongst their husbands and fathers, and hung about 'em, crying out, "Yield, yield; and leave Caesar to their revenge"; that by degrees the slaves abandoned Caesar, and left him only Tuscan and his heroic Imoinda; who, grown big as she was, did nevertheless press near her lord, having a bow and a quiver full of poisoned arrows, which she managed with such dexterity that she wounded several, and shot the governor into the shoulder; of which wound he had like to have died, but that an Indian woman, his mistress, sucked the wound and cleansed it from the venom. But however, he stirred not from the place till he had parleyed with Caesar, who he found was resolved to die fighting, and would not be taken; no more would Tuscan, or Imoinda. But he, more thirsting after revenge of another sort than that of depriving him of life, now made use of all his art of talking and dissembling, and besought Caesar to yield himself upon terms which he himself should propose, and should be sacredly assented to and kept by him. He told him, it was not that he any longer feared him, or could believe the force of two men, and a young heroine, could overcome all them, with all the slaves now on their side also; but it was the vast esteem he had for his person, the desire he had to serve so gallant a man, and to hinder himself from the reproach hereafter of having been the occasion of the death of a prince whose valor and magnanimity deserved the empire of the world. He protested to him, he looked upon this action as gallant and brave, however tending to the preju-

nation by settlers and slaves.
4. Swords with protective hilt guards. "Cat with nine tails": a whip with nine knotted lashes, used for punishment in the British navy and army until 1881.
5. Followed his own intelligence or judgment.

dice of his lord and master, who would by it have lost so considerable a number of slaves; that this flight of his should be looked on as a heat of youth, and rashness of a too forward courage, and an unconsidered impatience of liberty, and no more; and that he labored in vain to accomplish that which they would effectually perform as soon as any ship arrived that would touch on his coast. "So that if you will be pleased," continued he, "to surrender yourself, all imaginable respect shall be paid you; and yourself, your wife, and child, if it be here born, shall depart free out of our land."

But Caesar would hear of no composition;[6] though Byam urged, if he pursued and went on in his design, he would inevitably perish, either by great snakes, wild beasts, or hunger; and he ought to have regard to his wife, whose condition required ease, and not the fatigues of tedious travel, where she could not be secured from being devoured. But Caesar told him, there was no faith in the white men or the gods they adored, who instructed 'em in principles so false that honest men could not live amongst 'em; though no people professed so much, none performed so little; that he knew what he had to do when he dealt with men of honor, but with them a man ought to be eternally on his guard, and never to eat and drink with Christians without his weapon of defense in his hand; and for his own security, never to credit one word they spoke. As for the rashness and inconsiderateness of his action, he would confess the governor is in the right; and that he was ashamed of what he had done, in endeavoring to make those free who were by nature slaves, poor wretched rogues, fit to be used as Christian's tools; dogs, treacherous and cowardly, fit for such masters; and they wanted only but to be whipped into the knowledge of the Christian gods to be the vilest of all creeping things, to learn to worship such deities as had not power to make 'em just, brave, or honest. In fine, after a thousand things of this nature, not fit here to be recited, he told Byam he had rather die than live upon the same earth with such dogs. But Trefry and Byam pleaded and protested together so much that Trefry, believing the governor to mean what he said, and speaking very cordially himself, generously put himself into Caesar's hands, and took him aside and persuaded him, even with tears, to live, by surrendering himself, and to name his conditions. Caesar was overcome by his wit and reasons, and in consideration of Imoinda; and demanding what he desired, and that it should be ratified by their hands in writing, because he had perceived that was the common way of contract between man and man, amongst the whites. All this was performed, and Tuscan's pardon was put in, and they surrender to the governor, who walked peaceably down into the plantation with 'em, after giving order to bury their dead. Caesar was very much toiled with the bustle of the day, for he had fought like a fury; and what mischief was done he and Tuscan performed alone, and gave their enemies a fatal proof that they durst do anything and feared no mortal force.

But they were no sooner arrived at the place where all the slaves receive their punishments of whipping, but they laid hands on Caesar and Tuscan, faint with heat and toil; and surprising them, bound them to two several stakes, and whipped them in a most deplorable and inhuman manner, rending the very flesh from their bones; especially Caesar, who was not perceived

6. Settlement.

to make any moan or to alter his face, only to roll his eyes on the faithless governor, and those he believed guilty, with fierceness and indignation; and to complete his rage, he saw every one of those slaves, who but a few days before adored him as something more than mortal, now had a whip to give him some lashes, when he strove not to break his fetters; though if he had, it were impossible. But he pronounced a woe and revenge from his eyes, that darted fire that 'twas at once both awful and terrible to behold.

When they thought they were sufficiently revenged on him, they untied him, almost fainting with loss of blood from a thousand wounds all over his body, from which they had rent his clothes, and led him bleeding and naked as he was, and loaded him all over with irons; and then rubbed his wounds, to complete their cruelty, with Indian pepper, which had like to have made him raving mad; and in this condition made him so fast to the ground that he could not stir, if his pains and wounds would have given him leave. They spared Imoinda, and did not let her see this barbarity committed towards her lord, but carried her down to Parham and shut her up; which was not in kindness to her, but for fear she should die with the sight, or miscarry, and then they should lose a young slave and perhaps the mother.

You must know, that when the news was brought on Monday morning that Caesar had betaken himself to the woods and carried with him all the Negroes, we were possessed with extreme fear, which no persuasions could dissipate, that he would secure himself till night, and then that he would come down and cut all our throats. This apprehension made all the females of us fly down the river, to be secured; and while we were away they acted this cruelty. For I suppose I had authority and interest enough there, had I suspected any such thing, to have prevented it; but we had not gone many leagues but the news overtook us that Caesar was taken and whipped like a common slave. We met on the river with Colonel Martin, a man of great gallantry, wit, and goodness, and whom I have celebrated in a character of my new comedy[7] by his own name, in memory of so brave a man. He was wise and eloquent and, from the fineness of his parts, bore a great sway over the hearts of all the colony. He was a friend to Caesar, and resented this false dealing with him very much. We carried him back to Parham, thinking to have made an accommodation; when we came, the first news we heard was that the governor was dead of a wound Imoinda had given him; but it was not so well. But it seems he would have the pleasure of beholding the revenge he took on Caesar, and before the cruel ceremony was finished, he dropped down; and then they perceived the wound he had on his shoulder was by a venomed arrow, which, as I said, his Indian mistress healed by sucking the wound.

We were no sooner arrived but we went up to the plantation to see Caesar, whom we found in a very miserable and unexpressible condition; and I have a thousand times admired how he lived, in so much tormenting pain. We said all things to him that trouble, pity, and good nature could suggest, protesting our innocency of the fact and our abhorrence of such cruelties; making a thousand professions of services to him and begging as many pardons for the offenders, till we said so much that he believed we had no hand in his ill treatment; but told us he could never pardon Byam; as for Trefry, he

7. *The Younger Brother, or The Amorous Jilt*, not produced until 1696 despite this piece of promotion.

confessed he saw his grief and sorrow for his suffering, which he could not hinder, but was like to have been beaten down by the very slaves for speaking in his defense. But for Byam, who was their leader, their head—and should, by his justice and honor, have been an example to 'em—for him, he wished to live, to take a dire revenge of him, and said, "It had been well for him if he had sacrificed me, instead of giving me the contemptible[8] whip." He refused to talk much, but begging us to give him our hands, he took 'em, and protested never to lift up his to do us any harm. He had a great respect for Colonel Martin, and always took his counsel like that of a parent, and assured him he would obey him in anything but his revenge on Byam. "Therefore," said he, "for his own safety, let him speedily dispatch me; for if I could dispatch myself I would not, till that justice were done to my injured person, and the contempt of a soldier. No, I would not kill myself, even after a whipping, but will be content to live with that infamy, and be pointed at by every grinning slave, till I have completed my revenge; and then you shall see that Oroonoko scorns to live with the indignity that was put on Caesar." All we could do could get no more words from him; and we took care to have him put immediately into a healing bath to rid him of his pepper, and ordered a chirurgeon[9] to anoint him with healing balm, which he suffered; and in some time he began to be able to walk and eat. We failed not to visit him every day, and to that end had him brought to an apartment at Parham.

The governor was no sooner recovered, and had heard of the menaces of Caesar, but he called his council; who (not to disgrace them, or burlesque the government there) consisted of such notorious villains as Newgate[1] never transported; and possibly originally were such who understood neither the laws of God or man, and had no sort of principles to make 'em worthy the name of men; but at the very council table would contradict and fight with one another, and swear so bloodily that 'twas terrible to hear and see 'em. (Some of 'em were afterwards hanged when the Dutch took possession of the place, others sent off in chains.) But calling these special rulers of the nation together, and requiring their counsel in this weighty affair, they all concluded that (Damn 'em) it might be their own cases; and that Caesar ought to be made an example to all the Negroes, to fright 'em from daring to threaten their betters, their lords and masters; and at this rate no man was safe from his own slaves; and concluded, *nemine contradicente*,[2] that Caesar should be hanged.

Trefry then thought it time to use his authority, and told Byam his command did not extend to his lord's plantation, and that Parham was as much exempt from the law as Whitehall;[3] and that they ought no more to touch the servants of the Lord—(who there represented the King's person) than they could those about the King himself; and that Parham was a sanctuary; and though his lord were absent in person, his power was still in being there, which he had entrusted with him as far as the dominions of his particular plantations reached, and all that belonged to it; the rest of the country, as Byam was lieutenant to his lord, he might exercise his tyranny upon. Trefry had others as powerful, or more, that interested themselves in Caesar's life,

8. Showing contempt.
9. Surgeon.
1. The major London prison, from which criminals were transported to the colonies.

2. No one disagreeing (Latin).
3. The king's palace in London. Treffry stands as Lord Willoughby's deputy on his private land, Byam in the colony at large.

and absolutely said he should be defended. So turning the governor and his wise council out of the doors (for they sat at Parham House), they set a guard upon our landing place, and would admit none but those we called friends to us and Caesar.

The governor having remained wounded at Parham till his recovery was completed, Caesar did not know but he was still there; and indeed, for the most part his time was spent there, for he was one that loved to live at other people's expense; and if he were a day absent, he was ten present there, and used to play and walk and hunt and fish with Caesar. So that Caesar did not at all doubt, if he once recovered strength, but he should find an opportunity of being revenged on him. Though after such a revenge, he could not hope to live, for if he escaped the fury of the English mobile,[4] who perhaps would have been glad of the occasion to have killed him, he was resolved not to survive his whipping; yet he had, some tender hours, a repenting softness, which he called his fits of coward, wherein he struggled with Love for the victory of his heart, which took part with his charming Imoinda there; but for the most part his time was passed in melancholy thought and black designs. He considered, if he should do this deed and die, either in the attempt or after it, he left his lovely Imoinda a prey, or at best a slave, to the enraged multitude; his great heart could not endure that thought. "Perhaps," said he, "she may be first ravished by every brute, exposed first to their nasty lusts and then a shameful death." No; he could not live a moment under that apprehension, too insupportable to be borne. These were his thoughts and his silent arguments with his heart, as he told us afterwards; so that now resolving not only to kill Byam but all those he thought had enraged him, pleasing his great heart with the fancied slaughter he should make over the whole face of the plantation, he first resolved on a deed, that (however horrid it at first appeared to us all), when we had heard his reasons, we thought it brave and just. Being able to walk and, as he believed, fit for the execution of his great design, he begged Trefry to trust him into the air, believing a walk would do him good, which was granted him; and taking Imoinda with him, as he used to do in his more happy and calmer days, he led her up into a wood, where, after (with a thousand sighs, and long gazing silently on her face, while tears gushed, in spite of him, from his eyes) he told her his design first of killing her, and then his enemies, and next himself, and the impossibility of escaping, and therefore he told her the necessity of dying, he found the heroic wife faster pleading for death than he was to propose it, when she found his fixed resolution, and on her knees besought him not to leave her a prey to his enemies. He (grieved to death) yet pleased at her noble resolution, took her up, and embracing her with all the passion and languishment of a dying lover, drew his knife to kill this treasure of his soul, this pleasure of his eyes; while tears trickled down his cheeks, hers were smiling with joy she should die by so noble a hand, and be sent in her own country (for that's their notion of the next world) by him she so tenderly loved and so truly adored in this; for wives have a respect for their husbands equal to what any other people pay a deity, and when a man finds any occasion to quit his wife, if he love her, she dies by his hand; if not, he sells her, or suffers some other to kill her. It being thus, you may believe the deed was soon resolved on; and

4. Common people or mob.

'tis not to be doubted but the parting, the eternal leave-taking of two such lovers, so greatly born, so sensible,[5] so beautiful, so young, and so fond, must be very moving, as the relation of it was to me afterwards.

All that love could say in such cases being ended, and all the intermitting irresolutions being adjusted, the lovely, young, and adored victim lays herself down before the sacrificer; while he, with a hand resolved and a heart breaking within, gave the fatal stroke; first cutting her throat, and then severing her yet smiling face from that delicate body, pregnant as it was with fruits of tenderest love. As soon as he had done, he laid the body decently on leaves and flowers, of which he made a bed, and concealed it under the same coverlid[6] of nature; only her face he left yet bare to look on. But when he found she was dead and past all retrieve, never more to bless him with her eyes and soft language, his grief swelled up to rage; he tore, he raved, he roared, like some monster of the wood, calling on the loved name of Imoinda. A thousand times he turned the fatal knife that did the deed toward his own heart, with a resolution to go immediately after her; but dire revenge, which now was a thousand times more fierce in his soul than before, prevents him; and he would cry out, "No; since I have sacrificed Imoinda to my revenge, shall I lose that glory which I have purchased so dear as at the price of the fairest, dearest, softest creature that ever nature made? No, no!" Then, at her name, grief would get the ascendant of rage, and he would lie down by her side and water her face with showers of tears, which never were wont to fall from those eyes. And however bent he was on his intended slaughter, he had not power to stir from the sight of this dear object, now more beloved and more adored than ever.

He remained in this deploring condition for two days, and never rose from the ground where he had made his sad sacrifice. At last, rousing from her side, and accusing himself with living too long now Imoinda was dead, and that the deaths of those barbarous enemies were deferred too long, he resolved now to finish the great work; but offering to rise, he found his strength so decayed that he reeled to and fro, like boughs assailed by contrary winds; so that he was forced to lie down again, and try to summons all his courage to his aid. He found his brains turned round, and his eyes were dizzy, and objects appeared not the same to him they were wont to do; his breath was short, and all his limbs surprised with a faintness he had never felt before. He had not eat in two days, which was one occasion of this feebleness, but excess of grief was the greatest; yet still he hoped he should recover vigor to act his design, and lay expecting it yet six days longer, still mourning over the dead idol of his heart, and striving every day to rise, but could not.

In all this time you may believe we were in no little affliction for Caesar and his wife; some were of opinion he was escaped never to return; others thought some accident had happened to him. But however, we failed not to send out an hundred people several ways to search for him; a party of about forty went that way he took, among whom was Tuscan, who was perfectly reconciled to Byam. They had not gone very far into the wood but they smelt an unusual smell, as of a dead body; for stinks must be very noisome that can be distinguished among such a quantity of natural sweets as every inch

5. Sensitive. 6. Coverlet.

of that land produces. So that they concluded they should find him dead, or somebody that was so. They passed on towards it, as loathsome as it was, and made such a rustling among the leaves that lie thick on the ground, by continual falling, that Caesar heard he was approached; and though he had during the space of these eight days endeavored to rise, but found he wanted strength, yet looking up and seeing his pursuers, he rose and reeled to a neighboring tree, against which he fixed his back; and being within a dozen yards of those that advanced and saw him, he called out to them and bid them approach no nearer, if they would be safe. So that they stood still, and hardly believing their eyes, that would persuade them that it was Caesar that spoke to 'em, so much was he altered, they asked him what he had done with his wife, for they smelt a stink that almost struck them dead. He, pointing to the dead body, sighing, cried, "Behold her there." They put off the flowers that covered her with their sticks, and found she was killed, and cried out, "Oh, monster! that hast murdered thy wife." Then asking him why he did so cruel a deed, he replied, he had no leisure to answer impertinent questions. "You may go back," continued he, "and tell the faithless governor he may thank fortune that I am breathing my last, and that my arm is too feeble to obey my heart in what it had designed him." But his tongue faltering, and trembling, he could scarce end what he was saying. The English, taking advantage by his weakness, cried, "Let us take him alive by all means." He heard 'em; and as if he had revived from a fainting, or a dream, he cried out, "No, gentlemen, you are deceived; you will find no more Caesars to be whipped, no more find a faith in me. Feeble as you think me, I have strength yet left to secure me from a second indignity." They swore all anew, and he only shook his head and beheld them with scorn. Then they cried out, "Who will venture on this single man? Will nobody?" They stood all silent while Caesar replied, "Fatal will be the attempt to the first adventurer, let him assure himself," and at that word, held up his knife in a menacing posture. "Look ye, ye faithless crew," said he, " 'tis not life I seek, nor am I afraid of dying," and at that word cut a piece of flesh from his own throat, and threw it at 'em; "yet still I would live if I could, till I had perfected my revenge. But oh! it cannot be; I feel life gliding from my eyes and heart, and if I make not haste, I shall yet fall a victim to the shameful whip." At that, he ripped up his own belly, and took his bowels and pulled 'em out, with what strength he could; while some, on their knees imploring, besought him to hold his hand. But when they saw him tottering, they cried out, "Will none venture on him?" A bold English cried, "Yes, if he were the devil" (taking courage when he saw him almost dead); and swearing a horrid oath for his farewell to the world, he rushed on him; Caesar, with his armed hand, met him so fairly as stuck him to the heart, and he fell dead at his feet. Tuscan, seeing that, cried out, "I love thee, O Caesar, and therefore will not let thee die, if possible." And running to him, took him in his arms; but at the same time warding a blow that Caesar made at his bosom, he received it quite through his arm; and Caesar having not the strength to pluck the knife forth, though he attempted it, Tuscan neither pulled it out himself nor suffered it to be pulled out, but came down with it sticking in his arm; and the reason he gave for it was, because the air should not get into the wound. They put their hands across, and carried Caesar between six of 'em, fainted as he was, and they thought dead, or just dying; and they brought him to Parham, and laid

him on a couch, and had the chirurgeon immediately to him, who dressed his wounds and sewed up his belly, and used means to bring him to life, which they effected. We ran all to see him, and if before we thought him so beautiful a sight, he was now so altered that his face was like a death's head blacked over, nothing but teeth and eyeholes. For some days we suffered nobody to speak to him, but caused cordials to be poured down his throat, which sustained his life; and in six or seven days he recoevered his senses. For you must know that wounds are almost to a miracle cured in the Indies, unless wounds in the legs, which rarely ever cure.

When he was well enough to speak, we talked to him, and asked him some questions about his wife, and the reasons why he killed her; and he then told us what I have related of that resolution, and of his parting; and he besought us we would let him die, and was extremely afflicted to think it was possible he might live; he assured us if we did not dispatch him, he would prove very fatal to a great many. We said all we could to make him live, and gave him new assurances; but he begged we would not think so poorly of him, or of his love to Imoinda, to imagine we could flatter him to life again; but the chirurgeon assured him he could not live, and therefore he need not fear. We were all (but Caesar) afflicted at this news; and the sight was gashly;[7] his discourse was sad, and the earthly smell about him so strong that I was persuaded to leave the place for some time (being myself but sickly, and very apt to fall into fits of dangerous illness upon any extraordinary melancholy). The servants and Trefry and the chirurgeons promised all to take what possible care they could of the life of Caesar, and I, taking boat, went with other company to Colonel Martin's, about three days' journey down the river; but I was no sooner gone, but the governor taking Trefry about some pretended earnest business a day's journey up the river, having communicated his design to one Banister, a wild Irishman and one of the council, a fellow of absolute barbarity, and fit to execute any villainy, but was rich: he came up to Parham, and forcibly took Caesar, and had him carried to the same post where he was whipped; and causing him to be tied to it, and a great fire made before him, he told him he should die like a dog, as he was. Caesar replied, this was the first piece of bravery that ever Banister did, and he never spoke sense till he pronounced that word; and if he would keep it, he would declare, in the other world, that he was the only man of all the whites that ever he heard speak truth. And turning to the men that bound him, he said, "My friends, am I to die, or to be whipped?" And they cried, "Whipped! No, you shall not escape so well." And then he replied, smiling, "A blessing on thee," and assured them they need not tie him, for he would stand fixed like a rock, and endure death so as should encourage them to die. "But if you whip me," said he, "be sure you tie me fast."

He had learned to take tobacco; and when he was assured he should die, he desired they would give him a pipe in his mouth, ready lighted, which they did; and the executioner came, and first cut off his members,[8] and threw them into the fire; after that, with an ill-favored knife, they cut his ears, and his nose, and burned them; he still smoked on, as if nothing had touched him. Then they hacked off one of his arms, and still he bore up, and held his pipe; but at the cutting off the other arm, his head sunk, and his pipe dropped, and he gave up the ghost, without a groan or a reproach. My mother

7. Ghastly. 8. Genitals.

and sister were by him all the while, but not suffered to save him, so rude and wild were the rabble, and so inhuman were the justices, who stood by to see the execution, who after paid dearly enough for their insolence. They cut Caesar in quarters, and sent them to several of the chief plantations. One quarter was sent to Colonel Martin, who refused it, and swore he had rather see the quarters of Banister and the governor himself than those of Caesar on his plantations, and that he could govern his Negroes without terrifying and grieving them with frightful spectacles of a mangled king.

Thus died this great man, worthy of a better fate, and a more sublime wit than mine to write his praise; yet, I hope, the reputation of my pen is considerable enough to make his glorious name to survive to all ages, with that of the brave, the beautiful, and the constant Imoinda.

1688

LADY MARY CHUDLEIGH
1656–1710

In the preface to her *Poems on Several Occasions* (1703), Lady Mary Chudleigh explained that readers would discover in her verse "a picture of my mind, my sentiments all laid open to their view." "To the Ladies" suggests that she was unhappily married to Sir George Chudleigh, of Ashton, Devon. But as the critic Joanna Lipking has argued, the poem's technical expertise also places it in a highly stylized genre, whose poetic conventions Chudleigh may be expertly following. Little is known about her personal life except that she suffered over her daughter's dying young. Yet Lady Mary also reveals her strikingly feminist sentiments in *The Ladies' Defense* (1701) and *Essays upon Several Subjects* (1710). These books—the former in verse and the latter in prose—respond to a minister, John Sprint, whose wedding sermon *The Bride-Woman's Counselor* (1700) argued that a wife's whole duty was to love, honor, and obey her husband. Indignant that women are "debarred from knowledge, banished from the schools, / And with the utmost industry bred fools," Lady Mary scorns the "mean low trivial cares of life," asserting that women must "read and think, and think and read again, / And on our minds bestow the utmost pain." Although she attained some renown in her day—her *Poems* and her book of essays went through several editions—at her death Chudleigh left a number of works unpublished. Some of them appear in the modern collection of her writing edited by Margaret J. M. Ezell.

From The Ladies' Defense: Or, a Dialogue between Sir John Brute, Sir William Loveall, Melissa, and a Parson

Melissa's Answer

* * *

'Tis hard we should be by the men despised,
Yet kept from knowing what would make us prized:
Debarred from knowledge, banished from the schools,
515 And with the utmost industry bred fools.

Laughed out of reason, jested out of sense,
And nothing left but native innocence:
Then told we are incapable of wit,[1]
And only for the meanest drudgeries fit:
520 Made slaves to serve their luxury and pride,
And with innumerable hardships tried,
Till pitying heaven release us from our pain,
Kind heaven to whom alone we dare complain.
Th' ill-natured world will no compassion show;
525 Such as are wretched, it would still have so:
It gratifies its envy and its spite;
The most in others' miseries take delight.
While we are present they some pity spare,
And feast us on a thin repast of air:
530 Look grave and sigh, when we our wrongs relate,
And in a complement accuse[2] our fate:
Blame those to whom we our misfortunes owe,
And all the signs of real friendship show.
But when we're absent, we their sport are made,
535 They fan the flame, and our oppressors aid;
Join with the stronger, the victorious side,
And all our sufferings, all our griefs deride.
Those generous few, whom kinder thoughts inspire,
And who the happiness of all desire;
540 Who wish we were from barbarous usage free,
Exempt from toils, and shameful slavery,
Yet let us unreproved, misspend our hours,
And to mean purposes employ our nobler powers.
They think if we our thoughts can but express,
545 And know but how to work, to dance and dress,
It is enough, as much as we should mind,
As if we were for nothing else designed,
But made, like puppets, to divert mankind.
O that my sex would all such toys despise;
550 And only study to be good, and wise:
Inspect themselves, and every blemish find,
Search all the close recesses of the mind,
And leave no vice, no ruling passion there,
Nothing to raise a blush, or cause a fear:
555 Their memories with solid notions fill,
And let their reason dictate to their will.
Instead of novels, histories peruse,
And for their guides the wiser ancients choose,
Through all the labyrinths of learning go,
560 And grow more humble, as they more do know.
By doing this, they will respect procure,
Silence the men, and lasting fame secure;
And to themselves the best companions prove,
And neither fear their malice, nor desire their love.

1701

1. Intelligence. "Native": innate. 2. Reveal, disclose. "Complement": compliment.

To the Ladies

<div>
Wife and servant are the same,

But only differ in the name:

For when that fatal knot is tied,

Which nothing, nothing can divide:

5 When she the word obey has said,

And man by law supreme has made,

Then all that's kind is laid aside,

And nothing left but state[1] and pride:

Fierce as an Eastern prince he grows,

10 And all his innate rigor shows:

Then but to look, to laugh, or speak,

Will the nuptial contract break.

Like mutes she signs alone must make,

And never any freedom take:

15 But still be governed by a nod,

And fear her husband as her God:

Him still must serve, him still obey,

And nothing act, and nothing say,

But what her haughty lord thinks fit,

20 Who with the power, has all the wit.[2]

Then shun, oh! shun that wretched state,

And all the fawning flatt'rers hate:

Value your selves, and men despise,

You must be proud, if you'll be wise.

</div>

1703

1. Pomp. 2. Intelligence.

ANNE KILLIGREW
1660–1685

The author of a small but skillful body of verse, Anne Killigrew is best known today as the subject of John Dryden's famous elegy "To the Pious Memory of the Accomplished Young Lady Mrs. Anne Killigrew" (1686). Born in London shortly before the Restoration, she was the daughter of Dr. Henry Killigrew, chaplain to the duke of York and himself a dramatist whose genius, Dryden declared, had been "transfused into [her] blood." Because of her father's position, she was raised in an atmosphere where female talent was encouraged: she frequented court circles, produced portraits of important nobles along with paintings of classical subjects, and became maid of honor to Mary Modena, duchess of York. But though, when Killigrew died of smallpox at the age of twenty-five, Dryden praised her as a modern equivalent of the famous Greek woman poet Sappho, her literary career cannot have been quite as successful as his ceremonial eulogy suggested. Certainly her complaint in "Upon the Saying That My Verses Were Made by Another" ("Th'Envious Age, only to Me alone / Will not allow, what I do write, my Own") implies a literary anxiety comparable with Anne Bradstreet's fear that "If what I do prove well, it won't advance, / They'll say it's stolen, or else it was by chance." At the same time, the elaborate modesty of "To My Lord

Colrane" suggests that her nervousness about attacks from others inevitably inspired considerable self-doubt. The hazards of female authorship were not insignificant, even in an age when women intellectuals were beginning to gain some strength.

Yet despite Killigrew's literary anxieties, she expressed a counterbalancing aesthetic self-confidence in her succinct "Epitaph Upon Myself": "When I am Dead, few Friends attend my Hearse, / And for a Monument, I leave my VERSE." Nor was this faith entirely unjustified. After her untimely death, her father quickly arranged for her poems to appear in a book, noting in a letter to a friend that "if there had not been more true history in her praises, than Complement, I should never have suffered [her verse] to passé the Presse." Similarly, as if responding to her resentment of suspicions voiced by the "envious age," Dryden flatly declared, "Such noble vigour did her verse adorn, / That it seem'd borrow'd where 'twas only born."

Upon the Saying That My Verses Were Made by Another

Next heaven,[1] my vows to thee, O sacred Muse!
I offered up, nor didst thou them refuse.

O queen of verse, said I, if thou'lt inspire,
And warm my soul with thy poetic fire,
No love of gold shall share with thee my heart,
Or yet ambition in my breast have part,
5 More rich, more noble I will ever hold
The Muse's laurel,[2] than a crown of gold.
An undivided sacrifice I'll lay
Upon thine altar, soul and body pay;
Thou shalt my pleasure, my employment be,
10 My all I'll make a holocaust[3] to thee.

The deity that ever does attend
Prayers so sincere, to mine did condescend.[4]
I writ, and the judicious praised my pen:
Could any doubt ensuing glory then?
15 What pleasing raptures filled my ravished sense,
How strong, how sweet, fame, was thy influence!
And thine, false hope, that to my flattered sight
Did'st glories represent so near and bright!
By thee deceived, methought each verdant tree
20 Apollo's transformed Daphne[5] seemed to be;
And every fresher branch, and every bough,
Appeared as garlands to empale[6] my brow.
The learn'd in love say, thus the winged boy[7]
Does first approach, dressed up in welcome joy;
25 At first he to the cheated[8] lover's sight
Nought represents but rapture and delight,
Alluring hopes, soft fears, which stronger bind
Their hearts, than when they more assurance find.

1. I.e., next to heaven.
2. Leaves of a tree traditionally associated with poets and with victors.
3. Burnt offering.
4. Assent. "Attend": hear.
5. In classical myth, the nymph who was trans-

formed into a laurel tree (*daphnē*, in Greek) to escape the lecherous pursuit of Apollo, god of the sun and of poetry.
6. Surround.
7. Eros or Cupid, the god of love.
8. Deceived.

Emboldened thus, to fame I did commit
30 (By some few hands,) my most unlucky wit.[9]
But ah, the sad effects that from it came!
What ought t'have brought me honor, brought me shame!
Like Aesop's painted jay,[1] I seemed to all,
Adorned in plumes, I not my own could call:
35 Rifled like her, each one my feathers tore,
And, as they thought, unto the owner bore.
My laurels thus another's brow adorned,
My numbers[2] they admired, but me they scorned:
Another's brow, that had so rich a store
40 Of sacred wreaths that circled it before;
While mine quite lost (like a small stream that ran
Into a vast and boundless ocean,)
Was swallowed up with what it joined, and drowned.
And that abyss yet no accession[3] found.

45 Orinda (Albion's[4] and her sex's grace)
Owed not her glory to a beauteous face;
It was her radiant soul that shone within,
Which struck a luster through her outward skin;
That did her lips and cheeks with roses dye,
50 Advanced[5] her height, and sparkled in her eye.
Nor did her sex at all obstruct her fame,
But higher 'mong the stars it fixed her name;
What she did write, not only all allowed,[6]
But every laurel to her laurel bowed!

55 The envious age, only to me alone,
Will not allow what I do write, my own;
But let them rage, and 'gainst a maid conspire,
So deathless numbers from my tuneful lyre
Do ever flow; so, Phoebus,[7] I by thee
60 Divinely inspired and possessed may be,
I willingly accept Cassandra's[8] fate,
To speak the truth, although believed too late.

1686

To My Lord Colrane, In Answer to His Complemental[1] Verses Sent Me under the Name of Cleanor

Long my dull muse in heavy slumbers lay,
Indulging sloth, and to soft ease gave way,
Her fill of rest resolving to enjoy,
Or fancying little worthy her employ.

9. Imagination. "Some few hands": i.e., those who helped to circulate her work.
1. In one of Aesop's fables, a jay adorns himself in a peacock's feathers and is angrily attacked by the other birds.
2. Meter; more generally, poetry.
3. Addition.
4. England's. "Orinda": i.e., the poet Katherine Philips (1632–1664); see p. 169.

5. Increased.
6. Acknowledged.
7. Apollo.
8. A Trojan princess gifted by Apollo with prophecy; in anger at being spurned by her, he made certain that no one believed her predictions.
1. Complimentary. "Lord Colrane": Henry Hare, second baron Colraine (1636–1708).

5 When noble Cleanor's obliging strains
Her, the neglected lyre to tune, constrains.
Confused at first, she raised her drowsy head,
Pondered a while, then pleased, forsook her bed.
Surveyed each line with fancy richly fraught,
10 Re-read, and then revolved them in her thought.

 And can it be? she said, and can it be?
That 'mong the Great Ones I a poet see?
The Great Ones? who their ill-spent time divide,
'Twixt dangerous politics, and formal pride,
15 Destructive vice, expensive vanity,
In worse ways yet, if worse there any be:
Leave to inferiors the despised arts,
Let their retainers be the Men of Parts.[2]
But here with wonder and with joy I find,
20 I'th' noble born, a no less noble mind;
One, who on ancestors, does not rely
For fame, in merit, as in title, high!

 The Severe Goddess thus approved the lays:[3]
Yet too much pleased, alas, with her own praise.
25 But to vain pride, my muse, cease to give place,
Virgil's immortal numbers once did grace
A Smothered Gnat:[4] by high applause is shown,
If undeserved, the praisers' worth alone:
Nor that you should believ't, is't always meant,[5]
30 'Tis often for instruction only sent,
To praise men to amendment, and display,
By its perfection, where their weakness lay.
This use of these applauding numbers make
Them for example, not encomium, take.

1686

2. I.e., of ability or talent.
3. Poems.
4. A mock-heroic poem once thought to be by the
Roman poet Virgil (70–19 B.C.E.), paraphrased by

Edmund Spenser as *Virgil's Gnat* (1591). "Numbers": verses.
5. I.e., you should not always believe it is meant.

ANNE FINCH, COUNTESS OF WINCHILSEA
1661–1720

The very first poem in Anne Finch's 1713 collection of verse—the only volume she published in her lifetime—outlines her gloomy vision of the literary woman's situation. Accomplished artist though she was, Finch had every reason to feel bitterness, for she had long been, in the words of the critic Cora Kaplan, "a prime butt for anti-'bluestocking' jokes on the stage and in verse." Even her sometime friend Alexander Pope, for instance, had caricatured her in a 1717 play called *Three Hours after Mar-*

riage (coauthored with John Gay and John Arbuthnot) as a mad poetess named "Phoebe Clinket;" and as late as 1954 Sylvia Plath, herself destined to become one of the twentieth century's major literary women, was amused by that character's "high flown and very funny ambitions to write poetry." Nor is there any evidence that Plath, who played the part of Phoebe Clinket in a Cambridge University production of Pope's comedy, ever read the verse written by Anne Finch herself.

Yet this woman who feared she would be thought "a presumptuous creature" was a perceptive and productive poet. Her work was admired by many in her own day, and after her death discriminating readers from William Wordsworth to Virginia Woolf continued to celebrate her talent. The daughter of Sir William Kingsmill and Anne Haslewood, both members of wealthy upper-class families, she was raised in aristocratic circles. Carefully nurtured and well educated, she went to court in 1683 as a maid of honor—an attendant—to Mary Modena, duchess of York, a position in which she may well have known Anne Killigrew, who was also one of the duchess's ladies-in-waiting. Apparently, the young Anne Kingsmill was charming and beautiful; when Heneage Finch, also a royal attendant—a "gentleman of the bedchamber"— met her in those years, he courted her vigorously. The couple wed in 1684, and their marriage was a happy one, as many of Finch's poems—for instance, her "Letter to Daphnis"—testify.

After the former duke of York, now King James II, was exiled in the late 1680s and replaced as king by William of Orange, the Finches remained stubbornly loyal to their former patron and his wife. Swept out of court, they lived in comparative poverty among their relatives, in a kind of political exile of their own. With the accession of Queen Anne to the throne in 1702, however, the couple returned to London, where they eventually purchased a house and Anne Finch began circulating and publishing her poems. In 1712, Heneage Finch's nephew, the earl of Winchilsea, died without heirs, and the former gentleman of the bedchamber inherited his title and his luxurious estate at Eastwell, in Kent, along with considerable debts and legal problems. Despite their financial vexations, Anne and Heneage Finch divided their time between London and the Kentish countryside, where they settled into a life of comfortable retirement, with Anne writing many poems in praise of rural pleasures. Her "Nocturnal Reverie," for instance, with its vivid evocation of nighttime meadows and groves, reveals how attentively she observed the pastoral world she loved so much and explains why William Wordsworth, the great Romantic poet of nature, was to remark in 1815 that this poem contained almost the only "new image[s] of external nature" produced between Milton's *Paradise Lost* (1667) and Thomson's *The Seasons* (1730).

For Anne Finch, however, the serenity of the English landscape was more than an emblem of nature's beauty; it symbolized relief from a society where "all's confused"— and where the role of a literary woman was particularly confusing. Even during her days in the service of Mary Modena, this imaginative woman had written poetry. But, perhaps mindful of Anne Killigrew's fate, she had refused to publish it, explaining later that "I was not so far abandoned by my prudence as, out of mistaken vanity, to let any attempts of mine in poetry show themselves while I lived in such a public place as the court, where every one would have made their remarks upon a versifying maid of honor, and far the greater number with prejudice, if not contempt." Living and writing at Eastwell, though, she became the center of a circle of intellectual friends not unlike the group that had gathered around Katherine Philips a few decades earlier, and her poems were read in manuscript by many of these people. But while the reputation she thus achieved brought a good deal of admiration, it also brought from some quarters exactly the "prejudice, if not contempt," that she had earlier feared. No wonder, then, that in many of her verses she meditated with some bitterness on woman's lot. "How are we fallen, fallen by mistaken rules?" she asked in "The Introduction," wondering, as Mary Wollstonecraft was also to wonder, if women are "education's more than nature's fools." Moreover, just as Anne Bradstreet had mused nostalgically on the reign of Queen Elizabeth, when it was "treason" to consider the

female sex "void of reason," Finch dreamed of an age when women were not "fallen" and wished to be told "fables of women that excelled of old"—stories of such exemplary biblical heroines as Miriam and Deborah, for instance.

Perhaps because her sense of woman's "fall" was so keen, Finch was often prey to melancholy as well as bitterness. Some of her most famous works brood on the state of depression and anxiety that her contemporaries called "the spleen," and others, like "Ardelia to Melancholy," try to combat such feelings. To Woolf, considering this poet's career in *A Room of One's Own*, it seemed "a thousand pities that [her mind] should have been forced to [such] anger and bitterness," yet sympathetic readers can see now that even spleen became an important source of inspiration for Finch. In addition, we can see that her spleen was at least partly justified. Even today, more than 285 years after her death, there is no complete edition of her works. Ironically, her grieving husband had carefully transcribed and preserved her verses, declaring in an eloquent obituary that she was "a fine writer and an excellent Poet." Nevertheless, some of the poems he collected did not appear in print until the late 1990s.

A Letter to Daphnis,[1] April 2, 1685

This to the crown and blessing of my life,
The much loved husband of a happy wife,
To him whose constant passion found the art[2]
To win a stubborn and ungrateful heart;
5 And to the world by tenderest proof discovers[3]
They err, who say that husbands can't be lovers.
With such return of passion, as is due,
Daphnis I love, Daphnis my thoughts pursue,
Daphnis, my hopes, my joys, are bounded all in you:
10 Even I, for Daphnis, and my promise[4] sake,
What I in women censure,[5] undertake.
But this from love, not vanity, proceeds;
You know who writes; and I who 'tis that reads.
Judge not my passion by my want of skill,
15 Many love well, though they express it ill;
And I your censure could with pleasure bear,
Would you but soon return, and speak it here.

1685 1713

The Introduction

Did I my lines intend for public view,
How many censures[1] would their faults pursue,
Some would, because such words they do affect,

1. Finch's neoclassical name for her husband, Heneage Finch (d. 1726).
2. Skill.
3. Reveals.

4. I.e., her wedding vows.
5. Criticize, namely servility, devotion.
1. Severe criticisms.

Cry they're insipid, empty, uncorrect.
5 And many have attained, dull and untaught,
The name of wit[2] only by finding fault.
True judges might condemn their want of wit,[3]
And all might say they're by a woman writ.
Alas! a woman that attempts the pen
10 Such an intruder on the rights of men,
Such a presumptuous creature is esteemed,
The fault can by no virtue be redeemed.
They tell us we mistake our sex and way;
Good breeding, fashion, dancing, dressing, play
15 Are the accomplishments we should desire;
To write, or read, or think, or to enquire
Would cloud our beauty, and exhaust our time,
And interrupt the conquests of our prime;[4]
Whilst the dull manage of a servile house[5]
20 Is held by some our utmost art, and use.
 Sure 'twas not ever thus, nor are we told
Fables,[6] of women that excelled of old;
To whom, by the diffusive[7] hand of Heaven
Some share of wit and poetry was given.
25 On that glad day on which the Ark[8] returned,
The holy pledge for which the land had mourned,
The joyful tribes attend it on the way,
The Levites do the sacred charge[9] convey,
Whilst various instruments before it play;
30 Here holy virgins in the concert join,
The louder notes to soften and refine,
And with alternate verse complete the hymn divine.[1]
Lo! the young poet, after God's own heart,
By Him inspired, and taught the Muses' art,[2]
35 Returned from conquest, a bright chorus meets,
That sing his slain ten thousand in the streets.
In such loud numbers[3] they his acts declare,
Proclaim the wonders of his early war,
That Saul upon the vast applause does frown,
40 And feels its mighty thunder shake the crown.
What, can the threatened judgment now prolong?[4]
Half of the kingdom[5] is already gone;
The fairest half, whose influence guides the rest,
Have David's empire o'er their hearts confessed.

2. A learned person.
3. Intelligence, learning. "Want": lack.
4. Maturity. "Conquests": i.e., amorous triumphs.
5. A house full of servants.
6. Falsehoods.
7. Scattering.
8. The Ark of the Covenant, a chest containing the Ten Commandments, carried into Jerusalem amid great celebration (1 Chronicles 15).
9. I.e., the Ark. "Levites": a religious caste among the ancient Hebrews.
1. I.e., the virgins' voices alternate with the men's in song.

2. I.e., poetry and song (the Muses are Greek goddesses who preside over the arts and all intellectual pursuits). "Young poet": David, a young Israelite musician and warrior, who slew the giant Goliath and defeated the Philistine army, earning the love of his people and the jealousy of Saul, king of Israel (1 Samuel 17–18).
3. Verses. "His slain ten thousand": see 1 Samuel 18.7.
4. Be prolonged; Saul's doom had been foreshadowed.
5. I.e., the women.

45 A woman here leads fainting Israel on,
 She fights, she wins, she triumphs with a song,[6]
 Devout, majestic, for the subject fit,
 And far above her arms exalts her wit,
 Then to the peaceful, shady palm withdraws,
50 And rules the rescued nation with her laws.
 How are we fallen, fallen by mistaken rules?
 And education's, more than nature's fools,
 Debarred from all improvements of the mind,
 And to be dull, expected and designed;[7]
55 And if some one would soar above the rest,
 With warmer fancy[8] and ambition pressed,
 So strong th'opposing faction still appears.
 The hopes to thrive can ne'er outweigh the fears.
 Be cautioned then my Muse, and still retired;[9]
60 Nor be despised, aiming to be admired;
 Conscious of wants, still with contracted wing,
 To some few friends and to thy sorrows sing;
 For groves of laurel[1] thou wert never meant;
 Be dark enough thy shades, and be thou there content.

1689? 1713

The Spleen[1]

A Pindaric Poem[2]

What art thou, Spleen, which ev'ry thing dost ape.[3]
 Thou Proteus[4] to abused mankind;
 Who never yet thy real cause could find,
Or fix thee to remain in one continued[5] shape
5 Still varying thy perplexing form,
 Now a Dead Sea[6] thou'lt represent,
 A calm of stupid discontent,
Then, dashing on the rocks, wilt rage into a storm.
 Trembling sometimes thou dost appear,
10 Dissolved into a panic fear;
 On sleep intruding dost thy shadows spread,
 Thy gloomy terrors round the silent bed,
And crowd with boding[7] dreams the melancholy head;
 Or, when the midnight hour is told,[8]

6. Deborah, a prophet and judge, led her people in battle and wrote a song celebrating their victory (Judges 4–5).
7. Intended, formed.
8. More intense imagination.
9. Withdrawn, restrained.
1. Tree whose leaves are associated with poetic achievement.
1. One of the four humors, a bodily fluid thought to cause depression or melancholy.
2. A poetic form derived from the complex odes of

the Greek poet Pindar (ca. 518–438 B.C.E.), generally addressed to some spiritual or material object.
3. Imitate.
4. In Greek mythology, a divinity of the sea who was capable of changing shape at will.
5. Constant, unchanging.
6. A lake in the Middle East, lacking tidal movement and too salty to sustain life.
7. Foreboding, menacing.
8. Tolled, as by a bell.

15 And drooping lids thou still dost waking hold,
 Thy fond delusions cheat[9] the eyes:
 Before them antic[1] spectres dance,
 Unusual fires their pointed heads advance,
 And airy phantoms rise.
20 Such was the monstrous vision seen,
 When Brutus (now beneath his cares oppressed,
 And all Rome's fortunes rolling on his breast,
 Before Philippi's latest field,
 Before his fate did to Octavius lead)
25 Was vanquished by the spleen.[2]

 Falsely the mortal part we blame
 Of our depressed and pond'rous frame,[3]
 Which, till the first degrading sin[4]
 Let thee, its dull attendant, in,
30 Still with the other[5] did comply,
 Nor clogged the active soul, disposed to fly,
 And range[6] the mansions of its native sky.
 Nor, whilst in his own heaven he dwelt,
 Whilst man his Paradise possessed,
35 His fertile garden in the fragrant east,
 And all united odors smelt,
 No arméd sweets,[7] until thy reign,
 Could shock the sense, or in the face
 A flushed unhandsome color place.
40 Now the jonquil[8] o'ercomes the feeble brain;
 We faint beneath the aromatic pain,
 Till some offensive scent thy pow'rs appease,
 And pleasure we resign[9] for short, and nauseous ease.

 In ev'ry one thou dost possess
45 New are thy motions,[1] and thy dress:
 Now in some grove a list'ning friend
 Thy false suggestions must attend,
 Thy whispered griefs, thy fancied[2] sorrows hear,
 Breathed in a sigh, and witnessed by a tear;
50 Whilst in the light and vulgar[3] crowd,
 Thy slaves, more clamorous and loud,
 By laughters unprovoked,[4] thy influence too confess.
 In the imperious wife thou vapors[5] art,

9. Deceive.
1. Fantastic, clownlike.
2. In Shakespeare's *Julius Caesar* (1599), the Roman leader Brutus is visited by the ghost of Caesar, whom he has helped assassinate, on the eve of his battle in 42 B.C.E. on the plains of Philippi with Anthony and Octavius, the ultimately successful claimant to Roman rule.
3. The body. "Mortal part": the flesh.
4. Eve and Adam's eating of the forbidden fruit in Eden (Genesis 3).
5. I.e., the soul.

6. Travel through. "Disposed": accustomed, desiring.
7. Painfully sweet fragrances.
8. A variety of daffodil.
9. Give up.
1. Effects.
2. Imagined. "Attend": listen to.
3. Frivolous and common. "Witnessed": confirmed, validated.
4. Without cause.
5. Brief attacks of faintness and dizziness to which 18th-century women were thought highly susceptible.

Which from o'er-heated passions rise
55 In clouds to the attractive brain,[6]
Until descending thence again,
Through the o'er-cast, and show'ring eyes,
Upon her husband's softened heart,
He the disputed point must yield,
60 Something resign of the contested field
Till lordly man, born to imperial sway,
Compounds[7] for peace, to make that right away,
And woman, armed with Spleen, does servilely obey.

The fool, to imitate the wits,
65 Complains of thy pretended fits,[8]
And dullness, born with him, would lay
Upon thy accidental[9] sway;
Because, sometimes, thou dost presume
Into the ablest heads to come:
70 That, often, men of thoughts refined,
Impatient of unequal sense,
Such slow returns, where they so much dispense,[1]
Retiring from the crowd, are to thy shades inclined.
O'er me alas! thou dost too much prevail:
75 I feel thy force, whilst I against thee rail;
I feel my verse decay, and my cramped numbers[2] fail.
Through thy black jaundice,[3] I all objects see,

As dark, and terrible as thee,
My lines decried, and my employment thought
80 An useless folly, or presumptuous fault:
Whilst in the Muses' paths I stray,
Whilst in their groves, and by their secret springs
My hand delights to trace unusual things,
And deviates from the known, and common way;
85 Nor will in fading silks compose[4]
Faintly th' inimitable rose,
Fill up an ill-drawn bird, or paint on glass
The sov'reign's blurred and undistinguished face,
The threat'ning angel, and the speaking ass.[5]

90 Patron thou art to ev'ry gross abuse,[6]
The sullen husband's feigned excuse,
When the ill humor with his wife he spends,
And bears recruited[7] wit and spirits to his friends.

6. I.e., the brain attracts vapors from the bodily "passions" or emotions.
7. Makes a concession.
8. I.e., falsely complains of fits of spleen. "Wits": the learned.
9. Not innate, but circumstantial. "Dullness": stupidity. "Lay": blame.
1. I.e., impatient at receiving so little intellectual stimulation when they provide so much.
2. Bad verse.

3. I.e., discoloration of the tissues (usually yellow) caused by accumulation of bile; but spleen is black bile.
4. Embroider.
5. I.e., undertake "artistic" activities thought suitable for women (for the speaking ass, Numbers 22).
6. Blatant wrongdoing.
7. Replenished. "Ill humor": spleen. "Spends": exhausts.

The son of Bacchus[8] pleads thy pow'r,
95 As to the glass he still repairs,[9]
 Pretends but to remove thy cares,
Snatch from thy shades one gay and smiling hour,
And drown thy kingdom in a purple show'r.
When the coquette, whom ev'ry fool admires,
100 Would in variety be fair,
 And, changing hastily the scene
 From light, impertinent, and vain,
 Assumes a soft, a melancholy air,
And of her eyes rebates[1] the wand'ring fires,
105 The careless posture, and the head reclined,
 The thoughtful, and composéd face,
 Proclaiming the withdrawn, the absent mind,
 Allows the fop more liberty to gaze,
 Who gently for the tender cause enquires:
110 The cause, indeed, is a defect in sense,
Yet is the Spleen alleged[2] and still the dull pretense.
 But these are thy fantastic[3] harms,
 The tricks of thy pernicious stage,
 Which do the weaker sort engage;
115 Worse are the dire effects of thy more pow'rful charms.
 By thee religion, all we know,
 That should enlighten here below,
 Is veiled in darkness, and perplexed
 With anxious doubts, with endless scruples[4] vexed,
120 And some restraint implied from each perverted text[5]
 Whilst touch not, taste not, what is freely giv'n,
Is but thy niggard[6] voice, disgracing bounteous heav'n.
 From speech restrained, by thy deceits abused,
 To deserts banished, or in cells reclused
125 Mistaken vot'ries[7] to the Powers Divine,
 Whilst they a purer sacrifice design,[8]
Do but the Spleen obey, and worship at thy shrine.
 In vain to chase thee ev'ry art we try,
 In vain all remedies apply,
130 In vain the Indian leaf infuse,
 Or the parched eastern berry[9] bruise;
Some pass, in vain, those bounds, and nobler liquors use.
 Now harmony, in vain, we bring,
 Inspire the flute and touch the string.
135 From harmony no help is had;
Music but soothes thee, if too sweetly sad,
And if too light, but turns thee gaily mad.
 Though the physician's greatest gains,
 Although his growing wealth he sees

8. I.e., one who follows the Roman god of wine and revelry.
9. Turns, resorts.
1. Reduces.
2. Blamed. "Sense": intelligence.
3. Arising from the imagination.
4. Hesitations of conscience.

5. I.e., prohibitions inferred from distorted readings of the Bible.
6. Miserly.
7. Persons bound by religious vows.
8. Intend.
9. Coffee bean. "Indian leaf": tea.

140 Daily increased by ladies' fees,
Yet dost thou baffle all his studious pains.
 Not skilful Lower[1] thy source could find,
Or, through the well-dissected body trace
The secret, the mysterious ways,
145 By which thou dost surprise, and prey upon the mind.
 Though in the search, too deep for human thought,
 With unsuccessful toil he wrought,
 Till thinking thee to've catched, himself by thee caught,
 Retained thy pris'ner, thy acknowledged slave,
150 And sank beneath thy chain to a lamented grave.

1701 1713

To the Nightingale

Exert thy voice, sweet harbinger of spring!
 This moment is thy time to sing,
 This moment I attend[1] to praise,
And set my numbers to thy lays.[2]
5 Free as thine shall be my song;
 As thy music, short, or long.
Poets, wild as thee, were born,
 Pleasing best when unconfined,
 When to please is least designed,
10 Soothing but their cares to rest;[3]
 Cares do still their thoughts molest,
 And still th'unhappy poet's breast,
Like thine, when best he sings, is placed against a thorn.
She begins. Let all be still!
15 Muse, thy promise now fulfill!
Sweet, oh! sweet, still sweeter yet
Can thy words such accents fit,[4]
Canst thou syllables refine,
Melt a sense that shall retain
20 Still some spirit of the brain,[5]
Till with sounds like these it join.
 'Twill not be! then change thy note;
 Let division[6] shake thy throat.
Hark! Division now she tries;
25 Yet as far the muse outflies.
 Cease then, prithee, cease thy tune;
 Trifler wilt thou sing till June?

1. Richard Lower (1631–1691), famous British physiologist who studied the human nervous system.
1. Devote.
2. Songs. "Numbers": verses.
3. I.e., they intend only to soothe their own cares, not to please others.
4. I.e., can the muse's poetry match the bird's music.
5. The speaker asks her muse for a more musical strain of poetry that will keep an intellectual content. The metaphor is of refining or melting base ore into purer metals.
6. A series of rapid decorative runs or variations on a melody (a term from music).

Till thy business all lies waste,
And the time of building's past!
30 Thus we poets that have speech,
Unlike what thy forests teach,
 If a fluent vein be shown
 That's transcendent[7] to our own,
Criticize, reform, or preach,
35 Or censure what we cannot reach.

1702? 1713

The Circuit of Apollo[1]

Apollo as lately a circuit he made
Through the lands of the muses when Kent[2] he surveyed
And saw there that poets were not very common,
But most that pretended to verse[3] were the women,
5 Resolved to encourage the few that he found,
And she that writ best with a wreath[4] should be crowned.
A summons sent out was obeyed but by four,
When Phoebus, afflicted[5] to meet with no more,
And standing where sadly he now might descry
10 From the banks of the Stoure the desolate Wye,[6]
He lamented for Behn[7] o'er that place of her birth,
And said amongst femens[8] was not on the earth
Her superior in fancy, in language, or wit,[9]
Yet owned that a little too loosely[1] she writ,
15 Since the art of the muse is to stir up soft thoughts,
Yet to make all hearts beat without blushes or faults.

But now to proceed, and their merits to know
Before he on any the bays[2] would bestow,
He ordered them each in their several[3] way
20 To show him their papers, to sing or to say
Whate'er they thought best, their pretensions might prove,
When Alinda began, with a song upon love.
So easy the verse, yet composed with such art,
That not one expression fell short of the heart.
25 Apollo himself did their influence obey;
He catched up his lyre, and a part[4] he would play,
Declaring no harmony else could be found
Fit to wait upon[5] words of so moving a sound.

7. Superior.
1. I.e., the circular journey of the Greek god of
the sun and of poetry.
2. The county in southeast England where Finch
lived. "Muses": in Greek mythology, nine daugh-
ters of Memory who preside over the arts and all
intellectual pursuit.
3. Claimed to be poets.
4. Of laurel.
5. Pained, saddened. "Phoebus": Apollo.

6. Two rivers that flow through Kent.
7. Aphra Behn (1640?–1689), English poet (see
p. 178).
8. Women.
9. Intelligence. "Fancy": imagination.
1. With too much sexual explicitness.
2. Leaves of the laurel.
3. Individual, distinct.
4. Melody.
5. Accompany.

The wreath he reached out, to have placed on her head,
30 If Laura not quickly a paper had read,
Wherein she Orinda[6] has praiséd so high,
He owned it had reached him while yet in the sky,
That he thought with himself when it first struck his ear,
Whoe'er could write that ought the laurel to wear.
35 Betwixt them he stood in a musing suspense,
Till Valeria withdrew him a little from thence,
And told him as soon as she'd got him aside
Her works by no other but him should be tried;[7]
Which so often he read, and with still new delight,
40 That judgment 'twas thought would not pass till 'twas night;
Yet at length he restored them, but told her withal[8]
If she kept it still close, he'd the talent recall.
Ardelia[9] came last as expecting least praise,
Who writ for her pleasure and not for the bays,
45 But yet, as occasion or fancy should sway,
Would sometimes endeavor to pass a dull day
In composing a song, or a scene of a play
Not seeking for fame, which so little does last
That ere we can taste it the pleasure is past.
50 But Apollo replied, though so careless[1] she seemed,
Yet the bays, if her share, would be highly esteemed.

And now he was going to make an oration,
Had thrown by one lock with a delicate fashion,
Upon the left foot most genteelly did stand,
55 Had drawn back the other and waved his white hand,
When calling to mind how the prize, although given
By Paris[2] to her who was fairest in heaven,
Had pulled on the rash, inconsiderate boy
The fall of his house, with the ruin of Troy;
60 Since in wit or in beauty it never was heard
One female could yield to have another preferred,
He changed his design, and divided his praise,
And said that they all had a right to the bays,
And that 'twere injustice one brow to adorn
65 With a wreath which so fitly by each might be worn;
Then smiled to himself, and applauded his art,[3]
Who thus nicely[4] has acted so subtle a part
Four women to wheedle, but found 'em too many,
For who would please all can never please any.
70 In vain then he thought it, there longer to stay,
But told them he now must go drive on the day,[5]

6. I.e., Katherine Philips (1632–1664), English poet (see p. 169).
7. Judged.
8. Nevertheless.
9. Finch's neoclassical pen name. The other names in the poem may refer to women Finch knew.
1. Indifferent.
2. The son of King Priam of Troy, he was asked to decide which of the three goddesses Hera, Aph-
rodite, and Athena was the most beautiful. Paris chose Aphrodite in return for the most beautiful woman in the world. His abduction of Helen, wife of the Greek Menelaus, instigated the Trojan War and ultimately brought about the fall of his city and dynasty ("house").
3. Skill.
4. Cleverly, prudently.
5. In Greek mythology, Apollo drove the chariot that pulled the sun across the sky.

Yet the case to Parnassus[6] should soon be referred,
And there in a council of muses be heard,
Who of their own sex best the title might try,
75 Since no man upon earth, nor Himself in the sky
Would be so imprudent, so dull, or so blind,
To lose three parts in four amongst womankind.

1702

Adam Posed[1]

Could our first father, at his toilsome plough,
Thorns in his path, and labor on his brow,
Clothed only in a rude, unpolished skin,
Could he a vain fantastic nymph[2] have seen,
5 In all her airs, in all her antic graces,
Her various fashions, and more various faces;
How had it posed that skill, which late assigned
Just appellations to each several kind,[3]
A right idea of the sight to frame;
10 T'have guessed from what new element she came;
T'have hit[4] the wavering form, or given this thing a name!

1709

Friendship between Ephelia and Ardelia[1]

Eph. What friendship is, Ardelia, show.
Ard. 'Tis to love, as I love you.
Eph. This account, so short (though kind)
 Suits not my inquiring mind.
5 Therefore farther now repeat:
 What is friendship when complete?[2]
Ard. 'Tis to share all joy and grief;
 'Tis to lend all due relief
 From the tongue, the heart, the hand;
10 'Tis to mortgage house and land;
 For a friend be sold a slave;
 'Tis to die upon a grave,
 If a friend therein do lie.
Eph. This indeed, though carried high,
15 This, though more than e'er was done
 Underneath the rolling sun,
 This has all been said before.

6. The mountain where the Muses lived.
1. Puzzled.
2. Fanciful woman of fashion.
3. Adam was given the task of naming all living

creatures (Genesis 2.19–20).
4. Exactly suited.
1. Finch's neoclassical pen name.
2. Perfect.

Can Ardelia say no more?
Ard. Words indeed no more can show:
20 But 'tis to love, as I love you.

1713

A Nocturnal Reverie

In such a night, when every louder wind
Is to its distant cavern safe confined;
And only gentle Zephyr[1] fans his wings,
And lonely Philomel,[2] still waking, sings;
5 Or from some tree, famed for the owl's delight,
She, hollowing clear, directs the wanderer right:
In such a night, when passing clouds give place,[3]
Or thinly veil the heavens' mysterious face;
When in some river, overhung with green,
10 The waving moon and trembling leaves are seen;
When freshened grass now bears itself upright,
And makes cool banks to pleasing rest invite,
Whence springs the woodbind, and the bramble-rose,
And where the sleepy cowslip sheltered grows;
15 Whilst now a paler hue the foxglove takes,
Yet checkers still with red the dusky brakes;[4]
When scattered glow-worms, but in twilight fine,[5]
Show trivial beauties watch their hour to shine;
Whilst Salisbury[6] stands the test of every light,
20 In perfect charm and perfect virtue bright:
When odors, which declined repelling day,
Through temperate air uninterrupted stray;
When darkened groves their softest shadows wear,
And falling waters we distinctly hear;
25 When through the gloom more venerable shows
Some ancient fabric, awful[7] in repose,
While sunburnt hills their swarthy looks conceal,
And swelling haycocks thicken up the vale:
When the loosed horse now, as his pasture leads,
30 Comes slowly grazing through th'adjoining meads.[8]
Whose stealing pace and lengthened shade we fear,
Till torn up forage in his teeth we hear:
When nibbling sheep at large pursue their food,
And unmolested kine[9] rechew the cud;
35 When curlews cry beneath the village-walls,
And to her straggling brood the partridge calls;

1. The west wind.
2. A nightingale (from the classical myth in which a sorrowing woman, Philomela, was changed into that bird).
3. Disappear. "Hollowing": sounding.
4. Thickets.
5. Handsome; i.e., the glowworms demonstrate that small beauties must choose their moment to be seen.
6. An allusion to Finch's friend Anne Tafton, countess of Salisbury.
7. Awesome. "Fabric": building, structure.
8. Meadows.
9. Cattle.

Their shortlived jubilee the creatures keep,
Which but endures, whilst tyrant-man does sleep;
When a sedate content the spirit feels,
40 And no fierce light disturbs, whilst it reveals;
But silent musings urge the mind to seek
Something, too high for syllables to speak;
Till the free soul to a composedness charmed,
Finding the elements of rage disarmed,
45 O'er all below a solemn quiet grown,
Joys in th'inferior world,[1] and thinks it like her own:
In such a night let me abroad remain,
Till morning breaks, and all's confused again;
Our cares, our toils, our clamors are renewed,
50 Or pleasures, seldom reached, again pursued.

1713

The Apology[1]

'Tis true I write and tell me by what rule
I am alone forbid to play the fool:
To follow through the groves a wandering muse
And feigned[2] ideas for my pleasures choose.
5 Why should it in my pen be held a fault
Whilst Mira paints her face, to paint a thought;
Whilst Lamia to the manly bumper[3] flies
And borrowed spirits sparkle in her eyes;
Why should it be in me a thing so vain
10 To heat with poetry my colder brain?
But I write ill and therefore should forbear.
Does Flavia cease now at her fortieth year
In every place to let that face be seen
Which all the town rejected at fifteen?
15 Each woman has her weakness; mine indeed
Is still to write though hopeless to succeed.
Nor to the men is this so easy found
Even in most works with which the wits abound.
(So weak are all since our first breach[4] with Heaven)
20 There's less to be applauded than forgiven.

1713

1. The material world, thought to be lower than the spiritual world.
1. Defense.
2. Invented, imagined.

3. Large glass of wine.
4. The disobedience of Adam and Eve in eating the forbidden fruit from the tree of knowledge (Genesis 3). "Wits": intelligent people.

The Answer

[*TO POPE'S* "IMPROMPTU"][1]

Disarmed with so genteel an air,
 The contest I give o'er;
Yet, Alexander, have a care,
 And shock the sex[2] no more.
5 We rule the world our life's whole race,[3]
 Men but assume[4] that right;
First slaves to every tempting face,
 Then martyrs to our spite.
You of one Orpheus[5] sure have read,
10 Who would like you have writ
Had he in London town been bred,
 And polished too his wit;
But he poor soul thought all was well,
 And great should be his fame,
15 When he had left his wife in hell,
 And birds and beasts could tame.
Yet venturing then with scoffing rhymes
 The women to incense,
Resenting heroines[6] of those times
20 Soon punished his offense.
And as the Hebrus[7] rolled his skull
 And harp besmeared with blood,
They clashing as the waves grew full
 Still harmonized the flood.
25 But you our follies gently[8] treat,
 And spin so fine the thread,
You need not fear his awkward fate,
 The lock won't cost the head.[9]
Our admiration you command
30 For all that's gone before;
What next we look for at your hand
 Can only raise it more.

1. A short poem by Alexander Pope (1688–1744) addressed to Finch, with the subtitle "Occasioned by four satirical verses on women wits in *The Rape of the Lock*." The lines from Pope's great mock-epic (4.59–62), which slyly suggest that some women "scribble plays" as a manifestation of the same disorder that causes others to "take physic" (medicine) and that female discontent expresses itself alternately in "the hysteric or poetic fit," seem to have elicited an argument on female talent from Finch, a friend of Pope's. Pope responded with his brief "Impromptu" (improvisation), in which he flattered Finch by claiming that all the examples of female poets she cites pale beside her own accomplishments. "The Answer" is Finch's correspondingly deferential reply.
2. I.e., the female sex.

3. Length.
4. Claim without truly possessing.
5. Mythical Greek poet whose singing charmed wild animals and won back his dead wife, Eurydice, from the underworld—on the condition (which he does not keep) that he not look back at her until they are on the earth's surface.
6. A band of frenzied women, who tore Orpheus to pieces.
7. River into which Orpheus's head and lyre were cast after he was dismembered (see Ovid's *Metamorphoses* [ca. 10 C.E.], 11.50–53).
8. Genteelly, wittily.
9. A reference to *The Rape of the Lock* (1714), in which a lock of hair is stolen from Belinda, the heroine.

Yet sooth[1] the ladies I advise
(As me too pride has wrought[2]),
35 We're born to wit, but to be wise
By admonitions taught.

1717

1. Truly. 2. Shaped, influenced.

SARAH KEMBLE KNIGHT
1666–1727

A document prized by colonial historians, Sarah Kemble Knight's episodic travel journal graphically and comically describes the backwoods settlements, taverns, dinners, swamps, slaves, ferries, dialects, posts, canoes, oysters, Indians, sheep, drunks, and harbors she encountered in the roundtrip business venture that took her from Boston to New York and back between 1704 and 1705. As the literary historian Julia Stern has pointed out, Knight introduced ethnography into the travelogue: some eighty-five years before Benjamin Franklin's *Autobiography,* she thereby transformed the soul-searching Puritan diary into a secular record of worldly transactions. The first daughter of the merchant Thomas Kemble and Elizabeth Trerice Kemble of Boston, Sarah Kemble married a sometime sea captain, sometime businessman; Richard Knight's frequent absences from home lent her authority as the head not only of their household but also of a boardinghouse and a school. Just as unusual as her 1704–05 journey, Sarah Kemble Knight's skills at settling estates, writing business letters, and copying legal documents helped her to maintain her independence. Her daughter was born in 1689; her husband probably died in 1706; when, after marriage, her daughter moved to New London, Connecticut, Knight apparently followed her and continued her business activities there, running an inn and making advantageous property investments. Transcribed and edited by Theodore Dwight, Knight's journal was first published in 1825.

From The Private Journal of a Journey from Boston to New York

* * *

Tuesday, October the Third

About 8 in the morning, I with the post proceeded forward without observing anything remarkable; and about two, afternoon, arrived at the post's second stage,[1] where the western post met him and exchanged letters. Here, having called for something to eat, the woman brought in a twisted thing

1. A stopping place for post-riders where mail was passed on to a new rider or horses were changed.

like a cable, but something[2] whiter; and laying it on the board, tugged for life to bring it into a capacity to spread; which having with great pains accomplished, she served in a dish of pork and cabbage, I suppose the remains of dinner. The sauce was of a deep purple, which I thought was boiled in her dye kettle; the bread was Indian and everything on the table service agreeable to these. I, being hungry, got a little down; but my stomach was soon cloyed, and what cabbage I swallowed served me for a cud the whole day after.

Having here discharged the ordinary[3] for self and guide (as I understood was the custom), about three, afternoon, went on with my third guide, who rode very hard; and having crossed Providence ferry, we come to a river which they generally ride through. But I dare not venture; so the post got a lad and canoe to carry me to t'other side, and he ride through and led my horse. The canoe was very small and shallow, so that when we were in, she seemed ready to take in water, which greatly terrified me, and caused me to be very circumspect, sitting with my hands fast on each side, my eyes steady, not daring so much as to lodge my tongue a hair's breadth more on one side of my mouth than t'other nor so much as think on Lot's wife,[4] for a wry thought would have overset our wherry:[5] but was soon put out of this pain, by feeling the canoe on shore, which I as soon almost saluted with my feet; and rewarding my sculler, again mounted and made the best of our way forwards. The road here was very even and the day pleasant, it being now near sunset. But the post told me we had near 14 miles to ride to the next stage (where we were to lodge). I asked him of the rest of the road, foreseeing we must travail in the night. He told me there was a bad river we were to ride through, which was so very fierce a horse could sometimes hardly stem it: but it was but narrow, and we should soon be over. I cannot express the concern of mind this relation set me in: no thoughts but those of the dangerous river could entertain my imagination, and they were as formidable as various, still tormenting me with blackest ideas of my approaching fate—sometimes seeing myself drowning, otherwhiles drowned, and at the best, like a holy sister just come out of a spiritual bath in dripping garments.

Now was the glorious luminary, with his swift coursers arrived at his stage,[6] leaving poor me with the rest of this part of the lower world in darkness, with which we were soon surrounded. The only glimmering we now had was from the spangled skies, whose imperfect reflections rendered every object formidable. Each lifeless trunk, with its shattered limbs, appeared an armed enemy; and every little stump like a ravenous devourer. Nor could I so much as discern my guide, when at any distance, which added to the terror.

Thus, absolutely lost in thought, and dying with the very thoughts of drowning, I come up with the post, who I did not see till even with his horse: he told me he stopped for me, and we rode on very deliberately a few paces, when we entered a thicket of trees and shrubs, and I perceived by the horse's going, we were on the descent of a hill, which, as we come nearer the bottom, 'twas totally dark with the trees that surrounded it. But I knew by the going of the horse we had entered the water, which my guide told me was the hazardous river he had told me of; and he, riding up close to my side, bid

2. Somewhat.
3. A meal served at an inn or public house. "Discharged": paid for.
4. I.e., not daring to look back. When Sodom was being destroyed, Lot's wife looked back and was turned into a pillar of salt (Genesis 19.26).
5. Small boat.
6. I.e., it was night. The "glorious luminary" is the sun god Apollo, who rides across the sky in a chariot pulled by horses.

me not fear—we should be over immediately. I now rallied all the courage I was mistress of, knowing that I must either venture my fate of drowning, or be left like the children in the wood.[7] So, as the post bid me, I gave reins to my nag; and sitting as steady as just before in the canoe, in a few minutes got safe to the other side, which he told me was the Narragansett country.

Here we found great difficulty in travailing,[8] the way being very narrow, and on each side the trees and bushes gave us very unpleasant welcomes with their branches and boughs, which we could not avoid, it being so exceeding dark. My guide, as before so now, put on harder than I, with my weary bones, could follow; so left me and the way behind him. Now returned my distressed apprehensions of the place where I was: the dolesome woods, my company next to none, going I knew not whither, and encompassed with terrifying darkness; the least of which was enough to startle a more masculine courage. Added to which the reflections, as in the afternoon of the day that my call[9] was very questionable, which, till then I had not so prudently as I ought considered. Now, coming to the foot of a hill, I found great difficulty in ascending; but being got to the top, was there amply recompensed with the friendly appearance of the kind conductress of the night, just then advancing above the horizontal line. The raptures which the sight of that fair planet produced in me, caused me, for the moment, to forget my present weariness and past toils; and inspired me for most of the remaining way with very diverting thoughts, some of which, with the other occurrences of the day, I reserved to note down when I should come to my stage. My thoughts on the sight of the moon were to this purpose:

> Fair Cynthia,[1] all the homage that I may
> Unto a creature, unto thee I pay;
> In lonesome woods to meet so kind a guide,
> To me's more worth than all the world beside.
> Some joy I feel just now, when safe got o'er
> Yon surly river to this rugged shore,
> Deeming rough welcomes from these clownish trees
> Better than lodgings with Nereides.[2]
> Yet swelling fears surprise; all dark appears—
> Nothing but light can dissipate those fears.
> My fainting vitals can't lend strength to say,
> But softly whisper, O I wish 'twere day.
> The murmur hardly warmed the ambient air,
> E're thy bright aspect rescues from despair:
> Makes the old hag[3] her sable mantle loose,
> And a bright joy does through my soul diffuse.
> The boisterous trees now lend a passage free,
> And pleasant prospects thou giv'st light to see.

From hence we kept on, with more ease than before: the way being smooth and even, the night warm and serene, and the tall and thick trees at a distance, especially when the moon glared light through the branches, filled my

7. Or babes in the wood; a reference to a ballad in which two children are taken out to be murdered and instead are left in the woods, where they die during the night.
8. Traveling.
9. Mission.

1. The moon personified (in classical mythology, the goddess of the moon was born on Mt. Cynthus).
2. Sea nymphs, daughters of Nereus.
3. I.e., night.

imagination with the pleasant delusion of a sumptuous city, filled with famous buildings and churches, with their spiring steeples, balconies, galleries and I know not what: grandeurs which I had heard of, and which the stories of foreign countries had given me the idea of.

> Here stood a lofty church—there is a steeple,
> And there the grand parade—O see the people!
> That famous castle there, were I but nigh,
> To see the mote[4] and bridge and walls so high—
> They're very fine! says my deluded eye.

Being thus agreeably entertained without a thought of anything but thoughts themselves, I on a sudden was roused from these pleasing imaginations, by the post's sounding his horn, which assured me he was arrived at the stage, where we were to lodge: and that music was then most musical and agreeable to me.

Being come to Mr. Havens', I was very civilly received, and courteously entertained, in a clean comfortable house; and the good woman was very active in helping off my riding clothes, and then asked what I would eat. I told her I had some chocolate, if she would prepare it; which with the help of some milk, and a little clean brass kettle, she soon effected to my satisfaction. I then betook me to my apartment, which was a little room parted from the kitchen by a single board partition; where, after I had noted the occurrences of the past day, I went to bed, which, though pretty hard, yet neat and handsome. But I could get no sleep, because of the clamor of some of the town topers in next room, who were entered into strong debate concerning the signification of the name of their country (viz.) Narragansett. One said it was named so by the Indians, because there grew a brier there, of a prodigious height and bigness, the like hardly ever known, called by the Indians narragansett; and quotes an Indian of so barbarous a name for his author, that I could not write it. His antagonist replied no—it was from a spring it had its name, which he well knew where it was, which was extreme cold in summer, and as hot as could be imagined in the winter, which was much resorted to by the natives, and by them called Narragansett (hot and cold), and that was the original of their place's name—with a thousand impertinances not worth notice, which he uttered with such a roaring voice and thundering blows with the fist of wickedness on the table, that it pierced my very head. I heartily fretted, and wished 'um tongue-tied; but with as little success as a friend of mine once, who was (as she said) kept a whole night awake, on a journey, by a country left, and a sergeant, insigne[5] and a deacon, contriving how to bring a triangle into a square. They kept calling for t'other gill,[6] which while they were swallowing, was some intermission; but presently, like oil to fire, increased the flame. I set my candle on a chest by the bed side, and setting up, fell to my old way of composing my resentments, in the following manner:

> I ask thy aid, O potent rum!
> To charm these wrangling topers dumb.
> Thou hast their giddy brains possessed—

4. Hill on which a castle stands.
5. I.e., ensign, lowest grade of commissioned
officer. "Left": lieutenant.
6. A measure of wine.

The man confounded with the beast—
And I, poor I, can get no rest.
Intoxicate them with thy fumes:
O still their tongues' till morning comes!

And I know not but my wishes took effect; for the dispute soon ended with t'other dram; and so good night! * * *

Friday, October the Sixth

I got up very early, in order to hire somebody to go with me to New Haven, being in great perplexity at the thoughts of proceeding alone; which my most hospitable entertainer observing, himself went, and soon returned with a young gentleman of the town, who he could confide in to go with me; and about eight this morning, with Mr. Joshua Wheeler my new guide, taking leave of this worthy gentleman, we advanced on towards Saybrook. The roads all along this way are very bad, encumbered with rocks and mountainous passages, which were very disagreeable to my tired carcass; but we went on with a moderate pace which made the journey more pleasant. But after about eight miles riding, in going over a bridge under which the river run very swift, my horse stumbled, and very narrowly escaped falling over into the water; which extremely frightened me. But through God's goodness I met with no harm, and mounting again, in about half a mile's riding, come to an ordinary, were well entertained by a woman of about seventy and vantage,[7] but of as sound intellectuals as one of seventeen. She entertained Mr. Wheeler with some passages of a wedding awhile ago at a place hard by, the bride's groom being about her age or something above, saying his children was dreadfully against their father's marrying, which she condemned them extremely for.

From hence we went pretty briskly forward, and arrived at Saybrook ferry about two of the clock afternoon; and crossing it, we called at an inn to bait[8] (foreseeing we should not have such another opportunity till we come to Killingsworth). Landlady come in, with her hair about her ears, and hands at full pay[9] scratching. She told us she had some mutton which she would broil, which I was glad to hear; but I suppose forgot to wash her scratches; in a little time she brought it in; but it being pickled, and my guide said it smelled strong of head[1] sauce, we left it, and paid sixpence a piece for our dinners, which was only smell.

So we put forward with all speed, and about seven at night come to Killingsworth, and were tolerably well with travelers' fare, and lodged there that night.

We set out early in the morning and being something unacquainted with the way, having asked it of some we met, they told us we must ride a mile or two and turn down a lane on the right hand, and by their direction we rode on but not yet coming to the turning, we met a young fellow and asked him how far it was to the lane which turned down towards Guilford [Connecticut]. He said we must ride a little further and turn down by the corner of Uncle Sam's lot. My guide vented his spleen at the lubber,[2] and we soon

7. I.e., or more. "Ordinary": here, an inn; a place where meals are served.
8. Refresh themselves and feed the horses.

9. I.e., busily.
1. I.e., head cheese, a jellied loaf of meat parts.
2. Clumsy fellow.

after came into the road, and keeping still on, without anything further remarkable, about two o'clock afternoon we arrived at New Haven, where I was received with all possible respects and civility. Here I discharged Mr. Wheeler with a reward to his satisfaction, and took some time to rest after so long and toilsome a journey, and informed myself of the manners and customs of the place and at the same time employed myself in the affair I went there upon.

They are governed by the same laws as we in Boston (or little differing) throughout this whole colony of Connecticut, and much the same way of church government, and many of them good, sociable people, and I hope religious too. But a little too much independent in their principles, and, as I have been told, were formerly in their zeal very rigid in their administrations towards such as their laws made offenders, even to a harmless kiss or innocent merriment among young people, whipping being a frequent and counted an easy punishment, about which as other crimes, the judges were absolute in their sentences. They told me a pleasant story about a pair of justices in those parts, which I may not omit the relation of.

A negro slave belonging to a man in the town stole a hogshead[3] from his master and gave or sold it to an Indian, native of the place. The Indian sold it in the neighborhood, and so the theft was found out. Thereupon the heathen[4] was seized and carried to the justice's house to be examined. But his Worship (it seems) was gone into the field, with a brother in office to gather in his pompions.[5] Whither the malefactor is hurried, and complaint made and satisfaction in the name of justice demanded. Their Worships can't proceed in form without a bench: whereupon they order one to be immediately erected, which, for want of fitter materials, they made with pompions— which being finished, down sets their Worships, and the malefactor called and by the senior Justice interrogated after the following manner: You, Indian, why did you steal from this man? You shouldn't do so—it's a grandy wicked thing to steal. "Hol't, hol't," cries Justice junior. "Brother, you speak negro to him. I'll ask him." "You, sirrah, why did you steal this man's hogshead?" "Hogshead?" (replies the Indian), "Me no stomany."[6] "No?" says his Worship, and pulling off his hat, patted his own head with his hand, says, "Tatapa—you, Tatapa—you; all one this. Hogshead all one this." "Hah!" says Netop, "Now me stomany that." Whereupon the company fell into a great fit of laughter, even to roaring. Silence is commanded, but to no effect: for they continued perfectly shouting. "Nay," says his Worship in an angry tone, "If it be so, *take me off the bench.*"

Their diversions in this part of the country are on lecture days and training days[7] mostly: on the former there is riding from town to town.

And on training days the youth divert themselves by shooting at the target, as they call it (but it very much resembles a pillory[8]), where he that hits nearest the white has some yards of red ribbon presented him which being tied to his hatband, the two ends streaming down his back, he is led away in triumph with great applause as the winners of the Olympiack games. They

3. A large barrel or cask.
4. I.e., the Indian.
5. Pumpkins.
6. Understand.
7. Days set aside for military exercises. "Lecture

days": days when a less formal sermon was offered than the one prepared for Sundays.
8. A wooden frame on a post with holes through which offenders' head and arms were put while they were displayed as public punishment.

generally marry very young: the males oftener, as I am told, under twenty than above. They generally make public weddings and have a way something singular (as they say) in some of them, *viz.* just before joining hands the bridegroom quits the place, who is soon followed by the bridesmen and, as it were, dragged back to duty—being the reverse to the former practice among us, to steel[9] man's pride.

There are great plenty of oysters all along by the seaside as far as I rode in the colony and those very good. And they generally lived very well and comfortably in their families. But too indulgent (especially the farmers) to their slaves, suffering too great familiarity from them, permitting them to sit at table and eat with them (as they say, to save time), and into the dish goes the black hoof as freely as the white hand. They told me that there was a farmer lived near the town where I lodged who had some difference with his slave concerning something the master had promised him and did not punctually perform, which caused some hard words between them. But at length they put the matter to arbitration and bound themselves to stand to the award of such as they named—which done, the arbitrators having heard the allegations of both parties, order the master to pay 40[s1] to black face and acknowledge his fault. And so the matter ended, the poor master very honestly standing to[2] the award.

There are everywhere in the towns as I passed a number of Indians the natives of the country, and are the most savage[3] of all the savages of that kind that I had ever seen: little or no care taken (as I heard upon inquiry) to make them otherwise. They have in some places lands of their own, and governed by laws of their own making;—they marry many wives and at pleasure put them away, and on the least dislike or fickle humor, on either side. Saying *"stand away"* to one another is a sufficient divorce. And, indeed, those uncomely *"stand aways"* are too much in vogue among the English in this (indulgent colony) as their records plentifully prove, and that on very trivial matters, of which some have been told me, but are not proper to be related by a female pen, though some of that foolish sex have had too large a share in the story.

If the natives commit any crime on their own precincts among themselves the English takes no cognezens[4] of. But if on the English ground they are punishable by our laws. They mourn for their dead by blacking their faces and cutting their hair after an awkerd and frightful manner, but can't bear you should mention the names of their dead relations to them. They trade most for rum, for which they would hazard their very lives, and the English fit[5] them generally as well by seasoning it plentifully with water.

They give the title of merchant to every trader who rate their goods according to the time and spetia[6] they pay in: *viz.* pay, money, pay as money, and trusting. *Pay* is grain, pork, beef, &c. at the prices set by the General Court that year; *money* is pieces of eight, rials, or Boston or Bay shillings[7] (as they call them,) or good hard money, as sometimes silver coin is termed by them;

9. Make determined.
1. Shillings, or two English pounds.
2. I.e., paying.
3. Uncivilized.
4. Recognition (i.e., "cognizance").
5. Fix; cheat.

6. Actual coin or money (specie). "Rate": calculate the price of.
7. Coin minted in the Massachusetts Bay Colony. "Pieces of eight": Spanish silver coins. "Rials": former English gold coins worth 10 shillings.

also wampum, *viz.* Indian beads which serves for change. *Pay as money* is provisions, as aforesaid, one third cheaper than as the Assembly or General Court sets it, and *trust* as they and the merchant agree for time.

Now, when the buyer comes to ask for a commodity, sometimes before the merchant answers that he has it, he says, *"Is your pay ready?"* Perhaps the chap replies "Yes." "What do you pay in?" says the merchant. The buyer having answered, then the price is set; as suppose he wants a sixpenny knife, in pay it is 12d[8]—in pay as money eight pence, and hard money its own price, *viz.* 6d. It seems a very intricate way of trade and what *Lex Mercatoria*[9] had not thought of.

Being at a merchant's house, in comes a tall country fellow, with his alfogeos[1] full of tobacco; for they seldom lose their cud, but keep chewing and spitting as long as their eyes are open. He advanced to the middle of the room, makes an awkward nod, and spitting a large deal of aromatic tincture, he gave a scrape with his shovel-like shoe, leaving a small shovel full of dirt on the floor, made a full stop, hugging his own pretty body with his hands under his arms, stood staring round him like a cat let out of a basket. At last, like the creature Balaam rode on,[2] he opened his mouth and said: "Have you any ribinen for hatbands to sell, I pray?" The questions and answers about the pay being passed, the ribin is brought and opened. Bumpkin simpers, cries "It's confounded gay I vow"; and beckning to the door, in comes Joan Tawdry, dropping about 50 curtsies, and stands by him. He shows her the ribin. *"Law, you,"* says she, *"it's right gent,* do you take it, *tis dreadful*[3] *pretty."* Then she inquires *"Have you any hood silk*[4] *I pray?"* which being brought and bought, "Have you any *thread silk to sew it with?"* says she, which being accommodated with they departed. They generally stand after they come in a great while speechless, and sometimes don't say a word till they are asked what they want, which I impute to the awe they stand in of the merchants, who they are constantly almost indebted to, and must take what they bring without liberty to choose for themselves. But they serve them as well,[5] making the merchants stay long enough for their pay.

We may observe here the great necessity and benefit both of education and conversation; for these people have as large a portion of mother wit,[6] and sometimes a larger, than those who have been brought up in cities, but for want of improvements render themselves almost ridiculous, as above. I should be glad if they would leave such follies and am sure all that love clean houses (at least) would be glad on't too.

They are generally very plain in their dress, throughout all the colony, as I saw, and follow one another in their modes,[7] that you may know where they belong, especially the women, meet them where you will.

Their chief red-letter day is St. Election,[8] which is annually observed according to charter, to choose their government, a blessing they can never be thankful enough for, as they will find if ever it be their hard fortune to lose it. The present governor in Connecticut is the Honorable John Win-

8. Pence; from the Latin *denarius*, "penny."
9. The law of merchants (Latin).
1. Saddlebag-like cheeks; from the Spanish *alforges,* "pouch."
2. The ass of the prophet Balaam spoke to him (Numbers 22).
3. Extremely (slang). "Gent": genteel (slang),

stylish.
4. Silk cloth suitable for a hood to cover her head.
5. I.e., treat them equally badly.
6. Native intelligence.
7. Characteristic fashions.
8. I.e., election day, here humorously depicted as a sacred religious observance.

throp, Esq. A gentleman of an ancient and honorable family whose father was governor here sometime before, and his grandfather had been governor of the Massachusetts.[9] This gentleman is a very courteous and affable person, much given to hospitality, and has by his good services gained the affection of the people as much as any who had been before him in that post.

From *December the Sixth*

<center>✳ ✳ ✳</center>

The city of New York is a pleasant, well-compacted place, situated on a commodious river which is a fine harbor for shipping. The buildings brick generally, very stately and high, though not altogether like ours in Boston. The bricks in some of the houses are of divers colors and laid in checkers, being glazed look very agreeable. The inside of them are neat to admiration, the wooden work, for only the walls are plastered, and the sumers and gist[1] are planed and kept very white scowered as so is all the partitions if made of boards. The fireplaces have no jambs[2] (as ours have) but the backs run flush with the walls, and the hearth is of tiles and is as far out into the room at the ends as before the fire, which is generally five foot in the lower rooms, and the piece over where the mantle tree should be is made as ours with joiners[3] work, and as I suppose is fastened to iron rods inside. The house where the vendue[4] was, had chimney corners like ours, and they and the hearths were laid with the finest tile that I ever see, and the staircases laid all with white tile which is ever clean, and so are the walls of the kitchen which had a brick floor. They were making great preparations to receive their governor, Lord Cornbury from the Jerseys,[5] and for that end raised the militia to guard him on shore to the fort.

They are generally of the Church of England and have a New England gentleman for their minister, and a very fine church set out with all customary requisites. There are also a Dutch and divers conventicles as they call them, *viz.* Baptist, Quakers, etc. They are not strict in keeping the Sabbath as in Boston and other places where I had been, but seem to deal with great exactness as far as I see or deal with. They are sociable to one another and courteous and civil to strangers and fare well in their houses. The English go very fashionable in their dress. But the Dutch, especially the middling sort, differ from our women, in their habit go loose, wear French muchets which are like a cap and a headband in one, leaving their ears bare, which are set out with jewels of a large size and many in number. And their fingers hooped with rings, some with large stones in them of many colors as were their pendants in their ears, which you should see very old women wear as well as young.

They have vendues very frequently and make their earnings very well by them, for they treat with good liquor liberally, and the customers drink as

9. In 1704 Fitz-John Winthrop (1638–1707) was the governor of Connecticut. His father, John Winthrop (1606–1676), founded New London and was governor from 1659 to 1676. Fitz-John Winthrop's grandfather, John Winthrop (1588–1649), was the first governor of the Massachusetts Bay Colony.
1. Main beams and joists.

2. Side pieces on which the fireplace lintel rests.
3. Craftsmen who constructed things by joining pieces of wood together. Their work was more finished than a carpenter's.
4. Auction.
5. Edward Hyde (1661–1723), royal governor of New York and New Jersey from 1702 to 1708.

liberally and generally pay for't as well, by paying for that which they bid up briskly for, after the sack[6] has gone plentifully about, though sometimes good penny worths' are got there. Their diversions in the winter is riding sleighs about three or four miles out of town, where they have houses of entertainment at a place called the Bowery, and some go to friends' houses who handsomely treat them. Mr. Burroughs carried his spouse and daughter and myself out to one Madame Dowes, a gentlewoman that lived at a farm house, who gave us a handsome entertainment of five or six dishes and choice beer and metheglin,[7] cider, etc. all which she said was the produce of her farm. I believe we met 50 or 60 sleighs that day—they fly with great swiftness and some are so furious that they'll turn out of the path for none except a loaden cart. Nor do they spare for any diversion the place affords, and sociable to a degree, their tables being as free to their neighbors as to themselves.

Having here transacted the affair I went upon and some other that fell in the way, after about a fortnight's stay there I left New York with no little regret[.] * * *

January the Sixth

Being now well recruited[8] and fit for business I discoursed the person I was concerned with, that we might finish in order to my return to Boston. They delayed as they had hitherto done hoping to tire my patience. But I was resolute to stay and see an end of the matter let it be never so much to my disadvantage—So January 9th they come again and promise the Wednesday following to go through with the distribution of the estate which they delayed till Thursday and then come with new amusements.[9] But at length by the mediation of that holy good gentleman, the Rev. Mr. James Pierpont, the minister of New Haven, and with the advice and assistance of other our good friends we come to an accommodation and distribution, which having finished though not till February, the man that waited on me to York taking the charge of me I set out for Boston. We went from New Haven upon the ice (the ferry being not passable thereby) and the Rev. Mr. Pierpont with Madam Prout, cousin Trowbridge and divers others were taking leave, we went onward without anything remarkable till we come to New London and lodged again at Mr. Saltonstall's—and here I dismissed my guide, and my generous entertainer provided me Mr. Samuel Rogers of that place to go home with me—I stayed a day here longer than intended by the commands of the honorable Governor Winthrop to stay and take a supper with him whose wonderful civility I may not omit. The next morning I crossed the ferry to Groton, having had the honor of the company, of Madam Livingston (who is the governor's daughter) and Mary Christophers and divers others to the boat—and that night lodged at Stonington and had roast beef and pumpkin sauce for supper. The next night at Haven's and had roast fowl, and the next day we come to a river which by reason of the freshets coming down was swelled so high we feared it impassable and the rapid stream was very terrifying—However we must over and that in a small canoe. Mr. Rogers assuring me of his good conduct,[1] I after a stay of near an hour on the shore

6. Wine; specifically, white wine imported from Spain or the Canaries.
7. A spiced variety of mead. The cider offered was probably also alcoholic.

8. Restored.
9. I.e., trifles that caused further delays.
1. Company for safekeeping.

for consultation, went into the canoe, and Mr. Rogers paddled about 100 yards up the creek by the shore side, turned into the swift stream and dexterously steering her in a moment we come to the other side as swiftly passing as an arrow shot out of the bow by a strong arm. I stayed on the shore till he returned to fetch our horses, which he caused to swim over, himself bringing the furniture[2] in the canoe. But it is past my skill to express the exceeding fright all their transactions formed in me. We were now in the colony of Massachusetts and taking lodgings at the first inn we come to, had a pretty difficult passage the next day which was the second of March by reason of the sloughy[3] ways then thawed by the sun. Here I met Capt. John Richards of Boston who was going home, so being very glad of his company we rode something harder than hitherto, and missing my way in going up a very steep hill, my horse dropped down under me as dead; this new surprise no little hurt me, meeting it just at the entrance into Dedham from whence we intended to reach home that night. But was now obliged to get another horse there and leave my own, resolving for Boston that night if possible. But in going over the causeway at Dedham the Bridge being overflowed by the high waters coming down, I very narrowly escaped falling over into the river horse and all which 'twas almost a miracle I did not—now it grew late in the afternoon and the people having very much discouraged us about the sloughy way which they said we should find very difficult and hazardous, it so wrought on me being tired and dispirited and disappointed of my desires of going home, that I agreed to lodge there that night which we did at the house of one Draper, and the next day being March 3d we got safe home to Boston, where I found my aged and tender mother and my dear and only child in good health with open arms ready to receive me, and my kind relations and friends flocking in to welcome me and hear the story of my transactions and travails, I having this day been five months from home and now I cannot fully express my joy and satisfaction. But desire sincerely to adore my great Benefactor for thus graciously carrying forth and returning in safety his unworthy handmaid.

1704–05 1825

2. The horses' harnesses. 3. Muddy.

MARY ASTELL
1666–1731

In her preface to a collection of Lady Mary Wortley Montagu's Turkish Embassy letters (1724), Mary Astell compared them favorably with the travel literature composed by men and encouraged women readers to "be pleased that a *woman* triumphs." The mutual esteem of these two learned friends, evidenced not only by Astell's pride in Lady Mary's epistolary triumphs but also by Lady Mary's financial support of Astell's writing career, epitomizes the ideal that had earlier impelled Astell to write *A Serious Proposal to the Ladies* (1694), her project to establish a retreat in which women could educate themselves even as they pursued the "blessings" of friendship. Clearly Astell's description of this intellectual community of women was a response

to the frequent attacks on the vanity of female wishes in Restoration literature: while a number of satiric poems and plays criticized flirtatiousness and dilettantism as inherently female, Astell believed that religious and philosophic training could correct such feminine failings.

Astell's proposal, therefore, begins by arguing that women have been debarred from advantages, which they are later reproached for not having, and inculcated with vices, for which they are then upbraided. Uncompromising as she was in this claim, Astell accepted the legal, vocational, and economic subordination of women. Although she was quite conservative in subsequent essays on the inalterable subjugation of wives to husbands, in her proposal she could insist, by emphasizing the moral benefits of what amounts to a Protestant convent, on women's natural equality with men. Thus, as Katharine M. Rogers has argued in *Feminism in Eighteenth-Century England,* "Astell was able to combine acceptance of the external status quo with radical questioning of the alleged natural superiority on which men based their prerogatives," and she was able to do so, in part, because she limited her claims to single women.

Significantly, Astell herself remained single, and in *A Serious Proposal to the Ladies,* which went through several editions, she attempted to provide other women with a feasible alternative to marriage. Although this daughter of a Newcastle merchant must have counted herself lucky to be given an education by an uncle who was a clergyman, she dedicated her quiet life in Chelsea to championing other women's right to learn. Eighteen years old when she composed the poem "Ambition," she consistently sought to debate those "Who falsely say that women have no soul," publishing under the pseudonym "a Lover of her Sex." Anthologized in *The Ladies Library* (1714) by Richard Steele and satirized in *The Tatler* by Jonathan Swift, she established a considerable reputation within her own lifetime.

Ambition

Mar 30. 1684

I

What's this that with such vigor fills my breast?
 Like the first mover[1] finds no rest,
 And with its force does all things draw,
Makes all submit to its imperial law!
5 Sure 'tis a spark 'bove what Prometheus[2] stole,
 Kindled by a heavenly coal,
 Their sophistry I can control,[3]
Who falsely say that women have no soul.

II

Vile greatness! I disdain to bow to thee,
10 Thou art below even lowly me,
 I would no fame, no titles have,
And no more land than what will make a grave.
I scorn to weep for worlds, may I but reign

1. In the medieval astronomical system that pictured the heavens as concentric spheres, the *primum mobile* was the outermost moving sphere, which communicates its motion to all the others.
2. According to Greek legend, the Titan stole fire

from the gods for humanity (whom he had created).
3. Challenge; call to account. "Sophistry": clever but deceptive argumentation.

And empire o'er my self obtain,
15 In Caesar's throne I'd not sit down,
Nor would I stoop for Alexander's[4] crown.

III

Let me obscured be, and never known.
Or pointed at about the town,
Short-winded fame shall not transmit
20 My name, that the next age may censure it:
If I write sense no matter what they say,
Whether they call it dull, or pay
A reverence such as Virgil claims,
Their breath's infectious,[5] I have higher aims.

IV

25 Mean-spirited men! that bait at honor, praise,
A wreath of laurel or of bays,[6]
How short's their immortality!
But oh a crown of glory ne'er will die!
This I'm ambitious of, no pains will spare
30 To have a higher mansion[7] there,
There all are kings, here let me be,
Great O my God, great in humility.

1689 1988

From A Serious Proposal to the Ladies

[A RELIGIOUS RETIREMENT]

Now as to the proposal, it is to erect a monastery, or if you will (to avoid giving offence to the scrupulous and injudicious, by names which though innocent in themselves, have been abused by superstitious practices),[1] we will call it a religious retirement, and such as shall have a double aspect, being not only a retreat from the world for those who desire that advantage, but likewise, an institution and previous discipline,[2] to fit us to do the greatest good in it; such an institution as this (if I do not mightily deceive my self) would be the most probable method to amend the present, and improve the future age. * * *

You are therefore ladies, invited into a place, where you shall suffer no other confinement, but to be kept out of the road of sin: * * * Happy retreat!

4. Alexander the Great (356–323 B.C.E.), king of Macedon and conqueror of Greece and Persia. "Caesar's throne": *Caesar* was the name taken by Roman emperors from the first, Augustus (ruled 29 B.C.E.–14), to Domitian (ruled 81–96).
5. Morally contaminating. Virgil (70–19 B.C.E.), whose poetry includes the epic *The Aeneid*, is the dominant poet in Latin literature and was particularly highly regarded through the Middle Ages.

6. In classical Greece, victors were crowned with a wreath of laurel; bay is a kind of laurel. "Bait": stop.
7. I.e., a dwelling in heaven; see John 14.2: "In my Father's house are many mansions."
1. Monks had acquired a reputation among English anti-Papists for dabbling in the supernatural.
2. Discipline leading the way.

which will be the introducing you into such a paradise as your mother Eve forfeited,[3] where you shall feast on pleasures, that do not, like those of the world, disappoint your expectations, pall your appetites, and by the disgust they give you put you on the fruitless search after new delights, which when obtained are as empty as the former; but such as will make you truly happy now, and prepare you to be perfectly so hereafter. Here are no serpents to deceive you, whilst you entertain your selves in these delicious gardens. No provocations will be given in this amicable society, but to love and to good works, which will afford such an entertaining employment, that you'll have as little inclination as leisure to pursue those follies, which in the time of your ignorance passed with you under the name of love, although there is not in nature two more different things, than true love and that brutish passion, which pretends to ape it. Here will be no rivalling but for the love of God, no ambition but to procure his favour, to which nothing will more effectually recommend you, than a great and dear affection to each other. * * *

One great end of this institution shall be, to expel that cloud of ignorance which custom has involved us in, to furnish our minds with a stock of solid and useful knowledge, that the souls of women may no longer be the only unadorned and neglected things. It is not intended that our religious should waste their time, and trouble their heads about such unconcerning matters, as the vogue of the world has turned up for learning, the impertinency of which has been excellently exposed by an ingenious pen,[4] but busy themselves in a serious inquiry after necessary and perfective truths, something which it concerns them to know, and which tends to their real interest and perfection, and what that is the excellent author just now mentioned will sufficiently inform them. Such a course of study will neither be too troublesome nor out of the reach of a female virtuoso;[5] for it is not intended she should spend her hours in learning words but things, and therefore no more languages than are necessary to acquaint her with useful authors. Nor need she trouble her self in turning over a great number of books, but take care to understand and digest a few well chosen and good ones. Let her but obtain right ideas, and be truly acquainted with the nature of those objects that present themselves to her mind, and then no matter whether or no she be able to tell what fanciful people have said about them: And thoroughly to understand Christianity as professed by the Church of England,[6] will be sufficient to confirm her in the truth, though she have not a catalogue of those particular errors which oppose it. Indeed a learned education of the women will appear so unfashionable, that I began to startle at the singularity of the proposition, but was extremely pleased when I found a late ingenious author (whose book I met with since the writing of this) agree with me in my opinion.[7] For speaking of the repute that learning was in about 150 years ago, "It was so very modish," says he "that the fair sex seemed to believe that Greek and Latin added to their charms: and Plato and Aristotle untranslated, were frequent ornaments of their closets.[8] One would think by the effects,

3. Eve was cast out of the Garden of Eden with Adam after she was persuaded by the serpent to eat the fruit from the tree of knowledge (Genesis 3.6).
4. Astell's note cites John Norris's *Reflections upon the Conduct of Human Life* (1690). "Unconcerning": unimportant, irrelevant.

5. Scholar.
6. The Church of England set itself against the doctrines and ceremonies of the Catholic Church.
7. Astell's note cites William Wotton's *Reflections upon Ancient and Modern Learning* (1691).
8. Private chambers, studies. The "untranslated" works of the Greek philosophers Plato (ca. 427–

that it was a proper way of educating them, since there are no accounts in history of so many great women in any one age, as are to be found between the years 15 and 1600."

For since God has given women as well as men intelligent souls, why should they be forbidden to improve them? Since he has not denied us the faculty of thinking, why should we not (at least in gratitude to him) employ our thoughts on himself their noblest object, and not unworthily bestow them on trifles and gaieties and secular affairs? Being[9] the soul was created for the contemplation of truth as well as for the fruition of good, is it not as cruel and unjust to exclude women from the knowledge of the one as from the enjoyment of the other? Especially since the will is blind, and cannot choose but by the direction of the understanding; or to speak more properly, since the soul always wills according as she understands, so that if she understands amiss, she wills amiss. And as exercise enlarges and exalts any faculty, so through want of using it becomes cramp[1] and lessened; if therefore we make little or no use of our understandings, we shall shortly have none to use; and the more contracted and unemployed the deliberating and directive power is, the more liable is the elective to unworthy and mischievous choices. What is it but the want of an ingenious[2] education, that renders the generality of feminine conversations so insipid and foolish and their solitude so insupportable? Learning is therefore necessary to render them more agreeable and useful in company, and to furnish them with becoming entertainments when alone, that so they may not be driven to those miserable shifts,[3] which too many make use of to put off their time, that precious talent[4] that never lies on the hands of a judicious person. And since our happiness in the next world, depends so far on those dispositions which we carry along with us out of this, that without a right habitude and temper of mind we are not capable of felicity; and seeing our beatitude consists in the contemplation of the divine truth and beauty, as well as in the fruition of his goodness, can ignorance be a fit preparative for Heaven? Is't likely that she whose understanding has been busied about nothing but froth and trifles, should be capable of delighting her self in noble and sublime truths? Let such therefore as deny us the improvement of our intellectuals, either take up his[5] Paradox, who said that women have no souls, which at a time when the most contend to have them allowed to brutes, would be as unphilosophical as it is unmannerly, or else let them permit us to cultivate and improve them. There is a sort of learning indeed which is worse than the greatest ignorance: A woman may study plays and romances all her days, and be a great deal more knowing but never a jot the wiser. Such a knowledge as this serves only to instruct and put her forward in the practice of the greatest follies, yet how can they justly blame her who forbid, or at least won't afford opportunity of better? A rational mind will be employed, it will never be satisfied in doing nothing, and if you neglect to furnish it with good materials, 'tis like to take up with such as come to hand.

We pretend not that women should teach in the church, or usurp authority where it is not allowed them; permit us only to understand our own duty,

ca. 327 B.C.E.) and Aristotle (384–322 B.C.E.) were rediscovered in the Renaissance.
9. I.e., given that.
1. Contracted. "Want": lack.
2. Befitting a wellborn person.
3. Expedients, here evidently referring to women's

traditional leisure activities, such as music, embroidery, etc.
4. Treasure.
5. Perhaps the Prophet Muhammed (ca. 570–632 C.E.), who was commonly thought to have claimed in the Qur'an that women lack souls.

and not be forced to take it upon trust from others; to be at least so far learned, as to be able to form in our minds a true idea of Christianity, it being so very necessary to fence[6] us against the danger of these last and perilous days, in which deceivers a part of whose character is to lead captive silly women, need not creep into houses since they have authority to proclaim their errors on the housetop. And let us also acquire a true practical knowledge, such as will convince us of the absolute necessity of holy living as well as of right believing, and that no heresy is more dangerous than that of an ungodly and wicked life. And since the French tongue is understood by most ladies, methinks they may much better improve it by the study of philosophy (as I hear the French ladies do) Descartes, Malebranche[7] and others, than by reading idle novels and romances. 'Tis strange we shou'd be so forward to imitate their fashions and fopperies, and have no regard to what really deserves our imitation. And why shall it not be thought as genteel to understand French philosophy, as to be accoutred in a French mode? Let therefore the famous Madam D'acier, Scudery, &c, and our own incomparable Orinda,[8] excite the emulation of the English ladies.

The ladies, I'm sure, have no reason to dislike this proposal, but I know not how the men will resent it to have their enclosure broke down, and women invited to taste of that tree of knowledge they have so long unjustly monopolized. But they must excuse me, if I be as partial to my own sex as they are to theirs, and think women as capable of learning as men are, and that it becomes them as well. For I cannot imagine wherein the hurt lies, if instead of doing mischief to one another, by an uncharitable and vain conversation, women be enabled to inform and instruct those of their own sex at least; the holy ghost having left it on record, that Priscilla as well as her husband, catechized the eloquent Apollos[9] and the great Apostle found no fault with her. It will therefore be very proper for our ladies to spend part of their time in this retirement, in adorning their minds with useful knowledge.

1694

6. Protect, shield.
7. René Descartes (1596–1650) and Nicholas de Malebranche (1638–1715), well-known 17th-century philosophers.
8. Katherine Philips (1631–1664), English poet known as "the Matchless Orinda" (see p. 169). Anne Lefebvre Dacier (1647–1720), French clas-

sical scholar who translated the *Iliad* and *Odyssey*. Madeleine de Scudéry (1607–1701), French poet and novelist.
9. A preacher who knows only the teachings of John the Baptist; he is educated in Christianity by Priscilla and her husband Aquila, two followers of the apostle Paul (Acts 18.26).

LADY MARY WORTLEY MONTAGU
1689–1762

At twenty-one years of age, Lady Mary Pierrepont sent her translation of the *Enchiridion of Epictetus* to her mentor, Bishop Burnet, with a letter in which she explained, "My sex is usually forbid studies of this nature, and folly reckoned so much our proper sphere, that we are sooner pardoned any excesses of that, than the least pretensions to reading or good sense." Although she knew that "there is hardly a character in the

world more despicable, or more liable to universal ridicule than that of a learned woman," through her witty conversation and the candid letters and sardonic poems she circulated to friends, the woman who became Lady Mary Wortley Montagu went on to attain a reputation for learning that gained her staunch friends and merciless foes. Writing in the age of great epistolary productions, Lady Mary fashioned her letters into a fascinating record of women's customs and conduct both in England and abroad. The explicit sexual themes she addressed in her poems made her vulnerable to scandalous rumors, but she was also hailed by contemporaries as a "she meteor" or "the female traveler."

Almost every major event in Lady Mary's life was recorded in letters to her sister, her husband, and her daughter. It was a life of privilege and publicity. Her father was a wealthy Whig peer, Evelyn Pierrepont, who became fifth earl of Kingston in 1690 and first duke of Kingston in 1713; her mother, Mary Fielding, died when Lady Mary was five years old. The education she pursued in her father's library was stimulated by her uncle and Bishop Burnet, as well as by two close friends, Mary Astell and Anne Montagu. After Montagu's death in 1709, her brother continued this correspondence. When it turned into a courtship, which Lady Mary's father opposed, Edward Wortley Montagu and Lady Mary eloped in 1712. Montagu was made ambassador to Constantinople in 1716, and for two years Lady Mary sent letters home describing her journeys and adventures in Turkey, where she explored Constantinople in disguise and even visited a harem. On her return to England, she helped to popularize smallpox inoculation by having her own two children inoculated: a 1724 article in *The Plaindealer* viewed her education of an antagonistic medical profession as proof "that England has owed to women the greatest blessings she has been distinguished by."

Throughout her adult life, Lady Mary was active at the center of London's cultural coteries: she helped advance the career of her cousin, the dramatist and novelist Henry Fielding; she maintained friendships with Joseph Addison and Richard Steele, the author-editors of the influential periodical *The Spectator*; in 1717 she received Alexander Pope's "Eloisa to Abelard," which was addressed to her as to a close friend; and in 1735 she withstood Pope's furious attack on her as a slovenly "Sappho" in "Epistle 2: To a Lady." Partly motivated by her anger at Pope, her verse attack on Jonathan Swift lambasted his scurrilous "The Lady's Dressing Room."

After a bitter political feud with Pope and the marriage of her daughter in 1739, Lady Mary fell in love with Francesco Algarotti, a young writer she followed to Italy. She never established a lasting relationship with him, but she remained separated from her husband, returning to England only after his death in 1761 for the remaining year of her own life. A year after her death, the Turkish Embassy letters consolidated her literary reputation; she had prepared them for publication herself, keeping copies of those she mailed and deleting the more personal passages. Forty years later, her other correspondences began to appear in print, and today they total almost nine hundred letters. A number of her poems—*Town Eclogues* and *Court Poems*— appeared in a pirated volume in 1716, a portion of which was reprinted in 1747. In 1837, Lord Wharncliffe produced an edition of her *Letters and Works*. But her poems have only recently begun to receive the attention they deserve. Satires on feminine narcissism and on masculine arrogance, urbane assessments of urban life, and savvy evaluations of literary fashions, the poems of Lady Mary Wortley Montagu deploy traditional neoclassical forms with exceptional vigor and notable skill.

Saturday—The Small-Pox[1]

Flavia

The wretched Flavia, on her couch reclined;
Thus breathed the anguish of a wounded mind,
A glass[2] reversed in her right hand she bore,
For now she shunned the face she sought before.
5 "How am I changed! alas! how am I grown
A frightful spectre to myself unknown!
Where's my complexion? where my radiant bloom,
That promised happiness for years to come?
Then with what pleasure I this face surveyed!
10 To look once more, my visits oft delayed!
Charmed with the view, a fresher red would rise,
And a new life shot sparkling from my eyes!
 "Ah! faithless glass, my wonted bloom restore;
Alas! I rave, that bloom is now no more!
15 The greatest good the gods on men bestow,
Even youth itself, to me is useless now.
There was a time (oh! that I could forget!)
When opera-tickets poured before my feet;
And at the ring,[3] where brightest beauties shine,
20 The earliest cherries of the spring were mine.
Witness, O Lilly; and thou, Motteux, tell,
How much japan[4] these eyes have made ye sell.
With what contempt ye saw me oft despise
The humble offer of the raffled prize;
25 For at each raffle still each prize I bore,
With scorn rejected, or with triumph wore!
Now beauty's fled, and presents are no more!
 "For me the patriot has the House[5] forsook,
And left debates to catch a passing look:
30 For me the soldier has soft verses writ:
For me the beau has aimed to be a wit.
For me the wit to nonsense was betrayed;
The gamester has for me his dun delayed,
And overseen[6] the card he would have played.
35 The bold and haughty, by success made vain,
Awed by my eyes have trembled to complain:
The bashful 'squire, touched by a wish unknown,
Has dared to speak with spirit not his own:
Fired by one wish, all did alike adore;
40 Now beauty's fled, and lovers are no more!
 "As round the room I turn my weeping eyes,

1. Lady Mary herself contracted smallpox (1715), though she was not badly marked. Later she worked to introduce into England the practice of inoculation against smallpox, which she had observed in Turkey.
2. Mirror.
3. A circular course in London's Hyde Park.
4. I.e., Japanese goods. Charles Lillie, performer and an agent who sold the influential periodicals *The Tatler* (published 1709–11) and *The Spectator* (1712–15). Peter Motteux (1660–1718), translator and dramatist; he also dealt in tea and Chinese and Indian wares.
5. I.e., the House of Commons, the lower house of Parliament.
6. Overlooked. "Dun": debt collector.

New unaffected scenes of sorrow rise.
Far from my sight that killing picture[7] bear,
The face disfigure, and the canvas tear:
45 That picture which with pride I used to show,
The lost resemblance but upbraids me now.
And thou, my toilette![8] where I oft have sat,
While hours unheeded passed in deep debate
How curls should fall, or where a patch to place;
50 If blue or scarlet best became my face:
Now on some happier nymph your aid bestow;
On fairer heads, ye useless jewels, glow!
No borrowed lustre can my charms restore;
Beauty is fled, and dress is now no more!
55 "Ye meaner beauties, I permit ye shine;
Go, triumph in the hearts that once were mine:
But 'midst your triumphs with confusion know,
'Tis to my ruin all your charms ye owe.
Would pitying heaven restore my wonted mien,
60 Ye still might move unthought of and unseen:
But oh, how vain, how wretched is the boast
Of beauty faded, and of empire lost!
What now is left but, weeping, to deplore
My beauty fled, and empire now no more!
65 "Ye cruel chemists, what withheld your aid?
Could no pomatum[9] save a trembling maid?
How false and trifling is that art ye boast!
No art can give me back my beauty lost.
In tears, surrounded by my friends, I lay
70 Masked o'er, and trembled at the sight of day;
Mirmillio came my fortune to deplore
(A golden-headed cane well carved he bore),
Cordials, he cried, my spirits must restore!
Beauty is fled, and spirit is no more!
75 "Galen, the grave officious Squirt was there.
With fruitless grief and unavailing care;
Machaon[1] too, the great Machaon, known
By his red cloak and his superior frown;
And why, he cried, this grief and this despair?
80 You shall again be well, again be fair;
Believe my oath (with that an oath he swore);
False was his oath; my beauty was no more!
 "Cease, hapless maid, no more thy tale pursue,
Forsake mankind, and bid the world adieu!
85 Monarchs and beauties rule with equal sway:
All strive to serve, and glory to obey:
Alike unpitied when deposed they grow,
Men mock the idol of their former vow.

7. I.e., a painting that "kills" her with its "unaffected scenes" because it shows her face unscarred by smallpox.
8. Dressing table.
9. Scented ointment. "Chemists": druggists.

1. The son of Asclepius (the Greek god of healing) and one of the Greek heroes in the Trojan War; he healed many fellow soldiers. Galen (129–ca. 199 C.E.), Greek physician whose writings were authoritative for centuries. "Squirt": doctor (slang).

"Adieu! ye parks—in some obscure recess,
90 Where gentle streams will weep at my distress,
Where no false friend will in my grief take part,
And mourn my ruin with a joyful heart;
There let me live in some deserted place,
There hide in shades this lost inglorious face.
95 Plays, operas, circles,[2] I no more must view!
My toilette, patches, all the world adieu!"

1715 1716

Epitaph

Here lies John Hughs and Sarah Drew.
Perhaps you'll say, what's that to you?
Believe me, friend, much may be said
On this poor couple that are dead.
5 On Sunday next they should have married;
But see how oddly things are carried.
On Thursday last it rained and lightened,[1]
These tender lovers sadly frightened
Sheltered beneath the cocking hay[2]
10 In hopes to pass the storm away.
But the bold thunder found them out
(Commissioned for that end no doubt)
And seizing on their trembling breath
Consigned them to the shades of death.
15 Who knows if 'twas not kindly done?
For had they seen the next year's sun
A beaten wife and cuckold swain[3]
Had jointly cursed the marriage chain.
Now they are happy in their doom
20 For P. has wrote upon their tomb.[4]

1718 1763

An Answer to a Love Letter in Verse[1]

Is it to me, this sad-lamenting strain?
Are heaven's choicest gifts bestowed in vain?
A plenteous fortune, and a beauteous bride,
Your love rewarded, and content your pride!
5 Yet leaving her—'tis me that you pursue,
Without one single charm, but being new.

2. Tiers of seats in a theater.
1. I.e., there was a lightning storm.
2. I.e., haycocks.
3. A rustic, especially a lover in pastoral poetry.
4. In 1718, Alexander Pope (1688–1744), English poet, wrote three epitaphs on lovers killed by lightning, John Hewet and Sarah Drew, two of which

were highly sentimental in emphasizing the pair's purity and faithfulness; it is to these that Lady Mary is responding.
1. Lady Mary was replying to a letter from a "Mr. T." or "Mr. T——n." One "sad-lamenting" suitor sent her a verse epistle dated May 31, 1725; there were no doubt others.

How vile is man! How I detest the ways
Of artful falsehood, and designing praise!
Tasteless, an easy Happiness you slight,
10　Ruin your joy, and mischief your delight.
Why should poor Pug[2] (the mimic of your kind)
Wear a rough chain, and be to box confined?
Some cup perhaps he breaks, or tears a fan,
While moves unpunished the destroyer, man.
15　Not bound by vows, and unrestrained by shame,
In sport you break the heart, and rend the fame.[3]
Not that your art can be successful here,
Th'already plundered need no robber fear,
Nor sighs, nor charms, nor flattery can move,
20　Too well secured against a second love,
Once, and but once, that devil charmed my mind,
To reason deaf, to observation blind,
I idly hoped (what cannot love persuade?)
My fondness equaled, and my truth repaid,
25　Slow to distrust, and willing to believe,
Long hushed my doubts, and would my self deceive;
But oh too soon—this tale would ever last,
Sleep, sleep my wrongs and let me think 'em past.
　　For you who mourn with counterfeited grief
30　And ask so boldly like a begging thief;
May soon some other nymph inflict the pain
You know so well, with cruel art to feign,
Though long you've sported with Don Cupid's[4] dart,
You may see eyes, and you may feel a heart.
35　So the brisk wits[5] who stop the evening coach
Laugh at the fear that follows their approach,
With idle mirth, and haughty scorn despise
The passenger's pale cheek, and staring eyes;
But seized by justice, find a fright no jest
40　And all the terror doubled in their breast.

1720　　　　　　　　　　　　　　　　　　　　　　　　　1750

Epistle from Mrs. Yonge to Her Husband[1]

Think not this paper comes with vain pretense
To move your pity, or to mourn th' offense.
Too well I know that hard obdurate heart;
No softening mercy there will take my part,

2. A monkey.
3. Reputation.
4. Roman god of love, who shoots his victims with arrows. "Don": master (archaic).
5. I.e., highway robbers.
1. The editors gratefully acknowledge the permission of Lawrence Lipking to use information contained in his notes to this poem in *The Norton Anthology of English Literature*. In this epistle, or verse letter, Lady Mary assumes the role of Mary Yonge, a woman who, having separated from her adulterous husband, William, herself took a lover and was then publicly disgraced by the divorce proceedings that her husband instigated. Intimate details of her relationship with her lover were revealed during the trial, and the court awarded Mr. Yonge his wife's dowry and the greater part of her fortune.

5 Nor can a woman's arguments prevail.
When even your patron's[2] wise example fails.
But this last privilege I still retain;
Th' oppressed and injured always may complain.
 Too, too severely laws of honor bind
10 The weak submissive sex of womankind.
If sighs have gained or force compelled our hand,
Deceived by art,[3] or urged by stern command,
Whatever motive binds the fatal tie,
The judging world expects our constancy.
15 Just heaven! (for sure in heaven does justice reign,
Though tricks below that sacred name profane)
To you appealing I submit my cause,
Nor fear a judgment from impartial laws.
All bargains but conditional[4] are made;
20 The purchase void, the creditor unpaid,
Defrauded servants are from service free;
A wounded slave regains his liberty.
For wives ill used[5] no remedy remains,
To daily racks condemned, and to eternal chains.
25 From whence is this unjust distinction grown?
Are we not formed with passions like your own?
Nature with equal fire our souls endued,[6]
Our minds as haughty, and as warm our blood;
O'er the wide world your pleasures you pursue,
30 The change is justified by something new;
But we must sigh in silence—and be true.
Our sex's weakness you expose and blame
(Of every prattling fop the common theme),
Yet from this weakness you suppose is due
35 Sublimer virtue than your Cato[7] knew.
Had heaven designed us trials so severe,
It would have formed our tempers them to bear.[8]
 And I have borne (oh what have I not borne!)
The pang of jealousy, the insults of scorn.
40 Wearied at length, I from your sight remove,
And place my future hopes in secret love.
In the gay bloom of glowing youth retired,
I quit[9] the woman's joy to be admired,
With that small pension your hard heart allows,
45 Renounce your fortune, and release your vows.
To custom (though unjust) so much is due;
I hide my frailty from the public view.
My conscience clear, yet sensible of shame,
My life I hazard, to preserve my fame.

2. Sir Robert Walpole (1676–1745), a powerful friend of William Yonge's at court, who was said to tolerate his own wife's infidelity.
3. Artifice.
4. Only conditionally.
5. Poorly treated.
6. Endowed.
7. Two Roman statesmen of this name were known for their honesty and self-discipline; Cato the Elder (234–159 B.C.E.) is famous for his severe morals, while his great-grandson Cato the Younger (95–46 B.C.E.) is famed for his nobly tragic death.
8. I.e., capable of bearing such trials. "Tempers": characters.
9. Gave up.

50 And I prefer this low inglorious state
 To vile dependence on the thing I hate—
 But you pursue me to this last retreat.
 Dragged into light, my tender crime is shown
 And every circumstance of fondness known.
55 Beneath the shelter of the law you stand,
 And urge my ruin with a cruel hand,
 While to my fault thus rigidly severe,
 Tamely submissive to the man you fear.[1]
 This wretched outcast, this abandoned wife,
60 Has yet this joy to sweeten shameful life:
 By your mean conduct, infamously loose,[2]
 You are at once my accuser and excuse.
 Let me be damned by the censorious prude
 (Stupidly dull, or spiritually lewd),
65 My hapless case will surely pity find
 From every just and reasonable mind.
 When to the final sentence I submit,
 The lips condemn me, but their souls acquit.
 No more my husband, to your pleasures go,
70 The sweets of your recovered freedom know.
 Go: court the brittle friendship of the great,
 Smile at his board or at his levee[3] wait;
 And when dismissed, to madam's toilet fly,[4]
 More than her chambermaids, or glasses,[5] lie,
75 Tell her how young she looks, how heavenly fair,
 Admire the lilies and the roses there.
 Your high ambition may be gratified,
 Some cousin of her own be made your bride,
 And you the father of a glorious race
80 Endowed with Ch—l's strength and Low—r's face.[6]

1724 1972

The Reasons That Induced Dr. Swift to Write a Poem Called
the Lady's Dressing Room[1]

 The Doctor in a clean starched band,[2]
 His golden snuff box in his hand,
 With care his diamond ring displays
 And artful shows its various rays,

1. I.e., Walpole.
2. Immoral (i.e., adulterous). "Mean": low.
3. Morning reception of visitors. "Board": dining table.
4. It was fashionable for upper-class women to receive visitors during the last stages of dressing (their "toilet").
5. Mirrors.
6. General Charles Churchill (ca. 1679–1745) was rumored to have had an affair with Lady Walpole, and Antony Lowther (d. 1741) was a notori-

ous ladies' man. Lady Mary insinuates that Yonge's next wife may be as untrue as his first.
1. In "The Lady's Dressing Room" (1732), Jonathan Swift had asked, "Should I the queen of love refuse / Because she rose from stinking ooze?" His view of this excremental Venus clearly infuriated Lady Mary Wortley Montagu, who replied in a style that mimics Swift's.
2. Clerical collar (Swift was dean of St. Patrick's Cathedral in Dublin).

5 While grave he stalks down ——— Street,
His dearest Betty ——— to meet.
 Long had he waited for this hour,
Nor gained admittance to the bower,
Had joked and punned, and swore and writ,

10 Tried all his gallantry and wit,
Had told her oft what part he bore
In Oxford's[3] schemes in days of yore,
But bawdy, politics, nor satyr[4]
Could move this dull hard-hearted creature.

15 Jenny her maid could taste a rhyme
And grieved to see him lose his time,
Had kindly whispered in his ear,
"For twice two pound you enter here;
My lady vows without that sum

20 It is in vain you write or come."
 The destined offering now he brought
And in a paradise of thought
With a low bow approached the dame
Who smiling heard him preach his flame.

25 His gold she takes (such proofs as these
Convince most unbelieving shes)
And in her trunk rose up to lock it
(Too wise to trust it in her pocket)
And then, returned with blushing grace,

30 Expects the Doctor's warm embrace.
 But now this is the proper place
Where morals stare me in the face
And for the sake of fine expression
I'm forced to make a small digression.

35 Alas for wretched humankind,
With learning mad, with wisdom blind!
The ox thinks he's for saddle fit
(As long ago friend Horace[5] writ)
And men their talents still mistaking,

40 The stutterer fancies his is speaking.
With admiration oft we see
Hard features heightened by toupée,
The beau affects the politician,
Wit is the citizen's[6] ambition,

45 Poor Pope philosophy displays on
With so much rhyme and little reason,
And though he argues ne'er so long
That all is right, his head is wrong.[7]
 None strive to know their proper merit

50 But strain for wisdom, beauty, spirit,
And lose the praise that is their due

3. Robert Harley, earl of Oxford (1661–1724); he employed Swift as a political writer and served as prime minister (1711–14).
4. Satire.
5. Roman poet and satirist (65–8 B.C.E.); the allu-

sion is to his *Epistles* (ca. 20 B.C.E.), 1.14.43.
6. "A townsman; a man of trade; not a gentleman" (Samuel Johnson's *Dictionary*, 1755).
7. A parody of *An Essay on Man* (1734), 1. 294, by Alexander Pope (1688–1744).

While they've the impossible in view.
So have I seen the injudicious heir
To add one window the whole house impair.
55 Instinct the hound does better teach
Who never undertook to preach;
The frighted hare from dogs does run
But not attempts to bear a gun.
Here many noble thoughts occur
60 But I prolixity abhor,
And will pursue the instructive tale
To show the wise in some things fail.
 The reverend lover with surprise
Peeps in her bubbies,[8] and her eyes,
65 And kisses both, and tries—and tries.
The evening in this hellish play,
Beside his guineas thrown away,
Provoked the priest to that degree
He swore, "The fault is not in me.
70 Your damned close stool[9] so near my nose,
Your dirty smock, and stinking toes,
Would make a Hercules[1] as tame
As any beau that you can name."
 The nymph grown furious roared, "By God!
75 The blame lies all in sixty odd,"
And scornful pointing to the door
Cried, "Fumbler, see my face no more."
"With all my heart I'll go away,
But nothing done, I'll nothing pay.
80 Give back the money."—"How," cried she,
"Would you palm such a cheat on me!
For poor four pound to roar and bellow,
Why sure you want some new Prunella?"[2]
"I'll be revenged, you saucy quean"[3]
85 (Replies the disappointed Dean),
"I'll so describe your dressing room
The very Irish shall not come."[4]
She answered short, "I'm glad you'll write,
You'll furnish paper when I shite."

1734

8. Breasts.
9. Chamber pot.
1. The greatest hero of classical mythology.
2. The name of a prostitute; also, the dark worsted

cloth used for clergymen's gowns.
3. Whore.
4. A mocking attack on the Irish (and thus Swift)
as coarse and unrefined.

ELIZA HAYWOOD
1693?–1756

Prolific even by eighteenth-century standards, Eliza Haywood authored more than sixty titles—including short fiction, novels, plays, periodicals, political works, and poetry—in a career that spanned nearly forty years. Yet her early life remains shrouded in obscurity. Apparently abandoned by her husband before she was twenty-one, Haywood pursued a theater career, as an actress first at Dublin's Smock Alley theater and later in London. There she turned to fiction, and from the date of her first publication—the best-selling *Love in Excess; or, The Fatal Inquiry* (1719–20)—she was quickly established in literary London as the figure whom Henry Fielding dubbed "Mrs. Novel." In part, Haywood acquired a significant readership in the 1720s with a series of often racy popular novels; perhaps as a result, too, she also acquired critics such as Alexander Pope, who lampooned her for immorality and commercial sensationalism in *The Dunciad* (1728).

Haywood's later career was more circumspect, but even more versatile. Within a year of the publication of Samuel Richardson's best-selling novel *Pamela* (1740), she had produced both a satire and an imitation in *Anti-Pamela: Or, Feign'd Innocence Detected* (1741) and *The Virtuous Villager: Or, Virgin's Victory* (1742). Her later works included periodicals (*The Female Spectator*, 1744–46), allegorical prose (*Life's Progress through the Passions: Or, The Adventures of Natura*, 1748), a political pamphlet for which she was briefly jailed (*A Letter from H— G—, Esq.*, 1750), and advice manuals (*The Wife* and *The Husband*, 1756). With its moralistic message, *The History of Miss Betsy Thoughtless* (1751) proves that Haywood could alter her tone and themes to adjust to the prevailing tastes of the literary marketplace. At her death in 1756, Haywood was working on her last periodical, *The Young Lady*.

Fantomina; or, Love in a Maze (1724) was written at the height of Haywood's early career. As the scholar Christine Blouch explains, "An unnamed protagonist uses the occasion of attending the theater to create her own drama, which is a swiftly and intricately staged series of progressive identities that transgress social and sexual boundaries. *Fantomina* is about a young woman who decides to become mistress of her own identity." Of particular interest to contemporary readers is Haywood's depiction of a desirous female character whose brilliant masquerades easily dupe a gullible man. Yet just as fascinating as her analysis of the rhythms of dawning and dwindling desire is Haywood's gloomy conviction that at the story's end her impudent heroine must be severely punished for such erotic transgressions and impersonations.

Fantomina; or, Love in a Maze[1]

In love the victors from the vanquished fly.
They fly that wound, and they pursue that die.
Waller[2]

A young lady of distinguished birth, beauty, wit, and spirit, happened to be in a box one night at the playhouse; where, though there were a great number of celebrated toasts,[3] she perceived several gentlemen extremely pleased themselves with entertaining a woman who sat in a corner of the pit

1. We are indebted to Marah Gubar for bringing this text to our attention.
2. Edmund Waller (1606–1687), from "To A. H.,

of the Different Successes of Their Loves" (1645).
3. Women toasted by gentlemen; the belles of the season.

and, by her air and manner of receiving them, might easily be known to be one of those who come there for no other purpose, than to create acquaintance with as many as seem desirous of it. She could not help testifying her contempt of men who, regardless either of the play or circle,[4] threw away their time in such a manner, to some ladies that sat by her. But they, either less surprised by being more accustomed to such sights than she who had been bred for the most part in the country, or not of a disposition to consider anything very deeply, took but little notice of it. She still thought of it, however; and the longer she reflected on it, the greater was her wonder that men, some of whom she knew were accounted to have wit,[5] should have tastes so very depraved.—This excited a curiosity in her to know in what manner these creatures were addressed.—She was young, a stranger to the world, and consequently to the dangers of it; and having nobody in town, at that time, to whom she was obliged to be accountable for her actions, did in everything as her inclinations or humors rendered most agreeable to her: therefore thought it not in the least a fault to put in practice a little whim which came immediately into her head, to dress herself as near as she could in the fashion of those women who make sale of their favors, and set herself in the way of being accosted as such a one, having at that time no other aim than the gratification of an innocent curiosity.—She no sooner designed this frolic than she put it in execution; and muffling her hoods over her face, went the next night into the gallery-box, and practicing, as much as she had observed at that distance, the behavior of that woman, was not long before she found her disguise had answered the ends she wore it for.—A crowd of purchasers of all degrees and capacities were in a moment gathered about her, each endeavoring to outbid the other, in offering her a price for her embraces.— She listened to 'em all, and was not a little diverted in her mind at the disappointment she should give to so many, each of which thought himself secure of gaining her.—She was told by 'em all, that she was the most lovely woman in the world; and some cried, *Gad, she is mighty like my fine Lady Such-a-one*—naming her own name. She was naturally vain, and received no small pleasure in hearing herself praised, though in the person of another, and a supposed prostitute; but she dispatched as soon as she could all that had hitherto attacked her, when she saw the accomplished *Beauplaisir*[6] was making his way through the crowd as fast as he was able, to reach the bench she sat on. She had often seen him in the drawing-room, had talked with him; but then her quality and reputed virtue kept him from using her with that freedom she now expected he would do, and had discovered[7] something in him which had made her often think she should not be displeased, if he would abate some part of his reserve.—Now was the time to have her wishes answered.—He looked in her face, and fancied, as many others had done, that she very much resembled that lady whom she really was; but the vast disparity there appeared between their characters prevented him from entertaining even the most distant thought that they could be the same.—He addressed her at first with the usual salutations of her pretended profession, as, *Are you engaged, Madam?—Will you permit me to wait on you home after*

4. Tier of seats in the theater. "Testifying": asserting.
5. Intelligence.

6. "Good pleasure" (French).
7. Caught sight of. "Quality": high birth.

the play?—By Heaven, you are a fine girl!—How long have you used this house?—and such like questions; but perceiving she had a turn of wit, and a genteel manner in her raillery, beyond what is frequently to be found among those wretches, who are for the most part gentlewomen but by necessity, few of 'em having had an education suitable to what they affect to appear, he changed the form of his conversation, and showed her it was not because he understood no better, that he had made use of expressions so little polite.—In fine, they were infinitely charmed with each other. He was transported to find so much beauty and wit in a woman who he doubted not but on very easy terms he might enjoy; and she found a vast deal of pleasure in conversing with him in this free and unrestrained manner. They passed their time all the play with an equal satisfaction; but when it was over, she found herself involved in a difficulty which before never entered into her head, but which she knew not well how to get over.—The passion he professed for her was not of that humble nature which can be content with distant adorations.—He resolved not to part from her without the gratifications of those desires she had inspired; and presuming on the liberties which her supposed function allowed of, told her she must either go with him to some convenient house of his procuring, or permit him to wait on her to her own lodgings.—Never had she been in such a *dilemma*. Three or four times did she open her mouth to confess her real quality; but the influence of her ill stars prevented it, by putting an excuse into her head which did the business as well, and at the same time did not take from her the power of seeing and entertaining him a second time with the same freedom she had done this.—She told him, she was under obligations to a man who maintained her, and whom she durst not disappoint, having promised to meet him that night at a house hard by.—This story so like what those ladies sometimes tell, was not at all suspected by *Beauplaisir*; and assuring her he would be far from doing her a prejudice,[8] desired that in return for the pain he should suffer in being deprived of her company that night, that she would order her affairs, so as not to render him unhappy the next. She gave a solemn promise to be in the same box on the morrow evening, and they took leave of each other; he to the tavern to drown the remembrance of his disappointment; she in a hackney-chair[9] hurried home to indulge contemplation on the frolic she had taken, designing nothing less on her first reflections than to keep the promise she had made him, and hugging herself with joy, that she had the good luck to come off undiscovered.

But these cogitations were but of a short continuance, they vanished with the hurry of her spirits, and were succeeded by others vastly different and ruinous.—All the charms of *Beauplaisir* came fresh into her mind; she languished, she almost died for another opportunity of conversing with him; and not all the admonitions of her discretion were effectual to oblige her to deny laying hold of that which offered itself the next night.—She depended on the strength of her virtue to bear her fate through trials more dangerous than she apprehended this to be, and never having been addressed by him as Lady—, was resolved to receive his devoirs as a town-mistress,[1] imagining a world of satisfaction to herself in engaging him in the character of such a

8. An injury from misjudgment.
9. A hired closed vehicle for one person, carried
on two poles by two bearers.
1. Prostitute. "Devoirs": courteous attentions.

one observing the surprise he would be in to find himself refused by a woman and in who he supposed granted her favors without exception.—Strange and unaccountable were the whimsies she was possessed of—wild and incoherent her desires—unfixed and undetermined her resolutions, but in that of seeing *Beauplaisir* in the manner she had lately done. As for her proceedings with him, or how a second time to escape him without discovering[2] who she was, she could neither assure herself, nor whether or not in the last extremity she would do so.—Bent, however, on meeting him, whatever should be the consequence, she went out some hours before the time of going to the playhouse, and took lodgings in a house not very far from it, intending, that if he should insist on passing some part of the night with her, to carry him there, thinking she might with more security to her honor entertain him at a place where she was mistress than at any of his own choosing.

The appointed hour being arrived, she had the satisfaction to find his love in his assiduity. He was there before her; and nothing could be more tender than the manner in which he accosted her. But from the first moment she came in, to that of the play being done, he continued to assure her no consideration should prevail with him to part from her again, as she had done the night before; and she rejoiced to think she had taken that precaution of providing herself with a lodging, to which she thought she might invite him, without running any risk, either of her virtue or reputation.—Having told him she would admit of his accompanying her home, he seemed perfectly satisfied; and leading her to the place, which was not above twenty houses distant, would have ordered a collation[3] to be brought after them. But she would not permit it, telling him she was not one of those who suffered themselves to be treated at their own lodgings; and as soon she was come in, sent a servant, belonging to the house, to provide a very handsome supper and wine, and everything was served to table in a manner which showed the director neither wanted money, nor was ignorant how it should be laid out.

This proceeding, though it did not take from him the opinion that she was what she appeared to be, yet it gave him thoughts of her which he had not before.—He believed her a *mistress,* but believed her to be one of a superior rank, and began to imagine the possession of her would be much more expensive than at first he had expected. But not being of a humor to grudge anything for his pleasures, he gave himself no farther trouble than what were occasioned by fears of not having money enough to reach her price about him.

Supper being over, which was intermixed with a vast deal of amorous conversation, he began to explain himself more than he had done; and both by his words and behavior let her know he would not be denied that happiness the freedoms she allowed had made him hope.—It was in vain; she would have retracted the encouragement she had given.—In vain she endeavored to delay, till the next meeting, the fulfilling of his wishes.— She had now gone too far to retreat.—*He* was bold;—he was resolute. *She* fearful—confused, altogether unprepared to resist in such encounters, and rendered more so, by the extreme liking she had to him.—Shocked, however, at the apprehension of really losing her honor, she struggled all she could, and was just going to reveal the whole secret of her name and quality, when

2. Revealing. 3. Light meal.

the thoughts of the liberty he had taken with her, and those he still continued to prosecute,[4] prevented her, with representing the danger of being exposed, and the whole affair made a theme for public ridicule.—Thus much, indeed, she told him, that she was a virgin, and had assumed this manner of behavior only to engage him. But that he little regarded, or if he had, would have been far from obliging him to desist;—nay, in the present burning eagerness of desire, 'tis probable, that had he been acquainted both with who and what she really was, the knowledge of her birth would not have influenced him with respect sufficient to have curbed the wild exuberance of his luxurious[5] wishes, or made him in that longing, that impatient moment, change the form of his addresses. In fine, she was undone; and he gained a victory, so highly rapturous, that had he known over whom, scarce could he have triumphed more. Her tears, however, and the distraction she appeared in, after the ruinous ecstasy was past, as it heightened his wonder, so it abated his satisfaction.—He could not imagine for what reason a woman, who, if she intended not to be a *mistress*, had counterfeited the part of one, and taken so much pains to engage him, should lament a consequence which she could not but expect, and till the last test, seemed inclinable to grant; and was both surprised and troubled at the mystery.—He omitted nothing that he thought might make her easy; and still retaining an opinion that the hope of interest[6] had been the chief motive which had led her to act in the manner she had done, and believing that she might know so little of him as to suppose, now she had nothing left to give, he might not make that recompense she expected for her favors: to put her out of that pain, he pulled out of his pocket a purse of gold, entreating her to accept of that as an earnest of what he intended to do for her; assuring her, with ten thousand protestations, that he would spare nothing which his whole estate could purchase, to procure her content and happiness. This treatment made her quite forget the part she had assumed, and throwing it from her with an air of disdain, Is this a reward (*said she*) for condescensions,[7] such as I have yielded to?—Can all the wealth you are possessed of make a reparation for my loss of honor?— Oh! no, I am undone beyond the power of heaven itself to help me!—She uttered many more such exclamations; which the amazed *Beauplaisir* heard without being able to reply to, till by degrees sinking from that rage of temper, her eyes resumed their softening glances, and guessing at the consternation he was in, No, my dear *Beauplaisir*, (*added she*) your love alone can compensate for the shame you have involved me in; be you sincere and constant, and I hereafter shall, perhaps, be satisfied with my fate, and forgive myself the folly that betrayed me to you.

Beauplaisir thought he could not have a better opportunity than these words gave him of inquiring who she was, and wherefore she had feigned herself to be of a profession which he was now convinced she was not; and after he had made her a thousand vows of an affection as inviolable and ardent as she could wish to find in him, entreated she would inform him by what means his happiness had been brought about, and also to whom he was indebted for the bliss he had enjoyed.—Some remains of yet unextinguished modesty, and sense of shame, made her blush exceedingly at this

4. Persist in, carry on.
5. Lascivious.
6. Profit.
7. Stooping to unworthy acts.

demand; but recollecting herself in a little time, she told him so much of the truth, as to what related to the frolic she had taken of satisfying her curiosity in what manner *mistresses,* of the sort she appeared to be, were treated by those who addressed them; but forbore discovering her true name and quality, for the reasons she had done before, resolving, if he boasted of this affair, he should not have it in his power to touch her character. She therefore said she was the daughter of a country gentleman, who was come to town to buy clothes, and that she was called *Fantomina.* He had no reason to distrust the truth of this story, and was therefore satisfied with it; but did not doubt by the beginning of her conduct, but that[8] in the end she would be in reality, the thing she so artfully had counterfeited; and had good nature enough to pity the misfortunes he imagined would be her lot. But to tell her so, or offer his advice in that point, was not his business, at least, as yet.

They parted not till towards morning; and she obliged him to a willing vow of visiting her the next day at three in the afternoon. It was too late for her to go home that night, therefore she contented herself with lying there. In the morning she sent for the woman of the house to come up to her; and easily perceiving, by her manner, that she was a woman who might be influenced by gifts, made her a present of a couple of broad pieces,[9] and desired her, that if the gentleman who had been there the night before should ask any questions concerning her, that he should be told, she was lately come out of the country, had lodged there about a fortnight, and that her name was *Fantomina.* I shall (*also added she*) lie but seldom here; nor, indeed, ever come but in those times when I expect to meet him. I would, therefore, have you order it so, that he may think I am but just gone out, if he should happen by any accident to call when I am not here; for I would not, for the world, have him imagine I do not constantly lodge here. The landlady assured her she would do everything as she desired, and gave her to understand she wanted[1] not the gift of secrecy.

Everything being ordered at this home for the security of her reputation, she repaired to the other, where she easily excused to an unsuspecting aunt, with whom she boarded, her having been abroad all night, saying, she went with a gentleman and his lady in a barge to a little country seat of theirs up the river, all of them designing to return the same evening; but that one of the bargemen happening to be taken ill on the sudden, and no other waterman to be got that night, they were obliged to tarry till morning. Thus did this lady's wit and vivacity assist her in all, but where it was most needed.—She had discernment to foresee and avoid all those ills which might attend the loss of her *reputation,* but was wholly blind to those of the ruin of her *virtue;* and having managed her affairs so as to secure the *one,* grew perfectly easy with the remembrance she had forfeited the *other.*—The more she reflected on the merits of *Beauplaisir,* the more she excused herself for what she had done; and the prospect of that continued bliss she expected to share with him took from her all remorse for having engaged in an affair which promised her so much satisfaction, and in which she found not the least danger of misfortune.—If he is really (*said she, to herself*) the faithful, the constant lover he has sworn to be, how charming will be our amour?—And

8. I.e., her conduct never made him doubt that. 1. Lacked.
9. Gold coins.

if he should be false, grow satiated, like other men, I shall but, at the worst, have the private vexation of knowing I have lost him;—the intrigue being a secret, my disgrace will be so too.—I shall hear no whispers as I pass,—She is forsaken.—The odious word *forsaken* will never wound my ears; nor will my wrongs excite either the mirth or pity of the talking world.—It would not be even in the power of my undoer himself to triumph over me; and while he laughs at, and perhaps despises the fond, the yielding *Fantomina,* he will revere and esteem the virtuous, the reserved lady.—In this manner did she applaud her own conduct, and exult with the imagination that she had more prudence than all her sex beside. And it must be confessed, indeed, that she preserved an economy[2] in the management of this intrigue beyond what almost any woman but herself ever did: in the first place, by making no person in the world a confidant in it; and in the next, in concealing from *Beauplaisir* himself the knowledge who she was; for though she met him three or four days in a week at that lodging she had taken for that purpose, yet as much as he employed her time and thoughts, she was never missed from any assembly she had been accustomed to frequent.—The business of her love has engrossed her till six in the evening, and before seven she has been dressed in a different habit, and in another place.—Slippers, and a night-gown loosely flowing, has been the garb in which he has left the languishing *Fantomina;*—laced and adorned with all the blaze of jewels has he, in less than an hour after, beheld at the royal chapel, the palace gardens, drawing-room, opera, or play, the haughty awe-inspiring lady.—A thousand times has he stood amazed at the prodigious likeness between his little mistress and this court beauty; but was still as far from imagining they were the same as he was the first hour he had accosted her in the playhouse, though it is not impossible but that her resemblance to this celebrated lady might keep his inclination alive something longer than otherwise they would have been; and that it was to the thoughts of this (as he supposed) unenjoyed charmer she owed in great measure the vigor of his latter caresses.

But he varied not so much from his sex as to be able to prolong desire to any great length after possession. The rifled charms of *Fantomina* soon lost their poignancy[3] and grew tasteless and insipid; and when the season of the year inviting the company to the *Bath,*[4] she offered to accompany him, he made an excuse to go without her. She easily perceived his coldness, and the reason why he pretended her going would be inconvenient, and endured as much from the discovery as any of her sex could do. She dissembled it, however, before him, and took her leave of him with the show of no other concern than his absence occasioned. But this she did to take from him all suspicion of her following him, as she intended, and had already laid a scheme for.—From her first finding out that he designed to leave her behind, she plainly saw it was for no other reason, than that being tired of her conversation,[5] he was willing to be at liberty to pursue new conquests; and wisely considering that complaints, tears, swoonings, and all the extravagancies which women make use of in such cases have little prevalence over a heart inclined to rove, and only serve to render those who practice them

2. Ordering by rules.
3. Piquancy. "Rifled": stolen.
4. A fashionable resort town, notable for its hot

mineral springs, about 100 miles west from London.
5. Society; also, sexual intimacy.

more contemptible, by robbing them of that beauty which alone can bring back the fugitive lover, she resolved to take another course; and remembering the height of transport she enjoyed when the agreeable *Beauplaisir* kneeled at her feet, imploring her first favors, she longed to prove the same again. Not but a woman of her beauty and accomplishments might have beheld a thousand in that condition *Beauplaisir* had been; but with her sex's modesty, she had not also thrown off another virtue equally valuable, though generally unfortunate, *constancy.* She loved *Beauplaisir;* it was only he whose solici- tations could give her pleasure; and had she seen the whole species[6] despair- ing, dying for her sake, it might, perhaps, have been a satisfaction to her pride, but none to her more tender inclination.—Her design was once more to engage him; to hear him sigh, to see him languish, to feel the strenuous pressures of his eager arms, to be compelled, to be sweetly forced to what she wished with equal ardor, was what she wanted, and what she had formed a stratagem to obtain, in which she promised herself success.

 She no sooner heard he had left the town, than making a pretense to her aunt, that she was going to visit a relation in the country, went towards *Bath,* attended but by two servants, who she found reasons to quarrel with on the road and discharged. Clothing herself in a habit she had brought with her, she forsook the coach and went into a wagon, in which equipage she arrived at *Bath.* The dress she was in was a round-eared cap, a short red petticoat, and a little jacket of gray stuff; all the rest of her accoutrements were answer- able to[7] these, and joined with a broad country dialect, a rude unpolished air, which she, having been bred in these parts, knew very well how to imitate, with her hair and eye-brows blacked, made it impossible for her to be known, or taken for any other than what she seemed. Thus disguised did she offer herself to service in the house where *Beauplaisir* lodged, having made it her business to find out immediately where he was. Notwithstanding this meta- morphosis she was still extremely pretty; and the mistress of the house hap- pening at that time to want a maid, was very glad of the opportunity of taking her. She was presently[8] received into the family; and had a post in it (such as she would have chose, had she been left at her liberty), that of making the gentlemen's beds, getting them their breakfasts, and waiting on them in their chambers. Fortune in this exploit was extremely on her side; there were no others of the male sex in the house than an old gentleman who had lost the use of his limbs with the rheumatism, and had come thither for the benefit of the waters, and her beloved *Beauplaisir;* so that she was in no apprehensions of any amorous violence, but where she wished to find it. Nor were her designs disappointed. He was fired with the first sight of her; and though he did not presently take any farther notice of her than giving her two or three hearty kisses, yet she, who now understood that language but too well, easily saw they were the prelude to more substantial joys.—Coming the next morning to bring his chocolate, as he had ordered, he catched her by the pretty leg, which the shortness of her petticoat did not in the least oppose; then pulling her gently to him, asked her, how long she had been at service?—How many sweethearts she had? If she had ever been in love? and many other such questions, befitting one of the degree[9] she appeared to be:

6. I.e., of men. "Solicitations": sexual entreaties.
7. In agreement with.

8. Immediately.
9. Social class.

all which she answered with such seeming innocence, as more enflamed the amorous heart of him who talked to her. He compelled her to sit in his lap; and gazing on her blushing beauties, which, if possible, received addition from her plain and rural dress, he soon lost the power of containing himself.—His wild desires burst out in all his words and actions: he called her little angel, cherubim, swore he must enjoy her, though death were to be the conseqence, devoured her lips, her breasts with greedy kisses, held to his burning bosom her half-yielding, half-reluctant body, nor suffered her to get loose till he had ravaged all, and glutted each rapacious sense with the sweet beauties of the pretty *Celia*, for that was the name she bore in this second expedition.—Generous as liberality itself to all who gave him joy this way, he gave her a handsome sum of gold, which she durst not now refuse, for fear of creating some mistrust, and losing the heart she so lately had regained; therefore taking it with an humble courtesy, and a well counterfeited show of surprise and joy, cried, O law, Sir! what must I do for all this? He laughed at her simplicity, and kissing her again, though less fervently than he had done before, bad[1] her not be out of the way when he came home at night. She promised she would not, and very obediently kept her word.

His stay at *Bath* exceeded not a month; but in that time his supposed country lass had persecuted him so much with her fondness that in spite of the eagerness with which he first enjoyed her, he was at last grown more weary of her, than he had been of *Fantomina*: which she perceiving, would not be troublesome, but quitting her service, remained privately in the town till she heard he was on his return; and in that time provided herself of another disguise to carry on a third plot, which her inventing brain had furnished her with, once more to renew his twice-decayed ardors. The dress she had ordered to be made was such as widows wear in their first mourning, which, together with the most afflicted and penitential countenance that ever was seen, was no small alteration to her who used to seem all gaiety.—To add to this, her hair, which she was accustomed to wear very loose, both when *Fantomina* and *Celia*, was now tied back so straight, and her pinners[2] coming so very forward, that there was none of it to be seen. In fine, her habit and her air were so much changed, that she was not more difficult to be known in the rude country *girl*, than she was now in the sorrowful *widow*.

She knew that *Beauplaisir* came alone in his chariot to the *Bath*, and in the time of her being servant in the house where he lodged, heard nothing of any body that was to accompany him to *London*, and hoped he would return in the same manner he had gone. She therefore hired horses and a man to attend her to an inn about ten miles on this side of *Bath*, where having discharged them, she waited till the chariot should come by; which when it did, and she saw that he was alone in it, she called to him that drove it to stop a moment, and going to the door saluted the master with these words:

The distressed and wretched, Sir (*said she*), never fail to excite compassion in a generous mind; and I hope I am not deceived in my opinion that yours is such.—You have the appearance of a gentleman, and cannot, when you hear my story, refuse that assistance which is in your power to give to an

1. I.e., bade. 2. Long flaps on the sides of a headdress.

unhappy woman, who without it may be rendered the most miserable of all created beings.

It would not be very easy to represent the surprise so odd an address created in the mind of him to whom it was made.—She had not the appearance of one who wanted charity; and what other favor she required he could not conceive: but telling her she might command any thing in his power, gave her encouragement to declare herself in this manner. You may judge (*resumed she*), by the melancholy garb I am in, that I have lately lost all that ought to be valuable to womankind; but it is impossible for you to guess the greatness of my misfortune, unless you had known my husband, who was master of every perfection to endear him to a wife's affections.—But, notwithstanding. I look on myself as the most unhappy of my sex in out-living him, I must so far obey the dictates of my discretion as to take care of the little fortune he left behind him, which being in the hands of a brother of his in *London,* will be all carried off to *Holland,* where he is going to settle; if I reach not the town before he leaves it, I am undone for ever.—To which end I left *Bristol,* the place where we lived, hoping to get a place in the stage[3] at *Bath,* but they were all taken up before I came; and being, by a hurt I got in a fall, rendered incapable of traveling any long journey on horseback, I have no way to go to *London,* and must be inevitably ruined in the loss of all I have on earth, without[4] you have good nature enough to admit me to take part of your chariot.

Here the feigned widow ended her sorrowful tale, which had been several times interrupted by a parenthesis of sighs and groans; and *Beauplaisir,* with a complaisant[5] and tender air, assured her of his readiness to serve her in things of much greater consequence than what she desired of him; and told her it would be an impossibility of denying a place in his chariot to a lady, who he could not behold without yielding one in his heart. She answered the compliments he made her but with tears, which seemed to stream in such abundance from her eyes that she could not keep her handkerchief from her face one moment. Being come into the chariot, *Beauplaisir* said a thousand handsome things to persuade her from giving way to so violent a grief, which, he told her, would not only be destructive to her beauty, but likewise her health. But all his endeavors for consolement appeared ineffectual, and he began to think he should have but a dull journey, in the company of one who seemed so obstinately devoted to the memory of her dead husband that there was no getting a word from her on any other theme.—But bethinking himself of the celebrated story of the *Ephesian* matron,[6] it came into his head to make trial, she who seemed equally susceptible of *sorrow,* might not also be so too of *love:* and having began a discourse on almost every other topic, and finding her still incapable of answering, resolved to put it to the proof, if this would have no more effect to rouse her sleeping spirits.—With a gay air, therefore, though accompanied with the greatest modesty and respect, he turned the conversation, as though without design, on that joy-giving passion, and soon discovered that was indeed the subject she was best pleased to be entertained with; for on his giving her a hint to

3. Stagecoach.
4. Unless.
5. Indulgent.
6. See *Satyricon* 111–12 (ca. 60 C.E.), by the

Roman author Petronius, which relates how an Ephesian widow grieving in her husband's tomb was quickly seduced by a soldier.

begin upon, never any tongue run more voluble than hers, on the prodigious power it had to influence the souls of those possessed of it, to actions even the most distant from their intentions, principles, or humors.—From that she passed to a description of the happiness of mutual affection;—the unspeakable ecstasy of those who meet with equal ardency; and represented it in colors so lively, and disclosed by the gestures with which her words were accompanied, and the accent of her voice so true a feeling of what she said, that *Beauplaisir,* without being as stupid as he was really the contrary, could not avoid perceiving there were seeds of fire not yet extinguished, in this fair widow's soul, which wanted but the kindling breath of tender sighs to light into a blaze.—He now thought himself as fortunate, as some moments before he had the reverse; and doubted not but that before they parted, he should find a way to dry the tears of this lovely mourner, to the satisfaction of them both. He did not, however, offer, as he had done to *Fantomina* and *Celia,* to urge his passion directly to her, but by a thousand little softening artifices, which he well knew how to use, gave her leave to guess he was enamored. When they came to the inn where they were to lie, he declared himself somewhat more freely, and perceiving she did not resent it past forgiveness, grew more encroaching still.—He now took the liberty of kissing away her tears, and catching the sighs as they issued from her lips; telling her if grief was infectious, he was resolved to have his share; protesting he would gladly exchange passions with her, and be content to bear her load of *sorrow,* if she would as willingly ease the burden of his *love.*—She said little in answer to the strenuous pressures with which at last he ventured to enfold her, but not thinking it decent, for the character she had assumed, to yield so suddenly, and unable to deny both his and her own inclinations, she counterfeited a fainting, and fell motionless upon his breast.—He had no great notion that she was in a real fit, and the room they supped in happening to have a bed in it, he took her in his arms and laid her on it, believing that whatever her distemper was, that was the most proper place to convey her to.—He laid himself down by her, and endeavored to bring her to herself; and she was too grateful to her kind physician at her returning sense, to remove from the posture he had put her in, without his leave.

It may, perhaps, seem strange that *Beauplaisir* should in such near intimacies continue still deceived: I know there are men who will swear it is an impossibility, and that no disguise could hinder them from knowing a woman they had once enjoyed. In answer to these scruples, I can only say, that besides the alteration which the change of dress made in her, she was so admirably skilled in the art of feigning that she had the power of putting on almost what face she pleased, and knew so exactly how to form her behavior to the character she represented that all the comedians[7] at both playhouses are infinitely short of her performances. She could vary her very glances, tune her voice to accents the most different imaginable from those in which she spoke when she appeared herself.—These aids from nature, joined to the wiles of art, and the distance between the places where the imagined *Fantomina* and *Celia* were, might very well prevent his having any thought that they were the same, or that the fair *widow* was either of them. It never so much as entered his head, and though he did fancy he observed in the

7. Actors.

face of the latter, features which were not altogether unknown to him, yet he could not recollect when or where he had known them;—and being told by her, that from her birth, she had never removed from *Bristol,* a place where he never was, he rejected the belief of having seen her, and supposed his mind had been deluded by an idea of some other, whom she might have a resemblance of.

They passed the time of their journey in as much happiness as the most luxurious gratification of wild desires could make them; and when they came to the end of it, parted not without a mutual promise of seeing each other often.—He told her to what place she should direct a letter to him; and she assured him she would send to let him know where to come to her, as soon as she was fixed in lodgings.

She kept her promise; and charmed with the continuance of his eager fondness, went not home but into private lodgings, whence she wrote to him to visit her the first opportunity, and inquire for the Widow *Bloomer.*—She had no sooner dispatched this billet[8] than she repaired to the house where she had lodged as *Fantomina,* charging the people if *Beauplaisir* should come there, not to let him know she had been out of town. From thence she wrote to him, in a different hand, a long letter of complaint, that he had been so cruel in not sending one letter to her all the time he had been absent, entreated to see him, and concluded with subscribing herself his unalterably affectionate *Fantomina.* She received in one day answers to both these. The first contained these lines:

To the Charming Mrs. BLOOMER,

It would be impossible, my Angel! for me to express the thousandth part of that infinity of transport, the sight of your dear letter gave me.—Never was woman formed to charm like you: never did any look like you,—write like you,—bless like you;—nor did ever man adore as I do.—Since yesterday we parted, I have seemed a body without a soul; and had you not by this inspiring billet, gave me new life, I know not what by tomorrow I should have been.— I will be with you this evening about five.—O, 'tis an age till then!—But the cursed formalities of duty oblige me to dine with my lord—who never rises from table till that hour;—therefore adieu till then sweet lovely mistress of the soul and all the faculties of

Your most faithful,

BEAUPLAISIR.

The other was in this manner:
To the Lovely FANTOMINA,

If you were half so sensible as you ought of your own power of charming, you would be assured, that to be unfaithful or unkind to you would be among the things that are in their very natures impossibilities.—It was my misfortune, not my fault, that you were not persecuted every post with a declaration of my unchanging passion; but I had unluckily forgot the name of the woman at whose house you are, and knew not how to form a direction that it might come safe to your hands.—And, indeed, the reflection how you might misconstrue

8. Letter.

my silence, brought me to town some weeks sooner than I intended—If you knew how I have languished to renew those blessings I am permitted to enjoy in your society, you would rather pity than condemn

Your ever faithful,

Beauplaisir.

P.S. *I fear I cannot see you till tomorrow; some business has unluckily fallen out that will engross my hours till then.—Once more, my dear,* Adieu.

Traitor! (*cried she*) as soon as she had read them, 'tis thus our silly, fond, believing sex are served when they put faith in man. So had I been deceived and cheated, had I like the rest believed, and sat down mourning in absence, and vainly waiting recovered tendernesses.—How do some women (*continued she*) make their life a hell, burning in fruitless expectations, and dreaming out their days in hopes and fears, then wake at last to all the horror of despair?—But I have outwitted even the most subtle of the deceiving kind, and while he thinks to fool me, is himself the only beguiled person.

She made herself, most certainly, extremely happy in the reflection on the success of her stratagems; and while the knowledge of his inconstancy and levity of nature kept her from having that real tenderness for him she would else have had, she found the means of gratifying the inclination she had for his agreeable person in as full a manner as she could wish. She had all the sweets of love, but as yet had tasted none of the gall, and was in a state of contentment which might be envied by the more delicate.

When the expected hour arrived, she found that her lover had lost no part of the fervency with which he had parted from her; but when the next day she received him as *Fantomina*, she perceived a prodigious difference; which led her again into reflections on the unaccountableness of men's fancies, who still[9] prefer the last conquest, only because it is the last.—Here was an evident proof of it; for there could not be a difference in merit, because they were the same person; but the Widow *Bloomer* was a more new acquaintance than *Fantomina*, and therefore esteemed more valuable. This, indeed, must be said of *Beauplaisir*, that he had a greater share of good nature than most of his sex, who, for the most part, when they are weary of an intrigue, break it entirely off, without any regard to the despair of the abandoned nymph. Though he retained no more than a bare pity and complaisance[1] for *Fantomina*, yet believing she loved him to an excess, would not entirely forsake her, though the continuance of his visits was now become rather a penance than a pleasure.

The Widow *Bloomer* triumphed some time longer over the heart of this inconstant, but at length her sway was at an end, and she sunk in this character, to the same degree of tastelessness as she had done before in that of *Fantomina* and *Celia*.—She presently perceived it, but bore it as she had always done; it being but what she expected, she had prepared herself for it, and had another project in *embryo*, which she soon ripened into action. She did not, indeed, complete it altogether so suddenly as she had done the others, by reason there must be persons employed in it; and the aversion

9. Invariably. 1. Politeness.

she had to any *confidants* in her affairs, and the caution with which she had hitherto acted, and which she was still determined to continue, made it very difficult for her to find a way without breaking through that resolution to compass what she wished.—She got over the difficulty at last, however, by proceeding in a manner, if possible, more extraordinary than all her former behavior.—Muffling herself up in her hood one day, she went into the park about the hour when there are a great many necessitous gentlemen, who think themselves above doing what they call little things for a maintenance, walking in the *Mall,* to take a *Camelion* treat,[2] and fill their stomachs with air instead of meat. Two of those, who by their physiognomy she thought most proper for her purpose, she beckoned to come to her; and taking them into a walk more remote from company, began to communicate the business she had with them in these words: I am sensible, gentlemen (*said she*), that, through the blindness of fortune and partiality of the world, merit frequently goes unrewarded, and that those of the best pretensions meet with the least encouragement.—I ask your pardon (*continued she*), perceiving they seemed surprised, if I am mistaken in the notion, that you two may, perhaps, be of the number of those who have reason to complain of the injustice of fate; but if you are such as I take you for, I have a proposal to make you which may be of some little advantage to you. Neither of them made any immediate answer, but appeared buried in consideration for some moments. At length, We should, doubtless, madam (*said one of them*), willingly come into any measures to oblige you, provided they are such as may bring us into no danger, either as to our persons or reputations. That which I require of you (*resumed she*), has nothing in it criminal. All that I desire is *secrecy* in what you are entrusted, and to disguise yourselves in such a manner as you cannot be known, if hereafter seen by the person on whom you are to impose.—In fine, the business is only an innocent frolic, but if blazed abroad might be taken for too great a freedom in me.—Therefore, if you resolve to assist me, here are five pieces to drink my health, and assure you, that I have not discoursed you on an affair I design not to proceed in; and when it is accomplished fifty more lie ready for your acceptance. These words, and above all the money, which was a sum which, 'tis probable, they had not seen of a long time, made them immediately assent to all she desired, and press for the beginning of their employment. But things were not yet ripe for execution; and she told them, that the next day they should be let into the secret, charging them to meet her in the same place at an hour she appointed. 'Tis hard to say, which of these parties went away best pleased; *they,* that fortune had sent them so unexpected a windfall; or *she,* that she had found persons who appeared so well qualified to serve her.

Indefatigable in the pursuit of whatsoever her humor was bent upon, she had no sooner left her new-engaged emissaries, than she went in search of a house for the completing of her project.—She pitched on one very large, and magnificently furnished, which she hired by the week, giving them the money beforehand to prevent any inquiries. The next day she repaired to the park, where she met the punctual squires of low degree; and ordering them to follow her to the house she had taken, told them they must condescend

2. Chameleons were thought to live on air. "Necessitous": poor, needy. "The Mall": a walk in London's St. James Park that was a fashionable promenade.

to appear like servants, and gave each of them a very rich livery. Then writing a letter to *Beauplaisir,* in a character vastly different from either of those she had made use of as *Fantomina,* or the fair Widow *Bloomer,* ordered one of them to deliver it into his own hands, to bring back an answer, and to be careful that he sifted out nothing of the truth.—I do not fear (*said she*), that you should discover to him who I am, because that is a secret of which you yourselves are ignorant; but I would have you be so careful in your replies, that he may not think the concealment springs from any other reasons than your great integrity to your trust.—Seem therefore to know my whole affairs; and let your refusing to make him partaker in the secret, appear to be only the effect of your zeal for my interest and reputation. Promises of entire fidelity on the one side, and reward on the other, being past, the messenger made what haste he could to the house of *Beauplaisir;* and being there told where he might find him, performed exactly the injunction that had been given him. But never astonishment exceeding that which *Beauplaisir* felt at the reading this billet, in which he found these lines:

To the All-conquering Beauplaisir.

I imagine not that 'tis a new thing to you, to be told you are the greatest charm in nature to our sex: I shall therefore, not to fill up my letter with any impertinent praises on your wit or person, only tell you that I am infinite in love with both, and if you have a heart not too deeply engaged, should think myself the happiest of my sex in being capable of inspiring it with some tenderness.—There is but one thing in my power to refuse you, which is the knowledge of my name, which believing the sight of my face will render no secret, you must not take it ill that I conceal from you.—The bearer of this is a person I can trust; send by him your answer; but endeavor not to dive into the meaning of this mystery, which will be impossible for you to unravel, and at the same time very much disoblige me.—But that you may be in no apprehensions of being imposed on by a woman unworthy of your regard, I will venture to assure you, the first and greatest men in the kingdom would think themselves blessed to have that influence over me you have, though unknown to yourself acquired.—But I need not go about to raise your curiosity, by giving you any idea of what my person is; if you think fit to be satisfied, resolve to visit me tomorrow about three in the afternoon; and though my face is hid, you shall not want sufficient demonstration that she who takes these unusual measures to commence a friendship with you is neither old, nor deformed. Till then I am,

Yours,

Incognita.

He had scarce come to the conclusion before he asked the person who brought it, from what place he came;—the name of the lady he served;—if she were a wife, or widow, and several other questions directly opposite to the directions of the letter; but silence would have availed him as much as did all those testimonies of curiosity. No *Italian Bravo,*[3] employed in a business of the like nature, performed his office with more artifice; and the

3. Hired fighter or killer.

impatient inquirer was convinced, that nothing but doing as he was desired could give him any light into the character of the woman who declared so violent a passion for him; and little fearing any consequence which could ensue from such an encounter, resolved to rest satisfied till[4] he was informed of everything from herself, not imagining this *Incognita* varied so much from the generality of her sex as to be able to refuse the knowledge of anything to the man she loved with that transcendency of passion she professed, and which his many successes with the ladies gave him encouragement enough to believe. He therefore took pen and paper, and answered her letter in terms tender enough for a man who had never seen the person to whom he wrote. The words were as follows:

To the Obliging and Witty[5] INCOGNITA.

Though to tell me I am happy enough to be liked by a woman such, as by your manner of writing, I imagine you to be, is an honor which I can never sufficiently acknowledge, yet I know not how I am able to content myself with admiring the wonders of your wit alone. I am certain a soul like yours must shine in your eyes with a vivacity, which must bless all they look on.—I shall, however, endeavor to restrain myself in those bounds you are pleased to set me, till by the knowledge of my inviolable fidelity, I may be thought worthy of gazing on that heaven I am now but to enjoy in contemplation.—You need not doubt my glad compliance with your obliging summons. There is a charm in your lines which gives too sweet an idea of their lovely author to be resisted.—I am all impatient for the blissful moment which is to throw me at your feet, and give me an opportunity of convincing you that I am,

Your everlasting slave,

BEAUPLAISIR.

Nothing could be more pleased than she to whom it was directed, at the receipt of this letter; but when she was told how inquisitive he had been concerning her character and circumstances, she could not forbear laughing heartily to think of the tricks she had played him, and applauding her own strength of genius and force of resolution, which by such unthought-of ways could triumph over her lover's inconstancy, and render that very temper,[6] which to other women is the greatest curse, a means to make herself more blessed.—Had he been faithful to me (*said she, to herself*), either as *Fantomina*, or *Celia*, or the Widow *Bloomer*, the most violent passion, if it does not change its object, in time will wither. Possession naturally abates the vigor of desire, and I should have had, at best, but a cold, insipid, husband-like lover in my arms; but by these arts of passing on him as a new mistress whenever the ardor, which alone makes love a blessing, begins to diminish for the former one, I have him always raving, wild, impatient, longing, dying.—O that all neglected wives, and fond abandoned nymphs would take this method!—Men would be caught in their own snare, and have no cause to scorn our easy, weeping, wailing sex! Thus did she pride herself as if secure she never should have any reason to repent the present gaiety of her humor. The hour drawing near in which he was to come, she dressed herself in as

magnificent a manner as if she were to be that night at a ball at court, endeavoring to repair the want of those beauties which the vizard[7] should conceal, by setting forth the others with the greatest care and exactness. Her fine shape, and air, and neck appeared to great advantage; and by that which was to be seen of her, one might believe the rest to be perfectly agreeable. *Beauplaisir* was prodigiously charmed, as well with her appearance as with the manner she entertained him. But though he was wild with impatience for the sight of a face which belonged to so exquisite a body, yet he would not immediately press for it, believing before he left her he should easily obtain that satisfaction.—A noble collation being over, he began to sue for the performance of her promise of granting everything he could ask, excepting the sight of her face, and knowledge of her name. It would have been a ridiculous piece of affectation in her to have seemed coy in complying with what she herself had been the first in desiring. She yielded without even a show of reluctance: and if there be any true felicity in an amour such as theirs, both here enjoyed it to the full. But not in the height of all their mutual raptures could he prevail on her to satisfy his curiosity with the sight of her face: she told him that she hoped he knew so much of her as might serve to convince him, she was not unworthy of his tenderest regard; and if he could not content himself with that which she was willing to reveal, and which was the conditions of their meeting, dear as he was to her, she would rather part with him for ever, than consent to gratify an inquisitiveness which, in her opinion, had no business with his love. It was in vain that he endeavored to make her sensible of her mistake; and that this restraint was the greatest enemy imaginable to the happiness of them both. She was not to be persuaded, and he was obliged to desist his solicitations, though determined in his mind to compass what he so ardently desired, before he left the house. He then turned the discourse wholly on the violence of the passion he had for her; and expressed the greatest discontent in the world at the apprehensions of being separated;—swore he could dwell for ever in her arms, and with such an undeniable earnestness pressed to be permitted to tarry with her the whole night, that had she been less charmed with his renewed eagerness of desire, she scarce would have had the power of resisting him; but in granting this request, she was not without a thought that he had another reason for making it besides the extremity of his passion, and had it immediately in her head how to disappoint him.

The hours of repose being arrived, he begged she would retire to her chamber; to which she consented, but obliged him to go to bed first; which he did not much oppose, because he supposed she would not lie in her mask, and doubted not but the morning's dawn would bring the wished discovery.—The two imagined servants ushered him to his new lodging; where he lay some moments in all the perplexity imaginable at the oddness of this adventure. But she suffered[8] not these cogitations to be of any long continuance. She came, but came in the dark; which being no more than he expected by the former part of her proceedings, he said nothing of; but as much satisfaction as he found in her embraces, nothing ever longed for the approach of day with more impatience than he did. At last it came; but how great was his disappointment, when by the noises he heard in the street, the hurry of

7. Mask. 8. Allowed.

the coaches, and the cries of penny-merchants,[9] he was convinced it was night nowhere but with him? He was still in the same darkness as before; for she had taken care to blind the windows in such a manner, that not the least chink was left to let in day.—He complained of her behavior in terms that she would not have been able to resist yielding to, if she had not been certain it would have been the ruin of her passion.—She therefore answered him only as she had done before; and getting out of the bed from him, flew out of the room with too much swiftness for him to have overtaken her, if he had attempted it. The moment she left him, the two attendants entered the chamber, and plucking down the implements which had screened him from the knowledge of that which he so much desired to find out, restored his eyes once more to day.—They attended[1] to assist him in dressing, brought him tea, and by their obsequiousness, let him see there was but one thing which the mistress of them would not gladly oblige him in.—He was so much out of humor, however, at the disappointment of his curiosity, that he resolved never to make a second visit.—Finding her in an outer room, he made no scruple of expressing the sense he had of the little trust she reposed in him, and at last plainly told her, he could not submit to receive obligations from a lady, who thought him uncapable of keeping a secret, which she made no difficulty of letting her servants into.—He resented—he once more entreated—he said all that man could do, to prevail on her to unfold the mystery; but all his adjurations were fruitless; and he went out of the house determined never to re-enter it, till she should pay the price of his company with the discovery of her face and circumstances.—She suffered him to go with this resolution, and doubted not but he would recede from it, when he reflected on the happy moments they had passed together; but if he did not, she comforted herself with the design of forming some other stratagem, with which to impose on him a fourth time.

She kept the house, and her gentlemen-equipage for about a fortnight, in which time she continued to write to him as *Fantomina* and the Widow *Bloomer,* and received the visits he sometimes made to each; but his behavior to both was grown so cold, that she began to grow as weary of receiving his now insipid caresses as he was of offering them. She was beginning to think in what manner she should drop these two characters, when the sudden arrival of her mother, who had been some time in a foreign country, obliged her to put an immediate stop to the course of her whimsical adventures.— That lady, who was severely virtuous, did not approve of many things she had been told of the conduct of her daughter; and though it was not in the power of any person in the world to inform her of the truth of what she had been guilty of, yet she heard enough to make her keep her afterwards in a restraint, little agreeable to her humor, and the liberties to which she had been accustomed.

But this confinement was not the greatest part of the trouble of this now afflicted lady. She found the consequences of her amorous follies would be, without almost a miracle, impossible to be concealed.—She was with child; and though she would easily have found means to have screened even this from the knowledge of the world, had she been at liberty to have acted with the same unquestionable authority over herself as she did before the coming

9. Street vendors. 1. Waited upon him.

of her mother, yet now all her invention was at a loss for a stratagem to impose on a woman of her penetration.—By eating little, lacing prodigious straight,[2] and the advantage of a great hoop-petticoat, however, her bigness was not taken notice of, and, perhaps, she would not have been suspected till the time of her going into the country, where her mother designed to send her, and from whence she intended to make her escape to some place where she might be delivered with secrecy, if the time of it had not happened much sooner than she expected.—A ball being at court, the good old lady was willing she should partake of the diversion of it as a farewell to the town.—It was there she was seized with those pangs, which none in her condition are exempt from:—she could not conceal the sudden rack[3] which all at once invaded her; or had her tongue been mute, her wildly rolling eyes, the distortion of her features, and the convulsions which shook her whole frame, in spite of her, would have revealed she labored under some terrible shock of nature.—Everybody was surprised, everybody was concerned, but few guessed at the occasion.—Her mother grieved beyond expression, doubted not but she was struck with the hand of death; and ordered her to be carried home in a chair,[4] while herself followed in another.—A physician was immediately sent for; but he presently perceiving what was her distemper, called the old lady aside, and told her, it was not a doctor of his sex, but one of her own, her daughter stood in need of.—Never was astonishment and horror greater than that which seized the soul of this afflicted parent at these words: she could not for a time believe the truth of what she heard; but he insisting on it, and conjuring[5] her to send for a midwife, she was at length convinced of it.—All the pity and tenderness she had been for some moment before possessed of now vanished, and were succeeded by an adequate[6] shame and indignation.—She flew to the bed where her daughter was lying, and telling her what she had been informed of, and which she was now far from doubting, commanded her to reveal the name of the person whose insinuations[7] had drawn her to this dishonor.—It was a great while before she could be brought to confess anything, and much longer before she could be prevailed on to name the man whom she so fatally had loved; but the rack of nature growing more fierce, and the enraged old lady protesting no help should be afforded her while she persisted in her obstinacy, she, with great difficulty and hesitation in her speech, at last pronounced the name of *Beauplaisir*. She had no sooner satisfied her weeping mother, than that sorrowful lady sent messengers at the same time, for a midwife, and for that gentleman who had occasioned the other's being wanted.—He happened by accident to be at home, and immediately obeyed the summons, though prodigiously surprised what business a lady so much a stranger to him could have to impart.—But how much greater was his amazement, when taking him into her closet,[8] she there acquainted him with her daughter's misfortune, of the discovery she had made, and how far he was concerned in it?—All the idea one can form of wild astonishment was mean to what he felt.—He assured her that the young lady her daughter was a person whom he had never, more than at a distance, admired:—that he had indeed, spoke

2. I.e., strait, tightly.
3. Acute pain.
4. A sedan chair (a closed vehicle for one, carried on two poles by two bearers).

5. Entreating.
6. Equal in magnitude.
7. Subtle ingratiations.
8. Private room.

to her in public company, but that he never had a thought which tended to her dishonor.—His denials, if possible, added to the indignation she was before enflamed with.—She had no longer patience; and carrying him into the chamber, where she was just delivered of a fine girl, cried out, I will not be imposed on: the truth by one of you shall be revealed.—*Beauplaisir* being brought to the bedside, was beginning to address himself to the lady in it, to beg she would clear the mistake her mother was involved in; when she, covering herself with the cloths, and ready to die a second time with the inward agitations of her soul, shrieked out, Oh, I am undone!—I cannot live, and bear this shame!—But the old lady believing that now or never was the time to dive into the bottom of this mystery, forcing her to rear her head, told her, she should not hope to escape the scrutiny of a parent she had dishonored in such a manner, and pointing to *Beauplaisir,* Is this the gentleman (*said she*), to whom you owe your ruin? or have you deceived me by a fictitious tale? Oh! no (*resumed the trembling creature*), he is, indeed, the innocent cause of my undoing.—Promise me your pardon (*continued she*), and I will relate the means. Here she ceased, expecting what she would reply, which, on hearing *Beauplaisir* cry out, What mean you, madam? I your undoing, who never harbored the least design on you in my life, she did in these words: Though the injury you have done your family (*said she*), is of a nature which cannot justly hope forgiveness, yet be assured, I shall much sooner excuse you when satisfied of the truth, than while I am kept in a suspense, if possible, as vexatious as the crime itself is to me. Encouraged by this she related the whole truth. And 'tis difficult to determine, if *Beauplaisir,* or the lady, were most surprised at what they heard; he, that he should have been blinded so often by her artifices; or she, that so young a creature should have the skill to make use of them. Both sat for some time in a profound reverie; till at length she broke it first in these words: Pardon, sir (*said she*), the trouble I have given you: I must confess it was with a design to oblige you to repair the supposed injury you had done this unfortunate girl, by marrying her, but now I know not what to say.—The blame is wholly hers, and I have nothing to request further of you, than that you will not divulge the distracted folly she has been guilty of.—He answered her in terms perfectly polite; but made no offer of that which, perhaps, she expected, though could not, now informed of her daughter's proceedings, demand. He assured her, however, that if she would commit the newborn lady to his care, he would discharge it[9] faithfully. But neither of them would consent to that; and he took his leave, full of cogitations, more confused than ever he had known in his whole life. He continued to visit there, to inquire after her health every day; but the old lady perceiving there was nothing likely to ensue from these civilities but, perhaps, a renewing of the crime, she entreated him to refrain; and as soon as her daughter was in a condition, sent her to a monastery in *France,* the abbess of which had been her particular friend. And thus ended an intrigue which, considering the time it lasted, was as full of variety as any, perhaps, that many ages has produced.

1724

9. Perform his duty.

ANNE INGRAM, VISCOUNTESS IRWIN
ca. 1696–1764

"She wrote poetry, and every body was afraid of her," remembered a contemporary who had known Anne Ingram, Viscountess Irwin. And indeed, the polished versification and accomplished argumentation of Irwin's "Epistle to Mr. Pope" reveal that this noblewoman of letters was as feisty as she was aristocratic. A daughter of the third earl of Carlisle, the young Lady Anne was raised at Castle Howard, her father's magnificent Yorkshire estate, which is still one of England's stateliest homes. As an adult, she celebrated its groves and fields, along with her father's stewardship, in a poem titled "Castle Howard, the Seat of the Right Honourable Charles, Earl of Carlisle," noting that "[t]he heavenly Venus only here inspires / All modest Wishes and all chaste Desires" for "this Wood / Subdues all vicious Thoughts and raises only good."

In 1717 Lady Anne married Richard Ingram, fifth Viscount Irwin, whose death from smallpox just four years later left her so devastated that she was rebuked for her excessive display of grief in verse by her friend and contemporary Lady Mary Wortley Montagu. Eventually, however, the young widow recovered enough of her spirit to travel alone in Holland and France, and later still she became a lady-in-waiting to the princess of Wales, although she disliked the intrigues of the court, claiming that she needed the writings of Alexander Pope and Joseph Addison as "antidotes to preserve me from the contagion" of such a life. But if some of Pope's works had warded off the "contagion" of the court, others seemed in themselves poisonous to Ingram—in particular, his "Epistle to a Lady," with its assertion that while "Men . . . to business [or] to pleasure take, . . . every woman is at heart a rake." Stressing the same problems posed by female education that Anne Finch, countess of Winchilsea, had isolated when she exclaimed "How are we fallen! fallen by mistaken rules, / And education's, more than nature's fools," Ingram insisted that there is "Nothing so like as male and female youth, / Nothing so like as man and woman old" but "In education all the difference lies." Her shrewd emphasis on the ways girls are "[m]isled by custom (folly's fruitful heir)" to believe in little more than charm and beauty also paralleled the views of such predecessors and descendants as Mary Astell and Mary Wollstonecraft.

An Epistle to Mr. Pope,

Occasioned by his Characters of Women[1]

Nec rude quid prosit video ingenium.[2]

> By custom doomed to folly, sloth and ease,
> No wonder Pope such female triflers sees.
> But would the satirist confess the truth,
> Nothing so like as male and female youth,
> 5 Nothing so like as man and woman old,
> Their joys, their loves, their hates, if truly told.
> Though different acts seem different sex's growth,
> 'Tis the same principle impels them both.
> View daring men stung with ambition's fire,

1. "Epistle 2: To a Lady" (1735), by the English poet Alexander Pope (1688–1744).
2. Nor do I see what good can come of untrained natural ability (Latin; Horace, *Ars Poetica* [ca. 10 B.C.E.], 1.410).

10 The conquering hero, or the youthful 'squire,
 By different deeds aspire to deathless fame,
 One murthers³ man, the other murthers game.
 View a fair nymph blest with superior charms,
 Whose tempting form the coldest bosom warms;
15 No eastern monarch more despotic reigns
 Than this fair tyrant of the Cyprian⁴ plains.
 Whether a crown or bauble we desire,
 Whether to learning or to dress aspire,
 Whether we wait with joy the trumpet's call,
20 Or wish to shine the fairest at a ball,
 In either sex the appetite's the same,
 For love of power is still the love of fame.⁵
 Women must in a narrow orbit move,
 But power alike both males and females love.
25 What makes the difference then, you may inquire,
 Between the hero and the rural 'squire,
 Between the maid bred up with courtly care,
 Or she who earns by toil her daily fare?
 Their power is stinted, but not so their will;
30 Ambitious thoughts the humblest cottage fill;
 Far as they can they push their little fame,
 And try to leave behind a deathless name.
 In education all the difference lies;
 Women, if taught, would be as bold and wise
35 As haughty man, improved by art and rules;
 Where God makes one, neglect makes twenty fools.
 And though *Nugatrixes*⁶ are daily found,
 Flutt'ring *Nugators* equally abound;
 Such heads are toyshops,⁷ filled with trifling ware,
40 And can each folly with each female share.
 A female mind like a rude⁸ fallow lies;
 No seed is sown, but weeds spontaneous rise.
 As well might we expect, in winter, spring,
 As land untilled a fruitful crop should bring;
45 As well might we expect Peruvian ore
 We should possess, yet dig not for the store.
 Culture improves all fruits, all sorts we find,
 Wit,⁹ judgment, sense—fruits of the human mind.
 Ask the rich merchant, conversant in trade,
50 How nature operates in the growing blade;
 Ask the philosopher the price of stocks,
 Ask the gay courtier how to manage flocks;
 Inquire the dogmas of the learned schools
 (From Aristotle down to Newton's rules),¹

3. Murders.
4. Of Aphrodite, Greek goddess of love, whose most important temple was in Paphos, on Cyprus.
5. An echo and contradiction of Pope's "Epistle 2," ll. 208–10. "Still": always.
6. Female triflers (like *nugator*, the male equivalent, *nugatrix* is a rare word borrowed from Latin).
7. An allusion to Pope's *The Rape of the Lock*

(1714), 1.100.
8. Uncultivated.
9. Intelligence. "Culture": cultivation.
1. Sir Isaac Newton (1642–1727), English physicist and mathematician who discovered many fundamental rules of science; up to the Renaissance, the Greek philosopher Aristotle (384–322 B.C.E.) had been the dominant figure in science.

55 Of the rough soldier, bred to boisterous war,
Or one still rougher, a true British tar:[2]
They'll all reply, unpracticed in such laws,
The effect they know, though ignorant of the cause.
The sailor may perhaps have equal parts[3]
60 With him bred up to sciences and arts;
And he who at the helm or stern is seen,
Philosopher or hero might have been.
The whole in application is comprised,
Reason's not reason, if not exercised;
65 Use, not possession, real good affords;
No miser's rich that dares not touch his hoards.
 Can female youth, left to weak woman's care,
Misled by custom (folly's fruitful heir),
Told that their charms a monarch may enslave,
70 That beauty like the gods can kill or save;
Taught the arcanas,[4] the mysterious art
By ambush dress to catch unwary hearts;
If wealthy born, taught to lisp French and dance,
Their morals left (Lucretius-like) to chance;[5]
75 Strangers to reason and reflection made,
Left to their passions, and by them betrayed;
Untaught the noble end of glorious truth,
Bred to deceive even from their earliest youth;
Unused to books, nor virtue taught to prize;
80 Whose mind a savage waste unpeopled lies,
Which to supply, trifles fill up the void,
And idly busy, to no end employed—
Can these, from such a school, more virtue show,
Or tempting vice treat like a common foe?
85 Can they resist, when soothing pleasure woos;
Preserve their virtue, when their fame[6] they lose?
Can they on other themes converse or write,
Than what they hear all day, and dream all night?
 Not so the Roman female fame was spread;
90 Not so was Clelia, or Lucretia bred;
Not so such heroines true glory sought;
Not so was Portia, or Cornelia taught.[7]
Portia! the glory of the female race;
Portia! more lovely by her mind than face.
95 Early informed by truth's unerring beam,
What to reject, what justly to esteem.

2. Sailor.
3. Talents.
4. Secret things (the usual plural is *arcana*).
5. The Roman poet Lucretius (ca. 94–55 B.C.E.), a follower of the philosopher Epicurus, attributed free will to the random swerve of atoms (see *On the Nature of Things* 2.216–93).
6. Reputation.
7. Ingram names Roman women who were exemplars in classical writers. Clelia (Cloelia) escaped from the Etruscan to whom she had been given as a hostage; Lucretia committed suicide after being raped by the son of the last king of Rome (the pop-

ular uprising that followed led to the founding of the Republic). Portia (Porcia) was the daughter of Cato the Younger (95–46 B.C.E.), famous for the honesty of his life and for the nobility of his suicide; to show her worthiness to learn the secrets of her husband Brutus (ca. 85–42 B.C.E.), who conspired to assassinate Caesar, she stabbed herself in the thigh and silently bore the pain. Cornelia (fl. 2nd century B.C.E.) was famous for devoting herself to the education of her two sons, the notable statemen and social reformers Tiberius and Caius Gracchus.

Taught by philosophy all moral good,
How to repel in youth the impetuous blood,
How her most favorite passions to subdue,
100 And fame through virtue's avenues pursue,
She tries herself, and finds even dolorous pain
Can't the close secret from her breast obtain.
To Cato born, to noble Brutus joined,
She shines invincible in form and mind.
105 No more such generous sentiments we trace
In the gay moderns of the female race,
No more, alas! heroic virtue's shown;
Since knowledge ceased, philosophy's unknown.
No more can we expect our modern wives
110 Heroes should breed, who lead such useless lives.
Would you, who know the arcana of the soul,
The secret springs which move and guide the whole,
Would you, who can instruct as well as please,
Bestow some moments of your darling ease,
115 To rescue woman from this Gothic[8] state,
New passions raise, their minds anew create,
Then for the Spartan virtue[9] we might hope;
For who stands unconvinced by generous Pope?
Then would the British fair perpetual bloom,
120 And vie in fame with ancient Greece and Rome.

1736

8. Barbarous.
9. Women in Sparta, who had many more rights and freedoms than women elsewhere in ancient Greece, were known for being courageous, modest, and active and wise in politics.

MARY LEAPOR
1722–1746

Born into a working-class family in Northamptonshire and set to work as a scullery maid when she was still in her mid-teens, the indefatigably productive Mary Leapor created a large body of vivacious and skillful verse in her short lifetime. Although she had no formal schooling, she educated herself, studying classical myths, the Bible, and contemporary poetry—especially the works of Alexander Pope, whose witty couplets she adopted and adapted to her own use in such finely crafted poems as "Mira's Will," "Epistle to a Lady," and "Man the Monarch." According to one account, Leapor wrote "while the jack [machine for turning a spit] was standing still and the meat scorching"; indeed, she herself has the fictional "Deborah Dough" censoriously report that her "neighbor Mary—who, they say, / Sits scribble-scrabble all the day, . . . throws away her precious time / In scrawling nothing else but rhyme."

After her mother died in 1742, Leapor left domestic service, but her hard labors continued, for she now had to keep house for her father, a gardener, and assist him in his nursery. Yet though, as she put it in her "Epistle to a Lady," she found herself waking daily "to Business and to Woes / To sweep her Kitchen and to mend her

Clothes," she persisted in creating verses in a range of genres, including satires, pastorals, elegies, and country-house poems. Shortly before she died of measles, at the early age of twenty-four, readers to whom she showed her writings had begun to plan a collection of her poems; and after she died, a local patroness arranged the publication of two volumes. Admirers of the work included such luminaries as Samuel Richardson, Colley Cibber, and Christopher Smart. Recently, some scholars of eighteenth-century literature have claimed that Leapor may have been the most important female poet of her era. Certainly she was one of the most precocious and prolific. Tellingly, moreover, she was one of only a few artists who recorded in print the always marginalized and usually disregarded perspectives of women laborers—the housemaid scrubbing the stair landing, the cook stirring the pot in the kitchen, the seamstress darning stockings, the laundress bent over a tub of soiled linen.

Mira's Will

Imprimis[1]—my departed shade I trust
To Heaven—my body to the silent dust;
My name to public censure I submit,
To be disposed of as the world thinks fit;
My vice and folly let oblivion close,[2]
The world already is o'erstocked with those;
My wit I give, as misers give their store,
To those who think they had enough before.
Bestow my patience to compose the lives
Of slighted virgins and neglected wives;
To modish[3] lovers I resign my truth,
My cool reflection to unthinking youth;
And some good-nature give ('tis my desire)
To surly husbands, as their needs require;
And first discharge[4] my funeral—and then
To the small poets I bequeath my pen.

Let a small sprig (true emblem of my rhyme)
Of blasted laurel[5] on my hearse recline;
Let some grave wight,[6] that struggles for renown,
By chanting dirges through a market-town,
With gentle step precede the solemn train;
A broken flute upon his arm shall lean.
Six comic poets may the corpse surround,
And all free-holders,[7] if they can be found:
Then follow next the melancholy throng,
As shrewd instructors, who themselves are wrong.
The virtuoso, rich in sun-dried weeds,[8]
The politician, whom no mortal heeds,
The silent lawyer, chambered all the day,
And the stern soldier that receives no pay.
But stay—the mourners should be first our care,

1. First (used to introduce a list).
2. Bring to an end.
3. Fashionable (a disparaging term).
4. Perform; pay for.
5. Tree associated with poetry ("blasted" because

the poet is dead).
6. Person.
7. Men who own their land outright or have life leases.
8. Clothes. "Virtuoso": scholar.

Let the freed prentice lead the miser's heir;
Let the young relict[9] wipe her mournful eye,
And widowed husbands o'er their garlic cry.

35 All this let my executors fulfil,
And rest assured that this is Mira's will,
Who was, when she these legacies designed,
In body healthy, and composed in mind.

1748

The Epistle of Deborah Dough

Dearly beloved Cousin, these[1]
Are sent to thank you for your cheese;
The price of oats is greatly fell:
I hope your children all are well
5 (Likewise the calf you take delight in),
As I am at this present writing.
But I've no news to send you now;
Only I've lost my brindled[2] cow,
And that has greatly sunk my dairy.
10 But I forgot our neighbor Mary;
Our neighbor Mary—who, they say,
Sits scribble-scribble all the day,
And making—what—I can't remember;
But sure 'tis something like December;
15 A frosty morning—let me see—
O! now I have it to a T:
She throws away her precious time
In scrawling nothing else but rhyme;
Of which, they say, she's mighty proud,
20 And lifts her nose above the crowd;
Though my young daughter Cicely
Is taller by a foot than she,
And better learned (as people say);
Can knit a stocking in a day;
25 Can make a pudding, plump and rare;[3]
And boil her bacon to an hair;[4]
Will coddle apples nice and green,
And fry her pancakes—like a queen.

But there's a man, that keeps a dairy,
30 Will clip the wings of neighbor Mary:
Things wonderful they talk of him,
But I've a notion 'tis a whim.
Howe'er, 'tis certain he can make
Your rhymes as thick as plums in cake;

9. Widow.
1. I.e., these lines.
2. Marked with streaks.

3. With the utmost exactness. "Rare": remarkably good.
4. Stew.

35 Nay more, they say that from the pot
 He'll take his porridge, scalding hot,
 And drink 'em down;—and yet they tell ye
 Those porridge shall not burn his belly;
 A cheesecake o'er his head he'll throw,
40 And when 'tis on the stones below,
 It shan't be found so much as quaking,
 Provided 'tis of his wife's making.
 From this some people would infer
 That this good man's a conjuror:[5]
45 But I believe it is a lie;
 I never thought him so, not I,
 Though Win'fred Hobble who, you know,
 Is plagued with corns on every toe,
 Sticks on his verse with fastening spittle,
50 And says it helps her feet a little.
 Old Frances too his paper tears,
 And tucks it close behind his ears;
 And (as she told me t'other day)
 It charmed her toothache quite away.[6]

55 Now as thou'rt better learned than me,
 Dear Cos', I leave it all to thee
 To judge about this puzzling man,
 And ponder wisely—for you can.

 Now Cousin, I must let you know
60 That, while my name is Deborah Dough,
 I shall be always glad to see ye,
 And what I have, I'll freely gi' ye.

 'Tis one o'clock, as I'm a sinner;
 The boys are all come home to dinner,
65 And I must bid you now farewell.
 I pray remember me to Nell;
 And for your friend I'd have you know
 Your loving Cousin,

<div align="right">DEBORAH DOUGH</div>

ca. 1746 1751

Strephon to Celia[1]

A Modern Love-Letter

MADAM,
 I hope you'll think it's true,
 I deeply am in Love with you,

5. Someone who does magic.
6. I.e., the verses worked like a magic charm, but by touch rather than by being spoken.

1. Conventional names of lovers in pastoral poetry.

When I assure you t'other Day,
As I was musing on my way,
5 At thought of you I tumbl'd down
Directly in a deadly Swoon:
And tho' 'tis true I'm something better,[2]
Yet I can hardly spell my Letter:
And as the latter you may view,
10 I hope you'll think the former true.
You need not wonder at my Flame,[3]
For you are not a mortal Dame:
I saw you dropping from the Skies;
And let dull Idiots swear your Eyes
15 With Love their glowing Breast inspire,
I tell you they are Flames of Fire,
That scortch my Forehead to a Cinder,
And burn my very Heart to Tinder.
Your Breast so mighty cold I trow,
20 Is made of nothing else but Snow:
Your Hands (no wonder they have Charms)
Are made of Iv'ry like your Arms.
Your Cheeks that look as if they bled,
Are nothing else but Roses red.
25 Your Lips are Coral very bright,
Your Teeth—tho' Numbers out of spite,
May say they're Bones—yet 'twill appear
They're Rows of Pearl exceeding dear.

 Now, Madam, as the Chat goes round,
30 I hear you have ten thousand Pound:
But that I as a Trifle hold,
Give me your Person, dem[4] your Gold;
Yet for your own Sake 'tis secured,
I hope—your Houses too ensur'd,
35 I'd have you take a special Care,
And of false Mortgages beware;
You've Wealth enough 'tis true, but yet
You want a Friend to manage it.
Now such a Friend you soon might have,
40 By fixing on your humble Slave;
Not that I mind a stately House,
Or value Mony of a Louse;[5]
But your Five hundred Pounds a Year,
I wou'd secure it for my Dear:
45 Then smile upon your Slave, that lies
Half murder'd by your radiant Eyes;
Or else this very Moment dies—

Strephon.

1748

2. I.e., somewhat recovered.
3. Burning passion.
4. Damn.

5. I.e., put any value on money. "Mind": pay atten-
tion to, care about.

Proserpine's Ragout

As once grave Pluto[1] drove his royal wheels
O'er the large confines of the Stygian fields:
With kingly port he sat, and by his side
Rode his fair captive, now his awful[2] bride;
5 But from the lakes a sulphurous mist invades,
And strikes the fainting empress of the shades.
The trembling queen is seized with sickly yawns,
With griping colics,[3] and with feverish qualms.
'Back to the palace!' was the general cry:
10 Before the lash her sable coursers fly:
There rests the dame, and sought her royal bed,
Where the soft pillows raised her drooping head:
Restoring lenitives[4] were sought in vain
To cool her vitals and assuage her pain.
15 On nothing would the peevish matron feed:
Then useful Mercury[5] was called with speed,
And sent on earth some curious[6] dish to frame
Of light digestion for the sickly dame.
To earth he posted,[7] where he quickly found
20 Proper ingredients on our fertile ground.
Here first he seized, as nonsubstantial foods,
The courtier's friendship and the zeal of prudes,
The sighs of widowers, and blends with those
The vows of lovers and the brains of beaux,
25 The miser's charity, the drunkard's cares,
The wealth of poets, and the tears of heirs,
Philander's patience, when his lord denies,
The frowns of Celia, when her heart complies:
Then with a breath along the air he drives
30 The love of husbands and the charms of wives;
Where trifles dwell sagacious Hermes knew:
The wingèd youth to lordly senates flew,
From thence debates and long harangues to cull,
And steeped them softly in a statesman's skull.
35 And now the frothy dish began to seem
A proper viand for his sickly queen.
To crown the rest, he met by lucky chance
The wit of England, and the truth of France.

ca. 1746 1748

1. In Roman mythology, king of the underworld (which includes the river Styx). He kidnapped his bride, Proserpina, who was the daughter of Ceres, the goddess of the harvest and fertility.
2. Awe-inspiring, because queen of the dead.
3. Spasmodic pains in the bowels.
4. Palliatives, soothing medicines (especially laxatives).
5. In Roman mythology, the swift messenger of the gods, often portrayed with winged sandals (and called Hermes by the Greeks).
6. Exquisite, choice; also, odd. The ingredients of this "ragout" are all items of no or little substance.
7. Traveled in haste.

LUCY TERRY
ca. 1724–1821

A curious catalogue of the men and women massacred in an Indian raid on August 25, 1746, Lucy Terry's "Bars Fight" was handed down orally for one hundred years before it was printed in Josiah Holland's *History of Western Massachusetts* (1855). The word *bars* was a colonial term for meadow, though its contemporary meanings add resonance to this earliest known literary work by an African American. In oddly jaunty couplets that were probably meant to be sung as a sort of ballad, Lucy Terry mourns the deaths of two white families. Each reader will of course have a different sense of how far the ostensibly sorrowful elegy is at odds with the sprightly tone—in such lines as "And though he was so brave and bold, / His face no more shall we behold"; but Lucy Terry had good cause to share the Indians' rage against the colonists. Kidnapped as an infant in Africa, she was sold into slavery around 1730. Her master, Ensign Ebenezer Wells of Bristol, Rhode Island, brought her to the outpost settlement of Deerfield, Massachusetts, where the Indian ambush occurred. After converting to Christianity, in 1756 she married a free black named Obijah Prince, who purchased her freedom. Most of her married life seems to have been spent in Guilford, Vermont, where legends began to abound about her efforts to gain education for her six children, her storytelling abilities, her involvement in legal disputes over land, and her advocacy of civil rights for African Americans. Most accounts of her life mention that she spent three hours before the trustees of Williams College, pleading for the admission of one of her sons. Though unsuccessful in that case, she won a land dispute that made its way to the Supreme Court, whose presiding justice praised her argument as superior to that of any he had heard from Vermont lawyers. The critic Frances Smith Foster has pointed out that in "Bars Fight" Lucy Terry assumes "the role of historiographer without acknowledging this as an unusual position for one of her sex, race, and class": "The absence of racially explicit references does not so much imply misconceptions about her social status as it indicates that on this occasion, in this speech act, Lucy Terry chose to speak as significantly as possible."

Bars[1] Fight

August, 'twas the twenty-fifth,
Seventeen hundred forty-six,
The Indians did in ambush lay,
Some very valient men to slay,
5 The names of whom I'll not leave out:
Samuel Allen like a hero fout,[2]
And though he was so brave and bold,
His face no more shall we behold.

Eleazer Hawks was killed outright,
10 Before he had time to fight,—
Before he did the Indians see,
Was shot and killed immediately.

Oliver Amsden he was slain,
Which caused his friends much grief and pain.

1. Meadow. 2. I.e., fought.

15 Simeon Amsden they found dead
Not many rods distant from his head.

Adonijah Gillett, we do hear,
Did lose his life which was so dear.
John Sadler fled across the water,
20 And thus escaped the dreadful slaughter.

Eunice Allen see the Indians coming,
And hopes to save herself by running;
And had not her petticoats stopped her,
The awful creatures had not catched her,
25 Nor tommy hawked[3] her on the head,
And left her on the ground for dead.
Young Samuel Allen, Oh, lack-a-day!
Was taken and carried to Canada.

1855 1746

3. Struck with a tomahawk.

MARY ALCOCK
1742–1798

"She never held herself up as a writer," wrote Mary Alcock's niece, Joanna Hughes, who edited the posthumously published volume of her works, titled *Poetical Writer* (1799), adding that when Alcock "resorted to her pen it was either to amuse a leisure hour, to gratify an absent friend, or for the more sublime purpose of pouring out her heart in praise and thanksgiving to God." Nevertheless, reticent though she may have wished to seem, Alcock produced vigorous verse polemics in which she engaged with many of the most significant issues of her era. In particular, as one recent commentator has noted, a number of her most interesting poems "satirize reform efforts in England." *The Air Balloon; or The Flying Mortal,* for instance—a seven-page work that Alcock published as a pamphlet in 1784—bore an "Advertisement" chastising those who "wish TO EVADE THE LAWS OF THEIR KING OR COUNTRY," implicitly comparing such rebels against the established order of society with "AERIAL BEINGS" who try to escape the earth. Another poem, "Instructions, Supposed to be Written in Paris, for the Mob in England," even more frankly rebukes revolutionary movements by sardonically claiming "Freedom to seize and keep what'er I can."

 Born to a distinguished Northamptonshire family, Alcock was the granddaughter of Richard Bentley, a well-known classical scholar and master of Trinity College, Cambridge. Her brother, Richard Cumberland, was a playwright who numbered among his friends such luminaries as David Garrick, Joshua Reynolds, and Oliver Goldsmith. She herself appears to have been active in the literary world; besides publishing *The Air Balloon,* she is listed as a contributor to poetry sessions in Bath, and records suggest that she was married to John Alcock, archdeacon of Raphoe. Her "A Receipt for Writing a Novel" is milder than some of her more politically charged poems, but in its lighthearted way it does adopt a conservative stance while ridiculing the romances so popular among women writers and readers in this period.

A Receipt[1] for Writing a Novel

Would you a fav'rite novel make,
Try hard your reader's heart to break,
For who is pleas'd, if not tormented?
(Novels for that were first invented).
5 'Gainst nature, reason, sense, combine
To carry on your bold design,
And those ingredients I shall mention,
Compounded with your own invention,[2]
I'm sure will answer my intention.
10 Of love take first a due proportion—
It serves to keep the heart in motion:
Of jealousy a powerful zest,[3]
Of all tormenting passions best;
Of horror mix a copious share,
15 And duels you must never spare;
Hysteric fits at least a score,
Or, if you find occasion, more;
But fainting fits you need not measure,
The fair ones have them at their pleasure;
20 Of sighs and groans take no account,
But throw them in to vast amount;
A frantic fever you may add,
Most authors make their lovers mad;
Rack well your hero's nerves and heart,
25 And let your heroine take her part;
Her fine blue eyes were made to weep,
Nor should she ever taste of sleep;
Ply her with terrors day or night,
And keep her always in a fright,
30 But in a carriage when you get her,
Be sure you fairly overset her;[4]
If she will break her bones—why let her:
Again, if e'er she walks abroad,
Of course you bring some wicked lord,
35 Who with three ruffians snaps[5] his prey,
And to a castle speeds away;
There, close confin'd in haunted tower,
You leave your captive in his power,
Till dead with horror and dismay,
40 She scales the walls and flies away.

Now you contrive the lovers meeting,
To set your reader's heart abeating,
But ere they've had a moment's leisure,
Be sure to interrupt their pleasure;
45 Provide yourself with fresh alarms

1. Recipe.
2. Choice of subject. "Compounded": combined.
3. Something that imparts a relish or piquant
flavor.
4. I.e., turn her upside down.
5. Snatches.

To tear 'em from each other's arms;
No matter by what fate they're parted,
So that you keep them broken-hearted.

A cruel father some prepare
50 To drag her by her flaxen hair;
Some raise a storm, and some a ghost,
Take either, which may please you most.
But this you must with care observe,
That when you've wound up every nerve
55 With expectation, hope and fear,
Hero and heroine must disappear.
Some fill one book, some two without 'em,
And ne'er concern their heads about 'em,
This greatly rests the writer's brain,
60 For any story, that gives pain,
You now throw in—no matter what,
However foreign to the plot,
So it but serves to swell the book,
You foist it in with desperate hook—
65 A masquerade, a murder'd peer,
His throat just cut from ear to ear—
A rake turn'd hermit—a fond maid
Run mad, by some false loon[6] betray'd—
These stores supply the female pen,
70 Which writes them o'er and o'er again,
And readers likewise may be found
To circulate them round and round.

Now at your fable's close devise
Some grand event to give surprize—
75 Suppose your hero knows no mother—
Suppose he proves the heroine's brother—
This at one stroke dissolves each tie,
Far as from east to west they fly:
At length when every woe's expended,
80 And your last volume's nearly ended,
Clear the mistake, and introduce
Some tatt'ling nurse to cut the noose,
The spell is broke—again they meet
Expiring at each other's feet;
85 Their friends lie breathless on the floor—
You drop your pen; you can no more—
And ere your reader can recover,
They're married—and your history's over.

1799

6. Rogue; lout. "Fond": foolish.

ANNA LETITIA BARBAULD
1743–1825

An indefatigable and phenomenally productive essayist, pamphleteer, and poet, Anna Letitia Aiken was brought up in a family of Dissenters—religious nonconformists who encouraged her to read; write; and learn French, Italian, Latin, and Greek. With her clergyman husband, Rochemont Barbauld, whom she married in 1774, she ran a boys' school in Suffolk while publishing poems, essays, and works for children, some written in collaboration with her brother John. After the school was sold in 1785, the pace of her literary activity quickened: her works included a poem combating the slave trade ("Epistle to William Wilberforce," 1791), a controversial antiwar poem ("Eighteen Hundred and Eleven," 1811), and political pamphlets, one of which deplored England's declaration of war against the French Republic (*Sins of Government, Sins of the Nation,* 1793). At the same time, she edited the poetry of Mark Akenside (1794) and William Collins (1797), as well as the letters of Samuel Richardson; a fifty-volume edition of *The British Novelists* (1810); and *The Female Speaker* (1811), a collection of prose and poetry intended for young women readers.

In 1808, Barbauld's husband became insane and killed himself; though she was deeply grieved, she valiantly continued her literary work. Never a feminist, she declined to run a girls' school because, as her sardonic "The Rights of Woman" implies, she thought women should be "good wives or agreeable companions" rather than bluestockings. Yet she herself belonged to a circle of learned ladies that included such notable intellectuals as the playwright Joanna Baillie, the novelist Maria Edgeworth, and the essayist Hannah More.

The Rights of Woman

Yes, injured Woman! rise, assert thy right!
Woman! too long degraded, scorned, oppressed;
O born to rule in partial Law's despite,[1]
Resume thy native empire[2] o'er the breast!

5 Go forth arrayed in panoply divine,
That angel pureness which admits no stain;
Go, bid proud Man his boasted rule resign
And kiss the golden sceptre of thy reign.

Go, gird thyself with grace, collect thy store
10 Of bright artillery glancing from afar;
Soft melting tones thy thundering cannon's roar,
Blushes and tears thy magazine of war.

Thy rights are empire; urge no meaner claim,—
Felt, not defined, and if debated, lost;
15 Like sacred mysteries, which withheld from fame,
Shunning discussion, are revered the most.

1. In defiance of unfair law. 2. Innate rule.

Try all that wit and art suggest to bend
Of thy imperial foe the stubborn knee;
Make treacherous Man thy subject, not thy friend;
20 Thou mayest command, but never canst be free.

Awe the licentious and restrain the rude;
Soften the sullen, clear the cloudy brow:
Be, more than princes' gifts, thy favors sued;[3]—
She hazards all, who will the least allow.

25 But hope not, courted idol of mankind,
On this proud eminence secure to stay;
Subduing and subdued, thou soon shalt find
Thy coldness soften, and thy pride give way.

Then, then, abandon each ambitious thought;
30 Conquest or rule thy heart shall feebly move,
In Nature's school, by her soft maxims taught
That separate rights are lost in mutual love.

1795 1825

Washing-Day

The Muses are turned gossips; they have lost
The buskined[1] step, and clear high-sounding phrase,
Language of gods. Come then, domestic Muse,
In slipshod measure[2] loosely prattling on
5 Of farm or orchard, pleasant curds and cream,
Or drowning flies, or shoe lost in the mire
By little whimpering boy, with rueful face;
Come, Muse, and sing the dreaded Washing-Day.
Ye who beneath the yoke of wedlock bend,
10 With bowed soul, full well ye ken[3] the day
Which week, smooth sliding after week, brings on
Too soon;—for to that day nor[4] peace belongs
Nor comfort; ere the first gray streak of dawn,
The red-armed washers come and chase[5] repose.
15 Nor pleasant smile, nor quaint device of mirth,
E'er visited that day: the very cat,
From the wet kitchen scared, and reeking hearth,
Visits the parlor,—an unwonted guest.
The silent breakfast-meal is soon dispatched;
20 Uninterrupted, save by anxious looks
Cast at the lowering[6] sky, if sky should lower.

3. Sought.
1. Buskins were the high boots worn by actors of ancient Greek tragedies. "Muses": goddesses not just of tragedy but of the arts and learning more generally.

2. Meter.
3. Know.
4. Neither.
5. I.e., chase away.
6. Gloomy, threatening.

From that last evil, O preserve us, heavens!
For should the skies pour down, adieu to all
Remains of quiet: then expect to hear
25 Of sad disasters—dirt and gravel stains
Hard to efface, and loaded lines at once
Snapped short—and linen-horse[7] by dog thrown down,
And all the petty miseries of life.
Saints have been calm while stretched upon the rack,
30 And Guatimozin[8] smiled on burning coals;
But never yet did housewife notable
Greet with a smile a rainy washing-day.
—But grant the welkin[9] fair, require not thou
Who call'st thyself perchance the master there,
35 Or[1] study swept, or nicely dusted coat,
Or usual 'tendance[2]—ask not, indiscreet,
Thy stockings mended, though the yawning rents
Gape wide as Erebus[3] nor hope to find
Some snug recess impervious: shouldst thou try
40 The 'customed garden walks, thine eye shall rue
The budding fragrance of thy tender shrubs,
Myrtle or rose, all crushed beneath the weight
Of coarse-checked apron—with impatient hand
Twitched off when showers impend: or crossing lines
45 Shall mar thy musings, as the wet cold sheet
Flaps in thy face abrupt. Woe to the friend
Whose evil stars have urged him forth to claim
On such a day the hospitable rites![4]
Looks, blank at best, and stinted courtesy,
50 Shall he receive. Vainly he feeds his hopes
With dinner[5] of roast chicken, savory pie,
Or tart or pudding:—pudding he nor tart
That day shall eat: nor, though the husband try.
Mending what can't be helped, to kindle mirth
55 From cheer deficient, shall his consort's brow
Clear up propitious:—the unlucky guest
In silence dines, and early slinks away.
I well remember, when a child, the awe
This day struck into me; for then the maids,
60 I scarce knew why, looked cross, and drove me from them:
Nor soft caress could I obtain, nor hope
Usual indulgencies; jelly or creams,
Relic[6] of costly suppers, and set by
For me their petted one; or buttered toast,
65 When butter was forbid: or thrilling tale
Of ghost, or witch, or murder—so I went
And sheltered me beside the parlor fire:

7. A wooden frame on which linen is dried.
8. Cuauhtémoc (ca. 1495–1522), the last Aztec emperor; his stoicism and refusal to speak became proverbial.
9. Sky.
1. Either.
2. Attendance, service.
3. In Greek mythology, the place of darkness between the earth and the underworld.
4. Hospitality (a mock-epic expression).
5. The midday meal.
6. Leftover food. "Jelly": a dessert made from fruit juice, gelatin, and boiling water.

There my dear grandmother, eldest of forms,
Tended the little ones, and watched from harm,
70 Anxiously fond, though oft her spectacles
With elfin cunning hid, and oft the pins
Drawn from her ravelled stocking, might have soured
One less indulgent.—
At intervals my mother's voice was heard,
75 Urging dispatch: briskly the work went on,
All hands employed to wash, to rinse, to wring,
To fold, and starch, and clap, and iron, and plait.
Then would I sit me down, and ponder much
Why washings were. Sometimes through hollow bowl
80 Of pipe amused we blew, and sent aloft
The floating bubbles; little dreaming then
To see, Montgolfier,[7] thy silken ball
Ride buoyant through the clouds—so near approach
The sports of children and the toils of men.
85 Earth, air, and sky, and ocean, hath its bubbles,
And verse is one of them—this most of all.

1797

Epistle to William Wilberforce Esq.[1] on the Rejection of the Bill for Abolishing the Slave Trade, 1791

Cease, Wilberforce, to urge thy generous aim!
Thy Country knows the sin, and stands the shame!
The Preacher, Poet, Senator in vain
Has rattled in her sight the Negro's chain;
5 With his deep groans assailed her startled ear,
And rent the veil that hid his constant tear;
Forced her averted eyes his stripes to scan,
Beneath the bloody scourge laid bare the man,
Claimed Pity's tear, urged Conscience' strong controul,
10 And flashed conviction on her shrinking soul.
The Muse too, soon awaked, with ready tongue
At Mercy's shrine applausive pæans[2] rung;
And Freedom's eager sons in vain foretold
A new Astrean reign, an age of gold:[3]
15 She knows and she persists—Still Afric[4] bleeds,
Unchecked, the human traffic still proceeds;
She stamps her infamy to future time,
And on her hardened forehead seals the crime.

7. Joseph Michel Montgolfier (1740–1810) and his brother, Jacques Étienne (1745–1799), together invented the first practical hot-air balloon in 1783.
1. English Evangelical politican and philanthropist (1759–1833), instrumental in the abolition of the British slave trade (1807) and, ultimately, slavery itself in the British Empire (1833). In 1791, his motion for abolition was defeated in the House of Commons by a vote of 163 to 88.
2. Hymns of triumph loudly expressing approval.
3. Astraea, Greek goddess of justice, was the last of the immortals to leave the earth when the Golden Age ended; her return would thus herald a new golden age.
4. I.e., Africa (the continent, like England, is personified).

In vain, to thy white standard gathering round,
20 Wit, Worth, and Parts[5] and Eloquence are found:
In vain, to push to birth thy great design,
Contending chiefs, and hostile virtues join;
All, from conflicting ranks, of power possesst
To rouse, to melt, or to inform the breast.
25 Where seasoned tools of Avarice prevail,
A Nation's eloquence, combined, must fail:
Each flimsy sophistry by turns they try;
The plausive argument, the daring lie,
The artful gloss,[6] that moral sense confounds,
30 The' acknowledged thirst of gain that honour wounds;
Bane of ingenuous minds!—the' unfeeling sneer,
Which sudden turns to stone the falling tear:
They search assiduous, with inverted skill,[7]
For forms of wrong, and precedents of ill;
35 With impious mockery wrest the sacred page,
And glean up[8] crimes from each remoter age:
Wrung Nature's tortures shuddering, while you tell,
From scoffing fiends bursts forth the laugh of hell;
In Britain's senate,[9] Misery's pangs give birth
40 To jests unseemly, and to horrid mirth—
Forbear!—thy virtues but provoke our doom,
And swell the' account of vengeance yet to come;
For, not unmarked in Heaven's impartial plan,
Shall man, proud worm, contemn[1] his fellow-man!
45 And injured Afric, by herself redresst,
Darts her own serpents at her tyrant's breast.
Each vice, to minds depraved by bondage known,
With sure contagion fastens on his own;
In sickly languors melts his nerveless frame.
50 And blows to rage impetuous Passion's flame:
Fermenting swift, the fiery venom gains
The milky innocence of infant veins;
There swells the stubborn will, damps learning's fire,
The whirlwind wakes of uncontrouled desire,
55 Sears the young heart to images of woe,
And blasts the buds of Virtue as they blow.[2]

Lo! where reclined, pale Beauty courts the breeze,
Diffused on sofas of voluptuous ease;
With anxious awe her menial train around
60 Catch her faint whispers of half-uttered sound;
See her, in monstrous fellowship, unite
At once the Scythian and the Sybarite![3]
Blending repugnant vices, misallied,
Which frugal nature purposed to divide;

5. Abilities. "Wit": intelligence.
6. A deliberately false interpretation. "Plausive": plausible.
7. I.e., skill perverted in its use.
8. Gather together. "Wrest the sacred page": misinterpret the Bible.
9. I.e., Parliament.

1. Treat with contempt.
2. Bloom.
3. The fierce and the indolent (see line 65): Scythians, a nomadic people near the Black Sea, were famed for their bravery in war; the inhabitants of Sybaris, a Greek city in south Italy, were proverbial for their luxurious living.

65 See her, with indolence to fierceness joined,
Of body delicate, infirm of mind,
With languid tones imperious mandates urge;
With arm recumbent wield the household scourge;
And with unruffled mien, and placid sounds,
70 Contriving torture, and inflicting wounds.

Nor, in their palmy walks and spicy groves,
The form benign of rural Pleasure roves;
No milk-maid's song, or hum of village talk,
Soothes the lone poet in his evening walk:
75 No willing arm the flail unwearied plies,
Where the mixed sounds of cheerful labour rise;
No blooming maids and frolic swains[4] are seen
To pay gay homage to their harvest queen:
No heart-expanding scenes their eyes must prove
80 Of thriving industry and faithful love:
But shrieks and yells disturb the balmy air,
Dumb sullen looks of woe announce despair,
And angry eyes through dusky features glare.
Far from the sounding lash the Muses[5] fly,
85 And sensual riot drowns each finer joy.

Nor less from the gay East, on essenced[6] wings,
Breathing unnamed perfumes, Contagion springs;
The soft luxurious plague alike pervades
The marble palaces and rural shades;
90 Hence thronged Augusta[7] builds her rosy bowers,
And decks in summer-wreaths her smoky towers;
And hence, in summer bowers, Art's costly hand
Pours courtly splendours o'er the dazzled land:
The manners melt;—one undistinguished blaze
95 O'erwhelms the sober pomp of elder days;
Corruption follows with gigantic stride,
And scarce vouchsafes his shameless front[8] to hide:
The spreading leprosy taints every part,
Infects each limb, and sickens at the heart.
100 Simplicity, most dear of rural maids,
Weeping resigns her violated shades:
Stern Independence from his glebe[9] retires,
And anxious Freedom eyes her drooping fires;
By foreign wealth are British morals changed,
105 And Afric's sons, and India's, smile avenged:

For you, whose tempered ardour long has borne
Untired the labour, and unmoved the scorn;
In Virtue's fasti[1] be inscribed your fame,

4. Merry peasants.
5. The nine Muses represent not just poetry but all arts and intellectual pursuits.
6. Scented. "East": India.
7. London (a name associated with the city under

the Roman Empire).
8. Face; effrontery.
9. Field, land.
1. Calendar; annals.

And uttered yours with Howard's[2] honoured name;
110 Friends of the friendless—Hail, ye generous band!
Whose efforts yet arrest Heaven's lifted hand,
Around whose steady brows, in union bright,
The civic wreath and Christian's palm unite:
Your merit stands, no greater and no less,
115 Without, or with the varnish of success:
But seek no more to break a nation's fall,
For ye have saved yourselves—and that is all.
Succeeding times your struggles, and their fate,
With mingled shame and triumph shall relate;
120 While faithful History, in her various page,
Marking the features of this motley age,
To shed a glory, and to fix a stain,
Tells how you strove, and that you strove in vain.

1792, 1825

2. John Howard (1726–1790), English philanthropist and prison reformer.

ABIGAIL ADAMS
1744–1818

Born in Weymouth, Massachusetts, to a wealthy Congregational minister and his wife, Abigail Adams was kept out of school because of her poor health and therefore always felt herself to be uneducated. Yet she had access to her father's library, and she received an informal education from her grandmother. After marriage in 1764 to John Adams, then a lawyer, she raised their four children and helped run the family farm. In 1774, her husband became a delegate to the first Continental Congress and their voluminous correspondence began, eventually totaling more than three hundred letters. A lively, active correspondent whose letters have been in print since her grandson published a selection in 1840, she chronicled the turbulent years of the Revolutionary War and early republican era. Yet this eighteenth-century New Englander frequently asked the recipients of her "rough unpolished" messages to burn them. Perhaps they were originally preserved because her husband became the second president of the United States and her son, John Quincy Adams, the sixth. In any case, her comments on patriotism and citizenship, on education and religion, on household and national economies, and on her marriage of fifty-four years contribute to a portrait of an independent yet dedicated wife, one who learned to undertake the family's business enterprises when her husband's attention was consumed by public service. According to the historian Linda K. Kerber, in the many letters Adams wrote she remained "a shrewd commentator on the political scene, assuming as active an obligation to judge good and evil as if she were called upon annually to vote."

LETTERS TO JOHN ADAMS

[Man Is a Dangerous Creature][1]

November 27 1775

Tis a fortnight to Night since I wrote you a line during which, I have been confined with the Jaundice, Rhumatism and a most violent cold; I yesterday took a puke[2] which has relieved me, and I feel much better to day. Many, very many people who have had the dysentery, are now afflicted both with the Jaundice and Rhumatism, some it has left in Hecticks, some in dropsies.[3]

The great and incessant rains we have had this fall (the like cannot be recollected) may have occasiond some of the present disorders. The Jaundice is very prevelant in the Camp.[4] We have lately had a week of very cold weather, as cold as January, and a flight of snow, which I hope will purify the air of some of the noxious vapours. It has spoild many hundreds of Bushels of Apples, which were designd for cider, and which the great rains had prevented people from making up. Suppose[5] we have lost 5 Barrels by it.

Col. Warren[6] returnd last week to Plymouth, so that I shall not hear any thing from you till he goes back again which will not be till the last of this month.

He Damp'd my Spirits greatly by telling me that the Court[7] had prolonged your Stay an other month. I was pleasing myself with the thoughts that you would soon be upon your return. Tis in vain to repine. I hope the publick will reap what I sacrifice.

I wish I knew what mighty things were fabricating. If a form of Goverment is to be established here what one will be assumed? Will it be left to our assemblies to chuse one? and will not many men have many minds? and shall we not run into Dissentions among ourselves?

[I am more and more convinced that Man is a dangerous creature, and that power whether vested in many or a few is ever grasping, and like the grave cries give, give.[8]]The great fish swallow up the small, and he who is most strenuous for the Rights of the people, when vested with power, is as eager after the perogatives[9] of Goverment. You tell me of degrees of perfection to which Humane Nature is capable of arriving, and I believe it, but at the same time lament that our admiration should arise from the scarcity of the instances.

The Building up a Great Empire, which was only hinted at by my correspondent may now I suppose be realized even by the unbelievers. Yet will not ten thousand Difficulties arise in the formation of it? The Reigns of Goverment have been so long slakned, that I fear the people will not quietly submit to those restraints which are necessary for the peace, and security, of the community; if we separate from Brittain, what Code of Laws will be established. How shall we be governd so as to retain our Liberties? Can any goverment be free which is not administred by general stated Laws? Who

1. Adams's spelling has been preserved.
2. An emetic (an agent to induce vomiting).
3. Edemas, accumulation of fluid. "Heckticks": wasting fevers.
4. Army.

5. I.e., I suppose.
6. James Warren (1726–1808).
7. I.e., the Congress then meeting in Philadelphia.
8. An allusion to Proverbs 30.15–16.
9. I.e., prerogatives; special powers or rights.

shall frame these Laws? Who will give them force and energy? Tis true your Resolution[s] as a Body have heithertoo had the force of Laws. But will they continue to have?

When I consider these things and the prejudices of people in favour of Ancient customs and Regulations, I feel anxious for the fate of our Monarchy or Democracy or what ever is to take place. I soon get lost in a Labyrinth of perplexities, but whatever occurs, may justice and righteousness be the Stability of our times, and order arise out of confusion. Great difficulties may be surmounted, by patience and perseverance.

I believe I have tired you with politicks. As to news we have not any at all. I shudder at the approach of winter when I think I am to remain desolate. Suppose your weather is warm yet. Mr. Mason and Thaxter[1] live with me, and render some part of my time less disconsolate. Mr. Mason is a youth who will please you, he has Spirit, taste and Sense. His application to his Studies is constant and I am much mistaken if he does not make a very good figure in his profession.

I have with me now, the only Daughter[2] of your Brother; I feel a tenderer affection for her as she has lost a kind parent. Though too young to be sensible of her own loss, I can pitty her. She appears to be a child of a very good Disposition—only wants to be a little used to company.

Our Little ones send Duty to pappa and want much to see him. Tom says he[3] wont come home till the Battle is over—some strange notion he has got into his head. He has got a political cread to say to him when he returns.

I must bid you good night. Tis late for one who am much of an invalid. I was dissapointed last week in receiving a packet by the post, and upon unsealing it found only four news papers. I think you are more cautious than you need be. All Letters I believe have come safe to hand. I have Sixteen from you, and wish I had as many more. Adieu. Yours. 7

[Remember the Ladies]

Braintree March 31 1776

I wish you would ever write me a Letter half as long as I write you; and tell me if you may where your Fleet are gone? What sort of Defence Virginia can make against our common Enemy? Whether it is so situated as to make an able Defence? Are not the Gentery Lords and the common people vassals, are they not like the uncivilized Natives Brittain represents us to be? I hope their Riffel Men[1] who have shewen themselves very savage and even Blood thirsty; are not a specimen of the Generality of the people.

I am willing to allow the Colony great merit for having produced a Washington but they have been shamefully duped by a Dunmore.[2]

1. Jonathan Mason Jr. and John Thaxter Jr., law clerks.
2. Susanna (1766–1826), daughter of Elihu Adams, who died March 18, 1776.
3. I.e., John Adams.
1. Virginians played an important part in the 18th-century French and Indian Wars.

2. John Morris, earl of Dunmore (1732–1809), colonial governor of Virginia (1771–76), attempted to disarm the colonists and declared martial law after the Massachusetts battle of Lexington and Concord in 1775. George Washington was born in Virginia.

I have sometimes been ready to think that the passion for Liberty cannot be Eaquelly Strong in the Breasts of those who have been accustomed to deprive their fellow Creatures of theirs. Of this I am certain that it is not founded upon that generous and christian principal of doing to others as we would that others should do unto us.

Do not you want to see Boston;[3] I am fearfull of the small pox, or I should have been in before this time. I got Mr. Crane to go to our House and see what state it was in. I find it has been occupied by one of the Doctors of a Regiment, very dirty, but no other damage has been done to it. The few things which were left in it are all gone. Cranch has the key which he never deliverd up. I have wrote to him for it and am determined to get it cleand as soon as possible and shut it up. I look upon it a new acquisition of property, a property which one month ago I did not value at a single Shilling, and could with pleasure have seen it in flames.

The Town in General is left in a better state than we expected, more oweing to a percipitate flight than any Regard to the inhabitants, tho some individuals discoverd a sense of honour and justice and have left the rent of the Houses in which they were, for the owners and the furniture unhurt, or if damaged sufficient to make it good.

Others have committed abominable Ravages. The Mansion House of your President is safe and the furniture unhurt whilst both the House and Furniture of the Solisiter General[4] have fallen a prey to their own merciless party. Surely the very Fiends feel a Reverential awe for Virtue and patriotism, whilst they Detest the paricide and traitor.

I feel very differently at the approach of spring to what I did a month ago. We knew not then whether we could plant or sow with safety, whether when we had toild we could reap the fruits of our own industery, whether we could rest in our own Cottages, or whether we should not be driven from the sea coasts to seek shelter in the wilderness, but now we feel as if we might sit under our own vine and eat the good of the land.

I feel a gaieti de Coar[5] to which before I was a stranger. I think the Sun looks brighter, the Birds sing more melodiously, and Nature puts on a more chearfull countanance. We feel a temporary peace, and the poor fugitives are returning to their deserted habitations.

Tho we felicitate ourselves, we sympathize with those who are trembling least the Lot of Boston should be theirs. But they cannot be in similar circumstances unless pusilanimity and cowardise should take possession of them. They have time and warning given them to see the Evil and shun it.—I long to hear that you have declared an independancy—and by the way in the new Code of Laws which I suppose it will be necessary for you to make I desire you would Remember the Ladies, and be more generous and favourable to them than your ancestors. Do not put such unlimited power into the hands of the Husbands. Remember all Men would be tyrants if they could. If perticuliar care and attention is not paid to the Laidies we are determined to foment a Rebelion, and will not hold ourselves bound by any Laws in which we have no voice, or Representation.

3. In response to the Boston Tea Party of December 1773, British troops occupied the city from May 1774 until they were driven out in March 1776.
4. Samuel Quincy (1735–1789), solicitor general of the province of Massachusetts, who was himself a loyalist. "Your President": John Hancock (1737–1793), who presided over the First and Second Congresses of Massachusetts.
5. I.e., *gaieté de coeur*: cheerfulness (French).

That your Sex are Naturally Tyrannical is a Truth so thoroughly established as to admit of no dispute, but such of you as wish to be happy willingly give up the harsh title of Master for the more tender and endearing one of Friend. Why then, not put it out of the power of the vicious and the Lawless to use us with cruelty and indignity with impunity. Men of Sense in all Ages abhor those customs which treat us only as the vassals of your Sex. Regard us then as Beings placed by providence under your protection and in immitation of the Supreem Being make use of that power only for our happiness.

<div align="right">April 5</div>

Not having an opportunity of sending this I shall add a few lines more; tho not with a heart so gay. I have been attending the sick chamber of our Neighbour Trot whose affliction I most sensibly feel but cannot discribe, striped of two lovely children in one week. Gorge the Eldest died on wedensday and Billy the youngest on fryday, with the Canker fever,[6] a terible disorder so much like the thr[o]at distemper, that it differs but little from it. Betsy Cranch has been very bad, but upon the recovery. Becky Peck they do not expect will live out the day. Many grown person[s] are now sick with it, in this [street?] 5. It rages much in other Towns. The Mumps too are very frequent. Isaac is now confined with it. Our own little flock are yet well. My Heart trembles with anxiety for them. God preserve them.

I want to hear much oftener from you than I do. March 8 was the last date of any that I have yet had.—You inquire of whether I am making Salt peter.[7] I have not yet attempted it, but after Soap making believe I shall make the experiment. I find as much as I can do to manufacture cloathing for my family which would else be Naked. I know of but one person in this part of the Town who has made any, that is Mr. Tertias Bass as he is calld who has got very near an hundred weight which has been found to be very good. I have heard of some others in the other parishes. Mr. Reed of Weymouth has been applied to, to go to Andover to the mills which are now at work, and has gone. I have lately seen a small Manuscrip de[s]cribing the proportions for the various sorts of powder, fit for cannon, small arms and pistols. If it would be of any Service your way I will get it transcribed and send it to you.—Every one of your Friend[s] send their Regards, and all the little ones. Your Brothers youngest child lies bad with convulsion fitts.[8] Adieu. I need not say how much I am Your ever faithfull Friend.

[Absolute Power over Wives]

<div align="right">B[raintre]e May 7 1776</div>

How many are the solitary hours I spend, ruminating upon the past, and anticipating the future, whilst you overwhelmd with the cares of State, have but few moments you can devote to any individual. All domestick pleasures and injoyments are absorbed in the great and important duty you owe your

6. An ulcerated throat.
7. A substance used in medicine and preserving food (as well as in gunpowder).

8. Susanna, daughter of Peter Boylston Adams, died within the month at less than a year of age.

Country "for our Country is as it were a secondary God, and the First and greatest parent. It is to be preferred to Parents, Wives, Children, Friends and all things the Gods only excepted. For if our Country perishes it is as imposible to save an Individual, as to preserve one of the fingers of a Mortified Hand." Thus do I supress every wish, and silence every Murmer, acquiesceing in a painfull Seperation from the companion of my youth, and the Friend of my Heart.

I believe tis near ten days since I wrote you a line. I have not felt in a humour to entertain you. If I had taken up my pen perhaps some unbecomeing invective might have fallen from it; the Eyes of our Rulers have been closed and a Lethargy has seazd almost every Member. I fear a fatal Security has taken possession of them. Whilst the Building is on flame they tremble at the expence of water to quench it, in short two months has elapsed since the evacuation of Boston, and very little has been done in that time to secure it, or the Harbour from future invasion till the people are all in a flame; and no one among us that I have heard of even mentions expence, they think universally that there has been an amaizing neglect some where. Many have turnd out as volunteers to work upon Nodles Island, and many more would go upon Nantaskit if it was once set on foot.[1] "Tis a Maxim of state That power and Liberty are like Heat and moisture; where they are well mixt every thing prospers, where they are single, they are destructive."[2] A Goverment of more Stability is much wanted in this colony, and they are ready to receive it from the Hands of the Congress, and since I have begun with Maxims of State I will add an other viz. that a people may let a king fall, yet still remain a people, but if a king let his people slip from him, he is no longer a king. And as this is most certainly our case, why not proclaim to the World in decisive terms your own importance?

Shall we not be dispiced by foreign powers for hesitateing so long at a word?

I can not say that I think you very generous to the Ladies, for whilst you are proclaiming peace and good will to Men, Emancipating all Nations, you insist upon retaining an absolute power over Wives. But you must remember that Arbitrary power is like most other things which are very hard, very liable to be broken—and notwithstanding all your wise Laws and Maxims we have it in our power not only to free ourselves but to subdue our Masters, and without voilence throw both your natural and legal authority at our feet—

> "Charm by accepting, by submitting sway
> Yet have our Humour most when we obey."[3]

I thank you for several Letters which I have received since I wrote Last. They alleviate a tedious absence, and I long earnestly for a Saturday Evening, and experience a similar pleasure to that which I used to find in the return of my Friend upon that day after a weeks absence. The Idea of a year dissolves all my Phylosophy.

Our Little ones whom you so often recommend to my care and instruction shall not be deficient in virtue or probity if the precepts of a Mother have their desired Effect, but they would be doubly inforced could they be

1. I.e., put into action.
2. Quoted from *Maxims of State* (ca. 1692) by George Savile, first marquess of Halifax, English

politician and essayist.
3. Slightly misquoted from Alexander Pope's "Epistle 2: To a Lady" (1735), lines 263–64.

indulged with the example of a Father constantly before them; I often point them to their Sire

> "engaged in a corrupted State
> Wrestling with vice and faction."[4]

May 9

I designd to have finished the sheet, but an opportunity offering I close only just inform you that May the 7 our privateers took two prises in the Bay in fair sight of the Man of war, one a Brig from Irland the other from fyall [Faial][5] loaded with wine Brandy and the other Beef &c. The wind was East and a flood tide, so that the tenders could not get out tho they tried several times, the Light house fired Signal guns, but all would not do, they took them in triumph and carried them into Lyn.

Johnny and Charls have the Mumps, a bad disorder, but they are not very bad. Pray be kind enough to remember me at all times and write as often as you possibly can to your

Portia[6]

4. Joseph Addison, *Cato* (1713), act 4.
5. An island in the Azores.
6. Adams used this signature fairly often after May 1775. Portia (Porcia), daughter of the statesman Cato who was the subject of Addison's tragedy, was a Roman model of female virtue: to show her worthiness to share equally in the plots of her husband, a conspirator hoping to restore the Republic by assassinating Caesar, she stabbed herself in the thigh and silently bore the pain.

HANNAH MORE
1745–1833

The woman whom Samuel Johnson called "the most powerful versifatrix in the English language" produced popular plays in the 1770s; moral discourse and books advocating educational reforms in the 1780s and '90s, including the frequently reprinted *Strictures on the Modern System of Female Education* (1799); and political poems in the opening decades of the nineteenth century. Her best-known work, the didactic novel *Calebs in Search of a Wife* (1809), elaborates on her pedagogical themes by presenting Calebs interviewing prospective candidates until he finds his mate in the eminently reasonable but also morally exemplary Lucilla. Phenomenal financial success enabled the dying More to bequeath the £30,000 her books had earned to charities. Yet at the appearance of Mary Wollstonecraft's *Vindication of the Rights of Woman* (1792), More had jeered, "We shall be hearing of the Rights of Children next!" Conservative in her advocacy of separate spheres for men and women, in her criticism of the political philosophies behind the French and American revolutions, and in her Evangelical preaching of humility to the poor, More nevertheless protested fervently against the immorality of slavery; she also made a lasting mark as a pioneer in establishing Sunday schools to combat illiteracy and poverty in working-class communities.

The fourth of five daughters, Hannah More benefited from the education in Latin she received from her father, who was a master of the Free School of Fishponds, and

from the school opened by her oldest sister in Bristol, where she studied French, Italian, and Spanish and briefly taught. She became engaged, but the would-be groom balked at the marriage. As compensation for the broken-off engagement, More accepted an annual sum of £200 that gave her the means and determination to embark on an independent career in London; she had already written one drama, *The Search after Happiness* (1773), that found great success in girls' schools. As a member of a social circle that included the literary critic Dr. Johnson, the bluestocking Elizabeth Montagu, the painter Joshua Reynolds, and the actor David Garrick, More produced such sentimental plays as *The Inflexible Captive* (1774) and *Percy* (1778). After her removal from the London stage, either because she was charged with plagiarism or because she felt the theater inimical to her Christian values, she composed long poems about slavery and sentiment as well as best-selling tracts intended to reform the manners of the great and to edify the poor. Retired with her sisters, she devoted the rest of her life to educational, religious, and political publications that contributed to an extraordinary posthumous reputation during the Victorian period—a high regard that diminished considerably in the twentieth century.

From The Slave Trade

* * *

<div style="padding-left:2em">

Strange pow'r of song! the strain that warms the heart
Seems the same inspiration to impart;
Touch'd by th' extrinsic energy alone,
60 We think the flame which melts us is our own;
Deceiv'd, for genius we mistake delight,
Charm'd as we read, we fancy we can write.
 Tho' not to me, sweet Bard, thy pow'rs belong,
The cause I plead shall sanctify my song.
65 The Muse awakes no artificial[1] fire,
For Truth rejects what Fancy wou'd inspire:
Here Art wou'd weave her gayest flow'rs in vain,
The bright invention Nature wou'd disdain.
For no fictitious ills these numbers[2] flow,
70 But living anguish, and substantial woe;
No individual griefs my bosom melt,
For millions feel what Oronoko[3] felt:
Fir'd by no single wrongs, the countless host
I mourn, by rapine dragg'd from Afric's coast.
75 Perish th' illiberal thought which wou'd debase
The native genius of the sable race!
Perish the proud philosophy, which sought
To rob them of the pow'rs of equal thought!
What! does th' immortal principle within
80 Change with the casual colour of a skin?
Does matter govern spirit? or is MIND
Degraded by the form to which 'tis join'd?
No: they have heads to think, and hearts to feel,

</div>

1. Fictitious. "Muse": one of the nine Greek goddesses of arts and learning, often invoked as a source of inspiration or knowledge.

2. Verses.

3. The enslaved hero of Aphra Behn's novel *Oroonoko* (1688; see p. 186, above).

And souls to act, with firm, tho' erring zeal;
85 For they have keen affections, soft desires,
Love strong as death, and active patriot fires:
All the rude energy, the fervid flame
Of high-soul'd passion, and ingenuous[4] shame:
Strong, but luxuriant virtues, boldly shoot
90 From the wild vigour of a savage root.
 Nor weak their sense of honour's proudcontrol,
For pride is virtue in a Pagan soul;
A sense of worth, a conscience of desert,
A high, unbroken haughtiness of heart;
95 That self-same stuff which erst proud empires sway'd,
Of which the conquerors of the world were made.
Capricious fate of men! that very pride
In Afric scourg'd, in Rome was deify'd.
 No Muse, O Qua-shi![5] shall thy deeds relate,
100 No statue snatch thee from oblivious fate!
For thou wast born where never gentle Muse
On Valour's grave the flow'rs of Genius strews;
And thou wast born where no recording page
Plucks the fair deed from Time's devouring rage.
105 Had Fortune plac'd thee on some happier coast,
Where *polish'd* Pagans souls heroic boast,
To thee, who sought'st a voluntary grave,
Th' uninjur'd honours of thy name to save,
Whose generous arm thy barbarous Master spar'd,
110 Altars had smok'd, and temples had been rear'd.
 Whene'er to Afric's shores I turn my eyes,
Horrors of deepest, deadliest guilt arise;
I see, by more than Fancy's mirror shewn,
The burning village, and the blazing town:
115 See the dire victim torn from social life,
See the scar'd infant, hear the shrieking wife!
She, wretch forlorn! is dragg'd by hostile hands,
To distant tyrants sold, in distant lands!
Transmitted miseries, and successive chains,
120 The sole sad heritage her child obtains!
E'en this last wretched boon their foes deny,
To weep together, or together die.
By felon hands, by one relentless stroke,

4. High-minded; artless, frank.
5. It is a point of honour among Negroes of a high spirit to die rather than to suffer their glossy skin to bear the mark of the whip. Qua-shi had somehow offended his master, a young planter with whom he had been bred up in the endearing intimacy of a play-fellow. His services had been faithful; his attachment affectionate. The master resolved to punish him, and pursued him for that purpose. In trying to escape, Qua-shi stumbled and fell; the master fell upon him: they wrestled long with doubtful victory; at length Qua-shi got uppermost, and, being firmly seated on his master's breast, he secured his legs with one hand, and with the other drew a sharp knife; then said, "Master, I have been bred up with you from a child; I have loved you as myself; in return, you have condemned me to a punishment of which I must ever have borne the marks—thus only I can avoid them"; so saying, he drew the knife with all his strength across his own throat, and fell down dead, without a groan, on his master's body.—RAMSAY's *Essay on the Treatment of African Slaves* [More's note]. *An Essay on the Treatment and Conversion of African Slaves in the British Sugar Colonies* (1784), by James Ramsay (1733–1789), Scottish-born naval surgeon who became an Anglican minister; his service in a church in the Caribbean strengthened his commitment to abolitionism.

See the fond vital links of Nature broke!
125 The fibres twisting round a parent's heart,
Torn from their grasp, and bleeding as they part.

 * * *

 1788, 1836

From The Gin-Shop;[1] or, A Peep into Prison

Come, neighbour, take a walk with me
 Through many a London street,
And see the cause of penury
 In hundreds we shall meet.

45 We shall not need to travel far—
 Behold that great man's door;
He well discerns that idle crew
 From the deserving poor.

He will relieve with liberal hand
50 The child of honest thrift;
But where long scores at Gin-Shops stand
 He will withhold his gift.

Behold that shivering female there,
 Who plies her woeful trade!
55 'Tis ten to one you'll find that Gin
 That hopeless wretch has made.

Look down these steps, and view below
 Yon cellar under ground;
There every want and every woe,
60 And every sin is found.

Those little wretches, trembling there
 With hunger and with cold,
Were by their parents' love of Gin
 To sin and misery sold.

 * * *

To prison dire misfortune oft
 The guiltless debtor brings;
Yet oftener far it will be found
 From Gin the misery springs.

85 See the pale manufacturer there,
 How lank and lean he lies!

1. Gin became hugely popular in England in the 18th century; because it can be produced relatively simply and cheaply, it was a favorite drink of the urban poor.

How haggard is his sickly cheek!
 How dim his hollow eyes!

He plied the loom with good success,
90 His wages still were high;
Twice what the village-labourer gains
 His master did supply.

No book-debts[2] kept him from his cash,
95 All paid as soon as due;
His wages on the Saturday
 To fail he never knew.

How amply had his gains sufficed,
 On wife and children spent!
But all must for his pleasures go;
100 All to the Gin-Shop went.

See that apprentice, young in years,
 But hackneyed long in[3] sin;
What made him rob his master's till?
 Alas! 'twas love of Gin.

105 That serving-man—I knew him once,
 So jaunty, spruce and smart!
Why did he steal, then pawn the plate?
 'Twas Gin ensnared his heart.

But hark! what dismal sound is that?
110 'Tis Saint Sepulchre's bell![4]
It tolls, alas! for human guilt,
 Some malefactor's knell.

O! woeful sound, O! what could cause
 Such punishment and sin?
115 Hark! hear his words, he owns the cause—
 Bad Company and Gin.

And when the future lot is fixed
 Of darkness, fire and chains,
How can the drunkard hope to 'scape
120 Those everlasting pains?

For if the murderer's doomed to woe,
 As holy writ declares,
The drunkard with Self-murderers
 That dreadful portion shares.

1795

2. A debt owed, as recorded in an accounting book.
3. Long habituated in.

4. St. Sepulchre was the church across the road from London's Newgate prison; its bell would ring on the morning of executions.

CHARLOTTE SMITH
1749–1806

"It is on the Poetry I have written that I trust for the little reputation I may hereafter have," declared Charlotte Smith in a letter she wrote to her publishers in 1805, adding, a few weeks later, "I will not affect to say I am not conscious of being some degrees above most of the Lady-writers of the day." In fact, until she was supplanted as England's best-selling female novelist by Anne Radcliffe, the author of the Gothic classic *The Mysteries of Udolpho* (1794), Smith was enormously popular because of such fictions as *Emmeline* (1788) and *Ethelinda* (1789), both of which were so famous that they were the subjects of heated literary debate in early works by Jane Austen, one of her admirers. "You have read Mrs. Smith's Novels, I suppose?" inquires a character in Austen's "Catherine, or the Bower." "Oh! Yes, . . . I am quite delighted with them," replies her friend. "They are the sweetest things in the world"—and then the first speaker goes on to interrogate the second as to which book she prefers and why.

Yet though the romantic novel was a lucrative genre for Charlotte Smith, she rightly valued her contribution to Romantic poetry. Describing herself in *Beachy Head* (1807) as "an early worshipper at Nature's shrine," this poet-novelist was an important precursor of such major Romantics as William Wordsworth and Samuel Taylor Coleridge as well as a significant ancestor of the Victorian poet Elizabeth Barrett Browning. Though she was largely forgotten for most of the twentieth century, her productivity was extraordinary, as was her pioneering turn to the sonnet, a form that had fallen into disfavor by the early eighteenth century. Even while bearing and rearing ten children, Smith wrote and published more than twenty novels and books of verse, many of which were as influential as they were popular. Her groundbreaking *Elegiac Sonnets, and Other Essays* (1784) had gone through eleven editions by 1851, although Wordsworth's prophecy that she was "a lady to whom English verse is under greater obligations than are likely to be either acknowledged or remembered" was to prove all too true.

At sixteen, after a comfortable childhood at Bignor Park in Sussex—near the cliffs she was to celebrate in her influential poem *Beachy Head*—Charlotte Turner had married Benjamin Smith, the extravagant son of a London merchant. From the start, the marriage was an unhappy one, though she stayed by his side, even accompanying him during his incarceration when he was at one point sent to debtors' prison. By 1787, however, Benjamin's behavior became so abusive that his wife left him, and he fled to Scotland to escape his debtors. Burdened with the responsibility of supporting her children, she undertook to write and publish both poetry and prose fiction to survive. Her many novels after *Emmeline* and *Ethelinde* included *The Old Manor House* (1793) as well as the more doctrinaire political works *Desmond* (1792) and *The Young Philosopher* (1798), both of which show the influence of the philosopher Jean Jacques Rousseau and an enthusiastic sympathy with the ideals that motivated the French Revolution of 1789.

Smith's sonnet "Pressed by the Moon, Mute Arbitress of Tides" reveals a Romantic tendency toward self-analysis, even self-dramatization, that is quite consistent with the spirit of many of her novels. Her witty and genial "Thirty-Eight" is more surprising, coming as it does from an artist whose struggle for financial solvency was lifelong and sometimes desperate. Perhaps most characteristic are such ambitious, long blank-verse poems as *The Emigrants* (1793) and *Beachy Head,* both of which shaped and were shaped by what the critic Stuart Curran calls "an alternate Romanticism that seeks not to transcend or to absorb nature but to contemplate and honor" it. Though Smith's life was a hard one and her literary reputation was obscured for many years, she did survive—first through the effect her proto-Romantic modes had on disparate

but unquestionably major descendants, from Wordsworth and Coleridge to Barrett Browning, and more recently through the work of recovery that has been undertaken in numerous revisionary examinations of Romanticism itself. At the present writing, many of her novels and poems are in print or available on the Web, and a collection of her letters was published in 2003.

[Pressed by the moon, mute arbitress of tides]

Written in the churchyard at Middleton in Sussex

Pressed by the moon, mute arbitress of tides,
 While the loud equinox[1] its power combines,
 The sea no more its swelling surge confines,
But o'er the shrinking land sublimely rides.
5 The wild blast, rising from the western cave,
 Drives the huge billows from their heaving bed,
 Tears from their grassy tombs the village dead,
And breaks the silent sabbath[2] of the grave!
With shells and seaweed mingled, on the shore
10 Lo! their bones whiten in the frequent wave;
 But vain to them the winds and waters rave;
They hear the warring elements no more:
While I am doomed—by life's long storm oppressed,
To gaze with envy on their gloomy rest.

1786

Thirty-Eight

Addressed to Mrs. H—y

In early youth's unclouded scene,
The brilliant morning of eighteen,
With health and sprightly joy elate
 We gazed on life's enchanting spring,
5 Nor thought how quickly time would bring
The mournful period[1]—Thirty-eight.

Then the starch[2] maid or matron sage,
Already of that sober age,
We viewed with mingled scorn and hate,
10 In whose sharp words or sharper face
 With thoughtless mirth we loved to trace
The sad effects of—Thirty-eight.

Till saddening, sickening at the view,
We learned to dread what time might do;

1. I.e., a gale occurring at the time of the fall equinox.
2. I.e., rest.

1. Portion of time; conclusion.
2. Stiff, unbending.

15 And then preferred³ a prayer to fate
 To end our days ere that arrived,
 When (power and pleasure long survived)
We met neglect and—Thirty-eight.

But time, in spite of wishes, flies,
20 And fate our simple prayer denies,
And bids us death's own hour await:
 The auburn locks are mixed with gray,
 The transient roses fade away,
But reason comes at—Thirty-eight.

25 Her voice the anguish contradicts
That dying vanity inflicts;
Her hand new pleasures can create.
 For us she opens to the view
 Prospects less bright—but far more true,
30 And bids us smile at—Thirty-eight.

No more shall scandal's breath destroy
The social converse we enjoy
With bard or critic tête à tête;⁴
 O'er youth's bright blooms her blights shall pour,
35 But spare the improving friendly hour
That science⁵ gives to—Thirty-eight.

Stripped of their gaudy hues by truth,
We view the glitt'ring toys of youth,
And blush to think how poor the bait
40 For which to public scenes we ran
 And scorned of sober sense the plan
Which gives content at—Thirty-eight.

Though time's inexorable sway
Has torn the myrtle⁶ bands away,
45 For other wreaths 'tis not too late;
 The amaranth's purple glow survives,
 And still Minerva's olive⁷ lives
On the calm brow of—Thirty-eight.

With eye more steady we engage
50 To contemplate approaching age,
And life more justly estimate.
 With firmer souls and stronger powers,
 With reason, faith, and friendship ours,
 We'll not regret the stealing hours
55 That lead from Thirty—even to Forty-eight.

1786

3. Offered.
4. In privacy (French).
5. I.e., knowledge.
6. A plant sacred to Venus, Roman goddess of love.
7. A tree sacred to Minerva, Roman goddess of wisdom. "Amaranth": legendary flower that never faded.

Written near a Port on a Dark Evening

Huge vapors brood above the clifted shore,
 Night on the Ocean settles, dark and mute,
Save where is heard the repercussive roar
 Of drowsy billows, on the rugged foot
5 Of rocks remote; or still more distant tone
 Of seamen in the anchored bark[1] that tell
The watch reliéved; or one deep voice alone
 Singing the hour, and bidding "Strike the bell."[2]
All is black shadow, but the lucid line
10 Marked by the light surf on the level sand,
Or where afar the ship-lights faintly shine
 Like wandering fairy fires,[3] that oft on land
Mislead the Pilgrim—Such the dubious ray
That wavering Reason lends, in life's long darkling way.

 1797

Written in October

The blasts of Autumn as they scatter round
 The faded foliage of another year,
And muttering many a sad and solemn sound,
 Drive the pale fragments o'er the stubble sere,[1]
5 Are well attuned to my dejected mood;
 (Ah! better far than airs that breathe of Spring!)
 While the high rooks, that hoarsely clamoring
Seek in black phalanx[2] the half-leafless wood,
 I rather hear, than that enraptured lay[3]
10 Harmonious, and of Love and Pleasure born,
 Which from the golden furze,[4] or flowering thorn
 Awakes the Shepherd in the ides of May;[5]
Nature delights *me* most when most she mourns,
For never more to me the Spring of Hope returns!

 1797

1. Ship.
2. Traditionally, bells are struck to mark time on a ship—once at the beginning of a four-hour watch, then one more time each half hour until eight bells mark the watch's end.
3. Ignes fatui, or lights from the combustion of marsh gas.

1. Dry, withered.
2. I.e., a closely arrayed group of crows ("rooks"); literally, a battle line of infantry.
3. Song.
4. An evergreen shrub often found in wasteland in Europe.
5. May 15.

Nepenthe[1]

Oh! for imperial Polydamna's art,
 Which to bright Helen was in Egypt taught,
 To mix with magic power the oblivious draught[2]
Of force to staunch the bleeding of the heart,
5 And to Care's wan and hollow cheek impart
 The smile of happy youth, uncursed with thought.
Potent indeed the charm that could appease
 Affection's ceaseless anguish, doomed to weep
O'er the cold grave; or yield even transient ease
10 By soothing busy Memory to sleep!
—Around me those who surely must have tried
 Some charm of equal power, I daily see,
But still to *me* Oblivion is denied,
 There's no Nepenthe, now, on earth for me.

1797

On Being Cautioned against Walking on an Headland Overlooking the Sea, Because It Was Frequented by a Lunatic

Is there a solitary wretch who hies
 To the tall cliff, with starting pace or slow,
And, measuring, views with wild and hollow eyes
 Its distance from the waves that chide below;
5 Who, as the sea-born gale with frequent sighs
 Chills his cold bed upon the mountain turf,
With hoarse, half-utter'd lamentation, lies
 Murmuring responses to the dashing surf?
In moody sadness, on the giddy brink,
10 I see him more with envy than with fear;
He has no *nice felicities*[1] that shrink
 From giant horrors; wildly wandering here,
He seems (uncursed with reason) not to know
The depth or the duration of his woe.

1797

The Sea View[1]

The upland shepherd, as reclined he lies
 On the soft turf that clothes the mountain brow,

1. A potion that induces forgetfulness of pain and sorrow. According to Homer (*Odyssey* 4.220–32), Helen had been given the drug by Polydamna (wife of the king of Egypt, in some accounts) when she and her husband Menelaus were making their way home to Greece after the end of the Trojan War.

2. Potion bringing oblivion.
1. Refined delights.
1. Suggested by the recollection of having seen, some years since, on a beautiful evening of Summer, an engagement between two armed ships, from the high down called the Beacon Hill, near

Marks the bright sea-line mingling with the skies;
 Or from his course celestial, sinking slow,
5 The summer-sun in purple radiance low,
Blaze on the western waters; the wide scene
 Magnificent, and tranquil, seems to spread
Even o'er the rustic's breast a joy serene,
 When, like dark plague-spots by the Demons shed,
10 Charged deep with death, upon the waves, far seen,
 Move the war-freighted ships; and fierce and red,
 Flash their destructive fire.—The mangled dead
And dying victims then pollute the flood.
Ah! thus man spoils Heaven's glorious works with blood!

1797

From Beachy Head[1]

[IMPERIAL LORD OF THE HIGH SOUTHERN COAST]

On thy stupendous summit, rock sublime!
That o'er the channel reared, halfway at sea
The mariner at early morning hails,
I would recline; while Fancy should go forth,
5 And represent the strange and awful hour
Of vast concussion; when the Omnipotent
Stretched forth his arm, and rent the solid hills,
Bidding the impetuous main flood rush between
The rifted shores, and from the continent
10 Eternally divided this green isle.
Imperial lord of the high southern coast!
From thy projecting headland I would mark
Far in the east the shades of night disperse,
Melting and thinned, as from the dark blue wave
15 Emerging, brilliant rays of arrowy light
Dart from the horizon; when the glorious sun
Just lifts above it his resplendent orb.
Advances now, with feathery silver touched,
The rippling tide of flood; glisten the sands,
20 While, inmates of the chalky clefts that scar
Thy sides precipitous, with shrill harsh cry,
Their white wings glancing in the level beam,
The terns, and gulls, and tarrocks,[2] seek their food,
And thy rough hollows echo to the voice
25 Of the gray choughs, and ever restless daws,[3]
With clamor, not unlike the chiding hounds,
While the lone shepherd, and his baying dog,
Drive to thy turfy crest his bleating flock.

Brighthelmstone [Smith's note]. Brighthelmstone is the small fishing village that became Brighton, a town and seaside resort on the English Channel, 50 miles south of London.
1. "In crossing the Channel from the coast of France, Beachy-Head is the first land made" [Smith's note]. These high chalk cliffs are on the south coast of Sussex.
2. Seabirds.
3. "Choughs" and "daws" are crows.

The high meridian of the day is past,
30 And Ocean now, reflecting the calm Heaven,
Is of cerulean hue; and murmers low
The tide of ebb, upon the level sands.
The sloop, her angular canvas shifting still,
Catches the light and variable airs
35 That but a little crisp the summer sea,
Dimpling its tranquil surface.

* * *

[AN EARLY WORSHIPPER AT NATURE'S SHRINE]

255 Ah! who *is* happy? Happiness! a word—
That like false fire,[4] from marsh effluvia born,
Misleads the wanderer, destined to contend
In the world's wilderness, with want or woe—
Yet *they* are happy, who have never asked
260 What good or evil means. The boy
That on the river's margin gaily plays,
Has heard that Death is there[.]—He knows not Death,
And therefore fears it not; and venturing in
He gains a bullrush, or a minnow—then,
265 At certain peril, for a worthless prize,
A crow's, or raven's nest, he climbs the boll[5]
Of some tall pine; and of his prowess proud,
Is for a moment happy. Are *your* cares,
Ye who despise him, never worse applied?
270 The village girl is happy, who sets forth
To distant fair, gay in her Sunday suit,
With cherry colored knots, and flourished shawl,
And bonnet newly purchased. So is he
Her little brother, who his mimic drum
275 Beats, till he drowns her rural lovers' oaths
Of constant faith, and still increasing love;
Ah! yet a while, and half those oaths believed,
Her happiness is vanished; and the boy
While yet a stripling, finds the sound he loved
280 Has led him on,[6] till he has given up
His freedom, and his happiness together.
I once was happy, when while yet a child,
I learned to love these upland solitudes,
And, when elastic as the mountain air,
285 To my light spirit, care was yet unknown
And evil unforeseen:—Early it came,
And childhood scarcely passed, I was condemned,
A guiltless exile, silently to sigh,
While Memory, with faithful pencil, drew
290 The contrast; and regretting, I compared

4. I.e., ignis fatuus. 6. I.e., to becoming a soldier.
5. Tree trunk.

With the polluted smoky atmosphere
And dark and stifling streets, the southern hills
That to the setting Sun, their graceful heads
Rearing, o'erlook the frith, where Vecta[7] breaks
295 With her white rocks, the strong impetuous tide,
When western winds the vast Atlantic urge
To thunder on the coast[.]—Haunts of my youth!
Scenes of fond daydreams, I behold ye yet!
Where 'twas so pleasant by thy northern slopes
300 To climb the winding sheep-path, aided oft
By scattered thorns: whose spiny branches bore
Small woolly tufts, spoils of the vagrant lamb
There seeking shelter from the noonday sun;
And pleasant, seated on the short soft turf,
305 To look beneath upon the hollow way
While heavily upward moved the laboring wain,[8]
And stalking slowly by, the sturdy hind[9]
To ease his panting team, stopped with a stone
The grating wheel.

 Advancing higher still
310 The prospect widens, and the village church
But little, o'er the lowly roofs around
Rears its gray belfry, and its simple vane;
Those lowly roofs of thatch are half concealed
By the rude arms of trees,[1] lovely in spring,
315 When on each bough, the rosy-tinctured bloom
Sits thick, and promises autumnal plenty.
For even those orchards round the Norman Farms,
Which, as their owners mark the promised fruit,
Console them for the vineyards of the south,
Surpass not these.

320 Where woods of ash, and beech,
And partial copses, fringe the green hill foot,
The upland shepherd rears his modest home,
There wanders by, a little nameless stream
That from the hill wells forth, bright now and clear,
325 Or after rain with chalky mixture gray,
But still refreshing in its shallow course
The cottage garden; most for use designed,
Yet not of beauty destitute. The vine
Mantles the little casement; yet the briar
330 Drops fragrant dew among the July flowers;
And pansies rayed, and freaked[2] and mottled pinks
Grow among balm, and rosemary and rue
There honeysuckles flaunt, and roses blow
Almost uncultured:[3] Some with dark green leaves

7. The Isle of Wight. "Frith": or firth, an arm of
the sea.
8. Cart.
9. Agricultural laborer.

1. Apple trees, which blossom in the spring and
are harvested in the autumn.
2. Streaked with color.
3. Uncultivated. "Blow": blossom.

335 Contrast their flowers of pure unsullied white;
 Others, like velvet robes of regal state
 Of richest crimson, while in thorny moss
 Enshrined and cradled, the most lovely, wear
 The hues of youthful beauty's glowing cheek.—
340 With fond regret I recollect e'en now
 In Spring and Summer, what delight I felt
 Among these cottage gardens, and how much
 Such artless nosegays, knotted with a rush
 By village housewife or her ruddy maid,
345 Were welcome to me; soon and simple pleased.

 An early worshipper at Nature's shrine,
 I loved her rudest scenes—warrens, and heaths,[4]
 And yellow commons, and birch-shaded hollows,
 And hedge rows, bordering unfrequented lanes
350 Bowered with wild roses, and the clasping woodbine
 Where purple tassels of the tangling vetch
 With bittersweet, and bryony inweave,
 And the dew fills the silver bindweed's cups—
 I loved to trace the brooks whose humid banks
355 Nourish the harebell, and the freckled pagil;[5]
 And stroll among o'ershadowing woods of beech,
 Lending in Summer, from the heats of noon
 A whispering shade; while haply there reclines
 Some pensive lover of uncultured flowers,
360 Who, from the tumps[6] with bright green mosses clad,
 Plucks the wood sorrel, with its light thin leaves,
 Heart-shaped, and triply folded; and its root
 Creeping like beaded coral; or who there
 Gathers, the copse's pride, anemones,
365 With rays like golden studs on ivory laid
 Most delicate: but touched with purple clouds,
 Fit crown for April's fair but changeful brow.

 Ah! hills so early loved! in fancy still
 I breathe your pure keen air; and still behold
370 Those widely spreading views, mocking alike
 The Poet and the Painter's utmost art.
 And still, observing objects more minute,
 Wondering remark the strange and foreign forms
 Of seashells; with the pale calcareous[7] soil
375 Mingled, and seeming of resembling substance.
 Though surely the blue Ocean (from the heights
 Where the downs westward trend, but dimly seen)
 Here never rolled its surge. Does Nature then
 Mimic, in wanton mood, fantastic shapes
380 Of bivalves, and inwreathed volutes,[8] that cling
 To the dark sea-rock of the wat'ry world?

4. Open, uncultivated ground. "Warrens": uncultivated ground where rabbits breed.
5. These are all particular plants and wildflowers.
6. Hillocks.
7. Chalky (compare line 20, "chalky clefts").
8. Shellfish with spiral shells.

Or did this range of chalky mountains, once
Form a vast bason,[9] where the Ocean waves
Swelled fathomless? What time these fossil shells,
385 Buoyed on their native element, were thrown
Among the imbedding calx:[1] when the huge hill
Its giant bulk heaved, and in strange ferment
Grew up a guardian barrier, 'twixt the sea
And the green level of the sylvan weald.[2]

390 Ah! very vain is Science' proudest boast,
And but a little light its flame yet lends
To its most ardent votaries; since from whence
These fossil forms are seen, is but conjecture,
Food for vague theories, or vain dispute,
395 While to his daily task the peasant goes,
Unheeding such inquiry; with no care
But that the kindly change of sun and shower,
Fit for his toil the earth he cultivates.
As little recks[3] the herdsman of the hill,
400 Who on some turfy knoll, idly reclined,
Watches his wether[4] flock, that deep beneath
Rest the remains of men, of whom is left
No traces in the records of mankind,
Save what these half obliterated mounds
405 And half filled trenches doubtfully impart
To some lone antiquary; who on times remote,
Since which two thousand years have rolled away,
Loves to contemplate. He perhaps may trace,
Or fancy he can trace, the oblong square
410 Where the mailed legions, under Claudius,[5] reared
The rampire, or excavated fossé[6] delved;
What time the huge unwieldy Elephant[7]
Auxiliary reluctant, hither led,
From Afric's forest glooms and tawny sands,
415 First felt the Northern blast, and his vast frame
Sunk useless; whence in after ages found,
The wondering hinds, on those enormous bones
Gazed; and in giants dwelling on the hills
Believed and marvelled—

Hither, Ambition come!
420 Come and behold the nothingness of all
For which you carry through the oppressed Earth,
War, and its train of horrors—see where tread
The innumerous hoofs of flocks above the works
By which the warrior sought to register
425 His glory, and immortalize his name[.]—

9. I.e., basin.
1. Lime.
2. Forest.
3. Is aware, is concerned.
4. Castrated sheep.
5. Roman emperor (41–54 C.E.), who in 43 invaded Britain, which he made a province.

6. Ditch, trench. "Rampire": rampart.
7. In the year 1740, some workmen digging in the part at Burton in Sussex, discovered, nine feet below the surface, the teeth and bones of an elephant. . . . The Romans under the Emperor Claudius probably brought elephants into Britain [Smith's note].

The pirate Dane,[8] who from his circular camp
Bore in destructive robbery, fire and sword
Down through the vale, sleeps unremembered here;
And here, beneath the green sward, rests alike
430 The savage native, who his acorn meal
Shared with the herds, that ranged the pathless woods;
And the centurion, who on these wide hills
Encamping, planted the Imperial Eagle.[9]
All, with the lapse of Time, have passed away,
435 Even as the clouds, with dark and dragon shapes,
Or like vast promontories crowned with towers,
Cast their broad shadows on the downs: then sail
Far to the northward, and their transient gloom
Is soon forgotten.

* * *

1807

8. The incursions of the Danes were for many ages
the scourge of this island [Smith's note]. These
raids and invasions occurred between the 8th and
11th centuries.

9. The standard of a subdivision of a Roman
legion, whose officers were centurions.

JUDITH SARGENT MURRAY
1751–1820

More than a decade before Mary Wollstonecraft published *A Vindication of the Rights of Woman* (1792), Judith Sargent Murray drafted "On the Equality of the Sexes," though the essay was not published until 1790, under the name "Constantia." Its argument that education, not nature, renders men and women unequal anticipates Wollstonecraft's. And just as Wollstonecraft was inspired by the French Revolution to advocate equal rights for women, so Murray connected her faith in women's equality with her commitment to an America dedicated to egalitarianism, an allegiance probably fostered by the active role that the men in her family played in the Revolutionary War. It is education that enables Murray's novelistic paragon Margaretta to evade the misery attendant upon the seduction and abandonment plot and instead receive the happily-ever-after of virtue rewarded: included in the three-volume compilation of Murray's work, *The Gleaner* (1798), *The Story of Margaretta* accords with Wollstonecraft's and Murray's shared view that sentimentality or emotionalism—the product of female miseducation—will disappear when women are given the opportunity to exercise their rational faculties. *The Gleaner,* dedicated to Abigail Adams and her husband, was Murray's most successful publication, a miscellany that deploys a male persona finally unmasked to reveal the author's female identity.

That at an early age Judith Sargent studied science and literature, math and classical languages along with her brother may have shaped her later views and her commitment to publicizing them in poems, plays, and magazine articles. Brought up in Gloucester, Massachusetts, Judith Sargent profited from her parents' decision to hire a clergyman to tutor her brother, who was studying for entrance to Harvard College, and to allow his older sister to participate in the lessons. She also benefited from their

adherence to Universalism, for the Universalist church, one of the first Protestant denominations to ordain women as ministers, preached universal salvation and individual religious liberty. While married to the trader and sea captain John Stevens, she published her first essay, *Desultory Thoughts upon the Utility of Encouraging a Degree of Self-Complacency, Especially in Female Bosoms* (1784), an important precursor of her subsequent work. Two years after its publication, Stevens died in the West Indies, and in 1788 she married John Murray, a preacher of Universalism and a friend of her parents. The couple's move to Boston facilitated her writing many essays for journals like the *Massachusetts Magazine*, in which "On the Equality of the Sexes" appeared, as well as two plays: *The Medium, or Virtue Triumphant* (1795) and *The Traveller Returned* (1796). Following her husband's stroke in 1809, she edited his letters and sermons; after his death, she completed his autobiography before retiring to Natchez, then part of the Mississippi Territory, where she died in her daughter's home. According to Sharon M. Harris, who has edited Murray's selected writings, "Perhaps no American woman writer until Margaret Fuller equaled Murray in intellectual powers, in the breadth of genres in which she wrote, or in public recognition."

On the Equality of the Sexes[1]

Part I

<div style="margin-left:2em">

That minds are not alike, full well I know,
This truth each day's experience will show.
To heights surprising some great spirits soar,
With inborn strength mysterious depths explore;
5 Their eager gaze surveys the path of light,
Confessed it stood to Newton's[2] piercing sight.
 Deep science, like a bashful maid retires,
And but[3] the *ardent* breast her worth inspires;
By perseverance the coy fair is won,
10 And Genius, led by Study, wears the crown.
 But some there are who wish not to improve,
Who never can the path of knowledge love,
Whose souls almost with the dull body one,
With anxious care each mental pleasure shun.
15 Weak is the leveled,[4] enervated mind,
And but while here to vegetate designed.
The torpid spirit mingling with its clod
Can scarcely boast its origin from God.
Stupidly dull—they move progressing on—
20 They eat, and drink, and all their work is done,
While others, emulous of sweet applause,
Industrious seek for each event a cause,
Tracing the hidden springs whence knowledge flows,
Which nature all in beauteous order shows.
25 Yet cannot I their sentiments imbibe
Who this distinction to the sex ascribe,

</div>

1. The text used here is taken from *The Massachusetts Magazine, or Monthly Museum of Knowledge and Rational Entertainment*, March and April 1790.
2. Sir Isaac Newton (1642–1727), English mathematician and physicist who discovered that white light contains all colors of the spectrum and whose *Opticks* (1704) presented his influential theory that light is composed of particles.
3. Only.
4. Lowered.

As if a woman's form must needs enroll
A weak, a servile, an inferior soul;
And that the guise of man must still proclaim
30 Greatness of mind, and him, to be the same.
Yet as the hours revolve fair proofs arise
Which the bright wreath of growing fame supplies,
And in past times some men have *sunk* so *low*,
That female records nothing *less* can show.
35 But imbecility is still confined,[5]
And by the lordly sex to us consigned.
They rob us of the power t'improve,
And then declare we only trifles love.
Yet haste the era when the world shall know
40 That such distinctions only dwell below.
The soul unfettered to no sex confined,
Was for the abodes of cloudless day designed.
 Meantime we emulate their manly fires,
Though erudition all their thoughts inspires,
45 Yet nature with *equality* imparts,
And *noble passions*, swell e'en *female hearts*.

Is it upon mature consideration we adopt the idea that nature is thus partial in her distributions? Is it indeed a fact that she hath yielded to one half of the human species so unquestionable a mental superiority? I know that to both sexes elevated understandings, and the reverse, are common. But, suffer[6] me to ask, in what the minds of females are so notoriously deficient, or unequal? May not the intellectual powers be ranged under these four heads—imagination, reason, memory and judgment? The province of imagination hath long since been surrendered up to us, and we have been crowned undoubted sovereigns of the regions of fancy. Invention is perhaps the most arduous effort of the mind; this branch of imagination hath been particularly ceded to us, and we have been time out of mind invested with that creative faculty. Observe the variety of fashions (here I bar the contemptuous smile) which distinguish and adorn the female world; how continually are they changing, insomuch that they almost render the wise man's assertion problematical, and we are ready to say, *there is something new under the sun*.[7] Now what a playfulness, what an exuberance of fancy, what strength of inventive imagination, doth this continual variation discover?[8] Again, it hath been observed that if the turpitude of the conduct of our sex hath been ever so enormous, so extremely ready are we, that the very first thought presents us with an apology so plausible as to produce[9] our actions even in an amiable light. Another instance of our creative powers is our talent for slander. How ingenious are we at inventive scandal? What a formidable story can we in a moment fabricate merely from the force of a prolific imagination? How many reputations in the fertile brain of a female have been utterly despoiled? How industrious are we at improving[1] a hint? Suspicion how easily do we convert into conviction, and conviction, embellished by the power of eloquence, stalks abroad to the surprise and confusion of unsuspecting inno-

5. I.e., limited to one sex.
6. Allow.
7. Cf. Ecclesiastes 1.8: "There is no new thing under the sun."

8. Reveal.
9. Exhibit. "Apology": defense.
1. Magnifying.

cence. Perhaps it will be asked if I furnish these facts as instances of excellency in our sex. Certainly not; but as proofs of a creative faculty, of a lively imagination. Assuredly great activity of mind is thereby discovered, and was this activity properly directed what beneficial effects would follow. Is the needle and kitchen sufficient to employ the operations of a soul thus organized? I should conceive not. Nay, it is a truth that those very departments leave the intelligent principle vacant, and at liberty for speculation. Are we deficient in reason? We can only reason from what we know, and if an opportunity of acquiring knowledge hath been denied us, the inferiority of our sex cannot fairly be deduced from thence. Memory, I believe, will be allowed us in common, since every one's experience must testify that a loquacious old woman is as frequently met with as a communicative old man; their subjects are alike drawn from the fund of other times, and the transactions of their youth, or of maturer life, entertain, or perhaps fatigue you, in the evening of their lives. "But our judgment is not so strong—we do not distinguish so well."—Yet it may be questioned, from what doth this superiority in this determining faculty of the soul, proceed? May we not trace its source in the difference of education, and continued advantages? Will it be said that the judgment of a male of two years old is more sage than that of a female's of the same age? I believe the reverse is generally observed to be true. But from that period what partiality! How is the one exalted and the other depressed by the contrary modes of education which are adopted! The one is taught to aspire and the other is early confined and limited. As their years increase the sister must be wholly domesticated, while the brother is led by the hand through all the flowery paths of science.[2] Grant that their minds are by nature equal, yet who shall wonder at the *apparent* superiority, if indeed custom becomes *second nature*; nay if it taketh place of nature, and that it doth the experience of each day will evince. At length arrived at womanhood, the uncultivated fair one feels a void which the employments allotted her are by no means capable of filling. What can she do? To books she may not apply; or if she doth, *to those only of the novel kind,*[3] lest she merit the appellation of a *learned lady*; and what ideas have been affixed to this term, the observation of many can testify. Fashion, scandal, and sometimes what is still more reprehensible are then called in to her relief; and who can say to what lengths the liberties she takes may proceed. Meantime she herself is most unhappy; she feels the want of a cultivated mind. Is she single, she in vain seeks to fill up time from sexual employments or amusements.[4] Is she united to a person whose soul nature made equal to her own, education hath set him so far above her that in those entertainments which are productive of such rational felicity she is not qualified to accompany him. She experiences a mortifying consciousness of inferiority which embitters every enjoyment. Doth the person to whom her adverse fate hath consigned her possess a mind incapable of improvement, she is equally wretched in being so closely connected with an individual whom she cannot but despise. Now was she permitted the same instructors as her brother (with an eye however to their particular departments[5]) for the employment of a rational mind an ample field would be opened. In astronomy she might catch a glimpse of the

2. Knowledge.
3. I.e., fiction.
4. I.e., with activities appropriate for the (female)
sex.
5. Duties assigned to each.

immensity of the Deity and thence she would form amazing conceptions of the August and supreme Intelligence. In geography she would admire Jehovah in the midst of His benevolence; thus adapting this globe to the various wants and amusements of its inhabitants. In natural philosophy she would adore the infinite majesty of heaven, clothed in condescension[6] and as she traversed the reptile world, she would hail the goodness of a creating God. A mind thus filled would have little room for the trifles with which our sex are, with too much justice, accused of amusing themselves, and they would thus be rendered fit companions for those who should one day wear them as their crown. Fashions, in their variety, would then give place to conjectures, which might perhaps conduce to the improvement of the literary world; and there would be no leisure for slander or detraction. Reputation would not then be blasted, but serious speculations would occupy the lively imaginations of the sex. Unnecessary visits would be precluded, and that custom would only be indulged by way of relaxation, or to answer the demands of consanguinity and friendship. Females would become discreet, their judgments would be invigorated, and their partners for life being circumspectly chosen, an unhappy Hymen[7] would then be as rare as is now the reverse.

Will it be urged that those acquirements would supersede our domestic duties? I answer that every requisite in female economy[8] is easily attained; and, with truth, I can add that when once attained they require no further *mental attention*. Nay, while we are pursuing the needle, or the superintendency of the family, I repeat, that our minds are at full liberty for reflection; that imagination may exert itself in full vigor; and that if a just foundation is early laid, our ideas will then be worthy of rational beings. If we were industrious we might easily find time to arrange them upon paper, or should avocations press too hard for such an indulgence, the hours allotted for conversation would at least become more refined and rational. Should it still be vociferated, "Your domestic employments are sufficient"—I would calmly ask, is it reasonable that a candidate for immortality, for the joys of heaven, an intelligent being, who is to spend an eternity in contemplating the works of Deity, should at present be so degraded as to be allowed no other ideas than those which are suggested by the mechanism of a pudding, or the sewing the seams of a garment? Pity that all such censures of female improvement do not go one step further and deny their future existence;[9] to be consistent they surely ought.

Yes, ye lordly, ye haughty sex, our souls are by nature *equal* to yours; the same breath of God animates, enlivens, and invigorates us; and that we are not fallen lower than yourselves, let those witness who have greatly towered above the various discouragements by which they have been so heavily oppressed. And though I am unacquainted with the list of celebrated characters on either side, yet from the observations I have made in the contracted circle in which I have moved, I dare confidently believe that from the commencement of time to the present day there hath been as many females, as males, who, by the *mere force of natural powers*, have merited the crown of

6. Courteous disregard of higher rank. "Natural philosophy": science.
7. Marriage (in classical mythology, the god of marriage).
8. Household management.
9. I.e., deny that women have immortal souls.

applause; who, *thus unassisted*, have seized the wreath of fame. I know there are who assert that as the animal powers of the one sex are superior of course their mental faculties also must be stronger; thus attributing strength of mind to the transient organization of this earth born tenement. But if this reasoning is just, man must be content to yield the palm [to] many of the brute creation, since by not a few of his brethren of the field he is far surpassed in bodily strength. Moreover, was this argument admitted, it would prove too much, for ocular demonstration evinceth that there are many robust masculine ladies, and effeminate gentlemen. Yet I fancy that Mr. Pope,[1] though clogged with an enervated body, and distinguished by a diminutive stature, could nevertheless lay claim to greatness of soul, and perhaps there are many other instances which might be adduced to combat so unphilosophical an opinion. Do we not often see that when the clay built tabernacle[2] is well nigh dissolved, when it is just ready to mingle with the parent soil, the immortal inhabitant aspires to and even attaineth heights the most sublime and which were before wholly unexplored? Besides, were we to grant that animal strength proved anything, taking into consideration the accustomed impartiality of nature, we should be induced to imagine that she had invested the female mind with superior strength as an equivalent for the bodily powers of man. But waving[3] this however palpable advantage, for *equality only*, we wish to contend.

Part II

I am aware that there are many passages in the sacred oracles which seem to give the advantage to the other sex, but I consider all these as wholly metaphorical. Thus David was a man after God's own heart, yet see him enervated by his licentious passions![4] Behold him following Uriah to the death and show me wherein could consist the immaculate Being's complacency. Listen to the curses which Job bestoweth upon the day of his nativity,[5] and tell me where is his perfection, where his patience—*literally* it existed not. David and Job were types of Him[6] who was to come; and the superiority of man, as exhibited in scripture, being also emblematical, all arguments deduced from thence of course fall to the ground. The exquisite delicacy of the female mind proclaimeth the exactness of its texture, while its nice[7] sense of honor announceth its innate, its native grandeur. And indeed, in one respect, the preeminence seems to be tacitly allowed us, for after an education which limits and confines, and employments and recreations which naturally tend to enervate the body and debilitate the mind, after we have from early youth been adorned with ribbons and other gew-gaws, dressed out like the ancient victims previous to a sacrifice, being taught by the care of our parents in collecting the most showy materials that the ornamenting our exterior ought to be the principal object of our attention; after, I say, fifteen years thus spent, we are introduced into the world amid the united

1. Alexander Pope (1688–1744), a major English poet, was crippled in childhood by disease and was only four and a half feet tall.
2. I.e., the body, originally formed from dust (Genesis 2.7); cf. "earth born tenement," above.
3. I.e., waiving.
4. I.e., his lust for Bathsheba; King David ensured

that her husband, Uriah, would be killed in battle so that he might marry her (2 Samuel 11). David is called a man after the Lord's own heart in 1 Samuel 13.14.
5. Job 5.
6. Prefigurations of Jesus.
7. Scrupulous. "Exactness": consummate finish.

adulation of every beholder. Praise is sweet to the soul; we are immediately intoxicated by large draughts[8] of flattery, which being plentifully administered, is to the pride of our hearts the most acceptable incense. It is expected that with the other sex we should commence immediate war, and that we should triumph over the machinations of the most artful. We must be constantly upon our guard; prudence and discretion must be our characteristics, and we must rise superior to, and obtain a complete victory over, those who have been long adding to the native strength of their minds by an unremitted study of men and books, and who have, moreover, conceived from the loose characters which they have seen portrayed in the extensive variety of their reading a most contemptible opinion of the sex. Thus unequal, we are, notwithstanding, forced to the combat, and the infamy which is consequent upon the smallest deviation in our conduct proclaims the high idea which was formed of our native strength; and thus, indirectly at least, is the preference acknowledged to be our due. And if we are allowed an equality of acquirement, let serious studies equally employ our minds and we will bid our souls arise to equal strength. We will meet upon even ground the despot man; we will rush with alacrity to the combat, and, crowned by success, we shall then answer the exalted expectations which are formed. Though sensibility, soft compassion, and gentle commiseration are inmates in the female bosom, yet against every deep laid art, altogether fearless of the event, we will set them in array;[9] for assuredly the wreath of victory will encircle the spotless brow. If we meet an equal, a sensible friend, we will reward him with the hand of amity, and through life we will be assiduous to promote his happiness; but from every deep laid scheme for our ruin, retiring into ourselves, amid the flowery paths of science, we will indulge in all the refined and sentimental pleasures of contemplation. And should it still be urged that the studies thus insisted upon would interfere with our more peculiar department, I must further reply that *early hours* and close application will do wonders; and to her who is from the first dawn of reason taught to fill up time rationally, both the requisites will be easy. I grant that niggard[1] fortune is too generally unfriendly to the mind; and that much of that valuable treasure, time, is necessarily expended upon the wants of the body; but it should be remembered that in embarrassed circumstances our companions have as little leisure for literary improvement as is afforded to us; for most certainly their provident care[2] is at least as requisite as our exertions. Nay, we have even more leisure for sedentary pleasures, as our avocations are more retired, much less laborious, and, as hath been observed, by no means require that avidity of attention which is proper to the employments of the other sex. In high life, or, in other words, where the parties are in possession of affluence, the objection respecting time is wholly obviated, and, of course, falls to the ground. And it may also be repeated that many of those hours which are at present swallowed up in fashion and scandal might be redeemed were we habituated to useful reflections. But in one respect, O ye arbiters of our fate! we confess that the superiority is indubitably yours; you are by nature formed for our protectors; we pretend not to vie with you in bodily strength; upon this point we will never contend for victory. Shield us then, we beseech you,

8. Drinks.
9. In battle lines.

1. Stingly, miserly.
2. I.e., men's care in providing for their families.

from external evils, and in return *we* will transact *your* domestic affairs. Yes, *your*, for are you not equally interested in those matters with ourselves? Is not the elegancy of neatness as agreeable to your sight as to ours; is not the well favored viand equally delightful to your taste; and doth not your sense of hearing suffer as much from the discordant sounds prevalent in an ill regulated family produced by the voices of children and many *et ceteras*?

<div align="right">CONSTANTIA.[3]</div>

By way of supplement to the foregoing pages, I subjoin the following extract from a letter, wrote to a friend in the December of 1780.

And now assist me, O thou genius of my sex, while I undertake the arduous task of endeavoring to combat that vulgar, that almost universal error, which hath, it seems, enlisted even Mr. P—under its banners. The superiority of your sex hath, I grant, been time out of mind esteemed a truth incontrovertible; in consequence of which persuasion every plan of education hath been calculated to establish this favorite tenet. Not long since, weak and presuming as I was, I amused myself with selecting some arguments from nature, reason, and experience, against this so generally received idea. I confess that to sacred testimonies[4] I had not recourse. I held them to be merely metaphorical and thus regarding them, I could not persuade myself that there was any propriety in bringing them to decide in this *very important debate*. However, as you, sir, confine yourself entirely to the sacred oracles, I mean to bend the whole of my artillery against those supposed proofs which you have from thence provided, and from which you have formed an entrenchment *apparently* so invulnerable. And first, to begin with our great progenitors;[5] but here, suffer me to premise, that it is for mental strength I mean to contend, for with respect to animal powers, I yield them undisputed to that sex, which enjoys them in common with the lion, the tiger, and many other beasts of prey; therefore your observations respecting the *rib under the arm*,[6] *at a distance from the head*, etc., etc., in no sort militate against my view. Well, but the woman was first in the transgression. Strange how blind *self love* renders you men. Were you not wholly absorbed in a partial admiration of your own abilities, you would long since have acknowledged the force of what I am now going to urge. It is true some ignoramuses have absurdly enough informed us that the beauteous fair of paradise was seduced from her obedience by a malignant demon *in the guise of a baleful serpent*; but we, who are better informed, know that the fallen spirit presented himself to her view *a shining angel still*; for thus, saith the critics in the Hebrew tongue, ought the word to be rendered.[7] Let us examine her motive—Hark! the seraph declares that she shall attain a perfection of knowledge; for is there aught which is not comprehended under one or other of the terms *good* and *evil*.[8] It doth not appear that she was governed by any one sensual appe-

3. Murray's pen name. "*Et ceteras*": other things.
4. I.e., the Bible.
5. Adam and Eve, viewed as the ancestors of all humanity.
6. Genesis 2.21–22 describes woman as created from man's rib.
7. The Hebrew word translated "serpent" in Genesis 3.1 is *nachash*, usually linked to a root meaning "to hiss"; some scholars point to a similar root,

meaning "to shine." Morton may also be alluding to Paul's claim that Satan can disguise himself, "transformed into an angel of light" (1 Corinthians 11.14), for the serpent in the garden was popularly identified with Satan.
8. The serpent urges the woman to eat the forbidden fruit of the tree of knowledge: "ye shall be as gods, knowing good and evil" (Genesis 3.5). "Seraph": angel.

tite, but merely by a desire of adorning her mind. A laudable ambition fired her soul and a thirst for knowledge impelled the predilection so fatal in its consequences. Adam could not plead the same deception; assuredly he was not deceived; nor ought we to admire his superior strength, or wonder at his sagacity, when we so often confess that example is much more influential than precept. His gentle partner stood before him, a melancholy instance of the direful effects of disobedience; he saw her not possessed of that wisdom which she had fondly hoped to obtain, but he beheld the once blooming female disrobed of that innocence which had heretofore rendered her so lovely. To him, then, deception became impossible, as he had proof positive of the fallacy of the argument which the deceiver had suggested. What then could be his inducement to burst the barriers, and to fly directly in the face of that command, which *immediately* from the mouth of deity *he* had received,[9] since, I say, he could not plead that fascinating stimulus, the accumulation of knowledge, as indisputable conviction was so visibly portrayed before him. What mighty cause impelled him to sacrifice myriads of beings yet unborn, and by one impious act, which *he saw* would be productive of such fatal effects, entail undistinguished ruin upon a race of beings which he was yet to produce. Blush, ye vaunters of fortitude, ye boasters of resolution, ye haughty lords of the creation; blush when ye remember that he was influenced by no other motive than a bare pusillanimous attachment to a woman! by sentiments so exquisitely soft that all his sons have from that period, when they have designed to degrade them, described as highly feminine. Thus it should seem that all the arts of the grand deceiver (since means adequate to the purpose are, I conceive, invariably pursued) were requisite to mislead our general mother, while the father of mankind forfeited his own, and relinquished the happiness of posterity, merely in compliance with the blandishments of a female. The subsequent subjection the apostle Paul explains as a figure; after enlarging upon the subject, he adds, *"This is a great mystery; but I speak concerning Christ and the church."*[1] Now we know with what consummate wisdom the unerring father of eternity hath formed his plans; all the types which he hath displayed he hath permitted *materially* to fail, in the very virtue for which *they* were famed. The reason for this is obvious; we might otherwise mistake his economy and render that honor to the creature which is due only to the creator. I know that Adam was a figure[2] of Him who was to come. The Grace contained in this figure is the reason of my rejoicing, and while I am very far from prostrating before the shadow, I yield joyfully in all things the preeminence to the Second Federal Head.[3] Confiding[4] faith is prefigured by Abraham, yet he exhibits a contrast to affiance when he says of his fair companion, she is my sister.[5] Gentleness was the characteristic of Moses,[6] yet he hesitated not to reply to Jehovah Himself. With unsaintlike tongue he murmured at the waters of strife, and with rash

9. Genesis 2.16–17. "Immediately": directly.
1. Ephesians 5.32.
2. Prefiguration; image.
3. I.e., to Jesus, who is the second, after Adam, to make a covenant (the root meaning of "federal") with God.
4. Trusting. Abraham, the first patriarch, proved his faith by his willingness to sacrifice his son Isaac (Genesis 22.1–18).

5. Fearing that the Egyptians would kill him so that his beautiful wife would be free to marry, Abraham asked her to say that she was his sister, and she was taken into the Pharaoh's household as a concubine (Genesis 12.11–19). "Affiance": trust; pledging of faith in marriage.
6. Moses, who led the Israelites out of their Egyptian bondage, is described in Numbers 12.3 as meeker than any other man.

hands he break the Tables[7] which were inscribed by the finger of divinity. David, dignified with the title of the man after God's own heart, and yet how stained was his life. Solomon was celebrated for wisdom, but folly is wrote in legible characters upon his almost every action.[8] Lastly, let us turn our eyes to man in the aggregate. He is manifested as the figure of strength, but that we may not regard him as any thing more than a figure, his soul is formed in no sort superior, but every way equal to the mind of her who is the emblem of weakness and whom he hails the gentle companion of his better days.

<div align="right">1790, 1995</div>

7. The tablets on which were inscribed the Ten Commandments, written by God; Moses broke the first set given to him in anger at the idolatry of the people (Exodus 32.16, 19). For "the waters of strife," see Exodus 17.1–7; Psalm 106.32–33.

8. David's son Solomon, who "exceeded all the kings of the earth for riches and for wisdom," nevertheless drew God's anger by having hundreds of wives and concubines and by worshipping false gods (1 Kings 10.23, 11.1–10).

FRANCES BURNEY
1752–1840

At fifteen years of age, with her twelve-year-old sister Susan sobbing by her side, Frances Burney burned all of her early writing because her stepmother felt that a reputation for scribbling would harm the girl's marriage prospects and because she herself was early impressed "with ideas that fastened degradation to this class of composition" then, as now, called the novel. Soon after, however, Burney began to keep a secret journal addressed to "A Certain Miss Nobody," because "to Nobody can I be wholly unreserved." While she would eventually write her diary for the members of her family, her early determination to counterpoint decorous public submission with private literary assertion was to play a crucial role in her life.

The third of six children, Burney was eight years old when the family moved from King's Lynn to London, and ten years old when she lost her mother, Esther (Sleepe) Burney. She became greatly attached to her father, the historian of music Dr. Charles Burney, and to his friend Samuel ("Daddy") Crisp, the recipient of many of her early confidences. Although she was said to be shy and had received only a few months of formal schooling, through her gregarious father she met a number of artists and intellectuals. Her first and most important novel, *Evelina* (1778), explored the social development of a heroine who proves herself worthy of her wellborn suitor. Published anonymously when Burney was twenty-six, this epistolary fiction was an instant success. After its author's identity became known, first to her family and then to the public, it won Burney such prominent friends as the essayist and lexicographer Samuel Johnson, his companion Mrs. Hester Thrale, the painter Sir Joshua Reynolds, the playwright Richard Sheridan, and the philosopher Edmund Burke, all of whom appear in the *Diary*. With the encouragement of these supporters, her father, and Daddy Crisp, Burney next published *Cecilia; or, Memoirs of an Heiress* (1782). While not as popular as *Evelina*, it also analyzed the social and economic problems of women. In both of these novels, Burney self-consciously tried to raise the status of the novel by combining verisimilitude with instruction. In the process, she helped establish a new genre, the novel of manners. Indeed, she conveyed the manners and morals of polite society with a relish for the ridiculous and a respect for the conventional that explain why Jane Austen found both the theme and the title of *Pride and Prejudice* in the concluding chapter of *Cecilia*.

In spite of enthusiastic reviews, Burney felt she had exhausted her subject with *Cecilia* and, again with the encouragement of her father, she accepted a place at court in 1786. Although the position of second keeper of the robes to Queen Charlotte secured her a salary of two hundred pounds a year, it involved such official duties as mixing the queen's snuff and attending to her dressing, even as it placed Burney under the grating supervision of the first keeper of the robes, a Mrs. Schwellenberg. In 1791 Burney was allowed to retire with a pension of one hundred pounds, and two years later, at the age of forty-one, she married a penniless French exile, General Alexandre D'Arblay. She continued to publish, first *Brief Revelations Relative to the Emigrant French Clergy* (1793), and later *Camilla; or, Female Difficulties* (1796) and *The Wanderer* (1814). From 1802 to 1812, she lived with her husband and their son in France, where she received the title of countess from Louis XVIII. After fleeing to Brussels during Napoleon's Hundred Days, she returned with her family to London. She remained in retirement after her husband's death in 1818, editing her father's memoirs (1832). Three years after her death, her niece, Charlotte Frances Barrett, began issuing the *Diary and Letters*, but the *Early Diary* was not published until 1889. The first selection printed here from the *Diary and Letters of Madame d'Arblay* (12 volumes) demonstrates Burney's ear for dialogue and her eye for social detail. The second captures her honesty about the anxiety and pain she suffered before and during breast surgery.

From The Diary and Letters of Madame D'Arblay

Letter from Miss F. Burney to Mrs. Phillips[1] *[Authoress of "Evelina"]*

February 1782

I thank you most heartily for your two sweet letters, my ever dearest Susy, and equally for the kindness they contain and the kindness they accept. And, as I have a frank[2] and a subject, I will leave my *brothers,* and write you and my dear brother Molesworth a little account of a *rout* I have just been at, at the house of Mr. Paradise.[3]

You will wonder, perhaps, in this time of hurry, why I went thither; but when I tell you Pacchierotti[4] was there, you will not think it surprising.

There was a crowd of company; Charlotte[5] and I went together; my father came afterwards. Mrs. Paradise received us very graciously, and led me immediately up to Miss Thrale, who was sitting by the Pac.[6] The Miss Kirwans, you may be sure, were not far off, and so I did pretty well. There was nobody else I knew but Dr. Solander, Mr. Coxe, the traveller, Sir Sampson and Lady Gideon (Streatham acquaintances), Mr. Sastres, and Count Zenobia, a noble Venetian, whom I have often met lately at Mrs. Thrale's.[7]

We were very late, for we had waited cruelly for the coach, and Pac. had sung a song out of *Artaxerxes,* composed for a tenor, which we lost, to my infinite regret.[8] Afterwards he sang "Dolce speme,"[9] set by Bertoni, less ele-

1. Susan Burney Phillips, the author's sister.
2. An envelope marked or signed by an official so that it can be mailed without postage.
3. An acquaintance in polite society. "Rout": fashionable gathering.
4. A well-known operatic singer (1740–1821).
5. Burney's youngest sister.
6. I.e., Pacchierotti.

7. Hester Lynch Thrale (1741–1821), later Piozzi, British writer who was Samuel Johnson's close friend.
8. I.e., they arrived too late to hear it. "*Artaxerxes*": an opera (1761) by the English composer Thomas Arne.
9. Sweet hope (Italian).

gantly than by Sacchini, but more expressively for the words. He sang it delightfully. It was but the second time I have heard him in a room since his return to England.

After this he went into another room, to try if it would be cooler; and Mrs. Paradise, leaning over the Kirwans and Charlotte, who hardly got a seat all night for the crowd, said she begged to speak to me. I squeezed my great person out, and she then said,

"Miss Burney, Lady Say and Sele[1] desires the honor of being introduced to you."

Her ladyship stood by her side. She seems pretty near fifty—at least turned forty; her head was full of feathers, flowers, jewels, and gee-gaws, and as high as Lady Archer's; her dress was trimmed with beads, silver, persian sashes, and all sort of fine fancies; her face is thin and fiery, and her whole manner spoke a lady all alive.

"Miss Burney," cried she, with great quickness, and a look all curiosity, "I am very happy to see you; I have longed to see you a great while; I have read your performance,[2] and I am quite delighted with it. I think it's the most elegant novel I ever read in my life. Such a style! I am quite surprised at it. I can't think where you got so much invention!"

You may believe this was a reception not to make me very loquacious. I did not know which way to turn my head.

"I must introduce you," continued her ladyship, "to my sister; she'll be quite delighted to see you. She has written a novel herself; so you are sister authoresses. A most elegant thing it is, I assure you; almost as pretty as yours, only not quite so elegant. She has written two novels, only one is not so pretty as the other. But I shall insist upon your seeing them. One is in letters, like yours, only yours is prettiest; it's called the *Mausoleum of Julia!*"

What unfeeling things, thought I, are *my* sisters! I'm sure I never heard them go about thus praising *me!*

Mrs. Paradise then again came forward, and taking my hand, led me up to her ladyship's sister, Lady Hawke, saying aloud, and with a courteous smirk, "Miss Burney, ma'am, authoress of *Evelina.*"

"Yes," cried my friend, Lady Say and Sele, who followed me close, "it's the authoress of *Evelina;* so you are sister authoresses!"

Lady Hawke arose and curtsied. She is much younger than her sister, and rather pretty; extremely languishing, delicate, and pathetic;[3] apparently accustomed to be reckoned the genius of her family, and well contented to be looked upon as a creature dropped from the clouds.

I was then seated between their ladyships, and Lady S. and S., drawing as near to me as possible, said,

"Well, and so you wrote this pretty book!—and pray did your papa know of it?"

"No, ma'am; not till some months after the publication."

"So I've heard; it's surprising! I can't think how you invented it!—there's a vast deal of invention in it! And you've got so much humor, too! Now my sister has no humor—hers is all sentiment. You can't think how I was entertained with that old grandmother and her son!"

I suppose she meant Tom Branghton for the son.

1. A title, not a name; her husband is the Baron Say and Sele.
2. Burney's first published novel, *Evelina* (1778).
3. I.e., arousing sympathy, tenderness.

"How much pleasure you must have had in writing it; had not you?"

"Y—e—s, ma'am."

"So has my sister; she's never without a pen in her hand; she can't help writing for her life. When Lord Hawke is travelling about with her, she keeps writing all the way."

"Yes," said Lady Hawke; "I really can't help writing. One has great pleasure in writing the things; has not one, Miss Burney?"

"Y—e—s, ma'am."

"But your novel," cried Lady Say and Sele, "is in such a style!—so elegant! I am vastly glad you made it end happily. I hate a novel that don't end happy."

"Yes," said Lady Hawke, with a languid smile, "I was vastly glad when she married Lord Orville. I was sadly afraid it would not have been."

"My sister intends," said Lady Say and Sele, "to print her *Mausoleum,* just for her own friends and acquaintances."

"Yes," said Lady Hawke, "I have never printed yet."

"I saw Lady Hawke's name," quoth I to my first friend, "ascribed to the play of *Variety.*"[4]

"Did you indeed?" cried Lady Say, in an ecstasy. "Sister! do you know Miss Burney saw your name in the newspapers, about the play!"

"Did she?" said Lady Hawke, smiling complacently. "But I really did not write it; I never wrote a play in my life."

"Well," cried Lady Say, "but do repeat that sweet part that I am so fond of—you know what I mean; Miss Burney *must* hear it,—out of your novel, you know!"

Lady H.—No, I can't; I have forgot it.

Lady S.—Oh no! I am sure you have not; I insist upon it.

Lady H.—But I know you can repeat it yourself; you have so fine a memory; I am sure you can repeat it.

Lady S.—Oh, but I should not do it justice! that's all,—I should not do it justice!

Lady Hawke then bent forward, and repeated—" 'If, when he made the declaration of his love, the sensibility[5] that beamed in his eyes was felt in his heart, what pleasing sensations and soft alarms might not that tender avowal awaken!' "

"And from what, ma'am," cried I, astonished, and imagining I had mistaken them, "is this taken?"

"From my sister's novel!" answered the delighted Lady Say and Sele, expecting my raptures to be equal to her own; "it's in the *Mausoleum,*—did not you know that? Well, I can't think how you can write these sweet novels! And it's all just like that part. Lord Hawke himself says it's all poetry. For my part, I'm sure I never could write so. I suppose, Miss Burney, you are producing another,—a'n't you?"

"No, ma'am."

"Oh, I daresay you are. I daresay you are writing one at this very minute!"

Mrs. Paradise now came up to me again, followed by a square man, middle-aged, and humdrum, who, I found, was Lord Say and Sele, afterwards

4. I.e., a play by the name of *Variety,* anonymously produced at Drury Lane in 1782. The author was actually Richard Griffith.

5. Sensitivity, emotion.

from the Kirwans; for though they introduced him to me, I was so confounded by their vehemence and their manners, that I did not hear his name.

"Miss Burney," said Mrs. P., presenting me to him, "authoress of *Evelina*."

"Yes," cried Lady Say and Sele, starting up, " 'tis the authoress of *Evelina*!"

"Of what?" cried he.

"Of *Evelina*. You'd never think it,—she looks so young, to have so much invention, and such an elegant style! Well, I could write a play, I think, but I'm sure I could never write a novel."

"Oh yes, you could, if you would try," said Lady Hawke.

"Oh no, I could not," answered she; "I could not get a style—that's the thing—I could not tell how to get a style! and a novel's nothing without a style, you know!"

"Why no," said Lady Hawke; "that's true. But then you write such charming letters, you know!"

"Letters!" repeated Lady S. and S., simpering; "do you think so? Do you know I wrote a long letter to Mrs. Ray just before I came here, this very afternoon,—quite a long letter! I did, I assure you!"

Here Mrs. Paradise came forward with another gentleman, younger, slimmer, and smarter, and saying to me, "Sir Gregory Page Turner," said to him, "Miss Burney, authoress of *Evelina*."

At which Lady Say and Sele, in fresh transport, again arose, and rapturously again repeated—"Yes, she's authoress of *Evelina*! Have you read it?"

"No; is it to be had?"[6]

"Oh dear, yes! it's been printed these two years! You'd never think it! But it's the most elegant novel I ever read in my life. Writ in such a style!"

"Certainly," said he, very civilly; "I have every inducement to get it. Pray where is it to be had? everywhere, I suppose?"

"Oh, nowhere, I hope!" cried I, wishing at that moment it had been never in human ken.[7]

My *square* friend, Lord Say and Sele, then putting his head forward, said, very solemnly, "I'll purchase it!"

His lady then mentioned to me a hundred novels that I had never heard of, asking my opinion of them, and whether I knew the authors; Lady Hawke only occasionally and languidly joining in the discourse: and then Lady S. and S., suddenly arising, begged me not to move, for she should be back again in a minute, and flew to the next room.

I took, however, the first opportunity of Lady Hawke's casting down her eyes, and reclining her delicate head, to make away from this terrible set; and, just as I was got by the piano-forte, where I hoped Pacchierotti would soon present himself, Mrs. Paradise again came to me, and said,

"Miss Burney, Lady Say and Sele wishes vastly to cultivate your acquaintance, and begs to know if she may have the honor of your company to an assembly at her house next Friday?—and I will do myself the pleasure to call for you, if you will give me leave."

"Her ladyship does me much honor, but I am unfortunately engaged," was my answer, with as much promptness as I could command. F.B.

6. For sale. 7. Range of vision or knowledge.

[A MASTECTOMY]

<div align="right">Paris, March 22, 1812[8]</div>

Separated as I have now so long—long been from my dearest father—brothers—sisters—nieces, & native friends, I would spare, at least, their kind hearts any grief for me but what they must inevitably feel in reflecting upon the sorrow of such an absence to one so tenderly attached to all her first and forever so dear & regretted ties—nevertheless, if they should hear that I have been dangerously ill from any hand but my own, they might have doubts of my perfect recovery which my own alone can obviate. And how can I hope they will escape hearing what has reached Seville to the south, and Constantinople to the east? from both I have had messages—yet nothing could urge me to this communication till I heard that M. de Boinville had written it to his wife,[9] without any precaution, because in ignorance of my plan of silence. Still I must hope it may never travel to my dearest father—But to you, my beloved Esther, who, living more in the world, will surely hear it ere long, to you I will write the whole history, certain that, from the moment you know any evil has befallen me your kind kind heart will be constantly anxious to learn its extent, & its circumstances, as well as its termination.

About August, in the year 1810, I began to be annoyed by a small pain in my breast, which went on augmenting from week to week, yet, being rather heavy than acute, without causing me any uneasiness with respect to the consequences: Alas, *"what was the ignorance?"* The most sympathizing of partners, however, was more disturbed: not a start, not a wry face, not a movement that indicated pain was unobserved, & he early conceived apprehensions to which I was a stranger. He pressed me to see some surgeon; I revolted from the idea, & hoped, by care & warmth, to make all succor unnecessary. Thus passed some months, during which Madame de Maisonneuve, my particularly intimate friend, joined with M. d'Arblay to press me to consent to an examination. I thought their fears groundless, and could not make so great a conquest over my repugnance. I relate this false confidence, now, as a warning to my dear Esther—my sisters & nieces, should any similar sensations excite similar alarm. M. d'A. now revealed his uneasiness to another of our kind friends, Mme. de Tracy, who wrote to me a long & eloquent letter upon the subject, that began to awaken very unpleasant surmises; & a conference with her ensued, in which her urgency & representations, aided by her long experience of disease, & most miserable existence by art,[1] subdued me, and, most painfully & reluctantly, I ceased to object, & M. d'A. summoned a physician—M. Bourdois? Maria will cry;—No, my dear Maria, I would not give your beau frere[2] that trouble; not him, but Dr. Jouart, the physician of Miss Potts. Thinking but slightly of my statement, he gave me some directions that produced no fruit—on the contrary, I grew worse, & M. d'A. now would take no denial to my consulting M. Dubois, who had already attended & cured me in an abscess of which Maria, my dearest Esther, can give you the history. M. Dubois, the most celebrated

8. This letter was sent to Burney's older sister Esther.
9. An Englishwoman, making it likely that news of Burney's illness would reach her family.

1. Skill (i.e., of a physician).
2. Brother-in-law (French). Esther's daughter Maria had married Antoine Bourdois, brother of a prominent French physician.

surgeon of France, was then appointed accoucheur to the empress, & already lodged in the Tuilleries, & in constant attendance: but nothing could slacken the ardor of M. d'A. to obtain the first advice.[3] Fortunately for his kind wishes, M. Dubois had retained a partial regard for me from the time of his former attendance, &, when applied to through a third person, he took the first moment of liberty, granted by a *promenade* taken by the empress, to come to me. It was now I began to perceive my real danger. M. Dubois gave me a prescription to be pursued for a month, during which time he could not undertake to see me again, & pronounced nothing—but uttered so many charges to me to be tranquil, & to suffer no uneasiness, that I could not but suspect there was room for terrible inquietude. My alarm was increased by the nonappearance of M. d'A. after his departure. They had remained together some time in the book room, & M. d'A. did not return—till, unable to bear the suspense, I begged him to come back. He, also, sought then to tranquilize me—but in words only; his looks were shocking! his features, his whole face displayed the bitterest woe. I had not, therefore, much difficulty in telling myself what he endeavored not to tell me—that a small operation would be necessary to avert evil consequences!—Ah, my dearest Esther, for this I felt no courage—my dread & repugnance, from a thousand reasons *besides* the pain, almost shook all my faculties, &, for some time, I was rather confounded & stupified than affrighted.—Direful, however, was the effect of this interview; the pains became quicker & more violent, & the hardness of the spot affected increased. I took, but vainly, my prescription, & every symptom grew more serious. At this time, M. de Narbonne spoke to M. d'A. of a surgeon of great eminence, M. Larrey, who had cured a polonoise[4] lady of his acquaintance of a similar malady; &, as my horror of an operation was insuperable, M. de Narbonne strongly recommended that I should have recourse to M. Larrey. I thankfully caught at any hope; & another friend of M. d'A. gave the same counsel at the same instant, which other, M. Barbier Neuville, has an influence irresistible over this M. Larrey, to whom he wrote the most earnest injunction that he would use every exertion to rescue me from what I so much dreaded. M. Larrey came, though very unwillingly, & full of scruples concerning M. Dubois; nor would he give me his services till I wrote myself to state my affright at the delay of attendance occasioned by the present high office & royal confinement of M. Dubois, & requesting that I might be made over to M. Larrey. An answer such as might be expected arrived, & I was now put upon a new *regime*, & animated by the fairest hopes.—M. Larrey has proved one of the worthiest, most disinterested, & singularly excellent of men, endowed with real genius in his profession, though with an ignorance of the world & its usages that induces a *naïveté* that leads those who do not see him thoroughly to think him not alone simple, but weak. They are mistaken; but his attention & thoughts having exclusively turned one way, he is hardly awake any other. His directions seemed all to succeed, for though I had still cruel seizures of terrible pain, the fits were shorter & more rare, & my spirits revived, & I went out almost daily, & quite daily received in my apartment some friend or intimate acquaintance, contrarily to my usual mode of *sauvagerie*[5]—and what friends

3. I.e., advice from the foremost doctor. "Accoucheur": male midwife. "The empress": Marie Louise (1791–1847), second wife of Napoleon; their son was born in 1811. "The Tuilleries": royal palace in Paris, used by Napoleon as his chief residence.
4. Polish. Dominique-Jean Larrey (1766–1842), French military surgeon.
5. Savageness; unsociability (French, as are all translated phrases in these notes).

have I found! what kind, consoling, zealous friends during all this painful period! In fine, I was much better, & every symptom of alarm abated. My good M. Larrey was enchanted, yet so anxious, that he forced me to see le Docteur Ribe, the first anatomist,[6] he said, in France, from his own fear lest he was under any delusion, from the excess of his desire to save me. I was as rebellious to the first visit of this famous anatomist as Maria will tell you I had been to that of M. Dubois, so odious to me was this sort of process: however, I was obliged to submit: & M. Ribe confirmed our best hopes—— Here, my dearest Esther, I must grow brief, for my theme becomes less pleasant—Sundry circumstances, too long to detail, combined to counteract all my flattering expectations, & all the skill, & all the cares of my assiduous & excellent surgeon. * * * A physician was now called in, Dr. Moreau, to hear if he could suggest any new means: but Dr. Larrey had left him no resources untried. A formal consultation now was held, of Larrey, Ribe, & Moreau—&, in fine, I was formally condemned to an operation by all three. I was as much astonished as disappointed—for the poor breast was no where discolored, & not much larger than its healthy neighbor. Yet I felt the evil to be deep, so deep, that I often thought if it could not be dissolved, it could only with life be extirpated. I called up, however, all the reason I possessed, or could assume, & told them—that if they saw no other alternative, I would not resist their opinion & experience:—the good Dr. Larrey, who, during his long attendance had conceived for me the warmest friendship, had now tears in his eyes; from my dread he had expected resistance. He proposed again calling in M. Dubois. * * *—M. Dubois behaved extremely well, no pique intervened with the interest he had professed in my well-doing, & his conduct was manly & generous. It was difficult still to see him, but he appointed the earliest day in his power for a general & final consultation. I was informed of it only on the same day, to avoid useless agitation. He met here Drs. Larrey, Ribe, & Moreau. The case, I saw, offered uncommon difficulties, or presented eminent danger, but, the examination over, they desired to consult together. I left them—what an half hour I passed alone!—M. d'A. was at his office. Dr. Larrey then came to summon me. He did not speak, but looked very like my dear brother James, to whom he has a personal resemblance that has struck M. d'A. as well as myself. I came back, & took my seat, with what calmness I was able. All were silent, & Dr. Larrey, I saw, hid himself nearly behind my sofa. My heart beat fast: I saw all hope was over. I called upon them to speak. M. Dubois then, after a long & unintelligible harangue, from his own disturbance, pronounced my doom. I now saw it was inevitable, and abstained from any further effort. They received my formal consent, & retired to fix a day.

All hope of escaping this evil being now at an end, I could only console or employ my mind in considering how to render it less dreadful to M. d'A. M. Dubois had pronounced "il faut s'attendre à souffrir. Je ne veux pas vous trompez—Vous souffrirez—vous souffrirez *beaucoup!*—"[7] M. Ribe had *charged* me to cry! to withhold or restrain myself might have seriously bad consequences, he said. M. Moreau, in echoing this injunction, inquired whether I had cried or screamed at the birth of Alexander—Alas, I told him,

6. One who dissects the human body. "Enchanted": delighted.
7. You must expect to suffer. I do not want to mislead you—you will suffer—you will suffer *a great deal.* The use of anesthetics in surgery began only in the mid–19th century.

it had not been possible to do otherwise; Oh then, he answered, there is no fear!—What terrible inferences were here to be drawn! I desired, therefore, that M. d'A. might be kept in ignorance of the day till the operation should be over. To this they agreed, except M. Larrey, with high approbation; M. Larrey looked dissentient,[8] but was silent. M. Dubois protested he would not undertake to act, after what he had seen of the agitated spirits of M. d'A. if he were present; nor would he suffer me to know the time myself over night. I obtained with difficulty a promise of 4 hours warning, which were essential to me for sundry regulations.

From this time, I assumed the best spirits in my power, *to meet the coming blow;*—& support my too sympathizing partner. They would let me make no preparations, refusing to inform me what would be necessary; I have known, since, that Madame de Tessé, an admirable old friend of M. d'A, now mine, equally, & one of the first of her sex, in any country, for uncommon abilities, & nearly universal knowledge, had insisted upon sending all that might be necessary, & of keeping me in ignorance. M. d'A filled a closet with charpie,[9] compresses, & bandages—All that to *me* was owned, as wanting, was an armchair & some towels.—Many things, however, joined to the depth of my pains, assured me the business was not without danger. I therefore made my will—unknown, to this moment, to M. d'A. * * *

After sentence thus passed, I was in hourly expectation of a summons to execution; judge, then, my surprise to be suffered to go on full 3 weeks in the same state! M. Larrey from time to time visited me, but pronounced nothing, & was always melancholy. At length, M. d'A. was told that he waited himself for a summons! & that, a formal one, & in writing! *I* could not give one; a *consent* was my utmost effort. But poor M. d'A. wrote a desire that the operation, if necessary, might take place without further delay. In my own mind, I had all this time been persuaded there were hopes of a cure; why else, I thought, let me know my doom thus long? But here I must account for this apparently useless, & therefore cruel measure, though I only learnt it myself 2 months afterwards. M. Dubois had given his opinion that the evil was too far advanced for any remedy; that the cancer was already internally declared;[1] that I was inevitably destined to that most frightful of deaths, & that an operation would but accelerate my dissolution. Poor M. Larrey was so deeply affected by this sentence, that—as he has lately told me—he regretted to his soul ever having known me, & was upon the point of demanding a commission to the furthest end of France in order to force me into other hands. I had said, however, he remembered, once, that I would far rather suffer a quick end without, than a lingering life with this dreadfullest of maladies; he finally, therefore, considered it might be possible to save me by the trial, but that without it my case was desperate, & resolved to make the attempt. Nevertheless, the responsibility was too great to rest upon his own head entirely; & therefore he waited the formal summons.— In fine, one morning—the last of September, 1811, while I was still in bed, & M. d'A. was arranging some papers for his office—I received a letter written by M. de Lally to a journalist, in vindication of the honored memory of

8. Dissenting from the majority opinion. 1. Manifest.
9. Old linen used for surgical dressings.

his father against the assertions of Madame du Deffand.[2] I read it aloud to my Alexanders,[3] with tears of admiration & sympathy, & then sent it by Alex to its excellent author, as I had promised the preceding evening. I then dressed, aided, as usual for many months, by my maid, my right arm being condemned to total inaction; but not yet was the grand business over, when another letter was delivered to me—another, indeed!—'twas from M. Larrey, to acquaint me that at 10 o'clock he should be with me, properly accompanied, & to exhort me to rely as much upon his sensibility & his prudence, as upon his dexterity & his experience; he charged to secure the absence of M. d'A.; & told me that the young physician who would deliver me this *announce*, would prepare for the operation, in which he must lend his aid; & also that it had been the decision of the consultation[4] to allow me but two hours notice.—Judge, my Esther, if I read this unmoved!—yet I had to disguise my sensations & intentions from M. d'A.!—Dr. Aumont, the messenger & terrible herald, was in waiting; M. d'A. stood by my bed side; I affected to be long reading the note, to gain time for forming some plan, & such was my terror of involving M. d'A. in the unavailing wretchedness of witnessing what I must go through, that it conquered every other, & gave me the force to act as if I were directing some third person. * * * Sundry necessary works & orders filled up my time entirely till one o'clock. When all was ready—— but Dr. Moreau then arrived, with news that M. Dubois could not attend till three. Dr. Aumont went away—& the coast was clear. This, indeed, was a dreadful interval. I had no longer any thing to do—I had only to think—TWO HOURS thus spent seemed never-ending. I would fain have written to my dearest father—to you, my Esther—to Charlotte, James, Charles—Amelia Lock—but my arm prohibited me. I strolled to the salon—I saw it fitted with preparations, & I recoiled—But I soon returned; to what effect disguise from myself what I must so soon know?—yet the sight of the immense quantity of bandages, compresses, sponges, lint——made me a little sick.—I walked backwards & forwards till I quieted all emotion, & became, by degrees, nearly stupid—torpid, without sentiment or consciousness;—& thus I remained till the clock struck three. A sudden spirit of exertion then returned—I defied my poor arm, no longer worth sparing, & took my long banished pen to write a few words to M. d'A.—& a few more for Alex, in case of a fatal result. These short billets I could only deposit safely, when the cabriolets[5]—one— two—three—four—succeeded rapidly to each other in stopping at the door. Dr. Moreau instantly entered my room, to see if I were alive. He gave me a wine cordial, & went to the salon. I rang for my maid & nurses—but before I could speak to them, my room, without previous message, was entered by 7 men in black, Dr. Larrey, M. Dubois, Dr. Moreau, Dr. Aumont, Dr. Ribe, & a pupil of Dr. Larrey, & another of M. Dubois. I was now awakened from my stupor—& by a sort of indignation—Why so many? & without leave?— But I could not utter a syllable. M. Dubois acted as commander in chief. Dr. Larrey kept out of sight; M. Dubois ordered a bedstead into the middle of the room. Astonished, I turned to Dr. Larrey, who had promised that an

2. Marie du Deffand (1697–1780), who hosted a brilliant salon; her letters were published in 1809. She had written approvingly of the 1766 execution of M. de Lally's father, the Comte de Lally, who had been made the scapegoat for a military disaster.

3. I.e., Burney's husband and son.
4. Conference. "*Announce*": announcement, notification (*announce*, French).
5. Light two-wheeled carriages.

armchair would suffice; but he hung his head, & would not look at me. Two *old mattresses* M. Dubois then demanded, & an old sheet. I now began to tremble violently, more with distaste & horror of the preparations even than of the pain. These arranged to his liking, he desired me to mount the bedstead. I stood suspended, for a moment, whether I should not abruptly escape—I looked at the door, the windows—I felt desperate—but it was only for a moment, my reason then took the command, & my fears & feelings struggled vainly against it. I called to my maid—she was crying, & the two nurses stood, transfixed, at the door. "Let those women all go!" cried M. Dubois. This order recovered me my voice—"No," I cried, "let them stay! *qu'elles restent!*"[6] This occasioned a little dispute, that re-animated me. The maid, however, & one of the nurses ran off—I charged the other to approach, & she obeyed. M. Dubois now tried to issue his commands *en militaire,*[7] but I resisted all that were resistible—I was compelled, however, to submit to taking off my long robe de chambre,[8] which I had meant to retain—Ah, then, how did I think of my sisters!—not one, at so dreadful an instant, at hand, to protect—adjust—guard me—I regretted that I had refused Mme de Maisonneuve—Mme Chastel—no one upon whom I could rely—my departed angel![9]—how did I think of her!—how did I long—long for my Esther—my Charlotte!—My distress was, I suppose, apparent, though not my wishes, for M. Dubois himself now softened, & spoke soothingly. "Can *you,*" I cried, "feel for an operation that, to *you,* must seem so trivial?"—"Trivial?" he repeated—taking up a bit of paper, which he tore, unconsciously, into a million of pieces, *"oui—c'est peu de chose—mais—"*[1] he stammered, & could not go on. No one else attempted to speak, but I was softened myself, when I saw even M. Dubois grow agitated, while Dr. Larrey kept always aloof, yet a glance showed me he was pale as ashes. I knew not, positively, then, the immediate danger, but everything convinced me danger was hovering about me, & that this experiment could alone save me from its jaws. I mounted, therefore, unbidden, the bedstead—& M. Dubois placed me upon the mattress, & spread a cambric handkerchief upon my face. It was transparent, however, & I saw, through it, that the bedstead was instantly surrounded by the 7 men & my nurse. I refused to be held; but when, bright through the cambric, I saw the glitter of polished steel—I closed my eyes. I would not trust to convulsive fear the sight of the terrible incision. A silence the most profound ensued, which lasted for some minutes, during which, I imagine, they took their orders by signs, & made their examination—Oh what a horrible suspension!—I did not breathe—& M. Dubois tried vainly to find any pulse. This pause, at length, was broken by Dr. Larrey, who, in a voice of solemn melancholy, said "Qui me tiendra ce sein?—"[2]

No one answered; at least not verbally; but this aroused me from my passively submissive state, for I feared they imagined the whole breast infected—feared it too justly—for, again through the cambric, I saw the hand of M. Dubois held up, while his forefinger first described a straight line from top to bottom of the breast, secondly a cross, & thirdly a circle; intimating that the WHOLE was to be taken off. Excited by this idea, I started up, threw

6. They [female] remain.
7. In military fashion.
8. Dressing gown.
9. Susanna, Burney's favorite sister, who had died

in 1800.
1. Yes—it is a small thing—but.
2. Who will hold this breast for me?

off my veil, &, in answer to the demand "Qui me tiendra ce sein?" cried "C'est moi, monsieur!"[3] & I held my hand under it, & explained the nature of my sufferings, which all sprang from one point, though they darted into every part. I was heard attentively, but in utter silence, & M. Dubois then re-placed[4] me as before, &, as before, spread my veil over my face. How vain, alas, my representation! immediately again I saw the fatal finger describe the cross—& the circle. Hopeless, then, desperate, & self-given up, I closed once more my eyes, relinquishing all watching, all resistance, all interference, & sadly resolute to be wholly resigned.

My dearest Esther, & all my dears to whom she communicates this doleful ditty,[5] will rejoice to hear that this resolution once taken, was firmly adhered to, in defiance of a terror that surpasses all description, & the most torturing pain. Yet—when the dreadful steel was plunged into the breast—cutting through veins—arteries—flesh—nerves—I needed no injunctions not to restrain my cries. I began a scream that lasted unintermittingly during the whole time of the incision—& I almost marvel that it rings not in my ears still! so excruciating was the agony. When the wound was made, & the instrument was withdrawn, the pain seemed undiminished, for the air that suddenly rushed into those delicate parts felt like a mass of minute but sharp & forked poniards,[6] that were tearing the edges of the wound—but when again I felt the instrument—describing a curve—cutting against the grain, if I may so say, while the flesh resisted in a manner so forcible as to oppose & tire the hand of the operator, who was forced to change from the right to the left—then, indeed, I thought I must have expired. I attempted no more to open my eyes,—they felt as if hermetically shut, & so firmly closed, that the eyelids seemed indented into the cheeks. The instrument this second time withdrawn, I concluded the operation over. Oh no! presently the terrible cutting was renewed—& worse than ever, to separate the bottom, the foundation of this dreadful gland from the parts to which it adhered. Again all description would be baffled—yet again all was not over.—Dr. Larrey rested but his own hand, &—Oh heaven!—I then felt the knife rackling[7] against the breast bone—scraping it!—This performed, while I yet remained in utterly speechless torture, I heard the voice of Mr. Larrey (all others guarded a dead silence) in a tone nearly tragic, desire every one present to pronounce if any thing more remained to be done. The general voice was Yes—but the finger of Mr. Dubois—which I literally *felt* elevated over the wound, though I saw nothing, & though he touched nothing, so indescribably sensitive was the spot—pointed to some further requisition—& again began the scraping!—and, after this, Dr. Moreau thought he discerned a peccant[8] atom—and still, & still, M. Dubois demanded atom after atom. My dearest Esther, not for days, not for weeks, but for months I could not speak of this terrible business without nearly again going through it! I could not *think* of it with impunity! I was sick, I was disordered by a single question—even now, 9 months after it is over, I have a headache from going on with the account! & this miserable account, which I began 3 months ago, at least, I dare not revise, nor read, the recollection is still so painful.

3. I, sir!
4. Repositioned.
5. Subject, theme.
6. Daggers.

7. Scraping (apparently Burney's coinage, from the French verb *racler*).
8. Disease-inducing. "Requisition": necessity.

To conclude, the evil was so profound, the case so delicate, & the precautions necessary for preventing a return so numerous, that the operation, including the treatment & the dressing, lasted 20 minutes! a time, for sufferings so acute, that was hardly supportable. However, I bore it with all the courage I could exert, & never moved, nor stopped them, nor resisted, nor remonstrated, nor spoke—except once or twice, during the dressings, to say "Ah Messieurs! que je vous plains!—"[9] for indeed I was sensible to the feeling concern with which they all saw what I endured, though my speech was principally—*very* principally meant for Dr. Larrey. Except this, I uttered not a syllable, save, when so often they recommenced, calling out "Avertissez moi,[1] Messieurs! avertissez moi!—" Twice, I believe, I fainted; at least, I have two total chasms in my memory of this transaction, that impede my tying together what passed. When all was done, & they lifted me up that I might be put to bed, my strength was so totally annihilated, that I was obliged to be carried, & could not even sustain my hands & arms, which hung as if I had been lifeless; while my face, as the nurse has told me, was utterly colorless. This removal made me open my eyes—& I then saw my good Dr. Larrey, pale nearly as myself, his face streaked with blood, & its expression depicting grief, apprehension, & almost horror.

When I was in bed, my poor M. d'Arblay—who ought to write you himself his own history of this morning—was called to me—& afterwards our Alex.—

[M. D'ARBLAY'S POSTSCRIPT]

No! No my dearest & ever more dear friends, I shall not make a fruitless attempt. No language could convey what I felt in the deadly course of these seven hours. Nevertheless, every one *of you, my dearest dearest friends*, can guess, must even know it. Alexander had no less feeling, but showed more fortitude. He, perhaps, will be more able to describe to you, nearly at least, the torturing state of my poor heart & soul. Besides, I must own, to you, that these details which were, till just now, quite unknown to me, have almost killed me, & I am only able to thank God that this more than half angel has had the sublime courage to deny herself the comfort I might have offered her, to spare me, not the sharing of her excruciating pains, that was impossible, but the witnessing so terrific a scene, & perhaps the remorse to have rendered it more tragic. For I don't flatter myself I could have got through it—I must confess it.

Thank heaven! She is now surprisingly well, & in good spirits, & we hope to have many many still happy days. May that of peace soon arrive, and enable me to embrace better than with my pen my beloved & ever ever more dear friends of the town & country. Amen. Amen!

9. Ah sirs! how I pity you! 1. Warn me.

PHILLIS WHEATLEY
ca. 1753–1784

Just enough is known about Phillis Wheatley's life to suggest the extent of her poetic talent, for she developed her literary art against great odds. The time and place of Wheatley's birth are as unknown as her African name, but she probably came from what is now called Senegal or Gambia. When she was purchased directly off a slave ship in Boston by a wealthy tailor, John Wheatley, in 1761, she was losing her first teeth, and so she was believed to be about seven years of age. Because of her precocity, the girl, who became Mrs. Susannah Wheatley's personal servant, was treated beneficently by the standards of the time. She learned English in sixteen months, and soon studied Latin, as well as the Bible and English poetry by John Milton, Alexander Pope, and Thomas Gray. She began writing religious verse when she was thirteen, and she could not have been more than seventeen years old when she published one of her first poems, an elegy on the death of the English evangelical preacher George Whitefield. In 1773, in poor health, she was sent to England with the Wheatleys' son, and there her only book, *Poems on Various Subjects, Religious and Moral,* was published. After she returned to Boston to witness first Mrs. and then Mr. Wheatley's death, she was manumitted and married John Peters, a freedman who seems later to have been imprisoned for debt. Two of her three children died, and eventually Wheatley worked in a dilapidated lodging house to support herself and the third child, who died soon after she did.

Even the scanty information we have about Wheatley's career implies that she lived the life of a prodigy. Whether praised as an exemplary figure or scrutinized as a strange aberration, she was famous for her wit in conversation, her modesty, and her social poise. Certainly, her poems are decorous and pious in their stylistic use of conventional neoclassical couplets and in their thematic focus on spiritual salvation achieved through Christ. She was the guest of the countess of Huntingdon in London and met General George Washington after publishing a poem about him in the April 1776 issue of the *Philadelphia Magazine.* The volume of verse the countess of Huntingdon helped publish contains a foreword attesting to Wheatley's talents and is signed by eighteen prominent Massachusetts men, including John Hancock. Yet none of these testimonials saved her from the obscurity and destitution of her life after slavery. *Poems on Various Subjects* was published in America in 1786. But Wheatley's fame as the first black American woman poet was not established until Margaretta M. Odell published a *Memoir* in her 1834 edition of the *Poems.* Only recently has Wheatley received the scholarly attention her unprecedented achievement deserves. As the critic Henry Louis Gates Jr. has pointed out, her poetry marks the simultaneous literary origin of two aesthetic lineages: the black American literary tradition and the black female literary tradition. At the same time, her work is marked by a confident eloquence suggesting that she felt herself to be very much part of an intellectual mainstream in her addresses to such diverse figures as "S. M., a young African painter" and "His Excellency General Washington."

[Letter Sent by the Author's Master to the Publisher]

Phillis was brought from *Africa* to *America*, in the year 1761, between seven and eight years of age. Without any assistance from school education, and by only what she was taught in the family, she, in sixteen months time from her arrival, attained the English language, to which she was an utter stranger

before, to such a degree, as to read any, the most difficult parts of the sacred writings,[1] to the great astonishment of all who heard her.

As to her writing, her own curiosity led her to it; and this she learnt in so short a time, that in the year 1765, she wrote a letter to the Rev. Mr. Occom,[2] the *Indian* minister, while in *England*.

She has a great inclination to learn the Latin tongue, and has made some progress in it. This relation is given by her master who bought her, and with whom she now lives.

<div align="right">John Wheatley[3]</div>

Boston, Nov. 14, 1772

On Being Brought from Africa to America

'Twas mercy brought me from my pagan land,
Taught my benighted[1] soul to understand
That there's a God, that there's a Savior too:
Once I redemption neither sought nor knew.
5 Some view that sable race with scornful eye:
"Their color is a diabolic dye."
Remember, Christians, Negroes black as Cain[2]
May be refined and join the angelic strain.[3]

<div align="right">1773</div>

To the Right Honorable William, Earl of Dartmouth,[1] His Majesty's Principal Secretary of State for North America, Etc.

Hail, happy day, when, smiling like the morn,
Fair Freedom rose New England to adorn:
The northern clime[2] beneath her genial ray,
Dartmouth, congratulates thy blissful sway:[3]
5 Elate with hope her race no longer mourns,
Each soul expands, each grateful bosom burns,
While in thine hand with pleasure we behold
The silken reins, and Freedom's charms unfold.
Long lost to realms beneath the northern skies
10 She shines supreme, while hated Faction dies:
Soon as appeared the goddess[4] long desired,
Sick at the view, she[5] languished and expired;

1. I.e., the Bible.
2. Samson Occom (1723–1792), a Mohegan who had become an ordained Presbyterian minister and was a friend of the Wheatleys.
3. A Boston merchant (d. 1778).
1. Unenlightened.
2. After Cain murdered his brother Abel, God "marked" him so that no one would kill him (Genesis 4.15). This story was at times interpreted as explaining the origin of blacks.
3. Race. "Refined": purified (possibly a punning allusion to cane sugar).

1. The second earl of Dartmouth (1731–1801), who was appointed secretary in charge of the American colonies in August 1772, replacing the stern Lord Hillsborough. American sympathizers in England were hopeful that Dartmouth would prove to be more amenable to the colonies' grievances.
2. Region.
3. Reign, leadership.
4. I.e., Freedom.
5. I.e., Faction (internal conflict).

Thus from the splendors of the morning light
The owl in sadness seeks the caves of night.

15 No more, America, in mournful strain[6]
Of wrongs, and grievance unredressed complain,
No longer shalt thou dread the iron chain
Which wanton Tyranny with lawless hand
Had made, and with it meant to enslave the land.

20 Should you, my lord, while you peruse my song,
Wonder from whence my love of Freedom sprung,
Whence flow these wishes for the common good,
By feeling hearts alone best understood,
I, young in life, by seeming cruel fate,
25 Was snatched from Afric's fancied happy seat:[7]
What pangs excruciating must molest,
What sorrows labor in my parents' breast?
Steeled was that soul and by no misery moved
That from a father seized his babe beloved:
30 Such, such my case. And can I then but pray
Others may never feel tyrannic sway?

For favors past, great Sir, our thanks are due,
And thee we ask thy favors to renew,
Since in thy power,[8] as in thy will before,
35 To soothe the griefs which thou didst once deplore.
May heavenly grace the sacred sanction give
To all thy works, and thou forever live
Not only on the wings of fleeting Fame,
Though praise immortal crowns the patriot's[9] name,
40 But to conduct to heaven's refulgent fane,[1]
May fiery coursers sweep the ethereal plain,[2]
And bear thee upwards to that blessed abode,
Where, like the prophet,[3] thou shalt find thy God.

1773

To S. M.,[1] A Young *African* Painter, on Seeing His Works

To show the laboring bosom's deep intent,
And thought in living characters to paint,
When first thy pencil did those beauties give,
And breathing figures learnt from thee to live,

6. Passage of song or poetry.
7. Place of abode. "Fancied": imagined.
8. I.e., since it is in thy power. The line draws a distinction between Dartmouth's powerless state of sympathy for the colonies before his appointment, and his newfound ability to help them.
9. I.e., Dartmouth's.

1. Shining temple.
2. Heaven. "Coursers": swift horses.
3. Elijah, who was borne up into heaven on a chariot of fire (2 Kings 2.11).
1. Scipio Moorhead, a servant of Rev. John Moorhead in Boston.

5 How did those prospects give my soul delight,
 A new creation rushing on my sight?
 Still, wond'rous youth! each noble path pursue,
 On deathless glories fix thine ardent view:
 Still may the painter's and the poet's fire
10 To aid thy pencil, and thy verse conspire!
 And may the charms of each seraphic theme
 Conduct thy footsteps to immortal fame!
 High to the blissful wonders of the skies
 Elate thy soul, and raise thy wishful eyes.
15 Thrice happy, when exalted to survey
 That splendid city, crowned with endless day,
 Whose twice six gates on radiant hinges ring:
 Celestial Salem[2] blooms in endless spring.

 Calm and serene thy moments glide along,
20 And may the muse inspire each future song!
 Still, with the sweets of contemplation blessed,
 May peace with balmy wings your soul invest!
 But when these shades of time are chased away,
 And darkness ends in everlasting day,
25 On what seraphic pinions[3] shall we move,
 And view the landscapes in the realms above?
 There shall thy tongue in heavenly murmurs flow,
 And there my muse with heavenly transport glow:
 No more to tell of Damon's tender sighs,
30 Or rising radiance of Aurora's[4] eyes,
 For nobler themes demand a nobler strain,
 And purer language on the ethereal plain.[5]
 Cease, gentle muse! the solemn gloom of night
 Now seals the fair creation from my sight.

1773

To His Excellency, General Washington[1]

The following letter *and* verses, *were written by the famous* Phillis Wheatley, *the African Poetess, and presented to his Excellency Gen.* Washington.

Sir,

I have taken the freedom to address your Excellency in the enclosed poem, and entreat your acceptance, though I am not insensible of its inaccuracies. Your being appointed by the Grand Continental Congress to be Generalissimo of the armies of North America, together with the fame of your virtues,

2. I.e., Jerusalem in heaven, believed to have twelve gates (see Revelation 21.12).
3. Angels' wings.
4. Damon and Aurora are the subjects of a conventional love poem, unsuited to heaven.

5. In the heavens.
1. After reading this poem, Washington invited Wheatley to meet him in Cambridge, Massachusetts, in February 1776.

excite sensations not easy to suppress. Your generosity, therefore, I presume, will pardon the attempt. Wishing your Excellency all possible success in the great cause you are so generously engaged in. I am,

Your Excellency's most obedient humble servant,
Phillis Wheatley

Providence, Oct. 26, 1775
His Excellency Gen. Washington

> Celestial choir! enthroned in realms of light,
> Columbia's[2] scenes of glorious toils I write.
> While freedom's cause her anxious breast alarms,
> She flashes dreadful in refulgent arms.
> 5 See mother earth her offspring's fate bemoan,
> And nations gaze at scenes before unknown!
> See the bright beams of heaven's revolving light
> Involved in sorrows and the veil of night!
> The goddess[3] comes, she moves divinely fair,
> 10 Olive and laurel binds her golden hair:
> Wherever shines this native of the skies,
> Unnumbered charms and recent graces rise.
> Muse! bow propitious while my pen relates
> How pour her armies through a thousand gates:
> 15 As when Eolus[4] heaven's fair face deforms,
> Enwrapped in tempest and a night of storms;
> Astonished ocean feels the wild uproar,
> The refluent surges beat the sounding shore;
> Or thick as leaves in Autumn's golden reign,
> 20 Such, and so many, moves the warrior's train.
> In bright array they seek the work of war,
> Where high unfurled the ensign[5] waves in air.
> Shall I to Washington their praise recite?
> Enough thou knowest them in the fields of fight.
> 25 Thee, first in place and honors,—we demand
> The grace and glory of thy martial band.
> Famed for thy valor, for thy virtues more,
> Hear every tongue thy guardian aid implore!
> One century scarce performed its destined round,
> 30 When Gallic[6] powers Columbia's fury found;
> And so may you, whoever dares disgrace
> The land of freedom's heaven-defended race!
> Fixed are the eyes of nations on the scales,
> For in their hopes Columbia's arm prevails.
> 35 Anon Britannia droops the pensive head,
> While round increase the rising hills of dead.
> Ah! cruel blindness to Columbia's state!

2. America's.
3. Probably Liberty personified, here associated (in line 10) with the goddess of wisdom, Athena ("olive"), and with victory ("laurel").
4. God of winds. "Muse": goddess of art and learning, conventionally invoked for inspiration and information.

5. Banner, flag.
6. French. The reference is the colonial wars waged between France and Great Britain in North America. The final French and Indian War (1754–63) formed Washington's entire pre-Revolutionary military career.

Lament thy thirst of boundless power too late.
Proceed, great chief, with virtue on thy side,
40 Thy every action let the goddess guide.
A crown, a mansion, and a throne that shine,
With gold unfading, WASHINGTON! be thine.

1775–76 1776, 1834

To the University of Cambridge, in New England[1]

While an intrinsic ardor prompts to write,
The muses[2] promise to assist my pen;
'Twas not long since I left my native shore
The land of errors, and Egyptian gloom:[3]
5 Father of mercy, 'twas Thy gracious hand
Brought me in safety from those dark abodes.

Students, to you 'tis given to scan the heights
Above, to traverse the ethereal space,
And mark the systems of revolving worlds.
10 Still more, ye sons of science[4] ye receive
The blissful news by messengers from Heav'n,
How Jesus' blood for your redemption flows.
See Him with hands outstretched upon the cross;
Immense compassion in His bosom glows;
15 He hears revilers, nor resents their scorn:
What matchless mercy in the Son of God!
When the whole human race by sin had fall'n,
He deigned to die that they might rise again,
And share with Him in the sublimest skies,
20 Life without death, and glory without end.

Improve[5] your privileges while they stay,
Ye pupils, and each hour redeem, that bears
Or[6] good or bad report of you to Heav'n.
Let sin, that baneful evil to the soul,
25 By you be shunned, nor once remit your guard;
Suppress the deadly serpent in its egg.
Ye blooming plants of human race divine,
An Ethiop[7] tells you 'tis your greatest foe;
Its transient sweetness turns to endless pain,
30 And in immense perdition sinks the soul.

1773

1. Harvard.
2. In Greek mythology, nine daughters of Memory who preside over the arts and all intellectual pursuits.
3. Cf. Exodus 10.21–23, which describes "thick darkness" as one of the plagues inflicted by God on the Egyptians. "Errors": theological errors, because the Africans are not Christian.
4. Knowledge.
5. Take advantage of.
6. Either.
7. Ethiopian; i.e., a black person.

MARY ROBINSON
1758–1800

A famous beauty somewhat sardonically labeled "pretty, charming 'Perdita' " by Oscar Wilde, Mary Robinson led an adventurous life as wife, mother, actress, mistress, and prolific woman of letters. Born in Bristol and raised in London, she married Thomas Robinson in 1774, when she was still a teenager. She soon gave birth to a daughter, and when her husband was imprisoned for debt she spent ten months in prison with him and her baby. There she wrote a collection of poems that appeared in 1775, earning the patronage of the duchess of Devonshire. On leaving prison, she began a successful career as an actress, with the sponsorship of the famous actor David Garrick, whose attention she had caught even before her marriage. When she was only fifteen, she later remembered in her memoirs, "Garrick was delighted with everything I did. He would sometimes dance a minuet with me . . . but the circumstance which most pleased him was my tone of voice."

Robinson's glamorous performance as Perdita in Shakespeare's *The Winter's Tale* earned her a permanent pseudonym and charmed the seventeen-year-old prince of Wales; he made her royal mistress for a year, but then abandoned her with little compensation and an unsavory reputation. Unwilling to return to the stage, she began writing in earnest after several other romantic relationships failed—in particular a fifteen-year liaison with the rakish Colonel Banastre Tarleton, a gambling crony of the prince's—and a miscarriage left her partially paralyzed. Wide-ranging, lively, and lucrative, her literary output included several collections of poetry, among them an erotic sonnet sequence inspired by her passion for Tarleton (*Sappho and Phaon*, 1796); a satiric comedy (*Nobody*, 1794); a verse tragedy (*The Sicilian Lover*, 1796); eight novels, among them the best-selling gothic romance *Vicenza, or the Dangers of Credulity*, 1796); and a feminist polemic (*A Letter to the Woman of England on the Injustice of Mental Subordination*, 1799).

"Every event of my life has more or less been marked by the progressive evils of a too acute sensibility," Robinson declared in her memoir, but by the end of her career she had become both more acerbic and more politically assertive, insisting in her *Letter to the Women of England* that the "barbarity of custom's law in this *enlightened* country, has long been exercised to the prejudice of women [and] even the laws of honour have been perverted to oppress her." Movivng in intellectual circles that included William Wordsworth, Samuel Taylor Coleridge, Mary Wollstonecraft, and William Godwin, Robinson had been painted at the height of her social and theatrical popularity by such major contemporary artists as George Romney, Thomas Gainsborough, and Sir Joshua Reynolds. She enjoyed many triumphs, but she died at the relatively early age of forty-two, after years of ill health and of a disillusionment that she expressed not only in her feminist *Letter* but earlier, in "January, 1795," where she deplored a world of "Authors who can't earn a dinner; / Many a subtle rogue a winner" and "Taste and talents quite deserted; / All the laws of truth perverted."

London's Summer Morning

Who has not waked to list the busy sounds
Of summer's morning, in the sultry smoke
Of noisy London? On the pavement hot
The sooty chimney-boy, with dingy face
5 And tattered covering, shrilly bawls his trade,
Rousing the sleepy housemaid. At the door
The milk-pail rattles, and the tinkling bell

Proclaims the dustman's office;[1] while the street
Is lost in clouds impervious. Now begins
10 The din of hackney-coaches,[2] wagons, carts;
While tinmen's shops, and noisy trunk-makers,
Knife-grinders, coopers,[3] squeaking cork-cutters,
Fruit-barrows, and the hunger-giving cries
Of vegetable venders, fill the air.
15 Now every shop displays its varied trade,
And the fresh-sprinkled pavement cools the feet
Of early walkers. At the private door
The ruddy housemaid twirls the busy mop,
Annoying the smart 'prentice, or neat girl,
20 Tripping with band-box[4] lightly. Now the sun
Darts burning splendor on the glittering pane,
Save where the canvas awning throws a shade
On the gay merchandise. Now, spruce and trim,
In shops (where beauty smiles with industry)
25 Sits the smart damsel; while the passenger
Peeps through the window, watching every charm.
Now pastry dainties catch the eye minute
Of humming insects, while the limy snare[5]
Waits to enthrall them. Now the lamp-lighter
30 Mounts the tall ladder, nimbly venturous,
To trim the half-filled lamp; while at his feet
The pot-boy[6] yells discordant! All along
The sultry pavement, the old-clothes-man cries
In tone monotonous, and side-long views
35 The area for his traffic: now the bag
Is slyly opened, and the half-worn suit
(Sometimes the pilfered treasure of the base
Domestic spoiler[7]), for one half its worth,
Sinks in the green abyss. The porter now
40 Bears his huge load along the burning way;
And the poor poet wakes from busy dreams,
To paint the summer morning.

1794 1806

January, 1795

Pavement slippery, people sneezing,
Lords in ermine, beggars freezing;
Titled gluttons dainties carving,
Genius in a garret starving.

5 Lofty mansions, warm and spacious;
Courtiers cringing and voracious;[1]

1. I.e., carting away garbage. "Office": duty, function.
2. Hired carriages.
3. Those who make barrels and buckets.
4. Hat box.
5. Spread with bird lime, a sticky substance.
6. A boy who carries beer to customers outside the pub.
7. I.e., a thieving servant.
1. Greedy.

Misers scarce the wretched heeding;
Gallant soldiers fighting, bleeding.

Wives who laugh at passive spouses;
10 Theatres, and meeting-houses;[2]
Balls, where simpering misses languish;
Hospitals, and groans of anguish.

Arts and sciences bewailing;
Commerce drooping, credit failing;
15 Placemen[3] mocking subjects loyal;
Separations, weddings royal.

Authors who can't earn a dinner;
Many a subtle rogue a winner;
Fugitives for shelter seeking;
20 Misers hoarding, tradesmen breaking.[4]

Taste and talents quite deserted;
All the laws of truth perverted;
Arrogance o'er merit soaring;
Merit silently deploring.

25 Ladies gambling night and morning;
Fools the works of genius scorning;
Ancient dames for girls mistaken,
Youthful damsels quite forsaken.

Some in luxury delighting;
30 More in talking than in fighting;
Lovers old, and beaux decrepit;
Lordlings empty and insipid.

Poets, painters, and musicians;
Lawyers, doctors, politicians;
35 Pamphlets, newspapers, and odes,
Seeking fame by different roads.

Gallant souls with empty purses,
Generals only fit for nurses;
School-boys, smit with martial spirit,
40 Taking place of veteran merit.

Honest men who can't get places,
Knaves who show unblushing faces;
Ruin hastened, peace retarded;
Candor spurned, and art[5] rewarded.

1795 1806

2. Places of worship of Nonconformists or Dis-
senters.
3. A disparaging term for those with appointed
positions in government.

4. I.e., "breaking" them financially by not paying
them.
5. I.e., craftiness, cunning.

To the Poet Coleridge[1]

RAPT in the visionary theme!
 SPIRIT DIVINE! with THEE I'll wander,
Where the blue, wavy, lucid stream,
 'Mid forest glooms, shall slow meander!
5 With THEE I'll trace the circling bounds
 Of thy NEW PARADISE[2] extended;
And listen to the varying sounds
 Of winds, and foamy torrents blended.

Now by the source which laboring heaves
10 The mystic fountain, bubbling, panting,
While gossamer its network weaves,
 Adown the blue lawn slanting!
I'll mark thy *sunny dome,*[3] and view
Thy *Caves of Ice,* thy fields of dew!
15 Thy ever-blooming mead, whose flower
Waves to the cold breath of the moonlight hour![4]
Or when the day-star,[5] peering bright
On the gray wing of parting night;
While more than vegetating power[6]
20 Throbs grateful to the burning hour,
As summer's whispered sighs unfold
Her million, million buds of gold;
Then will I climb the breezy bounds,
 Of thy NEW PARADISE extended,
25 And listen to the distant sounds
 Of winds, and foamy torrents blended!

SPIRIT DIVINE! with THEE I'll trace
Imagination's boundless space!
With thee, beneath thy *sunny dome,*
30 I'll listen to the minstrel's lay,
 Hymning the gradual close of day;
In *Caves of Ice* enchanted roam,
Where on the glittering entrance plays
The moon's-beam with its silvery rays;
35 Or, when glassy stream,
 That through the deep dell flows,
Flashes the noon's hot beam;
 The noon's hot beam, that midway shows
Thy flaming Temple, studded o'er

1. Samuel Taylor Coleridge (1772–1834), poet and critic, who, along with his friend William Wordsworth, is most often linked with the beginnings of Romantic poetry in England. Coleridge was strongly influenced by German philosophy in his ideas of aesthetics and the imaginative process.
2. Perhaps a reference to the last line of Coleridge's "Kubla Khan" (written ca. 1797–98; published 1816) as well as to a construction of the poets' imaginations.
3. The speaker in "Kubla Khan" wishes he could build with music "That sunny dome! those caves of ice!"
4. Two of Coleridge's best-known poems, "Frost at Midnight" (1798) and "Dejection: A Ode" (1802), are set in moonlight. "Mead": meadow.
5. The sun.
6. Growing power; the phrase also has the sense of "the power that causes vegetation."

40 With all PERUVIA's[7] lustrous store!
There will I trace the circling bounds
 Of thy NEW PARADISE extended!
And listen to the awful sounds,
 Of winds, and foamy torrents blended!

45 And now I'll pause to catch the moan
 Of distant breezes, cavern-pent;
Now, ere the twilight tints are flown,
Purpling the landscape, far and wide,
On the dark promontory's side
50 I'll gather wild flowers, dew besprent,
And weave a crown for THEE,
GENIUS OF HEAVEN-TAUGHT POESY!
While, opening to my wondering eyes,
Thou bidst a new creation rise,
55 I'll raptured trace the circling bounds
 Of thy RICH PARADISE extended,
And listen to the varying sounds
 Of winds, and foaming torrents blended.

And now, with lofty tones inviting,
60 Thy nymph,[8] her dulcimer swift smiting,
Shall wake me in ecstatic measures!
Far, far removed from mortal pleasures!
 In cadence rich, in cadence strong,
Proving the wondrous witcheries of song!
65 I hear her voice! thy *sunny dome,*
Thy *caves of ice,* loud repeat,
Vibrations, maddening sweet,
 Calling the visionary wanderer home.
She sings of THEE, O favored child
70 Of *Minstrelsy,* SUBLIMELY WILD![9]
Of thee, whose soul can feel the tone
Which gives to airy dreams *a magic* ALL THY OWN!

1797

The Poor Singing Dame

Beneath an old wall, that went round an old castle,
 For many a year, with brown ivy o'erspread,
A neat little hovel, its lowly roof raising,
 Defied the wild winds that howl'd over its shed:
5 The turrets, that frown'd on the poor simple dwelling,
 Were rock'd to and fro, when the tempest would roar,
And the river, that down the rich valley was swelling,
 Flow'd swiftly beside the green step of its door.

7. I.e., Peru, whose chief mineral, copper, would
make a building "flame."
8. The "damsel with a dulcimer" in the last stanza
of "Kubla Khan."
9. Coleridge's description in "Kubla Khan" of a

"deep romantic chasm" provides a fine example of
the late-18th-century notion of the sublime: the
grand and lofty—in nature associated with the
fearful, wild, and violent—to which we respond
emotionally.

The summer sun gilded the rushy roof slanting,
10 The bright dews bespangled its ivy-bound hedge,
And above, on the ramparts, the sweet birds were chanting,
And wild buds thick dappled the clear river's edge,
When the castle's rich chambers were haunted and dreary,
 The poor little hovel was still and secure;
15 And no robber e'er enter'd, nor goblin nor fairy,
 For the splendors of pride had no charms to allure.

The Lord of the castle, a proud surly ruler,
 Oft heard the low dwelling with sweet music ring,
For the old Dame that liv'd in the little hut cheerly,
20 Would sit at her wheel,[1] and would merrily sing:
When with revels the castle's great hall was resounding,
 The old Dame was sleeping, not dreaming of fear;
And when over the mountains the huntsmen were bounding
She would open her lattice, their clamors to hear.

25 To the merry-ton'd horn she would dance on the threshold,
 And louder, and louder, repeat her old song:
And when winter its mantle of frost was displaying,
 She caroll'd, undaunted, the bare woods among:
She would gather dry fern, ever happy and singing,
30 With her cake of brown bread, and her jug of brown beer,
And would smile when she heard the great castle-bell ringing,
 Inviting the proud—to their prodigal cheer.

Thus she liv'd, ever patient and ever contented,
 Till envy the Lord of the castle possess'd,
35 For he hated that poverty should be so cheerful,
 While care could the fav'rites of fortune molest;
He sent his bold yeomen with threats to prevent[2] her,
 And still would she carol her sweet roundelay;
At last, an old steward relentless he sent her—
40 Who bore her, all trembling, to prison away!

Three weeks did she languish, then died broken-hearted,
 Poor Dame! how the death-bell did mournfully sound!
And along the green path six young bachelors bore her,
 And laid her for ever beneath the cold ground!
45 And the primroses pale 'mid the long grass were growing,
 The bright dews of twilight bespangled her grave,
And morn heard the breezes of summer soft blowing
 To bid the fresh flow'rets in sympathy wave.

The Lord of the castle, from that fatal moment
50 When poor singing Mary was laid in her grave,
Each night was surrounded by screech-owls appalling,
 Which o'er the black turrets their pinions would wave!
On the ramparts that frown'd on the river, swift flowing,
 They hover'd, still hooting a terrible song,

1. I.e., spinning wheel. 2. Confront; balk.

55 When his windows would rattle, the winter blast blowing,
 They would shriek like a ghost, the dark alleys among!

 Wherever he wander'd they follow'd him crying,
 At dawnlight, at eve, still they haunted his way!
 When the moon shone across the wide common they hooted,
60 Nor quitted his path till the blazing of day.
 His bones began wasting, his flesh was decaying,
 And he hung his proud head, and he perish'd with shame;
 And the tomb of rich marble, no soft tear displaying,
 O'ershadows the grave of the Poor Singing Dame!

1799–1800 1800

MARY WOLLSTONECRAFT
1759–1797

"It is time to effect a revolution in female manners—time to restore to them their lost dignity—and make them, as part of the human species, labor by reforming themselves, to reform the world": Mary Wollstonecraft's fervent radicalism extended from a critique of private property and political oppression to a protest against the subjection of women. Her most famous book, *A Vindication of the Rights of Woman* (1792), is a justification of women's rights and an attack against the wrongs inflicted on women, in which this author claims that women's manners have been corrupted by a culture that exalts feminine inferiority. Vanity, triviality, duplicity, and selfishness are the secondary characteristics of a creature, called female, who has been constructed to suit society. It is in this context that *A Vindication of the Rights of Woman* presents the first fully elaborated feminist criticism of misogynist images of women in literature as well as the first sustained argument for female political, economic, and legal equality. To be sure, a number of polemical tracts on the injustice of women's situation preceded Wollstonecraft's, with Catharine Macaulay's *Letters on Education,* which Wollstonecraft reviewed, published only two years earlier. But Wollstonecraft's impassioned plea against the miseducation of women constituted a groundbreaking demonstration of how the very protection offered women confines them to the vices and virtues of an inferior class and thereby inhibits both women and men from establishing their common humanity.

 Wollstonecraft's own education seems to have been acquired in spite of the impoverishment and instability of her family, but the energy of her revolt against injustice was very much shaped by her struggle for independence from that family. The woman who would dedicate her philosophical inquiries to a protest against arbitrary tyranny found political impetus in the personal injustices she both witnessed and experienced. The second of five children, Wollstonecraft suffered from the brutality of her father and the submissiveness of her mother. Although Edward John Wollstonecraft inherited a fortune from his father, a weaver, he lost it in a succession of farming failures that led to drunken physical abuse of his wife. Wollstonecraft tried to protect her mother, sleeping on the landing outside her mother's room on more than one occasion; however, she was regarded or regarded herself as second to her older brother in her mother's affections. As the family moved from London to Yorkshire to Wales, and back to London, Wollstonecraft suffered from the financial constraints that eventu-

ally led her father to use up most of the money settled on his daughters. To relieve him from debt and to extricate herself from his intolerable rule, she left home in 1778, at the age of nineteen, earning her living as a companion to a widow in Bath. Later, she would strive for her independence by opening a school and by becoming a governess. The school failed and the mother of her charges discharged her, but Wollstonecraft pursued her education, teaching herself both French and German, even as she sustained and was sustained by a succession of friendships.

In contrast to the violence she identified with her parents' marriage, friendships provided the bonds of affection in Wollstonecraft's life. At the age of eleven, in Beverley, for example, she wrote vivid letters to her best friend, Jane Arden, whom she would see again in Bath. She met her most cherished friend, Fanny Blood, in 1774, and their relationship flourished when, two years later, Wollstonecraft's father brought the family to Walworth. Two years older than Wollstonecraft, Fanny Blood lived in almost as difficult a home, with an improvident father and a patient mother who took in sewing to eke out a living for the family. When, in 1782, Wollstonecraft's mother died, Wollstonecraft, then twenty-three, joined the Blood family, where she sewed with Mrs. Blood and Fanny from sunrise to sunset.

During this same period, the two friends joined forces to rescue one of Wollstonecraft's younger sisters from a marriage she found intolerable: after giving birth to a child, Eliza Wollstonecraft Bishop suffered a severe emotional breakdown; Fanny Blood moved Eliza's belongings, while Mary Wollstonecraft removed Eliza from her husband and child. Whether the friends' audacious plan was heartless and foolhardy (the child died later that year) or redemptive and courageous (divorce was difficult for women to obtain), it illustrates Wollstonecraft's rebellious independence and her identification with women's suffering. Both traits are evident in her continued commitment to Fanny Blood. When, in 1785, Fanny Blood was pregnant in a foreign country, Wollstonecraft undertook the arduous voyage to Lisbon to be with her friend for the delivery. The despondency she experienced after the subsequent death of Fanny would haunt her for the rest of her life, although she continued to give financial support to her friend's relatives as well as to her own.

It was not until Wollstonecraft arrived in London in 1787 that she identified her ambitions with the profession of writing. Earlier, at her girls' school in Newington Green, she had benefited from the intellectual companionship of Richard Price, a famous liberal author of the period, and she had written *Thoughts on the Education of Daughters* on her return from Portugal. But under the auspices of Joseph Johnson, the mainstay of publishing associated with the revolutionary movements in France and America, she earned her living by writing essays for his *Analytic Review* and by translating Jacques Necker's *Of the Importance of Religious Opinions* (1788) and Christian Salzmann's *Elements of Morality* (1790). The appearances of her first novel, *Mary, a Fiction*; her children's book, *Original Stories*; and her no longer extant anthology, *The Female Reader*, in 1788 and 1789 were followed in 1790 by the instantaneous success of her *Vindication of the Rights of Men*. Wollstonecraft had clearly profited from the intellectual stimulation of Johnson's circle of acquaintances—such men as the mystic poet William Blake, who illustrated the second edition of *Original Stories*; the physician Dr. George Fordyce, a fellow of the Royal Society; the revolutionary theorist Tom Paine; and the Romantic painter Henry Fuseli.

Although later readers of *A Vindication of the Rights of Men* have faulted the book as disorganized, and although it was obscured by the subsequent popularity of Tom Paine's *The Rights of Man* (1791–92), it was the first rebuttal of the political theorist Edmund Burke's *Reflections on the Revolution in France* (1790). Wollstonecraft responded to Burke's eloquent attack on the French Revolution and his conservative idealization of England by defending the radical principles of her friend Price and by analyzing the exploitation of the working class and the disproportionate privileges of the propertied class in England. Her next work, *A Vindication of the Rights of Woman*, can be read as a sequel to *A Vindication of the Rights of Men*, an extension

of her enthusiastic response to the French Revolution. Written in six weeks, it was dedicated to the revolutionary French statesman Talleyrand to argue that the goals of liberty, equality, and fraternity would be undermined by the exclusion of women and their rights from programs for social reform. By the time she published her second *Vindication,* Wollstonecraft had joined the ranks of such professional literary women as Frances Burney and Hannah More. Indeed, she had exceeded them, for the philosophic breadth of her writing established links between radicalism, Romanticism, and feminism that would be of lasting importance.

Throughout her career, Wollstonecraft confronted the discrepancy between her revolutionary theories and the material realities they sought to address and redress. Nowhere is this more evident than in the tension between the ideal of male-female friendship in her polemical writing and the torment of romantic thralldom she suffered in her life. In spite of her growing reputation, after she had analyzed the destructiveness of romance in her second *Vindication,* Wollstonecraft left England when it became clear that she could not join the household of Fuseli, the married man she had begun to love. Escaping to France to witness the Revolution firsthand, she fell in love with an American, Gilbert Imlay, and was registered as his wife to gain the protection of American citizenship. Yet she refused the legal claim of marriage. Imlay had been an officer in the American Revolutionary army and had published a book about the Kentucky wilderness, but he was engaged in shady political and financial intrigues about which Wollstonecraft knew little or nothing. When he abandoned her in Paris under dangerous circumstances—with her baby daughter, Fanny, during the Reign of Terror—she wrote numerous letters lamenting his lack of feeling. When she returned to London from a trip through the Scandinavian countries, which he had arranged for her, she discovered his infidelity and tried to kill herself by throwing herself off Putney Bridge into the Thames. Astonishingly, however, she never stopped writing during this period, publishing *A Historical and Moral View of the Origins and Progress of the French Revolution* in 1794, the same year she gave birth to a daughter, and *Letters Written during a Short Residence in Sweden, Norway, and Denmark* in 1796, less than a year after her suicide attempt. Indeed, this book was constructed out of letters to Imlay, which were returned at her request.

The next year Wollstonecraft went to visit William Godwin. The already-established philosopher and novelist had met her earlier at Johnson's, but now Godwin was looking for a lifelong companion. Their ideas and careers meshed, and in spite of their principles, they decided to legalize the relationship when Wollstonecraft became pregnant for the second time. Tragically, however, their marriage lasted less than a year: Wollstonecraft died at thirty-six of puerperal fever, eleven days after she gave birth to Mary Wollstonecraft Godwin. The physicians, who may have caused blood poisoning in their efforts to remove the placenta, were hampered by the primitive state of medicine in this period. They could counteract the painful effects of Wollstonecraft's infection only with wine, of her lactation only with puppies brought in to draw the milk from her breasts. She had been unable to complete her last project, a novel titled *Maria; or, The Wrongs of Women.*

The gruesome irony of Wollstonecraft's personal tragedies when viewed from the perspective of her pioneering principles is also apparent in the use made of Godwin's laudatory *Memoirs of the Author of "A Vindication of the Rights of Woman"* (1798) and his edition of her *Posthumous Works* (1798), in which he reprinted her love letters to Imlay. The scandal that resulted caused Wollstonecraft to be castigated as a "hyena in petticoats" and a "philosophical wanton." It also effectively erased her philosophic achievement for more than a century. Yet women from George Eliot to Ruth Benedict continued to be fascinated by Wollstonecraft's life. The personal suffering that she dramatized in her novels and the visionary reforms for which she called in her political writing are twin aspects of what she saw as the injustice of a social system that defined women as male property. While in *A Vindication of the Rights of Woman* she condemned John Milton, Alexander Pope, Lord Chesterfield, and Jean-Jacques Rousseau for promulgating pernicious images of women, she was equally contemptuous of the

reading habits of women, whose addiction to romance seemed to her to propagate only ignorance and further dependency. In all these respects, Wollstonecraft became a foremother, not only for her biological daughter Mary Wollstonecraft Godwin Shelley, who read her parents' books while sitting by her mother's grave, but also for literary women from Margaret Fuller and Florence Nightingale to Charlotte Perkins Gilman, Olive Schreiner, Virginia Woolf, and Adrienne Rich, all of whom have extended the tradition of feminist polemic she established.

From A Vindication of the Rights of Woman[1]

Introduction

After considering the historic page, and viewing the living world with anxious solicitude, the most melancholy emotions of sorrowful indignation have depressed my spirits, and I have sighed when obliged to confess, that either nature has made a great difference between man and man, or that the civilization which has hitherto taken place in the world has been very partial. I have turned over various books written on the subject of education, and patiently observed the conduct of parents and the management of schools; but what has been the result?—a profound conviction that the neglected education of my fellow-creatures is the grand source of the misery I deplore; and that women, in particular, are rendered weak and wretched by a variety of concurring causes, originating from one hasty conclusion. The conduct and manners of women, in fact, evidently prove that their minds are not in a healthy state; for, like the flowers which are planted in too rich a soil, strength and usefulness are sacrificed to beauty; and the flaunting leaves, after having pleased a fastidious eye, fade, disregarded on the stalk, long before the season when they ought to have arrived at maturity.—One cause of this barren blooming I attribute to a false system of education, gathered from the books written on this subject by men who, considering females rather as women than human creatures, have been more anxious to make them alluring mistresses than affectionate wives and rational mothers; and the understanding of the sex has been so bubbled[2] by this specious homage, that the civilized women of the present century, with a few exceptions, are only anxious to inspire love, when they ought to cherish a nobler ambition, and by their abilities and virtues exact respect.

In a treatise, therefore, on female rights and manners, the works which have been particularly written for their improvement must not be overlooked; especially when it is asserted, in direct terms, that the minds of women are enfeebled by false refinement; that the books of instruction, written by men of genius, have had the same tendency as more frivolous productions; and that, in the true style of Mahometanism, they are treated as a kind of subordinate beings,[3] and not as a part of the human species, when improveable reason is allowed to be the dignified distinction which raises men above the brute creation, and puts a natural sceptre in a feeble hand.

1. The text is from the second revised edition of 1792, as edited by Carol H. Poston from the Norton Critical Edition of *A Vindication* (1975). The editors gratefully acknowledge Poston's permission to make use of the information in her annotations.

2. Deceived by "bubbles," i.e., insubstantial fictions.
3. Europeans commonly though mistakenly assumed that the Qur'an, the sacred text of Muslims, teaches that women have no souls.

Yet, because I am a woman, I would not lead my readers to suppose that I mean violently to agitate the contested question respecting the equality or inferiority of the sex; but as the subject lies in my way, and I cannot pass it over without subjecting the main tendency of my reasoning to misconstruction, I shall stop a moment to deliver, in a few words, my opinion.—In the government of the physical world it is observable that the female in point of strength is, in general, inferior to the male. This is the law of nature; and it does not appear to be suspended or abrogated in favor of women. A degree of physical superiority cannot, therefore, be denied—and it is a noble prerogative! But not content with this natural pre-eminence, men endeavor to sink us still lower, merely to render us alluring objects for a moment; and women, intoxicated by the adoration which men, under the influence of their senses, pay them, do not seek to obtain a durable interest in their hearts, or to become the friends of the fellow creatures who find amusement in their society.

I am aware of an obvious inference:—from every quarter have I heard exclamations against masculine women; but where are they to be found? If by this appellation men mean to inveigh against their ardor in hunting, shooting, and gaming, I shall most cordially join in the cry; but if it be against the imitation of manly virtues, or, more properly speaking, the attainment of those talents and virtues, the exercise of which ennobles the human character, and which raise females in the scale of animal being, when they are comprehensively termed mankind;—all those who view them with a philosophic eye must, I should think, wish with me, that they may every day grow more and more masculine.

This discussion naturally divides the subject. I shall first consider women in the grand light of human creatures, who, in common with men, are placed on this earth to unfold their faculties; and afterwards I shall more particularly point out their peculiar designation.

I wish also to steer clear of an error which many respectable writers have fallen into; for the instruction which has hitherto been addressed to women, has rather been applicable to *ladies,* if the little indirect advice, that is scattered through Sandford and Merton,[4] be excepted; but, addressing my sex in a firmer tone, I pay particular attention to those in the middle class, because they appear to be in the most natural state.[5] Perhaps the seeds of false-refinement, immorality, and vanity, have ever been shed by the great. Weak, artificial beings, raised above the common wants and affections of their race, in a premature unnatural manner, undermine the very foundation of virtue, and spread corruption through the whole mass of society! As a class of mankind they have the strongest claim to pity; the education of the rich tends to render them vain and helpless, and the unfolding mind is not strengthened by the practice of those duties which dignify the human character.—They only live to amuse themselves, and by the same law which in nature invariably produces certain effects, they soon only afford barren amusement.

But as I purpose taking a separate view of the different ranks of society, and of the moral character of women, in each, this hint is, for the present, sufficient; and I have only alluded to the subject, because it appears to me

4. The popular children's story *The History of Sandford and Merton,* by Thomas Day, was published in three volumes (1786–89). The tutor in it frequently cites the moral superiority of Harry Sandford, son of a poor farmer, over Tommy Merton, the son of a rich family.
5. The middle class is here considered more "natural" than the rich because uncorrupted by titles, property, and wealth.

to be the very essence of an introduction to give a cursory account of the contents of the work it introduces.

My own sex, I hope, will excuse me, if I treat them like rational creatures, instead of flattering their *fascinating* graces, and viewing them as if they were in a state of perpetual childhood, unable to stand alone. I earnestly wish to point out in what true dignity and human happiness consists—I wish to persuade women to endeavor to acquire strength, both of mind and body, and to convince them that the soft phrases, susceptibility of heart, delicacy of sentiment, and refinement of taste, are almost synonymous with epithets of weakness, and that those beings who are only the objects of pity and that kind of love, which has been termed its sister, will soon become objects of contempt.

Dismissing then those pretty feminine phrases, which the men condescendingly use to soften our slavish dependence, and despising that weak elegancy of mind, exquisite sensibility, and sweet docility of manners, supposed to be the sexual characteristics of the weaker vessel,[6] I wish to shew that elegance is inferior to virtue, that the first object of laudable ambition is to obtain a character as a human being, regardless of the distinction of sex; and that secondary views should be brought to this simple touchstone.

This is a rough sketch of my plan; and should I express my conviction with the energetic emotions that I feel whenever I think of the subject, the dictates of experience and reflection will be felt by some of my readers. Animated by this important object, I shall disdain to cull[7] my phrases or polish my style;—I aim at being useful, and sincerity will render me unaffected; for, wishing rather to persuade by the force of my arguments, than dazzle by the elegance of my language, I shall not waste my time in rounding periods,[8] or in fabricating the turgid bombast of artificial feelings, which, coming from the head, never reach the heart.—I shall be employed about things, not words!—and, anxious to render my sex more respectable members of society, I shall try to avoid that flowery diction which has slided from essays into novels, and from novels into familiar letters and conversation.

These pretty superlatives, dropping glibly from the tongue, vitiate the taste, and create a kind of sickly delicacy that turns away from simple unadorned truth, and a deluge of false sentiments and overstretched feelings, stifling the natural emotions of the heart, render the domestic pleasures insipid, that ought to sweeten the exercise of those severe duties, which educate a rational and immortal being for a nobler field of action.

The education of women has, of late, been more attended to than formerly; yet they are still reckoned a frivolous sex, and ridiculed or pitied by the writers who endeavor by satire or instruction to improve them. It is acknowledged that they spend many of the first years of their lives in acquiring a smattering of accomplishments; meanwhile strength of body and mind are sacrificed to libertine notions of beauty, to the desire of establishing themselves,—the only way women can rise in the world,—by marriage. And this desire making mere animals of them, when they marry they act as such children may be expected to act:—they dress; they paint, and nickname God's creatures.[9]—

6. A common description of women (see 1 Peter 3.7).
7. Be selective in.
8. I.e., in constructing elaborate sentences ("periods" are formal sentences made up of balanced clauses).
9. Hamlet accuses Ophelia of "female" faults: "You jig, you amble, and you lisp, and nickname God's creatures [ca. 1600], and make your wantonness your ignorance" (*Hamlet* 143–45).

Surely these weak beings are only fit for a seraglio![1]—Can they be expected to govern a family with judgment, or take care of the poor babes whom they bring into the world?

If then it can be fairly deduced from the present conduct of the sex, from the prevalent fondness for pleasure which takes place of ambition and those nobler passions that open and enlarge the soul; that the instruction which women have hitherto received has only tended, with the constitution of civil society, to render them insignificant objects of desire—mere propagators of fools!—if it can be proved that in aiming to accomplish them,[2] without cultivating their understandings, they are taken out of their sphere of duties, and made ridiculous and useless when the short-lived bloom of beauty is over,[3] I presume that *rational* men will excuse me for endeavoring to persuade them to become more masculine and respectable.

Indeed the word masculine is only a bugbear: there is little reason to fear that women will acquire too much courage or fortitude; for their apparent inferiority with respect to bodily strength, must render them, in some degree, dependent on men in the various relations of life, but why should it be increased by prejudices that give a sex to virtue, and confound simple truths with sensual reveries?

Women are, in fact, so much degraded by mistaken notions of female excellence, that I do not mean to add a paradox when I assert, that this artificial weakness produces a propensity to tyrannize, and gives birth to cunning, the natural opponent of strength, which leads them to play off those contemptible infantine airs that undermine esteem even whilst they excite desire. Let men become more chaste and modest, and if women do not grow wiser in the same ratio, it will be clear that they have weaker understandings. It seems scarcely necessary to say, that I now speak of the sex in general. Many individuals have more sense than their male relatives; and, as nothing preponderates where there is a constant struggle for an equilibrium, without[4] it has naturally more gravity, some women govern their husbands without degrading themselves, because intellect will always govern.

From *Chapter II*

THE PREVAILING OPINION OF A SEXUAL CHARACTER DISCUSSED

To account for, and excuse the tyranny of man, many ingenious arguments have been brought forward to prove, that the two sexes, in the acquirement of virtue, ought to aim at attaining a very different character: or, to speak explicitly, women are not allowed to have sufficient strength of mind to acquire what really deserves the name of virtue. Yet it should seem, allowing them to have souls, that there is but one way appointed by Providence to lead *mankind* to either virtue or happiness.

If then women are not a swarm of ephemeron[5] triflers, why should they be kept in ignorance under the specious name of innocence? Men complain, and with reason, of the follies and caprices of our sex, when they do not

1. Harem, the women's quarters in a Muslim palace.
2. Perfect them in personal graces.
3. A lively writer, I cannot recollect his name, asks what business women turned of forty have to do in the world? [Wollstonecraft's note]. In her edition of the *Vindication*, Poston suggests that the pas-

sage may be from Frances Burney's *Evelina* (1778), a novel in which a licentious lord exclaims, "I don't know what the devil a woman lives for after thirty; she is only in other folks' way."
4. Unless.
5. A flying insect that lives only one day.

keenly satirize our headstrong passions and groveling vices.—Behold, I should answer, the natural effect of ignorance! The mind will ever be unstable that has only prejudices to rest on, and the current will run with destructive fury when there are no barriers to break its force. Women are told from their infancy, and taught by the example of their mothers, that a little knowledge of human weakness, justly termed cunning, softness of temper, *outward* obedience, and a scrupulous attention to a puerile kind of propriety, will obtain for them the protection of man; and should they be beautiful, everything else is needless, for, at least, twenty years of their lives.

Thus Milton[6] describes our first frail mother; though when he tells us that women are formed for softness and sweet attractive grace, I cannot comprehend his meaning, unless, in the true Mahometan strain, he meant to deprive us of souls and insinuate that we were beings only designed by sweet attractive grace, and docile blind obedience, to gratify the senses of man when he can no longer soar on the wing of contemplation.

How grossly do they insult us who thus advise us only to render ourselves gentle, domestic brutes![7] For instance, the winning softness so warmly, and frequently, recommended, that governs by obeying. What childish expressions, and how insignificant is the being—can it be an immortal one? who will condescend to govern by such sinister methods! "Certainly," says Lord Bacon, "man is of kin to the beasts by his body; and if he be not of kin to God by his spirit, he is a base and ignoble creature!"[8] Men, indeed, appear to me to act in a very unphilosophical manner when they try to secure the good conduct of women by attempting to keep them always in a state of childhood. Rousseau[9] was more consistent when he wished to stop the progress of reason in both sexes, for if men eat of the tree of knowledge, women will come in for a taste but, from the imperfect cultivation which their understandings now receive, they only attain a knowledge of evil.

Children, I grant, should be innocent; but when the epithet is applied to men, or women, it is but a civil[1] term for weakness. For if it be allowed that women were destined by Providence to acquire human virtues, and by the exercise of their understandings, that stability of character which is the firmest ground to rest our future hopes upon, they must be permitted to turn to the fountain of light, and not forced to shape their course by the twinkling of a mere satellite.[2] Milton, I grant, was of a very different opinion; for he only bends to the indefeasible right of beauty, though it would be difficult to render two passages which I now mean to contrast, consistent. But into similar inconsistencies are great men often led by their senses.

> To whom thus Eve with *perfect beauty* adorned.
> My Author and Disposer, what thou bidst
> *Unargued* I obey; So God ordains;
> God is thy *law, thou mine:*—to know no more
> Is Woman's *happiest* knowledge and her *praise.*[3]

6. John Milton (1608–1674), English poet; the allusion is to his description of Eve in *Paradise Lost* (1667, 1674), 4.297–99: "For contemplation he and valor formed, / For softness she and sweet attractive grace, / He for God only, she for God in him."
7. Purely physical beings, lacking reason and intelligence.
8. Quoted from *Of Atheism* (1597) by the English philosopher Francis Bacon (1561–1626).

9. Jean-Jacques Rousseau (1712–1778), the Swiss-born French political philosopher who advocated intuition and instinct over rationality. His views on the education of women, alluded to throughout Wollstonecraft's treatise, are set forth in *Émile* (1762), especially in Book 5: "Sophy; or, Woman."
1. Polite; euphemistic.
2. Any body that orbits a larger body.
3. *Paradise Lost* 4.634–38 (Wollstonecraft's italics).

These are exactly the arguments that I have used to children; but I have added, your reason is now gaining strength, and, till it arrives at some degree of maturity, you must look up to me for advice—then you ought to *think*, and only rely on God.

Yet in the following lines Milton seems to coincide with me; when he makes Adam thus expostulate with his Maker.

> Hast thou not made me here thy substitute,
> And these inferior far beneath me set?
> Among *unequals* what society
> Can sort, what harmony or true delight?
> Which must be mutual, in proportion due
> Giv'n and *received*; but in *disparity*
> The one intense, the other still remiss
> Cannot well suit with either, but soon prove
> Tedious alike: of *fellowship* I speak
> Such as I seek, fit to participate
> All rational delight—[4]

In treating, therefore, of the manners of women, let us, disregarding sensual arguments, trace what we should endeavor to make them in order to cooperate, if the expression be not too bold, with the supreme Being.

By individual education, I mean, for the sense of the word is not precisely defined, such an attention to a child as will slowly sharpen the senses, form the temper,[5] regulate the passions as they begin to ferment, and set the understanding to work before the body arrives at maturity; so that the man may only have to proceed, not to begin, the important task of learning to think and reason.

To prevent any misconstruction, I must add, that I do not believe that a private education can work the wonders which some sanguine writers have attributed to it. Men and women must be educated, in a great degree, by the opinions and manners of the society they live in. In every age there has been a stream of popular opinion that has carried all before it, and given a family character, as it were, to the century. It may then fairly be inferred, that, till society be differently constituted, much cannot be expected from education. It is, however, sufficient for my present purpose to assert, that, whatever effect circumstances have on the abilities, every being may become virtuous by the exercise of its own reason; for if but one being was created with vicious inclinations, that is positively bad, what can save us from atheism? or if we worship a god, is not that god a devil?

Consequently, the most perfect education, in my opinion, is such an exercise of the understanding as is best calculated to strengthen the body and form the heart. Or, in other words, to enable the individual to attain such habits of virtue as will render it independent. In fact, it is a farce to call any being virtuous whose virtues do not result from the exercise of its own reason. This was Rousseau's opinion respecting men: I extend it to women, and confidently assert that they have been drawn out of their sphere by false refinement, and not by an endeavor to acquire masculine qualities. Still the regal homage which they receive is so intoxicating, that till the manners of

4. *Paradise Lost* 8.381–91 (Wollstonecraft's italics). 5. Temperament, character.

the times are changed, and formed on more reasonable principles, it may be impossible to convince them that the illegitimate power, which they obtain, by degrading themselves, is a curse, and that they must return to nature and equality, if they wish to secure the placid satisfaction that unsophisticated affections impart. But for this epoch we must wait—wait, perhaps, till kings and nobles, enlightened by reason, and, preferring the real dignity of man to childish state[6] throw off their gaudy hereditary trappings: and if then women do not resign the arbitrary power of beauty—they will prove that they have *less* mind than man.

I may be accused of arrogance; still I must declare what I firmly believe, that all the writers who have written on the subject of female education and manners from Rousseau to Dr. Gregory,[7] have contributed to render women more artificial, weak characters, than they would otherwise have been, and, consequently, more useless members of society. I might have expressed this conviction in a lower key; but I am afraid it would have been the whine of affectation, and not the faithful expression of my feelings, of the clear result, which experience and reflection have led me to draw. When I come to that division of the subject, I shall advert to the passages that I more particularly disapprove of, in the works of the authors I have just alluded to; but it is first necessary to observe, that my objection extends to the whole purport of those books, which tend, in my opinion, to degrade one half of the human species, and render women pleasing at the expense of every solid virtue.

Though, to reason on Rousseau's ground, if man did attain a degree of perfection of mind when his body arrived at maturity, it might be proper, in order to make a man and his wife *one*,[8] that she should rely entirely on his understanding: and the graceful ivy, clasping the oak that supported it, would form a whole in which strength and beauty would be equally conspicuous. But, alas! husbands, as well as their helpmates, are often only overgrown children: nay, thanks to early debauchery, scarcely men in their outward form—and if the blind lead the blind, one need not come from heaven to tell us the consequence.[9]

Many are the causes that, in the present corrupt state of society, contribute to enslave women by cramping their understandings and sharpening their senses. One, perhaps, that silently does more mischief than all the rest, is their disregard of order.

To do everything in an orderly manner, is a most important precept, which women, who, generally speaking, receive only a disorderly kind of education, seldom attend to with that degree of exactness that men, who from their infancy are broken into method, observe. This negligent kind of guess-work, for what other epithet can be used to point out the random exertions of a sort of instinctive common sense, never brought to the test of reason? prevents their generalizing matters of fact—so they do today, what they did yesterday, merely because they did it yesterday.

This contempt of the understanding in early life has more baneful consequences than is commonly supposed; for the little knowledge which women of strong minds attain, is, from various circumstances, of a more

6. Pomp, rich display.
7. John Gregory (1724–1773), author of a popular book on the education of women, *A Father's Legacy to His Daughters* (1774).
8. According to Genesis 2.24, man and wife "shall be one flesh."
9. I.e., both will fall into the ditch, a parable of Jesus (Matthew 15.14; Luke 6.39).

desultory kind than the knowledge of men, and it is acquired more by sheer observations on real life, than from comparing what has been individually observed with the results of experience generalized by speculation. Led by their dependent situation and domestic employments more into society, what they learn is rather by snatches; and as learning is with them, in general, only a secondary thing, they do not pursue any one branch with that persevering ardor necessary to give vigor to the faculties, and clearness to the judgment. In the present state of society, a little learning is required to support the character of a gentleman; and boys are obliged to submit to a few years of discipline. But in the education of women, the cultivation of the understanding is always subordinate to the acquirement of some corporeal accomplishment: even while enervated by confinement and false notions of modesty, the body is prevented from attaining that grace and beauty which relaxed half-formed limbs never exhibit. Besides, in youth their faculties are not brought forward by emulation; and having no serious scientific study, if they have natural sagacity it is turned too soon on life and manners. They dwell on effects, and modifications, without tracing them back to causes; and complicated rules to adjust behavior are a weak substitute for simple principles.

As a proof that education gives this appearance of weakness to females, we may instance the example of military men, who are, like them, sent into the world before their minds have been stored with knowledge or fortified by principles. The consequences are similar; soldiers acquire a little superficial knowledge, snatched from the muddy current of conversation, and, from continually mixing with society, they gain, what is termed a knowledge of the world; and this acquaintance with manners and customs has frequently been confounded with a knowledge of the human heart. But can the crude fruit of casual observation, never brought to the test of judgment, formed by comparing speculation and experience, deserve such a distinction? Soldiers, as well as women, practice the minor virtues with punctilious politeness. Where is then the sexual difference, when the education has been the same? All the difference that I can discern, arises from the superior advantage of liberty, which enables the former to see more of life.

* * *

Probably the prevailing opinion, that woman was created for man, may have taken its rise from Moses's poetical story;[1] yet, as very few, it is presumed, who have bestowed any serious thought on the subject, ever supposed that Eve was, literally speaking, one of Adam's ribs, the deduction must be allowed to fall to the ground; or, only be so far admitted as it proves that man, from the remotest antiquity, found it convenient to exert his strength to subjugate his companion, and his invention to shew that she ought to have her neck bent under the yoke, because the whole creation was only created for his convenience or pleasure.

Let it not be concluded that I wish to invert the order of things; I have already granted, that, from the constitution of their bodies, men seem to be designed by Providence to attain a greater degree of virtue.[2] I speak collec-

1. I.e., the story of Eve's creation from one of the ribs of Adam (Genesis 2.18–22). Authorship of the first five books of the Bible was traditionally attributed to Moses.

2. I.e., men have more passions and greater physical strength than women and must, therefore, exercise greater restraint.

tively of the whole sex; but I see not the shadow of a reason to conclude that their virtues should differ in respect to their nature. In fact, how can they, if virtue has only one eternal standard? I must therefore, if I reason consequentially, as strenuously maintain that they have the same simple direction, as that there is a God.

It follows then that cunning should not be opposed to wisdom, little cares to great exertions, or insipid softness, varnished over with the name of gentleness, to that fortitude which grand views alone can inspire.

I shall be told that woman would then lose many of her peculiar graces, and the opinion of a well known poet might be quoted to refute my unqualified assertion. For Pope has said, in the name of the whole male sex,

> Yet ne'er so sure our passion to create,
> As when she touched the brink of all we hate.[3]

In what light this sally places men and women, I shall leave to the judicious to determine: meanwhile I shall content myself with observing, that I cannot discover why, unless[4] they are mortal, females should always be degraded by being made subservient to love or lust.

To speak disrespectfully of love is, I know, high treason against sentiment and fine feelings; but I wish to speak the simple language of truth, and rather to address the head than the heart. To endeavor to reason love out of the world, would be to out Quixote Cervantes,[5] and equally offend against common sense; but an endeavor to restrain this tumultuous passion, and to prove that it should not be allowed to dethrone superior powers, or to usurp the sceptre which the understanding should ever coolly wield, appears less wild.

Youth is the season for love in both sexes; but in those days of thoughtless enjoyment provision should be made for the more important years of life, when reflection takes place of sensation. But Rousseau, and most of the male writers who have followed his steps, have warmly inculcated that the whole tendency of female education ought to be directed to one point:—to render them pleasing.

Let me reason with the supporters of this opinion who have any knowledge of human nature, do they imagine that marriage can eradicate the habitude of life? The woman who has only been taught to please will soon find that her charms are oblique sun-beams, and that they cannot have much effect on her husband's heart when they are seen every day, when the summer is passed and gone. Will she then have sufficient native[6] energy to look into herself for comfort, and cultivate her dormant faculties? or, is it not more rational to expect that she will try to please other men; and, in the emotions raised by the expectation of new conquests, endeavor to forget the mortification her love or pride has received? When the husband ceases to be a lover—and the time will inevitably come, her desire of pleasing will then grow languid, or become a spring of bitterness; and love, perhaps, the most evanescent of all passions, gives place to jealousy or vanity.

I now speak of women who are restrained by principle or prejudice; such women, though they would shrink from an intrigue[7] with real abhorrence, yet, nevertheless, wish to be convinced by the homage of gallantry that they

3. *Moral Essays*, "Epistle 2: To a Lady" (1735), lines 51–52, by the English poet Alexander Pope (1688–1744).
4. Except that.
5. I.e., to outdo the hero of Cervantes's *Don Quixote* (1605) in attempting the impossible.
6. Innate.
7. An extramarital affair.

are cruelly neglected by their husbands; or, days and weeks are spent in dreaming of the happiness enjoyed by congenial souls till their health is undermined and their spirits broken by discontent. How then can the great art of pleasing be such a necessary study? It is only useful to a mistress; the chaste wife, and serious mother, should only consider her power to please as the polish of her virtues, and the affection of her husband as one of the comforts that render her task less difficult and her life happier.—But, whether she be loved or neglected, her first wish should be to make herself respectable[8] and not to rely for all her happiness on a being subject to like infirmities with herself.

The worthy Dr. Gregory fell into a similar error. I respect his heart; but entirely disapprove of his celebrated *Legacy to His Daughters*.

He advises them to cultivate a fondness for dress, because a fondness for dress, he asserts, is natural to them. I am unable to comprehend what either he or Rousseau mean, when they frequently use this indefinite term.[9] If they told us that in a pre-existent state the soul was fond of dress, and brought this inclination with it into a new body, I should listen to them with a half smile, as I often do when I hear a rant about innate elegance.—But if he only meant to say that the exercise of the faculties will produce this fondness—I deny it—It is not natural, but arises, like false ambition in men, from a love of power.

Dr. Gregory goes much further; he actually recommends dissimulation, and advises an innocent girl to give the lie to her feelings, and not dance with spirit, when gaiety of heart would make her feel eloquent without making her gestures immodest. In the name of truth and common sense, why should not one woman acknowledge that she can take more exercise than another? or, in other words, that she has a sound constitution; and why, to damp innocent vivacity, is she darkly to be told that men will draw conclusions which she little thinks of?[1]—Let the libertine draw what inference he pleases; but, I hope, that no sensible mother will restrain the natural frankness of youth by instilling such indecent cautions. Out of the abundance of the heart the mouth speaketh;[2] and a wiser than Solomon hath said, that the heart should be made clean,[3] and not trivial ceremonies observed, which it is not very difficult to fulfill with scrupulous exactness when vice reigns in the heart.

Women ought to endeavor to purify their heart; but can they do so when their uncultivated understandings make them entirely dependent on their senses for employment and amusement, when no noble pursuit sets them above the little vanities of the day, or enables them to curb the wild emotions that agitate a reed over which every passing breeze has power? To gain the affections of a virtuous man is affectation necessary? Nature has given woman a weaker frame[4] than man; but, to ensure her husband's affections,

8. I.e., morally worthy of respect.
9. I.e., natural.
1. Gregory, in *A Father's Legacy to His Daughters,* writes: "I would have you to dance with spirit; but never allow yourselves to be so far transported with mirth, as to forget the delicacy of your sex.—Many a girl dancing in the gaiety and innocence of her heart, is thought to discover [reveal] a spirit she little dreams of."

2. Matthew 12.34.
3. Psalm 24.3–4: "Who shall ascend into the hill of the Lord? Or who shall stand in his holy place? He that hath clean hands, and a pure heart." The psalm is attributed to David, the "wiser than Solomon." Solomon is described as exceeding all kings of the earth in wisdom (1 Kings 10.23).
4. Body.

must a wife, who by the exercise of her mind and body whilst she was discharging the duties of a daughter, wife, and mother, has allowed her constitution to retain its natural strength, and her nerves a healthy tone, is she, I say, to condescend to use art[5] and feign a sickly delicacy in order to secure her husband's affection? Weakness may excite tenderness, and gratify the arrogant pride of man; but the lordly caresses of a protector will not gratify a noble mind that pants for, and deserves to be respected. Fondness is a poor substitute for friendship!

In a seraglio, I grant, that all these arts are necessary; the epicure[6] must have his palate tickled, or he will sink into apathy, but have women so little ambition as to be satisfied with such a condition? Can they supinely dream life away in the lap of pleasure, or the languor of weariness, rather than assert their claim to pursue reasonable pleasures and render themselves conspicuous[7] by practising the virtues which dignify mankind? Surely she has not an immortal soul who can loiter life away merely employed to adorn her person, that she may amuse the languid hours, and soften the cares of a fellow-creature who is willing to be enlivened by her smiles and tricks, when the serious business of life is over.

Besides, the woman who strengthens her body and exercises her mind will, by managing her family and practicing various virtues, become the friend, and not the humble dependent of her husband; and if she, by possessing such substantial qualities, merit his regard, she will not find it necessary to conceal her affection, nor to pretend to an unnatural coldness of constitution to excite her husband's passions. In fact, if we revert to history, we shall find that the women who have distinguished themselves have neither been the most beautiful nor the most gentle[8] of their sex.

Nature, or, to speak with strict propriety, God, has made all things right; but man has sought him out many inventions to mar the work. I now allude to that part of Dr. Gregory's treatise, where he advises a wife never to let her husband know the extent of her sensibility or affection. Voluptuous precaution, and as ineffectual as absurd.—Love, from its very nature, must be transitory. To seek for a secret that would render it constant, would be as wild a search as for the philosopher's stone, or the grand panacea[9] and the discovery would be equally useless, or rather pernicious to mankind. The most holy band of society is friendship. It has been well said, by a shrewd satirist, "that rare as true love is, true friendship is still rarer."[1]

This is an obvious truth, and the cause not lying deep, will not elude a slight glance of inquiry.

Love, the common passion,[2] in which chance and sensation take place of choice and reason, is, in some degree, felt by the mass of mankind; for it is not necessary to speak, at present, of the emotions that rise above or sink below love. This passion, naturally increased by suspense and difficulties, draws the mind out of its accustomed state, and exalts the affections; but the security of marriage, allowing the fever of love to subside, a healthy

5. Artifice, deceit.
6. I.e., a person devoted to sensual pleasure; here, the sultan catered to sexually by his harem ("seraglio").
7. Eminent.
8. Genteel, refined.

9. A medicine reputed to cure all illness. "Philosopher's stone": substance that alchemists believed could transform base matter into gold.
1. Maxim 473 of François de La Rochefoucauld (1613–1680), great French epigrammist.
2. Emotion.

temperature is thought insipid, only by those who have not sufficient intellect to substitute the calm tenderness of friendship, the confidence of respect instead of blind admiration, and the sensual emotions of fondness.

This is, must be, the course of nature.—Friendship or indifference inevitably succeeds love.—And this constitution seems perfectly to harmonize with the system of government which prevails in the moral world. Passions are spurs to action, and open the mind; but they sink into mere appetites, become a personal and momentary gratification, when the object is gained, and the satisfied mind rests in enjoyment. The man who had some virtue whilst he was struggling for a crown, often becomes a voluptuous tyrant when it graces his brow; and, when the lover is not lost in the husband, the dotard, a prey to childish caprices, and fond jealousies, neglects the serious duties of life, and the caresses which should excite confidence in his children are lavished on the overgrown child, his wife.

In order to fulfill the duties of life, and to be able to pursue with vigor the various employments which form the moral character, a master and mistress of a family ought not to continue to love each other with passion. I mean to say, that they ought not to indulge those emotions which disturb the order of society, and engross the thoughts that should be otherwise employed. The mind that has never been engrossed by one object wants[3] vigor—if it can long be so, it is weak.

A mistaken education, a narrow, uncultivated mind, and many sexual[4] prejudices, tend to make women more constant than men; but, for the present, I shall not touch on this branch of the subject. I will go still further, and advance, without dreaming of a paradox, that an unhappy marriage is often very advantageous to a family, and that the neglected wife is, in general, the best mother.[5] And this would almost always be the consequence if the female mind were more enlarged: for, it seems to be the common dispensation of Providence, that what we gain in present enjoyment should be deducted from the treasure of life, experience; and that when we are gathering the flowers of the day and revelling in pleasure, the solid fruit of toil and wisdom should not be caught at the same time. The way lies before us, we must turn to the right or left; and he who will pass life away in bounding from one pleasure to another, must not complain if he acquire neither wisdom nor respectability of character.

Supposing, for a moment, that the soul is not immortal, and that man was only created for the present scene,—I think we should have reason to complain that love, infantine fondness, ever grew insipid and palled upon the sense. Let us eat, drink, and love, for tomorrow we die, would be, in fact, the language of reason, the morality of life; and who but a fool would part with a reality for a fleeting shadow? But, if awed by observing the improbable[6] powers of the mind, we disdain to confine our wishes or thoughts to such a comparatively mean[7] field of action; that only appears grand and important, as it is connected with a boundless prospect and sublime hopes, what necessity is there for falsehood in conduct, and why must the sacred majesty of

3. Lacks.
4. Characteristic of the (female) sex.
5. Wollstonecraft sounds somewhat more cynical about married love here than she really is; she simply means that a woman not completely preoccu-

pied with her husband has more time and energy for her children.
6. Poston suggests that this is a misprint in the second edition for "improvable," i.e., unknowable.
7. Low, inferior.

truth be violated to detain a deceitful good that saps the very foundation of virtue? Why must the female mind be tainted by coquetish arts to gratify the sensualist, and prevent love from subsiding into friendship, or compassionate tenderness, when there are not qualities on which friendship can be built? Let the honest heart shew itself, and *reason* teach passion to submit to necessity; or, let the dignified, pursuit of virtue and knowledge raise the mind above those emotions which rather embitter than sweeten the cup of life, when they are not restrained within due bounds.

I do not mean to allude to the romantic passion,[8] which is the concomitant of genius.—Who can clip its wing? But that grand passion not proportioned to the puny enjoyments of life, is only true to the sentiment, and feeds on itself. The passions which have been celebrated for their durability have always been unfortunate. They have acquired strength by absence and constitutional melancholy.—The fancy[9] has hovered round a form of beauty dimly seen—but familiarity might have turned admiration into disgust; or, at least, into indifference, and allowed the imagination leisure to start fresh game. With perfect propriety, according to this view of things, does Rousseau make the mistress of his soul, Eloisa, love St. Preux when life was fading before her;[1] but this is no proof of the immortality of the passion.

Of the same complexion is Dr. Gregory's advice respecting delicacy of sentiment, which he advises a woman not to acquire, if she have determined to marry. This determination, however, perfectly consistent with his former advice, he calls *indelicate,* and earnestly persuades his daughters to conceal it, though it may govern their conduct;—as if it were indelicate to have the common appetites of human nature.

Noble morality! and consistent with the cautious prudence of a little soul that cannot extend its views beyond the present minute division of existence. If all the faculties of woman's mind are only to be cultivated as they respect her dependence on man; if, when a husband be obtained, she have arrived at her goal, and meanly proud rests satisfied with such a paltry crown, let her grovel contentedly, scarcely raised by her employments above the animal kingdom; but, if, struggling for the prize of her high calling, she look beyond the present scene, let her cultivate her understanding without stopping to consider what character the husband may have whom she is destined to marry. Let her only determine, without being too anxious about present happiness, to acquire the qualities that ennoble a rational being, and a rough inelegant husband may shock her taste without destroying her peace of mind. She will not model her soul to suit the frailties of her companion, but to bear with them: his character may be a trial, but not an impediment to virtue.

If Dr. Gregory confined his remark to romantic expectations of constant love and congenial feelings, he should have recollected that experience will banish what advice can never make us cease to wish for, when the imagination is kept alive at the expense of reason.

I own it frequently happens that women who have fostered a romantic unnatural delicacy of feeling, waste their[2] lives in *imagining* how happy they

8. I.e., the creative imagination.
9. The imagination.
1. In Rousseau's novel *Julie; ou, La Nouvelle Héloise* (1761), Julie reveals on her deathbed to her husband, Wolmar, that her real, passionate love is

for her former lover St. Preux. Julie or "Eloisa" was thought to represent a woman with whom Rousseau was in love at the time.
2. For example, the herd of Novelists [Wollstonecraft's note]. Wollstonecraft is referring both to

should have been with a husband who could love them with a fervid increasing affection every day, and all day. But they might as well pine married as single—and would not be a jot more unhappy with a bad husband than longing for a good one. That a proper education; or, to speak with more precision, a well stored mind, would enable a woman to support a single life with dignity, I grant; but that she should avoid cultivating her taste, lest her husband should occasionally shock it, is quitting a substance for a shadow. To say the truth, I do not know of what use is an improved taste, if the individual be not rendered more independent of the casualties[3] of life; if new sources of enjoyment, only dependent on the solitary operations of the mind, are not opened. People of taste, married or single, without distinction, will ever be disgusted by various things that touch not less observing minds. On this conclusion the argument must not be allowed to hinge; but in the whole sum of enjoyment is taste to be denominated a blessing?

The question is, whether it procures most pain or pleasure? The answer will decide the propriety of Dr. Gregory's advice, and shew how absurd and tyrannic it is thus to lay down a system of slavery; or to attempt to educate moral beings by any other rules than those deduced from pure reason, which apply to the whole species.

Gentleness of manners, forbearance and long-suffering, are such amiable Godlike qualities, that in sublime poetic strains the Deity has been invested with them; and perhaps, no representation of his goodness so strongly fastens on the human affections as those that represent him abundant in mercy and willing to pardon. Gentleness, considered in this point of view, bears on its front all the characteristics of grandeur, combined with the winning graces of condescension;[4] but what a different aspect it assumes when it is the submissive demeanor of dependence, the support of weakness that loves, because it wants protection, and is forbearing, because it must silently endure injuries; smiling under the lash at which it dare not snarl. Abject as this picture appears, it is the portrait of an accomplished woman, according to the received opinion of female excellence, separated by specious reasoners from human excellence. Or, they[5] kindly restore the rib, and make one moral being a man and woman; not forgetting to give her all the "submissive charms."[6]

How women are to exist in that state where there is to be neither marrying nor giving in marriage,[7] we are not told. For though moralists have agreed that the tenor of life seems to prove that man is prepared by various circumstances for a future state, they constantly concur in advising *woman* only to provide for the present. Gentleness, docility, and a spaniel-like affection are, on this ground, consistently recommended as the cardinal virtues of the sex; and, disregarding the arbitrary economy of nature, one writer has declared that it is masculine for a woman to be melancholy.[8] She was created to be

women who base their expectations in love on the distortions of sentimental novels and to women who indulge their fantasies by writing such novels.
3. Chance occurrences.
4. Gracious disregard of difference. "Front": face.
5. *Vide* [see] Rousseau and Swedenborg [Wollstonecraft's note]. Rousseau asserted that a married couple formed a single unit. Emmanuel Swedenborg (1688–1772), Swedish theologian, believed that in heaven, husband and wife are united in a single body.

6. *Paradise Lost* 4.497–99: "he in delight / Both of her beauty and submissive charms / Smiled with superior love."
7. "For in the resurrection they neither marry, nor are given in marriage, but are as the angels of God in heaven" (Matthew 22.30).
8. Perhaps a reference to Edmund Burke's *A Philosophical Enquiry into the Origins of Our Ideas of the Sublime and Beautiful* (1757), where he associates melancholy with the nonfeminine.

the toy of man, his rattle, and it must jingle in his ears whenever, dismissing reason, he chooses to be amused.

To recommend gentleness, indeed, on a broad basis is strictly philosophical. A frail being should labor to be gentle. But when forbearance confounds[9] right and wrong, it ceases to be a virtue; and, however convenient it may be found in a companion—that companion will ever be considered as an inferior, and only inspire a vapid tenderness, which easily degenerates into contempt. Still, if advice could really make a being gentle, whose natural disposition admitted not of such a fine polish, something towards the advancement of order would be attained; but if, as might quickly be demonstrated, only affectation be produced by this indiscriminate counsel, which throws a stumbling-block in the way of gradual improvement, and true melioration of temper, the sex is not much benefited by sacrificing solid virtues to the attainment of superficial graces, though for a few years they may procure the individuals regal sway.

As a philosopher, I read with indignation the plausible[1] epithets which men use to soften their insults, and, as a moralist, I ask what is meant by such heterogeneous associations, as fair defects, amiable weaknesses, &c.?[2] If there be but one criterion of morals, but one archetype for man, women appear to be suspended by destiny, according to the vulgar tale of Mahomet's coffin,[3] they have neither the unerring instinct of brutes, nor are allowed to fix the eye of reason on a perfect model. They were made to be loved, and must not aim at respect, lest they should be hunted out of society as masculine.

But to view the subject in another point of view. Do passive indolent women make the best wives? Confining our discussion to the present moment of existence, let us see how such weak creatures perform their part? Do the women who, by the attainment of a few superficial accomplishments, have strengthened the prevailing prejudice, merely contribute to the happiness of their husbands? Do they display their charms merely to amuse them? And have women, who have early imbibed notions of passive obedience, sufficient character to manage a family or educate children? So far from it, that, after surveying the history of woman, I cannot help, agreeing with the severest satirist, considering the sex as the weakest as well as the most oppressed half of the species. What does history disclose but marks of inferiority, and how few women have emancipated themselves from the galling yoke of sovereign man?—So few, that the exceptions remind me of an ingenious conjecture respecting Newton: that he was probably a being of a superior order, accidentally caged in a human body.[4] Following the same train of thinking, I have been led to imagine that the few extraordinary women who have rushed in eccentrical directions out of the orbit prescribed to their sex, were *male* spirits, confined by mistake in female frames. But if it be not philosophical to think of sex when the soul is mentioned, the inferiority must depend on the organs; or the heavenly fire, which is to ferment the clay, is not given in equal portions.

9. Confuses.
1. Ingratiating.
2. *Paradise Lost* 10.891–92: "This fair defect / Of nature," and Pope's "Epistle 2: To a Lady," line 44: "Fine by defect, and delicately weak."
3. According to popular ("vulgar") legend, Muhammed's coffin hovers magically inside his tomb.

4. Wollstonecraft may be recalling Pope's *An Essay on Man* (1733), 2.31–34: "Superior beings . . . / Admired such wisdom in an earthly shape, / And showed a Newton as we show an ape." Isaac Newton (1642–1727), great English scientist who founded modern physics.

But avoiding, as I have hitherto done, any direct comparison of the two sexes collectively, or frankly acknowledging the inferiority of woman, according to the present appearance of things, I shall only insist that men have increased that inferiority till women are almost sunk below the standard of rational creatures. Let their faculties have room to unfold, and their virtues to gain strength, and then determine where the whole sex must stand in the intellectual scale. Yet let it be remembered, that for a small number of distinguished women I do not ask a place.

* * *

From *Chapter XIII*

SOME INSTANCES OF THE FOLLY WHICH THE IGNORANCE OF WOMEN
GENERATES; WITH CONCLUDING REFLECTIONS ON THE MORAL
IMPROVEMENT THAT A REVOLUTION IN FEMALE MANNERS MIGHT
NATURALLY BE EXPECTED TO PRODUCE

Another instance of that feminine weakness of character, often produced by a confined education, is a romantic twist of the mind, which has been very properly termed *sentimental.*

Women subjected by ignorance to their sensations, and only taught to look for happiness in love, refine on[5] sensual feelings, and adopt metaphysical notions respecting that passion, which lead them shamefully to neglect the duties of life, and frequently in the midst of these sublime refinements they plump into actual vice.

These are the women who are amused by the reveries of the stupid novelists, who, knowing little of human nature, work up stale tales, and describe meretricious scenes, all retailed[6] in a sentimental jargon, which equally tend to corrupt the taste, and draw the heart aside from its daily duties. I do not mention the understanding, because never having been exercised, its slumbering energies rest inactive, like the lurking particles of fire which are supposed universally to pervade matter.[7]

Females, in fact, denied all political privileges, and not allowed, as married women, excepting in criminal cases, a civil existence,[8] have their attention naturally drawn from the interest of the whole community to that of the minute parts, though the private duty of any member of society must be very imperfectly performed when not connected with the general good. The mighty business of female life is to please, and restrained from entering into more important concerns by political and civil oppression, sentiments become events, and reflection deepens what it should, and would have effaced, if the understanding had been allowed to take a wider range.

But, confined to trifling employments, they naturally imbibe opinions which the only kind of reading calculated to interest an innocent frivolous

5. Intensify, heighten.
6. Recounted.
7. Popular belief held that all matter was made up of four elements in varying proportions: air, earth, fire, and water.
8. According to William Blackstone's influential

Commentaries on the Laws of England (1765), "By marriage, the husband and wife are one person in law: that is, the very being or legal existence of the woman is suspended during the marriage, or at least is incorporated and consolidated into that of the husband."

mind, inspires. Unable to grasp any thing great, is it surprising that they find the reading of history a very dry task, and disquisitions addressed to the understanding intolerably tedious, and almost unintelligible? Thus are they necessarily dependent on the novelist for amusement. Yet, when I exclaim against novels, I mean when contrasted with those works which exercise the understanding and regulate the imagination.—For any kind of reading I think better than leaving a blank still[9] a blank, because the mind must receive a degree of enlargement and obtain a little strength by a slight exertion of its thinking powers; besides, even the productions that are only addressed to the imagination, raise the reader a little above the gross gratification of appetites, to which the mind has not given a shade of delicacy.

This observation is the result of experience; for I have known several notable women, and one in particular, who was a very good woman—as good as such a narrow mind would allow her to be, who took care that her daughters (three in number) should never see a novel. As she was a woman of fortune and fashion, they had various masters to attend them, and a sort of menial governess to watch their footsteps. From their masters they learned how tables, chairs, &c. were called in French and Italian; but as the few books thrown in their way were far above their capacities, or devotional, they neither acquired ideas nor sentiments, and passed their time, when not compelled to repeat *words,* in dressing, quarrelling with each other, or conversing with their maids by stealth, till they were brought into company as marriageable.

Their mother, a widow, was busy in the meantime in keeping up her connections, as she termed a numerous acquaintance, lest her girls should want a proper introduction into the great world. And these young ladies, with minds vulgar in every sense of the word, and spoiled tempers, entered life puffed up with notions of their own consequence, and looking down with contempt on those who could not vie with them in dress and parade.[1]

With respect to love, nature, or their nurses, had taken care to teach them the physical meaning of the word; and, as they had few topics of conversation, and fewer refinements of sentiment, they expressed their gross[2] wishes not in very delicate phrases, when they spoke freely, talking of matrimony.

Could these girls have been injured by the perusal of novels? I almost forgot a shade[3] in the character of one of them; she affected a simplicity bordering on folly, and with a simper would utter the most immodest remarks and questions, the full meaning of which she had learned whilst secluded from the world, and afraid to speak in her mother's presence, who governed with a high hand: they were all educated, as she prided herself, in a most exemplary manner; and read their chapters[4] and psalms before breakfast, never touching a silly novel.

This is only one instance; but I recollect many other women who, not led by degrees to proper studies, and not permitted to choose for themselves, have indeed been overgrown children; or have obtained, by mixing in the world, a little of what is termed common sense: that is, a distinct manner of

9. Always.
1. Ostentation.
2. Unrefined, blatant.

3. Mark, flaw.
4. I.e., of the Bible.

seeing common occurrences, as they stand detached: but what deserves the name of intellect, the power of gaining general or abstract ideas, or even intermediate ones, was out of the question. Their minds were quiescent, and when they were not roused by sensible objects and employments of that kind, they were low-spirited, would cry, or go to sleep.

When, therefore, I advise my sex not to read such flimsy works, it is to induce them to read something superior; for I coincide in opinion with a sagacious man, who, having a daughter and niece under his care, pursued a very different plan with each.

The niece, who had considerable abilities, had, before she was left to his guardianship, been indulged in desultory reading. Her he endeavored to lead, and did lead to history and moral essays; but his daughter, whom a fond weak mother had indulged, and who consequently was averse to every thing like application, he allowed to read novels: and used to justify his conduct by saying, that if she ever attained a relish for reading them, he should have some foundation to work upon; and that erroneous opinions were better than none at all.

In fact the female mind has been so totally neglected, that knowledge was only to be acquired from this muddy source, till from reading novels some women of superior talents learned to despise them.

The best method, I believe, that can be adopted to correct a fondness for novels is to ridicule them: not indiscriminately, for then it would have little effect; but, if a judicious person, with some turn for humor, would read several to a young girl, and point out both by tones, and apt comparisons with pathetic[5] incidents and heroic characters in history how foolishly and ridiculously they caricatured human nature, just opinions might be substituted instead of romantic sentiments.

In one respect, however, the majority of both sexes resemble, and equally show a want of taste and modesty. Ignorant women, forced to be chaste to preserve their reputation, allow their imagination to revel in the unnatural and meretricious scenes sketched by the novel writers of the day, slighting as insipid the sober dignity and matron graces of history[6] whilst men carry the same vitiated taste into life, and fly for amusement to the wanton, from the unsophisticated charms of virtue, and the grave respectability of sense.

Besides, the reading of novels makes women, and particularly ladies of fashion, very fond of using strong expressions and superlatives in conversation; and, though the dissipated artificial life which they lead prevents their cherishing any strong legitimate passion, the language of passion in affected tones slips forever from their glib tongues, and every trifle produces those phosphoric bursts which only mimic in the dark the flame of passion.

* * *

1792

5. Stirring.
6. I am not now alluding to that superiority of mind which leads to the creation of ideal beauty, when he, surveyed with a penetrating eye, appears a tragicomedy, in which little can be seen to satisfy the heart without the help of fancy [Wollstonecraft's note]. "He" refers to the superior person, presumably an artist or poet.

SARAH WENTWORTH MORTON
1759–1846

Between Anne Bradstreet and Emily Dickinson stands the less well-known American woman poet who published under the pen name "Constantia" until she realized that the pseudonym was already being used by Judith Sargent Murray. Sarah Wentworth Morton thenceforth signed herself as "Philenia, a Lady of Boston." After making a reputation for herself in the pages of the *Massachusetts Magazine*, Morton devoted herself to public themes in her "noble savage" verse narrative, *Ouâbi: or the Virtues of Nature, An Indian Tale* (1790), which was later set to music, and in two epic poems about the American Revolution: *Beacon Hill, a Local Poem, Historic and Descriptive* (1797) and *The Virtues of Society: A Tale Founded on Fact* (1799). But most often cited, by later abolitionists and in schoolbooks, was her shorter poem "The African Chief" (1792). The list of subscribers for her collection of poems and essays, *My Mind and Its Thoughts* (1823)—the first publication printed under her own name— reflects her illustrious social connections. All these efforts bear the impress of Sarah Wentworth Morton's determination to contribute to a newly evolving and distinctly American literary history.

One of eleven children of affluent loyalists, Sarah Apthorp was born in Boston but soon moved with her family to her father's farm in what is now Quincy, Massachusetts. Later she took her mother's maiden name as her own middle name in order to pay tribute to her maternal origins. In 1781, she married the lawyer and orator Perez Morton, who would become attorney general of Massachusetts. Together they committed themselves to the Revolutionary cause, engaged in a lively social life with prominent patriots, and produced six children, all of whom died before she did. An early grief occurred seven years after the marriage: her sister Fanny poisoned herself, reportedly because she had borne Perez Morton a child. Whether or not the allegation was true—Sarah Wentworth Morton sided with the statesman John Adams and the former governor James Bowdoin, who helped clear her husband of the accusations made by her father—William Hill Brown's novel *The Power of Sympathy* (1789) broadcast the scandal. That her writing first appeared in the *Massachusetts Magazine* during the same period as Brown's novel proves that the thirty-year-old was never silenced by the troubling series of events, though they may have contributed to the melancholy tone of some of the verse she went on to produce.

The African Chief[1]

See how the black ship cleaves the main,[2]
 High bounding o'er the dark blue wave,
Remurmuring with the groans of pain,
 Deep freighted with the princely slave!

5 Did all the gods of Afric sleep,
 Forgetful of their guardian love,
When the white tyrants of the deep,
 Betrayed him in the palmy grove?

1. Taken in arms, fighting for his freedom, and inhumanly butchered by his conquerors! This affecting event was fully delineated in the various gazettes of that period [Morton's note].
2. Sea.

A chief of Gambia's golden shore,
10 Whose arm the band of warriors led,
Or more—the lord of generous power,
 By whom the foodless poor were fed.

Does not the voice of reason cry:
 Claim the first right that nature gave,
15 From the red scourge of bondage fly,
 Nor deign to live a burdened slave!

Has not his suffering offspring clung,
 Desponding round his fettered knee;
On his worn shoulder, weeping hung,
20 And urged one effort to be free!

His wife by nameless wrongs subdued,
 His bosom's friend to death resigned,
The flinty pathway drenched in blood,
 He saw with cold and frenzied mind.

25 Strong in despair, then sought the plain,
 To heaven was raised his steadfast eye,
Resolved to burst the crushing chain,
 Or mid the battle's blast to die.

First of his race, he led the band,
30 Guardless of[3] danger, hurling round,
Till by his red avenging hand,
 Full many a despot stained the ground.

When erst Messenia's[4] sons oppressed,
 Flew desperate to the sanguine[5] field,
35 With iron clothed each injured breast,
 And saw the cruel Spartan yield.

Did not the soul to heaven allied,
 With the proud heart as greatly swell,
As when the Roman Decius died,
40 Or when the Grecian victim fell?[6]

Do later deeds quick rapture raise,
 The boom Batavia's William won,

3. I.e., disregarding.

4. The *Messenians* being conquered by the *Spartans*, and agreeably to the custom of the age, the miserable remnant led into slavery, under these circumstances were so inhumanly oppressed, that rising, and united in arms, they seized upon a Spartan fortress and after innumerable injuries, inflicted and reciprocated, finally obtained their freedom [Morton's note]. By the 7th century B.C.E., the inhabitants of Messenia, a region in southwest Greece, had become helots—a slave population controlled but not individually owned

by Spartans. Messenia regained its independence in 369 B.C.E. (largely because in 371 the Spartans had suffered a stunning defeat by a Theban army).

5. Bloody.

6. Leonidas [Morton's note]. King of Sparta (d. 480 B.C.E.), Leonidas was famous for his heroic death: he and all the Spartans in his command fell in the unsuccessful defense of the pass at Thermopylae against a much larger Persian army. According to tradition, Decius deliberately charged into the enemy's ranks (340 B.C.E.), believing that his death would ensure Rome's victory.

Paoli's time-enduring praise,
　　Or the yet greater Washington![7]

45　If these exalt thy sacred zeal,
　　To hate oppression's mad control,
For bleeding Afric learn to feel,
　　Whose Chieftain claimed a kindred soul.

Ah, mourn the last disastrous hour,
50　　Lift the full eye of bootless[8] grief,
While victory treads the sultry shore,
　　And tears from hope the captive Chief,

While the hard race of pallid hue,
　　Unpracticed in the power to feel,
55　Resign him to the murderous crew,
　　The horrors of the quivering wheel.[9]

Let sorrow bathe each blushing cheek,
　　Bend piteous o'er the tortured slave,
Whose wrongs compassion cannot speak,
60　　Whose only refuge was the grave.

1792, 1823

From Ouâbi: or the Virtues of Nature, An Indian Tale in Four Cantos

Canto I

'Tis not the court, in dazzling splendor gay,
Where soft luxuriance spreads her silken arms,
Where garish fancy leads the soul astray,
And languid nature mourns her slighted charms;

5　'Tis not the golden hill, nor flowr'y dale,
Which lends my simple muse[1] her artless theme;
But the black forest and uncultur'd vale,
The savage warrior, and the lonely stream.

Where MISSISSIPPI[2] rolls his *parent flood*,
10　With slope impetuous to the surgy main,[3]

7. Morton names three men viewed as liberators: William III (1650–1702) was ruler of the Netherlands ("Batavia") when, after the Glorious Revolution of 1688, Parliament offered him the English crown (ruled, 1689–1702); Pasquale Paoli (1725–1807), a Corsican patriot, led a successful revolt against the Genoese and served as Corsica's president (1755–69) until the French took over the island; and George Washington (1732–1799) led the Continental armies against the British and was chosen as first president of the United States in 1789.

8. Unavailing; to no purpose.
9. An instrument of torture.
1. Goddess of art and learning, conventionally invoked for inspiration and information.
2. Mississippi, an Indian name, signifying the great father of all rivers. It is subject to no tides, but from its source in the north of the American Continent flows with rapid force, till it empties itself into the Gulph of Mexico [Morton's note]. The Ojibwe and Algonquin names for the river, which are close to *Mississippi*, mean "great river."
3. Swelling sea.

The desert's painted chiefs explore the wood,
Or with the thund'ring war-whoop[4] shake the plain.

There the fierce sachems[5] raise the battle's din,
Or in the stream their active bodies lave,
15 Or midst the flames their fearless songs begin[6]—
PAIN HAS NO TERRORS TO THE TRULY BRAVE.

There young CELARIO, Europe's fairest boast,[7]
In hopeless exile mourn'd the tedious day;
Now wand'ring slowly o'er the oozy coast,
20 Now thro the wild woods urg'd his anxious way.

Where the low stooping branch excludes the light,
A piercing shriek assail'd his wounded ear;
Swift as the winged arrow speeds its flight,
He seeks the piteous harbinger of fear.

25 There a tall Huron rais'd his threat'ning arm,
While round his knees a beauteous captive clung,
Striving to move him with her matchless form,
Or charm him by the magic of her tongue.

Soon as Celario viewed the murd'rous scene,
30 Quick from his vest the deathful tube[8] he drew;
Its leaden vengeance thunder'd o'er the green,
While from the savage hand the ling'ring hatchet flew.

Low at his feat the breathless warrior lies;
Still the soft captive sickens with alarms,
35 Calls on OUABI's name with streaming eyes,
While the young victor lives upon her charms.

Her limbs were straighter than the mountain pine,
Her hair far blacker than the raven's wing;
Beauty had lent her form the waving[9] line,
40 Her breath gave fragrance to the balmy spring.

Each bright perfection open'd on her face,
Her flowing garment wanton'd in the breeze,
Her slender feet the glitt'ring sandals grace,
Her look was dignity, her movement ease.

45 With spendid beads her braided tresses shone,
Her bending waist a modest girdle bound,

4. "War-whoop," the cry of battle, with which they always make their onset [Morton's note]. "Onset": assault.
5. Chiefs (used especially of Native Americans on the east coast).
6. The American Indians, after exhausting every species of cruelty and torture upon their most distinguished prisoners, bind them by a distant fire; who expire singing songs of glory and and defiance [Morton's note].
7. Person boasted about.
8. I.e., a gun.
9. See Hogarth's Line of Beauty [Morton's note]. In *The Analysis of Beauty* (1753), the English artist and art theorist William Hogarth (1697–1764) calls "the waving line" the "line of beauty."

Her pearly teeth outvi'd the cygnet's down—
She spoke—and music follow'd in the sound.

SHE.

Great ruler of the winged hour,[1]

50 AXÂKIA trembles at thy pow'r;
While from thy hand the thunders roll,
Thy charms with lightnings pierce the soul;
Ah! how unlike our sable race,
The snowy lustre of thy face!
55 That hair of beaming Cynthia's hue,[2]
Those shining eyes of heav'nly blue!
Ah! didst thou leave thy blissful land,
To save me from the murd'rer's hand?

And is Ouâbi still thy care,
60 The dauntless chief, unknown to fear?

HE.

Cease to call Ouâbi's name,
Give Celario all his claim.
No divinity is here: Spare thy praises, quit thy fear:
Bend no more that beauteous knee,
65 For I am a slave to thee:
Let my griefs thy pity move,
Heal them with the balm of love.
Far beyond the orient main,[3]
By my rage a youth was slain;
70 He this daring arm defied,
By this arm the ruffian died:
Exil'd from my native home,
Thro the desert wild I roam;
But if only blest by thee,
75 All the desert smiles on me.

SHE.

See a graceful form arise![4]
Now it fills my ravish'd eyes,
Brighter than the morning star,
'Tis Ouâbi, fam'd in war:
80 Close before my bosom spread,
O'er thy preference casts a shade,

Full on him these eyes recline,
And his person shuts out thine.

1. It is presumed that Azâkia had never before seen an European, or heard the report of a pistol, as she considers one a deity, and the other his thunder [Morton's note].
2. Pale blond. Cynthia is an epithet of Artemis (born on Mount Cynthus), Greek goddess of the moon.

3. Eastern sea.
4. The Indian women of America are very chaste after marriage, and if any person makes love to them, they answer, "The friend that is before my eyes, prevents my seeing you" [Morton's note]. "Makes love to": woos.

Let us to his home retire,
85 Where he lights the social[5] fire;
Do not thro the desert roam,
Find with me his gen'rous home;
There the Illinois obey Great Ouâbi's chosen sway.

1790

5. Friendly.

HELEN MARIA WILLIAMS
1762?–1827

After the death of her father, a Welsh army officer, Helen Maria Williams was educated with her two sisters at home in Berwick-on-Tweed by her Scots mother. At the age of nineteen, Williams set out for London with her first long poem completed, and in her twenties she began publishing sonnets, political poems against slavery, and sentimental fiction. An invitation from a French acquaintance led to a visit to France, which resulted in the first of her influential accounts of events across the Channel—*Letters Written from France in the Summer of 1790*—and eventually resulted in her decision to live out most of the rest of her life in France.

In thirteen volumes describing thirty years of French history, Helen Maria Williams retained her sympathy for the principles of the Revolution. Her letters attracted attention because of their emotional immediacy and because of her personal engagement in political events. In 1793, during the general arrest of British subjects, Williams was herself briefly imprisoned; in 1794, she moved to Switzerland out of fear of reprisals for her writings against the Jacobin Terror; after the fall of Robespierre, she returned to Paris, maintaining her libertarian ideals despite the atrocities she had witnessed and recorded. Her salon attracted a number of travelers, including Tom Paine, Mary Wollstonecraft, and William Wordsworth. But her view that "liberty is innocent of the outrages committed under its borrowed sanction" meant that her reputation with the British reading public suffered as her English contemporaries reacted with alarm to the violence of the Reign of Terror and the rise of Napoléon.

Williams's prestige continued to decline during the writing of the later volumes of *Letters from France,* when she entertained extensively in Paris, gaining notoriety not only for the large parties she generously sprinkled with social and artistic celebrities but also because of her decision to live with a divorced man, John Hurford Stone, whom she may have secretly married in 1794. Although she continued to publish books about French history as well as a number of English translations of French works, she had clearly alienated many of her readers. Yet when the first and most successful volume of *Letters from France* appeared in 1790, Williams's sympathetic description of the fall of the Bastille was widely admired and taken by some as an answer to Edmund Burke's criticism of the uprising in his *Reflections on the Revolution in France* (1790). About Williams's accounts, the critic Mary Favret has claimed that "despite their initial dependence on sentimental and romantic fictions," they "eventually serve as registers for political rather than emotional turbulence. They become the instruments probing the inner workings of power structures." An incisive observer, an astute commentator, and a sophisticated expatriate, Williams was a pio-

neering woman journalist who mediated between two cultures with subtlety and verve. In addition, she was a poet whose verse was admired by Wordsworth, who praised her in a sonnet of his own.

Sonnet to the Moon

The glitt'ring colours of the day are fled;
Come, melancholy orb! that dwell'st with night,
 Come! and o'er earth thy wand'ring lustre shed,
Thy deepest shadow, and thy softest light;
5 To me congenial is the gloomy grove,
When with faint light the sloping uplands shine;
 That gloom, those pensive rays alike I love,
Whose sadness seems in sympathy with mine!
 But most for this, pale orb! thy beams are dear,
10 For this, benignant orb! I hail thee most:
That while I pour the unavailing tear,
And mourn that hope to me in youth is lost,
 Thy light can visionary thoughts impart,
 And lead the Muse[1] to soothe a suff'ring heart.

1790

Sonnet: To the Torrid Zone[1]

Pathway of light! o'er thy empurpled zone
With lavish charms perennial summer strays;
Soft 'midst thy spicy groves the zephyr[2] plays,
While far around the rich perfumes are thrown;
5 The amadavid-bird[3] for thee alone
Spreads his gay plumes, that catch thy vivid rays:
For thee the gems with liquid lustre blaze,
And Nature's various wealth is all thy own.
But, ah! not thine is twilight's doubtful gloom,
10 Those mild gradations, mingling day with night;
Here instant darkness shrouds thy genial bloom,[4]
Nor leaves my pensive soul that ling'ring light,
When musing mem'ry would each trace resume
Of fading pleasures in successive flight.

1795

1. Goddess of art and learning, conventionally invoked for inspiration and information.
1. The region bounded by the Tropic of Cancer north of the equator, and the Tropic of Capricorn to the south.

2. West wind.
3. An Indian songbird.
4. Twilight is much shorter in the tropics than in more northern latitudes (though nightfall is not "instant").

From On the Bill Which Was Passed in England for Regulating the Slave Trade; a Short Time before Its Abolition[1]

The hollow winds of night no more
In wild, unequal cadence pour,
On musing fancy's wakeful ear,
The groan of agony severe
5 From yon dark vessel, which contains
The wretch new bound in hopeless chains!
Whose soul with keener anguish bleeds,
As Afric's less'ning shore recedes—
No more where Ocean's unseen bound
10 Leaves a drear world of waters round,
Between the howling gust, shall rise
The stifled captive's latest sighs!—
No more shall suffocating death
Seize the pent victim's sinking breath;
15 The pang of that convulsive hour,
Reproaching man's insatiate power;
Man! who to Afric's shore has past,
Relentless, as the annual blast
That sweeps the Western Isles,[2] and flings
20 Destruction from its furious wings!—
And woman, she, too weak to bear
The galling chain, the tainted air,—
Of mind too feeble to sustain
The vast, accumulated pain,—
25 No more, in desperation wild,
Shall madly strain her gasping child;
With all the mother at her soul,
With eyes where tears have ceas'd to roll,
Shall catch the livid infant's breath,
30 Then sink in agonizing death!
Britain! the noble, blest decree
That soothes despair, is fram'd by thee!
Thy powerful arm has interpos'd,
And *one* dire scene for ever clos'd;
35 Its horror shall no more belong
To that foul drama, deep with wrong.
O, first of Europe's polish'd lands
To ease the captive's iron bands;[3]
Long, as thy glorious annals shine,
40 This proud distinction shall be thine!
Not first alone when valour leads
To rush on danger's noblest deeds;
When mercy calls thee to explore

1. Though a committee was appointed in 1788 to investigate the slave trade, it was not abolished in England until 1807.
2. The exposed western and northern coasts of both Britain and Ireland are subject to winter gales.
3. The first European power to abolish the slave trade was in fact Denmark, by royal order (issued in 1792, it took effect at the end of 1802).

A gloomy path, untrod before,
45 Thy ardent spirit springs to heal,
And, greatly gen'rous, dares to feel!—
Valour is like the meteor's light,
Whose partial flash leaves deeper night;
While Mercy, like the lunar ray,
50 Gilds the thick shade with softer day.
 Blest deed! that met consenting minds
In all but those whom av'rice binds,—
Who creep in interest's crooked ways,
Nor ever pass her narrow maze;
55 Or those whom hard indiff'rence steels
To every pang another feels.
For *them* has fortune round their bowers
Twin'd, partial nymph! her lavish flowers;
For *them* from unsunn'd caves, she brings
60 Her summer ice; for *them* she springs
To climes where hotter suns produce
The richer fruit's delicious juice;
While *they*, whom wasted blessings tire,
Nor leave *one* want to feed desire,
65 With cool, insulting ease demand
Why, for yon hopeless, captive band,
Is ask'd, to mitigate despair,
The mercy of the common air?
The boon of larger space to breathe,
70 While coop'd that hollow deck beneath?
A lengthen'd plank, on which to throw
Their shackled limbs, while fiercely glow
The beams direct, that on each head
The fury of contagion shed?—
75 And dare presumptuous, guilty man,
Load with offence his fleeting span?
Deform creation with the gloom
Of crimes that blot its cheerful bloom?
Darken a work so perfect made,
80 And cast the universe in shade?—
Alas! to Afric's fetter'd race
Creation wears no form of grace!

* * *

1788, 1823

JOANNA BAILLIE
1762–1851

The daughter of an eminent Scottish family that claimed descent from the legendary William Wallace, Joanna Baillie was one of the most prolific and popular playwrights of her time. Praised and sponsored by (most notably) Sir Walter Scott, her dramas were performed in London, Liverpool, Edinburgh, and Dublin with casts featuring such luminaries as the actor John Kemble and his sister Mrs. Siddons; the works were widely read in the United States as well. Indeed, the success of Baillie's dramas both onstage and off prompted the often misogynistic Lord Byron to declare her the only exception to Voltaire's rule that "the composition of a tragedy requires *testicles*." "If this be true Lord knows what Joanna Baillie does," he joked in a letter to a friend, adding "I suppose she borrows them."

Usually characterized as a genteel, reserved, and pious lady, Baillie disapproved of the rakish Byron, whose brooding heroes she claimed to dislike. Yet the intensity that infuses his Romantic writings was arguably inspired at least in part by Baillie's ambitious three-volume *Series of Plays, in which it is attempted to delineate the stranger passions of the mind* (1798–1812), a sequence in which she proposed to offer a tragedy and a comedy on each of the major human emotions—for instance, *Basil, a tragedy on Love* and *DeMontfort, a tragedy on Hatred*. As sweeping in its ambition as the project itself was the "Introductory Discourse" with which this sometimes reclusive woman prefaced her first volume. A theoretical essay that may well have influenced William Wordsworth's "Preface to *Lyrical Ballads*" (1800), Baillie's treatise argued for "natural" diction, realistic subject matter, and a plain, relatively unembellished style "less constrained by that lofty seriousness which [had] generally been considered as necessary" by her contemporaries and precursors.

Baillie was raised in Glasgow, where her father was a professor of divinity and her maternal uncles were the noted surgeons William and John Hunter. At the boarding school where she was educated, she was a diligent student yet "full of merriment and playful trick," organizing amateur theatricals for which she herself designed costumes. After her father died and her brother completed a medical training, she moved with her family to London, where she anonymously published her first book, a slim collection titled *Poems: Wherein it is attempted to describe CERTAIN VIEWS OF NATURE and of RUSTIC MANNERS* (1790). Although the volume was barely noticed in the press, it marked the debut of a writer whose keen observations of both landscape and character would ultimately find an appreciative audience. Though Baillie's plays no longer have the charisma that they held for Scott and Byron, such vividly detailed verses as "A Mother to Her Waking Infant" and "London" reveal a sensibility that is still as appealing as her grander projects were in the nineteenth century.

After the deaths of her mother and brother, the unmarried Baillie lived for the remainder of her life with her older sister. In her later years she became increasingly devout, composing hymns and meditations on scripture while also maintaining her many literary friendships in London. To the end, however, she remained a loyal Scot, like her compatriot and contemporary Robert Burns, who might himself have written her charming "Woo'd and Married and A'." Wrote one Victorian biographer, "she clung obstinately to every association of her Scottish home," and though she was a "writer of fine English she nevertheless scorned the attempt to become a fine English lady."

A Mother to Her Waking Infant

Now in thy dazzling[1] half-oped eye,
Thy curlèd nose and lip awry,
Thy up-hoist arms and noddling[2] head,
And little chin with crystal spread,
5　Poor helpless thing! what do I see,
　　That I should sing of thee?

From thy poor tongue no accents come,
Which can but rub thy toothless gum;
Small understanding boasts thy face,
10　Thy shapeless limbs nor step nor grace;
A few short words thy feats may tell,
　　And yet I love thee well.

When sudden wakes the bitter shriek,
And redder swells thy little cheek;
15　When rattled keys thy woes beguile,
And through the wet eye gleams the smile,
Still for thy weakly self is spent
　　Thy little silly plaint.

But when thy friends are in distress,
20　Thou'lt laugh and chuckle ne'er the less;
Nor e'en with sympathy be smitten,
Though all are sad but thee and kitten;
Yet little varlet[3] that thou art,
　　Thou twitchest at the heart.

25　Thy rosy cheek so soft and warm;
Thy pinky[4] hand and dimpled arm;
Thy silken locks that scantly peep,
With gold-tipped ends, where circles deep
Around thy neck in harmless grace
30　So soft and sleekly hold their place,
Might harder hearts with kindness fill,
　　And gain our right good will.

Each passing clown[5] bestows his blessing,
Thy mouth is worn with old wives' kissing:
35　E'en lighter looks the gloomy eye
Of surly sense, when thou art by;
And yet I think whoe'er they be,
　　They love thee not like me.

1. Dazed.
2. Quickly nodding.
3. Rascal.
4. Pink-tinged.
5. Countryman, rustic.

Perhaps when time shall add a few
40 Short years to thee, thou'lt love me too.
Then wilt thou through life's weary way
Become my sure and cheering stay:
Wilt care for me, and be my hold,
 When I am weak and old.

45 Thou'lt listen to my lengthened tale,
And pity me when I am frail—
But see, the sweepy spinning fly
Upon the window takes thine eye.
Go to thy little senseless play—
50 Thou dost not heed my lay.[6]

1790

Song: Woo'd and Married and A'

The bride she is winsome and bonny,
 Her hair it is snooded[1] sae sleek,
And faithfu' and kind is her Johnny,
 Yet fast fa' the tears on her cheek.
5 New pearlins are cause of her sorrow,
New pearlins and plenishing[2] too,
The bride that has a' to borrow,
 Has e'en right mickle[3] ado,
 Woo'd and married and a'!
10 Woo'd and married and a'!
Is na' she very weel aff
 To be woo'd and married at a'?

Her mither then hastily spak,
 "The lassie is glaikit[4] wi' pride;
15 In my pouch I had never a plack[5]
 On the day when I was a bride.
E'en tak' to your wheel, and be clever,
 And draw out your thread in the sun;
The gear that is gifted,[6] it never
20 Will last like the gear that is won.[7]
 Woo'd and married and a'!
 Wi' havins and toucher[8] sae sma',
I think ye are very weel aff,
 To be woo'd and married at a'!"

25 "Toot, toot!" quo' her gray-headed faither,
 "She's less o' a bride than a bairn;

6. Song.
1. Bound with a hairband or ribbon.
2. Household furnishings; the bride's contribution to setting up house. "Pearlins": clothes trimmed with lace.
3. Much.

4. Foolish; giddy.
5. A small copper coin of little value, formerly used in Scotland. "Pouch": purse.
6. Given. "Gear": household necessaries; wealth.
7. Earned.
8. Dowry (tocher). "Havins": possessions.

She's ta'en like a cout[9] frae the heather,
 Wi' sense and discretion to learn.
Half husband, I trow, and half daddy,
30 As humor inconstantly leans,
The chiel maun[1] be patient and steady,
 That yokes wi' a mate in her teens.
 A kerchief sae douce[2] and sae neat,
 O'er her locks that the winds used to blaw!
35 I'm baith like to laugh and to greet,[3]
 When I think o' her married at a'!"

Then out spak' the wily bridegroom;
 Weel waled were his wordies, I ween[4]—
"I'm rich, though my coffer be toom,
40 Wi' the blinks o' your bonny blue een.[5]
I'm prouder o' thee by my side,
 Though thy ruffles or ribbons be few,
Than if Kate o' the Croft were my bride,
 Wi' purfles[6] and pearlins enow.
45 Dear and dearest of ony!
 Ye're woo'd and buikit[7] and a'!"
And do ye think scorn o' your Johnny,
 And grieve to be married at a'?"

She turn'd, and she blush'd, and she smiled,
50 And she looket sae bashfully down;
The pride o' her heart was beguiled,
 And she played wi' the sleeves o' her gown;
She twirled the tag o' her lace,
 And she nippet[8] her boddice sae blue,
55 Syne blinket sae sweet in his face,
 And aff like a maukin[9] she flew.
 Woo'd and married and a'!
 Wi' Johnny to roose[1] her and a'!
 She thinks hersel very weel aff,
60 To be woo'd and married at a'!

 1822

London

It is a goodly sight through the clear air,
From Hampstead's heathy height[1] to see at once
England's vast capital in fair expanse,

9. Colt. "Bairn": child.
1. The man must.
2. Sober, sedate.
3. Weep.
4. Think, believe. "Waled": chosen, selected.
5. Eyes. "Toom": empty.
6. Embroidered edges. "Croft": an agricultural holding worked by the tenant.
7. Booked; i.e., their names have been officially recorded as betrothed.
8. Pinched. "Tag": end.
9. Hare (malkin). "Syne": then, at the next moment.
1. Praise, extrol.
1. Hampstead Heath, the city's highest open space, offers excellent views of central London, 4 miles to the southeast.

Towers, belfries, lengthen'd streets, and structures fair.
5 St. Paul's high dome[2] amidst the vassal bands
Of neighb'ring spires, a regal chieftain stands,
And over fields of ridgy roofs appear,
With distance softly tinted, side by side,
In kindred grace, like twain of sisters dear,
10 The Towers of Westminster, her Abbey's pride;[3]
While, far beyond, the hills of Surrey[4] shine
Through thin soft haze, and show their wavy line.
View'd thus, a goodly sight! but when survey'd
Through denser air when moisten'd winds prevail,
15 In her grand panoply of smoke array'd,
While clouds aloft in heavy volumes sail,
She is sublime.—She seems a curtain'd gloom
Connecting heaven and earth,—a threat'ning sign of doom.
With more than natural height, rear'd in the sky
20 'Tis then St. Paul's arrests the wondering eye;
The lower parts in swathing mist conceal'd,
The higher through some half spent shower reveal'd,
So far from earth removed, that well, I trow,[5]
Did not its form man's artful structure show,
25 It might some lofty alpine peak be deem'd,
The eagle's haunt, with cave and crevice seam'd.
Stretch'd wide on either hand, a rugged screen,
In lurid dimness, nearer streets are seen
Like shoreward billows of a troubled main,[6]
30 Arrested in their rage. Through drizzly rain,
Cataracts of tawny sheen pour from the skies,
Of furnace smoke black curling columns rise,
And many tinted vapours, slowly pass
O'er the wide draping of that pictured mass.

35 So shows by day this grand imperial town,
And, when o'er all the night's black stole is thrown,
The distant traveller doth with wonder mark
Her luminous canopy athwart the dark,
Cast up, from myriads of lamps that shine
40 Along her streets in many a starry line:—
He wondering looks from his yet distant road,
And thinks the northern streamers[7] are abroad.
'What hollow sound is that?' approaching near,
The roar of many wheels breaks on his ear.
45 It is the flood of human life in motion!
It is the voice of a tempestuous ocean!
With sad but pleasing awe his soul is fill'd,

2. St. Paul's Cathedral, built between 1675 and 1710, rises more than 350 feet from the ground (the only higher church dome in the world is St. Peter's in Rome).
3. Westminster Abbey, the Gothic church where British monarchs are crowned, has two western towers built between 1722 and 1740.
4. County southwest of London.
5. Believe.
6. Sea.
7. I.e., the northern lights, or aurora borealis.

Scarce heaves his breast, and all within is still'd,
As many thoughts and feelings cross his mind,—
50 Thoughts, mingled, melancholy, undefined,
Of restless, reckless man, and years gone by,
And Time fast wending to Eternity.

1840, 1851

Literature of the Nineteenth Century

THE WORLD OF THE NINETEENTH CENTURY

"There can be no question that the present epoch is initiating an empire of the higher reason, of arts, affections, aspirations; and for that epoch the genius of woman has been reserved," declared Thomas Wentworth Higginson in 1859. The editor of the *Atlantic Monthly* and the sometime mentor of the American poet Emily Dickinson, Higginson was neither alone nor eccentric in holding such a belief. For both in England and America, the nineteenth century saw unprecedented changes in the conditions of women's lives as well as the consolidation of a powerful female literary tradition. Battling for the vote; demanding the right to own property and retain custody of their children after divorce; entering institutions of higher education; studying to be physicians and nurses, lawyers and journalists; forming trade unions; establishing businesses; and writing best sellers, women at home and abroad had become so dramatically visible that by the end of the century the so-called Woman Question—the issue of just what woman's "place" ought to be in a proper society—had begun to obsess a startling range of thinkers. That for three-quarters of a century, one woman—Queen Victoria—had occupied a place of extraordinary international significance may have added to the intensity with which such matters were discussed, for, though she was no feminist, the increasingly bulky figure of the queen loomed ever larger as the age progressed.

The nineteenth century was in any case an era of remarkable, even shocking cultural transformation. In London for Victoria's 1897 Diamond Jubilee, sixty years after she had ascended the throne in 1837, the American writer Mark Twain mused that though "British history is two thousand years old . . . in a good many ways the world has moved farther ahead since the Queen was born than it moved in all the rest of the two thousand put together." His observation applied with special force to the "moves" experienced or imagined for the first time by women. Yet those particular changes were inextricably related to more general changes. As the feminist historian Ray Strachey wrote in *The Cause* (1928), her account of the British struggle for female emancipation, "The true history of the Woman's Movement is the whole history of the nineteenth century; nothing which occurred in those years could be irrelevant to the great social change which was going on, and nothing was without its share of influence upon it." No doubt she was referring to exactly the kinds of sociocultural shifts Twain himself was contemplating: revolutionary upheaval, industrialization, imperialist expansion, political reform, and the so-called disappearance of God.

Revolutionary Ideologies

The eighteenth century had ended with two revolutions that radically redefined Western politics. The American Revolution (1776) revised the relationship between the Old World and the New. The French Revolution (1789), at least partly influenced by recent events in North America, brought the threat of such changes dramatically, and in the end bloodily, home to Europe. Together, the two revolutions reminded both the ruling class and the intellectual class whom the French called the "third estate" that old hierarchies were inexorably disintegrating. Neither the middle class (rising merchants and professionals) nor the proletariat (the peasant and working classes) were willing to continue to acquiesce in a system that taxed or oppressed them while denying them the power to make significant decisions about their own futures. Though the American Revolution has been seen by some commentators as upper-middle-class or even aristocratic in its origins while the French Revolution seems to many historians to represent a more genuine rising of "the people," the events share an ideology based for the first time on a passionately articulated vision of what Enlightenment thinkers from the French Jean-Jacques Rousseau to the American Thomas Paine called "the Rights of Man."

To men of letters, such a vision was profoundly inspiring, and they greeted, in William Blake's phrases, the "stiff shudderings" that "shook the heavenly thrones" of European tradition with outbursts of enthusiasm. Blake himself acclaimed the passing of the old order and the coming of the new, while William Wordsworth, describing the hopes for social metamorphosis that had been aroused in the early days of the uprising in France, recalled that "bliss was it in that dawn to be alive / But to be young was very heaven." Similarly, to such literary women as Mary Robinson, Mary Wollstonecraft, Charlotte Smith, and Helen Maria Williams, this revolutionary "dawn" seemed at first to promise major cultural transformations. And though these and other writers were later to be in various degrees disillusioned by the failures of both revolutions to live up to the great expectations they had elicited, the common ideology that both events dramatized was, as we will see, to be profoundly influential throughout the nineteenth century and up to our own day, affecting not only middle-of-the-road political movements like the one that led to the first Reform Act of 1832 but also more radical movements such as Chartism, abolitionism, and women's suffrage.

Industrialization and Its Implications

These movements were equally, and just as urgently, impelled by a very different revolution: the so-called Industrial Revolution. As early as the mid-eighteenth century, methods of manufacturing had begun to become more technologically sophisticated, especially in England and particularly in the production of textiles, one of the country's major industries. By the 1760s, the invention of the steam engine and the spinning jenny had pointed the way to an age when the work of spinning and weaving would go on in large, centralized factories rather than individual cottages and when such work would require ever larger amounts of coal to fire the engines that drove increasingly complex machines. At the same time, the English Enclosure Acts of the mid-eighteenth century had transformed communally worked lands into private agricultural businesses, forcing many small farmers to

migrate to urban centers, where they joined the new class of industrial laborers required by the burgeoning factory system; the opening of textile mills, paper factories, and other industries had begun to create a similar working class in America.

The striking metamorphoses of both England and America (but, again, especially England) from essentially agrarian nations to modern states commanding all the resources of power looms, printing presses, railroads, steamships, and telegraphs fostered a virtual religion of progress, which was exhilarating to many, not least to a number of writers. In 1823, for instance, the poet-playwright Joanna Baillie composed "Address to a Steamvessel," celebrating the ship's liberation from the vagaries of the weather: "Thou hold'st thy course in independent pride; / No leave ask'st thou of either wind or tide." Similarly, in 1833 William Wordsworth, the sometime celebrant of pastoral nature, wrote "Steamboats, Viaducts, and Railways," a sonnet praising their wonders, while in "Locksley Hall" (1842) Alfred, Lord Tennyson created a speaker who glorified the achievements of "men the workers, ever reaping something new." Some decades later, Walt Whitman in America wrote his paean "To a Locomotive in Winter" (1876), in which he exulted in the great engine as a "type of the modern—emblem of motion and power," and his reclusive contemporary Emily Dickinson admitted to comparable feelings about what was then called "the iron horse," confiding that "I like to see it lap the Miles" (ca. 1862). At the same time, however, even the earliest of these prophets of progress expressed certain misgivings about the technology that fascinated them. Baillie, for one, admitted that "light skiffs," dependent on the "breezy air," were "dearer to fancy" and that gazing on her steamship she felt "Half sad, half proud, half angry, and half pleased." And Wordsworth, too, had mixed feelings about the consequences of the steamboats, viaducts, and railways whose wonders he had praised; in later life, he campaigned against the construction of the Kendal and Windermere Railway, fearing that the visitors it brought to the Lake District would "deface" the countryside he loved.

Soon enough, indeed, industrial "progress" began to reveal its darker side, as numerous commentators noted. Quite early in the nineteenth century, sensitive observers had become aware of the dreadful conditions under which many of their contemporaries lived and worked. In the first decade of the new age, William Blake had inveighed against "dark Satanic Mills," the products of an unbridled rationalism that he saw threatening to disfigure "England's green and pleasant Land." The meaning of such mills was more forcefully brought home to those who labored in them for what were practically starvation wages as well as to those whose traditional employments as handloom weavers, spinners, dyers, and other craftsworkers were annihilated by their technology. In the 1810s, a number of workers, both those who were exploited by the new system and those who were dispossessed by it, tried sporadically to unite, in some cases actually attempting to destroy the machines that were oppressing them, in others holding mass meetings to demand reform. But their efforts were unsuccessful. Conservative governments in both England and America believed that socioeconomic factors should and would adjust themselves optimally without governmental intervention; this policy, known as "laissez-faire" (let it be), was advocated by many contemporary thinkers. In 1812 England's House of Lords passed a

bill requiring the death penalty for anyone who destroyed the apparatus used in the stocking industry, and in 1819 British troops charged a huge but peaceful crowd that had gathered at St. Peter's Fields, Manchester, to press for reform; in what became known as the "Peterloo massacre" (an allusion to the British defeat of Napoleon at Waterloo), the soldiers killed nine demonstrators and injured hundreds of others.

By the 1840s, the situation in England, particularly in the industrial north, was appalling: in the slums of Manchester and Liverpool, hungry families were packed into filthy hovels; five-year-old children and pregnant women worked like mules for fifteen-hour days, dragging loads of coal in the mines outside Nottingham; London seamstresses toiled for eighteen hours at a time during the height of the four-month social "season" and starved for the rest of the year; for workers who inhaled the polluted air of badly ventilated mills and factories, the death rate from tuberculosis was double the national average; and protective tariffs known as the "Corn Laws" kept foreign grain from entering the country so that the price of the bread made from English wheat could be inflated to exorbitant levels.

Friedrich Engels's radical *Condition of the Working Class in England* (1845) meticulously documented many of these problems, but even an "establishment" politician like Benjamin Disraeli raised his voice in dismay, arguing in the subtitle of his 1845 novel, *Sybil*, that there were really "two nations" in England—the rich and the poor. For of course what made the situation of the workers even more poignant was the fact that their labor had contributed to the steady rise of a newly rich group of capitalist entrepreneurs—tradesmen and factory owners, stockbrokers and professional managers—who were anything but hungry. It was this comfortable middle class, prosperous and often piously smug, that set the tone of nineteenth-century society in both England and America, decorously imitating what they believed to be the manners of the aristocracy, furnishing their parlors with ornate bric-a-brac, dressing their women in expensively complicated costumes—and, more often than not, ignoring or scorning the sufferings of the poor.

If conditions for the workers in the United States were not quite as extreme as they were in England, that was because the possibility of westward migration often acted as an escape valve. Nevertheless, even as it created a newly wealthy middle class in centers such as Boston and New York, industrialization took its toll in Britain's former colony, particularly in the factory towns of New England, where workers in the textile and paper industries, among others—frequently young girls from poor rural families or recent refugees from the great Irish potato famine—labored from sunup to sundown for meager wages. Not surprisingly, then, many writers on both sides of the Atlantic indited passionate protests against the abuses fostered by the new technology and by the capitalist system that sponsored it, decrying the powerlessness and pain of the poor as well as the insensitivity and materialism of the rich. As early as 1819, Percy Bysshe Shelley had responded to the massacre at St. Peter's Fields with his hortatory "A Song: 'Men of England,' " in which he demanded, "Wherefore plough / For the lords who lay ye low?" As time passed and conditions deteriorated further, other writers took up the theme, if not quite so radically. Such works as Charles Dickens's *Bleak House* (1853), along with Elizabeth Gaskell's *Mary Barton* (1848), Charlotte

Brontë's *Shirley* (1849), and Rebecca Harding Davis's *Life in the Iron Mills* (1861), incisively portrayed both the wretchedness and the rebellion of the laboring classes, while Herman Melville's sardonic tale "The Paradise of Bachelors and the Tartarus of Maids" (1855) set the comfortably "heavenly" lives of the wealthy—in this case a group of bachelors dwelling in London's Inns of Court—against the metaphorically infernal existence of New England factory girls.

Imperialism and Reform

A religion of progress and a reaction against technology's discontents were contradictory consequences of the Industrial Revolution, but a third was equally problematic. Creating a need for fresh markets as well as a demand for raw materials that could not be supplied at home, the new age of the machine inevitably led to the definitive expansion of the British Empire into "underdeveloped" parts of the globe that was called imperialism. Africa, Egypt, India—all previously colonized, to be sure—now became crucially interdependent segments of a new international organism, administered in London, Cairo, Calcutta, and elsewhere by a class of bureaucrats who felt it was, in the words of the late-nineteenth-century writer Rudyard Kipling, "the white man's burden" to bring civilization to supposedly barbaric natives. Even those who had expressed doubts about the efficacy of nineteenth-century progress often pledged allegiance to this enterprise; as the speaker of Tennyson's "Locksley Hall" declared, "Better fifty years of Europe than a cycle of Cathay."

At the same time, the only recently "United" States, themselves former colonies, were engaging in similar efforts of expansion and colonization. Following the eighteenth-century English philosopher George Berkeley's dictum that "Westward the course of Empire takes its way," Americans of European descent set out to conquer the wild frontiers of the New World they saw as their own, in the process exterminating or subordinating countless Native American peoples. Furthermore, to acquire laborers to work the vast cotton and tobacco plantations they had established in the South, American settlers purchased black slaves from traders who ruthlessly raided the coast of West Africa to steal or purchase human "raw materials" in a grim apotheosis of the imperialist impulse. By 1800, such activity had been going on for more than a century, and though in 1808 both England and the United States had officially prohibited the importation of slaves, the practice continued unabated: traders often "dumped" their manacled cargo (sometimes as many as 500 to 570 men and women) overboard if a patrol ship were sighted. By 1830, scholars estimate that there were approximately two million "assimilated" slaves—Africans who had learned to speak English and to do plantation work—in the United States; by 1860, shortly before the Civil War began, there were almost four million, and in a number of Southern states, such as Virginia and North Carolina, the "major cash crop," as the historian Eleanor Flexner has remarked, "was not cotton, or tobacco—but slaves," for black laborers were bred like cattle to reproduce more laborers, and young women in particular were prized for their "generating qualities."

Given the predatory impulses on which the imperialist imperatives of expansion and exploitation were based, their triggering of wars and uprisings in Europe, North America, and elsewhere was probably inevitable. These

clashes ranged from struggles between competing imperial powers (such as the Crimean War of 1850 to 1853, in which England and France attempted to wrest control of portions of the disintegrating Ottoman Empire from Russia) to wars of colonial conquest (such as the so-called Indian wars in the American West) and native insurrections (such as the sporadic mutinies in nineteenth-century British India and the continuing battle for home rule in colonial Ireland). But perhaps the most dramatic of all was the American Civil War (1861–65), which combined elements of several different kinds of struggles, representing at the same time a war of liberation for the enslaved blacks and a conflict of economic interests between two quasi-imperial powers, the industrial North and the agrarian South.

The American Civil War was preceded and at least in part generated by a reiteration of the ideology of human rights that was earlier associated with the American and French revolutions, an ideology that was rapidly to become crucial to leaders of liberation movements in colonized countries around the world and to the founders of the British and American women's suffrage movements. Expressing their horror at what Melville called "man's foulest crime"—black slavery—white writers of both sexes on both sides of the Atlantic, from Henry David Thoreau and John Stuart Mill to Walt Whitman, from Anna Letitia Barbauld, Helen Maria Williams, Harriet Beecher Stowe, and Elizabeth Barrett Browning to Louisa May Alcott, argued for human dignity, freedom, and self-determination; at the same time, a new generation of black writers and speakers, including Frederick Douglass, Sojourner Truth, Harriet Jacobs (writing as "Linda Brent"), Harriet E. Wilson, and Frances E. W. Harper, arose in the United States to testify from personal experience about the iniquity of slavery. Their commitment to justice was finally rewarded when, after a tragic and bloody five-year struggle, the Union defeated the Confederacy, and the Congress of the newly reunited country enacted the Thirteenth Amendment to the Constitution, which permanently outlawed slavery, thereby freeing all slaves and, within a few years, leading to the Fifteenth Amendment, which enfranchised all black men.

Yet dramatic as it was, the widespread protest of intellectuals against slavery and the major constitutional amendments to which it led were symptomatic of quieter protests that were also based on the ideology of human rights and that fostered important, if less sweeping, political reforms throughout the nineteenth century. Chief among these were the moves in England to extend the vote to middle- and working-class men and to repeal the Corn Laws. In 1832 the first Reform Bill was passed, enfranchising all men owning property worth £10 or more in annual rent; in 1867, after much agitation from a working-class party known as the Chartists (because they proposed a "People's Charter" allowing for universal suffrage), the second Reform Bill was enacted, which in effect extended the right to vote to all English men; and in 1846 the Corn Laws were repealed, reducing tariffs on imported grain and alleviating the inflationary conditions that had made the lives of the poor not only harsh but hungry.

The Disappearance of God

The agitations and anxieties that surrounded such vast social changes soon took their toll on the spiritual serenity of those bred in an old order that was rapidly giving way to a new one. As factories darkened the landscape of England and battles of "brother against brother" raged in the valleys of Amer-

ica, it no longer seemed possible to share the philosophical confidence in the destined progress of humanity that had marked the thinking of the eighteenth century. Indeed, despite the proclamations of some nineteenth-century optimists that, as one of Robert Browning's characters observes, "the best is yet to be" and the insistence of others that social and industrial advances sped humanity ever closer to what Tennyson called the "one far-off divine event, / To which the whole creation moves," many thinkers had difficulty believing in God or in the divine at all. Writing in "The Scholar Gypsy" (1853) about "this strange disease of modern life," Matthew Arnold warned of "the infection of our mental strife," and in "Dover Beach" (1867) he described the "melancholy, long, withdrawing roar" of "the Sea of Faith." He was responding to what the critic J. Hillis Miller has called the "disappearance of God" from the intellectual horizon of many contemporary thinkers.

There were, it is true, a number of figures who tried desperately to revive and revise old creeds—including such American Transcendentalists as Emerson and Thoreau, who substituted a belief in the luminous beneficence of Nature for more orthodox faiths, and such British conservatives as John Henry, Cardinal Newman, who argued for the redemptive powers of a return to Roman Catholic traditions. But many poets were haunted by a nightmarish refrain like that of Arthur Hugh Clough's *Dipsychus* (1865)—"Ting, ting, there is no God; ting, ting—/ Dong, there is no God; dong"—and they were convinced that the supposed piety of their more conventional middle-class countrymen was merely hypocritical, even mercenary in its motives. What intensified the skepticism of such thinkers was precisely the industrial "progress" of which so many nineteenth-century citizens were proud. For more often than not, such advances issued in social and scientific research that subverted the very foundations of traditional faith. The "condition of the working class" as described by Engels, after all, had inexorably led to the *Communist Manifesto* (1847), coauthored by Engels and Karl Marx, a document that severely questioned what had once seemed to be the almost divine rights of rulers and property owners. Similarly, the empirical impulses that fostered the invention of steamships and railways led just as inexorably to the discoveries of Charles Darwin, whose *Origin of Species* (1859) supplanted the old idea of a six-day divine creation of Adam and Eve with the new and unnerving concept of human evolution from lower organisms. In a world in which a man seemed no "higher" than an animal, and men treated each other (as well as women and children) like animals, it is no wonder that Tennyson had an anxious vision of "Nature red in tooth and claw." Though the Victorian poet laureate (official national poet) himself recovered from his moment of doubt, many of his contemporaries could not free themselves from such pessimism and skepticism. Thus the changes that Mark Twain observed—the moves ahead the world had made in Queen Victoria's lifetime—were both radical and radically unsettling.

WOMAN'S SPHERE

For women, though the nineteenth century's startling changes often triggered considerable unease, such shifts were always significant and frequently beneficial. In 1800, however, eight years after the publication of Mary Woll-

stonecraft's *A Vindication of the Rights of Woman* (1792), nothing could have seemed less likely than the possibility that, in Higginson's words, for this "epoch the genius of woman has been reserved." Indeed, despite the new conceptions of human rights dramatized by the American and French revolutions and the arguments for women's rights eloquently advanced by Wollstonecraft and earlier by writers such as Hannah More and Anne Finch, almost all women were still confined by law and custom in a secondary, private "sphere." Worse still, even some of the most liberal thinkers of the age helped formulate a concept of a "woman's sphere" that was in its way no less oppressive than the misogyny of medieval monks and the antifeminism of Augustan wits.

The Ideology of Femininity

Ironically enough, in the middle of the eighteenth century the French philosopher Jean-Jacques Rousseau, whose demands for human liberty had been influential on a number of movements for political reform, forcefully articulated some of the most restrictive tenets of what can be called the nineteenth century's ideology of femininity, declaring in *Émile* (1762) that "the whole education of women ought to be relative to men. To please them, to be useful to them, to make themselves loved and honored by them, to educate them when young, to care for them when grown, to counsel them, to console them, and to make life sweet and agreeable to them—these are the duties of women at all times, and what should be taught them from their infancy." The ideal woman he thus envisioned—a pure, submissive, decorous, and even angelic creature—was only one particularly notable representative of a standard against which every middle- and upper-class woman's conduct was measured, and other writers, female as well as male, elaborated on the virtues of such an ideal.

In 1844, for instance, the selflessness of the model woman was discussed by the English writer Mrs. Sarah Ellis, who admonished readers of her conduct books (volumes of advice on manners and morals) that " 'What shall I do to gratify myself—to be admired—or to vary the tenor of my existence?' are not the questions which a woman of right feelings asks on first waking to the avocations of the day. Much more congenial to the highest attributes of woman's character are inquiries such as these: 'How shall I endeavor through this day to turn the time, the health and the means permitted me to enjoy to the best account?' " In 1854, in a long and very popular poem about femininity with the telling title *The Angel in the House*, Coventry Patmore described such selflessness more extravagantly, casting it in terms that suggest self-sacrifice, even self-immolation:

> Man must be pleased; but him to please
> Is woman's pleasure; down the gulf
> Of his condoled necessities
> She casts her best, she flings herself.

In fact, for many writers, such a self-sacrificing and angelic woman became the paradigm of renunciatory Christian love. Working out of a tradition that went back at least as far as the German poet-novelist Goethe, whose Faust (in *Faust*, 1808–32) is redeemed by the "Eternal Feminine" (*das Ewige Weibliche*) that draws man's mind to "higher" things, such thinkers employed a

rhetoric drawn from religion to characterize the good mother as a sort of Madonna and the dutiful maiden as a virginal angel. Significantly, as the critic Nina Auerbach has observed, it was only in the nineteenth century that painters began regularly portraying angels as female; perhaps even more significantly, as Auerbach has also noted, the Victorian cult of the "angel in the house" can be associated with the "disappearance of God" we discussed earlier, with its theological imagery arising in part from a displacement of traditional metaphors for the sacred onto the secular figure of the woman.

Where some writers characterized the feminine ideal through a vocabulary drawn from religion, others used a rhetoric of chivalry. If for such thinkers the model woman was not an "angel," she was at least a "queen." John Ruskin's "Of Queens' Gardens" (1865), with its assertion that woman's "great function is Praise; she enters into no contest but infallibly judges the crown of contest," implicitly alludes to medieval jousts and tournaments to characterize the regal lady whose "intellect is not for invention or creation" but who "rules" man's home so that it is "the place of Peace." Just a few years later the American writer Louisa May Alcott—herself a feisty, self-supporting suffragist—would argue in similar terms in *Little Women* (1869) that "a woman's happiest kingdom is home."

Whether a selfless angel or a serene queen, the model woman was often seen by both British and American ideologists of femininity as delicate, frail, ethereal. To certify her spirituality and refinement, she must look and act like a fragile creature. Instructions as to how a young girl, or even an older woman, was to manage such a task often ranged from the ridiculous to the bizarre. Marriageable maidens on both sides of the Atlantic drank vinegar to cultivate an "interesting" pallor, tight-laced themselves into narrow corsets so as to achieve an uncannily slender waist (eighteen inches was the ideal), and practiced the "art" of fainting to remind beaux of their delicacy. More problematic still, many medical men and laymen believed that a "good"— that is, a well-bred middle- or upper-class—woman was essentially passionless: if men were beasts ruled by sexual desire, their pure wives and daughters knew nothing of such matters. To be sure, as the historian Peter Gay has documented, a number of nineteenth-century women both experienced and expressed erotic pleasure. Nevertheless, in public it was generally agreed that on her wedding night, the angelic virgin should in one way or another behave in accordance with what was said to have been Queen Victoria's advice to her daughters: "Close your eyes and think of England." As for childbirth, the details of confinement and delivery constituted a secret knowledge that was to be limited only to those who had already delivered, and even for such initiates they were "functions" not to be dwelt upon at any length, certainly not in public.

At its most extreme, this nineteenth-century ideal of the frail, even sickly female ultimately led to a glorification of the dead or dying woman. The most fruitful subject for literature, announced the American romancer Edgar Allan Poe in 1846, is "the death . . . of a beautiful woman"; and four years later, in "The Blessed Damozel" (1850), the English poet Dante Gabriel Rossetti offered a postmortem vision of a seductive angel-lady leaning over the golden walls of heaven and yearning toward her earthly lover. But while dead women were fascinating, dying girl-children were even more enthralling: the extravagantly sentimental death scenes of Charles Dickens's "Little

Nell" (in *The Old Curiosity Shop*, 1840) and Harriet Beecher Stowe's "Little Eva" (in *Uncle Tom's Cabin*, 1851–52) are only two examples of brilliantly morbid melodramas that center on such figures. These episodes seem to bring to the surface an extraordinary imperative that underlay much of the nineteenth-century ideology of femininity: in one way or another, woman must be "killed" into passivity for her to acquiesce in what Rousseau and others considered her duty of self-abnegation "relative to men."

But what of women who refused to be passive or, just as problematic, were forced by circumstance into "unwomanly" activity? For nineteenth-century ideologists of femininity, these fell into two categories: subordinate working-class women and insubordinate middle- or upper-class ladies. About the first category, most ideologists had comparatively little to say: although the working-class woman could never be a lady—and indeed the verbal distinction between "woman" and "lady" was a crucial one—at her best she could reflect the lady's virtues. Though neither angelically delicate nor gracefully regal, she could still mimic the characteristics of such figures by making herself into a proletarian Madonna who submerged her own interests in those of husband and children, as Rousseau had advised the more-educated woman to do. Were she single, however, her situation was far more perilous, for whether she worked on a farm or in a factory, as a kitchen helper or a parlor maid, moralists feared that she was constantly in danger of becoming a "fallen woman," a prostitute. Dante Gabriel Rossetti's 1870 poem "Jenny" brilliantly articulates the horror felt by a representative middle-class speaker at the "poor flower" of "lazy laughing, languid Jenny, / Fond of a kiss and fond of a guinea," a golden-haired whore whose favors he himself has just enjoyed. The idealized lady was in some sense "sick"—fragile, pale, ethereal—but her fallen contemporary was figuratively sickening: her "beauty goads / A man tonight to think of toads!" And even the virtue of the lady is finally put in question by Jenny's troublesome vice. Though the young prostitute is "like a rose shut in a book / In which pure women may not look," the speaker confesses his belief that she and her respectable counterpart are really sisters under the skin: "Of the same lump (it has been said) / For honor and dishonor made, / Two sister vessels."

The anxious notion that the angel and the whore might be counterparts was a crucial one. Rossetti implicitly conceded that Jenny and others of her class may have been forced to "fall" by poverty or ignorance, but what of those who fell by their own free will? More particularly, what of those who fell not merely by demanding the sexual liberty that the Victorian double standard gave to men and forbade to women but by asserting just those emotional and intellectual needs that Rousseau thought should be sacrificed to the claims of husbands, fathers, and sons? As if to warn against such female insubordination, nineteenth-century novelists and poets, in both England and America, frequently counterpointed glowing portraits of angelic ladies with fearful depictions of demonic madwomen and murderesses or, less extravagantly but just as censoriously, biting portrayals of scheming sorceresses, social climbers, and female intellectuals.

Thackeray's delineation of the ambitious Becky Sharp in *Vanity Fair* (1848) was a fairly typical example of the way in which a number of nineteenth-century writers perceived a sharp-witted woman's refusal to be selfless as ultimately pernicious. Paralleling the figure of Amelia Sedley, an

almost maddeningly angelic heroine (at whom Thackeray also pokes fun), Becky is an apparently realistic character, embedded in the scrupulously observed minutiae of Victorian society. Yet her shrewd charm cracks open when Thackeray derisively reminds his readers that he hasn't "showed the monster's [i.e., Becky's] hideous tail above water." More explicitly fantastic portraits of unladylike ladies were juxtaposed to pictures of ethereal maidens to make similar points in other novels. For instance, the passionate self-will of Zenobia, the dark heroine of Nathaniel Hawthorne's *Blithedale Romance* (1852), is unfavorably compared to the spiritual self-abnegation of her half-sister Priscilla, and the first of these women is punished with a hideous death by drowning when she fails to accept her sometime lover's dictum that "woman is a monster . . . without man as her acknowledged principal." Similarly, Charles Dickens's fallen aristocrat, Lady Dedlock, is contrasted to her illegitimate but virtuous daughter, Esther Summerson, and horribly murdered in *Bleak House* (1853); the reader is clearly meant to understand that her punishment appropriately fits her early crime of sexual indulgence. Fictions by women were also haunted by such double images of female self-assertion and self-abnegation: Charlotte Brontë's Bertha Mason Rochester, the madwoman in *Jane Eyre* (1847), is the counterpart of the novel's decorous heroine, Jane, and Elizabeth Barrett Browning's Lady Waldemar, the villainness of *Aurora Leigh* (1857), is set against the poem's noble protagonist, Aurora. For both sexes, these sometimes stereotypical figures originated in an ideology of femininity that stipulated the moral possibilities of "woman's sphere" by defining conflicting extremes: angel and monster, virgin and whore.

The Reality of Female Life

Were Victorian wives and daughters in fact angels and queens, monsters and madwomen? A reading of the literature of the period would at first suggest that such sentimental or melodramatic figures were to be found in every other British and American drawing room. Yet although a few women no doubt tried to replicate some of these fictional prototypes in their own lives, it is unlikely that many succeeded, given the intransigent facts of their social, economic, and cultural status. Qualified, to be sure, by class and (in the United States and the British colonies) by race, the female situation in England and America continued to be as problematic as ever for most of the century.

Despite her ostensible power to rule, even the most queenly or angelic married lady had few legal rights. On her marriage, she, like her ancestresses from the Middle Ages on, became what the eighteenth-century English jurist Sir William Blackstone described as a *feme covert* (a "covered" woman, in Anglo-Norman), a phrase also used by earlier legal commentators. "By marriage," Blackstone declared in a magisterial passage that was repeatedly cited throughout the nineteenth century, "the very being or legal existence of a woman is suspended, or at least it is incorporated or consolidated into that of the husband, under whose wing, protection, and cover she performs everything, and she is therefore called in our law a feme covert." Such an obliteration of legal reality—or "civil death," as it was sometimes termed—was also the lot of American married women, for the traditions of English common law were long the foundations of colonial jurisprudence.

Practically speaking, the consequences of such a definition of the wife's status were drastic indeed. In the year 1800 and long into the century that followed, a married woman could not own property, even what she herself might have brought to the marriage or inherited after she was wed. Furthermore, her husband could, and sometimes did, will his estate—including what had been her own inheritance—away from her. Finally, if he died without having made a will, her rights in the property they might have jointly accumulated were minimal; the historian Eleanor Flexner has reported that in New York State, for instance, a widow was allowed nothing but the family Bible and a few other books, some cattle and household goods, and, no matter how many children she had, "one table, six chairs, six knives and forks, six tea-cups and saucers, one sugar dish, one milk-pot, one tea-pot, and six spoons." In addition, a husband's power over his wife's property extended to power over her earnings, such as they were.

A woman's children, too, were her husband's: he had sole rights in their guardianship if the couple were separated for any reason, including his moral turpitude. Nor was it easy for wives to escape even the worst husbands: until past the middle of the nineteenth century, divorce was virtually unobtainable in both England and America, except by extraordinary legislative or parliamentary decrees (almost all of which were enacted at the behest of husbands), and a woman did not even have an inalienable entitlement to her own physical liberty; as the British suffragist Ray Strachey pointed out, in England "the right of a man to imprison his wife in his own house was not questioned till 1891." Finally, the married woman's moral as well as legal obliteration was signaled by her inability until fairly late in the nineteenth century to either sue or be sued: her husband was held responsible for all her acts and debts as if she were minor, defective, or mentally ill.

In addition to legal denials and constraints, severe restrictions were imposed on women by education and social custom. On the face of it, Rousseau's prescription that a girl be taught to subordinate her interests to men's should not necessarily entail the relegation of young women to almost total ignorance. To converse intelligently with gentlemen, after all, it might seem that a girl would have to be taught history, mathematics, classics—all subjects her brothers had studied and of which presumably they might like to speak. In practice, though, middle- and upper-class female education meant a minimal instruction in modern languages and a study of drawing or watercoloring, embroidery, and music; joined to these was a strict training in "propriety," which, wrote the influential educator Hannah More in 1799, "is to a woman what the great Roman critic says action is to an orator: it is the first, the second, the third requisite."

As for more serious subjects, such fields as classics or mathematics were considered absolutely improper for women, though a few, notably Elizabeth Barrett Browning and George Eliot, were privileged to study them on their own. Rather, to complete the lady's training and render her figure "elegant," she was often strapped to a "backboard"—an iron collar fastened to a board and fixed over the shoulders—for many hours every day, while her less aristocratic but almost equally genteel middle-class sister might be obliged to spend many tedious hours embroidering homiletic samplers and reading aloud from the Bible. How a spirited upper-class girl responded to such an education is made clear in Barrett Browning's *Aurora Leigh*, where the poet-heroine describes the "cage-bird life" for which her aristocratic English aunt

educated her. Similarly, the reaction of a lively middle-class girl to the lugu-brious education in "propriety" offered by a charitable boarding school is dramatized in the great Lowood episode of Charlotte Brontë's *Jane Eyre*, in which pedagogical humiliations that the Brontë sisters themselves had to endure are vividly and movingly recounted.

Where law and education restricted many possibilities of intellectual development for nineteenth-century ladies, custom closed off almost all the rest. The very doctrine of woman's "sphere," for instance, implied that there was an almost unbridgeable gulf between the public world of politics and business, ruled by men, and the domestic world of the household, ostensibly "ruled" but, more accurately, inhabited by women. "Man for the field and woman for the hearth, / Man for the sword and for the needle she; / Man with the head and woman with the heart, / Man to command and woman to obey," intones a solidly old-fashioned king in Tennyson's *The Princess* (1847), and his precepts aptly summarize the guidelines by which middle- and upper-class married women lived: a lady could not go out alone, espe-cially not in the city and certainly not at night; her days were to be spent supervising her servants, doing needlework, and making or receiving visits; her mind was to be occupied largely with fashion and society and perhaps to some small extent with charitable projects.

To be sure, she did have to bear children, and she often bore a great many. Despite efforts by a few radical physicians on both sides of the Atlantic to educate the public about birth control, contraceptive methods were still primitive as well as obscure in the nineteenth century, so that if in theory a lady was an angel, she was often in practice transformed by multiple preg-nancies into a "poor animal," as Jane Austen pityingly described one young female relative. Once her children were born, however, and if they sur-vived—for infant mortality rates remained high throughout the century—they were handed over to nurses and governesses who did the major work of raising them, depriving the lady of at least one meaningful function she might have had. As the Industrial Revolution progressed and more newly wealthy entrepreneurial families rose into the middle and upper classes, moreover, the division of woman's sphere from man's became increasingly sharp. With more money to pay more servants, the lady's household duties virtually disappeared, and with man's work—once done in or near the home and shared by wives on farms or in family trades—now located in offices and factories, the two spheres were geographically as well as socially separated.

No wonder, then, that Florence Nightingale complained in 1852 that "women's life is spent in pastime, men's in business," adding bitterly:

> A married woman's life consists in superintending what she does not know how to do. . . . [She] is to direct the servants, who are to provide conveniences and luxuries not thought of formerly. She has never learnt, and does not know how, but she must take care to provide them. She must superintend the nurse, and the governess of her children, though she knows nothing and has learnt nothing of the nurse's work. And the governess . . . what is she to do? She must direct the characters of her pupils. How is she fit for it? . . . Over her, so little prepared, the mother so little prepared is to preside.

Nightingale's mention of the "little prepared" governess reminds us that it was not only married upper- and middle-class women who suffered from the

constraints of law, education, and custom: the situation of the unmarried woman of "gentle" birth was equally if not more difficult. She could only comparatively rarely, and in unusual circumstances, inherit property. Most fortunes in England (and America as well) devolved on eldest sons, and in England great estates were frequently "entailed" on the male line, so that in the absence of sons some distant male relative would inherit a man's property—precisely the situation that triggers the comic action of Jane Austen's *Pride and Prejudice* (1813). Under the circumstances, it is not surprising that most women would prefer the subjugation of matrimony to the uncertainties of spinsterhood, not surprising that mothers struggled, often desperately, to further their daughters' chances on the "marriage market." In *Pride and Prejudice*, Elizabeth Bennet's close friend Charlotte Lucas marries the obnoxious Reverend Collins for security rather than love, out of—as the author explained—the "pure and disinterested desire of an establishment." For, commented Austen in a letter, "Single women have a dreadful propensity for being poor, which is one very strong argument in favor of matrimony." And in fact, no matter how gentle her birth, a portionless young woman who did not wed was frequently obliged to live as a maiden aunt on the goodwill of male relations or married sisters, or else she survived on a meager income as what with uncharacteristic bitterness Austen called a "ridiculous old maid, the proper sport of boys and girls."

Worse still, if she had neither charitable relations nor a modest income of her own, such a woman was generally obliged to turn to the only genteel careers open to her: in England, governessing, and in England and America, schoolteaching. Ill-paid, badly trained, and overworked, both governesses and schoolteachers often lived lives of quiet desperation, dreaming of matrimonial rescue. The governess's lot was especially difficult: while the schoolteacher at least had some authority in her classroom, the governess, living with a single family, was continually subject to the whims of her employers, who often insisted that in addition to her instructional tasks she care for infants, do much of the family sewing, and perform countless other miscellaneous chores. What made the governess's situation even more problematic was her tendency to suffer from an anxiety that one social historian has termed "status incongruence": since she was herself of "good birth," she felt equal and akin to the family in which she lived, yet she was, after all, as much a servant as any kitchen maid. A contemporary observer commented that though "the Governess is a class rapidly on the increase" because such employment is "the only recourse left to young girls in the highest ranks of society who are forced to earn their living," the sorrowful practitioner of that profession "may be known at a glance from her plain and quiet style of dress" and from "a fixed sad look of despair" on her face.

One reason why the governess represented a class "on the increase" was the phenomenon of so-called redundant women in Victorian England. Historians speculate that the emigration of large numbers of single men to America and to the Commonwealth colonies had left nineteenth-century England with a disproportionate mass of single women: according to the Victorian social critic W. R. Greg, 30 out of every 100 British women were unmarried in 1851, and 12 were widows; altogether, he estimated that 1,148,000 women in England and Wales were, as he put it, "unnaturally" single. The problem of such female "redundancy" was endlessly discussed in

newspapers and magazines; according to contemporary statistics at least 25,000 of these hapless "old maids" mournfully resolved their difficulties by becoming governesses.

But as much as they may have deviated from the nineteenth-century ideology of femininity, the real lives of nineteenth-century upper- and middle-class women did not swerve quite so radically from literary stereotypes as did the lives of their working-class sisters. Whether married or single, working-class women were usually expected, indeed obliged, to labor in both the private and the public spheres. Before the Industrial Revolution, such women had lived hard enough lives—spinning, sewing, cooking, and sharing farmwork with their husbands, fathers, or brothers—but after 1800 their situation became even more difficult, in both England and America. Because women were often willing to work for lower wages and longer hours than men, factories in both countries depended heavily on female labor, a fact that aroused considerable male resentment. As the historian Sheila Rowbotham has observed, "One of the frequent complaints in the early stages of the Industrial Revolution was that although women and children could find work, the men could not." Whether a husband was employed or unemployed, however, the working-class wife was still his property—and his servant. After long hours of factory work, she still had her domestic duties to do; in addition, if her children were not old enough to go into factories themselves, she had to arrange for their care. Nursing mothers often rushed home during factory breaks to breast-feed their infants, but many, inevitably, weaned their babies as early as they could, feeding them what Rowbotham describes as "watered-down, often infected cow's milk," a formula that accounts, at least in part, for the high infant mortality rate among the working classes.

Women who labored in dressmaking or in the mines struggled with equally harsh conditions. Young seamstresses often worked virtually around the clock during the London season, crowded into dark, ill-ventilated rooms that one contemporary witness described as "worse than in the worst-conducted factories." "The dressmakers themselves," added this commentator, "state their belief that 'no man could sustain the labor which is imposed on these young and delicate women.' " The situation of women in the mines was, if anything, more extreme: according to a Mines Commission report (1842), even in the advanced stages of pregnancy, they "always did the lifting or heavy part of the work, and neither they nor the children [who labored alongside them] were treated like human beings." Testified one woman worker: "I have a belt round my waist and a chain passing between my legs and go on my hands and feet [pulling loads of coal]. . . . I have drawn till I have had the skin off me; the belt and chain is worse when we are in the family way."

Though the working conditions of female domestic servants (of whom there were 750,000 in England alone in 1851) were not so extreme, they were arduous, marked by low pay, long hours, and little leisure time—usually only one half day per week. Worse still, of course, were the living and working conditions of black slaves in America. Bred like cattle to produce crops of new workers, subject to sexual exploitation and harassment by their white masters, frequently separated from husbands and children, forced to perform endless hours of unpaid labor in cotton fields and plantation houses, these women were no doubt the most oppressed of all nineteenth-century female workers. Yet paradoxically, such diverse writers as the black memoirist Har-

riet Jacobs and the white novelist Harriet Beecher Stowe frequently see these women—forced to be single and to sustain families against overwhelming odds—as repositories of strength, even as heroic figures. And indeed, the career of the legendary Harriet Tubman, a former slave who became a "conductor" on the "Underground Railroad" that funneled southern blacks to freedom in the North, more than supported such a view. Called "Moses" by her contemporaries, Tubman undertook some nineteen journeys into slave territory and liberated at least three hundred people.

Along with black heroines like Harriet Tubman, the only women workers who might seem to have achieved a rough equality with men and some control over their own lives were the pioneer women who labored to settle the American West. These women worked together with their husbands, as agricultural women traditionally had in England; and while they were frequently exhausted by the hardships they encountered, they could at least in some sense reap the rewards of their labor. The French writer Alexis de Tocqueville described one such woman with admiration, praising her energetic offspring as "true children of the wilderness" and noting that "she does not regret what [their upbringing has] cost her." But the American suffrage leader Anna Howard Shaw was less celebratory in her recollection of her own mother's first encounter with the primitive cabin in the backwoods of Michigan where her father (who remained in Massachusetts to work in a textile mill) had sent his family: "Something within her seemed to give way and she sank upon the floor. She could not realize . . . that this was really the place father had prepared for us, that here he expected us to live."

If the married lady had no rights, the working-class woman had none either. The wages she earned were her husband's money, and she had no reciprocal claim on his earnings, nor did she have the right to leave or divorce him. On the contrary, as Ray Strachey reminds us, "If a man was displeased with the way his wife worked for him—or with any other aspect of her conduct—he had a perfect right to beat her with a stick, provided it was not thicker than his own thumb." Moreover, if the lady's education was a training in submissive "propriety," the working-class woman's education—if she had any at all—was a training in industrious submission. In England, parish or "ragged" schools, charitable institutions for poor children, taught girls sewing, knitting, and other household skills, along with just enough reading to enable them to study the Bible; at one such institution, children over five worked from 5:00 A.M. to 6:00 P.M. at a "manufactory" and then attended school. Similarly, in America poor girls were expected to sew and knit while their brothers studied arithmetic and other subjects. Moreover, for many girls in both countries—but especially in England—a job as a domestic "apprentice" took the place of formal schooling altogether. Theoretically, such children were being trained to be good servants, but in fact most were simply exploited as household "slaveys," expected at the ages of seven or eight to do a full day's work in the kitchen or the laundry. As for the young black girls who were slaves in America, they generally received no education at all but worked alongside their parents in the cotton fields and cookhouses of the South.

Considering how few attractive vocational or personal alternatives working-class women had in the nineteenth century, it is surprising that more did not "fall," like Rossetti's "languid Jenny," into a life of prostitution. In the

middle of the century, some contemporary observers estimated that there were approximately fifty thousand "streetwalkers" in London alone, and proportionally similar numbers may have been concentrated in other urban centers like Edinburgh, New York, Chicago, and New Orleans. The "unskilled daughters of the unskilled classes," as one historian has defined them, these were mostly young women who turned to what was called "the life" when they could not support themselves as seamstresses and domestics, or in the hope—futile, as they usually discovered—of earning extra luxuries and mimicking the glittering fashions of upper-class ladies. Many rapidly contracted syphilis and other venereal diseases; some married and retired or established businesses, including brothels, of their own; few achieved even the small comforts Rossetti characterizes his Jenny as possessing, and fewer still looked as stylish as the heroine of Thomas Hardy's sardonic "The Ruined Maid" (1866), who boasts to a roughly clad country cousin with chapped hands and a sunburned face that she is elegantly dressed and fair-complexioned because she is "ruined."

In fact, tattered and ill, most prostitutes were seen not only as diseased but as a source of disease, and worse still, every working-class woman was defined as potentially a prostitute. In England in 1864, 1866, and 1869 Parliament passed what were known as the Contagious Diseases Acts, legislation that empowered the police in certain districts to arrest any working-class woman on suspicion of prostitution and subject her to enforced gynecological examinations. If a woman refused such an examination, it was generally assumed she was guilty; if she consented to it, that acquiescence proved her culpability as well. (Men who might have been the customers of such women were not subject to similar treatment, though they too, of course, might be considered responsible for the spread of venereal disease.) Enforcing a double standard of morality that humiliated women while encouraging male sexual exploitation, the Contagious Diseases Acts may encapsulate the problematic reality that shadowed the nineteenth century's ideology of femininity. In particular, an anxiety about the female body led, on the one hand, to fantasies about the upper-class woman's rare spirituality and, on the other hand, to imaginings of the working-class woman's corrosive sexuality.

WOMAN'S REVOLUTION

The history of Western culture had always been marked by a notable dissonance between what we have here been calling the ideology of femininity and what we have just defined as the reality of women's lives. During the nineteenth century, however, this discrepancy between fiction and fact became so striking that it created precisely the revolution to which Higginson was alluding when he claimed in 1859 that "now Cinderella [is thinking] of putting on her royal robes." Historians have speculated that the egalitarian ideologies with which the era began, along with the impulses toward political reform that accompanied such ideologies, were essential to the battle for women's rights and votes that marked this century. Similarly, the demands of women for higher education and their eagerness to enter trades and professions were fostered by those radical ideas about the world; and the large-

scale social changes impelled by the Industrial Revolution forced many working-class women out of the home and into the factory, at the same time making a number of middle- and upper-class women unpleasantly aware of just how unproductive a "lady's" leisure was. Finally, the rebelliousness of even the most religious women was implicitly encouraged by the newly anti-hierarchical thinking associated with the so-called disappearance of God.

Rights and Votes

It is not surprising that women, and some men as well, should early have understood the feminist implications of the intellectual assumptions that underlay the French Revolution and also, to some extent, the American War for Independence. As early as 1819, the Chartists who assembled at the disastrous St. Peter's Fields meeting near Manchester to demand government attention to their plight included not only a number of working-class women but also some men who supported their right to join in political protests. By the early 1830s, French socialist and utopian thinkers had begun to proselytize in England for causes that included "the emancipation of women." Among the middle classes, too, similar ideas were stirring: in 1831, the *Westminster Review* published an anonymous article advocating female suffrage, and in 1832 a Member of Parliament presented a petition to the House of Commons, asking that "every unmarried female possessing the necessary pecuniary qualification . . . be allowed to vote."

At the same time, even the most apparently privileged aristocratic women had begun to become aware of the disadvantages of their sex, and as Ray Strachey observes, one of them brought about "the first legislative attempt to improve the position of women in England": Lady Caroline Norton, a dashing and witty London hostess, was divorced by her husband and denied custody of her children in 1836; in despair, she wrote a series of fierce pamphlets, including *The Natural Right of a Mother to the Custody of Her Child* (1837), which finally resulted in Parliament's passage of the Infants' Custody Act of 1839. Though "a timid and hesitating measure," as Strachey remarks, this bill was nevertheless a legal landmark: it actually conceded some rights to women, who had hitherto had none.

In the United States, it was the antislavery movement that most dramatically inaugurated a feminist groundswell. Beginning in the 1830s, countless American women were active in the struggle to emancipate the blacks in the South. Their participation ranged from work in the Underground Railroad, which helped escaping slaves to find their way to freedom, to membership in the first National Female Anti-Slavery Society, founded in 1837. Among the most prominent speakers for the abolitionist cause were the Grimké sisters, Sarah and Angelina, who early saw a connection between their own political powerlessness and the subjugation of slaves. If women were not allowed to speak in the public sphere, they argued, how could they bear witness to what they knew was just? "I surrender not our claim to equality," declared Sarah Grimké in 1838, emphasizing her belief that *"whatsoever it is morally right for a man to do, it is morally right for a woman to do."* In a sardonic poem titled "The Times That Try Men's Souls" (1837), her contemporary and co-worker Maria Weston Chapman surfaced the protofeminist beliefs that informed such a statement—women, she exclaimed with mock horror, have begun to assert their wishes and complaints:

They've mounted the rostrum; the termagent elves,
. . . taken a notion to speak for themselves,
And are wielding the tongue and the pen;
They've mounted the rostrum; the termagent elves,
And—oh horrid!—are talking to men!

A few years after Chapman wrote these lines, the untenable position of both American and English women who wanted to speak for the rights of slaves was powerfully dramatized by an event that occurred in London. A group of American women were denied the right to be seated as delegates to the 1840 World Anti-Slavery Convention. Nothing could have more effectively clarified the disparity between the male abolitionists' transatlantic rhetoric of liberation and the reality of their misogyny, a misogyny that seemed to their female colleagues a shocking shadow of more general social feelings about women. Eight years later, in 1848, two of the would-be delegates to the London Anti-Slavery Convention—Lucretia Mott and Elizabeth Cady Stanton—were among five women who called a meeting of their own at Seneca Falls, in New York State. The resulting Woman's Rights Convention revised the American Declaration of Independence to support the proposition that sometimes "in the course of human events it becomes necessary for one portion of the family of man to assume among the people of the earth a position different from that they have hitherto occupied."

Many other nineteenth-century women contributed to the feminist effort. In the United States, for instance, Margaret Fuller published her impassioned and influential *Woman in the Nineteenth Century* in 1845, while Lucy Stone began a brilliant career as what Eleanor Flexner calls a lecturer "on behalf of the oppressed," declaring: "I expect to plead not for the slave only, but for suffering humanity everywhere. ESPECIALLY DO I MEAN TO LABOR FOR THE ELEVATION OF MY SEX." By 1851, Susan B. Anthony had joined Stone, Mott, and Stanton as one of the leaders of the suffrage movement; Sojourner Truth had risen in Akron, Ohio, to speak for the rights of black women; Frances E. W. Harper had begun to write eloquent poetry demanding the liberation of slaves and women; and countless other American women, black and white, of all ages and classes, had become converts to "the cause." Their work was slow and arduous. They wrote pamphlets, made speeches, carried petitions from house to house in villages, towns, and cities throughout the nation; testified before legislative bodies that were frequently amused or hostile; and marched in demonstrations. Their struggle—the longest single political battle in American history—did not gain them the vote nationally for more than three-quarters of a century. Yet they did make progress in achieving some rights for women. By 1860, Married Women's Property Acts had been passed in fourteen states, including Massachusetts, New York, and Illinois, while a few states and territories (for instance, Wyoming and Utah in 1870, Colorado in 1893, and Idaho in 1896) gradually extended voting rights to women.

The U.S. movement had a specific transatlantic impact through a story about the first Worcester (Massachusetts) Women's Rights convention that was written in 1851 for the *Westminster Review* by Harriet Taylor, a young Englishwoman, who described the proceedings and stated the case for women's rights. In the same year, Taylor married the philosopher John Stuart

Mill, and in 1861 her husband composed his intensely feminist *The Subjection of Women*. Published in 1869, this influential work formulated arguments for female equality that became central to the British women's movement. The book's ideas, insisted Mill, were "acquired mainly through [his wife's] teaching." Though some critics have disputed this claim, it is at least clear that the couple had an egalitarian relationship, which was essential in shaping Mill's thought; and it was clear, too, that Taylor had lucidly summarized some important American feminist concepts.

Even before Mill had started to draft his feminist treatise, a number of Englishwomen had begun to organize committees for women's rights roughly comparable to the groups working in America. Foremost among these early pioneers was Barbara Leigh Smith, later Barbara Bodichon: in 1855 she undertook to circulate petitions in support of a Married Women's Property Act; in 1857 she was instrumental in founding a feminist paper called *The Englishwoman's Journal*; and in 1865, at a meeting of a Kensington Ladies' Discussion Society, she adopted a strong position in favor of women's suffrage, a position that led to the formation of England's first Women's Suffrage Committee. In 1866, a year after John Stuart Mill had been elected to Parliament, this group presented him with several petitions, containing thousands of signatures in support of votes for women, which enabled him to bring about the first parliamentary debate on women's suffrage—an action he himself defined as "by far the most important public service" he performed during his membership in the House of Commons.

Still, despite the energy and enthusiasm of Bodichon, Mill, and others, the progress of the woman's "revolution" was as slow in England as in America. The first Married Women's Property Act was defeated in 1856, and Parliament passed a far more conservative Marriage and Divorce Law in 1857, an act that served to defuse demands for the much-needed property bill. Similarly, the Contagious Diseases Acts of the 1860s, legislation that, as we noted, allowed the harassment of countless working-class women, were stubbornly defended by the government for several decades. Finally, despite a brilliant speech by Mill, the 1866 bill for women's suffrage received comparatively few votes. It was not until 1882 that a serious and effective Married Women's Property Act was passed in England, and not until 1886 that the Contagious Diseases Acts were formally repealed, after a long and vigorous campaign led by Josephine Butler. As for suffrage, by the 1870s and 1880s the battle in England had barely been joined; like their American sisters, Englishwomen would have to wait for the vote until after World War I.

Education, Trades, and Professions

Though feminist political and legal advances came only gradually and sporadically, nineteenth-century women did make extraordinary progress in other ways. The philosophy of human rights that shaped so many of the suffrage and abolition movements' assumptions proved an equally crucial influence on theories about women's education. In the United States, such thinkers as Emma Willard, Frances Wright, and Catherine Beecher, each in her own way, insisted on demanding serious training for girls, and in 1833 what is now Oberlin College became the first institution to admit young women "coeds." Perhaps an even more important milestone in the history of

women's fight for learning was the founding of Mount Holyoke in 1837. Mary Lyon, the school's principal, was determined to teach her students such varied (and heretofore masculine) subjects as rhetoric and logic, human physiology and "intellectual philosophy," astronomy and chemistry. A number of interested observers in New England and elsewhere were impressed, for the establishment of Mount Holyoke was followed by the opening of Vassar in 1865, of Smith and Wellesley in 1875, of the "Harvard Annex" (Radcliffe) in 1879, and of Bryn Mawr in 1885.

During these years, similar struggles for educational opportunities were being waged by women in England. In the 1840s, Christian Socialists concerned about the condition of governesses founded a Governesses' Benevolent Institution, designed to provide annuities for "ladies in temporary distress," but they discovered they could hardly meet the needs of all those who applied for assistance. Reasoning that if such women "could teach better they could command higher salaries," the founders initiated a series of "Lectures to Ladies," which by 1848 had evolved into Queens College for Women in London, a kind of adult education school that offered basic courses in literature, science, and philosophy.

In addition, just as American feminists fought for admission to Harvard and managed to establish Radcliffe as its "annex," so British feminists laid siege to the great universities of Cambridge and Oxford. Their leader in this struggle was Emily Davies, who worked for years to persuade first London University, and then Cambridge to admit women. Though she did not achieve her goal in London, she triumphed when in 1870 Girton College for Women, now part of Cambridge University, was established. A year later, Anne Jemima Clough, another pioneering educator, was instrumental in founding what is now Newnham College, Cambridge, and in the 1870s and 1880s two women's colleges—Somerville and Lady Margaret Hall—were established at Oxford. By 1884, women were allowed to study at both major British universities—though they were still, for many years, denied the right to earn formal degrees.

A natural consequence of women's entrance into higher education was an intensification of female interest in joining the professions. Perhaps its most dramatic manifestation was the fight of a few courageous young women to enter medical schools and become practicing physicians. Again, it was an American who led this battle: despite much opposition, Elizabeth Blackwell gained admission to Geneva College (in Geneva, New York) as a medical student and graduated at the head of her class in 1849. Journeying to Europe for further training, she met and was influenced by the young Florence Nightingale, and later she returned to England, where she supported the long but ultimately successful struggles of two English women, Elizabeth Garrett and Sophia Jex-Blake, to gain medical degrees of their own.

Of course, such accomplishments as medical degrees and university study were largely the prerogative of upper- and middle-class women. But working-class women, too, began to fight for their rights and to unite in newly vital ways during the nineteenth century, for the philosophy of human rights preached by Chartists in England and similar reformers in America influenced all classes. In Lowell, Massachusetts, textile workers edited and published a widely known magazine, *The Lowell Offering,* and, even more important, organized the Female Labor Reform Association, which served as

a model for a number of comparable groups that sprang up in other New England mill towns. Although working-class women were not quite so active in England, similar organizations were also established there throughout the century. In the 1830s, as Sheila Rowbotham notes, Female Reform Societies and Female Political Unions supported the protests of male workers, while in 1874 Emma Paterson formed the Women's Protective and Provident League and the National Union of Working Women to encourage female trade unionism. The passion for justice of these activist women on both sides of the Atlantic, like the feminist principles of their middle- and upper-class sisters, was aptly expressed by what Eleanor Flexner explains was "a parody on an old song, *I Can't Be a Nun*," which striking factory girls in Lowell, Massachusetts, sang as they marched through the town in 1836:

> For I'm so fond of liberty
> Oh, I cannot be a slave,
> I will not be a slave,
> For I'm so fond of liberty
> That I cannot be a slave.

A GOLDEN AGE OF WOMEN'S LITERATURE

It is no coincidence that this century of feminist revolution was a golden age of women's literature. In the nineteenth century, after a female—and, more particularly, a feminist—tradition had earlier begun to establish itself in the words and works of such writers as Anne Bradstreet, Anne Finch, and Mary Wollstonecraft, the female imagination flourished. Significantly, the women Virginia Woolf called "the four great novelists"—Jane Austen, Charlotte and Emily Brontë, and George Eliot—were all nineteenth-century artists and artists very much of their time. Similarly, the era produced such major poets as Emily Dickinson, Elizabeth Barrett Browning, and Christina Rossetti. Equally influential in their time, however, were popular writers who are now less canonical. In England these included the best-selling poets and novelists Charlotte Smith, Ann Radcliffe, Felicia Hemans, Letitia Landon ("L.E.L.") and Mary Elizabeth Braddon as well as the much-admired playwright-poet Joanna Baillie. Among their American counterparts were such widely-read writers as Lydia Sigourney, "Fanny Fern," Helen Hunt Jackson, and Louisa May Alcott. In addition, the century fostered the work of a range of political or quasi-political figures—Margaret Fuller, Harriet Beecher Stowe, Harriet Martineau, Frances E. W. Harper, and Florence Nightingale—as well as the compelling fiction of Mary Shelley, the wife of Percy Shelley and daughter of Mary Wollstonecraft and William Godwin, along with the work of the novelists Maria Edgeworth and Elizabeth Gaskell, whose achievements appear "minor" only when they are set against the extraordinary accomplishments of the Brontës, Austen, and Eliot. Clearly, the spirit of the age that motivated such activists as Mott and Stanton, Bodichon and Blackwell also inspired the imaginings of their literary sisters. Indeed, as their texts suggest, nineteenth-century women writers were no less haunted than American and English suffragists by the discrepancy between ideology and reality, a discrepancy that frequently forced these artists to tell tales of pain even while

it fueled their fantasies of freedom. Still, though the writings of nineteenth-century women in England and America often drew, implicitly or explicitly, on precisely the impulses that energized the contemporary women's movement, the nature of those writings cannot be completely understood in isolation from the literary achievements of nineteenth-century men.

Male and Female Traditions

As in earlier eras, women writers in the nineteenth century worked both with and against the grain of male aesthetic assumptions and practices. There were no toweringly great women Romantic poets contemporary with William Wordsworth and Samuel Taylor Coleridge, Percy Bysshe Shelley, Lord Byron, and John Keats, for instance, yet some women artists did write poetry that can clearly be identified as Romantic in its praise of the unspoiled beauty of wild landscapes, its commitment to the power of the imagination, and its philosophy of what the critic M. H. Abrams, following Thomas Carlyle, has called "Natural Supernaturalism." The poet-novelist Charlotte Smith, for instance, produced *Beachy Head* (1807), a long blank-verse meditation on nature; as well as *Elegiac Sonnets* (1784) that revived a verse form which had fallen into disuse while also pioneering the formation of the Romantic aesthetic. Similarly, the poet Mary Tighe authored a Spenserian narrative titled *Cupid and Psyche* (1805), which influenced John Keats's famous "Ode to Psyche" (1820).

At the same time, a number of the ideas articulated by the male Romantics (and earlier by Smith and Tighe), as well as some recurrent Romantic themes and images, had considerable impact on the nineteenth-century female contemporaries and descendants of writers such as Wordsworth and Byron. Obviously, the writings of such relatives of poets as Dorothy Wordsworth and Mary Shelley would reveal these influences: Dorothy Wordsworth's journals are marked by (and themselves influenced) exactly the steady, detailed, and reverent observations of nature that characterize her brother William's *Lyrical Ballads* (1798) and *The Prelude* (1850), while Mary Shelley's tales and novels, especially *Frankenstein* (1818), exhibit just the concern with issues of liberty and authority, will and imagination, that are dramatized in her husband Percy's *Prometheus Unbound* (1820) and *The Triumph of Life* (1824). Yet even Jane Austen, notable for preferring "sense" to "sensibility" (as her 1811 novel titled *Sense and Sensibility* demonstrates), had to confront questions about the world that were raised by both male and female Romantics: in her early, parodic *Northanger Abbey* (composed before 1803), for instance, she comically yet seriously considered the implications for women of the Gothic romances (most famously authored by Ann Radcliffe) that obsessed many of her contemporaries as well as the cult of the picturesque that so influenced the Romantics, while in her late *Persuasion* (1818) she meditated on just the relationships between individual desire and social authority that also interested her male contemporaries.

Paradoxically, however, it is in the work of such midcentury novelists as Charlotte and Emily Brontë that we can find the most vivid traces of Romanticism as it was defined by male poets from Blake to Byron and Shelley. *Jane Eyre*'s impassioned plea for social and spiritual liberty is, after all, both a Byronic assertion of the claims of the self and a Shelleyan demand for social transformation, while the characterization of Jane's darkly brooding lover,

Edward Rochester, clearly draws on the traits of such haunting Byronic heroes as Manfred and Childe Harold. In fact, the Byronic hero—a dashing yet Satanic rebel who seized the imagination of readers throughout Europe in the first decades of the nineteenth century—provided a model of simultaneously tempting and terrifying masculinity for many women writers, including, besides Charlotte Brontë, Charlotte's sister Emily. Heathcliff, the mysteriously demonic foundling whose vengeful passions trigger the plot of *Wuthering Heights* (1847), clearly derives much of his power from that Romantic paradigm even while his hellish energies recall the subversive intensity of earlier, quasi-mythic figures such as William Blake's Orc and Los.

At the same time, the Byronic hero also provided a pattern for a new character type: a Byronic *heroine*. Charlotte Brontë's rebellious Jane Eyre and Emily Brontë's fierce Catherine Earnshaw are each in her own way revisions of this brooding outcast who rejects any cultural commandments that fail to meet the needs of his or her own soul. Similarly, Elizabeth Barrett Browning's Aurora Leigh, at least at the moment when she refuses to acquiesce in Romney's demand that she abnegate her own ambition to become his helpmate, argues with defiant passion for the authority of her own desire, while Emily Dickinson, in a number of her most intensely rebellious poems, assumes a posture of Byronic alienation from God and man alike. Considering that most of these women artists were confronting exactly the dissonance between ideology and reality that their feminist-activist contemporaries were, it is not surprising that they should have adopted such a revolutionary stance. What is impressive is the inventiveness with which they transformed a male figure into a female (and implicitly feminist) model.

But of course Byronic Romanticism was only a single strain in the literary chorus heard by nineteenth-century women writers on both sides of the Atlantic. In the United States, that strain, modified by the writings of the Victorian sage Thomas Carlyle and by the ideas of German Romantic philosophers, modulated into the concept of "self-reliance," which was central to such Transcendentalists as Ralph Waldo Emerson and Henry David Thoreau, a concept that Margaret Fuller turned to feminist purposes in the brilliant polemics of "The Great Lawsuit," later published as *Woman in the Nineteenth Century*. In England, the questioning of authority that had marked the texts of all the British Romantics evolved into a Victorian skepticism about received theology and a commitment to serious public service in the complex world of the "here and now" that often nearly replaced traditional religious faith not only in the writings of Tennyson, Browning, and Carlyle himself but also in the works of George Eliot and Elizabeth Barrett Browning. In other words, throughout the century the male and female literary traditions in England and America continued to be both intertwined and interdependent.

Yet those traditions could not be identical, despite the connections that we can trace between them. For one thing, although a number of literary women did manage to achieve not only greatness but fame in the course of the age, most continued to experience precisely the anxieties about literary authority that had been expressed by such precursors as Anne Bradstreet and Anne Finch. That the powerful novelists Charlotte and Emily Brontë and Marian Evans had to publish their works under male pseudonyms (respectively, Currer and Ellis Bell and George Eliot) is one indication that such

anxieties persisted. That the ambitious poets Elizabeth Barrett Browning, Emily Dickinson, and Christina Rossetti had, in various degrees, to withdraw from the public world is another indication: Barrett Browning confined herself to a sickroom for more than a decade; Dickinson not only imprisoned herself in her "Father's house" (as she put it) but refused to publish; and Rossetti, at least metaphorically, immured herself in the convent of her own soul.

Finally, that a number of these writers, both novelists and poets, frequently followed Byronic assertions of ambition with qualifying avowals of renunciation—a phenomenon we can see in the works of women from Jane Austen to Emily Dickinson, from Charlotte Brontë to Christina Rossetti—is yet another sign of continuing anxiety. After all, if a "lady" was supposed to be an angel in the house, how could she allow herself to make the self-confident claims for her own creativity that empowered her male contemporaries? "I think I shall be among the English Poets after my death," John Keats had written in 1818, but his American descendant, Emily Dickinson—who may have felt equal certainty—had to be more careful in her self-definitions: calling herself "the slightest in the House," she remarked ironically that "they shut me up in Prose . . . Because they liked me 'still.' " Similarly, Christina Rossetti reminded herself in "The Lowest Room" that it was best to be "last," and George Eliot defined Dorothea Brooke, the protagonist of *Middlemarch* (1872) and perhaps this novelist's favorite heroine, as "the foundress of nothing."

Nevertheless, even while expressing and enacting such striking conflicts, these women did continue to write and, as we have already observed, they created what was in some sense a golden age of the female imagination. How did they do it? Clearly, they were energized by the unprecedented fact that they *did* have female precursors as well as a growing number of highly visible female contemporaries.

For novelists from Austen and the Brontës to Stowe, Eliot, and Alcott, there was a newly viable—and popular—genre in which they could work, a genre that had been developed by such precursors as Frances (Fanny) Burney and Anne Radcliffe, and that was in their own century to be exploited with great commercial success by best-selling writers including (in England) the sensational novelists Mary Elizabeth Braddon and Rhoda Broughton, and (in America) the sentimental novelists Susan Warner and Maria Cummins. That a sensational work like Braddon's *Lady Audley's Secret* (1862) was often scorned by elite male critics as merely a "thriller" and that a sentimental work like Warner's *The Wide, Wide World* (1850) was frequently dismissed as little more than a tearjerker could not disguise from readers of both sexes the fact that the female authors of these and other novels had become key presences in a literary marketplace hitherto primarily dominated by male writers and editors. Nathaniel Hawthorne's complaint in 1855 that his art was threatened by a "damned mob of scribbling women" represents the reaction of many men of letters to this new female commercial power, but— despite George Eliot's diatribe "Silly Novels by Lady Novelists"—many women of letters must have been encouraged rather than disturbed by such power.

Similarly, poets including Barrett Browning, Rossetti, and Dickinson must have been heartened by the examples of such well-known women poets as

Felicia Hemans, Letitia Landon (known as "L.E.L."), and many more. That some of these artists, like the popular novelists Braddon and Warner, were scorned as effusive and sentimental (the American Lydia Sigourney, for instance, was labeled "the Sweet Singer of Hartford") does not mean that their presence was not in some sense a strengthening one for, say, Barrett Browning and Rossetti (both of whom wrote elegies on the death of L.E.L.) and even for Dickinson (who frequently attempted to "rewrite" in her own style the hearts-and-flowers verses of women poets whose works she read in the *Springfield Gazette*). In addition, of course, ambitious writers like Dickinson and Rossetti were profoundly inspired by the powerful example of Barrett Browning, a poet whose work, unlike that of Sigourney and L.E.L., was so widely admired in the nineteenth century that she was very seriously considered for the position of English poet laureate after William Wordsworth died in 1850.

Besides the existence of significant precursors and contemporaries, however, the revolutionary social changes to which Mark Twain was referring when he remarked that the world had been transformed over the course of Queen Victoria's reign affected women writers at least as strongly as they affected male artists. Some of these women—for instance, the legendary speaker Sojourner Truth, the escaped slave Harriet Jacobs, and the feminist orator Elizabeth Cady Stanton—were integrally involved in the various public movements that brought about these changes. But even those women who lived less overtly political lives saw that the tumult of the age required a record, and Elizabeth Barrett Browning provided one in her verse-novel *Aurora Leigh* just as George Eliot did in *Middlemarch*, Rebecca Cox Jackson in her journal, Harriet Beecher Stowe in *Uncle Tom's Cabin*, Harriet Wilson in *Our Nig*, Florence Nightingale in *Cassandra*, and Rebecca Harding Davis in *Life in the Iron-Mills*. Working in all the forms in which their aesthetic brothers worked—the novel, the essay, the long poem, the sonnet, the lyric—these diverse artists wrote their way out of the female "sphere" to which they had been confined.

As their texts show, such nineteenth-century women writers were often only covertly subversive, producing decorous surfaces that erupted to reveal indecorous, even Byronic, passions for liberty, as if many had decided to follow Emily Dickinson's dictum to "Tell all the Truth but tell it slant." Yet their power was irrepressible. With Elizabeth Barrett Browning's poet-heroine Aurora Leigh, each would have asserted that "every creature, female as the male, / Stands single in responsible act and thought," and, also with Aurora, each would have insisted that "I too have my vocation,—work to do, . . . Most serious work, most necessary work / As any of the economists." Significantly, it was Barrett Browning herself who once lamented that she looked "everywhere for [poetic] grandmothers, and found none." But after she and the other female artists of her century had made their enduring contributions to our culture, no aspiring young woman writer would ever have to level such a complaint again. At least in literature, what Thomas Wentworth Higginson called an "epoch" reserved for "the genius of woman" had finally begun—an era that certainly did not exclude the contributions of men but at last also, definitively, included women's achievements.

MARIA EDGEWORTH
1768–1849

Maria Edgeworth was born at Black Bourton, Oxfordshire, the second of the twenty-one children of Richard Lovell Edgeworth, a brilliant, if eccentric, inventor and educator of Anglo-Irish descent. Her mother, Anna Maria Elers, was apparently the least loved of his several wives, and after her death in 1773, Maria Edgeworth grew up under the care of three successive stepmothers. After attending one school at Derby and another in London, she accompanied her father and her current stepmother to Ireland in 1782. On the family estate, Edgeworthstown, Richard Edgeworth completed her education first by instructing her himself, then by involving her in local politics, and finally by collaborating with her on *Practical Education* (1798), a book that demonstrates his interest in the pedagogic theories of the French philosopher Jean-Jacques Rousseau. Maria Edgeworth had already begun to teach her younger siblings and, at her father's request, to translate works of the conservative moralist Madame de Genlis.

When the publication of Edgeworth's translation of Genlis's *Adelaide and Théodore* was canceled because of the appearance of another English version, her father's friend Thomas Day wrote a congratulatory letter, for, as Maria Edgeworth explained later, he was basically of the opinion "that the extent of a woman's erudition should consist in her knowing her simple letters, without their mischievous combinations." Her first signed work, *Letters for Literary Ladies* (1795), appropriately begins with an exchange of letters between a liberal father and his conservative friend on the subject of female authorship. Although these figures, modeled on Richard Edgeworth and Day, contend over the propriety of women writing, they agree that women are meant to be wives and mothers, two roles Edgeworth would extol in her fiction and avoid in her life. Just as her early efforts repeat her father's opinions in fictional forms, her later work would gloss his social theories. Under the supervision of her father, she produced financially successful moral tales and children's stories that contemporary reviewers praised for their instructiveness. Although many critics have viewed her father's influence as a form of control, Marilyn Butler has argued that such a perspective derives from a hostile Victorian reading of his character and that he played a "subordinate position of supplier of detail, or the less exalted role of proof-reader."

During the same period in which she was writing *Letters for Literary Ladies,* Edgeworth entertained her family with specimens of the speech of their Irish steward. An early dramatic monologue grew into her most famous novel, *Castle Rackrent* (1800), a humorous but telling critique of exploitative Irish landlords recounted by a shrewdly observant family retainer. Her realism in portraying Irish customs and speech was unprecedented. It also shaped the later novel *The Absentee* (1812), which criticized absentee Irish gentry ashamed of their origins. By the end of her life, when she helped relieve sufferers during the Irish potato famine of 1845 to 1850, Edgeworth had become an honorary member of the Irish Royal Academy. Her contribution to Irish literature led Sir Walter Scott to declare that he hoped to attain for his country—Scotland—"the rich humor, pathetic tenderness, and admirable taste" she had "so fortunately achieved for Ireland."

Edgeworth had begun writing, she explained, "to please my father," and "to please him I continued." Although she traveled several times to London, France, and Switzerland, where, on one occasion, she rejected a marriage proposal, she focused in her novels on the conventions of the domestic life she led. With the publication of *Belinda* (1801) and *Ormond* (1817), Edgeworth extended the tradition first established in Frances Burney's novel of manners and later perfected in Jane Austen's comic fiction. Like Austen, Edgeworth wrote in the common sitting room; in fact, she sat at a desk on which her father later inscribed his view that "in these works which were chiefly

written to please me," his daughter had "improved and amused her own mind, and gratified her heart, which I do believe is better than her head." After his death, she completed only one novel and his *Memoirs of Richard Lovell Edgeworth, Esq.* (1820): without his presence she seemed to lack a motive for writing. But for the youthful Austen, Maria Edgeworth, like Burney, had succeeded in securing the status of the novel by producing works "in which the greatest powers of the mind are displayed, in which the most thorough knowledge of human nature, the happiest delineation of its varieties, the liveliest effusions of wit and humor, are conveyed to the world in the best-chosen language."

In its topical subject and subtle rhetorical maneuvers, "The Grateful Negro" demonstrates how Edgeworth became one of the most incisive as well as one of the most commercially successful novelists of her time. The work's analysis of moral issues pertaining to family ties, domestic responsibilities, and social duties extends this artist's characteristic concerns to the more exotic locale of Jamaica and the more atypical subject of a slave rebellion. Like many later literary women, Edgeworth uses her own high valuation of the family to critique a slave economy that abrogates family ties. Just as interesting is Edgeworth's analysis of the complex ethical effects of gratitude, affection, sympathy, and sentiment on master-slave relationships. Since Edgeworth's character Caesar achieves through his high moral sense the status of a royal slave, he bears comparison with Aphra Behn's hero in *Oroonoko.*

The Grateful Negro

In the island of Jamaica there lived two planters, whose methods of managing their slaves were as different as possible. Mr. Jefferies considered the Negroes as an inferior species, incapable of gratitude, disposed to treachery, and to be roused from their natural indolence only by force; he treated his slaves, or rather suffered his overseer to treat them, with the greatest severity.

Jefferies was not a man of a cruel, but of a thoughtless and extravagant temper. He was of such a sanguine disposition, that he always calculated upon having a fine season, and fine crops on his plantation; and never had the prudence to make allowance for unfortunate accidents: he required, as he said, from his overseer produce and not excuses.

Durant, the overseer, did not scruple to use the most[1] cruel and barbarous methods of forcing the slaves to exertions beyond their strength. Complaints of his brutality, from time to time, reached his master's ears; but though Mr. Jefferies was moved to momentary compassion, he shut his heart against conviction: he hurried away to the jovial banquet, and drowned all painful reflections in wine.

He was this year much in debt; and, therefore, being more than usually anxious about his crop, he pressed his overseer to exert himself to the utmost.

The wretched slaves upon his plantation thought themselves still more unfortunate when they compared their condition with that of the Negroes on the estate of Mr. Edwards. This gentleman treated his slaves with all possible humanity and kindness. He wished that there was no such thing as

1. *The Negro Slaves* [1796]—a fine drama, by [August von] Kotzebue. It is to be hoped that such horrible instances of cruelty are not now to be found in nature. Bryan Edwards, in his *History of Jamaica* [1793], says that most of the planters are humane; but he allows that some facts can be cited in contradiction of this assertion [Edgeworth's note]. Edwards's *The History, Civil and Commercial, of the British Colonies in the West Indies* contains a lengthy section on Jamaica.

slavery in the world; but he was convinced, by the arguments of those who have the best means of obtaining information, that the sudden emancipation of the Negroes would rather increase than diminish their miseries. His benevolence, therefore, confined itself within the bounds of reason. He adopted those plans for the amelioration of the state of the slaves which appeared to him the most likely to succeed without producing any violent agitation or revolution.[2] For instance, his Negroes had reasonable and fixed daily tasks; and when these were finished, they were permitted to employ their time for their own advantage or amusement. If they chose to employ themselves longer for their master, they were paid regular wages for their extra work. This reward, for as such it was considered, operated most powerfully upon the slaves. Those who are animated by hope can perform what would seem impossibilities to those who are under the depressing influence of fear. The wages which Mr. Edwards promised, he took care to see punctually paid.

He had an excellent overseer, of the name of Abraham Bayley, a man of a mild but steady temper, who was attached not only to his master's interests but to his virtues; and who, therefore, was more intent upon seconding his humane views than upon squeezing from the labor of the Negroes the utmost produce. Each Negro had, near his cottage, a portion of land, called his provision-ground; and one day in the week was allowed for its cultivation.

It is common in Jamaica for the slaves to have provision-grounds, which they cultivate for their own advantage; but it too often happens, that, when a good Negro has successfully improved his little spot of ground, when he has built himself a house, and begins to enjoy the fruits of his industry, his acquired property is seized upon by the sheriff's officer for the payment of his master's debts; he is forcibly separated from his wife and children, dragged to public auction, purchased by a stranger, and perhaps sent to terminate his miserable existence in the mines of Mexico; excluded forever from the light of heaven; and all this without any crime or imprudence on his part, real or pretended. He is punished because his master is unfortunate!

To this barbarous injustice the Negroes on Mr. Edwards' plantation were never exposed. He never exceeded his income; he engaged in no wild speculations; he contracted no debts; and his slaves, therefore, were in no danger of being seized by a sheriff's officer: their property was secured to them by the prudence as well as by the generosity of their master.

One morning, as Mr. Edwards was walking in that part of his plantation which joined to Mr. Jefferies' estate, he thought he heard the voice of distress at some distance. The lamentations grew louder and louder as he approached the cottage, which stood upon the borders of Jefferies' plantation.

This cottage belonged to a slave of the name of Caesar, the best Negro in Mr. Jefferies' possession. Such had been his industry and exertion, that, notwithstanding the severe tasks imposed by Durant, the overseer, Caesar found means to cultivate his provision-ground to a degree of perfection no where else to be seen on this estate. Mr. Edwards had often admired this poor fellow's industry, and now hastened to inquire what misfortune had befallen him.

2. [Edward's] *History of the West Indies*, from which these ideas are adopted—not stolen [Edgeworth's note].

When he came to the cottage, he found Caesar standing with his arms folded, and his eyes fixed upon the ground. A young and beautiful female Negro was weeping bitterly, as she knelt at the feet of Durant, the overseer, who regarding her with a sullen aspect, repeated, "He must go. I tell you, woman, he must go. What signifies all this nonsense?"

At the sight of Mr. Edwards, the overseer's countenance suddenly changed, and assumed an air of obsequious civility. The poor woman retired to the farther corner of the cottage, and continued to weep. Caesar never moved. "Nothing is the matter, sir," said Durant, "but that Caesar is going to be sold. That is what the woman is crying for. They were to be married; but we'll find Clara another husband, I tell her; and she'll get the better of her grief, you know, sir, as I tell her, in time."

"Never! never!" said Clara.

"To whom is Caesar going to be sold? and for what sum?"

"For what can be got for him," replied Durant, laughing; "and to whoever will buy him. The sheriff's officer is here, who has seized him for debt, and must make the most of him at market."

"Poor fellow!" said Mr. Edwards; "and must he leave this cottage which he has built, and these bananas which he has planted?"

Caesar now for the first time looked up, and fixing his eyes upon Mr. Edwards for a moment, advanced with an intrepid rather than an imploring countenance, and said, "Will you be my master? Will you be her master? Buy both of us. You shall not repent of it. Caesar will serve you faithfully."

On hearing these words Clara sprang forward, and clasping her hands together, repeated, "Caesar will serve you faithfully."

Mr. Edwards was moved by their entreaties, but he left them without declaring his intentions. He went immediately to Mr. Jefferies, whom he found stretched on a sofa, drinking coffee. As soon as Mr. Edwards mentioned the occasion of his visit, and expressed his sorrow for Caesar, Jefferies exclaimed, "Yes, poor devil! I pity him from the bottom of my soul. But what can I do? I leave all those things to Durant. He says the sheriff's officer has seized him; and there's an end of the matter. You know, money must be had. Besides, Caesar is not worse off than any other slave sold for debt. What signifies talking about the matter, as if it were something that never happened before! Is not it a case that occurs every day in Jamaica?"

"So much the worse," replied Mr. Edwards.

"The worse for them, to be sure," said Jefferies. "But, after all, they are slaves, and are used to be treated as such; and they tell me the Negroes are a thousand times happier here, with us, than they ever were in their own country."

"Did the Negroes tell you so themselves?"

"No; but people better informed than Negroes have told me so; and, after all, slaves there must be; for indigo,[3] and rum, and sugar, we must have."

"Granting it to be physically impossible that the world should exist without rum, sugar, and indigo, why could they not be produced by freemen as well as by slaves? If we hired Negroes for laborers, instead of purchasing them for slaves, do you think they would not work as well as they do now? Does

3. A blue dye made from plants.

any Negro, under the fear of the overseer, work harder than a Birmingham journeyman,[4] or a Newcastle collier, who toil for themselves and their families?"

"Of that I don't pretend to judge. All I know is, that the West India planters would be ruined if they had no slaves; and I am a West India planter."

"So am I; yet I do not think they are the only people whose interests ought to be considered in this business."

"Their interests, luckily, are protected by the laws of the land; and though they are rich men, and white men, and freemen, they have as good a claim to their rights as the poorest black slave on any of our plantations."

"The law, in our case, seems to make the right; and the very reverse ought to be done—the right should make the law."

"Fortunately for us planters, we need not enter into such nice distinctions. You could not, if you would, abolish the trade. Slaves would be smuggled into the islands."

"What! if nobody would buy them? You know that you cannot smuggle slaves into England. The instant a slave touches English ground he becomes free. Glorious privilege! Why should it not be extended to all her dominions? If the future importation of slaves into these islands were forbidden by law, the trade must cease. No man can either sell or possess slaves without its being known: they cannot be smuggled like lace or brandy."

"Well, well!" retorted Jefferies, a little impatiently, "as yet the law is on our side. I can do nothing in this business, nor can you."

"Yes, we can do something; we can endeavor to make our Negroes as happy as possible."

"I leave the management of these people to Durant."

"That is the very thing of which they complain; forgive me for speaking to you with the frankness of an old acquaintance."

"Oh! you can't oblige me more: I love frankness of all things! To tell you the truth, I have heard complaints of Durant's severity; but I make it a principle to turn a deaf ear to them, for I know nothing can be done with these fellows without it. You are partial to Negroes; but even you must allow they are a race of beings naturally inferior to us. You may in vain think of managing a black as you would a white. Do what you please for a Negro, he will cheat you the first opportunity he finds. You know what their maxim is: 'God gives black men what white men forget.' "

To these common-place desultory observations Mr. Edwards made no reply; but recurred to poor Caesar, and offered to purchase both him and Clara, at the highest price the sheriff's officer could obtain for them at market. Mr. Jefferies, with the utmost politeness to his neighbor, but with the most perfect indifference to the happiness of those whom he considered of a different species from himself, acceded to this proposal. Nothing could be more reasonable, he said; and he was happy to have it in his power to oblige a gentleman for whom he had such a high esteem.

The bargain was quickly concluded with the sheriff's officer; for Mr. Edwards willingly paid several dollars more than the market price for the two

4. One who works for another for day wages (Birmingham, England, experienced great industrial development and population growth in the 17th century).

slaves. When Caesar and Clara heard that they were not to be separated, their joy and gratitude were expressed with all the ardor and tenderness peculiar to their different characters. Clara was an Eboe, Caesar a Koromantyn[5] Negro: the Eboes are soft, languishing, and timid; the Koromantyns are frank, fearless, martial, and heroic.

Mr. Edwards took his new slaves home with him, desired Bayley, his overseer, to mark out a provision-ground for Caesar, and to give him a cottage, which happened at this time to be vacant.

"Now, my good friend," said he to Caesar, "you may work for yourself, without fear that what you earn may be taken from you; or that you should ever be sold, to pay your master's debts. If he does not understand what I am saying," continued Mr. Edwards, turning to his overseer, "you will explain it to him."

Caesar perfectly understood all that Mr. Edwards said; but his feelings were at this instant so strong that he could not find expression for his gratitude: he stood like one stupefied! Kindness was new to him; it overpowered his manly heart; and at hearing the words "my good friend," the tears gushed from his eyes: tears which no torture could have extorted! Gratitude swelled in his bosom; and he longed to be alone, that he might freely yield to his emotions.

He was glad when the conch-shell sounded to call the Negroes to their daily labor, that he might relieve the sensations of his soul by bodily exertion. He performed his task in silence; and an inattentive observer might have thought him sullen.

In fact, he was impatient for the day to be over, that he might get rid of a heavy load which weighed upon his mind.

The cruelties practiced by Durant, the overseer of Jefferies' plantation, had exasperated the slaves under his dominion.

They were all leagued together in a conspiracy, which was kept profoundly secret. Their object was to extirpate every white man, woman, and child, in the island. Their plans were laid with consummate art; and the Negroes were urged to execute them by all the courage of despair.

The confederacy extended to all the Negroes in the island of Jamaica, excepting those on the plantation of Mr. Edwards. To them no hint of the dreadful secret had yet been given; their countrymen, knowing the attachment they felt to their master, dared not trust them with these projects of vengeance. Hector, the Negro who was at the head of the conspirators, was the particular friend of Caesar, and had imparted to him all his designs. These friends were bound to each other by the strongest ties. Their slavery and their sufferings began in the same hour; they were both brought from their own country in the same ship. This circumstance alone forms, among the Negroes, a bond of connection not easily to be dissolved. But the friendship of Caesar and Hector commenced even before they were united by the sympathy of misfortune; they were both of the same nation, both Koromantyns. In Africa they had both been accustomed to command; for they had signalized themselves by superior fortitude and courage. They respected each other for excelling in all which they had been taught to consider as virtuous; and with them revenge was a virtue!

5. I.e., from Africa's Gold Coast. "Eboe": from Benin, a former kingdom of West Africa.

Revenge was the ruling passion of Hector: in Caesar's mind it was rather a principle instilled by education. The one considered it as a duty, the other felt it as a pleasure. Hector's sense of injury was acute in the extreme; he knew not how to forgive. Caesar's sensibility was yet more alive to kindness than to insult. Hector would sacrifice his life to extirpate an enemy. Caesar would devote himself for the defense of a friend; and Caesar now considered a white man as his friend.

He was now placed in a painful situation. All his former friendships, all the solemn promises by which he was bound to his companions in misfortune, forbade him to indulge that delightful feeling of gratitude and affection, which, for the first time, he experienced for one of that race of beings whom he had hitherto considered as detestable tyrants—objects of implacable and just revenge!

Caesar was most impatient to have an interview with Hector, that he might communicate his new sentiments, and dissuade him from those schemes of destruction which he meditated. At midnight, when all the slaves except himself were asleep, he left his cottage, and went to Jefferies' plantation, to the hut in which Hector slept. Even in his dreams Hector breathed vengeance. "Spare none! Sons of Africa, spare none!" were the words he uttered in his sleep, as Caesar approached the mat on which he lay. The moon shone full upon him. Caesar contemplated the countenance of his friend, fierce even in sleep. "Spare none! Oh, yes! There is one that must be spared. There is one for whose sake all must be spared."

He wakened Hector by this exclamation. "Of what were you dreaming?" said Caesar.

"Of that which, sleeping or waking, fills my soul—revenge! Why did you waken me from my dream? It was delightful. The whites were weltering in their blood! But silence! we may be overheard."

"No; everyone sleeps but ourselves," replied Caesar. "I could not sleep without speaking to you on—a subject that weighs upon my mind. You have seen Mr. Edwards?"

"Yes. He that is now your master."

"He that is now my benefactor—my friend!"

"Friend! Can you call a white man friend?" cried Hector, starting up with a look of astonishment and indignation.

"Yes," replied Caesar, with firmness. "And you would speak, ay, and would feel, as I do, Hector, if you knew this white man. Oh, how unlike he is to all of his race, that we have ever seen! Do not turn from me with so much disdain. Hear me with patience, my friend."

"I cannot," replied Hector, "listen with patience to one who between the rising and the setting sun can forget all his resolutions, all his promises; who by a few soft words can be so wrought upon as to forget all the insults, all the injuries he has received from this accursed race; and can even call a white man friend!"

Caesar, unmoved by Hector's anger, continued to speak of Mr. Edwards with the warmest expressions of gratitude; and finished by declaring he would sooner forfeit his life than rebel against such a master. He conjured Hector to desist from executing his designs; but all was in vain. Hector sat with his elbows fixed upon his knees, leaning his head upon his hands, in gloomy silence.

Caesar's mind was divided between love for his friend and gratitude to his master: the conflict was violent and painful. Gratitude at last prevailed: he repeated his declaration, that he would rather die than continue in a conspiracy against his benefactor!

Hector refused to except him from the general doom. "Betray us if you will!" cried he. "Betray our secrets to him whom you call your benefactor! to him whom a few hours have made your friend! To him sacrifice the friend of your youth, the companion of your better days, of your better self! Yes, Caesar, deliver me over to the tormentors: I can endure more than they can inflict. I shall expire without a sigh, without a groan. Why do you linger here, Caesar? Why do you hesitate? Hasten this moment to your master; claim your reward for delivering into his power hundreds of your countrymen! Why do you hesitate? Away! The coward's friendship can be of use to none. Who can value his gratitude? Who can fear his revenge?"

Hector raised his voice so high, as he pronounced these words, that he wakened Durant, the overseer, who slept in the next house. They heard him call out suddenly, to inquire who was there: and Caesar had but just time to make his escape, before Durant appeared. He searched Hector's cottage; but finding no one, again retired to rest. This man's tyranny made him constantly suspicious; he dreaded that the slaves should combine against him; and he endeavored to prevent them, by every threat and every stratagem he could devise, from conversing with each other.

They had, however, taken their measures, hitherto, so secretly, that he had not the slightest idea of the conspiracy which was forming in the island. Their schemes were not yet ripe for execution; but the appointed time approached. Hector, when he coolly reflected on what had passed between him and Caesar, could not help admiring the frankness and courage with which he had avowed his change of sentiments. By this avowal, Caesar had in fact exposed his own life to the most imminent danger, from the vengeance of the conspirators, who might be tempted to assassinate him who had their lives in his power. Notwithstanding the contempt with which, in the first moment of passion, he had treated his friend, he was extremely anxious that he should not break off all connection with the conspirators. He knew that Caesar possessed both intrepidity and eloquence, and that his opposition to their schemes would perhaps entirely frustrate their whole design. He therefore determined to use every possible means to bend him to their purposes.

He resolved to have recourse to one of those persons who, among the Negroes, are considered as sorceresses.[6] Esther, an old Koromantyn Negress, had obtained by her skill in poisonous herbs, and her knowledge of venomous reptiles, a high reputation among her countrymen. She soon taught them to believe her to be possessed of supernatural powers; and she then worked their imagination to what pitch and purpose she pleased.

She was the chief instigator of this intended rebellion. It was she who had stimulated the revengeful temper of Hector almost to frenzy. She now promised him that her arts should be exerted over his friend; and it was not long before he felt their influence. Caesar soon perceived an extraordinary change in the countenance and manner of his beloved Clara. A melancholy hung

6. Those knowledgeable in *obeah* practices of sorcery and magic ritual.

over her, and she refused to impart to him the cause of her dejection. Caesar was indefatigable in his exertions to cultivate and embellish the ground near his cottage, in hopes of making it an agreeable habitation for her; but she seemed to take no interest in any thing. She would stand beside him immovable, in a deep reverie; but when he inquired whether she was ill, she would answer no, and endeavor to assume an air of gaiety: but this cheerfulness was transient; she soon relapsed into despondency. At length, she endeavored to avoid her lover, as if she feared his farther inquiries.

Unable to endure this state of suspense, he one evening resolved to bring her to an explanation. "Clara," said he, "you once loved me: I have done nothing, have I, to forfeit your confidence?"

"I once loved you!" said she, raising her languid eyes, and looking at him with reproachful tenderness; "and can you doubt my constancy? Oh, Caesar, you little know what is passing in my heart! You are the cause of my melancholy!"

She paused and hesitated, as if afraid that she had said too much; but Caesar urged her with so much vehemence, and so much tenderness, to open to him her whole soul, that, at last, she could not resist his eloquence. She reluctantly revealed to him that secret of which she could not think without horror. She informed him, that unless he complied with what was required of him by the sorceress Esther, he was devoted[7] to die. What it was that Esther required of him, Clara knew not: she knew nothing of the conspiracy. The timidity of her character was ill-suited to such a project; and everything relating to it had been concealed from her with the utmost care.

When she explained to Caesar the cause of her dejection, his natural courage resisted these superstitious fears; and he endeavored to raise Clara's spirits. He endeavored in vain: she fell at his feet; and with tears, and the most tender supplications, conjured him to avert the wrath of the sorceress, by obeying her commands, whatever they might be!

"Clara," replied he, "you know not what you ask!"

"I ask you to save your life!" said she. "I ask you, for my sake, to save your life, while yet it is in your power!"

"But would you, to save my life, Clara, make me the worst of criminals? Would you make me the murderer of my benefactor?"

Clara started with horror.

"Do you recollect the day, the moment, when we were on the point of being separated forever, Clara? Do you remember the white man's coming to my cottage? Do you remember his look of benevolence—his voice of compassion? Do you remember his generosity? Oh! Clara, would you make me the murderer of this man?"

"Heaven forbid!" said Clara. "This cannot be the will of the sorceress!"

"It is," said Caesar. "But she shall not succeed, even though she speaks with the voice of Clara. Urge me no further; my resolution is fixed. I should be unworthy of your love if I were capable of treachery and ingratitude."

"But is there no means of averting the wrath of Esther?" said Clara. "Your life—"

"Think, first, of my honor," interrupted Caesar. "Your fears deprive you of reason. Return to this sorceress, and tell her that I dread not her wrath. My

7. Doomed.

hands shall never be imbrued in the blood of my benefactor. Clara! can you forget his look when he told us that we should never more be separated?"

"It went to my heart," said Clara, bursting into tears. "Cruel, cruel Esther!" Why do you command us to destroy such a generous master?

The conch sounded to summon the Negroes to their morning's work. It happened this day, that Mr. Edwards, who was continually intent upon increasing the comforts and happiness of his slaves, sent his carpenter, while Caesar was absent, to fit up the inside of his cottage; and when Caesar returned from work, he found his master pruning the branches of a tamarind tree that over-hung the thatch. "How comes it, Caesar," said he, "that you have not pruned these branches?"

Caesar had no knife. "Here is mine for you," said Mr. Edwards. "It is very sharp," added he, smiling; "but I am not one of those master who are afraid to trust their Negroes with sharp knives."

These words were spoken with perfect simplicity: Mr. Edwards had no suspicion, at this time, of what was passing in the Negro's mind. Caesar received the knife without uttering a syllable; but no sooner was Mr. Edwards out of sight than he knelt down, and, in a transport of gratitude, swore that, with this knife, he would stab himself to the heart sooner than betray his master!

The principle of gratitude conquered every other sensation. The mind of Caesar was not insensible to the charms of freedom: he knew the Negro conspirators had so taken their measures that there was the greatest probability of their success. His heart beat high at the idea of recovering his liberty: but he was not to be seduced from his duty, not even by this delightful hope; nor was he to be intimidated by the dreadful certainty that his former friends and countrymen, considering him as a deserter from their cause, would become his bitterest enemies. The loss of Hector's esteem and affection was deeply felt by Caesar. Since the night that the decisive conversation relative to Mr. Edwards passed, Hector and he had never exchanged a syllable.

This visit proved the cause of much suffering to Hector, and to several of the slaves on Jefferies' plantation. We mentioned that Durant had been awakened by the raised voice of Hector. Though he could not find anyone in the cottage, yet his suspicions were not dissipated; and an accident nearly brought the whole conspiracy to light. Durant had ordered one of the Negroes to watch a boiler of sugar: the slave was overcome by the heat, and fainted. He had scarcely recovered his senses when the overseer came up, and found that the sugar had fermented, by having remained a few minutes too long in the boiler. He flew into a violent passion, and ordered that the Negro should receive fifty lashes. His victim bore them without uttering a groan; but, when his punishment was over, and when he thought the overseer was gone, he exclaimed, "It will soon be our turn!"

Durant was not out of hearing. He turned suddenly, and observed that the Negro looked at Hector when he pronounced these words, and this confirmed the suspicion that Hector was carrying on some conspiracy. He immediately had recourse to that brutality which he considered as the only means of governing black men: Hector and three other Negroes were lashed unmercifully; but no confessions could be extorted.

Mr. Jefferies might perhaps have forbidden such violence to be used, if he had not been at the time carousing with a party of jovial West Indians, who thought of nothing but indulging their appetites in all the luxuries that art

and nature could supply. The sufferings which had been endured by many of the wretched Negroes to furnish out this magnificent entertainment were never once thought of by these selfish epicures. Yet so false are the general estimates of character, that all these gentlemen passed for men of great feeling and generosity! The human mind, in certain situations, becomes so accustomed to ideas of tyranny and cruelty, that they no longer appear extraordinary or detestable: they rather seem part of the necessary and immutable order of things.

Mr. Jefferies was stopped, as he passed from his dining-room into his drawing-room, by a little Negro child, of about five years old, who was crying bitterly. He was the son of one of the slaves who were at this moment under the torturer's hand. "Poor little devil!" said Mr. Jeffries, who was more than half intoxicated. "Take him away; and tell Durant, some of ye, to pardon his father—if he can."

The child ran, eagerly, to announce his father's pardon; but he soon returned, crying more violently than before. Durant would not hear the boy; and it was now no longer possible to appeal to Mr. Jefferies, for he was in the midst of an assembly of fair ladies, and no servant belonging to the house dared to interrupt the festivities of the evening. The three men, who were so severely flogged to extort from them confessions, were perfectly innocent: they knew nothing of the confederacy; but the rebels seized the moment when their minds were exasperated by this cruelty and injustice, and they easily persuaded them to join the league. The hope of revenging themselves upon the overseer was a motive sufficient to make them brave death in any shape.

Another incident, which happened a few days before the time destined for the revolt of the slaves, determined numbers who had been undecided. Mrs. Jefferies was a languid beauty, or rather a languid fine lady who had been a beauty, and who spent all that part of the day which was not devoted to the pleasures of the table, or to reclining on a couch, in dress. She was one day extended on a sofa, fanned by four slaves, two at her head and two at her feet, when news was brought that a large chest, directed to her, was just arrived from London.

This chest contained various articles of dress of the newest fashions. The Jamaica ladies carry their ideas of magnificence to a high pitch: they willingly give a hundred guineas[8] for a gown, which they perhaps wear but once or twice. In the elegance and variety of her ornaments, Mrs. Jefferies was not exceeded by any lady in the island, except by one who had lately received a cargo from England. She now expected to outshine her competitor, and desired that the chest should be unpacked in her presence.

In taking out one of the gowns, it caught on a nail in the lid, and was torn. The lady, roused from her natural indolence by this disappointment to her vanity, instantly ordered that the unfortunate female slave should be severely chastised. The woman was the wife of Hector; and this fresh injury worked up his temper, naturally vindictive, to the highest point. He ardently longed for the moment when he might satiate his vengeance.

The plan the Negroes had laid was to set fire to the canes,[9] at one and the same time, on every plantation; and when the white inhabitants of the island

8. Gold coins worth 21 shillings (i.e., a pound and a shilling), and the units in which luxury items were normally priced.
9. Sugarcanes.

should run to put out the fire, the blacks were to seize this moment of confusion and consternation to fall upon them, and make a general massacre. The time when this scheme was to be carried into execution was not known to Caesar; for the conspirators had changed their day, as soon as Hector told them that his friend was no longer one of the confederacy. They dreaded he should betray them; and it was determined that he and Clara should both be destroyed, unless they could be prevailed upon to join the conspiracy.

Hector wished to save his friend, but the desire of vengeance overcame every other feeling. He resolved, however, to make an attempt, for the last time, to change Caesar's resolution.

For this purpose, Esther was the person he employed: she was to work upon his mind by means of Clara. On returning to her cottage one night, she found suspended from the thatch one of those strange fantastic charms with which the Indian[1] sorceresses terrify those whom they have prescribed. Clara, unable to conquer her terror, repaired again to Esther, who received her first in mysterious silence; but, after she had implored her forgiveness for the past, and with all possible humility conjured her to grant her future protection, the sorceress deigned to speak. Her commands were that Clara should prevail upon her lover to meet her, on this awful spot, the ensuing night.

Little suspecting what was going forward on the plantation of Jefferies, Mr. Edwards that evening gave his slaves a holiday. He and his family came out at sunset, when the fresh breeze had sprung up, and seated themselves under a spreading palm-tree, to enjoy the pleasing spectacle of this Negro festival. His Negroes were all well clad, and in the gayest colors, and their merry countenances suited the gaiety of their dress. While some were dancing, and some playing on the tambourine, others appeared among the distant trees, bringing baskets of avocado pears, grapes, and pineapples, the produce of their own provision-grounds; and others were employed in spreading their clean trenchers, or the calabashes,[2] which served for plates and dishes. The Negroes continued to dance and divert themselves till late in the evening. When they separated and retired to rest, Caesar, recollecting his promise to Clara, repaired secretly to the habitation of this sorceress. It was situated in the recess of a thick wood. When he arrived there, he found the door fastened; and he was obliged to wait some time before it was opened by Esther.

The first object he beheld was his beloved Clara, stretched on the ground, apparently a corpse! The sorceress had thrown her into a trance by a preparation of deadly nightshade. The hag burst into an infernal laugh, when she beheld the despair that was painted in Caesar's countenance. "Wretch!" cried she, "you have defied my power; behold its victim!"

Caesar, in a transport of rage, seized her by the throat: but his fury was soon checked.

"Destroy me," said the fiend, "and you destroy your Clara. She is not dead: but she lies in the sleep of death, into which she has been thrown by magic art, and from which no power but mine can restore her to the light of life. Yes! look at her, pale and motionless! Never will she rise from the earth, unless, within one hour, you obey my commands. I have administered to

1. I.e., West Indian.
2. Hollowed gourds. "Trenchers": wooden platters.

Hector and his companions the solemn fetish oath, at the sound of which every Negro in Africa trembles? You know my object."

"Fiend, I do!" replied Caesar, eyeing her sternly; "but, while I have life, it shall never be accomplished."

"Look yonder!" cried she, pointing to the moon; "in a few minutes that moon will set: at that hour Hector and his friends will appear. They come armed—armed with weapons which I shall steep in poison for their enemies. Themselves I will render invulnerable. Look again!" continued she; "if my dim eyes mistake not, yonder they come. Rash man, you die if they cross my threshold."

"I wish for death," said Caesar. "Clara is dead!"

"But you can restore her to life by a single word."

Caesar, at this moment, seemed to hesitate.

"Consider! Your heroism is vain," continued Esther. "You will have the knives of fifty of the conspirators in your bosom, if you do not join them; and, after you have fallen, the death of your master is inevitable. Here is the bowl of poison, in which the Negro knives are to be steeped. Your friends, your former friends, your countrymen, will be in arms in a few minutes; and they will bear down everything before them—Victory, Wealth, Freedom, and Revenge, will be theirs."

Caesar appeared to be more and more agitated. His eyes were fixed upon Clara. The conflict in his mind was violent: but his sense of gratitude and duty could not be shaken by hope, fear, or ambition; nor could it be vanquished by love. He determined, however, to appear to yield. As if struck with panic, at the approach of the confederate Negroes, he suddenly turned to the sorceress, and said, in a tone of feigned submission, "It is in vain to struggle with fate. Let my knife, too, be dipped in your magic poison."

The sorceress clapped her hands with infernal joy in her countenance. She bade him instantly give her his knife, that she might plunge it to the hilt in the bowl of poison, to which she turned with savage impatience. His knife was left in his cottage, and, under pretence of going in search of it, he escaped. Esther promised to prepare Hector and all his companions to receive him with their ancient cordiality on his return. Caesar ran with the utmost speed along a bye-path out of the wood, met none of the rebels, reached his master's house, scaled the wall of his bed-chamber, got in at the window, and wakened him, exclaiming, "Arm—arm yourself, my dear master! Arm all your slaves! They will fight for you, and die for you; as I will the first. The Koromantyn yell of war will be heard in Jefferies plantation this night! Arm—arm yourself, my dear master, and let us surround the rebel leaders while it is yet time. I will lead you to the place where they are all assembled, on condition that their chief, who is my friend, shall be pardoned."

Mr. Edwards armed himself and the Negroes on his plantation, as well as the whites; they were all equally attached to him. He followed Caesar into the recesses of the wood.

They proceeded with all possible rapidity, but in perfect silence, till they reached Esther's habitation: which they surrounded completely, before they were perceived by the conspirators.

Mr. Edwards looked through a hole in the wall; and, by the blue flame of a cauldron, over which the sorceress was stretching her shriveled hands, he saw Hector and five stout Negroes standing, intent upon her incantations.

These Negroes held their knives in their hands, ready to dip them into the bowl of poison. It was proposed, by one of the whites, to set fire immediately to the hut, and thus to force the rebels to surrender. The advice was followed; but Mr. Edwards charged his people to spare their prisoners. The moment the rebels saw that the thatch of the hut was in flames, they set up the Koromantyn yell of war, and rushed out with frantic desperation.

"Yield! You are pardoned, Hector," cried Mr. Edwards, in a loud voice.

"You are pardoned, my friend!" repeated Caesar.

Hector, incapable at this instant of listening to anything but revenge, sprang forwards, and plunged his knife into the bosom of Caesar. The faithful servant staggered back a few paces: his master caught him in his arms. "I die content," said he. "Bury me with Clara."

He swooned from loss of blood as they were carrying him home; but when his wound was examined, it was found not to be mortal. As he recovered from his swoon, he stared wildly round him, trying to recollect where he was, and what had happened. He thought that he was still in a dream, when he saw his beloved Clara standing beside him. The opiate, which the pretended sorceress had administered to her, had ceased to operate; she wakened from her trance just at the time the Koromantyn yell commenced. Caesar's joy!— we must leave that to the imagination.

In the meantime, what became of the rebel Negroes, and Mr. Edwards?

The taking the chief conspirators prisoners did not prevent the Negroes upon Jefferies' plantation from insurrection. The moment they heard the war-whoop, the signal agreed upon, they rose in a body; and, before they could be prevented, either by the whites on the estate, or by Mr. Edwards' adherents, they had set fire to the overseer's house, and to the canes. The overseer was the principal object of their vengeance—he died in tortures, inflicted by the hands of those who had suffered most by his cruelties. Mr. Edwards, however, quelled the insurgents before rebellion spread to any other estates in the island. The influence of his character, and the effect of his eloquence upon the minds of the people, were astonishing: nothing but his interference could have prevented the total destruction of Mr. Jefferies and his family, who, as it was computed, lost this night upwards of fifty thousand pounds. He was never afterwards able to recover his losses, or to shake off his constant fear of a fresh insurrection among his slaves. At length, he and his lady returned to England, where they were obliged to live in obscurity and indigence. They had no consolation in their misfortunes but that of railing at the treachery of the whole race of slaves. Our readers, we hope, will think that at least one exception may be made, in favor of THE GRATEFUL NEGRO.

March 1802 1804

DOROTHY WORDSWORTH
1771–1855

"She did not cultivate the graces which preside over the person and its carriage," wrote Thomas De Quincy, remembering Dorothy Wordsworth, "But, on the other hand, she was a person of very remarkable endowments intellectually [and] what she knew and had really mastered lay where it could not be disturbed—in the temple of her own most fervid heart." As for her brother, William, one of the greatest of the Romantics, he declared in his autobiographical poem, *The Prelude*, that his sister, had "preserved me still a Poet." Earlier, in "Tintern Abbey" (1798), his powerful meditation on the redemptive powers of nature, he was more explicit. Addressing Dorothy as his "dearest Friend," he told her that "in thy voice I catch / The language of my former heart, and read / My former pleasures in the shooting lights / Of thy wild eyes."

Though she was hardly as childlike as that last quotation implies, the woman who elicited such praise was in fact her brother's "dearest Friend" for most of his life. Born in 1771, the only girl among five Wordsworth children, Dorothy Wordsworth was twenty-one months William's junior. After their mother's death when Dorothy was quite young, the girl was raised by various relatives and saw her brothers only occasionally. But in 1795, when she was twenty-four, William came into a legacy that enabled the two to settle together permanently, first in a cottage in Dorsetshire and then at Grasmere, in the English Lake District Wordsworth was to celebrate throughout his poetic career.

At Alfoxden, in Dorsetshire, Dorothy began the journals that she later continued at Grasmere and that constitute the achievement on which her own reputation chiefly rests today: she began them because, as she noted, "I shall give William Pleasure" by undertaking such a task. For many readers, then—as for Dorothy herself—the principal virtue of these works inheres in the source material they provided for the writer's brother, along with the William Wordsworth biography they record. As the critic Helen Darbishire once observed, they are important documents that show us "the life of a great poet." At the same time, however, Dorothy's diaries are extraordinarily compelling in and of themselves.

Vividly observed, often passionately frank, these journals are written with a hasty energy that perfectly captures the kaleidoscope of the Wordsworths' rural yet literary world. Though outwardly serene, that world was full of variety and vitality, as Dorothy continually demonstrates. Daily life alternated arduous domesticity with outdoor adventure: Dorothy baked pies, broiled beefsteaks, and climbed craggy hillsides in rainy weather. William brooded on new poems, and Dorothy soothed his headaches, then wandered along country roads where she met a host of beggars, tinkers, and other itinerants who would provide him with subjects for more poems and her with further observations. Throughout the *Journals*, her narration of such matters is unfailingly brisk yet extraordinarily meticulous. On parting with her brother, for instance, she noted that "after a flood of tears my heart was easier," then demonstrated her recovery with keen observations of wildflowers and of "a blind man, driving a very large beautiful Bull and a cow." Nor did she ever yield to excessive sentimentality, even about her adored William: she could not, for example, resist recording an episode in a meadow when the poet "took a sheep for me, and then me for a sheep."

On the day in October 1802 when William Wordsworth married Dorothy's best friend, Mary Hutchinson, his sister was so affected and conflicted—as her journal entry, included here, reveals—that she could not attend the wedding. Yet after the couple returned to Grasmere, Dorothy went on living with them, and there is every indication that the family was harmonious. Not only did Dorothy continue to "preserve" her brother as a poet but she became a fond nurse to his children, for whom

she wrote some accomplished verses. As these works suggest, and as the piece titled "Grasmere—A Fragment" also indicates, she may well have had considerable poetic ability of her own. Why she did not produce more verse than she did is thus a troublesome question, for, as her journals make clear, she was never merely her brother's literary handmaiden, though critics have often defined her that way. Perhaps, as Virginia Woolf was to speculate in *A Room of One's Own,* she turned her talents to prose because "the poetry" is often "denied outlet" in women. In any case, she continued writing her lively and scrupulously detailed journals until 1828. In 1829, she suffered a serious illness, and in several poignant poems included here—"Thoughts on My Sick-Bed" and "When Shall I Tread Your Garden Path?"—she laments her consequent frailty. By the mid-1830s, however, she was irreversibly afflicted with what seems to have been senile dementia, though she lingered on in what M. H. Abrams has called a kind of "half-life" for another twenty years, nursed by the sister-in-law to whom she had herself been such a faithful helper (despite her initial ambivalence about William's marriage) and also attended, for much of the time, by the brother to whom her own devotion had long been so important.

From The Grasmere Journals

1800

May 14 [Wednesday]. Wm and John set off into Yorkshire after dinner at ½ past 2 o'clock, cold pork in their pockets.[1] I left them at the turning of the Low-wood bay under the trees. My heart was so full that I could hardly speak to W. when I gave him a farewell kiss. I sate a long time upon a stone at the margin of the lake, and after a flood of tears my heart was easier. The lake looked to me I knew not why dull and melancholy, and the weltering on the shores seemed a heavy sound. I walked as long as I could amongst the stones of the shore. The wood rich in flowers. A beautiful yellow, palish yellow flower, that looked thick round and double, and smelt very sweet—I supposed it was a ranunculus—Crowfoot, the grassy-leaved Rabbit-toothed white flower, strawberries, geranium—scentless violet, anemones two kinds, orchises, primroses. The heckberry very beautiful, the crab coming out as a low shrub. Met a blind man, driving a very large beautiful Bull and a cow—he walked with two sticks. Came home by Clappersgate. The valley very green, many sweet views up to Rydale head when I could juggle away the fine houses,[2] but they disturbed me even more than when I have been happier. One beautiful view of the Bridge, without Sir Michael's.[3] Sat down very often, though it was cold. I resolved to write a journal of the time till W. and J. return, and I set about keeping my resolve because I will not quarrel with myself, and because I shall give Wm Pleasure by it when he comes home again. At Rydale a woman of the village, stout and well dressed, begged a halfpenny—she had never she said done it before, but these hard times—— Arrived at home with a bad headache, set some slips of privett.[4] The evening cold, had a fire—my face now flame-coloured. It is nine o'clock. I shall soon

1. The poet William Wordsworth (1770–1850) and his younger brother John (1772–1805), were on the way to visit Mary Hutchinson (1770–1859), whom William would marry two years later.
2. I.e., keep them out of view.

3. Rydal Hall, the estate of Sir Michael le Fleming (1748–1806).
4. I.e., arranged cuttings from a privet, a shrub commonly used in hedges.

go to bed. A young woman begged at the door—she had come from Manchester on Sunday morn with two shillings and a slip of paper which she supposed a Bank note—it was a cheat. She had buried her husband and three children within a year and a half—all in one grave—burying very dear—paupers all put in one place—20 shillings paid for as much ground as will bury a man—a stone to be put over it or the right will be lost—each time the ground is opened. Oh! that I had a letter from William!

* * *

1801

November 27 [*Friday*]. Snow upon the ground thinly scattered. It snowed after we got up and then the sun shone and it was very warm though frosty—now the sun shines sweetly. A woman came who was travelling with her husband—he had been wounded and was going with her to live at Whitehaven. She had been at Ambleside the night before, offered 4d[5] at the Cock for a bed—they sent her to one Harrison's where she and her husband had slept upon the hearth and bought a pennyworth of chips for a fire. Her husband was gone before very lame—"Aye" says she "I was once an officer's wife I, as you see me now. My first husband married me at Appleby. I had 18£ a year for teaching a school and because I had no fortune his father turned him out of doors. I have been in the West Indies. I lost the use of this finger just before he died he came to me and said he must bid farewell to his dear children and me. I had a muslin gown on like yours—I seized hold of his coat as he went from me and slipped the joint of my finger. He was shot directly. I came to London and married this man. He was clerk to Judge Chambray, *that man,* that man that's going on the Road now.[6] If he, Judge Chambray, had been at Kendal he would [have] given us a guinea[7] or two and made nought of it, for he is very generous." Before dinner we set forward to walk intending to return to dinner. But as we had got as far as Rydale Wm thought he would go on to Mr Luff's. We accompanied him under Loughrigg, and parted near the stepping stones.

* * *

December 22 [*Tuesday*]. Still thaw. I washed my head. Wm and I went to Rydale for letters. The road was covered with dirty snow, rough and rather slippery. We had a melancholy letter from C.,[8] for he had been very ill, though he was better when he wrote. We walked home almost without speaking. Wm composed a few lines of the Pedlar. We talked about Lamb's Tragedy[9] as we went down the White Moss. We stopped a long time in going to watch a little bird with a salmon coloured breast—a white cross or T upon its wings, and a brownish back with faint stripes. It was pecking the scattered Dung upon the road. It began to peck at the distance of 4 yards from us and advanced nearer and nearer till it came within the length of Wm's stick

5. Fourpence.
6. Journeying.
7. A gold coin worth 21 shillings (i.e., a pound and a shilling).
8. Samuel Taylor Coleridge (1772–1834), poet and friend of the Wordsworths.
9. *John Woodvil* (1802), by the essayist Charles Lamb (1775–1834). "The Pedlar": the poem later published as *The Excursion* (1814).

without any apparent fear of us. As we came up the White Moss we met an old man, who I saw was a beggar by his two bags hanging over his shoulder, but from a half laziness, half indifference and a wanting to try him if he would speak I let him pass. He said nothing, and my heart smote me. I turned back and said You are begging? "Ay," says he. I gave him a halfpenny. William, judging from his appearance joined in, I suppose you were a sailor? "Ay," he replied, "I have been 57 years at sea, 12 of them on board a man-of-war[1] under Sir Hugh Palmer." Why have you not a pension? "I have no pension, but I could have got into Greenwich hospital[2] but all my officers are dead." He was 75 years of age, had a freshish colour in his cheeks, grey hair, a decent hat with a binding round the edge, the hat worn brown and glossy, his shoes were small thin shoes low in the quarters, pretty good. They had belonged to a gentleman. His coat was blue, frock shaped coming over his thighs, it had been joined up at the seams behind with paler blue to let it out, and there were three Bell-shaped patches of darker blue behind where the buttons had been. His breeches were either of fustian or grey cloth, with strings hanging down, whole and tight; he had a checked shirt on, and a small coloured handkerchief tied round his neck. His bags were hung over each shoulder and lay on each side of him, below his breast. One was brownish and of coarse stuff, the other was white with meal[3] on the outside, and his blue waist-coat was whitened with meal. In the coarse bag I guessed he put his scraps of meat etc. He walked with a slender stick decently stout, but his legs bowed outwards. We overtook old Fleming[4] at Rydale, leading his little Dutchmanlike grandchild along the slippery road. The same pace seemed to be natural to them both, the old man and the little child, and they went hand in hand, the grandfather cautious, yet looking proud of his charge.

* * *

December 29 [*Tuesday*]. A fine morning. A thin fog upon the hills which soon disappeared. The sun shone. Wilkinson went with us to the top of the hill. We turned out of the road at the 2nd mile stone and passed a pretty cluster of houses at the foot of St. John's Vale. The houses were among tall trees partly of Scotch fir, and some naked forest trees. We crossed a Bridge just below these houses and the river winded sweetly along the meadows. Our road soon led us along the sides of dreary bare hills, but we had a glorious prospect to the left of Saddleback, half way covered with snow and underneath the comfortable white houses and the village of Threlkeld. These houses and the village want trees about them. Skiddaw was behind us and dear Coleridge's desert[5] home——As we ascended the hills it grew very cold and slippery. Luckily the wind was at our backs and helped us on. A sharp hail shower gathered at the head of Matterdale and the view upwards was very grand—the wild cottages seen through the hurrying hail shower. The wind drove and eddied about and about and the hills looked large and swelling through the storm. We thought of Coleridge. O the bonny nooks and windings and curlings of the Beck[6] down at the bottom of the steep green mossy Banks.

* * *

1. A warship.
2. The royal hospital for seamen.
3. Flour.

4. Thomas Fleming, an innkeeper at Rydale.
5. Deserted.
6. Creek.

1802

January 31 [Sunday]. William had slept very ill—he was tired and had a bad headache. We walked round the two lakes. Grasmere was very soft and Rydale was extremely beautiful from the pasture side. Nab Scar was just topped by a cloud which cutting it off as high as it could be cut off made the mountain look uncommonly lofty. We sate down a long time in different places. I always love to walk that way because it is the way I first came to Rydale and Grasmere, and because our dear Coleridge did also. When I came with Wm 6½ years ago it was just at sunset. There was a rich yellow light on the waters and the Islands were reflected there. Today it was grave and soft but not perfectly calm. William says it was much such a day as when Coleridge came with him. The sun shone out before we reached Grasmere. We sate by the roadside at the foot of the Lake close to Mary's dear name which she had cut herself upon the stone. William cut at it with his knife to make it plainer. We amused ourselves for a long time in watching the Breezes some as if they came from the bottom of the lake spread in a circle, brushing along the surface of the water, and growing more delicate, as it were thinner and of a *paler* colour till they died away. Others spread out like a peacock's tail, and some went right forward this way and that in all directions. The lake was still where these breezes were not, but they made it all alive. I found a strawberry blossom in a rock. The little slender flower had more courage than the green leaves, for *they* were but half expanded and half grown, but the blossom was spread full out. I uprooted it rashly, and I felt as if I had been committing an outrage, so I planted it again. It will have but a stormy life of it, but let it live if it can. * * * Mr Simpson drank tea with us. We payed our rent to Benson. William's head bad after Mr S. was gone. I petted him on the carpet and began a letter to Sara.

* * *

February 14 [Sunday]. * * * After dinner a little before sunset I walked out. About 20 yards above glowworm Rock I met a Carman, a Highlander I suppose, with 4 carts, the first 3 belonging to himself, the last evidently to a man and his family who had joined company with him and who I guessed to be Potters. The carman was cheering his horses and talking to a little lass about 10 years of age who seemed to make him her companion. She ran to the Wall and took up a large stone to support the wheel of one of his carts and ran on before with it in her arms to be ready for him. She was a beautiful creature and there was something uncommonly impressive in the lightness and joyousness of her manner. Her business seemed to be all pleasure—pleasure in her own motions—and the man looked at her as if he too was pleased and spoke to her in the same tone in which he spoke to his horses. There was a wildness in her whole figure, not the wildness of a Mountain lass but a *Road* lass, a traveller from her Birth, who had wanted[7] neither food nor clothes. Her Mother followed the last cart with a lovely child, perhaps about a year old, at her Back and a good-looking girl about 15 years old walked beside her. All the children were like the mother. She had a very fresh complexion, but she was blown with fagging up the hill with the steep-

7. Lacked.

ness of the hill and the Bairn[8] that she carried. Her husband was helping
the horse to drag the cart up by pushing it with his Shoulder. I got tea when
I reached home and read German till about 9 o'clock. Then Molly went away
and I wrote to Coleridge. Went to bed at about 12 o'clock. I slept in Wm's
bed, and I slept badly, for my thoughts were full of William.

* * *

March 4 [*Thursday*]. Before we had quite finished Breakfast Calvert's man
brought the horses for Wm.[9] We had a deal to do to shave—pens to make—
poems to put in order for writing, to settle the dress pack up etc. The man
came before the pens were made and he was obliged to leave me with only
two. Since he has left me (at ½ past 11) it is now 2 I have been putting the
Drawers into order, laid by his clothes which we had thrown here and there
and everywhere, filed two months' newspapers and got my dinner 2 boiled
eggs and 2 apple tarts. I have set Molly on to clear the garden a little, and I
myself have helped. I transplanted some snowdrops—The Bees are busy—
Wm has a nice bright day. It was hard frost in the night. The Robins are
singing sweetly. Now for my walk. I *will* be busy, I *will* look well and be well
when he comes back to me. O the Darling! Here is one of his bitten apples!
I can hardly find in my heart to throw it into the fire. I must wash myself,
then off—I walked round the two Lakes crossed the stepping stones at
Rydale Foot. Sate down where we always sit. I was full of thoughts about my
darling. Blessings on him. I came home at the foot of our own hill under
Loughrigg. They are making sad ravages in the woods. Benson's Wood is
going and the wood above the River. The wind has blown down a [?small]
fir tree on the Rock that terminates John's path—I suppose the wind of
Wednesday night. I read German after my return till tea time. After tea I
worked and read the LB, enchanted with the Idiot Boy.[1] Wrote to Wm then
went to Bed. It snowed when I went to Bed.

* * *

March 18 [*Thursday*]. A very fine morning. The sun shone but it was far
colder than yesterday. I felt myself weak, and William charged me not to go
to Mrs Lloyd's. I seemed indeed, to myself unfit for it but when he was gone[2]
I thought I would get the visit over if I could—So I ate a Beef-steak thinking
it would strengthen me so it did, and I went off. I had a very pleasant walk.
Rydale vale was full of life and motion. The wind blew briskly and the lake
was covered all over with Bright silver waves that were there each the twin-
kling of an eye, then others rose up and took their place as fast as they went
away. The Rocks glittered in the sunshine, the crows and the ravens were
busy, and the thrushes and little Birds sang. I went through the fields, and
sate ½ an hour afraid to pass a Cow. The Cow looked at me and I looked at
the Cow and whenever I stirred the Cow gave over eating. I was not very
much tired when I reached Lloyds, I walked in the garden. Charles is all for
agriculture. Mrs L. in her kindest way. A parcel came in from Birmingham,
with Lamb's play for us and for C. They came with me as far as Rydale. As

8. Baby. "Blown with fagging": i.e., tired out with
struggling.
9. In preparation for an expedition to Keswick, to
meet Coleridge.

1. One of William's contributions to *Lyrical Bal-
lads*, the book of poems that Wordsworth and Cole-
ridge published together in 1798.
2. To Keswick.

we came along Ambleside vale in the twilight—it was a grave evening—there was something in the air that compelled me to serious thought. The hills were large, closed in by the sky. It was nearly dark when I parted from the Lloyds that is, night was come on and the moon came out from behind a mountain mass of Black clouds—O the unutterable darkness of the sky and the earth below the moon! and the glorious brightness of the moon itself! There was a vivid sparkling streak of light at this end of Rydale water but the rest was very dark and Loughrigg fell and Silver How were white and bright as if they were covered with hoar frost. The moon retired again and appeared and disappeared several times before I reached home. Once there was no moonlight to be seen but upon the Island house and the promontory of the Island where it stands, "That needs must be a holy place"[3] etc. etc. I had many very exquisite feelings and when I saw this lowly Building in the waters among the Dark and lofty hills, with that bright soft light upon it, it made me more than half a poet. I was tired when I reached home. I could not sit down to reading and tried to write verses but alas! I gave up expecting William and went soon to bed. Fletcher's carts came home late.

* * *

April 15 [Thursday]. It was a threatening misty morning—but mild. We set off after dinner from Eusemere. * * * When we were in the woods beyond Gowbarrow park we saw a few daffodils close to the water side. We fancied that the lake had floated the seeds ashore and that the little colony had so sprung up. But as we went along there were more and yet more and at last under the boughs of the trees, we saw that there was a long belt of them along the shore, about the breadth of a country turnpike road. I never saw daffodils so beautiful they grew among the mossy stones about and about them, some rested their heads upon these stones as on a pillow for weariness and the rest tossed and reeled and danced and seemed as if they verily laughed with the wind that blew upon them over the lake, they looked so gay ever glancing ever changing. This wind blew directly over the lake to them. There was here and there a little knot and a few stragglers a few yards higher up but they were so few as not to disturb the simplicity and unity and life of that one busy highway.[4] We rested again and again. The Bays were stormy, and we heard the waves at different distances and in the middle of the water like the sea.

* * *

April 29 [Thursday]. A beautiful morning. The sun shone and all was pleasant. * * * We * * * went to John's Grove, sate a while at first. Afterwards William lay, and I lay in the trench under the fence—he with his eyes shut and listening to the waterfalls and the Birds. There was no one waterfall above another—it was a sound of waters in the air—the voice of the air. William heard me breathing and rustling now and then but we both lay still, and unseen by one another. He thought that it would be as sweet thus to lie so in the grave, to hear the *peaceful* sounds of the earth and just to know that our dear friends were near. The Lake was still. There was a Boat out.

3. Source unknown; possibly from an early version of Coleridge's "Kubla Khan" (1816).
4. Two years later William wrote a poem about the daffodils, "I Wandered Lonely as a Cloud," which appears to rely heavily on Dorothy's prose description.

Silver How reflected with delicate purple and yellowish hues as I have seen Spar. Lambs on the island and running races together by the half dozen in the round field near us. The copses greenish, hawthorn green.—Came home to dinner then went to Mr. Simpson. We rested a long time under a wall. Sheep and lambs were in the field—cottages smoking. As I lay down on the grass, I observed the glittering silver line on the ridges of the Backs of the sheep, owing to their situation respecting the Sun—which made them look beautiful but with something of strangeness, like animals of another kind— as if belonging to a more splendid world.

* * *

September 24. Mary first met us in the avenue. She looked so fat and well that we were made very happy by the sight of her. Then came Sara, and last of all Joanna.[5] Tom was forking corn[6] standing upon the corn cart. We dressed ourselves immediately and got tea—the garden looked gay with asters and sweet peas. I looked at everything with tranquility and happiness— was ill on Saturday and on Sunday and continued to be during most of the time of our stay. Jack and George came on Friday Evening 1st October. On Saturday 2nd we rode to Hackness, William Jack George and Sara single, I behind Tom. On Sunday 3rd Mary and Sara were busy packing. On Monday 4th October 1802, my Brother William was married to Mary Hutchinson. I slept a good deal of the night and rose fresh and well in the morning. At a little after 8 o'clock I saw them go down the avenue towards the Church. William had parted from me upstairs. I gave him the wedding ring—with how deep a blessing! I took it from my forefinger where I had worn it the whole of the night before—he slipped it again onto my finger and blessed me fervently. When they were absent my dear little Sara prepared the breakfast. I kept myself as quiet as I could, but when I saw the two men running up the walk, coming to tell us it was over, I could stand it no longer and threw myself on the bed where I lay in stillness, neither hearing or seeing anything, till Sara came upstairs to me and said "They are coming" This forced me from the bed where I lay and I moved I knew not how straight forward, faster than my strength could carry me till I met my beloved William and fell upon his bosom. He and John Hutchinson led me to the house and there I stayed to welcome my dear Mary. As soon as we had breakfasted we departed.[7] It rained when we set off. Poor Mary was much agitated when she parted from her Brothers and Sisters and her home. Nothing particular occurred till we reached Kirby. We had sunshine and showers, pleasant talk, love and cheerfulness. * * * It rained very hard when we reached Windermere. We sate in the rain at Wilcock's to change horses, and arrived at Grasmere at about 6 o'clock on Wednesday Evening, the 6th of October 1802. Molly was overjoyed to see us, for my part I cannot describe what I felt, and our dear Mary's feelings would I dare say not be easy to speak of. We went by candle light into the garden and were astonished at the growth of the Brooms, Portugal Laurels, etc. etc. etc. The next day, Thursday, we

5. The occasion is the marriage of William and Mary. All of Mary's sisters and brothers were present, but only three attended the wedding, apparently because Dorothy was overwrought.

6. Wheat.
7. Dorothy traveled back to Grasmere Cottage with William and Mary.

unpacked the Boxes. On Friday 8th we baked Bread, and Mary and I walked, first upon the Hill side, and then in John's Grove, then in view of Rydale, the first walk that I had taken with my Sister.

1800–03 1971

Grasmere—A Fragment

Peaceful our valley, fair and green;
 And beautiful the cottages
Each in its nook, its sheltered hold,
 Or underneath its tuft of trees.

5 Many and beautiful they are;
 But there is one that I love best,
A lowly roof in truth it is,
 A brother of the rest.

Yet when I sit on rock or hill
10 Down-looking on the valley fair,
That cottage with its grove of trees
 Summons my heart; it settles there.

Others there are whose small domain
 Of fertile fields with hedgerows green
15 Might more seduce the traveler's mind
 To wish that there his home had been.

Such wish be his! I blame him not,
 My fancies they, perchance, are wild;
I love that house because it is
20 The very mountain's child.

Fields hath it of its own, green fields;
 But they are craggy, steep, and bare;
Their fence is of the mountain stone,
 And moss and lichen flourish there.

25 And when the storm comes from the North
 It lingers near that pastoral spot,
And piping through the mossy walls,
 It seems delighted with its lot.

And let it take its own delight,
30 And let it range the pastures bare
Until it reach that grove of trees
 —It may not enter there!

A green unfading grove it is,
 Skirted with many a lesser tree,
35 Hazel and holly, beech and oak,
 A fair and flourishing company!

Precious the shelter of those trees!
 They screen the cottage that I love;
The sunshine pierces to the roof
40 And the tall pine trees tower above.

When first I saw that dear abode
 It was a lovely winter's day:
After a night of perilous storm
 The West wind ruled with gentle sway;

45 A day so mild, it might have been
 The first day of the gladsome spring;
The robins warbled; and I heard
 One solitary throstle sing:

A stranger in the neighborhood,
50 All faces then to me unknown,
I left my sole companion-friend
 To wander out alone.

Lured by a little winding path,
 I quitted soon the public road,
55 A smooth and tempting path it was
 By sheep and shepherds trod.

Eastward, toward the mighty hills
 This pathway led me on,
Until I reached a lofty Rock
60 With velvet moss o'ergrown.

With russet Oak and tufts of Fern
 Its top was richly garlanded;
Its sides adorned with Eglantine
 Bedropped with hips of glossy red.

65 There too in many a sheltered chink
 The foxglove's broad leaves flourished fair,
And silver birch whose purple twigs
 Bend to the softest breathing air.

Beneath that rock my course I stayed
70 And, looking to its summit high,
"Thou wear'st," said I, "a splendid garb,
 Here winter keeps his revelry.

"I've been a dweller on the plains,
 Have sighed when summer days were gone;
75 No more I'll sigh; for winter here
 Hath gladsome gardens of his own.

"What need of flowers? The splendid moss
 Is gayer than an April mead;
More rich its hues of various green,
80 Orange and gold and glowing red."

—Beside that gay and lovely rock
 There came with merry voice
A foaming streamlet glancing by,
 It seemed to say "Rejoice!"

85 My youthful wishes all fulfilled
 Wishes matured by thoughtful choice,
I stood an Inmate[1] of this vale,
 How could I but rejoice?

<div align="right">1892</div>

Thoughts on My Sick-Bed

And has the remnant of my life
Been pilfered of this sunny Spring?
And have its own prelusive[1] sounds
Touched in my heart no echoing string?

5 Ah! say not so—the hidden life
Couchant[2] within this feeble frame
Hath been enriched by kindred gifts,
That, undesired, unsought-for, came

With joyful heart in youthful days
10 When fresh each season in its Round
I welcomed the earliest Celandine
Glittering upon the mossy ground;

With busy eyes I pierced the lane
In quest of known and *un*known things,
15 —The primrose a lamp on its fortress rock,
The silent butterfly spreading its wings,

1. Inhabitant.

1. Introductory; perhaps an allusion to William Wordsworth's *Prelude* (not published until 1850, but undoubtedly known to Dorothy in the two ear-lier versions of 1798–99 and 1805).

2. Lying. "Hidden life": the phrase also appears in Samuel Taylor Coleridge's "To William Wordsworth" (1817), line 17.

The violet betrayed by its noiseless breath,
The daffodil dancing in the breeze,[3]
The carolling thrush, on his naked perch,
20 Towering above the budding trees.

Our cottage-heath no longer our home,
Companions of Nature were we,
The Stirring, the Still, the Loquacious, the Mute—
To all we gave our sympathy.

25 Yet never in those careless days
When spring-time in rock, field, or bower
Was but a fountain of earthly hope
A promise of fruits & the *splendid* flower.

No! then I never felt a bliss
30 That might with *that* compare
Which, piercing to my couch of rest,
Came on the vernal air.

When loving Friends an offering brought,
The first flowers of the year,
35 Culled from the precincts of our home,
From nooks to Memory dear.

With some sad thoughts the work was done,
Unprompted and unbidden,
But joy it brought to my *hidden* life,
40 To consciousness no longer hidden.

I felt a Power unfelt before,
Controlling weakness, languor, pain;
It bore me to the Terrace walk
I trod the Hills again;—

45 No prisoner in this lonely room,
I *saw* the green Banks of the Wye,
Recalling thy prophetic words,
Bard, Brother, Friend from infancy![4]

No need of motion, or of strength,[5]
50 Or even the breathing air:
—I thought of Nature's loveliest scenes;
And with Memory I was there.

May 1832 1978

3. An allusion to William's "I wandered lonely as a cloud" (1807); see also Dorothy's journal above, p. 451.
4. See William's "Tintern Abbey" (1798), lines 114–46.
5. Compare William's "A slumber did my spirit seal" (1800), line 5.

[When shall I tread your garden path?]

When shall I tread your garden path?
Or climb your sheltering hill?
When shall I wander, free as air,
And track the foaming rill?

5 A prisoner on my pillowed couch
Five years in feebleness I've lain,
Oh! shall I e'er with vigorous step
Travel the hills again?

1835 1978

JANE AUSTEN
1775–1817

In 1816, writing to her nephew about his fiction and her own, Jane Austen asked, "What should I do with your strong, manly spirited sketches, full of variety and glow?—How could I possibly join them on to the little bit (two inches wide) of ivory on which I work with so fine a brush, as produces little effect after much labor?" This modest deprecation of her miniature art recalls the discreet figure Virginia Woolf evokes in *A Room of One's Own*, an Austen who sits writing in the common sitting room, readying herself for inevitable interruptions by providing herself with a blotter under which she can hide her manuscript. Yet by the time Austen was corresponding with J. Edward Austen at her desk in the common sitting room, she had already published four of the six novels that would gain her immediate and lasting acclaim. *Northanger Abbey* (1818), *Sense and Sensibility* (1811), *Pride and Prejudice* (1813), *Mansfield Park* (1814), *Emma* (1816), and *Persuasion* (1818) are unprecedented achievements inaugurating the great novelistic tradition that continues in the work of Mary Shelley, the Brontës, George Eliot, and Virginia Woolf herself.

Although Austen did not publish until she was thirty-six years old, she had two periods of literary productivity, first in her father's rectory when she was in her teens and early twenties, and second at Chawton, during the last decade of her life. Though shrouded in obscurity, the biographical background of her achievement has always been considered singularly uneventful. The daughter of George Austen, a rector and schoolteacher, and Cassandra (Leigh) Austen, the niece of the master of Balliol College, Oxford, Jane Austen was the seventh of eight children. Five of her six brothers married, and their children participated in the lively correspondence Austen maintained throughout her life. But her most intimate companion and correspondent was her older sister, Cassandra, a painter who was also, according to Austen, "the finest comic writer of the present age." Although Jane, beginning at six, and Cassandra, at nine, were sent away briefly to three different schools, they received most of their education at home from their father. When Mr. Austen discontinued his school, the two sisters shared a sitting room, which included Jane's piano and notebooks and Cassandra's drawing implements. From this period, 1787–93, date such precocious juvenilia as *Love and Freindship* (Austen's youthful spelling) and *The Beautiful Cassandra*. Four years later, Austen also drafted *First Impressions* (1797), which was the

original version of *Pride and Prejudice*; *Elinor and Marianne* (begun in 1795), the original of *Sense and Sensibility*; and *Northanger Abbey* (begun in 1788 and sold in 1803 but not published in her lifetime). Whether performing in home theatricals or circulating her manuscripts, Austen found in her immediate family her first and most enthusiastic audience. And Austen's characters would be drawn almost entirely from her family's class, the country gentry that distinguished itself from both the growing commercial class and the wealthier aristocracy.

In 1801, Mr. Austen gave his Steventon living (his church office and the revenue attached to it) over to his eldest son, and moved with his wife and daughters to Bath. Either before or directly after leaving Steventon—the evidence is contradictory and unclear—Austen may have been in love with a young man who died, exactly the experience Cassandra had apparently endured in 1797. In any case, the subsequent death of her father in 1805 left her mother with an inadequate income of £210 a year, which was later raised by her brothers to the barely adequate sum of £450. After a short stay in Southampton, Mrs. Austen and her daughters settled down in a cottage on Edward Austen's estate. In what must have been confining circumstances at Chawton—living with her mother, Cassandra, an unmarried friend, and occasionally her brother James's daughter—Austen began revising and publishing her novels in rapid succession. Although she published anonymously, the immediate success of her fiction led to the identification of its author. Yet Austen managed to maintain a life of obscurity that Cassandra abetted after her sister's death by burning many of her letters. A year of an undetermined illness ended Austen's life when she was forty-two years of age. She was mourned by many relatives, but by none more grievously than her sister, who wrote, "She was the sun of my life, the gilder of every pleasure, the soother of every sorrow, I had not a thought concealed from her, and it is as if I had lost a part of myself."

Modesty and a desire for anonymity characterize Austen's most famous pronouncements, whether she is describing her subject ("three or four families in a country village") or defining herself ("the most unlearned and uninformed female who ever dared to be an authoress"). Yet she was well read in the eighteenth-century and Romantic classics of Richardson, Fielding, Pope, Goldsmith, Hume, Johnson, Scott, Cowper, and Byron. She was also an avid reader of books by her female contemporaries, especially Frances Burney, Mary Brunton, Ann Radcliffe, and Maria Edgeworth. Indeed, in works like *Love and Freindship, Volume the First,* and *Northanger Abbey,* she began to define herself as a writer by self-consciously satirizing not only the female tradition in literature but also its effects on the growth and development of the female imagination: focusing either on the sentimental romance and the epistolary form or the Gothic novel, Austen comically criticized the overvaluation of love, the miseducation of women, the subterfuges of the marriage market, the rivalry among women for male approval, the female cult of weakness and dependency, the discrepancy between women's private sphere and public (male) history. Precisely these themes, moreover, would inform her major novels.

From *Sense and Sensibility* to *Persuasion,* Austen delineated the lot of upper-middle-class girls who can escape the constraints of family life only by marrying. Just as the Dashwood sisters of *Sense and Sensibility* watch the family's fortune going to their half-brother, the Bennet daughters realize that their father's property has been entailed to a male cousin in *Pride and Prejudice,* Fanny Price in *Mansfield Park* is a poor dependent, and Anne Elliot of *Persuasion* is resigned to an impoverished spinsterhood. Even Austen's peremptory Emma, the heroine "whom no one but myself will much like," must learn to respect the ethical and economic authority of the well-named Mr. Knightley. Given the financial, social, and political power of men, Austen implies, female survival depends on gaining male approval and protection. As each heroine learns to distinguish among several apparently eligible suitors, Austen satirizes the bombastic self-importance of some clergymen, the autocratic pride of many aristocrats, the crudity of the nouveau riche, and, always, the flightiness of girls who

delude themselves into thinking they are the masters of their own or anyone else's fate. Beneath the bright, sparkling tone of the narrator's voice, then, Austen's "two inches of ivory" become, in Dorothy Van Ghent's phrase, "a lady's fan," which is "in substance an elephant's tusk; it is a savagely probing instrument as well as a master-piece of refinement." And Austen seems supremely confident about the scope and subject of her comedy. When, after the publication of *Emma*, the prince regent trans-mitted a message to her that she could "dedicate any future book to H.R.H." and his librarian suggested that it be "an historical romance illustrative of the august House of Cobourg," Austen explained, "I could not sit down seriously to write a serious romance under any motive than to save my life; and if it were indispensable for me to keep it up and never relax into laughing at myself or at any other, I am sure I should be hung before I finished the first chapter. I must keep to my own style and go on in my own way."

The limits Austen set for her art are exactly the limits she perceived as imposed on female experience. By analyzing the manners and morals of women whose lives were confined to the common sitting room, with exuberant hilarity in the juvenilia and a more ironic wit in the mature fiction, Austen provides a subtle portrayal of female values, a precise examination of female grief and joy. While a few readers, most famously Mark Twain and Ralph Waldo Emerson, took her own assessment at face value and faulted her fiction for its limitations, most have followed the example of such dissimilar artists as Scott, Macaulay, Tennyson, Trollope, Kipling, and Woolf in placing Austen's accomplishment next to Shakespeare's. For Woolf, Austen is ulti-mately "a mistress of much deeper emotion than appears upon the surface. She stim-ulates us to provide what is not there. What she offers is, apparently, a trifle, yet is composed of something that expands in the reader's mind and endows with the endur-ing form of life scenes which are outwardly trivial." Austen is, therefore, "the most perfect artist among women." Although fine television and film adaptations of Aus-ten's narratives have proliferated at the turn of the twenty-first century, *Love and Freindship* makes manifest the eminently literary qualities of her humor.

Love and Freindship: A Novel in a Series of Letters[1]

"Deceived in Freindship & Betrayed in Love"

Letter the First. From Isabel to Laura

How often, in answer to my repeated intreaties that you would give my Daughter a regular detail of the Misfortunes and Adventures of your Life, have you said "No, my freind never will I comply with your request till I may be no longer in Danger of again experiencing such dreadful ones." Surely that time is now at hand. You are this Day 55. If a woman may ever be said to be in safety from the determined Perseverance of disagreable Lovers and the cruel Persecutions of obstinate Fathers, surely it must be at such a time of Life.

Isabel

1. The epistolary novel (i.e., a novel cast as a series of letters) was a popular form in the 18th century, the most famous example being Samuel Richard-son's *Clarissa*; (1747–48) Austen is satirizing this extremely sentimental genre. Following R. W. Chapman, we have retained Austen's idiosyncratic spelling and capitalization throughout this text.

Letter 2d. Laura to Isabel

Altho' I cannot agree with you in supposing that I shall never again be exposed to Misfortunes as unmerited as those I have already experienced, yet to avoid the imputation of Obstinacy or ill-nature, I will gratify the curiosity of your daughter; and may the fortitude with which I have suffered the many Afflictions of my past Life, prove to her a useful Lesson for the support of those which may befall her in her own.

<div align="right">Laura</div>

Letter 3d. Laura to Marianne

As the Daughter of my most intimate friend I think you entitled to that knowledge of my unhappy Story, which your Mother has so often solicited me to give you.

My Father was a native of Ireland & an inhabitant of Wales; My Mother was the natural Daughter of a Scotch Peer by an italian Opera-girl[2]—I was born in Spain & received my Education at a Convent in France.

When I had reached my eighteenth Year I was recalled by my Parents to my paternal roof in Wales. Our mansion was situated in one of the most romantic parts of the Vale of Uske. Tho' my Charms are now considerably softened and somewhat impaired by the Misfortunes I have undergone, I was once beautiful. But lovely as I was the Graces of my Person were the least of my Perfections. Of every accomplishment accustomary to my sex, I was Mistress. When in the Convent, my progress had always exceeded my instructions, my Acquirements had been wonderfull for my Age, and I had shortly surpassed my Masters.

In my Mind, every Virtue that could adorn it was centered; it was the Rendezvous of every good Quality & of every noble sentiment.

A sensibility[3] too tremblingly alive to every affliction of my Freinds, my Acquaintance and particularly to every affliction of my own, was my only fault, if a fault it could be called. Alas! how altered now! Tho' indeed my own misfortunes do not make less impression on me than they ever did, yet now I never feel for those of an other. My accomplishments too, begin to fade—I can neither sing so well nor Dance so gracefully as I once did and I have entirely forgot the *Minuet Dela Cour*[4]

<div align="right">Adeiu</div>

<div align="right">Laura</div>

Letter 4th. Laura to Marianne

Our neighbourhood was small, for it consisted only of your mother. She may probably have already told you that being left by her Parents in indigent Circumstances she had retired into Wales on eoconomical motives. There it

2. Dancer in the ballet, which was then a regular part of all operas; these performers were thought to be of loose morals. "Natural": illegitimate.
3. A strong capacity for emotional response, highly valued especially by upper-class women.
4. "Minuet of the court," an elegant French dance popular at the time.

was, our freindship first commenced. Isabel was then one and twenty—Tho'
pleasing both in her Person and Manners (between ourselves) she never
possessed the hundredth part of my Beauty or Accomplishments. Isabel had
seen the World. She had passed 2 Years at one of the first Boarding schools
in London; had spent a fortnight in Bath & had supped one night in
Southampton.[5]

"Beware my Laura (she would often say) Beware of the insipid Vanities
and idle Dissipations of the Metropolis of England; Beware of the unmeaning
Luxuries of Bath & of the Stinking fish of Southampton."

"Alas! (exclaimed I) how am I to avoid those evils I shall never be exposed
to? What probability is there of my ever tasting the Dissipations of London,
the Luxuries of Bath or the stinking Fish of Southampton? I who am doomed
to waste my Days of Youth & Beauty in an humble Cottage in the Vale of
Uske."

Ah! little did I then think I was ordained so soon to quit that humble
Cottage for the Deceitfull Pleasures of the World.

<div align="right">

Adeui

Laura

</div>

Letter 5th. Laura to Marianne

One Evening in December as my Father, my Mother and myself, were
arranged in social converse round our Fireside, we were on a sudden, greatly
astonished, by hearing a violent knocking on the outward Door of our rustic
Cot.[6]

My Father started—"What noise is that," (said he.) "It sounds like a loud
rapping at the Door"—(replied my Mother.) "it does indeed." (cried I.) "I am
of your opinion; (said my Father) it certainly does appear to proceed from
some uncommon violence exerted against our unoffending Door." "Yes
(exclaimed I) I cannot help thinking it must be somebody who knocks for
Admittance."

"That is another point (replied he;) We must not pretend to determine on
what motive the person may knock—tho' that someone *does* rap at the Door,
I am partly convinced."

Here, a 2d tremendous rap interrupted my Father in his speech and some-
what alarmed my Mother and me.

"Had we not better go and see who it is,? (said she) the Servants are out."
"I think we had." (replied I.) "Certainly, (added my Father) by all means."
"Shall we go now?" (said my Mother.) "The sooner the better." (answered
he). "Oh! let no time be lost." (cried I.)

A third more violent Rap than ever again assaulted our ears. "I am certain
there is somebody knocking at the Door." (said my Mother.) "I think there
must," (replied my Father) "I fancy the Servants are returned; (said I) I think
I hear Mary going to the Door." "I'm glad of it (cried my Father) for I long
to know who it is."

I was right in my Conjecture; for Mary instantly entering the Room,

5. An English port city. Bath is an English resort 6. Cottage.
famous for its mineral springs.

informed us that a young Gentleman & his Servant were at the Door, who had lossed their way, were very cold and begged leave to warm themselves by our fire.

"Wont you admit them?" (said I) "You have no objection, my Dear?" (said my Father.) "None in the World." (replied my Mother.)

Mary, without waiting for any further commands immediately left the room and quickly returned introducing the most beauteous and amiable Youth, I had ever beheld. The servant, She kept to herself.

My natural Sensibility had already been greatly affected by the sufferings of the unfortunate Stranger and no sooner did I first behold him, than I felt that on him the happiness or Misery of my future Life must depend.

<div align="right">

Adeui

Laura

</div>

Letter 6th. Laura to Marianne

The noble Youth informed us that his name was Lindsay—for particular reasons however I shall conceal it under that of Talbot. He told us that he was the son of an English Baronet,[7] that his Mother had been many years no more and that he had a Sister of the middle size. "My Father (he continued) is a mean and mercenary wretch—it is only to such particular freinds as this Dear Party that I would thus betray his failings. Your Virtues my amiable Polydore (addressing himself to my father) yours Dear Claudia and yours my Charming Laura call on me to repose in you, my Confidence." We bowed. "My Father, seduced by the false glare of Fortune and the Deluding Pomp of Title, insisted on my giving my hand to Lady Dorothea. No never exclaimed I. Lady Dorothea is lovely and Engaging; I prefer no woman to her; but know Sir, that I scorn to marry her in compliance with your wishes. No! Never shall it be said that I obliged my Father."

We all admired the noble Manliness of his reply. He continued.

"Sir Edward was surprized; he had perhaps little expected to meet with so spirited an opposition to his will.

Where Edward in the name of wonder (said he) did you pick up this unmeaning Gibberish? You have been studying Novels I suspect.

I scorned to answer: it would have been beneath my Dignity. I mounted my Horse and followed by my faithful William set forwards for my Aunts."

"My Father's house is situated in Bedfordshire my Aunt's in Middlesex, and tho' I flatter myself with being a tolerable proficienz in Geography, I know not how it happened, but I found myself entering this beautiful Vale which I find is in South Wales, when I had expected to have reached my Aunts.[8]

"After having wandered some time on the Banks of the Uske without knowing which way to go, I began to lament my cruel Destiny in the bitterest and most pathetic Manner. It was now perfectly dark, not a single Star was there to direct my steps, and I know not what might have befallen me had I not at length discerned thro' the solemn Gloom that surrounded me a distant Light, which as I approached it, I discovered to be the chearfull Blaze of your fire. Impelled by the combination of Misfortunes under which I laboured, namely

7. One of the less prestigious British titles.
8. Instead of traveling south less than 40 miles, he went almost 100 miles west.

Fear, Cold and Hunger I hesitated not to ask admittance which at length I have gained; and now my Adorable Laura (continued he taking my Hand) when may I hope to receive that reward of all the painfull sufferings I have undergone during the course of my Attachment to you, to which I have ever aspired? Oh! when will you reward me with Yourself?"

"This instant, Dear and Amiable Edward." (replied I.). We were immediately united by my Father, who tho' he had never taken orders had been bred to the Church.

<div align="right">Adeui</div>

<div align="right">Laura</div>

Letter 7th. Laura to Marianne

We remained but a few Days after our Marriage, in the Vale of Uske. After taking an affecting Farewell of my father, my Mother and my Isabel, I accompanied Edward to his Aunt's in Middlesex. Philippa received us both with every expression of affectionate Love. My arrival was indeed a most agreable surprize to her as she had not only been totally ignorant of my Marriage with her Nephew, but had never even had the slightest idea of there being such a person in the World.

Augusta, the sister of Edward was on a visit to her when we arrived. I found her exactly what her Brother had described her to be—of the middle size. She received me with equal surprize though not with equal Cordiality, as Philippa. There was a Disagreable Coldness and Forbidding Reserve in her reception of me which was equally Distressing and Unexpected. None of that interesting Sensibility or amiable Simpathy in her Manners and Address to me which should have Distinguished our introduction to each other. Her Language was neither warm, nor affectionate, her expressions of regard were neither animated nor cordial; her arms were not opened to receive me to her Heart, tho' my own were extended to press her to mine.

A short Conversation between Augusta and her Brother, which I accidentally overheard encreased my Dislike to her, and convinced me that her Heart was no more formed for the soft ties of Love than for the endearing intercourse of Freindship.

"But do you think that my Father will ever be reconciled to this imprudent connection?" (said Augusta.)

"Augusta (replied the noble Youth) I thought you had a better opinion of me, than to imagine I would so abjectly degrade myself as to consider my Father's Concurrence in any of my Affairs, either of Consequence or concern to me. Tell me Augusta tell me with sincerity; did you ever know me consult his inclinations or follow his Advice in the least trifling Particular since the age of fifteen?"

"Edward (replied she) you are surely too diffident in your own praise. Since you were fifteen only!—My Dear Brother since you were five years old, I entirely acquit you of ever having willingly contributed to the Satisfaction of your Father. But still I am not without apprehensions of your being shortly obliged to degrade yourself in your own eyes by seeking a Support for your Wife in the Generosity of Sir Edward."

"Never, never Augusta will I so demean myself. (said Edward). Support! What Support will Laura want which she can receive from him?"

"Only those very insignificant ones of Victuals and Drink." (answered she.)

"Victuals and Drink! (replied my Husband in a most nobly contemtuous Manner) and dost thou then imagine that there is no other support for an exalted Mind (such as is my Laura's) than the mean and indelicate employment of Eating and Drinking?"

"None that I know of, so efficacious." (returned Augusta).

"And did you then never feel the pleasing Pangs of Love, Augusta? (replied my Edward). Does it appear impossible to your vile and corrupted Palate, to exist on Love? Can you not conceive the Luxury of living in every Distress that Poverty can inflict, with the object of your tenderest Affection?"

"You are too ridiculous (said Augusta) to argue with; perhaps however you may in time be convinced that. . . ."

Here I was prevented from hearing the remainder of her Speech, by the Appearance of a very Handsome Young Woman, who was ushered into the Room at the Door of which I had been listening. On hearing her announced by the Name of "Lady Dorothea", I instantly quitted my Post and followed her into the Parlour, for I well remembered that she was the Lady, proposed as a Wife for my Edward by the Cruel and Unrelenting Baronet.

Altho' Lady Dorothea's visit was nominally to Philippa and Augusta, yet I have some reason to imagine that (acquainted with the Marriage and arrival of Edward) to see me was a principal motive to it.

I soon perceived that though lovely and Elegant in her Person and tho' Easy and Polite in her Address, she was of that inferior order of Beings with regard to Delicate feeling, tender Sentiments, and refined Sensibility, of which Augusta was one.

She staid but half an hour and neither in the Course of her Visit, confided to me any of her Secret thoughts, nor requested me to confide in her, any of mine. You will easily imagine therefore my Dear Marianne that I could not feel any ardent Affection or very sincere Attachment for Lady Dorothea.

<div style="text-align: right">

Adeiu

Laura

</div>

Letter 8th. Laura to Marianne, in continuation

Lady Dorothea had not left us long before another visitor as unexpected a one as her Ladyship, was announced. It was Sir Edward, who informed by Augusta of her Brother's marriage, came doubtless to reproach him for having dared to unite himself to me without his Knowledge. But Edward foreseeing his Design, approached him with heroic fortitude as soon as he entered the Room, and addressed him in the following Manner.

"Sir Edward, I know the motive of your Journey here—You come with the base Design of reproaching me for having entered into an indissoluble engagement with my Laura without your Consent—But Sir, I glory in the Act—. It is my greatest boast that I have incurred the Displeasure of my Father!"

So saying, he took my hand and whilst Sir Edward, Philippa, and Augusta were doubtless reflecting with Admiration on his undaunted Bravery, led me from the Parlor to his Father's Carriage, which yet remained at the Door and in which we were instantly conveyed from the pursuit of Sir Edward.

The Postilions[9] had at first received orders only to take the London road; as soon as we had sufficiently reflected However, we ordered them to Drive to M——, the seat of Edward's most particular freind, which was but a few miles distant.

At M——. we arrived in a few hours; and on sending in our names were immediately admitted to Sophia, the Wife of Edward's freind. After having been deprived during the course of 3 weeks of a real freind (for such I term your Mother) imagine my transports[1] at beholding one, most truly worthy of the Name. Sophia was rather above the middle size; most elegantly formed. A soft Languor spread over her lovely features, but increased their Beauty.— It was the Charectarestic of her Mind—. She was all Sensibility and Feeling. We flew into each others arms & after having exchanged vows of mutual Freindship for the rest of our Lives, instantly unfolded to each other the most inward Secrets of our Hearts—. We were interrupted in this Delightfull Employment by the entrance of Augustus, (Edward's freind) who was just returned from a solitary ramble.

Never did I see such an affecting Scene as was the meeting of Edward and Augustus.

"My Life! my Soul!" (exclaimed the former) "My Adorable Angel!" (replied the latter) as they flew into each other's arms. It was too pathetic for the feelings of Sophia and myself—We fainted Alternately on a Sofa.

<div align="right">Adeiu</div>

<div align="right">Laura</div>

Letter the 9th. From the Same to the Same

Towards the close of the Day we received the following Letter from Philippa.

"Sir Edward is greatly incensed by your abrupt departure; he has taken back Augusta with him to Bedfordshire. Much as I wish to enjoy again your charming society, I cannot determine to snatch you from that, of such dear & deserving Freinds—When your Visit to them is terminated, I trust you will return to the arms of your"

<div align="right">"Philippa."</div>

We returned a suitable answer to this affectionate Note & after thanking her for her kind invitation assured her that we would certainly avail ourselves of it, whenever we might have no other place to go to. Tho' certainly nothing could to any reasonable Being, have appeared more satisfactory, than so gratefull[2] a reply to her invitation, yet I know not how it was, but she was certainly capricious enough to be displeased with our behaviour and in a few weeks after, either to revenge our Conduct, or releive her own solitude, married a young and illiterate Fortune-hunter. This imprudent Step (tho' we were sensible that it would probably deprive us of that fortune which Philippa had ever taught us to expect) could not on our own accounts, excite from our exalted Minds a single sigh; yet fearfull lest it might prove a source of endless misery to the deluded Bride, our trembling Sensibility was greatly

9. Riders who guide the horses drawing a coach. 2. Pleasing, agreeable.
1. Joy.

affected when we were first informed of the Event. The affectionate Entreaties of Augustus and Sophia that we would for ever consider their House as our Home, easily prevailed on us to determine never more to leave them—. In the Society of my Edward & this Amiable Pair, I passed the happiest moments of my Life: Our time was most delightfully spent, in mutual Protestations of Freindship, and in vows of unalterable Love, in which we were secure from being interrupted, by intruding & disagreable Visitors, as Augustus & Sophia had on their first Entrance in the Neighbourhood, taken due care to inform the surrounding Families, that as their Happiness centered wholly in themselves, they wished for no other society. But alas! my Dear Marianne such Happiness as I then enjoyed was too perfect to be lasting. A most severe & unexpected Blow at once destroyed every Sensation of Pleasure. Convinced as you must be from what I have already told you concerning Augustus & Sophia, that there never were a happier Couple, I need not I imagine inform you that their union had been contrary to the inclinations of their Cruel & Mercenary Parents; who had vainly endeavoured with obstinate Perseverance to force them into a Marriage with those whom they had ever abhorred, but with an Heroic Fortitude worthy to be related & Admired, they had both, constantly refused to submit to such despotic Power.

After having so nobly disentangled themselves from the Shackles of Parental Authority, by a Clandestine Marriage, they were determined never to forfeit the good opinion they had gained in the World, in so doing, by accepting any proposals of reconciliation that might be offered them by their Fathers—to this farther tryal of their noble independance however they never were exposed.

They had been married but a few months when our visit to them commenced during which time they had been amply supported by a considerable sum of Money which Augustus had gracefully purloined from his Unworthy father's Escritoire,[3] a few days before his union with Sophia.

By our arrival their Expences were considerably encreased tho' their means for supplying them were then nearly exhausted. But they, Exalted Creatures! scorned to reflect a moment on their pecuniary Distresses & would have blushed at the idea of paying their Debts.—Alas! what was their Reward for such disinterested Behaviour. The beautifull Augustus was arrested and we were all undone. Such perfidious Treachery in the merciless perpetrators of the Deed will shock your gentle nature Dearest Marianne as much as it then affected the Delicate Sensibility of Edward, Sophia, your Laura, & of Augustus himself. To compleat such unparalelled Barbarity we were informed that an Execution[4] in the House would shortly take place. Ah! what could we do but what we did! We sighed & fainted on the Sofa.

<div style="text-align: right">Adeiu</div>

<div style="text-align: right">Laura</div>

Letter 10th. Laura in continuation

When we were somewhat recovered from the overpowering Effusions of our Grief, Edward desired that we would consider what was the most prudent step to be taken in our unhappy situation while he repaired to his imprisoned

3. Writing desk.

4. Legal seizure of property to pay bad debts.

freind to lament over his misfortunes. We promised that we would, & he set forwards on his Journey to Town. During his Absence we faithfully complied with his Desire & after the most mature Deliberation, at length agreed that the best thing we could do was to leave the House; of which we every moment expected the Officers of Justice to take possession. We waited therefore with the greatest impatience, for the return of Edward in order to impart to him the result of our Deliberations—. But no Edward appeared—. In vain did we count the tedious Moments of his Absence—in vain did we weep—in vain even did we sigh—no Edward returned—. This was too cruel, too unexpected a Blow to our Gentle Sensibility—. we could not support it—we could only faint—. At length collecting all the Resolution I was Mistress of, I arose & after packing up some necessary Apparel for Sophia & myself, I dragged her to a Carriage I had ordered & instantly we set out for London. As the Habitation of Augustus was within twelve miles of Town, it was not long e'er we arrived there, & no sooner had we entered Holbourn than letting down one of the Front Glasses I enquired of every decent-looking Person that we passed "If they had seen my Edward"?

But as we drove too rapidly to allow them to answer my repeated Enquiries, I gained little, or indeed, no information concerning him. "Where am I to Drive?" said the Postilion. "To Newgate[5] Gentle Youth (replied I), to see Augustus." "Oh! no, no, (exclaimed Sophia) I cannot go to Newgate; I shall not be able to support the sight of my Augustus in so cruel a confinement— my feelings are sufficiently shocked by the *recital,* of his Distress, but to behold it will overpower my Sensibility." As I perfectly agreed with her in the Justice of her Sentiments the Postilion was instantly directed to return into the Country. You may perhaps have been somewhat surprised my Dearest Marianne, that in the Distress I then endured, destitute of any Support, & unprovided with any Habitation, I should never once have remembered my Father & Mother or my paternal Cottage in the Vale of Uske. To account for this seeming forgetfullness I must inform you of a trifling Circumstance concerning them which I have as yet never mentioned—. The death of my Parents a few weeks after my Departure, is the circumstance I allude to. By their decease I became the lawfull Inheritress of their House & Fortune. But alas! the House had never been their own & their Fortune had only been an Annuity[6] on their own Lives. Such is the Depravity of the World! To your Mother I should have returned with Pleasure, should have been happy to have introduced to her, my Charming Sophia & should have with Chearfullness have passed the remainder of my Life in their dear Society in the Vale of Uske, had not one obstacle to the execution of so agreable a Scheme, intervened; which was the Marriage & Removal of your Mother to a Distant part of Ireland.

Adeiu

Laura

Letter 11th. Laura in continuation

"I have a Relation in Scotland (said Sophia to me as we left London) who I am certain would not hesitate in receiving me." "Shall I order the Boy to

5. London's chief prison. 6. A sum of money paid annually for life.

drive there?" said I—but instantly recollecting myself, exclaimed "Alas I fear it will be too long a Journey for the Horses." Unwilling however to act only from my own inadequate Knowledge of the Strength & Abilities of Horses, I consulted the Postilion, who was entirely of my Opinion concerning the Affair. We therefore determined to change Horses at the next Town & to travel Post[7] the remainder of the Journey.—. When we arrived at the last Inn we were to stop at, which was but a few miles from the House of Sophia's Relation, unwilling to intrude our Society on him unexpected & unthought of, we wrote a very elegant & well-penned Note to him containing an Account of our Destitute & melancholy Situation, and of our intention to spend some months with him in Scotland. As soon as we had dispatched this letter, we immediately prepared to follow it in person & were stepping into the Carriage for that Purpose when our Attention was attracted by the Entrance of a coroneted Coach & 4[8] into the Inn-yard. A Gentleman considerably advanced in years, descended from it—. At his first Appearance my Sensibility was wonderfully affected & e'er I had gazed at him a 2d time, an instinctive Sympathy whispered to my Heart, that he was my Grandfather.

Convinced that I could not be mistaken in my conjecture I instantly sprang from the Carriage I had just entered, & following the Venerable Stranger into the Room he had been shewn to, I threw myself on my knees before him & besought him to acknowledge me as his Grand Child.—He started, & after having attentively examined my features, raised me from the Ground & throwing his Grand-fatherly arms around my neck, exclaimed, "Acknowledge thee! Yes dear resemblance of my Laurina & my Laurina's Daughter, sweet image of my Claudia & my Claudia's Mother, I do acknowledge thee as the Daughter of the one & the Grandaughter of the other." While he was thus tenderly embracing me, Sophia astonished at my precipitate Departure, entered the Room in search of me—. No sooner had she caught the eye of the venerable Peer, than he exclaimed with every mark of Astonishment— "Another Grandaughter! Yes, yes, I see you are the Daughter of my Laurina's eldest Girl; Your resemblance to the beauteous Matilda sufficiently proclaims it." "Oh.!" replied Sophia, "when I first beheld you the instinct of Nature whispered me that we were in some degree related—But whether Grandfathers, or Grandmothers, I could not pretend to determine." He folded her in his arms, and whilst they were tenderly embracing, the Door of the Apartment opened and a most beautifull Young Man appeared. On perceiving him Lord St. Clair started and retreating back a few paces, with uplifted Hands, said, "Another Grandchild! What an unexpected Happiness is this! to discover in the space of 3 minutes, as many of my Descendants! This, I am certain is Philander[9] the son of my Laurina's 3d Girl the amiable Bertha; there wants now but the presence of Gustavus to compleat the Union of my Laurina's Grand-Children."

"And here he is; (said a Gracefull Youth who that instant entered the room) here is the Gustavus you desire to see. I am the son of Agatha your Laurina's 4th & Youngest Daughter." "I see you are indeed; replied Lord St. Clair— But tell me (continued he looking fearfully towards the Door) tell me, have I any other Grand-Children in the House." "None my Lord." "Then I will

7. In relays, changing horses at intervals.
8. A fancy coach drawn by four horses. "Coro-
neted": marked with a crown denoting nobility.
9. Traditional name for a lover or flirt.

provide for you all without further delay—Here are 4 Banknotes of 50£ each—Take them & remember I have done the Duty of a Grandfather—." He instantly left the Room & immediately afterwards the House.

Adeiu

Laura

Letter the 12th. Laura in continuation

You may imagine how greatly we were surprised by the sudden departure of Lord St. Clair. "Ignoble Grand-sire!" exclaimed Sophia. "Unworthy Grandfather!" said I, & instantly fainted in each other's arms. How long we remained in this situation I know not; but when we recovered we found ourselves alone, without either Gustavus, Philander or the Bank-notes. As we were deploring our unhappy fate, the Door of the Apartment opened & "Macdonald" was announced. He was Sophia's cousin. The haste with which he came to our relief so soon after the receipt of our Note, spoke so greatly in his favour that I hesitated not to pronounce him at first sight, a tender & Simpathetic Freind. Alas! he little deserved the name—for though he told us that he was much concerned at our Misfortunes, yet by his own account it appeared that the perusal of them, had neither drawn from him a single sigh, nor induced him to bestow one curse on our vindictive Stars.—. He told Sophia that his Daughter depended on her returning with him to Macdonald-Hall, & that as his Cousin's freind he should be happy to see me there also. To Macdonald-Hall, therefore, we went, and were received with great kindness by Janetta the daughter of Macdonald, & the Mistress of the Mansion. Janetta was then only fifteen; naturally well disposed, endowed with a susceptible Heart, and a simpathetic Disposition, she might, had these amiable Qualities been properly encouraged, have been an ornament to human Nature; but unfortunately her Father possessed not a soul sufficiently exalted to admire so promising a Disposition, and had endeavoured by every means in his power to prevent its encreasing with her Years. He had actually so far extinguished the natural noble Sensibility of her Heart, as to prevail on her to accept an offer from a young man of his Recommendation. They were to be married in a few months, and Graham, was in the House when we arrived. We soon saw through his Character.—. He was just such a Man as one might have expected to be the choice of Macdonald. They said he was Sensible, well-informed, and Agreable; we did not pretend to Judge of such trifles, but as we were convinced he had no soul, that he had never read the *Sorrows of Werter*,[1] & that his Hair bore not the slightest resemblance to Auburn, we were certain that Janetta could feel no affection for him, or at least that she ought to feel none. The very circumstance of his being her father's choice too, was so much in his disfavour, that had he been deserving her, in every other respect yet *that* of itself ought to have been a sufficient reason in the Eyes of Janetta for rejecting him. These considerations we were determined to represent to her in their proper light & doubted not of meeting with the desired success from one naturally so well disposed,

1. *The Sorrows of Young Werther* (1774), an extremely influential sentimental novel by Johann Wolfgang von Goethe; it records the brief and stormy life of a passionate young man.

whose errors in the Affair had only arisen from a want of proper confidence in her own opinion, & a suitable contempt of her father's. We found her indeed all that our warmest wishes could have hoped for; we had no difficulty to convince her that it was impossible she could love Graham, or that it was her duty to disobey her Father; the only thing at which she rather seemed to hesitate was our assertion that she must be attached to some other Person. For some time, she persevered in declaring that she knew no other young Man for whom she had the smallest Affection; but upon explaining the impossibility of such a thing she said that she believed she *did like* Captain M'Kenzie better than any one she knew besides. This confession satisfied us and after having enumerated the good Qualities of M'Kenzie & assured her that she was violently in love with him, we desired to know whether he had ever in any wise declared his Affection to her.

"So far from having ever declared it, I have no reason to imagine that he has ever felt any for me." said Janetta. "That he certainly adores you (replied Sophia) there can be no doubt—. The Attachment must be reciprocal—. Did he never gaze on you with Admiration—tenderly press your hand—drop an involuntary tear—& leave the room abruptly?" "Never (replied She) that I remember—he has always left the room indeed when his visit has been ended, but has never gone away particularly abruptly or without making a bow". "Indeed my Love (said I) you must be mistaken—: for it is absolutely impossible that he should ever have left you but with Confusion, Despair, & Precipitation[2]—. Consider but for a moment Janetta, & you must be convinced how absurd it is to suppose that he could ever make a Bow, or behave like any other Person." Having settled this Point to our satisfaction, the next we took into consideration was, to determine in what manner we should inform M'Kenzie of the favourable Opinion Janetta entertained of him.—. We at length agreed to acquaint him with it by an anonymous Letter which Sophia drew up in the following Manner.

"Oh! happy Lover of the beautifull Janetta, oh! enviable Possessor of her Heart whose hand is destined to another, why do you thus delay a confession of your Attachment to the amiable Object of it? Oh! consider that a few weeks will at once put an end to every flattering Hope that you may now entertain, by uniting the unfortunate Victim of her father's Cruelty to the execrable & detested Graham."

"Alas! why do you thus so cruelly connive at the projected Misery of her & of yourself by delaying to communicate that scheme which had doubtless long possessed your imagination? A secret Union will at once secure the felicity of both."

The amiable M'Kenzie, whose modesty as he afterwards assured us had been the only reason of his having so long concealed the violence of his affection for Janetta, on receiving this Billet[3] flew on the wings of Love to Macdonald-Hall, and so powerfully pleaded his Attachment to her who inspired it, that after a few more private interviews, Sophia & I experienced the Satisfaction of seeing them depart for Gretna-Green,[4] which they chose

2. I.e., tears.
3. Note.
4. A Scottish border village, famous for runaway

marriages (couples eloped there from England, where marriage laws were much stricter).

for the celebration of their Nuptials, in preference to any other place although it was at a considerable distance from Macdonald-Hall.

Adeiu

Laura

Letter the 13th. Laura in Continuation

They had been gone nearly a couple of Hours, before either Macdonald or Graham had entertained any suspicion of the affair—. And they might not even then have suspected it, but for the following little Accident. Sophia happening one Day to open a private Drawer in Macdonald's Library with one of her own keys, discovered that it was the Place where he kept his Papers of consequence & amongst them some bank notes of considerable amount. This discovery she imparted to me; and having agreed together that it would be a proper treatment of so vile a Wretch as Macdonald to deprive him of money, perhaps dishonestly gained, it was determined that the next time we should either of us happen to go that way, we would take one or more of the Bank notes from the drawer. This well-meant Plan we had often successfully put in Execution; but alas! on the very day of Janetta's Escape, as Sophia was majestically removing the 5th Bank-note from the Drawer to her own purse, she was suddenly most impertinently interrupted in her employment by the entrance of Macdonald himself, in a most abrupt & precipitate Manner. Sophia (who though naturally all winning sweetness could when occasions demanded it call forth the Dignity of her Sex) instantly put on a most forbidding look, & darting an angry frown on the undaunted Culprit, demanded in a haughty tone of voice "Wherefore her retirement[5] was thus insolently broken in on?" The unblushing Macdonald, without even endeavouring to exculpate himself from the crime he was charged with, meanly endeavoured to reproach Sophia with ignobly defrauding him of his Money. The dignity of Sophia was wounded; "Wretch (exclaimed she, hastily replacing the Bank-note in the Drawer) how darest thou to accuse me of an Act, of which the bare idea makes me blush?" The base wretch was still unconvinced & continued to upbraid the justly-offended Sophia in such opprobrious Language, that at length he so greatly provoked the gentle sweetness of her Nature, as to induce her to revenge herself on him by informing him of Janetta's Elopement, and of the active Part we had both taken in the Affair. At this period of their Quarrel I entered the Library and was as you may imagine equally offended as Sophia at the ill-grounded Accusations of the malevolent and contemptible Macdonald. "Base Miscreant (cried I) how canst thou thus undauntedly endeavour to sully the spotless reputation of such bright Excellence? Why dost thou not suspect my innocence as soon?" "Be satisfied Madam (replied he) I do suspect it, & therefore must desire that you will both leave this House in less than half an hour."

"We shall go willingly; (answered Sophia) our hearts have long detested thee, & nothing but our freindship for thy Daughter could have induced us to remain so long beneath thy roof."

"Your Freindship for my Daughter has indeed been most powerfully

5. Privacy, solitude.

exerted by throwing her into the arms of an unprincipled Fortune-hunter."
(replied he)

"Yes, (exclaimed I) amidst every misfortune, it will afford us some conso-
lation to reflect that by this one act of Freindship to Janetta, we have amply
discharged every obligation that we have received from her father."

"It must indeed be a most gratefull reflection, to your exalted minds." (said
he.)

As soon as we had packed up our wardrobe & valuables, we left Macdonald
Hall, & after having walked about a mile & a half we sate down by the side
of a clear limpid stream to refresh our exhausted limbs. The place was suited
to meditation.—. A Grove of full-grown Elms sheltered us from the East—.
A Bed of full-grown Nettles from the West—. Before us ran the murmuring
brook & behind us ran the turn-pike road. We were in a mood for contem-
plation & in a Disposition to enjoy so beautifull a spot. A mutual Silence
which had for some time reigned between us, was at length broke by my
exclaiming—"What a lovely Scene! Alas why are not Edward & Augustus
here to enjoy its Beauties with us?"

"Ah! my beloved Laura (cried Sophia) for pity's sake forbear recalling to
my remembrance the unhappy situation of my imprisoned Husband. Alas,
what would I not give to learn the fate of my Augustus! to know if he is still
in Newgate, or if he is yet hung. But never shall I be able so far to conquer
my tender sensibility as to enquire after him. Oh! do not I beseech you ever
let me again hear you repeat his beloved name—. It affects me too deeply—.
I cannot bear to hear him mentioned, it wounds my feelings."

"Excuse me my Sophia for having thus unwillingly offended you—" replied
I—and then changing the conversation, desired her to admire the Noble
Grandeur of the Elms which Sheltered us from the Eastern Zephyr.[6] "Alas!
my Laura (returned she) avoid so melancholy a subject, I intreat you.—Do
not again wound my Sensibility by Observations on those elms. They remind
me of Augustus—. He was like them, tall, magestic—he possessed that noble
grandeur which you admire in them."

I was silent, fearfull lest I might any more unwillingly distress her by fixing
on any other subject of conversation which might again remind her of
Augustus.

"Why do you not speak my Laura?" (said she after a short pause) "I cannot
support this silence—you must not leave me to my own reflections; they ever
recur to Augustus."

"What a beautifull Sky! (said I) How charmingly is the azure varied by
those delicate streaks of white!"

"Oh! my Laura (replied she hastily withdrawing her Eyes from a momen-
tary glance at the sky) do not thus distress me by calling my Attention to an
object which so cruelly reminds me of my Augustus's blue sattin Waist-coat
striped with white! In pity to your unhappy freind avoid a subject so distress-
ing." What could I do? The feelings of Sophia were at that time so exquisite,
& the tenderness she felt for Augustus so poignant that I had not the power
to start any other topic, justly fearing that it might in some unforseen manner
again awaken all her sensibility by directing her thoughts to her Husband.—
Yet to be silent would be cruel; She had intreated me to talk.

6. Gentle breeze.

From this Dilemma I was most fortunately releived by an accident truly apropos; it was the lucky overturning of a Gentleman's Phaeton,[7] on the road which ran murmuring behind us. It was a most fortunate Accident as it diverted the Attention of Sophia from the melancholy reflections which she had been before indulging. We instantly quitted our seats & ran to the rescue of those who but a few moments before had been in so elevated a situation as a fashionably high Phaeton, but who were now laid low and sprawling in the Dust—. "What an ample subject for reflection on the uncertain Enjoyments of this World, would not that Phaeton & the Life of Cardinal Wolsey[8] afford a thinking Mind!" said I to Sophia as we were hastening to the field of Action.

She had not time to answer me for every thought was now engaged by the horrid Spectacle before us. Two Gentlemen most elegantly attired but weltering in their blood was what first struck our Eyes—we approached—they were Edward & Augustus—Yes dearest Marianne they were our Husbands. Sophia shreiked & fainted on the Ground—I screamed and instantly ran mad—. We remained thus mutually deprived of our Senses some minutes, & on regaining them were deprived of them again—. For an Hour & a Quarter did we continue in this unfortunate Situation—Sophia fainting every moment & I running Mad as often. At length a Groan from the hapless Edward (who alone retained any share of Life) restored us to ourselves—. Had we indeed before imagined that either of them lived, we should have been more sparing of our Greif—but as we had supposed when we first beheld them that they were no more, we knew that nothing could remain to be done but what we were about—. No sooner therefore did we hear my Edward's groan than postponing our Lamentations for the present, we hastily ran to the Dear Youth and kneeling on each side of him implored him not to die—. "Laura (said He fixing his now languid Eyes on me) I fear I have been overturned."

I was overjoyed to find him yet sensible—.

"Oh! tell me Edward (said I) tell me I beseech you before you die, what has befallen you since that unhappy Day in which Augustus was arrested & we were separated—"

"I will" (said he) and instantly fetching a Deep sigh, expired—. Sophia immediately sunk again into a swoon—. My Greif was more audible, My voice faltered, My Eyes assumed a vacant Stare, My face became as pale as Death, and my Senses were considerably impaired—.

"Talk not to me of Phaetons (said I, raving in a frantic, incoherent manner)—Give me a violin—. I'll play to him & sooth him in his melancholy Hours—Beware ye gentle Nymphs of Cupid's Thunderbolts, avoid the piercing Shafts of Jupiter[9]—Look at that Grove of Firs—I see a Leg of Mutton—They told me Edward was not Dead; but they deceived me—they took him for a Cucumber—" Thus I continued wildly exclaiming on my Edward's death—. For two Hours did I rave thus madly and should not then have left off, as I was not in the least fatigued, had not Sophia who was just recovered

7. A light, open carriage.
8. Thomas Wolsey (ca. 1475–1530), British cardinal who fell from power as a result of a quarrel with Henry VIII.
9. Cupid is the god of love in Roman mythology,

traditionally armed with arrows, while Jupiter is the sovereign god who brandishes thunderbolts; Laura has confused the two. "Nymphs": mythical female spirits, but the word may also refer to young girls in general.

from her swoon, intreated me to consider that Night was now approaching and that the Damps began to fall. "And whither shall we go (said I) to shelter us from either"? "To that white Cottage." (replied she pointing to a neat building which rose up amidst the Grove of Elms & which I had not before observed—) I agreed & we instantly walked to it—we knocked at the door—it was opened by an old Woman; on being requested to afford us a Night's Lodging, she informed us that her House was but small, that she had only two Bed-rooms, but that However we should be wellcome to one of them. We were satisfied & followed the good Woman into the House where we were greatly cheered by the sight of a comfortable fire—. She was a Widow & had only one Daughter, who was then just Seventeen—One of the best of ages; but alas! she was very plain & her name was Bridget . . .

. . . Nothing therefore could be expected from her—she could not be supposed to posses either exalted Ideas, Delicate Feelings or refined Sensibilities —She was nothing more than a mere good-tempered, civil & obliging Young Woman; as such we could scarcely dislike her—she was only an Object of Contempt—.

<div align="right">

Adeiu

Laura

</div>

Letter the 14th. Laura in continuation

Arm yourself my amiable Young Freind with all the philosophy you are Mistress of; summon up all the fortitude you possess, for Alas! in the perusal of the following Pages your sensibility will be most severely tried. Ah! what were the Misfortunes I had before experienced & which I have already related to you, to the one I am now going to inform you of. The Death of my Father, my Mother, and my Husband though almost more than my gentle Nature could support, were trifles in comparison to the misfortune I am now proceeding to relate. The morning after our arrival at the Cottage, Sophia complained of a violent pain in her delicate limbs, accompanied with a disagreable Head-ake. She attributed it to a cold caught by her continued faintings in the open Air as the Dew was falling the Evening before. This I feared was but too probably the case; since how could it be otherwise accounted for that I should have escaped the same indisposition, but by supposing that the bodily Exertions I had undergone in my repeated fits of frenzy, had so effectually circulated & warmed my Blood as to make me proof against the chilling Damps of Night, whereas, Sophia lying totally inactive on the Ground must have been exposed to all their Severity. I was most seriously alarmed by her illness which trifling as it may appear to you, a certain instinctive Sensibility whispered me, would in the End be fatal to her.

Alas! my fears were but too fully justified; she grew gradually worse & I daily became more alarmed for her.—At length she was obliged to confine herself solely to the Bed allotted us by our worthy Landlady—. Her disorder turned to a galloping Consumption[1] & in a few Days carried her off. Amidst all my Lamentations for her (& violent you may suppose they were) I yet

1. Tuberculosis.

received some consolation in the reflection of my having paid every Attention to her, that could be offered, in her illness. I had wept over her every Day—had bathed her sweet face with my tears & had pressed her fair Hands continually in mine—. "My beloved Laura (said she to me a few Hours before she died) take warning from my unhappy End & avoid the imprudent conduct which has occasioned it . . . beware of fainting-fits . . . Though at the time they may be refreshing & Agreable yet beleive me they will in the end, if too often repeated & at improper seasons, prove destructive to your Constitution.. . . .My fate will teach you this . . . I die a Martyr to my greif for the loss of Augustus. . . . One fatal swoon has cost me my Life. . . . Beware of swoons Dear Laura . . . A frenzy fit is not one quarter so pernicious; it is an exercise to the Body & if not too violent, is I dare say conducive to Health in its consequences—Run mad as often as you chuse; but do not faint—".

These were the last words she ever adressed to me . . . It was her dieing Advice to her afflicted Laura, who has ever most faithfully adhered to it.

After having attended my lamented freind to her Early Grave, I immediately (tho' late at night) left the detested Village in which she died, & near which had expired my Husband & Augustus. I had not walked many yards from it before I was overtaken by a Stage-Coach, in which I instantly took a place, determined to proceed in it to Edinburgh, where I hoped to find some kind pitying Freind who would receive and comfort me in my Afflictions.

It was so dark when I entered the Coach that I could not distinguish the Number of my Fellow-travellers; I could only perceive that they were Many. Regardless however of any thing concerning them, I gave myself up to my own sad Reflections. A general Silence prevailed—A Silence, which was by nothing interrupted but by the loud & repeated snores of one of the Party.

"What an illiterate villain must that Man be! (thought I to myself) What a total Want of delicate refinement must he have who can thus shock our senses by such a brutal Noise! He must I am certain be capable of every bad Action! There is no crime too black for such a Character!" Thus reasoned I within myself, & doubtless such were the reflections of my fellow travellers.

At length, returning Day enabled me to behold the unprincipled Scoundrel who had so violently disturbed my feelings. It was Sir Edward the father of my Deceased Husband. By his side, sate Augusta, & on the same seat with me were your Mother & Lady Dorothea. Imagine my Surprise at finding myself thus seated amongst my old Acquaintance. Great as was my astonishment, it was yet increased, when on look out of Windows, I beheld the Husband of Philippa, with Philippa by his side, on the Coach-box, & when on looking behind, I beheld, Philander & Gustavus in the Basket.[2] "Oh! Heavens, (exclaimed I) is it possible that I should so unexpectedly be surrounded by my nearest Relations and Connections"? These words roused the rest of the Party, and every eye was directed to the corner in which I sat. "Oh! my Isabel (continued I throwing myself across Lady Dorothea into her arms) receive once more to your Bosom the unfortunate Laura. Alas! when we last parted in the Vale of Usk, I was happy in being united to the best of Edwards; I had then a Father and a Mother, & had never known misfortunes—But now deprived of every freind but you—"

2. The rear compartment of a coach.

"What! (interrupted Augusta) is my Brother dead then? Tell us I intreat you what is become of him?" "Yes, cold & insensible Nymph, (replied I) that luckless Swain[3] your Brother, is no more, & you may now glory in being the Heiress of Sir Edward's fortune."

Although I had always despised her from the Day I had overheard her conversation with my Edward, yet in civility I complied with hers & Sir Edward's intreaties that I would inform them of the whole melancholy Affair. They were greatly shocked—Even the obdurate Heart of Sir Edward & the insensible one of Augusta, were touched with Sorrow, by the unhappy tale. At the request of your Mother I related to them every other misfortune which had befallen me since we parted. Of the imprisonment of Augustus & the absence of Edward—of our arrival in Scotland—of our unexpected Meeting with our Grandfather and our cousins—of our visit to Macdonald-Hall—of the singular Service we there performed towards Janetta—of her Fathers ingratitude for it.. . . .of his inhuman Behaviour, unaccountable suspicions, & barbarous treatment of us, in obliging us to leave the House.. . . .of our Lamentations on the loss of Edward & Augustus & finally of the melancholy Death of my beloved Companion.

Pity & Surprise were strongly depictured in your Mother's Countenance, during the whole of my narration, but I am sorry to say, that to the eternal reproach of her Sensibility, the latter infinitely predominated. Nay, faultless as my Conduct had certainly been during the whole Course of my late Misfortunes & Adventures, she pretended to find fault with my Behaviour in many of the situations in which I had been placed. As I was sensible myself, that I had always behaved in a manner which reflected Honour on my Feelings & Refinement, I paid little attention to what she said, & desired her to satisfy my Curiosity by informing me how she came there, instead of wounding my spotless reputation with unjustifiable Reproaches. As soon as she had complyed with my wishes in this particular & had given me an accurate detail of every thing that had befallen her since our separation (the particulars of which if you are not already acquainted with, your Mother will give you) I applied to Augusta for the same information respecting herself, Sir Edward & Lady Dorothea.

She told me that having a considerable taste for the Beauties of Nature, her curiosity to behold the delightful scenes it exhibited in that part of the World had been so much raised by Gilpin's Tour to the Highlands,[4] that she had prevailed on her Father to undertake a Tour of Scotland & had persuaded Lady Dorothea to accompany them. That they had arrived at Edinburgh a few days before & from thence had made daily Excursions into the Country around in the Stage Coach they were then in, from one of which Excursions they were at that time returning. My next enquiries were concerning Philippa & her Husband, the latter of whom I learned having spent all her fortune, had recourse for subsistance to the talent in which, he had always most excelled, namely, Driving, & that having sold every thing which

3. "Nymph" and "swain" are terms derived from pastoral poetry, where they designate young women and men (often lovers).
4. *Observations, Relative Chiefly to Picturesque Beauty, Made in the Year 1776, on Several Parts of* *Great Britain, Particulary the High-Lands of Scotland* (1789), by William Gilpin (1724–1804), a British clergyman who wrote a number of works on landscapes and helped to begin the 18th-century cult of the "picturesque."

belonged to them except their Coach, had converted it into a Stage,[5] & in order to be removed from any of his former Acquaintance, had driven it to Edinburgh from whence he went to Sterling every other Day; That Philippa still retaining her affection for her ungratefull Husband, had followed him to Scotland & generally accompanied him in his little Excursions to Sterling. "It has only been to throw a little money into their Pockets (continued Augusta) that my Father has always travelled in their Coach to veiw the beauties of the Country since our arrival in Scotland—for it would certainly have been much more agreable to us, to visit the Highlands in a Postchaise[6] than merely to travel from Edinburgh to Sterling & from Sterling to Edinburgh every other Day in a crouded & uncomfortable Stage." I perfectly agreed with her in her sentiments on the Affair, & secretly blamed Sir Edward for thus sacrificing his Daughter's pleasure for the sake of a ridiculous old Woman whose folly in marrying so young a Man ought to be punished. His Behaviour however was entirely of a piece with his general Character; for what could be expected from a Man who possessed not the smallest atom of Sensibility, who scarcely knew the meaning of Simpathy, & who actually snored—.

<div align="right">

Adeiu

Laura

</div>

Letter the 15th. Laura in continuation

When we arrived at the town where we were to Breakfast, I was determined to speak with Philander & Gustavus, & to that purpose as soon as I left the Carriage, I went to the Basket & tenderly enquired after their Health, expressing my fears of the uneasiness of their Situation. At first they seemed rather confused at my Appearance dreading no doubt that I might call them to account for the money which our Grandfather had left me & which they had unjustly deprived me of, but finding that I mentioned nothing of the Matter, they desired me to step into the Basket as we might there converse with greater case. Accordingly I entered & whilst the rest of the party were devouring Green tea & buttered toast, we feasted ourselves in a more refined & Sentimental Manner by a confidential Conversation. I informed them of every thing which had befallen me during the course of my Life, and at my request they related to me every incident of theirs.

"We are the sons as you already know, of the two youngest Daughters which Lord St. Clair had by Laurina an italian opera girl. Our mothers could neither of them exactly ascertain who were our fathers; though it is generally believed that Philander, is the son of one Philip Jones a Bricklayer and that my father was Gregory Staves a Staymaker of Edinburgh. This is however of little consequence, for as our Mothers were certainly never married to either of them, it reflects no Dishonour on our Blood which is of a most ancient & unpolluted kind. Bertha (the Mother of Philander) & Agatha (my own Mother) always lived together. They were neither of them very rich; their united fortunes had originally amounted to nine thousand Pounds, but as

5. A coach that carries passengers for money.
6. A closed carriage that transports mail and passengers.

they had always lived upon the principal of it, when we were fifteen it was diminished to nine Hundred. This nine Hundred, they always kept in a Drawer in one of the Tables which stood in our common sitting Parlour, for the Convenience of having it always at Hand. Whether it was from this circumstance, of its being easily taken, or from a wish of being independant, or from an excess of Sensibility (for which we were always remarkable) I cannot now determine, but certain it is that when we had reached our 15th year, we took the Nine Hundred Pounds & ran away. Having obtained this prize we were determined to manage it with eoconomy & not to spend it either with folly or Extravagance. To this purpose we therefore divided it into nine parcels, one of which we devoted to Victuals, the 2d to Drink, the 3d to Housekeeping, the 4th to Carriages, the 5th to Horses, the 6th to Servants, the 7th to Amusements, the 8th to Cloathes & the 9th to Silver Buckles. Having thus arranged our Expences for two Months (for we expected to make the nine Hundred Pounds last as long) we hastened to London & had the good luck to spend it in 7 weeks & a Day which was 6 Days sooner than we had intended. As soon as we had thus happily disencumbered ourselves from the weight of so much Money, we began to think of returning to our Mothers, but accidentally hearing that they were both starved to death, we gave over the design & determined to engage ourselves to some strolling Company of Players, as we had always a turn for the Stage. Accordingly we offered our services to one & were accepted; our Company was indeed rather small, as it consisted only of the Manager his wife & ourselves, but there were fewer to pay and the only inconvenience attending it was the Scarcity of Plays which for want of People to fill the Characters, we could perform.—. We did not mind trifles however—. One of our most admired Performances was *Macbeth,* in which we were truly great. The Manager always played *Banquo* himself, his Wife my *Lady Macbeth.* I did the *Three Witches* & Philander acted *all the rest.* To say the truth this tragedy was not only the Best, but the only Play we ever performed; & after having acted it all over England, and Wales, we came to Scotland to exhibit it over the remainder of Great Britain. We happened to be quartered in that very Town, where you came and met your Grandfather—. We were in the Inn-yard when his Carriage entered & perceiving by the Arms to whom it belonged, & knowing that Lord St. Clair was our Grandfather, we agreed to endeavour to get something from him by discovering the Relationship—. You know how well it succeeded—. Having obtained the two Hundred Pounds, we instantly left the Town, leaving our Manager & his wife to act *Macbeth* by themselves, & took the road to Sterling, where we spent our little fortune with great *eclat.* We are now returning to Edinburgh to get some preferment[7] in the Acting way; & such my Dear Cousin is our History."

I thanked the amiable Youth for his entertaining Narration, & after expressing my Wishes for their Welfare & Happiness, left them in their little Habitation & returned to my other Freinds who impatiently expected me.

My Adventures are now drawing to a close my dearest Marianne; at least for the present.

When we arrived at Edinburgh Sir Edward told me that as the Widow of his Son, he desired I would accept from his Hands of four Hundred a year. I graciously promised that I would, but could not help observing that the

7. Employment. "Eclat": flamboyance, conspicuousness.

unsimpathetic Baronet offered it more on account of my being the Widow of Edward than in being the refined & Amiable Laura.

I took up my Residence in a romantic Village in the Highlands of Scotland, where I have ever since continued, & where I can uninterrupted by unmeaning Visits, indulge in a melancholy solitude, my unceasing Lamentations for the Death of my Father, my Mother, my Husband & my Freind.

Augusta has been for several Years united to Graham the Man of all others most suited to her; she became acquainted with him during her stay in Scotland.

Sir Edward in hopes of gaining an Heir to his Title & Estate, at the same time married Lady Dorothea—. His wishes have been answered.

Philander & Gustavus, after having raised their reputation by their Performances in the Theatrical Line at Edinburgh, removed to Covent Garden,[8] where they still Exhibit under the assumed names of *Lewis* & *Quick*.

Philippa has long paid the Debt of Nature,[9] Her Husband however still continues to drive the Stage-Coach from Edinburgh to Sterling:—

<div align="right">Adeiu my Dearest Marianne</div>

<div align="right">Laura</div>

June 13th 1790 1922

8. A theater in London. 9. I.e., has long since died.

FELICIA DOROTHEA HEMANS
1793–1835

"The boy stood on the burning deck / Whence all but he had fled; / The flame that lit the battle's wreck / Shone round him o'er the dead": countless schoolchildren in countless British and American classrooms, assemblies, and parlors recited these lines, which were first celebrated as a stirring portrait of bravery, then parodied as bad poetry or lambasted as puerile claptrap. Only at the end of the twentieth century did feminist scholars began to interpret "Casabianca" as a subtle critique of patriotism and the destructive submission it inculcates even in the very young. The boy who went down with his ship perished in the 1789 Battle of the Nile, when the British fleet, commanded by Horatio Nelson, proved victorious against Napoléon in Egypt. Composed fourteen years after her marriage to Captain Alfred Hemans and eight years after he had left her and their family for Italy, the poem may draw on her husband's experiences during the Peninsular Campaign, in which two of her brothers also served. At the same time, perhaps the son's plaintive but unanswered pleas— "Say, Father, say," young Casabianca calls out, and again "Speak, Father!"—reflect the abandonment Hemans had felt not only when her husband decided to leave her and her five sons but also eight years earlier, when her father deserted her mother and their children. Many of her other poems first gained her popularity and then notoriety for their pathos as well as their idealization of domesticity and maternity, though Hemans also created a number of murderous heroines who hardly conform to the cult of submission preached elsewhere in her verse.

Of course, abandonment, martyred innocence, and sentimentality characterize the writings of the authors Cheryl Walker has placed in the "nightingale" tradition; cer-

tainly, too, Hemans's murderous heroines take up violence to right terrible wrongs or to save themselves from fates far worse than death. Hemans, who may have capitalized on the desertion theme, is the very model of a nineteenth-century best-selling, prolific, and quintessentially feminine "poetess." In large part, she accomplished the task through the offices of a supportive mother who educated her at home. Felicia Hemans was born Felicia Browne in Liverpool, but was raised in North Wales. Her productivity began at an early age and continued throughout her life: at fifteen, she had published her first two books of verse, and from the age of twenty-three until near her death she produced new books of poetry almost annually. Before her marriage and after her husband's departure, her mother played a formative role in encouraging Hemans, helping her cope with the demands of an active literary career and an equally demanding domestic life. Although mocked by Lord Byron, who viewed her popularity as a personal challenge, she was eulogized by a host of celebrated authors after her death. But her uncanny business acumen—coupled with her ability to gain a wide audience through the patriotic, religious, and domestic themes she addressed—only sealed her doom with a number of modern readers, who grouped her with L.E.L. and Lydia Sigourney as prototypes of blatantly sappy and silly nineteenth-century poetasters. The research of such feminist scholars as Stuart Curran, Isobel Armstrong, Tricia Lootens, and Susan Wolfson has given us a more historically contextualized and aesthetically complicated portrait of Hemans as one of the most commercially successful women artists of her time.

Casabianca[1]

The boy stood on the burning deck
 Whence all but he had fled;
The flame that lit the battle's wreck
 Shone round him o'er the dead.

5 Yet beautiful and bright he stood,
 As born to rule the storm;
A creature of heroic blood,
 A proud, though childlike form.

The flames roll'd on—he would not go
10 Without his father's word;
That father, faint in death below,
 His voice no longer heard.

He call'd aloud:—"Say, Father, say
 If yet my task is done?"
15 He knew not that the chieftain lay
 Unconscious of his son.

1. Young Casabianca, a boy about thirteen years old, son to the Admiral of the *Orient*, remained at his post (in the Battle of the Nile) after the ship had taken fire, and all the guns had been abandoned, and perished in the explosion of the vessel, when the flames had reached the powder [Hemans's note]. In the Battle of the Nile, which took place on August 1, 1798, British ships commanded by Horatio Nelson decisively defeated a French fleet in Abu Kir Bay; the captain of the French admiral's ship, *L'Orient*, was Louis de Casabianca.

"Speak, Father!" once again he cried,
 "If I may yet be gone!"
And but the booming shots replied,
20 And fast the flames roll'd on.

Upon his brow he felt their breath,
 And in his waving hair,
And look'd from that lone post of death
 In still, yet brave despair.

25 And shouted but once more aloud,
 "My Father! must I stay?"
While o'er him fast, through sail and shroud,
 The wreathing fires made way.

They wrapt the ship in splendour wild,
30 They caught the flag on high,
And stream'd above the gallant child,
 Like banners in the sky.

There came a burst of thunder sound—
 The boy—oh! where was he?
35 Ask of the winds that far around
 With fragments strew'd the sea!—

With mast, and helm, and pennon fair,
 That well had borne their part,
But the noblest thing which perish'd there
40 Was that young faithful heart!

 1826

The Homes of England

> Where's the coward that would not dare
> To fight for such a land?
> —*Marmion*[1]

The stately Homes of England,
 How beautiful they stand!
Amidst their tall ancestral trees,
 O'er all the pleasant land.
5 The deer across their greensward bound
 Through shade and sunny gleam,
And the swan glides past them with the sound
 Of some rejoicing stream.

1. Sir Walter Scott's *Marmion* (1808), 4.633–34. Originally, the poem had an epigraph from another Scottish writer, Joanna Baillie (*Ethwald: A Tragedy*, part 2 [1802], 1.2.76–82).

The merry Homes of England!
 Around their hearths by night,
What gladsome looks of household love
 Meet in the ruddy light!
There woman's voice flows forth in song,
 Or childhood's tale is told,
Or lips move tunefully along
 Some glorious page of old.

The blessed Homes of England!
 How softly on their bowers
Is laid the holy quietness
 That breathes from Sabbath-hours!
Solemn, yet sweet, the church-bell's chime
 Floats through their woods at morn;
All other sounds, in that still time,
 Of breeze and leaf are born.

The Cottage Homes of England!
 By thousands on her plains,
They are smiling o'er the silvery brooks,
 And round the hamlet-fanes.²
Through glowing orchards forth they peep,
 Each from its nook of leaves,
And fearless there the lowly sleep,
 As the bird beneath their eaves.

The free, fair Homes of England!
 Long, long, in hut and hall,
May hearts of native proof be rear'd
 To guard each hallow'd wall!
And green for ever be the groves,
 And bright the flowery sod,
Where first the child's glad spirit loves
 Its country and its God!

1827

2. Churches in small villages.

Joan of Arc, in Rheims[1]

Jeanne d'Arc avait eu la joie de voir à Chàlons quelques amis de son enfance. Une joie plus ineffable encore l'attendoit à Rheims, au sein de son triomphe. [La respectable] Jacques d'Arc, son père, [. . .] y se trouva, aussitôt que de troupes de Charles VII y furent entrées; et comme les deux frères de notre héroïne l'avoient accompagnée, elle se vit, pour un instant, au milieu de sa famille, dans les bras d'un père vertueux.

—Vie de Jeanne d'Arc.[2]

Thou hast a charmed cup, O Fame!
A draught that mantles high,
And seems to lift this earth-born frame
Above mortality:
Away! to me—a woman—bring
Sweet waters from affection's spring.[3]

That was a joyous day in Rheims of old,
When peal on peal of mighty music roll'd
Forth from her throng'd cathedral; while around,
A multitude, whose billows made no sound,
5 Chain'd to a hush of wonder, tho' elate
With victory, listen'd at their temple's gate.
And what was done within?—within, the light
 Thro' the rich gloom of pictured windows flowing,
Tinged with soft awfulness a stately sight,
10 The chivalry of France, their proud heads bowing
In martial vassalage!—while midst that ring,
And shadow'd by ancestral tombs, a king
Receiv'd his birthright's crown. For this, the hymn
 Swell'd out like rushing waters, and the day
15 With the sweet censer's misty breath grew dim,
 As thro' long aisles it floated o'er th' array
Of arms and sweeping stoles. But who, alone
And unapproach'd, beside the altar-stone,
With the white banner, forth like sunshine streaming,
20 And the gold helm, thro' clouds of fragrance gleaming,
Silent and radiant stood?—the helm was rais'd,
And the fair face reveal'd, that upward gaz'd,
 Intensely worshipping:—a still, clear face,
Youthful, but brightly solemn!—Woman's cheek

1. Joan of Arc (Jeanne d'Arc, ca. 1412–1431), French saint and national heroine, was at the height of her success at Rheims. Led by voices to offer aid to the French dauphin in the Hundred Years War against the English, she and the troops she was given raised the siege of Orléans and took several English posts; she persuaded the dauphin to be crowned Charles VII in Rheims. As the war continued, she was captured by the Burgundians, sold to the English, and forced to stand trial for witchcraft and heresy in Rouen before French clerics who supported the English. She was found guilty and burned at the stake.
2. At Chalons, Joan of Arc had the pleasure of see-ing some of her childhood friends. An even more ineffable pleasure awaited her at Rheims, in the bosom of her triumph. [The worthy] Jacques d'Arc, her father, was there, at the moment that the troops of Charles VII entered; and as the two brothers of our heroine had accompanied him, she found herself, for a moment, in the middle of her family, in the arms of a virtuous father (French). Slightly misquoted from "Jeanne d'Arc ou La Pucelle d'Orléans," in *Almanach de Gotha pour l'Année 1822* (1822).
3. From Hemans's own "Woman and Fame," not published until 1829.

25 And brow were there, in deep devotion meek,
 Yet glorified with inspiration's trace
 On its pure paleness; while, enthron'd above,
 The pictur'd virgin, with her smile of love,
 Seem'd bending o'er her votaress.—That slight form!
30 Was that the leader thro' the battle storm?
 Had the soft light in that adoring eye,
 Guided the warrior where the swords flash'd high?
 'Twas so, even so!—and thou, the shepherd's child,
 Joanne, the lowly dreamer of the wild!
35 Never before, and never since that hour,
 Hath woman, mantled with victorious power,
 Stood forth as *thou* beside the shrine didst stand,
 Holy amidst the knighthood of the land;
 And beautiful with joy and with renown,
40 Lift thy white banner o'er the olden crown,
 Ransom'd for France by thee!
 The rites are done.
 Now let the dome with trumpet-notes be shaken,
 And bid the echoes of the tombs awaken,
 And come thou forth, that Heaven's rejoicing sun
45 May give thee welcome from thine own blue skies,
 Daughter of victory!—A triumphant strain,
 A proud rich stream of warlike melodies,
 Gush'd thro' the portals of the antique fane,[4]
 And forth she came.—Then rose a nation's sound[5]
50 Oh! what a power to bid the quick heart bound,
 The wind bears onward with the stormy cheer
 Man gives to glory on her high career!
 Is there indeed such power?—far deeper dwells
 In one kind household voice, to reach the cells
55 Whence happiness flows forth!—The shouts that fill'd
 The hollow heaven tempestuously, were still'd
 One moment; and in that brief pause, the tone,
 As of a breeze that o'er her home had blown,
 Sank on the bright maid's heart.—"Joanne!"—Who spoke
60 Like those whose childhood with *her* childhood grew
 Under one roof?—"Joanne!"—*that* murmur broke
 With sounds of weeping forth!—She turn'd—she knew
 Beside her, mark'd from all the thousands there,
 In the calm beauty of his silver hair,
65 The stately shepherd; and the youth, whose joy
 From his dark eye flash'd proudly; and the boy,
 The youngest-born, that ever lov'd her best:
 "Father! and ye, my brothers!"—On the breast
 Of that grey sire she sank—and swiftly back,
70 Ev'n in an instant, to their native track
 Her free thoughts flowed.—She saw the pomp no more—

4. Ancient temple. The cathedral, built 1211–
1311, replaced a 9th-century structure that had
been destroyed by fire.
5. Though Charles VII had been crowned, his rule

in fact extended over only a small area; France did
not take its modern form as a nation until the rule
of Louis XIV (1643–1715).

The plumes, the banners:—to her cabin-door,
And to the Fairy's fountain in the glade,[6]
Where her young sisters by her side had play'd,
75 And to her hamlet's chapel, where it rose
Hallowing the forest unto deep repose,
Her spirit turn'd.—The very wood-note, sung
 In early spring-time by the bird, which dwelt
Where o'er her father's roof the beech-leaves hung,
80 Was in her heart; a music heard and felt,
Winning her back to nature.—She unbound
 The helm of many battles from her head,
And, with her bright locks bow'd to sweep the ground,
 Lifting her voice up, wept for joy, and said,—
85 "Bless me, my father, bless me! and with thee,
To the still cabin and the beechen-tree,
Let me return!"
 Oh! never did thine eye
Thro' the green haunts of happy infancy
Wander again, Joanne!—too much of fame
90 Had shed its radiance on thy peasant-name;
And bought alone by gifts beyond all price,
The trusting heart's repose, the paradise
Of home with all its loves, doth fate allow
The crown of glory unto woman's brow.

1826, 1828

Indian Woman's Death-Song

*An Indian woman, driven to despair by her husband's desertion of
her for another wife, entered a canoe with her children, and rowed
it down the Mississippi towards a cataract. Her voice was heard from
the shore singing a mournful death-song, until overpowered by the
sound of the waters in which she perished. The tale is related in Long's
"Expedition to the Source of St. Peter's River."*[1]

*Non, je ne puis vivre avec un coeur brisé. Il faut que je retrouve la
joie, et que je m'unisse avec les esprits libres de l'air.*
 —Bride of Messina, *Translated by Madame De Stael*[2]

Let not my child be a girl, for very sad is the life of a woman.
 —The Prairie[3]

6. A beautiful fountain near Domremi, believed to
be haunted by fairies, and a favourite resort of
Jeanne d'Arc in her childhood [Hemans's note].
Domrémy, a village in northeast France (in Vosges,
Lorraine), was her birthplace.
1. *Narrative of an Expedition to the Source of St.
Peter's River* (1824), by William Hypolitus Keating,
recounted an expedition from Chicago to Prairie
Du Chien, Wisconsin, led by the American army
officer and explorer Stephen Harriman Long
(1784–1864).

2. "No, I cannot live with a broken heart. I must
find joy again, and unite myself with the free spirits
of the air." Translated into French by the French-
Swiss woman of letters Germaine de Staël (1766–
1817) from Friedrich Schiller's *Die Braut von Mes-
sina* (1803).
3. Slightly misquoted from James Fenimore Coo-
per's *The Prairie* (1827), chap. 26; the words are
spoken by a Dakota wife whose husband now
favors another.

Down a broad river of the western wilds,
Piercing thick forest glooms, a light canoe
Swept with the current: fearful was the speed
Of the frail bark, as by a tempest's wing
5 Borne leaf-like on to where the mist of spray
Rose with the cataract's thunder.—Yet within,
Proudly, and dauntlessly, and all alone,
Save that a babe lay sleeping at her breast,
A woman stood: upon her Indian brow
10 Sat a strange gladness, and her dark hair wav'd
As if triumphantly. She press'd her child,
In its bright slumber, to her beating heart,
And lifted her sweet voice, that rose awhile
Above the sound of waters, high and clear,
15 Wafting a wild proud strain, her song of death.

Roll swiftly to the Spirit's land, thou mighty stream and free!
Father of ancient waters,[4] roll! and bear our lives with thee!
The weary bird that storms have toss'd, would seek the sunshine's
 calm,
And the deer that hath the arrow's hurt, flies to the woods of balm.

20 Roll on!—my warrior's eye hath look'd upon another's face,
And mine hath faded from his soul, as fades a moonbeam's trace;
My shadow comes not o'er his path, my whisper to his dream,
He flings away the broken reed—roll swifter yet, thou stream!

The voice that spoke of other days is hush'd within *his* breast,
25 But *mine* its lonely music haunts, and will not let me rest;
It sings a low and mournful song of gladness that is gone,
I cannot live without that light—Father of waves! roll on!

Will he not miss the bounding step that met him from the chase?
The heart of love that made his home an ever sunny place?
30 The hand that spread the hunter's board, and deck'd his couch of
 yore?—
He will not!—roll, dark foaming stream, on to the better shore!

Some blessed fount amidst the woods of that bright land must flow,
Whose waters from my soul may lave the memory of this wo;
Some gentle wind must whisper there, whose breath may waft away
35 The burden of the heavy night, the sadness of the day.

And thou, my babe! tho' born, like me, for woman's weary lot,
Smile!—to that wasting of the heart, my own! I leave thee not;
Too bright a thing art *thou* to pine in aching love away,
Thy mother bears thee far, young Fawn! from sorrow and decay.

4. "Father of waters," the Indian name for the Mississippi [Hemans's note]. The Ojibwe and Algonquin names for the river, which are close to *Mississippi*, mean "great river."

40 She bears thee to the glorious bowers where none are heard to weep,
And where th' unkind one hath no power again to trouble sleep;
And where the soul shall find its youth, as wakening from a dream,—
One moment, and that realm is ours—On, on, dark rolling stream!

1828

REBECCA COX JACKSON
1795–1871

In a moving account of her self-education, the Shaker visionary and preacher Rebecca Jackson remembered a moment when her shame at her own illiteracy "pierced my soul like a sword" so that she "could not keep from crying." But then, she explained, "these words were spoken in my heart, 'Be faithful, and the time shall come when you can write.' " Not long after that, she added, an inner voice reminded her that God, "who learned the first man to read . . . can learn you," and in fact, apparently quite miraculously, she started that very day to read the Bible. Some years later, she began to write the striking spiritual autobiography excerpted here, and she continued composing this memoir on and off throughout her ministry.

Jackson was a free black woman. She was born just outside Philadelphia and for many years worked as a seamstress, a job that brought her some financial independence. Her husband, Samuel J. Jackson, lived with her, her older brother, Joseph Cox, and her brother's children in a comfortable house in Philadelphia. Jackson renounced the security of this life, however, after being profoundly transformed by a powerful experience of religious "awakening" that seized her during a thunderstorm in July 1830. Suddenly feeling herself to be an instrument of divine authority, she chose— like such earlier women as the fourteenth-century visionary Margery Kempe or the seventeenth-century mystic Jane Lead—to leave her husband, her home, and her family for a life of spiritual commitment. After having achieved considerable success as an itinerant preacher whose "gift," according to a contemporary witness, "was to travel some and speak to the people," she joined the radical sect known as the Shakers, a group of Protestant believers who advocated the Motherhood as well as the Father-hood of God and who seemed to her, with their austere dress and communal ways, to be "living to live forever." Throughout these years, she resided and journeyed through the countryside with a younger woman disciple named Rebecca Perot; known as "the two Rebeccas," the women were evidently both inseparable and inspiring. Together they founded and sustained an African American Philadelphia Shakers community.

Around 1843, Jackson undertook to write her memoirs, including a series of dreams and visions. Although these remained unpublished until the historian Jean McMahon Humez edited them in 1981, Shaker scholars transcribed and preserved them during the nineteenth century. In their dramatizations of violence as well as in their magical meditations on domesticity, such passages as "The Dream of Slaughter," "The Dream of the Cakes," and "The Dream of Washing Quilts" suggest the intensity with which an apparently unschooled woman could enrich her inner life with imagery drawn from "ordinary" reality. Moreover, in the simultaneous sense of peril and resistance that these dreams convey as well as in their sometimes haunted consciousness of racial difference, Jackson's memoirs imply that even for a supposedly "free" black woman, nineteenth-century America was hardly an unthreatening place. As another

nineteenth-century black woman preacher, Amanda Smith, remarked, "Some people would understand the quintessence of sanctifying grace if they could be black about twenty-four hours."

From Gifts of Power

A Dream of Slaughter

In a night or two after I had this dream,[1] I also dreamed I was in a house, entered in at the south door. I heard a footstep quick behind me and looked at the east window and saw a man coming. I run upstairs, told the child's nurse a robber was in the house. She fled. I went to the east window, then to the west, to jump out. I found in so doing I should kill myself, so I sat down on a chair by the west window with my face to the north. He came up and came right to me. He took a lance and laid my nose open and then he cut my head on the right side, from the back to the front above my nose, and pulled the skin down over that side. Then he cut the left, did the same way, and pulled the skin down. The skin and blood covered me like a veil from my head to my lap. All my body was covered with blood. Then he took a long knife and cut my chest open in the form of the cross and took all my bowels out and laid them on the floor by my right side, and then went in search of all the rest of the family. This was a family that I sewed in. When the lance was going through my nose it felt like a feather was going over my nose. I sat in silent prayer all the time saying these words in my mind, "Lord Jesus, receive my spirit."

After I found he was gone I thought I would make my escape before he returned. I was afraid if he found me alive he would want to treat me more cruel. But a voice above my head told me to sit still, as though I was dead, for that was the only thing that would save me. And this was the way I sat all the time he was amangling my body—as though I was dead. So in a moment after those words were spoken to me, he came in and came to me as if he was agoing to do something else to me, and I was afraid. I thought I would implore his mercy to save my life, but the same voice spoke to me and said, "He can show no mercy." And in the same moment, the same voice from above spoke to him and asked, "What is your occupation?" (and also the man that was with him). He said the man rid[2] the entrails but he opened the heart. And He commanded him not to touch me again. And they both fled from before me by the power of that voice. And then I found what it was that keep me alive. He had not as yet taken out my heart, but my entrails were laying all this time by my right side on the floor.

And then I awoke and my dream troubled me. I was so faint when I woke I could not get up for sometime. And when I did I cried, "I shall die! I shall die!" Samuel said, "What is the matter?" "Oh my dream! My dream!" And I was all in a tremble. And these words were spoken to me, "Thy life is hid in Christ. Thy life is hid in Christ. Thy life is hid in Christ." Three times these words were spoken to me. And I was strengthened and my soul filled with

1. She has just recounted a dream in which, by her own interpretation, she has learned to resist carnal pleasures and to follow God.

2. Removed.

the love of God. And I began to walk the floor back and forth apraising the Lord as though nothing had been.

* * *

The Dream of the Cakes

A dream. I thought I was going to bake some cakes. A sister come in that belonged to the Covenant. I said, "I am glad you have come!" "Why?" "Because I am going to bake some cakes." I sat down on a low stool before the griddle. It laid on two bricks, the fire under it. It stood in the northeast corner of the room on the floor. The fireplace was on the west side of the room. However, I greased the griddle, put on a little batter, about a tablespoonful. It run all over the griddle, a beautiful brown on both sides, though I did not turn it. And in a moment the people ate it all up—they were all white.[3] I did not see them before I saw them eating my cake. I knowed not where they came from—I looked at the sister. "Did you see that? Well, I will try it again."

I poured on another. It run all over, under, and into the fire. They ate it out of the fire and off of the griddle. And the people increased as the cake enlarged. I put on the third. It run all over the griddle, on the fire, under it, on the ashes, under it, and spread about one yard around. The people ate it off the griddle, off the fire, from under it, off the ashes, under the ashes. They ate it all, except a little piece about one inch in length, a half inch in width. This little piece lay before my right foot in the ashes. It was all I seen. I picked it up and said, "Let us taste it. They ate it so good." I broke it and put the piece in my mouth. It was the sweetest I ever tasted. I gave her the other, said, "Here, taste. No wonder they ate it up!"

So the people increased at the baking of the third cake to a large multitude.[4] I don't think I put on more than a spoonful each time—it is my manner in baking any kind of batter cakes to try the griddle with batter enough to make a cake the size of a half a dollar, so that if it sticks, then there is not much batter wasted.

And I woke in the morning. I told my dream. My dreams became a burden to my family. I shall only mention a few of them in this writing in order to show how it pleased God in His wisdom to lead a poor unlearned ignorant woman, without the aid of mortal.

The Dream of Washing Quilts

A dream. I was washing. I was squatting down, washing three bed quilts and singing as I was awashing. And this same sister[5] came to the south door and said, "What are you adoing here?" "I am awashing." "Ain't you afraid to be here?" "No." "Why, you are in great danger."

I then looked and saw I was in a place walled all around with stone. The place was four square. I was in the center of it. There was no window in it,

3. According to one editor, this dream reflects the fact that Jackson's early congregation were largely white.
4. Compare Jesus' feeding of thousands with a few loaves and fishes (e.g., Mark 6.37–44).
5. Jackson reveals later that this "sister" (the same who appeared in the previous dream) is jealous of her influence over the Covenant Meeting.

only one door. That was in the southwest corner, opened in. The south door she stood in, which brought her behind me, rather to my left. My face was east. Under me was a pool of water. This walled place was full of water like a bowl. Nobody could get to me. There were three pieces of boards about one yard in length. They were all one size. On one of them I sat. On the one at my right side sat a tub. In it was two quilts, which I had washed in this pool, though I knowed not I was in such a dangerous place till she spoke. Yet I did not feel to move till I had done my washing. So I sat still singing until I was done.

Then I picked up my tub with my three clean quilts in, put the tub on my head, came out with great ease and went eastward, came into a street ran north and south. I then stopped, turned around to see where I had come from, found I was standing by a gate as though I had come through it, saw a bridge alongside the gate. This bridge was over a stream of water. I could not tell whether I had come through this gate or over the bridge.

While I stood here awonder, I looked up, saw the gate post on the south side had a steeple on it, and on the top of the steeple was a gold ball. As I looked from the top to where I stood, I found a little white cord hanging right by my right hand. I caught hold of it, made a squat, then leaped into the air, placed my right foot on the ball, with my left foot swinging in the air. I was above all earthly things. I saw three cities, one in the east, one in the south, one in the west. These cities were clean and beautiful. Then I leaped down with as great ease as I ascended.

Then I heard this same sister speak behind me. "What are you doing here?" "Why, I have been on that pinnacle." She doubted. I caught hold of the cord and leaped upon it again. This I done three times—I had done it twice before she came. I then went through the gate and along this stream of water until I headed it. This was the same way I had come with my clean quilts in the tub upon my head, but I did not see this water nor this gate nor this bridge until I got into the street that ran north and south. This street which I came in from the washing ran east and west. Now as I returned the same way, it brought me westward, and when I headed this stream, I went south—but when I found myself at that gate, I had no tub nor quilts.

So now I went south. After I got far in the south, I looked up to the heavens, saw three pictures all of one size and of one appearance, very majestic, long, and beautiful, of the male order. They were some distance apart. They faced the north. Each one was on a black cloud. And there was three heavy claps of thunder. Each clap came out of each cloud. I found I had traveled a long distance—no house nor shelter near, as far as my eyes could see, and I saw a heavy thunderstorm rising. I wondered what I should do. It was said, "Turn back." I turned, and when I turned in the same road that I came—for I never turned out of the road in all my journey—being turned on my right (that is, on my right hand side off the road, east), I saw a beautiful white cottage into which I was told to enter, which I did. And when I found myself in so beautiful a house, sheltered from the storm, I was filled with joy and rejoicing. And it was said to me, "This is yours."

Then I heard this sister holler behind the cottage, "What are you adoing here?" "Why, I live here." "You live here?" "Yes, I live here." "Why, how can you live here? Nobody lives here." "Why, this is my cottage, and I am as happy as a lord." "Why, the sun never rises here." "The sun never rises here?"

As I made this reply I advanced to the door which I came in at, which was in the south side of the cottage. (She was on the north side which made her behind the cottage—I only heard her voice.) And when I went out and looked in the west, I saw the fourth picture, like the three I saw in the south—same size, same height in the heavens—and it faced the east and it was on a black cloud. And as I kept repeating, "The sun never rises here? No? Why, yonder she is arising—arising now!" "Well, she has only rose to you."

The sun, while I looked in the faces of the pictures, rose from behind the picture as though it came out of the cloud. And it rose out on the south side of this fourth picture, bearing her course toward these three pictures in the south, out of which came three claps of heavy thunder. The thunder out of the three black clouds behind the three pictures in the south, the sun out of the black cloud behind the fourth picture in the west. Then I waked.

1843–45 1981

MARY SHELLEY
1797–1851

Mary Wollstonecraft Godwin Shelley, wrote her friend Leigh Hunt in his "Blue-Stocking Revels" (1837), was "four-famed—for her parents, her lord, / And the poor lone impossible monster abhorred." Amiably sardonic though it is, this couplet tersely summarizes some of the major facts of this author's remarkable career. The daughter of the feminist theoretician Mary Wollstonecraft (famous for her *Vindication of the Rights of Woman,* 1792) and the rationalist philosopher William Godwin (equally well known for his *Enquiry Concerning Political Justice,* 1793), she eloped with the Romantic poet Percy Bysshe Shelley when she was only seventeen, and when she was merely nineteen she wrote *Frankenstein,* perhaps the most memorable and influential science fiction fantasy ever published in English.

Putting aside the intellectual achievements of her mother and father, Mary Shelley's existence was marked from the first by emotional extremes. Though her parents were radically opposed to marriage (Godwin had called it "the worst of all laws" and Wollstonecraft had defined it as "legalized prostitution"), they had somewhat embarrassedly wed not only to legitimize the birth of their child but also with every expectation of a peaceful life together. But Wollstonecraft died of puerperal fever just after giving birth to her daughter Mary, and Godwin, left in charge of his motherless infant as well as Wollstonecraft's illegitimate daughter, Fanny Imlay, was plunged into gloom. Nor did conditions substantially improve after Mary's father remarried, when she was four. His new wife was an adventuress named Mary Jane Vial, who proclaimed herself to be a widowed "Mrs. Clairmont." Described by one of Godwin's friends as a "clever, bustling, second-rate woman, glib of tongue and pen," she had two children of her own, Charles and Jane, to whom she was clearly partial, so that Mary soon began to feel like a rebellious Cinderella. Idolizing her scholarly but distant father, she grew up headstrong and literary, educating herself through voracious reading, scorning her stepmother, and making long brooding pilgrimages to her mother's grave.

Sent to live with family friends in Scotland when she was fifteen, Mary spent a good deal of time "scribbling." On her return to London in 1814, when she was nearly seventeen, she was immediately drawn to a young friend of her father's, the poet

Percy Bysshe Shelley, who was equally drawn to her. Injudiciously married at the age of nineteen to the sixteen-year-old Harriet Westbrook, Shelley was now twenty-two, the scion of an aristocratic family, who had glamorously repudiated his heritage to devote himself to art and ideas. In a few years, however, he had wearied of the comparatively ordinary wife who had already borne him one child and was about to give birth to another; evidently he was ready for amorous redemption. A disciple of Godwin's, Shelley had also long venerated the by now mythical Mary Wollstonecraft, and no doubt Mary Godwin's physical charm—in surviving portraits, she has a classic, cool beauty—together with her imaginative power and her fascinating heritage enthralled him as rapidly as his poetic charisma enchanted her. Within a month, the pair had confessed their feelings to each other, appropriately enough at Wollstonecraft's grave, and fled to the Continent together, bringing Mary's stepsister Jane—who had now renamed herself "Claire"—Clairmont with them; Mary was already pregnant with their first child.

It is an understatement to say that Mary's years with Shelley were hectic ones. Almost from the beginning, they were tragic. At the age of seventeen, she gave birth to her first child, a premature daughter who died in two weeks. Her journal entries from this period are hauntingly evocative. Indeed, as the feminist critic Ellen Moers has pointed out, their preoccupation with death and resurrection prefigures some of the central concerns of *Frankenstein*. "Dream that my little baby came to life again," she wrote on Sunday, March 19, 1815; "that it had been only cold, and that we rubbed it before the fire, and it lived." An imaginative, theatrical girl, Mary Shelley was being gradually transformed into a woman subject to genuine terrors. In 1816, both Fanny Imlay and Harriet Shelley committed suicide. Now Shelley was able to wed Mary, but to his distress he was never considered respectable enough to be given custody of his two children by Harriet. Married at last, the young couple wandered between England, Switzerland, and Italy, often impoverished and always beset by importunate friends and relatives. At the same time, many of their relationships were richly rewarding: John Keats, Lord Byron, Leigh Hunt, Thomas Love Peacock, James Hogg, Edward Trelawney, and other notable Romantics enlivened their social circle, and their growing intellectual as well as emotional dependence on each other seems also to have helped them cope with a range of difficulties, including the strains that Shelley's commitment to an ideology of "free love" put on the marriage.

Though problems must often have appeared unremitting, then, the Shelleys did have respites of relative calm. It was during one of these periods that Mary began the composition of *Frankenstein*. Summering in Geneva in 1816, she, Shelley, their six-month-old son William, and Claire occupied a small house near Byron's grander Villa Diodati; Claire was embroiled in a fitful affair with Byron, and Shelley, too, had become close to the aristocratic poet, who was already celebrated, even notorious, for both his work and his womanizing. Years later, in her wonderfully vivid introduction to the 1831 edition of the book, reprinted here, Mary was to respond to a question that, she explained, she was often asked: "How I, then a young girl, came to think of . . . so very hideous an idea?" One night, she recalled, the group—which also included Byron's eccentric young Italian physician, William Polidori—were regaling each other with tales of the supernatural in the villa's candlelit salon when Byron suddenly declared, "We will each write a ghost story." Mary was at first frustratingly empty of inspiration, but after brooding for a few days, she had a terrifying nightmare about a "pale student of unhallowed arts" who employed a "powerful engine" to awaken "the hideous phantasm of a man." Almost at once she understood that this horrifying dream might be the basis of "my ghost story—my tiresome, unlucky ghost story!" for she longed to "contrive [a tale] which would frighten my reader as I myself had been frightened that night!"

Frightening *Frankenstein* certainly is, but as readers from 1818 to the present have generally realized, it is considerably more than that. Subtitled *The Modern Prometheus* and prefaced with an epigraph from Milton's *Paradise Lost* (1667, 1674) in which the

fallen Adam reproaches God for having abandoned him, the novel openly meditates on large issues of responsibility and desire, science and sinfulness. Far more covertly, it reimagines Aeschylus's overreachingly ambitious Prometheus (whom Shelley himself was later to vindicate in his great verse drama *Prometheus Unbound*, 1820) and Milton's arrogantly vengeful Satan to consider questions about woman's anatomy and destiny that had always concerned Mary's own mother. For in "giving life" to a monster assembled from parts of corpses dug up in a nearby graveyard, the novel's protagonist, Victor Frankenstein, not only usurps the creative function of God, he enacts the maternal role of a woman, while, in experiencing himself as a lonely outcast, barred from education and inheritance, the book's nameless monster represents in exaggerated form some of the feelings a nineteenth-century daughter might well have had about her own place in a society where she had only the most minimal rights. Although such interpretations did not occur to the tale's earliest critics, most knew at once that they were encountering a work that was almost inexplicably resonant, and Mary Shelley herself was driven to contemplate the mysterious origins of her "hideous" idea. The explanation of these origins, as a number of recent writers have suggested, lay at least partly in the way early traumas of loss and sexuality, maternity and death had become intertwined in her life.

After the popular success of *Frankenstein*, such traumas unfortunately continued unabated. In the fall of 1817, six months before the publication of her novel, Mary had given birth to a daughter, Clara Everina; in the fall of 1818, six months after the book's appearance, the child died of dysentery in Venice. A year and a half later, in June 1819, the Shelleys' three-year-old son William succumbed to a similar malady in Rome. Mary, in particular, was devastated, and to distract herself she began a novel, *Mathilda*, which was unpublished in her lifetime but which served "to quell my wretchedness temporarily." Even more therapeutic was the birth of her son Percy Florence in November of the same year. He was the only one among her children to survive, and though he grew up to be a comparatively ordinary man—unworthy, as some thought, of the Godwin-Wollstonecraft-Shelley heritage—he soon became his mother's only consolation. For, two and a half years later, in the summer of 1822, Shelley himself, along with his friend Edward Williams, drowned in the bay of Lerici when the poet's boat, the *Don Juan*, was overturned.

Shortly before the catastrophe, Mary herself had suffered a miscarriage; overwrought and exhausted, she had parted with her husband coldly before he embarked on his fateful voyage—a failing for which she was never to forgive herself. But in any case this last blow was almost overwhelmingly heavy. A journal entry she wrote shortly after Shelley's death hardly seems to overstate the intensity of the dramas through which she had lived in the eight years since her elopement:

> I am now on the eve of completing my five & twentieth year—how drearily young for one so lost as I! How young in years for one lives ages each day in sorrow— think you that these moments are counted in my life as in other people's?—oh no! . . . what I have suffered . . . will write years on my brow & intrench them in my heart.

Despite such grief, Mary was to live some thirty more years after Shelley's death, and in those years she remained consistently productive, publishing a number of tales, five more novels—*Valperga* (1823), *The Last Man* (1826), *Perkin Warbeck* (1830), *Lodore* (1835), and *Falkner* (1837)—essays, travel sketches, and a series of biographies, as well as a set of useful and perceptive notes to her husband's poems. Vigorously inventive, her prose continued to enthrall many readers, though only *The Last Man* and *Falkner* begin to compare with *Frankenstein* in force and originality. *The Last Man* in particular has special biographical reference. Like her brief tale "The Mortal Immortal," this novel dramatizes the writer's anguished sense of having survived what seemed to be the deaths of almost everyone around her. And indeed she had, for not only were her husband and three of her children gone but so were her

half-sister Fanny Imlay, who had committed suicide in 1816; Shelley's friend Keats, who had died in Rome not long before Shelley himself drowned; and the couple's friend Byron, who died at Missolonghi in 1824, where he had gone to fight for the cause of Greek independence.

Yet Mary herself stubbornly endured, writing, raising her son Percy, recovering from smallpox, and refusing to remarry, with the proud explanation that she wanted the name "Mary Shelley" to be engraved on her tombstone. Always conscious of her maternal inheritance, she once declared: "If I have never written to vindicate the rights of women, I have ever befriended women when oppressed. At every risk I have befriended and supported victims to the social system." But she need not have struggled to justify herself, for with her imaginative energy she had accomplished at least as much as her mother had.

Introduction to *Frankenstein*

The Publishers of the Standard Novels, in selecting "Frankenstein" for one of their series, expressed a wish that I should furnish them with some account of the origin of the story. I am the more willing to comply, because I shall thus give a general answer to the question, so very frequently asked me—"How I, then a young girl, came to think of, and to dilate upon,[1] so very hideous an idea?" It is true that I am very averse to bringing myself forward in print; but as my account will only appear as an appendage to a former production, and as it will be confined to such topics as have connection with my authorship alone, I can scarcely accuse myself of a personal intrusion.

It is not singular that, as the daughter of two persons of distinguished literary celebrity,[2] I should very early in life have thought of writing. As a child I scribbled; and my favorite pastime, during the hours given me for recreation, was to "write stories." Still I had a dearer pleasure than this, which was the formation of castles in the air—the indulging in waking dreams—the following up trains of thought, which had for their subject the formation of a succession of imaginary incidents. My dreams were at once more fantastic and agreeable than my writings. In the latter I was a close imitator—rather doing as others had done, than putting down the suggestions of my own mind. What I wrote was intended at least for one other eye—my childhood's companion and friend; but my dreams were all my own; I accounted for them to nobody; they were my refuge when annoyed—my dearest pleasure when free.

I lived principally in the country as a girl, and passed a considerable time in Scotland. I made occasional visits to the more picturesque parts; but my habitual residence was on the blank and dreary northern shores of the Tay, near Dundee. Blank and dreary on retrospection I call them; they were not so to me then. They were the aerie[3] of freedom, and the pleasant region where unheeded I could commune with the creatures of my fancy. I wrote then—but in a most commonplace style. It was beneath the trees of the grounds belonging to our house, or on the bleak sides of the woodless mountains near, that my true compositions, the airy flights of my imagination, were born and fostered. I did not make myself the heroine of my tales. Life

1. Describe at length.
2. Mary Wollstonecraft (1759–1797) and William Godwin (1756–1836), both well-known authors.

3. The nest of a bird on a cliff or mountaintop, or any isolated or secluded dwelling.

appeared to me too commonplace an affair as regarded myself. I could not figure to myself that romantic woes or wonderful events would ever be my lot; but I was not confined to my own identity, and I could people the hours with creations far more interesting to me at that age, than my own sensations.

After this my life became busier, and reality stood in place of fiction. My husband,[4] however, was from the first, very anxious that I should prove myself worthy of my parentage, and enroll myself on the page of fame. He was forever inciting me to obtain literary reputation, which even on my own part I cared for then, though since I have become infinitely indifferent to it. At this time he desired that I should write, not so much with the idea that I could produce anything worthy of notice, but that he might himself judge how far I possessed the promise of better things hereafter. Still I did nothing. Traveling, and the cares of a family, occupied my time; and study, in the way of reading, or improving my ideas in communication with his far more cultivated mind, was all of literary employment that engaged my attention.

In the summer of 1816, we visited Switzerland, and became the neighbors of Lord Byron. At first we spent our pleasant hours on the lake, or wandering on its shores; and Lord Byron, who was writing the third canto of *Childe Harold*,[5] was the only one among us who put his thoughts upon paper. These, as he brought them successively to us, clothed in all the light and harmony of poetry, seemed to stamp as divine the glories of heaven and earth, whose influences we partook with him.

But it proved a wet, ungenial summer, and incessant rain often confined us for days to the house. Some volumes of ghost stories, translated from the German into French, fell into our hands. There was *The History of the Inconstant Lover*, who, when he thought to clasp the bride to whom he had pledged his vows, found himself in the arms of the pale ghost of her whom he had deserted. There was the tale of the sinful founder of his race, whose miserable doom it was to bestow the kiss of death on all the younger sons of his fated house, just when they reached the age of promise. His gigantic, shadowy form, clothed like the ghost in *Hamlet*, in complete armor, but with the beaver[6] up, was seen at midnight, by the moon's fitful beams, to advance slowly along the gloomy avenue. The shape was lost beneath the shadow of the castle walls; but soon a gate swung back, a step was heard, the door of the chamber opened, and he advanced to the couch of the blooming youths, cradled in healthy sleep. Eternal sorrow sat upon his face as he bent down and kissed the forehead of the boys, who from that hour withered like flowers snapped upon the stalk. I have not seen these stories since then; but their incidents are as fresh in my mind as if I had read them yesterday.

"We will each write a ghost story," said Lord Byron; and his proposition was acceded to. There were four of us. The noble author began a tale, a fragment of which he printed at the end of his poem of *Mazeppa*.[7] Shelley, more apt to embody ideas and sentiments in the radiance of brilliant imagery, and in the music of the most melodious verse that adorns our language, than to invent the machinery of a story, commenced one founded on the experiences of his early life. Poor Polidori[8] had some terrible idea about a skull-

4. The poet Percy Bysshe Shelley (1792–1822).
5. The first two cantos of the long poem *Childe Harold* by Lord Byron (1788–1824) were published to enormous popular acclaim in 1812; canto 3 appeared in 1816.

6. The piece of armor helmet that protects the lower part of the face.
7. *Mazeppa, a Poem* (1819).
8. John William Polidori (1795–1821), Byron's doctor and friend, whose other attempts to write

headed lady, who was so punished for peeping through a key-hole—what to see I forget—something very shocking and wrong of course; but when she was reduced to a worse condition than the renowned Tom of Coventry, he did not know what to do with her, and was obliged to despatch her to the tomb of the Capulets,[9] the only place for which she was fitted. The illustrious poets also, annoyed by the platitude of prose, speedily relinquished their uncongenial task.

I busied myself *to think of a story,*—a story to rival those which had excited us to this task. One which would speak to the mysterious fears of our nature, and awaken thrilling horror—one to make the reader dread to look round, to curdle the blood, and quicken the beatings of the heart. If I did not accomplish these things, my ghost story would be unworthy of its name. I thought and pondered—vainly. I felt that blank incapability of invention which is the greatest misery of authorship, when dull Nothing replies to our anxious invocations. *Have you thought of a story?* I was asked each morning, and each morning I was forced to reply with a mortifying negative.

Everything must have a beginning, to speak in Sanchean phrase;[1] and that beginning must be linked to something that went before. The Hindus give the world an elephant to support it, but they make the elephant stand upon a tortoise. Invention, it must be humbly admitted, does not consist in creating out of void, but out of chaos; the materials must, in the first place, be afforded: it can give form to dark, shapeless substances, but cannot bring into being the substance itself. In all matters of discovery and invention, even of those that appertain to the imagination, we are continually reminded of the story of Columbus and his egg.[2] Invention consists in the capacity of seizing on the capabilities of a subject, and in the power of molding and fashioning ideas suggested to it.

Many and long were the conversations between Lord Byron and Shelley, to which I was a devout but nearly silent listener. During one of these, various philosophical doctrines were discussed, and among others the nature of the principle of life, and whether there was any probability of its ever being discovered and communicated. They talked of the experiments of Dr. Darwin[3] (I speak not of what the Doctor really did, or said that he did, but, as more to my purpose, of what was then spoken of as having been done by him), who preserved a piece of vermicelli in a glass case, till by some extraordinary means it began to move with voluntary motion. Not thus, after all, would life be given. Perhaps a corpse would be reanimated; galvanism[4] had given token of such things: perhaps the component parts of a creature might be manufactured, brought together, and endued with vital warmth.

Night waned upon this talk, and even the witching hour had gone by, before we retired to rest. When I placed my head on my pillow, I did not

also met with little success.

9. Shakespeare's *Romeo and Juliet* ends with the unhappy pair dead in the tomb of Juliet's family. Tom of Coventry was the "peeping Tom" who alone looked at Lady Godiva when, according to legend, in the 12th century she rode naked through Coventry (so that her husband would lift a tax); his eyes shriveled in his head.

1. I.e., in a way befitting the down-to-earth and practical squire in Cervantes's *Don Quixote* (1605, 1615); perhaps a direct allusion to Sancho Panza's statement about the importance of beginnings in

Part 2, chapter 33.

2. The story that Christopher Columbus, when told that others could find the Indies, challenged the listeners to stand an egg on its end. When none could, he struck the egg on the table and left it standing on its broken end, to prove that the way would be easy to follow once he had shown it.

3. Erasmus Darwin (1731–1802), physician, poet, and scientist.

4. Application of electricity developed by chemical action, especially to stimulate plants or muscles.

sleep, nor could I be said to think. My imagination, unbidden, possessed and guided me, gifting the successive images that arose in my mind with a vividness far beyond the usual bounds of reverie. I saw—with shut eyes, but acute mental vision,—I saw the pale student of unhallowed arts kneeling beside the thing he had put together. I saw the hideous phantasm of a man stretched out, and then, on the working of some powerful engine, show signs of life, and stir with an uneasy, half vital motion. Frightful must it be; for supremely frightful would be the effect of any human endeavor to mock the stupendous mechanism of the Creator of the world. His success would terrify the artist; he would rush away from his odious handiwork, horror-stricken. He would hope that, left to itself, the slight spark of life which he had communicated would fade; that this thing, which had received such imperfect animation, would subside into dead matter; and he might sleep in the belief that the silence of the grave would quench for ever the transient existence of the hideous corpse which he had looked upon as the cradle of life. He sleeps; but he is awakened; he opens his eyes; behold the horrid thing stands at his bedside, opening his curtains, and looking on him with yellow, watery, but speculative eyes.

I opened mine in terror. The idea so possessed my mind, that a thrill of fear ran through me, and I wished to exchange the ghastly image of my fancy for the realities around. I see them still; the very room, the dark *parquet*,[5] the closed shutters, with the moonlight struggling through, and the sense I had that the glassy lake and white high Alps were beyond. I could not so easily get rid of my hideous phantom; still it haunted me. I must try to think of something else. I recurred to my ghost story,—my tiresome unlucky ghost story! O! if I could only contrive one which would frighten my reader as I myself had been frightened that night!

Swift as light and as cheering was the idea that broke in upon me. "I have found it! What terrified me will terrify others; and I need only describe the specter which had haunted my midnight pillow." On the morrow I announced that I had *thought of a story*. I began that day with the words, *It was on a dreary night of November,* making only a transcript of the grim terrors of my waking dream.

At first I thought but of a few pages—of a short tale; but Shelley urged me to develop the idea at greater length. I certainly did not owe the suggestion of one incident, nor scarcely of one train of feeling, to my husband, and yet but for his incitement, it would never have taken the form in which it was presented to the world. From this declaration I must except the preface. As far as I can recollect, it was entirely written by him.

And now, once again, I bid my hideous progeny go forth and prosper. I have an affection for it, for it was the offspring of happy days, when death and grief were but words, which found no true echo in my heart. Its several pages speak of many a walk, many a drive, and many a conversation, when I was not alone; and my companion was one who, in this world, I shall never see more. But this is for myself; my readers have nothing to do with these associations.

I will add but one word as to the alterations I have made. They are principally those of style. I have changed no portion of the story, nor introduced

5. Patterned wooden floor.

any new ideas of circumstances. I have mended the language where it was so bald[6] as to interfere with the interest of the narrative; and these changes occur almost exclusively in the beginning of the first volume. Throughout they are entirely confined to such parts as are mere adjuncts to the story, leaving the core and substance of it untouched.

1831

The Mortal Immortal

A Tale

July 16, 1833.—This is a memorable anniversary for me; on it I complete my three hundred and twenty-third year!

The Wandering Jew?[1]—certainly not. More than eighteen centuries have passed over his head. In comparison with him, I am a very young immortal.

Am I, then, immortal? This is a question which I have asked myself, by day and night, for now three hundred and three years, and yet cannot answer it. I detected a gray hair amidst my brown locks this very day—that surely signifies decay. Yet it may have remained concealed there for three hundred years—for some persons have become entirely white-headed before twenty years of age.

I will tell my story, and my reader shall judge for me. I will tell my story, and so contrive to pass some few hours of a long eternity, become so wearisome to me. Forever! Can it be? to live forever! I have heard of enchantments, in which the victims were plunged into a deep sleep, to wake, after a hundred years, as fresh as ever: I have heard of the Seven Sleepers[2]—thus to be immortal would not be so burthensome: but, oh! the weight of never-ending time—the tedious passage of the still-succeeding hours! How happy was the fabled Nourjahad![3]—But to my task.

All the world has heard of Cornelius Agrippa.[4] His memory is as immortal as his arts have made me. All the world has also heard of his scholar, who, unawares, raised the foul fiend during his master's absence, and was destroyed by him. The report, true or false, of this accident, was attended with many inconveniences to the renowned philosopher. All his scholars at once deserted him—his servants disappeared. He had no one near him to put coals on his ever-burning fires while he slept, or to attend to the changeful colors of his medicines while he studied. Experiment after experiment failed, because one pair of hands was insufficient to complete them: the dark spirits laughed at him for not being able to retain a single mortal in his service.

I was then very young—very poor—and very much in love. I had been for about a year the pupil of Cornelius, though I was absent when this accident

6. Unadorned, graceless.
1. According to medieval legend, a Jew who mocked Jesus on his way to be crucified was condemned to wander through the world until Judgment Day.
2. A legend about seven noble Christian youths of Ephesus who slept in a cave for some 200 years to

escape persecution.
3. The hero of Frances Sherwood's *History of Nourjahad* (1767) was happy because he safely learned how undesirable immortality is.
4. Heinrich Cornelius Agrippa von Nettesheim (1486–1535), German occult philosopher and alchemist.

took place. On my return, my friends implored me not to return to the alchemist's abode. I trembled as I listened to the dire tale they told; I required no second warning; and when Cornelius came and offered me a purse of gold if I would remain under his roof, I felt as if Satan himself tempted me. My teeth chattered—my hair stood on end:—I ran off as fast as my trembling knees would permit.

My failing steps were directed whither for two years they had every evening been attracted,—a gently bubbling spring of pure living waters, beside which lingered a dark-haired girl, whose beaming eyes were fixed on the path I was accustomed each night to tread. I cannot remember the hour when I did not love Bertha; we had been neighbors and playmates from infancy—her parents, like mine, were of humble life, yet respectable—our attachment had been a source of pleasure to them. In an evil hour, a malignant fever carried off both her father and mother, and Bertha became an orphan. She would have found a home beneath my paternal roof, but, unfortunately, the old lady of the near castle, rich, childless, and solitary, declared her intention to adopt her. Henceforth Bertha was clad in silk—inhabited a marble palace— and was looked on as being highly favored by fortune. But in her new situation among her new associates, Bertha remained true to the friend of her humbler days; she often visited the cottage of my father, and when forbidden to go thither, she would stray towards the neighboring wood, and meet me beside its shady fountain.

She often declared that she owed no duty to her new protectress equal in sanctity to that which bound us. Yet still I was too poor to marry, and she grew weary of being tormented on my account. She had a haughty but an impatient spirit, and grew angry at the obstacles that prevented our union. We met now after an absence, and she had been sorely beset while I was away; she complained bitterly, and almost reproached me for being poor. I replied hastily,—

"I am honest, if I am poor!—were I not, I might soon become rich!"

This exclamation produced a thousand questions. I feared to shock her by owning[5] the truth, but she drew it from me; and then, casting a look of disdain on me, she said—

"You pretend to love, and you fear to face the Devil for my sake!"

I protested that I had only dreaded to offend her;—while she dwelt on the magnitude of the reward that I should receive. Thus encouraged—shamed by her—led on by love and hope, laughing at my late fears, with quick steps and a light heart, I returned to accept the offers of the alchemist, and was instantly installed in my office.

A year passed away. I became possessed of no insignificant sum of money. Custom had banished my fears. In spite of the most painful vigilance, I had never detected the trace of a cloven foot;[6] nor was the studious silence of our abode ever disturbed by demoniac howls. I still continued my stolen interviews with Bertha, and Hope dawned on me—Hope—but not perfect joy; for Bertha fancied that love and security were enemies, and her pleasure was to divide them in my bosom. Though true of heart, she was somewhat of a coquette in manner; and I was jealous as a Turk. She slighted me in a

5. Admitting.
6. A feature thought to be possessed by the devil and his servants.

thousand ways, yet would never acknowledge herself to be in the wrong. She would drive me mad with anger, and then force me to beg her pardon. Sometimes she fancied that I was not sufficiently submissive, and then she had some story of a rival, favored by her protectress. She was surrounded by silk-clad youths—the rich and gay—What chance had the sad-robed scholar of Cornelius compared with these?

On one occasion, the philosopher made such large demands upon my time, that I was unable to meet her as I was wont. He was engaged in some mighty work, and I was forced to remain, day and night, feeding his furnaces and watching his chemical preparations. Bertha waited for me in vain at the fountain. Her haughty spirit fired at this neglect; and when at last I stole out during the few short minutes allotted to me for slumber, and hoped to be consoled by her, she received me with disdain, dismissed me in scorn, and vowed that any man should possess her hand rather than he who could not be in two places at once for her sake. She would be revenged!—And truly she was. In my dingy retreat I heard that she had been hunting, attended by Albert Hoffer. Albert Hoffer was favored by her protectress, and the three passed in cavalcade before my smoky window. Methought that they mentioned my name—it was followed by a laugh of derision, as her dark eyes glanced contemptuously towards my abode.

Jealousy, with all its venom, and all its misery, entered my breast. Now I shed a torrent of tears, to think that I should never call her mine; and, anon,[7] I imprecated a thousand curses on her inconstancy. Yet, still I must stir the fires of the alchemist, still attend on the changes of his unintelligible medicines.

Cornelius had watched for three days and nights, nor closed his eyes. The progress of his alembics[8] was slower than he expected: in spite of his anxiety, sleep weighed upon his eyelids. Again and again he threw off drowsiness with more than human energy; again and again it stole away his senses. He eyed his crucibles wistfully. "Not ready yet," he murmured; "will another night pass before the work is accomplished? Winzy,[9] you are vigilant—you are faithful—you have slept, my boy—you slept last night. Look at that glass vessel. The liquid it contains is of a soft rose-color: the moment it begins to change its hue, awaken me—till then I may close my eyes. First, it will turn white, and then emit golden flashes; but wait not till then; when the rose-color fades, rouse me." I scarcely heard the last words, muttered, as they were, in sleep. Even then he did not quite yield to nature. "Winzy, my boy," he again said, "do not touch the vessel—do not put it to your lips; it is a philter—a philter to cure love; you would not[1] cease to love your Bertha—beware to drink!"

And he slept. His venerable head sunk on his breast, and I scarce heard his regular breathing. For a few minutes I watched the vessel—the rosy hue of the liquid remained unchanged. Then my thoughts wandered—they visited the fountain, and dwelt on a thousand charming scenes never to be renewed—never! Serpents and adders were in my heart as the word "Never!" half formed itself on my lips. False girl!—false and cruel! Never more would she smile on me as that evening she smiled on Albert. Worthless, detested

7. Shortly afterward.
8. Apparatus used for distilling fluids.

9. The name of the narrator.
1. Do not wish to. "Philter": a potion or charm.

woman! I would not remain unrevenged—she should see Albert expire at her feet—she should die beneath my vengeance. She had smiled in disdain and triumph—she knew my wretchedness and her power. Yet what power had she?—the power of exciting my hate—my utter scorn—my—oh, all but indifference! Could I attain that—could I regard her with careless eyes, transferring my rejected love to one fairer and more true, that were indeed a victory!

A bright flash darted before my eyes. I had forgotten the medicine of the adept;[2] I gazed on it with wonder: flashes of admirable beauty, more bright than those which the diamond emits when the sun's rays are on it, glanced from the surface of the liquid; an odor the most fragrant and grateful stole over my sense; the vessel seemed one globe of living radiance, lovely to the eye, and most inviting to the taste. The first thought, instinctively inspired by the grosser sense, was, I will—I must drink. I raised the vessel to my lips. "It will cure me of love—of torture!" Already I had quaffed half of the most delicious liquor ever tasted by the palate of man, when the philosopher stirred. I started—I dropped the glass—the fluid flamed and glanced along the floor, while I felt Cornelius's grip at my throat, as he shrieked aloud, "Wretch! you have destroyed the labor of my life!"

The philosopher was totally unaware that I had drunk any portion of his drug. His idea was, and I gave a tacit assent to it, that I had raised the vessel from curiosity, and that, frighted at its brightness, and the flashes of intense light it gave forth, I had let it fall. I never undeceived him. The fire of the medicine was quenched—the fragrance died away—he grew calm, as a philosopher should under the heaviest trials, and dismissed me to rest.

I will not attempt to describe the sleep of glory and bliss which bathed my soul in paradise during the remaining hours of that memorable night. Words would be faint and shallow types[3] of my enjoyment, or of the gladness that possessed my bosom when I woke. I trod air—my thoughts were in heaven. Earth appeared heaven, and my inheritance upon it was to be one trance of delight. "This it is to be cured of love," I thought; "I will see Bertha this day, and she will find her lover cold and regardless; too happy to be disdainful, yet how utterly indifferent to her!"

The hours danced away. The philosopher, secure that he had once succeeded, and believing that he might again, began to concoct the same medicine once more. He was shut up with his books and drugs, and I had a holiday. I dressed myself with care; I looked in an old but polished shield, which served me for a mirror; methought my good looks had wonderfully improved. I hurried beyond the precincts of the town, joy in my soul, the beauty of heaven and earth around me. I turned my steps towards the castle—I could look on its lofty turrets with lightness of heart, for I was cured of love. My Bertha saw me afar off, as I came up the avenue. I know not what sudden impulse animated her bosom, but at the sight, she sprung with a light fawn-like bound down the marble steps, and was hastening towards me. But I had been perceived by another person. The old high-born hag, who called herself her protectress, and was her tyrant, had seen me, also; she hobbled, panting, up the terrace; a page, as ugly as herself, held up

2. An alchemist who has learned the secrets of the art.

3. Signs, prefigurations.

her train, and fanned her as she hurried along, and stopped my fair girl with a "How, now, my bold mistress? whither so fast? Back to your cage—hawks are abroad!"

Bertha clasped her hands—her eyes were still bent on my approaching figure. I saw the contest. How I abhorred the old crone who checked the kind impulses of my Bertha's softening heart. Hitherto, respect for her rank had caused me to avoid the lady of the castle; now I disdained such trivial considerations. I was cured of love, and lifted above all human fears; I hastened forwards, and soon reached the terrace. How lovely Bertha looked! her eyes flashing fire, her cheeks glowing with impatience and anger, she was a thousand times more graceful and charming than ever—I no longer loved— Oh! no, I adored—worshiped—idolized her!

She had that morning been persecuted, with more than usual vehemence, to consent to an immediate marriage with my rival. She was reproached with the encouragement that she had shown him—she was threatened with being turned out of doors with disgrace and shame. Her proud spirit rose in arms at the threat; but when she remembered the scorn that she had heaped upon me, and how, perhaps, she had thus lost one whom she now regarded as her only friend, she wept with remorse and rage. At that moment I appeared. "O, Winzy!" she exclaimed, "take me to your mother's cot;⁴ swiftly let me leave the detested luxuries and wretchedness of this noble dwelling—take me to poverty and happiness."

I clasped her in my arms with transport. The old lady was speechless with fury, and broke forth into invective only when we were far on our road to my natal cottage. My mother received the fair fugitive, escaped from a gilt cage to nature and liberty, with tenderness and joy; my father, who loved her, welcomed her heartily; it was a day of rejoicing, which did not need the addition of the celestial potion of the alchemist to steep me in delight.

Soon after this eventful day, I became the husband of Bertha. I ceased to be the scholar of Cornelius, but I continued his friend. I always felt grateful to him for having, unawares, procured me that delicious draught of a divine elixir, which, instead of curing me of love (sad cure! solitary and joyless remedy for evils which seem blessings to the memory), had inspired me with courage and resolution, thus winning for me an inestimable treasure in my Bertha.

I often called to mind that period of trance-like inebriation with wonder. The drink of Cornelius had not fulfilled the task for which he affirmed that it had been prepared, but its effects were more potent and blissful than words can express. They had faded by degrees, yet they lingered long—and painted life in hues of splendor. Bertha often wondered at my lightness of heart and unaccustomed gaiety; for, before, I had been rather serious, or even sad, in my disposition. She loved me the better for my cheerful temper, and our days were winged by joy.

Five years afterwards I was suddenly summoned to the bedside of the dying Cornelius. He had sent for me in haste, conjuring my instant presence. I found him stretched on his pallet,⁵ enfeebled even to death; all of life that yet remained animated his piercing eyes, and they were fixed on a glass vessel, full of a roseate liquid.

4. Cottage. 5. Thin mattress.

"Behold," he said, in a broken and inward voice, "the vanity of human wishes! a second time my hopes are about to be crowned, a second time they are destroyed. Look at that liquor—you remember five years ago I had prepared the same, with the same success;—then, as now, my thirsting lips expected to taste the immortal elixir—you dashed it from me! and at present it is too late."

He spoke with difficulty, and fell back on his pillow. I could not help saying,—

"How, revered master, can a cure for love restore you to life?"

A faint smile gleamed across his face as I listened earnestly to his scarcely intelligible answer.

"A cure for love and for all things—the Elixir of Immortality. Ah! if now I might drink, I should live for ever!"

As he spoke, a golden flash gleamed from the fluid; a well-remembered fragrance stole over the air; he raised himself, all weak as he was—strength seemed miraculously to reenter his frame—he stretched forth his hand—a loud explosion startled me—a ray of fire shot up from the elixir, and the glass vessel which contained it was shivered to atoms! I turned my eyes towards the philosopher; he had fallen back—his eyes were glassy—his features rigid—he was dead!

But I lived, and was to live forever! So said the unfortunate alchemist, and for a few days I believed his words. I remembered the glorious drunkenness that had followed my stolen draught. I reflected on the change I had felt in my frame—in my soul. The bounding elasticity of the one—the buoyant lightness of the other. I surveyed myself in a mirror, and could perceive no change in my features during the space of the five years which had elapsed. I remembered the radiant hues and grateful scent of that delicious beverage—worthy the gift it was capable of bestowing—I was, then, IMMORTAL!

A few days after I laughed at my credulity. The old proverb, that "a prophet is least regarded in his own country," was true with respect to me and my defunct master. I loved him as a man—I respected him as a sage—but I derided the notion that he could command the powers of darkness, and laughed at the superstitious fears with which he was regarded by the vulgar.[6] He was a wise philosopher, but had no acquaintance with any spirits but those clad in flesh and blood. His science was simply human; and human science, I soon persuaded myself, could never conquer nature's laws so far as to imprison the soul for ever within its carnal habitation. Cornelius had brewed a soul-refreshing drink—more inebriating than wine—sweeter and more fragrant than any fruit: it possessed probably strong medicinal powers, imparting gladness to the heart and vigor to the limbs; but its effects would wear out; already were they diminished in my frame. I was a lucky fellow to have quaffed health and joyous spirits, and perhaps long life, at my master's hands; but my good fortune ended there: longevity was far different from immortality.

I continued to entertain this belief for many years. Sometimes a thought stole across me—Was the alchemist indeed deceived? But my habitual credence was, that I should meet the fate of all the children of Adam[7] at my

6. Common, uneducated people.
7. According to Genesis 3, the first man, who brought death into the world when he and Eve ate the forbidden fruit in Eden.

appointed time—a little late, but still at a natural age. Yet it was certain that I retained a wonderfully youthful look. I was laughed at for my vanity in consulting the mirror so often, but I consulted it in vain—my brow was untrenched[8]—my cheeks—my eyes—my whole person continued as untarnished as in my twentieth year.

I was troubled. I looked at the faded beauty of Bertha—I seemed more like her son. By degrees our neighbors began to make similar observations, and I found at last that I went by the name of the Scholar bewitched. Bertha herself grew uneasy. She became jealous and peevish, and at length she began to question me. We had no children; we were all in all to each other; and though, as she grew older, her vivacious spirit became a little allied to ill-temper, and her beauty sadly diminished, I cherished her in my heart as the mistress I had idolized, the wife I had sought and won with such perfect love.

At last our situation became intolerable: Bertha was fifty—I twenty years of age. I had, in very shame, in some measure adopted the habits of a more advanced age; I no longer mingled in the dance among the young and gay, but my heart bounded along with them while I restrained my feet; and a sorry figure I cut among the Nestors[9] of our village. But before the time I mention, things were altered—we were universally shunned; we were—at least, I was—reported to have kept up an iniquitous acquaintance with some of my former master's supposed friends. Poor Bertha was pitied, but deserted. I was regarded with horror and detestation.

What was to be done? we sat by our winter fire—poverty had made itself felt, for none would buy the produce of my farm; and often I had been forced to journey twenty miles, to some place where I was not known, to dispose of our property. It is true we had saved something for an evil day—that day was come.

We sat by our lone fireside—the old-hearted youth and his antiquated wife. Again Bertha insisted on knowing the truth; she recapitulated all she had ever heard said about me, and added her own observations. She conjured me to cast off the spell; she described how much more comely gray hairs were than my chestnut locks; she descanted[1] on the reverence and respect due to age—how preferable to the slight regard paid to mere children: could I imagine that the despicable gifts of youth and good looks outweighed disgrace, hatred, and scorn? Nay, in the end I should be burned as a dealer in the black art, while she, to whom I had not deigned to communicate any portion of my good fortune, might be stoned as my accomplice. At length she insinuated that I must share my secret with her, and bestow on her like benefits to those I myself enjoyed, or she would denounce me—and then she burst into tears.

Thus beset, methought it was the best way to tell the truth. I revealed it as tenderly as I could, and spoke only of *a very long life,* not of immortality—which representation, indeed, coincided best with my own ideas. When I ended, I rose and said,

"And now, my Bertha, will you denounce the lover of your youth?—You will not, I know. But it is too hard, my poor wife, that you should suffer from

8. Unwrinkled.
9. Old men; Nestor was an aged counselor in

Homer's *Iliad.*
1. Discoursed.

my ill-luck and the accursed arts of Cornelius. I will leave you—you have wealth enough, and friends will return in my absence. I will go; young as I seem, and strong as I am, I can work and gain my bread among strangers, unsuspected and unknown. I loved you in youth; God is my witness that I would not desert you in age, but that your safety and happiness require it."

I took my cap and moved towards the door; in a moment Bertha's arms were round my neck, and her lips were pressed to mine. "No, my husband, my Winzy," she said, "you shall not go alone—take me with you; we will remove from this place, and, as you say, among strangers we shall be unsuspected and safe. I am not so very old as quite to shame you, my Winzy; and I dare say the charm will soon wear off, and, with the blessing of God, you will become more elderly-looking, as is fitting; you shall not leave me."

I returned the good soul's embrace heartily. "I will not, my Bertha; but for your sake I had not thought of such a thing.[2] I will be your true, faithful husband while you are spared to me, and do my duty by you to the last."

The next day we prepared secretly for our emigration. We were obliged to make great pecuniary sacrifices—it could not be helped. We realized a sum sufficient, at least, to maintain us while Bertha lived; and, without saying adieu to any one, quitted our native country to take refuge in a remote part of western France.

It was a cruel thing to transport poor Bertha from her native village, and the friends of her youth, to a new country, new language, new customs. The strange secret of my destiny rendered this removal immaterial to me; but I compassionated her deeply, and was glad to perceive that she found compensation for her misfortunes in a variety of little ridiculous circumstances. Away from all tell-tale chroniclers, she sought to decrease the apparent disparity of our ages by a thousand feminine arts—rouge, youthful dress, and assumed juvenility of manner. I could not be angry—Did not I myself wear a mask? Why quarrel with hers, because it was less successful? I grieved deeply when I remembered that this was my Bertha, whom I had loved so fondly, and won with such transport—the dark-eyed, dark-haired girl, with smiles of enchanting archness and a step like a fawn—this mincing, simpering, jealous old woman. I should have revered her gray locks and withered cheeks; but thus!—It was my work, I knew; but I did not the less deplore this type of human weakness.

Her jealousy never slept. Her chief occupation was to discover that, in spite of outward appearances, I was myself growing old. I verily believe that the poor soul loved me truly in her heart, but never had woman so tormenting a mode of displaying fondness. She would discern wrinkles in my face and decrepitude in my walk, while I bounded along in youthful vigor, the youngest looking of twenty youths. I never dared address another woman: on one occasion, fancying that the belle of the village regarded me with favoring eyes, she bought me a gray wig. Her constant discourse among her acquaintances was, that though I looked so young, there was ruin at work within my frame; and she affirmed that the worst symptom about me was my apparent health. My youth was a disease, she said, and I ought at all times to prepare, if not for a sudden and awful death, at least to awake some morning white-headed, and bowed down with all the marks of advanced years. I let her

2. I.e., I thought of it only for your sake.

talk—I often joined in her conjectures. Her warnings chimed in with my never-ceasing speculations concerning my state, and I took an earnest, though painful, interest in listening to all that her quick wit and excited imagination could say on the subject.

Why dwell on these minute circumstances? We lived on for many long years. Bertha became bed-rid and paralytic: I nursed her as a mother might a child. She grew peevish, and still harped upon one string—of how long I should survive her. It has ever been a source of consolation to me, that I performed my duty scrupulously towards her. She had been mine in youth, she was mine in age, and at last, when I heaped the sod over her corpse, I wept to feel that I had lost all that really bound me to humanity.

Since then how many have been my cares and woes, how few and empty my enjoyments! I pause here in my history—I will pursue it no further. A sailor without rudder or compass, tossed on a stormy sea—a traveller lost on a wide-spread heath, without landmark or star to guide him—such have I been: more lost, more hopeless than either. A nearing ship, a gleam from some far cot, may save them; but I have no beacon except the hope of death.

Death! mysterious, ill-visaged friend of weak humanity! Why alone of all mortals have you cast me from your sheltering fold?[3] O, for the peace of the grave! the deep silence of the iron-bound tomb! that thought would cease to work in my brain, and my heart beat no more with emotions varied only by new forms of sadness!

Am I immortal? I return to my first question. In the first place, is it not more probable that the beverage of the alchemist was fraught rather with longevity than eternal life? Such is my hope. And then be it remembered, that I only drank *half* of the potion prepared by him. Was not the whole necessary to complete the charm? To have drained half the Elixir of Immortality is but to be half immortal—my Forever is thus truncated and null.

But again, who shall number the years of the half of eternity? I often try to imagine by what rule the infinite may be divided. Sometimes I fancy age advancing upon me. One gray hair I have found. Fool! do I lament? Yes, the fear of age and death often creeps coldly into my heart; and the more I live, the more I dread death, even while I abhor life. Such an enigma is man—born to perish—when he wars, as I do, against the established laws of his nature.

But for this anomaly of feeling surely I might die: the medicine of the alchemist would not be proof against[4] fire—sword—and the strangling waters. I have gazed upon the blue depths of many a placid lake, and the tumultuous rushing of many a mighty river, and have said, peace inhabits those waters; yet I have turned my steps away, to live yet another day. I have asked myself, whether suicide would be a crime in one to whom thus only the portals of the other world could be opened. I have done all, except presenting myself as a soldier or duelist, an object of destruction to my—no, *not* my fellow-mortals, and therefore I have shrunk away. They are not my fellows. The inextinguishable power of life in my frame, and their ephemeral existence, place us wide as the poles asunder. I could not raise a hand against the meanest[5] or the most powerful among them.

3. An enclosure for sheep. Christ is traditionally represented as a shepherd; here Shelley places Death in that protective role.

4. Able to resist or repel.
5. Lowest.

Thus I have lived on for many a year—alone, and weary of myself—desirous of death, yet never dying—a mortal immortal. Neither ambition nor avarice can enter my mind, and the ardent love that gnaws at my heart, never to be returned—never to find an equal on which to expend itself—lives there only to torment me.

This very day I conceived a design by which I may end all—without self-slaughter, without making another man a Cain[6]—an expedition, which mortal frame can never survive, even endued[7] with the youth and strength that inhabits mine. Thus I shall put my immortality to the test, and rest for ever—or return, the wonder and benefactor of the human species.

Before I go, a miserable vanity has caused me to pen these pages. I would not die, and leave no name behind. Three centuries have passed since I quaffed the fatal beverage: another year shall not elapse before, encountering gigantic dangers—warring with the powers of frost in their home—beset by famine, toil, and tempest—I yield this body, too tenacious a cage for a soul which thirsts for freedom, to the destructive elements of air and water—or, if I survive, my name shall be recorded as one of the most famous among the sons of men; and, my task achieved, I shall adopt more resolute means, and, by scattering and annihilating the atoms that compose my frame, set at liberty the life imprisoned within, and so cruelly prevented from soaring from this dim earth to a sphere more congenial to its immortal essence.

1833 1834

6. I.e., a murderer. In Genesis 4, Cain, the son of cast out into the world.
Adam and Eve, murders his brother Abel and is 7. Endowed; embued.

SOJOURNER TRUTH
ca. 1797–1883

Our understanding of both the life and the art of Sojourner Truth is limited, for this woman, who by all accounts became a brilliant speechmaker, exemplifies an oral tradition only partially preserved. As Erlene Stetson and Linda David have demonstrated, "illiteracy did not exclude Truth from political discourse," because she relied on access to the written word, especially the Bible and newspapers, which she heard read aloud and which she refashioned in her remarkable speeches. Born into slavery in Hurley, Ulster County, New York, she was called Isabella, and after she fled to freedom in 1827, she took the last name of the family that protected her. Isabella Van Wagenen had already witnessed the sale of two of her four surviving children when she settled as a domestic servant with her son in New York City in or around 1829. There she worked with the evangelical preacher Elijah Pierson, who encouraged her efforts to convert prostitutes, and with Robert Matthew, whose communal household, "Zion Hill" in Sing Sing, New York, was her home for two years. In 1843, mystical visions and voices gave her the new name "Sojourner Truth." So christened, she sojourned alone to speak the truth on tours that would make her famous throughout the United States.

Her religious zeal was linked to abolitionist goals when, at a communal farm in Northampton, Massachusetts, in that first winter of her travels, she came into contact with George W. Benson, brother-in-law of the newspaper editor William Lloyd Gar-

rison. Subsequently hailed by abolitionist leaders, she toured Ohio, Indiana, Missouri, and Kansas throughout the 1850s, singing gospel songs, engaging large crowds with her charismatic speeches, and selling the *Narrative of Sojourner Truth* (1850), an autobiographical account transcribed and edited by Olive Gilbert. Illiterate all of her life, speaking an English accented with her original language, Dutch, Sojourner Truth was effective even with hostile audiences. In an essay in the April 1863 issue of the *Atlantic Monthly*, Harriet Beecher Stowe described the subtle power of this "sibyl" who had found enough charity to declare, "Lord, Lord, I can love *even de white folk!*" During the postwar period, encouraged by Elizabeth Cady Stanton, Sojourner Truth began speaking for the cause of women's suffrage, but she never relinquished her spiritual and racial themes. Her later call for a "Negro State" met with no success; however, she continued to lecture and sing in many eastern and midwestern states until, in her mid-eighties, she retired to Battle Creek, Michigan, where she died.

As one of the most effective female orators of her time, Sojourner Truth spoke for oppressed people with humor and courage that are evident, too, in the story of her response to allegations that she was a man: she was said to have bared her breast at a women's rights convention. Although we must depend on the records of her white friends, in her speeches Sojourner Truth emerges, as the scholar Sterling Stuckey has observed, with the vitality of a great blues singer who sustains the most essential values of her people.

We are indebted to Miriam Schneir for her modernization of Truth's speeches in *Feminism: The Essential Historical Writings* (1972); the speeches were originally recorded in Elizabeth Cady Stanton et al., *The History of Woman Suffrage* (1881–87).

Ain't I a Woman?

Well, children, where there is so much racket there must be something out of kilter. I think that 'twixt the negroes of the South and the women at the North, all talking about rights, the white men will be in a fix pretty soon. But what's all this here talking about?

That man over there says that women need to be helped into carriages, and lifted over ditches, and to have the best place everywhere. Nobody ever helps me into carriages, or over mud-puddles, or gives me any best place! And ain't I a woman? Look at me! Look at my arm! I have ploughed and planted, and gathered into barns, and no man could head[1] me! And ain't I a woman? I could work as much and eat as much as a man—when I could get it—and bear the lash as well! And ain't I a woman? I have borne thirteen children, and seen them most all sold off to slavery, and when I cried out with my mother's grief, none but Jesus heard me! And ain't I a woman?

Then they talk about this thing in the head; what's this they call it? [Intellect, someone whispers.] That's it, honey. What's that got to do with women's rights or negro's rights? If my cup won't hold but a pint, and yours holds a quart, wouldn't you be mean not to let me have my little half-measure full?

Then that little man in black there, he says women can't have as much rights as men, 'cause Christ wasn't a woman! Where did your Christ come from? Where did your Christ come from? From God and a woman! Man had nothing to do with Him.

1. Get in front of, surpass.

If the first woman God ever made was strong enough to turn the world upside down all alone, these women together ought to be able to turn it back, and get it right side up again! And now they is asking to do it, the men better let them.

Obliged to you for hearing me, and now old Sojourner ain't got nothing more to say.

1851 1881

What Time of Night It Is

Is it not good for me to come and draw forth a spirit,[1] to see what kind of spirit people are of? I see that some of you have got the spirit of a goose, and some have got the spirit of a snake. I feel at home here. I come to you, citizens of New York, as I suppose you ought to be. I am a citizen of the state of New York; I was born in it, and I was a slave in the state of New York; and now I am a good citizen of this state. I was born here, and I can tell you I feel at home here. I've been lookin' round and watchin' things, and I know a little mite 'bout Woman's Rights, too. I come forth to speak 'bout Woman's Rights, and want to throw in my little mite, to keep the scales a-movin'. I know that it feels a kind o' hissin' and ticklin' like to see a colored woman get up and tell you about things, and Woman's Rights. We have all been thrown down so low that nobody thought we'd ever get up again; but we have been long enough trodden now; we will come up again, and now I am here.

I was a-thinkin', when I see women contendin' for their rights, I was a-thinkin' what a difference there is now, and what there was in old times. I have only a few minutes to speak; but in the old times the kings of the earth would[n't] hear a woman. There was a king in the Scriptures;[2] and then it was the kings of the earth would kill a woman if she come into their presence; but Queen Esther come forth, for she was oppressed, and felt there was a great wrong, and she said I will die or I will bring my complaint before the king. Should the king of the United States be greater, or more crueler, or more harder? But the king, he raised up his sceptre and said: "Thy request shall be granted unto thee—to the half of my kingdom will I grant it to thee!" Then he said he would hang Haman on the gallows he had made up high. But that is not what women come forward to contend. The women want their rights as Esther. She only wanted to explain her rights. And he was so liberal that he said, "the half of my kingdom shall be granted to thee," and he did not wait for her to ask, he was so liberal with her.

Now, women do not ask half of a kingdom, but their rights, and they don't get 'em. When she comes to demand 'em, don't you hear how sons hiss their mothers like snakes because they ask for their rights; and can they ask for anything less? The king ordered Haman to be hung on the gallows which he prepared to hang others; but I do not want any man to be killed, but I am

1. An energetic response.
2. King Ahasuerus (Xerxes, king of Persia, r. 486–465 B.C.E.); men and women who came before him uncalled were put to death unless he held out his golden scepter, as he did to Esther, his Jewish queen, who saved her people from a massacre planned by Haman (see the Book of Esther, which this paragraph echoes).

sorry to see them so short-minded. But we'll have our rights; see if we don't; and you can't stop us from them; see if you can. You may hiss as much as you like, but it is comin'. Women don't get half as much rights as they ought to; we want more, and we will have it. Jesus says: "What I say to one, I say to all—watch!"[3] I'm a-watchin'. God says: "Honor your father and your mother."[4] Sons and daughters ought to behave themselves before their mothers, but they do not. I can see them a-laughin', and pointin' at their mothers up here on the stage. They hiss when an aged woman comes forth. If they'd been brought up proper they'd have known better than hissin' like snakes and geese. I'm 'round watchin' these things, and I wanted to come up and say these few things to you, and I'm glad of the hearin' you give me. I wanted to tell you a mite about Woman's Rights, and so I came out and said so. I am sittin' among you to watch; and every once and awhile I will come out and tell you what time of night it is.

1853 1881

Keeping the Thing Going while Things Are Stirring

My friends, I am rejoiced that you are glad, but I don't know how you will feel when I get through. I come from another field—the country of the slave. They have got their liberty—so much good luck to have slavery partly destroyed; not entirely. I want it root and branch destroyed. Then we will all be free indeed. I feel that if I have to answer for the deeds done in my body just as much as a man, I have a right to have just as much as a man. There is a great stir about colored men getting their rights,[1] but not a word about the colored women; and if colored men get their rights, and not colored women theirs, you see the colored men will be masters over the women, and it will be just as bad as it was before. So I am for keeping the thing going while things are stirring; because if we wait till it is still, it will take a great while to get it going again. White women are a great deal smarter, and know more than colored women, while colored women do not know scarcely anything. They go out washing, which is about as high as a colored woman gets, and their men go about idle, strutting up and down; and when the women come home, they[2] ask for their money and take it all, and then scold because there is no food. I want you to consider on that, chil'n. I call you chil'n; you are somebody's chil'n, and I am old enough to be mother of all that is here. I want women to have their rights. In the courts women have no right, no voice; nobody speaks for them.[3] I wish woman to have her voice there among the pettifoggers.[4] If it is not a fit place for women, it is unfit for men to be there.

I am above eighty years old; it is about time for me to be going. I have

3. Compare Mark 13:37: "And what I say unto you I say unto all, Watch."
4. One of the Ten Commandments (Exodus 20.2–17), which, according to the Bible, were issued by God to Moses on Mt. Sinai.
1. The Fourteenth and Fifteenth Amendments to the Constitution, proposed in 1866 and adopted in

1868, gave blacks the vote but omitted any reference to women.
2. I.e., the men.
3. In the 1860s, the rights of married women in most states were extremely limited.
4. Unscrupulous lawyers.

been forty years a slave and forty years free, and would be here forty years more to have equal rights for all. I suppose I am kept here because something remains for me to do; I suppose I am yet to help to break the chain. I have done a great deal of work; as much as a man, but did not get so much pay. I used to work in the field and bind grain, keeping up with the cradler;[5] but men doing no more, got twice as much pay; so with the German women. They work in the field and do as much work, but do not get the pay. We do as much, we eat as much, we want as much. I suppose I am about the only colored woman that goes about to speak for the rights of the colored women. I want to keep the thing stirring, now that the ice is cracked. What we want is a little money. You men know that you get as much again as women when you write, or for what you do. When we get our rights we shall not have to come to you for money, for then we shall have money enough in our own pockets; and may be you will ask us for money. But help us now until we get it. It is a good consolation to know that when we have got this battle once fought we shall not be coming to you any more. You have been having our rights so long, that you think, like a slave-holder, that you own us. I know that it is hard for one who has held the reins for so long to give up; it cuts like a knife. It will feel all the better when it closes up again. I have been in Washington about three years, seeing about these colored people. Now colored men have the right to vote. There ought to be equal rights now more than ever, since colored people have got their freedom. I am going to talk several times while I am here; so now I will do a little singing. I have not heard any singing since I came here.

1867 1882

5. A worker who reaps grain and lays it flat.

LETITIA ELIZABETH LANDON ("L.E.L.")
1802–1838

The prolific young writer who was known to early-nineteenth-century audiences mainly as "L.E.L." produced collections of poetry, novels, plays, and children's stories that ranked her among the best-selling authors of her era. Yet after her death she was quickly forgotten and even derided as a "luckless, and transient Sappho." Still, as one scholar notes, she was venerated by the early Victorians. Recalling his years at Cambridge, the well-known literary sage Edward Bulwer-Lytton remembered that "at college, lavishing our golden years [there was] a rush every Saturday afternoon for the 'Literary Gazette;' and an impatient anxiety to hasten at once to that corner of the sheet which contained the three magical letters 'L.E.L.' And all of us praised the verse, and all of us guessed at the author. We soon learned it was a female, and our admiration was doubled, and our conjectures tripled. She was young? She was pretty?"

Indeed, the woman known as L.E.L. was both young and pretty. Born and bred in London, she was a precociously talented poet whose neighbor, William Jerdan, editor of the *Literary Gazette*, arranged for her earliest verses to appear in his magazine when she was just seventeen. Thereafter, she wrote continually and published con-

sistently throughout her relatively short career, eventually becoming the chief support of her family after her father's business failure and subsequent death in 1824. Landon's extraordinary initial successes included numerous volumes of verse, most of which went through many printings, with one—*The Improvisatrice* (1824)—sailing through six editions in a single year. In addition to her creative work, L.E.L. produced countless book reviews and many versions of the specialized literary albums, gift books, and anthologies that were popular with late Romantic and early Victorian audiences.

Despite her success and glamour, however—or perhaps even because of it—Landon was victimized by gossip almost as soon as she gained fame. Like a female Byron, she focused much of her writing on brooding representations of romantic passion and its vicissitudes—and like her male counterpart, she was considered at best rakish, at worst (more terrible for a woman) "fallen." Her engagement in 1835 to the editor John Forster, who would later become the biographer of Charles Dickens, was cut short because of her suspiciously shady background. And her marriage to George Maclean, governor of the British colony at Cape Coast Castle in Africa (now Ghana), was brief, belated, and beleaguered. In 1838, just a few months after she had settled in Africa with her new husband, L.E.L. died of mysterious causes: an inquest determined that her demise resulted from an overdose of prussic acid, but how, why, and by whom such an overdose was administered has never become clear.

Although Landon's death was almost as theatrical as the circumstances—and productions—of her literary career had been, for better or worse she contributed to a developing image of the "poetess" as a heroine whose writings recorded the fluctuating moods of an impassioned, notably "feminine" consciousness. One of Landon's most important volumes included a sequence titled "Subjects for Pictures," a series of poems exploring the perspectives of mythological, legendary, and historical women. As her poems titled "Queen Victoria," "The Factory," and "The Marriage Pact" indicate, she could write with sardonic, and sometimes grim, wit about the circumstances of women and children in nineteenth-century England. At the same time, her dramatic examinations and impersonations of female protagonists explain why her earliest publication, *The Fate of Adelaide, A Swiss Romantic Tale; and Other Poems* (1821), was partly financed by—and dedicated to—the great Victorian actress Mrs. Siddons.

Ironically enough, however, it now seems that at least some of Landon's apparently stagy self-presentations were shaped and shadowed by a secret romance whose plotline has only recently come to light. In 2000, Cynthia Lawford, an American scholar working in England, discovered compelling evidence that there was in fact some truth to the rumors about Landon's love life. According to Lawford, the young poet had been involved in an affair with her mentor, William Jerdan—a married man twenty years her senior—from quite early in her career. Together, writes Lawford, the pair had three children: Ella Stuart, Fred Stuart, and Laura Landon. "I was told about the three children by Ella Stuart's great-great-grandson, Michael Gorman," adds Lawford, noting that "Landon's portrait hung in the drawing-room of his boyhood home."

Revenge

Ay, gaze upon her rose-wreathed hair,
 And gaze upon her smile;
Seem as you drank the very air
 Her breath perfumed the while:

5 And wake for her the gifted line,
 That wild and witching lay,[1]
And swear your heart is as a shrine,
 That only owns her sway.

'Tis well: I am revenged at last,—
10 Mark you that scornful cheek,—
The eye averted as you pass'd,
 Spoke more than words could speak.

Ay, now by all the bitter tears
 That I have shed for thee,—
15 The racking doubts, the burning fears,—
 Avenged they well may be—

By the nights pass'd in sleepless care,
 The days of endless woe;
All that you taught my heart to bear,
20 All that yourself will know.

I would not wish to see you laid
 Within an early tomb;
I should forget how you betray'd,
 And only weep your doom:

25 But this is fitting punishment,
 To live and love in vain,—
Oh my wrung heart, be thou content,
 And feed upon his pain.

Go thou and watch her lightest sigh,—
30 Thine own it will not be;
And bask beneath her sunny eye,—
 It will not turn on thee.

'Tis well: the rack, the chain, the wheel,
 Far better had'st thou proved;
35 Ev'n I could almost pity feel,
 For thou art not beloved.

1829, 1873

1. Song; poem, ballad.

The Little Shroud

She put him on a snow-white shroud,
 A chaplet on his head;
And gather'd early primroses
 To scatter o'er the dead.

5 She laid him in his little grave—
 'Twas hard to lay him there,
When spring was putting forth its flowers,
 And every thing was fair.

She had lost many children—now
10 The last of them was gone;
And day and night she sat and wept
 Beside the funeral stone.

One midnight, while her constant tears
 Were falling with the dew,
15 She heard a voice, and lo! her child
 Stood by her weeping too!

His shroud was damp, his face was white:
 He said,—"I cannot sleep,
Your tears have made my shroud so wet;
20 Oh, mother, do not weep!"

Oh, love is strong!—the mother's heart
 Was filled with tender fears:
Oh, love is strong!—and for her child
 Her grief restrained its tears.

25 One eve a light shone round her bed,
 And there she saw him stand—
Her infant, in his little shroud,
 A taper in his hand.

"Lo! mother, see my shroud is dry,
30 And I can sleep once more!"
And beautiful the parting smile
 The little infant wore.

And down within the silent grave
 He laid his weary head;
35 And soon the early violets
 Grew o'er his grassy bed.

1832

The Princess Victoria[1]

And art thou a Princess?—in sooth, we may well
Go back to the days of the sign and the spell,
When a young queen sat on an ivory throne
In a shining hall, whose windows shone
5 With colours its crystals caught from the sky,
Or the roof which a thousand rubies dye;
Where the summer garden was spread around,
With the date and the palm and the cedar crowned;
Where fountains played with the rainbow showers,
10 Touched with the hues of their comrade flowers;
Where the tulip and rose grew side by side,
One like a queen, and one like a bride;
One with its own imperial flush,
The other reddening with love's sweet blush;
15 When silver stuffs for her step were unrolled,
And the citron was served on a plate of gold;
When perfumes arose from pearl caskets filled
With odours from all sweet things distilled;
When a fairy guarded the throne from ill,
20 And she knew no rule but her own glad will:
Those were the days for a youthful queen,
And such, fair Princess, thou should'st have been.

But now thou wilt fill a weary throne,
What with rights of the people, and rights of thy own:
25 An ear-trumpet now thy sceptre should be,
Eternal debate is the future for thee.
Lord Brougham[2] will make a six-hours' oration,
On the progress of knowledge, the mind of the nation;
Lord Grey[3] one yet longer, to state that his place
30 Is perhaps less dear to himself than his race;
O'Connell[4] will tell Ireland's griefs and her wrongs,
In speech, the mac-adamized prose of Moore's songs;[5]
Good patience! how weary the young queen will be
Of 'the flower of the earth, and the gem of the sea!'[6]
35 Mr Hume,[7] with his watchwords 'Retrenchment and Waste',
Will insist that your wardrobe in his care be placed;
The silk he will save! the blond[8] he will spare—
I wish he may leave Your Grace any to wear.

1. Victoria (1819–1901) became queen of England in 1837.
2. Henry Peter Brougham (1778–1868), British jurist and member of Parliament whose famous 1831 speech helped pass the Reform Bill of 1832.
3. Charles Grey (1764–1845), prime minister of Britain (1830–34) and active supporter of electoral and other reform.
4. Daniel O'Connell (1775–1847), Irish leader in the struggle for Catholic civil rights; he was elected to Parliament in 1828.
5. Verse of the Irish poet Thomas Moore (1779–1852), some of whose writings were published set to music. "Mac-adamized": rendered flat and even, like a paved road.
6. See Moore's "Remember Thee!": "Wert thou all that I wish thee, great, glorious and free, / First flower of the earth, and first gem of the sea."
7. Joseph Hume (1775–1855), Scottish physician and politician, famous as a member of Parliament for questioning every item of public expenditure.
8. A silk lace, formed in hexagonal meshes.

That feminine fancy, a will of your own,
40 Is a luxury wholly denied to a throne;
And this is your future—how soon time will trace
A change and a sign on that fair and young face!
Methinks the best wish to be offered thee now,
Is—God keep the crown long from that innocent brow!

1832

The Factory[1]

'Tis an accursed thing!

There rests a shade above yon town,
 A dark funereal shroud:
'Tis not the tempest hurrying down,
 'Tis not a summer cloud.

5 The smoke that rises on the air
 Is as a type and sign;
A shadow flung by the despair
 Within those streets of thine.

That smoke shuts out the cheerful day
10 The sunset's purple hues,
The moonlight's pure and tranquil ray,
 The morning's pearly dews.

Such is the moral atmosphere
 Around thy daily life;
15 Heavy with care, and pale with fear,
 With future tumult rife.

There rises on the morning wind
 A low appealing cry,
A thousand children are resign'd
20 To sicken and to die!

We read of Moloch's sacrifice,[2]
 We sicken at the name,
And seem to hear the infant cries—
 And yet we do the same;—

25 And worse—'twas but a moment's pain
 The heathen altar gave,
But we give years,—our idol, Gain,
 Demands a living grave!

1. Child labor was common in England in the nineteenth century, especially in the textile industry; an act of 1819 set the minimum working age at 9, and the maximum working hours at 12.
2. I.e., the burning of children in worship of the god Moloch (see Leviticus 18.21; 2 Kings 23. 10).

How precious is the little one,
30 Before his mother's sight,
With bright hair dancing in the sun,
 And eyes of azure light!

He sleeps as rosy as the south,
 For summer days are long;
35 A prayer upon the little mouth,
 Lull'd by his nurse's song.

Love is around him, and his hours
 Are innocent and free;
His mind essays its early powers
40 Beside his mother's knee.

When afteryears of trouble come,
 Such as await man's prime,
How will he think of that dear home,
 And childhood's lovely time!

45 And such should childhood ever be,
 The fairy well; to bring
To life's worn, weary memory
 The freshness of its spring.

But here the order is reversed,
50 And infancy, like age,
Knows of existence but its worst,
 One dull and darken'd page;—

Written with tears and stamp'd with toil,
 Crush'd from the earliest hour,
55 Weeds darkening on the bitter soil
 That never knew a flower.

Look on yon child, it droops the head,
 Its knees are bow'd with pain;
It mutters from its wretched bed,
60 'O, let me sleep again!'

Alas! 'tis time, the mother's eyes
 Turn mournfully away;
Alas! 'tis time, the child must rise,
 And yet it is not day.

65 The lantern's lit—she hurries forth,
 The spare cloak's scanty fold
Scarce screens her from the snowy north,
 The child is pale and cold.

And wearily the little hands
70 Their task accustom'd ply;

While daily, some 'mid those pale bands,
 Droop, sicken, pine, and die.

Good God! to think upon a child
 That has no childish days,
75 No careless play, no frolics wild,
 No words of prayer and praise!

Man from the cradle—'tis too soon
 To earn their daily bread,
And heap the heat and toil of noon
80 Upon an infant's head.

To labour ere their strength be come,
 Or starve,—such is the doom
That makes of many an English home
 One long and living tomb!

85 Is there no pity from above,—
 No mercy in those skies;
Hath then the heart of man no love,
 To spare such a sacrifice?

O, England! though thy tribute waves
90 Proclaim three great and free,
While those small children pine like slaves,
 There is a curse on thee!

 1838, 1873

The Marriage Vow

The altar, 'tis of death! for there are laid
The sacrifice of all youth's sweetest hopes.
It is a dreadful thing for woman's lip
To swear the heart away; yet know that heart.
5 Annuls the vow while speaking, and shrinks back
From the dark future that it dares not face.
The service read above the open grave
Is far less terrible than that which seals
The vow that binds the victim, not the will:
10 For in the grave is rest.

 1841, 1873

ELIZABETH BARRETT BROWNING
1806–1861

Elizabeth Barrett Browning was probably best known once for her romance with Robert Browning. Her *Sonnets from the Portuguese,* a series of love poems dedicated to him, are still popular, while the dramatic elopement of the two writers has been the subject of many books and at least one play, *The Barretts of Wimpole Street* (1930) by Rudolf Besier. Yet in her own era this prolific, scholarly, and highly political poet was considered a major author rather than a romance heroine. After her death, a writer for the *Cornhill Magazine* declared that "Sensibility and intuition, those endowments of supereminent importance to individuals whose greatness is to grow in proportion to their understanding and interpretation of human life, were in her united in a degree seldom witnessed." But even during her lifetime she was a literary star. Older and more famous than the husband whose reputation has since eclipsed hers, Barrett Browning was seriously mentioned for the post of poet laureate when William Wordsworth died in 1850. Admired by such diverse figures as William Makepeace Thackeray and Harriet Martineau, Edgar Allan Poe and Harriet Beecher Stowe, Alfred, Lord Tennyson and Margaret Fuller, she was an accomplished student and translator of Greek, the center of a lively circle of English expatriates in mid-nineteenth-century Florence, a committed abolitionist, a powerful supporter of the movement for Italian unification, and a strong feminist. Indeed, nothing could be more misleading than the twentieth-century image of "Mrs. Browning" as a swooning Victorian invalid, languishing on a sofa, smelling salts in one hand and sentimental verses in the other.

Born on a pleasant estate at Durham in Herefordshire, Elizabeth Barrett was the oldest of eleven children. Her father, Edward Moulton Barrett, owned extensive plantations in Jamaica, from which the family fortune derived, though Elizabeth herself was later to be troubled by the link with slavery such holdings represented. Iron-willed and autocratic, he dominated the household, and Elizabeth's submissive mother, Mary Barrett, was evidently an appropriate wife for him: she was "one of those women," the poet later wrote, who "in . . . bowing themselves make a mark, a plait, within—a sign of suffering." Yet Elizabeth clearly loved and admired her; after Mrs. Barrett's death in 1828, she indicated in letters and journals that, like her heroine Aurora Leigh, she "felt a mother-want about the world."

A precocious child, Barrett Browning started to write poetry early. According to some reports, she composed verses at the age of four, and when she was fourteen her father—whose patriarchal sternness did not prevent him from taking pride in his oldest child's accomplishments—had her "epic," *The Battle of Marathon,* privately printed. At the age of sixteen, she wrote a long philosophical poem, *An Essay on Mind,* and around this time she began studying Greek, with special attention to the Greek Christian poets. Her life was not entirely carefree, however. In 1821 she suffered what was defined as a "nervous collapse"; her general health had, in any case, always been precarious, although at least one biographer has associated her mysteriously persistent illness with a "need to escape from the family" and perhaps the concomitant obligations of domesticity. In any case, whatever the medical facts may have been— and there has been considerable speculation about them—it is clear that quite early the poet began dosing herself, as so many other nineteenth-century invalids did, with what she called "muriate of morphine . . . in a combination with ether," an opiate designed to ease both physical pain and mental distress. For much of her adult life, especially her years of confinement in the famous house at 50 Wimpole Street from which Browning rescued her, she seems to have been virtually dependent on such drugs.

Despite these problems, Barrett Browning's earliest years at Wimpole Street were by no means bleak. After some financial losses, the family had moved there in 1838,

just as Elizabeth was beginning to establish a considerable literary reputation with her first books, a translation of Aeschylus's *Prometheus Bound* (1833) and a collection of her own verse, *The Seraphim and Other Poems* (1838). After her mother's death, she and her father had become particularly close—she was evidently always a special favorite of his—and she was also devoted to her brothers and sisters, especially her brother Edward ("Bro"), the sibling closest to her in age. In addition, she had formed friendships with a number of notable literary figures, including the essayist Mary Russell Mitford, the dramatist Richard Horne, and the man of letters John Kenyon. Her health continued to be poor, however, and in 1838 she was advised by doctors to vacation in Cornwall, where the climate was supposed to be good for invalids. She persuaded her father that Bro should accompany her there, and in what may well have been the major catastrophe of her life, the young man was drowned that year in a sailing accident off Torquay. Earlier in the year, her brother Samuel had also died, and the loss of Bro, coming so soon after another fatality, dealt her a terrible blow. Plunged into "hopeless grief," feeling herself to be "dead before death," and "living on the outside of my life," she retired into the notorious sickroom at Wimpole Street, from which she was not to emerge for another five years.

Still, although she was ill and in mourning, Barrett Browning continued her indefatigable correspondence and her vigorous composition. In 1844 she published a two-volume collection of her poems, with an American edition that had an introduction by Edgar Allan Poe. Friends visited her, she maintained a lively interest in London's literary world, and she continued her study of Greek; her *Account of the Greek Christian Poets* appeared serially in the *Athenaeum*, a major British periodical, in 1842. Finally, in 1845, she received a surprising letter from an admirer, Robert Browning, a little-known but increasingly well-regarded poet whose veneration of her work was to change her life. "I do . . . love these books with all my heart—and I love you too," he wrote, imploring her for the privilege of a meeting. At their first encounter, and thereafter, the two poets discovered many mutual affinities; within a year and a half of Browning's first letter to Elizabeth Barrett, they eloped to the Continent together.

Six years younger than his wife-to-be, Browning was a struggling experimental writer when the pair met. Because he was extraordinarily intellectual, his work was often considered "obscure," but in an effort to surmount such judgments he had been trying to write popular dramas, a labor that no doubt influenced his later mastery of the dramatic monologue and that must also have left its mark on his wife's work, perhaps enhancing her interest in capturing the theatrical intensity of immediate events. Because Elizabeth Barrett was far more established than Robert Browning at the time of their first meeting, however, it is just as likely that her stylistic inventiveness influenced his writing. Certainly, even in his first letter to her, he expressed his respect for her work, defining himself "as a loyal fellow-craftsman." Their flight from the dark house at Wimpole Street to the sunnier streets of France and Italy was obviously romantic: Edward Moulton Barrett had long refused to allow any of his children to marry, so the couple had to wed furtively in a London church, with only Elizabeth's maid and a cousin of Robert's as witnesses. But what was ultimately more crucial than the crisis of their love was the seriousness of their aesthetic as well as emotional engagement with each other and the psychological support that the poet formerly known as Elizabeth Barrett was to derive from that many-leveled relationship.

That she did derive such support from Browning is made clear by the intensity of the verse she wrote in the fifteen years of her marriage, years when the couple lived primarily in Florence at the house called Casa Guidi, which she memorialized in *Casa Guidi Windows* (1851), her brilliant meditation on the successes and setbacks of the Italian nationalist movement. Traveling through France, where Elizabeth insisted on meeting and doing homage to the novelist George Sand—about whom she had already written several sonnets—the Brownings came to Italy, the land that was to become

a significant second home for both. Here the two began to write what were obviously major works. Elizabeth, for instance, produced her *Poems* of 1850, which included such fierce political statements as "The Runaway Slave at Pilgrim's Point." Shortly thereafter, she published *Sonnets from the Portuguese,* a sequence that adapted the usually male-oriented genre of the sonnet cycle to female requirements, telling the story of a love affair from a woman's, instead of a man's, point of view. Then, in 1851, she produced *Casa Guidi Windows,* and in 1857 her "epic-novel" *Aurora Leigh* appeared. Finally, in 1860, she published *Poems before Congress,* a collection of frankly political manifestos dedicated to the cause of Italian unification; and in 1862, the year after her death from complications of bronchitis, her *Last Poems* were assembled by her husband. To the end, she had been vital and productive.

Aesthetically energized, Barrett Browning had also been socially and intellectually refreshed by her new life. In Florence she made many friends, including the American writers Harriet Beecher Stowe and Margaret Fuller as well as the increasingly eccentric English poet Walter Savage Landor, and she developed new interests, including— along with the Italian "cause"—the popular spiritualist movement. Most important, in Florence in 1849, after several miscarriages, she gave birth to a son, Robert Wiedeman Barrett-Browning, called "Pennini" (or "Pen" for short). Like marriage, maternity seemed only to enhance her creative imagination. Her "own young Florentine" with "brave blue English eyes" appears as a redemptive figure at the conclusion of *Casa Guidi Windows,* and again, thinly disguised, as a sacramental child in *Aurora Leigh.* Gracing poems and romping in parlors, he seems to have been a muse rather than an encumbrance for his forty-three-year-old mother.

If her own real child functioned as a herald of art as well as reality for Barrett Browning, however, that is because, especially during her Italian years, she had evolved a keenly felt aesthetic of reality. In *Aurora Leigh,* her heroine, a poet like herself, articulates this creed, and following such beliefs, Barrett Browning wrote with commitment about the problem of slavery in the United States, an issue she dramatized in "The Runaway Slave at Pilgrim's Point," and about the pain of impoverished children in England, a matter she had already begun to treat in the early polemics of "The Cry of the Children" and that she later took up in "A Song for the Ragged Schools of London" (1854). More elaborately, she recorded not only her aesthetic of reality but also her protofeminist philosophy in the book-length versenovel *Aurora Leigh,* where she attacked the degrading education received by most nineteenth-century women received and defended their right to intellectual self-determination. About this ambitious work, Virginia Woolf was to declare that its protagonist, "with her passionate interest in the social questions, her conflict as artist and woman, her longing for knowledge and freedom, is the true daughter of her age." But the author of *Aurora Leigh,* emerging from invalidism into aesthetic innovation and political activism, was equally a heroine of her era. Attempting a range of forms and meters—the sonnet and the verse drama, the ballad and the blank verse epic— Barrett Browning constantly tested herself against the highest standards of male-defined poetic genres, as if to declare, with her Aurora, "I too have my vocation— work to do . . . most serious work."

A True Dream

(Dreamed at Sidmouth[1] 1833)

I had not an evil end in view,
 Though I trod the evil way;
And why I practiced the magic art,
 My dream it did not say.

5 I unsealed the vial mystical,
 I outpoured the liquid thing,
And while the smoke came wreathing out,
 I stood unshuddering.

The smoke came wreathing, wreathing out,
10 All mute, and dark, and slow,
Till its cloud was stained with a fleshly hue,
 And a fleshly form 'gan show.

Then paused the smoke—the fleshly form
 Looked steadfast in mine ee,[2]
15 His beard was black as a thundercloud,
 But I trembled not to see.[3]

I unsealed the vial mystical,
 I outpoured the liquid thing,
And while the smoke came wreathing out,
20 I stood unshuddering.

The smoke came wreathing, wreathing out,
 All mute, and dark, and slow,
Till its cloud was stained with a fleshly hue,
 And a fleshly form 'gan show.

25 Then paused the smoke—but the mortal form
 A garment swart[4] did veil,
I looked on it with fixèd heart,
 Yea—not a pulse did fail!

I unsealed the vial mystical,
30 I outpoured the liquid thing,
And while the smoke came wreathing out,
 I stood unshuddering.

The smoke came wreathing, wreathing out,
 And now it was faster and lighter,
35 And it bore on its folds the rainbow's hues,
 Heaven could not show them brighter.

1. An English seaside town.
2. Archaic form of "eye"; here, Barrett Browning is evoking both the language and form of old English ballads like "Sir Patrick Spens."
3. I.e., did not tremble to see him.
4. Black or dark colored.

Then paused the smoke, the rainbow's hues
 Did a childish face express—
The rose in the cheek, the blue in the eyne,[5]
40 The yellow in the tress.

The fair young child shook back her hair,
 And round me her arms did wreathe,
Her lips were hard and cold as stone,
 They sucked away my breath.

45 I cast her off as she clung to me,
 With hate and shuddering;
I brake the vials, and foresware
 The cursèd, cursèd thing.

Anon[6] outspake a brother of mine—
50 "Upon the pavement, see,
Besprent with noisome[7] poison slime,
 Those twining serpents three."

Anon outspake my wildered[8] heart
 As I saw the serpent train—
55 "I have called up three existences
 I cannot quench again."

"Alas! with unholy company,
 My lifetime they will scathe;
They will hiss in the storm, and on sunny days
60 Will gleam and thwart my path."

Outspake that pitying brother of mine—
 "Now nay, my sister, nay,
I will pour on them oil of vitriol,[9]
 And burn their lives away."

65 "Now nay, my brother, torture not,
 Now hold thine hand, and spare."
He poured on them oil of vitriol,
 And did not heed my prayer.

I saw the drops of torture fall;
70 I heard the shriekings rise,
While the serpents writhed in agony
 Beneath my dreaming eyes.

And while they shrieked, and while they writhed,
 And inward and outward wound,
75 They waxèd larger, and their wail
 Assumed a human sound.

5. Eyes.
6. Then, shortly after.
7. Repulsive. "Besprent": sprinkled.

8. Bewildered.
9. A caustic chemical substance.

And glared their eyes, and their slimy scales
 Were roundly and redly bright,
Most like the lidless sun, what time[1]
80 Through the mist he meets your sight.

And larger and larger they waxèd still,
 And longer still and longer;
And they shrieked in their pain, "Come, come to us,
 We are stronger, we are stronger."

85 Upon the ground I laid mine head,
 And heard the wailing sound;
I did not wail, I did not writhe—
 I laid me on the ground.

And larger and larger they waxèd still
90 And longer still and longer;
And they shrieked in their pangs, "Come, come to us,
 We are stronger, we are stronger."

Then up I raised my burning brow,
 My quiv'ring arms on high;
95 I spake in prayer, and I named aloud
 The name of sanctity.

And as in my anguish I prayed and named
 Aloud the holy name,
The impious mocking serpent voice
100 Did echo back the same.

And larger and larger they waxèd still,
 And stronger still and longer!
And they shrieked in their pangs, "Come, come to us,
 We are stronger, we are stronger."

105 Then out from among them arose a form
 In shroud of death indued[2]—
I fled from him with wings of wind,
 With whirlwinds he pursued.

 * * *

I stood by a chamber door, and thought
110 Within its gloom to hide;
I locked the door, and the while forgot
 That I stood on the outer side.

1. When. "Lidless sun": the sun is compared to an eye with no lid.

2. I.e., wrapped or covered.

And the knell of mine heart was wildly tolled
 While I graspèd still the key;
115 For I felt beside me the icy breath,
 And knew that *that* was *he*.

I heard these words, "Who'er doth *taste*,
 Will *drink* the magic bowl;
So her body may do my mission here
120 Companioned by her soul."

Mine hand was cold as the key it held,
 Mine heart had an iron weight;
I saw a gleam, I heard a sound—
 The clock was striking eight.

1833 1913

The Cry of the Children[1]

Φεῦ, φεῦ, τί προσδέρκεσθέ μ' ὄμμασιν, τέκνα;[2]
—*Medea*.

I

Do ye hear the children weeping, O my brothers,
 Ere the sorrow comes with years?
They are leaning their young heads against their mothers,
 And *that* cannot stop their tears.
5 The young lambs are bleating in the meadows,
 The young birds are chirping in the nest,
The young fawns are playing with the shadows,
 The young flowers are blowing[3] toward the west—
But the young, young children, O my brothers,
10 They are weeping bitterly!
They are weeping in the playtime of the others,
 In the country of the free.

II

Do you question the young children in the sorrow
 Why their tears are falling so?
15 The old man may weep for his tomorrow
 Which is lost in long ago;
The old tree is leafless in the forest,
 The old year is ending in the frost,
The old wound, if stricken, is the sorest,
20 The old hope is hardest to be lost:

1. This poem was inspired by a government report on the employment of children in mines and factories, one of the major social issues in England at the time.
2. Alas, alas, why do you look at me with your eyes, children? (Greek). Spoken by Medea (Euripides, *Medea* 1040) shortly before she kills her children; the title quotes the chorus (line 1271).
3. Blooming.

But the young, young children, O my brothers,
 Do you ask them why they stand
Weeping sore before the bosoms of their mothers,
 In our happy fatherland?

III

25 They look up with their pale and sunken faces,
 And their looks are sad to see,
 For the man's hoary[4] anguish draws and presses
 Down the cheeks of infancy;
 "Your old earth," they say, "is very dreary,
30 Our young feet," they say, "are very weak;
 Few paces have we taken, yet are weary—
 Our grave-rest is very far to seek:
 Ask the aged why they weep, and not the children,
 For the outside earth is cold,
35 And we young ones stand without, in our bewildering,
 And the graves are for the old.

IV

"True," say the children, "it may happen
 That we die before our time:
Little Alice died last year, her grave is shapen
40 Like a snowball, in the rime.[5]
We looked into the pit prepared to take her:
 Was no room for any work in the close clay!
From the sleep wherein she lieth none will wake her,
 Crying, 'Get up, little Alice! it is day.'
45 If you listen by that grave, in sun and shower,
 With your ear down, little Alice never cries;
Could we see her face, be sure we should not know her,
 For the smile has time for growing in her eyes:
And merry go her moments, lulled and stilled in
50 The shroud by the kirk-chime.[6]
It is good when it happens," say the children,
 "That we die before our time."

V

Alas, alas, the children! they are seeking
 Death in life, as best to have:
55 They are binding up their hearts away from breaking,
 With a cerement[7] from the grave.
Go out, children, from the mine and from the city,
 Sing out, children, as the little thrushes do;
Pluck your handfuls of the meadow-cowslips pretty.

4. White-haired, extremely old.
5. Frost.
6. Church bell.

7. Shroud for the dead. "Binding up": wrapping to
strengthen or reinforce.

60 Laugh aloud, to feel your fingers let them through!
 But they answer, "Are your cowslips of the meadows
 Like our weeds anear the mine?
 Leave us quiet in the dark of the coal-shadows,
 From your pleasures fair and fine!

VI

65 "For oh," say the children, "we are weary,
 And we cannot run or leap;
 If we cared for any meadows, it were merely
 To drop down in them and sleep.
 Our knees tremble sorely in the stooping,
70 We fall upon our faces, trying to go;
 And, underneath our heavy eyelids drooping
 The reddest flower would look as pale as snow.
 For, all day, we drag our burden tiring
 Through the coal-dark, underground;
75 Or, all day, we drive the wheels of iron
 In the factories, round and round.

VII

 "For all day the wheels are droning, turning;
 Their wind comes in our faces,
 Till our hearts turn, our heads with pulses burning,
80 And the walls turn in their places:
 Turns the sky in the high window, blank and reeling,
 Turns the long light that drops adown the wall,
 Turn the black flies that crawl along the ceiling:
 All are turning, all the day, and we with all.
85 And all day the iron wheels are droning,
 And sometimes we could pray,
 'O ye wheels' (breaking out in a mad moaning),
 'Stop! be silent for today!' "

VIII

 Ay, be silent! Let them hear each other breathing
90 For a moment, mouth to mouth!
 Let them touch each other's hands, in a fresh wreathing
 Of their tender human youth!
 Let them feel that this cold metallic motion
 Is not all the life God fashions or reveals:
95 Let them prove[8] their living souls against the notion
 That they live in you, or under you, O wheels!
 Still, all day, the iron wheels go onward,
 Grinding life down from its mark;
 And the children's souls, which God is calling sunward,
100 Spin on blindly in the dark.

8. Test.

IX

Now tell the poor young children, O my brothers,
 To look up to Him and pray;
So the blessèd One who blesseth all the others,
 Will bless them another day.
105 They answer, "Who is God that He should hear us,
 While the rushing of the iron wheels is stirred?
When we sob aloud, the human creatures near us
 Pass by, hearing not, or answer not a word.
And we hear not (for the wheels in their resounding)
110 Strangers speaking at the door:
Is it likely God, with angels singing round Him,
 Hears our weeping anymore?

X

"Two words, indeed, of praying we remember,
 And at midnight's hour of harm.
115 'Our Father,'[9] looking upward in the chamber,
 We say softly for a charm.
We know no other words except 'Our Father,'
 And we think that, in some pause of angels' song,
God may pluck them with the silence sweet to gather,
120 And hold both within his right hand which is strong.
'Our Father!' If He heard us, He would surely
 (For they call Him good and mild)
Answer, smiling down the steep world very purely,
 'Come and rest with me, my child.'

XI

125 "But, no!" say the children, weeping faster,
 "He is speechless as a stone:
And they tell us, of His image is the master[1]
 Who commands us to work on.
Go to!" say the children,—"up in Heaven,
130 Dark, wheel-like, turning clouds are all we find.
Do not mock us; grief has made us unbelieving:
 We look up for God, but tears have made us blind."
Do you hear the children weeping and disproving,
 O my brothers, what ye preach?
135 For God's possible is taught by his world's loving,
 And the children doubt of each.

9. The first words of the Lord's Prayer (Matthew 6.9–13).

1. Even the cruel taskmaster of the children was made in God's image.

XII

And well may the children weep before you!
 They are weary ere they run;
They have never seen the sunshine, nor the glory
140 Which is brighter than the sun.
They know the grief of man, without its wisdom;
 They sink in man's despair, without its calm;
Are slaves, without the liberty in Christdom,
 Are martyrs, by the pang without the palm:[2]
145 Are worn as if with age, yet unretrievingly
 The harvest of its memories cannot reap,—
Are orphans of the earthly love and heavenly.
 Let them weep! let them weep!

XIII

They look up with their pale and sunken faces,
150 And their look is dread to see,
For they mind[3] you of their angels in high places,
 With eyes turned on Deity.
"How long," they say, "how long, O cruel nation,
 Will you stand, to move the world, on a child's heart,—
155 Stifle down with a mailèd heel its palpitation,
 And tread onward to your throne amid the mart?[4]
Our blood splashes upward, O goldheaper,
 And your purple[5] shows your path!
But the child's sob in the silence curses deeper
160 Than the strong man in his wrath." 1843

Grief

I tell you, hopeless grief is passionless;
That only men incredulous of despair,
Half-taught in anguish, through the midnight air
Beat upward to God's throne in loud access[1]
5 Of shrieking and reproach. Full desertness,
In souls as countries, lieth silent-bare
Under the blanching, vertical eye-glare
Of the absolute heavens. Deep-hearted man, express
Grief for thy dead in silence like to death—
10 Most like a monumental statue set
In everlasting watch and moveless woe
Till itself crumble to the dust beneath.
Touch it; the marble eyelids are not wet:
If it could weep, it could arise and go. 1844

2. Symbol of triumph; thus martyrs by their suffering only, not by their redemption.
3. Remind.
4. Market.

5. I.e., the blood left in their trail after trampling the children.
1. Outburst.

To George Sand[1]

A Desire

Thou large-brained woman and large-hearted man,
Self-called George Sand! whose soul, amid the lions[2]
Of thy tumultuous senses, moans defiance
And answers roar for roar, as spirits can:
5 I would some mild miraculous thunder ran
Above the applauded circus, in appliance
Of thine own nobler nature's strength and science,
Drawing two pinions,[3] white as wings of swan,
From thy strong shoulders, to amaze the place
10 With holier light! that thou to woman's claim
And man's, mightst join beside the angel's grace
Of a pure genius sanctified from blame,
Till child and maiden pressed to thine embrace
To kiss upon thy lips a stainless fame.[4]

1844

To George Sand[1]

A Recognition

True genius, but true woman! dost deny
The woman's nature with a manly scorn,
And break away the gauds[2] and armlets worn
By weaker women in captivity?
5 Ah, vain denial! that revolted cry
Is sobbed in by a woman's voice forlorn,—
Thy woman's hair, my sister, all unshorn
Floats back disheveled strength in agony,
Disproving thy man's name: and while before
10 The world thou burnest in a poet-fire,
We[3] see thy woman-heart beat evermore
Through the large flame. Beat purer, heart, and higher,
Till God unsex thee on the heavenly shore
Where unincarnate spirits purely aspire!

1844

1. French female novelist (1804–1876) whose novels and style of life were considered immoral by some.
2. In the ancient Roman "circus" or arena, slaves were pitted against lions for the amusement of spectators.
3. Wings.

4. I.e., a fame unstained by immorality.
1. See note to the previous poem.
2. Ornaments, here representing womanly things Sand has rejected, such as a woman's name and the role of a wife.
3. I.e., chiefly Barrett Browning herself, perhaps along with a select few who see Sand's true nature.

The Runaway Slave at Pilgrim's Point[1]

I

I stand on the mark beside the shore
 Of the first white pilgrim's bended knee,
Where exile turned to ancestor,[2]
 And God was thanked for liberty.
5 I have run through the night, my skin is as dark,
I bend my knee down on this mark:
 I look on the sky and the sea.

II

O pilgrim-souls, I speak to you!
 I see you come proud and slow
10 From the land of the spirits pale as dew
 And round me and round me ye go.
O pilgrims, I have gasped and run
All night long from the whips of one
 Who in your names works sin and woe!

III

15 And thus I thought that I would come
 And kneel here where ye knelt before,
And feel your souls around me hum
 In undertone to the ocean's roar;
And lift my black face, my black hand,
20 Here, in your names, to curse this land
 Ye blessed in freedom's, evermore.

IV

I am black, I am black,
 And yet God made me, they say:
But if He did so, smiling back
25 He must have cast his work away
Under the feet of his white creatures,
 With a look of scorn, that the dusky features
 Might be trodden again to clay.

V

And yet He has made dark things
30 To be glad and merry as light:
There's a little dark bird sits and sings,
 There's a dark stream ripples out of sight,

1. The point at Plymouth Rock, Massachusetts, where the Puritans, fleeing persecution in England, first landed their ships in the 17th century.

2. I.e., where the pilgrims, exiled from one nation, became ancestors to a new one.

And the dark frogs chant in the safe morass,[3]
And the sweetest stars are made to pass
35 O'er the face of the darkest night.

VI

But we who are dark, we are dark!
Ah God, we have no stars!
About our souls in care and cark[4]
Our blackness shuts like prison-bars:
40 The poor souls crouch so far behind
That never a comfort can they find
 By reaching through the prison-bars.

VII

Indeed we live beneath the sky,
That great smooth Hand of God stretched out
45 On all his children fatherly,
To save them from the dread and doubt
Which would be if, from this low place,
All opened straight up to his face
 Into the grand eternity.

VIII

50 And still God's sunshine and his frost,
They make us hot, they make us cold,
As if we were not black and lost;
 And the beasts and birds, in wood and fold,
Do fear and take us for very men:
55 Could the whippoorwill or the cat of the glen
 Look into my eyes and be bold?

IX

I am black, I am black!
But, once, I laughed in girlish glee,
For one of my color stood in the track
60 Where the drivers drove, and looked at me,
And tender and full was the look he gave—
Could a slave look so at another slave?—
 I look at the sky and the sea.

X

And from that hour our spirits grew
65 As free as if unsold, unbought:
Oh, strong enough, since we were two,
 To conquer the world, we thought.

3. Swamp. 4. Distress.

The drivers drove us day by day;
 We did not mind, we went one way,
70 And no better a freedom sought.

XI

In the sunny ground between the canes,[5]
 He said "I love you" as he passed;
When the shingle-roof rang sharp with the rains,
 I heard how he vowed it fast:
75 While others shook he smiled in the hut,
 As he carved me a bowl of the coconut
 Through the roar of the hurricanes.

XII

I sang his name instead of a song,
 Over and over I sang his name,
80 Upward and downward I drew it along
 My various notes,—the same, the same!
I sang it low, that the slave-girls near
Might never guess, from aught they could hear,
 It was only a name—a name.

XIII

85 I look on the sky and the sea.
 We were two to love and two to pray:
Yes, two, O God, who cried to Thee,
 Though nothing didst Thou say!
Coldly Thou sat'st behind the sun:
90 And now I cry who am but one,
 Thou wilt not speak today.

XIV

We were black, we were black,
 We had no claim to love and bliss,
What marvel if each went to wrack?[6]
95 They wrung my cold hands out of his,
They dragged him—where? I crawled to touch
His blood's mark in the dust . . . not much,
 Ye pilgrim-souls, though plain as *this*![7]

XV

Wrong, followed by a deeper wrong!
100 Mere grief's too good for such as I:
So the white men brought the shame ere long

5. Sugarcanes; the two worked on a sugar plantation.
6. Destruction.

7. The "mark beside the shore" where the speaker stands.

To strangle the sob of my agony.
They would not leave me for my dull
Wet eyes!—it was too merciful
105 To let me weep pure tears and die.

XVI

I am black, I am black!
 I wore a child upon my breast,
An amulet that hung too slack,
 And, in my unrest, could not rest:
110 Thus we went moaning, child and mother,
One to another, one to another,
 Until all ended for the best.

XVII

For hark! I will tell you low, low,
 I am black, you see,—
115 And the babe who lay on my bosom so,
 Was far too white, too white for me;
As white as the ladies who scorned to pray
Beside me at church but yesterday,
 Though my tears had washed a place for my knee.

XVIII

120 My own, own child! I could not bear
 To look in his face, it was so white;
I covered him up with a kerchief there,
 I covered his face in close and tight:
And he moaned and struggled, as well might be,
125 For the white child wanted his liberty—
 Ha, ha! he wanted the master-right.

XIX

He moaned and beat with his head and feet,
 His little feet that never grew;
He struck them out, as it was meet,[8]
130 Against my heart to break it through:
I might have sung and made him mild,
But I dared not sing to the white-faced child
 The only song I knew.

XX

I pulled the kerchief very close:
135 He could not see the sun, I swear,

8. Fitting.

More, then, alive, than now he does
 From between the roots of the mango . . . where?
I know where. Close! A child and mother
Do wrong to look at one another
140 When one is black and one is fair.

XXI

Why, in that single glance I had
 Of my child's face, . . . I tell you all,
I saw a look that made me mad!
 The *master's* look, that used to fall
145 On my soul like his lash . . . or worse!
And so, to save it from my curse,
 I twisted it round in my shawl.

XXII

And he moaned and trembled from foot to head,
 He shivered from head to foot;
150 Till after a time, he lay instead
 Too suddenly still and mute.
I felt, beside, a stiffening cold:
I dared to lift up just a fold,
 As in lifting a leaf of the mango-fruit.

XXIII

155 But *my* fruit . . . ha, ha!—there, had been
 (I laugh to think on't at this hour!)
Your fine white angels (who have seen
 Nearest the secret of God's power)
And plucked my fruit to make them wine,
160 And sucked the soul of that child of mine
 As the hummingbird sucks the soul of the flower.

XXIV

Ha, ha, the trick of the angels white!
 They freed the white child's spirit so.
I said not a word, but day and night
165 I carried the body to and fro,
And it lay on my heart like a stone, as chill.
—The sun may shine out as much as he will:
 I am cold, though it happened a month ago.

XXV

From the white man's house, and the black man's hut,
170 I carried the little body on:
The forest's arms did round us shut,

And silence through the trees did run:
They asked no question as I went,
They stood too high for astonishment,
175 They could see God sit on his throne.

XXVI

My little body, kerchiefed fast,
 I bore it on through the forest, on;
And when I felt it was tired at last,
 I scooped a hole beneath the moon:
180 Through the forest-tops the angels far,
With a white sharp finger from every star,
 Did point and mock at what was done.

XXVII

Yet when it was all done aright,—
 Earth, 'twixt me and my baby, strewed,—
185 All, changed to black earth,—nothing white,—
 A dark child in the dark!—ensued
Some comfort, and my heart grew young;
I sate down smiling there and sung
 The song I learnt in my maidenhood.

XXVIII

190 And thus we two were reconciled,
 The white child and black mother, thus;
For as I sang it soft and wild,
 The same song, more melodious,
Rose from the grave whereon I sate:
195 It was the dead child singing that,
 To join the souls of both of us.

XXIX

I look on the sea and the sky.
 Where the pilgrims' ships first anchored lay
The free sun rideth gloriously,
200 But the pilgrim ghosts have slid away
Through the earliest streaks of the morn:
My face is black, but it glares with a scorn
 Which they dare not meet by day.

XXX

Ha!—in their stead, their hunter sons!
205 Ha, ha! they are on me—they hunt in a ring!
Keep off! I brave you all at once,
 I throw off your eyes like snakes that sting!
You have killed the black eagle at nest, I think:

Did you ever stand still in your triumph, and shrink
210 From the stroke of her wounded wing?

XXXI

(Man, drop that stone you dared to lift!—)
 I wish you who stand there five abreast,
Each, for his own wife's joy and gift,
 A little corpse as safely at rest
215 As mine in the mangoes! Yes, but *she*
May keep live babies on her knee,
 And sing the song she likes the best.

XXXII

I am not mad: I am black.
 I see you staring in my face—
220 I know you staring, shrinking back,
 Ye are born of the Washington-race,[9]
And this land is the free America,
And this mark on my wrist—(I prove[1] what I say)
 Ropes tied me up here to the flogging-place.

XXXIII

225 You think I shrieked then? Not a sound.
 I hung, as a gourd hangs in the sun;
I only cursed them all around
 As softly as I might have done
My very own child: from these sands
230 Up to the mountains, lift your hands,
 O slaves, and end what I begun!

XXXIV

Whips, curses; these must answer those!
 For in this union you have set
Two kinds of men in adverse rows,
235 Each loathing each; and all forget
The seven wounds in Christ's body fair,
While He sees gaping everywhere
 Our countless wounds that pay no debt.[2]

XXXV

Our wounds are different. Your white men
240 Are, after all, not gods indeed,
Nor able to make Christs again
 Do good with bleeding. We who bleed
(Stand off!) we help not in our loss!

9. I.e., the race of George Washington.
1. Demonstrate.

2. I.e., that were not suffered in payment for the sins of humanity.

We are too heavy for our cross,
245 And fall and crush you and your seed.

XXXVI

I fall, I swoon![3] I look at the sky.
 The clouds are breaking on my brain;
I am floated along, as if I should die
 Of liberty's exquisite pain.
250 In the name of the white child waiting for me
In the death-dark where we may kiss and agree,
White men, I leave you all curse-free
 In my broken heart's disdain!

1850

Hiram Powers' "Greek Slave"[1]

They say ideal beauty cannot enter
The house of anguish. On the threshold stands
An alien image with enshackled hands,
Called the Greek Slave! as if the artist meant her
5 (That passionless perfection which he lent her,
Shadowed not darkened where the sill expands)[2]
To so confront man's crimes in different lands
With man's ideal sense. Pierce to the center,
Art's fiery finger, and break up ere long
10 The serfdom of this world. Appeal, fair stone,
From God's pure heights of beauty against man's wrong!
Catch up in thy divine face, not alone
East griefs but west,[3] and strike and shame the strong,
By thunders of white silence, overthrown.

1850

From Sonnets from the Portuguese[1]

V

I lift my heavy heart up solemnly,
 As once Electra[2] her sepulchral urn,
And, looking in thine eyes, I overturn

3. Possibly an echo of Percy Shelley's "Ode to the West Wind" (1820): "I fall upon the thorns of life! I bleed!"

1. The work of an American sculptor (1805–1873) who became a close friend of the Brownings while they were living in Florence.

2. I.e., where the threshold to the house of anguish begins; her beauty is not lessened by that threshold, only given a more somber cast.

3. Greek slavery was a grief of the East; Barrett Browning may be thinking here of American slavery as a grief of the West.

1. All the sonnets in the sequence are addressed to Elizabeth's husband, Robert, himself a famous poet.

2. In Sophocles' play *Electra*, the heroine's brother, Orestes, disguises himself and presents his sister with a funeral urn that he claims contains her brother's ashes.

The ashes at thy feet. Behold and see
5 What a great heap of grief lay hid in me,
And how the red wild sparkles dimly burn
Through the ashen grayness. If thy foot in scorn
Could tread them out to darkness utterly,
It might be well perhaps. But if instead
10 Thou wait beside me for the wind to blow
The gray dust up, . . . those laurels[3] on thine head,
O my Belovèd, will not shield thee so,
That none of all the fires shall scorch and shred
The hair beneath. Stand farther off then! go.

XXII

When our two souls stand up erect and strong,
Face to face, silent, drawing nigh[4] and nigher,
Until the lengthening wings break into fire
At either curvéd point,—what bitter wrong
5 Can the earth do to us, that we should not long
Be here contented? Think. In mounting higher,
The angels would press on us and aspire
To drop some golden orb[5] of perfect song
Into our deep, dear silence. Let us stay
10 Rather on earth, Belovèd,—where the unfit
Contrarious moods of men recoil away
And isolate pure spirits, and permit
A place to stand and love in for a day,
With darkness and the death-hour rounding it.

XLIII

How do I love thee? Let me count the ways.
I love thee to the depth and breadth and height
My soul can reach, when feeling out of sight
For the ends of Being and ideal Grace.
5 I love thee to the level of everyday's
Most quiet need, by sun and candle light.
I love thee freely, as men strive for Right;
I love thee purely, as they turn from Praise.
I love thee with the passion put to use[6]
10 In my old griefs, and with my childhood's faith.
I love thee with a love I seemed to lose
With my lost saints,—I love thee with the breath,
Smiles, tears, and all my life!—and, if God choose,
I shall but love thee better after death.

1850

3. Leaves associated with poetic achievement.
4. Near.
5. Ball or sphere. The image may recall the old notion of the "music of the spheres," created by the motions of stars and planets.
6. I.e., a natural reserve of passion that had formerly been directed to grief, now transformed to love.

Story of a young woman artist that also tells of a gender role change ("a people")

tons of color @ first...

Mom is the muse.

From Aurora Leigh

Book I

[AURORA'S PARENTS][1]

* * *My mother was a Florentine,[2]
30 Whose rare blue eyes were shut from seeing me
When scarcely I was four years old, my life
A poor spark snatched up from a failing lamp
Which went out therefore. She was weak and frail;
She could not bear the joy of giving life,
35 The mother's rapture slew her. If her kiss
Had left a longer weight upon my lips
It might have steadied the uneasy breath,
And reconciled and fraternized my soul
With the new order.[3] As it was, indeed,
40 I felt a mother-want about the world,
And still went seeking, like a bleating lamb
Left out at night in shutting up the fold,[4]—
As restless as a nest-deserted bird
Grown chill through something being away, though what
45 It knows not.* * *

65 My father was an austere Englishman,
Who, after a dry lifetime spent at home
In college-learning, law, and parish talk,
Was flooded with a passion unaware,
His whole provisioned and complacent past
70 Drowned out from him that moment. As he stood
In Florence, where he had come to spend a month
And note the secret of Da Vinci's drains,[5]
He musing somewhat absently perhaps
Some English question . . . whether men should pay
75 The unpopular but necessary tax
With left or right hand—in the alien sun
In that great square of the Santissima[6]
There drifted past him (scarcely marked enough
To move his comfortable island scorn)
80 A train of priestly banners, cross and psalm,
The white-veiled rose-crowned maidens holding up
Tall tapers, weighty for such wrists, aslant
To the blue luminous tremor of the air,
And letting drop the white wax as they went
85 To eat the bishop's wafer at the church;[7]

1. In Book I, the poet-to-be Aurora, born in Italy of an Italian mother and an English father, is orphaned early and brought to England, where she is raised and educated by her father's sister, an austere British lady. The first selection from Book I covers her memories of her mother, and the second records some of her reactions to her Victorian training in decorum.
2. Florence was a center of Renaissance art and culture.
3. I.e., her motherless state.

4. An enclosure for sheep.
5. Leonardo da Vinci (1452–1519), artist, scientist, and engineer, devised a system of irrigation for the plains of Lombardy.
6. The *piazza* or square before the 13th-century Church of Santissima Annunziata.
7. I.e., to receive Holy Communion—in which a wafer and wine, thought to make present the body and blood of Christ, are consumed—from the bishop.

From which long trail of chanting priests and girls,
A face flashed like a cymbal on his face
And shook with silent clangor brain and heart,
Transfiguring him to music. Thus, even thus,
90 He too received his sacramental gift
With eucharistic[8] meanings; for he loved.

92 And thus beloved, she died.* * *

120 * * *Father, then, and child,
We lived among the mountains many years,
God's silence on the outside of the house,
And we who did not speak too loud within,
And old Assunta to make up the fire,
125 Crossing herself whene'er a sudden flame
Which lightened from the firewood, made alive
That picture of my mother on the wall.

The painter drew it after she was dead,
And when the face was finished, throat and hands,
130 Her cameriera[9] carried him, in hate
Of the English-fashioned shroud, the last brocade
She dressed in at the Pitti;[1] "he should paint
No sadder thing than that," she swore, "to wrong
Her poor signora." Therefore very strange
135 The effect was. I, a little child, would crouch
For hours upon the floor with knees drawn up,
And gaze across them, half in terror, half
In adoration, at the picture there,—
That swan-like supernatural white life
140 Just sailing upward from the red stiff silk
Which seemed to have no part in it nor power
To keep it from quite breaking out of bounds.
For hours I sat and stared. Assunta's awe
And my poor father's melancholy eyes
145 Still pointed that way. That way went my thoughts
When wandering beyond sight. And as I grew
In years, I mixed, confused, unconsciously,
Whatever I last read or heard or dreamed,
Abhorrent, admirable, beautiful,
150 Pathetical, or ghastly, or grotesque,
With still that face . . . which did not therefore change,
But kept the mystic level of all forms,
Hates, fears, and admirations, was by turns
Ghost, fiend, and angel, fairy, witch, and sprite,
155 A dauntless Muse who eyes a dreadful Fate,
A loving Psyche who loses sight of Love,
A still Medusa[2] with mild milky brows

8. Relating to Holy Communion.
9. Lady's maid (Italian).
1. The Pitti Palace in Florence, once occupied by nobility.
2. In mythology, a female monster with snakes for hair; the sight of her face turned living creatures to stone. A muse is a goddess of the arts and learning. The Fates are three sisters who decide the destiny of each human being. Psyche, according to Greek myth, was a beautiful maiden who was wooed by Eros (Love) by night, until she attempted to catch sight of him, and he fled.

All curdled and all clothed upon with snakes
Whose slime falls fast as sweat will; or anon
160 Our Lady of the Passion, stabbed with swords[3]
Where the Babe sucked; or Lamia[4] in her first
Moonlighted pallor, ere she shrunk and blinked
And shuddering wriggled down to the unclean;
Or my own mother, leaving her last smile
165 In her last kiss upon the baby-mouth
My father pushed down on the bed for that,—
Or my dead mother, without smile or kiss,
Buried at Florence.* * *

[AURORA'S JOURNEY TO ENGLAND AND EDUCATION THERE BY
HER FATHER'S SISTER]

270 I think I see my father's sister stand
Upon the hall-step of her country-house
To give me welcome. She stood straight and calm,
Her somewhat narrow forehead braided tight
As if for taming accidental thoughts
275 From possible pulses,[5] brown hair pricked with gray
By frigid use of life (she was not old,
Although my father's elder by a year),
A nose drawn sharply, yet in delicate lines;
A close mild mouth, a little soured about
280 The ends, through speaking unrequited loves
Or peradventure[6] niggardly half-truths;
Eyes of no color,—once they might have smiled,
But never, never have forgot themselves
In smiling; cheeks, in which was yet a rose
285 Of perished summers, like a rose in a book,
Kept more for ruth[7] than pleasure,—if past bloom,
Past fading also.
 She had lived, we'll say,
A harmless life, she called a virtuous life,
A quiet life, which was not life at all
290 (But that, she had not lived enough to know),
Between the vicar and the country squires,
The lord-lieutenant looking down sometimes
From the empyrean[8] to assure their souls
Against chance vulgarisms, and, in the abyss,
295 The apothecary, looked on once a year
To prove their soundness of humility.
The poor-club[9] exercised her Christian gifts
Of knitting stockings, stitching petticoats,
Because we are of one flesh, after all,
300 And need one flannel (with a proper sense

3. The Virgin Mary, "stabbed" with grief by her
son Jesus' Crucifixion and suffering (the Passion).
4. In John Keats's poem *Lamia* (1820), a young
man falls in love with a beautiful woman who is
then revealed to be a serpent.

5. Excitements.
6. Perhaps.
7. Pity, remorse.
8. The highest reaches of heaven.
9. Charitable organization.

Or difference in the quality)—and still
The book-club, guarded from your modern trick
Of shaking dangerous questions from the crease,[1]
Preserved her intellectual. She had lived
305 A sort of cage-bird life, born in a cage,
Accounting that to leap from perch to perch
Was act and joy enough for any bird.
Dear heaven, how silly are the things that live
In thickets, and eat berries!
 I, alas,
310 A wild bird scarcely fledged, was brought to her cage,
And she was there to meet me. Very kind.
Bring the clean water, give out the fresh seed.

quoting her aunt, calling wild bird silly

* * *

385 I broke the copious curls upon my head
In braids, because she liked smooth-ordered hair.
I left off saying my sweet Tuscan words[2]
Which still at any stirring of the heart
Came up to float across the English phrase
390 As lilies (*Bene* or *Che che*[3]), because
She liked my father's child to speak his tongue
I learnt the collects and the catechism,
The creeds, from Athanasius back to Nice,
The Articles, the Tracts[4] *against* the times
395 (By no means Buonaventure's "Prick of Love"),
And various popular synopses of
Inhuman doctrines never taught by John,[5]
Because she liked instructed piety.
I learnt my complement of classic French
400 (Kept pure of Balzac and neologism[6])
And German also, since she liked a range
Of liberal education,—tongues, not books,
I learnt a little algebra, a little
Of the mathematics,—brushed with extreme flounce[7]
405 The circle of the sciences, because
She misliked women who are frivolous.
I learnt the royal genealogies
Of Oviedo,[8] the internal laws
Of the Burmese empire,—by how many feet

aunt was impatient about sciences

1. I.e., of finding subversive ideas hidden in books.
2. The dialect of Tuscany, the region of Italy where Florence is located.
3. What's the matter? "*Bene*": good.
4. The Thirty-Nine Articles are the creed of the Church of England. "Collects": opening prayers in the Anglican Church, which vary with the day. "Creeds": articles of Christian faith; the Athanasian creed, pertaining to the doctrines of the Trinity and the Incarnation, apparently dates to 361 C.E., while the Nicene creed, a profession of Christian faith, took its final form in 381.
5. All the works in this list are strict religious primers and treatises. "Tracts against the times" is a humorous reference to *Tracts for the Times* (1834) by John Henry Newman, Edward Pusey, and John Keble, which condemned Anglican Church reform. The *Prick of Love*, a devotional poem wrongly attributed to St. Bonaventure (1221–1274), focuses on love as more important than reason. John, author of one of the Gospels, did not concern himself with fine technical points of theology.
6. New words. Honoré de Balzac (1799–1850) wrote many popular novels dealing with the corruption of Parisian society.
7. Abruptness, impatience.
8. Gonzalo Fernández de Oviedo (1478–1557), Spanish historian. All the facts mentioned in this passage are noteworthy only for being esoteric, unrelated to Aurora's real concerns.

410　Mount Chimborazo outsoars Teneriffe,[9]
　　　What navigable river joins itself
　　　To Lara,[1] and what census of the year five
　　　Was taken at Klagenfurt,[2]—because she liked
　　　A general insight into useful facts.
415　I learnt much music,—such as would have been
　　　As quite impossible in Johnson's day[3]
　　　As still it might be wished—fine sleights of hand
　　　And unimagined fingering, shuffling off
　　　The hearer's soul through hurricanes of notes
420　To a noisy Tophet; and I drew . . . costumes
　　　From French engravings, nereids[4] neatly draped
　　　(With smirks of simmering godship): I washed in[5]
　　　Landscapes from nature (rather say, washed out).
　　　I danced the polka and Cellarius,[6]
425　Spun glass, stuffed birds, and modelled flowers in wax,
　　　Because she liked accomplishments in girls.
　　　I read a score of books on womanhood
　　　To prove, if women do not think at all,
　　　They may teach thinking (to a maiden aunt
430　Or else the author),—books that boldly assert
　　　Their right of comprehending husband's talk
　　　When not too deep, and even of answering
　　　With pretty "may it please you," or "so it is,"—
　　　Their rapid insight and fine aptitude,
435　Particular worth and general missionariness,[7]
　　　As long as they keep quiet by the fire
　　　And never say "no" when the world says "ay,"
　　　For that is fatal,—their angelic reach[8]
　　　Of virtue, chiefly used to sit and darn,
440　And fatten household sinners,—their, in brief,
　　　Potential faculty in everything
　　　Of abdicating power in it: she owned
　　　She liked a woman to be womanly,
　　　And English women, she thanked God and sighed
445　(Some people always sigh in thanking God),
　　　Were models to the universe. And last
　　　I learnt cross-stitch, because she did not like
　　　To see me wear the night with empty hands
　　　A-doing nothing. So, my shepherdess
450　Was something after all (the pastoral saints
　　　Be praised for't), leaning lovelorn with pink eyes
　　　To match her shoes, when I mistook the silks;
　　　Her head uncrushed by that round weight of hat

[handwritten marginal note:] image of the angel in the house. The woman does not assert herself, but is an embodiment of virtue that influences all around her

9. A mountain in the Canary Islands. Mount Chimborazo is a high peak in the Andes (in Ecuador).
1. A region in Spain on the river Arlanza.
2. A city in Austria.
3. The time of Samuel Johnson (1709–1784), English lexicographer. When a piece of music played by a young lady was described to him as very difficult, he is said to have answered, "I would it had been impossible."
4. Sea nymphs. "Tophet": hell.
5. Painted watercolors.
6. A kind of waltz.
7. I.e., desire to convert others to virtue.
8. Coventry Patmore's popular book-length poem *The Angel in the House* (1854) celebrated the ideals of domestic virtue.

So strangely similar to the tortoise shell
Which slew the tragic poet.[9]

455 By the way,
The works of women are symbolical. *→ Symbolical of the worth of woman.*
We sew, sew, prick our fingers, dull our sight,
Producing what? A pair of slippers, sir,
To put on when you're weary—or a stool
460 To stumble over and vex you . . . "curse that stool!"
Or else at best, a cushion, where you lean
And sleep, and dream of something we are not
But would be for your sake. Alas, alas!
This hurts most, this—that, after all, we are paid
The worth of our work, perhaps
465 In looking down
Those years of education (to return)
I wonder if Brinvilliers[1] suffered more
In the water-torture . . . flood succeeding flood
To drench the incapable throat and split the veins . . .
470 Than I did. Certain of your feebler souls
Go out[2] in such a process; many pine
To a sick, inodorous light; my own endured:
I had relations in the Unseen, and drew
The elemental nutriment and heat
475 From nature, as earth feels the sun at nights,
Or as a babe sucks surely in the dark.
I kept the life thrust on me, on the outside
Of the inner life with all its ample room
For heart and lungs, for will and intellect,
480 Inviolable by conventions. God,
I thank thee for that grace of thine!

 * * *

Book II

[ROMNEY'S PROPOSAL OF MARRIAGE TO AURORA AND HER REFUSAL][3]

 "Then, must it be
 Indeed farewell? And was I so far wrong *Aurora refuses*
420 In hope and in illusion, when I took *Romney's proposal.*
The woman to be nobler than the man,
Yourself the noblest woman, in the use[4]
And comprehension of what love is,—love,
That generates the likeness of itself
425 Through all heroic duties? so far wrong,

9. The Greek tragedian Aeschylus (526–456
B.C.E.) was reputedly killed when an eagle dropped
a tortoise on his head.
1. The Marquise de Brinvilliers (ca. 1630–1676);
she was tortured by having water forced down her
throat, because she allegedly murdered her hus-
band's relatives to win his fortune for herself and
her lover.
2. I.e., die.
3. In this selection Aurora's cousin Romney Leigh,

now the head of the family, has proposed to her,
arguing that it would be better for her to join him
in working for social welfare than to continue with
her plan to become a poet, since he believes that
women cannot write effective verse. In lines 418–
32, Romney is speaking. In the next paragraph,
Aurora reiterates her refusal, insisting on her com-
mitment to her chosen vocation.
4. Practice.

[handwritten left margin: Romney thinks she refuses him because of how he is proposing.]

[handwritten top right: Am I so wrong to say]

In saying bluntly, venturing truth on love,
'Come, human creature, love and work with me,'—
Instead of 'Lady, thou art wondrous fair,
And, where the Graces[5] walk before, the Muse

[handwritten right: should I have said]

430 Will follow at the lightning of their eyes,
And where the Muse walks, lovers need to creep:
Turn round and love me, or I die of love.' "
With quiet indignation I broke in.
"You misconceive the question like a man,

435 Who sees the woman as the complement
Of his sex merely. You forget too much
That every creature, female as the male,
Stands single in responsible act and thought
As also in birth and death. Whoever says

[handwritten right: she says his work is not her work.]

440 To a loyal woman, 'Love and work with me,'
Will get fair answers if the work and love,
Being good themselves, are good for her—the best
She was born for. Women of a softer mood,
Surprised by men when scarcely awake to life,

445 Will sometimes only hear the first word, love,
And catch up with it any kind of work,
Indifferent, so that dear love go with it.
I do not blame such women, though, for love,
They pick much oakum;[6] earth's fanatics make

450 Too frequently heaven's saints. But *me* your work
Is not the best for,—nor your love the best,
Nor able to commend the kind of work
For love's sake merely. Ah, you force me, sir,
To be overbold in speaking of myself:

455 I too have my vocation,—work to do,
The heavens and earth have set me since I changed
My father's face for theirs, and, though your world
Were twice as wretched as you represent,
Most serious work, most necessary work

460 As any of the economists'.[7] Reform,
Make trade a Christian possibility,
And individual right no general wrong;
Wipe out earth's furrows of the Thine and Mine,
And leave one green for men to play at bowls,[8]

465 With innings for them all! . . . What then, indeed,
If mortals are not greater by the head
Than any of their prosperities? what then,
Unless the artist keep up open roads
Betwixt the seen and unseen,—bursting through

470 The best of your conventions with his best,
The speakable, imaginable best
God bids him speak, to prove what lies beyond
Both speech and imagination? A starved man
Exceeds a fat beast: we'll not barter, sir,

5. Greek goddesses of charm and beauty.
6. Loose hemp or fiber derived from untwisting old rope; i.e., they are condemned to hard labor.

7. The economists wished to reform British trade; Aurora hopes to reform the British soul.
8. Lawn bowling.

475 The beautiful for barley.—And, even so,
 I hold you will not compass your poor ends
 Of barley-feeding and material ease,
 Without a poet's individualism
 To work your universal. It takes a soul,
480 To move a body: it takes a high-souled man,
 To move the masses, even to a cleaner stye:[9]
 It takes the ideal, to blow a hair's-breadth off
 The dust of the actual.—Ah, your Fouriers[1] failed,
 Because not poets enough to understand
485 That life develops from within.—For me,
 Perhaps I am not worthy, as you say,
 Of work like this: perhaps a woman's soul
 Aspires, and not creates: yet we aspire,
 And yet I'll try out your perhapses, sir,
490 And if I fail . . . why, burn me up my straw
 Like other false works—I'll not ask for grace;
 Your scorn is better, cousin Romney. I
 Who love my art, would never wish it lower
 To suit my stature. I may love my art.
495 You'll grant that even a woman may love art,
 Seeing that to waste true love on anything
 Is womanly, past question."

* * *

Book V

[AURORA'S THEORIES OF POETRY][2]

 The critics say that epics have died out
140 With Agamemnon and the goat-nursed gods;[3]
 I'll not believe it. I could never deem
 As Payne Knight did (the mythic mountaineer
 Who traveled higher than he was born to live,
 And showed sometimes the goiter[4] in his throat
145 Discoursing of an image seen through fog),
 That Homer's heroes measured twelve feet high.
 They were but men:—his Helen's[5] hair turned gray
 Like any plain Miss Smith's who wears a front;[6]
 And Hector's infant[7] whimpered at a plume
150 As yours last Friday at a turkey-cock.
 All actual heroes are essential men,

9. Enclosure for pigs.
1. François Fourier (1772–1837), French social theorist who advocated communal property as a basis for social harmony.
2. In this selection, Aurora, now a struggling poet living in London, formulates her artistic beliefs and goals, distinguishing her ideas about poetry from those of her contemporaries. In a sense, this aesthetic manifesto will prove to be the foundation of the success she achieves later in Barrett Browning's verse-novel.
3. In some accounts, the god Zeus was nursed by

a goat. Agamemnon: king of Mycenae, who led the Greeks in the war against Troy (the subject of Homer's epic poem *The Iliad*).
4. A disease often found in mountainous areas, where the diet lacks iodine. Richard Payne Knight (1750–1824), a classical scholar.
5. Helen of Troy, the most beautiful woman in the world; her abduction caused the Trojan War.
6. A hairpiece.
7. Astyanax, terrified of his father's armor and the crest of his helmet (*Iliad* 6.467–70). Hector was the greatest of the Trojan warriors.

And all men possible heroes: every age,
Heroic in proportions, double-faced,
Looks backward and before, expects a morn
And claims an epos.[8]

155 Ay, but every age
Appears to souls who live in't (ask Carlyle[9])
Most unheroic. Ours, for instance, ours:
The thinkers scout it, and the poets abound
Who scorn to touch it with a fingertip:
160 A pewter age[1]—mixed metal, silver-washed;
An age of scum, spooned off the richer past.
An age of patches for old gaberdines,
An age of mere transition,[2] meaning nought
Except that what succeeds must shame it quite
165 If God please. That's wrong thinking, to my mind,
And wrong thoughts make poor poems.

 Every age,
Through being beheld too close, is ill-discerned
By those who have not lived past it. We'll suppose
Mount Athos[3] carved, as Alexander schemed,
170 To some colossal statue of a man.
The peasants, gathering brushwood in his ear,
Had guessed as little as the browsing goats
Of form or feature of humanity
Up there,—in fact, had traveled five miles off
175 Or ere the giant image broke on them,
Full human profile, nose and chin distinct,
Mouth, muttering rhythms of silence up the sky
And fed at evening with the blood of suns;
Grand torso,—hand, that flung perpetually
180 The largesse of a silver river down
To all the country pastures. 'Tis even thus
With times we live in,—evermore too great
To be apprehended near.

 But poets should
Exert a double vision; should have eyes
185 To see near things as comprehensively
As if afar they took their point of sight,
And distant things as intimately deep
As if they touched them. Let us strive for this.
I do distrust the poet who discerns
190 No character or glory in his times,
And trundles back his soul five hundred years,
Past moat and drawbridge, into a castle-court,
To sing—oh, not of lizard or of toad

8. Epic poem.
9. Thomas Carlyle (1795–1881), Scottish historian and essayist who celebrated the heroic ideal in such works as *Heroes and Hero-Worship* and *Past and Present.*
1. An allusion to the classical idea of civilization's decline from a golden age through silver, bronze, and so on. Pewter is a metal alloy.
2. In *The Spirit of the Age* (1831), J. S. Mill called the present age "an age of transition." "Gaberdines": coats made of gabardine, a twilled fabric.
3. A mountain in northern Greece that an architect-builder proposed to carve into a likeness of Alexander the Great (356–323 B.C.E.)

Alive i' the ditch there,—'t were excusable,
195 But of some black chief, half knight, half sheep-lifter,
Some beauteous dame, half chattel[4] and half queen,
As dead as must be, for the greater part,
The poems made on their chivalric bones;
And that's no wonder: death inherits death.

200 Nay, if there's room for poets in this world
A little overgrown (I think there is),
Their sole work is to represent the age,
Their age, not Charlemagne's,[5]—this live, throbbing age,
That brawls, cheats, maddens, calculates, aspires,
205 And spends more passion, more heroic heat,
Betwixt the mirrors of its drawing-rooms,
Than Roland[6] with his knights at Roncesvalles.
To flinch from modern varnish, coat or flounce,
Cry out for togas and the picturesque,
210 Is fatal,—foolish too. King Arthur's self
Was commonplace to Lady Guenever;
And Camelot to minstrels seemed as flat
As Fleet Street[7] to our poets. Never flinch,
But still, unscrupulously epic, catch
215 Upon the burning lava of a song
The full-veined, heaving, double-breasted Age:
That, when the next shall come, the men of that
May touch the impress[8] with reverent hand, and say
"Behold,—behold the paps[9] we all have sucked!
220 This bosom seems to beat still, or at least
It sets ours beating: this is living art,
Which thus presents and thus records true life."

* * *

1857

A Curse for a Nation[1]

Prologue

I heard an angel speak last night,
 And he said "Write!
Write a Nation's curse for me,
 And send it over the Western Sea."

4. Property. "Sheep-lifter": thief of livestock.
5. King of the Franks (724–818 C.E.) who created an empire and became a hero of legend and poetry.
6. A knight and nephew of Charlemagne, killed in battle at Roncesvalles and immortalized in the 11th-century poem *Chanson de Roland*.
7. The London street where newspaper offices were concentrated. "Camelot": legendary British seat of King Arthur and his knights.
8. The image is of a molten substance being molded by the present age, which leaves its "impress" in the metal.
9. Breasts.
1. The nation is the United States, then practicing slavery.

5 I faltered, taking up the word:
 "Not so, my lord!
If curses must be, choose another
To send thy curse against my brother.

"For I am bound by gratitude,
10 By love and blood,
To brothers of mine across the sea,
Who stretch out kindly hands to me."

"Therefore," the voice said, "shalt thou write
 My curse tonight.
15 From the summits of love a curse is driven,
As lightning is from the tops of heaven."

"Not so," I answered. "Evermore
 My heart is sore
For my own land's sins: for little feet
20 Of children bleeding along the street:

"For parked-up² honors that gainsay
 The right of way:
For almsgiving through a door that is
Not open enough for two friends to kiss:

25 "For love of freedom which abates
 Beyond the Straits:³
For patriot virtue starved to vice on
Self-praise, self-interest, and suspicion:

"For an oligarchic parliament,⁴
30 And bribes well-meant.
What curse to another land assign,
When heavy-souled for the sins of mine?"

"Therefore," the voice said, "shalt thou write
 My curse tonight.
35 Because thou hast strength to see and hate
A foul thing done *within* thy gate."

"Not so," I answered once again.
 "To curse, choose men.
For I, a woman, have only known
40 How the heart melts and the tears run down."

"Therefore," the voice said, "shalt thou write
 My curse tonight.

2. Gathered in one place.
3. The Strait of Gibraltar, which divides Europe from Africa, where England had extensive colonies

and imperial interests.
4. I.e., a parliament controlled by an aristocratic elite.

Some women weep and curse, I say
(And no one marvels), night and day.

45 "And thou shalt take their part tonight,
 Weep and write.
 A curse from the depths of womanhood
 Is very salt, and bitter, and good."

 So thus I wrote, and mourned indeed,
50 What all may read.
 And thus, as was enjoined on me,
 I send it over the Western Sea.

The Curse

I

 Because ye have broken your own chain
 With the strain
55 Of brave men climbing a Nation's height,
 Yet thence bear down with brand and thong
 On souls of others,—for this wrong
 This is the curse. Write.

 Because yourselves are standing straight
60 In the state
 Of Freedom's foremost acolyte,
 Yet keep calm footing all the time
 On writhing bond-slaves,—for this crime
 This is the curse. Write.

65 Because ye prosper in God's name,
 With a claim
 To honor in the old world's sight,
 Yet do the fiend's work perfectly
 In strangling martyrs,—for this lie
70 This is the curse. Write.

II

 Ye shall watch while kings conspire
 Round the people's smouldering fire
 And, warm for your part,
 Shall never dare—O shame!
75 To utter the thought into flame
 Which burns at your heart.
 This is the curse. Write.

 Ye shall watch while nations strive
 With the bloodhounds, die or survive,
80 Drop faint from their jaws,
 Or throttle them backward to death;

And only under your breath
 Shall favor the cause.
 This is the curse. Write.

85 Ye shall watch while strong men draw
The nets of feudal law
 To strangle the weak;
And, counting the sin for a sin,
Your soul shall be sadder within
90 Than the word ye shall speak.
 This is the curse. Write.

When good men are praying erect
That Christ may avenge his elect
 And deliver the earth,
95 The prayer in your ears, said low,
Shall sound like the tramp of a foe
 That's driving you forth.
 This is the curse. Write.

When wise men give you their praise,
100 They shall pause in the heat of the phrase,
 As if carried too far.
When ye boast your own charters kept true,
Ye shall blush; for the thing which ye do
 Derides what ye are.
105 This is the curse. Write.

When fools cast taunts at your gate,
Your scorn ye shall somewhat abate
 As ye look o'er the wall;
For your conscience, tradition, and name
110 Explode with a deadlier blame
 Than the worst of them all.
 This is the curse. Write.

Go, wherever ill deeds shall be done,
Go, plant your flag in the sun
115 Beside the ill-doers!
And recoil from clenching the curse
Of God's witnessing Universe
 With a curse of yours.
 THIS is the curse. Write.

1860

Mother and Poet

Turin, after News from Gaeta, 1861[1]

1

Dead! One of them shot by the sea in the east,
 And one of them shot in the west by the sea.
Dead! both my boys! When you sit at the feast
 And are wanting a great song for Italy free,
5 Let none look at *me!*

2

Yet I was a poetess only last year,
 And good at my art, for a woman, men said;
But *this* woman, *this,* who is agonized here,
 —The east sea and west sea rhyme on in her head
10 For ever instead.

3

What art can a woman be good at? Oh, vain!
 What art *is* she good at, but hurting her breast
With the milk-teeth of babes, and a smile at the pain?
 Ah boys, how you hurt! you were strong as you pressed,
15 And I proud, by that test.

4

What art's for a woman? To hold on her knees
 Both darlings! to feel all their arms round her throat,
Cling, strangle a little! to sew by degrees
 And 'broider the long-clothes and neat little coat;
20 To dream and to doat.

5

To teach them . . . It stings there! *I* made them indeed
 Speak plain the word *country. I* taught them, no doubt,
That a country's a thing men should die for at need.
 I prated of liberty, rights, and about
25 The tyrant cast out.

6

And when their eyes flashed . . . O my beautiful eyes! . . .
 I exulted: nay, let them go forth at the wheels
Of the guns, and denied not. But then the surprise
 When one sits quite alone! Then one weeps, then one kneels!
30 God, how the house feels!

1. "The mother was Laura Savio of Turin, poet and patriot, whose two sons were killed at Ancona and Gaeta" [Browning's note]. At this time Italy was struggling to free itself from foreign rule and become a unified state. Ancona is a port on the Adriatic, Gaeta, a fortified port north of Naples, was the last stronghold of the Neapolitan government.

7

At first, happy news came, in gay letters moiled[2]
 With my kisses,—of camp-life and glory, and how
They both loved me; and, soon coming home to be spoiled
 In return would fan off every fly from my brow
35 With their green laurel-bough.

8

Then was triumph at Turin: "Ancona was free!"
 And someone came out of the cheers in the street,
With a face pale as stone, to say something to me.
 My Guido was dead! I fell down at his feet,
40 While they cheered in the street.

9

I bore it; friends soothed me; my grief looked sublime
 As the ransom of Italy. One boy remained
To be leant on and walked with, recalling the time
 When the first grew immortal, while both of us strained
45 To the height he had gained.

10

And letters still came, shorter, sadder, more strong,
 Writ now but in one hand, "I was not to faint,—
One loved me for two—would be with me ere long:
 And *Viva l'Italia!*[3]—he died for, our saint,
50 Who forbids our complaint."

11

My Nanni would add, "he was safe, and aware
 Of a presence that turned off the balls,[4]—was imprest
It was Guido himself, who knew what I could bear,
 And how 'twas impossible, quite dispossessed
55 To live on for the rest."

12

On which, without pause, up the telegraph line
 Swept smoothly the next news from Gaeta:—*Shot.*
Tell his mother. Ah, ah, "his," "their" mother,—not "mine,"
 No voice says "*My* mother" again to me. What!
60 You think Guido forgot?

13

Are souls straight so happy that, dizzy with Heaven,
 They drop earth's affections, conceive not of woe?
I think not. Themselves were too lately forgiven

2. Smeared.
3. Long live Italy!

4. Bullets.

Through THAT Love and Sorrow which reconciled so
65 The Above and Below.[5]

14

O Christ of the five wounds, who look'dst through the dark
To the face of thy mother! consider, I pray,
How we common mothers stand desolate, mark,
Whose sons, not being Christs, die with eyes turned away,
70 And no last word to say!

15

Both boys dead? but that's out of nature. We all
Have been patriots, yet each house must always keep one.
'Twere imbecile, hewing out roads to a wall;
And, when Italy's made, for what end is it done
75 If we have not a son?

16

Ah, ah, ah! when Gaeta's taken, what then?
When the fair wicked queen sits no more at her sport
Of the fire-balls of death crashing souls out of men?
When the guns of Cavalli[6] with final retort
80 Have cut the game short?

17

When Venice and Rome keep their new jubilee,
When your flag takes all heaven for its white, green, and red,[7]
When *you* have your country from mountain to sea,
When King Victor[8] has Italy's crown on his head,
85 (And I have my dead)—

18

What then? Do not mock me. Ah, ring your bells low,
And burn your lights faintly! *My* country is *there,*
Above the star pricked by the last peak of snow:
My Italy's there, with my brave civic pair,
90 To disfranchise despair!

19

Forgive me. Some women bear children in strength,
And bite back the cry of their pain in self-scorn;
But the birth-pangs of nations will wring us at length
Into wail such as this—and we sit on forlorn
95 When the man-child is born.

5. I.e., the love and sorrow of Jesus.
6. Giovanni Cavelli (1808–1879), commander of the artillery who improved cannon technology. "The fair wicked queen" was Maria Sophia (1841–1925), wife of Francis II, the last Neapolitan ruler.

7. The colors of the new Italian flag, symbolizing national unity.
8. Victor Emmanuel II (1820–1878), who in 1861 became the first king of a united Italy.

20
Dead! One of them shot by the sea in the east,
 And one of them shot in the west by the sea.
Both! both my boys! If in keeping the feast
 You want a great song for your Italy free,[9]
100 Let none look at *me!*

1862

9. I.e., the holiday celebrating the unification of Italy.

MARGARET FULLER
1810–1850

After Margaret Fuller's untimely death at forty years of age, Elizabeth Barrett Browning honored her "truth and courage," Ralph Waldo Emerson mourned that he had "lost in her my audience," Nathaniel Hawthorne censured her as "a great humbug" in his journal and as Zenobia in *The Blithedale Romance* (1852), Henry James brooded over the "haunting Margaret-ghost," and Henry David Thoreau spent five days on Fire Island, New York, searching for the remains of her body and her last book. Whether they castigated or praised her, however, all agreed that, in Barrett Browning's words, her "writings [were] curiously inferior to . . . her conversation." Indeed, their mixed response of awe at her personal power and uncertainty about the written evidence of that power typifies the problem Fuller poses for contemporary readers as well. But her prose nevertheless struggles to effect a cultural transformation that would reflect her own search for fulfillment, a search of epic proportions: "Such a predetermination to eat this big Universe as her oyster or egg," the English essayist and historian Thomas Carlyle wrote, "I have not before seen in any human soul."

Fuller's mother, Margaret (Crane) Fuller, was notable for her patient submissiveness as she bore nine children and raised the seven who survived past infancy. Her father, Timothy Fuller, was an energetic and independent graduate of Harvard, the speaker of the Massachusetts House of Representatives, a Unitarian in religion, and a Jeffersonian in politics. He taught his precocious first child Latin and English grammar at an early age, even as he encouraged direct discourse and discouraged stereotypically "feminine" hesitation, apology, or euphemism. This strenuous education produced a child prodigy who read Virgil, Ovid, and Horace at the age of seven, and who suffered terrifying nightmares and recurrent headaches for most of her life. Torn between her training as her father's "son" and her knowledge of her female self, Fuller felt that womanhood was "too straitly bounded" to give her scope, but she suffered feelings of inauthenticity when she "played" the part of the great man.

After a short stay at the Misses Prescott's School in Groton, Massachusetts, presumably designed to address this dilemma, Fuller continued her education at home in Cambridgeport until, after a move to Groton, her father died. To support the family, she taught at Bronson Alcott's experimental school in Boston and then at the Greene Street School in Providence. At both establishments she began to cultivate the friendships that would play a prominent role throughout her life. After more than one adolescent infatuation with female friends, she began her "conversations," meetings

or classes usually composed of an elite group of Bostonians who discussed such topics as ethics, fine arts, education, and Greek mythology. From 1839 to 1840, New England's version of the salon took place in Elizabeth Peabody's bookstore, where Fuller could draw on the connections she had already established in Cambridge intellectual society, which was composed of Transcendentalists such as Frederic Henry Hedge, W. E. Channing, and James Freeman Clarke. From 1840 to 1842, with the encouragement of Emerson, she edited the Transcendentalists' magazine, *The Dial*. In 1844, Horace Greeley, editor of the *New York Daily Tribune,* hired her to write literary criticism and moved her to New York.

As the first self-supporting American woman journalist, the translator of Johann Peter Eckermann's *Conversations with Goethe* (1839), and the author of *Summer on the Lakes* (1844), Fuller undertook to mediate between American society and European culture, represented by such figures as the German poet-dramatist Goethe, the Romantic poet Lord Byron, and the French novelist George Sand. While her *Papers on Literature and Art,* published in 1846, consolidated her reputation, her fame today depends largely on *Woman in the Nineteenth Century* (1845). Originally a *Dial* essay titled "The Great Lawsuit" (1843), this feminist polemic applied to women Transcendentalist tenets regarding the sacred duty of self-development, but it also solved the problem of Fuller's own sense of self-division: "there is no wholly masculine man," she proclaimed, "no purely feminine woman." Hortatory in tone, *Woman in the Nineteenth Century* resembles a sermon, insisting, as it does, that men and women alike must fulfill their potential for the greater spiritual good of both sexes. Although her prose is sometimes marred by strained rhetoric, the broadly based humanism Fuller stressed here was to inform the rest of her life as she widened her concerns from feminism to the politics of liberation.

Already, in New York, she had helped establish a "halfway house" for convicts and translated one of the earliest discussions of Karl Marx and Friedrich Engels to be offered in the United States. After she sailed for Europe as a foreign correspondent for the *Tribune,* she met Giuseppe Mazzini, the Italian patriot in exile, as well as two artists associated with sexual liberation, the French novelist George Sand and the exiled Polish writer Adam Mickiewicz. Eventually, she settled in Italy, where she took Giovanni Angelo, marchese d'Ossoli, as her lover. Ten years her junior, he was instrumental in consolidating her commitment to the cause of Italian independence. Her son, Angelo Eugene, was born on September 5, 1848, and in November Fuller left him to rejoin Ossoli in Rome. There she witnessed and reported on the arrival of the Italian nationalist Giuseppe Garibaldi, the proclamation of the Roman Republic, and the intervention of the French on behalf of the pope. During the French siege, she took over an emergency hospital, but when the Republic was overthrown in July, she fled with Ossoli and her child, first to Florence and then to America. It is unclear whether the two married before leaving Italy, although it is known that Fuller was working on a history of the Roman revolution at this time.

Just outside of New York's harbor, the ship bearing Fuller, Ossoli, and their child drove into a sandbar during a storm. The baby's body was washed ashore, but neither Margaret Fuller nor Ossoli was ever found. In spite of the fame Fuller had attained during her relatively short lifetime, the contemporary scholars Bell Gale Chevigny and Marie Olesen Urbanski have demonstrated how subsequent editors and biographers trivialized this activist literary woman's image. Yet, as Chevigny and Urbanski also show, Fuller continued to exert a profound influence on the growing American women's movement. In the words of the nineteenth-century suffragist Ednah Cheney, "Whatever she spoke of revealed a hidden meaning, and everything seemed to be put into true relation. . . . I was no longer the limitation of myself, but I felt that the whole wealth of the universe was open to me." Cheney understood, as did many of her contemporaries, that Fuller's famous presumption—her saying, for example, "I accept the universe"—could be misinterpreted as conceit, but what it truly signified was "consciousness of the illimitable ego, the divinity in the soul."

From Woman in the Nineteenth Century

[PREJUDICE AGAINST WOMEN]

* * *Knowing that there exists in the minds of men a tone of feeling toward women as toward slaves, such as is expressed in the common phrase, "Tell that to women and children"; that the infinite soul[1] can only work through them in already ascertained limits; that the gift of reason, Man's highest prerogative, is allotted to them in much lower degree; that they must be kept from mischief and melancholy by being constantly engaged in active labor, which is to be furnished and directed by those better able to think, etc., etc.,—we need not multiply instances, for who can review the experience of last week without recalling words which imply, whether in jest or earnest, these views, or views like these,—knowing this, can we wonder that many reformers think that measures are not likely to be taken in behalf of women, unless their wishes could be publicly represented by women?

"That can never be necessary," cry the other side. "All men are privately influenced by women; each has his wife, sister, or female friends, and is too much biased by these relations to fail of representing their interests; and, if this is not enough, let them propose and enforce their wishes with the pen. The beauty of home would be destroyed, the delicacy of the sex be violated, the dignity of halls of legislation degraded, by an attempt to introduce them there. Such duties are inconsistent with those of a mother;" and then we have ludicrous pictures of ladies in hysterics at the polls, and senate-chambers filled with cradles.

But if, in reply, we admit as truth that Woman seems destined by nature rather for the inner circle, we must add that the arrangements of civilized life have not been, as yet, such as to secure it to her. Her circle, if the duller, is not the quieter. If kept from "excitement," she is not from drudgery. Not only the Indian squaw carries the burdens of the camp, but the favorites of Louis XIV[2] accompany him in his journeys, and the washerwoman stands at her tub, and carries home her work at all seasons, and in all states of health. Those who think the physical circumstances of Woman would make a part in the affairs of national government unsuitable, are by no means those who think it impossible for negresses to endure fieldwork, even during pregnancy, or for sempstresses to go through their killing labors.

As to the use of the pen, there was quite as much opposition to Woman's possessing herself of that help to free agency as there is now to her seizing on the rostrum or the desk; and she is likely to draw, from a permission to plead her cause that way, opposite inferences to what might be wished by those who now grant it.

As to the possibility of her filling with grace and dignity any such position, we should think those who had seen the great actresses, and heard the Quaker preachers of modern times, would not doubt that Woman can express publicly the fulness of thought and creation, without losing any of the peculiar beauty of her sex. What can pollute and tarnish is to act thus from any motive except that something needs to be said or done. Woman

1. A Transcendentalist concept probably derived from: Ralph Waldo Emerson's "The Over-Soul" (1841).

2. Women in favor at the court of the French king (1638–1715; r. 1643–1715).

could take part in the processions, the songs, the dances of old religion; no one fancied her delicacy was impaired by appearing in public for such a cause.

As to her home, she is not likely to leave it more than she now does for balls, theatres, meetings for promoting missions, revival meetings, and others to which she flies, in hope of an animation for her existence commensurate with what she sees enjoyed by men. Governors of ladies'-fairs are no less engrossed by such a charge, than the governor of a state by his; presidents of Washingtonian societies[3] no less away from home than presidents of conventions. If men look straitly to it, they will find that, unless their lives are domestic, those of the women will not be. A house is no home unless it contain food and fire for the mind as well as for the body. The female Greek, of our day, is as much in the street as the male to cry, "What news?"[4] We doubt not it was the same in Athens of old. The women, shut out from the marketplace, made up for it at the religious festivals. For human beings are not so constituted that they can live without expansion. If they do not get it in one way, they must in another, or perish.

As to men's representing women fairly at present, while we hear from men who owe to their wives not only all that is comfortable or graceful, but all that is wise, in the arrangement of their lives, the frequent remark, "You cannot reason with a woman,"—when from those of delicacy, nobleness, and poetic culture, falls the contemptuous phrase "women and children," and that in no light sally of the hour, but in works intended to give a permanent statement of the best experiences,—when not one man, in the million, shall I say? no, not in the hundred million, can rise above the belief that Woman was made *for Man*,[5]—when such traits as these are daily forced upon the attention, can we feel that Man will always do justice to the interests of Woman? Can we think that he takes a sufficiently discerning and religious view of her office and destiny ever to do her justice, except when prompted by sentiment,—accidentally or transiently, that is, for the sentiment will vary according to the relations in which he is placed? The lover, the poet, the artist, are likely to view her nobly. The father and the philosopher have some chance of liberality; the man of the world, the legislator for expediency, none.

Under these circumstances, without attaching importance, in themselves, to the changes demanded by the champions of Woman, we hail them as signs of the times. We would have every arbitrary barrier thrown down. We would have every path laid open to Woman as freely as to Man. Were this done, and a slight temporary fermentation allowed to subside, we should see crystallizations more pure and of more various beauty. We believe the divine energy would pervade nature to a degree unknown in the history of former ages, and that no discordant collision, but a ravishing harmony of the spheres,[6] would ensue.

Yet, then and only then will mankind be ripe for this, when inward and outward freedom for Woman as much as for Man shall be acknowledged as a *right*, not yielded as a concession. As the friend of the Negro assumes that

3. Temperance groups. "Ladies'-fairs": bazaars organized by women.
4. Greek men were satirized for newsmongering, just as the Latin *quid nunc* (what now) became a term for male busybodies.

5. See Genesis 2.18.
6. A music of perfect order that, according to ancient astronomical belief, was created by the motions of the stars and planets.

one man cannot by right hold another in bondage, so should the friend of Woman assume that Man cannot by right lay even well-meant restrictions on Woman. If the Negro be a soul, if the woman be a soul, apparelled in flesh, to one Master only are they accountable. There is but one law for souls, and, if there is to be an interpreter of it, he must come not as man, or son of man, but as son of God.

Were thought and feeling once so far elevated that Man should esteem himself the brother and friend, but nowise the lord and tutor, of Woman,— were he really bound with her in equal worship,—arrangements as to function and employment would be of no consequence. What Woman needs is not as a woman to act or rule, but as a nature to grow, as an intellect to discern, as a soul to live freely and unimpeded, to unfold such powers as were given her when we left our common home. If fewer talents were given her, yet if allowed the free and full employment of these, so that she may render back to the giver his own with usury,[7] she will not complain; nay, I dare to say she will bless and rejoice in her earthly birth-place, her earthly lot. Let us consider what obstructions impede this good era, and what signs give reason to hope that it draws near.

I was talking on this subject with Miranda,[8] a woman, who, if any in the world could, might speak without heat and bitterness of the position of her sex. Her father was a man who cherished no sentimental reverence for Woman, but a firm belief in the equality of the sexes. She was his eldest child, and came to him at an age when he needed a companion. From the time she could speak and go alone, he addressed her not as a plaything, but as a living mind. Among the few verses he ever wrote was a copy addressed to this child, when the first locks were cut from her head; and the reverence expressed on this occasion for that cherished head, he never belied. It was to him the temple of immortal intellect. He respected his child, however, too much to be an indulgent parent. He called on her for clear judgment, for courage, for honor and fidelity; in short, for such virtues as he knew. In so far as he possessed the keys to the wonders of this universe, he allowed free use of them to her, and, by the incentive of a high expectation, he forbade, so far as possible, that she should let the privilege lie idle.

Thus this child was early led to feel herself a child of the spirit. She took her place easily, not only in the world of organized being, but in the world of mind. A dignified sense of self-dependence was given as all her portion, and she found it a sure anchor. Herself securely anchored, her relations with others were established with equal security. She was fortunate in a total absence of those charms which might have drawn to her bewildering flatteries, and in a strong electric[9] nature, which repelled those who did not belong to her, and attracted those who did. With men and women her relations were noble,—affectionate without passion, intellectual without coldness. The world was free to her, and she lived freely in it. Outward adversity came, and inward conflict; but that faith and self-respect had early been awakened which must always lead, at last, to an outward serenity and an inward peace.

Of Miranda I had always thought as an example, that the restraints upon

7. Interest.
8. An idealized representation of Fuller's own

experiences and opinions.
9. Highly charged, exciting.

the sex were insuperable only to those who think them so, or who noisily strive to break them. She had taken a course of her own, and no man stood in her way. Many of her acts had been unusual, but excited no uproar. Few helped, but none checked her; and the many men who knew her mind and her life, showed to her confidence as to a brother, gentleness as to a sister. And not only refined, but very coarse men approved and aided one in whom they saw resolution and clearness of design. Her mind was often the leading one, always effective.

When I talked with her upon these matters, and had said very much what I have written, she smilingly replied: "And yet we must admit that I have been fortunate, and this should not be.[1] My good father's early trust gave the first bias, and the rest followed, of course. It is true that I have had less outward aid, in after years, than most women; but that is of little consequence. Religion was early awakened in my soul,—a sense that what the soul is capable to ask it must attain, and that, though I might be aided and instructed by others, I must depend on myself as the only constant friend. This self-dependence, which was honored in me, is deprecated as a fault in most women. They are taught to learn their rule from without, not to unfold it from within.

"This is the fault of Man, who is still vain, and wishes to be more important to Woman than, by right, he should be."

"Men have not shown this disposition toward you," I said.

"No; because the position I early was enabled to take was one of self-reliance.[2] And were all women as sure of their wants as I was, the result would be the same. But they are so overloaded with precepts by guardians, who think that nothing is so much to be dreaded for a woman as originality of thought or character, that their minds are impeded by doubts till they lose their chance of fair, free proportions. The difficulty is to get them to the point from which they shall naturally develop self-respect, and learn self-help.

"Once I thought that men would help to forward this state of things more than I do now. I saw so many of them wretched in the connections[3] they had formed in weakness and vanity. They seemed so glad to esteem women whenever they could.

" 'The soft arms of affection,' said one of the most discerning spirits, 'will not suffice for me, unless on them I see the steel bracelets of strength.'

"But early I perceived that men never, in any extreme of despair, wished to be women. On the contrary, they were ever ready to taunt one another, at any sign of weakness, with,

Art thou not like the women, who,—

The passage ends various ways, according to the occasion and rhetoric of the speaker. When they admired any woman, they were inclined to speak of her as 'above her sex.' Silently I observed this, and feared it argued a rooted scepticism, which for ages had been fastening on the heart, and which only an age of miracles could eradicate. Ever I have been treated with great sin-

1. I.e., I would not be as I am without my good fortune.
2. Another Emersonian concept, expressing a faith in individualism.
3. Marriages, relationships.

cerity; and I look upon it as a signal instance of this, that an intimate friend of the other sex said, in a fervent moment, that I 'deserved in some star to be a man.' He was much surprised when I disclosed my view of my position and hopes, when I declared my faith that the feminine side, the side of love, of beauty, of holiness, was now to have its full chance, and that, if either were better, it was better now to be a woman; for even the slightest achievement of good was furthering an especial work of our time. He smiled incredulously. 'She makes the best she can of it,' thought he. 'Let Jews believe the pride of Jewry, but I am of the better sort, and know better.'

"Another used as highest praise, in speaking of a character in literature, the words 'a manly woman.'

"So in the noble passage of Ben Jonson:[4]

> I meant the day-star should not brighter ride,
>> Nor shed like influence from its lucent seat;
> I meant she should be courteous, facile, sweet,
>> Free from that solemn vice of greatness, pride;
> I meant each softest virtue there should meet,
>> Fit in that softer bosom to abide,
> Only a learned and a manly soul
>> I purposed her, that should with even powers
> The rock, the spindle, and the shears control
> Of destiny,[5] and spin her own free hours."

"Methinks," said I, "you are too fastidious in objecting to this. Jonson, in using the word 'manly,' only meant to heighten the picture of this, the true, the intelligent fate, with one of the deeper colors."

"And yet," said she, "so invariable is the use of this word where a heroic quality is to be described, and I feel so sure that persistence and courage are the most womanly no less than the most manly qualities, that I would exchange these words for others of a larger sense, at the risk of marring the fine tissue of the verse.[6] Read, 'A heavenward and instructed soul,' and I should be satisfied. Let it not be said, wherever there is energy or creative genius, 'She has a masculine mind.' "

[MUSE AND MINERVA]

There are two aspects of Woman's nature, represented by the ancients as Muse and Minerva.[7] It is the former to which the writer in the Pathfinder[8] looks. It is the latter which Wordsworth has in mind, when he says,

> With a placid brow,
> Which woman ne'er should forfeit, keep thy vow.[9]

4. English poet (1572–1637). The passage is slightly misquoted from Epigrams 76: "On Lucy, Countess of Bedford" (1616).
5. In classical mythology, the Fates spin out the thread of each person's destiny, cutting it when the time of death arrives.
6. I.e., its prosody.
7. A muse is a goddess of the arts and learning,

conventionally invoked for inspiration; Minerva is the Roman goddess of handicrafts, war, and wisdom, conflated with the Greek goddess Athena.
8. A weekly journal that began publication in New York in 1843.
9. Slightly misquoted from "Liberty: Sequel to the Preceding" (1835), by the English poet William Wordsworth (1770–1850).

The especial genius of Woman I believe to be electrical in movement, intuitive in function, spiritual in tendency. She excels not so easily in classification, or recreation,[1] as in an instinctive seizure of causes, and a simple breathing out of what she receives, that has the singleness of life, rather than the selecting and energizing of art.

More native is it to her to be the living model of the artist than to set apart from herself any one form in objective reality; more native to inspire and receive the poem, than to create it. In so far as soul is in her completely developed, all soul is the same; but in so far as it is modified in her as Woman, it flows, it breathes, it sings, rather than deposits soil, or finishes work; and that which is especially feminine flushes, in blossom, the face of earth, and pervades, like air and water, all this seeming solid globe, daily renewing and purifying its life. Such may be the especially feminine element spoken of as Femality. But it is no more the order of nature that it should be incarnated pure in any form, than that the masculine energy should exist unmingled with it in any form.

Male and female represent the two sides of the great radical dualism. But, in fact, they are perpetually passing into one another. Fluid hardens to solid, solid rushes to fluid. There is no wholly masculine man, no purely feminine woman.

History jeers at the attempts of physiologists to bind great original laws by the forms which flow from them. They make a rule; they say from observation what can and cannot be. In vain! Nature provides exceptions to every rule. She sends women to battle, and sets Hercules[2] spinning; she enables women to bear immense burdens, cold, and frost; she enables the man, who feels maternal love, to nourish his infant like a mother. Of late she plays still gayer pranks. Not only she deprives organizations, but organs, of a necessary end. She enables people to read with the top of the head, and see with the pit of the stomach. Presently she will make a female Newton, and a male Siren.[3]

Man partakes of the feminine in the Apollo,[4] Woman of the masculine as Minerva.

What I mean by the Muse is that unimpeded clearness of the intuitive powers, which a perfectly truthful adherence to every admonition of the higher instincts would bring to a finely organized human being. It may appear as prophecy or as poesy. It enabled Cassandra to foresee the results of actions passing round her; the Seeress[5] to behold the true character of the person through the mask of his customary life. (Sometimes she saw a feminine form behind the man, sometimes the reverse.) It enabled the daughter of Linnaeus to see the soul of the flower exhaling from the flower.[6] It gave a man, but a

1. I.e., re-creation (after careful analysis).
2. The greatest hero of classical mythology; for a time he was forced to serve the queen of Lydia, who made him dress in women's clothes and work with her maids.
3. One of three female monsters whose beautiful singing lured sailors to a deadly collision with the rocks around their island. Sir Isaac Newton (1642–1727), English physicist and mathematician.
4. Classical god of the sun and of poetry.
5. Prophetess or clairvoyant. The prophecies of Cassandra, daughter of the king of Troy, were true

but never believed.
6. The daughter of Linnaeus states, that, while looking steadfastly at the red lily, she saw its spirit hovering above it, as a red flame. It is true, this, like many fair spirit-stories, may be explained away as an optical illusion, but its poetic beauty and meaning would, even then, make it valuable, as an illustration of the spiritual fact [Fuller's note]. Linnaeus (Carl von Linné, 1707–1778), Swedish botanist who created the modern system of botanical nomenclature.

poet-man, the power of which he thus speaks: "Often in my contemplation of nature, radiant intimations, and as it were sheaves of light, appear before me as to the facts of cosmogony, in which my mind has, perhaps, taken especial part." He wisely adds, "but it is necessary with earnestness to verify the knowledge we gain by these flashes of light." And none should forget this. Sight must be verified by light before it can deserve the honors of piety and genius. Yet sight comes first, and of this sight of the world of causes, this approximation to the region of primitive motions, women I hold to be especially capable. Even without equal freedom with the other sex, they have already shown themselves so; and should these faculties have free play, I believe they will open new, deeper and purer sources of joyous inspiration than have as yet refreshed the earth.

Let us be wise, and not impede the soul. Let her work as she will. Let us have one creative energy, one incessant revelation. Let it take what form it will, and let us not bind it by the past to man or woman, black or white. Jove sprang from Rhea, Pallas from Jove.[7] So let it be.

If it has been the tendency of these remarks to call Woman rather to the Minerva side,—if I, unlike the more generous writer, have spoken from society no less than the soul,—let it be pardoned! It is love that has caused this,— love for many incarcerated souls, that might be freed, could the idea of religious self-dependence be established in them, could the weakening habit of dependence on others be broken up.

Proclus[8] teaches that every life has, in its sphere, a totality or wholeness of the animating powers of the other spheres; having only, as its own characteristic, a predominance of some one power. Thus Jupiter comprises, within himself, the other twelve powers,[9] which stand thus: The first triad is *demiurgic* or *fabricative*, that is, Jupiter, Neptune, Vulcan; the second, *defensive*, Vesta, Minerva, Mars; the third, *vivific*,[1] Ceres, Juno, Diana; and the fourth, Mercury, Venus, Apollo, *elevating and harmonic*. In the sphere of Jupiter, energy is predominant—with Venus, beauty; but each comprehends and apprehends all the others.

When the same community of life and consciousness of mind begin among men, humanity will have, positively and finally, subjugated its brute elements and Titanic childhood;[2] criticism will have perished; arbitrary limits and ignorant censure be impossible; all will have entered upon the liberty of law,[3] and the harmony of common growth.

Then Apollo will sing to his lyre what Vulcan forges on the anvil, and the Muse weave anew the tapestries of Minerva.

It is, therefore, only in the present crisis that the preference is given to Minerva. The power of continence must establish the legitimacy of freedom, the power of self-poise the perfection of motion.

Every relation, every gradation of nature is incalculably precious, but only

7. Another name for Jupiter, the chief of the Olympian gods (identified with the Greek Zeus), whose mother was the Titan Rhea; Pallas Athena was born, fully armed, from his head.
8. Greek philosopher and mystic (412–485 C.E.).
9. I.e., the Olympian gods, here given their Roman names: Neptune, god of the sea; Vulcan, god of fire and metalworking; Vesta, goddess of the hearth; Mars, god of war; Ceres, goddess of agriculture; Juno, goddess of birth and marriage

(Jupiter's sister and consort); Diana, goddess of the moon and the hunt; Mercury, god of commerce (and messenger of the gods); and Venus, goddess of love.
1. Life-giving.
2. I.e., moved beyond its primitive beginnings. The Titans, primeval deities born from Heaven and Earth, were overthrown by Jupiter (Zeus) and his brothers.
3. Natural law or necessity.

to the soul which is poised upon itself, and to whom no loss, no change, can bring dull discord, for it is in harmony with the central soul.[4]

<div align="center">* * *</div>

Women must leave off asking [men] and being influenced by them, but retire within themselves, and explore the ground-work of life till they find their peculiar secret. Then, when they come forth again, renovated and baptized, they will know how to turn all dross to gold, and will be rich and free though they live in a hut, tranquil if in a crowd. Then their sweet singing shall not be from passionate impulse, but the lyrical overflow of a divine rapture, and a new music shall be evolved from this many-chorded world.

Grant her, then, for a while, the armor and the javelin. Let her put from her the press of other minds, and meditate in virgin loneliness. The same idea shall reappear in due time as Muse, or Ceres, the all-kindly, patient Earth-Spirit.

[THE FUTURE OF WOMEN]

And now I have designated in outline, if not in fulness, the stream which is ever flowing from the heights of my thought.

In the earlier tract[5] I was told I did not make my meaning sufficiently clear. In this I have consequently tried to illustrate it in various ways, and may have been guilty of much repetition. Yet, as I am anxious to leave no room for doubt, I shall venture to retrace, once more, the scope of my design in points, as was done in old-fashioned sermons.

Man is a being of two-fold relations, to nature beneath, and intelligences above him. The earth is his school, if not his birth-place; God his object; life and thought his means of interpreting nature, and aspiring to God.

Only a fraction of this purpose is accomplished in the life of any one man. Its entire accomplishment is to be hoped only from the sum of the lives of men, or Man considered as a whole.

As this whole has one soul and one body, any injury or obstruction to a part, or to the meanest member, affects the whole. Man can never be perfectly happy or virtuous, till all men are so.

To address[6] Man wisely, you must not forget that his life is partly animal, subject to the same laws with Nature.

But you cannot address him wisely unless you consider him still more as soul, and appreciate the conditions and destiny of soul.

The growth of Man is twofold, masculine and feminine.

So far as these two methods can be distinguished, they are so as

Energy and Harmony;

Power and Beauty;

Intellect and Love;

or by some such rude classification; for we have not language primitive and pure enough to express such ideas with precision.

These two sides are supposed to be expressed in Man and Woman, that

4. Another reference to the Emersonian doctrine of the over-soul.
5. Her first version of this work, "The Great Law-

suit," was criticized when it appeared in the *Dial* (1843).
6. Consider.

is, as the more and the less, for the faculties have not been given pure to either, but only in preponderance. There are also exceptions in great number, such as men of far more beauty than power, and the reverse. But, as a general rule, it seems to have been the intention to give a preponderance on the one side, that is called masculine, and on the other, one that is called feminine.

There cannot be a doubt that, if these two developments were in perfect harmony, they would correspond to and fulfill one another, like hemispheres, or the tenor and bass in music.

But there is no perfect harmony in human nature; and the two parts answer one another only now and then; or, if there be a persistent consonance, it can only be traced at long intervals, instead of discoursing an obvious melody.

What is the cause of this?

Man, in the order of time, was developed first; as energy comes before harmony; power before beauty.

Woman was therefore under his care as an elder. He might have been her guardian and teacher.

But, as human nature goes not straightforward, but by excessive action and then reaction in an undulated course, he misunderstood and abused his advantages, and became her temporal master instead of her spiritual sire.

On himself came the punishment. He educated Woman more as a servant than a daughter, and found himself a king without a queen.

The children of this unequal union showed unequal natures, and, more and more, men seemed sons of the handmaid, rather than princess.

At last, there were so many Ishmaelites that the rest grew frightened and indignant. They laid the blame on Hagar,[7] and drove her forth into the wilderness.

But there were none the fewer Ishmaelites for that.

At last men became a little wiser, and saw that the infant Moses was, in every case, saved by the pure instincts of Woman's breast.[8] For, as too much adversity is better for the moral nature than too much prosperity, Woman, in this respect, dwindled less than Man, though in other respects still a child in leading-strings.[9]

So Man did her more and more justice, and grew more and more kind.

But yet—his habits and his will corrupted by the past—he did not clearly see that Woman was half himself; that her interests were identical with his; and that, by the law of their common being, he could never reach his true proportions while she remained in any wise shorn[1] of hers.

And so it has gone on to our day; both ideas developing, but more slowly than they would under a clearer recognition of truth and justice, which would have permitted the sexes their due influence on one another, and mutual improvement from more dignified relations.

Wherever there was pure love, the natural influences were, for the time, restored.

7. I.e., the "handmaid" of Sarah, who temporarily drove her into the wilderness after she showed contempt for Sarah's barrenness. The son Hagar bore to Abraham, Sarah's husband, was Ishmael, who would become "a wild man" (Exodus 16.11); the Ishmaelites are his descendants. After Sarah bore Isaac, both Hagar and Ishmael were sent into the wilderness (21.9–21).

8. Moses was found floating in a basket on the river Nile by the pharaoh's daughter, who rescued him (Exodus 2.1–6).

9. Strings used to support a child who is learning to walk.

1. In any way deprived.

Wherever the poet or artist gave free course to his genius, he saw the truth, and expressed it in worthy forms, for these men especially share and need the feminine principle. The divine birds need to be brooded[2] into life and song by mothers.

Wherever religion (I mean the thirst for truth and good, not the love of sect and dogma) had its course, the original design was apprehended in its simplicity, and the dove presaged sweetly from Dodona's oak.[3]

I have aimed to show that no age was left entirely without a witness of the equality of the sexes in function, duty, and hope.

Also that, when there was unwillingness or ignorance, which prevented this being acted upon, women had not the less power for their want of light and noble freedom. But it was power which hurt alike them and those against whom they made use of the arms of the servile,—cunning, blandishment, and unreasonable emotion.

That now the time has come when a clearer vision and better action are possible—when Man and Woman may regard one another as brother and sister, the pillars of one porch, the priests of one worship.

I have believed and intimated that this hope would receive an ampler fruition, than ever before, in our own land.

And it will do so if this land carry out the principles from which sprang our national life.

I believe that, at present, women are the best helpers of one another.

Let them think; let them act; till they know what they need.

We only ask of men to remove arbitrary barriers. Some would like to do more. But I believe it needs that Woman show herself in her native dignity, to teach them how to aid her; their minds are so encumbered by tradition.

When Lord Edward Fitzgerald[4] travelled with the Indians, his manly heart obliged him at once to take the packs from the squaws and carry them. But we do not read that the red men followed his example, though they are ready enough to carry the pack of the white woman, because she seems to them a superior being.

Let Woman appear in the mild majesty of Ceres, and rudest churls[5] will be willing to learn from her.

You ask, what use will she make of liberty, when she has so long been sustained and restrained?

I answer; in the first place, this will not be suddenly given. I read yesterday a debate of this year on the subject of enlarging women's rights over property. It was a leaf from the class-book that is preparing for the needed instruction. The men learned visibly as they spoke. The champions of Woman saw the fallacy of arguments on the opposite side, and were startled by their own convictions. With their wives at home, and the readers of the paper, it was the same. And so the stream flows on; thought urging action, and action leading to the evolution of still better thought.

But, were this freedom to come suddenly, I have no fear of the consequences. Individuals might commit excesses, but there is not only in the sex

2. Hatched.
3. An ancient Greek oracle; the rustling oak leaves revealed Zeus's message. The tree's sanctity had been made known by a dove that spoke.
4. Irish revolutionary (1763–1798); as a major in a British regiment based in New Brunswick, he undertook an expedition through the Canadian wilderness and subsequently down the Mississippi.
5. Uneducated men.

a reverence for decorums and limits inherited and enhanced from generation to generation, which many years of other life could not efface, but a native love, in Woman as Woman, of proportion, of "the simple art of not too much,"—a Greek moderation,[6] which would create immediately a restraining party, the natural legislators and instructors of the rest, and would gradually establish such rules are are needed to guard, without impeding, life.

The Graces[7] would lead the choral dance, and teach the rest to regulate their steps to the measure of beauty.

But if you ask me what offices they may fill, I reply—any. I do not care what case you put; let them be sea-captains, if you will. I do not doubt there are women well fitted for such an office, and, if so, I should be as glad to see them in it, as to welcome the maid of Saragossa, or the maid of Missolonghi, or the Suliote heroine, or Emily Plater.[8]

I think women need, especially at this juncture, a much greater range of occupation than they have, to rouse their latent powers. A party of travelers lately visited a lonely hut on a mountain. There they found an old woman, who told them she and her husband had lived there forty years. "Why," they said, "did you choose so barren a spot?" She "did not know; *it was the man's notion.*"

And, during forty years, she had been content to act, without knowing why, upon "the man's notion." I would not have it so.

In families that I know, some little girls like to saw wood, others to use carpenters' tools. Where these tastes are indulged, cheerfulness and good-humor are promoted. Where they are forbidden, because "such things are not proper for girls," they grow sullen and mischievous.

Fourier[9] had observed these wants of women, as no one can fail to do who watches the desires of little girls, or knows the ennui that haunts grown women, except where they make to themselves a serene little world by art of some kind. He, therefore, in proposing a great variety of employments, in manufactures or the care of plants and animals, allows for one third of women as likely to have a taste for masculine pursuits, one third of men for feminine.

Who does not observe the immediate glow and serenity that is diffused over the life of women, before restless or fretful, by engaging in gardening, building, or the lowest department of art? Here is something that is not routine, something that draws forth life towards the infinite.

I have no doubt, however, that a large proportion of women would give themselves to the same employments as now, because there are circumstances that must lead them. Mothers will delight to make the nest soft and warm. Nature would take care of that; no need to clip the wings of any bird that wants to soar and sing, or finds in itself the strength of pinion[1] for a migratory flight unusual to its kind. The difference would be that *all* need not be constrained to employments for which *some* are unfit.

6. A reference to the Greek temple of Apollo at Delphi, on whose wall was inscribed "Nothing too much" (often translated "Everything in moderation").
7. Three Greek goddesses of beauty and charm.
8. A Polish countess who commanded a company in the Polish army fighting against Russia (1831). The Maid of Saragossa was Maria Austin, who fought against the French in Spain (1808). The

Maid of Missolonghi, an unidentified Greek, fought during the Turkish sieges of 1822 or 1826. The Suliote heroine was probably Moscha, who led a band of women during the siege of Souli in Albania (1803).
9. François Fourier (1772–1837), French social theorist.
1. Wing.

I have urged upon the sex self-subsistence in its two forms of self-reliance and self-impulse, because I believe them to be the needed means of the present juncture.

I have urged on Woman independence of Man, not that I do not think the sexes mutually needed by one another, but because in Woman this fact has led to an excessive devotion, which has cooled love, degraded marriage, and prevented either sex from being what it should be to itself or the other.

I wish Woman to live, *first* for God's sake. Then she will not make an imperfect man her god, and thus sink to idolatry. Then she will not take what is not fit for her from a sense of weakness and poverty. Then, if she finds what she needs in Man embodied, she will know how to love, and be worthy of being loved.

By being more a soul, she will not be less Woman, for nature is perfected through spirit.

Now there is no woman, only an overgrown child.

That her hand may be given with dignity, she must be able to stand alone. I wish to see men and women capable of such relations as are depicted by Landor[2] in his Pericles and Aspasia, where grace is the natural garb of strength, and the affections are calm, because deep. The softness is that of a firm tissue, as when

> The gods approve
> The depth, but not the tumult of the soul,
> A fervent, not ungovernable love.[3]

A profound thinker has said, "No married woman can represent the female world, for she belongs to her husband. The idea of Woman must be represented by a virgin."

But that is the very fault of marriage, and of the present relation between the sexes, that the woman *does* belong to the man, instead of forming a whole with him. Were it otherwise, there would be no such limitation to the thought.

Woman, self-centered, would never be absorbed by any relation; it would be only an experience to her as to man. It is a vulgar error that love, a love, to Woman is her whole existence;[4] she also is born for Truth and Love in their universal energy. Would she but assume her inheritance, Mary would not be the only virgin mother. Not Manzoni[5] alone would celebrate in his wife the virgin mind with the maternal wisdom and conjugal affections. The soul is ever young, ever virgin.

And will not she soon appear?—the woman who shall vindicate their birthright for all women; who shall teach them what to claim, and how to use what they obtain? Shall not her name be for her era Victoria, for her country and life Virginia?[6] Yet predictions are rash; she herself must teach us to give her the fitting name.

<div align="right">1845</div>

2. Walter Savage Lander (1775–1864), English poet. *Pericles and Aspasia* (1836) is a work of prose consisting of imaginary letters between the Athenian statesman Pericles (ca. 495–429 B.C.E.) and his mistress, the courtesan Aspasia, who was renowned for her learning.
3. From Wordsworth's "Laodamia" (1815).
4. See, e.g., Lord Byron's *Don Juan* (1819):"Man's

love of man's life a thing apart, / 'Tis a woman's whole existence" (Canto 1, stanza 194).
5. Alessandro Manzoni (1785–1873), Italian novelist and poet.
6. Victoria (1819–1901; r. 1837–1901) was then queen of England; Virginia is a reference both to America, where Fuller sees woman's future lying, and to the virginity of soul she celebrates here.

ELIZABETH CLEGHORN GASKELL
1810–1865

Although she was born in London, the woman who gained fame as "Mrs. Gaskell" was destined to become one of the nineteenth century's foremost recorders of life in England's provinces during the height of the Industrial Revolution. Her father, William Stevenson, a sometime Unitarian minister, had come to the capital to take up a position as keeper of the records to the treasury, but soon after his wife's death, when Elizabeth—the last of eight children—was still very young, he sent this youngest daughter to live with an aunt at Knutsford, the small rural town that inspired her later depictions of isolated, pastoral "Cranford." There, at the age of twenty-one, she married the Reverend William Gaskell, also a Unitarian minister, with whom she was to live happily for the rest of her life.

After their marriage, the Gaskells settled in the industrial city of Manchester, where the Reverend Gaskell had his church, and within a decade or so the couple were the parents of four children, whose upbringing constituted a full-time job for Elizabeth Gaskell until 1845. In that year, her son William died, and although she had another child within a year, she may have begun writing what was to be her first novel, *Mary Barton* (1848), to "divert her mind," as one biographer puts it, from the pain of her loss. Even before she started to take herself seriously as a potential novelist, however, Gaskell had clearly developed the observational skills that give her works such force. Manchester in the 1840s was a city in turmoil, with furiously expanding factories dominating both the town and the lives of its enormous, increasingly impoverished population. In 1843, the historian-philosopher Thomas Carlyle published his *Past and Present,* a work that addressed itself in part to the crises afflicting such cities; in 1845, the German thinker Friedrich Engels, who was later to coauthor with Karl Marx *The Communist Manifesto* (1848), produced *The Condition of the Working Class in England,* which offered an extended analysis of the plight of Manchester's industrial laborers. Like these men—or perhaps even—to a greater degree, Gaskell had countless opportunities to observe the misery that lay all around her. She had collaborated with her husband on the beginning of a series titled *Sketches among the Poor* in 1837; in addition, as the wife of a minister, she was frequently obliged to visit and console sufferers; as a nascent novelist, too, she had a keen sense of the drama that marked the lives of the working class.

Not surprisingly, then, *Mary Barton* constituted a memorable portrait of a series of those lives at the same time that it offered a detailed examination of the tensions between industrial leaders and industrial laborers that shadowed and sometimes shattered the public world of Manchester. In later novels, moreover—particularly *Ruth* (1853), the story of an unwed working-class mother, and *North and South* (1855), a tale that explicitly compared the industrialized north of England to the more agrarian south—Gaskell continued to undertake fictional studies of what nineteenth-century writers called the "condition of England" question.

Set against Gaskell's other works, *Cranford* (1853) may at first appear to be little more than a nostalgic idyll of village life in the early Victorian period. Yet this writer's loving descriptions of the "elegant economy" practiced by her heroines of gentle birth but slender means are as incisive in their way as her more obviously analytical evocations of class conflict in Manchester. Begun as a series of sketches commissioned by Charles Dickens for *Household Words,* a weekly journal he founded in 1850, *Cranford* quickly evolved from a quietly comic memoir to a more searching but still humorous consideration of the relationship between old and new ways of life in a society that was rapidly changing. Disturbed by critics who argued that in *Mary Barton* she had been guilty of class prejudice, preferring the workers to their employers, Gaskell clearly set out in *Cranford* to show the trials of a vanishing genteel class even while she both celebrated and satirized foibles.

As she honed the novelistic skills she displayed in books as diverse as *Mary Barton* and *Cranford*, Gaskell quickly became one of England's most successful writers and the friend of such notables as Charles Dickens, Harriet Beecher Stowe, John Ruskin, and Florence Nightingale. But her most important literary relationship was with Charlotte Brontë, whom she met in 1850, when the author of *Jane Eyre* was at the height of her fame. Although the two women saw each other only a few times, they corresponded regularly, and Gaskell was increasingly moved by Brontë's sufferings and her fortitude. "Such a life as Miss B's I never heard of before [it was] described . . . to me," she wrote in awe to one of her friends, shortly after learning about the hardships of the novelist's history from a mutual acquaintance. After Brontë's death in 1855, Gaskell explored the conditions of that existence more fully when the Reverend Patrick Brontë asked her to write a life of his daughter, and the work she produced, despite inaccuracies and omissions designed to spare the feelings of the family, is a classic of English biography.

Gaskell's special ability to enter with sensitivity and sympathy into circumstances so different from her own constitutes yet another indication of the range of her literary talents. Some critics have considered those talents as distinctively "womanly" because of their delineation of "women's oddities," but Gaskell's skills might just as easily be defined as distinctively humane in their combination of scrupulous observation and compassionate imagination. Given her novelistic energy, she must certainly have been planning more works when she died quite suddenly at The Lawn, a country house she had just purchased as a retirement gift for her husband. She was buried in the town she had memorialized as "Cranford."

A gothic tale probably influenced by the Brontë writings Gaskell so much admired, "The Old Nurse's Story" was first published in 1852 by Charles Dickens in his journal *Household Words*; Gaskell later included it in her collection titled *Lizzie Leigh, and Other Tales* (1855).

The Old Nurse's Story

You know, my dears, that your mother was an orphan, and an only child; and I dare say you have heard that your grandfather was a clergyman up in Westmoreland, where I come from. I was just a girl in the village school, when, one day, your grandmother came in to ask the mistress if there was any scholar there who would do for a nurse-maid; and mighty proud I was, I can tell ye, when the mistress called me up, and spoke to my being a good girl at my needle, and a steady honest girl, and one whose parents were very respectable, though they might be poor. I thought I should like nothing better than to serve the pretty young lady, who was blushing as deep as I was, as she spoke of the coming baby, and what I should have to do with it. However, I see you don't care so much for this part of my story, as for what you think is to come, so I'll tell you at once I was engaged, and settled at the parsonage before Miss Rosamond (that was the baby, who is now your mother) was born. To be sure, I had little enough to do with her when she came, for she was never out of her mother's arms, and slept by her all night long; and proud enough was I sometimes when missis trusted her to me. There never was such a baby before or since, though you've all of you been fine enough in your turns; but for sweet winning ways, you've none of you come up to your mother. She took after her mother, who was a real lady born; a Miss Furnivall, a granddaughter of Lord Furnivall's in Northumberland. I believe she had neither brother nor sister, and had been brought up in my lord's family till she had married your grandfather, who was just a curate, son to a shop-

keeper in Carlisle—but a clever fine gentleman as ever was—and one who was a right-down hard worker in his parish, which was very wide, and scattered all abroad over the Westmoreland Fells. When your mother, little Miss Rosamond, was about four or five years old, both her parents died in a fortnight—one after the other. Ah! that was a sad time. My pretty young mistress and me was looking for another baby, when my master came home from one of his long rides, wet and tired, and took the fever he died of; and then she never held up her head again, but just lived to see her dead baby, and have it laid on her breast before she sighed away her life. My mistress had asked me, on her death-bed, never to leave Miss Rosamond; but if she had never spoken a word, I would have gone with the little child to the end of the world.

The next thing, and before we had well stilled our sobs, the executors and guardians came to settle the affairs. They were my poor young mistress's own cousin, Lord Furnivall, and Mr. Esthwaite, my master's brother, a shopkeeper in Manchester; not so well to do then, as he was afterwards, and with a large family rising about him. Well! I don't know if it were their settling, or because of a letter my mistress wrote on her death-bed to her cousin, my lord; but somehow it was settled that Miss Rosamond and me were to go to Furnivall Manor House, in Northumberland, and my lord spoke as if it had been her mother's wish that she should live with his family, and as if he had no objections, for that one or two more or less could make no difference in so grand a household. So, though that was not the way in which I should have wished the coming of my bright and pretty pet to have been looked at— who was like a sunbeam in any family, be it never so grand—I was well pleased that all the folks in the Dale should stare and admire, when they heard I was going to be young lady's maid at my Lord Furnivall's at Furnivall Manor.

But I made a mistake in thinking we were to go and live where my lord did. It turned out that the family had left Furnivall Manor House fifty years or more. I could not hear that my poor young mistress had ever been there, though she had been brought up in the family; and I was sorry for that, for I should have liked Miss Rosamond's youth to have passed where her mother's had been.

My lord's gentleman, from whom I asked as many questions as I durst, said that the Manor House was at the foot of the Cumberland Fells, and a very grand place; that an old Miss Furnivall, a great-aunt of my lord's, lived there, with only a few servants; but that it was a very healthy place, and my lord had thought that it would suit Miss Rosamond very well for a few years, and that her being there might perhaps amuse his old aunt.

I was bidden by my lord to have Miss Rosamond's things ready by a certain day. He was a stern, proud man, as they say all the Lord Furnivalls were; and he never spoke a word more than was necessary. Folk did say he had loved my young mistress; but that, because she knew that his father would object, she would never listen to him, and married Mr. Esthwaite; but I don't know. He never married at any rate. But he never took much notice of Miss Rosamond; which I thought he might have done if he had cared for her dead mother. He sent his gentleman with us to the Manor House, telling him to join him at Newcastle that same evening; so there was no great length of time for him to make us known to all the strangers before he, too, shook us off; and we were left, two lonely young things (I was not eighteen), in the

great old Manor House. It seems like yesterday that we drove there. We had left our own dear parsonage very early, and we had both cried as if our hearts would break, though we were travelling in my lord's carriage, which I had thought so much of once. And now it was long past noon on a September day, and we stopped to change horses for the last time at a little smoky town, all full of colliers and miners. Miss Rosamond had fallen asleep, but Mr. Henry told me to waken her, that she might see the park and the Manor House as we drove up. I thought it rather a pity; but I did what he bade me, for fear he should complain of me to my lord. We had left all signs of a town or even a village, and were then inside the gates of a large wild park—not like the parks here in the south, but with rocks, and the noise of running water, and gnarled thorn-trees, and old oaks, all white and peeled with age.

The road went up about two miles, and then we saw a great and stately house, with many trees close around it, so close that in some places their branches dragged against the walls when the wind blew; and some hung broken down; for no one seemed to take much charge of the place;—to lop the wood, or to keep the moss-covered carriage-way in order. Only in front of the house all was clear. The great oval drive was without a weed; and neither tree nor creeper was allowed to grow over the long, many-windowed front; at both sides of which a wing projected, which were each the ends of other side fronts; for the house, although it was so desolate, was even grander than I expected. Behind it rose the Fells, which seemed unenclosed and bare enough; and on the left hand of the house as you stood facing it, was a little old-fashioned flower-garden, as I found out afterward. A door opened out upon it from the west front; it had been scooped out of the thick dark wood for some old Lady Furnivall; but the branches of the great forest trees had grown and overshadowed it again, and there were very few flowers that would live there at that time.

When we drove up to the great front entrance, and went into the hall I thought we should be lost—it was so large, and vast, and grand. There was a chandelier all of bronze, hung down from the middle of the ceiling; and I had never seen one before, and looked at it all in amaze. Then, at one end of the hall, was a great fire-place, as large as the sides of the houses in my country, with massy andirons and dogs[1] to hold the wood; and by it were heavy old-fashioned sofas. At the opposite end of the hall, to the left as you went in—on the western side—was an organ built into the wall, and so large that it filled up the best part of that end. Beyond it, on the same side, was a door; and opposite, on each side of the fire-place, were also doors leading to the east front; but those I never went through as long as I stayed in the house, so I can't tell you what lay beyond.

The afternoon was closing in, and the hall, which had no fire lighted in it, looked dark and gloomy; but we did not stay there a moment. The old servant who had opened the door for us bowed to Mr. Henry, and took us in through the door at the further side of the great organ, and led us through several smaller halls and passages into the west drawing-room, where he said that Miss Furnivall was sitting. Poor little Miss Rosamond held very tight to me, as if she were scared and lost in that great place, and, as for myself, I was not much better. The west drawing-room was very cheerful-looking, with a

1. Metal log supports (i.e., andirons). "Country": native region or district.

warm fire in it, and plenty of good comfortable furniture about. Miss Furnivall was an old lady not far from eighty, I should think, but I do not know. She was thin and tall, and had a face as full of fine wrinkles as if they had been drawn all over it with a needle's point. Her eyes were very watchful, to make up, I suppose, for her being so deaf as to be obliged to use a trumpet.[2] Sitting with her, working at the same great piece of tapestry, was Mrs. Stark, her maid and companion, and almost as old as she was. She had lived with Miss Furnivall ever since they both were young, and now she seemed more like a friend than a servant; she looked so cold and grey, and stony, as if she had never loved or cared for any one; and I don't suppose she did care for any one, except her mistress; and, owing to the great deafness of the latter, Mrs. Stark treated her very much as if she were a child. Mr. Henry gave some message from my lord, and then he bowed good-bye to us all,—taking no notice of my sweet little Miss Rosamond's out-stretched hand—and left us standing there, being looked at by the two old ladies through their spectacles.

I was right glad when they rung for the old footman who had shown us in at first, and told him to take us to our rooms. So we went out of that great drawing-room, and into another sitting-room, and out of that, and then up a great flight of stairs, and along a broad gallery—which was something like a library, having books all down one side, and windows and writing-tables all down the other—till we came to our rooms, which I was not sorry to hear were just over the kitchens; for I began to think I should be lost in that wilderness of a house. There was an old nursery, that had been used for all the little lords and ladies long ago, with a pleasant fire burning in the grate, and the kettle boiling on the hob, and tea things spread out on the table; and out of that room was the night-nursery, with a little crib for Miss Rosamond close to my bed. And old James called up Dorothy, his wife, to bid us welcome; and both he and she were so hospitable and kind, that by-and-by Miss Rosamond and me felt quite at home; and by the time tea was over, she was sitting on Dorothy's knee, and chattering away as fast as her little tongue could go. I soon found out that Dorothy was from Westmoreland, and that bound her and me together, as it were; and I would never wish to meet with kinder people than were old James and his wife. James had lived pretty nearly all his life in my lord's family, and thought there was no one so grand as they. He even looked down a little on his wife; because, till he had married her, she had never lived in any but a farmer's household. But he was very fond of her, as well he might be. They had one servant under them, to do all the rough work. Agnes they called her; and she and me, and James and Dorothy, with Miss Furnivall and Mrs. Stark, made up the family; always remembering my sweet little Miss Rosamond! I used to wonder what they had done before she came, they thought so much of her now. Kitchen and drawing-room, it was all the same. The hard, sad Miss Furnivall, and the cold Mrs. Stark, looked pleased when she came fluttering in like a bird, playing and pranking hither and thither, with a continual murmur, and pretty prattle of gladness. I am sure, they were sorry many a time when she flitted away into the kitchen, though they were too proud to ask her to stay with them, and were a little surprised at her taste; though, to be sure, as Mrs.

2. A funnel-shaped device that amplifies sound when the narrow end is placed in the ear.

Stark said, it was not to be wondered at, remembering what stock her father had come of. The great, old rambling house, was a famous place for little Miss Rosamond. She made expeditions all over it, with me at her heels; all, except the east wing, which was never opened, and whither we never thought of going. But in the western and northern part was many a pleasant room; full of things that were curiosities to us, though they might not have been to people who had seen more. The windows were darkened by the sweeping boughs of the trees, and the ivy which had overgrown them: but, in the green gloom, we could manage to see old China jars and carved ivory boxes, and great heavy books, and, above all, the old pictures!

Once, I remember, my darling would have Dorothy go with us to tell us who they all were; for they were all portraits of some of my lord's family, though Dorothy could not tell us the names of every one. We had gone through most of the rooms, when we came to the old state drawing-room over the hall, and there was a picture of Miss Furnivall; or, as she was called in those days, Miss Grace, for she was the younger sister. Such a beauty she must have been! but with such a set, proud look, and such scorn looking out of her handsome eyes, with her eyebrows just a little raised, as if she wondered how any one could have the impertinence to look at her; and her lip curled at us, as we stood there gazing. She had a dress on, the like of which I had never seen before, but it was all the fashion when she was young; a hat of some soft white stuff like beaver, pulled a little over her brows, and a beautiful plume of feathers sweeping round it on one side; and her gown of blue satin was open in front to a quilted white stomacher.[3]

"Well, to be sure!" said I, when I had gazed my fill. "Flesh is grass,[4] they do say; but who would have thought that Miss Furnivall had been such an out-and-out beauty, to see her now?"

"Yes," said Dorothy. "Folks change sadly. But if what my master's father used to say was true, Miss Furnivall, the elder sister, was handsomer than Miss Grace. Her picture is here somewhere; but, if I show it you, you must never let on, even to James, that you have seen it. Can the little lady hold her tongue, think you?" asked she.

I was not so sure, for she was such a little sweet, bold, open-spoken child, so I set her to hide herself; and then I helped Dorothy to turn a great picture, that leaned with its face towards the wall, and was not hung up as the others were. To be sure, it beat Miss Grace for beauty; and, I think, for scornful pride, too, though in that matter it might be hard to choose. I could have looked at it an hour, but Dorothy seemed half frightened of having shown it to me, and hurried it back again, and bade me run and find Miss Rosamond, for that there were some ugly places about the house, where she should like ill for the child to go. I was a brave, high-spirited girl, and thought little of what the old woman said, for I liked hide-and-seek as well as any child in the parish; so off I ran to find my little one.

As winter drew on, and the days grew shorter, I was sometimes almost certain that I heard a noise as if some one was playing on the great organ in the hall. I did not hear it every evening; but, certainly, I did very often; usually when I was sitting with Miss Rosamond, after I had put her to bed, and

3. Embroidered center front of a bodice. "Beaver": a heavy cloth made of wool and fur.

4. See Isaiah 40.6: "All flesh is grass."

keeping quite still and silent in the bedroom. Then I used to hear it booming and swelling away in the distance. The first night, when I went down to my supper, I asked Dorothy who had been playing music, and James said very shortly that I was a gowk to take the wind soughing[5] among the trees for music; but I saw Dorothy look at him very fearfully, and Bessy, the kitchen-maid, said something beneath her breath, and went quite white. I saw they did not like my question, so I held my peace till I was with Dorothy alone, when I knew I could get a good deal out of her. So, the next day, I watched my time, and I coaxed and asked her who it was that played the organ; for I knew that it was the organ and not the wind well enough, for all I had kept silence before James. But Dorothy had had her lesson, I'll warrant, and never a word could I get from her. So then I tried Bessy, though I had always held my head rather above her, as I was evened[6] to James and Dorothy, and she was little better than their servant. So she said I must never, never tell; and, if I ever told, I was never to say *she* had told me; but it was a very strange noise, and she had heard it many a time, but most of all on winter nights, and before storms; and folks did say, it was the old lord playing on the great organ in the hall, just as he used to do when he was alive; but who the old lord was, or why he played, and why he played on stormy winter evenings in particular, she either could not or would not tell me. Well! I told you I had a brave heart; and I thought it was rather pleasant to have that grand music rolling about the house, let who would be the player; for now it rose above the great gusts of wind, and wailed and triumphed just like a living creature, and then it fell to a softness most complete; only it was always music and tunes, so it was nonsense to call it the wind. I thought, at first, it might be Miss Furnivall who played, unknown to Bessy; but, one day when I was in the hall by myself, I opened the organ and peeped all about it, and around it, as I had done to the organ in Crosthwaite Church once before, and I saw it was all broken and destroyed inside, though it looked so brave[7] and fine; and then, though it was noon-day, my flesh began to creep a little, and I shut it up, and ran away pretty quickly to my own bright nursery; and I did not like hearing the music for some time after that, any more than James and Dorothy did. All this time Miss Rosamond was making herself more and more beloved. The old ladies liked her to dine with them at their early dinner; James stood behind Miss Furnivall's chair, and I behind Miss Rosamond's, all in state; and, after dinner, she would play about in a corner of the great drawing-room, as still as any mouse, while Miss Furnivall slept, and I had my dinner in the kitchen. But she was glad enough to come to me in the nursery afterwards; for, as she said, Miss Furnivall was so sad, and Mrs. Stark so dull; but she and I were merry enough; and, by-and-by, I got not to care for that weird rolling music, which did one no harm, if we did not know where it came from.

That winter was very cold. In the middle of October the frosts began, and lasted many, many weeks. I remember, one day at dinner, Miss Furnivall lifted up her sad, heavy eyes, and said to Mrs. Stark, "I am afraid we shall have a terrible winter," in a strange kind of meaning way. But Mrs. Stark pretended not to hear, and talked very loud of something else. My little lady and I did not care for[8] the frost;—not we! As long as it was dry we climbed

5. Moaning. "Gowk": a fool.
6. Treated as an equal.
7. Splendid, handsome.
8. Care about.

up the steep brows, behind the house, and went up on the Fells, which were bleak and bare enough, and there we ran races in the fresh, sharp air; and once we came down by a new path that took us past the two old gnarled holly-trees, which grew about half-way down by the east side of the house. But the days grew shorter and shorter; and the old lord, if it was he, played away more and more stormily and sadly on the great organ. Once Sunday afternoon,—it must have been towards the end of November—I asked Dorothy to take charge of little Missey when she came out of the drawing-room, after Miss Furnivall had had her nap; for it was too cold to take her with me to church, and yet I wanted to go. And Dorothy was glad enough to promise, and was so fond of the child that all seemed well; and Bessy and I set off very briskly, though the sky hung heavy and black over the white earth, as if the night had never fully gone away; and the air, though still, was very biting and keen.

"We shall have a fall of snow," said Bessy to me. And sure enough, even while we were in church, it came down thick, in great large flakes, so thick it almost darkened the windows. It had stopped snowing before we came out, but it lay soft, thick and deep beneath our feet, as we tramped home. Before we got to the hall the moon rose, and I think it was lighter then,—what with the moon, and what with the white dazzling snow—than it had been when we went to church, between two and three o'clock. I have not told you that Miss Furnivall and Mrs. Stark never went to church: they used to read the prayers together, in their quiet gloomy way; they seemed to feel the Sunday very long without their tapestry-work to be busy at. So when I went to Dorothy in the kitchen, to fetch Miss Rosamond and take her up-stairs with me, I did not much wonder when the old woman told me that the ladies had kept the child with them, and that she had never come to the kitchen, as I had bidden her, when she was tired of behaving pretty in the drawing-room. So I took off my things and went to find her, and bring her to her supper in the nursery. But when I went into the best drawing-room, there sat the two old ladies, very still and quiet, dropping out a word now and then, but looking as if nothing so bright and merry as Miss Rosamond had ever been near them. Still I thought she might be hiding from me; it was one of her pretty ways; and that she had persuaded them to look as if they knew nothing about her; so I went softly peeping under this sofa, and behind that chair, making believe I was sadly frightened at not finding her.

"What's the matter, Hester?" said Mrs. Stark sharply. I don't know if Miss Furnivall had seen me, for, as I told you, she was very deaf, and she sat quite still, idly staring into the fire, with her hopeless face. "I'm only looking for my little Rosy-Posy," replied I, still thinking that the child was there, and near me, though I could not see her.

"Miss Rosamond is not here," said Mrs. Stark. "She went away more than an hour ago to find Dorothy." And she too turned and went on looking into the fire.

My heart sank at this, and I began to wish I had never left my darling. I went back to Dorothy and told her. James was gone out for the day, but she and me and Bessy took lights, and went up into the nursery first and then we roamed over the great large house, calling and entreating Miss Rosamond to come out of her hiding place, and not frighten us to death in that way. But there was no answer; no sound.

"Oh!" said I at last, "Can she have got into the east wing and hidden there?"

But Dorothy said it was not possible, for that she herself had never been in there; that the doors were always locked, and my lord's steward had the keys, she believed; at any rate, neither she nor James had ever seen them: so, I said I would go back and see it, after all, she was not hidden in the drawing-room, unknown to the old ladies; and if I found her there, I said, I would whip her well for the fright she had given me; but I never meant to do it. Well, I went back to the west drawing-room, and I told Mrs. Stark we could not find her anywhere, and asked for leave to look all about the furniture there, for I thought now, that she might have fallen asleep in some warm hidden corner; but no! we looked, Miss Furnivall got up and looked, trembling all over, and she was no where there; then we set off again, every one in the house, and looked in all the places we had searched before, but we could not find her. Miss Furnivall shivered and shook so much, that Mrs. Stark took her back into the warm drawing-room; but not before they had made me promise to bring her to them when she was found. Well-a-day! I began to think she never would be found, when I bethought me to look out into the great front court, all covered with snow. I was up-stairs when I looked out; but, it was such clear moonlight, I could see quite plain two little footprints, which might be traced from the hall door, and round the corner of the east wing. I don't know how I got down, but I tugged open the great, stiff hall door; and, throwing the skirt of my gown over my head for a cloak, I ran out. I turned the east corner, and there a black shadow fell on the snow; but when I came again into the moonlight, there were the little footmarks going up—up to the Fells. It was bitter cold; so cold that the air almost took the skin off my face as I ran, but I ran on, crying to think how my poor little darling must be perished[9] and frightened. I was within sight of the holly-trees, when I saw a shepherd coming down the hill, bearing something in his arms wrapped in his maud.[1] He shouted to me, and asked me if I had lost a bairn;[2] and, when I could not speak for crying, he bore towards me, and I saw my wee bairnie lying still, and white, and stiff, in his arms, as if she had been dead. He told me he had been up the Fells to gather in his sheep, before the deep cold of night came on, and that under the holly-trees (black marks on the hill-side, where no other bush was for miles around) he had found my little lady—my lamb—my queen—my darling—stiff and cold, in the terrible sleep which is frost-begotten. Oh! the joy, and the tears of having her in my arms once again! for I would not let him carry her; but took her, maud and all, into my own arms, and held her near my own warm neck and heart, and felt the life stealing slowly back again into her little gentle limbs. But she was still insensible when we reached the hall, and I had no breath for speech. We went in by the kitchen door.

"Bring the warming-pan," said I; and I carried her up-stairs and began undressing her by the nursery fire, which Bessy had kept up. I called my little lammie all the sweet and playful names I could think of,—even while my eyes were blinded by my tears; and at last, oh! at length she opened her large blue eyes. Then I put her into her warm bed, and sent Dorothy down to tell Miss Furnivall that all was well; and I made up my mind to sit by my darling's bedside the live-long night. She fell away into a soft sleep as soon

9. Near death from the cold.
1. A long piece of woolen cloth, used as an outer

wrap in southern Scotland.
2. Child.

as her pretty head had touched the pillow, and I watched by her till morning light; when she wakened up bright and clear—or so I thought at first—and, my dears, so I think now.

She said, that she had fancied that she should like to go to Dorothy, for that both the old ladies were asleep, and it was very dull in the drawing-room; and that, as she was going through the west lobby, she saw the snow through the high window falling—falling—soft and steady; but she wanted to see it lying pretty and white on the ground; so she made her way into the great hall; and then, going to the window, she saw it bright and soft upon the drive; but while she stood there, she saw a little girl, not so old as she was, "but so pretty," said my darling, "and this little girl beckoned to me to come out; and oh, she was so pretty and so sweet, I could not choose but go." And then this other little girl had taken her by the hand, and side by side the two had gone round the east corner.

"Now you are a naughty little girl, and telling stories," said I. "What would your good mamma, that is in heaven, and never told a story in her life, say to her little Rosamond, if she heard her—and I dare say she does—telling stories!"

"Indeed, Hester," sobbed out my child; "I'm telling you true. Indeed I am."

"Don't tell me!" said I, very stern. "I tracked you by your foot-marks through the snow; there were only yours to be seen: and if you had had a little girl to go hand-in-hand with you up the hill, don't you think the foot-prints would have gone along with yours?"

"I can't help it, dear, dear Hester," said she, crying, "if they did not; I never looked at her feet, but she held my hand fast and tight in her little one, and it was very, very cold. She took me up the Fell-path, up to the holly trees; and there I saw a lady weeping and crying; but when she saw me, she hushed her weeping, and smiled very proud and grand, and took me on her knees, and began to lull me to sleep; and that's all, Hester—but that is true; and my dear mamma knows it is," said she, crying. So I thought the child was in a fever, and pretended to believe her, as she went over her story—over and over again, and always the same. At last Dorothy knocked at the door with Miss Rosamond's breakfast; and she told me the old ladies were down in the eating-parlour, and that they wanted to speak to me. They had both been into the night-nursery the evening before, but it was after Miss Rosamond was asleep; so they had only looked at her—not asked me any questions.

"I shall catch it," thought I to myself, as I went along the north gallery. "And yet," I thought, taking courage, "it was in their charge I left her; and it's they that's to blame for letting her steal away unknown and unwatched." So I went in boldly, and told my story. I told it all to Miss Furnivall, shouting it close to her ear; but when I came to the mention of the other little girl out in the snow, coaxing and tempting her out, and willing her up to the grand and beautiful lady by the Holly-tree, she threw her arms up—her old and withered arms—and cried aloud, "Oh! Heaven, forgive! Have mercy!"

Mrs. Stark took hold of her; roughly enough, I thought; but she was past Mrs. Stark's management, and spoke to me, in a kind of wild warning and authority.

"Hester! keep her from that child! It will lure her to her death! That evil child! Tell her it is a wicked, naughty child." Then, Mrs. Stark hurried me out of the room; where, indeed, I was glad enough to go; but Miss Furnivall

kept shrieking out, "Oh! have mercy! Wilt Thou never forgive! It is many a long year ago———"

I was very uneasy in my mind after that. I durst never leave Miss Rosamond, night or day, for fear lest she might slip off again, after some fancy or other; and all the more, because I thought I could make out that Miss Furnivall was crazy, from their odd ways about her; and I was afraid lest something of the same kind (which might be in the family, you know) hung over my darling. And the great frost never ceased all this time; and, whenever it was a more stormy night than usual, between the gusts, and through the wind, we heard the old lord playing on the great organ. But, old lord, or not, wherever Miss Rosamond went, there I followed; for my love for her, pretty helpless orphan, was stronger than my fear for the grand and terrible sound. Besides, it rested with me to keep her cheerful and merry, as beseemed her age. So we played together, and wandered together, here and there, and everywhere; for I never dared to lose sight of her again in that large and rambling house. And so it happened, that one afternoon, not long before Christmas day, we were playing together on the billiard-table in the great hall (not that we knew the right way of playing, but she liked to roll the smooth ivory balls with her pretty hands, and I liked to do whatever she did); and, by-and-bye, without our noticing it, it grew dusk indoors, though it was still light in the open air, and I was thinking of taking her back into the nursery, when, all of a sudden, she cried out:

"Look, Hester! look! there is my poor little girl out in the snow!"

I turned towards the long narrow windows, and there, sure enough, I saw a little girl, less than my Miss Rosamond—dressed all unfit to be out-of-doors such a bitter night—crying, and beating against the window-panes, as if, she wanted to be let in. She seemed to sob and wail, till Miss Rosamond could bear it no longer, and was flying to the door to open it, when, all of a sudden, and close upon us, the great organ pealed out so loud and thundering, it fairly made me tremble; and all the more, when I remembered me that, even in the stillness of that dead-cold weather, I had heard no sound of little battering hands upon the window-glass, although the Phantom Child had seemed to put forth all its force; and, although I had seen it wail and cry, no faintest touch of sound had fallen upon my ears. Whether I remembered all this at the very moment, I do not know; the great organ sound had so stunned me into terror; but this I know, I caught up Miss Rosamond before she got the hall-door opened, and clutched her, and carried her away, kicking and screaming, into the large bright kitchen, where Dorothy and Agnes were busy with their mince-pies.

"What is the matter with my sweet one?" cried Dorothy, as I bore in Miss Rosamond, who was sobbing as if her heart would break.

"She won't let me open the door for my little girl to come in; and she'll die if she is out on the Fells all night. Cruel, naughty Hester," she said, slapping me; but she might have struck harder, for I had seen a look of ghastly terror on Dorothy's face, which made my very blood run cold.

"Shut the back kitchen door fast, and bolt it well," said she to Agnes. She said no more; she gave me raisins and almonds to quiet Miss Rosamond: but she sobbed about the little girl in the snow, and would not touch any of the good things. I was thankful when she cried herself to sleep in bed. Then I stole down to the kitchen, and told Dorothy I had made up my mind. I would

carry my darling back to my father's house in Applethwaite; where, if we lived humbly, we lived at peace. I said I had been frightened enough with the old lord's organ-playing; but now, that I had seen for myself this little moaning child, all decked out as no child in the neighborhood could be, beating and battering to get in, yet always without any sound or noise—with the dark wound on its right shoulder; and that Miss Rosamond had known it again for the phantom that had nearly lured her to her death (which Dorothy knew was true); I would stand it no longer.

I saw Dorothy change color once or twice. When I had done, she told me she did not think I could take Miss Rosamond with me, for that she was my lord's ward, and I had no right over her; and she asked me, would I leave the child that I was so fond of, just for sounds and sights that could do me no harm; and that they had all had to get used to in their turns? I was all in a hot, trembling passion; and I said it was very well for her to talk, that knew what these sights and noises betokened, and that had, perhaps, had something to do with the Spectre-child while it was alive. And I taunted her so, that she told me all she knew, at last; and then I wished I had never been told, for it only made me more afraid than ever.

She said she had heard the tale from old neighbors, that were alive when she was first married; when folks used to come to the hall sometimes, before it had got such a bad name on the country side: it might not be true, or it might, what she had been told.

The old lord was Miss Furnivall's father—Miss Grace, as Dorothy called her, for Miss Maude was the elder, and Miss Furnivall by rights. The old lord was eaten up with pride. Such a proud man was never seen or heard of; and his daughters were like him. No one was good enough to wed them, although they had choice enough; for they were the great beauties of their day, as I had seen by their portraits, where they hung in the state drawing-room. But, as the old saying is, "Pride will have a fall;" and these two haughty beauties fell in love with the same man, and he no better than a foreign musician, whom their father had down from London to play music with him at the Manor House. For, above all things, next to his pride, the old lord loved music. He could play on nearly every instrument that ever was heard of; and it was a strange thing it did not soften him; but he was a fierce dour old man, and had broken his poor wife's heart with his cruelty, they said. He was mad after music, and would pay any money for it. So he got this foreigner to come; who made such beautiful music, that they said the very birds on the trees stopped their singing to listen. And, by degrees, this foreign gentleman got such a hold over the old lord, that nothing would serve him but that he must come every year; and it was he that had the great organ brought from Holland and built up in the hall, where it stood now. He taught the old lord to play on it; but many and many a time, when Lord Furnivall was thinking of nothing but his fine organ, and his finer music, the dark foreigner was walking abroad in the woods with one of the young ladies; now Miss Maude, and then Miss Grace.

Miss Maude won the day and carried off the prize, such as it was; and he and she were married, all unknown to any one; and before he made his next yearly visit, she had been confined of[3] a little girl at a farm-house on the

3. Had given birth to.

Moors, while her father and Miss Grace thought she was away at Doncaster Races. But though she was a wife and a mother, she was not a bit softened, but as haughty and as passionate as ever; and perhaps more so, for she was jealous of Miss Grace, to whom her foreign husband paid a deal of court— by way of blinding her—as he told his wife. But Miss Grace triumphed[4] over Miss Maude, and Miss Maude grew fiercer and fiercer, both with her husband and with her sister; and the former—who could easily shake off what was disagreeable, and hide himself in foreign countries—went away a month before his usual time that summer, and half threatened that he would never come back again. Meanwhile, the little girl was left at the farm-house, and her mother used to have her horse saddled and gallop wildly over the hills to see her once every week, at the very least—for where she loved, she loved; and where she hated, she hated. And the old lord went on playing—playing on his organ; and the servants thought the sweet music he made had soothed down his awful temper, of which (Dorothy said) some terrible tales could be told. He grew infirm too, and had to walk with a crutch; and his son—that was the present Lord Furnivall's father—was with the army in America, and the other son at sea; so Miss Maude had it pretty much her own way, and she and Miss Grace grew colder and bitterer to each other every day; till at last they hardly ever spoke, except when the old lord was by. The foreign musician came again the next summer, but it was for the last time; for they led him such a life with their jealousy and their passions, that he grew weary, and went away, and never was heard of again. And Miss Maude, who had always meant to have her marriage acknowledged when her father should be dead, was left now a deserted wife—whom nobody knew to have been married—with a child that she dared not own, although she loved it to distraction; living with a father whom she feared, and a sister whom she hated. When the next summer passed over and the dark foreigner never came, both Miss Maude and Miss Grace grew gloomy and sad; they had a haggard look about them, though they looked handsome as ever. But by and by Miss Maude brightened; for her father grew more and more infirm, and more than ever carried away by his music; and she and Miss Grace lived almost entirely apart, having separate rooms, the one on the west side—Miss Maude on the east—those very rooms which were now shut up. So she thought she might have her little girl with her, and no one need ever know except those who dared not speak about it, and were bound to believe that it was, as she said, a cottager's child she had taken a fancy to. All this, Dorothy said, was pretty well known; but what came afterwards no one knew, except Miss Grace, and Mrs. Stark, who was even then her maid, and much more of a friend to her than ever her sister had been. But the servants supposed, from words that were dropped, that Miss Maude had triumphed over Miss Grace, and told her that all the time the dark foreigner had been mocking her with pretended love—he was her own husband; the color left Miss Grace's cheek and lips that very day for ever, and she was heard to say many a time that sooner or later she would have her revenge; and Mrs. Stark was for ever spying about the east rooms.

One fearful night, just after the New Year had come in, when the snow was lying thick and deep, and the flakes were still falling—fast enough to

4. Exulted.

blind any one who might be out and abroad—there was a great and violent noise heard, and the old lord's voice above all, cursing and swearing awfully,—and the cries of a little child,—and the proud defiance of a fierce woman,—and the sound of a blow,—and a dead stillness,—and moans and wailings dying away on the hill-side! Then the old lord summoned all his servants, and told them, with terrible oaths, and words more terrible, that his daughter had disgraced herself, and that he had turned her out of doors,—her, and her child,—and that if ever they gave her help,—or food— or shelter,—he prayed that they might never enter Heaven. And, all the while, Miss Grace stood by him, white and still as any stone; and when he had ended she heaved a great sigh, as much as to say her work was done, and her end was accomplished. But the old lord never touched his organ again, and died within the year; and no wonder! for, on the morrow of that wild and fearful night, the shepherds, coming down the Fell side, found Miss Maude sitting, all crazy and smiling, under the holly-trees, nursing a dead child,—with a terrible mark on its right shoulder. "But that was not what killed it," said Dorothy; "it was the frost and the cold—every wild creature was in its hole, and every beast in its fold,—while the child and its mother were turned out to wander on the Fells! And now you know all! and I wonder if you are less frightened now?"

I was more frightened than ever; but I said I was not. I wished Miss Rosamond and myself well out of that dreadful house for ever; but I would not leave her, and I dared not take her away. But oh! how I watched her, and guarded her! We bolted the doors, and shut the window-shutters fast, an hour or more before dark, rather than leave them open five minutes too late. But my little lady still heard the weird child crying and mourning; and not all we could do or say, could keep her from wanting to go to her, and let her in from the cruel wind and the snow. All this time, I kept away from Miss Furnivall and Mrs. Stark, as much as ever I could; for I feared them—I knew no good could be about them, with their grey hard faces, and their dreamy eyes, looking back into the ghastly years that were gone. But, even in my fear, I had a kind of pity—for Miss Furnivall, at least. Those gone down to the pit can hardly have a more hopeless look than that which was ever on her face. At last I even got so sorry for her—who never said a word but what was quite forced from her—that I prayed for her; and I taught Miss Rosamond to pray for one who had done a deadly sin; but often when she came to those words, she would listen, and start up from her knees, and say, "I hear my little girl plaining and crying very sad—Oh! let her in, or she will die!"

One night—just after New Year's Day had come at last, and the long winter had taken a turn as I hoped—I heard the west drawing-room bell ring three times, which was the signal for me. I would not leave Miss Rosamond alone, for all she was asleep—for the old lord had been playing wilder than ever— and I feared lest my darling should waken to hear the spectre child; see her I knew she could not, I had fastened the windows too well for that. So, I took her out of her bed and wrapped her up in such outer clothes as were most handy, and carried her down to the drawing-room, where the old ladies sat at their tapestry work as usual. They looked up when I came in, and Mrs. Stark asked, quite astounded, "Why did I bring Miss Rosamond there, out of her warm bed?" I had begun to whisper, "Because I was afraid of her being

tempted out while I was away, by the wild child in the snow," when she stopped me short (with a glance at Miss Furnivall) and said Miss Furnivall wanted me to undo some work she had done wrong, and which neither of them could see to unpick. So, I laid my pretty dear on the sofa, and sat down on a stool by them, and hardened my heart against them as I heard the wind rising and howling.

Miss Rosamond slept on sound, for all the wind blew so; and Miss Furnivall said never a word, nor looked round when the gusts shook the windows. All at once she started up to her full height, and put up one hand as if to bid us listen.

"I hear voices!" said she. "I hear terrible screams—I hear my father's voice!"

Just at that moment, my darling wakened with a sudden start: "My little girl is crying, oh, how she is crying!" and she tried to get up and go to her, but she got her feet entangled in the blanket, and I caught her up; for my flesh had begun to creep at these noises, which they heard while we could catch no sound. In a minute or two the noises came, and gathered fast, and filled our ears; we, too, heard voices and screams, and no longer heard the winter's wind that raged abroad. Mrs. Stark looked at me, and I at her, but we dared not speak. Suddenly Miss Furnivall went towards the door, out into the ante-room, through the west lobby, and opened the door into the great hall. Mrs. Stark followed, and I durst not be left, though my heart almost stopped beating for fear. I wrapped my darling tight in my arms, and went out with them. In the hall the screams were louder than ever; they sounded to come from the east wing—nearer and nearer—close on the other side of the locked-up doors—close behind them. Then I noticed that the great bronze chandelier seemed all alight, though the hall was dim, and that a fire was blazing in the vast hearth-place, though it gave no heat; and I shuddered up with terror, and folded my darling closer to me. But as I did so, the east door shook, and she, suddenly struggling to get free from me, cried, "Hester! I must go! My little girl is there; I hear her; she is coming! Hester, I must go!"

I held her tight with all my strength; with a set will, I held her. If I had died, my hands would have grasped her still; I was so resolved in my mind. Miss Furnivall stood listening, and paid no regard to my darling, who had got down to the ground, and whom I, upon my knees now, was holding with both my arms clasped round her neck; she still striving and crying to get free.

All at once, the east door gave way with a thundering crash, as if torn open in a violent passion, and there came into that broad and mysterious light, the figure of a tall old man, with grey hair and gleaming eyes. He drove before him, with many a relentless gesture of abhorrence, a stern and beautiful woman, with a little child clinging to her dress.

"Oh Hester! Hester!" cried Miss Rosamond. "It's the lady! the lady below the holly-trees; and my little girl is with her. Hester! Hester! let me go to her; they are drawing me to them. I feel them—I feel them. I must go!"

Again she was almost convulsed by her efforts to get away; but I held her tighter and tighter; till I feared I should do her a hurt; but rather that than let her go towards those terrible phantoms. They passed along towards the great hall-door, where the winds howled and ravened for their prey; but

before they reached that, the lady turned; and I could see that she defied the old man with a fierce and proud defiance; but then she quailed—and then she threw up her arms wildly and piteously to save her child—her little child—from a blow from his uplifted crutch.

And Miss Rosamond was torn as by a power stronger than mine, and writhed in my arms, and sobbed (for by this time the poor darling was growing faint).

"They want me to go with them on to the Fells—they are drawing me to them. Oh, my little girl! I would come, but cruel, wicked Hester holds me very tight." But when she saw the uplifted crutch she swooned away, and I thanked God for it. Just at this moment—when the tall old man, his hair streaming as in the blast of a furnace, was going to strike the little shrinking child—Miss Furnivall, the old woman by my side, cried out, "Oh, father! father! spare the little innocent child!" But just then I saw—we all saw—another phantom shape itself, and grow clear out of the blue and misty light that filled the hall; we had not seen her till now, for it was another lady who stood by the old man, with a look of relentless hate and triumphant scorn. That figure was very beautiful to look upon, with a soft white hat drawn down over the proud brows, and a red and curling lip. It was dressed in an open robe of blue satin. I had seen that figure before. It was the likeness of Miss Furnivall in her youth; and the terrible phantoms moved on, regardless of old Miss Furnivall's wild entreaty,—and the uplifted crutch fell on the right shoulder of the little child, and the younger sister looked on, stony and deadly serene. But at that moment, the dim lights, and the fire that gave no heat, went out of themselves, and Miss Furnivall lay at our feet stricken down by the palsy—death-stricken.

Yes! she was carried to her bed that night never to rise again. She lay with her face to the wall, muttering low but muttering alway: "Alas! alas! what is done in youth can never be undone in age! What is done in youth can never be undone in age!"

1852

FANNY FERN (SARA WILLIS PARTON)
1811–1872

A leading columnist, journalist, novelist, and activist, Sara Willis Parton was born in Maine; she was married twice, widowed, divorced, and the mother of three by the time she published her first collection of essays. Originally written for Boston newspapers under the pseudonym "Fanny Fern," *Fern Leaves from Fanny's Port-folio* (1853) became an instant best seller and was followed by several other equally successful books, whose popularity earned their author a prominent position as a regular weekly columnist for the New York *Ledger*. Married for a third time—to James Parton, himself a well-known literary man—Fanny Fern settled in New York City, where she wielded considerable influence as a commentator on current affairs, with a special interest in social inequities and women's issues.

Besides her celebrated columns, most of which were collected in such other volumes as *Fresh Leaves* (1857), *Folly as It Flies* (1868), *Ginger Snaps* (1870), and *Caper Sauce* (1872), Fern produced two novels, *Ruth Hall* (1855) and *Rose Clark* (1856). Her work was admired by Nathaniel Hawthorne (who praised *Ruth Hall*) and Walt Whitman (who imitated the cover design of *Fern Leaves* in the first edition of his *Leaves of Grass*, 1855). Sometimes sentimental, sometimes satiric, she was first and foremost an incisive observer of her culture's foibles, and she had an intense commitment to women's rights. Even in such a brief sketch as "Mrs. Adolphus Smith Sporting the 'Blue Stocking' " she dramatized the obstacles confronting female intellectual ambition with comic verve, while in more substantial pieces—for example, her discussion of the prostitutes incarcerated on Blackwells Island ("Blackwell's Island III," 1858) and "The Working-Girls of New York"—she was an impassioned feminist polemicist.

Mrs. Adolphus Smith Sporting the "Blue Stocking"[1]

Well, I think I'll finish that story for the editor of the "Dutchman." Let me see; where did I leave off? The setting sun was just gilding with his last ray— "Ma, I want some bread and molasses"—(yes, dear,) gilding with his last ray the church spire—"Wife, where's my Sunday pants?" (*Under the bed, dear,*) the church spire of Inverness, when a—"There's nothing under the bed, dear, but your lace cap"—(Perhaps they are in the coal hod[2] in the closet,) when a horseman was seen approaching—"Ma'am, the *pertators* is out;[3] not one for dinner"—(Take some turnips,) approaching, covered with dust, and— "Wife! the baby has swallowed a button"—(*Reverse him,* dear—take him by the heels,) and waving in his hand a banner, on which was written—"Ma! I've torn my pantaloons"—liberty or death! The inhabitants rushed *en masse*—"Wife! *will* you leave off scribbling?" (Don't be disagreeable, Smith, I'm just getting inspired,) to the public square, where De Begnis, who had been secretly—"Butcher wants to see you, ma'am"—secretly informed of the traitors'—"Forgot *which* you said, ma'am, sausages or mutton chop"—movements, gave orders to fire; not less than twenty—"My gracious! Smith, you haven't been *reversing* that child all this time; he's as black as your coat; and that boy of *yours* has torn up the first sheet of my manuscript. There! it's no use for a married woman to cultivate her intellect.—Smith, hand me those twins."

1853

Mr. Pipkin's Ideas of Family Retrenchment

Mrs. Pipkin, I am under the disagreeable necessity of informing you, that our family expenses are getting to be enormous. I see that carpet woman charged you a dollar for one day's work. Why, that is positively a man's wages;

1. Derisive term for an intellectual or literary woman (from an 18th-century literary society).
2. Coal scuttle (pail).
3. I.e., they are out of potatoes.

—such presumption is intolerable. Pity you did not make it yourself, Mrs. Pipkin; wives ought to lift their end of the yoke; that's my creed.

Little Tom Pipkin.—Papa, may I have this bit of paper on the floor? it is your tailor's bill—says, "$400 for your last year's clothes."

Mr. Pipkin.—Tom, go to bed, and learn never to interrupt your father when he is talking. Yes, as I was saying, Mrs. Pipkin, wives should hold up their end of the yoke; and it is high time there was a little retrenchment here; superfluities must be dispensed with.

Bridget.—Please, sir, there are three baskets of champagne just come for you, and four boxes of cigars.

Mr. Pipkin.—Will you please lock that door, Mrs. Pipkin, till I can get a chance to say what I have to say to you on this subject. I was thinking today, that you might dispense with your nursery maid, and take care of baby yourself. He don't cry much, except nights; and since I've slept alone upstairs, I don't hear the little tempest at all. It is really quite a relief—that child's voice is a perfect ear-splitter.

I think I shall get you, too, to take charge of the marketing and providing, (on a stipulated allowance from me, of course,) it will give me so much more time to—attend to *business,* Mrs. Pipkin. I shall take my own dinners down town at the——House. I hear Stevens is an excellent "caterer"; (though that's nothing to me, of course, as my only object in going is to meet business acquaintances from different parts of the Union, to drive a bargain, etc., etc.)

Well—it will cost you and the children little or nothing for your dinners. There's nothing so disgusting to a man of refinement, like myself, as to see a *woman* fond of eating; and as to children, any fool knows they ought not to be allowed to stuff their skins, like little anacondas.[1] Yes, our family expenses are enormous. My partner sighed like a pair of bellows at that last baby you had, Mrs. Pipkin; oh, it's quite ruinous—but I can't stop to talk now, I'm going to try a splendid horse which is offered me at a bargain— (too frisky for you to ride, my dear, but just the thing for me.)

You had better dismiss your nursery girl this afternoon; that will begin to look like retrenchment. Good-by; if I am not home till late, don't sit up for me, as I have ordered a supper at——House for my old friend, Tom Hillar, of New Orleans. We'll drink this toast, my dear: "Here's hoping the last little Pipkin may never have his nose put out of joint."

1853

Moral Molasses; or, Too Sweet by Half

The most thorough emetic[1] I know of, is in the shape of "Guide to Young Wives," and kindred books; as if one rule could, by any possibility, apply to all persons; as if every man living did not require different management (bless me, I did not intend to use that torpedo word,[2] but it is out now); as if, when things go wrong, a wife had only to fly upstairs, read a chapter in the "Young

1. Constrictors, snakes that swallow their prey whole.

1. A substance that induces vomiting.
2. I.e., an explosive word.

Wife's Guide," supposed to be suited to her complaint, and then go downstairs and apply the worthless plaster to the matrimonial sore. Pshaw! as well might a doctor send a peck of pills into a hospital, to be distributed by the hands of the nurse, to any and every male patient brought there, without regard to complaints or constitutional tendencies. I have no patience with such matrimonial nostrums.

"Always meet your husband with a smile." That is one of them. Suppose we put the boot on the other foot, and require the men to come grinning home? no matter how many of their notes may have been protested; no matter how, like Beelzebub,[3] their business partner may have tormented them; no matter how badly elections go—when they do it, may I be there to see! Nor should they. Passing over the everlasting monotony of that everlasting "Guide Book" smile, let us consider, brethren (sisters not admitted), what matrimony was intended for. As I look at it, as much to share each other's sorrows as to share each other's joys; neither of the twain to shoulder wholly the one or the other. Those of you, brethren, who agree with me in this lucid view of the subject, please to signify it by rising.

'Tis a vote.

Well then, do people in moments of perplexity generally grin? Is it not asking too much of female, and too much of male nature, to do it when a man's store burns down, and there is no insurance? or when a misguided and infatuated baby stuffs beans up its nose, while its mamma is putting new cuffs on her husband's coat, hearing Katy say her lesson, and telling the cook about dinner? And when this sorely afflicted couple meet, would it not be best to make a clean breast of their troubles, sympathize together over them, have a nice matrimonial cry on each other's shoulders, and wind up with a first-class kiss?

'Tis a vote.

Well then—to the mischief with your grinning over a volcano;—erupt, and have done with it! so shall you love each other more for your very sorrows; so shall you avoid hypocrisy and kindred bedevilments, and pull evenly in the matrimonial harness. I speak as unto *wise* men.

Lastly, brethren, what I particularly admire, is the indirect compliment to your sex, which this absurd rule I have quoted implies; the devotion, magnanimity, fortitude, and courage, it gives *you* fair-weather sailors credit for! But what is the use of talking about it? These guide books are mainly written by sentimental old maids; who, had they ever been within kissing distance of a beard, would not so abominably have wasted pen, ink, and paper; or, by some old bachelor, tip-toeing on the outskirts of the promised land, without a single clear idea of its resources and requirements, or courage enough to settle there if he had.

1853

3. The devil.

A Law More Nice Than Just

Here I have been sitting twiddling the morning paper between my fingers this half hour, reflecting upon the following paragraph in it: "Emma Wilson was arrested yesterday for wearing man's apparel."[1] Now, why this should be an actionable offense is past my finding out, or where's the harm in it, I am as much at a loss to see. Think of the old maids (and weep) who have to stay at home evening after evening, when, if they provided themselves with a coat, pants and hat, they might go abroad, instead of sitting there with their noses flattened against the window-pane, looking vainly for "the Coming Man."[2] Think of the married women who stay at home after their day's toil is done, waiting wearily for their thoughtless, truant husbands, when they might be taking the much needed independent walk in trowsers, which custom forbids to petticoats. And this, I fancy, may be the secret of this famous law—who knows? It *wouldn't* be pleasant for some of them to be surprised by a touch on the shoulder from some dapper young fellow, whose familiar treble voice belied his corduroys. That's it, now. What a fool I was not to think of it—not to remember that men who make the laws, make them to meet all these little emergencies.

Everybody knows what an everlasting drizzle of rain we have had lately, but nobody but a woman, and a woman who lives on fresh air and out-door exercise, knows the thraldom of taking her daily walk through a three weeks' rain, with skirts to hold up, and umbrella to hold down, and puddles to skip over, and gutters to walk round, and all the time in a fright lest, in an unguarded moment, her calves should become visible to some one of those rainy-day philanthropists who are interested in the public study of female anatomy.

One evening, after a long rainy day of scribbling, when my nerves were in double-twisted knots, and I felt as if myriads of little ants were leisurely traveling over me, and all for want of the walk which is my daily salvation, I stood at the window, looking at the slanting, persistent rain, and took my resolve. *"I'll do it,"* said I, audibly, planting my slipper upon the carpet. "Do what?" asked Mr. Fern, looking up from a big book. "Put on a suit of your clothes and take a tramp with you," was the answer. "You dare not," was the rejoinder; "you are a little coward, only saucy on paper." It was the work of a moment, with such a challenge, to fly up stairs and overhaul my philosopher's wardrobe. Of course we had fun. Tailors must be a stingy set, I remarked, to be so sparing of their cloth, as I struggled into a pair of their handiwork, undeterred by the vociferous laughter of the wretch who had solemnly vowed to "cherish me" through all my tribulations. "Upon my word, everything seems to be narrow where it ought to be broad, and the waist of this coat might be made for a hogshead; and, ugh! this shirt-collar is cutting my ears off, and you have not a decent cravat in the whole lot, and your vests are frights, and what am I to do with my hair?" Still no reply from Mr. Fern, who lay on the floor, faintly ejaculating, between his fits of laughter, "Oh, my! by Jove!—oh! by Jupiter!"

1. Into the 20th century, some municipalities had laws prohibiting women from wearing men's clothing.

2. I.e., a suitor who is up-and-coming, likely to be a success in life.

Was that to hinder me? Of course not. Strings and pins, woman's never-failing resort, soon brought broadcloth and kerseymere[3] to terms. I parted my hair on one side, rolled it under, and then secured it with hair-pins; chose the best fitting coat, and capping the climax with one of those soft, cosy hats, looked in the glass, where I beheld the very facsmile of a certain musical gentleman, whose photograph hangs this minute in Brady's entry.[4]

Well, Mr. Fern seized his hat, and out we went together. "Fanny," said he, "you must not take my arm; you are a fellow." "True," said I, "I forgot; "and you must not help me over the puddles, as you did just now, and do, for mercy's sake, stop laughing. There, there goes your hat—I mean *my* hat; confound the wind! and down comes my hair; lucky 'tis dark, isn't it?" But oh, the delicious freedom of that walk, after we were well started! No skirts to hold up, or to draggle their wet folds against my ankles; no stifling vail flapping in my face, and blinding my eyes; no umbrella to turn inside out, but instead, the cool rain driving slap into my face, and the resurrectionized blood coursing through my veins, and tingling in my cheeks. To be sure, Mr. Fern occasionally loitered behind, and leaned up against the side of a house to enjoy a little private "guffaw," and I could now and then hear a gasping "Oh, Fanny!" "oh, my!" but none of these things moved me, and if I don't have a nicely-fitting suit of my own to wear rainy evenings, it is because—well, there *are* difficulties in the way. Who's the best tailor?

Now, if any male or female Miss Nancy[5] who reads this feels shocked, let 'em! Any woman who likes, may stay at home during a three weeks' rain, till her skin looks like parchment, and her eyes like those of a dead fish, or she may go out and get a consumption dragging round wet petticoats; I won't—I positively declare I won't. I shall begin *evenings* when *that* suit is made, and take private walking lessons with Mr. Fern, and they who choose may crook their backs at home for fashion, and then send for the doctor to straighten them; I prefer to patronize my shoe-maker and tailor. I've as good a right to preserve the healthy body God gave me, as if I were not a woman.

1858

Blackwell's Island[1]

Number III

You can step aside, Mrs. Grundy;[2] what I am about to write is not for your over-fastidious ear. *You*, who take by the hand the polished roue, and welcome him with a sweet smile to the parlor where sit your young, trusting daughters; you, who "have no business with his private life, so long as his

3. A fine woolen fabric used in making suits (then usually spelled *cassimere*).
4. The New York City studio of the photographer Mathew Brady (1823?–1896); the "musical gentleman" was probably Fern's brother Richard Storrs Willis, a prominent music critic.
5. Prude.
1. A 2-mile-long island in the East River, between Manhattan and Queens (later called Welfare Island and, beginning in 1973, Roosevelt Island);

in the 19th century it held hospitals, lunatic asylum, workhouses for the poor, and prisons. After visiting the island, Fern published three articles in the New York *Ledger* on the plight of the women in its various institutions.
2. Someone who persistently judges others' behavior by highly conventional standards; from a character alluded to in the British comedy *Speed the Plow* (1798) by Thomas Morton.

manners are gentlemanly;" you who, while saying this, turn away with bitter, unwomanly words from his penitent, writhing victim. I ask no leave of *you* to speak of the wretched girls picked out of the gutters of New York streets, to inhabit those cells at Blackwell's Island. I speak not to *you* of what was tugging at my heartstrings as I saw them, that beautiful summer afternoon, file in, two by two, to their meals, followed by a man carrying a cowhide[3] in his hand, by way of reminder; all this would not interest you; but when you tell me that these women are not to be named to ears polite, that our sons and our daughters should grow up ignorant of their existence, I stop my ears. As if they could, or did! As if they can take a step in the public streets without being jostled or addressed by them, or pained by their passing ribaldry; as if they could return from a party or concert at night, without meeting droves of them; as if they could, even in broad daylight, sit down to an ice-cream without having one for a vis-a-vis.[4] As if they could ride in a car or omnibus,[5] or cross in a ferry-boat, or go to a watering-place, without being unmistakably confronted by them. No, Mrs. Grundy; you know all this as well as I do. You would push them "anywhere out of the world," as unfit to live, as unfit to die; *they*, the weaker party, while their partners in sin, for whom you claim greater mental superiority, and who, by your own finding, should be much better able to learn and *to teach* the lesson of self-control—to them you extend perfect absolution.[6] Most consistent Mrs. Grundy, get out of my way while I say what I was going to, without fear or favor of yours.

If I believed, as legislators, and others with whom I have talked on this subject, pretend to believe, they best know why, that God ever made one of those girls for the life they lead, for this is plain Saxon is what their talk amounts to, I should curse Him. If I could temporise as they do about it, as "a necessary evil," and "always has been, and always will be," and (then add this beautiful tribute to manhood) "that pure women would not be safe were it not so"—and all the other budget of excuses which this sin makes to cover its deformity—I would forswear my manhood.

You say their intellects are small, they are mere animals, naturally coarse and groveling. Answer me this—are they, or are they not *immortal*? Decide the question whether *this* life is to be *all* to them. Decide before you shoulder the responsibility of such a girl's future. Granted she has only *this* life. God knows how much misery may be crowded into that. But you say, "Bless your soul, why do you talk to *me*? I have nothing to do with it; I am as virtuous as St. Paul." St. Paul was a bachelor, and of course is not my favorite apostle;[7] but waiving that, I answer, you *have* something to do with it when you talk thus, and throw your influence on the wrong side. No matter how outwardly correct your past life may have been, if you *really believe* what you say, I would not give a fig for your virtue if temptation and opportunity favored; and if you talk so for talk's sake, and do not believe it, you had better "tarry at Jericho till your beard be grown."[8]

But you say to me, "Oh, you don't know anything about it; men are differently constituted from women; woman's sphere is home." That don't sus-

3. I.e., a whip.
4. A companion (literally, "face-to-face"; French).
5. Horse-drawn public bus. "Car": coach on a rail or trolley line.
6. I.e., only prostitutes, and not their customers, deserve punishment.
7. Fern is apparently among those who view Paul's writings as misogynist. He urged all to follow his model and live in chastity (1 Corinthians 7.1, 8).
8. 2 Samuel 10.5.

pend the laws of her being. That don't make it that she don't need sympathy and appreciation. That don't make it that she is never weary and needs amusement to restore her. Fudge.[9] I believe in no difference that makes this distinction. Women lead, most of them, lives of unbroken monotony, and have much more need of exhilarating influences than men, whose life is out of doors in the breathing, active world. Don't tell me of shoemakers at their lasts, and tailors at their needles. Do either ever have to lay down their customers' coats and shoes fifty times a day, and wonder when the day is over why their work is *not* done, though they have struggled through fire and water to finish it? Do not both tailor and shoemaker have at least the variation of a walk to or from the shop to their meals? Do not their customers talk their beloved politics to them while they stitch, and do not their "confreres"[1] run for a bottle of ale and crack merry jokes with them as their work progresses? Sirs! if monotony is to be avoided in man's life as injurious; if "variety" and exhilaration must always be the spice to his pursuits, how much more must it be necessary to a sensitively organized woman? If home is not sufficient, (and I will persist that any *industrious, virtuous, unambitious* man, may have a home if he chooses); if home is not sufficient for him, why should it suffice for her? whose work is never done—who can have literally *no* such thing as system, (and here's where a mother's discouragement comes in), while her babes are in their infancy; who often says to herself at night, though she would not for worlds part with one of them—"I can't tell what I have accomplished to-day, and yet I have not been idle a minute;" and day after day passes on in this way, and perhaps for weeks she does not pass the threshold for a breath of air, and yet men talk of "monotony!" and being "differently constituted," and needing amusement and exhilaration; and "business" is the broad mantle which it is not always safe for a wife to lift. I have no faith in putting women in a pound,[2] that men may trample down the clover in a forty-acre lot. But enough for that transparent excuse.

The great Law-giver made no distinction of sex, as far as I can find out, when he promulgated the seventh commandment,[3] nor should we. You tell me "society makes a difference;" more shame to it—more shame to the women who help to perpetuate it. You tell me that infidelity on the wife's part involves an unjust claim upon the husband and provider; and I ask you, on the other hand, if a good and virtuous wife has not a right to expect *healthy* children?

Let both be equally pure; let every man look upon every woman, whatsoever her rank or condition, as a sister whom his manhood is bound to protect, even, if need be, against herself, and let every woman turn the cold shoulder to any man of her acquaintance, how polished soever he may be, who would degrade her sex. Then this vexed question would be settled; there would be no such libels upon womanhood as I saw at Blackwell's Island, driven in droves to their cells. No more human traffic in those gilded palaces, which our children must not hear mentioned, forsooth! though their very fathers may help to support them, and which our tender-hearted legislators "can't

9. Poppycock (an exclamation of annoyed disbelief).
1. Colleagues (French).

2. A place of confinement.
3. "Thou shalt not commit adultery" (Exodus 20.14).

see their way clear about." Then our beautiful rivers would no longer toss upon our island shores the "dead bodies of unfortunate young females."

1858

The Working-Girls of New York

Nowhere more than in New York does the contest between squalor and splendor so sharply present itself. This is the first reflection of the observing stranger who walks its streets. Particularly is this noticeable with regard to its women. Jostling on the same pavement with the dainty fashionist is the care-worn working-girl. Looking at both these women, the question arises, which lives the more miserable life—she whom the world styles "fortunate," whose husband belongs to three clubs, and whose only meal with his family is an occasional breakfast, from year's end to year's end; who is as much a stranger to his own children as to the reader; whose young son of seventeen has already a detective on his track employed by his father to ascertain where and how he spends his nights and his father's money; swift retribution for that father who finds food, raiment, shelter, equipages for his household; but love, sympathy, companionship—never? Or she—this other woman— with a heart quite as hungry and unappeased, who also faces day by day the same appalling question: *Is this all life has for me?*

A great book is yet unwritten about women. Michelet[1] has aired his wax-doll theories regarding them. The defender of "woman's rights" has given us her views. Authors and authoresses of little, and big repute, have expressed themselves on this subject, and none of them as yet have begun to grasp it: men—because they lack spirituality, rightly and justly to interpret women; women—because they dare not, or will not, tell us that which most interests us to know. Who shall write this bold, frank, truthful book remains to be seen. Meanwhile woman's millennium is yet a great way off; and while it slowly progresses, conservatism and indifference gaze through their spectacles at the seething elements of to-day, and wonder "what ails all our women?"

Let me tell you what ails the working-girls. While yet your breakfast is progressing, and your toilet unmade comes forth through Chatham Street and the Bowery,[2] a long procession of them by twos and threes to their daily labor. Their breakfast, so called, has been hastily swallowed in a tenement house, where two of them share, in a small room, the same miserable bed. Of its quality you may better judge, when you know that each of these girls pays but three dollars a week for board, to the working man and his wife where they lodge.

The room they occupy is close and unventilated, with no accommodations for personal cleanliness, and so near to the little Flinegans[3] that their Celtic night-cries are distinctly heard. They have risen unrefreshed, as a matter of

1. Jules Michelet (1798–1874), French historian; in his writings (especially *Woman*, 1860), he depicted women as children.
2. Streets on the Lower East Side of Manhattan were many cheap lodgings were located (Chatham Street is now called East Broadway).
3. I.e., the children of poor Irish immigrants, who had streamed into New York following Ireland's potato famine of 1845–50.

course, and their ill-cooked breakfast does not mend the matter. They emerge from the doorway where their passage is obstructed by "nanny goats" and ragged children rooting together in the dirt, and pass out in into the street. They shiver as the sharp wind of early morning strikes their temples. There is no look of youth on their faces; hard lines appear there. Their brows are knit; their eyes are sunken; their dress is flimsy, and foolish and tawdry; always a hat; and feather or soiled artificial flower upon it; the hair dressed with an abortive attempt at style; a soiled petticoat; a greasy dress, a well-worn sacque⁴ or shawl, and a gilt breast-pin and earrings.

Now follow them to the large, black-looking building, where several hundred of them are manufacturing hoop-skirts. If you are a woman you have worn plenty; but you little thought what passed in the heads of these girls as their busy fingers glazed the wire, or prepared the spools for covering them, or secured the tapes which held them in their places. You could not stay five minutes in that room, where the noise of the machinery used is so deafening, that only by the motion of the lips could you comprehend a person speaking.

Five minutes! Why, these young creatures bear it, from seven in the morning till six in the evening; week after week, month after month, with only half an hour at midday to eat their dinner of a slice of bread and butter or an apple, which they usually eat in the building, some of them having come a long distance. As I said, the roar of machinery in that room is like the roar of Niagara. Observe them as you enter. Not one lifts her head. They might as well be machines, for any interest or curiosity they show, save always to know *what o'clock it is*. Pitiful! pitiful, you almost sob to yourself, as you look at these young girls. *Young!* Alas! it is only in years that they are young.

––––––––

"Only three dollars a week do they earn," said I to a brawny woman in a tenement house near where some of them boarded. "Only three dollars a week, and all of that goes for their board. How, then, do they clothe themselves?" Hell has nothing more horrible than the cold, sneering indifference of her reply: *"Ask the dry-goods men."*⁵

Perhaps you ask, why do not these girls go out to service? Surely it were better to live in a clean, nice house, in a healthy atmosphere, with respectable people, who might take other interest in them than to wring out the last particle of their available bodily strength. It were better surely to live in a house cheerful and bright, where merry voices were sometimes heard, and clean, wholesome food was given them. Why do they not? First, because, unhappily, they look down upon the position of a servant, even from *their* miserable stand-point. But chiefly, and mainly, because when six o'clock in the evening comes they are their own mistresses, without hinderance or questioning, till another day of labor begins. They do not sit in an underground kitchen, watching the bell-wire,⁶ and longing to see what is going on out of doors. More's the pity, that the street is their only refuge from the squalor and quarrelling and confusion of their tenement-house home. More's the pity, that as yet there are no sufficiently decent, cleanly boarding-houses, within their means, where their self-respect would not inevitably wither and die.

4. Loose-fitting coat.
5. Sellers of clothing and textiles.

6. I.e., waiting for the signal that their employer needs them.

As it is, they stroll the streets; and who can blame them? *There* are gay lights, and fine shop-windows. It costs nothing to *wish* they could have all those fine things. They look longingly into the theatres, through whose doors happier girls of their own age pass, radiant and smiling, with their lovers. Glimpses of Paradise come through those doors as they gaze. Back comes the old torturing question: Must my young life *always* be toil? *nothing* but toil? They stroll on. Music and bright lights from the underground "Concert Saloons," where girls like themselves get fine dresses and good wages, and flattering words and smiles beside. Alas! the future is far away; the present only is tangible. Is it a wonder if they never go back to the dark, cheerless tenement-house, or to the "manufactory" which sets their poor, weary bodies aching, till they feel forsaken of God and man? Talk of virtue! Live this life of toil, and starvation, and friendlessness, and "unwomanly rags," and learn charity. Sometimes they rush for escape into ill-sorted marriages, with coarse rough fellows, and go back to the old tenement-house life again, with this difference, that their toil does *not* end at six o'clock, and that from *this* bargain there is no release but death.

But there are other establishments than those factories where working-girls are employed. There is "Madame——, Modiste."[7] Surely the girls working there must fare better. Madame pays six thousand dollars rent for the elegant mansion in that fashionable street, in the basement or attic of which they work. Madame cuts and makes dresses, but she takes in none of the materials for that purpose. Not she. She coolly tells you that she will make you a very nice *plain* black silk dress, and find everything, for two hundred dollars. This is modest, at a clear profit to herself of one hundred dollars on every such dress, particularly as she buys all her material by the wholesale, and pays her girls, at the highest rate of compensation, not more than six dollars a week. At this rate of small wages and big profits, you can well understand how she can afford not only to keep up this splendid establishment, but another still more magnificent for her own *private* residence in quite as fashionable a neighborhood. Another "modiste" who *did* "take in material for dresses," and—ladies also! was in the habit of telling the latter that thirty-two yards of any material was required where sixteen would have answered. The remaining yards were then in all cases thrown into a rag-pen; from which, through contract with a man in her employ, she furnished herself with all the crockery, china, glass, tin and iron ware needed in her household. This same modiste employed twenty-five girls at the starvation price of three dollars and a half a week. The room in which they worked was about nine feet square, with only one window in it, and whoso came early enough to secure a seat by that window saved her eyesight by the process. Three sewing-machines whirred constantly by day in this little room, which at night was used as a sleeping apartment. As the twenty-five working-girls were ushered in to their day's labor in the morning before that room was ventilated, you would not wonder that by four in the afternoon dark circles appeared under their eyes, and they stopped occasionally to press their hands upon their aching temples. Not often, but *sometimes*, when the pain and exhaustion became intolerable.

One of the twenty-five was an orphan girl named Lizzy, only fifteen years

7. Maker of fashionable dresses.

of age. Not even this daily martyrdom had quenched her abounding spirits, in that room where never a smile was seen on another face—where never a jest was ventured on, not even when Madame's back was turned. Always Lizzie's hair was nicely smoothed, and though the clean little creature went without her breakfast—for a deduction of wages was the penalty of being late—yet had she always on a clean dark calico dress, smoothed by her own deft little fingers. In that dismal, smileless room she was the only sunbeam. But one day the twenty-five were startled; their needles dropped from their fingers. Lizzie was worn out at last! Her pretty face blanched, and with a low baby cry she threw her arms over her face and sobbed: "Oh, I *cannot* bear this life—I cannot bear it any longer. George *must* come and take me away from this." That night she was privately married to "George," who was an employee on the railroad. The next day while on the train attending to his duties, he broke his arm, and neither of the bridal pair having any money, George was taken to the hospital. The little bride, with starvation before her, went back that day to Madame, and concealing the fact of her marriage, begged humbly to be taken back, apologizing for her conduct on the day before, on the plea that she had such a violent pain in her temples that she knew not what she said. As she was a handy little workwoman, her request was granted, and she worked there for several weeks, during her honeymoon, at the old rate of pay. The day George was pronounced well, she threw down her work, clapped her little palms together, and announced to the astonished twenty-five that they had a married woman among them, and that she should not return the next morning. Being the middle of the week, and not the end, she had to go without her wages for that week. Romance was not part or parcel of Madame's establishment. Her law was as the Medes and Persians, which changed not.[8] Little Lizzie's future was no more to her than her past had been—no more than that of another young thing in that work-room, who begged a friend, each day, to bring her ever so little ardent spirits, at the half hour allotted to their miserable dinner, lest she should fail in strength to finish the day's work, upon which so much depended.

Oh! if the ladies who wore the gay robes manufactured in that room knew the tragedy of those young lives, would they not be to them like the penance robes of which we read, piercing, burning, torturing?

There is still another class of girls, who tend in the large shops in New York. Are they not better remunerated and lodged? We shall see. The additional dollar or two added to their wages is offset by the necessity of their being always nicely apparelled, and the necessity of a better lodging-house, and consequently a higher price for board, so that unless they are fortunate enough to have a parent's roof over their heads, they will not, except in rare cases, where there is a special gift as an accountant, or an artist-touch in the fingers, to twist a ribbon or frill a lace, be able to save any more than the class of which I have been speaking. They are allowed, however, by their employers, to purchase any article in the store at first cost,[9] which is something in their favor.

But, you say, is there no bright side to this dark picture? Are there no cases in which these girls battle bravely with penury? I have one in my mind now; a girl, I should say a lady; one of nature's ladies, with a face as refined and delicate as that of any lady who bends over these pages; who has been

8. Proverbial, from Daniel 6.12.

9. I.e., the cost to the store of a given item.

through this harrowing experience of the working-girl, and after years of patience, virtuous toil, has no more at this day than when she began, *i.e.,* her wages day by day. Of the wretched places she has called "home," I will not pain you by speaking. Of the rough words she has borne, that she was powerless, through her poverty, to resent. Of the long walks she has taken to obtain wages due, and failed to secure them at last. Of the weary, wakeful nights, and heart-breaking days, borne with a heroism and trust in God, that was truly sublime. Of the little remittances from time to time forwarded to old age and penury, in "the old country," when she herself was in want of comfortable clothing; when she herself had no shelter in case of sickness, save the hospital or the almshouse. Surely, such virtue and integrity, will have more enduring record than in these pages.

Humanity has not slept on this subject, though it has as yet accomplished little. A boarding-house has been established in New York for working-girls, excellent in its way, but intended mainly for those who "have seen better days," and not for the most needy class of which I have spoken. A noble institution, however, called "The Working Woman's Protective Union,"[1] has sprung up, for the benefit of this latter class, their object being to find places *in the country,* for such of these girls as will leave the overcrowded city, not as servants, but as operatives on sewing-machines, and to other similar revenues of employment. Their places are secured before they are sent. The person who engages them pays their expenses on leaving, and the consent of parents, or guardians, or friends, is always obtained before they leave. A room is to be connected with this institution, containing several sewing-machines, where gratuitous instruction will be furnished to those who desire it. A lawyer of New York has generously volunteered his services also, to collect the too tardy wages of these girls, due from flinty-hearted employers. Many of the girls who have applied here are under fifteen. At first, they utterly refused to go into the country, which to them was only another name for dullness; even preferring to wander up and down the streets of the city, half-fed and half-clothed, in search of employment, than to leave its dear kaleidoscope delights. But after a little, when letters came from some who had gone, describing in glowing terms, their pleasant homes; the wages that one could live and save money on; their kind treatment; the good, wholesome food and fresh air; their hearty, jolly country fun; and more than all, when it was announced that one of their number had actually married an ex-governor, the matter took another aspect. And, though all may not marry governors, and some may not marry at all; it still remains, that *inducing them to go to the country is striking a brave blow at the root of the evil;* for we all know, that human strength and human virtue have their limits; and the dreadful pressure of temptations and present ease, upon the discouragement, poverty and friendlessness of the working-girls of New York, must be gratifying to the devil. I do not hesitate to say, that there is no institution of the present day, more worthy to be sustained, or that more imperatively challenges the good works and good wishes of the benevolent, than "The New York Working Woman's Protective Union." May God speed it!

1868

1. The Working Women's Protective Union, an organization led by middle- and upper-class women, was founded in 1863.

fought against fugitive slave act...
slaves escaping to North had to be sent
back by Northerners w/out fair trial.

HARRIET BEECHER STOWE
1811–1896

Claims God
wrote "Uncle Tom's Cabin"

Harriet Beecher Stowe is still one of the most popular of the women novelists who published best sellers in America during the mid–nineteenth century. Approximately 350,000 copies of *Uncle Tom's Cabin; or, Life among the Lowly* (1851–52) were purchased during the first year of its printing, bringing its author $10,000 in just the first three months. While the book, which sold more than a million pirated copies in England, earned Stowe celebrity as well as such friends as George Eliot and Charles Dickens, within three years it had given rise to some thirty anti–*Uncle Tom* novels by Southern sympathizers. As a protest against the Fugitive Slave Act, which denied runaway slaves sanctuary and made it criminal to assist them, Stowe's novel preached the evils of slavery to a nation shown to be in need of Christian humility. By now *Uncle Tom's Cabin* has transcended both the partisanship of Northern abolitionists, who used it for propaganda purposes during the Civil War, and the more recent critical reaction of African American scholars, who have objected to the docility of "Uncle Tomism." Yet its controversial reception may have been responsible for obscuring the fact that Stowe published more than twenty-five other novels, essays, and stories.

To what familial influences can Stowe's prolific career be attributed? First, most biographers agree, Stowe's father, the eminent Congregational minister Lyman Beecher, was instrumental in instilling a sense of mission in his children: the eleven who survived to adulthood were all educated, according to his Calvinist values, for a life of public service as ministers or mothers, depending on their sex. Stowe received a theological education from her father, and all her life she struggled with despair over her inability to meet his spiritual standards, even as she sought to emulate the conversion work she saw him effecting in his church in her childhood hometown of Litchfield, Connecticut, and in the Lane Theological Seminary in Cincinnati, Ohio, where the family moved in 1832 when he became president of Lane. Stowe's mother, Roxana (Foote) Beecher, exerted her influence more as an absence than a presence: dead by the time her seventh child reached the age of four, she was remembered and cherished as a pious, devoted mother. Stowe was also imbued with a sense of the moral power of women by her older sister, Catharine Beecher, who took over their mother's household duties in 1815. After Harriet graduated from Miss Sarah Pierce's school in Litchfield, she attended the female seminary established by Catharine in Hartford. There she learned the lesson Catharine Beecher taught throughout her prominent career, the doctrine that women in their traditional roles could transform and redeem American culture through their exemplary Christian benevolence.

If the Beecher inheritance sustained and shaped the ethical impulse informing Stowe's subsequent fiction, her marriage to Calvin Ellis Stowe in 1836 provided her with a financial impetus for writing. This professor of biblical Hebrew at Lane shared her New England background, as well as her propensity for nervous depression and religious compunction. Never well paid, by 1844 he handed over the management of the family's finances to his wife, who discovered, to her relief, that she could lighten the load of what she considered "domestic slavery" by hiring a helper with the money she gained from publishing stories. In 1850, after six pregnancies and the death in infancy of her sixth baby, and with a seventh child on the way, Stowe moved with her husband to Maine, where he taught at Bowdoin College and where she experienced what she later called her "vision" of the death scene of Uncle Tom.

Her reading of abolitionist literature; the letters of her brother Charles, which recorded the voice of a sadistic Louisiana overseer he knew; the sermons of her other two brothers, Edward and Henry Ward, who denounced the Fugitive Slave Act from their pulpits; and the threat to one of her servants, who was claimed as a slave and

managed to escape through the help of the family—all of these contributed to Stowe's growing reaction against slavery, as had the death of her six-month-old baby, which taught her, she later explained, "what a poor slave mother may feel when her child is torn from her." If Stowe's pattern of imagery in *Uncle Tom's Cabin* is any index, she was haunted by a feeling of maternal loss—the loss of her infant and the earlier death of her mother—that she brilliantly described as the by-product of slavery. The faith in Christian humility she preached was associated with the spiritual agency of women, for her portraits of the submissive Tom, the angelic little Eva, and the maternal Quaker Rachel dramatized her attack on a slave system that divided mother and child. When *Uncle Tom's Cabin* was met by a storm of protests, she answered with *A Key to Uncle Tom's Cabin* (1853), documenting the horror of slavery she had fictionalized so effectively. After a triumphal European tour, recorded in *Sunny Memories of Foreign Lands* (1854), she wrote *Dred* (1856), a novel that depicts the disabling ethical effects of slavery on the white race.

Throughout her life, Stowe continued to support her family with writings that contributed to the formation of a national American literature. Turning to her native New England, she fashioned a regionalist perspective marked by respect for women's domestic sphere, a perspective that would later characterize the stories of Sarah Orne Jewett and Mary Wilkins Freeman. *The Minister's Wooing* (1859), *The Pearl of Orr's Island* (1862), *Oldtown Folks* (1869), and *Poganuc People* (1878) contain her finest portraits of New Englanders, dramatized through dialect, set in a somber physical landscape, and infused with a sometimes severe Calvinist spiritual atmosphere. "The Minister's Housekeeper," which is reprinted here from *Sam Lawson's Oldtown Fireside Stories* (1872), is narrated by a lazy but lively village storyteller Stowe had created in *Oldtown Folks* for comic relief. In the Oldtown tales, as in her children's stories, housekeeping manuals, and journalism, she achieved remarkable popularity and diversity.

Stowe had purchased an orange plantation in Mandarin, Florida, to escape Hartford winters after Calvin Stowe retired and to provide a rehabilitating occupation for her alcoholic son, Frederick William. She continued to support this son, her husband, and two unmarried daughters until her husband died in 1886. Suffering from senility and depression, she spent the last ten years of her life in Hartford. Seven years after her death, the Stowe cabinet in the library of the Woman's Building at the World's Columbian Exposition in Chicago contained a complete set of her works in twenty volumes, forty-two translations of *Uncle Tom's Cabin*, and a bust of the author done by the successful Boston sculptor Anne Whitney. The display was a fitting tribute to Stowe's achievement.

From Uncle Tom's Cabin

Chapter XXX. The Slave Warehouse

A slave warehouse! Perhaps some of my readers conjure up horrible visions of such a place. They fancy some foul, obscure den, some horrible *Tartarus "informis, ingens, ad lumen ademptum."*[1] But no, innocent friend; in these days men have learned the art of sinning expertly and genteelly, so as not to shock the eyes and senses of respectable society. Human property is high in the market; and is, therefore, well fed, well cleaned, tended, and looked after, that it may come to sale sleek, and strong, and shining. A slave-warehouse

1. Tartarus "hideous, huge, without light" (Latin); in Virgil's *Aeneid* 3.658 a similar phrase is applied to the blinded Cyclops, Polyphemus. Tartarus is the place of punishment in the underworld.

in New Orleans is a house externally not much unlike many others, kept with neatness; and where every day you may see arranged, under a sort of shed along the outside, rows of men and women, who stand there as a sign of the property sold within.

Then you shall be courteously entreated to call and examine, and shall find an abundance of husbands, wives, brothers, sisters, fathers, mothers, and young children, to be "sold separately, or in lots to suit the convenience of the purchaser;" and that soul immortal, once bought with blood and anguish by the Son of God, when the earth shook, and the rocks rent, and the graves were opened,[2] can be sold, leased, mortgaged, exchanged for groceries or dry goods, to suit the phases of trade, or the fancy of the purchaser.

It was a day or two after the conversation between Marie and Miss Ophelia, that Tom, Adolph, and about half a dozen others of the St. Clare estate, were turned over to the loving kindness of Mr. Skeggs, the keeper of a depot on _____ street, to await the auction, next day.

Tom had with him quite a sizable trunk full of clothing, as had most others of them. They were ushered, for the night, into a long room, where many other men, of all ages, sizes, and shades of complexion, were assembled, and from which roars of laughter and unthinking merriment were proceeding.

"Ah, ha! that's right. Go it, boys,—go it!" said Mr. Skeggs, the keeper. "My people are always so merry! Sambo, I see!" he said, speaking approvingly to a burly negro who was performing tricks of low buffoonery, which occasioned the shouts which Tom had heard.

As might be imagined, Tom was in no humor to join these proceedings; and, therefore, setting his trunk as far as possible from the noisy group, he sat down on it, and leaned his face against the wall.

The dealers in the human article make scrupulous and systematic efforts to promote noisy mirth among them, as a means of drowning reflection, and rendering them insensible to their condition. The whole object of the training to which the negro is put, from the time he is sold in the northern market till he arrives south, is systematically directed towards making him callous, unthinking, and brutal. The slave-dealer collects his gang in Virginia or Kentucky, and drives them to some convenient, healthy place,—often a watering place,—to be fattened. Here they are fed full daily; and, because some incline to pine, a fiddle is kept commonly going among them, and they are made to dance daily; and he who refuses to be merry—in whose soul thoughts of wife, or child, or home, are too strong for him to be gay—is marked as sullen and dangerous, and subjected to all the evils which the ill will of an utterly irresponsible and hardened man can inflict upon him. Briskness, alertness, and cheerfulness of appearance, especially before observers, are constantly enforced upon them, both by the hope of thereby getting a good master, and the fear of all that the driver may bring upon them, if they prove unsalable.

"What dat ar nigger doin here?" said Sambo, coming up to Tom, after Mr. Skeggs had left the room. Sambo was a full black, of great size, very lively, voluble, and full of trick and grimace.

"What you doin here?" said Sambo, coming up to Tom, and poking him facetiously in the side. "Meditatin', eh?"

2. A reference to the Harrowing of Hell, the story that Christ descended into Hell after his death and before his resurrection to release the souls held there.

"I am to be sold at the auction, to-morrow!" said Tom, quietly.

"Sold at auction,—haw! haw! boys, an't this yer fun? I wish't I was gwine that ar way!—tell ye, would n't I make em laugh? But how is it,—dis yer whole lot gwine tomorrow?" said Sambo, laying his hand freely on Adolph's shoulder.

"Please to let me alone!" said Adolph, fiercely, straightening himself up, with extreme disgust.

"Law, now, boys! dis yer's one o' yer white niggers,—kind o' cream color, ye know, scented!" said he, coming up to Adolph and snuffing. "O, Lor! he'd do for a tobaccer-shop; they could keep him to scent snuff! Lor, he'd keep a whole shop agwine,—he would!"

"I say, keep off, can't you?" said Adolph, enraged.

"Lor, now, how touchy we is,—we white niggers! Look at us, now!" and Sambo gave a ludicrous imitation of Adolph's manner; "here's de airs and graces. We's been in a good family, I specs."

"Yes," said Adolph; "I had a master that could have bought you all for old truck!"[3]

"Laws, now, only think," said Sambo, "the gentlemens that we is!"

"I belonged to the St. Clare family," said Adolph, proudly.

"Lor, you did! Be hanged if they ar' n't lucky to get shet of ye. Spects they 's gwine to trade ye off with a lot o' cracked tea-pots and sich like!" said Sambo, with a provoking grin.

Adolph, enraged at this taunt, flew furiously at his adversary, swearing and striking on every side of him. The rest laughed and shouted, and the uproar brought the keeper to the door.

"What now, boys? Order,—order!" he said, coming in and flourishing a large whip.

All fled in different directions, except Sambo, who, presuming on the favor which the keeper had to him as a licensed wag, stood his ground, ducking his head with a facetious grin, whenever the master made a dive at him.

"Lor, Mas'r, 'tan't us,—we's reglar stiddy,—it's these yer new hands; they's real aggravatin',—kinder pickin' at us, all time!"

The keeper, at this, turned upon Tom and Adolph, and distributing a few kicks and cuffs without much inquiry, and leaving general orders for all to be good boys and go to sleep, left the apartment.

While this scene was going on in the men's sleeping-room, the reader may be curious to take a peep at the corresponding apartment allotted to the women. Stretched out in various attitudes over the floor, he may see numberless sleeping forms of every shade of complexion, from the purest ebony to white, and of all years, from childhood to old age, lying now asleep. Here is a fine bright girl, of ten years, whose mother was sold out yesterday, and who to-night cried herself to sleep when nobody was looking at her. Here, a worn old negress, whose thin arms and callous fingers tell of hard toil, waiting to be sold to-morrow, as a cast-off article, for what can be got for her; and some forty or fifty others, with heads variously enveloped in blankets or articles of clothing, lie stretched around them. But, in a corner, sitting apart from the rest, are two females of a more interesting appearance than common. One of these is a respectably-dressed mulatto woman between forty

3. Odds and end, trash.

and fifty, with soft eyes and a gentle and pleasing physiognomy. She has on her head a high-raised turban, made of a gay red Madras handkerchief, of the first quality, and her dress is neatly fitted, and of good material, showing that she has been provided for with a careful hand. By her side, and nestling closely to her, is a young girl of fifteen,—her daughter. She is a quadroon,[4] as may be seen from her fairer complexion, though her likeness to her mother is quite discernible. She has the same soft, dark eye, with longer lashes, and her curling hair is of a luxuriant brown. She also is dressed with great neatness, and her white, delicate hands betray very little acquaintance with servile toil. These two are to be sold tomorrow, in the same lot with the St. Clare servants; and the gentleman to whom they belong, and to whom the money for their sale is to be transmitted, is a member of a Christian church in New York, who will receive the money, and go thereafter to the sacrament of his Lord and theirs, and think no more of it.

These two, whom we shall call Susan and Emmeline, had been the personal attendants of an amiable and pious lady of New Orleans, by whom they had been carefully and piously instructed and trained. They had been taught to read and write, diligently instructed in the truths of religion, and their lot had been as happy an one as in their condition it was possible to be. But the only son of their protectress had the management of her property; and, by carelessness and extravagance involved it to a large amount, and at last failed. One of the largest creditors was the respectable firm of B. & Co., in New York. B & Co. wrote to their lawyer in New Orleans, who attached the real estate (these two articles and a lot of plantation hands formed the most valuable part of it), and wrote word to that effect to New York. Brother B., being, as we have said, a Christian man, and a resident in a free State, felt some uneasiness on the subject. He didn't like trading in slaves and souls of men,—of course, he didn't; but, then, there were thirty thousand dollars in the case, and that was rather too much money to be lost for a principle; and so, after much considering, and asking advice from those that he knew would advise to suit him, Brother B. wrote to his lawyer to dispose of the business in the way that seemed to him the most suitable, and remit the proceeds.

The day after the letter arrived in New Orleans, Susan and Emmeline were attached, and sent to the depot to await a general auction on the following morning; and as they glimmer faintly upon us in the moonlight which steals through the grated window, we may listen to their conversation. Both are weeping, but each quietly, that the other may not hear.

"Mother, just lay your head on my lap, and see if you can't sleep a little," says the girl, trying to appear calm.

"I haven't any heart to sleep, Em; I can't; it's the last night we may be together!"

"O, mother, don't say so! perhaps we shall get sold together,—who knows?"

"If 't was anybody's else case, I should say so, too, Em," said the woman; "but I'm so feard of losin' you that I don't see anything but the danger."

"Why, mother, the man said we were both likely, and would sell well."

Susan remembered the man's looks and words. With a deadly sickness at her heart, she remembered how he had looked at Emmeline's hands, and lifted up her curly hair, and pronounced her a first-rate article. Susan had

been trained as a Christian, brought up in the daily reading of the Bible, and had the same horror of her child's being sold to a life of shame that any other Christian mother might have; but she had no hope,—no protection.

"Mother, I think we might do first rate, if you could get a place as cook, and I as chamber-maid or seamstress, in some family. I dare say we shall. Let's both look as bright and lively as we can, and tell all we can do, and perhaps we shall," said Emmeline.

"I want you to brush your hair all back straight, tomorrow," said Susan.

"What for, mother? I don't look near so well, that way."

"Yes, but you'll sell better so."

"I don't see why!" said the child.

"Respectable families would be more apt to buy you, if they saw you looked plain and decent, as if you wasn't trying to look handsome. I know their ways better 'n you do," said Susan.

"Well, mother, then I will."

"And, Emmeline, if we shouldn't ever see each other again, after tomorrow,—if I'm sold way up on a plantation somewhere, and you somewhere else,—always remember how you've been brought up, and all Missis has told you; take your Bible with you, and your hymn-book; and if you're faithful to the Lord, he'll be faithful to you."

So speaks the poor soul, in sore discouragement; for she knows that tomorrow any man, however vile and brutal, however godless and merciless, if he only has money to pay for her, may become owner of her daughter, body and soul; and then, how is the child to be faithful? She thinks of all this, as she holds her daughter in her arms, and wishes that she were not handsome and attractive. It seems almost an aggravation to her to remember how purely and piously, how much above the ordinary lot, she has been brought up. But she has no resort but to *pray*; and many such prayers to God have gone up from those same trim, neatly-arranged, respectable slave-prisons,—prayers which God has not forgotten, as a coming day shall show; for it is written, "Who causeth one of these little ones to offend, it were better for him that a mill-stone were hanged about his neck, and that he were drowned in the depths of the sea."[5]

The soft, earnest, quiet moonbeam looks in fixedly, marking the bars of the grated windows on the prostrate, sleeping forms. The mother and daughter are singing together a wild and melancholy dirge, common as a funeral hymn among the slaves:

> "O, where is weeping Mary?
> O, where is weeping Mary?
> 'Rived in the goodly land.
> She is dead and gone to Heaven;
> She is dead and gone to Heaven;
> 'Rived in the goodly land."

These words, sung by voices of a peculiar and melancholy sweetness, in an air which seemed like the sighing of earthly despair after heavenly hope, floated through the dark prison rooms with a pathetic cadence, as verse after verse was breathed out:

5. Compare Luke 17.2: "It were better for him that a millstone were hanged about his neck, and he cast into the sea."

"O, where are Paul and Silas?
O, where are Paul and Silas?
Gone to the the goodly land.
They are dead and gone to Heaven;
They are dead and gone to Heaven;
'Rived in the goodly land."

Sing on, poor souls! The night is short, and the morning will part you forever!

But now it is morning, and everybody is astir; and the worthy Mr. Skeggs is busy and bright, for a lot of goods is to be fitted out for auction. There is a brisk look-out on the toilet; injunctions passed around to every one to put on their best face and be spry; and now all are arranged in a circle for a last review, before they are marched up to the Bourse.[6]

Mr. Skeggs, with his palmetto on and his cigar in his mouth, walks around to put farewell touches on his wares.

"How's this?" he said, stepping in front of Susan and Emmeline. "Where's your curls, gal?"

The girl looked timidly at her mother, who, with the smooth adroitness common among her class, answers,

"I was telling her, last night, to put up her hair smooth and neat, and not havin' it flying about in curls; looks more respectable so."

"Bother!" said the man, peremptorily, turning to the girl; "you go right along, and curl yourself real smart!" He added, giving a crack to a rattan he held in his hand, "And be back in quick time, too!"

"You go and help her," he added, to the mother. "Them curls may make a hundred dollars difference in the sale of her."

Beneath a splendid dome were men of all nations, moving to and fro, over the marble pave. On every side of the circular area were little tribunes, or stations, for the use of speakers and auctioneers. Two of these, on opposite sides of the area, were now occupied by brilliant and talented gentlemen, enthusiastically forcing up, in English and French commingled, the bids of connoisseurs in their various wares. A third one, on the other side, still unoccupied, was surrounded by a group, waiting the moment of sale to begin. And here we may recognize the St. Clare servants,—Tom, Adolph, and others; and there, too, Susan and Emmeline, awaiting their turn with anxious and dejected faces. Various spectators, intending to purchase, or not intending, as the case might be, gathered around the group, handling, examining, and commenting on their various points and faces with the same freedom that a set of jockeys discuss the merits of a horse.

"Hulloa, Alf! what brings you here?" said a young exquisite, slapping the shoulder of a sprucely-dressed young man, who was examining Adolph through an eye-glass.

"Well, I was wanting a valet, and I heard that St. Clare's lot was going. I thought I'd just look at his—"

"Catch me ever buying any of St. Clare's people! Spoilt niggers, every one. Impudent as the devil!" said the other.

"Never fear that!" said the first. "If I get 'em, I'll soon have their airs out of them; they'll soon find that they've another kind of master to deal with

6. Exchange, market.

than Monsieur St. Clare. 'Pon my word, I'll buy that fellow. I like the shape of him."

"You'll find it'll take all you've got to keep him. He's deucedly extravagant!"

"Yes, but my lord will find that he *can't* be extravagant with *me*. Just let him be sent to the calaboose[7] a few times, and thoroughly dressed down! I'll tell you if it don't bring him to a sense of his ways! O, I'll reform him, up hill and down,—you'll see. I buy him, that's flat!"

Tom had been standing wistfully examining the multitude of faces throng-ing around him, for one whom he would wish to call master. And if you should ever be under the necessity, sir, of selecting, out of two hundred men, one who was to become your absolute owner and disposer, you would, per-haps, realize, just as Tom did, how few there were that you would feel at all comfortable in being made over to. Tom saw abundance of men,—great, burly, gruff men; little, chirping, dried men; long-favored, lank, hard men; and every variety of stubbed-looking, commonplace men, who pick up their fellow-men as one picks up chips, putting them into the fire or a basket with equal unconcern, according to their convenience; but he saw no St. Clare.

A little before the sale commenced, a short, broad, muscular man, in a checked shirt considerably open at the bosom, and pantaloons much the worse for dirt and wear, elbowed his way through the crowd, like one who is going actively into a business; and, coming up to the group, began to examine them systematically. From the moment that Tom saw him approaching, he felt an immediate and revolting horror at him, that increased as he came near. He was evidently, though short, of gigantic strength. His round, bullet head, large, light-gray eyes, with their shaggy, sandy eye-brows, and stiff, wiry, sun-burned hair, were rather unprepossessing items, it is to be con-fessed; his large, coarse mouth was distended with tobacco, the juice of which, from time to time, he ejected from him with great decision and explo-sive force; his hands were immensely large, hairy, sun-burned, freckled, and very dirty, and garnished with long nails, in a very foul condition. This man proceeded to a very free personal examination of the lot. He seized Tom by the jaw, and pulled open his mouth to inspect his teeth; made him strip up his sleeve, to show his muscle; turned him round, made him jump and spring, to show his paces.

"Where was you raised?" he added, briefly, to these investigations.

"In Kintuck, Mas'r," said Tom, looking about, as if for deliverance.

"What have you done?"

"Had care of Mas'r's farm," said Tom.

"Likely story!" said the other, shortly, as he passed on. He paused a moment before Dolph; then spitting a discharge of tobacco-juice on his well-blacked boots, and giving a contemptuous umph, he walked on. Again he stopped before Susan and Emmeline. He put out his heavy, dirty hand, and drew the girl towards him; passed it over her neck and bust, felt her arms, looked at her teeth, and then pushed her back against her mother, whose patient face showed the suffering she had been going through at every motion of the hideous stranger.

The girl was frightened, and began to cry.

"Stop that, you minx!" said the salesman; "no whimpering here,—the sale is going to begin." And accordingly the sale begun.

7. Jail.

Adolph was knocked off, at a good sum, to the young gentleman who had previously stated his intention of buying him; and the other servants of the St. Clare lot went to various bidders.

"Now, up with you, boy! d 'ye hear?" said the auctioneer to Tom.

Tom stepped upon the block, gave a few anxious looks round; all seemed mingled in a common, indistinct noise,—the clatter of the salesman crying off his qualifications in French and English, the quick fire of French and English bids; and almost in a moment came the final thump of the hammer, and the clear ring on the last syllable of the word *"dollars,"* as the auctioneer announced his price, and Tom was made over.—He had a master!

He was pushed from the block;—the short, bullet-headed man seizing him roughly by the shoulder, pushed him to one side, saying, in a harsh voice, "Stand there, *you*!"

Tom hardly realized anything; but still the bidding went on,—rattling, clattering, now French, now English. Down goes the hammer again,—Susan is sold! She goes down from the block, stops, looks wistfully back,—her daughter stretches her hands towards her. She looks with agony in the face of the man who has bought her,—a respectable middle-aged man, of benevolent countenance.

"O, Mas'r, please do buy my daughter!"

"I'd like to, but I'm afraid I can't afford it!" said the gentleman, looking, with painful interest, as the young girl mounted the block, and looked around her with a frightened and timid glance.

The blood flushes painfully in her otherwise colorless cheek, her eye has a feverish fire, and her mother groans to see that she looks more beautiful than she ever saw her before. The auctioneer sees his advantage, and expatiates volubly in mingled French and English, and bids rise in rapid succession.

"I'll do anything in reason," said the benevolent-looking gentleman, pressing in and joining with the bids. In a few moments they have run beyond his purse. He is silent; the auctioneer grows warmer; but bids gradually drop off. It lies now between an aristocratic old citizen and our bullet-headed acquaintance. The citizen bids for a few turns, contemptuously measuring his opponent; but the bullet-head has the advantage over him, both in obstinacy and concealed length of purse, and the controversy lasts but a moment; the hammer falls,—he has got the girl, body and soul, unless God help her!

Her master is Mr. Legree, who owns a cotton plantation on the Red river. She is pushed along into the same lot with Tom and two other men, and goes off, weeping as she goes.

The benevolent gentleman is sorry; but, then, the thing happens every day! One sees girls and mothers crying, at these sales, *always*! it can't be helped, etc.; and he walks off, with his acquisition, in another direction.

Two days after, the lawyer of the Christian firm of B & Co., New York, sent on their money to them. On the reverse of that draft, so obtained, let them write these words of the great Paymaster, to whom they shall make up their account in a future day: *"When he maketh inquisition for blood, he forgetteth not the cry of the humble!"*[8]

1852

8. See Psalm 9.12.

The Minister's Housekeeper[1]

SCENE.—*The shady side of a blueberry-pasture.—Sam Lawson with the boys, picking blueberries.—Sam, loq.*[2]

"Wal, you see, boys, 't was just here,—Parson Carryl's wife she died along in the forepart o' March: my cousin Huldy she undertook to keep house for him. The way on 't was, that Huldy she went to take care o' Mis' Carryl in the fust on 't, when she fust took sick. Huldy was a tailoress by trade; but then she was one o' these 'ere facultized[3] persons that has a gift for most anything, and that was how Mis' Carryl come to set sech store by her, that, when she was sick, nothin' would do for her but she must have Huldy round all the time: and the minister he said he'd make it good to her all the same, and she shouldn't lose nothin' by it. And so Huldy she stayed with Mis' Carryl full three months afore she died, and got to seein' to everything pretty much round the place.

"Wal, arter Mis' Carryl died, Parson Carryl he'd got so kind o' used to hevin' on her round, takin' care o' things, that he wanted her to stay along a spell; and so Huldy she stayed along a spell, and poured out his tea, and mended his close, and made pies and cakes, and cooked and washed and ironed, and kep' everything as neat as a pin. Huldy was a dreeful chipper sort o' gal; and work sort o' rolled off from her like water off a duck's back. There wa'n't no gal in Sherburne that could put sich a sight o' work through as Huldy; and yet, Sunday mornin', she always come out in the singers' seat[4] like one o' these 'ere June roses, lookin' so fresh and smilin', and her voice was jest as clear and sweet as a meadow lark's—Lordy massy! I 'member how she used to sing some o' them 'ere places where the treble and counter[5] used to go together: her voice kind o' trembled a little, and it sort o' went through and through a feller! tuck him right where he lived!"

Here Sam leaned contemplatively back with his head in a clump of sweet-fern, and refreshed himself with a chew of young wintergreen. "This 'ere young wintergreen, boys, is jest like a feller's thoughts o' things that happened when he was young: it comes up jest so fresh and tender every year, the longest time you hev to live; and you can't help chawin' on 't though 't is sort o' stingin'. I don't never get over likin' young wintergreen."

"But about Huldah, Sam?"

"Oh yes! about Huldy. Lordy massy! when a feller is Indianin' round,[6] these 'ere pleasant summer days, a feller's thoughts gits like a flock o' young partridges: they's up and down and everywhere; 'cause one place is jest about as good as another, when they's all so kind o' comfortable and nice. Wal, about Huldy,—as I was a-sayin'. She was jest as handsome a gal to look at as a feller could have; and I think a nice, well-behaved young gal in the singers' seat of a Sunday is a means o' grace: it's sort o' drawin' to the unregenerate, you know. Why, boys, in them days, I've walked ten miles over to Sherburne of a Sunday mornin', jest to play the bass-viol in the same singers' seat with Huldy. She was very much respected, Huldy was; and, when she

1. This is part of a series of stories narrated by Sam Lawson, the village loafer in a New England town.
2. *Loquitur*; i.e., Sam speaks (Latin).
3. A hybrid word, apparently of Sam's invention,

meaning multitalented.
4. The pew in a church where the choir sits.
5. Harmony.
6. Loafing.

went out to tailorin', she was allers bespoke[7] six months ahead, and sent for in waggins up and down for ten miles round; for the young fellers was allers 'mazin' anxious to be sent after Huldy, and was quite free to offer to go for her. Wal, after Mis' Carryl died, Huldy got to be sort o' housekeeper at the minister's, and saw to everything, and did everything: so that there wa'n't a pin out o' the way.

"But you know how 'tis in parishes: there allers is women that thinks the minister's affairs belongs to them, and they ought to have the rulin' and guidin' of 'em; and, if a minister's wife dies, there's folks that allers has their eyes open on providences,[8]—lookin' out who's to be the next one.

"Now, there was Mis' Amaziah Pipperidge, a widder with snappin' black eyes, and a hook nose,—kind o' like a hawk; and she was one o' them up-and-down commandin' sort o' women, that feel that they have a call to be seein' to everything that goes on in the parish, and 'specially to the minister.

"Folks did say that Mis' Pipperidge sort o' sot her eye on the Parson for herself: wal, now that 'ere might 'a' been, or it might not. Some folks thought it was a very suitable connection. You see, she hed a good property of her own, right nigh to the minister's lot, and was allers kind o' active and busy; so, takin' one thing with another, I shouldn't wonder if Mis' Pipperidge should a thought that Providence p'inted that way. At any rate, she went up to Deakin[9] Blodgett's wife, and they two sort o' put their heads together a-mournin' and condolin' about the way things was likely to go on at the minister's now Mis' Carryl was dead. Ye see, the parson's wife, she was one of them women who hed their eyes everywhere and on everything. She was a little thin woman, but tough as Inger rubber,[1] and smart as a steel trap; and there wa'n't a hen laid an egg, or cackled, but Mis' Carryl was right there to see about it; and she hed the garden made in the spring, and the medders mowed in summer, and the cider made, and the corn husked, and the apples got in the fall; and the doctor, he hedn't nothin' to do but jest sit stock-still a-meditatin' on Jerusalem and Jericho and them things that ministers think about. But Lordy massy! he didn't know nothin' about where anything he eat or drunk or wore come from or went to: his wife jest led him round in temporal things[2] and took care on him like a baby.

"Wal, to be sure, Mis' Carryl looked up to him in spirituals, and thought all the world on him; for there wa'n't a smarter minister nowhere round. Why, when he preached on decrees and election,[3] they used to come clear over from South Parish, and West Sherburne, and Oldtown to hear him; and there was sich a row o' waggins tied along by the meetin'-house that the stables was all full, and all the hitchin'-posts was full clean up to the tavern, so that folks said the doctor made the town look like a gineral trainin' day[4] a Sunday.

"He was gret on texts, the doctor was. When he hed a p'int to prove, he'd jest go through the Bible, and drive all the texts ahead o' him like a flock o' sheep; and then, if there was a text that seemed agin him, why, he'd come

<hr />

7. Hired or engaged beforehand. "Went out to tailorin' ": hired herself out as a seamstress.
8. Opportunities, presumed to be "provided" by God.
9. Deacon, a church administrator.
1. India rubber.

2. Worldly matters, as opposed to the eternal.
3. Divine choice in Puritan theology, the belief in predestination.
4. Day for training or parade by a volunteer military company.

out with his Greek and Hebrew, and kind o' chase it round a spell, jest as ye see a feller chase a contrary bell-wether,[5] and make him jump the fence arter the rest. I tell you, there wa'n't no text in the Bible that could stand agin the doctor when his blood was up. The year arter the doctor was app'inted to preach the 'lection sermon in Boston, he made such a figger that the Brattle Street Church sent a committee right down to see if they couldn't get him to Boston; and then the Sherburne folks, they up and raised his salary; ye see, there ain't nothin' wakes folks up like somebody else's wantin' what you've got. Wal, that fall they made him a Doctor o' Divinity at Cambridge College,[6] and so they sot more by him than ever. Wal, you see, the doctor, of course he felt kind o' lonesome and afflicted when Mis' Carryl was gone; but railly and truly, Huldy was so up to everything about house, that the doctor didn't miss nothin' in a temporal way. His shirt-bosoms was pleated finer than they ever was, and them ruffles round his wrists was kep' like the driven snow; and there wa'n't a brack[7] in his silk stockin's, and his shoe-buckles was kep' polished up, and his coats brushed, and then there wa'n't no bread and biscuit like Huldy's; and her butter was like solid lumps o' gold; and there weren't no pies to equal hers; and so the doctor never felt the loss o' Mis' Carryl at table. Then there was Huldy allers oppisite to him, with her blue eyes and her cheeks like two fresh peaches. She was kind o' pleasant to look at; and the more the doctor looked at her the better he liked her; and so things seemed to be goin' on quite quiet and comfortable ef it hadn't been that Mis' Pipperidge and Mis' Deakin Blodgett and Mis' Sawin got their heads together a-talkin' about things.

" 'Poor man,' says Mis' Pipperidge, 'what can that child that he's got there do towards takin' the care of all that place? It takes a mature woman,' she says, 'to tread in Mis' Carryl's shoes.'

" 'That it does,' said Mis' Blodgett; 'and, when things once get to runnin' downhill, there ain't no stoppin' on 'em,' says she.

"Then Mis' Sawin she took it up. (Ye see, Mis' Sawin used to go out to dressmakin', and was sort o' jealous, 'cause folks sot more by Huldy than they did by her.) 'Well,' says she, 'Huldy Peters is well enough at her trade. I never denied that, though I do say I never did believe in her way o' makin' buttonholes; and I must say, if 't was the dearest friend I hed, that I thought Huldy tryin' to fit Mis' Kittridge's plum-colored silk was a clear piece o' presumption; the silk was jist sp'iled, so 't wa'n't fit to come into the meetin'-house.[8] I must say, Huldy's a gal that's always too ventersome about takin' 'sponsibilities she don't know nothin' about.'

" 'Of course she don't,' said Mis' Deakin Blodgett. 'What does she know about all the lookin' and seein' to that there ought to be in guidin' the minister's house. Huldy's well meanin', and she's good at her work, and good in the singers' seat; but Lordy massy! she hain't got no experience. Parson Carryl ought to have an experienced woman to keep house for him. There's the spring house-cleanin' and the fall house-cleanin' to be seen to, and the things to be put away from the moths; and then the gettin' ready for the Association[9] and all the ministers' meetin's; and the makin' the soap and the candles, and

5. The sheep that leads a flock.
6. Harvard University in Cambridge, Massachusetts.
7. Flaw.
8. House of worship.
9. Regional association of churches.

settin' the hens and turkeys, watchin' the calves, and seein' after the hired men and the garden; and there that 'ere blessed man jist sets there at home as serene, and has nobody round but that 'ere gal, and don't even know how things must be a-runnin' to waste!'

"Wal, the upshot on't was, they fussed and fuzzled and wuzzled[1] till they'd drinked up all the tea in the teapot; and then they went down and called on the parson, and wuzzled him all up talkin' about this, that, and t'other that wanted lookin' to, and that it was no way to leave everything to a young chit[2] like Huldy, and that he ought to be lookin' about for an experienced woman. The parson he thanked 'em kindly, and said he believed their motives was good, but he didn't go no further. He didn't ask Mis' Pipperidge to come and stay there and help him, nor nothin' o' that kind; but he said he'd attend to matters himself. The fact was, the parson had got such a likin' for havin' Huldy round, that he couldn't think o' such a thing as swappin' her off for the Widder Pipperidge.

"But he thought to himself, 'Huldy is a good girl; but I oughtn't to be a-leavin' everything to her,—it's too hard on her. I ought to be instructin' and guidin' and helpin' of her; 'cause't ain't everybody could be expected to know and do what Mis' Carryl did;' and so at it he went; and Lordy massy! didn't Huldy hev a time on't when the minister began to come out of his study, and want to tew round and see to things? Huldy, you see, thought all the world of the minister, and she was 'most afraid to laugh; but she told me she couldn't, for the life of her, help it when his back was turned, for he wuzzled things up in the most singular way. But Huldy she'd jest say, 'Yes, sir,' and get him off into his study, and go on her own way.

" 'Huldy,' says the minister one day, 'you ain't experienced outdoors; and, when you want to know anything, you must come to me.'

" 'Yes, sir,' says Huldy.

" 'Now, Huldy,' says the parson, 'you must be sure to save the turkey-eggs, so that we can have a lot of turkeys for Thanksgiving.'

" 'Yes, sir,' says Huldy; and she opened the pantry-door, and showed him a nice dishful she'd been a-savin' up. Wal, the very next day the parson's hen-turkey was found killed up to old Jim Scroggs's barn. Folks said Scroggs killed it; though Scroggs he stood to it he didn't: at any rate, the Scroggses they made a meal on't; and Huldy she felt bad about it, 'cause she'd set her heart on raisin' the turkeys; and says she, 'Oh, dear! I don't know what I shall do. I was just ready to set her.' "[3]

" 'Do, Huldy?' says the parson. 'Why, there's the other turkey, out there by the door; and a fine bird, too, he is.'

"Sure enough, there was the old tom-turkey a-struttin' and a-sidlin' and a-quitterin', and a-floutin' his tail-feathers in the sun, like a lively young widower, all ready to begin life over ag'in.

" 'But,' says Huldy, 'you know *he* can't set on eggs.'

" 'He can't? I'd like to know why,' says the parson. 'He shall set on eggs, and hatch 'em too.'

1. I.e., gossipped and worried.
2. Pert young woman.

3. I.e., allow her to hatch her eggs by sitting on them.

" 'O doctor!' says Huldy, all in a tremble; 'cause, you know, she didn't want to contradict the minister, and she was afraid she should laugh,—'I never heard that a tom-turkey would set on eggs.'

" 'Why, they ought to,' said the parson, getting quite 'arnest; 'what else be they good for? you just bring out the eggs, now, and put 'em in the nest, and I'll make him set on 'em.'

"So Huldy she thought there weren't no way to convince him but to let him try: so she took the eggs out, and fixed 'em all nice in the nest; and then she come back and found old Tom a-skirmishin' with the parson pretty lively, I tell ye. Ye see, old Tom he didn't take the idee at all; and he flopped and gobbled, and fit the parson; and the parson's wig got round so that his cue[4] stuck straight out over his ear, but he'd got his blood up. Ye see, the old doctor was used to carryin' his p'ints o' doctrine; and he hadn't fit the Arminians and Socinians[5] to be beat by a tom-turkey; so finally he made a dive, and ketched him by the neck in spite o' his floppin', and stroked him down, and put Huldy's apron round him.

" 'There, Huldy,' he says, quite red in the face, 'we've got him now;' and he *traveled* off to the barn with him as lively as a cricket.

"Huldy came behind jist chokin' with laugh, and afraid the minister would look round and see her.

" 'Now, Huldy, we'll crook his legs, and set him down,' says the parson, when they got him to the nest; 'you see he is getting quiet, and he'll set there all right.'

"And the parson he sot him down; and old Tom he sot there solemn enough, and held his head down all droopin', lookin' like a rail pious old cock, as long as the parson sot by him.

" 'There! you see how still he sets,' says the parson to Huldy.

"Huldy was 'most dyin' for fear she should laugh. 'I'm afraid he'll get up,' says she, 'when you do.'

" 'Oh no, he won't!' says the parson, quite confident. 'There, there,' says he, layin' his hands on him, as if pronouncin' a blessin'. But when the parson riz up, old Tom he riz up too, and began to march over the eggs.

" 'Stop, now!' says the parson. 'I'll make him get down ag'in: hand me that corn-basket; we'll put that over him.'

"So he crooked old Tom's legs, and got him down ag'in; and they put the corn-basket over him, and then they both stood and waited.

" 'That'll do the thing, Huldy,' said the Parson.

" 'I don't know about it,' says Huldy.

" 'Oh yes, it will, child! I understand,' says he.

"Just as he spoke, the basket rïz right up and stood, and they could see old Tom's long legs.

" 'I'll make him stay down, confound him,' says the parson; for, ye see, parsons is men, like the rest on us, and the doctor had got his spunk up.

" 'You just hold him a minute, and I'll get something that'll make him stay, I guess;' and out he went to the fence, and brought in a long, thin, flat stone, and laid it on old Tom's back.

4. I.e., queue—the braid of his wig.
5. Two religious sects that opposed parts of the Calvinist doctrine of religious faith.

"Old Tom he wilted down considerable under this, and looked railly as if he was goin' to give in. He stayed still there a good long spell, and the minister and Huldy left him there and come up to the house; but they hadn't more than got in the door before they see Tom a-hippin' along, as high-steppin' as ever, sayin', 'Talk! talk! and quitter! quitter!' and struttin' and gobblin' as if he'd come through the Red Sea, and got the victory.[6]

" 'Oh, my eggs!' says Huldy. 'I'm afraid he's smashed 'em!'

"And sure enough, there they was, smashed flat enough under the stone.

" 'I'll have him killed,' said the parson: 'we won't have such a critter round.'

"But the parson he slep' on't, and then didn't do it; he only come out next Sunday with a tiptop sermon on the 'Riginal Cuss' that was pronounced on things in gineral, when Adam fell,[7] and showed how everything was allowed to go contrary ever since. There was pigweed, and pusley, and Canady thistles, cut-worms, and bag-worms, and canker-worms, to say nothin' of rattle-snakes. The doctor made it very impressive and sort o' improvin'; but Huldy she told me, goin' home, that she hardly could keep from laughin' two or three times in the sermon when she thought of old Tom a-standin' up with the corn-basket on his back.

"Wal, next week Huldy she jist borrowed the minister's horse and side-saddle, and rode over to South Parish to her Aunt Bascome's,—Widder Bascome's, you know, that lives there by the trout-brook,—and got a lot o' turkey-eggs o' her, and come back and set a hen on 'em, and said nothin'; and in good time there was as nice a lot o' turkey-chicks as ever ye see.

"Huldy never said a word to the minister about his experiment, and he never said a word to her; but he sort o' kep' more to his books, and didn't take it on him to advise so much.

"But not long arter he took it into his head that Huldy ought to have a pig to be a-fattin' with the buttermilk. Mis' Pipperidge set him up to it; and jist then old Tim Bigelow, out to Juniper Hill, told him if he'd call over he'd give him a little pig.

"So he sent for a man, and told him to build a pig-pen right out by the well, and have it all ready when he came home with his pig.

"Huldy she said she wished he might put a curb round the well out there, because in the dark, sometimes, a body might stumble into it; and the parson he told him he might do that.

"Wal, old Aikin, the carpenter, he didn't come till most the middle of the arternoon; and then he sort o' idled, so that he didn't get up the well-curb till sundown; and then he went off and said he'd come and do the pig-pen next day.

"Wal, arter dark, Parson Carryl he driv into the yard, full chizel,[8] with his pig. He'd tied up his mouth to keep him from squealin'; and he see what he thought was the pig-pen,—he was rather near-sighted,—and so he ran and threw piggy over; and down he dropped into the water, and the minister put out his horse and pranced off into the house quite delighted.

6. Moses led the Israelites across the Red Sea and defeated the Egyptians, who pursued them (Exodus 14.19–31).
7. In Genesis Adam falls from grace by eating a fruit from the Tree of Knowledge, thus bringing the curse of death and labor on himself and his descendants (Genesis 3). " 'Riginal Cuss": Original Curse or Sin.
8. Full speed.

" 'There, Huldy, I've got you a nice little pig.'

" 'Dear me!' says Huldy: 'where have you put him?'

" 'Why, out there in the pig-pen, to be sure.'

" 'Oh dear me!' says Huldy: 'that's the well-curb. There ain't no pig-pen built,' says she.

" 'Lordy massy!' says the parson: 'then I've thrown the pig in the well!'

"Wal, Huldy she worked and worked, and finally she fished piggy out in the bucket, but he was dead as a door-nail; and she got him out o' the way quietly, and didn't say much; and the parson he took to a great Hebrew book in his study; and says he, 'Huldy, I ain't much in temporals,' says he. Huldy says she kind o' felt her heart go out to him, he was so sort o' meek and helpless and larned; and says she, 'Wal, Parson Carryl, don't trouble your head no more about it; I'll see to things;' and sure enough, a week arter there was a nice pen, all ship-shape, and two little white pigs that Huldy bought with the money for the butter she sold at the store.

" 'Wal, Huldy,' said the parson, 'you are a most amazin' child: you don't say nothin',' but you do more than most folks.'

"Arter that the parson set sich store by Huldy that he come to her and asked her about everything, and it was amazin' how everything she put her hand to prospered. Huldy planted marigolds and larkspurs, pinks and carnations, all up and down the path to the front door, and trained up mornin'-glories and scarlet-runners round the windows. And she was always a-gettin' a root here, and a sprig there, and a seed from somebody else,—for Huldy was one o' them that has the gift, so that ef you jist give 'em the leastest sprig of anything they make a great bush out of it right away; so that in six months Huldy had roses and geraniums and lilies, sich as it would a took a gardener to raise. The parson he took no notice at fust; but when the yard was all ablaze with flowers he used to come and stand in a kind o' maze[9] at the front door, and say, 'Beautiful, beautiful! Why, Huldy, I never see anything like it.' And then when her work was done arternoons, Huldy would sit with her sewin' in the porch, and sing and trill away till she'd draw the meadow larks and the bobolinks and the orioles to answer her, and the great big elm-tree overhead would get perfectly rackety with the birds; and the parson, settin' there in his study, would git to kind o' dreamin' about the angels, and golden harps, and the New Jerusalem;[1] but he wouldn't speak a word, 'cause Huldy she was jist like them wood-thrushes, she never could sing so well when she thought folks was hearin'. Folks noticed, about this time, that the parson's sermons got to be like Aaron's rod, that budded and blossomed;[2] there was things in 'em about flowers and birds, and more 'special about the music o' heaven. And Huldy she noticed, that ef there was a hymn run in her head while she was round a-workin' the minister was sure to give it out next Sunday. You see, Huldy was jist like a bee: she always sung when she was workin', and you could hear her trillin', now down in the corn-patch, while she was pickin' the corn; and now in the buttery, while she was

9. State of amazement.
1. Holy city where redeemed souls abide.
2. In Numbers 17.1–10 the high priest Aaron's rod is caused to blossom by Moses as a sign of God's favor to Aaron and the priests.

workin' the butter; and now she'd go singin' down cellar, and then she'd be singin' up overhead, so that she seemed to fill a house chock full o' music.

"Huldy was so sort o' chipper and fair-spoken that she got the hired men all under her thumb: they come to her and took her orders jist as meek as so many calves; and she traded at the store, and kep' the accounts, and she hed her eyes everywhere, and tied up all the ends so tight that there wa'n't no gettin' round her. She wouldn't let nobody put nothin' off on[3] Parson Carryl, 'cause he was a minister. Huldy was allers up to anybody that wanted to make a hard bargain; and, afore he knew jist what he was about, she'd got the best end of it, and everybody said that Huldy was the most capable gal that they'd ever traded with.

"Wal, come to the meetin' of the Association, Mis' Deakin Blodgett and Mis' Pipperidge come callin' up to the Parson's, all in a stew, and offerin' their services to get the house ready; but the doctor he jist thanked 'em quite quiet, and turned 'em over to Huldy; and Huldy she told 'em that she'd got everything ready, and showed 'em her pantries, and her cakes and her pies and her puddin's, and took 'em all over the house; and they went peekin' and pokin', openin' cupboard doors, and lookin' into drawers; and they couldn't find so much as a thread out o' the way, from garret to cellar, and so they went off quite discontented. Arter that the women set a new trouble a-brewin'. Then they begun to talk that it was a year now since Mis' Carryl died; and it railly wasn't proper such a young gal to be stayin' there, who everybody could see was a-settin' her cap for the minister.

"Mis' Pipperidge said that, so long as she looked on Huldy as the hired gal, she hadn't thought much about it; but Huldy was railly takin' on airs as an equal, and appearin' as mistress o' the house in a way that would make talk if it went on. And Mis' Pipperidge she driv round up to Deakin Abner Snow's, and down to Mis' Lijah Perry's, and asked them if they wasn't afraid that the way the parson and Huldy was a-goin' on might make talk. And they said they hadn't thought on't before, but now, come to think on't, they was sure it would; and they all went and talked with somebody else, and asked them if they didn't think it would make talk. So come Sunday, between meetin's there wa'n't nothin' else talked about; and Huldy saw folks a-noddin' and a-winkin', and a-look-in' arter her, and she begun to feel drefful sort o' disagreeable. Finally Mis' Sawin she says to her, 'My dear, didn't you never think folks would talk about you and the minister?'

" 'No: why should they?' says Huldy, quite innocent.

" 'Wal, dear,' says she, 'I think it's a shame; but they say you're tryin' to catch him, and that it's so bold and improper for you to be courtin' of him right in his own house,—you know folks will talk,—I thought I'd tell you 'cause I think so much of you,' says she.

"Huldy was a gal of spirit, and she despised the talk, but it made her drefful uncomfortable; and when she got home at night she sat down in the mornin'-glory porch, quite quiet, and didn't sing a word.

"The minister he had heard the same thing from one of his deakins that day; and when he saw Huldy so kind o' silent, he says to her, 'Why don't you sing, my child?'

3. Cheat.

"He hed a pleasant sort o' way with him, the minister had, and Huldy had got a likin' to be with him, and it all come over her that perhaps she ought to go away; and her throat kind o' filled up so she couldn't hardly speak; and, says she, 'I can't sing tonight.'

"Says he, 'You don't know how much good your singin' has done me, nor how much good *you* have done me in all ways, Huldy. I wish I knew how to show my gratitude.'

" 'O sir!' says Huldy, '*is* it improper for me to be here?'

" 'No dear,' says the minister, 'but ill-natured folks will talk; but there is one way we can stop it, Huldy—if you will marry me. You'll make me very happy, and I'll do all I can to make you happy. Will you?'

"Wal, Huldy never told me jist what she said to the minister,—gals never does give you the particulars of them 'ere things jist as you'd like 'em,—only I know the upshot and the hull on't was, that Huldy she did a consid'able lot o' clear starchin' and ironin' the next two days; and the Friday o' next week the minister and she rode over together to Dr. Lothrop's in Oldtown; and the doctor, he jist made 'em man and wife, 'spite of envy of the Jews,' as the hymn says.[4] Wal, you'd better believe there was a-starin' and a-wonderin' next Sunday mornin' when the second bell was a-tollin', and the minister walked up the broad aisle with Huldy, all in white, arm in arm with him, and he opened the minister's pew, and handed her in as if she was a princess; for, you see, Parson Carryl come of a good family, and was a born gentleman, and ad a sort o' grand way o' bein' polite to womenfolks. Wal, I guess there was a-rus'lin' among the bunnets. Mis' Pipperidge gin a great bounce, like corn poppin' on a shovel, and her eyes glared through her glasses at Huldy as if they'd'a' sot her afire; and everybody in the meetin'-house was a-starin', I tell yew. But they couldn't none of 'em say nothin' agin Huldy's looks; for there wa'n't a crimp nor a frill about her that wa'n't jis' so; and her frock was white as the driven snow, and she had her bunnet all trimmed up with white ribbins; and all the fellows said the old doctor had stole a march, and got the handsomest gal in the parish.

"Wal, arter meetin' they all come round the parson and Huldy at the door, shakin' hands and laughin'; for by that time they was about agreed that they'd got to let putty well alone.

" 'Why, Parson Carryl,' says Mis' Deakin Blodgett, 'how you've come it over us.'[5]

" 'Yes,' says the parson, with a kind o' twinkle in his eye. 'I thought,' says he, 'as folks wanted to talk about Huldy and me, I'd give 'em somethin' wuth talkin' about.' "

1872

4. Slightly misquoted from "Psalm 118" by Isaac Watts (1674–1748).

5. I.e., fooled or surprised us.

HARRIET JACOBS
ca. 1813–1897

"Slavery is terrible for men; but it is far more terrible for women. Superadded to the burden common to all, *they* have wrongs, and sufferings, and mortifications peculiarly their own": Harriet Jacobs, under the pseudonym "Linda Brent," dramatically documented this claim in her 1861 autobiography, *Incidents in the Life of a Slave Girl.* From her description of her sexual harassment by her owner, Dr. Flint, to her account of how she was prevented from marrying, Jacobs used her narrator and fictionalized surrogate, Brent, to analyze the wrongs inflicted on slave women. In spite of Victorian taboos against so-called indelicate subjects, she also explained why women like her were drawn into sexual relationships with white men other than their masters ("It seems less degrading to give one's self, than to submit to compulsion"), and the difficulty these women had in obtaining freedom for their children. Although both the names and the locations in her narrative are fictitious (to protect the safety of those who helped her), she deals directly with the racial impact of slave revolts like the Nat Turner uprising of 1831 and legislation like the Fugitive Slave Act of 1850, which subjected runaways in the North to forcible removal back to the South.

As the scholarship of Jean Fagan Yellin has demonstrated, Harriet Jacobs fashioned her life story into Linda Brent's first-person account of a heroic mother and a fallen woman who endured twenty-seven years of slavery. After the death of her parents, Brent was nurtured by her maternal grandmother, a freed slave of extraordinary industry and piety. At fifteen years of age, Brent began resisting her owner's efforts at sexual exploitation as well as his wife's harassment. Much to Dr. Flint's outrage, she gave birth to a son and a daughter, both fathered by a white man she calls Mr. Sands, who promised to buy them for her. Much of her narrative is taken up with her efforts to secure freedom from both Dr. Flint and Mr. Sands for herself and her children. More than ten years after her escape, Brent's author met the white historical novelist and abolitionist Lydia Maria Child, who introduced and edited Jacobs's account. "With trifling exceptions, both the ideas and the language are her own," Child explained, adding that Brent's first mistress taught her how to read and write. For both Child and Jacobs, the publication of *Incidents in the Life of a Slave Girl* was a political effort to help other "sisters in bondage."

Despite its pointed rhetorical aims, *Incidents in the Life of a Slave Girl* follows the real-life trajectory of its author. The father of Harriet Jacobs was a carpenter who, despite slavery, managed to live together with his wife in Edenton, North Carolina, until her death. At that time, in 1825, father and daughter were bought by Dr. and Mrs. James Norcom, the prototypes for the Flints. Possibly in an effort to gain protection, Harriet Jacobs became involved with the white attorney Samuel Tredwell Sawyer, the model for Mr. Sands, and they had two children. Like her fictionalized surrogate, Harriet Jacobs hid for years in the home of her maternal grandmother, escaped to the North, and later managed to arrange for the freedom of her children. In 1853, while she was beginning to compose her narrative, the white abolitionist family for whom Jacobs worked succeeded in freeing her from slavery. With the help of Lydia Maria Child, Harriet Jacobs published a book that received quite a bit of attention among antislavery groups in England and America, but that went out of print after the Civil War.

The first selections printed here record Linda Brent's efforts to grapple with the sexual jealousies and aggression of her owners. As the critic Hortense Spillers has pointed out in "Mama's Baby, Papa's Maybe," the slave girl becomes vulnerable to white female as well as white male modes of domination and surveillance. The next excerpts are taken from the point in the narrative when Linda Brent has convinced the Flints that she has fled to New York. Actually, after running away to a swamp,

where she encountered "large, venomous snakes [that] were less dreadful to my imagination than the white men in that community called civilization," she has hidden out in the same southern town in which the Flints and Mr. Sands live, at her grandmother's house. Determined to shield herself and her children from harm, she has not revealed to her son or daughter her presence in the house where they, too, are living.

From Incidents in the Life of a Slave Girl

Chapter V. The Trials of Girlhood

During the first years of my service in Dr. Flint's family, I was accustomed to share some indulgences with the children of my mistress. Though this seemed to me no more than right, I was grateful for it, and tried to merit the kindness by the faithful discharge of my duties. But I now entered on my fifteenth year—a sad epoch in the life of a slave girl. My master began to whisper foul words in my ear. Young as I was, I could not remain ignorant of their import. I tried to treat them with indifference or contempt. The master's age, my extreme youth, and the fear that his conduct would be reported to my grandmother, made him bear this treatment for many months. He was a crafty man, and resorted to many means to accomplish his purposes. Sometimes he had stormy, terrific ways, that made his victims tremble; sometimes he assumed a gentleness that he thought must surely subdue. Of the two, I preferred his stormy moods, although they left me trembling. He tried his utmost to corrupt the pure principles my grandmother had instilled. He peopled my young mind with unclean images, such as only a vile monster could think of. I turned from him with disgust and hatred. But he was my master. I was compelled to live under the same roof with him—where I saw a man forty years my senior daily violating the most sacred commandments of nature. He told me I was his property; that I must be subject to his will in all things. My soul revolted against the mean tyranny. But where could I turn for protection? No matter whether the slave girl be as black as ebony or as fair as her mistress. In either case, there is no shadow of law to protect her from insult, from violence, or even from death; all these are inflicted by fiends who bear the shape of men. The mistress, who ought to protect the helpless victim, has no other feelings towards her but those of jealousy and rage. The degradation, the wrongs, the vices, that grow out of slavery, are more than I can describe. They are greater than you would willingly believe. Surely, if you credited one half the truths that are told you concerning the helpless millions suffering in this cruel bondage, you at the north would not help to tighten the yoke. You surely would refuse to do for the master, on your own soil, the mean and cruel work which trained bloodhounds and the lowest class of whites do for him at the south.[1]

Every where the years bring to all enough of sin and sorrow; but in slavery the very dawn of life is darkened by these shadows. Even the little child, who is accustomed to wait on her mistress and her children, will learn, before she is twelve years old, why it is that her mistress hates such and such a one

1. A reference to the Fugitive Slave Law of 1850, which required citizens of free as well as slave states to assist in catching fugitive slaves, who were denied jury trials.

among the slaves. Perhaps the child's own mother is among those hated ones. She listens to violent outbreaks of jealous passion, and cannot help understanding what is the cause. She will become prematurely knowing in evil things. Soon she will learn to tremble when she hears her master's footfall. She will be compelled to realize that she is no longer a child. If God has bestowed beauty upon her, it will prove her greatest curse. That which commands admiration in the white woman only hastens the degradation of the female slave. I know that some are too much brutalized by slavery to feel the humiliation of their position; but many slaves feel it most acutely, and shrink from the memory of it. I cannot tell how much I suffered in the presence of these wrongs, nor how I am still pained by the retrospect. My master met me at every turn, reminding me that I belonged to him, and swearing by heaven and earth that he would compel me to submit to him. If I went out for a breath of fresh air, after a day of unwearied toil, his footsteps dogged me. If I knelt by my mother's grave, his dark shadow fell on me even there. The light heart which nature had given me became heavy with sad forebodings. The other slaves in my master's house noticed the change. Many of them pitied me; but none dared to ask the cause. They had no need to inquire. They knew too well the guilty practices under that roof; and they were aware that to speak of them was an offence that never went unpunished.

I longed for some one to confide in. I would have given the world to have laid my head on my grandmother's faithful bosom, and told her all my troubles. But Dr. Flint swore he would kill me, if I was not as silent as the grave. Then, although my grandmother was all in all to me, I feared her as well as loved her. I had been accustomed to look up to her with a respect bordering upon awe. I was very young, and felt shamefaced about telling her such impure things, especially as I knew her to be very strict on such subjects. Moreover, she was a woman of a high spirit. She was usually very quiet in her demeanor; but if her indignation was once roused, it was not very easily quelled. I had been told that she once chased a white gentleman with a loaded pistol, because he insulted one of her daughters. I dreaded the consequences of a violent outbreak; and both pride and fear kept me silent. But though I did not confide in my grandmother, and even evaded her vigilant watchfulness and inquiry, her presence in the neighborhood was some protection to me. Though she had been a slave, Dr. Flint was afraid of her. He dreaded her scorching rebukes. Moreover, she was known and patronized by many people;[2] and he did not wish to have his villainy made public. It was lucky for me that I did not live on a distant plantation, but in a town not so large that the inhabitants were ignorant of each other's affairs. Bad as are the laws and customs in a slaveholding community, the doctor, as a professional man, deemed it prudent to keep up some outward show of decency.

O, what days and nights of fear and sorrow that man caused me! Reader, it is not to awaken sympathy for myself that I am telling you truthfully what I suffered in slavery. I do it to kindle a flame of compassion in your hearts for my sisters who are still in bondage, suffering as I once suffered.

I once saw two beautiful children playing together. One was a fair white child; the other was her slave, and also her sister. When I saw them embracing each other, and heard their joyous laughter, I turned sadly away from

2. Brent's grandmother, who was freed late in her life, was an accomplished cook and seamstress.

the lovely sight. I foresaw the inevitable blight that would fall on the little slave's heart. I knew how soon her laughter would be changed to sighs. The fair child grew up to be a still fairer woman. From childhood to womanhood her pathway was blooming with flowers, and overarched by a sunny sky. Scarcely one day of her life had been clouded when the sun rose on her happy bridal morning.

How had those years dealt with her slave sister, the little playmate of her childhood? She, also, was very beautiful; but the flowers and sunshine of love were not for her. She drank the cup of sin, and shame, and misery, whereof her persecuted race are compelled to drink.

In view of these things, why are ye silent, ye free men and women of the north? Why do your tongues falter in maintenance of the right? Would that I had more ability! But my heart is so full, and my pen is so weak! There are noble men and women who plead for us, striving to help those who cannot help themselves. God bless them! God give them strength and courage to go on! God bless those, every where, who are laboring to advance the cause of humanity!

Chapter VI. The Jealous Mistress

I would ten thousand times rather that my children should be the half-starved paupers of Ireland[3] than to be the most pampered among the slaves of America. I would rather drudge out my life on a cotton plantation, till the grave opened to give me rest, than to live with an unprincipled master and a jealous mistress. The felon's home in a penitentiary is preferable. He may repent, and turn from the error of his ways, and so find peace; but it is not so with a favorite slave. She is not allowed to have any pride of character. It is deemed a crime in her to wish to be virtuous.

Mrs. Flint possessed the key to her husband's character before I was born. She might have used this knowledge to counsel and to screen the young and the innocent among her slaves; but for them she had no sympathy. They were the objects of her constant suspicion and malevolence. She watched her husband with unceasing vigilance; but he was well practised in means to evade it. What he could not find opportunity to say in words he manifested in signs. He invented more than were ever thought of in a deaf and dumb asylum. I let them pass, as if I did not understand what he meant; and many were the curses and threats bestowed on me for my stupidity. One day he caught me teaching myself to write. He frowned, as if he was not well pleased; but I suppose he came to the conclusion that such an accomplishment might help to advance his favorite scheme. Before long, notes were often slipped into my hand. I would return them, saying, "I can't read them, sir." "Can't you?" he replied; "then I must read them to you." He always finished the reading by asking, "Do you understand?" Sometimes he would complain of the heat of the tea room, and order his supper to be placed on a small table in the piazza. He would seat himself there with a well-satisfied smile, and tell me to stand by and brush away the flies. He would eat very slowly, pausing between the mouthfuls. These intervals were employed in describing the happiness I was so foolishly throwing away, and in threatening

3. The potato famine in Ireland (1845–50) killed a million or more people.

me with the penalty that finally awaited my stubborn disobedience. He boasted much of the forbearance he had exercised towards me, and reminded me that there was a limit to his patience. When I succeeded in avoiding opportunities for him to talk to me at home, I was ordered to come to his office, to do some errand. When there, I was obliged to stand and listen to such language as he saw fit to address to me. Sometimes I so openly expressed my contempt for him that he would become violently enraged, and I wondered why he did not strike me. Circumstanced as he was, he probably thought it was better policy to be forbearing. But the state of things grew worse and worse daily. In desperation I told him that I must and would apply to my grandmother for protection. He threatened me with death, and worse than death, if I made any complaint to her. Strange to say, I did not despair. I was naturally of a buoyant disposition, and always I had a hope of somehow getting out of his clutches. Like many a poor, simple slave before me, I trusted that some threads of joy would yet be woven into my dark destiny.

I had entered my sixteenth year, and every day it became more apparent that my presence was intolerable to Mrs. Flint. Angry words frequently passed between her and her husband. He had never punished me himself, and he would not allow any body else to punish me. In that respect, she was never satisfied; but, in her angry moods, no terms were too vile for her to bestow upon me. Yet I, whom she detested so bitterly, had far more pity for her than he had, whose duty it was to make her life happy. I never wronged her, or wished to wrong her; and one word of kindness from her would have brought me to her feet.

After repeated quarrels between the doctor and his wife, he announced his intention to take his youngest daughter, then four years old, to sleep in his apartment.[4] It was necessary that a servant should sleep in the same room, to be on hand if the child stirred. I was selected for that office, and informed for what purpose that arrangement had been made. By managing to keep within sight of people, as much as possible, during the day time, I had hitherto succeeded in eluding my master, though a razor was often held to my throat to force me to change this line of policy. At night I slept by the side of my great aunt, where I felt safe. He was too prudent to come into her room. She was an old woman, and had been in the family many years. Moreover, as a married man, and a professional man, he deemed it necessary to save appearances in some degree. But he resolved to remove the obstacle in the way of his scheme; and he thought he had planned it so that he should evade suspicion. He was well aware how much I prized my refuge by the side of my old aunt, and he determined to dispossess me of it. The first night the doctor had the little child in his room alone. The next morning, I was ordered to take my station as nurse the following night. A kind Providence interposed in my favor. During the day Mrs. Flint heard of this new arrangement, and a storm followed. I rejoiced to hear it rage.

After a while my mistress sent for me to come to her room. Her first question was, "Did you know you were to sleep in the doctor's room?"

"Yes, ma'am."

"Who told you?"

"My master."

4. Room.

"Will you answer truly all the questions I ask?"

"Yes, ma'am."

"Tell me, then, as you hope to be forgiven, are you innocent of what I have accused you?"

"I am."

She handed me a Bible, and said, "Lay your hand on your heart, kiss this holy book, and swear before God that you tell me the truth."

I took the oath she required, and I did it with a clear conscience.

"You have taken God's holy word to testify your innocence," said she. "If you have deceived me, beware! Now take this stool, sit down, look me directly in the face, and tell me all that has passed between your master and you."

I did as she ordered. As I went on with my account her color changed frequently, she wept, and sometimes groaned. She spoke in tones so sad, that I was touched by her grief. The tears came to my eyes; but I was soon convinced that her emotions arose from anger and wounded pride. She felt that her marriage vows were desecrated, her dignity insulted; but she had no compassion for the poor victim of her husband's perfidy. She pitied herself as a martyr; but she was incapable of feeling for the condition of shame and misery in which her unfortunate, helpless slave was placed.

Yet perhaps she had some touch of feeling for me; for when the conference was ended, she spoke kindly, and promised to protect me. I should have been much comforted by this assurance if I could have had confidence in it; but my experiences in slavery had filled me with distrust. She was not a very refined woman, and had not much control over her passions. I was an object of her jealousy, and, consequently, of her hatred; and I knew I could not expect kindness or confidence from her under the circumstances in which I was placed. I could not blame her. Slaveholders' wives feel as other women would under similar circumstances. The fire of her temper kindled from small sparks, and now the flame became so intense that the doctor was obliged to give up his intended arrangement.

I knew I had ignited the torch, and I expected to suffer for it afterwards; but I felt too thankful to my mistress for the timely aid she rendered me to care much about that. She now took me to sleep in a room adjoining her own. There I was an object of her especial care, though not of her especial comfort, for she spent many a sleepless night to watch over me. Sometimes I woke up, and found her bending over me. At other times she whispered in my ear, as though it was her husband who was speaking to me, and listened to hear what I would answer. If she startled me, on such occasions, she would glide stealthily away; and the next morning she would tell me I had been talking in my sleep, and ask who I was talking to. At last, I began to be fearful for my life. It had been often threatened; and you can imagine, better than I can describe, what an unpleasant sensation it must produce to wake up in the dead of night and find a jealous woman bending over you. Terrible as this experience was, I had fears that it would give place to one more terrible.

My mistress grew weary of her vigils; they did not prove satisfactory. She changed her tactics. She now tried the trick of accusing my master of crime, in my presence, and gave my name as the author of the accusation. To my utter astonishment, he replied, "I don't believe it: but if she did acknowledge it, you tortured her into exposing me." Tortured into exposing him! Truly, Satan had no difficulty in distinguishing the color of his soul! I understood

his object in making this false representation. It was to show me that I gained nothing by seeking the protection of my mistress; that the power was still all in his own hands. I pitied Mrs. Flint. She was a second wife, many years the junior of her husband; and the hoary-headed miscreant was enough to try the patience of a wiser and better woman. She was completely foiled, and knew not how to proceed. She would gladly have had me flogged for my supposed false oath; but, as I have already stated, the doctor never allowed any one to whip me. The old sinner was politic. The application of the lash might have led to remarks that would have exposed him in the eyes of his children and grandchildren. How often did I rejoice that *I* lived in a town where all the inhabitants knew each other! If I had been on a remote plantation, or lost among the multitude of a crowded city, I should not be a living woman at this day.

The secrets of slavery are concealed like those of the Inquisition.[5] My master was, to my knowledge, the father of eleven slaves. But did the mothers dare to tell who was the father of their children? Did the other slaves dare to allude to it, except in whispers among themselves? No, indeed! They knew too well the terrible consequences.

My grandmother could not avoid seeing things which excited her suspicions. She was uneasy about me, and tried various ways to buy me; but the never changing answer was always repeated: "Linda does not belong to *me*. She is my daughter's property, and I have no legal right to sell her." The conscientious man! He was too scrupulous to *sell* me; but he had no scruples whatever about committing a much greater wrong against the helpless young girl placed under his guardianship, as his daughter's property. Sometimes my persecutor would ask me whether I would like to be sold. I told him I would rather be sold to any body than to lead such a life as I did. On such occasions he would assume the air of a very injured individual, and reproach me for my ingratitude. "Did I not take you into the house, and make you the companion of my own children?" he would say. "Have I ever treated you like a negro? I have never allowed you to be punished, not even to please your mistress. And this is the recompense I get, you ungrateful girl!" I answered that he had reasons of his own for screening me from punishment, and that the course he pursued made my mistress hate me and persecute me. If I wept, he would say, "Poor child! Don't cry! don't cry! I will make peace for you with your mistress. Only let me arrange matters in my own way. Poor, foolish girl! you don't know what is for your own good. I would cherish you. I would make a lady of you. Now go, and think of all I have promised you."

I did think of it.

Reader, I draw no imaginary pictures of southern homes. I am telling you the plain truth. Yet when victims make their escape from this wild beast of Slavery, northerners consent to act the part of bloodhounds, and hunt the poor fugitive back into his den, "full of dead men's bones, and all uncleanness."[6] Nay, more, they are not only willing, but proud, to give their daughters in marriage to slaveholders. The poor girls have romantic notions of a sunny clime, and of the flowering vines that all the year round shade a happy home.

5. The Inquisition—a medieval tribunal established by the Catholic Church to investigate heresy—always conducted trials secretly.

6. Jesus' denunciation of the scribes and Pharisees as hypocrites (Matthew 23.27).

To what disappointments are they destined! The young wife soon learns that the husband in whose hands she has placed her happiness pays no regard to his marriage vows. Children of every shade of complexion play with her own fair babies, and too well she knows that they are born unto him of his own household. Jealousy and hatred enter the flowery home, and it is ravaged of its loveliness.

Southern women often marry a man knowing that he is the father of many little slaves. They do not trouble themselves about it. They regard such children as property, as marketable as the pigs on the plantation; and it is seldom that they do not make them aware of this by passing them into the slave-trader's hands as soon as possible, and thus getting them out of their sight. I am glad to say there are some honorable exceptions.

I have myself known two southern wives who exhorted their husbands to free those slaves towards whom they stood in a "parental relation;" and their request was granted. These husbands blushed before the superior nobleness of their wives' natures. Though they had only counselled them to do that which it was their duty to do, it commanded their respect, and rendered their conduct more exemplary. Concealment was at an end, and confidence took the place of distrust.

Though this bad institution deadens the moral sense, even in white women, to a fearful extent, it is not altogether extinct. I have heard southern ladies say of Mr. Such a one, "He not only thinks it no disgrace to be the father of those little niggers, but he is not ashamed to call himself their master. I declare, such things ought not to be tolerated in any decent society!"

Chapter XXI. The Loophole of Retreat

A small shed had been added to my grandmother's house years ago. Some boards were laid across the joists at the top, and between these boards and the roof was a very small garret, never occupied by anything but rats and mice. It was a pent[7] roof, covered with nothing but shingles, according to the southern custom for such buildings. The garret was only nine feet long and seven wide. The highest part was three feet high, and sloped down abruptly to the loose board floor. There was no admission for either light or air. My uncle Phillip, who was a carpenter, had very skilfully made a concealed trap-door, which communicated with the storeroom. He had been doing this while I was waiting in the swamp. The storeroom opened upon a piazza. To this hole I was conveyed as soon as I entered the house. The air was stifling; the darkness total. A bed had been spread on the floor. I could sleep quite comfortably on one side; but the slope was so sudden that I could not turn on the other without hitting the roof. The rats and mice ran over my bed; but I was weary, and I slept such sleep as the wretched may, when a tempest has passed over them. Morning came. I knew it only by the noises I heard; for in my small den day and night were all the same. I suffered for air even more than for light. But I was not comfortless. I heard the voices of my children. There was joy and there was sadness in the sound. It made my tears flow. How I longed to speak to them! I was eager to look on their faces;

7. Sloping.

but there was no hole, no crack, through which I could peep. This continued darkness was oppressive. It seemed horrible to sit or lie in a cramped position day after day, without one gleam of light. Yet I would have chosen this, rather than my lot as a slave, though white people considered it an easy one; and it was so compared with the fate of others. I was never cruelly overworked; I was never lacerated with the whip from head to foot; I was never so beaten and bruised that I could not turn from one side to the other; I never had my heel-strings cut to prevent my running away; I was never chained to a log and forced to drag it about, while I toiled in the fields from morning till night; I was never branded with hot iron, or torn by bloodhounds. On the contrary, I had always been kindly treated, and tenderly cared for, until I came into the hands of Dr. Flint. I had never wished for freedom till then. But though my life in slavery was comparatively devoid of hardships, God pity the woman who is compelled to lead such a life!

My food was passed up to me through the trap-door my uncle had contrived; and my grandmother, my uncle Phillip, and aunt Nancy would seize such opportunities as they could, to mount up there and chat with me at the opening. But of course this was not safe in the daytime. It must all be done in darkness. It was impossible for me to move in an erect position, but I crawled about my den for exercise. One day I hit my head against something, and found it was a gimlet. My uncle had left it sticking there when he made the trap-door. I was as rejoiced as Robinson Crusoe[8] could have been at finding such a treasure. It put a lucky thought into my head. I said to myself, "Now I will have some light. Now I will see my children." I did not dare to begin my work during the daytime, for fear of attracting attention. But I groped round; and having found the side next the street, where I could frequently see my children, I stuck the gimlet in and waited for evening. I bored three rows of holes, one above another; then I bored out the interstices between. I thus succeeded in making one hole about an inch long and an inch broad. I sat by it till late into the night, to enjoy the little whiff of air that floated in. In the morning I watched for my children. The first person I saw in the street was Dr. Flint. I had a shuddering, superstitious feeling that it was a bad omen. Several familiar faces passed by. At last I heard the merry laugh of children, and presently two sweet little faces were looking up at me, as though they knew I was there, and were conscious of the joy they imparted. How I longed to tell them I was there!

My condition was now a little improved. But for weeks I was tormented by hundreds of little red insects, fine as a needle's point, that pierced through my skin, and produced an intolerable burning. The good grandmother gave me herb teas and cooling medicines, and finally I got rid of them. The heat of my den was intense, for nothing but thin shingles protected me from the scorching summer's sun. But I had my consolations. Through my peeping-hole I could watch the children, and when they were near enough, I could hear their talk. Aunt Nancy brought me all the news she could hear at Dr. Flint's. From her I learned that the doctor had written to New York to a colored woman, who had been born and raised in our neighborhood, and had breathed his contaminating atmosphere. He offered her a reward if she could find out any thing about me. I know not what was the nature of her

8. Shipwrecked hero of the novel (1719) by Daniel Defoe. "Gimlet": a small tool used for boring holes.

reply; but he soon after started for New York in haste, saying to his family that he had business of importance to transact. I peeped at him as he passed on his way to the steamboat. It was a satisfaction to have miles of land and water between us, even for a little while; and it was a still greater satisfaction to know that he believed me to be in the Free States. My little den seemed less dreary than it had done. He returned, as he did from his former journey to New York, without obtaining any satisfactory information. When he passed our house next morning, Benny[9] was standing at the gate. He had heard them say that he had gone to find me, and he called out, "Dr. Flint, did you bring my mother home? I want to see her." The doctor stamped his foot at him in a rage, and exclaimed, "Get out of the way, you little damned rascal! If you don't, I'll cut off your head."

Benny ran terrified into the house, saying, "You can't put me in jail again. I don't belong to you now." It was well that the wind carried the words away from the doctor's ear. I told my grandmother of it, when we had our next conference at the trap-door; and begged of her not to allow the children to be impertinent to the irascible old man.

Autumn came, with a pleasant abatement of heat. My eyes had become accustomed to the dim light, and by holding my book or work in a certain position near the aperture I contrived to read and sew. That was a great relief to the tedious monotony of my life. But when winter came, the cold penetrated through the thin shingle roof, and I was dreadfully chilled. The winters there are not so long, or so severe, as in northern latitudes; but the houses are not built to shelter from cold, and my little den was peculiarly comfortless. The kind grandmother brought me bed-clothes and warm drinks. Often I was obliged to lie in bed all day to keep comfortable; but with all my precautions, my shoulders and feet were frostbitten. O, those long, gloomy days, with no object for my eye to rest upon, and no thoughts to occupy my mind, except the dreary past and the uncertain future! I was thankful when there came a day sufficiently mild for me to wrap myself up and sit at the loophole to watch the passers by. Southerners have the habit of stopping and talking in the streets, and I heard many conversations not intended to meet my ears. I heard slave-hunters planning how to catch some poor fugitive. Several times I heard allusions to Dr. Flint, myself, and the history of my children, who, perhaps, were playing near the gate. One would say, "I wouldn't move my little finger to catch her, as old Flint's property," Another would say, "I'll catch *any* nigger for the reward. A man ought to have what belongs to him, if he *is* a damned brute." The opinion was often expressed that I was in the Free States. Very rarely did any one suggest that I might be in the vicinity. Had the least suspicion rested on my grandmother's house, it would have been burned to the ground. But it was the last place they thought of. Yet there was no place, where slavery existed, that could have afforded me so good a place of concealment.

Dr. Flint and his family repeatedly tried to coax and bribe my children to tell something they had heard said about me. One day the doctor took them into a shop, and offered them some bright little silver pieces and gay handkerchiefs if they would tell where their mother was. Ellen shrank away from him, and would not speak; but Benny spoke up, and said, "Dr. Flint, I don't

9. Brent's son. Her daughter's name is Ellen.

know where my mother is. I guess she's in New York; and when you go there again, I wish you'd ask her to come home, for I want to see her; but if you put her in jail, or tell her you'll cut her head off, I'll tell her to go right back."

From *Chapter XXIX. Preparations for Escape*[1]

I hardly expect that the reader will credit me, when I affirm that I lived in that little dismal hole, almost deprived of light and air, and with no space to move my limbs, for nearly seven years. But it is a fact; and to me a sad one, even now; for my body still suffers from the effects of that long imprisonment, to say nothing of my soul. Members of my family, now living in New York and Boston, can testify to the truth of what I say.

Countless were the nights that I sat late at the little loophole scarcely large enough to give me a glimpse of one twinkling star. There, I heard the patrols and slave-hunters conferring together about the capture of runaways, well knowing how rejoiced they would be to catch me.

Season after season, year after year, I peeped at my children's faces, and heard their sweet voices, with a heart yearning all the while to say, "Your mother is here." Sometimes it appeared to me as if ages had rolled away since I entered upon that gloomy, monotonous existence. At times, I was stupefied and listless; at other times I became very impatient to know when these dark years would end, and I should again be allowed to feel the sunshine, and breathe the pure air. * * *

* * * My restlessness increased. I had lived too long in bodily pain and anguish of spirit. Always I was in dread that by some accident, or some contrivance, slavery would succeed in snatching my children from me. This thought drove me nearly frantic, and I determined to steer for the North Star[2] at all hazards. At this crisis, Providence opened an unexpected way for me to escape. My friend Peter came one evening, and asked to speak with me. "Your day has come, Linda," said he. "I have found a chance for you to go to the Free States. You have a fortnight to decide." The news seemed too good to be true; but Peter explained his arrangements, and told me all that was necessary was for me to say I would go.[3] * * *

The anticipation of being a free woman proved almost too much for my weak frame. The excitement stimulated me, and at the same time bewildered me. I made busy preparations for my journey, and for my son to follow me. I resolved to have an interview with him before I went, that I might give him cautions and advice, and tell him how anxiously I should be waiting for him at the north. Grandmother stole up to me as often as possible to whisper words of counsel. She insisted upon my writing to Dr. Flint, as soon as I arrived in the Free States, and asking him to sell me to her. She said she would sacrifice her house, and all she had in the world, for the sake of having me safe with my children in any part of the world. If she could only live to know *that* she could die in peace. I promised the dear old faithful friend that

1. In the omitted chapters, Brent reveals herself to her daughter, Ellen, who subsequently escapes to the North.
2. "This was the only guide of many a fleeing slave, hiding by day and running by night" [note by Walter Teller, editor of our text].

3. In the omitted passage, Brent at first hesitates to escape because of her son but is persuaded by her uncle Phillip to "seize the chance so unexpectedly offered"; Phillip also tells her grandmother.

I would write to her as soon as I arrived, and put the letter in a safe way to reach her; but in my own mind I resolved that not another cent of her hard earnings should be spent to pay rapacious slave-holders for what they called their property. And even if I had not been unwilling to buy what I had already a right to possess, common humanity would have prevented me from accepting the generous offer, at the expense of turning my aged relative out of house and home, when she was trembling on the brink of the grave.

I was to escape in a vessel; but I forbear to mention any further particulars.[4] * * *

I made all my arrangements to go on board as soon as it was dusk. The intervening time I resolved to spend with my son. I had not spoken to him for seven years, though I had been under the same roof, and seen him every day, when I was well enough to sit at the loophole. I did not dare to venture beyond the storeroom; so they brought him there, and locked us up together, in a place concealed from the piazza door. It was an agitating interview for both of us. After we had talked and wept together for a little while, he said, "Mother, I'm glad you're going away. I wish I could go with you. I knew you was here; and I have been so afraid they would come and catch you!"

I was greatly surprised, and asked him how he had found it out.

He replied, "I was standing under the eaves, one day, before Ellen went away, and I heard somebody cough up over the wood shed. I don't know what made me think it was you, but I did think so. I missed Ellen, the night before she went away; and grandmother brought her back into the room in the night;[5] and I thought maybe she'd been to see *you*, before she went, for I heard grandmother whisper to her, 'Now go to sleep; and remember never to tell.'"

I asked him if he ever mentioned his suspicions to his sister. He said he never did; but after he heard the cough, if he saw her playing with other children on that side of the house, he always tried to coax her round to the other side, for fear they would hear me cough, too. He said he had kept a close lookout for Dr. Flint, and if he saw him speak to a constable, or a patrol, he always told grandmother. I now recollected that I had seen him manifest uneasiness, when people were on that side of the house, and I had at the time been puzzled to conjecture a motive for his actions. Such prudence may seem extraordinary in a boy of twelve years, but slaves, being surrounded by mysteries, deceptions, and dangers, early learn to be suspicious and watchful, and prematurely cautious and cunning. He had never asked a question of grandmother, or uncle Phillip, and I had often heard him chime in with other children, when they spoke of my being at the north.

I told him I was now really going to the Free States, and if he was a good, honest boy, and a loving child to his dear old grandmother, the Lord would bless him, and bring him to me, and we and Ellen would live together.

1861

4. In the omitted passage, Brent's grandmother is frightened by the murder of another fugitive slave. Brent, therefore, at first decides to remain with her grandmother and sends her friend Fanny to the ship in her place; Brent is, however, discovered by a neighbor when talking to her grandmother, who now tells her that she must go, too.
5. Ellen had spent her last night in North Carolina with her mother.

ELIZABETH CADY STANTON
1815–1902

"In thought and sympathy we were one," Elizabeth Cady Stanton wrote about herself and Susan B. Anthony, "and in the division of labor we exactly complemented each other. I am the better writer, she the better critic. She supplied the facts and statistics, I the philosophy and rhetoric, and, together, we have made arguments that stood unshaken through the storms of long years; arguments that no one has answered. Our speeches may be considered the united product of our two brains." Through Anthony's efficiency and Stanton's eloquence, these two reformers managed to dislodge feminist demands from the margins of other liberal movements. As different as they were temperamentally, together they formed the National Woman Suffrage Association (NWSA), which shaped the women's movement in America.

The woman who took literary responsibility for this effective collaboration was the fourth child of Daniel and Margaret (Livingston) Cady. After studying at home in Johnstown, New York, at the Johnstown Academy, and later at Emma Willard's Troy Female Seminary, Elizabeth Cady married Henry Brewster Stanton, a journalist and reformer, in 1840, and they attended the World Anti-Slavery Convention in London on their honeymoon. There, with Lucretia Mott, Stanton became involved in a protest against the exclusion of women delegates, and planned a women's rights convention that was to take place on July 19, 1848, at Seneca Falls, New York. Stanton's draft of the "Declaration of Sentiments" for the Seneca Falls Convention initiated a writing career that included the articles she published under the pseudonym "Sun Flower" in Amelia Bloomer's paper, the *Lily,* and the numerous speeches she delivered first in New York and later during several trips to the western states, tours that were undertaken, in part, to finance the education of her seven children. Stanton had met Anthony in 1851, when they began working together in the temperance and abolitionist movements. Before, during, and after the Civil War, they devoted themselves to the cause of women, organizing women's rights conventions and editing the weekly paper *Revolution.* As the president of NWSA for twenty-one years, Stanton became the major spokesperson for the women's movement. After the death of her husband in 1887, she extended her interest beyond suffrage, especially in her controversial feminist critique of the masculine bias in Judeo-Christian tradition, *The Woman's Bible* (1895, 1898). At this time, too, she published her lively autobiography, *Eighty Years and More* (1898). She continued lecturing on divorce, religion, and women's rights until she died in her sleep at the age of eighty-six, just after writing a letter to President Theodore Roosevelt in which she urged him to support women's suffrage.

✗ *From* Address to the New York State Legislature, 1860[1]

You who have read the history of nations, from Moses[2] down to our last election, where have you ever seen one class looking after the interests of another? Any of you can readily see the defects in other governments, and pronounce sentence against those who have sacrificed the masses to themselves; but when we come to our own case, we are blinded by custom and

1. This speech, delivered by Stanton, was the result of intense collaboration with Susan B. Anthony. Anthony declared that it was up to Stanton to "move the hearts of our law-makers at this time"; moreover, she came to live with Stanton to write the speech with her and to help in the household.
2. Biblical leader who guided the Israelites out of Egypt to the Promised Land.

self-interest. Some of you who have no capital can see the injustice which the laborer suffers; some of you who have no slaves, can see the cruelty of his oppression; but who of you appreciate the galling humiliation, the refinements of degradation, to which women (the mothers, wives, sisters, and daughters of freemen) are subject, in this the last half of the nineteenth century? How many of you have ever read even the laws concerning them that now disgrace your statute-books? In cruelty and tyranny, they are not surpassed by any slaveholding code in the Southern states; in fact they are worse, by just so far as woman, from her social position, refinement, and education, is on a more equal ground with the oppressor.

Allow me just here to call the attention of that party now so much interested in the slave of the Carolinas, to the similarity in his condition and that of the mothers, wives, and daughters of the Empire State.[3] The Negro has no name. He is Cuffy Douglas or Cuffy Brooks, just whose Cuffy he may chance to be. The woman has no name. She is Mrs. Richard Roe or Mrs. John Doe, just whose Mrs. she may chance to be. Cuffy has no right to his earnings; he can not buy or sell, or lay up anything that he can call his own. Mrs. Roe has no right to her earnings; she can neither buy nor sell, make contracts, nor lay up anything that she can call her own. Cuffy has no right to his children; they can be sold from him at any time. Mrs. Roe has no right to her children; they may be bound out to cancel a father's debts of honor. The unborn child, even, by the last will of the father, may be placed under the guardianship of a stranger and a foreigner. Cuffy has no legal existence; he is subject to restraint and moderate chastisement. Mrs. Roe has no legal existence; she has not the best right to her own person. The husband has the power to restrain, and administer moderate chastisement.

Blackstone[4] declares that the husband and wife are one, and learned commentators have decided that that one is the husband. In all civil codes, you will find them classified as one. Certain rights and immunities, such and such privileges are to be secured to white male citizens. What have women and Negroes to do with rights? What know they of government, war, or glory?

The prejudice against color, of which we hear so much, is no stronger than that against sex. It is produced by the same cause, and manifested very much in the same way. The Negro's skin and the woman's sex are both *prima facie* evidence that they were intended to be in subjection to the white Saxon man. The few social privileges which the man gives the woman, he makes up to the Negro in civil rights. The woman may sit at the same table and eat with the white man; the free Negro may hold property and vote. The woman may sit in the same pew with the white man in church; the free Negro may enter the pulpit and preach. Now, with the black man's right to suffrage, the right unquestioned, even by Paul, to minister at the altar,[5] it is evident that the prejudice against sex is more deeply rooted and more unreasonably maintained than that against color. * * *

Just imagine an inhabitant of another planet entertaining himself some pleasant evening in searching over our great national compact, our Declaration of Independence, our Constitutions, or some of our statute-books;

3. New York State.
4. Sir William Blackstone (1723–1780), author of the influential *Commentaries on the Laws of England* (1765–69), had articulated the principle that "by marriage the very being or legal existence of a woman is suspended."
5. In 1 Timothy 2.12, St. Paul refuses to allow "a woman to teach"; she must "be in silence."

what would he think of those "women and Negroes" that must be so fenced in, so guarded against? Why, he would certainly suppose we were monsters, like those fabulous giants or Brobdingnagians[6] of olden times, so dangerous to civilized man, from our size, ferocity, and power. Then let him take up our poets, from Pope down to Dana;[7] let him listen to our Fourth of July toasts, and some of the sentimental adulations of social life, and no logic could convince him that this creature of the law, and this angel of the family altar, could be one and the same being. Man is in such a labyrinth of contradictions with his marital and property rights; he is so befogged on the whole question of maidens, wives, and mothers, that from pure benevolence we should relieve him from this troublesome branch of legislation. We should vote, and make laws for ourselves. Do not be alarmed, dear ladies! You need spend no time reading Grotius, Coke, Puffendorf, Blackstone, Bentham, Kent, and Story[8] to find out what you need. We may safely trust the shrewd selfishness of the white man, and consent to live under the same broad code where he has so comfortably ensconced himself. Any legislation that will do for man, we may abide by most cheerfully. * * *

Now do not think, gentlemen, we wish you to do a great many troublesome things for us. We do not ask our legislators to spend a whole session in fixing up a code of laws to satisfy a class of most unreasonable women. We ask no more than the poor devils in the Scripture asked, "Let us alone."[9] In mercy, let us take care of ourselves, our property, our children, and our homes. True, we are not so strong, so wise, so crafty as you are, but if any kind friend leaves us a little money, or we can by great industry earn fifty cents a day, we would rather buy bread and clothes for our children than cigars and champagne for our legal protectors. There has been a great deal written and said about protection. We, as a class, are tired of one kind of protection, that which leaves us everything to do, to dare, and to suffer, and strips us of all means for its accomplishment. We would not tax man to take care of us. No, the Great Father has endowed all his creatures with the necessary powers for self-support, self-defense, and protection. We do not ask man to represent us; it is hard enough in times like these for man to carry backbone enough to represent himself. So long as the mass of men spend most of their time on the fence, not knowing which way to jump, they are surely in no condition to tell us where we had better stand. In pity for man, we would no longer hang like a mill-stone round his neck. Undo what man did for us in the Dark Ages, and strike out all special legislation for us; strike the words "white male" from all your constitutions, and then, with fair sailing, let us sink or swim, live or die, survive or perish together.

1860 1881

6. The race of giants in Jonathan Swift's *Gulliver's Travels* (1726).
7. Alexander Pope (1688–1744) and Richard Henry Dana Sr. (1787–1879), male authors who wrote about women either satirically or romantically.
8. All writers on the law: Hugo Grotius (Huigh de Groot, 1583–1645), Dutch scholar; Sir Edward

Coke (1552–1632), English jurist; Samuel von Puffendorf (1632–1694), German jurist and historian; Jeremy Bentham (1748–1832), English jurist and philosopher; James Kent (1763–1847), American jurist; and Joseph Story (1779–1845), American jurist.
9. Mark 1.24 (spoken by "an unclean spirit" possessing a man).

CHARLOTTE BRONTË
1816–1855

"Ten years ago we professed an orthodox system of novel-making. Our lovers were humble and devoted," remembered the Victorian journalist Margaret Oliphant in 1855, "when suddenly, without warning, *Jane Eyre* stole upon the scene, and the most alarming revolution of modern times has followed the invasion of *Jane Eyre*." When she spoke of "orthodox . . . novel-making," Oliphant no doubt meant to refer to the sentimental novels of manners that had been so popular in the earlier decades of the century. Certainly nothing could have been more different from such books than *Jane Eyre*. Indeed, although in our own century this revolutionary work has usually been thought of as a romance, the model for hundreds of best-selling love stories about darkly mysterious heroes and frail but feisty heroines, it is considerably more than that, as its first readers quickly understood. "Jane Eyre is throughout the personification of an unregenerate and undisciplined spirit," declared the reviewer Elizabeth Rigney in 1848, four years after the novel was published; and in 1853, another reviewer, Anne Mozley, recalled that the book seemed to many to have been written by "an alien . . . from society [who was] amenable to none of its laws."

The author of this electrifying best seller was born on April 21, 1816, the third child of Patrick Brontë, a clergyman of Irish descent, and his wife, Maria Branwell. In 1820, the family settled in the small Yorkshire town of Haworth, where the Reverend Brontë was curate of the local church. Both parents were evidently literary—Reverend Brontë produced several books of poetry, a novel, and a collection of sermons, and his wife wrote essays—but what might, despite modest means, have been a pleasant home became sorrowful when Mrs. Brontë died of cancer after giving birth to six children in rapid succession. Her husband tried in vain to remarry and finally invited his wife's sister, Elizabeth Branwell, to help care for his orphaned family. A strict and forbidding woman, "Aunt Branwell" lived with the Brontës until her death in 1842, but she seems never to have provided the warmth that they lost with their mother's death. Another catastrophe added further gloom to the household: in 1824, seeking to enrich his children's lives, Reverend Brontë sent his four oldest girls to Clergy Daughters' School at Cowan Bridge, a charitable institution for the daughters of impoverished clergymen that Charlotte Brontë was later to memorialize as *Jane Eyre*'s grim Lowood. By all accounts, her description in the novel was unfailingly accurate. Not only were the students subject to a tyrannical disciplinary system, they were so badly fed and housed that many became ill. Among the sickest were the Brontës. Maria and Elizabeth, the two oldest girls, succumbed to a combination of typhoid fever and consumption before their anxious relatives realized how dangerous conditions were; Charlotte and Emily were withdrawn from the school just in time to save their lives.

Isolated in their north England village on the edge of the Yorkshire moors, the four surviving children—Charlotte, Branwell, Emily, and Anne—drew together for comfort and eventually transformed Reverend Brontë's lonely parsonage into their own literary community. When their father brought Branwell a set of wooden soldiers, each child chose one, named it, and invented a history for it. Soon the tales they wove around these visionary beings evolved into a series of continuing fantasies about two imaginary kingdoms, "Angria" and "Gondal." Eventually, Branwell and Charlotte began to collaborate in recording the chronicles of Angria, while Emily and Anne transcribed the history of Gondal. Voracious readers, the four young scribes reproduced the styles and themes of writers they admired, most notably the popular Scottish novelist Sir Walter Scott and the Romantic poet Lord Byron, as well as the formats of journals like *Blackwood's,* in tiny volumes "printed" in a microscopic hand so as to look like miniaturized versions of real books.

What is more striking still, the Brontës continued creating and transcribing these romantic tales even after Charlotte had once again been sent away to school—this time, in 1831–32, to Roe Head, a far more comfortable and convenient establishment than Cowan Bridge had been—and even after she had returned to Roe Head in 1835 as a member of the teaching staff. In fact, in some ways Brontë's fantasizings about Angria intensified as she entered the workaday world of the schoolroom, where, as she noted, she had to toil in "irritation and weariness" to teach recalcitrant pupils "the distinction between an article and a substantive." Feeling herself trapped in "wretched bondage" to a career for which she had no natural vocation, she confided to her journal, "I should be agonised if I had not the dream [of Angria] to repose on," and in moments of "divine leisure" she transcribed the "fascinating spell" that the "infernal world" of her daydreams cast on her, writing in a kind of trance, with her eyes closed and her mind full of visions.

Despite Charlotte Brontë's sense that as a teacher or governess she was in "bondage," she knew that such jobs offered the only source of income to genteel but impoverished young women. As the unmarried daughter of a country clergyman with small means, Brontë had to find a way of supporting herself. Marriage was always, of course, a solution to a spinster's financial problems, but this independent young woman was determined to marry only a man she could respect, and though she had several proposals, none came from such a person. Inevitably, then, she was consigned to the schoolroom or the nursery. After teaching at Roe Head, she went on to several "situations" as private governess, and it is no doubt from these that she learned a truth that stands behind so many of the pained exclamations of her governess-heroine, Jane Eyre: "a private governess has no existence, is not considered as a living and rational being except as connected with the wearisome duties she has to fulfill."

In the summer of 1842, however, Charlotte Brontë and her younger sister Emily were suddenly given a chance for escape from such "wearisome duties." Troubled by her nieces' dilemma, the Brontës' severe Aunt Branwell quite unexpectedly offered them a small sum of money so that they could open a school of their own. But if they were to attempt such an enterprise, they would have to be better educated than they were, and so a second plan was set in motion: Charlotte and Emily were to be sent to Brussels, to a finishing school for young ladies called the Pensionnat Héger, where they would acquire the facility in foreign languages and the Continental polish that would fit them to be self-employed headmistresses.

Run by Constantin Héger, an impetuous but brilliant teacher, and his wife, Zoë, the daughter of a cultivated French emigré family, the Pensionnat was a small but exceptionally enlightened educational institution. It was here, however, that Charlotte Brontë found herself involved in real life in the kind of romantic struggle that she had up till now only encountered in her Angrian daydreams. For, perhaps within a few months of her arrival in Brussels, she began to fall in love with M. Héger, although, as a married man and a devout Catholic, he gave no sign of returning her feelings. At the end of a year, Aunt Branwell died and the sisters returned to Haworth, where Emily decided to stay and keep house for her father. But Charlotte could not repress her feelings; in the words of her fine biographer Winifred Gérin, she was drawn as by a "somnambulist's compulsion" to return to Brussels, where she spent a year as a teacher at the Pensionnat and where both the charisma and the increasing coolness of the "master" she loved gave her what was to become essential material for all four of her novels.

Those novels were not begun until two years after Charlotte had retreated to England in an effort to cure her unrequited passion. Still hoping to begin their school, the Brontë sisters drew up circulars and mailed them to prospective pupils, while in the meantime Charlotte wrote a series of pathetic letters to Héger, declaring that her correspondence with him was now her "only joy on earth." But there was little or no response to either the school circulars or the love letters. Not a single pupil expressed interest in "The Misses Brontë's Establishment," and Héger replied to Charlotte's

pleas for understanding at first with perfunctory friendliness and then with prolonged silence. By 1845, it was clear that this rebellious governess would not find redemption either in romance or in private enterprise. Her salvation lay in the writing that had always been her vocation, and in the community of imagination that she shared with her sisters, Anne and Emily.

It was Emily who provided the first impulse toward the creative resurrection that marked the years 1845 to 1848 for Charlotte Brontë. Accidentally discovering some of the verses the author-to-be of *Wuthering Heights* had been composing for years about the inhabitants of *her* fantasy kingdom, Gondal, Charlotte was struck by their distinctive intensity. Always decisive when she thought she saw a way out of the poverty in which the sisters were ensnared, she resolved at once to send the poems to a publisher, adding some works of her own and Anne's for good measure. Before doing so, she rechristened the three newly professional writers with noms de plume that were deliberately ambiguous in gender: Charlotte, Emily, and Anne Brontë became Currer, Ellis, and Acton Bell, ostensibly because, as Charlotte was somewhat disingenuously to explain later, "What author would be without the advantage of being able to walk invisible?" but more likely because women's works were not usually received with sufficient seriousness by reviewers.

The volume called *Poems by Currer, Ellis, and Acton Bell* was hardly received at all, in any case, for it sold only two copies in the year after its publication. Undaunted by this failure, however, the three Brontës turned to fiction, and here Charlotte's painful love for Héger, together with her years of transforming her daydreams about Angria into vivid romances, stood her in good stead. Her first novel, *The Professor* (published posthumously), drew directly on her experiences in Brussels, although it was told by a male narrator, as if its author were trying to disguise her own pain from herself. Her third novel, *Shirley* (1849), featured a hero who was a French tutor. Her fourth, *Villette* (1853), was set again in Brussels, and it was in good part devoted to an extraordinarily accurate portrait of the "master" she loved. Despite a surface realism, however, all three works were infused by Romantic and Gothic elements—dreams, visions, dramatic encounters—as well as by an energy of imagination that transformed biographical materials into compelling art.

But it was in Charlotte Brontë's second novel, *Jane Eyre* (1847), that all the elements of her life were most effectively transmuted into a powerful work of fiction. Her early trauma at Cowan Bridge, her hardships as a governess, and her love for Héger—all these experiences helped shape the fictional autobiography of a heroine who, like Brontë herself, seemed small, plain, and decorous even while her apparently "unregenerate spirit" brought about "the most alarming revolution of modern times." At the same time, this book in which a determined female narrator spoke with what was in 1847 surprising authority about a woman's desire for liberty—"for liberty I gasped; for liberty I uttered a prayer"—was also shaped and strengthened by a fantastic subplot for which there was no real-life precedent: the story of Bertha Mason Rochester. As if commenting on Jane's apparent decorum, Bertha's fierce mutterings and secret midnight wanderings suggest more sinister and subversive strategies to which women might be driven in their search for "liberty."

When *Jane Eyre* appeared, this unprecedented romance—combining an account of an independent woman's dreams and desires with a fantasy about explosive madness—took the reading public by storm. Shy by nature and profoundly unused to the sophistication of London circles, "Currer Bell" found herself almost overnight a literary lion. Years later Anne Ritchie, the daughter of the novelist William Makepeace Thackeray, still remembered her father's first meeting with the acclaimed author, and Elizabeth Gaskell reverently recorded her first impressions of Charlotte Brontë in a letter she later reprinted in her 1857 *Life of Charlotte Brontë*, noting that this new acquaintance appeared "to have gone through suffering enough to have taken out every spark of merriment, and to be shy and silent from the habit of extreme, intense solitude"—for indeed, added Gaskell, "Such a life as Miss Brontë's I never

heard of before," since the author dwelt "on the north side of a bleak moor, looking over sweeps of bleak moors" with the sky as a "companion." Despite the fact that she continued to live in the quiet isolation of Haworth, the governess who had seemed to have "no existence" had now a dramatic public life.

For Brontë herself, however, such success was bittersweet. Soon after the publication of *Jane Eyre,* her brother Branwell died in painful circumstances. Ostensibly an art student and painter, he had for years been both an alcoholic and a drug addict, and like his sister Charlotte but without her resilience, he had endured the pains of unrequited love. Within months, his death was followed by the deaths from tuberculosis of Emily and Anne. Bereft of the siblings who had constituted the only literary society she really wanted to join, Charlotte could not be consoled by her newly won fame. A determined survivor, she went on writing and keeping house for her father, but the Brontë parsonage was now lonelier and more sorrowful than ever, so that when Mrs. Gaskell visited in 1853 she was as struck by the silence as by the "exquisite" cleanliness of the household.

Perhaps in an attempt to cheer her solitude and her father's, Charlotte Brontë married Arthur Bell Nicholls, the Reverend Brontë's curate, in 1854. The marriage seems to have been reasonably content, although the new Mrs. Nicholls did complain to a friend that "the married woman can call but a very small portion of each day her own." Toward the end of the year, however, she became pregnant and suffered so severe a case of what it is almost an understatement to call "morning sickness" that by March of 1855 she was bedridden and emaciated. Some biographers have speculated that her illness was complicated by the same tuberculosis that killed her sisters; others have suggested that she could no longer continue the life that had consumed so many of those she loved. Whatever the medical causes, she died on March 31, 1855, and was buried near her sisters and brother in Haworth churchyard.

If Brontë's body could not rise to the task of survival, however, her imagination had been more than equal to that job. "Imagination is a strong, restless faculty which claims to be heard and exercised: are we to be quite deaf to her cry and insensate to her struggles?" she once wrote to the man of letters George Henry Lewes. For her, such a question had only one answer. Through all the hardships of an exceptionally difficult life, Brontë herself had attended with special intensity to the claims of imagination, so that, as Virginia Woolf declared seventy years after this writer's death, even now when we read *Jane Eyre* "we are steeped through and through with the genius, the vehemence, the indignation of Charlotte Brontë."

Jane Eyre[1]

Chapter I

There was no possibility of taking a walk that day. We had been wandering, indeed, in the leafless shrubbery an hour in the morning; but since dinner (Mrs. Reed, when there was no company, dined early) the cold winter wind had brought with it clouds so somber, and a rain so penetrating, that further outdoor exercise was now out of the question.

I was glad of it: I never liked long walks, especially on chilly afternoons: dreadful to me was the coming home in the raw twilight, with nipped fingers and toes, and a heart saddened by the chidings of Bessie, the nurse, and

1. We are indebted to Richard J. Dunn for information contained in his notes to the Norton Critical Edition of *Jane Eyre.*

humbled by the consciousness of my physical inferiority to Eliza, John, and Georgiana Reed.

The said Eliza, John, and Georgiana were now clustered round their mamma in the drawing-room: she lay reclined on the sofa by the fireside, and with her darlings about her (for the time neither quarreling nor crying) looked perfectly happy. Me, she had dispensed from joining the group; saying, "She regretted to be under the necessity of keeping me at a distance; but that until she heard from Bessie and could discover by her own observation that I was endeavoring in good earnest to acquire a more sociable and childlike disposition, a more attractive and sprightly manner—something lighter, franker, more natural, as it were—she really must exclude me from privileges intended only for contented, happy, little children."

"What does Bessie say I have done?" I asked.

"Jane, I don't like cavilers or questioners: besides, there is something truly forbidding in a child taking up her elders in that manner. Be seated somewhere; and until you can speak pleasantly, remain silent."

A small breakfast-room adjoined the drawing-room. I slipped in there. It contained a bookcase: I soon possessed myself of a volume, taking care that it should be one stored with pictures. I mounted into the window-seat: gathering up my feet, I sat cross-legged like a Turk; and, having drawn the red moreen curtain nearly close, I was shrined in double retirement.

Folds of scarlet drapery shut in my view to the right hand; to the left were the clear panes of glass, protecting, but not separating me from the drear November day. At intervals, while turning over the leaves of my book, I studied the aspect of that winter afternoon. Afar, it offered a pale blank of mist and cloud; near, a scene of wet lawn and storm-beat shrub, with ceaseless rain sweeping away wildly before a long and lamentable blast.

I returned to my book—Bewick's *History of British Birds:* the letterpress[2] thereof I cared little for, generally speaking; and yet there were certain introductory pages that, child as I was, I could not pass quite as a blank. They were those which treat of the haunts of sea-fowl; of "the solitary rocks and promontories" by them only inhabited; of the coast of Norway, studded with isles from its southern extremity, the Lindeness, or Naze, to the North Cape——

> Where the Northern Ocean, in vast whirls,
> Boils round the naked, melancholy isles
> Of farthest Thule; and the Atlantic surge
> Pours in among the stormy Hebrides.[3]

Nor could I pass unnoticed the suggestion of the bleak shores of Lapland, Siberia, Spitzbergen, Nova Zembla, Iceland, Greenland, with the "vast sweep of the Arctic Zone, and those forlorn regions of dreary space—that reservoir of frost and snow, where firm fields of ice, the accumulation of centuries of winters, glazed in Alpine heights above heights, surround the pole, and concentre the multiplied rigors of extreme cold." Of these death-white realms I formed an idea of my own: shadowy, like all the half-comprehended notions that float dim through children's brains, but strangely impressive. The words

2. I.e., the text, as distinct from the pictures, of Thomas Bewick, *History of British Birds* (1804).

3. From James Thomson's *Seasons, Autumn* (1730), lines 862–65.

in these introductory pages connected themselves with the succeeding vignettes,[4] and gave significance to the rock standing up alone in a sea of billow and spray; to the broken boat stranded on a desolate coast; to the cold and ghastly moon glancing through bars of cloud at a wreck just sinking.

I cannot tell what sentiment haunted the quite solitary churchyard, with its inscribed headstone; its gate, its two trees, its low horizon, girdled by a broken wall, and its newly-risen crescent, attesting the hour of eventide.

The two ships becalmed on a torpid sea I believed to be marine phantoms.

The fiend pinning down the thief's pack behind him I passed over quickly: it was an object of terror.

So was the black, horned thing seated aloof on a rock, surveying a distant crowd surrounding a gallows.

Each picture told a story; mysterious often to my undeveloped understanding and imperfect feelings, yet ever profoundly interesting: as interesting as the tales Bessie sometimes narrated on winter evenings, when she chanced to be in good humor; and when, having brought her ironing-table to the nursery-hearth, she allowed us to sit about it, and while she got up Mrs. Reed's lace frills, and crimped her night-cap borders, fed our eager attention with passages of love and adventure taken from old fairy tales and older ballads; or (as at a later period I discovered) from the pages of "Pamela," and "Henry, Earl of Moreland."[5]

With Bewick on my knee, I was then happy: happy at least in my way. I feared nothing but interruption and that came too soon. The breakfast-room door opened.

"Bah! Madame Mope!" cried the voice of John Reed; then he paused: he found the room apparently empty.

"Where the dickens is she?" he continued. "Lizzy! Georgy! (calling to his sisters) Joan[6] is not here: tell mamma she is run out into the rain—bad animal!"

"It is well I drew the curtain," thought I; and I wished fervently he might not discover my hiding-place: nor would John Reed have found it out himself; he was not quick either of vision or conception; but Eliza just put her head in at the door, and said at once:—"She is in the window-seat, to be sure, Jack."

And I came out immediately, for I trembled at the idea of being dragged forth by the said Jack.

"What do you want?" I asked, with awkward diffidence.

"Say, 'what do you want, Master Reed?' " was the answer. "I want you to come here"; and sitting himself in an arm-chair, he intimated by a gesture that I was to approach and stand before him.

John Reed was a schoolboy of fourteen years old; four years older than I, for I was but ten; large and stout for his age, with a dingy and unwholesome skin; thick lineaments in a spacious visage, heavy limbs and large extremities. He gorged himself habitually at table, which made him bilious, and gave him a dim and bleared eye and flabby cheeks. He ought now to have been at school; but his mamma had taken him home for a month or two, "on account

4. Engravings.
5. The popular novel (1740) by Samuel Richardson and a 1781 abridgement of *The Fool of Quality*

(1766–70) by Henry Brooke.
6. "Jane" is a variant of "Joan."

of his delicate health." Mr. Miles, the master, affirmed that he would do very well if he had fewer cakes and sweetmeats sent him from home; but the mother's heart turned from an opinion so harsh, and inclined rather to the more refined idea that John's sallowness was owing to over-application and, perhaps, to pining after home.

John had not much affection for his mother and sisters, and an antipathy to me. He bullied and punished me; not two or three times in the week, nor once or twice in the day, but continually: every nerve I had feared him, and every morsel of flesh on my bones shrank when he came near. There were moments when I was bewildered by the terror he inspired, because I had no appeal whatever against either his menaces or his inflictions; the servants did not like to offend their young master by taking my part against him, and Mrs. Reed was blind and deaf on the subject: she never saw him strike or heard him abuse me, though he did both now and then in her very presence; more frequently, however, behind her back.

Habitually obedient to John, I came up to his chair: he spent some three minutes in thrusting out his tongue at me as far as he could without damaging the roots: I knew he would soon strike, and while dreading the blow, I mused on the disgusting and ugly appearance of him who would presently deal it. I wonder if he read that notion in my face; for, all at once, without speaking, he struck suddenly and strongly. I tottered, and regaining my equilibrium retired back a step or two from his chair.

"That is for your impudence in answering mamma a while since," said he, "and for your sneaking way of getting behind curtains, and for the look you had in your eyes two minutes since, you rat!"

Accustomed to John Reed's abuse, I never had an idea of replying to it; my care was how to endure the blow which would certainly follow the insult.

"What were you doing behind the curtain?" he asked.

"I was reading."

"Show the book."

I returned to the window and fetched it thence.

"You have no business to take our books; you are a dependent, mamma says; you have no money; your father left you none; you ought to beg, and not live here with gentlemen's children like us, and eat the same meals we do, and wear clothes at our mamma's expense. Now, I'll teach you to rummage my book-shelves: for they *are* mine; all the house belongs to me, or will do in a few years. Go and stand by the door, out of the way of the mirror and the windows."

I did so, not at first aware what was his intention; but when I saw him lift and poise the book and stand in act to hurl it, I instinctively started aside with a cry of alarm: not soon enough, however; the volume was flung, it hit me, and I fell, striking my head against the door and cutting it. The cut bled, the pain was sharp: my terror had passed its climax; other feelings succeeded.

"Wicked and cruel boy!" I said. "You are like a murderer—you are like a slave-driver—you are like the Roman emperors!"

I had read Goldsmith's *History of Rome*,[7] and had formed my opinion of

7. Oliver Goldsmith's *The Roman History* (1769); the emperors named are the most notoriously erratic and cruel.

Nero, Caligula, etc. Also I had drawn parallels in silence, which I never thought thus to have declared aloud.

"What! what!" he cried. "Did she say that to me? Did you hear her, Eliza and Georgiana? Won't I tell mamma? but first———"

He ran headlong at me: I felt him grasp my hair and my shoulder: he had closed with a desperate thing. I really saw in him a tyrant: a murderer. I felt a drop or two of blood from my head trickle down my neck, and was sensible of somewhat pungent suffering: these sensations for the time predominated over fear, and I received him in frantic sort. I don't very well know what I did with my hands, but he called me "Rat! rat!" and bellowed out aloud. Aid was near him: Eliza and Georgiana had run for Mrs. Reed, who was gone upstairs; she now came upon the scene, followed by Bessie and her maid Abbot. We were parted: I heard the words:—"Dear! dear! What a fury to fly at Master John!"

"Did ever anybody see such a picture of passion!"

Then Mrs. Reed subjoined:—"Take her away to the red-room, and lock her in there." Four hands were immediately laid upon me, and I was borne upstairs.

Chapter II

I resisted all the way: a new thing for me, and a circumstance which greatly strengthened the bad opinion Bessie and Miss Abbot were disposed to entertain of me. The fact is, I was a trifle beside myself; or rather *out* of myself, as the French would say: I was conscious that a moment's mutiny had already rendered me liable to strange penalties, and, like any other rebel slave, I felt resolved, in my desperation, to go all lengths.

"Hold her arms, Miss Abbot: she's like a mad cat."

"For shame! for shame!" cried the lady's-maid. "What shocking conduct, Miss Eyre, to strike a young gentleman, your benefactress's son! Your young master."

"Master! How is he my master? Am I a servant?"

"No; you are less than a servant, for you do nothing for your keep. There, sit down, and think over your wickedness."

They had got me by this time into the apartment indicated by Mrs. Reed, and had thrust me upon a stool: my impulse was to rise from it like a spring; their two pairs of hands arrested me instantly.

"If you don't sit still, you must be tied down," said Bessie. "Miss Abbot, lend me your garters; she would break mine directly."

Miss Abbot turned to divest a stout leg of the necessary ligature. This preparation for bonds, and the additional ignominy it inferred, took a little of the excitement out of me.

"Don't take them off," I cried; "I will not stir."

In guarantee whereof I attached myself to my seat by my hands.

"Mind you don't," said Bessie; and when she had ascertained that I was really subsiding, she loosened her hold of me; then she and Miss Abbot stood with folded arms, looking darkly and doubtfully on my face, as incredulous of my sanity.

"She never did so before," at last said Bessie, turning to the Abigail.[8]

8. A lady's personal servant (after a character in *The Scornful Lady* [1671], a play by Francis Beaumont and John Fletcher).

"But it was always in her," was the reply. "I've told Missis often my opinion about the child, and Missis agreed with me. She's an underhand little thing: I never saw a girl of her age with so much cover."[9]

Bessie answered not; but ere long, addressing me, she said:

"You ought to be aware, Miss, that you are under obligations to Mrs. Reed: she keeps you: if she were to turn you off,[1] you would have to go to the poor-house."

I had nothing to say to these words: they were not new to me: my very first recollections of existence included hints of the same kind. This reproach of my dependence had become a vague singsong in my ear; very painful and crushing, but only half intelligible. Miss Abbot joined in:—"And you ought not to think yourself on an equality with the Misses Reed and Master Reed, because Missis kindly allows you to be brought up with them. They will have a great deal of money, and you will have none: it is your place to be humble, and to try to make yourself agreeable to them."

"What we tell you is for your good," added Bessie, in no harsh voice: "you should try to be useful and pleasant, then, perhaps, you would have a home here; but if you become passionate and rude, Missis will send you away, I am sure."

"Besides," said Miss Abbot, "God will punish her: He might strike her dead in the midst of her tantrums, and then where would she go? Come, Bessie, we will leave her: I wouldn't have her heart for anything. Say your prayers, Miss Eyre, when you are by yourself; for if you don't repent, something bad might be permitted to come down the chimney, and fetch you away."

They went, shutting the door, and locking it behind them.

The red-room was a spare chamber, very seldom slept in; I might say never, indeed, unless when a chance influx of visitors at Gateshead Hall rendered it necessary to turn to account all the accommodation it contained: yet it was one of the largest and stateliest chambers in the mansion. A bed supported on massive pillars of mahogany, hung with curtains of deep red damask, stood out like a tabernacle in the center; the two large windows, with their blinds always drawn down, were half shrouded in festoons and falls of similar drapery; the carpet was red; the table at the foot of the bed was covered with a crimson cloth; the walls were a soft fawn color, with a blush of pink in it; the wardrobe, the toilet-table, the chairs were of darkly-polished old mahogany. Out of these deep surrounding shades rose high, and glared white, the piled-up mattresses and pillows of the bed, spread with a snowy Marseilles counterpane. Scarcely less prominent was an ample, cushioned easy-chair near the head of the bed, also white, with a footstool before it; and looking, as I thought, like a pale throne.

This room was chill, because it seldom had a fire; it was silent, because remote from the nursery and kitchens; solemn, because it was known to be so seldom entered. The housemaid alone came here on Saturdays, to wipe from the mirrors and the furniture a week's quiet dust: and Mrs. Reed herself, at far intervals, visited it to review the contents of a certain secret drawer in the wardrobe, where were stored divers parchments, her jewel-casket, and a miniature of her deceased husband; and in those last words lies the secret of the red-room—the spell which kept it so lonely in spite of its grandeur.

Mr. Reed had been dead nine years: it was in this chamber he breathed

9. Deception. 1. Turn you out.

his last; here he lay in state; hence his coffin was borne by the undertaker's men; and, since that day, a sense of dreary consecration had guarded it from frequent intrusion.

My seat, to which Bessie and the bitter Miss Abbot had left me riveted, was a low ottoman near the marble chimney-piece; the bed rose before me; to my right hand there was the high, dark wardrobe, with subdued, broken reflections varying the gloss of its panels; to my left were the muffled windows; a great looking-glass between them repeated the vacant majesty of the bed and room. I was not quite sure whether they had locked the door; and, when I dared move, I got up, and went to see. Alas! yes: no jail was ever more secure. Returning, I had to cross before the looking-glass; my fascinated glance involuntarily explored the depth it revealed. All looked colder and darker in that visionary hollow than in reality: and the strange little figure there gazing at me, with a white face and arms specking the gloom, and glittering eyes of fear moving where all else was still, had the effect of a real spirit: I thought it like one of the tiny phantoms, half fairy, half imp, Bessie's evening stories represented as coming out of lone, ferny dells in moors, and appearing before the eyes of belated travelers. I returned to my stool.

Superstition was with me at that moment; but it was not yet her hour for complete victory: my blood was still warm; the mood of the revolted slave was still bracing me with its bitter vigor; I had to stem a rapid rush of retrospective thought before I quailed to the dismal present.

All John Reed's violent tyrannies, all his sisters' proud indifference, all his mother's aversion, all the servant's partiality, turned up in my disturbed mind like a dark deposit in a turbid well. Why was I always suffering, always browbeaten, always accused, forever condemned? Why could I never please? Why was it useless to try to win any one's favor? Eliza, who was headstrong and selfish, was respected. Georgiana, who had a spoiled temper, a very acrid spite, a captious and insolent carriage, was universally indulged. Her beauty, her pink cheeks and golden curls, seemed to give delight to all who looked at her, and to purchase indemnity for every fault. John, no one thwarted, much less punished; though he twisted the necks of the pigeons, killed the little pea-chicks,[2] set the dogs at the sheep, stripped the hothouse vines of their fruit, and broke the buds off the choicest plants in the conservatory: he called his mother "old girl," too; sometimes reviled her for her dark skin, similar to his own; bluntly disregarded her wishes; not unfrequently tore and spoiled her silk attire; and he was still "her own darling." I dared commit no fault; I strove to fulfill every duty; and I was termed naughty and tiresome, sullen and sneaking, from morning to noon, and from noon to night.

My head still ached and bled with the blow and fall I had received: no one had reproved John for wantonly striking me; and because I had turned against him to avert farther irrational violence, I was loaded with general opprobrium.

"Unjust!—unjust!" said my reason, forced by the agonizing stimulus into precocious though transitory power; and Resolve, equally wrought up, instigated some strange expedient to achieve escape from insupportable oppression—as running away, or, if that could not be effected, never eating or drinking more, and letting myself die.

2. Peacock chicks.

What a consternation of soul was mine that dreary afternoon! How all my brain was in tumult, and all my heart in insurrection! Yet in what darkness, what dense ignorance, was the mental battle fought! I could not answer the ceaseless inward question—*why* I thus suffered; now, at the distance of—I will not say how many years, I see it clearly.

I was a discord in Gateshead Hall; I was like nobody there; I had nothing in harmony with Mrs. Reed or her children, or her chosen vassalage. If they did not love me, in fact, as little did I love them. They were not bound to regard with affection a thing that could not sympathize with one amongst them; a heterogeneous thing, opposed to them in temperament, in capacity, in propensities; a useless thing, incapable of serving their interest, or adding to their pleasure; a noxious thing, cherishing the germs of indignation at their treatment, of contempt of their judgment. I know that had I been a sanguine, brilliant, careless, exacting, handsome, romping child—though equally dependent and friendless—Mrs. Reed would have endured my presence more complacently; her children would have entertained for me more of the cordiality of fellow-feeling; the servants would have been less prone to make me the scapegoat of the nursery.

Daylight began to forsake the red-room; it was past four o'clock, and the beclouded afternoon was tending to drear twilight. I heard the rain still beating continuously on the staircase window, and the wind howling in the grove behind the hall; I grew by degrees cold as a stone, and then my courage sank. My habitual mood of humiliation, self-doubt, forlorn depression, fell damp on the embers of my decaying ire. All said I was wicked, and perhaps I might be so: what thought had I been but just conceiving of starving myself to death? That certainly was a crime: and was I fit to die? Or was the vault under the chancel of Gateshead Church an inviting bourne? In such vault I had been told did Mr. Reed lie buried; and led by this thought to recall his idea, I dwelt on it with gathering dread. I could not remember him; but I knew that he was my own uncle—my mother's brother—that he had taken me when a parentless infant to his house; and that in his last moments he had required a promise of Mrs. Reed that she would rear and maintain me as one of her own children. Mrs. Reed probably considered she had kept this promise; and so she had, I dare say, as well as her nature would permit her; but how could she really like an interloper not of her race,[3] and unconnected with her, after her husband's death, by any tie? It must have been most irksome to find herself bound by a hard-wrung pledge to stand in the stead of a parent to a strange child she could not love, and to see an uncongenial alien permanently intruded on her own family group.

A singular notion dawned upon me. I doubted not—never doubted—that if Mr. Reed had been alive he would have treated me kindly; and now, as I sat looking at the white bed and overshadowed walls—occasionally also turning a fascinated eye towards the dimly gleaming mirror—I began to recall what I had heard of dead men, troubled in their graves by the violation of their last wishes, revisiting the earth to punish the perjured and avenge the oppressed; and I thought Mr. Reed's spirit, harassed by the wrongs of his sister's child, might quit its abode—whether in the church vault, or in the unknown world of the departed—and rise before me in this chamber. I wiped

3. I.e., family.

my tears and hushed my sobs, fearful lest any sign of violent grief might waken a preternatural voice to comfort me, or elicit from the gloom some haloed face, bending over me with strange pity. This idea, consolatory in theory, I felt would be terrible if realized: with all my might I endeavored to stifle it—I endeavored to be firm. Shaking my hair from my eyes, I lifted my head and tried to look boldly round the dark room. At this moment a light gleamed on the wall. Was it, I asked myself, a ray from the moon penetrating some aperture in the blind? No; moonlight was still, and this stirred; while I gazed, it glided up to the ceiling and quivered over my head. I can now conjecture readily that this streak of light was, in all likelihood, a gleam from a lantern, carried by some one across the lawn: but then, prepared as my mind was for horror, shaken as my nerves were by agitation, I thought the swift-darting beam was a herald of some coming vision from another world. My heart beat thick, my head grew hot; a sound filled my ears, which I deemed the rushing of wings: something seemed near me; I was oppressed, suffocated: endurance broke down; I rushed to the door and shook the lock in desperate effort. Steps came running along the outer passage; the key turned, Bessie and Abbot entered.

"Miss Eyre, are you ill?" said Bessie.

"What a dreadful noise! it went quite through me!" exclaimed Abbot.

"Take me out! let me go into the nursery!" was my cry.

"What for? Are you hurt? Have you seen something?" again demanded Bessie.

"Oh! I saw a light, and I thought a ghost would come." I had now got hold of Bessie's hand, and she did not snatch it from me.

"She has screamed out on purpose," declared Abbot, in some disgust. "And what a scream! If she had been in great pain one would have excused it, but she only wanted to bring us all here: I know her naughty tricks."

"What is all this?" demanded another voice, peremptorily; and Mrs. Reed came along the corridor, her cap flying wide, her gown rustling stormily. "Abbot and Bessie, I believe I gave orders that Jane Eyre should be left in the red-room till I came to her myself."

"Miss Jane screamed so loud, ma'am," pleaded Bessie.

"Let her go," was the only answer. "Loose Bessie's hand, child: you cannot succeed in getting out by these means, be assured. I abhor artifice, particularly in children; it is my duty to show you that tricks will not answer: you will now stay here an hour longer, and it is only on condition of perfect submission and stillness that I shall liberate you then."

"Oh aunt, have pity! Forgive me! I cannot endure it—let me be punished some other way! I shall be killed if———"

"Silence! This violence is all most repulsive": and so, no doubt, she felt it. I was a precocious actress in her eyes: she sincerely looked on me as a compound of virulent passions, mean spirit, and dangerous duplicity.

Bessie and Abbot having retreated, Mrs. Reed, impatient of my now frantic anguish and wild sobs, abruptly thrust me back and locked me in, without farther parley. I heard her sweeping away; and soon after she was gone I suppose I had a species of fit: unconsciousness closed the scene.

Chapter III

The next thing I remember is, waking up with a feeling as if I had had a frightful nightmare, and seeing before me a terrible red glare, crossed with thick black bars. I heard voices, too, speaking with a hollow sound, as if muffled by a rush of wind or water: agitation, uncertainty, and an all-predominating sense of terror confused my faculties. Ere long I became aware that some one was handling me; lifting me up and supporting me in a sitting posture, and that more tenderly than I had ever been raised or upheld before. I rested my head against a pillow or an arm, and felt easy.

In five minutes more the cloud of bewilderment dissolved: I knew quite well that I was in my own bed, and that the red glare was the nursery fire. It was night: a candle burned on the table; Bessie stood at the bed-foot with a basin in her hand, and a gentleman sat in a chair near my pillow, leaning over me.

I felt an inexpressible relief, a soothing conviction of protection and security, when I knew that there was a stranger in the room, an individual not belonging to Gateshead, and not related to Mrs. Reed. Turning from Bessie (though her presence was far less obnoxious to me than that of Abbot, for instance, would have been), I scrutinized the face of the gentleman: I knew him; it was Mr. Lloyd, an apothecary, sometimes called in by Mrs. Reed when the servants were ailing: for herself and the children she employed a physician.

"Well, who am I?" he asked.

I pronounced his name, offering him at the same time my hand: he took it, smiling and saying, "We shall do very well by-and-by." Then he laid me down, and addressing Bessie, charged her to be very careful that I was not disturbed during the night. Having given some further directions, and intimated that he should call again the next day, he departed—to my grief: I felt so sheltered and befriended while he sat in the chair near my pillow; and as he closed the door after him all the room darkened and my heart again sank: inexpressible sadness weighed it down.

"Do you feel as if you should sleep, Miss?" asked Bessie, rather softly.

Scarcely dared I answer her; for I feared the next sentence might be rough. "I will try."

"Would you like to drink, or could you eat anything?"

"No, thank you, Bessie."

"Then I think I shall go to bed, for it is past twelve o'clock; but you may call me if you want anything in the night."

Wonderful civility this! It emboldened me to ask a question.

"Bessie, what is the matter with me? Am I ill?"

"You fell sick, I suppose, in the red-room with crying; you'll be better soon, no doubt."

Bessie went into the housemaid's apartment, which was near. I heard her say—"Sarah, come and sleep with me in the nursery; I daren't for my life be alone with that poor child tonight; she might die; it's such a strange thing she should have that fit: I wonder if she saw anything. Missis was rather too hard."

Sarah came back with her; they both went to bed; they were whispering together for half an hour before they fell asleep. I caught scraps of their

conversation, from which I was able only too distinctly to infer the main subject discussed.

"Something passed her, all dressed in white, and vanished"—"A great black dog behind him"—"Three loud raps on the chamber door"—"A light in the churchyard just over his grave"—etc. etc.

At last both slept: the fire and the candle went out. For me, the watches of that long night passed in ghastly wakefulness; ear, eye, and mind were alike strained by dread: such dread as children only can feel.

No severe or prolonged bodily illness followed this incident of the red-room: it only gave my nerves a shock, of which I feel the reverberation to this day. Yes, Mrs. Reed, to you I owe some fearful pangs of mental suffering. But I ought to forgive you, for you knew not what you did:[4] while rending my heart-strings, you thought you were only uprooting my bad propensities.

Next day, by noon, I was up and dressed, and sat wrapped in a shawl by the nursery hearth. I felt physically weak and broken down; but my worst ailment was an unutterable wretchedness of mind: a wretchedness which kept drawing from me silent tears; no sooner had I wiped one salt drop from my cheek than another followed. Yet I thought I ought to have been happy, for none of the Reeds were there, they were all gone out in the carriage with their mamma: Abbot, too, was sewing in another room, and Bessie, as she moved hither and thither, putting away toys and arranging drawers, addressed to me every now and then a word of unwonted kindness. This state of things should have been to me a paradise of peace, accustomed as I was to a life of ceaseless reprimand and thankless fagging;[5] but, in fact, my racked nerves were now in such a state that no calm could soothe, and no pleasure excite them agreeably.

Bessie had been down into the kitchen, and she brought up with her a tart on a certain brightly painted china plate, whose bird of paradise, nestling in a wreath of convolvuli and rosebuds, had been wont to stir in me a most enthusiastic sense of admiration; and which plate I had often petitioned to be allowed to take in my hand in order to examine it more closely, but had always hitherto been deemed unworthy of such a privilege. This precious vessel was now placed on my knee, and I was cordially invited to eat the circlet of delicate pastry upon it. Vain favor! coming, like most other favors long deferred and often wished for, too late! I could not eat the tart: and the plumage of the bird, the tints of the flowers, seemed strangely faded: I put both plate and tart away. Bessie asked if I would have a book: the word *book* acted as a transient stimulus, and I begged her to fetch *Gulliver's Travels*[6] from the library. This book I had again and again perused with delight. I considered it a narrative of facts and discovered in it a vein of interest deeper than what I found in fairy tales: for as to the elves, having sought them in vain among foxglove leaves and bells, under mushrooms and beneath the ground-ivy mantling old wall-nooks, I had at length made up my mind to the sad truth, that they were all gone out of England to some savage country where the woods were wilder and thicker, and the population more scant; whereas, Lilliput and Brobdingnag being, in my creed, solid parts of the

4. An echo of Jesus' words on the cross: "Father, forgive them; for they know not what they do" (Luke 23.34).

5. Hard work.
6. Jonathan Swift's *Gulliver's Travels* (1726).

earth's surface, I doubted not that I might one day, by taking a long voyage, see with my own eyes the little fields, houses, and trees, the diminutive people, the tiny cows, sheep, and birds of the one realm; and the corn-fields forest-high, the mighty mastiffs, the monster cats, the tower-like men and women, of the other. Yet when this cherished volume was now placed in my hand—when I turned over its leaves, and sought in its marvelous pictures the charm I had, till now, never failed to find—all was eerie and dreary; the giants were gaunt goblins, the pigmies malevolent and fearful imps, Gulliver a most desolate wanderer in most dread and dangerous regions. I closed the book, which I dared no longer peruse, and put it on the table, beside the untasted tart.

Bessie had now finished dusting and tidying the room, and having washed her hands, she opened a certain little drawer, full of splendid shreds of silk and satin, and began making a new bonnet for Georgiana's doll. Meantime she sang: her song was—

> In the days when we went gipsying,
> A long time ago.[7]

I had often heard the song before, and always with lively delight; for Bessie had a sweet voice—at least I thought so. But now, though her voice was still sweet, I found in its melody an indescribable sadness. Sometimes, preoccupied with her work, she sang the refrain very low, very lingeringly; "A long time ago" came out like the saddest cadence of a funeral hymn. She passed into another ballad, this time a really doleful one.

> My feet they are sore, and my limbs they are weary;
> Long is the way, and the mountains are wild;
> Soon will the twilight close moonless and dreary
> Over the path of the poor orphan child.
>
> Why did they send me so far and so lonely,
> Up where the moors spread and gray rocks are piled?
> Men are hard-hearted, and kind angels only
> Watch o'er the steps of a poor orphan child.
>
> Yet distant and soft the night-breeze is blowing,
> Clouds there are none, and clear stars beam mild;
> God, in His mercy, protection is showing,
> Comfort and hope to the poor orphan child.
>
> Ev'n should I fall o'er the broken bridge passing,
> Or stray in the marshes, by false lights beguiled,
> Still will my Father, with promise and blessing,
> Take to His bosom the poor orphan child.
>
> There is a thought that for strength should avail me,
> Though both of shelter and kindred despoiled;
> Heaven is a home, and a rest will not fail me;
> God is a friend to the poor orphan child.

7. A popular song of the period.

"Come, Miss Jane, don't cry," said Bessie, as she finished. She might as well have said to the fire, "don't burn!" but how could she divine the morbid suffering to which I was a prey? In the course of the morning Mr. Lloyd came again.

"What, already up!" said he, as he entered the nursery. "Well, nurse, how is she?"

Bessie answered that I was doing very well.

"Then she ought to look more cheerful. Come here, Miss Jane; your name is Jane, is it not?"

"Yes, sir, Jane Eyre."

"Well, you have been crying, Miss Jane Eyre; can you tell me what about? Have you any pain?"

"No, sir."

"Oh! I daresay she is crying because she could not go out with Missis in the carriage," interposed Bessie.

"Surely not! why, she is too old for such pettishness."

I thought so too; and my self-esteem being wounded by the false charge, I answered promptly, "I never cried for such a thing in my life: I hate going out in the carriage. I cry because I am miserable."

"Oh fie, Miss!" said Bessie.

The good apothecary appeared a little puzzled. I was standing before him; he fixed his eyes on me very steadily: his eyes were small and gray: not very bright, but I daresay I should think them shrewd now: he had a hard-featured yet good-natured looking face. Having considered me at leisure, he said: "What made you ill yesterday?"

"She had a fall," said Bessie, again putting in her word.

"Fall! why that is like a baby again! Can't she manage to walk at her age? She must be eight or nine years old."

"I was knocked down," was the blunt explanation jerked out of me by another pang of mortified pride: "but that did not make me ill," I added; while Mr. Lloyd helped himself to a pinch of snuff.

As he was returning the box to his waistcoat pocket, a loud bell rang for the servants' dinner; he knew what it was. "That's for you, nurse," said he; "you can go down; I'll give Miss Jane a lecture till you come back."

Bessie would rather have stayed, but she was obliged to go, because punctuality at meals was rigidly enforced at Gateshead Hall.

"The fall did not make you ill; what did, then?" pursued Mr. Lloyd, when Bessie was gone.

"I was shut up in a room where there is a ghost till after dark."

I saw Mr. Lloyd smile and frown at the same time: "Ghost! What, you are a baby after all! You are afraid of ghosts?"

"Of Mr. Reed's ghost I am: he died in that room, and was laid out there. Neither Bessie nor any one else will go into it at night, if they can help it; and it was cruel to shut me up alone without a candle,—so cruel that I think I shall never forget it."

"Nonsense! And is it that makes you so miserable? Are you afraid now in daylight?"

"No: but night will come again before long: and besides,—I am unhappy,—very unhappy, for other things."

"What other things? Can you tell me some of them?"

How much I wished to reply fully to this question! How difficult it was to frame any answer. Children can feel, but they cannot analyze their feelings; and if the analysis is partially effected in thought, they know not how to express the result of the process in words. Fearful, however, of losing this first and only opportunity of relieving my grief by imparting it, I, after a disturbed pause, contrived to frame a meager, though, as far as it went, true response.

"For one thing, I have no father or mother, brothers or sisters."

"You have a kind aunt and cousins."

Again I paused; then bunglingly enounced: "But John Reed knocked me down, and my aunt shut me up in the red-room."

Mr. Lloyd a second time produced his snuff-box.

"Don't you think Gateshead Hall a very beautiful house?" asked he. "Are you not very thankful to have such a fine place to live at?"

"It is not my house, sir; and Abbot says I have less right to be here than a servant."

"Pooh! you can't be silly enough to wish to leave such a splendid place?"

"If I had anywhere else to go, I should be glad to leave it; but I can never get away from Gateshead till I am a woman."

"Perhaps you may—who knows? Have you any relations besides Mrs. Reed?"

"I think not, sir."

"None belonging to your father?"

"I don't know: I asked aunt Reed once, and she said possibly I might have some poor, low relations called Eyre, but she knew nothing about them."

"If you had such, would you like to go to them?"

I reflected. Poverty looks grim to grown people; still more so to children: they have not much idea of industrious, working, respectable poverty; they think of the word only as connected with ragged clothes, scanty food, fireless grates, rude manners, and debasing vices: poverty for me was synonymous with degradation.

"No; I should not like to belong to poor people," was my reply.

"Not even if they were kind to you?"

I shook my head: I could not see how poor people had the means of being kind; and then to learn to speak like them, to adopt their manners, to be uneducated, to grow up like one of the poor women I saw sometimes nursing their children or washing their clothes at the cottage doors of the village of Gateshead: no, I was not heroic enough to purchase liberty at the price of caste.

"But are your relatives so very poor? Are they working people?"

"I cannot tell; aunt Reed says, if I have any, they must be a beggarly set: I should not like to go a begging."

"Would you like to go to school?"

Again I reflected: I scarcely knew what school was; Bessie sometimes spoke of it as a place where young ladies sat in the stocks, wore backboards,[8] and were expected to be exceedingly genteel and precise: John Reed hated his school, and abused his master; but John Reed's tastes were no rule for mine,

8. Boards to which 19th-century young women were strapped to improve their posture. "Stocks": a pillory-like contrivance then used in girls' schools (intended to beautify the hands and feet).

and if Bessie's accounts of school discipline (gathered from the young ladies of a family where she had lived before coming to Gateshead) were somewhat appalling, her details of certain accomplishments attained by these same young ladies were, I thought, equally attractive. She boasted of beautiful paintings of landscapes and flowers by them executed; of songs they could sing and pieces they could play, of purses they could net, of French books they could translate; till my spirit was moved to emulation as I listened. Besides, school would be a complete change: it implied a long journey, an entire separation from Gateshead, an entrance into a new life.

"I should indeed like to go to school," was the audible conclusion of my musings.

"Well, well; who knows what may happen?" said Mr. Lloyd, as he got up: "The child ought to have change of air and scene," he added, speaking to himself; "nerves not in a good state."

Bessie now returned; at the same moment the carriage was heard rolling up the gravel-walk.

"Is that your mistress, nurse?" asked Mr. Lloyd. "I should like to speak to her before I go."

Bessie invited him to walk into the breakfast-room, and led the way out. In the interview which followed between him and Mrs. Reed, I presume, from after-occurrences, that the apothecary ventured to recommend my being sent to school; and the recommendation was no doubt readily enough adopted; for as Abbot said, in discussing the subject with Bessie when both sat sewing in the nursery one night, after I was in bed, and, as they thought, asleep, "Missis was, she dared say, glad enough to get rid of such a tiresome, ill-conditioned child, who always looked as if she were watching everybody, and scheming plots underhand." Abbot, I think, gave me credit for being a sort of infantine Guy Fawkes.[9]

On that same occasion I learned, for the first time, from Miss Abbot's communications to Bessie, that my father had been a poor clergyman; that my mother had married him against the wishes of her friends, who considered the match beneath her; that my grandfather Reed was so irritated at her disobedience, he cut her off without a shilling; that after my mother and father had been married a year, the latter caught the typhus fever while visiting among the poor of a large manufacturing town where his curacy was situated, and where that disease was then prevalent; that my mother took the infection from him, and both died within a month of each other.

Bessie, when she heard this narrative, sighed and said, "Poor Miss Jane is to be pitied, too, Abbot."

"Yes," responded Abbot, "if she were a nice, pretty child, one might compassionate her forlornness; but one really cannot care for such a little toad as that."

"Not a great deal, to be sure," agreed Bessie: "at any rate, a beauty like Miss Georgiana would be more moving in the same condition."

"Yes, I doat on Miss Georgiana!" cried the fervent Abbot. "Little darling!— with her long curls and her blue eyes, and such a sweet color as she has; just as if she were painted!—Bessie, I could fancy a Welsh rabbit for supper."

"So could I—with a roast onion. Come, we'll go down." They went.

9. Famous 16th-century English traitor who conspired to blow up the houses of Parliament.

Chapter IV

From my discourse with Mr. Lloyd, and from the above-reported conference between Bessie and Abbot, I gathered enough of hope to suffice as a motive for wishing to get well: a change seemed near,—I desired and waited it in silence. It tarried, however: days and weeks passed: I had regained my normal state of health, but no new allusion was made to the subject over which I brooded. Mrs. Reed surveyed me at times with a severe eye, but seldom addressed me: since my illness she had drawn a more marked line of separation than ever between me and her own children; appointing me a small closet[1] to sleep in by myself, condemning me to take my meals alone, and pass all my time in the nursery, while my cousins were constantly in the drawing-room. Not a hint, however, did she drop about sending me to school: still I felt an instinctive certainty that she would not long endure me under the same roof with her; for her glance, now more than ever, when turned on me, expressed an insuperable and rooted aversion.

Eliza and Georgiana, evidently acting according to orders, spoke to me as little as possible: John thrust his tongue in his cheek whenever he saw me, and once attempted chastisement; but as I instantly turned against him, roused by the same sentiment of deep ire and desperate revolt which had stirred my corruption before, he thought it better to desist, and ran from me, uttering execrations, and vowing I had burst his nose. I had indeed leveled at that prominent feature as hard a blow as my knuckles could inflict; and when I saw that either that or my look daunted him, I had the greatest inclination to follow up my advantage to purpose; but he was already with his mamma. I heard him in a blubbering tone commence the tale of how "that nasty Jane Eyre" had flown at him like a mad cat: he was stopped rather harshly—"Don't talk to me about her, John: I told you not to go near her; she is not worthy of notice; I do not choose that either you or your sisters should associate with her."

Here, leaning over the banister, I cried out suddenly, and without at all deliberating on my words,—"They are not fit to associate with me."

Mrs. Reed was rather a stout woman; but on hearing this strange and audacious declaration, she ran nimbly up the stair, swept me like a whirlwind into the nursery, and crushing me down on the edge of my crib, dared me in an emphatic voice to rise from that place, or utter one syllable, during the remainder of the day.

"What would uncle Reed say to you, if he were alive?" was my scarcely voluntary demand. I say scarcely voluntary, for it seemed as if my tongue pronounced words without my will consenting to their utterance: something spoke out of me over which I had no control.

"What?" said Mrs. Reed under her breath: her usually cold composed gray eye became troubled with a look like fear; she took her hand from my arm, and gazed at me as if she really did not know whether I were child or fiend. I was now in for it.[2]

"My uncle Reed is in heaven, and can see all you do and think; and so can papa and mamma: they know how you shut me up all day long, and how you wish me dead."

1. Small bedroom. 2. Committed to a course of action.

Mrs. Reed soon rallied her spirits: she shook me most soundly, she boxed both my ears, and then left me without a word. Bessie supplied the hiatus by a homily of an hour's length, in which she proved beyond a doubt that I was the most wicked and abandoned child ever reared under a roof. I half believed her; for I felt indeed only bad feelings surging in my breast.

November, December, and half of January passed away. Christmas and the New Year had been celebrated at Gateshead with the usual festive cheer; presents had been interchanged, dinners and evening parties given. From every enjoyment I was, of course, excluded: my share of the gaiety consisted in witnessing the daily apparelling of Eliza and Georgiana, and seeing them descend to the drawing-room, dressed out in thin muslin frocks and scarlet sashes, with hair elaborately ringletted; and afterwards, in listening to the sound of the piano or the harp played below, to the passing to and fro of the butler and footman, to the jingling of glass and china as refreshments were handed, to the broken hum of conversation as the drawing-room doors opened and closed. When tired of this occupation, I would retire from the stairhead to the solitary and silent nursery: there, though somewhat sad, I was not miserable. To speak truth, I had not the least wish to go into company, for in company I was very rarely noticed; and if Bessie had but been kind and companionable, I should have deemed it a treat to spend the evenings quietly with her, instead of passing them under the formidable eye of Mrs. Reed, in a room full of ladies and gentlemen. But Bessie, as soon as she had dressed her young ladies, used to take herself off to the lively regions of the kitchen and the house-keeper's room, generally bearing the candle along with her. I then sat with my doll on my knee, till the fire got low, glancing round occasionally to make sure that nothing worse than myself haunted the shadowy room; and when the embers sank to a dull red, I undressed hastily, tugging at knots and strings as I best might, and sought shelter from cold and darkness in my crib. To this crib I always took my doll; human beings must love something, and in the dearth of worthier objects of affection, I contrived to find a pleasure in loving and cherishing a faded graven image, shabby as a miniature scarecrow. It puzzles me now to remember with what absurd sincerity I doated on this little toy, half fancying it alive and capable of sensation. I could not sleep unless it was folded in my nightgown; and when it lay there safe and warm, I was comparatively happy, believing it to be happy likewise.

Long did the hours seem while I waited the departure of the company, and listened for the sound of Bessie's step on the stairs: sometimes she would come up in the interval to seek her thimble or her scissors, or perhaps to bring me something by way of supper—a bun or a cheese-cake—then she would sit on the bed while I ate it, and when I had finished, she would tuck the clothes round me, and twice she kissed me, and said, "Good night, Miss Jane." When thus gentle, Bessie seemed to me the best, prettiest, kindest being in the world; and I wished most intensely that she would always be so pleasant and amiable, and never push me about, or scold, or task me unreasonably, as she was too often wont to do. Bessie Lee must, I think, have been a girl of good natural capacity, for she was smart in all she did, and had a remarkable knack of narrative; so, at least, I judge from the impression made on me by her nursery tales. She was pretty, too, if my recollections of her face and person are correct. I remember her as a slim young woman, with

black hair, dark eyes, very nice features, and good, clear complexion; but she had a capricious and hasty temper, and indifferent ideas of principle or justice: still, such as she was, I preferred her to any one else at Gateshead Hall.

It was the fifteenth of January, about nine o'clock in the morning: Bessie was gone down to breakfast; my cousins had not yet been summoned to their mamma; Eliza was putting on her bonnet and warm garden-coat to go and feed her poultry, an occupation of which she was fond: and not less so of selling the eggs to the housekeeper and hoarding up the money she thus obtained. She had a turn for traffic,[3] and a marked propensity for saving; shown not only in the vending of eggs and chickens, but also in driving hard bargains with the gardener about flower-roots, seeds, and slips of plants; that functionary having orders from Mrs. Reed to buy of his young lady all the products of her parterre[4] she wished to sell: and Eliza would have sold the hair off her head if she could have made a handsome profit thereby. As to her money, she first secreted it in odd corners, wrapped in a rag or an old curl-paper; but some of these hoards having been discovered by the housemaid, Eliza, fearful of one day losing her valued treasure, consented to entrust it to her mother, at a usurious rate of interest—fifty or sixty per cent.; which interest she exacted every quarter, keeping her accounts in a little book with anxious accuracy.

Georgiana sat on a high stool, dressing her hair at the glass, and interweaving her curls with artificial flowers and faded feathers, of which she had found a store in a drawer in the attic. I was making my bed, having received strict orders from Bessie to get it arranged before she returned (for Bessie now frequently employed me as a sort of under-nurserymaid, to tidy the room, dust the chairs, etc.). Having spread the quilt, and folded my nightdress, I went to the window-seat to put in order some picture-books and doll's house furniture scattered there; an abrupt command from Georgiana to let her playthings alone (for the tiny chairs and mirrors, the fairy plates and cups were her property) stopped my proceedings; and then, for lack of other occupation, I fell to breathing on the frost-flowers with which the window was fretted, and thus clearing a space in the glass through which I might look out on the grounds, where all was still and petrified under the influence of a hard frost.

From this window were visible the porter's lodge and the carriage-road, and just as I had dissolved so much of the silver-white foliage veiling the panes as left room to look out, I saw the gates thrown open and a carriage roll through. I watched it ascending the drive with indifference: carriages often came to Gateshead, but none ever brought visitors in whom I was interested; it stopped in front of the house, the door-bell rang loudly, the new-comer was admitted. All this being nothing to me, my vacant attention soon found livelier attraction in the spectacle of a little hungry robin, which came and chirruped on the twigs of the leafless cherry-tree nailed against the wall near the casement. The remains of my breakfast of bread and milk stood on the table, and having crumbled a morsel of roll, I was tugging at the sash to put out the crumbs on the window-sill, when Bessie came running upstairs into the nursery.

"Miss Jane, take off your pinafore: what are you doing there? Have you

3. Trade 4. Ornamental garden.

washed your hands and face this morning?" I gave another tug before I answered, for I wanted the bird to be secure of its bread: the sash yielded; I scattered the crumbs, some on the stone sill, some on the cherry-tree bough, then, closing the window, I replied:—"No, Bessie; I have only just finished dusting."

"Troublesome, careless child! and what are you doing now? You look quite red, as if you had been about some mischief: what were you opening the window for?"

I was spared the trouble of answering, for Bessie seemed in too great a hurry to listen to explanations: she hauled me to the wash-stand, inflicted a merciless, but happily brief scrub on my face and hands with soap, water, and a coarse towel; disciplined my head with a bristly brush, denuded me of my pinafore, and then, hurrying me to the top of the stairs, bid me go down directly, as I was wanted in the breakfast-room.

I would have asked who wanted me: I would have demanded if Mrs. Reed was there; but Bessie was already gone, and had closed the nursery-door upon me: I slowly descended. For nearly three months I had never been called to Mrs. Reed's presence: restricted so long to the nursery, the breakfast, dining, and drawing-rooms were become for me awful regions, on which it dismayed me to intrude.

I now stood in the empty hall; before me was the breakfast-room door, and I stopped, intimidated and trembling. What a miserable little poltroon had fear, engendered of unjust punishment, made of me in those days! I feared to return to the nursery, and feared to go forward to the parlor; ten minutes I stood in agitated hesitation: the vehement ringing of the breakfast-room bell decided me; I *must* enter.

"Who could want me?" I asked inwardly, as with both hands I turned the stiff door-handle, which, for a second or two, resisted my efforts. "What should I see besides aunt Reed in the apartment?—a man or a woman?" The handle turned, the door unclosed, and passing through and curtseying low I looked up at—a black pillar! such, at least, appeared to me, at first sight, the straight, narrow, sable-clad shape standing erect on the rug: the grim face at the top was like a carved mask, placed above the shaft by way of capital.

Mrs. Reed occupied her usual seat by the fireside: she made a signal to me to approach: I did so, and she introduced me to the stony stranger with the words: "This is the little girl respecting whom I applied to you."

He, for it was a man, turned his head slowly towards where I stood, and having examined me with the two inquisitive-looking gray eyes which twinkled under a pair of bushy brows, said solemnly, and in a bass voice: "Her size is small: what is her age?"

"Ten years."

"So much?" was the doubtful answer; and he prolonged his scrutiny for some minutes. Presently he addressed me:

"Your name, little girl?"

"Jane Eyre, sir."

In uttering these words I looked up: he seemed to me a tall gentleman; but then I was very little: his features were large, and they and all the lines of his frame were equally harsh and prim.

"Well, Jane Eyre, and are you a good child?"

Impossible to reply to this in the affirmative: my little world held a contrary

opinion: I was silent. Mrs. Reed answered for me by an expressive shake of the head, adding soon, "Perhaps the less said on that subject the better, Mr. Brocklehurst."

"Sorry indeed to hear it! she and I must have some talk;" and bending from the perpendicular, he installed his person in the arm-chair, opposite Mrs. Reed's. "Come here," he said.

I stepped across the rug; he placed me square and straight before him. What a face he had, now that it was almost on a level with mine! what a great nose! and what a mouth! and what large prominent teeth!

"No sight so sad as that of a naughty child," he began, "especially a naughty little girl. Do you know where the wicked go after death?"

"They go to hell," was my ready and orthodox answer.

"And what is hell? Can you tell me that?"

"A pit full of fire."

"And should you like to fall into that pit, and to be burning there forever?"

"No, sir."

"What must you do to avoid it?"

I deliberated a moment; my answer, when it did come, was objectionable: "I must keep in good health and not die."

"How can you keep in good health? Children younger than you die daily. I buried a little child of five years old only a day or two since,—a good little child, whose soul is now in heaven. It is to be feared the same could not be said of you, were you to be called hence."

Not being in a condition to remove his doubt, I only cast my eyes down on the two large feet planted on the rug, and sighed, wishing myself far enough away.

"I hope that sigh is from the heart, and that you repent of ever having been the occasion of discomfort to your excellent benefactress."

"Benefactress! benefactress!" said I, inwardly: "they all call Mrs. Reed my benefactress; if so, a benefactress is a disagreeable thing."

"Do you say your prayers night and morning?" continued my interrogator.

"Yes, sir."

"Do you read your Bible?"

"Sometimes."

"With pleasure? Are you fond of it?"

"I like Revelations, and the book of Daniel, and Genesis and Samuel, and a little bit of Exodus, and some parts of Kings and Chronicles, and Job and Jonah."

"And the Psalms? I hope you like them?"

"No, sir."

"No? Oh, shocking! I have a little boy, younger than you, who knows six Psalms by heart: and when you ask him which he would rather have, a gingerbread-nut to eat, or a verse of a Psalm to learn he says: 'Oh! the verse of a Psalm! angels sing Psalms,' says he; 'I wish to be a little angel here below'; he then gets two nuts in recompense for his infant piety."

"Psalms are not interesting," I remarked.

"That proves you have a wicked heart; and you must pray to God to change it: to give you a new and clean one: to take away your heart of stone and give you a heart of flesh."

I was about to propound a question, touching the manner in which that

operation of changing my heart was to be performed, when Mrs. Reed interposed, telling me to sit down; she then proceeded to carry on the conversation herself.

"Mr. Brocklehurst, I believe I intimated in the letter which I wrote to you three weeks ago, that this little girl has not quite the character and disposition I could wish: should you admit her into Lowood school, I should be glad if the superintendent and teachers were requested to keep a strict eye on her, and above all, to guard against her worst fault, a tendency to deceit. I mention this in your hearing, Jane, that you may not attempt to impose on Mr. Brocklehurst."

Well might I dread, well might I dislike Mrs. Reed; for it was her nature to wound me cruelly: never was I happy in her presence: however carefully I obeyed, however strenuously I strove to please her, my efforts were still repulsed and repaid by such sentences as the above. Now, uttered before a stranger, the accusation cut me to the heart: I dimly perceived that she was already obliterating hope from the new phase of existence which she destined me to enter; I felt, though I could not have expressed the feeling, that she was sowing aversion and unkindness along my future path; I saw myself transformed under Mr. Brocklehurst's eye into an artful noxious child, and what could I do to remedy the injury?

"Nothing, indeed," thought I, as I struggled to repress a sob, and hastily wiped away some tears, the impotent evidences of my anguish.

"Deceit is, indeed, a sad fault in a child," said Mr. Brocklehurst "it is akin to falsehood, and all liars will have their portion in the lake burning with fire and brimstone: she shall, however, be watched, Mrs. Reed; I will speak to Miss Temple and the teachers."

"I should wish her to be brought up in a manner suiting her prospects," continued my benefactress; "to be made useful, to be kept humble: as for the vacations, she will, with your permission, spend them always at Lowood."

"Your decisions are perfectly judicious, madam," returned Mr. Brocklehurst. "Humility is a Christian grace, and one peculiarly appropriate to the pupils of Lowood: I, therefore, direct that especial care shall be bestowed on its cultivation among them. I have studied how best to mortify in them the worldly sentiment of pride; and, only the other day, I had a pleasing proof of my success. My second daughter, Augusta, went with her mamma to visit the school, and on her return she exclaimed: 'Oh, dear papa, how quiet and plain all the girls at Lowood look; with their hair combed behind their ears, and their long pinafores, and those little holland⁵ pockets outside their frocks—they are almost like poor people's children! and,' said she, 'they looked at my dress and mamma's, as if they had never seen a silk gown before.' "

"This is the state of things I quite approve," returned Mrs. Reed; "had I sought all England over, I could scarcely have found a system more exactly fitting a child like Jane Eyre. Consistency, my dear Mr. Brocklehurst; I advocate consistency in all things."

"Consistency, madam, is the first of Christian duties; and it has been observed in every arrangement connected with the establishment of Lowood:

5. Plain-weave heavy fabric.

plain fare, simple attire, unsophisticated accommodations, hardy and active habits; such is the order of the day in the house and its inhabitants."

"Quite right, sir. I may then depend upon this child being received as a pupil at Lowood, and there being trained in conformity to her position and prospects?"

"Madam, you may: she shall be placed in that nursery of chosen plants— and I trust she will show herself grateful for the inestimable privilege of her election."

"I will send her, then, as soon as possible, Mr. Brocklehurst; for, I assure you, I feel anxious to be relieved of a responsibility that was becoming too irksome."

"No doubt, no doubt, madam, and now I wish you good morning. I shall return to Brocklehurst Hall in the course of a week or two: my good friend, the Archdeacon, will not permit me to leave him sooner. I shall send Miss Temple notice that she is to expect a new girl, so that there will be no difficulty about receiving her. Good-bye."

"Good-bye, Mr. Brocklehurst; remember me to Mrs. and Miss Brocklehurst, and to Augusta and Theodore, and Master Broughton Brocklehurst."

"I will, madam. Little girl, here is a book entitled the 'Child's Guide';[6] read it with prayer, especially that part containing 'an account of the awfully sudden death of Martha G——, a naughty child addicted to falsehood and deceit.' "

With these words Mr. Brocklehurst put into my hand a thin pamphlet sewn in a cover, and having rung for his carriage he departed.

Mrs. Reed and I were left alone: some minutes passed in silence: she was sewing, I was watching her. Mrs. Reed might be at that time some six or seven and thirty; she was a woman of robust frame, square-shouldered and strong-limbed, not tall, and, though stout, not obese: she had a somewhat large face, the under-jaw being much developed and very solid; her brow was low, her chin large and prominent, mouth and nose sufficiently regular; under her light eyebrows glimmered an eye devoid of ruth; her skin was dark and opaque, her hair nearly flaxen; her constitution was sound as a bell— illness never came near her; she was an exact, clever manager, her household and tenantry were thoroughly under her control; her children, only, at times defied her authority, and laughed it to scorn; she dressed well, and had a presence and port[7] calculated to set off handsome attire.

Sitting on a low stool, a few yards from her arm-chair, I examined her figure; I perused her features. In my hand I held the tract containing the sudden death of the Liar: to which narrative my attention had been pointed as to an appropriate warning. What had just passed; what Mrs. Reed had said concerning me to Mr. Brocklehurst; the whole tenor of their conversation, was recent, raw, and stinging in my mind; I had felt every word as acutely as I had heard it plainly, and a passion of resentment fomented now within me.

Mrs. Reed looked up from her work; her eye settled on mine, her fingers at the same time suspended their nimble movements.

6. One of the heavily didactic and religious children's magazines of the period, such as The *Children's Friend.*

7. Manner.

"Go out of the room; return to the nursery," was her mandate. My look or something else must have struck her as offensive, for she spoke with extreme, though suppressed irritation. I got up, I went to the door; I came back again; I walked to the window, across the room, then close up to her.

Speak I must; I had been trodden on severely, and *must* turn: but how? What strength had I to dart retaliation at my antagonist? I gathered my energies and launched them in this blunt sentence:—"I am not deceitful: if I were, I should say I loved *you;* but I declare I do not love you: I dislike you the worst of anybody in the world except John Reed; and this book about the liar, you may give to your girl, Georgiana, for it is she who tells lies, and not I."

Mrs. Reed's hands still lay on her work inactive: her eye of ice continued to dwell freezingly on mine.

"What more have you to say?" she asked, rather in the tone in which a person might address an opponent of adult age than such as is ordinarily used to a child.

That eye of hers, that voice stirred every antipathy I had. Shaking from head to foot, thrilled with ungovernable excitement, I continued:—"I am glad you are no relation of mine: I will never call you aunt again as long as I live. I will never come to see you when I am grown up; and if any one asks me how I liked you, and how you treated me, I will say the very thought of you makes me sick, and that you treated me with miserable cruelty."

"How dare you affirm that, Jane Eyre?"

"How dare I, Mrs. Reed? How dare I? Because it is the *truth*. You think I have no feelings, and that I can do without one bit of love or kindness; but I cannot live so: and you have no pity. I shall remember how you thrust me back—roughly and violently thrust me back—into the red-room, and locked me up there, to my dying day; though I was in agony; though I cried out, while suffocating with distress, 'Have mercy! Have mercy, aunt Reed!' And that punishment you made me suffer because your wicked boy struck me—knocked me down for nothing. I will tell anybody who asks me questions this exact tale. People think you a good woman, but you are bad; hard-hearted. *You* are deceitful!"

Ere I had finished this reply my soul began to expand, to exult, with the strangest sense of freedom, of triumph, I ever felt. It seemed as if an invisible bond had burst, and that I had struggled out into unhoped-for liberty. Not without cause was this sentiment: Mrs. Reed looked frightened; her work had slipped from her knee; she was lifting up her hands, rocking herself to and fro, and even twisting her face as if she would cry.

"Jane, you are under a mistake: what is the matter with you? Why do you tremble so violently? Would you like to drink some water?"

"No, Mrs. Reed."

"Is there anything else you wish for, Jane? I assure you, I desire to be your friend."

"Not you. You told Mr. Brocklehurst I had a bad character, a deceitful disposition; and I'll let everybody at Lowood know what you are, and what you have done."

"Jane, you don't understand these things: children must be corrected for their faults."

"Deceit is not my fault!" I cried out in a savage, high voice.

"But you are passionate, Jane, that you must allow: and now return to the nursery—there's a dear—and lie down a little."

"I am not your dear; I cannot lie down: send me to school soon, Mrs. Reed, for I hate to live here."

"I will indeed send her to school soon," murmured Mrs. Reed, *sotto voce;* and gathering up her work, she abruptly quitted the apartment.

I was left there alone—winner of the field. It was the hardest battle I had fought, and the first victory I had gained: I stood awhile on the rug, where Mr. Brocklehurst had stood, and I enjoyed my conqueror's solitude. First, I smiled to myself and felt elate; but this fierce pleasure subsided in me as fast as did the accelerated throb of my pulses. A child cannot quarrel with its elders, as I had done; cannot give its furious feelings uncontrolled play, as I had given mine, without experiencing afterwards the pang of remorse and the chill of reaction. A ridge of lighted heath, alive, glancing, devouring, would have been a meet[8] emblem of my mind when I accused and menaced Mrs. Reed: the same ridge, black and blasted after the flames are dead, would have represented as meetly my subsequent condition, when half an hour's silence and reflection had shown me the madness of my conduct, and the dreariness of my hated and hating position.

Something of vengeance I had tasted for the first time; as aromatic wine it seemed, on swallowing, warm and racy: its afterflavor, metallic and corroding, gave me a sensation as if I had been poisoned. Willingly would I now have gone and asked Mrs. Reed's pardon; but I knew, partly from experience and partly from instinct, that was the way to make her repulse me with double scorn, thereby re-exciting every turbulent impulse of my nature.

I would fain exercise some better faculty than that of fierce speaking; fain find nourishment for some less fiendish feeling than that of sombre indignation. I took a book—some Arabian tales; I sat down and endeavored to read. I could make no sense of the subject; my own thoughts swam always between me and the page I had usually found fascinating. I opened the glass-door in the breakfast-room: the shrubbery was quite still: the black frost reigned, unbroken by sun or breeze, through the grounds. I covered my head and arms with the skirt of my frock, and went out to walk in a part of the plantation which was quite sequestered: but I found no pleasure in the silent trees, the falling fir-cones, the congealed relics of autumn, russet leaves, swept by past winds in heaps, and now stiffened together. I leaned against a gate, and looked into an empty field where no sheep were feeding, where the short grass was nipped and blanched. It was a very gray day; a most opaque sky, "onding on snaw,"[9] canopied all; thence flakes fell at intervals, which settled on the hard path and on the hoary lea without melting. I stood, a wretched child enough, whispering to myself over and over again, "What shall I do?—what shall I do?"

All at once I heard a clear voice call, "Miss Jane! where are you? Come to lunch!"

It was Bessie, I knew well enough; but I did not stir; her light step came tripping down the path.

"You naughty little thing!" she said. "Why don't you come when you are called?"

8. Proper.　　　　　　　　　　9. Appearing ready to snow (northern dialect).

Bessie's presence, compared with the thoughts over which I had been brooding, seemed cheerful; even though, as usual, she was somewhat cross. The fact is, after my conflict with and victory over Mrs. Reed, I was not disposed to care much for the nursemaid's transitory anger; and I was disposed to bask in her youthful lightness of heart. I just put my two arms round her, and said, "Come, Bessie! don't scold."

The action was more frank and fearless than any I was habituated to indulge in: somehow it pleased her.

"You are a strange child, Miss Jane," she said, as she looked down at me: "a little, roving, solitary thing: and you are going to school, I suppose?"

I nodded.

"And won't you be sorry to leave poor Bessie?"

"What does Bessie care for me? She is always scolding me."

"Because you're such a queer, frightened, shy, little thing. You should be bolder."

"What! to get more knocks?"

"Nonsense! But you are rather put upon, that's certain. My mother said, when she came to see me last week, that she would not like a little one of her own to be in your place. Now, come in, and I've some good news for you."

"I don't think you have, Bessie."

"Child! what do you mean? What sorrowful eyes you fix on me! Well! but Missis and the young ladies and Master John are going out to tea this afternoon, and you shall have tea with me. I'll ask cook to bake you a little cake, and then you shall help me to look over your drawers; for I am soon to pack your trunk. Missis intends you to leave Gateshead in a day or two, and you shall choose what toys you like to take with you."

"Bessie, you must promise not to scold me any more till I go."

"Well, I will: but mind you are a very good girl, and don't be afraid of me. Don't start when I chance to speak rather sharply: it's so provoking."

"I don't think I shall ever be afraid of you again, Bessie, because I have got used to you; and I shall soon have another set of people to dread."

"If you dread them, they'll dislike you."

"As you do, Bessie?"

"I don't dislike you, Miss; I believe I am fonder of you than of all the others."

"You don't show it."

"You little sharp thing! you've got quite a new way of talking. What makes you so venturesome and hardy?"

"Why, I shall soon be away from you, and besides—" I was going to say something about what had passed between me and Mrs. Reed; but on second thoughts I considered it better to remain silent on that head.

"And so you're glad to leave me?"

"Not at all, Bessie; indeed, just now I am rather sorry."

"Just now! and rather! How coolly my little lady says it! I daresay now if I were to ask you for a kiss you wouldn't give it me: you'd say you'd *rather* not."

"I'll kiss you and welcome: bend your head down." Bessie stooped; we mutually embraced, and I followed her into the house quite comforted. That afternoon lapsed in peace and harmony; and in the evening Bessie told me some of her most enchanting stories, and sang me some of her sweetest songs. Even for me life had its gleams of sunshine.

Chapter V

Five o'clock had hardly struck on the morning of the 19th of January, when Bessie brought a candle into my closet, and found me already up and nearly dressed. I had risen half an hour before her entrance, and had washed my face, and put on my clothes by the light of a half-moon just setting, whose rays streamed through the narrow window near my crib. I was to leave Gateshead that day by a coach which passed the lodge gates at six A.M. Bessie was the only person yet risen; she had lit a fire in the nursery, where she now proceeded to make my breakfast. Few children can eat when excited with the thoughts of a journey; nor could I. Bessie, having pressed me in vain to take a few spoonfuls of the boiled milk and bread she had prepared for me, wrapped up some biscuits in a paper and put them into my bag; then she helped me on with my pelisse[1] and bonnet, and wrapping herself in a shawl, she and I left the nursery. As we passed Mrs. Reed's bedroom, she said, "Will you go in and bid Missis good-bye?"

"No, Bessie: she came to my crib last night when you were gone down to supper, and said I need not disturb her in the morning, or my cousins either; and she told me to remember that she had always been my best friend, and to speak of her and be grateful to her accordingly."

"What did you say, Miss?"

"Nothing: I covered my face with the bed-clothes, and turned from her to the wall."

"That was wrong, Miss Jane."

"It was quite right, Bessie: your Missis has not been my friend: she has been my foe."

"Oh, Miss Jane! don't say so!"

"Good-bye to Gateshead!" cried I, as we passed through the hall and went out at the front door.

The moon was set, and it was very dark; Bessie carried a lantern, whose light glanced on wet steps and gravel road sodden by a recent thaw. Raw and chill was the winter morning: my teeth chattered as I hastened down the drive. There was a light in the porter's lodge: when we reached it, we found the porter's wife just kindling her fire: my trunk, which had been carried down the evening before, stood corded at the door. It wanted but a few minutes of six, and shortly after that hour had struck the distant roll of wheels announced the coming coach; I went to the door, and watched its lamps approach rapidly through the gloom.

"Is she going by herself?" asked the porter's wife.

"Yes."

"And how far is it?"

"Fifty miles."

"What a long way! I wonder Mrs. Reed is not afraid to trust her so far alone."

The coach drew up; there it was at the gates with its four horses and its top laden with passengers: the guard and coachman loudly urged haste; my trunk was hoisted up; I was taken from Bessie's neck, to which I clung with kisses.

1. Long coat or cloak.

"Be sure and take good care of her," cried she to the guard, as he lifted me into the inside.

"Ay, ay!" was the answer: the door was slapped to, a voice exclaimed, "All right," and on we drove. Thus was I severed from Bessie and Gateshead: thus whirled away to unknown, and, as I then deemed, remote and mysterious regions.

I remember but little of the journey: I only know that the day seemed to me of a preternatural length, and that we appeared to travel over hundreds of miles of road. We passed through several towns, and in one, a very large one, the coach stopped; the horses were taken out, and the passengers alighted to dine. I was carried into an inn, where the guard wanted me to have some dinner; but, as I had no appetite, he left me in an immense room with a fire-place at each end, a chandelier pendent from the ceiling, and a little red gallery high up against the wall filled with musical instruments. Here I walked about for a long time, feeling very strange, and mortally apprehensive of some one coming in and kidnapping me; for I believed in kidnappers, their exploits having frequently figured in Bessie's fireside chronicles. At last the guard returned: once more I was stowed away in the coach, my protector mounted his own seat, sounded his hollow horn, and away we rattled over the "stony street" of L——.

The afternoon came on wet and somewhat misty: as it waned into dusk I began to feel that we were getting very far indeed from Gateshead: we ceased to pass through towns; the country changed; great gray hills heaved up round the horizon: as twilight deepened we descended a valley, dark with wood, and long after night had overclouded the prospect I heard a wild wind rushing amongst trees.

Lulled by the sound, I at last dropped asleep: I had not long slumbered when the sudden cessation of motion awoke me; the coach-door was open, and a person like a servant was standing at it: I saw her face and dress by the light of the lamps.

"Is there a little girl called Jane Eyre here?" she asked. I answered "Yes," and was then lifted out; my trunk was handed down, and the coach instantly drove away.

I was stiff with long sitting, and bewildered with the noise and motion of the coach: gathering my faculties, I looked about me. Rain, wind, and darkness filled the air; nevertheless, I dimly discerned a wall before me and a door open in it; through this door I passed with my new guide: she shut and locked it behind her. There was now visible a house or houses—for the building spread far—with many windows, and lights burning in some; we went up a broad pebbly path, splashing wet, and were admitted at a door; then the servant led me through a passage into a room with a fire, where she left me alone.

I stood and warmed my numbed fingers over the blaze, then I looked round; there was no candle, but the uncertain light from the hearth showed, by intervals, papered walls, carpet, curtains, shining mahogany furniture: it was a parlour, not so spacious or splendid as the drawing-room at Gateshead, but comfortable enough. I was puzzling to make out the subject of a picture on the wall, when the door opened, and an individual carrying a light entered; another followed close behind.

The first was a tall lady with dark hair, dark eyes, and a pale and large

forehead; her figure was partly enveloped in a shawl, her countenance was grave, her bearing erect.

"The child is very young to be sent alone," said she, putting her candle down on the table. She considered me attentively for a minute or two, then further added:

"She had better be put to bed soon; she looks tired: are you tired?" she asked, placing her hand on my shoulder.

"A little, ma'am."

"And hungry too, no doubt: let her have some supper before she goes to bed, Miss Miller. Is this the first time you have left your parents to come to school, my little girl?"

I explained to her that I had no parents. She inquired how long they had been dead; then how old I was, what was my name, whether I could read, write, and sew a little: then she touched my cheek gently with her forefinger, and saying, "She hoped I should be a good child," dismissed me along with Miss Miller.

The lady I had left might be about twenty-nine; the one who went with me appeared some years younger: the first impressed me by her voice, look, and air. Miss Miller was more ordinary; ruddy in complexion, though of a careworn countenance; hurried in gait and action, like one who had always a multiplicity of tasks on hand: she looked, indeed, what I afterwards found she really was, an under-teacher. Led by her, I passed from compartment to compartment, from passage to passage, of a large and irregular building; till, emerging from the total and somewhat dreary silence pervading that portion of the house we had traversed, we came upon the hum of many voices, and presently entered a wide, long room, with great deal tables, two at each end, on each of which burnt a pair of candles, and seated all round on benches a congregation of girls of every age, from nine or ten to twenty. Seen by the dim light of the dips, their number to me appeared countless, though not in reality exceeding eighty; they were uniformly dressed in brown stuff frocks of quaint fashion, and long holland pinafores. It was the hour of study; they were engaged in conning over[2] their tomorrow's task, and the hum I had heard was the combined result of their whispered repetitions.

Miss Miller signed to me to sit on a bench near the door, then walking up to the top of the long room, she cried out:

"Monitors, collect the lesson-books and put them away!"

Four tall girls arose from different tables, and going round, gathered the books and removed them. Miss Miller again gave the word of command:

"Monitors, fetch the supper-trays!"

The tall girls went out, and returned presently, each bearing a tray, with portions of something, I knew not what, arranged thereon, and a pitcher of water and mug in the middle of each tray. The portions were handed round; those who liked took a draught of the water, the mug being common to all. When it came to my turn, I drank, for I was thirsty, but did not touch the food, excitement and fatigue rendering me incapable of eating: I now saw, however, that it was a thin oaten cake, shared into fragments.

The meal over, prayers were read by Miss Miller, and the classes filed off, two and two, upstairs. Overpowered by this time with weariness, I scarcely

2. Committing to memory. "Stuff": a woollen fabric.

noticed what sort of a place the bedroom was; except that, like the school-room, I saw it was very long. Tonight I was to be Miss Miller's bedfellow; she helped me to undress: when laid down I glanced at the long rows of beds, each of which was quickly filled with two occupants; in ten minutes the single light was extinguished; amidst silence and complete darkness, I fell asleep.

The night passed rapidly: I was too tired even to dream; I only once awoke to hear the wind rave in furious gusts, and the rain fall in torrents, and to be sensible that Miss Miller had taken her place by my side. When I again unclosed my eyes, a loud bell was ringing: the girls were up and dressing; day had not yet begun to dawn, and a rush-light or two burned in the room. I too rose reluctantly; it was bitter cold, and I dressed as well as I could for shivering, and washed when there was a basin at liberty, which did not occur soon, as there was but one basin to six girls on the stands down the middle of the room. Again the bell rang: all formed in file, two and two, and in that order descended the stairs and entered the cold and dimly-lit schoolroom: here prayers were read by Miss Miller; afterwards she called out:—"Form classes!"

A great tumult succeeded for some minutes, during which Miss Miller repeatedly exclaimed, "Silence!" and "Order!" When it subsided, I saw them all drawn up in four semicircles, before four chairs, placed at the four tables; all held books in their hands, and a great book, like a Bible, lay on each table, before the vacant seat. A pause of some seconds succeeded, filled up by the low, vague hum of numbers; Miss Miller walked from class to class, hushing this indefinite sound.

A distant bell tinkled: immediately three ladies entered the room, each walked to a table and took her seat; Miss Miller assumed the fourth vacant chair, which was that nearest the door, and around which the smallest of the children were assembled: to this inferior class I was called, and placed at the bottom of it.

Business now began: the day's Collect[3] was repeated, then certain texts of Scripture were said, and to these succeeded a protracted reading of chapters in the Bible, which lasted an hour. By the time that exercise was terminated day had fully dawned. The indefatigable bell now sounded for the fourth time: the classes were marshalled and marched into another room to break-fast: how glad I was to behold a prospect of getting something to eat! I was now nearly sick from inanition, having taken so little the day before.

The refectory was a great, low-ceiled, gloomy room; on two long tables smoked basins of something hot, which, however, to my dismay, sent forth an odor far from inviting. I saw a universal manifestation of discontent when the fumes of the repast met the nostrils of those destined to swallow it: from the van of the procession, the tall girls of the first class, rose the whispered words:—"Disgusting! The porridge is burned again!"

"Silence!" ejaculated a voice; not that of Miss Miller, but one of the upper teachers, a little and dark personage, smartly dressed, but of somewhat morose aspect, who installed herself at the top of one table, while a more buxom lady presided at the other. I looked in vain for her I had first seen the night before; she was not visible: Miss Miller occupied the foot of the table

3. A short morning prayer, which varies with the days.

where I sat, and a strange, foreign looking, elderly lady, the French teacher, as I afterwards found, took the corresponding seat at the other board. A long grace was said and a hymn sung; then a servant brought in some tea for the teachers, and the meal began.

Ravenous, and now very faint, I devoured a spoonful or two of my portion without thinking of its taste; but the first edge of hunger blunted, I perceived I had got in hand a nauseous mess: burned porridge is almost as bad as rotten potatoes; famine itself soon sickens over it. The spoons were moved slowly: I saw each girl taste her food and try to swallow it; but in most cases the effort was soon relinquished. Breakfast was over, and none had breakfasted. Thanks being returned for what we had not got, and a second hymn chanted, the refectory was evacuated for the schoolroom. I was one of the last to go out, and in passing the tables, I saw one teacher take a basin of the porridge and taste it; she looked at the others; all their countenances expressed displeasure, and one of them, the stout one, whispered:—"Abominable stuff! How shameful!"

A quarter of an hour passed before lessons again began, during which the schoolroom was in a glorious tumult; for that space of time, it seemed to be permitted to talk loud and more freely, and they used their privilege. The whole conversation ran on the breakfast, which one and all abused roundly. Poor things! it was the sole consolation they had. Miss Miller was now the only teacher in the room: a group of great girls standing about her, spoke with serious and sullen gestures. I heard the name of Mr. Brocklehurst pronounced by some lips; at which Miss Miller shook her head disapprovingly; but she made no great effort to check the general wrath: doubtless she shared in it.

A clock in the schoolroom struck nine; Miss Miller left her circle, and standing in the middle of the room, cried:—"Silence! To your seats!"

Discipline prevailed: in five minutes the confused throng was resolved into order, and comparative silence quelled the Babel clamor of tongues. The upper teachers now punctually resumed their posts: but still, all seemed to wait. Ranged on benches down the sides of the room, the eighty girls sat motionless and erect: a quaint assemblage they appeared, all with plain locks combed from their faces, not a curl visible; in brown dresses, made high and surrounded by a narrow tucker about the throat, with little pockets of holland (shaped something like a Highlander's purse) tied in front of their frocks, and destined to serve the purpose of a work-bag: all too wearing woolen stockings and country-made shoes, fastened with brass buckles. Above twenty of those clad in this costume were full-grown girls, or rather young women; it suited them ill, and gave an air of oddity even to the prettiest.

I was still looking at them, and also at intervals examining the teachers— none of whom precisely pleased me; for the stout one was a little coarse, the dark one not a little fierce, the foreigner harsh and grotesque, and Miss Miller, poor thing! looked purple, weatherbeaten, and overworked—when, as my eye wandered from face to face, the whole school rose simultaneously, as if moved by a common spring.

What was the matter? I had heard no order given: I was puzzled. Ere I had gathered my wits, the classes were again seated: but as all eyes were now turned to one point, mine followed the general direction, and encountered the personage who had received me last night. She stood at the bottom of

the long room, on the hearth; for there was a fire at each end: she surveyed the two rows of girls silently and gravely. Miss Miller approaching, seemed to ask her a question, and having received her answer, went back to her place, and said aloud,—"Monitor of the first class, fetch the globes!"

While the direction was being executed, the lady consulted moved slowly up the room. I suppose I have a considerable organ of Veneration,[4] for I retain yet the sense of admiring awe with which my eyes traced her steps. Seen now, in broad daylight, she looked tall, fair, and shapely; brown eyes, with a benignant light in their irids,[5] and a fine penciling of long lashes round, relieved the whiteness of her large front; on each of her temples her hair, of a very dark brown, was clustered in round curls, according to the fashion of those times, when neither smooth bands nor long ringlets were in vogue; her dress, also in the mode of the day, was of purple cloth, relieved by a sort of Spanish trimming of black velvet; a gold watch (watches were not so common then as now) shone at her girdle. Let the reader add, to complete the picture, refined features; a complexion, if pale, clear; and a stately air and carriage, and he will have, at least, as clearly as words can give it, a correct idea of the exterior of Miss Temple—Maria Temple, as I afterwards saw the name written in a prayer-book entrusted to me to carry to church.

The superintendent of Lowood (for such was this lady) having taken her seat before a pair of globes placed on one of the tables, summoned the first class round her, and commenced giving a lesson in geography; the lower classes were called by the teachers: repetitions in history, grammar, etc., went on for an hour; writing and arithmetic succeeded, and music lessons were given by Miss Temple to some of the elder girls. The duration of each lesson was measured by the clock, which at last struck twelve. The superintendent rose:—"I have a word to address to the pupils," said she.

The tumult of cessation from lessons was already breaking forth, but it sank at her voice. She went on:—"You had this morning a breakfast which you could not eat; you must be hungry. I have ordered that a lunch of bread and cheese shall be served to all."

The teachers looked at her with a sort of surprise.

"It is to be done on my responsibility," she added, in an explanatory tone to them, and immediately afterwards left the room.

The bread and cheese was presently brought in and distributed, to the high delight and refreshment of the whole school. The order was now given, "To the garden!" Each put on a coarse straw bonnet, with strings of colored calico, and a cloak of gray frieze. I was similarly equipped, and, following the stream, I made my way into the open air.

The garden was a wide enclosure, surrounded with walls so high as to exclude every glimpse of prospect; a covered verandah ran down one side, and broad walks bordered a middle space divided into scores of little beds: these beds were assigned as gardens for the pupils to cultivate, and each bed had an owner. When full of flowers they would doubtless look pretty; but now, at the latter end of January, all was wintry blight and brown decay. I

4. A reference to the "science" of phrenology, much in vogue in the 19th century, according to which a person's mental and moral character could be determined by the shape of the skull.
5. Plural of *iris*.

shuddered as I stood and looked around me: it was an inclement day for outdoor exercise; not positively rainy, but darkened by a drizzling yellow fog; all underfoot was still soaking wet with the floods of yesterday. The stronger among the girls ran about and engaged in active games, but sundry pale and thin ones herded together for shelter and warmth in the veranda; and among these, as the dense mist penetrated to their shivering frames, I heard frequently the sound of a hollow cough.

As yet I had spoken to no one, nor did anybody seem to take notice of me; I stood lonely enough: but to that feeling of isolation I was accustomed; it did not oppress me much. I leant against a pillar of the veranda, drew my gray mantle close about me, and trying to forget the cold which nipped me without, and the unsatisfied hunger which gnawed me within, delivered myself up to the employment of watching and thinking. My reflections were too undefined and fragmentary to merit record: I hardly yet knew where I was; Gateshead and my past life seemed floated away to an immeasurable distance; the present was vague and strange, and of the future I could form no conjecture. I looked round the convent-like garden, and then up at the house; a large building, half of which seemed gray and old, the other half quite new. The new part, containing the schoolroom and dormitory, was lit by mullioned and latticed windows, which gave it a church-like aspect; a stone tablet over the door, bore this inscription:—

LOWOOD INSTITUTION.

THIS PORTION WAS REBUILT A.D.—, BY NAOMI BROCKLEHURST, OF BROCKLEHURST HALL, IN THIS COUNTY.

"Let your light so shine before men that they may see your good works, and glorify your Father which is in heaven."
—St. Matt. V. 16.

I read these words over and over again: I felt that an explanation belonged to them, and was unable fully to penetrate their import. I was still pondering the signification of "Institution," and endeavoring to make out a connection between the first words and the verse of Scripture, when the sound of a cough close behind me, made me turn my head. I saw a girl sitting on a stone bench near; she was bent over a book, on the perusal of which she seemed intent: from where I stood I could see the title—it was Rasselas[6]; a name that struck me as strange, and consequently attractive. In turning a leaf she happened to look up, and I said to her directly:—"Is your book interesting?" I had already formed the intention of asking her to lend it to me some day.

"I like it," she answered, after a pause of a second or two, during which she examined me.

"What is it about?" I continued. I hardly know where I found the hardihood thus to open a conversation with a stranger; the step was contrary to my nature and habits: but I think her occupation touched a chord of sympathy

6. *The History of Rasselas, Prince of Abyssinia* (1759), a popular didactic romance by Samuel Johnson.

somewhere; for I too liked reading, though of a frivolous and childish kind; I could not digest or comprehend the serious or substantial.

"You may look at it," replied the girl, offering me the book.

I did so; a brief examination convinced me that the contents were less taking than the title: *Rasselas* looked dull to my trifling taste; I saw nothing about fairies, nothing about genii; no bright variety seemed spread over the closely printed pages. I returned it to her; she received it quietly, and without saying anything she was about to relapse into her former studious mood: again I ventured to disturb her:—"Can you tell me what the writing on that stone over the door means? What is Lowood Institution?"

"This house where you are come to live."

"And why do they call it Institution? Is it in any way different from other schools?"

"It is partly a charity-school: you and I, and all the rest of us, are charity children. I suppose you are an orphan: are not either your father or your mother dead?"

"Both died before I can remember."

"Well, all the girls here have lost either one or both parents, and this is called an institution for educating orphans."

"Do we pay no money? Do they keep us for nothing?"

"We pay, or our friends pay, fifteen pounds a year for each."

"Then why do they call us charity children?"

"Because fifteen pounds is not enough for board and teaching, and the deficiency is supplied by subscription."

"Who subscribes?"

"Different benevolent-minded ladies and gentlemen in this neighborhood and in London."

"Who was Naomi Brocklehurst?"

"The lady who built the new part of this house as that tablet records, and whose son overlooks and directs everything here."

"Why?"

"Because he is treasurer and manager of the establishment."

"Then this house does not belong to that tall lady who wears a watch, and who said we were to have some bread and cheese?"

"To Miss Temple? Oh, no! I wish it did: she has to answer to Mr. Brocklehurst for all she does. Mr. Brocklehurst buys all our food and all our clothes."

"Does he live here?"

"No—two miles off, at a large hall."

"Is he a good man?"

"He is a clergyman, and is said to do a great deal of good."

"Did you say that tall lady was called Miss Temple?"

"Yes."

"And what are the other teachers called?"

"The one with red cheeks is called Miss Smith; she attends to the work, and cuts out—for we make our own clothes, our frocks, and pelisses, and everything; the little one with black hair is Miss Scatcherd; she teaches history and grammar, and hears the second class repetitions; and the one who wears a shawl, and has a pocket-handkerchief tied to her side with a yellow

riband, is Madame Pierrot: she comes from Lisle, in France, and teaches French."

"Do you like the teachers?"

"Well enough."

"Do you like the little black one, and the Madame ————?—I cannot pronounce her name as you do."

"Miss Scatcherd is hasty—you must take care not to offend her; Madame Pierrot is not a bad sort of person."

"But Miss Temple is the best—isn't she?"

"Miss Temple is very good, and very clever: she is above the rest, because she knows far more than they do."

"Have you been long here?"

"Two years."

"Are you an orphan?"

"My mother is dead."

"Are you happy here?"

"You ask rather too many questions. I have given you answers enough for the present: now I want to read."

But at the moment the summons sounded for dinner: all reentered the house. The odor which now filled the refectory was scarcely more appetizing than that which had regaled our nostrils at breakfast: the dinner was served in two huge tin-plated vessels, whence rose a strong steam redolent of rancid fat. I found the mess to consist of indifferent potatoes and strange shreds of rusty meat, mixed and cooked together. Of this preparation a tolerably abundant plateful was opportioned to each pupil. I ate what I could, and wondered within myself whether every day's fare would be like this.

After dinner, we immediately adjourned to the schoolroom: lessons recommenced, and were continued till five o'clock.

The only marked event of the afternoon was, that I saw the girl with whom I had conversed in the veranda, dismissed in disgrace, by Miss Scatcherd, from a history class, and sent to stand in the middle of the large schoolroom. The punishment seemed to me in a high degree ignominious, especially for so great a girl—she looked thirteen or upwards. I expected she would show signs of great distress and shame; but to my surprise she neither wept nor blushed: composed, though grave, she stood, the central mark of all eyes. "How can she bear it so quietly—so firmly?" I asked of myself. "Were I in her place, it seems to me I should wish the earth to open and swallow me up. She looks as if she were thinking of something beyond her punishment—beyond her situation: of something not round her nor before her. I have heard of daydreams—is she in a daydream now? Her eyes are fixed on the floor, but I am sure they do not see it—her sight seems turned in, gone down into her heart: she is looking at what she can remember, I believe; not at what is really present. I wonder what sort of a girl she is—whether good or naughty?"

Soon after five P.M. we had another meal, consisting of a small mug of coffee, and half a slice of brown bread. I devoured my bread and drank my coffee with relish; but I should have been glad of as much more—I was still hungry. Half an hour's recreation succeeded, then study: then the glass of water and the piece of oat-cake, prayers and bed. Such was my first day at Lowood.

Chapter VI

The next day commenced as before, getting up and dressing by rush-light; but this morning we were obliged to dispense with the ceremony of washing: the water in the pitchers was frozen. A change had taken place in the weather the preceding evening, and a keen north-east wind, whistling through the crevices of our bed-room windows all night long, had made us shiver in our beds, and turned the contents of the ewers to ice.

Before the long hour and a half of prayers and Bible reading was over, I felt ready to perish with cold. Breakfast-time came at last, and this morning the porridge was not burned; the quality was eatable, the quantity small; how small my portion seemed! I wished it had been doubled.

In the course of the day I was enrolled a member of the fourth class, and regular tasks and occupations were assigned me: hitherto, I had only been a spectator of the proceedings at Lowood, I was now to become an actor therein. At first, being little accustomed to learn by heart, the lessons appeared to me both long and difficult: the frequent change from task to task, too, bewildered me; and I was glad, when, about three o'clock in the afternoon, Miss Smith put into my hands a border of muslin two yards long, together with needle, thimble, etc., and sent me to sit in a quiet corner of the schoolroom, with directions to hem the same. At that hour most of the others were sewing likewise; but one class still stood round Miss Scatcherd's chair reading, and as all was quiet, the subject of their lessons could be heard, together with the manner in which each girl acquitted herself, and the animadversions[7] or commendations of Miss Scatcherd on the performance. It was English history: among the readers, I observed my acquaintance of the veranda: at the commencement of the lesson, her place had been at the top of the class, but for some error of pronunciation or some inattention to stops, she was suddenly sent to the very bottom. Even in that obscure position, Miss Scatcherd continued to make her an object of constant notice: she was continually addressing to her such phrases as the following:—

"Burns" (such it seems was her name: the girls here were all called by their surnames, as boys are elsewhere), "Burns, you are standing on the side of your shoe, turn your toes out immediately." "Burns, you poke your chin out most unpleasantly, draw it in." "Burns, I insist on your holding your head up: I will not have you before me in that attitude," etc., etc.

A chapter having been read through twice, the books were closed and the girls examined. The lesson had comprised part of the reign of Charles I, and there were sundry questions about tonnage and poundage, and ship-money, which most of them appeared unable to answer; still, every little difficulty was solved instantly when it reached Burns: her memory seemed to have retained the substance of the whole lesson, and she was ready with answers on every point. I kept expecting that Miss Scatcherd would praise her attention; but, instead of that, she suddenly cried out:—

"You dirty, disagreeable girl! you have never cleaned your nails this morning!"

Burns made no answer: I wondered at her silence.

7. Critical remarks.

"Why," thought I, "does she not explain that she could neither clean her nails nor wash her face, as the water was frozen?"

My attention was now called off by Miss Smith desiring me to hold a skein of thread: while she was winding it, she talked to me from time to time, asking whether I had ever been at school before, whether I could mark,[8] stitch, knit, etc.; till she dismissed me, I could not pursue my observations on Miss Scatcherd's movements. When I returned to my seat, that lady was just delivering an order, of which I did not catch the import; but Burns immediately left the class, and, going into the small inner room where the books were kept, returned in half a minute, carrying in her hand a bundle of twigs tied together at one end. This ominous tool she presented to Miss Scatcherd with a respectful curtsy; then she quietly, and without being told, unloosed her pinafore, and the teacher instantly and sharply inflicted on her neck a dozen strokes with the bunch of twigs. Not a tear rose to Burns' eye; and, while I paused from my sewing, because my fingers quivered at this spectacle with a sentiment of unavailing and impotent anger, not a feature of her pensive face altered its ordinary expression.

"Hardened girl!" exclaimed Miss Scatcherd; "nothing can correct you of your slatternly habits: carry the rod away."

Burns obeyed: I looked at her narrowly as she emerged from the book-closet; she was just putting back her handkerchief into her pocket, and the trace of a tear glistened on her thin cheek.

The play-hour in the evening I thought the pleasantest fraction of the day at Lowood: the bit of bread, the draught of coffee swallowed at five o'clock had revived vitality, if it had not satisfied hunger; the long restraint of the day was slackened; the schoolroom felt warmer than in the morning—its fires being allowed to burn a little more brightly to supply, in some measure, the place of candles, not yet introduced; the ruddy gloaming,[9] the licensed uproar, the confusion of many voices, gave one a welcome sense of liberty.

On the evening of the day on which I had seen Miss Scatcherd flog her pupil, Burns, I wandered as usual among the forms and tables and laughing groups without a companion, yet not feeling lonely; when I passed the windows, I now and then lifted a blind and looked out; it snowed fast, a drift was already forming against the lower panes; putting my ear close to the window, I could distinguish from the gleeful tumult within, the disconsolate moan of the wind outside.

Probably, if I had lately left a good home and kind parents, this would have been the hour when I should most keenly have regretted the separation: that wind would then have saddened my heart; this obscure chaos would have disturbed my peace: as it was, I derived from both a strange excitement, and reckless and feverish, I wished the wind to howl more wildly, the gloom to deepen to darkness, and the confusion to rise to clamor.

Jumping over forms,[1] and creeping under tables, I made my way to one of the fire-places: there, kneeling by the high wire fender, I found Burns, absorbed, silent, abstracted from all round her by the companionship of a book, which she read by the dim glare of the embers.

"Is it still *Rasselas*?" I asked, coming behind her.

8. Embroider.
9. Twilight, dusk.

1. Benches.

"Yes," she said, "and I have just finished it."

And in five minutes more she shut it up. I was glad of this.

"Now," thought I, "I can perhaps get her to talk." I sat down by her on the floor.

"What is your name besides Burns?"

"Helen."

"Do you come a long way from here?"

"I come from a place further north; quite on the borders of Scotland."

"Will you ever go back?"

"I hope so; but nobody can be sure of the future."

"You must wish to leave Lowood?"

"No: why should I? I was sent to Lowood to get an education; and it would be of no use going away until I have attained that object."

"But that teacher, Miss Scatcherd, is so cruel to you?"

"Cruel? Not at all! She is severe: she dislikes my faults."

"And if I were in your place I should dislike her; I should resist her; if she struck me with that rod, I should get it from her hand; I should break it under her nose."

"Probably you would do nothing of the sort: but if you did, Mr. Brocklehurst would expel you from the school; that would be a great grief to your relations. It is far better to endure patiently a smart which nobody feels but yourself, than to commit a hasty action whose evil consequences will extend to all connected with you; and, besides, the Bible bids us return good for evil."[2]

"But then it seems disgraceful to be flogged, and to be sent to stand in the middle of a room full of people; and you are such a great girl: I am far younger than you, and I could not bear it."

"Yet it would be your duty to bear it, if you could not avoid it: it is weak and silly to say you *cannot bear* what it is your fate to be required to bear."

I heard her with wonder: I could not comprehend this doctrine of endurance; and still less could I understand or sympathize with the forbearance she expressed for her chastiser. Still I felt that Helen Burns considered things by a light invisible to my eyes. I suspected she might be right and I wrong; but I would not ponder the matter deeply: like Felix, I put it off to a more convenient season.[3]

"You say you have faults, Helen: what are they? To me you seem very good."

"Then learn from me, not to judge by appearances: I am, as Miss Scatcherd said, slatternly; I seldom put, and never keep, things in order; I am careless; I forget rules; I read when I should learn my lessons; I have no method; and sometimes I say, like you, I cannot *bear* to be subjected to systematic arrangements. This is all very provoking to Miss Scatcherd, who is naturally neat, punctual, and particular."

"And cross and cruel," I added; but Helen Burns would not admit my addition: she kept silence.

"Is Miss Temple as severe to you as Miss Scatcherd?"

2. For this teaching of Jesus, see Matthew 5.38–48, Luke 6.27–36; see also 1 Peter 3.8–9.

3. Felix, the Roman governor of Judea, was impressed by the eloquence of the apostle Paul, and so put off his trial to "a convenient season" (Acts 24.24–27).

At the utterance of Miss Temple's name, a soft smile flitted over her grave face.

"Miss Temple is full of goodness: it pains her to be severe to anyone, even the worst in the school; she sees my errors, and tells me of them gently; and, if I do anything worthy of praise, she gives me my meed liberally. One strong proof of my wretchedly defective nature is, that even her expostulations, so mild, so rational, have not influence to cure me of my faults; and even her praise, though I value it most highly, cannot stimulate me to continued care and foresight."

"That is curious," said I: "it is so easy to be careful."

"For *you* I have no doubt it is. I observed you in your class this morning, and saw you were closely attentive: your thoughts never seemed to wander while Miss Miller explained the lesson and questioned you. Now, mine continually rove away: when I should be listening to Miss Scatcherd, and collecting all she says with assiduity, often I lose the very sound of her voice; I fall into a sort of dream. Sometimes I think I am in Northumberland, and that the noises I hear round me are the bubbling of a little brook which runs through Deepden near our house;—then, when it comes to my turn to reply, I have to be wakened; and, having heard nothing of what was read for listening to the visionary brook, I have no answer ready."

"Yet how well you replied this afternoon."

"It was mere chance: the subject on which we had been reading had interested me. This afternoon, instead of dreaming of Deepden, I was wondering how a man who wished to do right could act so unjustly and unwisely as Charles the First sometimes did; and I thought what a pity it was that, with his integrity and conscientiousness, he could see no farther than the prerogatives of the crown. If he had but been able to look to a distance, and see to what they call the spirit of the age was tending! Still, I like Charles—I respect him—I pity him, poor murdered king![4] Yes, his enemies were the worst: they shed blood they had no right to shed. How dared they kill him!"

Helen was talking to herself now: she had forgotten I could not very well understand her—that I was ignorant, or nearly so, of the subject she discussed. I recalled her to my level.

"And when Miss Temple teaches you, do your thoughts wander then?"

"No, certainly, not often; because Miss Temple has generally something to say which is newer than my own reflections: her language is singularly agreeable to me, and the information she communicates is often just what I wished to gain."

"Well, then, with Miss Temple you are good?"

"Yes, in a passive way: I make no effort; I follow as inclination guides me. There is no merit in such goodness."

"A great deal: you are good to those who are good to you. It is all I ever desire to be. If people were always kind and obedient to those who are cruel and unjust, the wicked people would have it all their own way; they would never feel afraid, and so they would never alter, but would grow worse and worse. When we are struck at without a reason, we should strike back again

4. The reign of the Charles I (1600–1649; r. 1625–1649) led to the English Civil War, which ended in his beheading after he was tried before the House of Commons.

very hard; I am sure we should—so hard as to teach the person who struck us never to do it again."

"You will change your mind, I hope, when you grow older: as yet you are but a little untaught girl."

"But I feel this, Helen: I must dislike those who, whatever I do to please them, persist in disliking me; I must resist those who punish me unjustly. It is as natural as that I should love those who show me affection, or submit to punishment when I feel it is deserved."

"Heathens and savage tribes hold that doctrine; but Christians and civilized nations disown it."

"How? I don't understand."

"It is not violence that best overcomes hate—nor vengeance that most certainly heals injury."

"What then?"

"Read the New Testament, and observe what Christ says, and how he acts; make his word your rule, and his conduct your example."

"What does he say?"

"Love your enemies; bless them that curse you; do good to them that hate you and despitefully use you."[5]

"Then I should love Mrs. Reed, which I cannot do; I should bless her son John, which is impossible."

In her turn, Helen Burns asked me to explain, and I proceeded forthwith to pour out, in my own way, the tale of my sufferings and resentments. Bitter and truculent when excited, I spoke as I felt, without reserve or softening.

Helen heard me patiently to the end: I expected she would then make a remark, but she said nothing.

"Well," I asked impatiently, "is not Mrs. Reed a hard-hearted, bad woman?"

"She has been unkind to you, no doubt; because, you see, she dislikes your cast of character, as Miss Scatcherd does mine: but how minutely you remember all she has done and said to you! What a singularly deep impression her injustice seems to have made on your heart! No ill-usage so brands its record on my feelings. Would you not be happier if you tried to forget her severity, together with the passionate emotions it excited? Life appears to me too short to be spent in nursing animosity, or registering wrongs. We are, and must be, one and all, burdened with faults in this world: but the time will soon come when, I trust, we shall put them off in putting off our corruptible bodies; when debasement and sin will fall from us with this cumbrous frame of flesh, and only the spark of the spirit will remain,—the impalpable principle of life and thought, pure as when it left the Creator to inspire the creature: whence it came it will return; perhaps again to be communicated to some being higher than man—perhaps to pass through gradations of glory, from the pale human soul to brighten to the seraph! Surely it will never, on the contrary, be suffered to degenerate from man to fiend? No; I cannot believe that: I hold another creed; which no one ever taught me, and which I seldom mention; but in which I delight, and to which I cling: for it extends hope to all: it makes Eternity a rest—a mighty home, not a terror and an abyss. Besides, with this creed, I can so clearly distinguish

5. Matthew 5.44.

between the criminal and his crime; I can so sincerely forgive the first while I abhor the last: with this creed revenge never worries my heart, degradation never too deeply disgusts me, injustice never crushes me too low: I live in calm, looking to the end."

Helen's head, always drooping, sank a little lower as she finished this sentence. I saw by her look she wished no longer to talk to me, but rather to converse with her own thoughts. She was not allowed much time for meditation: a monitor, a great rough girl, presently came up, exclaiming in a strong Cumberland accent,—

"Helen Burns, if you don't go and put your drawer in order, and fold up your work this minute, I'll tell Miss Scatcherd to come and look at it!"

Helen sighed as her reverie fled, and getting up, obeyed the monitor without reply as without delay.

Chapter VII

My first quarter at Lowood seemed an age; and not the golden age either: it comprised an irksome struggle with difficulties in habituating myself to new rules and unwonted tasks. The fear of failure in these points harassed me worse than the physical hardships of my lot; though these were no trifles.

During January, February, and part of March, the deep snows, and, after their melting, the almost impassable roads, prevented our stirring beyond the garden walls, except to go to church; but within these limits we had to pass an hour every day in the open air. Our clothing was insufficient to protect us from the severe cold: we had no boots, the snow got into our shoes and melted there; our ungloved hands became numbed and covered with chilblains, as were our feet: I remember well the distracting irritation I endured from this cause every evening, when my feet inflamed; and the torture of thrusting the swelled, raw, and stiff toes into my shoes in the morning. Then the scanty supply of food was distressing: with the keen appetites of growing children, we had scarcely sufficient to keep alive a delicate invalid. From this deficiency of nourishment resulted an abuse, which pressed hardly on the younger pupils: whenever the famished great girls had an opportunity, they would coax or menace the little ones out of their portion. Many a time I have shared between two claimants the precious morsel of brown bread distributed at tea-time; and after relinquishing to a third, half the contents of my mug of coffee, I have swallowed the remainder with an accompaniment of secret tears, forced from me by the exigency of hunger.

Sundays were dreary days in that wintry season. We had to walk two miles to Brocklebridge Church, where our patron officiated. We set out cold, we arrived at church colder: during the morning service we became almost paralyzed. It was too far to return to dinner, and an allowance of cold meat and bread, in the same penurious proportion observed in our ordinary meals, was served round between the services.

At the close of the afternoon service we returned by an exposed and hilly road, where the bitter winter wind, blowing over a range of snowy summits to the north, almost flayed the skin from our faces.

I can remember Miss Temple walking lightly and rapidly along our drooping line, her plaid cloak, which the frosty wind fluttered, gathered close about her, and encouraging us, by precept and example, to keep up our spirits, and

march forward, as she said, "like stalwart soldiers." The other teachers, poor things, were generally themselves too much dejected to attempt the task of cheering others.

How we longed for the light and heat of a blazing fire when we got back! But, to the little ones at least, this was denied: each hearth in the schoolroom was immediately surrounded by a double row of great girls, and behind them the younger children crouched in groups, wrapping their starved[6] arms in their pinafores.

A little solace came at tea-time, in the shape of a double ration of bread—a whole, instead of a half, slice—with the delicious addition of a thin scrape of butter: it was the hebdomadal treat to which we all looked forward from Sabbath to Sabbath. I generally contrived to reserve a moiety[7] of this bounteous repast for myself; but the remainder I was invariably obliged to part with.

The Sunday evening was spent in repeating, by heart, the Church Catechism, and the fifth, sixth, and seventh chapters of St. Matthew; and in listening to a long sermon, read by Miss Miller, whose irrepressible yawns attested her weariness. A frequent interlude of these performances was the enactment of the part of Eutychus by some half dozen of little girls; who, overpowered with sleep, would fall down, if not out of the third loft, yet off the fourth form, and be taken up half dead.[8] The remedy was, to thrust them forward into the center of the schoolroom, and oblige them to stand there till the sermon was finished. Sometimes their feet failed them, and they sank together in a heap; they were then propped up with the monitors' high stools.

I have not yet alluded to the visits of Mr. Brocklehurst; and indeed that gentleman was from home during the greater part of the first month after my arrival; perhaps prolonging his stay with his friend the archdeacon: his absence was a relief to me. I need not say that I had my own reasons for dreading his coming: but come he did at last.

One afternoon (I had then been three weeks at Lowood), as I was sitting with a slate in my hand, puzzling over a sum in long division, my eyes, raised in abstraction to the window, caught sight of a figure just passing: I recognized almost instinctively that gaunt outline; and when two minutes after, all the school, teachers included, rose *en masse*, it was not necessary for me to look up in order to ascertain whose entrance they thus greeted. A long stride measured the schoolroom, and presently beside Miss Temple, who herself had risen, stood the same black column which had frowned on me so ominously from the hearth-rug of Gateshead. I now glanced sideways at this piece of architecture. Yes, I was right: it was Mr. Brocklehurst, buttoned up in a surtout,[9] and looking longer, narrower, and more rigid than ever.

I had my own reasons for being dismayed at this apparition: too well I remembered the perfidious hints given by Mrs. Reed about my disposition, etc.; the promise pledged by Mr. Brocklehurst to apprise Miss Temple and the teachers of my vicious nature. All along I had been dreading the fulfillment of this promise,—I had been looking out daily for the "Coming Man," whose information respecting my past life and conversation was to brand me

6. Frozen: literally, starved for warmth.
7. Half. "Hebdomadal": weekly.
8. Eutychus fell asleep while listening to the apos-

tle Paul and consequently fell from a third-story window ("third loft") (Acts 20.7–12).
9. Long, close-fitting overcoat.

as a bad child forever: now there he was. He stood at Miss Temple's side; he was speaking low in her ear: I did not doubt he was making disclosures of my villainy; and I watched her eye with painful anxiety, expecting every moment to see its dark orb turn on me a glance of repugnance and contempt. I listened too; and as I happened to be seated quite at the top of the room, I caught most of what he said: its import relieved me from immediate apprehension.

"I suppose, Miss Temple, the thread I bought at Lowton will do; it struck me that it would be just of the quality for the calico chemises, and I sorted the needles to match. You may tell Miss Smith that I forgot to make a memorandum of the darning needles, but she shall have some papers sent in next week; and she is not, on any account, to give out more than one at a time to each pupil: if they have more, they are apt to be careless and lose them. And, oh ma'am! I wish the woolen stockings were better looked to!—when I was here last, I went into the kitchen-garden and examined the clothes drying on the line; there was a quantity of black hose in a very bad state of repair: from the size of the holes in them I was sure they had not been well mended from time to time."

He paused.

"Your directions shall be attended to, sir," said Miss Temple.

"And, ma'am," he continued, "the laundress tells me some of the girls have two clean tuckers[1] in the week: it is too much; the rules limit them to one."

"I think I can explain that circumstance, sir. Agnes and Catherine Johnstone were invited to take tea with some friends at Lowton last Thursday, and I gave them leave to put on clean tuckers for the occasion."

Mr. Brocklehurst nodded.

"Well, for once it may pass; but please not to let the circumstance occur too often. And there is another thing which surprised me: I find, in settling accounts with the housekeeper, that a lunch, consisting of bread and cheese, has twice been served out to the girls during the past fortnight. How is this? I look over the regulations, and I find no such meal as lunch mentioned. Who introduced this innovation? and by what authority?"

"I must be responsible for the circumstance, sir," replied Miss Temple: "the breakfast was so ill-prepared that the pupils could not possibly eat it; and I dared not allow them to remain fasting till dinnertime."

"Madam, allow me an instant. You are aware that my plan in bringing up these girls is, not to accustom them to habits of luxury and indulgence, but to render them hardy, patient, self-denying. Should any little accidental disappointment of the appetite occur, such as the spoiling of a meal, the under or the over dressing of a dish, the incident ought not to be neutralized by replacing with something more delicate the comfort lost, thus pampering the body and obviating the aim of this institution; it ought to be improved to the spiritual edification of the pupils, by encouraging them to evince fortitude under the temporary privation. A brief address on those occasions would not be mistimed, wherein a judicious instructor would take the opportunity of referring to the sufferings of the primitive Christians; to the torments of martyrs; to the exhortations of our blessed Lord himself, calling upon his disciples to take up their cross and follow him; to his warnings that man

1. Pieces of cloth in the neckline of a dress.

shall not live by bread alone, but by every word that proceedeth out of the mouth of God; to his divine consolations, 'if ye suffer hunger or thirst for my sake, happy are ye.'[2] Oh, madam, when you put bread and cheese, instead of burned porridge, into these children's mouths, you may indeed feed their vile bodies, but you little think how you starve their immortal souls!"

Mr. Brocklehurst again paused—perhaps overcome by his feelings. Miss Temple had looked down when he first began to speak to her; but she now gazed straight before her, and her face, naturally pale as marble, appeared to be assuming also the coldness and fixity of that material; especially her mouth, closed as if it would have required a sculptor's chisel to open it, and her brow settled gradually into petrified severity.

Meantime, Mr. Brocklehurst, standing on the hearth with his hands behind his back, majestically surveyed the whole school. Suddenly his eye gave a blink, as if it had met something that either dazzled or shocked its pupil; turning, he said in more rapid accents than he had hitherto used:— "Miss Temple, Miss Temple, what—*what* is that girl with curled hair? Red hair, ma'am, curled—curled all over?" And extending his cane he pointed to the awful object, his hand shaking as he did so.

"It is Julia Severn," replied Miss Temple, very quietly.

"Julia Severn, ma'am! And why has she, or any other, curled hair? Why, in defiance of every precept and principle of this house, does she conform to the world so openly—here in an evangelical, charitable establishment— as to wear her hair one mass of curls?"

"Julia's hair curls naturally," returned Miss Temple, still more quietly.

"Naturally! Yes, but we are not to conform to nature: I wish these girls to be the children of Grace: and why that abundance? I have again and again intimated that I desire the hair to be arranged closely, modestly, plainly. Miss Temple, that girl's hair must be cut off entirely; I will send a barber tomorrow: and I see others who have far too much of the excrescence—that tall girl, tell her to turn round. Tell all the first form to rise up and direct their faces to the wall."

Miss Temple passed her handkerchief over her lips, as if to smooth away the involuntary smile that curled them; she gave the order, however, and when the first class could take in what was required of them, they obeyed. Leaning a little back on my bench, I could see the looks and grimaces with which they commented on this maneuver: it was a pity Mr. Brocklehurst could not see them too; he would perhaps have felt that, whatever he might do with the outside of the cup and platter, the inside was further beyond his interference than he imagined.[3]

He scrutinized the reverse of these living medals some five minutes, then pronounced sentence. These words fell like the knell of doom:—"All those top-knots must be cut off."

Miss Temple seemed to remonstrate.

"Madam," he pursued, "I have a master to serve whose kingdom is not of this world: my mission is to mortify in these girls the lusts of the flesh; to

2. Brocklehurst misquotes Matthew 5.6: "Blessed are they which do hunger and thirst after righteousness: for they shall be filled." For man not living by bread alone, see Deuteronomy 8.3; Matthew 4.4; Luke 4.4.

3. "Woe to you, scribes and Pharisees, hypocrites! for ye make clean the outside of the cup and of the platter, but within they are full of extortion and excess" (Matthew 23.25).

teach them to clothe themselves with shamefacedness and sobriety, not with braided hair and costly apparel; and each of the young persons before us has a string of hair twisted in plaits which vanity itself might have woven: these, I repeat, must be cut off; think of the time wasted, of——"

Mr. Brocklehurst was here interrupted: three other visitors, ladies, now entered the room. They ought to have come a little sooner to have heard his lecture on dress, for they were splendidly attired in velvet, silk, and furs. The two younger of the trio (fine girls of sixteen and seventeen) had gray beaver hats, then in fashion, shaded with ostrich plumes, and from under the brim of this graceful head-dress fell a profusion of light tresses, elaborately curled; the elder lady was enveloped in a costly velvet shawl, trimmed with ermine, and she wore a false front[4] of French curls.

These ladies were deferentially received by Miss Temple, as Mrs. and the Misses Brocklehurst, and conducted to seats of honor at the top of the room. It seems they had come in the carriage with their reverend relative, and had been conducting a rummaging scrutiny of the rooms upstairs, while he transacted business with the housekeeper, questioned the laundress, and lectured the superintendent. They now proceeded to address divers remarks and reproofs to Miss Smith, who was charged with the care of the linen and the inspection of the dormitories: but I had no time to listen to what they said; other matters called off and enchained my attention.

Hitherto, while gathering up the discourse of Mr. Brocklehurst and Miss Temple, I had not, at the same time, neglected precautions to secure my personal safety; which I thought would be effected, if I could only elude observation. To this end, I had sat well back on the form, and while seeming to be busy with my sum, had held my slate in such a manner as to conceal my face: I might have escaped notice, had not my treacherous slate somehow happened to slip from my hand and falling with an obtrusive crash, directly drawn every eye upon me; I knew it was all over now, and, as I stooped to pick up the two fragments of slate, I rallied my forces for the worst. It came.

"A careless girl!" said Mr. Brocklehurst, and immediately after—"It is the new pupil, I perceive." And before I could draw breath, "I must not forget I have a word to say respecting her." Then aloud: how loud it seemed to me! "Let the child who broke her slate, come forward!"

Of my own accord, I could not have stirred: I was paralyzed: but the two great girls who sat on each side of me, set me on my legs and pushed me towards the dread judge, and then Miss Temple gently assisted me to his very feet, and I caught her whispered counsel,—"Don't be afraid, Jane, I saw it was an accident; you shall not be punished."

The kind whisper went to my heart like a dagger.

"Another minute, and she will despise me for a hypocrite," thought I; and an impulse of fury against Reed, Brocklehurst, and Co. bounded in my pulses at the conviction. I was no Helen Burns. "Fetch that stool," said Mr. Brocklehurst, pointing to a very high one from which a monitor had just risen: it was brought.

"Place the child upon it"

And I was placed there, by whom I don't know: I was in no condition to note particulars: I was only aware that they had hoisted me up to the height

4. Hairpiece. "Beaver": a heavy fabric made of wool and fur.

of Mr. Brocklehurst's nose, that he was within a yard of me, and that a spread of shot orange and purple silk pelisses, and a cloud of silvery plumage extended and waved below me.

Mr. Brocklehurst hemmed.

"Ladies," said he, turning to his family; "Miss Temple, teachers, and children, you all see this girl?"

Of course they did; for I felt their eyes directed like burning-glasses against my scorched skin.

"You see she is yet young; you observe she possesses the ordinary form of childhood; God has graciously given her the shape that he has given to all of us; no signal deformity points her out as a marked character. Who would think that the Evil One had already found a servant and agent in her? Yet such, I grieve to say, is the case."

A pause—in which I began to steady the palsy of my nerves, and to feel that the Rubicon was passed;[5] and that the trial, no longer to be shirked, must be firmly sustained.

"My dear children," pursued the black marble clergyman, with pathos, "this is a sad, a melancholy occasion; for it becomes my duty to warn you, that this girl, who might be one of God's own lambs, is a little castaway: not a member of the true flock, but evidently an interloper and an alien. You must be on your guard against her; you must shun her example: if necessary, avoid her company, exclude her from your sports, and shut her out from your converse. Teachers, you must watch her: keep your eyes on her movements, weigh well her words, scrutinize her actions, punish her body to save her soul: if, indeed, such salvation be possible, for (my tongue falters while I tell it) this girl, this child, the native of a Christian land, worse than many a little heathen who says its prayers to Brahma and kneels before Juggernaut[6]—this girl is—a liar!"

Now came a pause of ten minutes; during which I, by this time in perfect possession of my wits, observed all the female Brocklehursts produce their pocket-handkerchiefs and apply them to their optics, while the elderly lady swayed herself to and fro, and the two younger ones whispered, "How shocking!"

Mr. Brocklehurst resumed.

"This I learned from her benefactress; from the pious and charitable lady who adopted her in her orphan state, reared her as her own daughter, and whose kindness, whose generosity the unhappy girl repaid by an ingratitude so bad, so dreadful, that at last her excellent patroness was obliged to separate her from her own young ones, fearful lest her vicious example should contaminate their purity: she has sent her here to be healed, even as the Jews of old sent their diseased to the troubled pool of Bethesda;[7] and, teachers, superintendent, I beg of you not to allow the waters to stagnate round her."

With this sublime conclusion, Mr. Brocklehurst adjusted the top button of his surtout, muttered something to his family, who rose, bowed to Miss Temple, and then all the great people sailed in state from the room. Turning

5. I.e., the point of no return was crossed.
6. Hindu gods.

7. Bethesda, literally, "house of grace," was the pool where Jesus healed an invalid (John 5.2–9).

at the door, my judge said:—"Let her stand half an hour longer on that stool, and let no one speak to her during the remainder of the day."

There was I, then, mounted aloft: I, who had said I could not bear the shame of standing on my natural feet in the middle of the room, was now exposed to general view on a pedestal of infamy. What my sensations were, no language can describe: but just as they all rose, stifling my breath and constricting my throat, a girl came up and passed me: in passing, she lifted her eyes. What a strange light inspired them! What an extraordinary sensation that ray sent through me! How the new feeling bore me up! It was as if a martyr, a hero, had passed a slave or victim, and imparted strength in the transit. I mastered the rising hysteria, lifted up my head, and took a firm stand on the stool. Helen Burns asked some slight question about her work of Miss Smith, was chidden for the triviality of the inquiry, returned to her place, and smiled at me as she again went by. What a smile! I remember it now, and I know that it was the effluence of fine intellect, of true courage; it lit up her marked lineaments, her thin face, her sunken gray eye, like a reflection from the aspect of an angel. Yet at that moment Helen Burns wore on her arm the "untidy badge"; scarcely an hour ago I had heard her condemned by Miss Scatcherd to a dinner of bread and water on the morrow, because she had blotted an exercise in copying it out. Such is the imperfect nature of man! such spots are there on the disc of the clearest planet; and eyes like Miss Scatcherd's can only see those minute defects, and are blind to the full brightness of the orb.

Chapter VIII

Ere the half-hour ended, five o'clock struck; school was dismissed and all were gone into the refectory to tea. I now ventured to descend: it was deep dusk; I retired into a corner and sat down on the floor. The spell by which I had been so far supported began to dissolve; reaction took place, and soon, so overwhelming was the grief that seized me, I sank prostrate with my face to the ground. Now I wept: Helen Burns was not here; nothing sustained me; left to myself I abandoned myself, and my tears watered the boards. I had meant to be so good, and to do so much at Lowood: to make so many friends, to earn respect, and win affection. Already I had made visible progress: that very morning I had reached the head of my class; Miss Miller had praised me warmly; Miss Temple had smiled approbation; she had promised to teach me drawing, and to let me learn French, if I continued to make similar improvement two months longer: and then I was well-received by my fellow-pupils; treated as an equal by those of my own age, and not molested by any; now, here I lay again crushed and trodden on; and could I ever rise more?

"Never," I thought; and ardently I wished to die. While sobbing out this wish in broken accents, someone approached: I started up—again Helen Burns was near me; the fading fires just showed her coming up the long, vacant room; she brought my coffee and bread.

"Come, eat something," she said; but I put both away from me, feeling as if a drop or a crumb would have choked me in my present condition. Helen regarded me, probably with surprise: I could not now abate my agitation, though I tried hard; I continued to weep aloud. She sat down on the ground

near me, embraced her knees with her arms, and rested her head upon them; in that attitude she remained silent as an Indian. I was the first who spoke:— "Helen, why do you stay with a girl whom everybody believes to be a liar?"

"Everybody, Jane? Why, there are only eighty people who have heard you called so, and the world contains hundreds of millions."

"But what have I to do with millions? The eighty I know despise me."

"Jane, you are mistaken: probably not one in the school either despises or dislikes you: many, I am sure, pity you much."

"How can they pity me after what Mr. Brocklehurst said?"

"Mr. Brocklehurst is not a god: nor is he even a great and admired man: he is little liked here; he never took steps to make himself liked. Had he treated you as an especial favorite, you would have found enemies, declared or covert, all around you: as it is, the greater number would offer you sympathy if they dared. Teachers and pupils may look coldly on you for a day or two, but friendly feelings are concealed in their hearts; and if you persevere in doing well, these feelings will ere long appear so much the more evident for their temporary suppression. Besides, Jane,"—she paused.

"Well, Helen?" said I, putting my hand into hers: she chafed my fingers gently to warm them, and went on:—

"If all the world hated you, and believed you wicked, while your own conscience approved you, and absolved you from guilt, you would not be without friends."

"No; I know I should think well of myself; but that is not enough: if others don't love me, I would rather die than live—I cannot bear to be solitary and hated, Helen. Look here; to gain some real affection from you, or Miss Temple, or any other whom I truly love, I would willingly submit to have the bone of my arm broken, or to let a bull toss me, or to stand behind a kicking horse, and let it dash its hoof at my chest,"—

"Hush, Jane! you think too much of the love of human beings, you are too impulsive, too vehement: the sovereign hand that created your frame, and put life into it, has provided you with other resources than your feeble self, or than creatures feeble as you. Besides this earth, and besides the race of men, there is an invisible world and a kingdom of spirits: that world is round us, for it is everywhere; and those spirits watch us, for they are commissioned to guard us; and if we were dying in pain and shame, if scorn smote us on all sides, and hatred crushed us, angels see our tortures, recognize our innocence (if innocent we be: as I know you are of this charge which Mr. Brocklehurst has weakly and pompously repeated at second-hand from Mrs. Reed; for I read a sincere nature in your ardent eyes and on your clear front), and God waits only the separation of spirit from flesh to crown us with a full reward. Why, then, should we ever sink overwhelmed with distress, when life is so soon over, and death is so certain an entrance to happiness—to glory?"

I was silent: Helen had calmed me; but in the tranquility she imparted there was an alloy of inexpressible sadness. I felt the impression of woe as she spoke, but I could not tell whence it came; and when, having done speaking, she breathed a little fast and coughed a short cough, I momentarily forgot my own sorrows to yield to a vague concern for her.

Resting my head on Helen's shoulder, I put my arms round her waist; she drew me to her, and we reposed in silence. We had not sat long thus, when

another person came in. Some heavy clouds, swept from the sky by a rising wind, had left the moon bare; and her light, streaming in through a window near, shone full both on us and on the approaching figure, which we at once recognized as Miss Temple.

"I came on purpose to find you, Jane Eyre," said she; "I want you in my room; and as Helen Burns is with you, she may come too."

We went; following the superintendent's guidance, we had to thread some intricate passages, and mount a staircase before we reached her apartment; it contained a good fire, and looked cheerful. Miss Temple told Helen Burns to be seated in a low arm-chair on one side of the hearth, and herself taking another, she called me to her side.

"Is it all over?" she asked, looking down at my face. "Have you cried your grief away?"

"I am afraid I never shall do that."

"Why?"

"Because I have been wrongly accused; and you, ma'am, and everybody else will now think me wicked."

"We shall think you what you prove yourself to be, my child. Continue to act as a good girl, and you will satisfy me."

"Shall I, Miss Temple?"

"You will," said she, passing her arm round me. "And now tell me who is the lady whom Mr. Brocklehurst called your benefactress?"

"Mrs. Reed, my uncle's wife. My uncle is dead, and left me to her care."

"Did she not, then, adopt you of her own accord?"

"No, ma'am; she was sorry to have to do it: but my uncle, as I have often heard the servants say, got her to promise before he died, that she would always keep me."

"Well, now, Jane, you know, or at least I will tell you, that when a criminal is accused, he is always allowed to speak in his own defence. You have been charged with falsehood; defend yourself to me as well as you can. Say whatever your memory suggests as true; but add nothing and exaggerate nothing."

I resolved, in the depth of my heart, that I would be most moderate—most correct; and, having reflected a few minutes in order to arrange coherently what I had to say, I told her all the story of my sad childhood. Exhausted by emotion, my language was more subdued than it generally was when it developed that sad theme; and mindful of Helen's warnings against the indulgence of resentment, I infused into the narrative far less of gall and wormwood than ordinary. Thus restrained and simplified, it sounded more credible: I felt as I went on that Miss Temple fully believed me.

In the course of the tale I had mentioned Mr. Lloyd as having come to see me after the fit: for I never forgot the, to me, frightful episode of the red-room; in detailing which, my excitement was sure, in some degree, to break bounds; for nothing could soften in my recollection the spasm of agony which clutched my heart when Mrs. Reed spurned my wild supplication for pardon, and locked me a second time in the dark and haunted chamber.

I had finished: Miss Temple regarded me a few minutes in silence; she then said:—"I know something of Mr. Lloyd; I shall write to him; if his reply agrees with your statement, you shall be publicly cleared from every imputation: to me, Jane, you are clear now."

She kissed me, and still keeping me at her side (where I was well contented

to stand, for I derived a child's pleasure from the contemplation of her face, her dress, her one or two ornaments, her white forehead, her clustered and shining curls, and beaming dark eyes), she proceeded to address Helen Burns.

"How are you tonight, Helen? Have you coughed much today?"

"Not quite so much, I think, ma'am."

"And the pain in your chest?"

"It is a little better."

Miss Temple got up, took her hand and examined her pulse; then she returned to her own seat: as she resumed it, I heard her sigh low. She was pensive a few minutes, then rousing herself, she said cheerfully:—"But you two are my visitors tonight; I must treat you as such." She rang her bell.

"Barbara," she said to the servant who answered it, "I have not yet had tea; bring the tray, and place cups for these two young ladies."

And a tray was soon brought. How pretty, to my eyes, did the china cups and bright teapot look, placed on the little round table near the fire! How fragrant was the steam of the beverage, and the scent of the toast! of which, however, I, to my dismay (for I was beginning to be hungry), discerned only a very small portion: Miss Temple discerned it too:—"Barbara," said she, "can you not bring a little more bread and butter? There is not enough for three."

Barbara went out: she returned soon:—"Madam, Mrs. Harden says she has sent up the usual quantity."

Mrs. Harden, be it observed, was the housekeeper: a woman after Mr. Brocklehurst's own heart, made up of equal parts of whalebone and iron.

"Oh, very well!" returned Miss Temple; "we must make it do, Barbara, I suppose." And as the girl withdrew, she added, smiling, "Fortunately, I have it in my power to supply deficiencies for this once."

Having invited Helen and me to approach the table, and placed before each of us a cup of tea with one delicious but thin morsel of toast, she got up, unlocked a drawer, and taking from it a parcel wrapped in paper, disclosed presently to our eyes a good-sized seed-cake.

"I meant to give each of you some of this to take with you," said she; "but as there is so little toast, you must have it now," and she proceeded to cut slices with a generous hand.

We feasted that evening as on nectar and ambrosia; and not the least delight of the entertainment was the smile of gratification with which our hostess regarded us, as we satisfied our famished appetites on the delicate fare she liberally supplied. Tea over and the tray removed, she again summoned us to the fire; we sat one on each side of her, and now a conversation followed between her and Helen, which it was indeed a privilege to be admitted to hear.

Miss Temple had always something of serenity in her air, of state in her mien, of refined propriety in her language, which precluded deviation into the ardent, the excited, the eager: something which chastened the pleasure of those who looked on her and listened to her, by a controlling sense of awe; and such was my feeling now; but as to Helen Burns, I was struck with wonder.

The refreshing meal, the brilliant fire, the presence and kindness of her beloved instructress, or, perhaps, more than all these, something in her own

unique mind, had roused her powers within her. They woke, they kindled: first, they glowed in the bright tint of her cheek, which till this hour I had never seen but pale and bloodless; then they shone in the liquid luster of her eyes, which had suddenly acquired a beauty more singular than that of Miss Temple's—a beauty neither of fine color nor long eyelash, nor penciled brow, but of meaning, of movement, of radiance. Then her soul sat on her lips, and language flowed, from what source I cannot tell: has a girl of fourteen a heart large enough, vigorous enough, to hold the swelling spring of pure full, fervid eloquence? Such was the characteristic of Helen's discourse on that, to me, memorable evening; her spirit seemed hastening to live within a very brief span as much as many live during a protracted existence.

They conversed of things I had never heard of: of nations and times past; of countries far away: of secrets of nature discovered or guessed at: they spoke of books: how many they had read! What stores of knowledge they possessed! Then they seemed so familiar with French names and French authors: but my amazement reached its climax when Miss Temple asked Helen if she sometimes snatched a moment to recall the Latin her father had taught her, and taking a book from a shelf, bade her read and construe a page of "Virgil"; and Helen obeyed, my organ of Veneration expanding at every sounding line. She had scarcely finished ere the bell announced bedtime: no delay could be admitted; Miss Temple embraced us both, saying, as she drew us to her heart:—"God bless you, my children!"

Helen she held a little longer than me: she let her go more reluctantly; it was Helen her eye followed to the door; it was for her she a second time breathed a sad sigh; for her she wiped a tear from her cheek.

On reaching the bedroom, we heard the voice of Miss Scatcherd: she was examining drawers; she had just pulled out Helen Burns' and when we entered Helen was greeted with a sharp reprimand, and told that tomorrow she should have half a dozen of untidily-folded articles pinned to her shoulder.

"My things were indeed in shameful disorder," murmured Helen to me, in a low voice: "I intended to have arranged them, but I forgot."

Next morning, Miss Scatcherd wrote in conspicuous characters on a piece of pasteboard the word "Slattern," and bound it like a phylactery[8] round Helen's large, mild, intelligent, and benign-looking forehead. She wore it till evening, patient, unresentful, regarding it as a deserved punishment. The moment Miss Scatcherd withdrew after afternoon-school, I ran to Helen, tore it off, and thrust it into the fire: the fury of which she was incapable had been burning in my soul all day, and tears, hot and large, had continually been scalding my cheek; for the spectacle of her sad resignation gave me an intolerable pain at the heart.

About a week subsequently to the incidents above narrated, Miss Temple, who had written to Mr. Lloyd, received his answer: it appeared that what he said went to corroborate my account. Miss Temple, having assembled the whole school, announced that inquiry had been made into the charges alleged against Jane Eyre, and that she was most happy to be able to pronounce her completely cleared from every imputation. The teachers then

8. Box containing scriptural passages, worn by Orthodox Jewish men during some prayers.

shook hands with me and kissed me, and a murmur of pleasure ran through the ranks of my companions.

Thus relieved of a grievous load, I from that hour set to work afresh, resolved to pioneer my way through every difficulty: I toiled hard, and my success was proportionate to my efforts; my memory, not naturally tenacious, improved with practice: exercise sharpened my wits; in a few weeks I was promoted to a higher class; in less than two months I was allowed to commence French and drawing. I learned the first two tenses of the verb Etre,[9] and sketched my first cottage (whose walls, by-the-by, outrivaled in slope those of the leaning tower of Pisa), on the same day. That night, on going to bed, I forgot to prepare in imagination the Barmecide[1] supper of hot roast potatoes, or white bread and new milk, with which I was wont to amuse my inward cravings: I feasted instead on the spectacle of ideal drawings, which I saw in the dark; all the work of my own hands: freely pencilled houses and trees, picturesque rocks and ruins, Cuyplike groups of cattle, sweet paintings of butterflies hovering over unblown[2] roses, of birds picking at ripe cherries, of wrens' nests enclosing pearl-like eggs, wreathed about with young ivy sprays. I examined, too, in thought, the possibility of my ever being able to translate currently[3] a certain little French story-book which Madame Pierrot had that day shown me; nor was the problem solved to my satisfaction ere I fell sweetly asleep.

Well has Solomon said—"Better is a dinner of herbs where love is, than a stalled ox and hatred therewith."[4]

I would not now have exchanged Lowood with all its privations, for Gateshead and its daily luxuries.

Chapter IX

But the privations, or rather the hardships, of Lowood lessened. Spring drew on: she was indeed already come; the frosts of winter had ceased; its snows were melted, its cutting winds ameliorated. My wretched feet, flayed and swollen to lameness by the sharp air of January, began to heal and subside under the gentler breathings of April; the nights and mornings no longer by their Canadian temperature froze the very blood in our veins; we could now endure the play-hour passed in the garden: sometimes on a sunny day it began even to be pleasant and genial, and a greenness grew over those brown beds, which, freshening daily, suggested the thought that Hope traversed them at night, and left each morning brighter traces of her steps. Flowers peeped out amongst the leaves; snowdrops, crocuses, purple auriculas, and golden-eyed pansies. On Thursday afternoons (half-holidays) we now took walks, and found still sweeter flowers opening by the wayside, under the hedges.

I discovered, too, that a great pleasure, an enjoyment which the horizon only bounded, lay all outside the high and spike-guarded walls of our garden: this pleasure consisted in prospect of noble summits girdling a great hill-hollow, rich in verdure and shadow; in a bright beck,[5] full of dark stones and

9. To be (French).
1. A wealthy man in The Arabian Nights who invites a beggar to an imaginary banquet.
2. Unblossomed. Albert Cuyp (1620–1691), Dutch landscape painter.
3. Fluently (a translation of the French couramment).
4. Proverbs 15.17.
5. Brook.

sparkling eddies. How different had this scene looked when I viewed it laid out beneath the iron sky of winter, stiffened in frost, shrouded with snow!—when mists as chill as death wandered to the impulse of east winds along those purple peaks, and rolled down "ing" and holm[6] till they blended with the frozen fog of the beck. That beck itself was then a torrent, turbid and curbless: it tore asunder the wood, and sent a raving sound through the air, often thickened with wild rain or whirling sleet; and for the forest on its banks, *that* showed only ranks of skeletons.

April advanced to May: a bright, serene May it was; days of blue sky, placid sunshine, and soft western or southern gales filled up its duration. And now vegetation matured with vigor; Lowood shook loose its tresses; it became all green, all flowery; its great elm, ash, and oak skeletons were restored to majestic life; woodland plants sprang up profusely in its recesses; unnumbered varieties of moss filled its hollows, and it made a strange ground-sunshine out of the wealth of its wild primrose plants: I have seen their pale gold gleam in overshadowed spots like scatterings of the sweetest luster. All this I enjoyed often and fully, free, unwatched, and almost alone: for this unwonted liberty and pleasure there was a cause, to which it now becomes my task to advert.

Have I not described a pleasant site for a dwelling, when I speak of it as bosomed in hill and wood, and rising from the verge of a stream? Assuredly, pleasant enough: but whether healthy or not is another question.

That forest-dell, where Lowood lay, was the cradle of fog and fog-bred pestilence; which, quickening with the quickening spring, crept into the Orphan Asylum, breathed typhus through its crowded school-room and dormitory, and, ere May arrived, transformed the seminary into a hospital.

Semistarvation and neglected colds had predisposed most of the pupils to receive infection: forty-five out of the eighty girls lay ill at one time. Classes were broken up, rules relaxed. The few who continued well were allowed almost unlimited license; because the medical attendant insisted on the necessity of frequent exercise to keep them in health: and had it been otherwise, no one had leisure to watch or restrain them. Miss Temple's whole attention was absorbed by the patients: she lived in the sick-room, never quitting it except to snatch a few hours' rest at night. The teachers were fully occupied with packing up and making other necessary preparations for the departure of those girls who were fortunate enough to have friends and relations able and willing to remove them from the seat of contagion. Many, already smitten, went home only to die: some died at the school, and were buried quietly and quickly, the nature of the malady forbidding delay.

While disease had thus become an inhabitant of Lowood, and death its frequent visitor; while there was gloom and fear within its walls; while its rooms and passages steamed with hospital smells, the drug and the pastille striving vainly to overcome the effluvia[7] of mortality, that bright May shone unclouded over the bold hills and beautiful woodland out of doors. Its garden, too, glowed with flowers; hollyhocks had sprung up tall as trees, lilies had opened, tulips and roses were in bloom; the borders of the little beds were gay with pink thrift and crimson double-daisies; the sweetbriers gave out, morning and evening, their scent of spice and apples; and these fragrant

6. Meadow and low ground beside a brook.
7. Offensive smells. "Pastille": an aromatic paste for fumigating a room's air.

treasures were all useless for most of the inmates of Lowood, except to furnish now and then a handful of herbs and blossoms to put in a coffin.

But I, and the rest who continued well, enjoyed fully the beauties of the scene and season: they let us ramble in the wood, like gipsies, from morning till night; we did what we liked, went where we liked: we lived better too. Mr. Brocklehurst and his family never came near Lowood now: household matters were not scrutinized into; the cross housekeeper was gone, driven away by the fear of infection; her successor, who had been matron at the Lowton Dispensary, unused to the ways of her new abode, provided with comparative liberality. Besides, there were fewer to feed: the sick could eat little; our breakfast-basins were better filled: when there was no time to prepare a regular dinner, which often happened, she would give us a large piece of cold pie, or a thick slice of bread and cheese, and this we carried away with us to the wood, where we each chose the spot we liked best, and dined sumptuously.

My favorite seat was a smooth and broad stone, rising white and dry from the very middle of the beck, and only to be got at by wading through the water; a feat I accomplished barefoot. The stone was just broad enough to accommodate, comfortably, another girl and me, at that time my chosen comrade—one Mary Ann Wilson; a shrewd, observant personage, whose society I took pleasure in, partly because she was witty and original, and partly because she had a manner which set me at my ease. Some years older than I, she knew more of the world, and could tell me many things I liked to hear: with her my curiosity found gratification: to my faults also she gave ample indulgence, never imposing curb or rein on anything I said. She had a turn for narrative, I for analysis; she liked to inform, I to question; so we got on swimmingly together, deriving much entertainment, if not much improvement, from our mutual intercourse.

And where, meantime, was Helen Burns? Why did I not spend these sweet days of liberty with her? Had I forgotten her? or was I so worthless as to have grown tired of her pure society? Surely the Mary Ann Wilson I have mentioned was inferior to my first acquaintance: she could only tell me amusing stories, and reciprocate any racy and pungent gossip I chose to indulge in; while, if I have spoken truth of Helen, she was qualified to give those who enjoyed the privilege of her converse, a taste of far higher things.

True, reader; and I knew and felt this: and though I am a defective being, with many faults and few redeeming points, yet I never tired of Helen Burns; nor ever ceased to cherish for her a sentiment of attachment, as strong, tender, and respectful as any that ever animated my heart. How could it be otherwise, when Helen, at all times and under all circumstances, evinced for me a quiet and faithful friendship, which ill-humor never soured, nor irritation ever troubled? But Helen was ill at present: for some weeks she had been removed from my sight to I knew not what room upstairs. She was not, I was told, in the hospital portion of the house with the fever patients; for her complaint was consumption,[8] not typhus: and by consumption I, in my ignorance, understood something mild, which time and care would be sure to alleviate.

I was confirmed in this idea by the fact of her once or twice coming downstairs on very warm sunny afternoons, and being taken by Miss Temple into

8. Tuberculosis.

the garden: but, on these occasions, I was not allowed to go and speak to her; I only saw her from the schoolroom window, and then not distinctly; for she was much wrapped up, and sat at a distance under the veranda.

One evening, in the beginning of June, I had stayed out very late with Mary Ann in the wood; we had, as usual, separated ourselves from the others and had wandered far: so far that we lost our way, and had to ask it at a lonely cottage, where a man and woman lived, who looked after a herd of half-wild swine that fed on the mast[9] in the wood. When we got back it was after moon-rise: a pony, which we knew to be the surgeon's, was standing at the garden door. Mary Ann remarked that she supposed some one must be very ill, as Mr. Bates had been sent for at that time of the evening. She went into the house; I stayed behind a few minutes to plant in my garden a handful of roots I had dug up in the forest, and which I feared would wither if I left them till the morning. This done, I lingered yet a little longer: the flowers smelt so sweet as the dew fell; it was such a pleasant evening, so serene, so warm; the still glowing west promised so fairly another fine day on the morrow; the moon rose with such majesty in the grave east. I was noting these things and enjoying them as a child might, when it entered my mind as it had never done before:—

"How sad to be lying now on a sick bed, and to be in danger of dying! This world is pleasant—it would be dreary to be called from it, and to have to go who knows where?"

And then my mind made its first earnest effort to comprehend what had been infused into it concerning heaven and hell: and for the first time it recoiled, baffled; and for the first time glancing behind, on each side, and before it, it saw all round an unfathomed gulf: it felt the one point where it stood—the present; all the rest was formless cloud and vacant depth: and it shuddered at the thought of tottering, and plunging amid that chaos. While pondering this new idea, I heard the front door open; Mr. Bates came out, and with him was a nurse. After she had seen him mount his horse and depart, she was about to close the door, but I ran up to her.

"How is Helen Burns?"

"Very poorly," was the answer.

"Is it her Mr. Bates has been to see?"

"Yes."

"And what does he say about her?"

"He says she'll not be here long."

This phrase, uttered in my hearing yesterday, would have only conveyed the notion that she was about to be removed to Northumberland, to her own home. I should not have suspected that it meant she was dying; but I knew instantly now: it opened clear on my comprehension that Helen Burns was numbering her last days in this world, and that she was going to be taken to the region of spirits, if such region there were. I experienced a shock of horror, then a strong thrill of grief, then a desire—a necessity to see her, and I asked in what room she lay.

"She is in Miss Temple's room," said the nurse.

"May I go up and speak to her?"

"Oh, no, child! It is not likely[1]; and now it is time for you to come in; you'll catch the fever if you stop out when the dew is falling."

9. Nuts on the forest floor. 1. Appropriate.

The nurse closed the front door; I went in by the side entrance which led to the schoolroom: I was just in time; it was nine o'clock, and Miss Miller was calling the pupils to go to bed.

It might be two hours later, probably near eleven, when I—not having been able to fall asleep, and deeming, from the perfect silence of the dormitory, that my companions were all wrapt in profound repose—rose softly, put on my frock over my night-dress, and, without shoes, crept from the apartment, and set off in quest of Miss Temple's room. It was quite at the other end of the house; but I knew my way; and the light of the unclouded summer moon, entering here and there at passage windows, enabled me to find it without difficulty. An odor of camphor and burned vinegar warned me when I came near the fever room: and I passed its door quickly, fearful lest the nurse who sat up all night should hear me. I dreaded being discovered and sent back; for I *must* see Helen,—I must embrace her before she died,—I must give her one last kiss, exchange with her one last word.

Having descended a staircase, traversed a portion of the house below, and succeeded in opening and shutting, without noise, two doors, I reached another flight of steps; these I mounted, and then just opposite to me was Miss Temple's room. A light shone through the key-hole, and from under the door; a profound stillness pervaded the vicinity. Coming near, I found the door slightly ajar; probably to admit some fresh air into the close abode of sickness. Indisposed to hesitate, and full of impatient impulses—soul and senses quivering with keen throes—I put it back and looked in. My eye sought Helen, and feared to find death.

Close by Miss Temple's bed, and half covered with its white curtains, there stood a little crib. I saw the outline of a form under the clothes, but the face was hid by the hangings: the nurse I had spoken to in the garden sat in an easy-chair, asleep; an unsnuffed candle burned dimly on the table. Miss Temple was not to be seen: I knew afterwards that she had been called to a delirious patient in the fever-room. I advanced; then paused by the crib side: my hand was on the curtain, but I preferred speaking before I withdrew it. I still recoiled at the dread of seeing a corpse.

"Helen!" I whispered softly, "are you awake?"

She stirred herself, put back the curtain, and I saw her face, pale, wasted, but quite composed: she looked so little changed that my fear was instantly dissipated.

"Can it be you, Jane?" she asked in her own gentle voice.

"Oh!" I thought, "she is not going to die: they are mistaken: she could not speak and look so calmly if she were."

I got on to her crib and kissed her: her forehead was cold, and her cheek both cold and thin, and so were her hand and wrist; but she smiled as of old.

"Why are you come here, Jane? It is past eleven o'clock: I heard it strike some minutes since."

"I came to see you, Helen: I heard you were very ill, and I could not sleep till I had spoken to you."

"You came to bid me good-bye, then: you are just in time probably."

"Are you going somewhere, Helen? Are you going home?"

"Yes; to my long home—my last home."

"No, no, Helen!" I stopped distressed. While I tried to devour my tears, a fit of coughing seized Helen; it did not, however, wake the nurse; when it

was over, she lay some minutes exhausted; then she whispered:—"Jane, your little feet are bare; lie down and cover yourself with my quilt."

I did so: she put her arm over me, and I nestled close to her. After a long silence, she resumed; still whispering,—

"I am very happy, Jane; and when you hear that I am dead, you must be sure and not grieve: there is nothing to grieve about. We all must die one day, and the illness which is removing me is not painful; it is gentle and gradual: my mind is at rest. I leave no one to regret me much: I have only a father; and he is lately married, and will not miss me. By dying young, I shall escape great sufferings. I had not qualities or talents to make my way very well in the world; I should have been continually at fault."

"But where are you going to, Helen? Can you see? Do you know?"

"I believe: I have faith: I am going to God."

"Where is God? What is God?"

"My Maker and yours, who will never destroy what he created. I rely implicitly on his power, and confide wholly in his goodness: I count the hours till that eventful one arrives which shall restore me to him, reveal him to me."

"You are sure, then, Helen, that there is such a place as heaven; and that our souls can get to it when we die?"

"I am sure there is a future state; I believe God is good; I can resign my immortal part to him without any misgiving. God is my father; God is my friend: I love him; I believe he loves me."

"And shall I see you again, Helen, when I die?"

"You will come to the same region of happiness: be received by the same mighty, universal Parent, no doubt, dear Jane."

Again I questioned; but this time only in thought. "Where is that region? Does it exist?" And I clasped my arms closer round Helen; she seemed dearer to me than ever; I felt as if I could not let her go; I lay with my face hidden on her neck. Presently she said in the sweetest tone,—"How comfortable I am! That last fit of coughing has tired me a little; I feel as if I could sleep: but don't leave me, Jane; I like to have you near me."

"I'll stay with you, *dear* Helen: no one shall take me away."

"Are you warm, darling?"

"Yes."

"Goodnight, Jane."

"Good-night, Helen."

She kissed me, and I her; and we both soon slumbered.

When I awoke it was day: an unusual movement roused me, I looked up; I was in somebody's arms; the nurse held me; she was carrying me through the passage back to the dormitory. I was not reprimanded for leaving my bed; people had something else to think about: no explanation was afforded then to my many questions; but a day or two afterwards I learned that Miss Temple, on returning to her own room at dawn, had found me laid in a little crib; my face against Helen Burns' shoulder, my arms around her neck. I was asleep, and Helen was—dead.

Her grave is in Brocklebridge churchyard: for fifteen years after her death it was only covered by a grassy mound; but now a gray marble tablet marks the spot, inscribed with her name, and the word "Resurgam."[2]

2. I shall rise again (Latin).

Chapter X

Hitherto I have recorded in detail the events of my insignificant existence: to the first ten years of my life, I have given almost as many chapters. But this is not to be a regular autobiography: I am only bound to invoke memory where I know her responses will possess some degree of interest; therefore I now pass a space of eight years almost in silence: a few lines only are necessary to keep up the links of connection.

When the typhus fever had fulfilled its mission of devastation at Lowood, it gradually disappeared from thence; but not till its virulence and the number of its victims had drawn public attention on the school. Inquiry was made into the origin of the scourge, and by degrees various facts came out which excited public indignation in a high degree. The unhealthy nature of the site; the quantity and quality of the children's food; the brackish, fetid water used in its preparation; the pupils' wretched clothing and accommodation: all these things were discovered; and the discovery produced a result mortifying to Mr. Brocklehurst, but beneficial to the institution.

Several wealthy and benevolent individuals in the county subscribed largely for the erection of a more convenient building in a better situation; new regulations were made; improvements in diet and clothing introduced; the funds of the school were entrusted to the management of a committee. Mr. Brocklehurst, who, from his wealth and family connections, could not be overlooked, still retained the post of treasurer; but he was aided in the discharge of his duties by gentlemen of rather more enlarged and sympathizing minds: his office of inspector, too, was shared by those who knew how to combine reason with strictness, comfort with economy, compassion with uprightness. The school, thus improved, became in time a truly useful and noble institution. I remained an inmate of its walls, after its regeneration, for eight years: six as pupil, and two as teacher; and in both capacities I bear my testimony to its value and importance.

During these eight years my life was uniform: but not unhappy, because it was not inactive. I had the means of an excellent education placed within my reach. A fondness for some of my studies, and a desire to excel in all, together with a great delight in pleasing my teachers, especially such as I loved, urged me on: I availed myself fully of the advantages offered me. In time I rose to be the first girl of the first class; then I was invested with the office of teacher; which I discharged with zeal for two years; but at the end of that time I altered.

Miss Temple, through all changes, had thus far continued superintendent of the seminary: to her instruction I owed the best part of my acquirements; her friendship and society had been my continual solace: she had stood me in the stead of mother, governess, and, latterly, companion. At this period she married, removed with her husband (a clergyman, an excellent man, almost worthy of such a wife) to a distant county, and consequently was lost to me.

From the day she left I was no longer the same: with her was gone every settled feeling, every association that had made Lowood in some degree a home to me. I had imbibed from her something of her nature and much of her habits: more harmonious thoughts: what seemed better-regulated feelings had become the inmates of my mind. I had given in allegiance to duty

and order; I was quiet; I believed I was content: to the eyes of others, usually even to my own, I appeared a disciplined and subdued character.

But destiny, in the shape of the Rev. Mr. Nasmyth, came between me and Miss Temple: I saw her in her traveling dress step into a post-chaise, shortly after the marriage ceremony; I watched the chaise mount the hill and disappear beyond its brow; and then retired to my own room, and there spent in solitude the greatest part of the half-holiday granted in honour of the occasion.

I walked about the chamber most of the time. I imagined myself only to be regretting my loss, and thinking how to repair it; but when my reflections were concluded, and I looked up and found that the afternoon was gone, and evening far advanced, another discovery dawned on me, namely, that in the interval I had undergone a transforming process; that my mind had put off all it had borrowed of Miss Temple—or rather that she had taken with her the serene atmosphere I had been breathing in her vicinity—and that now I was left in my natural element, and beginning to feel the stirring of old emotions. It did not seem as if a prop were withdrawn, but rather as if a motive were gone; it was not the power to be tranquil which had failed me, but the reason for tranquility was no more. My world had for some years been in Lowood: my experience had been of its rules and systems; now I remembered that the real world was wide, and that a varied field of hopes and fears, of sensations and excitements, awaited those who had courage to go forth into its expanse, to seek real knowledge of life amid its perils.

I went to my window, opened it, and looked out. There were the two wings of the building; there was the garden; there were the skirts of Lowood; there was the hilly horizon. My eye passed all other objects to rest on those most remote, the blue peaks: it was those I longed to surmount; all within their boundary of rock and heath seemed prison-ground, exile limits. I traced the white road winding round the base of one mountain, and vanishing in a gorge between two: how I longed to follow it further! I recalled the time when I had traveled that very road in a coach; I remembered descending that hill at twilight: an age seemed to have elapsed since the day which brought me first to Lowood, and I had never quitted it since. My vacations had all been spent at school: Mrs. Reed had never sent for me to Gateshead; neither she nor any of her family had ever been to visit me. I had had no communication by letter or message with the outer world: school-rules, school-duties, school-habits and notions, and voices, and faces, and phrases, and costumes, and preferences, and antipathies: such was what I knew of existence. And now I felt that it was not enough: I tired of the routine of eight years in one afternoon. I desired liberty; for liberty I gasped; for liberty I uttered a prayer; it seemed scattered on the wind then faintly blowing. I abandoned it and framed a humbler supplication; for change, stimulus: that petition, too, seemed swept off into vague space: "Then," I cried, half desperate, "grant me at least a new servitude!"

Here a bell, ringing the hour of supper, called me downstairs.

I was not free to resume the interrupted chain of my reflections till bedtime: even then a teacher who occupied the same room with me kept me from the subject to which I longed to recur, by a prolonged effusion of small talk. How I wished sleep would silence her! It seemed as if, could I but go

back to the idea which had last entered my mind as I stood at the window, some inventive suggestion would rise for my relief.

Miss Gryce snored at last; she was a heavy Welshwoman, and till now her habitual nasal strains had never been regarded by me in any other light than as a nuisance; tonight I hailed the first deep notes with satisfaction; I was debarrassed[3] of interruption; my half-effaced thought instantly revived.

"A new servitude! There is something in that," I soliloquized (mentally, be it understood; I did not talk aloud). "I know there is, because it does not sound too sweet; it is not like such words as Liberty, Excitement, Enjoyment: delightful sounds truly; but no more than sounds for me; and so hollow and fleeting that it is mere waste of time to listen to them. But Servitude! That must be matter of fact. Any one may serve: I have served here eight years; now all I want is to serve elsewhere. Can I not get so much of my own will? Is not the thing feasible? Yes—yes—the end is not so difficult; if I had only a brain active enough to ferret out the means of attaining it."

I sat up in bed by way of arousing this said brain: it was a chilly night; I covered my shoulders with a shawl, and then I proceeded to *think* again with all my might.

"What do I want? A new place, in a new house, amongst new faces, under new circumstances: I want this because it is of no use wanting anything better. How do people do to get a new place? They apply to friends, I suppose: I have no friends. There are many others who have no friends, who must look about for themselves and be their own helpers; and what is their resource?"

I could not tell: nothing answered me; I then ordered my brain to find a response, and quickly. It worked and worked faster: I felt the pulses throb in my head and temples; but for nearly an hour it worked in chaos, and no result came of its efforts. Feverish with vain labor, I got up and took a turn in the room; undrew the curtain, noted a star or two, shivered with cold, and again crept to bed.

A kind fairy, in my absence, had surely dropped the required suggestion on my pillow; for as I lay down it came quietly and naturally to my mind:—"Those who want situations advertise; you must advertise in the ——shire *Herald*."

"How? I know nothing about advertising."

Replies rose smooth and prompt now:—"You must inclose the advertisement and the money to pay for it under a cover directed to the Editor of the *Herald*; you must put it, the first opportunity you have, into the post at Lowton; answers must be addressed to J. E. at the post-office there: you can go and inquire in about a week after you send your letter, if any are come, and act accordingly."

This scheme I went over twice, thrice; it was then digested in my mind: I had it in a clear practical form; I felt satisfied, and fell asleep.

With earliest day I was up: I had my advertisement written, inclosed, and directed before the bell rang to rouse the school: it ran thus:—

"A young lady accustomed to tuition" (had I not been a teacher two years?) "is desirous of meeting with a situation in a private family where the children are under fourteen" (I thought that as I was barely eighteen, it would not do

3. Relieved, freed (from the French *debarrassée*, literally "disencumbered").

to undertake the guidance of pupils nearer my own age). "She is qualified to teach the usual branches of a good English education, together with French, Drawing, and Music" (in those days, reader, this now narrow catalog of accomplishments would have been held tolerably comprehensive). "Address, J. E., Post-office, Lowton, ——shire."

This document remained locked in my drawer all day: after tea, I asked leave of the new superintendent to go to Lowton, in order to perform some small commissions for myself and one or two of my fellow-teachers; permission was readily granted: I went. It was a walk of two miles, and the evening was wet, but the days were still long; I visited a shop or two, slipped the letter into the post-office, and came back through heavy rain, with streaming garments, but with a relieved heart.

The succeeding week seemed long: it came to an end at last, however, like all sublunary things, and once more, towards the close of a pleasant autumn day, I found myself afoot on the road to Lowton. A picturesque track it was, by the way, lying along the side of the beck and through the sweetest curves of the dale: but that day I thought more of the letters, that might or might not be awaiting me at the little burgh whither I was bound, than of the charms of lea and water.

My ostensible errand on this occasion was to get measured for a pair of shoes; so I discharged that business first, and when it was done, I stepped across the clean and quiet little street from the shoemaker's to the post-office; it was kept by an old dame, who wore horn spectacles on her nose and black mittens on her hands.

"Are there any letters for J. E.?" I asked.

She peered at me over her spectacles, and then she opened a drawer, and fumbled among its contents for a long time—so long that my hopes began to falter. At last, having held a document before her glasses for nearly five minutes, she presented it across the counter, accompanying the act by another inquisitive and mistrustful glance—it was for J. E.

"Is there only one?" I demanded.

"There are no more," said she; and I put it in my pocket and turned my face homeward: I could not open it then; rules obliged me to be back by eight, and it was already half-past seven.

Various duties awaited me on my arrival: I had to sit with the girls during their hour of study; then it was my turn to read prayers; to see them to bed: afterwards I supped with the other teachers. Even when we finally retired for the night, the inevitable Miss Gryce was still my companion: we had only a short end of candle in our candlestick, and I dreaded lest she should talk till it was all burnt out: fortunately, however, the heavy supper she had eaten produced a soporific effect: she was already snoring before I had finished undressing. There still remained an inch of candle: I now took out my letter; the seal was an initial F.; I broke it: the contents were brief.

"If J. E., who advertised in the ——shire Herald of last Thursday, possesses the acquirements mentioned, and if she is in a position to give satisfactory references as to character and competency; a situation can be offered her where there is but one pupil—a little girl, under ten years of age—and where the salary is thirty pounds per annum. J. E. is requested to send references, name, address, and all particulars to the direction, 'Mrs. Fairfax, Thornfield, near Millcote, ——shire.' "

I examined the document long: the writing was old-fashioned and rather uncertain, like that of an elderly lady. This circumstance was satisfactory: a private fear had haunted me that, in thus acting for myself, and by my own guidance, I ran the risk of getting into some scrape! and, above all things, I wished the result of my endeavors to be respectable, proper, *en règle*.[4] I now felt that an elderly lady was no bad ingredient in the business I had on hand. Mrs. Fairfax! I saw her in a black gown and widow's cap,—frigid, perhaps, but not uncivil: a model of elderly English respectability. Thornfield! that, doubtless, was the name of her house—a neat, orderly spot, I was sure, though I failed in my efforts to conceive a correct plan of the premises. Millcote, ——shire. I brushed up my recollections of the map of England; yes, I saw it, both the shire and the town. ——shire was seventy miles nearer London than the remote county where I now resided; that was a recommendation to me. I longed to go where there was life and movement. Millcote was a large manufacturing town on the banks of the A——: a busy place, enough, doubtless: so much the better; it would be a complete change at least. Not that my fancy was much captivated by the idea of long chimneys and clouds of smoke—"but," I argued, "Thornfield will, probably, be a good way from the town."

Here the socket of the candle dropped, and the wick went out.

Next day new steps were to be taken; my plans could no longer be confined to my own breast; I must impart them in order to achieve their success. Having sought and obtained an audience of the superintendent during the noontide recreation, I told her I had a prospect of getting a new situation where the salary would be double what I now receive (for at Lowood I only got fifteen pounds per annum), and requested she would break the matter for me to Mr. Brocklehurst, or some of the committee, and ascertain whether they would permit me to mention them as references. She obligingly consented to act as mediatrix in the matter. The next day she laid the affair before Mr. Brocklehurst, who said that Mrs. Reed must be written to, as she was my natural guardian. A note was accordingly addressed to that lady, who returned for answer, that "I might do as I pleased: she had long relinquished all interference in my affairs." This note went the round of the committee, and, at last, after what appeared to me most tedious delay, formal leave was given me to better my condition if I could; and an assurance added that, as I had always conducted myself well, both as teacher and pupil, at Lowood, a testimonial of character and capacity, signed by the inspectors of that institution, should forthwith be furnished me.

This testimonial I accordingly received in about a month, forwarded a copy of it to Mrs. Fairfax, and got that lady's reply, stating that she was satisfied, and fixing that day fortnight as the period for my assuming the post of governess in her house.

I now busied myself in preparations: the fortnight passed rapidly. I had not a very large wardrobe, though it was adequate to my wants; and the last day sufficed to pack my trunk,—the same I had brought with me eight years ago from Gateshead.

The box was corded, the card nailed on. In half an hour the carrier was to call for it to take it to Lowton, whither I myself was to repair at an early hour

4. By the rule (French).

the next morning to meet the coach. I had brushed my black stuff traveling dress, prepared my bonnet, gloves, and muff; sought in all my drawers to see that no article was left behind; and now, having nothing more to do, I sat down and tried to rest. I could not, though I had been on foot all day—I could not now repose an instant—I was too much excited. A phase of my life was closing tonight, a new one opening tomorrow: impossible to slumber in the interval; I must watch feverishly while the change was being accomplished.

"Miss," said a servant who met me in the lobby, where I was wandering like a troubled spirit, "a person below wishes to see you."

"The carrier, no doubt," I thought, and ran downstairs without inquiry. I was passing the back parlour, or teachers' sitting-room, the door of which was half-open, to go to the kitchen, when someone ran out.

"It's her, I am sure!—I could have told her anywhere!" cried the individual who stopped my progress and took my hand.

I looked. I saw a woman attired like a well-dressed servant, matronly, yet still young; very good-looking, with black hair and eyes, and lively complexion.

"Well, who is it?" she asked, in a voice and with a smile I half recognized! "You've not quite forgotten me, I think, Miss Jane?"

In another second I was embracing and kissing her rapturously. "Bessie! Bessie! Bessie!" that was all I said; whereat she half laughed, half cried, and we both went into the parlor. By the fire stood a little fellow of three years old, in plaid frock and trousers.

"That is my little boy," said Bessie, directly.

"Then you are married, Bessie?"

"Yes: nearly five years since, to Robert Leaven, the coachman, and I've a little girl besides Bobby there that I've christened Jane."

"And you don't live at Gateshead?"

"I live at the lodge: the old porter has left."

"Well, and how do they all get on? Tell me everything about them, Bessie: but sit down first; and, Bobby, come and sit on my knee, will you?" But Bobby preferred sidling over to his mother.

"You're not grown so very tall, Miss Jane, nor so very stout," continued Mrs. Leaven. "I dare say they've not kept you too well at school: Miss Reed is the head and shoulders taller than you are; and Miss Georgiana would make two of you in breadth."

"Georgiana is handsome, I suppose, Bessie?"

"Very. She went up to London last winter with her mamma, and there everybody admired her, and a young lord fell in love with her: but his relations were against the match; and—what do you think?—he and Miss Georgiana made it up to run away: but they were found out and stopped. It was Miss Reed that found them out: I believe she was envious; and now she and her sister lead a cat and dog life together; they are always quarrelling."

"Well, and what of John Reed?"

"Oh, he is not doing so well as his mamma could wish. He went to college, and he got—plucked,[5] I think they call it: and then his uncles wanted him

5. Expelled for failing examinations.

to be a barrister, and study the law: but he is such a dissipated young man, they will never make much of him, I think."

"What does he look like?"

"He is very tall: some people call him a fine-looking young man; but he has such thick lips."

"And Mrs. Reed?"

"Missis looks stout and well enough in the face, but I think she's not quite easy in her mind: Mr. John's conduct does not please her—he spends a deal of money."

"Did she send you here, Bessie?"

"No, indeed: but I have long wanted to see you, and when I heard that there had been a letter from you, and that you were going to another part of the country, I thought I'd just set off, and get a look at you before you were quite out of my reach."

"I am afraid you are disappointed in me, Bessie." I said this laughing: I perceived that Bessie's glance, though it expressed regard, did in no shape denote admiration.

"No, Miss Jane, not exactly: you are genteel enough; you look like a lady, and it is as much as ever I expected of you: you were no beauty as a child."

I smiled at Bessie's frank answer: I felt that it was correct, but I confess I was not quite indifferent to its import: at eighteen most people wish to please, and the conviction that they have not an exterior likely to second that desire brings anything but gratification.

"I dare say you are clever, though," continued Bessie, by way of solace. "What can you do? Can you play on the piano?"

"A little."

There was one in the room; Bessie went and opened it, and then asked me to sit down and give her a tune: I played a waltz or two, and she was charmed.

"The Miss Reeds could not play as well!" said she exultingly. "I always said you would surpass them in learning: and can you draw?"

"That is one of my paintings over the chimney-piece." It was a landscape in watercolors, of which I had made a present to the superintendent, in acknowledgment of her obliging mediation with the committee on my behalf, and which she had framed and glazed.

"Well, that is beautiful, Miss Jane! It is as fine a picture as any Miss Reed's drawing-master could paint, let alone the young ladies themselves, who could not come near it: and have you learnt French?"

"Yes, Bessie, I can both read it and speak it."

"And you can work on muslin and canvas?"

"I can."

"Oh, you are quite a lady, Miss Jane! I knew you would be: you will get on whether your relations notice you or not. There was something I wanted to ask you. Have you ever heard anything from your father's kinsfolk, the Eyres?"

"Never in my life."

"Well, you know Missis always said they were poor and quite despicable: and they may be poor; but I believe they are as much gentry as the Reeds are; for one day, nearly seven years ago, a Mr. Eyre came to Gateshead and wanted to see you. Missis said you were at school fifty miles off. He seemed

so much disappointed, for he could not stay: he was going on a voyage to a foreign country, and the ship was to sail from London in a day or two. He looked quite a gentleman, and I believe he was your father's brother."

"What foreign country was he going to, Bessie?"

"An island thousands of miles off, where they make wine—the butler did tell me"—

"Madeira?" I suggested.

"Yes, that is it—that is the very word."

"So he went?"

"Yes; he did not stay many minutes in the house: Missis was very high with him; she called him afterwards a 'sneaking tradesman.' My Robert believes he was a wine-merchant."

"Very likely," I returned; "or perhaps clerk or agent to a wine-merchant."

Bessie and I conversed about old times an hour longer, and then she was obliged to leave me. I saw her again for a few minutes the next morning at Lowton, while I was waiting for the coach. We parted finally at the door of the "Brocklehurst Arms" there. Each went our separate way: she set off for the brow of Lowood Fell to meet the conveyance which was to take her back to Gateshead; I mounted the vehicle which was to bear me to new duties and a new life in the unknown environs of Millcote.

Chapter XI

A new chapter in a novel is something like a new scene in a play: and when I draw up the curtain this time, reader, you must fancy you see a room in the "George Inn" at Millcote, with such large figured papering on the walls as inn rooms have; such a carpet, such furniture, such ornaments on the mantelpiece, such prints; including a portrait of George the Third, and another of the Prince of Wales, and a representation of the death of Wolfe.[6] All this is visible to you by the light of an oil lamp hanging from the ceiling, and by that of an excellent fire, near which I sit in my cloak and bonnet; my muff and umbrella lie on the table, and I am warming away the numbness and chill contracted by sixteen hours' exposure to the rawness of an October day: I left Lowton at four o'clock A.M., and the Millcote town clock is now just striking eight.

Reader, though I look comfortably accommodated, I am not very tranquil in my mind. I thought when the coach stopped here there would be someone to meet me; I looked anxiously round as I descended the wooden steps the "boots" placed for my convenience, expecting to hear my name pronounced, and to see some description of carriage waiting to convey me to Thornfield. Nothing of the sort was visible; and when I asked a waiter if any one had been to inquire after a Miss Eyre, I was answered in the negative: so I had no resource but to request to be shown into a private room: and here I am waiting, while all sorts of doubts and fears are troubling my thoughts.

It is a very strange sensation to inexperienced youth to feel itself quite alone in the world, cut adrift from every connection, uncertain whether the

6. James Wolfe (1727–1759), British army officer who commanded the 1759 expedition against Quebec; though the French were routed, he died, as famously portrayed in the 1770 painting by Benjamin West, *The Death of Wolfe*. George III (1738–1820) assumed the rule in 1760; his son the Prince of Wales (1762–1830), later George IV, became prince regent in 1811.

port to which it is bound can be reached, and prevented by many impediments from returning to that it has quitted. The charm of adventure sweetens that sensation, the glow of pride warms it; but then the throb of fear disturbs it; and fear with me became predominant, when half an hour elapsed and still I was alone. I bethought myself to ring the bell.

"Is there a place in this neighborhood called Thornfield?" I asked of the waiter who answered the summons.

"Thornfield? I don't know, ma'am; I'll inquire at the bar." He vanished, but reappeared instantly:—"Is your name Eyre, Miss?"

"Yes."

"Person here waiting for you."

I jumped up, took my muff and umbrella, and hastened into the inn-passage: a man was standing by the open door, and in the lamp-lit street I dimly saw a one-horse conveyance.

"This will be your luggage, I suppose?" said the man rather abruptly when he saw me, pointing to my trunk in the passage.

"Yes." He hoisted it on to the vehicle, which was a sort of car,[7] and then I got in: before he shut me up I asked him how far it was to Thornfield.

"A matter of six miles."

"How long shall we be before we get there?"

"Happen an hour and a half."

He fastened the car door, climbed to his own seat outside, and we set off. Our progress was leisurely, and gave me ample time to reflect; I was content to be at length so near the end of my journey; and as I leaned back in the comfortable though not elegant conveyance, I meditated much at my ease.

"I suppose," thought I, "judging from the plainness of the servant and carriage, Mrs. Fairfax is not a very dashing person: so much the better; I never lived among fine people but once, and I was very miserable with them. I wonder if she lives alone except this little girl; if so, and if she is in any degree amiable, I shall surely be able to get on with her! I will do my best: it is a pity that doing one's best does not always answer. At Lowood, indeed, I took that resolution, kept it, and succeeded in pleasing; but with Mrs. Reed, I remember, my best was always spurned with scorn. I pray God Mrs. Fairfax may not turn out a second Mrs. Reed; but if she does, I am not bound to stay with her: let the worst come to the worst, I can advertise again. How far are we on our road now, I wonder?"

I let down the window and looked out: Millcote was behind us; judging by the number of its lights, it seemed a place of considerable magnitude, much larger than Lowton. We were now, as far as I could see, on a sort of common; but there were houses scattered all over the district; I felt we were in a different region to Lowood, more populous, less picturesque; more stirring, less romantic.

The roads were heavy, the night misty; my conductor let his horse walk all the way, and the hour and a half extended, I verily believe, to two hours; at last he turned in his seat and said: "You're noan so far fro' Thornfield now."

Again I looked out: we were passing a church: I saw its low broad tower against the sky, and its bell was tolling a quarter; I saw a narrow galaxy of

7. Carriage.

lights too, on a hillside, marking a village or hamlet. About ten minutes after the driver got down and opened a pair of gates; we passed through, and they clashed to behind us. We now slowly ascended a drive, and came upon the long front of a house: candle-light gleamed from one curtained bow-window; all the rest were dark. The car stopped at the front door; it was opened by a maidservant; I alighted and went in.

"Will you walk this way, ma'am," said the girl; and I followed her across a square hall with high doors all round: she ushered me into a room whose double illumination of fire and candle at first dazzled me, contrasting as it did with the darkness to which my eyes had been for two hours inured; when I could see, however, a cozy and agreeable picture presented itself to my view.

A snug, small room; a round table by a cheerful fire; an arm-chair high-backed and old-fashioned, wherein sat the neatest imaginable little elderly lady, in widow's cap, black silk gown, and snowy muslin apron: exactly like what I had fancied Mrs. Fairfax, only less stately and milder-looking. She was occupied in knitting; a large cat sat demurely at her feet; nothing in short was wanting to complete the beau ideal[8] of domestic comfort. A more reassuring introduction for a new governess could scarcely be conceived: there was no grandeur to overwhelm, no stateliness to embarrass; and then, as I entered, the old lady got up, and promptly and kindly came forward to meet me.

"How do you do, my dear? I am afraid you have had a tedious ride; John drives so slowly: you must be cold; come to the fire."

"Mrs. Fairfax, I suppose?" said I.

"Yes, you are right: do sit down."

She conducted me to her own chair, and then began to remove my shawl and untie my bonnet-strings. I begged she would not give herself so much trouble.

"Oh, it is no trouble; I dare say your own hands are almost numbed with cold. Leah, make a little hot negus[9] and cut a sandwich or two: here are the keys of the storeroom."

And she produced from her pocket a most housewifely bunch of keys, and delivered them to the servant.

"Now, then, draw nearer to the fire," she continued. "You've brought your luggage with you, haven't you, my dear?"

"Yes, ma'am."

"I'll see it carried into your room," she said, and bustled out.

"She treats me like a visitor," thought I. "I little expected such a reception; I anticipated only coldness and stiffness: this is not like what I have heard of the treatment of governesses; but I must not exult too soon."

She returned, with her own hands cleared her knitting apparatus and a book or two from the table, to make room for the tray which Leah now brought, and then herself handed me the refreshments. I felt rather confused at being the object of more attention than I had ever before received, and that, too, shown by my employer and superior; but as she did not herself seem to consider she was doing anything out of her place, I thought it better to take her civilities quietly.

8. The perfect type or model (French). 9. A wine punch.

"Shall I have the pleasure of seeing Miss Fairfax tonight?" I asked, when I had partaken of what she offered me.

"What did you say, my dear? I am a little deaf," returned the good lady, approaching her ear to my mouth.

I repeated the question more distinctly.

"Miss Fairfax? Oh, you mean Miss Varens! Varens is the name of your future pupil."

"Indeed! Then she is not your daughter?"

"No,—I have no family."

I should have followed up my first inquiry by asking in what way Miss Varens was connected with her; but I recollected it was not polite to ask too many questions: besides, I was sure to hear in time.

"I am so glad," she continued, as she sat down opposite to me, and took the cat on her knee; "I am so glad you are come; it will be quite pleasant living here now with a companion. To be sure it is pleasant at any time; for Thornfield is a fine old hall, rather neglected of late years perhaps, but still it is a respectable place; yet you know in winter time one feels dreary quite alone, in the best quarters. I say alone—Leah is a nice girl to be sure, and John and his wife are very decent people; but then you see they are only servants, and one can't converse with them on terms of equality: one must keep them at due distance, for fear of losing one's authority. I'm sure last winter (it was a very severe one, if you recollect, and when it did not snow, it rained and blew) not a creature but the butcher and postman came to the house from November till February; and I really got quite melancholy with sitting night after night alone. I had Leah in to read to me sometimes; but I don't think the poor girl liked the task much: she felt it confining. In spring and summer one got on better: sunshine and long days make such a differ-ence; and then, just at the commencement of this autumn, little Adela Var-ens came and her nurse: a child makes a house alive all at once; and now you are here I shall be quite gay."

My heart really warmed to the worthy lady as I heard her talk: and I drew my chair a little nearer to her, and expressed my sincere wish that she might find my company as agreeable as she anticipated.

"But I'll not keep you sitting up late tonight," said she; "it is on the stroke of twelve now, and you have been traveling all day: you must feel tired. If you have got your feet well warmed I'll show you your bedroom. I've had the room next to mine prepared for you; it is only a small apartment, but I thought you would like it better than one of the large front chambers: to be sure they have finer furniture, but they are so dreary and solitary, I never sleep in them myself."

I thanked her for her considerate choice, and as I really felt fatigued with my long journey, expressed my readiness to retire. She took her candle, and I followed her from the room. First she went to see if the hall-door was fastened; having taken the key from the lock, she led the way upstairs. The steps and banisters were of oak; the staircase window was high and latticed; both it and the long gallery into which the bedroom doors opened looked as if they belonged to a church rather than a house. A very chill and vaultlike air pervaded the stairs and gallery, suggesting cheerless ideas of space and solitude; and I was glad when finally ushered into my chamber to find it of small dimensions, and furnished in ordinary modern style.

When Mrs. Fairfax had bidden me a kind good-night, and I had fastened my door, gazed leisurely round, and in some measure effaced the eerie impression made by that wide hall, that dark and spacious staircase, and that long, cold gallery, by the livelier aspect of my little room, I remembered that after a day of bodily fatigue and mental anxiety I was now at last in safe haven. The impulse of gratitude swelled my heart, and I knelt down at the bedside, and offered up thanks where thanks were due; not forgetting, ere I rose, to implore aid on my further path, and the power of meriting the kindness which seemed so frankly offered me before it was earned. My couch had no thorns in it that night; my solitary room no fears. At once weary and content, I slept soon and soundly: when I awoke it was broad day.

The chamber looked such a bright little place to me as the sun shone in between the gay blue chintz window curtains, showing papered walls and a carpeted floor, so unlike the bare planks and stained plaster of Lowood that my spirits rose at the view. Externals have a great effect on the young: I thought that a fairer era of life was beginning for me, one that was to have its flowers and pleasures, as well as its thorns and toils. My faculties, roused by the change of scene, the new field offered to hope, seemed all astir. I cannot precisely define what they expected, but it was something pleasant: not perhaps that day or that month, but at an indefinite future period.

I rose; I dressed myself with care: obliged to be plain—for I had no article of attire that was not made with extreme simplicity—I was still by nature solicitous to be neat. It was not my habit to be disregardful of appearance, or careless of the impression I made: on the contrary, I ever wished to look as well as I could, and to please as much as my want of beauty would permit. I sometimes regretted that I was not handsomer: I sometimes wished to have rosy cheeks, a straight nose, and small cherry mouth; I desired to be tall, stately, and finely developed in figure; I felt it a misfortune that I was so little, so pale, and had features so irregular and so marked. And why had I these aspirations and these regrets? It would be difficult to say: I could not then distinctly say it to myself; yet I had a reason, and a logical, natural reason too. However, when I had brushed my hair very smooth, and put on my black frock—which, Quaker-like as it was, at least had the merit of fitting to a nicety—and adjusted my clean white tucker, I thought I should do respectably enough to appear before Mrs. Fairfax; and that my new pupil would not at least recoil from me with antipathy. Having opened my chamber window, and seen that I left all things straight and neat on the toilet table, I ventured forth.

Traversing the long and matted gallery, I descended the slippery steps of oak; then I gained the hall: I halted there a minute: I looked at some pictures on the walls (one I remember represented a grim man in a cuirass, and one a lady with powdered hair and a pearl necklace), at a bronze lamp pendent from the ceiling, at a great clock whose case was of oak curiously carved, and ebon black with time and rubbing. Everything appeared very stately and imposing to me: but then I was so little accustomed to grandeur. The hall-door, which was half of glass, stood open; I stepped over the threshold. It was a fine autumn morning; the early sun shone serenely on embrowned groves and still green fields: advancing on to the lawn, I looked up and surveyed the front of the mansion. It was three stories high, of proportions not vast, though considerable: a gentleman's manor-house, not a nobleman's

seat: battlements round the top gave it a picturesque look. Its gray front stood out well from the background of a rookery, whose cawing tenants were now on the wing: they flew over the lawn and grounds to alight in a great meadow, from which these were separated by a sunk fence, and where an array of mighty old thorn trees, strong, knotty, and broad as oaks, at once explained the etymology of the mansion's designation. Farther off were hills: not so lofty as those round Lowood, nor so craggy, nor so like barriers of separation from the living world; but yet quiet and lonely hills enough, and seeming to embrace Thornfield with a seclusion I had not expected to find existent so near the stirring locality of Millcote. A little hamlet whose roofs were blent with trees straggled up the side of one of these hills; the church of the district stood nearer Thornfield: its old tower-top looked over a knoll between the house and gates.

I was yet enjoying the calm prospect and pleasant fresh air, yet listening with delight to the cawing of the rooks, yet surveying the wide, hoary front of the hall, and thinking what a great place it was for one lonely little dame like Mrs. Fairfax to inhabit, when that lady appeared at the door.

"What! out already?" said she. "I see you are an early riser." I went up to her, and was received with an affable kiss and shake of the hand.

"How do you like Thornfield?" she asked. I told her I liked it very much.

"Yes," she said, "it is a pretty place: but I fear it will be getting out of order, unless Mr. Rochester should take it into his head to come and reside here permanently; or, at least, visit it rather oftener: great houses and fine grounds require the presence of the proprietor."

"Mr. Rochester!" I exclaimed. "Who is he?"

"The owner of Thornfield," she responded quietly. "Did you not know he was called Rochester?"

Of course I did not—I had never heard of him before; but the old lady seemed to regard his existence as a universally understood fact, with which everybody must be acquainted by instinct.

"I thought," I continued, "Thornfield belonged to you."

"To me? Bless you, child; what an idea! To me? I am only the house-keeper—the manager. To be sure I am distantly related to the Rochesters by the mother's side; or, at least, my husband was: he was a clergyman, incumbent of Hay—that little village yonder on the hill—and that church near the gates was his. The present Mr. Rochester's mother was a Fairfax, and second cousin to my husband; but I never presume on the connection—in fact it is nothing to me; I consider myself quite in the light of an ordinary house-keeper: my employer is always civil, and I expect nothing more."

"And the little girl—my pupil?"

"She is Mr. Rochester's ward; he commissioned me to find a governess for her. He intends to have her brought up in ——shire, I believe. Here she comes with her 'bonne,' as she calls her nurse." The enigma then was explained: this affable and kind little widow was no great dame, but a dependent like myself. I did not like her the worse for that; on the contrary, I felt better pleased than ever. The equality between her and me was real; not the mere result of condescension on her part: so much the better—my position was all the freer.

As I was meditating on this discovery, a little girl, followed by her attendant, came running up the lawn. I looked at my pupil, who did not at first

appear to notice me: she was quite a child, perhaps seven or eight years old, slightly built, with a pale, small-featured face, and a redundancy of hair falling in curls to her waist.

"Good-morning, Miss Adela," said Mrs. Fairfax. "Come and speak to the lady who is to teach you, and to make you a clever woman some day." She approached.

"C'est là ma gouvernante?" said she, pointing to me, and addressing her nurse; who answered: "Mais oui, certainement."[1]

"Are they foreigners?" I inquired, amazed at hearing the French language.

"The nurse is a foreigner, and Adela was born on the Continent, and, I believe, never left it till within six months ago. When she first came here she could speak no English; now she can make shift to talk it a little: I don't understand her, she mixes it so with French; but you will make out her meaning very well, I daresay."

Fortunately I had had the advantage of being taught French by a French lady; and as I had always made a point of conversing with Madame Pierrot as often as I could, and had, besides, during the last seven years, learnt a portion of French by heart daily—applying myself to take pains with my accent, and imitating as closely as possible the pronunciation of my teacher—I had acquired a certain degree of readiness and correctness in the language, and was not likely to be much at a loss with Mademoiselle Adela. She came and shook hands with me when she heard that I was her governess; and as I led her into breakfast I addressed some phrases to her in her own tongue: she replied briefly at first, but after we were seated at the table, and she had examined me some ten minutes with her large hazel eyes, she suddenly commenced chattering fluently.

"Ah!" cried she, in French, "you speak my language as well as Mr. Rochester does: I can talk to you as I can to him, and so can Sophie. She will be glad: nobody here understands her: Madame Fairfax is all English. Sophie is my nurse; she came with me over the sea in a great ship with a chimney that smoked—how it did smoke!—and I was sick, and so was Sophie, and so was Mr. Rochester. Mr. Rochester lay down on a sofa in a pretty room called the salon, and Sophie and I had little beds in another place. I nearly fell out of mine; it was like a shelf. And Mademoiselle—what is your name?"

"Eyre—Jane Eyre."

"Aire?[2] Bah! I cannot say it. Well: our ship stopped in the morning, before it was quite daylight, at a great city—a huge city, with very dark houses and all smoky; not at all like the pretty clean town I came from; and Mr. Rochester carried me in his arms over a plank to the land, and Sophie came after, and we all got into a coach, which took us to a beautiful large house, larger than this and finer, called an hotel. We stayed there nearly a week. I and Sophie used to walk every day in a great green place full of trees, called the Park; and there were many children there besides me, and a pond with beautiful birds in it, that I fed with crumbs."

"Can you understand her when she runs on so fast?" asked Mrs. Fairfax.

1. "That is my governess?" ... "But of course" (French, as are all subsequent translations, unless otherwise specified.).

2. Threshing ground, nest for a bird of prey, or area.

I understood her very well, for I had been accustomed to the fluent tongue of Madame Pierrot.

"I wish," continued the good lady, "you would ask her a question or two about her parents: I wonder if she remembers them?"

"Adèle," I inquired, "with whom did you live when you were in that pretty clean town you spoke of?"

"I lived long ago with mamma; but she is gone to the Holy Virgin. Mamma used to teach me to dance and sing, and to say verses. A great many gentlemen and ladies came to see mamma, and I used to dance before them, or to sit on their knees and sing to them: I liked it. Shall I let you hear me sing now?"

She had finished her breakfast, so I permitted her to give a specimen of her accomplishments. Descending from her chair, she came and placed herself on my knee; then, folding her little hands demurely before her, shaking back her curls and lifting her eyes to the ceiling, she commenced singing a song from some opera. It was the strain of a forsaken lady, who, after bewailing the perfidy of her lover, calls pride to her aid; desires her attendant to deck her in her brightest jewels and richest robes, and resolves to meet the false one that night at a ball, and prove to him, by the gaiety of her demeanor, how little his desertion has affected her.

The subject seemed strangely chosen for an infant singer; but I suppose the point of the exhibition lay in hearing the notes of love and jealousy warbled with the lisp of childhood; and in very bad taste that point was: at least I thought so.

Adèle sang the canzonette[3] tunefully enough, and with the naïveté of her age. This achieved, she jumped from my knee and said, "Now, Mademoiselle, I will repeat you some poetry."

Assuming an attitude, she began "La Ligue des Rats: fable de la Fontaine."[4] She then declaimed the little piece with an attention to punctuation and emphasis, a flexibility of voice and an appropriateness of gesture, very unusual indeed at her age, and which proved she had been carefully trained.

"Was it your mamma who taught you that piece?" I asked.

"Yes; and she just used to say it in this way: 'Qu'avez vous donc? lui dit un de ces rats; parlez!'[5] She made me lift my hand—so—to remind me to raise my voice at the question. Now shall I dance for you?"

"No, that will do: but after your mamma went to the Holy Virgin, as you say, with whom did you live then?"

"With Madame Frédéric and her husband: she took care of me, but she is nothing related to me. I think she is poor, for she had not so fine a house as mamma. I was not long there. Mr. Rochester asked me if I would like to go and live with him in England, and I said yes; for I knew Mr. Rochester before I knew Madame Frédéric, and he was always kind to me and gave me pretty dresses and toys. But you see he has not kept his word, for he has brought me to England, and now he is gone back again himself, and I never see him."

After breakfast Adèle and I withdrew to the library; which room, it appears, Mr. Rochester had directed should be used as the schoolroom. Most of the

3. Short song.
4. "The League of Rats," a fable by the French poet Jean de La Fontaine (1621–1695).

5. What's the matter? says one of the rats to her; speak!

books were locked up behind glass doors; but there was one bookcase left open, containing everything that could be needed in the way of elementary works, and several volumes of light literature, poetry, biography, travels, a few romances, etc. I suppose he had considered that these were all the governess would require for her private perusal; and, indeed, they contented me amply for the present; compared with the scanty pickings I had now and then been able to glean at Lowood, they seemed to offer an abundant harvest of entertainment and information. In this room, too, there was a cabinet piano,[6] quite new and of superior tone; also an easel for painting, and a pair of globes.

I found my pupil sufficiently docile, though disinclined to apply: she had not been used to regular occupation of any kind. I felt it would be injudicious to confine her too much at first; so, when I had talked to her a great deal, and got her to learn a little, and when the morning had advanced to noon, I allowed her to return to her nurse. I then proposed to occupy myself till dinner-time in drawing some little sketches for her use.

As I was going upstairs to fetch my portfolio and pencils, Mrs. Fairfax called to me: "Your morning school-hours are over now, I suppose," said she. She was in a room the folding-doors of which stood open: I went in when she addressed me. It was a large, stately apartment, with purple chairs and curtains, a Turkey carpet, walnut-paneled walls, one vast window rich in stained glass, and a lofty ceiling, nobly molded. Mrs. Fairfax was dusting some vases of fine purple spar, which stood on a sideboard.

"What a beautiful room!" I exclaimed, as I looked round; for I had never before seen any half so imposing.

"Yes; this is the dining-room. I have just opened the window, to let in a little air and sunshine; for everything gets so damp in apartments that are seldom inhabited: the drawing-room yonder feels like a vault."

She pointed to a wide arch corresponding to the window, and hung like it with a Tyrian-dyed[7] curtain, now looped up. Mounting to it by two broad steps and looking through, I thought I caught a glimpse of a fairy place, so bright to my novice eyes appeared the view beyond. Yet it was merely a very pretty drawing-room, and within it a boudoir, both spread with white carpets, on which seemed laid brilliant garlands of flowers; both ceiled with snowy moldings of white grapes and vine-leaves, beneath which glowed in rich contrast crimson couches and ottomans; while the ornaments on the pale Parian mantelpiece were of sparkling Bohemian glass, ruby red; and between the windows large mirrors repeated the general blending of snow and fire.

"In what order you keep these rooms, Mrs. Fairfax!" said I. "No dust, no canvas coverings: except that the air feels chilly, one would think they were inhabited daily."

"Why, Miss Eyre, though Mr. Rochester's visits here are rare, they are always sudden and unexpected; and as I observed that it put him out to find everything swathed up, and to have a bustle of arrangement on his arrival, I thought it best to keep the rooms in readiness."

"Is Mr. Rochester an exacting, fastidious sort of man?"

"Not particularly so; but he has a gentleman's tastes and habits, and he expects to have things managed in conformity to them."

"Do you like him? Is he generally liked?"

6. Small upright piano.　　　　　　　　7. Purple or crimson.

"Oh, yes; the family have always been respected here. Almost all the land in this neighborhood, as far as you can see, has belonged to the Rochesters time out of mind."

"Well, but, leaving his land out of the question, do you like him? Is he liked for himself?"

"I have no cause to do otherwise than like him; and I believe he is considered a just and liberal landlord by his tenants: but he has never lived much amongst them."

"But has he no peculiarities? What, in short, is his character?"

"Oh! his character is unimpeachable, I suppose. He is rather peculiar, perhaps: he has traveled a great deal, and seen a great deal of the world, I should think. I daresay he is clever: but I never had much conversation with him."

"In what way is he peculiar?"

"I don't know—it is not easy to describe—nothing striking, but you feel it when he speaks to you: you cannot be always sure whether he is in jest or earnest, whether he is pleased or the contrary; you don't thoroughly understand him, in short—at least, I don't: but it is of no consequence, he is a very good master."

This was all the account I got from Mrs. Fairfax of her employer and mine. There are people who seem to have no notion of sketching a character, or observing and describing salient points, either in persons or things: the good lady evidently belonged to this class; my queries puzzled, but did not draw her out. Mr. Rochester was Mr. Rochester in her eyes; a gentleman, a landed proprietor—nothing more: she inquired and searched no further, and evidently wondered at my wish to gain a more definite notion of his identity.

When we left the dining-room, she proposed to show me over the rest of the house; and I followed her upstairs and downstairs, admiring as I went; for all was well arranged and handsome. The large front chambers I thought especially grand; and some of the third-story rooms, though dark and low, were interesting from their air of antiquity. The furniture once appropriated to the lower apartments had from time to time been removed here, as fashions changed; and the imperfect light entering by their narrow casements showed bedsteads of a hundred years old; chests in oak or walnut, looking with their strange carvings of palm branches and cherubs' heads, like types of the Hebrew ark;[8] rows of venerable chairs, high-backed and narrow; stools still more antiquated, on whose cushioned tops were yet apparent traces of half-effaced embroideries, wrought by fingers that for two generations had been coffin-dust. All these relics gave to the third story of Thornfield Hall the aspect of a home of the past: a shrine of memory. I liked the hush, the gloom, the quaintness of these retreats in the day; but I by no means coveted a night's repose on one of those wide and heavy beds: shut in, some of them, with doors of oak; shaded, others, with wrought old-English hangings crusted with thick work, portraying effigies of strange flowers, and stranger birds, and strangest human beings,—all which would have looked strange, indeed, by the pallid gleam of moonlight.

"Do the servants sleep in these rooms?" I asked.

"No; they occupy a range of smaller apartments to the back; no one ever

8. The sacred chest containing the Ten Commandments, described in Exodus 25.10–22.

sleeps here: one would almost say that, if there were a ghost at Thornfield Hall, this would be its haunt."

"So I think: you have no ghost, then?"

"None that I ever heard of," returned Mrs. Fairfax, smiling.

"Nor any traditions of one? no legends or ghost stories?"

"I believe not. And yet it is said the Rochesters have been rather a violent than a quiet race in their time: perhaps, though, that is the reason they rest tranquilly in their graves now."

"Yes—'after life's fitful fever they sleep well,' "[9] I muttered. "Where are you going now, Mrs. Fairfax?" for she was moving away.

"On to the leads;[1] will you come and see the view from thence?" I followed still, up a very narrow staircase to the attics, and thence by a ladder and through a trap-door to the roof of the hall. I was now on a level with the crow colony, and could see into their nests. Leaning over the battlements and looking far down, I surveyed the grounds laid out like a map: the bright and velvet lawn closely girdling the gray base of the mansion; the field, wide as a park, dotted with its ancient timber; the wood, dun and sere, divided by a path visibly overgrown, greener with moss than the trees were with foliage; the church at the gates, the road, the tranquil hills, all reposing in the autumn day's sun: the horizon bounded by a propitious sky, azure, marbled with pearly white. No feature in the scene was extraordinary, but all was pleasing. When I turned from it and repassed the trap-door, I could scarcely see my way down the ladder: the attic seemed black as a vault compared with that arch of blue air to which I had been looking up, and to that sunlit scene of grove, pasture, and green hill of which the hall was the center, and over which I had been gazing with delight.

Mrs. Fairfax stayed behind a moment to fasten the trap-door; I, by dint of groping, found the outlet from the attic, and proceeded to descend the narrow garret staircase. I lingered in the long passage to which this led, separating the front and back rooms of the third story: narrow, low, and dim, with only one little window at the far end, and looking, with its two rows of small black doors all shut, like a corridor in some Bluebeard's castle.[2]

While I paced softly on the last sound I expected to hear in so still a region, a laugh, struck my ear. It was a curious laugh; distinct, formal, mirthless. I stopped: the sound ceased, only for an instant; it began again louder: for at first, though distinct, it was very low. It passed off in a clamorous peal that seemed to wake an echo in every lonely chamber; though it originated but in one, and I could have pointed out the door whence the accents issued.

"Mrs. Fairfax!" I called out: for I now heard her descending the great stairs. "Did you hear that loud laugh? Who is it?"

"Some of the servants, very likely," she answered: "perhaps Grace Poole."

"Did you hear it?" I again inquired.

"Yes, plainly: I often hear her; she sews in one of these rooms. Sometimes Leah is with her: they are frequently noisy together."

The laugh was repeated in its low, syllabic tone, and terminated in an odd murmur.

9. See Shakespeare's *Macbeth* 3.2.25.
1. Roof.
2. In the fairy tale *Bluebeard,* by Charles Perrault

(1628–1703), the young wife is allowed to enter all the rooms in her husband's castle but one, where the bodies of his former wives are kept.

"Grace!" exclaimed Mrs. Fairfax.

I really did not expect any Grace to answer; for the laugh was as tragic, as preternatural a laugh as any I ever heard; and, but that it was high noon, and that no circumstance of ghostliness accompanied the curious cachinnation, but that neither scene nor season favored fear, I should have been superstitiously afraid. However, the event showed me I was a fool for entertaining a sense even of surprise.

The door nearest me opened, and a servant came out,—a woman of between thirty and forty; a set, square-made figure, red-haired, and with a hard, plain face: any apparition less romantic or less ghostly could scarcely be conceived.

"Too much noise, Grace," said Mrs. Fairfax. "Remember directions!" Grace curtseyed silently and went in.

"She is a person we have to sew and assist Leah in her house-maid's work," continued the widow; "not altogether unobjectionable in some points, but she does well enough. By-the-by, how have you got on with your new pupil this morning?"

The conversation, thus turned on Adèle, continued till we reached the light and cheerful region below. Adèle came running to meet us in the hall, exclaiming,—"Mesdames, vous êtes servies!" adding, "J'ai bien faim, moi!"[3]

We found dinner ready and waiting for us in Mrs. Fairfax's room.

Chapter XII

The promise of a smooth career, which my first calm introduction to Thornfield Hall seemed to pledge, was not belied on a longer acquaintance with the place and its inmates. Mrs. Fairfax turned out to be what she appeared, a placid-tempered, kind-natured woman, of competent education and average intelligence. My pupil was a lively child, who had been spoiled and indulged, and therefore was sometimes wayward; but as she was committed entirely to my care, and no injudicious interference from any quarter ever thwarted my plans for her improvement, she soon forgot her little freaks, and became obedient and teachable. She had no great talents, no marked traits of character, no peculiar development of feeling or taste which raised her one inch above the ordinary level of childhood; but neither had she any deficiency or vice which sunk her below it. She made reasonable progress, entertained for me a vivacious, though perhaps not very profound, affection; and by her simplicity, gay prattle, and efforts to please, inspired me, in return, with a degree of attachment sufficient to make us both content in each other's society.

This, par parenthèse,[4] will be thought cool language by persons who entertain solemn doctrines about the angelic nature of children, and the duty of those charged with their education to conceive for them an idolatrous devotion: but I am not writing to flatter parental egotism, to echo cant, or prop up humbug; I am merely telling the truth. I felt a conscientious solicitude for Adèle's welfare and progress, and a quiet liking to her little self; just as I cherished towards Mrs. Fairfax a thankfulness for her kindness, and a plea-

3. My ladies, dinner is served! . . . I am very hungry! 4. Parenthetically.

sure in her society proportionate to the tranquil regard she had for me, and the moderation of her mind and character.

Anybody may blame me who likes when I add further that now and then, when I took a walk by myself in the grounds, when I went down to the gates and looked through them along the road, or when, while Adèle played with her nurse, and Mrs. Fairfax made jellies[5] in the store-room, I climbed the three staircases, raised the trap-door of the attic, and having reached the leads, looked out afar over sequestered field and hill, and along dim sky-line—that then I longed for a power of vision which might overpass that limit; which might reach the busy world, towns, regions full of life I had heard of but never seen: that then I desired more of practical experience than I possessed; more of intercourse with my kind, of acquaintance with variety of character, than was here within my reach. I valued what was good in Mrs. Fairfax, and what was good in Adèle; but I believed in the existence of other and more vivid kinds of goodness, and what I believed in I wished to behold.

Who blames me? Many, no doubt; and I shall be called discontented. I could not help it: the restlessness was in my nature; it agitated me to pain sometimes. Then my sole relief was to walk along the corridor of the third story, backwards and forwards, safe in the silence and solitude of the spot and allow my mind's eye to dwell on whatever bright visions rose before it—and, certainly, they were many and glowing; to let my heart be heaved by the exultant movement, which, while it swelled it in trouble, expanded it with life; and, best of all, to open my inward ear to a tale that was never ended—a tale my imagination created, and narrated continuously; quickened with all of incident, life, fire, feeling, that I desired and had not in my actual existence.

It is in vain to say human beings ought to be satisfied with tranquillity: they must have action; and they will make it if they cannot find it. Millions are condemned to a stiller doom than mine, and millions are in silent revolt against their lot. Nobody knows how many rebellions besides political rebellions ferment in the masses of life which people earth. Women are supposed to be very calm generally: but women feel just as men feel; they need exercise for their faculties and a field for their efforts as much as their brothers do; they suffer from too rigid a restraint, too absolute a stagnation, precisely as men would suffer; and it is narrow-minded in their more privileged fellow-creatures to say that they ought to confine themselves to making puddings and knitting stockings, to playing on the piano and embroidering bags. It is thoughtless to condemn them, or laugh at them, if they seek to do more or learn more than custom has pronounced necessary for their sex.

When thus alone I not unfrequently heard Grace Poole's laugh: the same peal, the same low, slow ha! ha! which, when first heard, had thrilled me: I heard, too, her eccentric murmurs; stranger than her laugh. There were days when she was quite silent; but there were others when I could not account for the sounds she made. Sometimes I saw her; she would come out of her room with a basin, or a plate, or a tray in her hand, go down to the kitchen, and shortly return, generally (oh, romantic reader, forgive me for telling the plain truth:) bearing a pot of porter.[6] Her appearance always acted as a

5. A gelatin-based dessert, or a small sweet made from gelatin. 6. A dark brown, bitter beer.

damper to the curiosity raised by her oral oddities: hard-featured and staid, she had no point to which interest could attach. I made some attempts to draw her into conversation, but she seemed a person of few words: a monosyllabic reply usually cut short every effort of that sort.

The other members of the household, viz. John and his wife, Leah the housemaid, and Sophie the French nurse, were decent people: but in no respect remarkable. With Sophie I used to talk French, and sometimes I asked her questions about her native country; but she was not of a descriptive or narrative turn, and generally gave such vapid and confused answers as were calculated rather to check than encourage inquiry.

October, November, December passed away. One afternoon in January Mrs. Fairfax had begged a holiday for Adèle because she had a cold; and, as Adèle seconded the request with an ardor that reminded me how precious occasional holidays had been to me in my own childhood, I accorded it, deeming that I did well in showing pliability on the point. It was a fine, calm day, though very cold; I was tired of sitting still in the library through a whole long morning: Mrs. Fairfax had just written a letter which was waiting to be posted, so I put on my bonnet and cloak and volunteered to carry it to Hay; the distance, two miles, would be a pleasant winter afternoon walk. Having seen Adèle comfortably seated in her little chair by Mrs. Fairfax's parlor fireside, and given her her best wax doll (which I usually kept enveloped in silver paper in a drawer) to play with, and a story-book for change of amusement; and having replied to her "Revenez bientôt, ma bonne amie, ma chère Mdlle. Jeannette,"[7] with a kiss, I set out.

The ground was hard, the air was still, my road was lonely; I walked fast till I got warm, and then I walked slowly to enjoy and analyze the species of pleasure brooding for me in the hour and situation. It was three o'clock; the church bell tolled as I passed under the belfry: the charm of the hour lay in its approaching dimness, in the low-gliding and pale-beaming sun. I was a mile from Thornfield, in a lane noted for wild roses in summer, for nuts and blackberries in autumn, and even now possessing a few coral treasures in hips and haws, but whose best winter delight lay in its utter solitude and leafless repose. If a breath of air stirred, it made no sound here; for there was not a holly, not an evergreen to rustle, and the stripped hawthorn and hazel bushes were as still as the white, worn stones which causewayed the middle of the path. Far and wide, on each side, there were only fields, where no cattle now browsed; and the little brown birds, which stirred occasionally in the hedge, looked like single russet leaves that had forgotten to drop.

This lane inclined uphill all the way to Hay: having reached the middle I sat down on a stile which led thence into a field. Gathering my mantle about me, and sheltering my hands in my muff, I did not feel the cold, though it froze keenly; as was attested by a sheet of ice covering the causeway, where a little brooklet, now congealed, had overflowed after a rapid thaw some days since. From my seat I could look down on Thornfield: the gray and battlemented hall was the principal object in the vale below me; its woods and dark rookery rose against the west. I lingered till the sun went down among the trees, and sank crimson and clear behind them. I then turned eastward.

On the hilltop above me sat the rising moon; pale yet as a cloud, but

7. Come back soon, my good friend, my dear Miss Janie.

brightening momently: she looked over Hay, which, half lost in trees, sent up a blue smoke from its few chimneys; it was yet a mile distant, but in the absolute hush I could hear plainly its thin murmurs of life. My ear too felt the flow of currents; in what dales and depths I could not tell: but there were many hills beyond Hay, and doubtless many becks threading their passes. That evening calm betrayed alike the tinkle of the nearest streams, the sough of the most remote.

A rude noise broke on these fine ripplings and whisperings, at once so far away and so clear: a positive tramp, tramp; a metallic clatter, which effaced the soft wave-wanderings; as, in a picture, the solid mass of a crag, or the rough boles of a great oak, drawn in dark and strong on the foreground, efface the aërial distance of azure hill, sunny horizon, and blended clouds, where tint melts into tint.

The din was on the causeway; a horse was coming; the windings of the lane yet hid it, but it approached. I was just leaving the stile; yet, as the path was narrow, I sat still to let it go by. In those days I was young, and all sorts of fancies bright and dark tenanted my mind: the memories of nursery stories were there amongst other rubbish; and when they recurred, maturing youth added to them a vigor and vividness beyond what childhood could give. As this horse approached, and as I watched for it to appear through the dusk, I remembered certain of Bessie's tales, wherein figured a North-of-England spirit, called a "Gytrash," which, in the form of horse, mule, or large dog, haunted solitary ways, and sometimes came upon belated travelers, as this horse was now coming upon me.

It was very near, but not yet in sight, when, in addition to the tramp, tramp, I heard a rush under the hedge, and close down by the hazel stems glided a great dog, whose black and white color made him a distinct object against the trees. It was exactly one mask of Bessie's Gytrash,—a lion-like creature with long hair and a huge head: it passed me, however, quietly enough; not staying to look up, with strange pretercanine[8] eyes, in my face, as I half expected it would. The horse followed,—a tall steed, and on its back a rider. The man, the human being, broke the spell at once. Nothing ever rode the Gytrash: it was always alone; and goblins, to my notions, though they might tenant the dumb carcasses of beasts, could scarce covet shelter in the common-place human form. No Gytrash was this,—only a traveler taking the short cut to Millcote. He passed, and I went on: a few steps, and I turned: a sliding sound and an exclamation of "What the deuce is to do now?" and a clattering tumble, arrested my attention. Man and horse were down; they had slipped on the sheet of ice which glazed the causeway. The dog came bounding back, and seeing his master in a predicament, and hearing the horse groan, barked till the evening hills echoed the sound, which was deep in proportion to his magnitude. He snuffed round the prostrate group, and then he ran up to me; it was all he could do,—there was no other help at hand to summon. I obeyed him, and walked down to the traveler, by this time struggling himself free of his steed. His efforts were so vigorous I thought he could not be much hurt; but I asked him the question:—"Are you injured, sir?"

8. More than canine.

I think he was swearing, but am not certain; however, he was pronouncing some formula which prevented him from replying to me directly.

"Can I do anything?" I asked again.

"You must just stand on one side," he answered as he rose, first to his knees, and then to his feet. I did; whereupon began a heaving, stamping, clattering process, accompanied by a barking and baying which removed me effectually some yards' distance; but I would not be driven quite away till I saw the event.[9] This was finally fortunate; the horse was re-established, and the dog was silenced with a "Down, Pilot!" The traveler now, stooping, felt his foot and leg, as if trying whether they were sound; apparently something ailed them, for he halted to the stile whence I had just risen, and sat down.

I was in the mood for being useful, or at least officious, I think, for I now drew near him again.

"If you are hurt, and want help, sir, I can fetch some one either from Thornfield Hall or from Hay."

"Thank you; I shall do: I have no broken bones—only a sprain"; and again he stood up and tried his foot, but the result extorted an involuntary "Ugh!"

Something of daylight still lingered, and the moon was waxing bright: I could see him plainly. His figure was enveloped in a riding cloak, fur collared, and steel clasped; its details were not apparent, but I traced the general points of middle height, and considerable breadth of chest. He had a dark face, with stern features and a heavy brow; his eyes and gathered eyebrows looked ireful and thwarted just now; he was past youth, but had not reached middle age; perhaps he might be thirty-five. I felt no fear of him, and but little shyness. Had he been a handsome, heroic-looking young gentleman, I should not have dared to stand thus questioning him against his will, and offering my services unasked. I had hardly ever seen a handsome youth; never in my life spoken to one. I had a theoretical reverence and homage for beauty, elegance, gallantry, fascination; but had I met those qualities incarnate in masculine shape, I should have known instinctively that they neither had nor could have sympathy with anything in me, and should have shunned them as one would fire, lightning, or anything else that is bright but antipathetic.

If even this stranger had smiled and been good-humored to me when I addressed him; if he had put off my offer of assistance gaily and with thanks, I should have gone on my way and not felt any vocation to renew inquiries: but the frown, the roughness of the traveler, set me at my ease: I retained my station when he waved to me to go, and announced:—"I cannot think of leaving you, sir, at so late an hour, in this solitary lane, till I see you are fit to mount your horse."

He looked at me when I said this: he had hardly turned his eyes in my direction before.

"I should think you ought to be at home yourself," said he, "if you have a home in this neighborhood: where do you come from?"

"From just below; and I am not at all afraid of being out late when it is moonlight: I will run over to Hay for you with pleasure, if you wish it; indeed, I am going there to post a letter."

"You live just below—do you mean at that house with the battlements?"

9. What happened, how things turned out.

pointing to Thornfield Hall, on which the moon cast a hoary gleam, bringing it out distinct and pale from the woods, that, by contrast with the western sky, now seemed one mass of shadow.

"Yes, sir."

"Whose house is it?"

"Mr. Rochester's."

"Do you know Mr. Rochester?"

"No, I have never seen him."

"He is not resident, then?"

"No."

"Can you tell me where he is?"

"I cannot."

"You are not a servant at the hall, of course. You are—" He stopped, ran his eye over my dress, which, as usual, was quite simple: a black merino cloak, a black beaver bonnet: neither of them half fine enough for a lady's maid. He seemed puzzled to decide what I was: I helped him.

"I am the governess."

"Ah, the governess!" he repeated; "deuce take me, if I had not forgotten! The governess!" and again my raiment underwent scrutiny. In two minutes he rose from the stile: his face expressed pain when he tried to move.

"I cannot commission you to fetch help," he said; "but you may help me a little yourself, if you will be so kind."

"Yes, sir."

"You have not an umbrella that I can use as a stick?"

"No."

"Try to get hold of my horse's bridle and lead him to me: you are not afraid!"

I should have been afraid to touch a horse when alone, but when told to do it I was disposed to obey. I put down my muff on the stile, and went up to the tall steed; I endeavored to catch the bridle, but it was a spirited thing, and would not let me come near its head; I made effort on effort, though in vain: meantime, I was mortally afraid of its trampling fore-feet. The traveler waited and watched for some time, and at last he laughed.

"I see," he said, "the mountain will never be brought to Mahomet, so all you can do is to aid Mahomet to go to the mountain; I must beg of you to come here."[1]

I came. "Excuse me," he continued: "necessity compels me to make you useful." He laid a heavy hand on my shoulder, and leaning on me with some stress, limped to his horse. Having once caught the bridle, he mastered it directly, and sprang to his saddle; grimacing grimly as he made the effort, for it wrenched his sprain.

"Now," said he, releasing his under lip from a hard bite, "just hand me my whip; it lies there under the hedge."

I sought it and found it.

"Thank you: now make haste with the letter to Hay, and return as fast as you can."

1. According to legend, the prophet Muhammad summoned Mount Safa to come to him, in order to display his powers. When the mountain did not come, he told the spectators he would go to it.

A touch of a spurred heel made his horse first start and rear, and then bound away; the dog rushed in his traces: all three vanished,

> Like heath that, in the wilderness,
> The wild wind whirls away.[2]

I took up my muff and walked on. The incident had occurred and was gone for me: it *was* an incident of no moment, no romance, no interest in a sense; yet it marked with change one single hour of a monotonous life. My help had been needed and claimed; I had given it: I was pleased to have done something; trivial, transitory though the deed was, it was yet an active thing, and I was weary of an existence all passive. The new face, too, was like a new picture introduced to the gallery of memory; and it was dissimilar to all the others hanging there: firstly, because it was masculine; and, secondly, because it was dark, strong, and stern. I had it still before me when I entered Hay, and slipped the letter into the post-office; I saw it as I walked fast down hill all the way home. When I came to the stile, I stopped a minute, looked round and listened, with an idea that a horse's hoof might ring on the causeway again, and that a rider in a cloak, and a Gytrash-like Newfoundland dog, might be again apparent: I saw only the hedge and a pollard willow before me, rising up still and straight to meet the moonbeams; I heard only the faintest waft of wind roaming fitful among the trees round Thornfield, a mile distant; and when I glanced down in the direction of the murmur, my eye, traversing the hall-front, caught a light kindling in a window: it reminded me that I was late, and I hurried on.

I did not like reentering Thornfield. To pass its threshold was to return to stagnation; to cross the silent hall, to ascend the darksome staircase, to seek my own lonely little room, and then to meet tranquil Mrs. Fairfax, and spend the long winter evening with her, and her only, was to quell wholly the faint excitement wakened by my walk,—to slip again over my faculties the viewless fetters of an uniform and too still existence; of an existence whose very privileges of security and ease I was becoming incapable of appreciating. What good it would have done me at that time to have been tossed in the storms of an uncertain struggling life, and to have been taught by rough and bitter experience to long for the calm amid which I now repined! Yes, just as much good as it would do a man tired of sitting still in a "too easy chair"[3] to take a long walk; and just as natural was the wish to stir, under my circumstances, as it would be under his.

I lingered at the gates; I lingered on the lawn; I paced backwards and forwards on the pavement: the shutters of the glass door were closed; I could not see into the interior; and both my eyes and spirit seemed drawn from the gloomy house—from the gray hollow filled with rayless cells, as it appeared to me—to that sky expanded before me,—a blue sea absolved from taint of cloud; the moon ascending it in solemn march; her orb seeming to look up as she left the hilltops, from behind which she had come, far and farther below her, and aspired to the zenith, midnight-dark in its fathomless depth and measureless distance: and for those trembling stars that followed her course; they made my heart tremble, my veins glow when I viewed them.

2. From Thomas Moore's "Fallen Is Thy Throne," *Sacred Songs* (1816). 3. Alexander Pope's *The Dunciad* (1743), 4.342.

Little things recall us to earth: the clock struck in the hall; that sufficed; I turned from moon and stars, opened a side door, and went in.

The hall was not dark, nor yet was it lit, only by the high-hung bronze lamp: a warm glow suffused both it and the lower steps of the oak staircase. This ruddy shine issued from the great dining-room, whose two-leaved door stood open, and showed a genial fire in the grate, glancing on marble hearth and brass fire-irons, and revealing purple draperies and polished furniture, in the most pleasant radiance. It revealed, too, a group near the mantelpiece: I had scarcely caught it, and scarcely become aware of a cheerful mingling of voices, amongst which I seemed to distinguish the tones of Adèle, when the door closed.

I hastened to Mrs. Fairfax's room: there was a fire there too, but no candle, and no Mrs. Fairfax. Instead, all alone, sitting upright on the rug, and gazing with gravity at the blaze, I beheld a great black and white long-haired dog, just like the Gytrash of the lane. It was so like it that I went forward and said—"Pilot," and the thing got up and came to me and snuffed me. I caressed him, and he wagged his great tail: but he looked an eerie creature to be alone with, and I could not tell whence he had come. I rang the bell, for I wanted a candle; and I wanted, too, to get an account of this visitant. Leah entered.

"What dog is this?"

"He came with master."

"With whom?"

"With master—Mr. Rochester—he is just arrived."

"Indeed! and is Mrs. Fairfax with him?"

"Yes, and Miss Adèle; they are in the dining-room, and John is gone for a surgeon: for master has had an accident; his horse fell and his ankle is sprained."

"Did the horse fall in Hay Lane?"

"Yes, coming down hill; it slipped on some ice."

"Ah! Bring me a candle, will you, Leah?"

Leah brought it; she entered, followed by Mrs. Fairfax, who repeated the news; adding that Mr. Carter the surgeon was come, and was now with Mr. Rochester: then she hurried out to give orders about tea, and I went upstairs to take off my things.

Chapter XIII

Mr. Rochester, it seems, by the surgeon's orders, went to bed early that night; nor did he rise soon next morning. When he did come down, it was to attend to business: his agent and some of his tenants were arrived, and waiting to speak with him.

Adèle and I had now to vacate the library: it would be in daily requisition as a reception-room for callers. A fire was lit in an apartment upstairs, and there I carried our books, and arranged it for the future schoolroom. I discerned in the course of the morning that Thornfield Hall was a changed place: no longer silent as a church, it echoed every hour or two to a knock at the door, or a clang of the bell; steps, too, often traversed the hall, and new voices spoke in different keys below; a rill from the outer world was flowing through it; it had a master: for my part I liked it better.

Adèle was not easy to teach that day; she could not apply: she kept running to the door and looking over the banisters to see if she could get a glimpse of Mr. Rochester; then she coined pretexts to go downstairs, in order, as I shrewdly suspected, to visit the library, where I knew she was not wanted; then, when I got a little angry, and made her sit still, she continued to talk incessantly of her "ami, Monsieur Edouard Fairfax *de* Rochester,"[4] as she dubbed him (I had not before heard his prenomens[5]), and to conjecture what presents he had brought her: for it appears he had intimated the night before, that when his luggage came from Millcote there would be found among it a little box in whose contents she had an interest.

"Et cela doit signifier," said she, "qu'il y aura là dedans un cadeau pour moi, et peut-être pour vous aussi, mademoiselle. Monsieur a parlé de vous: il m'a demandé le nom de ma gouvernante, et si elle n'était pas une petite personne, assez mince et un peu pâle. J'ai dit qu'oui: car c'est vrai, n'est-ce pas, mademoiselle?"[6]

I and my pupil dined as usual in Mrs. Fairfax's parlor; the afternoon was wild and snowy, and we passed it in the schoolroom. At dark I allowed Adèle to put away books and work, and to run downstairs; for, from the comparative silence below, and from the cessation of appeals to the doorbell, I conjectured that Mr. Rochester was now at liberty. Left alone, I walked to the window; but nothing was to be seen thence: twilight and snowflakes together thickened the air, and hid the very shrubs on the lawn. I let down the curtain and went back to the fireside.

In the clear embers I was tracing a view, not unlike a picture I remembered to have seen of the castle of Heidelberg, on the Rhine, when Mrs. Fairfax came in, breaking up by her entrance the fiery mosaic I had been piecing together, and scattering too some heavy unwelcome thoughts that were beginning to throng on my solitude.

"Mr. Rochester would be glad if you and your pupil would take tea with him in the drawing-room this evening," said she: "he has been so much engaged all day that he could not ask to see you before."

"When is his tea-time?" I inquired.

"Oh, at six o'clock: he keeps early hours in the country. You had better change your frock now; I will go with you and fasten it. Here is a candle."

"Is it necessary to change my frock?"

"Yes, you had better: I always dress for the evening when Mr. Rochester is here."

This additional ceremony seemed somewhat stately: however, I repaired to my room, and, with Mrs. Fairfax's aid, replaced my black stuff dress by one of black silk: the best and the only additional one I had, except one of light gray, which, in my Lowood notions of the toilette, I thought too fine to be worn, except on first-rate occasions.

"You want a brooch," said Mrs. Fairfax. I had a single little pearl ornament which Miss Temple gave me as a parting keepsake: I put it on, and then we went downstairs. Unused as I was to strangers, it was rather a trial to appear

4. She adds the "de" as a sign of nobility. "Ami": friend.
5. Praenomens, or personal names.
6. "And that must mean," said she, "that there will be a present inside for me, and perhaps for you, too, Miss Eyre. Mr. Rochester talked about you; he asked me my governess's name and if she wasn't a small person, rather thin and a little pale. I said yes: because it's true, isn't it, Miss Eyre?"

thus formally summoned in Mr. Rochester's presence. I let Mrs. Fairfax precede me into the dining-room, and kept in her shade as we crossed that apartment; and, passing the arch, whose curtain was now dropped, entered the elegant recess beyond.

Two wax candles stood lighted on the table, and two on the mantelpiece; basking in the light and heat of a superb fire lay Pilot—Adèle knelt near him. Half reclined on a couch appeared Mr. Rochester, his foot supported by the cushion; he was looking at Adèle and the dog: the fire shone full on his face. I knew my traveler with his broad and jetty eyebrows; his square forehead, made squarer by the horizontal sweep of his black hair. I recognized his decisive nose, more remarkable for character than beauty; his full nostrils, denoting, I thought, choler;[7] his grim mouth, chin, and jaw—yes, all three were very grim, and no mistake. His shape, now divested of cloak, I perceived harmonized in squareness with his physiognomy: I suppose it was a good figure in the athletic sense of the term—broad-chested and thin-flanked, though neither tall nor graceful.

Mr. Rochester must have been aware of the entrance of Mrs. Fairfax and myself; but it appeared he was not in the mood to notice us, for he never lifted his head as we approached.

"Here is Miss Eyre, sir," said Mrs. Fairfax, in her quiet way. He bowed, still not taking his eyes from the group of the dog and child.

"Let Miss Eyre be seated," said he: and there was something in the forced stiff bow, in the impatient yet formal tone, which seemed further to express, "What the deuce is it to me whether Miss Eyre be there or not? At this moment I am not disposed to accost her."

I sat down quite disembarrassed. A reception of finished politeness would probably have confused me: I could not have returned or repaid it by answering grace and elegance on my part; but harsh caprice laid me under no obligation; on the contrary, a decent quiescence, under the freak of manner, gave me advantage. Besides, the eccentricity of the proceeding was piquant: I felt interested to see how he would go on.

He went on as a statue would, that is, he neither spoke nor moved. Mrs. Fairfax seemed to think it necessary that some one should be amiable, and she began to talk. Kindly, as usual—and, as usual, rather trite—she condoled with him on the pressure of business he had had all day; on the annoyance it must have been to him with that painful sprain: then she commended his patience and perseverance in going through with it.

"Madam, I should like some tea," was the sole rejoinder she got. She hastened to ring the bell; and, when the tray came, she proceeded to arrange the cups, spoons, etc., with assiduous celerity. I and Adèle went to the table; but the master did not leave his couch.

"Will you hand Mr. Rochester's cup?" said Mrs. Fairfax to me; "Adèle might perhaps spill it."

I did as requested. As he took the cup from my hand, Adèle, thinking the moment propitious for making a request in my favor, cried out:—"N'est-ce pas, monsieur, qu'il y a un cadeau pour Mademoiselle Eyre, dans votre petit coffre?"[8]

7. Anger (originally, one of the four humors thought to dominate a person's makeup).

8. Isn't it so, sir, that there is a present for Miss Eyre, in your little chest?

"Who talks of cadeaux?" said he gruffly: "did you expect a present, Miss Eyre? Are you fond of presents?" and he searched my face with eyes that I saw were dark, irate, and piercing.

"I hardly know, sir; I have little experience of them: they are generally thought pleasant things."

"Generally thought? But what do you think?"

"I should be obliged to take time, sir, before I could give you an answer worthy of your acceptance: a present has many faces to it, has it not? and one should consider all before pronouncing an opinion as to its nature."

"Miss Eyre, you are not so unsophisticated as Adèle: she demands a 'cadeau,' clamorously, the moment she sees me: you beat about the bush."

"Because I have less confidence in my deserts than Adèle has: she can prefer the claim of old acquaintance, and the right too of custom; for she says you have always been in the habit of giving her playthings; but if I had to make a case I should be puzzled, since I am a stranger, and have done nothing to entitle me to an acknowledgment."

"Oh, don't fall back on over-modesty! I have examined Adèle, and find you have taken great pains with her; she is not bright, she has no talents; yet in a short time she has made much improvement."

"Sir, you have now given me my 'cadeau'; I am obliged to you: it is the meed teachers most covet; praise of their pupil's progress."

"Humph!" said Mr. Rochester, and he took his tea in silence.

"Come to the fire," said the master, when the tray was taken away, and Mrs. Fairfax had settled into a corner with her knitting; while Adèle was leading me by the hand round the room, showing me the beautiful books and ornaments on the consoles and chiffonnières. We obeyed, as in duty bound; Adèle wanted to take a seat on my knee, but she was ordered to amuse herself with Pilot.

"You have been resident in my house three months?"

"Yes, sir."

"And you come from ——?"

"From Lowood school, in ——shire."

"Ah! a charitable concern.—How long were you there?"

"Eight years."

"Eight years! you must be tenacious of life. I thought half the time in such a place would have done up any constitution! No wonder you have rather the look of another world. I marveled where you had got that sort of face. When you came on me in Hay Lane last night, I thought unaccountably of fairy tales, and had half a mind to demand whether you had bewitched my horse: I am not sure yet. Who are your parents?"

"I have none."

"Nor ever had, I suppose: do you remember them?"

"No."

"I thought not. And so you were waiting for your people when you sat on the stile?"

"For whom, sir?"

"For the men in green: it was a proper moonlight evening for them. Did I break through one of your rings,[9] that you spread that damned ice on the causeway?"

9. Enchanted circles where fairies dance.

I shook my head. "The men in green all forsook England a hundred years ago," said I, speaking as seriously as he had done. "And not even in Hay Lane, or the fields about it, could you find a trace of them. I don't think either summer or harvest, or winter moon, will ever shine on their revels more."

Mrs. Fairfax had dropped her knitting, and, with raised eyebrows, seemed wondering what sort of talk this was.

"Well," resumed Mr. Rochester, "if you disown parents you must have some sort of kinsfolk: uncles and aunts?"

"No; none that I ever saw."

"And your home"

"I have none."

"Where do your brothers and sisters live?"

"I have no brothers and sisters."

"Who recommended you to come here?"

"I advertised, and Mrs. Fairfax answered my advertisement."

"Yes," said the good lady, who now knew what ground we were upon, "and I am daily thankful for the choice Providence led me to make. Miss Eyre has been an invaluable companion to me, and a kind and careful teacher to Adèle."

"Don't trouble yourself to give her a character," returned Mr. Rochester: "eulogiums will not bias me; I shall judge for myself. She began by felling my horse."

"Sir?" said Mrs. Fairfax.

"I have to thank her for this sprain."

The widow looked bewildered.

"Miss Eyre, have you ever lived in a town?"

"No, sir."

"Have you seen much society?"

"None but the pupils and teachers of Lowood; and now the inmates of Thornfield."

"Have you read much?"

"Only such books as came in my way; and they have not been numerous or very learned."

"You have lived the life of a nun: no doubt you are well drilled in religious forms;—Brocklehurst, who I understand directs Lowood, is a parson, is he not?"

"Yes, sir."

"And you girls probably worshipped him, as a convent full of religieuses[1] would worship their director?"

"Oh, no."

"You are very cool! No! What! A novice not worship her priest! That sounds blasphemous."

"I disliked Mr. Brocklehurst; and I was not alone in the feeling. He is a harsh man; at once pompous and meddling: he cut off our hair; and for economy's sake bought us bad needles and thread, with which we could hardly sew."

1. Nuns.

"That was very false economy," remarked Mrs. Fairfax, who now again caught the drift of the dialogue.

"And was that the head and front of his offending?"[2] demanded Mr. Rochester.

"He starved us when he had the sole superintendence of the provision department, before the committee was appointed; and he bored us with long lectures once a week, and with evening readings from books of his own inditing,[3] about sudden deaths and judgments, which made us afraid to go to bed."

"What age were you when you went to Lowood?"

"About ten."

"And you stayed there eight years: you are now, then, eighteen?"

I assented.

"Arithmetic, you see, is useful; without its aid I should hardly have been able to guess your age. It is a point difficult to fix where the features and countenance are so much at variance as in your case. And now, what did you learn at Lowood? Can you play?"

"A little."

"Of course: that is the established answer. Go into the library—I mean, if you please. (Excuse my tone of command; I am used to say 'Do this,' and it is done: I cannot alter my customary habits for one new inmate.) Go then, into the library; take a candle with you; leave the door open; sit down to the piano, and play a tune."

I departed, obeying his directions.

"Enough!" he called out in a few minutes. "You play a *little,* I see, like any other English schoolgirl: perhaps rather better than some, but not well."

I closed the piano and returned. Mr. Rochester continued:

"Adèle showed me some sketches this morning which she said were yours. I don't know whether they were entirely of your doing: probably a master aided you?"

"No, indeed!" I interjected.

"Ah! that pricks pride. Well, fetch me your portfolio, if you can vouch for its contents being original; but don't pass your word unless you are certain: I can recognize patchwork."

"Then I will say nothing, and you shall judge for yourself, sir."

I brought the portfolio from the library.

"Approach the table," said he; and I wheeled it to his couch. Adèle and Mrs. Fairfax drew near to see the pictures.

"No crowding," said Mr. Rochester: "take the drawings from my hand as I finish with them; but don't push your faces up to mine."

He deliberately scrutinized each sketch and painting. Three he laid aside; the others, when he had examined them, he swept from him.

"Take them off to the other table, Mrs. Fairfax," said he, "and look at them with Adèle;—you" (glancing at me) "resume your seat, and answer my ques-

2. Paraphrased from Shakespeare's *Othello* 1.3.80. 3. Written by him.

tions. I perceive these pictures were done by one hand: was that hand yours?"

"Yes."

"And when did you find time to do them? They have taken much time, and some thought."

"I did them in the last two vacations I spent at Lowood, when I had no other occupation."

"Where did you get your copies?"

"Out of my head."

"That head I see now on your shoulders?"

"Yes, sir."

"Has it other furniture of the same kind within?"

"I should think it may have: I should hope—better."

He spread the pictures before him, and again surveyed them alternately.

While he is so occupied I will tell you, reader, what they are: and first, I must premise that they are nothing wonderful. The subjects had, indeed, risen vividly on my mind. As I saw them with the spiritual eye, before I attempted to embody them, they were striking; but my hand would not second my fancy, and in each case it had wrought out but a pale portrait of the thing I had conceived.

These pictures were in watercolors. The first represented clouds low and livid, rolling over a swollen sea: all the distance was in eclipse; so, too, was the foreground; or, rather, the nearest billows, for there was no land. One gleam of light lifted into relief a half-submerged mast, on which sat a cormorant, dark and large, with wings flecked with foam: its beak held a gold bracelet, set with gems, that I had touched with as brilliant tints as my palette could yield, and as glittering distinctness as my pencil could impart. Sinking below the bird and mast, a drowned corpse glanced through the green water; a fair arm was the only limb clearly visible, whence the bracelet had been washed or torn.

The second picture contained for foreground only the dim peak of a hill, with grass and some leaves slanting as if by a breeze. Beyond and above spread an expanse of sky, dark blue as at twilight: rising into the sky was a woman's shape to the bust, portrayed in tints as dusk and soft as I could combine. The dim forehead was crowned with a star; the lineaments below were seen as through the suffusion of vapor; the eyes shone dark and wild; the hair streamed shadowy, like a beamless cloud torn by storm or by electric travail. On the neck lay a pale reflection like moonlight; the same faint luster touched the train of thin clouds from which rose and bowed this vision of the Evening Star.

The third showed the pinnacle of an iceberg piercing a polar winter sky: a muster of northern lights reared their dim lances, close serried, along the horizon. Throwing these into distance, rose, in the foreground, a head,—a colossal head, inclined towards the iceberg, and resting against it. Two thin hands, joined under the forehead, and supporting it, drew up before the lower features a sable veil; a brow quite bloodless, white as bone, and an eye hollow and fixed, blank of meaning but for the glassiness of despair, alone were visible. Above the temples, amidst wreathed turban folds of black drapery, vague in its character and consistency as cloud, gleamed a ring of white flame, gemmed with sparkles of a more lurid tinge. This pale crescent

was "The likeness of a Kingly Crown"; what it diademed was "the shape which shape had none."[4]

"Were you happy when you painted these pictures?" asked Mr. Rochester, presently.

"I was absorbed, sir: yes, and I was happy. To paint them, in short, was to enjoy one of the keenest pleasures I have ever known."

"That is not saying much. Your pleasures, by your own account, have been few; but I daresay you did exist in a kind of artist's dreamland while you blent and arranged these strange tints. Did you sit at them long each day?"

"I had nothing else to do, because it was the vacation, and I sat at them from morning till noon, and from noon till night: the length of the midsummer days favored my inclination to apply."

"And you felt self-satisfied with the result of your ardent labors?"

"Far from it. I was tormented by the contrast between my idea and my handiwork: in each case I had imagined something which I was quite powerless to realize."

"Not quite: you have secured the shadow of your thought: but no more, probably. You had not enough of the artist's skill and science to give it full being: yet the drawings are, for a schoolgirl, peculiar. As to the thoughts, they are elfish. These eyes in the Evening Star you must have seen in a dream. How could you make them look so clear, and yet not at all brilliant? for the planet above quells their rays. And what meaning is that in their solemn depth? And who taught you to paint wind? There is a high gale in that sky, and on this hilltop. Where did you see Latmos?[5] For that is Latmos. There,— put the drawings away!"

I had scarce tied the strings of the portfolio, when, looking at his watch, he said abruptly,—"It is nine o'clock: what are you about, Miss Eyre, to let Adèle sit up so long? Take her to bed."

Adèle went to kiss him before quitting the room: he endured the caress, but scarcely seemed to relish it more than Pilot would have done, nor so much.

"I wish you all good-night, now," said he, making a movement of the hand towards the door, in token that he was tired of our company, and wished to dismiss us. Mrs. Fairfax folded up her knitting: I took my portfolio: we curtseyed to him, received a frigid bow in return, and so withdrew.

"You said Mr. Rochester was not strikingly peculiar, Mrs. Fairfax," I observed, when I rejoined her in her room, after putting Adèle to bed.

"Well, is he?"

"I think so: he is very changeful and abrupt."

"True: no doubt he may appear so to a stranger, but I am so accustomed to his manner I never think of it; and then, if he has peculiarities of temper, allowance should be made."

"Why?"

"Partly because it is his nature—and we can none of us help our nature;

4. From Milton's *Paradise Lost* (1667–74), 2.666–73. These lines are a description of Death, the son of Satan.

5. A mountain in Caria (in present-day Turkey), mythic scene of the story of Selene (the Moon) and her lover Endymion.

and, partly, he has painful thoughts, no doubt, to harass him, and make his spirits unequal."

"What about?"

"Family troubles, for one thing."

"But he has no family."

"Not now, but he has had—or, at least, relatives. He lost his elder brother a few years since."

"His *elder* brother?"

"Yes. The present Mr. Rochester has not been very long in possession of the property; only about nine years."

"Nine years is a tolerable time. Was he so very fond of his brother as to be still inconsolable for his loss?"

"Why, no—perhaps not. I believe there were some misunderstandings between them. Mr. Rowland Rochester was not quite just to Mr. Edward; and, perhaps, he prejudiced his father against him. The old gentleman was fond of money, and anxious to keep the family estate together. He did not like to diminish the property by division, and yet he was anxious that Mr. Edward should have wealth too, to keep up the consequence of the name; and, soon after he was of age, some steps were taken that were not quite fair, and made a great deal of mischief. Old Mr. Rochester and Mr. Rowland combined to bring Mr. Edward into what he considered a painful position, for the sake of making his fortune: what the precise nature of that position was I never clearly knew, but his spirit could not brook what he had to suffer in it. He is not very forgiving: he broke with his family, and now for many years he has led an unsettled kind of life. I don't think he has ever been resident at Thornfield for a fortnight together since the death of his brother without a will left him master of the estate; and, indeed, no wonder he shuns the old place."

"Why should he shun it?"

"Perhaps he thinks it gloomy."

The answer was evasive—I should have liked something clearer; but Mrs. Fairfax either could not, or would not, give me more explicit information of the origin and nature of Mr. Rochester's trials. She averred they were a mystery to herself, and that what she knew was chiefly from conjecture. It was evident, indeed, that she wished me to drop the subject, which I did accordingly.

Chapter XIV

For several subsequent days I saw little of Mr. Rochester. In the mornings he seemed much engaged with business, and in the afternoon gentlemen from Millcote or the neighborhood called, and sometimes stayed to dine with him. When his sprain was well enough to admit of horse exercise, he rode out a good deal; probably to return these visits, as he generally did not come back till late at night.

During this interval even Adèle was seldom sent for to his presence, and all my acquaintance with him was confined to an occasional rencontre in the hall, on the stairs, or in the gallery, when he would sometimes pass me haughtily and coldly, just acknowledging my presence by a distant nod or a

cool glance, and sometimes bow and smile with gentlemanlike affability. His changes of mood did not offend me, because I saw that I had nothing to do with their alternation; the ebb and flow depended on causes quite disconnected with me.

One day he had had company to dinner, and had sent for my portfolio; in order, doubtless, to exhibit its contents. The gentlemen went away early, to attend a public meeting at Millcote, as Mrs. Fairfax informed me; but the night being wet and inclement, Mr. Rochester did not accompany them. Soon after they were gone, he rang the bell: a message came that I and Adèle were to go downstairs. I brushed Adèle's hair and made her neat, and having ascertained that I was myself in my usual Quaker trim, where there was nothing to retouch—all being too close and plain, braided locks included, to admit of disarrangement—we descended, Adèle wondering whether the *petit coffre* was at length come; for, owing to some mistake, its arrival had hitherto been delayed. She was gratified: there it stood, a little carton, on the table when we entered the dining-room. She appeared to know it by instinct.

"Ma boîte! ma boîte!"[6] exclaimed she, running towards it.

"Yes—there is your 'boîte' at last: take it into a corner, you genuine daughter of Paris, and amuse yourself with disemboweling it," said the deep and rather sarcastic voice of Mr. Rochester, proceeding from the depths of an immense easy-chair at the fireside. "And mind," he continued, "don't bother me with any details of the anatomical process, or any notice of the condition of the entrails: let your operation be conducted in silence: tiens-toi tranquille, enfant; comprends-tu?"[7]

Adèle seemed scarcely to need the warning; she had already retired to a sofa with her treasure, and was busy untying the cord which secured the lid. Having removed this impediment, and lifted certain silvery envelopes of tissue-paper, she merely exclaimed:—"Oh ciel! Que c'est beau!"[8] and then remained absorbed in ecstatic contemplation.

"Is Miss Eyre there?" now demanded the master, half rising from his seat to look round to the door, near which I still stood.

"Ah! well; come forward: be seated here." He drew a chair near his own. "I am not fond of the prattle of children," he continued; "for, old bachelor as I am, I have no pleasant associations connected with their lisp. It would be intolerable to me to pass a whole evening *tête-à-tête* with a brat. Don't draw that chair further off, Miss Eyre; sit down exactly where I placed it— if you please, that is. Confound these civilities! I continually forget them. Nor do I particularly affect simple-minded old ladies. By-the-bye, I must have mine in mind; it won't do to neglect her; she is a Fairfax, or wed to one; and blood is said to be thicker than water."

He rang and dispatched an invitation to Mrs. Fairfax, who soon arrived, knitting-basket in hand.

"Good-evening, madam; I sent to you for a charitable purpose: I have forbidden Adèle to talk to me about her presents, and she is bursting with repletion; have the goodness to serve her as auditress and interlocutrice:[9] it will be one of the most benevolent acts you ever performed."

Adèle, indeed, no sooner saw Mrs. Fairfax than she summoned her to the

6. My box.
7. Keep still, child; do you understand?

8. Oh heavens! How beautiful!
9. Female interlocutor or fellow speaker.

sofa, and there quickly filled her lap with the porcelain, the ivory, the waxen contents of her "boîte"; pouring out, meantime, explanations and raptures in such broken English as she was mistress of.

"Now I have performed the part of a good host," pursued Mr. Rochester, "put my guests into the way of amusing each other, I ought to be at liberty to attend to my own pleasure. Miss Eyre, draw your chair still a little further forward: you are yet too far back; I cannot see you without disturbing my position in this comfortable chair, which I have no mind to do."

I did as I was bid, though I would much rather have remained somewhat in the shade: but Mr. Rochester had such a direct way of giving orders, it seemed a matter of course to obey him promptly.

We were, as I have said, in the dining-room: the luster,[1] which had been lit for dinner, filled the room with a festal breadth of light; the large fire was all red and clear; the purple curtains hung rich and ample before the lofty windows and loftier arch; everything was still, save the subdued chat of Adèle (she dared not speak loud), and, filling up each pause, the beating of winter rain against the panes.

Mr. Rochester, as he sat in his damask-covered chair, looked different to what I had seen him look before; not quite so stern—much less gloomy. There was a smile on his lips, and his eyes sparkled, whether with wine or not I am not sure; but I think it very probable. He was, in short, in his after-dinner mood; more expanded and genial, and also more self-indulgent than the frigid and rigid temper of the morning: still he looked preciously grim, cushioning his massive head against the swelling back of his chair, and receiving the light of the fire on his granite-hewn features, and in his great, dark eyes; for he had great, dark eyes, and very fine eyes too—not without a certain change in their depths sometimes, which, if it was not softness, reminded you, at least, of that feeling.

He had been looking two minutes at the fire, and I had been looking the same length of time at him, when turning suddenly, he caught my gaze fastened on his physiognomy.

"You examine me, Miss Eyre," said he: "do you think me handsome?"

I should, if I had deliberated, have replied to this question by something conventionally vague and polite; but the answer somehow slipped from my tongue before I was aware:—"No, sir."

"Ah! By my word! there is something singular about you," said he: "you have the air of a little nonnette,[2] quaint, quiet, grave, and simple, as you sit with your hands before you, and your eyes generally bent on the carpet (except, by-the-bye, when they are directed piercingly to my face; as just now, for instance); and when one asks you a question, or makes a remark to which you are obliged to reply, you rap out a round rejoinder, which, if not blunt, is at least brusque. What do you mean by it?"

"Sir, I was too plain: I beg your pardon. I ought to have replied that it was not easy to give an impromptu answer to a question about appearances; that tastes differ; that beauty is of little consequence, or something of that sort."

"You ought to have replied no such thing. Beauty of little consequence, indeed! And so, under pretence of softening the previous outrage, of stroking and soothing me into placidity, you stick a sly penknife under my ear! Go

1. Chandelier.　　　　　　　　　　2. A young nun.

on: what fault do you find with me, pray? I suppose I have all my limbs and all my features like any other man?"

"Mr. Rochester, allow me to disown my first answer. I intended no pointed repartee: it was only a blunder."

"Just so: I think so: and you shall be answerable for it. Criticize me: does my forehead not please you?"

He lifted up the sable waves of hair which lay horizontally over his brow, and showed a solid enough mass of intellectual organs, but an abrupt deficiency where the suave sign of benevolence should have risen.

"Now, ma'am, am I a fool?"

"Far from it, sir. You would, perhaps, think me rude if I inquired in return whether you are a philanthropist?"

"There again! Another stick of the penknife, when she pretended to pat my head: and that is because I said I did not like the society of children and old women (low be it spoken!). No, young lady, I am not a general philanthropist; but I bear a conscience"; and he pointed to the prominences which are said to indicate that faculty, and which, fortunately for him, were sufficiently conspicuous; giving, indeed, a marked breadth to the upper part of his head: "and, besides, I once had a kind of rude tenderness of heart. When I was as old as you I was a feeling fellow enough; partial to the unfledged, unfostered, and unlucky; but fortune has knocked me about since: she has even kneaded me with her knuckles, and now I flatter myself I am hard and tough as an India-rubber ball; pervious, though, through a chink or two still, and with one sentient point in the middle of the lump. Yes: does that leave hope for me?"

"Hope of what, sir?"

"Of my final retransformation from India-rubber back to flesh?"

"Decidedly he has had too much wine," I thought; and I did not know what answer to make to his queer question: how could I tell whether he was capable of being re-transformed?

"You look very much puzzled, Miss Eyre; and though you are not pretty any more than I am handsome, yet a puzzled air becomes you; besides, it is covenient, for it keeps those searching eyes of yours away from my physiognomy, and busies them with the worsted flowers of the rug; so puzzle on. Young lady, I am disposed to be gregarious and communicative tonight."

With this announcement he rose from his chair, and stood, leaning his arm on the marble mantelpiece: in that attitude his shape was seen plainly as well as his face; his unusual breadth of chest, disproportionate almost to his length of limb. I am sure most people would have thought him an ugly man; yet there was so much unconscious pride in his port; so much ease in his demeanor; such a look of complete indifference to his own external appearance; so haughty a reliance on the power of other qualities, intrinsic or adventitious, to atone for the lack of mere personal attractiveness, that, in looking at him, one inevitably shared the indifference, and, even in a blind, imperfect sense, put faith in the confidence.

"I am disposed to be gregarious and communicative tonight," he repeated; "and that is why I sent for you: the fire and the chandelier were not sufficient company for me; nor would Pilot have been, for none of these can talk. Adèle is a degree better, but still far below the mark; Mrs. Fairfax ditto; you, I am persuaded, can suit me if you will: you puzzled me the first evening I invited

you down here. I have almost forgotten you since: other ideas have driven yours from my head; but tonight I am resolved to be at ease; to dismiss what importunes, and recall what pleases. It would please me now to draw you out—to learn more of you—therefore speak."

Instead of speaking, I smiled; and not a very complacent or submissive smile either.

"Speak," he urged.

"What about, sir?"

"Whatever you like. I leave both the choice of subject and the manner of treating it entirely to yourself."

Accordingly I sat and said nothing: "If he expects me to talk for the mere sake of talking and showing off, he will find he has addressed himself to the wrong person," I thought.

"You are dumb, Miss Eyre."

I was dumb still. He bent his head a little towards me, and with a single hasty glance seemed to dive into my eyes.

"Stubborn?" he said, "and annoyed. Ah, it is consistent. I put my request in an absurd, almost insolent form. Miss Eyre, I beg your pardon. The fact is, once for all, I don't wish to treat you like an inferior: that is (correcting himself), I claim only such superiority as must result from twenty years' difference in age and a century's advance in experience. This is legitimate, et j'y tiens,[3] as Adèle would say; and it is by virtue of this superiority and this alone that I desire you to have the goodness to talk to me a little now, and divert my thoughts, which are galled with dwelling on one point—cankering as a rusty nail."

He had deigned an explanation; almost an apology: I did not feel insensible to his condescension, and would not seem so.

"I am willing to amuse you if I can, sir: quite willing; but I cannot introduce a topic, because how do I know what will interest you? Ask me questions, and I will do my best to answer them."

"Then, in the first place, do you agree with me that I have a right to be a little masterful, abrupt; perhaps exacting, sometimes, on the grounds I stated; namely, that I am old enough to be your father, and that I have battled through a varied experience with many men of many nations, and roamed over half the globe, while you have lived quietly with one set of people in one house?"

"Do as you please, sir."

"That is no answer; or rather it is a very irritating, because a very evasive one; reply clearly."

"I don't think, sir, you have a right to command me merely because you are older than I, or because you have seen more of the world than I have; your claim to superiority depends on the use you have made of your time and experience."

"Humph! Promptly spoken. But I won't allow that, seeing that it would never suit my case; as I have made an indifferent, not to say a bad, use of both advantages. Leaving superiority out of the question, then, you must still agree to receive my orders now and then, without being piqued or hurt by the tone of command—will you?"

3. And I accept it.

I smiled: I thought to myself Mr. Rochester is peculiar—he seems to forget that he pays me £30 per annum for receiving his orders.

"The smile is very well," said he, catching instantly the passing expression; "but speak too."

"I was thinking, sir, that very few masters would trouble themselves to inquire whether or not their paid subordinates were piqued and hurt by their orders."

"Paid subordinates! What, you are my paid subordinate, are you? Oh, yes, I had forgotten the salary! Well, then, on that mercenary ground, will you agree to let me hector a little?"

"No, sir, not on that ground: but, on the ground that you did forget it, and that you care whether or not a dependent is comfortable in his dependency, I agree heartily."

"And will you consent to dispense with a great many conventional forms and phrases, without thinking that the omission arises from insolence?"

"I am sure, sir, I should never mistake informality for insolence: one I rather like, the other nothing free-born would submit to, even for a salary."

"Humbug! Most things free-born will submit to anything for a salary; therefore, keep to yourself, and don't venture on generalities of which you are intensely ignorant. However, I mentally shake hands with you for your answer, despite its inaccuracy; and as much for the manner in which it was said as for the substance of the speech: the manner was frank and sincere; one does not often see such a manner: no, on the contrary, affectation, or coldness, or stupid, coarse-minded misapprehension of one's meaning are the usual rewards of candor. Not three in three thousand raw school-girl governesses would have answered me as you have just done. But I don't mean to flatter you: if you are cast in a different mold to the majority, it is no merit of yours: Nature did it. And then, after all, I go too fast in my conclusions: for what I yet know, you may be no better than the rest; you may have intolerable defects to counterbalance your few good points."

"And so may you," I thought. My eye met his as the idea crossed my mind: he seemed to read the glance, answering as if its import had been spoken as well as imagined:—

"Yes, yes, you are right," said he; "I have plenty of faults of my own: I know it, and I don't wish to palliate them, I assure you. God wot I need not be too severe about others; I have a past existence, a series of deeds, a color of life to contemplate within my own breast, which might well call my sneers and censures from my neighbors to myself. I started, or rather (for, like other defaulters, I like to lay half the blame on ill fortune and adverse circumstances) was thrust on to a wrong tack at the age of one-and-twenty, and have never recovered the right course since: but I might have been very different; I might have been as good as you—wiser, almost as stainless. I envy you your peace of mind, your clean conscience, your unpolluted memory. Little girl, a memory without blot or contamination must be an exquisite treasure—an inexhaustible source of pure refreshment: is it not?"

"How was your memory when you were eighteen, sir?"

"All right then; limpid, salubrious: no gush of bilge water had turned it to fetid puddle. I was your equal at eighteen—quite your equal. Nature meant me to be, on the whole, a good man, Miss Eyre: one of the better kind; and you see I am not so. You would say you don't see it: at least I flatter myself

I read as much in your eye (beware, by-the-bye, what you express with that organ, I am quick at interpreting its language). Then take my word for it,—I am not a villain: you are not to suppose that—not to attribute to me any such bad eminence; but, owing, I verily believe, rather to circumstances than to my natural bent, I am a trite commonplace sinner, hackneyed in all the poor petty dissipations with which the rich and worthless try to put on life. Do you wonder that I avow this to you? Know, that in the course of your future life you will often find yourself elected the involuntary confidant of your acquaintances' secrets: people will instinctively find out, as I have done, that it is not your forte to tell of yourself, but to listen while others talk of themselves; they will feel, too, that you listen with no malevolent scorn of their indiscretion, but with a kind of innate sympathy; not the less comforting and encouraging because it is very unobstrusive in its manifestations."

"How do you know?—how can you guess all this, sir?"

"I know it well; therefore I proceed almost as freely as if I were writing my thoughts in a diary. You would say, I should have been superior to circumstances; so I should—so I should; but you see I was not. When fate wronged me, I had not the wisdom to remain cool: I turned desperate; then I degenerated. Now, when any vicious simpleton excites my disgust by his paltry ribaldry, I cannot flatter myself that I am better than he: I am forced to confess that he and I are on a level. I wish I had stood firm—God knows I do! Dread remorse when you are tempted to err, Miss Eyre: remorse is the poison of life."

"Repentance is said to be its cure, sir."

"It is not its cure. Reformation may be its cure; and I could reform—I have strength yet for that—if—but where is the use of thinking of it, hampered, burdened, cursed as I am? Besides, since happiness is irrevocably denied me, I have a right to get pleasure out of life: and I *will* get it, cost what it may."

"Then you will degenerate still more, sir."

"Possibly: yet why should I, if I can get sweet, fresh pleasure? And I may get it as sweet and fresh as the wild honey the bee gathers on the moor."

"It will sting—it will taste bitter, sir."

"How do you know?—you never tried it. How very serious—how very solemn you look: and you are as ignorant of the matter as this cameo head" (taking one from the mantelpiece). "You have no right to preach to me, you neophyte, that have not passed the porch of life, and are absolutely unacquainted with its mysteries."

"I only remind you of your own words, sir: you said error brought remorse, and you pronounced remorse the poison of existence."

"And who talks of error now? I scarcely think the notion that flitted across my brain was an error. I believe it was an inspiration rather than a temptation: it was very genial, very soothing,—I know that. Here it comes again! It is no devil, I assure you; or if it be, it has put on the robes of an angel of light. I think I must admit so fair a guest when it asks entrance to my heart."

"Distrust it, sir, it is not a true angel."

"Once more, how do you know? By what instinct do you pretend to distinguish between a fallen seraph of the abyss and a messenger from the eternal throne—between a guide and a seducer?"

"I judged by your countenance, sir; which was troubled: when you said the

suggestion had returned upon you. I feel sure it will work you more misery if you listen to it."

"Not at all—it bears the most gracious message in the world: for the rest, you are not my conscience-keeper, so don't make yourself uneasy. Here, come in, bonny wanderer!"

He said this as if he spoke to a vision, viewless to any eye but his own; then, folding his arms, which he had half extended, on his chest, he seemed to enclose in their embrace the invisible being.

"Now," he continued, again addressing me, "I have received the pilgrim—a disguised deity, as I verily believe. Already it has done me good: my heart was a sort of charnel; it will now be a shrine."

"To speak truth, sir, I don't understand you at all: I cannot keep up the conversation, because it has got out of my depth. Only one thing I know: you said you were not as good as you should like to be, and that you regretted your own imperfection;—one thing I can comprehend: you intimated that to have a sullied memory was a perpetual bane. It seems to me, that if you tried hard, you would in time find it possible to become what you yourself would approve; and that if from this day you began with resolution to correct your thoughts and actions, you would in a few years have laid up a new and stainless store of recollections, to which you might revert with pleasure."

"Justly thought; rightly said, Miss Eyre; and, at this moment, I am paving hell with energy."

"Sir?"

"I am laying down good intentions, which I believe durable as flint. Certainly, my associates and pursuits shall be other than they have been."

"And better?"

"And better—so much better as pure ore is than foul dross. You seem to doubt me; I don't doubt myself: I know what my aim is, what my motives are; and at this moment I pass a law, unalterable as that of the Medes and Persians,[4] that both are right."

"They cannot be, sir, if they require a new statute to legalize them."

"They are, Miss Eyre, though they absolutely require a new statute; unheard-of combinations of circumstances demand unheard-of-rules."

"That sounds a dangerous maxim, sir; because one can see at once that it is liable to abuse."

"Sententious sage! so it is: but I swear by my household gods not to abuse it."

"You are human and fallible."

"I am: so are you—what then?"

"The human and fallible should not arrogate a power with which the divine and perfect alone can be safely entrusted."

"What power?"

"That of saying of any strange, unsanctioned line of action,—'Let it be right.' "

" 'Let it be right'—the very words: you have pronounced them."

"*May* it be right then," I said, as I rose, deeming it useless to continue a discourse which was all darkness to me; and, besides, sensible that the character of my interlocutor was beyond my penetration; at least, beyond its

4. Inhabitants of Media and Persia (modern Iran), whose law "altereth not" (Daniel 6.8, 12).

present reach; and feeling the uncertainty, the vague sense of insecurity, which accompanies a conviction of ignorance.

"Where are you going?"

"To put Adèle to bed: it is past her bedtime."

"You are afraid of me, because I talk like a Sphinx."[5]

"Your language is enigmatical, sir: but though I am bewildered, I am certainly not afraid."

"You *are* afraid—your self-love dreads a blunder."

"In that sense I do feel apprehensive—I have no wish to talk nonsense."

"If you did, it would be in such a grave, quiet manner, I should mistake it for sense. Do you never laugh, Miss Eyre? Don't trouble yourself to answer— I see, you laugh rarely; but you can laugh very merrily: believe me, you are not naturally austere, any more than I am naturally vicious. The Lowood constraint still clings to you somewhat; controlling your features, muffling your voice, and restricting your limbs; and you fear in the presence of a man and a brother—or father, or master, or what you will—to smile too gaily, speak too freely, or move too quickly: but, in time, I think you will learn to be natural with me, as I find it impossible to be conventional with you; and then your looks and movements will have more vivacity and variety than they dare offer now. I see at intervals the glance of a curious sort of bird through the close-set bars of a cage; a vivid, restless, resolute captive is there; were it but free, it would soar cloud-high. You are still bent on going?"

"It has struck nine, sir."

"Never mind,—wait a minute: Adèle is not ready to go to bed yet. My position, Miss Eyre, with my back to the fire, and my face to the room, favors observation. While talking to you, I have also occasionally watched Adèle; (I have my own reasons for thinking her a curious study,—reasons that I may, nay that I shall, impart to you some day;) she pulled out of her box, about ten minutes ago, a little pink silk frock; rapture lit her face as she unfolded it; coquetry runs in her blood, blends with her brains, and seasons the marrow of her bones. 'Il faut que je l'essaie,' cried she; 'et à l'instant même!'[6] and she rushed out of the room. She is now with Sophie, undergoing a robing process: in a few minutes she will reenter; and I know what I shall see,—a miniature of Céline Varens, as she used to appear on the boards at the rising of——: but never mind that. However, my tenderest feelings are about to receive a shock: such is my presentiment; stay now, to see whether it will be realized."

Ere long Adèle's little foot was heard tripping across the hall. She entered, transformed as her guardian had predicted. A dress of rose-colored satin, very short, and as full in the skirt as it could be gathered, replaced the brown frock she had previously worn; a wreath of rosebuds circled her forehead; her feet were dressed in silk stockings and small white satin sandals.

"Est-ce que ma robe va bien?" cried she, bounding forwards; "et mes souliers? et mes bas? Tenez, je croix que je vais danser."[7]

And spreading out her dress, she chasséed across the room; till, having

5. I.e., one who speaks in riddles, like the mythical Greek monster.

6. I must try it, . . . and this very instant!

7. Is my dress all right? . . . and my shoes? and my stockings? Wait, I think I'm going to dance.

reached Mr. Rochester, she wheeled lightly round before him on tiptoe, then dropped on one knee at his feet, exclaiming:—

"Monsieur, je vous remercie mille fois de votre bonté"; then rising, she added, "C'est comme cela que maman faisait, n'est-ce pas, monsieur?"[8]

"Pre-cise-ly!" was the answer; "and, 'comme cela,'[9] she charmed my English gold out of my British breeches pocket. I have been green, too, Miss Eyre,—ay, grass green: not a more vernal tint freshens you now than once freshened me. My Spring is gone, however: but it has left me that French floweret on my hands; which, in some moods, I would fain be rid of. Not valuing now the root whence it sprang; having found that it was of a sort which nothing but gold dust could manure, I have but half a liking to the blossom: especially when it looks so artificial as just now. I keep it and rear it rather on the Roman Catholic principle of expiating numerous sins, great or small, by one good work. I'll explain all this some day. Good-night."

Chapter XV

Mr. Rochester did, on a future occasion, explain it.

It was one afternoon, when he chanced to meet me and Adèle in the grounds; and while she played with Pilot and her shuttlecock, he asked me to walk up and down a long beech avenue within sight of her.

He then said that she was the daughter of a French opera-dancer, Céline Varens, towards whom he had once cherished what he called a "grande passion."[1] This passion Céline had professed to return with even superior ardor. He thought himself her idol; ugly as he was: he believed, as he said, that she preferred his "taille d'athlète" to the elegance of the Apollo Belvidere.[2]

"And, Miss Eyre, so much was I flattered by this preference of the Gallic sylph for her British gnome, that I installed her in an hotel; gave her a complete establishment of servants, a carriage, cashmeres, diamonds, dentelles, etc. In short, I began the process of ruining myself in the received style, like any other spoony.[3] I had not, it seems, the originality to chalk out a new road to shame and destruction, but trod the old track with stupid exactness not to deviate an inch from the beaten center. I had—as I deserved to have— the fate of all other spoonies. Happening to call one evening when Céline did not expect me, I found her out; but it was a warm night, and I was tired with strolling through Paris, so I sat down in her boudoir; happy to breathe the air consecrated so lately by her presence. No,—I exaggerate; I never thought there was any consecrating virtue about her: it was rather a sort of pastille perfume she had left, a scent of musk and amber, than an odor of sanctity. I was just beginning to stifle with the fumes of conservatory flowers and sprinkled essences, when I bethought myself to open the window and step out on to the balcony. It was moonlight and gas-light besides, and very still and serene. The balcony was furnished with a chair or two; I sat down, took out a cigar,—I will take one now, if you will excuse me."

Here ensued a pause, filled up by the producing and lighting of a cigar;

8. Sir, I thank you a thousand times for your goodness; . . . It's just as Mamma used to do it, isn't it, sir?
9. Like that.
1. Great passion.

2. A famous statue of the god Apollo (the Greek ideal of mature male beauty), housed in the Belvedere wing of the Vatican. "Taille d'athlète": athletic figure.
3. Fool. "Dentelles": laces.

having placed it to his lips and breathed a trail of Havannah incense on the freezing and sunless air, he went on:—

"I liked bonbons too, in those days, Miss Eyre, and I was *croquant*—overlook the barbarism—*croquant*[4] chocolate comfits, and smoking alternately, watching meantime the equipages that rolled along the fashionable streets towards the neighboring opera-house, when in an elegant close carriage drawn by a beautiful pair of English horses, and distinctly seen in the brilliant city-night, I recognized the 'voiture'[5] I had given Céline. She was returning: of course my heart thumped with impatience against the iron rails I leaned upon. The carriage stopped, as I had expected, at the hotel door; my flame (that is the very word for an opera inamorata[6]) alighted: though muffled in a cloak—an unnecessary encumbrance, by-the-bye, on so warm a June evening—I knew her instantly by her little foot, seen peeping from the skirt of her dress, as she skipped from the carriage-step. Bending over the balcony, I was about to murmur, 'Mon ange'[7]—in a tone, of course, which should be audible to the ear of love alone—when a figure jumped from the carriage after her; cloaked also; but that was a spurred heel which had rung on the pavement, and that was a hatted head which now passed under the arched *porte-cochère* of the hotel.

"You never felt jealousy, did you, Miss Eyre? Of course not: I need not ask you: because you never felt love. You have both sentiments yet to experience: your soul sleeps; the shock is yet to be given which shall waken it. You think all existence lapses in as quiet a flow as that in which your youth has hitherto slid away. Floating on with closed eyes and muffled ears, you neither see the rocks bristling not far off in the bed of the flood, nor hear the breakers boil at their base. But I tell you—and you may mark my words—you will come some day to a craggy pass of the channel, where the whole of life's stream will be broken up into whirl and tumult, foam and noise: either you will be dashed to atoms on crag points, or lifted up and borne on by some master wave into a calmer current—as I am now.

"I like this day: I like that sky of steel; I like the sternness and stillness of the world under this frost. I like Thornfield: its antiquity; its retirement; its old crow-trees and thorn-trees; its gray façade, and lines of dark windows reflecting that metal welkin: and yet how long have I abhorred the very thought of it; shunned it like a great plague-house! How I do still abhor——"

He ground his teeth and was silent: he arrested his step and struck his boot against the hard ground. Some hated thought seemed to have him in its grip, and to hold him so tightly that he could not advance.

We were ascending the avenue when he thus paused; the hall was before us. Lifting his eye to its battlements, he cast over them a glare such as I never saw before or since. Pain, shame, ire—impatience, disgust, detestation—seemed momentarily to hold a quivering conflict in the large pupil dilating under his ebon eyebrow. Wild was the wrestle which should be paramount; but another feeling rose and triumphed: something hard and cynical; self-willed and resolute: it settled his passion and petrified his countenance: he went on:—"During the moment I was silent, Miss Eyre, I

4. Crunching. Rochester's "barbarism" may be his use of an English grammatical construction with a French verb.

5. Carriage.
6. Beloved woman.
7. My angel.

was arranging a point with my destiny. She stood there, by that beech-trunk—a hag like one of those who appeared to 'Macbeth' on the heath of Forres. 'You like Thornfield?' she said, lifting her finger; and then she wrote in the air a memento, which ran in lurid hieroglyphics all along the house-front, between the upper and lower row of windows. 'Like it if you can! Like it if you dare!'

" 'I will like it,' said I. 'I dare like it'; and (he subjoined moodily) I will keep my word: I will break obstacles to happiness, to goodness—yes, goodness; I wish to be a better man than I have been; than I am—as Job's leviathan broke the spear, the dart and the habergeon, hindrances which others count as iron and brass I will esteem but straw and rotten wood."[8]

Adèle here ran before him with her shuttlecock. "Away!" he cried harshly; "keep at a distance, child; or go in to Sophie!" Continuing then to pursue his walk in silence, I ventured to recall him to the point whence he had abruptly diverged:—"Did you leave the balcony, sir," I asked, "when Mdlle. Varens entered?"

I almost expected a rebuff for this hardly well-timed question: but, on the contrary, waking out of his scowling abstraction, he turned his eyes towards me, and the shade seemed to clear off his brow. "Oh, I had forgotten Céline! Well, to resume. When I saw my charmer thus come in accompanied by a cavalier, I seemed to hear a hiss, and the green snake of jealousy, rising on undulating coils from the moonlit balcony, glided within my waistcoat, and ate its way in two minutes to my heart's core. Strange!" he exclaimed, suddenly starting again from the point. "Strange that I should choose you for the confidant of all this, young lady: passing strange that you should listen to me quietly, as if it were the most usual thing in the world for a man like me to tell stories of his opera-mistresses to a quaint, inexperienced girl like you! But the last singularity explains the first, as I intimated once before: you, with your gravity, considerateness, and caution, were made to be the recipient of secrets. Besides, I know what sort of a mind I have placed in communication with my own: I know it is one not liable to take infection: it is a peculiar mind; it is an unique one. Happily I do not mean to harm it: but, if I did, it would not take harm from me. The more you and I converse, the better; for while I cannot blight you, you may refresh me." After this digression, he proceeded:—"I remained in the balcony. 'They will come to her boudoir, no doubt,' thought I: 'let me prepare an ambush.' So putting my hand in through the open window, I drew the curtain over it, leaving only an opening through which I could take observations; then I closed the case-ment, all but a chink just wide enough to furnish an outlet to lovers' whis-pered vows: then I stole back to my chair; and as I resumed it the pair came in. My eye was quickly at the aperture. Céline's chambermaid entered, lit a lamp, left it on the table, and withdrew. The couple were thus revealed to me clearly: both removed their cloaks, and there was 'the Varens'[9] shining in satin and jewels,—my gifts of course,—and there was her companion in an officer's uniform; and I knew him for a young roué of a vicomte[1]—a brainless and vicious youth whom I had sometimes met in society, and had

8. Job 41.26–27.
9. Literal translation of the French "la Varens": a common Gallic idiom was to identify a well-known

female stage performer by using her last name, pre-ceded by "la."
1. Viscount: a nobleman.

never thought of hating because I despised him so absolutely. On recognizing him, the fang of the snake, jealousy, was instantly broken; because at the same moment my love for Céline sank under an extinguisher. A woman who could betray me for such a rival was not worth contending for: she deserved only scorn; less, however, than I, who had been her dupe.

"They began to talk; their conversation eased me completely: frivolous, mercenary, heartless, and senseless, it was rather calculated to weary than enrage a listener. A card of mine lay on the table; this being perceived, brought my name under discussion. Neither of them possessed energy or wit to belabor me soundly; but they insulted me as coarsely as they could in their little way: especially Céline; who even waxed rather brilliant on my personal defects—deformities she termed them. Now it had been her custom to launch out into fervent admiration of what she called my 'beauté mâle':[2] wherein she differed diametrically from you, who told me point-blank, at the second interview, that you did not think me handsome. The contrast struck me at the time, and—"

Adéle here came running up again.

"Monsieur, John has just been to say that your agent has called and wishes to see you."

"Ah! in that case I must abridge. Opening the window, I walked in upon them; liberated Céline from my protection; gave her notice to vacate her hotel; offered her a purse for immediate exigencies; disregarded screams, hysterics, prayers, protestations, convulsions; made an appointment with the vicomte for a meeting at the Bois de Boulogne. Next morning I had the pleasure of encountering him; left a bullet in one of his poor etiolated arms, feeble as the wing of a chicken in the pip, and then thought I had done with the whole crew. But unluckily the Varens, six months before, had given me this filette[3] Adéle; who she affirmed was my daughter; and perhaps she may be, though I see no proofs of such grim paternity written in her countenance. Pilot is more like me than she. Some years after I had broken with the mother she abandoned her child and ran away to Italy with a musician or singer. I acknowledged no natural claim on Adéle's part to be supported by me; nor do I now acknowledge any, for I am not her father; but hearing that she was quite destitute, I e'en took the poor thing out of the slime and mud of Paris, and transplanted it here, to grow up clean in the wholesome soil of an English country garden. Mrs. Fairfax found you to train it; but now you know that it is the illegitimate offspring of a French opera-girl, you will perhaps think differently of your post and protégée. You will be coming to me some day with notice that you have found another place—that you beg me to look out for a new governess, etc.—eh?"

"No. Adéle is not answerable for either her mother's faults or yours. I have a regard for her, and now that I know she is, in a sense, parentless—forsaken by her mother and disowned by you, sir—I shall cling closer to her than before. How could I possibly prefer the spoilt pet of a wealthy family, who would hate her governess as a nuisance, to a lonely little orphan, who leans towards her as a friend?"

"Oh, that is the light in which you view it! Well, I must go in now; and you too: it darkens."

2. Masculine beauty. 3. Little girl.

But I stayed out a few minutes longer with Adèle and Pilot—ran a race with her, and played a game of battledore and shuttlecock.[4] When we went in, and I had removed her bonnet and coat, I took her on my knee; kept her there an hour, allowing her to prattle as she liked, not rebuking even some little freedoms and trivialities into which she was apt to stray when much noticed; and which betrayed in her a superficiality of character, inherited probably from her mother, hardly congenial to an English mind. Still she had her merits; and I was disposed to appreciate all that was good in her to the utmost. I sought in her countenance and features a likeness to Mr. Rochester, but found none—no trait, no turn of expression announced relationship. It was a pity: if she could but have been proved to resemble him, he would have thought more of her.

It was not till after I had withdrawn to my own chamber for the night that I steadily reviewed the tale Mr. Rochester had told me. As he had said, there was probably nothing at all extraordinary in the substance of the narrative itself—a wealthy Englishman's passion for a French dancer, and her treachery to him, were everyday matters enough, no doubt, in society—but there was something decidedly strange in the paroxysm of emotion which had suddenly seized him, when he was in the act of expressing the present contentment of his mood, and his newly-revived pleasure in the old hall and its environs. I meditated wonderingly on this incident: but gradually quitting it, as I found it for the present inexplicable, I turned to the consideration of my master's manner to myself. The confidence he had thought fit to repose in me seemed a tribute to my discretion. I regarded and accepted it as such. His deportment had now for some weeks been more uniform towards me than at the first. I never seemed in his way; he did not take fits of chilling hauteur; when he met me unexpectedly, the encounter seemed welcome— he had always a word and sometimes a smile for me; when summoned by formal invitation to his presence, I was honored by a cordiality of reception that made me feel I really possessed the power to amuse him, and that these evening conferences were sought as much for his pleasure as for my benefit.

I, indeed, talked comparatively little; but I heard him talk with relish. It was his nature to be communicative—he liked to open to a mind unacquainted with the world glimpses of its scenes and ways (I do not mean its corrupt scenes and wicked ways, but such as derived their interest from the great scale on which they were acted, the strange novelty by which they were characterised); and I had a keen delight in receiving the new ideas he offered, in imagining the new pictures he portrayed, and following him in thought through the new regions he disclosed, never startled or troubled by one noxious allusion.

The ease of his manner freed me from painful restraint; the friendly frankness, as correct as cordial, with which he treated me, drew me to him. I felt at times as if he were my relation, rather than my master: yet he was imperious sometimes still; but I did not mind that; I saw it was his way. So happy, so gratified did I become with this new interest added to life, that I ceased to pine after kindred. My thin crescent-destiny seemed to enlarge; the blanks of existence were filled up; my bodily health improved; I gathered flesh and strength.

4. Badminton.

And was Mr. Rochester now ugly in my eyes? No, reader. Gratitude, and many associations, all pleasurable and genial, made his face the object I best liked to see; his presence in a room was more cheering than the brightest fire. Yet I had not forgotten his faults—indeed, I could not, for he brought them frequently before me. He was proud, sardonic, harsh to inferiority of every description. In my secret soul I knew that his great kindness to me was balanced by unjust severity to many others. He was moody, too—unaccountably so. I more than once, when sent for to read to him, found him sitting in his library alone, with his head bent on his folded arms; and, when he looked up, a morose, almost a malignant scowl, blackened his features. But I believed that his moodiness, his harshness, and his former faults of morality (I say *former,* for now he seemed corrected of them) had their source in some cruel cross of fate. I believed he was naturally a man of better tendencies, higher principles, and purer tastes than such as circumstances had developed, education instilled, or destiny encouraged. I thought there were excellent materials in him; though for the present they hung together somewhat spoiled and tangled. I cannot deny that I grieved for his grief, whatever that was, and would have given much to assuage it.

Though I had now extinguished my candle and was laid down in bed, I could not sleep for thinking of his look when he paused in the avenue, and told how his destiny had risen up before him, and dared him to be happy at Thornfield.

"Why not?" I asked myself. "What alienates him from the house? Will he leave it again soon? Mrs. Fairfax said he seldom stayed here longer than a fortnight at a time, and he has now been resident eight weeks. If he does go, the change will be doleful. Suppose he should be absent spring, summer, and autumn: how joyless sunshine and fine days will seem."

I hardly know whether I had slept or not after this musing; at any rate, I started wide awake on hearing a vague murmur, peculiar and lugubrious, which sounded, I thought, just above me. I wished I had kept my candle burning: the night was drearily dark; my spirits were depressed. I rose and sat up in bed, listening. The sound was hushed.

I tried again to sleep; but my heart beat anxiously: my inward tranquillity was broken. The clock, far down in the hall, struck two. Just then it seemed my chamber-door was touched; as if fingers had swept the panels in groping a way along the dark gallery outside. I said, "Who is there?" Nothing answered. I was chilled with fear.

All at once I remembered that it might be Pilot: who, when the kitchen-door chanced to be left open, not unfrequently found his way up to the threshold of Mr. Rochester's chamber: I had seen him lying there myself, in the mornings. The idea calmed me somewhat: I lay down. Silence composes the nerves; and as an unbroken hush now reigned again through the whole house, I began to feel the return of slumber. But it was not fated that I should sleep that night. A dream had scarcely approached my ear, when it fled affrighted, scared by a marrow-freezing incident enough.

This was a demoniac laugh—low, suppressed, and deep—uttered, as it seemed, at the very key-hole of my chamber-door. The head of my bed was near the door, and I thought at first the goblin-laughter stood at my bedside—or rather, crouched by my pillow: but I rose, looked round, and could see nothing; while, as I still gazed, the unnatural sound was reiterated: and

I knew it came from behind the panels. My first impulse was to rise and fasten the bolt; my next again, to cry out, "Who is there?"

Something gurgled and moaned. Ere long, steps retreated up the gallery towards the third story staircase: a door had lately been made to shut in that staircase; I heard it open and close, and all was still.

"Was that Grace Poole? and is she possessed with a devil?" thought I. Impossible now to remain longer by myself: I must go to Mrs. Fairfax. I hurried on my frock and a shawl; I withdrew the bolt, and opened the door with a trembling hand. There was a candle burning just outside, left on the matting in the gallery. I was surprised at this circumstance: but still more was I amazed to perceive the air quite dim, as if filled with smoke; and, while looking to the right hand and left, to find whence these blue wreaths issued, I became further aware of a strong smell of burning.

Something creaked: it was a door ajar; and that door was Mr. Rochester's, and the smoke rushed in a cloud from thence. I thought no more of Mrs. Fairfax; I thought no more of Grace Poole or the laugh: in an instant, I was within the chamber. Tongues of flame darted round the bed: the curtains were on fire. In the midst of blaze and vapor, Mr. Rochester lay stretched motionless, in deep sleep.

"Wake! wake!" I cried—I shook him, but he only murmured and turned: the smoke had stupefied him. Not a moment could be lost: the very sheets were kindling. I rushed to his basin and ewer; fortunately, one was wide and the other deep, and both were filled with water. I heaved them up, deluged the bed and its occupant, flew back to my own room, brought my own water-jug, baptized the couch afresh, and, by God's aid, succeeded in extinguishing the flames which were devouring it.

The hiss of the quenched element, the breakage of a pitcher which I flung from my hand when I had emptied it, and, above all, the splash of the shower-bath I had liberally bestowed, roused Mr. Rochester at last. Though it was now dark, I knew he was awake; because I heard him fulminating strange anathemas[5] at finding himself lying in a pool of water.

"Is there a flood?" he cried.

"No, sir," I answered; "but there has been a fire: get up, do, you are quenched now; I will fetch you a candle."

"In the name of all the elves in Christendom, is that Jane Eyre?" he demanded. "What have you done with me, witch, sorceress? Who is in the room beside you? Have you plotted to drown me?"

"I will fetch you a candle, sir; and, in Heaven's name, get up. Somebody has plotted something: you cannot too soon find out who and what it is."

"There—I am up now; but at your peril you fetch a candle yet: wait two minutes till I get into some dry garments, if any dry there be—yes, here is my dressing-gown. Now run!"

I did run; I brought the candle which still remained in the gallery. He took it from my hand, held it up, and surveyed the bed, all blackened and scorched, the sheets drenched, the carpet round swimming in water.

"What is it? and who did it?" he asked.

I briefly related to him what had transpired: the strange laugh I had heard in the gallery: the step ascending to the third story; the smoke,—the smell

5. Curses.

of fire which had conducted me to his room; in what state I had found matters there, and how I had deluged him with all the water I could lay hands on.

He listened very gravely; his face, as I went on, expressed more concern than astonishment; he did not immediately speak when I had concluded.

"Shall I call Mrs. Fairfax?" I asked.

"Mrs. Fairfax? No: what the deuce would you call her for? What can she do? Let her sleep unmolested."

"Then I will fetch Leah, and wake John and his wife."

"Not at all: just be still. You have a shawl on? If you are not warm enough, you may take my cloak yonder; wrap it about you, and sit down in the arm-chair: there,—I will put it on. Now place your feet on the stool, to keep them out of the wet. I am going to leave you a few minutes. I shall take the candle. Remain where you are till I return: be as still as a mouse. I must pay a visit to the third story. Don't move, remember, or call any one."

He went: I watched the light withdraw. He passed up the gallery very softly, unclosed the staircase door with as little noise as possible, shut it after him, and the last ray vanished. I was left in total darkness. I listened for some noise, but heard nothing. A very long time elapsed. I grew weary: it was cold, in spite of the cloak; and then I did not see the use of staying, as I was not to rouse the house. I was on the point of risking Mr. Rochester's displeasure, by disobeying his orders, when the light once more gleamed dimly on the gallery-wall, and I heard his unshod feet tread the matting. "I hope it is he," thought I, "and not something worse."

He reentered, pale and very gloomy. 'I have found it all out,' said he, setting his candle down on the wash-stand; "it is as I thought."

"How, sir?"

He made no reply, but stood with his arms folded, looking on the ground. At the end of a few minutes, he inquired in rather a peculiar tone:—"I forget whether you said you saw anything when you opened your chamber door."

"No, sir, only the candlestick on the ground."

"But you heard an odd laugh? You have heard that laugh before, I should think, or something like it?"

"Yes, sir: there is a woman who sews here, called Grace Poole—she laughs in that way. She is a singular person."

"Just so. Grace Poole—you have guessed it. She is, as you say, singular,— very. Well, I shall reflect on the subject. Meantime, I am glad that you are the only person, besides myself, acquainted with the precise details of tonight's incident. You are no talking fool: say nothing about it. I will account for this state of affairs (pointing to the bed): and now return to your own room. I shall do very well on the sofa in the library for the rest of the night. It is near four:—in two hours the servants will be up."

"Good-night, then, sir," said I, departing.

He seemed surprised—very inconsistently so, as he had just told me to go.

"What!" he exclaimed, "are you quitting me already: and in that way?"

"You said I might go, sir."

"But not without taking leave; not without a word or two of acknowledg-ment and good will: not, in short, in that brief, dry fashion. Why, you have saved my life!—snatched me from a horrible and excruciating death!—and you walk past me as if we were mutual strangers! At least shake hands."

He held out his hand; I gave him mine: he took it first in one, then in both his own.

"You have saved my life: I have a pleasure in owing you so immense a debt. I cannot say more. Nothing else that has being would have been tolerable to me in the character of creditor for such an obligation: but you: it is different;—I feel your benefits no burden, Jane."

He paused; gazed at me: words almost visible trembled on his lips,—but his voice was checked.

"Good night again, sir. There is no debt, benefit, burden, obligation, in the case."

"I knew," he continued, "you would do me good in some way, at some time;—I saw it in your eyes when I first beheld you: their expression and smile did not—(again he stopped)—did not (he proceeded hastily) strike delight to my very inmost heart so for nothing. People talk of natural sympathies; I have heard of good genii—there are grains of truth in the wildest fable. My cherished preserver, good night!"

Strange energy was in his voice, strange fire in his look.

"I am glad I happened to be awake," I said; and then I was going.

"What! you *will* go?"

"I am cold, sir."

"Cold? Yes,—and standing in a pool! Go, then, Jane; go!" But he still retained my hand, and I could not free it. I bethought myself of an expedient.

"I think I hear Mrs. Fairfax move, sir," said I.

"Well, leave me." He relaxed his fingers, and I was gone.

I regained my couch, but never thought of sleep. Till morning dawned I was tossed on a buoyant but unquiet sea, where billows of trouble rolled under surges of joy. I thought sometimes I saw beyond its wild waters a shore, sweet as the hills of Beulah; and now and then a freshening gale wakened by hope, bore my spirit triumphantly towards the bourne;[6] but I could not reach it, even in fancy,—a counteracting breeze blew off land, and continually drove me back. Sense would resist delirium, judgment would warn passion. Too feverish to rest, I rose as soon as day dawned.

Chapter XVI

I both wished and feared to see Mr. Rochester on the day which followed this sleepless night. I wanted to hear his voice again, yet feared to meet his eye. During the early part of the morning, I momentarily expected his coming. He was not in the frequent habit of entering the schoolroom; but he did step in for a few minutes sometimes, and I had the impression that he was sure to visit it that day.

But the morning passed just as usual. Nothing happened to interrupt the quiet course of Adèle's studies; only, soon after breakfast, I heard some bustle in the neighborhood of Mr. Rochester's chamber, Mrs. Fairfax's voice, and Leah's, and the cook's—that is, John's wife—and even John's own gruff tones. There were exclamations of, "What a mercy master was not burned in his bed!" "It is always dangerous to keep a candle lit at night." "How

6. Destination. "Beulah": name (meaning "married") given to the Jews' land restored after their exile in Babylon (Isaiah 62:4).

providential that he had presence of mind to think of the water-jug!" "I won-
der he waked nobody!" "It is to be hoped he will not take cold with sleeping
on the library sofa," etc.

To much confabulation succeeded a sound of scrubbing and setting to
rights; and when I passed the room, in going downstairs to dinner, I saw
through the open door that all was again restored to complete order—only
the bed was stripped of its hangings. Leah stood up in the window-seat,
rubbing the panes of glass dimmed with smoke. I was about to address her,
for I wished to know what account had been given of the affair; but, on
advancing, I saw a second person in the chamber—a woman sitting on a
chair by the bedside, and sewing rings to new curtains. That woman was no
other than Grace Poole.

There she sat, staid and taciturn-looking, as usual, in her brown stuff
gown, her check apron, white handkerchief, and cap. She was intent on her
work, in which her whole thoughts seemed absorbed. On her hard forehead,
and in her commonplace features, was nothing either of the paleness or
desperation one would have expected to see marking the countenance of a
woman who had attempted murder, and whose intended victim had followed
her last night to her lair, and (as I believed) charged her with the crime she
wished to perpetrate. I was amazed—confounded. She looked up, while I
still gazed at her: no start, no increase or failure of color betrayed emotion,
consciousness of guilt, or fear of detection. She said, "Good morning, Miss,"
in her usual phlegmatic and brief manner; and taking up another ring and
more tape, went on with her sewing.

"I will put her to some test," thought I. "Such absolute impenetrability is
past comprehension."

"Good morning, Grace," I said. "Has anything happened here? I thought
I heard the servants all talking together a while ago."

"Only master had been reading in his bed last night. He fell asleep with
his candle lit, and the curtains got on fire; but, fortunately, he awoke before
the bed-clothes or the wood-work caught, and contrived to quench the flame
with the water in the ewer."

"A strange affair!" I said, in a low voice; then, looking at her fixedly, "Did
Mr. Rochester wake nobody? Did no one hear him move?"

She again raised her eyes to me; and this time there was something of
consciousness in their expression. She seemed to examine me warily; then
she answered, "The servants sleep so far off, you know, Miss, they would not
be likely to hear. Mrs. Fairfax's room and yours are the nearest to master's;
but Mrs. Fairfax said she heard nothing: when people get elderly, they often
sleep heavy." She paused, and then added, with a sort of assumed indiffer-
ence, but still in a marked and significant tone, "But you are young, Miss,
and I should say a light sleeper. Perhaps you may have heard a noise?"

"I did," said I, dropping my voice, so that Leah, who was still polishing the
panes, could not hear me, "and at first I thought it was Pilot; but Pilot cannot
laugh, and I am certain I heard a laugh, and a strange one."

She took a new needleful of thread, waxed it carefully, threaded her needle
with a steady hand, and then observed, with perfect composure,—"It is hard-
ly likely master would laugh, I should think, Miss, when he was in such
danger: you must have been dreaming."

"I was not dreaming," I said, with some warmth, for her brazen coolness

provoked me. Again she looked at me, and with the same scrutinizing and conscious eye.

"Have you told master that you heard a laugh?" she inquired.

"I have not had the opportunity of speaking to him this morning."

"You did not think of opening your door and looking out into the gallery?" she further asked.

She appeared to be cross-questioning me—attempting to draw from me information unawares. The idea struck me that if she discovered I knew or suspected her guilt, she would be playing off some of her malignant pranks on me. I thought it advisable to be on my guard.

"On the contrary," said I, "I bolted my door."

"Then you are not in the habit of bolting your door every night before you get into bed?"

"Fiend! she wants to know my habits, that she may lay her plans accordingly!" Indignation again prevailed over prudence; I replied sharply, "Hitherto I have often omitted to fasten the bolt: I did not think it necessary. I was not aware any danger or annoyance was to be dreaded at Thornfield Hall; but in future" (and I laid marked stress on the words) "I shall take good care to make all secure before I venture to lie down."

"It will be wise so to do," was her answer. "This neighborhood is as quiet as any I know, and I never heard of the hall being attempted by robbers since it was a house though there are hundreds of pounds' worth of plate in the plate-closet, as is well known. And you see, for such a large house, there are very few servants, because master has never lived here much, and when he does come, being a bachelor, he needs little waiting on; but I always think it best to err on the safe side: a door is soon fastened, and it is as well to have a drawn bolt between one and any mischief that may be about. A deal of people, Miss, are for trusting all to Providence; but I say Providence will not dispense with the means, though He often blesses them when they are used discreetly." And here she closed her harangue: a long one for her, and uttered with the demureness of a Quakeress.

I still stood absolutely dumfounded at what appeared to me her miraculous self-possession and most inscrutable hypocrisy, when the cook entered.

"Mrs. Poole," said she, addressing Grace, "the servants' dinner will soon be ready. Will you come down?"

"No. Just put my pint of porter and bit of pudding on a tray, and I'll carry it upstairs."

"You'll have some meat?"

"Just a morsel, and a taste of cheese, that's all."

"And the sago?"[7]

"Never mind it at present. I shall be coming down before tea-time. I'll make it myself."

The cook here turned to me, saying that Mrs. Fairfax was waiting for me: so I departed.

I hardly heard Mrs. Fairfax's account of the curtain conflagration during dinner, so much was I occupied in puzzling my brains over the enigmatical character of Grace Poole, and still more in pondering the problem of her position at Thornfield; in questioning why she had not been given into cus-

7. A cereal, eaten in the West Indies, made from palm tree trunks.

tody that morning, or, at the very least, dismissed from her master's service. He had almost as much as declared his conviction of her criminality last night: what mysterious cause withheld him from accusing her? Why had he enjoined me, too, to secrecy? It was strange—a bold, vindictive, and haughty gentleman seemed somehow in the power of one of the meanest of his dependants; so much in her power, that even when she lifted her hand against his life, he dared not openly charge her with the attempt, much less punish her for it.

Had Grace been young and handsome, I should have been tempted to think that tenderer feelings than prudence or fear influenced Mr. Rochester in her behalf; but, hard-favored and matronly as she was, the idea could not be admitted. "Yet," I reflected, "she has been young once; her youth would be contemporary with her master's. Mrs. Fairfax told me once she had lived here many years. I don't think she can ever have been pretty; but, for aught I know, she may possess originality and strength of character to compensate for the want of personal advantages. Mr. Rochester is an amateur of the decided and eccentric—Grace is eccentric at least. What if a former caprice (a freak very possible to a nature so sudden and headstrong as his) has delivered him into her power, and she now exercises over his actions a secret influence, the result of his own indiscretion, which he cannot shake off, and dare not disregard?" But, having reached this point of conjecture, Mrs. Poole's square, flat figure, and uncomely, dry, even coarse face, recurred so distinctly to my mind's eye, that I thought, "No; impossible! my supposition cannot be correct. Yet," suggested the secret voice which talks to us in our own hearts, "you are not beautiful either, and perhaps Mr. Rochester approves you—at any rate, you have often felt as if he did; and last night— remember his words; remember his look; remember his voice!"

I well remembered all—language, glance, and tone seemed at the moment vividly renewed. I was now in the schoolroom. Adèle was drawing. I bent over her and directed her pencil. She looked up with a sort of start.

"Qu'avez-vous, mademoiselle?" said she; "Vos doigts tremblent comme la feuille, et vos joues sont rouges: mais, rouges comme des cerises!"[8]

"I am hot, Adèle, with stooping!" She went on sketching, I went on thinking.

I hastened to drive from my mind the hateful notion I had been conceiving respecting Grace Poole: it disgusted me. I compared myself with her, and found we were different. Bessie Leaven had said I was quite a lady; and she spoke truth: I was a lady. And now I looked much better than I did when Bessie saw me: I had more color and more flesh; more life, more vivacity; because I had brighter hopes and keener enjoyments.

"Evening approaches," said I, as I looked towards the window. "I have never heard Mr. Rochester's voice or step in the house today; but surely I shall see him before night: I feared the meeting in the morning: now I desire it, because expectation has been so long baffled that it is grown impatient."

When dusk actually closed, and when Adèle left me to go and play in the nursery with Sophie, I did most keenly desire it. I listened for the bell to ring below; I listened for Leah coming up with a message; I fancied sometimes I

8. What's wrong, miss? . . . Your fingers are trembling like a leaf, and your cheeks are red: red as cherries!

heard Mr. Rochester's own tread, and I turned to the door, expecting it to open and admit him. The door remained shut: darkness only came in through the window. Still it was not late: he often sent for me at seven and eight o'clock, and it was yet but six. Surely I should not be wholly disappointed tonight, when I had so many things to say to him! I wanted again to introduce the subject of Grace Poole, and to hear what he would answer; I wanted to ask him plainly if he really believed it was she who had made last night's hideous attempt; and if so, why he kept her wickedness a secret. It little mattered whether my curiosity irritated him; I knew the pleasure of vexing and soothing him by turns; it was one I chiefly delighted in, and a sure instinct always prevented me from going too far: beyond the verge of provocation I never ventured; on the extreme brink I liked well to try my skill. Retaining every minute form of respect, every propriety of my station, I could still meet him in argument without fear or uneasy restraint: this suited both him and me.

A tread creaked on the stairs at last; Leah made her appearance, but it was only to intimate that tea was ready in Mrs. Fairfax's room. Thither I repaired, glad at least to go downstairs, for that brought me, I imagined, nearer to Mr. Rochester's presence.

"You must want your tea," said the good lady, as I joined her, "you ate so little at dinner. I am afraid," she continued, "you are not well to-day, you looked flushed and feverish."

"Oh, quite well! I never felt better."

"Then you must prove it by evincing a good appetite; will you fill the teapot while I knit off this needle?" Having completed her task, she rose to draw down the blind which she had hitherto kept up, by way, I suppose, of making the most of daylight: though dusk was now fast deepening into total obscurity.

"It is fair tonight," said she, as she looked through the panes, "though not starlight; Mr. Rochester has, on the whole, had a favorable day for his journey."

"Journey!—Is Mr. Rochester gone anywhere? I did not know he was out."

"Oh, he set off the moment he had breakfasted! He is gone to the Leas, Mr. Eshton's place, ten miles on the other side Millcote; I believe there is quite a party assembled there—Lord Ingram, Sir George Lynn, Colonel Dent, and others."

"Do you expect him back tonight?"

"No—nor tomorrow either; I should think he is very likely to stay a week or more. When these fine, fashionable people get together, they are so surrounded by elegance and gaiety, so well provided with all that can please and entertain, they are in no hurry to separate. Gentlemen, especially, are often in request on such occasions; and Mr. Rochester is so talented and so lively in society, that I believe he is a general favorite—the ladies are very fond of him—though you would not think his appearance calculated to recommend him particularly in their eyes; but I suppose his acquirements and abilities, perhaps his wealth and good blood, make amends for any little fault of looks."

"Are there ladies at the Leas?"

"There are Mrs. Eshton and her three daughters—very elegant young ladies, indeed; and there are the Honorable Blanche and Mary Ingram—most beautiful women, I suppose: indeed, I have seen Blanche, six or seven

years since, when she was a girl of eighteen. She came here to a Christmas
ball and party Mr. Rochester gave. You should have seen the dining-room
that day—how richly it was decorated, how brilliantly lit up! I should think
there were fifty ladies and gentlemen present—all of the first county families;
and Miss Ingram was considered the belle of the evening."

"You saw her, you say, Mrs. Fairfax: what was she like?"

"Yes, I saw her. The dining-room doors were thrown open, and, as it was
Christmas-time, the servants were allowed to assemble in the hall, to hear
some of the ladies sing and play. Mr. Rochester would have me to come in,
and I sat down in a quiet corner and watched them. I never saw a more
splendid scene: the ladies were magnificently dressed; most of them—at least
most of the younger ones—looked handsome, but Miss Ingram was certainly
the queen."

"And what was she like?"

"Tall, fine bust, sloping shoulders, long, graceful neck; olive complexion,
dark and clear; noble features; eyes rather like Mr. Rochester's, large and
black, and as brilliant as her jewels. And then she had such a fine head of
hair, raven-black, and so becomingly arranged; a crown of thick plaits
behind, and in front the longest, the glossiest curls I ever saw. She was
dressed in pure white, an amber-colored scarf was passed over her shoulder
and across her breast, tied at the side, and descending in long, fringed ends
below her knee. She wore an amber-colored flower, too, in her hair: it con-
trasted well with the jetty mass of her curls."

"She was greatly admired, of course?"

"Yes, indeed, and not only for her beauty, but for her accomplishments.
She was one of the ladies who sang; a gentleman accompanied her on the
piano. She and Mr. Rochester sang a duet."

"Mr. Rochester? I was not aware he could sing."

"Oh! he has a fine bass voice, and an excellent taste for music."

"And Miss Ingram, what sort of a voice had she?"

"A very rich and powerful one—she sang delightfully—it was a treat to
listen to her; and she played afterwards. I am no judge of music, but Mr.
Rochester is, and I heard him say her execution was remarkably good."

"And this beautiful and accomplished lady is not yet married?"

"It appears not: I fancy neither she nor her sister have very large fortunes.
Old Lord Ingram's estates were chiefly entailed, and the eldest son came in
for everything almost."

"But I wonder no wealthy nobleman or gentleman has taken a fancy to
her: Mr. Rochester, for instance. He is rich, is he not?"

"Oh! yes. But you see there is a considerable difference in age: Mr. Roch-
ester is near forty; she is but twenty-five."

"What of that? More unequal matches are made every day."

"True: yet I should scarcely fancy Mr. Rochester would entertain an idea
of the sort. But you eat nothing: you have scarcely tasted since you began
tea."

"No: I am too thirsty to eat. Will you let me have another cup?"

I was about again to revert to the probability of a union between Mr.
Rochester and the beautiful Blanche; but Adèle came in, and the conver-
sation was turned into another channel.

When once more alone, I reviewed the information I had got; looked into

my heart, examined its thoughts and feelings, and endeavored to bring back with a strict hand such as had been straying through imagination's boundless and trackless waste, into the safe fold of common sense.

Arraigned at my own bar, Memory having given her evidence of the hopes, wishes, sentiments I had been cherishing since last night—of the general state of mind in which I had indulged for nearly a fortnight past; Reason having come forward and told in her own quiet way, a plain, unvarnished tale, showing how I had rejected the real, and rabidly devoured the ideal;—I pronounced judgment to this effect:—That a greater fool than Jane Eyre had never breathed the breath of life: that a more fantastic idiot had never surfeited herself on sweet lies, and swallowed poison as if it were nectar.

"*You,*" I said, "a favorite with Mr. Rochester? You gifted with the power of pleasing him? *You* of importance to him in any way? Go! your folly sickens me. And you have derived pleasure from occasional tokens of preference—equivocal tokens, shown by a gentleman of family, and a man of the world, to a dependant and a novice. How dared you? Poor stupid dupe!—Could not even self-interest make you wiser? You repeated to yourself this morning the brief scene of last night?—Cover your face and be ashamed! He said something in praise of your eyes, did he? Blind puppy! Open their bleared lids and look on your own accursed senselessness! It does good to no woman to be flattered by her superior, who cannot possibly intend to marry her; and it is madness in all women to let a secret love kindle within them, which, if unreturned and unknown, must devour the life that feeds it; and, if discovered and responded to, must lead, *ignis-fatuus*-like,[9] into miry wilds, whence there is no extrication.

"Listen, then, Jane Eyre, to your sentence: tomorrow, place the glass before you, and draw in chalk your own picture, faithfully; without softening one defect: omit no harsh line, smooth away no displeasing irregularity; write under it, 'Portrait of a Governess, disconnected, poor, and plain.'

"Afterwards, take a piece of smooth ivory—you have one prepared in your drawing-box: take your palette, mix your freshest, finest, clearest tints; choose your most delicate camel-hair pencils; delineate carefully the loveliest face you can imagine; paint it in your softest shades and sweetest hues, according to the description given by Mrs. Fairfax of Blanche Ingram: remember the raven ringlets, the Oriental eye;—what! you revert to Mr. Rochester as a model! Order! No snivel!—no sentiment!—no regret! I will endure only sense and resolution. Recall the august yet harmonious lineaments, the Grecian neck and bust: let the round and dazzling arm be visible, and the delicate hand; omit neither diamond ring nor gold bracelet; portray faithfully the attire, aërial lace and glistening satin, graceful scarf and golden rose: call it 'Blanche, an accomplished lady of rank.'

"Whenever, in future, you should chance to fancy Mr. Rochester thinks well of you, take out these two pictures and compare them: say, 'Mr. Rochester might probably win that noble lady's love, if he chose to strive for it; is it likely he would waste a serious thought on this indigent and insignificant plebian?' "

"I'll do it," I resolved: and having framed this determination, I grew calm, and fell asleep.

9. Like a will-o'-the-wisp.

I kept my word. An hour or two sufficed to sketch my own portrait in crayons; and in less than a fortnight I had completed an ivory miniature of an imaginary Blanche Ingram. It looked a lovely face enough, and when compared with the real head in chalk, the contrast was as great as self-control could desire. I derived benefit from the task: it had kept my head and hands employed, and had given force and fixedness to the new impressions I wished to stamp indelibly on my heart.

Ere long, I had reason to congratulate myself on the course of wholesome discipline to which I had thus forced my feelings to submit: thanks to it, I was able to meet subsequent occurrences with a decent calm; which, had they found me unprepared, I should probably have been unequal to maintain, even externally.

Chapter XVII

A week passed, and no news arrived of Mr. Rochester: ten days, and still he did not come. Mrs. Fairfax said she should not be surprised if he were to go straight from the Leas to London, and thence to the Continent and not show his face again at Thornfield for a year to come: he had not unfrequently quitted it in a manner quite as abrupt and unexpected. When I heard this I was beginning to feel a strange chill and failing at the heart. I was actually permitting myself to experience a sickening sense of disappointment: but rallying my wits, and recollecting my principles, I at once called my sensations to order; and it was wonderful how I got over the temporary blunder—how I cleared up the mistake of supposing Mr. Rochester's movements a matter in which I had any cause to take a vital interest. Not that I humbled myself by a slavish notion of inferiority: on the contrary, I just said—"You have nothing to do with the master of Thornfield, further than to receive the salary he gives you for teaching his protégée, and to be grateful for such respectful and kind treatment as, if you do your duty, you have a right to expect at his hands. Be sure that is the only tie he seriously acknowledges between you and him: so don't make him the object of your fine feelings, your raptures, agonies, and so forth. He is not of your order: keep to your caste, and be too self-respecting to lavish the love of the whole heart, soul, and strength, where such a gift is not wanted and would be despised."

I went on with my day's business tranquilly, but ever and anon vague suggestions kept wandering across my brain of reasons why I should quit Thornfield; and I kept involuntarily framing advertisements and pondering conjectures about new situations; these thoughts I did not think it necessary to check; they might germinate and bear fruit if they could.

Mr. Rochester had been absent upwards of a fortnight, when the post brought Mrs. Fairfax a letter.

"It is from the master," said she as she looked at the direction. "Now I suppose we shall know whether we are to expect his return or not."

And while she broke the seal and perused the document, I went on taking my coffee (we were at breakfast); it was hot, and I attributed to that circumstance a fiery glow which suddenly rose to my face. Why my hand shook, and why I involuntarily spilt half the contents of my cup into my saucer, I did not choose to consider.

"Well—I sometimes think we are too quiet; but we run a chance of being

busy enough now: for a little while at least," said Mrs. Fairfax, still holding the note before her spectacles.

Ere I permitted myself to request an explanation, I tied the string of Adèle's pinafore, which happened to be loose: having helped her also to another bun, and refilled her mug with milk, I said, nonchalantly:—"Mr. Rochester is not likely to return soon, I suppose?"

"Indeed, he is—in three days, he says; that will be next Thursday; and not alone either. I don't know how many of the fine people at the Leas are coming with him. He sends directions for all the best bedrooms to be prepared; and the library and drawing-rooms are to be cleaned out; and I am to get more kitchen hands from the George Inn, at Millcote, and from wherever else I can; and the ladies will bring their maids and the gentlemen their valets: so we shall have a full house of it." And Mrs. Fairfax swallowed her breakfast and hastened away to commence operations.

The three days were, as she had foretold, busy enough. I had thought all the rooms at Thornfield beautifully clean and well-arranged, but it appears I was mistaken. Three women were got to help; and such scrubbing, such brushing, such washing of paint and beating of carpets, such taking down and putting up of pictures, such polishing of mirrors and lusters, such lighting of fires in bedrooms, such airing of sheets and feather-beds on hearths, I never beheld either before or since. Adèle ran quite wild in the midst of it: the preparations for company, and the prospect of their arrival, seemed to throw her into ecstasies. She would have Sophie to look over all her "toilettes," as she called frocks; to furbish up any that were "passées,"[1] and to air and arrange the new. For herself, she did nothing but caper about in the front chambers, jump on and off the bedsteads, and lie on the mattresses and piled-up bolsters and pillows before the enormous fires roaring in the chimneys. From school duties she was exonerated: Mrs. Fairfax had pressed me into her service, and I was all day in the storeroom, helping (or hindering) her and the cook; learning to make custards and cheesecakes and French pastry, to truss game and garnish dessert dishes.

The party were expected to arrive on Thursday afternoon, in time for dinner at six. During the intervening period I had no time to nurse chimeras; and I believe I was as active and gay as anybody—Adèle excepted. Still, now and then, I received a damping check to my cheerfulness; and was, in spite of myself, thrown back on the region of doubts and portents, and dark conjectures. This was when I chanced to see the third story staircase door (which of late had always been kept locked) open slowly, and give passage to the form of Grace Poole, in prim cap, white apron, and handerchief; when I watched her glide along the gallery, her quiet tread muffled in a list[2] slipper; when I saw her look into the bustling, topsy-turvy bedrooms,—just say a word, perhaps, to the charwoman about the proper way to polish a grate, or clean a marble mantlepiece, or take stains from papered walls, and then pass on. She would thus descend to the kitchen once a day, eat her dinner, smoke a moderate pipe on the hearth, and go back, carrying her pot of porter with her, for her private solace, in her own gloomy, upper haunt. Only one hour in the twenty-four did she pass with her fellow-servants below; all the rest of her time was spent in some low-ceiled, oaken chamber of the third story:

1. Out of style. 2. Made of the heavy material used to edge cloth.

there she sat and sewed—and probably laughed drearily to herself—as companionless as a prisoner in his dungeon.

The strangest thing of all was, that not a soul in the house, except me, noticed her habits, or seemed to marvel at them; no one discussed her position or employment; no one pitied her solitude or isolation. I once, indeed, overheard part of a dialogue between Leah and one of the charwomen, of which Grace formed the subject. Leah had been saying something I had not caught, and the charwoman remarked—"She gets good wages, I guess?"

"Yes," said Leah; "I wish I had as good; not that mine are to complain of,—there's no stinginess at Thornfield; but they're not one-fifth of the sum Mrs. Poole receives. And she is laying by: she goes every quarter to the bank at Millcote. I should not wonder but she has saved enough to keep her independent if she liked to leave; but I suppose she's got used to the place; and then she's not forty yet, and strong and able for anything. It is too soon for her to give up business."

"She is a good hand, I daresay," said the charwoman.

"Ah! she understands what she has to do,—nobody better,"—rejoined Leah, significantly; "and it is not every one could fill her shoes; not for all the money she gets."

"That it is not!" was the reply. "I wonder whether master——"

The charwoman was going on; but here Leah turned and perceived me, and she instantly gave her companion a nudge.

"Doesn't she know?" I heard the woman whisper.

Leah shook her head, and the conversation was of course dropped. All I had gathered from it amounted to this,—that there was a mystery at Thornfield; and that from participation in that mystery I was purposely excluded.

Thursday came: all work had been completed the previous evening; carpets were laid down, bed-hangings festooned, radiant white counterpanes spread, toilet-tables arranged, furniture rubbed, flowers piled in vases: both chambers and saloons[3] looked as fresh and bright as hands could make them. The hall, too, was scoured; and the great carved clock, as well as the steps and banisters of the staircase, were polished to the brightness of glass: in the dining-room, the sideboard flashed resplendent with plate; in the drawing-room and boudoir, vases of exotics bloomed on all sides.

Afternoon arrived: Mrs. Fairfax assumed her best black satin gown, her gloves, and her gold watch; for it was her part to receive the company—to conduct the ladies to their rooms, etc. Adèle, too, would be dressed: though I thought that she had little chance of being introduced to the party that day, at least. However, to please her, I allowed Sophie to apparel her in one of her short, full muslin frocks. For myself, I had no need to make any change; I should not be called upon to quit my sanctum of the schoolroom; for a sanctum it was now become to me—"a very pleasant refuge in time of trouble."[4]

It had been a mild, serene spring day; one of those days which, towards the end of March or the beginning of April, rise shining over the earth as heralds of summer. It was drawing to an end now; but the evening was even warm, and I sat at work in the schoolroom with the window open.

"It gets late," said Mrs. Fairfax, entering in rustling state. "I am glad I

3. Bedchambers and common rooms. 4. Misquoted from Psalm 46:1.

ordered dinner an hour after the time Mr. Rochester mentioned; for it is past six now. I have sent John down to the gates to see if there is anything on the road: one can see a long way from thence in the direction of Millcote." She went to the window. "Here he is!" said she. "Well, John" (leaning out), "any news?"

"They're coming, ma'am," was the answer. "They'll be here in ten minutes."

Adèle flew to the window. I followed; taking care to stand on one side, so that, screened by the curtain, I could see without being seen.

The ten minutes John had given seemed very long, but at last wheels were heard; four equestrians galloped up the drive, and after them came two open carriages. Fluttering veils and waving plumes filled the vehicles; two of the cavaliers were young, dashing-looking gentlemen; the third was Mr. Rochester, on his black horse, Mesrour;[5] Pilot bounding before him: at his side rode a lady, and he and she were the first of the party. Her purple riding-habit almost swept the ground, her veil streamed long on the breeze; mingling with its transparent folds, and gleaming through them, shone rich raven ringlets.

"Miss Ingram!" exclaimed Mrs. Fairfax, and away she hurried to her post below.

The cavalcade, following the sweep of the drive, quickly turned the angle of the house, and I lost sight of it. Adèle now petitioned to go down; but I took her on my knee and gave her to understand that she must not on any account think of venturing in sight of the ladies, either now or at any other time, unless expressly sent for; that Mr. Rochester would be very angry, etc. "Some natural tears she shed"[6] on being told this; but as I began to look very grave, she consented at last to wipe them.

A joyous stir was now audible in the hall; gentlemen's deep tones and ladies' silvery accents blent harmoniously together, and distinguishable above all, though not loud, was the sonorous voice of the master of Thornfield Hall, welcoming his fair and gallant guests under its roof. Then light steps ascended the stairs; and there was a tripping through the gallery, and soft cheerful laughs, and opening and closing doors, and for a time, a hush.

"Elles changent de toilettes,"[7] said Adèle; who, listening attentively, had followed every movement; and she sighed.

"Chez maman," said she, "quand il y avait du monde, je le suivais partout, au salon et à leurs chambres; souvent je regardais les femmes de chambre coiffer et habiller les dames, et c'était si amusant: comme cela on apprend."[8]

"Don't you feel hungry, Adèle?"

"Mais oui, mademoiselle: voilà cinq ou six heures que nous n'avons pas mangé."[9]

"Well now, while the ladies are in their rooms, I will venture down and get you something to eat."

And issuing from my asylum with precaution, I sought a backstairs which conducted directly to the kitchen. All in that region was fire and commotion;

5. The name of a royal executioner in *The Arabian Nights*.
6. *Paradise Lost* 12.645.
7. They [the women] are changing clothes.
8. At mama's, . . . when there were a lot of people, I would follow them everywhere, in the drawing room and to their rooms; I often watched the maids dress and groom the ladies, and it was so amusing: that is how one learns.
9. Yes, of course, miss: it's been five or six hours since we've eaten.

the soup and fish were in the last stage of projection, and the cook hung over her crucibles in a frame of mind and body threatening spontaneous combustion.[1] In the servants' hall two coachmen and three gentlemen's gentlemen stood or sat round the fire; the Abigails, I suppose, were upstairs with their mistresses: the new servants that had been hired from Millcote were bustling about everywhere. Threading this chaos, I at last reached the larder; there I took possession of a cold chicken, a roll of bread, some tarts, a plate or two, and a knife and fork: with this booty I made a hasty retreat. I had regained the gallery, and was just shutting the back-door behind me, when an accelerated hum warned me that the ladies were about to issue from their chambers. I could not proceed to the schoolroom without passing some of their doors, and running the risk of being surprised with my cargo of victualage; so I stood still at this end, which, being windowless, was dark: quite dark now, for the sun was set and twilight gathering.

Presently the chambers gave up their fair tenants one after another; each came out gaily and airily, with dress that gleamed lustrous through the dusk. For a moment they stood grouped together at the other extremity of the gallery, conversing in a key of sweet subdued vivacity; they then descended the staircase almost as noiselessly as a bright mist rolls down a hill. Their collective appearance had left on me an impression of high-born elegance, such as I had never before received.

I found Adèle peeping through the schoolroom door, which she held ajar. "What beautiful ladies!" cried she in English. "Oh, I wish I might go to them! Do you think Mr. Rochester will send for us by-and-by, after dinner?"

"No, indeed, I don't; Mr. Rochester has something else to think about. Never mind the ladies tonight; perhaps you will see them tomorrow; here is your dinner."

She was really hungry, so the chicken and tarts served to divert her attention for a time. It was well I secured this forage; or both she, I and Sophie, to whom I conveyed a share of our repast, would have run a chance of getting no dinner at all: every one downstairs was too much engaged to think of us. The dessert was not carried out till after nine; and at ten footmen were still running to and fro with trays and coffee-cups. I allowed Adèle to sit up much later than usual; for she declared she could not possibly go to sleep while the doors kept opening and shutting below, and people bustling about. Besides, she added, a message might possibly come from Mr. Rochester when she was undressed; "et alors quel dommage!"[2]

I told her stories as long as she would listen to them; and then for a change I took her out into the gallery. The hall lamp was now lit, and it amused her to look over the balustrade and watch the servants passing backwards and forwards. When the evening was far advanced, a sound of music issued from the drawing-room, whither the piano had been removed. Adèle and I sat down on the top step of the stairs to listen. Presently a voice blent with the rich tones of the instrument; it was a lady who sang, and very sweet her notes were. The solo over, a duet followed, and then a glee: a joyous conversational murmur filled up the intervals. I listened long: suddenly I discovered that my ear was wholly intent on analysing the mingled sounds, and trying to

1. A playful reference to alchemy, in which metals and powders are placed in crucibles in an attempt to make gold.
2. And then what a shame!

discriminate amidst the confusion of accents those of Mr. Rochester; and when it caught them, which it soon did, it found a further task in framing the tones, rendered by distance inarticulate, into words.

The clock struck eleven. I looked at Adèle, whose head leant against my shoulder; her eyes were waxing heavy, so I took her up in my arms and carried her off to bed. It was near one before the gentlemen and ladies sought their chambers.

The next day was as fine as its predecessor; it was devoted by the party to an excursion to some sight in the neighborhood. They set out early in the forenoon, some on horseback, the rest in carriages; I witnessed both the departure and the return. Miss Ingram, as before, was the only lady equestrian; and, as before, Mr. Rochester galloped at her side; the two rode a little apart from the rest. I pointed out this circumstance to Mrs. Fairfax, who was standing at the window with me:—"You said it was not likely they should think of being married," said I, "but you see Mr. Rochester evidently prefers her to any of the other ladies."

"Yes; I daresay: no doubt he admires her."

"And she him," I added; "look how she leans her head towards him as if she were conversing confidentially; I wish I could see her face; I have never had a glimpse of it yet."

"You will see her this evening," answered Mrs. Fairfax. "I happened to remark to Mr. Rochester how much Adèle wished to be introduced to the ladies, and he said: 'Oh! let her come into the drawing-room after dinner; and request Miss Eyre to accompany her.'"

"Yes—he said that from mere politeness: I need not go, I am sure," I answered.

"Well, I observed to him that as you were unused to company, I did not think you would like appearing before so gay a party—all strangers—and he replied, in his quick way: 'Nonsense! If she objects, tell her it is my particular wish; and if she resists, say I shall come and fetch her in case of contumacy.'"[3]

"I will not give him that trouble," I answered. "I will go, if no better may be: but I don't like it. Shall you be there, Mrs. Fairfax?"

"No; I pleaded off, and he admitted my plea. I'll tell you how to manage so as to avoid the embarrassment of making a formal entrance, which is the most disagreeable part of the business. You must go into the drawing-room while it is empty, before the ladies leave the dinner-table; choose your seat in any quiet nook you like; you need not stay long after the gentlemen come in, unless you please: just let Mr. Rochester see you are there and then slip away—nobody will notice you."

"Will these people remain long, do you think?"

"Perhaps two or three weeks; certainly not more. After the Easter recess, Sir George Lynn, who was lately elected member for Millcote, will have to go up to town and take his seat; I daresay Mr. Rochester will accompany him: it surprises me that he has already made so protracted a stay at Thornfield."

It was with some trepidation that I perceived the hour approach when I was to repair with my charge to the drawing-room. Adèle had been in a state

3. Stubborn resistance to authority.

of ecstasy all day, after hearing she was to be presented to the ladies in the evening; and it was not till Sophie commenced the operation of dressing her that she sobered down. Then the importance of the process quickly steadied her; and by the time she had her curls arranged in well-smoothed, drooping clusters, her pink satin frock put on, her long sash tied, and her lace mittens adjusted, she looked as grave as any judge. No need to warn her not to disarrange her attire: when she was dressed, she sat demurely down in her little chair, taking care previously to lift up the satin skirt for fear she should crease it, and assured me she would not stir thence till I was ready. This I quickly was; my best dress (the silver-gray one, purchased for Miss Temple's wedding, and never worn since) was soon put on; my hair was soon smoothed; my sole ornament, the pearl brooch, soon assumed. We descended.

Fortunately there was another entrance to the drawing-room than that through the saloon where they were all seated at dinner. We found the apartment vacant, a large fire burning silently on the marble hearth, and wax candles shining in bright solitude, amid the exquisite flowers with which the tables were adorned. The crimson curtain hung before the arch: slight as was the separation this drapery formed from the party in the adjoining saloon, they spoke in so low a key that nothing of their conversation could be distinguished beyond a soothing murmur.

Adèle, who appeared to be still under the influence of a most solemnizing impression, sat down, without a word, on the footstool I pointed out to her. I retired to a window-seat, and, taking a book from a table near, endeavored to read. Adèle brought her stool to my feet; ere long she touched my knee.

"What is it, Adèle?"

"Est-ce que je ne puis pas prendre une seule de ces fleurs magnifiques, mademoiselle? Seulement pour compléter ma toilette."[4]

"You think too much of your 'toilette,' Adèle, but you may have a flower." And I took a rose from a vase and fastened it in her sash. She sighed a sigh of ineffable satisfaction, as if her cup of happiness were now full. I turned my face away to conceal a smile I could not suppress: there was something ludicrous as well as painful in the little Parisienne's earnest and innate devotion to matters of dress.

A soft sound of rising now became audible; the curtain was swept back from the arch; through it appeared the dining-room, with its lit luster pouring down light on the silver and glass of a magnificent dessert-service covering a long table; a band of ladies stood in the opening; they entered, and the curtain fell behind them.

There were but eight, yet somehow as they flocked in, they gave the impression of a much larger number. Some of them were very tall, many were dressed in white, and all had a sweeping amplitude of array that seemed to magnify their persons as a mist magnifies the moon. I rose and curtseyed to them; one or two bent their heads in return, the others only stared at me.

They dispersed about the room, reminding me, by the lightness and buoyancy of their movements, of a flock of white plumy birds. Some of them threw themselves in half-reclining positions on the sofas and ottomans, some bent over the tables and examined the flowers and books, the rest gathered

4. Couldn't I take just one of these magnificent flowers, miss? Just to complete my costume.

in a group round the fire—all talked in a low but clear tone which seemed habitual to them. I knew their names afterwards, and may as well mention them now.

First there was Mrs. Eshton and two of her daughters. She had evidently been a handsome woman, and was well preserved still. Of her daughters, the eldest, Amy, was rather little; naïve, and childlike in face and manner, and piquant in form: her white muslin dress and blue sash became her well. The second, Louisa, was taller and more elegant in figure, with a very pretty face, of that order the French term "minois chiffonné":[5] both sisters were fair as lilies.

Lady Lynn was a large and stout personage of about forty, very erect, very haughty-looking, richly dressed in a satin robe of changeful sheen: her dark hair shone glossily under the shade of an azure plume, and within the circlet of a band of gems.

Mrs. Colonel Dent was less showy, but, I thought, more ladylike. She had a slight figure, a pale, gentle face, and fair hair. Her black satin dress, her scarf of rich foreign lace, and her pearl ornaments, pleased me better than the rainbow radiance of the titled dame.

But the three most distinguished—partly, perhaps, because the tallest figures of the band—were the Dowager Lady Ingram and her daughters, Blanche and Mary. They were all three of the loftiest stature of woman. The dowager might be between forty and fifty; her shape was still fine; her hair (by candlelight at least) still black; her teeth, too, were still apparently perfect. Most people would have termed her a splendid woman of her age: and so she was, no doubt, physically speaking; but then there was an expression of almost insupportable haughtiness in her bearing and countenance. She had Roman features and a double chin, disappearing into a throat like a pillar: these features appeared to me not only inflated and darkened, but even furrowed with pride; and the chin was sustained by the same principle, in a position of almost preternatural erectness. She had, likewise, a fierce and a hard eye: it reminded me of Mrs. Reed's; she mouthed her words in speaking; her voice was deep, its inflections very pompous, very dogmatical— very intolerable, in short. A crimson velvet robe, and a shawl turban of some gold-wrought Indian fabric, invested her (I suppose she thought) with a truly imperial dignity.

Blanche and Mary were of equal stature—straight and tall as poplars. Mary was too slim for her height; but Blanche was molded like a Dian.[6] I regarded her, of course, with special interest. First, I wished to see whether her appearance accorded with Mrs. Fairfax's description; secondly, whether it at all resembled the fancy miniature I had painted of her; and thirdly—it will out!—whether it were such as I should fancy likely to suit Mr. Rochester's taste.

As far as person went, she answered point for point, both to my picture and Mrs. Fairfax's description. The noble bust, the sloping shoulders, the graceful neck, the dark eyes and black ringlets were all there—but her face? Her face was like her mother's; a youthful unfurrowed likeness: the same low brow, the same high features, the same pride. It was not, however, so

5. A sweet, slightly petulant face.
6. I.e., Diana, beautiful Roman virgin goddess of hunting.

saturnine a pride: she laughed continually; her laugh was satirical, and so was the habitual expression of her arched and haughty lip.

Genius is said to be self-conscious: I cannot tell whether Miss Ingram was a genius, but she was self-conscious—remarkably self-conscious indeed. She entered into a discourse on botany with the gentle Mrs. Dent. It seems Mrs. Dent had not studied that science: though, as she said, she liked flowers, "especially wild ones"; Miss Ingram had, and she ran over its vocabulary with an air. I presently perceived she was (what is vernacularly termed) *trailing* Mrs. Dent; that is playing on her ignorance; her *trail* might be clever, but it was decidedly not good-natured. She played; her execution was brilliant; she sang; her voice was fine; she talked French apart to her mamma; and she talked it well, with fluency and with a good accent.

Mary had a milder and more open countenance than Blanche; softer features too, and a skin some shades fairer (Miss Ingram was dark as a Spaniard)—but Mary was deficient in life; her face lacked expression, her eye lustre; she had nothing to say, and having once taken her seat, remained fixed like a statue in its niche. The sisters were both attired in spotless white.

And did I now think Miss Ingram such a choice as Mr. Rochester would be likely to make? I could not tell—I did not know his taste in female beauty. If he liked the majestic, she was the very type of majesty: then she was accomplished, sprightly. Most gentlemen would admire her, I thought; and that he *did* admire her, I already seemed to have obtained proof: to remove the last shade of doubt, it remained but to see them together.

You are not to suppose, reader, that Adèle has all this time been sitting, motionless, on the stool at my feet: no; when the ladies entered, she rose, advanced to meet them, made a stately reverence, and said, with gravity,— "Bon jour, mesdames."[7]

And Miss Ingram had looked down at her with a mocking air, and exclaimed, "Oh, what a little puppet!"

Lady Lynn had remarked, "It is Mr. Rochester's ward, I suppose—the little French girl he was speaking of."

Mrs. Dent had kindly taken her hand, and given her a kiss. Amy and Louisa Eshton had cried out simultaneously—

"What a love of a child!"

And then they had called her to a sofa, where she now sat, ensconced between them, chattering alternately in French and broken English: absorbing not only the young ladies' attention, but that of Mrs. Eshton and Lady Lynn, and getting spoiled to her heart's content.

At last coffee is brought in, and the gentlemen are summoned. I sit in the shade—if any shade there be in this brilliantly-lit apartment; the window curtain half hides me. Again the arch yawns: they come. The collective appearance of the gentlemen, like that of the ladies, is very imposing: they are all costumed in black; most of them are tall, some young. Henry and Frederick Lynn are very dashing sparks, indeed; and Colonel Dent is a fine soldierly man. Mr. Eshton, the magistrate of the district, is gentleman-like: his hair is quite white, his eyebrows and whiskers still dark, which gives him something of the appearance of a "père noble de théâtre."[8] Lord Ingram, like

7. Hello, ladies.
8. Distinguished old gentleman, as portrayed in the theater.

his sisters, is very tall; like them, also, he is handsome; but he shares Mary's apathetic and listless look: he seems to have more length of limb than vivacity of blood or vigour of brain.

And where is Mr. Rochester?

He comes in last: I am not looking at the arch, yet I see him enter. I try to concentrate my attention on those netting-needles, on the meshes of the purse I am forming—I wish to think only of the work I have in my hands, to see only the silver beads and silk threads that lie in my lap; whereas, I distinctly behold his figure, and I inevitably recall the moment when I last saw it: just after I had rendered him, what he deemed an essential service—and he, holding my hand, and looking down on my face, surveyed me with eyes that revealed a heart full and eager to overflow; in whose emotions I had a part. How near had I approached him at that moment! What had occurred since, calculated to change his and my relative positions? Yet now, how distant, how far estranged we were! So far estranged, that I did not expect him to come and speak to me. I did not wonder, when, without looking at me, he took a seat at the other side of the room, and began conversing with some of the ladies.

No sooner did I see that his attention was riveted on them, and that I might gaze without being observed, than my eyes were drawn involuntarily to his face: I could not keep their lids under control: they would rise, and the irids would fix on him. I looked, and had an acute pleasure in looking,—a precious, yet poignant pleasure; pure gold, with a steely point of agony: a pleasure like what the thirst-perishing man might feel who knows the well to which he has crept is poisoned, yet stoops and drinks divine draughts nevertheless.

Most true is it that "beauty is in the eye of the gazer." My master's colorless, olive face, square, massive brow, broad and jetty eyebrows, deep eyes, strong features, firm, grim mouth,—all energy, decision, will,—were not beautiful, according to rule; but they were more than beautiful to me: they were full of an interest, an influence that quite mastered me,—that took my feelings from my own power and fettered them in his. I had not intended to love him: the reader knows I had wrought hard to extirpate from my soul the germs of love there detected; and now, at the first renewed view of him, they spontaneously revived, green and strong! He made me love him without looking at me.

I compared him with his guests. What was the gallant grace of the Lynns, the languid elegance of Lord Ingram,—even the military distinction of Colonel Dent, contrasted with his look of native pith and genuine power? I had no sympathy with their appearance, their expression; yet I could imagine that most observers would call them attractive, handsome, imposing; while they would pronounce Mr. Rochester at once harsh-featured and melancholy-looking. I saw them smile, laugh—it was nothing; the light of the candles had as much soul in it as their smile; the tinkle of the bell as much significance as their laugh. I saw Mr. Rochester smile—his stern features softened; his eye grew both brilliant and gentle, its ray both searching and sweet. He was talking, at the moment, to Louisa and Amy Eshton. I wondered to see them receive with calm that look which seemed to me so penetrating; I expected their eyes to fall, their color to rise under it; yet I was glad when I found they were in no sense moved. "He is not to them what he

is to me," I thought: "he is not of their kind. I believe he is of mine;—I am sure he is,—I feel akin to him,—I understand the language of his countenance and movements; though rank and wealth sever us widely, I have something in my brain and heart, in my blood and nerves, that assimilates me mentally to him. Did I say, a few days since, that I had nothing to do with him but to receive my salary at his hands? Did I forbid myself to think of him in any other light than as a paymaster? Blasphemy against nature! Every good, true, vigorous feeling I have, gathers impulsively round him. I know I must conceal my sentiments; I must smother hope; I must remember that he cannot care much for me. For when I say that I am of his kind, I do not mean that I have his force to influence, and his spell to attract; I mean only that I have certain tastes and feelings in common with him. I must then repeat continually that we are for ever sundered;—and yet, while I breathe and think I must love him."

Coffee is handed. The ladies, since the gentlemen entered, have become lively as larks; conversation waxes brisk and merry. Colonel Dent and Mr. Eshton argue on politics; their wives listen. The two proud dowagers, Lady Lynn and Lady Ingram, confabulate together. Sir George—whom, by-the-by, I have forgotten to describe—a very big and very fresh-looking country gentleman, stands before their sofa, coffee-cup in hand, and occasionally puts in a word. Mr. Frederick Lynn has taken a seat beside Mary Ingram, and is showing her the engravings of a splendid volume; she looks, smiles now and then, but apparently says little. The tall and phlegmatic[9] Lord Ingram leans with folded arms on the chair-back of the little and lively Amy Eshton; she glances up at him, and chatters like a wren: she likes him better than she does Mr. Rochester. Henry Lynn has taken possession of an ottoman at the feet of Louisa; Adèle shares it with him: he is trying to talk French with her, and Louisa laughs at his blunders. With whom will Blanche Ingram pair? She is standing alone at the table, bending gracefully over an album. She seems waiting to be sought; but she will not wait too long: she herself selects a mate.

Mr. Rochester, having quitted the Eshtons, stands on the hearth as solitary as she stands by the table; she confronts him, taking her station on the opposite side of the mantlepiece.

"Mr. Rochester, I thought you were not fond of children?"

"Nor am I."

"Then, what induced you to take charge of such a little doll as that?" (pointing to Adèle). "Where did you pick her up?"

"I did not pick her up, she was left on my hands."

"You should have sent her to school."

"I could not afford it; schools are so dear."

"Why, I suppose you have a governess for her; I saw a person with her just now—is she gone? Oh, no, there she is still behind the window-curtain. You pay her, of course. I should think it quite as expensive—more so, for you have them both to keep in addition."

I feared—or should I say, hoped—the allusion to me would make Mr. Rochester glance my way; and I involuntarily shrank further into the shade; but he never turned his eyes.

9. Slow and unemotional; phlegm was one of the four humors (see n. 7, p. 719).

"I have not considered the subject," said he indifferently, looking straight before him.

"No—you men never do consider economy and common sense. You should hear mamma on the chapter of governess. Mary and I have had, I should think, a dozen at least in our day; half of them detestable and the rest ridiculous, and all incubi[1]—were they not, mamma?"

"Did you speak, my own?"

The young lady thus claimed as the dowager's special property reiterated her question with an explanation.

"My dearest, don't mention governesses; the word makes me nervous. I have suffered a martyrdom from their incompetency and caprice; I thank Heaven I have now done with them!"

Mrs. Dent here bent over to the pious lady, and whispered something in her ear; I suppose, from the answer elicited, it was a reminder that one of the anathematised race was present.

"Tant pis!"[2] said her ladyship, "I hope it may do her good." Then, in a lower tone, but still loud enough for me to hear, "I noticed her; I am a judge of physiognomy, and in hers I see all the faults of her class."

"What are they, madam?" inquired Mr. Rochester aloud.

"I will tell you in your private ear," replied she, wagging her turban three times with portentous significancy.

"But my curiosity will be past its appetite; it craves food now."

"Ask Blanche; she is nearer you than I."

"Oh, don't refer him to me, mamma! I have just one word to say of the whole tribe; they are a nuisance. Not that I ever suffered much from them; I took care to turn the tables. What tricks Theodore and I used to play on our Miss Wilsons, and Mrs. Greys, and Madame Jouberts! Mary was always too sleepy to join in a plot with spirit. The best fun was with Madame Joubert. Miss Wilson was a poor sickly thing, lachrymose and low-spirited: not worth the trouble of vanquishing, in short; and Mrs. Grey was coarse and insensible: no blow took effect on her. But poor Madame Joubert! I see her yet in her raging passions, when we had driven her to extremities—spilled our tea, crumbled our bread and butter, tossed our books up to the ceiling, and played a charivari[3] with the ruler and desk, the fender and fire-irons. Theodore, do you remember those merry days?"

"Yaas, to be sure I do," drawled Lord Ingram; "and the poor old stick used to cry out, 'Oh, you villains[4] childs!' and then we sermonized her on the presumption of attempting to teach such clever blades as we were, when she was herself so ignorant."

"We did; and Tedo, you know I helped you in prosecuting (or persecuting) your tutor, whey-faced Mr. Vining—the parson in the pip,[5] as we used to call him. He and Miss Wilson took the liberty of falling in love with each other—at least Tedo and I thought so; we surprised sundry tender glances and sighs which we interpreted as tokens of 'la belle passion,'[6] and I promise you the public soon had the benefit of our discovery; we employed it as a sort of lever to hoist our dead-weights from the house. Dear mamma, there,

1. Evil spirits.
2. Too bad!
3. A noisy serenade to newlyweds.
4. Naughty.
5. Like a chick in its shell.
6. The beautiful passion.

as soon as she got an inkling of the business, found out that it was of an immoral tendency. Did you not, my lady-mother?"

"Certainly, my best. And I was quite right, depend on that: there are a thousand reasons why liaisons between governesses and tutors should never be tolerated a moment in any well-regulated house; firstly, ——."

"Oh, gracious, mamma! Spare us the enumeration! Au reste,[7] we all know them: danger of bad example to innocence of childhood—distractions and consequent neglect of duty on the part of the attached—mutual alliance and reliance; confidence thence resulting—insolence accompanying—mutiny and general blow-up. Am I right, Baroness Ingram, of Ingram Park?"

"My lily-flower, you are right now, as always."

"Then no more need be said; change the subject."

Amy Eshton, not hearing or not heeding this dictum, joined in with her soft infantine tone: "Louisa and I used to quiz[8] our governess too; but she was such a good creature, she would bear anything; nothing put her out. She was never cross with us; was she, Louisa?"

"No, never; we might do what we pleased—ransack her desk and her work-box, and turn her drawers inside out; and she was so good-natured, she would give us anything we asked for."

"I suppose now," said Miss Ingram, curling her lips sarcastically, "we shall have an abstract of the memoirs of all the governesses extant; in order to avert such a visitation, I again move the introduction of a new topic. Mr. Rochester, do you second my motion?"

"Madam, I support you on this point as on every other."

"Then on me be the onus of bringing it forward. Signor Eduardo, are you in voice tonight?"

"Donna Bianca,[9] if you command it, I will be."

"Then, signor, I lay on you my sovereign behest to furbish up your lungs and other vocal organs, as they will be wanted on my royal service."

"Who would not be the Rizzio of so divine a Mary?"

"A fig for Rizzio!" cried she, tossing her head with all its curls, as she moved to the piano. "It is my opinion the fiddler David must have been an insipid sort of fellow; I like black Bothwell better. To my mind a man is nothing without a spice of the devil in him; and history may say what it will of James Hepburn,[1] but I have a notion he was just the sort of wild, fierce, bandit hero whom I could have consented to gift with my hand."

"Gentlemen, you hear! Now which of you most resembles Bothwell?" cried Mr. Rochester.

"I should say the preference lies with you," responded Colonel Dent.

"On my honor, I am much obliged to you," was the reply.

Miss Ingram, who had now seated herself with proud grace at the piano, spreading out her snowy robes in queenly amplitude, commenced a brilliant prelude; talking meantime. She appeared to be on her high-horse tonight; both her words and her air seemed intended to excite not only the admira-

7. At any rate.
8. Mock. A "quiz" is an eccentric person.
9. Mr. Edward . . . Miss Blanche (Italian).
1. David Rizzio (ca. 1533–1566) was an Italian who joined the household of Mary, Queen of Scots (1542–1587), as a singer, then became the queen's

confidant and lover. Her second husband, Lord Darnley, had Rizzio killed. James Hepburn, fourth earl of Bothwell (1536–1578), in turn had Darnley murdered and married the queen, becoming her third husband.

tion, but the amazement of her auditors; she was evidently bent on striking them as something very dashing and daring indeed.

"Oh, I am so sick of the young men of the present day!" exclaimed she, rattling away at the instrument. "Poor puny things not fit to stir a step beyond papa's park-gates: nor to go even so far without mamma's permission and guardianship! Creatures so absorbed in care about their pretty faces and their white hands, and their small feet; as if a man had anything to do with beauty! As if loveliness were not the special prerogative of woman—her legitimate appanage[2] and heritage! I grant an ugly *woman* is a blot on the fair face of creation; but as to the *gentlemen,* let them be solicitous to possess only strength and valour: let their motto be—Hunt, shoot, and fight; the rest is not worth a fillip. Such should be my device, were I a man."

"Whenever I marry," she continued after a pause which none interrupted, "I am resolved my husband shall not be a rival, but a foil to me. I will suffer no competitor near the throne; I shall exact an undivided homage; his devotions shall not be shared between me and the shape he sees in his mirror. Mr. Rochester, now sing, and I will play for you."

"I am all obedience," was the response.

"Here then is a Corsair-song. Know that I doat on Corsairs; and for that reason, sing it 'con spirito.' "[3]

"Commands from Miss Ingram's lips would put spirit into a mug of milk and water."

"Take care, then: if you don't please me, I will shame you by showing how such things *should* be done."

"That is offering a premium on incapacity; I shall now endeavor to fail."

"Gardez-vous en bien![4] If you err wilfully, I shall devise a proportionate punishment."

"Miss Ingram ought to be clement, for she has it in her power to inflict a chastisement beyond mortal endurance."

"Ha! explain!" commanded the lady.

"Pardon me, madam; no need of explanation; your own fine sense must inform you that one of your frowns would be a sufficient substitute for capital punishment."

"Sing!" said she, and again touching the piano, she commenced an accompaniment in spirited style.

"Now is my time to slip away," thought I; but the tones that then severed the air arrested me. Mrs. Fairfax had said Mr. Rochester possessed a fine voice; he did—a mellow powerful bass, into which he threw his own feeling, his own force; finding a way through the ear to the heart, and there waking sensation strangely. I waited till the last deep and full vibration had expired— till the tide of talk, checked an instant, had resumed its flow; I then quitted my sheltered corner and made my exit by the side-door, which was fortunately near. Thence a narrow passage led into the hall; in crossing it, I perceived my sandal was loose; I stopped to tie it, kneeling down for that purpose on the mat at the foot of the staircase. I heard the dining-room door unclose; a gentleman came out; rising hastily, I stood face to face with him; it was Mr. Rochester.

2. I.e., endowment.
3. With spirit (Italian).
4. Be very careful.

"How do you do?" he asked.

"I am very well, sir."

"Why did you not come and speak to me in the room?"

I thought I might have retorted the question on him who put it; but I would not take that freedom. I answered:—"I did not wish to disturb you, as you seemed engaged, sir."

"What have you been doing during my absence?"

"Nothing particular; teaching Adèle as usual."

"And getting a good deal paler than you were—as I saw at first sight. What is the matter?"

"Nothing at all, sir."

"Did you take any cold that night you half drowned me?"

"Not the least."

"Return to the drawing-room; you are deserting too early."

"I am tired, sir."

He looked at me for a minute.

"And a little depressed," he said. "What about? Tell me."

"Nothing—nothing, sir. I am not depressed."

"But I affirm that you are: so much depressed that a few more words would bring tears to your eyes—indeed, they are there now, shining and swimming; and a bead has slipped from the lash and fallen on to the flag. If I had time, and was not in mortal dread of some prating prig of a servant passing, I would know what all this means. Well, tonight I excuse you; but understand that so long as my visitors stay, I expect you to appear in the drawing-room every evening; it is my wish; don't neglect it. Now go, and send Sophie for Adèle. Good-night, my——" He stopped, bit his lip, and abruptly left me.

Chapter XVIII

Merry days were these at Thornfield Hall; and busy days too: how different from the first three months of stillness, monotony, and solitude I had passed beneath its roof! All sad feelings seemed now driven from the house, all gloomy associations forgotten: there was life everywhere, movement all day long. You could not now traverse the gallery, once so hushed, nor enter the front chambers, once so tenantless, without encountering a smart lady's maid, or a dandy valet.

The kitchen, the butler's pantry, the servants' hall, the entrance hall, were equally alive; and the saloons were only left void and still when the blue sky and halcyon sunshine of the genial spring weather called their occupants out into the grounds. Even when that weather was broken, and continuous rain set in for some days, no damp seemed cast over enjoyment; indoor amusements only became more lively and varied, in consequence of the stop put to outdoor gaiety.

I wondered what they were going to do the first evening a change of entertainment was proposed; they spoke of "playing charades," but in my ignorance I did not understand the term. The servants were called in, the dining-room tables wheeled away, the lights otherwise disposed, the chairs placed in a semicircle opposite the arch. While Mr. Rochester and the other gentlemen directed these alterations, the ladies were running up and down stairs ringing for their maids. Mrs. Fairfax was summoned to give information

respecting the resources of the house in shawls, dresses, draperies of any kind; and certain wardrobes of the third story were ransacked, and their contents, in the shape of brocaded and hooped petticoats, satin sacques, black modes, lace lappets,[5] etc., were brought down in armfuls by the Abigails; then a selection was made, and such things as were chosen were carried to the boudoir within the drawing-room.

Meantime, Mr. Rochester had again summoned the ladies round him, and was selecting certain of their number to be of his party. "Miss Ingram is mine, of course," said he; afterwards he named the two Misses Eshton, and Mrs. Dent. He looked at me; I happened to be near him, as I had been fastening the clasp of Mrs. Dent's bracelet, which had got loose.

"Will you play?" he asked. I shook my head. He did not insist, which I rather feared he would have done; he allowed me to return quietly to my usual seat.

He and his aids now withdrew behind the curtain; the other party, which was headed by Colonel Dent, sat down on the crescent of chairs. One of the gentlemen, Mr. Eshton, observing me, seemed to propose that I should be asked to join them; but Lady Ingram instantly negatived the notion.

"No," I heard her say: "she looks too stupid for any game of the sort."

Ere long, a bell tinkled, and the curtain drew up. Within the arch the bulky figure of Sir George Lynn, whom Mr. Rochester had likewise chosen, was seen enveloped in a white sheet; before him, on a table, lay open a large book; and at his side stood Amy Eshton, draped in Mr. Rochester's cloak, and holding a book in her hand. Somebody, unseen, rang the bell merrily; then Adèle (who had insisted on being one of her guardian's party), bounded forward, scattering round her the contents of a basket of flowers she carried on her arm. Then appeared the magnificent figure of Miss Ingram, clad in white, a long veil on her head, and a wreath of roses round her brow; by her side walked Mr. Rochester, and together they drew near the table. They knelt, while Mrs. Dent and Louisa Eshton, dressed also in white, took up their stations behind them. A ceremony followed, in dumb show, in which it was easy to recognize the pantomime of a marriage. At its termination Colonel Dent and his party consulted in whispers for two minutes, then the Colonel called out,—"Bride!" Mr. Rochester bowed, and the curtain fell.

A considerable interval elapsed before it again rose. Its second rising displayed a more elaborately prepared scene than the last. The drawing-room, as I have before observed, was raised two steps above the dining-room, and on the top of the upper step, placed a yard or two back within the room, appeared a large marble basin, which I recognized as an ornament of the conservatory—where it usually stood, surrounded by exotics, and tenanted by gold fish—and whence it must have been transported with some trouble, on account of its size and weight.

Seated on the carpet, by the side of this basin, was seen Mr. Rochester, costumed in shawls, with a turban on his head. His dark eyes and swarth skin and Paynim features suited the costume exactly: he looked the very model of an Eastern emir; an agent or a victim of the bowstring. Presently advanced into view Miss Ingram. She, too, was attired in Oriental fashion:

5. Streamers attached to headgear. "Sacques": loose gowns. "Modes": clothing made of thin, light silk.

a crimsom scarf tied sashlike round the waist; an embroidered handkerchief knotted about her temples; her beautifully-molded arms bare, one of them up-raised in the act of supporting a pitcher, poised gracefully on her head. Both her cast of form and feature, her complexion and her general air, suggested the idea of some Israelitish princess of the patriarchal days; and such was doubtless the character she intended to represent.

She approached the basin, and bent over it as if to fill her pitcher; she again lifted it to her head. The personage on the well-brink now seemed to accost her; to make some request,—"She hasted, let down her pitcher on her hand and gave him to drink." From the bosom of his robe he then produced a casket, opened it and showed magnificent bracelets and earrings; she acted astonishment and admiration; kneeling, he laid the treasure at her feet; incredulity and delight were expressed by her looks and gestures; the stranger fastened the bracelets on her arms, and the rings in her ears. It was Eliezer and Rebecca; the camels only were wanting.[6]

The divining party again laid their heads together; apparently they could not agree about the word or syllable this scene illustrated. Colonel Dent, their spokesman, demanded "the tableau of the Whole";[7] whereupon the curtain again descended.

On its third rising only a portion of the drawing-room was disclosed; the rest being concealed by a screen, hung with some sort of dark and coarse drapery. The marble basin was removed; in its place stood a deal[8] table and a kitchen chair: these objects were visible by a very dim light proceeding from a horn lantern, the wax candles being all extinguished.

Amidst this sordid scene sat a man with his clenched hands resting on his knees, and his eyes bent on the ground. I knew Mr. Rochester; though the begrimed face, the disordered dress (his coat hanging loose from one arm, as if it had been almost torn from his back in a scuffle), the desperate and scowling countenance, the rough, bristling hair might well have disguised him. As he moved a chain clanked; to his wrists were attached fetters.

"Bridewell!"[9] exclaimed Colonel Dent, and the charade was solved.

A sufficient interval having elapsed for the performers to resume their ordinary costume, they reentered the dining-room. Mr. Rochester led in Miss Ingram; she was complimenting him on his acting.

"Do you know," said she, "that, of the three characters, I liked you in the last best? Oh, had you but lived a few years earlier, what a gallant gentleman-highwayman you would have made!"

"Is all the soot washed from my face?" he asked, turning it towards her.

"Alas, yes; the more's the pity! Nothing could be more becoming to your complexion than that ruffian's rouge."

"You would like a hero of the road then?"

"An English hero of the road would be the next best thing to an Italian bandit; and that could only be surpassed by a Levantine pirate."

"Well, whatever I am, remember you are my wife; we were married an

6. A servant of Abraham was instructed to find a wife for Abraham's son Isaac; the servant resolved to approach the first woman who was willing to serve water to him and his camels. In this way he met and wooed Rebecca, who became Isaac's wife (Genesis 24.14–67; quotation, 18).

7. A depiction of a scene representing the entire word, rather than a single syllable.

8. Pine or fir wood.

9. A prison.

hour since, in the presence of all these witnesses." She giggled, and her color rose.

"Now, Dent," continued Mr. Rochester, "it is your turn." And as the other party withdrew, he and his band took the vacated seats. Miss Ingram placed herself at her leader's right hand; the other diviners filled the chairs on each side of him and her. I did not now watch the actors; I no longer waited with interest for the curtain to rise; my attention was absorbed by the spectators; my eyes, erewhile fixed on the arch, were now irresistibly attracted to the semicircle of chairs. What charade Colonel Dent and his party played, what word they chose, how they acquitted themselves, I no longer remember; but I still see the consultation which followed each scene: I see Mr. Rochester turn to Miss Ingram, and Miss Ingram to him; I see her incline her head towards him till the jetty curls almost touch his shoulder and wave against his cheek; I hear their mutual whisperings; I recall their interchanged glances; and something even of the feeling roused by the spectacle returns in memory at this moment.

I have told you, reader, that I had learned to love Mr. Rochester; I could not unlove him now, merely because I found that he had ceased to notice me—because I might pass hours in his presence and he would never once, turn his eyes in my direction—because I saw all his attentions appropriated by a great lady, who scorned to touch me with the hem of her robes as she passed; who, if ever her dark and imperious eye fell on me by chance, would withdraw it instantly as from an object too mean to merit observation. I could not unlove him, because I felt sure he would soon marry this very lady— because I read daily in her a proud security in his intentions respecting her— because I witnessed hourly in him a style of courtship which, if careless and choosing rather to be sought than to seek, was yet, in its very carelessness, captivating, and in its very pride, irresistible.

There was nothing to cool or banish love in these circumstances; though much to create despair. Much too, you will think, reader, to engender jealousy; if a woman, in my position, could presume to be jealous of a woman in Miss Ingram's. But I was not jealous; or very rarely;—the nature of the pain I suffered could not be explained by that word. Miss Ingram was a mark beneath jealousy: she was too inferior to excite the feeling. Pardon the seeming paradox; I mean what I say. She was very showy, but she was not genuine: she had a fine person, many brilliant attainments; but her mind was poor, her heart barren by nature; nothing bloomed spontaneously on that soil; no unforced natural fruit delighted by its freshness. She was not good; she was not original: she used to repeat sounding phrases from books: she never offered, nor had, an opinion of her own. She advocated a high tone of sentiment; but she did not know the sensations of sympathy and pity; tenderness and truth were not in her. Too often she betrayed this, by the undue vent she gave to a spiteful antipathy she had conceived against little Adèle: pushing her away with some contumelious[1] epithet if she happened to approach her; sometimes ordering her from the room, and always treating her with coldness and acrimony. Other eyes besides mine watched these manifestations of character—watched them closely, keenly, shrewdly. Yes: the future bridegroom, Mr. Rochester himself, exercised over his intended a ceaseless

1. Humiliating.

surveillance: and it was from this sagacity—this guardedness of his—this perfect, clear consciousness of his fair one's defects—this obvious absence of passion in his sentiments towards her, that my ever-torturing pain arose.

I saw he was going to marry her, for family, perhaps political reasons; because her rank and connections suited him; I felt he had not given her his love, and that her qualifications were ill adapted to win from him that treasure. This was the point—this was where the nerve was touched and teased—this was where the fever was sustained and fed: *she could not charm him.*

If she had managed the victory at once, and he had yielded and sincerely laid his heart at her feet, I should have covered my face, turned to the wall, and (figuratively) have died to them. If Miss Ingram had been a good and noble woman, endowed with force, fervor, kindness, sense, I should have had one vital struggle with two tigers—jealousy and despair: then, my heart torn out and devoured, I should have admired her—acknowledged her excellence, and been quiet for the rest of my days: and the more absolute her superiority, the deeper would have been my admiration—the more truly tranquil my quiescence. But as matters really stood, to watch Miss Ingram's efforts at fascinating Mr. Rochester; to witness their repeated failure—herself unconscious that they did fail; vainly fancying that each shaft launched hit the mark, and infatuatedly pluming herself on success, when her pride and self-complacency repelled further and further what she wished to allure—to witness *this,* was to be at once under ceaseless excitation and ruthless restraint.

➜ Because, when she failed, I saw how she might have succeeded. Arrows that continually glanced off from Mr. Rochester's breast and fell harmless at his feet, might, I knew, if shot by a surer hand, have quivered keen in his proud heart—have called love into his stern eye and softness into his sardonic face; or, better still, without weapons a silent conquest might have been won.

"Why can she not influence him more, when she is privileged to draw so near to him?" I asked myself. "Surely she cannot truly like him, or not like him with true affection. If she did, she need not coin her smiles so lavishly, flash her glances so unremittingly, manufacture airs so elaborate, graces so multitudinous. It seems to me that she might, by merely sitting quietly at his side, saying little and looking less, get nigher his heart. I have seen in his face a far different expression from that which hardens it now while she is so vivaciously accosting him; but then it came of itself, it was not elicited by meretricious arts and calculated manuevers; and one had but to accept it—to answer what he asked without pretension, to address him when needful without grimace—and it increased and grew kinder and more genial, and warmed one like a fostering sunbeam. How will she manage to please him when they are married? I do not think she will manage it; and yet it might be managed and his wife might, I verily believe, be the very happiest woman the sun shines on."

I have not yet said anything condemnatory of Mr. Rochester's project of marrying for interest and connections. It surprised me when I first discovered that such was his intention; I had thought him a man unlikely to be influenced by motives so commonplace in his choice of a wife; but the longer I considered the position, education, etc., of the parties, the less I felt justified in judging and blaming either him or Miss Ingram, for acting in conformity

to ideas and principles instilled into them, doubtless, from their childhood. All their class held these principles; I supposed, then, they had reasons for holding them such as I could not fathom. It seemed to me that, were I a gentleman like him, I would take to my bosom only such a wife as I could love; but the very obviousness of the advantages to the husband's own happiness, offered by this plan, convinced me that there must be arguments against its general adoption of which I was quite ignorant; otherwise I felt sure all the world would act as I wished to act.

But in other points, as well as this, I was growing very lenient to my master: I was forgetting all his faults, for which I had once kept a sharp look-out. It had formerly been my endeavor to study all sides of his character; to take the bad with the good; and from the just weighing of both to form an equitable judgment. Now I saw no bad. The sarcasm that had repelled, the harshness that had startled me once, were only like keen condiments in a choice dish: their presence was pungent, but their absence would be felt as comparatively insipid. And as for the vague something—was it a sinister or a sorrowful, a designing or a desponding expression?—that opened upon a careful observer, now and then, in his eye and closed again before one could fathom the strange depth partially disclosed; that something which used to make me fear and shrink, as if I had been wandering amongst volcanic-looking hills, and had suddenly felt the ground quiver, and seen it gape; that something I at intervals beheld still, and with throbbing heart, but not with palsied nerves. Instead of wishing to shun, I longed only to dare—to divine it; and I thought Miss Ingram happy, because one day she might look into the abyss at her leisure, explore its secrets, and analyse their nature.

Meantime, while I thought only of my master and his future bride—saw only them, heard only their discourse, and considered only their movements of importance—the rest of the party were occupied with their own separate interests and pleasures. The ladies Lynn and Ingram continued to consort in solemn conferences, when they nodded their two turbans at each other, and held up their four hands in confronting gestures of surprise, or mystery, or horror, according to the theme on which their gossip ran, like a pair of magnified puppets. Mild Mrs. Dent talked with good-natured Mrs. Eshton; and the two sometimes bestowed a courteous word or smile on me. Sir George Lynn, Colonel Dent, and Mr. Eshton discussed politics, or county affairs, or justice business. Lord Ingram flirted with Amy Eshton; Louisa played and sang to and with one of the Messrs. Lynn; and Mary Ingram listened languidly to the gallant speeches of the other. Sometimes all, as with one consent, suspended their by-play to observe and listen to the principal actors; for, after all, Mr. Rochester, and—because closely connected with him—Miss Ingram, were the life and soul of the party. If he was absent from the room an hour, a perceptible dulness seemed to steal over the spirits of his guests, and his re-entrance was sure to give a fresh impulse to the vivacity of conversation.

The want of his animating influence appeared to be peculiarly felt one day that he had been summoned to Millcote on business, and was not likely to return till late. The afternoon was wet: a walk the party had proposed to take to see a gipsy camp, lately pitched on a common beyond Hay, was consequently deferred. Some of the gentlemen were gone to the stables; the younger ones, together with the younger ladies, were playing billiards in the

billiard-room. The dowagers Ingram and Lynn sought solace in a quiet game at cards. Blanche Ingram, after having repelled, by supercilious taciturnity, some efforts of Mrs. Dent and Mrs. Eshton to draw her into conversation, had first murmured over some sentimental tunes and airs on the piano, and then, having fetched a novel from the library, had flung herself in haughty listlessness on a sofa, and prepared to beguile, by the spell of fiction, the tedious hours of absence. The room and the house were silent; only now and then the merriment of the billiard players was heard from above.

It was verging on dusk, and the clock had already given warning of the hour to dress for dinner, when little Adèle, who knelt by me in the drawing-room window-seat, exclaimed,—"Voilà Monsieur Rochester, qui revient!"[2]

I turned, and Miss Ingram darted forwards from her sofa; the others, too, looked up from their several occupations; for at the same time a crunching of wheels, and a splashing tramp of horse-hoofs became audible on the wet gravel. A post-chaise was aproaching.

"What can possess him to come home in that style?" said Miss Ingram. "He rode Mesrour (the black horse), did he not, when he went out? and Pilot was with him,—what has he done with the animals?"

As she said this, she approached her tall person and ample garments so near the window, that I was obliged to bend back almost to the breaking of my spine; in her eagerness she did not observe me at first, but when she did, she curled her lip and moved to another casement. The post-chaise stopped, the driver rang the door bell, and a gentleman alighted, attired in traveling garb; but it was not Mr. Rochester; it was a tall, fashionable-looking man, a stranger.

"Provoking!" exclaimed Miss Ingram: "you tiresome monkey!" (apostrophizing Adèle) "who perched you up in the window to give false intelligence?" and she cast on me an angry glance, as if I were in fault.

Some parleying was audible in the hall, and soon the new-comer entered. He bowed to Lady Ingram, as deeming her the eldest lady present.

"It appears I come at an inopportune time, madam," said he; "when my friend, Mr. Rochester, is from home; but I arrive from a very long journey, and I think I may presume so far on old and intimate acquaintance as to instal myself here till he returns."

His manner was polite; his accent, in speaking, struck me as being somewhat unusual,—not precisely foreign, but still not altogether English; his age might be about Mr. Rochester's,—between thirty and forty; his complexion was singularly sallow; otherwise he was a fine-looking man, at first sight especially. On closer examination you detected something in his face that displeased; or rather, that failed to please. His features were regular, but too relaxed; his eye was large and well cut, but the life looking out of it was a tame, vacant life—at least so I thought.

The sound of the dressing-bell dispersed the party. It was not till after dinner that I saw him again; he then seemed quite at his ease. But I liked his physiognomy even less than before; it struck me as being, at the same time, unsettled and inanimate. His eye wandered, and had no meaning in its wandering; this gave him an odd look, such as I never remembered to have seen. For a handsome and not an unamiable-looking man, he repelled me

2. Here is Mr. Rochester, he's returned!

exceedingly; there was no power in that smooth-skinned face of a full oval shape; no firmness in that aquiline nose, and small cherry mouth; there was no thought on the low, even forehead; no command in that blank, brown eye.

As I sat in my usual nook, and looked at him with the light of the girandoles[3] on the mantelpiece beaming full over him—for he occupied an armchair, drawn close to the fire, and kept shrinking still nearer, as if he were cold—I compared him with Mr. Rochester. I think (with deference be it spoken) the contrast could not be much greater between a sleek gander and a fierce falcon: between a meek sheep and the rough-coated keen-eyed dog, its guardian.

He had spoken of Mr. Rochester as an old friend. A curious friendship theirs must have been: a pointed illustration, indeed, of the old adage that "extremes meet."

Two or three of the gentlemen sat near him, and I caught at times scraps of their conversation across the room. At first I could not make much sense of what I heard; for the discourse of Louisa Eshton and Mary Ingram, who sat nearer to me, confused the fragmentary sentences that reached me at intervals. These last were discussing the stranger: they both called him a "beautiful man." Louisa said he was "a love of a creature," and she "adored him": and Mary instanced his "pretty little mouth, and nice nose," as her ideal of the charming.

"And what a sweet-tempered forehead he has!" cried Louisa,—"so smooth—none of those frowning irregularities I dislike so much: and such a placid eye and smile!"

And then, to my great relief, Mr. Henry Lynn summoned them to the other side of the room, to settle some point about the deferred excursion to Hay Common.

I was now able to concentrate my attention on the group by the fire, and I presently gathered that the new-comer was called Mr. Mason: then I learned that he was but just arrived in England, and that he came from some hot country: which was the reason, doubtless, his face was so sallow, and that he sat so near the hearth, and wore a surtout in the house. Presently the words, Jamaica, Kingston, Spanish Town, indicated the West Indies as his residence; and it was with no little surprise I gathered, ere long, that he had there first seen and become acquainted with Mr. Rochester. He spoke of his friend's dislike of the burning heats, the hurricanes, and rainy seasons of that region. I knew Mr. Rochester had been a traveler: Mrs. Fairfax had said so; but I thought the continent of Europe had bounded his wanderings: till now I had never heard a hint given of visits to more distant shores.

I was pondering these things, when an incident, and a somewhat unexpected one, broke the thread of my musing. Mr. Mason, shivering as some one chanced to open the door, asked for more coal to be put on the fire, which had burned out its flame, though its mass of cinder still shone hot and red. The footman who brought in the coal, in going out, stopped near Mr. Eshton's chair, and said something to him in a low voice, of which I heard only the words, "old woman,"—"quite troublesome."

"Tell her she shall be put in the stocks if she does not take herself off," replied the magistrate.

3. Branched supports for candles.

"No—stop!" interrupted Colonel Dent. "Don't send her away, Eshton; we might turn the thing to account; better consult the ladies." And speaking aloud, he continued, "Ladies, you talked of going to Hay Common to visit the gipsy camp; Sam, here, says that one of the old Mother Bunches[4] is in the servants' hall at this moment, and insists upon being brought in before 'the quality,' to tell them their fortunes. Would you like to see her?"

"Surely, colonel," cried Lady Ingram, "you would not encourage such a low impostor. Dismiss her, by all means, at once!"

"But I cannot persuade her to go away, my lady," said the footman; "nor can any of the servants: Mrs. Fairfax is with her just now, entreating her to be gone; but she has taken a chair in the chimney-corner, and says nothing shall stir her from it till she gets leave to come in here."

"What does she want?" asked Mrs. Eshton.

" 'To tell the gentry their fortunes,' she says, ma'am; and she swears she must and will do it."

"What is she like?" inquired the Misses Eshton in a breath.

"A shockingly ugly old creature, miss; almost as black as a crock."

"Why, she's a real sorceress!" cried Frederick Lynn. "Let us have her in, of course."

"To be sure," rejoined his brother; "it would be a thousand pities to throw away such a chance of fun."

"My dear boys, what are you thinking about?" exclaimed Mrs. Lynn.

"I cannot possibly countenance any such inconsistent proceeding," chimed in the Dowager Ingram.

"Indeed, mamma, but you can—and will," pronounced the haughty voice of Blanche, as she turned round on the piano-stool; where till now she had sat silent, apparently examining sundry sheets of music. "I have a curiosity to hear my fortune told: therefore, Sam, order the beldame[5] forwards."

"My darling Blanche! recollect——"

"I do—I recollect all you can suggest; and I must have my will—quick, Sam!"

"Yes—yes—yes!" cried all the juveniles, both ladies and gentlemen. "Let her come—it will be excellent sport!"

The footman still lingered. "She looks such a rough one," said he.

"Go!" ejaculated Miss Ingram, and the man went.

Excitement instantly seized the whole party: a running fire of raillery and jests was proceeding when Sam returned.

"She won't come now," said he. "She says it's not her mission to appear before the 'vulgar herd' (them's her words). I must show her into a room by herself, and then those who wish to consult her must go to her one by one."

"You see now, my queenly Blanche," began Lady Ingram, "she encroaches. Be advised, my angel girl—and——"

"Show her into the library, of course," cut in the "angel girl." "It is not my mission to listen to her before the vulgar herd either: I mean to have her all to myself. Is there a fire in the library?"

"Yes, ma'am—but she looks such a tinker."[6]

"Cease that chatter, blockhead! and do my bidding."

4. A 16th-century London keeper of an alehouse whose name was used in many 17th-century jest-books.
5. Old woman.
6. Itinerant metal-worker, often a gypsy; a vaga-bond, a tramp.

Again Sam vanished; and mystery, animation, expectation rose to full flow once more.

"She's ready now," said the footman, as he reappeared. "She wishes to know who will be her first visitor."

"I think I had better just look in upon her before any of the ladies go," said Colonel Dent.

"Tell her, Sam, a gentleman is coming."

Sam went and returned.

"She says, sir, that she'll have no gentlemen; they need not trouble themselves to come near her: nor," he added, with difficulty suppressing a titter, "any ladies either, except the young and single."

"By Jove, she has taste!" exclaimed Henry Lynn.

Miss Ingram rose solemnly: "I go first," she said, in a tone which might have befitted the leader of a forlorn hope, mounting a breach in the van of his men.

"Oh, my best! oh, my dearest! pause—reflect!" was her mamma's cry; but she swept past her in stately silence, passed through the door which Colonel Dent held open, and we heard her enter the library.

A comparative silence ensued. Lady Ingram thought it "le cas"[7] to wring her hands: which she did accordingly. Miss Mary declared she felt, for her part, she never dared venture. Amy and Louisa Eshton tittered under their breath, and looked a little frightened.

The minutes passed very slowly: fifteen were counted before the library-door again opened. Miss Ingram returned to us through the arch.

Would she laugh? Would she take it as a joke? All eyes met her with a glance of curiosity, and she met all eyes with one of rebuff and coldness: she looked neither flurried nor merry; she walked stiffly to her seat, and took it in silence.

"Well, Blanche?" said Lord Ingram.

"What did she say, sister?" asked Mary.

"What did you think? How do you feel? Is she a real fortune-teller?" demanded the Misses Eshton.

"Now, now, good people," returned Miss Ingram, "don't press upon me. Really your organs of wonder and credulity are easily excited: you seem by the importance you all—my good mamma included—ascribe to this matter—absolutely to believe we have a genuine witch in the house, who is in close alliance with the old gentleman.[8] I have seen a gipsy-vagabond; she has practiced in hackneyed fashion the science of palmistry, and told me what such people usually tell. My whim is gratified; and now I think Mr. Eshton will do well to put the hag in the stocks tomorrow morning, as he threatened."

Miss Ingram took a book, leant back in her chair, and so declined further conversation. I watched her for nearly half an hour: during all that time she never turned a page, and her face grew momently darker, more dissatisfied, and more sourly expressive of disappointment. She had obviously not heard anything to her advantage: and it seemed to me, from her prolonged fit of gloom and taciturnity, that she herself, notwithstanding her professed indifference, attached undue importance to whatever revelations had been made her.

7. The right moment. 8. I.e., the devil.

Meantime, Mary Ingram, Amy and Louisa Eshton, declared they dared not go alone; and yet they all wished to go. A negotiation was opened through the medium of the ambassador, Sam; and after much pacing to and fro, till, I think, the said Sam's calves must have ached with the exercise, permission was at last, with great difficulty extorted from the rigorous Sibyl,[9] for the three to wait upon her in a body.

Their visit was not so still as Miss Ingram's had been: we heard hysterical giggling and little shrieks proceeding from the library; and at the end of about twenty minutes they burst the door open, and came running across the hall, as if they were half-scared out of their wits.

"I'm sure she is something not right!" they cried one and all. "She told us such things! She knows all about us!" and they sank breathless into the various seats the gentlemen hastened to bring them.

Pressed for further explanation they declared she had told them of things they had said and done when they were mere children; described books and ornaments they had in their boudoirs at home; keepsakes that different relations had presented to them. They affirmed that she had even divined their thoughts, and had whispered in the ear of each the name of the person she liked best in the world, and informed them of what they most wished for.

Here the gentlemen interposed with earnest petitions to be further enlightened on these two last-named points; but they got only blushes, ejaculations, tremors, and titters, in return for their importunity. The matrons, meantime, offered vinaigrettes[1] and wielded fans; and again and again reiterated the expression of their concern that their warning had not been taken in time; and the elder gentlemen laughed, and the younger urged their services on the agitated fair ones.

In the midst of the tumult, and while my eyes and ears were fully engaged in the scene before me, I heard a hem close at my elbow: I turned and saw Sam.

"If you please, miss, the gipsy declares that there is another young single lady in the room who has not been to her yet, and she swears she will not go till she has seen all. I thought it must be you: there is no one else for it. What shall I tell her?"

"Oh, I will go by all means," I answered; and I was glad of the unexpected opportunity to gratify my much-excited curiosity. I slipped out of the room, unobserved by any eye—for the company were gathered in one mass about the trembling trio just returned—and I closed the door quietly behind me.

"If you like, miss," said Sam, "I'll wait in the hall for you; and if she frightens you, just call and I'll come in."

"No, Sam, return to the kitchen: I am not in the least afraid." Nor was I; but I was a good deal interested and excited.

Chapter XIX

The library looked tranquil enough as I entered it, and the Sibyl—if Sibyl she were—was seated snugly enough in an easy chair at the chimney-corner. She had on a red cloak and a black bonnet: or rather, a broad-brimmed gipsy

9. Prophetess.
1. Small ornamental bottles, often containing smelling salts.

hat, tied down with a striped handkerchief under her chin. An extinguished candle stood on the table: she was bending over the fire, and seemed reading in a little black book, like a prayer-book, by the light of the blaze: she muttered the words to herself, as most old women do, while she read; she did not desist immediately on my entrance: it appeared she wished to finish a paragraph.

I stood on the rug and warmed my hands, which were rather cold with sitting at a distance from the drawing-room fire. I felt now as composed as ever I did in my life: there was nothing indeed in the gipsy's appearance to trouble one's calm. She shut her book and slowly looked up; her hat-brim partially shaded her face, yet I could see as she raised it, that it was a strange one. It looked all brown and black: elf-locks bristled out from beneath a white band which passed under her chin, and came half over her cheeks or rather jaws; her eye confronted me at once, with a bold and direct gaze.

"Well, and you want your fortune told?" she said in a voice as decided as her glance, as harsh as her features.

"I don't care about it, mother; you may please yourself; but I ought to warn you, I have no faith."

"It's like your impudence to say so: I expected it of you; I heard it in your step as you crossed the threshold."

"Did you? You've a quick ear."

"I have; and a quick eye, and a quick brain."

"You need them all in your trade."

"I do; especially when I've customers like you to deal with. Why don't you tremble?"

"I'm not cold."

"Why don't you turn pale?"

"I am not sick."

"Why don't you consult my art?"

"I'm not silly."

The old crone "nichered" a laugh under her bonnet and bandage: she then drew out a short, black pipe, and lighting it began to smoke. Having indulged a while in this sedative, she raised her bent body, took the pipe from her lips, and while gazing steadily at the fire, said very deliberately:—"You are cold; you are sick; and you are silly."

"Prove it," I rejoined.

"I will; in few words. You are cold, because you are alone: no contact strikes the fire from you that is in you. You are sick: because the best of feelings, the highest and the sweetest given to man, keeps far away from you. You are silly, because, suffer as you may, you will not beckon it to approach; nor will you stir one step to meet it where it waits you."

She again put her short, black pipe to her lips, and renewed her smoking with vigor.

"You might say all that to almost any one who, you knew, lived as a solitary dependant in a great house."

"I might say it to almost any one; but would it be true of almost any one?"

"In my circumstances."

"Yes; just so, in *your* circumstances: but find me another precisely placed as you are."

"It would be easy to find you thousands."

"You could scarcely find me one. If you knew it, you are peculiarly situated: very near happiness; yes; within reach of it. The materials are all prepared; there only wants a movement to combine them. Chance laid them somewhat apart; let them be once approached and bliss results."

"I don't understand enigmas. I never could guess a riddle in my life."

"If you wish me to speak more plainly, show me your palm."

"And I must cross it with silver, I suppose?"

"To be sure."

I gave her a shilling: she put it into an old stocking-foot which she took out of her pocket, and having tied it round and returned it, she told me to hold out my hand. I did. She approached her face to the palm, and pored over it without touching it.

"It is too fine," said she. "I can make nothing of such a hand as that; almost without lines: besides, what is in a palm? Destiny is not written there."

"I believe you," said I.

"No," she continued, "it is in the face: on the forehead, about the eyes, in the eyes themselves, in the lines of the mouth. Kneel, and lift up your head."

"Ah! now you are coming to reality," I said as I obeyed her. "I shall begin to put some faith in you presently."

I knelt within half a yard of her. She stirred the fire, so that a ripple of light broke from the disturbed coal: the glare, however, as she sat, only threw her face into deeper shadow: mine, it illumined.

"I wonder with what feelings you came to me tonight," she said, when she had examined me a while. "I wonder what thoughts are busy in your heart during all the hours you sit in yonder room with the fine people flitting before you like shapes in a magic lantern: just as little sympathetic communion passing between you and them, as if they were really mere shadows of human forms and not the actual substance."

"I feel tired often, sleepy sometimes; but seldom sad."

"Then you have some secret hope to buoy you up and please you with whispers of the future?"

"Not I. The utmost I hope is, to save money enough out of my earnings to set up a school some day in a little house rented by myself."

"A mean nutriment for the spirit to exist on: and sitting in that window-seat (you see I know your habits)——"

"You have learned them from the servants."

"Ah! you think yourself sharp. Well—perhaps I have: to speak truth, I have an acquaintance with one of them—Mrs. Poole——"

I started to my feet when I heard the name.

"You have—have you?" thought I; "there is diablerie[2] in the business after all, then!"

"Don't be alarmed," continued the strange being; "she's a safe hand, is Mrs. Poole: close and quiet: any one may repose confidence in her. But, as I was saying: sitting in that window-seat, do you think of nothing but your future school? Have you no present interest in any of the company who occupy the sofas and chairs before you? Is there not one face you study? One figure whose movements you follow with, at least, curiosity?"

"I like to observe all the faces, and all the figures."

2. Devilry.

"But do you never single one from the rest—or it may be, two?"

"I do frequently; when the gestures or looks of a pair seem telling a tale: it amuses me to watch them."

"What tale do you like best to hear?"

"Oh, I have not much choice! They generally run on the same theme— courtship; and promise to end in the same catastrophe—marriage."

"And do you like that monotonous theme?"

"Positively, I don't care about it: it is nothing to me."

"Nothing to you? When a lady, young and full of life and health, charming with beauty and endowed with the gifts of rank and fortune, sits and smiles in the eyes of a gentleman you——"

"I what?"

"You know—and, perhaps, think well of?"

"I don't know the gentlemen here. I have scarcely interchanged a syllable with one of them; and as to thinking well of them, I consider some respectable and stately, and middle-aged, and others young, dashing, handsome and lively: but certainly they are all at liberty to be the recipients of whose smiles they please, without my feeling disposed to consider the transaction of any moment to me."

"You don't know the gentlemen here? You have not exchanged a syllable with one of them? Will you say that of the master of the house?"

"He is not at home."

"A profound remark! A most ingenious quibble! He went to Millcote this morning, and will be back here tonight, or tomorrow: does that circumstance exclude him from the list of your acquaintance—blot him, as it were, out of existence?"

"No: but I can scarcely see what Mr. Rochester has to do with the theme you had introduced."

"I was talking of ladies smiling in the eyes of gentlemen; and of late so many smiles have been shed into Mr. Rochester's eyes that they overflow like two cups filled above the brim: have you never remarked that?"

"Mr. Rochester has a right to enjoy the society of his guests."

"No question about his right: but have you never observed that, of all the tales told here about matrimony, Mr. Rochester has been favored with the most lively and the most continuous?"

"The eagerness of a listener quickens the tongue of a narrator." I said this rather to myself than to the gipsy; whose strange talk, voice, manner, had by this time wrapped me in a kind of dream. One unexpected sentence came from her lips after another, till I got involved in a web of mystification; and wondered what unseen spirit had been sitting for weeks by my heart watching its workings and taking record of every pulse.

"Eagerness of a listener!" repeated she: "yes; Mr. Rochester has sat by the hour, his ear inclined to the fascinating lips that took such delight in their task of communicating; and Mr. Rochester was so willing to receive and looked so grateful for the pastime given him: you have noticed this?"

"Grateful! I cannot remember detecting gratitude in his face."

"Detecting! You have analyzed, then. And what did you detect, if not gratitude?"

I said nothing.

"You have seen love: have you not?—and, looking forward, you have seen him married and beheld his bride happy?"

"Humph! Not exactly. Your witch's skill is rather at fault sometimes."

"What the devil have you seen, then?"

"Never mind: I came here to inquire, not to confess. Is it known that Mr. Rochester is to be married?"

"Yes; and to the beautiful Miss Ingram."

"Shortly?"

"Appearances would warrant that conclusion; and, no doubt (though, with an audacity that wants chastising out of you, you seem to question it), they will be a superlatively happy pair. He must love such a handsome, noble, witty, accomplished lady; and probably she loves him: or, if not his person, at least his purse. I know she considers the Rochester estate eligible to the last degree; though (God pardon me!) I told her something on that point about an hour ago, which made her look wondrous grave: the corners of her mouth fell half an inch. I would advise her blackaviced[3] suitor to look out: if another comes with a longer, or clearer rent-roll,—he's dished——"

"But, mother, I did not come to hear Mr. Rochester's fortune: I came to hear my own; and you have told me nothing of it."

"Your fortune is yet doubtful: when I examined your face, one trait contradicted another. Chance has meted you a measure of happiness: that I know. I knew it before I came here this evening. She has laid it carefully on one side for you. I saw her do it. It depends on yourself to stretch out your hand, and take it up; but whether you will do so, is the problem I study. Kneel again on the rug."

"Don't keep me long; the fire scorches me."

I knelt. She did not stoop towards me, but only gazed leaning back in her chair. She began muttering,—"The flame flickers in the eye, the eye shines like dew: it looks soft and full of feeling; it smiles at my jargon: it is susceptible; impression follows impression through its clear sphere; where it ceases to smile, it is sad; an unconscious lassitude weighs on the lid: that signifies melancholy resulting from loneliness. It turns from me; it will not suffer farther scrutiny; it seems to deny, by a mocking glance, the truth of the discoveries I have already made,—to disown the charge both of sensibility and chagrin: its pride and reserve only confirm me in my opinion. The eye is favorable.

"As to the mouth, it delights at times in laughter; it is disposed to impart all that the brain conceives; though I daresay it would be silent on much the heart experiences. Mobile and flexible, it was never intended to be compressed in the eternal silence of solitude: it is a mouth which should speak much and smile often and have human affection for its interlocutor. That feature too is propitious.

"I see no enemy to a fortunate issue but in the brow; and that brow professes to say,—'I can live alone, if self-respect and circumstances require me so to do. I need not sell my soul to buy bliss. I have an inward treasure, born with me, which can keep me alive if all extraneous delights should be withheld; or offered only at a price I cannot afford to give.' The forehead declares, 'Reason sits firm and holds the reins, and she will not let the feelings burst away and hurry her to wild chasms. The passions may rage furiously, like true heathens, as they are; and the desires may imagine all sorts of vain things: but judgment shall still have the last word in every argument, and

3. I.e., blackavised, i.e., of a dark complexion.

the casting vote in every decision. Strong wind, earthquake-shock, and fire may pass by: but I shall follow the guiding of that still small voice which interprets the dictates of conscience.'

"Well said, forehead; your declaration shall be respected. I have formed my plans—right plans I deem them—and in them I have attended to the claims of conscience, the counsels of reason. I know how soon youth would fade and bloom perish, if, in the cup of bliss offered, but one dreg of shame, or one flavor of remorse were detected; and I do not want sacrifice, sorrow, dissolution—such is not my taste. I wish to foster, not to blight—to earn gratitude, not to wring tears of blood—no, nor of brine: my harvest must be in smiles, in endearments, in sweet—That will do. I think I rave in a kind of exquisite delirium. I should wish now to protract this moment *ad infinitum*; but I dare not. So far I have governed myself thoroughly. I have acted as I inwardly swore I would act; but farther might try me beyond my strength. Rise, Miss Eyre: leave me; 'the play is played out.' "[4]

Where was I? Did I wake or sleep? Had I been dreaming? Did I dream still? The old woman's voice had changed: her accent, her gesture, and all were familiar to me as my own face in a glass—as the speech of my own tongue. I got up, but did not go. I looked; I stirred the fire, and I looked again: but she drew her bonnet and her bandage closer about her face, and again beckoned me to depart. The flame illuminated her hand stretched out: roused now, and on the alert for discoveries, I at once noticed that hand. It was no more the withered limb of eld than my own; it was a rounded supple member, with smooth fingers, symmetrically turned; a broad ring flashed on the little finger, and stooping forward, I looked at it, and saw a gem I had seen a hundred times before. Again I looked at the face; which was no longer turned from me—on the contrary, the bonnet was doffed, the bandage displaced, the head advanced.

"Well, Jane, do you know me?" asked the familiar voice.

"Only take off the red cloak, sir, and then———"

"But the string is in a knot—help me."

"Break it, sir."

"There, then—'Off, ye lendings!' "[5]

And Mr. Rochester stepped out of his disguise.

"Now, sir, what a strange idea!"

"But well carried out, eh? Don't you think so?"

"With the ladies you must have managed well."

"But not with you?"

"You did not act the character of a gipsy with me."

"What character did I act? My own?"

"No; some unaccountable one. In short, I believe you have been trying to draw me out—or in; you have been talking nonsense to make me talk nonsense. It is scarcely fair, sir."

"Do you forgive me, Jane?"

"I cannot tell till I have thought it all over. If, on reflection, I find I have fallen into no great absurdity, I shall try to forgive you; but it was not right."

"Oh! you have been very correct—very careful, very sensible."

4. The next to last line of Shakespeare's *Twelfth Night* is "But that's all one, our play is done"; see

also *I Henry IV* 2.5.442, "Play out the play."
5. Shakepeare, *King Lear* 3.4.100.

I reflected, and thought, on the whole, I had. It was a comfort; but, indeed, I had been on my guard almost from the beginning of the interview. Something of masquerade I suspected. I knew gipsies and fortune-tellers did not express themselves as this seeming old woman had expressed herself; besides, I had noted her feigned voice, her anxiety to conceal her features. But my mind had been running on Grace Poole—that living enigma, that mystery of mysteries, as I considered her. I had never thought of Mr. Rochester.

"Well," said he, "what are you musing about? What does that grave smile signify?"

"Wonder and self-congratulation, sir. I have your permission to retire now, I suppose?"

"No; stay a moment; and tell me what the people in the drawing-room yonder are doing."

"Discussing the gipsy, I daresay."

"Sit down!—Let me hear what they said about me."

"I had better not stay long, sir; it must be near eleven o'clock. Oh! are you aware, Mr. Rochester, that a stranger has arrived here since you left this morning?"

"A stranger!—no; who can it be? I expected no one; is he gone?"

"No; he said he had known you long, and that he could take the liberty of installing himself here till you returned."

"The devil he did! Did he give his name?"

"His name is Mason, sir; and he comes from the West Indies; from Spanish Town, in Jamaica, I think."

Mr. Rochester was standing near me; he had taken my hand, as if to lead me to a chair. As I spoke, he gave my wrist a convulsive grip; the smile on his lips froze: apparently a spasm caught his breath.

"Mason!—the West Indies!" he said, in the tone one might fancy a speaking automaton to enounce its single words; "Mason!—the West Indies!" he reiterated; and he went over the syllables three times, growing, in the intervals of speaking, whiter than ashes: he hardly seemed to know what he was doing.

"Do you feel ill, sir?" I inquired.

"Jane, I've got a blow;—I've got a blow, Jane!" he staggered.

"Oh!—lean on me, sir."

"Jane, you offered me your shoulder once before; let me have it now."

"Yes, sir, yes; and my arm."

He sat down, and made me sit beside him. Holding my hand in both his own, he chafed it; gazing on me, at the same time, with the most troubled and dreary look.

"My little friend!" said he, "I wish I were in a quiet island with only you; and trouble, and danger, and hideous recollections removed from me."

"Can I help you, sir?—I'd give my life to serve you."

"Jane, if aid is wanted, I'll seek it at your hands; I promise you that."

"Thank you, sir; tell me what to do,—I'll try, at least, to do it."

"Fetch me now, Jane, a glass of wine from the dining-room; they will be at supper there; and tell me if Mason is with them, and what he is doing."

I went. I found all the party in the dining-room at supper, as Mr. Rochester had said; they were not seated at table,—the supper was arranged on the

side-board; each had taken what he chose, and they stood about here and there in groups, their plates and glasses in their hands. Every one seemed in high glee; laughter and conversation were general and animated. Mr. Mason stood near the fire, talking to Colonel and Mrs. Dent, and appeared as merry as any of them. I filled a wine-glass (I saw Miss Ingram watch me frowningly as I did so: she thought I was taking a liberty, I daresay), and I returned to the library.

Mr. Rochester's extreme pallor had disappeared, and he looked once more firm and stern. He took the glass from my hand.

"Here is to your health, ministrant spirit!" he said: he swallowed the contents and returned it to me. "What are they doing, Jane?"

"Laughing and talking, sir."

"They don't look grave and mysterious, as if they had heard something strange?"

"Not at all—they are full of jests and gaiety."

"And Mason?"

"He was laughing too."

"If all these people came in a body and spat at me, what would you do, Jane?"

"Turn them out of the room, sir, if I could."

He half smiled. "But if I were to go to them, and they only looked at me coldly, and whispered sneeringly among each other, and then drop off and left me one by one, what then? Would you go with them?"

"I rather think not, sir: I should have more pleasure in staying with you."

"To comfort me?"

"Yes, sir, to comfort you, as well as I could."

"And if they laid you under a ban for adhering to me?"

"I, probably, should know nothing about their ban; and if I did, I should care nothing about it."

"Then, you could dare censure for my sake?"

"I could dare it for the sake of any friend who deserved my adherence; as you, I am sure, do."

"Go back now into the room; step quietly up to Mason, and whisper in his ear that Mr. Rochester is come and wishes to see him: show him in here and then leave me."

"Yes, sir."

I did his behest. The company all stared at me as I passed straight among them. I sought Mr. Mason, delivered the message, and preceded him from the room: I ushered him into the library, and then I went upstairs.

At a late hour, after I had been in bed some time, I heard the visitors repair to their chambers: I distinguished Mr. Rochester's voice, and heard him say, "This way, Mason; this is your room."

He spoke cheerfully: the gay tones set my heart at ease. I was soon asleep.

Chapter XX

I had forgotten to draw my curtain,[6] which I usually did; and also to let down my window-blind. The consequence was, that when the moon, which

6. I.e., the curtain on her poster bed.

was full and bright (for the night was fine), came in her course to that space in the sky opposite my casement, and looked in at me through the unveiled panes, her glorious gaze roused me. Awaking in the dead of night, I opened my eyes on her disk—silver-white and crystal-clear. It was beautiful, but too solemn: I half rose, and stretched my arm to draw the curtain.

Good God! What a cry!

The night—its silence—its rest, was rent in twain, by a savage, a sharp, a shrilly sound that ran from end to end of Thornfield Hall.

My pulse stopped: my heart stood still; my stretched arm was paralyzed. The cry died, and was not renewed. Indeed, whatever being uttered that fearful shriek could not soon repeat it: not the widest-winged condor on the Andes could, twice in succession, send out such a yell from the cloud shrouding his eyrie. The thing delivering such utterance must rest ere it could repeat the effort.

It came out of the third story; for it passed overhead. And overhead—yes, in the room just above my chamber ceiling—I now heard a struggle: a deadly one it seemed from the noise; and a half-smothered voice shouted—"Help! help! help!" three times rapidly.

"Will no one come?" it cried; and then, while the staggering and stamping went on wildly, I distinguished through plank and plaster:—"Rochester! Rochester! for God's sake, come!"

A chamber door opened: some one ran, or rushed, along the gallery. Another step stamped on the flooring above, and something fell; and there was silence.

I had put on some clothes, though horror shook all my limbs: I issued from my apartment. The sleepers were all aroused: ejaculations, terrified murmurs, sounded in every room; door after door unclosed: one looked out and another looked out; the gallery filled. Gentlemen and ladies alike had quitted their beds; and "Oh! what is it?"—"Who is hurt?"—"What has happened?"—"Fetch a light!"—"Is it fire?"—"Are there robbers?"—"Where shall we run?" was demanded confusedly on all hands. But for the moonlight they would have been in complete darkness. They ran to and fro; they crowded together; some sobbed, some stumbled: the confusion was inextricable.

"Where the devil is Rochester?" cried Colonel Dent. "I cannot find him in his bed."

"Here! here!" was shouted in return. "Be composed, all of you: I'm coming."

And the door at the end of the gallery opened, and Mr. Rochester advanced with a candle: he had just descended from the upper story. One of the ladies ran to him directly; she seized his arm: it was Miss Ingram.

"What awful event has taken place?" said she. "Speak! let us know the worst at once!"

"But don't pull me down or strangle me," he replied: for the Misses Eshton were clinging about him now; and the two dowagers, in vast white wrappers, were bearing down on him like ships in full sail.

"All's right!—all's right!" he cried. "It's a mere rehearsal of Much Ado About Nothing. Ladies, keep off; or I shall wax dangerous."

And dangerous he looked: his black eyes darted sparks. Calming himself by an effort, he added:—"A servant has had the nightmare; that is all. She's an excitable, nervous person: she construed her dream into an apparition, or

something of that sort, no doubt; and has taken a fit with fright. Now, then, I must see you all back into your rooms; for, till the house is settled she cannot be looked after. Gentlemen, have the goodness to set the ladies the example. Miss Ingram, I am sure you will not fail in evincing superiority to idle terrors. Amy and Louisa, return to your nests like a pair of doves, as you are. Mesdames" (to the dowagers), "you will take cold to a dead certainty, if you stay in this chill gallery any longer."

And so, by dint of alternate coaxing and commanding, he contrived to get them all once more enclosed in their separate dormitories. I did not wait to be ordered back to mine; but retreated unnoticed: as unnoticed I had left it.

Not, however, to go to bed: on the contrary, I began and dressed myself carefully. The sounds I had heard after the scream, and the words that had been uttered, had probably been heard only by me; for they had proceeded from the room above mine: but they assured me that it was not a servant's dream which had thus struck horror through the house; and that the explanation Mr. Rochester had given was merely an invention framed to pacify his guests. I dressed, then, to be ready for emergencies. When dressed, I sat a long time by the window, looking out over the silent grounds and silvered fields, and waiting for I knew not what. It seemed to me that some event must follow the strange cry, struggle, and call.

No: stillness returned: each murmur and movement ceased gradually, and in about an hour Thornfield Hall was again as hushed as a desert. It seemed that sleep and night had resumed their empire. Meantime the moon declined: she was about to set. Not liking to sit in the cold and darkness, I thought I would lie down on my bed, dressed as I was. I left the window, and moved with little noise across the carpet; as I stooped to take off my shoes, a cautious hand tapped low at the door.

"Am I wanted?" I asked.

"Are you up?" asked the voice I expected to hear, viz. my master's.

"Yes, sir."

"And dressed?"

"Yes."

"Come out, then, quietly."

I obeyed. Mr. Rochester stood in the gallery, holding a light.

"I want you," he said: "come this way: take your time and make no noise."

My slippers were thin: I could walk the matted floor as softly as a cat. He glided up the gallery and up the stairs, and stopped in the dark, low corridor of the fateful third story: I had followed and stood at his side.

"Have you a sponge in your room?" he asked in a whisper.

"Yes, sir."

"Have you any salts—volatile salts?"

"Yes."

"Go back and fetch both."

I returned, sought the sponge on the wash-stand, the salts in my drawer, and once more retraced my steps. He still waited; he held a key in his hand: approaching one of the small, black doors, he put it in the lock; he paused and addressed me again.

"You don't turn sick at the sight of blood?"

"I think I shall not: I have never been tried yet."

I felt a thrill while I answered him; but no coldness, and no faintness.

"Just give me your hand," he said; "it will not do to risk a fainting fit."

I put my fingers into his. "Warm and steady," was his remark: he turned the key and opened the door.

I saw a room I remembered to have seen before; the day Mrs. Fairfax showed me over the house: it was hung with tapestry; but the tapestry was now looped up in one part, and there was a door apparent, which had then been concealed. This door was open; a light shone out of the room within: I heard thence a snarling, snatching sound, almost like a dog quarreling. Mr. Rochester, putting down his candle, said to me, "Wait a minute," and he went forward to the inner apartment. A shout of laughter greeted his entrance; noisy at first, and terminating in Grace Poole's own goblin ha! ha! She then was there. He made some sort of arrangement, without speaking; though I heard a low voice address him: he came out and closed the door behind him.

"Here, Jane!" he said; and I walked round to the other side of a large bed, which with its drawn curtains concealed a considerable portion of the chamber. An easy-chair was near the bed-head: a man sat in it, dressed with the exception of his coat; he was still; his head leaned back; his eyes were closed. Mr. Rochester held the candle over him; I recognised in his pale and seemingly lifeless face—the stranger, Mason: I saw too that his linen on one side, and one arm, was almost soaked in blood.

"Hold the candle," said Mr. Rochester, and I took it; he fetched a basin of water from the wash-stand: "Hold that," said he. I obeyed. He took the sponge, dipped it in and moistened the corpse-like face: he asked for my smelling-bottle, and applied it to the nostrils. Mr. Mason shortly unclosed his eyes; he groaned. Mr. Rochester opened the shirt of the wounded man, whose arm and shoulder were bandaged: he sponged away blood, trickling fast down.

"Is there immediate danger?" murmured Mr. Mason.

"Pooh! No—a mere scratch. Don't be so overcome, man: bear up! I'll fetch a surgeon for you now, myself: you'll be able to be removed by morning, I hope. Jane," he continued.

"Sir?"

"I shall have to leave you in this room with this gentleman, for an hour, or perhaps two hours; you will sponge the blood as I do when it returns: if he feels faint, you will put the glass of water on that stand to his lips, and your salts to his nose. You will not speak to him on any pretext—and— Richard—it will be at the peril of your life if you speak to her: open your lips—agitate yourself—and I'll not answer for the consequences."

Again the poor man groaned: he looked as if he dared not move: fear, either of death or of something else, appeared almost to paralyze him. Mr. Rochester put the now bloody sponge into my hand, and I proceeded to use it as he had done. He watched me a second, then saying, "Remember!—No conversation," he left the room. I experienced a strange feeling as the key grated in the lock, and the sound of his retreating step ceased to be heard.

Here then I was in the third story, fastened into one of its mystic cells; night around me; a pale and bloody spectacle under my eyes and hands; a murderess hardly separated from me by a single door: yes—that was appalling—the rest I could bear; but I shuddered at the thought of Grace Poole bursting out upon me.

I must keep to my post, however. I must watch this ghastly countenance—these blue, still lips forbidden to unclose—these eyes now shut, now opening, now wandering through the room, now fixing on me, and ever glazed with the dulness of horror. I must dip my hand again and again in the basin of blood and water, and wipe away the trickling gore. I must see the light of the unsnuffed candle wane on my employment; the shadows darken on the wrought-antique tapestry round me, and grow black under the hangings of the vast old bed, and quiver strangely over the doors of a great cabinet opposite—whose front, divided into twelve panels, bore in grim design the heads of the twelve apostles, each inclosed in its separate panel as in a frame; while above them at the top rose an ebon crucifix and a dying Christ.

According as the shifting obscurity and flickering gleam hovered here or glanced there, it was now the bearded physician, Luke, that bent his brow; now St. John's long hair that waved; and anon the devilish face of Judas, that grew out of the panel, and seemed gathering life and threatening a revelation of the arch-traitor—of Satan himself—in his subordinate's form.

Amidst all this, I had to listen as well as watch: to listen for the movements of the wild beast or the fiend in yonder side den. But since Mr. Rochester's visit it seemed spell-bound: all the night I heard but three sounds at three long intervals,—a step creak, a momentary renewal of the snarling, canine noise, and a deep human groan.

Then my own thoughts worried me. What crime was this, that lived incarnate in this sequestered mansion, and could neither be expelled nor subdued by the owner?—What mystery, that broke out, now in fire and now in blood, at the deadest hours of night? What creature was it, that, masked in an ordinary woman's face and shape, uttered the voice, now of a mocking demon, and anon of a carrion-seeking bird of prey?

And this man I bent over—this commonplace, quiet stranger—how had he become involved in the web of horror? and why had the Fury[7] flown at him? What made him seek this quarter of the house at an untimely season, when he should have been asleep in bed? I had heard Mr. Rochester assign him an apartment below—what brought him here? And why, now, was he so tame under the violence or treachery done him? Why did he so quietly submit to the concealment Mr. Rochester enforced? Why *did* Mr. Rochester enforce this concealment? His guest had been outraged, his own life on a former occasion had been hideously plotted against; and both attempts he smothered in secrecy and sank in oblivion! Lastly, I saw Mr. Mason was submissive to Mr. Rochester; that the impetuous will of the latter held complete sway over the inertness of the former: the few words which had passed between them assured me of this. It was evident that in their former intercourse, the passive disposition of the one had been habitually influenced by the active energy of the other: whence then had arisen Mr. Rochester's dismay when he heard of Mr. Mason's arrival? Why had the mere name of this unresisting individual—whom his word now sufficed to control like a child—fallen on him, a few hours since, as a thunderbolt might fall on an oak?

Oh! I could not forget his look and his paleness when he whispered: "Jane, I have got a blow—I have got a blow, Jane." I could not forget how the arm had trembled which he had rested on my shoulder: and it was no light matter

7. Greek female spirit of vengeance.

which could thus bow the resolute spirit and thrill the vigorous frame of Fairfax Rochester.

"When will he come? When will he come?" I cried inwardly, as the night lingered and lingered—as my bleeding patient drooped, moaned, sickened: and neither day nor aid arrived. I had, again and again, held the water to Mason's white lips; again and again offered him the stimulating salts: my efforts seemed ineffectual: either bodily or mental suffering, or loss of blood, or all three combined, were fast prostrating his strength. He moaned so, and looked so weak, wild, and lost, I feared he was dying; and I might not even speak to him.

The candle, wasted at last, went out; as it expired, I perceived streaks of gray light edging the window curtains: dawn was then approaching. Presently I heard Pilot bark far below, out of his distant kennel in the courtyard: hope revived. Nor was it unwarranted: in five minutes more the grating key, the yielding lock, warned me my watch was relieved. It could not have lasted more than two hours: many a week has seemed shorter.

Mr. Rochester entered, and with him the surgeon he had been to fetch.

"Now, Carter, be on the alert," he said to this last: "I give you but half an hour for dressing the wound, fastening the bandages, getting the patient downstairs and all."

"But is he fit to move, sir?"

"No doubt of it; it is nothing serious: he is nervous, his spirits must be kept up. Come, set to work."

Mr. Rochester drew back the thick curtain, drew up the holland blind, let in all the daylight he could; and I was surprised and cheered to see how far dawn was advanced: what rosy streaks were beginning to brighten the east. Then he approached Mason, whom the surgeon was already handling.

"Now, my good fellow, how are you?" he asked.

"She's done for me, I fear," was the faint reply.

"Not a whit!—courage! This day fortnight you'll hardly be a pin the worse of it: you've lost a little blood; that's all. Carter, assure him there's no danger."

"I can do that conscientiously," said Carter, who had now undone the bandages; "only I wish I could have got here sooner: he would not have bled so much—but how is this? The flesh on the shoulder is torn as well as cut. This wound was not done with a knife: there have been teeth here!"

"She bit me," he murmured. "She worried me like a tigress, when Rochester got the knife from her."

"You should not have yielded: you should have grappled with her at once," said Mr. Rochester.

"But under such circumstances, what could one do?" returned Mason. "Oh, it was frightful!" he added, shuddering. "And I did not expect it: she looked so quiet at first."

"I warned you," was his friend's answer; "I said—be on your guard when you go near her. Besides, you might have waited till tomorrow, and had me with you: it was mere folly to attempt the interview tonight and alone."

"I thought I could have done some good."

"You thought! you thought! Yes; it makes me impatient to hear you: but, however, you have suffered, and are likely to suffer enough for not taking my advice; so I'll say no more. Carter—hurry!—hurry! The sun will soon rise, and I must have him off."

"Directly, sir; the shoulder is just bandaged. I must look to this other wound in the arm: she has had her teeth here too, I think."

"She sucked the blood: she said she'd drain my heart," said Mason.

I saw Mr. Rochester shudder: a singularly marked expression of disgust, horror, hatred, warped his countenance almost to distortion; but he only said:—"Come, be silent, Richard, and never mind her gibberish: don't repeat it."

"I wish I could forget it," was the answer.

"You will when you are out of the country: when you get back to Spanish Town, you may think of her as dead and buried—or rather, you need not think of her at all."

"Impossible to forget this night!"

"It is not impossible: have some energy, man. You thought you were as dead as a herring two hours since, and you are all alive and talking now. There!—Carter has done with you or nearly so; I'll make you decent in a trice. Jane" (he turned to me for the first time since his reentrance), "take this key: go down into my bedroom, and walk straight forward into my dressing-room; open the top drawer of the wardrobe and take out a clean shirt and neck-handkerchief: bring them here; and be nimble."

I went; sought the repository he had mentioned, found the articles named and returned with them.

"Now," said he, "go to the other side of the bed while I order his toilet; but don't leave the room: you may be wanted again."

I retired as directed.

"Was anybody stirring below when you went down, Jane?" inquired Mr. Rochester, presently.

"No, sir; all was very still."

"We shall get you off cannily, Dick: and it will be better, both for your sake, and for that of the poor creature in yonder. I have striven long to avoid exposure, and I should not like it to come at last. Here, Carter, help him on with his waistcoat. Where did you leave your furred cloak? You can't travel a mile without that, I know, in this damned cold climate. In your room?— Jane, run down to Mr. Mason's room,—the one next mine,—and fetch a cloak you will see there."

Again I ran, and again returned, bearing an immense mantle lined and edged with fur.

"Now I've another errand for you," said my untiring master; "you must away to my room again. What a mercy you are shod with velvet, Jane!—a clod-hopping messenger would never do at this juncture. You must open the middle drawer of my toilet-table and take out a little phial and a little glass you will find there,—quick!"

I flew thither and back, bringing the desired vessels.

"That's well! Now, doctor, I shall take the liberty of administering a dose myself; on my own responsibility. I got this cordial at Rome of an Italian charlatan—a fellow you would have kicked, Carter. It is not a thing to be used indiscriminately, but it is good upon occasion: as now, for instance. Jane, a little water."

He held out the tiny glass, and I half filled it from the water bottle on the wash-stand.

"That will do—now wet the lip of the phial."

I did so: he measured twelve drops of a crimson liquid, and presented it to Mason.

"Drink, Richard: it will give you the heart you lack, for an hour or so."

"But will it hurt me?—is it inflammatory?"

"Drink! drink! drink!"

Mr. Mason obeyed, because it was evidently useless to resist. He was dressed now: he still looked pale, but he was no longer gory and sullied. Mr. Rochester let him sit three minutes after he had swallowed the liquid; he then took his arm.

"Now I am sure you can get on your feet," he said—"try."

The patient rose.

"Carter, take him under the other shoulder. Be of good cheer, Richard; step out—that's it!"

"I do feel better," remarked Mr. Mason.

"I am sure you do. Now, Jane, trip on before us away to the back-stairs; unbolt the side-passage door, and tell the driver of the post-chaise you will see in the yard—or just outside, for I told him not to drive his rattling wheels over the pavement—to be ready; we are coming: and, Jane, if any one is about, come to the foot of the stairs and hem."[8]

It was by this time half-past five, and the sun was on the point of rising; but I found the kitchen still dark and silent. The side-passage door was fastened; I opened it with as little noise as possible: all the yard was quiet; but the gates stood wide open, and there was a post-chaise, with horses ready harnessed, and driver seated on the box, stationed outside. I approached him, and said the gentlemen were coming; he nodded: then I looked carefully round and listened. The stillness of early morning slumbered everywhere; the curtains were yet drawn over the servants' chamber windows; little birds were just twittering in the blossom-blanched orchard trees, whose boughs drooped like white garlands over the wall enclosing one side of the yard; the carriage horses stamped from time to time in their closed stables: all else was still.

The gentlemen now appeared. Mason, supported by Mr. Rochester and the surgeon, seemed to walk with tolerable ease: they assisted him into the chaise; Carter followed.

"Take care of him," said Mr. Rochester to the latter, "and keep him at your house till he is quite well: I shall ride over in a day or two to see how he gets on. Richard, how is it with you?"

"The fresh air revives me, Fairfax."

"Leave the window open on his side, Carter; there is no wind—good-bye, Dick."

"Fairfax—"

"Well, what is it?"

"Let her be taken care of; let her be treated as tenderly as may be: let her—" he stopped and burst into tears.

"I do my best; and have done it, and will do it," was the answer: he shut up the chaise door, and the vehicle drove away.

"Yet would to God there was an end of all this!" added Mr. Rochester, as he closed and barred the heavy yard-gates. This done, he moved with slow

8. Cough.

step and abstracted air towards a door in the wall bordering the orchard. I, supposing he had done with me, prepared to return to the house; again, however, I heard him call "Jane!" He had opened the portal and stood at it, waiting for me.

"Come where there is some freshness, for a few moments," he said; "that house is a mere dungeon: don't you feel it so?"

"It seems to me a splendid mansion, sir."

"The glamor of inexperience is over your eyes," he answered; "and you see it through a charmed medium: you cannot discern that the gilding is slime and the silk draperies cobwebs; that the marble is sordid slate, and the polished woods mere refuse chips and scaly bark. Now *here*" (he pointed to the leafy enclosure we had entered) "all is real, sweet, and pure."

He strayed down a walk edged with box;[9] with apple trees, pear trees, and cherry trees on one side, and a border on the other, full of all sorts of old-fashioned flowers, stocks, sweet-williams, primroses, pansies, mingled with southern-wood, sweet-briar, and various fragrant herbs. They were fresh now as a succession of April showers and gleams, followed by a lovely spring morning, could make them: the sun was just entering the dappled east, and his light illumined the wreathed and dewy orchard trees and shone down the quiet walks under them.

"Jane, will you have a flower?"

He gathered a half-blown[1] rose, the first on the bush, and offered it to me.

"Thank you, sir."

"Do you like this sunrise, Jane? That sky with its high and light clouds which are sure to melt away as the day waxes warm—this placid and balmy atmosphere?"

"I do, very much."

"You have passed a strange night, Jane."

"Yes, sir."

"And it has made you look pale—were you afraid when I left you alone with Mason?"

"I was afraid of some one coming out of the inner room."

"But I had fastened the door—I had the key in my pocket: I should have been a careless shepherd if I had left a lamb—my pet lamb—so near a wolf's den, unguarded: you were safe."

"Will Grace Poole live here still, sir?"

"Oh, yes! don't trouble your head about her—put the thing out of your thoughts."

"Yet it seems to me your life is hardly secure while she stays."

"Never fear—I will take care of myself."

"Is the danger you apprehended last night gone by now sir?"

"I cannot vouch for that till Mason is out of England: nor even then. To live, for me, Jane, is to stand on a crater-crust which may crack and spue fire any day."

"But Mr. Mason seems a man easily led. Your influence, sir, is evidently potent with him: he will never set you at defiance, or wilfully injure you."

"Oh, no! Mason will not defy me; nor, knowing it, will he hurt me—but,

9. A shrub used for hedges. 1. Half-blossomed.

unintentionally, he might in a moment, by one careless word, deprive me, if not of life, yet for ever of happiness."

"Tell him to be cautious, sir: let him know what you fear, and show him how to avert the danger."

He laughed sardonically, hastily took my hand, and as hastily threw it from him.

"If I could do that, simpleton, where would the danger be? Annihilated in a moment. Ever since I have known Mason I have only had to say to him 'Do that,' and the thing has been done. But I cannot give him orders in this case: I cannot say 'Beware of harming me, Richard'; for it is imperative that I should keep him ignorant that harm to me is possible. Now you look puzzled; and I will puzzle you farther. You are my little friend, are you not?"

"I like to serve you, sir, and to obey you in all that is right."

"Precisely: I see you do. I see genuine contentment in your gait and mien, your eye and face, when you are helping me and pleasing me—working for me, and with me, in, as you characteristically say, 'all that is right': for if I bid you do what you thought wrong, there would be no light-footed running, no neat-handed alacrity, no lively glance and animated complexion. My friend would then turn to me, quiet and pale, and would say, 'No, sir; that is impossible: I cannot do it, because it is wrong'; and would become immutable as a fixed star. Well, you too have power over me, and may injure me: yet I dare not show you where I am vulnerable, lest, faithful and friendly as you are, you should transfix me at once."

"If you have no more to fear from Mr. Mason than you have from me, sir, you are very safe."

"God grant it may be so! Here, Jane, is an arbour; sit down."

The arbor was an arch in the wall, lined with ivy; it contained a rustic seat. Mr. Rochester took it, leaving room, however, for me: but I stood before him.

"Sit," he said; "the bench is long enough for two. You don't hesitate to take a place at my side, do you? Is that wrong, Jane?"

I answered him by assuming it: to refuse would, I felt, have been unwise.

"Now, my little friend, while the sun drinks the dew—while all the flowers in this old garden awake and expand, and the birds fetch their young ones' breakfast out of the cornfield, and the early bees do their first spell of work— I'll put a case to you; which you must endeavor to suppose your own: but first, look at me, and tell me you are at ease, and not fearing that I err in detaining you, or that you err in staying."

"No, sir; I am content."

"Well then, Jane, call to aid your fancy—suppose you were no longer a girl well reared and disciplined, but a wild boy indulged from childhood upwards; imagine yourself in a remote foreign land; conceive that you there commit a capital error, no matter of what nature or from what motives, but one whose consequences must follow you through life and taint all your existence. Mind, I don't say a *crime*; I am not speaking of shedding of blood or any other guilty act, which might make the perpetrator amenable to the law: my word is *error*. The results of what you have done become in time to you utterly insupportable; you take measures to obtain relief: unusual measures, but neither unlawful nor culpable. Still you are miserable; for hope has quitted you on the very confines of life: your sun at noon darkens in an eclipse, which you feel will not leave it till the time of setting. Bitter

and base associations have become the sole food of your memory: you wander here and there, seeking rest in exile: happiness in pleasure—I mean in heartless, sensual pleasure—such as dulls intellect and blights feeling. Heart-weary and soul-withered, you come home after years of voluntary banishment; you make a new acquaintance—how or where no matter: you find in this stranger much of the good and bright qualities which you have sought for twenty years, and never before encountered; and they are all fresh, healthy, without soil and without taint. Such society revives, regenerates: you feel better days come back—higher wishes, purer feelings; you desire to recommence your life, and to spend what remains to you of days in a way more worthy of an immortal being. To attain this end, are you justified in overleaping an obstacle of custom—a mere conventional impediment, which neither your conscience sanctifies nor your judgment approves?"

He paused for an answer: and what was I to say? Oh, for some good spirit to suggest a judicious and satisfactory response! Vain aspiration! The west wind whispered in the ivy round me; but no gentle Ariel[2] borrowed its breath as a medium of speech: the birds sang in the tree-tops; but their song, however sweet, was inarticulate.

Again Mr. Rochester propounded his query.

"Is the wandering and sinful, but now rest-seeking and repentant, man justified in daring the world's opinion, in order to attach to him for ever this gentle, gracious, genial stranger; thereby securing his own peace of mind and regeneration of life?"

"Sir," I answered, "a wanderer's repose or a sinner's reformation should never depend on a fellow-creature. Men and women die; philosophers falter in wisdom, and Christians in goodness: if any one you know has suffered and erred, let him look higher than his equals for strength to amend, and solace to heal."

"But the instrument—the instrument! God, who does the work, ordains the instrument. I have myself—I tell it you without parable—been a worldly, dissipated, restless man; and I believe I have found the instrument for my cure, in—"

He paused: the birds went on caroling, the leaves lightly rustling. I almost wondered they did not check their songs and whispers to catch the suspended revelation: but they would have had to wait many minutes—so long was the silence protracted. At last I looked up at the tardy speaker: he was looking eagerly at me.

"Little friend," said he, in quite a changed tone—while his face changed too; losing all its softness and gravity, and becoming harsh and sarcastic—"you have noticed my tender penchant for Miss Ingram: don't you think if I married her she would regenerate me with a vengeance?"

He got up instantly, went quite to the other end of the walk, and when he came back he was humming a tune.

"Jane, Jane," said he, stopping before me, "you are quite pale with your vigils: don't you curse me for disturbing your rest?"

"Curse you? No sir."

"Shake hands in confirmation of the word. What cold fingers! They were

2. Spirit (in Shakespeare's *Tempest*).

warmer last night when I touched them at the door of the mysterious chamber. Jane, when will you watch with me again?"

"Whenever I can be useful, sir."

"For instance, the night before I am married! I am sure I shall not be able to sleep. Will you promise to sit up with me to bear me company? To you I can talk of my lovely one: for now you have seen her and know her."

"Yes, sir."

"She's a rare one, is she not, Jane?"

"Yes, sir."

"A strapper—a real strapper, Jane: big, brown, and buxom; with hair just such as the ladies of Carthage[3] must have had. Bless me! there's Dent and Lynn in the stables! Go in by the shrubbery, through that wicket."

As I went one way, he went another, and I heard him in the yard, saying cheeringly:—"Mason got the start of you all this morning; he was gone before sunrise: I rose at four to see him off."

Chapter XXI

Presentiments are strange things! and so are sympathies; and so are signs: and the three combined make one mystery to which humanity has not yet found the key. I never laughed at presentiments in my life; because I have had strange ones of my own. Sympathies, I believe, exist: (for instance, between far-distant, long-absent, wholly estranged relatives; asserting, notwithstanding their alienation, the unity of the source to which each traces his origin) whose workings baffle mortal comprehension. And signs, for aught we know, may be but the sympathies of Nature with man.

When I was a little girl, only six years old, I, one night, heard Bessie Leaven say to Martha Abbot that she had been dreaming about a little child; and that to dream of children was a sure sign of trouble, either to one's self or one's kin. The saying might have worn out of my memory, had not a circumstance immediately followed which served indelibly to fix it there. The next day Bessie was sent for home to the deathbed of her little sister.

Of late I had often recalled this saying and this incident; for during the past week scarcely a night had gone over my couch that had not brought with it a dream of an infant: which I sometimes hushed in my arms, sometimes dandled on my knee, sometimes watched playing with daisies on a lawn; or again, dabbling its hands in running water. It was a wailing child this night, and a laughing one the next: now it nestled close to me, and now it ran from me; but whatever mood the apparition evinced, whatever aspect it wore, it failed not for seven successive nights to meet me the moment I entered the land of slumber.

I did not like this iteration of one idea—this strange recurrence of one image; and I grew nervous as bedtime approached, and the hour of the vision drew near. It was from companionship with this baby-phantom I had been roused on that moonlight night when I heard the cry; and it was on the afternoon of the day following I was summoned downstairs by a message

3. An ancient city-state in North Africa, and later a city in Tunisia; perhaps an allusion to the complaint of St. Cyprian of Carthage (d. 258 C.E.) that women had become too concerned about their hairstyles.

that some one wanted me in Mrs. Fairfax's room. On repairing thither, I found a man waiting for me, having the appearance of a gentleman's servant: he was dressed in deep mourning, and the hat he held in his hand was surrounded with a crape band.

"I daresay you hardly remember me, miss," he said, rising as I entered; "but my name is Leaven: I lived coachman with Mrs. Reed when you were at Gateshead eight or nine years since, and I live there still."

"Oh, Robert! how do you do? I remember you very well: you used to give me a ride sometimes on Miss Georgiana's bay pony. And how is Bessie? You are married to Bessie?"

"Yes, miss: my wife is very hearty, thank you; she brought me another little one about two months since—we have three now—and both mother and child are thriving."

"And are the family well at the house, Robert?"

"I am sorry I can't give better news of them, miss: they are very badly at present—in great trouble."

"I hope no one is dead," I said glancing at his black dress. He too looked down at the crape round his hat and replied,—"Mr. John died yesterday was a week, at his chambers in London."

"Mr. John?"

"Yes."

"And how does his mother bear it?"

"Why you see, Miss Eyre, it is not a common mishap: his life has been very wild: these last three years he gave himself up to strange ways; and his death was shocking."

"I heard from Bessie he was not doing well."

"Doing well! He could not do worse: he ruined his health and his estate amongst the worst men and the worst women. He got into debt and into jail: his mother helped him out twice, but as soon as he was free he returned to his old companions and habits. His head was not strong: the knaves he lived amongst fooled him beyond anything I ever heard. He came down to Gateshead about three weeks ago and wanted Missis to give up all to him. Missis refused: her means have long been much reduced by his extravagance; so he went back again, and the next news was that he was dead. How he died, God knows!—they say he killed himself."

I was silent: the tidings were frightful. Robert Leaven resumed:—"Missis had been out of health herself for some time: she had got very stout, but was not strong with it; and the loss of money and fear of poverty were quite breaking her down. The information about Mr. John's death and the manner of it came too suddenly: it brought on a stroke. She was three days without speaking; but last Tuesday she seemed rather better: she appeared as if she wanted to say something, and kept making signs to my wife and mumbling. It was only yesterday morning, however, that Bessie understood she was pronouncing your name; and at last she made out the words, 'Bring Jane— fetch Jane Eyre: I want to speak to her.' Bessie is not sure whether she is in her right mind, or means anything by the words; but she told Miss Reed and Miss Georgiana, and advised them to send for you. The young ladies put it off at first: but their mother grew so restless, and said, 'Jane, Jane,' so many times, that at last they consented. I left Gateshead yesterday; and if you can get ready, miss, I should like to take you back with me early tomorrow morning."

"Yes, Robert, I shall be ready: it seems to me that I ought to go."

"I think so too, miss. Bessie said she was sure you would not refuse: but I suppose you will have to ask leave before you can get off?"

"Yes; and I will do it now"; and having directed him to the servants' hall, and recommended him to the care of John's wife, and the attentions of John himself, I went in search of Mr. Rochester.

He was not in any of the lower rooms; he was not in the yard, the stables, or the grounds. I asked Mrs. Fairfax if she had seen him;—yes: she believed he was playing billiards with Miss Ingram. To the billiard-room I hastened: the click of balls and the hum of voices resounded thence: Mr. Rochester, Miss Ingram, the two Misses Eshton, and their admirers, were all busied in the game. It required some courage to disturb so interesting a party; my errand, however, was one I could not defer, so I approached the master where he stood at Miss Ingram's side. She turned as I drew near and looked at me haughtily: her eyes seemed to demand, "What can the creeping creature want now?" and when I said, in a low voice, "Mr. Rochester," she made a movement as if tempted to order me away. I remember her appearance at the moment,—it was very graceful and very striking: she wore a morning robe of sky-blue crape; a gauzy azure scarf was twisted in her hair. She had been all animation with the game, and irritated pride did not lower the expression of her haughty lineaments.

"Does that person want you?" she inquired of Mr. Rochester; and Mr. Rochester turned to see who the "person" was. He made a curious grimace,—one of his strange and equivocal demonstrations—threw down his cue and followed me from the room.

"Well, Jane?" he said, as he rested his back against the schoolroom door, which he had shut.

"If you please, sir, I want leave of absence for a week or two."

"What to do?—Where to go?"

"To see a sick lady who has sent for me."

"What sick lady?—Where does she live?"

"At Gateshead, in ——shire."

"——shire? That is a hundred miles off! Who may she be that sends for people to see her that distance?"

"Her name is Reed, sir,—Mrs. Reed."

"Reed of Gateshead? There was a Reed of Gateshead, a magistrate."

"It is his widow, sir."

"And what have you to do with her? How do you know her?"

"Mr. Reed was my uncle,—my mother's brother."

"The deuce he was! You never told me that before: you always said you had no relations."

"None that would own me, sir. Mr. Reed is dead, and his wife cast me off."

"Why?"

"Because I was poor, and burdensome, and she disliked me."

"But Reed left children?—you must have cousins? Sir George Lynn was talking of a Reed of Gateshead, yesterday—who, he said, was one of the veriest rascals in town; and Ingram was mentioning a Georgiana Reed of the same place, who was much admired for her beauty, a season or two ago, in London."

"John Reed is dead, too, sir: he ruined himself and half-ruined his family,

and is supposed to have committed suicide. The news so shocked his mother that it brought on an apoplectic attack."

"And what good can you do her? Nonsense, Jane! I would never think of running a hundred miles to see an old lady who will, perhaps, be dead before you reach her: besides, you say she cast you off."

"Yes, sir, but that is long ago; and when her circumstances were very different: I could not be easy to neglect her wishes now."

"How long will you stay?"

"As short a time as possible, sir."

"Promise me only to stay a week———"

"I had better not pass my word: I might be obliged to break it."

"At all events you *will* come back: you will not be induced under any pretext to take up a permanent residence with her."

"Oh, no! I shall certainly return if all be well."

"And who goes with you? You don't travel a hundred miles alone."

"No, sir, she has sent her coachman."

"A person to be trusted?"

"Yes, sir, he has lived ten years in the family."

Mr. Rochester meditated. "When do you wish to go?"

"Early tomorrow morning, sir."

"Well, you must have some money; you can't travel without money, and I daresay you have not much: I have given you no salary yet. How much have you in the world, Jane?" he asked, smiling.

I drew out my purse; a meager thing it was. "Five shillings, sir." He took the purse, poured the hoard into his palm and chuckled over it as if its scantiness pleased him. Soon he produced his pocket-book: "Here," said he, offering me a note: it was fifty pounds, and he owed me but fifteen. I told him I had no change.

"I don't want change: you know that. Take your wages."

I declined accepting more than was my due. He scowled at first; then, as if recollecting something, he said:—"Right, right! Better not give you all now: you would, perhaps, stay away three months if you had fifty pounds. There are ten: is it not plenty?"

"Yes, sir, but now you owe me five."

"Come back for it then: I am your banker for forty pounds."

"Mr. Rochester, I may as well mention another matter of business to you while I have the opportunity."

"Matter of business? I'm curious to hear it."

"You have as good as informed me, sir, that you are going shortly to be married?"

"Yes: what then?"

"In that case, sir, Adèle ought to go to school: I am sure you will perceive the necessity of it."

"To get her out of my bride's way; who might otherwise walk over her rather too emphatically. There's sense in the suggestion; not a doubt of it: Adèle, as you say, must go to school; and you, of course, must march straight to—the devil?"

"I hope not, sir: but I must seek another situation somewhere."

"In course!" he exclaimed, with a twang of voice and a distortion of features equally fantastic and ludicrous. He looked at me some minutes.

"And old Madam Reed, or the Misses, her daughters, will be solicited by you to seek a place, I suppose?"

"No, sir; I am not on such terms with my relatives as would justify me in asking favors of them—but I shall advertise."

"You shall walk up the pyramids of Egypt!" he growled. "At your peril you advertise! I wish I had only offered you a sovereign instead of ten pounds. Give me back nine pounds, Jane; I've a use for it."

"And so have I, sir," I returned, putting my hands and my purse behind me. "I could not spare the money on any account."

"Little niggard!" said he, "refusing me a pecuniary request! Give me five pounds, Jane."

"Not five shillings, sir; nor five pence."

"Just let me look at the cash."

"No, sir; you are not to be trusted."

"Jane!"

"Sir?"

"Promise me one thing."

"I'll promise you anything, sir, that I think I am likely to perform."

"Not to advertise: and to trust this quest of a situation to me. I'll find you one in time."

"I shall be glad so to do, sir, if you, in your turn, will promise that I and Adèle shall be both safe out of the house before your bride enters it"

"Very well! very well! I'll pledge my word on it. You go tomorrow, then?"

"Yes, sir; early."

"Shall you come down to the drawing-room after dinner?"

"No, sir, I must prepare for the journey."

"Then you and I must bid good-bye for a little while?"

"I suppose so, sir."

"And how do people perform that ceremony of parting, Jane? Teach me; I'm not quite up to it."

"They say, Farewell; or any other form they prefer."

"Then say it."

"Farewell, Mr. Rochester, for the present."

"What must I say?"

"The same, if you like, sir."

"Farewell, Miss Eyre, for the present: is that all?"

"Yes."

"It seems stingy, to my notions, and dry and unfriendly. I should like something else: a little addition to the rite. If one shook hands, for instance; but no—that would not content me either. So you'll do no more than say Farewell, Jane?"

"It is enough, sir: as much good will may be conveyed in one hearty word as in many."

"Very likely; but it is blank and cool—'farewell.' "

"How long is he going to stand with his back against the door?" I asked myself; "I want to commence my packing." The dinner-bell rang, and suddenly away he bolted, without another syllable: I saw him no more during the day, and was off before he had risen in the morning.

I reached the lodge at Gateshead about five o'clock in the afternoon of the first of May: I stepped in there before going up to the hall. It was very clean

and neat: the ornamental windows were hung with little white curtains; the floor was spotless; the grate and fire-irons were burnished bright, and the fire burned clear. Bessie sat on the hearth nursing her last-born, and Robert and his sister played quietly in a corner.

"Bless you!—I knew you would come!" exclaimed Mrs. Leaven, as I entered.

"Yes, Bessie," said I, after I had kissed her; "and I trust I am not too late. How is Mrs. Reed?—Alive still, I hope."

"Yes, she is alive; and more sensible and collected than she was. The doctor says she may linger a week or two yet; but he hardly thinks she will finally recover."

"Has she mentioned me lately?"

"She was talking of you only this morning, and wishing you would come: but she is sleeping now; or was ten minutes ago, when I was up at the house. She generally lies in a kind of lethargy all the afternoon, and wakes up about six or seven. Will you rest yourself here an hour, miss, and then I will go up with you?"

Robert here entered, and Bessie laid her sleeping child in the cradle and went to welcome him: afterwards she insisted on my taking off my bonnet and having some tea; for she said I looked pale and tired. I was glad to accept her hospitality; and I submitted to be relieved of my travelling garb just as passively as I used to let her undress me when a child.

Old times crowded fast back on me as I watched her bustling about—setting out the tea-tray with her best china, cutting bread-and-butter, toasting a tea-cake, and, between whiles, giving little Robert or Jane an occasional tap or push, just as she used to give me in former days. Bessie had retained her quick temper as well as her light foot and good looks.

Tea ready, I was going to approach the table; but she desired me to sit still, quite in her old, peremptory tones. I must be served at the fireside, she said; and she placed before me a little round stand with my cup and a plate of toast, absolutely as she used to accommodate me with some privately purloined dainty on a nursery chair: and I smiled and obeyed her as in bygone days.

She wanted to know if I was happy at Thornfield Hall, and what sort of a person the mistress was; and when I told her there was only a master, whether he was a nice gentleman, and if I liked him. I told her he was rather an ugly man, but quite a gentleman; and that he treated me kindly, and I was content. Then I went on to describe to her the gay company that had lately been staying at the house: and to these details Bessie listened with interest: they were precisely of the kind she relished.

In such conversation an hour was soon gone: Bessie restored to me my bonnet, etc., and, accompanied by her, I quitted the lodge for the hall. It was also accompanied by her that I had, nearly nine years ago, walked down the path I was now ascending. On a dark, misty, raw morning in January, I had left a hostile roof with a desperate and embittered heart—a sense of outlawry and almost of reprobation—to seek the chilly harborage of Lowood: that bourne so far away and unexplored. The same hostile roof now again rose before me: my prospects were doubtful yet; and I had yet an aching heart. I still felt as a wanderer on the face of the earth; but I experienced firmer trust in myself and my own powers, and less withering dread of oppres-

sion. The gaping wound of my wrongs, too, was now quite healed; and the flame of resentment extinguished.

"You shall go into the breakfast-room first," said Bessie, as she preceded me through the hall; "the young ladies will be there."

In another moment I was within that apartment. There was every article of furniture looking just as it did on the morning I was first introduced to Mr. Brocklehurst: the very rug he had stood upon still covered the hearth. Glancing at the book-cases, I thought I could distinguish the two volumes of *Bewick's British Bird*s occupying their old place on the third shelf, and *Gulliver's Travels* and the *Arabian Nights* ranged just above. The inanimate objects were not changed: but the living things had altered past recognition. Two young ladies appeared before me; one very tall, almost as tall as Miss Ingram,—very thin too, with a sallow face and severe mien. There was something ascetic in her look, which was augmented by the extreme plainness of a straight-skirted, black, stuff dress, a starched linen collar, hair combed away from the temples, and the nun-like ornament of a string of ebony beads and a crucifix. This I felt sure was Eliza, though I could trace little resemblance to her former self in that elongated and colorless visage.

The other was as certainly Georgiana: but not the Georgiana I remembered —the slim and fairy-like girl of eleven. This was a full-blown, very plump damsel, fair as wax-work; with handsome and regular features, languishing blue eyes, and ringleted yellow hair. The hue of her dress was black too; but its fashion was so different from her sister's—so much more flowing and becoming—it looked as stylish as the other's looked puritanical.

In each of the sisters there was one trait of the mother—and only one: the thin and pallid elder daughter had her parent's Cairngorm[4] eye: the blooming and luxuriant younger girl had her contour of jaw and chin,—perhaps a little softened, but still imparting an indescribable hardness to the countenance, otherwise so voluptuous and buxom.

Both ladies, as I advanced, rose to welcome me, and both addressed me by the name of "Miss Eyre." Eliza's greeting was delivered in a short, abrupt voice, without a smile; and then she sat down again, fixed her eyes on the fire, and seemed to forget me. Georgiana added to her "How d'ye do?" several common-places about my journey, the weather and so on, uttered in rather a drawling tone: and accompanied by sundry side-glances that measured me from head to foot—now traversing the folds of my drab merino pelisse, and now lingering on the plain trimming of my cottage bonnet. Young ladies have a remarkable way of letting you know that they think you a "quiz" without actually saying the words. A certain superciliousness of look, coolness of manner, nonchalance of tone, express fully their sentiments on the point, without committing them by any positive rudeness in word or deed.

A sneer, however, whether covert or open, had now no longer that power over me it once possessed: as I sat between my cousins, I was surprised to find how easy I felt under the total neglect of the one and the semi-sarcastic attentions of the other—Eliza did not mortify, nor Georgiana ruffle me. The fact was, I had other things to think about; within the last few months feelings had been stirred in me so much more potent than any they could raise— pains and pleasures so much more acute and exquisite had been excited,

4. Smoky brown (literally, a variety of quartz).

than any it was in their power to inflict or bestow—that their airs gave me no concern either for good or bad.

"How is Mrs. Reed?" I asked soon, looking calmly at Georgiana; who thought fit to bridle at the direct address, as if it were an unexpected liberty.

"Mrs. Reed? Ah! mama you mean; she is extremely poorly: I doubt if you can see her tonight."

"If," said I, "you would just step upstairs and tell her I am come, I should be much obliged to you."

Georgiana almost started, and she opened her blue eyes wild and wide. "I know she had a particular wish to see me," I added, "and I would not defer attending to her desire longer than is absolutely necessary."

"Mama dislikes being disturbed in an evening," remarked Eliza. I soon rose, quietly took off my bonnet and gloves, uninvited, and said I would just step out to Bessie—who was, I dared say, in the kitchen—and ask her to ascertain whether Mrs. Reed was disposed to receive me or not tonight. I went, and having found Bessie and despatched her on my errand, I proceeded to take further measures. It had heretofore been my habit always to shrink from arrogance: received as I had been today, I should, a year ago, have resolved to quit Gateshead the very next morning; now, it was disclosed to me all at once, that that would be a foolish plan. I had taken a journey of a hundred miles to see my aunt, and I must stay with her till she was better—or dead: as to her daughters' pride or folly, I must put it on one side; make myself independent of it. So I addressed the house-keeper; asked her to show me a room, told her I should probably be a visitor here for a week or two, had my trunk conveyed to my chamber, and followed it thither myself: I met Bessie on the landing.

"Missis is awake," said she; "I have told her you are here: come and let us see if she will know you."

I did not need to be guided to the well-known room: to which I had so often been summoned for chastizement or reprimand in former days. I hastened before Bessie, I softly opened the door: a shaded light stood on the table, for it was now getting dark. There was the great four-post bed with amber hangings as of old: there the toilet-table, the arm-chair, and the foot-stool: at which I had a hundred times been sentenced to kneel, to ask pardon for offences, by me uncommitted. I looked into a certain corner near, half-expecting to see the slim outline of a once-dreaded switch; which used to lurk there, waiting to leap out imp-like and lace my quivering palm or shrinking neck. I approached the bed; I opened the curtains and leaned over the high-piled pillows.

Well did I remember Mrs. Reed's face, and I eagerly sought the familiar image. It is a happy thing that time quells the longings of vengeance, and hushes the promptings of rage and aversion: I had left this woman in bitterness and hate, and I came back to her now with no other emotion than a sort of ruth for her great sufferings, and a strong yearning to forget and forgive all injuries—to be reconciled and clasp hands in amity.

The well-known face was there: stern, relentless as ever—there was that peculiar eye which nothing could melt; and the somewhat raised, imperious, despotic eyebrow. How often had it lowered on me menace and hate! and how the recollection of childhood's terrors and sorrows revived as I traced its harsh line now! And yet I stooped down and kissed her: she looked at me.

"Is this Jane Eyre?" she said.

"Yes, aunt Reed. How are you, dear aunt?"

I had once vowed that I would never call her aunt again: I thought it no sin to forget and break that vow now. My fingers had fastened on her hand which lay outside the sheet: had she pressed mine kindly, I should at that moment have experienced true pleasure. But unimpressionable natures are not so soon softened, nor are natural antipathies so readily eradicated: Mrs. Reed took her hand away, and, turning her face rather from me, she remarked that the night was warm. Again she regarded me, so icily, I felt at once that her opinion of me—her feeling towards me—was unchanged, and unchangeable. I knew by her stony eye—opaque to tenderness, indissoluble to tears—that she was resolved to consider me bad to the last; because to believe me good, would give her no generous pleasure: only a sense of mortification.

I felt pain, and then I felt ire; and then I felt a determination to subdue her—to be her mistress in spite both of her nature and her will. My tears had risen, just as in childhood: I ordered them back to their source. I brought a chair to the bed-head: I sat down and leaned over the pillow.

"You sent for me," I said, "and I am here; and it is my intention to stay till I see how you get on."

"Oh, of course! You have seen my daughters?"

"Yes."

"Well, you may tell them I wish you to stay till I can talk some things over with you I have on my mind: tonight it is too late, and I have a difficulty in recalling them. But there was something I wished to say—let me see——"

The wandering look and changed utterance told what wreck had taken place in her once-vigorous frame. Turning restlessly, she drew the bed-clothes round her; my elbow, resting on a corner of the quilt, fixed it down: she was at once irritated.

"Sit up!" said she; "don't annoy me with holding the clothes fast—are you Jane Eyre?"

"I am Jane Eyre."

"I have had more trouble with that child than anyone would believe. Such a burden to be left on my hands—and so much annoyance as she caused me, daily and hourly, with her incomprehensible disposition, and her sudden starts of temper, and her continual, unnatural watchings of one's movements! I declare she talked to me once like something mad, or like a fiend—no child ever spoke or looked as she did; I was glad to get her away from the house. What did they do with her at Lowood? The fever broke out there, and many of the pupils died. She, however, did not die: but I said she did—I wish she had died!"

"A strange wish, Mrs. Reed: why do you hate her so?"

"I had a dislike to her mother always; for she was my husband's only sister, and a great favorite with him: he opposed the family's disowning her when she made her low marriage; and when news came of her death, he wept like a simpleton. He would send for the baby; though I entreated him rather to put it out to nurse and pay for its maintenance. I hated it the first time I set my eyes on it—a sickly, whining, pining thing! It would wail in its cradle all night long—not screaming heartily like any other child, but whimpering and moaning. Reed pitied it; and he used to nurse it and notice[5] it as if it had

5. Treat with favor.

been his own: more, indeed, than he ever noticed his own at that age. He would try to make my children friendly to the little beggar: the darlings could not bear it, and he was angry with them when they showed their dislike. In his last illness, he had it brought continually to his bedside; and but an hour before he died, he bound me by vow to keep the creature. I would as soon have been charged with a pauper brat out of a workhouse: but he was weak, naturally weak. John does not at all resemble his father, and I am glad of it: John is like me and like my brothers—he is quite a Gibson. Oh, I wish he would cease tormenting me with letters for money! I have no more money to give him: we are getting poor. I must send away half the servants and shut up part of the house; or let it off. I can never submit to do that—yet how are we to get on? Two-thirds of my income goes in paying the interest of mortgages. John gambles dreadfully, and always loses—poor boy! He is beset by sharpers: John is sunk and degraded—his look is frightful—I feel ashamed for him when I see him."

She was getting much excited. "I think I had better leave her now," said I to Bessie, who stood on the other side of the bed.

"Perhaps you had, miss: but she often talks in this way towards night—in the morning she is calmer."

I rose. "Stop!" exclaimed Mrs. Reed. "There is another thing I wished to say. He threatens me—he continually threatens me with his own death, or mine: and I dream sometimes that I see him laid out with a great wound in his throat, or with a swollen and blackened face. I am come to a strange pass: I have heavy troubles. What is to be done? How is the money to be had?"

Bessie now endeavored to persuade her to take a sedative draught: she succeeded with difficulty. Soon after, Mrs. Reed grew more composed, and sank into a dozing state. I then left her.

More than ten days elapsed before I had again any conversation with her. She continued either delirious or lethargic; and the doctor forbade every thing which could painfully excite her. Meantime, I got on as well as I could with Georgiana and Eliza. They were very cold, indeed, at first. Eliza would sit half the day sewing, reading, or writing, and scarcely utter a word either to me or her sister. Georgiana would chatter nonsense to her canary bird by the hour, and take no notice of me. But I was determined not to seem at a loss for occupation or amusement: I had brought my drawing materials with me, and they served me for both.

Provided with a case of pencils, and some sheets of paper, I used to take a seat apart from them, near the window, and busy myself in sketching fancy vignettes, representing any scene that happened momentarily to shape itself in the ever-shifting kaleidoscope of imagination: a glimpse of sea between two rocks; the rising moon, and a ship crossing its disk; a group of reeds and water-flags, and a naiad's[6] head crowned with lotus-flowers, rising out of them; an elf sitting in a hedge-sparrow's nest, under a wreath of hawthorn-bloom.

One morning I fell to sketching a face: what sort of a face it was to be, I did not care or know. I took a soft black pencil, gave it a broad point, and

6. River nymph.

worked away. Soon I had traced on the paper a broad and prominent fore-head, and a square lower outline of visage: that contour gave me pleasure; my fingers proceeded actively to fill it with features. Strongly-marked hori-zontal eyebrows must be traced under that brow; then followed, naturally, a well-defined nose, with a straight ridge and full nostrils; then a flexible-looking mouth, by no means narrow; then a firm chin with a decided cleft down the middle of it: of course, some black whiskers were wanted, and some jetty hair, tufted on the temples, and waved above the forehead. Now for the eyes: I had left them to the last, because they required the most careful working. I drew them large; I shaped them well: the eyelashes I traced long and sombre; the irids lustrous and large. "Good! but not quite the thing," I thought, as I surveyed the effect: "They want more force and spirit;" and I wrought the shades blacker, that the lights might flash more brilliantly—a happy touch or two secured success. There, I had a friend's face under my gaze; and what did it signify that those young ladies turned their backs on me? I looked at it; I smiled at the speaking likeness: I was absorbed and content.

"Is that a portrait of some one you know?" asked Eliza, who had approached me unnoticed. I responded that it was merely a fancy head, and hurried it beneath the other sheets. Of course, I lied: it was, in fact, a very faithful representation of Mr. Rochester. But what was that to her, or to any one but myself? Georgiana also advanced to look. The other drawings pleased her much, but she called that "an ugly man." They both seemed surprised at my skill. I offered to sketch their portraits; and each, in turn, sat for a pencil outline. Then Georgiana produced her album. I promised to contribute a water-color drawing: this put her at once into good humor. She proposed a walk in the grounds. Before we had been out two hours, we were deep in a confidential conversation: she had favored me with a description of the brilliant winter she had spent in London two seasons ago—of the admiration she had there excited—the attention she had received: and I even got hints of the titled conquest she had made. In the course of the afternoon and evening these hints were enlarged on: various soft conversations were reported, and sentimental scenes represented; and, in short, a volume of a novel of fashionable life was that day improvised by her for my benefit. The communications were renewed from day to day: they always ran on the same theme—herself, her loves, and woes. It was strange she never once adverted either to her mother's illness, or her brother's death, or the present gloomy state of the family prospects. Her mind seemed wholly taken up with remi-niscences of past gaiety, and aspirations after dissipations to come. She passed about five minutes each day in her mother's sick-room and no more.

Eliza still spoke little: she had evidently no time to talk. I never saw a busier person than she seemed to be: yet it was difficult to say what she did: or rather, to discover any result of her diligence. She had an alarum to call her up early. I know not how she occupied herself before breakfast, but after that meal she divided her time into regular portions; and each hour had its allotted task. Three times a day she studied a little book, which I found, on inspection, was a Common Prayer-book. I asked her once what was the great attraction of that volume, and she said "the Rubric."[7] Three hours she gave

7. The section stating the rules for services.

to stitching, with gold thread, the border of a square crimson cloth, almost large enough for a carpet. In answer to my inquiries after the use of this article, she informed me it was a covering for the altar of a new church lately erected near Gateshead. Two hours she devoted to her diary; two to working by herself in the kitchen-garden; and one to the regulation of her accounts. She seemed to want no company; no conversation. I believe she was happy in her way: this routine sufficed to her; and nothing annoyed her so much as the occurrence of any incident which forced her to vary its clock-work regularity.

She told me one evening, when more disposed to be communicative than usual, that John's conduct, and the threatened ruin of the family, had been a source of profound affliction to her: but she had now, she said, settled her mind, and formed her resolution. Her own fortune she had taken care to secure; and when her mother died,—and it was wholly improbable, she tranquilly remarked, that she should either recover or linger long,—she would execute a long-cherished project: seek a retirement where punctual habits would be permanently secured from disturbance, and place safe barriers between herself and a frivolous world. I asked if Georgiana would accompany her.

"Of course not. Georgiana and she had nothing in common: they never had had. She would not be burdened with her society for any consideration. Georgiana should take her own course; and she, Eliza, would take hers."

Georgiana, when not unburdening her heart to me, spent most of her time in lying on the sofa, fretting about the dulness of the house, and wishing over and over again that her aunt Gibson would send her an invitation up to town. "It would be so much better," she said, "if she could only get out of the way for a month or two, till all was over." I did not ask what she meant by "all being over," but I suppose she referred to the expected decease of her mother and the gloomy sequel of funeral rites. Eliza generally took no more notice of her sister's indolence and complaints than if no such murmuring, lounging object had been before her. One day, however, as she put away her account book, and unfolded her embroidery, she suddenly took her up thus:
—"Georgiana, a more vain and absurd animal than you, was certainly never allowed to cumber the earth. You had no right to be born: for you make no use of life. Instead of living for, in, and with yourself, as a reasonable being ought, you seek only to fasten your feebleness on some other person's strength: if no one can be found willing to burden her or himself with such a fat, weak, puffy, useless thing, you cry out that you are ill-treated, neglected, miserable. Then, too, existence for you must be a scene of continual change and excitement, or else the world is a dungeon: you must be admired, you must be courted, you must be flattered—you must have music, dancing, and society—or you languish, you die away. Have you no sense to devise a system which will make you independent of all efforts, and all wills, but your own? Take one day; share it into sections; to each section apportion its task: leave no stray unemployed quarters of an hour, ten minutes, five minutes, include all; do each piece of business in its turn with method, with rigid regularity. The day will close almost before you are aware it has begun; and you are indebted to no one for helping you to get rid of one vacant moment; you have had to seek no one's company, conversation, sympathy,

forbearance: you have lived, in short, as an independent being ought to do. Take this advice: the first and last I shall offer you; then you will not want me or anyone else, happen what may. Neglect it—go on as heretofore, craving, whining, and idling—and suffer the results of your idiocy, however bad and insufferable they may be. I tell you this plainly; and listen: for though I shall no more repeat what I am now about to say, I shall steadily act on it. After my mother's death, I wash my hands of you: from the day her coffin is carried to the vault in Gateshead Church, you and I will be as separate as if we had never known each other. You need not think that because we chanced to be born of the same parents, I shall suffer you to fasten me down by even the feeblest claim; I can tell you this—if the whole human race, ourselves excepted, were swept away, and we two stood alone on the earth, I would leave you in the old world, and betake myself to the new."

She closed her lips.

"You might have spared yourself the trouble of delivering that tirade," answered Georgiana. "Everybody knows you are the most selfish, heartless creature in existence: and I know your spiteful hatred towards me; I have had a specimen of it before in the trick you played me about Lord Edwin Vere: you could not bear me to be raised above you, to have a title, to be received into circles where you dare not show your face, and so you acted the spy and informer, and ruined my prospects for ever." Georgiana took out her handkerchief and blew her nose for an hour afterwards; Eliza sat cold, impassible, and assiduously industrious.

True, generous feeling is made small account of by some: but here were two natures rendered, the one intolerably acrid, the other despicably savourless for the want of it. Feeling without judgment is a washy draught indeed; but judgment untempered by feeling is too bitter and husky a morsel for human deglutition.[8]

It was a wet and windy afternoon: Georgiana had fallen asleep on the sofa over the perusal of a novel; Eliza was gone to attend a saint's-day service at the new church—for in matters of religion she was a rigid formalist: no weather ever prevented the punctual discharge of what she considered her devotional duties: fair or foul, she went to church thrice every Sunday, and as often on week-days as there were prayers.

I bethought myself to go upstairs and see how the dying woman sped, who lay there almost unheeded: the very servants paid her but a remittent attention: the hired nurse, being little looked after, would slip out of the room whenever she could. Bessie was faithful; but she had her own family to mind, and could only come occasionally to the hall. I found the sick-room unwatched, as I had expected: no nurse was there; the patient lay still, and seemingly lethargic; her livid face sunk in the pillows: the fire was dying in the grate. I renewed the fuel, re-arranged the bed-clothes, gazed awhile on her who could not now gaze on me, and then I moved away to the window.

The rain beat strongly against the panes, the wind blew tempestuously: "One lies there," I thought, "who will soon be beyond the war of earthly elements. Whither will that spirit—now struggling to quit its material tenement—flit when at length released?"

8. Swallowing.

In pondering the great mystery, I thought of Helen Burns, recalled her dying words—her faith—her doctrine of equality of disembodied souls. I was still listening in thought to her well-remembered tones—still picturing her pale and spiritual aspect, her wasted face and sublime gaze, as she lay on her placid deathbed, and whispered her longing to be restored to her divine Father's bosom—when a feeble voice murmured from the couch behind: "Who is that?"

I knew Mrs. Reed had not spoken for days: was she reviving? I went up to her.

"It is I, aunt Reed."

"Who—I?" was her answer. "Who are you?" looking at me with surprise and a sort of alarm, but still not wildly. "You are quite a stranger to me—where is Bessie?"

"She is at the lodge, aunt."

"Aunt!" she repeated. "Who calls me aunt? You are not one of the Gibsons; and yet I know you—that face, and the eyes and forehead are quite familiar to me: you are like—why you are like Jane Eyre!"

I said nothing: I was afraid of occasioning some shock by declaring my identity.

"Yet," said she, "I am afraid it is a mistake: my thoughts deceive me. I wished to see Jane Eyre, and I fancy a likeness where none exists: besides, in eight years she must be so changed."

I now gently assured her that I was the person she supposed and desired me to be: and seeing that I was understood, and that her senses were quite collected, I explained how Bessie had sent her husband to fetch me from Thornfield.

"I am very ill, I know," she said ere long. "I was trying to turn myself a few minutes since, and find I cannot move a limb. It is as well I should ease my mind before I die: what we think little of in health, burdens us at such an hour as the present is to me. Is the nurse here? or is there no one in the room but you?"

I assured her we were alone.

"Well, I have twice done you a wrong which I regret now. One was in breaking the promise which I gave my husband to bring you up as my own child; the other—" she stopped. "After all it is of no great importance, perhaps," she murmured to herself: "and then I may get better; and to humble myself so to her is painful."

She made an effort to alter her position, but failed: her face changed; she seemed to experience some inward sensation—the precursor, perhaps, of the last pang.

"Well: I must get it over. Eternity is before me: I had better tell her.—Go to my dressing-case, open it, and take out a letter you will see there."

I obeyed her directions.

"Read the letter," she said.

It was short and thus conceived:

"Madam,—

"Will you have the goodness to send me the address of my niece, Jane Eyre, and to tell me how she is: it is my intention to write shortly and desire her to come to me at Madeira. Providence has blessed my endeavors to secure a

competency; and as I am unmarried and childless, I wish to adopt her during my life, and bequeath her at my death whatever I may have to leave.

I am, Madam, etc. etc.

John Eyre, Madeira."

It was dated three years back.

"Why did I never hear of this?" I asked.

"Because I disliked you too fixedly and thoroughly ever to lend a hand in lifting you to prosperity. I could not forget your conduct to me, Jane—the fury with which you once turned on me; the tone in which you declared you abhorred me the worst of anybody in the world; the unchildlike look and voice with which you affirmed that the very thought of me made you sick, and asserted that I had treated you with miserable cruelty. I could not forget my own sensations when you thus started up and poured out the venom of your mind: I felt fear, as if an animal that I had struck or pushed had looked up at me with human eyes and cursed me in a man's voice.—Bring me some water! Oh, make haste!"

"Dear Mrs. Reed," said I, as I offered her the draught she required, "think no more of all this, let it pass away from your mind. Forgive me for my passionate language: I was a child then; eight, nine years have passed since that day."

She heeded nothing of what I said; but when she had tasted the water and drawn breath, she went on thus:—"I tell you I could not forget it; and I took my revenge: for you to be adopted by your uncle, and placed in a state of ease and comfort, was what I could not endure. I wrote to him; I said I was sorry for his disappointment, but Jane Eyre was dead: she had died of typhus fever at Lowood. Now act as you please: write and contradict my assertion—expose my falsehood as soon as you like. You were born, I think, to be my torment: my last hour is racked by the recollection of a deed which, but for you, I should never have been tempted to commit."

"If you could but be persuaded to think no more of it, aunt, and to regard me with kindness and forgiveness"——

"You have a very bad disposition," said she, "and one to this day I feel it impossible to understand: how for nine years you could be patient and quiescent under any treatment, and in the tenth break out all fire and violence, I can never comprehend."

"My disposition is not so bad as you think: I am passionate, but not vindictive. Many a time, as a little child, I should have been glad to love you if you would have let me; and I long earnestly to be reconciled to you now: kiss me, aunt."

I approached my cheek to her lips: she would not touch it. She said I oppressed her by leaning over the bed; and again demanded water. As I laid her down—for I raised her and supported her on my arm while she drank—I covered her ice-cold and clammy hand with mine: the feeble fingers shrank from my touch—the glazing eyes shunned my gaze.

"Love me, then, or hate me, as you will," I said at last; "you have my full and free forgiveness: ask now for God's; and be at peace."

Poor, suffering woman! it was too late for her to make now the effort to change her habitual frame of mind: living, she had ever hated me—dying, she must hate me still.

The nurse now entered, and Bessie followed. I yet lingered half an hour longer, hoping to see some sign of amity: but she gave none. She was fast relapsing into stupor; nor did her mind again rally: at twelve o'clock that night she died. I was not present to close her eyes; nor were either of her daughters. They came to tell us the next morning that all was over. She was by that time laid out. Eliza and I went to look at her: Georgiana, who had burst out into loud weeping, said she dared not go. There was stretched Sarah Reed's once robust and active frame, rigid and still: her eye of flint was covered with its cold lid; her brow and strong traits wore yet the impress of her inexorable soul. A strange and solemn object was that corpse to me. I gazed on it with gloom and pain: nothing soft, nothing sweet, nothing pitying, or hopeful, or subduing, did it inspire; only a grating anguish for *her* woes—not my loss— and a somber tearless dismay at the fearfulness of death in such a form.

Eliza surveyed her parent calmly. After a silence of some minutes she observed, "With her constitution she should have lived to a good old age: her life was shortened by trouble." And then a spasm constricted her mouth for an instant: as it passed away she turned and left the room, and so did I. Neither of us had dropped a tear.

Chapter XXII

Mr. Rochester had given me but one week's leave of absence: yet a month elapsed before I quitted Gateshead. I wished to leave immediately after the funeral; but Georgiana entreated me to stay till she could get off to London: whither she was now at last invited by her uncle, Mr. Gibson; who had come down to direct his sister's interment and settle the family affairs. Georgiana said she dreaded being left alone with Eliza; from her she got neither sympathy in her dejection, support in her fears, nor aid in her preparations; so I bore with her feeble-minded quailings, and selfish lamentations, as well as I could, and did my best in sewing for her, and packing her dresses. It is true that while I worked she would idle; and I thought to myself, "If you and I were destined to live always together, cousin, we would commence matters on a different footing. I should not settle tamely down into being the forbearing party; I should assign you your share of labor, and compel you to accomplish it, or else it should be left undone: I should insist, also, on your keeping some of those drawling, half-insincere complaints hushed in your own breast. It is only because our connection happens to be very transitory, and comes at a peculiarly mournful season, that I consent thus to render it so patient and compliant on my part."

At last I saw Georgiana off; but now it was Eliza's turn to request me to stay another week. Her plans required all her time and attention, she said: she was about to depart for some unknown bourne; and all day long she stayed in her own room, her door bolted within, filling trunks, emptying drawers, burning papers, and holding no communication with anyone. She wished me to look after the house, to see callers, and answer notes of condolence.

One morning she told me I was at liberty. "And," she added, "I am obliged to you for your valuable services and discreet conduct! There is some difference between living with such a one as you, and with Georgiana: you perform you own part in life, and burden no one. Tomorrow," she continued, "I set

out for the Continent. I shall take up my abode in a religious house near Lisle—a nunnery you would call it: there I shall be quiet and unmolested. I shall devote myself for a time to the examination of the Roman Catholic dogmas, and to a careful study of the workings of their system; if I find it to be, as I half suspect it is, the one best calculated to ensure the doing of all things decently and in order, I shall embrace the tenets of Rome and probably take the veil."

I neither expressed surprise at this resolution nor attempted to dissuade her from it. "The vocation will fit you to a hair," I thought: "much good may it do you!"

When we parted, she said: "Good-bye, cousin Jane Eyre; I wish you well: you have some sense."

I then returned: "You are not without sense, cousin Eliza; but what you have I suppose in another year will be walled up alive in a French convent. However, it is not my business, and so it suits you—I don't much care."

"You are in the right," said she: and with these words we each went our separate way. As I shall not have occasion to refer either to her or her sister again, I may as well mention here that Georgiana made an advantageous match with a wealthy worn-out man of fashion; and that Eliza actually took the veil, and is at this day superior of the convent where she passed the period of her novitiate: and which she endowed with her fortune.

How people feel when they are returning home from an absence, long or short, I did not know: I had never experienced the sensation. I had known what it was to come back to Gateshead when a child, after a long walk—to be scolded for looking cold or gloomy; and later, what it was to come back from church to Lowood—to long for a plenteous meal and a good fire, and to be unable to get either. Neither of these returnings were very pleasant or desirable: no magnet drew me to a given point, increasing in its strength of attraction the nearer I came. The return to Thornfield was yet to be tried.

My journey seemed tedious—very tedious: fifty miles one day, a night spent at an inn; fifty miles the next day. During the first twelve hours I thought of Mrs. Reed in her last moments; I saw her disfigured and discolored face, and heard her strangely altered voice. I mused on the funeral day, the coffin, the hearse, the black train of tenants and servants—few was the number of relatives—the gaping vault, the silent church, the solemn service. Then I thought of Eliza and Georgiana: I beheld one the cynosure[9] of a ball-room, the other the inmate of a convent cell; and I dwelt on and analyzed their separate peculiarities of person and character. The evening arrival at the great town of —— scattered these thoughts; night gave them quite another turn: laid down on my traveller's bed, I left reminiscence for anticipation.

I was going back to Thornfield: but how long was I to stay there? Not long; of that I was sure. I had heard from Mrs. Fairfax in the interim of my absence: the party at the hall was dispersed; Mr. Rochester had left for London three weeks ago, but he was then expected to return in a fortnight. Mrs. Fairfax surmised that he was gone to make arrangements for his wedding, as he had talked of purchasing a new carriage: she said the idea of his marrying Miss Ingram still seemed strange to her; but from what everybody said, and from

9. Center of attention.

what she had herself seen, she could no longer doubt that the event would shortly take place. "You would be strangely incredulous if you did doubt it," was my mental comment. "I don't doubt it."

The question followed, "Where was I to go?" I dreamt of Miss Ingram all the night: in a vivid morning dream I saw her closing the gates of Thornfield against me and pointing me out another road; and Mr. Rochester looked on with his arms folded—smiling sardonically, as it seemed, at both her and me.

I had not notified to Mrs. Fairfax the exact day of my return; for I did not wish either car or carriage to meet me at Millcote. I proposed to walk the distance quietly by myself; and very quietly, after leaving my box in the ostler's[1] care, did I slip away from the George Inn, about six o'clock of a June evening, and take the old road to Thornfield: a road which lay chiefly through fields, and was now little frequented.

It was not a bright or splendid summer evening, though fair and soft: the haymakers were at work all along the road; and the sky, though far from cloudless, was such as promised well for the future: its blue—where blue was visible—was mild and settled, and its cloud strata high and thin. The west, too, was warm: no watery gleam chilled it—it seemed as if there was a fire lit, an altar burning behind its screen of marbled vapor, and out of apertures shone a golden redness.

I felt glad as the road shortened before me: so glad that I stopped once to ask myself what that joy meant: and to remind reason that it was not to my home I was going, or to a permanent resting-place, or to a place where fond friends looked out for me and waited my arrival. "Mrs. Fairfax will smile you a calm welcome, to be sure," said I; "and little Adèle will clap her hands and jump to see you; but you know very well you are thinking of another than they; and that he is not thinking of you."

But what is so headstrong as youth? What so blind as inexperience? These affirmed that it was pleasure enough to have the privilege of again looking on Mr. Rochester, whether he looked on me or not; and they added—"Hasten! hasten! be with him while you may: but a few more days or weeks, at most, and you are parted with him for ever!" And then I strangled a new-born agony—a deformed thing which I could not persuade myself to own and rear—and ran on.

They are making hay, too, in Thornfield meadows: or, rather, the laborers are just quitting their work, and returning home with their rakes on their shoulders: now, at the hour I arrive. I have but a field or two to traverse, and then I shall cross the road and reach the gates. How full the hedges are of roses! But I have no time to gather any; I want to be at the house. I passed a tall briar, shooting leafy and flowery branches across the path; I see the narrow stile with stone steps; and I see—Mr. Rochester sitting there, a book and a pencil in his hand: he is writing.

Well, he is not a ghost; yet every nerve I have is unstrung: for a moment I am beyond my own mastery. What does it mean? I did not think I should tremble in this way when I saw him—or lose my voice or the power of motion in his presence. I will go back as soon as I can stir: I need not make an

1. The man who cares for horses at an inn.

absolute fool of myself. I know another way to the house. It does not signify if I knew twenty ways; for he has seen me.

"Hallo!" he cries; and he puts up his book and his pencil. "There you are! Come on, if you please."

I suppose I do come on; though in what fashion I know not: being scarcely cognizant of my movements, and solicitous only to appear calm; and, above all, to control the working muscles of my face—which I feel rebel insolently against my will, and struggle to express what I had resolved to conceal. But I have a veil—it is down: I may make shift yet to behave with decent composure.

"And this is Jane Eyre? Are you coming from Millcote, and on foot? Yes—just one of your tricks: not to send for a carriage, and come clattering over the street and road like a common mortal, but to steal into the vicinage of your home along with twilight, just as if you were a dream or a shade. What the deuce have you done with yourself this last month?"

"I have been with my aunt, sir, who is dead."

"A true Janian reply! Good angels be my guard! She comes from the other world—from the abode of people who are dead; and tells me so when she meets me alone here in the gloaming! If I dared, I'd touch you, to see if you are substance or shadow, you elf!—but I'd as soon offer to take hold of a blue *ignis fatuus* light[2] in a marsh. Truant! truant!" he added, when he had paused an instant. "Absent from me a whole month: and forgetting me quite, I'll be sworn!"

I knew there would be pleasure in meeting my master again; even though broken by the fear that he was so soon to cease to be my master, and by the knowledge that I was nothing to him: but there was ever in Mr. Rochester (so at least I thought) such a wealth of the power of communicating happiness, that to taste but of the crumbs he scattered to stray and stranger birds like me was to feast genially. His last words were balm: they seemed to imply that it imported something to him whether I forgot him or not. And he had spoken of Thornfield as my home—would that it were my home!

He did not leave the stile, and I hardly liked to ask to go by. I inquired soon if he had not been to London.

"Yes: I suppose you found that out by second-sight."

"Mrs. Fairfax told me in a letter."

"And did she inform you what I went to do?"

"Oh, yes, sir! Everybody knew your errand."

"You must see the carriage, Jane, and tell me if you don't think it will suit Mrs. Rochester exactly; and whether she won't look like Queen Boadicea,[3] leaning back against those purple cushions. I wish, Jane, I were a trifle better adapted to match with her externally. Tell me now, fairy as you are,—can't you give me a charm, or a philter,[4] or something of that sort, to make me a handsome man?"

"It would be past the power of magic, sir;" and, in thought, I added, "A loving eye is all the charm needed: to such you are handsome enough; or rather, your sternness has a power beyond beauty."

Mr. Rochester had sometimes read my unspoken thoughts with an acumen

2. Light from marsh gas.
3. Early British queen (d. 60 C.E.), who led a revolt against the Romans.
4. A potion.

to me incomprehensible: in the present instance he took no notice of my abrupt vocal response; but he smiled at me with a certain smile he had of his own, and which he used but on rare occasions. He seemed to think it too good for common purposes: it was the real sunshine of feeling—he shed it over me now.

"Pass, Janet," said he, making room for me to cross the stile: "go up home, and stay your weary little wandering feet at a friend's threshold."

All I had now to do was to obey him in silence: no need for me to colloquize further. I got over the stile without a word, and meant to leave him calmly. An impulse held me fast,—a force turned me round. I said—or something in me said for me, and in spite of me:—

"Thank you, Mr. Rochester, for your great kindness. I am strangely glad to get back again to you; and wherever you are is my home—my only home."

I walked on so fast that even he could hardly have overtaken me had he tried. Little Adèle was half wild with delight when she saw me. Mrs. Fairfax received me with her usual plain friendliness. Leah smiled; and even Sophie bid me "bon soir"[5] with glee. This was very pleasant: there is no happiness like that of being loved by your fellow creatures, and feeling that your presence is an addition to their comfort.

I, that evening, shut my eyes resolutely against the future: I stopped my ears against the voice that kept warning me of near separation and coming grief. When tea was over and Mrs. Fairfax had taken her knitting, and I had assumed a low seat near her, and Adèle, kneeling on the carpet, had nestled close up to me, and a sense of mutual affection seemed to surround us with a ring of golden peace, I uttered a silent prayer that we might not be parted far or soon; but when, as we thus sat, Mr. Rochester entered, unannounced, and looking at us, seemed to take pleasure in the spectacle of a group so amicable—when he said he supposed the old lady was all right now that she had got her adopted daughter back again, and added that he saw Adèle was "prête à croquer sa petite maman Anglaise"[6]—I half ventured to hope that he would, even after his marriage, keep us together somewhere under the shelter of his protection, and not quite exiled from the sunshine of his presence.

A fortnight of dubious calm succeeded my return to Thornfield Hall. Nothing was said of the master's marriage, and I saw no preparation going on for such an event. Almost every day I asked Mrs. Fairfax if she had yet heard anything decided: her answer was always in the negative. Once, she said, she had actually put the question to Mr. Rochester as to when he was going to bring his bride home; but he had answered her only by a joke, and one of his queer looks, and she could not tell what to make of him.

One thing specially surprised me, and that was, there were no journeyings backward and forward, no visits to Ingram Park: to be sure it was twenty miles off, on the borders of another county; but what was that distance to an ardent lover? To so practiced and indefatigable a horseman as Mr. Rochester it would be but a morning's ride. I began to cherish hopes I had no right to conceive: that the match was broken off; that rumor had been mistaken; that one or both parties had changed their minds. I used to look at my master's face to see if it were sad or fierce; but I could not remember the

5. Good evening. 6. Ready to devour her little English mother.

time when it had been so uniformly clear of clouds or evil feelings. If, in the moments I and my pupil spent with him, I lacked spirits and sank into inevitable dejection, he became even gay. Never had he called me more frequently to his presence; never been kinder to me when there—and, alas! never had I loved him so well.

Chapter XXIII

A splendid Midsummer shone over England: skies so pure, suns so radiant as were then seen in long succession, seldom favor, even singly, our wave-girt land. It was as if a band of Italian days had come from the South, like a flock of glorious passenger birds, and lighted to rest them on the cliffs of Albion.[7] The hay was all got in; the fields round Thornfield were green and shorn; the roads white and baked; the trees were in their dark prime; hedge and wood, full-leaved and deeply tinted, contrasted well with the sunny hue of the cleared meadows between.

On Midsummer-eve, Adèle, weary with gathering wild strawberries in Hay Lane half the day, had gone to bed with the sun. I watched her drop asleep, and when I left her I sought the garden.

It was now the sweetest hour of the twenty-four:—"Day its fervid fires had wasted,"[8] and dew fell cool on panting plain and scorched summit. Where the sun had gone down in simple state—pure of the pomp of clouds—spread a solemn purple, burning with the light of red jewel and furnace flame at one point, on one hill-peak, and extending high and wide, soft and still softer, over half heaven. The east had its own charm of fine, deep blue, and its own modest gem, a rising and solitary star: soon it would boast the moon; but she was yet beneath the horizon.

I walked a while on the pavement; but a subtle, well-known scent—that of a cigar—stole from some window; I saw the library casement open a hand-breath; I knew I might be watched thence; so I went apart into the orchard. No nook in the grounds more sheltered and more Eden-like; it was full of trees, it bloomed with flowers: a very high wall shut it out from the court, on one side; on the other, a beech avenue screened it from the lawn. At the bottom was a sunk fence; its sole separation from lonely fields; a winding walk, bordered with laurels and terminating in a giant horse-chestnut, circled at the base by a seat, led down to the fence. Here one could wander unseen. While such honey-dew fell, such silence reigned, such gloaming gathered, I felt as if I could haunt such shade for ever: but in threading the flower and fruit parterres at the upper part of the enclosure, enticed there by the light the now-rising moon casts on this more open quarter, my step is stayed—not by sound, not by sight, but once more by a warning fragrance.

Sweet briar and southernwood, jasmine, pink, and rose, have long been yielding their evening sacrifice of incense: this new scent is neither of shrub nor flower; it is—I know it well—it is Mr. Rochester's cigar. I look round, and I listen. I see trees laden with ripening fruit. I hear a nightingale warbling in a wood half a mile off; no moving form is visible, no coming step audible; but that perfume increases: I must flee. I make for the wicket leading to the

7. England.
8. From Thomas Campbell's "The Turkish Lady" (1805).

shrubbery, and I see Mr. Rochester entering. I step aside into the ivy recess; he will not stay long: he will soon return whence he came, and if I sit still he will never see me.

But no—eventide is as pleasant to him as to me, and this antique garden as attractive; and he strolls on, now lifting the gooseberry tree branches to look at the fruit, large as plums, with which they are laden; now taking a ripe cherry from the wall; now stooping towards a knot of flowers, either to inhale their fragrance or to admire the dew-beads on their petals. A great moth goes humming by me; it alights on a plant at Mr. Rochester's foot: he sees it, and bends to examine it.

"Now he has his back towards me," thought I, "and he is occupied too; perhaps, if I walk softly, I can slip away unnoticed."

I trod on an edging of turf that the crackle of the pebbly gravel might not betray me: he was standing among the beds at a yard or two distant from where I had to pass; the moth apparently engaged him. "I shall get by very well," I meditated. As I crossed his shadow, thrown long over the garden by the moon, not yet risen high, he said quietly without turning:—"Jane, come and look at this fellow."

I had made no noise: he had not eyes behind—could his shadow feel? I started at first, and then I approached him.

"Look at his wings," said he; "he reminds me rather of a West Indian insect; one does not often see so large and gay a night-rover in England: there! he is flown."

The moth roamed away. I was sheepishly retreating also; but Mr. Rochester followed me, and when we reached the wicket, he said:—"Turn back: on so lovely a night it is a shame to sit in the house; and surely no one can wish to go to bed while sunset is thus at meeting with moonrise."

It is one of my faults that, though my tongue is sometimes prompt enough at an answer, there are times when it sadly fails me in framing an excuse; and always the lapse occurs at some crisis, when a facile word or plausible pretext is specially wanted to get me out of painful embarrassment. I did not like to walk at this hour alone with Mr. Rochester in the shadowy orchard; but I could not find a reason to allege for leaving him. I followed with lagging step, and thoughts busily bent on discovering a means of extrication; but he himself looked so composed, and so grave also, I became ashamed of feeling any confusion: the evil—if evil existent or prospective there was—seemed to lie with me only; his mind was unconscious and quiet.

"Jane," he recommenced, as we entered the laurel walk, and slowly strayed down in the direction of the sunk fence and the horse-chestnut, "Thornfield is a pleasant place in summer, is it not?"

"Yes, sir."

"You must have become in some degree attached to the house,—you, who have an eye for natural beauties, and a good deal of the organ of Adhesiveness?"

"I am attached to it, indeed."

"And though I don't comprehend how it is, I perceive you have acquired a degree of regard for that foolish little child, Adèle, too; and even for simple dame Fairfax?"

"Yes, sir; in different ways, I have an affection for both."

"And would be sorry to part with them?"

"Yes."

"Pity!" he said, and sighed and paused. "It is always the way of events in this life," he continued presently: "no sooner have you got settled in a pleasant resting-place, than a voice calls out to you to rise and move on, for the hour of repose is expired."

"Must I move on, sir?" I asked. "Must I leave Thornfield?"

"I believe you must, Jane. I am sorry, Janet, but I believe indeed you must."

This was a blow: but I did not let it prostrate me.

"Well, sir, I shall be ready when the order to march comes."

"It is come now—I must give it tonight."

"Then you are going to be married, sir?"

"Ex-act-ly—pre-cise-ly: with your usual acuteness, you have hit the nail straight on the head."

"Soon, sir?"

"Very soon, my——that is, Miss Eyre: and you'll remember, Jane, the first time I, or Rumor, plainly intimated to you that it was my intention to put my old bachelor's neck into the sacred noose, to enter into the holy estate of matrimony—to take Miss Ingram to my bosom, in short (she's an extensive armful: but that's not to the point—one can't have too much of such a very excellent thing as my beautiful Blanche): well, as I was saying—listen to me, Jane! You're not turning your head to look after more moths, are you? That was only a lady-clock,[9] child, 'flying away home.' I wish to remind you that it was you who first said to me, with that discretion I respect in you—with that foresight, prudence, and humility which befit your responsible and dependent position—that in case I married Miss Ingram—both you and little Adèle had better trot forthwith. I pass over the sort of slur conveyed in this suggestion on the character of my beloved; indeed, when you are far away, Janet, I'll try to forget it: I shall notice only its wisdom; which is such that I have made it my law of action. Adèle must go to school; and you, Miss Eyre, must get a new situation."

"Yes, sir, I will advertise immediately: and meantime, I suppose"——I was going to say, "I suppose I may stay here till I find another shelter to betake myself to:" but I stopped, feeling it would not do to risk a long sentence, for my voice was not quite under command.

"In about a month I hope to be a bridegroom," continued Mr. Rochester; "and in the interim I shall myself look out for employment and an asylum for you."

"Thank you, sir; I am sorry to give——"

"Oh, no need to apologize! I consider that when a dependent does her duty as well as you have done yours, she has a sort of claim upon her employer for any little assistance he can conveniently render her; indeed I have already, through my future mother-in-law, heard of a place that I think will suit: it is to undertake the education of the five daughters of Mrs. Dionysius O'Gall, of Bitternutt Lodge, Connaught, Ireland. You'll like Ireland, I think: they're such warm-hearted people there, they say."

"It is a long way off, sir."

"No matter—a girl of your sense will not object to the voyage or the distance."

9. Ladybug.

"Not the voyage, but the distance: and then the sea is a barrier——"

"From what, Jane?"

"From England and from Thornfield: and——"

"Well?"

"From *you*, sir."

I said this almost involuntarily; and, with as little sanction of free will, my tears gushed out. I did not cry so as to be heard, however; I avoided sobbing. The thought of Mrs. O'Gall and Bitternutt Lodge struck cold to my heart; and colder the thought of all the brine and foam, destined, as it seemed, to rush between me and the master at whose side I now walked! and coldest the remembrance of the wider ocean—wealth, caste, custom intervened between me and what I naturally and inevitably loved.

"It is a long way," I again said.

"It is to be sure; and when you get to Bitternutt Lodge, Connaught, Ireland, I shall never see you again, Jane: that's morally certain. I never go over to Ireland, not having myself much of a fancy for the country. We have been good friends, Jane; have we not?"

"Yes, sir."

"And when friends are on the eve of separation, they like to spend the little time that remains to them close to each other. Come—we'll talk over the voyage and the parting quietly, half an hour or so, while the stars enter into their shining life up in heaven yonder: here is the chestnut tree: here is the bench at its old roots. Come, we will sit there in peace tonight, though we should never more be destined to sit there together." He seated me and himself.

"It is a long way to Ireland, Janet, and I am sorry to send my little friend on such weary travels; but if I can't do better, how is it to be helped? Are you anything akin to me, do you think, Jane?"

I could risk no sort of answer by this time: my heart was full.

"Because," he said, "I sometimes have a queer feeling with regard to you—especially when you are near me, as now: it is as if I had a string somewhere under my left ribs, tightly and inextricably knotted to a similar string situated in the corresponding quarter of your little frame. And if that boisterous channel, and two hundred miles or so of land come broad between us, I am afraid that cord of communion will be snapped; and then I've a nervous notion I should take to bleeding inwardly. As for you—you'd forget me."

"That I *never* should, sir: you know"——impossible to proceed.

"Jane, do you hear that nightingale singing in the wood? Listen!"

In listening, I sobbed convulsively; for I could repress what I endured no longer; I was obliged to yield, and I was shaken from head to foot with acute distress. When I did speak, it was only to express an impetuous wish that I had never been born, or never come to Thornfield.

"Because you are sorry to leave it?"

The vehemence of emotion, stirred by grief and love within me, was claiming mastery, and struggling for full sway; and asserting a right to predominate: to overcome, to live, rise, and reign at last; yes,—and to speak.

"I grieve to leave Thornfield: I love Thornfield—I love it, because I have lived in it a full and delightful life,—momentarily at least. I have not been trampled on. I have not been petrified. I have not been buried with inferior minds, and excluded from every glimpse of communion with what is bright

and energetic, and high. I have talked, face to face, with what I reverence;
with what I delight in,—with an original, a vigorous, an expanded mind. I
have known you, Mr. Rochester; and it strikes me with terror and anguish
to feel I absolutely must be torn from you for ever. I see the necessity of
departure; and it is like looking on the necessity of death."

"Where do you see the necessity?" he asked, suddenly.

"Where? You, sir, have placed it before me."

"In what shape?"

"In the shape of Miss Ingram; a noble and beautiful woman,—your bride."

"My bride! What bride? I have no bride!"

"But you will have."

"Yes;—I will!—I will!" He set his teeth.

"Then I must go—you have said it yourself."

"No: you must stay! I swear it—and the oath shall be kept."

"I tell you I must go!" I retorted, roused to something like passion. "Do
you think I can stay to become nothing to you? Do you think I am an autom-
aton?—a machine without feelings? and can bear to have my morsel of bread
snatched from my lips, and my drop of living water dashed from my cup? Do
you think, because I am poor, obscure, plain, and little, I am soulless and
heartless? You think wrong!—I have as much soul as you,—and full as much
heart! And if God had gifted me with some beauty and much wealth, I should
have made it as hard for you to leave me, as it is now for me to leave you. I
am not talking to you now through the medium of custom, conventionalities,
nor even of mortal flesh—it is my spirit that addresses your spirit; just as if
both had passed through the grave, and we stood at God's feet, equal,—as
we are!"

[margin annotation: blows up @ him finally just like @ miss feed]

"As we are!" repeated Mr. Rochester—"so," he added, enclosing me in his
arms, gathering me to his breast, pressing his lips on my lips: "So, Jane!"

"Yes, so, sir," I rejoined: "and yet not so; for you are a married man—or
as good as a married man, and wed to one inferior to you—to one with whom
you have no sympathy—whom I do not believe you truly love; for I have seen
and heard you sneer at her. I would scorn such a union: therefore I am better
than you—let me go!"

"Where, Jane? To Ireland?"

"Yes—to Ireland. I have spoken my mind, and can go anywhere now."

"Jane, be still; don't struggle so, like a wild, frantic bird that is rending its
own plumage in its desperation."

"I am no bird; and no net ensnares me: I am a free human being with an
independent will; which I now exert to leave you."

Another effort set me at liberty, and I stood erect before him.

"And your will shall decide your destiny," he said: "I offer you my hand,
my heart, and a share of all my possessions."

"You play a farce, which I merely laugh at."

"I ask you to pass through life at my side—to be my second self, and best
earthly companion."

"For that fate you have already made your choice, and must abide by it."

"Jane, be still a few moments; you are over-excited: I will be still too."

A waft of wind came sweeping down the laurel walk, and trembled through
the boughs of the chestnut: it wandered away—away—to an indefinite dis-
tance—it died. The nightingale's song was then the only voice of the hour:

in listening to it, I again wept. Mr. Rochester sat quiet, looking at me gently and seriously. Some time passed before he spoke; he at last said:—"Come to my side, Jane, and let us explain and understand one another."

"I will never again come to your side: I am torn away now, and cannot return."

"But, Jane, I summon you as my wife: it is you only I intend to marry."

I was silent: I thought he mocked me.

"Come, Jane—come hither."

"Your bride stands between us."

He rose, and with a stride reached me.

"My bride is here," he said, again drawing me to him, "because my equal is here, and my likeness. Jane, will you marry me?"

Still I did not answer, and still I writhed myself from his grasp: for I was still incredulous.

"Do you doubt me, Jane?"

"Entirely."

"You have no faith in me?"

"Not a whit."

"Am I a liar in your eyes?" he asked passionately. "Little sceptic, you *shall* be convinced. What love have I for Miss Ingram? None: and that you know. What love has she for me? None: as I have taken pains to prove; I caused a rumor to reach her that my fortune was not a third of what was supposed, and after that I presented myself to see the result; it was coldness both from her and her mother. I would not—I could not—marry Miss Ingram. You— you strange—you almost unearthly thing!—I love as my own flesh. You— poor and obscure, and small and plain as you are—I entreat to accept me as a husband."

"What, me!" I ejaculated: beginning in his earnestness—and especially in his incivility—to credit his sincerity: "me who have not a friend in the world but you—if you are my friend: not a shilling but what you have given me?"

"You, Jane. I must have you for my own—entirely my own. Will you be mine? Say yes, quickly."

"Mr. Rochester, let me look at your face: turn to the moonlight."

"Why?"

"Because I want to read your countenance; turn!"

"There: you will find it scarcely more legible than a crumpled, scratched page. Read on: only make haste, for I suffer."

His face was very much agitated and very much flushed, and there were strong workings in the features, and strange gleams in the eyes.

"Oh, Jane, you torture me!" he exclaimed. "With that searching and yet faithful and generous look, you torture me!"

"How can I do that? If you are true, and your offer real, my only feelings to you must be gratitude and devotion—they cannot torture."

"Gratitude!" he ejaculated; and added wildly—"Jane, accept me quickly. Say, Edward—give me my name—Edward—I will marry you."

"Are you in earnest?—Do you truly love me? Do you sincerely wish me to be your wife?"

"I do; and if an oath is necessary to satisfy you, I swear it."

"Then, sir, I will marry you."

"Edward—my little wife!"

"Dear Edward!"

"Come to me—come to me entirely now," said he: and added, in his deepest tone, speaking in my ear as his cheek was laid on mine, "Make my happiness—I will make yours."

"God pardon me!" he subjoined ere long; "and man meddle not with me: I have her, and will hold her."

"There is no one to meddle, sir. I have no kindred to interfere."

"No—that is the best of it," he said.

And if I loved him less I should have thought his accent and look of exultation savage; but, sitting by him, roused from the nightmare of parting—called to the paradise of union—I thought only of the bliss given me to drink in so abundant a flow. Again and again he said, "Are you happy, Jane?" and again and again I answered, "Yes." After which he murmured, "It will atone—it will atone. Have I not found her friendless, and cold, and comfortless? Will I not guard, and cherish, and solace her? Is there not love in my heart, and constancy in my resolves? It will expiate at God's tribunal. I know my Maker sanctions what I do. For the world's judgment—I wash my hands thereof. For man's opinion—I defy it."

But what had befallen the night? The moon was not yet set, and we were all in shadow: I could scarcely see my master's face, near as I was. And what ailed the chestnut tree? it writhed and groaned; while wind roared in the laurel walk, and came sweeping over us.

"We must go in," said Mr. Rochester: "the weather changes. I could have sat with thee till morning, Jane."

"And so," thought I, "could I with you." I should have said so, perhaps, but a livid, vivid spark leapt out of a cloud at which I was looking, and there was a crack, a crash, and a close rattling peal; and I thought only of hiding my dazzled eyes against Mr. Rochester's shoulder.

The rain rushed down. He hurried me up the walk, through the grounds, and into the house; but we were quite wet before we could pass the threshold. He was taking off my shawl in the hall, and shaking the water out of my loosened hair, when Mrs. Fairfax emerged from her room. I did not observe her at first, nor did Mr. Rochester. The lamp was lit. The clock was on the stroke of twelve.

"Hasten to take off your wet things," said he; "and before you go, good-night—good-night, my darling!"

He kissed me repeatedly. When I looked up, on leaving his arms, there stood the widow, pale, grave, and amazed. I only smiled at her, and ran upstairs. "Explanation will do for another time," thought I. Still, when I reached my chamber, I felt a pang at the idea that she should even temporarily misconstrue what she had seen. But joy soon effaced every other feeling; and loud as the wind blew, near and deep as the thunder crashed, fierce and frequent as the lightning gleamed, cataract-like as the rain fell during a storm of two hours' duration, I experienced no fear, and little awe. Mr. Rochester came thrice to my door in the course of it, to ask if I was safe and tranquil: and that was comfort, that was strength for anything.

Before I left my bed in the morning, little Adèle came running in to tell me that the great horse-chestnut at the bottom of the orchard had been struck by lightning in the night, and half of it split away.

Chapter XXIV

As I rose and dressed, I thought over what had happened, and wondered if it were a dream. I could not be certain of the reality till I had seen Mr. Rochester again, and heard him renew his words of love and promise.

While arranging my hair, I looked at my face in the glass, and felt it was no longer plain: there was hope in its aspect, and life in its color; and my eyes seemed as if they had beheld the fount of fruition, and borrowed beams from the lustrous ripple. I had often been unwilling to look at my master, because I feared he could not be pleased at my look; but I was sure I might lift my face to his now, and not cool his affection by its expression. I took a plain but clean and light summer dress from my drawer and put it on: it seemed no attire had ever so well become me; because none had I ever worn in so blissful a mood.

I was not surprised, when I ran down into the hall, to see that a brilliant June morning had succeeded to the tempest of the night; and to feel, through the open glass door, the breathing of a fresh and fragrant breeze. Nature must be gladsome when I was so happy. A beggar-woman and her little boy— pale, ragged objects both—were coming up the walk, and I ran down and gave them all the money I happened to have in my purse—some three or four shillings: good or bad, they must partake of my jubilee. The rooks cawed, and blither birds sang; but nothing was so merry or so musical as my own rejoicing heart.

Mrs. Fairfax surprised me by looking out of the window with a sad countenance, and saying gravely:—"Miss Eyre, will you come to breakfast?" During the meal she was quiet and cool: but I could not undeceive her then. I must wait for my master to give explanations; and so must she. I ate what I could, and then I hastened upstairs. I met Adèle leaving the school-room.

"Where are you going? It is time for lessons."

"Mr. Rochester has sent me away to the nursery."

"Where is he?"

"In there," pointing to the apartment she had left; and I went in, and there he stood.

"Come and bid me good-morning," said he. I gladly advanced; and it was not merely a cold word now, or even a shake of the hand that I received, but an embrace and a kiss. It seemed natural; it seemed genial to be so well-loved, so caressed by him.

"Jane, you look blooming, and smiling, and pretty," said he: "truly pretty this morning. Is this my pale, little elf? Is this my mustard-seed?[1] This little sunny-faced girl with the dimpled cheek and rosy lips; the satin-smooth hazel hair, and the radiant hazel eyes?" (I had green eyes, reader; but you must excuse the mistake: for him they were new-dyed, I suppose.)

"It is Jane Eyre, sir."

"Soon to be Jane Rochester," he added: "in four weeks, Janet, not a day more. Do you hear that?"

I did, and I could not quite comprehend it: it made me giddy. The feeling, the announcement sent through me, was something stronger than was con-

1. Name of one of the fairies in Shakespeare's *A Midsummer Night's Dream*.

sistent with joy—something that smote and stunned: it was, I think, almost fear.

"You blushed, and now you are white, Jane: what is that for?"

"Because you gave me a new name—Jane Rochester; and it seems so strange."

"Yes, Mrs. Rochester," said he; "young Mrs. Rochester—Fairfax Rochester's girl-bride."

"It can never be, sir; it does not sound likely. Human beings never enjoy complete happiness in this world. I was not born for a different destiny to the rest of my species: to imagine such a lot befalling me is a fairy tale—a day-dream."

"Which I can and will realize. I shall begin today. This morning I wrote to my banker in London to send me certain jewels he has in his keeping,—heirlooms for the ladies of Thornfield. In a day or two I hope to pour them into your lap: for every privilege, every attention shall be yours, that I would accord a peer's daughter, if about to marry her."

"Oh, sir!—never mind jewels! I don't like to hear them spoken of. Jewels for Jane Eyre sounds unnatural and strange: I would rather not have them."

"I will myself put the diamond chain round your neck, and the circlet on your forehead,—which it will become: for nature, at least, has stamped her patent of nobility on this brow, Jane; and I will clasp the bracelets on these fine wrists, and load these fairy-like fingers with rings."

"No, no, sir! think of other subjects, and speak of other things, and in another strain. Don't address me as if I were a beauty; I am your plain, Quakerish governess."

"You are a beauty, in my eyes; and a beauty just after the desire of my heart,—delicate and aërial."

"Puny and insignificant, you mean. You are dreaming, sir,—or you are sneering. For God's sake, don't be ironical!"

"I will make the world acknowledge you a beauty too," he went on, while I really became uneasy at the strain he had adopted; because I felt he was either deluding himself, or trying to delude me. "I will attire my Jane in satin and lace, and she shall have roses in her hair; and I will cover the head I love best with a priceless veil."

"And then you won't know me, sir; and I shall not be your Jane Eyre any longer, but an ape in a harlequin's[2] jacket,—a jay in borrowed plumes. I would as soon see you, Mr. Rochester, tricked out in stage-trappings, as myself clad in a court-lady's robe; and I don't call you handsome, sir, though I love you most dearly: far too dearly to flatter you. Don't flatter me."

He pursued his theme, however, without noticing my deprecation. "This very day I shall take you in the carriage to Millcote, and you must choose some dresses for yourself. I told you we shall be married in four weeks. The wedding is to take place quietly, in the church down below yonder; and then I shall waft you away at once to town. After a brief stay there, I shall bear my treasure to regions nearer the sun: to French vineyards and Italian plains; and she shall see whatever is famous in old story and in modern record: she shall taste, too, of the life of cities; and she shall learn to value herself by just comparison with others."

2. I.e., clown's.

"Shall I travel?—and with you, sir?"

"You shall sojourn at Paris, Rome, and Naples: at Florence, Venice, and Vienna: all the ground I have wandered over shall be retrodden by you: wherever I stamped my hoof, your sylph's[3] foot shall step also. Ten years since, I flew through Europe half mad; with disgust, hate, and rage, as my companions; now I shall revisit it healed and cleansed, with a very angel as my comforter."

I laughed at him as he said this. "I am not an angel," I asserted; "and I will not be one till I die: I will be myself. Mr. Rochester, you must neither expect nor exact anything celestial of me—for you will not get it, any more than I shall get it of you: which I do not at all anticipate."

"What do you anticipate of me?"

"For a little while you will perhaps be as you are now,—a very little while; and then you will turn cool; and then you will be capricious; and then you will be stern, and I shall have much ado to please you: but when you get well used to me, you will perhaps like me again—*like* me, I say, not *love* me. I suppose your love will effervesce in six months, or less. I have observed in books written by men, that period assigned as the farthest to which a husband's ardor extends. Yet, after all, as a friend and companion, I hope never to become quite distasteful to my dear master."

"Distasteful! and like you again! I think I shall like you again and yet again: and I will make you confess I do not only *like*, but *love* you—with truth, fervor, constancy."

"Yet are you not capricious, sir?"

"To women who please me only by their faces, I am the very devil when I find out they have neither souls nor hearts—when they open to me a perspective of flatness, triviality, and perhaps imbecility, coarseness, and ill-temper: but to the clear eye and eloquent tongue, to the soul made of fire, and the character that bends but does not break—at once supple and stable, tractable and consistent—I am ever tender and true."

"Had you ever experience of such a character, sir? Did you ever love such an one?"

"I love it now."

"But before me: if I, indeed, in any respect come up to that difficult standard?"

"I never met your likeness. Jane: you please me, and you master me—you seem to submit, and I like the sense of pliancy you impart: and while I am twining the soft, silken skein round my finger, it sends a thrill up my arm to my heart. I am influenced—conquered; and the influence is sweeter than I can express; and the conquest I undergo has a witchery beyond any triumph I can win. Why do you smile, Jane? What does that inexplicable, that uncanny turn of countenance mean?"

"I was thinking, sir (you will excuse the idea; it was involuntary), I was thinking of Hercules and Samson[4] with their charmers——"

"You were, you little elfish——"

"Hush, sir! You don't talk very wisely just now; any more than those gen-

3. A being who inhabits air.
4. He was charmed by Delilah, who betrayed him to his enemies (Judges 16). In classical mythology, Hercules was "charmed" by various women, espe-
cially by his wife, Deianira, who was responsible for his death. Both men were renowned for their strength.

tlemen acted very wisely. However, had they been married, they would no doubt by their severity as husbands have made up for their softness as suitors; and so will you, I fear. I wonder how you will answer me a year hence, should I ask a favor it does not suit your convenience or pleasure to grant."

"Ask me something now, Janet—the least thing: I desire to be entreated——"

"Indeed, I will, sir; I have my petition all ready."

"Speak! But if you look up and smile with that countenance, I shall swear concession before I know to what, and that will make a fool of me."

"Not at all, sir; I ask only this: don't send for the jewels, and don't crown me with roses: you might as well put a border of gold lace round that plain pocket handkerchief you have there."

"I might as well 'gild refined gold.'[5] I know it: your request is granted then—for the time. I will remand the order I despatched to my banker. But you have not yet asked for anything; you have prayed a gift to be withdrawn: try again."

"Well, then, sir; have the goodness to gratify my curiosity, which is much piqued on one point."

He looked disturbed. "What? what?" he said hastily. "Curiosity is a dangerous petition: it is well I have not taken a vow to accord every request——"

"But there can be no danger in complying with this, sir."

"Utter it, Jane: but I wish that instead of a mere inquiry into perhaps, a secret, it was a wish for half my estate."

"Now, king Ahasuerus![6] What do I want with half your estate? Do you think I am a Jew-usurer, seeking good investment in land? I would much rather have all your confidence. You will not exclude me from your confidence, if you admit me to your heart?"

"You are welcome to all my confidence that is worth having, Jane: but for God's sake don't desire a useless burden! Don't long for poison—don't turn out a downright Eve[7] on my hands!"

"Why not, sir? You have just been telling me how much you like to be conquered, and how pleasant over-persuasion is to you. Don't you think I had better take advantage of the confession, and begin and coax, and entreat—even cry and be sulky if necessary for the sake of a mere essay of my power?"

"I dare you to any such experiment. Encroach, presume, and the game is up."

"Is it, sir? You soon give in. How stern you look now! Your eyebrows have become as thick as my finger, and your forehead resembles, what, in some very astonishing poetry, I once saw styled 'a blue-piled thunderloft.'[8] That will be your married look, sir, I suppose?"

"If that will be *your* married look, I, as a Christian, will soon give up the notion of consorting with a mere sprite or salamander.[9] But what had you to ask, thing?—out with it!"

"There, you are less than civil now; and I like rudeness a great deal better than flattery. I had rather be a *thing* than an angel. This is what I have to

5. Shakespeare's *King John* 4.2 line 11.
6. Xerxes, king of Persia (r. 486–465 B.C.E.), described in the Book of Esther as fabulously rich.
7. I.e., one desiring forbidden and harmful knowledge.
8. Perhaps from the Brontës' own poetry.
9. A mythical being that can inhabit fire.

ask:—Why did you take such pains to make me believe you wished to marry Miss Ingram?"

"Is that all? Thank God, it is no worse!"

And now he unknit his black brows; looked down, smiling at me, and stroked my hair, as if well pleased at seeing a danger averted.

"I think I may confess," he continued, "even although I should make you a little indignant, Jane—and I have seen what a fire-spirit you can be when you are indignant. You glowed in the cool moonlight last night, when you mutinied against fate, and claimed your rank as my equal. Janet, by-the-by, it was you who made me the offer."

"Of course, I did. But to the point if you please, sir—Miss Ingram?"

"Well, I feigned courtship of Miss Ingram, because I wished to render you as madly in love with me as I was with you; and I knew jealousy would be the best ally I could call in for the furtherance of that end."

"Excellent!—now you are small—not one whit bigger than the end of my little finger. It was a burning shame, and a scandalous disgrace to act in that way. Did you think nothing of Miss Ingram's feelings, sir?"

"Her feelings are concentrated in one—pride; and that needs humbling. Were you jealous, Jane?"

"Never mind, Mr. Rochester: it is in no way interesting to you to know that. Answer me truly once more. Do you think Miss Ingram will not suffer from your dishonest coquetry? Won't she feel forsaken and deserted?"

"Impossible!—when I told you how she, on the contrary, deserted me: the idea of my insolvency cooled, or rather extinguished, her flame in a moment."

"You have a curious designing mind, Mr. Rochester. I am afraid your principles on some points are eccentric."

"My principles were never trained, Jane: they may have grown a little awry for want of attention."

"Once again, seriously; may I enjoy the great good that has been vouchsafed to me, without fearing that any one else is suffering the bitter pain I myself felt a while ago?"

"That you may, my good little girl: there is not another being in the world has the same pure love for me as yourself—for I lay that pleasant unction to my soul, Jane, a belief in your affection."

I turned my lips to the hand that lay on my shoulder. I loved him very much—more than I could trust myself to say—more than words had power to express.

"Ask something more," he said presently; "it is my delight to be entreated, and to yield."

I was again ready with my request.

"Communicate your intentions to Mrs. Fairfax, sir: she saw me with you last night in the hall, and she was shocked. Give her some explanation before I see her again. It pains me to be misjudged by so good a woman."

"Go to your room, and put on your bonnet," he replied. "I mean you to accompany me to Millcote this morning; and while you prepare for the drive, I will enlighten the old lady's understanding. Did she think, Janet, you had given the world for love, and considered it well lost?"[1]

"I believe she thought I had forgotten my station, and yours, sir."

1. *All for Love; or, The World Well Lost* (1678) is the title of a heroic tragedy by John Dryden.

"Station! station!—your station is in my heart, and on the necks of those who would insult you, now or hereafter—Go."

I was soon dressed; and when I heard Mr. Rochester quit Mrs. Fairfax's parlor, I hurried down to it. The old lady had been reading her morning portion of Scripture—the lesson for the day; her Bible lay open before her, and her spectacles were upon it. Her occupation, suspended by Mr. Rochester's announcement, seemed now forgotten: her eyes, fixed on the blank wall opposite, expressed the surprise of a quiet mind, stirred by unwonted tidings. Seeing me, she roused herself: she made a sort of effort to smile, and framed a few words of congratulation; but the smile expired, and the sentence was abandoned unfinished. She put up her spectacles, shut the Bible, and pushed her chair back from the table.

"I feel so astonished," she began, "I hardly know what to say to you, Miss Eyre. I have surely not been dreaming, have I? Sometimes I half fall asleep when I am sitting alone, and fancy things that have never happened. It has seemed to me more than once when I have been in a doze, that my dear husband, who died fifteen years since, has come in and sat down beside me; and that I have even heard him call me by my name, Alice, as he used to do. Now, can you tell me whether it is actually true that Mr. Rochester has asked you to marry him? Don't laugh at me. But I really thought he came in here five minutes ago, and said, that in a month you would be his wife."

"He has said the same thing to me," I replied.

"He has! Do you believe him? Have you accepted him?"

"Yes."

She looked at me bewildered.

"I could never have thought it. He is a proud man: all the Rochesters were proud: and his father, at least, liked money. He, too, has always been called careful. He means to marry you?"

"He tells me so."

She surveyed my whole person: in her eyes I read that they had there found no charm powerful enough to solve the enigma.

"It passes me!" she continued: "but no doubt it is true since you say so. How it will answer, I cannot tell: I really don't know. Equality of position and fortune is often advisable in such cases; and there are twenty years of difference in your ages. He might almost be your father."

"No, indeed, Mrs. Fairfax!" exclaimed I, nettled: "he is nothing like my father! No one, who saw us together, would suppose it for an instant. Mr. Rochester looks as young, and is as young, as some men at five-and-twenty."

"Is it really for love he is going to marry you?" she asked.

I was so hurt by her coldness and scepticism that the tears rose to my eyes.

"I am sorry to grieve you," pursued the widow; "but you are so young, and so little acquainted with men, I wished to put you on your guard. It is an old saying that 'all is not gold that glitters'; and in this case I do fear there will be something found to be different to what either you or I expect."

"Why?—am I a monster?" I said: "is it impossible that Mr. Rochester should have a sincere affection for me?"

"No: you are very well; and much improved of late: and Mr. Rochester, I daresay, is fond of you. I have always noticed that you were a sort of pet of his. There are times when, for your sake, I have been a little uneasy at his marked preference, and have wished to put you on your guard: but I did not

like to suggest even the possibility of wrong. I knew such an idea would shock, perhaps offend you; and you were so discreet, and so thoroughly modest and sensible, I hoped you might be trusted to protect yourself. Last night I cannot tell you what I suffered when I sought all over the house, and could find you nowhere, nor the master either; and then, at twelve o'clock, saw you come in with him."

"Well, never mind that now," I interrupted impatiently: "it is enough that all was right."

"I hope all will be right in the end," she said: "but believe me, you cannot be too careful. Try and keep Mr. Rochester at a distance: distrust yourself as well as him. Gentlemen in his station are not accustomed to marry their governesses."

I was growing truly irritated: happily, Adèle ran in.

"Let me go,—let me go to Millcote too!" she cried. "Mr. Rochester won't: though there is so much room in the new carriage. Beg him to let me go, mademoiselle."

"That I will, Adèle," and I hastened away with her, glad to quit my gloomy monitress. The carriage was ready: they were bringing it round to the front, and my master was pacing the pavement, Pilot following him backwards and forwards.

"Adèle may accompany us, may she not, sir?"

"I told her no. I'll have no brats!—I'll have only you."

"Do let her go, Mr. Rochester, if you please: it would be better."

"Not it: she will be a restraint."

He was quite peremptory, both in look and voice. The chill of Mrs. Fairfax's warnings, and the damp of her doubts were upon me: something of unsubstantiality and uncertainty had beset my hopes. I half lost the sense of power over him. I was about mechanically to obey him, without further remonstrance; but as he helped me into the carriage, he looked at my face.

"What is the matter?" he asked; "all the sunshine is gone. Do you really wish the bairn to go? Will it annoy you if she is left behind?"

"I would far rather she went, sir."

"Then off for your bonnet, and back, like a flash of lightning!" cried he to Adèle.

She obeyed him with what speed she might.

"After all, a single morning's interruption will not matter much," said he, "when I mean shortly to claim you—your thoughts, conversation, and company—for life."

Adèle, when lifted in, commenced kissing me, by way of expressing her gratitude for my intercession: she was instantly stowed away into a corner on the other side of him. She then peeped round to where I sat; so stern a neighbor was too restrictive: to him, in his present fractious mood she dared whisper no observations, nor ask of him any information.

"Let her come to me," I entreated: "she will, perhaps, trouble you, sir: there is plenty of room on this side."

He handed her over as if she had been a lap-dog; "I'll send her to school yet," he said, but now he was smiling.

Adèle heard him, and asked if she was to go school "sans mademoiselle."

"Yes," he replied, "absolutely sans mademoiselle; for I am to take mademoiselle to the moon, and there I shall seek a cave in one of the white valleys

among the volcano-tops, and mademoiselle shall live with me there, and only me."

"She will have nothing to eat: you will starve her," observed Adèle.

"I shall gather manna for her morning and night: the plains and hillsides in the moon are bleached with manna, Adèle."

"She will want to warm herself: what will she do for a fire?"

"Fire rises out of the lunar mountains: when she is cold, I'll carry her up to a peak and lay her down on the edge of a crater."

"Oh, qu'elle y sera mal—peu confortable![2] And her clothes, they will wear out: how can she get new ones?"

Mr. Rochester professed to be puzzled. "Hem?" said he. "What would you do, Adèle? Cudgel your brains for an expedient. How would a white or a pink cloud answer for a gown, do you think? And one could cut a pretty enough scarf out of a rainbow."

"She is far better as she is," concluded Adèle, after musing some time: "besides, she would get tired of living with only you in the moon. If I were mademoiselle, I would never consent to go with you."

"She has consented: she has pledged her word."

"But you can't get her there: there is no road to the moon: it is all air; and neither you nor she can fly."

"Adèle, look at that field." We were now outside Thornfield gates, and bowling lightly along the smooth road to Millcote, where the dust was well-laid by the thunder-storm, and where the low hedges and lofty timber trees on each side glistened green, and rain-refreshed.

"In that field, Adèle, I was walking late one evening about a fortnight since—the evening of the day you helped me to make hay in the orchard meadows; and as I was tired with raking swaths, I sat down to rest me on a stile; and there I took out a little book and a pencil, and began to write about a misfortune that befell me long ago and a wish I had for happy days to come: I was writing away very fast, though daylight was fading from the leaf, when something came up the path and stopped two yards off me. I looked at it. It was a little thing with a veil of gossamer on its head. I beckoned it to come near me; it stood soon at my knee. I never spoke to it, and it never spoke to me, in words: but I read its eyes, and it read mine; and our speechless colloquy was to this effect:—It was a fairy, and come from Elf-land, it said; and its errand was to make me happy: I must go with it out of the common world to a lonely place—such as the moon, for instance—and it nodded its head towards her horn, rising over Hay-hill: it told me of the alabaster cave and silver vale where we might live. I said I should like to go; but reminded it, as you did me, that I had no wings to fly.

" 'Oh,' returned the fairy, 'that does not signify! Here is a talisman will remove all difficulties;' and she held out a pretty gold ring. 'Put it,' she said, 'on the fourth finger of my left hand, and I am yours, and you are mine; and we shall leave earth, and make our own heaven yonder.' She nodded again at the moon. The ring, Adèle, is in my breeches-pocket, under the disguise of a sovereign[3]: but I mean soon to change it to a ring again."

"But what has mademoiselle to do with it? I don't care for the fairy: you said it was mademoiselle you would take to the moon?"——

2. Oh, she'll be uncomfortable there! 3. A gold coin worth 1 pound.

"Mademoiselle is a fairy," he said, whispering mysteriously. Whereupon I told her not to mind his badinage; and she, on her part, evinced a fund of genuine French scepticism: denominating Mr. Rochester "un vrai menteur,"[4] and assuring him that she had made no account whatever of his "Contes de fée," and that "du reste, il n'y avait pas de fées, et quand même il y en avait,"[5] she was sure they would never appear to him, nor ever give him rings, or offer to live with him in the moon. The hour spent at Millcote was a somewhat harassing one to me. Mr. Rochester obliged me to go to a certain silk warehouse: there I was ordered to choose half a dozen dresses. I hated the business, I begged leave to defer it: no—it should be gone through with now. By dint of entreaties expressed in energetic whispers I reduced the half-dozen to two: these, however, he vowed he would select himself. With anxiety I watched his eye rove over the gay stores: he fixed on a rich silk of the most brilliant amethyst dye, and a superb pink satin. I told him in a new series of whispers, that he might as well buy me a gold gown and a silver bonnet at once: I should certainly never venture to wear his choice. With infinite difficulty, for he was stubborn as a stone, I persuaded him to make an exchange in favor of a sober black satin and pearl-gray silk. "It might pass for the present," he said; "but he would yet see me glittering like a parterre."

Glad was I to get him out of the silk warehouse, and then out of a jeweller's shop: the more he bought me, the more my cheek burned with a sense of annoyance and degradation. As we reentered the carriage, and I sat back feverish and fagged, I remembered what in the hurry of events, dark and bright, I had wholly forgotten—the letter of my uncle, John Eyre, to Mrs. Reed: his intention to adopt me and make me his legatee. "It would, indeed, be a relief," I thought, "if I had ever so small an independency; I never can bear being dressed like a doll by Mr. Rochester, or sitting like a second Danae with the golden shower falling daily round me.[6] I will write to Madeira the moment I get home, and tell my uncle John I am going to be married, and to whom: if I had but a prospect of one day bringing Mr. Rochester an accession of fortune, I could better endure to be kept by him now." And somewhat relieved by this idea (which I failed not to execute that day), I ventured once more to meet my master's and lover's eye; which most pertinaciously sought mine, though I averted both face and gaze. He smiled; and I thought his smile was such as a sultan might, in a blissful and fond moment, bestow on a slave his gold and gems had enriched: I crushed his hand, which was ever hunting mine, vigorously, and thrust it back to him red with the passionate pressure—

"You need not look in that way," I said: "if you do I'll wear nothing but my old Lowood frocks to the end of the chapter. I'll be married in this lilac gingham—you may make a dressing-gown for yourself out of the pearl-gray silk, and an infinite series of waist-coats out of the black satin."

He chuckled; he rubbed his hands: "Oh, it is rich to see and hear her!" he exclaimed. "Is she original? Is she piquant? I would not exchange this one little English girl for the grand Turk's whole seraglio;[7] gazelle-eyes, houri forms, and all!"

4. A real liar.
5. Fairy tales, and that furthermore, there were no fairies, and even so there were some (*quand même* may be Brontë's error for *même se*, "even if").
6. Zeus, as a shower of gold, made love to Danae.
7. I.e., harem.

The Eastern allusion bit me again: "I'll not stand you an inch in the stead of a seraglio," I said; "so don't consider me an equivalent for one; if you have a fancy for anything in that line, away with you, sir, to the bazaars of Stamboul without delay; and lay out in extensive slave-purchases some of that spare cash you seem at a loss to spend satisfactorily here."

"And what will you do, Janet, while I am bargaining for so many tons of flesh and such an assortment of black eyes?"

"I'll be preparing myself to go out as a missionary to preach liberty to them that are enslaved—your harem inmates amongst the rest. I'll get admitted there, and I'll stir up mutiny; and you, three-tailed bashaw[8] as you are, sir, shall in a trice find yourself fettered amongst our hands: nor will I, for one, consent to cut your bonds till you have signed a charter, the most liberal that despot ever yet conferred."

"I would consent to be at your mercy, Jane."

"I would have no mercy, Mr. Rochester, if you supplicated for it with an eye like that. While you looked so, I should be certain that whatever charter you might grant under coercion, your first act, when released, would be to violate its conditions."

"Why, Jane, what would you have? I fear you will compel me to go through a private marriage ceremony, besides that performed at the altar. You will stipulate, I see, for peculiar terms—what will they be?"

"I only want an easy mind, sir; not crushed by crowded obligations. Do you remember what you said of Céline Varens?—of the diamonds, the cashmeres you gave her? I will not be your English Céline Varens. I shall continue to act as Adèle's governess; by that I shall earn my board and lodging, and thirty pounds a year besides, I'll furnish my own wardrobe out of that money, and you shall give me nothing but"——

"Well, but what?"

"Your regard: and if I give you mine in return, that debt will be quit."

"Well, for cool native impudence, and pure innate pride, you haven't your equal," said he. We were now approaching Thornfield. "Will it please you to dine with me today?" he asked, as we re-entered the gates.

"No, thank you, sir."

"And what for, 'no, thank you,' if one may inquire?"

"I never have dined with you, sir: and I see no reason why I should now: till"——

"Till what? You delight in half-phrases."

"Till I can't help it."

"Do you suppose I eat like an ogre, or a ghoul, that you dread being the companion of my repast?"

"I have formed no supposition on the subject, sir; but I want to go on as usual for another month."

"You will give up your governessing slavery at once."

"Indeed! begging your pardon, sir, I shall not. I shall just go on with it as usual. I shall keep out of your way all day, as I have been accustomed to do: you may send for me in the evening, when you feel disposed to see me, and I'll come then; but at no other time."

8. Pasha (a grand Turk). The phrase "three-tailed Pasha" appears in William Makepeace Thackeray's *The Book of Snobs* (1846–47), ch. 3.

"I want a smoke, Jane, or a pinch of snuff, to comfort me under all this, 'pour me donner une contenance,'[9] as Adèle would say: and unfortunately I have neither my cigar-case, nor my snuff-box. But listen—whisper—it is your time now, little tyrant, but it will be mine presently: and when once I have fairly seized you, to have and to hold, I'll just—figuratively speaking—attach you to a chain like this" (touching his watch-guard).

"Yes, bonny wee thing, I'll wear you in my bosom, lest my jewel I should tyne."[1]

He said this as he helped me to alight from the carriage; and while he afterwards lifted out Adèle, I entered the house, and made good my retreat upstairs.

He duly summoned me to his presence in the evening. I had prepared an occupation for him; for I was determined not to spend the whole time in a *tête-à-tête* conversation. I remembered his fine voice; I knew he liked to sing—good singers generally do. I was no vocalist myself, and, in his fastidious judgment, no musician either; but I delighted in listening when the performance was good. No sooner had twilight, that hour of romance, begun to lower her blue and starry banner over the lattice, than I rose, opened the piano, and entreated him, for the love of heaven, to give me a song. He said I was a capricious witch, and that he would rather sing another time; but I averred that no time was like the present.

"Did I like his voice?" he asked.

"Very much." I was not fond of pampering that susceptible vanity of his; but for once, and from motives of expediency, I would e'en soothe and stimulate it.

"Then, Jane, you must play the accompaniment."

"Very well, sir; I will try."

I did try, but was presently swept off the stool and denominated "a little bungler." Being pushed unceremoniously to one side—which was precisely what I wished—he unsurped my place, and proceeded to accompany himself: for he could play as well as sing. I hied me to the window-recess; and while I sat there and looked out on the still trees and dim lawn, to a sweet air was sung in mellow tones the following strain:—

> The truest love that ever heart
> Felt at its kindled core
> Did through each vein, in quickened start,
> The tide of being pour.
>
> Her coming was my hope each day,
> Her parting was my pain;
> The chance that did her steps delay
> Was ice in every vein.
>
> I dreamed it would be nameless bliss,
> As I loved, loved to be;
> And to this object did I press
> As blind as eagerly.

9. To steady me. 1. Lose.

But wide as pathless was the space
 That lay, our lives, between,
And dangerous as the foamy race
 Of ocean-surges green.

And haunted as a robber-path
 Through wilderness or wood;
For Might and Right, and Woe and Wrath,
 Between our spirits stood.

I dangers dared; I hind'rance scorned;
 I omens did defy:
Whatever menaced, harassed, warned,
 I passed impetuous by.

On sped my rainbow, fast as light;
 I flew as in a dream;
For glorious rose upon my sight
 That child of Shower and Gleam.

Still bright on clouds of suffering dim
 Shines that soft, solemn joy;
Nor care I now, how dense and grim
 Disasters gather nigh.

I care not in this moment sweet,
 Though all I have rushed o'er
Should come on pinion, strong and fleet,
 Proclaiming vengeance sore:

Though haughty Hate should strike me down,
 Right, bar approach to me,
And grinding Might, with furious frown,
 Swear endless enmity.

My love has placed her little hand
 With noble faith in mine,
And vowed that wedlock's sacred band
 Our nature shall entwine.

My love has sworn, with sealing kiss,
 With me to live—to die;
I have at last my nameless bliss:
 As I love—loved am I!

He rose and came towards me, and I saw his face all kindled, and his full falcon-eye flashing, and tenderness and passion in every lineament. I quailed momentarily—then I rallied. Soft scene, daring demonstration, I would not have; and I stood in peril of both: a weapon of defence must be prepared—I whetted my tongue: as he reached me, I asked with asperity, "whom he was going to marry now?"

"That was a strange question to be put by his darling Jane."

"Indeed! I considered it a very natural and necessary one: he had talked of his future wife dying with him. What did he mean by such a pagan idea? I had no intention of dying with him—he might depend on that."

"Oh, all he longed, all he prayed for, was that I might live with him! Death was not for such as I."

"Indeed it was: I had as good a right to die when my time came as he had: but I should bide that time, and not be hurried away in a suttee."[2]

"Would I forgive him for the selfish idea, and prove my pardon by a reconciling kiss?"

"No: I would rather be excused."

Here I heard myself apostrophized as a "hard little thing;" and it was added, "any other woman would have been melted to marrow at hearing such stanzas crooned in her praise."

I assured him I was naturally hard—very flinty, and that he would often find me so; and that, moreover, I was determined to show him divers rugged points in my character before the ensuing four weeks elapsed: he should know fully what sort of a bargain he had made, while there was yet time to rescind it.

"Would I be quiet, and talk rationally?"

"I would be quiet if he liked; and as to talking rationally, I flattered myself I was doing that now."

He fretted, pished and pshawed. "Very good," I thought; "you may fume and fidget as you please: but this is the best plan to pursue with you, I am certain. I like you more than I can say; but I'll not sink into a bathos of sentiment: and with this needle of repartee I'll keep you from the edge of the gulf too; and, moreover, maintain by its pungent aid that distance between you and myself most conducive to our real mutual advantage."

From less to more, I worked him up to considerable irritation; then, after he had retired, in dudgeon, quite to the other end of the room, I got up, and saying, "I wish you good-night, sir," in my natural and wonted respectful manner, I slipped out by the side-door and got away.

The system thus entered on I pursued during the whole season of probation; and with the best success. He was kept, to be sure, rather cross and crusty: but on the whole I could see he was excellently entertained; and that a lamb-like submission and turtle-dove sensibility, while fostering his despotism more, would have pleased his judgment, satisfied his common-sense, and even suited his taste, less.

In other people's presence I was, as formerly, deferential and quiet; any other line of conduct being uncalled for: it was only in the evening conferences I thus thwarted and afflicted him. He continued to send for me punctually the moment the clock struck seven; though when I appeared before him now, he had no such honeyed terms as "love" and "darling" on his lips: the best words at my service were "provoking puppet," "malicious elf," "sprite," "changeling," etc. For caresses, too, I now got grimaces; for a pressure of the hand, a pinch on the arm; for a kiss on the cheek, a severe tweak of the ear. It was all right: at present I decidedly preferred these fierce favors to anything more tender. Mrs. Fairfax, I saw, approved me: her anxiety on my account vanished; therefore I was certain I did well. Meantime, Mr.

2. Custom according to which a Hindu widow was cremated on her husband's funeral pyre.

Rochester affirmed I was wearing him to skin and bone, and threatened awful vengeance for my present conduct at some period fast coming. I laughed in my sleeve at his menaces: "I can keep you in reasonable check now," I reflected; "and I don't doubt to be able to do it hereafter: if one expedient loses its virtue, another must be devised."

Yet after all my task was not an easy one; often I would rather have pleased than teased him. My future husband was becoming to me my whole world; and more than the world: almost my hope of heaven. He stood between me and every thought of religion, as an eclipse intervenes between man and the broad sun. I could not, in those days, see God for his creature: of whom I had made an idol.

Chapter XXV

The month of courtship had wasted: its very last hours were being numbered. There was no putting off the day that advanced—the bridal day; and all preparations for its arrival were complete. I, at least, had nothing more to do: there were my trunks, packed, locked, corded, ranged in a row along the wall of my little chamber: to-morrow, at this time, they would be far on their road to London: and so should I (D.V.³),—or rather, not I, but one Jane Rochester, a person whom as yet I knew not. The cards of address alone remained to nail on: they lay, four little squares, on the drawer. Mr. Rochester had himself written the direction, "Mrs. Rochester, ——— Hotel, London," on each: I could not persuade myself to affix them, or to have them affixed. Mrs. Rochester! She did not exist: she would not be born till tomorrow, some time after eight o'clock A.M.; and I would wait to be assured she had come into the world alive before I assigned to her all that property. It was enough that in yonder closet, opposite my dressing-table, garments said to be hers had already displaced my black stuff Lowood frock and straw bonnet: for not to me appertained that suit of wedding raiment, the pearl-colored robe, the vapory veil, pendent from the usurped portmanteau. I shut the closet, to conceal the strange, wraith-like apparel it contained; which, at this evening hour—nine o'clock—gave out certainly a most ghostly shimmer through the shadow of my apartment.

"I will leave you by yourself, white dream," I said. "I am feverish: I hear the wind blowing: I will go out of doors and feel it."

It was not only the hurry of preparation that made me feverish; not only the anticipation of the great change—the new life which was to commence to-morrow: both these circumstances had their share, doubtless, in producing that restless, excited mood which hurried me forth at this late hour into the darkening grounds; but a third cause influenced my mind more than they.

I had at heart a strange and anxious thought. Something had happened which I could not comprehend; no one knew of or had seen the event but myself: it had taken place the preceding night. Mr. Rochester that night was absent from home; nor was he yet returned: business had called him to a small estate of two or three farms he possessed thirty miles off—business it was requisite he should settle in person, previously to his meditated depar-

3. *Deo volente* (God willing; Latin).

ture from England. I waited now his return; eager to disburthen my mind, and to seek of him the solution of the enigma that perplexed me. Stay till he comes, reader; and, when I disclose my secret to him, you shall share the confidence.

I sought the orchard: driven to its shelter by the wind, which all day had blown strong and full from the south; without, however, bringing a speck of rain. Instead of subsiding as night drew on, it seemed to augment its rush and deepen its roar: the trees blew steadfastly one way, never writhing round, and scarcely tossing back their boughs once in an hour; so continuous was the strain bending their branchy heads northward—the clouds drifted from pole to pole, fast following, mass on mass: no glimpse of blue sky had been visible that July day.

It was not without a certain wild pleasure I ran before the wind delivering my trouble of mind to the measureless air-torrent thundering through space. Descending the laurel-walk, I faced the wreck of the chestnut-tree; it stood up, black and riven: the trunk, split down the center, gasped ghastly. The cloven halves were not broken from each other, for the firm base and strong roots kept them unsundered below; though community of vitality was destroyed—the sap could flow no more: their great boughs on each side were dead, and next winter's tempests would be sure to fell one or both to earth: as yet, however, they might be said to form one tree—a ruin, but an entire ruin.

"You did right to hold fast to each other," I said: as if the monster splinters were living things, and could hear me. "I think, scathed as you look, and charred and scorched, there must be a little sense of life in you yet; rising out of that adhesion at the faithful, honest roots: you will never have green leaves more—never more see birds making nests and singing idyls in your boughs; the time of pleasure and love is over with you; but you are not desolate: each of you has a comrade to sympathize with him in his decay." As I looked up at them, the moon appeared momentarily in that part of the sky which filled their fissure; her disk was blood-red and half overcast; she seemed to throw on me one bewildered, dreary glance, and buried herself again instantly in the deep drift of cloud. The wind fell, for a second, round Thornfield; but far away over wood and water, poured a wild, melancholy wail: it was sad to listen to, and I ran off again.

Here and there I strayed through the orchard, gathered up the apples with which the grass round the tree roots was thickly strewn: then I employed myself in dividing the ripe from the unripe; I carried them into the house and put them away in the store-room. Then I repaired to the library to ascertain whether the fire was lit; for, though summer, I knew on such a gloomy evening Mr. Rochester would like to see a cheerful hearth when he came in: yes, the fire had been kindled some time, and burnt well. I placed his armchair by the chimney-corner: I wheeled the table near it: I let down the curtain, and had the candles brought in ready for lighting. More restless than ever, when I had completed these arrangements I could not sit still, nor even remain in the house: a little timepiece in the room and the old clock in the hall simultaneously struck ten.

"How late it grows!" I said: "I will run down to the gates: it is moonlight at intervals; I can see a good way on the road. He may be coming now, and to meet him will save some minutes of suspense."

The wind roared high in the great trees which enbowered the gates; but the road as far as I could see, to the right hand and the left, was all still and solitary: save for the shadows of clouds crossing it at intervals, as the moon looked out, it was but a long pale line, unvaried by one moving speck.

A puerile tear dimmed my eye while I looked—a tear of disappointment and impatience: ashamed of it, I wiped it away. I lingered; the moon shut herself wholly within her chamber, and drew close her curtain of dense cloud; the night grew dark; rain came driving fast on the gale.

"I wish he would come! I wish he would come!" I exclaimed, seized with hypochondriac foreboding. I had expected his arrival before tea; now it was dark: what could keep him? Had an accident happened? The event of last night again recurred to me. I interpreted it as a warning of disaster. I feared my hopes were too bright to be realized; and I had enjoyed so much bliss lately that I imagined my fortune had passed its meridian, and must now decline.

"Well, I cannot return to the house," I thought; "I cannot sit by the fireside while he is abroad in inclement weather: better tire my limbs than strain my heart; I will go forward and meet him."

I set out; I walked fast, but not far: ere I had measured a quarter of a mile I heard the tramp of hoofs; a horseman came on, full gallop; a dog ran by his side. Away with evil presentiment! It was he: here he was, mounted on Mesrour, followed by Pilot. He saw me; for the moon had opened a blue field in the sky, and rode in it watery bright: he took his hat off, and waved it round his head. I now ran to meet him.

"There!" he exclaimed, as he stretched out his hand and bent from the saddle: "You can't do without me, that is evident. Step on my boot-toe; give me both hands: mount!"

I obeyed; joy made me agile: I sprang up before him. A hearty kissing I got for a welcome; and some boastful triumph; which I swallowed as well as I could. He checked himself in his exultation to demand, "But is there anything the matter, Janet, that you come to meet me at such an hour? Is there anything wrong?"

"No; but I thought you would never come. I could not bear to wait in the house for you, especially with this rain and wind."

"Rain and wind, indeed! Yes, you are dripping like a mermaid; pull my cloak round you: but I think you are feverish, Jane: both your cheek and hand are burning hot. I ask again, is there anything the matter?"

"Nothing, now: I am neither afraid nor unhappy."

"Then you have been both?"

"Rather: but I'll tell you all about it by-and-by, sir; and I daresay you will only laugh at me for my pains."

"I'll laugh at you heartily when tomorrow is past; till then I dare not: my prize is not certain. This is you; who have been as slippery as an eel this last month, and as thorny as a briar-rose. I could not lay a finger anywhere but I was pricked; and now I seem to have gathered up a stray lamb in my arms: you wandered out of the fold to seek your shepherd, did you, Jane?"

"I wanted you: but don't boast. Here we are at Thornfield: now let me get down."

He landed me on the pavement. As John took his horse, and he followed me into the hall, he told me to make haste and put something dry on, and

then return to him in the library; and he stopped me, as I made for the staircase, to extort a promise that I would not be long: nor was I long: in five minutes I rejoined him. I found him at supper.

"Take a seat and bear me company, Jane: please God, it is the last meal but one you will eat at Thornfield Hall for a long time."

I sat down near him; but told him I could not eat.

"Is it because you have the prospect of a journey before you, Jane? Is it the thoughts of going to London that takes away your appetite?"

"I cannot see my prospects clearly tonight, sir; and I hardly know what thoughts I have in my head. Everything in life seems unreal."

"Except me: I am substantial enough:—touch me."

"You, sir, are the most phantom-like of all: you are a mere dream."

He held out his hand, laughing: "Is that a dream?" said he, placing it close to my eyes. He had a rounded, muscular, and vigorous hand, as well as a long, strong arm.

"Yes; though I touch it, it is a dream," said I, as I put it down from before my face. "Sir, have you finished supper?"

"Yes, Jane."

I rang the bell, and ordered away the tray. When we were again alone, I stirred the fire, and then took a low seat at my master's knee.

"It is near midnight," I said.

"Yes: but remember, Jane, you promised to wake with me the night before my wedding."

"I did; and I will keep my promise, for an hour or two at least: I have no wish to go to bed."

"Are all your arrangements complete?"

"All, sir."

"And on my part, likewise," he returned.

"I have settled everything; and we shall leave Thornfield tomorrow, within half an hour after our return from church."

"Very well, sir."

"With what an extraordinary smile you uttered that word—'very well,' Jane! What a bright spot of color you have on each cheek! and how strangely your eyes glitter! Are you well?"

"I believe I am."

"Believe! What is the matter?—Tell me what you feel."

"I could not, sir: no words could tell you what I feel. I wish this present hour would never end: who knows with what fate the next may come charged?"

"This is hypochondria, Jane. You have been over-excited, or over-fatigued."

"Do you, sir, feel calm and happy?"

"Calm?—no: but happy—to the heart's core."

I looked up at him to read the signs of bliss in his face: it was ardent and flushed.

"Give me your confidence, Jane," he said: "relieve your mind of any weight that oppresses it by imparting it to me. What do you fear?—that I shall not prove a good husband?"

"It is the idea farthest from my thoughts."

"Are you apprehensive of the new sphere you are about to enter?—of the new life into which you are passing?"

"No."

"You puzzle me, Jane: your look and tone of sorrowful audacity perplex and pain me. I want an explanation."

"Then, sir—listen. You were from home last night?"

"I was: I know that; and you hinted a while ago at something which had happened in my absence:—nothing, probably, of consequence; but, in short, it has disturbed you. Let me hear it. Mrs. Fairfax has said something, perhaps? or you have overheard the servants talk?—your sensitive self-respect has been wounded?"

"No, sir." It struck twelve—I waited till the timepiece had concluded its silver chime, and the clock its hoarse, vibrating stroke, and then I proceeded.

"All day yesterday I was very busy, and very happy in my ceaseless bustle; for I am not, as you seem to think, troubled by any haunting fears about the new sphere, et cetera: I think it a glorious thing to have the hope of living with you, because I love you. No, sir, don't caress me now—let me talk undisturbed. Yesterday I trusted well in Providence, and believed that events were working together for your good and mine: it was a fine day, if you recollect—the calmness of the air and sky forbade apprehensions respecting your safety or comfort on your journey. I walked a little while on the pavement after tea, thinking of you; and I beheld you in imagination so near me I scarcely missed your actual presence. I thought of the life that lay before me—*your* life, sir—an existence more expansive and stirring than my own: as much more so as the depths of the sea to which the brook runs are than the shallows of its own strait channel. I wondered why moralists call this world a dreary wilderness; for me it blossomed like a rose. Just at sunset the air turned cold and the sky cloudy: I went in. Sophie called me upstairs to look at my wedding-dress, which they had just brought; and under it in the box I found your present—the veil which, in your princely extravagance, you sent for from London: resolved, I suppose, since I would not have jewels, to cheat me into accepting something as costly. I smiled as I unfolded it, and devised how I would tease you about your aristocratic tastes, and your efforts to masque your plebeian bride in the attributes of a peeress. I thought how I would carry down to you the square of unembroidered blond[4] I had myself prepared as a covering for my low-born head, and ask if that was not good enough for a woman who could bring her husband neither fortune, beauty, nor connections. I saw plainly how you would look; and heard your impetuous republican answers, and your haughty disavowal of any necessity on your part to augment your wealth, or elevate your standing, by marrying either a purse or a coronet."

"How well you read me, you witch!" interposed Mr. Rochester; "but what did you find in the veil besides its embroidery? Did you find poison, or a dagger, that you look so mournful now?"

"No, no, sir; besides the delicacy and richness of the fabric, I found nothing save Fairfax Rochester's pride; and that did not scare me, because I am used to the sight of the demon. But, sir, as it grew dark the wind rose: it blew yesterday evening, not as it blows now—wild and high—but 'with a sullen, moaning sound'[5] far more eerie. I wished you were at home. I came

4. A kind of silk lace.
5. Sir Walter Scott's *The Lay of the Last Minstrel* (1805), 1.13.1.

into this room, and the sight of the empty chair and fireless hearth chilled me. For some time after I went to bed I could not sleep—a sense of anxious excitement distressed me. The gale still rising seemed to my ear to muffle a mournful under-sound; whether in the house or abroad I could not at first tell, but it recurred, doubtful, yet doleful at every lull: at last I made out it must be some dog howling at a distance. I was glad when it ceased. On sleeping, I continued in dreams the idea of a dark and gusty night. I continued also the wish to be with you, and experienced a strange, regretful consciousness of some barrier dividing us. During all my first sleep I was following the windings of an unknown road; total obscurity environed me; rain pelted me; I was burdened with the charge of a little child: a very small creature, too young and feeble to walk, and which shivered in my cold arms and wailed piteously in my ear. I thought, sir, that you were on the road a long way before me; and I strained every nerve to over take you, and made effort on effort to utter your name and entreat you to stop—but my movements were fettered; and my voice still died away inarticulate; while you, I felt, withdrew farther and farther every moment."

"And these dreams weigh on your spirits now, Jane, when I am close to you? Little nervous subject! Forget visionary woe, and think only of real happiness! You say you love me, Janet: yes—I will not forget that; and you cannot deny it. *Those* words did not die inarticulate on your lips. I heard them clear and soft: a thought too solemn perhaps, but sweet as music—'I think it is a glorious thing to have the hope of living with you, Edward, because I love you.'—Do you love me, Jane? Repeat it."

"I do, sir.—I do with my whole heart."

"Well," he said, after some minutes' silence, "it is strange; but that sentence has penetrated my breast painfully. Why? I think because you said it with such an earnest, religious energy: and because your upward gaze at me now is the very sublime of faith, truth, and devotion: it is too much as if some spirit were near me. Look wicked, Jane; as you know well how to look; coin one of your wild, shy, provoking smiles; tell me you hate me—tease me, vex me; do anything but move me: I would rather be incensed than saddened."

"I will tease you and vex you to your heart's content when I have finished my tale: but hear me to the end."

"I thought, Jane, you had told me all. I thought I had found the source of your melancholy in a dream!"

I shook my head. "What! is there more? But I will not believe it to be anything important. I warn you of incredulity beforehand. Go on."

The disquietude of his air, the somewhat apprehensive impatience of his manner, surprised me: but I proceeded.

"I dreamt another dream, sir: that Thornfield Hall was a dreary ruin, the retreat of bats and owls. I thought that of all the stately front nothing remained but a shell-like wall, very high, and very fragile-looking. I wandered, on a moonlight night, through the grass-grown enclosure within: here I stumbled over a marble hearth, and there over a fallen fragment of cornice. Wrapped up in a shawl, I still carried the unknown little child: I might not lay it down anywhere, however tired were my arms—however much its weight impeded my progress, I must retain it. I heard the gallop of a horse at a distance on the road: I was sure it was you; and you were departing for

many years, and for a distant country. I climbed the thin wall with frantic, perilous haste, eager to catch one glimpse of you from the top: the stones rolled from under my feet, the ivy branches I grasped gave way, the child clung round my neck in terror, and almost strangled me: at last I gained the summit. I saw you like a speck on a white track, lessening every moment. The blast blew so strong I could not stand. I sat down on the narrow ledge; I hushed the scared infant in my lap: you turned an angle of the road; I bent forward to take a last look; the wall crumbled; I was shaken; the child rolled from my knee, I lost my balance, fell, and woke."

"Now, Jane, that is all."

"All the preface, sir; the tale is yet to come. On waking, a gleam dazzled my eyes: I thought—oh, it is daylight! But I was mistaken: it was only candlelight. Sophie, I supposed, had come in. There was a light on the dressing-table, and the door of the closet, where, before going to bed, I had hung my wedding-dress and veil, stood open: I heard a rustling there. I asked, 'Sophie, what are you doing?' No one answered; but a form emerged from the closet: it took the light, held it aloft, and surveyed the garments pendent from the portmanteau. 'Sophie! Sophie!' I again cried: and still it was silent. I had risen up in bed; I bent forward: first, surprise, then bewilderment, came over me; and then my blood crept cold through my veins. Mr. Rochester, this was not Sophie, it was not Leah, it was not Mrs. Fairfax: It was not—no, I was sure of it, and am still—it was not even that strange woman, Grace Poole."

"It must have been one of them," interrupted my master.

"No, sir, I solemnly assure you to the contrary. The shape standing before me had never crossed my eyes within the precincts of Thornfield Hall before; the height, the contour, were new to me."

"Describe it, Jane."

"It seemed, sir, a woman, tall and large, with thick and dark hair hanging long down her back. I know not what dress she had on: it was white and straight; but whether gown, sheet, or shroud, I cannot tell."

"Did you see her face?"

"Not at first. But presently she took my veil from its place; she held it up, gazed at it long, and then she threw it over her own head, and turned to the mirror. At that moment I saw the reflection of the visage and features quite distinctly in the dark oblong glass."

"And how were they?"

"Fearful and ghastly to me—oh, sir, I never saw a face like it! It was a discolored face—it was a savage face. I wish I could forget the roll of the red eyes and the fearful blackened inflation of the lineaments."

"Ghosts are usually pale, Jane."

"This, sir, was purple: the lips were swelled and dark; the brow furrowed; the black eyebrows widely raised over the bloodshot eyes. Shall I tell you of what it reminded me?"

"You may."

"Of the foul German specter—the Vampire."

"Ah?—What did it do?"

"Sir, it removed my veil from its gaunt head, rent it in two parts, and flinging both on the floor, trampled on them."

"Afterwards?"

"It drew aside the window-curtain and looked out: perhaps it saw dawn

approaching, for, taking the candle, it retreated to the door. Just at my bed-side the figure stopped: the fiery eye glared upon me—she thrust up her candle close to my face, and extinguished it under my eyes. I was aware her lurid visage flamed over mine, and I lost consciousness: for the second time in my life—only the second time—I became insensible from terror."

"Who was with you when you revived?"

"No one, sir; but the broad day. I rose, bathed my head and face in water, drank a long draught; felt that though enfeebled I was not ill, and determined that to none but you would I impart this vision. Now, sir, tell me who and what that woman was?"

"The creature of an over-stimulated brain; that is certain. I must be careful of you, my treasure: nerves like yours were not made for rough handling."

"Sir, depend on it, my nerves were not in fault; the thing was real: the transaction actually took place."

"And your previous dreams: were they real too? Is Thornfield Hall a ruin? Am I severed from you by insuperable obstacles? Am I leaving you without a tear—without a kiss—without a word?"

"Not yet."

"Am I about to do it?—Why, the day is already commenced which is to bind us indissolubly; and when we are once united, there shall be no recurrence of these mental terrors: I guarantee that."

"Mental terrors, sir! I wish I could believe them to be only such: I wish it more now than ever; since even you cannot explain to me the mystery of that awful visitant."

"And since I cannot do it, Jane, it must have been unreal."

"But, sir, when I said so to myself on rising this morning, and when I looked round the room to gather courage and comfort from the cheerful aspect of each familiar object in full daylight, there—on the carpet—I saw what gave the distinct lie to my hypothesis,—the veil, torn from top to bottom, in two halves!"

I felt Mr. Rochester start and shudder; he hastily flung his arms round me.

"Thank God!" he exclaimed, "that if anything malignant did come near you last night, it was only the veil that was harmed.—Oh, to think what might have happened!"

He drew his breath short, and strained me so close to him I could scarcely pant. After some minutes' silence, he continued, cheerily:—"Now, Janet, I'll explain to you all about it. It was half dream, half reality: a woman did, I doubt not, enter your room: and that woman was—must have been—Grace Poole. You call her a strange being yourself: from all you know you have reason so to call her—what did she do to me? what to Mason? In a state between sleeping and waking you noticed her entrance and her actions; but feverish, almost delirious as you were, you ascribed to her goblin appearance different from her own: the long dishevelled hair, the swelled black face, the exaggerated stature, were figments of imagination; results of nightmare: the spiteful tearing of the veil was real: and it is like her. I see you would ask why I keep such a woman in my house: when we have been married a year and a day, I will tell you; but not now. Are you satisfied, Jane? Do you accept my solution of the mystery?"

I reflected, and in truth it appeared to me the only possible one: satisfied I was not, but to please him I endeavored to appear so—relieved, I certainly

did feel; so I answered him with a contented smile. And now, as it was long past one, I prepared to leave him.

"Does not Sophie sleep with Adèle in the nursery?" he asked, as I lit my candle.

"Yes, sir."

"And there is room enough in Adèle's little bed for you. You must share it with her tonight, Jane: it is no wonder that the incident you have related should make you nervous, and I would rather you did not sleep alone: promise me to go to the nursery."

"I shall be very glad to do so, sir."

"And fasten the door securely on the inside. Wake Sophie when you go upstairs, under pretence of requesting her to rouse you in good time tomorrow; for you must be dressed and have finished breakfast before eight. And now, no more somber thoughts: chase dull care away, Janet. Don't you hear to what soft whispers the wind has fallen? and there is no more beating of rain against the window-panes: look here" (he lifted up the curtain)—"it is a lovely night!"

It was. Half heaven was pure and stainless: the clouds, now trooping before the wind, which had shifted to the west, were filing off eastward in long, silvered columns. The moon shone peacefully.

"Well," said Mr. Rochester, gazing inquiringly into my eyes, "how is my Janet now?"

"The night is serene, sir; and so am I."

"And you will not dream of separation and sorrow tonight; but of happy love and blissful union."

This prediction was but half fulfilled: I did not indeed dream of sorrow, but as little did I dream of joy; for I never slept at all. With little Adèle in my arms, I watched the slumber of childhood—so tranquil, so passionless, so innocent—and waited for the coming day: all my life was awake and astir in my frame; and as soon as the sun rose I rose too. I remember Adèle clung to me as I left her; I remember I kissed her as I loosened her little hands from my neck; and I cried over her with strange emotion, and quitted her because I feared my sobs would break her still sound repose. She seemed the emblem of my past life; and he, I was now to array myself to meet, the dread, but adored, type of my unknown future day.

Chapter XXVI

Sophie came at seven to dress me; she was very long indeed in accomplishing her task—so long that Mr. Rochester, grown, I suppose, impatient of my delay, sent up to ask why I did not come. She was just fastening my veil (the plain square of blond after all) to my hair with a brooch; I hurried from under her hands as soon as I could.

"Stop!" she cried in French. "Look at yourself in the mirror: you have not taken one peep."

So I turned at the door: I saw a robed and veiled figure, so unlike my usual self that it seemed almost the image of a stranger. "Jane!" called a voice, and I hastened down. I was received at the foot of the stairs by Mr. Rochester.

"Lingerer," he said, "my brain is on fire with impatience; and you tarry so long!"

He took me into the dining-room, surveyed me keenly all over, pronounced

me "fair as a lily, and not only the pride of his life, but the desire of his eyes," and then, telling me he would give me but ten minutes to eat some breakfast, he rang the bell. One of his lately hired servants, a footman, answered it.

"Is John getting the carriage ready?"

"Yes, sir."

"Is the luggage brought down?"

"They are bringing it down, sir."

"Go you to the church: see if Mr. Wood (the clergyman) and the clerk are there: return and tell me."

The church, as the reader knows, was but just beyond the gates; the footman soon returned.

"Mr. Wood is in the vestry, sir, putting on his surplice."

"And the carriage?"

"The horses are harnessing."

"We shall not want it to go to church; but it must be ready the moment we return, all the boxes and luggage arranged and strapped on, and the coachman in his seat."

"Yes, sir."

"Jane, are you ready?"

I rose. There were no groomsmen, no bridesmaids, no relatives to wait for or marshal: none but Mr. Rochester and I. Mrs. Fairfax stood in the hall as we passed. I would fain have spoken to her, but my hand was held by a grasp of iron: I was hurried along by a stride I could hardly follow; and to look at Mr. Rochester's face was to feel that not a second of delay would be tolerated for any purpose. I wonder what other bridegroom ever looked as he did—so bent up to a purpose, so grimly resolute: or who, under such steadfast brows, ever revealed such flaming and flashing eyes.

I know not whether the day was fair or foul; in descending the drive, I gazed neither on sky nor earth; my heart was with my eyes; and both seemed migrated into Mr. Rochester's frame. I wanted to see the invisible thing on which, as we went along, he appeared to fasten a glance fierce and fell.[6] I wanted to feel the thoughts whose force he seemed breasting and resisting.

At the churchyard wicket he stopped: he discovered I was quite out of breath.

"Am I cruel in my love?" he said. "Delay an instant: lean on me, Jane."

And now I can recall the picture of the gray old house of God rising calm before me, of a rook wheeling round the steeple, of a ruddy morning sky beyond. I remember something, too, of the green grave-mounds; and I have not forgotten, either, two figures of strangers, straying among the low hillocks, and reading the mementoes graven on the few mossy head-stones. I noticed them, because, as they saw us, they passed round to the back of the church; and I doubted not they were going to enter by the side-aisle door, and witness the ceremony. By Mr. Rochester they were not observed; he was earnestly looking at my face, from which the blood had, I daresay, momentarily fled: for I felt my forehead dewy, and my cheeks and lips cold. When I rallied, which I soon did, he walked gently with me up the path to the porch.

We entered the quiet and humble temple; the priest waited in his white

6. Piercing, terrible.

surplice at the lowly altar, the clerk beside him. All was still: two shadows only moved in a remote corner. My conjecture had been correct: the strangers had slipped in before us, and they now stood by the vault of the Rochesters, their backs towards us, viewing through the rails the old time-stained marble tomb, where a kneeling angel guarded the remains of Damer de Rochester, slain at Marston Moor[7] in the time of the civil wars; and of Elizabeth, his wife.

Our place was taken at the communion rails. Hearing a cautious step behind me, I glanced over my shoulder: one of the strangers—a gentleman, evidently—was advancing up the chancel. The service began. The explanation of the intent of matrimony was gone through; and then the clergyman came a step further forward, and, bending slightly towards Mr. Rochester, went on.

"I require and charge you both (as ye will answer at the dreadful day of judgment, when the secrets of all hearts shall be disclosed), that if either of you know any impediment why ye may not lawfully be joined in matrimony, ye do now confess it; for be ye well assured that so many as are coupled together otherwise than God's word doth allow, are not joined together by God, neither is their matrimony lawful."

He paused, as the custom is. When is the pause after that sentence ever broken by reply? Not, perhaps, once in a hundred years. And the clergyman, who had not lifted his eyes from his book, and had held his breath but for a moment, was proceeding: his hand was already stretched towards Mr. Rochester, as his lips unclosed to ask, "Wilt thou have this woman for thy wedded wife?"—when a distinct and near voice said:—"The marriage cannot go on: I declare the existence of an impediment."

The clergyman looked up at the speaker, and stood mute; the clerk did the same; Mr. Rochester moved slightly, as if an earthquake had rolled under his feet: taking a firmer footing, and not turning his head or eyes; he said, "Proceed."

Profound silence fell when he had uttered that word, with deep but low intonation. Presently Mr. Wood said:—"I cannot proceed without some investigation into what has been asserted, and evidence of its truth or falsehood."

"The ceremony is quite broken off," subjoined the voice behind us. "I am in a condition to prove my allegation: an insuperable impediment to this marriage exists."

Mr. Rochester heard, but heeded not: he stood stubborn and rigid: making no movement, but to possess himself of my hand. What a hot and strong grasp he had!—and how like quarried marble was his pale, firm, massive front at this moment! How his eye shone, still, watchful, and yet wild beneath!

Mr. Wood seemed at a loss.

"What is the nature of the impediment?" he asked. "Perhaps it may be got over—explained away?"

"Hardly," was the answer: "I have called it insuperable, and I speak advisedly."

7. Parliamentarian victory over the Royalists (July 2, 1644) during the English civil war.

The speaker came forwards, and leaned on the rails. He continued, uttering each word distinctly, calmly, steadily, but not loudly.

"It simply consists in the existence of a previous marriage. Mr. Rochester has a wife now living."

My nerves vibrated to those low-spoken words as they had never vibrated to thunder—my blood felt their subtle violence as it had never felt frost or fire: but I was collected, and in no danger of swooning. I looked at Mr. Rochester: I made him look at me. His whole face was colorless rock: his eye was both spark and flint. He disavowed nothing: he seemed as if he would defy all things. Without speaking, without smiling, without seeming to recognize in me a human being, he only twined my waist with his arm, and riveted me to his side.

"Who are you?" he asked of the intruder.

"My name is Briggs—a solicitor of——Street, London."

"And you would thrust on me a wife?"

"I would remind you of your lady's existence, sir; which the law recognizes, if you do not."

"Favor me with an account of her—with her name, her parentage, her place of abode."

"Certainly." Mr. Briggs calmly took a paper from his pocket, and read out in a sort of official, nasal voice:—

" 'I affirm and can prove that on the 20th of October, A.D. —— (a date of fifteen years back), Edward Fairfax Rochester, of Thornfield Hall, in the county of ——, and of Ferndean Manor, in ——shire, England, was married to my sister, Bertha Antoinetta Mason, daughter of Jonas Mason, merchant, and of Antoinetta his wife, a Creole—at ——church, Spanish Town, Jamaica. The record of the marriage will be found in the register of that church—a copy of it is now in my possession. Signed, Richard Mason.' "

"That—if a genuine document—may prove I have been married, but it does not prove that the woman mentioned therein as my wife is still living."

"She was living three months ago," returned the lawyer.

"How do you know?"

"I have a witness to the fact, whose testimony even you, sir, will scarcely controvert."

"Produce him—or go to hell."

"I will produce him first—he is on the spot: Mr. Mason, have the goodness to step forward."

Mr. Rochester, on hearing the name, set his teeth; he experienced, too, a sort of strong convulsive quiver; near to him as I was, I felt the spasmodic movement of fury or despair run through his frame. The second stranger, who had hitherto lingered in the background, now drew near; a pale face looked over the solicitor's shoulder—yes, it was Mason himself. Mr. Rochester turned and glared at him. His eye, as I have often said, was a black eye: it had now a tawny, nay a bloody light in its gloom; and his face flushed—olive cheek and hueless forehead received a glow, as from spreading, ascending heart-fire: and he stirred, lifted his strong arm—he could have struck Mason—dashed him on the church-floor—shocked by ruthless blow the breath from his body—but Mason shrank away, and cried faintly, "Good God!" Contempt fell cool on Mr. Rochester—his passion died as if a blight had shrivelled it up: he only asked, "What have *you* to say?"

An inaudible reply escaped Mason's white lips.

"The devil is in it if you cannot answer distinctly. I again demand, what have *you* to say?"

"Sir—sir"—interrupted the clergyman, "do not forget you are in a sacred place." Then, addressing Mason, he inquired gently, "Are you aware, sir, whether or not this gentleman's wife is still living?"

"Courage," urged the lawyer,—"speak out."

"She is now living at Thornfield Hall," said Mason, in more articulate tones: "I saw her there last April. I am her brother."

"At Thornfield Hall!" ejaculated the clergyman. "Impossible! I am an old resident in this neighbourhood, sir, and I never heard of a Mrs. Rochester at Thornfield Hall."

I saw a grim smile contort Mr. Rochester's lip, and he muttered:—"No—by God! I took care that none should hear of it—or of her under that name." He mused—for ten minutes he held counsel with himself: he formed his resolve, and announced it:—"Enough—all shall bolt out at once, like a bullet from the barrel.—Wood, close your book, and take off your surplice; John Green (to the clerk) leave the church: there will be no wedding today:" the man obeyed.

Mr. Rochester continued, hardily and recklessly: "Bigamy is an ugly word!—I meant, however, to be a bigamist; but fate has outmaneuvered me; or Providence has checked me,—perhaps the last. I am little better than a devil at this moment; and, as my pastor there would tell me, deserve no doubt the sternest judgments of God,—even to the quenchless fire and deathless worm. Gentlemen, my plan is broken up!—what this lawyer and his client say is true: I have been married; and the woman to whom I was married lives! You say you never heard of a Mrs. Rochester at the house up yonder, Wood: but I dare say you have many a time inclined your ear to gossip about the mysterious lunatic kept there under watch and ward. Some have whispered to you that she is my bastard half-sister: some, my cast-off mistress; I now inform you that she is my wife, whom I married fifteen years ago,—Bertha Mason by name; sister of this resolute personage, who is now, with his quivering limbs and white cheeks, showing you what a stout heart men may bear. Cheer up, Dick!—never fear me!—I'd almost as soon strike a woman as you. Bertha Mason is mad; and she came of a mad family;—idiots and maniacs through three generations! Her mother, the Creole,[8] was both a mad-woman and a drunkard!—as I found out after I had wed the daughter: for they were silent on family secrets before. Bertha, like a dutiful child, copied her parent in both points. I had a charming partner—pure, wise, modest: you can fancy I was a happy man.—I went through rich scenes! Oh! my experience has been heavenly, if you only knew it! But I owe you no further explanation. Briggs, Wood, Mason,—I invite you all to come up to the house and visit Mrs. Poole's patient, and *my wife!* You shall see what sort of a being I was cheated into espousing, and judge whether or not I had a right to break the compact, and seek sympathy with something at least human. This girl," he continued, looking at me, "knew no more than you, Wood, of the disgusting secret: she thought all was fair and legal; and never dreamt she was going to

8. In the West Indies, a person of European descent.

be entrapped into a feigned union with a defrauded wretch, already bound to a bad, mad, and embruted partner! Come, all of you, follow."

Still holding me fast, he left the church: the three gentlemen came after. At the front door of the hall we found the carriage.

"Take it back to the coach-house, John," said Mr. Rochester, coolly; "it will not be wanted today."

At our entrance Mrs. Fairfax, Adèle, Sophie, Leah, advanced to meet and greet us.

"To the right about—every soul!" cried the master: "away with your congratulations! Who wants them?—Not I!—they are fifteen years too late!"

He passed on and ascended the stairs, still holding my hand, and still beckoning the gentlemen to follow him; which they did. We mounted the first staircase, passed up the gallery, proceeded to the third storey: the low, black door, opened by Mr. Rochester's master key, admitted us to the tapestried room, with its great bed and its pictorial cabinet.

"You know this place, Mason," said our guide; "she bit and stabbed you here."

He lifted the hangings from the wall, uncovering the second door: this, too, he opened. In a room without a window there burned a fire, guarded by a high and strong fender, and a lamp suspended from the ceiling by a chain. Grace Poole bent over the fire, apparently cooking something in a saucepan. In the deep shade, at the further end of the room, a figure ran backwards and forwards. What it was, whether beast or human being, one could not, at first sight, tell: it grovelled, seemingly, on all fours; it snatched and growled like some strange wild animal: but it was covered with clothing; and a quantity of dark, grizzled hair, wild as a mane, hid its head and face.

"Good-morrow, Mrs. Poole!" said Mr. Rochester. "How are you? and how is your charge today?"

"We're tolerable, sir, I thank you," replied Grace, lifting the boiling mess carefully on to the hob: "rather snappish, but not 'rageous."

A fierce cry seemed to give the lie to her favorable report: the clothed hyena rose up, and stood tall on its hind feet.

"Ah, sir, she sees you!" exclaimed Grace: "you'd better not stay."

"Only a few moments, Grace: you must allow me a few moments."

"Take care then, sir!—for God's sake, take care!"

The maniac bellowed: she parted her shaggy locks from her visage, and gazed wildly at her visitors. I recognized well that purple face—those bloated features. Mrs. Poole advanced.

"Keep out of the way," said Mr. Rochester, thrusting her aside: "she has no knife now, I suppose? and I'm on my guard."

"One never knows what she has, sir: she is so cunning: it is not in mortal discretion to fathom her craft."

"We had better leave her," whispered Mason.

"Go to the devil!" was his brother-in-law's recommendation.

" 'Ware!" cried Grace. The three gentlemen retreated simultaneously. Mr. Rochester flung me behind him: the lunatic sprang and grappled his throat viciously, and laid her teeth to his cheek: they struggled. She was a big woman, in stature almost equaling her husband, and corpulent besides: she showed virile force in the contest—more than once she almost throttled him, athletic as he was. He could have settled her with a well-planted blow; but

he would not strike: he would only wrestle. At last he mastered her arms; Grace Poole gave him a cord, and he pinioned them behind her: with more rope, which was at hand, he bound her to a chair. The operation was performed amidst the fiercest yells and the most convulsive plunges. Mr. Rochester then turned to the spectators: he looked at them with a smile both acrid and desolate.

"That is *my wife*," said he. "Such is the sole conjugal embrace I am ever to know—such are the endearments which are to solace my leisure hours! And *this* is what I wished to have" (laying his hand on my shoulder): "this young girl, who stands so grave and quiet at the mouth of hell, looking collectedly at the gambols of a demon. I wanted her just as a change after that fierce ragout. Wood and Briggs, look at the difference! Compare these clear eyes with the red balls yonder—this face with that mask—this form with that bulk; then judge me, priest of the gospel and man of the law, and remember, with what judgment ye judge ye shall be judged![9] Off with you now. I must shut up my prize."

We all withdrew. Mr. Rochester stayed a moment behind us to give some further order to Grace Poole. The solicitor addressed me as he descended the stair.

"You, madam," said he, "are cleared from all blame: your uncle will be glad to hear it—if, indeed, he should be still living—when Mr. Mason returns to Madeira."

"My uncle! What of him? Do you know him?"

"Mr. Mason does: Mr. Eyre has been the Funchal correspondent of[1] his house for some years. When your uncle received your letter intimating the contemplated union between yourself and Mr. Rochester, Mr. Mason, who was staying at Madeira to recruit his health, on his way back to Jamaica, happened to be with him. Mr. Eyre mentioned the intelligence; for he knew that my client here was acquainted with a gentleman of the name of Rochester. Mr. Mason, astonished and distressed as you may suppose, revealed the real state of matters. Your uncle, I am sorry to say, is now on a sick bed; from which, considering the nature of his disease—decline—and the stage it has reached, it is unlikely he will ever rise. He could not then hasten to England himself, to extricate you from the snare into which you had fallen, but he implored Mr. Mason to lose no time in taking steps to prevent the false marriage. He referred him to me for assistance. I used all despatch, and am thankful I was not too late: as you, doubtless, must be also. Were I not morally certain that your uncle will be dead ere you reach Madeira, I would advise you to accompany Mr. Mason back: but as it is, I think you had better remain in England till you can hear further, either from or of Mr. Eyre. Have we anything else to stay for?" he inquired of Mr. Mason.

"No, no—let us be gone," was the anxious reply; and without waiting to take leave of Mr. Rochester, they made their exit at the hall door. The clergyman stayed to exchange a few sentences, either of admonition or reproof, with his haughty parishioner: this duty done, he too departed.

I heard him go as I stood at the half-open door of my own room, to which I had now withdrawn. The house cleared, I shut myself in, fastened the bolt

9. Matthew 7.1–2.
1. The person in a regular business relationship

with. "Funchal": capital of the Madeira Islands, Portugal.

that none might intrude, and proceeded—not to weep, not to mourn, I was yet too calm for that, but—mechanically to take off the wedding-dress, and replace it by the stuff gown I had worn yesterday, as I thought, for the last time. I then sat down: I felt weak and tired. I leaned my arms on a table, and my head dropped on them. And now I thought: till now I had only heard, seen, moved—followed up and down where I was led or dragged—watched event rush on event, disclosure open beyond disclosure: but *now, I thought.*

The morning had been a quiet morning enough—all except the brief scene with the lunatic: the transaction in the church had not been noisy; there was no explosion of passion, no loud altercation, no dispute, no defiance or challenge, no tears, no sobs: a few words had been spoken, a calmly pronounced objection to the marriage made; some stern, short questions put by Mr. Rochester; answers, explanations given, evidence adduced; an open admission of the truth had been uttered by my master; then the living proof had been seen: the intruders were gone, and all was over.

I was in my own room as usual—just myself, without obvious change: nothing had smitten me, or scathed me, or maimed me. And yet, where was the Jane Eyre of yesterday?—where was her life?—where were her prospects?

Jane Eyre, who had been an ardent, expectant woman—almost a bride— was a cold, solitary girl again: her life was pale; her prospects were desolate. A Christmas frost had come at midsummer; a white December storm had whirled over June; ice glazed the ripe apples, drifts crushed the blowing roses; on hay-field and corn-field lay a frozen shroud: lanes which last night blushed full of flowers, today were pathless with untrodden snow; and the woods, which twelve hours since waved leafy and fragrant as groves between the tropics, now spread, waste, wild, and white as pine-forests in wintry Norway. My hopes were all dead—struck with a subtle doom, such as in one night, fell on all the first-born in the land of Egypt.[2] I looked on my cherished wishes, yesterday so blooming and glowing: they lay stark, chill, livid corpses that could never revive. I looked at my love: that feeling which was my master's—which he had created; it shivered in my heart, like a suffering child in a cold cradle; sickness and anguish had seized it; it could not seek Mr. Rochester's arms—it could not derive warmth from his breast. Oh, never more could it turn to him; for faith was blighted—confidence destroyed! Mr. Rochester was not to me what he had been; for he was not what I had thought him. I would not ascribe vice to him; I would not say he had betrayed me: but the attribute of stainless truth was gone from his idea; and from his presence I must go; *that* I perceived well. When—how—whither, I could not yet discern; but he himself, I doubted not, would hurry me from Thornfield. Real affection, it seemed, he could not have for me; it had been only fitful passion: that was balked; he would want me no more. I should fear even to cross his path now: my view must be hateful to him. Oh, how blind had been my eyes! How weak my conduct!

My eyes were covered and closed: eddying darkness seemed to swim round me, and reflection came in as black and confused a flow. Self-abandoned, relaxed, and effortless, I seemed to have laid me down in the dried-up bed of a great river; I heard a flood loosened in remote mountains, and felt the torrent come: to rise I had no will, to flee I had no strength. I lay faint;

2. Exodus 12.

longing to be dead. One idea only still throbbed life-like within me—a remembrance of God: it begot an unuttered prayer: these words went wandering up and down in my rayless mind, as something that should be whispered; but no energy was found to express them:—"Be not far from me, for trouble is near: there is none to help."[3]

It was near: and as I had lifted no petition to Heaven to avert it—as I had neither joined my hands, nor bent my knees, nor moved my lips—it came: in full, heavy swing the torrent poured over me. The whole consciousness of my life lorn, my love lost, my hope quenched, my faith death-struck, swayed full and mighty above me in one sullen mass. That bitter hour cannot be described: in truth, "the waters came into my soul; I sank in deep mire: I felt no standing; I came into deep waters; the floods overflowed me."[4]

Chapter XXVII

Some time in the afternoon I raised my head, and looking round and seeing the western sun gilding the sign of its decline on the wall, I asked, "What am I to do?"

But the answer my mind gave—"Leave Thornfield at once"—was so prompt, so dread, that I stopped my ears: I said, I could not bear such words now. "That I am not Edward Rochester's bride is the least part of my woe," I alleged: "that I have wakened out of most glorious dreams, and found them all void and vain, is a horror I could bear and master; but that I must leave him decidedly, instantly, entirely, is intolerable. I cannot do it."

But, then, a voice within me averred that I could do it; and foretold that I should do it. I wrestled with my own resolution: I wanted to be weak that I might avoid the awful passage of further suffering I saw laid out for me; and conscience, turned tyrant, held passion by the throat, told her tauntingly she had yet but dipped her dainty foot in the slough, and swore that with that arm of iron he would thrust her down to unsounded depths of agony.

"Let me be torn away, then!" I cried. "Let another help me!"

"No; you shall tear yourself away, none shall help you: you shall, yourself, pluck out your right eye: yourself cut off your right hand: your heart shall be the victim; and you, the priest, to transfix it."[5]

I rose up suddenly, terror-struck at the solitude which so ruthless a judge haunted,—at the silence which so awful a voice filled. My head swam as I stood erect: I perceived that I was sickening from excitement and inanition; neither meat nor drink had passed my lips that day, for I had taken no breakfast. And, with a strange pang, I now reflected that, long as I had been shut up here, no message had been sent to ask how I was, or to invite me to come down: not even little Adèle had tapped at the door; not even Mrs. Fairfax had sought me. "Friends always forget those whom fortune forsakes," I murmured, as I undrew the bolt and passed out. I stumbled over an obstacle: my head was still dizzy, my sight was dim, and my limbs were feeble. I could not soon recover myself. I fell, but not on to the ground; an out-stretched arm

3. Psalm 22.11.
4. Psalm 69.1–2.
5. In Matthew 5.27–30 Jesus redefines the Old Testament concept of adultery to include one's thoughts and uses similar language to describe the necessary response.

caught me; I looked up—I was supported by Mr. Rochester, who sat in a chair across my chamber threshold.

"You come out at last," he said. "Well, I have been waiting for you long, and listening: yet not one movement have I heard, nor one sob: five minutes more of that death-like hush, and I should have forced the lock like a burglar. So, you shun me?—you shut yourself up and grieve alone! I would rather you had come and upbraided me with vehemence. You are passionate: I expected a scene of some kind. I was prepared for the hot rain of tears; only I wanted them to be shed on my breast: now a senseless floor has received them, or your drenched handkerchief. But I err: you have not wept at all! I see a white cheek and a faded eye, but no trace of tears. I suppose, then, your heart has been weeping blood?

"Well, Jane; not a word of reproach? Nothing bitter—nothing poignant? Nothing to cut a feeling or sting a passion? You sit quietly where I have placed you, and regard me with a weary, passive look.

"Jane, I never meant to wound you thus. If the man who had but one little ewe lamb that was dear to him as a daughter, that ate of his bread and drank of his cup, and lay in his bosom, had by some mistake slaughtered it at the shambles, he would not have rued his bloody blunder more than I now rue mine.[6] Will you ever forgive me?"

Reader!—I forgave him at the moment, and on the spot. There was such deep remorse in his eye, such true pity in his tone, such manly energy in his manner; and, besides, there was such unchanged love in his whole look and mien—I forgave him all: yet not in words, not outwardly; only at my heart's core.

"You know I am a scoundrel, Jane?" ere long he inquired wistfully—wondering, I suppose, at my continued silence and tameness: the result rather of weakness than of will.

"Yes, sir."

"Then tell me so roundly and sharply—don't spare me."

"I cannot: I am tired and sick. I want some water." He heaved a sort of shuddering sigh, and taking me in his arms, carried me downstairs. At first I did not know to what room he had borne me; all was cloudy to my glazed sight: presently I felt the reviving warmth of a fire; for, summer as it was, I had become icy cold in my chamber. He put wine to my lips; I tasted it and revived; then I ate something he offered me, and was soon myself. I was in the library—sitting in his chair—he was quite near. "If I could go out of life now, without too sharp a pang, it would be well for me," I thought; "then I should not have to make the effort of cracking my heart-strings in rending them from among Mr. Rochester's. I must leave him, it appears. I do not want to leave him—I cannot leave him."

"How are you now, Jane?"

"Much better, sir: I shall be well soon."

"Taste the wine again, Jane."

I obeyed him; then he put the glass on the table, stood before me, and looked at me attentively. Suddenly he turned away, with an inarticulate exclamation, full of passionate emotion of some kind; he walked fast through

6. 2 Samuel 12.1–4 tells of the rich man's deliberate slaughter of the poor man's well-loved lamb. "Shambles": slaughterhouse.

the room and came back: he stooped towards me as if to kiss me; but I remembered caresses were now forbidden. I turned my face away, and put his aside.

"What!—How is this?" he exclaimed hastily. "Oh, I know! you won't kiss the husband of Bertha Mason? You consider my arms filled and my embraces appropriated?"

"At any rate, there is neither room nor claim for me, sir."

"Why, Jane? I will spare you the trouble of much talking: I will answer for you—because I have a wife already, you would reply.—I guess rightly?"

"Yes."

"If you think so, you must have a strange opinion of me: you must regard me as a plotting profligate—a base and low rake who has been simulating disinterested love in order to draw you into a snare deliberately laid, and strip you of honor, and rob you of self-respect. What do you say to that? I see you can say nothing: in the first place, you are faint still, and have enough to do to draw your breath; in the second place, you cannot yet accustom yourself to accuse and revile me; and, besides, the flood-gates of tears are opened, and they would rush out if you spoke much; and you have no desire to expostulate, to upbraid, to make a scene: you are thinking how to *act,—talking,* you consider, is of no use. I know you—I am on my guard."

"Sir, I do not wish to act against you," I said; and my unsteady voice warned me to curtail my sentence.

"Not in *your* sense of the word, but in *mine,* you are scheming to destroy me. You have as good as said that I am a married man—as a married man you will shun me, keep out of my way: just now you have refused to kiss me. You intend to make yourself a complete stranger to me; to live under this roof only as Adèle's governess: if ever I say a friendly word to you, if ever a friendly feeling inclines you again to me, you will say,—'That man had nearly made me his mistress: I must be ice and rock to him'; and ice and rock you will accordingly become."

I cleared and steadied my voice to reply: "All is changed about me, sir; I must change too—there is no doubt of that; and to avoid fluctuations of feeling, and continual combats with recollections and associations, there is only one way—Adèle must have a new governess, sir."

"Oh, Adèle will go to school—I have settled that already; nor do I mean to torment you with the hideous associations and recollections of Thornfield Hall—this accursed place—this tent of Achan[7]—this insolent vault, offering the ghastliness of living death to the light of the open sky—this narrow stone hell, with its one real fiend, worse than a legion of such as we imagine.—Jane, you shall not stay here, nor will I. I was wrong ever to bring you to Thornfield Hall, knowing as I did how it was haunted. I charged them to conceal from you, before I ever saw you, all knowledge of the curse of the place; merely because I feared Adèle never would have a governess to stay if she knew with what inmate she was housed, and my plans would not permit me to remove the maniac elsewhere—though I possess an old house, Fern-dean Manor, even more retired and hidden than this, where I could have lodged her safely enough, had not a scruple about the unhealthiness of the situation, in the heart of a wood, made my conscience recoil from the

7. Achan concealed stolen treasure in his tent (Joshua 7).

arrangement. Probably those damp walls would soon have eased me of her charge: but to each villain his own vice; and mine is not a tendency to indirect assassination, even of what I most hate.

"Concealing the mad-woman's neighborhood from you, however, was something like covering a child with a cloak, and laying it down near a upas-tree:[8] that demon's vicinage is poisoned, and always was. But I'll shut up Thornfield Hall: I'll nail up the front door, and board the lower windows; I'll give Mrs. Poole two hundred a year to live here with *my wife*, as you term that fearful hag: Grace will do much for money, and she shall have her son, the keeper at Grimsby Retreat, to bear her company and be at hand to give her aid in the paroxysms when *my wife* is prompted by her familiar to burn people in their beds at night, to stab them, to bite their flesh from their bones, and so on"—

"Sir," I interrupted him, "you are inexorable for that unfortunate lady: you speak of her with hate—with vindictive antipathy. It is cruel—she cannot help being mad."

"Jane, my little darling (so I will call you, for so you are), you don't know what you are talking about; you misjudge me again: it is not because she is mad I hate her. If you were mad, do you think I should hate you?"

"I do indeed, sir."

"Then you are mistaken, and you know nothing about me, and nothing about the sort of love of which I am capable. Every atom of your flesh is as dear to me as my own: in pain and sickness it would still be dear. Your mind is my treasure, and if it were broken, it would be my treasure still: if you raved, my arms should confine you, and not a strait waistcoat—your grasp, even in fury, would have a charm for me: if you flew at me as wildly as that woman did this morning, I should receive you in an embrace at least as fond as it would be restrictive. I should not shrink from you with disgust as I did from her: in your quiet moments you should have no watcher and no nurse but me; and I could hang over you with untiring tenderness, though you gave me no smile in return; and never weary of gazing into your eyes, though they had no longer a ray of recognition for me.—But why do I follow that train of ideas? I was talking of removing you from Thornfield. All, you know, is prepared for prompt departure: tomorrow you shall go. I only ask you to endure one more night under this roof, Jane: and then, farewell to its miseries and terrors for ever! I have a place to repair to which will be a secure sanctuary from hateful reminiscences, from unwelcome intrusion—even from falsehood and slander."

"And take Adèle with you, sir," I interrupted; "she will be a companion for you."

"What do you mean, Jane? I told you I would send Adèle to school: and what do I want with a child for a companion? and not my own child,—a French dancer's bastard. Why do you importune me about her? I say, why do you assign Adèle to me for a companion?"

"You spoke of a retirement, sir; and retirement and solitude are dull: too dull for you."

"Solitude! solitude!" he reiterated, with irritation. "I see I must come to

8. A tree of Java that, according to legend, killed all life around it (in fact, its sap can be used to make poison).

an explanation. I don't know what sphinx-like expression is forming in your countenance. *You* are to share my solitude. Do you understand?"

I shook my head: it required a degree of courage, excited as he was becoming, even to risk that mute sign of dissent. He had been walking fast about the room, and he stopped, as if suddenly rooted to one spot. He looked at me long and hard: I turned my eyes from him, fixed them on the fire, and tried to assume and maintain a quiet, collected aspect.

"Now for the hitch in Jane's character," he said at last, speaking more calmly than from his look I had expected him to speak. "The reel of silk has run smoothly enough so far; but I always knew there would come a knot and a puzzle: here it is. Now for vexation, and exasperation, and endless trouble! By God! I long to exert a fraction of Samson's strength, and break the entanglement like tow!"[9]

He recommenced his walk: but soon again stopped, and this time just before me.

"Jane! will you hear reason?" (he stooped and approached his lips to my ear) "because, if you won't, I'll try violence." His voice was hoarse; his look that of a man who is just about to burst an insufferable bond and plunge headlong into wild license. I saw that in another moment, and with one impetus of frenzy more, I should be able to do nothing with him. The present—the passing second of time—was all I had in which to control and restrain him: a movement of repulsion, flight, fear, would have sealed my doom,—and his. But I was not afraid: not in the least. I felt an inward power; a sense of influence, which supported me. The crisis was perilous; but not without its charm: such as the Indian, perhaps, feels when he slips over the rapid in his canoe. I took hold of his clenched hand; loosened the contorted fingers, and said to him, soothingly,—"Sit down; I'll talk to you as long as you like, and hear all you have to say, whether reasonable or unreasonable."

He sat down: but he did not get leave to speak directly. I had been struggling with tears for some time; I had taken great pains to repress them, because I knew he would not like to see me weep. Now, however, I considered it well to let them flow as freely and as long as they liked. If the flood annoyed him, so much the better. So I gave way and cried heartily.

Soon I heard him earnestly entreating me to be composed. I said I could not while he was in such a passion.

"But I am not angry, Jane: I only love you too well; and you had steeled your little pale face with such a resolute, frozen look, I could not endure it. Hush, now, and wipe your eyes."

His softened voice announced that he was subdued; so I, in my turn, became calm. Now he made an effort to rest his head on my shoulder; but I would not permit it. Then he would draw me to him: no.

"Jane! Jane!" he said, in such an accent of bitter sadness it thrilled along every nerve I had, "you don't love me, then? It was only my station, and the rank of my wife, that you valued? Now that you think me disqualified to become your husband you recoil from my touch as if I were some toad or ape."

These words cut me: yet what could I do or say? I ought probably to have

9. Flax or other fiber used to make twine; in Scottish dialect, a rope or, specifically, a hangman's rope.

done or said nothing: but I was so tortured by a sense of remorse at thus hurting his feelings I could not control the wish to drop balm where I had wounded.

"I *do* love you," I said, "more than ever: but I must not show or indulge the feeling: and this is the last time I must express it."

"The last time, Jane! What! do you think you can live with me, and see me daily, and yet, if you still love me, be always cold and distant?"

"No, sir; that I am certain I could not; and therefore I see there is but one way: but you will be furious if I mention it."

"Oh, mention it! If I storm, you have the art of weeping."

"Mr. Rochester, I must leave you."

"For how long, Jane? For a few minutes, while you smooth your hair— which is somewhat dishevelled; and bathe your face—which looks feverish?"

"I must leave Adèle and Thornfield. I must part with you for my whole life: I must begin a new existence amongst strange faces and strange scenes."

"Of course: I told you you should. I pass over the madness about parting from me. You mean you must become a part of me. As to the new existence, it is all right: you shall yet be my wife: I am not married. You shall be Mrs. Rochester—both virtually and nominally. I shall keep only to you so long as you and I live. You shall go to a place I have in the south of France: a white-washed villa on the shores of the Mediterranean. There you shall live a happy, and guarded, and most innocent life. Never fear that I wish to lure you into error—to make you my mistress. Why do you shake your head? Jane, you must be reasonable; or in truth I shall again become frantic."

His voice and hand quivered; his large nostrils dilated; his eye blazed; still I dared to speak:—"Sir, your wife is living: that is a fact acknowledged this morning by yourself. If I lived with you as you desire, I should then be your mistress: to say otherwise is sophistical—is false."

"Jane, I am not a gentle-tempered man—you forget that: I am not long-enduring; I am not cool and dispassionate. Out of pity to me and yourself, put your finger on my pulse, feel how it throbs, and—beware!"

He bared his wrist and offered it to me: the blood was forsaking his cheek and lips; they were growing livid; I was distressed on all hands. To agitate him thus deeply, by a resistance he so abhorred, was cruel: to yield was out of the question. I did what human beings do instinctively when they are driven to utter extremity—looked for aid to one higher than man: the words "God help me!" burst involuntarily from my lips.

"I am a fool!" cried Mr. Rochester suddenly. "I keep telling her I am not married, and do not explain to her why. I forget she knows nothing of the character of that woman, or of the circumstances attending my infernal union with her. Oh, I am certain Jane will agree with me in opinion when she knows all that I know! Just put your hand in mine, Janet, that I may have the evidence of touch as well as sight to prove you are near me—and I will in a few words show you the real state of the case. Can you listen to me?"

"Yes, sir; for hours if you will."

"I ask only minutes. Jane, did you ever hear or know that I was not the eldest son of my house; that I had once a brother older than I?"

"I remember Mrs. Fairfax told me so once."

"And did you ever hear that my father was an avaricious grasping man?"

"I have understood something to that effect."

"Well, Jane, being so, it was his resolution to keep the property together; he could not bear the idea of dividing his estate and leaving me a fair portion: all, he resolved, should go to my brother Rowland. Yet as little could he endure that a son of his should be a poor man. I must be provided for by a wealthy marriage. He sought me a partner betimes. Mr. Mason, a West India planter and merchant, was his old acquaintance. He was certain his possessions were real and vast: he made inquiries. Mr. Mason, he found, had a son and daughter; and he learned from him that he could and would give the latter a fortune of thirty thousand pounds: that sufficed. When I left college I was sent out to Jamaica, to espouse a bride already courted for me. My father said nothing about her money: but he told me Miss Mason was the boast of Spanish Town for her beauty: and this was no lie. I found her a fine woman, in the style of Blanche Ingram; tall, dark, and majestic. Her family wished to secure me, because I was of a good race; and so did she. They showed her to me in parties, splendidly dressed. I seldom saw her alone, and had very little private conversation with her. She flattered me, and lavishly displayed for my pleasure her charms and accomplishments. All the men in her circle seemed to admire her and envy me. I was dazzled, stimulated: my senses were excited; and being ignorant, raw, and inexperienced, I thought I loved her. There is no folly so besotted that the idiotic rivalries of society, the prurience, the rashness, the blindness of youth, will not hurry a man to its commission. Her relatives encouraged me; competitors piqued me; she allured me: a marriage was achieved almost before I knew where I was. Oh, I have no respect for myself when I think of that act!—an agony of inward contempt masters me. I never loved, I never esteemed, I did not even know her. I was not sure of the existence of one virtue in her nature: I had marked neither modesty, nor benevolence, nor candor, nor refinement in her mind or manners—and, I married her:—gross, groveling, mole-eyed[1] blockhead that I was! With less sin I might have—but let me remember to whom I am speaking.

"My bride's mother I had never seen: I understood she was dead. The honeymoon over, I learned my mistake; she was only mad, and shut up in a lunatic asylum. There was a younger brother, too, a complete dumb idiot. The elder one, whom you have seen (and whom I cannot hate, whilst I abhor all his kindred, because he has some grains of affection in his feeble mind; shown in the continued interest he takes in his wretched sister, and also in a dog-like attachment he once bore me), will probably be in the same state one day. My father, and my brother Rowland, knew all this; but they thought only of the thirty thousand pounds, and joined in the plot against me.

"These were vile discoveries; but, except for the treachery of concealment, I should have made them no subject of reproach to my wife: even when I found her nature wholly alien to mine; her tastes obnoxious to me; her cast of mind common, low, narrow, and singularly incapable of being led to anything higher, expanded to anything larger—when I found that I could not pass a single evening, nor even a single hour of the day, with her in comfort: that kindly conversation could not be sustained between us, because whatever topic I started immediately received from her a turn at once coarse and trite, perverse and imbecile—when I perceived that I should never have a

1. I.e., nearly blind.

quiet or settled household, because no servant would bear the continued outbreaks of her violent and unreasonable temper, or the vexations of her absurd, contradictory, exacting orders—even then I restrained myself: I eschewed upbraiding, I curtailed remonstrance; I tried to devour my repentance and disgust in secret; I repressed the deep antipathy I felt.

"Jane, I will not trouble you with abominable details: some strong words shall express what I have to say. I lived with that woman upstairs four years, and before that time she had tried me indeed: her character ripened and developed with frightful rapidity; her vices sprang up fast and rank: they were so strong, only cruelty could check them; and I would not use cruelty. What a pigmy intellect she had—and what giant propensities! How fearful were the curses those propensities entailed on me! Bertha Mason,—the true daughter of an infamous mother,—dragged me through all the hideous and degrading agonies which must attend a man bound to a wife at once intemperate and unchaste.

"My brother in the interval was dead; and at the end of the four years my father died too. I was rich enough now—yet poor to hideous indigence: a nature the most gross, impure, depraved, I ever saw, was associated with mine, and called by the law and by society a part of me. And I could not rid myself of it by any legal proceedings: for the doctors now discovered that *my wife* was mad—her excesses had prematurely developed the germs of insanity:—Jane, you don't like my narrative; you look almost sick—shall I defer the rest to another day?"

"No, sir, finish it now: I pity you—I do earnestly pity you."

"Pity, Jane, from some people is a noxious and insulting sort of tribute, which one is justified in hurling back in the teeth of those who offer it; but that is the sort of pity native to callous, selfish hearts: it is a hybrid, egotistical pain at hearing of woes, crossed with ignorant contempt for those who have endured them. But that is not your pity, Jane: it is not the feeling of which your whole face is full at this moment—with which your eyes are now almost overflowing—with which your heart is heaving—with which your hand is trembling in mine. Your pity, my darling, is the suffering mother of love: its anguish is the very natal pang of the divine passion. I accept it, Jane; let the daughter have free advent—my arms wait to receive her."

"Now, sir, proceed: what did you do when you found she was mad?"

"Jane—I approached the verge of despair: a remnant of self-respect was all that intervened between me and the gulf. In the eyes of the world I was doubtless covered with grimy dishonor: but I resolved to be clean in my own sight—and to the last I repudiated the contamination of her crimes, and wrenched myself from connection with her mental defects. Still, society associated my name and person with hers! I yet saw her and heard her daily: something of her breath (faugh!) mixed with the air I breathed; and, besides, I remembered I had once been her husband—that recollection was then, and is now, inexpressibly odious to me: moreover, I knew that while she lived I could never be the husband of another and better wife; and though five years my senior (her family and her father had lied to me even in the particular of her age), she was likely to live as long as I, being as robust in frame as she was infirm in mind. Thus, at the age of twenty-six, I was hopeless.

"One night I had been awakened by her yells—(since the medical men had pronounced her mad she had of course been shut up)—it was a fiery

West Indian night; one of the description that frequently precede the hurricanes of those climates; being unable to sleep in bed, I got up and opened the window. The air was like sulfur-steams—I could find no refreshment anywhere. Mosquitoes came buzzing in and hummed sullenly round the room; the sea, which I could hear from thence, rumbled dull like an earthquake—black clouds were casting up over it; the moon was setting in the waves, broad and red, like a hot cannon-ball—she threw her last bloody glance over a world quivering with the ferment of tempest. I was physically influenced by the atmosphere and scene, and my ears were filled with the curses the maniac still shrieked out; wherein she momentarily mingled my name with such a tone of demon-hate, with such language!—no professed harlot ever had a fouler vocabulary than she: though two rooms off, I heard every word—the thin partitions of the West India house opposing but slight obstruction to her wolfish cries.

" 'This life,' said I at last, 'is hell! this is the air—those are the sounds of the bottomless pit! I have a right to deliver myself from it if I can. The sufferings of this mortal state will leave me with the heavy flesh that now cumbers my soul. Of the fanatic's burning eternity I have no fear; there is not a future state worse than this present one—let me break away, and go home to God!'

"I said this whilst I knelt down at and unlocked a trunk which contained a brace of loaded pistols: I meant to shoot myself. I only entertained the intention for a moment; for not being insane, the crisis of exquisite and unalloyed despair which had originated the wish and design of self-destruction was past in a second.

"A wind fresh from Europe blew over the ocean and rushed through the open casement: the storm broke, streamed, thundered, blazed, and the air grew pure. I then framed and fixed a resolution. While I walked under the dripping orange-trees of my wet garden, and among its drenched pomegranates and pineapples, and while the refulgent dawn of the tropics kindled round me—I reasoned thus, Jane:—and now listen; for it was true Wisdom that consoled me in that hour, and showed me the right path to follow.

"The sweet wind from Europe was still whispering in the refreshed leaves, and the Atlantic was thundering in glorious liberty; my heart, dried up and scorched for a long time, swelled to the tone, and filled with living blood— my being longed for renewal—my soul thirsted for a pure draught. I saw Hope revive—and felt Regeneration possible. From a flowery arch at the bottom of my garden I gazed over the sea—bluer than the sky: the old world was beyond; clear prospects opened thus:—

" 'Go,' said Hope, 'and live again in Europe: there it is not known what a sullied name you bear, nor what a filthy burden is bound to you. You may take the maniac with you to England; confine her with due attendance and precautions at Thornfield: then travel yourself to what clime you will, and form what new tie you like. That woman, who has so abused your long-suffering—so sullied your name; so outraged your honor; so blighted your youth—is not your wife; nor are you her husband. See that she is cared for as her condition demands, and you have done all that God and Humanity require of you. Let her identity, her connection with yourself, be buried in oblivion: you are bound to impart them to no living being. Place her in safety and comfort: shelter her degradation with secrecy, and leave her.'

"I acted precisely on this suggestion. My father and brother had not made my marriage known to their acquaintance; because, in the very first letter I wrote to apprise them of the union—having already begun to experience extreme disgust of its consequences; and from the family character and constitution seeing a hideous future opening to me—I added an urgent charge to keep it secret; and very soon the infamous conduct of the wife my father had selected for me was such as to make him blush to own her as his daughter-in-law. Far from desiring to publish the connection, he became as anxious to conceal it as myself.

"To England, then, I conveyed her; a fearful voyage I had with such a monster in the vessel. Glad was I when I at last got her to Thornfield, and saw her safely lodged in that third-story room, of whose secret inner cabinet she has now for ten years made a wild beast's den—a goblin's cell. I had some trouble in finding an attendant for her: as it was necessary to select one on whose fidelity dependence could be placed; for her ravings would inevitably betray my secret: besides, she had lucid intervals of days—sometimes weeks—which she filled up with abuse of me. At last I hired Grace Poole, from the Grimsby Retreat. She and the surgeon, Carter (who dressed Mason's wounds that night he was stabbed and worried), are the only two I have ever admitted to my confidence. Mrs. Fairfax may indeed have suspected something; but she could have gained no precise knowledge as to facts. Grace has, on the whole, proved a good keeper; though, owing partly to a fault of her own, of which it appears nothing can cure her, and which is incident to her harassing profession,[2] her vigilance has been more than once lulled and baffled. The lunatic is both cunning and malignant; she has never failed to take advantage of her guardian's temporary lapses; once to secrete the knife with which she stabbed her brother, and twice to possess herself of the key of her cell, and issue therefrom in the night-time. On the first of these occasions she perpetrated the attempt to burn me in my bed; on the second she paid that ghastly visit to you. I thank Providence, who watched over you, that she then spent her fury on your wedding apparel; which perhaps brought back vague reminiscences of her own bridal days; but on what might have happened I cannot endure to reflect. When I think of the thing which flew at my throat this morning hanging its black and scarlet visage over the nest of my dove my blood curdles"——

"And what, sir," I asked, while he paused, "did you do when you had settled her here? Where did you go?"

"What did I do, Jane? I transformed myself into a Will-o'-the-wisp. Where did I go? I pursued wanderings as wild as those of the March-spirit. I sought the Continent, and went devious through all its lands. My fixed desire was to seek and find a good and intelligent woman whom I could love: a contrast to the fury I left at Thornfield"——

"But you could not marry, sir."

"I had determined, and was convinced that I could and ought. It was not my original intention to deceive, as I have deceived you. I meant to tell my tale plainly, and make my proposals openly: and it appeared to me so absolutely rational that I should be considered free to love and be loved, I never

2. Nurses were widely believed to be especially fond of drink.

doubted some woman might be found willing and able to understand my case and accept me, in spite of the curse with which I was burdened."

"Well, sir?"

"When you are inquisitive, Jane, you always make me smile. You open your eyes like an eager bird, and make every now and then a restless movement; as if answers in speech did not flow fast enough for you, and you wanted to read the tablet of one's heart. But before I go on tell me what you mean by your 'Well, sir?' It is a small phrase very frequent with you; and which many a time has drawn me on and on through interminable talk: I don't very well know why."

"I mean—What next? How did you proceed? What came of such an event?"

"Precisely: and what do you wish to know now?"

"Whether you found any one you liked: whether you asked her to marry you; and what she said."

"I can tell you whether I found any one I liked, and whether I asked her to marry me: but what she said is yet to be recorded in the book of Fate. For ten long years I roved about, living first in one capital, then another: sometimes in St. Petersburg; oftener in Paris; occasionally in Rome, Naples, and Florence. Provided with plenty of money and the passport of an old name, I could choose my own society: no circles were closed against me. I sought my ideal of a woman among English ladies, French countesses, Italian signoras, and German gräfinnen.[3] I could not find her. Sometimes, for a fleeting moment, I thought I caught a glance, heard a tone, beheld a form, which announced the realization of my dream: but I was presently undeceived. You are not to suppose that I desired perfection either of mind or person. I longed only for what suited me—for the antipodes of the Creole: and I longed vainly. Amongst them all I found not one whom, had I been ever so free, I—warned as I was of the risks, the horrors, the loathings of incongruous unions—would have asked to marry me. Disappointment made me reckless. I tried dissipation—never debauchery: that I hated, and hate. That was my Indian Messalina's[4] attribute: rooted disgust at it and her restrained me much, even in pleasure. Any enjoyment that bordered on riot seemed to approach me to her and her vices, and I eschewed it.

"Yet I could not live alone; so I tried the companionship of mistresses. The first I chose was Céline Varens—another of those steps which make a man spurn himself when he recalls them. You already know what she was, and how my liaison with her terminated. She had two successors: an Italian, Giacinta, and a German, Clara; both considered singularly handsome. What was their beauty to me in a few weeks? Giacinta was unprincipled and violent: I tired of her in three months. Clara was honest and quiet; but heavy, mindless, unimpressible: not one whit to my taste. I was glad to give her a sufficient sum to set her up in a good line of business, and so get decently rid of her. But, Jane, I see by your face you are not forming a very favorable opinion of me just now. You think me an unfeeling, loose-principled rake: don't you?"

"I don't like you so well as I have done sometimes, indeed, sir. Did it not

3. Countesses.
4. Cruel and licentious wife (ca. 22–48 C.E.) of the Roman emperor Claudius. "Antipodes": exact opposites.

seem to you in the least wrong to live in that way: first with one mistress and then another? You talk of it as a mere matter of course."

"It was with me: and I did not like it. It was a groveling fashion of existence: I should never like to return to it. Hiring a mistress is the next worst thing to buying a slave: both are often by nature, and always by position, inferior; and to live familiarly with inferiors is degrading. I now hate the recollection of the time I passed with Céline, Giacinta, and Clara."

I felt the truth of these words; and I drew from them the certain inference, that if I were so far to forget myself and all the teaching that had ever been instilled into me as—under any pretext—with any justification—through any temptation—to become the successor of these poor girls, he would one day regard me with the same feeling which now in his mind desecrated their memory. I did not give utterance to this conviction: it was enough to feel it. I impressed it on my heart, that it might remain there to serve me as aid in the time of trial.

"Now, Jane, why don't you say 'Well, sir?' I have not done. You are looking grave. You disapprove of me still, I see. But let me come to the point. Last January, rid of all mistresses—in a harsh, bitter frame of mind, the result of a useless, roving, lonely life—corroded with disappointment, sourly disposed against all men, and especially against all *woman*kind (for I began to regard the notion of an intellectual, faithful, loving woman as a mere dream), recalled by business, I came back to England.

"On a frosty winter afternoon I rode in sight of Thornfield Hall. Abhorred spot! I expected no peace—no pleasure there. On a stile in Hay Lane I saw a quiet little figure sitting by itself. I passed it as negligently as I did the pollard willow opposite to it; I had no presentiment of what it would be to me; no inward warning that the arbitress of my life—my genius for good or evil—waited there in humble guise. I did not know it even when, on the occasion of Mesrour's accident, it came up and gravely offered me help. Childish and slender creature! It seemed as if a linnet had hopped on my foot and proposed to bear me on its tiny wing. I was surly; but the thing would not go: it stood by me with strange perseverance, and looked and spoke with a sort of authority. I must be aided, and by that hand: and aided I was.

"When once I had pressed the frail shoulder, something new—a fresh sap and sense—stole into my frame. It was well I had learnt that this elf must return to me—that it belonged to my house down below—or I could not have felt it pass away from under my hand, and seen it vanish behind the dim hedge, without singular regret. I heard you come home that night, Jane: though probably you were not aware that I thought of you, or watched for you. The next day I observed you—myself unseen—for half an hour, while you played with Adèle in the gallery. It was a snowy day, I recollect, and you could not go out of doors. I was in my room; the door was ajar: I could both listen and watch. Adèle claimed your outward attention for a while; yet I fancied your thoughts were elsewhere: but you were very patient with her, my little Jane; you talked to her and amused her a long time. When at last she left you, you lapsed at once into deep reverie: you betook yourself slowly to pace the gallery. Now and then, in passing a casement you glanced out at the thick-falling snow; you listened to the sobbing wind, and again you paced gently on and dreamed. I think those day visions were not dark; there was a pleasurable illumination in your eye occasionally, a soft excitement in your

aspect, which told of no bitter, bilious, hypochondriac brooding: your look revealed rather the sweet musings, of youth, when its spirit follows on willing wings the flight of Hope, up and on to an ideal heaven. The voice of Mrs. Fairfax, speaking to a servant in the hall, wakened you: and how curiously you smiled to and at yourself, Janet! There was much sense in your smile: it was very shrewd, and seemed to make light of your own abstraction. It seemed to say—'My fine visions are all very well, but I must not forget they are absolutely unreal. I have a rosy sky, and a green flowery Eden in my brain; but without, I am perfectly aware, lies at my feet a rough tract to travel, and around me gather black tempests to encounter.' You ran downstairs and demanded of Mrs. Fairfax some occupation: the weekly house accounts to make up, or something of that sort, I think it was. I was vexed with you for getting out of my sight.

"Impatiently I waited for evening, when I might summon you to my presence. An unusual—to me—a perfectly new character I suspected was yours: I desired to search it deeper, and know it better. You entered the room with a look and air at once shy and independent: you were quaintly dressed— much as you are now. I made you talk—ere long I found you full of strange contrasts. Your garb and manner were restricted by rule; your air was often diffident, and altogether that of one refined by nature, but absolutely unused to society, and a good deal afraid of making herself disadvantageously conspicuous by some solecism or blunder; yet when addressed you lifted a keen, a daring, and a glowing eye to your interlocutor's face: there was penetration and power in each glance you gave; when plied by close questions, you found ready and round[5] answers. Very soon you seemed to get used to me; I believe you felt the existence of sympathy between you and your grim and cross master, Jane; for it was astonishing to see how quickly a certain pleasant ease tranquilized your manner: snarl as I would, you showed no surprise, fear, annoyance, or displeasure at my moroseness; you watched me, and now and then smiled at me with a simple yet sagacious grace I cannot describe. I was at once content and stimulated with what I saw: I liked what I had seen, and wished to see more. Yet, for a long time, I treated you distantly, and sought your company rarely. I was an intellectual epicure, and wished to prolong the gratification of making this novel and piquant acquaintance: besides, I was for a while troubled with a haunting fear that if I handled the flower freely its bloom would fade—the sweet charm of freshness would leave it. I did not then know that it was no transitory blossom; but rather the radiant resemblance of one, cut in an indestructible gem. Moreover, I wished to see whether you would seek me if I shunned you—but you did not: you kept in the school-room as still as your own desk and easel; if by chance I met you, you passed me as soon, and with as little token of recognition, as was consistent with respect. Your habitual expression in those days, Jane, was a thoughtful look; not despondent, for you were not sickly; but not buoyant, for you had little hope, and no actual pleasure. I wondered what you thought of me—or if you ever thought of me; to find this out I resumed my notice of you. There was something glad in your glance and genial in your manner when you conversed: I saw you had a social heart; it was the silent schoolroom—it was the tedium of your life—that made you mournful. I

5. Straightforward.

permitted myself the delight of being kind to you; kindness stirred emotion soon: your face became soft in expression, your tones gentle; I liked my name pronounced by your lips in a grateful, happy accent. I used to enjoy a chance meeting with you, Jane, at this time: there was a curious hesitation in your manner: you glanced at me with a slight trouble—a hovering doubt: you did not know what my caprice might be—whether I was going to play the master and be stern, or the friend and be benignant. I was now too fond of you often to stimulate the first whim; and, when I stretched my hand out cordially, such bloom and light and bliss rose to your young, wistful features, I had much ado often to avoid straining you then and there to my heart."

"Don't talk any more of those days, sir," I interrupted, furtively dashing away some tears from my eyes; his language was torture to me; for I knew what I must do—and do soon—and all these reminiscences and these revelations of his feelings only made my work more difficult.

"No, Jane," he returned: "what necessity is there to dwell on the Past, when the Present is so much surer—the Future so much brighter?"

I shuddered to hear the infatuated assertion.

"You see now how the case stands—do you not?" he continued. "After a youth and manhood passed half in unutterable misery and half in dreary solitude, I have for the first time found what I can truly love—I have found *you*. You are my sympathy—my better self—my good angel—I am bound to you with a strong attachment. I think you good, gifted, lovely: a fervent, a solemn passion is conceived in my heart; it leans to you, draws you to my center and spring of life, wraps my existence about you—and, kindling in pure, powerful flame, fuses you and me in one.

"It was because I felt and knew this that I resolved to marry you. To tell me that I had already a wife is empty mockery: you know now that I had but a hideous demon. I was wrong to attempt to deceive you; but I feared a stubbornness that exists in your character. I feared early instilled prejudice: I wanted to have you safe before hazarding confidences. This was cowardly: I should have appealed to your nobleness and magnanimity at first, as I do now—opened to you plainly my life of agony—described to you my hunger and thirst after a higher and worthier existence—shown to you, not my *resolution* (that word is weak), but my resistless *bent* to love faithfully and well where I am faithfully and well loved in return. Then I should have asked you to accept my pledge of fidelity, and to give me yours: Jane—give it me now."

A pause.

"Why are you silent, Jane?"

I was experiencing an ordeal: a hand of fiery iron grasped my vitals. Terrible moment: full of struggle, blackness, burning! Not a human being that ever lived could wish to be loved better than I was loved; and him who thus loved me I absolutely worshiped: and I must renounce love and idol. One drear word comprised my intolerable duty—"Depart!"

"Jane, you understand what I want of you? Just this promise—'I will be yours, Mr. Rochester.' "

"Mr. Rochester, I will *not* be yours."

Another long silence.

"Jane!" recommenced he, with a gentleness that broke me down with grief, and turned me stone-cold with ominous terror—for this still voice was the pant of a lion rising—"Jane, do you mean to go one way in the world, and to let me go another?"

"I do."

"Jane" (bending towards and embracing me), "do you mean it now?"

"I do."

"And now?" softly kissing my forehead and cheek.

"I do"—extricating myself from restraint rapidly and completely.

"Oh, Jane, this is bitter! This—this is wicked. It would not be wicked to love me."

"It would to obey you."

A wild look raised his brows—crossed his features: he rose; but he forbore yet. I laid my hand on the back of the chair for support: I shook, I feared—but I resolved.

"One instant, Jane. Give one glance to my horrible life when you are gone. All happiness will be torn away with you. What then is left? For a wife I have but the maniac upstairs: as well might you refer me to some corpse in yonder churchyard. What shall I do, Jane? Where turn for a companion, and for some hope?"

"Do as I do: trust in God and yourself. Believe in heaven. Hope to meet again there."

"Then you will not yield?"

"No."

"Then you condemn me to live wretched, and to die accursed?" His voice rose.

"I advise you to live sinless; and I wish you to die tranquil."

"Then you snatch love and innocence from me? You fling me back on lust for a passion—vice for an occupation?"

"Mr. Rochester, I no more assign this fate to you than I grasp at it for myself. We were born to strive and endure—you as well as I: do so. You will forget me before I forget you."

"You make me a liar by such language: you sully my honor. I declared I could not change: you tell me to my face I shall change soon. And what a distortion in your judgment, what a perversity in your ideas, is proved by your conduct! Is it better to drive a fellow-creature to despair than to transgress a mere human law—no man being injured by the breach? For you have neither relatives nor acquaintances whom you need fear to offend by living with me."

This was true: and while he spoke my very conscience and reason turned traitors against me, and charged me with crime in resisting him. They spoke almost as loud as Feeling: and that clamored wildly. "Oh, comply!" it said. "Think of his misery; think of his danger—look at his state when left alone; remember his headlong nature; consider the recklessness following on despair—soothe him; save him; love him; tell him you love him and will be his. Who in the world cares for *you*? or who will be injured by what you do?"

Still indomitable was the reply—"*I care for myself.* The more solitary, the more friendless, the more unsustained I am, the more I will respect myself. I will keep the law given by God; sanctioned by man. I will hold to the principles received by me when I was sane, and not mad—as I am now. Laws and principles are not for the times when there is no temptation: they are for such moments as this, when body and soul rise in mutiny against their rigor; stringent are they; inviolate they shall be. If at my individual convenience I might break them, what would be their worth? They have a worth—so I have always believed; and if I cannot believe it now, it is because I am

insane—quite insane: with my veins running fire, and my heart beating faster than I can count its throbs. Preconceived opinions, foregone determinations, are all I have at this hour to stand by: there I plant my foot."

I did. Mr. Rochester, reading my countenance, saw I had done so. His fury was wrought to the highest: he must yield to it for a moment, whatever followed; he crossed the floor and seized my arm, and grasped my waist. He seemed to devour me with his flaming glance: physically, I felt, at the moment, powerless as stubble exposed to the draught and glow of a furnace—mentally, I still possessed my soul, and with it the certainty of ultimate safety. The soul, fortunately, has an interpreter—often an unconscious, but still a truthful interpreter—in the eye. My eye rose to his; and while I looked in his fierce face, I gave an involuntary sigh: his grip was painful, and my overtasked strength almost exhausted.

"Never," said he, as he ground his teeth, "never was anything at once so frail and so indomitable. A mere reed she feels in my hand!" (And he shook me with the force of his hold.) "I could bend her with my finger and thumb: and what good would it do if I bent, if I uptore, if I crushed her? Consider that eye: consider the resolute, wild, free thing looking out of it, defying me, with more than courage—with a stern triumph. Whatever I do with its cage, I cannot get at it—the savage, beautiful creature! If I tear, if I rend the slight prison, my outrage will only let the captive loose. Conqueror I might be of the house; but the inmate would escape to heaven before I could call myself possessor of its clay dwelling-place. And it is you, spirit—with will and energy, and virtue and purity—that I want: not alone your brittle frame. Of yourself, you could come with soft flight and nestle against my heart, if you would: seized against your will you will elude the grasp like an essence—you will vanish ere I inhale your fragrance. Oh! come, Jane, come!"

As he said this he released me from his clutch, and only looked at me. The look was far worse to resist than the frantic strain: only an idiot, however, would have succumbed now. I had dared and baffled his fury; I must elude his sorrow: I retired to the door.

"You are going, Jane?"

"I am going, sir."

"You are leaving me?"

"Yes."

"You will not come?—You will not be my comforter, my rescuer?—My deep love, my wild woe, my frantic prayer, are all nothing to you?"

What unutterable pathos was in his voice! How hard it was to reiterate firmly, "I am going."

"Jane!"

"Mr. Rochester!"

"Withdraw, then,—I consent—but remember, you leave me here in anguish. Go up to your own room; think over all I have said, and, Jane, cast a glance on my sufferings—think of me."

He turned away; he threw himself on his face on the sofa. "Oh, Jane! my hope—my love—my life!" broke in anguish from his lips. Then came a deep, strong sob.

I had already gained the door: but, reader, I walked back—walked back as determinedly as I had retreated. I knelt down by him; I turned his face from the cushion to me; I kissed his cheek; I smoothed his hair with my hand.

"God bless you, my dear master!" I said. "God keep you from harm and wrong—direct you, solace you—reward you well for your past kindness to me."

"Little Jane's love would have been my best reward," he answered: "without it, my heart is broken. But Jane will give me her love: yes—nobly, generously."

Up the blood rushed to his face; forth flashed the fire from his eyes; erect he sprang; he held his arms out; but I evaded the embrace, and at once quitted the room.

"Farewell!" was the cry of my heart as I left him. Despair added, "Farewell, for ever!"

That night I never thought to sleep; but a slumber fell on me as soon as I lay down in bed. I was transported in thought to the scenes of childhood; I dreamed I lay in the red-room at Gateshead; that the night was dark, and my mind impressed with strange fears. The light that long ago had struck me into syncope,[6] recalled in this vision, seemed glidingly to mount the wall, and tremblingly to pause in the center of the obscured ceiling. I lifted up my head to look: the roof resolved to clouds, high and dim; the gleam was such as the moon imparts to vapors she is about to sever. I watched her come—watched with the strangest anticipation; as though some word of doom were to be written on her disk. She broke forth as never moon yet burst from cloud: a hand first penetrated the sable folds and waved them away; then, not a moon, but a white human form shone in the azure, inclining a glorious brow earthward. It gazed and gazed and gazed on me. It spoke to my spirit: immeasurably distant was the tone, yet so near, it whispered in my heart—"My daughter, flee temptation!"

"Mother, I will."

So I answered after I had waked from the trance-like dream. It was yet night, but July nights are short: soon after midnight dawn comes. "It cannot be too early to commence the task I have to fulfill," thought I. I rose: I was dressed; for I had taken off nothing but my shoes. I knew where to find in my drawers some linen, a locket, a ring. In seeking these articles I encountered the beads of a pearl necklace Mr. Rochester had forced me to accept a few days ago. I left that; it was not mine: it was the visionary bride's, who had melted in air. The other articles I made up in a parcel; my purse, containing twenty shillings (it was all I had), I put in my pocket: I tied on my straw bonnet, pinned my shawl, took the parcel and my slippers, which I would not put on yet, and stole from my room.

"Farewell, kind Mrs. Fairfax!" I whispered, as I glided past her door. "Farewell, my darling Adèle!" I said, as I glanced towards the nursery. No thought could be admitted of entering to embrace her. I had to deceive a fine ear: for aught I knew, it might now be listening.

I would have got past Mr. Rochester's chamber without a pause; but my heart momentarily stopping its beat at that threshold, my foot was forced to stop also. No sleep was there: the inmate was walking restlessly from wall to wall; and again and again he sighed while I listened. There was a heaven—a temporary heaven—in this room for me, if I chose: I had but to go in and

6. A faint.

to say—"Mr. Rochester, I will love you and live with you through life till death," and a fount of rapture would spring to my lips. I thought of this.

That kind master, who could not sleep now, was waiting with impatience for day. He would send for me in the morning; I should be gone. He would have me sought for: vainly. He would feel himself forsaken; his love rejected: he would suffer; perhaps grow desperate. I thought of this too. My hand moved towards the lock; I caught it back, and glided on.

Drearily I wound my way downstairs: I knew what I had to do, and I did it mechanically. I sought the key of the side-door in the kitchen; I sought, too, a phial of oil and a feather; I oiled the key and the lock. I got some water, I got some bread: for perhaps I would have to walk far; and my strength, sorely shaken of late, must not break down. All this I did without one sound. I opened the door, passed out, shut it softly. Dim dawn glimmered in the yard. The great gates were closed and locked; but a wicket in one of them was only latched. Through that I departed: it, too, I shut; and now I was out of Thornfield.

A mile off, beyond the fields, lay a road which stretched in the contrary direction to Millcote; a road I had never traveled, but often noticed, and wondered where it led: thither I bent my steps. No reflection was to be allowed now: not one glance was to be cast back; not even one forward. Not one thought was to be given either to the past or the future. The first was a page so heavenly sweet—so deadly sad—that to read one line of it would dissolve my courage and break down my energy. That last was an awful blank: something like the world when the deluge was gone by.

I skirted fields, and hedges, and lanes, till after sunrise. I believe it was a lovely summer morning: I know my shoes, which I had put on when I left the house, were soon wet with dew. But I looked neither to rising sun, nor smiling sky, nor wakening nature. He who is taken out to pass through a fair scene to the scaffold thinks not of the flowers that smile on his road, but of the block and axe-edge; of the disseverment of bone and vein; of the grave gaping at the end: and I thought of drear flight and homeless wandering—and, oh! with agony I thought of what I left. I could not help it. I thought of him now—in his room—watching the sunrise; hoping I should soon come to say I would stay with him, and be his. I longed to be his; I panted to return: it was not too late; I could yet spare him the bitter pang of bereavement. As yet my flight, I was sure, was undiscovered. I could go back and be his comforter—his pride; his redeemer from misery; perhaps from ruin. Oh, that fear of his self-abandonment—far worse than my abandonment—how it goaded me! It was a barbed arrow-head in my breast; it tore me when I tried to extract it; it sickened me when remembrance thrust it further in. Birds began singing in brake and copse: birds were faithful to their mates; birds were emblems of love. What was I? In the midst of my pain of heart, and frantic effort of principle, I abhorred myself. I had no solace from self appro-bation: none even from self-respect. I had injured—wounded—left my mas-ter. I was hateful in my own eyes. Still I could not turn, nor retrace one step. God must have led me on. As to my own will or conscience, impassioned grief had trampled one and stifled the other. I was weeping wildly as I walked along my solitary way: fast, fast I went, like one delirious. A weakness, begin-ning inwardly, extending to the limbs, seized me, and I fell: I lay on the ground some minutes, pressing my face to the wet turf. I had some fear—or

hope—that here I should die: but I was soon up; crawling forwards on my hands and knees, and then again raised to my feet—as eager and as determined as ever to reach the road.

When I got there I was forced to sit to rest me under the hedge; and while I sat, I heard wheels, and saw a coach come on. I stood up and lifted my hand; it stopped. I asked where it was going: the driver named a place a long way off, and where I was sure Mr. Rochester had no connections. I asked for what sum he would take me there; he said thirty shillings; I answered I had but twenty; well, he would try to make it do. He further gave me leave to get into the inside, as the vehicle was empty: I entered, was shut in, and it rolled on its way.

Gentle reader, may you never feel what I then felt! May your eyes never shed such stormy, scalding, heart-wrung tears as poured from mine. May you never appeal to Heaven in prayers so hopeless and so agonised as in that hour left my lips: for never may you, like me, dread to be the instrument of evil to what you wholly love.

Chapter XXVIII

Two days are passed. It is a summer evening; the coachman has set me down at a place called Whitcross; he could take me no farther for the sum I had given, and I was not possessed of another shilling in the world. The coach is a mile off by this time; I am alone. At this moment I discover that I forgot to take my parcel out of the pocket of the coach, where I had placed it for safety; there it remains, there it must remain; and now, I am absolutely destitute.

Whitcross is no town, nor even a hamlet; it is but a stone pillar set up where four roads meet: white-washed, I suppose, to be more obvious at a distance and in darkness. Four arms spring from its summit: the nearest town to which these point is, according to the inscription, distant ten miles; the farthest, above twenty. From the well-known names of these towns I learn in what county I have lighted; a north-midland shire, dusk with moorland, ridged with mountain: this I see. There are great moors behind and on each hand of me; there are waves of mountains far beyond that deep valley at my feet. The population here must be thin, and I see no passengers on these roads: they stretch out east, west, north, and south—white, broad, lonely; they are all cut in the moor, and the heather grows deep and wild to their very verge. Yet a chance traveler might pass by; and I wish no eye to see me now: strangers would wonder what I am doing, lingering here at the sign-post, evidently objectless and lost. I might be questioned: I could give no answer but what would sound incredible and excite suspicion. Not a tie holds me to human society at this moment—not a charm or hope calls me where my fellow-creatures are—none that saw me would have a kind thought or a good wish for me. I have no relative but the universal mother, Nature: I will seek her breast and ask repose.

I struck straight into the heath; I held on to a hollow I saw deeply furrowing the brown moorside; I waded knee-deep in its dark growth; I turned with its turnings, and finding a moss-blackened granite crag in a hidden angle, I sat down under it. High banks of moor were about me; the crag protected my head: the sky was over that.

Some time passed before I felt tranquil even here: I had a vague dread that wild cattle might be near, or that some sportsman or poacher might discover me. If a gust of wind swept the waste, I looked up, fearing it was the rush of a bull; if a plover whistled, I imagined it a man. Finding my apprehensions unfounded, however, and calmed by the deep silence that reigned as evening declined at nightfall, I took confidence. As yet I had not thought; I had only listened, watched, dreaded; now I regained the faculty of reflection.

What was I to do? Where to go? Oh, intolerable questions, when I could do nothing and go nowhere!—when a long way must yet be measured by my weary, trembling limbs, before I could reach human habitation—when cold charity must be entreated before I could get a lodging: reluctant sympathy importuned: almost certain repulse incurred: before my tale could be listened to, or one of my wants relieved!

I touched the heath: it was dry, and yet warm with the heat of the summer-day. I looked at the sky; it was pure: a kindly star twinkled just above the chasm ridge. The dew fell, but with propitious softness; no breeze whispered. Nature seemed to me benign and good; I thought she loved me, outcast as I was; and I, who from man could anticipate only mistrust, rejection, insult, clung to her with filial fondness. Tonight, at least, I would be her guest—as I was her child: my mother would lodge me without money and without price. I had one morsel of bread yet: the remnant of a roll I had bought in a town we passed through at noon with a stray penny—my last coin. I saw ripe bilberries gleaming here and there, like jet beads in the heath: I gathered a handful and ate them with the bread. My hunger, sharp before, was, if not satisfied, appeased by this hermit's meal. I said my evening prayers at its conclusion, and then chose my couch.

Beside the crag the heath was very deep: when I lay down my feet were buried in it; rising high on each side, it left only a narrow space for the night-air to invade. I folded my shawl double, and spread it over me for a coverlet; a low, mossy swell was my pillow. Thus lodged, I was not, at least at the commencement of the night, cold.

My rest might have been blissful enough, only a sad heart broke it. It plained of its gaping wounds, its inward bleeding, its riven chords, It trembled for Mr. Rochester and his doom: it bemoaned him with bitter pity; it demanded him with ceaseless longing: and, impotent as a bird with both wings broken, it still quivered its shattered pinions in vain attempts to seek him.

Worn out with this torture of thought, I rose to my knees. Night was come, and her planets were risen: a safe, still night; too serene for the companionship of fear. We know that God is everywhere; but certainly we feel His presence most when His works are on the grandest scale spread before us: and it is in the unclouded night-sky, where His worlds wheel their silent course, that we read clearest His infinitude, His omnipotence, His omnipresence. I had risen to my knees to pray for Mr. Rochester. Looking up, I, with tear-dimmed eyes, saw the mighty Milky Way. Remembering what it was—what countless systems there swept space like a soft trace of light—I felt the might and strength of God. Sure was I of His efficiency to save what He had made: convinced I grew that neither earth should perish nor one of the souls it treasured. I turned my prayer to thanksgiving: the Source of Life

was also the Savior of spirits. Mr. Rochester was safe: he was God's, and by God would he be guarded. I again nestled to the breast of the hill; and ere long, in sleep, forgot sorrow.

But next day Want came to me, pale and bare. Long after the little birds had left their nests; long after bees had come in the sweet prime of day to gather the heath honey before the dew was dried—when the long morning shadows were curtailed, and the sun filled earth and sky—I got up, and I looked round me.

What a still, hot, perfect day! What a golden desert this spreading moor! Everywhere sunshine. I wished I could live in it and on it. I saw a lizard run over the crag; I saw a bee busy among the sweet bilberries. I would fain at the moment have become bee or lizard, that I might have found fitting nutriment, permanent shelter here. But I was a human being, and had a human being's wants: I must not linger where there was nothing to supply them. I rose; I looked back at the bed I had left. Hopeless of the future, I wished but this—that my Maker had that night thought good to require my soul of me while I slept; and that this weary frame, absolved by death from further conflict with fate, had now but to decay quietly, and mingle in peace with the soil of this wilderness. Life, however, was yet in my possession; with all its requirements, and pains, and responsibilities. The burden must be carried; the want provided for; the suffering endured; the responsibility fulfilled. I set out.

Whitcross regained, I followed a road which led from the sun, now fervent and high. By no other circumstance had I will to decide my choice. I walked a long time, and when I thought I had nearly done enough, and might conscientiously yield to the fatigue that almost overpowered me—might relax this forced action, and, sitting down on a stone I saw near, submit resistlessly to the apathy that clogged heart and limb—I heard a bell chime—a church bell.

I turned in the direction of the sound, and there, amongst the romantic hills, whose changes and aspect I had ceased to note an hour ago, I saw a hamlet and a spire. All the valley at my right hand was full of pasture-fields, and corn-fields, and wood; and a glittering stream ran zig-zag through the varied shades of green, the mellowing grain, the sombre wood-land, the clear and sunny lea. Recalled by the rumbling of wheels to the road before me, I saw a heavily-laden waggon laboring up the hill; and not far beyond were two cows and their drover. Human life and human labor were near. I must struggle on: strive to live and bend to toil like the rest.

About two o'clock P.M. I entered the village. At the bottom of its one street there was a little shop with some cakes of bread in the window. I coveted a cake of bread. With that refreshment I could perhaps regain a degree of energy; without it, it would be difficult to proceed. The wish to have some strength and some vigour returned to me as soon as I was amongst my fellow-beings. I felt it would be degrading to faint with hunger on the causeway of a hamlet. Had I nothing about me I could offer in exchange for one of these rolls? I considered. I had a small silk handkerchief tied round my throat; I had my gloves. I could hardly tell how men and women in extremities of destitution proceeded. I did not know whether either of these articles would be accepted: probably they would not; but I must try.

I entered the shop: a woman was there. Seeing a respectably-dressed per-

son, a lady as she supposed, she came forward with civility. How could she serve me? I was seized with shame: my tongue would not utter the request I had prepared. I dared not offer her the half-worn gloves, the creased handkerchief: besides, I felt it would be absurd. I only begged permission to sit down a moment, as I was tired. Disappointed in the expectation of a customer, she coolly acceded to my request. She pointed to a seat; I sank into it. I felt sorely urged to weep; but conscious how unseasonable such a manifestation would be, I restrained it. Soon I asked her, "if there were any dressmaker or plain-work-woman in the village?"

"Yes; two or three. Quite as many as there was employment for."

I reflected. I was driven to the point now. I was brought face to face with Necessity. I stood in the position of one without a resource: without a friend; without a coin. I must do something. What? I must apply somewhere. Where?

"Did she know of any place in the neighborhood where a servant was wanted?"

"Nay; she couldn't say."

"What was the chief trade in this place? What did most of the people do?"

"Some were farm laborers; a good deal worked at Mr. Oliver's needle-factory, and at the foundry."

"Did Mr. Oliver employ women?"

"Nay; it was men's work."

"And what do the women do?"

"I knawn't," was the answer. "Some does one thing, and some another. Poor folk mun get on as they can."

She seemed to be tired of my questions: and, indeed, what claim had I to importune her? A neighbor or two came in; my chair was evidently wanted. I took leave.

I passed up the street, looking as I went at all the houses to the right hand and to the left: but I could discover no pretext, nor see an inducement, to enter any. I rambled round the hamlet, going sometimes to a little distance and returning again, for an hour or more. Much exhausted, and suffering greatly now for want of food, I turned aside into a lane and sat down under the hedge. Ere many minutes had elapsed I was again on my feet, however, and again searching for something—a resource, or at least an informant. A pretty little house stood at the top of the lane, with a garden before it; exquisitely neat, and brilliantly blooming. I stopped at it. What business had I to approach the white door or touch the glittering knocker? In what way could it possibly be the interest of the inhabitants of that dwelling to serve me? Yet I drew near and knocked. A mild-looking, cleanly-attired young woman opened the door. In such a voice as might be expected from a hopeless heart and fainting frame—a voice wretchedly low and faltering—I asked if a servant was wanted here?

"No," said she; "we do not keep a servant."

"Can you tell me where I could get employment of any kind?" I continued. "I am a stranger, without acquaintance, in this place. I want some work: no matter what."

But it was not her business to think for me, or to seek a place for me: besides, in her eyes, how doubtful must have appeared my character, position, tale. She shook her head; she "was sorry she could give me no infor-

mation," and the white door closed, quite gently and civilly: but it shut me out. If she had held it open a little longer, I believe I should have begged a piece of bread; for I was now brought low.

I could not bear to return to the sordid village; where, besides, no prospect of aid was visible. I should have longed rather to deviate to a wood I saw not far off, which appeared in its thick shade to offer inviting shelter; but I was so sick, so weak, so gnawed with nature's cravings, instinct kept me roaming round abodes where there was a chance of food. Solitude would be no solitude—rest no rest—while the vulture, hunger, thus sank beak and talons in my side.

I drew near houses; I left them, and came back again, and again I wandered away: always repelled by the consciousness of having no claim to ask—no right to expect interest in my isolated lot. Meantime the afternoon advanced, while I thus wandered about like a lost and starving dog. In crossing a field I saw the church spire before me: I hastened towards it. Near the churchyard, and in the middle of a garden, stood a well-built though small house, which I had no doubt was the parsonage. I remembered that strangers who arrive at a place where they have no friends, and who want employment, sometimes apply to the clergyman for introduction and aid. It is the clergyman's function to help—at least with advice—those who wished to help themselves. I seemed to have something like a right to seek counsel here. Renewing, then, my courage, and gathering my feeble remains of strength, I pushed on. I reached the house, and knocked at the kitchen-door. An old woman opened: I asked was this the parsonage?

"Yes."

"Was the clergyman in?"

"No."

"Would he be in soon?"

"No, he was gone from home."

"To a distance?"

Not so far—happen three mile. He had been called away by the sudden death of his father: he was at Marsh End now, and would very likely stay there a fortnight longer.

"Was there any lady of the house?"

"Nay, there was naught but her, and she was housekeeper;" and of her, reader, I could not bear to ask the relief for want of which I was sinking; I could not yet beg; and again I crawled away.

Once more I took off my handkerchief—once more I thought of the cakes of bread in the little shop. Oh, for but a crust! for but one mouthful to allay the pang of famine! Instinctively I turned my face again to the village; I found the shop again, and I went in; and though others were there besides the woman, I ventured the request: "Would she give me a roll for this handkerchief?"

She looked at me with evident suspicion: "Nay, she never sold stuff i' that way."

Almost desperate, I asked for half a cake; she again refused. "How could she tell where I had got the handkerchief?" she said.

"Would she take my gloves?"

"No! what could she do with them?"

Reader, it is not pleasant to dwell on these details. Some say there is

enjoyment in looking back to painful experience past; but at this day I can scarcely bear to review the times to which I allude: the moral degradation, blent with the physical suffering, form too distressing a recollection ever to be willingly dwelt on. I blamed none of those who repulsed me. I felt it was what was to be expected, and what could not be helped: an ordinary beggar is frequently an object of suspicion; a well-dressed beggar inevitably so. To be sure what I begged was employment: but whose business was it to provide me with employment? Not, certainly, that of persons who saw me then for the first time, and who knew nothing about my character. And as to the woman who would not take my handkerchief in exchange for her bread, why, she was right; if the offer appeared to her sinister, or the exchange unprofitable. Let me condense now. I am sick of the subject.

A little before dark I passed a farm-house, at the open door of which the farmer was sitting, eating his supper of bread and cheese; I stopped, and said:—"Will you give me a piece of bread? for I am very hungry." He cast on me a glance of surprise; but without answering he cut a thick slice from his loaf, and gave it to me. I imagine he did not think I was a beggar, but only an eccentric sort of lady, who had taken a fancy to his brown loaf. As soon as I was out of sight of his house, I sat down and ate it.

I could not hope to get a lodging under a roof, and sought it in the wood I have before alluded to. But my night was wretched, my rest broken: the ground was damp, the air cold: besides intruders passed near me more than once, and I had again and again to change my quarters: no sense of safety or tranquillity befriended me. Towards morning it rained; the whole of the following day was wet. Do not ask me, reader, to give a minute account of that day; as before, I sought work; as before, I was repulsed; as before, I starved; but once did food pass my lips. At the door of a cottage I saw a little girl about to throw a mess of cold porridge into a pig trough. "Will you give me that?" I asked.

She stared at me. "Mother!" she exclaimed; "there is a woman wants me to give her this porridge."

"Well, lass," replied a voice within, "give it her if she's a beggar. T' pig doesn't want[7] it."

The girl emptied the stiffened mold into my hand, and I devoured it ravenously.

As the wet twilight deepened, I stopped in a solitary bridle-path, which I had been pursuing an hour or more.

"My strength is quite failing me," I said, in soliloquy. "I feel I cannot go much further. Shall I be an outcast again this night? While the rain descends so, must I lay my head on the cold, drenched ground? I fear I cannot do otherwise: for who will receive me? But it will be very dreadful: with this feeling of hunger, faintness, chill, and this sense of desolation—this total prostration of hope. In all likelihood, though, I should die before morning. And why cannot I reconcile myself to the prospect of death? Why do I struggle to retain a valueless life? Because I know, or believe, Mr. Rochester is still living: and then, to die of want and cold, is a fate to which nature cannot submit passively. Oh, Providence! sustain me a little longer! Aid—direct me!"

My glazed eye wandered over the dim and misty landscape. I saw I had

7. Need.

strayed far from the village: it was quite out of sight. The very cultivation surrounding it had disappeared. I had, by cross-ways and by-paths, once more drawn near the tract of moorland; and now, only a few fields, almost as wild and unproductive as the heath from which they were scarcely reclaimed, lay between me and the dusky hill.

"Well, I would rather die yonder than in a street, or on a frequented road," I reflected. "And far better that crows and ravens—if any ravens there be in these regions—should pick my flesh from my bones, than that they should be prisoned in a workhouse coffin and moulder in a pauper's grave."

To the hill, then, I turned. I reached it. It remained now only to find a hollow where I could lie down, and feel at least hidden, if not secure: but all the surface of the waste looked level. It showed no variation but of tint; green, where rush and moss overgrew the marshes; black, where the dry soil bore only heath. Dark as it was getting, I could still see these changes; though but as mere alternations of light and shade: for color had faded with the daylight.

My eye still roved over the sullen swell, and along the moor-edge, vanishing amidst the wildest scenery; when at one dim point, far in among the marshes and the ridges, a light sprang up. "That is an *ignis fatuus*," was my first thought; and I expected it would soon vanish. It burned on, however, quite steadily; neither receding nor advancing. "Is it, then, a bonfire just kindled?" I questioned. I watched to see whether it would spread: but no; as it did not diminish, so it did not enlarge. "It may be a candle in a house," I then conjectured: "but if so, I can never reach it. It is much too far away: and were it within a yard of me, what would it avail? I should but knock at the door to have it shut in my face."

And I sank down where I stood, and hid my face against the ground. I lay still a while: the night-wind swept over the hill and over me, and died moaning in the distance; the rain fell fast, wetting me afresh to the skin. Could I but have stiffened to the still frost—the friendly numbness of death—it might have pelted on: I should not have felt it; but my yet living flesh shuddered to its chilling influence. I rose ere long.

The light was yet there: shining dim, but constant, through the rain. I tried to walk again: I dragged my exhausted limbs slowly towards it. It led me aslant over the hill, through a wide bog; which would have been impassable in winter, and was splashy and shaking even now, in the height of summer. Here I fell twice; but as often I rose and rallied my faculties. This light was my forlorn hope: I must gain it.

Having crossed the marsh, I saw a trace of white over the moor. I approached it; it was a road or a track: it led straight up to the light, which now beamed from a sort of knoll, amid a clump of trees—firs, apparently, from what I could distinguish of the character of their forms and foliage through the gloom. My star vanished as I drew near: some obstacle had intervened between me and it. I put out my hand to feel the dark mass before me; I discriminated the rough stones of a low wall—above it, something like palisades, and within, a high and prickly hedge. I groped on. Again a whitish object gleamed before me: it was a gate—a wicket; it moved on its hinges as I touched it. On each side stood a sable bush—holly or yew.

Entering the gate and passing the shrubs, the silhouette of a house rose to view; black, low, and rather long; but the guiding light shone nowhere.

All was obscurity. Were the inmates retired to rest? I feared it must be so. In seeking the door, I turned an angle: there shot out the friendly gleam again, from the lozenged panes of a very small latticed window, within a foot of the ground; made still smaller by the growth of ivy or some other creeping plant, whose leaves clustered thick over the portion of the house wall in which it was set. The aperture was so screened and narrow that curtain or shutter had been deemed unnecessary; and when I stooped down and put aside the spray of foliage shooting over it, I could see all within. I could see clearly a room with a sanded floor, clean scoured; a dresser of walnut, with pewter plates ranged in rows, reflecting the redness and radiance of a glowing peat-fire. I could see a clock, a white deal table, some chairs. The candle, whose ray had been my beacon, burnt on the table; and by its light an elderly woman, somewhat rough-looking, but scrupulously clean, like all about her, was knitting a stocking.

I noticed these objects cursorily only—in them there was nothing extraordinary. A group of more interest appeared near the hearth, sitting still amidst the rosy peace and warmth suffusing it. Two young, graceful women—ladies in every point—sat, one in a low rocking-chair, the other on a lower stool; both wore deep mourning of crape and bombazeen, which sombre garb singularly set off very fair necks and faces: a large old pointer dog rested its massive head on the knee of one girl—in the lap of the other was cushioned a black cat.

A strange place was this humble kitchen for such occupants! Who were they? They could not be the daughters of the elderly person at the table; for she looked like a rustic, and they were all delicacy and cultivation. I had nowhere seen such faces as theirs: and yet, as I gazed on them, I seemed intimate with every lineament. I cannot call them handsome—they were too pale and grave for the word: as they each bent over a book, they looked thoughtful almost to severity. A stand between them supported a second candle and two great volumes, to which they frequently referred; comparing them seemingly with the smaller books they held in their hands, like people consulting a dictionary to aid them in the task of translation. This scene was as silent as if all the figures had been shadows, and the fire-lit apartment a picture: so hushed was it, I could hear the cinders fall from the grate, the clock tick in its obscure corner; and I even fancied I could distinguish the click-click of the woman's knitting-needles. When, therefore, a voice broke the strange stillness at last, it was audible enough to me.

"Listen, Diana," said one of the absorbed students; "Franz and old Daniel are together in the night-time, and Franz is telling a dream from which he has awakened in terror—listen!" And in a low voice she read something, of which not one word was intelligible to me; for it was in an unknown tongue—neither French nor Latin. Whether it were Greek or German I could not tell.

"That is strong," she said, when she had finished: "I relish it." The other girl, who had lifted her head to listen to her sister, repeated, while she gazed at the fire, a line of what had been read. At a later day, I knew the language and the book; therefore I will here quote the line: though when I first heard it it was only like a stroke on sounding brass to me—conveying no meaning:
—" 'Da trat hervor Einer, anzusehen wie die Sternen Nacht.' Good! good!" she exclaimed, while her dark and deep eye sparkled. "There you have a dim and mighty archangel fitly set before you! The line is worth a hundred pages

of fustian. 'Ich wäge die Gedanken in der Schale meines Zornes und die Werke mit dem Gewichte meines Grimms.'[8] I like it!"

Both were again silent.

"Is there ony country where they talk i' that way?" asked the old woman, looking up from her knitting.

"Yes, Hannah—a far larger country than England; where they talk in no other way."

"Well, for sure case, I knawn't how they can understand t' one t' other: and if either o' ye went there, ye could tell what they said, I guess?"

"We could probably tell something of what they said, but not all—for we are not as clever as you think us, Hannah. We don't speak German, and we cannot read it without a dictionary to help us."

"And what good does it do you?"

"We mean to teach it some time—or at least the elements, as they say; and then we shall get more money than we do now."

"Varry like: but give ower studying: ye've done enough for tonight."

"I think we have: at least I'm tired. Mary, are you?"

"Mortally: after all, it's tough work fagging away at a language with no master but a lexicon."

"It is: especially such a language as this crabbed but glorious Deutsch. I wonder when St. John will come home."

"Surely he will not be long now: it is just ten" (looking at a little gold watch she drew from her girdle). "It rains fast. Hannah, will you have the goodness to look at the fire in the parlor?"

The woman rose: she opened a door, through which I dimly saw a passage: soon I heard her stir a fire in an inner room; she presently came back.

"Ah, childer!" said she, "it fair troubles me to go into yond' room now: it looks so lonesome wi' the chair empty and set back in a corner."

She wiped her eyes with her apron: the two girls, grave before, looked sad now.

"But he is in a better place," continued Hannah: "we shouldn't wish him here again. And then, nobody need to have a quieter death nor he had."

"You say he never mentioned us?" inquired one of the ladies.

"He hadn't time, bairn: he was gone in a minute—was your father. He had been a bit ailing like the day before, but naught to signify; and when Mr. St. John asked if he would like either o' ye to be sent for, he fair laughed at him. He began again with a bit of a heaviness in his head the next day—that is, a fortnight sin"—and he went to sleep and niver wakened: he wor' a'most stark[9] when your brother went into t' chamber and fand him. Ah, childer! that's t' last o' t' old stock—for ye and Mr. St. John is like of a different soart to them 'at's gone; for all your mother wor mich i' your way; and a'most as book-learned. She wor the pictur' o' ye, Mary: Diana is more like your father."

I thought them so similar I could not tell where the old servant (for such I now concluded her to be) saw the difference. Both were fair complexioned and slenderly made; both possessed faces full of distinction and intelligence. One, to be sure, had hair a shade darker than the other, and there was a

8. Then there stepped forth one, in appearance like the starry sky. . . . I weigh thoughts in the scale of my anger, and deeds with the weight of my wrath! From Friedrich Schiller's *The Robbers* (1781), 5.1. "Fustian": pretentious writing.
9. Rigid in death.

difference in their style of wearing it: Mary's pale brown locks were parted and braided smooth; Diana's duskier tresses covered her neck with thick curls. The clock struck ten.

"Ye'll want your supper, I am sure," observed Hannah; "and so will Mr. St. John when he comes in."

And she proceeded to prepare the meal. The ladies rose; they seemed about to withdraw to the parlor. Till this moment I had been so intent on watching them, their appearance and conversation had excited in me so keen an interest, I had half-forgotten my own wretched position: now it recurred to me. More desolate, more desperate than ever, it seemed from contrast. And how impossible did it appear to touch the inmates of this house with concern on my behalf; to make them believe in the truth of my wants and woes—to induce them to vouchsafe a rest for my wanderings! As I groped out the door, and knocked at it hesitatingly, I felt that last idea to be a mere chimera. Hannah opened.

"What do you want?" she inquired, in a voice of surprise, as she surveyed me by the light of the candle she held.

"May I speak to your mistresses?" I said.

"You had better tell me what you have to say to them. Where do you come from?"

"I am a stranger."

"What is your business here at this hour?"

"I want a night's shelter in an outhouse or anywhere, and a morsel of bread to eat."

Distrust, the very feeling I dreaded, appeared in Hannah's face. "I'll give you a piece of bread," she said, after a pause; "but we can't take in a vagrant to lodge. It isn't likely."

"Do let me speak to your mistresses."

"No; not I. What can they do for you? You should not be roving about now; it looks very ill."

"But where shall I go if you drive me away? What shall I do?"

"Oh, I'll warrant you know where to go, and what to do. Mind you don't do wrong, that's all. Here is a penny; now go"——

"A penny cannot feed me, and I have no strength to go farther. Don't shut the door:—oh, don't, for God's sake!"

"I must; the rain is driving in"——

"Tell the young ladies.—Let me see them"——

"Indeed, I will not. You are not what you ought to be or you wouldn't make such a noise. Move off."

"But I must die if I am turned away."

"Not you. I'm fear'd you have some ill plans agate,[1] that bring you about folk's houses at this time o' night. If you've any followers—housebreakers or such like—anywhere near, you may tell them we are not by ourselves in the house; we have a gentleman, and dogs, and guns." Here the honest but inflexible servant clapped the door to and bolted it within.

This was the climax. A pang of exquisite suffering—a throe of true despair—rent and heaved my heart. Worn out, indeed, I was; not another step could I stir. I sank on the wet door-step: I groaned—I wrung my hands—

1. Under way (literally, "on gate").

I wept in utter anguish. Oh, this specter of death! Oh, this last hour, approaching in such horror! Alas, this isolation—this banishment from my kind! Not only the anchor of home, but the footing of fortitude was gone—at least for a moment: but the last I soon endeavored to regain.

"I can but die," I said, "and I believe in God. Let me try to wait His will in silence."

These words I not only thought, but uttered; and thrusting back all my misery into my heart, I made an effort to compel it to remain there—dumb and still.

"All men must die," said a voice quite close at hand; "but all are not condemned to meet a lingering and premature doom, such as yours would be if you perished here of want."

"Who or what speaks?" I asked, terrified at the unexpected sound, and incapable now of deriving from any occurrence a hope of aid. A form was near—what form the pitch-dark night and my enfeebled vision prevented me from distinguishing. With a loud long knock the new comer appealed to the door.

"Is it you, Mr. St. John?" cried Hannah.

"Yes—yes; open quickly."

"Well, how wet and cold you must be, such a wild night as it is! Come in—your sisters are quite uneasy about you, and I believe there are bad folks about. There has been a beggar-woman—I declare she is not gone yet!—laid down there. Get up! for shame! Move off, I say!"

"Hush, Hannah! I have a word to say to the woman. You have done your duty in excluding, now let me do mine in admitting her. I was near, and listened to both you and her. I think this is a peculiar case—I must at least examine into it. Young woman, rise, and pass before me into the house."

With difficulty I obeyed him. Presently I stood within that clean, bright kitchen—on the very hearth—trembling, sickening; conscious of an aspect in the last degree ghastly, wild and weatherbeaten. The two ladies, their brother, Mr. St. John, the old servant, were all gazing at me.

"St. John, who is it?" I heard one ask.

"I cannot tell: I found her at the door," was the reply.

"She does look white," said Hannah.

"As white as clay or death," was responded. "She will fall: let her sit."

And indeed my head swam: I dropped; but a chair received me. I still possessed my senses; though just now I could not speak.

"Perhaps a little water would restore her. Hannah, fetch some. But she is worn to nothing. How very thin, and how very bloodless!"

"A mere specter!"

"Is she ill, or only famished?"

"Famished, I think. Hannah, is that milk? Give it me, and a piece of bread."

Diana (I knew her by the long curls which I saw drooping between me and the fire as she bent over me) broke some bread, dipped it in milk, and put it to my lips. Her face was near mine: I saw there was pity in it, and I felt sympathy in her hurried breathing. In her simple words, too, the same balm-like emotion spoke: "Try to eat."

"Yes—try," repeated Mary gently; and Mary's hand removed my sodden bonnet and lifted my head. I tasted what they offered me: feebly at first, eagerly soon.

"Not too much at first—restrain her," said the brother; "she has had enough." And he withdrew the cup of milk and the plate of bread.

"A little more, St. John—look at the avidity in her eyes."

"No more at present, sister. Try if she can speak now—ask her her name."

I felt I could speak, and I answered—"My name is Jane Elliott." Anxious as ever to avoid discovery, I had before resolved to assume an *alias*.

"And where do you live? Where are your friends?"

I was silent.

"Can we send for any one you know?"

I shook my head.

"What account can you give of yourself?"

Somehow, now that I had once crossed the threshold of this house, and once was brought face to face with its owners, I felt no longer outcast, vagrant, and disowned by the wide world. I dared to put off the mendicant—to resume my natural manner and character. I began once more to know myself; and when Mr. St. John demanded an account—which at present I was far too weak to render—I said after a brief pause,—"Sir, I can give you no details tonight."

"But what, then," said he, "do you expect me to do for you?"

"Nothing," I replied. My strength sufficed for but short answers. Diana took the word:—

"Do you mean," she asked, "that we have now given you what aid you require? and that we may dismiss you to the moor and the rainy night?"

I looked at her. She had, I thought, a remarkable countenance; instinct both with power and goodness. I took sudden courage. Answering her compassionate gaze with a smile, I said: "I will trust you. If I were a masterless and stray dog, I know that you would not turn me from your hearth tonight: as it is, I really have no fear. Do with me and for me as you like; but excuse me from much discourse—my breath is short—I feel a spasm when I speak." All three surveyed me, and all three were silent.

"Hannah," said Mr. St. John at last, "let her sit there at present, and ask her no questions; in ten minutes more, give her the remainder of that milk and bread. Mary and Diana, let us go into the parlor and talk the matter over."

They withdrew. Very soon one of the ladies returned—I could not tell which. A kind of pleasant stupor was stealing over me as I sat by the genial fire. In an undertone she gave some directions to Hannah. Ere long, with the servant's aid, I contrived to mount a staircase; my dripping clothes were removed; soon a warm, dry bed received me. I thanked God—experienced amid unutterable exhaustion a glow of grateful joy—and slept.

Chapter XXIX

The recollection of about three days and nights succeeding this is very dim in my mind. I can recall some sensations felt in that interval; but few thoughts framed, and no actions performed. I knew I was in a small room, and in a narrow bed. To that bed I seemed to have grown; I lay on it motionless as a stone; and to have torn me from it would have been almost to kill me. I took no note of the lapse of time—of the change from morning to noon, from noon to evening. I observed when any one entered or left the

apartment; I could even tell who they were; I could understand what was said when the speaker stood near to me; but I could not answer; to open my lips or move my limbs was equally impossible. Hannah, the servant, was my most frequent visitor. Her coming disturbed me. I had a feeling that she wished me away: that she did not understand me or my circumstances: that she was prejudiced against me. Diana and Mary appeared in the chamber once or twice a day. They would whisper sentences of this sort at my bed-side:—

"It is very well we took her in."

"Yes; she would certainly have been found dead at the door in the morning, had she been left out all night. I wonder what she has gone through?"

"Strange hardships, I imagine—poor, emaciated, pallid wanderer!"

"She is not an uneducated person, I should think, by her manner of speaking; her accent was quite pure; and the clothes she took off, though splashed and wet, were little worn and fine."

"She has a peculiar face; fleshless and haggard as it is, I rather like it; and when in good health and animated, I can fancy her physiognomy would be agreeable."

Never once in their dialogues did I hear a syllable of regret at the hospitality they had extended to me; or of suspicion of, or aversion to, myself. I was comforted.

Mr. St. John came but once: he looked at me, and said my state of lethargy was the result of reaction from excessive and protracted fatigue. He pronounced it needless to send for a doctor: nature, he was sure, would manage best left to herself. He said every nerve had been overstrained in some way, and the whole system must sleep torpid awhile. There was no disease. He imagined my recovery would be rapid enough when once commenced. These opinions he delivered in a few words, in a quiet, low voice; and added, after a pause, in the tone of a man little accustomed to expansive comment, "rather an unusual physiognomy; certainly not indicative of vulgarity or degradation."

"Far otherwise," responded Diana. "To speak truth, St. John, my heart rather warms to the poor little soul. I wish we may be able to benefit her permanently."

"That is hardly likely," was the reply. "You will find she is some young lady who has had a misunderstanding with her friends and has probably injudiciously left them. We may, perhaps, succeed in restoring her to them, if she is not obstinate: but I trace lines of force in her face which make me sceptical of her tractability." He stood considering me some minutes; then added, "She looks sensible, but not at all handsome."

"She is so ill, St. John."

"Ill or well, she would always be plain. The grace and harmony of beauty are quite wanting in those features."

On the third day I was better; on the fourth, I could speak, move, rise in bed, and turn. Hannah had brought me some gruel and dry toast, about, as I supposed, the dinner hour. I had eaten with relish: the food was good—void of the feverish flavor which had hitherto poisoned what I had swallowed. When she left me, I felt comparatively strong and revived; ere long satiety of repose and desire for action stirred me. I wished to rise; but what could I put on? Only my damp and bemired apparel, in which I had slept on the

ground and fallen in the marsh. I felt ashamed to appear before my bene-
factors so clad. I was spared the humiliation.

On a chair by the bedside were all my own things, clean and dry. My black
silk frock hung against the wall. The traces of the bog were removed from
it; the creases left by the wet smoothed out: it was quite decent. My very
shoes and stockings were purified and rendered presentable. There were the
means of washing in the room, and a comb and brush to smooth my hair.
After a weary process, and resting every five minutes, I succeeded in dress-
ing myself. My clothes hung loose on me, for I was much wasted; but I
covered deficiencies with a shawl, and once more, clean and respectable-
looking—no speck of the dirt, no trace of the disorder I so hated, and which
seemed so to degrade me, left—I crept down a stone staircase with the aid
of the banisters to a narrow low passage, and found my way presently to the
kitchen.

It was full of the fragrance of new bread and the warmth of a generous
fire. Hannah was baking. Prejudices, it is well known, are most difficult to
eradicate from the heart whose soil has never been loosened or fertilized by
education: they grow there, firm as weeds among stones. Hannah had been
cold and stiff, indeed, at the first: latterly she had begun to relent a little;
and when she saw me come in tidy and well-dressed, she even smiled.

"What, you have got up?" she said. "You are better, then. You may sit you
down in my chair on the hearthstone, if you will."

She pointed to the rocking-chair: I took it. She bustled about, examining
me every now and then with the corner of her eye. Turning to me, as she
took some loaves from the oven, she asked, bluntly—"Did you ever go a-
begging afore you came here?"

I was indignant for a moment; but remembering that anger was out of the
question, and that I had indeed appeared as a beggar to her, I answered
quietly, but still not without a certain marked firmness—"You are mistaken
in supposing me a beggar: any more than yourself or your
young ladies."

After a pause, she said, "I dunnut understand that: you've like no house,
nor no brass, I guess?"

"The want of house or brass (by which I suppose you mean money) does
not make a beggar in your sense of the word."

"Are you book-learned?" she inquired, presently.

"Yes, very."

"But you've never been to a boarding-school!"

"I was at a boarding-school eight years."

She opened her eyes wide.

"Whatever cannot ye keep yourself for, then?"

"I have kept myself; and, I trust, shall keep myself again. What are you
going to do with these gooseberries?" I inquired, as she brought out a basket
of the fruit.

"Mak'em into pies."

"Give them to me and I'll pick them."

"Nay; I dunnut want ye to do nought."

"But I must do something. Let me have them."

She consented; and she even brought me a clean towel to spread over my
dress, "lest," as she said, "I should mucky it."

"Ye've not been used to a sarvant's wark, I see by your hands," she remarked. "Happen ye've been a dressmaker."

"No, you are wrong. And, now, never mind what I have been: don't trouble your head further about me; but tell me the name of the house where we are."

"Some calls it Marsh End, and some calls it Moor House."

"And the gentleman who lives here is called Mr. St. John?"

"Nay; he doesn't live here: he is only staying a while. When he is at home, he in his own parish at Morton."

"That village a few miles off?"

"Aye."

"And what is he?"

"He is a parson."

I remembered the answer of the old housekeeper at the parsonage, when I had asked to see the clergyman. "This, then, was his father's residence?"

"Aye; old Mr. Rivers lived here, and his father, and grandfather, and gurt (great) grandfather afore him."

"The name, then, of that gentleman is Mr. St. John Rivers?"

"Aye; St. John is like his kirstened name."

"And his sisters are called Diana and Mary Rivers?"

"Yes."

"Their father is dead?"

"Dead three weeks sin' of a stroke."

"They have no mother?"

"The mistress has been dead this mony a year."

"Have you lived with the family long?"

"I've lived here thirty year. I nursed them all three."

"That proves you must have been an honest and faithful servant. I will say so much for you, though you have had the incivility to call me a beggar."

She again regarded me with a surprised stare. "I believe," she said, "I was quite mista'en in my thoughts of you: but there is so mony cheats goes about, you mun forgie me."

"And though," I continued, rather severely, "you wished to turn me from the door, on a night when you should not have shut out a dog."

"Well, it was hard: but what can a body do? I thought more o' th' childer nor of mysel': poor things! They've like nobody to tak' care on 'em but me. I'm like to look sharpish."

I maintained a grave silence for some minutes.

"You munnut think too hardly of me," she again remarked.

"But I do think hardly of you," I said; "and I'll tell you why—not so much because you refused to give me shelter, or regarded me as an impostor, as because you just now made it a species of reproach that I had no 'brass,' and no house. Some of the best people that ever lived have been as destitute as I am; and if you are a Christian, you ought not to consider poverty a crime."

"No more I ought," said she: "Mr. St. John tells me so too; and I see I wor wrang—but I've clear a different notion on you now to what I had. You look a raight down dacent little crater."

"That will do—I forgive you now. Shake hands."

She put her floury and horny hand into mine: another and heartier smile illumined her rough face: and from that moment we were friends.

Hannah was evidently fond of talking. While I picked the fruit and she made the paste for the pies, she proceeded to give me sundry details about her deceased master and mistress, and "the childer," as she called the young people.

Old Mr. Rivers, she said, was a plain man enough; but a gentleman, and of as ancient a family as could be found. Marsh End had belonged to the Rivers' ever since it was a house: and it was, she affirmed, "aboon two hundred year old—for all it looked but a small, humble place, naught to compare wi' Mr. Oliver's grand hall down i' Morton Vale. But she could remember Bill Oliver's father a journeyman needle-maker; and th' Rivers' wor gentry i' thi' owd days o' th' Henrys, as onybody might see by looking into th' registers i' Morton Church vestry." Still, she allowed, "the owd maister was like other folk—naught mich out o' t' common way: stark mad o' shooting, and farming, and sich like." The mistress was different. She was a great reader, and studied a deal; and the "bairns" had taken after her. There was nothing like them in these parts, nor ever had been; they had liked learning, all three, almost from the time they could speak; and they had always been "of a mak' of their own." Mr. St. John, when he grew up, would go to college and be a parson; and the girls, as soon as they left school, would seek places as governesses: for they had told her their father had some years ago lost a great deal of money by a man he had trusted turning bankrupt; and as he was now not rich enough to give them fortunes, they must provide for themselves. They had lived very little at home for a long while, and were only come now to stay a few weeks on account of their father's death: but they did so like Marsh End and Morton, and all these moors and hills about. They had been in London, and many other grand towns; but they always said there was no place like home; and then they were so agreeable with each other—never fell out nor "threaped."[2] She did not know where there was such a family for being united.

Having finished my task of gooseberry picking, I asked where the two ladies and their brother were now.

"Gone over to Morton for a walk; but they would be back in half an hour to tea."

They returned within the time Hannah had allotted them: they entered by the kitchen door. Mr. St. John, when he saw me, merely bowed and passed through; the two ladies stopped: Mary, in a few words, kindly and calmly expressed the pleasure she felt in seeing me well enough to be able to come down; Diana took my hand: she shook her head at me.

"You should have waited for my leave to descend," she said. "You still look very pale—and so thin! Poor child!—poor girl!"

Diana had a voice toned, to my ear, like the cooing of a dove. She possessed eyes whose gaze I delighted to encounter. Her whole face seemed to me full of charm. Mary's countenance was equally intelligent—her features equally pretty: but her expression was more reserved; and her manners, though gentle, more distant. Diana looked and spoke with a certain authority: she had a will, evidently. It was my nature to feel pleasure in yielding to an authority supported like hers: and to bend, where my conscience and self-respect permitted, to an active will.

2. Quarreled.

"And what business have you here?" she continued. "It is not your place. Mary and I sit in the kitchen sometimes, because at home we like to be free, even to licence—but you are a visitor, and must go into the parlor."

"I am very well here."

"Not at all—with Hannah bustling about and covering you with flour."

"Besides, the fire is too hot for you," interposed Mary.

"To be sure," added her sister. "Come, you must be obedient." And still holding my hand, she made me rise, and led me into the inner room.

"Sit there," she said, placing me on the sofa, "while we take our things off and get the tea ready; it is another privilege we exercise in our little moorland home—to prepare our own meals when we are so inclined; or when Hannah is baking, brewing, washing, or ironing."

She closed the door, leaving me solus with Mr. St. John, who sat opposite, a book or newspaper in his hand. I examined, first, the parlor, and then its occupant.

The parlor was rather a small room, very plainly furnished; yet comfortable, because clean and neat. The old-fashioned chairs were very bright, and the walnut-wood table was like a looking-glass. A few strange antique portraits of the men and women of other days decorated the stained walls; a cupboard with glass doors contained some books and an ancient set of china. There was no superfluous ornament in the room—not one modern piece of furniture, save a brace of work-boxes and a lady's desk in rosewood, which stood on a side-table: everything—including the carpet and curtains—looked at once well worn and well saved.

Mr. St. John—sitting as still as one of the dusky pictures on the walls, keeping his eyes fixed on the page he perused and his lips mutely sealed, was easy enough to examine. Had he been a statue instead of a man, he could not have been easier. He was young—perhaps from twenty-eight to thirty—tall, slender; his face riveted the eye; it was like a Greek face, very pure in outline: quite a straight, classic nose; quite an Athenian mouth and chin. It is seldom, indeed, an English face comes so near the antique models as did his. He might well be a little shocked at the irregularity of my lineaments, his own being so harmonious. His eyes were large and blue, with brown lashes; his high forehead, colorless as ivory, was partially streaked over by careless locks of fair hair.

This is a gentle delineation, is it not, reader? Yet he whom it describes scarcely impressed one with the idea of a gentle, a yielding, an impressible, or even a placid nature. Quiescent as he now sat, there was something about his nostril, his mouth, his brow, which, to my perceptions, indicated elements within either restless, or hard, or eager. He did not speak to me one word, nor even direct to me one glance, till his sisters returned. Diana, as she passed in and out in the course of preparing tea, brought me a little cake, baked on the top of the oven.

"Eat that now," she said: "you must be hungry. Hannah says you have had nothing but some gruel since breakfast."

I did not refuse it, for my appetite was awakened and keen. Mr. Rivers now closed his book, approached the table, and, as he took a seat, fixed his blue pictorial-looking eyes full on me. There was an unceremonious directness, a searching, decided steadfastness in his gaze now, which told that intention, and not diffidence, had hitherto kept it averted from the stranger.

"You are very hungry," he said.

"I am, sir." It is my way—it always was my way, by instinct—ever to meet the brief with brevity, the direct with plainness.

"It is well for you that a low fever has forced you to abstain for the last three days: there would have been danger in yielding to the cravings of your appetite at first. Now you may eat; though still not immoderately."

"I trust I shall not eat long at your expense, sir," was my very clumsily-contrived, unpolished answer.

"No," he said coolly: "when you have indicated to us the residence of your friends, we can write to them, and you may be restored to home."

"That, I must plainly tell you, is out of my power to do; being absolutely without home and friends."

The three looked at me, but not distrustfully; I felt there was no suspicion in their glances: there was more of curiosity. I speak particularly of the young ladies. St. John's eyes, though clear enough in a literal sense, in a figurative one were difficult to fathom. He seemed to use them rather as instruments to search other people's thoughts, than as agents to reveal his own: the which combination of keenness and reserve was considerably more calculated to embarrass than to encourage.

"Do you mean to say," he asked, "that you are completely isolated from every connection?"

"I do. Not a tie links me to any living thing: not a claim do I possess to admittance under any roof in England."

"A most singular position at your age!"

Here I saw his glance directed to my hands, which were folded on the table before me. I wondered what he sought there: his words soon explained the quest.

"You have never been married? You are a spinster?"

Diana laughed.

"Why, she can't be above seventeen or eighteen years old, St. John," said she.

"I am near nineteen: but I am not married. No."

I felt a burning glow mount to my face; for bitter and agitating recollections were awakened by the allusion to marriage. They all saw the embarrassment and the emotion. Diana and Mary relieved me by turning their eyes elsewhere than to my crimsoned visage; but the colder and sterner brother continued to gaze, till the trouble he had excited forced out tears as well as color.

"Where did you last reside?" he now asked.

"You are too inquisitive, St. John," murmured Mary, in a low voice; but he leaned over the table and required an answer by a second firm and piercing look.

"The name of the place where, and of the person with whom I lived, is my secret," I replied, concisely.

"Which, if you like, you have, in my opinion, a right to keep both from St. John and every other questioner," remarked Diana.

"Yet if I know nothing about you or your history, I cannot help you," he said. "And you need help: do you not?"

"I need it, and I seek it; so far, sir, that some true philanthropist will put

me in the way of getting work which I can do, and the remuneration for which will keep me: if but in the barest necessaries of life."

"I know not whether I am a true philanthropist; yet I am willing to aid you to the utmost of my power, in a purpose so honest. First, then, tell me what you have been accustomed to do, and what you *can* do."

I had now swallowed my tea. I was mightily refreshed by the beverage; as much so as a giant with wine: it gave new tone to my unstrung nerves, and enabled me to address this penetrating young judge steadily.

"Mr. Rivers," I said, turning to him, and looking at him, as he looked at me, openly and without diffidence, "you and your sisters have done me a great service—the greatest man can do his fellow-being; you have rescued me, by your noble hospitality, from death. This benefit conferred gives you an unlimited claim on my gratitude; and a claim, to a certain extent, on my confidence. I will tell you as much of the history of the wanderer you have harbored as I can tell without compromising my own peace of mind—my own security, moral and physical, and that of others.

"I am an orphan; the daughter of a clergyman. My parents died before I could know them. I was brought up a dependent; educated in a charitable institution. I will even tell you the name of the establishment where I passed six years as a pupil and two as a teacher—Lowood Orphan Asylum, —— shire: you will have heard of it, Mr. Rivers?—the Rev. Robert Brocklehurst is the treasurer."

"I have heard of Mr. Brocklehurst, and I have seen the school."

"I left Lowood nearly a year since to become a private governess. I obtained a good situation, and was happy. This place I was obliged to leave four days before I came here. The reason of my departure I cannot and ought not to explain: it would be useless—dangerous; and would sound incredible. No blame attached to me; I am as free from culpability as any one of you three. Miserable I am, and must be for a time; for the catastrophe which drove me from a house I had found a paradise was of a strange and direful nature. I observed but two points in planning my departure—speed, secrecy: to secure these I had to leave behind me everything I possessed except a small parcel; which, in my hurry and trouble of mind, I forgot to take out of the coach that brought me to Whitcross. To this neighborhood, then, I came, quite destitute. I slept two nights in the open air, and wandered about two days without crossing a threshold: but twice in that space of time did I taste food; and it was when brought by hunger, exhaustion and despair almost to the last gasp that you, Mr. Rivers, forbade me to perish of want at your door, and took me under the shelter of your roof. I know all your sisters have done for me since—for I have not been insensible during my seeming torpor— and I owe to their spontaneous, genuine, genial compassion, as large a debt as to your evangelical charity."

"Don't make her talk any more now, St. John," said Diana, as I paused; "she is evidently not yet fit for excitement. Come to the sofa, and sit down now, Miss Elliott."

I gave an involuntary half-start at hearing the alias; I had forgotten my new name. Mr. Rivers, whom nothing seemed to escape, noticed it at once.

"You said your name was Jane Elliott?" he observed.

"I did say so; and it is the name by which I think it expedient to be called

at present: but it is not my real name, and when I hear it, it sounds strange to me."

"Your real name you will not give?"

"No: I fear discovery above all things; and whatever disclosure would lead to it, I avoid."

"You are quite right, I am sure," said Diana. "Now do, brother, let her be at peace a while."

But when St. John had mused a few moments, he recommenced, as imperturbably, and with as much acumen as ever.

"You would not like to be long dependent on our hospitality—you would wish, I see, to dispense as soon as may be with my sisters' compassion; and, above all, with my *charity* (I am quite sensible of the distinction drawn, nor do I resent it—it is just): you desire to be independent of us?"

"I do: I have already said so. Show me how to work, or how to seek work: that is all I now ask; then let me go, if it be but to the meanest cottage—but *till then* allow me to stay here: I dread another essay of the horrors of homeless destitution."

"Indeed, you *shall* stay here," said Diana, putting her white hand on my head.

"You *shall*," repeated Mary, in the tone of undemonstrative sincerity which seemed natural to her.

"My sisters, you see, have a pleasure in keeping you," said Mr. St. John, "as they would have a pleasure in keeping and cherishing a half-frozen bird some wintry wind might have driven through their casement. *I* feel more inclination to put you in the way of keeping yourself: and shall endeavor to do so: but observe, my sphere is narrow. I am but the incumbent of a poor country parish: my aid must be of the humblest sort. And if you are inclined to despise the day of small things, seek some more efficient succour than such as I can offer."

"She has already said that she is willing to do anything honest she *can* do," answered Diana for me; "and you know, St. John, she has no choice of helpers: she is forced to put up with such crusty people as you."

"I will be a dressmaker: I will be a plain-work-woman; I will be a servant, a nurse-girl, if I can be no better," I answered.

"Right," said Mr. St. John, quite coolly. "If such is your spirit, I promise to aid you; in my own time and way."

He now resumed the book with which he had been occupied before tea. I soon withdrew; for I had talked as much, and sat up as long, as my present strength would permit.

Chapter XXX

The more I knew of the inmates of Moor House, the better I liked them. In a few days I had so far recovered my health that I could sit up all day, and walk out sometimes. I could join with Diana and Mary in all their occupations; converse with them as much as they wished, and aid them when and where they would allow me. There was a reviving pleasure in this intercourse, of a kind now tasted by me for the first time—the pleasure arising from perfect congeniality of tastes, sentiments, and principles.

I liked to read what they liked to read: what they enjoyed, delighted me;

what they approved, I reverenced. They loved their sequestered home. I, too, in the gray, small, antique structure, with its low roof, its latticed casements, its moldering walls, its avenue of aged firs—all grown aslant under the stress of mountain winds; its garden, dark with yew and holly—and where no flowers but of the hardiest species would bloom—found a charm both potent and permanent. They clung to the purple moors behind and around their dwelling—to the hollow vale into which the pebbly bridle-path leading from their gate descended; and which wound between fern-banks first, and then amongst a few of the wildest little pasture-fields that ever bordered a wilderness of heath, or gave sustenance to a flock of gray moorland sheep, with their little mossy-faced lambs:—they clung to this scene, I say, with a perfect enthusiasm of attachment. I could comprehend the feeling, and share both its strength and truth. I saw the fascination of the locality. I felt the consecration of its loneliness: my eye feasted on the outline of swell and sweep—on the wild coloring communicated to ridge and dell by moss, by heath-bell, by flower-sprinkled turf, by brilliant bracken and mellow granite crag. These details were just to me what they were to them—so many pure and sweet sources of pleasure. The strong blast and the soft breeze; the rough and the halcyon day; the hours of sunrise and sunset; the moonlight and the clouded night, developed for me, in these regions, the same attraction as for them—wound round my faculties the same spell that entranced theirs.

Indoors we agreed equally well. They were both more accomplished and better read than I was: but with eagerness I followed in the path of knowledge they had trodden before me. I devoured the books they lent me: then it was full satisfaction to discuss with them in the evening what I had perused during the day. Thought fitted thought; opinion met opinion: we coincided, in short, perfectly.

If in our trio there was a superior and a leader, it was Diana. Physically, she far excelled me: she was handsome; she was vigorous. In her animal spirits there was an affluence of life and certainty of flow, such as excited my wonder, while it baffled my comprehension. I could talk a while when the evening commenced: but the first gush of vivacity and fluency gone, I was fain to sit on a stool at Diana's feet, to rest my head on her knee, and listen alternately to her and Mary; while they sounded thoroughly the topic on which I had but touched. Diana offered to teach me German. I liked to learn of her: I saw the part of instructress pleased and suited her; that of scholar pleased and suited me no less. Our natures dovetailed: mutual affection—of the strongest kind—was the result. They discovered I could draw: their pencils and color-boxes were immediately at my service. My skill, greater in this one point than theirs, surprised and charmed them. Mary would sit and watch me by the hour together: then she would take lessons; and a docile, intelligent, assiduous pupil she made. Thus occupied, and mutually entertained, days passed like hours and weeks like days.

As to Mr. St. John, the intimacy which had arisen so naturally and rapidly between me and his sisters did not extend to him. One reason of the distance yet observed between us was that he was comparatively seldom at home: a large proportion of his time appeared devoted to visiting the sick and poor among the scattered population of his parish.

No weather seemed to hinder him in these pastoral excursions: rain or fair, he would, when his hours of morning study were over, take his hat, and,

followed by his father's old pointer Carlo, go out on his mission of love or duty—I scarcely know in which light he regarded it. Sometimes, when the day was very unfavourable, his sisters would expostulate. He would then say, with a peculiar smile, more solemn than cheerful,—"And if I let a gust of wind or a sprinkling of rain turn me aside from these easy tasks, what preparation would such sloth be for the future I propose to myself?"

Diana and Mary's general answer to this question was a sigh, and some minutes of apparently mournful meditation.

But besides his frequent absences, there was another barrier to friendship with him: he seemed of a reserved, an abstracted, and even of a brooding nature. Zealous in his ministerial labors, blameless in his life and habits, he yet did not appear to enjoy that mental serenity, that inward content, which should be the reward of every sincere Christian and practical philanthropist. Often, of an evening, when he sat at the window, his desk and papers before him, he would cease reading or writing, rest his chin on his hand, and deliver himself up to I know not what course of thought; but that it was perturbed and exciting might be seen in the frequent flash and changeful dilation of his eye.

I think, moreover, that Nature was not to him that treasury of delight it was to his sisters. He expressed once, and but once in my hearing, a strong sense of the rugged charm of the hills, and an inborn affection for the dark roof and hoary walls he called his home; but there was more of gloom than pleasure in the tone and words in which the sentiment was manifested; and never did he seem to roam the moors for the sake of their soothing silence— never seek out or dwell upon the thousand peaceful delights they could yield.

Incommunicative as he was, some time elapsed before I had an opportunity of gauging his mind. I first got an idea of its caliber when I heard him preach in his own church at Morton. I wish I could describe that sermon; but it is past my power. I cannot even render faithfully the effect it produced on me.

It began calm—and indeed, as far as delivery and pitch of voice went, it was calm to the end: an earnestly felt, yet strictly restrained zeal breathed soon in the distinct accents, and prompted the nervous language. This grew to force—compressed, condensed, controlled. The heart was thrilled, the mind astonished, by the power of the preacher: neither was softened. Throughout there was a strange bitterness; an absence of consolatory gentleness; stern allusions to Calvinistic doctrines—election, predestination, reprobation—were frequent; and each reference to these points sounded like a sentence pronounced for doom. When he had done, instead of feeling better, calmer, more enlightened by his discourse, I experienced an inexpressible sadness; for it seemed to me—I know not whether equally so to others—that the eloquence to which I had been listening had sprung from a depth where lay turbid dregs of disappointment—where moved troubling impulses of insatiate yearnings and disquieting aspirations. I was sure St. John Rivers—pure-lived, conscientious, zealous as he was—had not yet found that peace of God which passeth all understanding;[3] he had no more found it, I thought, then had I; with my concealed and racking regrets for my broken idol and lost elysium[4]—regrets to which I have latterly avoided referring; but which possessed me and tyrannized over me ruthlessly.

3. Philippians 4.7. 4. I.e., paradise.

Meantime a month was gone. Diana and Mary were soon to leave Moor House, and return to the far different life and scene which awaited them, as governesses in a large, fashionable, south-of-England city; where each held a situation in families, by whose wealthy and haughty members they were regarded only as humble dependents, and who neither knew nor sought one of their innate excellences, and appreciated only their acquired accomplishments as they appreciated the skill of their cook or the taste of their waiting-woman. Mr. St. John had said nothing to me yet about the employment he had promised to obtain for me; yet it became urgent that I should have a vocation of some kind. One morning, being left alone with him a few minutes in the parlor, I ventured to approach the window-recess—which his table, chair, and desk consecrated as a kind of study—and I was going to speak; though not very well knowing in what words to frame my inquiry—for it is at all times difficult to break the ice of reserve glassing over such natures as his—when he saved me the trouble by being the first to commence a dialogue.

Looking up as I drew near—"You have a question to ask of me?" he said.

"Yes; I wish to know whether you have heard of any service I can offer myself to undertake."

"I found or devised something for you three weeks ago; but as you seemed both useful and happy here—as my sisters had evidently become attached to you, and your society gave them unusual pleasure—I deemed it inexpedient to break in on your mutual comfort till their approaching departure from Marsh End should render yours necessary."

"And they will go in three days now?" I said.

"Yes; and when they go I shall return to the parsonage at Morton: Hannah will accompany me; and this old house will be shut up."

I waited for a few moments, expecting he would go on with the subject first broached; but he seemed to have entered another train of reflection; his look denoted abstraction from me and my business. I was obliged to recall him to a theme which was of necessity one of close and anxious interest to me.

"What is the employment you had in view, Mr. Rivers? I hope this delay will not have increased the difficulty of securing it."

"Oh, no; since it is an employment which depends only on me to give, and you to accept."

He again paused: there seemed a reluctance to continue. I grew impatient: a restless movement or two, and an eager and exacting glance fastened on his face, conveyed the feeling to him as effectually as words could have done, and with less trouble.

"You need be in no hurry to hear," he said; "let me frankly tell you, I have nothing eligible or profitable to suggest. Before I explain, recall, if you please, my notice, clearly given, that if I helped you, it must be as the blind man would help the lame. I am poor; for I find that, when I have paid my father's debts, all the patrimony remaining to me will be this crumbling grange, the row of scathed firs behind, and the patch of moorish soil, with the yew-trees and holly-bushes in front. I am obscure: Rivers is an old name; but of the three sole descendants of the race, two earn the dependent's crust among strangers, and the third considers himself an alien from his native country— not only for life, but in death. Yes, and deems, and is bound to deem, himself honored by the lot, and aspires but after the day when the cross of separation

from fleshly ties shall be laid on his shoulders, and when the Head of that church-militant, of whose humblest members he is one, shall give the word, 'Rise, follow Me!' "

St. John said these words as he pronounced his sermons, with a quiet, deep voice; with an unflushed cheek, and a coruscating radiance of glance. He resumed:—"And since I am myself poor and obscure, I can offer you but a service of poverty and obscurity. *You* may even think it degrading—for I see now your habits have been what the world calls refined: your tastes lean to the ideal; and your society has at least been amongst the educated—but I consider that no service degrades which can better our race. I hold that the more arid and unreclaimed the soil where the Christian laborer's task of tillage is appointed him—the scantier the meed his toil brings—the higher the honor. His, under such circumstances, is the destiny of the pioneer; and the first pioneers of the Gospel were the Apostles—their captain was Jesus, the Redeemer, Himself."

"Well?" I said, as he again paused—"proceed."

He looked at me before he proceeded: indeed, he seemed leisurely to read my face, as if its features and lines were characters on a page. The conclusions drawn from this scrutiny he partially expressed in his succeeding observations.

"I believe you will accept the post I offer you," said he; "and hold it for a while: not permanently, though: any more than I could permanently keep the narrow and narrowing—the tranquil, hidden office of English country incumbent: for in your nature is an alloy as detrimental to repose as that in mine; though of a different kind."

"Do explain," I urged, when he halted once more.

"I will; and you shall hear how poor the proposal is,—how trivial—how cramping. I shall not stay long at Morton, now that my father is dead, and that I am my own master. I shall leave the place probably in the course of a twelve-month: but while I do stay I will exert myself to the utmost for its improvement. Morton, when I came to it two years ago, had no school: the children of the poor were excluded from every hope of progress. I established one for boys: I mean now to open a second school for girls. I have hired a building for the purpose, with a cottage of two rooms attached to it for the mistress's house. Her salary will be thirty pounds a year; her house is already furnished, very simply, but sufficiently, by the kindness of a lady, Miss Oliver; the only daughter of the sole rich man in my parish—Mr. Oliver, the proprietor of a needle-factory and iron-foundry in the valley. The same lady pays for the education and clothing of an orphan from the workhouse; on condition that she shall aid the mistress in such menial offices connected with her own house and the school as her occupation of teaching will prevent her having time to discharge in person. Will you be this mistress?"

He put the question rather hurriedly; he seemed half to expect an indignant, or at least a disdainful, rejection of the offer: not knowing all my thoughts and feelings, though guessing some, he could not tell in what light the lot would appear to me. In truth it was humble—but then it was sheltered, and I wanted a safe asylum: it was plodding—but then, compared with that of a governess in a rich house, it was independent; and the fear of servitude with strangers entered my soul like iron: it was not ignoble—not unworthy—not mentally degrading. I made my decision.

"I thank you for the proposal, Mr. Rivers; and I accept it with all my heart."

"But you comprehend me?" he said. "It is a village school; your scholars will be only poor girls—cottagers' children—at the best, farmers' daughters. Knitting, sewing, reading, writing, cyphering, will be all you will have to teach. What will you do with your accomplishments? What with the largest portion of your mind—sentiments—tastes?"

"Save them till they are wanted. They will keep."

"You know what you undertake; then?"

"I do."

He now smiled: and not a bitter or a sad smile, but one well pleased and deeply gratified.

"And when will you commence the exercise of your function?"

"I will go to my house tomorrow; and open the school, if you like, next week."

"Very well: so be it."

He rose and walked through the room. Standing still, he again looked at me. He shook his head.

"What do you disapprove of, Mr. Rivers?" I asked.

"You will not stay at Morton long: no, no!"

"Why! What is your reason for saying so?"

"I read it in your eye; it is not of that description which promises the maintenance of an even tenor in life."

"I am not ambitious."

He started at the word "ambitious." He repeated, "No. What made you think of ambition? Who is ambitious? I know I am: but how did you find it out?"

"I was speaking of myself."

"Well, if you are not ambitious, you are"——He paused.

"What?"

"I was going to say, impassioned: but perhaps you would have misunderstood the word, and been displeased. I mean, that human affections and sympathies have a most powerful hold on you. I am sure you cannot long be content to pass your leisure in solitude, and to devote your working hours to a monotonous labor wholly void of stimulus; any more than I can be content," he added, with emphasis, "to live here buried in morass, pent in with mountain—my nature, that God gave me, contravened; my faculties, heaven-bestowed, paralyzed—made useless. You hear now how I contradict myself. I, who preached contentment with a humble lot, and justified the vocation even of hewers of wood, and drawers of water, in God's service—I, His ordained minister, almost rave in my restlessness. Well, propensities and principles must be reconciled by some means."

He left the room. In this brief hour I had learnt more of him than in the whole previous month: yet still he puzzled me.

Diana and Mary Rivers became more sad and silent as the day approached for leaving their brother and their home. They both tried to appear as usual; but the sorrow they had to struggle against was one that could not be entirely conquered or concealed. Diana intimated that this would be a different parting from any they had ever yet known. It would probably, as far as St. John was concerned, be a parting for years: it might be a parting for life.

"He will sacrifice all to his long-framed resolves," she said: "natural affec-

tion and feelings more potent still. St. John looks quiet, Jane; but he hides a fever in his vitals. You would think him gentle, yet in some things he is inexorable as death; and the worst of it is, my conscience will hardly permit me to dissuade him from his severe decision: certainly, I cannot for a moment blame him for it. It is right, noble, Christian: yet it breaks my heart." And the tears gushed to her fine eyes. Mary bent her head low over her work.

"We are now without father: we shall soon be without home and brother," she murmured.

At that moment a little accident supervened which seemed decreed by fate purposely to prove the truth of the adage that "misfortunes never come singly": and to add to their distresses the vexing one of the slip between the cup and the lip. St. John passed the window reading a letter. He entered.

"Our uncle John is dead," said he.

Both the sisters seemed struck: not shocked or appalled; the tidings appeared in their eyes rather momentous than afflicting.

"Dead?" repeated Diana.

"Yes."

She riveted a searching gaze on her brother's face. "And what then?" she demanded, in a low voice.

"What then, Di?" he replied, maintaining a marble immobility of feature. "When then? Why—nothing. Read."

He threw the letter into her lap. She glanced over it, and handed it to Mary. Mary perused it in silence, and returned it to her brother. All three looked at each other, and all three smiled—a dreary, pensive smile enough.

"Amen! We can yet live," said Diana at last.

"At any rate, it makes us no worse off than we were before," remarked Mary.

"Only it forces rather strongly on the mind the picture of what *might have been*," said Mr. Rivers; "and contrasts it somewhat too vividly with what *is*."

He folded the letter, locked it in his desk, and again went out.

For some minutes no one spoke. Diana then turned to me.

"Jane, you will wonder at us and our mysteries," she said, "and think us hard-hearted beings not to be more moved at the death of so near a relation as an uncle; but we have never seen him or known him. He was my mother's brother. My father and he quarreled long ago. It was by his advice that my father risked most of his property in the speculation that ruined him. Mutual recrimination passed between them: they parted in anger, and were never reconciled. My uncle engaged afterwards in more prosperous undertakings: it appears he realized a fortune of twenty thousand pounds. He was never married, and had no near kindred but ourselves, and one other person, not more closely related than we. My father always cherished the idea that he would atone for his error by leaving his possessions to us: that letter informs us that he has bequeathed every penny to the other relation; with the exception of thirty guineas, to be divided between St. John, Diana, and Mary Rivers, for the purchase of three mourning rings. He had a right, of course, to do as he pleased: and yet a momentary damp is cast on the spirits by the receipt of such news. Mary and I would have esteemed ourselves rich with a thousand pounds each; and to St. John such a sum would have been valuable, for the good it would have enabled him to do."

This explanation given, the subject was dropped, and no further reference

made to it, by either Mr. Rivers or his sisters. The next day I left Marsh End
for Morton. The day after, Diana and Mary quitted it for distant B——. In
a week, Mr. Rivers and Hannah repaired to the parsonage: and so the old
grange was abandoned.

Chapter XXXI

My home, then,—when I at last find a home,—is a cottage: a little room
with white-washed walls and a sanded floor; containing four painted chairs
and a table, a clock, a cupboard, with two or three plates and dishes, and a
set of tea-things in delf.[5] Above, a chamber of the same dimensions as the
kitchen, with a deal bedstead, and chest of drawers; small, yet too large to
be filled with my scanty wardrobe: though the kindness of my gentle and
generous friends has increased that by a modest stock of such things as are
necessary.

It is evening. I have dismissed, with the fee of an orange, the little orphan
who serves me as a handmaid. I am sitting alone on the hearth. This morning
the village school opened. I had twenty scholars. But three of the number
can read: none write or cypher. Several knit, and a few sew a little. They
speak with the broadest accent of the district. At present they and I have a
difficulty in understanding each other's language. Some of them are unman-
nered, rough, intractable, as well as ignorant; but others are docile, have a
wish to learn, and evince a disposition that pleases me. I must not forget that
these coarsely-clad little peasants are of flesh and blood as good as the scions
of gentlest genealogy; and that the germs of native excellence, refinement,
intelligence, kind feeling, are as likely to exist in their hearts as in those of
the best-born. My duty will be to develop these germs: surely I shall find
some happiness in discharging that office. Much enjoyment I do not expect
in the life opening before me: yet it will, doubtless, if I regulate my mind,
and exert my powers as I ought, yield me enough to live on from day to day.

Was I very gleeful, settled, content, during the hours I passed in yonder
bare, humble schoolroom this morning and afternoon? Not to deceive
myself, I must reply—No: I felt desolate to a degree. I felt—yes, idiot that I
am—I felt degraded. I doubted I had taken a step which sank instead of
raising me in the scale of social existence. I was weakly dismayed at the
ignorance, the poverty, the coarseness of all I heard and saw round me. But
let me not hate and despise myself too much for these feelings: I know them
to be wrong—that is a great step gained; I shall strive to overcome them.
Tomorrow, I trust, I shall get the better of them partially; and in a few weeks,
perhaps, they will be quite subdued. In a few months, it is possible, the
happiness of seeing progress, and a change for the better in my scholars,
may substitute gratification for disgust.

Meantime, let me ask myself one question—Which is better?—To have
surrendered to temptation; listened to passion; made no painful effort—no
struggle;—but to have sunk down in the silken snare; fallen asleep on the
flowers covering it; wakened in a southern clime, among the luxuries of a
pleasure villa: to have been now living in France, Mr. Rochester's mistress;
delirious with his love half my time—for he would—oh, yes, he would have

5. I.e., delft, Dutch pottery.

loved me well for a while. He *did* love me—no one will ever love me so again. I shall never more know the sweet homage given to beauty, youth, and grace—for never to anyone else shall I seem to possess these charms. He was fond and proud of me—it is what no man besides will ever be.—But where am I wondering, and what am I saying; and, above all, feeling? Whether is it better, I ask, to be a slave in a fool's paradise at Marseilles— fevered with delusive bliss one hour—suffocating with the bitterest tears of remorse and shame the next—or to be a village schoolmistress, free and honest, in a breezy mountain nook in the healthy heart of England?

Yes; I feel now that I was right when I adhered to principle and law, and scorned and crushed the insane promptings of a frenzied moment. God directed me to a correct choice: I thank His providence for the guidance.

Having brought my eventide musings to this point, I rose, went to my door, and looked at the sunset of the harvest-day, and at the quiet fields before my cottage; which, with the school, was distant half a mile from the village. The birds were singing their last strains—

> "The air was mild; the dew was balm."[6]

While I looked, I thought myself happy, and was surprised to find myself ere long weeping—and why? For the doom which had reft me from adhesion to my master: for him I was no more to see; for the desperate grief and fatal fury—consequences of my departure—which might now, perhaps, be drag- ging him from the path of right, too far to leave hope of ultimate restoration thither. At this thought, I turned my face aside from the lovely sky of eve and lonely vale of Morton—I say *lonely,* for in that bend of it visible to me there was no building apparent save the church and the parsonage, half-hid in trees; and, quite at the extremity, the roof of Vale Hall, where the rich Mr. Oliver and his daughter lived. I hid my eyes, and leant my head against the stone frame of my door; but soon a slight noise near the wicket which shut in my tiny garden from the meadow beyond it made me look up. A dog—old Carlo, Mr. Rivers' pointer, as I saw in a moment—was pushing the gate with his nose, and St. John himself leaned upon it with folded arms; his brow knit, his gaze, grave almost to displeasure, fixed on me. I asked him to come in.

"No, I cannot stay; I have only brought you a little parcel my sisters left for you. I think it contains a color-box, pencils, and paper."

I approached to take it: a welcome gift it was. He examined my face, I thought, with austerity, as I came near: the traces of tears were doubtless very visible upon it.

"Have you found your first day's work harder than you expected?" he asked.

"Oh, no! On the contrary, I think in time I shall get on with my scholars very well."

"But perhaps your accommodations—your cottage—your furniture— have disappointed your expectations? They are, in truth, scanty enough; but——"

I interrupted:—"My cottage is clean and weather-proof; my furniture suf- ficient and commodious. All I see has made me thankful, not despondent. I am not absolutely such a fool and sensualist as to regret the absence of a carpet, a sofa, and silver plate: besides, five weeks ago I had nothing—I was

6. From Sir Walter Scott's *The Lay of the Last Minstrel* 3.24.3–4.

an outcast, a beggar, a vagrant; now I have acquaintance, a home, a business. I wonder at the goodness of God; the generosity of my friends; the bounty of my lot. I do not repine."

"But you feel solitude an oppression? The little house there behind you is dark and empty."

"I have hardly had time yet to enjoy a sense of tranquillity, much less to grow impatient under one of loneliness."

"Very well; I hope you feel the content you express: at any rate, your good sense will tell you that it is too soon yet to yield to the vacillating fears of Lot's wife.[7] What you had left before I saw you, of course I do not know; but I counsel you to resist, firmly, every temptation which would incline you to look back: pursue your present career steadily, for some months at least."

"It is what I mean to do," I answered.

St. John continued:—"It is hard work to control the workings of inclination, and turn the bent of nature: but that it may be done I know from experience. God has given us, in a measure, the power to make our own fate; and when our energies seem to demand a sustenance they cannot get—when our will strains after a path we may not follow—we need neither starve from inanition, nor stand still in despair: we have but to seek another nourishment for the mind, as strong as the forbidden fruit it longed to taste—and perhaps purer; and to hew out for the adventurous foot a road as direct and broad as the one Fortune has blocked up against us, if rougher than it.

"A year ago I was myself intensely miserable, because I thought I had made a mistake in entering the ministry: its uniform duties wearied me to death. I burnt for the more active life of the world—for the more exciting toils of a literary career—for the destiny of an artist, author, orator; anything rather than that of a priest: yes, the heart of a politician, of a soldier, of a votary of glory, a lover of renown, a luster after power, beat under my curate's surplice. I considered; my life was so wretched, it must be changed, or I must die. After a season of darkness and struggling, light broke and relief fell: my cramped existence all at once spread out to a plain without bounds—my powers heard a call from heaven to rise, gather their full strength, spread their wings, and mount beyond ken. God had an errand for me; to bear which afar, to deliver it well, skill and strength, courage and eloquence, the best qualifications of soldier, statesman, and orator, were all needed: for these all center in the good missionary.

"A missionary I resolved to be. From that moment my state of mind changed; the fetters dissolved and dropped from every faculty, leaving nothing of bondage but its galling soreness—which time only can heal. My father, indeed, opposed the determination, but since his death I have not a legitimate obstacle to contend with; some affairs settled, a successor for Morton provided, an entanglement or two of the feelings broken through or cut asunder—a last conflict with human weakness, in which I know I shall overcome, because I have vowed that I *will* overcome—and I leave Europe for the East."

He said this in his peculiar, subdued, yet emphatic voice; looking, when he had ceased speaking, not at me, but at the setting sun, at which I looked too. Both he and I had our backs towards the path leading up the field to

7. Fleeing the destruction of Sodom, Lot's wife looked backward and was turned into a pillar of salt (Genesis 19.24–26).

the wicket. We had heard no step on that grass-grown track; the water running in the vale was the one lulling sound of the hour and scene; we might well then start when a gay voice, sweet as a silver bell, exclaimed:—"Good evening, Mr. Rivers. And good evening, old Carlo. Your dog is quicker to recognize his friends than you are, sir; he pricked his ears and wagged his tail when I was at the bottom of the field, and you have your back towards me now."

It was true. Though Mr. Rivers had started at the first of those musical accents, as if a thunderbolt had split a cloud over his head, he stood yet, at the close of the sentence, in the same attitude in which the speaker had surprised him—his arm resting on the gate, his face directed towards the west. He turned at last, with measured deliberation. A vision, as it seemed to me, had risen at his side. There appeared, within three feet of him, a form clad in pure white—a youthful, graceful form: full, yet fine in contour; and when, after bending to caress Carlo, it lifted up its head, and threw back a long veil, there bloomed under his glance a face of perfect beauty. Perfect beauty is a strong expression; but I do not retrace or qualify it: as sweet features as ever the temperate clime of Albion molded; as pure hues of rose and lily as ever her humid gales and vapory skies generated and screened justified, in this instance, the term. No charm was wanting, no defect was perceptible; the young girl had regular and delicate lineaments; eyes shaped and colored as we see them in lovely pictures, large, and dark, and full; the long and shadowy eyelash which encircles a fine eye with so soft a fascination; the penciled brow which gives such clearness; the white, smooth forehead which adds such repose to the livelier beauties of tint and ray; the cheek, oval, fresh, and smooth; the lips, fresh too, ruddy, healthy, sweetly formed; the even and gleaming teeth without flaw; the small dimpled chin; the ornament of rich, plenteous tresses—all advantages, in short, which, combined, realize the ideal of beauty were fully hers. I wondered, as I looked at this fair creature: I admired her with my whole heart. Nature had surely formed her in a partial mood; and, forgetting her usual stinted stepmother dole of gifts, had endowed this, her darling, with a granddame's bounty.

What did St. John Rivers think of this earthly angel? I naturally asked myself that question as I saw him turn to her and look at her; and, as naturally, I sought the answer to the inquiry in his countenance. He had already withdrawn his eye from the Peri,[8] and was looking at a humble tuft of daisies which grew by the wicket.

"A lovely evening, but late for you to be out alone," he said, as he crushed the snowy heads of the closed flowers with his foot.

"Oh, I only came home from S———" (she mentioned the name of a large town some twenty miles distant) "this afternoon. Papa told me you had opened your school, and that the new mistress was come; and so I put on my bonnet after tea, and ran up the valley to see her: this is she?" pointing to me.

"It is," said St. John.

"Do you think you shall like Morton?" she asked of me, with a direct and naïve simplicity of tone and manner, pleasing, if childlike.

"I hope I shall. I have many inducements to do so."

8. Fairy, beautiful girl.

"Did you find your scholars as attentive as you expected?"

"Quite."

"Do you like your house?"

"Very much."

"Have I furnished it nicely?"

"Very nicely indeed."

"And made a good choice of an attendant for you in Alice Wood?"

"You have, indeed. She is teachable and handy." (This, then, I thought, is Miss Oliver, the heiress; favored, it seems, in the gifts of fortune, as well as in those of nature! What happy combination of the planets presided over her birth, I wonder?)

"I shall come up and help you to teach sometimes," she added. "It will be a change for me to visit you now and then; and I like a change. Mr. Rivers, I have been so gay during my stay at S——. Last night, or rather this morning, I was dancing till two o'clock. The ——th regiment are stationed there since the riots; and the officers are the most agreeable men in the world: they put all our young knife-grinders and scissor merchants to shame."

It seemed to me that Mr. St. John's under lip protruded, and his upper lip curled a moment. His mouth certainly looked a good deal compressed, and the lower part of his face unusually stern and square, as the laughing girl gave him this information. He lifted his gaze, too, from the daisies, and turned it on her. An unsmiling, a searching, a meaning gaze it was. She answered it with a second laugh, and laughter well became her youth, her roses, her dimples, her bright eyes.

As he stood, mute and grave, she again fell to caressing Carlo. "Poor Carlo loves me," said she. "*He* is not stern and distant to his friends; and if he could speak, he would not be silent."

As she patted the dog's head, bending with native grace before his young and austere master, I saw a glow rise to that master's face. I saw his solemn eye melt with sudden fire, and flicker with resistless emotion. Flushed and kindled thus, he looked nearly as beautiful for a man as she for a woman. His chest heaved once, as if his large heart, weary of despotic constriction, had expanded, despite the will, and made a vigorous bound for the attainment of liberty. But he curbed it, I think, as a resolute rider would curb a rearing steed. He responded neither by word nor movement to the gentle advances made him.

"Papa says you never come to see us now," continued Miss Oliver, looking up. "You are quite a stranger at Vale Hall. He is alone this evening, and not very well: will you return with me and visit him?"

"It is not a seasonable hour to intrude on Mr. Oliver," answered St. John.

"Not a seasonable hour! But I declare it is. It is just the hour when papa most wants company: when the works are closed, and he has no business to occupy him. Now, Mr. Rivers, *do* come. Why are you so very shy, and so very somber?"

She filled up the hiatus his silence left by a reply of her own.

"I forgot!" she exclaimed, shaking her beautiful curled head, as if shocked at herself. "I am so giddy and thoughtless! *Do* excuse me. It had slipped my memory that you have good reasons to be indisposed for joining in my chatter. Diana and Mary have left you, and Moor House is shut up, and you are so lonely. I am sure I pity you. Do come and see papa."

"Not tonight, Miss Rosamond, not tonight."

Mr. St. John spoke almost like an automaton: himself only knew the effort it cost him thus to refuse.

"Well, if you are so obstinate, I will leave you; for I dare not stay any longer: the dew begins to fall. Good-evening!"

She held out her hand. He just touched it. "Good-evening!" he repeated, in a voice low and hollow as an echo. She turned; but in a moment returned.

"Are you well?" she asked. Well might she put the question: his face was blanched as her gown.

"Quite well," he enunciated; and, with a bow, he left the gate. She went one way; he another. She turned twice to gaze after him, as she tripped fairy-like down the field; he, as he strode firmly across, never turned at all.

This spectacle of another's suffering and sacrifice rapt my thoughts from exclusive meditation on my own. Diana Rivers had designated her brother "inexorable as death." She had not exaggerated.

Chapter XXXII

I continued the labors of the village-school as actively and faithfully as I could. It was truly hard work at first. Some time elapsed before, with all my efforts, I could comprehend my scholars and their nature. Wholly untaught, with faculties quite torpid, they seemed to me hopelessly dull; and, at first sight, all dull alike: but I soon found I was mistaken. There was a difference among them as among the educated; and when I got to know them, and they me, this difference rapidly developed itself. Their amazement at me, my language, my rules, and ways, once subsided, I found some of these heavy-looking, gaping rustics wake up into sharp-witted girls enough. Many showed themselves obliging, and amiable too; and I discovered among them not a few examples of natural politeness and innate self-respect, as well as of excellent capacity, that won both my goodwill and my admiration. These soon took a pleasure in doing their work well; in keeping their persons neat; in learning their tasks regularly; in acquiring quiet and orderly manners. The rapidity of their progress, in some instances, was even surprising; and an honest and happy pride I took in it: besides, I began personally to like some of the best girls; and they liked me. I had among my scholars several farmers' daughters: young women grown, almost. These could already read, write, and sew; and to them I taught the elements of grammar, geography, history, and the finer kinds of needlework. I found estimable characters among them—characters desirous of information, and disposed for improvement—with whom I passed many a pleasant evening hour in their own homes. Their parents then (the farmer and his wife) loaded me with attentions. There was an enjoyment in accepting their simple kindness, and in repaying it by a consideration—a scrupulous regard to their feelings—to which they were not, perhaps, at all times accustomed, and which both charmed and benefited them; because, while it elevated them in their own eyes, it made them emulous to merit the deferential treatment they received.

I felt I became a favorite in the neighborhood. Whenever I went out, I heard on all sides cordial salutations, and was welcomed with friendly smiles. To live amid general regard, though it be but the regard of working-people,

is like "sitting in sunshine, calm and sweet:"[9] serene inward feelings bud and bloom under the ray. At this period of my life my heart far oftener swelled with thankfulness than sank with dejection: and yet, reader, to tell you all, in the midst of this calm, this useful existence—after a day passed in honorable exertion among my scholars, an evening spent in drawing or reading contentedly alone—I used to rush into strange dreams at night: dreams many-colored, agitated, full of the ideal, the stirring, the stormy—dreams where, amid unusual scenes, charged with adventure, with agitating risk and romantic chance, I still again and again met Mr. Rochester, always at some exciting crisis; and then the sense of being in his arms, hearing his voice, meeting his eye, touching his hand and cheek, loving him, being loved by him—the hope of passing a lifetime at his side, would be renewed, with all its first force and fire. Then I awoke. Then I recalled where I was, and how situated. Then I rose up on my curtainless bed, trembling and quivering; and then the still, dark night witnessed the convulsion of despair and heard the burst of passion. By nine o'clock the next morning I was punctually opening the school; tranquil, settled, prepared for the steady duties of the day.

Rosamond Oliver kept her word in coming to visit me. Her call at the school was generally made in the course of her morning ride. She would canter up to the door on her pony, followed by a mounted livery servant. Anything more exquisite than her appearance, in her purple habit, with her Amazon's cap of black velvet placed gracefully above the long curls that kissed her cheek and floated to her shoulders, can scarcely be imagined: and it was thus she would enter the rustic building, and glide through the dazzled ranks of the village children. She generally came at the hour when Mr. Rivers was engaged in giving his daily catechising lesson. Keenly, I fear, did the eye of the visitress pierce the young pastor's heart. A sort of instinct seemed to warn him of her entrance, even when he did not see it; and when he was looking quite away from the door, if she appeared at it his cheek would glow and his marble-seeming features, though they refused to relax, changed indescribably: and in their very quiescence became expressive of a repressed fervor, stronger than working muscle or darting glance could indicate.

Of course she knew her power: indeed, he did not, because he could not, conceal it from her. In spite of his Christian stoicism, when she went up and addressed him, and smiled gaily, encouragingly, even fondly in his face, his hand would tremble and his eye burn. He seemed to say, with his sad and resolute look, if he did not say it with his lips, "I love you, and I know you prefer me. It is not despair of success that keeps me dumb. If I offered my heart, I believe you would accept it. But that heart is already laid on a sacred altar: the fire is arranged round it. It will soon be no more than a sacrifice consumed."

And then she would pout like a disappointed child; a pensive cloud would soften her radiant vivacity; she would withdraw her hand hastily from his, and turn in transient petulance from his aspect, at once so heroic and so martyr-like. St. John, no doubt, would have given the world to follow, recall, retain her, when she thus left him: but he would not give one chance of Heaven; nor relinquish, for the elysium of her love, one hope of the true,

9. From Thomas Moore's *Lalla Rookh* (1817), *Third Day*, 346.

eternal Paradise. Besides, he could not bound all that he had in his nature—
the rover, the aspirant, the poet, the priest—in the limits of a single passion.
He could not—he would not—renounce his wide field of mission warfare
for the parlors and the peace of Vale Hall. I learnt so much from himself, in
an inroad I once, despite his reserve, had the daring to make on his
confidence.

Miss Oliver already honored me with frequent visits to my cottage. I had
learnt her whole character; which was without mystery or disguise: she was
coquettish, but not heartless; exacting, but not worthlessly selfish. She had
been indulged from her birth, but was not absolutely spoiled. She was hasty,
but good-humored; vain (she could not help it, when every glance in the
glass showed her such a flush of loveliness), but not affected; liberal-handed;
innocent of the pride of wealth; ingenuous; sufficiently intelligent; gay, lively,
and unthinking: she was very charming, in short, even to a cool observer of
her own sex like me; but she was not profoundly interesting or thoroughly
impressive. A very different sort of mind was hers from that, for instance, of
the sisters of St. John. Still, I liked her almost as I liked my pupil Adèle:
except that for a child whom we have watched over and taught a closer
affection is engendered than we can give an equally attractive adult
acquaintance.

She had taken an amiable caprice to me. She said I was like Mr. Rivers
(only, certainly, she allowed, "not one-tenth so handsome: though I was a
nice neat little soul enough, but he was an angel"). I was, however, good,
clever, composed, and firm, like him. I was a *lusus naturae,*[1] she affirmed, as
a village schoolmistress: she was sure my previous history, if known, would
make a delightful romance.

One evening, while, with her usual childlike activity, and thoughtless yet
not offensive inquisitiveness, she was rummaging the cupboard and the
table-drawer of my little kitchen, she discovered first two French books, a
volume of Schiller, a German grammar and dictionary; and then my drawing-
materials and some sketches, including a pencil-head of a pretty little
cherub-like girl, one of my scholars, and sundry views from nature, taken in
the Vale of Morton and on the surrounding moors. She was first transfixed
with surprise, and then electrified with delight.

"Had I done these pictures? Did I know French and German? What a
love—what a miracle I was! I drew better than her master in the first school
in S——. Would I sketch a portrait of her, to show to papa?"

"With pleasure," I replied; and I felt a thrill of artist-delight at the idea of
copying from so perfect and radiant a model. She had then on a dark-blue
silk dress; her arms and her neck were bare; her only ornament was her
chestnut tresses, which waved over her shoulders with all the wild grace of
natural curls. I took a sheet of fine cardboard, and drew a careful outline. I
promised myself the pleasure of coloring it; and, as it was getting late then,
I told her she must come and sit another day.

She made such a report of me to her father that Mr. Oliver himself accom-
panied her next evening—a tall, massive-featured, middle-aged, and gray-
headed man, at whose side his lovely daughter looked like a bright flower
near a hoary turret. He appeared a taciturn, and perhaps a proud personage;

1. Sport of nature (Latin).

but he was very kind to me. The sketch of Rosamond's portrait pleased him highly: he said I must make a finished picture of it. He insisted, too, on my coming the next day to spend the evening at Vale Hall.

I went. I found it a large, handsome residence, showing abundant evidences of wealth in the proprietor. Rosamond was full of glee and pleasure all the time I stayed. Her father was affable; and when he entered into conversation with me after tea, he expressed in strong terms his approbation of what I had done in Morton school; and said he only feared, from what he saw and heard, I was too good for the place, and would soon quit it for one more suitable.

"Indeed!" cried Rosamond, "she is clever enough to be a governess in a high family, papa."

I thought—I would far rather be where I am than in any high family in the land. Mr. Oliver spoke of Mr. Rivers—of the Rivers family—with great respect. He said it was a very old name in that neighborhood; that the ancestors of the house were wealthy; that all Morton had once belonged to them, that even now he considered the representative of that house might, if he liked, make an alliance with the best. He accounted it a pity that so fine and talented a young man should have formed the design of going out as a missionary; it was quite throwing a valuable life away. It appeared, then, that her father would throw no obstacle in the way of Rosamond's union with St. John. Mr. Oliver evidently regarded the young clergyman's good birth, old name, and sacred profession as sufficient compensation for the want of fortune.

It was the 5th of November, and a holiday.[2] My little servant, after helping me to clean my house, was gone, well satisfied with the fee of a penny for her aid. All about me was spotless and bright—scoured floor, polished grate, and well-rubbed chairs. I had also made myself neat, and had now the afternoon before me to spend as I would.

The translation of a few pages of German occupied an hour; then I got my palette and pencils, and fell to the more soothing, because easier occupation, of completing Rosamond Oliver's miniature. The head was finished already: there was but the background to tint and the drapery to shade off; a touch of carmine, too, to add to the ripe lips—a soft curl here and there to the tresses—a deeper tinge to the shadow of the lash under the azured eyelid. I was absorbed in the execution of these nice details when, after one rapid tap, my door unclosed, admitting St. John Rivers.

"I am come to see how you are spending your holiday," he said. "Not, I hope, in thought? No, that is well: while you draw you will not feel lonely. You see, I mistrust you still: though you have borne up wonderfully so far. I have brought you a book for evening solace," and he laid on the table a new publication—a poem: one of those genuine productions so often vouchsafed to the fortunate public of those days—the golden age of modern literature. Alas! the readers of our era are less favored. But, courage! I will not pause either to accuse or repine. I know poetry is not dead, nor genius lost; nor has Mammon[3] gained power over either, to bind or slay: they will both assert their existence, their presence, their liberty and strength again one day. Pow-

2. I.e., Guy Fawkes Day, anniversary of the ill-fated Gunpowder Plot (to blow up the houses of Parliament) of 1605.

3. I.e., money.

erful angels, safe in heaven! they smile when sordid souls triumph, and feeble ones weep over their destruction. Poetry destroyed? Genius banished? No! Mediocrity, no: do not let envy prompt you to the thought. No; they not only live, but reign, and redeem: and without their divine influence spread everywhere you would be in hell—the hell of your own meanness.

While I was eagerly glancing at the bright pages of Marmion[4] (for Marmion it was) St. John stooped to examine my drawing. His tall figure sprang erect again with a start: he said nothing. I looked up at him: he shunned my eye. I knew his thoughts well, and could read his heart plainly; at the moment I felt calmer and cooler than he: I had then temporarily the advantage of him; and I conceived an inclination to do him some good, if I could.

"With all his firmness and self-control," thought I, "he tasks himself too far: locks every feeling and pang within—expresses, confesses, imparts nothing. I am sure it would benefit him to talk a little about this sweet Rosamond, whom he thinks he ought not to marry: I will make him talk."

I said first: "Take a chair, Mr. Rivers." But he answered, as he always did, that he could not stay. "Very well," I responded, mentally, "stand if you like; but you shall not go just yet, I am determined: solitude is at least as bad for you as it is for me. I'll try if I cannot discover the secret spring of your confidence, and find an aperture in that marble breast through which I can shed one drop of the balm of sympathy."

"Is this portrait like?" I asked bluntly.

"Like! Like whom? I did not observe it closely."

"You did, Mr. Rivers."

He almost started at my sudden and strange abruptness: he looked at me astonished. "Oh, that is nothing yet," I muttered within. "I don't mean to be baffled by a little stiffness on your part; I'm prepared to go to considerable lengths." I continued, "You observed it closely and distinctly: but I have no objection to your looking at it again," and I rose and placed it in his hand.

"A well-executed picture," he said; "very soft, clear colouring; very graceful and correct drawing."

"Yes, yes; I know all that. But what of the resemblance? Who is it like?"

Mastering some hesitation, he answered, "Miss Oliver, I presume."

"Of course. And now, sir, to reward you for the accurate guess I will promise to paint you a careful and faithful duplicate of this very picture, provided you admit that the gift would be acceptable to you. I don't wish to throw away my time and trouble on an offering you would deem worthless."

He continued to gaze at the picture: the longer he looked, the firmer he held it, the more he seemed to covet it. "It is like!" he murmured; "the eye is well managed: the colour, light, expression, are perfect. It smiles!"

"Would it comfort or would it wound you to have a similar painting? Tell me that. When you are at Madagascar, or at the Cape, or in India, would it be a consolation to have that memento in your possession? or would the sight of it bring recollections calculated to enervate and distress?"

He now furtively raised his eyes: he glanced at me, irresolute, disturbed; he again surveyed the picture.

"That I should like to have it is certain: whether it would be judicious or wise is another question."

4. Sir Walter Scott's *Marmion* (1808).

Since I had ascertained that Rosamond really preferred him, and that her father was not likely to oppose the match, I—less exalted in my views than St. John—had been strongly disposed in my own heart to advocate their union. It seemed to me that, should he become the possessor of Mr. Oliver's large fortune, he might do as much good with it as if he went and laid his genius out to wither and his strength to waste under a tropical sun. With this persuasion I now answered:—"As far as I can see, it would be wiser and more judicious if you were to take to yourself the original at once."

By this time he had sat down: he had laid the picture on the table before him, and with his brow supported on both hands hung fondly over it. I discerned he was now neither angry nor shocked at my audacity. I saw even that to be thus frankly addressed on a subject he had deemed unapproachable—to hear it thus freely handled—was beginning to be felt by him as a new pleasure—an unhoped-for relief. Reserved people often really need the frank discussion of their sentiments and griefs more than the expansive. The sternest-seeming stoic is human after all; and to "burst" with boldness and goodwill into "the silent sea"[5] of their souls is often to confer on them the first of obligations.

"She likes you, I am sure," said I, as I stood behind his chair, "and her father respects you. Moreover, she is a sweet girl—rather thoughtless; but you would have sufficient thought for both yourself and her. You ought to marry her."

"*Does* she like me?" he asked.

"Certainly; better than she likes any one else. She talks of you continually: there is no subject she enjoys so much or touches upon so often."

"It is very pleasant to hear this," he said—"very: go on for another quarter of an hour." And he actually took out his watch and laid it upon the table to measure the time.

"But where is the use of going on," I asked, "when you are probably preparing some iron blow of contradiction, or forging a fresh chain to fetter your heart?"

"Don't imagine such hard things. Fancy me yielding and melting, as I am doing: human love rising like a freshly opened fountain in my mind and overflowing with sweet inundation all the field I have so carefully, and with such labour prepared—so assiduously sown with the seeds of good intentions, of self-denying plans. And now it is deluged with a nectarous flood—the young germs swamped—delicious poison cankering them: now I see myself stretched on an ottoman in the drawing-room at Vale Hall, at my bride Rosamond Oliver's feet: she is talking to me with her sweet voice—gazing down on me with those eyes your skilful hand has copied so well—smiling at me with these coral lips. She is mine—I am hers—this present life and passing world suffice to me. Hush! say nothing—my heart is full of delight—my senses are entranced—let the time I marked pass in peace."

I humored him: the watch ticked on: he breathed fast and low: I stood silent. Amidst this hush the quarter sped; he replaced the watch, laid the picture down, rose, and stood on the hearth.

"Now," said he, "that little space was given to delirium and delusion. I rested my temples on the breast of temptation, and put my neck voluntarily

5. Samuel Taylor Coleridge's *The Rime of the Ancient Mariner* (1798), lines 105–6.

under her yoke of flowers; I tasted her cup. The pillow was burning; there is an asp in the garland; the wine has a bitter taste; her promises are hollow—her offers false; I see and know all this."

I gazed at him in wonder.

"It is strange," pursued he, "that while I love Rosamond Oliver so wildly—with all the intensity, indeed, of a first passion, the object of which is exquisitely beautiful, graceful, and fascinating—I experience at the same time a calm, unwarped consciousness that she would not make me a good wife; that she is not the partner suited to me; that I should discover this within a year after marriage; and that to twelve months' rapture would succeed a lifetime of regret. This I know."

"Strange, indeed!" I could not help ejaculating.

"While something in me," he went on, "is acutely sensible to her charms, something else is as deeply impressed with her defects; they are such that she could sympathize in nothing I aspired to—cooperate in nothing I undertook. Rosamond a sufferer, a laborer, a female apostle? Rosamond a missionary's wife? No!"

"But you need not be a missionary. You might relinquish that scheme."

"Relinquish! What! my vocation? My great work? My foundation laid on earth for a mansion[6] in heaven? My hopes of being numbered in the band who have merged all ambition in the glorious one of bettering their race—of carrying knowledge into the realms of ignorance—of substituting peace for war—freedom for bondage—religion for superstition—the hope of heaven for the fear of hell? Must I relinquish that? It is dearer than the blood in my veins. It is what I have to look forward to and to live for."

After a considerable pause, I said,—"And Miss Oliver? Are her disappointment and sorrow of no interest to you?"

"Miss Oliver is ever surrounded by suitors and flatterers; in less than a month my image will be effaced from her heart. She will forget me; and will marry, probably some one who will make her far happier than I should do."

"You speak coolly enough; but you suffer in the conflict. You are wasting away."

"No. If I get a little thin, it is with anxiety about my prospects, yet unsettled—my departure, continually procrastinated. Only this morning I received intelligence that the successor, whose arrival I have been so long expecting, cannot be ready to replace me for three months to come yet; and perhaps the three months may extend to six."

"You tremble and become flushed whenever Miss Oliver enters the schoolroom."

Again the surprised expression crossed his face. He had not imagined that a woman would dare to speak so to a man. For me, I felt at home in this sort of discourse. I could never rest in communication with strong, discreet, and refined minds, whether male or female, till I had passed the outworks of conventional reserve, and crossed the threshold of confidence, and won a place by their heart's very hearthstone.

"You *are* original," said he, "and not timid. There is something brave in your spirit, as well as penetrating in your eye; but allow me to assure you that you partially misinterpret my emotions. You think them more profound

6. A dwelling place (see John 14.2).

and potent than they are. You give me a larger allowance of sympathy than I have a just claim to. When I colour, and when I shake before Miss Oliver, I do not pity myself. I scorn the weakness. I know it is ignoble; a mere fever of the flesh: not, I declare, a convulsion of the soul. *That* is just as fixed as a rock firm set in the depths of a restless sea. Know me to be what I am—a cold, hard man."

I smiled incredulously.

"You have taken my confidence by storm," he continued: "and now it is much at your service. I am simply, in my original state—stripped of that blood-bleached robe with which Christianity covers human deformity—a cold, hard, ambitious man. Natural affection only, of all the sentiments, has permanent power over me. Reason, and not Feeling, is my guide: my ambition is unlimited; my desire to rise higher, to do more than others, insatiable. I honor endurance, perseverance, industry, talent; because these are the means by which men achieve great ends and mount to lofty eminence. I watch your career with interest, because I consider you a specimen of a diligent, orderly, energetic woman; not because I deeply compassionate what you have gone through, or what you still suffer."

"You would describe yourself as a mere pagan philosopher," I said.

"No. There is this difference between me and deistic philosophers: I believe; and I believe the Gospel. You missed your epithet. I am not a pagan, but a Christian philosopher—a follower of the sect of Jesus. As His disciple I adopt His pure, His merciful, His benignant doctrines. I advocate them: I am sworn to spread them. Won in youth to religion, she has cultivated my original qualities thus:—From the minute germ, natural affection, she has developed the overshadowing tree, philanthropy. From the wild, stringy root of human uprightness, she has reared a due sense of the Divine justice. Of the ambition to win power and renown for my wretched self, she has formed the ambition to spread my Master's kingdom; to achieve victories for the standard of the cross. So much has religion done for me; turning the original materials to the best account; pruning and training nature. But she could not eradicate nature: nor will it be eradicated 'till this mortal shall put on immortality.' "[7]

Having said this, he took his hat, which lay on the table beside my palette. Once more he looked at the portrait.

"She *is* lovely," he murmured. "She is well named the Rose of the World,[8] indeed!"

"And may I not paint one like it for you?"

"*Cui bono?*[9] No."

He drew over the picture the sheet of thin paper on which I was accustomed to rest my hand in painting to prevent the cardboard from being sullied. What he suddenly saw on this blank paper it was impossible for me to tell: but something had caught his eye. He took it up with a snatch; he looked at the edge; then shot a glance at me, inexpressibly peculiar and quite incomprehensible: a glance that seemed to take and make note of every point in my shape, face, and dress; for it traversed all, quick, keen as lightning. His

7. 1 Corinthians 15.53–54.
8. In Latin, *rosa mundi*.

9. Who stands to benefit? (Latin).

lips parted, as if to speak: but he checked the coming sentence, whatever it was.

"What is the matter?" I asked.

"Nothing in the world," was the reply; and, replacing the paper, I saw him dexterously tear a narrow slip from the margin. It disappeared in his glove; and, with one hasty nod and "good-afternoon," he vanished.

"Well!" I exclaimed, using an expression of the district, "that caps the globe,[1] however!"

I, in my turn, scrutinized the paper, but saw nothing on it save a few dingy stains of paint where I had tried the tint in my pencil. I pondered the mystery a minute or two; but finding it insolvable, and being certain it could not be of much moment, I dismissed and soon forgot it.

Chapter XXXIII

When Mr. St. John went it was beginning to snow; the whirling storm continued all night. The next day a keen wind brought fresh and blinding falls; by twilight the valley was drifted up and almost impassable. I had closed my shutter, laid a mat to the door to prevent the snow from blowing in under it, trimmed my fire, and after sitting nearly an hour on the hearth listening to the muffled fury of the tempest, I lit a candle, took down Marmion, and beginning—

> Day set on Norham's castled steep,
> And Tweed's fair river broad and deep,
> And Cheviot's mountains lone;
> The massive towers, the donjon keep,
> The flanking walls that round them sweep,
> In yellow luster shone,

I soon forgot storm in music.

I heard a noise: the wind, I thought, shook the door. No; it was St. John Rivers, who, lifting the latch, came in out of the frozen hurricane—the howling darkness—and stood before me: the cloak that covered his tall figure all white as a glacier. I was almost in consternation; so little had I expected any guest from the blocked-up vale that night.

"Any ill news?" I demanded. "Has anything happened?"

"No. How very easily alarmed you are!" he answered, removing his cloak and hanging it up against the door, towards which he again coolly pushed the mat which his entrance had deranged. He stamped the snow from his boots.

"I shall sully the purity of your floor," said he, "but you must excuse me for once." Then he approached the fire: "I have had hard work to get here, I assure you," he observed, as he warmed his hands over the flame. "One drift took me up to the waist; happily the snow is quite soft yet."

"But why are you come?" I could not forbear saying.

"Rather an inhospitable question to put to a visitor; but since you ask it, I answer simply to have a little talk with you; I got tired of my mute books and empty rooms. Besides, since yesterday I have experienced the excitement

1. Tops everything.

of a person to whom a tale has been half-told, and who is impatient to hear the sequel."

He sat down. I recalled his singular conduct of yesterday, and really I began to fear his wits were touched. If he were insane, however, his was a very cool and collected insanity: I had never seen that handsome-featured face of his look more like chiseled marble than it did just now, as he put aside his snow-wet hair from his forehead and let the firelight shine free on his pale brow and cheek as pale, where it grieved me to discover the hollow trace of care or sorrow now so plainly graved. I waited, expecting he would say something I could at least comprehend; but his hand was now at his chin, his finger on his lip: he was thinking. It struck me that his hand looked wasted like his face. A perhaps uncalled-for gush of pity came over my heart: I was moved to say:—"I wish Diana or Mary would come and live with you: it is too bad that you should be quite alone; and you are recklessly rash about your own health."

"Not at all," said he: "I care for myself when necessary; I am well now. What do you see amiss in me?"

This was said with a careless, abstracted indifference, which showed that my solicitude was, at least in his opinion, wholly superfluous. I was silenced.

He still slowly moved his finger over his upper lip, and still his eye dwelt dreamily on the glowing grate. Thinking it urgent to say something, I asked him presently if he felt any cold draught from the door, which was behind him.

"No, no," he responded, shortly and somewhat testily.

"Well," I reflected, "if you won't talk, you may be still; I'll let you alone now, and return to my book."

So I snuffed the candle, and resumed the perusal of Marmion. He soon stirred; my eye was instantly drawn to his movements; he only took out a morocco pocket-book, thence produced a letter, which he read in silence, folded it, put it back, relapsed into meditation. It was vain to try to read with such an inscrutable fixture before me; nor could I, in my impatience, consent to be dumb; he might rebuff me if he liked, but talk I would.

"Have you heard from Diana and Mary lately?"

"Not since the letter I showed you a week ago."

"There has not been any change made about your own arrangements? You will not be summoned to leave England sooner than you expected?"

"I fear not, indeed: such chance is too good to befall me." Baffled so far I changed my ground—I bethought myself to talk about the school and my scholars.

"Mary Garrett's mother is better, and Mary came back to the school this morning, and I shall have four new girls next week from the Foundry Close—they would have come today but for the snow."

"Indeed!"

"Mr. Oliver pays for two."

"Does he?"

"He means to give the whole school a treat at Christmas."

"I know."

"Was it your suggestion?"

"No."

"Whose, then?"

"His daughter's, I think."

"It is like her: she is so good-natured."

"Yes."

Again came the blank of a pause: the clock struck eight strokes. It aroused him; he uncrossed his legs, sat erect, turned to me.

"Leave your book a moment, and come a little nearer the fire," he said.

Wondering, and of my wonder finding no end, I complied.

"Half an hour ago," he pursued, "I spoke of my impatience to hear the sequel of a tale: on reflection, I find the matter will be better managed by my assuming the narrator's part, and converting you into a listener. Before commencing it is but fair to warn you that the story will sound somewhat hackneyed in your ears: but stale details often regain a degree of freshness when they pass through new lips. For the rest, whether trite or novel, it is short.

"Twenty years ago a poor curate—never mind his name at this moment—fell in love with a rich man's daughter; she fell in love with him, and married him, against the advice of all her friends; who consequently disowned her immediately after the wedding. Before two years passed the rash pair were both dead, and laid quietly side by side under one slab. (I have seen their grave; it formed part of the pavement of a huge churchyard surrounding the grim, soot-black old cathedral of an overgrown manufacturing town in———shire.) They left a daughter, which, at its very birth, Charity received in her lap—cold as that of the snow-drift I almost stuck fast in to-night. Charity carried the friendless thing to the house of its rich maternal relations; it was reared by an aunt-in-law called (I come to names now) Mrs. Reed, of Gateshead—you start—did you hear a noise? I daresay it is only a rat scrambling along the rafters of the adjoining schoolroom: it was a barn before I had it repaired and altered, and barns are generally haunted by rats.—To proceed. Mrs. Reed kept the orphan ten years: whether it was happy or not with her I cannot say, never having been told; but at the end of that time she transferred it to a place you know—being no other than Lowood School, where you so long resided yourself. It seems her career there was very honorable: from a pupil she became a teacher, like yourself—really it strikes me there are parallel points in her history and yours—she left it to be a governess: there, again, your fates were analogous; she undertook the education of the ward of a certain Mr. Rochester."

"Mr. Rivers!" I interrupted.

"I can guess your feelings," he said, "but restrain them for a while: I have nearly finished; hear me to the end. Of Mr. Rochester's character I know nothing, but the one fact that he professed to offer honorable marriage to this young girl, and that at the very altar she discovered he had a wife yet alive, though a lunatic. What his subsequent conduct and proposals were is a matter of pure conjecture; but when an event transpired which rendered inquiry after the governess necessary, it was discovered she was gone—no one could tell when, where, or how. She had left Thornfield Hall in the night; every research after her course had been vain: the country had been scoured far and wide; no vestige of information could be gathered respecting her. Yet that she should be found is become a matter of serious urgency: advertisements have been put in all the papers; I myself have received a letter from one Mr. Briggs, a solicitor, communicating the details I have just imparted. Is it not an odd tale?"

"Just tell me this," said I, "and since you know so much you surely *can* tell it me—what of Mr. Rochester? How and where is he? What is he doing? Is he well?"

"I am ignorant of all concerning Mr. Rochester: the letter never mentions him but to narrate the fraudulent and illegal attempt I have adverted to. You should rather ask the name of the governess—the nature of the event which requires her appearance."

"Did no one go to Thornfield Hall then? Did no one see Mr. Rochester?"

"I suppose not."

"But they wrote to him?"

"Of course."

"And what did he say? Who has his letters?"

"Mr. Briggs intimates that the answer to his application was not from Mr. Rochester, but from a lady: it is signed 'Alice Fairfax.' "

I felt cold and dismayed: my worst fears then were probably true: he had in all probability left England, and rushed in reckless desperation to some former haunt on the Continent. And what opiate for his severe sufferings—what object for his strong passions—had he sought there? I dared not answer the question. Oh, my poor master—once almost my husband—whom I had often called "my dear Edward!"

"He must have been a bad man," observed Mr. Rivers.

"You don't know him—don't pronounce an opinion upon him," I said, with warmth.

"Very well," he answered, quietly: "and indeed my head is otherwise occupied than with him: I have my tale to finish. Since you won't ask the governess's name, I must tell it of my own accord—stay—I have it here—it is always more satisfactory to see important points written down, fairly committed to black and white."

And the pocket-book was again deliberately produced, opened, sought through; from one of its compartments was extracted a shabby slip of paper, hastily torn off: I recognized in its texture and its stains of ultramarine and lake and vermilion the ravished margin of the portrait-cover. He got up, held it close to my eyes: and I read, traced in Indian ink, in my own handwriting, the words "Jane Eyre"—the work doubtless of some moment of abstraction.

"Briggs wrote to me of a Jane Eyre," he said; "the advertisements demanded a Jane Eyre: I knew a Jane Elliott.—I confess I had my suspicions, but it was only yesterday afternoon they were at once resolved into certainty. You own the name and renounce the *alias*?"

"Yes—yes—but where is Mr. Briggs? He perhaps knows more of Mr. Rochester than you do."

"Briggs is in London; I should doubt his knowing anything at all about Mr. Rochester; it is not in Mr. Rochester he is interested. Meantime you forget essential points in pursuing trifles: you do not inquire why Mr. Briggs sought after you—what he wanted with you."

"Well, what did he want?"

"Merely to tell you that your uncle, Mr. Eyre of Madeira, is dead; that he has left you all his property, and that you are now rich—merely that—nothing more."

"I! rich?"

"Yes, you, rich—quite an heiress."

Silence succeeded.

"You must prove your identity, of course," resumed St. John, presently: "a step which will offer no difficulties: you can then enter on immediate possession. Your fortune is vested in the English funds; Briggs has the will and the necessary documents."

Here was a new card turned up! It is a fine thing, reader, to be lifted in a moment from indigence to wealth—a very fine thing: but not a matter one can comprehend, or consequently enjoy, all at once. And then there are other chances in life far more thrilling and rapture-giving; *this* is solid, an affair of the actual world, nothing ideal about it: all its associations are solid and sober, and its manifestations are the same. One does not jump, and spring, and shout hurrah! at hearing one has got a fortune; one begins to consider responsibilities and to ponder business; on a base of steady satisfaction rise certain grave cares—and we contain ourselves, and brood over our bliss with a solemn brow.

Besides, the words Legacy, Bequest, go side by side with the words Death, Funeral. My uncle I had heard was dead—my only relative; ever since being made aware of his existence I had cherished the hope of one day seeing him: now, I never should. And then this money came only to me: not to me and a rejoicing family, but to my isolated self. It was a grand boon doubtless; and independence would be glorious—yes, I felt that—*that* thought swelled my heart.

"You unbend your forehead at last," said Mr. Rivers: "I thought Medusa[2] had looked at you, and that you were turning to stone—perhaps now you will ask how much you are worth?"

"How much am I worth?"

"Oh, a trifle! Nothing of course to speak of—twenty thousand pounds, I think they say—but what is that?"

"Twenty thousand pounds?"

Here was a new stunner—I had been calculating on four or five thousand. This news actually took my breath for a moment: Mr. St. John, whom I had never heard laugh before, laughed now.

"Well," said he, "if you had committed a murder, and I had told you your crime was discovered, you could scarcely look more aghast."

"It is a large sum—don't you think there is a mistake?"

"No mistake at all."

"Perhaps you have read the figures wrong—it may be 2,000!"

"It is written in letters, not figures,—twenty thousand."

I again felt rather like an individual of but average gastronomical powers sitting down to feast alone at a table spread with provisions for a hundred. Mr. Rivers rose now and put his cloak on.

"If it were not such a very wild night," he said, "I would send Hannah down to keep you company: you look too desperately miserable to be left alone. But Hannah, poor woman! could not stride the drifts so well as I: her legs are not quite so long: so I must e'en leave you to your sorrows. Goodnight."

He was lifting the latch: a sudden thought occurred to me.

"Stop one minute!" I cried.

"Well?"

2. Mythological Gorgon, a female snake-haired monster who turned to stone all who looked at her.

"It puzzles me to know why Mr. Briggs wrote to you about me; or how he knew you, or could fancy that you, living in such an out-of-the-way place, had the power to aid in my discovery."

"Oh! I am a clergyman," he said; "and the clergy are often appealed to about odd matters."

Again the latch rattled.

"No: that does not satisfy me!" I exclaimed: and, indeed, there was something in the hasty and unexplanatory reply which, instead of allaying, piqued my curiosity more than ever.

"It is a very strange piece of business," I added. "I must know more about it."

"Another time."

"No: tonight!—tonight!" and as he turned from the door I placed myself between it and him. He looked rather embarrassed.

"You certainly shall not go till you have told me all!" I said.

"I would rather not, just now."

"You shall!—you must!"

"I would rather Diana or Mary informed you."

Of course these objections wrought my eagerness to a climax: gratified it must be, and that without delay; and I told him so.

"But I apprised you that I was a hard man," said he; "difficult to persuade."

"And I am a hard woman,—impossible to put off."

"And then," he pursued, "I am cold: no fervor infects me."

"Whereas I am hot, and fire dissolves ice. The blaze there has thawed all the snow from your cloak; by the same token it has streamed on to my floor, and made it like a trampled street. As you hope ever to be forgiven, Mr. Rivers, the high crime and misdemeanor of spoiling a sanded kitchen, tell me what I wish to know."

"Well, then," he said, "I yield; if not to your earnestness, to your perseverance: as stone is worn by continual dropping. Besides, you must know some day,—as well now as later. Your name is Jane Eyre?"

"Of course: that was all settled before."

"You are not, perhaps, aware that I am your namesake?—that I was christened St. John Eyre Rivers?"

"No, indeed! I remember now seeing the letter E comprised in your initials written in books you have at different times lent me; but I never asked for what name it stood. But what then? Surely"——

I stopped: I could not trust myself to entertain, much less to express, the thought that rushed upon me—that embodied itself,—that, in a second, stood out a strong, solid probability. Circumstances knit themselves, fitted themselves, shot into order: the chain that had been lying hitherto a formless lump of links was drawn out straight,—every ring was perfect, the connection complete. I knew, by instinct, how the matter stood before St. John had said another word: but I cannot expect the reader to have the same intuitive perception, so I must repeat his explanation.

"My mother's name was Eyre; she had two brothers; one a clergyman, who married Miss Jane Reed, of Gateshead; the other, John Eyre, Esq., merchant, late of Funchal, Madeira. Mr. Briggs, being Mr. Eyre's solicitor, wrote to us last August to inform us of our uncle's death; and to say that he had left his property to his brother the clergyman's orphan daughter; overlooking us, in

consequence of a quarrel, never forgiven, between him and my father. He wrote again a few weeks since, to intimate that the heiress was lost; and asking if we knew anything of her. A name casually written on a slip of paper has enabled me to find her out. You know the rest." Again he was going, but I set my back against the door.

"Do let me speak," I said; "let me have one moment to draw breath and reflect." I paused—he stood before me, hat in hand, looking composed enough. I resumed: "Your mother was my father's sister?"

"Yes."

"My aunt, consequently?"

He bowed.

"My uncle John was your uncle John? You, Diana and Mary, are his sister's children; as I am his brother's child?"

"Undeniably."

"You three, then, are my cousins; half our blood on each side flows from the same source?"

"We are cousins; yes."

I surveyed him. It seemed I had found a brother: one I could be proud of,—one I could love; and two sisters whose qualities were such that, when I knew them but as mere strangers, they had inspired me with genuine affection and admiration. The two girls on whom, kneeling down on the wet ground, and looking through the low, latticed window of Moor House kitchen, I had gazed with so bitter a mixture of interest and despair were my near kinswomen; and the young and stately gentleman who had found me almost dying at his threshold was my blood relation. Glorious discovery to a lonely wretch! This was wealth indeed!—wealth to the heart!—a mine of pure, genial affections. This was a blessing, bright, vivid, and exhilarating;— not like the ponderous gift of gold: rich and welcome enough in its way, but sobering from its weight. I now clapped my hands in sudden joy—my pulse bounded, my veins thrilled.

"Oh, I am glad!—I am glad!" I exclaimed.

St. John smiled. "Did I not say you neglected essential points to pursue trifles?" he asked. "You were serious when I told you you had got a fortune; and now, for a matter of no moment, you are excited."

"What *can* you mean? It may be of no moment to you; you have sisters, and don't care for a cousin; but I had nobody; and now three relations,—or two, if you don't choose to be counted,—are born into my world full grown. I say again, I am glad!"

I walked fast through the room: I stopped, half suffocated with the thoughts that rose faster than I could receive, comprehend, settle them:— thoughts of what might, could, would, and should be, and that ere long. I looked at the blank wall: it seemed a sky, thick with ascending stars,—every one lit me to a purpose or delight. Those who had saved my life, whom till this hour I had loved barrenly, I could now benefit. They were under a yoke: I could free them: they were scattered,—I could reunite them—the independence, the affluence which was mine might be theirs too. Were we not four? Twenty thousand pounds shared equally would be five thousand each, enough and to spare: justice would be done,—mutual happiness secured. Now the wealth did not weigh on me: now it was not a mere bequest of coin,—it was a legacy of life, hope, enjoyment.

How I looked while these ideas were taking my spirit by storm I cannot tell; but I perceived soon that Mr. Rivers had placed a chair behind me, and was gently attempting to make me sit down on it. He also advised me to be composed: I scorned the insinuation of helplessness and distraction, shook off his hand, and began to walk about again.

"Write to Diana and Mary tomorrow," I said, "and tell them to come home directly; Diana said they would both consider themselves rich with a thousand pounds, so with five thousand they will do very well."

"Tell me where I can get you a glass of water," said St. John; "you must really make an effort to tranquilize your feelings."

"Nonsense! and what sort of an effect will the bequest have on you? Will it keep you in England, induce you to marry Miss Oliver, and settle down like an ordinary mortal?"

"You wander: your head becomes confused. I have been too abrupt in communicating the news; it has excited you beyond your strength."

"Mr. Rivers! you quite put me out of patience; I am rational enough; it is you who misunderstand; or rather who affect to misunderstand."

"Perhaps if you explained yourself a little more fully I should comprehend better."

"Explain! What is there to explain? You cannot fail to see that twenty thousand pounds, the sum in question, divided equally between the nephew and three nieces of our uncle will give five thousand to each? What I want is, that you should write to your sisters and tell them of the fortune that has accrued to them."

"To you, you mean."

"I have intimated my view of the case: I am incapable of taking any other. I am not brutally selfish, blindly unjust, or fiendishly ungrateful. Besides, I am resolved I will have a home and connections. I like Moor House, and I will live at Moor House; I like Diana and Mary, and I will attach myself for life to Diana and Mary. It would please and benefit me to have five thousand pounds; it would torment and oppress me to have twenty thousand; which, moreover, could never be mine in justice, though it might in law. I abandon to you, then, what is absolutely superfluous to me. Let there be no opposition, and no discussion about it; let us agree among each other, and decide the point at once."

"This is acting on first impulses; you must take days to consider such a matter, ere your word can be regarded as valid."

"Oh! if all you doubt is my sincerity, I am easy: you see the justice of the case?"

"I *do* see a certain justice; but it is contrary to all custom. Besides, the entire fortune is your right: my uncle gained it by his own efforts; he was free to leave it to whom he would: he left it to you. After all, justice permits you to keep it: you may, with a clear conscience, consider it absolutely your own."

"With me," said I, "it is fully as much a matter of feeling as of conscience: I must indulge my feelings; I so seldom have had an opportunity of doing so. Were you to argue, object, and annoy me for a year, I could not forego the delicious pleasure of which I have caught a glimpse—that of repaying, in part, a mighty obligation, and winning to myself life-long friends."

"You think so now," rejoined St. John; "because you do not know what it

is to possess, nor consequently to enjoy wealth: you cannot form a notion of the importance twenty thousand pounds would give you; of the place it would enable you to take in society; of the prospects it would open to you: you cannot——"

"And you," I interrupted, "cannot at all imagine the craving I have for fraternal and sisterly love. I never had a home, I never had brothers and sisters; I must and will have them now: you are not reluctant to admit me and own me, are you?"

"Jane: I will be your brother—my sisters will be your sisters—without stipulating for this sacrifice of your just rights."

"Brother? Yes; at the distance of a thousand leagues! Sisters? Yes; slaving amongst strangers! I, wealthy—gorged with gold I never earned and do not merit! You, penniless! Famous equality and fraternization! Close union! Intimate attachment!"

"But, Jane, your aspirations after family ties and domestic happiness may be realised otherwise than by the means you contemplate: you may marry."

"Nonsense again! Marry! I don't want to marry, and never shall marry."

"That is saying too much: such hazardous affirmations are a proof of the excitement under which you labor."

"It is not saying too much: I know what I feel, and how averse are my inclinations to the bare thought of marriage. No one would take me for love; and I will not be regarded in the light of a mere money-speculation. And I do not want a stranger—unsympathizing alien, different from me; I want my kindred: those with whom I have full fellow-feeling. Say again you will be my brother: when you uttered the words I was satisfied, happy; repeat them, if you can repeat them sincerely."

"I think I can. I know I have always loved my own sisters; and I know on what my affection for them is grounded,—respect for their worth and admiration of their talents. You too have principle and mind: your tastes and habits resemble Diana's and Mary's; your presence is always agreeable to me; in your conversation I have already for some time found a salutary solace. I feel I can easily and naturally make room in my heart for you, as my third and youngest sister."

"Thank you: that contents me for tonight. Now you had better go; for if you stay longer you will perhaps irritate me afresh by some mistrustful scruple."

"And the school, Miss Eyre? It must now be shut up, I suppose?"

"No. I will retain my post of mistress till you get a substitute."

He smiled approbation: we shook hands, and he took leave.

I need not narrate in detail the further struggles I had and arguments I used to get matters regarding the legacy settled as I wished. My task was a very hard one: but, as I was absolutely resolved—as my cousins saw at length that my mind was really and immutably fixed on making a just division of the property—as they would have done precisely what I wished to do—they yielded at length so far as to consent to put the affair to arbitration. The judges chosen were Mr. Oliver and an able lawyer: both coincided in my opinion: I carried my point. The instruments of transfer were drawn out: St. John, Diana, Mary, and I, each became possessed of a competency.[3]

3. I.e., sufficient money.

Chapter XXXIV

It was near Christmas by the time all was settled: the season of general holiday approached. I now closed Morton school, taking care that the parting should not be barren on my side. Good fortune opens the hand as well as the heart wonderfully; and to give somewhat when we have largely received, is but to afford a vent to the unusual ebullition of the sensations. I had long felt with pleasure that many of my rustic scholars liked me, and when we parted that consciousness was confirmed: they manifested their affection plainly and strongly. Deep was my gratification to find I had really a place in their unsophisticated hearts: I promised them that never a week should pass in future that I did not visit them, and give them an hour's teaching in their school.

Mr. Rivers came up, as—having seen the classes, now numbering sixty girls, file out before me, and locked the door—I stood with the key in my hand, exchanging a few words of special farewell with some half-dozen of my best scholars: as decent, respectable, modest, and well-informed young women as could be found in the ranks of the British peasantry. And that is saying a great deal; for after all the British peasantry are the best taught, best mannered, most self-respecting of any in Europe: since those days I have seen paysannes and Bäuerinnen:[4] and the best of them seemed to me ignorant, coarse, and besotted, compared with my Morton girls.

"Do you consider you have got your reward for a season of exertion?" asked Mr. Rivers when they were gone. "Does not the consciousness of having done some real good in your day and generation give pleasure?"

"Doubtless."

"And you have only toiled a few months! Would not a life devoted to the task of regenerating your race be well spent?"

"Yes," I said; "but I could not go on for ever so: I want to enjoy my own faculties as well as to cultivate those of other people. I must enjoy them now; don't recall either my mind or body to the school: I am out of it, and disposed for full holiday."

He looked grave. "What now? What sudden eagerness is this you evince? What are you going to do?"

"To be active: as active as I can. And first I must beg you to set Hannah at liberty, and get somebody else to wait on you."

"Do you want her?"

"Yes, to go with me to Moor House: Diana and Mary will be at home in a week, and I want to have everything in order against their arrival."

"I understand: I thought you were for flying off on some excursion. It is better so: Hannah shall go with you."

"Tell her to be ready by tomorrow then; and here is the schoolroom key: I will give you the key of my cottage in the morning."

He took it. "You give it up very gleefully," said he: "I don't quite understand your light-heartedness; because I cannot tell what employment you propose to yourself as a substitute for the one you are relinquishing. What aim, what purpose, what ambition in life have you now?"

"My first aim will be to *clean down* (do you comprehend the full force of

4. Peasant women (French and German).

the expression?) to *clean down* Moor House from chamber to cellar; my next to rub it up with beeswax, oil, and an indefinite number of cloths, till it glitters again; my third, to arrange every chair, table, bed, carpet, with mathematical precision; afterwards I shall go near to ruin you in coals and peat to keep up good fires in every room; and lastly, the two days preceding that on which your sisters are expected will be devoted by Hannah and me to such a beating of eggs, sorting of currants, grating of spices, compounding of Christmas cakes, chopping up of materials for mince-pies, and solemnizing of other culinary rites, as words can convey but an inadequate notion of to the uninitiated like you. My purpose, in short, is to have all things in an absolutely perfect state of readiness for Diana and Mary before next Thursday; and my ambition is to give them a beau-ideal of a welcome when they come."

St. John smiled slightly: still he was dissatisfied.

"It is all very well for the present," said he: "but seriously, I trust that when the first flush of vivacity is over you will look a little higher than domestic endearments and household joys."

"The best things the world has!" I interrupted.

"No, Jane, no: this world is not the scene of fruition; do not attempt to make it so: nor of rest; do not turn slothful."

"I mean, on the contrary, to be busy."

"Jane, I excuse you for the present: two months' grace I allow you for the full enjoyment of your new position, and for pleasing yourself with this late-found charm of relationship; but *then* I hope you will begin to look beyond Moor House and Morton, and sisterly society, and the selfish calm and sensual comfort of civilised affluence. I hope your energies will then once more trouble you with their strength."

I looked at him with surprise.

"St. John," I said, "I think you are almost wicked to talk so. I am disposed to be as content as a queen, and you try to stir me up to restlessness! To what end?"

"To the end of turning to profit the talents which God has committed to your keeping; and of which He will surely one day demand a strict account. Jane, I shall watch you closely and anxiously—I warn you of that. And try to restrain the disproportionate fervor with which you throw yourself into common-place home pleasures. Don't cling so tenaciously to ties of the flesh; save your constancy and ardor for an adequate cause; forbear to waste them on trite transient objects. Do you hear, Jane?"

"Yes; just as if you were speaking Greek. I feel I have adequate cause to be happy, and I *will* be happy. Good-bye!"

Happy at Moor House I was, and hard I worked; and so did Hannah: she was charmed to see how jovial I could be amidst the bustle of a house turned topsy-turvy—how I could brush, and dust, and clean, and cook. And really after a day or two of confusion worse confounded it was delightful, by degrees, to invoke order from the chaos ourselves had made. I had previously taken a journey to S——to purchase some new furniture: my cousins having given me carte blanche to effect what alterations I pleased, and a sum having been set aside for that purpose. The ordinary sitting-room and bedrooms I left much as they were: for I knew Diana and Mary would derive more pleasure from seeing again the old homely tables and chairs and beds than from

the spectacle of the smartest innovations. Still some novelty was necessary, to give to their return the piquancy with which I wished it to be invested. Dark handsome new carpets and curtains, an arrangement of some carefully selected antique ornaments in porcelain and bronze, new coverings, and mirrors, and dressing-cases for the toilet-tables, answered the end: they looked fresh without being glaring. A spare parlor and bedroom I refurnished entirely with old mahogany and crimson upholstery: I laid canvas on the passage and carpets on the stairs. When all was finished, I thought Moor House as complete a model of bright modest snugness within as it was, at this season, a specimen of wintry waste and desert dreariness without.

The eventful Thursday at length came. They were expected about dark, and ere dusk fires were lit upstairs and below; the kitchen was in perfect trim; Hannah and I were dressed, and all was in readiness.

St. John arrived first. I had entreated him to keep quite clear of the house till everything was arranged: and, indeed, the bare idea of the commotion, at once sordid and trivial, going on within its walls sufficed to scare him to estrangement. He found me in the kitchen, watching the progress of certain cakes for tea, then baking. Approaching the hearth, he asked, "If I was at last satisfied with housemaid's work?" I answered by inviting him to accompany me on a general inspection of the result of my labours. With some difficulty I got him to make the tour of the house. He just looked in at the doors I opened; and when he had wandered upstairs and downstairs, he said I must have gone through a great deal of fatigue and trouble to have effected such considerable changes in so short a time: but not a syllable did he utter indicating pleasure in the improved aspect of his abode.

This silence damped me. I thought perhaps the alterations had disturbed some old associations he valued. I inquired whether this was the case: no doubt in a somewhat crestfallen tone.

"Not at all; he had, on the contrary, remarked that I had scrupulously respected every association: he feared, indeed, I must have bestowed more thought on the matter than it was worth. How many minutes, for instance, had I devoted to studying the arrangement of this very room?—By-the-bye, could I tell him where such a book was?"

I showed him the volume on the shelf: he took it down, and withdrawing to his accustomed window recess, he began to read it.

Now, I did not like this, reader. St. John was a good man; but I began to feel he had spoken truth of himself when he said he was hard and cold. The humanities and amenities of life had no attraction for him—its peaceful enjoyments no charm. Literally, he lived only to aspire—after what was good and great, certainly; but still he would never rest; nor approve of others resting round him. As I looked at his lofty forehead, still and pale as a white stone—at his fine lineaments fixed in study—I comprehended all at once that he would hardly make a good husband: that it would be a trying thing to be his wife. I understood, as by inspiration, the nature of his love for Miss Oliver; I agreed with him that it was but a love of the senses. I comprehended how he should despise himself for the feverish influence it exercised over him; how he should wish to stifle and destroy it; how he should mistrust its ever conducing permanently to his happiness, or hers. I saw he was of the material from which nature hews her heroes—Christian and Pagan—her lawgivers, her statesmen, her conquerors; a steadfast bulwark for great inter-

ests to rest upon; but, at the fireside, too often a cold cumbrous column, gloomy and out of place.

"This parlor is not his sphere," I reflected; "the Himalayan ridge, or Caffre[5] bush, even the plague-cursed Guinea Coast swamp, would suit him better. Well may he eschew the calm of domestic life; it is not his element: there his faculties stagnate—they cannot develop or appear to advantage. It is in scenes of strife and danger—where courage is proved, and energy exercised, and fortitude tasked—that he will speak and move, the leader and superior. A merry child would have the advantage of him on this hearth. He is right to choose a missionary's career—I see it now."

"They are coming! they are coming!" cried Hannah, throwing open the parlour door. At the same moment old Carlo barked joyfully. Out I ran. It was now dark: but a rumbling of wheels was audible. Hannah soon had a lantern lit. The vehicle had stopped at the wicket; the driver opened the door: first one well-known form, then another, stepped out. In a minute I had my face under their bonnets, in contact first with Mary's soft cheek, then with Diana's flowing curls. They laughed—kissed me—then Hannah: patted Carlo, who was half wild with delight, asked eagerly if all was well; and being assured in the affirmative, hastened into the house.

They were stiff with their long and jolting drive from Whitcross, and chilled with the frosty night-air; but their pleasant countenances expanded to the cheerful fire-light. While the driver and Hannah brought in the boxes, they demanded St. John. At this moment he advanced from the parlor. They both threw their arms round his neck at once. He gave each one quiet kiss, said in a low tone a few words of welcome, stood a while to be talked to, and then, intimating that he supposed they would soon rejoin him in the parlor, withdrew there as to a place of refuge.

I had lit their candles to go upstairs, but Diana had first to give hospitable orders respecting the driver; this done, both followed me. They were delighted with the renovation and decoration of their rooms; with the new drapery, and fresh carpets, and rich tinted china vases: they expressed their gratification ungrudgingly. I had the pleasure of feeling that my arrangements met their wishes exactly; and that what I had done added a vivid charm to their joyous return home.

Sweet was that evening. My cousins, full of exhilaration, were so eloquent in narrative and comment, that their fluency covered St. John's taciturnity: he was sincerely glad to see his sisters; but in their glow of fervour and flow of joy he could not sympathize. The event of the day—that is, the return of Diana and Mary—pleased him; but the accompaniments of that event, the glad tumult, the garrulous glee of reception, irked him: I saw he wished the calmer morrow was come. In the very meridian of the night's enjoyment, about an hour after tea, a rap was heard at the door. Hannah entered with the intimation that "a poor lad was come, at that unlikely time, to fetch Mr. Rivers to see his mother, who was drawing away."

"Where does she live, Hannah?"

"Clear up at Whitcross Brow, almost four miles off; and moor and moss all the way."

"Tell him I will go."

<hr>

5. Kaffir, African.

"I'm sure, sir, you had better not. It's the worst road to travel after dark that can be: there's no track at all over the bog. And then it is such a bitter night—the keenest wind you ever felt. You had better send word, sir, that you will be there in the morning."

But he was already in the passage, putting on his cloak; and without one objection, one murmur, he departed. It was then nine o'clock: he did not return till midnight. Starved and tired enough he was: but he looked happier than when he set out. He had performed an act of duty; made an exertion; felt his own strength to do and deny, and was on better terms with himself.

I am afraid the whole of the ensuing week tried his patience. It was Christmas week: we took to no settled employment, but spent it in a sort of merry domestic dissipation. The air of the moors, the freedom of home, the dawn of prosperity, acted on Diana and Mary's spirits like some life-giving elixir: they were gay from morning till noon, and from noon till night. They could always talk; and their discourse, witty, pithy, original, had such charms for me, that I preferred listening to, and sharing in it, to doing anything else. St. John did not rebuke our vivacity; but he escaped from it: he was seldom in the house; his parish was large, the population scattered, and he found daily business in visiting the sick and poor in its different districts.

One morning, at breakfast, Diana, after looking a little pensive for some minutes, asked him, "If his plans were yet unchanged?"

"Unchanged and unchangeable," was the reply. And he proceeded to inform us that his departure from England was now definitively fixed for the ensuing year.

"And Rosamond Oliver?" suggested Mary: the words seeming to escape her lips involuntarily: for no sooner had she uttered them, than she made a gesture as if wishing to recall them. St. John had a book in his hand—it was his unsocial custom to read at meals—he closed it, and looked up.

"Rosamond Oliver," said he, "is about to be married to Mr. Granby; one of the best connected and most estimable residents in S——, grandson and heir to Sir Frederic Granby: I had the intelligence from her father yesterday."

His sisters looked at each other, and at me; we all three looked at him: he was serene as glass.

"The match must have been got up hastily," said Diana: "they cannot have known each other long."

"But two months: they met in October at the county ball at S——. But where there are no obstacles to a union, as in the present case, where the connection is in every point desirable, delays are unnecessary: they will be married as soon as S——Place, which Sir Frederic gives up to them, can be refitted for their reception."

The first time I found St. John alone after this communication, I felt tempted to inquire if the event distressed him: but he seemed so little to need sympathy, that, so far from venturing to offer him more, I experienced some shame at the recollection of what I had already hazarded. Besides, I was out of practice in talking to him: his reserve was again frozen over, and my frankness was congealed beneath it. He had not kept his promise of treating me like his sisters; he continually made little chilling differences between us, which did not at all tend to the development of cordiality: in short, now that I was acknowledged his kinswoman, and lived under the same roof with him, I felt the distance between us to be far greater than when he

had known me only as the village schoolmistress. When I remembered how far I had once been admitted to his confidence, I could hardly comprehend his present frigidity.

Such being the case, I felt not a little surprised when he raised his head suddenly from the desk over which he was stooping, and said:—"You see, Jane, the battle is fought and the victory won."

Startled at being thus addressed, I did not immediately reply: after a moment's hesitation I answered:—"But are you sure you are not in the position of those conquerors whose triumphs have cost them too dear? Would not such another ruin you?"

"I think not; and if I were, it does not much signify; I shall never be called upon to contend for such another. The event of the conflict is decisive: my way is now clear; I thank God for it!" So saying, he returned to his papers and his silence.

As our mutual happiness (i.e. Diana's, Mary's, and mine) settled into a quieter character, and we resumed our usual habits and regular studies, St. John stayed more at home: he sat with us in the same room, sometimes for hours together. While Mary drew, Diana pursued a course of encyclopaedic reading she had (to my awe and amazement) undertaken, and I fagged away at German, he pondered a mystic lore of his own: that of some Eastern tongue, the acquisition of which he thought necessary to his plans.

Thus engaged, he appeared, sitting in his own recess, quiet and absorbed enough; but that blue eye of his had a habit of leaving the outlandish-looking grammar, and wandering over, and sometimes fixing upon us, his fellow students, with a curious intensity of observation: if caught, it would be instantly withdrawn; yet ever and anon it returned searchingly to our table. I wondered what it meant: I wondered, too, at the punctual satisfaction he never failed to exhibit on an occasion that seemed to me of small moment, namely,—my weekly visit to Morton school; and still more was I puzzled when, if the day was unfavorable, if there was snow, or rain, or high wind, and his sisters urged me not to go, he would invariably make light of their solicitude, and encourage me to accomplish the task without regard to the elements.

"Jane is not such a weakling as you would make her," he would say: "she can bear a mountain blast, or a shower, or a few flakes of snow, as well as any of us. Her constitution is both sound and elastic;—better calculated to endure variations of climate than many more robust."

And when I returned, sometimes a good deal tired and not a little weather-beaten, I never dared complain, because I saw that to murmur would be to vex him: on all occasions fortitude pleased him; the reverse was a special annoyance.

One afternoon, however, I got leave to stay at home, because I really had a cold. His sisters were gone to Morton in my stead: I sat reading Schiller; he, deciphering his crabbed Oriental scrolls. As I exchanged a translation for an exercise, I happened to look his way: there I found myself under the influence of the ever-watchful blue eye. How long it had been searching me through and through, and over and over, I cannot tell: so keen was it, and yet so cold, I felt for the moment superstitious—as if I were sitting in the room with something uncanny.

"Jane, what are you doing?"

"Learning German."

"I want you to give up German, and learn Hindostanee."

"You are not in earnest?"

"In such earnest that I must have it so: and I will tell you why."

He then went on to explain that Hindostanee was the language he was himself at present studying: that, as he advanced, he was apt to forget the commencement; that it would assist him greatly to have a pupil with whom he might again and again go over the elements, and so fix them thoroughly in his mind; that his choice had hovered for some time between me and his sisters; but that he had fixed on me, because he saw I could sit at a task the longest of the three. Would I do him this favor? I should not, perhaps, have to make the sacrifice long; as it wanted now barely three months to his departure.

St. John was not a man to be lightly refused: you felt that every impression made on him, either for pain or pleasure, was deep-graved and permanent. I consented. When Diana and Mary returned, the former found her scholar transferred from her to her brother: she laughed; and both she and Mary agreed that St. John should never have persuaded them to such a step. He answered, quietly: "I know it."

I found him a very patient, very forbearing, and yet an exacting master: he expected me to do a great deal; and when I fulfilled his expectations, he, in his own way, fully testified his approbation. By degrees, he acquired a certain influence over me that took away my liberty of mind: his praise and notice were more restraining than his indifference. I could no longer talk or laugh freely when he was by, because a tiresomely importunate instinct reminded me that vivacity (at least in me) was distasteful to him. I was so fully aware that only serious moods and occupations were acceptable, that in his presence every effort to sustain or follow any other became vain: I fell under a freezing spell. When he said "go," I went; "come," I came; "do this," I did it. But I did not love my servitude: I wished, many a time, he had continued to neglect me.

One evening when, at bedtime, his sisters and I stood round him, bidding him good-night, he kissed each of them, as was his custom; and, as was equally his custom, he gave me his hand. Diana, who chanced to be in a frolicsome humor (*she* was not painfully controlled by his will; for hers, in another way, was as strong), exclaimed:—"St. John! you used to call Jane your third sister, but you don't treat her as such: you should kiss her too."

She pushed me towards him. I thought Diana very provoking, and felt uncomfortably confused; and while I was thus thinking and feeling, St. John bent his head; his Greek face was brought to a level with mine, his eyes questioned my eyes piercingly—he kissed me. There are no such things as marble kisses, or ice kisses, or I should say my ecclesiastical cousin's salute belonged to one of these classes; but there may be experiment kisses, and his was an experiment kiss. When given, he viewed me to learn the result; it was not striking: I am sure I did not blush; perhaps I might have turned a little pale, for I felt as if this kiss were a seal affixed to my fetters. He never omitted the ceremony afterwards, and the gravity and quiescence with which I underwent it seemed to invest it for him with a certain charm.

As for me, I daily wished more to please him: but to do so, I felt daily more and more that I must disown half my nature, stifle half my faculties, wrest

my tastes from their original bent, force myself to the adoption of pursuits for which I had no natural vocation. He wanted to train me to an elevation I could never reach; it racked me hourly to aspire to the standard he uplifted. The thing was as impossible as to mold my irregular features to his correct and classic pattern, to give to my changeable green eyes the sea-blue tint and solemn lustre of his own.

Not his ascendancy alone, however, held me in thrall at present. Of late it had been easy enough for me to look sad: a cankering evil sat at my heart and drained my happiness at its source—the evil of suspense.

Perhaps you think I had forgotten Mr. Rochester, reader, amid these changes of place and fortune. Not for a moment. His idea was still with me; because it was not a vapor sunshine could disperse; nor a sand-traced effigy storms could wash away: it was a name graven on a tablet, fated to last as long as the marble it inscribed. The craving to know what had become of him followed me everywhere; when I was at Morton, I reentered my cottage every evening to think of that: and now at Moor House, I sought my bedroom each night to brood over it.

In the course of my necessary correspondence with Mr. Briggs about the will, I had inquired if he knew anything of Mr. Rochester's present residence and state of health; but, as St. John had conjectured, he was quite ignorant of all concerning him. I then wrote to Mrs. Fairfax, entreating information on the subject. I had calculated with certainty on this step answering my end: I felt sure it would elicit an early answer. I was astonished when a fortnight passed without reply; but when two months wore away, and day after day the post arrived and brought nothing for me, I fell a prey to the keenest anxiety.

I wrote again: there was a chance of my first letter having missed. Renewed hope followed renewed effort: it shone like the former for some weeks, then, like it, it faded, flickered: not a line, not a word reached me. When half a year wasted in vain expectancy my hope died out: and then I felt dark indeed.

A fine spring shone round me, which I could not enjoy. Summer approached; Diana tried to cheer me: she said I looked ill, and wished to accompany me to the sea-side. This St. John opposed; he said I did not want dissipation, I wanted employment; my present life was too purposeless, I required an aim; and, I suppose, by way of supplying deficiencies, he prolonged still further my lessons in Hindostanee, and grew more urgent in requiring their accomplishment: and I, like a fool, never thought of resisting him—I could not resist him.

One day I had come to my studies in lower spirits than usual; the ebb was occasioned by a poignantly felt disappointment: Hannah had told me in the morning there was a letter for me, and when I went down to take it, almost certain that the long looked-for tidings were vouchsafed me at last, I found only an unimportant note from Mr. Briggs on business. The bitter check had wrung from me some tears; and now as I sat poring over the crabbed characters and flourishing tropes of an Indian scribe, my eyes filled again.

St. John called me to his side to read; in attempting to do this my voice failed me: words were lost in sobs. He and I were the only occupants of the parlour: Diana was practicing her music in the drawing-room, Mary was gardening—it was a very fine May-day, clear, sunny, and breezy. My companion expressed no surprise at this emotion, nor did he question me as to

its cause; he only said:—"We will wait a few minutes, Jane, till you are more composed." And while I smothered the paroxysm with all haste, he sat calm and patient, leaning on his desk and looking like a physician watching with the eye of science an expected and fully understood crisis in a patient's malady. Having stifled my sobs, wiped my eyes, and muttered something about not being very well that morning, I resumed my task, and succeeded in completing it. St. John put away my books and his, locked his desk, and said:— "Now, Jane, you shall take a walk; and with me."

"I will call Diana and Mary."

"No. I want only one companion this morning, and that must be you: put on your things; go out by the kitchen door; take the road towards the head of Marsh Glen: I will join you in a moment."

I know no medium: I never in my life have known any medium in my dealings with positive, hard characters, antagonistic to my own, between absolute submission and determined revolt. I have always faithfully observed the one, up to the very moment of bursting, sometimes with volcanic vehemence, into the other; and as neither present circumstances warranted, nor my present mood inclined me to mutiny, I observed careful obedience to St. John's directions; and in ten minutes I was treading the wild track of the glen, side by side with him.

The breeze was from the west: it came over the hill, sweet with scents of heath and rush; the sky was of stainless blue; the stream descending the ravine, swelled with past spring rains, poured along plentiful and clear, catching golden gleams from the sun, and sapphire tints from the firmament. As we advanced and left the track, we trod a soft turf, mossy fine and emerald green, minutely enamelled with a tiny white flower and spangled with a starlike yellow blossom: the hills, meantime, shut us quite in; for the glen, towards its head, wound to the very core.

"Let us rest here," said St. John, as we reached the first stragglers of a battalion of rocks, guarding a sort of pass, beyond which the beck rushed down a waterfall; and where, still a little further, the mountain shook off turf and flower, had only heath for raiment, and crag for gem—where it exaggerated the wild to the savage, and exchanged the fresh for the frowning— where it guarded the forlorn hope of solitude, and a last refuge for silence.

I took a seat: St. John stood near me. He looked up the pass and down the hollow; his glance wandered away with the stream, and returned to traverse the unclouded heaven which colored it; he removed his hat, let the breeze stir his hair and kiss his brow. He seemed in communion with the genius of the haunt: with his eye he bade farewell to something.

"And I shall see it again," he said aloud, "in dreams, when I sleep by the Ganges: and again, in a more remote hour—when another slumber overcomes me—on the shore of a darker stream."

Strange words of a strange love! An austere patriot's passion for his fatherland! He sat down; for half an hour we never spoke; neither he to me nor I to him: that interval past, he recommenced:—"Jane, I go in six weeks; I have taken my berth in an East Indiaman which sails on the twentieth of June."

"God will protect you; for you have undertaken His work," I answered.

"Yes," said he, "there is my glory and joy. I am the servant of an infallible master. I am not going out under human guidance, subject to the defective laws and erring control of my feeble fellow-worms: my king, my lawgiver, my

captain, is the All-perfect. It seems strange to me that all round me do not burn to enlist under the same banner,—to join in the same enterprise."

"All have not your powers: and it would be folly for the feeble to wish to march with the strong."

"I do not speak to the feeble, or think of them: I address only such as are worthy of the work, and competent to accomplish it."

"Those are few in number, and difficult to discover."

"You say truly: but when found, it is right to stir them up—to urge and exhort them to the effort—to show them what their gifts are, and why they were given—to speak Heaven's message in their ear,—to offer them, direct from God, a place in the ranks of His chosen."

"If they are really qualified for the task, will not their own hearts be the first to inform them of it?"

I felt as if an awful charm was framing round and gathering over me: I trembled to hear some fatal word spoken which would at once declare and rivet the spell.

"And what does *your* heart say?" demanded St. John.

"My heart is mute,—my heart is mute," I answered, struck and thrilled.

"Then I must speak for it," continued the deep, relentless voice. "Jane, come with me to India: come as my help-meet and fellow laborer."

The glen and sky spun round: the hills heaved! It was as if I had heard a summons from Heaven—as if a visionary messenger, like him of Macedonia, had enounced, "Come over and help us!"[6] But I was no apostle,—I could not behold the herald,—I could not receive his call.

"Oh, St. John!" I cried, "have some mercy!"

I appealed to one who, in the discharge of what he believed his duty, knew neither mercy nor remorse. He continued:—"God and nature intended you for a missionary's wife. It is not personal, but mental endowments they have given you: you are formed for labor, not for love. A missionary's wife you must—shall be. You shall be mine: I claim you—not for my pleasure, but for my Sovereign's service."

"I am not fit for it: I have no vocation," I said.

He had calculated on these first objections: he was not irritated by them. Indeed, as he leaned back against the crag behind him, folded his arms on his chest, and fixed his countenance, I saw he was prepared for a long and trying opposition, and had taken in a stock of patience to last him to its close—resolved, however, that that close should be conquest for him.

"Humility, Jane," said he, "is the groundwork of Christian virtues: you say right that you are not fit for the work. Who is fit for it? Or who, that ever was truly called, believed himself worthy of the summons? I, for instance, am but dust and ashes. With St. Paul, I acknowledge myself the chiefest of sinners:[7] but I do not suffer this sense of my personal vileness to daunt me. I know my Leader: that He is just as well as mighty; and while He has chosen a feeble instrument to perform a great task, He will, from the boundless stores of His providence, supply the inadequacy of the means to the end. Think like me, Jane—trust like me. It is the Rock of Ages I ask you to lean on: do not doubt but it will bear the weight of your human weakness."

6. A Macedonian appeared in a vision to Paul, asking him to come and help the Macedonians (Acts 16.9).
7. 1 Timothy 1.15.

"I do not understand a missionary life: I have never studied missionary labors."

"There, I, humble as I am, can give you the aid you want: I can set you your task from hour to hour; stand by you always; help you from moment to moment. This I could do in the beginning: soon (for I know your powers) you would be as strong and apt as myself, and would not require my help."

"But my powers—where are they for this undertaking? I do not feel them. Nothing speaks or stirs in me while you talk. I am sensible of no light kindling—no life quickening—no voice counseling or cheering. Oh, I wish I could make you see how much my mind is at this moment like a rayless dungeon, with one shrinking fear fettered in its depths—the fear of being persuaded by you to attempt what I cannot accomplish!"

"I have an answer for you—hear it. I have watched you ever since we first met: I have made you my study for ten months. I have proved you in that time by sundry tests: and what have I seen and elicited? In the village school I found you could perform well, punctually, uprightly, labor uncongenial to your habits and inclinations; I saw you could perform it with capacity and tact: you could win while you controlled. In the calm with which you learnt you had become suddenly rich, I read a mind clear of the vice of Demas:—lucre had no undue power over you.[8] In the resolute readiness with which you cut your wealth into four shares, keeping but one to yourself, and relinquishing the three others to the claim of abstract justice, I recognized a soul that reveled in the flame and excitement of sacrifice. In the tractability with which, at my wish, you forsook a study in which you were interested, and adopted another because it interested me; in the untiring assiduity with which you have since persevered in it—in the unflagging energy and unshaken temper with which you have met its difficulties—I acknowledge the complement of the qualities I seek. Jane, you are docile, diligent, disinterested, faithful, constant, and courageous; very gentle, and very heroic: cease to mistrust yourself—I can trust you unreservedly. As a conductress of Indian schools, and a helper amongst Indian women, your assistance will be to me invaluable."

My iron shroud contracted round me; persuasion advanced with slow sure step. Shut my eyes as I would, these last words of his succeeded in making the way, which had seemed blocked up, comparatively clear. My work, which had appeared so vague, so hopelessly diffuse, condensed itself as he proceeded, and assumed a definite form under his shaping hand. He waited for an answer. I demanded a quarter of an hour to think, before I again hazarded a reply.

"Very willingly," he rejoined: and rising, he strode a little distance up the pass, threw himself down on a swell of heath, and there lay still.

"I *can* do what he wants me to do: I am forced to see and acknowledge that," I meditated—"That is, if life be spared me. But I feel mine is not the existence to be long protracted under an Indian sun.—What then? He does not care for that: when my time came to die he would resign me, in all serenity and sanctity, to the God who gave me. The case is very plain before me. In leaving England, I should leave a loved but empty land—Mr. Rochester is not there: and if he were, what is, what can that ever be to me? My

8. Demas's love of the world made him desert Paul (2 Timothy 4.10).

business is to live without him now: nothing so absurd, so weak as to drag on from day to day, as if I were waiting some impossible change in circumstances, which might reunite me to him. Of course (as St. John once said) I must seek another interest in life to replace the one lost: is not the occupation he now offers me truly the most glorious man can adopt or God assign? Is it not, by its noble cares and sublime results, the one best calculated to fill the void left by uptorn affections and demolished hopes? I believe I must say, Yes—and yet I shudder. Alas! If I join St. John, I abandon half myself: if I go to India, I go to premature death. And how will the interval between leaving England for India, and India for the grave, be filled? Oh, I know well! That, too, is very clear to my vision. By straining to satisfy St. John till my sinews ache, I *shall* satisfy him—to the finest central point and farthest outward circle of his expectations. If I *do* go with him—if I *do* make the sacrifice he urges, I will make it absolutely: I will throw all on the altar—heart, vitals, the entire victim. He will never love me; but he shall approve me; I will show him energies he has not yet seen, resources he was never suspected. Yes: I can work as hard as he can; and with as little grudging.

"Consent, then, to his demand is possible: but for one item—one dreadful item. It is—that he asks me to be his wife, and has no more of a husband's heart for me than that frowning giant of a rock, down which the stream is foaming in yonder gorge. He prizes me as a soldier would a good weapon; and that is all. Unmarried to him, this would never grieve me; but can I let him complete his calculations—coolly put into practice his plans—go through the wedding ceremony? Can I receive from him the bridal ring, endure all the forms of love (which I doubt not he would scrupulously observe) and know that the spirit was quite absent? Can I bear the consciousness that every endearment he bestows is a sacrifice made on principle? No: such a martyrdom would be monstrous. I will never undergo it. As his sister, I might accompany him—not as his wife: I will tell him so."

I looked toward the knoll: there he lay, still as a prostrate column; his face turned to me: his eye beaming, watchful, and keen. He started to his feet, and approached me.

"I am ready to go to India, if I may go free."

"Your answer requires a commentary," he said; "it is not clear."

"You have hitherto been my adopted brother: I, your adopted sister; let us continue as such: you and I had better not marry."

He shook his head. "Adopted fraternity will not do in this case. If you were my real sister it would be different: I should take you and seek no wife. But as it is, either our union must be consecrated and sealed by marriage, or it cannot exist: practical obstacles oppose themselves to any other plan. Do you not see it, Jane? Consider a moment—your strong sense will guide you."

I did consider: and still my sense, such as it was, directed me only to the fact that we did not love each other as man and wife should; and therefore it inferred we ought not to marry. I said so. "St. John," I returned, "I regard you as a brother—you, me as a sister: so let us continue."

"We cannot—we cannot," he answered, with short, sharp determination: "it would not do. You have said you will go with me to India: remember—you have said that."

"Conditionally."

"Well—well. To the main point—the departure with me from England,

the cooperation with me in my future labors—you do not object. You have already as good as put your hand to the plow: you are too consistent to withdraw it. You have but one end to keep in view—how the work you have undertaken can best be done. Simplify your complicated interests, feelings, thoughts, wishes, aims; merge all considerations in one purpose: that of fulfilling with effect—with power—the mission of your great Master. To do so, you must have a coadjutor—not a brother; that is a loose tie: but a husband. I, too, do not want a sister; a sister might any day be taken from me. I want a wife: the sole helpmeet I can influence efficiently in life and retain absolutely till death."

I shuddered as he spoke: I felt his influence in my marrow—his hold on my limbs.

"Seek one elsewhere than in me, St. John: seek one fitted to you."

"One fitted to my purpose, you mean—fitted to my vocation. Again I tell you it is not the insignificant private individual—the mere man, with the man's selfish senses—I wish to mate: it is the missionary."

"And I will give the missionary my energies—it is all he wants—but not myself: that would be only adding the husk and shell to the kernel. For them he has no use: I retain them."

"You cannot—you ought not. Do you think God will be satisfied with half an oblation?[9] Will He accept a mutilated sacrifice? It is the cause of God I advocate: it is under His standard I enlist you. I cannot accept on His behalf a divided allegiance: it must be entire."

"Oh! I will give my heart to God," I said. "*You* do not want it."

I will not swear, reader, that there was not something of repressed sarcasm both in the tone in which I uttered this sentence, and in the feeling that accompanied it. I had silently feared St. John till now, because I had not understood him. He had held me in awe, because he had held me in doubt. How much of him was saint, how much mortal, I could not heretofore tell: but revelations were being made in this conference: the analysis of his nature was proceeding before my eyes. I saw his fallibilities: I comprehended them. I understood that, sitting there where I did, on the bank of heath, and with that handsome form before me, I sat at the feet of a man, erring as I. The veil fell from his hardness and despotism. Having felt in him the presence of these qualities, I felt his imperfection, and took courage. I was with an equal—one with whom I might argue—one whom, if I saw good, I might resist.

He was silent after I had uttered the last sentence, and I presently risked an upward glance at his countenance. His eye, bent on me, expressed at once stern surprise and keen inquiry. "Is she sarcastic, and sarcastic to *me*!" it seemed to say. "What does this signify?"

"Do not let us forget that this is a solemn matter," he said ere long: "one of which we may neither think nor talk lightly without sin. I trust, Jane, you are in earnest when you say you will give your heart to God: it is all I want. Once wrench your heart from man, and fix it on your Maker, the advancement of that Maker's spiritual kingdom on earth will be your chief delight and endeavor; you will be ready to do at once whatever furthers that end. You will see what impetus would be given to your efforts and mine by our

9. Offering.

physical and mental union in marriage: the only union that gives a character of permanent conformity to the destinies and designs of human beings: and, passing over all minor caprices—all trivial difficulties and delicacies of feeling—all scruple about the degree, kind, strength or tenderness of mere personal inclination—you will hasten to enter into that union at once."

"Shall I?" I said briefly; and I looked at his features, beautiful in their harmony, but strangely formidable in their still severity; at his brow, commanding but not open; at his eyes, bright and deep, and searching, but never soft; at his tall, imposing figure; and fancied myself in idea *his wife*. Oh! it would never do! As his curate, his comrade, all would be right: I would cross oceans with him in that capacity; toil under eastern suns, in Asia deserts with him in that office; admire and emulate his courage and devotion, and vigor; accommodate quietly to his masterhood; smile undisturbed at his ineradicable ambition; discriminate the Christian from the man: profoundly esteem the one, and freely forgive the other. I should suffer often, no doubt, attached to him only in this capacity: my body would be under rather a stringent yoke, but my heart and mind would be free. I should still have my unblighted self to turn to: my natural unenslaved feelings with which to communicate in moments of loneliness. There would be recesses in my mind which would be only mine, to which he never came; and sentiments growing there fresh and sheltered, which his austerity could never blight, nor his measured warrior-march trample down: but as his wife—at his side always, and always restrained, and always checked—forced to keep the fire of my nature continually low, to compel it to burn inwardly and never utter a cry, though the imprisoned flame consumed vital after vital—*this* would be unendurable.

"St. John!" I exclaimed, when I had got so far in my meditation.

"Well?" he answered icily.

"I repeat: I freely consent to go with you as your fellow-missionary; but not as your wife; I cannot marry you and become part of you."

"A part of me you must become," he answered steadily; "otherwise the whole bargain is void. How can I, a man not yet thirty, take out with me to India a girl of nineteen, unless she be married to me? How can we be for ever together—sometimes in solitudes, sometimes amid savage tribes—and unwed?"

"Very well," I said shortly; "under the circumstances, quite as well as if I were either your real sister, or a man and a clergyman like yourself."

"It is known that you are not my sister; I cannot introduce you as such: to attempt it would be to fasten injurious suspicions on us both. And for the rest, though you have a man's vigorous brain, you have a woman's heart, and—it would not do."

"It would do," I affirmed with some disdain, "perfectly well. I have a woman's heart; but not where you are concerned; for you I have only a comrade's constancy; a fellow-soldier's frankness, fidelity, fraternity, if you like; a neophyte's respect and submission to his hierophant:[1] nothing more—don't fear."

"It is what I want," he said, speaking to himself; "it is just what I want. And there are obstacles in the way: they must be hewn down. Jane, you would

1. Priest (in ancient Greece). "Neophyte": new convert.

not repent marrying me; be certain of that; we *must* be married. I repeat it: there is no other way; and undoubtedly enough of love would follow upon marriage to render the union right even in your eyes."

"I scorn your idea of love," I could not help saying, as I rose up and stood before him, leaning my back against the rock. "I scorn the counterfeit sentiment you offer: yes, St. John, and I scorn you when you offer it."

He looked at me fixedly: compressing his well-cut lips while he did so. Whether he was incensed or surprised, or what, it was not easy to tell: he could command his countenance thoroughly.

"I scarcely expected to hear that expression from you," he said: "I think I have done and uttered nothing to deserve scorn."

I was touched by his gentle tone, and overawed by his high, calm mien.

"Forgive me the words, St. John: but it is your own fault that I have been roused to speak so unguardedly. You have introduced a topic on which our natures are at variance—a topic we should never discuss: the very name of love is an apple of discord[2] between us—if the reality were required what should we do? How should we feel? My dear cousin, abandon your scheme of marriage—forget it."

"No," said he; "it is a long-cherished scheme, and the only one which can secure my great end: but I shall urge you no further at present. Tomorrow I leave home for Cambridge: I have many friends there to whom I should wish to say farewell. I shall be absent a fortnight—take that space of time to consider my offer: and do not forget that if you reject it, it is not me you deny, but God. Through my means, He opens to you a noble career; as my wife only can you enter upon it. Refuse to be my wife, and you limit yourself for ever to a track of selfish ease and barren obscurity. Tremble lest in that case you should be numbered with those who have denied the faith, and are worse than infidels!"

He had done. Turning from me, he once more

Looked to river, looked to hill:[3]

But this time his feelings were all pent in his heart: I was not worthy to hear them uttered. As I walked by his side homeward, I read well in his iron silence all he felt towards me: the disappointment of an austere and despotic nature, which has met resistance where it expected submission—the disapprobation of a cool, inflexible judgment, which has detected in another feelings and views in which it has no power to sympathize: in short, as a man, he would have wished to coerce me into obedience: it was only as a sincere Christian he bore so patiently with my perversity, and allowed so long a space for reflection and repentance.

That night, after he had kissed his sisters, he thought proper to forget even to shake hands with me; but left the room in silence. I—who, though I had no love, had much friendship for him—was hurt by the marked omission: so much hurt that tears started to my eyes.

"I see you and St. John have been quarreling, Jane," said Diana, "during your walk on the moor. But go after him; he is now lingering in the passage, expecting you—he will make it up."

2. Mythical apple thrown among the Greek goddesses by Eris, goddess of strife.

3. Sir Walter Scott's *The Lay of the Last Minstrel* 5.26.1

I have not much pride under such circumstances: I would always rather be happy than dignified; and I ran after him—he stood at the foot of the stairs.

"Good-night, St. John," said I.

"Good-night, Jane," he replied calmly.

"Then shake hands," I added.

What a cold, loose touch he impressed on my fingers! He was deeply displeased by what had occurred that day: cordiality would not warm, nor tears move him. No happy reconciliation was to be had with him—no cheering smile or generous word: but still the Christian was patient and placid; and when I asked him if he forgave me, he answered that he was not in the habit of cherishing the remembrance of vexation; that he had nothing to forgive: not having been offended.

And with that answer he left me. I would much rather he had knocked me down.

Chapter XXXV

He did not leave for Cambridge the next day, as he had said he would. He deferred his departure a whole week; and during that time he made me feel what severe punishment a good yet stern, a conscientious yet implacable man can inflict on one who has offended him. Without one overt act of hostility, one upbraiding word, he contrived to impress me momently with the conviction that I was put beyond the pale of his favor.

Not that St. John harbored a spirit of unchristian vindictiveness—not that he would have injured a hair of my head, if it had been fully in his power to do so. Both by nature and principle he was superior to the mean gratification of vengeance: he had forgiven me for saying I scorned him and his love, but he had not forgotten the words; and as long as he and I lived he never would forget them. I saw by his look, when he turned to me, that they were always written on the air between me and him; whenever I spoke, they sounded in my voice to his ear; and their echo toned every answer he gave me.

He did not abstain from conversing with me: he even called me as usual each morning to join him at his desk; and I fear the corrupt man within him had a pleasure unimparted to, and unshared by, the pure Christian, in evincing with what skill he could, while acting and speaking apparently just as usual, extract from every deed and every phrase the spirit of interest and approval which had formerly communicated a certain austere charm to his language and manner. To me, he was in reality become no longer flesh, but marble; his eye was a cold, bright, blue gem; his tongue, a speaking instrument—nothing more.

All this was torture to me—refined, lingering torture. It kept up a slow fire of indignation, and a trembling trouble of grief, which harassed and crushed me altogether. I felt how, if I were his wife, this good man, pure as the deep sunless source, could soon kill me: without drawing from my veins a single drop of blood, or receiving on his own crystal conscience the faintest stain of crime. Especially I felt this when I made any attempt to propitiate him. No ruth met my ruth. *He* experienced no suffering from estrangement—no yearning after reconciliation; and though, more than once, my fast falling tears blistered the page over which we both bent, they produced no more effect on him than if his heart had been really a matter of stone or metal.

To his sisters, meantime, he was somewhat kinder than usual: as if afraid that mere coldness would not sufficiently convince me how completely I was banished and banned, he added the force of contrast: and this I am sure he did, not by malice, but on principle.

The night before he left home, happening to see him walking in the garden about sunset, and remembering, as I looked at him, that this man, alienated as he now was, had once saved my life, and that we were near relations, I was moved to make a last attempt to regain his friendship. I went out and approached him, as he stood leaning over the little gate: I spoke to the point at once.

"St. John, I am unhappy, because you are still angry with me. Let us be friends."

"I hope we are friends," was the unmoved reply; while he still watched the rising of the moon, which he had been contemplating as I approached.

"No, St. John, we are not friends as we were. You know that."

"Are we not? That is wrong. For my part, I wish you no ill and all good."

"I believe you, St. John; for I am sure you are incapable of wishing anyone ill: but, as I am your kinswoman, I should desire somewhat more of affection than that sort of general philanthropy you extend to mere strangers."

"Of course," he said. "Your wish is reasonable; and I am far from regarding you as a stranger."

This, spoken in a cool, tranquil tone, was mortifying and baffling enough. Had I attended to the suggestions of pride and ire, I should immediately have left him: but something worked within me more strongly than those feelings could. I deeply venerated my cousin's talent and principle. His friendship was of value to me: to lose it tried me severely. I would not so soon relinquish the attempt to reconquer it.

"Must we part in this way, St. John? And when you go to India, will you leave me so, without a kinder word than you have yet spoken?"

He now turned quite from the moon, and faced me.

"When I go to India, Jane, will I leave you? What! do you not go to India?"

"You said I could not, unless I married you."

"And you will not marry me? You adhere to that resolution?"

Reader, do you know, as I do, what terror those cold people can put into the ice of their questions? How much of the fall of the avalanche is in their anger? of the breaking up of the frozen sea in their displeasure?

"No, St. John, I will not marry you. I adhere to my resolution."

The avalanche had shaken and slid a little forward; but it did not yet crash down.

"Once more, why this refusal?" he asked.

"Formerly," I answered, "because you did not love me; now, I reply, because you almost hate me. If I were to marry you, you would kill me. You are killing me now."

His lips and cheeks turned white—quite white.

"*I should kill you—I am killing you?* Your words are such as ought not to be used: violent, unfeminine, and untrue. They betray an unfortunate state of mind: they merit severe reproof: they would seem inexcusable; but that it is the duty of man to forgive his fellow, even until seventy-and-seven times."[4]

I had finished the business now. While earnestly wishing to erase from his

4. Matthew 18:21–22.

mind the trace of my former offence, I had stamped on that tenacious surface another and far deeper impression: I had burned it in.

"Now, you will indeed hate me," I said. "It is useless to attempt to conciliate you: I see I have made an eternal enemy of you."

A fresh wrong did these words inflict: the worse because they touched on the truth. That bloodless lip quivered to a temporary spasm. I knew the steely ire I had whetted. I was heart-wrung.

"You utterly misinterpret my words," I said, at once seizing his hand: "I have no intention to grieve or pain you—indeed, I have not."

Most bitterly he smiled—most decidedly he withdrew his hand from mine. "And now you recall your promise, and will not go to India at all, I presume?" said he, after a considerable pause.

"Yes I will, as your assistant," I answered.

A very long silence succeeded. What struggle there was in him between Nature and Grace in this interval I cannot tell; only singular gleams scintillated in his eyes, and strange shadows passed over his face. He spoke at last.

"I before proved to you the absurdity of a single woman of your age proposing to accompany abroad a single man of mine. I proved it to you in such terms as, I should have thought, would have prevented your ever again alluding to the plan. That you have done so, I regret—for your sake."

I interrupted him. Anything like a tangible reproach gave me courage at once.

"Keep to common sense, St. John: you are verging on nonsense. You pretend to be shocked by what I have said. You are not really shocked; for, with your superior mind, you cannot be either so dull or so conceited as to misunderstand my meaning. I say again, I will be your curate, if you like, but never your wife."

Again he turned lividly pale; but, as before, controlled his passion perfectly. He answered emphatically, but calmly: "A female curate, who is not my wife, would never suit me. With me, then, it seems, you cannot go: but if you are sincere in your offer, I will, while in town, speak to a married missionary, whose wife needs a coadjutor. Your own fortune will make you independent of the Society's aid; and thus you may still be spared the dishonor of breaking your promise, and deserting the band you engaged to join."

Now I never had, as the reader knows, either given any formal promise, or entered into any engagement; and this language was all much too hard, and much too despotic for the occasion. I replied: "There is no dishonor; no breach of promise; no desertion in the case. I am not under the slightest obligation to go to India: especially with strangers. With you I would have ventured much; because I admire, confide in, and, as a sister, I love you: but I am convinced that, go when and with whom I would, I should not live long in that climate."

"Ah! you are afraid of yourself," he said, curling his lip.

"I am. God did not give me my life to throw away; and to do as you wish me would, I begin to think, be almost equivalent to committing suicide. Moreover, before I definitively resolve in quitting England, I will know for certain whether I cannot be of greater use by remaining in it than by leaving it."

"What do you mean?"

"It would be fruitless to attempt to explain: but there is a point on which

I have long endured painful doubt; and I can go nowhere till by some means that doubt is removed."

"I know where your heart turns and to what it clings. The interest you cherish is lawless and unconsecrated. Long since you ought to have crushed it: now you should blush to allude to it. You think of Mr. Rochester?"

It was true. I confessed it by silence.

"Are you going to seek Mr. Rochester?"

"I must find out what is become of him."

"It remains for me, then," he said, "to remember you in my prayers; and to entreat God for you, in all earnestness, that you may not indeed become a castaway. I had thought I recognized in you one of the chosen. But God sees not as man sees: *His* will be done."

He opened the gate, passed through it, and strayed away down the glen. He was soon out of sight.

On reentering the parlor, I found Diana standing at the window, looking very thoughtful. Diana was a great deal taller than I: she put her hand on my shoulder, and, stooping, examined my face.

"Jane," she said, "you are always agitated and pale now. I am sure there is something the matter. Tell me what business St. John and you have on hand. I have watched you this half-hour from the window: you must forgive my being such a spy, but for a long time I have fancied I hardly know what. St. John is a strange being——"

She paused—I did not speak: soon she resumed:—"That brother of mine cherishes peculiar views of some sort respecting you, I am sure: he has long distinguished you by a notice and interest he never showed to any one else— to what end? I wish he loved you—does he Jane?"

I put her cool hand to my hot forehead: "No, Di, not one whit."

"Then why does he follow you so with his eyes—and get you so frequently alone with him, and keep you so continually at his side? Mary and I had both concluded he wished you to marry him."

"He does—he has asked me to be his wife."

Diana clapped her hands. "That is just what we hoped and thought! And you will marry him, Jane, won't you? And then he will stay in England."

"Far from that, Diana; his sole idea in proposing to me is to procure a fitting fellow-laborer in his Indian toils."

"What! He wishes you to go to India?"

"Yes."

"Madness!" she exclaimed. "You would not live three months there, I am certain. You never shall go: you have not consented—have you, Jane?"

"I have refused to marry him——"

"And have consequently displeased him?" she suggested.

"Deeply: he will never forgive me, I fear: yet I offered to accompany him as his sister."

"It was frantic folly to do so, Jane. Think of the task you undertook—one of incessant fatigue: where fatigue kills even the strong; and you are weak. St. John—you know him—would urge you to impossibilities: with him there would be no permission to rest during the hot hours; and unfortunately, I have noticed, whatever he exacts, you force yourself to perform. I am astonished you found courage to refuse his hand. You do not love him then, Jane?"

"Not as a husband."

"Yet he is a handsome fellow."

"And I am so plain, you see, Di. We should never suit."

"Plain! You? Not at all. You are much too pretty, as well as too good, to be grilled alive in Calcutta." And again she earnestly conjured me to give up all thoughts of going out with her brother.

"I must, indeed," I said; "for when just now I repeated the offer of serving him for a deacon, he expressed himself shocked at my want of decency. He seemed to think I had committed an impropriety in proposing to accompany him unmarried: as if I had not from the first hoped to find in him a brother; and habitually regarded him as such."

"What makes you say he does not love you, Jane?"

"You should hear himself on the subject. He has again and again explained that it is not himself, but his office he wishes to mate. He has told me I am formed for labor—not for love: which is true, no doubt. But, in my opinion, if I am not formed for love, it follows that I am not formed for marriage. Would it not be strange, Di, to be chained for life to a man who regarded one but as a useful tool?"

"Insupportable—unnatural—out of the question!"

"And then," I continued, "though I have only sisterly affection for him now, yet, if forced to be his wife, I can imagine the possibility of conceiving an inevitable, strange, torturing kind of love for him: because he is so talented; and there is often a certain heroic grandeur in his look, manner, and conversation. In that case, my lot would become unspeakably wretched. He would not want me to love him; and if I showed the feeling, he would make me sensible that it was a superfluity, unrequired by him, unbecoming in me. I know he would."

"And yet St. John is a good man," said Diana.

"He is a good and a great man: but he forgets, pitilessly, the feelings and claims of little people, in pursuing his own large views. It is better, therefore, for the insignificant to keep out of his way; lest, in his progress, he should trample them down. Here he comes! I will leave you, Diana." And I hastened upstairs, as I saw him entering the garden.

But I was forced to meet him again at supper. During that meal he appeared just as composed as usual. I had thought he would hardly speak to me, and I was certain he had given up the pursuit of his matrimonial scheme: the sequel showed I was mistaken on both points. He addressed me precisely in his ordinary manner; or what had, of late, been his ordinary manner; one scrupulously polite. No doubt he had invoked the help of the Holy Spirit to subdue the anger I had roused in him, and now believed he had forgiven me once more.

For the evening reading before prayers, he selected the twenty-first chapter of Revelation. It was at all times pleasant to listen while from his lips fell the words of the Bible: never did his fine voice sound at once so sweet and full—never did his manner become so impressive in its noble simplicity, as when he delivered the oracles of God: and tonight that voice took a more solemn tone—that manner a more thrilling meaning—as he sat in the midst of his household circle (the May moon shining in through the uncurtained window, and rendering almost unnecessary the light of the candle on the table): as he sat there, bending over the great old Bible, and described from its page the vision of the new heaven and the new earth—told how God would come

to dwell with men, how He would wipe away all tears from their eyes, and promised that there should be no more death, neither sorrow nor crying, nor any more pain, because the former things were passed away.

The succeeding words thrilled me strangely as he spoke them: especially as I felt, by the slight, indescribable alteration in sound, that in uttering them, his eye had turned on me.

"He that overcometh shall inherit all things; and I will be his God, and he shall be my son. But," was slowly, distinctly read, "the fearful, the unbelieving, etc. shall have their part in the lake which burneth with fire and brimstone, which is the second death."

Henceforth I knew what fate St. John feared for me.

A calm, subdued triumph, blent with a longing earnestness, marked his enunciation of the last glorious verses of that chapter. The reader believed his name was already written in the Lamb's book of life, and he yearned after the hour which should admit him to the city to which the kings of the earth bring their glory and honor; which has no need of sun or moon to shine in it, because the glory of God lightens it, and the Lamb is the light thereof.

In the prayer following the chapter, all his energy gathered—all his stern zeal woke: he was in deep earnest, wrestling with God, and resolved on a conquest. He supplicated strength for the weak-hearted; guidance for wanderers from the fold: a return, even at the eleventh hour, for those whom the temptations of the world and the flesh were luring from the narrow path. He asked, he urged, he claimed the boon of a brand snatched from the burning. Earnestness is ever deeply solemn: first, as I listened to that prayer, I wondered at his; then, when it continued and rose, I was touched by it, and at last awed. He felt the greatness and goodness of his purpose so sincerely: others who heard him plead for it, could not but feel it too.

The prayer over, we took leave of him: he was to go at a very early hour in the morning. Diana and Mary having kissed him, left the room—in compliance, I think, with a whispered hint from him: I tendered my hand, and wished him a pleasant journey.

"Thank you, Jane. As I said, I shall return from Cambridge in a fortnight: that space, then, is yet left you for reflection. If I listened to human pride, I should say no more to you of marriage with me; but I listen to my duty, and keep steadily in view my first aim—to do all things to the glory of God. My Master was long-suffering: so will I be. I cannot give you up to perdition as a vessel of wrath: repent—resolve; while there is yet time. Remember, we are bid to work while it is day—warned that 'the night cometh when no man shall work.'[5] Remember the fate of Dives,[6] who had his good things in this life. God give you strength to choose that better part which shall not be taken from you!"

He laid his hand on my head as he uttered the last words. He had spoken earnestly, mildly: his look was not, indeed, that of a lover beholding his mistress; but it was that of a pastor recalling his wandering sheep—or better, of a guardian angel watching the soul for which he is responsible. All men of talent, whether they be men of feeling or not; whether they be zealots, or aspirants, or despots—provided only they be sincere—have their sublime

5. John 9.4.
6. In Luke 16.19–31, Dives, the rich man, goes to hell.

moments: when they subdue and rule. I felt veneration for St. John—veneration so strong that its impetus thrust me at once to the point I had so long shunned. I was tempted to cease struggling with him—to rush down the torrent of his will into the gulf of his existence, and there lose my own. I was almost as hard beset by him now as I had been once before, in a different way, by another. I was a fool both times. To have yielded then would have been an error of principle; to have yielded now would have been an error of judgment. So I think at this hour, when I look back to the crisis through the quiet medium of time: I was unconscious of folly at the instant.

I stood motionless under my hierophant's touch. My refusals were forgotten —my fears overcome—my wrestlings paralyzed. The impossible—*i.e.* my marriage with St. John—was fast becoming the Possible. All was changing utterly, with a sudden sweep. Religion called—Angels beckoned—God commanded—life rolled together like a scroll—death's gates opening, showed eternity beyond: it seemed, that for safety and bliss there, all here might be sacrificed in a second. The dim room was full of visions.

"Could you decide now?" asked the missionary. The inquiry was put in gentle tones: he drew me to him as gently. Oh, that gentleness! how far more potent is it than force! I could resist St. John's wrath: I grew pliant as a reed under his kindness. Yet I knew all the time, if I yielded now, I should not the less be made to repent, some day, of my former rebellion. His nature was not changed by one hour of solemn prayer: it was only elevated.

"I could decide if I were but certain," I answered: "were I but convinced that it is God's will I should marry you, I could vow to marry you here and now—come afterwards what would!"

"My prayers are heard!" ejaculated St. John. He pressed his hand firmer on my head, as if he claimed me: he surrounded me with his arm, *almost* as if he loved me (I say *almost*—I knew the difference—for I had felt what it was to be loved; but, like him, I had now put love out of the question, and thought only of duty): I contended with my inward dimness of vision, before which clouds yet rolled. I sincerely, deeply, fervently longed to do what was right; and only that. "Show me, show me the path!" I entreated of Heaven. I was excited more than I had ever been; and whether what followed was the effect of excitement, the reader shall judge.

All the house was still; for I believe all, except St. John and myself, were now retired to rest. The one candle was dying out: the room was full of moonlight. My heart beat fast and thick: I heard its throb. Suddenly it stood still to an inexpressible feeling that thrilled it through, and passed at once to my head and extremities. The feeling was not like an electric shock; but it was quite as sharp, as strange, as startling: it acted on my senses as if their utmost activity hitherto had been but torpor; from which they were now summoned, and forced to wake. They rose expectant: eye and ear waited, while the flesh quivered on my bones.

"What have you heard? What do you see?" asked St. John. I saw nothing: but I heard a voice somewhere cry—"Jane! Jane! Jane!" nothing more.

"Oh God! what is it?" I gasped.

I might have said, "Where is it?" for it did not seem in the room—nor in the house—nor in the garden: it did not come out of the air—nor from under the earth—nor from overhead. I had heard it—where, or whence, for ever impossible to know! And it was the voice of a human being—a known, loved,

well-remembered voice—that of Edward Fairfax Rochester; and it spoke in pain and woe wildly, eerily, urgently.

"I am coming!" I cried. "Wait for me! Oh, I will come!" I flew to the door, and looked into the passage: it was dark. I ran out into the garden: it was void.

"Where are you?" I exclaimed.

The hills beyond Marsh Glen sent the answer faintly back—"Where are you?" I listened. The wind sighed low in the firs: all was moorland loneliness and midnight hush.

"Down superstition!" I commented, as that specter rose up black by the black yew at the gate. "This is not thy deception, nor thy witchcraft: it is the work of nature. She was roused, and did—no miracle—but her best."

I broke from St. John, who had followed, and would have detained me. It was *my* time to assume ascendancy. *My* powers were in play, and in force. I told him to forbear question or remark; I desired him to leave me: I must, and would be alone. He obeyed at once. Where there is energy to command well enough, obedience never fails. I mounted to my chamber; locked myself in; fell on my knees; and prayed in my way—a different way to St. John's, but effective in its own fashion. I seemed to penetrate very near a Mighty Spirit; and my soul rushed out in gratitude at His feet. I rose from the thanksgiving—took a resolve—and lay down, unscared, enlightened—eager but for the daylight.

Chapter XXXVI

The daylight came. I rose at dawn. I busied myself for an hour or two with arranging my things in my chamber, drawers, and wardrobe, in the order wherein I should wish to leave them during a brief absence. Meantime, I heard St. John quit his room. He stopped at my door: I feared he would knock—no, but a slip of paper was passed under the door. I took it up. It bore these words—

"You left me too suddenly last night. Had you stayed but a little longer, you would have laid your hand on the Christian's cross and the angel's crown. I shall expect your clear decision when I return this day fortnight. Meantime, watch and pray that you enter not into temptation: the spirit, I trust, is willing, but the flesh, I see, is weak.[7] I shall pray for you hourly,—Yours, St. John."

"My Spirit," I answered mentally, "is willing to do what is right; and my flesh, I hope, is strong enough to accomplish the will of Heaven, when once that will is distinctly known to me. At any rate, it shall be strong enough to search—inquire—to grope an outlet from this cloud of doubt, and find the open day of certainty."

It was the first of June; yet the morning was overcast and chilly: rain beat fast on my casement. I heard the front-door open, and St. John pass out. Looking through the window, I saw him traverse the garden. He took the way over the misty moors in the direction of Whitcross—there he would meet the coach.

"In a few more hours I shall succeed you in that track, cousin," thought

7. Matthew 26.41.

I: "I too have a coach to meet at Whitcross. I too have some to see and ask after in England, before I depart for ever."

It wanted yet two hours of breakfast-time. I filled the interval in walking softly about my room, and pondering the visitation which had given my plans their present bent. I recalled that inward sensation I had experienced: for I could recall it, with all its unspeakable strangeness. I recalled the voice I had heard; again I questioned whence it came, as vainly as before: it seemed in *me*—not in the external world. I asked, was it a mere nervous impression—a delusion? I could not conceive or believe: it was more like an inspiration. The wondrous shock of feeling had come like the earthquake which shook the foundations of Paul and Silas's prison:[8] it had opened the doors of the soul's cell, and loosed its bands—it had wakened it out of its sleep, whence it sprang trembling, listening, aghast; then vibrated thrice a cry on my startled ear, and in my quaking heart, and through my spirit; which neither feared nor shook, but exulted as if in joy over the success of one effort it had been privileged to make, independent of the cumbrous body.

"Ere many days," I said, as I terminated my musings, "I will know something of him whose voice seemed last night to summon me. Letters have proved of no avail—personal inquiry shall replace them."

At breakfast I announced to Diana and Mary that I was going a journey, and should be absent at least four days.

"Alone, Jane?" they asked.

"Yes; it was to see, or hear news of, a friend about whom I had for some time been uneasy."

They might have said, as I have no doubt they thought, that they had believed me to be without any friends save them: for, indeed, I had often said so; but with their true natural delicacy, they abstained from comment; except that Diana asked me if I was sure I was well enough to travel. I looked very pale, she observed. I replied, that nothing ailed me save anxiety of mind, which I hoped soon to alleviate.

It was easy to make my further arrangements; for I was troubled with no inquiries—no surmises. Having once explained to them that I could not now be explicit about my plans, they kindly and wisely acquiesced in the silence with which I pursued them; according to me the privilege of free action I should, under similar circumstances, have accorded them.

I left Moor House at three o'clock P.M., and soon after four I stood at the foot of the sign-post of Whitcross, waiting the arrival of the coach which was to take me to distant Thornfield. Amid the silence of those solitary roads and desert hills, I heard it approach from a great distance. It was the same vehicle whence, a year ago, I had alighted one summer evening on this very spot—how desolate, and hopeless, and objectless! It stopped as I beckoned. I entered—not now obliged to part with my whole fortune as the price of its accommodation. Once more on the road to Thornfield, I felt like the messenger-pigeon flying home.

It was a journey of six-and-thirty hours. I had set out from Whitcross on a Tuesday afternoon, and early on the succeeding Thursday morning the coach stopped to water the horses at a wayside inn, situated in the midst of scenery whose green hedges and large fields and low pastoral hills (how mild

8. Acts 16.25–26.

of feature and verdant of hue compared with the stern north-midland moors
of Morton!) met my eye like the lineaments of a once familiar face. Yes, I
knew the character of this landscape: I was sure we were near my bourne.

"How far is Thornfield Hall from here?" I asked of the ostler.

"Just two miles, ma'am, across the fields."

"My journey is closed," I thought to myself. I got out of the coach, gave a
box I had into the ostler's charge, to be kept till I called for it; paid my fare;
satisfied the coachman, and was going: the brightening day gleamed on the
sign of the inn, and I read in gilt letters, "The Rochester Arms." My heart
leaped up: I was already on my master's very lands. It fell again: the thought
struck it:—

"Your master himself may be beyond the British Channel, for aught you
know: and then, if he is at Thornfield Hall, towards which you hasten, who
besides him is there? His lunatic wife: and you have nothing to do with him:
you dare not speak to him or seek his presence. You have lost your labor—
you had better go no farther," urged the monitor. "Ask information of the
people at the inn; they can give you all you seek: they can solve your doubts
at once. Go up to that man, and inquire if Mr. Rochester be at home."

The suggestion was sensible; and yet I could not force myself to act on it.
I so dreaded a reply that would crush me with despair. To prolong doubt was
to prolong hope. I might yet once more see the Hall under the ray of her
star. There was the stile before me—the very fields through which I had
hurried, blind, deaf, distracted, with a revengeful fury tracking and scourging
me, on the morning I fled from Thornfield: ere I well knew what course I
had resolved to take, I was in the midst of them. How fast I walked! How I
ran sometimes! How I looked forward to catch the first view of the well-
known woods! With what feelings I welcomed single trees I knew, and famil-
iar glimpses of meadow and hill between them!

At last the woods rose; the rookery clustered dark; a loud cawing broke
the morning stillness. Strange delight inspired me: on I hastened. Another
field crossed—a lane threaded—and there were the courtyard walls—the
back offices: the house itself, the rookery still hid. "My first view of it shall
be in front," I determined, "where its bold battlements will strike the eye
nobly at once, and where I can single out my master's very window: perhaps
he will be standing at it—he rises early: perhaps he is now walking in the
orchard, or on the pavement in front. Could I but see him!—but a moment!
Surely, in that case, I should not be so mad as to run to him? I cannot tell—I
am not certain. And if I did—what then? God bless him! What then? Who
would be hurt by my once more tasting the life his glance can give me?—I
rave: perhaps at this moment he is watching the sun rise over the Pyrenees,
or on the tideless sea of the south."

I had coasted along the lower wall of the orchard—turned its angle: there
was a gate just there, opening into the meadow, between two stone pillars,
crowned by stone balls. From behind one pillar I could peep round quietly
at the full front of the mansion. I advanced my head with precaution, desir-
ous to ascertain if any bedroom window-blinds were yet drawn up: battle-
ments, windows, long front—all from this sheltered station were at my
command.

The crows sailing overhead perhaps watched me while I took this survey.
I wonder what they thought: they must have considered I was very careful

and timid at first, and that gradually I grew very bold and reckless. A peep, and then a long stare; and then a departure from my niche and a straying out into the meadow; and a sudden stop full in front of the great mansion, and a protracted, hardy gaze towards it. "What affectation of diffidence was this at first?" they might have demanded. "What stupid regardlessness now?"

Hear an illustration, reader.

A lover finds his mistress asleep on a mossy bank; he wishes to catch a glimpse of her fair face without waking her. He steals softly over the grass, careful to make no sound; he pauses—fancying she has stirred: he withdraws; not for worlds would he be seen. All is still: he again advances: he bends above her; a light veil rests on her features: he lifts it, bends lower; now his eyes anticipate the vision of beauty—warm, and blooming, and lovely, in rest. How hurried was their first glance! But how they fix! How he starts! How he suddenly and vehemently clasps in both arms the form he dared not, a moment since, touch with his finger! How he calls aloud a name, and drops his burden, and gazes on it wildly! He thus grasps and cries, and gazes, because he no longer fears to waken by any sound he can utter—by any movement he can make. He thought his love slept sweetly: he finds she is stone-dead.

I looked with timorous joy towards a stately house: I saw a blackened ruin.

No need to cower behind a gate-post, indeed!—to peep up at chamber lattices, fearing life was astir behind them! No need to listen for doors opening—to fancy steps on the pavement or the gravel-walk! The lawn, the grounds were trodden and waste: the portal yawned void. The front was, as I had once seen it in a dream, but a shell-like wall, very high and very fragile looking, perforated with paneless windows: no roof, no battlements, no chimneys—all had crashed in.

And there was the silence of death about it: the solitude of a lonesome wild. No wonder that letters addressed to people here had never received an answer: as well despatch epistles to a vault in a church aisle. The grim blackness of the stones told by what fate the Hall had fallen—by conflagration: but how kindled? What story belonged to this disaster? What loss, besides mortar and marble and wood-work, had followed upon it? Had life been wrecked, as well as property? If so, whose? Dreadful question: there was no one here to answer it—not even dumb sign, mute token.

In wandering round the shattered walls and through the devastated interior, I gathered evidence that the calamity was not of late occurrence. Winter snows, I thought, had drifted through that void arch; winter rains beaten in at those hollow casements; for, amid the drenched piles of rubbish, spring had cherished vegetation: grass and weed grew here and there between the stones and fallen rafters. And oh! where, meantime, was the hapless owner of this wreck? In what land? Under what auspices? My eye involuntarily wandered to the gray church tower near the gates, and I asked, "Is he with Damer de Rochester, sharing the shelter of his narrow marble house?"

Some answer must be had to these questions. I could find it nowhere but at the inn, and thither, ere long, I returned. The host himself brought my breakfast into the parlor. I requested him to shut the door and sit down: I had some questions to ask him. But when he complied, I scarcely knew how to begin; such horror had I of the possible answers. And yet the spectacle of desolation I had just left prepared me in a measure for a tale of misery. The host was a respectable-looking, middle-aged man.

"You know Thornfield Hall, of course?" I managed to say at last.

"Yes, ma'am; I lived there once."

"Did you?" Not in my time, I thought: you are a stranger to me.

"I was the late Mr. Rochester's butler," he added.

The late! I seemed to have received with full force the blow I had been trying to evade.

"The late!" I gasped. "Is he dead?"

"I mean the present gentleman Mr. Edward's father," he explained.

I breathed again: my blood resumed its flow. Fully assured by these words that Mr. Edward—*my* Mr. Rochester (God bless him, wherever he was!)—was at least alive: was, in short, "the present gentleman." Gladdening words! It seemed I could hear all that was to come—whatever the disclosures might be—with comparative tranquillity. Since he was not in the grave, I could bear, I thought, to learn that he was at the Antipodes.

"Is Mr. Rochester living at Thornfield Hall now?" I asked, knowing, of course, what the answer would be, but yet desirous of deferring the direct question as to where he really was.

"No, ma'am—oh, no! No one is living there. I suppose you are a stranger in these parts, or you would have heard what happened last autumn,—Thornfield Hall is quite a ruin: it was burnt down just about harvest time. A dreadful calamity! such an immense quantity of valuable property destroyed: hardly any of the furniture could be saved. The fire broke out at dead of night, and before the engines arrived from Millcote, the building was one mass of flame. It was a terrible spectacle: I witnessed it myself."

"At dead of night!" I muttered. Yes, that was ever the hour of fatality at Thornfield. "Was it known how it originated?" I demanded.

"They guessed, ma'am: they guessed. Indeed, I should say it was ascertained beyond a doubt. You are not perhaps aware," he continued, edging his chair a little nearer the table, and speaking low, "that there was a lady,—a—a lunatic, kept in the house?"

"I have heard something of it."

"She was kept in very close confinement, ma'am; people even for some years was not absolutely certain of her existence. No one saw her: they only knew by rumor that such a person was at the Hall; and who or what she was it was difficult to conjecture. They said Mr. Edward had brought her from abroad; and some believed she had been his mistress. But a queer thing happened a year since—a very queer thing."

I feared now to hear my own story. I endeavored to recall him to the main fact.

"And this lady?"

"This lady, ma'am," he answered, "turned out to be Mr. Rochester's wife! The discovery was brought about in the strangest way. There was a young lady, a governess at the Hall, that Mr. Rochester fell in——"

"But the fire," I suggested.

"I'm coming to that, ma'am—that Mr. Edward fell in love with. The servants say they never saw anybody so much in love as he was: he was after her continually. They used to watch him—servants will, you know, ma'am—and he set store on her past everything: for all, nobody but him thought her so very handsome. She was a little small thing, they say, almost like a child. I never saw her myself; but I've heard Leah, the housemaid, tell of her. Leah liked her well enough. Mr. Rochester was about forty, and this governess not

twenty; and you see, when gentlemen of his age fall in love with girls, they are often like as if they were bewitched: well, he would marry her."

"You shall tell me this part of the story another time," I said; "but now I have a particular reason for wishing to hear all about the fire. Was it suspected that this lunatic, Mrs. Rochester, had any hand in it?"

"You've hit it, ma'am: it's quite certain that it was her and nobody but her, that set it going. She had a woman to take care of her called Mrs. Poole— an able woman in her line, and very trustworthy, but for one fault—a fault common to a deal of them nurses and matrons—*she kept a private bottle of gin by her,* and now and then took a drop over much. It is excusable, for she had a hard life of it: but still it was dangerous; for when Mrs. Poole was fast asleep, after the gin-and-water, the mad lady, who was as cunning as a witch, would take the keys out of her pocket, let herself out of her chamber, and go roaming about the house, doing any wild mischief that came into her head. They say she had nearly burned her husband in his bed once: but I don't know about that. However, on this night, she set fire first to the hangings of the room next her own; and then she got down to a lower story, and made her way to the chamber that had been the governess's—(she was like as if she knew somehow how matters had gone on, and had a spite at her)—and she kindled the bed there; but there was nobody sleeping in it fortunately. The governess had run away two months before; and for all Mr. Rochester sought her as if she had been the most precious thing he had in the world, he never could hear a word of her; and he grew savage—quite savage in his disappointment: he never was a wild man, but he got dangerous after he lost her. He would be alone, too. He sent Mrs. Fairfax, the housekeeper, away to her friends at a distance; but he did it handsomely, for he settled an annuity on her for life: and she deserved it—she was a very good woman. Miss Adèle, a ward he had, was put to school. He broke off acquaintance with all the gentry, and shut himself up, like a hermit, at the Hall."

"What! did he not leave England?"

"Leave England? Bless you, no! He would not cross the door-stones of the house; except at night, when he walked just like a ghost about the grounds and in the orchard as if he had lost his senses—which it is my opinion he had; for a more spirited, bolder, keener gentleman than he was before that midge of a governess crossed him, you never saw, ma'am. He was not a man given to wine, or cards, or racing, as some are, and he was not so very handsome; but he had a courage and a will of his own, if ever man had. I knew him from a boy, you see: and for my part I have often wished that Miss Eyre had been sunk in the sea before she came to Thornfield Hall."

"Then Mr. Rochester was at home when the fire broke out?"

"Yes, indeed was he; and he went up to the attics when all was burning above and below, and got the servants out of their beds and helped them down himself—and went back to get his mad wife out of her cell. And then they called out to him that she was on the roof; where she was standing, waving her arms, above the battlements, and shouting out till they could hear her a mile off; I saw her and heard her with my own eyes. She was a big woman, and had long black hair: we could see it streaming against the flames as she stood. I witnessed, and several more witnessed Mr. Rochester ascend through the skylight on to the roof; we heard him call 'Bertha!' We

saw him approach her; and then, ma'am, she yelled, and gave a spring, and the next minute she lay smashed on the pavement."

"Dead?"

"Dead? Ay, dead as the stones on which her brains and blood were scattered."

"Good God!"

"You may well say so, ma'am: it was frightful!"

He shuddered.

"And afterwards?" I urged.

"Well, ma'am, afterwards the house was burned to the ground: there are only some bits of walls standing now."

"Were any other lives lost?"

"No—perhaps it would have been better if there had."

"What do you mean?"

"Poor Mr. Edward!" he ejaculated, "I little thought ever to have seen it! Some say it was a just judgment on him for keeping his first marriage secret, and wanting to take another wife while he had one living: but I pity him, for my part."

"You said he was alive?" I exclaimed.

"Yes, yes: he is alive; but many think he had better be dead."

"Why? How?" My blood was again running cold. "Where is he?" I demanded. "Is he in England?"

"Ay—ay—he's in England; he can't get out of England, I fancy—he's a fixture now."

What agony was this! And the man seemed resolved to protract it.

"He is stone-blind," he said at last. "Yes—he is stone-blind—is Mr. Edward."

I had dreaded worse. I had dreaded he was mad. I summoned strength to ask what had caused this calamity.

"It was all his own courage, and a body may say, his kindness, in a way, ma'am: he wouldn't leave the house till every one else was out before him. As he came down the great staircase at last, after Mrs. Rochester had flung herself from the battlements, there was a great crash—all fell. He was taken out from under the ruins, alive, but sadly hurt: a beam had fallen in such a way as to protect him partly; but one eye was knocked out, and one hand so crushed that Mr. Carter, the surgeon, had to amputate it directly. The other eye inflamed: he lost the sight of that also. He is now helpless, indeed—blind and a cripple."

"Where is he? Where does he now live?"

"At Ferndean, a manor-house on a farm he has, about thirty miles off: quite a desolate spot."

"Who is with him?"

"Old John and his wife: he would have none else. He is quite broken down, they say."

"Have you any sort of conveyance?"

"We have a chaise, ma'am, a very handsome chaise."

"Let it be got ready instantly; and if your post-boy can drive me to Ferndean before dark this day, I'll pay both you and him twice the hire you usually demand."

Chapter XXXVII

The manor-house of Ferndean was a building of considerable antiquity, moderate size, and no architectural pretensions, deep buried in a wood. I had heard of it before. Mr. Rochester often spoke of it, and sometimes went there. His father had purchased the estate for the sake of the game covers. He would have let the house; but could find no tenant, in consequence of its ineligible and insalubrious site. Ferndean then remained uninhabited and unfurnished; with the exception of some two or three rooms fitted up for the accommodation of the squire when he went there in the season to shoot.

To this house I came, just ere dark, on an evening marked by the characteristics of sad sky, cold gale, and continued small, penetrating rain. The last mile I performed on foot, having dismissed the chaise and driver with the double remuneration I had promised. Even when within a very short distance of the manor-house you could see nothing of it; so thick and dark grew the timber of the gloomy wood about it. Iron gates between granite pillars showed me where to enter, and passing through them, I found myself at once in the twilight of close-ranked trees. There was a grass-grown track descending the forest aisle, between hoar and knotty shafts and under branched arches. I followed it, expecting soon to reach the dwelling; but it stretched on and on, it wound far and farther: no sign of habitation or grounds was visible.

I thought I had taken a wrong direction and lost my way. The darkness of natural as well as of sylvan dusk gathered over me. I looked round in search of another road. There was none: all was interwoven stem, columnar trunk, dense, summer foliage—no opening anywhere.

I proceeded: at last my way opened, the trees thinned a little: presently I beheld a railing, then the house—scarce, by this dim light, distinguishable from the trees; so dank and green were its decaying walls. Entering a portal, fastened only by a latch, I stood amidst a space of enclosed ground, from which the wood swept away in a semicircle. There were no flowers, no garden-beds; only a broad gravel-walk girdling a grass-plat, and this set in the heavy frame of the forest. The house presented two pointed gables in its front; the windows were latticed and narrow; the front door was narrow too, one step led up to it. The whole looked, as the host of the Rochester Arms had said, "quite a desolate spot." It was as still as a church on a week-day: the pattering rain on the forest leaves was the only sound audible in its vicinage.

"Can there be life here?" I asked.

Yes: life of some kind there was: for I heard a movement—that narrow front door was unclosing, and some shape was about to issue from the grange.

It opened slowly: a figure came out into the twilight and stood on the step; a man without a hat: he stretched forth his hand as if to feel whether it rained. Dusk as it was, I had recognized him—it was my master, Edward Fairfax Rochester, and no other.

I stayed my step, almost my breath, and stood to watch him—to examine him, myself unseen, and alas! to him invisible. It was a sudden meeting, and one in which rapture was kept well in check by pain. I had no difficulty in restraining my voice from exclamation, my step from hasty advance.

His form was of the same strong and stalwart contour as ever: his port was still erect, his hair was still raven-black; nor were his features altered or sunk: not in one year's space, by any sorrow, could his athletic strength be quelled, or his vigorous prime blighted. But in his countenance I saw a change: that looked desperate and brooding—that reminded me of some wronged and fettered wild beast or bird, dangerous to approach in his sullen woe. The caged eagle, whose gold-ringed eyes cruelty has extinguished, might look as looked that sightless Samson.

And, reader, do you think I feared him in his blind ferocity?—if you do, you little know me. A soft hope blent with my sorrow that soon I should dare to drop a kiss on that brow of rock, and on those lips so sternly sealed beneath it: but not yet. I would not accost him yet.

He descended the one step, and advanced slowly and gropingly towards the grass-plat. Where was his daring stride now? Then he paused, as if he knew not which way to turn. He lifted his hand and opened his eyelids; gazed blank, and with a straining effort, on the sky, and towards the amphitheatre of trees: one saw that all to him was void darkness. He stretched his right hand (the left arm, the mutilated one, he kept hidden in his bosom); he seemed to wish by touch to gain an idea of what lay around him: he met but vacancy still; for the trees were some yards off where he stood. He relinquished the endeavor, folded his arms, and stood quiet and mute in the rain, now falling fast on his uncovered head. At this moment John approached him from some quarter.

"Will you take my arm, sir?" he said; "there is a heavy shower coming on: had you not better go in?"

"Let me alone," was the answer.

John withdrew, without having observed me. Mr. Rochester now tried to walk about: vainly,—all was too uncertain. He groped his way back to the house, and, reentering it, closed the door.

I now drew near and knocked: John's wife opened for me. "Mary," I said, "how are you?"

She started as if she had seen a ghost: I calmed her. To her hurried "Is it really you, miss, come at this late hour to this 'only place?" I answered by taking her hand; and then I followed her into the kitchen, where John now sat by a good fire. I explained to them, in few words, that I had heard all which had happened since I left Thornfield, and that I was come to see Mr. Rochester. I asked John to go down to the turnpike-house, where I had dismissed the chaise, and bring my trunk, which I had left there: and then, while I removed my bonnet and shawl, I questioned Mary as to whether I could be accommodated at the Manor House for the night; and finding that arrangements to that effect, though difficult, would not be impossible, I informed her I should stay. Just at this moment the parlor-bell rang.

"When you go in," said I, "tell your master that a person wishes to speak to him, but do not give my name."

"I don't think he will see you," she answered; "he refuses everybody."

When she returned I inquired what he had said.

"You are to send in your name and your business," she replied. She then proceeded to fill a glass with water, and place it on a tray, together with candles.

"Is that what he rang for?" I asked.

"Yes: he always has candles brought in at dark, though he is blind."

"Give the tray to me, I will carry it in."

I took it from her hand: she pointed me out the parlor door. The tray shook as I held it; the water spilled from the glass; my heart struck my ribs loud and fast. Mary opened the door for me, and shut it behind me.

This parlor looked gloomy: a neglected handful of fire burned low in the grate; and, leaning over it, with his head supported against the high, old-fashioned mantelpiece, appeared the blind tenant of the room. His old dog, Pilot, lay on one side, removed out of the way, and coiled up as if afraid of being inadvertently trodden upon. Pilot pricked up his ears when I came in: then he jumped up with a yelp and a whine, and bounded towards me: he almost knocked the tray from my hands. I set it on the table; then patted him, and said softly, "Lie down!" Mr. Rochester turned mechanically to *see* what the commotion was: but as he *saw* nothing, he returned and sighed.

"Give me the water, Mary," he said.

I approached him with the now only half-filled glass. Pilot followed me, still excited.

"What is the matter?" he inquired.

"Down, Pilot!" I again said. He checked the water on its way to his lips, and seemed to listen: he drank, and put the glass down. "This is you, Mary, is it not?"

"Mary is in the kitchen," I answered.

He put out his hand with a quick gesture, but not seeing where I stood, he did not touch me. "Who is this? Who is this?" he demanded, trying, as it seemed, to *see* with those sightless eyes—unavailing and distressing attempt! "Answer me—speak again!" he ordered, imperiously and aloud.

"Will you have a little more water, sir? I spilled half of what was in the glass," I said.

"*Who* is it? *What* is it? Who speaks?"

"Pilot knows me, and John and Mary know I am here. I came only this evening," I answered.

"Great God!—what delusion has come over me? What sweet madness has seized me?"

"No delusion—no madness: your mind, sir, is too strong for delusion, your health too sound for frenzy."

"And where is the speaker? Is it only a voice? Oh! I *cannot* see, but I must feel, or my heart will stop and my brain burst. Whatever—whoever you are—be perceptible to the touch or I cannot live!"

He groped; I arrested his wandering hand, and prisoned it in both mine.

"Her very fingers!" he cried; "her small, slight fingers! If so, there must be more of her."

The muscular hand broke from my custody; my arm was seized, my shoulder—neck—waist—I was entwined and gathered to him.

"Is it Jane? *What* is it? This is her shape—this is her size——"

"And this her voice," I added. "She is all here: her heart, too. God bless you, sir! I am glad to be so near you again."

"Jane Eyre!—Jane Eyre!" was all he said.

"My dear master," I answered, "I am Jane Eyre: I have found you out—I am come back to you."

"In truth?—in the flesh? My living Jane?"

"You touch me, sir,—you hold me, and fast enough; I am not cold like a corpse, nor vacant like air, am I?"

"My living darling! These are certainly her limbs, and these her features; but I cannot be so blest, after all my misery. It is a dream; such dreams as I have had at night when I have clasped her once more to my heart, as I do now; and kissed her, as thus—and felt that she loved me, and trusted that she would not leave me."

"Which I never will, sir, from this day."

"Never will, says the vision? But I always woke and found it an empty mockery; and I was desolate and abandoned—my life dark, lonely, hopeless—my soul athirst and forbidden to drink—my heart famished and never to be fed. Gentle, soft dream, nestling in my arms now, you will fly, too, as your sisters have all fled before you: but kiss me before you go— embrace me, Jane."

"There, sir—and there!"

I pressed my lips to his once brilliant and now rayless eyes—I swept his hair from his brow, and kissed that too. He suddenly seemed to arouse himself: the conviction of the reality of all this seized him.

"It is you—is it Jane? You are come back to me then?"

"I am."

"And you do not lie dead in some ditch under some stream? And you are not a pining outcast amongst strangers?"

"No, sir; I am an independent woman now."

"Independent! What do you mean, Jane?"

"My uncle in Madeira is dead, and he left me five thousand pounds."

"Ah, this is practical—this is real!" he cried: "I should never dream that. Besides, there is that peculiar voice of hers, so animating and piquant, as well as soft: it cheers my withered heart; it puts life into it.—What, Janet! Are you an independent woman? A rich woman?"

"Quite rich, sir. If you won't let me live with you, I can build a house of my own close up to your door, and you may come and sit in my parlor when you want company of an evening."

"But as you are rich, Jane, you have now, no doubt, friends who will look after you, and not suffer you to devote yourself to a blind lameter[9] like me?"

"I told you I am independent, sir, as well as rich: I am my own mistress."

"And you will stay with me?"

"Certainly—unless you object. I will be your neighbor, your nurse, your housekeeper. I find you lonely: I will be your companion—to read to you, to walk with you, to sit with you, to wait on you, to be eyes and hands to you. Cease to look so melancholy, my dear master; you shall not be left desolate, so long as I live."

He replied not: he seemed serious—abstracted; he sighed; he half-opened his lips as if to speak: he closed them again. I felt a little embarrassed. Perhaps I had too rashly overleaped conventionalities; and he, like St. John, saw impropriety in my inconsiderateness. I had indeed made my proposal from the idea that he wished and would ask me to be his wife: an expectation, not the less certain because unexpressed, had buoyed me up, that he would claim me at once as his own. But no hint to that effect escaping him, and his

9. Cripple.

countenance becoming more overcast, I suddenly remembered that I might have been all wrong and was perhaps playing the fool unwittingly; and I began gently to withdraw myself from his arms—but he eagerly snatched me closer.

"No—no—Jane: you must not go. No—I have touched you, heard you, felt the comfort of your presence—the sweetness of your consolation: I cannot give up these joys. I have little left in myself—I must have you. The world may laugh—may call me absurd, selfish—but it does not signify. My very soul demands you: it will be satisfied: or it will take deadly vengeance on its frame."

"Well, sir, I will stay with you: I have said so."

"Yes—but you understand one thing by staying with me; and I understand another. You, perhaps, could make up your mind to be about my hand and chair—to wait on me as a kind little nurse (for you have an affectionate heart and a generous spirit, which prompt you to make sacrifices for those you pity), and that ought to suffice for me no doubt. I suppose I should now entertain none but fatherly feelings for you: do you think so? Come—tell me."

"I will think what you like, sir: I am content to be only your nurse, if you think it better."

"But you cannot always be my nurse, Janet: you are young—you must marry one day."

"I don't care about being married."

"You should care, Janet: if I were what I once was, I would try to make you care—but—a sightless block!"

He relapsed again into gloom. I, on the contrary, became more cheerful, and took fresh courage: these last words gave me an insight as to where the difficulty lay; and as it was no difficulty with me, I felt quite relieved from my previous embarrassment. I resumed a livelier vein of conversation.

"It is time some one undertook to rehumanize you," said I, parting his thick and long uncut locks; "for I see you are being metamorphosed into a lion, or something of that sort. You have 'a faux air' of Nebuchadnezzar in the fields[1] about you, that is certain: your hair reminds me of eagle's feathers; whether your nails are grown like bird's claws or not, I have not yet noticed."

"On this arm I have neither hand nor nails," he said, drawing the mutilated limb from his breast, and showing it to me. "It is a mere stump—a ghastly sight! Don't you think so, Jane?"

"It is a pity to see it; and a pity to see your eyes—and the scar of fire on your forehead: and the worst of it is, one is in danger of loving you too well for all this; and making too much of you."

"I thought you would be revolted, Jane, when you saw my arm and cicatrised[2] visage."

"Did you? Don't tell me so—lest I should say something disparaging to your judgment. Now, let me leave you an instant, to make a better fire, and have the hearth swept up. Can you tell when there is a good fire?"

"Yes, with the right eye I see a glow—a ruddy haze."

"And you see the candles?"

1. In Daniel 4.32–37 Nebuchadnezzar is driven into the fields to repent. "Faux air": semblance. 2. Scarred.

"Very dimly—each is a luminous cloud."

"Can you see me?"

"No, my fairy: but I am only too thankful to hear and feel you."

"When do you take supper?"

"I never take supper."

"But you shall have some tonight. I am hungry: so are you, I daresay, only you forget."

Summoning Mary, I soon had the room in more cheerful order: I prepared him, likewise, a comfortable repast. My spirits were excited, and with pleasure and ease I talked to him during supper, and for a long time after. There was no harassing restraint, no repressing of glee and vivacity with him; for with him I was at perfect ease, because I knew I suited him: all I said or did seemed either to console or revive him. Delightful consciousness! It brought to life and light my whole nature: in his presence I thoroughly lived; and he lived in mine. Blind as he was, smiles played over his face, joy dawned on his forehead; his lineaments softened and warmed.

After supper he began to ask me many questions, of where I had been, what I had been doing, how I had found him out; but I gave him only very partial replies: it was too late to enter into particulars that night. Besides, I wished to touch no deep-thrilling chord—to open no fresh well of emotion in his heart: my sole present aim was to cheer him. Cheered, as I have said, he was: and yet but by fits. If a moment's silence broke the conversation, he would turn restless, touch me, then say, "Jane."

"You are altogether a human being, Jane? You are certain of that?"

"I conscientiously believe so, Mr. Rochester."

"Yet how, on this dark and doleful evening, could you so suddenly rise on my lone hearth? I stretched my hand to take a glass of water from a hireling, and it was given me by you: I asked a question, expecting John's wife to answer me, and your voice spoke at my ear."

"Because I had come in, in Mary's stead, with the tray."

"And there is enchantment in the very hour I am now spending with you. Who can tell what a dark, dreary, hopeless life I have dragged on for months past? Doing nothing, expecting nothing; merging night in day; feeling but the sensation of cold when I let the fire go out, of hunger when I forgot to eat: and then a ceaseless sorrow, and, at times, a very delirium of desire to behold my Jane again. Yes: for her restoration I longed, far more than for that of my lost sight. How can it be that Jane is with me, and says she loves me? Will she not depart as suddenly as she came? Tomorrow, I fear, I shall find her no more."

A common-place, practical reply, out of the train of his own disturbed ideas, was, I was sure, the best and most reassuring for him in this frame of mind. I passed my finger over his eyebrows, and remarked that they were scorched, and that I would apply something which should make them grow as broad and black as ever.

"Where is the use of doing me good in any way, beneficent spirit, when, at some fatal moment, you will again desert me—passing like a shadow, whither and how to me unknown; and for me remaining afterwards undiscoverable?"

"Have you a pocket comb about you, sir?"

"What for, Jane?"

"Just to comb out this shaggy black mane. I find you rather alarming when I examine you close at hand: you talk of my being a fairy; but I am sure you are more like a brownie."[3]

"Am I hideous, Jane?"

"Very, sir: you always were, you know."

"Humph! The wickedness has not been taken out of you, wherever you have sojourned."

"Yet I have been with good people; far better than you: a hundred times better people; possessed of ideas and views you never entertained in your life: quite more refined and exalted."

"Who the deuce have you been with?"

"If you twist in that way you will make me pull the hair out of your head; and then I think you will cease to entertain doubts of my substantiality."

"Who have you been with, Jane?"

"You shall not get it out of me tonight, sir; you must wait till tomorrow; to leave my tale half told will, you know, be a sort of security that I shall appear at your breakfast table to finish it. By-the-bye, I must mind not to rise on your hearth with only a glass of water, then: I must bring an egg at the least, to say nothing of fried ham."

"You mocking changeling—fairy-born and human-bred! You make me feel as I have not felt these twelve months. If Saul could have had you for his David, the evil spirit would have been exorcised without the aid of the harp."[4]

"There, sir, you are redd up[5] and made decent. Now I'll leave you: I have been traveling these last three days, and I believe I am tired. Good-night."

"Just one word, Jane: were there only ladies in the house where you have been?"

I laughed and made my escape, still laughing as I ran upstairs. "A good idea!" I thought, with glee. "I see I have the means of fretting him out of his melancholy for some time to come."

Very early the next morning I heard him up and astir, wandering from one room to another. As soon as Mary came down I heard the question: "Is Miss Eyre here?" Then: "Which room did you put her into? Was it dry? Is she up? Go and ask if she wants anything; and when she will come down."

I came down as soon as I thought there was a prospect of breakfast. Entering the room very softly, I had a view of him before he discovered my presence. It was mournful indeed to witness the subjugation of that vigorous spirit to a corporeal infirmity. He sat in his chair,—still, but not at rest: expectant evidently; the lines of now habitual sadness marking his strong features.

His countenance reminded one of a lamp quenched, waiting to be relit— and alas! it was not himself that could now kindle the luster of animated expression: he was dependent on another for that office! I had meant to be gay and careless, but the powerlessness of the strong man touched my heart to the quick: still I accosted him with what vivacity I could: "It is a bright, sunny morning, sir," I said. "The rain is over and gone, and there is a tender shining after it: you shall have a walk soon."

I had wakened the glow: his features beamed.

3. A benevolent spirit, of shaggy appearance. 5. Tidied.
4. 1 Samuel 16.23.

"Oh, you are indeed there, my sky-lark! Come to me. You are not gone: not vanished? I heard one of your kind an hour ago, singing high over the wood: but its song had no music for me, any more than the rising sun had rays. All the melody on earth is concentrated in my Jane's tongue to my ear (I am glad it is not naturally a silent one): all the sunshine I can feel is in her presence."

The water stood in my eyes to hear this avowal of his dependence: just as if a royal eagle, chained to a perch, should be forced to entreat a sparrow to become its purveyor. But I would not be lachrymose: I dashed off the salt drops, and busied myself with preparing breakfast.

Most of the morning was spent in the open air. I led him out of the wet and wild wood into some cheerful fields: I described to him how brilliantly green they were; how the flowers and hedges looked refreshed; how sparkingly blue was the sky. I sought a seat for him in a hidden and lovely spot: a dry stump of a tree: nor did I refuse to let him, when seated, place me on his knee: why should I, when both he and I were happier near than apart? Pilot lay beside us: all was quiet. He broke out suddenly while clasping me in his arms: "Cruel, cruel deserter! Oh, Jane, what did I feel when I discovered you had fled from Thornfield, and when I could nowhere find you; and, after examining your apartment, ascertained that you had taken no money, nor anything which could serve as an equivalent! A pearl necklace I had given you lay untouched in its little casket; your trunks were left corded and locked as they had been prepared for the bridal tour. What could my darling do, I asked, left destitute and penniless? And what did she do? Let me hear now."

Thus urged, I began the narrative of my experience for the last year. I softened considerably what related to the three days of wandering and starvation, because to have told him all would have been to inflict unnecessary pain: the little I did say lacerated his faithful heart deeper than I wished.

I should not have left him thus, he said, without any means of making my way: I should have told him my intention. I should have confided in him: he would never have forced me to be his mistress. Violent as he had seemed in his despair, he, in truth, loved me far too well and too tenderly to constitute himself my tyrant: he would have given me half his fortune, without demanding so much as a kiss in return, rather than I should have flung myself friendless on the wide world. I had endured, he was certain, more than I had confessed to him.

"Well, whatever my sufferings had been, they were very short," I answered: and then I proceeded to tell him how I had been received at Moor House; how I had obtained the office of schoolmistress, etc. The accession of fortune, the discovery of my relations, followed in due order. Of course St. John Rivers' name came in frequently in the progress of my tale. When I had done that name was immediately taken up.

"This St. John, then, is your cousin?"

"Yes."

"You have spoken of him often: do you like him?"

"He was a very good man, sir; I could not help liking him."

"A good man? Does that mean a respectable, well-conducted man of fifty? Or what does it mean?"

"St. John was only twenty-nine, sir."

" 'Jeune encore,'[6] as the French say. Is he a person of low stature, phlegmatic, and plain? A person whose goodness consists rather in his guiltlessness of vice than in his prowess in virtue?"

"He is untiringly active. Great and exalted deeds are what he lives to perform."

"But his brain? That is probably rather soft? He means well: but you shrug your shoulders to hear him talk?"

"He talks little, sir: what he does say is ever to the point. His brain is first-rate, I should think not impressible, but vigorous."

"Is he an able man, then?"

"Truly able."

"A thoroughly educated man?"

"St. John is an accomplished and profound scholar."

"His manners, I think, you said are not to your taste?—priggish and parsonic?"

"I never mentioned his manners; but, unless I had a very bad taste, they must suit it; they are polished, calm, and gentlemanlike."

"His appearance,—I forget what description you gave of his appearance;—a sort of raw curate, half-strangled with his white neckcloth, and stilted up on his thick-soled high-lows,[7] eh?"

"St. John dresses well. He is a handsome man: tall, fair, with blue eyes and a Grecian profile."

(Aside.) "Damn him!"—(To me.) "Did you like him, Jane?"

"Yes, Mr. Rochester, I liked him: but you asked me that before."

I perceived, of course, the drift of my interlocutor. Jealousy had got hold of him: she stung him; but the sting was salutary: it gave him respite from the gnawing fang of melancholy. I would not, therefore, immediately charm the snake.

"Perhaps you would rather not sit any longer on my knee, Miss Eyre?" was the next somewhat unexpected observation.

"Why not, Mr. Rochester?"

"The picture you have just drawn is suggestive of a rather too overwhelming contrast. Your words have delineated very prettily a graceful Apollo: he is present to your imagination,—tall, fair, blue-eyed, and with a Grecian profile. Your eyes dwell on a Vulcan,[8]—a real blacksmith, brown, broad-shouldered; and blind and lame into the bargain."

"I never thought of it before; but you certainly are rather like Vulcan, sir."

"Well,—you can leave me, ma'am: but before you go" (and he retained me by a firmer grasp than ever), "you will be pleased just to answer me a question or two." He paused.

"What questions, Mr. Rochester?"

Then followed this cross-examination.

"St. John made you schoolmistress of Morton before he knew you were his cousin?"

"Yes."

"You would often see him? He would visit the school sometimes?"

6. Still young.
7. High-fastening shoes.
8. The lame god of fire who worked at a forge.

Apollo was the handsome sun god of classical mythology.

"Daily."

"He would approve of your plans, Jane? I know they would be clever, for you are a talented creature."

"He approved of them—yes."

"He would discover many things in you he could not have expected to find? Some of your accomplishments are not ordinary."

"I don't know about that."

"You had a little cottage near the school, you say: did he ever come there to see you?"

"Now and then."

"Of an evening?"

"Once or twice."

A pause.

"How long did you reside with him and his sisters after the cousinship was discovered?"

"Five months."

"Did Rivers spend much time with the ladies of his family?"

"Yes; the back parlor was both his study and ours: he sat near the window, and we by the table."

"Did he study much?"

"A good deal."

"What?"

"Hindostanee."

"And what did you do meantime?"

"I learned German, at first."

"Did he teach you?"

"He did not understand German."

"Did he teach you nothing?"

"A little Hindostanee."

"Rivers taught you Hindostanee?"

"Yes, sir."

"And his sisters also?"

"No."

"Only you?"

"Only me."

"Did you ask to learn?"

"No."

"He wished to teach you?"

"Yes."

A second pause.

"Why did he wish it? Of what use could Hindostanee be to you?"

"He intended me to go with him to India."

"Ah! here I reach the root of the matter. He wanted you to marry him?"

"He asked me to marry him."

"That is a fiction—an impudent invention to vex me."

"I beg your pardon, it is the literal truth: he asked me more than once, and was as stiff about urging his point as ever you could be."

"Miss Eyre, I repeat, you can leave me. How often am I to say the same thing? Why do you remain pertinaciously perched on my knee, when I have given you notice to quit?"

"Because I am comfortable there."

"No, Jane, you are not comfortable there, because your heart is not with me: it is with this cousin—this St. John. Oh, till this moment I thought my little Jane was all mine! I had a belief she loved me even when she left me: that was an atom of sweet in much bitter. Long as we have been parted, hot tears as I have wept over our separation, I never thought that while I was mourning her she was loving another! But it is useless grieving. Jane, leave me: go and marry Rivers."

"Shake me off, then, sir—push me away, for I'll not leave you of my own accord."

"Jane, I ever like your tone of voice: it still renews hope, it sounds so truthful. When I hear it, it carries me back a year. I forget that you have formed a new tie. But I am not a fool—go——"

"Where must I go, sir?"

"Your own way—with the husband you have chosen."

"Who is that?"

"You know—this St. John Rivers."

"He is not my husband, nor ever will be. He does not love me: I do not love him. He loves (as he *can* love, and that is not as you love) a beautiful young lady called Rosamond. He wanted to marry me only because he thought I should make a suitable missionary's wife, which she would not have done. He is good and great, but severe; and, for me, cold as an iceberg. He is not like you, sir: I am not happy at his side, nor near him, nor with him. He has no indulgence for me—no fondness. He sees nothing attractive in me; not even youth—only a few useful mental points.—Then I must leave you, sir, to go to him?"

I shuddered involuntarily, and clung instinctively closer to my blind but beloved master. He smiled.

"What, Jane! Is this true? Is such really the state of matters between you and Rivers?"

"Absolutely, sir. Oh, you need not be jealous! I wanted to tease you a little to make you less sad: I thought anger would be better than grief. But if you wish me to love you, could you but see how much I *do* love you, you would be proud and content. All my heart is yours, sir: it belongs to you; and with you it would remain were fate to exile the rest of me from your presence for ever."

Again, as he kissed me, painful thoughts darkened his aspect.

"My seared vision! my crippled strength!" he murmured regretfully.

I caressed, in order to soothe him. I knew of what he was thinking, and wanted to speak for him; but dared not. As he turned aside his face a minute I saw a tear slide from under the sealed eyelid, and trickle down the manly cheek. My heart swelled.

"I am no better than the old lightning-struck chestnut-tree in Thornfield orchard," he remarked ere long. "And what right would that ruin have to bid a budding woodbine cover its decay with freshness?"

"You are no ruin, sir—no lightning-struck tree: you are green and vigorous. Plants will grow about your roots, whether you ask them or not, because they take delight in your bountiful shadow; and as they grow they will lean towards you, and wind round you, because your strength offers them so safe a prop."

Again he smiled: I gave him comfort.

"You speak of friends, Jane?" he asked.

"Yes: of friends," I answered rather hesitatingly: for I knew I meant more than friends, but could not tell what other word to employ. He helped me.

"Ah! Jane. But I want a wife."

"Do you, sir?"

"Yes: is it news to you?"

"Of course: you said nothing about it before."

"Is it unwelcome news?"

"That depends on circumstances, sir—on your choice."

"Which you shall make for me, Jane. I will abide by your decision."

"Choose then, sir—*her who loves you best.*"

"I will at least choose—*her I love best.* Jane, will you marry me?"

"Yes, sir."

"A poor blind man, whom you will have to lead about by the hand?"

"Yes, sir."

"A crippled man, twenty years older than you, whom you will have to wait on?"

"Yes, sir."

"Truly, Jane?"

"Most truly, sir."

"Oh! my darling! God bless you and reward you!"

"Mr. Rochester, if ever I did a good deed in my life—if ever I thought a good thought—if ever I prayed a sincere and blameless prayer—if ever I wished a righteous wish,—I am rewarded now. To be your wife is, for me, to be as happy as I can be on earth."

"Because you delight in sacrifice."

"Sacrifice! What do I sacrifice? Famine for food, expectation for content. To be privileged to put my arms round what I value—to press my lips to what I love—to repose on what I trust: is that to make a sacrifice? If so, then certainly I delight in sacrifice."

"And to bear with my infirmities, Jane: to overlook my deficiencies."

"Which are none, sir, to me. I love you better now, when I can really be useful to you, than I did in your state of proud independence, when you disdained every part but that of the giver and protector."

"Hitherto I have hated to be helped—to be led: henceforth, I feel, I shall hate it no more. I did not like to put my hand into a hireling's, but it is pleasant to feel it circled by Jane's little fingers. I preferred utter loneliness to the constant attendance of servants; but Jane's soft ministry will be a perpetual joy. Jane suits me: do I suit her?"

"To the finest fiber of my nature, sir."

"The case being so, we have nothing in the world to wait for: we must be married instantly."

He looked and spoke with eagerness: his old impetuosity was rising.

"We must become one flesh without any delay, Jane: there is but the license to get—then we marry."

"Mr. Rochester, I have just discovered the sun is far declined from its meridian, and Pilot is actually gone home to his dinner. Let me look at your watch."

"Fasten it into your girdle, Janet, and keep it hence-forward: I have no use for it."

"It is nearly four o'clock in the afternoon, sir. Don't you feel hungry?"

"The third day from this must be our wedding-day, Jane. Never mind fine clothes and jewels now: all that is not worth a fillip."

"The sun has dried up all the rain-drops, sir. The breeze is still: it is quite hot."

"Do you know, Jane, I have your little pearl necklace at this moment fastened round my bronze scrag under my cravat? I have worn it since the day I lost my only treasure: as a memento of her."

"We will go home through the wood: that will be the shadiest way."

He pursued his own thoughts without heeding me.

"Jane! you think me, I daresay, an irreligious dog: but my heart swells with gratitude to the beneficent God of this earth just now. He sees not as man sees, but far clearer: judges not as man judges, but far more wisely. I did wrong: I would have sullied my innocent flower—breathed guilt on its purity: the Omnipotent snatched it from me. I, in my stiff-necked rebellion, almost cursed the dispensation: instead of bending to the decree, I defied it. Divine justice pursued its course; disasters came thick on me: I was forced to pass through the valley of the shadow of death. *His* chastisements are mighty; and one smote me which has humbled me for ever. You know I was proud of my strength; but what is it now, when I must give it over to foreign guidance, as a child does its weakness? Of late, Jane—only—only of late—I began to see and acknowledge the hand of God in my doom. I began to experience remorse, repentance; the wish for reconcilement to my Maker. I began sometimes to pray: very brief prayers they were, but very sincere.

"Some days since: nay, I can number them—four; it was last Monday night, a singular mood came over me: one in which grief replaced frenzy—sorrow, sullenness. I had long had the impression that since I could nowhere find you, you must be dead. Late that night—perhaps it might be between eleven and twelve o'clock—ere I retired to my dreary rest, I supplicated God that, if it seemed good to Him, I might soon be taken from this life, and admitted to that world to come, where there was still hope of rejoining Jane.

"I was in my own room, and sitting by the window, which was open: it soothed me to feel the balmy night-air: though I could see no stars and only by a vague, luminous haze, knew the presence of a moon. I longed for thee, Janet! Oh, I longed for thee both with soul and flesh! I asked of God, at once in anguish and humility, if I had not been long enough desolate, afflicted, tormented; and might not soon taste bliss and peace once more. That I merited all I endured I acknowledged—that I could scarcely endure more I pleaded; and the Alpha and Omega[9] of my heart's wishes broke involuntarily from my lips in the words—'Jane! Jane! Jane!' "

"Did you speak these words aloud?"

"I did, Jane. If any listener had heard me, he would have thought me mad: I pronounced them with such frantic energy."

"And it was last Monday night: somewhere near midnight?"

"Yes; but the time is of no consequence: what followed is the strange point. You will think me superstitious,—some superstition I have in my blood, and always had: nevertheless, this is true—true at least it is that I heard what I now relate.

9. I.e., the beginning and end (the first and last letters of the Greek alphabet).

"As I exclaimed 'Jane! Jane! Jane!' a voice—I cannot tell whence the voice came, but I know whose voice it was—replied, 'I am coming: wait for me;' and a moment after went whispering on the wind the words—'Where are you?'"

"I'll tell you, if I can, the idea, the picture these words opened to my mind: yet it is difficult to express what I want to express. Ferndean is buried, as you see, in a heavy wood, where sound falls dull, and dies unreverberating. 'Where are you?' seemed spoken among mountains; for I heard a hill-sent echo repeat the words. Cooler and fresher at the moment the gale seemed to visit my brow: I could have deemed that in some wild, lone scene, I and Jane were meeting. In spirit, I believe, we must have met. You no doubt were, at that hour, in unconscious sleep, Jane: perhaps your soul wandered from its cell to comfort mine; for those were your accents—as certain as I live— they were yours!"

Reader, it was on Monday night—near midnight—that I too had received the mysterious summons: those were the very words by which I replied to it. I listened to Mr. Rochester's narrative; but made no disclosure in return. The coincidence struck me as too awful and inexplicable to be communicated or discussed. If I told anything, my tale would be such as must necessarily make a profound impression on the mind of my hearer: and that mind, yet from its sufferings too prone to gloom, needed not the deeper shade of the supernatural. I kept these things then, and pondered them in my heart.[1]

"You cannot now wonder," continued my master, "that when you rose upon me so unexpectedly last night I had difficulty in believing you any other than a mere voice and vision: something that would melt to silence and annihilation, as the midnight whisper and mountain echo had melted before. Now, I thank God! I know it to be otherwise. Yes, I thank God!"

He put me off his knee, rose, and reverently lifting his hat from his brow, and bending his sightless eyes to the earth, he stood in mute devotion. Only the last words of the worship were audible.

"I thank my Maker that in the midst of judgment He has remembered mercy. I humbly entreat my Redeemer to give me strength to lead henceforth a purer life than I have done hitherto!"

Then he stretched his hand out to be led. I took that dear hand, held it a moment to my lips, then let it pass round my shoulder: being so much lower of stature than he, I served both for his prop and guide. We entered the wood, and wended homeward.

Chapter XXXVIII

CONCLUSION

Reader, I married him. A quiet wedding we had: he and I, the parson and clerk, were alone present. When we got back from church, I went into the kitchen of the manor-house, where Mary was cooking the dinner, and John cleaning the knives, and I said: "Mary, I have been married to Mr. Rochester this morning." The housekeeper and her husband were both of that decent

1. Luke 2.19 (said of the Virgin Mary).

phlegmatic order of people to whom one may at any time safely communicate a remarkable piece of news without incurring the danger of having one's ears pierced by some shrill ejaculation, and subsequently stunned by a torrent of wordy wonderment. Mary did look up, and she did stare at me: the ladle with which she was basting a pair of chickens roasting at the fire did for some three minutes hang suspended in air; and for the same space of time John's knives also had rest from the polishing process: but Mary, bending again over the roast, said only: "Have you, Miss? Well, for sure!"

A short time after she pursued: "I seed you go out with the master, but I didn't know you were gone to church to be wed;" and she basted away. John, when I turned to him, was grinning from ear to ear.

"I told Mary how it would be," he said: "I knew what Mr. Edward" (John was an old servant, and had known his master when he was the cadet[2] of the house, therefore he often gave him his Christian name)—"I knew what Mr. Edward would do; and I was certain he would not wait long neither: and he's done right, for aught I know. I wish you joy, Miss!" and he politely pulled his forelock.

"Thank you, John. Mr. Rochester told me to give you and Mary this." I put into his hand a five-pound note. Without waiting to hear more, I left the kitchen. In passing the door of that sanctum some time after I caught the words: "She'll happen do better for him nor ony o' t' grand ladies." And again, "If she ben't one o' th' handsomest, she's noan faâl and varry good-natured; and i' his een[3] she's fair beautiful, onybody may see that."

I wrote to Moor House and to Cambridge immediately to say what I had done: fully explaining also why I had thus acted. Diana and Mary approved the step unreservedly. Diana announced that she would just give me time to get over the honeymoon, and then she would come and see me.

"She had better not wait till then, Jane," said Mr. Rochester, when I read her letter to him; "if she does, she will be too late, for our honeymoon will shine our life-long: its beams will only fade over your grave or mine."

How St. John received the news I don't know; he never answered the letter in which I communicated it: yet six months after he wrote to me; without, however, mentioning Mr. Rochester's name, or alluding to my marriage. His letter was then calm: and though very serious, kind. He has maintained a regular, though not frequent correspondence ever since: he hopes I am happy, and trusts I am not of those who live without God in the world, and only mind earthly things.

You have not quite forgotten little Adèle, have you, reader? I had not; I soon asked and obtained leave of Mr. Rochester to go and see her at the school where he had placed her. Her frantic joy at beholding me again moved me much. She looked pale and thin: she said she was not happy. I found the rules of the establishment were too strict, its course of study too severe, for a child of her age: I took her home with me. I meant to become her governess once more; but I soon found this impracticable; my time and cares were now required by another—my husband needed them all. So I sought out a school conducted on a more indulgent system; and near enough to permit of my visiting her often, and bringing her home sometimes. I took care she should never want for anything that could contribute to her comfort: she soon set-

2. Younger son. 3. Eyes. "Noan faâl": no fool.

tled in her new abode, became very happy there, and made fair progress in her studies. As she grew up a sound English education corrected in a great measure her French defects; and when she left school I found in her a pleasing and obliging companion: docile, good-tempered, and well-principled. By her grateful attention to me and mine she has long since well repaid any little kindness I ever had in my power to offer her.

My tale draws to its close: one word respecting my experience of married life, and one brief glance at the fortunes of those whose names have most frequently recurred in this narrative, and I have done.

I have now been married ten years. I know what it is to live entirely for and with what I love best on earth. I hold myself supremely blest—blest beyond what language can express; because I am my husband's life as fully as he is mine. No woman was ever nearer to her mate than I am; ever more absolutely bone of his bone and flesh of his flesh.[4]

I know no weariness of my Edward's society: he knows none of mine, any more than we each do of the pulsation of the heart that beats in our separate bosoms; consequently, we are ever together. To be together is for us to be at once as free as in solitude, as gay as in company. We talk, I believe, all day long: to talk to each other is but a more animated and an audible thinking. All my confidence is bestowed on him, all his confidence is devoted to me; we are precisely suited in character—perfect concord is the result.

Mr. Rochester continued blind the first two years of our union: perhaps it was that circumstance that drew us so very near—that knit us so very close! for I was then his vision, as I am still his right hand. Literally, I was (what he often called me) the apple of his eye. He saw nature—he saw books through me; and never did I weary of gazing for his behalf, and of putting into words the effect of field, tree, town, river, cloud, sunbeam—of the landscape before us; of the weather round us—and impressing by sound on his ear what light could no longer stamp on his eye. Never did I weary of reading to him: never did I weary of conducting him where he wished to go: of doing for him what he wished to be done. And there was a pleasure in my services, most full, most exquisite, even though sad—because he claimed these services without painful shame or damping humiliation. He loved me so truly that he knew no reluctance in profiting by my attendance: he felt I loved him so fondly that to yield that attendance was to indulge my sweetest wishes.

One morning at the end of the two years, as I was writing a letter to his dictation, he came and bent over me, and said—"Jane, have you a glittering ornament round your neck?"

I had a gold watch-chain: I answered, "Yes."

"And have you a pale blue dress on?"

I had. He informed me then that for some time he had fancied the obscurity clouding one eye was becoming less dense; and that now he was sure of it.

He and I went up to London. He had the advice of an eminent oculist; and he eventually recovered the sight of that one eye. He cannot now see very distinctly: he cannot read or write much; but he can find his way without being led by the hand: the sky is no longer a blank to him—the earth no

4. Genesis 2.23.

longer a void. When his firstborn was put into his arms, he could see that the boy had inherited his own eyes, as they once were—large, brilliant, and black. On that occasion he again, with a full heart, acknowledged that God had tempered judgment with mercy.

My Edward and I, then, are happy: and the more so because those we most love are happy likewise. Diana and Mary Rivers are both married: alternately, once every year, they come to see us, and we go to see them. Diana's husband is a captain in the navy; a gallant officer and a good man. Mary's is a clergyman: a college friend of her brother's; and, from his attainments and principles, worthy of the connection. Both Captain Fitzjames and Mr. Wharton love their wives, and are loved by them.

As to St. John Rivers, he left England: he went to India. He entered on the path he had marked for himself; he pursues it still. A more resolute, indefatigable pioneer never wrought amidst rocks and dangers. Firm, faithful, and devoted; full of energy, and zeal, and truth, he labors for his race: he clears their painful way to improvement: he hews down like a giant the prejudices of creed and caste that encumber it. He may be stern; he may be exacting: he may be ambitious yet; but his is the sternness of the warrior Greatheart, who guards his pilgrim convoy from the onslaught of Apollyon.[5] His is the exaction of the apostle, who speaks but for Christ when he says— "Whosoever will come after Me, let him deny himself, and take up his cross and follow Me."[6] His is the ambition of the high master-spirit, which aims to fill a place in the first rank of those who are redeemed from the earth— who stand without fault before the throne of God; who share the last mighty victories of the Lamb; who are called, and chosen, and faithful.

St. John is unmarried: he never will marry now. Himself has hitherto sufficed to the toil; and the toil draws near its close: his glorious sun hastens to its setting. The last letter I received from him drew from my eyes human tears, and yet filled my heart with Divine joy: he anticipated his sure reward, his incorruptible crown. I know that a stranger's hand will write to me next, to say that the good and faithful servant has been called at length into the joy of his Lord. And why weep for this? No fear of death will darken St. John's last hour: his mind will be unclouded; his heart will be undaunted; his hope will be sure; his faith steadfast. His own words are a pledge of this: —"My Master," he says, "has forewarned me. Daily he announces more distinctly,—'Surely I come quickly!'[7] and hourly I more eagerly respond,— 'Amen; even so come, Lord Jesus!' "

1847

5. In John Bunyan's *The Pilgrim's Progress* (1678), Apollyon is the angel of the bottomless pit. Greatheart is the Christian warrior.

6. Mark 8.34.
7. Revelation 22.20, the next to last verse of the final book of the Bible.

EMILY BRONTË
1818–1848

"Stronger than a man, simpler than a child, her nature stood alone," wrote Charlotte Brontë of her sister Emily in a *Biographical Notice of Ellis and Acton Bell* that she published after the deaths of the authors of *Wuthering Heights* and *Agnes Grey*. A few years later, Constantin Héger, Emily's schoolmaster for a year in Brussels, added an equally striking tribute: "She should have been a man—a great navigator[;] . . . her strong, imperious will would never have been daunted by opposition or difficulty." Paradoxically, however, the woman who inspired such dramatic statements appeared to many as a shy yet practical housekeeper who baked bread that was "always light and excellent" while studying German and scribbling poems on odd scraps of paper. Perhaps, indeed, it is because of such contradictions that the life story of Emily Brontë has long haunted biographers as well as more casual readers of her work.

Born in 1818, Emily Brontë was the fifth child of Patrick Brontë, a literarily inclined clergyman, and his wife, Maria Branwell Brontë, a lively but fragile woman who died not long after the birth of her last child, Anne. Like her equally famous sister Charlotte, Emily was raised at Haworth Parsonage in Yorkshire by her mother's pious sister, Elizabeth Branwell, who moved from Cornwall to her brother-in-law's home in order to care for his motherless children when he failed to remarry after his wife's death. Like Charlotte, too, Emily was briefly enrolled in the Clergy Daughters' School at Cowan Bridge, where she was one of the youngest pupils and was summarily brought home after her older sisters, Maria and Elizabeth, fell ill and died of a combination of typhoid fever and tuberculosis. Unlike Charlotte, however, Emily appeared—at least on the surface—to have transcended that traumatic experience unscathed, or so the biographer Winifred Gérin has argued.

After the deaths of Maria and Elizabeth, Emily received a haphazard education at home, along with her older brother, Branwell, and her remaining sisters, Charlotte and Anne. Because their father was an intellectual and literarily inclined, the children had access to a library that included not only the works of writers such as John Milton, Lord Byron, and Sir Walter Scott but also *The Arabian Nights* and the latest issues of contemporary periodicals like *Blackwood's* magazine. Equally obsessed with politics and poetry, history and fiction, they began early to incorporate such matters into what Charlotte called their "Bed Plays"—elaborate fantasies, which were eventually to become more real to Emily than her daily life. Most notably, when their father brought Branwell a set of wooden soldiers, each child chose a figure with which to identify. Emily's was "Parry," named (as if in anticipation of Héger's later description of her) after her childhood hero William Edward Parry, the Arctic explorer, and at first this dashing character figured in "plays" primarily of Charlotte and Branwell's invention. Eventually, however, Emily, together with her sister Anne, incorporated his adventures into a series of sagas that were uniquely their own. These were the chronicles of "Gondal," an imaginary country in the North Pacific that was ruled by a tempestuous queen known, variously, as Augusta Geraldine Almeda, A. G. A., Rosina of Alcona, A. S., Sidonia's deity, and Gondal's queen. Astonishingly, these two young women sustained their involvement in the "history" of this imaginary country long past their teens: much of Emily Brontë's poetry, the critic Fannie Ratchford has shown, was conceived as part of a Gondal "cycle" whose prose portions have been lost.

What is perhaps even more impressive about Emily Brontë's commitment to Gondal is the way she was able both to extend and to elaborate her fantasy in the midst of an apparently prosaic reality. The "Diary Papers" she and her sister Anne wrote on their birthdays indicate the ease with which Emily moved from her existence as a housekeeping daughter to her imaginative experience as Gondal's queen. In 1834,

for instance, when she was just sixteen, she juxtaposed domestic detail and mysterious drama in a statement that began by noting "I fed Rainbow, Diamond Snowflake Jasper" (pet birds), went on to observe that "Taby" (the family servant) "said just now Come Anne pilloputate" (peel a potato), and then declared that "the Gondals are discovering the interior of Gaaldine" (their exotic continent). Rarely have English writers combined such minutely accurate transcriptions of ordinary life—kitchens and potato peels—with such imaginings of high adventure. Yet it is precisely this configuration of the prosaic and the poetic that gives Emily Brontë's one novel, *Wuthering Heights,* its distinctive power.

As her Diary Papers suggest, Emily's housekeeping life at Haworth Parsonage was by no means an imprisonment. Rather, she felt constrained and confined on the few occasions when she had to leave home. In 1835, she briefly attended Roe Head, a girls' boarding school where Charlotte was employed as a teacher, and in 1837 she herself spent some six months teaching at Law Hill, a similar institution. Both experiences were unpleasant, indeed almost disastrous, for her. "I felt in my heart she would die, if she did not go home," Charlotte remembered about her sister's days at Roe Head, explaining that "liberty was the breath of Emily's nostrils; without it, she perished." Nevertheless, despite her attachment to such "liberty"—which she evidently found only on the moors near Haworth—Emily accompanied Charlotte to Brussels in 1842, where the two studied at a Belgian school, the Pensionnat Héger, in the hope that they might prepare themselves to found an educational establishment of their own. In November 1842, however, receiving word that their "Aunt Branwell" had died, the sisters returned to Haworth, and although Charlotte went back to Brussels for another term, Emily was never really to leave home again.

Despite its apparent quietness, Emily's time in Yorkshire from 1842 to 1848 was eventful. According to one critic, her father "seems to have selected her as an honorary boy to be trusted with fire-arms in defence of the weak" so that her "life exemplifies a rough joy in itself," with "its war-games: its word games and its power to extend its own structuring vision out upon the given world." Her sister Charlotte clearly sensed this. In the autumn of 1845, she "accidentally alighted," as she later put it, "on a MS volume of verses in my sister Emily's handwriting," and finding that these works had "a peculiar music—wild, melancholy, and elevating," she conceived a plan to publish them, along with poems by herself and Anne; thus in 1846 a volume titled *Poems by Currer, Ellis, and Acton Bell* appeared in London. The pseudonyms had been chosen because they concealed the femininity of the three authors at the same time that they were "not positively masculine." Yet Ellis Bell's gender was an important factor in her sister's appreciation of her work: "I know no woman that ever lived who wrote such poetry before," she exclaimed in a letter to her publisher. No doubt she was referring to the "rough joy" and visionary sternness that set Emily's poems apart from the sentimental effusions that "ladies" were supposed to produce. But although a few reviewers received the verse of the Bells with approbation, and at least one singled out Ellis's "power of wing" for special praise, the reading public did not share either his admiration or Charlotte's. In the year after the Bells' *Poems* appeared, only two copies were sold.

Undaunted, the sisters set out to try their fortunes as fiction writers. The books they produced were Charlotte's *Jane Eyre;* Anne's *Agnes Grey;* and Emily's *Wuthering Heights,* a novel that was not greeted with anything like the wave of popular enthusiasm that met *Jane Eyre.* Some reviewers, generally the most sympathetic, thought it an early, immature work by "Currer Bell" himself. Others, shocked at the book's frank portrayals of passion and dissolution, commented that it was "a disagreeable story" and speculated that, like the novel, its author must be "dogged, brutal, and morose." In fact, *Wuthering Heights* is none of these: brilliantly organized by an interlocking series of first-person narratives, it is a tale of love, revenge, and redemption that comments on the tensions of nineteenth-century society even while it offers a vision of a spiritual region beyond ordinary "reality." Like William Wordsworth and

Thomas Carlyle, Brontë invested the world with a kind of "natural supernaturalism" that gave mystical radiance to the earthly realm of moors and cliffs, and even to the emotional relationships of men and women, parents and children. Like William Blake and Byron, she defined her visionary system as one that was beyond good and evil. Indeed, in *Wuthering Heights*'s satanic hero, Heathcliff, she created a figure who "stalked apart" from ordinary mortals and conventional morality as so many of Byron's heroes did, a figure whose fierce passions, like those of his beloved Catherine Earnshaw Linton, often seem to represent the author's own desire for the subversive *Marriage of Heaven and Hell* that Blake had imagined some fifty years earlier.

That Emily Brontë quite consciously shaped *Wuthering Heights* not just as a Gothic romance but also as a radically visionary work becomes quite clear when one studies her poems. Here, in verses spoken in her "own" voice as well as in dramatic monologues written for Gondalian characters such as A. G. A. and her band of troubled lovers, the poet expressed her own alienation from social conventions and her own yearning for the "dazzling sea" of infinity, her own defiance of time and mortality, and her own commitment to the inspiring "night wind" of imagination. "No Coward Soul Is Mine," perhaps her most famous poem, articulated the severe yet ecstatic creed by which she lived and that informs her other verses, along with her one novel. "No trembler in the world's storm-troubled sphere," she relied in true Romantic fashion on the "God within my breast" to redeem her from pain, and, in true mystical fashion, she saw that inner "God" as one with an outer spirit of "Undying Life." But at the same time, in a poem that her sister Charlotte published after her death, Emily Brontë insisted that she would not renounce the reality of nature, for "The earth that wakes *one* human heart to feeling / Can centre both the worlds of Heaven and Hell."

If she had experienced a terrestrial heaven on the moors, however, Brontë was destined to live through a domestic hell in her own household. Never a man of strong character, her brother, Branwell, had dramatically deteriorated over the years, and when he was rejected by a married woman with whom he had been in love, he declined into alcoholism and opium addiction. By all accounts, it was Emily who watched over him in his last days, waiting up night after night to lead him to bed when he came home drunk or drugged. In September 1848, "his constitution shattered," as Charlotte put it, he died; and October 1, the day of his funeral, was the last day on which Emily went out of her house. Apparently she caught a cold at the funeral service and thereby aggravated an underlying condition; she fell ill with consumption, whose course was possibly hastened by the trauma through which she had just lived. Characteristically, she refused to see a doctor and forced herself to go about her usual business during the entire two-month period of her fatal sickness. Even on the day of her death, she stubbornly rose and dressed. Yet the extent of her illness can be judged from the report of the carpenter who made her coffin in December 1848: he claimed he had never made so narrow a coffin for an adult; it was, he said, five feet six inches in length, sixteen inches in width.

Always stoic, Emily Brontë had sworn to the end that "I'll walk where my own nature would be leading: / It vexes me to choose another guide." After her death, such independence was to be recognized as one of the qualities that gave her writing extraordinary power. But even in her lifetime, those closest to her had recognized her special genius: her poems "stirred my heart like the sound of a trumpet when I read them alone and in secret," Charlotte once confided to a friend, "for Ellis Bell is of no . . . ordinary materials."

[Tell me, tell me, smiling child]

Tell me, tell me, smiling child,
What the past is like to thee?
"An Autumn evening soft and mild
With a wind that sighs mournfully."

5 Tell me, what is the present hour?
"A green and flowery spray
Where a young bird sits gathering its power
To mount and fly away."

And what is the future, happy one?
10 "A sea beneath a cloudless sun;
A mighty, glorious, dazzling sea
Stretching into infinity."

1836 1941

[I am the only being whose doom]

I am the only being whose doom[1]
No tongue would ask, no eye would mourn;
I never caused a thought of gloom,
A smile of joy, since I was born.

5 In secret pleasure, secret tears,
This changeful life has slipped away,
As friendless after eighteen years,
As lone as on my natal day.

There have been times I cannot hide,
10 There have been times when this was drear,
When my sad soul forgot its pride
And longed for one to love me here.

But those were in the early glow
Of feelings since subdued by care;
15 And they have died so long ago,
I hardly now believe they were.[2]

First melted off the hope of youth,
Then fancy's[3] rainbow fast withdrew;
And then experience told me truth
20 In mortal bosoms never grew.

1. Death or fate.
2. I.e., existed.

3. Imagination's.

'Twas grief enough to think mankind
All hollow, servile, insincere;
But worse to trust to my own mind
And find the same corruption there.

May 17, 1837 1910

[Alone I sat; the summer day]

Alone I sat; the summer day
Had died in smiling light away;
I saw it die, I watched it fade
From misty hill and breezeless glade:

5 And thoughts in my soul were gushing,
And my heart bowed beneath their power;
And tears within my eyes were rushing
Because I could not speak the feeling,
The solemn joy around me stealing
10 In that divine, untroubled hour.

I asked myself, "O why has heaven
Denied the precious gift to me,
The glorious gift to many given
To speak their thoughts in poetry?

15 "Dreams have encircled me," I said,
"From careless childhood's sunny time;
Visions by ardent fancy fed
Since life was in its morning prime."[1]

But now, when I had hoped to sing,
20 My fingers strike a tuneless string;
And still the burden of the strain[2]
Is "Strive no more; 'tis all in vain."

August 1837 1941

1. First hour, beginning. 2. Tune. "Burden": bass or accompanying part.

F. de Samara to A. G. A.[1]

Light up thy halls! 'Tis closing day;
I'm drear and lone and far away—
Cold blows on my breast the northwind's bitter sigh,
And oh, my couch is bleak beneath the rainy sky!

5 Light up thy halls—and think not of me;
That face is absent now, thou hast hated so to see—
Bright be thine eyes, undimmed their dazzling shine,
For never, never more shall they encounter mine!

The desert[2] moor is dark; there is tempest in the air;
10 I have breathed my only wish in one last, one burning prayer—
A prayer that would come forth, although it lingered long;
That set on fire my heart, but froze upon my tongue.

And now, it shall be done before the morning rise:
I will not watch the sun ascend in yonder skies.
15 One task alone remains—thy pictured face to view;
And then I go to prove[3] if God, at least, be true!

Do I not see thee now? Thy black resplendent hair;
Thy glory-beaming brow, and smile, how heavenly fair!
Thine eyes are turned away—those eyes I would not see;
20 Their dark, their deadly ray, would more than madden me.

There, go, Deceiver, go! My hand is streaming wet;
My heart's blood flows to buy the blessing—To forget!
Oh could that lost heart give back, back again to thine,
One tenth part of the pain that clouds my dark decline![4]

25 Oh could I see thy lids weighed down in cheerless woe;
Too full to hide their tears, too stern to overflow;
Oh could I know thy soul with equal grief was torn,
This fate might be endured—this anguish might be borne!

How gloomy grows the night! 'Tis Gondal's wind that blows;
30 I shall not tread again the deep glens where it rose—
I feel it on my face—"Where, wild blast, dost thou roam?
What do we, wanderer,[5] here, so far away from home?

"I do not need thy breath to cool my death-cold brow;
But go to that far land, where she is shining now;

1. A. G. A. is Augusta Geraldine Almeda, the heroine of an intricate dynastic story set in the mythological kingdom of Gondal. Both Anne and Emily Brontë participated in creating the story. The speaker of the poem is one of A. G. A.'s betrayed lovers. C. W. Hatfield argues that Emily Brontë made a mistake in copying the poem and that the speaker is really Lord Alfred of Aspin Castle,

A. G. A.'s deserted husband, and not the youth Fernando de Samara (see Hatfield's *The Complete Poems of Emily Jane Brontë*, p. 16).
2. Deserted.
3. Test.
4. End, death.
5. The speaker addresses the wind.

35 Tell Her my latest wish, tell Her my dreary doom;[6]
 Say that *my* pangs are past, but *Hers* are yet to come."

 Vain words—vain, frenzied thoughts! No ear can hear me call—
 Lost in the vacant air my frantic curses fall—
 And could she see me now, perchance her lip would smile,
40 Would smile in careless pride and utter scorn the while!

 And yet for all her hate, each parting glance would tell
 A stronger passion breathed, burned, in this last farewell.
 Unconquered in my soul the Tyrant[7] rules me still;
 Life bows to my control, but *Love* I cannot kill!

November 1, 1838 1941

The Night-Wind

 In summer's mellow midnight,
 A cloudless moon shone through
 Our open parlor window
 And rosetrees wet with dew.

5 I sat in silent musing,
 The soft wind waved my hair:
 It told me Heaven was glorious,
 And sleeping Earth was fair.

 I needed not its breathing
10 To bring such thoughts to me,
 But still it whispered lowly,
 "How dark the woods will be!

 "The thick leaves in my murmur
 Are rustling like a dream,
15 And all their myriad voices
 Instinct[1] with spirit seem."

 I said, "Go, gentle singer,
 Thy wooing voice is kind,
 But do not think its music
20 Has power to reach my mind.

 "Play with the scented flower,
 The young tree's supple bough,
 And leave my human feelings
 In their own course to flow."

6. The speaker's death or fate; also his curse. 1. Infused.
7. I.e., love.

25　The wanderer would not leave[2] me;
　　Its kiss grew warmer still—
　　"O come," it sighed so sweetly,
　　"I'll win thee 'gainst thy will.

　　"Have we not been from childhood friends?
30　Have I not loved thee long?
　　As long as thou hast loved the night
　　Whose silence wakes my song.

　　"And when thy heart is laid at rest
　　Beneath the church-yard stone
35　I shall have time enough to mourn
　　And thou to be alone."

September 11, 1840 1850

[Riches I hold in light esteem]

　　Riches I hold in light esteem
　　And Love I laugh to scorn
　　And lust of Fame was but a dream
　　That vanished with the morn—

5　And if I pray, the only prayer
　　That moves my lips for me
　　Is—"Leave the heart that now I bear
　　And give me liberty."

　　Yes, as my swift days near their goal
10　'Tis all that I implore—
　　Through life and death, a chainless soul
　　With courage to endure!

March 1, 1841 1846

[Aye, there it is! It wakes to-night][1]

　　Aye, there it[2] is! It wakes to-night
　　Sweet thoughts that will not die
　　And feeling's fires flash all as bright
　　As in the years gone by!

2. An alternative reading of the manuscript is
"heed."
1. Possibly addressed to one of Emily Brontë's sib-
lings. Charlotte Brontë supplied the following

note: "In these stanzas a louder gale has roused the
sleeper on her pillow: the wakened soul struggles
to blend with the storm by which it is swayed."
2. I.e., the gale wind.

5 And I can tell by thine altered cheek
 And by thy kindled gaze
 And by the words thou scarce dost speak,
 How wildly fancy[3] plays.

 Yes, I could swear that glorious wind
10 Has swept the world aside,
 Has dashed its memory from thy mind
 Like foam-bells[4] from the tide—

 And thou art now a spirit pouring
 Thy presence into all—
15 The essence of the Tempest's roaring
 And of the Tempest's fall—

 A universal influence
 From thine own influence free;
 A principle of life, intense,
20 Lost to mortality.

 Thus truly when that breast is cold
 Thy prisoned soul shall rise,
 The dungeon mingle with the mold[5]—
 The captive with the skies.

July 6, 1841 1850

A Day Dream

 On a sunny brae[1] alone I lay
 One summer afternoon;
 It was the marriage-time of May
 With her young lover, June.[2]

5 From her Mother's[3] heart seemed loath to part
 That queen of bridal charms,
 But her Father[4] smiled on the fairest child
 He ever held in his arms.

 The trees did wave their plumy crests,
10 The glad birds caroled clear;
 And I, of all the wedding guests,
 Was only[5] sullen there.

 There was not one but wished to shun
 My aspect void of cheer;

3. Imagination.
4. Bubbles.
5. Earth or decaying flesh in the earth.
1. Hillside along a river.

2. I.e., it was the end of May.
3. The earth's.
4. The sun.
5. Alone.

15 The very gray rocks, looking on,
 Asked, "What do you do here?"

 And I could utter no reply:
 In sooth I did not know
 Why I had brought a clouded eye
20 To greet the general glow.

 So, resting on a heathy bank,
 I took my heart to me;
 And we together sadly sank
 Into a reverie.

25 We thought, "When winter comes again,
 Where will these bright things be?
 All vanished, like a vision vain,
 An unreal mockery!

 "The birds that now so blithely sing,
30 Through deserts frozen dry,
 Poor spectres of the perished Spring
 In famished troops will fly.

 "And why should we be glad at all?
 The leaf is hardly green,
35 Before a token of the fall[6]
 Is on its surface seen."

 Now whether it were really so
 I never could be sure;
 But as, in fit of peevish woe,
40 I stretched me on the moor,

 A thousand thousand glancing fires
 Seemed kindling in the air;
 A thousand thousand silvery lyres
 Resounded far and near:

45 Methought the very breath I breathed
 Was full of sparks divine,
 And all my heather-couch was wreathed
 By that celestial shine.

 And while the wide Earth echoing rang
50 To their strange minstrelsy,
 The little glittering spirits sang,
 Or seemed to sing, to me:

 "O mortal, mortal, let them die;
 Let Time and Tears destroy,

6. Both autumn and the biblical Fall into sin of Adam and Eve.

55 That we may overflow the sky
 With universal joy.

 "Let Grief distract the sufferer's breast,
 And Night obscure his way;
 They hasten him to endless rest,
60 And everlasting day.

 "To Thee the world is like a tomb,
 A desert's naked shore;
 To us, in unimagined bloom,
 It brightens more and more.

65 "And could we lift the veil and give
 One brief glimpse to thine eye
 Thou would'st rejoice for those that live,
 Because they live to die."

 The music ceased—the noonday Dream
70 Like dream of night withdrew
 But Fancy still will sometimes deem
 Her fond⁷ creation true.

March 5, 1844 1846

R. Alcona to J. Brenzaida ¹

Cold in the earth, and the deep snow piled above thee!
Far, far removed, cold in the dreary grave!
Have I forgot, my Only Love, to love thee,
Severed at last by Time's all-wearing wave?

5 Now, when alone, do my thoughts no longer hover
Over the mountains on Angora's shore;
Resting their wings where heath and fern-leaves cover
That noble heart for ever, ever more?

Cold in the earth, and fifteen wild Decembers
10 From those brown hills have melted into spring—
Faithful indeed is the spirit that remembers
After such years of change and suffering!

Sweet Love of youth, forgive if I forget thee
While the World's tide is bearing me along:
15 Sterner desires and darker hopes beset me,
Hopes which obscure but cannot do thee wrong.

7. Foolish. "Fancy": imagination.
1. Rosina Alcona is another name for A. G. A., the heroine of the Gondal stories. C. W. Hatfield sug-

gests that Brenzaida may be A. G. A.'s first love as well as her last husband. Here he is deceased.

No other Sun has lightened up my heaven;
No other Star has ever shone for me:
All my life's bliss from thy dear life was given—
20 All my life's bliss is in the grave with thee.

But when the days of golden dreams had perished
And even Despair was powerless to destroy,
Then did I learn how existence could be cherished,
Strengthened and fed without the aid of joy;

25 Then did I check the tears of useless passion,
Weaned my young soul from yearning after thine;
Sternly denied its burning wish to hasten
Down to that tomb already more than mine!

And even yet, I dare not let it languish,
30 Dare not indulge in Memory's rapturous pain;
Once drinking deep of that divinest anguish,
How could I seek the empty world again?

March 3, 1845 1846

[Ah! why, because the dazzling sun]

Ah! why, because the dazzling sun
Restored my earth to joy
Have you[1] departed, every one,
And left a desert[2] sky?

5 All through the night, your glorious eyes
Were gazing down in mine,
And with a full heart's thankful sighs
I blessed that watch divine!

I was at peace, and drank your beams
10 As they were life to me
And revelled in my changeful dreams
Like petrel[3] on the sea.

Thought followed thought—star followed star
Through boundless regions on,
15 While one sweet influence, near and far,
Thrilled through and proved us one.

Why did the morning rise to break
So great, so pure a spell,
And scorch with fire the tranquil cheek
20 Where your cool radiance fell?

1. The speaker addresses the stars. 3. Seabirds.
2. Deserted.

Blood-red he[4] rose, and arrow-straight
His fierce beams struck my brow:
The soul of Nature sprang elate,
But mine sank sad and low!

25 My lids closed down—yet through their veil
I saw him blazing still;
And bathe in gold the misty dale,
And flash upon the hill.

I turned me to the pillow then
30 To call back Night, and see
Your worlds of solemn light, again
Throb with my heart and me!

It would not do—the pillow glowed
And glowed both roof and floor,
35 And birds sang loudly in the wood,
And fresh winds shook the door.

The curtains waved, the wakened flies
Were murmuring round my room,
Imprisoned there, till I should rise
40 And give them leave to roam.

O Stars and Dreams and Gentle Night;
O Night and Stars return!
And hide me from the hostile light
That does not warm, but burn—

45 That drains the blood of suffering men;
Drinks tears, instead of dew:
Let me sleep through his blinding reign,
And only wake with you!

April 14, 1845 1846

The Prisoner

A *Fragment*

In the dungeon crypts[1] idly did I stray,
Reckless of the lives wasting there away;
"Draw the ponderous bars! open, Warder stern!"
He dared not say me nay—the hinges harshly turn.

5 "Our guests are darkly lodged," I whispered, gazing through
The vault, whose grated eye showed heaven more gray than blue

4. The sun.
1. Underground vaults. The speaker, a man, is wandering through the dungeon in the castle of his father.

(This was when glad Spring laughed in awaking pride);
"Aye, darkly lodged enough!" returned my sullen guide.

Then, God forgive my youth! forgive my careless tongue!
10 I scoffed, as the chill chains on the damp flagstones rung:
"Confined in triple walls, art thou so much to fear,
That we must bind thee down and clench thy fetters here?"

The captive raised her face; it was as soft and mild
As sculptured marble saint; or slumbering unweaned child;
15 It was so soft and mild, it was so sweet and fair,
Pain could not trace a line, or grief a shadow there!

The captive raised her hand and pressed it to her brow;
"I have been struck," she said, "and I am suffering now;
Yet these are little worth, your bolts and irons strong:
20 And, were they forged in steel, they could not hold me long."

Hoarse laughed the jailor grim: "Shall I be won to hear;
Dost think, fond,² dreaming wretch, that I shall grant thy prayer?
Or, better still, wilt melt my master's heart with groans?
Ah! sooner might the sun thaw down these granite stones.

25 "My master's voice is low, his aspect bland and kind,
But hard as hardest flint the soul that lurks behind;
And I am rough and rude, yet not more rough to see
Than is the hidden ghost³ that has its home in me."

About her lips there played a smile of almost scorn.
30 "My friend," she gently said, "you have not heard me mourn;
When you my kindred's lives, my lost life can restore,
Then may I weep and sue—but never, friend, before!

"Still, let my tyrants know, I am not doomed to wear
Year after year in gloom, and desolate despair;
35 A messenger of Hope comes every night to me,
And offers for short life, eternal liberty.

"He comes with western winds, with evening's wandering airs,
With that clear dusk of heaven that brings the thickest stars,
Winds take a pensive tone, and stars a tender fire,
40 And visions rise, and change, that kill me with desire.

"Desire for nothing known in my maturer years,
When Joy grew mad with awe, at counting future tears.
When, if my spirit's sky was full of flashes warm,
I knew not whence they came, from sun or thunderstorm.

2. Foolish. 3. Soul.

45 "But, first, a hush of peace—a soundless calm descends;
The struggle of distress and fierce impatience ends;
Mute music soothes my breast—unuttered harmony,
That I could never dream, till Earth was lost to me.

"Then dawns the Invisible; the Unseen its truth reveals;
50 My outward sense is gone, my inward essence feels:
Its wings are almost free—its home, its harbor found,
Measuring the gulf, it stoops—and dares the final bound.

"Oh! dreadful is the check—intense the agony—
When the ear begins to hear, and the eye begins to see;
55 When the pulse begins to throb, the brain to think again;
The soul to feel the flesh, and the flesh to feel the chain.

"Yet I would lose no sting, would wish no torture less;
The more that anguish racks, the earlier it will bless;
And robed in fires of hell, or bright with heavenly shine,
60 If it but herald death, the vision is divine!"

She ceased to speak, and we, unanswering, turned to go—
We had no further power to work the captive woe:
Her cheek, her gleaming eye, declared that man had given
A sentence, unapproved, and overruled by Heaven.

October 9, 1845 1846

[No coward soul is mine][1]

No coward soul is mine
No trembler in the world's storm-troubled sphere
I see Heaven's glories shine
And Faith shines equal arming me from Fear

5 O God within my breast
Almighty ever-present Deity
Life, that in me hast rest
As I Undying Life, have power in Thee

Vain are the thousand creeds
10 That move men's hearts, unutterably vain,
Worthless as withered weeds
Or idlest froth amid the boundless main

To waken doubt in one
Holding so fast by thy infinity
15 So surely anchored on
The steadfast rock of Immortality

1. The following are the last lines my sister Emily ever wrote [Charlotte Brontë's note].

With wide-embracing love
Thy spirit animates eternal years
Pervades and broods above,
20 Changes, sustains, dissolves, creates and rears

Though Earth and moon were gone
And suns and universes ceased to be
And thou wert left alone
Every Existence would exist in thee

25 There is not room for Death
Nor atom that his might could render void
Since thou art Being and Breath
And what thou art may never be destroyed.

January 2, 1846 1850

Stanzas[1]

Often rebuked, yet always back returning
 To those first feelings that were born with me,
And leaving busy chase of wealth and learning
 For idle dreams of things which cannot be:

5 To-day, I will seek not the shadowy region;[2]
 Its unsustaining vastness waxes drear;
And visions rising, legion after legion,
 Bring the unreal world too strangely near.

I'll walk, but not in old heroic traces,[3]
10 And not in paths of high morality,
And not among the half-distinguished faces,
 The clouded forms of long-past history.

I'll walk where my own nature would be leading:
 It vexes[4] me to choose another guide:
15 Where the gray flocks in ferny glens are feeding;
 Where the wild wind blows on the mountain side.

What have those lonely mountains worth revealing?
 More glory and more grief than I can tell:
The earth that wakes *one* human heart to feeling
20 Can center both the worlds of Heaven and Hell.

 1850

1. As no manuscript exists for this poem, there is some speculation that Charlotte may have written it instead of Emily; however, the poem seems to summarize much of Emily's characteristic vision.
2. The shadowy world of the imagination, specif-
ically the private myth of Gondal.
3. Paths or, alternatively, straps that form a harness.
4. Provokes.

GEORGE ELIOT
1819–1880

Known as Mary Anne, Mary Ann, and Marian Evans to her family, "Clematis" (meaning mental beauty) to a youthful friend, "Deutera" (which *means* second and *sounds* a little like daughter") to her first scholarly mentor, Mrs. Lewes to her correspondents, "Our Lady" to the women she considered her spiritual daughters, "Mutter" to her adopted sons, and Mrs. John W. Cross to her eulogists, one of the most celebrated sages of Victorian England was best known to the reading public as "George Eliot." By adopting this name, she paid tribute to the man who nurtured her literary efforts, George Henry Lewes, but she also placed herself in a tradition that goes back to George Sand (Aurore Dupin Dudevant) and the Bells (the Brontës). It was the name George Eliot that her readers associated with the blend of compassion, wisdom, and humor that characterizes the omniscient voice of her novels. However, as Ruby Redinger has demonstrated in her biography, the very proliferation of feminine names by which Eliot was known dramatizes the problem she had to solve when she began to publish fiction under a male pseudonym at the age of thirty-eight. Although she would eventually attain the appropriate distinction of being represented in the English Men of Letters series, Eliot was aware that her identification with masculine achievement threatened to undermine her consciousness of herself as a woman: a talented but embittered female artist in Eliot's last novel exclaims, "You may try, but you cannot imagine what it is to have a man's force of genius in you, yet to suffer the slavery of being a girl." Nevertheless, one of Eliot's greatest accomplishments may have been her dramatization of just this contradiction.

In Eliot's most autobiographical novel, *The Mill on the Floss* (1860), Maggie Tulliver's acute sense of her own female "slavery" reflects some of the early frustration that resulted in the headaches, depressions, and sensitivity toward cold that Eliot suffered all of her adult life. Maggie's imaginative curiosity earns, from an otherwise affectionate father, the sardonic comment that "an over-'cute [over-acute] woman's no better nor a long-tailed sheep—she'll fetch none the bigger price for that." While Eliot's father was more prosperous as a farmer and agent for a neighboring estate than the miller who is Maggie's father, Robert Evans was just as traditional in his support of the Church of England, the Tory Party, and their implicitly conservative assumptions about the appropriate sphere of women. Maggie's mother, Mrs. Tulliver, seems more attached to her son, and even to her monographed linen, than to her daughter, just as Eliot always believed her own mother favored her older brother, Isaac. Similarly, in *The Mill on the Floss*, the sister who is destined never to receive the affection she craves from her brother associates her emotional deprivation with Lucy Dean, the conventionally pretty cousin who is as neat as Maggie is messy, as obedient as Maggie is rebellious; in Eliot's childhood this role was played by her older sister Chrissey. From her depiction of Maggie's angry torturing of her doll to her portrayal of the girl's voracious reading and her running away to become queen of the Gypsies, Eliot dramatizes the "hunger of the heart" for sympathy it never receives. Maggie's warring impulses—her desire for intellectual stimulation as opposed to her dutiful efforts at renunciation—reflect Eliot's own self-division as well as her awareness of the constraints of provincial life.

Yet looking backward on provincial life remained the motivating impulse and subject of most of Eliot's fiction. Her nostalgia for the everyday scenes of the preindustrial past turned them into "the mother tongue of our imagination," but what she herself humorously portrayed as the shrewd narrow-mindedness of rural characters was precisely what hindered her own development. From the age of five, Eliot attended three different schools, making friends with at least one headmistress, Maria Lewis. From the time she left school at fifteen, when her mother died, until she was thirty, when

her father died, however, she was hampered by the household and nursing duties she assiduously performed. At home, she continued to study Italian, German, and music, corresponding frequently with Miss Lewis, who developed an evangelical strain of puritanism in the young girl. Only when Isaac married and she moved with her father from Griff to a house in Coventry did Eliot begin to find acquaintances who would pose challenging philosophic questions to her.

People such as Charles Bray, the author of *The Philosophy of Necessity* (1841), and his wife, Caroline (Hennell) Bray, whose brother wrote *An Inquiry Concerning the Origin of Christianity* (1838), encouraged Eliot's intellectual development, which issued in a typically Victorian crisis of faith. After a painful struggle, she renounced traditional Christianity, but she could make peace with her father only by promising to accompany him to church on Sundays. During this time, she completed her first major translation, David Friedrich Strauss's *Das Leben Jesu* (*The Life of Jesus*, 1846). Published anonymously, it contributed, as did her other translations, to the belief that animated her subsequent fiction, "that the idea of God, so far as it has been a highly spiritual influence, is the ideal of a goodness entirely human." The struggle with her spiritual Father was an index of her struggle with her own father, whose death evoked contradictory responses: "What shall I be without my father?" Eliot mused during his dying. "It will seem as if part of my moral nature were gone. I had a vision of myself last night becoming earthly sensual and devilish for want of that purifying restraining influence." Retrospectively, however, her comment that his dying days were "the happiest" of her life indicates some intimation that his death meant her release.

After a recuperative trip to Switzerland, Eliot was introduced by the Brays to John Chapman, editor of the *Westminster Review,* and she moved to London, where she worked hard to become a member of the literary establishment. As assistant editor of the *Westminster,* she corresponded and negotiated with authors, read proofs, and wrote reviews of philosophic and religious books. She met such eminent Victorians as Charles Dickens, James Froude, Harriet Martineau, John Stuart Mill, and, most important, the philosopher Herbert Spencer. As the biographer Gordon Haight has demonstrated, her earlier propensity to glorify a father figure to whom she could dedicate her labor now meant that she did not receive the credit she deserved for turning the *Westminster* into one of England's leading reviews. Ensconced in Chapman's household, she found herself contending with his jealous wife and his mistress. In the presence of Chapman and Spencer, moreover, she became even more acutely self-conscious about what Hallam Tennyson would call her "strong masculine face."

This painful but stimulating period was ended when Spencer introduced Eliot to the writer and editor George Henry Lewes, a married man who had separated from his wife. After they began seeing each other, they made the highly unconventional decision to live together, despite the fact that Lewes could not obtain a divorce. Although she faced the censure not only of her brother, Isaac, but also of polite London society, Eliot went off to the Continent in 1854 to begin life with Lewes as an unmarried wife. No wonder, then, that she objected to the plot of *Jane Eyre,* specifically to Jane's refusal to live with the married Rochester: "All self-sacrifice is good," she characteristically conceded, "but one would like it to be in a somewhat nobler cause than a diabolical law which chains a man body and soul to a putrifying carcass." The number of those who refused to visit the woman who returned to London calling herself "Marian Lewes" should not be minimized: even so tolerant a writer as Mrs. Gaskell wrote to her, "I wish you *were* Mrs. Lewes."

By 1856 Eliot was clearly assessing the current state of fiction, specifically condemning "silly novels" by "lady novelists." In the *Westminster Review,* she asked, "Why can we not have pictures of religious life among the industrial classes in England, as interesting as Mrs. Stowe's pictures of religious life among the Negroes?" Not to be discounted in considering Eliot's late productivity is the intellectual stimulation that Lewes's own work supplied: a versatile physiologist, biographer, novelist, essayist, and

editor, he was the author of a *Biographical History of Philosophy* (1854–56) and an article titled "The Lady Novelists" (1852). It was he who encouraged her to compose and publish her first stories in *Blackwood's* "Maga," which were collected in *Scenes of Clerical Life* (1858). Here, as so often, her title was deceptive, for these three stories actually focus on three female characters: a patient but dying wife-mother, a foreign girl goaded into murderous rage by a faithless lover, and a woman who, having been physically abused by her husband, takes refuge in alcohol.

Lewes had believed that "people would have sniffed" at Eliot's first novel, *Adam Bede* (1859), "if they had known the writer to be a woman," and its instant success did place George Eliot in the ranks of major novelists such as Dickens and Thackeray. Even after her true identity became known, Lewes continued to protect her career, writing letters for her to publishers, keeping back unfavorable reviews that would have troubled her, and suggesting certain scenes for novels in progress. Because Lewes and Eliot had to support themselves and his three sons through their writing, they welcomed the £12,000 *Adam Bede* brought. *Silas Marner* (1861) was so popular that her publisher, Blackwood, had to double the original edition of four thousand copies within a month after publication. By this time Eliot had become a careful businesswoman who negotiated herself for the £7,000 she received for *Romola* (1863).

How are the private lives of men and women related to the public issues of culture and society? This question was the recurrent subject of Eliot's mature novels: *Felix Holt* (1866), *Middlemarch* (1871–72), and *Daniel Deronda* (1874–76). Perhaps *Middlemarch*, with its subtitle, *A Study of Provincial Life*, best exemplifies Eliot's panoramic range. Set in the 1830s, with its aristocratic landlords and clergymen, its middle-class bankers and doctors, and its working-class grocers and horse dealers, the novel insists on the complex interrelationships between the sexes and the classes by developing a metaphor of a web or labyrinth and even by elaborating an image of the multitudinous scratches on the surface of a pier glass (a mirror): "place now against it a lighted candle as a centre of illumination, and lo! the scratches will seem to arrange themselves in a fine series of concentric circles round that little sun." Eliot explained that this "parable" signifies the egoism produced by any single perspective, the "flattering illusion" of a concentric arrangement of events that both delights and deludes. For her narrator, who studies this "exclusive optical selection" with patient omniscience, the novel becomes a philosophic study of domestic incompatibility and religious hypocrisy, political discord and legal intrigue. As a composite of the novel's chorus of characters, the narrator maintains a tolerant tone and sympathetic stance that assume that even the most common lives illustrate how "the growing good of the world is partly dependent on unhistoric acts."

Of course the unhistoric acts of Eliot's heroine, Dorothea Brooke, play a central role in *Middlemarch*. As the critic Barbara Hardy has observed, the heroines of all of Eliot's novels share "the *ex-officio* disability of being a woman." For Dorothea, as for the others, this disability is associated with ignorance, the absence of a vocation, and the desire for knowledge "such as great men know." Married to an aging scholar because she wishes to become wise herself in order to do good works, Dorothea discovers not only that she cannot learn from her husband, the author of the projected *Key to All Mythologies*, but that he is hardly wise himself. Thus she becomes a "foundress of nothing," for Eliot consistently denied her heroines the worldly success she herself achieved. Yet, through her suffering, Dorothea attains the growth in sympathy that is always an index of ethical maturity in Eliot's world. For a contemporary like Emily Dickinson, Eliot's achievement was monumental: "What do I think of *Middlemarch*? What do I think of glory?" she wrote, adding that "the mysteries of human nature surpass the 'mysteries of redemption.' "

When Lewes died in 1878, Eliot went into mourning. Previously, in times of stress she had relied on a succession of close female friends: Maria Lewis, Sara Hennell, Barbara Smith Bodichon, and Edith Simcox. But if Eliot felt that her pseudonym

encoded her special dependency on Lewes ("To L—— I owe it"), then she must have known that no one could take his place and that her writing career was over. Yet, on May 6, 1880, much to her friends' surprise and dismay, Eliot announced her marriage to John Walter Cross. More than twenty years her junior, he had met her in 1867 when he was traveling on the Continent with his mother. The marriage ended seven months after the wedding, when Eliot died. Cross used her letters to write the first and most laudatory of her biographies, but in spite of his efforts, the next generation of readers considered Eliot's fiction too moralistic, earnest, and diffuse. Women writers from Eliza Linton and Mrs. Oliphant to Katherine Mansfield envied the protection Eliot had received from Lewes, but they distrusted her assumption of masculine superiority. Nevertheless, by integrating philosophy and fiction, Eliot exerted a profound influence on the shape of the novel as it was developed by writers as diverse as Henry James, D. H. Lawrence, and Margaret Drabble.

The selections printed here represent two different aspects of Eliot's career. The essay "Silly Novels by Lady Novelists" (1856), which was published anonymously in the *Westminster Review*, illuminates her attitudes toward gender and genre at the start of her literary career. The short story "The Lifted Veil" (1859), which appeared anonymously in *Blackwood's*, reflects her reaction to the lifting of her own veil of anonymity when the public was discovering her identity. Eccentric though it is in her oeuvre, the tale questions the ideal of sympathetic identification Eliot usually espoused, for, as a surrogate of the author, Latimer experiences nothing but pain from the telepathy that reveals to him the subjectivity of others. "The Lifted Veil" also extends the tradition of female Gothic established in Shelley's "The Mortal Immortal" and Brontë's *Jane Eyre*.

Silly Novels by Lady Novelists[1]

Silly Novels by Lady Novelists are a genus with many species, determined by the particular quality of silliness that predominates in them—the frothy, the prosy, the pious, or the pedantic. But it is a mixture of all these—a composite order of feminine fatuity, that produces the largest class of such novels, which we shall distinguish as the *mind-and-millinery* species. The heroine is usually an heiress, probably a peeress in her own right, with perhaps a vicious baronet, an amiable duke, and an irresistible younger son of a marquis as lovers in the foreground, a clergyman and a poet sighing for her in the middle distance, and a crowd of undefined adorers dimly indicated beyond. Her eyes and her wit are both dazzling; her nose and her morals are alike free from any tendency to irregularity; she has a superb *contralto* and a superb intellect; she is perfectly well-dressed and perfectly religious; she dances like a sylph,[2] and reads the Bible in the original tongues. Or it may be that the heroine is not an heiress—that rank and wealth are the only things in which she is deficient; but she infallibly gets into high society, she has the triumph of refusing many matches and securing the best, and she wears some family jewels or other as a sort of crown of righteousness at the end. Rakish men either bite their lips in impotent confusion at her repartees, or are touched to penitence by her reproofs, which, on appropriate occasions, rise to a lofty strain of rhetoric; indeed, there is a general propensity in her

1. Published anonymously in the *Westminster Review*.

2. An elemental being that inhabits the air.

to make speeches, and to rhapsodize at some length when she retires to her bedroom. In her recorded conversations she is amazingly eloquent, and in her unrecorded conversations, amazingly witty. She is understood to have a depth of insight that looks through and through the shallow theories of philosophers, and her superior instincts are a sort of dial by which men have only to set their clocks and watches, and all will go well. The men play a very subordinate part by her side. You are consoled now and then by a hint that they have affairs, which keeps you in mind that the working-day business of the world is somehow being carried on, but ostensibly the final cause of their existence is that they may accompany the heroine on her "starring" expedition through life. They see her at a ball, and are dazzled; at a flower-show, and they are fascinated; on a riding excursion, and they are witched[3] by her noble horsemanship; at church, and they are awed by the sweet solemnity of her demeanour. She is the ideal woman in feelings, faculties, and flounces. For all this, she as often as not marries the wrong person to begin with, and she suffers terribly from the plots and intrigues of the vicious baronet; but even death has a soft place in his heart for such a paragon, and remedies all mistakes for her just at the right moment. The vicious baronet is sure to be killed in a duel, and the tedious husband dies in his bed requesting his wife, as a particular favour to him, to marry the man she loves best, and having already dispatched a note to the lover informing him of the comfortable arrangement. Before matters arrive at this desirable issue our feelings are tried by seeing the noble, lovely, and gifted heroine pass through many *mauvais moments*,[4] but we have the satisfaction of knowing that her sorrows are wept into embroidered pocket-handkerchiefs, that her fainting from reclines on the very best upholstery, and that whatever vicissitudes she may undergo, from being dashed out of her carriage to having her head shaved in a fever, she comes out of them all with a complexion more blooming and locks more redundant[5] than ever.

We may remark, by the way, that we have been relieved from a serious scruple by discovering that silly novels by lady novelists rarely introduce us into any other than very lofty and fashionable society. We had imagined that destitute women turned novelists, as they turned governesses, because they had no other "lady-like" means of getting their bread. On this supposition, vacillating syntax and improbable incident had a certain pathos for us, like the extremely supererogatory pincushions and ill-devised nightcaps that are offered for sale by a blind man. We felt the commodity to be a nuisance, but we were glad to think that the money went to relieve the necessitous, and we pictured to ourselves lonely women struggling for a maintenance, or wives and daughters devoting themselves to the production of "copy" out of pure heroism,—perhaps to pay their husband's debts, or to purchase luxuries for a sick father. Under these impressions we shrank from criticising a lady's novel: her English might be faulty, but, we said to ourselves, her motives are irreproachable; her imagination may be uninventive, but her patience is untiring. Empty writing was excused by an empty stomach, and twaddle was consecrated by tears. But no! This theory of ours, like many other pretty theories, has had to give way before observation. Women's silly novels, we

3. Bewitched.
4. Bad moments (French).

5. Copious.

are now convinced, are written under totally different circumstances. The fair writers have evidently never talked to a tradesman except from a carriage window; they have no notion of the working-classes except as "dependents;" they think five hundred a-year a miserable pittance; Belgravia[6] and "baronial halls" are their primary truths; and they have no idea of feeling interest in any man who is not at least a great landed proprietor, if not a prime minister. It is clear that they write in elegant boudoirs, with violet-colored ink and a ruby pen; that they must be entirely indifferent to publishers' accounts, and inexperienced in every form of poverty except poverty of brains. It is true that we are constantly struck with the want of verisimilitude in their representations of the high society in which they seem to live; but then they betray no closer acquaintance with any other form of life. If their peers and peeresses are improbable, their literary men, tradespeople, and cottagers are impossible; and their intellect seems to have the peculiar impartiality of reproducing both what they *have* seen and heard, and what they have *not* seen and heard, with equal unfaithfulness.

* * *

Writers of the mind-and-millinery school are remarkably unanimous in their choice of diction. In their novels, there is usually a lady or gentleman who is more or less of a upas tree:[7] the lover has a manly breast; minds are redolent of various things; hearts are hollow; events are utilized; friends are consigned to the tomb; infancy is an engaging period; the sun is a luminary that goes to his western couch, or gathers the rain-drops into his refulgent bosom; life is a melancholy boon; Albion and Scotia[8] are conversational epithets. There is a striking resemblance, too, in the character of their moral comments, such, for instance, as that "It is a fact, no less true than melancholy, that all people, more or less, richer or poorer, are swayed by bad example;" that "Books, however trivial, contain some subjects from which useful information may be drawn;" that "Vice can too often borrow the language of virtue;" that "Merit and nobility of nature must exist, to be accepted, for clamour and pretension cannot impose upon those too well read in human nature to be easily deceived;" and that, "In order to forgive, we must have been injured." There is, doubtless, a class of readers to whom these remarks appear peculiarly pointed and pungent; for we often find them doubly and trebly scored with the pencil, and delicate hands giving in their determined adhesion to these hardy novelties by a distinct *très vrai*,[9] emphasized by many notes of exclamation. The colloquial style of these novels is often marked by much ingenious inversion, and a careful avoidance of such cheap phraseology as can be heard every day. Angry young gentlemen exclaim—" 'Tis ever thus, methinks;" and in the half-hour before dinner a young lady informs her next neighbour that the first day she read Shakespeare she "stole away into the park, and beneath the shadow of the greenwood tree, devoured with rapture the inspired page of the great magician." But the most remarkable efforts of the mind-and-millinery writers lie in their philosophic reflections. The authoress of "Laura Gay,"[1] for example, having

6. A fashionable and well-to-do neighborhood in London.
7. I.e., a poisonous influence; according to legend, this tree, native to Java, killed all life around it (in fact, its sap can be used to make poison).

8. Poetic names for England and Scotland.
9. Very true (French).
1. An 1856 novel by Laura Gay, which Eliot has satirized in the previous section.

married her hero and heroine, improves the event by observing that "if those sceptics, whose eyes have so long gazed on matter that they can no longer see aught else in man, could once enter with heart and soul into such bliss as this, they would come to say that the soul of man and the polypus[2] are not of common origin, or of the same texture." Lady novelists, it appears, can see something else besides matter; they are not limited to phenomena, but can relieve their eyesight by occasional glimpses of the *noumenon,*[3] and are, therefore, naturally better able than any one else to confound sceptics, even of that remarkable, but to us unknown school, which maintains that the soul of man is of the same texture as the polypus.

The most pitiable of all silly novels by lady novelists are what we may call the *oracular* species—novels intended to expound the writer's religious, philosophical, or moral theories. There seems to be a notion abroad among women, rather akin to the superstition that the speech and actions of idiots are inspired, and that the human being most entirely exhausted of common sense is the fittest vehicle of revelation. To judge from their writings, there are certain ladies who think that an amazing ignorance, both of science and of life, is the best possible qualification for forming an opinion on the knottiest moral and speculative questions. Apparently, their recipe for solving all such difficulties is something like this:—Take a woman's head, stuff it with a smattering of philosophy and literature chopped small, and with false notions of society baked hard, let it hang over a desk a few hours every day, and serve up hot in feeble English, when not required. You will rarely meet with a lady novelist of the oracular class who is diffident of her ability to decide on theological questions,—who has any suspicion that she is not capable of discriminating with the nicest[4] accuracy between the good and evil in all church parties,—who does not see precisely how it is that men have gone wrong hitherto,—and pity philosophers in general that they have not had the opportunity of consulting her. Great writers, who have modestly contented themselves with putting their experience into fiction, and have thought it quite a sufficient task to exhibit men and things as they are, she sighs over as deplorably deficient in the application of their powers. "They have solved no great questions"—and she is ready to remedy their omission by setting before you a complete theory of life and manual of divinity, in a love story, where ladies and gentlemen of good family go through genteel vicissitudes, to the utter confusion of Deists, Puseyites,[5] and ultra-Protestants, and to the perfect establishment of that particular view of Christianity which either condenses itself into a sentence of small caps, or explodes into a cluster of stars on the three hundred and thirtieth page. It is true, the ladies and gentlemen will probably seem to you remarkably little like any you have had the fortune or misfortune to meet with, for, as a general rule, the ability of a lady novelist to describe actual life and her fellow-men, is in inverse proportion to her confident eloquence about God and the other world, and the means by which she usually chooses to conduct you to true ideas of the invisible is a totally false picture of the visible.

2. Polyp.
3. That which is apprehended by thought (as opposed to things perceived by the senses, or phenomena).
4. Most strict or precise.
5. I.e., members of the Oxford Movement, which sought to revive certain Roman Catholic doctrines and rituals within the Anglican Church; the English theologian Edward Pusey (1800–1882) was one of its leaders. "Deists": those who found evidence for the existence of God in nature, rejected the supernatural, and avoided formal religion.

* * *

The epithet "silly" may seem impertinent, applied to a novel which indicates so much reading and intellectual activity as "The Enigma;"[6] but we use this epithet advisedly. If, as the world has long agreed, a very great amount of instruction will not make a wise man, still less will a very mediocre amount of instruction make a wise woman. And the most mischievous form of feminine silliness is the literary form, because it tends to confirm the popular prejudice against the more solid education of women. When men see girls wasting their time in consultations about bonnets and ball dresses, and in giggling or sentimental love-confidences, or middle-aged women mismanaging their children, and solacing themselves with acrid gossip, they can hardly help saying, "For Heaven's sake, let girls be better educated; let them have some better objects of thought—some more solid occupations." But after a few hours' conversation with an oracular literary woman, or a few hours' reading of her books, they are likely enough to say, "After all, when a woman gets some knowledge, see what use she makes of it! Her knowledge remains acquisition, instead of passing into culture; instead of being subdued into modesty and simplicity by a larger acquaintance with thought and fact, she has a feverish consciousness of her attainments; she keeps a sort of mental pocket-mirror, and is continually looking in it at her own 'intellectuality;' she spoils the taste of one's muffin by questions of metaphysics; 'puts down' men at a dinner table with her superior information; and seizes the opportunity of a *soirée* to catechise us on the vital question of the relation between mind and matter. And then, look at her writings! She mistakes vagueness for depth, bombast for eloquence, and affectation for originality; she struts on one page, rolls her eyes on another, grimaces in a third, and is hysterical in a fourth. She may have read many writings of great men, and a few writings of great women; but she is as unable to discern the difference between her own style and theirs as a Yorkshireman is to discern the difference between his own English and a Londoner's: rhodomontade[7] is the native accent of her intellect. No—the average nature of women is too shallow and feeble a soil to bear much tillage; it is only fit for the very lightest crops."

It is true that the men who come to such a decision on such very superficial and imperfect observation may not be among the wisest in the world; but we have not now to contest their opinion—we are only pointing out how it is unconsciously encouraged by many women who have volunteered themselves as representatives of the feminine intellect. We do not believe that a man was ever strengthened in such an opinion by associating with a woman of true culture, whose mind had absorbed her knowledge instead of being absorbed by it. A really cultured women, like a really cultured woman, like a really cultured man, is all the simpler and the less obtrusive for her knowledge; it has made her see herself and her opinions in something like just proportions; she does not make it a pedestal from which she flatters herself that she commands a complete view of men and things, but makes it a point of observation from which to form a right estimate of herself. She neither spouts poetry nor quotes Cicero[8] on slight provocation; not because she

6. *The Enigma: A Leaf from the Archives of Wolchorley House* (1856), an anonymously published novel just ridiculed by Eliot.
7. Inflated language, ranting. A Yorkshireman,

speaking dialect, is assumed to be unable to perceive the greater refinement and purity of a Londoner's speech.
8. Roman statesman and orator (106–43 B.C.E.).

thinks that a sacrifice must be made to the prejudices of men, but because that mode of exhibiting her memory and Latinity does not present itself to her as edifying or graceful. She does not write books to confound philosophers, perhaps because she is able to write books that delight them. In conversation she is the least formidable of women, because she understands you, without wanting to make you aware that you *can't* understand her. She does not give you information, which is the raw material of culture,—she gives you sympathy, which is its subtlest essence.

A more numerous class of silly novels than the oracular, (which are generally inspired by some form of High Church, or transcendental Christianity,) is what we may call the *white neck-cloth* species, which represent the tone of thought and feeling in the Evangelical party. This species is a kind of genteel tract on a large scale, intended as a sort of medicinal sweetmeat for Low Church young ladies; and Evangelical substitute for the fashionable novel, as the May Meetings[9] are a substitute for the Opera. Even Quaker children, one would think, can hardly have been denied the indulgence of a doll; but it must be a doll dressed in a drab gown and a coal-scuttle bonnet—not a worldly doll, in gauze and spangles. And there are no young ladies, we imagine,—unless they belong to the Church of the United Brethren, in which people are married without any love-making—who can dispense with love stories. Thus, for Evangelical young ladies there are Evangelical love stories, in which the vicissitudes of the tender passion are sanctified by saving views of Regeneration and the Atonement. These novels differ from the oracular ones, as a Low Churchwoman often differs from a High Churchwoman: they are a little less supercilious, and a great deal more ignorant, a little less correct in their syntax, and a great deal more vulgar.

The Orlando of Evangelical literature is the young curate, looked at from the point of view of the middle class, where cambric bands[1] are understood to have as thrilling an effect on the hearts of young ladies as epaulettes have in the classes above and below it. In the ordinary type of these novels, the hero is almost sure to be a young curate, frowned upon, perhaps, by worldly mammas, but carrying captive the hearts of their daughters, who can "never forget *that* sermon;" tender glances are seized from the pulpit stairs instead of the opera-box; *tête-à-têtes* are seasoned with quotations from Scripture, instead of quotations from the poets; and questions as to the state of the heroine's affections are mingled with anxieties as to the state of her soul. The young curate always has a background of well-dressed and wealthy, if not fashionable society;—for Evangelical silliness is as snobbish as any other kind of silliness; and the Evangelical lady novelist, while she explains to you the type of the scapegoat on one page, is ambitious on another to represent the manners and conversation of aristocratic people. Her pictures of fashionable society are often curious studies considered as efforts of the Evangelical imagination; but in one particular the novels of the White Neck-cloth School are meritoriously realistic,—their favourite hero, the Evangelical young curate, is always rather an insipid personage.

9. The annual spring meetings of the Church of England's Missionary Society; High Church Anglicans sympathized with the Oxford Movement, while Low Church Anglicans emphasized evangelical principles over ritual and ceremony.

1. The linen strips hanging down one's front, as part of clerical dress (as epaulettes are part of a military uniform). "Orlando": i.e., the romantic hero (from the character in Shakespeare's *As You Like it*).

* * *

But, perhaps, the least readable of silly women's novels, are the *modern-antique* species, which unfold to us the domestic life of Jannes and Jambres, the private love affairs of Sennacherib, or the mental struggles and ultimate conversion of Demetrius the silversmith.[2] From most silly novels we can at least extract a laugh; but those of the modern antique school have a ponderous, a leaden kind of fatuity, under which we groan. What can be more demonstrative of the inability of literary women to measure their own powers, than their frequent assumption of a task which can only be justified by the rarest concurrence of acquirement with genius? The finest effort to reanimate the past is of course only approximative—is always more or less an infusion of the modern spirit into the ancient form,—

> Was ihr den Geist der Zeiten heisst,
> Das ist im Grund der Herren eigner Geist,
> In dem die Zeiten sich bespiegeln.[3]

Admitting that genius which has familiarized itself with all the relics of an ancient period can sometimes, by the force of its sympathetic divination, restore the missing notes in the "music of humanity," and reconstruct the fragments into a whole which will really bring the remote past nearer to us, and interpret it to our duller apprehension,—this form of imaginative power must always be among the very rarest, because it demands as much accurate and minute knowledge as creative vigour. Yet we find ladies constantly choosing to make their mental mediocrity more conspicuous, by clothing it in a masquerade of ancient names; by putting their feeble sentimentality into the mouths of Roman vestals or Egyptian princesses, and attributing their rhetorical arguments to Jewish high-priests and Greek philosophers. * * *

"Be not a baker if your head be made of butter," says a homely proverb, which, being interpreted, may mean, let no woman rush into print who is not prepared for the consequences. We are aware that our remarks are in a very different tone from that of the reviewers who, with a perennial recurrence of precisely similar emotions, only paralleled, we imagine, in the experience of monthly nurses,[4] tell one lady novelist after another that they "hail" her productions "with delight." We are aware that the ladies at whom our criticism is pointed are accustomed to be told, in the choicest phraseology of puffery, that their pictures of life are brilliant, their characters well drawn, their style fascinating, and their sentiments lofty. But if they are inclined to resent our plainness of speech, we ask them to reflect for a moment on the chary praise, and often captious blame, which their panegyrists give to writers whose works are on the way to become classics. No sooner does a woman show that she has genius or effective talent, than she receives the tribute of being moderately praised and severely criticised. By a peculiar thermometric adjustment, when a woman's talent is at zero, journalistic approbation is at the boiling pitch; when she attains mediocrity, it is already at no more than

2. Demetrius roused his fellow craftsmen against Paul, whose presence in Ephesus, home of a major temple of Diana, was hurting their business of making silver shrines for the goddess (Acts 19.24–27). Jannes and Jambres were Egyptian magicians who stood against Moses at Pharaoh's court (2 Timothy 3.8). Sennacherib was a king of Assyria,

ruling from 704 to 681 B.C.E.
3. What they call the spirit of the age/Is at the base the gentlemen's own spirit,/In which the ages are reflected (German); Goethe's *Faust*, part I (1808), lines 577–79.
4. Women hired to nurse infants.

summer heat; and if ever she reaches excellence, critical enthusiasm drops to the freezing point. Harriet Martineau, Currer Bell, and Mrs. Gaskell[5] have been treated as cavalierly as if they had been men. And every critic who forms a high estimate of the share women may ultimately take in literature, will, on principle, abstain from any exceptional indulgence towards the productions of literary women. For it must be plain to every one who looks impartially and extensively into feminine literature, that its greatest deficiencies are due hardly more to the want of intellectual power than to the want of those moral qualities that contribute to literary excellence—patient diligence, a sense of the responsibility involved in publication, and an appreciation of the sacredness of the writer's art. In the majority of women's books you see that kind of facility which springs from the absence of any high standard; that fertility in imbecile combination or feeble imitation which a little self-criticism would check and reduce to barrenness; just as with a total want of musical ear people will sing out of tune, while a degree more melodic sensibility would suffice to render them silent. The foolish vanity of wishing to appear in print, instead of being counterbalanced by any consciousness of the intellectual or moral derogation implied in futile authorship, seems to be encouraged by the extremely false impression that to write *at all* is a proof of superiority in a woman. On this ground, we believe that the average intellect of women is unfairly represented by the mass of feminine literature, and that while the few women who write well are very far above the ordinary intellectual level of their sex, the many women who write ill are very far below it. So that, after all, the severer critics are fulfilling a chivalrous duty in depriving the mere fact of feminine authorship of any false prestige which may give it a delusive attraction, and in recommending women of mediocre faculties—as at least a negative service they can render their sex—to abstain from writing.

The standing apology for women who become writers without any special qualification is that society shuts them out from other spheres of occupation. Society is a very culpable entity, and has to answer for the manufacture of many unwholesome commodities, from bad pickles to bad poetry. But society, like "matter," and Her Majesty's Government, and other lofty abstractions, has its share of excessive blame as well as excessive praise. Where there is one woman who writes from necessity, we believe there are three women who write from vanity, and, besides, there is something so antiseptic in the mere healthy fact of working for one's bread, that the most trashy and rotten kind of feminine literature is not likely to have been produced under such circumstances. "In all labour there is profit,"[6] but ladies' silly novels, we imagine, are less the result of labour than of busy idleness.

Happily, we are not dependent on argument to prove that Fiction is a department of literature in which women can, after their kind, fully equal men. A cluster of great names, both living and dead, rush to our memories in evidence that women can produce novels not only fine, but among the very finest;—novels, too, that have a precious speciality, lying quite apart from masculine aptitudes and experience. No educational restrictions can

5. Leading women prose authors: Martineau (1802–1876) was known for her works of political economy as well as her fiction and children's tales, while Charlotte Brontë (1818–1855); see above,

p. 633) and Elizabeth Gaskell (1810–1865; see above, p. 572) were primarily novelists.
6. Proverbs 14.23.

shut women out from the materials of fiction, and there is no species of art which is so free from rigid requirements. Like crystalline masses, it may take any form, and yet be beautiful; we have only to pour in the right elements— genuine observation, humor, and passion. But it is precisely this absence of rigid requirement which constitutes the fatal seduction of novel-writing to incompetent women. Ladies are not wont to be very grossly deceived as to their power of playing on the piano; here certain positive difficulties of execution have to be conquered, and incompetence inevitably breaks down. Every art which has its absolute *technique* is, to a certain extent, guarded from the intrusions of mere left-handed imbecility. But in novel-writing there are no barriers for incapacity to stumble against, no external criteria to prevent a writer from mistaking foolish facility for mastery. And so we have again and again the old story of La Fontaine's ass, who puts his nose to the flute, and, finding that he elicits some sound, exclaims, "Moi, aussi, je joue de la flute;"[7]—a fable which we commend, at parting, to the consideration of any feminine reader who is in danger of adding to the number of "silly novels by lady novelists."

1856

The Lifted Veil

Give me no light, great Heaven, but such as turns
To energy of human fellowship;
No powers beyond the growing heritage
That makes completer manhood.[1]

Chapter I

The time of my end approaches. I have lately been subject to attacks of *angina pectoris;*[2] and in the ordinary course of things, my physician tells me, I may fairly hope that my life will not be protracted many months. Unless, then, I am cursed with an exceptional physical constitution, as I am cursed with an exceptional mental character, I shall not much longer groan under the wearisome burden of this earthly existence. If it were to be otherwise,—if I were to live on to the age most men desire and provide for,—I should for once have known whether the miseries of delusive expectation can outweigh the miseries of true prevision. For I foresee when I shall die, and everything that will happen in my last moments.

Just a month from this day, on the 20th of September, 1850, I shall be sitting in this chair, in this study, at ten o'clock at night, longing to die, weary of incessant insight and foresight, without delusions and without hope. Just as I am watching a tongue of blue flame rising in the fire, and my lamp is burning low, the horrible contraction will begin at my chest. I shall only have time to reach the bell, and pull it violently, before the sense of suffocation

7. "*I also play the flute*" (French). "The Ass and the Flute" is a fable by the French writer Jean-Pierre Florian (1755–1794), not his precedessor

Jean de La Fontaine (1621–1695).
1. The epigraph is by Eliot.
2. A painful heart disease.

will come. No one will answer my bell. I know why. My two servants are lovers, and will have quarreled. My housekeeper will have rushed out of the house in a fury, two hours before, hoping that Perry will believe she has gone to drown herself. Perry is alarmed at last, and is gone out after her. The little scullery-maid is asleep on a bench: she never answers the bell; it does not wake her. The sense of suffocation increases: my lamp goes out with a horrible stench: I make a great effort, and snatch at the bell again. I long for life, and there is no help. I thirsted for the unknown: the thirst is gone. O God, let me stay with the known, and be weary of it: I am content. Agony of pain and suffocation,—and all the while the earth, the fields, the pebbly brook at the bottom of the rookery,[3] the fresh scent after the rain, the light of the morning through my chamber-window, the warmth of the hearth after the frosty air,—will darkness close over them forever?

Darkness,—darkness,—no pain,—nothing but darkness: but I am passing on and on through the darkness: my thought stays in the darkness, but always with a sense of moving onward. . . .

Before that time comes, I wish to use my last hours of ease and strength in telling the strange story of my experience. I have never fully unbosomed myself to any human being; I have never been encouraged to trust much in the sympathy of my fellow-men. But we have all a chance of meeting with some pity, some tenderness, some charity, when we are dead: it is the living only who cannot be forgiven,—the living only from whom men's indulgence and reverence are held off, like the rain by the hard east wind. While the heart beats, bruise it,—it is your only opportunity; while the eye can still turn towards you with moist timid entreaty, freeze it with an icy unanswering gaze; while the ear, that delicate messenger to the inmost sanctuary of the soul, can still take in the tones of kindness, put it off with hard civility, or sneering compliment, or envious affectation of indifference; while the creative brain can still throb with the sense of injustice, with the yearning for brotherly recognition,—make haste,—oppress it with your ill-considered judgments, your trivial comparisons, your careless misrepresentations. The heart will by and by be still,—*ubi sæava indignatio ulterius cor lacerare nequit;*[4] the eye will cease to entreat; the ear will be deaf; the brain will have ceased from all wants as well as from all work. Then your charitable speeches may find vent; then you may remember and pity the toil and the struggle and the failure; then you may give due honor to the work achieved; then you may find extenuation for errors, and may consent to bury them.

That is a trivial schoolboy text; why do I dwell on it? It has little reference to me, for I shall leave no works behind me for men to honor. I have no near relatives who will make up, by weeping over my grave, for the wounds they inflicted on me when I was among them. It is only the story of my life that will perhaps win a little more sympathy from strangers when I am dead, than I ever believed it would obtain from my friends while I was living.

My childhood perhaps seems happier to me than it really was, by contrast with all the after-years. For then the curtain of the future was as impenetrable to me as to other children: I had all their delight in the present hour,

3. A nesting place of crows or ravens.
4. "Inscription on Swift's tombstone" [Eliot's note]. Where fierce indignation can no longer tear

his heart (Latin). Jonathan Swift (1667–1745), Anglo-Irish satirist.

their sweet indefinite hopes for the morrow; and I had a tender mother: even now, after the dreary lapse of long years, a slight trace of sensation accompanies the remembrance of her caress as she held me on her knee,—her arms round my little body, her cheek pressed on mine. I had a complaint of the eyes that made me blind for a little while, and she kept me on her knee from morning till night. That unequaled love soon vanished out of my life, and even to my childish consciousness it was as if that life had become more chill. I rode my little white pony with the groom by my side as before, but there were no loving eyes looking at me as I mounted, no glad arms opened to me when I came back. Perhaps I missed my mother's love more than most children of seven or eight would have done, to whom the other pleasures of life remained as before; for I was certainly a very sensitive child. I remember still the mingled trepidation and delicious excitement with which I was affected by the tramping of the horses on the pavement in the echoing stables, by the loud resonance of the grooms' voices, by the booming bark of the dogs as my father's carriage thundered under the archway of the courtyard, by the din of the gong as it gave notice of luncheon and dinner. The measured tramp of soldiery which I sometimes heard—for my father's house lay near a country town where there were large barracks—made me sob and tremble; and yet when they were gone past, I longed for them to come back again.

I fancy my father thought me an odd child, and had little fondness for me; though he was very careful in fulfilling what he regarded as a parent's duties. But he was already past the middle of life, and I was not his only son. My mother had been his second wife, and he was five-and-forty when he married her. He was a firm, unbending, intensely orderly man, in root and stem a banker, but with a flourishing graft[5] of the active landholder, aspiring to county influence: one of those people who are always like themselves from day to day, who are uninfluenced by the weather, and neither know melancholy nor high spirits. I held him in great awe, and appeared more timid and sensitive in his presence than at other times; a circumstance which, perhaps, helped to confirm him in the intention to educate me on a different plan from the prescriptive one with which he had complied in the case of my elder brother, already a tall youth at Eton.[6] My brother was to be his representative and successor; he must go to Eton and Oxford, for the sake of making connections, of course: my father was not a man to underrate the bearing of Latin satirists or Greek dramatists on the attainment of an aristocratic position. But, intrinsically, he had slight esteem for "those dead but sceptred spirits;" having qualified himself for forming an independent opinion by reading Potter's "Æschylus," and dipping into Francis's "Horace."[7] To this negative view he added a positive one, derived from a recent connection with mining speculations; namely, that a scientific education was the really useful training for a younger son. Moreover, it was clear that a shy, sensitive boy like me was not fit to encounter the rough experience of a public school. Mr. Letherall had said so very decidedly. Mr. Letherall was a large man in spectacles, who one day took my small head between his large hands, and pressed it here and there in an exploratory, suspicious manner,—then placed each

5. Part of a plant that has been attached to another plant of a different species.
6. Famous English private school (in Britain, called a "public school"), with a classical cur-
riculum.
7. English translations of the Greek tragedian and Roman poet.

of his great thumbs on my temples, and pushed me a little way from him, and stared at me with glittering spectacles. The contemplation appeared to displease him, for he frowned sternly, and said to my father, drawing his thumbs across my eyebrows,—

"The deficiency is there, sir,—there; and here," he added, touching the upper sides of my head,—"here is the excess. That must be brought out, sir, and this must be laid to sleep."[8]

I was in a state of tremor, partly at the vague idea that I was the object of reprobation, partly in the agitation of my first hatred,—hatred of this big, spectacled man, who pulled my head about as if he wanted to buy and cheapen it.

I am not aware how much Mr. Letherall had to do with the system afterwards adopted towards me, but it was presently clear that private tutors, natural history, science, and the modern languages were the appliances by which the defects of my organization were to be remedied. I was very stupid about machines, so I was to be greatly occupied with them; I had no memory for classification, so it was particularly necessary that I should study systematic zoölogy and botany; I was hungry for human deeds and human emotions, so I was to be plentifully crammed with the mechanical powers, the elementary bodies, and the phenomena of electricity and magnetism. A better-constituted boy would certainly have profited under my intelligent tutors, with their scientific apparatus; and would, doubtless, have found the phenomena of electricity and magnetism as fascinating as I was, every Thursday, assured they were. As it was, I could have paired off, for ignorance of whatever was taught me, with the worst Latin scholar that was ever turned out of a classical academy. I read Plutarch, and Shakespeare, and Don Quixote[9] by the sly, and supplied myself in that way with wandering thoughts, while my tutor was assuring me that "an improved man, as distinguished from an ignorant one, was a man who knew the reason why water ran down-hill." I had no desire to be this improved man; I was glad of the running water; I could watch it and listen to it gurgling among the pebbles, and bathing the bright green water-plants, by the hour together. I did not want to know *why* it ran; I had perfect confidence that there were good reasons for what was so very beautiful.

There is no need to dwell on this part of my life. I have said enough to indicate that my nature was of the sensitive, unpractical order, and that it grew up in an uncongenial medium, which could never foster it into happy, healthy development. When I was sixteen I was sent to Geneva[1] to complete my course of education; and the change was a very happy one to me, for the first sight of the Alps, with the setting sun on them, as we descended the Jura,[2] seemed to me like an entrance into heaven; and the three years of my life there were spent in a perpetual sense of exaltation, as if from a draught of delicious wine, at the presence of Nature in all her awful loveliness. You will think, perhaps, that I must have been a poet, from this early sensibility[3] to Nature. But my lot was not so happy as that. A poet pours forth his song

8. Letherall is practicing the "science" of phrenology, much in vogue in the later 19th century, according to which a person's mental character could be determined by the shape of his or her skull.
9. The comic novel (1605–15) by Miguel de Cer-

vantes. Plutarch (ca. 50–ca. 120 C.E.), a Greek historian and biographer.
1. A city in Switzerland known for its fine schools.
2. A mountain range along the border between France and Switzerland.
3. I.e., sensitivity. "Awful": awe-inspiring.

and *believes* in the listening ear and answering soul, to which his song will be floated sooner or later. But the poet's sensibility without his voice,—the poet's sensibility that finds no vent but in silent tears on the sunny bank, when the noonday light sparkles on the water or in an inward shudder at the sound of harsh human tones, the sight of a cold human eye,—this dumb passion brings with it a fatal solitude of soul in the society of one's fellow-men. My least solitary moments were those in which I pushed off in my boat, at evening, towards the center of the lake; it seemed to me that the sky, and the glowing mountain-tops, and the wide blue water surrounded me with a cherishing love such as no human face had shed on me since my mother's love had vanished out of my life. I used to do as Jean Jacques[4] did,—lie down in my boat and let it glide where it would, while I looked up at the departing glow leaving one mountain-top after the other, as if the prophet's chariot of fire[5] were passing over them on its way to the home of light. Then, when the white summits were all sad and corpse-like, I had to push homeward, for I was under careful surveillance, and was allowed no late wanderings. This disposition of mine was not favorable to the formation of intimate friendships among the numerous youths of my own age who are always to be found studying at Geneva. Yet I made *one* such friendship; and, singularly enough, it was with a youth whose intellectual tendencies were the very reverse of my own. I shall call him Charles Meunier; his real surname—an English one, for he was of English extraction—having since become celebrated. He was an orphan, who lived on a miserable pittance while he pursued the medical studies for which he had a special genius. Strange! that with my vague mind, susceptible and unobservant, hating inquiry and given up to contemplation, I should have been drawn towards a youth whose strongest passion was science. But the bond was not an intellectual one; it came from a source that can happily blend the stupid with the brilliant, the dreamy with the practical: it came from community of feeling. Charles was poor and ugly, derided by Genevese *gamins,*[6] and not acceptable in drawing-rooms. I saw that he was isolated, as I was, though from a different cause, and, stimulated by a sympathetic resentment, I made timid advances towards him. It is enough to say that there sprang up as much comradeship between us as our different habits would allow; and in Charles's rare holidays we went up the Salève together, or took the boat to Vevey, while I listened dreamily to the monologues in which he unfolded his bold conceptions of future experiment and discovery. I mingled them confusedly in my thought with glimpses of blue water and delicate floating cloud, with the notes of birds and the distant glitter of the glacier. He knew quite well that my mind was half absent, yet he liked to talk to me in this way; for don't we talk of our hopes and our projects even to dogs and birds, when they love us? I have mentioned this one friendship because of its connection with a strange and terrible scene which I shall have to narrate in my subsequent life.

This happier life at Geneva was put an end to by a severe illness, which is partly a blank to me, partly a time of dimly remembered suffering, with the presence of my father by my bed from time to time. Then came the languid

4. Jean-Jacques Rousseau (1712–1778), French philosopher who believed in the goodness of nature. This description of the power of nature also recalls William Wordsworth's *Prelude* (1850),
lines 351–400.
5. The prophet Elijah was carried into heaven on a flaming chariot (2 Kings 2).
6. Street urchins.

monotony of convalescence, the days gradually breaking into variety and distinctness as my strength enabled me to take longer and longer drives. On one of these more vividly remembered days, my father said to me, as he sat beside my sofa,—

"When you are quite well enough to travel, Latimer, I shall take you home with me. The journey will amuse you and do you good, for I shall go through the Tyrol and Austria, and you will see many new places. Our neighbors, the Filmores, are come; Alfred will join us at Basle, and we shall all go together to Vienna, and back by Prague—"

My father was called away before he had finished his sentence, and he left my mind resting on the word *Prague*, with a strange sense that a new and wondrous scene was breaking upon me: a city under the broad sunshine, that seemed to me as if it were the summer sunshine of a long-past century arrested in its course,—unrefreshed for ages by the dews of night or the rushing rain-cloud; scorching the dusty, weary, time-eaten grandeur of a people doomed to live on in the stale repetition of memories, like deposed and superannuated kings in their regal gold-inwoven tatters. The city looked so thirsty that the broad river seemed to me a sheet of metal; and the black-ened statues, as I passed under their blank gaze, along the unending bridge, with their ancient garments and their saintly crowns, seemed to me the real inhabitants and owners of this place, while the busy, trivial men and women, hurrying to and fro, were a swarm of ephemeral visitants infesting it for a day. It is such grim, stony beings as these, I thought, who are the fathers of ancient faded children, in those tanned time-fretted dwellings that crowd the steep before me; who pay their court in the worn and crumbling pomp of the palace which stretches its monotonous length on the height; who worship wearily in the stifling air of the churches, urged by no fear or hope, but compelled by their doom to be ever old and undying, to live on in the rigidity of habit, as they live on in perpetual mid-day, without the repose of night or the new birth of morning.

A stunning clang of metal suddenly thrilled through me, and I became conscious of the objects in my room again: one of the fire-irons had fallen as Pierre opened the door to bring me my draught.[7] My heart was palpitating violently, and I begged Pierre to leave my draught beside me; I would take it presently.

As soon as I was alone again, I began to ask myself whether I had been sleeping. Was this a dream,—this wonderfully distinct vision,—minute in its distinctness down to a patch of rainbow light on the pavement, transmitted through a colored lamp in the shape of a star,—of a strange city, quite unfamiliar to my imagination? I had seen no picture of Prague: it lay in my mind as a mere name, with vaguely remembered historical associations,—ill-defined memories of imperial grandeur and religious wars.

Nothing of this sort had ever occurred in my dreaming experience before, for I had often been humiliated because my dreams were only saved from being utterly disjointed and commonplace by the frequent terrors of night-mare. But I could not believe that I had been asleep, for I remembered distinctly the gradual breaking-in of the vision upon me, like the new images in a dissolving view, or the growing distinctness of the landscape as the sun

7. Dose of liquid medicine.

lifts up the veil of the morning mist. And while I was conscious of this incipient vision, I was also conscious that Pierre came to tell my father Mr. Filmore was waiting for him, and that my father hurried out of the room. No, it was not a dream; was it,—the thought was full of tremulous exultation,—was it the poet's nature in me, hitherto only a troubled yearning sensibility, now manifesting itself suddenly as spontaneous creation? Surely it was in this way that Homer saw the plain of Troy, that Dante saw the abodes of the departed, that Milton saw the earthward flight of the Tempter.[8] Was it that my illness had wrought some happy change in my organization,— given a firmer tension to my nerves,—carried off some dull obstruction? I had often read of such effects,—in works of fiction at least. Nay; in genuine biographies I had read of the subtilizing or exalting influence of some diseases on the mental powers. Did not Novalis feel his inspiration intensified under the progress of consumption?[9]

When my mind had dwelt for some time on this blissful idea, it seemed to me that I might perhaps test it by an exertion of my will. The vision had begun when my father was speaking of our going to Prague. I did not for a moment believe it was really a representation of that city; I believed—I hoped it was a picture that my newly liberated genius had painted in fiery haste, with the colours snatched from lazy memory. Suppose I were to fix my mind on some other place,—Venice, for example, which was far more familiar to my imagination than Prague: perhaps the same sort of result would follow. I concentrated my thoughts on Venice; I stimulated my imagination with poetic memories, and strove to feel myself present in Venice, as I had felt myself present in Prague. But in vain. I was only coloring the Canaletto[1] engravings that hung in my old bedroom at home; the picture was a shifting one, my mind wandering uncertainly in search of more vivid images; I could see no accident of form or shadow without conscious labor after the necessary conditions. It was all prosaic effort, not rapt passivity, such as I had experienced half an hour before. I was discouraged; but I remembered that inspiration was fitful.

For several days I was in a state of excited expectation, watching for a recurrence of my new gift. I sent my thoughts ranging over my world of knowledge, in the hope that they would find some object which would send a reawakening vibration through my slumbering genius. But no; my world remained as dim as ever, and that flash of strange light refused to come again, though I watched for it with palpitating eagerness.

My father accompanied me every day in a drive, and a gradually lengthening walk as my powers of walking increased; and one evening he had agreed to come and fetch me at twelve the next day, that we might go together to select a musical box, and other purchases rigorously demanded of a rich Englishman visiting Geneva. He was one of the most punctual of men and bankers, and I was always nervously anxious to be quite ready for him at the appointed time. But, to my surprise, at a quarter past twelve he had not appeared. I felt all the impatience of a convalescent who has nothing particular to do, and who has just taken a tonic[2] in the prospect of immediate exercise that would carry off the stimulus.

8. In the *Iliad*; the *Divine Comedy* (ca. 1308–21), by Dante Alighieri (1265–1321); and *Paradise Lost* (1667–74), by John Milton (1608–1674), which includes a description of Satan's fall from heaven.

9. Tuberculosis. Novalis (1772–1801), German Romantic poet.
1. Venetian painter (1697–1768).
2. An invigorating drug.

Unable to sit still and reserve my strength, I walked up and down the room, looking out on the current of the Rhone, just where it leaves the dark-blue lake; but thinking all the while of the possible causes that could detain my father.

Suddenly I was conscious that my father was in the room, but not alone: there were two persons with him. Strange! I had heard no footstep, I had not seen the door open; but I saw my father, and at his right hand our neighbor Mrs. Filmore, whom I remembered very well, though I had not seen her for five years. She was a commonplace middle-aged woman, in silk and cashmere; but the lady on the left of my father was not more than twenty, a tall, slim, willowy figure, with luxuriant blond hair, arranged in cunning braids and folds that looked almost too massive for the slight figure and the small-featured, thin-lipped face they crowned. But the face had not a girlish expression: the features were sharp, the pale gray eyes at once acute, restless, and sarcastic. They were fixed on me in half-smiling curiosity, and I felt a painful sensation as if a sharp wind were cutting me. The pale-green dress, and the green leaves that seemed to form a border about her pale blond hair, made me think of a Water-Nixie[3]—for my mind was full of German lyrics, and this pale, fatal-eyed woman, with the green weeds, looked like a birth from some cold sedgy stream, the daughter of an aged river.

"Well, Latimer, you thought me long," my father said. . . .

But while the last word was in my ears, the whole group vanished, and there was nothing between me and the Chinese painted folding-screen that stood before the door. I was cold and trembling; I could only totter forward and throw myself on the sofa. This strange new power had manifested itself again. . . . But *was* it a power? Might it not rather be a disease,—a sort of intermittent delirium, concentrating my energy of brain into moments of unhealthy activity, and leaving my saner hours all the more barren? I felt a dizzy sense of unreality in what my eye rested on; I grasped the bell convulsively, like one trying to free himself from nightmare, and rang it twice. Pierre came with a look of alarm in his face.

"Monsieur ne se trouve pas bien?"[4] he said anxiously.

"I'm tired of waiting, Pierre," I said, as distinctly and emphatically as I could, like a man determined to be sober in spite of wine; "I'm afraid something has happened to my father,—he's usually so punctual. Run to the Hôtel des Bergues and see if he is there."

Pierre left the room at once, with a soothing "Bien, Monsieur;" and I felt the better for this scene of simple, waking prose. Seeking to calm myself still further, I went into my bedroom, adjoining the *salon,* and opened a case of eau-de-Cologne; took out a bottle; went through the process of taking out the cork very neatly, and then rubbed the reviving spirit over my hands and forehead, and under my nostrils, drawing a new delight from the scent because I had procured it by slow details of labor, and by no strange sudden madness. Already I had begun to taste something of the horror that belongs to the lot of a human being whose nature is not adjusted to simple human conditions.

Still enjoying the scent, I returned to the *salon,* but it was not unoccupied, as it had been before I left it. In front of the Chinese folding-screen there was my father, with Mrs. Filmore on his right hand, and on his left, the slim

3. In Germanic folklore, a water sprite.
4. Monsieur is not well? (French).

blond-haired girl, with the keen face and the keen eyes fixed on me in half-smiling curiosity.

"Well, Latimer, you thought me long," my father said. . . .

I heard no more, felt no more, till I became conscious that I was lying with my head low on the sofa, Pierre and my father by my side. As soon as I was thoroughly revived, my father left the room, and presently returned, saying,—

"I've been to tell the ladies how you are, Latimer. They were waiting in the next room. We shall put off our shopping expedition to-day."

Presently he said, "That young lady is Bertha Grant, Mrs. Filmore's orphan niece. Filmore has adopted her, and she lives with them, so you will have her for a neighbor when we go home,—perhaps for a near relation; for there is a tenderness between her and Alfred, I suspect, and I should be gratified by the match, since Filmore means to provide for her in every way as if she were his daughter. It had not occurred to me that you knew nothing about her living with the Filmores."

He made no further allusion to the fact of my having fainted at the moment of seeing her, and I would not for the world have told him the reason: I shrank from the idea of disclosing to anyone what might be regarded as a pitiable peculiarity, most of all from betraying it to my father, who would have suspected my sanity ever after.

I do not mean to dwell with particularity on the details of my experience. I have described these two cases at length, because they had definite, clearly traceable results in my after-lot.

Shortly after this last occurrence—I think the very next day—I began to be aware of a phase in my abnormal sensibility, to which, from the languid and slight nature of my intercourse with others since my illness, I had not been alive before. This was the obtrusion on my mind of the mental process going forward in first one person, and then another, with whom I happened to be in contact: the vagrant, frivolous ideas and emotions of some uninteresting acquaintance—Mrs. Filmore, for example—would force themselves on my consciousness like an importunate, ill-played musical instrument, or the loud activity of an imprisoned insect. But this unpleasant sensibility was fitful, and left me moments of rest, when the souls of my companions were once more shut out from me, and I felt a relief such as silence brings to wearied nerves. I might have believed this importunate insight to be merely a diseased activity of the imagination, but that my prevision of incalculable words and actions proved it to have a fixed relation to the mental process in other minds. But this superadded consciousness, wearying and annoying enough when it urged on me the trivial experience of indifferent people, became an intense pain and grief when it seemed to be opening to me the souls of those who were in a close relation to me,—when the rational talk, the graceful attentions, the wittily turned phrases, and the kindly deeds, which used to make the web of their characters, were seen as if thrust asunder by a microscopic vision, that showed all the intermediate frivolities, all the suppressed egoism, all the struggling chaos of puerilities, meanness, vague capricious memories, and indolent make-shift thoughts, from which human words and deeds emerge like leaflets[5] covering a fermenting heap.

At Basle we were joined by my brother Alfred, now a handsome self-

5. Small leaves.

confident man of six-and-twenty,—a thorough contrast to my fragile, nervous, ineffectual self. I believe I was held to have a sort of half-womanish, half-ghostly beauty; for the portrait-painters, who are thick as weeds at Geneva, had often asked me to sit to them, and I had been the model of a dying minstrel in a fancy picture. But I thoroughly disliked my own *physique*, and nothing but the belief that it was a condition of poetic genius would have reconciled me to it. That brief hope was quite fled, and I saw in my face now nothing but the stamp of a morbid organization, framed for passive suffering,—too feeble for the sublime resistance of poetic production. Alfred, from whom I had been almost constantly separated, and who, in his present stage of character and appearance, came before me as a perfect stranger, was bent on being extremely friendly and brother-like to me. He had the superficial kindness of a good-humored, self-satisfied nature, that fears no rivalry, and has encountered no contrarieties. I am not sure that my disposition was good enough for me to have been quite free from envy towards him, even if our desires had not clashed, and if I had been in the healthy human condition which admits of generous confidence and charitable construction.[6] There must always have been an antipathy between our natures. As it was, he became in a few weeks an object of intense hatred to me; and when he entered the room, still more when he spoke, it was as if a sensation of grating metal had set my teeth on edge. My diseased consciousness was more intensely and continually occupied with his thoughts and emotions than with those of any other person who came in my way. I was perpetually exasperated with the petty promptings of his conceit and his love of patronage, with his self-complacent belief in Bertha Grant's passion for him, with his half-pitying contempt for me—seen not in the ordinary indications of intonation and phrase and slight action, which an acute and suspicious mind is on the watch for, but in all their naked skinless complication.

For we were rivals, and our desires clashed, though he was not aware of it. I have said nothing yet of the effect Bertha Grant produced in me on a nearer acquaintance. That effect was chiefly determined by the fact that she made the only exception, among all the human beings about me, to my unhappy gift of insight. About Bertha I was always in a state of uncertainty: I could watch the expression of her face, and speculate on its meaning; I could ask for her opinion with the real interest of ignorance; I could listen for her words and watch for her smile with hope and fear: she had for me the fascination of an unraveled destiny. I say it was this fact that chiefly determined the strong effect she produced on me: for, in the abstract, no womanly character could seem to have less affinity for that of a shrinking, romantic, passionate youth than Bertha's. She was keen, sarcastic, unimaginative, prematurely cynical, remaining critical and unmoved in the most impressive scenes, inclined to dissect all my favorite poems, and especially contemptuous towards the German lyrics which were my pet literature at that time. To this moment I am unable to define my feeling towards her: it was not ordinary boyish admiration, for she was the very opposite, even to the color of her hair, of the ideal woman who still remained to me the type[7] of loveliness; and she was without that enthusiasm for the great and good, which, even at the moment of her strongest dominion over me, I should have

6. Interpretation. 7. Standard, ideal.

declared to be the highest element of character. But there is no tyranny more complete than that which a self-centered negative nature exercises over a morbidly sensitive nature perpetually craving sympathy and support. The most independent people feel the effect of a man's silence in heightening their value for his opinion,—feel an additional triumph in conquering the reverence of a critic habitually captious and satirical: no wonder, then, that an enthusiastic self-distrusting youth should watch and wait before the closed secret of a sarcastic woman's face, as if it were the shrine of the doubtfully benignant deity who ruled his destiny. For a young enthusiast is unable to imagine the total negation in another mind of the emotions which are stirring his own: they may be feeble, latent, inactive, he thinks, but they are there,— they may be called forth; sometimes, in moments of happy hallucination, he believes they may be there in all the greater strength because he sees no outward sign of them. And this effect, as I have intimated, was heightened to its utmost intensity in me, because Bertha was the only being who remained for me in the mysterious seclusion of soul that renders such youthful delusion possible. Doubtless there was another sort of fascination at work,—that subtle physical attraction which delights in cheating our psychological predictions, and in compelling the men who paint sylphs to fall in love with some *bonne et brave femme*,[8] heavy-heeled and freckled.

Bertha's behavior towards me was such as to encourage all my illusions, to heighten my boyish passion, and make me more and more dependent on her smiles. Looking back with my present wretched knowledge, I conclude that her vanity and love of power were intensely gratified by the belief that I had fainted on first seeing her purely from the strong impression her person had produced on me. The most prosaic woman likes to believe herself the object of a violent, a poetic passion; and without a grain of romance in her, Bertha had that spirit of intrigue which gave piquancy to the idea that the brother of the man she meant to marry was dying with love and jealousy for her sake. That she meant to marry my brother was what at that time I did not believe; for though he was assiduous in his attentions to her, and I knew well enough that both he and my father had made up their minds to this result, there was not yet an understood engagement,—there had been no explicit declaration; and Bertha habitually, while she flirted with my brother, and accepted his homage in a way that implied to him a thorough recognition of its intention, made me believe, by the subtlest looks and phrases,—feminine nothings which could never be quoted against her,—that he was really the object of her secret ridicule; that she thought him, as I did, a coxcomb,[9] whom she would have pleasure in disappointing. Me she openly petted in my brother's presence, as if I were too young and sickly ever to be thought of as a lover; and that was the view he took of me. But I believe she must inwardly have delighted in the tremors into which she threw me by the coaxing way in which she patted my curls, while she laughed at my quotations. Such caresses were always given in the presence of our friends; for when we were alone together, she affected a much greater distance towards me, and now and then took the opportunity, by words or slight actions, to stimulate my foolish timid hope that she really preferred me. And why should she not

8. Good and hearty woman: (French). "Sylphs": elemental beings that inhabit the air. 9. A conceited young man.

follow her inclination? I was not in so advantageous a position as my brother, but I had fortune, I was not a year younger than she was, and she was an heiress, who would soon be of age to decide for herself.

The fluctuations of hope and fear, confined to this one channel, made each day in her presence a delicious torment. There was one deliberate act of hers which especially helped to intoxicate me. When we were at Vienna her twentieth birthday occurred, and as she was very fond of ornaments, we all took the opportunity of the splendid jewelers' shops in that Teutonic Paris to purchase her a birthday present of jewelry. Mine, naturally, was the least expensive; it was an opal ring,—the opal was my favorite stone, because it seems to blush and turn pale as if it had a soul. I told Bertha so when I gave it her, and said that it was an emblem of the poetic nature, changing with the changing light of heaven and of woman's eyes. In the evening she appeared elegantly dressed, and wearing conspicuously all the birthday presents except mine. I looked eagerly at her fingers, but saw no opal. I had no opportunity of noticing this to her during the evening; but the next day, when I found her seated near the window alone, after breakfast, I said: "You scorn to wear my poor opal. I should have remembered that you despised poetic natures, and should have given you coral, or turquoise, or some other opaque unresponsive stone." "Do I despise it?" she answered, taking hold of a delicate gold chain which she always wore round her neck and drawing out the end from her bosom with my ring hanging to it; "it hurts me a little, I can tell you," she said, with her usual dubious[1] smile, "to wear it in that secret place; and since your poetical nature is so stupid as to prefer a more public position, I shall not endure the pain any longer."

She took off the ring from the chain and put it on her finger, smiling still, while the blood rushed to my cheeks, and I could not trust myself to say a word of entreaty that she would keep the ring where it was before.

I was completely fooled by this, and for two days shut myself up in my own room whenever Bertha was absent, that I might intoxicate myself afresh with the thought of this scene and all it implied.

I should mention that during these two months,—which seemed a long life to me from the novelty and intensity of the pleasures and pains I underwent,—my diseased participation in other people's consciousness continued to torment me; now it was my father, and now my brother, now Mrs. Filmore or her husband, and now our German courier, whose stream of thought rushed upon me like a ringing in the ears not to be got rid of, though it allowed my own impulses and ideas to continue their uninterrupted course. It was like a preternaturally heightened sense of hearing, making audible to one a roar of sound where others find perfect stillness.[2] The weariness and disgust of this involuntary intrusion into other souls was counteracted only by my ignorance of Bertha, and my growing passion for her,—a passion enormously stimulated, if not produced, by that ignorance. She was my oasis of mystery in the dreary desert of knowledge. I had never allowed my diseased condition to betray itself, or to drive me into any unusual speech or action, except once, when, in a moment of peculiar bitterness against my brother, I

1. Ambiguous.
2. Eliot uses this simile again in a famous passage in *Middlemarch* (1871–72, chap. 28): "If we had a keen vision and feeling of all ordinary human life, it would be like hearing the grass grow and the squirrel's heart beat, and we should die of that roar which lies on the other side of silence."

had forestalled some words which I knew he was going to utter,—a clever observation, which he had prepared beforehand. He had occasionally a slightly affected hesitation in his speech, and when he paused an instant after the second word, my impatience and jealousy impelled me to continue the speech for him, as if it were something we had both learned by rote. He colored and looked astonished, as well as annoyed; and the words had no sooner escaped my lips than I felt a shock of alarm lest such an anticipation of words—very far from being words of course, easy to divine—should have betrayed me as an exceptional being, a sort of quiet energumen,[3] whom everyone, Bertha above all, would shudder at and avoid. But I magnified, as usual, the impression any word or deed of mine could produce on others; for no one gave any sign of having noticed my interruption as more than a rudeness, to be forgiven me on the score of my feeble nervous condition.

While this superadded consciousness of the actual was almost constant with me, I had never had a recurrence of that distinct prevision which I have described in relation to my first interview with Bertha; and I was waiting with eager curiosity to know whether or not my vision of Prague would prove to have been an instance of the same kind. A few days after the incident of the opal ring, we were paying one of our frequent visits to the Lichtenberg Palace. I could never look at many pictures in succession; for pictures, when they are at all powerful, affect me so strongly that one or two exhaust all my capability of contemplation. This morning I had been looking at Giorgione's picture of the cruel-eyed woman, said to be a likeness of Lucrezia Borgia.[4] I had stood long alone before it, fascinated by the terrible reality of that cunning, relentless face, till I felt a strange poisoned sensation, as if I had long been inhaling a fatal odor, and was just beginning to be conscious of its effects. Perhaps even then I should not have moved away, if the rest of the party had not returned to this room, and announced that they were going to the Belvedere Gallery to settle a bet which had arisen between my brother and Mr. Filmore about a portrait. I followed them dreamily, and was hardly alive to what occurred till they had all gone up to the gallery, leaving me below; for I refused to come within sight of another picture that day. I made my way to the Grand Terrace, since it was agreed that we should saunter in the gardens when the dispute had been decided. I had been sitting here a short space, vaguely conscious of trim gardens, with a city and green hills in the distance, when, wishing to avoid the proximity of the sentinel, I rose and walked down the broad stone steps, intending to seat myself farther on in the gardens. Just as I reached the gravel-walk, I felt an arm slipped within mine, and a light hand gently pressing my wrist. In the same instant a strange intoxicating numbness passed over me, like the continuance or climax of the sensation I was still feeling from the gaze of Lucrezia Borgia. The gardens, the summer sky, the consciousness of Bertha's arm being within mine, all vanished, and I seemed to be suddenly in darkness, out of which there gradually broke a dim firelight, and I felt myself sitting in my father's leather chair in the library at home. I knew the fireplace,—the dogs for the wood-fire,—the black marble chimney-piece with the white marble medallion of the dying Cleopatra[5] in the centre. Intense and hopeless misery was pressing

3. One who is possessed by a devil.
4. Borgia (1480–1519), member of a powerful Italian family famous for licentiousness, intrigue, and violence, whose second husband was mur-

dered. Giorgione (ca. 1478–1511), Italian painter.
5. Egyptian queen (69–30 B.C.E.; r. 51–30), who killed herself—according to legend, by letting a poisonous asp bite her. "Dogs": andirons.

on my soul; the light became stronger, for Bertha was entering with a candle in her hand,—Bertha, my wife,—with cruel eyes, with green jewels and green leaves on her white ball-dress; every hateful thought within her present to me. . . . "Madman, idiot! why don't you kill yourself, then?" It was a moment of hell. I saw into her pitiless soul,—saw its barren worldliness, its scorching hate,—and felt it clothe me round like an air I was obliged to breathe. She came with her candle and stood over me with a bitter smile of contempt; I saw the great emerald brooch on her bosom, a studded serpent with diamond eyes. I shuddered,—I despised this woman with the barren soul and mean thoughts; but I felt helpless before her, as if she clutched my bleeding heart, and would clutch it till the last drop of life-blood ebbed away. She was my wife, and we hated each other. Gradually the hearth, the dim library, the candle-light disappeared,—seemed to melt away into a background of light, the green serpent with the diamond eyes remaining a dark image on the retina. Then I had a sense of my eyelids quivering, and the living daylight broke in upon me; I saw gardens, and heard voices; I was seated on the steps of the Belvedere Terrace, and my friends were round me.

The tumult of mind into which I was thrown by this hideous vision made me ill for several days, and prolonged our stay at Vienna. I shuddered with horror as the scene recurred to me; and it recurred constantly, with all its minutiæ, as if they had been burnt into my memory; and yet, such is the madness of the human heart under the influence of its immediate desires, I felt a wild hell-braving joy that Bertha was to be mine; for the fulfilment of my former prevision concerning her first appearance before me, left me little hope that this last hideous glimpse of the future was the mere diseased play of my own mind, and had no relation to external realities. One thing alone I looked towards as a possible means of casting doubt on my terrible conviction,—the discovery that my vision of Prague had been false,—and Prague was the next city on our route.

Meanwhile I was no sooner in Bertha's society again, than I was as completely under her sway as before. What if I saw into the heart of Bertha, the matured woman,—Bertha, my wife? Bertha, the *girl*, was a fascinating secret to me still: I trembled under her touch; I felt the witchery of her presence; I yearned to be assured of her love. The fear of poison is feeble against the sense of thirst. Nay, I was just as jealous of my brother as before,—just as much irritated by his small patronizing ways; for my pride, my diseased sensibility, were there as they had always been, and winced as inevitably under every offence as my eye winced from an intruding mote. The future, even when brought within the compass of feeling by a vision that made me shudder, had still no more than the force of an idea, compared with the force of present emotion,—of my love for Bertha, of my dislike and jealousy towards my brother.

It is an old story, that men sell themselves to the tempter, and sign a bond with their blood, because it is only to take effect at a distant day; then rush on to snatch the cup their souls thirst after with an impulse not the less savage because there is a dark shadow beside them forevermore. There is no short cut, no patent tram-road[6] to wisdom: after all the centuries of invention, the soul's path lies through the thorny wilderness which must be still

6. A road made of metal rails for streetcars.

trodden in solitude, with bleeding feet, with sobs for help, as it was trodden by them of old time.

My mind speculated eagerly on the means by which I should become my brother's successful rival, for I was still too timid, in my ignorance of Bertha's actual feeling, to venture on any step that would urge from her an avowal of it. I thought I should gain confidence even for this, if my vision of Prague proved to have been veracious; and yet, the horror of that certitude! Behind the slim girl Bertha, whose words and looks I watched for, whose touch was bliss, there stood continually that Bertha with the fuller form, the harder eyes, the more rigid mouth,—with the barren selfish soul laid bare; no longer a fascinating secret, but a measured fact, urging itself perpetually on my unwilling sight. Are you unable to give me your sympathy,—you who read this? Are you unable to imagine this double consciousness at work within me, flowing on like two parallel streams which never mingle their waters and blend into a common hue? Yet you must have known something of the presentiments that spring from an insight at war with passion; and my visions were only like presentiments intensified to horror. You have known the powerlessness of ideas before the might of impulse; and my visions, when once they had passed into memory, were mere ideas,—pale shadows that beckoned in vain, while my hand was grasped by the living and the loved.

In after days I thought with bitter regret that if I had foreseen something more or something different,—if instead of that hideous vision which poisoned the passion it could not destroy, or if even along with it I could have had a foreshadowing of that moment when I looked on my brother's face for the last time, some softening influence would have been shed over my feeling towards him: pride and hatred would surely have been subdued into pity, and the record of those hidden sins would have been shortened. But this is one of the vain thoughts with which we men flatter ourselves. We try to believe that the egoism within us would have easily been melted, and that it was only the narrowness of our knowledge which hemmed in our generosity, our awe, our human piety, and hindered them from submerging our hard indifference to the sensations and emotions of our fellow. Our tenderness and self-renunciation seem strong when our egoism has had its day,—when, after our mean striving for a triumph that is to be another's loss, the triumph comes suddenly, and we shudder at it, because it is held out by the chill hand of death.

Our arrival in Prague happened at night, and I was glad of this, for it seemed like a deferring of a terribly decisive moment, to be in the city for hours without seeing it. As we were not to remain long in Prague, but to go on speedily to Dresden, it was proposed that we should drive out the next morning and take a general view of the place, as well as visit some of its specially interesting spots, before the heat became oppressive,—for we were in August, and the season was hot and dry. But it happened that the ladies were rather late at their morning toilet,[7] and to my father's politely repressed but perceptible annoyance, we were not in the carriage till the morning was far advanced. I thought with a sense of relief, as we entered the Jews' quarter, where we were to visit the old synagogue, that we should be kept in this flat, shut-up part of the city, until we should all be too tired and too warm to go

7. Bathing and dressing.

farther, and so we should return without seeing more than the streets through which we had already passed. That would give me another day's suspense,—suspense, the only form in which a fearful spirit knows the solace of hope. But as I stood under the blackened, groined arches of that old synagogue, made dimly visible by the seven thin candles in the sacred lamp, while our Jewish cicerone reached down the Book of the Law,[8] and read to us in its ancient tongue,—I felt a shuddering impression that this strange building, with its shrunken lights, this surviving withered remnant of mediæval Judaism, was of a piece with my vision. Those darkened dusty Christian saints, with their loftier arches and their larger candles, needed the consolatory scorn with which they might point to a more shrivelled death-in-life than their own.

As I expected, when we left the Jews' quarter the elders of our party wished to return to the hotel. But now, instead of rejoicing in this, as I had done beforehand, I felt a sudden overpowering impulse to go on at once to the bridge, and put an end to the suspense I had been wishing to protract. I declared, with unusual decision, that I would get out of the carriage and walk on alone; they might return without me. My father, thinking this merely a sample of my usual "poetic nonsense," objected that I should only do myself harm by walking in the heat; but when I persisted, he said angrily that I might follow my own absurd devices, but that Schmidt (our courier) must go with me. I assented to this, and set off with Schmidt towards the bridge. I had no sooner passed from under the archway of the grand old gate leading on to the bridge, than a trembling seized me, and I turned cold under the mid-day sun; yet I went on: I was in search of something,—a small detail which I remembered with special intensity as part of my vision. There it was,—the patch of rainbow light on the pavement transmitted through a lamp in the shape of a star.

Chapter II

Before the autumn was at an end, and while the brown leaves still stood thick on the beeches in our park, my brother and Bertha were engaged to each other, and it was understood that their marriage was to take place early in the next spring. In spite of the certainty I had felt from that moment on the bridge at Prague, that Bertha would one day be my wife, my constitutional timidity and distrust had continued to benumb me, and the words in which I had sometimes premeditated a confession of my love had died away unuttered. The same conflict had gone on within me as before,—the longing for an assurance of love from Bertha's lips, the dread lest a word of contempt and denial should fall upon me like a corrosive acid. What was the conviction of a distant necessity to me? I trembled under a present glance, I hungered after a present joy, I was clogged and chilled by a present fear. And so the days passed on: I witnessed Bertha's engagement and heard her marriage discussed as if I were under a conscious nightmare,—knowing it was a dream that would vanish, but feeling stifled under the grasp of hard-clutching fingers.

When I was not in Bertha's presence,—and I was with her very often, for

8. The Torah (the first five books of the Bible). "Cicerone": guide.

she continued to treat me with a playful patronage that wakened no jealousy in my brother,—I spent my time chiefly in wandering, in strolling, or taking long rides while the daylight lasted, and then shutting myself up with my unread books; for books had lost the power of chaining my attention. My self-consciousness was heightened to that pitch of intensity in which our own emotions take the form of a drama which urges itself imperatively on our contemplation, and we begin to weep, less under the sense of our suffering than at the thought of it. I felt a sort of pitying anguish over the pathos of my own lot: the lot of a being finely organized for pain, but with hardly any fibers that responded to pleasure,—to whom the idea of future evil robbed the present of its joy, and for whom the idea of future good did not still the uneasiness of a present yearning or a present dread. I went dumbly through that stage of the poet's suffering, in which he feels the delicious pang of utterance, and makes an image of his sorrows.

I was left entirely without remonstrance concerning this dreamy wayward life: I knew my father's thought about me: "That lad will never be good for anything in life: he may waste his years in an insignificant way on the income that falls to him: I shall not trouble myself about a career for him."

One mild morning in the beginning of November, it happened that I was standing outside the portico patting lazy old Cæsar, a Newfoundland almost blind with age, the only dog that ever took any notice of me,—for the very dogs shunned me, and fawned on the happier people about me,—when the groom brought up my brother's horse which was to carry him to the hunt, and my brother himself appeared at the door, florid, broad-chested, and self-complacent, feeling what a good-natured fellow he was not to behave insolently to us all on the strength of his great advantages.

"Latimer, old boy," he said to me in a tone of compassionate cordiality, "what a pity it is you don't have a run with the hounds now and then! The finest thing in the world for low spirits!"

"Low spirits!" I thought bitterly, as he rode away; "that is the sort of phrase with which coarse, narrow natures like yours think to describe experience of which you can know no more than your horse knows. It is to such as you that the good of this world falls: ready dulness, healthy selfishness, good-tempered conceit,—these are the keys to happiness."

The quick thought came, that my selfishness was even stronger than his,—it was only a suffering selfishness instead of an enjoying one. But then, again, my exasperating insight into Alfred's self-complacent soul, his freedom from all the doubts and fears, the unsatisfied yearnings, the exquisite tortures of sensitiveness, that had made the web of my life, seemed to absolve me from all bonds towards him. This man needed no pity, no love; those fine influences would have been as little felt by him as the delicate white mist is felt by the rock it caresses. There was no evil in store for *him*: if he was not to marry Bertha, it would be because he had found a lot pleasanter to himself.

Mr. Filmore's house lay not more than half a mile beyond our own gates, and whenever I knew my brother was gone in another direction, I went there for the chance of finding Bertha at home. Later on in the day I walked thither. By a rare accident she was alone, and we walked out in the grounds together, for she seldom went on foot beyond the trimly swept gravel-walks. I remember what a beautiful sylph she looked to me as the low November sun shone on her blond hair, and she tripped along teasing me with her usual

light banter, to which I listened half fondly, half moodily; it was all the sign Bertha's mysterious inner self ever made to me. Today perhaps the moodiness predominated, for I had not yet shaken off the access of jealous hate which my brother had raised in me by his parting patronage.[9] Suddenly I interrupted and startled her by saying, almost fiercely, "Bertha, how can you love Alfred?"

She looked at me with surprise for a moment, but soon her light smile came again, and she answered sarcastically, "Why do you suppose I love him?"

"How can you ask that, Bertha?"

"What! your wisdom thinks I must love the man I'm going to marry? The most unpleasant thing in the world. I should quarrel with him; I should be jealous of him; our *ménage*[1] would be conducted in a very ill-bred manner. A little quiet contempt contributes greatly to the elegance of life."

"Bertha, that is not your real feeling. Why do you delight in trying to deceive me by inventing such cynical speeches?"

"I need never take the trouble of invention in order to deceive you, my small Tasso"[2] (that was the mocking name she usually gave me). "The easiest way to deceive a poet is to tell him the truth."

She was testing the validity of her epigram in a daring way, and for a moment the shadow of my vision—the Bertha whose soul was no secret to me—passed between me and the radiant girl, the playful sylph whose feelings were a fascinating mystery. I suppose I must have shuddered, or betrayed in some other way my momentary chill of horror.

"Tasso!" she said, seizing my wrist and peeping round into my face, "are you really beginning to discern what a heartless girl I am? Why, you are not half the poet I thought you were; you are actually capable of believing the truth about me."

The shadow passed from between us, and was no longer the object nearest to me. The girl whose light fingers grasped me, whose elfish charming face looked into mine,—who, I thought, was betraying an interest in my feelings that she would not have directly avowed,—this warm-breathing presence again possessed my senses and imagination like a returning siren[3] melody which had been overpowered for an instant by the roar of threatening waves. It was a moment as delicious to me as the waking up to a consciousness of youth after a dream of middle age. I forgot everything but my passion, and said with swimming eyes,—

"Bertha, shall you love me when we are first married? I wouldn't mind if you really loved me only for a little while."

Her look of astonishment, as she loosed my hand and started away from me, recalled me to a sense of my strange, my criminal indiscretion.

"Forgive me," I said hurriedly, as soon as I could speak again; "I did not know what I was saying."

"Ah, Tasso's mad fit has come on, I see," she answered quietly, for she had recovered herself sooner than I had. "Let him go home and keep his head cool. I must go in, for the sun is setting."

9. I.e., patronizing remark. "Access": outburst.
1. Household.
2. Torquato Tasso (1544–1595), Italian poet, author of the epic *Gerusalemme Liberata*; he was twice confined as insane.
3. The sirens are mythological female monsters who lure sailors toward rocks by the beauty of their song.

I left her,—full of indignation against myself. I had let slip words which, if she reflected on them, might rouse in her a suspicion of my abnormal mental condition,—a suspicion which of all things I dreaded. And besides that, I was ashamed of the apparent baseness I had committed in uttering them to my brother's betrothed wife. I wandered home slowly, entering our park through a private gate instead of by the lodges.[4] As I approached the house, I saw a man dashing off at full speed from the stable-yard across the park. Had any accident happened at home? No; perhaps it was only one of my father's peremptory business errands that required this headlong haste. Nevertheless I quickened my pace without any distinct motive, and was soon at the house. I will not dwell on the scene I found there. My brother was dead,—had been pitched from his horse, and killed on the spot by a concussion of the brain.

I went up to the room where he lay, and where my father was seated beside him with a look of rigid despair. I had shunned my father more than any one since our return home, for the radical antipathy between our natures made my insight into his inner self a constant affliction to me. But now, as I went up to him, and stood beside him in sad silence, I felt the presence of a new element that blended us as we had never been blent before. My father had been one of the most successful men in the money-getting world: he had had no sentimental sufferings, no illness. The heaviest trouble that had befallen him was the death of his first wife. But he married my mother soon after; and I remember he seemed exactly the same, to my keen childish observation, the week after her death as before. But now, at last, a sorrow had come,—the sorrow of old age, which suffers the more from the crushing of its pride and its hopes, in proportion as the pride and hope are narrow and prosaic. His son was to have been married soon,—would probably have stood for the borough[5] at the next election. That son's existence was the best motive that could be alleged for making new purchases of land every year to round off the estate. It is a dreary thing to live on doing the same things year after year, without knowing why we do them. Perhaps the tragedy of disappointed youth and passion is less piteous than the tragedy of disappointed age and worldliness.

As I saw into the desolation of my father's heart, I felt a movement of deep pity towards him, which was the beginning of a new affection,—an affection that grew and strengthened in spite of the strange bitterness with which he regarded me in the first month or two after my brother's death. If it had not been for the softening influence of my compassion for him,—the first deep compassion I had ever felt,—I should have been stung by the perception that my father transferred the inheritance of an eldest son to me with a mortified sense that fate had compelled him to the unwelcome course of caring for me as an important being. It was only in spite of himself that he began to think of me with anxious regard. There is hardly any neglected child for whom death has made vacant a more favored place, who will not understand what I mean.

Gradually, however, my new deference to his wishes, the effect of that patience which was born of my pity for him, won upon his affection, and he

4. Small houses on large private estates used by caretakers, gamekeepers, and other servants.

5. I.e., have run as a parliamentary representative for his district.

began to please himself with the endeavor to make me fill my brother's place as fully as my feebler personality would admit. I saw that the prospect which by and by presented itself of my becoming Bertha's husband was welcome to him, and he even contemplated in my case what he had not intended in my brother's,—that his son and daughter-in-law should make one household with him. My softened feeling towards my father made this the happiest time I had known since childhood;—these last months in which I retained the delicious illusion of loving Bertha, of longing and doubting and hoping that she might love me. She behaved with a certain new consciousness and distance towards me after my brother's death; and I too was under a double constraint,—that of delicacy towards my brother's memory, and of anxiety as to the impression my abrupt words had left on her mind. But the additional screen this mutual reserve erected between us only brought me more completely under her power: no matter how empty the adytum,[6] so that the veil be thick enough. So absolute is our soul's need of something hidden and uncertain for the maintenance of that doubt and hope and effort which are the breath of its life, that if the whole future were laid bare to us beyond today, the interest of all mankind would be bent on the hours that lie between; we should pant after the uncertainties of our one morning and our one afternoon; we should rush fiercely to the Exchange[7] for our last possibility of speculation, of success, of disappointment; we should have a glut of political prophets foretelling a crisis or a no-crisis within the only twenty-four hours left open to prophecy. Conceive the condition of the human mind if all propositions whatsoever were self-evident except one, which was to become self-evident at the close of a summer's day, but in the mean time might be the subject of question, of hypothesis, of debate. Art and philosophy, literature and science, would fasten like bees on that one proposition which had the honey of probability in it, and be the more eager because their enjoyment would end with sunset. Our impulses, our spiritual activities, no more adjust themselves to the idea of their future nullity, than the beating of our heart, or the irritability of our muscles.

Bertha, the slim, fair-haired girl, whose present thoughts and emotions were an enigma to me amid the fatiguing obviousness of the other minds around me, was as absorbing to me as a single unknown today,—as a single hypothetic proposition to remain problematic till sunset; and all the cramped, hemmed-in belief and disbelief, trust and distrust, of my nature welled out in this one narrow channel.

And she made me believe that she loved me. Without ever quitting her tone of *badinage*[8] and playful superiority, she intoxicated me with the sense that I was necessary to her, that she was never at ease unless I was near her, submitting to her playful tyranny. It costs a woman so little effort to besot us in this way! A half-repressed word, a moment's unexpected silence, even an easy fit of petulance on our account, will serve us as *hashish* for a long while. Out of the subtlest web of scarcely perceptible signs, she set me weaving the fancy that she had always unconsciously loved me better than Alfred, but that, with the ignorant fluttered sensibility of a young girl, she had been imposed on by the charm that lay for her in the distinction of being admired

6. Innermost sanctuary of a temple.
7. The Royal Exchange in London, in whose large

courtyard merchants and tradesmen did business.
8. Joking, trifling.

and chosen by a man who made so brilliant a figure in the world as my brother. She satirized herself in a very graceful way for her vanity and ambition. What was it to me that I had the light of my wretched prevision on the fact that now it was I who possessed at least all but the personal part of my brother's advantages? Our sweet illusions are half of them conscious illusions, like effects of color that we know to be made up of tinsel, broken glass, and rags.

We were married eighteen months after Alfred's death, one cold, clear morning in April, when there came hail and sunshine both together; and Bertha, in her white silk and pale-green leaves, and the pale hues of her hair and face, looked like the spirit of the morning. My father was happier than he had thought of being again: my marriage, he felt sure, would complete the desirable modification of my character, and make me practical and worldly enough to take my place in society among sane men. For he delighted in Bertha's tact and acuteness, and felt sure she would be mistress of me, and make me what she chose: I was only twenty-one, and madly in love with her. Poor father! He kept that hope a little while after our first year of marriage, and it was not quite extinct when paralysis came and saved him from utter disappointment.

I shall hurry through the rest of my story, not dwelling so much as I have hitherto done on my inward experience. When people are well known to each other, they talk rather of what befalls them externally, leaving their feelings and sentiments to be inferred.

We lived in a round of visits for some time after our return home, giving splendid dinner-parties, and making a sensation in our neighborhood by the new luster of our equipage, for my father had reserved this display of his increased wealth for the period of his son's marriage; and we gave our acquaintances liberal opportunity for remarking that it was a pity I made so poor a figure as an heir and a bridegroom. The nervous fatigue of this existence, the insincerities and platitudes which I had to live through twice over,—through my inner and outward sense,—would have been maddening to me, if I had not had that sort of intoxicated callousness which came from the delights of a first passion. A bride and bride-groom, surrounded by all the appliances of wealth, hurried through the day by the whirl of society, filling their solitary moments with hastily snatched caresses, are prepared for their future life together as the *novice* is prepared for the cloister,—by experiencing its utmost contrast.

Through all these crowded excited months, Bertha's inward self remained shrouded from me, and I still read her thoughts only through the language of her lips and demeanor: I had still the human interest of wondering whether what I did and said pleased her, of longing to hear a word of affection, of giving a delicious exaggeration of meaning to her smile. But I was conscious of a growing difference in her manner towards me; sometimes strong enough to be called haughty coldness, cutting and chilling me as the hail had done that came across the sunshine on our marriage morning; sometimes only perceptible in the dexterous avoidance of a *tête-à-tête* walk or dinner to which I had been looking forward. I had been deeply pained by this,—had even felt a sort of crushing of the heart, from the sense that my brief day of happiness was near its setting; but still I remained dependent on Bertha, eager for the last rays of a bliss that would soon be gone forever,

hoping and watching for some after-glow more beautiful from the impending night.

I remember—how should I not remember?—the time when that dependence and hope utterly left me, when the sadness I had felt in Bertha's growing estrangement became a joy that I looked back upon with longing, as a man might look back on the last pains in a paralyzed limb. It was just after the close of my father's last illness, which had necessarily withdrawn us from society and thrown us more upon each other. It was the evening of my father's death. On that evening the veil which had shrouded Bertha's soul from me—had made me find in her alone among my fellow-beings the blessed possibility of mystery and doubt and expectation—was first withdrawn. Perhaps it was the first day since the beginning of my passion for her, in which that passion was completely neutralized by the presence of an absorbing feeling of another kind. I had been watching by my father's death-bed: I had been witnessing the last fitful yearning glance his soul had cast back on the spent inheritance of life,—the last faint consciousness of love he had gathered from the pressure of my hand. What are all our personal loves when we have been sharing in that supreme agony? In the first moments when we come away from the presence of death, every other relation to the living is merged, to our feeling, in the great relation of a common nature and a common destiny.

In that state of mind I joined Bertha in her private sitting-room. She was seated in a leaning posture on a settee, with her back towards the door; the great rich coils of her pale blond hair surmounting her small neck, visible above the back of the settee. I remember, as I closed the door behind me, a cold tremulousness seizing me, and a vague sense of being hated and lonely,—vague and strong, like a presentiment. I know how I looked at that moment, for I saw myself in Bertha's thought as she lifted her cutting gray eyes, and looked at me: a miserable ghost-seer, surrounded by phantoms in the noonday, trembling under a breeze when the leaves were still, without appetite for the common objects of human desire, but pining after the moonbeams. We were front to front with each other, and judged each other. The terrible moment of complete illumination had come to me, and I saw that the darkness had hidden no landscape from me, but only a blank prosaic wall: from that evening forth, through the sickening years which followed, I saw all round the narrow room of this woman's soul,—saw petty artifice and mere negation where I had delighted to believe in coy sensibilities and in wit at war with latent feeling,—saw the light floating vanities of the girl defining themselves into the systematic coquetry, the scheming selfishness, of the woman,—saw repulsion and antipathy harden into cruel hatred, giving pain only for the sake of wreaking itself.

For Bertha too; after her kind, felt the bitterness of disillusion. She had believed that my wild poet's passion for her would make me her slave; and that, being her slave, I should execute her will in all things. With the essential shallowness of a negative, unimaginative nature, she was unable to conceive the fact that sensibilities were anything else than weaknesses. She had thought my weaknesses would put me in her power, and she found them unmanageable forces. Our positions were reversed. Before marriage she had completely mastered my imagination, for she was a secret to me; and I created the unknown thought before which I trembled as if it were hers. But

now that her soul was laid open to me, now that I was compelled to share the privacy of her motives, to follow all the petty devices that preceded her words and acts, she found herself powerless with me, except to produce in me the chill shudder of repulsion,—powerless, because I could be acted on by no lever within her reach. I was dead to worldly ambitions, to social vanities, to all the incentives within the compass of her narrow imagination, and I lived under influences utterly invisible to her.

She was really pitiable to have such a husband, and so all the world thought. A graceful, brilliant woman, like Bertha, who smiled on morning callers, made a figure in ball-rooms, and was capable of that light repartee which, from such a woman, is accepted as wit, was secure of carrying off all sympathy from a husband who was sickly, abstracted, and, as some suspected, crack-brained. Even the servants in our house gave her the balance of their regard and pity. For there were no audible quarrels between us; our alienation, our repulsion from each other, lay within the silence of our own hearts; and if the mistress went out a great deal, and seemed to dislike the master's society, was it not natural, poor thing? The master was odd. I was kind and just to my dependants, but I excited in them a shrinking, half-contemptuous pity; for this class of men and women are but slightly determined in their estimate of others by general considerations, or even experience, of character. They judge of persons as they judge of coins, and value those who pass current at a high rate.

After a time I interfered so little with Bertha's habits, that it might seem wonderful how her hatred towards me could grow so intense and active as it did. But she had begun to suspect, by some involuntary betrayals of mine, that there was an abnormal power of penetration in me,—that fitfully, at least, I was strangely cognizant of her thoughts and intentions, and she began to be haunted by a terror of me, which alternated every now and then with defiance. She meditated continually how the incubus[9] could be shaken off her life,—how she could be freed from this hateful bond to a being whom she at once despised as an imbecile, and dreaded as an inquisitor. For a long while she lived in the hope that my evident wretchedness would drive me to the commission of suicide; but suicide was not in my nature. I was too completely swayed by the sense that I was in the grasp of unknown forces, to believe in my power of self-release. Towards my own destiny I had become entirely passive; for my one ardent desire had spent itself, and impulse no longer predominated over knowledge. For this reason I never thought of taking any steps towards a complete separation, which would have made our alienation evident to the world. Why should I rush for help to a new course, when I was only suffering from the consequences of a deed which had been the act of my intensest will? That would have been the logic of one who had desires to gratify, and I had no desires. But Bertha and I lived more and more aloof from each other. The rich find it easy to live married and apart.

That course of our life which I have indicated in a few sentences filled the space of years. So much misery, so slow and hideous a growth of hatred and sin, may be compressed into a sentence! And men judge of each other's lives through this summary medium. They epitomize[1] the experience of their fellow-mortal, and pronounce judgment on him in neat syntax, and feel them-

9. An evil spirit thought in medieval times to have sexual intercourse with women while they are asleep.
1. Summarize.

selves wise and virtuous,—conquerors over the temptations they define in well-selected predicates. Seven years of wretchedness glide glibly over the lips of the man who has never counted them out in moments of chill disappointment, of head and heart throbbings, of dread and vain wrestling, of remorse and despair. We learn *words* by rote, but not their meaning; *that* must be paid for with our life-blood, and printed in the subtle fibers of our nerves.

But I will hasten to finish my story. Brevity is justified at once to those who readily understand, and to those who will never understand.

Some years after my father's death, I was sitting by the dim firelight in my library one January evening,—sitting in the leather chair that used to be my father's,—when Bertha appeared at the door, with a candle in her hand, and advanced towards me. I knew the ball-dress she had on,—the white ball-dress with the green jewels, shone upon by the light of the wax candle which lit up the medallion of the dying Cleopatra on the mantelpiece. Why did she come to me before going out? I had not seen her in the library, which was my habitual place, for months. Why did she stand before me with the candle in her hand, with her cruel contemptuous eyes fixed on me, and the glittering serpent, like a familiar demon, on her breast? For a moment I thought this fulfillment of my vision at Vienna marked some dreadful crisis in my fate, but I saw nothing in Bertha's mind, as she stood before me, except scorn for the look of overwhelming misery with which I sat before her. . . . "Fool, idiot, why don't you kill yourself, then?"—that was her thought. But at length her thoughts reverted to her errand, and she spoke aloud. The apparently indifferent nature of the errand seemed to make a ridiculous anticlimax to my prevision and my agitation.

"I have had to hire a new maid. Fletcher is going to be married, and she wants me to ask you to let her husband have the public-house and farm at Molton. I wish him to have it. You must give the promise now, because Fletcher is going tomorrow morning,—and quickly, because I'm in a hurry."

"Very well; you may promise her," I said indifferently; and Bertha swept out of the library again.

I always shrank from the sight of a new person, and all the more when it was a person whose mental life was likely to weary my reluctant insight with worldly ignorant trivialities. But I shrank especially from the sight of this new maid, because her advent had been announced to me at a moment to which I could not cease to attach some fatality: I had a vague dread that I should find her mixed up with the dreary drama of my life,—that some new sickening vision would reveal her to me as an evil genius.[2] When at last I did unavoidably meet her, the vague dread was changed into definite disgust. She was a tall, wiry, dark-eyed woman, this Mrs. Archer, with a face handsome enough to give her coarse hard nature the odious finish of bold, selfconfident coquetry. That was enough to make me avoid her, quite apart from the contemptuous feeling with which she contemplated me. I seldom saw her; but I perceived that she rapidly became a favorite with her mistress, and, after the lapse of eight or nine months, I began to be aware that there had arisen in Bertha's mind towards this woman a mingled feeling of fear and dependence, and that this feeling was associated with ill-defined images

2. Spirit or influence.

of candle-light scenes in her dressing-room, and the locking up of something in Bertha's cabinet. My interviews with my wife had become so brief and so rarely solitary that I had no opportunity of perceiving these images in her mind with more definiteness. The recollections of the past become contracted in the rapidity of thought till they sometimes bear hardly a more distinct resemblance to the external reality than the forms of an oriental alphabet[3] to the objects that suggested them.

Besides, for the last year or more a modification had been going forward in my mental condition, and was growing more and more marked. My insight into the minds of those around me was becoming dimmer and more fitful, and the ideas that crowded my double consciousness became less and less dependent on any personal contact. All that was personal in me seemed to be suffering a gradual death, so that I was losing the organ through which the personal agitations and projects of others could affect me. But along with this relief from wearisome insight, there was a new development of what I concluded—as I have since found rightly,—to be a prevision of external scenes. It was as if the relation between me and my fellow-men was more and more deadened, and my relation to what we call the inanimate was quickened into new life. The more I lived apart from society, and in proportion as my wretchedness subsided from the violent throb of agonized passion into the dulness of habitual pain, the more frequent and vivid became such visions as that I had had of Prague,—of strange cities, of sandy plains, of gigantic ruins, of midnight skies with strange bright constellations, of mountain-passes, of grassy nooks flecked with the afternoon sunshine through the boughs: I was in the midst of such scenes, and in all of them one presence seemed to weigh on me in all these mighty shapes,—the presence of something unknown and pitiless. For continual suffering had annihilated religious faith within me: to the utterly miserable—the unloving and the unloved—there is no religion possible, no worship but a worship of devils. And beyond all these, and continually recurring, was the vision of my death,—the pangs, the suffocation, the last struggle, when life would be grasped at in vain.

Things were in this state near the end of the seventh year. I had become entirely free from insight, from my abnormal cognizance of any other consciousness than my own, and, instead of intruding involuntarily into the world of other minds, was living continually in my own solitary future. Bertha was aware that I was greatly changed. To my surprise she had of late seemed to seek opportunities of remaining in my society, and had cultivated that kind of distant yet familiar talk which is customary between a husband and wife who live in polite and irrevocable alienation. I bore this with languid submission, and without feeling enough interest in her motives to be roused into keen observation; yet I could not help perceiving something triumphant and excited in her carriage and the expression of her face,—something too subtle to express itself in words or tones, but giving one the idea that she lived in a state of expectation or hopeful suspense. My chief feeling was satisfaction that her inner self was once more shut out from me; and I almost revelled for the moment in the absent melancholy that made me answer her at cross purposes, and betray utter ignorance of what she had been saying.

3. I.e., the ideograms of the Chinese writing system.

I remember well the look and the smile with which she one day said, after a mistake of this kind on my part: "I used to think you were a clairvoyant, and that was the reason why you were so bitter against other clairvoyants, wanting to keep your monopoly; but I see now you have become rather duller than the rest of the world."

I said nothing in reply. It occurred to me that her recent obtrusion of herself upon me might have been prompted by the wish to test my power of detecting some of her secrets; but I let the thought drop again at once: her motives and her deeds had no interest for me, and whatever pleasures she might be seeking, I had no wish to balk her. There was still pity in my soul for every living thing, and Bertha was living,—was surrounded with possibilities of misery.

Just at this time there occurred an event which roused me somewhat from my inertia, and gave me an interest in the passing moment that I had thought impossible for me. It was a visit from Charles Meunier, who had written me word that he was coming to England for relaxation from too strenuous labor, and would like to see me. Meunier had now a European reputation; but his letter to me expressed that keen remembrance of an early regard, an early debt of sympathy, which is inseparable from nobility of character: and I too felt as if his presence would be to me like a transient resurrection into a happier preexistence.

He came, and as far as possible, I renewed our old pleasure of making *tête-à-tête* excursions, though, instead of mountains and glaciers and the wide blue lake, we had to content ourselves with mere slopes and ponds and artificial plantations. The years had changed us both, but with what different result! Meunier was now a brilliant figure in society, to whom elegant women pretended to listen, and whose acquaintance was boasted of by noblemen ambitious of brains. He repressed with the utmost delicacy all betrayal of the shock which I am sure he must have received from our meeting, or of a desire to penetrate into my condition and circumstances, and sought by the utmost exertion of his charming social powers to make our reunion agreeable. Bertha was much struck by the unexpected fascinations of a visitor whom she had expected to find presentable only on the score of his celebrity, and put forth all her coquetries and accomplishments. Apparently she succeeded in attracting his admiration, for his manner towards her was attentive and flattering. The effect of his presence on me was so benignant, especially in those renewals of our old *tête-à-tête* wanderings, when he poured forth to me wonderful narratives of his professional experience, that more than once, when his talk turned on the psychological relations of disease, the thought crossed my mind that, if his stay with me were long enough, I might possibly bring myself to tell this man the secrets of my lot. Might there not lie some remedy for *me*, too, in his science? Might there not at least lie some comprehension and sympathy ready for me in his large and susceptible mind? But the thought only flickered feebly now and then, and died out before it could become a wish. The horror I had of again breaking in on the privacy of another soul made me, by an irrational instinct, draw the shroud of concealment more closely around my own, as we automatically perform the gesture we feel to be wanting in another.

When Meunier's visit was approaching its conclusion, there happened an

event which caused some excitement in our household, owing to the sur-
prisingly strong effect it appeared to produce on Bertha,—on Bertha, the
self-possessed, who usually seemed inaccessible to feminine agitations, and
did even her hate in a self-restrained hygienic manner. This event was the
sudden severe illness of her maid, Mrs. Archer. I have reserved to this
moment the mention of a circumstance which had forced itself on my notice
shortly before Meunier's arrival, namely, that there had been some quarrel
between Bertha and this maid, apparently during a visit to a distant family,
in which she had accompanied her mistress. I had overheard Archer speaking
in a tone of bitter insolence, which I should have thought an adequate reason
for immediate dismissal. No dismissal followed; on the contrary, Bertha
seemed to be silently putting up with personal inconveniences from the exhi-
bitions of this woman's temper. I was the more astonished to observe that
her illness seemed a cause of strong solicitude to Bertha; that she was at the
bedside night and day, and would allow no one else to officiate as head-
nurse. It happened that our family doctor was out on a holiday, an accident
which made Meunier's presence in the house doubly welcome, and he appar-
ently entered into the case with an interest which seemed so much stronger
than the ordinary professional feeling, that one day when he had fallen into
a long fit of silence after visiting her, I said to him,—

"Is this a very peculiar case of disease, Meunier?"

"No," he answered, "it is an attack of peritonitis, which will be fatal, but
which does not differ physically from many other cases that have come under
my observation. But I'll tell you what I have on my mind. I want to make an
experiment on this woman, if you will give me permission. It can do her no
harm,—will give her no pain,—for I shall not make it until life is extinct to
all purposes of sensation. I want to try the effect of transfusing blood into
her arteries after the heart has ceased to beat for some minutes. I have tried
the experiment again and again with animals that have died of this disease,
with astounding results, and I want to try it on a human subject. I have the
small tubes necessary, in a case I have with me, and the rest of the apparatus
could be prepared readily. I should use my own blood,—take it from my own
arm. This woman won't live through the night, I'm convinced, and I want
you to promise me your assistance in making the experiment. I can't do
without another hand, but it would perhaps not be well to call in a medical
assistant from among your provincial doctors. A disagreeable foolish version
of the thing might get abroad."

"Have you spoken to my wife on the subject?" I said, "because she appears
to be peculiarly sensitive about this woman: she has been a favorite maid."

"To tell you the truth," said Meunier, "I don't want her to know about it.
There are always insuperable difficulties with women in these matters, and
the effect on the supposed dead body may be startling. You and I will sit up
together, and be in readiness. When certain symptoms appear I shall take
you in, and at the right moment we must manage to get every one else out
of the room."

I need not give our farther conversation on the subject. He entered very
fully into the details, and overcame my repulsion from them, by exciting in
me a mingled awe and curiosity concerning the possible results of his
experiment.

We prepared everything, and he instructed me in my part as assistant. He

had not told Bertha of his absolute conviction that Archer would not survive through the night, and endeavored to persuade her to leave the patient and take a night's rest. But she was obstinate, suspecting the fact that death was at hand, and supposing that he wished merely to save her nerves. She refused to leave the sick-room. Meunier and I sat up together in the library, he making frequent visits to the sick-room, and returning with the information that the case was taking precisely the course he expected. Once he said to me, "Can you imagine any cause of ill feeling this woman has against her mistress, who is so devoted to her?"

"I think there was some misunderstanding between them before her illness. Why do you ask?"

"Because I have observed for the last five or six hours,—since, I fancy, she has lost all hope of recovery,—there seems a strange prompting in her to say something which pain and failing strength forbid her to utter; and there is a look of hideous meaning in her eyes, which she turns continually towards her mistress. In this disease the mind often remains singularly clear to the last."

"I am not surprised at an indication of malevolent feeling in her," I said. "She is a woman who has always inspired me with distrust and dislike, but she managed to insinuate herself into her mistress's favor." He was silent after this, looking at the fire with an air of absorption, till he went upstairs again. He stayed away longer than usual, and on returning, said to me quietly, "Come now."

I followed him to the chamber where death was hovering. The dark hangings of the large bed made a background that gave a strong relief to Bertha's pale face as I entered. She started forward as she saw me enter, and then looked at Meunier with an expression of angry inquiry; but he lifted up his hand as if to impose silence, while he fixed his glance on the dying woman and felt her pulse. The face was pinched and ghastly, a cold perspiration was on the forehead, and the eyelids were lowered so as almost to conceal the large dark eyes. After a minute or two, Meunier walked round to the other side of the bed where Bertha stood, and with his usual air of gentle politeness towards her begged her to leave the patient under our care,—everything should be done for her,—she was no longer in a state to be conscious of an affectionate presence. Bertha was hesitating, apparently almost willing to believe his assurance and to comply. She looked round at the ghastly dying face, as if to read the confirmation of that assurance, when for a moment the lowered eyelids were raised again, and it seemed as if the eyes were looking towards Bertha, but blankly. A shudder passed through Bertha's frame, and she returned to her station near the pillow, tacitly implying that she would not leave the room.

The eyelids were lifted no more. Once I looked at Bertha as she watched the face of the dying one. She wore a rich *peignoir,* and her blond hair was half covered by a lace cap: in her attire she was, as always, an elegant woman, fit to figure in a picture of modern aristocratic life: but I asked myself how that face of hers could ever have seemed to me the face of a woman born of woman, with memories of childhood, capable of pain, needing to be fondled? The features at that moment seemed so preternaturally sharp, the eyes were so hard and eager,—she looked like a cruel immortal, finding her spiritual feast in the agonies of a dying race. For across those hard features there

came something like a flash when the last hour had been breathed out, and we all felt that the dark veil had completely fallen. What secret was there between Bertha and this woman? I turned my eyes from her with a horrible dread lest my insight should return, and I should be obliged to see what had been breeding about two unloving women's hearts. I felt that Bertha had been watching for the moment of death as the sealing of her secret: I thanked Heaven it could remain sealed for me.

Meunier said quietly, "She is gone." He then gave his arm to Bertha, and she submitted to be led out of the room.

I suppose it was at her order that two female attendants came into the room, and dismissed the younger one who had been present before. When they entered, Meunier had already opened the artery in the long thin neck that lay rigid on the pillow, and I dismissed them, ordering them to remain at a distance till we rang: the doctor, I said, had an operation to perform,—he was not sure about the death. For the next twenty minutes I forgot everything but Meunier and the experiment in which he was so absorbed that I think his senses would have been closed against all sounds or sights which had no relation to it. It was my task at first to keep up the artificial respiration in the body after the transfusion had been effected, but presently Meunier relieved me, and I could see the wondrous slow return of life; the breast began to heave, the inspirations became stronger, the eyelids quivered, and the soul seemed to have returned beneath them. The artificial respiration was withdrawn: still the breathing continued, and there was a movement of the lips.

Just then I heard the handle of the door moving: I suppose Bertha had heard from the women that they had been dismissed: probably a vague fear had arisen in her mind, for she entered with a look of alarm. She came to the foot of the bed and gave a stifled cry.

The dead woman's eyes were wide open, and met hers in full recognition,—the recognition of hate. With a sudden strong effort, the hand that Bertha had thought forever still was pointed towards her, and the haggard face moved. The gasping eager voice said,—

"You mean to poison your husband . . . the poison is in the black cabinet . . . I got it for you . . . you laughed at me, and told lies about me behind my back, to make me disgusting . . . because you were jealous . . . are you sorry . . . now?"

The lips continued to murmur, but the sounds were no longer distinct. Soon there was no sound,—only a slight movement: the flame had leaped out, and was being extinguished the faster. The wretched woman's heart-strings had been set to hatred and vengeance; the spirit of life had swept the chords for an instant, and was gone again forever. Great God! Is this what it is to live again . . . to wake up with our unstilled thirst upon us, with our unuttered curses rising to our lips, with our muscles ready to act out their half-committed sins?

Bertha stood pale at the foot of the bed, quivering and helpless, despairing of devices,[4] like a cunning animal whose hiding-places are surrounded by swift-advancing flame. Even Meunier looked paralyzed; life for that moment

4. I.e., losing hope in her plans.

ceased to be a scientific problem to him. As for me, this scene seemed of one texture with the rest of my existence: horror was my familiar,[5] and this new revelation was only like an old pain recurring with new circumstances.

Since then Bertha and I have lived apart,—she in her own neighborhood, the mistress of half our wealth; I as a wanderer in foreign countries, until I came to this Devonshire nest to die. Bertha lives pitied and admired; for what had I against that charming woman, whom every one but myself could have been happy with? There had been no witness of the scene in the dying room except Meunier, and while Meunier lived his lips were sealed by a promise to me.

Once or twice, weary of wandering, I rested in a favorite spot, and my heart went out towards the men and women and children whose faces were becoming familiar to me; but I was driven away again in terror at the approach of my old insight,—driven away to live continually with the one Unknown Presence revealed and yet hidden by the moving curtain of the earth and sky. Till at last disease took hold of me and forced me to rest here,—forced me to live in dependence on my servants. And then the curse of insight, of my double consciousness, came again, and has never left me. I know all their narrow thoughts, their feeble regard, their half-wearied pity.

It is the 20th of September, 1850. I know these figures I have just written, as if they were a long familiar inscription. I have seen them on this page in my desk unnumbered times, when the scene of my dying struggle has opened upon me. . . .

<div align="right">1859</div>

5. Familiar spirit or demon.

FLORENCE NIGHTINGALE
1820–1910

Florence Nightingale was famous in her lifetime as a nurse, hospital administrator, sanitation reformer, and founder of the Nightingale School for Nursing as well as the Training School for Midwives. She was also the author of a polemical tract titled *Cassandra*. The title of this protest against the feminization of women dramatizes Nightingale's anxious awareness that her own complaint might be just as ineffectual as that of Cassandra, the virgin priestess of Apollo whose divinely inspired prophecy is destined to go unheeded.

Nightingale's protest was part of a personal rebellion against her family's traditionally Victorian expectations for her. The family was extremely well-to-do, with residences in Derbyshire, the New Forest, and London's fashionable Mayfair district. It was her mother, Fanny, and her older sister, Parthenope, who represented a feminine ideal that Nightingale found stultifying. Although William Edward Nightingale educated his two children in Greek and Latin, history and philosophy, both girls were

clearly intended to grace a fairly typical upper-class household and to marry well. Florence Nightingale reacted to such values by falling into trances, depressions, and daydreams: "The whole occupation of Parthe and Mama," Nightingale later wrote, "was to lie on two sofas and tell one another not to get tired by putting flowers into water." In 1837 the first of what she described as four calls from God enjoined her to a life of active service. Strengthened in her resolve to defy the family's prescriptions, she rejected a marriage proposal from Richard Monckton Milnes, a prosperous social reformer. Between her seventeenth and thirty-second years she struggled to free herself from her mother's acceptance of Parthenope's extreme emotional dependency. In her guilt over this conflict, Nightingale resembled the speaker whose suicidal speeches frame Cassandra: "My present life is suicide," she wrote in her diary. "In my 31st year I see nothing desirable but death; What am I that their life is not good enough for me? Oh God what am I?"

Cassandra, which was originally part of a work titled Suggestions for Thought to Searchers after Religious Truth, dates from this period in 1851 and 1852 when Nightingale was struggling with the issue of her own self-definition. This three-volume book has never been publicly printed, and Cassandra was not available until 1928, when Ray Strachey included it in The Cause, her history of the women's movement. The writing of Suggestions for Thought, however, cleared a way for Nightingale herself: at thirty-two years of age, she left home to train as a nurse at the Institute for Deaconesses at Kaiserwerth on the Rhine. In spite of her family's disapprobation, in 1853 she returned to England to become the superintendent of the Institute for the Care of Sick Gentlewomen in Distressed Circumstances, when her father agreed to settle an annual £500 on her to ensure her independence. The next year she began her famous work at Scutari in the Crimea.

With ten Roman Catholic nuns, fourteen Anglican sisters, and fourteen hospital nurses, Nightingale confronted the cholera, typhus, gangrene, dysentery, and scurvy that were destroying the British army. In spite of the initial hostility of army officials, Nightingale was determined to help the thousands of men who were dying because of lack of sanitation, lack of equipment, and lack of space in the barracks hospital. She dispensed food and clothing, organized a laundry, built a new wing, and equipped it with everything from towels to arrowroot in huge milk pails. On her return, a national heroine at the age of thirty-six, the "Lady of the Lamp" suffered an illness that at least one scholar, George Pickering, concludes was "a weapon to protect herself from her family."

An invalid's life guaranteed Nightingale's privacy so she could devote herself to the two hundred-odd books and reports she wrote on world hunger, education, taxation, hospital construction, reform of the Poor Law, and the administration of the army in India. Significantly, too, after her mother's death in 1880 and Parthenope's in 1890, her health began to improve; however, she never relinquished her horror of what her mother and sister had represented. During her years of invalidism, she had worked through the agency of a succession of prominent men, including Sidney Herbert, Arthur Clough, and Sir John Sutherland. Friendly with each "exactly like two men," she had declared earlier to Harriet Martineau that "I am brutally indifferent to the wrongs or rights of my sex." Paradoxically, however, in Cassandra, the work that liberated her to reject the idleness of her mother and sister, Nightingale produced what the critic Elaine Showalter has aptly termed "a major text of English feminism, a link between Wollstonecraft and Woolf."

From Cassandra

[WOMEN'S TIME][1]

"Yet I would spare no pang,
Would wish no torture less,
The more that anguish racks,
The earlier it will bless."

Give us back our suffering, we cry to Heaven in our hearts—suffering rather than indifferentism; for out of nothing comes nothing.[2] But out of suffering may come the cure. Better have pain than paralysis! A hundred struggle and drown in the breakers. One discovers the new world. But rather, ten times rather, die in the surf, heralding the way to that new world, than stand idly on the shore!

Passion, intellect, moral activity—these three have never been satisfied in a woman. In this cold and oppressive conventional atmosphere, they cannot be satisfied. To say more on this subject would be to enter into the whole history of society, of the present state of civilization.

Look at that lizard—"It is not hot," he says, "I like it. The atmosphere which enervates you is life to me." The state of society which some complain of makes others happy. Why should these complain to those? *They* do not suffer. *They* would not understand it, any more than that lizard would comprehend the sufferings of a Shetland sheep.

The progressive[3] world is necessarily divided into two classes—those who take the best of what there is and enjoy it—those who wish for something better and try to create it. Without these two classes the world would be badly off. They are the very conditions of progress, both the one and the other. Were there none who were discontented with what they have, the world would never reach anything better. And, through the other class, which is constantly taking the best of what the first is creating for them, a balance is secured, and that which is conquered is held fast. But with neither class must we quarrel for not possessing the privileges of the other. The laws of the nature of each make it impossible.

Is discontent a privilege?

Yes, it is a privilege for you to suffer for your race—a privilege not reserved to the Redeemer,[4] and the martyrs alone, but one enjoyed by numbers in every age.

The common-place life of thousands; and in that is its only interest—its only merit as a history; viz. that it is the type of common sufferings—the story of one who has not the courage to resist nor to submit to the civilization of her time—is this.

Poetry and imagination begin life. A child will fall on its knees on the gravel walk at the sight of a pink hawthorn in full flower, when it is by itself, to praise God for it.

Then comes intellect. It wishes to satisfy the wants which intellect creates for it. But there is a physical, not moral, impossibility of supplying the wants of the intellect in the state of civilization at which we have arrived. The

1. Part II of *Cassandra*.
2. An echo of Shakespeare's *King Lear* 1.1.89: "Nothing will come of nothing."
3. I.e., progressing or developing.
4. Christ.

stimulus, the training, the time, are all three wanting to us; or, in other words, the means and inducements are not there.

Look at the poor lives we lead. It is a wonder that we are so good as we are, not that we are so bad. In looking round we are struck with the power of the organizations we see, not with their want[5] of power. Now and then, it is true, we are conscious that *there* is an inferior organization, but, in general, just the contrary. Mrs. A. has the imagination, the poetry of a Murillo,[6] and has sufficient power of execution to show that she might have had a great deal more. Why is she not a Murillo? From a material difficulty, not a mental one. If she has a knife and fork in her hands for three hours of the day, she cannot have a pencil or brush. Dinner is the great sacred ceremony of this day, the great sacrament. To be absent from dinner is equivalent to being ill. Nothing else will excuse us from it. Bodily incapacity is the only apology valid. If she has a pen and ink in her hands during other three hours, writing answers for the penny post, again, she cannot have her pencil,[7] and *so ad infinitum* through life. People have no type[8] before them in their lives, neither fathers nor mothers, nor the children themselves. They look at things in detail. They say, "It is very desirable that A., my daughter, should go to such a party, should know such a lady, should sit by such a person." It is true. But what standard have they before them of the nature and destination of man? The very words are rejected as pedantic. But might they not, at least, have a type in their minds that such an one might be a discoverer through her intellect, such another through her art, a third through her moral power?

Women often try one branch of intellect after another in their youth, *e.g.* mathematics. But that, least of all is compatible with the life of "society." It is impossible to follow up anything systematically. Women often long to enter some man's profession where they would find direction, competition (or rather opportunity of measuring the intellect with others) and, above all, time.

In those wise institutions, mixed as they are with many follies, which will last as long as the human race lasts, because they are adapted to the wants of the human race; those institutions which we call monasteries, and which, embracing much that is contrary to the laws of nature, are yet better adapted to the union of the life of action and that of thought than any other mode of life with which we are acquainted; in many such, four and a half hours, at least, are daily set aside for thought, rules are given for thought, training and opportunity afforded. Among us there is *no* time appointed for this purpose, and the difficulty is that, in our social life, we must be always doubtful whether we ought not to be with somebody else or be doing something else.

Are men better off than women in this?

If one calls upon a friend in London and sees her son in the drawing-room, it strikes one as odd to find a young man sitting idle in his mother's drawing-room in the morning. For men, who are seen much in those haunts, there is no end of the epithets we have: "knights of the carpet," "drawing-room heroes," "ladies' men." But suppose we were to see a number of men in the morning sitting round a table in the drawing-room, looking at prints, doing worsted work,[9] and reading little books, how we should laugh! A member of

5. Lack.
6. Bartolomé Murillo (1618–1682), Spanish painter of religious and peasant subjects.
7. Artist's pencil or brush.
8. Model.
9. Knitting, or doing embroidery.

the House of Commons was once known to do worsted work. Of another man was said, "His only fault is that he is too good; he drives out with his mother every day in the carriage, and if he is asked anywhere he answers that he must dine with his mother, but, if she can spare him, he will come in to tea, and he does not come."

Now, why is it more ridiculous for a man than for a woman to do worsted work and drive out every day in the carriage? Why should we laugh if we were to see a parcel of men sitting round a drawing-room table in the morning, and think it all right if they were women?

Is man's time more valuable than woman's? or is the difference between man and woman this, that woman has confessedly nothing to do?

Women are never supposed to have any occupation of sufficient importance *not* to be interrupted, except "suckling their fools";[1] and women themselves have accepted this, have written books to support it, and have trained themselves so as to consider whatever they do as *not* of such value to the world or to others, but that they can throw it up at the first "claim of social life." They have accustomed themselves to consider intellectual occupation as a merely selfish amusement, which it is their "duty" to give up for every trifler more selfish than themselves.

A young man (who was afterwards useful and known in his day and generation) when busy reading and sent for by his proud mother to shine in some morning visit, came; but, after it was over, he said, "Now, remember, this is not to happen again. I came that you might not think me sulky, but I shall not come again." But for a young woman to send such a message to her mother and sisters, how impertinent it would be! A woman of great administrative powers said that she never undertook anything which she "could not throw by at once, if necessary."

How do we explain then the many cases of women who have distinguished themselves in classics, mathematics, even in politics?

Widowhood, ill-health, or want of bread, these three explanations or excuses are supposed to justify a woman taking up an occupation. In some cases, no doubt, an indomitable force of character will suffice without any of these three, but such are rare.

But see how society fritters away the intellects of those committed to her charge! It is said that society is necessary to sharpen the intellect. But what do we seek society for? It does sharpen the intellect, because it is a kind of *tour-de-force* to say something at a pinch,—unprepared and uninterested with any subject, to improvise something under difficulties. But what "go we out for to seek"? To take the chance of some one having something to say which we want to hear? or of finding something to say which *they* want to hear? You have a little to say, but not much. You often make a stipulation with someone else, "Come in ten minutes, for I shall not be able to find enough to spin out longer than that." You are not to talk of anything very interesting, for the essence of society is to prevent any long conversations and all tête-à-têtes. *Glissez, n'appuyez pas* is its very motto. The praise of a good *maîtresse demaison*[2] consists in this, that she allows no one person to be too much absorbed in, or too long about, a conversation. She always

1. Iago on women's role: "To suckle fools, and chronicle small beer" (*Shakespeare, Othello* 2.1.162).

2. Mistress of the house (French). "*Glissez, n'appuyez pas*": slide, don't lean (French).

recalls them to their "duty." People do not go into the company of their fellow-creatures for what would seem a very sufficient reason, namely, that they have something to say to them, or something that they want to hear from them; but in the vague hope that they may find something to say.

Then as to solitary opportunities. Women never have an half-hour in all their lives (excepting before or after anybody is up in the house) that they can call their own, without fear of offending or of hurting someone. Why do people sit up so late, or, more rarely, get up so early? Not because the day is not long enough, but because they have "no time in the day to themselves."

If we do attempt to do anything in company, what is the system of literary exercise which we pursue? Everybody reads aloud out of their own book or newspaper—or, every five minutes, something is said. And what is it to be "read aloud to"? The most miserable exercise of the human intellect. Or rather, is it any exercise at all? It is like lying on one's back, with one's hands tied and having liquid poured down one's throat. Worse than that, because suffocation would immediately ensue and put a stop to this operation. But no suffocation would stop the other.

So much for the satisfaction of the intellect. Yet for a married woman in society, it is even worse. A married woman was heard to wish that she could break a limb that she might have a little time to herself. Many take advantage of the fear of "infection" to do the same.

It is a thing so accepted among women that they have nothing to do, that one woman has not the least scruple in saying to another, "I will come and spend the morning with you." And you would be thought quite surly and absurd, if you were to refuse it on the plea of occupation. Nay, it is thought a mark of amiability and affection, if you are "on such terms" that you can "come in" "any morning you please."

In a country house, if there is a large party of young people, "You will spend the morning with us," they say to the neighbors, "we will drive together in the afternoon," "tomorrow we will make an expedition, and we will spend the evening together." And this is thought friendly and spending time in a pleasant manner. So women play through life. Yet time is the most valuable of all things. If they had come every morning and afternoon and robbed us of half-a-crown we should have had redress from the police. But it is laid down, that our time is of no value. If you offer a morning visit to a professional man, and say, "I will just stay an hour with you, if you will allow me, till so and so comes back to fetch me"; it costs him the earnings of an hour, and therefore he has a right to complain. But women have no right, because it is "only their time."

Women have no means given them, whereby they can resist the "claims of social life." They are taught from their infancy upwards that it is a wrong, ill-tempered, and a misunderstanding of "woman's mission" (with a great M) if they do not allow themselves willingly to be interrupted at all hours. If a woman has once put in a claim to be treated as a man by some work of science or art or literature, which she can show as the "fruit of her leisure," then she will be considered justified in having leisure (hardly, perhaps, even then). But if not, not. If she has nothing to show, she must resign herself to her fate.

[THE SAVIOR OF HER RACE]

V

"L'enthousiasme est la faiblesse d'un temps où l'intelligence monte très haut, entrainée par l'imagination, et tombe très bas, écrasée par une réalité, sans poésie et sans grandeur."[3]

Women dream till they have no longer the strength to dream; those dreams against which they so struggle, so honestly, vigorously, and conscientiously, and so in vain, yet which are their life, without which they could not have lived; those dreams go at last. All their plans and visions seem vanished, and they know not where; gone, and they cannot recall them. They do not even remember them. And they are left without the food of reality or of hope.

Later in life, they neither desire nor dream, neither of activity, nor of love, nor of intellect. The last often survives the longest. They wish, if their experiences would benefit anybody, to give them to someone. But they never find an hour free in which to collect their thoughts, and so discouragement becomes ever deeper and deeper, and they less and less capable of undertaking anything.

It seems as if the female spirit of the world were mourning everlastingly over blessings, not *lost*, but which she has never had, and which, in her discouragement she feels that she never will have, they are so far off.

The more complete a woman's organization, the more she will feel it, till at last there shall arise a woman, who will resume,[4] in her own soul, all the sufferings of her race, and that woman will be the Savior of her race.

Jesus Christ raised women above the condition of mere slaves, mere ministers to the passions of the man, raised them by His sympathy, to be Ministers of God. He gave them moral activity. But the Age, the World, Humanity, must give them the means to exercise this moral activity, must give them intellectual cultivation, spheres of action.

There is perhaps no century where the woman shows so meanly as in this.[5] Because her education seems entirely to have parted company with her vocation; there is no longer unity between the woman as inwardly developed, and as outwardly manifested.

In the last century it was not so. In the succeeding one let us hope that it will no longer be so.

But now she is like the Archangel Michael as he stands upon Saint Angelo at Rome.[6] She has an immense provision of wings, which seem as if they would bear her over earth and heaven; but when she tries to use them, she is petrified into stone, her feet are grown into the earth, chained to the bronze pedestal.

Nothing can well be imagined more painful than the present position of

3. Enthusiasm is the weakness of a time when intelligence mounts very high, dragged by the imagination, and falls very low, crushed by a reality without poetry and without grandeur (French). From George Sand's 1839 preface to her novel *Lélia* (1833).
4. Encompass, go through in summary form.
5. At almost every period of social life, we find, as it were, two undercurrents running different ways. There is the noble woman who dreams the following out her useful vocation; but there is also the selfish dreamer now, who is ever turning to something new, regardless of the expectations she has voluntarily excited, who is ever talking about "making a life for herself," heedless that she is spoiling another life, undertaken, perhaps, at her own bidding. This is the ugly reverse of the medal [Nightingale's note].
6. The Castel Sant'Angelo (originally the tomb of Hadrian) is Rome's fortress; it takes its name from the 18-century statue of the archangel on its round top.

woman, unless, on the one hand, she renounces all outward activity and keeps herself within the magic sphere, the bubble of her dreams; or, on the other, surrendering all aspiration, she gives herself to her real life, soul and body. For those to whom it is possible, the latter is best; for out of activity may come thought, out of mere aspiration can come nothing.

But now—when the young imagination is so high and so developed, and reality is so narrow and conventional—there is no more parallelism between life in the thought and life in the actual than between the corpse, which lies motionless in its narrow bed, and the spirit, which, in our imagination, is at large among the stars.

The ideal life is passed in noble schemes of good consecutively followed up, of devotion to a great object, of sympathy given and received for high ideas and generous feelings. The actual life is passed in sympathy given and received for a dinner, a party, a piece of furniture, a house built or a garden laid out well, in devotion to your guests—(a too real devotion, for it implies that of all your time)—in schemes of schooling for the poor, which you follow up perhaps in an odd quarter of an hour, between luncheon and driving out in the carriage—broth and dripping are included in the plan[7]—and the rest of your time goes in ordering the dinner, hunting for a governess for your children, and sending pheasants and apples to your poorer relations. Is there anything in *this* life which can be called an Incarnation of the ideal life within? Is it a wonder that the unhappy woman should prefer to keep them entirely separate? not to take the bloom off her Ideal by mixing it up with her Actual; not to make her Actual still more unpalatable by trying to *inform* it with her Ideal? And then she is blamed, and her own sex unites against her, for not being content with the "day of small things."[8] She is told that "trifles make the sum of human things"; they do indeed. She is contemptuously asked, "Would she abolish domestic life?" Men are afraid that their houses will not be so comfortable, that their wives will make themselves "remarkable" women, that they will make themselves distasteful to men; they write books (and very wisely) to teach themselves to dramatize "little things," to persuade themselves that "domestic life is their sphere" and to idealize the "sacred hearth." Sacred it is indeed. Sacred from the touch of their sons almost as soon as they are out of childhood—from its dulness and its tyrannous trifling *these* recoil. Sacred from the grasp of their daughters' affections upon which it has so light a hold that they seize the first opportunity of marriage, *their* only chance of emancipation. The "sacred hearth"; sacred to their husband's sleep, their sons' absence in the body and their daughters' in mind.

Oh! mothers, who talk about this hearth, how much do you know of your son's real life, how much of your daughter's imaginary one? Awake, ye women, all ye that sleep, awake! If this domestic life were so very good, would your young men wander away from it, your maidens think of something else?

The time is come when women must do something more than the "domestic hearth," which means nursing the infants, keeping a pretty house, having a good dinner and an entertaining party.

7. I.e., little bits of time are intermingled like broth and dripping. 8. Zechariah 4.10.

You say, "It is true, our young men see visions, and our maidens dream dreams," but what of? Does not the woman intend to marry, and have over again what she has at home? and the man ultimately too? Yes, but not the same; she *will* have the same, that is, if circumstances are not altered to prevent it; but her *ideal* is very different, though that ideal and the reality will never come together to mould each other. And it is not only the unmarried woman who dreams. The married woman also holds long imaginary conversations but too often.

<div align="center">VI</div>

We live in the world, it is said, and must walk in its ways.

Was Christ called a complainer against the world? Yet all these great teachers and preachers must have had a most deep and ingrained sense, a continual feeling of the miseries and wrongs of the world. Otherwise they would not have been impelled to devote life and death to redress them. Christ, Socrates, Howard,[9] they must have had no ear for the joys, compared to that which they had for the sorrows of the world.

They acted, however, and we complain. The great reformers of the world turn into the great misanthropists, if circumstances or organization do not permit them to act. Christ, if He had been a woman, might have been nothing but a great complainer. Peace be with the misanthropists! They have made a step in progress; the next will make them great philanthropists; they are divided but by a line.

The next Christ will perhaps be a female Christ. But do we see one woman who looks like a female Christ? or even like "the messenger before" her "face,"[1] to go before her and prepare the hearts and minds for her?

To this will be answered that half the inmates of Bedlam begin in this way, by fancying that they are "the Christ."[2]

People talk about imitating Christ, and imitate Him in the little trifling formal things, such as washing the feet, saying His prayer, and so on; but if anyone attempts the real imitation of Him, there are no bounds to the outcry with which the presumption of that person is condemned.

For instance, Christ was saying something to the people one day, which interested Him very much, and interested them very much; and Mary and His brothers came in the middle of it, and wanted to interrupt Him, and take Him home to dinner, very likely—(how natural that story is! does it not speak more home than any historic evidences of the Gospel's reality?), and He, instead of being angry with their interruption of Him in such an important

<hr/>

9. Probably John Howard (1726–1790), an English prison reformer. Socrates (469–399 B.C.E.), Greek philosopher.
1. I.e., like John the Baptist; see Matthew 11.10.
2. It is quite true that insanity, sensuality, and monstrous fraud have constantly assumed to be "the Christ," *vide* the Agapemone and the Mormons. "Believing" a man of the name of Prince "to be the tabernacle of God on earth," poor deluded women transfer to him all their stock in the Three per Cents. We hear of the Mormons, etc., being the "recipients and mouthpieces of God's Spirit." They profess to be "incarnations of the Deity," "witnesses of the Almighty," "solely knowing God's will, and being the medium of communicating it to man," and so forth. It does not appear to us that this blasphemy is very dangerous to the cause of true religion in general, any more than forgery is very dangerous to commerce in general. It is the universal dishonesty in religion, as in trade, which is really dangerous [Nightingale's note]. The Agapemone was a group in England, founded in 1849 by Henry James Prince, made up of both sexes and based on community of goods. The religion of the Mormons (the Church of Jesus Christ of Latter-day Saints) was founded in New York State in 1830 by Joseph Smith.

work for some trifling thing, answers, "Who is my mother? and who are my brethren? Whosoever shall do the will of my Father which is in heaven, the same is my brother and sister and mother."[3] But if *we* were to say that, we should be accused of "destroying the family tie, of diminishing the obligation of the home duties."

He might well say, "Heaven and earth shall pass away, but my words shall not pass away."[4] His words will never pass away. If He had said, "Tell them that I am engaged at this moment in something very important; that the instruction of the multitude ought to go before any personal ties; that I will remember to come when I have done," no one would have been impressed by His words; but how striking is that, "Behold my mother and my brethren!"

<div align="center">VII</div>

The dying woman to her mourners:—"Oh! if you knew how gladly I leave this life, how much more courage I feel to take the chance of another, than of anything I see before me in this, you would put on your wedding-clothes instead of mourning for me!"

"But," they say, "so much talent! so many gifts! such good which you might have done!"

"The world will be put back some little time by my death," she says; "you see I estimate my powers at least as highly as you can; but it is by the death which has taken place some years ago in me, not by the death which is about to take place now." And so is the world put back by the death of every one who has to sacrifice the development of his or her peculiar gifts (which were meant, not for selfish gratification, but for the improvement of that world) to conventionality.

"My people were like children playing on the shore of the eighteenth century. I was their hobby-horse, their plaything; and they drove me to and fro, dear souls! never weary of the play themselves, till I, who had grown to woman's estate and to the ideas of the nineteenth century, lay down exhausted, my mind closed to hope, my heart to strength.

"Free—free—oh! divine freedom, art thou come at last? Welcome, beautiful death!"

Let neither name nor date be placed on her grave, still less the expression of regret or of admiration; but simply the words, "I believe in God."

1852–59 1928

3. Mark 3.33–35. The "three per cents" were Britain's public securities. Bedlam (originally the Hospital of St. Mary of Bethlehem, later Bethlem Royal Hospital) in London is England's oldest institution for the mentally ill.
4. Matthew 24.35.

FRANCES E. W. HARPER
1825–1911

Of the black women writers who contributed to the abolition movement, the one with the most successful publishing career was Frances Ellen Watkins Harper. Although her first collection of poetry and prose, *Forest Leaves* (ca. 1845), is no longer available, her volume of antislavery verse, *Poems on Miscellaneous Subjects* (1854), sold twelve thousand copies by 1858 and went through some twenty editions by 1874. Her narrative poems, which dramatized her protest against white injustice to blacks, were exceptionally popular with lecture audiences. Several of her novels, stories, and essays were effective diatribes against slavery and for temperance. Just as "The Two Offers" (*Anglo-African Magazine*, 1859) was described as "the first short story published by an American Negro," *Iola Leroy; or, Shadows Uplifted* (1892) was recognized as the first novel by a black author to describe Reconstruction. According to the African American scholar Hazel V. Carby, the novel—"rooted in the authority of Harper's experience as abolitionist, lecturer, poet, teacher, feminist, and black woman"— should be understood as an attempt to "re-arm the black intellectual and to contest the terrain of racist retrenchment." Throughout her life, Harper integrated her literary career with public service dedicated to the moral education of whites and blacks.

Born in Baltimore, Maryland, the only child of free black parents, Frances Watkins was orphaned at the age of three and raised by her uncle, the Reverend William Watkins. At fourteen, after attending his school for free blacks, she supported herself as a nursemaid and later as a seamstress and teacher. Through contacts with abolitionists involved in the Underground Railroad in the early 1850s, she lectured widely for antislavery societies in Massachusetts, Pennsylvania, Maine, New Jersey, New York, and Ohio, sometimes using the lecture podium for readings of her poetry. On November 22, 1860, she married Fenton Harper, a widower who died four years later. When she resumed her lecturing, she toured the South, addressing both black and mixed audiences. With Frederick Douglass and Susan B. Anthony, Harper organized the American Equal Rights Association, though she often questioned those advocating black rights only for black men as well as those advocating women's suffrage only for white women. From 1871, when she settled in Philadelphia with her daughter, until her death at eighty-five, Harper worked actively in social and civic organizations, as a participant in two conventions of the American Woman Suffrage Association, as the director of the American Association of Education of Colored Youth, and as the vice president of the National Association of Colored Women.

Her verse, written to dramatize her political commitments, was sometimes as sentimental as the poetry of Felicia Hemans, her contemporary. Yet, at her best, Harper sometimes used biblical characters and black dialect to define the terrible experience of slavery from the point of view of black women, and to record the subversive survival skills such women contributed to slave culture.

Ethiopia

Yes! Ethiopia yet shall stretch
Her bleeding hands abroad;
Her cry of agony shall reach
The burning throne of God,

5　The tyrant's yoke from off her neck,
　　　　His fetters from her soul,
　　The mighty hand of God shall break,
　　　　And spurn the base control.

　　Redeemed from dust and freed from chains,
10　　　Her sons shall lift their eyes;
　　From cloud-capt hills and verdant plains
　　　　Shall shouts of triumph rise.

　　Upon her dark, despairing brow,
　　　　Shall play a smile of peace;
15　For God shall bend unto her wo,
　　　　And bid her sorrows cease.

　　'Neath sheltering vines and stately palms
　　　　Shall laughing children play,
　　And aged sires with joyous psalms
20　　　Shall gladden every day.

　　Secure by night, and blest by day,
　　　　Shall pass her happy hours;
　　Nor human tigers hunt for prey
　　　　Within her peaceful bowers.

25　Then, Ethiopia! stretch, oh! stretch
　　　　Thy bleeding hands abroad;
　　Thy cry of agony shall reach
　　　　And find redress from God.

1854

The Slave Mother

　　Heard you that shriek? It rose
　　　　So wildly on the air,
　　It seemed as if a burdened heart
　　　　Was breaking in despair.

5　Saw you those hands so sadly clasped—
　　　　The bowed and feeble head—
　　The shuddering of that fragile form—
　　　　That look of grief and dread?

　　Saw you the sad, imploring eye?
10　　　Its every glance was pain,
　　As if a storm of agony
　　　　Were sweeping through the brain.

She is a mother, pale with fear,
 Her boy clings to her side,
15 And in her kirtle[1] vainly tries
 His trembling form to hide.

He is not hers, although she bore
 For him a mother's pains;
He is not hers, although her blood
20 Is coursing through his veins!

He is not hers, for cruel hands
 May rudely tear apart
The only wreath of household love
 That binds her breaking heart.

25 His love has been a joyous light
 That o'er her pathway smiled,
A fountain gushing ever new,
 Amid life's desert wild.

His lightest word has been a tone
30 Of music round her heart,
Their lives a streamlet blent in one—
 Oh, Father! must they part?

They tear him from her circling arms,
 Her last and fond embrace.
35 Oh! never more may her sad eyes
 Gaze on his mournful face.

No marvel, then, these bitter shrieks
 Disturb the listening air:
She is a mother, and her heart
40 Is breaking in despair.

1854

Vashti[1]

She leaned her head upon her hand
 And heard the king's decree—
"My lords are feasting in my halls,
 Bid Vashti come to me.

5 "I've shown the treasures of my house,
 My costly jewels rare,

1. Outer skirt.
1. The wife of Ahasuerus, who refused to dance before him and was therefore banished from his sight (Esther 1.9–19).

But with the glory of her eyes
 No rubies can compare.

"Adorned and crowned I'd have her come,
10 With all her queenly grace,
And, 'mid my lords and mighty men,
 Unveil her lovely face.

"Each gem that sparkles in my crown,
 Or glitters on my throne,
15 Grows poor and pale when she appears,
 My beautiful, my own!"

All waiting stood the chamberlains
 To hear the Queen's reply,
They saw her cheek grow deathly pale,
20 But light flash'd to her eye:

"Go, tell the King," she proudly said,
 "That I am Persia's Queen,
And by his crowds of merry men
 I never will be seen.

25 "I'll take the crown from off my head
 And tread it 'neath my feet
Before their rude and careless gaze
 My shrinking eyes shall meet.

"A queen unveiled before the crowd!—
30 Upon each lip my name!—
Why, Persia's women all would blush
 And weep for Vashti's shame!

"Go back!" she cried, and waved her hand,
 And grief was in her eye:
35 "Go, tell the King," she sadly said,
 "That I would rather die."

They brought her message to the King,
 Dark flashed his angry eye;
'Twas as the lightning ere the storm
40 Hath swept in fury by.

Then bitterly outspoke the King,
 Through purple lips of wrath—
"What shall be done to her who dares
 To cross your monarch's path?"

45 Then spake his wily counsellors—
 "O King of this fair land!
From distant Ind to Ethiop,
 All bow to thy command.

"But if, before thy servants' eyes,
50 This thing they plainly see,
That Vashti doth not heed thy will
 Nor yield herself to thee,

"The women, restive 'neath our rule,
 Would learn to scorn our name,
55 And from her deed to us would come
 Reproach and burning shame.

"Then, gracious King, sign with thy hand
 This stern but just decree,
That Vashti lay aside her crown,
60 Thy Queen no more to be."

She heard again the King's command,
 And left her high estate,[2]
Strong in her earnest womanhood,
 She calmly met her fate,

65 And left the palace of the King,
 Proud of her spotless name—
A woman who could bend to grief,
 But would not bow to shame.

<div align="right">1871</div>

Aunt Chloe's Politics

Of course, I don't know very much
 About these politics,
But I think that some who run 'em,
 Do mighty ugly tricks.

5 I've seen 'em honey-fugle[1] round,
 And talk so awful sweet,
That you'd think them full of kindness,
 As an egg is full of meat.[2]

Now I don't believe in looking
10 Honest people in the face,
And saying when you're doing wrong,
 That "I haven't sold my race."[3]

When we want to school our children,
 If the money isn't there,

2. Rank or standing in society.
1. Sweet-talk, deceive through empty rhetoric.

2. I.e., yolk and albumen.
3. I.e., wronged my people.

15 Whether black or white have took it,
 The love we all must share.

 And this buying up each other
 Is something worse than mean,
 Though I thinks a heap of voting,
20 I go for voting clean.[4]

1872

Learning to Read

 Very soon the Yankee teachers
 Came down and set up school;
 But, oh! how the Rebs[1] did hate it,—
 It was agin' their rule.

5 Our masters always tried to hide
 Book learning from our eyes;
 Knowledge didn't agree with slavery—
 'Twould make us all too wise.

 But some of us would try to steal
10 A little from the book,
 And put the words together,
 And learn by hook or crook.

 I remember Uncle Caldwell,
 Who took pot liquor fat[2]
15 And greased the pages of his book,
 And hid it in his hat

 And had his master ever seen
 The leaves upon his head,
 He'd have thought them greasy papers,
20 But nothing to be read.

 And there was Mr. Turner's Ben,
 Who heard the children spell,
 And picked the words right up by heart,
 And learned to read 'em well.

25 Well, the Northern folks kept sending
 The Yankee teachers down;
 And they stood right up and helped us,
 Though Rebs did sneer and frown.

4. After the Civil War, white politicians tried to buy black votes.
1. The southern "rebels." The poem takes place, during the period of Reconstruction, when Northern teachers came to the South to educate the newly freed slaves. It had been illegal to teach slaves to read.
2. The fat that floats to the top of the pot.

And, I longed to read my Bible,
30 For precious words it said;
But when I begun to learn it,
 Folks just shook their heads,

And said there is no use trying,
 Oh! Chloe, you're too late;
35 But as I was rising[3] sixty,
 I had no time to wait.

So I got a pair of glasses,
 And straight to work I went,
And never stopped till I could read
40 The hymns and Testament.

Then I got a little cabin
 A place to call my own—
And I felt as independent
 As the queen upon her throne.

 1872

An Appeal to My Country Women

You can sigh o'er the sad-eyed Armenian
 Who weeps in her desolate home.[1]
You can mourn o'er the exile of Russia
 From kindred and friends doomed to roam.

5 You can pity the men who have woven
 From passion and appetite chains
To coil with a terrible tension
 Around their heartstrings and brains.

You can sorrow o'er little children
10 Disinherited from their birth,
The wee waifs and toddlers neglected,
 Robbed of sunshine, music and mirth.

For beasts you have gentle compassion;
 Your mercy and pity they share.
15 For the wretched, outcast and fallen
 You have tenderness, love and care.

But hark! from our Southland are floating
 Sobs of anguish, murmurs of pain,
And women heart-stricken are weeping
20 Over their tortured and their slain.

3. Nearing.
1. Armenia, which was part of Russia, suffered

greatly from Turkish oppression between 1894 and
1915.

On their brows the sun has left traces;
 Shrink not from their sorrow in scorn.
When they entered the threshold of being
 The children of a King were born.

25 Each comes as a guest to the table
 The hands of our God has outspread,
To fountains that ever leap upward,
 To share in the soil we all tread.

When we plead for the wrecked and fallen,
30 The exile from far-distant shores,
Remember that men are still wasting
 Life's crimson around our own doors.

Have ye not, oh, my favored sisters,
 Just a plea, a prayer or a tear,
35 For mothers who dwell 'neath the shadows
 Of agony, hatred and fear?

Men may tread down the poor and lowly,
 May crush them in anger and hate,
But surely the mills of God's justice
40 Will grind out the grist of their fate.

Oh, people sin-laden and guilty,
 So lusty and proud in your prime,
The sharp sickles of God's retribution
 Will gather your harvest of crime.

45 Weep not, oh my well-sheltered sisters,
 Weep not for the Negro alone,
But weep for your sons who must gather
 The crops which their fathers have sown.

Go read on the tombstones of nations
50 Of chieftains who masterful trod,
The sentence which time has engraven,
 That they had forgotten their God.

'Tis the judgment of God that men reap
 The tares[2] which in madness they sow,
55 Sorrow follows the footsteps of crime,
 And Sin is the consort of Woe.

1900

2. Weeds (see Jesus' parable of the wheat and the tares, Matthew 13.24–30).

HARRIET E. ADAMS WILSON
1828?–1863?

Harriet E. Wilson was the first black woman to publish a novel in English and the first African American to publish a novel in the United States. Her sardonically entitled *Our Nig* was printed (apparently at her own expense) by the Massachusetts firm of George C. Rand and Avery in September 1859. Even more than the phrase "our nig"—a phrase that would have been as shocking in the nineteenth century as it is today—the book's full title emphasized the author's political motivation, as well as her irony, for it read:

OUR NIG.
or,
*Sketches from the
Life of a Free Black,*
In a Two-Story White House, North.
SHOWING THAT SLAVERY'S SHADOWS
FALL EVEN THERE.

by "OUR NIG."

Our Nig received no reviews, evidently had hardly any sales, and was almost completely forgotten until the scholar Henry Louis Gates Jr. reissued it in a facsimile edition in 1983.

As Gates observed, Wilson's use of the controversial, emotionally charged word *nig* in her title may in fact have been partly responsible for the obscurity into which the novel fell; in addition, he argues that the opening of the tale, which portrays a comparatively happy marriage between a black man and a white woman, may have made the work unacceptable to black and white readers alike. In any case, the book's failure undoubtedly accounts for the paucity of information about Wilson herself. She was born in Milford, New Hampshire, she may have been trained as a hatmaker, she married and was evidently deserted by a sailor named Thomas Wilson, and she subsequently gave birth in a "county house" (a poor house) to a child named George Mason Wilson, who died in 1860 at the age of seven: these are among the few facts known about her. Nevertheless, *Our Nig* itself offers a vivid picture of the kind of life she must have lived as a free black in New England, for the novel appears to be based on personal experiences.

The selection included here, for instance, recounts the circumstances of the childhood of "our nig," a mulatto girl named Alfrado, or "Frado" for short. When this passage begins, the child is seven, her father has died, and her mother has deserted her, leaving her with a wealthy white family, the Bellmonts, who have decided to keep her in the household as a servant. Frado's painful struggle for dignity and independence exposes the psychological and material impediments to racial equality in the so-called free north.

From Our Nig

[FRADO'S CHILDHOOD]

Frado was called early in the morning by her new mistress. Her first work was to feed the hens. She was shown how it was *always* to be done, and in no other way; any departure from this rule to be punished by a whipping.

She was then accompanied by Jack[1] to drive the cows to pasture, so she might learn the way. Upon her return she was allowed to eat her breakfast, consisting of a bowl of skimmed milk, with brown bread crusts, which she was told to eat, standing, by the kitchen table, and must not be over ten minutes about it. Meanwhile the family were taking their morning meal in the dining-room. This over, she was placed on a cricket[2] to wash the common dishes; she was to be in waiting always to bring wood and chips, to run hither and thither from room to room.

A large amount of dish-washing for small hands followed dinner. Then the same after tea and going after the cows finished her first day's work. It was a new discipline to the child. She found some attractions about the place, and she retired to rest at night more willing to remain. The same routine followed day after day, with slight variation; adding a little more work, and spicing the toil with "words that burn," and frequent blows on her head. These were great annoyances to Frado, and had she known where her mother was, she would have gone at once to her. She was often greatly wearied, and silently wept over her sad fate. At first she wept aloud, which Mrs. Bellmont noticed by applying a rawhide,[3] always at hand in the kitchen. It was a symptom of discontent and complaining which must be "nipped in the bud," she said.

Thus passed a year. No intelligence of Mag.[4] It was now certain Frado was to become a permanent member of the family. Her labors were multiplied; she was quite indispensable, although but seven years old. She had never learned to read, never heard of a school until her residence in the family.

Mrs. Bellmont was in doubt about the utility of attempting to educate people of color, who were incapable of elevation. This subject occasioned a lengthy discussion in the family, Mr. Bellmont, Jane and Jack arguing for Frado's education; Mary and her mother objecting. At last Mr. Bellmont declared decisively that she *should* go to school. He was a man who seldom decided controversies at home. The word once spoken admitted of no appeal; so, notwithstanding Mary's objection that she would have to attend the same school she did, the word became law.

It was to be a new scene to Frado, and Jack had many queries and conjectures to answer. He was himself too far advanced to attend the summer school, which Frado regretted, having had too many opportunities of witnessing Miss Mary's temper to feel safe in her company alone.

The opening day of school came. Frado sauntered on far in the rear of Mary, who was ashamed to be seen "walking with a nigger." As soon as she appeared, with scanty clothing and bared feet, the children assembled, noisily published her approach: "See that nigger," shouted one. "Look! look!" cried another. "I won't play with her," said one little girl. "Nor I neither," replied another.

Mary evidently relished these sharp attacks, and saw a fair prospect of lowering Nig where, according to her views, she belonged. Poor Frado, chagrined and grieved, felt that her anticipations of pleasure at such a place were far from being realized. She was just deciding to return home, and never come there again, when the teacher appeared, and observing the downcast

1. The son of the Bellmont family.
2. A footstool.
3. I.e., a whip.
4. Frado's mother.

looks of the child, took her by the hand, and led her into the school-room. All followed, and, after the bustle of securing seats was over. Miss Marsh inquired if the children knew "any cause for the sorrow of that little girl?" pointing to Frado. It was soon all told. She then reminded them of their duties to the poor and friendless; their cowardice in attacking a young innocent child; referred them to one who looks not on outward appearances, but on the heart. "She looks like a good girl; I think I shall love her, so lay aside all prejudice, and vie with each other in shewing kindness and good-will to one who seems different from you," were the closing remarks of the kind lady. Those kind words! The most agreeable sound which ever meets the ear of sorrowing, grieving childhood.

Example rendered her words efficacious. Day by day there was a manifest change of deportment towards "Nig." Her speeches often drew merriment from the children; no one could do more to enliven their favorite pastimes than Frado. Mary could not endure to see her thus noticed, yet knew not how to prevent it. She could not influence her schoolmates as she wished. She had not gained their effections by winning ways and yielding points of controversy. On the contrary, she was self-willed, domineering; every day reported "mad"[5] by some of her companions. She availed herself of the only alternative, abuse and taunts, as they returned from school. This was not satisfactory; she wanted to use physical force "to subdue her," to "keep her down."

There was, on their way home, a field intersected by a stream over which a single plank was placed for a crossing. It occurred to Mary that it would be a punishment to Nig to compel her to cross over; so she dragged her to the edge, and told her authoritatively to go over. Nig hesitated, resisted. Mary placed herself behind the child, and, in the struggle to force her over, lost her footing and plunged into the stream. Some of the larger scholars being in sight, ran, and thus prevented Mary from drowning and Frado from falling. Nig scampered home fast as possible, and Mary went to the nearest house, dripping, to procure a change of garments. She came loitering home, half crying, exclaiming, "Nig pushed me into the stream!" She then related the particulars. Nig was called from the kitchen. Mary stood with anger flashing in her eyes. Mr. Bellmont sat quietly reading his paper. He had witnessed too many of Miss Mary's outbreaks to be startled. Mrs. Bellmont interrogated Nig.

"I did n't do it! I did n't do it!" answered Nig, passionately, and then related the occurrence truthfully.

The discrepancy greatly enraged Mrs. Bellmont. With loud accusations and angry gestures she approached the child. Turning to her husband, she asked.

"Will you sit still, there, and hear that black nigger call Mary a liar?"

"How do we know but she has told the truth? I shall not punish her," he replied, and left the house, as he usually did when a tempest threatened to envelop him. No sooner was he out of sight than Mrs. B. and Mary commenced beating her inhumanly; then propping her mouth open with a piece of wood, shut her up in a dark room, without any supper. For employment, while the tempest raged within, Mr. Bellmont went for the cows, a task

5. Wild.

belonging to Frado, and thus unintentionally prolonged her pain. At dark Jack came in, and seeing Mary, accosted her with, "So you thought you'd vent your spite on Nig, did you? Why can't you let her alone? It was good enough for you to get a ducking, only you did not stay in half long enough."

"Stop!" said his mother. "You shall never talk so before me. You would have that little nigger trample on Mary, would you? She came home with a lie; it made Mary's story false."

"What was Mary's story?" asked Jack.

It was related.

"Now," said Jack, sallying into a chair, "the school-children happened to see it all, and they tell the same story Nig does. Which is most likely to be true, what a dozen agree they saw, or the contrary?"

"It is very strange you will believe what others say against your sister," retorted his mother, with flashing eye. "I think it is time your father subdued you."

"Father is a sensible man," argued Jack. "He would not wrong a dog. Where *is* Frado?" he continued.

"Mother gave her a good whipping and shut her up," replied Mary.

Just then Mr. Bellmont entered, and asked if Frado was "shut up yet."

The knowledge of her innocence, the perfidy of his sister, worked fearfully on Jack. He bounded from his chair, searched every room till he found the child; her mouth wedged apart, her face swollen, and full of pain.

How Jack pitied her! He relieved her jaws, brought her some supper, took her to her room, comforted her as well as he knew how, sat by her till she fell asleep, and then left for the sitting room. As he passed his mother, he remarked, "If that was the way Frado was to be treated, he hoped she would never wake again!" He then imparted her situation to his father, who seemed untouched, till a glance at Jack exposed a tearful eye. Jack went early to her next morning. She awoke sad, but refreshed. After breakfast Jack took her with him to the field, and kept her through the day. But it could not be so generally. She must return to school, to her household duties. He resolved to do what he could to protect her from Mary and his mother. He bought her a dog, which became a great favorite with both. The invalid, Jane, would gladly befriend her; but she had not the strength to brave the iron will of her mother. Kind words and affectionate glances were the only expressions of sympathy she could safely indulge in. The men employed on the farm were always glad to hear her prattle; she was a great favorite with them. Mrs. Bellmont allowed them the privilege of talking with her in the kitchen. She did not fear but she should have ample opportunity of subduing her when they were away. Three months of schooling, summer and winter, she enjoyed for three years. Her winter over-dress was a cast-off overcoat, once worn by Jack, and a sun-bonnet. It was a source of great merriment to the scholars, but Nig's retorts were so mirthful, and their satisfaction so evident in attributing the selection to "Old Granny Bellmont," that it was not painful to Nig or pleasurable to Mary. Her jollity was not to be quenched by whipping or scolding. In Mrs. Bellmont's presence she was under restraint; but in the kitchen, and among her schoolmates, the pent up fires burst forth. She was ever at some sly prank when unseen by her teacher, in school hours; not unfrequently some outburst of merriment, of which she was the original, was

charged upon some innocent mate, and punishment inflicted which she merited. They enjoyed her antics so fully that any of them would suffer wrongfully to keep open the avenues of mirth. She would venture far beyond propriety, thus shielded and countenanced.

The teacher's desk was supplied with drawers, in which were stored his books and other *et ceteras* of the profession. The children observed Nig very busy there one morning before school, as they flitted in occasionally from their play outside. The master came; called the children to order; opened a drawer to take the book the occasion required; when out poured a volume of smoke. "Fire! fire!" screamed he, at the top of his voice. By this time he had become sufficiently acquainted with the peculiar odor, to know he was imposed upon. The scholars shouted with laughter to see the terror of the dupe, who, feeling abashed at the needless fright, made no very strict investigation, and Nig once more escaped punishment. She had provided herself with cigars, and puffing, puffing away at the crack of the drawer, had filled it with smoke, and then closed it tightly to deceive the teacher, and amuse the scholars. The interim of terms was filled up with a variety of duties new and peculiar. At home, no matter how powerful the heat when sent to rake hay or guard the grazing herd, she was never permitted to shield her skin from the sun. She was not many shades darker than Mary now; what a calamity it would be ever to hear the contrast spoken of. Mrs. Bellmont was determined the sun should have full power to darken the shade which nature had first bestowed upon her as best befitting.

1859

EMILY DICKINSON
1830–1886

In 1881 a young woman named Mabel Loomis Todd wrote her parents about "the *character* of Amherst . . . a lady whom the people call the *'Myth'*: She has not been outside of her own house in fifteen years. . . . She dresses wholly in white, and her mind is said to be perfectly wonderful." So began the legend of Emily Dickinson, one of the greatest poets of the nineteenth century, who was for years portrayed by biographers and critics as an eccentric recluse, a "little home-keeping person," a mad spinster who had been disappointed in love. For, four years after this New England woman in white died in 1886, the same Mabel Loomis Todd brought out a volume containing selections from 1,776 strange and passionate poems, which had been found, neatly sewed into booklets, in her bureau drawers, and the imagination of the public was immediately seized by the mysterious discrepancy between what seemed to be the isolation of Dickinson's life and the intensity of her art. To many, indeed, the "case" of Emily Dickinson—only eight of whose poems had been published in her lifetime—seemed to offer a crucial model for the situation of the woman poet. Eccentricity, reclusiveness, and, most of all, thwarted romance—these appeared to be the conditions that might drive a woman to what was, for women, the perversity of writing verse.

Despite the equivocal glamour of the legend Todd helped create, however, the "Myth of Amherst" had a conventional enough childhood, and even in its apparent isolation her adult life was marked not so much by longing for lost love as by aesthetic and intellectual commitment to her art, in whose cause she continually demanded "severer service" of herself. The second child of Edward Dickinson, an austere but ambitious lawyer, and his retiring wife, Emily, she was born on December 10, 1830, into one of Amherst's leading families. With her older brother, Austin, and her younger sister, Lavinia, she seems to have had a cheerful home and, by the standards of her time and place, a good education at Amherst Academy. When she was seventeen, moreover, she even went for a year to what was to become one of the first women's colleges—Mount Holyoke Female Seminary, a few miles outside Amherst.

It was at Mount Holyoke that Dickinson's independence and imagination began to manifest themselves. Two episodes, in particular, tell us something about the kind of resourceful and rebellious girl she was. The first, about which Todd heard from the poet's sister, has to do with geometry: "When the [geometry] examination came and [Emily] had never studied it, she went to the blackboard and gave such a glib exposition of imaginary figures that the dazed teacher passed her with the highest mark." The second, which was reported by a classmate, has to do with religion: when Mary Lyon, the school principal, was proselytizing for an evangelical revival, she "asked all those who wanted to be Christians to rise," but because Emily could not "honestly accede to" the request, she, and only she, "remained seated."

Geometry may have been a subject that the young Dickinson was able to "imagine," but orthodox religious conversion evidently was not, and, as many biographers have speculated, it was quite possibly Lyon's evangelical revival that decided the poet on leaving Mount Holyoke, though her father's desire to have his older daughter back at home also played a part in the move. In any case, after only a year she left school, never to return, and from then on her life became increasingly withdrawn, as she slowly developed the fear of public places (known as agoraphobia) that marked her later years. Her trips out of town were few. As a girl, she traveled to Boston, Cambridge, and Worcester several times to vacation with relatives. In 1855, she and her sister "Vinnie" accompanied their congressman father to Washington and Philadelphia for a visit of almost two months. Finally, in 1864, she spent some weeks in Cambridge because she was being treated by a Boston specialist for what recent scholars have theorized was a bad case of an eye disorder called exotropia. Except for these excursions, she remained in Amherst—a kind of Yankee princess deliberately training herself to see, as she put it, "New Englandly"—until her death in 1886 of Bright's disease.

To be sure, throughout her career Dickinson maintained a voluminous, lively, and often brilliant correspondence with personal and family friends as well as literary acquaintances. Within her circle of intimates, moreover, she was evidently quite warmly nurtured both as a woman and as an artist by her sister-in-law, Susan Gilbert Dickinson, the especially beloved companion about whom she once wrote that "When my Hands are Cut, Her / fingers will be / found inside."

But even in Amherst, what Dickinson called the "circumference" of her daily life gradually narrowed. At first a high-spirited girl, helping to hostess her father's parties, paying visits to neighbors, and composing whimsical valentines for undergraduates at Amherst College, she eventually took to dressing "wholly in white," assured the editor Thomas Wentworth Higginson—one of her major correspondents—that "I do not cross my Father's ground to any house in town," refused for the most part to appear before callers, and even in her last illness allowed a doctor to "examine" her only as she walked past a partially opened door in the next room. Becoming a "Myth," she "manifested" her presence, like a priestess of some mysterious religion, only through tokens of flowers, cakes, and wine, transmitted by her sister or the family servant, or, as one famous story has it, through playful gifts of sweets to children, arranged in a basket let down from her bedroom window.

What could have accounted for such behavior in a woman who had been a witty and energetic girl? For years, biographers of Dickinson assumed that sometime in the early 1860s she had fallen hopelessly in love with a man whose identity has never been established, though the leading candidate for the position was long supposed to be the Reverend Charles Wadsworth, a magnetic but married clergyman, whom she was thought to have met during her 1855 stay in Philadelphia. A series of tormented, often frankly erotic letters to a man enigmatically addressed as "Master," in which Dickinson variously defines herself as a wounded bird, a childlike "Daisy," a "culprit," a "smaller life," reinforced the sense of such biographers that both this writer's withdrawal from the world and her impassioned art were inspired by a tragic romance.

More recently, however, critics have begun to question the sentimental assumptions on which such interpretations of her life and work were based. As these scholars concede, there may well have been an emotional event that inspired both Dickinson's poetry and her self-protectiveness, and some recent researchers—notably Lillian Faderman, Ellen Hart, and Martha Nell Smith—speculate that the romantic enthrallment underlying not only the "Master" letters but also many of the love poems may have more to do with the writer's passion for her sister-in-law Sue (about whom she wrote that she is "the Woman / whom I prefer") than with a charismatic mystery man. Nonetheless, the "Master" letters, with their deliberate effacement of the addressee's identity, are just as clearly explorations of the general relationship between male power and female powerlessness, male authority and female dependency, as they are pleas for erotic reassurance from a particular individual. Moreover, in these letters as in so many of her most impassioned verses, the poet is obviously both disguising and dramatizing herself, as if to document a crucial confession that she made to Higginson, the *Atlantic Monthly* editor who became her literary mentor: "When I state myself, as the Representative of the Verse—it does not mean—me—but a supposed person."

Anticipating modern theories of the poet's "persona," Dickinson's definition of herself as a "supposed person" reveals just how self-consciously literary she was, even while its suggestion of a commitment to fantasy recalls the imaginary geometry she sketched on a Mount Holyoke blackboard. In many other ways, moreover, her correspondence with Higginson reinforces these points, as contemporary critics have begun to notice. Struck by an essay titled "A Letter to a Young Contributor," which the *Atlantic* editor published in 1862, Dickinson began to write to Higginson in that year, inquiring if her verses were "alive" and asking if she might be his "scholar." Though his responses were sometimes equivocal—he often objected to her eccentric language or to the meters that she called "the Bells whose jingling cooled my tramp"— his basic reaction was encouraging, and in 1870 he even journeyed to Amherst to meet her, becoming one of the few visitors to whom she appeared in person in her later life. For all his faults of perception, he seems to have understood, as many Dickinson biographers after him did not, the extent and intensity of her aesthetic vocation.

A further indication of Dickinson's literary intensity—her professionalism, even— can be found in records of her reading. According to family members, the walls of this poet's bedroom were hung with pictures of favorite writers—George Eliot, Thomas Carlyle, Elizabeth Barrett Browning, a selection that reveals how she ranged from the male to the female literary traditions and from prose to poetry in her search for intellectual models. Most persistently, however, she defined herself as a woman writer, reading the works of female precursors with special care, attending to the implications of such novels as Charlotte Brontë's *Jane Eyre*, Emily Brontë's *Wuthering Heights*, and George Eliot's *Middlemarch* with the same absorbed delight that characterized her devotion to Elizabeth Barrett Browning's *Aurora Leigh*. Finally, then, the key to her enigmatic identity as a "supposed person" who was called the "Myth of Amherst" may rest not in investigations of her questionable romance but in studies of her unquestionably serious reading, as well as in analyses of her disquietingly

powerful writing. Elliptically phrased, intensely compressed, her poems are more linguistically innovative than any other nineteenth-century verses, with the possible exception of some works by Walt Whitman and Gerard Manley Hopkins, her two most radical male contemporaries. Throughout her largely secret but always brilliant career, moreover, she confronted precisely the questions about the individual and society, time and death, flesh and spirit, that major precursors from John Milton to John Keats had faced. Dreaming of "Amplitude and Awe," she recorded sometimes vengeful, sometimes mystical visions of social and personal transformation in poems as inventively phrased and imaginatively constructed as any in the English language.

Clearly such accomplishments required not only extraordinary talent but also some measure of freedom. Yet because she was the unmarried daughter of conservative New Englanders, Dickinson was obliged to take on many household tasks; as a nineteenth-century New England wife, she would have had the same number of obligations, if not more. Some of these she performed with pleasure; in 1856, for instance, she was judge of a bread-baking contest, and in 1857 she won a prize in that contest. But as Higginson's "scholar," as a voracious reader and an ambitious writer, Dickinson had to win herself time for "Amplitude and Awe," and it is increasingly clear that she did so through a strategic withdrawal from her ordinary world. A story related by her niece Martha Dickinson Bianchi reveals that the poet herself knew from the first what both the price and the prize might be: on one occasion, said Bianchi, Dickinson took her up to the room in which she regularly sequestered herself and, mimicking locking herself in, "thumb and forefinger closed on an imaginary key," said "with a quick turn of her wrist, 'It's just a turn—and freedom, Matty!' "

In the freedom of her solitary, but not lonely, room, Dickinson may have become what her Amherst neighbors saw as a bewildering "myth." Yet there, too, she created myths of her own. Reading the Brontës and Barrett Browning, studying Transcendentalism and the Bible, she contrived a theology that is powerfully expressed in many of her poems. That it was at its most hopeful a female-centered theology is revealed in verses like those she wrote about the women artists she admired, as well as in more general works like her gravely pantheistic address to the "Sweet Mountains" who "tell me no lie," with its definition of the hills around Amherst as "strong Madonnas" and its description of the writer herself as "The Wayward Nun—beneath the Hill—/ Whose service is to You—." As Dickinson's admirer and descendant Adrienne Rich has accurately observed, this passionate poet consistently chose to confront her society—to "have it out"—"on her own premises." But even among her contemporaries her literary reputation was not inconsiderable; indeed, by the time she died in 1886, her genius had had a profound impact on a significant circle of friends and admirers. At her funeral, Higginson read one of her favorite poems, Emily Brontë's "No Coward Soul is Mine," after announcing that this was a work "our friend who has just now put on Immortality, *and who seemed scarce ever to have taken it off*, used to read to her sister" (emphasis added). And in an obituary written for the *Springfield Republican*, the poet's beloved sister-in-law Sue wrote that her "talk and writings were like no one's else," adding that her "swift poetic rapture was like the long glistening note of a bird one hears in the June woods at high noon, but can never see."

The text and numbering of the poems follow the 1998 variorum edition of R. W. Franklin. The bracketed numbers to the right refer to the order established by Thomas H. Johnson in his edition of 1955.

13 [24]

There is a morn by men unseen -
Whose maids opon remoter green
Keep their seraphic[1] May -
And all day long, with dance and game,
And gambol I may never name -
Employ their holiday.

Here to light measure, move the feet
Which walk no more the village street -
Nor by the wood are found -
Here are the birds that sought the sun
When last year's distaff[2] idle hung
And summer's brows were bound.

Ne'er saw I such a wondrous scene -
Ne'er such a ring on such a green -
Nor so serene array -
As if the stars some summer night
Should swing their cups of Chrysolite[3] -
And revel till the day -

Like thee to dance - like thee to sing -
People opon that mystic green -
I ask, each new May morn.
I wait thy far - fantastic[4] bells -
Announcing me in other dells -
Unto the different dawn!

1858 1945

157 [103]

I have a King, who does not speak -
So - wondering - thro' the hours meek
I trudge the day away -
Half glad when it is night - and sleep -
If, haply, thro' a dream, to peep
In parlors, shut by day.

And if I do - when morning comes -
It is as if a hundred drums
Did round my pillow roll,
And shouts fill all my childish sky,

1. Angelic.
2. Staff that holds unspun wool.
3. A goldlike mineral.
4. Imaginary.

And Bells keep saying 'Victory'
From steeples in my soul!

And if I dont - the little Bird
Within the Orchard, is not heard,
15 And I omit to pray
'Father, thy will be done'[5] today
For my will goes the other way,
And it were perjury!

1860 1896

194 [1072]

Title divine, is mine.
The Wife without the Sign -
Acute Degree conferred on me -
Empress of Calvary[6] -
5 Royal, all but the Crown -
Betrothed, without the Swoon
God gives us Women -
When You hold Garnet[7] to Garnet -
Gold - to Gold -
10 Born - Bridalled - Shrouded -
In a Day -
Tri Victory -
"My Husband" - Women say
Stroking the Melody -
15 Is this the way -

1861 1924

201 [209]

With thee, in the Desert -
With thee in the thirst -
With thee in the Tamarind wood -
Leopard breathes - at last!

1861 1945

5. From the Lord's Prayer (see Matthew 6.10). 7. A dark red gemstone.
6. The hill on which Christ was crucified.

205 [*211*]

Come slowly - Eden!
Lips unused to Thee -
Bashful - sip thy Jessamines[8] -
As the fainting Bee -

5 Reaching late his flower,
Round her chamber hums -
Counts his nectars -
Enters - and is lost in Balms.[9]

1861 1890

260 [*288*]

I'm Nobody! Who are you?
Are you - Nobody - too?
Then there's a pair of us!
Dont tell! they'd advertise[1] - you know!

5 How dreary - to be - Somebody!
How public - like a Frog -
To tell one's name - the livelong June -
To an admiring Bog!

1861 1891

267 [*1737*]

Rearrange a "Wife's" Affection!
When they dislocate my Brain!
Amputate my freckled Bosom!
Make me bearded like a man!

5 Blush, my spirit, in thy Fastness[2] -
Blush, my unacknowledged clay[3] -
Seven years of troth[4] have taught thee
More than Wifehood ever may!

Love that never leaped it's socket -
10 Trust intrenched in narrow pain -
Constancy thro' fire - awarded -
Anguish - bare of anodyne![5]

Burden - borne so far triumphant -
None suspect me of the crown,
15 For I wear the "Thorns"[6] till *Sunset* -
Then - my Diadem put on.

8. Jasmines.
9. Perfumes.
1. Announce, publicize.
2. Firm, secure, or constrained position.
3. Flesh.

4. Fidelity, betrothal.
5. Medicine that relieves pain.
6. Jesus was made to wear a crown of thorns at his Crucifixion.

Big my Secret but it's *bandaged* -
It will never get away
Till the Day it's Weary Keeper
20 Leads it through the Grave to thee.

1861 1945

269 [249]

Wild nights - Wild nights!
Were I with thee
Wild nights should be
Our luxury!

5 Futile - the winds -
To a Heart in port -
Done with the Compass -
Done with the Chart!

10 Rowing in Eden -
Ah - the Sea!
Might I but moor - tonight -
In thee!

1861 1891

307 [271]

A solemn thing - it was - I said -
A Woman - white - to be -
And wear - if God should count me fit -
Her blameless mystery -

5 A hallowed thing - to drop a life
Into the purple well -
Too plummetless[7] - that it return -
Eternity - until -

I pondered how the bliss would look -
10 And would it feel as big -
When I could take it in my hand -
As hovering - seen - through fog -

And then - the size of this "small" life -
The Sages - call it small -
15 Swelled - like Horizons - in my vest[8] -
And I sneered - softly - "small"!

1862 1896

7. Bottomless. 8. Clothing.

320 [258]

There's a certain Slant of light,
Winter Afternoons -
That oppresses, like the Heft
Of Cathedral Tunes -

5 Heavenly Hurt, it gives us -
We can find no scar,
But internal difference -
Where the Meanings, are -

None may teach it - Any -
10 'Tis the Seal Despair -
An imperial affliction
Sent us of the Air -

When it comes, the Landscape listens -
Shadows - hold their breath -
15 When it goes,'tis like the Distance
On the look of Death -

1862 1890

325 [322]

There came a Day - at Summer's full -
Entirely for me -
I thought that such - were for the Saints -
Where Resurrections - be -

5 The Sun - as common - went abroad -
The Flowers - accustomed - blew⁹ -
As if no Soul the Solstice passed -
That maketh all things new.

The time was scarce profaned - by speech -
10 The symbol of a word
Was needless - as at Sacrament¹ -
The Wardrobe - of Our Lord -

Each was to each - the sealed church -
Permitted to commune - this time -
15 Lest we too awkward - show -
At "Supper of the Lamb."²

9. Bloomed.
1. One of the rites instituted by Jesus for his fol-
lowers' sanctification.
2. I.e., Jesus. "Sealed": authenticated.

The hours slid fast - as hours will -
Clutched tight - by greedy hands -
So - faces on two Decks - look back -
20 Bound to opposing Lands -

And so - when all the time had failed -
Without external sound -
Each - bound the other's Crucifix -
We gave no other bond -

25 Sufficient troth - that we shall rise -
Deposed - at length - the Grave -
To *that* New Marriage -
Justified - through Calvaries[3] of Love!

1862 1890

336 [327]

Before I got my eye put out -
I liked as well to see
As other creatures, that have eyes -
And know no other way -

5 But were it told to me, Today,
That I might have the Sky
For mine, I tell you that my Heart
Would split, for size of me -

The Meadows - mine -
10 The Mountains - mine -
All Forests - Stintless stars -
As much of noon, as I could take -
Between my finite eyes -

The Motions of the Dipping Birds -
15 The Morning's Amber Road -
For mine - to look at when I liked,
The news would strike me dead -

So safer - guess - with just my soul
Opon the window pane
20 Where other creatures put their eyes -
Incautious - of the Sun -

1862 1891

3. Intense sufferings (Calvary was the site of Jesus' Crucifixion). "Justified": judged worthy of salvation.

340 [280]

I felt a Funeral, in my Brain,
And Mourners to and fro
Kept treading - treading - till it seemed
That Sense was breaking through - [4]

5 And when they all were seated,
A Service, like a Drum -
Kept beating - beating - till I thought
My mind was going numb -

And then I heard them lift a Box
10 And creak across my Soul
With those same Boots of Lead, again,
Then Space - began to toll,

As all the Heavens were a Bell,
And Being, but an Ear,
15 And I, and Silence, some strange Race
Wrecked, solitary, here -

And then a Plank in Reason, broke,
And I dropped down, and down -
And hit a World, at every plunge,
20 And Finished knowing - then -

1862 1896

353 [508]

I'm ceded - I've stopped being Their's -
The name They dropped opon my face
With water,[5] in the country church
Is finished using, now,
5 And They can put it with my Dolls,
My childhood, and the string of spools,
I've finished threading - too -

Baptized, before, without the choice,
But this time, consciously, Of Grace -
10 Unto supremest name -
Called to my Full - The Crescent[6] dropped -

4. I.e., sense or reason was collapsing.
5. I.e., at baptism.
6. I.e., the crescent moon, symbolizing the imma-
ture self, compared with the full moon, represent-
ing maturity.

Existence's whole Arc, filled up,
With one - small Diadem -

My second Rank - too small the first -
15 Crowned - Crowing - on my Father's breast -
A half unconscious Queen -
But this time - Adequate - Erect,
With Will to choose,
Or to reject,
20 And I choose, just a Crown -

1862 1890

360 [512]

The Soul has Bandaged moments -
When too appalled to stir -
She feels some ghastly Fright come up
And stop to look at her -

5 Salute her, with long fingers -
Caress her freezing hair -
Sip, Goblin, from the very lips
The Lover - hovered - o'er -
Unworthy, that a thought so mean
10 Accost a Theme - so - fair -

The soul has moments of escape -
When bursting all the doors -
She dances like a Bomb, abroad,
And swings opon the Hours,

As do the Bee - delirious borne -
Long Dungeoned from his Rose -
Touch Liberty - then know no more -
But Noon, and Paradise -

The Soul's retaken moments -
When, Felon led along,
With shackles on the plumed feet,[7]
And staples, in the song,

The Horror welcomes her, again,
These, are not brayed of Tongue -

1862 1945

7. Bent rods to which rope can be attached. "Plumed": winged.

372 [*341*]

After great pain, a formal feeling comes -
The Nerves sit ceremonious, like Tombs -
The stiff Heart questions 'was it He, that bore,'
And 'Yesterday, or Centuries before'?

5 The Feet, mechanical, go round -
A Wooden way
Of Ground, or Air, or Ought -
Regardless grown,
A Quartz contentment, like a stone -

10 This is the Hour of Lead -
Remembered, if outlived,
As Freezing persons, recollect the Snow -
First - Chill - then Stupor - then the letting go -

1862 1929

382 [*425*]

Good Morning - Midnight -
I'm coming Home -
Day - got tired of Me -
How could I - of Him?

5 Sunshine was a sweet place -
I liked to stay -
But Morn - did'nt want me - now -
So - Good night - Day!

10 I can look - cant I -
When the East is Red?
The Hills - have a way - then -
That puts the Heart - abroad -

You - are not so fair - Midnight -
I chose - Day -
But - please take a little Girl -
He turned away!

1862 1929

<center>401</center> <div align="right">[365]</div>

Dare you see a Soul at the "White Heat"?
Then crouch within the door -
Red - is the Fire's common tint -
But when the vivid Ore

5 Has vanquished Flame's conditions -
It quivers from the Forge
Without a color, but the Light
Of unannointed Blaze -

Least[8] Village, boasts it's Blacksmith -
10 Whose Anvil's even ring
Stands symbol for the finer Forge
That soundless tugs - within -

Refining these impatient Ores
With Hammer, and with Blaze
15 Until the designated Light
Repudiate the Forge -

1862 1891

<center>407</center> <div align="right">[670]</div>

One need not be a Chamber - to be Haunted -
One need not be a House -
The Brain has Corridors - surpassing
Material Place -

5 Far safer, of a midnight meeting
External Ghost
Than it's interior confronting -
That cooler Host -

Far safer, through an Abbey gallop,
10 The Stones a'chase -
Than unarmed, one's a'self encounter -
In lonesome Place -

Ourself behind ourself, concealed -
Should startle most -
15 Assassin hid in our Apartment
Be Horror's least -

The Body - borrows a Revolver -
He bolts the Door -
O'erlooking a superior spectre -
20 Or More -

1862 1891

8. I.e., the smallest.

409 [303]

The Soul selects her own Society -
Then - shuts the Door -
To her divine Majority -
Present no more -

5 Unmoved - she notes the Chariots - pausing -
At her low Gate -
Unmoved - an Emperor be kneeling
Opon her Mat -

I've known her - from an ample nation -
10 Choose One -
Then - close the Valves of her attention -
Like Stone -

1862 1890

411 [528]

Mine - by the Right of the White Election!
Mine - by the Royal Seal!
Mine - by the sign in the Scarlet prison -
Bars - cannot conceal!

5 Mine - here - in Vision - and in Veto!
Mine - by the Grave's Repeal -
Titled - Confirmed -
Delirious Charter!
Mine - long as Ages steal!

1862 1890

439 [579]

I had been hungry, all the Years -
My Noon had Come - to dine -
I trembling drew the Table near -
And touched the Curious Wine -

5 'Twas this on Tables I had seen -
When turning, hungry, Home
I looked in Windows, for the Wealth
I could not hope - for Mine -

I did not know the ample Bread -
10 'Twas so unlike the Crumb

The Birds and I, had often shared
In Nature's - Dining Room -

The Plenty hurt me - 'twas so new -
Myself felt ill - and odd -
15 As Berry - of a Mountain Bush -
Transplanted - to the Road -

Nor was I hungry - so I found
That Hunger - was a way
Of persons Outside Windows -
20 The entering - takes away -

1862 1891

445 [613]

They shut me up in Prose -
As when a little Girl
They put me in the Closet -
Because they liked me "still" -

5 Still! Could themself have peeped -
And seen my Brain - go round -
They might as wise have lodged a Bird
For Treason - in the Pound[9] -

Himself has but to will
10 And easy as a Star
Look down opon Captivity -
And laugh - No more have I[1] -

1862 1935

455 [454]

It was given to me by the Gods -
When I was a little Girl -
They give us Presents most - you know -
When we are new - and small.
5 I kept it in my Hand -
I never put it down -
I did not dare to eat - or sleep -
For fear it would be gone -
I heard such words as "Rich" -
10 When hurrying to school -

9. An enclosure for animals, here roofless.
1. I.e., I have to do no more than the bird to be free.

From lips at Corners of the Streets -
And wrestled with a smile.
Rich! 'Twas Myself - was rich -
To take the name of Gold -
15 And Gold to own - in solid Bars -
The Difference - made me bold -

1862 1945

<center>458</center> [479]

She dealt her pretty words like Blades -
How glittering they shone -
And every One unbared a Nerve
Or wantoned[2] with a Bone -

5 She never deemed - she hurt -
That - is not Steel's Affair -
A vulgar grimace in the Flesh -
How ill the Creatures bear -

To Ache is human - not polite -
10 The Film opon the eye
Mortality's old Custom -
Just locking up - to Die -

1862 1929

<center>466</center> [657]

I dwell in Possibility -
A fairer House than Prose -
More numerous of Windows -
Superior - for Doors -

5 Of Chambers as the Cedars -
Impregnable of eye -
And for an everlasting Roof
The Gambrels[3] of the Sky -

Of Visitors - the fairest -
10 For Occupation[4] - This -
The spreading wide my narrow Hands
To gather Paradise -

1862 1929

2. Toyed.
3. Slanted roofs.

4. Principal business.

479 [712]

Because I could not stop for Death -
He kindly stopped for me -
The Carriage held but just Ourselves -
And Immortality.

5 We slowly drove - He knew no haste
And I had put away
My labor and my leisure too,
For His Civility -

We passed the School, where Children strove
10 At Recess - in the Ring -
We passed the Fields of Gazing Grain -
We passed the Setting Sun -

Or rather - He passed Us -
The Dews drew quivering and Chill -
15 For only Gossamer, my Gown -
My Tippet - only Tulle[5] -

We paused before a House that seemed
A Swelling of the Ground -
The Roof was scarcely visible -
20 The Cornice - in the Ground[6] -

Since then - 'tis Centuries - and yet
Feels shorter than the Day
I first surmised the Horses' Heads
Were toward Eternity -

1862 1890

517 [601]

A still - Volcano - Life -
That flickered in the night -
When it was dark enough to do
Without erasing sight -

5 A quiet - Earthquake style -
Too subtle to suspect
By natures this side Naples[7] -
The North cannot detect

5. A fine silk net. "Tippet": a feminine garment 7. The Italian city closest to the famous volcano
that covers the shoulders. Vesuvius.
6. I.e., a grave.

The solemn - Torrid - Symbol -
10 The lips that never lie -
Whose hissing Corals part - and shut -
And Cities - ooze away -

1863 1929

 519 [441]

This is my letter to the World
That never wrote to Me -
The simple News that Nature told -
With tender Majesty

5 Her[8] Message is committed
To Hands I cannot see -
For love of Her - Sweet - countrymen -
Judge tenderly - of Me

1863 1890

 533 [569]

I reckon[9] - When I count at all -
First - Poets - Then the Sun -
Then Summer - Then the Heaven of God -
And then - the List is done -

5 But, looking back - the First so seems
To Comprehend the Whole -
The Others look a needless Show -
So I write - Poets - All -

Their Summer - lasts a solid Year -
10 They can afford a Sun
The East - would deem extravagant -
And if the Further Heaven -

Be Beautiful as they prepare[1]
For Those who worship Them -
15 It is too difficult a Grace -
To justify the Dream -

1863 1929

8. I.e., Nature's.
9. Take into account, add up.

1. I.e., as the one that they prepare.

<center>559</center> <center>[392]</center>

Through the Dark Sod - as Education -
The Lily passes sure[2] -
Feels her White foot - no trepidation -
Her faith - no fear -

5 Afterward - in the Meadow -
Swinging her Beryl[3] Bell -
The Mold-life[4] - all forgotten - now -
In Extasy - and Dell -

1863 1929

<center>590</center> <center>[669]</center>

No Romance sold unto[5]
Could so enthrall a Man -
As the perusal of
His individual One -

5 'Tis Fiction's - to dilute to plausibility
Our - Novel. When 'tis small eno'
To credit[6] - 'Tis'nt true -

1863 1914

<center>591</center> <center>[465]</center>

I heard a Fly buzz - when I died -
The Stillness in the Room
Was like the Stillness in the Air -
Between the Heaves of Storm -

5 The Eyes around - had wrung them dry -
And Breaths were gathering firm
For that last Onset - when the King
Be witnessed - in the Room -

I willed my Keepsakes - Signed away
10 What portion of me be
Assignable - and then it was
There interposed a Fly -

2. Both the sod and the lily's passage through it
are comparable to education.
3. Blue.

4. Its life in the soil.
5. I.e., no fantastic tale sold to [a man].
6. Believe.

With Blue - uncertain - stumbling Buzz -
Between the light - and me -
15 And then the Windows failed - and then
I could not see to see -

1863 1896

600 [*312*]

Her - last Poems[7] -
Poets ended -
Silver - perished - with her Tongue -
Not on Record - bubbled Other -
5 Flute - or Woman - so divine -

Not unto it's Summer Morning -
Robin - uttered half the Tune -
Gushed too full for the adoring -
From the Anglo-Florentine[8] -

Late - the Praise - 'Tis dull - Conferring
On the Head too High - to Crown -
Diadem - or Ducal showing[9] -
Be it's Grave - sufficient Sign -

Nought - that We - No Poet's Kinsman -
Suffocate - with easy Wo -
What - and if Ourself a Bridegroom -
Put Her down - in Italy?[1]

1863 1914

620 [*435*]

Much Madness is divinest Sense -
To a discerning Eye -
Much Sense - the starkest Madness -
'Tis the Majority
5 In this, as all, prevail -
Assent - and you are sane -
Demur - you're straightway dangerous -
And handled with a Chain -

1863 1890

7. This poem is an homage to Elizabeth Barrett
Browning (1806–1861; see above, p. 521), whose
Last Poems were posthumously published in 1862.
8. Barrett Browning lived with her husband, Rob-
ert Browning, in Florence during the last fourteen
years of her life.
9. I.e., ducal crown.
1. I.e., how much would I grieve for her were I her
husband and had buried her in Italy?

627 [593]

I think I was enchanted
When first a sombre Girl -
I read that Foreign Lady[2] -
The Dark - felt beautiful -

5 And whether it was noon at night -
Or only Heaven - at noon -
For very Lunacy of Light
I had not power to tell -

The Bees - became as Butterflies -
10 The Butterflies - as Swans -
Approached - and spurned the narrow Grass -
And just the meanest Tunes

That Nature murmured to herself
To keep herself in Cheer -
15 I took for Giants - practising
Titanic Opera -

The Days - to Mighty Metres stept -
The Homeliest - adorned
As if unto a Jubilee
20 'Twere suddenly confirmed -

I could not have defined the change -
Conversion of the Mind
Like Sanctifying in the Soul -
Is witnessed - not explained -

25 'Twas a Divine Insanity -
The Danger to be sane
Should I again experience -
'Tis Antidote to turn -

To Tomes of Solid Witchcraft -
30 Magicians be asleep -
But Magic - hath an element
Like Deity - to keep -

1863 1935

2. A reference to the poet Elizabeth Barrett Browning (1806–1861; see above, p. 521).

649 [384]

No Rack[3] can torture me -
My Soul - at Liberty -
Behind this mortal Bone
There knits a bolder One[4] -

5 You cannot prick with Saw -
Nor pierce with Cimitar -
Two Bodies - therefore be -
Bind One - The Other fly -

10 The Eagle of his Nest
No easier divest[5] -
And gain the Sky
Than mayest Thou -

Except[6] Thyself may be
Thine Enemy -
15 Captivity is Consciousness -
So's Liberty -

1863 1890

656 [520]

I started Early - Took my Dog -
And visited the Sea -
The Mermaids in the Basement
Came out to look at me -

5 And Frigates - in the Upper Floor
Extended Hempen Hands -
Presuming Me to be a Mouse -
Aground - opon the Sands -

But no Man moved Me - till the Tide
10 Went past my simple Shoe -
And past my Apron - and my Belt
And past my Boddice - too -

And made as He would eat me up -
As wholly as a Dew
15 Opon a Dandelion's Sleeve -
And then - I started - too -

3. A device of torture on which the victim's body
is stretched.
4. I.e., bone.

5. I.e., it is no easier for the eagle to leave his nest.
6. Unless.

And He - He followed - close behind -
I felt His Silver Heel
Opon my Ancle - Then My Shoes
20 Would overflow with Pearl -

Until We met the Solid Town -
No One He seemed to know -
And bowing - with a Mighty look -
At me - The Sea withdrew -

1863 1891

675 [*401*]

What Soft - Cherubic Creatures -
These Gentlewomen are -
One would as soon assault a Plush[6] -
Or violate a Star -

5 Such Dimity[7] Convictions -
A Horror so refined
Of freckled Human Nature -
Of Deity - Ashamed -

It's such a common - Glory -
10 A Fisherman's[8] - Degree -
Redemption - Brittle Lady -
Be so - ashamed of Thee -

1863 1896

697 [*462*]

Why make it[9] doubt - it hurts it so -
So sick - to guess -
So strong - to know -
So brave - opon it's little Bed
5 To tell the very last They said
Unto Itself - and smile - And shake -
For that dear - distant - dangerous - sake -
But - the Instead - the Pinching fear
That Something - it did do - or dare -
10 Offend the Vision - and it flee -
And They no more remember me -
Nor ever turn to tell me why -
Oh, Master, This is Misery -

1863 1929

6. A thick, rich fabric.
7. A sheer cotton fabric.
8. An allusion to Christ.

9. For Dickinson's use of *it* to describe herself and for her reference to her *Master,* see letters 233 (p. 1070) and 248 (p. 1071).

709 [642]

Me from Myself - to banish -
Had I Art -
Invincible My Fortress
Unto All Heart -

5 But since Myself - assault Me -
How have I peace
Except by subjugating
Consciousness?

And since We're Mutual Monarch
10 How this be
Except by Abdication -
Me - of Me - ?

1863 1929

745 [722]

Sweet Mountains - Ye tell Me no lie -
Never deny Me - Never fly -
Those same unvarying Eyes
Turn on Me - When I fail - or feign,
5 Or take the Royal names in vain -
Their far - slow - Violet Gaze -

My Strong Madonnas[1] - Cherish still -
The Wayward Nun - beneath the Hill -
Whose service - is to You -
10 Her latest[2] Worship - When the Day
Fades from the Firmament away -
To lift Her Brows on You[3] -

1863 1945

764 [754]

My Life had stood - a Loaded Gun -
In Corners - till a Day
The Owner passed - identified -
And carried Me away -

5 And now We roam in Sovreign Woods -
And now We hunt the Doe -

1. Italian name for the Virgin Mary; not normally plural.
2. Last.
3. I.e., to look at you.

And every time I speak for Him
The Mountains straight reply -

And do I smile, such cordial light
10 Opon the Valley glow -
It is as a Vesuvian[4] face
Had let it's pleasure through -

And when at Night - Our good Day done -
I guard My Master's Head -
15 'Tis better than the Eider Duck's[5]
Deep Pillow - to have shared -

To foe of His - I'm deadly foe -
None stir the second time -
On whom I lay a Yellow Eye -
20 Or an emphatic Thumb -

Though I than He - may longer live
He longer must - than I -
For I have but the power to kill,
Without - the power to die -

1863 1929

788 [709]

Publication - is the Auction
Of the Mind of Man -
Poverty - be justifying
For so foul a thing

5 Possibly - but We - would rather
From Our Garret go
White - unto the White Creator -
Than invest - Our Snow -

Thought belong to Him who gave it -
10 Then - to Him Who bear
It's Corporeal illustration - sell
The Royal Air -

In the Parcel - Be the Merchant
Of the Heavenly Grace -
15 But reduce no Human Spirit
To Disgrace of Price -

1863 1929

4. Volcanic, after Mount Vesuvius in Italy. 5. The duck from which eiderdown is taken.

857 [732]

She rose to His Requirement - dropt
The Playthings of Her Life
To take the honorable Work
Of Woman, and of Wife -

5 If ought She missed in Her new Day,
Of Amplitude, or Awe -
Or first Prospective - or the Gold
In using, wear away,

It lay unmentioned - as the Sea
10 Develope Pearl, and Weed,
But only to Himself - be known
The Fathoms they abide -

1864 1890

1061 [858]

This Chasm, Sweet, opon my life
I mention it to you,
When Sunrise through a fissure drop
The Day must follow too.

5 If we demur, it's gaping sides
Disclose as 'twere a Tomb
Ourself am lying straight wherein
The Favorite of Doom -

When it has just contained a Life
10 Then, Darling, it will close
And yet so bolder every Day
So turbulent it grows

I'm tempted half to stitch it up
With a remaining Breath
15 I should not miss in yielding, though
To Him, it would be Death -

And so I bear it big about
My Burial - before
A Life quite ready to depart
20 Can harass me no more -

1865 1945

1072 [959]

A loss of something ever felt I -
The first that I could recollect
Bereft I was - of what I knew not
Too young that any should suspect

5 A Mourner walked among the children
I notwithstanding went about
As one bemoaning a Dominion
Itself[6] the only Prince cast out -

Elder, Today, A session wiser,
10 And fainter, too, as Wiseness is
I find Myself still softly searching
For my Delinquent[7] Palaces -

And a Suspicion, like a Finger
Touches my Forehead now and then
15 That I am looking oppositely
For the Site of the Kingdom of Heaven -

1865 1945

1096 [986]

A narrow Fellow in the Grass
Occasionally rides -
You may have met him? Did you not
His notice instant is -

5 The Grass divides as with a Comb -
A spotted Shaft is seen,
And then it closes at your Feet
And opens further on -

He likes a Boggy Acre -
10 A Floor too cool for Corn -
But when a Boy and Barefoot
I more than once at Noon

Have passed I thought a Whip Lash
Unbraiding in the Sun
15 When stooping to secure it
It wrinkled And was gone -

6. I.e., the one bemoaning. 7. Lost.

Several of Nature's People
I know and they know me
I feel for them a transport
20 Of Cordiality

But never met this Fellow
Attended or alone
Without a tighter Breathing
And Zero at the Bone.

1865 1866

1163 [*1138*]

A Spider sewed at Night
Without a Light
Opon an Arc of White -

If Ruff it was of Dame
5 Or Shroud of Gnome
Himself himself inform[8] -

Of Immortality
His strategy
Was physiognomy -

1869 1891

1263 [*1129*]

Tell all the truth but tell it slant -
Success in Circuit[9] lies
Too bright for our infirm Delight
The Truth's superb surprise
5 As Lightning to the Children eased
With explanation kind
The Truth must dazzle gradually
Or every man be blind -

1872 1945

8. I.e., only he could tell himself. 9. I.e., circuitousness.

<center>1311</center> <div align="right">[1282]</div>

A Art thou the thing I wanted?
 Begone - my Tooth has grown[1] -
 Supply the minor Palate
 That has not starved so long -
5 I tell thee while I waited
 The mystery of Food
 Increased till I abjured it
 And dine without
 Like God -

B Art thou the thing I wanted?
 Begone - my Tooth has grown -
 Affront a minor palate
 Thou did'st not goad so long -

5 I tell thee while I waited -

 The mystery of Food
 Increased till I abjured it
 Subsisting now like God -

1873 1945

<center>1332</center> <div align="right">[1317]</div>

 Abraham to kill him
 Was distinctly told -
 Isaac was an Urchin -
 Abraham was old -

5 Not a hesitation -
 Abraham complied -
 Flattered by Obeisance
 Tyranny demurred -

 Isaac - to his Children
10 Lived to tell the tale -
 Moral - with a Mastiff
 Manners may prevail.

1874 1945

1. Both "my taste has matured" and "I am longer in the tooth" (i.e., older).

<center>

1470 [*1445*]

</center>

Death is the supple Suitor
That wins at last -
It is a stealthy Wooing
5 Conducted first
By pallid innuendoes
And dim approach
But brave at last with Bugles
And a bisected Coach
It bears away in triumph
10 To Troth unknown
And Kinsmen as divulgeless
As Clans of Down -

1878 1945

<center>

1602 [*1562*]

</center>

Her[8] Losses make our Gains ashamed.
She bore Life's empty Pack
As gallantly as if the East
Were swinging at her Back -
5 Life's empty Pack is heaviest,
As every Porter knows -
In vain to punish Honey -
It only sweeter grows -

1883 1894

<center>

1691 [*1705*]

</center>

Volcanoes be in Sicily
And South America
I judge from my Geography
Volcano nearer here
5 A Lava step at any time
Am I inclined to climb
A Crater I may contemplate
Vesuvius[9] at Home

 1914

8. George Eliot's. Dickinson wrote this poem immediately after reading John Cross's biography of the late novelist (1819–1880; see above, p. 975) and enclosed it in a letter to the publisher Thomas Niles, in which she wrote, "The Life of Marian Evans had much I never knew. A Doom of Fruit without the Bloom, like the Niger Fig."
9. A volcano near Naples, Italy.

1715 [*1651*]

A word made Flesh[1] is seldom
And tremblingly partook
Nor then perhaps reported
But have I not mistook
5 Each one of us has tasted
With ecstasies of stealth
The very food debated
To our specific strength -

A word that breathes distinctly
10 Has not the power to die
Cohesive as the Spirit
It may expire if He -

"Made Flesh and dwelt among us"
Could condescension be
15 Like this consent of Language
This loved Philology[2]

1955

1734 [*1657*]

Eden is that old fashioned House
We dwell in every day
Without suspecting our abode
Until we drive away

5 How fair on looking back the Day
We sauntered from the Door
Unconscious our returning
But discover it no more

1914

1742 [*1670*]

In Winter in my Room
I came upon a Worm
Pink lank and warm
But as he was a worm
5 And worms presume
Not quite with him at home

1. A biblical description of Christ: "And the Word
was made flesh" (John 1.14).

2. The study of language.

Secured him by a string
To something neighboring
And went along -

10 A Trifle[3] afterward
A thing occurred
I'd not believe it if I heard
But state with creeping blood
A snake with mottles rare
15 Surveyed my chamber floor
In feature as the worm before
But ringed with power
The very string with which
I tied him - too -
20 When he was mean[4] and new
That string was there -

I shrank - "How fair you are"!
Propitiation's Claw -
"Afraid he hissed
25 Of me"?
"No Cordiality" -
He fathomed me -
Then to a Rhythm *Slim*
Secreted in his Form
As Patterns swim
30 Projected him.[5]

That time I flew
Both eyes his way
Lest he pursue
35 Nor ever ceased to run
Till in a distant Town
Towns on from mine
I set me down
This was a dream -

1914

1773 [1732]

My life closed twice before it's close;
It yet remains to see
If Immortality unveil
A third event to me,
5 So huge, so hopeless to conceive

3. Shortly.
4. Low, small.

5. I.e., he advanced.

As these that twice befell.
Parting is all we know of heaven,
And all we need of hell.

1896

Letters

233 [*Daisy and Her Master*]

To recipient unknown
ca. 1861

Master.

If you saw a bullet hit a Bird—and he told you he was'nt shot—you might weep at his courtesy, but you would certainly doubt his word.

One drop more from the gash that stains your Daisy's[1] bosom—then would you *believe*? Thomas' faith in Anatomy, was stronger than his faith in faith.[2] God made me—[Sir][3] Master—I did'nt be—myself. I dont know how it was done. He built the heart in me—Bye and bye it outgrew me—and like the little mother—with the big child—I got tired holding him. I heard of a thing called "Redemption"—which rested men and women. You remember I asked you for it—you gave me something else. I forgot the Redemption [in the Redeemed—I did'nt tell you for a long time, but I knew you had altered me—I] and was tired—no more—[so dear did this stranger become that were it, or my breath—the Alternative—I had tossed the fellow away with a smile.] I am older—tonight, Master—but the love is the same—so are the moon and the crescent. If it had been God's will that I might breathe where you breathed—and find the place—myself—at night—if I (can) never forget that I am not with you—and that sorrow and frost are nearer than I—if I wish with a might I cannot repress—that mine were the Queen's place—the love of the Plantagenet[4] is my only apology—To come nearer than presbyteries[5]—and nearer than the new Coat—that the Tailor made—the prank of the Heart at play on the Heart—in holy Holiday—is forbidden me—You make me say it over—I fear you laugh—when I do not see—[but] "Chillon"[6] is not funny. Have you the Heart in your breast—Sir—is it set like mine—a little to the left—has it the misgiving—if it wake in the night—perchance—itself to it—a timbrel[7] is it—itself to it a tune?

These things are [reverent] holy, Sir, I touch them [reverently] hallowed, but persons who pray—dare remark [our] "Father"! You say I do not tell you all—Daisy confessed—and denied not.

1. Dickinson's name for herself when writing to her "Master," whose identity is unknown.
2. In John 20.25, "doubting Thomas" refuses to believe in Christ's Resurrection until "I shall see in his hands the print of the nails, and put my finger into the print of the nails, and thrust my hand into his side."
3. Words which ED crossed out are here enclosed in brackets; alternative readings are in parentheses [note by Thomas H. Johnson, editor of the letters].

4. I.e., the love of royalty for royalty (the Plantagenets were royal family that ruled England from 1154 to 1391).
5. The parts of churches reserved for officiating clergy. There has been some speculation that the "Master" was a minister, the Reverend Charles Wadsworth.
6. A reference, probably, to Lord Byron's poem *The Prisoner of Chillon* (1816).
7. Small drum or tambourine.

Vesuvius dont talk—Etna dont—[Thy] one of them—said a syllable—a thousand years ago, and Pompeii[8] heard it, and hid forever—She could'nt look the world in the face, afterward—I suppose—Bashfull Pompeii! "Tell you of the want"—you know what a leech is, dont you—and [remember that] Daisy's arm is small—and you have felt the horizon hav'nt you—and did the sea—never come so close as to make you dance?

I dont know what you can do for it—thank you—Master—but if I had the Beard on my cheek—like you—and you—had Daisy's petals—and you cared so for me—what would become of you? Could you forget me in fight, or flight—or the foreign land? Could'nt Carlo,[9] and you and I walk in the meadows an hour—and nobody care but the Bobolink—and *his*—a *silver* scruple? I used to think when I died—I could see you—so I died as fast as I could—but the "Corporation"[1] are going Heaven too so [Eternity] wont be sequestered—now [at all]—Say I may wait for you—say I need go with no stranger to the to me—untried [country] fold—I waited a long time—Master—but I can wait more—wait till my hazel hair is dappled—and you carry the cane—then I can look at my watch—and if the Day is too far declined—we can take the chances [of] for Heaven—What would you do with me if I came "in white?" Have you the little chest to put the Alive—in?

I want to see you more—Sir—than all I wish for in this world—and the wish—altered a little—will be my only one—for the skies.

Could you come to New England—[this summer—could] would you come to Amherst—Would you like to come—Master?

[Would it do harm—yet we both fear God—] Would Daisy disappoint you—no—she would'nt—Sir—it were comfort forever—just to look in your face, while you looked in mine—then I could play in the woods till Dark—till you take me where Sundown cannot find us—and the true keep coming—till the town is full. [Will you tell me if you will?]

I did'nt think to tell you, you did'nt come to me "in white," nor ever told me why,

> No Rose, yet felt myself a'bloom,
> No Bird—yet rode in Ether.

248 [*Daisy Kneels a Culprit*]

To recipient unknown
early 1862?

Oh, did I offend it—[Did'nt it want me to tell it the truth] Daisy—Daisy—offend it—who bends her smaller life to his (it's) meeker (lower) every day—who only asks—a task—[who] something to do for love of it—some little way she cannot guess to make that master glad—

A love so big it scares her, rushing among her small heart—pushing aside the blood and leaving her faint (all) and white in the gust's arm—

Daisy—who never flinched thro' that awful parting, but held her life so tight he should not see the wound—who would have sheltered him in her childish bosom (Heart)—only it was'nt big eno' for a Guest so large—*this*

8. A Roman town, buried by an eruption of Mount Vesuvius in 79 C.E. Etna is also a volcano in Italy.

9. Dickinson's dog.
1. The ruling elders of a church.

Daisy—grieve her Lord—and yet it (she) often blundered—Perhaps she grieved (grazed) his taste—perhaps her odd—Backwoodsman [life] ways [troubled] teased his finer nature (sense). Daisy [fea] knows all that—but must she go unpardoned—teach her, preceptor grace—teach her majesty— Slow (Dull) at patrician things—Even the wren upon her nest learns (knows) more than Daisy dares—

Low at the knee that bore her once unto [royal] wordless rest [now] Daisy [stoops a] kneels a culprit—tell her her [offence] fault—Master—if it is [not so] small eno' to cancel with her life, [Daisy] she is satisfied—but punish [do not] dont banish her—shut her in prison, Sir—only pledge that you will forgive—sometime—before the grave, and Daisy will not mind—She will awake in [his] your likeness.

Wonder stings me more than the Bee—who did never sting me—but made gay music with his might wherever I [may] [should] did go—Wonder wastes my pound, you said I had no size to spare—

You send the water over the Dam in my brown eyes—

I've got a cough as big as a thimble—but I dont care for that—I've got a Tomahawk in my side but that dont hurt me much. [If you] Her master stabs her more—

Wont he come to her—or will he let her seek him, never minding [whatever] so long wandering [out] if to him at last.

Oh how the sailor strains, when his boat is filling—Oh how the dying tug, till the angel comes. Master—open your life wide, and take me in forever, I will never be tired—I will never be noisy when you want to be still. I will be [glad] [as the] your best little girl—nobody else will see me, but you—but that is enough—I shall not want any more—and all that Heaven only will disappoint me—will be because it's not so dear

260 [Say If My Verse Is Alive?]

To T. W. Higginson[2]
15 April 1862

Mr Higginson,

Are you too deeply occupied to say if my Verse is alive?

The Mind is so near itself—it cannot see, distinctly—and I have none to ask—

Should you think it breathed—and had you the leisure to tell me, I should feel quick gratitude—

If I make the mistake—that you dared to tell me—would give me sincerer honor—toward you—

I enclose my name—asking you, if you please—Sir—to tell me what is true?

That you will not betray me—it is needless to ask—since Honor is its own pawn—

2. Thomas Wentworth Higginson (1823–1911), a clergyman and then an essayist and lecturer, had published a "Letter to a Young Contributor" in the *Atlantic Monthly*. Dickinson wrote this letter in response, beginning a correspondence that lasted the rest of Dickinson's life.

261 [My "Companions"]

To T. W. Higginson
25 April 1862

Mr Higginson,

Your kindness claimed earlier gratitude—but I was ill—and write today, from my pillow.

Thank you for the surgery—it was not so painful as I supposed. I bring you others—as you ask—though they might not differ—

While my thought is undressed—I can make the distinction, but when I put them in the Gown—they look alike, and numb.

You asked how old I was? I made no verse—but one or two—until this winter—Sir—

I had a terror—since September—I could tell to none—and so I sing, as the Boy does by the Burying Ground—because I am afraid—You inquire my Books—For Poets—I have Keats—and Mr and Mrs Browning. For Prose— Mr Ruskin—Sir Thomas Browne—and the Revelations.[3] I went to school— but in your manner of the phrase—had no education. When a little Girl, I had a friend, who taught me Immortality—but venturing too near, himself— he never returned—Soon after, my Tutor, died—and for several years, my Lexicon—was my only companion—Then I found one more—but he was not contented I be his scholar—so he left the Land.

You ask of my Companions Hills—Sir—and the Sundown—and a Dog— large as myself, that my Father bought me—They are better than Beings— because they know—but do not tell—and the noise in the Pool, at Noon— excels my Piano. I have a Brother and Sister—My Mother does not care for thought—and Father, too busy with his Briefs—to notice what we do—He buys me many Books—but begs me not to read them—because he fears they joggle the Mind. They are religious—except me—and address an Eclipse, every morning—whom they call their "Father." But I fear my story fatigues you—I would like to learn—Could you tell me how to grow—or is it uncon- veyed—like Melody—or Witchcraft?

You speak of Mr Whitman[4]—I never read his Book—but was told that he was disgraceful—

I read Miss Prescott's[5] "Circumstance," but it followed me, in the Dark— so I avoided her—

Two Editors of Journals came to my Father's House, this winter—and asked me for my Mind—and when I asked them "Why," they said I was penurious—and they, would use it for the World—

I could not weigh myself—Myself—

My size felt small—to me—I read your Chapters in the Atlantic—and

3. Revelation, the visionary last book of the Bible. John Keats (1795–1821), English Romantic poet. Robert Browning (1812–1889) and Elizabeth Bar- rett Browning (1806–1861; see above, p. 521), English poets. John Ruskin (1819–1900), English art critic and essayist. Sir Thomas Browne (1605– 1682), English prose writer noted for his ornate style. Higginson's "Letter to a Young Contributor"

had mentioned Ruskin and Browne.
4. The American poet Walt Whitman (1819– 1892); a number of contemporary reviewers had attacked his sexually frank Leaves of Grass, which included poems described as "coarse," "vulgar," and "indecent."
5. Harriet Prescott (1835–1921), popular short story writer.

experienced honor for you—I was sure you would not reject a confiding question—

Is this—Sir—what you asked me to tell you?

Your friend,
E—Dickinson.

265 [*Fame*]

To T. W. Higginson
7 June 1862

Dear friend.

Your letter gave no Drunkenness, because I tasted Rum before—Domingo[6] comes but once—yet I have had few pleasures so deep as your opinion, and if I tried to thank you, my tears would block my tongue—

My dying Tutor told me that he would like to live till I had been a poet, but Death was much of Mob as I could master[7]—then—And when far afterward—a sudden light on Orchards, or a new fashion in the wind troubled my attention—I felt a palsy, here—the Verses just relieve—

Your second letter surprised me, and for a moment, swung—I had not supposed it. Your first—gave no dishonor, because the True—are not ashamed—I thanked you for your justice—but could not drop the Bells whose jingling cooled my Tramp—Perhaps the Balm, seemed better, because you bled me, first.

I smile when you suggest that I delay "to publish"—that being foreign to my thought, as Firmament to Fin—

If fame belonged to me, I could not escape her—if she did not, the longest day would pass me on the chase—and the approbation of my Dog, would forsake me—then—My Barefoot-Rank is better—

You think my gait "spasmodic"[8]—I am in danger—Sir—

You think me "uncontrolled"—I have no Tribunal.

Would you have time to be the "friend" you should think I need? I have a little shape—it would not crowd your Desk—nor make much Racket as the Mouse, that dents your Galleries—

If I might bring you what I do—not so frequent to trouble you—and ask you if I told it clear—'twould be control, to me—

The Sailor cannot see the North—but knows the Needle[9] can—

The "hand you stretch me in the Dark," I put mine in, and turn away—I have no Saxon,[1] now—

> And it should lift it's purple Dikes,
> As if I asked a common Alms,
> And in my wondering hand
> A Stranger pressed a Kingdom,
> And I, bewildered, stand—

6. Santo Domingo, capital of the Dominican Republic in the West Indies. Dickinson used the name in several poems; here it is invoked as a source of rum.
7. I.e., I was unable to write for a "mob"—a pop-ular audience.
8. I.e., fails to scan in proper measures.
9. Compass needle.
1. Language fails me [Johnson's note].

As if I asked the Orient
Had it for me a Morn—
And it should lift it's purple Dikes,
And shatter me with Dawn!

But, will you be my Preceptor, Mr Higginson?

Your friend
E Dickinson—

268 [*My Business Is Circumference*]

To T. W. Higginson
July 1862

Could you believe me—without? I had no portrait, now, but am small, like the Wren, and my Hair is bold, like the Chestnut Bur—and my eyes, like the Sherry in the Glass, that the Guest leaves—Would this do just as well?

It often alarms Father—He says Death might occur, and he has Molds[2] of all the rest—but has no Mold of me, but I noticed the Quick wore off those things, in a few days, and forestall the dishonor—You will think no caprice of me—

You said "Dark." I know the Butterfly—and the Lizard—and the Orchis[3]— Are not those *your* Countrymen?

I am happy to be your scholar, and will deserve the kindness, I cannot repay.

If you truly consent, I recite, now—

Will you tell me my fault, frankly as to yourself, for I had rather wince, than die. Men do not call the surgeon, to commend—the Bone, but to set it, Sir, and fracture within, is more critical. And for this, Preceptor, I shall bring you—Obedience—the Blossom from my Garden, and every gratitude I know. Perhaps you smile at me. I could not stop for that—My Business is Circumference[4]—An ignorance, not of Customs, but if caught with the Dawn—or the Sunset see me—Myself the only Kangaroo among the Beauty, Sir, if you please, it afflicts me, and I thought that instruction would take it away.

Because you have much business, beside the growth of me—you will appoint, yourself, how often I shall come—without your inconvenience. And if at any time—you regret you received me, or I prove a different fabric to that you supposed—you must banish me—

When I state myself, as the Representative of the Verse—it does not mean—me—but a supposed person. You are true, about the "perfection."

Today, makes Yesterday mean.

You spoke of Pippa Passes[5]—I never heard anybody speak of Pippa Passes—before.

2. I.e., photographs or pictures.
3. Small orchid; Higginson had written a number of nature essays.
4. This important Dickinsonian word has been defined by Johnson as "a projection of her imagination into all relationships of man, nature, and spirit."
5. Dramatic poem (1841) by Robert Browning.

You see my posture is benighted.
To thank you, baffles me. Are you perfectly powerful? Had I a pleasure
you had not, I could delight to bring it.

Your Scholar

CHRISTINA ROSSETTI
1830–1894

Admired by such varied contemporaries and descendants as Algernon Charles Swin-
burne and Gerard Manley Hopkins, Virginia Woolf and Edith Sitwell, Christina Ros-
setti has often been considered a sort of nun of art, a reclusive poet who lived an
uneventful life of austere piety. Yet this apparently retiring woman of letters began
her days as a rebelliously willful child, and what her brother referred to as her "hushed
life-drama" informed a long literary career marked by struggle and success. Born in
1830, Rossetti was the youngest of four children in an exuberant Anglo-Italian family.
Her father, Gabriele Rossetti, had been a famous poet and politician in Naples.
Forced to emigrate because he was a member of the Carbonari, a revolutionary group
seeking to establish a Neapolitan republic, he settled in London. There he taught
Italian, wrote long scholarly treatises on Dante, and married Frances Polidori, a lively
sometime governess who was the daughter of Gaetano Polidori, another distinguished
Italian emigré, and an Englishwoman named Anna Louisa Pierce. Not surprisingly,
all the children of the Rossetti marriage were energetic and ambitious. Maria, the
oldest, wrote her own study of Dante and eventually joined an Anglican sisterhood
devoted to social work; Dante Gabriel, the second child (known in the family as
Gabriel), became a poet and painter, one of the members of the so-called Pre-
Raphaelite Brotherhood, a group of young men whose radical ideas about aesthetic
style were to influence English art for several generations; and William Michael, the
third, became a well-known man of letters.

Like the four Brontë children, the four young Rossettis read voraciously and pro-
duced several family journals for which both Gabriel and Christina supplied poems
from an early age. Unlike the Brontës, however, the Rossetti children grew up in a
cosmopolitan setting. William later recalled that, bilingual from their youth, they
listened, fascinated, as numerous Italian expatriates "engaged in animated talk on the
affairs of Europe . . . with frequent and fervent recitations of poetry." In addition,
they spent many summers at the country cottage of their grandfather Polidori, who
introduced them to the pleasures of rural life and who, in 1847, when Christina was
seventeen, published her first volume of verses on his private printing press. Then,
in the summer of 1848, when Gabriel and six friends formed the Pre-Raphaelite
Brotherhood, Christina became romantically involved with James Collinson, a poet-
painter who was one of the "brothers," and the pair were engaged that autumn.
Though their relationship did not finally end in marriage, it is likely that through
Collinson, as well as through Gabriel, the young poet was exposed to some of the
most advanced cultural and aesthetic ideas then current in London, including a neo-
Romantic revival of medievalism that marked some of her early poems and ballads.
Certainly, her work appeared in several issues of *The Germ,* a short-lived journal that
was published by the Brotherhood, and she sometimes posed as a model for various
artists in the group.

Educated at home, Christina Rossetti was raised a strict Anglican, so strict that

one of her reasons for breaking her engagement to Collinson was said to be his conversion in 1850 to Roman Catholicism. But she began early to read secular as well as religious poetry from both the Italian and English traditions. Like her sister, Maria, she was meant to follow in her mother's footsteps and become a governess, but such employment seemed hopelessly dreary to her. Perhaps it was no coincidence, then, that in her adolescence she developed a number of mysterious ailments which made it difficult for her to work outside her home. As early as 1855, when she was temporarily employed as a governess, she confessed in a note to William that "I am rejoiced to feel that my health does really unfit me for miscellaneous governessing *en permanence.*"

From the 1850s on, therefore, Christina Rossetti lived mostly at home with her parents, helping to nurse her father, who had become seriously ill in 1843, and after his death in 1854 helping her mother to run the household. Still, she was by no means a recluse. From 1860 to 1870, she did social work at the St. Mary Magdalen Home for Fallen Women on Highgate Hill, and in 1854 she volunteered for service with Florence Nightingale's expedition of nurses to Scutari; evidently, it was only because of her youth that she was not accepted. Besides her involvement in welfare organizations, she led an active social life. In 1862, her brother Gabriel, who had been rootless and depressed after the 1861 suicide of his wife (and onetime mistress), the former Elizabeth Siddal, leased a luxurious residence called Tudor House. There he became the center of a glittering circle that included George Meredith, Swinburne, Robert Browning, and Lewis Carroll. Much admired by members of this set, Christina spent a good deal of time at Tudor House.

It was in the 1850s and 1860s, too, that Christina Rossetti had what seem to have been several love affairs whose vicissitudes she may have recorded in the stream of intensely erotic and sometimes painfully renunciatory poems that she produced in this period, including a sequence of love poems in Italian—*Il Rossegiao dell'oriente (The Reddening Dawn)*—that was discovered after her death. Her brother William consistently claimed that some of her most sorrowful poems were written about her failed relationship with James Collinson, and that others were responses to an amorous entanglement with Charles Bagot Cayley, who proposed to her (and was refused) in 1866. More recently, Lona Mosk Packer, the author of a 1963 biography, has argued that for much of her life Christina was hopelessly in love with William Bell Scott, a friend of the family and a married man, who only briefly returned her affection. Whatever the facts—and it is always possible that Christina's tragic "affair" was more imaginary than real—her poems suggest that at this time she was both scrupulous and sensual, both rigorously moral and richly romantic.

Most important, however, Rossetti's poems of this period reveal that she was already an accomplished artist. Her first collection, *Goblin Market, and Other Poems,* appeared in 1862, with a second edition in 1865. Her second book, *The Prince's Progress, and Other Poems,* was published in 1866. Both volumes included illustrations by her brother Gabriel, and both met with critical acclaim. Thus, by the 1870s Christina had become a seasoned writer with a considerable reputation. In 1870 she published a collection of short stories, in 1872 a book of inventive and charming nursery rhymes, and in 1874 a Lewis Carroll–like tale for children titled *Speaking Likenesses.* In addition, she produced four more books of poems in the course of her career as well as several essays on Dante and six volumes of religious essays. The subject of many critical tributes and the object of a few literary pilgrimages, she developed a briskly professional attitude toward her own work. At a time when there were not yet any international copyright laws to protect the interests of authors, she entered vigorously into royalty negotiations, pressed publishers to see that her books were issued promptly and printed properly, and energetically insisted on retaining what she called "my dear Copyright."

Such professional keenness may at first seem rather at odds with the character of the voice that emerges from Rossetti's poems. For the most part, her verses are

marked by a delicate austerity of style that appears incompatible with some of her businesslike correspondence. Yet it is important to remember that Rossetti was always a highly conscious craftswoman and that she came from a family of aesthetically sophisticated intellectuals, with her brothers, in particular, frequently helping her to revise her work and always helping to guard her professional interests. At the same time, it is important to consider the possibility that Rossetti was quite aware of the distinction between her own position in the world and that occupied by the very brothers for whose assistance she had often to be grateful. Though she had been glad to be liberated from the prison of "governessing *en permanence*," she was then obliged to live decorously at home, a chaste Victorian "spinster," while Gabriel, along with his Pre-Raphaelite Brothers, sowed wild oats and took London by storm, and William pursued a more sedate but equally unconstrained career as a critic and editor. "Beautiful, delightful, noble, memorable, as is the world you and yours frequent," she wrote William in 1888, "I yet am well content in my shady crevice: which crevice enjoys the unique advantage of being to my certain knowledge the place assigned me."

Despite this profession of contentment, however, Rossetti's poems suggest that she often had to struggle to renounce or at least moderate worldly ambition as well as to reconcile herself to losses in love. In their various ways, for instance, *Goblin Market* and "The World" meditate on the dangers of desire, especially the dangers of female desire, while "Shut Out," "Symbols," and "The Convent Threshold" explore the difficulties of renunciation. More specifically, "A Triad," "A Soul," "In an Artist's Studio," "Eve," and "Enrica, 1865" contemplate the limited (though sometimes enlivening) range of alternatives available to women, and such so-called mortuary verses as "After Death" and "Dead before Death"—verses written about or from the vantage point of the dead—mourn those limitations. Finally, "Winter: My Secret" suggests that its author is almost gleefully eager to guard her own privacy by withholding personal facts and feelings ("I tell my secret? No indeed, not I"), even while an exuberant fantasy like "Venus's Looking Glass" hints at the possibility of a transfigured world in which female power might be openly liberated and celebrated.

That Rossetti did allow herself to record hopeful visions is significant in view of the increasingly intense religiosity as well as the undeniable somberness that characterized her later life. In 1871 she suffered a severe attack of Graves' disease, a thyroid disorder that seriously disfigured and debilitated her, and around this time she began to write the devotional essays collected in six volumes published by the Society for the Propagation of Christian Knowledge. When she recovered, her brother William, with whom she, her mother, and two elderly aunts had been living, married Lucy Brown, the daughter of Ford Madox Brown, another one of the Pre-Raphaelite Brotherhood. Tensions arose between Christina and Lucy; though the poet tried hard to assuage these strains, within two years she, her mother, and her aunts established a separate household of their own.

After the three older women died, Christina was left alone, and in 1894 she succumbed to cancer. During the last weeks of her life, a neighbor complained that she could be heard screaming for several hours every evening, and one wonders if such outbursts—which her physician attributed to "hysteria" rather than pain—might represent some portion of the cost exacted by her long renunciation of desire. Nevertheless, though she may have suffered more than she admitted in the "shady crevice" of her renunciation, and though she herself often dreamed of dying into another, more spiritually loving world, the works of this woman whom an admirer once described as a "playful saint" won through to many significant aesthetic triumphs. "Death, oblivion, and rest lap round your songs with their dark wave," Virginia Woolf declared in a centennial essay addressed to the poet herself. But a "firm hand pruned your lines; a sharp ear tested their music. Nothing soft, otiose, irrelevant cumbered your pages. In a word, you were an artist."

Song

When I am dead, my dearest,
 Sing no sad songs for me;
Plant thou no roses at my head,
 Nor shady cypress tree:

5 Be the green grass above me
 With showers and dewdrops wet;
And if thou wilt, remember,
 And if thou wilt, forget.

 I shall not see the shadows,
10 I shall not feel the rain;
I shall not hear the nightingale
 Sing on, as if in pain:
And dreaming through the twilight
 That doth not rise nor set,
15 Haply[1] I may remember,
 And haply may forget.

1848 1862

Symbols

I watched a rosebud very long
 Brought on by dew and sun and shower,
 Waiting to see the perfect[1] flower:
Then, when I thought it should be strong,
5 It opened at the matin[2] hour
 And fell at evensong.

I watched a nest from day to day,
 A green nest full of pleasant shade,
 Wherein three speckled eggs were laid:
10 But when they should have hatched in May,
 The two old birds had grown afraid
 Or tired, and flew away.

Then in my wrath I broke the bough
 That I had tended so with care,
15 Hoping its scent should fill the air;
I crushed the eggs, not heeding how
 Their ancient promise had been fair:
 I would have vengeance now.

1. Perhaps; by chance.
1. Finished, full-grown.

2. Morning (*matins* and *evensong* are also morning and evening prayers).

But the dead branch spoke from the sod,[3]
20 And the eggs answered me again:
 Because we failed dost thou complain?
Is thy wrath just? And what if God,
 Who waiteth for thy fruits in vain,
 Should also take the rod?[4]

1849 1862

After Death

The curtains were half drawn, the floor was swept
And strewn with rushes, rosemary and may[1]
Lay thick upon the bed on which I lay,
Where thro' the lattice ivy-shadows crept.
5 He leaned above me, thinking that I slept
 And could not hear him; but I heard him say:
 "Poor child, poor child": and as he turned away
Came a deep silence, and I knew he wept.
He did not touch the shroud, or raise the fold
10 That hid my face, or take my hand in his,
 Or ruffle the smooth pillows for my head:
 He did not love me living; but once dead
He pitied me; and very sweet it is
To know he still is warm tho' I am cold.

1849 1862

A Soul

She stands as pale as Parian statues[1] stand;
Like Cleopatra when she turned at bay,
 And felt her strength above the Roman sway,[2]
And felt the aspic[3] writhing in her hand.
5 Her face is steadfast toward the shadowy land,
 For dim beyond it looms the land of day:
 Her feet are steadfast, all the arduous way
That foot-track doth not waver on the sand.
She stands there like a beacon through the night,
10 A pale clear beacon where the storm-drift is—
She stands alone, a wonder deathly-white:

3. In Genesis 4.10, God says to Cain, who has murdered his brother Abel, "the voice of thy brother's blood crieth unto me from the ground."
4. I.e., punish.
1. Green, flowering branches associated with spring.
1. Ancient statues made with the beautiful white marble from the Greek island of Paros.

2. Sovereign power. Cleopatra (69–30 B.C.E.), queen of Egypt, was captured by the Romans, who planned to parade her before the populace. Rather than become a public spectacle, she killed herself—according to legend, by letting a poisonous snake bite her; she feels her strength to be greater because she has taken control of her destiny.
3. Variation of "asp," a venomous Egyptian snake.

She stands there patient nerved with inner might,
 Indomitable in her feebleness,
 Her face and will athirst against the light.

1854 1896

The World

By day she[1] wooes me, soft, exceeding fair:
 But all night as the moon so changeth she;
 Loathsome and foul with hideous leprosy
And subtle serpents gliding in her hair.
5 By day she wooes me to the outer air,
 Ripe fruits, sweet flowers, and full satiety:
 But thro' the night, a beast she grins at me,
A very monster void of love and prayer.
By day she stands a lie: by night she stands
10 In all the naked horror of the truth
With pushing horns and clawed and clutching hands.
Is this a friend indeed; that I should sell
 My soul to her, give her my life and youth,
Till my feet, cloven[2] too, take hold on hell?

1854 1862

Dead before Death

Ah! changed and cold, how changed and very cold!
 With stiffened smiling lips and cold calm eyes:
 Changed, yet the same; much knowing, little wise;
This was the promise of the days of old!
5 Grown hard and stubborn in the ancient mold,[1]
 Grown rigid in the sham of lifelong lies:
 We hoped for better things as years would rise,
But it is over as a tale once told.
All fallen the blossom that no fruitage bore,
10 All lost the present and the future time,
All lost, all lost, the lapse[2] that went before:
So lost till death shut-to the opened door,
 So lost from chime to everlasting chime,
So cold and lost for ever evermore.

1854 1862

1. I.e., the world.
2. The devil is traditionally thought to have cloven hooves.
1. Both a hollow form in which something is given shape, and soil rich in decaying organic matter.
2. Fall (perhaps a reference to the biblical Fall into evil of Adam and Eve in Genesis).

Cobwebs

It is a land with neither night nor day,
 Nor heat nor cold, nor any wind nor rain,
 Nor hills nor valleys: but one even plain
Stretches through long unbroken miles away,
5 While through the sluggish air a twilight gray
 Broodeth: no moons or seasons wax and wane,
 No ebb and flow are there along the main,[1]
No bud-time, no leaf-falling, there for aye:[2]—
No ripple on the sea, no shifting sand,
10 No beat of wings to stir the stagnant space:
No pulse of life through all the loveless land
And loveless sea; no trace of days before,
 No guarded home, no toil-won resting-place,
No future hope, no fear for evermore.

1855 1896

Shut Out

The door was shut. I looked between
 Its iron bars; and saw it lie,
 My garden, mine, beneath the sky,
Pied[1] with all flowers bedewed and green:

5 From bough to bough the song-birds crossed,
 From flower to flower the moths and bees;
 With all its nests and stately trees
It had been mine, and it was lost.

A shadowless spirit kept the gate,
10 Blank and unchanging like the grave.
 I peering thro' said: "Let me have
Some buds to cheer my outcast state."

He answered not. "Or give me, then,
 But one small twig from shrub or tree;
15 And bid my home remember me
Until I come to it again."

The spirit was silent; but he took
 Mortar and stone to build a wall;
 He left no loophole great or small
20 Thro' which my straining eyes might look:

1. Sea.
2. Always.

1. Covered with multicolored patches.

So now I sit here quite alone
 Blinded with tears; nor grieve for that,
 For nought is left worth looking at
Since my delightful land is gone.

25 A violet bed is budding near,
 Wherein a lark has made her nest:
 And good they are, but not the best;
 And dear they are, but not so dear.

1856 1862

A Triad[1]

Three sang of love together: one with lips
 Crimson, with cheeks and bosom in a glow,
Flushed to the yellow hair and finger tips;
 And one there sang who soft and smooth as snow
5 Bloomed like a tinted hyacinth at a show;
And one was blue with famine after love,
 Who like a harpstring snapped rang harsh and low
The burden[2] of what those were singing of.
One shamed herself in love; one temperately
10 Grew gross[3] in soulless love, a sluggish wife;
One famished died for love. Thus two of three
 Took death for love and won him after strife;
One droned in sweetness like a fattened bee:
 All on the threshold, yet all short of life.

1856 1862

A Birthday

My heart is like a singing bird
 Whose nest is in a watered shoot;
My heart is like an apple tree
 Whose boughs are bent with thickset fruit;
5 My heart is like a rainbow shell
 That paddles in a halcyon sea;
My heart is gladder than all these
 Because my love is come to me.

Raise me a dais[1] of silk and down;
10 Hang it with vair[2] and purple dyes;
Carve it in doves and pomegranates,

1. A musical chord formed of three notes; also, simply a group of three.
2. In music, a bass part.
3. Fat.

1. A platform, often hung with cloth and ornately decorated.
2. Gray and white squirrel fur.

And peacocks with a hundred eyes;
Work it in gold and silver grapes,
 In leaves and silver fleurs-de-lys,[3]
15 Because the birthday of my life
 Is come, my love is come to me.

1857 1861

Winter: My Secret

I tell my secret? No indeed, not I:
Perhaps some day, who knows?
But not today; it froze, and blows, and snows,
And you're too curious: fie!
5 You want to hear it? well:
Only, my secret's mine, and I won't tell.

Or, after all, perhaps there's none:
Suppose there is no secret after all,
But only just my fun.
10 Today's a nipping day, a biting day;
In which one wants a shawl,
A veil, a cloak, and other wraps:
I cannot ope to every one who taps,
And let the draughts come whistling thro' my hall;
15 Come bounding and surrounding me,
Come buffeting, astounding me,
Nipping and clipping thro' my wraps and all.
I wear my mask for warmth: who ever shows
His nose to Russian snows
25 To be pecked at by every wind that blows?
You would not peck? I thank you for good will,
Believe, but leave that truth untested still.

Spring's an expansive time: yet I don't trust
March with its peck of dust,
30 Nor April with its rainbow-crowned brief showers,
Nor even May, whose flowers
One frost may wither thro' the sunless hours.

Perhaps some languid summer day,
When drowsy birds sing less and less,
35 And golden fruit is ripening to excess,
If there's not too much sun nor too much cloud,
And the warm wind is neither still nor loud,
Perhaps my secret I may say,
Or you may guess.

1857 1862

3. Conventionalized emblem of an iris, used in heraldry.

Up-hill

Does the road wind up-hill all the way?
 Yes, to the very end.
Will the day's journey take the whole long day?
 From morn to night, my friend.

5 But is there for the night a resting-place?
 A roof for when the slow dark hours begin.
May not the darkness hide it from my face?
 You cannot miss that inn.[1]

Shall I meet other wayfarers at night?
10 Those who have gone before.
Then must I knock, or call when just in sight?
 They will not keep you standing at that door.

Shall I find comfort, travel-sore and weak?
 Of labor you shall find the sum.
15 Will there be beds for me and all who seek?
 Yea, beds for all who come.

1858 1861

The Convent Threshold

There's blood between us, love, my love,
There's father's blood, there's brother's blood;
And blood's a bar I cannot pass:
I choose the stairs that mount above,
5 Stair after golden skyward stair,
To city and to sea of glass.
My lily feet are soiled with mud,
With scarlet mud which tells a tale
Of hope that was, of guilt that was,
10 Of love that shall not yet avail;
Alas, my heart, if I could bare
My heart, this selfsame stain is there:
I seek the sea of glass and fire[1]
To wash the spot, to burn the snare;[2]
15 Lo, stairs are meant to lift us higher:
Mount with me, mount the kindled stair.

Your eyes look earthward, mine look up.
I see the far-off city grand,
Beyond the hills a watered land,

1. I.e., death.
1. An image taken from St. John's vision of the Day of Judgment in Revelation 15.2.

2. The spot and the snare are emblems of worldly sin and temptation.

20 Beyond the gulf a gleaming strand
 Of mansions where the righteous sup;
 Who sleep at ease among their trees,
 Or wake to sing a cadenced hymn
 With Cherubim and Seraphim;[3]
25 They bore the Cross, they drained the cup,[4]
 Racked, roasted, crushed, wrenched limb from limb,
 They the offscouring[5] of the world:
 The heaven of starry heavens unfurled,
 The sun before their face is dim.

30 You looking earthward, what see you?
 Milk-white, wine-flushed among the vines,
 Up and down leaping, to and fro,
 Most glad, most full, made strong with wines,
 Blooming as peaches pearled with dew,
35 Their golden windy hair afloat,
 Love-music warbling in their throat,
 Young men and women come and go.

 You linger, yet the time is short:
 Flee for your life, gird up your strength
40 To flee; the shadows stretched at length
 Show that day wanes, that night draws nigh;
 Flee to the mountain, tarry not.
 Is this a time for smile and sigh,
 For songs among the secret trees
45 Where sudden blue birds nest and sport?
 The time is short and yet you stay:
 Today while it is called today
 Kneel, wrestle, knock, do violence, pray:
 Today is short, tomorrow nigh:
50 Why will[6] you die? why will you die?

 You sinned with me a pleasant sin:
 Repent with me, for I repent.
 Woe's me the lore I must unlearn!
 Woe's me that easy way we went,
55 So rugged when I would return!
 How long until my sleep begin,
 How long shall stretch these nights and days?
 Surely, clean Angels cry, she prays;
 She laves[7] her soul with tedious tears:
60 How long must stretch these years and years?

 I turn from you my cheeks and eyes,
 My hair which you shall see no more—
 Alas for joy that went before,

3. Two orders of angels in heaven.
4. I.e., the cup of communion, drunk in remembrance of Jesus (see, e.g., 1 Corinthians 11.25–26); and perhaps also the cup that Jesus identifies

with his crucifixion (see, e.g., Matthew 26.39, 42).
5. Garbage, filth.
6. I.e., do you wish?
7. Washes.

For joy that dies, for love that dies.
65 Only my lips still turn to you,
My livid lips that cry, Repent.
Oh weary life, Oh weary Lent,[8]
Oh weary time whose stars are few.

How should I rest in Paradise,
70 Or sit on steps of heaven alone?
If Saints and Angels spoke of love
Should I not answer from my throne:
Have pity upon me, ye my friends,
For I have heard the sound thereof:
75 Should I not turn with yearning eyes,
Turn earthwards with a pitiful pang?
Oh save me from a pang in heaven.
By all the gifts we took and gave,
Repent, repent, and be forgiven:
80 This life is long, but yet it ends;
Repent and purge your soul and save:
No gladder song the morning stars
Upon their birthday morning sang
Than Angels sing when one repents.

85 I tell you what I dreamed last night:
A spirit with transfigured face
Fire-footed clomb an infinite space.
I heard his hundred pinions[9] clang,
Heaven-bells rejoicing rang and rang,
90 Heaven-air was thrilled with subtle scents,
Worlds spun upon their rushing cars:[1]
He mounted shrieking: "Give me light."
Still light was poured on him, more light;
Angels, Archangels[2] he outstripped.

95 Exultant in exceeding might,
And trod the skirts of Cherubim.
Still "Give me light," he shrieked; and dipped
His thirsty face, and drank a sea,
Athirst with thirst it could not slake.
100 I saw him, drunk with knowledge, take
From aching brows the aureole[3] crown—
His locks writhed like a cloven snake—
He left his throne to grovel down
And lick the dust of Seraphs' feet:
105 For what is knowledge duly weighed?
Knowledge is strong, but love is sweet;
Yea all the progress he had made

8. In the Christian church, the period of forty days
before Easter observed with penitance and fasting
to recall Christ's fasting in the wilderness. More
generally, a time of pious self-deprivation.

9. Wings. "Clomb": climbed.
1. Chariots.
2. The highest order of angels.
3. Halo.

Was but to learn that all is small
Save love, for love is all in all.

110 I tell you what I dreamed last night:
It was not dark, it was not light,
Cold dews had drenched my plenteous hair
Thro' clay;[4] you came to seek me there.
And "Do you dream of me?" you said.
115 My heart was dust that used to leap
To you; I answered half asleep:
"My pillow is damp, my sheets are red,
There's a leaden tester[5] to my bed:
Find you a warmer playfellow,
120 A warmer pillow for your head,
A kinder love to love than mine."
You wrung your hands; while I like lead
Crushed downwards thro' the sodden earth:
You smote your hands but not in mirth,
125 And reeled but were not drunk with wine.

For all night long I dreamed of you:
I woke and prayed against my will,
Then slept to dream of you again.
At length I rose and knelt and prayed:
130 I cannot write the words I said,
My words were slow, my tears were few;
But thro' the dark my silence spoke
Like thunder. When this morning broke,
My face was pinched, my hair was gray,
135 And frozen blood was on the sill
Where stifling in my struggle I lay.

If now you saw me you would say:
Where is the face I used to love?
And I would answer: Gone before;
140 It tarries veiled in paradise.
When once the morning star shall rise,
When earth with shadow flees away
And we stand safe within the door,
Then you shall lift the veil thereof.
145 Look up, rise up: for far above
Our palms[6] are grown, our place is set;
There we shall meet as once we met
And love with old familiar love.

1858 1862

4. The clay of the grave.
5. Canopy; here the coffin's lid.

6. Trees whose leaves are associated with victory,
triumph.

Goblin Market

Morning and evening
Maids heard the goblins cry:
"Come buy our orchard fruits,
Come buy, come buy:
5 Apples and quinces,
Lemons and oranges,
Plump unpecked cherries,
Melons and raspberries,
Bloom-down-cheeked peaches,
10 Swart-headed[1] mulberries,
Wild free-born cranberries,
Crabapples, dewberries,
Pineapples, blackberries,
Apricots, strawberries;—
15 All ripe together
In summer weather,—
Morns that pass by,
Fair eyes that fly;
Come buy, come buy:
20 Our grapes fresh from the vine,
Pomegranates full and fine,
Dates and sharp bullaces,
Rare pears and greengages,
Damsons[2] and bilberries,
25 Taste them and try:
Currants and gooseberries,
Bright-fire-like barberries,
Figs to fill your mouth,
Citrons from the South,
30 Sweet to tongue and sound to eye;
Come buy, come buy."

Evening by evening
Among the brookside rushes,
Laura bowed her head to hear,
Lizzie veiled her blushes:
35 Crouching close together
In the cooling weather,
With clasping arms and cautioning lips,
With tingling cheeks and finger tips.
"Lie close," Laura said,
40 Pricking up her golden head:
"We must not look at goblin men,
We must not buy their fruits:
Who knows upon what soil they fed
Their hungry thirsty roots?"
45 "Come buy," call the goblins

1. Black-headed. 2. Bullaces, greengages, and damsons are plums.

Hobbling down the glen.
"Oh," cried Lizzie, "Laura, Laura,
You should not peep at goblin men."
Lizzie covered up her eyes,
50 Covered close lest they should look;
Laura reared her glossy head,
And whispered like the restless brook:
"Look, Lizzie, look, Lizzie,
Down the glen tramp little men.
55 One hauls a basket,
One bears a plate,
One lugs a golden dish
Of many pounds' weight.
How fair the vine must grow
60 Whose grapes are so luscious;
How warm the wind must blow
Through those fruit bushes."
"No," said Lizzie: "No, no, no;
Their offers should not charm us,
65 Their evil gifts would harm us."
She thrust a dimpled finger
In each ear, shut eyes and ran:
Curious Laura chose to linger
Wondering at each merchant man.
70 One had a cat's face,
One whisked a tail,
One tramped at a rat's pace,
One crawled like a snail,
One like a wombat prowled obtuse and furry,
75 One like a ratel³ tumbled hurry skurry.
She heard a voice like voice of doves
Cooing all together:
They sounded kind and full of loves
In the pleasant weather.

Laura stretched her gleaming neck
Like a rush-imbedded swan,
Like a lily from the beck,⁴
Like a moonlit poplar branch,
85 Like a vessel at the launch
When its last restraint is gone.

Backwards up the mossy glen
Turned and trooped the goblin men,
With their shrill repeated cry,
90 "Come buy, come buy."
When they reached where Laura was
They stood stock still upon the moss,
Leering at each other,
Brother with queer brother;

3. A badgerlike mammal of Africa, India, and the 4. Small brook.
Middle East.

95 Signaling each other,
 Brother with sly brother.
 One set his basket down,
 One reared his plate;
 One began to weave a crown
100 Of tendrils, leaves, and rough nuts brown
 (Men sell not such in any town);
 One heaved the golden weight
 Of dish and fruit to offer her:
 "Come buy, come buy," was still their cry.
105 Laura stared but did not stir,
 Longed but had no money.
 The whisk-tailed merchant bade her taste
 In tones as smooth as honey,
 The cat-faced purred,
110 The rat-paced spoke a word
 Of welcome, and the snail-paced even was heard;
 One parrot-voiced and jolly
 Cried "Pretty Goblin" still for "Pretty Polly";
 One whistled like a bird.

115 But sweet-tooth Laura spoke in haste:
 "Good Folk, I have no coin;
 To take were to purloin:
 I have no copper in my purse,
 I have no silver either,
120 And all my gold is on the furze[5]
 That shakes in windy weather
 Above the rusty heather."
 "You have much gold upon your head."
 They answered all together:
125 "Buy from us with a golden curl."
 She clipped a precious golden lock,
 She dropped a tear more rare than pearl,
 Then sucked their fruit globes fair or red.
 Sweeter than honey from the rock,
130 Stronger than man-rejoicing wine,[6]
 Clearer than water flowed that juice;
 She never tasted such before,
 How should it cloy with length of use?
 She sucked and sucked and sucked the more
135 Fruits which that unknown orchard bore,
 She sucked until her lips were sore;
 Then flung the emptied rinds away
 But gathered up one kernel stone,
 And knew not was it night or day
140 As she turned home alone.

 Lizzie met her at the gate
 Full of wise upbraidings:
 "Dear, you should not stay so late,

5. A spiny shrub. 6. See Psalms 81.16, 104.15.

Twilight is not good for maidens;
145 Should not loiter in the glen
In the haunts of goblin men.
Do you not remember Jeanie,
How she met them in the moonlight,
Took their gifts both choice and many,
150 Ate their fruits and wore their flowers
Plucked from bowers
Where summer ripens at all hours?
But ever in the noonlight
She pined and pined away;
155 Sought them by night and day,
Found them no more, but dwindled and grew gray;
Then fell with the first snow,
While to this day no grass will grow
Where she lies low:
160 I planted daisies there a year ago
That never blow.
You should not loiter so."
"Nay, hush," said Laura:
"Nay, hush, my sister:
165 I ate and ate my fill,
Yet my mouth waters still:
Tomorrow night I will
Buy more"; and kissed her.
"Have done with sorrow;
170 I'll bring you plums tomorrow
Fresh on their mother twigs,
Cherries worth getting;
You cannot think what figs
My teeth have met in,
175 What melons icy-cold
Piled on a dish of gold
Too huge for me to hold,
What peaches with a velvet nap,
Pellucid grapes without one seed:
180 Odorous indeed must be the mead
Whereon they grow, and pure the wave they drink
With lilies at the brink,
And sugar-sweet their sap."

Golden head by golden head,
185 Like two pigeons in one nest
Folded in each other's wings,
They lay down in their curtained bed:
Like two blossoms on one stem,
Like two flakes of new-fallen snow,
190 Like two wands of ivory
Tipped with gold for awful[7] kings.
Moon and stars gazed in at them,

7. Awe-inspiring.

Wind sang to them lullaby,
Lumbering owls forebore to fly,
195 Not a bat flapped to and fro
Round their nest:
Cheek to cheek and breast to breast
Locked together in one nest.

Early in the morning
200 When the first cock crowed his warning.
Neat like bees, as sweet and busy,
Laura rose with Lizzie:
Fetched in honey, milked the cows,
Aired and set to rights the house,
205 Kneaded cakes of whitest wheat,
Cakes for dainty mouths to eat,
Next churned butter, whipped up cream,
Fed their poultry, sat and sewed;
Talked as modest maidens should:
210 Lizzie with an open heart,
Laura in an absent dream,
One content, one sick in part;
One warbling for the mere bright day's delight,
One longing for the night.

215 At length slow evening came:
They went with pitchers to the reedy brook;
Lizzie most placid in her look,
Laura most like a leaping flame,
They drew the gurgling water from its deep.
220 Lizzie plucked purple and rich golden flags,
Then turning homeward said: "The sunset flushes
Those furthest loftiest crags;
Come, Laura, not another maiden lags.
No willful squirrel wags,
225 The beasts and birds are fast asleep."
But Laura loitered still among the rushes.
And said the bank was steep.

And said the hour was early still,
The dew not fallen, the wind not chill;
230 Listening ever, but not catching
The customary cry,
"Come buy, come buy,"
With its iterated jingle
Of sugar-baited words:
235 Not for all her watching
Once discerning even one goblin
Racing, whisking, tumbling, hobbling—
Let alone the herds
That used to tramp along the glen,
240 In groups or single,
Of brisk fruit-merchant men.

Till Lizzie urged, "O Laura, come;
I hear the fruit-call, but I dare not look:
You should not loiter longer at this brook:
245 Come with me home.
The stars rise, the moon bends her arc,
Each glow-worm winks her spark,
Let us get home before the night grows dark:
For clouds may gather
250 Though this is summer weather,
Put out the lights and drench us through;
Then if we lost our way what should we do?"

Laura turned cold as stone
To find her sister heard that cry alone,
255 That goblin cry,
"Come buy our fruits, come buy."
Must she then buy no more such dainty fruit?
Must she no more such succous pasture find,
Gone deaf and blind?
260 Her tree of life dropped from the root:
She said not one word in her heart's sore ache:
But peering through the dimness, nought discerning,
Trudged home, her pitcher dripping all the way;
So crept to bed, and lay
265 Silent till Lizzie slept;
Then sat up in a passionate yearning.
And gnashed her teeth for balked desire, and wept
As if her heart would break.

Day after day, night after night,
270 Laura kept watch in vain
In sullen silence of exceeding pain.
She never caught again the goblin cry,
"Come buy, come buy";—
She never spied the goblin men
275 Hawking their fruits along the glen:
But when the noon waxed bright
Her hair grew thin and gray;
She dwindled, as the fair full moon doth turn
To swift decay and burn
280 Her fire away.

One day remembering her kernelstone
She set it by a wall that faced the south:
Dewed it with tears, hoped for a root,
Watched for a waxing shoot,
285 But there came none.
It never saw the sun,
It never felt the trickling moisture run:
While with sunk eyes and faded mouth
She dreamed of melons, as a traveler sees
290 False waves in desert drouth

With shade of leaf-crowned trees,
And burns the thirstier in the sandful breeze.

She no more swept the house,
Tended the fowls or cows,
295 Fetched honey, kneaded cakes of wheat,
Brought water from the brook:
But sat down listless in the chimneynook
And would not eat.

Tender Lizzie could not bear
300 To watch her sister's cankerous care,[8]
Yet not to share.
She night and morning
Caught the goblins' cry:
"Come buy our orchard fruits,
305 Come buy, come buy":—
Beside the brook, along the glen,
She heard the tramp of goblin men,
The voice and stir
Poor Laura could not hear;
310 Longed to buy fruit to comfort her,
But feared to pay too dear.
She thought of Jeanie in her grave,
Who should have been a bride;
But who for joys brides hope to have
315 Fell sick and died
In her gay prime,
In earliest winter time,
With the first glazing rime,
With the first snow-fall of crisp winter time.

320 Till Laura dwindling
Seemed knocking at Death's door.
Then Lizzie weighed no more
Better and worse;
But put a silver penny in her purse,
325 Kissed Laura, crossed the heath with clumps of furze
At twilight, halted by the brook:
And for the first time in her life
Began to listen and look.

Laughed every goblin
330 When they spied her peeping:
Came towards her hobbling,
Flying, running, leaping,
Puffing and blowing,
Chuckling, clapping, crowing,
335 Cluckling and gobbling,
Mopping and mowing,

8. I.e., the care eating away at her.

Full of airs and graces,
Pulling wry faces,
Demure grimaces,
340 Cat-like and rat-like,
Ratel- and wombat-like,
Snail-paced in a hurry,
Parrot-voiced and whistler,
Helter skelter, hurry skurry,
345 Chattering like magpies,
Fluttering like pigeons,
Gliding like fishes,—
Hugged her and kissed her:
Squeezed and caressed her:
350 Stretched up their dishes,
Panniers, and plates:
"Look at our apples
Russet and dun,
Bob at our cherries,
355 Bite at our peaches,
Citrons and dates,
Grapes for the asking,
Pears red with basking
Out in the sun,
360 Plums on their twigs;
Pluck them and suck them,
Pomegranates, figs."—

"Good folk," said Lizzie,
Mindful of Jeanie:
365 "Give me much and many":—
Held out her apron,
Tossed them her penny
"Nay, take a seat with us,
Honor and eat with us,"
370 They answered grinning:
"Our feast is but beginning.
Night yet is early,
Warm and dew-pearly,
Wakeful and starry:
375 Such fruits as these
No man can carry;
Half their bloom would fly,
Half their dew would dry,
Half their flavor would pass by.
380 Sit down and feast with us,
Be welcome guest with us,
Cheer you and rest with us."—
"Thank you," said Lizzie: "But one waits
At home alone for me:
385 So without further parleying,
If you will not sell me any
Of your fruits though much and many,

Give me back my silver penny
I tossed you for a fee."—
390 They began to scratch their pates,
No longer wagging, purring,
But visibly demurring,
Grunting and snarling.
One called her proud,
395 Cross-grained, uncivil;
Their tones waxed loud,
Their looks were evil.
Lashing their tails
They trod and hustled her,
400 Elbowed and jostled her,
Clawed with their nails,
Barking, mewing, hissing, mocking,
Tore her gown and soiled her stocking,
Twitched her hair out by the roots,
405 Stamped upon her tender feet,
Held her hands and squeezed their fruits
Against her mouth to make her eat.

White and golden Lizzie stood,
Like a lily in a flood,—
410 Like a rock of blue-veined stone
Lashed by tides obstreperously,—
Like a beacon left alone
In a hoary roaring sea,
Sending up a golden fire,—
415 Like a fruit-crowned orange-tree
White with blossoms honey-sweet
Sore beset by wasp and bee,—
Like a royal virgin town
Topped with gilded dome and spire
420 Close beleaguered by a fleet
Mad to tug her standard down.

One may lead a horse to water,
Twenty cannot make him drink.
Though the goblins cuffed and caught her,
425 Coaxed and fought her,
Bullied and besought her,
Scratched her, pinched her black as ink,
Kicked and knocked her,
Mauled and mocked her,
430 Lizzie uttered not a word;
Would not open lip from lip
Lest they should cram a mouthful in:
But laughed in heart to feel the drip
Of juice that syruped all her face,
435 And lodged in dimples of her chin,
And streaked her neck which quaked like curd.
At last the evil people,

Worn out by her resistance,
Flung back her penny, kicked their fruit
440 Along whichever road they took,
Not leaving root or stone or shoot;
Some writhed into the ground,
Some dived into the brook
With ring and ripple,
445 Some scudded on the gale without a sound.
Some vanished in the distance.

In a smart, ache, tingle,
Lizzie went her way;
Knew not was it night or day;
450 Sprang up the bank, tore through the furze,
Threaded copse and dingle,
And heard her penny jingle
Bouncing in her purse,—
Its bounce was music to her ear.
455 She ran and ran
As if she feared some goblin man
Dogged her with gibe or curse
Or something worse:
But not one goblin skurried after,
460 Nor was she pricked by fear;
The kind heart made her windy-paced
That urged her home quite out of breath with haste
And inward laughter.

She cried, "Laura," up the garden,
465 "Did you miss me?
Come and kiss me.
Never mind my bruises,
Hug me, kiss me, suck my juices
Squeezed from goblin fruits for you,
470 Goblin pulp and goblin dew.
Eat me, drink me, love me;
Laura, make much of me;
For your sake I have braved the glen
And had to do with goblin merchant men."

475 Laura started from her chair,
Flung her arms up in the air,
Clutched her hair:
"Lizzie, Lizzie, have you tasted
For my sake the fruit forbidden?
480 Must your light like mine be hidden,
Your young life like mine be wasted,
Undone in mine undoing,
And ruined in my ruin,
Thirsty, cankered, goblin-ridden?"—
485 She clung about her sister,
Kissed and kissed and kissed her:

Tears once again
Refreshed her shrunken eyes,
Dropping like rain
490 After long sultry drouth;
Shaking with anguish, fear, and pain,
She kissed and kissed her with a hungry mouth.

Her lips began to scorch,
That juice was wormwood to her tongue,
495 She loathed the feast:
Writhing as one possessed she leaped and sung,
Rent all her robe, and wrung
Her hands in lamentable haste,
And beat her breast,
500 Her locks streamed like the torch
Borne by a racer at full speed,
Or like the mane of horses in their flight,
Or like an eagle when she stems⁹ the light
Straight toward the sun,
505 Or like a caged thing freed,
Or like a flying flag when armies run.

Swift fire spread through her veins, knocked at her heart,
Met the fire smoldering there
And overbore its lesser flame;
510 She gorged on bitterness without a name:
Ah fool, to choose such part
Of soul-consuming care!
Sense failed in the mortal strife:
Like the watch-tower of a town
515 Which an earthquake shatters down,
Like a lightning-stricken mast,
Like a wind-uprooted tree
Spun about,
Like a foam-topped waterspout
520 Cast down headlong in the sea,
She fell at last;
Pleasure past and anguish past,
Is it death or is it life?

Life out of death.
525 That night long Lizzie watched by her,
Counted her pulse's flagging stir,
Felt for her breath,
Held water to her lips, and cooled her face
With tears and fanning leaves.
530 But when the first birds chirped about their eaves,
And early reapers plodded to the place
Of golden sheaves,
And dew-wet grass

9. Makes headway against.

Bowed in the morning winds so brisk to pass,
535 And new buds with new day
Opened of cup-like lilies on the stream,
Laura awoke as from a dream,
Laughed in the innocent old way,
Hugged Lizzie but not twice or thrice;
540 Her gleaming locks showed not one thread of gray,
Her breath was sweet as May,
And light danced in her eyes.

Days, weeks, months, years
Afterwards, when both were wives
545 With children of their own;
Their mother-hearts beset with fears,
Their lives bound up in tender lives:
Laura would call the little ones
And tell them of her early prime,
550 Those pleasant days long gone
Of not-returning time:
Would talk about the haunted glen,
The wicked quaint fruit-merchant men,
Their fruits like honey to the throat
555 But poison in the blood
(Men sell not such in any town):
Would tell them how her sister stood
In deadly peril to do her good,
And win the fiery antidote:
560 Then joining hands to little hands
Would bid them cling together,—
"For there is no friend like a sister
In calm or stormy weather;
To cheer one on the tedious way,
565 To fetch one if one goes astray,
To lift one if one totters down,
To strengthen whilst one stands."

1859 1896

In an Artist's Studio

One face looks out from all his[1] canvases,
 One selfsame figure sits or walks or leans:
 We found her hidden just behind those screens,
 That mirror[2] gave back all her loveliness.
5 A queen in opal or in ruby dress,

1. Dante Gabriel Rossetti (1828–1882), Christina Rossetti's brother. The "face" is that of Elizabeth Siddal (1829–1862), whom Dante Gabriel later married. Christina herself also posed for many of his paintings.

2. The artist's eye and/or his painting. "Screens": the paintings; however, nude models were protected from the eyes of visitors to the artist's studio by screens, so the word creates an ambiguity throughout the poem.

A nameless girl in freshest summer-greens,
A saint, an angel—every canvas means
The same one meaning, neither more nor less.
He feeds upon her face by day and night,
10 And she with true kind eyes looks back on him,
Fair as the moon and joyful as the light:
　　Not wan with waiting, not with sorrow dim;
Not as she is, but was when hope shone bright;
　　Not as she is, but as she fills his dream.

1861 1896

Eve[1]

"While I sit at the door
Sick to gaze within
Mine eye weepeth sore
For sorrow and sin:
5 As a tree my sin stands
To darken all lands;
Death is the fruit it bore.

"How have Eden bowers grown
Without Adam to bend them!
10 How have Eden flowers blown[2]
Squandering their sweet breath
Without me to tend them!
The Tree of Life was ours,
Tree twelvefold-fruited,
15 Most lofty tree that flowers,
Most deeply rooted:
I chose the tree of death.

"Hadst thou but said me nay,
Adam, my brother,
20 I might have pined away;
I, but none other:
God might have let thee stay
Safe in our garden,
By putting me away
25 Beyond all pardon.

"I, Eve, sad mother
Of all who must live,
I, not another,
Plucked bitterest fruit to give

1. The first woman and wife of Adam, who, in Genesis 3, is cajoled by the serpent into eating fruit from the forbidden tree of knowledge and who then gives the fruit to Adam to eat, thus bringing about the expulsion from Eden and the emergence of death into the world.
2. Blossomed.

30 My friend, husband, lover;—
 O wanton eyes, run over;
 Who but I should grieve?—
 Cain hath slain his brother:[3]
 Of all who must die mother,
35 Miserable Eve!"

 Thus she sat weeping,
 Thus Eve our mother,
 Where one lay sleeping
 Slain by his brother.
40 Greatest and least
 Each piteous beast
 To hear her voice
 Forgot his joys
 And set aside his feast.

45 The mouse paused in his walk
 And dropped his wheaten stalk;
 Grave cattle wagged their heads
 In rumination;[4]
 The eagle gave a cry
50 From his cloud station;
 Larks on thyme beds
 Forbore to mount or sing;
 Bees drooped upon the wing;
 The raven perched on high
55 Forgot his ration;
 The conies[5] in their rock,
 A feeble nation,
 Quaked sympathetical;
 The mocking-bird left off to mock;
60 Huge camels knelt as if
 In deprecation;
 The kind hart's tears were falling;
 Chattered the wistful stork;
 Dove-voices with a dying fall[6]
65 Cooed desolation
 Answering grief by grief.

 Only the serpent in the dust
 Wriggling and crawling,
 Grinned an evil grin and thrust
70 His tongue out with its fork.

1865 1866

3. In Genesis 4, Adam and Eve's son Cain kills his brother, Abel.
4. Both cud chewing and, usually in human application, deep thought.

5. Rabbits.
6. Dying away, trailing off, but also with a suggestion of the Fall into sin of Adam and Eve.

Enrica, 1865[1]

She came among us from the South
 And made the North her home awhile;
 Our dimness brightened in her smile,
Our tongue[2] grew sweeter in her mouth.

5 We chilled beside her liberal[3] glow,
 She dwarfed us by her ampler scale,
 Her full-blown blossom made us pale,
She summer-like and we like snow.

We Englishwomen, trim, correct,
10 All minted[4] in the selfsame mold,
 Warm-hearted but of semblance cold,
All-courteous out of self-respect.

She woman in her natural grace,
 Less trammelled[5] she by lore of school,
15 Courteous by nature not by rule,
Warm-hearted and of cordial face.

So for awhile she made her home
 Among us in the rigid North,
 She who from Italy came forth
20 And scaled the Alps and crossed the foam.

But if she found us like our sea,
 Of aspect colorless and chill,
 Rock-girt; like it she found us still
Deep at our deepest, strong and free.

1865 1875

Venus's Looking-Glass

I marked where lovely Venus[1] and her court
 With song and dance and merry laugh went by;
 Weightless, their wingless feet seemed made to fly,
Bound from the ground and in mid air to sport.
5 Left far behind I heard the dolphins snort,
 Tracking their goddess with a wistful eye,
 Around whose head white doves rose, wheeling high
Or low, and cooed after their tender sort.
All this I saw in Spring. Thro' Summer heat

1. The poem is about a woman of Rossetti's acquaintance named Enrica Barile, who had been abandoned by her husband (a rather eccentric man who changed his name to Filopanti, "all-loving"), and subsequently moved to London.
2. Language.

3. Generous, abundant.
4. Stamped, like coins.
5. Confined, restrained.
1. The Roman name for Aphrodite, the Greek goddess of love; dolphins and doves were sacred to her. "Marked": saw.

10 I saw the lovely Queen of Love no more.
 But when flushed Autumn thro' the woodlands went
I spied sweet Venus walk amid the wheat:
 Whom seeing, every harvester gave o'er
 His toil, and laughed and hoped and was content.

1872 1875

REBECCA HARDING DAVIS
1831–1910

For Tillie Olsen, the twentieth-century working-class writer who recovered *Life in the Iron-Mills* from a century of critical neglect, Rebecca Harding Davis's novella represents the triumph of a "house-bound, class-bound, sex-bound" author who was somehow able to envision the grim realities of mid-nineteenth-century industrialization in America: labor's alienated relations with managers and owners, the degradation of ignored and unjust poverty, the pollution caused by industrial waste. *Life in the Iron-Mills,* which appeared anonymously in an 1861 issue of the *Atlantic Monthly,* was immediately acknowledged as a literary landmark by Nathaniel Hawthorne and Louisa May Alcott, Henry Ward Beecher, and Ralph Waldo Emerson. Some six years before the French novelist Émile Zola began publishing what were called "naturalistic" novels, a thirty-year-old Virginian had brilliantly dramatized the socioeconomic implications of environmental determinism. Yet, by the end of her life, this innovative writer was mainly remembered as the mother of the distinguished reporter Richard Harding Davis.

Little is known about the circumstances that turned Harding Davis into a sometimes inspired, always prolific author. The eldest of five children, she was born in Washington County, Pennsylvania, but moved with her family in 1836 to the city of Wheeling (then in Virginia and now in West Virginia). Wheeling not only was a center of the booming steel industry in the late 1850s but, inside a border state, was also increasingly involved in the turbulent antagonisms preceding the Civil War. The Harding family was middle class. Richard W. Harding, an Englishman from Ireland, was successful in business, conservative in his political views, and autocratic in his demands on the family. Rachel Leet (Wilson) Harding first educated her daughter at home and then sent her to the Washington Female Seminary in Pennsylvania. After graduating in 1848 with the highest honors in her class, Rebecca Harding returned to Wheeling and her family, educating the younger children, studying the books brought home by her brother, William, when he attended Washington College, and, perhaps most important, walking through the mills and factories of the town.

During this period, Harding sent *Life in the Iron-Mills* to the prestigious magazine that was run by James T. Fields. His acceptance letter, accompanied by $50, must have seemed like the beginning of an exciting new life, and in fact, it did lead to a longer work serialized in the *Atlantic* and later published in book form as *Margaret Howth* (1862), as well as to several dramatic stories about the devastating costs of the Civil War. It also resulted in a visit to Fields, which initiated a long-lasting friendship with his wife, Annie Fields, and shorter exchanges with Hawthorne and Emerson, among others. And it precipitated a correspondence with a reader-admirer whom Harding met in 1862 and married in 1863: three years her junior, Lemuel Clarke Davis was studying for the bar and writing journalism when he decided to settle with his wife in Philadelphia.

Although Harding Davis continued to pursue an ever more professional career in journalism and fiction, the rest of her life hardly met the expectations of those exciting years. First, nursing her father through a long illness, she found little refuge back at her new home, which was shared initially with her husband's sister and her children. Next, Harding Davis fell ill with what might have been nervous exhaustion. Then, to supplement the family's income, she began writing for magazines that could pay her more than the *Atlantic.* Subsequent novels suffered from the time pressures imposed by serialization. The late *Pro Ares et Focis—A Plea for Our Altars and Hearths* (1870) proclaimed the joys of domesticity; however, the author's own domestic life seems to have been arduous. With her husband increasingly occupied by abolitionist activities and by his duties as editor of the *Philadelphia Public Ledger,* she must have found it difficult to combine her position as contributing editor of the *New York Tribune* with the raising of their two sons and daughter. Yet, in her forties, she retained her earlier determination to extend the subject of fiction to wider social and economic issues: *Put Out of the Way* (1871), for example, focuses on the laws relating to lunacy; *Earthen Pitchers* (1873–74) on two young professional women; *John Andross* (1874) on monetary corruption in government. A number of short stories collected in *Silhouettes of American Life* (1892) further developed her self-defined literary project, "to dig into this commonplace, this vulgar American life, and see what is in it."

By the time she died at seventy-nine, Harding Davis had witnessed a decline of interest in her work. Yet she must have known that by writing *Life in the Iron-Mills,* she had herself confronted just the inhibitions to creativity that she had analyzed with such clarity in her portrait of a working-class sculptor's efforts to construct the form of his desire out of the refuse (the korl) of the iron mill. Tellingly, when her editor objected to the title she had chosen to give this tale, Harding Davis's alternative was "The Korl Woman" or "Beyond," for this huge figure of a woman imbued with longing signifies not only the thwarted work of the korl cutter but also Harding Davis's own protest against a world in which she saw that class, race, and gender could condemn human beings to frustration and pain.

Life in the Iron-Mills

"Is this the end?
O Life, as futile, then, as frail!
What hope of answer or redress?"[1]

A cloudy day: do you know what that is in a town of iron-works? The sky sank down before dawn, muddy, flat, immovable. The air is thick, clammy with the breath of crowded human beings. It stifles me. I open the window, and, looking out, can scarcely see through the rain the grocer's shop opposite, where a crowd of drunken Irishmen are puffing Lynchburg tobacco[2] in their pipes. I can detect the scent through all the foul smells ranging loose in the air.

The idiosyncrasy of this town is smoke. It rolls sullenly in slow folds from the great chimneys of the iron-foundries, and settles down in black, slimy pools on the muddy streets. Smoke on the wharves, smoke on the dingy boats, on the yellow river,—clinging in a coating of greasy soot to the house-front, the two faded poplars, the faces of the passers-by. The long train of mules, dragging masses of pig-iron[3] through the narrow street, have a foul vapor

1. The first line is Davis's; the next two are from Alfred, Lord Tennyson's *In Memoriam: A.H.H.* (1850), 56.25–27.

2. An inferior tobacco grown in Virginia.
3. Crude iron formed in blocks.

hanging to their reeking sides. Here, inside, is a little broken figure of an angel pointing upward from the mantel-shelf; but even its wings are covered with smoke, clotted and black. Smoke everywhere! A dirty canary chirps desolately in a cage beside me. Its dream of green fields and sunshine is a very old dream,—almost worn out, I think.

From the back-window I can see a narrow brick-yard sloping down to the river-side, strewed with rain-butts[4] and tubs. The river, dull and tawny-colored, (*la belle rivière!*[5]) drags itself sluggishly along, tired of the heavy weight of boats and coal-barges. What wonder? When I was a child, I used to fancy a look of weary, dumb appeal upon the face of the Negro-like river slavishly bearing its burden day after day. Something of the same idle notion comes to me to-day, when from the street-window I look on the slow stream of human life creeping past, night and morning, to the great mills. Masses of men, with dull, besotted[6] faces bent to the ground, sharpened here and there by pain or cunning; skin and muscle and flesh begrimed with smoke and ashes; stooping all night over boiling caldrons of metal, laired by day in dens of drunkenness and infamy; breathing from infancy to death an air saturated with fog and grease and soot, vileness for soul and body. What do you make of a case like that, amateur psychologist? You call it an altogether serious thing to be alive: to these men it is a drunken jest, a joke,—horrible to angels perhaps, to them commonplace enough. My fancy about the river was an idle one: it is no type of such a life. What if it be stagnant and slimy here? It knows that beyond there waits for it odorous sunlight,—quaint old gardens, dusky with soft, green foliage of apple-trees, and flushing crimson with roses,—air, and fields, and mountains. The future of the Welsh puddler[7] passing just now is not so pleasant. To be stowed away, after his grimy work is done, in a hole in the muddy graveyard, and after that,—*not* air, nor green fields, nor curious roses.

Can you see how foggy the day is? As I stand here, idly tapping the window-pane, and looking out through the rain at the dirty back-yard and the coal-boats below, fragments of an old story float up before me,—a story of this old house into which I happened to come today. You may think it a tiresome story enough, as foggy as the day, sharpened by no sudden flashes of pain or pleasure.—I know: only the outline of a dull life, that long since, with thousands of dull lives like its own, was vainly lived and lost: thousands of them,—massed, vile, slimy lives, like those of the torpid lizards in yonder stagnant water-butt.—Lost? There is a curious point for you to settle, my friend, who study psychology in a lazy, *dilettante* way. Stop a moment. I am going to be honest. This is what I want you to do. I want you to hide your disgust, take no heed to your clean clothes, and come right down with me,—here, into the thickest of the fog and mud and foul effluvia.[8] I want you to hear this story. There is a secret down here, in this nightmare fog, that has lain dumb for centuries: I want to make it a real thing to you. You, Egoist, or Pantheist, or Arminian,[9] busy in making straight paths for your feet on the hills, do not see it clearly,—this terrible question which men here have

4. Large casks for catching rainwater.
5. The beautiful river! (French)—an ironic recollection of the Ohio's former purity.
6. Stupid, especially with drunkenness.
7. One who "puddles," or refines metal by stirring

molten vats.
8. Offensive smells or waste by-products.
9. Respectively, one who believes in self-interest, one who believes that God is present in all things, and one who believes in free will.

gone mad and died trying to answer. I dare not put this secret into words. I told you it was dumb. These men, going by with drunken faces and brains full of unawakened power, do not ask it of Society or of God. Their lives ask it; their deaths ask it. There is no reply. I will tell you plainly that I have a great hope; and I bring it to you to be tested. It is this: that this terrible dumb question is its own reply; that it is not the sentence of death we think it, but, from the very extremity of its darkness, the most solemn prophecy which the world has known of the Hope to come. I dare make my meaning no clearer, but will only tell my story. It will, perhaps, seem to you as foul and dark as this thick vapor about us, and as pregnant with death; but if your eyes are free as mine are to look deeper, no perfume-tinted dawn will be so fair with promise of the day that shall surely come.

My story is very simple,—only what I remember of the life of one of these men,—a furnace-tender in one of Kirby & John's rolling-mills,[1]—Hugh Wolfe. You know the mills? They took the great order for the Lower Virginia railroads there last winter; run usually with about a thousand men. I cannot tell why I choose the half-forgotten story of this Wolfe more than that of myriads of these furnace-hands. Perhaps because there is a secret underlying sympathy between that story and this day with its impure fog and thwarted sunshine,—or perhaps simply for the reason that this house is the one where the Wolfes lived. There were the father and son,—both hands, as I said, in one of Kirby & John's mills for making railroad-iron,—and Deborah, their cousin, a picker[2] in some of the cotton-mills. The house was rented then to half a dozen families. The Wolfes had two of the cellar-rooms. The old man, like many of the puddlers and feeders[3] of the mills, was Welsh,—had spent half of his life in the Cornish tin-mines.[4] You may pick the Welsh emigrants, Cornish miners, out of the throng passing the windows, any day. They are a trifle more filthy; their muscles are not so brawny; they stoop more. When they are drunk, they neither yell, nor shout, nor stagger, but skulk along like beaten hounds. A pure, unmixed blood, I fancy: shows itself in the slight angular bodies and sharply-cut facial lines. It is nearly thirty years since the Wolfes lived here. Their lives were like those of their class: incessant labor, sleeping in kennel-like rooms, eating rank pork and molasses, drinking— God and the distillers only know what; with an occasional night in jail, to atone for some drunken excess. Is that all of their lives?—of the portion given to them and these their duplicates swarming the streets to-day?—nothing beneath?—all? So many a political reformer will tell you,—and many a private reformer, too, who has gone among them with a heart tender with Christ's charity, and come out outraged, hardened.

One rainy night, about eleven o'clock, a crowd of half-clothed women stopped outside of the cellar-door. They were going home from the cotton-mill.

"Good-night, Deb," said one, a mulatto,[5] steadying herself against the gas-post. She needed the post to steady her. So did more than one of them.

"Dah's a ball to Miss Potts' to-night. Ye'd best come."

1. Mills where metal is rolled into sheets, bars, and other forms.
2. Operator of a machine that separates cotton fibers.
3. Workers who feed more molten metal into the casting forms.
4. Cornwall is in southwest England, where much mining was done.
5. A person who is half black in ancestry.

"Inteet, Deb, if hur'll come, hur'll hef fun,"[6] said a shrill Welsh voice in the crowd.

Two or three dirty hands were thrust out to catch the gown of the woman, who was groping for the latch of the door.

"No."

"No? Where's Kit Small, then?"

"Begorra! on the spools.[7] Alleys behint, though we helped her, we dud. An wid ye! Let Deb alone! It's ondacent frettin' a quite body. Be the powers, an' we'll have a night of it! there'll be lashin's o' drink,—the Vargent[8] be blessed and praised for 't!"

They went on, the mulatto inclining for a moment to show fight, and drag the woman Wolfe off with them; but, being pacified, she staggered away.

Deborah groped her way into the cellar, and, after considerable stumbling, kindled a match, and lighted a tallow dip[9] that sent a yellow glimmer over the room. It was low, damp,—the earthen floor covered with a green, slimy moss,—a fetid air smothering the breath. Old Wolfe lay asleep on a heap of straw, wrapped in a torn horse-blanket. He was a pale, meek little man, with a white face and red rabbit-eyes. The woman Deborah was like him; only her face was even more ghastly, her lips bluer, her eyes more watery. She wore a faded cotton gown and a slouching bonnet. When she walked, one could see that she was deformed, almost a hunchback. She trod softly, so as not to waken him, and went through into the room beyond. There she found by the half-extinguished fire an iron saucepan filled with cold boiled potatoes, which she put upon a broken chair with a pint-cup of ale. Placing the old candlestick beside this dainty repast, she untied her bonnet, which hung limp and wet over her face, and prepared to eat her supper. It was the first food that had touched her lips since morning. There was enough of it, how-ever: there is not always. She was hungry,—one could see that easily enough,—and not drunk, as most of her companions would have been found at this hour. She did not drink, this woman,—her face told that, too,—nothing stronger than ale. Perhaps the weak, flaccid wretch had some stim-ulant in her pale life to keep her up,—some love or hope, it might be, or urgent need. When that stimulant was gone, she would take to whiskey. Man cannot live by work alone. While she was skinning the potatoes, and munch-ing them, a noise behind her made her stop.

"Janey!" she called, lifting the candle and peering into the darkness. "Janey, are you there?"

A heap of ragged coats was heaved up, and the face of a young girl emerged, staring sleepily at the woman.

"Deborah," she said, at last, "I'm here the night."

"Yes, child. Hur's welcome," she said, quietly eating on.

The girl's face was haggard and sickly; her eyes were heavy with sleep and hunger: real Milesian[1] eyes they were, dark, delicate blue, glooming out from black shadows with a pitiful fright.

"I was alone," she said, timidly.

6. Indeed, Deb, if you'll come, you'll have fun (Welsh dialect).
7. I.e., working on the spools where cotton is wound. "Begorra": by God (Irish euphemism).

8. The Virgin Mary. "Lashin's": plenty.
9. The least expensive kind of candle.
1. Irish.

"Where's the father?" asked Deborah, holding out a potato, which the girl greedily seized.

"He's beyant,—wid Haley,—in the stone house." (Did you ever hear the word *jail* from an Irish mouth?) "I came here. Hugh told me never to stay me-lone."

"Hugh?"

"Yes."

A vexed frown crossed her face. The girl saw it, and added quickly,—

"I have not seen Hugh the day, Deb. The old man says his watch[2] lasts till the mornin'."

The woman sprang up, and hastily began to arrange some bread and flitch[3] in a tin pail, and to pour her own measure of ale into a bottle. Tying on her bonnet, she blew out the candle.

"Lay ye down, Janey dear," she said, gently, covering her with the old rags. "Hur can eat the potatoes, if hur's hungry."

"Where are ye goin', Deb? The rain's sharp."

"To the mill, with Hugh's supper."

"Let him bide till th' morn. Sit ye down."

"No, no,"—sharply pushing her off. "The boy'll starve."

She hurried from the cellar, while the child wearily coiled herself up for sleep. The rain was falling heavily, as the woman, pail in hand, emerged from the mouth of the alley, and turned down the narrow street, that stretched out, long and black, miles before her. Here and there a flicker of gas lighted an uncertain space of muddy footwalk and gutter; the long rows of houses, except an occasional lager-bier shop, were closed; now and then she met a band of mill-hands skulking to or from their work.

Not many even of the inhabitants of a manufacturing town know the vast machinery of system by which the bodies of workmen are governed, that goes on unceasingly from year to year. The hands of each mill are divided into watches that relieve each other as regularly as the sentinels of an army. By night and day the work goes on, the unsleeping engines groan and shriek, the fiery pools of metal boil and surge. Only for a day in the week, in half-courtesy to public censure, the fires are partially veiled; but as soon as the clock strikes midnight, the great furnaces break forth with renewed fury, the clamor begins with fresh, breathless vigor, the engines sob and shriek like "gods in pain."

As Deborah hurried down through the heavy rain, the noise of these thousand engines sounded through the sleep and shadow of the city like far-off thunder. The mill to which she was going lay on the river, a mile below the city-limits. It was far, and she was weak, aching from standing twelve hours at the spools. Yet it was her almost nightly walk to take this man his supper, though at every square she sat down to rest, and she knew she should receive small word of thanks.

Perhaps, if she had possessed an artist's eye, the picturesque oddity of the scene might have made her step stagger less, and the path seem shorter; but to her the mills were only "summat deilish[4] to look at by night."

The road leading to the mills had been quarried from the solid rock, which

2. Workshift.
3. Rank salt pork.

4. Somewhat devilish.

rose abrupt and bare on one side of the cinder-covered road, while the river, sluggish and black, crept past on the other. The mills for rolling iron are simply immense tent-like roofs, covering acres of ground, open on every side. Beneath these roofs Deborah looked in on a city of fires, that burned hot and fiercely in the night. Fire in every horrible form: pits of flame waving in the wind; liquid metal-flames writhing in tortuous streams through the sand; wide caldrons filled with boiling fire, over which bent ghastly wretches stirring the strange brewing; and through all, crowds of half-clad men, looking like revengeful ghosts in the red light, hurried, throwing masses of glittering fire. It was like a street in Hell. Even Deborah muttered, as she crept through, " 'T looks like t' Devil's place!" It did,—in more ways than one.

She found the man she was looking for, at last, heaping coal on a furnace. He had not time to eat his supper; so she went behind the furnace, and waited. Only a few men were with him, and they noticed her only by a "Hyur comes t' hunchback, Wolfe."

Deborah was stupid with sleep; her back pained her sharply; and her teeth chattered with cold, with the rain that soaked her clothes and dripped from her at every step. She stood, however, patiently holding the pail, and waiting.

"Hout, woman! ye look like a drowned cat. Come near to the fire,"—said one of the men, approaching to scrape away the ashes.

She shook her head. Wolfe had forgotten her. He turned, hearing the man, and came closer.

"I did no' think; gi' me my supper, woman."

She watched him eat with a painful eagerness. With a woman's quick instinct, she saw that he was not hungry,—was eating to please her. Her pale, watery eyes began to gather a strange light.

"Is't good, Hugh? T'ale was a bit sour, I feared."

"No, good enough." He hesitated a moment. "Ye're tired, poor lass! Bide here till I go. Lay down there on that heap of ash, and go to sleep."

He threw her an old coat for a pillow, and turned to his work. The heap was the refuse of the burnt iron, and was not a hard bed; the half-smothered warmth, too, penetrated her limbs, dulling their pain and cold shiver.

Miserable enough she looked, lying there on the ashes like a limp, dirty rag,—yet not an unfitting figure to crown the scene of hopeless discomfort and veiled crime: more fitting, if one looked deeper into the heart of things,— at her thwarted woman's form, her colorless life, her waking stupor that smothered pain and hunger,—even more fit to be a type of her class. Deeper yet if one could look, was there nothing worth reading in this wet, faded thing, half-covered with ashes? no story of a soul filled with groping passionate love, heroic unselfishness, fierce jealousy? of years of weary trying to please the one human being whom she loved, to gain one look of real heart-kindness from him? If anything like this were hidden beneath the pale, bleared eyes, and dull, washed-out-looking face, no one had ever taken the trouble to read its faint signs: not the half-clothed furnace-tender, Wolfe, certainly. Yet he was kind to her: it was his nature to be kind, even to the very rats that swarmed in the cellar; kind to her in just the same way. She knew that. And it might be that very knowledge had given to her face its apathy and vacancy more than her low, torpid life. One sees that dead, vacant look steal sometimes over the rarest, finest of women's faces,—in the very midst, it may be, of their warmest summer's day; and then one can guess at

the secret of intolerable solitude that lies hid beneath the delicate laces and brilliant smile. There was no warmth, no brilliancy, no summer for this woman; so the stupor and vacancy had time to gnaw into her face perpetually. She was young, too, though no one guessed it; so the gnawing was the fiercer.

She lay quiet in the dark corner, listening, through the monotonous din and uncertain glare of the works, to the dull plash of the rain in the far distance,—shrinking back whenever the man Wolfe happened to look towards her. She knew, in spite of all his kindness, that there was that in her face and form which made him loathe the sight of her. She felt by instinct, although she could not comprehend it, the finer nature of the man, which made him among his fellow-workmen something unique, set apart. She knew, that, down under all the vileness and coarseness of his life, there was a groping passion for whatever was beautiful and pure,—that his soul sickened with disgust at her deformity, even when his words were kindest. Through this dull consciousness, which never left her, came, like a sting, the recollection of the dark blue eyes and lithe figure of the little Irish girl she had left in the cellar. The recollection struck through even her stupid intellect with a vivid glow of beauty and of grace. Little Janey, timid, helpless, clinging to Hugh as her only friend: that was the sharp thought, the bitter thought, that drove into the glazed eyes a fierce light of pain. You laugh at it? Are pain and jealousy less savage realities down here in this place I am taking you to than in your own house or your own heart,—your heart, which they clutch at sometimes? The note is the same, I fancy, be the octave high or low.

If you could go into this mill where Deborah lay, and drag out from the hearts of these men the terrible tragedy of their lives, taking it as a symptom of the disease of their class, no ghost Horror would terrify you more. A reality of soul-starvation, of living death, that meets you every day under the besotted faces on the street,—I can paint nothing of this, only give you the outside outlines of a night, a crisis in the life of one man: whatever muddy depth of soul-history lies beneath you can read according to the eyes God has given you.

Wolfe, while Deborah watched him as a spaniel its master, bent over the furnace with his iron pole, unconscious of her scrutiny, only stopping to receive orders. Physically, Nature had promised the man but little. He had already lost the strength and instinct vigor of a man, his muscles were thin, his nerves weak, his face (a meek, woman's face) haggard, yellow with consumption. In the mill he was known as one of the girl-men: "Molly Wolfe" was his *sobriquet*.[5] He was never seen in the cockpit, did not own a terrier,[6] drank but seldom; when he did, desperately. He fought sometimes, but was always thrashed, pommelled to a jelly. The man was game enough, when his blood was up: but he was no favorite in the mill; he had the taint of school-learning on him,—not to a dangerous extent, only a quarter or so in the free-school in fact,[7] but enough to ruin him as a good hand in a fight.

For other reasons, too, he was not popular. Not one of themselves, they

5. Nickname. "Consumption": tuberculosis.
6. Terriers were bred as hunters. "Cockpit": place where cockfights are held, a violent game in which roosters are made to kill each other.
7. Most workers in the mills were illiterate, public schools almost nonexistent [Tillie Olsen's note].

felt that, though outwardly as filthy and ash-covered; silent, with foreign thoughts and longings breaking out through his quietness in innumerable curious ways: this one, for instance. In the neighboring furnace-buildings lay great heaps of the refuse from the ore after the pig-metal is run. *Korl* we call it here: a light, porous substance, of a delicate, waxen, flesh-colored tinge. Out of the blocks of this korl, Wolfe, in his off-hours from the furnace, had a habit of chipping and moulding figures,—hideous, fantastic enough, but sometimes strangely beautiful: even the mill-men saw that, while they jeered at him. It was a curious fancy in the man, almost a passion. The few hours for rest he spent hewing and hacking with his blunt knife, never speaking, until his watch came again,—working at one figure for months, and, when it was finished, breaking it to pieces perhaps, in a fit of disappointment. A morbid, gloomy man, untaught, unled, left to feed his soul in grossness and crime, and hard, grinding labor.

I want you to come down and look at this Wolfe, standing there among the lowest of his kind, and see him just as he is, that you may judge him justly when you hear the story of this night. I want you to look back, as he does every day, at his birth in vice, his starved infancy; to remember the heavy years he has groped through as boy and man,—the slow, heavy years of constant, hot work. So long ago he began, that he thinks sometimes he has worked there for ages. There is no hope that it will ever end. Think that God put into this man's soul a fierce thirst for beauty,—to know it, to create it; to *be*—something, he knows not what,—other than he is. There are moments when a passing cloud, the sun glinting on the purple thistles, a kindly smile, a child's face, will rouse him to a passion of pain,—when his nature starts up with a mad cry of rage against God, man, whoever it is that has forced this vile, slimy life upon him. With all this groping, this mad desire, a great blind intellect stumbling through wrong, a loving poet's heart, the man was by habit only a coarse, vulgar laborer, familiar with sights and words you would blush to name. Be just: when I tell you about this night, see him as he is. Be just,—not like man's law, which seizes on one isolated fact, but like God's judging angel, whose clear, sad eye saw all the countless cankering days of this man's life, all the countless nights, when, sick with starving, his soul fainted in him, before it judged him for this night, the saddest of all.

I called this night the crisis of his life. If it was, it stole on him unawares. These great turning-days of life cast no shadow before, slip by unconsciously. Only a trifle, a little turn of the rudder, and the ship goes to heaven or hell.

Wolfe, while Deborah watched him, dug into the furnace of melting iron with his pole, dully thinking only how many rails the lump would yield. It was late,—nearly Sunday morning; another hour, and the heavy work would be done,—only the furnaces to replenish and cover for the next day. The workmen were growing more noisy, shouting, as they had to do, to be heard over the deep clamor of the mills. Suddenly they grew less boisterous,—at the far end, entirely silent. Something unusual had happened. After a moment, the silence came nearer; the men stopped their jeers and drunken choruses. Deborah, stupidly lifting up her head, saw the cause of the quiet. A group of five or six men were slowly approaching, stopping to examine each furnace as they came. Visitors often came to see the mills after night: except by growing less noisy, the men took no notice of them. The furnace where

Wolfe worked was near the bounds of the works; they halted there hot and tired: a walk over one of these great foundries is no trifling task. The woman, drawing out of sight, turned over to sleep. Wolfe, seeing them stop, suddenly roused from his indifferent stupor, and watched them keenly. He knew some of them: the overseer, Clarke,—a son of Kirby, one of the mill-owners,—and a Doctor May, one of the town-physicians. The other two were strangers. Wolfe came closer. He seized eagerly every chance that brought him into contact with this mysterious class that shone down on him perpetually with the glamour of another order of being. What made the difference between them? That was the mystery of his life. He had a vague notion that perhaps to-night he could find it out. One of the strangers sat down on a pile of bricks, and beckoned young Kirby to his side.

"This *is* hot, with a vengeance. A match, please?"—lighting his cigar. "But the walk is worth the trouble. If it were not that you must have heard it so often, Kirby, I would tell you that your works look like Dante's Inferno."[8]

Kirby laughed.

"Yes. Yonder is Farinata himself in the burning tomb,"[9]—pointing to some figure in the shimmering shadows.

"Judging from some of the faces of your men," said the other, "they bid fair to try the reality of Dante's vision, some day."

Young Kirby looked curiously around, as if seeing the faces of his hands for the first time.

"They're bad enough, that's true. A desperate set, I fancy. Eh, Clarke?"

The overseer did not hear him. He was talking of net profits just then,— giving, in fact, a schedule of the annual business of the firm to a sharp peering little Yankee, who jotted down notes on a paper laid on the crown of his hat: a reporter for one of the city-papers, getting up a series of reviews of the leading manufactories. The other gentlemen had accompanied them merely for amusement. They were silent until the notes were finished, drying their feet at the furnaces, and sheltering their faces from the intolerable heat. At last the overseer concluded with—"I believe that is a pretty fair estimate, Captain."

"Here, some of you men!" said Kirby, "bring up those boards. We may as well sit down, gentlemen, until the rain is over. It cannot last much longer at this rate."

"Pig-metal,"—mumbled the reporter,—"um!—coal facilities,—um!— hands employed, twelve hundred,—bitumen,—um!—all right, I believe, Mr. Clarke;—sinking-fund,—what did you say was your sinking-fund?"[1]

"Twelve hundred hands?" said the stranger, the young man who had first spoken. "Do you control their votes, Kirby?"

"Control? No." The young man smiled complacently. "But my father brought seven hundred votes to the polls for his candidate last November. No force-work, you understand,—only a speech or two, a hint to form themselves into a society, and a bit of red and blue bunting to make them a flag. The Invincible Roughs,—I believe that is their name. I forget the motto: 'Our country's hope,' I think."

8. I.e., the vision of hell in the *Inferno*, by Dante Alighieri (1265–1321).
9. Farinata degli Uberti, one of the heretics in

Canto 10 of the *Inferno*.
1. Money accumulated to pay off a corporate debt.

There was a laugh. The young man talking to Kirby sat with an amused light in his cool gray eye, surveying critically the half-clothed figures of the puddlers, and the slow swing of their brawny muscles. He was a stranger in the city,—spending a couple of months in the borders of a Slave State, to study the institutions of the South,[2]—a brother-in-law of Kirby's,—Mitchell. He was an amateur gymnast,—hence his anatomical eye; a patron, in a *blasé* way, of the prize-ring; a man who sucked the essence out of a science or philosophy in an indifferent, gentlemanly way; who took Kant, Novalis, Humboldt,[3] for what they were worth in his own scales; accepting all, despising nothing, in heaven, earth, or hell, but one-ideal men; with a temper yielding and brilliant as summer water, until his Self was touched, when it was ice, though brilliant still. Such men are not rare in the States.

As he knocked the ashes from his cigar, Wolfe caught with a quick pleasure the contour of the white hand, the blood-glow of a red ring he wore. His voice, too, and that of Kirby's, touched him like music,—low, even, with chording cadences. About this man Mitchell hung the impalpable atmosphere belonging to the thoroughbred gentleman. Wolfe, scraping away the ashes beside him, was conscious of it, did obeisance to it with his artist sense, unconscious that he did so.

The rain did not cease. Clark and the reporter left the mills; the others, comfortably seated near the furnace, lingered, smoking and talking in a desultory way. Greek would not have been more unintelligible to the furnace-tenders, whose presence they soon forgot entirely. Kirby drew out a newspaper from his pocket and read aloud some article, which they discussed eagerly. At every sentence, Wolfe listened more and more like a dumb, hopeless animal, with a duller, more stolid look creeping over his face, glancing now and then at Mitchell, marking acutely every smallest sign of refinement, then back to himself, seeing as in a mirror his filthy body, his more stained soul.

Never! He had no words for such a thought, but he knew now, in all the sharpness of the bitter certainty, that between them there was a great gulf never to be passed.[4] Never!

The bells of the mills rang for midnight. Sunday morning had dawned. Whatever hidden message lay in the tolling bells floated past these men unknown. Yet it was there. Veiled in the solemn music ushering the risen saviour was a key-note to solve the darkest secrets of a world gone wrong,—even this social riddle which the brain of the grimy puddler grappled with madly tonight.

The men began to withdraw the metal from the caldrons. The mills were deserted on Sundays, except by the hands who fed the fires, and those who had no lodgings and slept usually on the ash-heaps. The three strangers sat still during the next hour, watching the men cover the furnaces, laughing now and then at some jest of Kirby's.

"Do you know," said Mitchell, "I like this view of the works better than when the glare was fiercest? These heavy shadows and the amphitheatre of

2. I.e., slavery.
3. Three very different German thinkers: Immanuel Kant (1724–1804), philosopher of ethics and metaphysics; Novalis (1772–1801), Romantic poet; and Wilhelm von Humboldt (1767–1835),

statesman and philologist.
4. In Luke 16.26, Jesus speaks of the "great gulf fixed" between Dives, the rich man, in hell, and Lazarus, the beggar, in heaven.

smothered fires are ghostly, unreal. One could fancy these red smouldering lights to be the half-shut eyes of wild beasts, and the spectral figures their victims in the den."

Kirby laughed. "You are fanciful. Come, let us get out of the den. The spectral figures, as you call them, are a little too real for me to fancy a close proximity in the darkness,—unarmed, too."

The others rose, buttoning their over-coats, and lighting cigars.

"Raining, still," said Doctor May, "and hard. Where did we leave the coach, Mitchell?"

"At the other side of the works.—Kirby, what's that?"

Mitchell started back, half-frightened, as, suddenly turning a corner, the white figure of a woman faced him in the darkness,—a woman, white, of giant proportions, crouching on the ground, her arms flung out in some wild gesture of warning.

"Stop! Make that fire burn there!" cried Kirby, stopping short.

The flame burst out, flashing the gaunt figure into bold relief.

Mitchell drew a long breath.

"I thought it was alive," he said, going up curiously.

The others followed.

"Not marble, eh?" asked Kirby, touching it.

One of the lower overseers stopped.

"Korl, Sir."

"Who did it?"

"Can't say. Some of the hands; chipped it out in off-hours."

"Chipped to some purpose, I should say. What a flesh-tint the stuff has! Do you see, Mitchell?"

"I see."

He had stepped aside where the light fell boldest on the figure, looking at it in silence. There was not one line of beauty or grace in it: a nude woman's form, muscular, grown coarse with labor, the powerful limbs instinct[5] with some one poignant longing. One idea: there it was in the tense, rigid muscles, the clutching hands, the wild, eager face, like that of a starving wolf's. Kirby and Doctor May walked around it, critical, curious. Mitchell stood aloof, silent. The figure touched him strangely.

"Not badly done," said Doctor May. "Where did the fellow learn that sweep of the muscles in the arm and hand? Look at them! They are groping,—do you see?—clutching: the peculiar action of a man dying of thirst."

"They have ample facilities for studying anatomy," sneered Kirby, glancing at the half-naked figures.

"Look," continued the Doctor, "at this bony wrist, and the strained sinews of the instep! A working-woman,—the very type[6] of her class."

"God forbid!" muttered Mitchell.

"Why?" demanded May. "What does the fellow intend by the figure? I cannot catch the meaning."

"Ask him," said the other, dryly. "There he stands,"—pointing to Wolfe, who stood with a group of men, leaning on his ash-rake.

The Doctor beckoned him with the affable smile which kind-hearted men put on, when talking with these people.

5. Infused. 6. Typical specimen, representative.

"Mr. Mitchell has picked you out as the man who did this,—I'm sure I don't know why. But what did you mean by it?"

"She be hungry."

Wolfe's eyes answered Mitchell, not the Doctor.

"Oh-h! But what a mistake you have made, my fine fellow! You have given no sign of starvation to the body. It is strong,—terribly strong. It has the mad, half-despairing gesture of drowning."

Wolfe's stammered, glanced appealingly at Mitchell, who saw the soul of the thing, he knew. But the cool, probing eyes were turned on himself now,— mocking, cruel, relentless.

"Not hungry for meat," the furnace-tender said at last.

"What then? Whiskey?" jeered Kirby, with a coarse laugh.

Wolfe was silent a moment, thinking.

"I dunno," he said, with a bewildered look. "It mebbe. Summat to make her live, I think,—like you. Whiskey ull do it, in a way."

The young man laughed again. Mitchell flashed a look of disgust some-where,—not at Wolfe.

"May," he broke out impatiently, "are you blind? Look at that woman's face! It asks questions of God, and says, 'I have a right to know.' Good God, how hungry it is!"

They looked a moment; then May turned to the mill-owner:—

"Have you many such hands as this? What are you going to do with them? Keep them at puddling iron?"

Kirby shrugged his shoulders. Mitchell's look had irritated him.

"*Ce n'est pas mon affaire.*[7] I have no fancy for nursing infant geniuses. I suppose there are some stray gleams of mind and soul among these wretches. The Lord will take care of his own; or else they can work out their own salvation. I have heard you call our American system a ladder which any man can scale. Do you doubt it? Or perhaps you want to banish all social ladders, and put us all on a flat table-land,—eh, May?"

The Doctor looked vexed, puzzled. Some terrible problem lay hid in this woman's face, and troubled these men. Kirby waited for an answer, and, receiving none, went on, warming with his subject.

"I tell you, there's something wrong that no talk of '*Liberté*' or '*Égalité*'[8] will do away. If I had the making of men, these men who do the lowest part of the world's work should be machines,—nothing more,—hands. It would be kindness. God help them! What are taste, reason, to creatures who must live such lives as that?" He pointed to Deborah, sleeping on the ash-heap. "So many nerves to sting them to pain. What if God had put your brain, with all its agony of touch, into your fingers, and bid you work and strike with that?"

"You think you could govern the world better?" laughed the Doctor.

"I do not think at all."

"That is true philosophy. Drift with the stream, because you cannot dive deep enough to find bottom, eh?"

"Exactly," rejoined Kirby. "I do not think. I wash my hands of all social problems,—slavery, caste, white or black. My duty to my operatives[9] has a

7. That's not my business (French).
8. The slogan of the French Revolution was *Li-berté, Égalité, Fraternité* (Liberty, Equality, Broth-erhood).
9. Workers.

narrow limit,—the pay-hour on Saturday night. Outside of that, if they cut korl, or cut each other's throats, (the more popular amusement of the two,) I am not responsible."

The Doctor sighed,—a good honest sigh, from the depths of his stomach.

"God help us! Who is responsible?"

"Not I, I tell you," said Kirby, testily. "What has the man who pays them money to do with their souls' concerns, more than the grocer or butcher who takes it?"

"And yet," said Mitchell's cynical voice, "look at her! How hungry she is!"

Kirby tapped his boot with his cane. No one spoke. Only the dumb face of the rough image looking into their faces with the awful question, "What shall we do to be saved?"[1] Only Wolfe's face, with its heavy weight of brain, its weak, uncertain mouth, its desperate eyes, out of which looked the soul of his class,—only Wolfe's face turned towards Kirby's. Mitchell laughed,—a cool, musical laugh.

"Money has spoken!" he said, seating himself lightly on a stone with the air of an amused spectator at a play. "Are you answered?"—turning to Wolfe his clear, magnetic face.

Bright and deep and cold as Arctic air, the soul of the man lay tranquil beneath. He looked at the furnace-tender as he had looked at a rare mosaic in the morning; only the man was the more amusing study of the two.

"Are you answered? Why, May, look at him! '*De profundis clamavi.*'[2] Or, to quote in English, 'Hungry and thirsty, his soul faints in him.' And so Money sends back its answer into the depths through you, Kirby! Very clear the answer, too!—I think I remember reading the same words somewhere:—washing your hands in Eau de Cologne, and saying, 'I am innocent of the blood of this man. See ye to it!' "[3]

Kirby flushed angrily.

"You quote Scripture freely."

"Do I not quote correctly? I think I remember another line, which may amend my meaning: 'Inasmuch as ye did it unto one of the least of these, ye did it unto me.' Deist?[4] Bless you, man, I was raised on the milk of the Word. Now, Doctor, the pocket of the world having uttered its voice, what has the heart to say? You are a philanthropist, in a small way,—*n'est ce pas?*[5] Here, boy, this gentleman can show you how to cut korl better,—or your destiny. Go on, May!"

"I think a mocking devil possesses you to-night," rejoined the Doctor, seriously.

He went to Wolfe and put his hand kindly on his arm. Something of a vague idea possessed the Doctor's brain that much good was to be done here by a friendly word or two: a latent genius to be warmed into life by a waited-for sun-beam. Here it was: he had brought it. So he went on complacently:—

"Do you know, boy, you have it in you to be a great sculptor, a great man?—do you understand?" (talking down to the capacity of his hearer: it is a way people have with children, and men like Wolfe,)—"to live a better, stronger

1. An echo of the words of the keeper of the prison in Philippi after an earthquake opens the doors of his prison (Acts 16.30).
2. I have cried out of the deep [unto thee, O Lord] (Latin version of Psalm 130.1).
3. The words of Pontius Pilate, the Roman judge who permitted Christ to be crucified but refused

to take responsibility (Matthew 27.24).
4. Believer in a God who created the universe and its laws but who thereafter refrains from interfering with those laws. The quote is from Matthew 25.40.
5. Isn't that right? (French).

life than I, or Mr. Kirby here? A man may make himself anything he chooses. God has given you stronger powers than many men,—me, for instance."

May stopped, heated, glowing with his own magnanimity. And it was magnanimous. The puddler had drunk in every word, looking through the Doctor's flurry, and generous heat, and self-approval, into his will, with those slow, absorbing eyes of his.

"Make yourself what you will. It is your right."

"I know," quietly. "Will you help me?"

Mitchell laughed again. The Doctor turned now, in a passion,—

"You know, Mitchell, I have not the means. You know, if I had, it is in my heart to take this boy and educate him for"—

"The glory of God, and the glory of John May."

May did not speak for a moment; then, controlled, he said,—

"Why should one be raised, when myriads are left?—I have not the money, boy," to Wolfe, shortly.

"Money?" He said it over slowly, as one repeats the guessed answer to a riddle, doubtfully. "That is it? Money?"

"Yes, money,—that is it," said Mitchell, rising, and drawing his furred coat about him. "You've found the cure for all the world's diseases.—Come, May, find your good-humor, and come home. This damp wind chills my very bones. Come and preach your Saint-Simonian[6] doctrines to-morrow to Kirby's hands. Let them have a clear idea of the rights of the soul, and I'll venture next week they'll strike for higher wages. That will be the end of it."

"Will you send the coach-driver to this side of the mills?" asked Kirby, turning to Wolfe.

He spoke kindly: it was his habit to do so. Deborah, seeing the puddler go, crept after him. The three men waited outside. Doctor May walked up and down, chafed. Suddenly he stopped.

"Go back, Mitchell! You say the pocket and the heart of the world speak without meaning to these people. What has its head to say? Taste, culture, refinement? Go!"

Mitchell was leaning against a brick wall. He turned his head indolently, and looked into the mills. There hung about the place a thick, unclean odor. The slightest motion of his hand marked that he perceived it, and his insufferable disgust. That was all. May said nothing, only quickened his angry tramp.

"Besides," added Mitchell, giving a corollary to his answer, "it would be of no use. I am not one of them."

"You do not mean"—said May, facing him.

"Yes, I mean just that. Reform is born of need, not pity. No vital movement of the people's has worked down, for good or evil; fermented, instead, carried up the heaving, cloggy mass. Think back through history, and you will know it. What will this lowest deep—thieves, Magdalens,[7] negroes—do with the light filtered through ponderous Church creeds, Baconian theories, Goethe schemes? Some day, out of their bitter need will be thrown up their own light-bringer,—their Jean Paul, their Cromwell,[8] their Messiah."

6. Socialist; after Claude-Henri de Rouvroy, comte de Saint-Simon (1760–1825), French social theorist.

7. Prostitutes (from Mary Magdalen, traditionally

identified with the repentant prostitute who anointed Jesus' feet; see Luke 7.37–50).

8. Oliver Cromwell (1599–1658) led the revolt against the British monarchy. Francis Bacon

"Bah!" was the Doctor's inward criticism. However, in practice, he adopted the theory; for, when, night and morning, afterwards, he prayed that power might be given these degraded souls to rise, he glowed at heart, recognizing an accomplished duty.

Wolfe and the woman had stood in the shadow of the works as the coach drove off. The Doctor had held out his hand in a frank, generous way, telling him to "take care of himself, and to remember it was his right to rise." Mitchell had simply touched his hat, as to an equal, with a quiet look of thorough recognition. Kirby had thrown Deborah some money, which she found, and clutched eagerly enough. They were gone now, all of them. The man sat down on the cinder-road, looking up into the murky sky.

" 'T be late, Hugh. Wunnot hur come?"

He shook his head doggedly, and the woman crouched out of his sight against the wall. Do you remember rare moments when a sudden light flashed over yourself, your world, God? when you stood on a mountain-peak, seeing your life as it might have been, as it is? one quick instant, when custom lost its force and every-day usage? when your friend, wife, brother, stood in a new light? your soul was bared, and the grave,—a foretaste of the nakedness of the Judgment-Day? So it came before him, his life, that night. The slow tides of pain he had borne gathered themselves up and surged against his soul. His squalid daily life, the brutal coarseness eating into his brain, as the ashes into his skin: before, these things had been a dull aching into his consciousness; tonight, they were reality. He gripped the filthy red shirt that clung, stiff with soot, about him, and tore it savagely from his arm. The flesh beneath was muddy with grease and ashes,—and the heart beneath that! And the soul? God knows.

Then flashed before his vivid poetic sense the man who had left him,— the pure face, the delicate, sinewy limbs, in harmony with all he knew of beauty or truth. In his cloudy fancy he had pictured a Something like this. He had found it in this Mitchell, even when he idly scoffed at his pain: a Man all-knowing, all-seeing, crowned by Nature, reigning,—the keen glance of his eye falling like a sceptre on other men. And yet his instinct taught him that he too—He! He looked at himself with sudden loathing, sick, wrung his hands with a cry, and then was silent. With all the phantoms of his heated, ignorant fancy, Wolfe had not been vague in his ambitions. They were practical, slowly built up before him out of his knowledge of what he could do. Through years he had day by day made this hope a real thing to himself,— a clear, projected figure of himself, as he might become.

Able to speak, to know what was best, to raise these men and women working at his side up with him: sometimes he forgot this defined hope in the frantic anguish to escape,—only to escape,—out of the wet, the pain, the ashes, somewhere, anywhere,—only for one moment of free air on a hillside, to lie down and let his sick soul throb itself out in the sunshine. But to-night he panted for life. The savage strength of his nature was roused; his cry was fierce to God for justice.

"Look at me!" he said to Deborah, with a low, bitter laugh, striking his puny chest savagely. "What am I worth, Deb? Is it my fault that I am no better? My fault? My fault?"

(1561–1626), a philosopher, and Johann Wolfgang von Goethe (1749–1832), a poet, developed complicated abstract theories. Jean Paul Richter (1763–1825) was a German novelist.

He stopped, stung with a sudden remorse, seeing her hunchback shape writhing with sobs. For Deborah was crying thankless tears, according to the fashion of women.

"God forgi' me, woman! Things go harder wi' you nor me. It's a worse share."

He got up and helped her to rise; and they went doggedly down the muddy street, side by side.

"It's all wrong," he muttered, slowly,—"all wrong! I dunnot understan'. But it'll end some day."

"Come home, Hugh!" she said, coaxingly; for he had stopped, looking around bewildered.

"Home,—and back to the mill!" He went on saying this over to himself, as if he would mutter down every pain in this dull despair.

She followed him through the fog, her blue lips chattering with cold. They reached the cellar at last. Old Wolfe had been drinking since she went out, and had crept nearer the door. The girl Janey slept heavily in the corner. He went up to her, touching softly the worn white arm with his fingers. Some bitterer thought stung him, as he stood there. He wiped the drops from his forehead, and went into the room beyond, livid, trembling. A hope, trifling, perhaps, but very dear, had died just then out of the poor puddler's life, as he looked at the sleeping, innocent girl,—some plan for the future, in which she had borne a part. He gave it up that moment, then and forever. Only a trifle, perhaps, to us: his face grew a shade paler,—that was all. But, somehow, the man's soul, as God and the angels looked down on it, never was the same afterwards.

Deborah followed him into the inner room. She carried a candle, which she placed on the floor, closing the door after her. She had seen the look on his face, as he turned away: her own grew deadly. Yet, as she came up to him her eyes glowed. He was seated on an old chest, quiet, holding his face in his hands.

"Hugh!" she said, softly.

He did not speak.

"Hugh, did hur hear what the man said,—him with the clear voice? Did hur hear? Money, money,—that it wud do all?"

He pushed her away,—gently, but he was worn out; her rasping tone fretted him.

"Hugh!"

The candle flared a pale yellow light over the cobwebbed brick walls, and the woman standing there. He looked at her. She was young, in deadly earnest; her faded eyes, and wet, ragged figure caught from their frantic eagerness a power akin to beauty.

"Hugh, it is true! Money ull do it! Oh, Hugh, boy, listen till me! He said it true! It is money!"

"I know. Go back! I do not want you here."

"Hugh, it is t' last time. I'll never worrit hur again."[9]

There were tears in her voice now, but she choked them back.

"Hear till me only to-night! If one of t'witch people wud come, them we heard of t' home, and gif hur all hur wants, what then? Say, Hugh!"

9. I'll never bother you again (Welsh dialect).

"What do you mean?"

"I mean money."

Her whisper shrilled through his brain.

"If one of t' witch dwarfs wud come from t' lane moors to-night, and gif hur money, to go out,—*out*, I say,—out, lad, where t' sun shines, and t' heath grows, and t' ladies walk in silken gownds, and God stays all t' time,—where t' man lives that talked to us to-night,—Hugh knows,—Hugh could walk there like a king!"

He thought the woman mad, tried to check her, but she went on, fierce in her eager haste.

"If I were t' witch dwarf, if I had t' money, wud hur thank me? Wud hur take me out o' this place wid hur and Janey? I wud not come into the gran' house hur wud build, to vex hur wid t' hunch,—only at night, when t' shadows were dark, stand far off to see hur."

Mad? Yes! Are many of us mad in this way?

"Poor Deb! poor Deb!" he said, soothingly.

"It is here," she said, suddenly jerking into his hand a small roll. "I took it! I did it! Me, me!—not hur! I shall be hanged, I shall be burnt in hell, if anybody knows I took it! Out of his pocket, as he leaned against t' bricks. Hur knows?"

She thrust it into his hand, and then, her errand done, began to gather chips together to make a fire, choking down hysteric sobs.

"Has it come to this?"

That was all he said. The Welsh Wolfe blood was honest. The roll was a small green pocket-book containing one or two gold pieces, and a check for an incredible amount, as it seemed to the poor puddler. He laid it down, hiding his face again in his hands.

"Hugh, don't be angry wud me! It's only poor Deb,—hur knows?"

He took the long skinny fingers kindly in his.

"Angry? God help me, no! Let me sleep. I am tired."

He threw himself heavily down on the wooden bench, stunned with pain and weariness. She brought some old rags to cover him.

It was late on Sunday evening before he awoke. I tell God's truth, when I say he had then no thought of keeping this money. Deborah had hid it in his pocket. He found it there. She watched him eagerly, as he took it out.

"I must gif it to him," he said, reading her face.

"Hur knows," she said with a bitter sigh of disappointment. "But it is hur right to keep it."

His right! The word struck him. Doctor May had used the same. He washed himself, and went out to find this man Mitchell. His right! Why did this chance word cling to him so obstinately? Do you hear the fierce devils whisper in his ear, as he went slowly down the darkening street?

The evening came on, slow and calm. He seated himself at the end of an alley leading into one of the larger streets. His brain was clear to-night, keen, intent, mastering. It would not start back, cowardly, from any hellish temptation, but meet it face to face. Therefore the great temptation of his life came to him veiled by no sophistry, but bold, defiant, owning its own vile name, trusting to one bold blow for victory.

He did not deceive himself. Theft! That was it. At first the word sickened him, then he grappled with it. Sitting there on a broken cart-wheel, the fading

day, the noisy groups, the church-bells' tolling passed before him like a panorama,[1] while the sharp struggle went on within. This money! He took it out, and looked at it. If he gave it back, what then? He was going to be cool about it.

People going by to church saw only a sickly mill-boy watching them quietly at the alley's mouth. They did not know that he was mad, or they would not have gone by so quietly: mad with hunger; stretching out his hands to the world, that had given so much to them, for leave to live the life God meant him to live. His soul within him was smothering to death; he wanted so much, thought so much, and knew—nothing. There was nothing of which he was certain, except the mill and things there. Of God and heaven he had heard so little, that they were to him what fairy-land is to a child: something real, but not here; very far off. His brain, greedy, dwarfed, full of thwarted energy and unused powers, questioned these men and women going by, coldly, bitterly, that night. Was it not his right to live as they,—a pure life, a good, true-hearted life, full of beauty and kind words? He only wanted to know how to use the strength within him. His heart warmed, as he thought of it. He suffered[2] himself to think of it longer. If he took the money?

Then he saw himself as he might be, strong, helpful, kindly. The night crept on, as this one image slowly evolved itself from the crowd of other thoughts and stood triumphant. He looked at it. As he might be! What wonder, if it blinded him to delirium,—the madness that underlies all revolution, all progress, and all fall?

You laugh at the shallow temptation? You see the error underlying its argument so clearly,—that to him a true life was one of full development rather than self-restraint? that he was deaf to the higher tone in a cry of voluntary suffering for truth's sake than in the fullest flow of spontaneous harmony? I do not plead his cause. I only want to show you the mote in my brother's eye: then you can see clearly to take it out.[3]

The money,—there it lay on his knee, a little blotted slip of paper, nothing in itself; used to raise him out of the pit; something straight from God's hand. A thief! Well, what was it to be a thief? He met the question at last, face to face, wiping the clammy drops of sweat from his forehead. God made this money—the fresh air, too—for his children's use. He never made the difference between poor and rich. The Something who looked down on him that moment through the cool gray sky had a kindly face, he knew,—loved his children alike. Oh, he knew that!

There were times when the soft floods of color in the crimson and purple flames, or the clear depth of amber in the water below the bridge, had somehow given him a glimpse of another world than this,—of an infinite depth of beauty and of quiet somewhere,—somewhere,—a depth of quiet and rest and love. Looking up now, it became strangely real. The sun had sunk quite below the hills, but his last rays struck upward, touching the zenith. The fog had risen, and the town and river were steeped in its thick, gray damp; but overhead, the sun-touched smoke-clouds opened like a cleft ocean,—shifting, rolling seas of crimson mist, waves of billowy silver veined with blood-

1. I.e., like the continuous scenes painted on rolls of canvas that were unrolled before an audience; a popular 19th-century theatrical pastime.
2. Allowed.
3. An allusion to the Sermon on the Mount, where

Jesus criticizes our haste to judge others by comparing it to an eagerness to point to a mote, or bit of dust, in the eye of another while ignoring the beam, or large timber, in our own (Matthew 7.3–4).

scarlet, inner depths unfathomable of glancing light. Wolfe's artist-eye grew drunk with color. The gates of that other world! Fading, flashing before him now! What, in that world of Beauty, Content, and Right, were the pretty laws, the mine and thine, of mill-owners and mill-hands?

A consciousness of power stirred within him. He stood up. A man,—he thought, stretching out his hands,—free to work, to live, to love! Free! His right! He folded the scrap of paper in his hand. As his nervous fingers took it in, limp and blotted, so his soul took in the mean temptation, lapped it in fancied rights, in dreams of improved existences, drifting and endless as the cloud-seas of color. Clutching it, as if the tightness of his hold would strengthen his sense of possession, he went aimlessly down the street. It was his watch at the mill. He need not go, need never go again, thank God!— shaking off the thought with unspeakable loathing.

Shall I go over the history of the hours of that night? how the man wandered from one to another of his old haunts, with a half-consciousness of bidding them farewell,—lanes and alleys and back-yards where the mill-hands lodged,—noting, with a new eagerness, the filth and drunkenness, the pigpens, the ash-heaps covered with potato-skins, the bloated, pimpled woman at the doors,—with a new disgust, a new sense of sudden triumph, and, under all, a new, vague dread, unknown before, smothered down, kept under, but still there? It left him but once during the night, when, for the second time in his life, he entered a church. It was a sombre Gothic pile,[4] where the stained light lost itself in far-retreating arches; built to meet the requirements and sympathies of a far other class than Wolfe's. Yet it touched, moved him uncontrollably. The distances, the shadows, the still, marble figures, the mass of silent kneeling worshippers, the mysterious music, thrilled, lifted his soul with a wonderful pain. Wolfe forgot himself, forgot the new life he was going to live, the mean terror gnawing underneath. The voice of the speaker strengthened the charm; it was clear, feeling, full, strong. An old man, who had lived much, suffered much; whose brain was keenly alive, dominant; whose heart was summer-warm with charity. He taught it to-night. He held up Humanity in its grand total; showed the great world-cancer to his people. Who could show it better? He was a Christian reformer; he had studied the age thoroughly; his outlook at man had been free world-wide, over all time. His faith stood sublime upon the Rock of Ages;[5] his fiery zeal guided vast schemes by which the gospel was to be preached to all nations. How did he preach it to-night? In burning, light-laden words he painted the incarnate Life, Love, the universal Man: words that became reality in the lives of these people,—that lived again in beautiful words and actions, trifling, but heroic. Sin, as he defined it, was a real foe to them; their trials, temptations, were his. His words passed far over the furnace-tender's grasp, toned to suit another class of culture; they sounded in his ears a very pleasant song in an unknown tongue. He meant to cure this world-cancer with a steady eye that had never glared with hunger, and a hand that neither poverty nor strychnine-whiskey had taught to shake. In this morbid,[6] distorted heart of the Welsh puddler he had failed.

Wolfe rose at last, and turned from the church down the street. He looked

4. Large building.
5. I.e., strong Christian faith.
6. Diseased. "Strychnine-whiskey": a kind of cheap whisky (strychnine, which is highly poisonous, acts as a stimulant in small amounts).

up; the night had come on foggy, damp; the golden mists had vanished, and the sky lay dull and ash-colored. He wandered again aimlessly down the street, idly wondering what had become of the cloud-sea of crimson and scarlet. The trial-day of this man's life was over, and he had lost the victory. What followed was mere drifting circumstance,—a quicker walking over the path,—that was all. Do you want to hear the end of it? You wish me to make a tragic story out of it? Why, in the police-reports of the morning paper you can find a dozen such tragedies: hints of shipwrecks unlike any that ever befell on the high seas; hints that here a power was lost to heaven,—that there a soul went down where no tide can ebb or flow. Commonplace enough the hints are,—jocose sometimes, done up in rhyme.

Doctor May, a month after the night I have told you of, was reading to his wife at breakfast from this fourth column of the morning-paper: an unusual thing,—these police-reports not being, in general, choice reading for ladies; but it was only one item he read.

"Oh, my dear! You remember that man I told you of, that we saw at Kirby's mill?—that was arrested for robbing Mitchell? Here he is; just listen:—'Circuit Court. Judge Day. Hugh Wolfe, operative in Kirby & John's Loudon Mills. Charge, grand larceny. Sentence, nineteen years hard labor in penitentiary.'—Scoundrel! Serves him right! After all our kindness that night! Picking Mitchell's pocket at the very time!"

His wife said something about the ingratitude of that kind of people, and then they began to talk of something else.

Nineteen years! How easy that was to read! What a simple word for Judge Day to utter! Nineteen years! Half a lifetime![7]

Hugh Wolfe sat on the window-ledge of his cell, looking out. His ankles were ironed. Not usual in such cases; but he had made two desperate efforts to escape. "Well," as Haley, the jailer, said, "small blame to him! Nineteen years' imprisonment was not a pleasant thing to look forward to." Haley was very good-natured about it, though Wolfe had fought him savagely.

"When he was first caught," the jailer said afterwards, in telling the story, "before the trial, the fellow was cut down at once,—laid there on that pallet like a dead man, with his hands over his eyes. Never saw a man so cut down in my life. Time of the trial, too, came the queerest dodge of any customer I ever had. Would choose no lawyer. Judge gave him one, of course. Gibson it was. He tried to prove the fellow crazy; but it wouldn't go. Thing was plain as daylight: money found on him. 'Twas a hard sentence,—all the law allows; but it was for 'xample's sake. These mill-hands are gettin' onbearable. When the sentence was read, he just looked up, and said the money was his by rights, and that all the world had gone wrong. That night, after the trial, a gentleman came to see him here, name of Mitchell,—him as he stole from. Talked to him for an hour. Thought he came for curiosity, like. After he was gone, thought Wolfe was remarkable quiet, and went into his cell. Found him very low; bed all bloody. Doctor said he had been bleeding at the lungs. He was as weak as a cat; yet, if ye'll b'lieve me, he tried to get a-past me and get out. I just carried him like a baby, and threw him on the pallet. Three days after, he tried it again: that time reached the wall. Lord help you! he

7. Nineteen years was literally half a lifetime. Life expectancy for a male in the 1850's was thirty-seven years. Hugh Wolfe is nineteen years old, for all his "lifetime" in the mills, the "slow heavy years of constant hot work." As was common at the time, he had probably been in the mills since he was nine or ten [Olsen's note].

fought like a tiger,—giv' some terrible blows. Fightin' for life, you see; for he can't live long, shut up in the stone crib down yonder. Got a death-cough now. 'T took two of us to bring him down that day; so I just put the irons on his feet. There he sits, in there. Goin' to-morrow, with a batch more of 'em. That woman, hunchback, tried with him,—you remember?—she's only got three years. 'Complice. But *she's* a woman, you know. He's been quiet ever since I put on irons: giv' up, I suppose. Looks white, sick-lookin'. It acts different on 'em, bein' sentenced. Most of 'em gets reckless, devilish-like. Some prays awful, and sings them vile songs of the mills, all in a breath. That woman, now, she's desper't'. Been beggin' to see Hugh, as she calls him, for three days. I'm a-goin' to let her in. She don't go with him. Here she is in this next cell. I'm a-goin' now to let her in."

He let her in. Wolfe did not see her. She crept into a corner of the cell, and stood watching him. He was scratching the iron bars of the window with a piece of tin which he had picked up, with an idle, uncertain, vacant stare, just as a child or idiot would do.

"Tryin' to get out, old boy?" laughed Haley. "Them irons will need a crow-bar beside your tin, before you can open 'em."

Wolfe laughed, too, in a senseless way.

"I think I'll get out," he said.

"I believe his brain's touched," said Haley, when he came out.

The puddler scraped away with the tin for half an hour. Still Deborah did not speak. At last she ventured nearer, and touched his arm.

"Blood?" she said, looking at some spots on his coat with a shudder.

He looked up at her. "Why, Deb!" he said, smiling,—such a bright, boyish smile, that it went to poor Deborah's heart directly, and she sobbed and cried out loud.

"Oh, Hugh, lad! Hugh! dunnot look at me, when it wur my fault! To think I brought hur to it! And I loved hur so! Oh, lad, I dud!"

The confession, even in this wretch, came with the woman's blush through the sharp cry.

He did not seem to hear her,—scraping away diligently at the bars with the bit of tin.

Was he going mad? She peered closely into his face. Something she saw there made her draw suddenly back,—something which Haley had not seen, that lay beneath the pinched, vacant look it had caught since the trial, or the curious gray shadow that rested on it. That gray shadow,—yes, she knew what that meant. She had often seen it creeping over women's faces for months, who died at last of slow hunger or consumption. That meant death, distant, lingering: but this—Whatever it was the woman saw, or thought she saw, used as she was to crime and misery, seemed to make her sick with a new horror. Forgetting her fear of him, she caught his shoulders, and looked keenly, steadily, into his eyes.

"Hugh!" she cried, in a desperate whisper,—"oh, boy, not that! for God's sake, not *that!*"

The vacant laugh went off his face, and he answered her in a muttered word or two that drove her away. Yet the words were kindly enough. Sitting there on his pallet, she cried silently a hopeless sort of tears, but did not speak again. The man looked up furtively at her now and then. Whatever his own trouble was, her distress vexed him with a momentary sting.

It was market-day. The narrow window of the jail looked down directly on

the carts and wagons drawn up in a long line, where they had unloaded. He could see, too, and hear distinctly the clink of money as it changed hands, the busy crowd of whites and blacks shoving, pushing one another, and the chaffering[8] and swearing at the stalls. Somehow, the sound, more than anything else had done, wakened him up,—made the whole real to him. He was done with the world and the business of it. He let the tin fall, and looked out, pressing his face close to the rusty bars. How they crowded and pushed! And he,—he should never walk that pavement again! There came Neff Sanders, one of the feeders at the mill, with a basket on his arm. Sure enough, Neff was married the other week. He whistled, hoping he would look up; but he did not. He wondered if Neff remembered he was there,—if any of the boys thought of him up there, and thought that he never was to go down that old cinder-road again. Never again! He had not quite understood it before; but now he did. Not for days or years, but never!—that was it.

How clear the light fell on that stall in front of the market! and how like a picture it was, the dark-green heaps of corn, and the crimson beets, and golden melons! There was another with game: how the light flickered on that pheasant's breast, with the purplish blood dripping over the brown feathers! He could see the red shining of the drops, it was so near. In one minute he could be down there. It was just a step. So easy, as it seemed, so natural to go! Yet it could never be—not in all the thousands of years to come—that he should put his foot on that street again! He thought of himself with a sorrowful pity, as of some one else. There was a dog down in the market, walking after his master with such a stately, grave look!—only a dog, yet he could go backwards and forwards just as he pleased: he had good luck! Why, the very vilest cur, yelping there in the gutter, had not lived his life, had been free to act out whatever thought God had put into his brain; while he—No, he would not think of that! He tried to put the thought away, and to listen to a dispute between a countryman and a woman about some meat; but it would come back. He, what had he done to bear this?

Then came the sudden picture of what might have been, and now. He knew what it was to be in the penitentiary,—how it went with men there. He knew how in these long years he should slowly die, but not until soul and body had become corrupt and rotten,—how, when he came out, if he lived to come, even the lowest of the mill-hands would jeer him,—how his hands would be weak, and his brain senseless and stupid. He believed he was almost that now. He put his hand to his head, with a puzzled, weary look. It ached, his head, with thinking. He tried to quiet himself. It was only right, perhaps; he had done wrong. But was there right or wrong for such as he? What was right? And who had ever taught him? He thrust the whole matter away. A dark, cold quiet crept through his brain. It was all wrong; but let it be! It was nothing to him more than the others. Let it be!

The door grated, as Haley opened it.

"Come, my woman! Must lock up for t' night. Come, stir yerself!"

She went up and took Hugh's hand.

"Good-night, Deb," he said, carelessly.

She had not hoped he would say more; but the tired pain on her mouth just then was bitterer than death. She took his passive hand and kissed it.

8. Bargaining.

"Hur'll never see Deb again!" she ventured, her lips growing colder and more bloodless.

What did she say that for? Did he not know it? Yet he would not be impatient with poor old Deb. She had trouble of her own, as well as he.

"No, never again," he said, trying to be cheerful.

She stood just a moment, looking at him. Do you laugh at her, standing there, with her hunchback, her rags, her bleared, withered face, and the great despised love tugging at her heart?

"Come, you!" called Haley, impatiently.

She did not move.

"Hugh!" she whispered.

It was to be her last word. What was it?

"Hugh, boy, not THAT!"

He did not answer. She wrung—her hands, trying to be silent, looking in his face in an agony of entreaty. He smiled again, kindly.

"It is best, Deb. I cannot bear to be hurted any more."

"Hur knows," she said, humbly.

"Tell my father good-bye; and—and kiss little Janey."

She nodded, saying nothing, looked in his face again, and went out of the door. As she went, she staggered.

"Drinkin' to-day?" broke out Haley, pushing her before him. "Where the Devil did you get it? Here, in with ye!" and he shoved her into her cell, next to Wolfe's, and shut the door.

Along the wall of her cell there was a crack low down by the floor, through which she could see the light from Wolfe's. She had discovered it days before. She hurried in now, and, kneeling down by it, listened, hoping to hear some sound. Nothing buy the rasping of the tin on the bars. He was at his old amusement again. Something in the noise jarred on her ear, for she shivered as she heard it. Hugh rasped away at the bars. A dull old bit of tin, not fit to cut korl with.

He looked out of the window again. People were leaving the market now. A tall mulatto girl, following her mistress, her basket on her head, crossed the street just below, and looked up. She was laughing; but, when she caught sight of the haggard face peering out through the bars, suddenly grew grave, and hurried by. A free, firm, step, a clear-cut olive face, with a scarlet turban tied on one side, dark, shining eyes, and on the head the basket poised, filled with fruit and flowers, under which the scarlet turban and bright eyes looked out half-shadowed. The picture caught his eye. It was good to see a face like that. He would try to-morrow, and cut one like it. To-morrow! He threw down the tin, trembling, and covered his face with his hands. When he looked up again, the daylight was gone.

Deborah, crouching near by on the other side of the wall, heard no noise. He sat on the side of the low pallet, thinking. Whatever was the mystery which the woman had seen on his face, it came out now slowly, in the dark there, and became fixed,—a something never seen on his face before. The evening was darkening fast. The market had been over for an hour; the rumbling of the carts over the pavement grew more infrequent: he listened to each, as it passed, because he thought it was to be for the last time. For the same reason, it was, I suppose, that he strained his eyes to catch a glimpse of each passer-by, wondering who they were, what kind of homes they were

going to, if they had children,—listening eagerly to every chance word in the street, as if—(God be merciful to the man! what strange fancy was this?)—as if he never should hear human voices again.

It was quite dark at last. The street was a lonely one. The last passenger, he thought, was gone. No,—there was a quick step: Joe Hill, lighting the lamps. Joe was a good old chap; never passed a fellow without some joke or other. He remembered once seeing the place where he lived with his wife. "Granny Hill" the boys called her. Bedridden she was; but so kind as Joe was to her! kept the room so clean!—and the old woman, when he was there, was laughing at "some of t' lad's foolishness." The step was far down the street; but he could see him place the ladder, run up, and light the gas. A longing seized him to be spoken to once more.

"Joe!" he called, out of the grating. "Good-bye, Joe!"

The old man stopped a moment, listening uncertainly; then hurried on. The prisoner thrust his hand out of the window, and called again, louder; but Joe was too far down the street. It was a little thing; but it hurt him,—this disappointment.

"Good-bye, Joe!" he called, sorrowfully enough.

"Be quiet!" said one of the jailers, passing the door, striking on it with his club.

Oh, that was the last, was it?

There was an inexpressible bitterness on his face, as he lay down on the bed, taking the bit of tin, which he had rasped to a tolerable degree of sharpness, in his hand,—to play with, it may be. He bared his arms, looking intently at their corded veins and sinews. Deborah, listening in the next cell, heard a slight clicking sound, often repeated. She shut her lips tightly, that she might not scream, the cold drops of sweat broke over her, in her dumb agony.

"Hur knows best," she muttered at last, fiercely clutching the boards where she lay.

If she could have seen Wolfe, there was nothing about him to frighten her. He lay quite still, his arms outstretched, looking at the pearly stream of moonlight coming into the window. I think in that one hour that came then he lived back over all the years that had gone before. I think that all the low, vile life, all his wrongs, all his starved hopes, came then, and stung him with a farewell poison that made him sick unto death. He made neither moan nor cry, only turned his worn face now and then to the pure light, that seemed so far off, as one that said, "How long, O Lord? how long?"[9]

The hour was over at last. The moon, passing over her nightly path, slowly came nearer, and threw the light across his bed on his feet. He watched it steadily, as it crept up, inch by inch, slowly. It seemed to him to carry with it a great silence. He had been so hot and tired there always in the mills! The years had been so fierce and cruel! There was coming now quiet and coolness and sleep. His tense limbs relaxed, and settled in a calm languor. The blood ran fainter and slow from his heart. He did not think now with a savage anger of what might be and was not; he was conscious only of deep stillness creeping over him. At first he saw a sea of faces: the mill-men,—

9. From "The Marriage of Tirzah and Ahirad" (1827), a poem by Thomas Babington Macaulay. This also echoes Psalm 6.3 and Revelation 6.10.

women he had known, drunken and bloated,—Janeys timid and pitiful,—poor old Debs: then they floated together like a mist, and faded away, leaving only the clear, pearly moonlight.

Whether, as the pure light crept up the stretched-out figure, it brought with it calm and peace, who shall say? His dumb soul was alone with God in judgment. A Voice may have spoken for it from far-off Calvary, "Father, forgive them, for they know not what they do!"[1] Who dare say? Fainter and fainter the heart rose and fell, slower and slower the moon floated from behind a cloud, until, when at last its full tide of white splendor swept over the cell, it seemed to wrap and fold into a deeper stillness the dead figure that never should move again. Silence deeper than the Night! Nothing that moved, save the black nauseous stream of blood dripping slowly from the pallet to the floor!

There was outcry and crowd enough in the cell the next day. The coroner and his jury, the local editors, Kirby himself, and boys with their hands thrust knowingly into their pockets and heads on one side, jammed into the corners. Coming and going all day. Only one woman. She came late, and outstayed them all. A Quaker, or Friend,[2] as they call themselves. I think this woman was known by that name in heaven. A homely body, coarsely dressed in gray and white. Deborah (for Haley had let her in) took notice of her. She watched them all—sitting on the end of the pallet, holding his head in her arms—with the ferocity of a watch-dog, if any of them touched the body. There was no meekness, or sorrow, in her face; the stuff out of which murderers are made, instead. All the time Haley and the woman were laying straight the limbs and cleaning the cell, Deborah sat still, keenly watching the Quaker's face. Of all the crowd there that day, this woman alone had not spoken to her,—only once or twice had put some cordial to her lips. After they all were gone, the woman, in the same still, gentle way, brought a vase of wood-leaves and berries, and placed it by the pallet, then opened the narrow window. The fresh air blew in, and swept the woody fragrance over the dead face. Deborah looked up with a quick wonder.

"Did hur know my boy wud like it? Did hur know Hugh?"

"I know Hugh now."

The white fingers passed in a slow, pitiful way over the dead, worn face. There was a heavy shadow in the quiet eyes.

"Did hur know where they'll bury Hugh?" said Deborah in a shrill tone, catching her arm.

This had been the question hanging on her lips all day.

"In t' town-yard? Under t' mud and ash? T' lad'll smother, woman! He wur born on t' lane moor, where t' air is frick[3] and strong. Take hur out, for God's sake, take hur out where t' air blows!"

The Quaker hesitated, but only for a moment. She put her strong arm around Deborah and led her to the window.

"Thee sees the hills, friend, over the river? Thee sees how the light lies warm there, and the winds of God blow all the day? I live there,—where the blue smoke is, by the trees. Look at me." She turned Deborah's face to her

1. Christ's words on the cross (Luke 23.34).
2. A member of the Society of Friends, a religious

sect that began in 17th-century England.
3. Fresh.

own, clear and earnest. "Thee will believe me? I will take Hugh and bury him there to-morrow."

Deborah did not doubt her. As the evening wore on, she leaned against the iron bars, looking at the hills that rose far off, through the thick sodden clouds, like a bright, unattainable calm. As she looked, a shadow of their solemn repose fell on her face: its fierce discontent faded into a pitiful, humble quiet. Slow, solemn tears gathered in her eyes: the poor weak eyes turned so hopelessly to the place where Hugh was to rest, the grave heights looking higher and brighter and more solemn than ever before. The Quaker watched her keenly. She came to her at last, and touched her arm.

"When thee comes back," she said, in a low, sorrowful tone, like one who speaks from a strong heart deeply moved with remorse or pity, "thee shall begin thy life again,—there on the hills. I came too late; but not for thee,—by God's help, it may be."

Not too late. Three years after, the Quaker began her work. I end my story here. At evening-time it was light. There is no need to tire you with the long years of sunshine, and fresh air, and slow, patient Christ-love, needed to make healthy and hopeful this impure body and soul. There is a homely pine house, on one of these hills, whose windows overlook broad, wooded slopes and clover-crimsoned meadows,—niched into the very place where the light is warmest, the air freest. It is the Friends' meeting-house. Once a week they sit there, in their grave, earnest way, waiting for the Spirit of Love to speak, opening their simple hearts to receive His words. There is a woman, old, deformed, who takes a humble place among them: waiting like them: in her gray dress, her worn face, pure and meek, turned now and then to the sky. A woman much loved by these silent, restful people; more silent than they, more humble, more loving. Waiting: with her eyes turned to hills higher and purer than these on which she lives,—dim and far off now, but to be reached some day. There may be in her heart some latent hope to meet there the love denied her here,—that she shall find him whom she lost, and that then she will not be all-unworthy. Who blames her? Something is lost in the passage of every soul from one eternity to the other,—something pure and beautiful, which might have been and was not: a hope, a talent, a love, over which the soul mourns, like Esau[4] deprived of his birthright. What blame to the meek Quaker, if she took her lost hope to make the hills of heaven more fair?

Nothing remains to tell that the poor Welsh puddler once lived, but this figure of the mill-woman cut in korl. I have it here in a corner of my library. I keep it hid behind a curtain,—it is such a rough, ungainly thing. Yet there are about it touches, grand sweeps of outline, that show a master's hand. Sometimes,—to-night, for instance,—the curtain is accidentally drawn back, and I see a bare arm stretched out imploringly in the darkness, and an eager, wolfish face watching mine: a wan, woeful face, through which the spirit of the dead korl-cutter looks out, with its thwarted life, its mighty hunger, its unfinished work. Its pale, vague lips seem to tremble with a terrible question. "Is this the End?" they say,—"nothing beyond?—no more?" Why, you tell me you have seen that look in the eyes of dumb brutes,—horses dying under the lash. I know.

4. The son of Isaac and Rebecca, who sold his birthright to his brother Jacob (Genesis 25.31).

The deep of the night is passing while I write. The gas-light wakens from the shadows here and there the objects which lie scattered through the room: only faintly, though; for they belong to the open sunlight. As I glance at them, they each recall some task or pleasure of the coming day. A half-moulded child's head; Aphrodite;[5] a bough of forest-leaves; music; work; homely fragments, in which lie the secrets of all eternal truth and beauty. Prophetic all! Only this dumb, woeful face seems to belong to and end with the night. I turn to look at it. Has the power of its desperate need commanded the darkness away? While the room is yet steeped in heavy shadow, a cool, gray light suddenly touches its head like a blessing hand, and its groping arm points through the broken cloud to the far East, where, in the flickering, nebulous crimson, God has set the promise of the Dawn.

<div style="text-align: right">1861</div>

5. The Greek goddess of love.

LOUISA MAY ALCOTT
1832–1888

If American girls between 1870 and the present were to vote for their favorite fictional heroine, Louisa May Alcott's Jo March would be among the election's finalists. The central character of Alcott's *Little Women* (1869), high-spirited Jo is a literarily inclined tomboy, the second oldest of four sisters whose domestic adventures have had an enduring appeal for generations of young readers. Though the novel in which they appear is frequently didactic, drawing for both its narrative structure and its moral strictures on John Bunyan's allegorical *Pilgrim's Progress* (1678), it is continually enlivened by realistic details of New England home life during the Civil War period as well as by incisive depictions of the pressures associated with growing up female in nineteenth-century America. More specifically, the tale is made dramatic by its sympathetic examination of rambunctious Jo's initial rebellion against, and ultimate reconciliation to what the historian Nancy Cott has called "the bonds of womanhood."

No doubt one factor that gave this portrait of the artist as a "little woman" special force was that in many ways the tale of Jo's pilgrim's progress toward maturity was Alcott's own story. Born in 1832, Louisa May Alcott was, like Jo, the second of four sisters; and like Jo March, the young "Lu" was impetuous, even often obstreperous: she later remembered that "No boy could be my friend till I had beaten him in a race, and no girl if she refused to climb trees, leap fences." Lu's more decorous older sister, Anna, inspired the character of Jo's sister Meg; her younger sisters, Elizabeth and May, were depicted in barely disguised forms as Jo's sisters Beth and Amy. Like gentle philosophical Mr. March, who is away fighting in the Civil War for much of the book, Lu Alcott's father was an unworldly philosopher who was often absent from home on lecture and walking tours. The friend of such notable New England intellectuals as Emerson and Thoreau, Bronson Alcott was an experimental educator, a Transcendentalist, and a social reformer whose commitment to idealistic causes—for instance, the short-lived utopian community called "Fruitlands"—frequently left his family on the edge of poverty. Like *Little Women*'s patient and diligent "Marmee," his wife,

Abba, was a strong, supportive woman who kept the household going, both emotionally and financially, through all kinds of vicissitudes. Probably it was from her example that the young Louisa gained the determination to shoulder what *Little Women*, following *Pilgrim's Progress*, calls the "burdens" of life. Certainly it was to assist her overworked mother that she resolved, at the age of eighteen, to become self-supporting, and, more, to make enough money so that Abba Alcott could "have a lovely, quiet home . . . with no debts or troubles."

Although, as she herself observed, the range of careers available to nineteenth-century girls was severely limited, Alcott held positions as a seamstress, a domestic servant, a governess, a teacher, a lady's "companion," and an army nurse—all jobs whose oppressions and rewards she was later to describe not only in such essays as "How I Went Out to Service" but also in her novel *Work* (1873) and in several other volumes. Even while she labored at these often menial occupations, however, she was steadily writing fiction, poetry, and journalistic sketches. For like Jo, the young Lu was an imaginative girl who composed Gothic thrillers (which she published under the pseudonym A. M. Barnard) when she was still a teenager. And again like Jo—who learns to renounce her desire for romantic "blood and thunder" in a chapter of *Little Women* called "Literary Lessons"—Alcott moved during her career from romance to realism, from melodramatizing to moralizing. In 1863 she published a well-received collection titled *Hospital Sketches*, describing her experiences as a Civil War army nurse with poignant accuracy, and in 1864 she published a promising first novel, *Moods*. Then, early in 1868, she became the editor of *Merry's Museum*, a magazine for girls, and, when a Boston publisher suggested that she herself might write a novel for young people, she composed *Little Women* in two six-week periods. The book was an instant success, establishing her as one of America's best-selling writers. For the next twenty years, until her death in 1888, she was to maintain and enhance her reputation, producing, on the average, a book a year, including seven more novels for girls and two for adults, as well as sixteen collections of stories and sketches for children and adolescents.

Alcott's great contemporary, the novelist Henry James, somewhat patronizingly called her "the novelist of children . . . the Thackeray, the Trollope of the nursery and the schoolroom." Yet as recent critics have increasingly recognized, her children's books as well as her works for adults—including the "sensational" fictions that she published pseudonymously—were serious and complex. From *Little Women* onward, all her fiction reveals her continuing concern with social reform, especially her sense of the ways in which young women were exploited by a society that obliged them to support themselves but offered them few opportunities for self-improvement. Similarly, her early thrillers, collected in two volumes in the 1970s—*Behind a Mask* and *Plots and Counterplots*—frequently suggest a secret rage at female powerlessness, a rage that is briefly expressed by even the ever-patient Marmee in *Little Women*, when she confesses that "I have been angry every day of my life." At the same time, such a tale as "My Mysterious Mademoiselle," along with a number of other gender-bending stories of impersonation, enacts its author's rebellion against constricting roles and rules with wit and verve. "I am more than half-persuaded that I am a man's soul, put by some freak of nature into a woman's body," Alcott once told an interviewer. Not surprisingly, then, she was active in the nineteenth-century feminist movement. She was the first woman to register in Concord when Massachusetts gave women limited suffrage in 1879, for instance, and she helped facilitate the 1881 publication of Harriet Hanson Robinson's *Massachusetts in the Woman Suffrage Movement*, claiming that she took "more pride" in such gestures toward political reform "than in all the books I ever wrote." But as *Little Women* and other writings demonstrate, this impassioned feminist also inherited from her mother a more general sense of social responsibility for the welfare of those less fortunate than herself.

Perhaps, indeed, it was because her private as well as public responsibilities had been so heavy and of such long standing that Alcott's success as a writer brought her

comparatively little satisfaction. Though she was lionized on literary tours and treated as a celebrity in her hometown of Concord, she disliked the attentions of her many admirers, complaining that "I asked for bread, and got a stone,—in the shape of a pedestal." Alcott's last years were shadowed by numerous problems and sorrows. Her aging father and her widowed sister Anna continued to be financial and emotional burdens; she herself suffered from mercury poisoning, induced by medicine with which she was treated after contracting typhoid fever while working as a nurse during the Civil War; and she grieved the early death of her youngest sister, May, following childbirth. At the same time, her adoption in 1880 of her namesake, May's daughter Louisa May ("Lulu"), brought new pleasure into her life—though for a relatively brief period. Ironically, Louisa May Alcott died (from the mercury poisoning, scholars now believe) on the very day of her father's funeral. She was at the height of her fame: *Jo's Boys*, yet another in her sequence about the March family, appeared in the year of her death.

My Mysterious Mademoiselle

At Lyons I engaged a coupé,[1] laid in a substantial lunch, got out my novels and cigars, and prepared to make myself as comfortable as circumstances permitted; for we should not reach Nice till morning, and a night journey was my especial detestation. Nothing would have induced me to undertake it in mid-winter, but a pathetic letter from my sister, imploring me to come to her, as she was failing fast, and had a precious gift to bestow upon me before she died. This sister had mortally offended our father by marrying a Frenchman. The old man never forgave her, never would see her, and cut her off with a shilling in his will. I had been forbidden to have any communication with her on pain of disinheritance, and had obeyed, for I shared my father's prejudice, and made no attempt to befriend my sister, even when I learned that she was a widow, although my father's death freed me from my promise. For more than fifteen years we had been utterly estranged; but when her pleading letter came to me, my heart softened, and I longed to see her. My conscience reproached me, and, leaving my cozy bachelor establishment in London, I hurried away, hoping to repair the neglect of years by tardy tenderness and care.

My thoughts worried me that night, and the fear of being too late haunted me distressfully. I could neither read, sleep, nor smoke, and soon heartily wished I had taken a seat in a double carriage, where society of some sort would have made the long hours more endurable. As we stopped at a way-station, I was roused from a remorseful reverie by the guard, who put in his head to inquire, with an insinuating shrug and smile:

"Will monsieur permit a lady to enter? The train is very full, and no place remains for her in the first-class. It will be a great kindness if monsieur will take pity on the charming little mademoiselle."

He dropped his voice in uttering the last words, and gave a nod, which plainly expressed his opinion that monsieur would not regret the courtesy. Glad to be relieved from the solitude that oppressed me, I consented at once,

1. The end compartment in a railway carriage, with seating on only one side.

and waited with some curiosity to see what sort of companion I was to have for the next few hours.

The first glance satisfied me; but, like a true Englishman, I made no demonstration of interest beyond a bow and a brief reply to the apologies and thanks uttered in a fresh young voice as the new-comer took her seat. A slender girl of sixteen or so, simply dressed in black, with a little hat tied down over golden curls, and a rosy face, lit up by lustrous hazel eyes, at once arch, modest and wistful. A cloak and a plump traveling bag were all her luggage, and quickly arranging them, she drew out a book, sank back in her corner, and appeared to read, as if anxious to render me forgetful of her presence as soon as possible.

I liked that, and resolved to convince her at the first opportunity that I was no English bear, but a gentleman who could be very agreeable when he chose.

The opportunity did not arrive as soon as I hoped, and I began to grow impatient to hear the fresh young voice again. I made a few attempts at conversation, but the little girl seemed timid, for she answered in the briefest words, and fell to reading again, forcing me to content myself with admiring the long curled lashes, the rosy mouth, and the golden hair of this demure demoiselle.

She was evidently afraid of the big, black-bearded gentleman, and would not be drawn out, so I solaced myself by watching her in the windows opposite, which reflected every movement like a mirror.

Presently the book slipped from her hand, the bright eyes grew heavy, the pretty head began to nod, and sleep grew more and more irresistible. Half closing my eyes, I feigned slumber, and was amused at the little girl's evident relief. She peeped at first, then took a good look, then smiled to herself as if well pleased, yawned, and rubbed her eyes like a sleepy child, took off her hat, tied a coquettish rose-colored rigolette[2] over her soft hair, viewed herself in the glass, and laughed a low laugh, so full of merriment, that I found it difficult to keep my countenance. Then, with a roguish glance at me, she put out her hand toward the flask of wine lying on the leaf, with a half-open case of chocolate croquettes, which I had been munching, lifted the flask to her lips, put it hastily down again, took one bon-bon, and, curling herself up like a kitten, seemed to drop asleep at once.

"Poor little thing," I thought to myself, "she is hungry, cold, and tired; she longs for a warm sip, a sugar-plum, and a kind word, I dare say. She is far too young and pretty to be traveling alone. I must take care of her."

In pursuance of which friendly resolve I laid my rug lightly over her, slipped a soft shawl under her head, drew the curtains for warmth, and then repaid myself for these attentions by looking long and freely at the face encircled by the rosy cloud. Prettier than ever when flushed with sleep did it look, and I quite lost myself in the pleasant reverie which came to me while leaning over the young girl, watching the silken lashes lying quietly on the blooming cheeks, listening to her soft breath, touching the yellow curls that strayed over the arm of the seat, and wondering who the charming little person might be. She reminded me of my first sweetheart—a pretty cousin, who had captivated my boyish heart at eighteen, and dealt it a wound it never

2. A woman's scarflike headcovering (usually knit or crocheted of wool).

could forget. At five-and-thirty these little romances sometimes return to one's memory fresher and dearer for the years that have taught us the sweetness of youth—the bitterness of regret. In a sort of waking dream I sat looking at the stranger, who seemed to wear the guise of my first love, till suddenly the great eyes flashed wide open, the girl sprung up, and, clasping her hands, cried, imploringly:

"Ah, monsieur, do not hurt me, for I am helpless. Take my little purse: take all I have, but spare my life for my poor mother's sake!"

"Good heavens, child, do you take me for a robber?" I exclaimed, startled out of my sentimental fancies by this unexpected performance.

"Pardon; I was dreaming; I woke to find you bending over me, and I was frightened," she murmured, eying me timidly.

"That was also a part of your dream. Do I look like a rascal, mademoiselle?" I demanded, anxious to reassure her.

"Indeed, no; you look truly kind, and I trust you. But I am not used to traveling alone; I am anxious and timid, yet now I do not fear. Pardon, monsieur; pray, pardon a poor child who has no friend to protect her."

She put out her hand with an impulsive gesture, as the soft eyes were lifted confidingly to mine, and what could I do but kiss the hand in true French style, and smile back into the eyes with involuntary tenderness, as I replied, with unusual gallantry:

"Not without a friend to protect her, if mademoiselle will permit me the happiness. Rest tranquil, no one shall harm you. Confide in me, and you shall find that we 'cold English' have hearts, and my be trusted."

"Ah, so kind, so pitiful! A thousand thanks; but do not let me disturb monsieur. I will have no more panics, and can only atone for my foolish fancy by remaining quiet, that monsieur may sleep."

"Sleep! Not I: and the best atonement you can make is to join me at supper, and wile away this tedious night with friendly confidences. Shall it be so, mademoiselle?" I asked, assuming a paternal air to reassure her.

"That would be pleasant; for I confess I am hungry, and have nothing with me. I left in such haste I forgot—" She paused suddenly, turned scarlet, and drooped her eyes, as if on the point of betraying some secret.

I took no notice, but began to fancy that my little friend was engaged in some romance which might prove interesting. Opening my traveling-case, I set forth cold chicken, *tartines*,[3] wine, and sweetmeats, and served her as respectfully as if she had been a duchess, instead of what I suspected—a run-away school-girl. My manner put her at her ease, and she chatted away with charming frankness, though now and then she checked some word on her lips, blushed and laughed, and looked so merry and mysterious, that I began to find my school-girl a most captivating companion. The hours flew rapidly now; remorse and anxiety slept; I felt blithe and young again, for my lost love seemed to sit beside me; I forgot my years, and almost fancied myself an ardent lad again.

What mademoiselle thought of me I could only guess; but look, tone and manner betrayed the most flattering confidence. I enjoyed the little adventure without a thought of consequences.

At Toulon we changed cars, and I could not get a coupé, but fortunately

3. Slices of bread and butter (French, as are all translated terms in the story).

found places in a carriage, whose only occupant was a sleepy old woman. As I was about taking my seat, after bringing my companion a cup of hot coffee, she uttered an exclamation, dragged her vail over her face, and shrunk into the corner of our compartment.

"What alarms you?" I asked, anxiously, for her mystery piqued my curiosity.

"Look out and see if a tall young man is not promenading the platform, and looking into every carriage," returned mademoiselle, in good English, for the first time.

I looked out, saw the person described, watched him approach, and observed that he glanced eagerly into each car as he passed.

"He is there, and is about to favor us with an inspection. What are your commands, mademoiselle?" I asked.

"Oh, sir, befriend me; cover me up; say that I am ill; call yourself my father for a moment—I will explain it all. Hush, he is here!" and the girl clung to my arm with a nervous gesture, an imploring look, which I could not resist.

The stranger appeared, entered with a grave bow, seated himself opposite, and glanced from me to the muffled figure at my side. We were off in a moment, and no one spoke, till a little cough behind the veil gave the new-comer a pretext for addressing me.

"Mademoiselle is annoyed by the air; permit me to close the window."

"Madame[4] is an invalid, and will thank you to do so," I replied, taking a malicious satisfaction in disobeying the girl, for the idea of passing as her father disgusted me, and I preferred a more youthful title.

A sly pinch of the arm was all the revenge she could take; and, as I stooped to settle the cloaks about her, I got a glance from the hazel eyes, reproachful, defiant, and merry.

"Ah, she has spirit, this little wandering princess. Let us see what our friend opposite has to do with her," I said to myself, feeling almost jealous of the young man, who was a handsome, resolute-looking fellow, in a sort of uniform.

"Does he understand English, madame, my wife?" I whispered to the girl.

"Not a word," she whispered back, with another charming pinch.

"Good; then tell me all about him. I demand an explanation."

"Not now; not here, wait a little. Can you not trust me, when I confide so much to you?"

"No, I am burning with curiosity, and I deserve some reward for my good behavior. Shall I not have it, *ma amie?*"[5]

"Truly, you do, and I will give you anything by-and-by," she began.

"*Anything?*" I asked, quickly.

"Yes; I give you my word."

"I shall hold you to your promise. Come, we will make a little bargain. I will blindly obey you till we reach Nice, if you will frankly tell me the cause of all this mystery before we part."

"Done!" cried the girl, with an odd laugh.

"Done!" said I, feeling that I was probably making a fool of myself.

The young man eyed us sharply as we spoke, but said nothing, and, wishing

4. I.e., a married woman (in distinction to *made-moiselle*). 5. My friend.

to make the most of my bargain, I pillowed my little wife's head on my shoulder, and talked in whispers, while she nestled in shelter of my arm, and seemed to enjoy the escapade with all the thoughtless *abandon* of a girl. Why she went off into frequent fits of quiet laughter I did not quite understand, for my whispers were decidedly more tender than witty; but I fancied it hysterical, and, having made up my mind that some touching romance was soon to be revealed to me, I prepared myself for it, by playing my part with spirit, finding something very agreeable in my new *role* of devoted husband.

The remarks of our neighbors amused us immensely; for, the old lady, on waking, evidently took us for an English couple on a honeymoon trip, and confided her opinion of the "mad English" to the young man, who knit his brows and mused moodily.

To our great satisfaction, both of our companions quitted us at midnight; and the moment the door closed behind them, the girl tore off her vail, threw herself on the seat opposite me, and laughed till the tears rolled down her cheeks.

"Now, mademoiselle, I demand an explanation," I said, seriously, when her merriment subsided.

"You shall have it; but first tell me what do I look like?" and she turned her face toward me with a wicked smile, that puzzled me more than her words.

"Like a very charming young lady who has run way from school or *pension*,[6] either to escape from a lover or to meet one."

"My faith! but that is a compliment to my skill," muttered the girl, as if to herself; then aloud, and soberly, though her eyes still danced with irrepressible mirth: "Monsieur is right in one thing. I have run away from school, but not to meet or fly a lover. Ah, no; I go to find my mother. She is ill; they concealed it from me; I ran away, and would have walked from Lyons to Nice if old Justine had not helped me."

"And this young man—why did you dread him?" I asked, eagerly.

"He is one of the teachers. He goes to find and reclaim me; but, thanks to my disguise, and your kindness, he has not discovered me."

"But why should he reclaim you? Surely, if your mother is ill, you have a right to visit her, and she would desire it."

"Ah, it is a sad story! I can only tell you that we are poor. I am too young yet to help my mother. Two rich aunts placed me in a fine school, and support me till I am eighteen, on condition that my mother does not see me. They hate her, and I would have rejected their charity, but for the thought that soon I can earn my bread and support her. She wished me to go, and I obeyed, though it broke my heart. I study hard. I suffer many trials. I make no complaint; but I hope and wait, and when the time comes I fly to her, and never leave her any more."

What had come to the girl? The words poured from her lips with impetuous force; her eyes flashed; her face glowed; her voice was possessed with strange eloquence, by turns tender, defiant, proud, and pathetic. She clinched her hands, and dashed her little hat at her feet with a vehement gesture when speaking of her aunts. Her eyes shone through indignant tears when alluding

6. Boarding school.

to her trials; and, as she said, brokenly, "I fly to her, and never leave her any more," she opened her arms as if to embrace and hold her mother fast.

It moved me strangely; for, instead of a shallow, coquettish school-girl, I found a passionate, resolute creature, ready to do and dare anything for the mother she loved. I resolved to see the end of this adventure, and wished my sister had a child as fond and faithful to comfort and sustain her; but her only son had died a baby, and she was alone, for I had deserted her.

"Have you no friends but these cruel aunts?" I asked, compassionately.

"No, not one. My father is dead, my mother poor and ill, and I am powerless to help her," she answered, with a sob.

"Not quite; remember I am a friend."

As I spoke I offered my hand; but, to my intense surprise, the girl struck it away from her with a passionate motion, saying, almost fiercely:

"No; it is too late—to late! You should have come before."

"My poor child, calm yourself. I *am* indeed a friend; believe it, and let me help you. I can sympathize with your distress, for I, too, go to Nice to find one dear to me. My poor sister, whom I have neglected many years; but now I go to ask pardon, and to serve her with all my heart. Come, then, let us comfort one another, and go hopefully to meet those who love and long for us."

Still another surprise; for, with a face as sweetly penitent as it had been sternly proud before, this strange girl caught my hand in hers, kissed it warmly, and whispered, gratefully:

"I often dreamed of a friend like this, but never thought to find him so. God bless you, my—" She paused there, hid her face an instant, then looked up without a shadow in her eyes, saying more quietly, and with a smile I could not understand:

"What shall I give you to prove my thanks for your kindness to me?"

"When we part, you shall give me an English good-by."

"A kiss on the lips! Fie! monsieur will not demand that of me," cried the girl, whose changeful face was gay again.

"And, why not, since I am old enough to be called your father."

"Ah, that displeased you! Well, you had your revenge; rest content with that, *mon mari*,"[7] laughed the girl, retreating to a corner with a rebellious air.

"I shall claim my reward when we part; so resign yourself, mademoiselle. By-the-way, what name has my little friend?"

"I will tell you when I pay my debt. Now let me sleep. I am tired, and so are you. Good-night, Monsieur George Vane," and, leaving me to wonder how she had learned my name, the tormenting creature barricaded herself with cloaks and bags, and seemed to sleep tranquilly.

Tired with the long night, I soon dropped off into a doze, which must have been a long one; for, when I woke, I found myself in the dark.

"Where the deuce are we?" I exclaimed; for the lamp was out, and no sign of dawn visible, though I had seen a ruddy streak when I last looked out.

"In the long tunnel near Nice," answered a voice from the gloom.

7. My husband.

"Ah, mademoiselle is awake! Is she not afraid that I may demand payment now?"

"Wait till the light comes, and if you deserve it *then*, you shall have it," and I heard the little gipsy laughing in her corner. The next minute a spark glowed opposite me; the odor of my choice cigarettes filled the air, and the crackle of a bon-bon was heard.

Before I could make up my mind how to punish these freaks, we shot out of the tunnel, and I sat petrified with amazement, for there, opposite me, lounged, not my pretty blonde school-girl, but a handsome black-haired, mischievous lad, in the costume of a pupil of a French military academy; with his little cap rakishly askew, his blue coat buttoned smartly to the chin, his well-booted feet on the seat beside him, and his small hands daintily gloved, this young rascal lay staring at me with such a world of fun in his fine eyes, that I tingled all over with a shock of surprise which almost took my breath away.

"Have a light, uncle?" was the cool remark that broke the long silence.

"Where is the girl?" was all I could say, with a dazed expression.

"There, sir," pointing to the bag, with a smile that made me feel as if I was not yet awake, so like the girl's was it.

"And who the devil are you?" I cried, getting angry all at once.

Standing as straight as an arrow, the boy answered, with a military salute: "George Vane Vandeleur, at your service, uncle."

"My sister has no children; her boy died years ago, you young villain."

"He tried to, but they wouldn't let him. I'm sorry to contradict you, sir: but I'm your sister's son, and that will prove it."

Much bewildered, I took the letter he handed me, and found it impossible to doubt the boy's word. It was from my sister to her son, telling him that she had written to me, that I had answered kindly, and promised to come to her. She bade the boy visit her if possible, that I might see him, for she could not doubt that I would receive him for her sake, and free him from dependence on the French aunts who made their favors burdensome by reproach and separation.

As I read, I forgave the boy his prank, and longed to give him a hearty welcome; but recollections of my own part in that night's masquerade annoyed me so much that to conceal my chagrin I assumed a stern air, and demanded, coldly:

"Was it necessary to make a girl of yourself in order to visit your mother?"

"Yes, sir," answered the boy, promptly, adding, with the most engaging frankness: "I'll tell you how it was, uncle, and I know you will pardon me, because mamma has often told me of your pranks when a boy, and I made you my hero. See, then, mamma sends me this letter, and I am wild to go, that I may embrace her and see my uncle. But my aunts say, 'No,' and tell them at school that I am to be kept close. Ah, they are strict there; the boys are left no freedom, and my only chance was the one holiday when I go to my aunts. I resolved to run away; and walk to mamma, for nothing shall part us but her will. I had a little money, and I confided my plan to Justine, my old nurse. She is a brave one! She said:

" 'You shall go, but not as a beggar. See, I have money. Take it, my son, and visit your mother like a gentleman.'

"That was grand; but I feared to be caught before I could leave Lyons, so

I resolved to disguise myself, and then if they followed I should escape them. Often at school I have played girl-parts, because I am small, and have as yet no beard. So Justine dressed me in the skirt, cloak and hat of her grand-daughter. I had the blonde wig I wore on the stage, a little rouge, a soft tone, a modest air, and—*voilà mademoiselle!*"

"Exactly; it was well done, though at times you forgot the 'modest air,' nephew." I said, with as much dignity as suppressed merriment permitted.

"It was impossible to remember it at all times; and you did not seem to like mademoiselle the less for a little coquetry," replied the rogue, with a sly glance out of the handsome eyes that had bewitched me.

"Continue your story, sir. Was the young man we met really a teacher?"

"Yes, uncle; but you so kindly protected me that he could not even suspect your delicate wife."

The boy choked over the last word, and burst into a laugh so irresistibly infectious that I joined him, and lost my dignity for ever.

"George, you are a scapegrace," was the only reproof I had breath enough to make.

"But uncle pardons me, since he gives me my name, and looks at me so kindly that I must embrace him."

And with a demonstrative affection which an English boy would have died rather than betray, my French nephew threw his arms about my neck, and kissed me heartily on both cheeks. I had often ridiculed the fashion, but now I rather liked it, and began to think my prejudice ill-founded, as I listened to the lad's account of the sorrows and hardships they had been called on to suffer since his father died.

"Why was I never told of your existence?" I asked, feeling how much I had lost in my long ignorance of this bright boy, who was already dear to me.

"When I was so ill while a baby, mamma wrote to my grandfather, hoping to touch his heart: but he never answered her, and she wrote no more. If uncle had cared to find his nephew, he might easily have done so; the channel is not very wide."

The reproach in the last words went straight to my heart; but I only said, stroking the curly head:

"Did you never mean to make yourself known to me? When your mother was suffering, could you not try me?"

"I never could beg, even for her, and trusted to the good God, and we were helped. I did mean to make myself known to you when I had done something to be proud of; not before."

I knew where that haughty spirit came from, and was as glad to see it as I was to see how much the boy resembled my once lovely sister.

"How did you know me, George?" I asked, finding pleasure in uttering the familiar name, unspoken since my father died.

"I saw your name on your luggage at Marseilles, and thought you looked like the picture mamma cherishes so tenderly, and I resolved to try and touch your heart before you knew who I was. The guard put me into your coupé, for I bribed him, and then I acted my best; but it was so droll I nearly spoiled it all by some boy's word, or a laugh. My faith, uncle, I did not know the English were so gallant."

"It did not occur to you that I might be acting also, perhaps? I own I was

puzzled at first, but I soon made up my mind that you were some little adventuress out on a lark, as we say in England, and I behaved accordingly."

"If all little adventuresses got on as well as I did, I fancy many would go on this lark of yours. A talent for acting runs in the family, that is evident," said the boy.

"Hold your tongue, jackanapes!" sternly. "How old are you, my lad?" mildly.

"Fifteen, sir."

"That young to begin the world, with no friends but two cold-hearted old women!"

"Ah, no, I have the good God and my mother, and now—may I say an uncle who loves me a little, and permits me to love him with all my heart?"

Never mind what answer I made: I have recorded weaknesses enough already, so let that pass, as well as the conversation which left both pair of eyes a little wet, but both pair of hearts very happy.

As the train thundered into the station at Nice, just as the sun rose gloriously over the blue Mediterranean, George whispered to me, with the irrepressible impudence of a mischief-loving boy:

"Uncle, shall I give you 'the English good-by' now?"

"No, my lad: give me a hearty English welcome, and God bless you!" I answered, as we shook hands, manfully, and walked away together, laughing over the adventure with my mysterious mademoiselle.

1869

How I Went Out to Service

When I was eighteen I wanted[1] something to do. I had tried teaching for two years, and hated it; I had tried sewing, and could not earn my bread in that way, at the cost of health; I tried story-writing and got five dollars for stories which now bring a hundred; I had thought seriously of going upon the stage, but certain highly respectable relatives were so shocked at the mere idea that I relinquished my dramatic aspirations.

"What shall I do?" was still the question that perplexed me. I was ready to work, eager to be independent, and too proud to endure patronage. But the right task seemed hard to find, and my bottled energies were fermenting in a way that threatened an explosion before long.

My honored mother was a city missionary that winter, and not only served the clamorous poor, but often found it in her power to help decayed gentlefolk by quietly placing them where they could earn their bread without the entire sacrifice of taste and talent which makes poverty so hard for such to bear. Knowing her tact and skill, people often came to her for companions, housekeepers, and that class of the needy who do not make their wants known through an intelligence office.[2]

One day, as I sat dreaming splendid dreams, while I made a series of little

1. Was in need of.
2. An office where information can be obtained concerning servants.

petticoats out of the odds and ends sent in for the poor, a tall, ministerial gentleman appeared, in search of a companion for his sister. He possessed an impressive nose, a fine flow of language, and a pair of large hands, encased in black kid gloves. With much waving of these somber members, Mr. R.[3] set forth the delights awaiting the happy soul who should secure this home. He described it as a sort of heaven on earth. "There are books, pictures, flowers, a piano, and the best of society," he said. "This person will be one of the family in all respects, and only required to help about the lighter work, which my sister has done herself hitherto, but is now a martyr to neuralgia and needs a gentle friend to assist her."

My mother, who never lost her faith in human nature, in spite of many impostures, believed every word, and quite beamed with benevolent interest as she listened and tried to recall some needy young woman to whom this charming home would be a blessing. I also innocently thought:

"That sounds inviting. I like housework and can do it well. I should have time to enjoy the books and things I love, and D—is not far away from home. Suppose I try it."

So, when my mother turned to me, asking if I could suggest any one, I became as red as a poppy and said abruptly:

"Only myself."

"Do you really mean it?" cried my astonished parent.

"I really do if Mr. R. thinks I should suit," was my steady reply, as I partially obscured my crimson countenance behind a little flannel skirt, still redder.

The Reverend Josephus gazed upon me with the benign regard which a bachelor of five and thirty may accord a bashful damsel of eighteen. A smile dawned upon his countenance, "sicklied o'er with the pale cast of thought,"[4] or dyspepsia; and he softly folded the black gloves, as if about to bestow a blessing as he replied, with emphasis:

"I am sure you would, and we should think ourselves most fortunate if we could secure your society, and—ahem—services for my poor sister."

"Then I'll try it," responded the impetuous maid.

"We will talk it over a little first, and let you know to-morrow, sir," put in my prudent parent, adding, as Mr. R. arose: "What wages do you pay?"

"My dear madam, in a case like this let me not use such words as those. Anything you may think proper we shall gladly give. The labor is very light, for there are but three of us and our habits are of the simplest sort. I am a frail reed and may break at any moment; so is my sister, and my aged father cannot long remain; therefore, money is little to us, and any one who comes to lend her youth and strength to our feeble household will not be forgotten in the end, I assure you." And, with another pensive smile, a farewell wave of the impressive gloves, the Reverend Josephus bowed like a well-sweep and departed.

"My dear, are you in earnest?" asked my mother.

"Of course, I am. Why not try this experiment? It can but fail, like all the others."

"I have no objection; only I fancied you were rather too proud for this sort of thing."

3. In fact, Alcott's employer was James Richard-
son of Dedham, Mass.

4. Shakespeare's *Hamlet* 3.1.87.

"I am too proud to be idle and dependent, ma'am. I'll scrub floors and take in washing first. I do housework at home for love; why not do it abroad for money? I like it better than teaching. It is healthier than sewing and surer than writing. So why not try it?"

"It is going out to service, you know, though you are called a companion. How does that suit?"

"I don't care. Every sort of work that is paid for is service; and I don't mind being a companion, if I can do it well. I may find it is my mission to take care of neuralgic old ladies and lackadaisical clergymen. It does not sound exciting, but it's better than nothing," I answered, with a sigh; for it *was* rather a sudden downfall to give up being a Siddons and become a Betcinder.[5]

How my sisters laughed when they heard the new plan! But they soon resigned themselves, sure of fun, for Lu's adventures were the standing joke of the family. Of course, the highly respectable relatives held up their hands in holy horror at the idea of one of the clan degrading herself by going out to service. Teaching a private school was the proper thing for an indigent gentlewoman. Sewing even, if done in the seclusion of home and not mentioned in public, could be tolerated. Story-writing was a genteel accomplishment and reflected credit upon the name. But leaving the paternal roof to wash other people's teacups, nurse other people's ails, and obey other people's orders for hire—this, this was degradation; and headstrong Louisa would disgrace her name forever if she did it.

Opposition only fired the revolutionary blood in my veins, and I crowned my iniquity by the rebellious declaration:

"If doing this work hurts my respectability, I wouldn't give much for it. My aristocratic ancestors don't feed or clothe me and my democratic ideas of honesty and honor won't let me be idle or dependent. You need not know me if you are ashamed of me, and I won't ask you for a penny; so, if I never do succeed in anything, I shall have the immense satisfaction of knowing I am under no obligation to any one."

In spite of the laughter and the lamentation, I got ready my small wardrobe, consisting of two calico dresses and one delaine,[6] made by myself, also several large and uncompromising blue aprons and three tidy little sweeping-caps; for I had some English notions about housework and felt that my muslin hair-protectors would be useful in some of the "light labors" I was to undertake. It is needless to say they were very becoming. Then, firmly embracing my family, I set forth, one cold January day, with my little trunk, a stout heart, and a five-dollar bill for my fortune.

"She will be back in a week," was my sister's prophecy, as she wiped her weeping eye.

"No, she won't, for she has promised to stay the month out and she will keep her word," answered my mother, who always defended the black sheep of her flock.

I heard both speeches, and registered a tremendous vow to keep that promise, if I died in the attempt—little dreaming, poor innocent, what lay before me.

5. I.e., Cinderella. Sarah Siddons (1755–1831), notable British tragic actress.
6. A light fabric (generally cotton and wool) used for women's dresses; it is usually printed. "Calico": a coarse, printed cotton cloth.

Josephus meantime had written me several remarkable letters, describing the different members of the family I was about to enter. His account was peculiar, but I believed every word of it and my romantic fancy was much excited by the details he gave. The principal ones are as follows condensed from the voluminous epistles which he evidently enjoyed writing:

"You will find a stately mansion, fast falling to decay, for my father will have nothing repaired, preferring that the old house and its master should crumble away together. I have, however, been permitted to rescue a few rooms from ruin; and here I pass my recluse life, surrounded by the things I love. This will naturally be more attractive to you than the gloomy apartments my father inhabits, and I hope you will here allow me to minister to your young and cheerful nature when your daily cares are over. I need such companionship and shall always welcome you to my abode.

"Eliza, my sister, is a child at forty, for she has lived alone with my father and an old servant all her life. She is a good creature, but not lively, and needs stirring up, as you will soon see. Also I hope by your means to rescue her from the evil influence of Puah, who, in my estimation, is a *wretch*. She has gained entire control over Eliza, and warps her mind with great skill, prejudicing her against *me* and thereby desolating my home. Puah hates *me* and always has. Why I know not, except that I will not yield to her control. She ruled here for years while I was away, and my return upset all her nefarious plans. It will always be my firm opinion that she has tried to *poison me*, and may again. But even this dark suspicion will not deter me from my duty. I cannot send her away, for both my deluded father and my sister have entire faith in her, and I cannot shake it. She is faithful and kind to them, so I submit and remain to guard them, even at the risk of my life.

"I tell you these things because I wish you to know all and be warned, for this old hag has a specious tongue, and I should grieve to see you deceived by her lies. Say nothing, but watch her silently, and help me to thwart her evil plots; but do not trust her, or beware."

Now this was altogether romantic and sensational, and I felt as if about to enter one of those delightfully dangerous houses we read of in novels, where perils, mysteries, and sins freely disport themselves, till the newcomer sets all to rights, after unheard of trials and escapes.

I arrived at twilight, just the proper time for the heroine to appear; and, as no one answered my modest solo on the rusty knocker, I walked in and looked about me. Yes, here was the long, shadowy hall, where the ghosts doubtless walked at midnight. Peering in at an open door on the right, I saw a parlor full of ancient furniture, faded, dusty, and dilapidated. Old portraits stared at me from the walls and a damp child froze the marrow of my bones in the most approved style.

"The romance opens well," I thought, and, peeping in at an opposite door, beheld a luxurious apartment, full of the warm glow of firelight, the balmy breath of hyacinths and roses, the white glimmer of piano keys, and tempting rows of books along the walls.

The contrast between the two rooms was striking, and, after an admiring survey, I continued my explorations, thinking that I should not mind being "ministered to" in that inviting place when my work was done.

A third door showed me a plain, dull sitting room, with an old man napping in his easy-chair. I heard voices in the kitchen beyond, and, entering there,

beheld Puah the fiend. Unfortunately, for the dramatic effect of the tableaux, all I saw was a mild-faced old woman, buttering toast, while she conversed with her familiar, a comfortable gray cat.

The old lady greeted me kindly, but I fancied her faded blue eye had a weird expression and her amiable words were all a snare, though I own I was rather disappointed at the commonplace appearance of this humble Borgia.[7]

She showed me to a tiny room, where I felt more like a young giantess than ever, and was obliged to stow away my possessions as snugly as in a ship's cabin. When I presently descended, armed with a blue apron and "a heart for any fate,"[8] I found the old man awake and received from him a welcome full of ancient courtesy and kindliness. Miss Eliza crept in like a timid mouse, looking so afraid of her buxom companion that I forgot my own shyness in trying to relieve hers. She was so enveloped in shawls that all I could discover was that my mistress was a very nervous little woman, with a small button of pale hair on the outside of her head and the vaguest notions of work inside. A few spasmodic remarks and many awkward pauses brought me to teatime, when Josephus appeared, as tall, thin, and cadaverous as ever. After his arrival there was no more silence, for he preached all supertime something in this agreeable style.

"My young friend, our habits, as you see, are of the simplest. We eat in the kitchen, and all together, in the primitive fashion; for it suits my father and saves labor. I could wish more order and elegance; but *my* wishes are not consulted and I submit. I live above these petty crosses, and, though my health suffers from bad cookery, I do not murmur. Only, I must say, in passing, that if you *will* make your battercakes green with saleratus,[9] Puah, I shall feel it my duty to throw them out of the window. *I* am used to poison; but I cannot see the coals of this blooming girl's stomach destroyed, as mine have been. And, speaking of duties, I may as well mention to you, Louisa (I call you so in a truly fraternal spirit), that I like to find my study in order when I come down in the morning; for I often need a few moments of solitude before I face the daily annoyances of my life. I shall permit *you* to perform this light task, for *you* have some idea of order (I see it in the formation of your brow), and feel sure that *you* will respect the sanctuary of thought. Eliza is so blind she does not see dust, and Puah enjoys devastating the one poor refuge I can call my own this side the grave. We are all waiting for you, sir. My father keeps up the old formalities, you observe; and I endure them, though *my* views are more advanced."

The old gentleman hastily finished his tea and returned thanks, when his son stalked gloomily away, evidently oppressed with the burden of his wrongs, also, as I irreverently fancied, with the seven "green" flapjacks he had devoured during the sermon.

I helped wash up the cups, and during that domestic rite Puah chatted in what I should have considered a cheery, social way had I not been darkly warned against her wiles.

"You needn't mind half Josephus says, my dear. He likes to hear himself talk and always goes on so before folks. I sometimes thinks his books and

7. I.e., plotter, schemer; in 15th- and 16th-century Italy, the prominent Borgia family gained a reputation for greed, treachery, and murder, especially by poison.

8. From "A Psalm of Life" (1838), by the American poet Henry Wadsworth Longfellow.
9. Baking soda. "Battercakes": pancakes.

new ideas have sort of muddled his wits, for he is as full of notions as a paper is of pins; and he gets dreadfully put out if we don't give in to 'em. But, gracious me! they are so redicklus sometimes and so selfish I can't allow him to make a fool of himself or plague Lizy. She don't dare to say her soul is her own; so I have to stand up for her. His pa don't know half his odd doings; for I try to keep the old gentleman comfortable and have to manage 'em all, which is not an easy job I do assure you."

I had a secret conviction that she was right, but did not commit myself in any way, and we joined the social circle in the sitting room. The prospect was not a lively one, for the old gentleman nodded behind his newspaper; Eliza, with her head pinned up in a little blanket, slumbered on the sofa, Puah fell to knitting silently; and the plump cat dozed under the stove.[1] Josephus was visible, artistically posed in the luxurious recesses of his cell, with the light beaming on his thoughtful brow, as he pored over a large volume or mused with upturned eye.

Having nothing else to do, I sat and stared at him, till, emerging from a deep reverie, with an effective start, he became conscious of my existence and beckoned me to approach the "sanctuary of thought" with a dramatic waft of his large hand.

I went, took possession of an easy chair, and prepared myself for elegant conversation. I was disappointed, however; for Josephus showed me a list of his favorite dishes, sole fruit of all that absorbing thought, and, with an earnestness that flushed his saffron countenance, gave me hints as to the proper preparation of these delicacies.

I mildly mentioned that I was not a cook; but was effectually silenced by being reminded that I came to be generally useful, to take his sister's place, and see that the flame of life which burned so feebly in this earthly tabernacle was fed with proper fuel. Mince pies, Welsh rarebits, sausages, and strong coffee did not strike me as strictly spiritual fare; but I listened meekly and privately resolved to shift this awful responsibility to Puah's shoulders.

Detecting me in gape,[2] after an hour of this high converse, he presented me with an overblown rose, which fell to pieces before I got out of the room, pressed my hand, and dismissed me with a fervent "God bless you, child. Don't forget the dropped[3] eggs for breakfast."

I was up betimes next morning and had the study in perfect order before the recluse appeared, enjoying a good prowl among the books as I worked and becoming so absorbed that I forgot the eggs, till a gusty sigh startled me, and I beheld Josephus, in dressing gown and slippers, languidly surveying the scene.

"Nay, do not fly," he said, as I grasped my duster in guilty haste. "It pleases me to see you here and lends a sweet, domestic charm to my solitary room. I like that graceful cap, that housewifely apron, and I beg you to wear them often; for it refreshes my eye to see something tasteful, young, and womanly about me. Eliza makes a bundle of herself and Puah is simply detestable."

He sank languidly into a chair and closed his eyes, as if the mere thought of his enemy was too much for him. I took advantage of this momentary

1. I.e., a Franklin stove, used to heat the room.
2. A yawn.
3. Poached.

prostration to slip away, convulsed with laughter at the looks and words of this bald-headed sentimentalist.

After breakfast I fell to work with a will, eager to show my powers and glad to put things to rights, for many hard jobs had evidently been waiting for a stronger arm than Puah's and a more methodical head than Eliza's.

Everything was dusty, moldy, shiftless, and neglected, except the domain of Josephus. Up-stairs the paper was dropping from the walls, the ancient furniture was all more or less dilapidated, and every hold and corner was full of relics tucked away by Puah, who was a regular old magpie. Rats and mice reveled in the empty rooms and spiders wove their tapestry undisturbed, for the old man would have nothing altered or repaired and his part of the house was fast going to ruin.

I longed to have a grand "clearing up"; but was forbidden to do more than to keep things in livable order. On the whole, it was fortunate, for I soon found that my hands would be kept busy with the realms of Josephus, whose ethereal being shrank from dust, shivered at a cold breath, and needed much cosseting with dainty food, hot fires, soft beds, and endless service, else, as he expressed it, the frail reed would break.

I regret to say that a time soon came when I felt supremely indifferent as to the breakage, and very skeptical as to the fragility of a reed that ate, slept, dawdled, and scolded so energetically. The rose that fell to pieces so suddenly was a good symbol of the rapid disappearance of all the romantic delusions I had indulged in for a time. A week's acquaintance with the inmates of this old house quite settled my opinion, and further developments only confirmed it.

Miss Eliza was a nonentity and made no more impression on me than a fly. The old gentleman passed his days in a placid sort of doze and took no notice of what went on about him. Puah had been a faithful drudge for years, and, instead of being a "wretch," was, as I soon satisfied myself, a motherly old soul, with no malice in her. The secret of Josephus's dislike was that the reverend tyrant ruled the house, and all obeyed him but Puah, who had nursed him as a baby, boxed his ears as a boy, and was not afraid of him even when he became a man and a minister. I soon repented of my first suspicions, and grew fond of her, for without my old gossip I should have fared ill when my day of tribulation came.

At first I innocently accepted the fraternal invitations to visit the study, feeling that when my day's work was done I earned a right to rest and read. But I soon found that this was not the idea. I was not to read; but to be read to. I was not to enjoy the flowers, pictures, fire, and books; but to keep them in order for my lord to enjoy. I was also to be a passive bucket, into which he was to pour all manner of philosophic, metaphysical, and sentimental rubbish. I was to serve his needs, soothe his sufferings, and sympathize with all his sorrows—be a galley slave, in fact.

As soon as I clearly understood this, I tried to put an end to it by shunning the study and never lingering there an instant after my work was done. But it availed little, for Josephus demanded much sympathy and was bound to have it. So he came and read poems while I washed dishes, discussed his pet problems all meal-times, and put reproachful notes under my door, in which were comically mingled complaints of neglect and orders for dinner.

I bore it as long as I could, and then freed my mind in a declaration of independence, delivered in the kitchen, where he found me scrubbing the

hearth. It was not an impressive attitude for an orator, nor was the occupation one a girl would choose when receiving calls; but I have always felt grateful for the intense discomfort of that moment, since it gave me the courage to rebel outright. Stranded on a small island of mat, in a sea of soapsuds, I brandished a scrubbing brush, as I indignantly informed him that I came to be a companion to his sister, not to him, and I should keep that post or none. This I followed up by reproaching him with the delusive reports he had given me of the place and its duties, and assuring him that I should not stay long unless matters mended.

"But I offer you lighter tasks, and you refuse them," he began, still hovering in the doorway, whither he had hastily retired when I opened my batteries.

"But I don't like the tasks, and consider them much worse than hard work," was my ungrateful answer, as I sat upon my island, with the softsoap conveniently near.

"Do you mean to say you prefer to scrub the hearth to sitting in my charming room while I read Hegel[4] to you?" he demanded, glaring down upon me.

"Infinitely," I responded promptly, and emphasized my words by beginning to scrub with a zeal that made the bricks white with foam.

"Is it possible!" and, with a groan at my depravity, Josephus retired, full of ungodly wrath.

I remember that I immediately burst into jocund song, so that no doubt might remain in his mind, and continued to warble cheerfully till my task was done. I also remember that I cried heartily when I got to my room, I was so vexed, disappointed, and tired. But my bower was so small I should soon have swamped the furniture if I had indulged copiously in tears; therefore I speedily dried them up, wrote a comic letter home, and waited with interest to see what would happen next.

Far be it from me to accuse one of the nobler sex of spite or the small revenge of underhand annoyances and slights to one who could not escape and would not retaliate; but after that day a curious change came over the spirit of that very unpleasant dream. Gradually all the work of the house had been slipping into my hands; for Eliza was too poorly to help and direct, and Puah too old to do much besides the cooking. About this time I found that even the roughest work was added to my share, for Josephus was unusually feeble and no one was hired to do his chores. Having made up my mind to go when the month was out, I said nothing, but dug paths, brought water from the well, split kindlings, made fires, and sifted ashes, like a true Cinderella.

There never had been any pretense of companionship with Eliza, who spent her days mulling over the fire, and seldom exerted herself except to find odd jobs for me to do—rusty knives to clean, sheets to turn, old stockings to mend, and, when all else failed, some paradise of moths and mice to be cleared up; for the house was full of such "glory holds."[5]

If I remonstrated, Eliza at once dissolved into tears and said she must do as she was told; Puah begged me to hold on till spring, when things would be much better; and pity pleaded for the two poor souls. But I don't think I

4. Georg Wilhelm Friedrich Hegel (1770–1831), German idealist philosopher whose writings are very dense.

5. I.e., glory-holes, or places where things are simply heaped together.

could have stood it if my promise had not bound me, for when the fiend said "Budge" honor said "Budge not" and I stayed.

But, being a mortal worm, I turned[6] now and then when ireful Josephus trod upon me too hard, especially in the matter of boot-blacking. I really don't know why that is considered such humiliating work for a woman; but so it is, and there I drew the line. I would have cleaned the old man's shoes without a murmur; but he preferred to keep their native rustiness intact. Eliza never went out, and Puah affected carpet-slippers of the Chinese-junk[7] pattern. Josephus, however, plumed himself upon his feet, which, like his nose, were large, and never took his walks abroad without having his boots in a high state of polish. He had brushed them himself at first; but soon after the explosion I discovered a pair of muddy boots in the shed, set suggestively near the blacking-box. I did not take the hint; feeling instinctively that this amiable being was trying how much I would bear for the sake of peace.

The boots remained untouched; and another pair soon came to keep them company, whereat I smiled wickedly as I chopped just kindlings enough for my own use. Day after day the collection grew, and neither party gave in. Boots were succeeded by shoes, then rubbers gave a pleasing variety to the long line, and then I knew the end was near.

"Why are not my boots attended to?" demanded Josephus, one evening, when obliged to go out.

"I'm sure I don't know," was Eliza's helpless answer.

"I told Louizy I guessed you'd want some of 'em before long," observed Puah with an exasperating twinkle in her old eye.

"And what did she say?" asked my lord with an ireful whack of his velvet slippers as he cast them down.

"Oh! she said she was so busy doing your other work you'd have to do that yourself; and I thought she was about right."

"Louizy" heard it all through the slide, and could have embraced the old woman for her words, but kept still till Josephus had resumed his slippers with a growl and retired to the shed, leaving Eliza in tears, Puah chuckling, and the rebellious handmaid exulting in the china-closet.

Alas! for romance and the Christian virtues, several pairs of boots were cleaned that night, and my sinful soul enjoyed the spectacle of the reverend bootblack at his task. I even found my "fancy work," as I called the evening job of pairing[8] a bucketful of hard russets with a dull knife, much cheered by the shoe-brush accompaniment played in the shed.

Thunder-clouds rested upon the martyr's brow at breakfast, and I was as much ignored as the cat. And what a relief that was! The piano was locked up, so were the bookcases, the newspapers mysteriously disappeared, and a solemn silence reigned at table, for no one dared to talk when that gifted tongue was mute. Eliza fled from the gathering storm and had a comfortable fit of neuralgia in her own room, where Puah nursed her, leaving me to skirmish with the enemy.

It was not a fair fight, and that experience lessened my respect for mankind immensely. I did my best, however—grubbed about all day and amused my

6. I.e., turned on my attacker; compare Shakespeare's *3 Henry VI* 2.2.17: "The smallest worm will turn, being trodden on."

7. A flat-bottomed boat.
8. I.e., paring (she is peeling potatoes).

dreary evenings as well as I could; too proud even to borrow a book, lest it should seem like a surrender. What a long month it was, and how eagerly I counted the hours of that last week, for my time was up Saturday and I hoped to be off at once. But when I announced my intention such dismay fell upon Eliza that my heart was touched, and Puah so urgently begged me to stay till they could get some one that I consented to remain a few days longer, and wrote posthaste to my mother, telling her to send a substitute quickly or I should do something desperate.

That blessed woman, little dreaming of all the woes I had endured, advised me to be patient, to do the generous thing, and be sure I should not regret it in the end. I groaned, submitted, and did regret it all the days of my life.

Three mortal weeks I waited; for, though two other victims came, I was implored to set them going, and tried to do it. But both fled after a day or two, condemning the place as a very hard one and calling me a fool to stand it another hour. I entirely agreed with them on both points, and, when I had cleared up after the second incapable lady, I tarried not for the coming of a third, but clutched my property and announced my departure by the next train.

Of course, Eliza wept, Puah moaned, the old man politely regretted, and the younger one washed his hands of the whole affair by shutting himself up in his room and forbidding me to say farewell because "he could not bear it." I laughed, and fancied it done for effect then; but I soon understood it better and did not laugh.

At the last moment, Eliza nervously tucked a sixpenny pocketbook into my hand and shrouded herself in the little blanket with a sob. But Puah kissed me kindly and whispered, with an odd look: "Don't blame us for anything. Some folks is liberal and some ain't." I thanked the poor old soul for her kindness to me and trudged gayly away to the station, whither my property had preceded me on a wheelbarrow, hired at my own expense.

I never shall forget that day. A bleak March afternoon, a sloppy, lonely road, and one hoarse crow stalking about a field, so like Josephus that I could not resist throwing a snowball at him. Behind me stood the dull old house, no longer either mysterious or romantic in my disenchanted eyes; before me rumbled the barrow, bearing my dilapidated wardrobe; and in my pocket reposed what I fondly hoped was, if not a liberal, at least an honest return for seven weeks of the hardest work I ever did.

Unable to resist the desire to see what my earnings were, I opened the purse and beheld *four dollars.*

I have had a good many bitter minutes in my life; but one of the bitterest came to me as I stood there in the windy road, with the sixpenny pocket-book open before me, and looked from my poor chapped, grimy, chill-blained hands to the paltry sum that was considered reward enough for all the hard and humble labor they had done.

A girl's heart is a sensitive thing. And mine had been very full lately; for it had suffered many of the trials that wound deeply yet cannot be told; so I think it as but natural that my first impulse was to go straight back to that sacred study and fling this insulting money at the feet of him who sent it. But I was so boiling over with indignation that I could not trust myself in his presence, lest I should be unable to resist the temptation to shake him, in spite of his cloth.

No, I would go home, show my honorable wounds, tell my pathetic tale, and leave my parents to avenge my wrongs. I did so; but over that harrowing scene I drop a veil, for my feeble pen refuses to depict the emotions of my outraged family. I will merely mention that the four dollars went back and the reverend Josephus never heard the last of it in that neighborhood.

My experiment seemed a dire failure and I mourned it as such for years; but more than once in my life I have been grateful for that serio-comico experience, since it has taught me many lessons. One of the most useful of these has been the power of successfully making a companion, not a servant, of those whose aid I need, and helping to gild their honest wages with the sympathy and justice which can sweeten the humblest and lighten the hardest task.

1874

ADAH ISAACS MENKEN
1835–1868

Performing in an equestrian melodrama based on a poem by Lord Byron and titled *Mazeppa: or The Wild Horse of Tartary,* Adah Isaacs Menken stripped to a flesh-colored body stocking that made her look nude, then was strapped to a horse: astride the steed whipped to a gallop, she hurtled down a narrow ramp extending into the audience. This startling role brought international renown, which she promoted by means of all the publicity measures available to her: she distributed her photograph for display in the shop windows of the cities she toured, cropped her dark hair close to her head, smoked cigarettes ostentatiously in public, married four times (once to the heavyweight boxing champion of the world, John C. Heenan), and was reported to have been involved in compromising situations with the French author Alexandre Dumas and the English writer Algernon Swinburne, with the result that scandals erupted. For example, many of Swinburne's readers thought that Menken was the model for "Dolores," a poem infused with masochistic imagery. In wide currency among some Victorian circles was a rumor about why Menken broke off their relationship: to the poet Dante Gabriel Rossetti, she reportedly explained that "it was difficult to get Algernon 'up to scratch'" and "I can't make him understand that biting's no use." By the age of thirty-three, when she died in Paris, she and many others had fabricated multiple stories contributing to her bad-girl image, which has made it difficult for contemporary scholars to discern the facts about her life.

One controversy surrounds her religion, for some biographical accounts state that Menken was raised a Catholic by her parents in Louisiana, and that she converted to Judaism after marrying her first husband; however, she herself claimed to have been born Jewish and to have adhered to Judaism throughout her career. In any case, Menken did learn Hebrew so as to study classical Jewish texts, and she contributed poems as well as essays to the weekly *Israelite,* after she and her first husband, Alexander Isaacs Menken, moved to Cincinnati. In her second and her fourth marriage, Menken gave birth to sons—George Sand served as godmother to the second baby— but both died in infancy. A stage celebrity in America and Europe, Menken relished hobnobbing and corresponding with such literary luminaries as the young Samuel Clemens, Bret Harte, Charles Dickens, Rossetti, Dumas, and Swinburne. Although her last three husbands were gentile and George Sand had convinced her to baptize

her second baby, Menken was visited by a rabbi as she was dying (of peritonitis or tuberculosis, it is now believed), and she was buried in the Jewish section of Paris's Montparnasse Cemetery. The dramatic monologues "Judith," written from the perspective of a sensuous and wild woman who holds "with iron grasp the battle axe," like "Myself," appeared in Menken's only volume of verse, *Infelicia* (1868), which was published posthumously.

Judith[1]

> "Repent, or I will come unto thee quickly, and will fight thee with the sword of my mouth."
>
> —Revelation, ii.16.

I

Ashkelon[2] is not cut off with the remnant of a valley.
Baldness dwells not upon Gaza.
The field of the valley is mine, and it is clothed in verdure.
The steepness of Baal-perazim is mine;
5 And the Philistines[3] spread themselves in the valley of Rephaim.
They shall yet be delivered into my hands.
For the God of Battles has gone before me!
The sword of the mouth shall smite them to dust.
I have slept in the darkness—
10 But the seventh angel[4] woke me, and giving me a sword of flame,
 points to the blood-ribbed cloud, that lifts his reeking head above the mountain.
Thus am I the prophet.
I see the dawn that heralds to my waiting soul the advent of power.
 Power that will unseal the thunders!
 Power that will give voice to graves!
15 Graves of the living;
 Graves of the dying;
 Graves of the sinning;
 Graves of the loving;
 Graves of despairing;
20 And oh! graves of the deserted!
These shall speak, each as their voices shall be loosed.
And the day is dawning.

II

Stand back, ye Philistines!
Practise what ye preach to me;
25 I heed ye not, for I know ye all.

1. The story of Judith, clearly a work of fiction, is told in the Book of Judith. When the Assyrian army besieged the city of Bethulia (probably an invented name for Shechem, in the hill country of Israel), a beautiful widow, Judith, pretended to betray her people; she tricked Nebuchadnezzar's general, Holofernes, into entertaining her and, when he was in a drunken stupor, beheaded him.

2. A Mediterranean seaport just north of Gaza, capital of the Canaanite kings and later a major Philistine city; it was destroyed by Nebuchadnezzar, king of Assyria, in 604 B.C.E.
3. Enemies of the ancient Israelites.
4. The angel that announces Judgment Day (Revelation 10.1–7).

Ye are living burning lies, and profanation to the garments which with
 stately steps ye sweep your marble palaces.
Your palaces of Sin, around which the damning evidence of guilt
 hangs like a reeking vapor.
Stand back!
I would pass up the golden road of the world.
30 A place in the ranks awaits me.
I know that ye are hedged on the borders of my path.
Lie and tremble, for ye well know that I hold with iron grasp the battle
 axe.
Creep back to your dark tents in the valley.
Slouch back to your haunts of crime.
35 Ye do not know me, neither do ye see me.
But the sword of my mouth[5] is unsealed, and ye coil yourselves in
 slime and bitterness at my feet.
I mix your jewelled heads, and your gleaming eyes, and your hissing
 tongues with the dust.
My garments shall bear no mark of ye.
When I shall return this sword to the angel, your foul blood will not
 stain its edge.
40 It will glimmer with the light of truth, and the strong arm shall rest.

III

Stand back!
I am no Magdalene[6] waiting to kiss the hem of your garment.
It is mid-day.
See ye not what is written on my forehead?
45 I am Judith!
I wait for the head of my Holofernes!
Ere the last tremble of the conscious death agony shall have shud-
 dered, I will show it to ye with the long black hair clinging to the
 glazed eyes, and the great mouth opened in search of voice, and
 the strong throat all hot and reeking with blood, that will thrill
 me with wild unspeakable joy as it courses down my bare body
 and dabbles my cold feet!
My sensuous soul will quake with the burden of so much bliss.
Oh, what wild passionate kisses will I draw up from that bleeding
 mouth!
50 I will strangle this pallid throat of mine on the sweet blood!
I will revel in my passion.
At midnight I will feast on it in the darkness.
For it was that which thrilled its crimson tides of reckless passion
 through the blue veins of my life, and made them leap up in the
 wild sweetness of Love and agony of Revenge!
55 I am starving for this feast.
Oh forget not that I am Judith!
And I know where sleeps Holofernes.

1868

5. See Revelation 19.15: "And out of his mouth
goeth a sharp sword, that with it he should smite
the nations."
6. I.e., a prostitute; the Mary Magdalene healed

of evil spirits by Jesus (Luke 8.2) is traditionally
identified with the prostitute who kisses and
anoints his feet (Luke 7.37–48).

Myself

"La patience est amère; mais le fruit en est doux!"[1]

I

Away down into the shadowy depths of the Real I once lived.
I thought that to seem was to be.
But the waters of Marah[2] were beautiful, yet they were bitter.
I waited, and hoped, and prayed;
5 Counting the heart-throbs and the tears that answered them.
Through my earnest pleadings for the True, I learned that the mildest
 mercy of life was a smiling sneer;
And that the business of the world was to lash with vengeance all who
 dared to be what their God had made them.
Smother back tears to the red blood of the heart!
10 Crush out things called souls!
No room for them here!

II

Now I gloss my pale face with laughter, and sail my voice on with the
 tide.
Decked in jewels and lace, I laugh beneath the gaslight's glare, and
 quaff the purple wine.
But the minor-keyed soul is standing naked and hungry upon one of
 Heaven's high hills of light.
Standing and waiting for the blood of the feast!
15 Starving for one poor word!
Waiting for God to launch out some beacon on the boundless shores
 of this Night.
Shivering for the uprising of some soft wing under which it may creep,
 lizard-like, to warmth and rest.
Waiting! Starving and shivering!

III

Still I trim my white bosom with crimson roses; for none shall see the
 thorns.
20 I bind my aching brow with a jewelled crown, that none shall see the
 iron one beneath.
My silver-sandaled feet keep impatient time to the music, because I
 cannot be calm.
I laugh at earth's passion-fever of Love; yet I know that God is near to
 the soul on the hill, and hears the ceaseless ebb and flow of a
 hopeless love, through all my laughter.
But if I can cheat my heart with the old comfort, that love can be for-
 gotten, is it not better?

1. Patience is bitter; but its fruit is sweet!
(French). Slightly misquoted from Jean-Jacques
Rousseau's *Julie; or, The New Heloise* (1761).

2. Literally, "Bitterness"; these waters were made
sweet for the the people of Israel to drink after
Moses led them out of Egypt (Exodus 15.22–25).

After all, living is but to play a part!
25 The poorest worm would be a jewel-headed snake if she could!

IV

All this grandeur of glare and glitter has its nighttime.
The pallid eyelids must shut-out smiles and daylight.
Then I fold my cold hands, and look down at the restless rivers of a
 love that rushes through my life.
Unseen and unknown they tide on over black rocks and chasms of
 Death.
30 Oh, for one sweet word to bridge their terrible depths!
O jealous soul! why wilt thou crave and yearn for what thou canst not
 have?
And life is so long—so long.

V

With the daylight comes the business of living.
The prayers that I sent trembling up the golden thread of hope all
 come back to me.
35 I lock them close in my bosom, far under the velvet and roses of the
 world.
For I know that stronger than these torrents of passion is the soul that
 hath lifted itself up to the hill.
What care I for his careless laugh?
I do not sigh; but I know that God hears the life-blood dripping as I,
 too, laugh.
I would not be thought a foolish rose, that flaunts her red heart out to
 the sun.
40 Loving is not living!

VI

Yet through all this I know that night will roll back from the still, gray
 plain of heaven, and that my triumph shall rise sweet with the
 dawn!
When these mortal mists shall unclothe the world, then shall I be
 known as I am!
When I dare be dead and buried behind a wall of wings, then shall he
 know me!
When this world shall fall, like some old ghost, wrapped in the black
 skirts of the wind, down into the fathomless eternity of fire, then
 shall souls uprise!
45 When God shall lift the frozen seal[3] from struggling voices, then shall
 we speak!
When the purple-and-gold of our inner natures shall be lighted up in
 the Eternity of Truth, then will love be mine!
I can wait.

1868

3. An allusion to the seven seals opened at the Apocalypse (Revelation 6–10).

Turn-of-the-Century
Literature

A MAJOR SHIFT IN GENDER RELATIONS

Speaking about women's labor, the rebellious heroine of Olive Schreiner's *The Story of an African Farm* (1883) exclaims, "*we* bear the world, and *we* make it." Her brash affirmation of female creative primacy would be symbolized ten years later in America by the Woman's Building at the World's Columbian Exposition in Chicago. This building—the first that was funded, managed, and designed entirely by women—included Mary Cassatt's mural depicting "woman apart from her relations to man" and exhibits dedicated to British nurses, African American and Euro-American inventors, Continental artisans, and Eastern explorers as well as the first international collection of women's books gathered by women. Opening in 1893, the same year that New Zealand granted women the vote and the British Parliament passed the last of the Married Woman's Property Acts, the Woman's Building expressed the confidence that women felt in looking back on more than a century of unusual accomplishments.

Yet the antilynching journalist Ida B. Wells-Barnett was not alone in protesting the exclusion of African Americans from the opening ceremonies and governing committees of the Chicago's World Fair. Protests against the whiteness of what was often dubbed the "White City" led the World's Congress of Representative Women to invite such black activists as Frances E. W. Harper and Anna Julia Cooper to speak. Their inclusion typifies the ways in which womanhood began to be pluralized during a period when women from various ethnic and economic backgrounds began to publish. By 1900, women with diverse perspectives had become, in the words of the feminist historian Ray Strachey, "free both in their persons and their properties, their money and their consciences, their bodies and their souls." For this reason, as another cultural historian, Theodore Roszak, has demonstrated, "the 'woman problem' had become one of the most earthshattering debates in the Western world[;] . . . by the final decades of the century, it permeated everything." Between the 1880s and the outbreak of World War I in 1914, female lives and letters on both sides of the Atlantic were transformed by the entrance of large numbers of women into the labor force, by increased educational opportunities, and by the emergence of militant suffragism. It is hardly surprising, then, that many literary figures in this period felt that they were living between two worlds, one dead and the other struggling to be born. Nor is it surprising that both sexes frequently associated accelerating historical changes with the rapidly shifting situation of many differently positioned women. For as the Victorian age turned into the mod-

ern period, women's revolt was a dramatic component in a series of violent challenges to the social order that were posed by artists, workers, colonized peoples, social reformers, and freethinkers.

A Transitional Age

While it may be convenient to mark the end of the Victorian period as the year 1901, when Queen Victoria died after a sixty-four-year reign and Theodore Roosevelt began to make the White House his "bully pulpit," there was a growing realization throughout the last three decades of the nineteenth century and the first decade of the twentieth century that a major historical revolution was in the making. Already in 1873, Mark Twain and Charles Dudley Warner were calling the age "gilded" rather than golden, for they were appalled by the crass materialism that was turning America into a world power, a rival to England in industrial leadership. Many intellectuals agreed that Victorianism was dead, though they disagreed about the exact date of its demise: the English libertarian Edward Carpenter and the American historian Henry Adams associated this transition with the 1880s and 1890s, respectively; the poet William Butler Yeats triumphantly announced that "Victorianism had been defeated in the year 1900"; and the novelist Virginia Woolf dated that defeat to 1910, the year when Victoria's successor, King Edward VII, died. Some of Woolf's friends took the publication of Lytton Strachey's *Eminent Victorians* (1918) as the symbolic end of the nineteenth century, for Strachey's book attacked head-on the respectability, earnestness, industriousness, piety, and propriety of his parents' generation.

Strachey's scathing rejection of the bourgeois values he associated with Victorian complacency had been anticipated in the 1870s, when the novelist Samuel Butler criticized the patriarchal family, the church, the law, scientific theories based on evolution, and faith in progress through technology. Indeed, throughout the late nineteenth century, there were symptoms of a breakdown of certainty and a growing alienation of intellectuals from society. Late Victorians and early modernists alike confronted nineteenth-century economic prosperity from a disillusioned perspective, born in part of their dissatisfaction with the literary marketplace, because the rapid commercialization of literature—accelerated by the higher literacy rate associated with the growth of elementary school education, made compulsory in 1870—had led to the formation of a mass reading audience. Not a few writers echoed the protests of the novelist George Gissing, who deplored the mediocrity encouraged by the economics driving literary production. At the same time, however, a number of artists felt constrained by the moralistic standards still maintained by publishers. Outrage over the sexual explicitness of Thomas Hardy's *Jude the Obscure* (1895) so angered Hardy that he decided to devote himself exclusively to writing poetry. Thus authors and readers in both England and America began to witness a schism between a financially successful popular culture and what was considered genuine "high" art.

The writers who most flamboyantly thumbed their noses at respectable Victorian virtues, even as they sought to elevate the status of art by eliminating its utilitarian function, were the so-called aesthetes. In England, the aesthetic movement espoused the slogan "art for art's sake," the doctrine that the true artistic spirit eschews conventional morality to maintain the integrity of individual vision. As the phrase *fin de siècle* (end of the century)

itself suggests, the aesthetes' stylization of the self and of art was profoundly affected by French ideas, especially the ideas of poets such as Charles Baudelaire and Arthur Rimbaud, both of whom were represented in Arthur Symons's *The Symbolist Movement in Literature* (1899). According to these thinkers, the artist was not to preach societal reformation but, in the words of Walter Pater in *Studies in the History of the Renaissance* (1873), "to burn always with [a] hard gem-like flame," for "art comes to you proposing frankly to give nothing but the highest quality to your moments as they pass, and simply for those moments' sake."

The erotic poetry of Algernon Charles Swinburne, the baroque and sometimes pornographic drawings of Aubrey Beardsley, and the figure of the dandy began to epitomize what was considered the "decadence" of this movement, while Oscar Wilde's homosexuality became a notorious emblem of bohemian defiance that was castigated in America from countless pulpits. Wilde's hero in *The Picture of Dorian Gray* (1891) perfectly captured the era's mood of exhausted satiety when he responded to the *fin de siècle* by sighing, "I wish it were *fin du globe*." Throughout "the mauve decade" or "the gay nineties," such periodicals as *The Yellow Book* and *The Chap-Book* flaunted the quest for a deliberately abnormal, exotic, and titillating style. Frank Harris's long-banned four-volume history of his sexual escapades, *My Life and Loves* (1922–27), and the dances of the American Isadora Duncan, performed in free-flowing robes and bare feet, defied puritanical codes as assiduously as did the art of the aesthetes.

Of course, many writers rejected the sensationalism and world-weariness of the aesthetes, but even the eminent late Victorians George Meredith and Rudyard Kipling developed highly innovative styles: Meredith used an elaborately elliptical prose in novels that ridicule the presumption of masculine superiority, while Kipling wrote stories and poems in dialects that capture the unique perspectives of everyday soldiers and citizens. A major transformation in literary history was reflected, too, in the lyrical and novelistic experimentation of many other artists in this period. Throughout the 1870s and 1880s, Walt Whitman issued revised editions of *Leaves of Grass* (first published in 1855), to the acclaim of such English men of letters as William Michael Rossetti and Swinburne. Several years later, Emily Dickinson's unconventional lyrics began to appear in America, while in England the Jesuit poet Gerard Manley Hopkins revived archaic words, coined compound phrases, and invented a new theory of rhythm in startlingly alliterative poetry that would not be published until 1918. In addition, Henry James and Joseph Conrad exploited in their fiction and explained in their critical prefaces their own complex uses of multiple narrators and points of view, thus helping to transform the novel into a more self-consciously literary form than it had ever been before.

Like the modernists Ezra Pound, Gertrude Stein, and James Joyce, Henry James was an expatriate in an art world that defined itself as an international elite. International experimentation also characterized the age's music and painting. The art critic Roger Fry selected for exhibition in London canvases by impressionists such as Édouard Manet, Paul Cézanne, and Vincent Van Gogh, together with paintings by the postimpressionists Henri Matisse and Pablo Picasso. Through such different events in music history as the dramatist George Bernard Shaw's defense of Richard Wagner's mythically struc-

tured operas in *The Perfect Wagnerite* (1898) and Anton von Webern's creation of atonal scores (*Passacaglia*, 1908), conventional ideas of representation and reality were being broken down, as they were also in the literature that began to appear in newly created "little magazines." With the emergence of modernism in the years directly before the outbreak of World War I, many artists had begun to engage in an open rebellion against society at large, for they were demonstrating how all established forms of intellectual and moral certainty had lost their legitimacy.

Industrialization

What intensified such artists' feelings that they were living in a transitional time were the rise of the industrial city and the rapid advances in national wealth and population that were associated with the development of capitalism in this period. Both American and English societies were transformed by mass production techniques employed in large factories powered by ever more complicated machines. Exciting new technological prospects also opened up with the invention of the electric lightbulb (1879), the production of radio shortwaves (1887), the marketing of the Kodak camera (1888), the development of wireless telegraphy (1895), the discovery of radiation by the Curies (1897–1901), and the first flight by the Wright brothers (1903). In 1895, newly invented automobiles were entered in their first race (only six were able to start and their speed averaged 5.25 miles per hour) and the Underwood Typewriter Company began to market machines that enabled the typist to see what was being typed: both the car and the typewriter would quickly become enormously popular. Louis Sullivan's soaring office buildings, the construction of the Brooklyn Bridge (1869–83), and the Lumière brothers' first public screening of motion picture shorts (1895) were only the most dramatic signs of how the new technology would shape modern architecture and art. Exhilarated by unfolding possibilities for personal success, popular novelists like Horatio Alger continued to publish best-selling books promulgating an ethic of individual enterprise.

But many social critics felt that the replacement of the mid-nineteenth-century civil "war for freedom" by the "war for the dollar" dramatized all the inequities of industrialization. In America, a number of "robber barons" or captains of industry had amassed huge fortunes, which they displayed in the ornate mansions of New York and Chicago. Such ostentation led the American economist Thorstein Veblen to write *The Theory of the Leisure Class* (1899). For the American novelist Edith Wharton, the conspicuous consumption of New York high society—its lavish garden parties, silver-backed hairbrushes, visiting cards, and ostentatious boxes at the opera—illustrated the immorality of a class that considered only bankruptcy a sin. While industrial development in this period proceeded more slowly in England than in the United States, both countries witnessed the growth of joint stock companies, syndicates, trusts, mergers, holding companies, and interlocking boards of directors. With the growing use of electrical energy for domestic lighting and industrial power, as well as the introduction of diesel engines, subways, plastics, refrigeration, and canning, the Industrial Revolution began to bring comparative comfort to many people for the first time. But the extension of manhood suffrage, the institution of minimum wage laws,

and the passage of child labor laws did little to alleviate the economic suffering that resulted from recurrent unemployment, overproduction, and wage cutbacks.

Thus, although a number of religious leaders claimed that "God has intended the great to be great and the little to be little," and so-called social Darwinists argued that the poor had proven themselves to be "evolutionary misfits" who deserved to be destroyed by the economic system, the working class began in this period to organize for collective bargaining to attain job security, shorter hours, better conditions, and higher wages. Labor unions in England developed comparatively peacefully until 1906, when their effort to get working-class spokesmen into Parliament resulted in the creation of the Labour Party; but in America the rise of unions was dramatic and bloody. After more than 110,000 miles of railroad track were built across the American continent in the 1860s and 1870s, for example, the railroad strikes of 1877, 1886, and 1894 provoked judicial and governmental opposition. The Homestead, Pennsylvania, steel strike (1892) was matched in England by the 1888 strike of Bryant and May's match girls, many of whom suffered from a cancer called "phossy-jaw," caused by the phosphorus into which they dipped matches. Both skilled and unskilled workers in England and America used meetings, leaflets, lockouts, boycotts, picketing, strikes, syndicalism (general strikes), and legislative lobbying to cope with the exploitation and oppression that Karl Marx had outlined in *Das Kapital* (1867–94), that the socialists Beatrice and Sidney Webb had described in their jointly authored *The History of Trade Unionism* (1894) and *Industrial Democracy* (1897), and that Emma Goldman addressed in radical speeches as well as essays.

Besides leading to such public activity and political theory, utopian socialism was at least in part responsible for the growth of fantastic fiction at the turn of the century. On the one hand, H. G. Wells believed that the split between rich and poor had produced two distinct races, and in *The Time Machine* (1895), a pioneering science fiction novel, he implied that the working-class tenders of machines would cannibalize the effete and idle rich. Edward Bellamy, on the other hand, wrote a popular "fairy tale of social felicity" titled *Looking Backward* (1888), in which a future collectivity eradicates all the evils of private enterprise. In addition, the poet William Morris developed utopian ideas about the aesthetic manufacturing of furniture and home decorations, ideas that contributed to the formation of the Arts and Crafts movement.

Growing social militancy also resulted in an interest in literary "realism" and "naturalism." In France, the realistic presentation of average people in middle-class society by the novelist Honoré de Balzac (especially in the works making up *The Human Comedy,* 1830–50) had been succeeded by naturalism, the movement in fiction that approached working-class characters in terms of biological inheritance and economic determinism. The Goncourt brothers and Émile Zola attempted to present their readers "with a living model, or rather life itself with its entrails warm and active, its guts palpitating." As early as 1900, the Philadelphia painter Thomas Eakins discouraged his students from studying classical busts and took them instead to a bone-boiling establishment to dissect horses. George Moore, Arnold Bennett, and John Galsworthy carried on the realistic tradition in English novels

about the manners of the genteel and the morals of the poor, while Frank Norris, Upton Sinclair, and Theodore Dreiser developed naturalism in America.

Given their quasi-scientific interest in cultural subsections of the population, a number of these writers appeared to agree with the novelist William Dean Howells that "our life is too large for our art to be broad." Both in ethnic and in regional literature, turn-of-the-century artists charted rapid changes in society, which had affected different portions of the population in various ways. Ethnic voices began to articulate the special perspective of the some thirteen million immigrants who arrived in New York City between 1890 and 1919 from eastern Europe and southern Italy. Among Jewish writers, for example, Emma Lazarus wrote "The New Colossus," for the "huddled masses yearning to breathe free." The Danish American reformer Jacob Riis portrayed slum life in *How the Other Half Lives* (1890). Similarly, whether addressing the problems of rural villages in England or New England, such turn-of-the-century regionalists as Thomas Hardy and Mary E. Wilkins Freeman attempted to capture the uniqueness of the local customs and landscapes that frame their characters' lives. In poetry, too, A. E. Housman and Edwin Arlington Robinson described the obscure destinies of Shropshire lads and Maine butchers, while James Whitcomb Riley and Paul Laurence Dunbar gained popularity through dialect verse. Whether they were resigned or rebellious, writers had turned their attention to much distinctively new subject matter.

The Rise and Fall of Empire

Just as nineteenth-century monopoly capitalism had developed huge corporations, nineteenth-century imperialism had portioned the entire globe into spheres of influence. Strong national pride and economic expediency caused both the English and the American governments to consolidate their colonial holdings throughout this period. The rise of imperialist fervor was perhaps most striking in America, for the expanding United States strengthened its hold on the American West, even as it began to exert its influence over foreign states. On the domestic front, large firms controlled the many transcontinental railroad lines that, for the first time, connected the eastern states to what had been the western wilderness. A vast section of northern Oklahoma Territory was leased to settler-farmers in 1893, the year that Frederick Jackson Turner attended the World's Columbian Exposition to present his famous thesis about the closing of the frontier. In 1912, the last states of the original forty-eight—New Mexico and Arizona—were admitted to the Union.

The subjugation of Native Americans—a process that concluded in this period—was accompanied by opportunities for foreign conquest offered by a new policy of international imperialism. The Spanish-American War (1898) led to America's first acquisition of noncontiguous colonies with substantial populations: Hawaii, Puerto Rico, the Philippines, and Cuba were colonized in a course of action that President McKinley described as America's "manifest destiny." According to his successor, Theodore Roosevelt, "the nation that has trained itself to a career of unwarlike and isolated ease is bound, in the end, to go down before other nations which have not lost the manly and adventurous virtues." Although the Monroe Doctrine (1823) was supposed to prevent European intervention in the Western Hemisphere,

the construction of the Panama Canal (1904–14) demonstrated how this policy could be used to justify the intervention of the United States in Latin America. Countless legislators lauded the nobility of taking up what the British writer Rudyard Kipling called the "white man's burden."

As Kipling's famous phrase suggests, the glamorization of militaristic nationalism in America mirrored European jingoism. An ideology of aggression, which some historians associate with the international events that led to World War I, was implicit in the imperialist expansion of England. Benjamin Disraeli's "Big England" policy had resulted in the purchase of Suez Canal shares in 1875 and his proclamation of Queen Victoria as "Empress of India" in 1876. By 1894, England was signing the Congo Treaty with King Leopold II of Belgium, gaining both countries leases in Africa. In 1900 the British Empire covered nearly twenty million square miles and contained three hundred million people, and the newly created Girl Guides were themselves guided by a handbook that was subtitled *How Girls Can Help Build the Empire*.

Even in its heyday, however, there were strong reactions against empire building, among them the Indian Mutiny in 1857, the Jamaica Rebellion in 1865, and the massacre of General Gordon and his troops at Khartoum, in the Sudan, in 1885. The Anglo-Boer War in South Africa (1899–1902) not only showed that a small number of Dutch settlers could challenge English right and might but was also the first war protested by many British intellectuals. In 1905 the pamphlet *The Decline and Fall of the British Empire* sold thousands of copies in several months, reflecting widespread belief that the empire might have passed its peak. Moreover, just when it seemed that the sun literally could not set on the British Empire, Joseph Conrad provided one of the most scathing critiques of the European invasion of Africa in *Heart of Darkness* (1899): the "white man's burden," Conrad implied, was less an ennobling mission to civilize the native African populations than a mercenary effort to wrest wealth from them.

While Cecil Rhodes, prime minister of the Cape Colony (South Africa), and the South African writer Olive Schreiner were disagreeing about the moral influence of the English presence in Africa, a number of black intellectuals in America were redefining their situation through an effort to re-imagine their relationship to their ancestors' native continent. To some extent, the dialogues between such men as Booker T. Washington, W. E. B. Du Bois, and Marcus Garvey presented what in our time remain the parameters of African American identity. Certainly each confronted the racism rampant in America after the abolition of slavery: the Ku Klux Klan, first organized in 1866, was reborn much stronger in 1915; in 1896, *Plessy v. Ferguson* legalized public segregation; and between 1885 and 1910, more than thirty-five hundred lynchings occurred. To deal with their existence as in some sense a colonized people, Washington, Du Bois, and Garvey proposed to blacks different courses of liberation: integration with the dominant culture or an ideology of separatism. While in *Up from Slavery* (1901) Washington counseled self-improvement, which he gauged by white standards, Du Bois espoused "Pan-Africanism" during his editorship of the magazine *Crisis*, and Garvey headed the Universal Negro Improvement Association in an effort to raise racial pride and liberate Africa from colonial rule.

Both Du Bois and Garvey understood the need for cultural identity that

was informing the growth of jazz in black urban communities. By 1904 Ma Rainey was touring America in a song-and-dance team with her husband, and by 1907 Bessie Smith was singing the blues at the Ivory Theatre in Chattanooga, Tennessee. Similarly, on numerous reservations throughout the Southwest, American Indian communities attempted to preserve their traditional rituals and languages after the genocide perpetrated by the government's "pacification" programs. In 1879 Susette La Flesche (or Inshta Theumba, which means "Bright Eyes") began the lecture tours on behalf of Native American rights that would inspire Helen Hunt Jackson to write her indictments of governmental Indian policies, *A Century of Dishonor* (1881) and *Ramona* (1884).

At the same time that white supremacy was coming under attack in America, England experienced the growing dissent expressed by colonial rebellions that gained momentum throughout this period. Perhaps in response to such agitation, independence movements (which often excluded native populations) helped convert Canada into a federation in 1867, Australia into a commonwealth in 1900, and New Zealand into a separate dominion in 1907, as well as establishing the Union of South Africa in 1909. Most dramatically, in Ireland Charles Stewart Parnell led the Home Rule Party in its demands for a separate Irish legislature. Parnell suffered political disaster in 1890, after he was named as a co-respondent in a divorce suit; however, rising Irish protests against British rule continued up to the beginning of the century, when the radical Sinn Fein movement became more violent, and through World War I, when Irish patriots sought help from England's enemy, Germany. The Irish Literary Revival (or the Irish Renaissance, as it is sometimes called) was the literary expression of Irish nationalism.

Standish James O'Grady's histories of Ireland (1878, 1880) and Douglas Hyde's translations of Gaelic poetry shaped William Butler Yeats's poems on Irish heroic legends. Indeed, whether Yeats expressed disillusionment with public response to the nationalist movement ("romantic Ireland's dead and gone") or sympathy with the suffering of the militants ("a terrible beauty is born"), his poetry was as grounded in Celtic mythology and Irish politics as were the plays of Lady Augusta Gregory, the aristocrat who directed Dublin's Abbey Theatre with him. From the middle of the nineteenth century, when Oscar Wilde's mother wrote for *The Nation*, to 1914, when James Joyce's short stories, *Dubliners*, appeared in print, Ireland witnessed an extraordinary literary revival.

The Death of God

In the face of widespread discontent with the distribution of wealth and intense debates about the imperialist mission, organized religion also came under attack. Earlier in the century God might seem in some circles to have disappeared, but he was now declared "dead" by the German philosopher Friedrich Nietzsche (1844–1900). After several decades of Darwinian speculation on the origins of the universe and a quarter century of scholarship investigating the historical backgrounds of the Bible, even so conservative a writer as the British novelist Mrs. Humphrey Ward questioned the literal truth of revelation. Like Thomas Hardy, moreover, a number of artists felt "God-Forsaken" by a deity indifferent to human suffering or, again like Hardy, they believed the world to be determined by mere chance or "Crass Casualty." In England, but more especially in America, many intellectuals

and artists were disaffected by the crusading fervor of the evangelicalism that fueled the temperance and worldwide mission movements, for the rhetoric of some Protestant crusaders seemed dangerously antiforeigner, antiblack, anti-Catholic, and anti-Semitic. In the place of orthodox faith, what the American philosopher William James (1842–1910) called "varieties of religious experience" began to proliferate.

An explosion of interest in alternative religions was fostered by and in turn fostered the development of anthropology. Sir James Frazer's study of primitive rituals in *The Golden Bough* (1890–1915) and Andrew Lang's *Myth, Ritual, and Religion* (1887) contributed to the dethronement of religious orthodoxy through their analyses of pagan mythology and folklore. In addition, Madame Blavatsky, the founder of the Theosophical Society (1875), conflated Christianity and other religions when she argued in *The Secret Doctrine* (1888) that Jesus was an incarnation of Buddha. The Tarot, astrology, and the Kabbalah were studied in occult groups like the Golden Dawn, which supplied the poet Yeats—an inveterate attender of séances—with much of his esoteric imagery. At the same time, psychologists, and in particular psychologists of religion, emphasized the human origins of all faiths: not only did William James analyze how all religions seek to heal humanity's sense of unease but the philosopher George Santayana (1863–1952) claimed that "religion and poetry are identical in essence," elevating the human imagination to a redemptive force. And, of course, religious beliefs continued to remain an important subject of and inspiration for poetry in the work of such different writers as Alice Meynell, Amy Levy, and the pseudonymous Michael Field (Katherine Harris Bradley and her niece Edith Emma Cooper).

But, as the unconventional lives of the couple known as Michael Field attest, the so-called death of God also resulted in an ideology of sexual liberation. The birth control advocate Annie Besant, for example, was drawn to Eastern forms of mysticism that she viewed as less puritanical than Christianity. With the publication of Edward Carpenter's *Love's Coming of Age* (1896) and Havelock Ellis's *Studies in the Psychology of Sex* (1897–1928), the subject of human sexuality began to emerge as a field of scientific inquiry, one that was soon to be more closely studied by the Viennese psychoanalyst Sigmund Freud (1856–1939), whose dream interpretations and studies of hysteria began to be translated into English in the first two decades of the twentieth century. In part because of the discourse of "sexology," new words—*homosexual, lesbian, heterosexual*—began to circulate in medical, sociological, and literary circles. Arguing for toleration of homosexuality and for an acceptance of sexuality as part of human behavior, both Carpenter and Ellis saw themselves as liberating modern humanity from Victorian prudery. Although Carpenter, Ellis, and Freud were criticized or censured for their explicit treatment of desire, the complexities of sexual identity would quickly become major topics for poets and novelists.

IMAGES OF WOMEN

Not only did women participate in all the movements that challenged the balance of power among classes and nations but they were also in the process of fomenting a social revolution that would radically change the relationship

between the sexes. As the cultural historian Samuel Hynes has explained, this "revolution had many implications besides the sexual," for it "involved legal, political, and economic issues, and touched on property ownership, the franchise, higher education, the birth rate, laws of marriage and divorce, the protocol of the court, and the future of the empire—in short, on nearly every aspect of . . . society." In this context, it is hardly surprising that by 1920, when Arnold Bennett published *Our Women,* he was arguing that "sex-discord" had "noticeably developed since Coventry Patmore wrote *The Angel in the House*" (1858), a poem that celebrated the virtues of the ideal bride. Patmore's ideology of feminine renunciation and domesticity continued to be influential at the turn of the century, but artists and intellectuals tended to confront what the scholar Martha Vicinus has called women's "widening sphere" more directly and overtly, whether as opponents or as advocates, as the period progressed. While moralists, educators, and physicians continued to explain to women why they should lead decorous, selfless private lives as wives and mothers, a number of artists responded angrily or triumphantly to the fact that many women no longer did so.

Patmore's exemplary woman, for example, continued to haunt Henry Adams, who argued in *The Education of Henry Adams* (1907) that modern scientific energy, typified by the dynamo, had to be countered by the eternal beauty and potency he identified with the medieval figure of the Virgin. Though Adams viewed the demise of the Virgin and the rise of the dynamo with trepidation, countless writers argued that women could counter the evils of industrial life if they remained within the home. But domesticity was also assumed to constitute women's primary source of satisfaction. John Cordy Jeaffreson's popular novel *A Woman in Spite of Herself* (1872) dramatized the pleasure with which its heroine relinquishes the male costume circumstances had required of her; she is relieved to admit her femininity and accept a marriage proposal that will allow her to demonstrate "the never-ceasing, ever-active delight that a true woman feels" in being the "watchful ministrant, enthusiastic slave of the man to whom she has given her heart."

Even while works such as Jeaffreson's and Patmore's celebrated this angelic ministrant and slave, much late Victorian and early-twentieth-century literature anxiously meditated on her disappearance. Henry A. Jones's play *The Case of Rebellious Susan* (1894), for example, included a scene in which an older man lectures a henpecking, selfish wife who refuses to serve dinner "while the present inequalities between the sexes remain unredressed": "Nature's darling woman," he explains to her, "is a stay-at-home woman, a woman who wants to be a good wife and a good mother, and cares very little for anything else." "Go home!" he concludes, as if anticipating the defensive stridency of the hero in Harley Granville-Barker's play *The Madras House* (1910), who argues that "women haven't morals or intellect in our sense of the words. . . . Shut them away from public life and public exhibition."

At the same time, imperiled as the Victorian cult of feminine purity was felt to be, the ideology of separate sexual spheres was used to argue that women had feminized a previously virile culture. In countless adventure tales in which boys such as Mark Twain's Huck (in *The Adventures of Huckleberry Finn,* 1884) and Robert Louis Stevenson's Jim Hawkins (in *Treasure Island,* 1883) hear and respond to the call of the wild, they are fleeing from a society

associated not only with moralistic women but with women whose refinement symbolizes the confinement of civilization. Turn-of-the-century literature abounded with images of Mrs. Grundy, a priggish puritan whose excessive zeal for gentility makes life unendurable for real men. Yet women's supposed purity was still deployed by advocates and critics of women's increasingly active role in public life: legislators on both sides of the Atlantic argued, on the one hand, that women would purify politics if they were allowed to participate and, on the other hand, that women would be defiled by such participation. Moreover, even as women's angelic status was being characterized as repressive or endangered, the Victorian cult of feminine selflessness and fragility was also used to prove that, in the words of the antisuffragist James McGrigor Allan, "every woman is . . . always more or less an invalid."

Among the rapidly growing ranks of male gynecologists, obstetricians, and psychologists, hysteria, which was associated with women etymologically through the Greek root *hyster* (womb), was considered a female disease in which "the patient loses more and more of her energy and self-control, becoming capriciously fanciful about her health, imagining or feigning strange diseases." Indeed, late-nineteenth- and early-twentieth-century physicians such as Henry Maudsley and S. Weir Mitchell sought to demonstrate not just that menstruation, pregnancy, and lactation turned women into helpless invalids but also that higher education and physical or even mental labor would damage women's health. Mitchell prescribed what became popular as "the rest cure": only complete immobilization—bed rest, constant feeding, and enforced idleness—would center the woman on her primary function, reproduction, and heal her neurasthenic symptoms. Yet when the Victorian angel threatened to turn into an invalid, she came perilously close to functioning like her Victorian counterpart, the madwoman, for through illness she had exempted herself from her socially prescribed duties of childbearing, child rearing, and home management. By the turn of the century, however, the angel, the madwoman, and the invalid had all been upstaged by two distinct but related images of rebelliously assertive women: the femme fatale and the New Woman.

From the Pre-Raphaelite paintings of Edward Burne-Jones to the art nouveau illustrations of Aubrey Beardsley, from Swinburne's sadistic Faustine to Yeats's destructive "daughters of Herodias," the sinister but sensuous figure of the femme fatale evoked the same fascination that Walter Pater expressed about Leonardo da Vinci's *La Gioconda* (the *Mona Lisa*). In a famous passage of *Studies in the History of the Renaissance,* Pater portrayed an alluring woman who is "older than the rocks among which she sits; like the vampire, she has been dead many times, and learned the secrets of the grave." Imbued with the sins of the Borgias, the secrets of Leda (mother of Helen of Troy), and the sanctity of St. Anne (mother of the Virgin Mary), Pater's world-weary beauty is both a lustful vampire and a potent mother, and she therefore epitomizes the contradictory qualities of the fatal female. By the turn of the century, such a figure appeared in so much poetry and fiction that the cultural historian Mario Praz argued that "in no other literary period . . . has sex been so obviously the mainspring of works of imagination."

As a seductive rebel, for instance, the femme fatale emerged in such excep-

tionally popular late Victorian fantasies as H. Rider Haggard's best-selling *She* (1887) and George MacDonald's *Lilith* (1895). Endowed with amazing grace, Haggard's She-Who-Must-Be-Obeyed and MacDonald's Lilith are tormented, divided creatures, burning with insatiable, destructive desire and with a power that implies mounting male anxiety about female energy— specifically, those energies associated with the mother transformed into a monster. As if to illustrate this point, the hero of George Bernard Shaw's *Man and Superman* (1903) explains that "of all human struggles there is none so treacherous and remorseless as the struggle between the artist man and the mother woman. Which shall use up the other? That is the issue between them." More generally, the realistic novel in this period also dramatized growing male anxiety that men were losing the battle between the sexes. In *Sister Carrie* (1900), Theodore Dreiser described the rise of an actress who triumphs on the stage while her abandoned lover commits suicide. Even in comic or farcical literature, the female seemed indomitable. Max Beerbohm's *Zuleika Dobson* (1911) portrayed the havoc that ensues in Oxford after the entrance of one femme fatale: all the undergraduates kill themselves because of their adoration of a flirtatious coquette.

To be sure, a number of American and English writers responded quite differently to women's rising power, for they identified with what they perceived to be the growing rebelliousness of women. Following the feminist concerns of the Victorian philosopher John Stuart Mill (1806–1873), George Gissing, George Moore, and John Galsworthy composed novels that implicitly criticized existing divorce laws, custody provisions, punitive attitudes toward illegitimacy, and the impoverishment of single women. A host of books resembled Stephen Crane's *Maggie: A Girl of the Streets* (1893) in offering sympathetic treatments of the fallen woman. At the same time, the middle-class American girl emerged in much fiction as a lively representative of the independence of her culture. Praised by Rudyard Kipling, fictionalized by William Dean Howells, and caricatured as "the Gibson girl," she was to acquire spunky innocence, spontaneity, and intelligence in some of the novels of Henry James. In *The Portrait of a Lady* (1881), for example, where he located "the center of the subject in the young woman's own consciousness," James traced the fastidiousness with which his heroine moved from naive idealism to moral maturity.

Although Howells's and James's audacious innocents often ended up either dead or married, they contributed to the construction of a new character, the New Woman. In portraying this figure, who prefigures the modernist "flapper," many English and American writers used the novel and the theater to try to make the feminist cause their own. Much of their writing was influenced by the plays of Henrik Ibsen. With its concluding scene in which Nora slams the door as she leaves her husband and children, *A Doll's House* (1879) was only the most famous of the Norwegian dramatist's treatments of women's demands for release from the childish dependency and boredom of domesticity. Following Ibsen in England, Shaw brought imperious heroines onto the stage, represented by actresses such as Elizabeth Robins and Ellen Terry. Similarly, the novels of George Meredith (*Diana of the Crossways*, 1885) and Grant Allen (*The Woman Who Did*, 1895) focused on female characters who actively and articulately expressed their dissatisfaction with conventional feminine roles. Frequently as seductive and

divided as the femme fatale, the New Woman was a rebel who regarded marriage as incompatible with her emancipation but who just as frequently suffered a tragic penalty for her views, because even while she was often a locus for the male novelist's own discontent with sex roles, she was also often used to dramatize what many men of letters saw as the self-destructiveness of feminism.

For all the irony and ambiguity of Henry James's narrative tone, the suffrage movement is presented in *The Bostonians* (1886) in terms of a manipulative bonding between two women living in what James's hero calls "a feminine, a nervous, hysterical, chattering, canting age." Such a diagnosis of feminism reflected the views of men like Sir Almroth Wright, an eminent bacteriologist and author of *The Unexpurgated Case against Woman Suffrage* (1913). In a 1912 letter to the London *Times,* Wright argued that "there is mixed up with the woman's movement much mental disorder"; with a half million "excess women" in Britain, Wright believed that "physiological emergencies" motivated the behavior of the militant suffragist. The idea that the independent woman was sick informed even Havelock Ellis's defense of female homosexuality, for Ellis claimed that the "invert," as he called her, suffered the biological tragedy of being born into the wrong body. Similarly, despite Thomas Hardy's indisputable sympathies for the sufferings of his New Woman, Sue Bridehead, in *Jude the Obscure,* the plot of the novel implies that men will be destroyed by women, whether by a "mere female animal" like Arabella Donn or by the conflicted spirituality of a neurasthenic Sue.

If the New Woman was a source of much imaginative energy at the turn of the century, it may have been because writers like James believed that, in the words of the critic Larzer Ziff, "women, with their free use of leisure, were the chief consumers of novels and therefore were increasingly becoming producers of them. The feminine attitude, now disengaging itself from that of men, was in point of fact coming to be all that the novel was." At least some men responded to the prominence of women writers with attacks whose defensiveness ranged from the sardonic wit that marked Oscar Wilde's discussion of "English Poetesses" in London's *Queen* magazine (1888) to the satiric ferocity that characterized Mark Twain's portrait of the adolescent poet Emmeline Grangerford in *Huckleberry Finn.* Finally, then, the turn-of-the-century obsession with figures such as the femme fatale and the New Woman reflected not only the importance of women's issues in the public and private lives of Americans and Britons but also the growth of the female reading public and the visibility and success of women writers.

WOMEN'S LIVES

In an age when men stopped sporting beards and women started riding bicycles, one sign of the dramatic transformation of women's lives was the change in fashion that began to liberate women from the weight and confinement of crinolines and hoops, replacing them first with bustles and then with simpler, lighter skirts. By the beginning of World War I, many of the necessary conditions for female emancipation were present. As identified by the historian Gerda Lerner, these included a technology that permitted society

to remove food preparation and care of the sick from the home, the mechanization of heating and laundry, the spread of health care and birth control, and the availability of education to all children. Yet, while women by 1900 were, as the suffragist Ray Strachey claimed in *The Cause* (1928), "in the main, free," Strachey herself went on to point out that they were still "politically outcast and economically oppressed; under-educated and over-flattered; too much despised and too much admired."

Unlike her mother and her grandmother, the married woman in this period did have some control over her property and her children. By 1883 married women in England were as free as American women to own acquired or inherited property; and after 1886, the Guardianship of Infants Act provided that on a father's death, the mother would become either the sole or joint guardian of her offspring. Divorce laws, however, continued to treat the two sexes differently. In England the husband could sue solely by reason of his wife's adultery, but the wife had to prove cruelty or desertion as well as adultery. In the United States, too, the laws were inequitable: in the state of Minnesota, for instance, a woman who was divorced by reason of her adultery had to forfeit real estate that had been her own property, while a man so divorced did not. Still, changes in property, divorce, and custody laws did imply that wives were no longer assumed to be the possessions of their husbands.

Just as legal constraints confining women were being debated and sometimes even loosened, educational restrictions were being questioned, circumvented, and overturned. To be sure, from educators like Dr. Edward H. Clarke, a Harvard professor, women continued to hear that higher education would atrophy women's uteruses. But such claims were countered by M. Carey Thomas, president of Bryn Mawr College, who argued in 1913 that "we know that college women are not only not invalids, but that they are better physically than other women in their own class of life." At the same time, as the historians Barbara Ehrenreich and Deirdre English first demonstrated, the new subject of domestic science, or home economics, became a way of justifying higher education for women, who were now held to need scientific training to make housekeeping an efficient profession. As in America, where the daughters of the wealthy could attend Bryn Mawr, Oberlin, Vassar, or the new Harvard annex, Radcliffe, in England women could pursue their higher education not only at several Cambridge and Oxford colleges—Girton and Newnham, Somerville and Lady Margaret Hall—but also within London University; Oxford and Cambridge still did not grant women degrees, however. A few African American women were given the opportunity of higher education at schools like Bethune-Cookman College: established by Mary McLeod Bethune from sums she raised selling sweet potato pies and ice cream to workmen on construction jobs, this college was dedicated to Bethune's commitment that all black youngsters should be given a chance to prove their worth. In 1890 the African American reformer Anna Julia Cooper presented an important essay titled "The Higher Education of Women," which included a plea that such education should include "colored women."

After 1870, when both boys and girls were for the first time guaranteed an elementary school education by the passage of the Elementary Education Act, educational opportunities for the working class were enhanced in

England. But such opportunities were limited by the custom of training working-class daughters for domestic service. Public schools and churches in America, moreover, often channeled immigrant women into home economics programs in which they could acquire the laundering, cooking, housecleaning, and sewing skills that would prepare them for low-status, low-paying jobs. But a number of social workers tried to improve the quality of life for urban immigrant women. In 1889 Jane Addams established her famous pioneering settlement house in Chicago's slums. The women who ran Hull House—with its kindergarten, courses in arts and crafts, and lectures from the educator John Dewey and the architect Frank Lloyd Wright—provided social and intellectual opportunities for their community even as they helped establish social work as a profession.

Addams's co-workers also agitated along with labor unions for the first meaningful factory laws in Illinois. The number of women workers in America had increased dramatically from approximately 4 million in 1890 to 5.33 million in 1900 and 7.5 million in 1910. Many were in domestic occupations, but thousands of others were farm laborers, teachers, sales clerks, factory workers, and textile or garment workers as well as holders of white-collar jobs—cashiers, bookkeepers, accountants, typists, and stenographers. Between 1870 and 1914 in England, the number of women clerks in the civil service multiplied twenty times, and thousands of women entered textile factories. In spite of this drastic rise in the number of women workers, trade union leaders were often dubious about organizing women, not infrequently because they believed with the English trade unionist Henry Broadhurst that "wives should be in their proper place at home." Male fears of job competition also perpetuated the exclusion of women and thereby fostered low pay and limited job options for women.

Although women were not unionized at the same rate as men, many women on both sides of the Atlantic did participate in the trade union movement. One of the most important early strikes in the history of American unions took place in 1909–10 among shirtwaist makers in New York and Philadelphia. Early locals of what is now called the International Ladies' Garment Workers' Union organized in the Triangle Waist Company, which in 1911 was the site of a fire that killed 146 operatives. The terrible conditions created by the "sweating system"—overcrowded tenement buildings, low pay, job insecurity, dangerous and uninspected machinery, employment of very young children—were denounced by the labor organizer Ida M. Van Etten at the national convention of the American Federation of Labor in 1890 and by the English socialist Beatrice Potter (Webb), who wrote "Pages from a Work Girl's Diary" (1888) about London East End tailoring. While the populist orator Mary Elizabeth Lease urged farmers "to raise less corn and more hell" and the organizer Mary "Mother" Jones agitated among urban laborers, the activist Emma Goldman was repeatedly arrested and eventually deported for anarchist agitation.

That Goldman was eventually to include birth control and free love in her program for human liberation indicates how women were beginning to attempt to gain power over their own bodies. However, Goldman's emphasis in the second decade of the twentieth century on women's right to sexual pleasure was far removed from the grounds of earlier pleas for control over reproduction. As the historian Linda Gordon has shown, throughout the last

quarter of the nineteenth century women based their arguments for what they called "voluntary motherhood" on their hostility toward men and toward sex. The "fearful strain" of repeated pregnancies and childbirths led nineteenth-century suffragists to attack "the lustful domination of man," just as the threat of "social diseases" (syphilis, gonorrhea) later led to the suffrage slogan "Votes for Women and Purity for Men." Social purity campaigns, which emphasized the superior chastity of women, were also efforts to elevate the values of maternal tenderness, patience, and supportiveness. Of course, as in the Victorian era, most middle-class girls at the turn of the century were denied all information about reproduction on the grounds that exposure to it would be an affront to their purity. Thus Vera Brittain, who would grow up to become a feminist writer, remembers that as a schoolgirl she given newspapers from which all paragraphs about sex had been carefully excised.

When the increasing demand for contraceptive information became evident in this period, it immediately met legal opposition. In the 1870s in England, Annie Besant was arrested for publishing George Knowlton's *Fruits of Philosophy*, a book that contained descriptions of contraceptive methods, and in America the so-called Comstock Law (1873) prohibited the sale and the mailing "of obscene literature and articles of immoral use," including birth control information. Many moralists opposed the use of existing methods of contraception such as coitus interruptus, the vaginal sponge, the sheath, and the pessary (an intravaginal device). Just as adamantly, many medical men argued that "continence" (abstinence) was the only suitable form of birth control. Not only did ignorant physicians advise women as late as the 1880s and 1890s that the "safe" time for sex was midway between the periods of menstruation, but the medical attack on birth control also often warned that contraception led to such disasters as hardening of the uterus or moral degeneracy. Yet the use of lamb ceca (intestines) and rubber revolutionized the manufacturing of condoms and resulted in the invention of the Mensinga diaphragm; the developing birth control movement probably affected the rapidly falling birth rate, which in the United Kingdom dropped by nearly 30 percent between the mid-1880s and 1910.

The shift from social purity and continence to birth control in the struggle over reproductive rights paralleled a similar ideological shift in the struggle for political rights. Both in England and in America, the activist organizations of women in the 1870s and 1880s argued for reforms on the grounds of women's ethical superiority. In England, the protest led by Josephine Butler against the Contagious Diseases Acts, which forced accused prostitutes to submit to physical examinations, attacked laws that condoned (male) sexual immorality. Butler's reports of women who had been forced to submit to examinations dwelt on the indignities of "monstrous instruments" used coercively: "They seem to tear the passage open first with their hands," one victim testified, "and then they thrust in instruments, and they pull them out and push them in, and they turn and twist them about; and if you cry out they stifle you." The repeal of the Contagious Diseases Acts in 1886 was driven by an ideology of feminine purity that paradoxically involved many middle-class women in public discussions of prostitution and social diseases. Because of its emphasis on deviant or simply excessive male sexual demands, this campaign, like the social purity movement, may have also contributed

at the beginning of the twentieth century to what the scholar Lillian Faderman has described as the marked development of quasi-homosexual bonds (so-called Boston marriages) between women.

Just as committed to a standard of female-defined virtue, the Woman's Christian Temperance Union (WCTU), which grew to eight hundred thousand members between 1880 and 1920 in America, promoted the slogan "For God and Home and Native Land" to symbolize its effort to bring the purity associated with the home into the national arena. Focusing on temperance (abstinence and the legal prohibition of liquor), WCTU organizers argued that women suffered physically, psychologically, and economically from men's consumption of alcohol. Although Frances Willard, the union's president, eventually placed the temperance cause within a socialist and suffragist context, she never managed to persuade all her followers to look forward to "that day when the mothers, and daughters of America shall have a voice [i.e., vote] in the decision by which . . . the rum-shop is opened or shut beside their homes." Throughout the final decades of the nineteenth century, however, women attempted through reform groups, volunteer organizations, and clubs to extend their role as nurturers and moral teachers from the domestic to the public sphere. In this context, the sanctification of motherhood became part of the argument for the vote, for women justified their entrance into public life not only in terms of their domestic responsibilities and their superior morality but also in terms of their importance as bearers of the race: in spite of its racist overtones, eugenics—the science of improving humanity through genetic control of heredity—supplied a rhetoric that lent the mother a crucial role in the development of the species.

When women on both sides of the Atlantic began organizing with increased militancy to gain female enfranchisement, their opponents included the novelist Mary Ward, the poet Christina Rossetti, and even the socialist Beatrice Webb, all of whom signed in 1889 a protest against "an emancipating process [that] has now reached the limits fixed by the physical constitution of women." The turn-of-the-century suffragists against whom they argued saw that process as far from complete as they built on the work of early feminists such as Elizabeth Cady Stanton and Mary Wollstonecraft and on their own experiences in the socialist and labor movements as well as in social purity and temperance organizations.

While none of the existing political parties in England chose to advocate women's enfranchisement, the ideological underpinnings of the struggle for the vote were established by Olive Schreiner, whose novels and tracts identified women's secondary status with "the subjugation of large bodies of other human creatures, either as slaves, subject races, or classes." The granting of women's suffrage in New Zealand in 1893 and in South Australia in 1894 provided new impetus to the cause. After repeated efforts by the moderate National Union, led by Millicent Garrett Fawcett, had failed to get a suffrage bill through Parliament, Emmeline Pankhurst in 1903 formed a new suffrage society, the Women's Social and Political Union (WSPU). Annie Kenney, a mill hand from Oldham, and Christabel Pankhurst, one of Emmeline's daughters, were among the first to use the tactics—heckling, illegal speaking, seeking arrest, and enduring imprisonment—that would continue to characterize the growing militancy of the WSPU. Meetings and marches grew more frequent and larger as the militants began pouring acid into letter

boxes, throwing bricks and stones through shop windows, cutting telegraph wires, and slashing paintings.

Convinced that they would receive newspaper attention only through dramatic action, those militants sentenced to prison terms refused to eat, and jailors resorted to what was called the "forcible feeding" of hunger strikers. Wardens pinned the protester to a bed and physicians pushed twenty inches of tubing down her nostrils or throat; milk and eggs were poured through a funnel into the tube. Painful and dangerous, such treatments were publicly condemned when an aristocrat, Lady Constance Lytton, disguised as a working-class woman named "Jane Wharton," was paralyzed by the practice. Nevertheless, the government responded only with what became known as the Cat and Mouse Act (1913), an act that released sick hunger strikers and allowed them to be rearrested without a fresh warrant, to continue serving their sentences when they were well. Despite growing public support for women's suffrage during the renewed campaigns of 1913 and 1914, many moderates and socialists had been alienated by the Pankhursts' methods or by their exclusive focus on the vote. After the outbreak of war in August 1914, the movement was further split between those women who followed Mrs. Pankhurst in dedicating their energies to the war effort and others, like Olive Schreiner, who worked for world peace.

The splitting of the woman's movement into moderates and militants also occurred in America. Notwithstanding the new leadership of Carrie Chapman Catt and Anna Howard Shaw, the National American Woman Suffrage Association experienced what the historian Eleanor Flexner has called "the doldrums" between 1896 and 1910, for many suffragists were beginning to question their state-by-state strategy, which was both arduous and frequently unsuccessful. When the national movement lost several state campaigns, two splinter groups arose, led by women deeply influenced by their experience with the militant Pankhursts. Harriot Stanton Blatch, Elizabeth Cady Stanton's daughter, traveled back to the United States from England in 1902, dismayed by the comparative inertia of American suffrage organizations. While Blatch's Equality League of Self-Supporting Women began to hold open-air meetings and parades, Alice Paul, who had been jailed in England, undertaken a hunger strike, and undergone forcible feeding, returned to America in 1910 and began describing the British movement to American suffrage groups. With the pacifist Crystal Eastman and the historian Mary Beard, Paul started to campaign for a federal suffrage amendment. As different as Alice Paul's and Harriot Stanton Blatch's tactics were from those of Carrie Chapman Catt and Anna Howard Shaw, both militants and moderates depended for their intellectual framework on the analyses of female subordination provided by Charlotte Perkins Gilman, whose *Women and Economics* (1898) hailed "the woman's movement . . . as the best birth of our century." Even as the suffrage movement shaped the writing of women in this period, then, literary women also helped to clarify (and sometimes to contest) the aims of turn-of-the-century feminism.

THE WOMAN QUESTION AND WOMEN'S ARTISTIC QUEST

In W. S. Gilbert and Sir Arthur Sullivan's comic opera *The Mikado* (1885), one singer places "that singular anomaly, the lady novelist" on a list of char-

acters who "never would be missed"; in fact, women novelists (and, for that matter, female poets) were hardly anomalies by the turn of the century. Yet for many years their contributions were missing from the standard literary histories of this period; they had been relegated to the footnotes of literary history or placed in a predominantly male context. Indeed, only within the past several decades have scholars begun to bring back into print and study the works of late-nineteenth-century poets such as Sarah Morgan Bryan Piatt, Augusta Webster, and Amy Levy, although they were well received in their own day and made substantial contributions to the evolution of verse, especially in their approach to the dramatic monologue.

Not only the prominent role played by women of letters but also the uniqueness of their achievements become clearer when we take into account the centrality of the woman question in their lives and works. Inevitably, the impact of the suffrage movement was greatest on the production of polemical prose. In such books as *Woman and Labor* (1911) and *Women and Economics*, Olive Schreiner and Charlotte Perkins Gilman were contributing to the mass of expository writing that was being published by feminist and antifeminist women alike. In addition, a generation of what we would now call women's studies scholars began exploring women's cultural situation. Matilda Joslyn Gage's *Woman, Church and State* (1893) provided a female view of religious history, and Cicely Hamilton's *Marriage as a Trade* (1909) supplied a sociological analysis of the institutions that shaped women's lives. In 1910 Emma Goldman produced "The Traffic in Women," an essay that connects the exploitation of prostitutes with the subjugation of all women, and Emily James Putnam published *The Lady*, a book about that outmoded and "somewhat dangerous" social type. By 1912, when Harriet Shaw Weaver and Dora Marsden were editing the magazine *The Freewoman*, Anna Garlin Spencer had documented the contributions of women from primitive to modern times in *Woman's Share in Social Culture*. By this time, too, Alice Meynell, Mary Elizabeth Coleridge, Mathilda Blind, and Mrs. Oliphant had produced essays and biographies about literary women.

The effort to document women's cultural situation also led the anthropologist Ruth Underhill to take down the stories of the American Indian Maria Chona (published as *The Autobiography of a Papago Woman*, 1936), just as it impelled the folklorist Mary Austin to transcribe American Indian legends in *The Basket Woman* (1904). The author of two autobiographies, Austin was one of the many women in this period who published confessional accounts of their development. A number of Victorian women's diaries and journals were issued at the turn of the century: Elizabeth Cady Stanton's *Eighty Years and More*, which analyzed her role in the feminist movement, appeared in 1898; Mary Boykin Chesnut's diary, which described life on a Southern plantation during the Civil War, was published in an abbreviated form in 1905 as *A Diary from Dixie*; and the diaries of Marie Bashkirtseff (translated in 1890) and Mary MacLane (1902) were widely read. In many of these publications, women openly discussed their feelings about the female body, birth control, housework, female friendships, and aging. Alice James's *Diary*, which was privately printed several years after her death in 1892, describes not only her complex attitudes toward her famous brothers, Henry and William James, but also her resentment at a medical establishment that could not save her from an invalid's life. Just as personal and just as focused on the relationship between women and the medical establish-

ment, Charlotte Perkins Gilman's story "The Yellow Wallpaper" (1892) analyzed female madness in terms of women's ambivalent attitudes toward men and maternity.

Besides bringing to the surface the psychological problems that women writers confronted, the feminist movement also provided a utopian vision of a world in which women might experience complete freedom. In verse, drama, fiction, and expository prose, women began to translate the visionary rhetoric of suffragism into utopian works of art. As the literary critic Elaine Showalter has reminded readers, in *Gloriana; or, The Revolution of 1900* (1890), Lady Florence Dixie envisioned a girl who disguises herself as a boy in order to enter Oxford and Parliament, while "Ellis Ethelmer," in *Woman Free* (1893), imagined what would happen if the menstrual cycle were to end. Similarly, Cicely Hamilton and Christopher St. John's play *How the Vote Was Won* (1909) dramatized the conversion of patriarchal relatives to a triumphant suffrage cause. Elizabeth Robins, who also produced a play about the suffrage question, published *The Convert* (1907), a novel that presented suffragists who seem to be "speaking in an unknown tongue," for they desire "a world where beauty exists for beauty's sake—which is love's sake—and not for tricking money or power out of men," a future world that may be "beyond the imagining of many." Gilman herself was to focus on precisely such a world in her utopian fantasy *Herland* (1915), which describes an all-female community of women capable of reproducing themselves without the help of men.

Even when artistic works by women participated in the literary movements dominated or defined by their male contemporaries—for instance, symbolism, naturalism, and regionalism—the contributions of women were characterized by their focus on the issues associated with the turn-of-the-century woman question. Among poets, the women artists who were involved in a revolt against bourgeois conventionality wrote almost exclusively about their defiance of taboos placed on women. The American poet who renamed herself Renée Vivien, for example, lived most of her adult life in Paris, where she wrote French verse influenced by Baudelaire and Swinburne: Vivien, who flaunted her alienation from society through her identification with "decadence," undertook to mythologize the lesbian relationships she sustained with, among others, the expatriate writer Natalie Barney. In addition, the British poet Charlotte Mew used sensuous imagery in dramatic monologues frequently narrated by female characters who aspire to a spiritual grace they are destined never to receive; her contemporary Mary Elizabeth Coleridge portrayed the tormenting self-division of a woman who sees the "hideous wound" of "a woman, wild" in "The Other Side of the Mirror." Similar symbolist techniques were used by Olive Schreiner in allegorical meditations that explored the spiritual and aesthetic quests that shape women's dreams and dreads.

While such prose writers as Vernon Lee and Marie Corelli viewed the seductive femme fatale as an image of powerful female beauty, Schreiner analyzed in close detail the effects of narcissism and idleness on women robbed of all functions except the aesthetic. Indeed, her discussion in *Woman and Labor* of what she called "sex-parasitism" was partially an analysis of how the role of the femme fatale is fatal for women. Just as concerned with the pain experienced by the woman who is perceived as fatally attractive,

George Egerton (the pseudonym of Mary Chavelita Dunne) stunned London with what then seemed an erotically explicit volume of stories, *Keynotes* (1893), some of which deal with the frustration of female characters who are hampered by their distrust or ignorance of male sexuality. Like Kate Chopin, whose controversial novel *The Awakening* (1899) shocked American readers, Egerton wrote with unprecedented candor about female sexuality.

In one of her more successful stories, Egerton described the fantasy of a woman who imagines herself performing in front of a male audience that succumbs to her exotic charms. Significantly, the women who were most influenced by the idea of the femme fatale were female performers. The Italian actress Eleanora Duse (about whom Amy Lowell was to write a number of poems) and the English-speaking actresses Ellen Terry and Elizabeth Robins, both of whom starred in the plays of Ibsen and Shaw, led visibly eccentric lives, but they were less flamboyant than the very popular entertainer Sarah Bernhardt, who played the role of the femme fatale both on- and offstage. Attended by a menagerie of wild beasts, engaged in a series of notorious love affairs, sleeping in a satin-lined coffin, Bernhardt reputedly wore a necklace of petrified human eyes. Equally melodramatic, one of the theater's most notorious fallen women was created by Elizabeth Robins and Florence Bell: their play *Alan's Wife* (1893) features a murderous mother who goes off to her death defending her suffocation of her sickly son as an act of mercy. At the same time, among dancers, Loie Fuller became famous in art nouveau circles for her swirling veil dances and Isadora Duncan became internationally infamous not only for what she herself called the "fantastic sensuality and ecstasy" of her dances but also for her bohemian lifestyle.

Just as aestheticism had a distinctive impact on women's art at the turn of the century, so too the realistic and naturalistic traditions influenced women in a special way. The early writer of naturalistic fiction Rebecca Harding Davis continued publishing throughout this period. Similarly, Mary Ward wrote novels about the degrading conditions of the London poor. But many female writers analyzed social determinism in terms less of governmental or industrial corruption than of the private lives of women. Two African American novelists, Frances Harper and Pauline Hopkins, produced pioneering works of "racial uplift" to improve the public image of black women; Harper's *Iola Leroy* (1892) and Hopkins's *Contending Forces* (1900) protested against racial discrimination as well as sexual exploitation. At the same time, the educational and social liabilities of middle-class white women served as the mainspring of some of May Sinclair's and Edith Wharton's most successful fiction. Unlike those male contemporaries who portrayed the new freedom of the New Woman, female realists focused for the most part on the continuing confinement facing women in an increasingly acquisitive society. Wharton, in particular, analyzed the bondage of heroines who are trapped by materialistic societal conventions that turn them into valuable objects.

Like H. H. Richardson, who located a number of her stories and novels in her native Australia, and Wharton, who became famous for her delineations of wealthy New York society, many turn-of-the-century women writers analyzed the unique mores of the local communities that had shaped their own family histories, much as Lady Gregory did in her volumes of Irish legends and in the plays she wrote for the Abbey Theatre. Studying the ori-

gins of their own identities and their cultural roots, such authors help explain the importance of regionalism in turn-of-the-century literature by women. Unlike Bret Harte, whose stories about California are dominated by romantic gamblers and sentimental miners, the short story writers Sarah Orne Jewett and Mary E. Wilkins Freeman described the visiting, gossiping, cooking, and gardening that supplied a network of support for their communities of women. Like Emma Lazarus, who wrote about Jewish Americans, and Pauline Johnson, who described Native American populations, Jewett and Freeman implicitly provided a social history that might otherwise have gone unrecorded by traditional historians. Jewett's *The Country of the Pointed Firs* (1896), no less than Chopin's *Bayou Folk* (1894), set the private problems of daughters, single women, mothers, and widows into the context of economic and social issues at the turn of the century. At the same time, such regionalists sometimes also eulogized a pastoral, timeless realm in which women had established a harmonious, almost mythic, relationship with the physical landscape.

Reflecting the ways in which polemical, autobiographical, utopian, realistic, and regional writing by women concentrated on the situation of woman in nature and society, Chopin's important novel *The Awakening* focused on a twenty-eight-year-old, married mother of two children who is awakened socially and sexually to "her position in the universe as a human being." Indeed, this work functions not only polemically, as a plea for women's autonomy, and autobiographically, as a study of the competition between motherhood and artistry, but also as a fantasy of female sensuality, solitude, and self-discovery. Chopin had profited from her reading of Sarah Orne Jewett's stories, just as Jewett and Freeman had developed a tradition pioneered by Harriet Beecher Stowe. For although such American prose writers as Elizabeth Stuart Phelps Ward and Constance Fenimore Woolson published novels and short stories about the impossibility of being both a woman and an artist, many other turn-of-the-century women writers could begin to look back on a tradition of successful women authors.

During the span of years that witnessed the deaths of such Victorian sibyls as George Eliot and Harriet Beecher Stowe, women writers felt themselves to be living through a period of transition similar to yet somewhat different from that experienced by their male counterparts, for they were writing in an age when thousands of women were crossing the threshold from the private to the public sphere. Unlike many of their Victorian precursors, literary women no longer felt constrained to write covertly about their rebellion against socially prescribed roles. Rather, many of these artists were empowered to record both their protests and their pleas by the idea, articulated in *Woman and Labor,* that "it is the woman who is the final standard of the race." Although two classics of this period—*The Awakening* and "The Yellow Wallpaper"—are overtly pessimistic about women's fates, as are some of the stories of Woolson and Wharton, their pessimism is born of raised expectations for a fully integrated life. Whether the female contemporaries of Chopin and Gilman wrote about the possibility of industrialization ending the necessity of women's domestic service, about the tensions resulting from ethnic or racial discrimination and female subjugation, or about the significance for women of the death of a patriarchal God, they would have agreed with Henry Adams that "the proper study of mankind is woman."

SARAH MORGAN BRYAN PIATT
1836–1919

Sarah Morgan Bryan Piatt's verse "demands an apprehension which is denied to the many" because she writes in a language that is "wayward, abrupt, enigmatic, and prolific in innuendoes and questions it neglects to answer": so declared a reviewer of this lively poet's sixth collection, *Dramatic Persons and Moods* (1881). Perhaps for this reason, Piatt's reputation declined rapidly and radically after her death, despite her learning, industry, and voluminous output. Like her contemporary, the more reclusive (and even more innovative) Emily Dickinson, this author of "wayward" poems was producing difficult, serious, often rebelliously skeptical art in an era whose "poetesses" were usually dismissed as a sweetly "tuneful sisterhood." Such works as "The Palace-Burner," "Engaged Too Long," and "The Sorrows of Charlotte" challenge conventional nineteenth-century definitions of femininity, while such other poems as "A New Thanksgiving" and "The Coming of Eve" even more bitterly subvert contemporary pieties.

The woman who published controversial yet widely read poetry during her lifetime and then sank for so long into posthumous obscurity was born and raised in Kentucky, a descendant of pioneers (among them Daniel Boone) and southern plantation owners. After an exceptionally strong education at Henry Female College, she married John Piatt, an Ohioan who was also a poet. While rising seven children, she settled with him in the North, where he briefly held a government job in Washington, D.C., and then, during and after the Civil War, in Ohio. Perhaps because this last move coincided with the American struggle between the states, much of Piatt's writing is marked by skepticism and anger bred by that conflict. But later, too, when John Piatt worked for eleven years as an American consul in the Irish cities of Cork and Cobh, his wife complained that she felt "exiled" even while her poetry revealed that her imagination was deeply engaged by her new surroundings.

Throughout their travels, both poets continued publishing energetically; Sarah Piatt, in particular, composed some fifteen volumes of verse in the course of her literary career, including *The Nests of Washington and Other Poems* (1864), which she jointly authored with her husband, and, when she was in Ireland, *An Irish Garland* (1884) and *Pictures, Portraits, and People in Ireland* (1893). Ironically, although her work evoked ambivalent responses from American reviewers, it was much admired in Victorian England, where she was compared to such established luminaries as Christina Rossetti and Elizabeth Barrett Browning. Yet Sarah Piatt's often extraordinarily powerful poems were not really recovered for current readers on either side of the Atlantic until the early twenty-first century, when Paula Bernat Bennett edited *The Palace-Burner: The Selected Poetry of Sarah Piatt* (2001).

The Palace-Burner

(A Picture in a Newspaper.)

She has been burning palaces. "To see
 The sparks look pretty in the wind?" Well, yes—
And something more. But women brave as she
 Leave much for cowards such as I to guess.

5 But this is old, so old that everything
 Is ashes here—the woman and the rest.
 Two years are oh! so long. Now you may bring
 Some newer pictures. You like this one best?

 You wish that you had lived in Paris then?
10 You would have loved to burn a palace, too?
 But they had guns in France, and Christian men
 Shot wicked little Communists, like you.[1]

 You would have burned the palace? Just because
 You did not live in it yourself! Oh! why?
15 Have I not taught you to respect the laws?
 You would have burned the palace. Would not *I*?

 Would *I*? Go to your play. Would I, indeed?
 I? Does the boy not know my soul to be
 Languid and worldly, with a dainty need
20 For light and music? Yet he questions me.

 Can he have seen my soul more near than I?
 Ah! in the dusk and distance sweet she seems,
 With lips to kiss away a baby's cry,
 Hands fit for flowers, and eyes for tears and dreams.

25 Can he have seen my soul? And could she wear
 Such utter life upon a dying face,
 Such unappealing, beautiful despair,
 Such garments—soon to be a shroud—with grace?

 Has she a charm so calm that it could breathe
30 In damp, low places till some frightened hour;
 Then start, like a fair, subtle snake, and wreathe
 A stinging poison with a shadowy power?

 Would *I* burn palaces? The child has seen
 In this fierce creature of the Commune here,
35 So bright with bitterness and so serene,
 A being finer than my soul, I fear.

 1872

The Sorrows of Charlotte

The Sorrows of Werther,[1] that is the Book,
 Little girl of mine. Will I show you what
His sorrows were like? Such a brown-eyed look
 Could hardly see. Never mind, they were not
5 Such sorrows, I fancy, as yours or mine,
But such as in pictures look so fine,
 And such as can end—in a pistol shot.

"Is any one else in the Book?" (I knew
 She would ask me that.) Yes, Charlotte is there.
10 "Then is it the Sorrows of Charlotte too?"
 No, child, for never a man would care
To write such a long sad story, you see,
 As the—cutting of bread-and-butter would be;
 And never a woman had time to dare!

 1872

Engaged Too Long

Why do I grieve with summer here?
I want the flower that died last year;
I want the old drops of the dew,
And my old love, sir,—and not you.

5 Younger than you, nor quite so wise,
Was he who had your hair and eyes,—
Who said, "I love you" first, you see;
This you repeat, and weary me.

 1879

The Witch in the Glass

"My mother says I must not pass
 Too near that glass;[1]
She is afraid that I will see
A little witch that looks like me,
5 With a red, red mouth, to whisper low
The very thing I should not know!"

Alack for all your mother's care!
 A bird of the air,
A wistful wind, or (I suppose
10 Sent by some hapless boy) a rose,
With breath too sweet, will whisper low,
The very thing you should not know!

 1880, 1881

1. *The Sorrows of Young Werther* (1774), a sensationally popular short novel by Johann von Goethe. The artistic, sensitive Werther falls in love with a young woman named Charlotte who is engaged to a more conventional and wealthier man; she marries, and the book ends with Werther's death after he shoots himself in the head.
1. Mirror.

The Christening

In vain we broider cap and cloak, and fold
 The long robe, white and rare;
In vain we serve on dishes of red gold,
 Perhaps, the rich man's fare;
5 In vain we bid the fabled folk who bring
 All gifts the world holds sweet:
This one, forsooth, shall give the child to sing;
 To move like music this shall charm its feet;
 This help the cheek to blush, the heart to beat.

10 Unto the christening there shall surely come
 The Uninvited Guest,
The evil mother, weird[1] and wise, with some
 Sad purpose in her breast.
Yea and though every spinning-wheel be stilled
15 In all the country round,
Behold, her prophecy must be fulfilled;[2]
 The turret with the spindle will be found,
 And the white hand will reach and take the wound.

1884

The Coming of Eve

And What Came of It

God gave the world to Man in the Beginning.[1]
 Alone in Eden there and lord of all,
He mused:"There may be one thing worth the winning.
 (All else is mine.) When will that Apple fall?

5 "I weary of the Garden. Here are roses
 That bloom and die not. Oh, that they would die!
Without one thorn each bud its blush uncloses.
 (Perhaps the thorns will sharpen by and by!)

"In all this world of loveliness, I find not
10 One flower whose face seems fair at all to see.
I might endure—even Paradise, and mind not,
 Were Some One here to wear a rose for me.

1. Supernatural.
2. I.e., the prophecy in the fairy tale "Sleeping Beauty"; at the christening of this princess, the fairy whom the king and queen failed to invite predicted that the girl would pierce her hand with a spindle and fall down dead.
1. "In the beginning" are the first words of the Bible; its first chapters, Genesis 1–3, describe the creation of the heavens, the earth, and the living things on it, particularly the first man and woman and their expulsion from the Garden of Eden for eating the forbidden fruit of the tree of the knowledge of good and evil. In that account, the serpent persuaded Eve to eat the fruit (conventionally identified as an apple), which she then gave to Adam.

"Still, yonder fruit must mock me with its glitter!
 (The Woman—were there one!—might rob the Tree!)
15 It may be that the taste within is bitter,
 And this eternal sweetness tortures me."

He yawned himself to sleep. And then, (oh wonder!
 Oh beauty that made flower and star look dim!)
He woke, and lo! the Woman waited under
20 The Tree—whereon the Apple grew—for him.

"What would my lord?" the Vision sighed. "Command me.
 (Heaven for his pleasure made me—from his side[2]—
At least, not for my own!)" "You understand me?—
 I want yon Apple, Fairest!" he replied. . . .

25 Then, lo! the seraph's[3] sword of fire above them!—
 And lo! all Eden blackened at their feet!
With none on earth and none in Heaven to love them,
 Save one another, life at once grew sweet! . . .

God gave the world to Man. With eyes entreating,
30 The Woman said: "Hast Thou no gift for me?"
"Yea, Woman! In thy breast a Heart is beating!"
 The Father spake. "That is my gift to thee!" . . .

Eve—passing—left this gift to all her daughters.
 Is Man a wanderer from his home apart?
35 Do great winds hurl him over troubled waters?
 Faints he on sand? She follows with her Heart!

He goeth forth to battle and is wounded.
 She binds the wounds he dies from—or has made!
He sounds[4] the seas. She sounds the deeps unsounded—
40 The darker deeps from which he shrinks afraid!

She watches by the cradle, and so catches
 The first light of the soul, God's new-born star!
She watches by the grave—alone, she watches
 (Others forget) where death and silence are.

45 She helps her race as maid, as wife, as mother—
 With grace, with love, with sweetness, with her Heart! . . .
Yet women, sisters, helping one another,
 Most surely ye shall choose the better part.

2. Genesis 2.21–22 (the creation of Eve from Adam's rib).

3. Angel's. See Genesis 3.24.

4. Measures the depth of.

She has her little wrongs. To bear or mend them
50 Is what she—must! God gave the world to Man.
To her He gave—her troubles! He will end them!
But, meanwhile, let her help Him as she can!

1900 1903

A New Thanksgiving

For war, plague, pestilence, flood, famine, fire,
 For Christ discrowned, for false gods set on high;
For fools, whose hands must have their hearts' desire,
 We thank Thee—in the darkness—and so die.

5 For shipwreck: Oh, the sob of strangling seas!—
 No matter. For the snake that charms the dove;
And (is it not the bitterest of all these?)
 We thank Thee—in our blind faith—even for Love.

For breaking hearts; for all that breaks the heart;
10 For Death, the one thing after all the rest,
We thank Three, O our Father! Thou who art,
 And wast, and shalt be—knowing these are best.

1910

AUGUSTA WEBSTER
1837–1894

During the 1870s and 1880s, Augusta Webster worked for the National Committee for Women's Suffrage, served on the London School Board, and published poetry reviews for the *Athenaeum*. The scholar Patricia Rigg has cautioned that it would be a mistake to assume that Webster defined herself primarily as a writer of dramatic poetry, for she also translated Greek plays, published a novel as well as long narrative poems and verse dramas, and was writing the sonnet sequence *Mother and Daughter* at the end of her life. Just as important, many of these works were well received in her day. However, Webster's books soon went out of print and now, after her recent recovery, she is best known for dramatic monologues such as "Circe" and "A Castaway," which began to receive critical attention only in the 1990s. Like Robert Browning, whom she reviewed favorably and to whom she was compared in her day, Webster used the dramatic monologue to focus on the interaction between individual psychology and the social circumstances that it reflects or seeks to resist. The mythological figure of Circe allowed Webster to contrast female to male sexual desire, while the persona of a prostitute in "A Castaway" enabled Webster to enter into a central Victorian conversation about degeneracy, desire, and the sexual double standard.

Because literary historians have neither journals nor extensive letters on which to rely, biographical information about Webster is scant. She was born and named Julia Augusta Davies in Poole, Dorset, but spent most of her youth on board the ship of

her father, a vice admiral; the *Griper* was stationed in a number of ports in southern England. When her father was appointed chief constable of Cambridgeshire, the family moved to Cambridge, where she learned Greek, Italian, Spanish, and French and where she also attended the Cambridge School of Art. After publishing a volume of verse under the pseudonym Cecil Home in 1860, she wed Thomas Webster, a fellow and law lecturer at Trinity College, Cambridge, who moved with her to London in 1870 and began practicing law. During the early years of marriage, she gave birth to a daughter and published a novel under her pseudonym as well as five books of poetry and of translations under her married name. Webster's exclusion from the canon during the end of the nineteenth century and throughout most of the twentieth has been attributed to various factors: her lack of powerful literary patrons and friends, for instance, or the strong political content of her subjects. She herself noted that Elizabeth Barrett Browning was one of the few authors able to urge the righting of social wrongs in poetry that managed to survive the success of its causes.

Circe[1]

 The sun drops luridly into the west;
 Darkness has raised her arms to draw him down
 Before the time, not waiting as of wont[2]
 Till he has come to her behind the sea;
5 And the smooth waves grow sullen in the gloom
 And wear their threatening purple; more and more
 The plain of waters sways and seems to rise
 Convexly from its level of the shores;
 And low dull thunder rolls along the beach:
10 There will be storm at last, storm, glorious storm!

 Oh welcome, welcome, though it rend my bowers,
 Scattering my blossomed roses like the dust,
 Splitting the shrieking branches, tossing down
 My riotous vines with their young half-tinged grapes
15 Like small round amethysts or beryls strung
 Tumultuously in clusters; though it sate
 Its ravenous spite among my goodliest pines
 Standing there round and still against the sky
 That makes blue lakes between their sombre tufts,
20 Or harry from my silvery olive slopes
 Some hoary king whose gnarled fantastic limbs
 Wear rugged armour of a thousand years;
 Though it will hurl high on my flowery shores
 The hostile wave that rives at the poor sward
25 And drags it down the slants, that swirls its foam
 Over my terraces, shakes their firm blocks
 Of great bright marbles into tumbled heaps,
 And makes my pleached[3] and mossy labyrinths,
 Where the small odorous blossoms grow like stars

1. In Homer's *Odyssey* (book 10), a powerful enchantress who lived on an island off the coast of Italy; she was encountered by Odysseus as he attempted to return home after the Trojan War. She transformed his crew into swine, and he stayed with her for a year after persuading her to turn them back into men.
2. Was customary.
3. Tangled.

30 Strewn in the milky way, a briny marsh.
 What matter? let it come and bring me change,
 Breaking the sickly sweet monotony.

 I am too weary of this long bright calm;
 Always the same blue sky, always the sea
35 The same blue perfect likeness of the sky,
 One rose to match the other that has waned,
 To-morrow's dawn the twin of yesterday's;
 And every night the ceaseless crickets chirp
 The same long joy and the late strain of birds
40 Repeats their strain of all the even month;
 And changelessly the petty plashing surfs
 Bubble their chiming burden round the stones;
 Dusk after dusk brings the same languid trance
 Upon the shadowy hills, and in the fields
45 The waves of fireflies come and go the same,
 Making the very flash of light and stir
 Vex one like dronings of the shuttles[4] at task.

 Give me some change. Must life be only sweet,
 All honey-pap as babes would have their food?
50 And, if my heart must always be adrowse
 In a hush of stagnant sunshine, give me, then,
 Something outside me stirring; let the storm
 Break up the sluggish beauty, let it fall
 Beaten below the feet of passionate winds,
55 And then to-morrow waken jubilant
 In a new birth; let me see subtle joy
 Of anguish and of hopes, of change and growth.

 What fate is mine, who, far apart from pains
 And fears and turmoils of the cross-grained world,
60 Dwell like a lonely god in a charmed isle
 Where I am first and only, and, like one
 Who should love poisonous savours more than mead,[5]
 Long for a tempest on me and grow sick
 Of rest and of divine free carelessness!
65 Oh me, I am a woman, not a god;
 Yea, those who tend me, even, are more than I,
 My nymphs who have the souls of flowers and birds
 Singing and blossoming immortally.

 Ah me! these love a day and laugh again,
70 And loving, laughing, find a full content;
 But I know nought of peace, and have not loved.

 Where is my love? Does someone cry for me
 Not knowing whom he calls? Does his soul cry

4. I.e., of a loom.

For mine to grow beside it, grow in it?
75 Does he beseech the gods to give him me,
The one unknown rare woman by whose side
No other woman thrice as beautiful
Could once seem fair to him; to whose voice heard
In any common tones no sweetest sound
80 Of love made melody on silver lutes,
Or singing like Apollo's[6] when the gods
Grow pale with happy listening, might be peered
For making music to him; whom once found
There will be no more seeking anything?

85 Oh love, oh love, oh love, art not yet come
Out of the waiting shadows into life?
Art not yet come after so many years
That I have longed for thee? Come! I am here.

 Not yet. For surely I should feel a sound
90 Of his far answer if now in the world
He sought me who will seek me—Oh, ye gods,
Will he not seek me? Is it all a dream?
Will there be only these, these bestial things
Who wallow in their styes, or mop and mow
95 Among the trees, or munch in pens and byres,[7]
Or snarl and filch behind their wattled coops;
These things who had believed that they were men?

 Nay, but he *will* come. Why am I so fair,
And marvellously minded, and with sight
100 Which flashes suddenly on hidden things,
As the gods see, who do not need to look?
Why wear I in my eyes that stronger power
Than basilisks,[8] whose gaze can only kill,
To draw men's souls to me to live or die
105 As I would have them? Why am I given pride
Which yet longs to be broken, and this scorn,
Cruel and vengeful, for the lesser men
Who meet the smiles I waste for lack of him,
And grow too glad? Why am I who I am?
110 But for the sake of him whom fate will send
One day to be my master utterly,
That he should take me, the desire of all,
Whom only he in the world could bow to him.

 Oh, sunlike glory of pale glittering hairs,
115 Bright as the filmy wires my weavers take
To make me golden gauzes—Oh, deep eyes,
Darker and softer than the bluest dusk

6. In classical mythology, the god of poetry, music,
and the sun.
7. Cow barns.

8. Mythological monsters with the power to kill
with a glance.

Of August violets, darker and deep
Like crystal fathomless lakes in summer noons—
120 Oh, sad sweet longing smile—Oh, lips that tempt
My very self to kisses—oh, round cheeks
Tenderly radiant with the even flush
Of pale smoothed coral—perfect lovely face
Answering my gaze from out this fleckless pool—
125 Wonder of glossy shoulders, chiselled limbs—
Should I be so your lover as I am,
Drinking an exquisite joy to watch you thus
In all a hundred changes through the day,
But that I love you for him till he comes,
130 But that my beauty means his loving it?

Oh, look! a speck on this side of the sun,
Coming—yes, coming with the rising wind
That frays the darkening cloud-wrack on the verge
And in a little while will leap abroad,
135 Spattering the sky with rushing blacknesses,
Dashing the hissing mountainous waves at the stars.
'Twill drive me that black speck a shuddering hulk
Caught in the buffeting waves, dashed impotent
From ridge to ridge, will drive it in the night
140 With that dull jarring crash upon the beach,
And the cries for help and the cries of fear and hope.

And then tomorrow they will thoughtfully,
With grave low voices, count their perils up,
And thank the gods for having let them live
145 And tell of wives and mothers in their homes,
And children, who would have such loss in them
That they must weep (and maybe I weep too)
With fancy of the weepings had they died.
And the next morrow they will feel their ease
150 And sigh with sleek content, or laugh elate,
Tasting delight of rest and revelling,
Music and perfumes, joyaunce[9] for the eyes
Of rosy faces and luxurious pomps,
The savour of the banquet and the glow
155 And fragrance of the wine-cup; and they'll talk
How good it is to house in palaces
Out of the storms and struggles, and what luck
Strewed their good ship on our accessless coast.
Then the next day the beast in them will wake,
160 And one will strike and bicker, and one swell
With puffed-up greatness, and one gibe and strut
In apish pranks, and one will line his sleeve
With pilfered booties, and one snatch the gems
Out of the carven goblets as they pass,
165 One will grow mad with fever of the wine,

9. Delight.

And one will sluggishly besot himself,[1]
And one be lewd, and one be gluttonous;
And I shall sickly look and loathe them all.

170 Oh my rare cup! my pure and crystal cup,
With not one speck of colour to make false
The entering lights, or flaw to make them swerve!
My cup of Truth! How the lost fools will laugh
And thank me for my boon, as if I gave
Some momentary flash of the gods' joy,
175 To drink where *I* have drunk and touch the touch
Of *my* lips with their own! Aye, let them touch.

Too cruel, am I? And the silly beasts,
Crowding around me when I pass their way,
Glower on me and, although they love me still,
180 (With their poor sorts of love such as they could)
Call wrath and vengeance to their humid eyes
To scare me into mercy, or creep near
With piteous fawnings, supplicating bleats.
Too cruel? Did I choose them what they are?
185 Or change them from themselves by poisonous charms?
But any draught, pure water, natural wine,
Out of my cup, revealed them to themselves
And to each other. Change? there was no change;
Only disguise gone from them unawares:
190 And had there been one true right man of them
He would have drunk the draught as I had drunk,
And stood unharmed and looked me in the eyes,
Abashing me before him. But these things—
Why, which of them has even shown the kind
195 Of some one nobler beast? Pah! yapping wolves,
And pitiless stealthy wild-cats, curs, and apes,
And gorging swine, and slinking venomous snakes—
All false and ravenous and sensual brutes
That shame the Earth that bore them, these they are.

200 Lo, lo! the shivering blueness darting forth
On half the heavens, and the forked thin fire
Strikes to the sea: and hark, the sudden voice
That rushes through the trees before the storm,
And shuddering of the branches. Yet the sky
205 Is blue against them still, and early stars
Sparkle above the pine-tops; and the air
Clings faint and motionless around me here.

Another burst of flame—and the black speck
Shows in the glare, lashed onwards. It were well
210 I bade make ready for our guests to-night.

1870

1. Stupefy his mind.

A Castaway

Poor little diary, with its simple thoughts,
Its good resolves, its "Studied French an hour,"
"Read Modern History," "Trimmed up my grey hat,"
"Darned stockings," "Tatted," "Practiced my new song,"
5 "Went to the daily service," "Took Bess soup,"
"Went out to tea." Poor simple diary!
And did *I* write it? Was I this good girl,
This budding colourless young rose of home?
Did I so live content in such a life,
10 Seeing no larger scope, nor asking it,
Than this small constant round—old clothes to mend,
New clothes to make, then go and say my prayers,
Or carry soup, or take a little walk
And pick the ragged-robins[1] in the hedge?
15 Then, for ambition, (was there ever life
That could forego that?) To improve my mind
And know French better and sing harder songs;
For gaiety, to go, in my best white
Well washed and starched and freshened with new bows,
20 And take tea out to meet the clergyman.
No wishes and no cares, almost no hopes,
Only the young girl's hazed and golden dreams
That veil the Future from her.

 So long since:
And now it seems a jest to talk of me
25 As if I could be one with her, of me
Who am . . . me.

 And what is that? My looking-glass
Answers it passably; a woman sure,
No fiend, no slimy thing out of the pools,
A woman with a ripe and smiling lip
30 That has no venom in its touch I think,
With a white brow on which there is no brand;
A woman none dare call not beautiful,
Not womanly in every woman's grace.

 Aye, let me feed upon my beauty thus,
35 Be glad in it like painters when they see
At last the face they dreamed but could not find
Look from their canvas on them, triumph in it,
The dearest thing I have. Why,'tis my all,
Let me make much of it: is it not this,
40 This beauty, my own curse at once and tool
To snare men's souls, (I know what the good say
Of beauty in such creatures) is it not this
That makes me feel myself a woman still,

1. A fragrant English flower (an herb in the pink family).

With still some little pride, some little—
 Stop!
45 "Some little pride, some little"—Here's a jest!
What word will fit the sense but modesty?
A wanton I, but modest!

 Modest, true;
I'm not drunk in the streets, ply not for hire
At infamous corners with my likenesses
50 Of the humbler kind; yes, modesty's my word—
'Twould shape my mouth well too, I think I'll try:
"Sir, Mr. What-you-will, Lord Who-knows-what,
My present lover or my next to come,
Value me at my worth, fill your purse full,
55 For I am modest; yes, and honour me
As though your schoolgirl sister or your wife
Could let her skirts brush mine or talk of me;
For I am modest."

 Well, I flout myself:
But yet, but yet——

 Fie, poor fantastic fool,
60 Why do I play the hypocrite alone,
Who am no hypocrite with others by?
Where should be my "But yet"? I am that thing
Called half a dozen dainty names, and none
Dainty enough to serve the turn and hide
65 The one coarse English worst that lurks beneath:
Just that, no worse, no better.

 And, for me,
I say let no one be above her trade;
I own my kindredship with any drab[2]
Who sells herself as I, although she crouch
70 In fetid garrets and I have a home
All velvet and marqueterie and pastilles,[3]
Although she hide her skeleton in rags
And I set fashions and wear cobweb lace:
The difference lies but in my choicer ware,
75 That I sell beauty and she ugliness;
Our traffic's one——I'm no sweet slaver-tongue
To gloze upon it[4] and explain myself
A sort of fractious angel misconceived—
Our traffic's one: I own it. And what then?
80 I know of worse that are called honourable.
Our lawyers, who with noble eloquence
And virtuous outbursts lie to hang a man,
Or lie to save him, which[5] way goes the fee:

2. Slut, prostitute.
3. Perfumes. "Marqueterie": inlaid furniture.

4. Explain it away. "Slaver-tongue": nonsense talker.
5. I.e., whichever.

Our preachers, gloating on your future hell
85 For not believing what they doubt themselves:
Our doctors, who sort poisons out by chance
And wonder how they'll answer,[6] and grow rich:
Our journalists, whose business is to fib
And juggle truths and falsehoods to and fro:
90 Our tradesmen, who must keep unspotted names
And cheat the least like stealing that they can:
Our——all of them, the virtuous worthy men
Who feed on the world's follies, vices, wants,
And do their businesses of lies and shams
95 Honestly, reputably, while the world
Claps hands and cries "good luck," which of their trades,
Their honourable trades, barefaced like mine,
All secrets brazened out, would shew more white?[7]

And whom do I hurt more than they? as much?
100 The wives? Poor fools, what do I take from them
Worth crying for or keeping? If they knew
What their fine husbands look like seen by eyes
That may perceive there are more men than one!
But, if they can, let them just take the pains
105 To keep them: 'tis not such a mighty task
To pin an idiot to your apron-string;
And wives have an advantage over us,
(The good and blind ones have) the smile or pout
Leaves them no secret nausea at odd times.
110 Oh, they could keep their husbands if they cared,
But 'tis an easier life to let them go,
And whimper at it for morality.

Oh! those shrill carping virtues, safely housed
From reach of even a smile that should put red
115 On a decorous cheek, who rail at us
With such a spiteful scorn and rancorousness,
(Which maybe is half envy at the heart)
And boast themselves so measurelessly good
And us so measurelessly unlike them,
120 What is their wondrous merit that they stay
In comfortable homes whence not a soul
Has ever thought of tempting them, and wear
No kisses but a husband's upon lips
There is no other man desires to kiss—
125 Refrain in fact from sin impossible?
How dare they hate us so? what have they done,
What borne, to prove them other than we are?
What right have they to scorn us—glass-case saints,
Dianas[8] under lock and key—what right

6. Serve the purpose.
7. Innocent.

8. I.e., virgins (after Diana, the Roman virgin goddess of the hunt).

130 More than the well-fed helpless barn-door fowl
To scorn the larcenous wild-birds?

 Pshaw, let be!
Scorn or no scorn, what matter for their scorn?
I have outfaced my own—that's harder work.
Aye, let their virtuous malice dribble on—
135 Mock snowstorms on the stage—I'm proof⁹ long since:
I have looked coolly on my what and why,
And I accept myself.

 Oh I'll endorse
The shamefullest revilings mouthed at me,
Cry "True! Oh perfect picture! Yes, that's I!"
140 And add a telling blackness here and there,
And then dare swear you, every nine of ten,
My judges and accusers, I'd not change
My conscience against yours, you who tread out
Your devil's pilgrimage along the roads
145 That take in church and chapel, and arrange
A roundabout and decent way to hell.

 Well, mine's a short way and a merry one:
So says my pious hash of ohs and ahs,
Choice texts and choicer threats, appropriate names,
150 (Rahabs and Jezebels) some fierce Tartuffe¹
Hurled at me through the post. We had rare fun
Over that tract digested with champagne.
Where is it? where's my rich repertory
Of insults Biblical? '*I prey on souls*'—
155 Only my men have oftenest none I think:
'*I snare the simple ones*'²—but in these days
There seem to be none simple and none snared
And most men have their favourite sinnings planned
To do them civilly and sensibly:
160 '*I braid my hair*'—but braids are out of date:
'*I paint my cheeks*'³—I always wear them pale:
'*I*—'

 Pshaw! the trash is savourless to-day:
One cannot laugh alone. There, let it burn.
What, does the windy dullard think one needs
165 His wisdom dove-tailed on to Solomon's,⁴
His threats out-threatening God's, to teach the news
That those who need not sin have safer souls?

9. Impervious to them.
1. A religious hypocrite, after the title character of the 1664 comic drama by Molière. Rahab and Jezebel are both biblical figures: Rahab was a harlot of Jericho who protected two Israelite spies (Joshua 2, 6.18); and the name of Jezebel, the power-hungry wife of Ahab, became synonymous for a bold woman of loose morals (see 2 Kings 9.30).
2. For a "harlot" snaring a young man from "among the simple ones," see Proverbs 7.
3. As did Jezebel (2 Kings 9.30). Women are admonished not to braid their hair in 1 Timothy 2.9.
4. Biblical king whose wisdom was proverbial.

We know it, but we've bodies to save too;
And so we earn our living.

 Well lit, tract!
170 At least you've made me a good leaping blaze.
Up, up, how the flame shoots! and now 'tis dead.
Oh proper finish, preaching to the last—
No such bad omen either; sudden end,
And no sad withering horrible old age.
175 How one would clutch at youth to hold it tight!
And then to know it gone, to see it gone,
Be taught its absence by harsh careless looks,
To live forgotten, solitary, old—
The cruellest word that ever woman learns.
180 Old—that's to be nothing, or to be at best
A blurred memorial that in better days
There was a woman once with such a name.
No, no, I could not bear it: death itself
Shows kinder promise . . . even death itself,
Since it must come one day—

185 Oh this grey gloom!
This rain, rain, rain, what wretched thoughts it brings!
Death: I'll not think of it.

 Will no one come?
'Tis dreary work alone.

 Why did I read
That silly diary? Now, sing-song, ding-dong,
190 Come the old vexing echoes back again,
Church bells and nursery good-books, back again
Upon my shrinking ears that had forgotten—
I hate the useless memories: 'tis fools' work
Singing the hacknied dirge of 'better days':
195 Best take Now kindly, give the past good-bye,
Whether it were a better or a worse.

 Yes, yes, I listened to the echoes once,
The echoes and the thoughts from the old days.
The worse for me: I lost my richest friend,
200 And that was all the difference. For the world,
I would not have that flight known. How they'd roar:
"What! Eulalie, when she refused us all,
'Ill' and 'away,' was doing Magdalene,[5]
Tears, ashes, and her Bible, and then off
205 To hide her in a Refuge . . . for a week!"

5. Acting the part of a reformed prostitute (the Mary Magdalene healed of evil spirits by Jesus is traditionally identified with the prostitute who kisses and anoints his feet; see Luke 8.2, 7.37–48). Many Magdalene houses, intended to redeem prostitutes, were set up in Britain in the nineteenth century.

A wild whim that, to fancy I could change
My new self for my old because I wished!
Since then, when in my languid days there comes
That craving, like homesickness, to go back
210 To the good days, the dear old stupid days,
To the quiet and the innocence, I know
'Tis a sick fancy and try palliatives.

 What is it? You go back to the old home,
And 'tis not *your* home, has no place for you,
215 And, if it had, you could not fit you in it.
And could I fit me to my former self?
If I had had the wit, like some of us,
To sow my wild-oats into three per cents,[6]
Could I not find me shelter in the peace
220 Of some far nook where none of them would come,
Nor whisper travel from this scurrilous world
(That gloats, and moralizes through its leers)
To blast me with my fashionable shame?
There I might—oh my castle in the clouds!
225 And where's its rent?—but there, were there a there,
I might again live the grave blameless life
Among such simple pleasures, simple cares:
But could they be my pleasures, be my cares?
The blameless life, but never the content—
230 Never. How could I henceforth be content
With any life but one that sets the brain
In a hot merry fever with its stir?
What would there be in quiet rustic days,
Each like the other, full of time to think,
235 To keep one bold enough to live at all?
Quiet is hell, I say—as if a woman
Could bear to sit alone, quiet all day,
And loathe herself and sicken on her thoughts.

 They tried it at the Refuge, and I failed:
240 I could not bear it. Dreary hideous room,
Coarse pittance, prison rules, one might bear these
And keep one's purpose; but so much alone,
And then made faint and weak and fanciful
By change from pampering to half-famishing—
245 Good God, what thoughts come! Only one week more
And 'twould have ended: but in one day more
I must have killed myself. And I loathe death,
The dreadful foul corruption with who knows
What future after it.
 Well, I came back,
250 Back to my slough.[7] Who says I had my choice?
Could I stay there to die of some mad death?

6. The government securities of Great Britain.
7. Place of deep mud; state of moral degradation.
Perhaps the word is meant to evoke the Slough of

Despond of John Bunyan's *The Pilgrim's Progress*
(1678).

And if I rambled out into the world
Sinless but penniless, what else were that
But slower death, slow pining shivering death
255 By misery and hunger? Choice! what choice
Of living well or ill? could I have that?
And who would give it me? I think indeed
If some kind hand, a woman's—I hate men—
Had stretched itself to help me to firm ground,
260 Taken a chance and risked my falling back,
I could have gone my way not falling back:
But, let her be all brave, all charitable,
How could she do it? Such a trifling boon—
A little work to live by,'tis not much—
265 And I might have found will enough to last:
But where's the work? More sempstresses than shirts;
And defter hands at white work[8] than are mine
Drop starved at last: dressmakers, milliners,
Too many too they say; and then their trades
270 Need skill, apprenticeship. And who so bold
As hire me for their humblest drudgery?
Not even for scullery slut;[9] not even, I think,
For governess although they'd get me cheap.
And after all it would be something hard,
275 With the marts for decent women overfull,
If I could elbow in and snatch a chance
And oust some good girl so, who then perforce
Must come and snatch her chance among our crowd.

Why, if the worthy men who think all's done
280 If we'll but come where we can hear them preach,
Could bring us all, or any half of us,
Into their fold, teach all us wandering sheep,
Or only half of us, to stand in rows
And baa them hymns and moral songs, good lack,[1]
285 What would they do with us? what could they do?
Just think! with weren't but half of us on hand
To find work for . . . or husbands. Would they try
To ship us to the colonies for wives?[2]

Well, well, I know the wise ones talk and talk:
290 "Here's cause, here's cure:" "No, here it is, and here:"
And find society to blame, or law,
The Church, the men, the women, too few schools,
Too many schools, too much, too little taught:
Somewhere or somehow someone is to blame:
295 But I say all the fault's with God himself
Who puts too many women in the world.

8. Needlework.
9. Kitchen maids.
1. An exclamation.
2. For a long period of time, Great Britain trans-
ported many of its convicted criminals to penal col-
onies, first in North America (Georgia) and later in
Australia; transportation officially ended in 1868
(it had effectively stopped in 1857).

We ought to die off reasonably and leave
As many as the men want, none to waste.
Here's cause; the woman's superfluity:[3]
300 And for the cure, why, if it were the law,
Say, every year, in due percentages,
Balancing them with males as the times need,
To kill off female infants, 'twould make room;
And some of us would not have lost too much,
305 Losing life ere we know what it *can* mean.

 The other day I saw a woman weep
Beside her dead child's bed: the little thing
Lay smiling, and the mother wailed half mad,
Shrieking to God to give it back again.
310 I could have laughed aloud: the little girl
Living had but her mother's life to live;
There she lay smiling, and her mother wept
To know her gone!

 My mother would have wept.

 Oh, mother, mother, did you ever dream,
315 You good grave simple mother, you pure soul
No evil could come nigh, did you once dream
In all your dying cares for your lone girl
Left to fight out her fortune helplessly
That there would be *this* danger?—for *your* girl,
320 Taught by you, lapped in a sweet ignorance,
Scarcely more wise of what things sin could be
Than some young child a summer six months old,
Where in the north the summer makes a day,
Of what is darkness . . . darkness that will come
325 To-morrow suddenly. Thank God at least
For this much of my life, that when you died,
That when you kissed me dying, not a thought
Of this made sorrow for you, that I too
Was pure of even fear.

 Oh yes, I thought,
330 Still new in my insipid treadmill life,
(My father so late dead), and hopeful still,
There might be something pleasant somewhere in it,
Some sudden fairy come, no doubt, to turn
My pumpkin to a chariot,[4] I thought then
335 That I might plod and plod and drum the sounds
Of useless facts into unwilling ears,
Tease children with dull questions half the day
Then con[5] dull answers in my room at night

3. In 1862 W. R. Greg published a much-quoted article on "superfluous" women, "Why Are Women Redundant?"

4. I.e., to bring about a fairy-tale ending, as in the story of Cinderella.
5. Study; examine.

Ready for next day's questions, mend quill pens
340 And cut my fingers, add up sums done wrong
And never get them right; teach, teach, and teach—
What I half knew, or not at all—teach, teach
For years, a lifetime—*I!*

 And yet, who knows?
It might have been, for I was patient once,
345 And willing, and meant well; it might have been
Had I but still clung on in my first place[6]—
A safe dull place, where mostly there were smiles
But never merry-makings; where all days
Jogged on sedately busy, with no haste;
350 Where all seemed measured out, but margins broad:
A dull home but a peaceful, where I felt
My pupils would be dear young sisters soon,
And felt their mother take me to her heart,
Motherly to all lonely harmless things.
355 But I must have a conscience, must blurt out
My great discovery of my ignorance!
And who required it of me? And who gained?
What did it matter for a more or less
The girls learnt in their schoolbooks, to forget
360 In their first season?[7] We did well together:
They loved me and I them: but I went off
To housemaid's pay, six crossgrained[8] brats to teach,
Wrangles and jangles, doubts, disgrace . . . then this;
And they had a perfection found for them,
365 Who has all ladies' learning in her head
Abridged and scheduled, speaks five languages,
Knows botany and conchology[9] and globes,
Draws, paints, plays, sings, embroiders, teaches all
On a patent[1] method never known to fail:
370 And now they're finished and, I hear, poor things,
Are the worst dancers and worst dressers out.
And where's their profit of those prison years
All gone to make them wise in lesson-books?
Who wants his wife to know weeds' Latin names?
375 Who ever chose a girl for saying dates?
Or asked if she had learned to trace a map?

 Well, well, the silly rules this silly world
Makes about women! This is one of them.
Why must there be pretence of teaching them
380 What no one ever cares that they should know,
What, grown out of the schoolroom, they cast off
Like the schoolroom pinafore, no better fit

6. I.e., first position as a governess.
7. The time when fashionable society assembled in London, and when upper-class girls came out" (first appeared publicly) to begin searching for a husband.
8. Intractable, difficult to deal with.
9. The science of seashells.
1. Proprietary; patented.

For any use of real grown-up life,
For any use to her who seeks or waits
385 The husband and the home, for any use,
For any shallowest pretence of use,
To her who has them? Do I not know this,
I, like my betters, that a woman's life,
Her natural life, her good life, her one life,
390 Is in her husband, God on earth to her,
And what she knows and what she can and is
Is only good as it brings good to him?

 Oh God, do I not know it? I the thing
Of shame and rottenness, the animal
395 That feed men's lusts and prey on them, I, I,
Who should not dare to take the name of wife
On my polluted lips, who in the word
Hear but my own reviling, I know that.
I could have lived by that rule, how content:
400 My pleasure to make him some pleasure, pride
To be as he would have me, duty, care,
To fit all to his taste, rule my small sphere
To his intention; then to lean on him,
Be guided, tutored, loved—no not that word,
405 That *loved* which between men and women means
All selfishness, all cloying talk, all lust,
All vanity, all idiocy—not loved,
But cared for. I've been loved myself, I think,
Some once or twice since my poor mother died,
410 But *cared for*, never:—that's a word for homes,
Kind homes, good homes, where simple children come
And ask their mother is this right or wrong,
Because they know she's perfect, cannot err;
Their father told them so, and he knows all,
415 Being so wise and good and wonderful,
Even enough to scold even her at times
And tell her everything she does not know.
Ah the sweet nursery logic!

 Fool! thrice fool!
Do I hanker after that too? Fancy me
420 Infallible nursery saint, live code of law!
Me preaching! teaching innocence to be good!—
A mother!

 Yet the baby thing that woke
And wailed an hour or two, and then was dead,
Was mine, and had he lived . . . why then my name
425 Would have been mother. But 'twas well he died:
I could have been no mother, I, lost then
Beyond his saving. Had he come before
And lived, come to me in the doubtful days
When shame and boldness had not grown one sense,

430　For his sake, with the courage come of him,
　　I might have struggled back.

　　　　　　　　　　But how? But how?
　　His father would not then have let me go:
　　His time had not yet come to make an end
　　Of my 'for ever' with a hireling's fee
435　And civil light dismissal. None but him
　　To claim a bit of bread of if I went,
　　Child or no child: would he have given it me?
　　He! no; he had not done with me. No help,
　　No help, no help. Some ways can be trodden back,
440　But never our way, we who one wild day
　　Have given goodbye to what in our deep hearts
　　The lowest woman still holds best in life,
　　Good name—good name though given by the world
　　That mouths and garbles with its decent prate,
445　And wraps it in respectable grave shams,
　　And patches conscience partly by the rule
　　Of what one's neighbour thinks, but something more
　　By what his eyes are sharp enough to see.
　　How I could scorn it with its Pharisees,[2]
450　If it could not scorn me: but yet, but yet—
　　Oh God, if I could look it in the face!

　　　Oh I am wild, am ill, I think, to-night:
　　Will no one come and laugh with me? No feast,
　　No merriment to-night. So long alone!
　　Will no one come?

455　　　　　　　　　At least there's a new dress
　　To try, and grumble at—they never fit
　　To one's ideal. Yes, a new rich dress,
　　With lace like this too, that's a soothing balm
　　For any fretting woman, cannot fail;
460　I've heard men say it . . . and they know so well
　　What's in all women's hearts, especially
　　Women like me.

　　　　　　　　No help! no help! no help!
　　How could it be? It was too late long since—
　　Even at the first too late. Whose blame is that?
465　There are some kindly people in the world,
　　But what can *they* do? If one hurls oneself
　　Into a quicksand, what can be the end,
　　But that one sinks and sinks? Cry out for help?
　　Ah yes, and, if it came, who is so strong
470　To strain from the firm ground and lift one out?
　　And how, so firmly clutching the stretched hand
　　As death's pursuing terror bids, even so,

2. Hypocrites; literally, a sect of Jews who believed in strict separation from the heathen and who were attacked by Jesus for hypocrisy, greed, and blindness (Matthew 23.13–36).

How can one reach firm land, having to foot
The treacherous crumbling soil that slides and gives
475 And sucks one in again? Impossible path!
No, why waste struggles, I or any one?
What is must be. What then? I where I am,
Sinking and sinking; let the wise pass by
And keep their wisdom for an apter use,
480 Let me sink merrily as I best may.

 Only, I think my brother—I forgot;
He stopped his brotherhood some years ago—
But if he had been just so much less good
As to remember mercy. Did he think
485 How once I was his sister, prizing him
As sisters do, content to learn for him
The lesson girls with brothers all must learn,
To do without?

 I have heard girls lament
That doing so without all things one would,
490 But I saw never aught to murmur at,
For men must be made ready for their work
And women all have more or less their chance
Of husbands to work for them, keep them safe
Like summer roses in soft greenhouse air
495 That never guess 'tis winter out of doors:
No, I saw never aught to murmur at,
Content with stinted fare and shabby clothes
And cloistered silent life to save expense,
Teaching myself out of my borrowed books,
500 While he for some one pastime, (needful, true,
To keep him of his rank; 'twas not his fault)
Spent in a month what could have given me
My teachers for a year.

 'Twas no one's fault:
For could he be launched forth on the rude sea
505 Of this contentious world and left to find
Oars and the boatman's skill by some good chance?
'Twas no one's fault: yet still he might have thought
Of our so different youths and owned at least
'Tis pitiful when a mere nerveless girl
510 Untutored must put forth upon that sea,
Not in the woman's true place, the wife's place,
To trust a husband and be borne along,
But impotent blind pilot to herself.

 Merciless, merciless—like the prudent world
515 That will not have the flawed soul prank[3] itself
With a hoped second virtue, will not have
The woman fallen once lift up herself . . .

3. Dress up, adorn.

Lest she should fall again. Oh how his taunts,
His loathing fierce reproaches, scarred and seared
520　Like branding iron hissing in a wound!
And it was true—*that* killed me: and I felt
A hideous hopeless shame burn out my heart,
And knew myself for ever that he said,
That which I was—Oh it was true, true, true.

525　　No, not true then. I was not all that then.
Oh, I have drifted on before mad winds
And made ignoble shipwreck; not to-day
Could any breeze of heaven prosper me
Into the track again, nor any hand
530　Snatch me out of the whirlpool I have reached;
But then?

　　　　　　　　Nay, he judged very well: he knew
Repentance was too dear a luxury
For a beggar's buying, knew it earns no bread—
And knew me a too base and nerveless thing
535　To bear my first fault's sequel and just die.
And how could he have helped me? Held my hand,
Owned me for his, fronted the angry world
Clothed with my ignominy? Or maybe
Taken me to his home to damn him worse?
540　What did I look for? for what less would serve
That he could do, a man without a purse?
He meant me well, he sent me that five pounds,
Much to him then; and, if he bade me work
And never vex him more with news of me,
545　We both knew him too poor for pensioners.
I see he did his best; I could wish now
Sending it back I had professed some thanks.

　　But there! I was too wretched to be meek:
It seemed to me as if he, every one,
550　The whole great world, were guilty of my guilt,
Abettors and avengers: in my heart
I gibed them back their gibings; I was wild.

　　I see clear now and know one has one's life
In hand at first to spend or spare or give
555　Like any other coin; spend it, or give,
Or drop it in the mire, can the world see
You get your value for it, or bar off
The hurrying of its marts to grope it up
And give it back to you for better use?
560　And if you spend or give, that is your choice;
And if you let it slip, that's your choice too,
You should have held it firmer. Yours the blame,
And not another's, not the indifferent world's
Which goes on steadily, statistically,

565 And count by censuses not separate souls—
And if it somehow needs to its worst use
So many lives of women, useless else,
It buys us of ourselves; we could hold back,
Free all of us to starve, and some of us,
570 (Those who have done no ill, and are in luck)
To slave their lives out and have food and clothes
Until they grow unserviceably old.

 Oh, I blame no one—scarcely even myself.
It was to be: the very good in me
575 Has always turned to hurt; all I thought right
At the hot moment, judged of afterwards,
Shows reckless.

 Why, look at it, had I taken
The pay my dead child's father offered me
For having been its mother, I could then
580 Have kept life in me—many have to do it,
That swarm in the back alleys, on no more,
Cold sometimes, mostly hungry, but they live—
I could have gained a respite trying it,
And maybe found at last some humble work
585 To eke the pittance out. Not I, forsooth,
I must have spirit, must have womanly pride,
Must dash back his contemptuous wages, I
Who had not scorned to earn them, dash them back
The fiercer that he dared to count our boy
590 In my appraising: and yet now I think
I might have taken it for my dead boy's sake;
It would have been *his* gift.

 But I went forth
With my fine scorn, and whither did it lead?
Money's the root of evil do they say?[4]
595 Money is virtue, strength: money to me
Would then have been repentance: could I live
Upon my idiot's pride?

 Well, it fell soon.
I had prayed Clement might believe me dead,
And yet I begged of him—That's like me too,
600 Beg of him and then send him back his alms!
What if he gave as to a whining wretch
That holds her hand and lies? I am less to him
Than such a one; her rags do him no wrong,
But I, I wrong him merely that I live,
605 Being his sister. Could I not at least
Have still let him forget me? But 'tis past:
And naturally he may hope I am long dead.

4. According to the apostle Paul, "The love of money is the root of all evil" (1 Timothy 6.10).

Good God! to think that we were what we were
One to the other . . . and now!

 He has done well;
610 Married a sort of heiress, I have heard,
A dapper little madam dimple cheeked
And dimple brained, who makes him a good wife—
No doubt she'd never own but just to him,
And in a whisper, she can even suspect
615 That we exist, we other women things:
What would she say if she could learn one day
She has a sister-in-law? So he and I
Must stand apart till doomsday.

 But the jest,
To think how she would look!—Her fright, poor thing!
620 The notion!—I could laugh outright . . . or else,
For I feel near it, roll on the ground and sob.

Well, after all, there's not much difference
Between the two sometimes.

 Was that the bell?
Someone at last, thank goodness. There's a voice,
625 And that's a pleasure. Whose though? Ah, I know.
Why did she come alone, the cackling goose?
Why not have brought her sister?—she tells more
And titters less. No matter; half a loaf
Is better than no bread.

 Oh, is it you?
630 Most welcome, dear: one gets so moped⁵ alone.

 1870

From Mother and Daughter

XV

That some day Death who has us all for jest
 Shall hide me in the dark and voiceless mould,
 And him whose living hand has mine in hold,
Where loving comes not nor the looks that rest,
5 Shall make us nought where we are known the best,
 Forgotten things that leave their track untold
 As in the August night the sky's dropped gold—
This seems no strangeness, but Death's natural hest.¹

5. Melancholy; low-spirited. 1. Purpose.

But looking on the dawn that is her face
10 To know she too is Death's seems misbelief;[2]
She should not find decay, but, as the sun
Moves mightier from the veil that hides his place,
Keep ceaseless radiance. Life is Death begun:
But Death and her! That's strangeness passing grief.

XVII

And how could I grow old while she's so young?
 Methinks her heart sets time for mine to beat,
 We are so near; her new thoughts, incomplete,
Find their shaped wording happen on my tongue;
5 Like bloom on last year's winterings newly sprung
 My youth upflowers with hers, and must repeat
 Old joyaunces[3] in me nigh obsolete.
Could I grow older while my child's so young?

And there are tales how youthful blood instilled
10 Thawing frore[4] Age's veins gave life new course,
And quavering limbs and eyes made indolent
 Grew freshly eager with beginning force:
She so breathes impulse. Were my years twice spent,
Not burdening Age, with her, could make me chilled.

1895

2. Heresy.
3. Enjoyments.

4. Frozen.

CONSTANCE FENIMORE WOOLSON
1840–1894

Relatively little is known about the creative development of Constance Fenimore Woolson, who was born in Claremont, New Hampshire. She spent her school years in Cleveland, Ohio, and her summers at the family cottage on Mackinac Island, Michigan, the setting of her earliest stories, *Castle Nowhere: Lake Country Sketches* (1878), and of her first novel, *Anne* (1880). The great-niece of the novelist James Fenimore Cooper, Woolson traveled along the eastern seaboard with her mother after her father's death in 1869. Ten years later, when her mother died, she moved to Europe, where she lived for the remainder of her life, primarily in Italy and Switzerland. In Florence, she met Henry James in 1880 and either or both may have conceived what Leon Edel called a "virtuous attachment," though Edel's attribution of Woolson's later unhappiness to unrequited love for James has recently been questioned. For, despite her productivity—Woolson published four novels between 1883 and 1894—this writer had long felt herself to have inherited "a sort of depression that comes unexpectedly, and makes everything black."

The circumstances surrounding Woolson's death are controversial, but a number

of scholars believe that she committed suicide by throwing herself from her bedroom window in Venice. At her request, she was buried in the Protestant Cemetery in Rome. Imbued with the melancholy from which its author suffered, her subtly nuanced "Miss Grief" provides uncanny insight into the relationships between literary men and women. Composed before Woolson's own meeting with James, it has nevertheless been read as a comment on masterful men of letters like James and even as an influence on the famous author of such studies of artists' lives and problems as "The Aspern Papers" (1888) and "The Lesson of the Master" (1888). Not only a fascinating portrait of two quite different and competitive writers, Woolson's story also raises important questions about the basis of aesthetic judgments. How do we— why do we—term a work inspired or perverse, brilliant or flawed? On what bases are books accepted and printed by publishers? How are literary reputations established?

Miss Grief

"A conceited fool" is a not uncommon expression. Now, I know that I am not a fool, but I also know that I am conceited. But, candidly, can it be helped if one happens to be young, well and strong, passably good looking, with some money that one has inherited and more that one has earned—in all, enough to make life comfortable—and if upon this foundation rests also the pleasant superstructure of a literary success? The success is deserved, I think: certainly it was not lightly gained. Yet even with this I fully appreciate its rarity. Thus, I find myself very well entertained in life: I have all I wish in the way of society, and a deep, though of course carefully concealed, satisfaction in my own little fame; which fame I foster by a gentle system of non-interference. I know that I am spoken of as "that quiet young fellow who writes those delightful little studies of society, you know"; and I live up to that definition.

A year ago I was in Rome, and enjoying life particularly. I had a large number of my acquaintances there, both American and English, and no day passed without its invitation. Of course I understood it: it is seldom that you find a literary man who is good tempered, well dressed, sufficiently provided with money, and amiably obedient to all the rules and requirements of "society." "When found, make a note of it";[1] and the note was generally an invitation.

One evening, upon returning to my lodgings, my man Simpson informed me that a person had called in the afternoon, and upon learning that I was absent had left not a card, but her name—"Miss Grief." The title lingered— Miss Grief! "Grief has not so far visited me here," I said to myself, dismissing Simpson and seeking my little balcony for a final smoke, "and she shall not now. I shall take care to be 'not at home' to her if she continues to call." And then I fell to thinking of Isabel Abercrombie, in whose society I had spent that and many evenings: they were golden thoughts.

The next day there was an excursion; it was late when I reached my rooms, and again Simpson informed me that Miss Grief had called.

"Is she coming continuously?" I said, half to myself.

1. An allusion to a remark in Charles Dickens's *Dombey and Son* (1846–48): "When found, make a note of" (chapter 15).

"Yes, sir: she mentioned that she should call again."

"How does she look?"

"Well, sir, a lady, but not so prosperous as she was, I should say," answered Simpson, discreetly.

"Young?"

"No, sir."

"Alone?"

"A maid with her, sir."

But once outside in my little high-up balcony with my cigar, I again forgot Miss Grief and whatever she might represent. Who would not forget in that moonlight, with Isabel Abercrombie's face to remember?

The stranger came a third time, and I was absent; then she let two days pass, and began again. It grew to be a regular dialogue between Simpson and myself when I came in at night: "Grief today?"

"Yes, sir."

"What time?"

"Four, sir."

"Happy the man," I thought, "who can keep her confined to a particular hour!"

But I should not have treated my visitor so cavalierly if I had not felt sure that she was eccentric and unconventional—qualities extremely tiresome in a woman no longer young or attractive. If she were not eccentric, she would not have persisted in coming to my door day after day in this silent way, without stating her errand, leaving a note, or presenting her credentials in any shape. I made up my mind that she had something to sell—a bit of carving or some intaglio supposed to be antique. It was known that I had a fancy for oddities. I said to myself, "She has read or heard of my 'Old Gold' story, or else 'The Buried God,' and she thinks me an idealizing ignoramus upon whom she can impose. Her sepulchral name is at least not Italian; probably she is a sharp countrywoman of mine, turning, by means of the present aesthetic craze, an honest penny when she can."

She had called seven times during a period of two weeks without seeing me, when one day I happened to be at home in the afternoon, owing to a pouring rain and a fit of doubt concerning Miss Abercrombie. For I had constructed a careful theory of that young lady's characteristics in my own mind, and she had lived up to it delightfully until the previous evening, when with one word she had blown it to atoms and taken flight, leaving me standing, as it were, on a desolate shore, with nothing but a handful of mistaken inductions wherewith to console myself. I do not know a more exasperating frame of mind, at least for a constructor of theories. I could not write, and so I took up a French novel (I model myself a little on Balzac[2]). I had been turning over its pages but a few moments when Simpson knocked, and, entering softly, said, with just a shadow of a smile on his well-trained face, "Miss Grief." I briefly consigned Miss Grief to all the Furies,[3] and then, as he still lingered—perhaps not knowing where they resided—I asked where the visitor was.

2. Honoré de Balzac (1799–1850), whose novels and stories in *The Human Comedy*, his name for the whole body of his work, were early examples of social realism in fiction.

3. Greek female spirits of vengeance.

"Outside, sir—in the hall. I told her I would see if you were at home."

"She must be unpleasantly wet if she had no carriage."

"No carriage, sir: they always come on foot. I think she *is* a little damp, sir."

"Well, let her in; but I don't want the maid. I may as well see her now, I suppose, and end the affair."

"Yes, sir."

I did not put down my book. My visitor should have a hearing, but not much more: she had sacrificed her womanly claims by her persistent attacks upon my door. Presently Simpson ushered her in. "Miss Grief," he said, and then went out, closing the curtain behind him.

A woman—yes, a lady—but shabby, unattractive, and more than middle-aged.

I rose, bowed slightly, and then dropped into my chair again, still keeping the book in my hand. "Miss Grief?" I said interrogatively as I indicated a seat with my eyebrows.

"Not Grief," she answered—"Crief: my name is Crief."

She sat down, and I saw that she held a small flat box.

"Not carving, then," I thought—"probably old lace, something that belonged to Tullia or Lucrezia Borgia."[4] But, as she did not speak, I found myself obliged to begin: "You have been here, I think, once or twice before?"

"Seven times; this is the eighth."

A silence.

"I am often out; indeed, I may say that I am never in," I remarked carelessly.

"Yes; you have many friends."

"—Who will perhaps buy old lace," I mentally added. But this time I too remained silent; why should I trouble myself to draw her out? She had sought me; let her advance her idea, whatever it was, now that entrance was gained.

But Miss Grief (I preferred to call her so) did not look as though she could advance anything: her black gown, damp with rain, seemed to retreat fearfully to her thin self, while her thin self retreated as far as possible from me, from the chair, from everything. Her eyes were cast down; an old-fashioned lace veil with a heavy border shaded her face. She looked at the floor, and I looked at her.

I grew a little impatient, but I made up my mind that I would continue silent and see how long a time she would consider necessary to give due effect to her little pantomime. Comedy? Or was it tragedy? I suppose full five minutes passed thus in our double silence; and that is a long time when two persons are sitting opposite each other alone in a small still room.

At last my visitor, without raising her eyes, said slowly, "You are very happy, are you not, with youth, health, friends, riches, fame?"

It was a singular beginning. Her voice was clear, low, and very sweet as she thus enumerated my advantages one by one in a list. I was attracted by it, but repelled by her words, which seemed to me flattery both dull and bold.

4. Lucrezia Borgia (1480–1519), a member of a powerful Italian family famous for licentiousness, intrigue, and violence, whose second husband was murdered. According to the Roman historian Livy, Tullia (ca. 530 B.C.E.) conspired with Tarquinius Superbus to murder her husband and his wife (her sister), married Superbus, and then hounded him into deposing her father the king, over whose murdered body she drove her chariot.

"Thanks," I said, "for your kindness, but I fear it is undeserved. I seldom discuss myself even when with my friends."

"I am your friend," replied Miss Grief. Then, after a moment, she added slowly, "I have read every word you have written."

I curled the edges of my book indifferently; I am not a fop,[5] I hope, but—others have said the same.

"What is more, I know much of it by heart," continued my visitor. "Wait: I will show you"; and then, without pause, she began to repeat something of mine word for word, just as I had written it. On she went, and I—listened. I intended interrupting her after a moment, but I did not, because she was reciting so well, and also because I felt a desire gaining upon me to see what she would make of a certain conversation which I knew was coming—a conversation between two of my characters which was, to say the least, sphinx-like,[6] and somewhat incandescent as well. What won me a little, too, was the fact that the scene she was reciting (it was hardly more than that, though called a story) was secretly my favorite among all the sketches from my pen which a gracious public has received with favor. I never said so, but it was; and I had always felt a wondering annoyance that the aforesaid public, while kindly praising beyond their worth other attempts of mine, had never noticed the higher purpose of this little shaft, aimed not at the balconies and lighted windows of society, but straight up toward the distant stars. So she went on, and presently reached the conversation: my two people began to talk. She had raised her eyes now, and was looking at me soberly as she gave the words of the woman, quiet, gentle, cold, and the replies of the man, bitter, hot, and scathing. Her very voice changed, and took, though always sweetly, the different tones required, while no point of meaning, however small, no breath of delicate emphasis which I had meant, but which the dull types could not give, escaped an appreciative and full, almost overfull, recognition which startled me. For she had understood me—understood me almost better than I had understood myself. It seemed to me that while I had labored to interpret, partially, a psychological riddle, she, coming after, had comprehended its bearings better than I had, though confining herself strictly to my own words and emphasis. The scene ended (and it ended rather suddenly), she dropped her eyes, and moved her hand nervously to and fro over the box she held; her gloves were old and shabby, her hands small.

I was secretly much surprised by what I had heard, but my ill humor was deep-seated that day, and I still felt sure, besides, that the box contained something which I was expected to buy.

"You recite remarkably well," I said carelessly, "and I am much flattered also by your appreciation of my attempt. But it is not, I presume, to that alone that I owe the pleasure of this visit?"

"Yes," she answered, still looking down, "it is, for if you had not written that scene I should not have sought you. Your other sketches are interiors—exquisitely painted and delicately finished, but of small scope. *This* is a sketch in a few bold, masterly lines—work of entirely different spirit and purpose."

I was nettled by her insight. "You have bestowed so much of your kind attention upon me that I feel your debtor," I said, conventionally. "It may be

5. A conceited person.　　　　　6. Enigmatic, mysterious.

that there is something I can do for you—connected, possibly, with that little box?"

It was impertinent, but it was true; for she answered, "Yes."

I smiled, but her eyes were cast down and she did not see the smile.

"What I have to show you is a manuscript," she said after a pause which I did not break; "it is a drama. I thought that perhaps you would read it.

"An authoress! This is worse than old lace," I said to myself in dismay.— Then, aloud, "My opinion would be worth nothing, Miss Crief."

"Not in a business way, I know. But it might be—an assistance personally." Her voice had sunk to a whisper; outside, the rain was pouring steadily down. She was a very depressing object to me as she sat there with her box.

"I hardly think I have the time at present—" I began.

She had raised her eyes and was looking at me; then, when I paused, she rose and came suddenly toward my chair. "Yes, you will read it," she said with her hand on my arm—"you will read it. Look at this room; look at yourself; look at all you have. Then look at me, and have pity."

I had risen, for she held my arm, and her damp skirt was brushing my knees.

Her large dark eyes looked intently into mine as she went on: "I have no shame in asking. Why should I have? It is my last endeavor; but a calm and well-considered one. If you refuse I shall go away, knowing that Fate has willed it so. And I shall be content."

"She is mad," I thought. But she did not look so, and she had spoken quietly, even gently. "Sit down," I said, moving away from her. I felt as if I had been magnetized; but it was only the nearness of her eyes to mine, and their intensity. I drew forward a chair, but she remained standing.

"I cannot," she said in the same sweet, gentle tone, "unless you promise."

"Very well, I promise; only sit down."

As I took her arm to lead her to the chair, I perceived that she was trembling, but her face continued unmoved.

"You do not, of course, wish me to look at your manuscript now?" I said, temporizing; "it would be much better to leave it. Give me your address, and I will return it to you with my written opinion; though, I repeat, the latter will be of no use to you. It is the opinion of an editor or publisher that you want."

"It shall be as you please. And I will go in a moment," said Miss Grief, pressing her palms together, as if trying to control the tremor that had seized her slight frame.

She looked so pallid that I thought of offering her a glass of wine; then I remembered that if I did it might be a bait to bring her here again, and this I was desirous to prevent. She rose while the thought was passing through my mind. Her pasteboard box lay on the chair she had first occupied; she took it, wrote an address on the cover, laid it down, and then, bowing with a little air of formality, drew her black shawl round her shoulders and turned toward the door.

I followed, after touching the bell. "You will hear from me by letter," I said.

Simpson opened the door, and I caught a glimpse of the maid, who was waiting in the anteroom. She was an old woman, shorter than her mistress, equally thin, and dressed like her in rusty black. As the door opened she

turned toward it a pair of small, dim, blue eyes with a look of furtive suspense. Simpson dropped the curtain, shutting me into the inner room; he had no intention of allowing me to accompany my visitor further. But I had the curiosity to go to a bay window in an angle from whence I could command the street door, and presently I saw them issue forth in the rain and walk away side by side, the mistress, being the taller, holding the umbrella: probably there was not much difference in rank between persons so poor and forlorn as these.

It grew dark. I was invited out for the evening, and I knew that if I should go I should meet Miss Abercrombie. I said to myself that I would not go. I got out my paper for writing, I made my preparations for a quiet evening at home with myself; but it was of no use. It all ended slavishly in my going. At the last allowable moment I presented myself, and—as a punishment for my vacillation, I suppose—I never passed a more disagreeable evening. I drove homeward in a murky temper; it was foggy without, and very foggy within. What Isabel really was, now that she had broken through my elaborately built theories, I was not able to decide. There was, to tell the truth, a certain young Englishman—But that is apart from this story.

I reached home, went up to my rooms, and had a supper. It was to console myself; I am obliged to console myself scientifically once in a while. I was walking up and down afterward, smoking and feeling somewhat better, when my eye fell upon the pasteboard box. I took it up; on the cover was written an address which showed that my visitor must have walked a long distance in order to see me: "A. Crief."—"A Grief," I thought; "and so she is. I positively believe she has brought all this trouble upon me: she has the evil eye." I took out the manuscript and looked at it. It was in the form of a little volume, and clearly written; on the cover was the word "Armor" in German text,[7] and, underneath, a pen-and-ink sketch of a helmet, breastplate, and shield.

"Grief certainly needs armor," I said to myself, sitting down by the table and turning over the pages. "I may as well look over the thing now; I could not be in a worse mood." And then I began to read.

Early the next morning Simpson took a note from me to the given address, returning with the following reply: "No; I prefer to come to you; at four; A. Crief." These words, with their three semicolons, were written in pencil upon a piece of coarse printing paper, but the handwriting was as clear and delicate as that of the manuscript in ink.

"What sort of a place was it, Simpson?"

"Very poor, sir, but I did not go all the way up. The elder person came down, sir, took the note, and requested me to wait where I was."

"You had no chance, then, to make inquiries?" I said, knowing full well that he had emptied the entire neighborhood of any information it might possess concerning these two lodgers.

"Well, sir, you know how these foreigners will talk, whether one wants to hear or not. But it seems that these two persons have been there but a few weeks; they live alone, and are uncommonly silent and reserved. The people round there call them something that signifies 'the Madames American, thin and dumb.' "

7. I.e., in black letter (or Gothic) type.

At four the "Madames American" arrived; it was raining again, and they came on foot under their old umbrella. The maid waited in the anteroom, and Miss Grief was ushered into my bachelor's parlor. I had thought that I should meet her with great deference; but she looked so forlorn that my deference changed to pity. It was the woman that impressed me then, more than the writer—the fragile, nerveless body more than the inspired mind. For it was inspired; I had sat up half the night over her drama, and had felt thrilled through and through more than once by its earnestness, passion, and power.

No one could have been more surprised than I was to find myself thus enthusiastic. I thought I had outgrown that sort of thing. And one would have supposed, too (I myself should have supposed so the day before), that the faults of the drama, which were many and prominent, would have chilled any liking I might have felt, I being a writer myself, and therefore critical; for writers are as apt to make much of the "how," rather than the "what," as painters, who, it is well known, prefer an exquisitely rendered representation of a commonplace theme to an imperfectly executed picture of even the most striking subject. But in this case, on the contrary, the scattered rays of splendor in Miss Grief's drama had made me forget the dark spots, which were numerous and disfiguring; or, rather, the splendor had made me anxious to have the spots removed. And this also was a philanthropic state very unusual with me. Regarding unsuccessful writers, my motto had been "Væ victis!"[8]

My visitor took a seat and folded her hands; I could see, in spite of her quiet manner, that she was in breathless suspense. It seemed so pitiful that she should be trembling there before me—a woman so much older than I was, a woman who possessed the divine spark of genius, which I was by no means sure (in spite of my success) had been granted to me—that I felt as if I ought to go down on my knees before her, and entreat her to take her proper place of supremacy at once. But there! one does not go down on one's knees, combustively,[9] as it were, before a woman over fifty, plain in feature, thin, dejected, and ill dressed. I contented myself with taking her hands (in their miserable old gloves) in mine, while I said cordially, "Miss Crief, your drama seems to me full of original power. It has roused my enthusiasm: I sat up half the night reading it."

The hands I held shook, but something (perhaps a shame for having evaded the knees business) made me tighten my hold and bestow upon her also a reassuring smile. She looked at me for a moment, and then, suddenly and noiselessly, tears rose and rolled down her cheeks. I dropped her hands and retreated. I had not thought her tearful: on the contrary, her voice and face had seemed rigidly controlled. But now here she was bending herself over the side of the chair with her head resting on her arms, not sobbing aloud, but her whole frame shaken by the strength of her emotion. I rushed for a glass of wine; I pressed her to take it. I did not quite know what to do, but, putting myself in her place, I decided to praise the drama; and praise it I did. I do not know when I have used so many adjectives. She raised her head and began to wipe her eyes.

"Do take the wine," I said, interrupting myself in my cataract of language.

8. Woe to the defeated! (Latin).

9. I.e., in a manner to cause combustion.

"I dare not," she answered; then added humbly, "that is, unless you have a biscuit here or a bit of bread."

I found some biscuit; she ate two, and then slowly drank the wine, while I resumed my verbal Niagara. Under its influence—and that of the wine too, perhaps—she began to show new life. It was not that she looked radiant— she could not—but simply that she looked warm. I now perceived what had been the principal discomfort of her appearance heretofore: it was that she had looked all the time as if suffering from cold.

At last I could think of nothing more to say, and stopped. I really admired the drama, but I thought I had exerted myself sufficiently as an anti-hysteric, and that adjectives enough, for the present at least, had been administered. She had put down her empty wineglass, and was resting her hands on the broad cushioned arms of her chair with, for a thin person, a sort of expanded content.

"You must pardon my tears," she said, smiling; "it was the revulsion of feeling. My life was at a low ebb: if your sentence had been against me, it would have been my end."

"Your end?"

"Yes, the end of my life; I should have destroyed myself."

"Then you would have been a weak as well as wicked woman," I said in a tone of disgust. I do hate sensationalism.

"Oh no, you know nothing about it. I should have destroyed only this poor worn tenement of clay. But I can well understand how *you* would look upon it. Regarding the desirableness of life, the prince and the beggar may have different opinions. We will say no more of it, but talk of the drama instead." As she spoke the word "drama" a triumphant brightness came into her eyes.

I took the manuscript from a drawer and sat down beside her. "I suppose you know that there are faults," I said, expecting ready acquiescence.

"I was not aware that there were any," was her gentle reply.

Here was a beginning! After all my interest in her—and, I may say under the circumstances, my kindness—she received me in this way! However, my belief in her genius was too sincere to be altered by her whimsies; so I persevered. "Let us go over it together," I said. "Shall I read it to you, or will you read it to me?"

"I will not read it, but recite it."

"That will never do; you will recite it so well that we shall see only the good points, and what we have to concern ourselves with now is the bad ones."

"I will recite it," she repeated.

"Now, Miss Crief," I said bluntly, "for what purpose did you come to me? Certainly not merely to recite: I am no stage manager. In plain English, was it not your idea that I might help you in obtaining a publisher?"

"Yes, yes," she answered, looking at me apprehensively, all her old manner returning.

I followed up my advantage, opened the little paper volume and began. I first took the drama line by line, and spoke of the faults of expression and structure; then I turned back and touched upon two or three glaring impossibilities in the plot. "Your absorbed interest in the motive of the whole no doubt made you forget these blemishes," I said apologetically.

But, to my surprise, I found that she did not see the blemishes—that she

appreciated nothing I had said, comprehended nothing. Such unaccountable obtuseness puzzled me. I began again, going over the whole with even greater minuteness and care. I worked hard: the perspiration stood in beads upon my forehead as I struggled with her—what shall I call it—obstinacy? But it was not exactly obstinacy. She simply could not see the faults of her own work, any more than a blind man can see the smoke that dims a patch of blue sky. When I had finished my task the second time, she still remained as gently impassive as before. I leaned back in my chair exhausted, and looked at her.

Even then she did not seem to comprehend (whether she agreed with it or not) what I must be thinking. "It is such a heaven to me that you like it!" she murmured dreamily, breaking the silence. Then, with more animation, "And *now* you will let me recite it?"

I was too weary to oppose her; she threw aside her shawl and bonnet, and standing in the center of the room, began.

And she carried me along with her: all the strong passages were doubly strong when spoken, and the faults, which seemed nothing to her, were made by her earnestness to seem nothing to me, at least for that moment. When it was ended, she stood looking at me with a triumphant smile.

"Yes," I said, "I like it, and you see that I do. But I like it because my taste is peculiar. To me originality and force are everything—perhaps because I have them not to any marked degree myself—but the world at large will not overlook as I do your absolutely barbarous shortcomings on account of them. Will you trust me to go over the drama and correct it at my pleasure?" This was a vast deal for me to offer; I was surprised at myself.

"No," she answered softly, still smiling. "There shall not be so much as a comma altered." Then she sat down and fell into a reverie as though she were alone.

"Have you written anything else?" I said after a while, when I had become tired of the silence.

"Yes."

"Can I see it? Or is it *them*"

"It is *them*. Yes, you can see all."

"I will call upon you for the purpose."

"No, you must not," she said, coming back to the present nervously. "I prefer to come to you."

At this moment Simpson entered to light the room, and busied himself rather longer than was necessary over the task. When he finally went out, I saw that my visitor's manner had sunk into its former depression: the presence of the servant seemed to have chilled her.

"When did you say I might come?" I repeated, ignoring her refusal.

"I did not say it. It would be impossible."

"Well, then, when will you come here?" There was, I fear, a trace of fatigue in my tone.

"At your good pleasure, sir," she answered humbly.

My chivalry was touched by this: after all, she was a woman. "Come tomorrow," I said. "By the way, come and dine with me then; why not?" I was curious to see what she would reply.

"Why not, indeed? Yes, I will come. I am forty-three: I might have been your mother."

This was not quite true, as I am over thirty: but I look young, while she—

Well, I had thought her over fifty. "I can hardly call you 'mother,' but we might compromise upon 'aunt,' " I said, laughing. "Aunt what?"

"My name is Aaronna," she gravely answered. "My father was much disappointed that I was not a boy, and gave me as nearly as possible the name he had prepared—Aaron."

"Then come and dine with me tomorrow, and bring with you the other manuscripts, Aaronna," I said, amused at the quaint sound of the name. On the whole, I did not like "aunt."

"I will come," she answered.

It was twilight and still raining, but she refused all offers of escort or carriage, departing with her maid, as she had come, under the brown umbrella. The next day we had the dinner. Simpson was astonished—and more than astonished, grieved—when I told him that he was to dine with the maid; but he could not complain in words, since my own guest, the mistress, was hardly more attractive. When our preparations were complete, I could not help laughing: the two prim little tables, one in the parlor and one in the anteroom, and Simpson disapprovingly going back and forth between them, were irresistible.

I greeted my guest hilariously[1] when she arrived, and, fortunately, her manner was not quite so depressed as usual: I could never have accorded myself with a tearful mood. I had thought that perhaps she would make, for the occasion, some change in her attire; I have never known a woman who had not some scrap of finery, however small, in reserve for that unexpected occasion of which she is ever dreaming. But no: Miss Grief wore the same black gown, unadorned and unaltered. I was glad that there was no rain that day, so that the skirt did not at least look so damp and rheumatic.

She ate quietly, almost furtively, yet with a good appetite, and she did not refuse the wine. Then, when the meal was over and Simpson had removed the dishes, I asked for the new manuscripts. She gave me an old green copybook filled with short poems, and a prose sketch by itself; I lit a cigar and sat down at my desk to look them over.

"Perhaps you will try a cigarette?" I suggested, more for amusement than anything else, for there was not a shade of Bohemianism about her; her whole appearance was puritanical.

"I have not yet succeeded in learning to smoke."

"You have tried?" I said, turning round.

"Yes: Serena and I tried, but we did not succeed."

"Serena is your maid?"

"She lives with me."

I was seized with inward laughter, and began hastily to look over her manuscripts with my back toward her, so that she might not see it. A vision had risen before me of those two forlorn women, alone in their room with locked doors, patiently trying to acquire the smoker's art.

But my attention was soon absorbed by the papers before me. Such a fantastic collection of words, lines, and epithets I had never before seen, or even in dreams imagined. In truth, they were like the work of dreams: they were *Kubla Khan*,[2] only more so. Here and there was radiance like the flash of a diamond, but each poem, almost each verse and line, was marred by

1. Cheerfully.
2. Samuel Taylor Coleridge subtitled his poem (published in 1816) "a vision in a dream."

some fault or lack which seemed wilful perversity, like the work of an evil sprite. It was like a case of jeweller's wares set before you, with each ring unfinished, each bracelet too large or too small for its purpose, each breast-pin without its fastening, each necklace purposely broken. I turned the pages, marvelling. When about half an hour had passed, and I was leaning back for a moment to light another cigar, I glanced toward my visitor. She was behind me, in an easy chair before my small fire, and she was—fast asleep! In the relaxation of her unconsciousness I was struck anew by the poverty her appearance expressed; her feet were visible, and I saw the miserable worn old shoes which hitherto she had kept concealed.

After looking at her for a moment, I returned to my task and took up the prose story; in prose she must be more reasonable. She was less fantastic perhaps, but hardly more reasonable. The story was that of a profligate and commonplace man forced by two of his friends, in order not to break the heart of a dying girl who loves him, to live up to a high imaginary ideal of himself which her pure but mistaken mind has formed. He has a handsome face and sweet voice, and repeats what they tell them. Her long, slow decline and happy death, and his own inward ennui and profound weariness of the rôle he has to play, made the vivid points of the story. So far, well enough, but here was the trouble: through the whole narrative moved another character, a physician of tender heart and exquisite mercy, who practiced murder as a fine art, and was regarded (by the author) as a second Messiah! This was monstrous. I read it through twice, and threw it down; then, fatigued, I turned round and leaned back, waiting for her to wake. I could see her profile against the dark hue of the easy chair.

Presently she seemed to feel my gaze, for she stirred, then opened her eyes. "I have been asleep," she said, rising hurriedly.

"No harm in that, Aaronna."

But she was deeply embarrassed and troubled, much more so than the occasion required; so much so, indeed, that I turned the conversation back upon the manuscripts as a diversion. "I cannot stand that doctor of yours," I said, indicating the prose story; "no one would. You must cut him out."

Her self-possession returned as if by magic. "Certainly not," she answered haughtily.

"Oh, if you do not care—I had labored under the impression that you were anxious these things should find a purchaser."

"I am, I am," she said, her manner changing to deep humility with wonderful rapidity. With such alternations of feeling as this sweeping over her like great waves, no wonder she was old before her time.

"Then you must take out that doctor."

"I am willing, but do not know how," she answered, pressing her hands together helplessly. "In my mind he belongs to the story so closely that he cannot be separated from it."

Here Simpson entered, bringing a note for me: it was a line from Mrs. Abercrombie inviting me for that evening—an unexpected gathering, and therefore likely to be all the more agreeable. My heart bounded in spite of me; I forgot Miss Grief and her manuscripts for the moment as completely as though they had never existed. But, bodily, being still in the same room with her, her speech brought me back to the present.

"You have had good news?" she said.

"Oh no, nothing especial—merely an invitation."

"But good news also," she repeated. "And now, as for me, I must go."

Not supposing that she would stay much later in any case, I had that morning ordered a carriage to come for her at about that hour. I told her this. She made no reply beyond putting on her bonnet and shawl.

"You will hear from me soon," I said; "I shall do all I can for you."

She had reached the door, but before opening it she stopped, turned and extended her hand. "You are good," she said: "I give you thanks. Do not think me ungrateful or envious. It is only that you are young, and I am so—so old." Then she opened the door and passed through the anteroom without pause, her maid accompanying her and Simpson with gladness lighting the way. They were gone. I dressed hastily and went out—to continue my studies in psychology.

Time passed; I was busy, amused and perhaps a little excited (sometimes psychology is exciting). But, though much occupied with my own affairs, I did not altogether neglect my self-imposed task regarding Miss Grief. I began by sending her prose story to a friend, the editor of a monthly magazine, with a letter making a strong plea for its admittance. It should have a chance first on its own merits. Then I forwarded the drama to a publisher, also an acquaintance, a man with a taste for phantasms and a soul above mere common popularity, as his own coffers knew to their cost. This done, I waited with conscience clear.

Four weeks passed. During this waiting period I heard nothing from Miss Grief. At last one morning came a letter from my editor. "The story has force, but I cannot stand that doctor," he wrote. "Let her cut him out, and I might print it." Just what I myself had said. The package lay there on my table, travel worn and grimed; a returned manuscript is, I think, the most melancholy object on earth. I decided to wait, before writing to Aaronna, until the second letter was received. A week later it came. "Armor" was declined. The publisher had been "impressed" by the power displayed in certain passages, but the "impossibilities of the plot" rendered it "unavailable for publication"—in fact, would "bury it in ridicule" if brought before the public, a public "lamentably" fond of amusement, "seeking it, undaunted, even in the cannon's mouth." I doubt if he knew himself what he meant. But one thing, at any rate, was clear: "Armor" was declined.

Now, I am, as I have remarked before, a little obstinate. I was determined that Miss Grief's work should be received. I would alter and improve it myself, without letting her know: the end justified the means. Surely the sieve of my own good taste, whose mesh had been pronounced so fine and delicate, would serve for two. I began; and utterly failed.

I set to work first upon "Armor." I amended, altered, left out, put in, pieced, condensed, lengthened; I did my best, and all to no avail. I could not succeed in completing anything that satisfied me, or that approached, in truth, Miss Grief's own work just as it stood. I suppose I went over that manuscript twenty times: I covered sheets of paper with my copies. But the obstinate drama refused to be corrected; as it was it must stand or fall.

Wearied and annoyed, I threw it aside and took up the prose story: that would be easier. But, to my surprise, I found that that apparently gentle "doctor" would not out: he was so closely interwoven with every part of the tale that to take him out was like taking out one especial figure in a carpet:

that is, impossible, unless you unravel the whole. At last I did unravel the whole, and then the story was no longer good, or Aaronna's: it was weak, and mine. All this took time, for of course I had much to do in connection with my own life and tasks. But, though slowly and at my leisure, I really did try my best as regarded Miss Grief, and without success. I was forced at last to make up my mind that either my own powers were not equal to the task, or else that her perversities were as essential a part of her work as her inspirations, and not to be separated from it. Once during this period I showed two of the short poems to Isabel, withholding of course the writer's name. "They were written by a woman," I explained.

"Her mind must have been disordered, poor thing!" Isabel said in her gentle way when she returned them—"at least, judging by these. They are hopelessly mixed and vague."

Now, they were not vague so much as vast. But I knew that I could not make Isabel comprehend it, and (so complex a creature is man) I do not know that I wanted her to comprehend it. These were the only ones in the whole collection that I would have shown her, and I was rather glad that she did not like even these. Not that poor Aaronna's poems were evil: they were simply unrestrained, large, vast, like the skies or the wind. Isabel was bounded on all sides, like a violet in a garden bed. And I liked her so.

One afternoon, about the time when I was beginning to see that I could not "improve" Miss Grief, I came upon the maid. I was driving, and she had stopped on the crossing to let the carriage pass. I recognized her at a glance (by her general forlornness), and called to the driver to stop. "How is Miss Grief?" I said. "I have been intending to write to her for some time."

"And your note, when it comes," answered the old woman on the crosswalk fiercely, "she shall not see."

"What?"

"I say she shall not see it. Your patronizing face shows that you have no good news, and you shall not rack and stab her any more on *this* earth, please God, while I have authority."

"Who has racked or stabbed her, Serena?"

"Serena, indeed! Rubbish! I'm no Serena: I'm her aunt. And as to who has racked and stabbed her, I say you, *you*—YOU literary men!" She had put her old head inside my carriage, and flung out these words at me in a shrill, menacing tone. "But she shall die in peace in spite of you," she continued. "Vampires! you take her ideas and fatten on them, and leave her to starve. You know you do—*you* who have had her poor manuscripts these months and months!"

"Is she ill?" I asked in real concern, gathering that much at least from the incoherent tirade.

"She is dying," answered the desolate old creature, her voice softening and her dim eyes filling with tears.

"Oh, I trust not. Perhaps something can be done. Can I help you in any way?"

"In all ways if you would," she said, breaking down and beginning to sob weakly, with her head resting on the sill of the carriage window. "Oh, what have we not been through together, we two! Piece by piece I have sold all."

I am goodhearted enough, but I do not like to have old women weeping across my carriage door. I suggested, therefore, that she should come inside

and let me take her home. Her shabby old skirt was soon beside me, and, following her directions, the driver turned toward one of the most wretched quarters of the city, the abode of poverty, crowded and unclean. Here, in a large bare chamber up many flights of stairs, I found Miss Grief.

As I entered I was startled: I thought she was dead. There seemed no life present until she opened her eyes, and even then they rested upon us vaguely, as though she did not know who we were. But as I approached a light came into them: she recognized me, and this sudden revivification, this return of the soul to the almost deserted body, was the most wonderful thing I ever saw. "You have good news of the drama?" she whispered as I bent over her: "tell me. I *know* you have good news."

What was I to answer? Pray, what would you have answered, puritan?

"Yes, I have good news, Aaronna," I said. "The drama will appear." (And who knows? Perhaps it will in some other world.)

She smiled, and her now brilliant eyes did not leave my face.

"He knows I'm your aunt: I told him," said the old woman, coming to the bedside.

"Did you?" whispered Miss Grief, still gazing at me with a smile. "Then please, dear Aunt Martha, give me something to eat."

Aunt Martha hurried across the room, and I followed her. "It's the first time she's asked for food in weeks," she said in a husky tone.

She opened a cupboard door vaguely, but I could see nothing within. "What have you for her?" I asked with some impatience, though in a low voice.

"Please God, nothing!" answered the poor old woman, hiding her reply and her tears behind the broad cupboard door. "I was going out to get a little something when I met you."

"Good Heavens! is it money you need? Here, take this and send; or go yourself in the carriage waiting below."

She hurried out breathless, and I went back to the bedside, much disturbed by what I had seen and heard. But Miss Grief's eyes were full of life, and as I sat down beside her she whispered earnestly, "Tell me."

And I did tell her—a romance invented for the occasion. I venture to say that none of my published sketches could compare with it. As for the lie involved, it will stand among my few good deeds, I know, at the judgment bar.

And she was satisfied. "I have never known what it was," she whispered, "to be fully happy until now." She closed her eyes, and when the lids fell I again thought that she had passed away. But no, there was still pulsation in her small, thin wrist. As she perceived my touch she smiled. "Yes, I am happy," she said again, though without audible sound.

The old aunt returned; food was prepared, and she took some. I myself went out after wine that should be rich and pure. She rallied a little, but I did not leave her: her eyes dwelt upon me and compelled me to stay, or rather my conscience compelled me. It was a damp night, and I had a little fire made. The wine, fruit, flowers, and candles I had ordered made the bare place for the time being bright and fragrant. Aunt Martha dozed in her chair from sheer fatigue—she had watched many nights—but Miss Grief was awake, and I sat beside her.

"I make you my executor," she murmured, "as to the drama. But my other

manuscripts place, when I am gone, under my head, and let them be buried with me. They are not many—those you have and these. See!"

I followed her gesture, and saw under her pillows the edges of two more copybooks like the one I had. "Do not look at them—my poor dead children!" she said tenderly. "Let them depart with me—unread, as I have been."

Later she whispered, "Did you wonder why I came to you? It was the contrast. You were young—strong—rich—praised—loved—successful: all that I was not. I wanted to look at you—and imagine how it would feel. You had success—but I had the greater power. Tell me, did I not have it?"

"Yes, Aaronna."

"It is all in the past now. But I am satisfied."

After another pause she said with a faint smile, "Do you remember when I fell asleep in your parlor? It was the good and rich food. It was so long since I had had food like that!"

I took her hand and held it, conscience stricken, but now she hardly seemed to perceive my touch. "And the smoking?" she whispered. "Do you remember how you laughed? I saw it. But I had heard that smoking soothed—that one was no longer tired and hungry—with a cigar."

In little whispers of this sort, separated by long rests and pauses, the night passed. Once she asked if her aunt was asleep, and when I answered in the affirmative she said, "Help her to return home—to America: the drama will pay for it. I ought never to have brought her away."

I promised, and she resumed her bright-eyed silence.

I think she did not speak again. Toward morning the change came, and soon after sunrise, with her old aunt kneeling by her side, she passed away.

All was arranged as she had wished. Her manuscripts, covered with violets, formed her pillow. No one followed her to the grave save her aunt and myself; I thought she would prefer it so. Her name was not "Crief," after all, but "Moncrief"; I saw it written out by Aunt Martha for the coffin plate, as follows: "Aaronna Moncrief, aged forty-three years, two months, and eight days."

I never knew more of her history than is written here. If there was more that I might have learned, it remained unlearned, for I did not ask.

And the drama? I keep it here in this locked case. I could have had it published at my own expense; but I think that now she knows its faults herself, perhaps, and would not like it.

I keep it; and, once in a while, I read it over—not as a *memento mori*[3] exactly, but rather as a memento of my own good fortune, for which I should continually give thanks. The want of one grain made all her work void, and that one grain was given to me. She, with the greater power, failed—I, with the less, succeeded. But no praise is due to me for that. When I die "Armor" is to be destroyed unread: not even Isabel is to see it. For women will misunderstand each other; and, dear and precious to me as my sweet wife is, I could not bear that she or anyone should cast so much as a thought of scorn upon the memory of the writer, upon my poor dead, "unavailable," unaccepted "Miss Grief."

1880

3. A reminder of death (Latin; lit., "remember that you must die").

MICHAEL FIELD
[KATHERINE BRADLEY *and* EDITH COOPER]
1846–1914 1862–1913

The couple whom friends called the Michael Fields were aunt and niece but also collaborative poets and lifelong lovers. Katherine Bradley was the daughter of a tobacco manufacturer in Birmingham, who died when she was two years old. As a teenager, she traveled with her mother to the home of her mother's sister, a woman who shortly thereafter became an invalid. At Kenilworth, Warwickshire, the first child of that invalid, Edith Cooper, soon became the object of Katherine's devoted care. Katherine Bradley studied at Newnham College, Cambridge, and in Paris; published a volume of verse titled *The New Minnesinger* (1875) under the pseudonym Arran Leigh, a clear homage to Elizabeth Barrett Browning's *Aurora Leigh;* and then with Edith Cooper attended classes in classics and philosophy at Bristol University, where both worked in favor of votes for women and against animal vivisection. In 1881, their first joint volume, *Bellerophôn,* was published under the names Arran and Isla Leigh. The drama *Calirrhoë, and Fair Rosamund* (1884) came out under the single male pseudonym that they used in the more than twenty volumes they went on to publish together and that is still used today.

In its evocations and translations of the verse of Sappho, *Long Ago* (1889) reworks classical material that had been important to an earlier woman writer—Mary Robinson—and that would continue to inspire the modernist H. D. as well as such contemporary writers as Olga Broumas, Monique Wittig, and Jeanette Winterson. Perhaps the mythological importance of Sappho as the first source of song and as the first legendary lesbian explains why Robert Browning dubbed Michael Field "two dear Greek women." In *Victorian Sappho,* the contemporary scholar Yopie Prins has wondered, "How shall we read these poems written by two women writing as a man writing as Sappho?" She goes on to suggest that Bradley and Cooper "turn to Sappho, whom they certainly understand to be lesbian in more than the proper sense of the name, in order to develop a model of lyric authorship in which voice is the effect of an eroticized textual mediation between the two of them rather than the representation of an unmediated solitary utterance." Not composed as songs, their lyrics (they explained) were pieced together "like mosaic-work—the mingled, various product of our two brains."

As Katherine Bradley and Edith Cooper traveled through Germany, France, and Italy, and later as they settled down first in Reigate and then in Richmond, they gained a circle of acquaintances that sounds like a who's who of turn-of-the-century European culture: they knew the fiction writer Vernon Lee, the lecturer on aesthetics Walter Pater, the sexologist Havelock Ellis, the celebrity and wit Oscar Wilde, the poets Paul Verlaine and William Butler Yeats, the South African novelist Olive Schreiner, and the children's writer E. Nesbit, though in later life they rejected what they viewed as the decadence of the age and increasingly retired from it. To Ellis, a pioneer in studying the "intermediate" or "invert" sex he associated with homosexuality, Bradley and Cooper described the partnership that took up most of their time and attention: "we cross and interlace like a company of dancing summer flies; if one begins a character, his companion seizes and possesses it; if one conceives a scene or situation, the other corrects, completes, or murderously cuts away." Prolific in their composing of plays, poems, and diaries, Bradley and Cooper eventually converted to Roman Catholicism. When Edith Cooper was diagnosed with cancer in 1911, Katherine Bradley kept her own cancer a secret, but suffered a hemorrhage two days after her companion's funeral and died three years later. Pioneering lesbian scholars such as Jeannette H. Foster and Lillian Faderman helped bring critical attention back to a pair of writers who, despite their celebrity

connections and prolific publishing career, had all but vanished from history by the mid–twentieth century.

[Atthis, my darling]

Τὸ μέλημα τοὐμόν[1]

Atthis, my darling, thou did'st stray
A few feet to the rushy bed,
When a great fear and passion shook
My heart lest haply thou wert dead;
5 It grew so still about the brook,
As if a soul were drawn away.

Anon thy clear eyes, silver-blue,
Shone through the tamarisk-branches fine;
To pluck me iris thou had'st sprung
10 Through galingale and celandine;
Away, away, the flowers I flung
And thee down to my breast I drew.

My darling! Nay, our very breath
Nor light nor darkness shall divide;
15 Queen Dawn shall find us on one bed,
Nor must thou flutter from my side
An instant, lest I feel the dread,
Atthis, the immanence of death.

1889

[Maids, not to you my mind doth change]

Ταῖς κάλαις ἴμμιν [τὸ] νόημα τῶμον οὐ διάμειπτον[1]

Maids, not to you my mind doth change;
Men I defy, allure, estrange,
Prostrate, make bond or free:
Soft as the stream beneath the plane
5 To you I sing my love's refrain;
Between us is no thought of pain,
 Peril, satiety.

1. My darling (Greek); Sappho, fragment 126 Bergk. Atthis is addressed in a number of Sappho's fragmental poems (though not this one).

1. My mind is not changeable toward you, beautiful [women] (Greek); Sappho, fragment 14 Bergk.

Soon doth a lover's patience tire,
But ye to manifold desire
10 Can yield response, ye know
When for long, museful days I pine,
The presage at my heart divine;
To you I never breathe a sign
Of inward want or woe.

15 When injuries my spirit bruise,
Allaying virtue ye infuse
With unobtrusive skill:
And if care frets ye come to me
As fresh as nymph from stream or tree,[2]
20 And with your soft vitality
 My weary bosom fill.

 1889

[Come, Gorgo, put the rug in place]

Ἀλλὰ, μὴ μεγαλύνεο δακτυλίω πέρι[1]

Come, Gorgo, put the rug in place,
 And passionate recline;
I love to see thee in thy grace,
 Dark, virulent, divine.

5 But wherefore thus thy proud eyes fix
 Upon a jewelled band?
Art thou so glad the sardonyx
 Because thy shapely hand?

Bethink thee! 'Tis for such as thou
10 Zeus[2] leaves his lofty seat;
'Tis at thy beauty's bidding how
 Man's mortal life shall fleet;
Those fairest hands—dost thou forget
 Their power to thrill and cling?
15 O foolish woman, dost thou set
 Thy pride upon a ring?

 1889

2. Greek mythology distinguishes between nymphs identified with trees (dryads); freshwater streams, lakes, and fountains (naiads); and the sea (nereids).

1. But don't pride yourself on a ring (Greek); Sappho, fragment 35 Bergk. Gorgo is the object of witty invective in some of Sappho's fragments.
2. The king of the Greek gods.

A Pen-Drawing of Leda[1]

Sodoma[2]

The Grand Duke's Palace at Weimar[3]

'Tis Leda lovely, wild and free,
 Drawing her gracious Swan down through the grass to see
 Certain round eggs without a speck:
One hand plunged in the reeds and one dinting the downy neck,
5 Although his hectoring bill
 Gapes toward her tresses,
She draws the fondled creature to her will.

 She joys to bend in the live light
Her glistening body toward her love, how much more bright!
10 Though on her breast the sunshine lies
And spreads its affluence on the wide curves of her waist and thighs,
 To her meek, smitten gaze
 Where her hand presses
The Swan's white neck sink Heaven's concentred rays.

 1892

[A girl]

 A girl,
 Her soul a deep-wave pearl
Dim, lucent of all lovely mysteries;
 A face flowered for heart's ease,
5 A brow's grace soft as seas
 Seen through faint forest-trees:
 A mouth, the lips apart,
Like aspen-leaflets trembling in the breeze
From her tempestuous heart.
10 Such: and our souls so knit,
I leave a page half-writ—
 The work begun
Will be to heaven's conception done,
 If she come to it.

 1893

1. In Greek mythology, the queen of Sparta (the wife of Tyndareus); she was seduced by Zeus, who came to her in the form of a swan. In some accounts, she gave birth to two eggs, each containing one mortal and one half-immortal child: Castor and Polydeuces in one, and Helen and Clytemnes- tra in the other.
2. Giovanni Bazzi (1477–1549), Italian painter who worked mainly in Siena.
3. City in central Germany, formerly the capital of the grand duchy of Saxe-Weimar and a significant cultural center.

Unbosoming

The love that breeds
In my heart for thee!
As the iris is full, brimful of seeds,
And all that it flowered for among the reeds
5 Is packed in a thousand vermilion-beads
That push, and riot, and squeeze, and clip,
Till they burst the sides of the silver scrip,[1]
And at last we see
What the bloom, with its tremulous, bowery fold
15 Of zephyr-petal[2] at heart did hold:
So my breast is rent
With the burthen[3] and strain of its great content;
For the summer of fragrance and sighs is dead,
The harvest-secret is burning red,
20 And I would give thee, after my kind,
The final issues of heart and mind.

1893

[It was deep April]

It was deep April, and the morn
 Shakespere was born;[1]
The world was on us, pressing sore;
My Love and I took hands and swore,
5 Against the world, to be
Poets and lovers evermore,
To laugh and dream on Lethe's shore,
To sing to Charon[2] in his boat,
Heartening the timid souls afloat;
10 Of judgment never to take heed,
But to those fast-locked souls to speed,
Who never from Apollo[3] fled,
Who spent no hour among the dead;
 Continually
15 With them to dwell,
Indifferent to heaven and hell.

1893

1. Small bag or wallet.
2. The zephyr-flower, sephyranth.
3. Burden.
1. The conventionally assigned birth date of William Shakespeare is April 2, 1564 (he was baptized on April 26).

2. In classical mythology, the ferryman who carries the souls of the dead across the river Styx; Lethe (literally "Forgetfulness," in Greek) is another river of the underworld.
3. In classical mythology, god of poetry and the arts more generally.

To Christina Rossetti[1]

Lady, we would behold thee moving bright
As Beatrice or Matilda[2] mid the trees,
Alas! thy moan was as a moan for ease
And passage through cool shadows to the night:
5 Fleeing from love, hadst thou not poet's right
To slip into the universe? The seas
Are fathomless to rivers drowned in these,
And sorrow is secure in leafy light.
Ah, had this secret touched thee, in a tomb
10 Thou hadst not buried thy enchanting self,
As happy Syrinx[3] murmuring with the wind,
Or Daphne[4] thrilled through all her mystic bloom,
From safe recess as genius[5] or as elf,
Thou hadst breathed joy in earth and in thy kind.

1896

Eros[1]

O Eros of the mountains, of the earth,
One thing I know of thee that thou art old,
Far, sovereign, lonesome tyrant of the dearth
Of chaos,[2] ruler of the primal cold!
5 None gave thee nurture: chaos' icy rings
Pressed on thy plenitude. O fostering power,
Thine the first voice, first warmth, first golden wings,
First blowing zephyr,[3] earliest opened flower,
Thine the first smile of Time: thou hast no mate,
10 Thou art alone forever, giving all:
After thine image, Love, thou did'st create
Man to be poor, man to be prodigal;
And thus, O awful god, he is endued
With the raw hungers of thy solitude.

1908

1. English poet (1830–1894); see above, p. 1076.
2. In Dante's *Purgatorio* (1321), canto 28, the narrator enters the sacred wood of the earthly paradise and sees Matilda, who symbolizes the active spiritual life, picking flowers and singing. Beatrice, Dante's great love, represents the wisdom of faith and is his guide through Paradise.
3. In classical mythology, a river nymph pursued by Pan; she escaped him by turning into a reed, which he then cut into pieces of different lengths
to create the panpipes (*syrinx*, in Greek).
4. A river god's daughter who was turned into a laurel tree (*daphnē*, in Greek) as she fled the advances of Apollo.
5. The resident spirit of a place.
1. Greek god of love, conventionally portrayed as winged; also, the Greek word meaning "love."
2. The primordial void that begins Greek creation myths.
3. The west wind.

[Lo, my loved is dying]

Lo, my loved is dying, and the call
Is come that I must die,
All the leaves are dying, all
Dying, drifting by.
5 Every leaf is lonely in its fall,
Every flower has its speck and stain;
The birds from hedge and tree
Lisp mournfully,
And the great reconciliation of this pain
10 Lies in the full, soft rain.

1913 1930

ALICE MEYNELL
1847–1922

"Of all the crying evils in the depraved earth . . . the greatest, judged by all the laws of God and humanity, is the miserable selfishness of men that keeps women from work," wrote the poet Alice Thompson at the age of eighteen. The daughter of cultivated, independently wealthy parents—her mother was a pianist and artist, her father an amateur man of letters—this surprisingly feminist young woman was already beginning to write the elegant verse that would later in her life bring her considerable fame. Raised partly in Italy, where her family lived in what the critic Cora Kaplan has called a "relaxed bohemian style," she had been educated at home and had been taught, as her remark about work suggests, to take herself seriously. In addition, like her mother and sister, she was a convert to Catholicism, organizing her life as well as her art around a strong commitment to her faith.

Alice Thompson's first book of poetry, *Preludes,* appeared in 1875, and two years later she married a young Catholic journalist, Wilfred Meynell. With her husband, she founded and edited several magazines, one of which, *Merry England,* brought her the friendship of well-known contemporary poets such as Coventry Patmore, Hilaire Belloc, and Francis Thompson. Besides working on *Merry England,* she also wrote an impressive number of fine essays—many on literary subjects—for such periodicals as *The Spectator* and *The Saturday Review,* and she combined this activity with a busy domestic life: her egalitarian marriage produced eight children, seven of whom survived.

Meynell's most notable achievement, however, was a body of verse that seemed, in the words of one admirer, Vita Sackville-West, to have been written "with an etching pen." Austerely lyric, poems such as "A Father of Women," "The Sunderland Children," and "Parentage" reveal the aesthetic craft that elicited for Meynell the praise of such a major figure as John Ruskin. At the same time, the political, and often distinctively feminist, passion that infuses these works reminds us that they were written by the same woman who had longed for significant work at the age of eighteen. Not surprisingly, Meynell became a suffragist in her later years, and she drew on her deep-seated feminism in singularly powerful poems about the horrors of World War I, a conflict that she saw as having been brought about by cynical "fathers"—

for, as she had already observed in "Parentage" (1896), "Theirs are armies. Death is theirs." Perhaps impressed by such intensity, the American poet Amy Lowell remembered, after Meynell's death in 1922, that this English writer's words "rang . . . like bronze cathedral bells/Down ancient lawns."

The Sunderland Children

On the 183 Sunderland children who lost their lives in a panic
at the Victoria Hall, 16th June, 1883[1]

This was the surplus childhood, held as cheap!
 Not worth the care which shields
The lambs that are to stay, the corn[2] to reap—
 The promise of the fields.

5 The nation guards her future. Fruits and grass
 And vegetable life
Are fostered league by league. But oh, the mass
 Of childhood over-rife!
O mass, O units! Oh, the separate story
10 Planned for each breather of breath!
This futile young mankind, and transitory,
 Is left to stray to Death.

O promise, presage, menace! Upon these
 A certain seal is laid.
15 Unkept, unbroken, are the auguries
 These little children made.

For threat is bound with promise; and the nation
 Holds festival of regret
Over these dead—dead in their isolation—
20 Wisely. She feared their threat.

1883

1. At a Saturday afternoon entertainment in the English mining town of Sunderland, most of the children were sitting in the cheapest seats in the gallery—about 1,500, with very few adults. Prizes had been promised to all, and as they began to be distributed on the main floor at the end of the show, the children rushed down the stairs. Because the door to the lobby could open only 18 inches, hundreds of children became trapped on the last steps, jammed into a mass of bodies more than 6 feet high.
2. Wheat.

Parentage

"When Augustus Caesar[1] legislated against the unmarried citizens of Rome, he declared them to be, in some sort, slayers of the people."

Ah no! not these!
These, who were childless, are not they who gave
So many dead unto the journeying wave,
The helpless nurslings of the cradling seas;
5 Not they who doomed by infallible decrees
Unnumbered man to the innumerable grave.

But those who slay
Are fathers. Theirs are armies. Death is theirs—
The death of innocences and despairs;
10 The dying of the golden and the gray
The sentence, when these speak it, has no Nay.
And she who slays is she who bears, who bears.

1896

A Father of Women: Ad Sororem E. B.[1]

"Thy father was transfused into thy blood."
Dryden: *Ode to Mrs. Anne Killigrew*[2]

Our father works in us,
The daughters of his manhood. Not undone
Is he, not wasted, though transmuted thus,
And though he left no son.

5 Therefore on him I cry
To arm me: "For my delicate mind a casque,[3]
A breastplate for my heart, courage to die,
Of thee, captain, I ask.

"Nor strengthen only; press
10 A finger on this violent blood and pale,
Over this rash will let thy tenderness
A while pause, and prevail.

1. First emperor of Rome (63 B.C.E.–14 C.E.).
1. To Sister E. B. (Latin). E. B. is almost certainly Meynall's sister Elizabeth Thompson Butler (1844–1933), a painter of military and battle scenes.
2. A poet and painter (1660–1685; see above,

p. 233) whose father published sermons and a tragedy. John Dryden (1631–1700), author of the ode (1686), which first appeared in her sole volume of poems.
3. Helmet.

"And shepherd-father, thou
Whose staff folded[4] my thoughts before my birth,
15 Control them now I am of earth, and now
Thou art no more of earth.

"O liberal, constant, dear,
Crush in my nature the ungenerous art[5]
Of the inferior; set me high, and here,
20 Here garner up thy heart!"

Like to him now are they,
The million living fathers of the War[6]—
Mourning the crippled world, the bitter day—
Whose striplings are no more.

25 The crippled world! Come then,
Fathers of women with your honor in trust,
Approve, accept, know them daughters of men,
Now that your sons are dust.

1917

4. I.e., guided to the fold, an enclosure for sheep. 6. World War I, then called the Great War.
5. Artifice.

ALICE JAMES
1848–1892

The journal Alice James kept for the last three years of her life is acerbic about English customs and medical practices, witty about the gossip and books she received in her sickroom, and sensitively introspective. For the most part, it was dictated to her intimate companion, Katharine Peabody Loring. These two friends may have furnished the impetus for Alice's brother Henry's portrait of two emotionally involved suffragists in *The Bostonians* (1886). They had traveled to England to cure Katharine's sister and to visit Alice's novelist brother after the death of Alice's parents in 1882, but Alice's poor health prolonged their stay.

As the only daughter in the illustrious James family and the youngest of five siblings, Alice James was not well equipped to handle either her volatile father, who preached Christian mysticism and intellectual ambition to his children, or her mother, who was worshiped as a self-effacing madonna within the family. After a childhood punctuated by foreign travel, she grew up in Cambridge, Massachusetts. Her first mental breakdown occurred at sixteen. While her brothers William and Henry were preparing for their eminent careers in psychology and literature, she was treated for stomach pains, "heart attacks," fainting spells, and paralyzed limbs with the remedies of her time: "motor-therapy," "electricity," "blistering" baths, and "sulphuric ether." At thirty years of age, she was tempted to commit suicide during a profound depression, but her father's "permission"—his acknowledgment, on learning of her feelings, of her freedom to choose to die—made even that alternative seem impossible. Before and after her parents' death, she must have compared her own private suffering with her

brothers' public accomplishments. A late diary entry lists Henry's *The Tragic Muse* and *The American* along with her philosopher brother William's *Psychology*: "Not a bad show for one family!" she exulted, ominously adding, "especially if I get myself dead, the hardest job of all."

Because, as her brother Henry explained, "in our family group girls seem scarcely to have had a chance," he believed that Alice's "tragic health was, in a manner, the only solution for her of the practical problem of life." He had not known of the journal during her lifetime; however, Alice James had valued it sufficiently to ask that it be typed, and after Alice's death from breast cancer at forty-four, Loring privately printed a copy for each of the surviving brothers and one for herself. A 1934 edition was followed by Leon Edel's 1964 edition, from which the selections printed here were taken.

From The Diary

[*My First Journal!*]

May 31st, 1889

I think that if I get into the habit of writing a bit about what happens, or rather doesn't happen, I may lose a little of the sense of loneliness and desolation which abides with me. My circumstances allowing of nothing but the ejaculation of one-syllabled reflections, a written monologue by that most interesting being, *myself,* may have its yet to be discovered consolations. I shall at least have it all my own way and it may bring relief as an outlet to that geyser of emotions, sensations, speculations and reflections which ferments perpetually within my poor old carcass for its sins; so here goes, my first Journal!

[*My Microscopic Field*]

July 12th [1889]

* * *It's amusing to see how, even on my microscopic field, minute events are perpetually taking place illustrative of the broadest facts of human nature. Yesterday Nurse and I had a good laugh but I must allow that decidedly she "had" me. I was thinking of something that interested me very much and my mind was suddenly flooded by one of those luminous waves that sweep out of consciousness all but the living sense and overpower one with joy in the rich, throbbing complexity of life, when suddenly I looked up at Nurse, who was dressing me, and saw her primitive, rudimentary expression (so common here) as of no inherited quarrel with her destiny of putting petticoats over my head; the poverty and deadness of it contrasted to the tide of speculation that was coursing thro' my brain made me exclaim, "Oh! Nurse, don't you wish you were inside of *me!*"—her look of dismay and vehement disclaimer—"Inside of you, Miss, when you have just had a sick headache for five days!"—gave a greater blow to my vanity, than that much battered article has ever received. The headache had gone off in the night and I had clean forgotten it—when the little wretch confronted me with it, at this sublime moment when I was feeling within me the potency of a Bis-

marck,[1] and left me powerless before the immutable law that however great we may seem to our own consciousness no human being would exchange his for ours, and before the fact that *my* glorious role was to stand for *Sick headache* to mankind! What a grotesque I am to be sure! Lying in this room, with the resistance of a thistle-down, having illusory moments of throbbing with the pulse of the Race, the Mystery to be solved at the next breath and the fountain of all Happiness within me—the sense of vitality, in short, simply proportionate to the excess of weakness!—To sit by and watch these absurdities is amusing in its way and reminds me of how I used to *listen* to my "company manners" in the days when I had 'em, and how ridiculous they sounded.

Ah! Those strange people who have the courage to be unhappy! *Are* they unhappy, by-the-way?

[Pharasaism; Death]

February 17th [1890]

I find myself as the months pass more and more stifled by the all pervasive sense of pharasaism[2] in the British constitution of things. You don't feel it at first and you can't put your finger upon it in your friends, but as the days go by you unfold it with your *Standard*,[3] in the morn. It rises dense from the P.M.G. in the evening, it creeps thro' the cracks in the window frames like the fog and envelopes you thro' the day. I asked H.[4] once how it struck him from his wider and varied field not wanting my view to become cramped upon conclusions drawn from my centimeter of observation, he said that he didn't think it could be exaggerated. It's woven of a multiplicity of minute details and incidents which elude you in the telling but which seem to exist in the texture of things and leave a dent in the mind as they file past. A monarchy to which they bow down in its tinsel capacity only, denying to it a manly movement of any sort; a boneless Church broadening itself out, up to date; the hysterical legislation over a dog with a broken leg whilst Society is engaged making bags of 4,000 pheasants, etc. etc., or gloating over foxes torn to pieces by a pack of hounds;[5] the docility with which the classes enslave themselves to respectability or non-respectability as the "good-form"[6] of the moment may be; the "sense of their betters" in the masses; the passivity with which the working man allows himself to be patted and legislated out of all independence; thus the profound ineradicables in the bone and sinew conviction that outlying regions are their preserves, that they alone of human races massacre savages out of pure virtue. It would ill-become an American to reflect upon the treatment of aboriginal races; but I never heard it suggested that our hideous dealings with the Indians was brotherly love masquerading under the disguise of pure cussedness.

It would have been highly immoral, when Kath.[7] was here, not to get as

1. Otto von Bismarck (1815–1898), creator and first chancellor of the German Empire, noted for his strength and ruthlessness.
2. Strict adherence to the outward forms of moral and social strictures without regard to their spirit.
3. The *Morning Standard* and the *Pall Mall Gazette* ("P.M.G.") were two London newspapers of the period.
4. Alice's brother Henry James (1843–1916), the famous novelist.
5. I.e., so-called sporting hunting. "Bags": game-bags.
6. I.e., code of behavior.
7. Katharine P. Loring (1849–1943), James's intimate companion.

much work out of her as possible, so the second week she began upon Woking. I had got discouraged about cremation, having been told that it was very fussy and expensive, so she wrote for the circular[8] to be sent by the Cremation people, when, lo! it's as simple and inexpensive as possible, only six guineas[9] and one extra for a parson. Me ashes are to be put in an urn, and sent home, not as a parlor ornament for William's[1] new house, but to be buried beside Father and Mother in the cemetery at Cam[bridge],—so that we shall not be myths as Harry suggests we might otherwise become. 'Tis a great waste that I didn't die whilst K. was here; she could have carried home the urn in her top berth and as she lay convulsed with seasickness it would have greatly assuaged her grief to have such a palpable assurance that that portion of me hitherto so susceptible to the dread thing was reduced to ashes. It seems delightfully clean to elude in this way that early riser, the unpleasant wurrum, and I am greatly in hopes that

> "The worms crawled in
> And the worms crawled out,"[2]

will not be true of my return to dust.

Then we began upon my Will, which I wanted to make over again, leaving out, of course, those who had offended me since my last, as a cousin of Lilla Walsh's used to do, who re-made hers every few weeks. K. told me that as long as I indulged in no amateur legal terminology but confined myself strictly to my vernacular it would be all right, so she wouldn't allow me even one decorative bequeath. She wrote to the Consul at Birmingham to ask him if it had to be signed in his presence and he said yes, so hearing that Lizzie Putnam was at Banbury and was coming to spend a certain afternoon, K. telegraphed to the Consul, as it was so good to get a Boston witness. The arrival of this august personage the Consul naturally caused me to "go off" and I had to be put to bed—when the most amusing scene followed. I lay in a semi-faint, draped in as many frills as could be found for the occasion, with Nurse at my head with the thickest layer of her anxious-devoted-nurse expression on, as K. told me after, when thro' a mist I vaguely saw five black figures file into my little bower, headed by the most extraordinary little man, all gesticulation and grimace, who planted himself at the foot of the bed and stroking my knees began a long harangue to the effect that he and his wife had both "laid upon a bed of sickness" which seemed to constitute uncontrovertible reason for my immediate recovery. K. with difficulty restrained him from reading the Will aloud there and then—he has doubtless not forgiven this dam thrown across to arrest the flood of his eloquence—It was so curious for me, just like a nightmare effect and I felt as if I were assisting at the reading of my own Will, surrounded by the greedy relatives, as in novels. After they had filed in and out several times and become tangled in as much resounding red-tape as the creature could reel off for the occasion they went off downstairs to an "elegant" tea where the Consul entertained them with his whole history and the digestive processes of his domestic circle, which seem to be in a sadly disorganized condition. He asked K. whether she was related to "Our great Minister to Portugal Geo. B. Loring"[3]—imagine the

8. Advertising pamphlet.
9. A guinea was a gold coin worth 21 shillings (i.e., 1 pound and 1 shilling).
1. Alice's brother the psychologist and philosopher William James (1842–1910).

2. From a macabre children's song.
3. A Massachusetts politician (1817–1891) whose district was just north of Boston; he served as minister to Portugal from 1889 to 1890.

condition of a Peabody-Loring having such an insult hurled at her! And he also wanted to know whether Postmaster James and I were consanguineous.[4] I, not having been *born* (ahem!) was able to take things more easily, besides Mr. James, I believe, was a man to be related to whom would have been an honor. Miss Blanche Leppington, who had been asked to be a witness, told K. after that she hadn't looked at my face but that she felt as if she "ought to keep her eye fixed upon Miss James's *hand!*"—she also said the scene— "Will remain in my thoughts as the most pathetic I ever saw and in my imagination as the most picturesque and American!"—I can't complain of not being taken seriously and I think it is the first time that *picturesque* and *American,* which are usually supposed to neutralize one another so completely, were ever conjoined. In recounting the story to H. he said, "You can't say you've done nothing for your Race since you've brought that about in your own person."

[My "Hidden Self"]

October 26th [1890]

William uses an excellent expression when he says in his paper on the "Hidden Self" that the nervous victim "abandons" certain portions of his consciousness.[5] It may be the word commonly used by his kind. It is just the right one at any rate, altho' I have never unfortunately been able to abandon my consciousness and get five minutes' rest. I have passed thro' an infinite succession of conscious abandonments and in looking back now I see how it began in my childhood, altho' I wasn't conscious of the necessity until '67 or '68 when I broke down first, acutely, and had violent turns of hysteria. As I lay prostrate after the storm with my mind luminous and active and susceptible of the clearest, strongest impressions, I saw so distinctly that it was a fight simply between my body and my will, a battle in which the former was to be triumphant to the end. Owing to some physical weakness, excess of nervous susceptibility, the moral power *pauses,* as it were for a moment, and refuses to maintain muscular sanity, worn out with the strain of its constabulary functions. As I used to sit immovable reading in the library with waves of violent inclination suddenly invading my muscles taking some one of their myriad forms such as throwing myself out of the window, or knocking off the head of the benignant pater[6] as he sat with his silver locks, writing at his table, it used to seem to me that the only difference between me and the insane was that I had not only all the horrors and suffering of insanity but the duties of doctor, nurse, and strait-jacket imposed upon me, too. Conceive of never being without the sense that if you let yourself go for a moment your mechanism will fall into pie[7] and that at some given moment you must abandon it all, let the dykes break and the flood sweep in, acknowledging yourself abjectly impotent before the immutable laws. When all one's moral and natural stock in trade is a temperament forbidding the abandonment of an inch or the relaxation of a muscle, 'tis a never-ending fight. When the

4. Related. Thomas James, U.S. postmaster general, March 5–December 20, 1881.
5. William James had published an essay that year titled "The Hidden Self," in which he described "contractions in the field of consciousness" in hysterical patients.
6. Father (Latin); in this case, the eminent theologian Henry James Sr. (1811–1882).
7. Disorder (literally, printer's type that is spilled or mixed).

fancy took me of a morning at school to *study* my lessons by way of variety instead of shirking or wiggling thro' the most impossible sensations of upheaval, violent revolt in my head overtook me so that I had to "abandon" my brain, as it were. So it has always been, anything that sticks of itself is free to do so, but conscious and continuous cerebration is an impossible exercise and from just behind the eyes my head feels like a dense jungle into which no ray of light has ever penetrated. So, with the rest, you abandon the pit of your stomach, the palms of your hands, the soles of your feet, and refuse to keep them sane when you find in turn one moral impression after another producing despair in the one, terror in the other, anxiety in the third and so on until life becomes one long flight from remote suggestion and complicated eluding of the multifold traps set for your undoing.

[Going Downhill]

May 31st [1891]

To him who waits, all things come! My aspirations may have been eccentric, but I cannot complain now, that they have not been brilliantly fulfilled. Ever since I have been ill, I have longed and longed for some palpable disease, no matter how conventionally dreadful a label it might have, but I was always driven back to stagger alone under the monstrous mass of subjective sensations, which that sympathetic being "the medical man" had no higher inspiration than to assure me I was personally responsible for, washing his hands of me with a graceful complacency under my very nose. Dr. Torry was the only man who ever treated me like a rational being, who did not assume, because I was victim to many pains, that I was, of necessity, an arrested mental development too.

Nothwithstanding all the happiness and comfort here, I have been going downhill at a steady trot; so they sent for Sir Andrew Clark[8] four days ago, and the blessed being has endowed me not only with cardiac complications, but says that a lump that I have had in one of my breasts for three months, which has given me a great deal of pain, is a tumor, that nothing can be done for me but to alleviate pain, that it is only a question of time, etc. This with a delicate embroidery of "the most distressing case of nervous hyperaesthesia"[9] added to a spinal neurosis that has taken me off my legs for seven years; with attacks of rheumatic gout in my stomach for the last twenty, ought to satisfy the most inflated pathologic vanity. It is decidedly indecent to catalog oneself in this way, but I put it down in a scientific spirit, to show that though I have no productive worth, I have a certain value as an indestructible quantity.

[This Long Slow Dying]

February 2nd [1892]

This long slow dying is no doubt instructive, but it is disappointingly free from excitements: "naturalness" being carried to its supreme expression. One

8. Famous and fashionable British doctor (1826–1893); his practice included many prominent individuals.

9. Abnormal sensitivity to pain.

sloughs off the activities one by one, and never knows that they're gone, until one suddenly finds that the months have slipped away and the sofa will never more be laid upon, the morning paper read, or the loss of the new book regretted; one revolves with equal content within the narrowing circle until the vanishing point is reached, I suppose.

Vanity, however, maintains its undisputed sway, and I take satisfaction in feeling as much myself as ever, perhaps simply a more concentrated essence in this curtailment. If I could concern myself about the fate of my soul, it would give doubtless a savor of uncertainty to the fleeting moments, but I never felt so absolutely uninterested in the poor, shabby, old thing. The fact is, I have been dead so long and it has been simply such a grim shoving of the hours behind me as I faced a ceaseless possible horror, since that hideous summer of '78, when I went down to the deep sea, its dark waters closed over me and I knew neither hope nor peace;[1] that now it's only the shriveling of an empty pea pod that has to be completed.

A little while ago we had rather an amusing episode with the kind and usually understanding Tuckey,[2] who was led away into assuring me that I should live a good bit still—I was terribly shocked and when he saw the havoc that he wrought, he reassuringly said: "but you'll be comfortable, too," at which I exclaimed: "Oh I don't care about that, but boo-hoo, it's so *inconvenient!*" and the poor man burst into a roar of laughter. I was glad afterwards that it happened, as I was taken quite by surprise, and was able to test the sincerity of my mortuary inclinations. I have always *thought* that I wanted to die, but I felt quite uncertain as to what my muscular demonstrations might be at the moment of transition, for I occasionally have a quiver as of an expected dentistical wrench[3] when I fancy the actual moment. But my substance seemed equally outraged with my mind at Tuckey's dictum, so mayhap I shall be able to maintain a calm befitting so sublimated a spirit!—at any rate there is no humbuggy "strength of mind" about it, 'tis simply physical debility, 'twould be such a bore to be perturbed.

[Physical Pain]

March 4th [1892]

I am being ground slowly on the grim grindstone of physical pain, and on two nights I had almost asked for K.'s lethal dose, but one steps hesitantly along such unaccustomed ways and endures from second to second; and I feel sure that it can't be possible but what the bewildered little hammer[4] that keeps me going will very shortly see the decency of ending his distracted career; however this may be, physical pain however great ends in itself and falls away like dry husks from the mind, whilst moral discords and nervous horrors sear the soul. These last, Katharine has completely under the control of her rhythmic hand, so I go no longer in dread. Oh the wonderful moment when I felt myself floated for the first time into the deep sea of divine *cessation,* and saw all the dear old mysteries and miracles vanish into vapor!

1. She had suffered a serious nervous breakdown.
2. Charles Lloyd Tuckey, an English physician who wrote on the therapeutic effects of hypnotism.

3. I.e., like waiting for a tooth to be pulled.
4. I.e., her heart.

That first experience doesn't repeat itself, fortunately, for it might become a seduction.

Katharine can't help it, she's made that way, a simple embodiment of Health, as Baldwin[5] called her, "the New England Professor of doing things."

Final Entry by Katharine P. Loring

All through Saturday the 5th and even in the night, Alice was making sentences. One of the last things she said to me was to make a correction in the sentence of March 4th "moral discords and nervous horrors."

This dictation of March 4th was rushing about in her brain all day, and although she was very weak and it tired her much to dictate, she could not get her head quiet until she had had it written: then she was relieved and I finished Miss Woolson's story of "Dorothy"[6] to her.

1964

5. William Wilberforce Baldwin (1850–1910), American physician and friend of Henry James.
6. A story by the American-born writer Constance

Fenimore Woolson (1840–1894; see above, p. 1205), first published in the March 1892 *Harper's*.

EMMA LAZARUS
1849–1887

Poet, novelist, essayist, translator, dramatist, and social activist, Emma Lazarus is best known today for the last five lines of one of her sonnets, which in 1903 was inscribed on the pedestal of the Statue of Liberty. "The New Colossus" whom she defines as "Mother of Exiles" expresses a concern for the tired, poor, "huddled masses yearning to breathe free" that animated all the enterprises of her exceptionally privileged author. The child of well-to-do Sephardic parents, Lazarus was educated in languages, literature, and music by tutors in the New York City home she shared with her siblings. At her seventeenth birthday, her father privately printed her first book; it led to her meeting and then sustaining a correspondence with Ralph Waldo Emerson, who remained an important influence, as did various other prominent artists she visited during later tours of England, France, and Italy. In spite of these opportunities and contacts, a remark of Emerson's daughter Ellen—she described her excitement at encountering "a real unconverted Jew (who had no objections to calling herself one)"—illuminates the curiosity Lazarus must have realized she provoked in overwhelmingly gentile cultural circles. Around the time of Lazarus's birth, there were approximately 50,000 Jews in the United States; but by the turn of the century immigration, mainly from eastern Europe, brought the total to nearly two million.

As the visibility of Jews grew and along with it anti-Semitism, Lazarus began to tackle Christian prejudice in work that anticipated the later Zionist movement and was perhaps partly inspired by her reading of George Eliot's treatment of Jewish characters longing for a nation in *Daniel Deronda* (1876). That Lazarus brought her concern for social justice issues to the precarious situation of Jewish people is clear from her translations of Hebrew poetry in *Songs of a Semite* (1882), her play about the persecution of Jews in 1349 Thuringia; her *Century Magazine* and *American*

Hebrew articles urging the establishment of a Jewish homeland; her exertions for the Society for the Improvement of East European Jews and the Hebrew Immigrant Aid Society; and her book of prose poems, *By the Waters of Babylon* (1887). Although she has been faulted as assimilated and thus disdainful or ignorant of the rituals and traditions of the very people she sought to defend, the double vision of Jewish and American perspectives combines in her finest works: "In the Jewish Synagogue at Newport," for instance, responds to Henry Wadsworth Longfellow's poem "The Jewish Cemetery at Newport" (1854) by disputing his elegy on the death of the Jewish faith, while "1492" juxtaposes the expulsion of the Jews from Spain with the promise of inclusion held out by the discovery of America.

In the Jewish Synagogue at Newport[1]

Here, where the noises of the busy town,
 The ocean's plunge and roar can enter not,
We stand and gaze around with tearful awe,
 And muse upon the consecrated spot.

5 No signs of life are here: the very prayers
 Inscribed around are in a language dead;
The light of the "perpetual lamp"[2] is spent
 That an undying radiance was to shed.

What prayers were in this temple offered up,
10 Wrung from sad hearts that knew no joy on earth,
By these lone exiles of a thousand years,[3]
 From the fair sunrise land that gave them birth!

Now as we gaze, in this new world of light,
 Upon this relic of the days of old,
15 The present vanishes, and tropic bloom
 And Eastern towns and temples we behold.

Again we see the patriarch with his flocks,[4]
 The purple seas, the hot blue sky o'erhead,
The slaves of Egypt,—omens, mysteries,—
20 Dark fleeing hosts by flaming angels led.[5]

1. Newport, Rhode Island, a seaport, had a large Jewish community in the eighteenth century; Touro Synagogue, dedicated in 1763, was one of the earliest synagogues in America and is the oldest now standing.
2. A flame is always kept burning above the ark, which in every synagogue holds the scrolls of the Torah. "A language dead": Hebrew, which for centuries before the founding of the modern state of Israel was used only for prayers and sacred texts.
3. Jews lost control of Palestine when the Romans conquered the region in the first century B.C.E.; the destruction of the second temple in Jerusalem in 70 C.E. marked the beginning of the second exile (a sizable number of religious ceremonies can take place only in the temple).
4. The patriarchs of the Hebrew Bible—Abraham, Isaac, and Jacob—all had flocks of sheep.
5. The Book of Exodus describes the enslavement of the Israelites in Egypt; to persuade the pharaoh to release them, God sent ten supernatural plagues (rivers turned to blood, frogs covered the land, etc.). After they were freed, God led them through the desert "by day in a pillar of cloud, . . . and by night in a pillar of fire" (Exodus 13.21).

A wondrous light upon a sky-kissed mount,
 A man who reads Jehovah's written law,[6]
'Midst blinding glory and effulgence rare,
 Unto a people prone with reverent awe.

25 The pride of luxury's barbaric pomp
 In the rich court of royal Solomon[7]—
Alas! we wake: one scene alone remains,—
 The exiles by the streams of Babylon.[8]

Our softened voices send us back again
30 But mournful echoes through the empty hall;
Our footsteps have a strange, unnatural sound,
 And with unwonted gentleness they fall.

The weary ones, the sad, the suffering,
 All found their comfort in the holy place,
35 And children's gladness and men's gratitude
 Took voice and mingled in the chant of praise.

The funeral and the marriage, now, alas!
 We know not which is sadder to recall;
For youth and happiness have followed age,
40 And green grass lieth gently over all.

And still the sacred shrine is holy yet,
 With its lone floors where reverent feet once trod.
Take off your shoes as by the burning bush,[9]
 Before the mystery of death and God.

1867 1871

1492

Thou two-faced year,[1] Mother of Change and Fate,
Didst weep when Spain cast forth with flaming sword,[2]
The children of the prophets of the Lord,
Prince, priest, and people, spurned by zealot hate.
5 Hounded from sea to sea, from state to state,
The West refused them, and the East abhorred.
No anchorage the known world could afford,

6. I.e., Moses, who received the Ten Commandments from God (Jehovah, from the Hebrew word YHWH) on Mount Sinai. When he came down from the mountain to read them to the people as he was commanded, the skin on his face shone (Exodus 34).
7. King Solomon, revered for his wisdom and as the builder of the first temple in Jerusalem (1 Kings 6), also was notorious for his harem of 700 wives and 300 concubines (1 Kings 11.3).
8. Solomon's temple was destroyed by the Babylonians in 586 B.C.E., marking the beginning of the first exile; a few thousand Jews were taken to Babylon (see Psalm 137), and many more fled as refugees from the newly formed Babylonian provinces. Jerusalem was restored to Jewish rule in 538, and by 515 B.C.E. the temple had been rebuilt.
9. The bush through which God initially spoke to Moses, telling him first to take off his shoes because he was standing on holy ground (Exodus 3.2–5).
1. The year 1492 is both glorious (as the year when Columbus, bankrolled by King Ferdinand and Queen Isabella of Spain, landed in America) and infamous (as the year when the Jews were expelled from Spain, by the same monarchs).
2. An allusion to the expulsion of Adam and Eve from Eden (Genesis 3.24).

Close-locked was every port, barred every gate.
Then smiling, thou unveil'dst, O two-faced year,
10 A virgin world³ where doors of sunset part,
Saying, "Ho, all who weary, enter here!⁴
There falls each ancient barrier that the art
Of race or creed or rank devised, to rear
Grim bulwarked hatred between heart and heart!"

1883 1889

The New Ezekiel¹

What, can these dead bones² live, whose sap is dried
 By twenty scorching centuries of wrong?
Is this the House of Israel, whose pride
 Is as a tale that's told, an ancient song?
5 Are these ignoble relics all that live
 Of psalmist, priest, and prophet? Can the breath
Of very heaven bid these bones revive,
 Open the graves and clothe the ribs of death?

Yea, Prophesy, the Lord hath said. Again
10 Say to the wind, Come forth and breathe afresh,
Even that they may live upon these slain,
 And bone to bone shall leap, and flesh to flesh.³
The Spirit is not dead, proclaim the word,
 Where lay dead bones, a host of armed men stand!
15 I ope your graves, my people, saith the Lord,
 And I shall place you living in your land.⁴

1895(?)

The New Colossus¹

Not like the brazen giant of Greek fame,²
With conquering limbs astride from land to land;
Here at our sea-washed, sunset gates shall stand
A mighty woman with a torch, whose flame

3. America.
4. Compare "The New Colossus," lines 10–14 (below).
1. A priest who was a prophet of the Babylonian exile (586–538 B.C.E.); before the fall of Jerusalem, Ezekiel foretold the doom of the kingdom of Judah, and after it he promised restoration and healing.
2. God's question to Ezekiel in his vision of a valley of dry bones brought back to life (Ezekiel 37.1–14, esp. 3). The vision represented God's promise to bring the Jews "into the land of Israel," for "these bones are the whole house of Israel" (11–12).
3. See Ezekiel 37.5–10.
4. See Ezekiel 37.14.

1. Written in aid of the Bartholdi Pedestal Fund, 1883 [Lazarus's note]. Frédéric-Auguste Bartholdi (1834–1904), French sculptor who designed the 152-foot-tall Statue of Liberty (presented 1885, unveiled 1886), a gift from France to the United States. The pedestal, built with American funding, is 150 feet tall; this sonnet was affixed to it in 1903.
2. The Colossus of Rhodes, a bronze statue of Helios, the sun god, built between 191 and 280 B.C.E. It was more than 100 feet tall, and according to legend it stood astride the harbor; in fact, it stood on a promontory overlooking the harbor (it fell during an earthquake ca. 225 B.C.E.).

5 Is the imprisoned lightning, and her name
Mother of Exiles. From her beacon-hand
Glows world-wide welcome; her mild eyes command
The air-bridged harbor that twin cities frame.[3]
"Keep, ancient lands, your storied pomp!" cries she
10 With silent lips. "Give me your tired, your poor,
Your huddled masses yearning to breathe free,
The wretched refuse of your teeming shore.
Send these, the homeless, tempest-tost to me,
I lift my lamp beside the golden door!"

1883 1883, 1895

Venus of the Louvre[1]

Down the long hall she glistens like a star,
The foam-born mother of Love,[2] transfixed to stone,
Yet none the less immortal, breathing on.
Time's brutal hand hath maimed but could not mar.
5 When first the enthralled enchantress from afar
Dazzled mine eyes, I saw not her alone,
Serenely poised on her world-worshipped throne,
As when she guided once her dove-drawn car,[3]
But at her feet a pale, death-stricken Jew,
10 Her life adorer, sobbed farewell to love.
Here *Heine*[4] wept! Here still he weeps anew,
Nor ever shall his shadow lift or move,
While mourns one ardent heart, one poet-brain,
For vanished Hellas and Hebraic pain.[5]

ca. 1885 1895

3. The statue stands on Liberty Island (formerly Bedloe's Island) in Upper New York Harbor, between Jersey City and New York City; ships entering New York Harbor must pass it.
1. I.e., the Venus de Milo, a marble statue found in 1820 on the Greek island of Milos (or Milo), believed to depict the goddess of love and beauty (Venus to the Romans, Aphrodite to the Greeks). Created ca. 130 B.C.E., it is now missing both arms. It has been displayed in Paris in the Louvre, the foremost art museum in France, since 1821.
2. In Greek mythology, Aphrodite is the mother of Eros (Love); she was said to be born from the foam

around Uranus's severed genitals, which had been thrown into the sea by his son the Titan Cronos.
3. Chariot.
4. Heinrich Heine (1797–1856), German Jewish poet and critic, who moved to Paris in 1831. He visited the statue shortly before he died.
5. Perhaps a reference to Heine's pain at converting to Protestantism in 1825 in order to be eligible to have a career in civil service (barred to Jews). The juxtaposition of "Hellas" (ancient Greece) and "Hebraic" also suggests the dialectic between Hellenism and Hebraism that Matthew Arnold describes in *Culture and Anarchy* (1868).

SARAH ORNE JEWETT
1849–1909

In one of several tributes to Sarah Orne Jewett, Willa Cather recounted how the more experienced writer "once laughingly told me that her head was full of dear old houses and dear old women, and that when an old house and an old woman came together in her brain with a click, she knew that a story was under way." Jewett, who later advised Cather to relinquish "the masquerade" of her male narrator and write from a female point of view, crafted an art subtle enough to catch the idiomatic language and conservative values of the old women who inhabited the old houses of her native Maine, houses that often situated them in the elegiac splendor of a fading but beautiful world. No wonder, then, that Cather rated *The Country of the Pointed Firs* (1896), along with *The Scarlet Letter* and *Huckleberry Finn,* as one of the three enduring masterpieces of American literature. For, as Cather remarked, these chapters in what amounts to a lyrical novel "are living things caught in the open, with light and freedom and air-spaces about them." Like Jewett's other publications, "they melt into the land and the life of the land until they are not stories at all, but life itself."

That Jewett herself referred to her fiction as "sketches" illustrates her conscious substitution of a meditative lyricism for the neatly sustained conflicts of traditionally plotted stories. Such a focus also reflects the serenity of a life lived for the most part with a profound sense of rootedness, specifically in the southern portion of Maine. The second of the three daughters of Theodore Herman Jewett and Caroline Frances (Perry) Jewett, Theodora Sarah Orne Jewett quickly dropped her first name, which had been bestowed on her as a tribute to her father and her father's father. But she was born, was reared, and died in the pre-Revolutionary house in South Berwick that her grandfather, a prosperous shipbuilder, had bought. Both of her parents came from distinguished, well-educated families: her father, a physician, was descended from the first Bay Colony settlers, and her mother's father was a renowned surgeon. Because she was subject to ill health as a child, Jewett's father thought she would benefit from fresh air and so he took her on his rounds. Through her observation of his country patients, she acquired a deep respect for the everyday lives of common people and an equally sensitive appreciation of the region's landscape.

In her novel *The Country Doctor* (1884), she would present the struggles of a female character seeking to adopt the role of a father, who is clearly her most important mentor. Jewett's informal education with her own father was supplemented by Miss Olive Rayne's school in South Berwick and the Berwick Academy, from which she graduated in 1865. Three years later, under the pseudonym Alice or A. C. Eliot, she began publishing her first stories in the *Riverside Magazine for Young People* and the *Atlantic Monthly.* Her father's encouraging admonition—"Don't try to write *about* things: write the things themselves just as they are"—clearly shaped her aesthetic goals. By 1877 Jewett had accepted William Dean Howells's advice to collect her sketches about "things themselves," which had appeared in his *Atlantic,* in the volume she titled *Deephaven* (1877).

The letters and diaries of Jewett from this period in her life document her close relationships with a number of female friends. After her father's death in 1878, moreover, her acquaintance with Annie Adams Fields ripened into a thirty-year liaison, which the critic Josephine Donovan has placed in the context of other so-called Boston marriages: that is, female couples living together in a union comparable to marriage. Annie Fields was the wife of James T. Fields, a prominent Boston publisher who would also become the editor of the *Atlantic.* Fields was a hostess, an author, and a social welfare worker. The earliest letters between Fields and Jewett, which were omitted from Fields's 1911 edition of Jewett's letters, are dated 1877, when

Fields was forty-three and Jewett was twenty-eight. The correspondence quickly became affectionately intimate, and after the death of James Fields in 1881, the two women lived together, spending part of each year on Charles Street in Boston, part in Maine, and part traveling in western Europe.

Sustained by Fields's support and the models provided by her own wide reading in nineteenth-century fiction, Jewett produced such collections as *A White Heron, and Other Stories* (1886) and *The King of Folly Island* (1888). During her lifetime, she received public acknowledgment of her contribution to American letters from established writers including John Greenleaf Whittier and James Russell Lowell and from Bowdoin College, her father's alma mater, which made her a doctor of letters in 1901. For the last seven years of her life, she suffered the consequences of a spinal concussion caused by an accident in her carriage. By the time she died in her sixtieth year, however, she had succeeded in portraying the visionary resiliency with which women responded to the poverty and the physical splendor of rural New England. "The Town Poor" exemplifies Jewett's interest in the everyday lives of the often economically impoverished but psychologically resourceful women in her native region.

The Town Poor

Mrs. William Trimble and Miss Rebecca Wright were driving along Hampden east road, one afternoon in early spring. Their progress was slow. Mrs. Trimble's sorrel horse was old and stiff, and the wheels were clogged by clay mud. The frost was not yet out of the ground, although the snow was nearly gone, except in a few places on the north side of the woods, or where it had drifted all winter against a length of fence.

"There must be a good deal o' snow to the nor'ard of us yet," said weatherwise Mrs. Trimble. "I feel it in the air; 't is more than the ground-damp. We ain't goin' to have real nice weather till the up-country snow 's all gone."

"I heard say yesterday that there was good sleddin' yet, all up through Parsley," responded Miss Wright. "I should n't like to live in them northern places. My cousin Ellen's husband was a Parsley man, an' he was obliged, as you may have heard, to go up north to his father's second wife's funeral; got back day before yesterday. 'T was about twenty-one miles, an' they started on wheels; but when they 'd gone nine or ten miles, they found 't was no sort o' use, an' left their wagon an' took a sleigh. The man that owned it charged 'em four an' six,[1] too. I should n't have thought he would; they told him they was goin' to a funeral; an' they had their own buffaloes[2] an' everything."

"Well, I expect it's a good deal harder scratchin', up that way; they have to git money where they can; the farms is very poor as you go north," suggested Mrs. Trimble kindly. " 'T ain't none too rich a country where we be, but I've always been grateful I wa'n't born up to Parsley."

The old horse plodded along, and the sun, coming out from the heavy spring clouds, sent a sudden shine of light along the muddy road. Sister Wright drew her large veil forward over the high brim of her bonnet. She was not used to driving, or to being much in the open air; but Mrs. Trimble was an active business woman, and looked after her own affairs herself, in

1. Probably $4 and 6 bits (i.e., 75 cents). 2. Warm blankets made from buffalo skin.

all weathers. The late Mr. Trimble had left her a good farm, but not much ready money, and it was often said that she was better off in the end than if he had lived. She regretted his loss deeply, however; it was impossible for her to speak of him, even to intimate friends, without emotion, and nobody had ever hinted that this emotion was insincere. She was most warm-hearted and generous, and in her limited way played the part of Lady Bountiful[3] in the town of Hampden.

"Why, there's where the Bray girls lives, ain't it?" she exclaimed, as, beyond a thicket of witch-hazel and scrub-oak, they came in sight of a weather-beaten, solitary farmhouse. The barn was too far away for thrift or comfort, and they could see long lines of light between the shrunken boards as they came nearer. The fields looked both stony and sodden. Somehow, even Parsley itself could be hardly more forlorn.

"Yes 'm," said Miss Wright, "that 's where they live now, poor things. I know the place, though I ain't been up here for years. You don't suppose, Mis' Trimble—I ain't seen the girls out to meetin'[4] all winter. I've re'lly been covetin' "—

"Why, yes, Rebecca, of course we could stop," answered Mrs. Trimble heartily. "The exercises[5] was over earlier 'n I expected, an' you're goin' to remain over night long o' me, you know. There won't be no tea till we git there, so we can't be late. I'm in the habit o' sendin' a basket to the Bray girls when any o' our folks is comin' this way, but I ain't been to see 'em since they moved up here. Why, it must be a good deal over a year ago. I know 't was in the late winter they had to make the move. 'T was cruel hard, I must say, an' if I had n't been down with my pleurisy fever I'd have stirred round an' done somethin' about it. There was a good deal o' sickness at the time, an'—well, 't was kind o' rushed through, breakin' of 'em up, an' lots o' folks blamed the selec'men;[6] but when 't was done, 't was done, an' nobody took holt to undo it. Ann an' Mandy looked same 's ever when they come to meetin', 'long in the summer,—kind o' wishful, perhaps. They've always sent me word they was gittin' on pretty comfortable."

"That would be their way," said Rebecca Wright. "They never was any hand to complain, though Mandy's less cheerful than Ann. If Mandy 'd been spared such poor eyesight, an' Ann had n't got her lame wrist that wa'n't set right, they 'd kep' off the town fast enough. They both shed tears when they talked to me about havin' to break up, when I went to see 'em before I went over to brother Asa's. You see we was brought up neighbors, an' we went to school together, the Brays an' me. 'T was a special Providence brought us home this road, I've been so covetin' a chance to git to see 'em. My lameness hampers me."

"I'm glad we come this way, myself," said Mrs. Trimble.

"I'd like to see just how they fare," Miss Rebecca Wright continued. "They give their consent to goin' on the town because they knew they'd got to be dependent, an' so they felt 't would come easier for all than for a few to help 'em. They acted real dignified an' right-minded, contrary to what most do in

3. The munificent lady in a neighborhood; from a character in *The Beaux' Stratagem* (1707), by George Farquhar.
4. I.e., at the meetinghouse, or church.
5. Religious services.

6. Selectmen; in New England towns, these officials, chosen annually, administer local affairs. "Breakin' of 'em up": i.e., the breaking up of their household.

such cases, but they was dreadful anxious to see who would bid 'em off, town-meeting day; they did so hope 't would be somebody right in the village. I just sat down an' cried good when I found Abel Janes's folks had got hold of 'em. They always had the name of bein' slack an' poor-spirited, an' they did it just for what they got out o' the town. The selectmen this last year ain't what we have had. I hope they've been considerate about the Bray girls."

"I should have be'n more considerate about fetchin' of you over," apologized Mrs. Trimble. "I've got my horse, an' you're lame-footed; 't is too far for you to come. But time does slip away with busy folks, an' I forgit a good deal I ought to remember."

"There's nobody more considerate than you be," protested Miss Rebecca Wright.

Mrs. Trimble made no answer, but took out her whip and gently touched the sorrel horse, who walked considerably faster, but did not think it worth while to trot. It was a long, round-about way to the house, farther down the road and up a lane.

"I never had any opinion of the Bray girls' father, leavin' 'em as he did," said Mrs. Trimble.

"He was much praised in his time, though there was always some said his early life had n't been up to the mark," explained her companion. "He was a great favorite of our then preacher, the Reverend Daniel Longbrother. They did a good deal for the parish, but they did it their own way. Deacon Bray was one that did his part in the repairs without urging. You know 't was in his time the first repairs was made, when they got out the old soundin'-board an' them handsome square pews. It cost an awful sight o' money, too. They had n't done payin' up that debt when they set to alter it again an' git the walls frescoed. My grandmother was one that always spoke her mind right out, an' she was dreadful opposed to breakin' up the square pews where she'd always set. They was countin' up what 't would cost in parish meetin', an' she riz right up an' said 't would n't cost nothin' to let 'em stay, an' there wa'n't a house carpenter left in the parish that could do such nice work, an' time would come when the great-grandchildren would give their eye-teeth to have the old meetin'-house look just as it did then. But haul the inside to pieces they would and did."

"There come to be a real fight over it, did n't there?" agreed Mrs. Trimble soothingly. "Well, 't wa'n't good taste. I remember the old house well. I come here as a child to visit a cousin o' mother's, an' Mr. Trimble's folks was neighbors, an' we was drawed to each other then, young 's we was. Mr. Trimble spoke of it many's the time,—that first time he ever see me, in a leghorn hat[7] with a feather; 't was one that mother had, an' pressed over."

"When I think of them old sermons that used to be preached in that old meetin'-house of all, I'm glad it 's altered over, so 's not to remind folks," said Miss Rebecca Wright, after a suitable pause. "Them old brimstone discourses, you know, Mis' Trimble. Preachers is far more reasonable, nowadays. Why, I set an' thought, last Sabbath, as I listened, that if old Mr. Longbrother an' Deacon Bray could hear the difference they'd crack the ground over 'em like pole beans, an' come right up 'long side their headstones."

7. A straw hat made of bleached wheat imported from Leghorn, in Tuscany.

Mrs. Trimble laughed heartily, and shook the reins three or four times by way of emphasis. "There 's no gitting round you," she said, much pleased. "I should think Deacon Bray would want to rise, any way, if 't was so he could, an' knew how his poor girls was farin'. A man ought to provide for his folks he 's got to leave behind him, specially if they 're women. To be sure, they had their little home; but we 've seen how, with all their industrious ways, they had n't means to keep it. I s'pose he thought he 'd got time enough to lay by, when he give so generous in collections; but he did n't lay by, an' there they be. He might have took lessons from the squirrels: even them little wild creatur's makes them their winter hoards, an' menfolks ought to know enough if squirrels does. 'Be just before you are generous:' that's what was always set for the B's in the copy-books,[8] when I was to school, and it often runs through my mind."

"'As for man, his days are as grass,'[9]—that was for A; the two go well together," added Miss Rebecca Wright soberly. "My good gracious, ain't this a starved-lookin' place? It makes me ache to think them nice Bray girls has to brook it[1] here."

The sorrel horse, though somewhat puzzled by an unexpected deviation from his homeward way, willingly came to a stand by the gnawed corner of the door-yard fence, which evidently served as hitching-place. Two or three ragged old hens were picking about the yard, and at last a face appeared at the kitchen window, tied up in a handkerchief, as if it were a case of tooth-ache. By the time our friends reached the side door next this window, Mrs. Janes came disconsolately to open it for them, shutting it again as soon as possible, though the air felt more chilly inside the house.

"Take seats," said Mrs. Janes briefly. "You'll have to see me just as I be. I have been suffering these four days with the ague, and everything to do. Mrs. Janes is to court, on the jury. 'T was inconvenient to spare him. I should be pleased to have you lay off your things."

Comfortable Mrs. Trimble looked about the cheerless kitchen, and could not think of anything to say; so she smiled blandly and shook her head in answer to the invitation. "We'll just set a few minutes with you, to pass the time o' day, an' then we must go in an' have a word with the Miss Brays, bein' old acquaintance. It ain't been so we could git to call on 'em before. I don't know 's you 're acquainted with Miss R'becca Wright. She 's been out of town a good deal."

"I heard she was stopping over to Plainfields with her brother's folks," replied Mrs. Janes, rocking herself with irregular motion, as she sat close to the stove. "Got back some time in the fall, I believe?"

"Yes 'm," said Miss Rebecca, with an undue sense of guilt and conviction. "We've been to the installation[2] over to the East Parish, an' thought we'd stop in; we took this road home to see if 't was any better. How is the Miss Brays gettin' on?"

"They 're well 's common," answered Mrs. Janes grudgingly. "I was put out with Mr. Janes for fetchin' of 'em here, with all I've got to do, an' I own I

8. Books used in teaching penmanship; the examples for imitation often were biblical or other proverbs. In this case, the quotation appears as an "old proverb" in Richard Brinsley Sheridan's *The School for Scandal* (1777), 4.1.

9. Psalms 103.15.
1. I.e., endure living.
2. A ceremony in which a member of the clergy is installed in a church or other office.

was kind o' surly to 'em 'long to the first of it. He gits the money from the town, an' it helps him out; but he bid 'em off for five dollars a month, an' we can't do much for 'em at no such price as that. I went an' dealt with the selec'men, an' made 'em promise to find their firewood an' some other things extra. They was glad to get rid o' the matter the fourth time I went, an' would ha' promised 'most anything. But Mr. Janes don't keep me half the time in oven-wood, he's off so much, an' we was cramped o' room, any way. I have to store things up garrit[3] a good deal, an' that keeps me trampin' right through their room. I do the best for 'em I can, Mis' Trimble, but 't ain't so easy for me as 't is for you, with all your means to do with."

The poor woman looked pinched and miserable herself, though it was evident that she had no gift at house or home keeping. Mrs. Trimble's heart was wrung with pain, as she thought of the unwelcome inmates of such a place; but she held her peace bravely, while Miss Rebecca again gave some brief information in regard to the installation.

"You go right up them back stairs," the hostess directed at last. "I'm glad some o' you church folks has seen fit to come an' visit 'em. There ain't been nobody here this long spell, an' they've aged a sight since they come. They always send down a taste out of your baskets, Mis' Trimble, an' I relish it, I tell you. I'll shut the door after you, if you don't object. I feel every draught o' cold air."

"I've always heard she was a great hand to make a poor mouth. Wa'n't she from somewheres up Parsley way?" whispered Miss Rebecca, as they stumbled in the half-light.

"Poor meechin'[4] body, wherever she come from," replied Mrs. Trimble, as she knocked at the door.

There was silence for a moment after this unusual sound; then one of the Bray sisters opened the door. The eager guests stared into a small, low room, brown with age, and gray, too, as if former dust and cobwebs could not be made wholly to disappear. The two elderly women who stood there looked like captives. Their withered faces wore a look of apprehension, and the room itself was more bare and plain than was fitting to their evident refinement of character and self-respect. There was an uncovered small table in the middle of the floor, with some crackers on a plate; and, for some reason or other, this added a great deal to the general desolation.

But Miss Ann Bray, the elder sister, who carried her right arm in a sling, with piteously drooping fingers, gazed at the visitors with radiant joy. She had not seen them arrive.

The one window gave only the view at the back of the house, across the fields, and their coming was indeed a surprise. The next minute she was laughing and crying together. "Oh, sister!" she said, "if here ain't our dear Mis' Trimble!—an' my heart o' goodness,'t is 'Becca Wright, too! What dear good creatur's you be! I've felt all day as if something good was goin' to happen, an' was just sayin' to myself 't was most sundown now, but I would n't let on to Mandany I'd give up hope quite yet. You see, the scissors stuck in the floor this very mornin' an' it's always a reliable sign. There, I've got to kiss ye both again!"

"I don't know where we can all set," lamented sister Mandana. "There ain't

3. In the garret, the area under the roof. 4. Shrinking, retiring; complaining (dialect).

but the one chair an' the bed; t' other chair's too rickety; an' we've been promised another these ten days; but first they've forgot it, an' next Mis' Janes can't spare it,—one excuse an' another. I am goin' to git a stump o' wood an' nail a board on to it, when I can git outdoor again," said Mandana, in a plaintive voice. "There, I ain't goin' to complain o' nothin', now you've come," she added; and the guests sat down, Mrs. Trimble, as was proper, in the one chair.

"We've sat on the bed many's the time with you,'Becca, an' talked over our girl nonsense, ain't we? You know where 't was—in the little back bedroom we had when we was girls, an' used to peek out at our beaux through the strings o' mornin'-glories," laughed Ann Bray delightedly, her thin face shining more and more with joy. "I brought some o' them mornin'-glory seeds along when we come away, we'd raised 'em so many years; an' we got 'em started all right, but the hens found 'em out. I declare I chased them poor hens, foolish as 't was; but the mornin'-glories I'd counted on a sight to remind me o' home. You see, our debts was so large, after my long sickness an' all, that we did n't feel 't was right to keep back anything we could help from the auction."

It was impossible for any one to speak for a moment or two; the sisters felt their own uprooted condition afresh, and their guests for the first time really comprehended the piteous contrast between that neat little village house, which now seemed a palace of comfort, and this cold, unpainted upper room in the remote Janes farmhouse. It was an unwelcome thought to Mrs. Trimble that the well-to-do town of Hampden could provide no better for its poor than this, and her round face flushed with resentment and the shame of personal responsibility. "The girls shall be well settled in the village before another winter, if I pay their board myself," she made an inward resolution, and took another almost tearful look at the broken stove, the miserable bed, and the sisters' one hair-covered trunk, on which Mandana was sitting. But the poor place was filled with a golden spirit of hospitality.

Rebecca was again discoursing eloquently of the installation; it was so much easier to speak of general subjects, and the sisters had evidently been longing to hear some news. Since the late summer they had not been to church, and presently Mrs. Trimble asked the reason.

"Now, don't you go to pouring out our woes, Mandy!" begged little old Ann, looking shy and almost girlish, and as if she insisted upon playing that life was still all before them and all pleasure. "Don't you go to spoilin' their visit with our complaints! They know well's we do that changes must come, an' we'd been so wonted[5] to our home things that this come hard at first; but then they felt for us, I know just as well's can be. 'T will soon be summer again, an' 't is real pleasant right out in the fields here, when there ain't too hot a spell. I've got to know a sight o' singin' birds since we come."

"Give me the folks I've always known," sighed the younger sister, who looked older than Miss Ann, and less even-tempered. "You may have your birds, if you want 'em. I do re'lly long to go to meetin' an' see folks go by up the aisle. Now, I will speak of it, Ann, whatever you say. We need, each of us, a pair o' good stout shoes an' rubbers,—ours are all wore out; an' we 've asked an' asked, an' they never think to bring 'em, an' "—

5. Accustomed.

Poor old Mandana, on the trunk, covered her face with her arms and sobbed aloud. The elder sister stood over her, and patted her on the thin shoulder like a child, and tried to comfort her. It crossed Mrs. Trimble's mind that it was not the first time one had wept and the other had comforted. The sad scene must have been repeated many times in that long, drear winter. She would see them forever after in her mind as fixed as a picture, and her own tears fell fast.

"You did n't see Mis' Janes's cunning[6] little boy, the next one to the baby, did you?" asked Ann Bray, turning round quickly at last, and going cheerfully on with the conversation. "Now, hush, Mandy, dear; they'll think you're childish! He's a dear, friendly little creatur', an' likes to stay with us a good deal, though we feel 's if it 't was too cold for him, now we are waitin' to get us more wood."

"When I think of the acres o' woodland in this town!" groaned Rebecca Wright. "I believe I'm goin' to preach next Sunday,'stead o' the minister, an' I'll make the sparks fly. I've always heard the saying, 'What's everybody's business is nobody's business,' an' I've come to believe it."

"Now, don't you,'Becca. You've happened on a kind of a poor time with us, but we've got more belongings than you see here, an' a good large cluset, where we can store those things there ain't room to have about. You an' Miss Trimble have happened on a kind of poor day, you know. Soon 's I git me some stout shoes an' rubbers, as Mandy says, I can fetch home plenty o' little dry boughs o' pine; you remember I was always a great hand to roam in the woods? If we could only have a front room, so 't we could look out on the road an' see passin', an' was shod for meetin', I don' know 's we should complain. Now we're just goin' to give you what we've got, an' make out with a good welcome. We make more tea 'n we want in the mornin', an' then let the fire go down, since 't has been so mild. We've got a *good* cluset" (disappearing as she spoke), "an' I know this to be good tea,'cause it's some o' yourn, Mis' Trimble. An' here's our sprigged chiny cups that R'becca knows by sight, if Mis' Trimble don't. We kep' out four of 'em, an' put the even half dozen with the rest of the auction stuff. I've often wondered who'd got 'em, but I never asked, for fear 't would be somebody that would distress us. They was mother's, you know."

The four cups were poured, and the little table pushed to the bed, where Rebecca Wright still sat, and Mandana, wiping her eyes, came and joined her. Mrs. Trimble sat in her chair at the end, and Ann trotted about the room in pleased content for a while, and in and out of the closet, as if she still had much to do; then she came and stood opposite Mrs. Trimble. She was very short and small, and there was no painful sense of her being obliged to stand. The four cups were not quite full of cold tea, but there was a clean old tablecloth folded double, and a plate with three pairs of crackers neatly piled, and a small—it must be owned, a very small—piece of hard white cheese. Then, for a treat, in a glass dish, there was a little preserved peach, the last—Miss Rebecca knew it instinctively—of the household stores brought from their old home. It was very sugary, this bit of peach; and as she helped her guests and sister Mandy, Miss Ann Bray said, half unconsciously, as she often had said with less reason in the old days, "Our preserves

6. Clever.

ain't so good as usual this year; this is beginning to candy." Both the guests
protested, while Rebecca added that the taste of it carried her back, and
made her feel young again. The Brays had always managed to keep one or
two peach-trees alive in their corner of a garden. "I've been keeping this
preserve for a treat," said her friend. "I'm glad to have you eat some,'Becca.
Last summer I often wished you was home an' could come an' see us,'stead
o' being away off to Plainfields."

The crackers did not taste too dry. Miss Ann took the last of the peach on
her own cracker; there could not have been quite a small spoonful, after the
others were helped, but she asked them first if they would not have some
more. Then there was a silence, and in the silence a wave of tender feeling
rose high in the hearts of the four elderly women. At this moment the setting
sun flooded the poor plain room with light; the unpainted wood was all of a
golden-brown, and Ann Bray, with her gray hair and aged face, stood at the
head of the table in a kind of aureole. Mrs. Trimble's face was all aquiver as
she looked at her; she thought of the text about two or three being gathered
together,[7] and was half afraid.

"I believe we ought to 've asked Mis' Janes if she would n't come up," said
Ann. "She's real good feelin', but she's had it very hard, an gits discouraged.
I can't find that she's ever had anything real pleasant to look back to, as we
have. There, next time we'll make a good heartenin' time for her too."

The sorrel horse had taken a long nap by the gnawed fence-rail, and the
cool air after sundown made him impatient to be gone. The two friends jolted
homeward in the gathering darkness, through the stiffening mud, and nei-
ther Mrs. Trimble nor Rebecca Wright said a word until they were out of
sight as well as out of sound of the Janes house. Time must elapse before
they could reach a more familiar part of the road and resume conversation
on its natural level.

"I consider myself to blame," insisted Mrs. Trimble at last. "I have n't no
words of accusation for nobody else, an' I ain't one to take comfort in calling
names to the board o' selec'men. I make no reproaches, an' I take it all on
my own shoulders; but I'm goin' to stir about me, I tell you! I shall begin
early to-morrow. They're goin' back to their own house,—it's been standin'
empty all winter,—an' the town's goin' to give 'em the rent an' what firewood
they need; it won't come to more than the board's payin' out now. An' you
an' me'll take this same horse an' wagon, an' ride an go afoot by turns, an'
git means enough together to buy back their furniture an' whatever was sold
at that plaguey auction; an' then we'll put it all back, an' tell 'em they've got
to move to a new place, an' just carry 'em right back again where they come
from. An' don't you never tell, R'becca, but here I be a widow woman, layin'
up what I make from my farm for nobody knows who, an' I'm goin' to do for
them Bray girls all I'm a mind to. I should be sca't[8] to wake up in heaven,
an' hear anybody there ask how the Bray girls was. Don't talk to me about
the town o' Hampden, an' don't ever let me hear the name o' town poor! I'm
ashamed to go home an' see what's set out for supper. I wish I'd brought 'em
right along."

7. A reference to Jesus' words in Matthew 18.20:
"For where two or three are gathered together in

my name, there I am in the midst of them."
8. I.e., scared.

"I was goin' to ask if we could n't git the new doctor to go up an' do somethin' for poor Ann's arm," said Miss Rebecca. "They say he's very smart. If she could get so 's to braid straw⁹ or hook rugs again, she'd soon be earnin' a little somethin'. An' may be he could do somethin' for Mandy's eyes. They did use to live so neat an' ladylike. Somehow I could n't speak to tell 'em there that 't was I bought them six best cups an' saucers, time of the auction; they went very low, as everything else did, an' I thought I could save it some other way. They shall have 'em back an' welcome. You're real whole-hearted, Mis' Trimble. I expect Ann'll be sayin' that her father's child'n wa'n't goin' to be left desolate, an' that all the bread he cast on the water's¹ comin' back through you."

"I don't care what she says, dear creatur'!" exclaimed Mrs. Trimble. "I'm full o' regrets I took time for that installation, an' set there seepin' in a lot o' talk this whole day long, except for its kind of bringin' us to the Bray girls. I wish to my heart 't was to-morrow mornin' a'ready, an' I a-startin' for the selec'*men*."

<div align="right">1890</div>

9. E.g., for hats.
1. See Ecclesiastes 11.1: "Cast thy bread upon the waters: for thou shalt find it after many days."

KATE CHOPIN
1850–1904

When *The Awakening,* Kate Chopin's frank exploration of a late-nineteenth-century woman's growth toward sexual and emotional independence, appeared in 1899, critics assailed it. The novel "leaves one sick of human nature," declared one writer; "it is not a healthy book," complained another; "the purport of the story can hardly be described in language fit for publication," stormed a third. Within months, the libraries of Chopin's native city, St. Louis, had refused to carry the book, and the author herself was rebuffed by a number of acquaintances, though she had attempted to defend herself by playfully explaining in a newspaper article that "I never dreamed of Mrs. Pontellier [the novel's heroine] making such a mess of things and working out her own damnation as she did." In fact, though *The Awakening* has by now been recognized as an American classic, Chopin was never to reap the rewards of her achievement. In the years between 1899, when the work was published, and 1904, when she died, she earned hardly any royalties from the novel; her third collection of short stories was rejected by the firm that had published *The Awakening;* and—no doubt disheartened by these failures—she was able to compose only a few tales and poems. For more than three decades after Chopin's death, moreover, her allegedly scandalous masterpiece fell into oblivion; indeed, although one critic attempted to revive the book in the 1930s, *The Awakening* was not really to be recovered for readers until the 1960s.

The well-bred daughter of a wealthy St. Louis family, Katherine O'Flaherty would not have seemed likely to produce so controversial a work. On her mother's side, she was descended from French Creole aristocrats, while her father was an Irish immigrant who had become a singularly successful merchant before his death in an 1855

railway accident. Coming from such a background, Chopin received, at home, a typically Victorian training in decorum as well as, at school, a strict Catholic education. In 1868, when she made her debut in society, she was said to be "one of the acknowledged belles of St. Louis;" and after she married Oscar Chopin, a Creole cotton trader, in 1870, she was evidently a happy and dutiful wife whom one observer later described as the "conscientious mother" of six children. The young couple had first settled in New Orleans, and then, with their family, they had moved to a plantation near Cloutierville, in Natchitoches (pronounced *Nack-uh-tush*) parish, an area Chopin was eventually to memorialize in a series of brilliant stories and sketches. When her husband died of swamp fever in 1883, Chopin was said to be "inconsolable."

Painful as it was, however, Oscar's untimely death precipitated his widow into serious literary activity. She had apparently always "scribbled"—a diary as well as some sketches and poems from her youth are still held by the St. Louis Historical Society—but when she returned to her birthplace with her children, she began to write in earnest. Though they were at first received as "delightful sketches," even her earliest stories were more radical than many readers understood, suggesting that the "acknowledged belle" and the dutiful wife had always harbored a streak of rebelliousness, which was to find its fullest expression in *The Awakening*.

Chopin's family doctor, Frederick Kolbenheyer, had become one of her closest friends in these years, and according to the biographer Per Seyersted, he was a "determined agnostic" who persuaded her to read the writing of such pioneering Victorian thinkers as Charles Darwin and Thomas Henry Huxley and to renounce most of the main tenets of Catholicism. In addition, Chopin had begun to read extensively in contemporary fiction, studying, on the one hand, the works of American women regionalists such as Sarah Orne Jewett and Mary E. Wilkins Freeman, and, on the other hand, the works of French naturalists such as Émile Zola, Gustave Flaubert, and Guy de Maupassant. Maupassant, in particular, had become one of her literary idols, an artist whom she defined as "a man who had escaped from tradition and authority, who had entered into himself and looked out upon life through his own being and with his own eyes." In all her short fictions, Chopin, too, was enacting just such escapes from tradition and authority. A number of the tales that were eventually collected in *Bayou Folk* (1894) and *A Night in Acadie* (1897) examined the inequities of traditional marriage; some explored the arbitrary race distinctions that characterized southern culture; others questioned the class divisions that marked even so seemingly simple a world as that of Natchitoches parish; and one or two frankly imagined alternative ways in which society might be structured to allow individuals, especially women, more opportunities for emotional, sexual, and intellectual freedom. With comparable clarity, Chopin's first novel, *At Fault* (1890), explored an explosive love triangle, raising questions about marriage and divorce, guilt and responsibility.

But it is in *The Awakening* that Chopin most openly and vividly dramatized her own—as well as her heroine's—desire for freedom. Setting her novel in the Louisiana resort town of Grand Isle, where she herself had spent many summers as a young married woman, and in the kind of bourgeois New Orleans neighborhood where she had also lived during her marriage, she used a distinctively turn-of-the-century myth of female sexual independence to show how her protagonist, Edna Pontellier, was defined, and ultimately destroyed, by a society that could not conceive of allowing a woman—especially a wife and mother—the kind of autonomy for which she longed. Specifically, Chopin employed not only realistic strategies, learned from such cherished precursors as Jewett and Maupassant, but also images of desire and of the body's holiness, drawn from significant literary ancestors such as the English poet Algernon Charles Swinburne and the American poet Walt Whitman, to explore ideas about the relationship between female sexuality and female creativity that were, in her era, almost entirely forbidden—at least to women writers.

For Edna Pontellier, who explains to her lover, "I give myself where I please," a supposedly "proper" lady has as much right to experience desire as her gentlemanly

counterpart might; similarly, for Edna a lady has as much right to feel ambition as might any male peer. Nevertheless, the structure of Chopin's novel is profoundly pessimistic about such desires and ambitions: if Aphrodite, the Greek goddess of love (to whom Edna is at one point in the book compared), were reborn as a late Victorian woman, Chopin suggests, Edna's fate might be *her* fate. For though a number of critics from the earliest reviewers to the most recent scholars have felt, with the American novelist Willa Cather, that Edna Pontellier was no more than, in Cather's words, "a Creole Bovary"—a New World version of Flaubert's foolishly sentimental Madame Bovary—*The Awakening* seems to elaborate a shadowy story about female erotic freedom and even about feminist emotional independence.

Whether or not Chopin's death in her early fifties was related to the failure of her book, it represented a serious loss to American literature, for when she wrote *The Awakening* she was clearly at the height of her extraordinary power. Yet, despite the pain that she evidently put an end to her literary career, Chopin's passionate fantasy about her heroine's fantasizings has haunted a number of readers, at least since 1969, when the scholar Per Seyersted produced a definitive two-volume edition of her works, which reintroduced the novel to a wide audience of teachers, critics, and historians. Even Edna's final swim into the sea can be seen, after all, in terms of a metaphor Florence Nightingale had used in her visionary *Cassandra,* almost half a century before Chopin had begun to imagine this surprisingly liberated woman's ambiguously significant awakening: "rather, ten times, die in the surf, heralding the way to [a] new world, than stand idly on the shore."

The Awakening[1]

I

A green and yellow parrot, which hung in a cage outside the door, kept repeating over and over:

"*Allez vous-en! Allez vous-en! Sapristi!*[2] That's all right!"

He could speak a little Spanish, and also a language which nobody understood, unless it was the mocking-bird that hung on the other side of the door, whistling his fluty notes out upon the breeze with maddening persistence.

Mr. Pontellier, unable to read his newspaper with any degree of comfort, arose with an expression and an exclamation of disgust. He walked down the gallery and across the narrow "bridges" which connected the Lebrun cottages one with the other. He had been seated before the door of the main house. The parrot and the mocking-bird were the property of Madame Lebrun, and they had the right to make all the noise they wished. Mr. Pontellier had the privilege of quitting their society when they ceased to be entertaining.

He stopped before the door of his own cottage, which was the fourth one from the main building and next to the last. Seating himself in a wicker rocker which was there, he once more applied himself to the task of reading the newspaper. The day was Sunday; the paper was a day old. The Sunday papers had not yet reached Grand Isle.[3] He was already acquainted with the market reports, and he glanced restlessly over the editorials and bits of news

1. Notes to *The Awakening* owe much to the Norton Critical Edition prepared by Margo Culley and to the text prepared by Ronald Gottesman in *The Norton Anthology of American Literature.*

2. Go away! Go away! For God's sake! (French, as are all translated terms unless otherwise specified).
3. Resort island, between the Gulf of Mexico and Caminada Bay, south of New Orleans.

which he had not had time to read before quitting New Orleans the day before.

Mr. Pontellier wore eye-glasses. He was a man of forty, of medium height and slender build; he stooped a little. His hair was brown and straight, parted on one side. His beard was neatly and closely trimmed.

Once in a while he withdrew his glance from the newspaper and looked about him. There was more noise than ever over at the house. The main building was called "the house," to distinguish it from the cottages. The chattering and whistling birds were still at it. Two young girls, the Farival twins, were playing a duet from "Zampa"[4] upon the piano. Madame Lebrun was bustling in and out, giving orders in a high key to a yard-boy whenever she got inside the house, and directions in an equally high voice to a dining-room servant whenever she got outside. She was a fresh, pretty woman, clad always in white with elbow sleeves. Her starched skirts crinkled as she came and went. Farther down, before one of the cottages, a lady in black was walking demurely up and down, telling her beads. A good many persons of the *pension* had gone over to the *Chênière Caminada* in Beaudelet's lugger[5] to hear mass. Some young people were out under the water-oaks playing croquet. Mr. Pontellier's two children were there—sturdy little fellows of four and five. A quadroon[6] nurse followed them about with a far-away, meditative air.

Mr. Pontellier finally lit a cigar and began to smoke, letting the paper drag idly from his hand. He fixed his gaze upon a white sunshade[7] that was advancing at snail's pace from the beach. He could see it plainly between the gaunt trunks of the water-oaks and across the stretch of yellow camomile. The gulf looked far away melting hazily into the blue of the horizon. The sunshade continued to approach slowly. Beneath its pink-lined shelter were his wife, Mrs. Pontellier, and young Robert Lebrun. When they reached the cottage, the two seated themselves with some appearance of fatigue upon the step of the porch, facing each other, each leaning against a supporting post.

"What folly! to bathe[8] at such an hour in such heat!" exclaimed Mr. Pontellier. He himself had taken a plunge at daylight. That was why the morning seemed long to him.

"You are burnt beyond recognition," he added, looking at his wife as one looks at a valuable piece of personal property which has suffered some damage. She held up her hands, strong, shapely hands, and surveyed them critically, drawing up her lawn[9] sleeves above the wrists. Looking at them reminded her of her rings, which she had given to her husband before leaving for the beach. She silently reached out to him, and he, understanding, took the rings from his vest pocket and dropped them into her open palm. She slipped them upon her fingers; then clasping her knees, she looked across at Robert and began to laugh. The rings sparkled upon her fingers. He sent back an answering smile.

"What is it?" asked Pontellier, looking lazily and amused from one to the other. It was some utter nonsense; some adventure out there in the water,

4. A popular Romantic opera (1831) by the French composer Louis Hérold (1791–1833).
5. Passenger boat. "*Pension*": a bed-and-board hotel. *Chênière Caminada* is an island between Grande Isle and the Louisiana coast.

6. I.e., with one-quarter black ancestry.
7. Parasol.
8. Swim.
9. Fine, sheer muslin.

and they both tried to relate it at once. It did not seem half so amusing when told. They realized this, and so did Mr. Pontellier. He yawned and stretched himself. Then he got up, saying he had half a mind to go over to Klein's hotel and play a game of billiards.

"Come go along, Lebrun," he proposed to Robert. But Robert admitted quite frankly that he preferred to stay where he was and talk to Mrs. Pontellier.

"Well, send him about his business when he bores you, Edna," instructed her husband as he prepared to leave.

"Here, take the umbrella," she exclaimed, holding it out to him. He accepted the sunshade, and lifting it over his head descended the steps and walked away.

"Coming back to dinner?" his wife called after him. He halted a moment and shrugged his shoulders. He felt in his vest pocket; there was a ten-dollar bill there. He did not know; perhaps he would return for the early dinner and perhaps he would not. It all depended upon the company which he found over at Klein's and the size of "the game." He did not say this, but she understood it, and laughed, nodding good-by to him.

Both children wanted to follow their father when they saw him starting out. He kissed them and promised to bring them back bonbons and peanuts.

II

Mrs. Pontellier's eyes were quick and bright; they were a yellowish brown, about the color of her hair. She had a way of turning them swiftly upon an object and holding them there as if lost in some inward maze of contemplation or thought.

Her eyebrows were a shade darker than her hair. They were thick and almost horizontal, emphasizing the depth of her eyes. She was rather handsome than beautiful. Her face was captivating by reason of a certain frankness of expression and a contradictory subtle play of features. Her manner was engaging.

Robert rolled a cigarette. He smoked cigarettes because he could not afford cigars, he said. He had a cigar in his pocket which Mr. Pontellier had presented him with, and he was saving it for his after-dinner smoke.

This seemed quite proper and natural on his part. In coloring he was not unlike his companion. A clean-shaven face made the resemblance more pronounced than it would otherwise have been. There rested no shadow of care upon his open countenance. His eyes gathered in and reflected the light and languor of the summer day.

Mrs. Pontellier reached over for a palmleaf fan that lay on the porch and began to fan herself, while Robert sent between his lips light puffs from his cigarette. They chatted incessantly: about the things around them; their amusing adventure out in the water—it had again assumed its entertaining aspect; about the wind, the trees, the people who had gone to the *Chênière;* about the children playing croquet under the oaks, and the Farival twins, who were now performing the overture to "The Poet and Peasant."[1]

Robert talked a good deal about himself. He was very young, and did not

1. The 1846 operetta by the Austrian composer Franz von Suppé.

know any better. Mrs. Pontellier talked a little about herself for the same reason. Each was interested in what the other said. Robert spoke of his intention to go to Mexico in the autumn, where fortune awaited him. He was always intending to go to Mexico, but some way never got there. Meanwhile he held on to his modest position in a mercantile house in New Orleans, where an equal familiarity with English, French and Spanish gave him no small value as a clerk and correspondent.

He was spending his summer vacation, as he always did, with his mother at Grand Isle. In former times, before Robert could remember, "the house" had been a summer luxury of the Lebruns. Now flanked by its dozen or more cottages, which were always filled with exclusive visitors from the "*Quartier Français*,"[2] it enabled Madame Lebrun to maintain the easy and comfortable existence which appeared to be her birthright.

Mrs. Pontellier talked about her father's Mississippi plantation and her girlhood home in the old Kentucky blue-grass country. She was an American woman, with a small infusion of French which seemed to have been lost in dilution. She read a letter from her sister, who was away in the East, and who had engaged herself to be married. Robert was interested, and wanted to know what manner of girls the sisters were, what the father was like, and how long the mother had been dead.

When Mrs. Pontellier folded the letter it was time for her to dress for the early dinner.

"I see Léonce isn't coming back," she said, with a glance in the direction whence her husband had disappeared. Robert supposed he was not, as there were a good many New Orleans club men over at Klein's.

When Mrs. Pontellier left him to enter her room, the young man descended the steps and strolled over toward the croquet players, where, during the half-hour before dinner, he amused himself with the little Pontellier children, who were very fond of him.

III

It was eleven o'clock that night when Mr. Pontellier returned from Klein's hotel. He was in an excellent humor, in high spirits, and very talkative. His entrance awoke his wife, who was in bed and fast asleep when he came in. He talked to her while he undressed, telling her anecdotes and bits of news and gossip that he had gathered during the day. From his trousers pockets he took a fistful of crumpled bank notes and a good deal of silver coin, which he piled on the bureau indiscriminately with keys, knife, handkerchief, and whatever else happened to be in his pockets. She was overcome with sleep, and answered him with little half utterances.

He thought it very discouraging that his wife, who was the sole object of his existence, evinced so little interest in things which concerned him and valued so little his conversation.

Mr. Pontellier had forgotten the bonbons and peanuts for the boys. Notwithstanding he loved them very much, and went into the adjoining room where they slept to take a look at them and make sure that they were resting

2. The French Quarter of New Orleans, first settled by the French in the early 18th century and occupied at this time by wealthy established families.

comfortably. The result of his investigation was far from satisfactory. He turned and shifted the youngsters about in bed. One of them began to kick and talk about a basket full of crabs.

Mr. Pontellier returned to his wife with the information that Raoul had a high fever and needed looking after. Then he lit a cigar and went and sat near the open door to smoke it.

Mrs. Pontellier was quite sure Raoul had no fever. He had gone to bed perfectly well, she said, and nothing had ailed him all day. Mr. Pontellier was too well acquainted with fever symptoms to be mistaken. He assured her the child was consuming[3] at that moment in the next room.

He reproached his wife with her inattention, her habitual neglect of the children. If it was not a mother's place to look after children, whose on earth was it? He himself had his hands full with his brokerage business. He could not be in two places at once; making a living for his family on the street, and staying at home to see that no harm befell them. He talked in a monotonous, insistent way.

Mrs. Pontellier sprang out of bed and went into the next room. She soon came back and sat on the edge of the bed, leaning her head down on the pillow. She said nothing, and refused to answer her husband when he questioned her. When his cigar was smoked out he went to bed, and in half a minute he was fast asleep.

Mrs. Pontellier was by that time thoroughly awake. She began to cry a little, and wiped her eyes on the sleeve of her *peignoir*. Blowing out the candle, which her husband had left burning, she slipped her bare feet into a pair of satin *mules* at the foot of the bed and went out on the porch, where she sat down in the wicker chair and began to rock gently to and fro.

It was then past midnight. The cottages were all dark. A single faint light gleamed out from the hallway of the house. There was no sound abroad except the hooting of an old owl in the top of a water-oak, and the everlasting voice of the sea, that was not uplifted at that soft hour. It broke like a mournful lullaby upon the night.

The tears came so fast to Mrs. Pontellier's eyes that the damp sleeve of her *peignoir* no longer served to dry them. She was holding the back of her chair with one hand; her loose sleeve had slipped almost to the shoulder of her uplifted arm. Turning, she thrust her face, steaming and wet, into the bend of her arm, and she went on crying there, not caring any longer to dry her face, her eyes, her arms. She could not have told why she was crying. Such experiences as the foregoing were not uncommon in her married life. They seemed never before to have weighed much against the abundance of her husband's kindness and a uniform devotion which had come to be tacit and self-understood.

An indescribable oppression, which seemed to generate in some unfamiliar part of her consciousness, filled her whole being with a vague anguish. It was like a shadow, like a mist passing across her soul's summer day. It was strange and unfamiliar; it was a mood. She did not sit there inwardly upbraiding her husband, lamenting at Fate, which had directed her footsteps to the path which they had taken. She was just having a good cry all to herself. The

3. I.e., "consumptive," feverish.

mosquitoes made merry over her, biting her firm, round arms and nipping at her bare insteps.

The little stinging, buzzing imps succeeded in dispelling a mood which might have held her there in the darkness half a night longer.

The following morning Mr. Pontellier was up in good time to take the rockaway[4] which was to convey him to the steamer at the wharf. He was returning to the city to his business, and they would not see him again at the Island till the coming Saturday. He had regained his composure, which seemed to have been somewhat impaired the night before. He was eager to be gone, as he looked forward to a lively week in Carondelet Street.[5]

Mr. Pontellier gave his wife half the money which he had brought away from Klein's hotel the evening before. She liked money as well as most women, and accepted it with no little satisfaction.

"It will buy a handsome wedding present for Sister Janet!" she exclaimed, smoothing out the bills as she counted them one by one.

"Oh! we'll treat Sister Janet better than that, my dear," he laughed, as he prepared to kiss her good-by.

The boys were tumbling about, clinging to his legs, imploring that numerous things be brought back to them. Mr. Pontellier was a great favorite, and ladies, men, children, even nurses, were always on hand to say good-by to him. His wife stood smiling and waving, the boys shouting, as he disappeared in the old rockaway down the sandy road.

A few days later a box arrived for Mrs. Pontellier from New Orleans. It was from her husband. It was filled with *friandises*,[6] with luscious and toothsome bits—the finest of fruits, *pâtés*, a rare bottle or two, delicious syrups, and bonbons in abundance.

Mrs. Pontellier was always very generous with the contents of such a box; she was quite used to receiving them when away from home. The *pâtés* and fruit were brought to the dining-room; the bonbons were passed around. And the ladies, selecting with dainty and discriminating fingers and a little greedily, all declared that Mr. Pontellier was the best husband in the world. Mrs. Pontellier was forced to admit that she knew of none better.

IV

It would have been a difficult matter for Mr. Pontellier to define to his own satisfaction or any one else's wherein his wife failed in her duty toward their children. It was something which he felt rather than perceived, and he never voiced the feeling without subsequent regret and ample atonement.

If one of the little Pontellier boys took a tumble whilst at play, he was not apt to rush crying to his mother's arms for comfort; he would more likely pick himself up, wipe the water out of his eyes and the sand out of his mouth, and go on playing. Tots as they were, they pulled together and stood their ground in childish battles with doubled fists and uplifted voices, which usually prevailed against the other mother-tots. The quadroon nurse was looked upon as a huge encumbrance, only good to button up waists and panties and

4. Four-wheeled carriage.
5. The financial center of New Orleans.

6. Delicacies, sweets.

to brush and part hair; since it seemed to be a law of society that hair must be parted and brushed.

In short, Mrs. Pontellier was not a mother-woman. The mother-women seemed to prevail that summer at Grand Isle. It was easy to know them, fluttering about with extended, protecting wings when any harm, real or imaginary, threatened their precious brood. They were women who idolized their children, worshiped their husbands, and esteemed it a holy privilege to efface themselves as individuals and grow wings as ministering angels.

Many of them were delicious in the rôle; one of them was the embodiment of every womanly grace and charm. If her husband did not adore her, he was a brute, deserving of death by slow torture. Her name was Adèle Ratignolle. There are no words to describe her save the old ones that have served so often to picture the bygone heroine of romance and the fair lady of our dreams. There was nothing subtle or hidden about her charms; her beauty was all there, flaming and apparent: the spun-gold hair that comb nor confining pin could restrain; the blue eyes that were like nothing but sapphires; two lips that pouted, that were so red one could only think of cherries or some other delicious crimson fruit in looking at them. She was growing a little stout, but it did not seem to detract an iota from the grace of every step, pose, gesture. One would not have wanted her white neck a mite less full or her beautiful arms more slender. Never were hands more exquisite than hers, and it was a joy to look at them when she threaded her needle or adjusted her gold thimble to her taper[7] middle finger as she sewed away on the little night-drawers or fashioned a bodice or a bib.

Madame Ratignolle was very fond of Mrs. Pontellier, and often she took her sewing and went over to sit with her in the afternoons. She was sitting there the afternoon of the day the boy arrived from New Orleans. She had possession of the rocker, and she was busily engaged in sewing upon a diminutive pair of night drawers.

She had brought the pattern of the drawers for Mrs. Pontellier to cut out— a marvel of construction, fashioned to enclose a baby's body so effectually that only two small eyes might look out from the garment, like an Eskimo's. They were designed for winter wear, when treacherous drafts came down chimneys and insidious currents of deadly cold found their way through key-holes.

Mrs. Pontellier's mind was quite at rest concerning the present material needs of her children, and she could not see the use of anticipating and making winter night garments the subject of her summer meditations. But she did not want to appear unamiable and uninterested, so she had brought forth newspapers which she spread upon the floor of the gallery, and under Madame Ratignolle's directions she had cut a pattern of the impervious garment.

Robert was there, seated as he had been the Sunday before, and Mrs. Pontellier also occupied her former position on the upper step, leaning listlessly against the post. Beside her was a box of bonbons, which she held out at intervals to Madame Ratignolle.

That lady seemed at a loss to make a selection, but finally settled upon a stick of nugat, wondering if it were not too rich; whether it could possibly

7. I.e., tapered.

hurt her. Madame Ratignolle had been married seven years. About every two years she had a baby. At that time she had three babies, and was beginning to think of a fourth one. She was always talking about her "condition." Her "condition" was in no way apparent, and no one would have known a thing about it but for her persistence in making it the subject of conversation.

Robert started to reassure her, asserting that he had known a lady who had subsisted upon nugat during the entire—but seeing the color mount into Mrs. Pontellier's face he checked himself and changed the subject.

Mrs. Pontellier, though she had married a Creole,[8] was not thoroughly at home in the society of Creoles; never before had she been thrown so intimately among them. There were only Creoles that summer at Lebrun's. They all knew each other, and felt like one large family, among whom existed the most amicable relations. A characteristic which distinguished them and which impressed Mrs. Pontellier most forcibly was their entire absence of prudery. Their freedom of expression was at first incomprehensible to her, though she had no difficulty in reconciling it with a lofty chastity which in the Creole woman seems to be inborn and unmistakable.

Never would Edna Pontellier forget the shock with which she heard Madame Ratignolle relating to old Monsieur Farival the harrowing story of one of her accouchements,[9] withholding no intimate detail. She was growing accustomed to like shocks, but she could not keep the mounting color back from her cheeks. Oftener than once her coming had interrupted the droll story with which Robert was entertaining some amused group of married women.

A book had gone the rounds of the pension. When it came her turn to read it, she did so with profound astonishment. She felt moved to read the book in secret and solitude, though none of the others had done so—to hide it from view at the sound of approaching footsteps. It was openly criticised and freely discussed at table. Mrs. Pontellier gave over being astonished, and concluded that wonders would never cease.

V

They formed a congenial group sitting there that summer afternoon— Madame Ratignolle sewing away, often stopping to relate a story or incident with much expressive gesture of her perfect hands: Robert and Mrs. Pontellier sitting idle, exchanging occasional words, glances or smiles which indicated a certain advanced stage of intimacy and *camaraderie*.

He had lived in her shadow during the past month. No one thought anything of it. Many had predicted that Robert would devote himself to Mrs. Pontellier when he arrived. Since the age of fifteen, which was eleven years before, Robert each summer at Grand Isle had constituted himself the devoted attendant of some fair dame or damsel. Sometimes it was a young girl, again a widow; but as often as not it was some interesting married woman.

For two consecutive seasons he lived in the sunlight of Mademoiselle Duvigné's presence. But she died between summers; then Robert posed as

8. Someone descended from the original French and Spanish settlers of New Orleans; thus at this time, an aristocrat.
9. Childbirths.

an inconsolable, prostrating himself at the feet of Madame Ratignolle for whatever crumbs of sympathy and comfort she might be pleased to vouchsafe.

Mrs. Pontellier liked to sit and gaze at her fair companion as she might look upon a faultless Madonna.

"Could any one fathom the cruelty beneath that fair exterior?" murmured Robert. "She knew that I adored her once, and she let me adore her. It was 'Robert, come; go; stand up; sit down; do this; do that; see if the baby sleeps; my thimble, please, that I left God knows where. Come and read Daudet[1] to me while I sew.' "

"*Par exemple!*[2] I never had to ask. You were always there under my feet, like a troublesome cat."

"You mean like an adoring dog. And just as soon as Ratignolle appeared on the scene, then it *was* like a dog. '*Passez! Adieu! Allez vous-en!*'"[3]

"Perhaps I feared to make Alphonse jealous," she interjoined, with excessive naïveté. That made them all laugh. The right hand jealous of the left! The heart jealous of the soul! But for that matter, the Creole husband is never jealous; with him the gangrene passion is one which has become dwarfed by disuse.

Meanwhile Robert, addressing Mrs. Pontellier, continued to tell of his one time hopeless passion for Madame Ratignolle; of sleepless nights, of consuming flames till the very sea sizzled when he took his daily plunge. While the lady at the needle kept up a little running, contemptuous comment:

"*Blagueur—farceur—gros bête, va!*"[4]

He never assumed this serio-comic tone when alone with Mrs. Pontellier. She never knew precisely what to make of it; at that moment it was impossible for her to guess how much of it was jest and what proportion was earnest. It was understood that he had often spoken words of love to Madame Ratignolle, without any thought of being taken seriously. Mrs. Pontellier was glad he had not assumed a similar rôle toward herself. It would have been unacceptable and annoying.

Mrs. Pontellier had brought her sketching materials, which she sometimes dabbled with in an unprofessional way. She liked the dabbling. She felt in it satisfaction of a kind which no other employment afforded her.

She had long wished to try herself on Madame Ratignolle. Never had that lady seemed a more tempting subject than at that moment, seated there like some sensuous Madonna, with the gleam of the fading day enriching her splendid color.

Robert crossed over and seated himself upon the step below Mrs. Pontellier, that he might watch her work. She handled her brushes with a certain ease and freedom which came, not from long and close acquaintance with them, but from a natural aptitude. Robert followed her work with close attention, giving forth little ejaculatory expressions of appreciation in French, which he addressed to Madame Ratignolle.

"*Mais ce n'est pas mal! Elle s'y connait, elle a de la force, oui.*"[5]

During his oblivious attention he once quietly rested his head against Mrs.

1. Alphone Daudet (1840–1887), French novelist.
2. For goodness' sake!
3. Go on! Good-by! Go away!

4. Liar—comedian—silly, go on with you.
5. Why, that's not bad at all! She knows what she's doing; yes, she has talent.

Pontellier's arm. As gently she repulsed him. Once again he repeated the offense. She could not but believe it to be thoughtlessness on his part; yet that was no reason she should submit to it. She did not remonstrate, except again to repulse him quietly but firmly. He offered no apology.

The picture completed bore no resemblance to Madame Ratignolle. She was greatly disappointed to find that it did not look like her. But it was a fair enough piece of work, and in many respects satisfying.

Mrs. Pontellier evidently did not think so. After surveying the sketch critically she drew a broad smudge of paint across its surface, and crumpled the paper between her hands.

The youngsters came tumbling up the steps, the quadroon following at the respectful distance which they required her to observe. Mrs. Pontellier made them carry her paints and things into the house. She sought to detain them for a little talk and some pleasantry. But they were greatly in earnest. They had only come to investigate the contents of the bonbon box. They accepted without murmuring what she chose to give them, each holding out two chubby hands scoop-like, in the vain hope that they might be filled; and then away they went.

The sun was low in the west, and the breeze soft and languorous that came up from the south, charged with the seductive odor of the sea. Children, freshly befurbelowed,[6] were gathering for their games under the oaks. Their voices were high and penetrating.

Madame Ratignolle folded her sewing, placing thimble, scissors and thread all neatly together in the roll, which she pinned securely. She complained of faintness. Mrs. Pontellier flew for the cologne water and a fan. She bathed Madame Ratignolle's face with cologne, while Robert plied the fan with unnecessary vigor.

The spell was soon over, and Mrs. Pontellier could not help wondering if there were not a little imagination responsible for its origin, for the rose tint had never faded from her friend's face.

She stood watching the fair woman walk down the long line of galleries with the grace and majesty which queens are sometimes supposed to possess. Her little ones ran to meet her. Two of them clung about her white skirts, the third she took from its nurse and with a thousand endearments bore it along in her own fond, encircling arms. Though, as everybody well knew, the doctor had forbidden her to lift so much as a pin!

"Are you going bathing?" asked Robert of Mrs. Pontellier. It was not so much a question as a reminder.

"Oh, no," she answered, with a tone of indecision. "I'm tired; I think not." Her glance wandered from his face away toward the Gulf, whose sonorous murmur reached her like a loving but imperative entreaty.

"Oh, come!" he insisted. "You mustn't miss your bath. Come on. The water must be delicious; it will not hurt you. Come."

He reached up for her big, rough straw hat that hung on a peg outside the door, and put it on her head. They descended the steps, and walked away together toward the beach. The sun was low in the west and the breeze was soft and warm.

6. Dressed up.

VI

Edna Pontellier could not have told why, wishing to go to the beach with Robert, she should in the first place have declined, and in the second place have followed in obedience to one of the two contradictory impulses which impelled her.

A certain light was beginning to dawn dimly within her,—the light which, showing the way, forbids it.

At that early period it served but to bewilder her. It moved her to dreams, to thoughtfulness, to the shadowy anguish which had overcome her the midnight when she had abandoned herself to tears.

In short, Mrs. Pontellier was beginning to realize her position in the universe as a human being, and to recognize her relations as an individual to the world within and about her. This may seem like a ponderous weight of wisdom to descend upon the soul of a young woman of twenty-eight—perhaps more wisdom than the Holy Ghost is usually pleased to vouchsafe to any woman.

But the beginning of things, of a world especially, is necessarily vague, tangled, chaotic, and exceedingly disturbing. How few of us ever emerge from such beginning! How many souls perish in its tumult!

The voice of the sea is seductive; never ceasing, whispering, clamoring, murmuring, inviting the soul to wander for a spell in abysses of solitude; to lose itself in mazes of inward contemplation.

The voice of the sea speaks to the soul. The touch of the sea is sensuous, enfolding the body in its soft, close embrace.

VII

Mrs. Pontellier was not a woman given to confidences, a characteristic hitherto contrary to her nature. Even as a child she had lived her own small life all within herself. At a very early period she had apprehended instinctively the dual life—that outward existence which conforms, the inward life which questions.

That summer at Grand Isle she began to loose a little the mantle of reserve that had always enveloped her. There may have been—there must have been—influences, both subtle and apparent, working in their several ways to induce her to do this; but the most obvious was the influence of Adèle Ratignolle. The excessive physical charm of the Creole had first attracted her, for Edna had a sensuous susceptibility to beauty. Then the candor of the woman's whole existence, which everyone might read, and which formed so striking a contrast to her own habitual reserve—this might have furnished a link. Who can tell what metals the gods use in forging the subtle bond which we call sympathy, which we might as well call love.

The two women went away one morning to the beach together, arm in arm, under the huge white sunshade. Edna had prevailed upon Madame Ratignolle to leave the children behind, though she could not induce her to relinquish a diminutive roll of needlework, which Adèle begged to be allowed to slip into the depths of her pocket. In some unaccountable way they had escaped from Robert.

The walk to the beach was no inconsiderable one, consisting as it did of

a long, sandy path, upon which a sporadic and tangled growth that bordered it on either side made frequent and unexpected inroads. There were acres of yellow camomile reaching out on either hand. Further away still, vegetable gardens abounded, with frequent small plantations of orange or lemon trees intervening. The dark green clusters glistened from afar in the sun.

The women were both of goodly height, Madame Ratignolle possessing the more feminine and matronly figure. The charm of Edna Pontellier's physique stole insensibly upon you. The lines of her body were long, clean and symmetrical; it was a body which occasionally fell into splendid poses; there was no suggestion of the trim, stereotyped fashion-plate about it. A casual and indiscriminating observer, in passing, might not cast a second glance upon the figure. But with more feeling and discernment he would have recognized the noble beauty of its modeling, and the graceful severity of poise and movement, which made Edna Pontellier different from the crowd.

She wore a cool muslin that morning—white, with a waving vertical line of brown running through it; also a white linen collar and the big straw hat which she had taken from the peg outside the door. The hat rested any way on her yellow-brown hair, that waved a little, was heavy, and clung close to her head.

Madame Ratignolle, more careful of her complexion, had twined a gauze veil about her head. She wore dogskin gloves, white gauntlets that protected her wrists. She was dressed in pure white, with a fluffiness of ruffles that became her. The draperies and fluttering things which she wore suited her rich, luxuriant beauty as a greater severity of line could not have done.

There were a number of bath-houses along the beach, of rough but solid construction, built with small, protecting galleries facing the water. Each house consisted of two compartments, and each family at Lebrun's possessed a compartment for itself, fitted out with all the essential paraphernalia of the bath and whatever other conveniences the owners might desire. The two women had no intention of bathing; they had just strolled down to the beach for a walk and to be alone and near the water. The Pontellier and Ratignolle compartments adjoined one another under the same roof.

Mrs. Pontellier had brought down her key through force of habit. Unlocking the door of her bath-room she went inside, and soon emerged, bringing a rug, which she spread upon the floor of the gallery, and two huge hair pillows covered with crash,[7] which she placed against the front of the building.

The two seated themselves there in the shade of the porch, side by side, with their backs against the pillows and their feet extended. Madame Ratignolle removed her veil, wiped her face with a rather delicate handkerchief, and fanned herself with the fan which she always carried suspended somewhere about her person by a long, narrow ribbon. Edna removed her collar and opened her dress at the throat. She took the fan from Madame Ratignolle and began to fan both herself and her companion. It was very warm, and for a while they did nothing but exchange remarks about the heat, the sun, the glare. But there was a breeze blowing, a choppy stiff wind that whipped the water into froth. It fluttered the skirts of the two women and kept them for a while engaged in adjusting, readjusting, tucking in, securing hair-pins and

7. Heavy linen fabric. "Rug": blanket.

hat-pins. A few persons were sporting some distance away in the water. The beach was very still of human sound at that hour. The lady in black was reading her morning devotions on the porch of a neighboring bath-house. Two young lovers were exchanging their hearts' yearnings beneath the children's tent, which they had found unoccupied.

Edna Pontellier, casting her eyes about, had finally kept them at rest upon the sea. The day was clear and carried the gaze out as far as the blue sky went; there were a few white clouds suspended idly over the horizon. A lateen[8] sail was visible in the direction of Cat Island, and others to the south seemed almost motionless in the far distance.

"Of whom—of what are you thinking?" asked Adèle of her companion, whose countenance she had been watching with a little amused attention, arrested by the absorbed expression which seemed to have seized and fixed every feature into a statuesque repose.

"Nothing," returned Mrs. Pontellier, with a start, adding at once: "How stupid! But it seems to me it is the reply we make instinctively to such a question. Let me see," she went on, throwing back her head and narrowing her fine eyes till they shone like two vivid points of light. "Let me see. I was really not conscious of thinking of anything; but perhaps I can retrace my thoughts."

"Oh! never mind!" laughed Madame Ratignolle. "I am not quite so exacting. I will let you off this time. It is really too hot to think, especially to think about thinking."

"But for the fun of it," persisted Edna. "First of all, the sight of the water stretching so far away, those motionless sails against the blue sky, made a delicious picture that I just wanted to sit and look at. The hot wind beating in my face made me think—without any connection that I can trace—of a summer day in Kentucky, of a meadow that seemed as big as the ocean to the very little girl walking through the grass, which was higher than her waist. She threw out her arms as if swimming when she walked, beating the tall grass as one strikes out in the water. Oh, I see the connection now!"

"Where were you going that day in Kentucky, walking through the grass?"

"I don't remember now. I was just walking diagonally across a big field. My sun-bonnet obstructed the view. I could see only the stretch of green before me, and I felt as if I must walk on forever, without coming to the end of it. I don't remember whether I was frightened or pleased. I must have been entertained.

"Likely as not it was Sunday," she laughed; "and I was running away from from prayers, from the Presbyterian service, read in a spirit of gloom by my father that chills me yet to think of."

"And have you been running away from prayers ever since, *ma chère?*" asked Madame Ratignolle, amused.

"No! oh, no!" Edna hastened to say. "I was a little unthinking child in those days, just following a misleading impulse without question. On the contrary, during one period of my life religion took a firm hold upon me; after I was twelve and until—until—why, I suppose until now, though I never thought much about it—just driven along by habit. But do you know," she broke off, turning her quick eyes upon Madame Ratignolle and leaning for-

8. Triangular.

ward a little so as to bring her face quite close to that of her companion, "sometimes I feel this summer as if I were walking through the green meadow again; idly, aimlessly, unthinking and unguided."

Madame Ratignolle laid her hand over that of Mrs. Pontellier, which was near her. Seeing that the hand was not withdrawn, she clasped it firmly and warmly. She even stroked it a little, fondly, with the other hand, murmuring in an undertone, "*Pauvre chérie.*"[9]

The action was at first a little confusing to Edna, but she soon lent herself readily to the Creole's gentle caress. She was not accustomed to an outward and spoken expression of affection, either in herself or in others. She and her younger sister, Janet, had quarreled a good deal through force of unfortunate habit. Her older sister, Margaret, was matronly and dignified, probably from having assumed matronly and house-wifely responsibilities too early in life, their mother having died when they were quite young. Margaret was not effusive; she was practical. Edna had had an occasional girl friend, but whether accidentally or not, they seemed to have been all of one type—the self-contained. She never realized that the reserve of her own character had much, perhaps everything, to do with this. Her most intimate friend at school had been one of rather exceptional intellectual gifts, who wrote fine-sounding essays which Edna admired and strove to imitate; and with her she talked and glowed over the English classics, and sometimes held religious and political controversies.

Edna often wondered at one propensity which sometimes had inwardly disturbed her without causing any outward show or manifestation on her part. At a very early age—perhaps it was when she traversed the ocean of waving grass—she remembered that she had been passionately enamored of a dignified and sad-eyed cavalry officer who visited her father in Kentucky. She could not leave his presence when he was there, nor remove her eyes from his face which was something like Napoleon's, with a lock of black hair falling across the forehead.[1] But the cavalry officer melted imperceptibly out of her existence.

At another time her affections were deeply engaged by a young gentleman who visited a lady on a neighboring plantation. It was after they went to Mississippi to live. The young man was engaged to be married to the young lady, and they sometimes called upon Margaret, driving over of afternoons in a buggy. Edna was a little miss, just merging into her teens; and the realization that she herself was nothing, nothing, nothing to the engaged young man was a bitter affliction to her. But he, too, went the way of dreams.

She was a grown young woman when she was overtaken by what she supposed to be the climax of her fate. It was when the face and figure of a great tragedian began to haunt her imagination and stir her senses. The persistence of the infatuation lent it an aspect of genuineness. The hopelessness of it colored it with the lofty tones of a great passion.

The picture of the tragedian stood enframed upon her desk. Any one may possess the portrait of a tragedian without exciting suspicion or comment. (This was a sinister reflection which she cherished.) In the presence of others she expressed admiration for his exalted gifts, as she handed the photograph

9. Poor dear.
1. I.e., as Napoléon Bonaparte (1769–1821), emperor of the French, was often depicted in portraits.

around and dwelt upon the fidelity of the likeness. When alone she sometimes picked it up and kissed the cold glass passionately.

Her marriage to Léonce Pontellier was purely an accident, in this respect resembling many other marriages which masquerade as the decrees of Fate. It was in the midst of her secret great passion that she met him. He fell in love, as men are in the habit of doing, and pressed his suit with an earnestness and an ardor which left nothing to be desired. He pleased her; his absolute devotion flattered her. She fancied there was a sympathy of thought and taste between them, in which fancy she was mistaken. Add to this the violent opposition of her father and her sister Margaret to her marriage with a Catholic, and we need seek no further for the motives which led her to accept Monsieur Pontellier for her husband.

The acme of bliss, which would have been a marriage with the tragedian, was not for her in this world. As the devoted wife of a man who worshiped her, she felt she would take her place with a certain dignity in the world of reality, closing the portals forever behind her upon the realm of romance and dreams.

But it was not long before the tragedian had gone to join the cavalry officer and the engaged young man and a few others; and Edna found herself face to face with the realities. She grew fond of her husband, realizing with some unaccountable satisfaction that no trace of passion or excessive and fictitious warmth colored her affection, thereby threatening its dissolution.

She was fond of her children in an uneven, impulsive way. She would sometimes gather them passionately to her heart; she would sometimes forget them. The year before they had spent part of the summer with their grandmother Pontellier in Iberville.[2] Feeling secure regarding their happiness and welfare, she did not miss them except with an occasional intense longing. Their absence was a sort of relief, though she did not admit this, even to herself. It seemed to free her of a responsibility which she had blindly assumed and for which Fate had not fitted her.

Edna did not reveal so much as all this to Madame Ratignolle that summer day when they sat with faces turned to the sea. But a good part of it escaped her. She had put her head down on Madame Ratignolle's shoulder. She was flushed and felt intoxicated with the sound of her own voice and the unaccustomed taste of candor. It muddled her like wine, or like a first breath of freedom.

There was the sound of approaching voices. It was Robert, surrounded by a troop of children, searching for them. The two little Pontelliers were with him, and he carried Madame Ratignolle's little girl in his arms. There were other children beside, and two nursemaids followed, looking disagreeable and resigned.

The women at once rose and began to shake out their draperies and relax their muscles. Mrs. Pontellier threw the cushions and rug into the bathhouse. The children all scampered off to the awning, and they stood there in a line, gazing upon the intruding lovers, still exchanging their vows and sighs. The lovers got up, with only a silent protest, and walked slowly away somewhere else.

2. Rural parish (county) in Louisiana, west of Baton Rouge.

The children possessed themselves of the tent, and Mrs. Pontellier went over to join them.

Madame Ratignolle begged Robert to accompany her to the house; she complained of cramp in her limbs and stiffness of the joints. She leaned draggingly upon his arm as they walked.

VIII

"Do me a favor, Robert," spoke the pretty woman at his side, almost as soon as she and Robert had started on their slow, homeward way. She looked up in his face, leaning on his arm beneath the encircling shadow of the umbrella which he had lifted.

"Granted; as many as you like," he returned, glancing down into her eyes that were full of thoughtfulness and some speculation.

"I only ask for one; let Mrs. Pontellier alone."

"*Tiens!*" he exclaimed, with a sudden, boyish laugh. *"Voilà que Madame Ratignolle est jealouse!"*[3]

"Nonsense! I'm in earnest; I mean what I say. Let Mrs. Pontellier alone."

"Why?" he asked; himself growing serious at his companion's solicitation.

"She is not one of us; she is not like us. She might make the unfortunate blunder of taking you seriously."

His face flushed with annoyance, and taking off his soft hat he began to beat it impatiently against his leg as he walked. "Why shouldn't she take me seriously?" he demanded sharply. "Am I a comedian, a clown, a jack-in-the-box? Why shouldn't she? You Creoles! I have no patience with you! Am I always to be regarded as a feature of an amusing programme? I hope Mrs. Pontellier does take me seriously. I hope she has discernment enough to find in me something besides the *blagueur*.[4] If I thought there was any doubt—"

"Oh, enough, Robert!" she broke into his heated outburst. "You are not thinking of what you are saying. You speak with about as little reflection as we might expect from one of those children down there playing in the sand. If your attentions to any married women here were ever offered with any intention of being convincing, you would not be the gentleman we all know you to be, and you would be unfit to associate with the wives and daughters of the people who trust you."

Madame Ratignolle had spoken what she believed to be the law and the gospel. The young man shrugged his shoulders impatiently.

"Oh! well! That isn't it," slamming his hat down vehemently upon his head. "You ought to feel that such things are not flattering to say to a fellow."

"Should our whole intercourse consist of an exchange of compliments? *Ma foi!*[5]

"It isn't pleasant to have a woman tell you—" he went on, unheedingly, but breaking off suddenly: "Now if I were like Arobin—you remember Alcée Arobin and that story of the consul's wife at Biloxi?" And he related the story of Alcée Arobin and the consul's wife; and another about the tenor of the French Opera,[6] who received letters which should never have been written;

3. So, Madame Ratignolle is jealous!
4. Joker, liar.
5. For heaven's sake!
6. In New Orleans; perhaps the most distin-

guished American opera company of the time. Biloxi, in Mississippi, is a coastal resort town near New Orleans.

and still other stories, grave and gay, till Mrs. Pontellier and her possible propensity for taking young men seriously was apparently forgotten.

Madame Ratignolle, when they had regained her cottage, went in to take the hour's rest which she considered helpful. Before leaving her. Robert begged her pardon for the impatience—he called it rudeness—with which he had received her well-meant caution.

"You made one mistake, Adèle," he said, with a light smile; "there is no earthly possibility of Mrs. Pontellier ever taking me seriously. You should have warned me against taking myself seriously. Your advice might then have carried some weight and given me subject for some reflection. *Au revoir.* But you look tired," he added, solicitously. "Would you like a cup of bouillon? Shall I stir you a toddy? Let me mix you a toddy with a drop of Angostura."[7]

She acceded to the suggestion of bouillon, which was grateful[8] and acceptable. He went himself to the kitchen, which was a building apart from the cottages and lying to the rear of the house. And he himself brought her the golden-brown bouillon, in a dainty Sèvres[9] cup, with a flaky cracker or two on the saucer.

She thrust a bare, white arm from the curtain which shielded her open door, and received the cup from his hands. She told him he was a *bon garçon,*[1] and she meant it. Robert thanked her and turned away toward "the house."

The lovers were just entering the grounds of the *pension.* They were leaning toward each other as the water-oaks bent from the sea. There was not a particle of earth beneath their feet. Their heads might have been turned upside-down, so absolutely did they tread upon blue ether. The lady in black, creeping behind them, looked a trifle paler and more jaded than usual. There was no sign of Mrs. Pontellier and the children. Robert scanned the distance for any such apparition. They would doubtless remain away till the dinner hour. The young man ascended to his mother's room. It was situated at the top of the house, made up of odd angles and a queer, sloping ceiling. Two broad dormer windows looked out toward the Gulf, and as far across it as a man's eye might reach. The furnishings of the room were light, cool, and practical.

Madame Lebrun was busily engaged at the sewing-machine. A little black girl sat on the floor, and with her hands worked the treadle of the machine. The Creole woman does not take any chances which may be avoided of imperiling her health.

Robert went over and seated himself on the broad sill of one of the dormer windows. He took a book from his pocket and began energetically to read it, judging by the precision and frequency with which he turned the leaves. The sewing-machine made a resounding clatter in the room; it was of a ponderous, by-gone make. In the lulls, Robert and his mother exchanged bits of desultory conversation.

"Where is Mrs. Pontellier?"

"Down at the beach with the children."

"I promised to lend her the Goncourt.[2] Don't forget to take it down when

7. Aromatic bitters.
8. Pleasing.
9. Fine porcelain made in Sèvres, France.

1. Both "nice fellow" and "good waiter."
2. A French novel by Edmond de Goncourt (1822–1896).

you go; it's there on the bookshelf over the small table." Clatter, clatter, clatter, bang! for the next five or eight minutes.

"Where is Victor going with the rockaway?"

"The rockaway? Victor?"

"Yes; down there in front. He seems to be getting ready to drive away somewhere."

"Call him." Clatter, clatter!

Robert uttered a shrill, piercing whistle which might have been heard back at the wharf.

"He won't look up."

Madame Lebrun flew to the window. She called "Victor!" She waved a handkerchief and called again. The young fellow below got into the vehicle and started the horse off at a gallop.

Madame Lebrun went back to the machine, crimson with annoyance. Victor was the younger son and brother—a *tête montée*,[3] with a temper which invited violence and a will which no ax could break.

"Whenever you say the word I'm ready to thrash any amount of reason into him that he's able to hold."

"If your father had only lived!" Clatter, clatter, clatter, clatter, bang! It was a fixed belief with Madame Lebrun that the conduct of the universe and all things pertaining thereto would have been manifestly of a more intelligent and higher order had not Monsieur Lebrun been removed to other spheres during the early years of their married life.

"What do you hear from Montel?" Montel was a middle-aged gentleman whose vain ambition and desire for the past twenty years had been to fill the void which Monsieur Lebrun's taking off had left in the Lebrun household. Clatter, clatter, bang, clatter!

"I have a letter somewhere," looking in the machine drawer and finding the letter in the bottom of the work-basket. "He says to tell you he will be in Vera Cruz[4] the beginning of next month"—clatter, clatter!—"and if you still have the intention of joining him"—bang! clatter, clatter, bang!

"Why didn't you tell me so before, mother? You know I wanted—" Clatter, clatter, clatter!

"Do you see Mrs. Pontellier starting back with the children? She will be in late to luncheon again. She never starts to get ready for luncheon till the last minute." Clatter, clatter! "Where are you going?"

"Where did you say the Goncourt was?"

IX

Every light in the hall was ablaze; every lamp turned as high as it could be without smoking the chimney or threatening explosion. The lamps were fixed at intervals against the wall, encircling the whole room. Some one had gathered orange and lemon branches and with these fashioned graceful festoons between. The dark green of the branches stood out and glistened against the white muslin curtains which draped the windows, and which puffed, floated, and flapped at the capricious will of a stiff breeze that swept up from the Gulf.

3. An impulsive character. 4. A Mexican city on the Gulf of Mexico.

It was Saturday night a few weeks after the intimate conversation held between Robert and Madame Ratignolle on their way from the beach. An unusual number of husbands, fathers, and friends had come down to stay over Sunday; and they were being suitably entertained by their families, with the material help of Madame Lebrun. The dining tables had all been removed to one end of the hall, and the chairs ranged about in rows and in clusters. Each little family group had had its say and exchanged its domestic gossip earlier in the evening. There was now an apparent disposition to relax; to widen the circle of confidences and give a more general tone to the conversation.

Many of the children had been permitted to sit up beyond their usual bedtime. A small band of them were lying on their stomachs on the floor looking at the colored sheets of the comic papers which Mr. Pontellier had brought down. The little Pontellier boys were permitting them to do so, and making their authority felt.

Music, dancing, and a recitation or two were the entertainments furnished, or rather, offered. But there was nothing systematic about the programme, no appearance of prearrangement nor even premeditation.

At an early hour in the evening the Farival twins were prevailed upon to play the piano. They were girls of fourteen, always clad in the Virgin's colors, blue and white, having been dedicated to the Blessed Virgin at their baptism. They played a duet from "Zampa," and at the earnest solicitation of every one present followed it with the overture to "The Poet and the Peasant."

"Allez vous-en! Sapristi!" shrieked the parrot outside the door. He was the only being present who possessed sufficient candor to admit that he was not listening to these gracious performances for the first time that summer. Old Monsieur Farival, grandfather of the twins, grew indignant over the interruption, and insisted upon having the bird removed and consigned to regions of darkness. Victor Lebrun objected; and his decrees were as immutable as those of Fate. The parrot fortunately offered no further interruption to the entertainment, the whole venom of his nature apparently having been cherished up and hurled against the twins in that one impetuous outburst.

Later a young brother and sister gave recitations, which every one present had heard many times at winter evening entertainments in the city.

A little girl performed a skirt dance in the center of the floor. The mother played her accompaniments and at the same time watched her daughter with greedy admiration and nervous apprehension. She need have had no apprehension. The child was mistress of the situation. She had been properly dressed for the occasion in black tulle and black silk tights. Her little neck and arms were bare, and her hair, artificially crimped, stood out like fluffy black plumes over her head. Her poses were full of grace, and her little black-shod toes twinkled as they shot out and upward with a rapidity and a suddenness which were bewildering.

But there was no reason why every one should not dance. Madame Ratignolle could not, so it was she who gaily consented to play for the others. She played very well, keeping excellent waltz time and infusing an expression into the strains which was indeed inspiring. She was keeping up her music on account of the children she said; because she and her husband both considered it a means of brightening the home and making it attractive.

Almost every one danced but the twins, who could not be induced to

separate during the brief period when one or the other should be whirling around the room in the arms of a man. They might have danced together, but they did not think of it.

The children were sent to bed. Some went submissively; others with shrieks and protests as they were dragged away. They had been permitted to sit up till after the ice-cream, which naturally marked the limit of human indulgence.

The ice-cream was passed around with cake—gold and silver cake arranged on platters in alternate slices; it had been made and frozen during the afternoon back of the kitchen by two black women, under the supervision of Victor. It was pronounced a great success—excellent if it had only contained a little less vanilla or a little more sugar, if it had been frozen a degree harder, and if the salt might have been kept out of portions of it.[5] Victor was proud of his achievement, and went about recommending it and urging every one to partake of it to excess.

After Mrs. Pontellier had danced twice with her husband, once with Robert, and once with Monsieur Ratignolle, who was thin and tall and swayed like a reed in the wind when he danced, she went out on the gallery and seated herself on the low window-sill, where she commanded a view of all that went on in the hall and could look out toward the Gulf. There was a soft effulgence in the east. The moon was coming up, and its mystic shimmer was casting a million lights across the distant, restless water.

"Would you like to hear Mademoiselle Reisz play?" asked Robert, coming out on the porch where she was. Of course Edna would like to hear Mademoiselle Reisz play; but she feared it would be useless to entreat her.

"I'll ask her," he said. "I'll tell her that you want to hear her. She likes you. She will come." He turned and hurried away to one of the far cottages, where Mademoiselle Reisz was shuffling away. She was dragging a chair in and out of her room, and at intervals objecting to the crying of a baby, which a nurse in the adjoining cottage was endeavoring to put to sleep. She was a disagreeable little woman, no longer young, who had quarreled with almost every one, owing to a temper which was self-assertive and a disposition to trample upon the rights of others. Robert prevailed upon her without any too great difficulty.

She entered the hall with him during a lull in the dance. She made an awkward, imperious little bow as she went in. She was a homely woman, with a small weazened face and body and eyes that glowed. She had absolutely no taste in dress, and wore a batch of rusty black lace with a bunch of artificial violets pinned to the side of her hair.

"Ask Mrs. Pontellier what she would like to hear me play," she requested of Robert. She sat perfectly still before the piano, not touching the keys, while Robert carried her message to Edna at the window. A general air of surprise and genuine satisfaction fell upon every one as they saw the pianist enter. There was a settling down, and a prevailing air of expectancy everywhere. Edna was a trifle embarrassed at being thus signaled out for the imperious little woman's favor. She would not dare to choose, and begged that Mademoiselle Reisz would please herself in selections.

Edna was what she herself called very fond of music. Musical strains, well

5. I.e., some of the salt used in the process of freezing the ingredients got into the ice cream itself.

rendered, had a way of evoking pictures in her mind. She sometimes liked to sit in the room of mornings when Madame Ratignolle played or practiced. One piece which that lady played Edna had entitled "Solitude." It was a short, plaintive, minor strain. The name of the piece was something else, but she called it "Solitude." When she heard it there came before her imagination the figure of a man standing beside a desolate rock on the seashore. He was naked. His attitude was one of hopeless resignation as he looked toward a distant bird winging its flight away from him.

Another piece called to her mind a dainty young woman clad in an Empire gown, taking mincing dancing steps as she came down a long avenue between tall hedges. Again, another reminded her of children at play, and still another of nothing on earth but a demure lady stroking a cat.

The very first chords which Mademoiselle Reisz struck upon the piano sent a keen tremor down Mrs. Pontellier's spinal column. It was not the first time she had heard an artist at the piano. Perhaps it was the first time she was ready, perhaps the first time her being was tempered to take an impress of the abiding truth.

She waited for the material pictures which she thought would gather and blaze before her imagination. She waited in vain. She saw no pictures of solitude, of hope, of longing, or of despair. But the very passions themselves were aroused within her soul, swaying it, lashing it, as the waves daily beat upon her splendid body. She trembled, she was choking, and the tears blinded her.

Mademoiselle had finished. She arose, and bowing her stiff, lofty bow, she went away, stopping for neither thanks nor applause. As she passed along the gallery she patted Edna upon the shoulder.

"Well, how did you like my music?" she asked. The young woman was unable to answer; she pressed the hand of the pianist convulsively. Mademoiselle Reisz perceived her agitation and even her tears. She patted her again upon the shoulder as she said:

"You are the only one worth playing for. Those others? Bah!" and she went shuffling and sidling on down the gallery toward her room.

But she was mistaken about "those others." Her playing had aroused a fever of enthusiasm. "What passion!" "What an artist!" "I have always said no one could play Chopin like Mademoiselle Reisz!" "That last prelude! Bon Dieu![6] It shakes a man!"

It was growing late, and there was a general disposition to disband. But someone, perhaps it was Robert, thought of a bath at that mystic hour and under that mystic moon.

X

- At all events Robert proposed it, and there was not a dissenting voice. There was not one but was ready to follow when he led the way. He did not lead the way, however, he directed the way; and he himself loitered behind with the lovers, who had betrayed a disposition to linger and hold themselves apart. He walked between them, whether with malicious or mischievous intent was not wholly clear, even to himself.

6. "Good Lord!" Frédéric Chopin (1810–1849), Polish composer and piano virtuoso.

The Pontelliers and Ratignolles walked ahead; the women leaning upon the arms of their husbands. Edna could hear Robert's voice behind them, and could sometimes hear what he said. She wondered why he did not join them. It was unlike him not to. Of late he had sometimes held away from her for an entire day, redoubling his devotion upon the next and the next, as though to make up for hours that had been lost. She missed him the days when some pretext served to take him away from her, just as one misses the sun on a cloudy day without having thought much about the sun when it was shining.

The people walked in little groups toward the beach. They talked and laughed; some of them sang. There was a band playing down at Klein's hotel, and the strains reached them faintly, tempered by the distance. There were strange, rare odors abroad—a tangle of the sea smell and of weeds and damp, new-plowed earth, mingled with the heavy perfume of a field of white blossoms somewhere near. But the night sat light upon the sea and the land. There was no weight of darkness; there were no shadows. The white light of the moon had fallen upon the world like the mystery and the softness of sleep.

Most of them walked into the water as though into a native element. The sea was quiet now, and swelled lazily in broad billows that melted into one another and did not break except upon the beach in little foamy crests that coiled back like slow, white serpents.

Edna had attempted all summer to learn to swim. She had received instructions from both the men and women; in some instances from the children. Robert had pursued a system of lessons almost daily; and he was nearly at the point of discouragement in realizing the futility of his efforts. A certain ungovernable dread hung about her when in the water, unless there was a hand near by that might reach out and reassure her.

But that night she was like the little tottering, stumbling, clutching child, who of a sudden realizes its powers, and walks for the first time alone, boldly and with over-confidence. She could have shouted for joy. She did shout for joy, as with a sweeping stroke or two she lifted her body to the surface of the water.

A feeling of exultation overtook her, as if some power of significant import had been given her soul. She grew daring and reckless, overestimating her strength. She wanted to swim far out, where no woman had swum before.

Her unlooked-for achievement was the subject of wonder, applause, and admiration. Each one congratulated himself that his special teachings had accomplished this desired end.

"How easy it is!" she thought. "It is nothing," she said aloud: "why did I not discover before that it was nothing. Think of the time I have lost splashing about like a baby!" She would not join the groups in their sports and bouts, but intoxicated with her newly conquered power, she swam out alone.

She turned her face seaward to gather in an impression of space and solitude, which the vast expanse of water, meeting and melting with moonlit sky, conveyed to her excited fancy. As she swam she seemed to be reaching out for the unlimited in which to lose herself.

Once she turned and looked toward the shore, toward the people she had left there. She had not gone any great distance—that is, what would have been great distance for an experienced swimmer. But to her unaccustomed

vision the stretch of water behind her assumed the aspect of a barrier which her unaided strength would never be able to overcome.

A quick vision of death smote her soul, and for a second of time appalled and enfeebled her senses. But by an effort she rallied her staggering faculties and managed to regain the land.

She made no mention of her encounter with death and her flash of terror, except to say to her husband, "I thought I should have perished out there alone."

"You were not so very far, my dear; I was watching you," he told her.

Edna went at once to the bath-house, and she had put on her dry clothes and was ready to return home before the others had left the water. She started to walk away alone. They all called to her and shouted to her. She waved a dissenting hand, and went on paying no further heed to their renewed cries which sought to detain her.

"Sometimes I am tempted to think that Mrs. Pontellier is capricious," said Madame Lebrun, who was amusing herself immensely and feared that Edna's abrupt departure might put an end to the pleasure.

"I know she is," assented Mr. Pontellier; "sometimes, not often."

Edna had not traversed a quarter of the distance on her way home before she was overtaken by Robert.

"Did you think I was afraid?" she asked him, without a shade of annoyance.

"No; I knew you weren't afraid."

"Then why did you come? Why didn't you stay out there with the others?"

"I never thought of it."

"Thought of what?"

"Of anything. What difference does it make?"

"I'm very tired," she uttered, complainingly.

"I know you are."

"You don't know anything about it. Why should you know? I never was so exhausted in my life. But it isn't unpleasant. A thousand emotions have swept through me to-night. I don't comprehend half of them. Don't mind what I'm saying; I am just thinking aloud. I wonder if I shall ever be stirred again as Mademoiselle Reisz's playing moved me to-night. I wonder if any night on earth will ever again be like this one. It is like a night in a dream. The people about me are like some uncanny, half-human beings. There must be spirits abroad to-night."

"There are," whispered Robert. "Didn't you know this was the twenty-eighth of August?"

"The twenty-eighth of August?"

"Yes. On the twenty-eighth of August, at the hour of midnight, and if the moon is shining—the moon must be shining—a spirit that has haunted these shores for ages rises up from the Gulf. With its own penetrating vision the spirit seeks some one mortal worthy to hold him company, worthy of being exalted for a few hours into realms of the semi-celestials. His search has always hitherto been fruitless, and he has sunk back, disheartened, into the sea. But tonight he found Mrs. Pontellier. Perhaps he will never wholly release her from the spell. Perhaps she will never again suffer a poor, unworthy earthling to walk in the shadow of her divine presence."

"Don't banter me," she said, wounded at what appeared to be his flippancy. He did not mind the entreaty, but the tone with its delicate note of pathos

was like a reproach. He could not explain; he could not tell her that he had penetrated her mood and understood. He said nothing except to offer her his arm, for, by her own admission, she was exhausted. She had been walking alone with her arms hanging limp, letting her white skirts trail along the dewy path. She took his arm, but she did not lean upon it. She let her hand lie listlessly, as though her thoughts were elsewhere—somewhere in advance of her body, and she was striving to overtake them.

Robert assisted her into the hammock which swung from the post before her door out to the trunk of a tree.

"Will you stay out here and wait for Mr. Pontellier?" he asked.

"I'll stay out here. Good-night."

"Shall I get you a pillow?"

"There's one here," she said, feeling about, for they were in the shadow.

"It must be soiled; the children have been tumbling it about."

"No matter." And having discovered the pillow, she adjusted it beneath her head. She extended herself in the hammock with a deep breath of relief. She was not a supercilious or an over-dainty woman. She was not much given to reclining in the hammock, and when she did so it was with no cat-like suggestion of voluptuous ease, but with a beneficent repose which seemed to invade her whole body.

"Shall I stay with you till Mr. Pontellier comes?" asked Robert, seating himself on the outer edge of one of the steps and taking hold of the hammock rope which was fastened to the post.

"If you wish. Don't swing the hammock. Will you get my white shawl which I left on the window-sill over at the house?"

"Are you chilly?"

"No; but I shall be presently."

"Presently?" he laughed. "Do you know what time it is? How long are you going to stay out here?"

"I don't know. Will you get the shawl?"

"Of course I will," he said, rising. He went over to the house, walking along the grass. She watched his figure pass in and out of the strips of moonlight. It was past midnight. It was very quiet.

When he returned with the shawl she took it and kept it in her hand. She did not put it around her.

"Did you say I should stay till Mr. Pontellier came back?"

"I said you might if you wished to."

He seated himself again and rolled a cigarette, which he smoked in silence. Neither did Mrs. Pontellier speak. No multitude of words could have been more significant than those moments of silence, or more pregnant with the first-felt throbbings of desire.

When the voices of the bathers were heard approaching, Robert said good-night. She did not answer him. He thought she was asleep. Again she watched his figure pass in and out of the strips of moonlight as he walked away.

XI

"What are you doing out here, Edna? I thought I should find you in bed," said her husband, when he discovered her lying there. He had walked up with Madame Lebrun and left her at the house. His wife did not reply.

"Are you asleep?" he asked, bending down close to look at her.

"No." Her eyes gleamed bright and intense, with no sleepy shadows, as they looked into his.

"Do you know it is past one o'clock? Come on," and he mounted the steps and went into their room.

"Edna!" called Mr. Pontellier from within, after a few moments had gone by.

"Don't wait for me," she answered. He thrust his head through the door.

"You will take cold out there," he said, irritably. "What folly is this? Why don't you come in?"

"It isn't cold; I have my shawl."

"The mosquitoes will devour you."

"There are no mosquitoes."

She heard him moving about the room; every sound indicating impatience and irritation. Another time she would have gone in at his request. She would, through habit, have yielded to his desire; not with any sense of submission or obedience to his compelling wishes, but unthinkingly, as we walk, move, sit, stand, go through the daily treadmill of the life which has been portioned out to us.

"Edna, dear, are you not coming in soon?" he asked again, this time fondly, with a note of entreaty.

"No; I am going to stay out here."

"This is more than folly," he blurted out. "I can't permit you to stay out there all night. You must come in the house instantly."

With a writhing motion she settled herself more securely in the hammock. She perceived that her will had blazed up, stubborn and resistant. She could not at that moment have done other than denied and resisted. She wondered if her husband had ever spoken to her like that before, and if she had submitted to his command. Of course she had; she remembered that she had. But she could not realize why or how she should have yielded, feeling as she then did.

"Léonce, go to bed," she said. "I mean to stay out here. I don't wish to go in, and I don't intend to. Don't speak to me like that again; I shall not answer you."

Mr. Pontellier had prepared for bed, but he slipped on an extra garment. He opened a bottle of wine, of which he kept a small and select supply in a buffet[7] of his own. He drank a glass of the wine and went out on the gallery and offered a glass to his wife. She did not wish any. He drew up the rocker, hoisted his slippered feet on the rail, and proceeded to smoke a cigar. He smoked two cigars; then he went inside and drank another glass of wine. Mrs. Pontellier again declined to accept a glass when it was offered to her. Mr. Pontellier once more seated himself with elevated feet, and after a reasonable interval of time smoked some more cigars.

Edna began to feel like one who awakens gradually out of a dream, a delicious, grotesque, impossible dream, to feel again the realities pressing into her soul. The physical need for sleep began to overtake her; the exuberance which had sustained and exalted her spirit left her helpless and yielding to the conditions which crowded her in.

The stillest hour of the night had come, the hour before dawn, when the

7. Sideboard.

world seems to hold its breath. The moon hung low, and had turned from silver to copper in the sleeping sky. The old owl no longer hooted, and the water-oaks had ceased to moan as they bent their heads.

Edna arose, cramped from lying so long and still in the hammock. She tottered up the steps, clutching feebly at the post before passing into the house.

"Are you coming in, Léonce?" she asked, turning her face toward her husband.

"Yes, dear," he answered, with a glance following a misty puff of smoke. "Just as soon as I have finished my cigar."

XII

She slept but a few hours. They were troubled and feverish hours, disturbed with dreams that were intangible, that eluded her, leaving only an impression upon her half-awakened senses of something unattainable. She was up and dressed in the cool of the early morning. The air was invigorating and steadied somewhat her faculties. However, she was not seeking refreshment or help from any source either external or from within. She was blindly following whatever impulse moved her, as if she had placed herself in alien hands for direction, and freed her soul of responsibility.

Most of the people at that early hour were still in bed and asleep. A few, who intended to go over to the *Chênière* for mass, were moving about. The lovers, who had laid their plans the night before, were already strolling toward the wharf. The lady in black with her Sunday prayer book, velvet and gold-clasped, and her Sunday silver beads, was following them at no great distance. Old Monsieur Farival was up, and was more than half inclined to do anything that suggested itself. He put on his big straw hat, and taking his umbrella from the stand in the hall, followed the lady in black, never overtaking her.

The little negro girl who worked Madame Lebrun's sewing-machine was sweeping the galleries with long, absent-minded strokes of the broom. Edna sent her up into the house to awaken Robert.

"Tell him I am going to the Chênière. The boat is ready, tell him to hurry."

He had soon joined her. She had never sent for him before. She had never asked for him. She had never seemed to want him before. She did not appear conscious that she had done anything unusual in commanding his presence. He was apparently equally unconscious of anything extraordinary in the situation. But his face was suffused with a quiet glow when he met her.

They went together back to the kitchen to drink coffee. There was no time to wait for any nicety of service. They stood outside the window and the cook passed them their coffee and a roll, which they drank and ate from the window-sill. Edna said it tasted good. She had not thought of coffee nor of anything. He told her he had often noticed that she lacked forethought.

"Wasn't it enough to think of going to the *Chênière* and waking you up?" she laughed. "Do I have to think of everything?—as Léonce says when he's in a bad humor. I don't blame him; he'd never be in a bad humor if it weren't for me."

They took a short cut across the sands. At a distance they could see the curious procession moving toward the wharf—the lovers, shoulder to shoul-

der, creeping; the lady in black, gaining steadily upon them; old Monsieur
Farival, losing ground inch by inch, and a young barefooted Spanish girl,
with a red kerchief on her head and a basket on her arm, bringing up the
rear.

Robert knew the girl, and he talked to her a little in the boat. No one
present understood what they said. Her name was Mariequita. She had a
round, sly, piquant face and pretty black eyes. Her hands were small, and
she kept them folded over the handle of her basket. Her feet were broad and
coarse. She did not strive to hide them. Edna looked at her feet, and noticed
the sand and slime between her brown toes.

Beaudelet grumbled because Mariequita was there, taking up so much
room. In reality he was annoyed at having old Monsieur Farival, who con-
sidered himself the better sailor of the two. But he would not quarrel with
so old a man as Monsieur Farival, so he quarreled with Mariequita. The girl
was deprecatory at one moment, appealing to Robert. She was saucy the
next, moving her head up and down, making "eyes" at Robert and making
"mouths" at Beaudelet.

The lovers were all alone. They saw nothing, they heard nothing. The lady
in black was counting her beads[8] for the third time. Old Monsieur Farival
talked incessantly of what he knew about handling a boat, and of what Beau-
delet did not know on the same subject.

Edna liked it all. She looked Mariequita up and down, from her ugly brown
toes to her pretty black eyes, and back again.

"Why does she look at me like that?" inquired the girl of Robert.

"Maybe she thinks you are pretty. Shall I ask her?"

"No. Is she your sweetheart?"

"She's a married lady, and has two children."

"Oh! well! Francisco ran away with Sylvano's wife, who had four children.
They took all his money and one of the children and stole his boat."

"Shut up!"

"Does she understand?"

"Oh, hush!"

"Are those two married over there—leaning on each other?"

"Of course not," laughed Robert.

"Of course not," echoed Mariequita, with a serious, confirmatory bob of
the head.

The sun was high up and beginning to bite. The swift breeze seemed to
Edna to bury the sting of it into the pores of her face and hands. Robert held
his umbrella over her.

As they went cutting sidewise through the water, the sails bellied taut,
with the wind filling and overflowing them. Old Monsieur Farival laughed
sardonically at something as he looked at the sails, and Beaudelet swore at
the old man under his breath.

Sailing across the bay to the *Chênière Caminada*, Edna felt as if she were
being borne away from some anchorage which had held her fast, whose
chains had been loosening—had snapped the night before when the mystic
spirit was abroad, leaving her free to drift whithersoever she chose to set her
sails. Robert spoke to her incessantly; he no longer noticed Mariequita. The

8. I.e., praying; the "beads" are her rosary.

girl had shrimps in her bamboo basket. They were covered with Spanish moss. She beat the moss impatiently, and muttered to herself sullenly.

"Let us go to Grande Terre[9] to-morrow?" said Robert in a low voice.

"What shall we do there?"

"Climb up the hill to the old fort and look at the little wriggling gold snakes, and watch the lizards sun themselves."

She gazed away toward Grande Terre and thought she would like to be alone there with Robert, in the sun, listening to the ocean's roar and watching the slimy lizards writhe in and out among the ruins of the old fort.

"And the next day or the next we can sail to the Bayou Brulow,"[1] he went on.

"What shall we do there?"

"Anything—cast bait for fish."

"No; we'll go back to Grande Terre. Let the fish alone."

"We'll go wherever you like," he said. "I'll have Tonie come over and help me patch and trim my boat. We shall not need Beaudelet nor any one. Are you afraid of the pirogue?"[2]

"Oh, no."

"Then I'll take you some night in the pirogue when the moon shines. Maybe your Gulf spirit will whisper to you in which of these islands the treasures are hidden—direct you to the very spot, perhaps."

"And in a day we should be rich!" she laughed. "I'd give it all to you, the pirate gold and every bit of treasure we could dig up. I think you would know how to spend it. Pirate gold isn't a thing to be hoarded or utilized. It is something to squander and throw to the four winds, for the fun of seeing the golden specks fly."

"We'd share it, and scatter it together," he said. His face flushed.

They all went together up to the quaint little Gothic church of Our Lady of Lourdes, gleaming all brown and yellow with paint in the sun's glare.

Only Beaudelet remained behind, tinkering at his boat, and Mariequita walked away with her basket of shrimps, casting a look of childish ill-humor and reproach at Robert from the corner of her eye.

XIII

A feeling of oppression and drowsiness overcame Edna during the service. Her head began to ache, and the lights on the altar swayed before her eyes. Another time she might have made an effort to regain her composure; but her one thought was to quit the stifling atmosphere of the church and reach the open air. She arose, climbing over Robert's feet with a muttered apology. Old Monsieur Farival, flurried, curious, stood up, but upon seeing that Robert had followed Mrs. Pontellier, he sank back into his seat. He whispered an anxious inquiry of the lady in black, who did not notice him or reply, but kept her eyes fastened upon the pages of her velvet prayer-book.

"I felt giddy and almost overcome," Edna said, lifting her hands instinctively to her head and pushing her straw hat up from her forehead. "I couldn't

9. An island near Grande Isle.
1. A nearby village built on stilts or platforms in a

marshy area (bayou).
2. Canoe.

have stayed through the service." They were outside in the shadow of the church. Robert was full of solicitude.

"It was folly to have thought of going in the first place, let alone staying. Come over to Madame Antoine's; you can rest there." He took her arm and led her away, looking anxiously and continuously down into her face.

How still it was, with only the voice of the sea whispering through the reeds that grew in the salt-water pools! The long line of little gray, weather-beaten houses nestled peacefully among the orange trees. It must always have been God's day on that low, drowsy island, Edna thought. They stopped, leaning over a jagged fence made of sea-drift, to ask for water. A youth, a mild-faced Acadian,[3] was drawing water from the cistern, which was nothing more than a rusty buoy, with an opening on one side, sunk in the ground. The water which the youth handed to them in a tin pail was not cold to taste, but it was cool to her heated face, and it greatly revived and refreshed her.

Madame Antoine's cot[4] was at the far end of the village. She welcomed them with all the native hospitality, as she would have opened her door to let the sunlight in. She was fat, and walked heavily and clumsily across the floor. She could speak no English, but when Robert made her understand that the lady who accompanied him was ill and desired to rest, she was all eagerness to make Edna feel at home and to dispose of her comfortably.

The whole place was immaculately clean, and the big, four-posted bed, snow-white, invited one to repose. It stood in a small side room which looked out across a narrow grass plot toward the shed, where there was a disabled boat lying keel upward.

Madame Antoine had not gone to mass. Her son Tonie had, but she supposed he would soon be back, and she invited Robert to be seated and wait for him. But he went and sat outside the door and smoked. Madame Antoine busied herself in the large front room preparing dinner. She was boiling mullets[5] over a few red coals in the huge fireplace.

Edna, left alone in the little side room, loosened her clothes, removing the greater part of them. She bathed her face, her neck and arms in the basin that stood between the windows. She took off her shoes and stockings and stretched herself in the very center of the high, white bed. How luxurious it felt to rest thus in a strange, quaint bed, with its sweet country odor of laurel lingering about the sheets and mattress! She stretched her strong limbs that ached a little. She ran her fingers through her loosened hair for a while. She looked at her round arms as she held them straight up and rubbed them one after the other, observing closely, as if it were something she saw for the first time, the fine, firm quality and texture of her flesh. She clasped her hands easily above her head, and it was thus she fell asleep.

She slept lightly at first, half awake and drowsily attentive to the things about her. She could hear Madame Antoine's heavy, scraping tread as she walked back and forth on the sanded floor. Some chickens were clucking outside the windows, scratching for bits of gravel in the grass. Later she half heard the voices of Robert and Tonie talking under the shed. She did not stir. Even her eyelids rested numb and heavily over her sleepy eyes. The voices went on—Tonie's slow, Acadian drawl, Robert's quick, soft, smooth

3. A descendant of French Canadians expelled from Nova Scotia in 1755.

4. Cottage.

5. Small fish.

French. She understood French imperfectly unless directly addressed, and the voices were only part of the other drowsy, muffled sounds lulling her.

When Edna awoke it was with the conviction that she had slept long and soundly. The voices were hushed under the shed. Madame Antoine's step was no longer to be heard in the adjoining room. Even the chickens had gone elsewhere to scratch and cluck. The mosquito bar[6] was drawn over her; the old woman had come in while she slept and let down the bar. Edna arose quietly from the bed, and looking between the curtains of the window, she saw by the slanting rays of the sun that the afternoon was far advanced. Robert was out there under the shed, reclining in the shade against the sloping keel of the overturned boat. He was reading from a book. Tonie was no longer with him. She wondered what had become of the rest of the party. She peeped out at him two or three times as she stood washing herself in the little basin between the windows.

Madame Antoine had laid some coarse, clean towels upon a chair, and had placed a box of *poudre de riz*[7] within easy reach. Edna dabbed the powder upon her nose and cheeks as she looked at herself closely in the little distorted mirror which hung on the wall above the basin. Her eyes were bright and wide awake and her face glowed.

When she had completed her toilet she walked into the adjoining room. She was very hungry. No one was there. But there was a cloth spread upon the table that stood against the wall, and a cover was laid for one, with a crusty brown loaf and a bottle of wine beside the plate. Edna bit a piece from the brown loaf, tearing it with her strong, white teeth. She poured some of the wine into the glass and drank it down. Then she went softly out of doors, and plucking an orange from the low-hanging bough of a tree, threw it at Robert, who did not know she was awake and up.

And illumination broke over his whole face when he saw her and joined her under the orange tree.

"How many years have I slept?" she inquired. "The whole island seems changed. A new race of beings must have sprung up, leaving only you and me as past relics. How many ages ago did Madame Antoine and Tonie die? and when did our people from Grand Isle disappear from the earth?"

He familiarly adjusted a ruffle upon her shoulder.

"You have slept precisely one hundred years. I was left here to guard your slumbers; and for one hundred years I have been out under the shed reading a book. The only evil I couldn't prevent was to keep a broiled fowl from drying up."

"If it had turned to stone, still will I eat it," said Edna, moving with him into the house. "But really, what has become of Monsieur Farival and the others?"

"Gone hours ago. When they found that you were sleeping they thought it best not to awake you. Anyway, I wouldn't have let them. What was I here for?"

"I wonder if Léonce will be uneasy!" she speculated, as she seated herself at table.

"Of course not; he knows you are with me," Robert replied, as he busied

6. Bar holding mosquito netting attached to the bedframe.

7. Rice powder or talcum powder.

himself among sundry pans and covered dishes which had been left standing on the hearth.

"Where are Madame Antoine and her son?" asked Edna.

"Gone to Vespers,[8] and to visit some friends, I believe. I am to take you back in Tonie's boat whenever you are ready to go."

He stirred the smoldering ashes till the broiled fowl began to sizzle afresh. He served her with no mean repast, dripping the coffee anew and sharing it with her. Madame Antoine had cooked little else than the mullets, but while Edna slept Robert had foraged the island. He was childishly gratified to discover her appetite, and to see the relish with which she ate the food which he had procured for her.

"Shall we go right away?" she asked, after draining her glass and brushing together the crumbs of the crusty loaf.

"The sun isn't as low as it will be in two hours," he answered.

"The sun will be gone in two hours."

"Well, let it go; who cares!"

They waited a good while under the orange trees, till Madame Antoine came back, panting, waddling, with a thousand apologies to explain her absence. Tonie did not dare to return. He was shy, and would not willingly face any woman except his mother.

It was very pleasant to stay there under the orange trees, while the sun dipped lower and lower, turning the western sky to flaming copper and gold. The shadows lengthened and crept out like stealthy, grotesque monsters across the grass.

Edna and Robert both sat upon the ground—that is, he lay upon the ground beside her, occasionally picking at the hem of her muslin gown.

Madame Antoine seated her fat body, broad and squat, upon a bench beside the door. She had been talking all the afternoon, and had wound herself up to the story-telling pitch.

And what stories she told them! But twice in her life she had left the *Chênière Caminada,* and then for the briefest span. All her years she had squatted and waddled there upon the island, gathering legends of the Baratarians[9] and the sea. The night came on, with the moon to lighten it. Edna could hear the whispering voices of dead men and the click of muffled gold.

When she and Robert stepped into Tonie's boat, with the red lateen sail, misty spirit forms were prowling in the shadows and among the reeds, and upon the water were phantom ships, speeding to cover.

XIV

The youngest boy, Étienne, had been very naughty, Madame Ratignolle said, as she delivered him into the hands of his mother. He had been unwilling to go to bed and had made a scene; where upon she had taken charge of him and pacified him as well as she could. Raoul had been in bed and asleep for two hours.

The youngster was in his long white nightgown, that kept tripping him up as Madame Ratignolle led him along by the hand. With the other chubby

8. Evening church service.
9. Pirates active in the area of Barataria Bay— most notably, Jean Laffite (ca. 1780–ca. 1826) and his crew.

fist he rubbed his eyes, which were heavy with sleep and ill humor. Edna took him in her arms, and seating herself in the rocker, began to coddle and caress him, calling him all manner of tender names, soothing him to sleep.

It was not more than nine o'clock. No one had yet gone to bed but the children.

Léonce had been very uneasy at first, Madame Ratignolle said, and had wanted to start at once for the *Chênière*. But Monsieur Farival had assured him that his wife was only overcome with sleep and fatigue, that Tonie would bring her safely back later in the day; and he had thus been dissuaded from crossing the bay. He had gone over to Klein's, looking up some cotton broker whom he wished to see in regard to securities, exchanges, stocks, bonds, or something of the sort, Madame Ratignolle did not remember what. He said he would not remain away late. She herself was suffering from heat and oppression, she said. She carried a bottle of salts and a large fan. She would not consent to remain with Edna, for Monsieur Ratignolle was alone, and he detested above all things to be left alone.

When Étienne had fallen asleep Edna bore him into the back room, and Robert went and lifted the mosquito bar that she might lay the child comfortably in his bed. The quadroon had vanished. When they emerged from the cottage Robert bade Edna good-night. "Do you know we have been together the whole livelong day, Robert—since early this morning?" she said at parting.

"All but the hundred years when you were sleeping. Good-night."

He pressed her hand and went away in the direction of the beach. He did not join any of the others, but walked alone toward the Gulf.

Edna stayed outside, awaiting her husband's return. She had no desire to sleep or to retire; nor did she feel like going over to sit with the Ratignolles, or to join Madame Lebrun and a group whose animated voices reached her as they sat in conversation before the house. She let her mind wander back over her stay at Grand Isle; and she tried to discover wherein this summer had been different from any and every other summer of her life. She could only realize that she herself—her present self—was in some way different from the other self. That she was seeing with different eyes and making the acquaintance of new conditions in herself that colored and changed her environment, she did not yet suspect.

She wondered why Robert had gone away and left her. It did not occur to her to think he might have grown tired of being with her the livelong day. She was not tired, and she felt that he was not. She regretted that he had gone. It was so much more natural to have him stay, when he was not absolutely required to leave her.

As Edna waited for her husband she sang low a little song that Robert had sung as they crossed the bay. It began with "Ah! *Si tu savais*,"[1] and every verse ended with "*si tu savais*."

Robert's voice was not pretentious. It was musical and true. The voice, the notes, the whole refrain haunted her memory.

1. "Couldst Thou but Know," a song by Michael William Balfe (1808–1870).

XV

When Edna entered the dining-room one evening a little late, as was her habit, an unusually animated conversation seemed to be going on. Several persons were talking at once, and Victor's voice was predominating, even over that of his mother. Edna had returned late from her bath, had dressed in some haste, and her face was flushed. Her head, set off by the dainty white gown, suggested a rich, rare blossom. She took her seat at table between old Monsieur Farival and Madame Ratignolle.

As she seated herself and was about to begin to eat her soup, which had been served when she entered the room, several persons informed her simultaneously that Robert was going to Mexico. She laid her spoon down and looked about her bewildered. He had been with her, reading to her all the morning, and had never even mentioned such a place as Mexico. She had not seen him during the afternoon; she had heard some one say he was at the house, upstairs with his mother. This she had thought nothing of, though she was surprised when he did not join her later in the afternoon, when she went down to the beach.

She looked across at him, where he sat beside Madame Lebrun, who presided. Edna's face was a blank picture of bewilderment, which she never thought of disguising. He lifted his eyebrows with the pretext of a smile as he returned her glance. He looked embarrassed and uneasy.

"When is he going?" she asked of everybody in general, as if Robert were not there to answer for himself.

"To-night!" "This very evening!" "Did you ever!" "What possesses him!" some of the replies she gathered, uttered simultaneously in French and English.

"Impossible!" she exclaimed. "How can a person start off from Grand Isle to Mexico at a moment's notice, as if he were going over to Klein's or to the wharf or down to the beach?"

"I said all along I was going to Mexico; I've been saying so for years!" cried Robert, in an excited and irritable tone, with the air of a man defending himself against a swarm of stinging insects.

Madame Lebrun knocked on the table with her knife handle.

"Please let Robert explain why he is going, and why he is going to-night," she called out. "Really, this table is getting to be more and more like Bedlam[2] every day, with everybody talking at once. Sometimes—I hope God will forgive me—but positively, sometimes I wish Victor would lose the power of speech."

Victor laughed sardonically as he thanked his mother for her holy wish, of which he failed to see the benefit to anybody, except that it might afford her a more ample opportunity and license to talk herself.

Monsieur Farival thought that Victor should have been taken out in mid-ocean in his earliest youth and drowned. Victor thought there would be more logic in thus disposing of old people with an established claim for making themselves universally obnoxious. Madame Lebrun grew a trifle hysterical; Robert called his brother some sharp, hard names.

2. England's oldest institution for the mentally ill, in London (originally the Hospital of St. Mary of Bethlehem, later Bethlem Royal Hospital); by extension, any madhouse.

"There's nothing much to explain, mother," he said; though he explained, nevertheless—looking chiefly at Edna—that he could only meet the gentleman whom he intended to join at Vera Cruz by taking such and such a steamer, which left New Orleans on such a day; that Beaudelet was going out with his lugger[3]-load of vegetables that night, which gave him an opportunity of reaching the city and making his vessel in time.

"But when did you make up your mind to all this?" demanded Monsieur Farival.

"This afternoon," returned Robert, with a shade of annoyance.

"At what time this afternoon?" persisted the old gentleman, with nagging determination, as if he were cross-questioning a criminal in a court of justice.

"At four o'clock this afternoon. Monsieur Farival," Robert replied, in a high voice and with a lofty air, which reminded Edna of some gentleman on the stage.

She had forced herself to eat most of her soup, and now she was picking the flaky bits of a *court bouillon*[4] with her fork.

The lovers were profiting by the general conversation on Mexico to speak in whispers of matters which they rightly considered were interesting to no one but themselves. The lady in black had once received a pair of prayer-beads of curious workmanship from Mexico, with very special indulgence[5] attached to them, but she had never been able to ascertain whether the indulgence extended outside the Mexican border. Father Fochel of the Cathedral had attempted to explain it; but he had not done so to her satisfaction. And she begged that Robert would interest himself, and discover, if possible, whether she was entitled to the indulgence accompanying the remarkably curious Mexican prayer-beads.

Madame Ratignolle hoped that Robert would exercise extreme caution in dealing with the Mexicans, who, she considered, were a treacherous people, unscrupulous and revengeful. She trusted she did them no injustice in thus condemning them as a race. She had known personally but one Mexican, who made and sold excellent tamales, and whom she would have trusted implicitly, so soft-spoken was he. One day he was arrested for stabbing his wife. She never knew whether he had been hanged or not.

Victor had grown hilarious, and was attempting to tell an anecdote about a Mexican girl who served chocolate one winter in a restaurant in Dauphine Street. No one would listen to him but old Monsieur Farival, who went into convulsions over the droll story.

Edna wondered if they had all gone mad, to be talking and clamoring at that rate. She herself could think of nothing to say about Mexico or the Mexicans.

"At what time do you leave?" she asked Robert.

"At ten," he told her. "Beaudelet wants to wait for the moon."

"Are you all ready to go?"

"Quite ready. I shall only take a handbag, and shall pack my trunk in the city."

3. A small boat.
4. Broth in which fish is poached.
5. According to a Roman Catholic belief, some

religious articles, if specifically blessed, could remit part of the punishment after death for sins.

He turned to answer some question put to him by his mother and Edna, having finished her black coffee, left the table.

She went directly to her room. The little cottage was close and stuffy after leaving the outer air. But she did not mind; there appeared to be a hundred different things demanding her attention indoors. She began to set the toilet-stand to rights, grumbling at the negligence of the quadroon, who was in the adjoining room putting the children to bed. She gathered together stray garments that were hanging on the backs of chairs, and put each where it belonged in closet or bureau drawer. She changed her gown for a more comfortable and commodious wrapper. She rearranged her hair, combing and brushing it with unusual energy. Then she went in and assisted the quadroon in getting the boys to bed.

They were very playful and inclined to talk—to do anything but lie quiet and go to sleep. Edna sent the quadroon away to her supper and told her she need not return. Then she sat and told the children a story. Instead of soothing it excited them, and added to their wakefulness. She left them in heated argument, speculating about the conclusion of the tale which their mother promised to finish the following night.

The little black girl came in to say that Madame Lebrun would like to have Mrs. Pontellier go and sit with them over at the house till Mr. Robert went away. Edna returned answer that she had already undressed, that she did not feel quite well, but perhaps she would go over to the house later. She started to dress again, and got as far advanced as to remove her *peignoir*. But changing her mind once more she resumed the *peignoir,* and went outside and sat down before her door. She was overheated and irritable, and fanned herself energetically for a while. Madame Ratignolle came down to discover what was the matter.

"All that noise and confusion at the table must have upset me," replied Edna, "and moreover, I hate shocks and surprises. The idea of Robert starting off in such a ridiculously sudden and dramatic way! As if it were a matter of life and death! Never saying a word about it all morning when he was with me."

"Yes," agreed Madame Ratignolle. "I think it was showing us all—you especially—very little consideration. It wouldn't have surprised me in any of the others; those Lebruns are all given to heroics. But I must say I should never have expected such a thing from Robert. Are you not coming down? Come on, dear; it doesn't look friendly."

"No," said Edna, a little sullenly. "I can't go to the trouble of dressing again; I don't feel like it."

"You needn't dress; you look all right; fasten a belt around your waist. Just look at me!"

"No," persisted Edna; "but you go on. Madame Lebrun might be offended if we both stayed away."

Madame Ratignolle kissed Edna good-night, and went away, being in truth rather desirous of joining in the general and animated conversation which was still in progress concerning Mexico and the Mexicans.

Somewhat later Robert came up, carrying his hand-bag.

"Aren't you feeling well?" he asked.

"Oh, well enough. Are you going right away?"

He lit a match and looked at his watch. "In twenty minutes," he said. The

sudden and brief flare of the match emphasized the darkness for a while. He sat down upon a stool which the children had left out on the porch.

"Get a chair," said Edna.

"This will do," he replied. He put on his soft hat and nervously took it off again, and wiping his face with his handkerchief, complained of the heat.

"Take the fan," said Edna, offering it to him.

"Oh, no! Thank you. It does no good; you have to stop fanning some time, and feel all the more uncomfortable afterward."

"That's one of the ridiculous things which men always say. I have never known one to speak otherwise of fanning. How long will you be gone?"

"Forever, perhaps. I don't know. It depends upon a good many things."

"Well, in case it shouldn't be forever, how long will it be?"

"I don't know."

"This seems to me perfectly preposterous and uncalled for. I don't like it. I don't understand your motive for silence and mystery, never saying a word to me about it this morning." He remained silent, not offering to defend himself. He only said, after a moment:

"Don't part from me in an ill-humor. I never knew you to be out of patience with me before."

"I don't want to part in any ill-humor," said she. "But can't you understand? I've grown used to seeing you, to having you with me all the time, and your action seems unfriendly, even unkind. You don't even offer an excuse for it. Why, I was planning to be together, thinking of how pleasant it would be to see you in the city next winter."

"So was I," he blurted. "Perhaps that's the—" He stood up suddenly and held out his hand. "Good-by, my dear Mrs. Pontellier; good-by. You won't—I hope you won't completely forget me." She clung to his hand, striving to detain him.

"Write to me when you get there, won't you, Robert?" she entreated.

"I will, thank you. Good-by."

How unlike Robert! The merest acquaintance would have said something more emphatic than "I will, thank you; good-by," to such a request.

He had evidently already taken leave of the people over at the house, for he descended the steps and went to join Beaudelet, who was out there with an oar across his shoulder waiting for Robert. They walked away in the darkness. She could only hear Beaudelet's voice; Robert had apparently not even spoken a word of greeting to his companion.

Edna bit her handkerchief convulsively, striving to hold back and to hide, even from herself as she would have hidden from another the emotion which was troubling—tearing—her. Her eyes were brimming with tears.

For the first time she recognized anew the symptoms of infatuation which she felt incipiently as a child, as a girl in her earliest teens, and later as a young woman. The recognition did not lessen the reality, the poignancy of the revelation by any suggestion or promise of instability. The past was nothing to her; offered no lesson which she was willing to heed. The future was a mystery which she never attempted to penetrate. The present alone was significant; was hers, to torture her as it was doing then with the biting conviction that she had lost that which she had held, that she had been denied that which her impassioned, newly awakened being demanded.

XVI

"Do you miss your friend greatly?" asked Mademoiselle Reisz one morning as she came creeping up behind Edna, who had just left her cottage on her way to the beach. She spent much of her time in the water since she had acquired finally the art of swimming. As their stay at Grand Isle drew near its close, she felt that she could not give too much time to a diversion which afforded her the only real pleasurable moments that she knew. When Mademoiselle Reisz came and touched her upon the shoulder and spoke to her, the woman seemed to echo the thought which was ever in Edna's mind; or, better, the feeling which constantly possessed her.

Robert's going had some way taken the brightness, the color, the meaning out of everything. The conditions of her life were in no way changed, but her whole existence was dulled, like a faded garment which seems to be no longer worth wearing. She sought him everywhere—in others whom she induced to talk about him. She went up in the mornings to Madame Lebrun's room, braving the clatter of the old sewing-machine. She sat there and chatted at intervals as Robert had done. She gazed around the room at the pictures and photographs hanging upon the wall, and discovered in some corner an old family album, which she examined with the keenest interest, appealing to Madame Lebrun for enlightenment concerning the many figures and faces which she discovered between its pages.

There was a picture of Madame Lebrun with Robert as a baby, seated in her lap, a round-faced infant with a fist in his mouth. The eyes alone in the baby suggested the man. And that was he also in kilts, at the age of five, wearing long curls and holding a whip in his hand. It made Edna laugh, and she laughed, too, at the portrait in his first long trousers; while another interested her, taken when he left for college, looking thin, long-faced, with eyes full of fire, ambition and great intentions. But there was no recent picture, none which suggested the Robert who had gone away five days ago, leaving a void and wilderness behind him.

"Oh, Robert stopped having his pictures taken when he had to pay for them himself! He found wiser use for his money, he says," explained Madame Lebrun. She had a letter from him, written before he left New Orleans. Edna wished to see the letter, and Madame Lebrun told her to look for it either on the table or the dresser, or perhaps it was on the mantelpiece.

The letter was on the bookshelf. It possessed the greatest interest and attraction for Edna; the envelope, its size and shape, the postmark, the handwriting. She examined every detail of the outside before opening it. There were only a few lines, setting forth that he would leave the city that afternoon, that he had packed his trunk in good shape, that he was well, and sent her his love and begged to be affectionately remembered to all. There was no special message to Edna except a postscript saying that if Mrs. Pontellier desired to finish the book which he had been reading to her, his mother would find it in his room, among other books there on the table. Edna experienced a pang of jealousy because he had written to his mother rather than to her.

Every one seemed to take for granted that she missed him. Even her husband, when he came down the Saturday following Robert's departure, expressed regret that he had gone.

"How do you get on without him, Edna?" he asked.

"It's very dull without him," she admitted. Mr. Pontellier had seen Robert in the city, and Edna asked him a dozen questions or more. Where had they met? On Carondelet Street, in the morning. They had gone "in" and had a drink and a cigar together. What had they talked about? Chiefly about his prospects in Mexico, which Mr. Pontellier thought were promising. How did he look? How did he seem—grave, or gay, or how? Quite cheerful, and wholly taken up with the idea of his trip, which Mr. Pontellier found altogether natural in a young fellow about to seek fortune and adventure in a strange, queer country.

Edna tapped her foot impatiently, and wondered why the children persisted in playing in the sun when they might be under the trees. She went down and led them out of the sun, scolding the quadroon for not being more attentive.

It did not strike her as in the least grotesque that she should be making of Robert the object of conversation and leading her husband to speak of him. The sentiment which she entertained for Robert in no way resembled that which she felt for her husband, or had ever felt, or ever expected to feel. She had all her life long been accustomed to harbor thoughts and emotions which never voiced themselves. They had never taken the form of struggles. They belonged to her and were her own, and she entertained the conviction that she had a right to them and that they concerned no one but herself. Edna had once told Madame Ratignolle that she would never sacrifice herself for her children, or for any one. Then had followed a rather heated argument; the two women did not appear to understand each other or to be talking the same language. Edna tried to appease her friend, to explain.

"I would give up the unessential; I would give my money. I would give my life for my children; but I wouldn't give myself. I can't make it more clear; it's only something which I am beginning to comprehend, which is revealing itself to me."

"I don't know what you would call the essential, or what you mean by the unessential," said Madame Ratignolle, cheerfully; "but a woman who would give her life for her children could do no more than that—your Bible tells you so. I'm sure I couldn't do more than that."

"Oh, yes you could!" laughed Edna.

She was not surprised at Mademoiselle Reisz's question the morning that lady, following her to the beach, tapped her on the shoulder and asked if she did not greatly miss her young friend.

"Oh, good morning, Mademoiselle; it is you? Why, of course I miss Robert. Are you going down to bathe?"

"Why should I go down to bathe at the very end of the season when I haven't been in the surf all summer?" replied the woman, disagreeably.

"I beg your pardon," offered Edna, in some embarrassment, for she should have remembered that Mademoiselle Reisz's avoidance of the water had furnished a theme for much pleasantry. Some among them thought it was on account of her false hair, or the dread of getting the violets wet, while others attributed it to the natural aversion for water sometimes believed to accompany the artistic temperament. Mademoiselle offered Edna some chocolates in a paper bag, which she took from her pocket, by way of showing that she

bore no ill feeling. She habitually ate chocolates for their sustaining quality; they contained much nutriment in small compass, she said. They saved her from starvation, as Madame Lebrun's table was utterly impossible; and no one save so impertinent a woman as Madame Lebrun could think of offering such food to people and requiring them to pay for it.

"She must feel very lonely without her son," said Edna, desiring to change the subject. "Her favorite son, too. It must have been quite hard to let him go."

Mademoiselle laughed maliciously.

"Her favorite son! Oh dear! Who could have been imposing such a tale upon you? Aline Lebrun lives for Victor, and for Victor alone. She has spoiled him into the worthless creature he is. She worships him and the ground he walks on. Robert is very well in a way, to give up all the money he can earn to the family, and keep the barest pittance for himself. Favorite son, indeed! I miss the poor fellow myself, my dear. I liked to see him and to hear him about the place—the only Lebrun who is worth a pinch of salt. He comes to see me often in the city. I like to play to him. That Victor! hanging would be too good for him. It's a wonder Robert hasn't beaten him to death long ago."

"I thought he had great patience with his brother," offered Edna, glad to be talking about Robert, no matter what was said.

"Oh! he thrashed him well enough a year or two ago," said Mademoiselle. "It was about a Spanish girl, whom Victor considered that he had some sort of claim upon. He met Robert one day talking to the girl, or walking with her, or bathing with her, or carrying her basket—I don't remember what;— and he became so insulting and abusive that Robert gave him a thrashing on the spot that has kept him comparatively in order for a good while. It's about time he was getting another."

"Was her name Mariequita?" asked Edna.

"Mariequita—yes, that was it. Mariequita. I had forgotten. Oh, she's a sly one, and a bad one, that Mariequita!"

Edna looked down at Mademoiselle Reisz and wondered how she could have listened to her venom so long. For some reason she felt depressed, almost unhappy. She had not intended to go into the water; but she donned her bathing suit, and left Mademoiselle alone, seated under the shade of the children's tent. The water was growing cooler as the season advanced. Edna plunged and swam about with an abandon that thrilled and invigorated her. She remained a long time in the water, half hoping that Mademoiselle Reisz would not wait for her.

But Mademoiselle waited. She was very amiable during the walk back, and raved much over Edna's appearance in her bathing suit. She talked about music. She hoped that Edna would go to see her in the city, and wrote her address with the stub of a pencil on a piece of card which she found in her pocket.

"When do you leave?" asked Edna.

"Next Monday; and you?"

"The following week," answered Edna, adding, "It has been a pleasant summer, hasn't it, Mademoiselle?"

"Well," agreed Mademoiselle Reisz, with a shrug, "rather pleasant, if it hadn't been for the mosquitoes and the Farival twins."

XVII

The Pontelliers possessed a very charming home on Esplanade Street[6] in New Orleans. It was a large, double cottage, with a broad front veranda, whose round, fluted columns supported the sloping roof. The house was painted a dazzling white; the outside shutters, or jalousies, were green. In the yard, which was kept scrupulously neat, were flowers and plants of every description which flourishes in South Louisiana. Within doors the appointments were perfect after the conventional type. The softest carpets and rugs covered the floors; rich and tasteful draperies hung at doors and windows. There were paintings, selected with judgment and discrimination, upon the walls. The cut glass, the silver, the heavy damask which daily appeared upon the table were the envy of many women whose husbands were less generous than Mr. Pontellier.

Mr. Pontellier was very fond of walking about his house examining its various appointments and details, to see that nothing was amiss. He greatly valued his possessions, chiefly because they were his, and derived genuine pleasure from contemplating a painting, a statuette, a rare lace curtain—no matter what—after he had bought it and placed it among his household goods.

On Tuesday afternoons—Tuesday being Mrs. Pontellier's reception day[7]—there was a constant stream of callers—women who came in carriages or in the street cars, or walked when the air was soft and distance permitted. A light-colored mulatto boy, in dress coat and bearing a diminutive silver tray for the reception of cards, admitted them. A maid, in white fluted cap, offered the callers liqueur, coffee, or chocolate, as they might desire. Mrs. Pontellier, attired in a handsome reception gown, remained in the drawing-room the entire afternoon receiving her visitors. Men sometimes called in the evening with their wives.

This had been the programme which Mrs. Pontellier had religiously followed since her marriage, six years before. Certain evenings during the week she and her husband attended the opera or sometimes the play.

Mr. Pontellier left his home in the mornings between nine and ten o'clock, and rarely returned before half-past six or seven in the evening—dinner being served at half-past seven.

He and his wife seated themselves at table on Tuesday evening, a few weeks after their return from Grand Isle. They were alone together. The boys were being put to bed; the patter of their bare, escaping feet could be heard occasionally, as well as the pursuing voice of the quadroon, lifted in mild protest and entreaty. Mrs. Pontellier did not wear her usual Tuesday reception gown; she was in ordinary house dress. Mr. Pontellier who was observant about such things, noticed it, as he served the soup and handed it to the boy in waiting.

"Tired out, Edna? Whom did you have? Many callers?" he asked. He tasted his soup and began to season it with pepper, salt, vinegar, mustard—everything within reach.

6. The most exclusive address of the Creole aristocracy.

7. The day when a woman was "at home" to receive visitors.

"There were a good many," replied Edna, who was eating her soup with evident satisfaction. "I found their cards when I got home; I was out."

"Out!" exclaimed her husband, with something like genuine consternation in his voice as he laid down the vinegar cruet and looked at her through his glasses. "Why, what could have taken you out on Tuesday? What did you have to do?"

"Nothing. I simply felt like going out, and I went out."

"Well, I hope you left some suitable excuse," said her husband, somewhat appeased, as he added a dash of cayenne pepper to the soup.

"No, I left no excuse. I told Joe to say I was out, that was all."

"Why, my dear, I should think you'd understand by this time that people don't do such things; we've got to observe *les convenances*[8] if we ever expect to get on and keep up with procession. If you felt that you had to leave home this afternoon, you should have left some suitable explanation for your absence.

"This soup is really impossible; it's strange that woman hasn't learned yet to make a decent soup. Any free-lunch stand in town serves a better one. Was Mrs. Belthrop here?"

"Bring the tray with the cards, Joe. I don't remember who was here."

The boy retired and returned after a moment, bringing the tiny silver tray, which was covered with ladies' visiting cards. He handed it to Mrs. Pontellier.

"Give it to Mr. Pontellier," she said.

Joe offered the tray to Mr. Pontellier, and removed the soup.

Mr. Pontellier scanned the names of his wife's callers, reading some of them aloud, with comments as he read.

" 'The Misses Delasidas.' I worked a big deal in futures[9] for their father this morning; nice girls; it's time they were getting married. 'Mrs. Belthrop.' I tell you what it is, Edna; you can't afford to snub Mrs. Belthrop. Why, Belthrop could buy and sell us ten times over. His business is worth a good, round sum to me. You'd better write her a note. 'Mrs. James Highcamp.' Hugh! the less you have to do with Mrs. Highcamp, the better. 'Madame Laforcé.' Came all the way from Carrolton,[1] too, poor old soul. 'Miss Wiggs,' 'Mrs. Eleanor Boltons.' " He pushed the cards aside.

"Mercy!" exclaimed Edna, who had been fuming. "Why are you taking the thing so seriously and making such a fuss over it?"

"I'm not making any fuss over it. But it's just such seeming trifles that we've got to take seriously; such things count."

The fish was scorched. Mr. Pontellier would not touch it. Edna said she did not mind a little scorched taste. The roast was in some way not to his fancy, and he did not like the manner in which the vegetables were served.

"It seems to me," he said, "we spend money enough in this house to procure at least one meal a day which a man could eat and retain his self-respect."

"You used to think the cook was a treasure," returned Edna, indifferently.

"Perhaps she was when she first came; but cooks are only human. They need looking after, like any other class of persons that you employ. Suppose

8. The conventions.
9. A form of financial speculation.

1. A village to the west of New Orleans.

I didn't look after the clerks in my office, just let them run things their own way; they'd soon make a nice mess of me and my business."

"Where are you going?" asked Edna, seeing that her husband arose from table without having eaten a morsel except a taste of the highly-seasoned soup.

"I'm going to get my dinner at the club. Good night." He went into the hall, took his hat and stick from the stand, and left the house.

She was somewhat familiar with such scenes. They had often made her very unhappy. On a few previous occasions she had been completely deprived of any desire to finish her dinner. Sometimes she had gone into the kitchen to administer a tardy rebuke to the cook. Once she went to her room and studied the cookbook during an entire evening, finally writing out a menu for the week, which left her harassed with a feeling that, after all, she had accomplished no good that was worth the name.

But that evening Edna finished her dinner alone, with forced deliberation. Her face was flushed and her eyes flamed with some inward fire that lighted them. After finishing her dinner she went to her room, having instructed the boy to tell any other callers that she was indisposed.

It was a large, beautiful room, rich and picturesque in the soft, dim light which the maid had turned low. She went and stood at an open window and looked out upon the deep tangle of the garden below. All the mystery and witchery of the night seemed to have gathered there amid the perfumes and the dusky and tortuous outlines of flowers and foliage. She was seeking herself and finding herself in just such sweet, half-darkness which met her moods. But the voices were not soothing that came to her from the darkness and the sky above and the stars. They jeered and sounded mournful notes without promise, devoid even of hope. She turned back into the room and began to walk to and fro down its whole length, without stopping, without resting. She carried in her hands a thin handkerchief, which she tore into ribbons, rolled into a ball, and flung from her. Once she stopped, and taking off her wedding ring, flung it upon the carpet. When she saw it lying there, she stamped her heel upon it, striving to crush it. But her small boot heel did not make an indenture, not a mark upon the little glittering circlet.

In a sweeping passion she seized a glass vase from the table and flung it upon the tiles of the hearth. She wanted to destroy something. The crash and clatter were what she wanted to hear.

A maid, alarmed at the din of breaking glass, entered the room to discover what was the matter.

"A vase fell upon the hearth," said Edna. "Never mind; leave it till morning."

"Oh! you might get some of the glass in your feet, ma'am," insisted the young woman, picking up bits of the broken vase that were scattered upon the carpet. "And here's your ring, ma'am, under the chair."

Edna held out her hand, and taking the ring, slipped it upon her finger.

XVIII

The following morning Mr. Pontellier, upon leaving for his office, asked Edna if she would not meet him in town in order to look at some new fixtures for the library.

"I hardly think we need new fixtures, Léonce. Don't let us get anything new; you are too extravagant. I don't believe you ever think of saving or putting by."

"The way to become rich is to make money, my dear Edna, not to save it," he said. He regretted that she did not feel inclined to go with him and select new fixtures. He kissed her good-by, and told her she was not looking well and must take care of herself. She was unusually pale and very quiet.

She stood on the front veranda as he quitted the house, and absently picked a few sprays of jessamine that grew upon a trellis near by. She inhaled the odor of the blossoms and thrust them into the bosom of her white morning gown. The boys were dragging along the banquette[2] a small "express wagon," which they had filled with block and sticks. The quadroon was following them with little quick steps, having assumed a fictitious animation and alacrity for the occasion. A fruit vender was crying his wares in the street.

Edna looked straight before her with a self-absorbed expression upon her face. She felt no interest in anything about her. The street, the children, the fruit vender, the flowers growing there under her eyes, were all part and parcel of an alien world which had suddenly become antagonistic.

She went back into the house. She had thought of speaking to the cook concerning her blunders of the previous night; but Mr. Pontellier had saved her that disagreeable mission, for which she was so poorly fitted. Mr. Pontellier's arguments were usually convincing with those whom he employed. He left home feeling quite sure that he and Edna would sit down that evening, and possibly a few subsequent evenings, to a dinner deserving of the name.

Edna spent an hour or two in looking over some of her old sketches. She could see their shortcomings and defects, which were glaring in her eyes. She tried to work a little, but found she was not in the humor. Finally she gathered together a few of the sketches—those which she considered the least discreditable; and she carried them with her when, a little later, she dressed and left the house. She looked handsome and distinguished in her street gown. The tan of the seashore had left her face, and her forehead was smooth, white, and polished beneath her heavy, yellow-brown hair. There were a few freckles on her face, and a small, dark mole near the under lip and one on the temple, half-hidden in her hair.

As Edna walked along the street she was thinking of Robert. She was still under the spell of her infatuation. She had tried to forget him, realizing the inutility of remembering. But the thought of him was like an obsession, ever pressing itself upon her. It was not that she dwelt upon details of their acquaintance, or recalled in any special or peculiar way his personality; it was his being, his existence, which dominated her thought, fading sometimes as if it would melt into the mist of the forgotten, reviving again with an intensity which filled her with an incomprehensible longing.

Edna was on her way to Madame Ratignolle's. Their intimacy, begun at Grand Isle, had not declined, and they had seen each other with some frequency since their return to the city. The Ratignolles lived at no great distance from Edna's home, on the corner of a side street, where Monsieur Ratignolle owned and conducted a drug store which enjoyed a steady and

2. Sidewalk. "Jessamine": jasmine.

prosperous trade. His father had been in the business before him, and Monsieur Ratignolle stood well in the community and bore an enviable reputation for integrity and clear-headedness. His family lived in commodious apartments over the store, having an entrance on the side within the *porte cochère*.[3] There was something which Edna thought very French, very foreign, about their whole manner of living. In the large and pleasant salon which extended across the width of the house, the Ratignolles entertained their friends once a fortnight with a *soirée musicale*,[4] sometimes diversified by card-playing. There was a friend who played upon the 'cello. One brought his flute and another his violin, while there were some who sang and a number who performed upon the piano with various degrees of taste and agility. The Ratignolles' *soirées musicales* were widely known, and it was considered a privilege to be invited to them.

Edna found her friend engaged in assorting the clothes which had returned that morning from the laundry. She at once abandoned her occupation upon seeing Edna, who had been ushered without ceremony into her presence.

" 'Cité can do it as well as I; it is really her business," she explained to Edna, who apologized for interrupting her. And she summoned a young black woman, whom she instructed, in French, to be very careful in checking off the list which she handed her. She told her to notice particularly if a fine linen handkerchief of Monsieur Ratignolle's, which was missing last week, had been returned; and to be sure to set to one side such pieces as required mending and darning.

Then placing an arm around Edna's waist, she led her to the front of the house, to the salon, where it was cool and sweet with the odor of great roses that stood upon the hearth in jars.

Madame Ratignolle looked more beautiful than ever there at home, in a negligé which left her arms almost wholly bare and exposed the rich, melting curves of her white throat.

"Perhaps I shall be able to paint your picture some day," said Edna with a smile when they were seated. She produced the roll of sketches and started to unfold them. "I believe I ought to work again. I feel as if I wanted to be doing something. What do you think of them? Do you think it worth while to take it up again and study some more? I might study for a while with Laidpore."

She knew that Madame Ratignolle's opinion in such a matter would be next to valueless, that she herself had not alone decided, but determined; but she sought the words and praise and encouragement that would help her to put her heart into her venture.

"Your talent is immense, dear!"

"Nonsense!" protested Edna, well pleased.

"Immense, I tell you," persisted Madame Ratignolle, surveying the sketches one by one, at close range, then holding them at arm's length, narrowing her eyes, and dropping her head on one side. "Surely, this Bavarian peasant is worthy of framing; and this basket of apples! never have I seen anything more lifelike. One might almost be tempted to reach out a hand and take one."

3. A roofed structure extending from a building's entrance over its driveway, protecting travelers alighting from or boarding a vehicle.
4. Musical evening.

Edna could not control a feeling which bordered upon complacency at her friend's praise, even realizing, as she did, its true worth. She retained a few of the sketches, and gave all the rest to Madame Ratignolle, who appreciated the gift far beyond its value and proudly exhibited the pictures to her husband when he came up from the store a little later for his midday dinner.

Mr. Ratignolle was one of those men who are called the salt of the earth. His cheerfulness was unbounded, and it was matched by his goodness of heart, his broad charity, and common sense. He and his wife spoke English with an accent which was only discernible through its un-English emphasis and a certain carefulness and deliberation. Edna's husband spoke English with no accent whatever. The Ratignolles understood each other perfectly. If ever the fusion of two human beings into one has been accomplished on this sphere it was surely in their union.

As Edna seated herself at table with them she thought, "Better a dinner of herbs,"[5] though it did not take her long to discover that was no dinner of herbs, but a delicious repast, simple, choice, and in every way satisfying.

Monsieur Ratignolle was delighted to see her, though he found her looking not so well as at Grand Isle, and he advised a tonic. He talked a good deal on various topics, a little politics, some city news and neighborhood gossip. He spoke with an animation and earnestness that gave an exaggerated importance to every syllable he uttered. His wife was keenly interested in everything he said, laying down her fork the better to listen, chiming in, taking the words out of his mouth.

Edna felt depressed rather than soothed after leaving them. The little glimpse of domestic harmony which had been offered her gave her no regret, no longing. It was not a condition of life which fitted her, and she could see in it but an appalling and hopeless ennui. She was moved by a kind of commiseration for Madame Ratignolle,—a pity for that colorless existence which never uplifted its possessor beyond the region of blind contentment, in which no moment of anguish ever visited her soul, in which she would never have the taste of life's delirium. Edna vaguely wondered what she meant by "life's delirium." It had crossed her thought like some unsought, extraneous impression.

XIX

Edna could not help but think that it was very foolish, very childish, to have stamped upon her wedding ring and smashed the crystal vase upon the tiles. She was visited by no more outbursts, moving her to such futile expedients. She began to do as she liked and to feel as she liked. She completely abandoned her Tuesdays at home, and did not return the visits of those who had called upon her. She made no ineffectual efforts to conduct her household *en bonne ménagère,*[6] going and coming as it suited her fancy, and, so far as she was able, lending herself to any passing caprice.

Mr. Pontellier had been a rather courteous husband so long as he met a certain tacit submissiveness in his wife. But her new and unexpected line of conduct completely bewildered him. It shocked him. Then her absolute dis-

5. "Better is a dinner of herbs where love is, than a stalled ox and hatred therewith" (Proverbs 15:17).

6. As a good housewife.

regard for her duties as a wife angered him. When Mr. Pontellier became rude, Edna grew insolent. She had resolved never to take another step backward.

"It seems to me the utmost folly for a woman at the head of a household, and the mother of children, to spend in an atelier[7] days which would be better employed contriving for the comfort of her family."

"I feel like painting," answered Edna. "Perhaps I shan't always feel like it."

"Then in God's name paint! but don't let the family go to the devil. There's Madame Ratignolle; because she keeps up her music, she doesn't let everything go to chaos. And she's more of a musician than you are a painter."

"She isn't a musician, and I'm not a painter. It isn't on account of painting that I let things go."

"On account of what, then?"

"Oh! I don't know. Let me alone; you bother me."

It sometimes entered Mr. Pontellier's mind to wonder if his wife were not growing a little unbalanced mentally. He could see plainly that she was not herself. That is, he could not see that she was becoming herself and daily casting aside that fictitious self which we assume like a garment with which to appear before the world.

Her husband let her alone as she requested, and went away to his office. Edna went up to her atelier—a bright room in the top of the house. She was working with great energy and interest, without accomplishing anything, however, which satisfied her even in the smallest degree. For a time she had the whole household enrolled in the service of art. The boys posed for her. They thought it amusing at first, but the occupation soon lost its attractiveness when they discovered that it was not a game arranged especially for their entertainment. The quadroon sat for hours before Edna's palette, patient as a savage, while the house-maid took charge of the children, and the drawing-room went undusted. But the house-maid, too, served her term as model when Edna perceived that the young woman's back and shoulders were molded on classic lines, and that her hair, loosened from its confining cap, became an inspiration. While Edna worked she sometimes sang low the little air, "*Ah! si tu savais!*"

It moved her with recollections. She could hear again the ripple of the water, the flapping sail. She could see the glint of the moon upon the bay, and could feel the soft, gusty beating of the hot south wind. A subtle current of desire passed through her body, weakening her hold upon the brushes and making her eyes burn.

There were days when she was very happy without knowing why. She was happy to be alive and breathing, when her whole being seemed to be one with the sunlight, the color, the odors, the luxuriant warmth of some perfect Southern day. She liked then to wander alone into strange and unfamiliar places. She discovered many a sunny, sleepy corner, fashioned to dream in. And she found it good to dream and to be alone and unmolested.

There were days when she was unhappy, she did not know why,—when it did not seem worth while to be glad or sorry, to be alive or dead; when life appeared to her like a grotesque pandemonium and humanity like worms

7. Studio.

struggling blindly toward inevitable annihilation. She could not work on such a day, nor weave fancies to stir her pulses and warm her blood.

XX

It was during such a mood that Edna hunted up Mademoiselle Reisz. She had not forgotten the rather disagreeable impression left upon her by their last interview; but she nevertheless felt a desire to see her—above all, to listen while she played upon the piano. Quite early in the afternoon she started upon her quest for the pianist. Unfortunately she had mislaid or lost Mademoiselle Reisz's card, and looking up her address in the city directory, she found that the woman lived on Bienville Street, some distance away. The directory which fell into her hands was a year or more old, however, and upon reaching the number indicated, Edna discovered that the house was occupied by a respectable family of mulattoes who had *chambres garnies*[8] to let. They had been living there for six months, and knew absolutely nothing of a Mademoiselle Reisz. In fact, they knew nothing of any of their neighbors; their lodgers were all people of the highest distinction, they assured Edna. She did not linger to discuss class distinctions with Madame Pouponne, but hastened to a neighboring grocery store, feeling sure that Mademoiselle would have left her address with the proprietor.

He knew Mademoiselle Reisz a good deal better than he wanted to know her, he informed his questioner. In truth, he did not want to know her at all, anything concerning her—the most disagreeable and unpopular woman who ever lived in Bienville Street. He thanked heaven she had left the neighborhood, and was equally thankful that he did not know where she had gone.

Edna's desire to see Mademoiselle Reisz had increased tenfold since these unlooked for obstacles had arisen to thwart it. She was wondering who could give her the information she sought, when it suddenly occurred to her that Madame Lebrun would be the one most likely to do so. She knew it was useless to ask Madame Ratignolle, who was on the most distant terms with the musician, and preferred to know nothing concerning her. She had once been almost as emphatic in expressing herself upon the subject as the corner grocer.

Edna knew that Madame Lebrun had returned to the city, for it was the middle of November. And she also knew where the Lebruns lived, on Chartres Street.

Their home from the outside looked like a prison, with iron bars before the door and lower windows. The iron bars were a relic of the old *régime*,[9] and no one had ever thought of dislodging them. At the side was a high fence enclosing the garden. A gate or door opening upon the street was locked. Edna rang the bell at this side garden gate, and stood upon the banquette, waiting to be admitted.

It was Victor who opened the gate for her. A black woman, wiping her hands upon her apron, was close at his heels. Before she saw them Edna could hear them in altercation, the woman—plainly an anomaly—claiming the right to be allowed to perform her duties, one of which was to answer the bell.

8. Furnished rooms.

9. I.e., the Spanish regime (1766–1803).

Victor was surprised and delighted to see Mrs. Pontellier, and he made no attempt to conceal either his astonishment or his delight. He was a dark-browed, good-looking youngster of nineteen, greatly resembling his mother, but with ten times her impetuosity. He instructed the black woman to go at once and inform Madame Lebrun that Mrs. Pontellier desired to see her. The woman grumbled a refusal to do part of her duty when she had not been permitted to do it all, and started back to her interrupted task of weeding the garden. Whereupon Victor administered a rebuke in the form of a volley of abuse, which owing to its rapidity and incoherence, was all but incomprehensible to Edna. Whatever it was, the rebuke was convincing, for the woman dropped her hoe and went mumbling into the house.

Edna did not wish to enter. It was very pleasant there on the side porch, where there were chairs, a wicker lounge, and a small table. She seated herself, for she was tired from her long tramp; and she began to rock gently and smooth out the folds of her silk parasol. Victor drew up his chair beside her. He at once explained that the black woman's offensive conduct was all due to imperfect training, as he was not there to take her in hand. He had only come up from the island the morning before, expected to return next day. He stayed all winter at the island; he lived there, and kept the place in order and got things ready for the summer visitors.

But a man needed occasional relaxation, he informed Mrs. Pontellier, and every now and again he drummed up a pretext to bring him to the city. My! but he had had a time of it the evening before! He wouldn't want his mother to know, and he began to talk in a whisper. He was scintillant[1] with recollections. Of course, he couldn't think of telling Mrs. Pontellier all about it, she being a woman and not comprehending such things. But it all began with a girl peeping and smiling at him through the shutters as he passed by. Oh! but she was a beauty! Certainly he smiled back, and went up and talked to her. Mrs. Pontellier did not know him if she supposed he was one to let an opportunity like that escape him. Despite herself, the youngster amused her. She must have betrayed in her look some degree of interest or entertainment. The boy grew more daring, and Mrs. Pontellier might have found herself, in a little while, listening to a highly colored story but for the timely appearance of Madame Lebrun.

That lady was still clad in white, according to her custom of the summer. Her eyes beamed an effusive welcome. Would not Mrs. Pontellier go inside? Would she partake of some refreshment? Why had she not been there before? How was that dear Mr. Pontellier and how were those sweet children? Had Mrs. Pontellier ever known such a warm November?

Victor went and reclined on the wicker lounge behind his mother's chair, where he commanded a view of Edna's face. He had taken her parasol from her hands while he spoke to her, and he now lifted it and twirled it above him as he lay on his back. When Madame Lebrun complained that it was so dull coming back to the city; that she saw so few people now; that even Victor, when he came up from the island for a day or two, had so much to occupy him and engage his time, then it was that the youth went into contortions on the lounge and winked mischievously at Edna. She somehow felt like a confederate in crime, and tried to look severe and disapproving.

1. Sparkling.

There had been but two letters from Robert, with little in them they told her. Victor said it was really not worth while to go inside for the letters, when his mother entreated him to go in search of them. He remembered the contents, which in truth he rattled off very glibly when put to the test.

One letter was written from Vera Cruz and the other from the City of Mexico. He had met Montel, who was doing everything toward his advancement. So far, the financial situation was no improvement over the one he had left in New Orleans, but of course the prospects were vastly better. He wrote of the City of Mexico, the buildings, the people and their habits, the conditions of life which he found there. He sent his love to the family. He inclosed a check to his mother, and hoped she would affectionately remember him to all his friends. That was about the substance of the two letters. Edna felt that if there had been a message for her, she would have received it. The despondent frame of mind in which she had left home began again to overtake her, and she remembered that she wished to find Mademoiselle Reisz.

Madame Lebrun knew where Mademoiselle Reisz lived. She gave Edna the address, regretting that she would not consent to stay and spend the remainder of the afternoon, and pay a visit to Mademoiselle Reisz some other day. The afternoon was already well advanced.

Victor escorted her out upon the banquette, lifted her parasol, and held it over her while he walked to the car with her. He entreated her to bear in mind that the disclosures of the afternoon were strictly confidential. She laughed and bantered him a little, remembering too late that she should have been dignified and reserved.

"How handsome Mrs. Pontellier looked!" said Madame Lebrun to her son.

"Ravishing!" he admitted. "The city atmosphere has improved her. Some way she doesn't seem like the same woman."

XXI

Some people contended that the reason Mademoiselle Reisz always chose apartments up under the roof was to discourage the approach of beggars, peddlars and callers. There were plenty of windows in her little front room. They were for the most part dingy, but as they were nearly always open it did not make so much difference. They often admitted into the room a good deal of smoke and soot; but at the same time all the light and air that there was came through them. From her windows could be seen the crescent of the river, the masts of ships and the big chimneys of the Mississippi steamers. A magnificent piano crowded the apartment. In the next room she slept, and in the third and last she harbored a gasoline stove on which she cooked her meals when disinclined to descend to the neighboring restaurant. It was there also that she ate, keeping her belongings in a rare old buffet, dingy and battered from a hundred years of use.

When Edna knocked at Mademoiselle Reisz's front room door and entered, she discovered that person standing beside the window, engaged in mending or patching an old prunella gaiter.[2] The little musician laughed all over when she saw Edna. Her laugh consisted of a contortion of the face

2. A cloth button shoe.

and all the muscles of the body. She seemed strikingly homely, standing there in the afternoon light. She still wore the shabby lace and the artificial bunch of violets on the side of her head.

"So you remembered me at last," said Mademoiselle. "I had said to myself, 'Ah, bah! she will never come.'"

"Did you want me to come?" asked Edna with a smile.

"I had not thought much about it," answered Mademoiselle. The two had seated themselves on a little bumpy sofa which stood against the wall. "I am glad, however, that you came. I have the water boiling back there, and was just about to make some coffee. You will drink a cup with me. And how is *la belle dame*?[3] Always handsome! always healthy! always contented!" She took Edna's hand between her strong wiry fingers, holding it loosely without warmth, and executing a sort of double theme upon the back and palm.

"Yes," she went on; "I sometimes thought: 'She will never come. She promised as those women in society always do, without meaning it. She will not come.' For I really don't believe you like me, Mrs. Pontellier."

"I don't know whether I like you or not," replied Edna, gazing down at the little woman with a quizzical look.

The candor of Mrs. Pontellier's admission greatly pleased Mademoiselle Reisz. She expressed her gratification by repairing forthwith to the region of the gasoline stove and rewarding her guest with the promised cup of coffee. The coffee and the biscuit accompanying it proved very acceptable to Edna, who had declined refreshment at Madame Lebrun's and was now beginning to feel hungry. Mademoiselle set the tray which she brought in upon a small table near at hand, and seated herself once again on the lumpy sofa.

"I have had a letter from your friend," she remarked, as she poured a little cream into Edna's cup and handed it to her.

"My friend?"

"Yes, your friend Robert. He wrote to me from the City of Mexico."

"Wrote to *you*?" repeated Edna in amazement, stirring her coffee absently.

"Yes, to me. Why not? Don't stir all the warmth out of your coffee; drink it. Though the letter might as well have been sent to you; it was nothing but Mrs. Pontellier from beginning to end."

"Let me see it," requested the young woman, entreatingly.

"No; a letter concerns no one but the person who writes it and the one to whom it is written."

"Haven't you just said it concerned me from beginning to end?"

"It was written about you, not to you. 'Have you seen Mrs. Pontellier? How is she looking?' he asks. 'As Mrs. Pontellier says,' or 'as Mrs. Pontellier once said.' 'If Mrs. Pontellier should call upon you, play for her that Impromptu of Chopin's, my favorite. I heard it here a day or two ago, but not as you play it. I should like to know how it affects her,' and so on, as if he supposed we were constantly in each other's society."

"Let me see the letter."

"Oh, no."

"Have you answered it?"

"No."

"Let me see the letter."

3. The lovely lady.

"No, and again, no."

"Then play the Impromptu for me."

"It is growing late; what time do you have to be home?"

"Time doesn't concern me. Your question seems a little rude. Play the Impromptu."

"But you have told me nothing of yourself. What are you doing?"

"Painting!" laughed Edna. "I am becoming an artist. Think of it!"

"Ah! an artist! You have pretensions, Madame."

"Why pretensions? Do you think I could not become an artist?"

"I do not know you well enough to say. I do not know your talent or your temperament. To be an artist includes much; one must possess many gifts—absolute gifts—which have not been acquired by one's own effort. And, moreover, to succeed, the artist must possess the courageous soul."

"What do you mean by the courageous soul?"

"Courageous, *ma foi!*[4] The brave soul. The soul that dares and defies."

"Show me the letter and play for me the Impromptu. You see that I have persistence. Does that quality count for anything in art?"

"It counts with a foolish old woman whom you have captivated," replied Mademoiselle, with her wriggling laugh.

The letter was right there at hand in the drawer of the little table upon which Edna had just placed her coffee cup. Mademoiselle opened the drawer and drew forth the letter, the topmost one. She placed it in Edna's hands, and without further comment arose and went to the piano.

Mademoiselle played a soft interlude. It was an improvisation. She sat low at the instrument, and the lines of her body settled into ungraceful curves and angles that gave it an appearance of deformity. Gradually and imperceptibly the interlude melted into the soft opening minor chords of the Chopin Impromptu.

Edna did not know when the impromptu began or ended. She sat in the sofa corner reading Robert's letter by the fading light. Mademoiselle had glided from the Chopin into the quivering love-notes of Isolde's song,[5] and back again to the Impromptu with its soulful and poignant longing.

The shadows deepened in the little room. The music grew strange and fantastic—turbulent, insistent, plaintive and soft with entreaty. The shadows grew deeper. The music filled the room. It floated out upon the night, over the housetops, the crescent of the river, losing itself in the silence of the upper air.

Edna was sobbing, just as she had wept one midnight at Grand Isle when strange, new voices awoke in her. She arose in some agitation to take her departure. "May I come again, Mademoiselle?" she asked at the threshold.

"Come whenever you feel like it. Be careful; the stairs and landings are dark; don't stumble."

Mademoiselle reëntered and lit a candle. Robert's letter was on the floor. She stooped and picked it up. It was crumpled and damp with tears. Mademoiselle smoothed the letter out, restored it to the envelope, and replaced it in the table drawer.

4. In fact (literally, "my faith").

5. From Richard Wagner's opera *Tristan und Isolde* (1857–59); Isolde sings her *Liebestod* (lit-erally, "love-death"; German) as she bids her dead lover farewell and then dies in his arms.

XXII

One morning on his way into town Mr. Pontellier stopped at the house of his old friend and family physican, Doctor Mandelet. The Doctor was a semi-retired physician, resting, as the saying is, upon his laurels. He bore a reputation for wisdom rather than skill—leaving the active practice of medicine to his assistants and younger contemporaries—and was much sought for in matters of consultation. A few families, united to him by bonds of friendship, he still attended when they required the services of a physician. The Pontelliers were among these.

Mr. Pontellier found the Doctor reading at the open window of his study. His house stood rather far back from the street, in the center of a delightful garden, so that it was quiet and peaceful at the old gentleman's study window. He was a great reader. He stared up disapprovingly over his eyeglasses as Mr. Pontellier entered, wondering who had the temerity to disturb him at that hour of the morning.

"Ah, Pontellier! Not sick, I hope. Come and have a seat. What news do you bring this morning?" He was quite portly, with a profusion of gray hair, and small blue eyes which age had robbed of much of their brightness but none of their penetration.

"Oh! I'm never sick, Doctor. You know that I come of tough fiber—of that old Creole race of Pontelliers that dry up and finally blow away. I come to consult—no, not precisely to consult—to talk to you about Edna. I don't know what ails her."

"Madame Pontellier not well?" marveled the Doctor. "Why I saw her—I think it was a week ago—walking along Canal Street,[6] the picture of health, it seemed to me."

"Yes, yes; she seems quite well," said Mr. Pontellier, leaning forward and whirling his stick between his two hands; "but she doesn't act well. She's odd, she's not like herself. I can't make her out, and I thought perhaps you'd help me."

"How does she act?" inquired the doctor.

"Well, it isn't easy to explain," said Mr. Pontellier, throwing himself back in his chair. "She lets the housekeeping go to the dickens."

"Well, well; women are not all alike, my dear Pontellier. We've got to consider—"

"I know that; I told you I couldn't explain. Her whole attitude—toward me and everybody and everything—has changed. You know I have a quick temper, but I don't want to quarrel or be rude to a woman, especially my wife; yet I'm driven to it, and feel like ten thousand devils after I've made a fool of myself. She's making it devilishly uncomfortable for me," he went on nervously. "She's got some sort of notion in her head concerning the eternal rights of women; and—you understand—we meet in the morning at the breakfast table."

The old gentleman lifted his shaggy eyebrows, protruded his thick nether lip, and tapped the arms of his chair with his cushioned finger-tips.

"What have you been doing to her, Pontellier?"

"Doing! *Parbleu!*"[7]

"Has she," asked the Doctor, with a smile, "has she been associating of

6. The main street of downtown New Orleans. 7. For heaven's sake!

late with a circle of pseudo-intellectual women[8]—superspiritual superior beings? My wife has been telling me about them."

"That's the trouble," broke in Mr. Pontellier, "she hasn't been associating with any one. She has abandoned her Tuesdays at home, has thrown over all her acquaintances, and goes tramping about by herself, moping in the street-cars, getting in after dark. I tell you she's peculiar. I don't like it; I feel a little worried over it."

This was a new aspect for the Doctor. "Nothing hereditary?" he asked, seriously. "Nothing peculiar about her family antecedents, is there?"

"Oh, no, indeed! She comes of sound old Presbyterian Kentucky stock. The old gentleman, her father, I have heard, used to atone for his week-day sins with his Sunday devotions. I know for a fact, that his race horses literally ran away with the prettiest bit of Kentucky farming land I ever laid eyes upon. Margaret—you know Margaret—she has all the Presbyterianism undiluted. And the youngest is something of a vixen. By the way, she gets married in a couple of weeks from now."

"Send your wife up to the wedding," exclaimed the Doctor, foreseeing a happy solution. "Let her stay among her own people for a while; it will do her good."

"That's what I want her to do. She won't go to the marriage. She says a wedding is one of the most lamentable spectacles on earth. Nice thing for a woman to say to her husband!" exclaimed Mr. Pontellier, fuming anew at the recollection.

"Pontellier," said the Doctor, after a moment's reflection, "let your wife alone for a while. Don't bother her, and don't let her bother you. Woman, my dear friend, is a very peculiar and delicate organism—a sensitive and highly organized woman, such as I know Mrs. Pontellier to be, is especially peculiar. It would require an inspired psychologist to deal successfully with them. And when ordinary fellows like you and me attempt to cope with their idiosyncrasies the result is bungling. Most women are moody and whimsical. This is some passing whim of your wife, due to some cause or causes which you and I needn't try to fathom. But it will pass happily over, especially if you let her alone. Send her around to see me."

"Oh! I couldn't do that; there'd be no reason for it," objected Mr. Pontellier.

"Then I'll go around and see her," said the Doctor. "I'll drop in to dinner some evening *en bon ami*."[9]

"Do! by all means," urged Mr. Pontellier. "What evening will you come? Say Thursday. Will you come Thursday?" he asked, rising to take his leave.

"Very well; Thursday. My wife may possibly have some engagement for me Thursday. In case she has, I shall let you know. Otherwise, you may expect me."

Mr. Pontellier turned before leaving to say:

"I am going to New York on business very soon. I have a big scheme on hand, and want to be on the field proper to pull the ropes and handle the ribbons.[1] We'll let you in on the inside if you say so, Doctor," he laughed.

8. Women's clubs flourished during the late nineteenth century in America. They were a source of education for women as well as an arena for political organization. As the Doctor's remark indicates, the club movement was met with scorn in some quarters [Culley's note].
9. Like an old friend.
1. I.e., the reins.

"No, I thank you, my dear sir," returned the Doctor. "I leave such ventures to you younger men with the fever of life still in your blood."

"What I wanted to say," continued Mr. Pontellier, with his hand on the knob; "I may have to be absent a good while. Would you advise me to take Edna along?"

"By all means, if she wishes to go. If not, leave her here. Don't contradict her. The mood will pass, I assure you. It may take a month, two, three months—possibly longer, but it will pass; have patience."

"Well, good-by, à jeudi,"[2] said Mr. Pontellier, as he let himself out.

The Doctor would have liked during the course of conversation to ask, "Is there any man in the case?" but he knew his Creole too well to make such a blunder as that.

He did not resume his book immediately, but sat for a while meditatively looking out into the garden.

XXIII

Edna's father was in the city, and had been with them several days. She was not very warmly or deeply attached to him, but they had certain tastes in common, and when together they were companionable. His coming was in the nature of a welcome disturbance; it seemed to furnish a new direction for her emotions.

He had come to purchase a wedding gift for his daughter, Janet, and an outfit for himself in which he might make a creditable appearance at her marriage. Mr. Pontellier had selected the bridal gift, as every one immediately connected with him always deferred to this taste in such matters. And his suggestions on the question of dress—which too often assumes the nature of a problem—were of inestimable value to his father-in-law. But for the past few days the old gentleman had been upon Edna's hands, and in his society she was becoming acquainted with a new set of sensations. He had been a colonel in the Confederate army, and still maintained, with the title, the military bearing which had always accompanied it. His hair and mustache were white and silky, emphasizing the rugged bronze of his face. He was tall and thin, and wore his coats padded, which gave a fictitious breadth and depth to his shoulders and chest. Edna and her father looked very distinguished together, and excited a good deal of notice during their perambulations. Upon his arrival she began by introducing him to her atelier and making a sketch of him. He took the whole matter very seriously. If her talent had been ten-fold greater than it was, it would not have surprised him, convinced as he was that he had bequeathed to all of his daughters the germs of a masterful capability, which only depended upon their own efforts to be directed toward successful achievement.

Before her pencil he sat rigid and unflinching, as he had faced the cannon's mouth in days gone by. He resented the intrusion of the children, who gaped with wondering eyes at him, sitting so stiff up there in their mother's bright atelier. When they drew near he motioned them away with an expressive action of the foot, loath to disturb the fixed lines of his countenance, his arms, or his rigid shoulders.

2. Until Thursday.

Edna, anxious to entertain him, invited Mademoiselle Reisz to meet him, having promised him a treat in her piano playing; but Mademoiselle declined the invitation. So together they attended a *soirée musicale* at the Ratignolles'. Monsieur and Madame Ratignolle made much of the Colonel, installing him as the guest of honor and engaging him at once to dine with them the following Sunday, or any day which he might select. Madame coquetted with him in the most captivating and naïve manner, with eyes, gestures, and a profusion of compliments, till the Colonel's old head felt thirty years younger on his padded shoulders. Edna marveled, not comprehending. She herself was almost devoid of coquetry.

There were one or two men whom she observed at the *soirée musicale*; but she would never have felt moved to any kittenish display to attract their notice—to any feline or feminine wiles to express herself toward them. Their personality attracted her in an agreeable way. Her fancy selected them, and she was glad when a lull in the music gave them an opportunity to meet her and talk with her. Often on the street the glance of strange eyes had lingered in her memory, and sometimes had disturbed her.

Mr. Pontellier did not attend these *soirées musicales*. He considered them *bourgeois*, and found more diversion at the club. To Madame Ratignolle he said the music dispensed at her *soirées* was "too heavy," too far beyond his untrained comprehension. His excuse flattered her. But she disapproved of Mr. Pontellier's club, and she was frank enough to tell Edna so.

"It's a pity Mr. Pontellier doesn't stay home more in the evenings. I think you would be more—well, if you don't mind my saying it—more united, if he did."

"Oh! dear no!" said Edna, with a blank look in her eyes. "What should I do if he stayed home? We wouldn't have anything to say to each other."

She had not much of anything to say to her father, for that matter; but he did not antagonize her. She discovered that he interested her, though she realized that he might not interest her long; and for the first time in her life she felt as if she were thoroughly acquainted with him. He kept her busy serving him and ministering to his wants. It amused her to do so. She would not permit a servant or one of the children to do anything for him which she might do herself. Her husband noticed, and thought it was the expression of a deep filial attachment which he had never suspected.

The Colonel drank numerous "toddies" during the course of the day, which left him, however, imperturbed. He was an expert at concocting strong drinks. He had even invented some, to which he had given fantastic names, and for whose manufacture he required diverse ingredients that it devolved upon Edna to procure for him.

When Doctor Mandelet dined with the Pontelliers on Thursday he could discern in Mrs. Pontellier no trace of that morbid condition which her husband had reported to him. She was excited and in a manner radiant. She and her father had been to the race course, and their thoughts when they seated themselves at table were still occupied with the events of the afternoon, and their talk was still of the track. The Doctor had not kept pace with turf affairs. He had certain recollections of racing in what he called "the good old times" when the Lecompte stables flourished,[3] and he drew upon

3. New Orleans had been a celebrated racing center before the Civil War.

this fund of memories so that he might not be left out and seem wholly devoid of the modern spirit. But he failed to impose upon the Colonel, and was even far from impressing him with this trumped-up knowledge of bygone days. Edna had staked her father on his last venture, with the most gratifying results to both of them. Besides, they had met some very charming people, according to the Colonel's impressions. Mrs. Mortimer Merriman and Mrs. James Highcamp, who were there with Alcée Arobin, had joined them and had enlivened the hours in a fashion that warmed him to think of.

Mr. Pontellier himself had no particular leaning toward horse-racing, and was even rather inclined to discourage it as a pastime, especially when he considered the fate of that blue-grass farm in Kentucky. He endeavored, in a general way, to express a particular disapproval, and only succeeded in arousing the ire and opposition of his father-in-law. A pretty dispute followed in which Edna warmly espoused her father's cause and the Doctor remained neutral.

He observed his hostess attentively from under his shaggy brows, and noted a subtle change which had transformed her from the listless woman he had known into a being who, for the moment, seemed palpitant with the forces of life. Her speech was warm and energetic. There was no repression in her glance or gesture. She reminded him of some beautiful, sleek animal waking up in the sun.

The dinner was excellent. The claret was warm and the champagne was cold, and under their beneficent influence the threatened unpleasantness melted and vanished with the fumes of the wine.

Mr. Pontellier warmed up and grew reminiscent. He told some amusing plantation experiences, recollections of old Iberville and his youth, when he hunted 'possum in company with some friendly darky; thrashed the pecan trees, shot the grosbec,[4] and roamed the woods and fields in mischievous idleness.

The Colonel, with little sense of humor and of the fitness of things, related a somber episode of those dark and bitter days, in which he had acted a conspicuous part and always formed a central figure. Nor was the Doctor happier in his selection, when he told the old, ever new and curious story of the waning of a woman's love, seeking strange, new channels, only to return to its legitimate source after days of fierce unrest. It was one of the many little human documents which had been unfolded to him during his long career as a physician. The story did not seem especially to impress Edna. She had one of her own to tell, of a woman who paddled away with her lover one night in a pirogue and never came back. They were lost amid the Baratarian Islands, and no one ever heard of them or found trace of them from that day to this. It was a pure invention. She said that Madame Antoine had related it to her. That, also, was an invention. Perhaps it was a dream she had had. But every glowing word seemed real to those who listened. They could feel the hot breath of the Southern night; they could hear the long sweep of the pirogue through the glistening moonlit water, the beating of birds' wings, rising startled from among the reeds in the salt-water pools; they could see the faces of the lovers, pale, close together, rapt in oblivious forgetfulness, drifting into the unknown.

4. I.e., grosbeak, game birds with large bill (*gros bec*).

The champagne was cold, and its subtle fumes played fantastic tricks with Edna's memory that night.

Outside, away from the glow of the fire and the soft lamplight, the night was chill and murky. The Doctor doubled his old-fashioned cloak across his breast as he strode home through the darkness. He knew his fellow-creatures better than most men; knew that inner life which so seldom unfolds itself to unanointed eyes. He was sorry he had accepted Pontellier's invitation. He was growing old, and beginning to need rest and an imperturbed spirit. He did not want the secrets of other lives thrust upon him.

"I hope it isn't Arobin," he muttered to himself as he walked. "I hope to heaven it isn't Alcée Arobin."

XXIV

Edna and her father had a warm, and almost violent dispute upon the subject of her refusal to attend her sister's wedding. Mr. Pontellier declined to interfere, to interpose either his influence or his authority. He was following Doctor Mandelet's advice, and letting her do as she liked. The Colonel reproached his daughter for her lack of filial kindness and respect, her want of sisterly affection and womanly consideration. His arguments were labored and unconvincing. He doubted if Janet would accept any excuse—forgetting that Edna had offered none. He doubted if Janet would ever speak to her again, and he was sure Margaret would not.

Edna was glad to be rid of her father when he finally took himself off with his wedding garments and his bridal gifts, with his padded shoulders, his Bible reading, his "toddies" and ponderous oaths.

Mr. Pontellier followed him closely. He meant to stop at the wedding on his way to New York and endeavor by every means which money and love could devise to atone somewhat for Edna's incomprehensible action.

"You are too lenient, too lenient by far, Léonce," asserted the Colonel. "Authority, coercion are what is needed. Put your foot down good and hard; the only way to manage a wife. Take my word for it."

The Colonel was perhaps unaware that he had coerced his own wife into her grave. Mr. Pontellier had a vague suspicion of it which he thought it needless to mention at that late day.

Edna was not so consciously gratified at her husband's leaving home as she had been over the departure of her father. As the day approached when he was to leave her for a comparatively long stay, she grew melting and affectionate, remembering his many acts of consideration and his repeated expressions of an ardent attachment. She was solicitous about his health and his welfare. She bustled around, looking after his clothing, thinking about heavy underwear, quite as Madame Ratignolle would have done under similar circumstances. She cried when he went away, calling him her dear, good friend, and she was quite certain she would grow lonely before very long and go to join him in New York.

But after all, a radiant peace settled upon her when she at last found herself alone. Even the children were gone. Old Madame Pontellier had come herself and carried them off to Iberville with their quadroon. The old madame did not venture to say she was afraid they would be neglected during Léonce's absence; she hardly ventured to think so. She was hungry for

them—even a little fierce in her attachment. She did not want them to be wholly "children of the pavement," she always said when begging to have them for a space. She wished them to know the country, with its streams, its fields, its woods, its freedom, so delicious to the young. She wished them to taste something of the life their father had lived and known and loved when he, too, was a little child.

When Edna was at last alone, she breathed a big, genuine sigh of relief. A feeling that was unfamiliar but very delicious came over her. She walked all through the house, from one room to another, as if inspecting it for the first time. She tried the various chairs and lounges, as if she had never sat and reclined upon them before. And she perambulated around the outside of the house, investigating, looking to see if windows and shutters were secure and in order. The flowers were like new acquaintances; she approached them in a familiar spirit, and made herself at home among them. The garden walks were damp, and Edna called to the maid to bring out her rubber sandals. And there she stayed, and stooped, digging around the plants, trimming, picking dead, dry leaves. The children's little dog came out, interfering, getting in her way. She scolded him, laughing at him, played with him. The garden smelled so good and looked so pretty in the afternoon sunlight. Edna plucked all the bright flowers she could find, and went into the house with them, she and the little dog.

Even the kitchen assumed a sudden interesting character which she had never before perceived. She went in to give directions to the cook, to say that the butcher would have to bring much less meat, that they would require only half their usual quantity of bread, of milk and groceries. She told the cook that she herself would be greatly occupied during Mr. Pontellier's absence, and she begged her to take all thought and responsibility of the larder upon her own shoulders.

That night Edna dined alone. The candelabra, with a few candles in the center of the table, gave all the light she needed. Outside the circle of light in which she sat, the large dining-room looked solemn and shadowy. The cook, placed upon her mettle, served a delicious repast—a luscious tenderloin broiled à point. The wine tasted good; the marron glacé[5] seemed to be just what she wanted. It was so pleasant, too, to dine in a comfortable *peignoir*.

She thought a little sentimentally about Léonce and the children, and wondered what they were doing. As she gave a dainty scrap or two to the doggie, she talked intimately to him about Étienne and Raoul. He was beside himself with astonishment and delight over these companionable advances, and showed his appreciation by his little quick, snappy barks and a lively agitation.

Then Edna sat in the library after dinner and read Emerson[6] until she grew sleepy. She realized that she had neglected her reading, and determined to start anew upon a course of improving studies, now that her time was completely her own to do with as she liked.

After a refreshing bath, Edna went to bed. And as she snuggled comfort-

5. Glazed chestnuts. "À point": to a turn.
6. Ralph Waldo Emerson (1803–1882), American philosopher, essayist, and poet, whose works

emphasize individual intuition and the rejection of traditional authority.

ably beneath the eiderdown a sense of restfulness invaded her, such as she had not known before.

XXV

When the weather was dark and cloudy Edna could not work. She needed the sun to mellow and temper her mood to the sticking point. She had reached a stage when she seemed to be no longer feeling her way, working, when in the humor, with sureness and ease. And being devoid of ambition, and striving not toward accomplishment, she drew satisfaction from the work in itself.

On rainy or melancholy days Edna went out and sought the society of the friends she had made at Grand Isle. Or else she stayed indoors and nursed a mood with which she was becoming too familiar for her own comfort and peace of mind. It was not despair; but it seemed to her as if life were passing by, leaving its promise broken and unfulfilled. Yet there were other days when she listened, was led on and deceived by fresh promises which her youth held out to her.

She went again to the races, and again. Alcée Arobin and Mrs. Highcamp called for her one bright afternoon in Arobin's drag.[7]

Mrs. Highcamp was a worldly but unaffected, intelligent, slim, tall blonde woman in the forties, with an indifferent manner and blue eyes that stared. She had a daughter who served her as a pretext for cultivating the society of young men of fashion. Alcée Arobin was one of them. He was a familiar figure at the race course, the opera, the fashionable clubs. There was a perpetual smile in his eyes, which seldom failed to awaken a corresponding cheerfulness in any one who looked into them and listened to his good-humored voice. His manner was quiet, and at times a little insolent. He possessed a good figure, a pleasing face, not overburdened with depth of thought or feeling; and his dress was that of the conventional man of fashion.

He admired Edna extravagantly, after meeting her at the races with her father. He had met her before on other occasions, but she had seemed to him unapproachable until that day. It was at his instigation that Mrs. Highcamp called to ask her to go with them to the Jockey Club[8] to witness the turf event of the season.

There were possibly a few track men out there who knew the race horse as well as Edna, but there was certainly none who knew it better. She sat between her two companions as one having authority to speak. She laughed at Arobin's pretensions, and deplored Mrs. Highcamp's ignorance. The race horse was a friend and intimate associate of her childhood. The atmosphere of the stables and the breath of the blue grass paddock revived in her memory and lingered in her nostrils. She did not perceive that she was talking like her father as the sleek geldings ambled in review before them. She played for very high stakes, and fortune favored her. The fever of the game flamed in her cheeks and eyes, and it got into her blood and into her brain like an intoxicant. People turned their heads to look at her, and more than one lent an attentive ear to her utterances, hoping thereby to secure the elusive but ever-desired "tip." Arobin caught the contagion of excitement which drew

7. Heavy coach. 8. The exclusive New Louisiana Jockey Club.

him to Edna like a magnet. Mrs. Highcamp remained, as usual, unmoved, with her indifferent stare and uplifted eyebrows.

Edna stayed and dined with Mrs. Highcamp upon being urged to do so. Arobin also remained and sent away his drag.

The dinner was quiet and uninteresting, save for the cheerful efforts of Arobin to enliven things. Mrs. Highcamp deplored the absence of her daughter from the races, and tried to convey to her what she had missed by going to the "Dante reading" instead of joining them.[9] The girl held a geranium leaf up to her nose and said nothing, but looked knowing and noncommittal. Mr. Highcamp was a plain, bald-headed man, who only talked under compulsion. He was unresponsive. Mrs. Highcamp was full of delicate courtesy and consideration toward her husband. She addressed most of her conversation to him at table. They sat in the library after dinner and read the evening papers together under the drop-light;[1] while the younger people went into the drawing-room near by and talked. Miss Highcamp played some selections from Grieg[2] upon the piano. She seemed to have apprehended all of the composer's coldness and none of his poetry. While Edna listened she could not help wondering if she had lost her taste for music.

When the time came for her to go home, Mr. Highcamp grunted a lame offer to escort her, looking down at his slippered feet with tactless concern. It was Arobin who took her home. The car ride was long, and it was late when they reached Esplanade Street. Arobin asked permission to enter for a second to light his cigarette—his match safe[3] was empty. He filled his match safe, but did not light his cigarette until he left her, after she had expressed her willingness to go to the races with him again.

Edna was neither tired nor sleepy. She was hungry again, for the Highcamp dinner, though of excellent quality, had lacked abundance. She rummaged in the larder and brought forth a slice of "Gruyère"[4] and some crackers. She opened a bottle of beer which she found in the ice-box. Edna felt extremely restless and excited. She vacantly hummed a fantastic tune as she poked at the wood embers on the hearth and munched a cracker.

She wanted something to happen—something, anything; she did not know what. She regretted that she had not made Arobin stay a half hour to talk over the horses with her. She counted the money she had won. But there was nothing else to do, so she went to bed, and tossed there for hours in a sort of monotonous agitation.

In the middle of the night she remembered that she had forgotten to write her regular letter to her husband; and she decided to do so next day and tell him about her afternoon at the Jockey Club. She lay wide awake composing a letter which was nothing like the one which she wrote the next day. When the maid awoke her in the morning Edna was dreaming of Mr. Highcamp playing the piano at the entrance of a music store on Canal Street, while his wife was saying to Alcée Arobin, as they boarded an Esplanade Street car:

"What a pity that so much talent has been neglected! but I must go."

When a few days later, Alcée Arobin again called for Edna in his drag,

9. I.e., her daughter preferred intellectual activities. Dante Alighieri (1265–1321), Italian poet, wrote *The Divine Comedy*.
1. Gas lamp that could be lowered for reading.
2. Edvard Grieg (1843–1907), Norwegian composer.
3. I.e., matchbox.
4. A cheese originally made in Gruyère, a district in Switzerland.

Mrs. Highcamp was not with him. He said they would pick her up. But as the lady had not been apprised of his intention of picking her up, she was not at home. The daughter was just leaving the house to attend the meeting of a branch Folk Lore Society,[5] and regretted that she could not accompany them. Arobin appeared nonplused, and asked Edna if there were any one else she cared to ask.

She did not deem it worthwhile to go in search of any of the fashionable acquaintances from whom she had withdrawn herself. She thought of Madame Ratignolle, but knew that her fair friend did not leave the house, except to take a languid walk around the block with her husband after nightfall. Mademoiselle Reisz would have laughed at such a request from Edna. Madame Lebrun might have enjoyed the outing, but for some reason Edna did not want her. So they went alone, she and Arobin.

The afternoon was intensely interesting to her. The excitement came back upon her like a remittent fever. Her talk grew familiar and confidential. It was no labor to become intimate with Arobin. His manner invited easy confidence. The preliminary stage of becoming acquainted was one which he always endeavored to ignore when a pretty and engaging woman was concerned.

He stayed and dined with Edna. He stayed and sat beside the wood fire. They laughed and talked; and before it was time to go he was telling her how different life might have been if he had known her years before. With ingenuous frankness he spoke of what a wicked, ill-disciplined boy he had been, and impulsively drew up his cuff to exhibit upon his wrist the scar from a saber cut which he had received in a duel outside of Paris when he was nineteen. She touched his hand as she scanned the red cicatrice[6] on the inside of his white wrist. A quick impulse that was somewhat spasmodic impelled her fingers to close in a sort of clutch upon his hand. He felt the pressure of her pointed nails in the flesh of his palm.

She arose hastily and walked toward the mantel.

"The sight of a wound or scar always agitates and sickens me," she said. "I shouldn't have looked at it."

"I beg your pardon," he entreated, following her; "it never occurred to me that it might be repulsive."

He stood close to her, and the effrontery in his eyes repelled the old, vanishing self in her, yet drew all her awakening sensousness. He saw enough in her face to impel him to take her hand and hold it while he said his lingering good night.

"Will you go to the races again?" he asked.

"No," she said. "I've had enough of the races. I don't want to lose all the money I've won, and I've got to work when the weather is bright, instead of—"

"Yes; work; to be sure. You promised to show me your work. What morning may I come up to your atelier? To-morrow?"

"No!"

"Day after?"

"No, no."

5. The New Orleans Association of the American 6. Scar.
Folklore Society.

"Oh, please don't refuse me! I know something of such things, I might help you with a stray suggestion or two."

"No. Good night. Why don't you go after you have said good night? I don't like you," she went on in a high, excited pitch, attempting to draw away her hand. She felt that her words lacked dignity and sincerity, and she knew that he felt it.

"I'm sorry you don't like me. I'm sorry I offended you. How have I offended you? What have I done? Can't you forgive me?" And he bent and pressed his lips upon her hand as if he wished never more to withdraw them.

"Mr. Arobin," she complained, "I'm greatly upset by the excitement of the afternoon; I'm not myself. My manner must have misled you in some way. I wish you to go, please." She spoke in a monotonous, dull tone. He took his hat from the table, and stood with eyes turned from her, looking into the dying fire. For a moment or two he kept an impressive silence.

"Your manner has not misled me, Mrs. Pontellier," he said finally. "My own emotions have done that. I couldn't help it. When I'm near you, how could I help it? Don't think anything of it, don't bother, please. You see, I go when you command me. If you wish me to stay away, I shall do so. If you let me come back, I—oh! you will let me come back?"

He cast one appealing glance at her, to which she made no response. Alcée Arobin's manner was so genuine that it often deceived even himself.

Edna did not care or think whether it were genuine or not. When she was alone she looked mechanically at the back of her hand which he had kissed so warmly. Then she leaned her head down on the mantelpiece. She felt somewhat like a woman who in a moment of passion is betrayed into an act of infidelity, and realizes the significance of the act without being wholly awakened from its glamour. The thought was passing vaguely through her mind, "what would he think?"

She did not mean her husband; she was thinking of Robert Lebrun. Her husband seemed to her now like a person whom she had married without love as an excuse.

She lit a candle and went up to her room. Alcée Arobin was absolutely nothing to her. Yet his presence, his manners, the warmth of his glances, and above all the touch of his lips upon her hand had acted like a narcotic upon her.

She slept a languorous sleep, interwoven with vanishing dreams.

XXVI

Alcée Arobin wrote Edna an elaborate note of apology, palpitant with sincerity. It embarrassed her; for in a cooler, quieter moment it appeared to her absurd that she should have taken his action so seriously, so dramatically. She felt sure that the significance of the whole occurrence had lain in her own self-consciousness. If she ignored his note it would give undue importance to a trivial affair. If she replied to it in a serious spirit it would still leave in his mind the impression that she had in a susceptible moment yielded to his influence. After all, it was no great matter to have one's hand kissed. She was provoked at his having written the apology. She answered in as light and bantering a spirit as she fancied it deserved, and said she would

be glad to have him look in upon her at work whenever he felt the inclination and his business gave him the opportunity.

He responded at once by presenting himself at her home with all his disarming naïveté. And then there was scarcely a day which followed that she did not see him or was not reminded of him. He was prolific in pretexts. His attitude became one of good-humored subservience and tacit adoration. He was ready at all times to submit to her moods, which were as often kind as they were cold. She grew accustomed to him. They became intimate and friendly by imperceptible degrees, and then by leaps. He sometimes talked in a way that astonished her at first and brought the crimson into her face; in a way that pleased her at last, appealing to the animalism that stirred impatiently within her.

There was nothing which so quieted the turmoil of Edna's senses as a visit to Mademoiselle Reisz. It was then, in the presence of that personality which was offensive to her, that the woman, by her divine art, seemed to reach Edna's spirit and set it free.

It was misty, with heavy, lowering atmosphere, one afternoon, when Edna climbed the stairs to the pianist's apartments under the roof. Her clothes were dripping with moisture. She felt chilled and pinched as she entered the room. Mademoiselle was poking at a rusty stove that smoked a little and warmed the room indifferently. She was endeavoring to heat a pot of chocolate on the stove. The room looked cheerless and dingy to Edna as she entered. A bust of Beethoven, covered with a hood of dust, scowled at her from the mantelpiece.

"Ah! here comes the sunlight!" exclaimed Mademoiselle, rising from her knees before the stove. "Now it will be warm and bright enough; I can let the fire alone."

She closed the stove door with a bang, and approaching assisted in removing Edna's dripping mackintosh.

"You are cold; you look miserable. The chocolate will soon be hot. But would you rather have a taste of brandy? I have scarcely touched the bottle which you brought me for my cold." A piece of red flannel was wrapped around Mademoiselle's throat; a stiff neck compelled her to hold her head on one side.

"I will take some brandy," said Edna, shivering as she removed her gloves and overshoes. She drank the liquor from the glass as a man would have done. Then flinging herself upon the uncomfortable sofa she said, "Mademoiselle, I am going to move away from my house on Esplanade Street."

"Ah!" ejaculated the musician, neither surprised nor especially interested. Nothing ever seemed to astonish her very much. She was endeavoring to adjust the bunch of violets which had become loose from its fastening in her hair. Edna drew her down upon the sofa and taking a pin from her own hair, secured the shabby artificial flowers in their accustomed place.

"Aren't you astonished?"

"Passably. Where are you going? To New York? to Iberville? to your father in Mississippi? where?"

"Just two steps away," laughed Edna, "in a little four-room house around the corner. It looks so cozy, so inviting and restful, whenever I pass by; and it's for rent. I'm tired looking after that big house. It never seemed like mine,

anyway—like home. It's too much trouble. I have to keep too many servants. I am tired bothering with them."

"That is not your true reason, *ma belle*.[7] There is no use in telling me lies. I don't know your reason, but you have not told me the truth." Edna did not protest or endeavor to justify herself.

"The house, the money that provides for it, are not mine. Isn't that enough reason?"

"They are your husband's," returned Mademoiselle, with a shrug and a malicious elevation of the eyebrows.

"Oh! I see there is no deceiving you. Then let me tell you: it is a caprice. I have a little money of my own from my mother's estate, which my father sends me by driblets. I won a large sum this winter on the races, and I am beginning to sell my sketches. Laidpore is more and more pleased with my work; he says it grows in force and individuality. I cannot judge of that myself, but feel that I have gained in ease and confidence. However, as I said, I have sold a good many through Laidpore. I can live in the tiny house for little or nothing, with one servant. Old Celestine, who works occasionally for me, says she will come stay with me and do my work. I know I shall like it, like the feeling of freedom and independence.

"What does your husband say?"

"I have not told him yet. I only thought of it this morning. He will think I am demented, no doubt. Perhaps you think so."

Mademoiselle shook her head slowly. "Your reason is not yet clear to me," she said.

Neither was it quite clear to Edna herself; but it unfolded itself as she sat for a while in silence. Instinct had prompted her to put away her husband's bounty in casting off her allegiance. She did not know how it would be when he returned. There would have to be an understanding, an explanation. Conditions would some way adjust themselves, she felt, but whatever came, she had resolved never again to belong to another than herself.

"I shall give a grand dinner before I leave the old house!" Edna exclaimed. "You will have to come to it, Mademoiselle. I will give you everything that you like to eat and to drink. We shall sing and laugh and be merry for once." And she uttered a sigh that came from the very depth of her being.

If Mademoiselle happened to have received a letter from Robert during the interval of Edna's visits, she would give her the letter unsolicited. And she would seat herself at the piano and play as her humor prompted her while the young woman read the letter.

The little stove was roaring; it was red-hot, and the chocolate in the tin sizzled and sputtered. Edna went forward and opened the stove door, and Mademoiselle rising took a letter from under the bust of Beethoven and handed it to Edna.

"Another! so soon!" she exclaimed, her eyes filled with delight. "Tell me, Mademoiselle, does he know that I see his letters?"

"Never in the world! He would be angry and would never write to me again if he thought so. Does he write to you? Never a line. Does he send you a message? Never a word. It is because he loves you, poor fool, and is trying to forget you, since you are not free to listen to him or to belong to him."

7. My pretty.

"Why do you show me his letters, then?"

"Haven't you begged for them? Can I refuse you anything? Oh! you cannot deceive me," and Mademoiselle approached her beloved instrument and began to play. Edna did not at once read the letter. She sat holding it in her hand, while the music penetrated her whole being like an effulgence, warming and brightening the dark places of her soul. It prepared her for joy and exultation.

"Oh!" she exclaimed, letting the letter fall to the floor. "Why did you not tell me?" She went and grasped Mademoiselle's hands up from the keys. "Oh! unkind! malicious! Why did you not tell me?"

"That he was coming back? No great news, *ma foi*. I wonder he did not come long ago."

"But when, when?" cried Edna, impatiently. "He does not say when."

"He says 'very soon.' You know as much about it as I do, it is all in the letter."

"But why? Why is he coming? Oh, if I thought—" and she snatched the letters from the floor and turned the pages this way and that way, looking for the reason, which was left untold.

"If I were young and in love with a man," said Mademoiselle, turning on the stool and pressing her wiry hands between her knees as she looked down at Edna, who sat on the floor holding the letter, "it seems to me he would have to be some *grand esprit*,[8] a man with lofty aims and ability to reach them; one who stood high enough to attract the notice of his fellow-men. It seems to me if I were young and in love I should never deem a man of ordinary caliber worthy of my devotion."

"Now it is you who are telling lies and seeking to deceive me, Mademoiselle; or else you have never been in love, and know nothing about it. Why," went on Edna, clasping her knees and looking up into Mademoiselle's twisted face, "do you suppose a woman knows why she loves? Does she select? Does she say to herself: 'Go to! Here is a distinguished statesman with presidential possibilities: I shall proceed to fall in love with him.' Or, 'I shall set my heart upon this musician, whose fame is on every tongue?' Or, 'This financier, who controls the world's money markets?' "

"You are purposely misunderstanding me, *ma reine*.[9] Are you in love with Robert?"

"Yes," said Edna. It was the first time she had admitted it, and a glow overspread her face, blotching it with red spots.

"Why?" asked her companion. "Why do you love him when you ought not to?"

Edna, with a motion or two, dragged herself on her knees before Mademoiselle Reisz, who took the glowing face between her two hands.

"Why? Because his hair is brown and grows away from his temples; because he opens and shuts his eyes, and his nose is a little out of drawing; because he has two lips and a square chin, and a little finger which he can't straighten from having played baseball too energetically in his youth. Because—"

"Because you do, in short," laughed Mademoiselle. "What will you do when he comes back?" she asked.

8. Noble soul (literally, "grand spirit").　　　9. My queen.

"Do? Nothing, except feel glad and happy to be alive."

She was already glad and happy to be alive at the mere thought of his return. The murky, lowering sky, which had depressed her a few hours before, seemed bracing and invigorating as she splashed through the streets on her way home.

She stopped at a confectioner's and ordered a huge box of bonbons for the children in Iberville. She slipped a card in the box, on which she scribbled a tender message and sent an abundance of kisses.

Before dinner in the evening Edna wrote a charming letter to her husband, telling him of her intention to move for a while into the little house around the block, and to give a farewell dinner before leaving, regretting that he was not there to share it, to help her out with the menu and assist her in entertaining the guests. Her letter was brilliant and brimming with cheerfulness.

XXVII

"What is the matter with you?" asked Arobin that evening. "I never found you in such a happy mood." Edna was tired by that time, and was reclining on the lounge before the fire.

"Don't you know the weather prophet has told us we shall see the sun pretty soon?"

"Well, that ought to be reason enough," he acquiesced. "You wouldn't give me another if I sat here all night imploring you." He sat close to her on a low tabouret,[1] and as he spoke his fingers lightly touched the hair that fell a little over her forehead. She liked the touch of his fingers through her hair, and closed her eyes sensitively.

"One of these days," she said, "I'm going to pull myself together for a while and think—try to determine what character of a woman I am; for, candidly, I don't know. By all the codes which I am acquainted with, I am a devilishly wicked specimen of the sex. But some way I can't convince myself that I am. I must think about it."

"Don't. What's the use? Why should you bother thinking about it when I can tell you what manner of woman you are?" His fingers strayed occasionally down to her warm, smooth cheeks and firm chin, which was growing a little full and double.

"Oh, yes! You will tell me that I am adorable; everything that is captivating. Spare yourself the effort."

"No; I shan't tell you anything of the sort, though I shouldn't be lying if I did."

"Do you know Mademoiselle Reisz?" she asked irrelevantly.

"The pianist? I know her by sight. I've heard her play."

"She says queer things sometimes in a bantering way that you don't notice at the time and you feel yourself thinking about afterward."

"For instance?"

"Well, for instance, when I left her today, she put her arms around me and felt my shoulder blades, to see if my wings were strong, she said. 'The bird that would soar above the level plain of tradition and prejudice must have strong wings. It is a sad spectacle to see the weaklings bruised, exhausted, fluttering back to earth.' "

1. Cylindrical stool.

"Whither would you soar?"

"I'm not thinking of any extraordinary flights. I only half comprehend her."

"I've heard she's partially demented," said Arobin.

"She seems to me wonderfully sane," Edna replied.

"I'm told she's extremely disagreeable and unpleasant. Why have you introduced her at a moment when I desired to talk of you?"

"Oh! talk of me if you like," cried Edna, clasping her hands beneath her head; "but let me think of something else while you do."

"I'm jealous of your thoughts to-night. They're making you a little kinder than usual; but some way I feel as if they were wandering, as if they were not here with me." She only looked at him and smiled. His eyes were very near. He leaned upon the lounge with an arm extended across her, while the other hand still rested upon her hair. They continued silently to look into each other's eyes. When he leaned forward and kissed her, she clasped his head, holding his lips to hers.

It was the first kiss of her life to which her nature had really responded. It was a flaming torch that kindled desire.

XXVIII

Edna cried a little that night after Arobin left her. It was only one phase of the multitudinous emotions which had assailed her. There was with her an overwhelming feeling of irresponsibility. There was the shock of the unexpected and the unaccustomed. There was her husband's reproach looking at her from external existence. There was Robert's reproach making itself felt by a quicker, fiercer, more overpowering love, which had awakened within her toward him. Above all, there was understanding. She felt as if a mist had been lifted from her eyes, enabling her to look upon and comprehend the significance of life, that monster made up of beauty and brutality. But among the conflicting sensations which assailed her, there was neither shame nor remorse. There was a dull pang of regret because it was not the kiss of love which had inflamed her, because it was not love which had held this cup of life to her lips.

XXIX

Without even waiting for an answer from her husband regarding his opinion or wishes in the matter, Edna hastened her preparations for quitting her home on Esplanade Street and moving into the little house around the block. A feverish anxiety attended her every action in that direction. There was no moment of deliberation, no interval of repose between the thought and its fulfillment. Early upon the morning following those hours passed in Arobin's society, Edna set about securing her new abode and hurrying her arrangements for occupying it. Within the precincts of her home she felt like one who has entered and lingered within the portals of some forbidden temple in which a thousand muffled voices bade her begone.

Whatever was her own in the house, everything which she had acquired aside from her husband's bounty, she caused to be transported to the other house, supplying simple and meager deficiencies from her own resources.

Arobin found her with rolled sleeves, working in company with the housemaid when he looked in during the afternoon. She was splendid and robust,

and had never appeared handsomer than in the old blue gown, with a red silk handkerchief knotted at random around her head to protect her hair from the dust. She was mounted upon a high step-ladder, unhooking a picture from the wall when he entered. He had found the front door open, and had followed his ring by walking in unceremoniously.

"Come down!" he said. "Do you want to kill yourself?" She greeted him with affected carelessness, and appeared absorbed in her occupation.

If he had expected to find her languishing, reproachful, or indulging in sentimental tears, he must have been greatly surprised.

He was no doubt prepared for any emergency, ready for any one of the foregoing attitudes, just as he bent himself easily and naturally to the situation which confronted him.

"Please come down," he insisted, holding the ladder and looking up at her.

"No," she answered; "Ellen is afraid to mount the ladder. Joe is working at the 'pigeon house'—that's the name Ellen gives it, because it's so small and looks like a pigeon house—and some one has to do this."

Arobin pulled off his coat, and expressed himself ready and willing to tempt fate in her place. Ellen brought him one of her dustcaps, and went into contortions of mirth, which she found it impossible to control, which she saw him put it on before the mirror as grotesquely as he could. Edna herself could not refrain from smiling when she fastened it at his request. So it was he who in turn mounted the ladder, unhooking pictures and curtains, and dislodging ornaments as Edna directed. When he had finished he took off his dustcap and went out to wash his hands.

Edna was sitting on the tabouret, idly brushing the tips of a feather duster along the carpet when he came in again.

"Is there anything more you will let me do?" he asked.

"That is all," she answered. "Ellen can manage the rest." She kept the young woman occupied in the drawing-room, unwilling to be left alone with Arobin.

"What about the dinner?" he asked; "the grand event, the *coup d'état?*"

"It will be day after to-morrow. Why do you call it the '*coup d'état?*' Oh! it will be very fine; all my best of everything—crystal, silver and gold. Sèvres, flowers, music, and champagne to swim in. I'll let Léonce pay the bills. I wonder what he'll say when he sees the bills."

"And you ask me why I call it a *coup d'état?*" Arobin had put on his coat, and he stood before her and asked if his cravat was plumb. She told him it was, looking no higher than the tip of his collar.

"When do you go to the 'pigeon house?'—with all due acknowledgement to Ellen."

"Day after to-morrow, after the dinner. I shall sleep there."

"Ellen, will you very kindly get me a glass of water?" asked Arobin. "The dust in the curtains, if you will pardon me for hinting such a thing, has parched my throat to a crisp."

"While Ellen gets the water," said Edna, rising, "I will say good-by and let you go. I must get rid of this grime, and I have a million things to do and think of."

"When shall I see you?" asked Arobin, seeking to detain her, the maid having left the room.

"At the dinner, of course. You are invited."

"Not before?—not to-night or to-morrow morning or to-morrow noon or night? or the day after morning or noon? Can't you see yourself, without my telling you, what an eternity it is?"

He had followed her into the hall and to the foot of the stairway looking up at her as she mounted with her face half turned to him.

"Not an instant sooner," she said. But she laughed and looked at him with eyes that at once gave him courage to wait and made it torture to wait.

XXX

Though Edna had spoken of the dinner as a very grand affair, it was in truth a very small affair and very select, in so much as the invited were few and were selected with discrimination. She had counted upon an even dozen seating themselves at her round mahogany board, forgetting for the moment that Madame Ratignolle was to the last degree *souffrante*[2] and unpresentable, and not foreseeing that Madame Lebrun would send a thousand regrets at the last moment. So there were only ten, after all, which made a cozy, comfortable number.

There were Mr. and Mrs. Merriman, a pretty vivacious little woman in the thirties; her husband, a jovial fellow, something of a shallow-pate,[3] who laughed a good deal at other people's witticisms, and had thereby made himself extremely popular. Mrs. Highcamp had accompanied them. Of course, there was Alcée Arobin; and Mademoiselle Reisz had consented to come. Edna had sent her a fresh bunch of violets with black lace trimmings for her hair. Monsieur Ratignolle brought himself and his wife's excuses. Victor Lebrun, who happened to be in the city, bent upon relaxation, had accepted with alacrity. There was a Miss Mayblunt, no longer in her teens, who looked at the world through lorgnettes and with the keenest interest. It was thought and said that she was intellectual; it was suspected of her that she wrote under a *nom de guerre*.[4] She had come with a gentleman by the name of Gouvernail, connected with one of the daily papers, of whom nothing special could be said, except that he was observant and seemed quiet and inoffensive. Edna herself made the tenth, and at half-past eight they seated themselves at table, Arobin and Monsieur Ratignolle on either side of their hostess.

Mrs. Highcamp sat between Arobin and Victor Lebrun. Then came Mrs. Merriman, Mr. Gouvernail, Miss Mayblunt, Mr. Merriman, and Mademoiselle Reisz next to Monsieur Ratignolle.

There was something extremely gorgeous about the appearance of the table, an effect of splendor conveyed by a cover of pale yellow satin under strips of lace-work. There were wax candles in massive brass candelabra, burning softly under yellow silk shades; full, fragrant roses, yellow and red, abounded. There were silver and gold, as she had said there would be, and crystal which glittered like the gems which the women wore.

The ordinary stiff dining chairs had been discarded for the occasion and replaced by the most commodious and luxurious which could be collected throughout the house. Mademoiselle Reisz, being exceedingly diminutive,

2. Ill.
3. I.e., shallow-minded.

4. Pseudonym (usually nom de plume, for writers).

was elevated upon cushions, as small children are sometimes hoisted at table upon bulky volumes.

"Something new, Edna?" exclaimed Miss Mayblunt, with lorgnette directed toward a magnificent cluster of diamonds that sparkled, that almost sputtered, in Edna's hair, just over the center of her forehead.

"Quite new; 'brand' new, in fact; a present from my husband. It arrived this morning from New York. I may as well admit that this is my birthday, and that I am twenty-nine. In good time I expect you to drink my health. Meanwhile, I shall ask you to begin with this cocktail, composed—would you say 'composed?' " with an appeal to Miss Mayblunt—"composed by my father in honor of Sister Janet's wedding."

Before each guest stood a tiny glass that looked and sparkled like a garnet gem.

"Then, all things considered," spoke Arobin, "it might not be amiss to start out by drinking the Colonel's health in the cocktail which he composed, on the birthday of the most charming of women—the daughter whom he invented."

Mr. Merriman's laugh at this sally was such a genuine outburst and so contagious that it started the dinner with an agreeable swing that never slackened.

Miss Mayblunt begged to be allowed to keep her cocktail untouched before her, just to look at. The color was marvelous! She could compare it to nothing she had ever seen, and the garnet lights which it emitted were unspeakably rare. She pronounced the Colonel an artist, and stuck to it.

Monsieur Ratignolle was prepared to take things seriously; the *mets,* and *entre-mets,* the service, the decorations, even the people. He looked up from his pompono[5] and inquired of Arobin if he were related to the gentleman of that name who formed one of the firm of Laitner and Arobin, lawyers. The young man admitted that Laitner was a warm personal friend, who permitted Arobin's name to decorate the firm's letterheads and to appear upon a shingle that graced Perdido Street.

"There are so many inquisitive people and institutions abounding," said Arobin, "that one is really forced as a matter of convenience these days to assume the virtue of an occupation if he has it not."

Monsieur Ratignolle stared a little, and turned to ask Mademoiselle Reisz if she considered the symphony concerts up to the standard which had been set the previous winter. Mademoiselle Reisz answered Monsieur Ratignolle in French, which Edna thought a little rude, under the circumstances, but characteristic. Mademoiselle had only disagreeable things to say of the symphony concerts, and insulting remarks to make of all the musicians of New Orleans, singly and collectively. All her interest seemed to be centered upon the delicacies placed before her.

Mr. Merriman said that Mr. Arobin's remark about inquisitive people reminded him of a man from Waco[6] the other day at the St. Charles Hotel— but as Mr. Merriman's stories were always lame and lacking point, his wife seldom permitted him to complete them. She interrupted him to ask if he remembered the name of the author whose book she had bought the week

5. Or pompano fish, a southern delicacy. "*Mets,* 6. A town in Texas.
and *entre-mets*": main courses and side dishes.

before to send to a friend in Geneva. She was talking "books" with Mr. Gouvernail and trying to draw from him his opinion upon current literary topics. Her husband told the story of the Waco man privately to Miss May-blunt, who pretended to be greatly amused and to think it extremely clever.

Mrs. Highcamp hung with languid but unaffected interest upon the warm and impetuous volubility of her left-hand neighbor, Victor Lebrun. Her attention was never for a moment withdrawn from him after seating herself at table; and when he turned to Mrs. Merriman, who was prettier and more vivacious than Mrs. Highcamp, she waited with easy indifference for an opportunity to reclaim his attention. There was the occasional sound of music, of mandolins, sufficiently removed to be an agreeable accompaniment rather than an interruption to the conversation. Outside the soft, monotonous splash of a fountain could be heard; the sound penetrated into the room with the heavy odor of jessamine that came through the open windows.

The golden shimmer of Edna's satin gown spread in rich folds on either side of her. There was a soft fall of lace encircling her shoulders. It was the color of her skin, without the glow, the myriad living tints that one may sometimes discover in vibrant flesh. There was something in her attitude, in her whole appearance when she leaned her head against the high-backed chair and spread her arms, which suggested the regal woman, the one who rules, who looks on, who stands alone.

But as she sat there amid her guests, she felt the old ennui overtaking her; the hopelessness which so often assailed her, which came upon her like an obsession, like something extraneous, independent of volition. It was something which announced itself; a chill breath that seemed to issue from some vast cavern wherein discords wailed. There came over her the acute longing which always summoned into her spiritual vision the presence of the beloved one, overpowering her at once with a sense of the unattainable.

The moments glided on, while a feeling of good fellowship passed around the circle like a mystic cord, holding and binding these people together with jest and laughter. Monsieur Ratignolle was the first to break the pleasant charm. At ten o'clock he excused himself. Madame Ratignolle was waiting for him at home. She was *bien souffrante*,[7] and she was filled with vague dread, which only her husband's presence could allay.

Mademoiselle Reisz arose with Monsieur Ratignolle, who offered to escort her to the car. She had eaten well; she had tasted the good rich wines, and they must have turned her head, for she bowed pleasantly to all as she withdrew from table. She kissed Edna upon the shoulder, and whispered: "*Bonne nuit, ma reine; soyez sage.*"[8] She had been a little bewildered upon rising, or rather, descending from her cushions, and Monsieur Ratignolle gallantly took her arm and led her away.

Mrs. Highcamp was weaving a garland of roses, yellow and red. When she had finished the garland, she laid it lightly upon Victor's black curls. He was reclining far back in the luxurious chair, holding a glass of champagne to the light.

As if a magician's wand had touched him, the garland of roses transformed him into a vision of Oriental beauty. His cheeks were the color of crushed grapes, and his dusky eyes glowed with a languishing fire.

7. Very ill.　　　　8. Good night, my queen; be good.

"*Sapristi!*" exclaimed Arobin.

But Mrs. Highcamp had one more touch to add to the picture. She took from the back of her chair a white silken scarf, with which she had covered her shoulders in the early part of the evening. She draped it across the boy in graceful folds, and in a way to conceal his black, conventional evening dress. He did not seem to mind what she did to him, only smiled, showing a faint gleam of white teeth, while he continued to gaze with narrowing eyes at the light through his glass of champagne.

"Oh! to be able to paint in color rather than in words!" exclaimed Miss Mayblunt, losing herself in a rhapsodic dream as she looked at him.

"There was a graven image of Desire
Painted with red blood on a ground of gold' "[9]

murmured Gouvernail, under his breath.

The effect of the wine upon Victor was to change his accustomed volubility into silence. He seemed to have abandoned himself to a reverie, and to be seeing pleasing visions in the amber bead.

"Sing," entreated Mrs. Highcamp. "Won't you sing to us?"

"Let him alone," said Arobin.

"He's posing," offered Mr. Merriman; "let him have it out."

"I believe he's paralyzed," laughed Mrs. Merriman. And leaning over the youth's chair, she took the glass from his hand and held it to his lips. He sipped the wine slowly, and when he had drained the glass she laid it upon the table and wiped his lips with her little filmy handkerchief.

"Yes, I'll sing for you," he said, turning in his chair toward Mrs. Highcamp. He clasped his hands behind his head, and looking up at the ceiling began to hum a little, trying his voice like a musician tuning an instrument. Then, looking at Edna, he began to sing:

"Ah! si tu savais!"

"Stop!" she cried, "don't sing that. I don't want you to sing it," and she laid her glass so impetuously and blindly upon the table as to shatter it against a caraffe. The wine spilled over Arobin's legs and some of it trickled down upon Mrs. Highcamp's black gauze gown. Victor had lost all idea of courtesy, or else he thought his hostess was not in earnest, for he laughed and went on:

"Ah! si tu savais
Ce que tes yeux me disent"[1]—

"Oh! you mustn't! you mustn't," exclaimed Edna, and pushing back her chair she got up, and going behind him placed her hand over his mouth. He kissed the soft palm that pressed upon his lips.

"No, no, I won't, Mrs. Pontellier. I didn't know you meant it," looking up at her with caressing eyes. The touch of his lips was like a pleasing sting to her hand. She lifted the garland of roses from his head and flung it across the room.

"Come, Victor; you've posed long enough. Give Mrs. Highcamp her scarf."

9. The opening lines of "A Cameo" (1866), by the English poet Algernon Charles Swinburne.

1. Ah! if you knew what your eyes say to me.

Mrs. Highcamp undraped the scarf from about him with her own hands. Miss Mayblunt and Mr. Gouvernail suddenly conceived the notion that it was time to say good night. And Mr. and Mrs. Merriman wondered how it could be so late.

Before parting from Victor, Mrs. Highcamp invited him to call upon her daughter, who she knew would be charmed to meet him and talk French and sing French songs with him. Victor expressed his desire and intention to call upon Miss Highcamp at the first opportunity which presented itself. He asked if Arobin were going his way. Arobin was not.

The mandolin players had long since stolen away. A profound stillness had fallen upon the broad, beautiful street. The voices of Edna's disbanding guests jarred like a discordant note upon the quiet harmony of the night.

XXXI

"Well?" questioned Arobin, who had remained with Edna after the others had departed.

"Well," she reiterated, and stood up, stretching her arms, and feeling the need to relax her muscles after having been so long seated.

"What next?" he asked.

"The servants are all gone. They left when the musicians did. I have dismissed them. The house has to be closed and locked, and I shall trot around to the pigeon house, and shall send Celestine over in the morning to straighten things up."

He looked around, and began to turn out some of the lights.

"What about upstairs?" he inquired.

"I think it is all right: but there may be a window or two unlatched. We had better look; you might take a candle and see. And bring me my wrap and hat on the foot of the bed in the middle room."

He went up with the light, and Edna began closing doors and windows. She hated to shut in the smoke and the fumes of the wine. Arobin found her cape and hat, which he brought down and helped her to put on.

When everything was secured and the lights put out, they left through the front door, Arobin locking it and taking the key, which he carried for Edna. He helped her down the steps.

"Will you have a spray of jessamine?" he asked, breaking off a few blossoms as he passed.

"No; I don't want anything."

She seemed disheartened, and had nothing to say. She took his arm, which he offered her, holding up the weight of her satin train with the other hand. She looked down, noticing the black line of his leg moving in and out so close to her against the yellow shimmer of her gown. There was the whistle of a railway train somewhere in the distance, and the midnight bells were ringing. They met no one in their short walk.

The "pigeon-house" stood behind a locked gate, and a shallow *parterre*[2] that had been somewhat neglected. There was a small front porch, upon which a long window and the front door opened. The door opened directly

2. Ornamental garden.

into the parlor; there was no side entry. Back in the yard was a room for servants, in which old Celestine had been ensconced.

Edna had left a lamp burning low upon the table. She had succeeded in making the room look habitable and homelike. There were some books on the table and a lounge near at hand. On the floor was a fresh matting, covered with a rug or two; and on the walls hung a few tasteful pictures. But the room was filled with flowers. These were a surprise to her. Arobin had sent them, and had had Celestine distribute them during Edna's absence. Her bedroom was adjoining, and across a small passage were the dining-room and kitchen.

Edna seated herself with every appearance of discomfort.

"Are you tired?" he asked.

"Yes, and chilled and miserable. I feel as if I had been wound up to a certain pitch—too tight—and something inside of me had snapped." She rested her head against the table upon her bare arm.

"You want to rest," he said, "and to be quiet. I'll go; I'll leave you and let you rest."

"Yes," she replied.

He stood up beside her and smoothed her hair with his soft magnetic hand. His touch conveyed to her a certain physical comfort. She could have fallen quietly asleep there if he had continued to pass his hand over her hair. He brushed the hair upward from the nape of her neck.

"I hope you will feel better and happier in the morning," he said. "You have tried to do too much in the past few days. The dinner was the last straw; you might have dispensed with it."

"Yes," she admitted; "it was stupid."

"No, it was delightful; but it has worn you out." His hand had strayed to her beautiful shoulders, and he could feel the response of her flesh to his touch. He seated himself beside her and kissed her lightly upon the shoulder.

"I thought you were going away," she said, in an uneven voice.

"I am, after I have said good night."

"Good night," she murmured.

He did not answer, except to continue to caress her. He did not say good night until she had become supple to his gentle, seductive entreaties.

XXXII

When Mr. Pontellier learned of his wife's intention to abandon her home and take up her residence elsewhere, he immediately wrote her a letter of unqualified disapproval and remonstrance. She had given reasons which he was unwilling to acknowledge as adequate. He hoped she had not acted upon her rash impulse; and he begged her to consider first, foremost, and above all else, what people would say. He was not dreaming of scandal when he uttered this warning; that was a thing which would never have entered into his mind to consider in connection with his wife's name or his own. He was simply thinking of his financial integrity. It might get noised about that the Pontelliers had met with reverses, and were forced to conduct their *ménage*[3]

3. Household.

on a humbler scale than heretofore. It might do incalculable mischief to his business prospects.

But remembering Edna's whimsical turn of mind of late, and foreseeing that she had immediately acted upon her impetuous determination, he grasped the situation with his usual promptness and handled it with his well-known business tact and cleverness.

The same mail which brought to Edna his letter of disapproval carried instructions—the most minute instructions—to a well-known architect concerning the remodeling of his home, changes which he had long contemplated, and which he desired carried forward during his temporary absence.

Expert and reliable packers and movers were engaged to convey the furniture, carpets, pictures—everything movable, in short—to places of security. And in an incredibly short time the Pontellier house was turned over to the artisans. There was to be an addition—a small snuggery;[4] there was to be frescoing, and hardwood flooring was to be put into such rooms as had not yet been subjected to this improvement.

Furthermore, in one of the daily papers appeared a brief notice to the effect that Mr. and Mrs. Pontellier were contemplating a summer sojourn abroad, and that their handsome residence on Esplanade Street was undergoing sumptuous alterations, and would not be ready for occupancy until their return. Mr. Pontellier had saved appearances!

Edna admired the skill of his maneuver, and avoided any occasion to balk his intentions. When the situation as set forth by Mr. Pontellier was accepted and taken for granted, she was apparently satisfied that it should be so.

The pigeon-house pleased her. It at once assumed the intimate character of a home, while she herself invested it with a charm which it reflected like a warm glow. There was with her a feeling of having descended in the social scale, with a corresponding sense of having risen in the spiritual. Every step which she took toward relieving herself from obligations added to her strength and expansion as an individual. She began to look with her own eyes; to see and to apprehend the deeper undercurrents of life. No longer was she content to "feed upon opinion" when her own soul had invited her.

After a little while, a few days, in fact, Edna went up and spent a week with her children in Iberville. They were delicious February days, with all the summer's promises hovering in the air.

How glad she was to see the children! She wept for very pleasure when she felt their little arms clasping her; their hard, ruddy cheeks pressed against her own glowing cheeks. She looked into their faces with hungry eyes that could not be satisfied with looking. And what stories they had to tell their mother! About the pigs, the cows, the mules! About riding to the mill behind Gluglu; fishing back in the lake with their Uncle Jasper; picking pecans with Lidie's little black brood, and hauling chips in their express wagon. It was a thousand times more fun to haul real chips for old lame Susie's real fire than to drag painted blocks along the banquette on Esplanade Street!

She went with them herself to see the pigs and the cows, to look at the darkies laying the cane, to thrash the pecan trees, and catch fish in the back lake. She lived with them a whole week long, giving them all of herself, and

4. Den.

gathering and filling herself with their young existence. They listened, breathless, when she told them the house in Esplanade Street was crowded with workmen, hammering, nailing, sawing, and filling the place with clatter. They wanted to know where their bed was; what had been done with their rocking-horse; and where did Joe sleep, and where had Ellen gone, and the cook? But, above all, they were fired with a desire to see the little house around the block. Was there any place to play? Were there any boys next door? Raoul, with pessimistic foreboding, was convinced that there were only girls next door. Where would they sleep, and where would papa sleep? She told them the fairies would fix it all right.

The old Madame was charmed with Edna's visit, and showered all manner of delicate attentions upon her. She was delighted to know that the Esplanade Street house was in a dismantled condition. It gave her the promise and pretext to keep the children indefinitely.

It was with a wrench and a pang that Edna left her children. She carried away with her the sound of their voices and the touch of their cheeks. All along the journey homeward their presence lingered with her like the memory of a delicious song. But by the time she had regained the city the song no longer echoed in her soul. She was again alone.

XXXIII

It happened sometimes when Edna went to see Mademoiselle Reisz that the little musician was absent, giving a lesson or making some small necessary household purchase. The key was always left in a secret hiding-place in the entry, which Edna knew. If Mademoiselle happened to be away, Edna would usually enter and wait for her return.

When she knocked at Mademoiselle Reisz's door one afternoon there was no response; so unlocking the door, as usual, she entered and found the apartment deserted, as she had expected. Her day had been quite filled up, and it was for a rest, for a refuge, and to talk about Robert, that she sought out her friend.

She had worked at her canvas—a young Italian character study—all the morning, completing the work without the model; but there had been many interruptions, some incident to her modest housekeeping, and others of a social nature.

Madame Ratignolle had dragged herself over, avoiding the too public thoroughfares, she said. She complained that Edna had neglected her much of late. Besides, she was consumed with curiosity to see the little house and the manner in which it was conducted. She wanted to hear all about the dinner party; Monsieur Ratignolle had left so early. What had happened after he left? The champagne and grapes which Edna sent over were *too* delicious. She had so little appetite; they had refreshed and toned her stomach. Where on earth was she going to put Mr. Pontellier in that little house, and the boys? And then she made Edna promise to go to her when her hour of trial overtook her.

"At any time—any time of the day or night, dear," Edna assured her.

Before leaving Madame Ratignolle said:

"In some way you seem to me like a child, Edna. You seem to act without a certain amount of reflection which is necessary in this life. That is the

reason I want to say you mustn't mind if I advise you to be a little careful while you are living here alone. Why don't you have some one come and stay with you? Wouldn't Mademoiselle Reisz come?"

"No; she wouldn't wish to come, and I shouldn't want her always with me."

"Well, the reason—you know how evil-minded the world is—some one was talking of Alcée Arobin visiting you. Of course, it wouldn't matter if Mr. Arobin had not such a dreadful reputation. Monsieur Ratignolle was telling me that his attentions alone are considered enough to ruin a woman's name."

"Does he boast of his successes?" asked Edna, indifferently, squinting at her picture.

"No, I think not. I believe he is a decent fellow as far as that goes. But his character is so well known among the men. I shan't be able to come back and see you; it was very, very imprudent today."

"Mind the step!" cried Edna.

"Don't neglect me," entreated Madame Ratignolle; "and don't mind what I said about Arobin, or having some one to stay with you."

"Of course not," Edna laughed. "You may say anything you like to me." They kissed each other good-bye. Madame Ratignolle had not far to go, and Edna stood on the porch a while watching her walk down the street.

Then in the afternoon Mrs. Merriman and Mrs. Highcamp had made their "party call." Edna felt that they might have dispensed with the formality. They had also come to invite her to play *vingt-et-un*[5] one evening at Mrs. Merriman's. She was asked to go early, to dinner, and Mr. Merriman or Mr. Arobin would take her home. Edna accepted in a half-hearted way. She sometimes felt very tired of Mrs. Highcamp and Mrs. Merriman.

Late in the afternoon she sought refuge with Mademoiselle Reisz, and stayed there alone, waiting for her, feeling a kind of repose invade her with the very atmosphere of the shabby, unpretentious little room.

Edna sat at the window, which looked out over the house-tops and across the river. The window frame was filled with pots of flowers, and she sat and picked the dry leaves from a rose geranium. The day was warm, and the breeze which blew from the river was very pleasant. She removed her hat and laid it on the piano. She went on picking the leaves and digging around the plants with her hat pin. Once she thought she heard Mademoiselle Reisz approaching. But it was a young black girl, who came in, bringing a small bundle of laundry, which she deposited in the adjoining room, and went away.

Edna seated herself at the piano, and softly picked out with one hand the bars of a piece of music which lay open before her. A half-hour went by. There was the occasional sound of people going and coming in the lower hall. She was growing interested in her occupation of picking out the aria, when there was a second rap at the door. She vaguely wondered what these people did when they found Mademoiselle's door locked.

"Come in," she called. turning her face toward the door. And this time it was Robert Lebrun who presented himself. She attempted to rise; she could not have done so without betraying the agitation which mastered her at sight of him, so she fell back upon the stool, only exclaiming, "Why Robert!"

5. Twenty-one, a card game.

He came and clasped her hand, seemingly without knowing what he was saying or doing.

"Mrs. Pontellier! How do you happen—oh! how well you look! Is Mademoiselle Reisz not here? I never expected to see you."

"When did you come back?" asked Edna in an unsteady voice, wiping her face with her handkerchief. She seemed ill at ease on the piano stool, and he begged her to take the chair by the window. She did so, mechanically, while he seated himself on the stool.

"I returned day before yesterday," he answered, while he leaned his arm on the keys, bringing forth a crash of discordant sound.

"Day before yesterday!" she repeated, aloud, and went on thinking to herself, "day before yesterday," in a sort of an uncomprehending way. She had pictured him seeking her at the very first hour, and he had lived under the same sky since day before yesterday; while only by accident had he stumbled upon her. Mademoiselle must have lied when she said, "Poor fool, he loves you."

"Day before yesterday," she repeated, breaking off a spray of Mademoiselle's geranium; "then if you had not met me here to-day you wouldn't—when—that is, didn't you mean to come and see me?"

"Of course, I should have gone to see you. There have been so many things—" he turned the leaves of Mademoiselle's music nervously. "I started in at once yesterday with the old firm. After all there is as much chance for me here as there was there—that is, I might find it profitable some day. The Mexicans were not very congenial."

So he had come back because the Mexicans were not congenial; because business was as profitable here as there; because of any reason, and not because he cared to be near her. She remembered the day she sat on the floor, turning the pages of his letter, seeking the reason which was left untold.

She had not noticed how he looked—only feeling his presence; but she turned deliberately and observed him. After all, he had been absent but a few months, and was not changed. His hair—the color of hers—waved back from his temples in the same way as before. His skin was not more burned than it had been at Grand Isle. She found in his eyes, when he looked at her for one silent moment, the same tender caress, with an added warmth and entreaty which had not been there before—the same glance which had penetrated to the sleeping places of her soul and awakened them.

A hundred times Edna had pictured Robert's return, and imagined their first meeting. It was usually at her home, whither he had sought her out at once. She always fancied him expressing or betraying in some way his love for her. And here, the reality was that they sat ten feet apart, she at the window, crushing geranium leaves in her hand and smelling them, he twirling around on the piano stool, saying:

"I was very much surprised to hear of Mr. Pontellier's absence; it's a wonder Mademoiselle Reisz did not tell me; and your moving—mother told me yesterday. I should think you would have gone to New York with him, or to Iberville with the children, rather than be bothered here with housekeeping. And you are going abroad, too, I hear. We shan't have you at Grand Isle next summer; it won't seem—do you see much of Mademoiselle Reisz? She often spoke of you in the few letters she wrote."

"Do you remember that you promised to write to me when you went away?" A flush overspread his whole face.

"I couldn't believe that my letters would be of any interest to you."

"That is an excuse; it isn't the truth." Edna reached for her hat on the piano. She adjusted it, sticking the hat pin through the heavy coil of hair with some deliberation.

"Are you not going to wait for Mademoiselle Reisz?" asked Robert.

"No; I have found when she is absent this long, she is liable not to come back till late." She drew on her gloves, and Robert picked up his hat.

"Won't you wait for her?" asked Edna.

"Not if you think she will not be back till late," adding, as if suddenly aware of some discourtesy in his speech, "and I should miss the pleasure of walking home with you." Edna locked the door and put the key back in its hiding place.

They went together, picking their way across muddy streets and sidewalks encumbered with the cheap display of small tradesmen. Part of the distance they rode in the car, and after disembarking, passed the Pontellier mansion, which looked broken and half torn asunder. Robert had never known the house, and looked at it with interest.

"I never knew you in your home," he remarked.

"I am glad you did not."

"Why?" She did not answer. They went on around the corner, and it seemed as if her dreams were coming true after all, when he followed her into the little house.

"You must stay and dine with me, Robert. You see I am all alone, and it is so long since I have seen you. There is so much I want to ask you."

She took off her hat and gloves. He stood irresolute, making some excuse about his mother who expected him; he even muttered something about an engagement. She struck a match and lit the lamp on the table; it was growing dusk. When he saw her face in the lamplight, looking pained, with all the soft lines gone out of it, he threw his hat aside and seated himself.

"Oh! you know I want to stay if you will let me!" he exclaimed. All the softness came back. She laughed, and went and put her hand on his shoulder.

"This is the first moment you have seemed like the old Robert. I'll go tell Celestine." She hurried away to tell Celestine to set an extra place. She even sent her off in search of some added delicacy which she had not thought of for herself. And she recommended great care in dripping the coffee and having the omelet done to a proper turn.

When she reëntered, Robert was turning over magazines, sketches, and things that lay upon the table in great disorder. He picked up a photograph, and exclaimed:

"Alcée Arobin! What on earth is his picture doing here?"

"I tried to make a sketch of his head one day," answered Edna, "and he thought the photograph might help me. It was at the other house. I thought it had been left there. I must have picked it up with my drawing materials."

"I should think you would give it back to him if you have finished with it."

"Oh! I have a great many such photographs. I never think of returning them. They don't amount to anything." Robert kept on looking at the picture.

"It seems to me—do you think his head worth drawing? Is he a friend of Mr. Pontellier's? You never said you knew him."

"He isn't a friend of Mr. Pontellier's; he's a friend of mine. I always knew him—that is, it is only of late that I know him pretty well. But I'd rather talk about you, and know what you have been seeing and doing and feeling out there in Mexico." Robert threw aside the picture.

"I've been seeing the waves and the white beach of Grand Isle; the quiet, grassy street of the *Chênière*; the old fort at Grande Terre. I've been working like a machine, and feeling like a lost soul. There was nothing interesting."

She leaned her head upon her hand to shade her eyes from the light.

"And what have you been seeing and doing and feeling all these days?" he asked.

"I've been seeing the waves and the white beach of Grand Isle; the quiet, grassy street of the *Chênière Caminada*; the old sunny fort at Grande Terre. I've been working with little more comprehension than a machine, and still feeling like a lost soul. There was nothing interesting."

"Mrs. Pontellier, you are cruel," he said, with feeling, closing his eyes and resting his head back in his chair. They remained in silence till old Celestine announced dinner.

XXXIV

The dining-room was very small. Edna's round mahogany would have almost filled it. As it was there was but a step or two from the little table in the kitchen, to the mantel, the small buffet, and the side door that opened out on the narrow brick-paved yard.

A certain degree of ceremony settled upon them with the announcement of dinner. There was no return to personalities. Robert related incidents of his sojourn in Mexico, and Edna talked of events likely to interest him, which had occurred during his absence. The dinner was of ordinary quality, except for the few delicacies which she had sent out to purchase. Old Celestine, with a bandana *tignon* twisted about her head,[6] hobbled in and out, taking a personal interest in everything; and she lingered occasionally to talk *patois*[7] with Robert, whom she had known as a boy.

He went out to a neighboring cigar stand to purchase cigarette papers, and when he came back he found that Celestine had served the black coffee in the parlor.

"Perhaps I shouldn't have come back," he said. "When you are tired of me, tell me to go."

"You never tire me. You must have forgotten the hours and hours at Grand Isle in which we grew accustomed to each other and used to being together."

"I have forgotten nothing at Grand Isle," he said, not looking at her, but rolling a cigarette. His tobacco pouch, which he laid upon the table, was a fantastic embroidered silk affair, evidently the handiwork of a woman.

"You used to carry your tobacco in a rubber pouch," said Edna, picking up the pouch and examining the needlework.

"Yes; it was lost."

"Where did you buy this one? In Mexico?"

6. I.e., her hair is tied up with a scarf. 7. Dialect.

"It was given to me by a Vera Cruz girl; they are very generous," he replied, striking a match and lighting his cigarette.

"They are very handsome, I suppose, those Mexican women; very picturesque, with their black eyes and their lace scarfs."

"Some are; others are hideous. Just as you find women everywhere."

"What was she like—the one who gave you the pouch? You must have known her very well."

"She was very ordinary. She wasn't of the slightest importance. I knew her well enough."

"Did you visit at her house? Was it interesting? I should like to know and hear about the people you met, and the impressions they made on you."

"There are some people who leave impressions not so lasting as the imprint of an oar upon the water."

"Was she such a one?"

"It would be ungenerous for me to admit that she was of that order and kind." He thrust the pouch back in his pocket, as if to put away the subject with the trifle which had brought it up.

Arobin dropped in with a message from Mrs. Merriman, to say that the card party was postponed on account of the illness of one of her children.

"How do you do, Arobin?" said Robert, rising from the obscurity.

"Oh! Lebrun. To be sure! I heard yesterday you were back. How did they treat you down in Mexico?"

"Fairly well."

"But not well enough to keep you there. Stunning girls, though, in Mexico. I thought I should never get away from Vera Cruz when I was down there a couple of years ago."

"Did they embroider slippers and tobacco pouches and hat bands and things for you?" asked Edna.

"Oh! my! no! I didn't get so deep in their regard. I fear they made more impression on me than I made on them."

"You were less fortunate than Robert, then."

"I am always less fortunate than Robert. Has he been imparting tender confidences?"

"I've been imposing myself long enough," said Robert, rising, and shaking hands with Edna. "Please convey my regards to Mr. Pontellier when you write."

He shook hands with Arobin and went away.

"Fine fellow, that Lebrun," said Arobin when Robert had gone. "I never heard you speak of him."

"I knew him last summer at Grand Isle," she replied. "Here is that photograph of yours. Don't you want it?"

"What do I want with it? Throw it away." She threw it back on the table.

"I'm not going to Mrs. Merriman's," she said. "If you see her, tell her so. But perhaps I had better write. I think I shall write now, and say that I am sorry her child is sick, and tell her not to count on me."

"It would be a good scheme," acquiesced Arobin. "I don't blame you; stupid lot!"

Edna opened the blotter, and having procured paper and pen, began to write a note. Arobin lit a cigar and read the evening paper, which he had in his pocket.

"What is the date?" she asked. He told her.

"Will you mail this for me when you go out?"

"Certainly." He read to her little bits out of the newspaper, while she straightened things on the table.

"What do you want to do?" he asked, throwing aside the paper. "Do you want to go for a walk or a drive or anything? It would be a fine night to drive."

"No; I don't want to do anything but just be quiet. You go away and amuse yourself. Don't stay."

"I'll go away if I must; but I shan't amuse myself. You know that I only live when I am near you."

He stood up to bid her good night.

"Is that one of the things you always say to women?"

"I have said it before, but I don't think I ever came so near meaning it," he answered with a smile. There were no warm lights in her eyes; only a dreamy, absent look.

"Good night. I adore you. Sleep well," he said, and he kissed her hand and went away.

She stayed alone in a kind of reverie—a sort of stupor. Step by step she lived over every instant of the time she had been with Robert after he had entered Mademoiselle Reisz's door. She recalled his words, his looks. How few and meager they had been for her hungry heart! A vision—a transcendently seductive vision of a Mexican girl arose before her. She writhed with a jealous pang. She wondered when he would come back. He had not said he would come back. She had been with him, had heard his voice and touched his hand. But some way he had seemed nearer to her off there in Mexico.

XXXV

The morning was full of sunlight and hope. Edna could see before her no denial—only the promise of excessive joy. She lay in bed awake, with bright eyes full of speculation. "He loves you, poor fool." If she could but get that conviction firmly fixed in her mind, what mattered about the rest? She felt she had been childish and unwise the night before in giving herself over to despondency. She recapitulated the motives which no doubt explained Robert's reserve. They were not insurmountable; they would not hold if he really loved her; they could not hold against her own passion, which he must come to realize in time. She pictured him going to his business that morning. She even saw how he was dressed; how he walked down one street, and turned the corner of another; saw him bending over his desk, talking to people who entered the office, going to his lunch, and perhaps watching for her on the street. He would come to her in the afternoon or evening, sit and roll his cigarette, talk a little, and go away as he had done the night before. But how delicious it would be to have him there with her! She would have no regrets, nor seek to penetrate his reserve if he still chose to wear it.

Edna ate her breakfast only half dressed. The maid brought her a delicious printed scrawl from Raoul, expressing his love, asking her to send him some bonbons, and telling her they had found that morning ten tiny white pigs all lying in a row beside Lidie's big white pig.

A letter also came from her husband, saying he hoped to be back early in

March, and then they would get ready for that journey abroad which he had promised her so long, which he felt now fully able to afford; he felt able to travel as people should, without any thought of small economies—thanks to his recent speculations in Wall Street.

Much to her surprise she received a note from Arobin, written at midnight from the club. It was to say good morning to her, to hope that she had slept well, to assure her of his devotion, which he trusted she in some faintest manner returned.

All these letters were pleasing to her. She answered the children in a cheerful frame of mind, promising them bonbons, and congratulating them upon their happy find of the little pigs.

She answered her husband with friendly evasiveness,—not with any fixed design to mislead him, only because all sense of reality had gone out of her life, she had abandoned herself to Fate, and awaited the consequences with indifference.

To Arobin's note she made no reply. She put it under Celestine's stove-lid.

Edna worked several hours with much spirit. She saw no one but a picture dealer, who asked her if it were true that she was going abroad to study in Paris.

She said possibly she might, and he negotiated with her for some Parisian studies to reach him in time for the holiday trade in December.

Robert did not come that day. She was keenly disappointed. He did not come the following day, nor the next. Each morning she awoke with hope, and each night she was a prey to despondency. She was tempted to seek him out. But far from yielding to the impulse, she avoided any occasion which might throw her in his way. She did not go to Mademoiselle Reisz's nor pass by Madame Lebrun's, as she might have done if he had still been in Mexico.

When Arobin, one night, urged her to drive with him, she went—out to the lake, on the Shell Road.[8] His horses were full of mettle, and even a little unmanageable. She liked the rapid gait at which they spun along, and the quick, sharp sound of the horses' hoofs on the hard road. They did not stop anywhere to eat or to drink. Arobin was not needlessly imprudent. But they ate and they drank when they regained Edna's little dining-room—which was comparatively early in the evening.

It was late when he left her. It was getting to be more than a passing whim with Arobin to see her and be with her. He had detected the latent sensuality, which unfolded under his delicate sense of her nature's requirements like a torpid, torrid, sensitive blossom.

There was no despondency when she fell asleep that night; nor was there hope when she awoke in the morning.

XXXVI

There was a garden out in the suburbs; a small, leafy corner, with a few green tables under the orange trees. An old cat slept all day on the stone step in the sun, and an old *mulatresse*[9] slept her idle hours away in her chair

8. Road by Lake Pontchartrain.
9. A mulatto woman, of mixed black and white ancestry.

at the open window, till some one happened to knock on one of the green tables. She had milk and cream cheese to sell, and bread and butter. There was no one who could make such excellent coffee or fry a chicken so golden brown as she.

The place was too modest to attract the attention of people of fashion, and so quiet as to have escaped the notice of those in search of pleasure and dissipation. Edna had discovered it accidentally one day when the high-board gate stood ajar. She caught sight of a little green table, blotched with the checkered sunlight that filtered through the quivering leaves overhead. Within she had found the slumbering *mulatresse,* the drowsy cat, and a glass of milk which reminded her of the milk she had tasted in Iberville.

She often stopped there during her perambulations; sometimes taking a book with her, and sitting an hour or two under the trees when she found the place deserted. Once or twice she took a quiet dinner there alone, having instructed Celestine beforehand to prepare no dinner at home. It was the last place in the city where she would have expected to meet any one she knew.

Still she was not astonished when, as she was partaking of a modest dinner late in the afternoon, looking into an open book, stroking the cat, which had made friends with her—she was not greatly astonished to see Robert come in at the tall garden gate.

"I am destined to see you only by accident," she said, shoving the cat off the chair beside her. He was surprised, ill at ease, almost embarrassed at meeting her thus so unexpectedly.

"Do you come here often?" he asked.

"I almost live here," she said.

"I used to drop in very often for a cup of Catiche's good coffee. This is the first time since I came back."

"She'll bring you a plate, and you will share my dinner. There's always enough for two—even three." Edna had intended to be indifferent and as reserved as he when she met him; she had reached the determination by a laborious train of reasoning, incident to one of her despondent moods. But her resolve melted when she saw him before her, seated there beside her in the little garden, as if a designing Providence had led him into her path.

"Why have you kept away from me, Robert?" she asked, closing the book that lay open upon the table.

"Why are you so personal, Mrs. Pontellier? Why do you force me to idiotic subterfuges?" he exclaimed with sudden warmth. "I suppose there's no use telling you I've been very busy, or that I've been sick, or that I've been to see you and not found you at home. Please let me off with any one of those excuses."

"You are the embodiment of selfishness," she said. "You save yourself something—I don't know what—but there is some selfish motive, and in sparing yourself you never consider for a moment what I think, or how I feel your neglect and indifference. I suppose this is what you would call unwomanly; but I have got into a habit of expressing myself. It doesn't matter to me, and you may think me unwomanly if you like."

"No; I only think you cruel, as I said the other day. Maybe not intentionally cruel; but you seem to be forcing me into disclosures which can result in nothing; as if you would have me bare a wound for the pleasure of looking at it, without the intention or power of healing it."

"I'm spoiling your dinner, Robert; never mind what I say. You haven't eaten a morsel."

"I only came in for a cup of coffee." His sensitive face was all disfigured with excitement.

"Isn't this a delightful place?" she remarked. "I am so glad it has never actually been discovered. It is so quiet, so sweet here. Do you notice there is scarcely a sound to be heard? It's so out of the way; and a good walk from the car.[1] However, I don't mind walking. I always feel so sorry for women who don't like to walk; they miss so much—so many rare little glimpses of life; and we women learn so little of life on the whole.

"Catiche's coffee is always hot. I don't know how she manages it, here in the open air. Celestine's coffee gets cold bringing it from the kitchen to the dining-room. Three lumps! How can you drink it so sweet? Take some of the cress with your chop; it's so biting and crisp. Then there's the advantage of being able to smoke with your coffee out here. Now, in the city—aren't you going to smoke?"

"After a while," he said, laying a cigar on the table.

"Who gave it to you?" she laughed.

"I bought it. I suppose I'm getting reckless; I bought a whole box." She was determined not to be personal again and make him uncomfortable.

The cat made friends with him, and climbed into his lap when he smoked his cigar. He stroked her silky fur, and talked a little about her. He looked at Edna's book, which he had read; and he told her the end, to save her the trouble of wading through it, he said.

Again he accompanied her back to her home; and it was after dusk when they reached the little "pigeon-house." She did not ask him to remain, which he was grateful for, as it permitted him to stay without the discomfort of blundering through an excuse which he had no intention of considering. He helped her to light the lamp; then she went into her room to take off her hat and to bathe her face and hands.

When she came back Robert was not examining the pictures and magazines as before; he sat off in the shadow, leaning his head back on the chair as if in a reverie. Edna lingered a moment beside the table, arranging the books there. Then she went across the room to where he sat. She bent over the arm of his chair and called his name.

"Robert," she said, "are you asleep?"

"No," he answered, looking up at her.

She leaned over and kissed him—a soft, cool, delicate kiss, whose voluptuous sting penetrated his whole being—then she moved away from him. He followed, and took her in his arms, just holding her close to him. She put her hand up to his face and pressed his cheek against her own. The action was full of love and tenderness. He sought her lips again. Then he drew her down upon the sofa beside him and held her hand in both of his.

"Now you know," he said, "now you know what I have been fighting against since last summer at Grand Isle; what drove me away and drove me back again."

"Why have you been fighting against it?" she asked. Her face glowed with soft lights.

"Why? Because you were not free; you were Léonce Pontellier's wife. I

1. I.e., the nearest streetcar.

couldn't help loving you if you were ten times his wife, but so long as I went away from you and kept away I could help telling you so." She put her free hand up to his shoulder, and then against his cheek, rubbing it softly. He kissed her again. His face was warm and flushed.

"There in Mexico I was thinking of you all the time, and longing for you."

"But not writing to me," she interrupted.

"Something put into my head that you cared for me; and I lost my senses. I forgot everything but a wild dream of your some way becoming my wife."

"Your wife!"

"Religion, loyalty, everything would give way if only you cared."

"Then you must have forgotten that I was Léonce Pontellier's wife."

"Oh! I was demented, dreaming of wild, impossible things, recalling men who had set their wives free, we have heard of such things."

"Yes, we have heard of such things."

"I came back full of vague, mad intentions. And when I got here—"

"When you got here you never came near me!" She was still caressing his cheek.

"I realized what a cur I was to dream of such a thing, even if you had been willing."

She took his face between her hands and looked into it as if she would never withdraw her eyes more. She kissed him on the forehead, the eyes, the cheeks, and the lips.

"You have been a very, very foolish boy, wasting your time dreaming of impossible things when you speak of Mr. Pontellier setting me free! I am no longer one of Mr. Pontellier's possessions to dispose of or not. I give myself where I choose. If he were to say, 'Here, Robert, take her and be happy; she is yours,' I should laugh at you both."

His face grew a little white. "What do you mean?" he asked.

There was a knock at the door. Old Celestine came in to say that Madame Ratignolle's servant had come around the back way with a message that Madame had been taken sick and begged Mrs. Pontellier to go to her immediately.

"Yes, yes," said Edna, rising: "I promised. Tell her yes—to wait for me. I'll go back with her."

"Let me walk over with you," offered Robert.

"No," she said; "I will go with the servant." She went into her room to put on her hat, and when she came in again she sat once more upon the sofa beside him. He had not stirred. She put her arms about his neck.

"Good-by, my sweet Robert. Tell me good-by." He kissed her with a degree of passion which had not before entered into his caress, and strained her to him.

"I love you," she whispered, "only you; no one but you. It was you who awoke me last summer out of a life-long, stupid dream. Oh! you have made me so unhappy with your indifference. Oh! I have suffered, suffered! Now you are here we shall love each other, my Robert. We shall be everything to each other. Nothing else in the world is of any consequence. I must go to my friend; but you will wait for me? No matter how late; you will wait for me, Robert?"

"Don't go; don't go! Oh! Edna, stay with me," he pleaded. "Why should you go? Stay with me, stay with me."

"I shall come back as soon as I can; I shall find you here." She buried her face in his neck, and said good-by again. Her seductive voice, together with his great love for her, had enthralled his senses, had deprived him of every impulse but the longing to hold her and keep her.

XXXVII

Edna looked in at the drug store. Monsieur Ratignolle was putting up a mixture himself, very carefully, dropping a red liquid into a tiny glass. He was grateful to Edna for having come; her presence would be a comfort to his wife. Madame Ratignolle's sister, who had always been with her at such trying times, had not been able to come up from the plantation, and Adèle had been inconsolable until Mrs. Pontellier so kindly promised to come to her. The nurse had been with them at night for the past week, as she lived a great distance away. And Dr. Mandelet had been coming and going all the afternoon. They were then looking for him any moment.

Edna hastened upstairs by a private stairway that led from the rear of the store to the apartments above. The children were all sleeping in a back room. Madame Ratignolle was in the salon, whither she had strayed in her suffering impatience. She sat on the sofa, clad in an ample white *peignoir,* holding a handkerchief tight in her hand with a nervous clutch. Her face was drawn and pinched, her sweet blue eyes haggard and unnatural. All her beautiful hair had been drawn back and plaited. It lay in a long braid on the sofa pillow, coiled like a golden serpent. The nurse, a comfortable looking *Griffe*[2] woman in white apron and cap, was urging her to return to her bedroom.

"There is no use, there is no use," she said at once to Edna. "We must get rid of Mandelet; he is getting too old and careless. He said he would be here at half-past seven; now it must be eight. See what time it is, Joséphine."

The woman was possessed of a cheerful nature, and refused to take any situation too seriously, especially a situation with which she was so familiar. She urged Madame to have courage and patience. But Madame only set her teeth hard into her under lip, and Edna saw the sweat gather in beads on her white forehead. After a moment or two she uttered a profound sigh and wiped her face with the handkerchief rolled in a ball. She appeared exhausted. The nurse gave her a fresh handkerchief, sprinkled with cologne water.

"This is too much!" she cried. "Mandelet ought to be killed! Where is Alphonse? Is it possible I am to be abandoned like this—neglected by every one?"

"Neglected, indeed!" exclaimed the nurse. Wasn't she there? And here was Mrs. Pontellier leaving, no doubt, a pleasant evening at home to devote to her? And wasn't Monsieur Ratignolle coming that very instant through the hall? And Joséphine was quite sure she had heard Doctor Mandelet's coupé.[3] Yes, there it was, down at the door.

Adèle consented to go back to her room. She sat on the edge of a little low couch next to her bed.

Doctor Mandelet paid no attention to Madame Ratignolle's upbraidings.

2. The offspring of a mulatto and a black or an American Indian. 3. Closed carriage.

He was accustomed to them at such times, and was too well convinced of her loyalty to doubt it.

He was glad to see Edna, and wanted her to go with him into the salon and entertain him. But Madame Ratignolle would not consent that Edna should leave her for an instant. Between agonizing moments, she chatted a little, and said it took her mind off her sufferings.

Edna began to feel uneasy. She was seized with a vague dread. Her own like experiences seemed far away, unreal, and only half remembered. She recalled faintly an ecstasy of pain, the heavy odor of chloroform, a stupor which had deadened sensation, and an awakening to find a little new life to which she had given being, added to the great unnumbered multitude of souls that come and go.

She began to wish she had not come; her presence was not necessary. She might have invented a pretext for staying away; she might even invent a pretext now for going. But Edna did not go. With an inward agony, with a flaming, outspoken revolt against the ways of Nature, she witnessed the scene [of] torture.

She was still stunned and speechless with emotion when later she leaned over her friend to kiss her and softly say good-by. Adèle, pressing her cheek, whispered in an exhausted voice: "Think of the children, Edna. Oh think of the children! Remember them!"

XXXVIII

Edna still felt dazed when she got outside in the open air. The Doctor's coupé had returned for him and stood before the *porte cochère*. She did not wish to enter the coupé, and told Doctor Mandelet she would walk; she was not afraid, and would go alone. He directed his carriage to meet him at Mrs. Pontellier's, and he started to walk home with her.

Up—away up, over the narrow street between the tall houses, the stars were blazing. The air was mild and caressing, but cool with the breath of spring and the night. They walked slowly, the Doctor with a heavy, measured tread and his hands behind him; Edna, in an absent-minded way, as she had walked one night at Grand Isle, as if her thoughts had gone ahead of her and she was striving to overtake them.

"You shouldn't have been there, Mrs. Pontellier," he said. "That was no place for you. Adèle is full of whims at such times. There were a dozen women she might have had with her, unimpressionable women. I felt that it was cruel, cruel. You shouldn't have gone."

"Oh, well!" she answered, indifferently. "I don't know that it matters after all. One has to think of the children some time or other; the sooner the better."

"When is Léonce coming back?"

"Quite soon. Some time in March."

"And you are going abroad?"

"Perhaps—no, I am not going. I'm not going to be forced into doing things. I don't want to go abroad. I want to be let alone. Nobody has any right—except children, perhaps—and even then, it seems to me—or it did seem—" She felt that her speech was voicing the incoherency of her thoughts, and stopped abruptly.

"The trouble is," sighed the Doctor, grasping her meaning intuitively, "that youth is given up to illusions. It seems to be a provision of Nature; a decoy to secure mothers for the race. And Nature takes no account of moral consequences, of arbitrary conditions which we create, and which we feel obliged to maintain at any cost."

"Yes," she said. "The years that are gone seem like dreams—if one might go on sleeping and dreaming—but to wake up and find—oh! well! perhaps it is better to wake up after all, even to suffer, rather than to remain a dupe to illusions all one's life."

"It seems to me, my dear child," said the Doctor at parting, holding her hand, "you seem to me to be in trouble. I am not going to ask for your confidence. I will only say that if ever you feel moved to give it to me, perhaps I might help you. I know I would understand, and I tell you there are not many who would—not many, my dear."

"Some way I don't feel moved to speak of things that trouble me. Don't think I am ungrateful or that I don't appreciate your sympathy. There are periods of despondency and suffering which take possession of me. But I don't want anything but my own way. That is wanting a good deal, of course, when you have to trample upon the lives, the hearts, the prejudices of others—but no matter—still, I shouldn't want to trample upon the little lives. Oh! I don't know what I'm saying, Doctor. Good night. Don't blame me for anything."

"Yes, I will blame you if you don't come and see me soon. We will talk of things you never have dreamt of talking about before. It will do us both good. I don't want you to blame yourself, whatever comes. Good night, my child."

She let herself in at the gate, but instead of entering she sat upon the step of the porch. The night was quiet and soothing. All the tearing emotion of the last few hours seemed to fall away from her like a somber, uncomfortable garment, which she had but to loosen to be rid of. She went back to that hour before Adèle had sent for her; and her senses kindled afresh in thinking of Robert's words, the pressure of his arms, and the feeling of his lips upon her own. She could picture at that moment no greater bliss on earth than possession of the beloved one. His expression of love had already given him to her in part. When she thought that he was there at hand, waiting for her, she grew numb with the intoxication of expectancy. It was so late; he should be asleep perhaps. She would awaken him with a kiss. She hoped he would be asleep that she might arouse him with her caresses.

Still, she remembered Adèle's voice whispering, "Think of the children; think of them." She meant to think of them, that determination had driven into her soul like a death wound—but not to-night. To-morrow would be time to think of everything.

Robert was not waiting for her in the little parlor. He was nowhere at hand. The house was empty. But he had scrawled on a piece of paper that lay in the lamplight:

"I love you. Good-by—because I love you."

Edna grew faint when she read the words. She went and sat on the sofa. Then she stretched herself out there, never uttering a sound. She did not sleep. She did not go to bed. The lamp sputtered and went out. She was still awake in the morning, when Celestine unlocked the kitchen door and came in to light the fire.

XXXIX

Victor, with hammer and nails and scraps of scantling,[4] was patching a corner of one of the galleries. Mariequita sat near by, dangling her legs, watching him work, and handing him nails from the tool-box. The sun was beating down upon them. The girl had covered her head with her apron folded into a square pad. They had been talking for an hour or more. She was never tired of hearing Victor describe the dinner at Mrs. Pontellier's. He exaggerated every detail, making it appear a veritable Lucullean feast.[5] The flowers were in tubs, he said. The champagne was quaffed from huge golden goblets. Venus rising from the foam[6] could have presented no more entrancing a spectacle than Mrs. Pontellier, blazing with beauty and diamonds at the head of the board, while the other women were all of them youthful houris[7] possessed of incomparable charms.

She got it into her head that Victor was in love with Mrs. Pontellier, and he gave her evasive answers, framed so as to confirm her belief. She grew sullen and cried a little, threatening to go off and leave him to his fine ladies. There were a dozen men crazy about her at the *Chênière*; and since it was the fashion to be in love with married people, why she could run away any time she liked to New Orleans with Célina's husband.

Célina's husband was a fool, a coward, and a pig, and to prove it to her, Victor intended to hammer his head into a jelly the next time he encountered him. This assurance was very consoling to Mariequita. She dried her eyes, and grew cheerful at the prospect.

They were still talking of the dinner and the allurements of city life when Mrs. Pontellier herself slipped around the corner of the house. The two youngsters stayed dumb with amazement before what they considered to be an apparition. But it was really she in flesh and blood, looking tired and a little travel-stained.

"I walked up from the wharf," she said, "and heard the hammering. I supposed it was you, mending the porch. It's a good thing. I was always tripping over those loose planks last summer. How dreary and deserted everything looks!"

It took Victor some little time to comprehend that she had come in Beaudelet's lugger, that she had come alone, and for no purpose but to rest.

"There's nothing fixed up yet, you see. I'll give you my room; it's the only place."

"Any corner will do," she assured him.

"And if you can stand Philomel's cooking," he went on, "though I might try to get her mother while you are here. Do you think she would come?" turning to Mariequita.

Mariequita thought that perhaps Philomel's mother might come for a few days, and money enough.

Beholding Mrs. Pontellier make her appearance, the girl had at once suspected a lovers' rendezvous. But Victor's astonishment was so genuine, and Mrs. Pontellier's indifference so apparent, that the disturbing notion did not

4. Small bits of wood.
5. The Roman general Lucius Licinius Lucullus (ca. 177–ca. 57 B.C.E.) was noted for his extravagant banquets.

6. The Roman goddess of love and beauty was born out of the sea-foam.
7. Beautiful maidens in the Muslim paradise.

lodge long in her brain. She contemplated with the greatest interest this woman who gave the most sumptuous dinners in America, and who had all the men in New Orleans at her feet.

"What time will you have dinner?" asked Edna. "I'm very hungry; but don't get anything extra."

"I'll have it ready in little or no time," he said, bustling and packing away his tools. "You may go to my room to brush up and rest yourself. Mariequita will show you."

"Thank you," said Edna. "But, do you know, I have a notion to go down to the beach and take a good wash and even a little swim, before dinner?"

"The water is too cold!" they both exclaimed. "Don't think of it."

"Well, I might go down and try—dip my toes in. Why, it seems to me the sun is hot enough to have warmed the very depths of the ocean. Could you get me a couple of towels? I'd better go right away, so as to be back in time. It would be a little too chilly if I waited till this afternoon."

Mariequita ran over to Victor's room, and returned with some towels, which she gave to Edna.

"I hope you have fish for dinner," said Edna, as she started to walk away; "but don't do anything extra if you haven't."

"Run and find Philomel's mother," Victor instructed the girl. "I'll go to the kitchen and see what I can do. By Gimminy! Women have no consideration! She might have sent me word."

Edna walked on down to the beach rather mechanically, not noticing anything special except that the sun was hot. She was not dwelling upon any particular train of thought. She had done all the thinking which was necessary after Robert went away, when she lay awake upon the sofa till morning.

She had said over and over to herself: "To-day it is Arobin; tomorrow it will be some one else. It makes no difference to me, it doesn't matter about Léonce Pontellier—but Raoul and Étienne!" She understood now clearly what she had meant long ago when she said to Adèle Ratignolle that she would give up the unessential, but she would never sacrifice herself for her children.

Despondency had come upon her there in the wakeful night, and had never lifted. There was no one thing in the world that she desired. There was no human being whom she wanted near her except Robert; and she even realized that the day would come when he, too, and the thought of him would melt out of her existence, leaving her alone. The children appeared before her like antagonists who had overcome her; who had overpowered her and sought to drag her into the soul's slavery for the rest of her days. But she knew a way to elude them. She was not thinking of these things when she walked down to the beach.

The water of the Gulf stretched out before her gleaming with the million lights of the sun. The voice of the sea is seductive, never ceasing, whispering, clamoring, murmuring, inviting the soul to wander in abysses of solitude. All along the white beach, up and down, there was no living thing in sight. A bird with a broken wing was beating the air above, reeling, fluttering, circling disabled down, down to the water.

Edna had found her old bathing suit still hanging, faded, upon its accustomed peg.

She put it on, leaving her clothing in the bath-house. But when she was there beside the sea, absolutely alone, she cast the unpleasant, pricking garments from her, and for the first time in her life she stood naked in the open air, at the mercy of the sun, the breeze that beat upon her, and the waves that invited her.

How strange and awful it seemed to stand naked under the sky! how delicious! She felt like some new-born creature, opening its eyes in a familiar world that it had never known.

The foamy wavelets curled up to her white feet, and coiled like serpents about her ankles. She walked out. The water was chill, but she walked on. The water was deep, but she lifted her white body and reached out with a long, sweeping stroke. The touch of the sea is sensuous, enfolding the body in its soft, close embrace.

She went on and on. She remembered the night she swam far out, and recalled the terror that seized her at the fear of being unable to regain the shore. She did not look back now, but went on and on, thinking of the blue-grass meadow that she had traversed when a little child, believing that it had no beginning and no end.

Her arms and legs were growing tired.

She thought of Léonce and the children. They were a part of her life. But they need not have thought that they could possess her, body and soul. How Mademoiselle Reisz would have laughed, perhaps sneered, if she knew! "And you call yourself an artist! What pretensions, Madame! The artist must possess the courageous soul that dares and defies."

Exhaustion was pressing upon and over-powering her.

"Good-by—because, I love you." He did not know; he did not understand. He would never understand. Perhaps Doctor Mandelet would have understood if she had seen him—but it was too late; the shore was far behind her, and her strength was gone.

She looked into the distance, and the old terror flamed up for an instant, then sank again. Edna heard her father's voice and her sister Margaret's. She heard the barking of an old dog that was chained to the sycamore tree. The spurs of the cavalry officer clanged as he walked across the porch. There was the hum of bees, and the musky odor of pinks filled the air.

1899

MARY E. WILKINS FREEMAN
1852–1930

Mary E. Wilkins Freeman's finest short stories hauntingly explore the lives of aging New England women who confront their destitution with sturdy, even ferocious, independence. Whether, like Louisa Ellis of "A New England Nun," they refuse marriage in order to protect the seclusion and sanctity of virginity or, like Sarah Penn of "The Revolt of 'Mother,'" they assert their right to control the domestic sphere in which they have been placed, Freeman's heroines recognize their isolation and defi-

antly struggle to preserve their integrity against the demands of the importunate suitors, husbands, and preachers who represent all that is left of a dwindling Puritan culture. Like Sarah Orne Jewett, Freeman wrote in and about a region that had experienced a striking demographic change, namely the decline of the male population after the Civil War and the depression in New England's rural village economy.

The town in which Freeman spent most of her life, Randolph, Massachusetts, was populated by farmers, cottage workers in the shoe industry, and house carpenters like her father, Warren Wilkins. Both he and his wife, Eleanor (Lothrop) Wilkins, could trace their ancestry back to seventeenth-century New England settlers. Their first surviving infant, Mary Wilkins was seven years old when her sister was born. At this age, too, in the village school, she met Mary Wales, a friend she would cherish throughout her life. At fifteen, she moved to Brattleboro, Vermont, where her father hoped to improve the family's fortunes by becoming part-owner of a dry goods store. But the next sixteen years would be filled with disappointments. After graduating from Brattleboro High School in 1870 and spending one unhappy year at Mount Holyoke Female Seminary, Mary Wilkins apparently fell in love with one Hanson Tyler. While the biographical details of this failed relationship are obscure, it is clear that it was accompanied by a series of other difficulties: Mary Wilkins's father went out of business, her one friend left town, her younger sister died, and the family moved into the house of Hanson Tyler's father, with Eleanor Wilkins employed as the Reverend Tyler's housekeeper. When she died suddenly in 1880 and Warren Wilkins died three years later, the thirty-one-year-old Mary Wilkins found herself alone and impoverished.

What saved Freeman from destitution and depression was the literary success she had already begun to achieve. Children's poems in a local magazine, *Wide Awake,* had brought small sums, but in 1882 she had won a fifty-dollar prize offered by a leading Boston magazine for adult fiction, and that same year *Harper's Bazaar* sent her twenty-five dollars with an encouraging acceptance letter. Returning to Randolph, this time to live in the Wales household, Wilkins benefited for the next twenty years from the care of her childhood friend, for Mary Wales freed her from housekeeping chores and solaced her during the nightmares that frequently disturbed her sleep and that may have been responsible for her later addiction to sedatives. *A Humble Romance and Other Stories* (1887) and *A New England Nun and Other Stories* (1891) are usually considered Wilkins's best work. After 1895, when she began traveling to Brattleboro, Boston, Chicago, and Paris, she was well established as a "local color" realist.

In spite of her financial success and fame, one index of Wilkins's troubled state of mind was her decade-long indecision about whether or not to commit herself to marriage. She had met Dr. Charles Freeman, a nonpracticing physician, in 1892. She was forty-nine years old when, after breaking the engagement and postponing the wedding, she married him in 1902. During the first years of their marriage, he was supportive of her writing, and she published a number of stories about the local customs of her new home, Metuchen, New Jersey. But in 1909 Dr. Freeman entered a sanitarium for alcoholism, the first of a series of such confinements. Before his death, his wife had obtained a legal separation, and after it she successfully contested his will, in which he had left most of his property to someone else. Wealthy at the end of her life, she was awarded the Howells Medal for Fiction in 1926, the same year that she and Edith Wharton became the first women to be elected to membership in the National Institute of Arts and Letters. When she died at seventy-eight, Freeman had published twenty volumes of adult fiction—novels and short stories—as well as six volumes of children's stories. "The Revolt of 'Mother' " demonstrates the wit and verve of her best work, in which a traditional farmwife, Sarah Penn stages a surprising domestic insurrection, much to the consternation of her children and husband.

The Revolt of "Mother"

"Father!"

"What is it?"

"What are them men diggin' over there in the field for?"

There was a sudden dropping and enlarging of the lower part of the old man's face, as if some heavy weight had settled therein; he shut his mouth tight, and went on harnessing the great bay mare. He hustled the collar on to her neck with a jerk.

"Father!"

The old man slapped the saddle upon the mare's back.

"Look here, father, I want to know what them men are diggin' over in the field for, an' I'm goin' to know."

"I wish you'd go into the house, mother, an' 'tend to your own affairs," the old man said then. He ran his words together, and his speech was almost as inarticulate as a growl.

But the woman understood; it was her most native tongue. "I ain't goin' into the house till you tell me what them men are doin' over there in the field," said she.

Then she stood waiting. She was a small woman, short and straight-waisted like a child in her brown cotton gown. Her forehead was mild and benevolent between the smooth curves of gray hair; there were meek downward lines about her nose and mouth; but her eyes, fixed upon the old man, looked as if the meekness had been the result of her own will, never of the will of another.

They were in the barn, standing before the wide open doors. The spring air, full of the smell of growing grass and unseen blossoms, came in their faces. The deep yard in front was littered with farm wagons and piles of wood; on the edges, close to the fence and the house, the grass was a vivid green, and there were some dandelions.

The old man glanced doggedly at his wife as he tightened the last buckles on the harness. She looked as immovable to him as one of the rocks in his pasture-land, bound to the earth with generations of blackberry vines. He slapped the reins over the horse, and started forth from the barn.

"*Father!*" said she.

The old man pulled up. "What is it?"

"I want to know what them men are diggin' over there in that field for."

"They're diggin' a cellar, I s'pose, if you've got to know."

"A cellar for what?"

"A barn."

"A barn? You ain't goin' to build a barn over there where we was goin' to have a house, father?"

The old man said not another word. He hurried the horse into the farm wagon, and clattered out of the yard, jouncing as sturdily on his seat as a boy.

The woman stood a moment looking after him, then she went out of the barn across a corner of the yard to the house. The house, standing at right angles with the great barn and a long reach of sheds and out-buildings, was infinitesimal compared with them. It was scarcely as commodious for people as the little boxes under the barn eaves were for doves.

A pretty girl's face, pink and delicate as a flower, was looking out of one of the house windows. She was watching three men who were digging over in the field which bounded the yard near the road line. She turned quietly when the woman entered.

"What are they digging for, mother?" said she. "Did he tell you?"

"They're diggin' for—a cellar for a new barn."

"Oh, mother, he ain't going to build another barn?"

"That's what he says."

A boy stood before the kitchen glass combing his hair. He combed slowly and painstakingly, arranging his brown hair in a smooth hillock over his forehead. He did not seem to pay any attention to the conversation.

"Sammy, did you know father was going to build a new barn?" asked the girl.

The boy combed assiduously.

"Sammy!"

He turned, and showed a face like his father's under his smooth crest of hair. "Yes, I s'pose I did," he said, reluctantly.

"How long have you known it?" asked his mother.

" 'Bout three months, I guess."

"Why didn't you tell of it?"

"Didn't think 'twould do no good."

"I don't see what father wants another barn for," said the girl, in her sweet, slow voice. She turned again to the window, and stared out at the digging men in the field. Her tender, sweet face was full of a gentle distress. Her forehead was as bald and innocent as a baby's, with the light hair strained back from it in a row of curl-papers. She was quite large, but her soft curves did not look as if they covered muscles.

Her mother looked sternly at the boy. "Is he goin' to buy more cows?" said she.

The boy did not reply; he was tying his shoes.

"Sammy, I want you to tell me if he's goin' to buy more cows."

"I s'pose he is."

"How many?"

"Four, I guess."

His mother said nothing more. She went into the pantry, and there was a clatter of dishes. The boy got his cap from a nail behind the door, took an old arithmetic[1] from the shelf, and started for school. He was lightly built, but clumsy. He went out of the yard with a curious spring in the hips, that made his loose home-made jacket tilt up in the rear.

The girl went to the sink, and began to wash the dishes that were piled up there. Her mother came promptly out of the pantry, and shoved her aside. "You wipe 'em," said she; "I'll wash. There's a good many this mornin'."

The mother plunged her hands vigorously into the water, the girl wiped the plates slowly and dreamily. "Mother," said she, "don't you think it's too bad father's going to build that new barn, much as we need a decent house to live in?"

Her mother scrubbed a dish fiercely. "You ain't found out yet we're women-folks, Nanny Penn," said she. "You ain't seen enough of men-folks yet to.

1. Treatise on computation.

One of these days you'll find it out, an' then you'll know that we know only what men-folks think we do, so far as any use of it goes, an' how we'd ought to reckon men-folks in with Providence, an' not complain of what they do any more than we do of the weather."

"I don't care; I don't believe George is anything like that, anyhow," said Nanny. Her delicate face flushed pink, her lips pouted softly, as if she were going to cry.

"You wait an' see. I guess George Eastman ain't no better than other men. You hadn't ought to judge father, though. He can't help it,'cause he don't look at things jest the way we do. An' we've been pretty comfortable here, after all. The roof don't leak—ain't never but once—that's one thing. Father's kept it shingled right up."

"I do wish we had a parlor."

"I guess it won't hurt George Eastman any to come to see you in a nice clean kitchen. I guess a good many girls don't have as good a place as this. Nobody's ever heard me complain."

"I ain't complained either, mother."

"Well, I don't think you'd better, a good father an' a good home as you've got. S'pose your father made you go out an' work for your livin'? Lots of girls have to that ain't no stronger an' better able to than you be."

Sarah Penn washed the frying-pan with a conclusive air. She scrubbed the outside of it as faithfully as the inside. She was a masterly keeper of her box of a house. Her one living-room never seemed to have in it any of the dust which the friction of life with inanimate matter produces. She swept, and there seemed to be no dirt to go before the broom; she cleaned, and one could see no difference. She was like an artist so perfect that he has apparently no art. To-day she got out a mixing bowl and a board, and rolled some pies, and there was no more flour upon her than upon her daughter who was doing finer work. Nanny was to be married in the fall, and she was sewing on some white cambric and embroidery. She sewed industriously while her mother cooked, her soft milk-white hands and wrists showed whiter than her delicate work.

"We must have the stove moved out in the shed before long," said Mrs. Penn. "Talk about not havin' things, it's been a real blessin' to be able to put a stove up in that shed in hot weather. Father did one good thing when he fixed that stove-pipe out there."

Sarah Penn's face as she rolled her pies had that expression of meek vigor which might have characterized one of the New Testament saints. She was making mince-pies. Her husband, Adoniram Penn, liked them better than any other kind. She baked twice a week. Adoniram often liked a piece of pie between meals. She hurried this morning. It had been later than usual when she began, and she wanted to have a pie baked for dinner. However deep a resentment she might be forced to hold against her husband, she would never fail in sedulous attention to his wants.

Nobility of character manifests itself at loop-holes when it is not provided with large doors. Sarah Penn's showed itself to-day in flaky dishes of pastry. So she made the pies faithfully, while across the table she could see, when she glanced up from her work, the sight that rankled in her patient and steadfast soul—the digging of the cellar of the new barn in the place where Adoniram forty years ago had promised her their new house should stand.

The pies were done for dinner. Adoniram and Sammy were home a few minutes after twelve o'clock. The dinner was eaten with serious haste. There was never much conversation at the table in the Penn family. Adoniram asked a blessing, and they ate promptly, then rose up and went about their work.

Sammy went back to school, taking soft sly lopes out of the yard like a rabbit. He wanted a game of marbles before school, and feared his father would give him some chores to do. Adoniram hastened to the door and called after him, but he was out of sight.

"I don't see what you let him go for, mother," said he. "I wanted him to help me unload that wood."

Adoniram went to work out in the yard unloading wood from the wagon. Sarah put away the dinner dishes, while Nanny took down her curl-papers and changed her dress. She was going down to the store to buy some more embroidery and thread.

When Nanny was gone, Mrs. Penn went to the door. "Father!" she called.

"Well, what is it!"

"I want to see you jest a minute, father."

"I can't leave this wood nohow. I've got to git it unloaded an' go for a load of gravel afore two o'clock. Sammy had ought to helped me. You hadn't ought to let him go to school so early."

"I want to see you jest a minute."

"I tell ye I can't, nohow, mother."

"Father, you come here." Sarah Penn stood in the door like a queen; she held her head as if it bore a crown; there was that patience which makes authority royal in her voice. Adoniram went.

Mrs. Penn led the way into the kitchen, and pointed to a chair. "Sit down, father," said she; "I've got somethin' I want to say to you."

He sat down heavily; his face was quite stolid, but he looked at her with restive eyes. "Well, what is it, mother?"

"I want to know what you're buildin' that new barn for, father?"

"I ain't got nothin' to say about it."

"It can't be you think you need another barn?"

"I tell ye I ain't got nothin' to say about it, mother; an' I ain't goin' to say nothin'."

"Be you goin' to buy more cows?"

Adoniram did not reply; he shut his mouth tight.

"I know you be, as well as I want to. Now, father, look here"—Sarah Penn had not sat down; she stood before her husband in the humble fashion of a Scripture woman[2]—"I'm goin' to talk real plain to you; I never have sence I married you, but I'm goin' to now. I ain't never complained, an' I ain't goin' to complain now, but I'm goin' to talk plain. You see this room here, father; you look at it well. You see there ain't no carpet on the floor, an' you see the paper is all dirty, an' droppin' off the walls. We ain't had no new paper on it for ten year, an' then I put it on myself, an' it didn't cost but ninepence a roll. You see this room, father; it's all the one I've had to work in an' eat in an' sit in sence we was married. There ain't another woman in the whole town whose husband ain't got half the means you have but what's got better.

2. I.e., submissive, as several verses in the New Testament command. See especially Ephesians 5.21, Colossians 3.18: "Wives, submit yourselves unto your own husbands."

It's all the room Nanny's got to have her company in; an' there ain't one of her mates but what's got better, an' their fathers not so able as hers is. It's all the room she'll have to be married in. What would you have thought, father, if we had had our weddin' in a room no better than this? I was married in my mother's parlor, with a carpet on the floor, an' stuffed furniture, an' a mahogany card-table. An' this is all the room my daughter will have to be married in. Look here, father!"

Sarah Penn went across the room as though it were a tragic stage. She flung open a door and disclosed a tiny bedroom; only large enough for a bed and bureau, with a path between. "There, father," said she—"there's all the room I've had to sleep in forty year. All my children were born there—the two that died, an' the two that's livin'. I was sick with a fever there."

She stepped to another door and opened it. It led into the small, ill-lighted pantry. "Here," said she, "is all the buttery[3] I've got—every place I've got for my dishes, to set away my victuals in, an' to keep my milk-pans in. Father, I've been takin' care of the milk of six cows in this place, an' now you're goin' to build a new barn, an' keep more cows, an' give me more to do in it."

She threw open another door. A narrow crooked flight of stairs wound upward from it. "There, father," said she, "I want you to look at the stairs that go up to them two unfinished chambers that are all the places our son an' daughter have had to sleep in all their lives. There ain't a prettier girl in town nor a more ladylike one than Nanny, an' that's the place she has to sleep in. It ain't so good as your horse's stall; it ain't so warm an' tight."

Sarah Penn went back and stood before her husband. "Now, father," said she, "I want to know if you think you're doin' right an' accordin' to what you profess. Here, when we was married, forty year ago, you promised me faithful that we should have a new house built in a that lot over in the field before the year was out. You said you had money enough, an' you wouldn't ask me to live in no such place as this. It is forty year now, an' you've been makin' more money, an' I've been savin' of it for you ever since, an' you ain't built no house yet. You've built sheds an' cow-houses an' one new barn, an' now you're goin' to build another. Father, I want to know if you think it's right. You're lodgin' your dumb beasts better than you are your own flesh an' blood. I want to know if you think it's right."

"I ain't got nothin' to say."

"You can't say nothin' without ownin' it ain't right, father. An' there's another thing—I ain't complained; I've got along forty year, an' I s'pose I should forty more, if it wa'n't for that—if we don't have another house. Nanny she can't live with us after she's married. She'll have to go somewheres else to live away from us, an' it don't seem as if I could have it so, noways, father. She wa'n't ever strong. She's got considerable color, but there wa'n't never any backbone to her. I've always took the heft of everything off her, an' she ain't fit to keep house an' do everything herself. She'll be all worn out inside of a year. Think of her doin' all the washin' an' ironin' an' bakin' with them soft white hands an' arms, an' sweepin'! I can't have it so, noways, father."

Mrs. Penn's face was burning; her mild eyes gleamed. She had pleaded her little cause like a Webster;[4] she had ranged from severity to pathos; but

3. Pantry.
4. I.e., like Daniel Webster (1782–1852), American statesman and renowned orator.

her opponent employed that obstinate silence which makes eloquence futile with mocking echoes. Adoniram arose clumsily.

"Father, ain't you got nothin' to say?" said Mrs. Penn.

"I've got to go off after that load of gravel. I can't stan' here talkin' all day."

"Father, won't you think it over, an' have a house built there instead of a barn?"

"I ain't got nothin' to say."

Adoniram shuffled out. Mrs. Penn went into her bedroom. When she came out, her eyes were red. She had a roll of unbleached cotton cloth. She spread it out on the kitchen table, and began cutting out some shirts for her husband. The men over in the field had a team to help them this afternoon; she could hear their halloos. She had a scanty pattern for the shirts; she had to plan and piece the sleeves.

Nanny came home with her embroidery, and sat down with her needle-work. She had taken down her curl-papers, and there was a soft roll of fair hair like an aureole over her forehead; her face was as delicately fine and clear as porcelain. Suddenly she looked up, and the tender red flamed all over her face and neck. "Mother," said she.

"What say?"

"I've been thinking—I don't see how we're goin' to have any—wedding in this room. I'd be ashamed to have his folks come if we didn't have anybody else."

"Mebbe we can have some new paper before then; I can put it on. I guess you won't have no call to be ashamed of your belongin's."

"We might have the wedding in the new barn," said Nanny, with gentle pettishness. "Why, mother, what makes you look so?"

Mrs. Penn had started, and was staring at her with a curious expression. She turned again to her work, and spread out a pattern carefully on the cloth. "Nothin'," said she.

Presently Adoniram clattered out of the yard in his two-wheeled dump cart, standing as proudly upright as a Roman charioteer. Mrs. Penn opened the door and stood there a minute looking out; the halloos of the men sounded louder.

It seemed to her all through the spring months that she heard nothing but the halloos and the noises of saws and hammers. The new barn grew fast. It was a fine edifice for this little village. Men came on pleasant Sundays, in their meeting suits and clean shirt bosoms, and stood around it admiringly. Mrs. Penn did not speak of it, and Adoniram did not mention it to her, although sometimes, upon a return from inspecting it, he bore himself with injured dignity.

"It's a strange thing how your mother feels about the new barn," he said, confidentially, to Sammy one day.

Sammy only grunted after an odd fashion for a boy; he had learned it from his father.

The barn was all completed ready for use by the third week in July. Adoniram had planned to move his stock in on Wednesday; on Tuesday he received a letter which changed his plans. He came in with it early in the morning. "Sammy's been to the post-office," said he, "an' I've got a letter from Hiram." Hiram was Mrs. Penn's brother, who lived in Vermont.

"Well," said Mrs. Penn, "what does he say about the folks?"

"I guess they're all right. He says he thinks if I come up country right off there's a chance to buy jest the kind of a horse I want." He stared reflectively out of the window at the new barn.

Mrs. Penn was making pies. She went on clapping the rolling-pin into the crust, although she was very pale, and her heart beat loudly.

"I dun' know but what I'd better go," said Adoniram. "I hate to go off jest now, right in the midst of hayin', but the ten-acre lot's cut, an' I guess Rufus an' the others can git along without me three or four days. I can't get a horse round here to suit me, nohow, an' I've got to have another for all that wood-haulin' in the fall. I told Hiram to watch out, an' if he got wind of a good horse to let me know. I guess I'd better go."

"I'll get out your clean shirt an' collar," said Mrs. Penn calmly.

She laid out Adoniram's Sunday suit and his clean clothes on the bed in the little bedroom. She got his shaving-water and razor ready. At last she buttoned on his collar and fastened his black cravat.

Adoniram never wore his collar and cravat except on extra occasions. He held his head high, with a rasped dignity. When he was all ready, with his coat and hat brushed, and a lunch of pie and cheese in a paper bag, he hesitated on the threshold of the door. He looked at his wife, and his manner was defiantly apologetic. "If them cows come to-day, Sammy can drive 'em into the new barn," said he; "an' when they bring the hay up, they can pitch it in there."

"Well," replied Mrs. Penn.

Adoniram set his shaven face ahead and started. When he had cleared the door-step, he turned and looked back with a kind of nervous solemnity. "I shall be back by Saturday if nothin' happens," said he.

"Do be careful, father," returned his wife.

She stood in the door with Nanny at her elbow and watched him out of sight. Her eyes had a strange, doubtful expression in them; her peaceful forehead was contracted. She went in, and about her baking again. Nanny sat sewing. Her wedding-day was drawing nearer, and she was getting pale and thin with her steady sewing. Her mother kept glancing at her.

"Have you got that pain in your side this mornin'?" she asked.

"A little."

Mrs. Penn's face, as she worked, changed, her perplexed forehead smoothed, her eyes were steady, her lips firmly set. She formed a maxim for herself, although incoherently with her unlettered thoughts. "Unsolicited opportunities are the guide-posts of the Lord to the new roads of life," she repeated in effect, and she made up her mind to her course of action.

"S'posin' I *had* wrote to Hiram," she muttered once, when she was in the pantry—"s'posin' I had wrote, an' asked him if he knew of any horse? But I didn't, an' father's goin' wa'n't none of my doin'. It looks like a providence." Her voice rang out quite loud at the last.

"What you talkin' about, mother?" called Nanny.

"Nothin'."

Mrs. Penn hurried her baking; at eleven o'clock it was all done. The load of hay from the west field came slowly down the cart track, and drew up at the new barn. Mrs. Penn ran out. "Stop!" she screamed—"stop!"

The men stopped and looked; Sammy upreared from the top of the load, and stared at his mother.

"Stop!" she cried out again. "Don't you put the hay in that barn; put it in the old one."

"Why, he said to put it in here," returned one of the hay-makers, wonderingly. He was a young man, a neighbor's son, whom Adoniram hired by the year to help on the farm.

"Don't you put the hay in the new barn; there's room enough in the old one, ain't there?" said Mrs. Penn.

"Room enough," returned the hired man, in his thick, rustic tones. "Didn't need the new barn, nohow, far as room's concerned. Well, I s'pose he changed his mind." He took hold of the horses' bridles.

Mrs. Penn went back to the house. Soon the kitchen windows were darkened, and a fragrance like warm honey came into the room.

Nanny laid down her work. "I thought father wanted them to put the hay into the new barn?" she said, wonderingly.

"It's all right," replied her mother.

Sammy slid down from the load of hay, and came in to see if dinner was ready.

"I ain't goin' to get a regular dinner to-day, as long as father's gone," said his mother. "I've let the fire go out. You can have some bread an' milk an' pie. I thought we could get along." She set out some bowls of milk, some bread, and a pie on the kitchen table. "You'd better eat your dinner now," said she. "You might jest as well get through with it. I want you to help me afterward."

Nanny and Sammy stared at each other. There was something strange in their mother's manner. Mrs. Penn did not eat anything herself. She went into the pantry, and they heard her moving dishes while they ate. Presently she came out with a pile of plates. She got the clothes-basket out of the shed, and packed them in it. Nanny and Sammy watched. She brought out cups and saucers, and put them in with the plates.

"What you goin' to do, mother?" inquired Nanny, in a timid voice. A sense of something unusual made her tremble, as if it were a ghost. Sammy rolled his eyes over his pie.

"You'll see what I'm goin' to do," replied Mrs. Penn. "If you're through, Nanny, I want you to go up-stairs an' pack up your things; an' I want you, Sammy, to help me take down the bed in the bedroom."

"Oh, mother, what for?" gasped Nanny.

"You'll see."

During the next few hours a feat was performed by this simple, pious New England mother which was equal in its way to Wolfe's storming of the Heights of Abraham.[5] It took no more genius and audacity of bravery for Wolfe to cheer his wondering soldiers up those steep precipices, under the sleeping eyes of the enemy, than for Sarah Penn, at the head of her children, to move all their little household goods into the new barn while her husband was away.

Nanny and Sammy followed their mother's instructions without a murmur; indeed, they were overawed. There is a certain uncanny and superhuman quality about all such purely original undertakings as their mother's was

5. In the battle against the French that secured British control of North America, Major General James Wolfe (1727–1759) led his troops up the heights of the Plains of Abraham, just outside the city walls of Quebec; his mortal wounding on the field was the subject of a famous and much-reproduced painting.

to them. Nanny went back and forth with her light loads, and Sammy tugged with sober energy.

At five o'clock in the afternoon the little house in which the Penns had lived for forty years had emptied itself into the new barn.

Every builder builds somewhat for unknown purposes, and is in a measure a prophet. The architect of Adoniram Penn's barn, while he designed it for the comfort of four-footed animals, had planned better than he knew for the comfort of humans. Sarah Penn saw at a glance its possibilities. Those great box-stalls, with quilts hung before them, would make better bedrooms than the one she had occupied for forty years, and there was a tight carriage-room. The harness-room, with its chimney and shelves, would make a kitchen of her dreams. The great middle space would make a parlor, by-and-by, fit for a palace. Up stairs there was as much room as down. With partitions and windows, what a house would there be! Sarah looked at the row of stanchions[6] before the allotted space for cows, and reflected that she would have her front entry there.

At six o'clock the stove was up in the harness-room, the kettle was boiling, and the table set for tea. It looked almost as home-like as the abandoned house across the yard had ever done. The young hired man milked, and Sarah directed him calmly to bring the milk to the new barn. He came gaping, dropping little blots of foam from the brimming pails on the grass. Before the next morning he had spread the story of Adoniram Penn's wife moving into the new barn all over the little village. Men assembled in the store and talked it over, women with shawls over their heads scuttled into each other's houses before their work was done. Any deviation from the ordinary course of life in this quiet town was enough to stop all progress in it. Everybody paused to look at the staid, independent figure on the side track.[7] There was a difference of opinion with regard to her. Some held her to be insane; some, of a lawless and rebellious spirit.

Friday the minister went to see her. It was in the forenoon, and she was at the barn door shelling pease for dinner. She looked up and returned his salutation with dignity, then she went on with her work. She did not invite him in. The saintly expression of her face remained fixed, but there was an angry flush over it.

The minister stood awkwardly before her, and talked. She handled the pease as if they were bullets. At last she looked up, and her eyes showed the spirit that her meek front had covered for a lifetime.

"There ain't no use talkin', Mr. Hersey," said she. "I've thought it all over an' over, an' I believe I'm doin' what's right. I've made it the subject of prayer, an' it's betwixt me an' the Lord an' Adoniram. There ain't no call for nobody else to worry about it."

"Well, of course, if you have brought it to the Lord in prayer, and feel satisfied that you are doing right, Mrs. Penn," said the minister, helplessly. His thin gray-bearded face was pathetic. He was a sickly man; his youthful confidence had cooled; he had to scourge himself up to some of his pastoral duties as relentlessly as a Catholic ascetic, and then he was prostrated by the smart.

6. Devices that fit loosely around the cows' necks to limit their movement in the stalls.

7. Literally, a railway siding.

"I think it's right jest as much as I think it was right for our forefathers to come over from the old country 'cause they didn't have what belonged to 'em," said Mrs. Penn. She arose. The barn threshold might have been Plymouth Rock[8] from her bearing. "I don't doubt you mean well, Mr. Hersey," said she, "but there are things people hadn't ought to interfere with. I've been a member of the church for over forty year. I've got my own mind an' my own feet, an' I'm goin' to think my own thoughts an' go my own ways, an' nobody but the Lord is goin' to dictate to me unless I've a mind to have him. Won't you come in an' set down? How is Mis' Hersey?"

"She is well, I thank you," replied the minister. He added some more perplexed apologetic remarks; then he retreated.

He could expound the intricacies of every character study in the Scriptures, he was competent to grasp the Pilgrim Fathers and all historical innovators, but Sarah Penn was beyond him. He could deal with primal cases, but parallel ones worsted him. But, after all, although it was aside from his province, he wondered more how Adoniram Penn would deal with his wife than how the Lord would. Everybody shared the wonder. When Adoniram's four new cows arrived, Sarah ordered three to be put in the old barn, the other in the house shed where the cooking-stove had stood. That added to the excitement. It was whispered that all four cows were domiciled in the house.

Towards sunset on Saturday, when Adoniram was expected home, there was a knot of men in the road near the new barn. The hired man had milked, but he still hung around the premises. Sarah Penn had supper all ready. There were brown-bread and baked beans and a custard pie; it was the supper that Adoniram loved on a Saturday night. She had on a clean calico, and she bore herself imperturbably. Nanny and Sammy kept close at her heels. Their eyes were large, and Nanny was full of nervous tremors. Still there was to them more pleasant excitement than anything else. An inborn confidence in their mother over their father asserted itself.

Sammy looked out of the harness-room window. "There he is," he announced, in an awed whisper. He and Nanny peeped around the casing. Mrs. Penn kept on about her work. The children watched Adoniram leave the new horse standing in the drive while he went to the house door. It was fastened. Then he went around to the shed. That door was seldom locked, even when the family was away. The thought how her father would be confronted by the cow flashed upon Nanny. There was a hysterical sob in her throat. Adoniram emerged from the shed and stood looking about in a dazed fashion. His lips moved; he was saying something, but they could not hear what it was. The hired man was peeping around a corner of the old barn, but nobody saw him.

Adoniram took the new horse by the bridle and led him across the yard to the new barn. Nanny and Sammy slunk close to their mother. The barn doors rolled back, and there stood Adoniram, with the long mild face of the great Canadian farm horse looking over his shoulder.

Nanny kept behind her mother, but Sammy stepped suddenly forward, and stood in front of her.

8. The boulder in Plymouth, Massachusetts, on which, according to legend, the Pilgrims first set foot after disembarking from the *Mayflower* in 1620.

Adoniram stared at the group. "What on airth you all down here for?" said he. "What's the matter over to the house?"

"We've come here to live, father," said Sammy. His shrill voice quavered out bravely.

"What"—Adoniram sniffed—"what is it smells like cookin?" said he. He stepped forward and looked in the open door of the harness-room. Then he turned to his wife. His old bristling face was pale and frightened. "What on airth does this mean, mother?" he gasped.

"You come in here, father," said Sarah. She led the way into the harness-room and shut the door. "Now, father," said she, "you needn't be scared. I ain't crazy. There ain't nothin' to be upset over. But we've come here to live, an' we're goin' to live here. We've got jest as good a right here as new horses an' cows. The house wa'n't fit for us to live in any longer, an' I made up my mind I wa'n't goin' to stay there. I've done my duty by you forty year, an' I'm goin' to do it now; but I'm goin' to live here. You've got to put in some windows and partitions; an' you'll have to buy some furniture."

"Why, mother!" the old man gasped.

"You'd better take your coat off an' get washed—there's the wash-basin—an' then we'll have supper."

"Why, mother!"

Sammy went past the window, leading the new horse to the old barn. The old man saw him, and shook his head speechlessly. He tried to take off his coat, but his arms seemed to lack the power. His wife helped him. She poured some water into the tin basin, and put in a piece of soap. She got the comb and brush, and smoothed his thin gray hair after he had washed. Then she put the beans, hot bread, and tea on the table. Sammy came in, and the family drew up. Adoniram sat looking dazedly at his plate, and they waited.

"Ain't you goin' to ask a blessin', father?" said Sarah.

And the old man bent his head and mumbled.

All through the meal he stopped eating at intervals, and stared furtively at his wife; but he ate well. The home food tasted good to him, and his old frame was too sturdily healthy to be affected by his mind. But after supper he went out, and sat down on the step of the smaller door at the right of the barn, through which he had meant his Jerseys to pass in stately file, but which Sarah designed for her front house door, and he leaned his head on his hands.

After the supper dishes were cleared away and the milk-pans washed, Sarah went out to him. The twilight was deepening. There was a clear green glow in the sky. Before them stretched the smooth level of field; in the distance was a cluster of hay-stacks like the huts of a village; the air was very cool and calm and sweet. The landscape might have been an ideal one of peace.

Sarah bent over and touched her husband on one of his thin, sinewy shoulders. "Father!"

The old man's shoulders heaved: he was weeping.

"Why, don't do so, father," said Sarah.

"I'll—put up the—partitions, an'—everything you—want, mother."

Sarah put her apron up to her face; she was overcome by her own triumph.

Adoniram was like a fortress whose walls had no active resistance, and went down the instant the right besieging tools were used. "Why, mother," he said, hoarsely, "I hadn't no idee you was so set on't as all this comes to."

1891

OLIVE SCHREINER
1855–1920

South African novelist, feminist, anti-imperialist, socialist, and pacifist, Olive Schreiner was a celebrity in turn-of-the-century England. Her first published novel, *The Story of an African Farm* (1883), was a best seller; her first volume of allegorical fantasies, *Dreams* (1890), was reprinted twenty-four times by 1930; her protest against the racist atrocities of white "pioneers" in Africa, *Trooper Peter Halket* (1897), was quickly translated into German, Swedish, Danish, Dutch, and French; *Woman and Labor* (1911), like its American analogue, Charlotte Perkins Gilman's *Women and Economics* (1898), was hailed by suffragists for its analysis of the historical subjection of women. Yet not only did Schreiner continue to suffer the debilitating consequences of asthma, eating disorders, headaches, and a restlessness that denied her a home, but her most ambitious projects were left unfinished at her death. "Sometimes I don't seem to be alive at all," she admitted at the height of her fame. "No one wants me. I'm [in] no relation with the life or thought in England or Africa or anywhere else." If Schreiner's work is sometimes marred by the self-indulgence that characterizes this remark, it is also frankly ambitious in its effort to align the life and thought of England and colonial Africa with the idealism that imbued her own life and thought.

Such ambition seems especially remarkable given the bleak destitution of Schreiner's early childhood. Born in a Wesleyan mission house, Schreiner was the ninth child of Gottlieb and Rebecca (Lyndall) Schreiner. She was six when the family began to travel over the *karroo* (the South African plains). Her father, a deeply religious missionary, was eventually expelled from the rigid London Missionary Society when he was driven by the family's dire economic need to resort to private trading. While he was sternly orthodox and naively impractical, her mother was unbending in her belief in British superiority over black African natives and Boers (Dutch settlers in Africa) and in her commitment to conventionally Victorian ideas about female decorum.

Both Schreiner's early religious doubts and her feminism reflected prevailing intellectual trends in the late Victorian period, and she read widely in the philosophical works of Herbert Spencer, John Stuart Mill, and Ralph Waldo Emerson. But she received little formal schooling: at eleven, she was sent to live with an older brother and sister; at the age of fifteen, she took the first of a series of positions as governess in Boer farming families. In these inauspicious circumstances, she composed her first two novels, *Undine* and *The Story of an African Farm*. The latter, written under the pseudonym "Ralph Iron," she brought with her to England in 1881 when seeking to train herself as a doctor. Although poor health prevented her from gaining a medical education, the successful publication of *The Story of an African Farm* won her entrance into two pioneering intellectual organizations: the Fellowship of the New Life and the Men and Women's Club. Throughout the 1880s she lived in London

rooming houses, where she wrote essays on prostitution and birth control, planned an edition of Mary Wollstonecraft's *A Vindication of the Rights of Woman,* and spoke on and for the woman question.

At the age of thirty-four, Schreiner returned to South Africa, where she became involved in the antagonisms preceding the Anglo-Boer War (1899–1902). Samuel Cron Cronwright, also an anti-imperialist, was a successful cattle breeder when he and Schreiner decided to marry. Following her wishes, he took her last name and supported her efforts to write, but a series of catastrophes made writing nearly impossible. In 1895 Schreiner gave birth to a nine-pound, nine-ounce daughter, who died mysteriously after only sixteen hours of life. Subsequent miscarriages, imprisonment during the Anglo-Boer War (for her radical political stance), the looting of her Johannesburg home, and the burning of her lengthy manuscript on women and labor (presumably by British troops) only exacerbated her asthma and her writing difficulties. Still, she worked for women's suffrage and women's trade unions even after her return to London before World War I.

Perhaps it was both the pain and the courage of Schreiner's life that made her work so influential. Torn between her love for the physical beauty of Africa and her desire for the intellectual stimulation of England, she was also caught between Victorian certainties and modernist skepticism. As if to announce the advent of a new age, even before Schreiner embarked on her unconventional life she had created the most flamboyant representative of the so-called New Woman in *The Story of an African Farm.* Ironically or not, this rebellious heroine is endowed with Schreiner's mother's maiden name: Lyndall. Lyndall's rage against female socialization results in a diatribe analyzing how "the world makes men and women" out of the "little plastic beings" born into it: "To you," she explains to her male companion, "it says—*Work!* and to us it says—*Seem!*" Refusing such dissembling, Lyndall never relinquishes her faith in "a new time" that would liberate women and thereby bring about the fellowship between the sexes that Schreiner herself craved.

From Woman and Labor

[*Sex-parasitism*]

* * *There never has been, and as far as can be seen, there never will be, a time when the majority of the males in any society will be supported by the rest of the males in a condition of perfect mental and physical inactivity. *"Find labor or die,"* is the choice ultimately put before the human male today, as in the past; and *this* constitutes his labor problem.[1]

The labor of the man may not always be useful in the highest sense to his society, or it may even be distinctly harmful and antisocial, as in the case of the robber-barons of the Middle Ages, who lived by capturing and despoiling all who passed by their castles; or as in the case of the share speculators, stock-jobbers, ring-and-corner capitalists,[2] and monopolists of the present

1. The nearest approach to complete parasitism on the part of a vast body of males occurred, perhaps, in ancient Rome at the time of the decay and downfall of the Empire, when the bulk of the population, male as well as female, was fed on imported corn, wine, and oil, and supplied even with entertainment, almost entirely without exertion or labor of any kind; but this condition was of short duration, and speedily contributed to the downfall of the diseased Empire itself. Among the wealthy and so-called upper classes, the males of various aristocrats have frequently tended to become completely parasitic after a lapse of time, but such a condition has always been met by a short and sharp remedy; and the class has fallen, or become extinct. The condition of the males of the upper classes in France before the Revolution affords an interesting illustration of this point [Schreiner's note].
2. I.e., capitalists who attempt to control the market by price-fixing. "Stock-jobbers": stockbrokers.

day, who feed upon the productive labors of society without contributing anything to its welfare. But even males so occupied are compelled to expend a vast amount of energy and even a low intelligence in their callings; and, however injurious to their societies, they run no personal risk of handing down effete and enervated constitutions to their race. Whether beneficially or unbeneficially, the human male must, generally speaking, employ his intellect, or his muscle, or die.

The position of the unemployed modern female is one wholly different. The choice before her, as her ancient fields of domestic labor slip from her, is not generally or often at the present day the choice between finding new fields of labor, or death; but one far more serious in its ultimate reaction on humanity as a whole—it is the choice between finding new forms of labor or sinking slowly into a condition of more or less complete and passive *sex-parasitism!*[3]

Again and again in the history of the past, when among human creatures a certain stage of material civilization has been reached, a curious tendency has manifested itself for the human female to become more or less parasitic; social conditions tend to rob her of all forms of active conscious social labor, and to reduce her, like the field-bug, to the passive exercise of her sex functions alone. And the result of this parasitism has invariably been the decay in vitality and intelligence of the female, followed after a longer or shorter period by that of her male descendants and her entire society.

Nevertheless, in the history of the past the dangers of the sex-parasitism have never threatened more than a small section of the females of the human race, those exclusively of some dominant race or class; the mass of women beneath them being still compelled to assume many forms of strenuous activity. It is at the present day, and under the peculiar conditions of our modern civilization, that for the first time sex-parasitism has become a danger, more or less remote, to the mass of civilized women, perhaps ultimately to all.

In the very early stages of human growth, the sexual parasitism and degeneration of the female formed no possible source of social danger. Where the conditions of life rendered it inevitable that all the labor of a community should be performed by the members of that community for themselves, without the assistance of slaves or machinery, the tendency has always been

3. It is not without profound interest to note the varying phenomena of sex-parasitism as they present themselves in the animal world, both in the male and in the female form. Though among the greater number of species in the animal world the female form is larger and more powerful rather than the male (e.g.. among birds of prey. such as eagles, falcons, vultures, &c., and among fishes, insects, &c.), yet sex-parasitism appears among both sex forms. In certain sea-creatures, for example, the female carries about in the folds of her covering three or four minute and quite inactive males, who are entirely passive and dependent upon her.

Among termites, on the other hand, the female has so far degenerated that she has entirely lost the power of locomotion; she can no longer provide herself or her offspring with nourishment, or defend or even clean herself; she has become a mere passive, distended, bag of eggs, without intelligence or activity, she and her off-spring existing through the exertions of the slaves and workers of the community. Among other insects, such, for example, as certain ticks, another form of female parasitism prevails, and while the male remains a complex, highly active, and winged creature, the female, fastening herself by the head into the flesh of some living animal and sucking its blood, has lost wings and all activity, and power of locomotion, having become a mere distended bladder, which when filled with eggs bursts and ends a parasitic existence which has hardly been life. It is not impossible, and it appears, indeed, highly probable, that it has been this degeneration and parasitism on the part of the female which has set its limitation to the evolution of ants, creatures which, having reached a point of mental development in some respects almost as high as that of man, have yet become curiously and immovably arrested. The whole question of sex-parasitism among the lower animals is one throwing suggestive and instructive side-lights on human social problems, but is too extensive to be here entered on [Schreiner's note].

rather to throw an excessive amount of social labor on the female. Under no conditions, at no time, in no place, in the history of the world have the males of any period, of any nation, or of any class, shown the slightest inclination to allow their own females to become inactive or parasitic, so long as the actual muscular labor of feeding and clothing them would in that case have devolved upon *themselves!*

The parasitism of the human female becomes a possibility only when a point in civilization is reached (such as that which was attained in the ancient civilizations of Greece, Rome, Persia, Assyria, India, and such as today exists in many of the civilizations of the East, such as those of China and Turkey), when, owing to the extensive employment of the labor of slaves, or of subject races or classes, the dominant race or class has become so liberally supplied with the material goods of life that mere physical toil on the part of its own female members has become unnecessary.

It is when this point has been reached, and never before, that the symptoms of female parasitism have in the past almost invariably tended to manifest themselves, and have become a social danger. The males of the dominant class have almost always contrived to absorb to themselves the new intellectual occupations, which the absence of necessity for the old forms of physical toil made possible in their societies; and the females of the dominant class or race, for whose muscular labors there was now also no longer any need, not succeeding in grasping or attaining to these new forms of labor, have sunk into a state in which, performing no species of active social duty, they have existed through the passive performance of sexual functions alone, with how much or how little of discontent will now never be known, since no literary record has been made by the woman of the past, of her desires or sorrows. Then, in place of the active laboring woman, upholding society by her toil, has come the effete wife, concubine or prostitute, clad in fine raiment, the work of others' fingers; fed on luxurious viands, the result of others' toil, waited on and tended by the labor of others. The need for her physical labor having gone, and mental industry not having taken its place, she bedecked and scented her person, or had it bedecked and scented for her, she lay upon her sofa, or drove or was carried out in her vehicle, and, loaded with jewels, she sought by dissipations and amusements to fill up the inordinate blank left by the lack of productive activity. And the hand whitened and frame softened, till, at last, the very duties of motherhood, which were all the constitution of her life left her, became distasteful, and, from the instant when her infant came damp from her womb, it passed into the hands of others, to be tended and reared by them; and from youth to age her offspring often owed nothing to her personal toil. In many cases so complete was her enervation, that at last the very joy of giving life, the glory and beatitude of a virile womanhood, became distasteful; and she sought to evade it, not because of its interference with more imperious duties to those already born of her, or to her society, but because her existence of inactivity had robbed her of all joy in strenuous exertion and endurance in any form. Finely clad, tenderly housed, life became for her merely the gratification of her own physical and sexual appetites, and the appetites of the male, through the stimulation of which she could maintain herself. And, whether as kept wife, kept mistress, or prostitute, she contributed nothing to the active and sustaining labors of her society. She had attained to the

full development of that type which, whether in modern Paris or New York or London, or in ancient Greece, Assyria, or Rome, is essentially one in its features, its nature, and its results. She was the "fine lady," the human female parasite—the most deadly microbe which can make its appearance on the surface of any social organism.[4]

Wherever in the history of the past this type has reached its full development and has comprised the bulk of the females belonging to any dominant class or race, it has heralded its decay. In Assyria, Greece, Rome, Persia, as in Turkey today, the same material conditions have produced the same social disease among wealthy and dominant races; and again and again when the nation so affected has come into contact with nations more healthily constituted, this diseased condition has contributed to its destruction.

1911

4. The relation of female parasitism generally to the peculiar phenomenon of prostitution is fundamental. Prostitution can never be adequately dealt with, either from the moral or the scientific standpoint, unless its relation to the general phenomenon of female parasitism be fully recognized. It is the failure to do this which leaves so painful a sense of abortion on the mind, after listening to most modern utterances on the question, whether made from the emotional platform of the moral reformer, or the intellectual platform of the would-be scientist. We are left with a feeling that the matter has been handled but not dealt with: that the knife has not reached the core [Schreiner's note].

ANNA JULIA COOPER
1858?–1964

Born to a slave mother, Hannah Stanley Haywood, and a father presumed to be her mother's master, Anna Julia Cooper attended Saint Augustine's Normal School in North Carolina on a scholarship meant to train teachers of the formerly enslaved. Funded by the Episcopal Church, the award was auspicious, for Cooper dedicated her long life and activist career to the education of people she felt had been neglected, especially women of color. For two years, from 1877 until 1879, she was married to a theology student, George A. C. Cooper, who taught the first Greek class at Saint Augustine's; after his premature death, Anna Julia Cooper dedicated her affections to the students she instructed and fostered first as a teacher, then as principal of the Washington Colored High School (known as the M Street School) in the District of Columbia, as well as to the black women she addressed in her many lectures on female education. She alternated her subsequent formal training—at Oberlin College, where she received a B.A. and then an M.A. in math; at Columbia University; and later at the University of Paris, where she eventually earned a Ph.D. in French—with various teaching, administrative, lecturing, and editing positions; she was among the first African American women to receive higher degrees. Cooper published *A Voice from the South* in 1892, around the same time that she addressed the Women's Congress at the Chicago Columbian Exposition and was helping to organize Washington, D.C.'s Colored Women's League. In 1900 she participated with W.E.B. Du Bois at the Pan-African Conference held in London; in the 1920s she played a prominent role in the Colored Settlement House and the Colored Young Women's Christian Association; and in 1930 she became the president of Frelinghuysen University, a school established to serve working-class students. On her 100th birthday, she received congratulatory messages from President and Mrs. Dwight D. Eisenhower.

Despite such honors, Anna Julia Cooper repeatedly experienced racially motivated mortifications that brought home the need for fortitude in adversity. In 1905, for instance, a white school board accused Cooper of a sexual liaison with one of her foster children, a charge her editor Charles Lemert attributes to racist politics and calls a "dirty trick." Describing her recurrent lecture trips through the South, Cooper recalled dilapidated train stations at which she confronted "two dingy little rooms with 'FOR LADIES' swinging over one and 'FOR COLORED PEOPLE' over the other," signs that cause her to wonder "under which head I come." Facing such humiliations, Cooper never relinquished her efforts to bring about a time "when race, color, sex, condition, are realized to be the accidents, not the substance of life, and consequently as not obscuring or modifying the inalienable title to life, liberty, and pursuit of happiness." She consistently linked her exertions to "the woman's cause," which meant "not the white woman nor the black woman nor the red woman, but the cause of every man or woman who has writhed silently under mighty wrong." According to Cooper, "Only the BLACK WOMAN can say 'when and where I enter, in the quiet, undisputed dignity of my womanhood, without violence and without suing or special patronage, then and there the whole *Negro race enters with me.*' " With their oracular cadences, these quotations, from her lectures "Woman versus the Indian" (1891–92) and "Womanhood: A Vital Element in the Regeneration and Progress of a Race" (1886), typify the erudition and rhetorical power with which Cooper called for the progress toward racial equality that she believed black women could best bring about.

Womanhood: A Vital Element in the Regeneration and Progress of a Race[1]

The two sources from which, perhaps, modern civilization has derived its noble and ennobling ideal of woman are Christianity and the Feudal System.

In Oriental[2] countries woman has been uniformly devoted to a life of ignorance, infamy,[3] and complete stagnation. The Chinese shoe of to-day does not more entirely dwarf, cramp, and destroy her physical powers, than have the customs, laws, and social instincts, which from remotest ages have governed our Sister of the East, enervated and blighted her mental and moral life.

Mahomet makes no account of woman whatever in his polity. The Koran, which, unlike our Bible, was a product and not a growth,[4] tried to address itself to the needs of Arabian civilization as Mahomet with his circumscribed powers saw them. The Arab was a nomad. Home to him meant his present camping place. That deity who, according to our western ideals, makes and sanctifies the home, was to him a transient bauble to be toyed with so long as it gave pleasure and then to be thrown aside for a new one. As a personality, an individual soul, capable of eternal growth and unlimited development, and destined to mould and shape the civilization of the future to an incalculable extent, Mahomet did not know woman. There was no hereafter,

1. Read before the convocation of colored clergy of the Protestant Episcopal Church at Washington, D.C., 1886 [Cooper's note].
2. Middle Eastern, North African, and East Asian.
3. I.e., a shoe for a foot that has been bound, a process that left women barely able to walk.

4. Though its canonical text was established much more quickly than that of the Bible, the Qur'an— sacred writings accepted as divine revelation made to the Prophet Muhammed (ca. 570–632 C.E.)— was in fact not compiled as a single volume during his lifetime.

no paradise for her. The heaven of the Mussulman is peopled and made gladsome not by the departed wife, or sister, or mother, but by *houri*[5]—a figment of Mahomet's brain, partaking of the ethereal qualities of angels, yet imbued with all the vices and inanity of Oriental women. The harem here, and—"dust to dust" hereafter, this was the hope, the inspiration, the *summum bonum*[6] of the Eastern woman's life! With what result on the life of the nation, the "Unspeakable Turk," the "sick man" of modern Europe[7] can to-day exemplify.

Says a certain writer: "The private life of the Turk is vilest of the vile, unprogressive, unambitious, and inconceivably low." And yet Turkey is not without her great men. She has produced most brilliant minds; men skilled in all the intricacies of diplomacy and statesmanship; men whose intellects could grapple with the deep problems of empire and manipulate the subtle agencies which check-mate kings. But these minds were not the normal outgrowth of a healthy trunk. They seemed rather ephemeral excrescencies which shoot far out with all the vigor and promise, apparently, of strong branches; but soon alas fall into decay and ugliness because there is no soundness in the root, no life-giving sap, permeating, strengthening and perpetuating the whole. There is a worm at the core! The homelife is impure! and when we look for fruit, like apples of Sodom,[8] it crumbles within our grasp into dust and ashes.

It is pleasing to turn from this effete and immobile civilization to a society still fresh and vigorous, whose seed is in itself, and whose very name is synonymous with all that is progressive, elevating and inspiring, viz., the European bud and the American flower of modern civilization.

And here let me say parenthetically that our satisfaction in American institutions rests not on the fruition we now enjoy, but springs rather from the possibilities and promise that are inherent in the system, though as yet, perhaps, far in the future.

"Happiness," says Madame de Stael,[9] "consists not in perfections attained, but in a sense of progress, the result of our own endeavor under conspiring circumstances *toward* a goal which continually advances and broadens and deepens till it is swallowed up in the Infinite." Such conditions in embryo are all that we claim for the land of the West. We have not yet reached our ideal in American civilization. The pessimists even declare that we are not marching in that direction. But there can be no doubt that here in America is the arena in which the next triumph of civilization is to be won; and here too we find promise abundant and possibilities infinite.

Now let us see on what basis this hope for our country primarily and fundamentally rests. Can any one doubt that it is chiefly on the homelife and on the influence of good women in those homes? Says Macaulay:[1] "You may judge a nation's rank in the scale of civilization from the way they treat

5. Beautiful maidens who live with the blessed in paradise. "Mussulman": Muslim.
6. Highest good (Latin). "Dust to dust": see Genesis 3.19 (God speaking to Adam): "for dust thou art, and unto dust shalt thou return."
7. The Scottish historian Thomas Carlyle used the phrase "the unspeakable Turk" in a letter to a meeting of 1877 following Turkey's response to the rebellion of Bosnia and Herzegovina, and a number of famous individuals (including Czar Nicholas I in 1853) spoke of Turkey or the weakening Ottoman Empire as a "sick man."
8. A city said to have been destroyed by God in a rain of brimstone and fire because of its inequity and the wickedness of its people (Genesis 18.20–19.28).
9. Madame de Staël (1766–1817), French writer.
1. Thomas Babington Macaulay (1800–1859), British historian and politician.

their women." And Emerson,[2] "I have thought that a sufficient measure of civilization is the influence of good women." Now this high regard for woman, this germ of a prolific idea which in our own day is bearing such rich and varied fruit, was ingrafted into European civilization, we have said, from two sources, the Christian Church and the Feudal System. For although the Feudal System can in no sense be said to have originated the idea, yet there can be no doubt that the habits of life and modes of thought to which Feudalism gave rise, materially fostered and developed it; for they gave us chivalry, than which no institution has more sensibly magnified and elevated woman's position in society.

Tacitus[3] dwells on the tender regard for woman entertained by these rugged barbarians before they left their northern homes to overrun Europe. Old Norse legends too, and primitive poems, all breathe the same spirit of love of home and veneration for the pure and noble influence there presiding—the wife, the sister, the mother.

And when later on we see the settled life of the Middle Ages "oozing out," as M. Guizot[4] expresses it, from the plundering and pillaging life of barbarism and crystallizing into the Feudal System, the tiger of the field is brought once more within the charmed circle of the goddesses of his castle, and his imagination weaves around them a halo whose reflection possibly has not yet altogether vanished.

It is true the spirit of Christianity had not yet put the seal of catholicity on this sentiment. Chivalry, according to Bascom,[5] was but the toning down and softening of a rough and lawless period. It gave a roseate glow to a bitter winter's day. Those who looked out from castle windows revelled in its "amethyst tints." But God's poor, the weak, the unlovely, the commonplace were still freezing and starving none the less in unpitied, unrelieved loneliness.

Respect for woman, the much lauded chivalry of the Middle Ages, meant what I fear it still means to some men in our own day—respect for the elect few among whom they expect to consort.

The idea of the radical amelioration of womankind, reverence for woman as woman regardless of rank, wealth, or culture, was to come from that rich and bounteous fountain from which flow all our liberal and universal ideas—the Gospel of Jesus Christ.

And yet the Christian Church at the time of which we have been speaking would seem to have been doing even less to protect and elevate woman than the little done by secular society. The Church as an organization committed a double offense against woman in the Middle Ages. Making of marriage a sacrament and at the same time insisting on the celibacy of the clergy and other religious orders, she gave an inferior if not an impure character to the marriage relation, especially fitted to reflect discredit on woman. Would this were all or the worst! but the Church by the licentiousness of its chosen servants invaded the household and established too often as vicious connections those relations which it forbade to assume openly and in good faith.

2. Ralph Waldo Emerson (1803–1882), American philosopher, essayist, and poet; the quotation is from his essay "Civilization" (1862).
3. Cornelius Tacitus (ca. 55–ca. 100 C.E.), Roman historian; he praises the respect for women displayed by the German tribes in his *Germania*.

Northern "barbarians" sacked Rome in 410 C.E.
4. François-Pierre-Guillaume Guizot (1787–1874), French historian and politician.
5. John Bascom (1827–1911), American philosopher, college professor, and prolific writer.

"Thus," to use the words of our authority, "the religious corps became as numerous, as searching, and as unclean as the frogs of Egypt, which penetrated into all quarters, into the ovens and kneading troughs, leaving their filthy trail wherever they went." Says Chaucer[6] with characteristic satire, speaking of the Friars:

> 'Women may now go safely up and doun,
> In every bush, and under every tree,
> Ther is non other incubus[7] but he,
> And he ne will don hem no dishonour.'

Henry, Bishop of Liege, could unblushingly boast the birth of twenty-two children in fourteen years.[8]

It may help us under some of the perplexities which beset our way in "the one Catholic and Apostolic Church" to-day, to recall some of the corruptions and incongruities against which the Bride of Christ[9] has had to struggle in her past history and in spite of which she has kept, through many vicissitudes, the faith once delivered to the saints. Individuals, organizations, whole sections of the Church militant may outrage the Christ whom they profess, may ruthlessly trample under foot both the spirit and the letter of his precepts, yet not till we hear the voices audibly saying "Come let us depart hence," shall we cease to believe and cling to the promise, *I am with you to the end of the world.*"[1]

> "Yet saints their watch are keeping
> The cry goes up 'How long!'
> And soon the night of weeping
> Shall be the morn of song."[2]

However much then the facts of any particular period of history may seem to deny it, I for one do not doubt that the source of the vitalizing principle of woman's development and amelioration is the Christian Church, so far as that church is coincident with Christianity.

Christ gave ideals not formulæ. The Gospel is a germ requiring millennia for its growth and ripening. It needs and at the same time helps to form around itself a soil enriched in civilization, and perfected in culture and insight without which the embryo can neither be unfolded or comprehended. With all the strides our civilization has made from the first to the nineteenth century, we can boast not an idea, not a principle of action, not a progressive social force but was already mutely foreshadowed, or directly enjoined in that simple tale of a meek and lowly life. The quiet face of the Nazarene[3] is ever seen a little way ahead, never too far to come down to and touch the life of the lowest in days the darkest, yet ever leading onward, still onward, the tottering childish feet of our strangely boastful civilization.

By laying down for woman the same code of morality, the same standard of purity, as for man; by refusing to countenance the shameless and equally guilty monsters who were gloating over her fall,—graciously stooping in all

6. English poet (ca. 1343–1400); the quotation, modernized, is from *The Wife of Bath's Tale*, 884–87.
7. An evil spirit that copulates with women in their sleep.
8. Bascom [Cooper's note].

9. I.e., the Catholic Church.
1. Matthew 28.20.
2. From "The Church's Own Foundation," a hymn by the Anglican clergyman Samuel J. Stone (1839–1900).
3. Jesus.

the majesty of his own spotlessness to wipe away the filth and grime of her guilty past and bid her go in peace and sin no more; and again in the moments of his own careworn and footsore dejection, turning trustfully and lovingly, away from the heartless snubbing and sneers, away from the cruel malignity of mobs and prelates in the dusty marts of Jerusalem to the ready sympathy, loving appreciation and unfaltering friendship of that quiet home at Bethany; and even at the last, by his dying bequest to the disciple whom he loved,[4] signifying the protection and tender regard to be extended to that sorrowing mother and ever afterward to the sex she represented;—throughout his life and in his death he has given to men a rule and guide for the estimation of woman as an equal, as a helper, as a friend, and as a sacred charge to be sheltered and cared for with a brother's love and sympathy, lessons which nineteen centuries' gigantic strides in knowledge, arts, and sciences, in social and ethical principles have not been able to probe to their depth or to exhaust in practice.

It seems not too much to say then of the vitalizing, regenerating, and progressive influence of womanhood on the civilization of today, that, while it was foreshadowed among Germanic nations in the far away dawn of their history as a narrow, sickly and stunted growth, it yet owes its catholicity and power, the deepening of its roots and broadening of its branches to Christianity.

The union of these two forces, the Barbaric and the Christian, was not long delayed after the Fall of the Empire. The Church, which fell with Rome, finding herself in danger of being swallowed up by barbarism, with characteristic vigor and fertility of resources, addressed herself immediately to the task of conquering her conquerers. The means chosen does credit to her power of penetration and adaptability, as well as to her profound, unerring, all-compassing diplomacy; and makes us even now wonder if aught human can successfully and ultimately withstand her far-seeing designs and brilliant policy, or gainsay her well-earned claim to the word *Catholic*.[5]

She saw the barbarian, little more developed than a wild beast. She forbore to antagonize and mystify his warlike nature by a full blaze of the heart-searching and humanizing tenets of her great Head. She said little of the rule "If thy brother smite thee on one cheek, turn to him the other also;"[6] but thought it sufficient for the needs of those times, to establish the so-called "Truce of God" under which men were bound to abstain from butchering one another for three days of each week and on Church festivals. In other words, she respected their individuality: non-resistance pure and simple being for them an utter impossibility, she contented herself with less radical measures calculated to lead up finally to the full measure of the benevolence of Christ.

Next she took advantage of the barbarian's sensuous love of gaudy display and put all her magnificent garments on. She could not capture him by

4. See John 19.26–27, describing Jesus on the cross: "When Jesus therefore saw his mother, and the disciple standing by, whom he loved, he saith unto his mother, Woman, behold thy son! Then said he to the disciple, Behold thy mother! And from that hour that disciple took her unto his own home." "Bethany": a village less than 2 miles from Jerusalem where Jesus often met with his friends Mary, Martha, and Lazarus (see, e.g., Luke 10.38–39; John 11.1–2).
5. I.e., universal.
6. See Matthew 5.39.

physical force, she would dazzle him by gorgeous spectacles. It is said that Romanism[7] gained more in pomp and ritual during this trying period of the Dark Ages than throughout all her former history.

The result was she carried her point. Once more Rome laid her ambitious hand on the temporal power, and allied with Charlemagne,[8] aspired to rule the world through a civilization dominated by Christianity and permeated by the traditions and instincts of those sturdy barbarians.

Here was the confluence of the two streams we have been tracing, which, united now, stretch before us as a broad majestic river. In regard to woman it was the meeting of two noble and ennobling forces, two kindred ideas the resultant of which, we doubt not, is destined to be a potent force in the betterment of the world.

Now after our appeal to history comparing nations destitute of this force and so destitute also of the principle of progress, with other nations among whom the influence of woman is prominent coupled with a brisk, progressive, satisfying civilization,—if in addition we find this strong presumptive evidence corroborated by reason and experience, we may conclude that these two equally varying concomitants are linked as cause and effect; in other words, that the position of woman in society determines the vital elements of its regeneration and progress.

Now that this is so on *a priori* grounds all must admit. And this not because woman is better or stronger or wiser than man, but from the nature of the case, because it is she who must first form the man by directing the earliest impulses of his character.[9]

Byron and Wordsworth were both geniuses and would have stamped themselves on the thought of their age under any circumstances; and yet we find the one a savor of life unto life, the other of death unto death. "Byron, like a rocket, shot his way upward with scorn and repulsion, flamed out in wild, explosive, brilliant excesses and disappeared in darkness made all the more palpable."[1]

Wordsworth lent of his gifts to reinforce that "power in the Universe which makes for righteousness" by taking the harp handed him from Heaven and using it to swell the strains of angelic choirs. Two locomotives equally mighty stand facing opposite tracks; the one to rush headlong to destruction with all its precious freight, the other to toil grandly and gloriously up the steep embattlements to Heaven and to God. Who—who can say what a world of consequences hung on the first placing and starting of these enormous forces!

Woman, Mother,—your responsibility is one that might make angels tremble and fear to take hold! To trifle with it, to ignore or misuse it, is to treat lightly the most sacred and solemn trust ever confided by God to human kind. The training of children is a task on which an infinity of weal[2] or woe depends. Who does not covet it? Yet who does not stand awe-struck before its momentous issues! It is a matter of small moment, it seems to me, whether

7. I.e., Roman Catholicism.
8. The king of the Franks (742–814; r. 768–814), and the first Holy Roman emperor (800–814).
9. George Gordon, Lord Byron (1788–1824), and William Wordsworth (1770–1850), English

Romantic poets.
1. Bascom's Eng. Lit. p. 253 [Cooper's note]. Bascom's *Philosophy of English Literature: A Course of Lectures Delivered in the Lowell Institute* (1874).
2. Prosperity.

that lovely girl in whose accomplishments you take such pride and delight, can enter the gay and crowded salon with the ease and elegance of this or that French or English gentlewoman, compared with the decision as to whether her individuality is going to reinforce the good or the evil elements of the world. The lace and the diamonds, the dance and the theater, gain a new significance when scanned in their bearings on such issues. Their influence on the individual personality, and through her on the society and civilization which she vitalizes and inspires—all this and more must be weighed in the balance before the jury can return a just and intelligent verdict as to the innocence or banefulness of these apparently simple amusements.

Now the fact of woman's influence on society being granted, what are its practical bearings on the work which brought together this conference of colored clergy and laymen in Washington? "We come not here to talk." Life is too busy, too pregnant with meaning and far reaching consequences to allow you to come this far for mere intellectual entertainment.

The vital agency of womanhood in the regeneration and progress of a race, as a general question, is conceded almost before it is fairly stated. I confess one of the difficulties for me in the subject assigned lay in its obviousness. The plea is taken away by the opposite attorney's granting the whole question.

"Woman's influence on social progress"—who in Christendom doubts or questions it? One may as well be called on to prove that the sun is the source of light and heat and energy to this many-sided little world.

Nor, on the other hand, could it have been intended that I should apply the position when taken and proven, to the needs and responsibilities of the women of our race in the South. For is it not written, "Cursed is he that cometh after the king?"[3] and has not the King already preceded me in "The Black Woman of the South"?[4]

They have had both Moses and the Prophets in Dr. Crummell and if they hear not him, neither would they be persuaded though one came up from the South.

I would beg, however, with the Doctor's permission, to add my plea for the *Colored Girls* of the South:—that large, bright, promising fatally beautiful class that stand shivering like a delicate plantlet before the fury of tempestuous elements, so full of promise and possibilities, yet so sure of destruction; often without a father to whom they dare apply the loving term, often without a stronger brother to espouse their cause and defend their honor with his life's blood; in the midst of pitfalls and snares, waylaid by the lower classes of white men, with no shelter, no protection nearer than the great blue vault above, which half conceals and half reveals the one Care-Taker they know so little of. Oh, save them, help them, shield, train, develop, teach, inspire them! Snatch them, in God's name, as brands from the burning! There is material in them well worth your while, the hope in germ of a staunch, helpful, regenerating womanhood on which, primarily, rests the foundation stones of our future as a race.

It is absurd to quote statistics showing the Negro's bank account and rent

3. See Ecclesiastes 2.12: "for what can the man do that cometh after the king?"
4. *The Black Woman of the South: Her Neglects and Her Needs* (1883), a pamphlet reprinting a ser-

mon preached that year by Alexander Crummell (1819–1898), a black nationalist and Episcopal minister, then the leader of a church in Washington, D.C. (1873–94).

rolls, to point to the hundreds of newspapers edited by colored men and lists of lawyers, doctors, professors, D.D's, LL D's, etc., etc., etc., while the source from which the life-blood of the race is to flow is subject to taint and corruption in the enemy's camp.

True progress is never made by spasms. Real progress is growth. It must begin in the seed. Then, "first the blade, then the ear, after that the full corn in the ear."[5] There is something to encourage and inspire us in the advancement of individuals since their emancipation from slavery. It at least proves that there is nothing irretrievably wrong in the shape of the black man's skull,[6] and that under given circumstances his development, downward or upward, will be similar to that of other average human beings.

But there is no time to be wasted in mere felicitation. That the Negro has his niche in the infinite purposes of the Eternal, no one who has studied the history of the last fifty years in America will deny. That much depends on his own right comprehension of his responsibility and rising to the demands of the hour, it will be good for him to see; and how best to use his present so that the structure of the future shall be stronger and higher and brighter and nobler and holier than that of the past, is a question to be decided each day by every one of us.

The race is just twenty-one years removed from the conception and experience of a chattel, just at the age of ruddy manhood. It is well enough to pause a moment for retrospection, introspection, and prospection. We look back, not to become inflated with conceit because of the depths from which we have arisen, but that we may learn wisdom from experience. We look within that we may gather together once more our forces, and, by improved and more practical methods, address ourselves to the tasks before us. We look forward with hope and trust that the same God whose guiding hand led our fathers through and out of the gall and bitterness of oppression, will still lead and direct their children, to the honor of His name, and for their ultimate salvation.

But this survey of the failures or achievements of the past, the difficulties and embarrassments of the present, and the mingled hopes and fears for the future, must not degenerate into mere dreaming nor consume the time which belongs to the practical and effective handling of the crucial questions of the hour; and there can be no issue more vital and momentous than this of the womanhood of the race.

Here is the vulnerable point, not in the heel, but at the heart of the young Achilles;[7] and here must the defenses be strengthened and the watch redoubled.

We are the heirs of a past which was not our fathers' moulding. "Every man the arbiter of his own destiny" was not true for the American Negro of the past: and it is no fault of his that he finds himself to-day the inheritor of a manhood and womanhood impoverished and debased by two centuries and more of compression and degradation.

But weaknesses and malformations, which to-day are attributable to a

5. Mark 4.28.
6. A reference to phrenology, the "science" (popular in the nineteenth century) that linked character and mental faculties to the shape of one's skull.

7. In Greek mythology, the foremost Greek fighter in the Trojan War. Because his immortal mother had dipped him in the river Styx, he was invulnerable except for his heel, where she had held him.

vicious schoolmaster and a pernicious system, will a century hence be rightly regarded as proofs of innate corruptness and radical incurability.

Now the fundamental agency under God in the regeneration, the re-training of the race, as well as the ground work and starting point of its progress upward, must be the *black woman.*

With all the wrongs and neglects of her past, with all the weakness, the debasement, the moral thralldom of her present, the black woman of to-day stands mute and wondering at the Herculean task devolving upon her. But the cycles wait for her. No other hand can move the lever. She must be loosed from her bands and set to work.

Our meager and superficial results from past efforts prove their futility; and every attempt to elevate the Negro, whether undertaken by himself or through the philanthropy of others, cannot but prove abortive unless so directed as to utilize the indispensable agency of an elevated and trained womanhood.

A race cannot be purified from without. Preachers and teachers are helps, and stimulants and conditions as necessary as the gracious rain and sunshine are to plant growth. But what are rain and dew and sunshine and cloud if there be no life in the plant germ? We must go to the root and see that that is sound and healthy and vigorous; and not deceive ourselves with waxen flowers and painted leaves of mock chlorophyll.

We too often mistake individuals' honor for race development and so are ready to substitute pretty accomplishments for sound sense and earnest purpose.

A stream cannot rise higher than its source. The atmosphere of homes is no rarer and purer and sweeter than are the mothers in those homes. A race is but a total of families. The nation is the aggregate of its homes. As the whole is sum of all its parts, so the character of the parts will determine the characteristics of the whole. These are all axioms and so evident that it seems gratuitous to remark it; and yet, unless I am greatly mistaken, most of the unsatisfaction from our past results arises from just such a radical and pal-pable error as much almost on our own part as on that of our benevolent white friends.

The Negro is constitutionally hopeful and proverbially irrepressible; and naturally stands in danger of being dazzled by the shimmer and tinsel of superficials. We often mistake foliage for fruit and overestimate or wrongly estimate brilliant results.

The late Martin R. Delany,[8] who was an unadulterated black man, used to say when honors of state fell upon him, that when he entered the council of kings the black race entered with him; meaning, I suppose, that there was no discounting his race identity and attributing his achievements to some admixture of Saxon blood. But our present record of eminent men, when placed beside the actual status of the race in America to-day, proves that no man can represent the race. Whatever the attainments of the individual may be, unless his home has moved on *pari passu,*[9] he can never be regarded as identical with or representative of the whole.

Not by pointing to sun-bathed mountaintops do we prove that Phœbus[1]

8. Physician, writer, and soldier (1812–1885); like Crummell, Delany was proud of his purely African ancestry (Delany believed he was descended from royalty) and was a black nationalist who advocated emigration to Africa.
9. At an equal rate (literally, "with equal step": Latin).
1. A name of Apollo, classical god of the sun.

warms the valleys. We must point to homes, average homes, homes of the rank and file of horny handed toiling men and women of the South (where the masses are) lighted and cheered by the good, the beautiful, and the true,—then and not till then will the whole plateau be lifted into the sunlight.

Only the BLACK WOMAN can say "when and where I enter, in the quiet, undisputed dignity of my womanhood, without violence and without suing or special patronage, then and there the whole *Negro race enters with me.*" Is it not evident then that as individual workers for this race we must address ourselves with no half-hearted zeal to this feature of our mission. The need is felt and must be recognized by all. There is a call for workers, for missionaries, for men and women with the double consecration of a fundamental love of humanity and a desire for its melioration through the Gospel; but superadded to this we demand an intelligent and sympathetic comprehension of the interests and special needs of the Negro.

I see not why there should not be an organized effort for the protection and elevation of our girls such as the White Cross League[2] in England. English women are strengthened and protected by more than twelve centuries of Christian influences, freedom and civilization; English girls are dispirited and crushed down by no such all-levelling prejudice as that supercilious caste spirit in America which cynically assumes "A Negro woman cannot be a lady." English womanhood is beset by no such snares and traps as betray the unprotected, untrained colored girl of the South, whose only crime and dire destruction often is her unconscious and marvelous beauty. Surely then if English indignation is aroused and English manhood thrilled under the leadership of a Bishop of the English church to build up bulwarks around their wronged sisters, Negro sentiment cannot remain callous and Negro effort nerveless in view of the imminent peril of the mothers of the next generation. "*I am my Sister's keeper!*"[3] should be the hearty response of every man and woman of the race, and this conviction should purify and exalt the narrow, selfish and petty personal aims of life into a noble and sacred purpose.

We need men who can let their interest and gallantry extend outside the circle of their æsthetic appreciation; men who can be a father, a brother, a friend to every weak, struggling unshielded girl. We need women who are so sure of their own social footing that they need not fear leaning to lend a hand to a fallen or falling sister. We need men and women who do not exhaust their genius splitting hairs on aristocratic distinctions and thanking God they are not as others; but earnest, unselfish souls, who can go into the highways and byways, lifting up and leading, advising and encouraging with the truly catholic benevolence of the Gospel of Christ.

As Church workers we must confess our path of duty is less obvious; or rather our ability to adapt our machinery to our conception of the peculiar exigencies of this work as taught by experience and our own consciousness of the needs of the Negro, is as yet not demonstrable. Flexibility and aggressiveness are not such strong characteristics of the Church to-day as in the Dark Ages.

As a Mission field for the Church the Southern Negro is in some aspects

2. A temperance or social purity organization, also known as the White Cross Army, founded by Joseph Lightfoot, the Anglican bishop of Durham, England, in 1883.

3. An allusion to Cain's dismissive answer to God: "Am I my brother's keeper?" (Genesis 4.9).

most promising; in others, perplexing. Aliens neither in language and customs, nor in associations and sympathies, naturally of deeply rooted religious instincts and taking most readily and kindly to the worship and teachings of the Church, surely the task of proselytizing the American Negro is infinitely less formidable than that which confronted the Church in the Barbarians of Europe. Besides, this people already look to the Church as the hope of their race. Thinking colored men almost uniformly admit that the Protestant Episcopal Church with its quiet, chaste dignity and decorous solemnity, its instructive and elevating ritual, its bright chanting and joyous hymning, is eminently fitted to correct the peculiar faults of worship—the rank exuberance and often ludicrous demonstrativeness of their people. Yet, strange to say, the Church, claiming to be missionary and Catholic, urging that schism is sin and denominationalism inexcusable, has made in all these years almost no inroads upon this semi-civilized religionism.

Harvests from this over ripe field of home missions have been gathered in by Methodists, Baptists, and not least by Congregationalists, who were unknown to the Freedmen before their emancipation.

Our clergy numbers less than two dozen[4] priests of Negro blood and we have hardly more than one self-supporting colored congregation in the entire Southland. While the organization known as the A. M. E. Church[5] has 14,063 ministers, itinerant and local, 4,069 self-supporting churches, 4,275 Sunday-schools, with property valued at $7,772,284, raising yearly for church purposes $1,427,000.

Stranger and more significant than all, the leading men of this race (I do not mean demagogues and politicians, but men of intellect, heart, and race devotion, men to whom the elevation of their people means more than personal ambition and sordid gain—and the men of that stamp have not all died yet) the Christian workers for the race, of younger and more cultured growth, are noticeably drifting into sectarian churches, many of them declaring all the time that they acknowledge the historic claims of the Church, believe her apostolicity, and would experience greater personal comfort, spiritual and intellectual, in her revered communion. It is a fact which any one may verify for himself, that representative colored men, professing that in their heart of hearts they are Episcopalians, are actually working in Methodist and Baptist pulpits; while the ranks of the Episcopal clergy are left to be filled largely by men who certainly suggest the propriety of a *"perpetual* Diaconate"[6] if they cannot be said to have created the necessity for it.

Now where is the trouble? Something must be wrong. What is it?

A certain Southern Bishop of our Church reviewing the situation, whether in Godly anxiety or in "Gothic antipathy" I know not, deprecates the fact that the colored people do not seem *drawn* to the Episcopal Church, and comes to the sage conclusion that the Church is not adapted to the rude untutored minds of the Freedmen, and that they may be left to go to the Methodists and Baptists whither their racial proclivities undeniably tend.

4. The published report of '91 shows 26 priests for the entire country, including one not engaged in work and one a professor in a non-sectarian school, since made Dean of an Episcopal Annex to Howard University known and King Hall [Cooper's note]. Howard, a historically black institution in Wash- ington, D.C., was founded in 1867.
5. The African Methodist Episcopal Church, the largest body of black Methodists in the United States (founded in 1816).
6. An official body of deacons, holders of the initial level of ordination in the Episcopal Church.

How the good Bishop can agree that all-foreseeing Wisdom, and Catholic Love would have framed his Church as typified in his seamless garment and unbroken body, and yet not leave it broad enough and deep enough and loving enough to seek and save and hold seven millions of God's poor, I cannot see.

But the doctors while discussing their scientifically conclusive diagnosis of the disease, will perhaps not think it presumptuous in the patient if he dares to suggest where at least the pain is. If this be allowed, a *Black woman of the South* would beg to point out two possible oversights in this southern work which may indicate in part both a cause and a remedy for some failure. The first is *not calculating for the Black man's personality;* not having respect, if I may so express it, to his manhood or deferring at all to his conceptions of the needs of his people. When colored persons have been employed it was too often as machines or as manikins. There has been no disposition, generally, to get the black man's ideal or to let his individuality work by its own gravity, as it were. A conference of earnest Christian men have met at regular intervals for some years past to discuss the best methods of promoting the welfare and development of colored people in this country. Yet, strange as it may seem, they have never invited a colored man or even intimated that one would be welcome to take part in their deliberations. Their remedial contrivances are purely theoretical or empirical, therefore, and the whole machinery devoid of soul.

The second important oversight in my judgment is closely allied to this and probably grows out of it, and that is not developing Negro womanhood as an essential fundamental for the elevation of the race, and utilizing this agency in extending the work of the Church.

Of the first I have possibly already presumed to say too much since it does not strictly come within the province of my subject. However, Macaulay somewhere[7] criticises the Church of England as not knowing how to use fanatics, and declares that had Ignatius Loyola[8] been in the Anglican instead of the Roman communion, the Jesuits would have been schismatics instead of Catholics; and if the religious awakenings of the Wesleys[9] had been in Rome, she would have shaven their heads, tied ropes around their waists, and sent them out under her own banner and blessing. Whether this be true or not, there is certainly a vast amount of force potential for Negro evangelization rendered latent, or worse, antagonistic by the halting, uncertain, I had almost said, *trimming* policy of the Church in the South. This may sound both presumptuous and ungrateful. It is mortifying, I know, to benevolent wisdom, after having spent itself in the execution of well conned[1] theories for the ideal development of a particular work, to hear perhaps the weakest and humblest element of that work asking "what doest thou?"

Yet so it will be in life. The "thus far and no farther" pattern cannot be fitted to any growth in God's kingdom. The universal law of development is "onward and upward." It is God-given and inviolable. From the unfolding of the germ in the acorn to reach the sturdy oak, to the growth of a human soul

7. Cooper is paraphrasing from Macaulay's 1840 review of Leopold von Ranke's *History of the Popes.*
8. Spanish priest (1491–1556), a founder and first general of the Society of Jesus (the Jesuits).
9. John (1703–1791) and Charles Wesley (1707–1788), founders of Methodism, which—contrary to their original intention—broke away from the Anglican Church.
1. Closely studied.

into the full knowledge and likeness of its Creator, the breadth and scope of the movement in each and all are too grand, too mysterious, too like God himself, to be encompassed and locked down in human molds.

After all the Southern slave owners were right: either the very alphabet of intellectual growth must be forbidden[2] and the Negro dealt with absolutely as a chattel having neither rights nor sensibilities; or else the clamps and irons of mental and moral, as well as civil compression must be riven asunder and the truly enfranchised soul led to the entrance of that boundless vista through which it is to toil upwards to its beckoning God as the buried seed germ to meet the sun.

A perpetual colored diaconate, carefully and kindly superintended by the white clergy; congregations of shiny faced peasants with their clean white aprons and sunbonnets catechised at regular intervals and taught to recite the creed, the Lord's prayer[3] and the ten commandments—duty towards God and duty towards neighbor, surely such well tended sheep ought to be grateful to their shepherds and content in that station of life to which it pleased God to call them. True, like the old professor lecturing to his solitary student, we make no provision here for irregularities. "Questions must be kept till after class," or dispensed with altogether. That some do ask questions and insist on answers, in class too, must be both impertinent and annoying. Let not our spiritual pastors and masters however be grieved at such self-assertion as merely signifies we have a destiny to fulfill and as men and women we must *be about our Father's business.*[4]

It is a mistake to suppose that the Negro is prejudiced against a white ministry. Naturally there is not a more kindly and implicit follower of a white man's guidance than the average colored peasant. What would to others be an ordinary act of friendly or pastoral interest he would be more inclined to regard gratefully as a condescension.[5] And he never forgets such kindness. Could the Negro be brought near to his white priest or bishop, he is not suspicious. He is not only willing but often longs to unburden his soul to this intelligent guide. There are no reservations when he is convinced that you are his friend. It is a saddening satire on American history and manners that it takes something to convince him.

That our people are not "drawn" to a church whose chief dignitaries they see only in the chancel, and whom they reverence as they would a painting or an angel, whose life never comes down to and touches theirs with the inspiration of an objective reality, may be "perplexing" truly (American caste and American Christianity both being facts) but it need not be surprising. There must be something of human nature in it, the same as that which brought about that "the Word was made flesh and dwelt among us"[6] that He might "draw" us towards God.

Men are not "drawn" by abstractions. Only sympathy and love can draw, and until our Church in America realizes this and provides a clergy that can come in touch with our life and have a fellow feeling for our woes, without

2. In most Southern states, it was illegal to teach slaves to read or write.
3. Matthew 6.9–13. "The creed": the Apostle's Creed.
4. See Luke 2.49, where Jesus as a boy tells Mary and Joseph, "I must be about my Father's business."
5. The generous overlooking of difference in rank when dealing with an inferior.
6. John 1.14.

being imbedded and frozen up in their "Gothic antipathies," the good bishops are likely to continue "perplexed" by the sparsity of colored Episcopalians.

A colored priest of my acquaintance recently related to me, with tears in his eyes, how his reverend Father in God, the Bishop who had ordained him, had met him on the cars on his way to the diocesan convention and warned him, not unkindly, not to take a seat in the body of the convention with the white clergy. To avoid disturbance of their godly placidity he would of course please sit back and somewhat apart. I do not imagine that that clergyman had very much heart for the Christly (!) deliberations of that convention.

To return, however, it is not on this broader view of Church work, which I mentioned as a primary cause of its halting progress with the colored people, that I am to speak. My proper theme is the second oversight of which in my judgment our Christian propagandists have been guilty: or, the necessity of church training, protecting and uplifting our colored womanhood as indispensable to the evangelization of the race.

Apelles[7] did not disdain even that criticism of his lofty art which came from an uncouth cobbler; and may I not hope that the writer's oneness with her subject both in feeling and in being may palliate undue obtrusiveness of opinions here. That the race cannot be effectually lifted up till its women are truly elevated we take as proven. It is not for us to dwell on the needs, the neglects, and the ways of succor, pertaining to the black woman of the South. The ground has been ably discussed and an admirable and practical plan proposed by the oldest Negro priest in America, advising and urging that special organizations such as Church Sisterhoods and industrial schools be devised to meet her pressing needs in the Southland. That some such movements are vital to the life of this people and the extension of the Church among them, is not hard to see. Yet the pamphlet fell still-born from the press. So far as I am informed the Church has made no motion towards carrying out Dr. Crummell's suggestion.

The denomination which comes next [to] our own in opposing the proverbial emotionalism of Negro worship in the South, and which in consequence like ours receives the cold shoulder from the old heads, resting as we do under the charge of not "having religion" and not believing in conversion—the Congregationalists—have quietly gone to work on the young, have established industrial and training schools, and now almost every community in the South is yearly enriched by a fresh infusion of vigorous young hearts, cultivated heads, and helpful hands that have been trained at Fisk, at Hampton, in Atlanta University, and in Tuskegee, Alabama.[8]

These young people are missionaries actual or virtual both here and in Africa. They have learned to love the methods and doctrines of the Church which trained and educated them; and so Congregationalism surely and steadily progresses.

Need I compare these well known facts with results shown by the Church in the same field and during the same or even a longer time.

The institution of the Church in the South to which she mainly looks for the training of her colored clergy and for the help of the "Black Woman"

7. Greek painter (flourished 4th century B.C.E.). According to a story told in Pliny the Elder's *Natural History* 35.36 (77 C.E.), he corrected a work after a shoemaker criticized him for having made an error in representing the shoes.
8. Historically black schools, all founded between 1866 and 1868 except Tuskegee, which opened in 1881.

and "Colored Girl" of the South, has graduated since the year 1868, when the school was founded, *five young women;*[9] and while yearly numerous young men have been kept and trained for the ministry by the charities of the Church, the number of indigent females who have here been supported, sheltered and trained, is phenomenally small. Indeed, to my mind, the attitude of the Church toward this feature of her work is as if the solution of the problem of Negro missions depended solely on sending a quota of deacons and priests into the field, girls being a sort of *tertium quid*[1] whose development may be promoted if they can pay their way and fall in with the plans mapped out for the training of the other sex. Now I would ask in all earnestness, does not this force potential deserve by education and stimulus to be made dynamic? Is it not a solemn duty incumbent on all colored churchmen to make it so? Will not the aid of the Church be given to prepare our girls in head, heart, and hand for the duties and responsibilities that await the intelligent wife, the Christian mother, the earnest, virtuous, helpful woman, at once both the lever and the fulcrum for uplifting the race.

As Negroes and churchmen we cannot be indifferent to these questions. They touch us most vitally on both sides. We believe in the Holy Catholic Church. We believe that however gigantic and apparently remote the consummation, the Church will go on conquering and to conquer till the kingdoms of this world, not excepting the black man and the black woman of the South, shall have become the kingdoms of the Lord and of his Christ.

That past work in this direction has been unsatisfactory we must admit. That without a change of policy results in the future will be as meagre, we greatly fear. Our life as a race is at stake. The dearest interests of our hearts are in the scales. We must either break away from dear old landmarks and plunge out in any line and every line that enables us to meet the pressing need of our people, or we must ask the Church to allow and help us, untrammelled by the prejudices and theories of individuals, to work aggressively under her direction as we alone can, with God's help, for the salvation of our people.

The time is ripe for action. Self-seeking and ambition must be laid on the altar. The battle is one of sacrifice and hardship, but our duty is plain. We have been recipients of missionary bounty in some sort for twenty-one years. Not even the senseless vegetable is content to be a mere reservoir. Receiving without giving is an anomaly in nature. Nature's cells are all little workshops for manufacturing sunbeams, the product to be *given out* to earth's inhabitants in warmth, energy, thought, action. Inanimate creation always pays back an equivalent.

Now, *How much owest thou my Lord?* Will his account be overdrawn if he call for singleness of purpose and self-sacrificing labor for your brethren? Having passed through your drill school, will you refuse a general's commission even if it entail responsibility, risk and anxiety, with possibly some adverse criticism? Is it too much to ask you to step forward and direct the work for your race along those lines which you know to be of first and vital importance?

9. Five have been graduated since '86, two in '91, two in '92 [Cooper's note]. The "institution" is apparently Saint Augustine's Normal School, where Cooper was educated; though established in 1867, it received its first students in 1868.

1. Third thing [Latin].

Will you allow these words of Ralph Waldo Emerson? "In ordinary," says he, "we have a snappish criticism which watches and contradicts the opposite party. We want the will which advances and dictates [acts]. Nature has made up her mind that what cannot defend itself, shall not be defended. Complaining never so loud and with never so much reason, is of no use. What cannot stand must fall; *and the measure of our sincerity and therefore of the respect of men is the amount of health and wealth we will hazard in the defense of our right.*"[2]

1886

2. Quoted, with some omissions, from Emerson's *Society and Solitude* (1870); Cooper's emphasis.

PAULINE HOPKINS
1859–1930

At the start of her forties in 1900, Pauline Hopkins began publishing in the opening issues of the *Colored American* magazine, a Boston-based journal that advertised itself as "an outlet for books about Negroes and by Negro authorship." Three of her four novels were serialized in the groundbreaking magazine; she contributed essays as well as stories, served on its board of directors, edited its Women's Department, and took over the duties of literary editor in 1903. In these capacities, she helped facilitate the new black journalism of Frances E. W. Harper, Angelina Grimké, Benjamin Griffith Brawley, and William Stanley Braithwaite. After the *Colored American* was bought by Booker T. Washington, whose politics of assimilation Hopkins distrusted, she was forced to resign, though she went on to work for two other African American magazines—the *Voice of the South* and the *New Era*—and in 1905 published *A Primer of Facts Pertaining to the Early Greatness of the African Race and the Possibility of Restoration by Its Descendants—with Epilogue.* This title captures the urgency of her artistic efforts from the very beginning of her career. Her first creative effort consisted of a musical drama, *Peculiar Sam; or, the Underground Railroad* (1879), which was presented as *Slaves' Escape; or the Underground Railroad* at Boston's Oakland Garden in 1880.

Pauline Elizabeth Hopkins was born in Portland, Maine, the daughter of Sarah Allen and Northrup Hopkins. Raised by a mother whose relatives had helped found the historic St. Paul Baptist Church in Boston, and by a stepfather who was a veteran of the Civil War, she grew up in Boston and graduated from the Boston Girls High School. Secretarial training assured her an income at the beginning and ending of her literary career: before her stint with the *Colored American,* she became a stenographer for the Bureau of Statistics on the Massachusetts Census; and after contributing to the *New Era,* she worked as a stenographer for the Massachusetts Institute of Technology. Today she is best known for *Contending Forces: A Romance Illustrative of Negro Life North and South* (1900), a novel that has been faulted for elevating light-skinned over darker-skinned black characters but that has also been praised for confronting the family separations perpetuated by slavery. In such interracial love stories as *Hagar's Daughter, a Story of Southern Caste Prejudice* (1901–02), *Of One Blood; or, The Hidden Self* (1902–03), and *Winona: A Tale of Negro Life in the South and Southwest* (1902–03), Hopkins was able to consider the contending social and psychological forces promoted by ongoing racial prejudice.

Talma Gordon

The Canterbury Club of Boston was holding its regular monthly meeting at the palatial Beacon-street residence of Dr. William Thornton, expert medical practitioner and specialist. All the members were present, because some rare opinions were to be aired by men of profound thought on a question of vital importance to the life of the Republic, and because the club celebrated its anniversary in a home usually closed to society. The Doctor's winters, since his marriage, were passed at his summer home near his celebrated sanatorium. This winter found him in town with his wife and two boys. We had heard much of the beauty of the former, who was entirely unknown to social life, and about whose life and marriage we felt sure a romantic interest attached. The Doctor himself was too bright a luminary of the professional world to remain long hidden without creating comment. We had accepted the invitation to dine with alacrity, knowing that we should be welcomed to a banquet that would feast both eye and palate; but we had not been favored by even a glimpse of the hostess. The subject for discussion was: "Expansion; Its Effect upon the Future Development of the Anglo-Saxon throughout the World."

Dinner was over, but we still sat about the social board discussing the question of the hour. The Hon. Herbert Clapp, eminent jurist and politician, had painted in glowing colors the advantages to be gained by the increase of wealth and the exalted position which expansion would give the United States in the councils of the great governments of the world. In smoothly flowing sentences marshalled in rhetorical order, with compact ideas, and incisive argument, he drew an effective picture with all the persuasive eloquence of the trained orator.

Joseph Whitman, the theologian of world-wide fame, accepted the arguments of Mr. Clapp, but subordinated all to the great opportunity which expansion would give to the religious enthusiast. None could doubt the sincerity of this man, who looked once into the idealized face on which heaven had set the seal of consecration.

Various opinions were advanced by the twenty-five men present, but the host said nothing; he glanced from one to another with a look of amusement in his shrewd gray-blue eyes. "Wonderful eyes," said his patients who came under their magic spell. "A wonderful man and a wonderful mind," agreed his contemporaries, as they heard in amazement of some great cure of chronic or malignant disease which approached the supernatural.

"What do you think of this question, Doctor?" finally asked the president, turning to the silent host.

"Your arguments are good; they would convince almost anyone."

"But not Doctor Thornton," laughed the theologian.

"I acquiesce which ever way the result turns. Still, I like to view both sides of a question. We have considered but one tonight. Did you ever think that in spite of our prejudices against amalgamation, some of our descendants, indeed many of them, will inevitably intermarry among those far-off tribes of dark-skinned peoples, if they become a part of this great Union?"

"Among the lower classes that may occur, but not to any great extent," remarked a college president.

"My experience teaches me that it will occur among all classes, and to an appalling extent," replied the Doctor.

"You don't believe in intermarriage with other races?"

"Yes, most emphatically, when they possess decent moral development and physical perfection, for then we develop a superior being in the progeny born of the intermarriage. But if we are not ready to receive and assimilate the new material which will be brought to mingle with our pure Anglo-Saxon stream, we should call a halt in our expansion policy."

"I must confess, Doctor, that in the idea of amalgamation you present a new thought to my mind. Will you not favor us with a few of your main points?" asked the president of the club, breaking the silence which followed the Doctor's remarks.

"Yes, Doctor, give us your theories on the subject. We may not agree with you, but we are all open to conviction."

The Doctor removed the half-consumed cigar from his lips, drank what remained in his glass of the choice Burgundy, and leaning back in his chair contemplated the earnest faces before him.

We may make laws, but laws are but straws in the hands of Omnipotence.

> "There's a divinity that shapes our ends,
> Rough-hew them how we will."[1]

And no man may combat fate. Given a man, propinquity, opportunity fascinating femininity, and there you are. Black, white, green, yellow—nothing will prevent intermarriage. Position, wealth, family, friends—all sink into insignificance before the God-implanted instinct that made Adam, awakening from a deep sleep and finding the woman beside him, accept Eve as bone of his bone;[2] he cared not nor questioned whence she came. So it is with the sons of Adam ever since, through the law of heredity which makes us all one common family. And so it will be with us in our re-formation of this old Republic. Perhaps I can make my meaning clearer by illustration, and with your permission I will tell you a story which came under my observation as a practitioner.

Doubtless all of you heard of the terrible tragedy which occurred at Gordonville, Mass., some years ago, when Capt. Jonathan Gordon, his wife and little son were murdered. I suppose that I am the only man on his side the Atlantic, outside of the police, who can tell you the true story of that crime.

I knew Captain Gordon well; it was through his persuasions that I bought a place in Gordonville and settled down to spending my summers in that charming rural neighborhood. I had rendered the Captain what he was pleased to call valuable medical help, and I became his family physician. Captain Gordon was a retired sea captain, formerly engaged in the East India trade. All his ancestors had been such; but when the bottom fell out of that business he established the Gordonville Mills with his first wife's money, and settled down as a money-making manufacturer of cotton-cloth. The Gordons were old New England Puritans who had come over in the "Mayflower"; they had owned Gordon Hall for more than a hundred years. It was a baronial-like pile of granite with towers, standing on a hill which commanded a superb

1. Shakespeare, *Hamlet* 5.2.10–11.
2. See Genesis 2.21–23, which describes the creation of Eve from one of the ribs of Adam while he is in a deep sleep. On waking, he says, "This is now bone of my bones."

view of Massachusetts Bay and the surrounding country. I imagine the Gordon star was under a cloud about the time Captain Jonathan married his first wife, Miss Isabel Franklin of Boston, who brought to him the money which mended the broken fortunes of the Gordon house, and restored this old Puritan stock to its rightful position. In the person of Captain Gordon the austerity of manner and indomitable will-power that he had inherited were combined with a temper that brooked no contradiction.

The first wife died at the birth of her third child, leaving him two daughters, Jeannette and Talma. Very soon after her death the Captain married again. I have heard it rumored that the Gordon girls did not get on very well with their stepmother. She was a woman with no fortune of her own, and envied the large portion left by the first Mrs. Gordon to her daughters.

Jeannette was tall, dark, and stern like her father; Talma was like her dead mother, and possessed of great talent, so great that her father sent her to the American Academy at Rome, to develop the gift. It was the hottest of July days when her friends were bidden to an afternoon party on the lawn and a dance in the evening, to welcome Talma Gordon among them again. I watched her as she moved about among her guests, a fairylike blonde in floating white draperies, her face a study in delicate changing tints, like the heart of a flower, sparkling in smiles about the mouth to end in merry laughter in the clear blue eyes. There were all the subtle allurements of birth, wealth and culture about the exquisite creature:

> "Smiling, frowning evermore,
> Thou art perfect in love-lore,
> Ever varying Madeline,"[3]

quoted a celebrated writer as he stood apart with me, gazing upon the scene before us. He sighed as he looked at the girl.

"Doctor, there is genius and passion in her face. Sometime our little friend will do wonderful things. But is it desirable to be singled out for special blessings by the gods? Genius always carries with it intense capacity for suffering: "Whom the gods love die young.' "[4]

"Ah," I replied, "do not name death and Talma Gordon together. Cease your dismal croakings; such talk is rank heresy."

The dazzling daylight dropped slowly into summer twilight. The merriment continued; more guests arrived; the great dancing pagoda built for the occasion was lighted by myriads of Japanese lanterns.[5] The strains from the band grew sweeter and sweeter, and "all went merry as a marriage bell." It was a rare treat to have this party at Gordon Hall, for Captain Jonathan was not given to hospitality. We broke up shortly before midnight, with expressions of delight from all the guests.

I was a bachelor then, without ties. Captain Gordon insisted upon my having a bed at the Hall. I did not fall asleep readily; there seemed to be something in the air that forbade it. I was still awake when a distant clock struck the second hour of the morning. Suddenly the heavens were lighted

3. From "Madeline" (1830), by Alfred, Lord Tennyson (in the poem, the final line quoted here functions as a kind of refrain; it does not follow the initial couplet).
4. An aphorism at least as old as the Greek comic dramatist Menander (ca. 342–ca. 292 B.C.E.);

quoted as something said "of yore" in *Don Juan* (1819–24), 4.12, by George Gordon, Lord Byron, who attributed the sentiment to the Greek historian Herodotus.
5. Decorative lanterns, often made of paper.

by a sheet of ghastly light; a terrific midsummer thunderstorm was breaking over the sleeping town. A lurid flash lit up all the landscape, painting the trees in grotesque shapes against the murky sky, and defining clearly the sullen blackness of the waters of the bay breaking in grandeur against the rocky coast. I had arisen and put back the draperies from the windows, to have an unobstructed view of the grand scene. A low muttering coming nearer and nearer, a terrific roar, and then a tremendous downpour. The storm had burst.

Now the uncanny howling of a dog mingled with the rattling volleys of thunder. I heard the opening and closing of doors; the servants were about looking after things. It was impossible to sleep. The lightning was more vivid. There was a blinding flash of a greenish-white tinge mingled with the crash of falling timbers. Then before my startled gaze arose columns of red flames reflected against the sky. "Heaven help us!" I cried; "it is the left tower; it has been struck and is on fire!"

I hurried on my clothes and stepped into the corridor; the girls were there before me. Jeannette came up to me instantly with anxious face. "Oh, Doctor Thornton, what shall we do? papa and mamma and little Johnny are in the old left tower. It is on fire. I have knocked and knocked, but get no answer."

"Don't be alarmed," said I soothingly. "Jenkins, ring the alarm bell," I continued, turning to the butler who was standing near; "the rest follow me. We will force the entrance to the Captain's room."

Instantly, it seemed to me, the bell boomed out upon the now silent air, for the storm had died down as quickly as it arose; and as our little procession paused before the entrance to the old left tower, we could distinguish the sound of the fire engines already on their way from the village.

The door resisted all our efforts; there seemed to be a barrier against it which nothing could move. The flames were gaining headway. Still the same deathly silence within the rooms.

"Oh, will they never get here?" cried Talma, ringing her hands in terror. Jeannette said nothing, but her face was ashen. The servants were huddled together in a panic-stricken group. I can never tell you what a relief it was when we heard the first sound of the firemen's voices, saw their quick movements, and heard the ringing of the axes with which they cut away every obstacle to our entrance to the rooms. The neighbors who had just enjoyed the hospitality of the house were now gathered around offering all the assistance in their power. In less than fifteen minutes the fire was out, and the men began to bear the unconscious inmates from the ruins. They carried them to the pagoda so lately the scene of mirth and pleasure, and I took up my station there, ready to assume my professional duties. The Captain was nearest me; and as I stooped to make the necessary examination I reeled away from the ghastly sight which confronted me—*gentlemen, across the Captain's throat was a deep gash that severed the jugular vein!*

The Doctor paused, and the hand with which he refilled his glass trembled violently.

"What is it, Doctor?" cried the men, gathering about me.

"Take the women away; this is murder!"

"Murder!" cried Jeannette, as she fell against the side of the pagoda.

"Murder!" screamed Talma, staring at me as if unable to grasp my meaning.

I continued my examination of the bodies, and found that the same thing had happened to Mrs. Gordon and to little Johnny.

The police were notified; and when the sun rose over the dripping town he found them in charge of Gordon hall, the servants standing in excited knots talking over the crime, the friends of the family confounded, and the two girls trying to comfort each other and realize the terrible misfortune that had overtaken them.

Nothing in the rooms of the left tower seemed to have been disturbed. The door of communication between the rooms of the husband and wife was open, as they had arranged it for the night. Little Johnny's crib was placed beside his mother's bed. In it he was found as though never awakened by the storm. It was quite evident that the assassin was no common ruffian. The chief gave strict orders for a watch to be kept on all strangers or suspicious characters who were seen in the neighborhood. He made inquiries among the servants, seeing each one separately, but there was nothing gained from them. No one had heard anything suspicious; all had been awakened by the storm. The chief was puzzled. Here was a triple crime for which no motive could be assigned.

"What do you think of it?" I asked him, as we stood together on the lawn.

"It is my opinion that the deed was committed by one of the higher classes, which makes the mystery more difficult to solve. I tell you, Doctor, there are mysteries that never come to light, and this, I think, is one of them."

While we were talking Jenkins, the butler, an old and trusted servant, came up to the chief and saluted respectfully. "Want to speak with me, Jenkins?" he asked. The man nodded, and they walked away together.

The story of the inquest was short, but appalling. It was shown that Talma had been allowed to go abroad to study because she and Mrs. Gordon did not get on well together. From the testimony of Jenkins it seemed that Talma and her father had quarrelled bitterly about her lover, a young artist whom she had met at Rome, who was unknown to fame, and very poor. There had been terrible things said by each, and threats even had passed, all of which now rose up in judgment against the unhappy girl. The examination of the family solicitor revealed the fact that Captain Gordon intended to leave his daughters only a small annuity, the bulk of the fortune going to his son Jonathan, junior. This was a monstrous injustice, as everyone felt. In vain Talma protested her innocence. Someone must have done it. No one would be benefited so much by these deaths as she and her sister. Moreover, the will, together with other papers, was nowhere to be found. Not the slightest clue bearing upon the disturbing elements in this family, if any there were, was to be found. As the only surviving relatives, Jeannette and Talma became joint heirs to an immense fortune, which only for the bloody tragedy just enacted would, in all probability, have passed them by. Here was the motive. The case was very black against Talma. The foreman stood up. The silence was intense: We "find that Capt. Jonathan Gordon, Mary E. Gordon and Jonathan Gordon, junior, all deceased, came to their deaths by means of a knife or other sharp instrument in the hands of Talma Gordon." The girl was like one stricken with death. The flower-like mouth was drawn and pinched; the great sapphire-blue eyes were black with passionate anguish, terror and despair. She was placed in jail to await her trial at the fall session of the criminal court. The excitement in the hitherto quiet town rose to fever heat.

Many points in the evidence seemed incomplete to thinking men. The weapon could not be found, nor could it be divined what had become of it. No reason could be given for the murder except the quarrel between Talma and her father and the ill will which existed between the girl and her stepmother.

When the trial was called Jeannette sat beside Talma in the prisoner's dock; both were arrayed in deepest mourning. Talma was pale and careworn, but seemed uplifted, spiritualized, as it were. Upon Jeannette the full realization of her sister's peril seemed to weigh heavily. She had changed much too: hollow cheeks, tottering steps, eyes blazing with fever, all suggestive of rapid and premature decay. From far-off Italy Edward Turner, growing famous in the art world, came to stand beside his girl-love in this hour of anguish.

The trial was a memorable one. No additional evidence had been collected to strengthen the prosecution; when the attorney-general rose to open the case against Talma he knew, as everyone else did, that he could not convict solely on the evidence adduced. What was given did not always bear upon the case, and brought out strange stories of Captain Jonathan's methods. Tales were told of sailors who had sworn to take his life, in revenge for injuries inflicted upon them by his hand. One or two clues were followed, but without avail. The judge summed up the evidence impartially, giving the prisoner the benefit of the doubt. The points in hand furnished valuable collateral evidence, but were not direct proof. Although the moral presumption was against the prisoner, legal evidence was lacking to actually convict. The jury found the prisoner "Not Guilty," owing to the fact that the evidence was entirely circumstantial. The verdict was received in painful silence; then a murmur of discontent ran through the great crowd.

"She must have done it," said one; "who else has been benefited by the horrible deed?"

"A poor woman would not have fared so well at the hands of the jury, nor a homely one either, for that matter," said another.

The great Gordon trial was ended; innocent or guilty, Talma Gordon could not be tried again. She was free; but her liberty, with blasted prospects and fair fame gone forever, was valueless to her. She seemed to have but one object in her mind: to find the murderer or murderers of her parents and half-brother. By her direction the shrewdest of detectives were employed and money flowed like water, but to no purpose; the Gordon tragedy remained a mystery. I had consented to act as one of the trustees of the immense Gordon estates and business interests, and by my advice the Misses Gordon went abroad. A year later I received a letter from Edward Turner, saying that Jeannette Gordon had died suddenly at Rome, and that Talma, after refusing all his entreaties for an early marriage, had disappeared, leaving no clue as to her whereabouts. I could give the poor fellow no comfort, although I had been duly notified of the death of Jeannette by Talma, in a letter telling me where to forward her remittances, and at the same time requesting me to keep her present residence secret, especially from Edward.

I had established a sanitarium for the cure of chronic diseases at Gordonville, and absorbed in the cares of my profession I gave little thought to the Gordons. I seemed fated to be involved in mysteries.

A man claiming to be an Englishman, and fresh from the California gold

fields, engaged board and professional service at my retreat. I found him suffering in the grasp of the tubercle-fiend[6]—the last stages. He called himself Simon Cameron. Seldom have I seen so fascinating and wicked a face. The lines of the mouth were cruel, the eyes cold and sharp, the smile mocking and evil. He had money in plenty but seemed to have no friends, for he had received no letters and had had no visitors in the time he had been with us. He was an enigma to me; and his nationality puzzled me, for of course I did not believe his story of being English. The peaceful influence of the house seemed to sooth him in a measure, and make his last steps to the mysterious valley as easy as possible. For a time he improved, and would sit or walk about the grounds and sing sweet songs for the pleasure of the other inmates. Strange to say, his malady only affected his voice at times. He sang quaint songs in a silvery tenor of great purity and sweetness that was delicious to the listening ear:

> "A wet sheet and a flowing sea,
> A wind that follows fast,
> And fills the white and rustling sail
> And bends the gallant mast;
> And bends the gallant mast, my boys;
> While like the eagle free,
> Away the good ship flies, and leaves
> Old England on the lea."[7]

There are few singers on the lyric stage who could surpass Simon Cameron.

One night, a few weeks after Cameron's arrival, I sat in my office making up my accounts when the door opened and closed; I glanced up, expecting to see a servant. A lady advanced toward me! She threw back her veil, and then I saw that Talma Gordon, or her ghost, stood before me. After the first excitement of our meeting was over, she told me she had come direct from Paris, to place herself in my care. I had studied her attentively during the first moments of our meeting, and I felt that she was right; unless something unforeseen happened to arouse her from the stupor into which she seemed to have fallen, the last Gordon was doomed to an early death. The next day I told her I had cabled Edward Turner to come to her.

"It will do no good; I cannot marry him," was her only comment.

"Have you no feeling of pity for that faithful fellow?" I asked her sternly, provoked by her seeming indifference. I shall never forget the varied emotions depicted on her speaking face. Fully revealed to my gaze was the sight of a human soul tortured beyond the point of endurance; suffering all things, enduring all things, in the silent agony of despair.

In a few days Edward arrived, and Talma consented to see him and explain her refusal to keep her promise to him. You must be present, Doctor; it is due your long, tried friendship to know that I have not been fickle, but have acted from the best and strongest motives.

I shall never forget that day. It was directly after lunch that we met in the library. I was greatly excited, expecting I knew not what. Edward was agi-

6. I.e., tuberculosis.
7. A sea ballad (1825) by the Scottish poet Allan Cunningham.

tated, too. Talma was the only calm one. She handed me what seemed to be a letter, with the request that I would read it. Even now I think I can repeat every word of the document, so indelibly are the words engraved upon my mind:

MY DARLING SISTER TALMA: When you read these lines I shall be no more, for I shall not live to see your life blasted by the same knowledge that has blighted mine.

One evening, about a year before your expected return from Rome, I climbed into a hammock in one corner of the veranda outside the breakfast-room windows, intending to spend the twilight hours in lazy comfort, for it was very hot, enervating August weather. I fell asleep. I was awakened by voices. Because of the heat the rooms had been left in semi-darkness. As I lay there, lazily enjoying the beauty of the perfect summer night, my wandering thoughts were arrested by words spoken by our father to Mrs. Gordon, for they were the occupants of the breakfast-room.

"Never fear, Mary; Johnny shall have it all—money, houses, land and business."

"But if you do go first, Jonathan, what will happen if the girls contest the will? People will think that they ought to have the money as it appears to be theirs by law. I never could survive the terrible disgrace of the story."

"Don't borrow trouble; all you would need to do would be to show them papers I have drawn up, and they would be glad to take their annuity and say nothing. After all, I do not think it is so bad. Jeannette can teach; Talma can paint; six hundred dollars a year is quite enough for them."

I had been somewhat mystified by the conversation until now. This last remark solved the riddle. What could he mean? teach, paint, six hundred a year! With my usual impetuosity I sprang from my resting-place, and in a moment stood in the room confronting my father, and asking what he meant. I could see plainly that both were disconcerted by my unexpected appearance.

"Ah, wretched girl! you have been listening. But what could I expect of your mother's daughter?"

At these words I felt the indignant blood rush to my head in a torrent. So it had been all my life. Before you could remember, Talma, I had felt my little heart swell with anger at the disparaging hints and slurs concerning our mother. Now was my time. I determined that tonight I would know why she was looked upon as an outcast, and her children subjected to every humiliation. So I replied to my father in bitter anger:

"I was not listening; I fell asleep in the hammock. What do you mean by a paltry six hundred a year each to Talma and to me? 'My mother's daughter' demands an explanation from you, sir, of the meaning of the monstrous injustice that you have always practised toward my sister and me."

"Speak more respectfully to your father, Jeannette," broke in Mrs. Gordon.

"How is it, madam, that you look for respect from one whom you have delighted to torment ever since you came into this most unhappy family?"

"Hush, both of you," said Captain Gordon, who seemed to have recovered from the dismay into which my sudden appearance and passionate words had plunged him. "I think I may as well tell you as to wait. Since you know so much, you may as well know the whole miserable story." He motioned me to a seat. I could see that he was deeply agitated. I seated myself in a chair

he pointed out, in wonder and expectation,—expectation of I knew not what. I trembled. This was a supreme moment in my life; I felt it. The air was heavy with the intense stillness that had settled over us as the common sounds of day gave place to the early quiet of the rural evening. I could see Mrs. Gordon's face as she sat within the radius of the lighted hallway. There was a smile of triumph upon it. I clinched my hands and bit my lips until the blood came, in the effort to keep from screaming. What was I about to hear? At last he spoke:

"I was disappointed at your birth, and also at the birth of Talma. I wanted a male heir. When I knew that I should again be a father I was torn by hope and fear, but I comforted myself with the thought that luck would be with me in the birth of the third child. When the doctor brought me word that a son was born to the house of Gordon, I was wild with delight, and did not notice his disturbed countenance. In the midst of my joy he said to me:

"Captain Gordon, there is something strange about this birth. I want you to see this child."

Quelling my exultation I followed him to the nursery, and there, lying in the cradle, I saw a child dark as a mulatto, with the characteristic features of the Negro! I was stunned. Gradually it dawned upon me that there was something radically wrong. I turned to the doctor for an explanation.

"There is but one explanation, Captain Gordon; there is Negro blood in this child."

"There is no Negro blood in my veins," I said proudly. Then I paused— *the mother!*—I glanced at the doctor. He was watching me intently. The same thought was in his mind. I must have lived a thousand years in that cursed five seconds that I stood there confronting the physician and trying to think. "Come," said I to him, "let us end this suspense." Without thinking of consequences, I hurried away to your mother and accused her of infidelity to her marriage vows. I raved like a madman. Your mother fell into convulsions; her life was despaired of. I sent for Mr. and Mrs. Franklin, and then I learned the truth. They were childless. One year while on a Southern tour, they befriended an octoroon[8] girl who had been abandoned by her white lover. Her child was a beautiful girl baby. They, being Northern born, thought little of caste distinction because the child showed no trace of Negro blood. They determined to adopt it. They went abroad, secretly sending back word to their friends at a proper time, of the birth of a little daughter. No one doubted the truth of the statement. They made Isabel their heiress, and all went well until the birth of your brother. Your mother and the unfortunate babe died. This is the story which, if known, would bring dire disgrace upon the Gordon family.

To appease my righteous wrath, Mr. Franklin left a codicil to his will by which all the property is left at my disposal save a small annuity to you and your sister.

I sat there after he had finished his story, stunned by what I had heard. I understood, now, Mrs. Gordon's half contemptuous toleration and lack of consideration for us both. As I rose from my seat to leave the room I said to Captain Gordon:

8. Someone with one-eighth black blood.

"Still, in spite of all, sir, I am a Gordon, legally born. I will not tamely give up my birthright."

I left that room a broken-hearted girl, filled with a desire for revenge upon this man, my father, who by his manner disowned us without a regret. Not once in that remarkable interview did he speak of our mother as his wife; he quietly repudiated her and us with all the cold cruelty of relentless caste prejudice. I heard the treatment of your lover's proposal; I knew why Captain Gordon's consent to your marriage was withheld.

The night of the reception and dance was the chance for which I had waited, planned and watched. I crept from my window into the ivy-vines, and so down, down, until I stood upon the window-sill of Captain Gordon's room in the old left tower. How did I do it, you ask? I do not know. The house was silent after the revel; the darkness of the gathering storm favored me, too. The lawyer was there that day. The will was signed and put safely away among my father's papers. I was determined to have the will and the other documents bearing upon the case, and I would have revenge, too, for the cruelties we had suffered. With the old East Indian dagger firmly grasped I entered the room and found—that my revenge had been forestalled! The horror of the discovery I made that night restored me to reason and a realization of the crime I meditated. Scarce knowing what I did, I sought and found the papers, and crept back to my room as I had come. Do you wonder that my disease is past medical aid?"

I looked at Edward as I finished. He sat, his face covered with his hands. Finally he looked up with a glance of haggard despair: "God! Doctor, but this is too much. I could stand the stigma of murder, but add to that the pollution of Negro blood! No man is brave enough to face such a situation."

"It is as I thought it would be," said Talma sadly, while the tears poured over her white face. "I do not blame you, Edward."

He rose from his chair, rung my hand in a convulsive clasp, turned to Talma and bowed profoundly, with his eyes fixed upon the floor, hesitated, turned, paused, bowed again and abruptly left the room. So those two who had been lovers, parted. I turned to Talma, expecting her to give way. She smiled a pitiful smile, and said: "You see, Doctor, I knew best."

From that on she failed rapidly. I was restless. If only I could rouse her to an interest in life, she might live to old age. So rich, so young, so beautiful, so talented, so pure; I grew savage thinking of the injustice of the world. I had not reckoned on the power that never sleeps. Something was about to happen.

On visiting Cameron next morning I found him approaching the end. He had been sinking for a week very rapidly. As I sat by the bedside holding his emaciated hand, he fixed his bright, wicked eyes on me, and asked: "How long have I got to live?"

"Candidly, but a few hours."

"Thank you; well, I want death; I am not afraid to die. Doctor, Cameron is not my name."

"I never supposed it was."

"No? You are sharper than I thought. I heard all your talk yesterday with Talma Gordon. Curse the whole race!"

He clasped his bony fingers around my arm and gasped: "*I murdered the Gordons!*"

Had I the pen of a Dumas[9] I could not paint Cameron as he told his story. It is a question with me whether this wheeling planet, home of the suffering, doubting, dying, may not hold worse agonies on its smiling surface than those of the conventional hell. I sent for Talma and a lawyer. We gave him stimulants, and then with broken intervals of coughing and prostration we got the story of the Gordon murder. I give it to you in a few words:

"I am an East Indian, but my name does not matter, Cameron is as good as any. There is many a soul crying in heaven and hell for vengeance on Jonathan Gordon. Gold was his idol; and many a good man walked the plank, and many a gallant ship was stripped of her treasure, to satisfy his lust for gold. His blackest crime was the murder of my father, who was his friend, and had sailed with him for many a year as mate. One night these two went ashore together to bury their treasure. My father never returned from that expedition. His body was afterward found with a bullet through the heart on the shore where the vessel stopped that night. It was the custom then among pirates for the captain to kill the men who helped bury their treasure. Captain Gordon was no better than a pirate. An East Indian never forgets, and I swore by my mother's deathbed to hunt Captain Gordon down until I had avenged my father's murder. I had the plans of the Gordon estate, and fixed on the night of the reception in honor of Talma as the time for my vengeance. There is a secret entrance from the shore to the chambers where Captain Gordon slept; no one knew of it save the Captain and trusted members of his crew. My mother gave me the plans, and entrance and escape were easy."

"So the great mystery was solved. In a few hours Cameron was no more. We placed the confession in the hands of the police, and there the matter ended."

"But what became of Talma Gordon?" questioned the president. "Did she die?"

"Gentlemen," said the Doctor, rising to his feet and sweeping the faces of the company with his eagle gaze, "gentlemen, if you will follow me to the drawing-room, I shall have much pleasure in introducing you to my wife— *nee* Talma Gordon."

1900

9. Alexandre Dumas (1802–1870), French playwright and novelist who wrote such works of adventure as *The Three Musketeers* and *The Count of Monte Cristo*; Dumas was one-quarter black.

CHARLOTTE PERKINS GILMAN
1860–1935

In her autobiography, *The Living of Charlotte Perkins Gilman* (1935), Charlotte Perkins Gilman described the "dark fog" that enveloped her after she gave birth to her daughter, Katherine, and was treated by the prominent neurologist S. Weir Mitchell. This major proponent of the so-called rest cure put her to bed, where she was fed, bathed, massaged, advised to have her child with her at all times, and admonished her "never to touch pen, brush, or pencil again." Only further troubled by the treatment, the twenty-five-year-old wife and mother "made a rag baby, hung it on a

doorknob and played with it. I would crawl into remote closets and under beds—to hide from the grinding pressure of that profound distress." Two years later, in the fall of 1887, she knew that she had to choose "not . . . between going and staying" with her husband and child, "but between going, insane, and staying, sane." She left her husband in 1888, but this early nervous collapse marked the rest of her life, disrupting her concentration and draining her energies. Yet it also led to the writing of her now classic short story, "The Yellow Wallpaper" (1892), and to the lecturing and publishing that would establish her reputation during her lifetime as the leading feminist theorist in America.

Gilman's early breakdown, which might today be diagnosed as postpartum depression, probably had its origin in the emotional deprivation she suffered as a child. Born in 1860, in Hartford, Connecticut, she and her older brother were raised by their mother, Mary A. (Fitch) Perkins, after their father left the family because Mary had been warned against another pregnancy, or so Gilman suggests in her autobiography. In any case, the young girl found it difficult to sustain through letters a relationship with a father who was so remote, although she identified her own intellectual ambition with his relatives, the famous Beechers: "The word Father," she explained in her autobiography, "means nothing to me, save indeed in advice about books and the care of them—which seems more the librarian than the father." The great-niece of Catharine Beecher and Harriet Beecher Stowe, Gilman also suffered from her mother's poverty, a problem that caused the family to move nineteen times in eighteen years. Just as difficult to accept was Mary Perkins's apparently principled decision to spare her children the expectation of emotional fulfillment by refusing them any physical signs of tenderness: "She would not let me caress her, and would not caress me, unless I was asleep." Understandably, the young girl would keep herself awake, "even using pins to prevent dropping off," so as to feign sleep and gain the "raptur[ous]" enjoyment of "being gathered into her arms, held close and kissed."

For a short period of time, Gilman attended the Rhode Island School of Design, where she obtained the training that enabled her to work as an art teacher and governess. Her first husband, Charles Walter Stetson, was a Providence artist whom she married in 1884, although even during their courtship she was aware of the difficulty of combining marriage, motherhood, and work. After her breakdown, she moved with her daughter Katherine to Pasadena, California. There she obtained a divorce and decided to send Katherine to live with her ex-husband and his new wife, her friend Grace Ellery Channing. The resulting publicity, generated by Massachusetts and California newspapers, condemned Gilman as unfeeling and unnatural. In spite of her anguish over both the decision and the notoriety, she struggled to support herself first in Oakland and then in San Francisco by lecturing, editing, writing, and teaching. Many of her most effective polemical poems were composed and printed in this period. "The Yellow Wallpaper," which was published in May 1892 in *The New England Magazine* and later reprinted by William Dean Howells in *Great Modern American Stories* (1920), was followed by the feminist polemic *Women and Economics* (1898). Hailed as the Bible of the women's movement and translated into seven languages, the latter work established the argument Gilman would extend in many other publications: namely, the claim that women's economic dependency on men had arrested not only their intellectual and emotional growth but also the healthy development of the human species.

Two years after the publication of *Women and Economics*, Charlotte Perkins Stetson married George Houghton Gilman, a first cousin who had corresponded extensively with her about her doubts and desires concerning marriage. For the next three decades they lived together, first in New York and then in Norwich, Connecticut. His support, as well as the household help provided by Helen Campbell, a close friend she had made in California, allowed Gilman to develop more fully the socialist ideas of Edward Bellamy and the principles of the American sociologist Frank Ward. As in *Women and Economics*, she continued to argue that the subordination of the female sex had been necessary in the past for human evolution, but that in the twentieth

century masculine assertiveness had to be complemented by a female culture grounded in cooperation and nurturance. Attacking what she called a "masculinist" society, Gilman explored alternative social organizations to free women from domestic subservience: in *Concerning Children* (1900), *The Home* (1903), and *Human Work* (1904), she suggested day care centers; the professionalization of house cleaning, laundry, and sewing; and kitchenless houses. Later books such as *Man-Made World* (1911) and *His Religion and Hers* (1923) posit the female as the primary type of the human species, arguing that women's commitment to sustaining life; contrasts with men's engagement with war, an involvement that results in a theology of sacrificial violence. From 1909 until 1916, Gilman's editorials, poems, and fiction appeared in the *Forerunner,* the monthly magazine she edited and published. It was there that she serialized her feminist utopia, *Herland* (1915), a fantasy about a world of parthenogenetic women whose culture explicitly dramatizes the ecological and ethical superiority of matriarchy while implicitly demonstrating the inferiority of patriarchy.

Although Gilman played an important role in the feminist movement, addressing the International Suffrage Convention in Budapest in 1913 and helping to found the Woman's Peace Party in 1915, when that movement declined in the 1920s she began to lose her audience. After her husband's sudden death in 1934, she returned to California to live near her daughter. There she was joined by the widowed Grace Channing Stetson. After discovering that she was suffering from breast cancer, she ended her life with chloroform, not because of the pain she suffered, she explained, but because her career of service was over. After her death, Gilman and her work were relegated to a minor place in history. For almost fifty years, "The Yellow Wallpaper" went unprinted and unread. For more than sixty years, *Herland* was unavailable. The editorial and biographical work of Ann J. Lane, Gail Parker, Elaine R. Hedges, Carl Degler, Catherine Golden, and Mary A. Hill has made possible a critical reappraisal of this socialist-feminist whose fiction furnishes a poetics for the feminist politics she developed at the turn of the century.

She Walketh Veiled and Sleeping

> She walketh veiled and sleeping,
> For she knoweth not her power;
> She obeyeth but the pleading
> Of her heart, and the high leading
> 5 Of her soul, unto this hour.
> Slow advancing, halting, creeping,
> Comes the Woman to the hour!—
> She walketh veiled and sleeping,
> For she knoweth not her power.

1889

False Play

> "Do you love me?" asked the mother of her child,
> And the baby answered, "No!"
> Great Love listened and sadly smiled;
> He knew the love in the heart of the child—
> 5 That you could not wake it so.

"Do not love me?" the foolish mother cried,
 And the baby answered, "No!"
He knew the worth of the trick she tried—
Great Love listened, and grieving, sighed
10 That the mother scorned him so.

"Oh, poor mama!" and she played her part
 Till the baby's strength gave way:
He knew it was false in his inmost heart,
But he could not bear that her tears should start,
15 So he joined in the lying play.

"Then love mama!" and the soft lips crept
 To the kiss that his love should show,—
The mouth to speak while the spirit slept!
Great Love listened, and blushed, and wept
20 That they blasphemed him so.

 1893

The Mother's Charge

She raised her head. With hot and glittering eye,
"I know," she said, "that I am going to die.
Come here, my daughter, while my mind is clear.
Let me make plain to you your duty here;
5 My duty once—I never failed to try—
But for some reason I am going to die."
She raised her head, and, while her eyes rolled wild,
Poured these instructions on the gasping child:
"Begin at once—don't iron sitting down—
10 Wash your potatoes when the fat is brown—
Monday, unless it rains—it always pays
To get fall sewing done on the right days—
A carpet-sweeper and a little broom—
Save dishes—wash the summer dining-room
15 With soda—keep the children out of doors—
The starch is out—beeswax on all the floors—
If girls are treated like your friends they stay—
They stay, and treat you like their friends—the way
To make home happy is to keep a jar—
20 And save the prettiest pieces for the star
In the middle—blue's too dark—all silk is best—
And don't forget the corners—when they're dressed
Put them on ice—and always wash the chest
Three times a day, the windows every week—
25 We need more flour—the bedroom ceilings leak—
It's better than onion—keep the boys at home—
Gardening is good—a load, three loads of loam—
They bloom in spring—and smile, smile always, dear—
Be brave, keep on—I hope I've made it clear."

30 She died, as all her mothers died before.
 Her daughter died in turn, and made one more.

1894

The Yellow Wallpaper

It is very seldom that mere ordinary people like John and myself secure ancestral halls for the summer.

A colonial mansion, a hereditary estate, I would say a haunted house and reach the height of romantic felicity—but that would be asking too much of fate!

Still I will proudly declare that there is something queer about it.

Else, why should it be let so cheaply? And why have stood so long untenanted?

John laughs at me, of course, but one expects that.

John is practical in the extreme. He has no patience with faith, an intense horror of superstition, and he scoffs openly at any talk of things not to be felt and seen and put down in figures.

John is a physician, and *perhaps*—(I would not say it to a living soul, of course, but this is dead paper and a great relief to my mind)—*perhaps* that is one reason I do not get well faster.

You see, he does not believe I am sick! And what can one do?

If a physician of high standing, and one's own husband, assures friends and relatives that there is really nothing the matter with one but temporary nervous depression—a slight hysterical[1] tendency—what is one to do?

My brother is also a physician, and also of high standing, and he says the same thing.

So I take phosphates or phosphites—whichever it is—and tonics, and air and exercise, and journeys, and am absolutely forbidden to "work" until I am well again.

Personally, I disagree with their ideas.

Personally, I believe that congenial work, with excitement and change, would do me good.

But what is one to do?

I did write for a while in spite of them; but it *does* exhaust me a good deal—having to be so sly about it, or else meet with heavy opposition.

I sometimes fancy that in my condition, if I had less opposition and more society and stimulus—but John says the very worst thing I can do is to think about my condition, and I confess it always makes me feel bad.

So I will let it alone and talk about the house.

The most beautiful place! It is quite alone, standing well back from the road, quite three miles from the village. It makes me think of English places that you read about, for there are hedges and walls and gates that lock, and lots of separate little houses for the gardeners and people.

1. *Hysteria* was, at the time, a loose term covering various kinds of "female" emotional disorders—depression, anxiety, nervousness, and so on.

There is a *delicious* garden! I never saw such a garden—large and shady, full of box[2]-bordered paths, and lined with long grape-covered arbors with seats under them.

There were greenhouses, but they are all broken now.

There was some legal trouble, I believe, something about the heirs and co-heirs; anyhow, the place has been empty for years.

That spoils my ghostliness, I am afraid, but I don't care—there is something strange about the house—I can feel it.

I even said so to John one moonlight evening, but he said what I felt was a draught, and shut the window.

I get unreasonably angry with John sometimes. I'm sure I never used to be so sensitive. I think it is due to this nervous condition.

But John says if I feel so I shall neglect proper self-control; so I take pains to control myself—before him, at least, and that makes me very tired.

I don't like our room a bit. I wanted one downstairs that opened onto the piazza and had roses all over the window, and such pretty old-fashioned chintz hangings! But John would not hear of it.

He said there was only one window and not room for two beds, and no near room for him if he took another.

He is very careful and loving, and hardly lets me stir without special direction.

I have a schedule prescription for each hour in the day; he takes all care from me, and so I feel basely ungrateful not to value it more.

He said he came here solely on my account, that I was to have perfect rest and all the air I could get. "Your exercise depends on your strength, my dear," said he, "and your food somewhat on your appetite; but air you can absorb all the time." So we took the nursery at the top of the house.

It is a big, airy room, the whole floor nearly, with windows that look all ways, and air and sunshine galore. It was nursery first, and then playroom and gymnasium, I should judge, for the windows are barred for little children, and there are rings and things in the walls.

The paint and paper look as if a boys' school had used it. It is stripped off—the paper—in great patches all around the head of my bed, about as far as I can reach, and in a great place on the other side of the room low down. I never saw a worse paper in my life. One of those sprawling, flamboyant patterns committing every artistic sin.

It is dull enough to confuse the eye in following, pronounced enough constantly to irritate and provoke study, and when you follow the lame uncertain curves for a little distance they suddenly commit suicide—plunge off at outrageous angles, destroy themselves in unheard-of contradictions.

The color is repellent, almost revolting: a smouldering unclean yellow, strangely faded by the slow-turning sunlight. It is a dull yet lurid orange in some places, a sickly sulphur tint in others.

No wonder the children hated it! I should hate it myself if I had to live in this room long.

There comes John, and I must put this away—he hates to have me write a word.

2. I.e., boxwood.

We have been here two weeks, and I haven't felt like writing before, since that first day.

I am sitting by the window now, up in this atrocious nursery, and there is nothing to hinder my writing as much as I please, save lack of strength.

John is away all day, and even some nights when his cases are serious.

I am glad my case is not serious!

But these nervous troubles are dreadfully depressing.

John does not know how much I really suffer. He knows there is no reason to suffer, and that satisfies him.

Of course it is only nervousness. It does weigh on me so not to do my duty in any way!

I meant to be such a help to John, such a real rest and comfort, and here I am a comparative burden already!

Nobody would believe what an effort it is to do what little I am able—to dress and entertain, and order things.

It is fortunate Mary is so good with the baby. Such a dear baby!

And yet I *cannot* be with him, it makes me so nervous.

I suppose John never was nervous in his life. He laughs at me so about this wallpaper!

At first he meant to repaper the room, but afterward he said that I was letting it get the better of me, and that nothing was worse for a nervous patient than to give way to such fancies.

He said that after the wallpaper was changed it would be the heavy bedstead, and then the barred windows, and then that gate at the head of the stairs, and so on.

"You know the place is doing you good," he said, "and really, dear, I don't care to renovate the house just for a three months' rental."

"Then do let us go downstairs," I said. "There are such pretty rooms there."

Then he took me in his arms and called me a blessed little goose, and said he would go down cellar, if I wished, and have it whitewashed into the bargain.

But he is right enough about the beds and windows and things.

It is as airy and comfortable a room as anyone need wish, and, of course, I would not be so silly as to make him uncomfortable just for a whim.

I'm really getting quite fond of the big room, all but that horrid paper.

Out of one window I can see the garden—those mysterious deep-shaded arbors, the riotous old-fashioned flowers, and bushes and gnarly trees.

Out of another I get a lovely view of the bay and a little private wharf belonging to the estate. There is a beautiful shaded lane that runs down there from the house. I always fancy I see people walking in these numerous paths and arbors, but John has cautioned me not to give way to fancy in the least. He says that with my imaginative power and habit of story-making, a nervous weakness like mine is sure to lead to all manner of excited fancies, and that I ought to use my will and good sense to check the tendency. So I try.

I think sometimes that if I were only well enough to write a little it would relieve the press of ideas and rest me.

But I find I get pretty tired when I try.

It is so discouraging not to have any advice and companionship about my work. When I get really well, John says we will ask Cousin Henry and Julia

down for a long visit; but he says he would as soon put fireworks in my pillow-case as to let me have those stimulating people about now.

I wish I could get well faster.

But I must not think about that. This paper looks to me as if it *knew* what a vicious influence it had!

There is a recurrent spot where the pattern lolls like a broken neck and two bulbous eyes stare at you upside down.

I get positively angry with the impertinence of it and the everlastingness. Up and down and sideways they crawl, and those absurd unblinking eyes are everywhere. There is one place where two breadths didn't match, and the eyes go all up and down the line, one a little higher than the other.

I never saw so much expression in an inanimate thing before, and we all know how much expression they have! I used to lie awake as a child and get more entertainment and terror out of blank walls and plain furniture than most children could find in a toy-store.

I remember what a kindly wink the knobs of our big old bureau used to have, and there was one chair that always seemed like a strong friend.

I used to feel that if any of the other things looked too fierce I could always hop into that chair and be safe.

The furniture in this room is no worse than inharmonious, however, for we had to bring it all from downstairs. I suppose when this was used as a playroom they had to take the nursery things out, and no wonder! I never saw such ravages as the children have made here.

The wallpaper, as I said before, is torn off in spots, and it sticketh closer than a brother[3]—they must have had perseverance as well as hatred.

Then the floor is scratched and gouged and splintered, the plaster itself is dug out here and there, and this great heavy bed, which is all we found in the room, looks as if it had been through the wars.

But I don't mind it a bit—only the paper.

There comes John's sister. Such a dear girl as she is, and so careful of me! I must not let her find me writing.

She is a perfect and enthusiastic housekeeper, and hopes for no better profession. I verily believe she thinks it is the writing which made me sick!

But I can write when she is out, and see her a long way off from these windows.

There is one that commands the road, a lovely shaded winding road, and one that just looks off over the country. A lovely country, too, full of great elms and velvet meadows.

This wallpaper has a kind of sub-pattern in a different shade, a particularly irritating one, for you can only see it in certain lights, and not clearly then.

But in the places where it isn't faded and where the sun is just so—I can see a strange, provoking, formless sort of figure that seems to skulk about behind that silly and conspicuous front design.

There's sister on the stairs!

Well, the Fourth of July is over! The people are all gone, and I am tired out. John thought it might do me good to see a little company, so we just had Mother and Nellie and the children down for a week.

Of course I didn't do a thing. Jennie sees to everything now.

3. Proverbs 18.24.

But it tired me all the same.

John says if I don't pick up faster he shall send me to Weir Mitchell[4] in the fall.

But I don't want to go there at all. I had a friend who was in his hands once, and she says he is just like John and my brother, only more so!

Besides, it is such an undertaking to go so far.

I don't feel as if it was worthwhile to turn my hand over for anything, and I'm getting dreadfully fretful and querulous.

I cry at nothing, and cry most of the time.

Of course I don't when John is here, or anybody else, but when I am alone.

And I am alone a good deal just now. John is kept in town very often by serious cases, and Jennie is good and lets me alone when I want her to.

So I walk a little in the garden or down that lovely lane, sit on the porch under the roses, and lie down up here a good deal.

I'm getting really fond of the room in spite of the wallpaper. Perhaps *because* of the wallpaper.

It dwells in my mind so!

I lie here on this great immovable bed—it is nailed down, I believe—and follow that pattern about by the hour. It is as good as gymnastics, I assure you. I start, we'll say, at the bottom, down in the corner over there where it has not been touched, and I determine for the thousandth time that I *will* follow that pointless pattern to some sort of a conclusion.

I know a little of the principle of design, and I know this thing was not arranged on any laws of radiation, or alternation, or repetition, or symmetry, or anything else that I ever heard of.

It is repeated, of course, by the breadths, but not otherwise.

Looked at in one way, each breadth stands alone; the bloated curves and flourishes—a kind of "debased Romanesque" with delirium tremens[5]—go waddling up and down in isolated columns of fatuity.

But, on the other hand, they connect diagonally, and the sprawling outlines run off in great slanting waves of optic horror, like a lot of wallowing sea-weeds in full chase.

The whole thing goes horizontally, too, at least it seems so, and I exhaust myself trying to distinguish the order of its going in that direction.

They have used a horizontal breadth for a frieze, and that adds wonderfully to the confusion.

There is one end of the room where it is almost intact, and there, when the crosslights fade and the low sun shines directly upon it, I can almost fancy radiation after all—the interminable grotesque seems to form around a common center and rush off in headlong plunges of equal distraction.

It makes me tired to follow it. I will take a nap, I guess.

I don't know why I should write this.

I don't want to.

I don't feel able.

And I know John would think it absurd. But I *must* say what I feel and think in some way—it is such a relief!

But the effort is getting to be greater than the relief.

4. Silas Weir Mitchell (1829–1914), American nerve specialist, who popularized the "rest cure" and who treated Gilman herself.

5. Trembling delirium associated with alcoholism. "Romanesque": a highly decorative style of architecture.

Half the time now I am awfully lazy, and lie down ever so much. John says I mustn't lose my strength, and has me take cod liver oil and lots of tonics and things, to say nothing of ale and wine and rare meat.

Dear John! He loves me very dearly, and hates to have me sick. I tried to have a real earnest reasonable talk with him the other day, and tell him how I wish he would let me go and make a visit to Cousin Henry and Julia.

But he said I wasn't able to go, nor able to stand it after I got there; and I did not make out a very good case for myself, for I was crying before I had finished.

It is getting to be a great effort for me to think straight. Just this nervous weakness, I suppose.

And dear John gathered me up in his arms, and just carried me upstairs and laid me on the bed, and sat by me and read to me till it tired my head.

He said I was his darling and his comfort and all he had, and that I must take care of myself for his sake, and keep well.

He says no one but myself can help me out of it, that I must use my will and self-control and not let any silly fancies run away with me.

There's one comfort—the baby is well and happy, and does not have to occupy this nursery with the horrid wallpaper.

If we had not used it, that blessed child would have! What a fortunate escape! Why, I wouldn't have a child of mine, an impressionable little thing, live in such a room for worlds.

I never thought of it before, but it is lucky that John kept me here after all; I can stand it so much easier than a baby, you see.

Of course I never mention it to them any more—I am too wise—but I keep watch for it all the same.

There are things in that wallpaper that nobody knows about but me, or ever will.

Behind that outside pattern the dim shapes get clearer every day.

It is always the same shape, only very numerous.

And it is like a woman stooping down and creeping about behind that pattern. I don't like it a bit. I wonder—I begin to think—I wish John would take me away from here!

It is so hard to talk with John about my case, because he is so wise, and because he loves me so.

But I tried it last night.

It was moonlight. The moon shines in all around just as the sun does.

I hate to see it sometimes, it creeps so slowly, and always comes in by one window or another.

John was asleep and I hated to waken him, so I kept still and watched the moonlight on that undulating wallpaper till I felt creepy.

The faint figure behind seemed to shake the pattern, just as if she wanted to get out.

I got up softly and went to feel and see if the paper *did* move, and when I came back John was awake.

"What is it, little girl?" he said. "Don't go walking about like that—you'll get cold."

I thought it was a good time to talk, so I told him that I really was not gaining here, and that I wished he would take me away.

"Why, darling!" said he. "Our lease will be up in three weeks, and I can't see how to leave before.

"The repairs are not done at home, and I cannot possibly leave town just now. Of course, if you were in any danger, I could and would, but you really are better, dear, whether you can see it or not. I am a doctor, dear, and I know. You are gaining flesh and color, your appetite is better, I feel really much easier about you."

"I don't weigh a bit more," said I, "nor as much; and my appetite may be better in the evening when you are here but it is worse in the morning when you are away!"

"Bless her little heart!" said he with a big hug. "She shall be as sick as she pleases! But now let's improve the shining hours[6] by going to sleep, and talk about it in the morning!"

"And you won't go away?" I asked gloomily.

"Why, how can I, dear? It is only three weeks more and then we will take a nice little trip of a few days while Jennie is getting the house ready. Really, dear, you are better!"

"Better in body perhaps—" I began, and stopped short, for he sat up straight and looked at me with such a stern, reproachful look that I could not say another word.

"My darling," said he, "I beg of you, for my sake and for our child's sake, as well as for your own, that you will never for one instant let that idea enter your mind! There is nothing so dangerous, so fascinating, to a temperament like yours. It is a false and foolish fancy. Can you not trust me as a physician when I tell you so?"

So of course I said no more on that score, and we went to sleep before long. He thought I was asleep first, but I wasn't and lay there for hours trying to decide whether that front pattern and the back pattern really did move together or separately.

On a pattern like this, by daylight, there is a lack of sequence, a defiance of law, that is a constant irritant to a normal mind.

The color is hideous enough, and unreliable enough, and infuriating enough, but the pattern is torturing.

You think you have mastered it, but just as you get well under way in following, it turns a back-somersault and there you are. It slaps you in the face, knocks you down, and tramples upon you. It is like a bad dream.

The outside pattern is a florid arabesque,[7] reminding one of a fungus. If you can imagine a toadstool in joints, an interminable string of toadstools, budding and sprouting in endless convolutions—why, that is something like it.

That is, sometimes!

There is one marked peculiarity about this paper, a thing nobody seems to notice but myself, and that is that it changes as the light changes.

When the sun shoots in through the east window—I always watch for that first long, straight ray—it changes so quickly that I never can quite believe it.

That is why I watch it always.

6. From the popular moral poem by Isaac Watts "Against Idleness and Mischief" (1715): "How doth the little busy bee / Improve each shining hour, / And gather honey all the day / From every opening flower!"

7. An intricate pattern of interlaced lines.

By moonlight—the moon shines in all night when there is a moon—I wouldn't know it was the same paper.

At night in any kind of light, in twilight, candlelight, lamplight, and worst of all by moonlight, it becomes bars! The outside pattern, I mean, and the woman behind it is as plain as can be.

I didn't realize for a long time what the thing was that showed behind, that dim sub-pattern, but now I am quite sure it is a woman.

By daylight she is subdued, quiet. I fancy it is the pattern that keeps her so still. It is so puzzling. It keeps me quiet by the hour.

I lie down ever so much now. John says it is good for me, and to sleep all I can.

Indeed he started the habit by making me lie down for an hour after each meal.

It is a very bad habit, I am convinced, for you see, I don't sleep.

And that cultivates deceit, for I don't tell them I'm awake—oh, no!

The fact is I am getting a little afraid of John.

He seems very queer sometimes, and even Jennie has an inexplicable look.

It strikes me occasionally, just as a scientific hypothesis, that perhaps it is the paper!

I have watched John when he did not know I was looking, and come into the room suddenly on the most innocent excuses, and I've caught him several times *looking at the paper!* And Jennie too. I caught Jennie with her hand on it once.

She didn't know I was in the room, and when I asked her in a quiet, a very quiet voice, with the most restrained manner possible, what she was doing with the paper, she turned around as if she had been caught stealing, and looked quite angry—asked me why I should frighten her so!

Then she said that the paper stained everything it touched, that she had found yellow smooches on all my clothes and John's and she wished we would be more careful!

Did not that sound innocent? But I know she was studying that pattern, and I am determined that nobody shall find it out but myself!

Life is very much more exciting now than it used to be. You see, I have something more to expect, to look forward to, to watch. I really do eat better, and am more quiet than I was.

John is so pleased to see me improve! He laughed a little the other day, and said I seemed to be flourishing in spite of my wallpaper.

I turned it off with a laugh. I had no intention of telling him it was *because* of the wallpaper—he would make fun of me. He might even want to take me away.

I don't want to leave now until I have found it out. There is a week more, and I think that will be enough.

I'm feeling so much better!

I don't sleep much at night, for it is so interesting to watch developments; but I sleep a good deal during the daytime.

In the daytime it is tiresome and perplexing.

There are always new shoots on the fungus, and new shades of yellow all over it. I cannot keep count of them, though I have tried conscientiously.

It is the strangest yellow, that wallpaper! It makes me think of all the yellow

things I ever saw—not beautiful ones like buttercups, but old, foul, bad yellow things.

But there is something else about that paper—the smell! I noticed it the moment we came into the room, but with so much air and sun it was not bad. Now we have had a week of fog and rain, and whether the windows are open or not, the smell is here.

It creeps all over the house.

I find it hovering in the dining-room, skulking in the parlor, hiding in the hall, lying in wait for me on the stairs.

It gets into my hair.

Even when I go to ride, if I turn my head suddenly and surprise it—there is that smell!

Such a peculiar odor, too! I have spent hours in trying to analyze it, to find what it smelled like.

It is not bad—at first—and very gentle, but quite the subtlest, most enduring odor I ever met.

In this damp weather it is awful. I wake up in the night and find it hanging over me.

It used to disturb me at first. I thought seriously of burning the house—to reach the smell.

But now I am used to it. The only thing I can think of that it is like is the *color* of the paper! A yellow smell.

There is a very funny mark on this wall, low down, near the mopboard. A streak that runs round the room. It goes behind every piece of furniture, except the bed, a long, straight, even *smooch,* as if it had been rubbed over and over.

I wonder how it was done and who did it, and what they did it for. Round and round and round—round and round and round—it makes me dizzy!

I really have discovered something at last.

Through watching so much at night, when it changes so, I have finally found out.

The front pattern *does* move—and no wonder! The woman behind shakes it!

Sometimes I think there are a great many women behind, and sometimes only one, and she crawls around fast, and her crawling shakes it all over.

Then in the very bright spots she keeps still, and in the very shady spots she just takes hold of the bars and shakes them hard.

And she is all the time trying to climb through. But nobody could climb through that pattern—it strangles so; I think that is why it has so many heads.

They get through, and then the pattern strangles them off and turns them upside down, and makes their eyes white!

If those heads were covered or taken off it would not be half so bad.

I think that woman gets out in the daytime!

And I'll tell you why—privately—I've seen her!

I can see her out of every one of my windows!

It is the same woman, I know, for she is always creeping, and most women do not creep by daylight.

I see her in that long shaded lane, creeping up and down. I see her in those dark grape arbors, creeping all around the garden.

I see her on that long road under the trees, creeping along, and when a carriage comes she hides under the blackberry vines.

I don't blame her a bit. It must be very humiliating to be caught creeping by daylight!

I always lock the door when I creep by daylight. I can't do it at night, for I know John would suspect something at once.

And John is so queer now that I don't want to irritate him. I wish he would take another room! Besides, I don't want anybody to get that woman out at night but myself.

I often wonder if I could see her out of all the windows at once.

But, turn as fast as I can, I can only see out of one at one time.

And though I always see her, she *may* be able to creep faster than I can turn! I have watched her sometimes away off in the open country, creeping as fast as a cloud shadow in a wind.

If only that top pattern could be gotten off from the under one! I mean to try it, little by little.

I have found out another funny thing, but I shan't tell it this time! It does not do to trust people too much.

There are only two more days to get this paper off, and I believe John is beginning to notice. I don't like the look in his eyes.

And I heard him ask Jennie a lot of professional questions about me. She had a very good report to give.

She said I slept a good deal in the daytime.

John knows I don't sleep very well at night, for all I'm so quiet!

He asked me all sorts of questions, too, and pretended to be very loving and kind.

As if I couldn't see through him!

Still, I don't wonder he acts so, sleeping under this paper for three months.

It only interests me, but I feel sure John and Jennie are affected by it.

Hurrah! This is the last day, but it is enough. John is to stay in town over night, and won't be out until this evening.

Jennie wanted to sleep with me—the sly thing; but I told her I should undoubtedly rest better for a night all alone.

That was clever, for really I wasn't alone a bit! As soon as it was moonlight and that poor thing began to crawl and shake the pattern, I got up and ran to help her.

I pulled and she shook. I shook and she pulled, and before morning we had peeled off yards of that paper.

A strip about as high as my head and half around the room.

And then when the sun came and that awful pattern began to laugh at me, I declared I would finish it today!

We go away tomorrow, and they are moving all my furniture down again to leave things as they were before.

Jennie looked at the wall in amazement, but I told her merrily that I did it out of pure spite at the vicious thing.

She laughed and said she wouldn't mind doing it herself, but I must not get tired.

How she betrayed herself that time!

But I am here, and no person touches this paper but Me—not *alive!*

She tried to get me out of the room—it was too patent! But I said it was

so quiet and empty and clean now that I believed I would lie down again and sleep all I could, and not to wake me even for dinner—I would call when I woke.

So now she is gone, and the servants are gone, and the things are gone, and there is nothing left but that great bedstead nailed down, with the canvas mattress we found on it.

We shall sleep downstairs tonight, and take the boat home tomorrow.

I quite enjoy the room, now it is bare again.

How those children did tear about here!

This bedstead is fairly gnawed!

But I must get to work.

I have locked the door and thrown the key down into the front path.

I don't want to go out, and I don't want to have anybody come in, till John comes.

I want to astonish him.

I've got a rope up here that even Jennie did not find. If that woman does get out, and tries to get away, I can tie her!

But I forgot I could not reach far without anything to stand on!

This bed will *not* move!

I tried to lift and push it until I was lame, and then I got so angry I bit off a little piece at one corner—but it hurt my teeth.

Then I peeled off all the paper I could reach standing on the floor. It sticks horribly and the pattern just enjoys it! All those strangled heads and bulbous eyes and waddling fungus growths just shriek with derision!

I am getting angry enough to do something desperate. To jump out of the window would be admirable exercise, but the bars are too strong even to try.

Besides I wouldn't do it. Of course not. I know well enough that a step like that is improper and might be misconstrued.

I don't like to *look* out of the windows even—there are so many of those creeping women, and they creep so fast.

I wonder if they all come out of that wallpaper as I did?

But I am securely fastened now by my well-hidden rope—you don't get *me* out in the road there!

I suppose I shall have to get back behind the pattern when it comes night, and that is hard!

It is so pleasant to be out in this great room and creep around as I please!

I don't want to go outside. I won't, even if Jennie asks me to.

For outside you have to creep on the ground, and everything is green instead of yellow.

But here I can creep smoothly on the floor, and my shoulder just fits in that long smooch around the wall, so I cannot lose my way.

Why, there's John at the door!

It is no use, young man, you can't open it!

How he does call and pound!

Now he's crying to Jennie for an axe.

It would be a shame to break down that beautiful door!

"John, dear!" said I in the gentlest voice. "The key is down by the front steps, under a plantain[8] leaf!"

8. An herb that grows primarily as a weed.

That silenced him for a few moments.

Then he said, very quietly indeed, "Open the door, my darling!"

"I can't," said I. "The key is down by the front door under a plantain leaf!" And then I said it again, several times, very gently and slowly, and said it so often that he had to go and see, and he got it of course, and came in. He stopped short by the door.

"What is the matter?" he cried. "For God's sake, what are you doing!"

I kept on creeping just the same, but I looked at him over my shoulder.

"I've got out at last," said I, "in spite of you and Jane. And I've pulled off most of the paper, so you can't put me back!"

Now why should that man have fainted? But he did, and right across my path by the wall, so that I had to creep over him every time!

<div align="right">1892</div>

Why I Wrote The Yellow Wallpaper?

Many and many a reader has asked that. When the story first came out, in the *New England Magazine* about 1891, a Boston physician made protest in *The Transcript*. Such a story ought not to be written, he said; it was enough to drive anyone mad to read it.

Another physician, in Kansas I think, wrote to say that it was the best description of incipient insanity he had ever seen, and—begging my pardon—had I been there?

Now the story of the story is this:

For many years I suffered from a severe and continuous nervous breakdown tending to melancholia—and beyond. During about the third year of this trouble I went, in devout faith and some faint stir of hope, to a noted specialist in nervous diseases,[1] the best known in the country. This wise man put me to bed and applied the rest cure, to which a still good physique responded so promptly that he concluded there was nothing much the matter with me, and sent me home with solemn advice to "live as domestic a life as far as possible;" to "have but two hours' intellectual life a day," and "never to touch pen, brush or pencil again as long as I lived." This was in 1887.

I went home and obeyed those directions for some three months, and came so near the border line of utter mental ruin that I could see over.

Then, using the remnants of intelligence that remained, and helped by a wise friend, I cast the noted specialist's advice to the winds and went to work again—work, the normal life of every human being; work, in which is joy and growth and service, without which one is a pauper and a parasite; ultimately recovering some measure of power.

Being naturally moved to rejoicing by this narrow escape. I wrote *The Yellow Wallpaper*, with its embellishments and additions to carry out the ideal (I never had hallucinations or objections to my mural decorations) and sent a copy to the physician who so nearly drove me mad. He never acknowledged it.

1. Silas Weir Mitchell (1829–1914), Philadelphia-based physician who specialized in neurology and toxicology, with a particular interest in women's nervous ailments.

The little book is valued by alienists and as a good specimen of one kind of literature. It has to my knowledge saved one woman from a similar fate—so terrifying her family that they let her out into normal activity and she recovered.

But the best result is this. Many years later I was told that the great specialist had admitted to friends of his that he had altered his treatment of neurasthenia since reading *The Yellow Wallpaper.*

It was not intended to drive people crazy, but to save people from being driven crazy, and it worked.

1913

AMY LEVY
1861–1889

The word "minor" circulates throughout the poetry, criticism, and fiction of Amy Levy, as if to signal her modest aspirations or her awareness of the limitations inherent in the art she admired and created. It was an adjective W. H. Auden associated with authors who—rather than evolving through a series of styles—remained fixed in a single mode of writing or a single tonality. In an essay on one of her most important precursors, "James Thomson: A Minor Poet" (1883), Levy praises the "attitude of mind which we call Weltschmerz, Pessimism," and this is the recurrent feeling that tends to characterize the mental suffering articulated not only in his works but also in her own. Levy's three volumes of poetry—*Xantippe and Other Verse* (1881), *A Minor Poet and Other Verse* (1884), and *A London Plane-Tree* (1889)—contain numerous poems with various personae and speakers who brood on dejection or pain that often results in thoughts of despair or suicide. In addition, the critical prose she produced consistently voices dissatisfaction and distress. The essays she published in *The Jewish Chronicle,* for example, confess her fear that "We ourselves . . . are not very good Jews," record her awareness that Jewish humor usually grapples with tragic circumstances, and discuss her dismay that young Jewish women are instructed to look only toward marriage for fulfillment.

Anxiety about stultifying gender scripts informs not just Levy's poems and essays but also many of her fictional narratives. A number of the stories by Levy that Oscar Wilde published in his journal *Woman's World* are animated by cynicism about the game of marriage. According to the critic Deborah Epstein Nord, Levy's first novel, *The Romance of a Shop* (1888), dramatizes an "experience of marginality" that inevitably renders her "independent, idiosyncratic heroines" vulnerable. Levy's second novel, *Reuben Sachs* (1888), includes a Jewish character who surrenders her individual aspirations to social conventions. Although Wilde praised the "uncompromising truth" of this portrait of the middle-class Anglo-Jewish community, it was faulted by other readers and reviewers for stereotyping the English Jews of Bayswater, Kensington Gardens, and Maida Vale. The next year *The British Weekly* serialized her novella *Miss Meredith,* which reworks the plot of *Jane Eyre* for a heroine who "considered Mr. Rochester the most unpleasant person that ever a woman made herself miserable over."

The despair threaded throughout Amy Levy's works contrasts oddly with her privileged material circumstances, though it foreshadows the early suicide of this pioneering Anglo-Jewish artist. The second of seven children, Levy was born into a

well-off and assimilated family. Accounts of the Levy children producing home the-
atricals and literary magazines recall those of other talented children in the Victorian
period, like the Brontës. But unlike the Brontës, Levy was given the unusual oppor-
tunity of studying at Brighton High School and Newnham College, Cambridge, before
she began a literary life in London. There she socialized with prominent activists
promoting the rights of workers and women—radical thinkers such as Eleanor Marx,
Olive Schreiner, and Beatrice Potter (Webb). On one of her several trips to Europe,
Levy met the pseudonymous writer Vernon Lee (Violet Paget); the last sonnet Levy
composed, "To Vernon Lee," uses a male voice to express an unrequited passion for
the expatriate aesthete. Whether Amy Levy's despair was the result of anger at eco-
nomic injustices, frustration at gender biases, ambivalence about her Jewish origins,
or despair at breaking out of what Adrienne Rich calls "compulsory heterosexuality,"
two months before her twenty-eighth birthday she lit charcoal in her room and
inhaled the fumes that killed her. Her works were for the most part neglected until
they began to be reprinted and anthologized at the end of the twentieth century.

Magdalen[1]

All things I can endure, save one.
The bare, blank room where is no sun;
The parcelled hours; the pallet hard;
The dreary faces here within;
5 The outer women's cold regard;
The Pastor's iterated "sin";—
These things could I endure, and count
No overstrain'd, unjust amount;
No undue payment for such bliss—
10 Yea, all things bear, save only this:
That you, who knew what thing would be,
Have wrought this evil unto me.

It is so strange to think on still—
That you, that *you* should do me ill!
15 Not as one ignorant or blind,
But seeing clearly in your mind
How this must be which now has been,
Nothing aghast at what was seen.
Now that the tale is told and done,
20 It is so strange to think upon.

You were so tender with me, too!
One summer's night a cold blast blew,
Closer about my throat you drew
The half-slipt shawl of dusky blue.
25 And once my hand, on a summer's morn,
I stretched to pluck a rose; a thorn

1. A reformed prostitute or fallen women; the
Mary Magdalene healed of evil spirits by Jesus is
traditionally identified with the prostitute who
kisses and anoints his feet (see Luke 8.2, 7.37–48).
Many Magdalene houses, intended to redeem
prostitutes, were set up in Britain in the nineteenth
century.

Struck through the flesh and made it bleed
(A little drop of blood indeed!)
Pale grew your cheek; you stoopt and bound
30 Your handkerchief about the wound;
Your voice came with a broken sound;
With the deep breath your breast was riven;
I wonder, did God laugh in Heaven?

How strange, that *you* should work my woe!
35 How strange! I wonder, do you know
How gladly, gladly I had died
(And life was very sweet that tide[2])
To save you from the least, light ill?
How gladly I had borne your pain.
40 With one great pulse we seem'd to thrill,—
Nay, but we thrill'd with pulses twain.

Even if one had told me this,
"A poison lurks within your kiss,
Gall that shall turn to night his day:"
45 Thereon I straight had turned away—
Ay, tho' my heart had crack'd with pain—
And never kiss'd your lips again.

At night, or when the daylight nears,
I hear the other women weep;
50 My own heart's anguish lies too deep
For the soft rain and pain of tears.
I think my heart has turn'd to stone,
A dull, dead weight that hurts my breast;
Here, on my pallet-bed alone,
55 I keep apart from all the rest.
Wide-eyed I lie upon my bed,
I often cannot sleep all night;
The future and the past are dead,
There is no thought can bring delight.
60 All night I lie and think and think;
If my heart were not made of stone,
But flesh and blood, it needs must shrink
Before such thoughts. Was ever known
A woman with a heart of stone/

65 The doctor says that I shall die.
It may be so, yet what care I?
Endless reposing from the strife,
Death do I trust no more than life.
For one thing is like one arrayed,
70 And there is neither false nor true;
But in a hideous masquerade
All things dance on, the ages through.
And good is evil, evil good;

2. In that period.

Nothing is known or understood
75 Save only Pain. I have no faith
In God or Devil, Life or Death.

The doctor says that I shall die.
You, that I knew in days gone by,
I fain would see your face once more,
80 Con[3] well its features o'er and o'er;
And touch your hand and feel your kiss,
Look in your eyes and tell you this:
That all is done, that I am free;
That you, through all eternity,
85 Have neither part nor lot in me.

1884

Epitaph

(On a commonplace person who died in bed)

This is the end of him, here he lies:
The dust in his throat, the worm in his eyes,
The mould[1] in his mouth, the turf on his breast;
This is the end of him, this is best.
5 He will never lie on his couch awake,
Wide-eyed, tearless, till dim daybreak.
Never again will he smile and smile
When his heart is breaking all the while.
He will never stretch out his hands in vain
10 Groping and groping—never again.
Never ask for bread, get a stone instead,[2]
Never pretend that the stone is bread.
Never sway and sway 'twixt the false and true,
Weighing and noting the long hours through.
15 Never ache and ache with the chok'd-up sighs;
This is the end of him, here he lies.

1884

In the Mile End Road[1]

How like her! But 'tis she herself,
Comes up the crowded street,
How little did I think, the morn,
My only love to meet!

3. Examine; commit to memory.
1. Loose earth, especially of the grave.
2. See Matthew 7.9: "Or what man is there of you, whom if his son ask bread, will he give him a stone?"

1. A road in east London; it runs past the Spanish and Portuguese Jews' Hospital and an old Jewish cemetery.

5　Whose else that motion and that mien?
　　Whose else that airy tread?
　For one strange moment I forgot
　　My only love was dead.

1889

Ballade of an Omnibus[1]

To see my love suffices me.
—Ballades in Blue China.[2]

Some men to carriages aspire;
　On some the costly hansoms[3] wait;
Some seek a fly, on job or hire;
Some mount the trotting steed, elate.
5　I envy not the rich and great,
A wandering minstrel, poor and free,
I am contented with my fate—
An omnibus suffices me.

In winter days of rain and mire
10　I find within a corner strait;
The 'busmen know me and my lyre
From Brompton to the Bull-and-Gate.[4]
When summer comes, I mount in state
The topmost summit, whence I see
15　Crœsus[5] look up, compassionate—
An omnibus suffices me.

I mark, untroubled by desire,
Lucullus' phaeton[6] and its freight.
The scene whereof I cannot tire,
20　The human tale of love and hate,
The city pageant, early and late
Unfolds itself, rolls by, to be
A pleasure deep and delicate.
An omnibus suffices me.

25　Princess, your splendour you require,
I, my simplicity; agree
Neither to rate lower nor higher.
An omnibus suffices me.

1889

1. I.e., a city bus (literally, "for all"; Latin). These horse-drawn public conveyances were widely used in London by the mid-nineteenth century.
2. A collection (1880) by Andrew Lang; the quotation is from "Ballade Amoureuse: After Froissart."
3. Small, two-wheeled covered carriages with the driver's seat elevated behind (often used as cabs, available for hire).
4. The name of a pub (a corruption of "Boulogne

Gate" and thus signifying an honor to Henry VIII, who took Boulogne in 1544). "Brompton": a road near Hyde Park.
5. I.e., a rich man. Croesus was the proverbially wealthy last king of Lydia (r. ca. 560–546 B.C.E.).
6. A light four-wheeled horse-drawn carriage. Lucius Licinius Lucullus (ca. 177–ca. 57 B.C.E.), a Roman general known for his wealth and extravagant living.

MARY ELIZABETH COLERIDGE
1861–1907

The great-great-niece of the Romantic poet Samuel Taylor Coleridge, Mary Elizabeth Coleridge was once called "the tail of the comet S. T. C.," and she herself declared that "I have no fairy god-mother, but lay claim to a fairy great-great uncle, which is perhaps the reason that I am condemned to wander restlessly around the Gates of Fairyland, although I have never yet passed them." In fact, in a number of uncannily imaginative verses, this late Victorian woman does seem to have "passed" such gates to peer into the realm of fantasy that her Romantic ancestor inhabited. Yet although she began writing articles and reviews for major journals and newspapers when she was still in her twenties, she never sought to rival her great-great-uncle's reputation as a poet. She published five novels in her lifetime—the most successful was *The King with Two Faces* (1897)—but she refused to release, or even discuss, most of her verse until the poet Robert Bridges, a family friend, urged her to do so. In 1896, with his encouragement, she published a collection titled *Fancy's Following*, and the next year she brought out *Fancy's Guerdon*. Both volumes appeared under the pseudonym Anodos or "Wanderer" (literally, "having no road"), which was borrowed from a character in George MacDonald's *Phantastes* (1858); the remainder of her verse remained unpublished until 1908, the year after her death.

The daughter of a charitable, domestic mother, and a literary lawyer who frequently entertained such notables as Alfred Tennyson and Robert Browning, Coleridge lived all her life at home with her parents, and on the surface her existence was relatively uneventful. She was exceptionally well educated, however; according to her friend Edith Sichel, "by the time she was nineteen she was well versed in [Hebrew], as well as in German, French, Italian; and a little later she became a keen reader of Greek." In addition, she undertook ambitious studies of philosophy and literature; she participated vigorously in intellectual circles; she traveled widely on the Continent; and besides writing, stories and essays for *The Cornhill Magazine*, *The Times Literary Supplement*, *The Reflector*, and other journals, she taught English literature at a working women's college for the last twelve years of her life, immersing herself in that job with passionate commitment. When she died of appendicitis at the early age of forty-six, Coleridge left a substantial body of work, in particularly a series of visionary, luminously phrased poems. While such texts as "The Witch" and "The Other Side of a Mirror" suggest through their disturbing Gothic imagery that her career may not have been as serene as it appeared, "The White Women" outlines the feminist utopia of which she evidently dreamed.

A Clever Woman

You thought I had the strength of men,
 Because with men I dared to speak,
And courted Science now and then,
 And studied Latin for a week;
5 But woman's woman, even when
 She reads her Ethics[1] in the Greek.

1. The *Nichomachean Ethics* (ca. 330 B.C.E.), by the philosopher Aristotle.

You thought me wiser than my kind;
　　You thought me "more than common tall;"
You thought because I had a mind,
10　　That I could have no heart at all;
But woman's woman you will find,
　　Whether she be great or small.

And then you needs must die—ah, well!
　　I knew you not, you loved not me.
15　'Twas not because that darkness fell,
　　You saw not what there was to see.
But I that saw and could not tell—
　　O evil Angel, set me free!

1907

The Other Side of a Mirror

I sat before my glass one day,
　　And conjured up a vision bare,
Unlike the aspects glad and gay,
　　That erst were found reflected there—
5　The vision of a woman, wild
　　With more than womanly despair.

Her hair stood back on either side
　　A face bereft of loveliness.
It had no envy[1] now to hide
10　What once no man on earth could guess.
It formed the thorny aureole[2]
　　Of hard unsanctified distress.

Her lips were open—not a sound
　　Came through the parted lines of red.
15　Whate'er it was, the hideous wound
　　In silence and in secret bled.
No sigh relieved her speechless woe,
　　She had no voice to speak her dread.

And in her lurid eyes there shone
20　　The dying flame of life's desire,
Made mad because its hope was gone,
　　And kindled at the leaping fire
Of jealousy, and fierce revenge,
　　And strength that could not change nor tire.

25　Shade of a shadow in the glass,
　　O set the crystal surface free!
Pass—as the fairer visions pass—

1. Desire.　　　　　　　　　　2. Radiant light around the head.

Nor ever more return, to be
The ghost of a distracted hour,
30 That heard me whisper, "I am she!"

1882 1908

Regina[1]

My Queen her scepter did lay down,
She took from her head the golden crown
Worn by right of her royal birth.
Her purple robe she cast aside,
5 And the scarlet vestures of her pride,
That was the pride of the earth.
In her nakedness was she
Queen of the world, herself and me.

My Queen took up her scepter bright,
10 Her crown more radiant than the light,
The rubies gleaming out of the gold.
She donned her robe of purple rare,
And did a deed that none may dare,
That makes the blood run cold.
15 And in her bravery is she
Queen of herself, the world and me.

1884 1908

The Devil's Funeral

The Devil is dead, good people all!
Who are the bearers that bear the pall?

One of them thinks he has slain God too,
With the self-same sword that Satan slew.

5 One of them thinks he has saved God's life;
The Devil was ever the God of strife.

A purple pall above him spread!
A king it is that is lying dead.

The worst of kings never ruled so well
10 As this magnificent King of Hell.

What is the guerdon[1] of all his pains?
He is dead himself, but Hell remains.

1. Queen (Latin). 1. Reward.

He forged his coffin before he died.
'Twas made of gold that was seven times tried:[2]

15 The glittering golden words of those,
Who counted themselves his chiefest foes.

Where will you bury him? Not on earth!
In poison flowers he would come to birth.

We will not cast him into the sea.
20 The winds and the waves would set him free.

Lay him out straight on the funeral pyre!
All his life he has lived in fire.

And lo! as the crackling flame burns bright,
Satan transformed to an angel of light,

25 That he may work more utter woe
Than ever he worked when he dwelt below.

1890 1908

The Witch

I have walked a great while over the snow,
And I am not tall nor strong.
My clothes are wet, and my teeth are set,
And the way was hard and long.
5 I have wandered over the fruitful earth,
But I never came here before.
Oh, lift me over the threshold, and let me in at the door!

The cutting wind is a cruel foe.
I dare not stand in the blast.
10 My hands are stone, and my voice a groan,
And the worst of death is past.
I am but a little maiden still,
My little white feet are sore.
Oh, lift me over the threshold, and let me in at the door!

15 Her voice was the voice that women have,
Who plead for their heart's desire.
She came—she came—and the quivering flame
Sank and died in the fire.
It never was lit again on my hearth
20 Since I hurried across the floor,
To lift her over the threshold, and let her in at the door.

1892 1908

2. Tempered. "Seven": the number suggests a connection to the Apocalypse (see, e.g., Revelation 1.12–20, 8.1–10.7).

Doubt

Two forms of darkness are there. One is Night,
When I have been an animal, and feared
I knew not what, and lost my soul, nor dared
Feel aught save hungry longing for the light.
5 And one is Blindness. Absolute and bright,
The Sun's rays smote me till they masked the Sun;
The Light itself was by the light undone;
The day was filled with terrors and affright.

Then did I weep, compassionate of those
10 Who see no friend in God—in Satan's host no foes.

1892 1908

The White Women[1]

Where dwell the lovely, wild white women folk,
 Mortal to man?
They never bowed their necks beneath the yoke,
They dwelt alone when the first morning broke
5 And Time began.

Taller are they than man, and very fair,
 Their cheeks are pale,
At sight of them the tiger in his lair,
The falcon hanging in the azure air,
10 The eagles quail.

The deadly shafts their nervous hands let fly
 Are stronger than our strongest—in their form
Larger, more beauteous, carved amazingly,
And when they fight, the wild white women cry
15 The war-cry of the storm.

Their words are not as ours. If man might go
 Among the waves of Ocean when they break
And hear them—hear the language of the snow
Falling on torrents—he might also know
20 The tongue they speak.

Pure are they as the light; they never sinned,
 But when the rays of the eternal fire
Kindle the West, their tresses they unbind
And fling their girdles to the Western wind,
25 Swept by desire.

1. From a legend of Malay, told by Hugh Clifford [Coleridge's note]. Sir Hugh Charles Clifford (1866–1941), a colonial administrator who spent most of his career in the Protected Malay States (part of present-day Malaysia) and published many stories and essays about Malay life.

Lo, maidens to the maidens then are born,
 Strong children of the maidens and the breeze,
Dreams are not—in the glory of the morn,
Seen through the gates of ivory and horn[2]—
30 More fair than these.

And none may find their dwelling. In the shade
 Primeval of the forest oaks they hide.
One of our race, lost in an awful glade,
Saw with his human eyes a wild white maid,
35 And gazing, died.

1900 1908

Marriage

No more alone sleeping, no more alone waking,
 Thy dreams divided, thy prayers in twain;
Thy merry sisters to-night forsaking,
 Never shall we see thee, maiden, again.

5 Never shall we see thee, thine eyes glancing,
 Flashing with laughter and wild in glee,
Under the mistletoe kissing and dancing,
 Wantonly free.

There shall come a matron walking sedately,
10 Low-voiced, gentle, wise in reply.
Tell me, O tell me, can I love her greatly?
All for her sake must the maiden die!

1900 1908

2. The two gates through which false and true dreams pass up from the underworld, according to classical myth.

E. PAULINE JOHNSON (TEKAHIONWAKE)
1861–1913

According to one biographer, Emily Pauline Johnson, who also performed under the Mohawk name Tekahionwake, "swept into . . . remote communities like a vigorous and refreshing wind from civilization, bringing not only entertainment but a vision of Canada stretching from sea to sea." A poet and fiction writer with a dramatic stage presence, Johnson was born on the Six Nations Reserve near Brantford, Ontario, to a Mohawk chief, G. H. Johnson, and his English wife, Emily Susanna Howells. Deeply influenced by English literature, especially the Victorian poetry to which her

mother introduced her, she nevertheless identified most passionately with Native American culture. "I am an Indian," she is said to have once declared, "and my aim, my joy and my pride is to sing the glories of my own people."

Still, although Johnson was raised on the reserve, where she learned early to canoe and camp on the Grand River, she lived for most of her childhood and adolescence in Chiefwood, an English-style mansion that her father had built for his family in an area set off from the rest of the tribal settlement. Her sense of her Native American identity was therefore shaped both by the legends and songs she learned from Indian relatives and by the Europeanized surroundings in which she lived. Inevitably, the name *Tekahionwake* (pronounced dageh-eeon-wageh) had special meaning for Pauline Johnson: the word means "double wampum" or "double life," and such doubleness was certainly to mark her examinations of her mixed heritage.

When Johnson was in her early twenties, her father died, and the young writer—who had already begun to compose poems—moved with her mother, sister, and brothers to nearby Brantford, where she began publishing and reciting verses to help support the family. One of her earliest successes was "Cry from an Indian Wife" (1892), a work deploring the warfare between "our little band" and "the "white-faced warriors, marching West to quell / Our fallen tribe that rises to rebel." Rousingly dramatic, the poem quickly became one of the popular pieces that Johnson recited to increasing acclaim in her native Ontario. Within a few years, she was journeying around the country, touring New England and ultimately England, performing both in ball gowns and in a Native American buckskin costume before enthusiastic crowds. While undertaking such arduous tours, she also published six collections of poems and stories, including *The White Wampum* (1895) and *Canadian Born* (1903). Finally, in 1909 she retired from her travels and settled in Vancouver, where she remained such a celebrity that when she died of breast cancer in 1913 the flags of the city flew at half-mast on the day of her burial.

Like so many of Johnson's other works, "A Red Girl's Reasoning" captures the complexity of one of her principal subjects: the negotiations between a proud Native American culture and an indifferent or hostile society of conquering "white-faced warriors."

A Red Girl's Reasoning

"Be pretty good to her, Charlie, my boy, or she'll balk sure as shooting."

That was what old Jimmy Robinson said to his brand new son-in-law, while they waited for the bride to reappear.

"Oh! you bet, there's no danger of much else. I'll be good to her, help me Heaven," replied Charlie McDonald, brightly.

"Yes, of course you will," answered the old man, "but don't you forget, there's a good big bit of her mother in her, and," closing his left eye significantly, "you don't understand these Indians as I do."

"But I'm just as fond of them, Mr Robinson," Charlie said assertively, "and I get on with them too, now, don't I?"

"Yes, pretty well for a town boy; but when you have lived forty years among these people, as I have done; when you have had your wife as long as I have had mine—for there's no getting over it, Christine's disposition is as native as her mother's, every bit—and perhaps when you've owned for eighteen years a daughter as dutiful, as loving, as fearless, and, alas! as obstinate as that little piece you are stealing away from me to-day—I tell you, youngster, you'll know more than you know now. It is kindness for kindness, bullet for

bullet, blood for blood. Remember, what you are, she will be," and the old Hudson Bay trader[1] scrutinized Charlie McDonald's face like a detective.

It was a happy face, fair face, good to look at, with a certain ripple of dimples somewhere about the mouth, and eyes that laughed out the very sunniness of their owner's soul. There was not a severe nor yet a weak line anywhere. He was a well-meaning young fellow, happily dispositioned, and a great favourite with the tribe at Robinson's Post, whither he had gone in the service of the Department of Agriculture, to assist the local agent through the tedium of a long census-taking.

As a boy he had had the Indian relic-hunting craze, as a youth he had studied Indian archaeology and folk-lore, as a man he consummated his predilections for Indianology by loving, winning and marrying the quiet little daughter of the English trader, who himself had married a native woman some twenty years ago. The country was all backwoods, and the Post miles and miles from even the semblance of civilization, and the lonely young Englishman's heart had gone out to the girl who, apart from speaking a very few words of English, was utterly uncivilized and uncultured, but had withal that marvellously innate refinement so universally possessed by the higher tribes of North American Indians.

Like all her race, observant, intuitive, having horror of ridicule, consequently quick at acquirement and teachable in mental and social habits, she had developed from absolute pagan indifference into a sweet, elderly Christian woman, whose broken English, quiet manner, and still handsome copper-coloured face, were the joy of old Robinson's declining years.

He had given their daughter Christine all the advantages of his own learning—which, if truthfully told, was not universal; but the girl had a fair common education, and the native adaptability to progress.

She belonged to neither and still to both types of the cultured Indian. The solemn, silent, almost heavy manner of the one so commingled with the gesticulating Frenchiness and vivacity of the other, that one unfamiliar with native Canadian life would find it difficult to determine her nationality.

She looked very pretty to Charles McDonald's loving eyes, as she reappeared in the doorway, holding her mother's hand and saying some happy words of farewell. Personally she looked much the same as her sisters, all Canada through, who are the offspring of red and white parentage—olive-complexioned, grey-eyed, black-haired, with figure slight and delicate, and the wistful, unfathomable expression in her whole face that turns one so heart-sick as they glance at the young Indians of to-day—it is the forerunner too frequently of "the white man's disease," consumption[2]—but McDonald was pathetically in love, and thought her the most beautiful woman he had ever seen in his life.

There had not been much of a wedding ceremony. The priest had cantered through the service in Latin, pronounced the benediction in English, and congratulated the "happy couple" in Indian, as a compliment to the assem-

1. The Hudson's Bay Company, formed in 1670, was given a monopoly on fur trading in Canada and ownership of much of the territory south of Hudson Bay by the king of England, Charles II; by 1869, when its holdings became part of the newly federated country, it had gained control of most of the land in modern-day Canada.
2. Tuberculosis. The disease was indigenous in the New World, but Europeans brought with them a more virulent form to which the Native Americans had no immunity.

bled tribe in the little amateur structure that did service at the post as a sanctuary.

But the knot was tied as firmly and indissolubly as if all Charlie Mc-Donald's swell city friends had crushed themselves up against the chancel to congratulate him, and in his heart he was deeply thankful to escape the flower-pelting, white gloves, rice-throwing, and ponderous stupidity of a breakfast, and indeed all the regulation gimcracks of the usual marriage celebrations, and it was with a hand trembling with absolute happiness that he assisted his little Indian wife into the old muddy buckboard[3] that, hitched to an underbred-looking pony, was to convey them over the first stages of their journey. Then came more adieus, some hand-clasping, old Jimmy Robinson looking very serious just at the last, Mrs Jimmy, stout, stolid, betraying nothing of visible emotion, and then the pony, roughshod and shaggy, trudged on, while mutual handwaves were kept up until the old Hudson's Bay Post dropped out of sight, and the buckboard with its lightsome load of hearts, deliriously happy, jogged on over the uneven trail.

She was "all the rage" that winter at the provincial capital. The men called her a "deuced fine little woman." The ladies said she was "just the sweetest wildflower." Whereas she was really but an ordinary, pale, dark girl who spoke slowly and with a strong accent, who danced fairly well, sang acceptably, and never stirred outside the door without her husband.

Charlie was proud of her; he was proud that she had "taken" so well among his friends, proud that she bore herself so complacently in the drawing-rooms of the wives of pompous Government officials, but doubly proud of her almost abject devotion to him. If ever human being was worshipped that being was Charlie McDonald; it could scarcely have been otherwise, for the almost godlike strength of his passion for that little wife of his would have mastered and melted a far more invincible citadel than an already affectionate woman's heart.

Favourites socially, McDonald and his wife went everywhere. In fashionable circles she was "new"—a potent charm to acquire popularity, and the little velvet-clad figure was always the centre of interest among all the women in the room. She always dressed in velvet. No woman in Canada, has she but the faintest dash of native blood in her veins, but loves velvets and silks. As beef to the Englishman, wine to the Frenchman, fads to the Yankee, so are velvet and silk to the Indian girl, be she wild as prairie grass, be she on the borders of civilization, or, having stepped within its boundary, mounted the steps of culture even under its superficial heights.

"Such a dolling little appil blossom," said the wife of a local M.P., who brushed up her etiquette and English once a year at Ottawa. "Does she always laugh so sweetly, and gobble you up with those great big grey eyes of hers, when you are togetheah at home, Mr McDonald? If so, I should think youah pooah brothah would feel himself terribly *de trop*."[4]

He laughed lightly. "Yes, Mrs Stuart, there are not two of Christie; she is the same at home and abroad, and as for Joe, he doesn't mind us a bit; he's no end fond of her."

"I'm very glad he is. I always fancied he did not care for her, d'you know."

3. A four-wheeled open carriage with a seat attached to the boards running between the two axles.

4. Too much (French); superfluous.

If ever a blunt woman existed it was Mrs Stuart. She really meant nothing, but her remark bothered Charlie. He was fond of his brother, and jealous for Christie's popularity. So that night when he and Joe were having a pipe he said: "I've never asked you yet what you thought of her, Joe." A brief pause, then Joe spoke. "I'm glad she loves you."

"Why?"

"Because that girl has but two possibilities regarding humanity—love or hate."

"Humph! Does she love or hate *you*?"

"Ask her."

"You talk bosh. If she hated you, you'd get out. If she loved you I'd *make* you get out."

Joe McDonald whistled a little, then laughed. "Now that we are on the subject, I might as well ask—honestly, old man, wouldn't you and Christie prefer keeping house alone to having me always around?"

"Nonsense, sheer nonsense. Why, thunder, man, Christie's no end fond of you, and as for me—you surely don't want assurances from me?"

"No, but I often think a young couple—"

"Young couple be blowed! After a while when they want you and your old surveying chains, and spindle-legged tripod telescope kickshaws,[5] farther west, I venture to say the little woman will cry her eyes out—won't you, Christie?" This last in a higher tone, as through clouds of tobacco smoke he caught sight of his wife passing the doorway.

She entered. "Oh, no, I would not cry; I never do cry, but I would be heart-sore to lose you, Joe, and apart from that"—a little wickedly—"you may come in handy for an exchange some day, as Charlie does always say when he hoards up duplicate relics."

"Are Charlie and I duplicates?"

"Well—not exactly"—her head a little to one side, and eyeing them both merrily, while she slipped softly on to the arm of her husband's chair—"but, in the event of Charlie's failing me"—everyone laughed then. The "some day" that she spoke of was nearer than they thought. It came about in this wise.

There was a dance at the Lieutenant-Governor's, and the world and his wife were there. The nobs[6] were in great feather that night, particularly the women, who flaunted about in new gowns and much splendour. Christie McDonald had a new gown also, but wore it with the utmost unconcern, and if she heard any of the flattering remarks made about her she at least appeared to disregard them.

"I never dreamed you could wear blue so splendidly," said Captain Logan, as they sat out a dance together.

"Indeed she can, though," interposed Mrs Stuart, halting in one of her gracious sweeps down the room with her husband's private secretary.

"Don't shout so, captain. I can hear every sentence you uttah—of course Mrs McDonald can wear blue—she has a morning gown of cadet blue[7] that she is a picture in."

5. Toys.
6. Persons of wealth or social distinction.
7. A gray-tinted blue.

"You are both very kind," said Christie. "I like blue; it is the colour of all the Hudson's Bay posts, and the factor's residence is always decorated in blue."

"Is it really? How interesting—do tell us some more of your old home, Mrs McDonald; you so seldom speak of your life at the post, and we fellows so often wish to hear of it all," said Logan eagerly.

"Why do you not ask me of it, then?"

"Well—er, I'm sure I don't know; I'm fully interested in the Ind—in your people—your mother's people, I mean, but it always seems so personal, I suppose; and-a-a-"

"Perhaps you are, like all other white people, afraid to mention my nationality to me."

The captain winced, and Mrs Stuart laughed uneasily. Joe McDonald was not far off, and he was listening, and chuckling, and saying to himself, "That's you, Christie, lay 'em out; it won't hurt 'em to know how they appear once in a while."

"Well, Captain Logan" she was saying, "what is it you would like to hear—of my people, or my parents, or myself?"

"All, all, my dear," cried Mrs Stuart clamorously. "I'll speak for him—tell us of yourself and your mother—your father is delightful, I am sure—but then he is only an ordinary Englishman, not half as interesting as a foreigner, or—or, perhaps I should say, a native."

Christie laughed. "Yes," she said, "my father often teases my mother now about how very native she was when he married her; then, how could she have been otherwise? She did not know a word of English, and there was not another English-speaking person besides my father and his two companions within sixty miles."

"Two companions, eh? one a Catholic priest and the other a wine merchant, I suppose, and with your father in the Hudson's Bay, they were good representatives of the pioneers in the New World," remarked Logan, waggishly.

"Oh, no, they were all Hudson's Bay men. There were no rumsellers and no missionaries in that part of the country then."

Mrs Stuart looked puzzled. "No *missionaries?*" she repeated with an odd intonation.

Christie's insight was quick. There was a peculiar expression of interrogation in the eyes of her listeners, and the girl's blood leapt angrily up into her temples as she said hurriedly, "I know what you mean; I know what you are thinking. You are wondering how my parents were married—"

"Well—er, my dear, it seems peculiar—if there was no priest, and no magistrate, why—a—" Mrs Stuart paused awkwardly.

"The marriage was performed by Indian rites," said Christie.

"Oh, do tell me about it; is the ceremony very interesting and quaint—are your chieftains anything like Buddhist priests?" It was Logan who spoke.

"Why, no," said the girl in amazement at that gentleman's ignorance. "There is no ceremony at all, save a feast. The two people just agree to live only with and for each other, and the man takes his wife to his home, just as you do. There is no ritual to bind them; they need none; an Indian's word was his law in those days, you know."

Mrs Stuart stepped backwards. "Ah!" was all she said. Logan removed his eye-glass and stared blankly at Christie. "And did McDonald marry you in this singular fashion?" he questioned.

"Oh, no, we were married by Father O'Leary. Why do you ask?"

"Because if he had, I'd have blown his brains out to-morrow."

Mrs Stuart's partner, who had hitherto been silent, coughed and began to twirl his cuff stud nervously, but nobody took any notice of him. Christie had risen, slowly, ominously—risen, with the dignity and pride of an empress.

"Captain Logan," she said, "what do you dare to say to me? What do you dare to mean? Do you presume to think it would not have been lawful for Charlie to marry me according to my people's rites? Do you for one instant dare to question that my parents were not as legally—"

"Don't, dear, don't," interrupted Mrs Stuart hurriedly; "it is bad enough now, goodness knows; don't make—" Then she broke off blindly. Christie's eyes glared at the mumbling woman, at her uneasy partner, at the horrified captain. Then they rested on the McDonald brothers, who stood within ear-shot, Joe's face scarlet, her husband's white as ashes, with something in his eyes she had never seen before. It was Joe who saved the situation. Stepping quickly across towards his sister-in-law, he offered her his arm, saying, "The next dance is ours, I think, Christie."

Then Logan pulled himself together, and attempted to carry Mrs Stuart off for the waltz, but for once in her life that lady had lost her head. "It is shocking!" she said, "outrageously shocking! I wonder if they told Mr McDonald before he married her!" Then looking hurriedly round, she too saw the young husband's face and knew that they had not.

"Humph! deuced nice kettle of fish—poor old Charlie has always thought so much of honourable birth."

Logan thought he spoke in an undertone, but "poor old Charlie" heard him. He followed his wife and brother across the room. "Joe," he said, "will you see that a trap[8] is called?" Then to Christie, "Joe will see that you get home all right." He wheeled on his heel then and left the ballroom.

Joe *did* see.

He tucked a poor, shivering, pallid little woman into a cab, and wound her bare throat up in the scarlet velvet cloak that was hanging uselessly over her arm. She crouched down beside him, saying, "I am so cold, Joe; I am so cold," but she did not seem to know enough to wrap herself up. Joe felt all through this long drive that nothing this side of Heaven would be so good as to die, and he was glad when the poor little voice at his elbow said, "What is he so angry at, Joe?"

"I don't know exactly, dear," he said gently, "but I think it was what you said about this Indian marriage."

"But why should I not have said it? Is there anything wrong about it?" she asked pitifully.

"Nothing, that I can see—there was no other way; but Charlie is very angry, and you must be brave and forgiving with him, Christie, dear."

"But I did never see him like that before, did you?"

"Once."

8. A light carriage, usually drawn by one horse.

"When?"

"Oh, at college, one day, a boy tore his prayer-book in half, and threw it into the grate, just to be mean, you know. Our mother had given it to him at his confirmation."

"And did he look so?"

"About, but it all blew over in a day—Charlie's tempers are short and brisk. Just don't take any notice of him; run off to bed, and he'll have forgotten it by the morning."

They reached home at last. Christie said goodnight quietly, going directly to her room. Joe went to his room also, filled a pipe and smoked for an hour. Across the passage he could hear her slippered feet pacing up and down, up and down the length of her apartment. There was something panther-like in those restless footfalls, a meaning velvetyness that made him shiver, and again he wished he were dead—or elsewhere.

After a time the hall door opened, and someone came upstairs, along the passage, and to the little woman's room. As he entered, she turned and faced him.

"Christie," he said harshly, "do you know what you have done?"

"Yes," taking a step nearer him, her whole soul springing up into her eyes, "I have angered you, Charlie, and—"

"Angered me? You have disgraced me; and, moreover, you have disgraced yourself and both your parents."

"Disgraced?"

"Yes, *disgraced*; you have literally declared to the whole city that your father and mother were never married, and that you are the child of—what shall we call it—love? certainly not legality."

Across the hallway sat Joe McDonald, his blood freezing; but it leapt into every vein like fire at the awful anguish in the little voice that cried simply, "Oh! Charlie!"

"How could you do it, how could you do it, Christie, without shame either for yourself or for me, let alone your parents?"

The voice was like an angry demon's—not a trace was there in it of the yellow-haired, blue-eyed, laughing-lipped boy who had driven away so gaily to the dance five hours before.

"Shame? Why should I be ashamed of the rites of my people any more than you should be ashamed of the customs of yours—of a marriage more sacred and holy than half of your white man's mockeries?"

It was the voice of another nature in the girl—the love and the pleading were dead in it.

"Do you mean to tell me, Charlie—you who have studied my race and their laws for years—do you mean to tell me that, because there was no priest and no magistrate, my mother was not married? Do you mean to say that all my forefathers, for hundreds of years back, have been illegally born? If so, you blacken my ancestry beyond—beyond—beyond all reason."

"No, Christie, I would not be so brutal as that; but your father and mother live in more civilized times. Father O'Leary has been at the post for nearly twenty years. Why was not your father straight enough to have the ceremony performed when he *did* get the chance?"

The girl turned upon him with the face of a fury. "Do you suppose," she almost hissed, "that my mother would be married according to your *white*

rites after she had been five years a wife, and I had been born in the meantime? *No*, a thousand times I say, *no*. When the priest came with his notions of Christianizing, and talked to them of re-marriage by the Church, my mother arose and said, 'Never—never—I have never had but this one husband; he has had none but me for wife, and to have you re-marry us would be to say as much to the whole world as that we had never been married before.[9] You go away; *I* do not ask that *your* people be re-married; talk not so to me. I *am* married, and you or the Church cannot do or undo it."

"Your father was a fool not to insist upon the law, and so was the priest."

"Law? *My* people have *no* priest, and my nation cringes not to law. Our priest is purity, and our law is honour. Priest? Was there a *priest* at the most holy marriage known to humanity—that stainless marriage whose offspring is the God you white men told my pagan mother of?"

"Christie—you are *worse* than blasphemous; such a profane remark shows how little you understand the sanctity of the Christian faith—"

"I know what I *do* understand it; it is that you are hating me because I told some of the beautiful customs of my people to Mrs Stuart and those men."

"Pooh! who cares for them? It is not them; the trouble is they won't keep their mouths shut. Logan's a cad and will toss the whole tale about at the club before to-morrow night; and as for the Stuart woman, I'd like to know how I'm going to take you to Ottawa for presentation and the opening,[1] while she is blabbing the whole miserable scandal in every drawing-room, and I'll be pointed out as a romantic fool, and you as worse; I can't understand why your father didn't tell me before we were married; I at least might have warned you to never mention it." Something of recklessness rang up through his voice, just as the panther-likeness crept up from her footsteps and couched itself in hers. She spoke in tones quiet, soft, deadly.

"Before we were married! Oh! Charlie, would it have—made—any—difference?"

"God knows," he said, throwing himself into a chair, his blonde hair rumpled and wet. It was the only boyish thing about him now.

She walked towards him, then halted in the centre of the room. "Charlie McDonald," she said, and it was as if a stone had spoken, "look up." He raised his head, startled by her tone. There was a threat in her eyes that, had his rage been less courageous, his pride less bitterly wounded, would have cowed him.

"There was no such time as that before our marriage, for we *are not married now*. Stop," she said, outstretching her palms against him as he sprang to his feet, "I tell you we are not married. Why should I recognize the rites of your nation when you do not acknowledge the rites of mine? According to your own words, my parents should have gone through your church ceremony as well as through an Indian contract; according to my words, we should go through an Indian contract as well as through a church marriage. If their union is illegal, so is ours. If you think my father is living in dishonour with my mother, my people will think I am living in dishonour with you. How do I know when another nation will come and conquer you as you white men

9. Fact [Johnson's note].
1. I.e., the opening of parliament, an event of great ceremony.

conquered us? And they will have another marriage rite to perform, and they will tell us another truth, that you are not my husband, that you are but disgracing and dishonouring me, that you are keeping me here, not as your wife, but as your—your *squaw*."

The terrible word had never passed her lips before, and the blood stained her face to her very temples. She snatched off her wedding ring and tossed it across the room, saying scornfully, "That thing is as empty to me as the Indian rites to you."

He caught her by the wrists; his small white teeth were locked tightly, his blue eyes blazed into hers.

"Christine, do you dare to doubt my honour towards you? *you*, whom I should have died for; do you *dare* to think I have kept you here, not as my wife, but—"

"Oh, God! You are hurting me; you are breaking my arm," she gasped.

The door was flung open, and Joe McDonald's sinewy hands clinched like vices on his brother's shoulders.

"Charlie, you're mad, mad as the devil. Let go of her this minute."

The girl staggered backwards as the iron fingers loosed her wrists. "Oh, Joe," she cried, "I am not his wife, and he says I am born—nameless."

"Here," said Joe, shoving his brother towards the door. "Go downstairs till you can collect your senses. If ever a being acted like an infernal fool, you're the man."

The young husband looked from one to the other, dazed by his wife's insult, abandoned to a fit of ridiculously childish temper. Blind as he was with passion, he remembered long afterwards seeing them standing there, his brother's face darkened with a scowl of anger—his wife, clad in the mockery of her ball dress, her scarlet velvet cloak half covering her bare brown neck and arms, her eyes like flames of fire, her face like a piece of sculptured greystone.[2]

Without a word he flung himself furiously from the room, and immediately afterwards they heard the heavy hall door bang behind him.

"Can I do anything for you, Christie?" asked her brother-in-law calmly.

"No, thank you—unless—I think I would like a drink of water, please."

He brought her up a goblet filled with wine; her hand did not even tremble as she took it. As for Joe, a demon arose in his soul as he noticed she kept her wrists covered.

"Do you think he will come back?" she said.

"Oh, yes, of course; he'll be all right in the morning. Now go to bed like a good little girl, and—and, I say, Christie, you can call me if you want anything; I'll be right here, you know."

"Thank you, Joe; you are kind—and good."

He returned then to his apartment. His pipe was out, but he picked up a newspaper instead, threw himself into an armchair, and in a half-hour was in the land of dreams.

When Charlie came home in the morning, after a six-mile walk into the country and back again, his foolish anger was dead and buried. Logan's "Poor old Charlie" did not ring so distinctly in his ears. Mrs Stuart's horrified expression had faded considerably from his recollection. He thought only of

2. A gray volcanic rock.

that surprisingly tall, dark girl, whose eyes looked like coals, whose voice pierced him like a flint-tipped arrow. Ah, well, they would never quarrel again like that, he told himself. She loved him so, and would forgive him after he had talked quietly to her, and told her what an ass he was. She was simple-minded and awfully ignorant to pitch those old Indian laws at him in her fury, but he could not blame her. Oh, no, he could not for one moment blame her. He had been terribly severe and unreasonable, and the horrid McDonald temper had got the better of him; and he loved her so. Oh! he loved her so! She would surely feel that, and forgive him, and—He went straight to his wife's room. The blue velvet evening dress lay on the chair into which he had thrown himself when he doomed his life's happiness by those two words, "God knows." A bunch of dead daffodils and her slippers were on the floor, everything—but Christie.

He went to his brother's bedroom door.

"Joe," he called, rapping nervously thereon; "Joe, wake up; where's Christie, d'you know?"

"Good Lord, no," gasped that youth, springing out of his armchair and opening the door. As he did so a note fell from off the handle. Charlie's face blanched to his very hair while Joe read aloud, his voice weakening at every word:

> "DEAR OLD JOE—I went into your room at daylight to get that picture of the Post on your bookshelves. I hope you do not mind, but I kissed your hair while you slept; it was so curly, and yellow, and soft, just like his. Good-bye, Joe.
> CHRISTIE

And when Joe looked into his brother's face and saw the anguish settle in those laughing blue eyes, the despair that drove the dimples away from that almost girlish mouth; when he realized that this boy was but four-and-twenty years old, and that all his future was perhaps darkened and shadowed for ever, a great, deep sorrow arose in his heart, and he forgot all things, all but the agony that rang up through the voice of the fair, handsome lad as he staggered forward, crying, "Oh! Joe—what shall I do—what shall I do?"

It was months and months before he found her, but during all that time he had never known a hopeless moment; discouraged he often was, but despondent, never. The sunniness of his ever-boyish heart radiated with a warmth that would have flooded a much deeper gloom than that which settled within his eager young life. Suffer? ah! yes, he suffered, not with locked teeth and stony stoicism, not with the masterful self-command, the reserve, the conquered bitterness of the still-water sort of nature, that is supposed to run to such depths. He tried to be bright, and his sweet old boyish self. He would laugh sometimes in a pitiful, pathetic fashion. He took to petting dogs, looking into their large, solemn eyes with his wistful, questioning blue ones; he would kiss them, as women sometimes do, and call them "dear old fellow," in tones that had tears; and once in the course of his travels, while at a little way-station, he discovered a huge St Bernard imprisoned by some mischance in an empty freight car; the animal was nearly dead from starvation, and it seemed to salve his own sick heart to rescue back the dog's life. Nobody claimed the big starving creature, the train hands knew nothing of its owner,

and gladly handed it over to its deliverer. "Hudson," he called it, and afterwards when Joe McDonald would relate the story of his brother's life he invariably terminated it with, "And I really believe that big lumbering brute saved him." From what, he was never known to say.

But all things end, and he heard of her at last. She had never returned to the Post, as he at first thought she would, but had gone to the little town of B——, in Ontario, where she was making her living at embroidery and plain sewing.

The September sun had set redly when at last he reached the outskirts of the town, opened up the wicket gate, and walked up the weedy, unkept path leading to the cottage where she lodged.

Even through the twilight, he could see her there, leaning on the rail of the verandah—oddly enough she had about her shoulders the scarlet velvet cloak she wore when he had flung himself so madly from the room that night.

The moment the lad saw her his heart swelled with a sudden heat, burning moisture leapt into his eyes, and clogged his long, boyish lashes. He bounded up the steps—"Christie," he said, and the word scorched his lips like audible flame.

She turned to him, and for a second stood magnetized by his passionately wistful face; her peculiar greyish eyes seemed to drink the very life of his unquenchable love, though the tears that suddenly sprang into his seemed to absorb every pulse in his body through those hungry, pleading eyes of his that had, oh! so often, been blinded by her kisses when once her whole world lay in their blue depths.

"You will come back to me, Christie, my wife? My wife, you will let me love you again?"

She gave a singular little gasp, and shook her head. "Don't, oh! don't," he cried piteously. "You will come to me, dear? it is all such a bitter mistake— I did not understand. Oh! Christie, I did not understand, and you'll forgive me, and love me again, won't you—won't you?"

"No," said the girl with quick, indrawn breath.

He dashed the back of his hand across his wet eyelids. His lips were growing numb, and he bungled over the monosyllable "Why?"

"I do not like you," she answered quietly.

"God! Oh! God, what is there left?"

She did not appear to hear the heart-break in his voice; she stood like one wrapped in sombre thought; no blaze, no tear, nothing in her eyes; no hardness, no tenderness about her mouth. The wind was blowing her cloak aside, and the only visible human life in her whole body was once when he spoke the muscles of her brown arm seemed to contract.

"But, darling, you are mine—*mine*—we are husband and wife! Oh, heaven, you *must* love me, you *must* come to me again."

"You cannot *make* me come," said the icy voice, "neither church, nor law, nor even"—and the voice softened—"nor even love can make a slave of a red girl."

"Heaven forbid it," he faltered. "No, Christie, I will never claim you without your love. What reunion would that be? But, oh, Christie, you are lying to me, you are lying to yourself, you are lying to heaven."

She did not move. If only he could touch her he felt as sure of her yielding as he felt sure there was a hereafter. The memory of times when he had but

to lay his hand on her hair to call a most passionate response from her filled his heart with a torture that choked all words before they reached his lips; at the thought of those days he forgot she was unapproachable, forgot how forbidding were her eyes, how stony her lips. Flinging himself forward, his knee on the chair at her side, his face pressed hardly in the folds of the cloak on her shoulder, he clasped his arms about her with a boyish petulance, saying, "Christie, Christie, my little girl wife, I love you, I love you, and you are killing me."

She quivered from head to foot as his fair, wavy hair brushed her neck, his despairing face sank lower until his cheek, hot as fire, rested on the cool, olive flesh of her arm. A warm moisture oozed up through her skin, and as he felt it glowed he looked up. Her teeth, white and cold, were locked over her under lip, and her eyes were as grey stones.

Not murderers alone know the agony of a death sentence.

"Is it all useless? all useless, dear?" he said, with lips starving for hers.

"All useless," she repeated. "I have no love for you now. You forfeited me and my heart months ago, when you said *those two words*."

His arms fell away from her wearily, he arose mechanically, he placed his little grey checked cap on the back of his yellow curls, the old-time laughter was dead in the blue eyes that now looked scared and haunted, the boyishness and the dimples crept away for ever from the lips that quivered like a child's; he turned from her, but she had looked once into his face as the Law Giver[3] must have looked at the land of Canaan outspread at his feet. She watched him go down the long path and through the picket gate, she watched the big yellowish dog that had waited for him lumber up to its feet—stretch— then follow him. She was conscious of but two things, the vengeful lie in her soul, and a little space on her arm that his wet lashes had brushed.

It was hours afterwards when he reached his room. He had said nothing, done nothing—what use were words or deeds? Old Jimmy Robinson was right; she had "balked" sure enough.

What a bare, hotelish room it was! He tossed off his coat and sat for ten minutes looking blankly at the sputtering gas jet. Then his whole life, desolate as a desert, loomed up before him with appalling distinctness. Throwing himself on the floor beside his bed, with clasped hands and arms outstretched on the white counterpane, he sobbed, he sobbed. "Oh! God, dear God, I thought you loved me; I thought you'd let me have her again, but you must be tired of me, tired of loving me, too. I've nothing left now, nothing! it doesn't seem that I even have you to-night."

He lifted his face then, for his dog, big and clumsy and yellow, was licking at his sleeve.

1892

3. I.e., Moses, who, according to the Bible, led the people of Israel out of slavery in Egypt into the desert, where he received God's laws. He never entered Canaan, the promised land, but he saw it just before he died (Deuteronomy 32.48–52, 34).

The Song My Paddle Sings

West wind, blow from your prairie nest,
Blow from the mountains, blow from the west.
The sail is idle, the sailor too;
O! wind of the west, we wait for you.
5 Blow, blow!
I have wooed you so,
But never a favour you bestow.
You rock your cradle the hills between,
But scorn to notice my white lateen.[1]

10 I stow the sail, unship the mast:
I wooed you long but my wooing's past;
My paddle will lull you into rest.
O! drowsy wind of the drowsy west,
Sleep, sleep,
15 By your mountain steep,
Or down where the prairie grasses sweep!
Now fold in slumber your laggard wings,
For soft is the song my paddle sings.

August is laughing across the sky,
20 Laughing while paddle, canoe and I,
Drift, drift,
Where the hills uplift
On either side of the current swift.

The river rolls in its rocky bed;
25 My paddle is plying its way ahead;
Dip, dip,
While the waters flip
In foam as over their breast we slip.

And oh, the river runs swifter now;
30 The eddies circle about my bow.
Swirl, swirl!
How the ripples curl
In many a dangerous pool awhirl!

And forward far the rapids roar,
35 Fretting their margin for evermore.
Dash, dash,
With a mighty crash,
They seethe, and boil, and bound, and splash.

1. Triangular sail.

Be strong, O paddle! be brave, canoe!
40 The reckless waves you must plunge into.
Reel, reel,
On your trembling keel,
But never a fear my craft will feel.

We've raced the rapid, we're far ahead!
45 The river slips through its silent bed.
Sway, sway,
As the bubbles spray
And fall in tinkling tunes away.

And up on the hills against the sky,
50 A fir tree rocking its lullaby,
Swings, swings,
Its emerald wings,
Swelling the song that my paddle sings.

1895

Selected Bibliographies

For ease of reference, all the authors are listed in alphabetical order.

Abigail Adams

Adams's published correspondence consists of *Letters of Mrs. Adams* (1840) and *Familiar Letters of John Adams and His Wife, during the Revolution* (1876), both edited by her grandson Charles Adams; *The Book of Abigail and John* (1975), ed. L. H. Butterfield, who restored the original spelling and content that Charles Adams had edited; *New Letters of Abigail Adams* (1973), ed. Stewart Mitchell; and *The Adams Family Correspondence* (1964–73), ed. L. H. Butterfield. Frank Shuffleton has more recently edited and introduced *The Letters of John and Abigail Adams* (2004). Two useful biographies are Phyllis Lee Levin, *Abigail Adams, A Biography* (1987); and Edith Belle Gelles, *Portia: The World of Abigail Adams* (1992). A valuable full-length study is Rosemary Skinner Keller, *Patriotism and the Female Sex: Abigail Adams and the American Revolution* (1994). Helpful critical essays include two by Edith B. Gelles, "The Abigail Industry," *The William and Mary Quarterly* 45 (1988), and, " 'Remember the Ladies': Politics in the Letters of Abigail Adams," *Gender and Politics in the Age of Letter Writing, 1750–2000*, ed. Caroline Bland and Maire Cross (2003); as well as Frank Shuffleton, "In Different Voices: Gender in the American Republic of Letters," *Early American Literature* 25 (1990).

Louisa May Alcott

In addition to Alcott's famous children's novels, *Little Women* (1869), *Little Men* (1871), *Eight Cousins* (1875), *Jo's Boys* (1886), and many others, all currently available in many editions, numerous other Alcott works have been republished, including *Hospital Sketches* (1863; 1960, ed. Bessie Z. Jones); *Behind a Mask: The Unknown Thrillers of Louisa May Alcott* (1975), ed. and with an introduction by Madeline Stern; *Plots and Counterplots: More Unknown Thrillers of Louisa May Alcott* (1976) and *A Double Life: Newly Discovered Thrillers of Louisa May Alcott* (1988), both ed. Stern; *Louisa May Alcott: Selected Fiction* (1990), ed. Madeline Stern and Daniel Shealy; *Work: A Story of Experience* (1873; 1977, with an introduction by Elizabeth Hardwick); and *Alternative Alcott* (1988), ed. and with an introduction by Elaine Showalter.

See also *From Jo March's Attic: Stories of Intrigue and Suspense* (1993), ed. Stern and Shealy; *Louisa May Alcott Unmasked: Collected Thrillers* (1995), ed. and with an introduction by Madeline Stern; and *The Inheritance* (1997), ed. and with an afterword by Loel Myerson and Daniel Shealy. One useful compilation of Alcott's political writings is *Signature of Reform* (2002), ed. Madeleine B. Stern. Four anthologies of Alcott's writings are *Louisa May Alcott's Fairy Tales and Fantasy Stories* (1992), ed. Daniel Shealy; *The Feminist Alcott: Stories of a Woman's Power* (1996), ed. and with an introduction by Madeleine B. Stern; *Louisa May Alcott on Race, Sex, and Slavery* (1997), ed. and with an introduction by Sarah Elbert; and *The Portable Louisa May Alcott* (2000), ed. and with an introduction by Elizabeth Lennox Keyser. Alcott's work is also included in the collections *Fiction by Nineteenth Century Women Writers: A New England Sampler* (1999), ed. Thomas A. Maik, and *Fifty Major Thinkers on Education: From Confucius to Dewey* (2001), ed. Joy A. Palmer.

Valuable background information is included in *Louisa May Alcott, Her Life, Letters, and Journals* (1889), ed. Ednah D. Cheney; *The Journals of Louisa May Alcott* (1989), ed. Joel Myerson and Daniel Shealy; and *The Selected Letters of Louisa May Alcott* (1995), ed. Joel Myerson and Daniel Shealy. See also *Louisa May Alcott: An Intimate Anthology* (1997), 1st New York Public Library collector's edition, and *The Louisa May Alcott Encyclopedia* (2001), ed. Gregory Eiselein and Anne K. Phillips. The many biographies of Alcott include Katharine Susan Anthony, *Louisa May Alcott* (1939); Marjorie Worthington, *Miss Alcott of Concord, a Biography* (1958); Martha Sexton, *Louisa May Alcott: A Modern Biography* (1995); and Madeleine B. Stern, *Louisa May Alcott: A Biography* (1999).

Critical studies on Alcott include Cornelia Lynde Meigs, *Louisa May Alcott and the American Family Story* (1970); Ruth K. McDonald, *Louisa May Alcott* (1983); Sarah Elber, *Hunger for Home: Louisa May Alcott's Place in American Culture* (1987); and Elizabeth Lennox Keyser, *Whispers in the Dark: The Fiction of Louisa May Alcott* (1993). Also useful are Madeleine B.

Stern, *Louisa May Alcott: From Blood & Thunder to Hearth & Home* (1998), and Christine Doyle, *Louisa May Alcott & Charlotte Brontë: Transatlantic Translations* (2000). Important short analyses are Carolyn Heilbrun, "Louisa May Alcott: The Influence of *Little Women*," in *Women, the Arts, and the 1920's in Paris and New York* (1982), ed. Kenneth Wheeler and Virginia Lee Dussier; Nina Auerbach's discussion of *Little Women* in *Communities of Women* (1979); and Elaine Showalter, "Little Women: The American Female Myth," in her *Sister's Choice: Tradition and Change in American Women's Writing* (1991). See also Mary Rigsby, " 'So like women!': Louisa May Alcott's Work and the Ideology of Relations," in *Redefining the Political Novel: American Women Writers, 1797–1901* (1995), ed. Sharon M. Harris; Sandra Harbert Petrulionis, "By the Light of Her Mother's Lamp: Woman's Work Versus Man's Philosophy in Louisa May Alcott's 'Transcendental Wild Oats'," in *Studies in the American Renaissance* (1995), ed. Joel Myerson; Gail K. Smith, "Who Was That Masked Woman? Gender and Form in Louisa May Alcott's Confidence Stories," in *American Women Short-Story Writers: A Collection of Critical Essays* (1995), ed. Julie Brown; and Kathryn R. Kent, " 'Trying all kinds': Louisa May Alcott's Pedagogic Erotics," in her *Making Girls Into Women: American Women's Writing and the Rise of Lesbian Identity* (2003). Two bibliographies, Alma J. Payne, *Louisa May Alcott, a Reference Guide* (1980), and Ruth K. McDonald, "Recent Alcott Criticism," *Children's Literature* 9 (1981), are helpful, though somewhat outdated. One more recent bibliography is Beverly Lyon Clark, *Louisa May Alcott: The Contemporary Reviews* (2004). Two other useful articles are Janet S. Zehr, "The Response of Nineteenth-Century Audiences to Louisa May Alcott's Fiction," *American Transcendental Quarterly* 1 (1987), and Glenn Hendler, "The Limits of Sympathy: Louisa May Alcott and the Sentimental Novel," *American Literary History* 3 (1991).

Mary Astell

Besides *A Serious Proposal to the Ladies* (1694), Astell's works include *Letters Concerning the Love of God* (1695), *Some Reflections on Marriage* (1700), *Moderation Truly Stated* (1704), and *The Christian Religion as Professed by a Daughter of the Church of England* (1705). Bridget Hill edited a collection of Astell's work, *The First English Feminist: Reflections upon Marriage and Other Writings by Mary Astell* (1986), and Patricia Springborg has edited two modern editions of her work, *Political Writings* (1996) and *A Serious Proposal to the Ladies* (1997). The most useful critical study to date is Ruth Perry's *The Celebrated Mary Astell: An Early English Feminist* (1986). The only other

full-length study is the early *Mary Astell* (1916), by Florence M. Smith. Astell is discussed in Hilda Smith, *Reason's Disciples* (1982), and Joan Kinnaird writes about Astell in *Feminist Theorists* (1984), ed. Dale Spender. Useful essays on Astell and her work include Catherine Gallagher, "Embracing the Absolute: The Politics of the Female Subject in Seventeenth-Century England," *Genders* 1 (1988); Alessa Johns, "Mary Astell's 'Excited Needles': Theorizing Feminist Utopia in Seventeenth-Century England," *Utopia Studies* 7 (1996); Patricia Spainsborg, "Mary Astell and John Locke," in *English Literature, 1650–1740*, ed. Steven Zwicker (1998); and Penny A. Weiss, "Mary Astell: Including Women's Voices in Political Theory," *Hypatia* 19 (2004).

Jane Austen

The standard edition of Austen's work, including *Sense and Sensibility* (1811), *Pride and Prejudice* (1813), *Mansfield Park* (1814), *Emma* (1816), *Persuasion* (1818), and *Northanger Abbey* (1818), is *The Works of Jane Austen*, ed. R. W. Chapman, first published in the 1920s and reprinted in the 1970s with revisions by Mary Lascelles. Chapman also collected and edited *Jane Austen's Letters* (1979) and *Selected Letters, 1796–1817* (1985). The recently issued *Jane Austen's Manuscript Letters in Facsimile* (1990), ed. Jo Modert, includes Austen's every known letter, and *My Dear Cassandra: The Letters of Jane Austen* (1991), ed. Penelope Hughes-Hellet, contains a selection. Norton Critical Editions of *Emma*, ed. Stephen M. Parrish, *Pride and Prejudice*, ed. Donald J. Gray, and *Persuasion*, ed. Patricia Meyer Spacks, contain valuable secondary material. Useful biographical information can be found in William and Richard Austen-Leigh, *Jane Austen: Her Life and Letters* (1913); Mary A. Austen-Leigh, *Personal Aspects of Jane Austen* (1920); and James Edward Austen-Leigh, *Memoir of Jane Austen* (1926). Other biographies include Chapman, *Jane Austen, Facts and Problems* (1948); Margaret Kennedy, *Jane Austen* (1950); Marghanita Laski, *Jane Austen and Her World* (1969); Margaret Llewelyn, *Jane Austen: A Character Study* (1977); George H. Tucker, *A Goodly Heritage: A History of Jane Austen's Family* (1983); John Halperin, *The Life of Jane Austen* (1984); and Park Honan, *Jane Austen: Her Life* (1987). Several more recent biographies include Valerie Grosvenor-Myer, *Jane Austen: Obstinate Heart* (1997); Claire Tomalin, *Jane Austen: A Life* (1997); and Deirdre LeFaye, *Jane Austen* (1998).

Full-length critical studies of Austen's novels are numerous. Among the more influential are Mary Lascelles, *Jane Austen and Her Art* (1938); Marvin Mudrick, *Jane Austen: Irony as Defense and Discovery* (1952); Andrew H. Wright, *Jane*

Austen's Novels (1957); A. Walton Litz, *Jane Austen* (1965); Joseph Wiesenfarth, *The Errand of Form* (1967); Alistair M. Duckworth, *The Improvement of the Estate* (1971); and Stuart M. Tave, *Some Words of Jane Austen* (1973). Other helpful studies are Julia P. Brown, *Jane Austen's Novels: Social Change and Literary Form* (1979); Susan Morgan, *In the Meantime: Character and Perception in Jane Austen's Fiction* (1980); John Odmark, *An Understanding of Jane Austen's Novels: Character, Value, and Ironic Perspective* (1981); P. J. M. Scott, *Jane Austen, A Reassessment* (1982); Laura G. Mooneyham, *Romance, Language, and Education in Jane Austen's Novels* (1986); James Thompson, *Between Self and World: The Novels of Jane Austen* (1988); Roger Gard, *Jane Austen's Novels: The Art of Clarity* (1992); and Maaja A. Stewart, *Domestic Realities and Imperial Fictions: Jane Austen's Novels in Eighteenth-Century Contexts* (1993). Collections of essays include *Jane Austen Today* (1975), ed. Joel Weinscheimer; *Jane Austen: New Perspectives* (1983), ed. Janet Todd, a feminist collection; and *Jane Austen in Hollywood* (1998), ed. Linda Troost and Sayer Greenfield. Feminist approaches to Austen's work can be found in Jean Kennard, *Victims of Convention* (1977); Sandra M. Gilbert and Susan Gubar, *The Madwoman in the Attic* (1979); Mary Poovey, *The Proper Lady and the Woman Writer* (1984); Claudia L. Johnson, *Jane Austen: Women, Politics, and the Novel* (1988); Alison Sulloway, *Jane Austen and the Province of Womanhood* (1989); and Audrey Bilger, *Laughing Feminism: Subversive Comedy in Fanny Burney, Maria Edgeworth, and Jane Austen* (1998). Interesting recent critical essays are Janet Todd, "Jane Austen, Politics and Sensibility," in *Feminist Criticism: Theory and Practice* (1991), ed. Linda Hutcheon and Paul Perron; Christine Marshall, " 'Dull Elves' and Feminists: A Summary of Feminist Criticism of Jane Austen," *Persuasions* 14 (1992); and Mary Jean Corbett, " 'Cousins in Love &c.' in Jane Austen," *Tulsa Studies in Women's Literature* 23 (2004). For further references, see David Gibson's useful, though somewhat dated, *A Bibliography of Jane Austen* (1982).

Anna Letitia Barbauld

Barbauld's complete poems—only recently available in a modern edition—are assembled chronologically in *The Poems of Anna Laetitia Barbauld* (1994), ed. William McCarthy and Elizabeth Kraft, a collection that includes an informative introduction and meticulous textual notes. Barbauld's important prose works include *Lessons for Children* (1778) and *Hymns in Prose for Children* (1781), as well as two works written in collaboration with John Aiken: *Miscellaneous Pieces in Prose* (1773) and *Evenings at Home; or, the Juvenile Budget Opened*, 6 vols. (1792–96).

For the most comprehensive collection of her prose, and a selection of her poetry, see *Anna Letitia Barbauld: Selected Poetry and Prose* (2002), ed. William McCarthy and Elizabeth Kraft. Barbauld edited the six-volume *Correspondence of Samuel Richardson* (1804); a fifty-volume anthology, *British Novelists* (1810); and a collection of passages by English poets and prose writers, *The Female Speaker* (1811). The two-volume *Works of Anna Laetitia Barbauld*, ed. Lucy Aikin, was published posthumously in 1825, and *Letters of Maria Edgeworth and Anna Laetitia Barbauld*, ed. Sir Walter Sidney Scott, appeared in 1953. Barbauld's writings were included in *British Women Poets of the Romantic Era: An Anthology* (1997), ed. William McCarthy and Elizabeth Kraft.

Betsy Rodgers's valuable biography, *Georgian Chronicle: Barbauld and Her Family* (1958), contains previously unpublished letters. For a more recent biography, see Dick Wakefield, *Anna Laetitia Barbauld* (2001). Critical studies of Barbauld include Marilyn L. Williamson, "Who's Afraid of Mrs. Barbauld? The Blue-Stockings and Feminism," *International Journal of Women's Studies* 3 (1980); Ann Messenger, "Heroics and Mock-Heroics: John Milton, Alexander Pope, and Anna Laetitia Barbauld," in her *His and Hers: Essays in Restoration and Eighteenth-Century Literature* (1986); Catherine Moore, " 'Ladies . . . Taking the Pen in Hand': Mrs. Barbauld's Criticism of Eighteenth-Century Women Novelists," in *Fetter'd or Free? British Women Novelists, 1670–1815* (1986), ed. Mary Ann Schofield and Cecilia Macheski; Katherine Rogers, "Anna Barbauld's Criticism of Fiction: Johnsonian Mode, Female Vision," *Studies in Eighteenth-Century Culture* 21 (1991); and John M. Anderson, " 'The First Fire': Barbauld Rewrites the Greater Romantic Lyric," *Studies in English Literature, 1500–1900* 34 (1994). See also Laura Mandell's discussion of Barbauld in *Misogynous Economies: The Business of Literature in Eighteenth-Century Britain* (1999).

Aphra Behn

The four-volume edition of *The Works of Aphra Behn* (1992), ed. Janet M. Todd, is arranged as follows: I, *Poetry*; II, *Love-Letters Between a Nobleman and His Sister*; III, *The Fair Jilt and Other Stories*; IV, *Seneca Unmasked and Other Prose Translations*. *Five Plays*, selected and introduced by Maureen Duffy, appeared in 1990. The following editions of Behn's works are part of a Garland series called "Satire and Sense": *A Critical Old-Spelling Edition of Aphra Behn's The City Heiress* (1987) and *Aphra Behn's The Luckey Chance* (1687): *A Critical Edition* (1987), ed. Stephen Orgel. *Oroonoko, The Rover, and Other Stories*, ed. Duffy, was published in 1992. Malcolm Hicks edited and wrote an introduction to *Selected Poems* (1993). The

Norton Critical Edition of *Oroonoko*, ed. Joanna Lipking (1997), also includes select historical and critical work on Behn. Three biographies have appeared in recent decades: Duffy, *The Passionate Shepherdess: Aphra Behn, 1640–1689* (1977); Angeline Goreau, *Reconstructing Aphra: A Social Biography of Aphra Behn* (1980); and Todd, *The Secret Life of Aphra Behn* (1997). Todd has also edited *Aphra Behn Studies* (1996) and *Aphra Behn* (1999).

Good discussions of Behn's work are Laura Brown, "The Romance of Empire: *Oroonoko* and the Trade in Slaves," *The New Eighteenth Century: Theory, Politics, English Literature* (1987), eds. Brown and Felicity Nussbaum; Rosalind Ballaster, *Seductive Forms: Women's Amatory Fiction from 1684–1740: With Particular Reference to Aphra Behn, Delarivier Manley, and Eliza Haywood* (1992); *Rereading Aphra Behn: History, Theory, and Criticism* (1993), ed. Heidi Hutner; and M. L. Stapleton, *Admired and Understood: The Poetry of Aphra Behn* (2004). Margaret Ferguson examines Behn's work in "The Authorial Ciphers of Aphra Behn," *English Literature, 1650–1740*, ed. Steven N. Zwicker (1998), as well as in *Dido's Daughters: Literacy, Gender, and Empire in Early Modern England and France* (2003). Behn is also discussed by Fidelis Morgan in *The Female Wits* (1981), and by Angeline Goreau in *Feminist Theorists* (1984), ed. Dale Spender. Articles of interest are Judith Kegan Gardiner, "Aphra Behn: Sexuality and Self-Respect," *Women's Studies* 7 (1980), and in the same journal, Robert Adams Day, "Muses in the Mud: The Female Wits Anthropologically Considered." Three more recent articles are Patricia Pender, "Competing Conceptions: Rhetorics of Representation in Aphra Behn's *Oroonoko*," *Women's Writing* 8 (2001); Oddvar Holmesland, "Aphra Behn's *Oroonoko*: Cultural Dialectics and the Novel," *ELH* 68 (2001); and Warren Chernaik, "Captains and Slaves: Aphra Behn and the Rhetoric of Republicanism," *Seventeenth Century* 17 (2002). See also Mary Ann O'Donnell, *Aphra Behn: An Annotated Bibliography of Primary and Secondary Sources* (rev. 2004).

Juliana Berners

Although there is no complete modernized edition of the *Book of Saint Albans* (1468), originally published by the "Schoolmaster of St Albans," Middle English editions include *The Boke of Saint Albans by Dame Juliana Berners* (1901), a large facsimile of the 1468 edition, with an introduction by William Blades; *Julians Barnes: Boke of Huntyng* (1964), ed. Gunnar Tilander; and *English Hawking and Hunting in "The Boke of St Albans"* (1975), ed. Rachel Hands, which has a helpful critical introduction and textual notes. Berners is also discussed in E. F. Jacob, "The Book of St Albans," *BJRL* 28

(1944); A. L. Binns, "A Manuscript Source of *The Book of St Albans*," *BJRL* 33 (1950); Rachel Hands, "Juliana Berners and the *Boke of St. Albans*," *Review of English Studies* 18 (1967); and, most recently, Alexandra Barratt, ed., *Women's Writing in Middle English* (1992).

Anne Bradstreet

Jeannine Hensley's edition, *The Works of Anne Bradstreet* (1967), has an introduction by Adrienne Rich; this essay also appears, with a later preface, in Rich's *On Lies, Secrets, and Silence* (1979). *The Complete Works of Anne Bradstreet*, ed. Joseph McElrath and Allan Robb, came out in 1981, and Charles E. Hambrick-Stowe's edited collection, *Early New England Meditative Poetry: Anne Bradstreet and Edward Taylor*, was printed in 1988. The biography by Charlotte Gordon, *Mistress Bradstreet: The Untold Life of America's First Poet*, was published in 2005. Useful critical discussions may be found in Josephine Piercy, *Anne Bradstreet* (1965); Elizabeth W. White, *Anne Bradstreet: The Tenth Muse* (1971); Ann Stanford, *Anne Bradstreet: The Worldly Puritan* (1977); Albert J. Von Frank, *The Sacred Game: Provincialism and Frontier Consciousness in American Literature, 1639–1860* (1985); Douglas R. Anderson, *A House Undivided: Domesticity and Community in American Literature* (1990); Rob Wilson, *American Sublime: The Genealogy of a Poetic Genre* (1991); and Amanda Porterfield, *Female Piety in Puritan New England: The Emergence of Religious Humanism* (1992). An interesting recent study is Jeffrey A. Hammond, *Sinful Self, Saintly Self: The Puritan Experience of Poetry* (1993). See also Theresa Freda Nicolay, *Gender Roles, Literary Authority, and Three American Women Writers: Anne Dudley Bradstreet, Mercy Otis Warren, Margaret Fuller Ossoli* (1995); and Douglas Wilson, *Beyond Stateliest Marble: The Passionate Femininity of Anne Bradstreet* (2001). Feminist work appears in Wendy Martin, "Anne Bradstreet's Poetry: A Study of Subversive Piety," in *Shakespeare's Sisters* (1979), ed. Sandra M. Gilbert and Susan Gubar, and, also by Martin, *An American Triptych* (1984). Other helpful articles include Emily Stipes Watts, " 'The Posy Unity': Anne Bradstreet's Search for Order," in *Puritan Influences in American Literature* (1979), ed. Emory Elliott; Ellen B. Brandt, "Anne Bradstreet: The Erotic Component in Puritan Poetry," *Women's Studies* 7 (1980); and Eileen Margerum, "Anne Bradstreet's Public Poetry and the Tradition of Humility," *Early American Literature* 17 (1982). Also of interest are Beth M. Doriani, " 'Then Have I . . . Said with David': Anne Bradstreet's Andover Manuscript Poems and the Influence of the Psalm Tradition," *Early American Literature* 24 (1989); Jane D. Eberwein, "Civil War and Bradstreet's 'Monarchies,' " *Early American*

Literature 26 (1991); and Robert Boschman, "Anne Bradstreet and Elizabeth Bishop: Nature, Culture, and Gender in 'Contemplations' and 'At the Fishhouses,' " *Journal of American Studies* 26 (1992). Also useful are Carol Schilling, "Corresponding Figures: Embodying Sacred and Secular Commonplaces in Anne Bradstreet's Letters to Simon," *Literature and Belief* 15 (1995); Gina Bloom, ' "Walk in Darkness': The Practice of Duty in Anne Bradstreet's Marriage Poems," *Literature and Belief* 16 (1996); Nancy E. Wright, "Epitaphic Conventions and the Reception of Anne Bradstreet's Public Voice," *Early American Literature* 31 (1996); Jean Marie Lutes, "Negotiating Theology and Gynecology: Anne Bradstreet's Representations of the Female Body," *Signs* 22 (1997); Sara Eaton, "Anne Bradstreet's 'Personal' Protestant Poetics," *Women's Writing* 4 (1997); Carrie Galloway Blackstock, "Anne Bradstreet and Performativity: Self-Cultivation, Self-Deployment," *Early American Literature* 32 (1997); Bethany Reid, "'Unfit for Light': Anne Bradstreet's Monstrous Birth," *New England Quarterly* 71 (1998); Katharine Gillespie, " 'This Briny Ocean Will O'erflow Your Shore': Anne Bradstreet's 'Second World' Atlanticism and National Narratives of Literary History," *Symbiosis* 3 (1999); Lee Oser, "Almost a Golden World: Sidney, Spenser, and Puritan Conflict in Bradstreet's 'Contemplations'," *Renascence* 52 (2000); Tamara Harvey, " 'Now Sisters . . . Impart Your Usefulnesse, and Force': Anne Bradstreet's Feminist Functionalism in 'The Tenth Muse'," *Early American Literature* 35 (2000); and Christopher Ivic, " 'Our British Land': Anne Bradstreet's Atlantic Perspective," in *Archipelagic Identities: Literature and Identity in the Atlantic Archipelago, 1550–1800* (2004), ed. Philip Schwyzer and Simon Mealor. A useful bibliography is Raymond F. Dalle, *Anne Bradstreet: A Reference Guide* (1990). Raymond A. Craig's two-volume edition, *A Concordance to the Complete Works of Anne Bradstreet*, was published in 2000.

Charlotte Brontë

The standard edition of Brontë's work—including *Jane Eyre* (1847), *Shirley* (1849), *Villette* (1853), and *The Professor* (1857)—is *The Shakespeare Head Brontë* (1931–38), ed. Thomas James Wise and John Alexander Symington. The same editors also produced *The Brontës: Their Lives, Friendships, and Correspondence*, 4 vols. (1932). Brontë's juvenilia is included in *Legends of Angria* (1933), ed. Fannie E. Ratchford, with the collaboration of William Clyde DeVane, and *An Edition of the Early Writings of Charlotte Brontë, II: The Rise of Angria, 1833–1835*, 2 vols. (1991), ed. Christine Alexander. In addition, numerous editions of Brontë's individual novels exist, including a Penguin series with valuable introductions, which includes

Juvenilia, 1829–1835 (1996), ed. Juliet Barker. A Norton Critical Edition of *Jane Eyre* (2001), ed. Richard J. Dunn, contains a number of critical articles and a bibliography. See also *Five Novelettes* (1971), ed. Winifred Gérin, and *The Secret and Lily Hart: Two Tales* (1979), ed. William Holtz. *Poems by the Brontë Sisters* (1948) has an introduction by M. R. D. Seaward; *The Poems of Charlotte Brontë* (1985) has a new text and commentary by Victor A. Neufeldt; Christine Alexander edited *Something about Arthur* (1981); and *The Unfinished Novels* was published in 1993.

The best biographies are Elizabeth Gaskell's justly famous *The Life of Charlotte Brontë* (1857), available in several editions, and Winifred Gérin's *Charlotte Brontë: The Evolution of Genius* (1967); but Helene Moglen's critical biography, *Charlotte Brontë: The Self Conceived* (1976), also offers useful psychological insights. In addition, both Lyndall Gordon's recent biography, *Charlotte Brontë: A Passionate Life* (1994), and Jane Sellars's *Charlotte Brontë* (1997) are valuable resources. The two-volume *The Letters of Charlotte Brontë: with a Selection of Letters by Family and Friends*, ed. Margaret Smith, was published in 1995–2004. Critical works include Robert Bernard Martin, *The Accents of Persuasion* (1966); Earl A. Knies, *The Art of Charlotte Brontë* (1969); Margot Peters, *Charlotte Brontë: Style in the Novel* (1973); Lawrence Jay Dessner, *The Homely Web of Truth: A Study of Charlotte Brontë's Novels* (1973); Charles Burkhart, *Charlotte Brontë: A Psychosexual Study of Her Novels* (1973); Patricia Beer, *Reader, I Married Him* (1974); and Christine Alexander, *The Early Writings of Charlotte Brontë* (1983). See also Sally Shuttleworth, *Charlotte Brontë and Victorian Psychology* (1996); Marianne Thormählen, *The Brontës and Religion* (1999); Kathleen Constable, *A Stranger Within the Gates: Charlotte Brontë and Victorian Irishness* (2000); Heather Glen, *Charlotte Brontë: The Imagination in History* (2002); Jin-Ok Kim, *Charlotte Brontë and Female Desire* (2003); Liana F. Piehler, *Spatial Dynamics and Female Development in Victorian Art and Novels: Creating a Woman's Space* (2003); the thirtieth anniversary edition of Terence Eagleton, *Myths of Power: A Marxist Study of the Brontës* (2005); Diana Peschier, *Nineteenth-Century Anti-Catholic Discourses: The Case of Charlotte Brontë* (2005); and Beth E. Torgerson, *Reading the Brontë Body: Disease, Desire, and the Constraints of Culture* (2005). Feminist approaches can be found in Barbara Hill Rigney, *Madness and Sexual Politics in the Feminist Novel* (1978); Sandra M. Gilbert and Susan Gubar, *The Madwoman in the Attic* (1979); Judith Lowder Newton, *Women, Power, and Subversion* (1981); Dianne F. Sadoff, *Monsters of Affection: Dickens, Eliot, and Brontë on Fatherhood*

(1982); and Elaine Showalter, *A Literature of Their Own* (1999). Valuable chapter-length studies of Brontë's work include Mary Winkler, " 'But It Is a True Thing': Vision and Creation in the Work of Charlotte Brontë," in *Seeing and Saying: Self-referentiality in British and American Literature* (1998), ed. Detlev Gohrbandt; and Francis Fennell and Monica Fennell, " 'Ladies – Loaf Givers': Food, Women, and Society in the Novels of Charlotte Brontë and George Eliot," in *Keeping the Victorian House: A Collection of Essays* (1995), ed. Vanessa Dickerson. Interesting recent articles include Danieal F. Halloran, "Reader, I married him: Charlotte Brontë's Marriage Contract," *New Renaissance* 9 (1995); Artur P. Kmiecik, "Charlotte Brontë's heroines on the 'contraband appetite for unfeminine knowledge'," *Kwartalnik Neofilologiczny* 45 (1998); Kate E. Brown, "Catastrophe and the City: Charlotte Brontë as Urban Novelist," *Nineteenth-Century Literature* 57 (2002); and Kate E. Brown, "Beloved Objects: Mourning, Materiality, and Charlotte Brontë's 'Never-Ending Story'," *ELH: Journal of English Literary History* 65 (1998). Essay collections include *The Brontës: The Critical Heritage* (1974), ed. Miriam Allot; *The Brontës: A Collection of Critical Essays* (1970), ed. Ian Gregor; and *Critical Essays on Charlotte Brontë* (1990), Barbara Timm Gates. Also useful are Rebecca Crump, *Charlotte and Emily Brontë: A Reference Guide* (1982), and *The Cambridge Companion to the Brontës* (2002), ed. Heather Glen.

Emily Brontë
A definitive edition of Brontë's *The Complete Poems* was produced by C. W. Hatfield in 1941, while her Gondal narrative was reconstructed in Fannie E. Ratchford, *The Brontës' Web of Childhood* (1941), and in Ratchford, *Gondal's Queen: A Novel in Verse* (1955). A useful edition of *Wuthering Heights* (1847) is the Norton Critical Edition, ed. William M. Sale Jr. The recent translations and commentaries, *The Belgian Essays* (1996), ed. and trans. Sue Lonoff, are very useful. Also valuable is Lisa Paddock and Carl Rollyson, *The Brontës A to Z: The Essential Reference to their Lives and Work* (2003). An excellent biography is Winifred Gérin, *Emily Brontë* (1971). Four more recent biographies are Edward Chitham, *A Life of Emily Brontë* (1987); Katherine Frank, *A Chainless Soul: A Life of Emily Brontë* (1990); Steve Vine, *Emily Brontë* (1998); and Robert Barnard, *Emily Brontë* (2000).
Full-length critical studies include Margaret Lane, *The Drug-like Brontë Dream* (1980); Mary Visick, *The Genesis of Wuthering Heights* (1980); Stevie Davis, *Emily Brontë: The Artist as a Free Man* (1983); Meg Harris Williams, *A Strange Way of Killing: The Poetic Structure of*

Wuthering Heights (1987); Stevie Davis, *Emily Brontë* (1988); Maureen Peck-O'Toole, *Aspects of Lyric in the Poetry of Emily Brontë* (1988); Carol Jacobs, *Uncontainable Romanticism: Shelley, Brontë, Kleist* (1989); Irene Taylor, *Holy Ghosts: The Male Muses of Emily and Charlotte Brontë* (1990); Virginia Jill Dix Ghnassia, *Metaphysical Rebellion in the Works of Emily Brontë: A Reinterpretation* (1994); Beth E. Torgerson, *Reading the Brontë Body: Disease, Desire, and the Constraints of Culture* (2005); and Marianne Thormählen, *The Brontës and Religion* (1999). Feminist analyses appear in Sandra M. Gilbert and Susan Gubar, *The Madwoman in the Attic* (1979); Margaret Homans, *Women Writers and Poetic Identity* (1980); Christine Gallant, "The Archetypal Feminine in Emily Brontë's Poetry," *Women's Studies* 7 (1980); Nina Auerbach, *Romantic Imprisonment: Women and Other Glorified Outcasts* (1985); Homans, *Bearing the Word: Language and Female Experience in Nineteenth-Century Women's Writing* (1986); Judith Weissman, *Half Savage and Hardy and Free: Women and Rural Radicalism in the Nineteenth-Century Novel* (1987); Patricia Yaeger, *Honey-Mad Women: Emancipatory Strategies in Women's Writing* (1988); and Elsie B. Michie, *Outside the Pale: Cultural Exclusion, Gender Difference, and the Victorian Woman Writer* (1993). Four valuable collections of critical essays are *The Art of Emily Brontë* (1977), ed. Anne Smith; *The Brontës: Modern Critical Views* (1987), ed. Harold Bloom; *Emily Brontë's Wuthering Heights: Modern Critical Interpretations* (1987); and *Critical Essays on Emily Brontë* (1997), ed. Thomas John Winnifrith. Also helpful, though somewhat dated, is Janet M. Barclay, *Emily Brontë Criticism, 1900–1980: An Annotated Checklist* (1984). Also useful is *The Cambridge Companion to the Brontës* (2002), ed. Heather Glen.

Elizabeth Barrett Browning
Barrett Browning's works—including *An Essay on Mind, with Other Poems* (1826), *The Seraphim, and Other Poems* (1838), *Poems* (1844), *Sonnets from the Portuguese* (1850), *Casa Guidi Windows* (1851), *Aurora Leigh* (1857), *Poems before Congress* (1860), and *Last Poems* (1862)— have been collected in the standard *Complete Works of Elizabeth Barrett Browning*, 6 vols. (1900), ed. Charlotte Porter and Helen Clarke. In addition, Julia Markus's edition of *Casa Guidi Windows* (1977), Cora Kaplan's edition of *Aurora Leigh and Other Poems* (1978), and Margaret Forster's edition of *Selected Poems of Elizabeth Barrett Browning* (1988) are useful texts. Volumes of letters include *The Letters of Elizabeth Barrett Browning* (1899), ed. Frederic G. Kenyon; *Elizabeth Barrett to Mr. Boyd* (1955), ed. Barbara McCarthy; *The Letters of Robert Browning and Elizabeth Barrett, 1845–1846,*

2 vols. (1964); and *The Letters of Elizabeth Barrett Browning to Mary Russell Mitford, 1836–1854* (1983), ed. Meredith Raymond and Mary Rose Sullivan. Volumes 1 and 2 of *The Brownings' Correspondence*, ed. Philip Kelley and Ronald Hudson, appeared in 1984, and volume 3 in 1985. Other collections of correspondence include *Woman of Letters: Selected Letters of Elizabeth Barrett Browning and Mary Russell Mitford* (1987), ed. Meredith B. Raymond and Mary Rose Sullivan; *Robert Browning and Elizabeth Barrett: The Courtship Correspondence, 1845–1846: A Selection* (1989), ed. Daniel Karlin; and *The Letters of Elizabeth Barrett Browning to her Sister Arabella* (2002), ed. Scott Lewis.

Among biographies and biographical studies, the most helpful are Gardner B. Taplin, *The Life of Elizabeth Barrett Browning* (1957); Alethea Hayter, *Elizabeth Barrett Browning* (1965); Edward C. McAlzer, *The Brownings at Casa Guidi* (1979); Rosalie Mander, *Mrs. Browning: The Story of Elizabeth Barrett* (1980); Roy E. Gridley, *The Brownings and France: A Chronicle with Commentary* (1982); Margaret Forster, *Elizabeth Barrett Browning: A Biography* (1988); Daniel Karlin, *The Courtship of Robert Browning and Elizabeth Barrett* (1985); Joanna Richardson, *The Brownings: A Biography* (1986); Peter Dally, *Elizabeth Barrett Browning: A Psychological Portrait* (1989); Barbara Dennis, *Elizabeth Barrett Browning: The Hope End Years* (1996); R. A. Barrett, *The Barretts of Jamaica: The Family of Elizabeth Barrett Browning* (2000); Mary Sanders Pollock, *Elizabeth Barrett and Robert Browning: A Creative Partnership* (2003); and Simon Avery and Rebecca Stott, *Elizabeth Barrett Browning* (2003). For interesting interviews and comments from the Brownings' contemporaries, see *Elizabeth Barrett Browning and Robert Browning: Interviews and Recollections* (2000), ed. Martin Garrett. Full-length critical studies include Angela Leighton, *Elizabeth Barrett Browning* (1986); Helen Cooper, *Elizabeth Barrett Browning: Woman and Artist* (1988); Dorothy Mermin, *Elizabeth Barrett Browning: The Origins of a New Poetry* (1989); Glennis Stephenson, *Elizabeth Barrett Browning and the Poetry of Love* (1989); and Linda M. Lewis, *Elizabeth Barrett Browning's Spiritual Progress: Face to Face with God* (1998). Essays on Browning's work have been assembled in *Critical Essays on Elizabeth Barrett Browning* (1999), ed. Sandra Donaldson. A valuable feminist study is Deirdre David, *Intellectual Women and Victorian Patriarchy: Harriet Martineau, Elizabeth Barrett Browning, George Eliot* (1987). In addition, a number of essays have appeared in journals: Flavia Alaya, "The Ring, the Rescue and the Risorgimento: Reunifying the Brownings' Italy," *Browning Institute Studies* 6 (1978); Virginia Steinmetz,

"Beyond the Sun: Patriarchal Images in *Aurora Leigh*," *Studies in Browning and His Circle* 9 (1981); Barbara Gelpi, "*Aurora Leigh*: The Vocation of the Woman Poet," *Victorian Poetry* 19 (1981); Dorothy Mermin, "The Female Poet and the Embarrassed Reader: Elizabeth Barrett Browning's *Sonnets from the Portuguese*," *ELH* (1981); Dolores Rosenblum, "Face to Face: Elizabeth Barrett Browning's *Aurora Leigh* and 19th-Century Poetry," *Victorian Studies* 26 (1983); Sandra M. Gilbert, "From Patria to Matria: Elizabeth Barrett Browning's Risorgimento," *PMLA* (1984); Deborah Logan, "The Economics of Sexuality: Elizabeth Barrett Browning and the Victorian 'Bad Conscience'," *Women's Studies* 24 (1995); Vivienne Rundle, " 'The Inscription of These Volumes': The Prefatory Writings of Elizabeth Barrett Browning," *Victorian Poetry* 34 (1996); Ranen Omer, "Elizabeth Barrett Browning and Apocalypse: The Unraveling of Poetic Autonomy," *Texas Studies in Literature and Language* 39 (1997); Andrew M. Stauffer, "Elizabeth Barrett Browning's (Re)visions of Slavery," *English Language Notes* 34 (1997); Leigh Coral Harris, "From *mythos* to *logos*: Political Aesthetics and Liminal Poetics in Elizabeth Barrett Browning's *Casa Guidi Windows*," *Victorian Literature and Culture* 28 (2000); Linda Shires, "Elizabeth Barrett Browning: Cross-dwelling and the Reworking of Female Poetic Authority," *Victorian Literature and Culture* 30 (2002); and Christine Kenyon-Jones, " 'Some World's-Wonder in Chapel or Crypt': Elizabeth Barrett Browning and Disability," *Nineteenth Century Studies* 16 (2002). Helpful reference guides are Joseph Magoon, *A Bibliography of Writings about the Brownings: Robert Browning and Elizabeth Barrett Browning from 1980 to 1989* (1990), and Sandra Donaldson, *Elizabeth Barrett Browning: An Annotated Bibliography of the Commentary and Criticism, 1826–1990* (1993). Also useful is Sandra Donaldson's comprehensive guide, "Cumulative Index to the Annual Bibliographies on Robert and Elizabeth Barrett Browning for 1972–1998," *Victorian Literature and Culture* 31 (2003).

Frances Burney

Burney's works include *Evelina* (1778), *Cecilia* (1782), *Camilla* (1796), *The Wanderer; or, Female Difficulties* (1814), and *The Memoirs of Dr. Burney* (1832). Eight volumes of her *Journals and Letters* have been edited by Joyce Hemlow (1972–80); *Fanny Burney, Selected Letters and Journals*, edited by Hemlow, was published in 1986, and the three-volume work *The Early Journals and Letters of Fanny Burney*, ed. Lars Troide, was published in 1988. The most useful biography is Margaret Anne Doody's *Frances Burney: The Life in the Works* (1988). Many other biographies have been published, includ-

ing Emily Hahn, *A Degree of Prudery* (1950); Winifred Gérin, *The Young Fanny Burney* (1961); Michael E. Adelstein, *Fanny Burney* (1968); along with, more recently, Kate Chisolm, *Fanny Burney: Her Life, 1752–1840* (1998); Janice Farrar Thaddeus, *Frances Burney: A Literary Life* (2000); and Claire Harman, *Fanny Burney: A Biography* (2001).

Full-length critical studies include Kristina Straub, *Divided Fictions: Fanny Burney and Feminine Strategy* (1987); Julia Epstein, *The Iron Pen: Frances Burney and the Politics of Women's Writing* (1989); Tracy Daugherty, *Narrative Techniques in the Novels of Fanny Burney* (1989); Katharine M. Rogers, *Frances Burney: The World of "Female Difficulties"* (1990); and Joanne Cutting-Gray, *Woman as "Nobody" and the Novels of Fanny Burney* (1992). Claudia L. Johnson includes a useful discussion of Burney in *Equivocal Beings: Politics Gender, and Sentimentality in the 1790s* (1995), as does Audrey Bilger in *Laughing Feminism: Subversive Comedy in Fanny Burney, Maria Edgeworth, and Jane Austen* (1998). Two helpful essays are William Galperin, "What Happens when Jane Austen and Frances Burney Enter the Romantic Canon?" *Lessons of Romanticism*, ed. Thomas Pfau and Robert F. Gleckner (1998), and Mark Schoenfield, "Novel Marriages, Romantic Labor, and the Quarterly Press," *Prose Studies* 25 (2002). Also helpful is Joseph A. Grau, *Fanny Burney: An Annotated Bibliography* (1981).

Elizabeth Cary

Cary's dramas include *The Tragedy of Mariam, the Fair Queen of Jewry* (1613). A 1994 reprint, edited by Barry Weller and Margaret W. Ferguson, also includes *The Lady Falkland: Her Life*, a biography written by either Anne or Mary, Cary's daughters, as well as a valuable introduction, textual notes, and bibliography. Cary also composed *The History of Edward II* (1627), religious poetry, saints' lives, and translated Catholic polemical texts. Heather Wolfe edited *Lady Falkland: Life and Letters*, 2001. Two interesting biographies are Kenneth B. Murdock's *The Sun at Noon* (1939) and Ginger Roberts Brackett's *Elizabeth Cary: Writer of Conscience* (1996).

A recent essay collection is *Renaissance Women: The Plays of Elizabeth Cary and the Poems of Aemilia Lanier* (1994), ed. Diane Purkiss. For critical essays, see Sandra K. Fischer, "Elizabeth Cary and Tyranny, Domestic and Religious," in *Silent but for the Word: Tudor Women as Patrons, Translators, and Writers of Religious Works* (1985), ed. Margaret Patterson Hannay; Betty S. Travitsky, "The Feme Covert in Elizabeth Cary's *Mariam*," in *Ambiguous Realities: Women in the Middle Ages and Renaissance* (1987), ed. Carole Levin and Jeanie Watson; Tina Krontiris, "Style and Gender in Elizabeth Cary's *Edward II*," in *The Renaissance*

Englishwoman in Print (1990), ed. Anne M. Haselkorn and Betty S. Travitsky; Margaret W. Ferguson, "Running On with Almost Public Voice: The Case of 'E. C.,' " in *Tradition and the Talents of Women* (1991), ed. Florence Howe; Maureen Quilligan, "Staging Gender: William Shakespeare and Elizabeth Cary," in *Sexuality and Gender in Early Modern Europe: Institutions, Texts, Images* (1993), ed. James Grantham Turner; Louise Schleiner, "Lady Falkland's Reentry into Writing: Anglo-Catholic Consensual Discourse and Her *Edward II* as Historical Fiction," in *The Witness of Times: Manifestations of Ideology in Seventeenth-Century England* (1993), ed. Katherine Keller and Gerald Schiffhorst; and Kim Walker, " 'To Beg their Fees': The Emergence of the Professional Woman Writer," in *Women Writers of the English Renaissance* (1996). For the most recent discussions of Cary's work, see Naomi J. Miller, "Domestic Politics in Elizabeth Cary's *The Tragedy of Mariam*," *Studies in English Literature 1500–1900* 37 (1997); Andrew Hiscock, "The Hateful Cuckoo: Elizabeth Cary's *Tragedie of Mariam, A Renaissance Drama of Dispossession*," *Forum for Modern Language Studies* 33 (1997); Rosemary Kegl, "Theaters, Households, and a 'Kind of History' in Elizabeth Cary's *The Tragedy of Mariam*," in *Enacting Gender on the English Renaissance Stage* (1999), ed. Viviana Comensoli and Anne Russell; and Janet Starner-Wright and Susan M. Fitzmaurice, "Shaping a Drama Out of a History: Elizabeth Cary and the Story of Edward II," in *Critical Survey* 14 (2002).

Margaret Cavendish, Duchess of Newcastle

The most complete modern edition of Cavendish's work was edited by Kate Lilley, *Margaret Cavendish: The Description of a New World Called the Blazing World and Other Writings* (1992). Paul Salzmann also includes *The Blazing World* in his *Anthology of Seventeenth-Century Fiction* (1991). Plays by Cavendish can be found in *Convent Pleasures and Other Plays*, ed. Ann Shaver (1999); other selections of Cavendish's writing appear in *Women Writers of the Seventeenth-Century*, ed. Katharina Wilson and Frank J. Warnke, and in *Kissing the Rod: An Anthology of Seventeenth-Century Women's Verse* (1988), ed. Germaine Greer et al. Two other books have been reprinted in facsimile, *Sociable Letters* (1969), and *Poems and Fancies* (1972).

She is discussed in Reverend J. Granger, *Biographical History of England* (1824), and Louisa Costello, *Memoirs of Eminent Englishwomen* (1844). Critical studies of her life and work are Douglas Grant, *Margaret the First* (1957), and Kathleen Jones, *A Glorious Fame: The Life of Margaret Cavendish, Duchess of Newcastle, 1623–1673* (1988). See also John Rogers, *Mat-*

ter of Revolution: Science, Poetry, and Politics in the Age of Milton (1996), and Alice Fulton, *Feeling as a Foreign Language: The Good Strangeness of Poetry* (1999). In 2003 Line Cottegnies and Nancy Weitz edited a collection of essays, *Authorial Conquests: Essays on Genre in the Writings of Margaret Cavendish.* Other useful critical essays on Cavendish include Moira Ferguson, "A 'Wise, Wittie and Learned Lady': Margaret Lucas Cavendish," in *Women Writers of the Seventeenth Century* (1989), ed. Katharina M. Wilson; and Linda Payne, "Dramatic Dreamscape: Women's Dreams and Utopian Vision in the Works of Margaret Cavendish, Duchess of Newcastle," in *Curtain Calls: British and American Women and the Theater, 1660–1820,* ed. Mary Anne Schofield (1991). Journal articles of interest are Patricia A. Sullivan, "Female Writing beside the Rhetorical Tradition," *International Journal of Women's Studies* 3 (1981); Catherine Gallagher, "Embracing the Absolute: The Politics of the Female Subject in Seventeenth-Century England," *Genders* 1 (1989); Eve Keller, "Producing Petty Gods: Margaret Cavendish's Critique of Experimental Science," in *English Literary History* 64 (1997); and Kathryn Schwarz, "Chastity, Militant and Married: Cavendish's Romance, Milton's Masque," *PMLA* 118 (2003).

Kate Chopin

Chopin's works include *At Fault* (1890), *Bayou Folk* (1894), *A Night in Acadie* (1897), *The Awakening* (1899), and *A Vocation and a Voice: Stories* (1991), originally cancelled by her publisher and just recently issued. A new Norton Critical Edition of *The Awakening* appeared in 1994. A definitive *Complete Works of Kate Chopin* (1969) appeared in two volumes edited by Per Seyersted, who is also the author of *Kate Chopin: A Critical Biography* (1969); in addition, with Emily Toth, Seyersted edited *A Kate Chopin Miscellany* (1979). An early critical biography is Daniel Rankin, *Kate Chopin and Her Creole Stories* (1932), and two more recent biographies are Emily Toth, *Unveiling Kate Chopin* (1999), and Nancy A. Walker, *Kate Chopin: A Literary Life* (2001). Emily Toth also edited *Kate Chopin's Private Papers* (1998).

Complete critical volumes on Chopin include Bernard Koloski, *Kate Chopin: A Study of the Short Fiction* (1996); Bonnie James Shaker, *Coloring Locals: Racial Formation in Kate Chopin's Youth's Companion Stories* (2003); and Allen F. Stein, *Women and Autonomy in Kate Chopin's Short Fiction* (2005). Among important articles are Robert Cantwell, "*The Awakening* by Kate Chopin," *Georgia Review* 10 (1956); Larzer Ziff, "An Abyss of Inequality: Sarah Orne Jewett, Mary Wilkins Freeman, Kate Chopin," in *The American 1890s* (1966); George Spangler, "Kate Chopin's *The Awaken-*

ing: A Partial Dissent," *Novel* 3 (1970); Cynthia Griffin Wolff, "Thanatos and Eros: Kate Chopin's *The Awakening*," *American Quarterly* 25 (1973); Ruth Sullivan and Stewart Smith, "Narrative Stance in Kate Chopin's *The Awakening*," *Studies in American Fiction* 1 (1973); Otis B. Wheeler, "The Five Awakenings of Edna Pontellier," *The Southern Review* 11 (1975); Jane P. Tompkins, "*The Awakening*: An Evaluation," *Feminist Studies* 3 (1976); Emily Toth, "Kate Chopin's *The Awakening* as Feminist Criticism," *Louisiana Studies* 15 (1976); Priscilla Allen, "Old Critics and New: The Treatment of Chopin's *The Awakening,*" in *The Authority of Experience* (1977), ed. Arlyn Diamond and Lee R. Edwards; Lawrence Thornton, "*The Awakening*: A Political Romance," *American Literature* 52 (1980); Anne Goodwyn Jones, "Kate Chopin: The Life Behind the Mask," in *Tomorrow Is Another Day* by Jones (1981); and Sandra M. Gilbert, "The Second Coming of Aphrodite: Kate Chopin's Fantasy of Desire," *Kenyon Review* 5 (1983). For more recent work, see Yves Clemmen, "Photographic Politics: The Text and its Readings in Kate Chopin's *The Awakening*," *Southern Quarterly* 32 (1994); Heather Kirk Thomas, "Kate Chopin's Scribbling Women and the American Literary Marketplace," *Studies in American Fiction* 23 (1995); Gerri Brightwell, "Charting the Nebula: Gender, Language, and Power in Kate Chopin's *The Awakening*," *Women and Language* 18 (1995); Walter Taylor and Jo Ann B. Fineman, "Kate Chopin: Pre-Freudian Freudian," *Southern Literary Journal* 29 (1996); Ann C. Colley, "Kate Chopin's *The Awakening* as Displaced Conversion Narrative," *Anglica* 7 (1997); Rebecca Dickson, "Kate Chopin, Mrs Pontellier, and Narrative Control," *Southern Quarterly* 37 (1999); Gail Lippincott, "Thirty-nine Weeks: Pregnancy and Birth Imagery in Kate Chopin's *The Awakening*," in *This Giving Birth: Pregnancy and Childbirth in American Women's Writing* (2000), ed. Julie Tharp and Susan MacCallum-Whitcomb; Anthony P. Petruzzi, "Two Modes of Disclosure in Kate Chopin's *The Awakening*," *Lit: Literature, Interpretation, Theory* 13 (2002); Teresa Gibert, "The Role of Implicatures in Kate Chopin's Louisiana Short Stories," *Journal of the Short Story in English / Les Cahiers de la Nouvelle* 40 (2003); Mary Biggs, " 'Si tu savais': The Gay / Transgendered Sensibility of Kate Chopin's *The Awakening*," *Women's Studies* 33 (2004); and Erik Margraf, "Kate Chopin's *The Awakening* as a Naturalistic Novel," *American Literary Realism* 37 (2005). Two useful collections of critical essays on Chopin are *Kate Chopin Reconsidered: Beyond the Bayou* (1992), ed. Lynda S. Boren and Sara deSaussure Davis, and *Critical Essays on Kate Chopin* (1996), ed. Alice Hall Petry. Valuable, though now outdated, is Marlene Springer,

Edith Wharton and Kate Chopin: A Reference Guide (1976). Two helpful resources are Linda Wagner-Martin, "Recent Books on Kate Chopin," *Mississippi Quarterly* 42 (1989), and Suzanne Disheroon Green and David J. Caudle, *Kate Chopin: An Annotated Bibliography of Critical Works* (1999).

Lady Mary Chudleigh

Chudleigh's works include *The Female Advocate; or, A Plea for the Just Liberty of the Tender Sex and Particularly of Married Women* (1701), *The Ladies Defence; or, "The Bride-Woman's Counseller" Answer'd* (1701), and *Poems on Several Occasions* (1703). A modern collection, *The Poems and Prose of Mary, Lady Chudleigh*, ed. Margaret J. M. Ezell, appeared in 1993. For criticism of Chudleigh's work, see Carol Barash, " 'The Native Liberty . . . of the Subject': Configurations of Gender and Authority in the Works of Mary Chudleigh, Sarah Fye Egerton, and Mary Astell," *Women, Writing, History, 1640–1799*, ed. Isobel Grundy and Susan Wiseman (1992); Barbara Olive, "A Puritan Subject's Panegyrics to Queen Anne," *SEL* 42 (2002); and Rebecca M. Mills, "Mary, Lady Chudleigh (1656–1710): Poet, Protofeminist, and Patron," *Women and Poetry, 1660–1750*, ed. Sarah Prescott and David E. Shuttleton (2003).

Mary Elizabeth Coleridge

Theresa Whistler edited and introduced Coleridge's *Collected Poems* (1954), which includes verse from *Poems* (1908) and additional, previously unpublished material. Poems by Coleridge have appeared in a number of collections and anthologies: *Bread and Roses: Women's Poetry of the Nineteenth and Twentieth Centuries* (1982), ed. Diana Scott; *Sound the Deep Waters: Women's Romantic Poetry in the Victorian Age* (1991), ed. Pamela Norris; *Faith in Her Words: Six Centuries of Women's Poetry* (1991), ed. Veronica Zundel; *The Things That Matter: An Anthology of Women's Spiritual Poetry* (1992), ed. Julia Neuberger; and *Winged Words: Victorian Women's Poetry and Verse* (1994), ed. Catherine Reilly. Edith Sichel wrote a memoir that is included in *Gathered Leaves from the Prose of Mary E. Coleridge* (1910). Among Coleridge's other works are a novel, *The Seven Sleepers of Ephesus* (1893), and a biographical study, *Holman Hunt* (1908). Critical essays on Coleridge's writings include Katharine McGowran, "The Restless Wanderer at the Gates: Hosts, Guests and Ghosts in the Poetry of Mary E. Coleridge," in *Victorian Women Poets: A Critical Reader* (1996), ed. Angela Leighton, and Alison Chapman, "Mary Elizabeth Coleridge, Literary Influence and Technologies of the Uncanny," in *Victorian Gothic: Literary and Cultural Manifestations in the Nineteenth Century* (2000), ed. Ruth Robbins and Julian Wolfreys.

Anna Julia Cooper

Two useful reprints of Cooper's work are *A Voice from the South* (1988), ed. Mary Helen Washington and Charles Lemert and Esma Bhan, *The Voice of Anna Julia Cooper: Including "A Voice from the South"* (1998). Full-length biographical and critical studies of Cooper include Louise Daniel Hutchison, *Anna J. Cooper, A Voice from the South* (1981); Leona Gabel, *From Slavery to the Sorbonne and Beyond* (1982); and Karen A. Johnson, *Uplifting the Women and the Race: The Lives, Educational Philosophies and Social Activism of Anna Julia Cooper and Nannie Helen Burroughs* (1999). A useful essay is Elizabeth Alexander, " 'We Must Be about Our Father's Business': Anne Julia Cooper and the In-Corporation of the Nineteenth-Century African-American Intellectual," *Signs* 20 (1995).

Rebecca Harding Davis

Davis's most famous story, *Life in the Iron-Mills; or, The Korl Woman* (1861), was reissued by the Feminist Press in 1972, with a biographical interpretation by Tillie Olsen, and has been reprinted several times thereafter. Other works by Davis include *Margaret Howth* (1862), *Waiting for the Verdict* (1868), *Pro Aris et Focis—A Plea for Our Altars and Hearths* (1870), *John Andross* (1874), *Doctor Warrick's Daughters* (1896), and *Frances Waldeaux* (1896). Her autobiographical work was reissued in 2001 as *Rebecca Harding Davis: Writing Cultural Autobiography*, ed. Janice Milner Lasseter and Sharon M. Harris. For further biographical information, see Jean Pfaelzer, "Legacy Profile: Rebecca Harding Davis (1831–1910)," *Legacy* 7 (1990).

Three full-length studies of Davis are Sharon M. Harris, *Rebecca Harding Davis and American Realism* (1991); Jane Attenridge Rose, *Rebecca Harding Davis* (1993); and Jean Pfaelzer's *Parlor Radical: Rebecca Harding Davis and the Origins of American Social Realism* (1996). The increasing interest in Davis in recent decades has generated many critical articles, including Walter Hesford, "The Literary Context of *Life in the Iron-Mills*," *American Literature* 49 (1977); Pfaelzer, "Rebecca Harding-Davis: Domesticity, Social Order, and the Industrial Novel," *International Journal of Women's Studies* 4 (1981); Jean Fagan Yellin, "The 'Feminization' of Rebecca Harding Davis," *American Literary History* 2 (1990); Rose, "The Artist Manqué in the Fiction of Rebecca Harding Davis," in *Writing the Woman Artist: Essays on Poetics, Politics, and Portraiture* (1991), ed. Suzanne W. Jones; Amy Schrager Lang, "Class and the Strategies of Sympathy," *The Culture of Sentiment: Race, Gender, and Sentimentality in Nineteenth-Century America* (1992), ed. Shirley Samuels, which compares Davis and Harriet Beecher

Stowe; Eric Schocket, " 'Discovering Some New Race': Rebecca Harding Davis's *Life in the Iron Mills* and the Literary Emergence of Working-Class Whiteness," *PMLA* 115 (2000); and Stephen Knadler, " 'Miscegenated Whiteness': Rebecca Harding Davis, the 'Civil-izing War,' and Female Racism," *Nineteenth-Century Literature* 57 (2002). See also Pfaelzer's *A Rebecca Harding Davis Reader* (1995). A valuable resource is Rose, "A Bibliography of Fiction and Non-Fiction by Rebecca Harding Davis," *American Literary Realism, 1870–1910* 22 (1990).

Emily Dickinson

The Poems of Emily Dickinson (1955) was edited by Thomas H. Johnson, and he and Theodora Ward edited the three companion volumes, *The Letters of Emily Dickinson* (1958). More recently, Ralph W. Franklin has edited *The Manuscript Books of Emily Dickinson* (1981) and *The Master Letters of Emily Dickinson* (1986). *New Poems of Emily Dickinson* (1993), ed. William H. Shurr, Anna Dunlap, and Emily Grey Shurr, is a collection of poems gathered from Dickinson's letters. Also useful are *Open Me Carefully: Emily Dickinson's Intimate Letters to Susan Huntington Dickinson*, ed. Ellen Louise Hart and Martha Nell Smith (1998), and Cynthia MacKenzie, *A Concordance to the Letters of Emily Dickinson* (2000). Jay Leyda's compendious *The Years and Hours of Emily Dickinson* (1960) provides documents about the poet's life and time. Richard B. Sewall, *The Life of Emily Dickinson* (1994), is probably the most definitive biography, but Thomas H. Johnson, *Emily Dickinson: An Interpretive Biography* (1955), is also an important one. John Cody, *After Great Pain: The Inner Life of Emily Dickinson* (1971), is an interesting but controversial psychoanalytic study. Cynthia Griffin Wolff's biography, *Emily Dickinson,* appeared in 1986. Recent biographical sources include Douglas Westfall, *The Life of Emily Dickinson* (2000); Alfred Habegger, *My Wars Are Laid Away in Books: The Life of Emily Dickinson* (2001); Connie Ann Kirk, *Emily Dickinson: A Biography* (2004); and *A Historical Guide to Emily Dickinson* (2004), ed. Vivian R. Pollak.

Full-length critical works include Albert J. Gelpi, *Emily Dickinson: The Mind of the Poet* (1965); Brita Lindberg-Seyersted, *The Voice of the Poet: Aspects of Style in the Poetry of Emily Dickinson* (1968); Ruth Miller, *The Poetry of Emily Dickinson* (1968); Rebecca Patterson, *Emily Dickinson's Imagery* (1974); Robert Weisbuch, *Emily Dickinson's Poetry* (1975); Christopher E. G. Benfrey, *Emily Dickinson and the Problem of Others* (1985); Jane Donahue Eberwein, *Emily Dickinson: Strategies of Limitation* (1985); Wendy Barker, *Lunacy of Light: Emily Dickinson and the Experience of Metaphor* (1987); Christianne Miller, *Emily Dickinson: A Poet's Grammar* (1987); Elizabeth Phillips, *Emily Dickinson: Personae and Performance* (1988); Joanne Dobson, *Emily Dickinson and the Strategies of Reticence* (1989); Judy Jo Small, *Positive as Sound: Emily Dickinson's Rhyme* (1990); Gary Lee Stonum, *The Dickinson Sublime* (1990); and Sharon Cameron, *Choosing Not Choosing: Dickinson's Fascicles* (1992). See also Margaret Dickie, *Lyric Contingencies: Emily Dickinson and Wallace Stevens* (1991); James Olney, *The Language(s) of Poetry: Walt Whitman, Emily Dickinson, Gerard Manley Hopkins* (1993); Dorothy Huff Oberhaus, *Emily Dickinson's Fascicles: Method & Meaning* (1995); Claudia Ottlinger, *The Death-Motif in the Poetry of Emily Dickinson and Christina Rossetti* (1996); Beth Maclay Doriani, *Emily Dickinson: Daughter of Prophecy* (1996); Robert Graham Lambert, Jr., *A Critical Study of Emily Dickinson's Letters: The Prose of a Poet* (1996); Daneen Wardrop, *Emily Dickinson's Gothic: Goblin with a Gauge* (1996); Paul Crumbley, *Inflections of the Pen: Dash and Voice in Emily Dickinson* (1997); James R. Guthrie, *Emily Dickinson's Vision: Illness and Identity in Her Poetry* (1998); Morag Harris, *Emily Dickinson in Time: Experience and its Analysis in Progressive Verbal Form* (1999); James McIntosh, *Nimble Believing: Dickinson and the Unknown* (2000); Domhnall Mitchell, *Emily Dickinson: Monarch of Perception* (2000); Eleanor Elson Heginbotham, *Reading the Fascicles of Emily Dickinson: Dwelling in Possibilities* (2003); Richard E. Brantley, *Experience and Faith: The Late-Romantic Imagination of Emily Dickinson* (2004); Roger Lundin, *Emily Dickinson and the Art of Belief* (2004); and Domhnall Mitchell, *Measures of Possibility: Emily Dickinson's Manuscripts* (2005). Other studies include Paul J. Ferlazzo, *Emily Dickinson* (1976); Sharon Cameron, *Lyric Time* (1979); Karl Keller, *The Only Kangaroo among the Beauty: Emily Dickinson and America* (1979); and David Porter, *Dickinson: The Modern Idiom* (1981).

Feminist analyses of Dickinson's work are represented by Joanne Feit Diehl, *Dickinson and the Romantic Imagination* (1981); Barbara Clarke Mossberg, *Emily Dickinson: When a Writer Is a Daughter* (1982); Suzanne Juhasz, *The Undiscovered Continent: Emily Dickinson and the Space of the Mind* (1983); Vivian R. Pollak, *Dickinson: The Anxiety of Gender* (1984); Paula Bennett, *Emily Dickinson: Woman Poet* (1990); Mary Leoffelholz, *Dickinson and the Boundaries of Feminist Theory* (1990); Judith Farr, *The Passion of Emily Dickinson* (1992); Martha Nell Smith, *Rowing in Eden: Rereading Emily Dickinson* (1992); and Sabine Sielke, *Fashioning the Female Subject: The Intertextual Networking of Dickinson, Moore, and Rich* (1997). Valuable collections of critical essays are *Emily Dickinson: Modern Critical Views*

(1985), ed. Harold Bloom; *On Dickinson: The Best from American Literature* (1990), ed. Edwin H. Cady and Louis J. Budd; *Emily Dickinson's Open Folios: Scenes of Reading, Surfaces of Writing* (1995), ed. Marta L. Werner; *Emily Dickinson: A Collection of Critical Essays* (1996), ed. Judith Farr; and *Dickinson and Audience* (1996), ed. Martin Orzeck and Robert Weisbuch. Useful reference guides are Karen Dandurand, *Dickinson Scholarship: An Annotated Bibliography, 1965–1985* (1988); Jeanetta Boswell, *Emily Dickinson: A Bibliography of Secondary Sources, 1890–1987* (1989); Joseph Duchac, *The Poems of Emily Dickinson: An Annotated Guide to Commentary Published in English, 1978–1989* (1993); Fordyce R. Bennett, *A Reference Guide to the Bible in Emily Dickinson's Poetry* (1997); and *An Emily Dickinson Encyclopedia* (1998), ed. Jane Donahue Eberwein.

Maria Edgeworth

The most comprehensive collection of Edgeworth's work available is the twelve-volume *Novels and Selected Writings of Maria Edgeworth*, which appeared in 1999 as part of the Pickering Masters series. Ten volumes of Edgeworth's *Tales and Novels* (1893), including *Castle Rackrent* (1800), *Belinda* (1801), *Leonora* (1806), *Tales of Fashionable Life* (1809), and *The Absentee* (1812), were reprinted in 1967. *Belinda* and *Patronage* were reprinted in 1986, with introductions by Eva Figes. *Helen* was reprinted in 1987, with an introduction by Maggie Gee; *The Absentee* was reprinted in 1988, edited by W. J. McCormack and Kim Walker; *Castle Rackrent and Ennui* was reprinted in 1992, edited by Marilyn Butler; and *Dumb Andy* reappeared in 1992, edited by Jonathan Levy. Editions of her nonfiction and letters include *Letters from England, 1813–1844* (1971), ed. Christina Colvin; *Letters for Literary Ladies* (1974), with an introduction by Gina Luria; *The Education of the Heart: The Correspondence of Rachel Mordecai Lazarus and Maria Edgeworth* (1977), ed. Edgar E. MacDonald; and *The Early Lessons, Part 10* (1990), with an introduction by Mitzi Myers.

Among older biographical works are Isabel Constance Clarke, *Maria Edgeworth, Her Family and Friends* (1950); Marilyn Butler, *Maria Edgeworth* (1971). A slightly more recent biography is Oleta Elizabeth McWhorter Harden, *Maria Edgeworth* (1984). In addition, James Newcomer has two full-length studies, *Maria Edgeworth, the Novelist, 1767–1849* (1967), and *Maria Edgeworth* (1973), while other studies include Mark D. Hawthorne, *Doubt and Dogma in Maria Edgeworth* (1967); Michael Hurst, *Maria Edgeworth and the Public Scene* (1969); Harden, *Maria Edgeworth's Art of Prose Fiction* (1971). Edgeworth is also discussed by Vineta Colby in *Yesterday's Women* (1974), and by Patricia Voss-Clesly in *Tendencies of Character Depiction in the Domestic Novels of Burney, Edgeworth, and Austen* (1979). More recent discussions appear in Elizabeth Kowalski-Wallace, *Their Fathers' Daughters: Hannah More, Maria Edgeworth, and Patriarchal Complicity* (1991); Caroline Gonda, *Reading Daughters' Fictions 1709–1834: Novels and Society from Manley to Edgeworth* (1996); and Audrey Bilger, *Laughing Feminism: Subversive Comedy in Fanny Burney, Maria Edgeworth, and Jane Austen* (1998). Two useful critical essays are Mitzi Myers, "The Dilemmas of Gender as Double-Voiced Narrative; or, Maria Edgeworth Mothers the Bildungsroman," in *The Idea of the Novel in the Eighteenth Century* (1988), ed. Robert W. Uphaus, and W. J. McCormack, "Setting and Ideology: With Reference to the Fiction of Maria Edgeworth; A Collection of Interpretations," in *Ancestral Voices: The Big House in Anglo-Irish Literature* (1992), ed. Otto Rauchbauer.

George Eliot

Eliot's publications include *Scenes of Clerical Life* (1858), *Adam Bede* (1859), *The Mill on the Floss* (1860), *Silas Marner* (1861), *Romola* (1863), *Felix Holt the Radical* (1866), *The Spanish Gypsy* (1868), *Armgart* (1871), *Middlemarch* (1872), *Daniel Deronda* (1876), and *Impressions of Theophrastus Such* (1876). Ten volumes of her works were published by Blackwood in the 1890s. Gordon S. Haight edited *The George Eliot Letters, 1954–1978*, and in 1985 edited *Selections from George Eliot's Letters*, a sampling from the larger volumes. Joseph Wiesenfarth edited *A Writer's Notebook*, and *Uncollected Writings* (1981). Also useful is the three-volume *George Eliot's Life as Related in Her Letters and Journals* (1885), arranged and edited by her husband, J. W. Cross. There are, of course, numerous editions of the novels, some of which, like the Penguins, contain valuable introductions and notes. There are three recent collections of Eliot's work: *Collected Poems* (1989), with an introduction by Lucien Jenkins; *Selected Essays, Poems, and Other Writings* (1990), ed. A. S. Byatt and Nicholas Warren, with an introduction by Byatt; and *The Complete Shorter Poetry of George Eliot*, ed. Gerard Van den Broek and William Baker (2005). *Middlemarch* appears in a Norton Critical Edition, ed. Bert G. Hornback. There have been many biographies; the best of them is Gordon S. Haight, *George Eliot* (1968). Haight also wrote *George Eliot and John Chapman* (1969), and edited *A Century of George Eliot Critics* (1965). In addition, with Rosemary T. VanArsdel, he edited *George Eliot, A Centenary Tribute* (1982). Also useful are Ruby V.

Redinger's biography, *George Eliot: The Emergent Self* (1975), and Ina Taylor, *A Woman of Correspondence: The Life of George Eliot* (1989). Three more recent biographies are Frederick R. Karl, *George Eliot, Voice of a Century: A Biography* (1995); Rosemary Ashton, *George Eliot: A Life* (1997); and Tim Dolin, *George Eliot* (2005). *The Real Life of Mary Ann Evans: George Eliot, Her Letters, and Fiction*, ed. Rosemarie Bodenheimer (1994), contains both biographical and critical information.

Valuable full-length studies include Barbara Hardy, *The Novels of George Eliot: A Study in Form* (1959); U. C. Knoepflmacher, *George Eliot's Early Novels: The Limits of Realism* (1968); Felicia Bonaparte, *Will and Destiny: Morality and Tragedy in George Eliot's Novels* (1975); Joseph Wiesenfarth, *George Eliot's Mythmaking* (1977); Mary Ellen Doyle, *The Sympathetic Response: George Eliot's Fictional Rhetoric* (1981); Karen S. Mann, *The Language That Makes George Eliot's Fiction* (1983); Suzanne Graver, *George Eliot and Community: A Study in Social Theory and Fictional Form* (1984); Alan Perlis, *A Return to the Primal Self: Identity in the Fiction of George Eliot* (1989); Nancy Henry, *George Eliot and the British Empire* (2002); and Neil Hurtz, *George Eliot's Pulse* (2003). Gillian Beer discusses Eliot alongside Darwin in *Darwin's Plots: Evolutionary Narrative in Darwin, George Eliot, and Nineteenth-Century Fiction*, 2nd ed. (2000). Among feminist treatments are chapters in Patricia Meyer Spacks, *The Female Imagination* (1975); Elaine Showalter, *A Literature of Their Own* (1977); Sandra M. Gilbert and Susan Gubar, *The Madwoman in the Attic* (1979); Diane F. Sadoff, *Monsters of Affection* (1982); Phyllis Rose, *Parallel Lives: Five Victorian Marriages* (1983); and Carolyn Heilbrun, *Women's Lives: The View from the Threshold* (1999). Collections of critical essays include *Critical Essays on George Eliot* (1970), ed. Barbara Hardy; *George Eliot: A Collection of Critical Essays* (1970), ed. George R. Creeger; *George Eliot: The Critical Heritage* (1971), ed. David Carroll; *The Critical Response to George Eliot* (1994), ed. Karen L. Pangallo; *The Transformation of Rage: Mourning and Creativity in George Eliot's Fiction* (1994), ed. Peggy Fitzhugh Johnstone; *George Eliot and the Politics of National Inheritance* (1994), ed. Bernard Semmel; the two-volume *George Eliot: Critical Assessments*, ed. Stuart Hutchinson (1996); and *The Cambridge Companion to George Eliot*, ed. George Levine (2001). There are also numerous collections on individual Eliot novels, such as the helpful *This Particular Web: Essays on Middlemarch* (1975), ed. Ian Adams. A useful resource is *An Annotated Critical Biography of George Eliot* (1988), ed. Levine with Patricia O'Hara.

Queen Elizabeth I

The most comprehensive edition of Elizabeth's work is *Elizabeth I: Collected Works* (2000), ed. Leah S. Marcus, Jane Mueller, and Mary Beth Rose. The standard edition of the poems is Leicester Bradner, *The Poems of Queen Elizabeth I* (1964). There are many collections of her letters; the most inclusive is *The Letters of Queen Elizabeth* (1935), ed. G. B. Harrison, but forty previously unprinted letters were recently edited by E. I. Kouri and titled *Elizabethan England and Europe* (1982). George P. Rice Jr. published selected official addresses in *The Public Speaking of Queen Elizabeth* (1951).

Several literary figures have written about Elizabeth, including Thomas Heywood, *England's Elizabeth* (1631); Lytton Strachey, *Elizabeth and Essex, a Tragic History* (1928); and Edith Sitwell, *Fanfare for Elizabeth* (1946). Elizabeth Jenkins, *Elizabeth the Great* (1959), and *Elizabeth and Leicester* (1962), are valuable studies, as are Paul Johnson, *Elizabeth I: A Study in Power and Intellect* (1974), and Alison Plowden, *Elizabeth Regina: The Age of Triumph, 1588–1603* (1980). See also Wallace T. MacCaffery's recent biography, *Elizabeth I* (1993); Susan Doran's study *Elizabeth I and Religion, 1558–1603* (1994); Carole Levin, *"The Heart and Stomach of a King": Elizabeth I and the Politics of Sex and Power* (1994); and Helen Hackett, *Virgin Mother, Maiden Queen* (1995). Susan Frye's interesting book, *Elizabeth I: The Competition for Representation* (1993), discusses representations of the queen in literature. Steven W. May's article "Recent Studies in Elizabeth I," *English Literary Renaissance* 23 (1993), is a helpful resource.

Fanny Fern

Among the editions of Fern's collected newspaper articles are *Fern Leaves from Fanny's Portfolio* (1853), *Caper-Sauce: A Volume of Chit-Chat about Men, Women, and Things* (1872), and *Fanny Fern: A Memorial Volume* (1872). Her novel, *Ruth Hall*, was first published in 1855, and reissued in 1986 in the collection *Ruth Hall and Other Writings*, ed. Joyce W. Warren. A second novel, *Rose Clark*, was published in 1856. For interesting biographical information, see Joyce Warren's important full-length study of Fern's life and work, *Fanny Fern: An Independent Woman* (1992), as well as her profile of Fern in *Legacy* 2 (1985), and her critical introduction to *Ruth Hall and Other Writings* (1986). Useful critical articles are Lauren Berlant, "The Female Woman: Fanny Fern and the Form of Sentiment," *American Literary History* 3 (1991); Claire C. Pettengill, "Against Novels: Fanny Fern's Newspaper Fiction and the Reform of Print Culture," *American Periodicals* (1996); Carolyn Kitch, " 'The Courage to Call Things by their Right Names': Fanny Fern, Fem-

inine Sympathy, and Feminist Issues in Nineteenth-century American Journalism," *American Journalism* 13 (1996); Jaime Harker, " 'Pious Cant' and Blasphemy: Fanny Fern's Radicalized Sentiment," *Legacy* 18 (2001); Elizabeth A. Wright, "Open-ended Oratory: Fanny Fern's Use of the Periodical as a Rhetorical Platform," *American Journalism* 18 (2001); Wright, " 'Joking Isn't Safe': Fanny Fern, Irony, and Signifyin(g)," *Rhetoric Society Quarterly* 31 (2001); and Sonia Di Loreto, "Going Public: Fanny Fern's Writing in the Publishing World," in *Public and Private in American History: State, Family, Subjectivity in the Twentieth Century* (2003), ed. Raffaella Baritono.

Michael Field (Katherine Harris Bradley and Edith Emma Cooper)

Using the pen-name Arran Leigh, Bradley alone published *The New Minnesinger* (1875), while *Bellerophôn* (1881), the first jointly authored work of Bradley and Cooper, appeared under the names Arran and Isla Leigh. Beginning with *Calirrhoë, and Fair Rosamund* (1884), they published under the name Michael Field a number of plays and volumes of poetry, including their most notable collections *Long Ago* (1889), *Sight and Song* (1892), and *Underneath the Bough* (1893). Selections from the journal they kept jointly were published posthumously as *Works and Days: From the Journal of Michael Field* (1933), ed. T. and D. C. Moore. An early biography is Mary Sturgeon, *Michael Field* (1921).

More recent biographical and critical material can be found in Angela Leighton, *Victorian Women Poets: Writing Against the Heart* (1992). Yopie Prins includes an excellent discussion of Michael Field in *Victorian Sappho* (1999). Helpful essays are Holly Laird, "Contradictory Legacies: Michael Field and Feminist Restoration," *Victorian Poetry* 33 (1995); Ana Parejo Vadillo, "*Sight and Song*: Transparent Translations and a Manifesto for the Observer," *Victorian Poetry* 38 (2000); and Jill Ehnenn, "Looking Strategically: Feminist and Queer Aesthetics in Michael Field's *Sight and Song*," *Victorian Poetry* 42 (2004).

Anne Finch

Myra Reynolds's *The Poems of Anne, Countess of Winchilsea* (1903) is out of print, but Katharine M. Rogers edited *Selected Poems of Anne Finch* in 1979. Rogers also wrote an essay on Finch, "An Augustan Woman Poet," in *Shakespeare's Sisters* (1979), ed. Sandra M. Gilbert and Susan Gubar, as well as "Finch's 'Candid Account' vs. Eighteenth-Century Theories of the Spleen," *Mosaic* 22 (1989). In addition, Finch's work appears in Rogers's own anthology, *Before Their Time: Six Women Writers of the Eighteenth Century* (1979). Never previously published, the *Wellesley Manuscript Poems of*

Anne, Countess of Winchilsea, ed. J. M. Ellis d'Alessandro, became available to Finch scholars in 1988. A new selection with a useful introduction, *Selected Poems of Anne Finch*, ed. Denys Thompson, appeared in 1987. Elizabeth Hampsten has written the introduction, "Poems by Anne Finch," *Women's Studies* 7 (1980), and Barbara McGovern's valuable biography, *Anne Finch and Her Poetry*, was published in 1992.

One valuable critical study is Charles H. Hinnant, *The Poetry of Anne Finch: An Essay in Interpretation* (1994). Discussions of Finch's writings are also included in Hilda Smith, *Reason's Disciples* (1982); Ann Messenger, *His and Hers: Essays in Restoration and Eighteenth-Century Literature* (1986); Ruth Salvaggio, *Enlightened Absence: Neoclassical Configurations of the Feminine* (1988); Harriette Andreadis, *Sappho in Early Modern England: Female Same-Sex Literary Erotics, 1550–1714* (2001); and Ann Messenger, *Pastoral Tradition and the Female Talent: Studies in Augustan Poetry* (2001). Other useful articles include Lucy Brashear, "Finch's 'The Bird and the Arras,' " *Explicator* (1981); Ann Messenger, "Publishing without Perishing: Lady Winchilsea's Miscellany Poems of 1713," *Restoration* (1981); Dorothy Mermin, "Women Becoming Poets: Katherine Philips, Aphra Behn, Anne Finch," *ELH* 57 (1990); Jean Mallinson, "Anne Finch: A Woman Poet and the Tradition" in *Gender at Work: Four Women Writers of the Eighteenth Century* (1990), ed. Messenger; Charles H. Hinnant, "Song and Speech in Anne Finch's 'To the Nightingale,' " *Studies in English Literature, 1500–1900* 31 (1991); Hinnant, "Feminism and Femininity: A Reconsideration of Anne Finch's 'Ardelia's Answer to Ephelia,' " *The Eighteenth Century* 33 (1992); Douglas Lane Patey, "Anne Finch, John Dyer, and the Georgic Syntax of Nature," in *Augustan Subjects: Essays in Honor of Martin C. Battestin* (1997), ed. Albert J. Rivero; Jennifer Keith, "The Poetics of Anne Finch," *Studies in English Literature 1500–1900* 38 (1998); Peter Knox-Shaw, "Jane Austen's nocturnal and Anne Finch," *English Language Notes* 39 (2002); Martha Rainbolt, "Women Naming Women: The Use of Sobriquets by Aphra Behn, Anne Finch, and Katherine Philips," *Names* 50 (2002); and Christopher Miller, "Staying Out Late: Anne Finch's Poetics of Evening," *Studies in English Literature 1500–1900* 45 (2005).

Mary E. Wilkins Freeman

Of the six volumes of short stories Freeman published, the two best known are *A Humble Romance* (1887) and *A New England Nun* (1891). Three collections of Freeman's work are *The Best Stories of Mary E. Wilkins* (1927), ed. Henry W. Lanier; *Selected Stories of Mary E. Wilkins Freeman* (1983), ed. Marjorie Pryse;

and *The Uncollected Stories of Mary Wilkins Freeman* (1992), ed. Mary Reichardt. Freeman also wrote a number of novels, including *Pembroke* (1894), *By the Light of the Soul* (1906), *The Portion of Labor* (1901), and *The Shoulders of Atlas* (1908). A volume of Freeman's correspondence, *The Infant Sphinx: The Collected Letters of Mary E. Wilkins Freeman*, ed. Brent L. Kendrick, appeared in 1985.

Full-length critical/biographical studies include Edward Foster, *Mary E. Wilkins Freeman* (1956); Abigail Ann Hamblen, *The New England Art of Mary E. Wilkins Freeman* (1966); and Perry D. Westbrook, *Mary Wilkins Freeman* (1967). See also Marjorie Pryse, "Mary E. Wilkins Freeman," in *Modern American Women Writers* (1990), ed. Elaine Showalter. In recent years, Mary R. Reichardt has published widely on Freeman, see her useful full-length study *A Web of Relationship: Women in the Short Stories of Mary Wilkins Freeman* (1992) and her essays "Mary Wilkins Freeman: One Hundred Years of Criticism," *Legacy: A Journal of Nineteenth-Century American Women Writers* 4 (1987); "A Checklist of Uncollected Short Fiction by Mary Wilkins Freeman," *American Literary Realism, 1870–1910* 23 (1990), co-authored with Philip Eppard; " 'Friend of My Heart': Women as Friends and Rivals in the Short Stories of Mary Wilkins Freeman," *American Literary Realism, 1870–1910* 22 (1990); and "The Web of Self-Strangulation: Mothers, Daughters, and the Question of Marriage in the Short Stories of Mary Wilkins Freeman," in *Joinings and Disjoinings: The Significance of Marital Status in Literature* (1991), ed. JoAnna Stephens Mink and Janet Doubler Ward. Among other articles, especially useful are Ann Douglas Wood, "The Literature of Impoverishment: The Women Local Colorists in America, 1865–1914," *Women's Studies* 1 (1972); Alice G. Brand, "Mary Wilkins Freeman: Misanthropy as Propaganda," *New England Quarterly* 50 (1977); Joseph E. McElrath Jr., "The Artistry of Mary E. Wilkins Freeman's 'The Revolt,' " *Studies in Short Fiction* 17 (1980); Sarah W. Sherman, "The Great Goddess in New England: Mary Wilkins Freeman's 'Christmas Jenny,' " *Studies in Short Fiction* 17 (1980); Kate Gardner, "The Subversion of Genre in the Short Stories of Mary Wilkins Freeman," *The New England Quarterly* 65 (1992); Martha J. Cutter, "Beyond Stereotypes: Mary Wilkins Freeman's Radical Critique of Nineteenth-Century Cults of Femininity," *Women's Studies* 21 (1992); and Monika M. Elbert, "Mary Wilkins Freeman's Devious Women, *Harper's Bazaar*, and the Rhetoric of Advertising," *Essays in Literature* 20 (1993).

Margaret Fuller

Fuller's works include *Summer on the Lakes* (1844), *Woman in the Nineteenth Century* (1845), *Papers on Literature and Art* (1846), and numerous magazine essays and newspaper articles, some of which appear in the posthumous collections *At Home and Abroad* (1856) and *Life Without and Life Within* (1859), both edited by her brother, Arthur B. Fuller. *The Letters of Margaret Fuller*, 5 vols. (1983–88), was edited by Robert N. Hudspeth. The somewhat bowdlerized *Memoirs of Margaret Fuller Ossoli* (1852), was prepared by W. H. Channing, James Freeman Clarke, and Ralph Waldo Emerson; however, accurate and substantial recent collections of Fuller's writings are Bell Gale Chevigny, *The Woman and the Myth: Margaret Fuller's Life and Writings* (1994); *The Portable Margaret Fuller* (1994); and *Women in the Nineteenth Century and Other Writings* (1994). Biographies include Joseph J. Deiss, *The Roman Years of Margaret Fuller* (1969); Charles Capper, *Margaret Fuller: An American Romantic Life* (1992); Donna Dickenson, *Margaret Fuller: Writing a Woman's Life* (1993); and Eve Kornfield, *Margaret Fuller: A Brief Biography with Documents* (1997). The most comprehensive account of her life is Charles Capper's two-volume biography, *Margaret Fuller: An American Romantic Life*, vol. 1: *The Private Years* (1994), and vol. 2: *The Public Years* (2002).

Full-length critical studies include Paula Blanchard, *Margaret Fuller, from Transcendentalism to Revolution* (1978); Margaret Allen, *The Achievement of Margaret Fuller* (1979); Marie Urbanski, *Margaret Fuller's "Woman in the 19th Century": A Literary Study of Form and Content, of Sources and Influence* (1980); and Jeffery Steele, *Transfiguring America: Myth, Ideology, and Mourning in Margaret Fuller's Writing* (2001). For a discussion of Fuller's relation to Romanticism, see Julie K. Ellison, *Delicate Subjects: Romanticism, Gender, and the Ethics of Understanding* (1990). Another useful discussion of Fuller appears in Theresa F. Nicolay, *Gender Roles, Literary Authority, and Three American Writers: Anne Dudley Bradstreet, Mercy Otis Warren, and Margaret Fuller.* Joel Myerson has published annotated bibliographies of secondary material (1977) and of Fuller's own work (1978); more recently he also edited *Margaret Fuller: An Annotated Bibliography of Criticism, 1983–1995* (1998).

Elizabeth Gaskell

The standard edition of Gaskell's novels, including *Mary Barton* (1848), *Cranford* (1853), *Ruth* (1853), *North and South* (1955), *Sylvia's Lovers* (1863), and *Wives and Daughters* (1866), is *The Works of Mrs. Gaskell* (1906–20), with an introduction by A. W. Ward. In addition, much of this fiction, along with Gaskell's *The Life of Charlotte Brontë* (1857), has been published in modern editions, most notably a Penguin series with good critical introductions. The author's

letters appear in *The Letters of Mrs. Gaskell* (rev. 1997), ed. J. A. V. Chapple and Arthur Pollard; *Letters of Mrs. Gaskell and Charles Eliot Norton, 1855–1865* (1973), ed. with an introduction by Jane Whitehill; and *Elizabeth Gaskell: A Portrait in Letters* (1980), ed. J. A. V. Chapple. There are many biographies, the best of which is Winifred Gérin, *Elizabeth Gaskell* (1976). A helpful recent biography is Jennifer Uglow, *Elizabeth Gaskell: A Habit of Stories*, (1993).

Full-length critical studies include Aina Rubenius, *The Woman Question in Mrs. Gaskell's Life and Works* (1950); A. B. Hopkins, *Elizabeth Gaskell: Her Life and Work* (1952); Edgar Wright, *Mrs. Gaskell: The Basis for Reassessment* (1965); Margaret Ganz, *Elizabeth Gaskell: The Artist in Conflict* (1969); J. G. Sharps, *Mrs. Gaskell's Observation and Invention* (1970); Angus Easson, *Elizabeth Gaskell* (1979); Enid Lowry Duthie, *The Themes of Elizabeth Gaskell* (1980); Patsy Stoneman, *Elizabeth Gaskell* (1987); Hilary Margo Schor, *Scheherezade in the Marketplace: Elizabeth Gaskell and the Victorian Novel* (1992); and Linda K. Hughes and Michael Lund, *Victorian Publishing and Mrs. Gaskell's Work* (1999). Angus Easson edited *Elizabeth Gaskell: The Critical Heritage* in 1991. Nina Auerbach takes a feminist approach to *Cranford* in *Communities of Women: An Idea in Fiction* (1978); and valuable discussions of Gaskell appear in Pauline Nestor, *Female Friendships and Communities: Charlotte Brontë, George Eliot, Elizabeth Gaskell* (1985); Margaret Homans, *Bearing the Word: Language and Female Experience in Nineteenth-Century Women's Writing* (1986); Rosemarie Bodenheimer, *The Politics of Story in Victorian Social Fiction* (1988); and Elsie B. Michie, *Outside the Pale: Cultural Exclusion, Gender Difference, and the Victorian Woman Writer* (1993). Useful reference works are Robert L. Selig, *Elizabeth Gaskell: A Reference Guide* (1977), and Jeffrey Welch, *Elizabeth Gaskell: An Annotated Bibliography, 1929–1975* (1977).

Charlotte Perkins Gilman

A collection of Gilman's fiction is *The Charlotte Perkins Gilman Reader: The Yellow Wallpaper, and Other Fiction* (1980), ed. and with an introduction by Ann J. Lane, who also wrote the introduction for the 1979 Pantheon edition of *Herland* (1915). Another volume of Gilman's collected fiction is *"The Yellow Wall-Paper" and Selected Stories of Charlotte Perkins Gilman* (1994), ed. Denise D. Knight, and a recent collection of Gilman's nonfiction is *Charlotte Perkins Gilman: A Nonfiction Reader* (1991), ed. Larry Ceplair. Catherine J. Golden has edited *The Yellow Wall-Paper: A Sourcebook and a Critical Edition* (2004). Other reprinted works include the Feminist Press edition of the 1892 *The Yellow Wallpaper* (1973), with an afterword

by Elaine R. Hedges; *Women and Economics: A Study of the Economic Relation between Men and Women as a Factor in Social Evolution* (1898); *The Home, Its Work and Influence* (1903); and *The Man-Made World; or, Our Androcentric Culture* (1911). Of great interest is the writer's autobiography, *The Living of Charlotte Perkins Gilman* (1935). *The Diaries of Charlotte Perkins Gilman*, ed. Knight, appeared in two volumes in 1994, and in 1995 Mary A. Hill edited *A Journey from Within: The Love Letters of Charlotte Perkins Gilman, 1897–1900*. The standard biography is Lane, *To "Herland" and Beyond: The Life and Work of Charlotte Perkins Gilman* (1990).

Critical discussions of Gilman appear in Janet Beer, *Kate Chopin, Edith Wharton, and Charlotte Perkins Gilman: Studies in Short Fiction* (1997), and Thomas Peyser, *Utopia and Cosmopolis: Globalization in the Era of American Literary Realism* (1998). There are a number of useful collections of critical essays, including *Charlotte Perkins Gilman: The Woman and Her Work* (1989), ed. Sheryl L. Meyering; *Critical Essays on Charlotte Perkins Gilman* (1992), ed. Joanne B. Karpinski; *The Captive Imagination: A Casebook on "The Yellow Wallpaper"* (1992), ed. Catherine Golden; *A Very Different Story: Studies in the Fiction of Charlotte Perkins Gilman*, ed. Val Gough and Jill Rudd (1998); *Charlotte Perkins Gilman: Optimist Reformer* (1999); and *Charlotte Perkins Gilman and Her Contemporaries: Literary and Intellectual Contexts* (2004), ed. Cynthia J. Davis and Denise D. Knight. Helpful feminist studies are Carl N. Degler, "Charlotte Perkins Gilman on the Theory and Practice of Feminism," *American Quarterly* (1956); Mary A. Hill, "Charlotte Perkins Gilman: A Feminist Struggle with Womanhood," *Massachusetts Review* 23 (1980); Hill, *Charlotte Perkins Gilman: The Making of a Radical Feminist, 1860–1896*; Laura E. Donaldson, "The Eve of De-Struction: Charlotte Perkins Gilman and the Feminist Recreation of Paradise," *Women's Studies* 16 (1989); and Georgia Johnston, "Exploring Lack and Absence in the Body / Text: Charlotte Perkins Gilman Prewriting Irigaray," *Women's Studies* 21 (1992). Gilman is also discussed in *Modern American Women Writers* (1991), ed. Elaine Showalter. Two useful resources are Gary Scharnhorst, *Charlotte Perkins Gilman: A Bibliography* (1985), and Julie Bates Dock, "'But One Expects That': Charlotte Perkins Gilman's 'The Yellow Wallpaper' and the Shifting Light of Scholarship," *PMLA* (January 1996).

Frances E. W. Harper

Harper's published works include *Poems on Miscellaneous Subjects* (1854), *Poems* (1871), *Sketches of Southern Life* (1872), *Iola Leroy; or, Shadows Uplifted* (1892), and *The Martyr of Ala-*

bama and Other Poems (c. 1894). Her best-known work, *Iola Leroy*, was reissued in 1988 by the Schomburg Library of Nineteenth-Century Black Women Writers, with an introduction by Frances Smith Foster, and is also included in two collections: *Three Classic African-American Novels* (1990), ed. and with an introduction by Henry Louis Gates Jr., and *The African-American Novel in the Age of Reaction: Three Classics* (1992), ed. and with an introduction by William L. Andrews. *Minnie's Sacrifice, Sowing and Reaping and Trial and Triumph: Three Rediscovered Novels by Frances E. W. Harper* was published in 2000. *The Complete Poems of Frances E. W. Harper*, ed. Maryemma Graham, appeared in 1988, and *A Brighter Coming Day: A Frances Ellen Watkins Harper Reader*, ed. Frances Smith Foster, was issued in 1990. For a comprehensive biography of Harper, see Melba Joyce Boyd, *Discarded Legacy* (1994). Harper is also discussed in four broad studies: William H. Robinson Jr., *Early Black American Poets* (1971); Joan Sherman, *Invisible Poets: Afro-American Women of the Nineteenth Century* (1974); Gloria Hull, "Afro-American Women Poets: A Bio-Critical Survey," in *Shakespeare's Sisters* (1979), ed. Sandra M. Gilbert and Susan Gubar; and John Ernest, *Resistance and Reformation in Nineteenth-Century African-American Literature* (1995). She is also discussed within a narrower context by Elizabeth Ammons, *Conflicting Stories: American Women Writers at the Turn into the Twentieth Century* (1991).

A valuable essay is Patricia L. Hill, "Let Me Make the Songs for the People: A Study of Frances W. Harper's Poetry," *Black American Literature Forum* 15 (1981). See also the interesting essays by Paul Lauter, "Is Frances Ellen Watkins Harper Good Enough to Teach?" *Legacy* 5 (1988); Farah Jasmine Griffin, "Frances Ellen Watkins Harper in the Reconstruction South," *SAGE: A Scholarly Journal on Black Women* (1988); Claudia Tate, "Allegories of Black Female Desire; or, Rereading Nineteenth-Century Sentimental Narratives of Black Female Authority," in *Changing Our Words: Essays on Criticism, Theory, and Writing by Black Women* (1989), ed. Cheryl A. Wall; Lauren Berlant, "The Queen of America Goes to Washington City: Harriet Jacobs, Frances Harper, Anita Hill," *American Literature* 65 (1993); Shirley Wilson Logan, "Black Speakers, White Representations: Frances Ellen Watkins Harper and the Construction of a Public Persona," *African American Rhetoric(s): Interdisciplinary Perspectives*, ed. Elaine B. Richardson and Ronald L. Jackson (2004).

Eliza Haywood

Haywood's works include *The Fortunate Foundlings* (1744) and *The History of Miss Betsy Thoughtless*, with an introduction by Dale Spen-

der (1986). Mary Anne Schofield has introduced two collections of Haywood's novels: *The Masquerade Novels of Eliza Haywood* (1986), which includes *The Masqueraders, Fantomina, The Fatal Secret*, and *Idalia*, and *Four Novels of Eliza Haywood: Photoreprints* (1983). *The Plays of Eliza Haywood*, ed. Valerie C. Rudolph, appeared in 1983. Included in a recent flurry of modern editions are: *Selections from "The Female Spectator*," ed. Gabrielle M. Firmager (1993); *Love in Excess, or The Fatal Injury*, ed. David Oakleaf (1996); *The History of Miss Betsy Thoughtless*, ed. Christine Blouch (1998); *Adventures of Ivoaas, Princess of Ijaveo*, ed. Earla Wilputte (1999); *Anti-Pamela, or Feigned Innocence Detected* (2004), ed. Catherine Ingrassia. In 2000, the three-volume *Selected Works of Eliza Haywood* appeared. For a biography, see Mary Anne Schofield, *Eliza Haywood* (1985).

An interesting full-length study of Haywood is Juliette Merritt, *Beyond Spectacle: Eliza Haywood's Female Spectators* (2004). Kirsten T. Saxton and Rebecca P. Bocchicchio have edited a collection of essays titled *The Passionate Fictions of Eliza Haywood: Essays on Her Life and Work* (2000). Other critical articles include Schofield, "Exposé of the Popular Heroine: The Female Protagonists of Eliza Haywood," *Studies in Eighteenth-Century Culture* 12 (1983); Kathryn Shevelow, "Re-Writing the Moral Essay: Eliza Haywood's Female Spectator," *Reader* 13 (1985); April London, "Placing the Female: The Metonymic Garden in Amatory and Pious Narrative, 1700–1740," in *Fetter'd or Free? British Women Novelists, 1670–1815* (1986), ed. Mary Anne Schofield; Christine Blouch, "Eliza Haywood and the Romance of Obscurity," *Studies in English Literature, 1500–1900* 31 (1991); Polly Stevens Fields, "Manly Vigor and Women's Wit: Dialoguing Gender in the Plays of Eliza Haywood," in *Compendious Conversations: The Method of Dialogue in the Early Enlightenment* (1992), ed. Kevin L. Cope; William B. Warner, "Formulating Fiction: Romancing the General Reader in Early Modern Britain," in *Cultural Institutions of the Novel*, ed. Deidre Lynch and Warner (1996); Karen Haywood, "Eliza Haywood and the Gender of Print," *Eighteenth Century: Theory and Interpretation* 38 (1997); and Kathryn R. King, "Spying upon the Conjurer: Haywood, Curiosity, and 'the Novel' in the 1720s," *Studies in the Novel* 30 (1998).

Felicia Hemans

Poems, by Felicia Dorothea Browne appeared in 1808 when its author was just fifteen; she followed this volume with a number of other publications, including her two most acclaimed collections, *The Forest Sanctuary; and Other Poems* (1825) and *Records of Women: with Other Poems* (1828). A seven-volume edition of her complete works appeared posthumously in

1839. A useful modern edition is *Felicia Hemans: Selected Poems, Letters, Reception Materials* (2000), ed. Susan Wolfson.

Biographical and critical material can be found in Angela Leighton, *Victorian Women Poets: Writing Against the Heart* (1992). Further critical discussion of Hemans appears in Marlon Ross, *The Contours of Masculine Desire: Romanticism and the Rise of Women's Poetry* (1989), and Norma Clarke, *Ambitious Heights: Writing, Friendship, Love: The Jewsbury Sisters, Felicia Hemans, and Jane Welsh Carlyle* (1990). An excellent collection of essays is *Felicia Hemans: Reimagining Poetry in the Nineteenth Century* (2001), ed. Nanora Sweet and Julie Melnyk.

Mary Sidney Herbert, Countess of Pembroke
Herbert's published works include *The Psalms of Sir Philip Sidney and the Countess of Pembroke* (1963), ed. J. C. A. Rathmell; *Two Poems by the Countess of Pembroke* (1962), ed. Bent Juel-Jensen; *The Triumph of Death, and Other Unpublished and Uncollected Poems* (1977), ed. G. F. Waller; *The Countess of Pembroke's Antonie* (1897), ed. Alice Luce; and *The Countess of Pembroke's Emanuell*, ed. A. B. Grosart, in *Miscellanies* (1871). Her work was more recently collected in *The Collected Works of Mary Sidney Herbert, Countess of Pembroke* (1998), ed. Margaret P. Hannay, Noel J. Kinnamon, and Michael G. Brennan. Herbert is included in George Ballard, *Memoirs of Several Ladies of Great Britain* (1752), and Louisa Costello, *Memoirs of Eminent Englishwomen* (1844). Biographical materials include M. M. Bulloch, *Mary Sidney, Countess of Pembroke, an Elizabethan Historiette* (1895), and the useful Frances B. Young, *Mary Sidney, Countess of Pembroke* (1912). G. F. Waller has written the more recent *Mary Sidney, Countess of Pembroke, a Critical Study of Her Writings and Literary Milieu* (1979). Herbert's work is excerpted and discussed in *Readings in Renaissance Women's Drama: Criticism, History, and Performance, 1594–1998* (1998), ed. S. P. Cerasano and Marion Wynne-Davies. In addition, her work is discussed in Coburn Freer, "The Countess of Pembroke in a World of Words," *Style* 5 (1980); Margaret Hannay Patterson, " 'Doo What Men May Sing': Mary Sidney and the Tradition of Admonitory Dedication," in her *Silent but for the Word: Tudor Women as Patrons, Translators, and Writers of Religious Works* (1985); and Beth Wynne Fisken, " 'The Art of Sacred Parody' in Mary Sidney's Psalmes," *Tulsa Studies in Women's Literature* 8 (1989). A full-length study is Mary Ellen Lamb, *Gender and Authorship in the Sidney Circle* (1990).

Pauline Hopkins
A comprehensive collection of the novel-length fiction by Hopkins is *The Magazine Novels of Pauline Hopkins* (1988), ed. Hazel Carby which includes a useful introduction by Carby. Richard Yarborough's edition of *Contending Forces* also includes a helpful introduction.

Critical treatment of Hopkins and her work can be found in Ann Allen Schockley, "Pauline Elizabeth Hopkins: A Biographical Excursion into Obscurity," *Phylon* 33 (1972) as well as the collection of essays *The Unruly Voice: Rediscovering Pauline Elizabeth Hopkins* (1996), ed. John Cullen Greusser. Further discussion of Hopkins can be found in Carby, *Reconstructing Womanhood: The Emergence of the Afro-American Woman Novelist* (1987), and Claudia Tate, *Domestic Allegories of Political Desire* (1992).

Rebecca Cox Jackson
Jackson's work has been collected in *Gifts of Power: The Writings of Rebecca Jackson, Black Visionary, Shaker Eldress* (1981), ed. and with an introduction by Jean McMahon Humez. Richard E. Williams's biography, *Called and Chosen: The Story of Mother Rebecca Jackson and the Philadelphia Shakers*, has been edited by Cheryl Dorschner and republished in 1981. A valuable essay, occasioned by the publication of *Gifts of Power*, appears in Alice Walker's volume *In Search of Our Mothers' Gardens* (1983); and Diane Sasson's essay, "Life as Vision: The Autobiography of Mother Rebecca Jackson," appeared in *The Shaker Spiritual Narrative* (1983), ed. Sarah D. Sasson. Jackson is also discussed in Joanne Braxton, *Black Women Writing Autobiography* (1989), in Darlene Clark Hines, ed., *Black Women in America: An Historical Encyclopedia* (1993); and by Joyce L. Cherry in *African-American Authors, 1745–1945: A Bio-Bibliographical Critical Sourcebook*, ed. Emmanuel S. Nelson (2000).

Harriet Jacobs
A reprint of Jacobs's *Incidents in the Life of a Slave Girl* (1861) was edited by Walter Teller in 1973. In 1987 Jean Fagan Yellin edited an edition containing Yellin's valuable introduction and photographs of historical documents, which was reissued in 2000 to include the narrative of Harriet Jacobs's brother, John J. Jacobs. Harriet Jacobs is discussed in William L. Andrews, *To Tell a True Story: The First Century of Afro-American Autobiography, 1760–1865* (1986); Valerie Smith, *Self-Discovery and Authority in Afro-American Narrative* (1988); Sidonie Smith, "Resisting the Gaze of Embodiment: Women's Autobiography in the Nineteenth Century," in *American Women's Autobiography: Fea(s)ts of Memory* (1992), ed. Margo Culley; Frances Smith Foster, *Written by Herself: Literary Production of African American Women, 1746–1892* (1993); Karen Sanchez-Eppler, *Touching Liberty: Abolition, Feminism, and the Politics of the Body* (1993); Carla Kaplan, *The Erotics of Talk: Women's Writing and Feminist Paradigms*

(1996); and Yvonne Johnson, *Voices of African-American Women: The Use of Narrative and Authorial Voice in the Works of Harriet Jacobs, Zora Neale Hurston, and Alice Walker* (1998). Rafia Zafar and Deborah M. Garfield edited *Harriet Jacobs and "Incidents in the Life of a Slave Girl"*: *New Critical Essays* (1996), and Henry Louis Gates and Hollis Robbins edited *In Seach of Hanna Crafts: Critical Essays on* The Bondswoman's Narrative (2004). Other useful critical essays are Mary Ellen Washington, "Meditations on History: The Slave Narrative of Linda Brent," in her *Invented Lives: Narratives of Black Women, 1860–1960* (1987); Beth Maclay Doriani, "Black Womanhood in Nineteenth-Century America: Subversion and Self-Construction in Two Women's Autobiographies," *American Quarterly* 43 (1991), which discusses Jacobs and Harriet Wilson; and Kaplan, "Narrative Contracts and Emancipatory Readers: Incidents in the Life of a Slave Girl," *The Yale Journal of Criticism* 6 (1993).

Sarah Orne Jewett

Jewett's work includes *Deephaven* (1877), *A Country Doctor* (1884), *A White Heron and Other Stories* (1886), and *The Country of the Pointed Firs* (1896). Her *Stories and Tales* were published in seven volumes in 1910, but a more readily available collection, *The Best Stories of Sarah Orne Jewett* (1925), was edited in two volumes with a preface by Willa Cather. In 1988, Charles Waugh et al. edited another *The Best Stories*, with an introduction by Josephine Donovan. *The Country of the Pointed Firs, and Other Stories* was edited by Mary Ellen Chase in 1968 and reissued, with an introduction by Marjorie Pryse, in 1981. Richard Cary edited *The Uncollected Short Stories of Sarah Orne Jewett* (1971), as well as the *Sarah Orne Jewett Letters,* revised and enlarged in 1967. Critical biographies include F. O. Matthiessen, *Sarah Orne Jewett* (1929); Cary, *Sarah Orne Jewett* (1962); Margaret Thorp, *Sarah Orne Jewett* (1966); and Elizabeth Silverthorne, *Sarah Orne Jewett: A Writer's Life* (1993).

Other critical studies are Josephine Donovan, *Sarah Orne Jewett* (1980); Perry Westbrook, *Acres of Flint: Sarah Orne Jewett and Her Contemporaries* (1981); Sarah Way Sherman, *Sarah Orne Jewett: An American Persephone* (1989); Marilyn Sanders Mobley, *Folk Roots and Mythic Wings in Sarah Orne Jewett and Toni Morrison: The Cultural Functions of Narrative* (1991); Joseph Church, *Transcendent Daughters in Jewett's Country of the Painted Firs* (1995); and Margaret Roman, *Sarah Orne Jewett: Reconstructing Gender* (1997). Gwen L. Nagel has edited *Critical Essays on Sarah Orne Jewett* (1984), as well as a valuable reference guide, *Sarah Orne Jewett* (1978). Other helpful essay collections are Richard Cary, *Appreciation of Sarah Orne Jewett* (1973), and *Jewett and Her*

Contemporaries: Reshaping the Canon (1999), ed. Kren L. Kilcup and Thomas S. Edwards.

Julian of Norwich

Marion Glasscoe has edited a reliable edition of the Middle English text of Julian's *A Revelation of Divine Love* (1976), but a more readable modern version is *A Book of Showings* (1978), ed. and trans. Edmund Colledge and James Walsh. Two other editions have appeared in recent years, one edited by G. R. Crampton in 1994, which was designed for students, and another edited and translated by Julia Bolton Holloway in 2003.

P. Franklin Chambers, *Juliana of Norwich* (1955), and Paul Molinari, *Julian of Norwich* (1958), offer general introductions to her work; Robert Stone, *Middle English Prose Style* (1970), treats both Julian and Margery Kempe. More recent overviews are Grace Jantzen, *Julian of Norwich: Mystic and Theologian* (1988), and Nicholas Watson, "Julian of Norwich," *The Cambridge Companion to Medieval Women's Writing* (2003). Other useful critical works include Brant Pelphrey, *Love Was His Meaning: The Theology and Mysticism of Julian of Norwich* (1982); Jennifer P. Hummel, "God Is Our Mother": *Julian of Norwich, and the Medieval Image of Feminine Divinity* (1982); Denise N. Baker, *Julian of Norwich's Showings: From Vision to Book* (1994); and Sheila Upjohn, *Why Julian Now? A Voyage of Discovery* (1997). A useful collection is *Julian of Norwich: A Book of Essays* (1998), ed. Sandra J. McEntire. Other critical essays are Ritamary Bradley, "Mysticism in the Motherhood Similitude of Julian of Norwich," *Studia-Mystica* 8 (1985); Marion Glasscoe, "Visions and Revisions: A Further Look at the Manuscripts of Julian of Norwich," *Studies in Bibliography* 42 (1989); Lynn Staley Johnson, "The Trope of the Scribe and the Question of Literary Authority in the Works of Julian of Norwich and Margery Kempe," *Speculum* 66 (1991); Elizabeth Robertson, "Medieval Medical Views of Women and Female Spirituality in the *Ancrene Wisse* and Julian of Norwich's Showings," in *Feminist Approaches to the Body in Medieval Literature* (1993), ed. Linda Lomperis and Sarah Stanbury; and Nicholas Watson, " 'Yf Wommen Be Double Naturelly': Remaking 'Woman' in Julian of Norwich's *Revelation of Love*," *Exemplaria* 8 (1996). Mary Mason's useful article, "The Other Voice: Autobiography of Women Writers," in *Autobiography,* ed. James Olney (1980), puts Julian's work in the context of women's autobiography.

Margery Kempe

Colonel W. E. I. Butler-Bowdon edited and modernized *The Book of Margery Kempe* (1936). In 1940, Sanford Brown Meech edited a transcription of the Butler-Bowdon manuscript, which includes a prefatory note by Hope Emily

Allen; B. A. Windeatt edited an edition in 1985, while in 1996 L. Staley edited another edition designed for students.

Valuable introductions are Katharine Cholmeley, *Margery Kempe, Genius and Mystic* (1947); Martin Thornton, *Margery Kempe, an Example in the English Pastoral Tradition* (1960); Louise Collis, *Memoirs of a Medieval Woman: The Life and Times of Margery Kempe* (1964); Clarissa W. Atkinson, *Mystic and Pilgrim: The Book and the World of Margery Kempe* (1983); and Carolyn Dinshaw, "Margery Kempe," *The Cambridge Companion to Medieval Women's Writing* (2003). Three valuable full-length studies are Karma Lochrie, *Margery Kempe and Translations of the Flesh* (1991); Lynn Staley Johnson, *Margery Kempe's Dissenting Fictions* (1994); and Rosalynn Voaden, *God's Words, Women's Voices: The Discernment of Spirit in the Writings of Late-Medieval Women Visionaries* (1999). Robert Stone discusses her in his *Middle English Prose Style* (1970), as do Mary Mason in "The Other Voice: Autobiography of Women's Writers," in *Autobiography* (1980), ed. James Olney, and Hope Phyllis Weissman in "Margery Kempe in Jerusalem: *Hysterica Compassio* in the Late Middle Ages," in *Acts of Interpretation* (1982), ed. Mary J. Carruthers and Elizabeth D. Kirk. Sandra J. McEntire edited the collection *Margery Kempe: A Book of Essays* (1992). Other useful essays are François Le Saux, " 'Hir not Lettyrd': Margery Kempe and Writing," in *Writing and Culture* (1992), ed. Balz Engler; Robert C. Ross, "Oral Life, Written Text: The Genesis of the *Book of Margery Kempe*," *Yearbook of English Studies* 22 (1992); Lynn Staley Johnson, "Margery Kempe: Social Critic," *Journal of Medieval and Renaissance Studies* 22 (1992); and Wendy Harding, "Body into Text: *The Book of Margery Kempe*," in *Feminist Approaches to the Body in Medieval Literature* (1993), ed. Sarah Stansbury.

Anne Killigrew

Killigrew's work is collected in *Poems* (1686). A facsimile reproduction, with an introduction by Richard Morton, was published in 1967. A valuable essay on Killigrew's poetry is Kristina Straub, "Indecent Liberties with a Poet: Audience and the Metaphor of Rape in Killigrew's 'Upon the Saying That My Verses . . . ' and Pope's 'Arbuthnot,' " *Tulsa Studies in Women's Literature* 6 (1987). See also the discussions of Killigrew in Ann Messenger, *His and Hers: Essays in Restoration and Eighteenth-Century Literature* (1986); Elaine Hobby, *Virtue of Necessity: English Women's Writing, 1646–1688* (1988); and Harriette Andreadis, *Sappho in Early Modern England: Female Same-Sex Literary Erotics, 1550–1714* (2001).

Sarah Kemble Knight

G. P. Winthrop edited an edition of Knight's *Private Journal* in 1920 that contains Theodore Dwight's introduction to the first published edition of the journal (1825). Sidney Gunn wrote a useful biographical entry on Knight for *The Dictionary of American Biography* (1933).

Aemilia Lanyer

Lanyer's long poem, *Salve Deus Rex Judaeorum* (1611), appears as *The Poems of Shakespeare's Dark Lady* (1979), ed. and with an introduction by A. L. Rouse. Susanne Woods edited *The Poems of Aemilia Lanyer* in 1993. Some of Lanyer's work is included in *The Female Spectator* (1977), ed. Mary R. Mahl and Helene Koon. She is discussed in George Ballard, *Memoirs of Several Ladies of Great Britain* (1752); H. T. C. de la Fontaine, *The King's Musick* (1909); and Eric Blom, *Grove's Dictionary of Music and Musicians* (1954) (supplement 1961). Valuable biographical material can be found in Susanne Woods, *Lanyer: A Renaissance Woman Poet* (1999). One critical volume dedicated entirely to Lanyer's work is *Aemilia Lanyer: Gender, Genre, and the Canon* (1998), ed. Marshall Grossman. Helpful critical studies include Barbara K. Lewalski, "Of God and Good Women: The Poems of Aemilia Lanyer," in *Silent but for the Word: Tudor Women as Patrons, Translators, and Writers of Religious Works* (1985), ed. Margaret Patterson Hannay; Ann Baynes Coiro, "Writing in Service: Sexual Politics and Class Position in the Poetry of Aemilia Lanyer and Ben Jonson," *Criticism* 35 (1993); Lewalski, "Re-Writing Patriarchy and Patronage: Margaret Clifford, Anne Clifford, and Aemilia Lanyer," in *Patronage, Politics, and Literary Tradition in England, 1558–1578* (1993), ed. Cedric C. Brown; and Wendy Wall, "Our Bodies / Our Texts? Renaissance Women and the Trials of Authorship," in *Anxious Power: Reading, Writing, and Ambivalence in Narrative by Women* (1993), ed. Carol J. Singley and Susan Elizabeth Sweeney. Among much recent criticism, most noteworthy is Achsah Guibbory, "The Gospel According to Aemilia: Women and the Sacred in Aemilia Lanyer's Salve Deus Rex Judaeorum," in *Sacred and Profane: Secular and Devotional Interplay in Early Modern British Literature* (1996), ed. Helen Wilcox, Richard Todd, and Alasdair MacDonald; Lisa Schnell, " 'So Great a Difference Is There in Degree': Aemilia Lanyer and the Aims of Feminist Criticism," in *Modern Language Quarterly* 57 (1996); Hugh Jenkins, "Petitions for Absolute Retreat: Genre and Gender in the Country-House Poems of Aemilia Lanyer and Ann Finch," in his *Feigned Commonwealths: The Country-House Poem and the Fashioning of the Ideal Community* (1998); Richard Duerden, "Crossings: Class, Gender, Chiasmus, and the Cross in Aemilia Lanyer's *Salve Deus Rex Judaeorum*," in *Literature and Belief* 19 (1999); Susanne Woods, "Anne Lock and Aemilia Lanyer: a Tradition of Protestant Women Speaking," in *Form and Reform in*

Renaissance England: Essays in Honor of Barbara Kiefer Lewalski (2000), ed. Amy Boesky and Mary Thomas Crane; Marie H. Loughlin, " 'Fast Ti'd Unto Them in a Golden Chaine': Typology, Apocalypse, and Woman's Genealogy in Aemilia Lanyer's *Salve Deus Rex Judaeorum*," *Renaissance Quarterly* 53 (2000); John Rogers, "The Passion of a Female Literary Tradition: Aemilia Lanyer's *Salve Deus Rex Judaeorum*," *Huntington Library Quarterly* 63 (2000); Patricia Phillippy, "Sisters of Magdalen: Women's Mourning in Aemilia Lanyer's *Salve Deus Rex Judaeorum*," in *English Literary Renaissance* 31 (2001); Sharon Cadman Seelig, " 'To All Vertuous Ladies in Generall': Aemilia Lanyer's Community of Strong Women," in *Literary Circles and Cultural Communities in Renaissance England* (2001), ed. Claude J. Summers, Claude J. and Ted-Larry Pebworth; Colleen Shea, "Literary Authority as Cultural Criticism in Aemilia Lanyer's *The Authors Dreame*," in *English Literary Renaissance* 32 (2002); Micheline White, "A Woman with Saint Peter's Keys? Aemilia Lanyer's *Salve Deus Rex Judaeorum* (1611) and the Priestly Gifts of Women," *Criticism* 45 (2003); Pamela Joseph Benson, "The Stigma of Italy Undone: Aemilia Lanyer's Canonization of Lady Mary Sidney," in *Strong Voices, Weak History: Early Women Writers and Canons in England, France, and Italy* (2005), ed. Pamela Joseph Benson and Victoria Kirkham. Valuable discussions of Lanyer are also included in Elaine V. Beilin's *Redeeming Eve: Women Writers of the English Renaissance* (1987); Lynette McGrath, *Subjectivity and Women's Poetry in Early Modern England: Why on the Ridge Should She Desire to Go?* (2002); and Lyn Bennett, *Women Writing of Divinest Things: Rhetoric and the Poetry of Pembroke, Wroth and Lanyer* (2004).

Emma Lazarus

Poems of Emily Lazarus in Two Volumes originally appeared in 1888, although the standard edition of her work is now *Emma Lazarus: Selections from Her Poetry and Prose*, ed. Morris U. Schappes (1967). Several other titles by Lazarus have been reissued, including *An Epistle to the Hebrews*, ed. Morris Schappes (1987), and *Disraeli, the Jew: Essays by Emma Lazarus*, ed. Michael Selzer (1993).

Two somewhat dated although still helpful studies are H. E. Jacobs, *World of Emma Lazarus* (1949), and Eve Merriman, *Emma Lazarus: Woman with a Torch* (1956). More recent is Dan Vogel, *Emma Lazarus* (1980), while Jacob Rader Marcus, *The American Jewish Woman: A Documentary History* (1981), offers a useful background. Diane Lichtenstein discusses Lazarus in *Writing Their Nations: The Tradition of Nineteenth-Century American Jewish Women Writers* (1992) as well as in her entry on Lazarus in *Jewish Women in America: An Historical Encyclopedia* (1997), ed. Paula E. Hyman and Deborah Dash Moore. An important reading of her poetry is Shira Wolosky, "An American-Jewish Typology: Emma Lazarus and the Figure of Christ," *Prooftexts* 16 (1996).

Jane Lead

Lead's published works include *A Fountain of Gardens Watered by the River of Divine Pleasure and Springing Up in All Variety of Spiritual Plants* (1677–1701) and *Wars of David* (1700). Most of the studies are by Catherine F. Smith and include "A Note on Jane Lead with Selections from Her Writings," *Studia Mystica* 3; "Mysticism and Feminism: Jacob Boehme and Jane Lead," in *Women and Men: The Consequences of Power* (1977), ed. Dana V. Hiller and Robin Ann Sheets; "Jane Lead: The Feminist Mind and Art of a 17th-Century Protestant Mystic," in *Women of Spirit* (1979), ed. Rosemary Ruether and Eleanor McLaughlin; "Jane Lead: Mysticism and the Woman Clothed with the Sun," in *Shakespeare's Sisters* (1979), ed. Sandra M. Gilbert and Susan Gubar; "Jane Lead's Wisdom: Women and Prophecy in Seventeenth-Century England," in *Poetic Prophecy in Western Literature* (1984), ed. Jan Wojick and Raymond Jean Fontain; "Three Guineas: Virginia Woolf's Prophecy," in *Virginia Woolf and Bloomsbury: A Centenary Celebration* (1987), ed. Jane Marcus, which compares Woolf's prophetic writings with those of Lead; and Avra Kouffman, "Reflections on the Sacred: The Mystical Diaries of Jane Lead and Ann Bathurst," in *Things of the Spirit: Women Writers Constructing Spirituality* (2004), ed. Kristina K. Groover; and Theresa D. Kemp, " 'Here must a beheading go before': The Antirationalist Androgynist Theosophy of Jane Lead's *Revelation of Revelations*," *CLIO* 34 (2005).

Amy Levy

Levy produced three volumes of poetry: *Xantippe and Other Verse* (1881), *A Minor Poet and Other Poems* (1884), and *A London Plane-Tree and Other Verse* (1889). Her prose includes the novels *Reuben Sachs* (1888), *Miss Meredith* (1889), and *Romance of a Shop* (1889). A modern edition of her work is *The Complete Novels and Selected Writings of Amy Levy, 1861–1889* (1993), ed. Melvyn New. A biography is Linda Hunt Beckman, *Amy Levy: Her Life and Letters* (2000).

Cynthia Scheinberg discusses Levy in *Women's Poetry and Religion in Victorian England: Jewish Identity and Christian Culture* (2000). Useful essays on Levy include Scheinberg, "Canonizing the Jew: Amy Levy's Challenge to Victorian Poetic Identity," *Victorian Studies* 39 (1996); Emma Francis, "Amy Levy: Contradictions? Feminism and Semitic Discourse," *Women's Poetry, Late Romantic to Late Victorian: Gender and Genre, 1830–1900* (1999), ed. Isobel Armstrong and Virginia Blain;

and Ana Parejo Vadillo, "Phenomena in Flux: The Aesthetics and Politics of Traveling in Modernity," *Women's Experience of Modernity, 1875–1945* (2002), ed. Ann Ardis and Leslie Lewis.

Adah Isaacs Menken

Although Menken's one book of poetry, *Infelicia* (1868), has never been reissued, several of her poems appear in recent anthologies, including *Judith, Myself* and *Hear, O Israel!* in *The American Jewish Woman: A Documentary History* (1981), ed. Jacob R. Marcus; *Judith* in *American Women Poets of the Nineteenth Century* (1992), ed. Cheryl Walker; and *Drifts that Bar My Door* in *Four Centuries of Jewish Women's Spirituality* (1992), ed. Ellen Umansky and Dianne Ashton. Two biographies are Paul Lewis, *Queen of the Plaza: A Biography of Adah Isaacs Menken* (1964), and Wold Mankowitz, *Mazeppa: The Lives, Loves and Legends of Adah Isaacs Menken* (1982). Alan Ackerman contributed an entry on Menken in *Jewish Women in America: An Historical Encyclopedia* (1997), ed. Paula E. Hyman and Deborah Dash Moore. Further critical treatment can be found in the introduction by Umansky and Ashton to Part II of *Four Centuries of Jewish Women's Spirituality* (1992) and Shira Wolosky, "Women's Bibles: Biblical Interpretation in Nineteenth-Century American Women's Poetry," *Poetry and Public Discourse, The Cambridge History of American Literature*, vol. 3 (1994), ed. Sacvan Bercovitch.

Alice Meynell

Meynell's collected poems appear in *The Poems of Alice Meynell* (1923). *Alice Meynell, Prose and Poetry* (1947) is a centenary volume edited by Frederick Page, with a biographical and critical introduction by Vita Sackville-West. A centenary collection of her essays, with an introduction by Sir Francis Meynell, was reprinted in 1970. Another selection of her essays, edited and introduced by P. M. Fraser, is *The Wares of Autolycus* (1965).

For useful biographical information, see Viola Meynell, *Alice Meynell: A Memoir* (1929), and June Badeni, *The Slender Tree: A Life of Alice Meynell* (1981). A feminist approach is represented by Beverly Ann Schlack, "The 'Poetess of Poets': Alice Meynell Rediscovered," *Women's Studies* 7 (1980). Critical studies include John S. Anson, " 'The Wind Is Blind': Power and Constraint in the Poetry of Alice Meynell," *Studia Mystica* 9 (1986); Shelly J. Crisp, "Meynell's 'The Return to Nature': Histories of Modern Poetry," *The Explicator* 50 (1991); Sharon Smulders, "Feminism, Pacifism, and the Ethics of War: The Politics and Poetics of Alice Meynell's War Verse," *English Literature in Transition* 36 (1993); Maria Frawley, "Modernism and Maternity: Alice Meynell and the Politics of

Motherhood," in *Unmanning Modernism: Gendered Re-readings* (1997), ed. Elizabeth Jane Harrison and Shirley Peterson; Talia Schaffer, "Writing a Public Self: Alice Meynell's 'Unstable equilibrium'," in *Women's Experience of Modernity, 1875–1945* (2003), ed. Ann L. Ardis and Leslie W. Lewis; Vanessa Furse Jackson, " 'Tides of the Mind': Restraint and Renunciation in the Poetry of Alice Meynell," *Victorian Poetry* 36 (1998); Maria Frawley, " 'The Tides of the Mind': Alice Meynell's Poetry of Perception," *Victorian Poetry* 38 (2000); Talia Schaffer, "A Tethered Angel: The Martyrology of Alice Meynell," *Victorian Poetry* 38 (2000); and Kathleen Anderson, " 'I Make the Whole World Answer to My Art': Alice Meynell's Poetic Identity," *Victorian Poetry* 41 (2003). See also Angela Leighton's chapter on Meynell in her *Victorian Women Poets: Writing against the Heart* (1992), and Ana Parejo Vadillo's discussion of Meynell in her *Women Poets and Urban Aestheticism: Passengers of Modernity* (2005).

Lady Mary Wortley Montagu

Lord J. S. W. Wharncliffe, Montagu's great grandson, edited *The Letters and Works of Lady Mary Wortley Montagu* (1837). A modern edition of the *Complete Letters* is edited by Robert Halsband (1965), who also edited Montagu's *The Nonsense of Common Sense* (1947), and, with Isobel Grundy, *Essays and Poems of Lady Mary Wortley Montagu* (1977). A new edition of *Letters* was published by Everyman's Library in 1992; *Turkish Embassy Letters* appeared in 1993, edited by Malcolm Jack, and with an introduction by Anita Desai; and in 1996 Grundy published a new edition of the *Romance Letters*. Halsband also wrote a definitive biography, *The Life of Lady Mary Wortley Montagu* (1956); Grundy published another major biography in 1999, *Lady Mary Wortley Montagu: Comet of the Enlightenment*. Cynthia Lowenthal's *Lady Mary Wortley Montagu and the Eighteenth-Century Familiar Letter* (1994) is also a useful full-length study.

Critical articles include two by Isobel Grundy: "The Politics of Female Authorship: Lady Mary Wortley Montagu's Reaction to the Printing of Her Poems," *The Book Collector* (1982), and " 'Trash, Trumpery, and Idle Time': Lady Mary Wortley Montagu and Fiction," *Eighteenth-Century Fiction* 5 (1993). See also Jill Rubenstein, "Women's Biography as a Family Affair: Lady Louisa Stuart's 'Biographical Anecdotes' of Lady Wortley Montagu," *Prose Studies: History, Theory, Criticism* 9 (1986); Cynthia Lowenthal, "The Veil of Romance: Lady Mary's Embassy Letters," *Eighteenth-Century Life* 14 (1990); Cynthia Wall, "Editing Desire: Pope's Correspondence with (and without) Lady Mary," *Philological Quarterly* 71 (1992); and Jill Campbell, "Lady Mary Wortley Montagu and the Historical

Machinery of Female Identity," *History, Gender, and Eighteenth-Century Literature* (1994), ed. Beth Fowkes Tobin.

Hannah More
More wrote copious plays, poems, educational tracts, and pieces of social commentary, which were collected and published posthumously in the two-volume *Works of Hannah More* (1835). For a modern biography, see Charles H. Ford, *Hannah More: A Critical Biography*. Useful criticism includes Elizabeth Kowalski-Wallace, *Their Fathers' Daughters: Hannah More, Maria Edgeworth, and Patriarchal Complicity* (1991), and Patricia Demers, *The World of Hannah More* (1996).

Sarah Wentworth Morton
My Mind and Its Thoughts, in Sketches, Fragments, and Essays was reprinted with an introduction by W. K. Bottorff in 1975. The standard biography is Emily Pendleton and Milton Ellis, *Philenia: The Life and Works of Sarah Wentworth Morton, 1759–1846* (1931).

Martha Moulsworth
An edition of Moulsworth's text was edited, with annotations, analysis, and contextual discussion, by Robert C. Evans and Barbara Wiedemann as *"My Name Was Martha": A Renaissance Woman's Autobiographical Poem* (1993). For further critical discussion of her work, see *"The Muses Females Are": Martha Moulsworth and Other Women Writers of the English Renaissance* (1995), ed. Evans and Ann C. Little. See also Sara H. Mendleson, "Stuart Women's Diaries and Occasional Memoirs," *Women in English Society, 1500–1800* (1985), ed. Mary Prior, and *Her Own Life: Autobiographical Writings by Seventeenth-Century Englishwomen* (1989), ed. Elspeth Graham et al.

Judith Sargent Murray
The Gleaner was reprinted with an introduction by Nina Baym in 1992, while *Selected Writings* (1995), ed. Sharon M. Harris, also offers useful commentary on Murray's work. The standard biography is Vena Bernadette Field, *Constantia: A Study in the Life and Work of Judith Sargent Murray, 1751–1820* (1931).

Florence Nightingale
Lynn McDonald has recently edited *The Collected Works of Florence Nightingale* (2001). Nightingale's work is also available in *Florence Nightingale in Rome: Letters Written by Florence Nightingale in Rome in the Winter of 1847–1848* (1981), ed. Mary Keele; and *Cassandra*, which originally appeared in the appendices of Ray Strachey's *The Cause: A Short History of the Women's Movement in Great Britain* (1928), which has been published separately by the Feminist Press (1978), ed. Myra Stark, and which has been included in *Cassandra and Other Selections for Thought* (1992), ed. Mary Poovey. Also available are *"I Have Done My Duty": Florence Nightingale in the Crimean War, 1854–58* (1987), ed. Sue M. Goldie; *Notes on Hospitals: Florence Nightingale on Hospital Reform* (1989), ed. Charles E. Rosenberg; *Ever Yours, Florence Nightingale: Selected Letters* (1990), ed. Martha Vicinus and Bea Merngarrd; *Notes on Nursing: What It Is and What It Is Not* (1992), ed. Barbara Stevens Barnum; and *Selections for Thought* (1994), ed. Michael D. Calabria and Janet A. Macrae. Biographies include Sir Edward Tyas Cook, *The Life of Florence Nightingale* (1913); Cecil Woodham-Smith, *Florence Nightingale, 1820–1910* (1951); Elspeth Huxley, *Florence Nightingale* (1975); and Monica E. Baly, *Florence Nightingale and the Nursing Legacy* (1986), which is also a study of nursing in Great Britain.

Lytton Strachey wrote a famous essay on Nightingale in *Eminent Victorians* (1918), and more recently she is discussed in George Pickering, *Creative Malady* (1974), and in Mary Poovey, *Uneven Developments: The Ideological Work of Gender in Mid-Victorian England* (1988). Two full-length studies are Nancy Boyd, *Josephine Butler, Octavia Hill, Florence Nightingale: Three Victorian Women Who Changed Their World* (1982), and F. B. Smith, *Florence Nightingale: Reputation and Power* (1982). A useful collection of essays is *Florence Nightingale and Her Era: A Collection of New Scholarship* (1990), ed. Vern Bullough, Bonnie Bullough, and Marietta P. Stanton. A valuable feminist essay is Elaine Showalter, "Florence Nightingale's Feminist Complaint: Women, Religion, and Suggestions for Thought," *Signs* 6 (1981), and three recent interesting essays are George P. Landow, "Aggressive (Re) Interpretations of the Female Sage: Florence Nightingale's Cassandra," in *Victorian Sages and Cultural Discourse: Renegotiating Gender and Power* (1990), ed. Thais E. Morgan; Showalter, "Miranda and Cassandra: The Discourse of the Feminist Intellectual," in *Tradition and the Talents of Women* (1991), ed. Florence Howe; and Katherine V. Snyder, "From Novel to Essay: Gender and Revision in Florence Nightingale's 'Cassandra,'" in *The Politics of the Essay: Feminist Perspectives* (1993), ed. Ruth Ellen Boetcher Joeres and Elizabeth Mittman.

Katherine Philips
Philips's poems appear in *Poems by the Most Deservedly Admired Mrs. Katherine Philips, the Matchless Orinda* (1669); *Selected Poems* (1904–05), ed. L. I. Guiney; *Minor Poets of the Caroline Period*, vol. 1 (1905), ed. George Saintsbury. The definitive *Collected Works of Katherine Philips, the "Matchless Orinda"*

appeared in 1990; Patrick Thomas edited vols. 1 and 2 (poems and letters), and G. Greer and R. Little edited vol. 3 (translations). A facsimile edition of *Poems* (1667) was published in 1992. A full-length study is Philip Webster Sower, *The Matchless Orinda* (1931), but Philips is also included in Louisa Costello, *Memoirs of Eminent Englishwomen* (1844). Three critical essays by Claudia A. Limbert include important biographical information: "Two Poems and a Prose Receipt: The Unpublished Juvenilia of Katherine Philips," *ELR* 16 (1986); "Katherine Philips: Controlling a Life and Reputation," *South Atlantic Review* 56 (1991); and " 'The Unison of Well-Tun'd Hearts': Katherine Philips' Friendships with Male Writers," *English Language Notes* 29 (1991). Other useful discussions include Lucy Brashear, "The Forgotten Legacy of the 'Matchless Orinda,' " *Anglo-Welsh Review* 65; Catherine Cole Mambretti, " 'Fugitive Papers': A New Orinda Poem and Problems in Her Canon," *Papers of the Bibliographical Society of America* 71; Fidelis Morgan, *The Female Wits* (1981); Elizabeth H. Hagerman, "Katherine Philips: The Matchless Orinda," in *Women Writers of the Renaissance and Reformation* (1987), ed. Katharina M. Wilson; Harriette Andreadis, "The Sapphic Platonics of Katherine Philips, 1632–1644," *Signs* 15 (1989); Dorothy Mermin, "Women Becoming Poets: Katherine Philips, Aphra Behn, Anne Finch," *ELH* 57 (1990); Celia A. Easton, "Excusing the Breach of Nature's Laws: The Discourse of Denial and Disguise in Katherine Philips' Friendship Poetry," *Restoration* 14 (1990); Arlene Stiebel, "Subversive Sexuality: Masking the Erotic in Poems by Katherine Philips and Aphra Behn," in *Renaissance Discourses of Desire* (1993), ed. Claude J. Summers and Ted Larry Pebworth; Bronwen Price, " 'Spotless Passion': Public Face and Private Space in the Poetry of Katherine Philips, the 'Matchless Orinda'," *Poetry Wales* 33 (1997); Andrew Shifflett, " 'How Many Virtues Must I Hate': Katherine Philips and the Politics of Clemency," *Studies in Philology* 94 (1997); Ros Ballaster, "Restoring the Renaissance: Margaret Cavendish and Katherine Philips," in *Renaissance Configurations: Voices/Bodies/Spaces, 1580–1690* (1998), ed. Gordon McMullan; Susannah B. Mintz, "Katherine Philips and the Space of Friendship," *Restoration* 22 (1998); James Loxley, "Unfettered Organs: The Polemical Voices of Katherine Philips," in *This Double Voice: Gendered Writing in Early Modern England* (2000), ed. Danielle Clarke and Elizabeth Clarke; Harriette Andreadis, "An Emerging Sapphic Discourse: The Legacy of Katherine Philips—Literatures and Traditions of Friendship," in her *Sappho in Early Modern England: Female Same-Sex Literary Erotics, 1550–1714* (2001); Catherine Gray, "Katherine Philips and the Post-Courtly Coterie," *English Literary Renaissance* 32 (2002); Marie-Louise Coolahan, " 'We Live by Chance, and Slip into Events': Occasionality and the Manuscript Verse of Katherine Philips," *Eighteenth-Century Ireland / Iris an dá chultúr* 18 (2003); Elizabeth M.A. Hodgson, "Katherine Philips: Agent of Matchlessness," *Women's Writing* 10 (2003); Paula Loscocco, "Inventing the English Sappho: Katherine Philips's Donnean Poetry," *Journal of English and Germanic Philology* 102 (2003); Paul Trolander and Zeynep Tenger, "Katherine Philips and Coterie Critical Practices," *Eighteenth-Century Studies* 37 (2004). See also the helpful discussions of Philips in Elaine Hobby, *Virtue of Necessity: English Women's Writing, 1646–1688* (1988), and Hero Chalmers, *Royalist Women Writers, 1650–1689* (2004).

Mary Robinson

Robinson's novels include *Vancenza; or, The Dangers of Credulity* (1792), *Angelina* (1796), *Walsingham; or, The Pupil of Nature* (1797), *The Natural Daughter* (1799), and *The False Friend* (1799). Works of poetry include *Verses* (1775); three volumes of *Poems* (appearing in 1775, 1791, and 1794); a collection of sonnets, *Sappho and Phaon* (1796); and the posthumously published *The Poetical Works of the Late Mrs. Mary Robinson* (1806). Robinson also published a feminist essay, "Thoughts on the Condition of Women and on the Injustice of Mental Subordination" (1798). Her autobiography, *Memoirs of the Late Mrs. Mary Robinson, Written By Herself* (1801), appeared the year after her death. Although *Walsingham* was reprinted in 1974 (with an introduction by Gina Luria), Robinson's other works are not available in modern editions. M. J. Levy edited *Perdita: The Memoirs of Mary Robinson*, which appeared in 1994.

Most of the scholarship on Robinson focuses on her sensational life and on her circle of famous contemporaries. Biographical studies include Stanley Makower, *Perdita: A Romance in Biography* (1908); Robert Bass, *The Green Dragon: The Lives of Banastre Tarleton and Mary Robinson* (1957); Paula Byrne, *Perdita: The Life of Mary Robinson* (2004); Hester Davenport, *The Prince's Mistress: A Life of Mary Robinson* (2004); and Sarah Gristwood, *Perdita: Royal Mistress, Writer, Romantic* (2005). One comparative volume on Robinson's work is Eleanor Ty, *Empowering the Feminine: The Narratives of Mary Robinson, Jane West, and Amelia Opie, 1796–1812* (1998). Essays on Robinson and her circle include Donald H. Reiman, "The Beauty of Buttermere as Fact and Romantic Symbol," *Criticism* 26 (1984); Jan Fergus and Janice Farrar Thaddeus, "Women, Publishers, and Money, 1790–1820," *Studies in Eighteenth-Century Culture* 17 (1987); Martin J. Levy, "Coleridge,

Mary Robinson, and 'Kubla Khan,' " *The Charles Lamb Bulletin* 77 (1992); Judith Pascoe, "The Spectacular Flaneuse: Mary Robinson and the City of London," *The Wordsworth Circle* 23 (1992); Jacqueline Labbe, "Selling One's Sorrows: Charlotte Smith, Mary Robinson, and the Marketing of Poetry," *The Wordsworth Circle* 25 (1994); Eleanor Ty, "Engendering a Female Subject: Mary Robinson's (Re)presentations of the Self," *English Studies in Canada* 21 (1995); Lisa Vargo, "The Claims of 'Real Life and Manners': Coleridge and Mary Robinson," *Wordsworth Circle* 26 (1995); Daniel Robinson, "From 'Mingled Measure' to 'Ecstatic measures': Mary Robinson's Poetic Reading of *Kubla Khan*," *Wordsworth Circle* 26 (1995); Jerome McGann, "Mary Robinson and the Myth of Sappho," *Modern Language Quarterly* 56 (1995); Sharon Setzer, "Mary Robinson's Sylphid Self: The End of Feminine Self-Fashioning," *Philological Quarterly* 75 (1996); Adriana Craciun, "Violence Against Difference: Mary Wollstonecraft and Mary Robinson," *Bucknell Review* 42 (1998); Anne K. Mellor, "Mary Robinson and the Scripts of Female Sexuality," in *Representations of the Self from the Renaissance to Romanticism* (2000), ed. Patrick Coleman, Jayne Lewis, and Jill Kowalik; William D. Brewer, "Subverting Individuality: Mary Robinson and Polygraphs," in *Inventing the Individual: Romanticism and the Idea of Individualism* (2002), ed. Larry H. Peer; Claire Brock, " 'Then Smile and Know Thyself Supremely Great': Mary Robinson's Reputation and the Problem of Literary Debt," *Women's Writing* 9 (2002); Nikki Hessell, "Mary Robinson's Poetry and the London Newspapers," *Notes and Queries* 49 (2002); Anne Close, "Notorious: Mary Robinson and the Gothic," *Gothic Studies* 6 (2002); and Eugene Stelzig, " 'Spirit Divine: With Thee I'll Wonder': Mary Robinson and Coleridge in Poetic Dialogue," *Wordsworth Circle*, 35 (2004). Robinson's work is also discussed in *Re-Visioning Romanticism: British Women Writers, 1776–1837* (1994), ed. Carol Shiner Wilson and Joel Haefner, and Judith Pascoe, *Romantic Theatricality: Gender, Poetry, and Spectatorship* (1997).

Christina Rossetti

Rossetti's volumes—including *Goblin Market, and Other Poems* (1862), *The Prince's Progress* (1866), *Sing-Song* (1872), and *New Poems* (1896)—were collected in *The Poetical Works of Christina Rossetti* (1904), ed. W. M. Rossetti; and Rebecca Crump has edited three volumes of *The Complete Poems of Christina Rossetti*: vol. 1 appeared in 1979, vol. 2 in 1986, and vol. 3 in 1990. This variorum edition includes detailed textual notes. David A. Kent and P. G. Stanwood edited *Selected Prose of Christina Rossetti*, which appeared in 1998. *The Letters of Christina Ros-*

setti, edited by Antony H. Harrison, began production in four volumes in 1997. Biographical studies include Mackenzie Bell, *Christina Rossetti: A Biographical and Critical Study* (1898); Marya Zaturenska, *Christina Rossetti: A Portrait* (1949); Lona M. Packer, *Christina Rossetti* (1963); Georgina Battiscombe, *Christina Rossetti* (1965); Fredegond Shove, *Christina Rossetti: A Study* (1969); Margaret Sawtell, *Christina Rossetti: Her Life and Religion* (1974); Ralph A. Bellas, *Christina Rossetti* (1977); Georgina Battiscombe, *Christina Rossetti: A Divided Life* (1981); Kathleen Jones, *Learning Not to Be First: The Life of Christina Rossetti* (1990); and Jan Marsch, *Christina Rossetti: A Literary Biography* (1994).

Critical essays on her life and work include Virginia Woolf's appreciative " 'I Am Christina Rossetti,' " in *The Second Common Reader* (1932), as well as two pieces by Jerome J. McGann: "Christina Rossetti's Poems: A New Edition and Revaluation," *Victorian Studies* 23 (1980), and "The Religious Poetry of Christina Rossetti," *Critical Inquiry* 10 (1983). Two useful collections of essays are *The Achievement of Christina Rossetti* (1987), ed. David Kent, and *The Culture of Christina Rossetti: Female Poetics and Victorian Contexts* (1999), ed. Mary Arseneau, Antony H. Harrison, and Lorraine Janzen Kooistra. Full-length studies include Dolores Rosenblum, *Christina Rossetti: The Poetry of Endurance* (1986); Antony H. Harrison, *Christina Rossetti in Context* (1988); Katherine J. Mayberry, *Christina Rossetti and the Poetry of Discovery* (1990); Sharon Smulders, *Christina Rossetti Revisited* (1996); Kathryn Burlinson, *Christina Rossetti* (1998); Diane D. Amico, *Christina Rossetti: Faith, Gender, and Time* (1999); Alison Chapman, *The Afterlife of Christina Rossetti* (2000); Lorraine Janzen Kooistra, *Christina Rossetti and Illustration: A Publishing History* (2002); Lynda Palazzo, *Christina Rossetti's Feminist Theology* (2002); Mary Arseneau, *Recovering Christina Rossetti: Female Community and Incarnational Poetics* (2004); and Constance W. Hassett, *Christina Rossetti: The Patience of Style* (2005). Other helpful studies are Sharon Leder and Andrea Abbott, *The Language of Exclusion: The Poetry of Emily Dickinson and Christina Rossetti* (1987); Mary E. Finn, *Writing the Incommensurable: Kierkegaard, Rossetti, and Hopkins* (1992); Claudia Ottlinger, *The Death-Motif in the Poetry of Emily Dickinson and Christina Rossetti* (1996); and Eijun Senaha, *Sex, Drugs and Madness in Poetry From William Blake to Christina Rossetti: Women's Pain, Women's Pleasure* (1996). Feminist approaches are represented by a chapter in Ellen Moers, *Literary Women* (1976); by a chapter in Gilbert and Gubar, *The Madwoman in the Attic* (1979); by a section in Nina Auerbach, *Woman and the Demon* (1982); and by Sharon

Smulders, "Women's Enfranchisement in Christina Rossetti's Poetry," *Texas Studies in Literature and Language* 34 (1992). Rossetti's works also receive valuable consideration in Tricia Lootens, *Lost Saints: Silence, Gender, and Victorian Literary Canonization* (1996); Cynthia Scheinberg, *Women's Poetry and Religion in Victorian England* (2002); Kristina K. Groover, *Things of the Spirit: Women Writers Constructing Spirituality* (2004); and Alexis Easley, *First Person Anonymous: Women Writers and Victorian Print Media, 1830–70* (2004). Three useful reference works are Rebecca W. Crump, *Christina Rossetti: A Reference Guide* (1976); *The Bible and the Poetry of Christina Rossetti: A Concordance* (1979), comp. Nilda Jimenez; and Edna Kotin Charles, *Christina Rossetti: Critical Perspectives, 1862–1982* (1985).

Mary Rowlandson

Rowlandson's major work is *The Narrative of the Captivity and Restoration of Mrs. Mary Rowlandson* (1682). Richard Slotkin, *Regeneration through Violence* (1973), contains a useful discussion of her captivity. See also *Captives among the Indians* (1915), ed. Horace Kephart, and R. H. Pearce, "The Significances of the Captivity Narrative," *American Literature* 19 (1947). Among more recent critical studies of Rowlandson's life and work are Mitchell R. Breitwieser, *American Puritanism and the Defense of Mourning: Religion, Grief, and Ethnology in Mary White Rowlandson's Captivity Narrative* (1991), and Rebecca Blevins Faery, *Cartographies of Desire: Captivity, Race, and Sex in the Shaping of an American Nation* (1999). Essays include "The Captivity and Restoration of Mrs. Mary Rowlandson," in Susan Howe, *The Birth-Mark: Unsettling the Wilderness in American Literary History* (1993), and Christopher Castiglia, *Bound and Determined: Captivity, Culturecrossing, and White Womanhood from Mary Rowlandson to Patty Hearst* (1996). Useful journal articles are Tara Fitzpatrick, "The Figure of Captivity: The Cultural Work of the Puritan Captivity Narrative," *American Literary History* 3 (1991); Teresa Toulouse, "Mary Rowlandson and the 'Rhetoric of Ambiguity,' " in *Sacvan Bercovitch and the Puritan Imagination* (1992), ed. Michael Schuldiner; Toulouse, " 'My Own Credit': Strategies of (E)valuation in Mary Rowlandson's Captivity Narrative," *American Literature* 64 (1992); Pamela Lougheed, " 'Then Began He to Rant and Threaten': Indian Malice and Individual Liberty in Mary Rowlandson's Captivity Narrative," *American Literature* 74 (2002); and Tiffany Potter, "Writing Indigenous Femininity: Mary Rowlandson's Captivity Narrative," *Eighteenth-Century Studies* 36 (2003).

Olive Schreiner

Among the works published in Schreiner's lifetime, most important are *The Story of an African Farm* (1883), *Dreams* (1890), *Trooper Peter Halkett of Mashonoland* (1897), *Dream Life and Real Life* (1893, 1912), and *Woman and Labour* (1911); the last two have been reprinted by the Cassandra and Virago Presses, while *The Story of an African Farm* is available in a number of editions. *Stories, Dreams, and Allegories* (1924), *From Man to Man* (1926), and *Undine* (1919) were published posthumously and have also been reprinted. In addition, there are several collections of Schreiner's writing available: *Olive Schreiner, a Selection* (1968), ed. Uys Krige; *A Track to the Water's Edge: The Olive Schreiner Reader* (1973), ed. Howard Thurman; and *An Olive Schreiner Reader: Writings on Women and South Africa* (1987), ed. and with an introduction by Carol Barash, and an afterword by Nadine Gordimer. Yaffa Claire Drazin has edited *"My Other Self": The Letters of Olive Schreiner and Havelock Ellis, 1884–1920* (1992); and Richard Rive has edited *Olive Schreiner Letters* (1988).

Biographical and critical studies include Vera Buchanan-Gould, *Not Without Honor: The Life and Writings of Olive Schreiner* (1948); Daisy Lucie Hofman, *Olive Schreiner, Her Friends and Times* (1955); Joyce Avrech Berkman, *Olive Schreiner: Feminism on the Frontier* (1979); Ruth First and Ann Scott, *Olive Schreiner* (1980); First, *Olive Schreiner: A Biography* (1980); Douglas Ridley Beeton, *Facets of Olive Schreiner: A Manuscript Sourcebook* (1987); Berkman, *The Healing Imagination of Olive Schreiner: Beyond South African Colonialism* (1989); Carol Barash, "Virile Womanhood: Olive Schreiner's Narratives of a Master Race," in *Speaking of Gender* (1989), ed. Elaine Showalter; Gerald Monsman, *Olive Schreiner's Fiction: Landscape and Power* (1991); Cherry Clayton, *Olive Schreiner* (1997); and Carolyn Burdett, *Olive Schreiner and the Progress of Feminism: Evolution, Gender, Empire* (2001).

Mary Shelley

Although there is no collected edition of Mary Shelley's works, a number of titles have been republished. *Frankenstein* (1818) is available in many modern reprints; especially useful are the scholarly edition by James Rieger (1974) and the Norton Critical Edition edited by J. Paul Hunter (1996). *The Last Man* (1826) has been reprinted in an edition by Hugh J. Luke Jr. (1965); *Mathilda*, which the author left in manuscript, was printed for the first time by Elizabeth Nitchie (1959); and Shelley's short fiction has been edited by Charles E. Robinson in *Mary Shelley: Collected Tales and Stories* (1990). Robinson also edited *Mythological Dramas: Proserpine and Midas* (1992). The *Mary Shelley Reader*, ed. Betty T. Bennett and Robinson, contains *Frankenstein*, *Mathilda*, essays, reviews, and letters, and appeared in 1990. Her prefaces and notes to her husband's poems appear in *The Complete*

Poetical Works of Percy Bysshe Shelley (1970), ed. Thomas Hutchinson and rev. G. M. Matthews. More recent publications of individual works include *Valperga* in 1995, *Maurice, or, The Fisher's Tale* in 1998, and *Transformation* in 2004. *Mary Shelley's Literary Lives and Other Writings* appeared in 2002.

Frederick L. Jones edited *The Letters of Mary W. Shelley* (1946) and *Mary Shelley's Journal* (1947). Paula R. Feldman and Diana Scott-Kilvert edited *The Journals of Mary Shelley, 1814–1844* (1987). Betty T. Bennett edited two volumes of *The Letters of Mary Wollstonecraft Shelley* (1980, 1983); published "Finding Mary Shelley in Her Letters" in *Romantic Revisions* (1992), ed. Robert Brinkley and Keith Hanley; and most recently edited *Selected Letters of Mary Wollstonecraft Shelley* (1995) and published *Mary Wollstonecraft Shelley: An Introduction* (1998). Biographies include R. Glynn Grylls, *Mary Shelley: A Biography* (1938); Muriel Spark, *Child of Light: A Reassessment of Mary Shelley* (1951); Elizabeth Nitchie, *Mary Shelley, Author of "Frankenstein"* (1953); Jane Dunn, *Moon in Eclipse: A Life of Mary Shelley* (1978); Bonnie R. Neumann, *The Lonely Muse: A Critical Biography of Mary Shelley* (1979); John Williams, *Mary Shelley: A Literary Life* (1999); Miranda Seymour, *Mary Shelley* (2000); and Martin Barrett, *Mary Shelley* (2002). Also helpful is Martin Garret, *A Mary Shelley Chronology* (2002); and Lucy Morrison and Staci Stone, *A Mary Shelley Encyclopedia* (2003). Three valuable critical volumes dedicated to Shelley's work are Johanna M. Smith, *Mary Shelley* (1996); Radu Florescu, *In Search of Frankenstein: Exploring the Myths Behind Mary Shelley's Monster* (1998); and Debra Benita Shaw, *Women, Science, and Fiction: The Frankenstein Inheritance* (2000). Valuable collections of essays include *The Endurance of Frankenstein* (1979), ed. George Levine and U. C. Knoepflmacher; the St. Martin's Press 1992 edition of *Frankenstein*, which contains critical essays from five perspectives, including feminism, psychoanalysis, and cultural criticism; *The Other Mary Shelley: Beyond Frankenstein* (1993), ed. Audrey A. Fisch, Anne K. Mellor, and Esther H. Schor; the 1996 Norton volume *Frankenstein: The 1818 Text, Context, Nineteenth-Century Responses, Modern Criticism*, ed. Paul J. Hunter; *Iconoclastic Departures: Mary Shelley after Frankenstein* (1997), ed. Syndy M. Conger, Frederick S. Frank, and Gregory O'Dea; *Critical Essays on Mary Wollstonecraft Shelley* (1998), ed. Mary Lowe-Evans; *Mary Shelley in Her Times* (2000), ed. Betty T. Bennett and Stuart Curran; *Jane Austen and Mary Shelley and Their Sisters* (2000), ed. Laura Dabundo; *Mary Shelley's Fictions: From Frankenstein to Falkner* (2000), ed. Michael Eberle-Sinatra; and *Mary Wollstonecraft and Mary Shelley: Writing Lives* (2001), ed. Helen M. Buss. See also Mary A. Favret, "A

Woman Writes the Fiction of the Body in *Frankenstein*," *Genders* 14 (1992); Margo V. Perkins, "The Nature of Otherness: Class and Difference in Mary Shelley's *Frankenstein*," *Studies in the Humanities* 19 (1992); James P. Davis, "*Frankenstein* and the Subversion of the Masculine Voice," *Women's Studies: An Interdisciplinary Journal* 21 (1992); Bette London, "Mary Shelley, *Frankenstein*, and the Spectacle of Masculinity," *PMLA* 108 (1993); Colleen Hobbs, "Reading the Symptoms: An Exploration of Repression and Hysteria in Mary Shelley's *Frankenstein*," *Studies in the Novel* 25 (1993); Ashley J. Cross, " 'Indelible Impressions': Gender and Language in Mary Shelley's *Frankenstein*," *Women's Studies* 27 (1998); James A. Wohlpart, "A Tradition of Male Poetics: Mary Shelley's *Frankenstein* as an Allegory of Art," *Midwest Quarterly* 39 (1998); Nora Crook, "Sleuthing Toward a Mary Shelley Canon," *Women's Writing* 6 (1999); Ramona M. Ralston and Sid Sondergard, "Biodepictions of Mary Shelley: The Romantic Woman Artist as Mother of Monsters," in *Biofictions: The Rewriting of Romantic Lives in Contemporary Fiction and Drama* (1999), ed. Martin Middeke; Haidee Kotze, "Desire, Gender, Power, Language: A Psychoanalytic Reading of Mary Shelley's *Frankenstein*," *Literator* 21 (2000); Emma Liggins, "The Medical Gaze and the Female Corpse: Looking at Bodies in Mary Shelley's *Frankenstein*," *Studies in the Novel* 32 (2000); Cynthia Pon, " 'Passages' in Mary Shelley's *Frankenstein*: Toward a Feminist Figure of Humanity?" *Modern Language Studies* 30 (2000); Marjean D. Purinton, "Mary Shelley's Science Fiction Short Stories and the Legacy of Wollstonecraft's Feminism," *Women's Studies* 30 (2001); and Ann Frank Wake, "Justine's Trial Revisited: A Space for Women's Subculture in Mary Shelley's *Frankenstein*," *European Romantic Review* 12 (2001). Other feminist analyses are represented by chapters in Ellen Moers, *Literary Women* (1976); Sandra M. Gilbert and Susan Gubar, *The Madwoman in the Attic* (1979); and Mary Poovey, *The Proper Lady and the Woman Writer* (1984). Early references may be found in W. H. Lyles's somewhat outdated *Mary Shelley: An Annotated Bibliography* (1975), but a more recent reference guide is *A Routledge Literary Sourcebook on Mary Shelley's Frankenstein* (2002), ed. Timothy Morton.

Charlotte Smith

Among Smith's numerous novels are *Emmeline* (1788), *Ethelinde* (1789), *Celestina* (1791), *Desmond* (1792), *The Old Manor House* (1793), and *The Wanderings of Warwick* (1794). *The Old Manor House* was reprinted in 1969 with an introduction by Anne Henry Ehrenpreis, and more recently, a number of new editions have appeared: *Emmeline* (1988), with an introduction by Zoe Fairbairns; *The Old Manor House*

(1989), with an introduction by Judith Stanton; *Letters of a Solitary Wanderer* (1995); *Desmond* (1997), with an introduction by Antje Blank and Janet Todd; *The Young Philosopher* (1999), edited by Elizabeth Kraft; *Emmeline* (2003) and *Celestina* (2004), both edited by Loraine Fletcher. Smith also published poetry in *Elegiac Sonnets* (1784) and *Beachy Head: With Other Poems* (1807). A collection, *The Poems of Charlotte Smith*, ed. Stuart Curran, was issued in 1993. Two biographies are Florence May Anna Hillbish, *Charlotte Smith, Poet and Novelist* (1941), and Loraine Fletcher, *Charlotte Smith: A Critical Biography* (2001). Judith Phillips Stanton edited *The Collected Letters of Charlotte Smith*, which appeared in 2003. Three critical volumes featuring studies of Smith's writings are Carrol L. Fry, *Charlotte Smith* (1996); Diane Long Hoeveler, *Gothic Feminism: The Professionalization of Gender from Charlotte Smith to the Brontës* (1998); and Jacqueline M. Labbe, *Charlotte Smith: Romanticism, Poetry, and the Culture of Gender* (2003). Katharine M. Rogers includes a discussion of Smith in "Inhibitions in Eighteenth-Century Women Novelists," *Eighteenth-Century Studies* (1977), and in her anthology *Before Their Time* (1979). In addition, Smith is discussed in Margaret Doody, "English Women Novelists and the French Revolution," in *La Femme en Angleterre et dans les colonies Americaines aux XVIIe et XVIIIe siécles* (1975), and Matthew Bray's essay "Removing the Anglo-Saxon Yoke: The Francocentric Vision of Charlotte Smith's Later Works," *The Wordsworth Circle* 24 (1993), discusses the French influence on Smith's writing. Useful essays include Judith Phillips Stanton, "Charlotte Smith's 'Literary Business': Income, Patronage, and Indigence," *The Age of Johnson: A Scholarly Annual* 1 (1987); Sarah Zimmerman, "Charlotte Smith's Letters and the Practice of Self-Presentation," *Princeton University Library Chronicle* 53 (1991); Jacqueline Labbe, "Selling One's Sorrows: Charlotte Smith, Mary Robinson, and the Marketing of Poetry," *The Wordsworth Circle* 25 (1994); Donelle R. Rowe, "Charlotte Smith's Sublime: Feminine Poetics, Botany, and *Beachy Head*," *Prism(s)* 7 (1999); Joseph Rosenblum, "The Treatment of Women in the Novels of Charlotte Smith," in *Jane Austen and Mary Shelley and Their Sisters* (2000), ed. Laura Dabundo; Diane E. Boyd, " 'Professing Drudge': Charlotte Smith's Negotiation of a Mother-Writer Author Connection," *South Atlantic Review* 66 (2001); Kari E. Lokke, "Charlotte Smith and the Politics of Transcendence," in *Rebellious Hearts: British Women Writers and the French Revolution* (2001), ed. Adriana Craciun and Kari E. Lokke; Anne D. Wallace, "Picturesque Fossils, Sublime Geology? The Crisis of Authority in Charlotte Smith's *Beachy Head*," *European Romantic Review* 13 (2002); Maxwell Wheeler, "Charlotte

Smith's Historical Narratives and the English Subject," *Prism(s)* 10 (2002); Kandi Tayebi, "Charlotte Smith and the Quest for the Romantic Prophetic Voice," *Women's Writing* 11 (2004); and Kandi Tayebi, "Undermining the Eighteenth-Century Pastoral: Rewriting the Poet's Relationship to Nature in Charlotte Smith's Poetry," in *European Romantic Review* 15 (2004).

Rachel Speght

Barbara K. Lewalski has edited *The Polemics and Poems of Rachel Speght* (1996), and selections from her tracts are contained in both *The Women's Sharp Revenge: Five Women's Pamphlets from the Renaissance* (1985), ed. Simon Shepherd, as well as *Half Humankind: Contexts and Texts of the Controversy about Women in England, 1540–1640* (1985), ed. Katherine Henderson and Barbara McManus. Biographical and critical work on Speght can be found in Linda Woodbridge, *Women and the English Renaissance: Literature and the Nature of Womankind, 1540–1620* (1984); Ann Rosalind Jones, *The Renaissance Englishwoman in Print: Counterbalancing the Canon* (1990), ed. Anne M. Haselkorn and Betty Travitsky; Lewalski, *Writing Women in Jacobean England* (1993); *Women Writers in Renaissance England* (1997), ed. Randall Martin; and Lewalski, "Female Text, Male Reader Response: Contemporary Marginalia in Rachel Speght's *A Mouzell for Melastomus*," *Representing Women in Renaissance England* (1997), ed. Claudia J. Summers and Ted Larry Pebworth.

Elizabeth Cady Stanton

The three-volume *Selected Papers of Elizabeth Cady Stanton and Susan B. Anthony*, ed. Anne D. Gordon, appeared in 1997. Stanton's *History of Woman Suffrage* (1881–86), ed. with Susan B. Anthony and Matilda Joslyn Gage, was reprinted in 1969; *The Woman's Bible* (1895, 1898) has been republished as *The Original Feminist Attack on the Bible*, with an introduction by Barbara Welter (1974); *Elizabeth Cady Stanton* (1922), ed. Theodore Stanton and Harriot Stanton Blatch, was reissued in 1969; *Eighty Years and More (1815–1897): Reminiscences of Elizabeth Cady Stanton* (1898) was reprinted in 1970. Also useful is *Elizabeth Cady Stanton, Susan B. Anthony: Correspondence, Writing, Speeches* (1981), ed. and with critical commentary by Ellen Carol DuBois. Biographies include Alma Lutz, *Created Equal: A Biography of Elizabeth Cady Stanton, 1815–1902* (1940); Mary Ann B. Oakley, *Elizabeth Cady Stanton* (1972); Lois W. Banner, *Elizabeth Cady Stanton: A Radical for Women's Rights* (1980); and Elisabeth Griffith, *In Her Own Right: The Life of Elizabeth Cady Stanton* (1984).

Two full-length studies are Beth Marie Wag-

genspack, *The Search for Self-Sovereignty: The Oratory of Elizabeth Cady Stanton* (1989), and Judith Wellman, *The Road to Seneca Falls: Elizabeth Cady Stanton and the First Women's Rights Convention* (2004). Useful critical essays are Ellen DuBois, "The Limitations of Sisterhood: Elizabeth Cady Stanton and Division in the American Suffrage Movement, 1875–1902," in *Women and the Structure of Society* (1984), ed. Barbara Harris and JoAnn K. McNamara; Mary Loeffelholz, "Posing the Woman Citizen: The Contradictions of Stanton's Feminism," *Genders* 7 (1990); Sidonie Smith, "Resisting the Gaze of Embodiment: Women's Autobiography in the Nineteenth Century," in *American Women's Autobiography: Fea(s)ts of Memory* (1992), ed. Margo Culley, which compares Stanton's autobiography to Harriet Jacobs's; and Lisa S. Strange, "The Bicycle, Women's Rights, and Elizabeth Cady Stanton," *Women's Studies* 31 (2002). Stanton is also discussed in Lois J. Fowler and David H. Fowler, ed., *Revelations of Self: American Women in Autobiography* (1990), and Mary D. Pellauer, *Toward a Tradition of Feminist Theology* (1991), which examines Stanton's religious-social thought.

Harriet Beecher Stowe

Stowe's major works include *Uncle Tom's Cabin* (1851–52), *Sunny Memories of Foreign Lands* (1854), *Dred* (1856), *The Minister's Wooing* (1859), *The Pearl of Orr's Island* (1862), *Oldtown Folks* (1869), *Oldtown Fireside Stories* (1872), and *Poganuc People* (1878). *The Writings of Harriet Beecher Stowe*, 16 vols. (1896), is still the standard edition. More recently, John M. Moran edited *Collected Poems* (1967); while Margaret G. Mair, Earl A. French, and Diana Royce produced *The Papers of Harriet Beecher Stowe* (1977); and Joan D. Hedrick edited *The Harriet Beecher Stowe Reader* (1999). An excellent edition of *Uncle Tom's Cabin*, with an introduction by Ann Douglas, appeared in 1981. Elizabeth Ammons edited a Norton Critical Edition of *Uncle Tom's Cabin*, which was published in 1994. Several memoirs were written during Stowe's lifetime or soon after she died. While Robert Frost Wilson's *Crusader in Crinoline: The Life of Harriet Beecher Stowe* (1941), has been considered the standard biography, Joan D. Hedrick's more recent *Harriet Beecher Stowe: A Life* (1994), is also extremely useful. Johanna Johnston, *Runaway to Heaven: The Story of Harriet Beecher Stowe* (1963), is a good popular biography. Others include Edward Wagenknecht, *Harriet Beecher Stowe: The Known and the Unknown* (1965), and Noel B. Gerson, *Harriet Beecher Stowe: A Biography* (1976).

Critical studies include Charles H. Foster, *The Rungless Ladder: Harriet Beecher Stowe and New England Puritanism* (1954); John R.

Adams, *Harriet Beecher Stowe* (1963); Alice C. Crozier, *The Novels of Harriet Beecher Stowe* (1980); Gayle Kimball, *The Religious Ideas of Harriet Beecher Stowe: Her Gospel of Womanhood* (1982); and Jeanne Boydston, *The Limits of Sisterhood: The Beecher Sisters on Women's Rights and Women's Sphere* (1988). Two valuable feminist articles are Jane P. Tompkins, "Sentimental Power: Uncle Tom's Cabin and the Politics of Literary History," *Glyph* (1981), and Laurie Crumpacker, "Four Novels of Harriet Beecher Stowe: A Study in 19th-Century Androgyny," in *American Novelists Revisited: Essays in Feminist Criticism* (1982), ed. Fritz Fleischmann. Stowe's work is also treated in Ann Douglas, *The Feminization of American Culture* (1977); Leslie Fiedler, *The Inadvertent Epic: From "Uncle Tom's Cabin" to "Roots"* (1980); Thomas F. Gossett, *Uncle Tom's Cabin and American Culture* (1985); Gillian Brown, *Domestic Individualism: Imagining Self in Nineteenth-Century America* (1992); and Carolyn Heilbrun, *Women's Lives: The View from the Threshold* (1999). For other useful critical studies, see *New Essays on Uncle Tom's Cabin* (1986), ed. Eric J. Sundquist; Josephine Donovan, *Uncle Tom's Cabin: Evil, Affliction, and Redemptive Love* (1991); *Approaches to Teaching "Uncle Tom's Cabin,"* ed. Elizabeth Ammons and Susan Balesco (2000); *A Routledge Literary Sourcebook on Harriet Beecher Stowe's* Uncle Tom's Cabin, ed. Debra Rosenthal (2004); and *The Cambridge Companion to Harriet Beecher Stowe* (2004), ed. Cindy Weinstein.

Lucy Terry

A brief but reliable biography is David R. Proper, *Lucy Terry Prince: Singer of History* (1997). Other useful sources include George Sheldon, *A History of Deerfield, Massachusetts* (1895), and Lorenzo J. Green, *The Negro in Colonial England* (1942). A much more recent analysis of Terry's work can be found in Frances Smith Foster, *Written by Herself: Literary Productions of Early African American Writers* (1993).

Sojourner Truth

Truth's speeches can be found in Elizabeth Cady Stanton et al., *History of Woman Suffrage*, vols. I–III (1881–86). Truth's story is told in the *Narrative of Sojourner Truth, a Northern Slave, Emancipated from Bodily Servitude by the State of New York, in 1828*, an account written by Olive Gilbert in 1850 and reprinted several times, for instance, in 1991, with an introduction by Jeffrey C. Stewart, and in 1993, edited and with an introduction by Margaret Washington. Also reprinted is Arthur Huff Fauset, *Sojourner Truth: God's Faithful Pilgrim* (1938; 1971). More recent biographies are Jacqueline Bernard, *Journey toward Freedom: The Story of Sojourner Truth* (1967); Carleton Mabee,

Sojourner Truth, Slave, Prophet, Legend (1993); and Nell Irvin Painter, *Sojourner Truth: A Life, A Symbol* (1996).

An important interpretation of Truth's life and work is Linda David and Erlene Stetson, *Glorying in Tribulation: The Lifework of Sojourner Truth* (1994). Useful articles are Nell Irvin Painter, "Sojourner Truth in Life and Memory: Writing the Biography of an American Exotic," *Gender and History* 2 (1990); Drema R. Lipscomb, "Sojourner Truth: A Practical Public Discourse," *Reclaiming Rhetorica: Women in the Rhetorical Tradition*, ed. Andrea Lunsford (1995); Jean M. Humez, "Reading the *Narrative of Sojourner Truth* as a Collaborative Text," *Frontiers* 16 (1996); and Joann P. Krieg, "Whitman and Sojourner Truth," *Walt Whitman Quarterly Review* 16 (1998).

Augusta Webster

Webster's books of poetry are *Blanche Lisle and Other Poems* (1860), *Lillian Gray: A Poem* (1864), *Dramatic Studies* (1866), *A Woman Sold and Other Poems* (1867), *Portraits* (1870), *Yu-pe-Ya's Lute* (1874), *A Book of Rhyme* (1881), and *Mother and Daughter* (1895), an uncompleted sonnet sequence published posthumously. Her poems were collected as *Selections from the Verse of Augusta Webster* (1893), while a selection of her essays appeared as *A Housewife's Opinions* (1877). In addition to these, she also wrote several pieces of fiction, a number of plays, and translated the classical Greek dramas *Prometheus Bound* (1866) and *Medea* (1868). A modern collection of Webster's poetry and selections of her prose appear in *Augusta Webster: Portraits and Other Poems* (1999), ed. Christine Stuphin, a work that also features a short biography.

Other biographical and critical work on Webster appears in Angela Leighton, *Victorian Women Poets: Writing Against the Heart* (1992), and E. Warwick Slinn, *Poetry and Culture: Performativity and Critique* (2002). Useful essays include Christine Stuphin, "Human Tigresses, Fractious Angels, and Nursery Saints: Augusta Webster's 'A Castaway' and Victorian Discourses on Prostitution and Women's Sexuality," *Victorian Poetry* 38 (Winter 2000), and Patricia Rigg, "Augusta Webster and the Lyric Muse: *The Athenaeum* and Webster's Poetics," *Victorian Poetry* 42 (Summer 2004).

Phillis Wheatley

Wheatley's only book is *Poems on Various Subjects, Religious and Moral* (1773). The standard modern edition of her poetry and prose is *Complete Writings* (2001), ed. Vincent Carretta; another good current edition is the revised and enlarged *The Poems of Phillis Wheatley* (1989), ed. Julian D. Mason Jr. See also *The Collected Works of Phillis Wheatley* (1988), ed. John C.

Shields. Shirley Graham, *The Story of Phillis Wheatley* (1969); William G. Allen, *Wheatley, Banneker and Harton* (1970); and Merle Richmond, *Phillis Wheatley* (1988), are useful critical biographies. Dickson D. Bruce also includes a helpful discussion of Wheatley in *The Origins of African American Literature, 1680–1865* (2001).

William Henry Robinson has four important contributions: *Phillis Wheatley in the Black American Beginnings* (1975); *Phillis Wheatley: A Bio-Bibliography* (1981); *Critical Essays on Phillis Wheatley* (1982); and *Phillis Wheatley and Her Writings* (1984). Henry Louis Gates Jr. wrote about her in *The Trials of Phillis Wheatley: America's First Black Poet and Her Encounters with the Founding Fathers* (2003). Other helpful secondary sources are *Bid the Vassal Soar: Interpretive Essays on the Life and Poetry of Phillis Wheatley and George Moses* (1974), ed. M. A. Richmond; Helen Burke, "Problematizing American Dissent: The Subject of Phillis Wheatley," in *Cohesion and Dissent in America* (1994), ed. Carol Colabretta and Joseph Alkana; Carla Willard, "Wheatley's Turn of Praise: Heroic Entrapment and the Paradox of Revolution," *American Literature* 67 (1995); Paula Bennet, "Phillis Wheatley's Vocation and the Paradox of the 'Afric Muse,'" *PMLA* 113 (1998).

Isabella Whitney

Whitney's two published works consist of a poem, *The Copy of a Letter* (1567), and a collection of verse, *A Sweet Nosegay or Pleasant Posye* (1573), which includes a poetic rewriting of Hugh Plat's maxims from *The Floures of Philosophie* (1572); a series of verse letters; and Whitney's "Will and Testament." Biographical and critical approaches to her career appear in four book-length studies: Elaine V. Beilin, *Redeeming Eve: Women Writers of the English Renaissance* (1987); Ann Rosalind Jones, "Nets and Bridles: Early Modern Conduct Books and Sixteenth-Century Women's Lyrics," in *The Ideology of Conduct: Essays in Literature and the History of Sexuality* (1987), ed. Nancy Armstrong and Leonard Tennenhouse; Tina Krontiris, *Oppositional Voices: Women as Writers and Translators in the English Renaissance* (1992); and *Isabella Whitney, Mary Sidney, and Aemelia Lanyer: Renaissance Women Poets* (2000), ed. Danielle Clarke. See also "Isabella Whitney, Sir Hugh Plat, Geoffrey Whitney, and 'Sister Eldershae'," *English Language Notes* 21 (1983). Useful critical essays include Betty Travitsky, "The Lady Doth Protest: Protest in the Popular Writings of Renaissance Englishwomen," *English Literary Renaissance* 14 (1984); Wendy Wall, "Isabella Whitney and the Female Legacy," *English Literary History* 58 (1991); Ann Kothe, "Modest Incursions: The Production of

Writers and their Readers in the Early Modern Prefaces of Isabella Whitney and Margaret Tyler," *English Language Notes* 37 (1999); and Boyd M. Berry, " 'We Are Not All Alyke Nor of Complexion One': Truism and Isabella Whitney's Multiple Readers," *Renaissance Papers* 2000 (2000). Whitney's work is also discussed in Lynette McGrath, *Subjectivity and Women's Poetry in Early Modern England: Why on the Ridge Should She Desire to Go?* (2002).

Helen Maria Williams
Williams's work includes *An Ode on the Peace* (1783), *Peru: A Poem* (1784), *Poems* (1786), *Julia: A Novel* (1790), *Letters on the French Revolution* (1791–92), *Letters From France* (1794), *Letters Containing a Sketch on the Politics of France* (1796), *A Tour of Switzerland* (1798), *Poems: Moral, Elegant and Pathetic* (1801), *Sketches of the State of Manners and Opinions in the French Republic Towards the Close of the Eighteenth Century* (1801), *The History of Perourou, The Bellows-Mender* (1802), *A Narrative of the Events Which Have Taken Place In France* (1815), *Poems on Various Subjects* (1823), *Memoirs of the Reign of Robespierre* (1929), and *Four New Letters of Mary Wollstonecraft and Helen M. Williams* (1937), ed. Benjamin Kurtz and Carrie C. Autry. Williams also translated many books from the French, including Louis Sebastian Mercier, *Seraphina: A Novel* (1797); M. Ducray-Duminil, *Ambrose and Eleanor: of the Adventures of Two Children Deserted on an Uninhabited Island* (1799); Bernardin de Saint-Pierre, *Paul and Virginia* (1800); Francois Babie Barancy, *The Political and Confidential Correspondence of Lewis XVI* (1803); Alexander von Humboldt and Aime de Bonpland, *Researches Concerning the Institutions and Monuments of the Ancient Inhabitants of America* (1814); and von Humboldt and de Bonpland, *Personal Narrative of Travels to the Equinoctical Regions of the New Continent During the Years 1799–1804* (1815).

Critical work includes Gary Kelly, *Women, Writing and Revolution, 1790–1827* (1993). Williams is also treated in Mary Favret, *Romantic Correspondence: Women, Politics, and the Fiction of Letters* (1993), and Nicola Watson, *Revolution and the Form of the British Novel, 1790–1825* (1994). Useful essays on Williams include Deborah Kennedy, "Spectacle of the Guillotine: Helen Maria Williams and the Reign of Terror," *Philological Quarterly* 73 (1994); Mary A. Favret, "Spectatrice as Spectacle: Helen Maria Williams at Home in the Revolution," *Studies in Romanticism* 32 (1993).

Harriet E. Adams Wilson
Wilson's book *Our Nig* (1859) was discovered by Henry Louis Gates Jr. and republished by Vintage Books in 1983, rev. 2003, with a useful

critical and biographical introduction by Gates. *Our Nig* is also included in *Three Classic African-American Novels* (1990), ed. William L. Andrews. Important biographical material can be found in Barbara A. White, "*Our Nig* and the She-Devil: New Information about Harriet Wilson and the 'Bellmont' Family," *American Literature* 65 (1993).

A valuable essay on Wilson's novel is Gates, "Parallel Discursive Universes: Fictions of the Self in Harriet Wilson's *Our Nig*," in his *Figures in Black: Words, Signs, and the "Racial" Self* (1987). See also the discussions of Wilson in Bernard W. Bell, *The Afro-American Novel and Its Tradition* (1987); William L. Andrews, *To Tell a Free Story: The First Century of Afro-American Autobiography, 1760–1865* (1988); and Claudia Tate, *Domestic Allegories of Political Desire: The Black Heroine's Text at the Turn of the Century* (1992). Other useful studies include Frances S. Foster, "Adding Color and Contour to Early American Self-Portraitures: Autobiographical Writings of African-American Women," in *Conjuring: Black Women, Fiction, and Literary Tradition* (1985), ed. Marjorie Pryse and Hortense Spillers; Beth Maclay Doriani, "Black Womanhood in Nineteenth-Century America: Subversion and Self-Construction in Two Women's Autobiographies," *American Quarterly* 43 (1991); Elizabeth Breau, "Identifying Satire: *Our Nig*," *Callaloo* 16 (1993); Cynthia J. Davis, "Speaking of the Body's Pain: Harriet Wilson's *Our Nig*," *African American Review* 27 (1993); Karla Holloway, "Economies of Space: Markets and Marketability in *Our Nig* and *Iola Leroy*," in *The (Other) American Traditions: Nineteenth-Century Women Writers* (1993); and Margaret Lindgren, "Harriet Jacobs, Harriet Wilson, and the Redoubled Voice in Black Autobiography," *Obsidian II* 8 (1993).

Mary Wollstonecraft
The seven-volume edition of *The Works of Mary Wollstonecraft*, ed. Janet M. Todd and Marilyn Butler, was published in 1989 as part of the Pickering Masters series; it includes all of Wollstonecraft's work published during her lifetime or immediately after her death. Of these works, the most important are the following three political writings: *A Vindication of the Rights of Men* (1790), *A Vindication of the Rights of Woman* (1792), and *An Historical and Moral View of the French Revolution* (1794), all of which are also collected even more recently in *Political Writings* (1993), ed. Todd; and her two novels, *Mary, a Fiction* (1788) and *Maria; or, The Wrongs of Women* (1797), the second of which she left unfinished at her death. *The Collected Letters*, ed. Ralph M. Wardle, was published in 1979; Todd edited another version in 2003. Many biographers have drawn upon William Godwin's

"Memoirs of the Author of *A Vindication of the Rights of Women*" (1798). Modern critical biographies include Ralph Wardle, *Mary Wollstonecraft* (1951); Eleanor Flexner, *Mary Wollstonecraft: A Biography* (1972); Claire Tomlin, *The Life and Death of Mary Wollstonecraft* (1975, rev. 1992); Todd and Moira Ferguson, *Mary Wollstonecraft* (1984); and Lyndall Gordon, *Mary Wollstonecraft: A New Genus* (2005).

Interesting appreciative essays include Virginia Woolf, "Mary Wollstonecraft," in *The Second Common Reader* (1932), and Ruth Benedict, "Mary Wollstonecraft," in *An Anthropologist at Work* (1959), ed. Margaret Mead. Among more recent critical studies of Wollstonecraft's life and work are Moira Ferguson, *Mary Wollstonecraft* (1984); Virginia Sapiro, *A Vindication of Political Virtue: The Political Theory of Mary Wollstonecraft* (1992); Syndy M. Conger, *Mary Wollstonecraft and the Language of Sensibility* (1994); Jane Moore, *Mary Wollstonecraft* (1999); and Barbara Taylor, *Mary Wollstonecraft and the Feminist Imagination* (2003). Wollstonecraft is also treated in Mary Poovey, *The Proper Lady and the Woman Writer* (1984); Laurie Langbauer, "An Early Romance: Motherhood and Women's Writing in Mary Wollstonecraft's Novels," in *Romanticism and Feminism* (1988), ed. Anne Mellor; and Tom Furniss, "Mary Wollstonecraft (1759–97)," in *A Handbook to English Romanticism* (1992), ed. Jean Raimond and J. R. Watson. See also *Feminist Interpretations of Mary Wollstonecraft* (1996), ed. Maria J. Falco, and *The Cambridge Companion to Mary Wollstonecraft* (2003), ed. Esthor Schor. Janet M. Todd compiled an annotated bibliography, *Mary Wollstonecraft* (1976), and Leigh Williams and Rosemarie Johnstone produced *Updating Mary Wollstonecraft: A Bibliography of Criticism, 1976–1989, Bulletin of Bibliography* 48 (1991).

Constance Fenimore Woolson

Constance Fenimore Woolson: Selected Stories and Travel Narratives, ed. Victoria Brehm and Sharon L. Dean, appeared in 2004. Another edition of Woolson's stories, *Women Artists, Women Exiles: "Miss Grief" and Other Stories*, ed. Joan Myers Weimar, became available in 1988. Some of Woolson's correspondence has been published in Alice Hall Petry, ed., " 'Always, Your Attached Friend': The Unpublished Letters of Constance Fenimore Woolson to John and Clara Hay," *Books at Brown* 29–39 (1982–83). A valuable critical biography is Cheryl B. Torsney, *Constance Fenimore Woolson: The Grief of Artistry* (1989). Sharon Dean examines Woolson's literary, cultural, and historical context in *Constance Fenimore Woolson: Homeward Bound* (1995). One of the women Lyndall Gordon discusses in *Henry James: Two Women and His Art* (1999) is Woolson. Torsney

has also edited the useful collection *Critical Essays on Constance Fenimore Woolson* (1992); another valuable essay collection is *Constance Fenimore Woolson's Nineteenth Century: Essays* (2001), ed. Victoria Brehm.

Two critical articles are Sharon L. Dean, "Homeward Bound: The Novels of Constance Fenimore Woolson," *Legacy* 6 (1989), and Victoria Brehm, "Island Fortresses: The Landscape of the Imagination in the Great Lakes Fiction of Constance Fenimore Woolson," *American Literary Realism, 1870–1910* 22 (1990).

Dorothy Wordsworth

Mary Moorman edited *Journals: The Alfoxden Journal, 1798,* and *The Grasmere Journals, 1800–1803* (1971), with an introduction by Helen Darbishire. Pamela Woof edited an edition of *Grasmere Journals* (1991), and Paul Hamilton edited *Dorothy Wordsworth: Selections from the Journals* (1992). Her *Recollections of a Tour Made in Scotland* was reprinted in 1997, with notes and photographs by Carol Kyros Walker. Wordsworth's letters are collected with those of her brother in *The Letters of William Wordsworth and Dorothy Wordsworth*, 6 vols. (1935–39; rev. C. L. Shaver et al., 1967–82). The standard biography is Ernest de Selincourt, *Dorothy Wordsworth* (1933). More recent are Elizabeth Gunn, *A Passion for the Particular: Dorothy Wordsworth, a Portrait* (1981); Pamela Woof, *Dorothy Wordsworth, Writer* (1988); and *Dorothy Wordsworth: On a Wander by Ourselves* (1997). Also helpful are Sean Manley, *Dorothy and William Wordsworth: The Heart of a Circle of Friends* (1974), and *Prominent Sisters: Mary Lamb, Dorothy Wordsworth, and Sarah Disraeli* (1996). A book-length study of Wordsworth's literary influence is Susan Levin, *Dorothy Wordsworth and Romanticism* (1987). Noteworthy critical essays include Alexis Easley, "Wandering Women: Dorothy Wordsworth's *Grasmere Journals* and the Discourse on Female Vagrancy," *Women's Writing* 3 (1996); Richard G. Swartz, "Dorothy Wordsworth, Local Tourism, and the Anxiety (or Semiotics) of Description," *Prose Studies* 20 (1997); Jill Ehnnen, "Writing Against, Writing Through: Subjectivity, Vocation, and Authorship in the Work of Dorothy Wordsworth," *South Atlantic Review* 64 (1999); and Patricia Comitini, " 'More Than Half a Poet': Vocational Philanthropy and Dorothy Wordsworth's *Grasmere Journals*," *European Romantic Review* 14 (2003). For useful feminist approaches to this writer's career and works, see the chapter in Margaret Homans, *Women Writers and Poetic Identity* (1980); James Holt McGavran Jr., "Dorothy Wordsworth's Journals: Putting Herself Down," in *The Private Self: Theory and Practice of Women's Autobiographical Writings* (1988), ed. Shari Benstock; and Pamela Woof, "Dorothy Wordsworth's Journals

and the Engendering of Poetry," *Bucknell Review* 36 (1992).

Mary Wroth

The Poems of Lady Mary Wroth (1983), ed. Josephine Roberts, includes most of Wroth's poems, an informative introduction, and detailed notes (as well as an appendix with selections from Wroth's correspondence). R. E. Pritchard edited *Poems: Selections* by Wroth, which appeared in 1996. The first part of Wroth's romance, *The Countesse of Montgomeries Urania* (1621), is available in a modern edition edited by Josephine A. Roberts (1995). The sonnet sequence *Pamphilia to Amphilanthus* (originally appended to *Urania*) was edited by Gary Waller in 1977. Wroth's pastoral drama *Love's Victory* (unpublished in her lifetime) was edited by Michael G. Brennan in 1988.

Critical studies that provide interesting biographical background are Waller's *The Sidney Family Romance: Mary Wroth, William Herbert, and the Early Modern Construction of Gender* (1993), and Mary Ellen Lamb's *Gender and Authorship in the Sidney Circle* (1990). Full-length studies of Wroth's poetry are May N. Paulissen, *The Love Sonnets of Lady Mary Wroth: A Critical Introduction* (1982); Naomi J. Miller, *Changing the Subject: Mary Wroth and Figurations of Gender in Early Modern England* (1996); and Sheila T. Cavanagh, *Cherished Torment: The Emotional Geography of Lady Mary Wroth's Urania* (2001). Feminist perspectives on Wroth can be found in a useful collection of critical essays, *The Renaissance Englishwoman in Print: Counterbalancing the Canon* (1990). Another important collection, *Reading Mary Wroth: Representing Alternatives in Early Modern England*, ed. Naomi J. Miller and Gary Waller, appeared in 1991. See also the valuable discussions of Wroth in Paul Salzman, *English Prose Fiction, 1558–1700: A Critical History* (1985); Elaine V. Beilin, *Redeeming Eve: Women Writers of the English Renaissance* (1987); Ann Rosalind Jones, *The Currency of Eros: Women's Love Lyric in Europe, 1540–1620* (1990); Barbara Kiefer Lewalski, *Writing Women in Jacobean England* (1993); and Lyn Bennett, *Women Writing of Divinest Things: Rhetoric and the Poetry of Pembroke, Wroth and Lanyer* (2004). Josephine Roberts has published three notable articles on Wroth: "Lady Mary Wroth's Sonnets: A Labyrinth of the Mind," *Journal of Women's Studies in Literature* 1 (1979); "The Biographical Problem of *Pamphilia to Amphilanthus*," *Tulsa Studies in Women's Literature* 1 (1982); and "Labyrinths of Desire: Lady Mary Wroth's Reconstruction of Romance," *Women's Studies* 19 (1991). Two essays by Maureen Quilligan are also helpful: "Lady Mary Wroth: Female Authority and the Family Romance," in *Unfolded Tales: Essays on Renaissance Romance* (1989), ed. George Logan and Gordon Teskey, and "The Constant Subject: Instability and Female Authority in Wroth's *Urania* Poems," in *Soliciting Interpretation: Literary Theory and Seventeenth-Century Poetry* (1990), ed. Elizabeth D. Harvey and Katharine Eisaman Maus. Useful recent essays include Helen Hackett, " 'A Book, and Solitariness': Melancholia, Gender and Literary Subjectivity in Mary Wroth's *Urania*," in *Renaissance Configurations: Voices/Bodies/Spaces* (1998), ed. Gordon McMullan; Shannon Miller, "Constructing the Female Self: Architectural Structures in Mary Wroth's *Urania*," in *Renaissance Culture and the Everyday* (1999), ed. Patricia Fumerton and Simon Hunt; Linda L. Dove, "Mary Wroth and the Politics of the Household in *Pamphilia to Amphilanthus*," in *Women Writing and the Reproduction of Culture in Tudor and Stuart Britain* (2000), ed. Mary E. Burke; Bernadette Andrea, "Pamphilia's Cabinet: Gendered Authorship and Empire in Lady Mary Wroth's *Urania*," *ELH: Journal of English Literary History* 68 (2001); Emma Clark, "Metaphors of Motherhood: Claiming Back the Female Body in the Poems of Mary Sidney and Mary Wroth," *Women's Writing* 8 (2001); Christina Luckyj, "The Politics of Genre in Early Women's Writing: The Case of Lady Mary Wroth," *English Studies in Canada* 27 (2001); Akiko Kusunoki, "Female Selfhood and Male Violence in English Renaissance Drama: A View From Mary Wroth's *Urania*," in *Women, Violence, and English Renaissance Literature: Essays Honoring Paul Jorgensen* (2003), ed. Linda Woodbridge and Sharon Beehler; and Susan Lauffer O'Hara, "Sonnets as Theater: The Performance of Ideal Love and the Negation of Marriage in Mary Wroth's Masque," *Explorations in Renaissance Culture* 29 (2003).

Abigail Adams: Letters to John Adams reprinted by permission of the publishers from *The Adams Family Correspondence*, Vol. I, edited by L. H. Butterfield et al., Cambridge, Mass.: The Belknap Press of Harvard University Press. Copyright © 1963 by the Massachusetts Historical Society.

Aphra Behn: *Oroonoko, or the Royal Slave* by Aphra Behn. Published in 1993 by W. W. Norton & Company, Inc. Used with permission of W. W. Norton & Company.

Anne Bradstreet: "The Prologue," "In Honour of That High and Mighty Princess Queen Elizabeth of Happy Memory," "The Author to Her Book," "A Letter to Her Husband," "To Her Father with Some Verses for Deliverance from a Fever," "Meditations Divine and Moral," "Here Follows Some Verses Upon the Burning of Our House," "To My Dear and Loving Husband," "In Memory of My Dear Grandchild Anne Bradstreet," "In Reference to Her Children" reprinted by permission of the publisher from *The Works of Anne Bradstreet* edited by Jeannine Hensley, Cambridge Mass.: The Belknap Press of Harvard University Press. Copyright © 1967 by the President and Fellows of Harvard College.

Emily Brontë: "Tell me, Tell me, smiling child," "I am the only being whose doom," "Alone I sat; the summer day," F. de Samara to A. G. A. ("Light up thy halls! 'Tis closing day"), "The Night-Wind," "Riches I hold in light esteem," "Aye, there it is! It wakes to-night," "A Day Dream," R. Alcona to J. Brenzaida ("Cold in the earth, and the deep snow piled above thee!"), "Ah! why, because the dazzling sun," "The Prisoner: A Fragment," "No Coward soul is mine," stanzas ("Often rebuked, yet always back returning") from *The Complete Poems of Emily Brontë*, edited by C. Hatfield. Copyright © 1941 by Columbia University Press. Reprinted with permission of the publisher.

Frances Burney: "Mastectomy" from *The Journals and Letters of Fanny Burney*, volume 6, edited by Joyce Harlow. Reprinted by permission of Oxford University Press.

Elizabeth Cary: Excerpts from *Tragedy of Mariam: The Faire Queene of Jewry, With the Lady Falkland: Her Life By One of Her Daughter*, ed. B. Weller and M. Ferguson. Copyright © 1993 The Regents of the University of California. Reprinted by permission.

Emily Dickinson: Poems 13, 157, 194, 201, 205, 260, 267, 269, 307, 320, 325, 336, 340, 353, 360, 372, 382, 401, 407, 409, 411, 439, 445, 455, 458, 466, 479, 517, 519, 533, 559, 590, 591, 600, 620, 627, 649, 656, 675, 697, 709, 745, 764, 788, 857, 1061, 1072, 1096, 1163, 1263, 1311, 1332, 1470, 1602, 1691, 1715, 1734, 1742, and 1773 reprinted by permission of the publishers and Trustees of Amherst College from *The Poems of Emily Dickinson*, Ralph W. Franklin, ed., Cambridge, Mass.: The Belknap Press of Harvard University Press, copyright © 1998 by the President and Fellows of Harvard College, copyright © 1951, 1955, 1979, 1983 by the President and Fellows of Harvard College. Letters 233, 248, 260, 261, 265, 268 reprinted by permission of the publishers from *The Letters of Emily Dickinson*, edited by Thomas H. Johnson, Cambridge, Mass.: The Belknap Press of Harvard University Press, copyright © 1958, 1986 by the President and Fellows of Harvard College; 1914, 1924, 1932, 1942 by Martha Dickinson Bianchi; 1952 by Alfred Leete Hampson; 1960 by Mary L. Hampson.

Queen Elizabeth I: "Speech to the Troops at Tilbury" from *The Public Speaking of Queen Elizabeth*, edited by George P. Rice Jr. Reprinted by permission of Columbia University Press. "Ah Silly Pugge" by Queen Elizabeth. Reprinted by permission of the Honourable Society of the Inner Temple. "On Monsieur's Departure" and "The Doubt of Future Foes" from *The Poems of Queen Elizabeth I*, edited by Leicester Bradner. Copyright © 1964 by Brown University. Reprinted by permission of University of New England Press.

Michael Field: "Come Gorgo Put the Rug in Place," "A Girl," "It Was Deep April," "Eros", "Lo, My Loved is Dying," "Maids, Not to you my Mind Doth," "Unbosoming," and "To Christina Rossetti" by Michael Field. Reprinted by permission of Blackwell Publishing.

Mary Sidney Herbert: "Psalm 58" from *The Psalms of Sir Philip Sidney and the Countess of Pembroke*, edited by J. C. A. Rathmell. New York University Press, 1963. Reprinted by permission.

Rebecca Cox Jackson: "Gifts of Power," "A Dream of Slaughter," "The Dream of the Cakes," "The Dream of Washing Quilts" from *The Gifts of Power: The Writings of Rebecca Jackson, Black Visionary, Shaker Eldress*, edited by Jean McMahan Humez (1981). Reprinted by permission of the Shaker Manuscript Collection, The Western Reserve Historical Society.

Harriet Jacobs: Excerpts from *Incidents in the Life of a Slave Girl* reprinted by permission of the publisher from *Incidents in the Life of a Slave Girl, Written by Herself* by Harriet Jacobs, edited with

Index

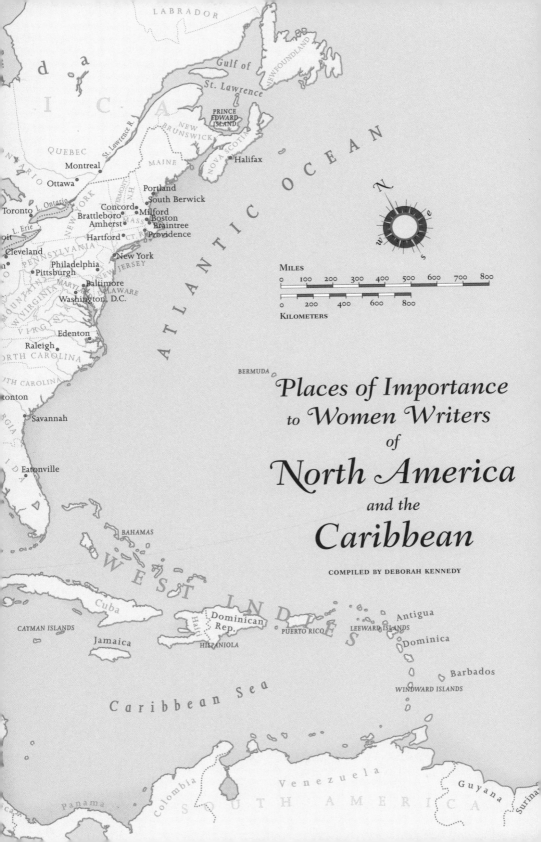

Places of Importance
to Women Writers
of
North America
and the
Caribbean

COMPILED BY DEBORAH KENNEDY